D1586053

'Meticulously-researched . . . addictively page-turning plot'
Jewish Chronicle

'Sex is handled with taste and evident relish . . . very readable'
Preview

'Having enjoyed all previous books by Shirley Eskapa, it came as no surprise to me that this latest publication is another winner . . . I loved every page and can highly recommend it . . . Many characters move through the pages but Saffity, Max and Colette will retain a special place in the reader's mind for some time'
Womanwise

'I finished reading *Scales of Passion* last week and found it wonderfully provocative, an absolute rollercoaster ride in its drama and intrigue and incredibly moving. I will write more about it later and give you my choices for casting. It could be a tremendous mini-series'
Brian Linehan

Shirley Eskapa writes about her subject better than any woman I know – because she knows her subject.
Allan Fotheringham

Scales of Passion

Shirley Eskapa is the author of the best-selling work of non-fiction *Woman Versus Woman*. Her widely acclaimed novels – among them *The Secret Keeper*, *The Seduction* and *Blood Fugue* – have been translated into nine languages. Married with three children, she has lived in Johannesburg, Geneva and Monte Carlo and is now settled in London.

Also by Shirley Eskapa
in Pan Books

Fiction
THE SEDUCTION
THE SECRET KEEPER

Non-fiction
WOMAN VERSUS WOMAN

Shirley Eskapa

Scales of Passion

Pan Books
in association with Macmillan

First published 1989 by Macmillan London Limited
This edition published 1990 by Pan Books Ltd,
Cavaye Place, London SW10 9PG
in association with Macmillan
9 8 7 6 5 4 3 2 1
© Shirley Eskapa 1989
ISBN 0 330 31211 1

Printed in England by Clays Ltd, St Ives plc

The characters in this novel and their actions are imaginary.
Their names and experiences have no relation to those of
actual people, living or dead, except by coincidence.

Acknowledgements

My endless gratitude to James Hale, Editorial Director of
Macmillan, for his inspired guidance.

I owe a huge debt of gratitude to Margaret Marshall of M & C
Word Processing, who typed and retyped this manuscript with
grace, curiosity and understanding.

I am more than thankful to my father-in-law, Pepo Eskapa, for
plying me with invaluable material on Salonika, Paris and
Johannesburg.

My profound thanks to my son-in-law, Richard Grosse, for his
expert legal advice.

Halina and George Szpiro's enthusiastic reading of the draft
manuscript inspired me onward.

Krista Wichman of the Wiener Library was unstintingly
generous and helpful.

The encouragement of Clive Beck, Rosalie Berwin, Deodata
Currie, Patrick Cosgrave, Lisa Kaye, David Elliot, Lola
Finkelstein, Jeanette Kupfurmann, Barbara Leser and Niza
Parente helped me more than they can ever know.

Thanks to Philip Chadbourne for recounting his experience as a
Jedburgher.

My husband Raymond lived long years with Saffity, Max and
Colette, and all four of us are eternally grateful.

To Rhona, my sister,
for the courage of her understanding;

and

To my children, Roy, Linda and Robert
for their surpassing kindness

All our ancestors are in us. Who can feel himself alone?

Beer-Hoffmann, *Schlafflied für Miriam*, 1898

Prologue

Extract from Sir Simon Saffity's letter to Max Blum, April 8th, 1973.

God can no more alter the geography of my birth than the history of my past. Too late and at too great a cost, I have learned that everyone's past is destined to eternity.

I believed I had murdered my origins and buried them in the soil of secrecy. I had already done so when you and I met in Paris in 1923. I wish I could blame it all on the passionate arrogance of a teenager, but the teenage syndrome had not yet been invented; besides, neither you nor I was ever a teenager in any sense of the word. That luxury – or curse – passed us by.

I must not digress.

When we were all émigrés together, Paris was the melting pot of Europe. You came from Poland, I came from Greece, and Colette came from the States, which – as you only recently discovered – was *her* secret.

You had no secret, but you did not know that. Still, you were a threat. So I used all my considerable resources and all my power to condemn you to a lifetime of guilty secrecy as a murderer. I never let up.

I got away with it for forty-five years.

For all those years Colette was my friend, my mentor and often my sanity.

What I did to you was – and is – unpardonable. You will not deny that what you did to me was – and is – equally unpardonable.

You matched me in the end.

Part One

1

Legends grow around some men, theories around others. It was said that Sir Simon Saffity was a legend born of a theory. But the truth was that in war-torn Salonika in 1917, when he was a nine-year-old Greek boy called Simon Saffarty, a few smiling British officers changed his life with a gift of tasteless white English bread.

Behind him Salonika burned. That summer of 1917 Greece was at last on the side of the Allies. The fire had begun more than twenty-four hours earlier, and had already burned more than half his ancient city. Now the fingers of flame stretched out to the sea and dissolved in a stinging mist.

The day before, a Saturday, the winds had been unusually fierce, and as the afternoon siesta ended the fire began. It was Sabbath – many of the stevedores were Jews – so the port and the town were more or less at a standstill.

When Simon's father Maurice first saw the flames, his usual poor judgement had led him to believe the roof of his great-aunt's house on the Rue Parallèle would be safe. Now, standing on the roof with a long-prepared, emergency sack of clothing slung over his shoulder, Simon watched his father and watched the fire. Maurice was clearly certain that the hot Vardar wind would blow the blaze in another direction. The sound of the flames, a huge, menacing roar, and the sight of the advancing red glow topped by pillars of smoke made the ill-tempered man speechless. This was no less shocking than the fire itself.

'We must move, father,' Simon wanted to say. 'We will not be safe.' But he waited respectfully for his father to speak.

From the street below people started calling, 'Get down! Get down! Already the flames are leaping over the Odos Egnatias.'

And Simon saw that his father was powerless. Fear dug into his heart like claws.

Above the wailing in the streets, the crashing buildings and the flaming crackle, he heard the rhythmical clicking of his father's ancient, rusty key against the small string of amber beads that warded off the evil eye. Nine years earlier, on the day Simon was born, the same key had been handed to his father, the key that had opened the front door of the Saffarty home in Spain until the Inquisition four hundred years before. The beads and the key clicked faster and faster, echoing his own heart-beat.

Below, the crowded street filled with thousands of people on bicycles, with sewing machines, with furniture, with broken mirrors. The sight of the precious sewing machines convinced Simon that the direction of the wind would not change, as his father had hoped. Somehow he had to force him off the roof. He trembled, more afraid of his father than of the fire. Then he did the unthinkable – he grabbed his father's hand and dragged him off the roof, pushing the bewildered man ahead of him.

In the narrow, snaking streets they found his mother Ruth among the frantic throng.

The heat of the great sheets of flame and wind drove everyone before it. In the rush, his father's ancient key and amber beads slipped out of his wet sweaty hands and Simon snatched them up.

At last they reached the *quartier de campagne* – the countryside – where they met other distraught relatives, and where the exhausted children could sleep safely in the open fields.

Simon rolled over onto his stomach, squeezed his eyes shut and put his hands to his ears yet, stubborn as pain, the image of his father on the roof stayed with him. The man he both feared and revered, whose fists constantly proved his strength to his son, had been as helpless as a baby. How could his own father be a coward? Simon's disappointment in him was so great that he took the shame as if it were his own. Still on his stomach, he removed his hands from his ears, flexed all his muscles and clenched his fists. His heart seemed to spread across his chest.

After a while his sense of shame turned to rage. He hated his father's weakness more than his cruelty. Well, he, Simon Saffarty was not a coward. Had he not forced his father from the roof? Only then did his brain allow his exhausted body to sleep.

The next day a small band of his older cousins was sent in search of bread, and Simon was allowed to join them. They went to an encampment of Serb soldiers, and another of French soldiers, but they had none; they were sold out. Simon felt the beginnings of real hunger, his first experience of the sensation. Of course he had known the other kind, the kind brought on by the spicy scents of cinnamon, and cloves and toasting figs.

Still it was not altogether unexpected, this hunger.

'Well,' his cousin Daniel, who was fourteen, said, 'we must try the British.'

'The British?' asked Isaac, the older cousin, scornfully. 'They will have nothing. The British are poor. Even their officers wear no medals, no braid.'

'The British have lorries,' Simon said firmly. 'They will also have bread.'

'What do *you* know, Simonico?' Isaac said, using the diminutive deliberately. 'What can a nine-year-old boy know?'

'I know that I am hungry,' Simon said swiftly. 'I saw the Saltiel family in a British lorry, with four drums of olive oil and even a sewing machine. Isaacino Saltiel was eating bread.'

'We will go to the British camp then,' Daniel said. He glanced at his young cousin, and his sad, intelligent black eyes flickered with understanding. He took the smaller boy's hand. 'Come with me, Simonico,' he said.

Under Daniel's leadership they made their way past the famous Monastir Road that had been built with stones broken by scores of Greek peasant women, to where a British brigade was stationed. There they found hundreds of fellow Salonikans who had been given sanctuary.

It was there too that they were given the soggy, tasteless white English bread.

Incomprehensibly, the precious bread was free, though the British soldiers could have charged as much as the French. At first, the boys thought the soldiers would not sell them the bread. They cast their eyes down, and silently abandoned their attempts to communicate with the soldiers in French, in Greek, in Turkish and in German. Finally, one of the soldiers laughingly called out, '*Baksheesh! Baksheesh!*'

'It is a gift,' Simon said quickly. 'Daniel, the bread is a gift!'

That the soldiers did not speak any of their languages made them strange enough. But their unmistakably friendly smiles were stranger still.

Victorious, the cousins raced homewards. As they drew nearer the smell of the dying fire burnt their nostrils. Suddenly Daniel stopped short, beside a melon-vendor. 'We were given money for bread, not for melon,' Isaac said.

'We will have both bread and melon,' Daniel answered carefully. 'Simonico is hungry. Aren't you, Simonico?'

Calmly Daniel paid, said the *bracha*, the ancient Hebrew blessing, and the boys began to eat.

Simon was no longer hungry. The moment the bread was in his hand his hunger had left him. But he chewed the sweet flesh of the melon slowly and thoughtfully. Those smiling soldiers had given them bread . . . but he knew his father would accuse him of having taken charity, like a beggar. He said, 'My father will beat me for this.'

'For eating melon?' Isaac said scornfully.

He passed his hand over his forehead. 'We took charity.'

A silence. 'Better be a servant in a heathen temple than take alms,' Daniel intoned.

'But if we do not mention the melon, we still will have spent all the money,' Simon pointed out.

'That's *clever*,' Daniel said admiringly.

'He's saving his skin, that's all,' Isaac said sharply.

Simon chose to say nothing. He knew the value of silence. He was thinking of the English officers who gave freely what they could have sold.

On the third day the fire was brought under control. By that time at least half the ancient city – where, on three consecutive sabbaths, the apostle St Paul was said to have preached in the synagogue – had been laid waste. Not even the church of St Demetrius, the patron saint of Salonika, was saved.

It was only five years since the Balkan Wars had turned the citizens of Salonika from Turks into Greeks. Some blamed the fire on the Turks, others on the Greeks.

Rumours, meanwhile, kept pace with the feverish work of putting out the fire. Salonika had always been a city of rumour, of espionage and counter-espionage. The Germans triumphantly called it their largest internment camp. It had not been necessary for them to take prisoners; almost half a million Allied troops were locked inside the city.

One rumour said that the fire had been started by a Turkish woman frying egg-plant in a narrow street. The French Commander-in-Chief of the Salonikan force, General Sarail, was cursed and blamed for having stopped all water supplies. At the same time everyone knew that the water supply and the fire-fighting equipment – three or four wooden boxes on wheels giving forth feeble jets of water – were pitifully inadequate. Yet it was also said that General Sarail had ordered dynamite to be used and the fire had thus been brought under control.

Many swore that it was thanks to the British that part of the city was saved.

They had brought up ships that sprayed water from the sea, and then driven in two red lorries, machines with pipes thousands of metres long to carry the water from the sea. This they sprayed for hours on end over the streets and the buildings, over everything that blazed.

And as they did so suddenly the wind abated. The hot Vardar wind was exhausted.

Simon's father claimed it was God who had ended the fire.

Watching the city smoulder Simon, normally a devout and religious child, listened but asked no questions. The evidence was there – had he not seen, with his own eyes, the power of the British?

On Thursday, five days after the fire had begun, Simon's father called him. 'Do you know how many people are homeless?' he demanded. *'Fifty thousand people have no homes.* But your father, Maurice Saffarty, has found lodgings for his family. Daniel's father is accepting the charity of the British camp.' He thundered, 'The Saffartys never take charity. Never forget that, boy!'

Simon shuffled his feet. Did he know about the English bread? He said, smiling, 'You found lodgings, father?'

There was no answering smile. Instead, his father was even grimmer than usual.

He was puffing on one of his interminable Turkish cigarettes and his greying moustache was edged with a yellow grime. Grey, yellow and black – the colours of the dead fish his father worked with. Mercifully, the strong Turkish cigarette blunted the smell of fish that was as permanent as a birth-mark.

He said, 'Two rooms in the house of a Turkish family. You will need to learn some Turkish to give them respect. For instance, before you enter the house, you will knock on the door and, in your loudest voice, you will call out, *"Kimse Olmasin* – whoever is there must veil herself." You are a male, and the Turkish women must conceal themselves from you. Is that clear?'

'Yes, father,' Simon said, and repeated, *'Kimse Olmasin.* Whoever is there must veil herself.'

'You learn quickly, my son.'

A compliment from a cruel father is alarming. Simon backed away, embarrassed. He could not forget those moments on the roof. His father's flattery added to his sense of shame – if it was a sin to think your own father a coward, it was a greater sin not to trust him. He said meekly, 'Thank you, father.' On impulse, he added eagerly, 'It will not be hard for me to learn Turkish.'

Turkish would be Simon's fifth language. Ladino, an ancient Castilian dialect, was his mother-tongue, French the language of his schooling, Greek the language of the streets, and Hebrew the language of his forefathers. His father, of course, spoke Turkish.

Ruth Saffarty counted her blessings as she adapted to her new surroundings.

No one in her family had been injured in the fire and, as she told Simon over and over again, 'Money wounds are not mortal.' But everything, all their possessions, had been lost. Change was better than catastrophe, she said, and the people of Salonika had grown used to change. The Balkan wars had seen to that. Simon had himself witnessed the triumphal march of the Greek army that put an end to four hundred and twenty years of Turkish rule. That, as far as Simon was concerned, was when men could wear a hat instead of a fez. Now, living with the Turkish family, Simon and his father exchanged their hats for the fez.

It grew colder now. Soon the delicious odour of *salep*, his favourite hot drink, a scalding liquid jelly flavoured with cinnamon and cloves, pervaded the entire household. At the door of the Turkish part Simon called out to the women to veil themselves, but other than that he did not speak to them.

He was a dutiful son. He asked few questions and kept his thoughts to himself.

It was a confusing time. Often Maurice Saffarty declared, 'Of what you hear believe nothing, and of what you see believe half.' And he would throw a taunting, knowing glance in his wife's direction.

Simon's father had a small interest in a wholesale fish business, but suspected that he was being cheated. So Ruth Saffarty worked even harder, slaving over their charcoal burner, constructed out of a fifty-litre petrol drum cut in half. In winter the alley ran with mud. She would add the charcoal to the cinders before carrying the brazier from the alley into their living quarters.

It was Ruth Saffarty's inspired cooking that had finally won her the acceptance of her second husband's disapproving family.

Ten years ago, at the age of nineteen, when she had been married for the second time, she had been considered a widow rather than a bride. If having no dowry was not bad enough, she was also a foreigner, an Ashkenazic Jewess from the Ukraine. Her first husband had scandalized everyone by not marrying a Sephardic Jewess; instead, he had chosen an Ashkenazi, a *Frenk*, a Westerner. It was generally believed that his sudden death from typhoid was not unrelated to his rash and reckless marriage. Dazed, grief-stricken and living with her bitter mother-in-law, Ruth would rise at dawn, trudge miles to an empty field in which dark, deeply red roses grew wild, and pick them while the dew was still on the petals. She turned them into a delicious jam. She made sesame and almond brittle, and stuffed dates with roasted almonds. News of her expertise spread through the family, and her dead husband's relatives came to test her delicacies for themselves. Her pickled peppers were pronounced unsurpassable.

She mastered Ladino, and two years later when her dead husband's cousin married her she was no longer regarded as an alien.

She was never idle. When she was not cooking and cleaning, she crocheted shawls which her new husband sold. The tall angular woman with the remote melancholy eyes was considered harmless. By the time Simon was born the following year, she had already discovered more than a few grey hairs and her foreign origins were no longer mentioned. Indeed, her shameful secret had never been divulged to Simon. Still, far from regretting her first marriage, she stubbornly and privately rejoiced in it, counting it among her blessings. Here, in this strange land she had encountered one other blessing.

There were no pogroms.

In Salonika it was said that the month of March smiles through the rain, while nature secretly prepares spring. It was in March, three years after the fire, that Simon's father found new lodgings: two rooms, a bedroom and a kitchen with a real oven. There was a hob, too, made of several charcoal fires. There, in that kitchen, damp despite the huge oven, Simon studied and slept. Under the padded quilts he pretended that he was in a safe, small room of his own. It seemed real enough; he was tall for his age and his narrow bed was almost too small for him.

And he had discovered football. He was part of a regular team, and on the muddy, vacant ground that served as a football field Simon discovered competition. There, in the mud, among other strong and fleet boys, Simon found some relief from the strict discipline and stricter gloom of school and home. Simon's eleventh birthday had come and gone, with nothing more than a grim reminder from his father that he would be a man soon, and then he would learn more about the hard struggle of living.

His grandfather's seventy-fifth birthday festivities, following so soon after his own birthday, set in train new terrors and, worse, a new premonition. For this birthday party was also a time of prayer, of giving thanks to the Almighty for having been allowed to reach such a great age. What set up a storm of terror in Simon's heart was the moment when he was compelled not only to see, but to touch the burial shroud his grandfather had bought to commemorate his seventy-five years of life.

His grandfather's corpse would be swathed in that shroud . . .

When the dreaded day finally arrived it was almost a relief. He realised at once that his grandfather was testing him, for the old man's eyes both dared and doubted him.

Simon stared at him and stared at the shroud, conscious of the silence that had suddenly fallen on the gathering. He felt his own father's mocking, commanding eyes. He heard his father's ancient key clicking against the string of amber beads.

10

Simon Saffarty was not a coward. He stroked the shroud slowly, as if it were ordinary linen and then, as though examining its quality, pinched it between his fingers.

The silence turned quickly to a murmur, and the murmur to sardonic laughter. Simon set his shoulders back squarely and said, 'A shroud has no pockets, grandfather.'

His grandfather looked at him keenly, as if committing his features to memory. 'Well said, my son. You would do well to remember that.' Then he placed his hand on Simon's head and blessed him.

At Yom Kippur, the Day of Atonement, the most holy day of the year, his grandfather wore his new shroud-coat in synagogue. Even though wearing it was customary among aged men on high holy days, it frightened Simon. The next day, to conceal his fear, he protested. 'You should have a silk shroud, grandfather.'

'Silk?' the old man questioned. 'Why silk?'

'Because it is softer than linen.' He swallowed hard, and continued. 'My grandfather deserves the best.'

'My son, in death all men are equal. An illiterate is equal to a scholar, a poor man is no different from a rich man.' He squinted into the distance. 'There is no best in death.'

'I don't want to be dead! I don't want to be equal!' Simon exploded. 'I want to be rich!'

The old man shook his head. 'A daydreamer yet.' Suddenly he grabbed Simon's wrist. 'I'm wrong. In daydreams lies also hope.' Under his breath he added, 'The more poverty the more hope.'

A week later, in accordance with Simon's premonition, his grandfather was dead.

Football, after that, became even more important. It was something of a miracle, Simon thought, the way a mere ball could make everything else vanish from his mind.

Though Simon continued to be top of his class, his father thought sport was an unprofitable way of spending time. 'You may have come first, but you could have better marks,' he grumbled. There had been no more compliments after the family had moved into their new quarters.

'I will try harder, father.'

'What can you learn from a foolish ball?'

Simon was silent.

'Speak, boy, speak. Let me hear the value of a ball — '

'A ball has no value, father. I will improve my studies.'

Yet Simon lived for football.

Winning did not count nearly as much as not losing. In another era and another place, he might well have been described as talented. He was tall, strong and agile, and had excellent ball control. He loved nothing better than deceiving his opponents dribbling or feinting past them.

And Simon had made friends with a boy on his football team, Odysseus Politis. Odysseus was two years older than him and came from another world. He had travelled; he had even been to France. The son of a grain merchant, Odysseus was rich. He had a room of his own that he called a study, and books lined his walls. What was more, his father had a real library where the works of famous French writers were to be found, and allowed Simon to make full use of it. Both Odysseus and Simon were at a French school, so they spoke nothing but French to one another – what better language in which to extol the virtues of Liberté, Egalité, Fraternité?

It was as they were discussing Zola that Odysseus suddenly said, 'We're moving to Paris, my father says. I am going to study law there in due course.'

'Paris?' Simon asked softly. The thought dazzled him. He began to prowl the rooms, and in tones of wonder said, 'I will get to Paris myself.' The possibility had never occurred to him before.

'How?'

'I'm not sure,' he said simply. 'I know only that I must!' Odysseus and Simon became firm friends, and met often. And after Paris . . . Britain? London? France was near England. People had even swum across the Channel from France to England . . .

Twice Simon stayed too long at the football ground, which meant that he was late for his Hebrew classes. He was warned that he would be punished if he was late again. Punishment was a certainty, not a risk. All the same one day Simon could not tear himself away from the game.

Even before he entered the airless classroom, with its black pock-marked desks, and its shrill, thick-lipped teacher, Monsieur Carasso, he could feel as much as hear the raw, uneasy hush that awaited him. He sighed and pushed open the door, and was making his way to his accustomed place when Monsieur Carasso shrilled, 'Ah – so Monsieur Saffarty has consented to honour us with his presence, after all.'

Simon kept silent.

'Answer me, boy! To what do I owe the honour of your appearance?'

Still Simon did not speak.

'Ah-ha!' the teacher shrilled, his thick lips wobbling with menace. 'Monsieur Saffarty is stubborn, too, I see. Fetch me my cure for stubbornness.'

Wordlessly, Simon handed him the foot-stocks, or *sepos*. Two hinged rings connected by a bar of iron locked Simon's ankles tighter than handcuffs. 'We'll see how well you kick that foolish ball now,' Monsieur Carasso said with the sly, falsetto laugh that the rest of the boys were expected to echo.

A brief, nervous titter exploded in the airless room. Simon struggled to suppress the beginnings of a scornful laugh. Better to act humiliated than to show his contempt. He had long since lost respect for his teacher, and these days had little respect for his class-mates, either.

Immobile in his foot-stocks, Simon stood in front of the class. He fixed his eye on a damp spot on the wall, and day-dreamed of Odysseus, of what Odysseus would say, of how he and Odysseus would laugh together afterwards. As if in a trance his mind seemed to float above the dank room, and the boys and the teacher in it, and his legs registered no pain. He imagined himself in Odysseus' study, saw the drawn green shutters and, beyond, the ordered loveliness of a rose garden with real roses, and paths and ferns and olive trees.

After two hours the foot-stocks were released and though Simon heard the iron clang he felt nothing, not even relief. He met Monsieur Carasso's satisfied eyes head-on and it was the teacher, not Simon, who looked away.

In bed that night Simon discovered that you could refuse to feel as you could refuse to speak.

Two days after the punishment with the foot-irons Simon's father was late for the evening meal. Simon's mother sent him to the Café Crystal, not to ask for him, she said, only to look. But neither his father nor his companions were there. When he returned home, his father was waiting for him. His mother's eye twitched in a frantic and wilder dance – an unmistakable signal of impending catastrophe.

'A laughing-stock,' his father roared. 'That's what the son of Maurice Saffarty has made his father. A laughing-stock!'

His head jerked with every syllable, as if he were trying to fling it off his neck. And his face was frighteningly, luminously pale.

'Father — ' Simon began.

'Shut up. Shut your mouth. Are you satisfied you've made me a laughing-stock? Made me look like a fool? By not telling me of your punishment, you doubled my humiliation. I had to hear about it from a stranger! From Isaac Fais!'

Simon's mother flinched, as if from a blow. Fais was more successful than her husband, and a hated competitor. The family knew these rages too well. They dreaded the ugly, loud repetitive voice that grew steadily higher until, part shriek, and part roar, it reached – and plundered – their every nerve. It made Simon's head swell.

'I'm sorry, father.'

'It's too easy to say sorry. You lied to me.'

'But I said nothing — '

'Concealing the truth is a lie.' Now his father's voice dropped ominously. Like the click of a tongue, his father's key clicked against the amber beads. 'I told that Isaac Fais, that piece of slime, that there will be no more football for my son. I forbid you to play.'

'I can't give up — '

'What's that you say? You *can't*?' his father interrupted roughly. 'Are you telling me you *can't*? Did I hear right?'

'Yes,' Simon said defiantly. 'You heard right. I'll study harder. Two more hours every day to make up for the time — '

But his father was not listening. At first he spoke in a whisper, but the whisper rose in a terrible crescendo. 'It's not enough to *humiliate* his father! It's not enough to make his father look like a fool! Now he *disobeys* his own father!'

Crazed now, perhaps by the hideous ceaseless howl of his own voice, and fairly skipping with rage, his only aim to connect with his son's flesh, Maurice Saffarty struck blindly. And even as Simon fell, lay still, and blood gushed, the terrible voice continued.

Simon's mother's ineffectual wailing turned to a shriek. 'Murderer!' she screamed. 'Murderer! You've killed him with your cursed key!'

14

His shouts turning to wails, Maurice Saffarty fell upon his son, crushing his body with the full weight of his own. His tears mingled with his son's blood. 'Simon. My son, my son, forgive me! Speak to me!'

Desperately, as if by reflex, his mother grabbed a jug and threw cold water over her husband's back. 'Leave him alone! Leave him to me!' She pressed her ear to Simon's chest. 'Thank God he's not dead,' she whispered.

Speedily wrapping Simon in her shawls, she scooped him up in her arms with the strength of desperation. The shawls did nothing to staunch the blood.

'He must go to the hospital,' she said decisively.

'The hospital?' Simon's father had never known anyone who had ever been inside a hospital. People only went there to die. 'The hospital?'

Already on her way out, she called out contemptuously, 'I will tell them it was an accident.'

At first the physical pain was agonising. His left eye, cut by the ancient rusty key, became like a new nerve-centre, as if the blow had forced his entire brain into the socket of a single eye. His cornea had been ruptured, and his eyelid had not escaped injury either. Behind the bandages that sealed both eyes the stitches in his eyelid pinched.

He lay still and silent. The minutest movement, they told him, might blind his left eye, and could harm his good eye too . . .

It would take six weeks – as long as the bandages were to be in place – before the doctors would know the result of their surgery. In the synagogue special prayers were said, and people marvelled at the dignity with which Maurice Saffarty received their sympathy. The nurses, the doctors, indeed everyone, thought Simon brave, and remarked on it. But pain had taken Simon beyond bravery, to a point where silence was safer than sound.

He lost all sense of time and space.

Three weeks after the accident a nurse told him, 'I have a package and a letter for you. Would you like me to read the letter first?'

He must not move. He hated to move his lips, even. Still, he whispered, 'Mistake — '

'No mistake,' the nurse insisted. 'It's addressed to Monsieur Simon Saffarty. I'll read it to you.'

She tore open the envelope, and the sound rasped his eye.

'Ah, it's written in French. I can't read it.' Her voice lifted. 'Shall I tell you who sent it?'

Simon nodded.

'Odysseus,' the nurse said. 'Odysseus sent it.' She began opening the package. 'It looks like it's a piece of material – red and blue cotton.' A moment later the nurse spread it out. 'It's the French flag,' she said, astonished. 'What a strange gift.'

'It's a joke,' Simon whispered.

The nurse left and soon returned with one of her colleagues who could speak French.

She read aloud.

Dear Friend,

I hope by now that you are recovered enough to receive this message of good wishes. Fear gripped my heart and sadness filled my soul when the news of the danger to your eyes reached me. Today I took myself to the hospital, but was told visitors were not permitted.

Be of good courage, my friend.

This small gift is a glorious reminder of the future, as well as a symbol of hope.

May you have the strength to equal your courage.

Your devoted friend,
Odysseus Politis

'You have a fine friend, Simon.' The nurse added, 'You are lucky.'

Simon did not answer. A dry, panting wheeze escaped his lips.

'What is it, Simon? What is it?'

'I am afraid of the tears,' Simon whispered. 'Tears might cause movement.'

A sudden surge of faith filled him with an overpowering joy, and his silent prayer of thanks was made through smiling lips.

Now Simon's darkness was alive with Odysseus, with his garden of real roses and olive trees. He thought of Odysseus' cool study, of the green shutters, of the books against the walls.

Once, Odysseus had shown him a *zarf*, a minute coffee cup in an ornamental filigree holder encrusted with white bright glass, which he said were real jewels, real diamonds. A gift to his father, he said. Odysseus was magic, and his home was a magic dream, as magical as Paris.

'That letter must have done you good,' the nurse said, two days later. 'The fever has gone down.'

At last the bandages were removed and though his left eye now squinted and the vision was poor, he could see.

He was not blind . . . He would not be blind . . .

The doctor concluded his examination by saying, 'My son, I have bad news for you.'

'Bad news?' Simon echoed.

'Bad news. No football ever again. Another injury could be fatal to that eye. It could blind it.'

'No football,' Simon repeated. 'Is that *all*? No football. Oh, how — ' Simon hesitated, searching for the right words, 'how – *trivial*,' he said, triumphantly.

'You are wise beyond your years,' the doctor said sharply. 'How did the accident happen? You never told me.'

'I can't remember. I'm sorry, doctor, I can't remember what happened.'

A few paces away from the bed the doctor called out, 'You have a bright future, my boy. You use your memory well!'

A little later, when all was quiet, he nervously looked at himself in the mirror. His eye tilted toward a distant direction; he could neither tell what it focused on, nor what it saw. Better a crooked eye than no eye, he told himself fiercely.

So this was his father's legacy to him – an eye that looked like a spy.

When Simon returned from the hospital, he found his mother much changed. The key to *la casa vieja* was locked away in a bank vault and the ominous click against the amber beads was silenced for ever. She did not flinch when Maurice Saffarty spoke. Her sad brown eyes were even more remote, but her cowering, shuffling walk had given way to a brave new stride, and her jaw tilted defiantly.

Proudly Simon showed her the French flag. 'I'll get to France one day,' he said fiercely.

'Of course you will, my son, my soul.'

'You think so?' he asked. 'What makes you so sure?'

Her answer was immediate. 'You have a strong will, my son, a

17

mighty will.' She leaned forward and with a graceful sweep of her hand, unusual to both, caressed his cheek. 'You are not yet thirteen, and already you are taller than a grown man. And no matter how strong, your body is only made of flesh and blood. But your will is made of flint!'

His hand flew to his eye. 'What can my will do for *this*?'

'With time, you will conquer that too,' she said. 'A man's will is his destiny.'

Though it was not uncommon for mothers to address their sons as 'my son, my soul', Ruth meant it every time she said it. Truly, Simon was her son, her soul, her life. Yet she had secluded herself from him, deliberately fashioning an invisible barrier between them; she was constantly on guard, weighing every word on the scales of her passion to protect him from her secret alien past. Why should he judge himself – and be judged – an oddity, a stranger, a mongrel, just because her different origins were held to be inferior?

There were no pogroms in France, either.

She was proud of his voracious reading. He could learn far more from books than from his mother, so why bother him with the chatter of a mindless woman? Though there had been a time when – just as greedily – she had read the works of Shalom Aleichem and Peretz herself.

They did not talk often; such conversation as there was, at meals, was governed by her frequently angry husband. But just as Simon had begun to speak far earlier than most other children, so had he talked about different things, and different countries like England and France. Sometimes she half thought that deep in his heart he knew he was different, and was tempted to reveal the truth of herself to him.

But two things stopped her. The first was obvious – his damaged eye.

Her second reason was based more on superstition: for as long as she could remember, her son had been abnormally wise for his years. It was not just a simple matter of walking, talking and counting ahead of his time.

Some months after the terrible fire Simon came to show her his cousin Daniel's bicycle's punctured tube which he had patched

18

successfully. 'Look at this tube,' he said in a low, pensive tone. 'I've fixed it, and it works the same as if it were new. But it is *not* the same. It has changed, like I have changed since the fire. I look the same, but I will never be the same again.'

It was a small thing but it told her that he was special. And because he was special, a terrible payment would be exacted. May the payment come only from her! It was safer not to think about such things.

She had done the washing and would set about pickling peppers. She said out loud, 'May God preserve him.'

The bitter satisfaction Simon took in his father's chastened behaviour was quickly overtaken by the news that the Politis family had left Salonika. Their departure had been too hurried for a single farewell – the grain business had failed, gone bankrupt. And it was whispered that Odysseus' father was, in truth, a Turkish spy, or perhaps a German agent, that the grain business was merely a front . . .

Simon missed Odysseus. All along he had sensed something unsettling in their friendship. Odysseus had given him a warm and comfortable feeling; in his dreamy eyes there was a certain, cosy intimacy. But Odysseus had also awoken him to another world – a world of cosmopolitan sophistication, of fine possessions, of other cultures: the world of his schoolbooks brought to life. And a world where wealth made all things possible, a world far removed from the bleak, austere poverty all around him in Salonika.

At least Odysseus would not see his crooked eye.

Simon grew more and more withdrawn – not sullen, only sad. He felt an inner chill that nothing could warm. By this time it was winter, and every afternoon, when he returned from school, *salep*, his favourite hot drink, awaited him. Every afternoon his mother watched and hovered over him. He had grown used to her watchfulness.

One day she said sharply, 'You are shivering with loneliness.'

Unused to her sharp tone, Simon put his cup down. 'What?' he said.

'You heard me. I said you are shivering with loneliness. You miss your friend Odysseus Politis.'

'You don't know him,' Simon said bitingly. 'You never met him.'

She put aside the copper pitcher she was polishing with powdered brick, and fidgeted with the folds of her long skirt. Her face twitched.

19

Simon looked at her impatiently. She said, 'The Politis family have moved to Syria. Here, this is their address.' She handed him a scrap of brown paper.

'A good friend is like a brother,' she continued slowly, 'but self-pity is as dangerous as quicksand. You may be lonely, but you are not alone.'

Simon made no answer, but she saw hope in his expression.

Of course, now that he had Odysseus' address he felt more secure, almost happy. Still, he delayed writing and when finally he composed a letter he had no expectation of a reply.

Soon he was thirteen, and ready for his *barmitzvah*. It was almost a year since he had been compelled to renounce football and, with it, his childhood.

In spite of his crooked eye he seemed at ease with himself, and at one with his God. The glory of the moment radiated from him, and his cheeks glowed. He stood tall, straight-backed and unafraid, and if at first sight his height made him look more like a young man than a fledgling teenager, a touchingly boyish vitality betrayed his true age. He handled his new prayer shawl proudly, and with authority.

'The boy excelled himself,' Monsieur Carasso, his hated Hebrew teacher, pronounced over and over again. 'I always knew he had it in him.'

'He's a fine-looking boy too,' someone said.

Monsieur Carasso nodded, but asked his wife yet again, 'How is it that a boy with a crooked eye can still be attractive?'

After the service they crowded round Simon and shook his hand, and though he towered over most of them, they could not but respond to his strong grip, and his warm smile. 'He's got something, that Simon Saffarty,' one murmured to another.

'He will do great things with his life,' his mother said later.

'When I was his age I was earning my own bread,' his father grumbled.

Simon turned his crooked gaze on his father and said nothing.

Odysseus did not answer Simon's letter. Sometimes Simon looked in on the Politis garden. Overgrown and wild, it reminded him of himself – wild with unthinkable longings, his body overgrown with hair. He had not yet found the brother his mother had spoken of, but was not without companionship, so it mattered less.

Besides, he had begun to make money. He had become an unofficial tutor, with a simple but efficient fee system. He charged a small fee for explaining mathematical problems, but the writing of essays took longer and Simon charged accordingly. Already he understood that the best way to learn is to teach . . . In any case, Simon could not get enough of French literature. He found the works of Racine, Victor Hugo and Molière almost unbearably moving.

For two years Simon brooded. Tall for his age, and growing out of his adolescent awkwardnesses, he walked the streets of Salonika like an animal in a cage. His hunched figure became a familiar sight to the longshoremen at the port, sitting shaped like a question mark on a bollard at twilight, staring out to sea.

The houses seemed to block him in. Slouching to school, or home again, he would kick the cobbles as if urging them out of his way.

It wasn't just his height that made other people small. Their chatter, their absorptions, their daily tasks, their ambitions – it was all small. The whole place was small. Was this for what he had been born?

He had to get out.

The spark that set Simon's smouldering on fire was the news that Aaron Touro – illiterate Aaron Touro, who couldn't speak a word of French – was being sent to Paris to join his brother Samuel, who worked there as a typographer.

Aaron Touro! The injustice! Simply because he was two years older, and his father Jacob had the money . . . Aaron didn't even *want* to go; his father wanted to be rid of the snivelling wretch.

Enraged, Simon ran all the way home from school and told his mother that he too was leaving.

'You – the only son – the only child – you would leave us!'

Simon flushed. He knew that what he wanted was a betrayal of sorts. To leave the family home for a distant city in a different country was no less of a sin, and almost as unthinkable, as beating his own mother. But he had a trump card, and he played it now. He said, 'The Greeks are forcing young boys into their army — '

'They won't want you. Not you.'

'Why not?'

'The accident. Your eye.'

'They'll put me in an office, then. I'll get killed in that army. You'll see. You'll be sorry.'

'Don't talk like that. You'll tempt the evil eye — '

'But you *told* me I would get to Paris,' he said puzzled.

'I must have tempted the evil eye,' she wailed. 'I meant you would travel there in ten or twenty years — '

'Aaron Touro is an ignorant fool, but he's seventeen, two years older than me. I've decided to travel with him.'

'*You've* decided?'

'Yes, I, Simon Saffarty, have decided. I will travel to Paris with him. There's a famous commercial school in Paris. I could learn about business.'

'Who will pay?'

'I don't know who will pay.' Suddenly, Simon began to weep, an avalanche of stored heartbreak that he could not stop. This perfect opportunity – travelling with Aaron Touro – had come to him, yet he would be condemned for ever to stay in Salonika, to work with his father, and stink, like his father, of fish. It was too much. Between sobs, he wailed, 'I want a better life . . . a better life . . . '

Like countless mothers before her, his mother would have done anything to put an end not only to his sorrow but to its source. She said, 'I will speak to your father. I will say I have given you my blessing. Drink this. You will need to be strong for your journey — '

They both knew, though neither of them said so, that Simon's crooked eye had won her the right to speak for him.

But for Maurice Saffarty, the shame of having his son leave his family for a distant country was as great as his shame over Simon's eye. He flatly refused, and then, to put an end to the argument, said, 'You don't know a living soul in Paris.'

'I know Samuel Touro.'

'You have never even met him.'

'It makes no difference. He is going to meet his brother Aaron at the station in Paris. He will meet me, too — '

Back and forth the argument went, back and forth, like a football. Agitation made his father sweat. The reek of fish strengthened, and with it Simon's determination.

'I will be studying how to be a businessman,' he said. 'How to construct a balance between profits and losses. How many times have you warned me about debt?'

'You will get me into debt, Simon. The fare alone is twice more than I can afford.'

He knew of only one way to defeat his father, and that was to find a cheaper fare. When, after a secret and thorough investigation, he presented his findings to his bewildered father, and to the incredulous Touros, he had cut the costs of their journey by more than sixty per cent.

'The money,' he told them gravely, 'is better in our pockets than in the pockets of the shipping company.'

It was logical enough for everyone to have assumed that it was cheaper to sail directly from their own port of Salonika, than to travel to Piraeus from their own front door. And yet, if they went by train to Athens, they would board a small steamer at Piraeus, and after five days at sea they would be in Marseilles. They would then take the train to Paris where Aaron's brother Samuel Touro would be waiting to welcome them.

'Because,' Simon explained, 'if you don't buy your ticket in advance, you pay much, much less.'

'How much less?'

'Sixty per cent!'

Of course, he had been warned that the ticket might not be available, but of this he made no mention. He merely weighed the risk, and it was with this risk that his career began. But so that everyone, and for that matter he himself, would believe there was no risk at all, he gave a definite departure date. They would sail for France on April 15th, 1923.

Meanwhile – so that Simon would never dishonour the family name – Maurice Saffarty set about immersing his son in the history of his family. He took him to what was left of the ancient gates of the city of Salonika, and reminded him that more than four hundred years ago it was a Saffarty who had persuaded the Sultan to give asylum to the Jews who were fleeing the tortures of the Spanish Inquisition.

They stopped beside a well and silently watched the young women drawing water into their goatskin buckets. Maurice Saffarty sighed heavily. Then, speaking in an unusually low voice, he began, 'You are going to a strange and distant land, my son. You will meet other Jews from other lands. They are not Sephardic Jews like us; they are called Ashkenazim, and they are from Europe. They are not proud as we are proud. For their ancestors did not serve as physicians and philosophers to kings as ours did. They do not speak Ladino, but another language.'

'Jews who do not speak Ladino?' Simon said, incredulous. 'What language do they speak? Have you heard it?'

'Their language is called Yiddish,' Simon's father said slowly. 'I have seldom heard it.'

He paused to light yet another cigarette. Perhaps this was the moment to tell Simon that his knowledge of the cossacks and the pogroms had come from the lips of Simon's own Ashkenazic mother, who had been born in the Ukraine. He thought better of it, and said only, 'Some of them come from Russia where, even now in 1923, it is a disgrace to be a Jew.' He stood up. 'But you, Simon, you are a Saffarty! You belong to the Jewish nobility!'

And, as his father spoke, Simon half thought that he was asking forgiveness for the accident. His heart longed to pretend respect, and to kiss his father's hand, but his head knew that to do so would have dishonoured not only his father's name, but his father himself.

His father was a failure.

Besides, always, always, that relentless stink of dead fish . . .

When the time came for Simon to leave, his mother did not go to Salonika station. 'I will take leave of my only son here, in the shrine of his own home,' she said, speaking quietly, and with great dignity. 'If I am never to see him again, it will not be in a public place that I last saw my son, my soul.'

She made sure that his French flag, and his French–English phrase manual, were included among his possessions.

The journey from his home to the station was a blur of excitement and sadness and fear. He wished he could have afforded to have taken an Italian steamer from Salonika. He wished he could have seen once more the stately White Tower, the red saddle roofs, and the needle minarets. He wished all that because he knew his mother was less fearful of the port than of the station. She had never ventured as far as the station. She would have accompanied him to the port.

Moments before he and Aaron boarded the train, his father gave a massive sigh and handed him his precious key. 'I may never see you again,' he said brokenly. He tried and failed to meet his son's crooked eye. As the train pulled away, he called out, 'Don't sell yourself, my son. If a boss thinks you are good enough for him, you'll know you are better off working for yourself.'

At last, but too late, though for the first time, Simon and his father were in absolute agreement.

Part Two

2

As soon as the train left the station Aaron began to set up a thin, watery wail. The carriage window was open and through the smoke a piece of grit had blown into his eye. Rubbing his eye frantically, Aaron kept repeating, 'Burned alive! I'll be burned alive!' Then the rhythm of his wails met the rhythm of the train, and presently he fell asleep.

Simon looked at him with contempt. Aaron was seventeen years old, a grown man, and yet here he was crying over a piece of grit. There was a saying, 'The cinder falls in the eye of the cross-eyed one,' but who, after all, was the one with the crooked eye? He studied the ancient key his father had passed into his custodianship. Now he knew why his mother had enlarged his trouser pockets.

When Aaron awoke Simon said at once, 'I saw how your pretty cousin, Sarica, was looking at you at the station. You're a lucky man!'

'How did she look?' Aaron flushed and his hard, red pimples glistened. 'What did you see?'

'She looked at you with great love in her eyes. She's got her eye on you, anyone could tell!'

'Nonsense. You talk like a child.'

'She's got a grand figure, your cousin Sarica,' Simon went on, etching the air with his hands. 'Yes, she's got a nice soft body, your cousin — '

'Yes,' Aaron said. 'Her figure — '

'She didn't kiss you like a cousin when she said goodbye, either,' Simon said slyly.

'How did my cousin kiss me?' Aaron asked, intrigued. 'Tell me.'

'Like a bride. Your cousin kissed you like a bride.'

Marriages between cousins were far from uncommon. Aaron leaned back and closed his eyes.

If he could keep Aaron happy until they boarded the steamer, Simon thought. Just until then, at least . . .

They chatted about Sarica's sisters, who were not as pretty as she, and the time passed, and with it Simon's fears.

At Piraeus Simon took over. He left Aaron in charge of the luggage while he bought their tickets. There would be no food on board, nor any sleeping accommodation. They would sleep on deck. So Simon dipped into his private fund earned from the tutoring, and bought bread and cheese and, of course, olives.

When the boat finally cast off Simon had no last lingering glances for his homeland, but stood in the bows staring out at the wide expanse of sea stretching ahead.

It was cold on the deck at night, and crowded; so many people, and so much seasickness. Aaron suffered for two days and two nights, groaning, unable to eat or drink. Simon, in search of water for himself, stumbled over a pair of grinning dentures that someone had removed in order to be sick. For a moment he was horrified; they were a macabre sight. Then he overheard a woman saying, 'Who would have guessed Maritt had false teeth? I'll never let her forget this – never!'

He began to laugh then, at first nervously, but suddenly those mouthless, grinning teeth were inexplicably funny, and his laughter deepened and spread, until it took control of his entire body and he laughed and laughed, and the tension of the journey slipped away.

He did his best for Aaron, holding his head, and covering his thin shaking shoulders with his own homespun blanket. He made friends with the fatherly cook, and when Aaron was well enough to take a hot drink Simon brought him a brew of honey and hot lemon. Aaron survived; Simon rejoiced in the salty freshness of the open deck, dipping into his French–English manual.

Early on Thursday morning they docked at Marseilles. Here there were confusion and customs, and an unfamiliar and at first unintelligible French. Why was the Marseilles accent so remote from the pure pronunciation of his schooling? Aaron was bewildered and tearful again; there were too many trains; would they find the right one? Yes, this must be right: 'See, Aaron, Paris, written up there?'

Now Aaron hesitated. No, he insisted stubbornly, it was the wrong train. No – nothing would make him get on the wrong train.

There was no alternative; Simon snatched Aaron's bag and flung it on the train. Then he grabbed Aaron like another piece of luggage and threw him in, too, following just as the train pulled out.

After a while Aaron said, 'I'm sorry, Simonico.'

Simon stayed silent.

'Simonico?' Aaron said nervously. 'I said I was sorry.'

'Be a man,' Simon replied angrily. 'Behave like a man.' His voice rose. 'And don't you ever call me Simonico again!'

'What must I call you – Simon?'

'No. You will call me Saffarty. That is what you will call me – Saffarty.'

He took out the huge rusty key, and stared at it for the thousandth time. This key had almost blinded him. Now it would bring him good luck. It was his lucky talisman, to be protected, if necessary, with his own life.

The Paris station, the Gare de Lyons, was large, beyond Simon's wildest imaginings. Large as an ocean is large, with waves made of rushing, crushing people.

How would Samuel find them? For the first time Simon felt lost and afraid. Suddenly he heard a shout, 'Aaron, Aaron,' and then that familiar trusted chattering of Ladino. Simon stared at the tall young man with a beret who talked and gestured with tears and laughter. He liked the beret, and decided at once that he must have one too.

'So this is young Simonico,' Samuel said, kissing Simon's cheeks. 'Simonico the bargain-finder, huh?'

'You must call him Saffarty,' Aaron said, mockingly. 'He ordered me to call him Saffarty.'

'Is that so?' Samuel grinned. 'Why? Why Saffarty?'

'Because Saffarty is my name.'

And yet he was not sure why – or even how – the idea had come to him. Perhaps he had sensed that at the beginning of his life, he should start as a man, and be called the way a man is called. He went on, 'I am a stranger here. Other than you and Aaron I know no one in France. My name is my only family!'

Samuel crushed his hand in his. 'Very well, Saffarty,' he said. 'Saffarty it shall be.'

They went at once to Samuel's rented room in Montmartre. Saffarty would share with the brothers for two nights; it would give him time to find a place of his own. The room was small but adequate. He could touch the low-slung ceiling without stretching.

Samuel was proud of the heating in the room, and prouder still of the Namias family who owned the apartment; Monsieur Namias was a concierge at one of the largest banks.

'And now, Saffarty,' Samuel boomed. 'We must eat. They're expecting us at the Café Rouge. They know all about my brother!'

Again, they made their way through the crowds of Montmartre. Saffarty wanted to stop and listen to the accordionist, but Samuel urged him on. 'I can't wait for you two to see the Café Rouge. It's the best value in Paris! And they know me there.'

It was a small restaurant, misty with smoke and alive with talk. The busy waiters wore long white aprons and each table was covered in a clean white cloth. Saffarty had never eaten in a restaurant in his life. Dazed, he sat down at the table and as he fingered and stroked the white linen he remembered his grandfather's burial shroud. He barely heard the waiter's welcome.

'It must be expensive,' he said, still dazed, almost talking to himself. 'Isn't it too expensive for us? I mean, too expensive for me? Well, perhaps, a treat tonight. But after tonight — '

A waiter brought them a carafe of red wine. Saffarty stared, hypnotized, as Samuel poured it into three glasses. A restaurant was already too much, but now, on top of that . . . wine? Well, he would brave it out. He'd eat nothing tomorrow, and perhaps even the next day.

'It's all included, Saffarty,' Samuel said, laughing. 'A glass of wine, and a four-course meal for three francs twenty-five centimes. It's the best value in Paris!' He lowered his voice. 'And if you're clever listen to me – you'll buy yourself a book of thirty tickets for ninety-five francs.'

'But that's a saving of seventy-two francs and fifty centimes.'

'Is your mind an adding machine, eh, Saffarty? Come, drink.'

A steaming bowl of soup, smelling strongly of leek, was set in front of him and suddenly Saffarty knew how hungry he had been. As he raised the spoon to his lips his fingers trembled embarrassingly. After the soup came a fried and unidentifiable fish. Simon and Aaron ate with the steady concentration of the famished. By the time their plates of *boeuf bourguignon* had arrived the hunger had gone, and they ate from choice, and not from need.

Here he was, thought Saffarty, drinking wine for the first time, eating in a restaurant for the first time, in Paris for the first time. A delicious freedom seeped through him; it all felt so right. He sat back in his chair. He had taken the *right* decision to come to Paris – and he could afford that book of thirty tickets for thirty meals. He listened to the laughter – for so long the sound of others' laughter had hurt him. He listened, now, and smiled.

At that moment Aaron said, 'Of course, the food we are eating is kosher — '

Samuel broke into a mocking, coughing laugh. 'You'll starve if you want to eat kosher food in Paris!' he said bitterly.

Saffarty was thunderstruck. Aaron's over-wrought eyes bored deep into his brother, who looked stricken; if he had been eating a living animal it could not have been more terrible.

Aaron said, hopelessly, 'But you couldn't have let me eat *trayf*! Not *trayf* – not *that*! My own brother could not have done that to me.'

'Of course it's not kosher here,' Samuel hissed. He said again, 'If you want to eat kosher food you'll starve!'

Saffarty laid down his fork. His hands went cold. At any moment he expected a terrible punishment, like being blinded. His insides felt bruised. Worse still, the food in his stomach began to rise upwards. The possibility of breaking the law by not eating kosher food had not as much as crossed his mind. Here he was, congratulating himself on being in the right place, at the right time, because of the right decision. And now suddenly . . .

Aaron covered his mouth with his hands. He said, 'I'm going to vomit! Get me out, get me out!'

The brothers rushed to the lavatory.

Saffarty remained seated. The sauce congealed on his plate. His belly felt heavy and sore, but the food stayed where it was. Through his pocket his fingers caressed the iron key. Self-loathing mingled with remorse. Hardly had he left Salonika than he had betrayed his father, his mother, his people and his name. *If you want to eat kosher in Paris, you'll starve!* Better to starve, then. Better, even, to return to Salonika . . . His great iron key, the key that was the living testimony to his forefathers who had survived the Inquisition, was like a dagger in his hand. He plunged it into his palm, but felt no pain.

There was no doubt in his mind that if he had broken his faith he no longer deserved to be a Jew.

The Touro brothers returned to the table. 'We're leaving,' Samuel said shortly. 'We're going back to my lodgings.' He jerked his head backward. 'Coming?' he said.

'But . . . shouldn't we pay?' Saffarty asked.

'I gave them three tickets yesterday,' Samuel said harshly, 'and this is how my snivelling idiot of a brother accepts my generosity!'

They walked, or rather marched, back to Aaron's room. No one spoke.

The chill among the three of them made Saffarty grateful for the warmth of the small room. Then he noticed that the walls were covered in orange roses. 'Walls of roses,' he said, awed. 'I've never seen anything like this before.'

'It's nothing,' Samuel said impatiently. 'It's only paper. You get wallpaper everywhere.' He began to gesticulate wildly. 'Never mind about the roses. This is a clean room, and warm in winter, and cheap. My brother doesn't know how lucky he is. Either he's a coward or he's an idiot.' His voice rose higher. 'He wants to go back to Salonika *tomorrow*!'

'Tomorrow?' Saffarty repeated, bewildered. 'Aaron wants to go back to Salonika tomorrow?'

'I will not eat *trayf*,' Aaron said.

'Well then, you can live on bread and cheese and olives,' Saffarty said quickly.

'Where's the lavatory?' Aaron said miserably. 'I'm sick.'

Left alone, Saffarty traced the outline of a large, full-blown rose. He had half a mind to travel back with Aaron, but the fat rose tempted him with how much else there was to see. And do. And be.

If he went back, and gave up, he would never leave Salonika again. He would stink of dead fish, like his father . . . Guilt washed over him again. True, he had sinned and worse, he would sin again. His skin prickled and his forehead was clammy. He opened the small window and the chill spring air rushed in. The ugly, rasping sound of Aaron retching carried upward.

He put his hands to his ears but could not stifle the inner clamour. He had sinned and would sin again. *He did not deserve to be a Jew.* Everything he had learned, and was, swayed in the confusion of his emotion and tottered under the force of his will. He would continue to eat non-kosher food. He would choose to sin again and again. Therefore there was no hope of atonement. But his own punishment would be secret, just and complete. He no longer deserved to be a Jew. Surely, if he made such a sacrifice, if he surrendered his Jewish soul, God would forgive him? He, of course, would never forgive himself, but he could no more bring himself to give up Paris than give up the key to his heritage.

He was only fifteen, he reminded himself; he was at the start of his life. But he knew himself well enough to know that once his mind was made up, there would be no turning back.

The risks were beyond calculation. They were as unknown, as unreal, as the life that lay in front of him. What had he to lose? How much had he not to gain?

He would cease to be a Jew . . .

With this spiritual decision Saffarty took charge of his destiny and laid the foundations of his career.

Samuel argued and wrangled, Aaron whimpered and snivelled, and the night passed sleeplessly. Samuel made several unsuccessful attempts to draw Saffarty into the quarrel, but he sat with his back to the wall and affected an exhausted sleep. Early in the morning Samuel left them to see Monsieur Namias, their landlord. As soon as his brother left Aaron fell into a deep sleep.

Saffarty waited anxiously; Samuel seemed to spend an eternity with the concierge.

When Samuel returned, he slammed the door loudly and said, 'Wake up, you two, wake up!'

Saffarty made as if he were only just beginning to stir, and Samuel, now obviously beside himself with anger, delivered several sharp prods to his shin.

Saffarty scrambled to his feet. 'What's going on?' he said. He rubbed his shin.

'I'm taking this wretched coward of a brother back to Marseilles myself. Then I'm going away – on business. Monsieur Namias has agreed to let you have my room while I'm away.'

'A thousand thanks.'

'You will have to pay the rent, of course – the same as I pay. Seventy-five francs.'

'Of course,' Saffarty said, he hoped, smoothly. Seventy-five francs – exactly twice as much as he had budgeted . . . Still, if he bought a book of restaurant tickets and had only one meal a day, he would buy the time to find a cheaper place. So far as he could see, his funds would last for two months. Then he would find a job. There was no alternative. He added quickly, 'I suppose I pay the rent directly to Monsieur Namias?'

Samuel whistled. 'You're sharp,' he said. 'Too sharp. With that eye of yours, who knows what you are thinking? Yes, give the money to Monsieur Namias, if you like.'

Saffarty could have sworn there was a hidden profit for Samuel in that rent; as much, if not more, than fifty francs? What could he do? Perhaps he could delay paying until tomorrow and find a cheaper place to stay?

'Go and pay Monsieur Namias, now. Before he goes to work!'

Samuel had got the better of him now but one day he, Saffarty, would even the score.

After the brothers had left for the station, and Monsieur Namias had been paid, Saffarty unlocked his suitcase so that he could put his sleepless night's plan into action. He located the velvet bag with his *tallit*, the prayer shawl, almost at once. It was packed beside the French flag Odysseus had given him. He unfolded the *tallit* and laid it across his bed like a blanket. The black bands edging each side of the shawl symbolised mourning for the destruction of the Temple nineteen hundred years earlier. He stared at it for a long while, and then with a great sigh gathered it up, and draped it over his shoulders. Then he took a deep breath, removed it, and crumpled it in his fists. He flung himself over the bed and he wept into the shawl. Gradually his weeping tailed off into a whimper.

His tears were for what he had done, and for what he was about to do.

Presently he grew calmer. 'I will do it now,' he said to himself. 'I will get it over with.'

He stuffed the prayer shawl back into its velvet bag, and then made his way downstairs and outside to the lavatory. It burned quickly on the tiles in a very short while. He waited until every trace of it had been flushed down the lavatory.

Then he returned to the room, lay down and fell into an exhausted sleep. Two hours later he awoke, lay back and surveyed the room, astonished to find that in spite of his drastic action he was still fascinated by his new environment.

It was shabby but cosy. The wardrobe still contained a few of Samuel's belongings, but there was room enough for Saffarty's things. It came to him, as he stared at the orange roses, that he really was altogether alone in Paris, unless he counted Monsieur Namias. Perhaps, if he talked to Madame Namias, perhaps she could tell him how to find his way to the Ecole Inter-Commercial, the commercial school? In Salonika, few of the streets were named, and still fewer houses were numbered. It did not occur to him that there might be a street map. He remembered the jars of rose jam that his mother had made for him before he left. He was to have presented them to Samuel – now, perhaps he could give them to Madame Namias?

He jumped off the bed, and went to inspect himself in the cracked mirror inside the wardrobe. He needed a shave and was, in any case, obliged to ask Madame Namias where he could do so. He changed his shirt and, carefully carrying three jars, went in search of her.

The Namiases' apartment consisted of four rooms over a dress shop. Besides Samuel's cubicle, there were two other bedrooms and a kitchen. A steel staircase had been attached to one of the exterior walls so that you could gain access to the flat without having to go through the shop.

Saffarty made his way through the dimly lit rooms by following his nose to the kitchen. Madame Namias was seated at the kitchen table, smoking a cigarette! A woman smoking! It made him draw his breath. He approached her timidly, saying 'I hope I am not disturbing you, madame. I have a gift of rose jam — '

'*Maash*' *Allah!* May God preserve you,' Madame Namias said, breaking immediately into Ladino. 'How kind! How kind!' She rose at once, and began busying herself at the stove. 'Sit down. We will have coffee together. Only this morning, mind; breakfast is not included in the rent.'

He sat down and let her chatter warm him. She was a slim woman, and moved quickly. She wore a dark green overall, and over that a heavily floral apron. He was aware of her keen, obviously appraising eyes.

A corner of the kitchen was curtained off for the shower and handbasin. He could take a shower once a week, on a Thursday morning, at seven o'clock, Madame Namias told him. Shaving? Had he not seen the bowl and jug in his room? He must fill the jug the night before.

'Oh,' he said, disappointed. 'It's Friday. I miss the shower by one day.'

'Well then, after that long journey, you may use the shower today. But just this once, do you understand?' She stopped, and looked more closely at him. 'What happened to your eye?' she said.

'An accident,' he said shortly.

'Oh, you poor one. Tonight you will join us for the Sabbath meal. Now, you want to know how to reach the Rue Pigier. Here, we'll have a look at the street map.' Madame Namias moved away. She laid a map on the table.

'A *street* map?' Saffarty said.

'Here in Paris all the streets have names All the buildings have numbers. What's your name, boy? I've forgotten it already.'

'Saffarty.'

'Not your family name. Your first name.'

'Everyone calls me Saffarty. I prefer it.'

'I see,' she said, looking at him shrewdly. 'Well then, Saffarty, see if you can read this map.'

Saffarty found the first shower of his life was also his first openly sensual moment. Until then all his bathing had been in the Turkish baths – all pungent chemicals and public exposure. Now, his flesh tingled and breathed. Afterwards he took the map Madame Namias had given him and went in search of the Ecole Inter-Commercial.

He discovered the Metro.

Trains, in tunnels under the earth, moving as smoothly and as easily as fish. He watched the people, small children travelling alone, and he inhaled the strong comforting Gauloise smoke, and, there, riding in those tunnels, like veins under the earth, he felt he was at the earth's centre, deep inside the heart of the world. He felt clean, in spite of his new secret, and even though he was undoubtedly beneath the earth he felt astonishingly safe.

That night, he joined the Namiases at their Sabbath meal, made the correct traditional responses, and his new sin did not explode his heart.

Instead he felt it strengthen.

On Monday he enrolled at the Ecole Inter-Commercial, paid his fees and began classes at once. He studied book-keeping, correspondence and shorthand. He thought shorthand no less miraculous than the Metro, another of those incredible Western inventions. He told himself to start thinking of himself as a Westerner. At school in Salonika all his instruction had been in French, and his tongue rapidly adjusted to the Parisian accent. Languages came as easily to Saffarty as arithmetic.

3

The rose jam had been his initiation into the art of bribery – it had bought him not only an extra bath, but an extra meal. Even so, two weeks later, Madame Namias' invitation to join them again at their Sabbath meal came as a surprise.

A further surprise awaited him. The Namiases had a visitor, a house-guest. Their niece, Judith, who lived in Marseilles, and who was a professional photographer, had arrived to spend a month in Paris. A professional photographer would have been stunning enough – but a *woman* professional photographer! How clever he had been to leave Salonika!

All through the meal he studied Judith, and made no attempt to conceal his appreciation of her. Everything about her pleased and amazed him, and he was glad that she spoke Ladino, for her harsh Marseilles accent might have spoilt everything.

He warmed to her quick, ready laugh that jiggled her full breasts, her rapid chatter, and the way she tilted her head to listen when he spoke. She knew Paris well, as well as she knew her own bed, she said, and was more than ready to be his guide. Her hands were large and workmanlike, and moved as she talked, and the heavy gold bangles above each wrist caught the shimmer of the Sabbath candles. He had seen hands like hers before; they reminded him of someone, though who he could not say. The talk turned to the advantages of shorthand; he said it was a machine in its own right, and his enthusiastic and convincing arguments persuaded her to pay him what he saw as the greatest compliment of his life.

'You've taught me something,' she said with her quick laugh. 'I will learn shorthand. Who knows, I might even become a real journalist?' She laughed again, even more heartily, and again her breasts jiggled.

Saffarty felt a heaviness in his loins, a brief stirring, and then an eruption into an erection. He crossed his legs. Did she know what was happening to him? He was sure she knew about her jiggling breasts, though – they didn't jiggle quite so markedly when she laughed with the others. She was taunting him, making fun of him. He had seen through her, and he was glad. She was mocking him, really, mocking his crossed eye. His erection subsided. He uncrossed his legs, and withdrew into an offended silence. Judith made several attempts to draw him out, but he refused to offer anything more than an excessively polite response.

Saffarty waited for the meal to end, and as soon as he was satisfied that the coffee cups had cooled he made his extravagant thanks and left.

Once in his room he undressed quickly and crawled between the sheets. He hated her; she had attacked his pride, and his manhood, and his sexual ignorance. Meanwhile his body ached for her in a way it had never ached for any woman – that is, any real, live woman. Judith was no fantasy. Judith was a real girl, almost a friend. His entire body vibrated with such fierce anguish that all hope of helping himself out, as he so often did, was extinguished. He turned over onto his stomach to cry, and instead of shame came sleep.

He was awakened by a clinking sound, and turned over. At first he thought he still dreamed; there, on his bed, black hair streaming over a flowing white nightgown, sat Judith. He jerked upright and she put her fingers over his lips. Her bangles clinked. 'Shh!' she said. 'Shh! Shh! It's me, Judith.' She rolled her bangles off. 'These things make too much noise.'

'Why are you here?' he asked suspiciously. 'What do you want?'

She leaned forward and stroked his hair. 'I was lonely,' she whispered. 'Why did you stop talking to me? Are you lonely, too?'

'No.'

'Are you never lonely?'

'No. Not any more.'

'How old are you?'

'Twenty.' The lie came easily, speedily.

'I guessed right — '

'You guessed how old I am?'

'Yes. I knew we were the same age. Twenty.' Judith laughed.

'Careful,' he said. 'They'll hear us.'

'I'm cold,' she whispered. 'It's freezing. They're too mean to turn on the heating.'

'They say they do in winter.'

'If I don't get under the blankets with you, I'll have to go back to my room. Can you move up a little?'

He moved quickly. 'It's a big bed,' he said.

She got in beside him. 'Oh, you're warm,' she said. 'Your body's so warm, so wonderfully, wonderfully warm.' Her own body shook, but whether with cold or with fright he couldn't tell.

Saffarty lay rigid, every muscle tense, afraid his bursting erection would be discovered.

'Do you like me, Saffarty?' she said.

'Yes.'

'Well then, kiss me.'

She took his mouth and slowly, but thoroughly, pore by pore, her tongue began to search out and then to caress his every nerve. Still he lay flat and kept his body rigid. Suddenly, she moaned and moved her body on top of his, and felt his hardness. 'Oh, you're so big. Wonderfully, wonderfully huge.' She wriggled. Suddenly she stopped. 'We must take our clothes off,' she said.

When they were both naked she whispered, 'Here, let me put this on for you. We have to catch all those millions of little Saffartys.' No sooner did her fingers connect with his flesh than, past caring, and long past all shame, the hot, spurting liquid that up until then had been a private, secret happening, gushed into her hands. She scooped the sticky stuff, smeared it over her breasts, her chest, returning again and again for more. Each touch of her fingers brought a renewed urgency. 'Here,' she whispered. 'Let's try again.'

While he was still on his back, she straddled him. Suddenly, without dislodging either of them, he rolled her onto her back, and now his tongue sought hers, and his breath whistled as he breathed only her breath. Even through the sheath, her sliding, searing warmth enveloped him, protected him and, because he was at its centre, isolated him from all the world. Invisible sensations overtook him; he knew that making love to a woman was like nothing else in the world.

'Sleep,' Judith said. 'Go to sleep now. You deserve to sleep! I'll stay right by you.'

A little later Saffarty awoke, and the heat of her body and the sound of her breathing told him it had not been a dream. Then he remembered whose hands Judith's had reminded him of – his mother's. He wanted Judith again, and with the same urgency. He tossed and turned and pretended to bump into her in his sleep. She put out a testing hand, and found him at once. 'Wait,' she said. 'Wait until I've put on another safe!'

And so it went on until dawn, until it was time for Judith to return to her own room before her aunt awoke. They arranged to meet for lunch at the Café Rouge.

That morning, when he arrived at school, the entire class was already seated at a huge oval table. Mercifully, Monsieur Mallet entered only moments after Saffarty was seated. When the *maître* took his seat on the high throne-like chair, Saffarty froze. He had forgotten all about his first accounting test. At once he willed himself to think of nothing else – to concentrate, concentrate! He must not let a woman distract him; and so he successfully banished Judith from his mind.

Later, Judith met him at the Café Rouge. They know me there, he had told her earlier that morning.

And so began the two glorious weeks that, forever after, Saffarty would see as the crucible, or the real beginning, of his life. Two weeks of laughter, of pure *joie de vivre*, of exquisite sensuality, and the beginnings of a love of beauty in all its forms, in women, in art and in nature. Of course he had laughed before, and not so long ago at that, when he had stumbled over those false teeth on the French steamer on the way to Marseilles. He told Judith about that, and her full, high-pitched laughter joined his. He told her, without embarrassment, about his shortage of funds and she said, 'Ah yes, well certainly you are still a student.' After that first meal he did not pay for her again. Still, they ate many meals at the Café Rouge, and the steamy, earthy bistro became their own, and the waiters gave them the smiles and the gestures they reserved for lovers.

They bought matching black berets, and Judith cut her hair in the new short bob, and Saffarty went with her to the *coiffeuse*. They went to the Salon des Indépendants, and just as surely as he had fallen in love with the Metro he fell in love with the art of the machine. Judith taught him how to look at the paintings with a photographer's eye. Judith was to photograph some of the ballerinas of the Diaghilev company; but, try as he might, Saffarty was unmoved by the ballet. Whereas the art of Léger, with its strong stress on machine forms, combined beauty with relevance, and was therefore meaningful. It involved both the present and the future, and the immediate future had become his prime concern. Léger had said he would make an iron bolt more beautiful than a rose, and this, Saffarty believed, was entirely possible.

At night the streets were often wet, but because they were not Salonican streets they were not muddy, and reflected the lights. Now *that*, Saffarty said, *that* was ballet of a sort.

And all the while they looked for new lodgings for Saffarty. It was not easy within his price range, and he was determined he would pay no more than half his present rent. Finally they settled on a minute box of a room in the tiny Hôtel Ouisseau. It had heating, and contained the usual zinc bucket, jug and chamber pot, and it was also clean.

They found it a week before Judith had to return to Marseilles. She told her somewhat suspicious aunt that she was leaving Paris earlier, for an important photographic assignment. Now, in their new and private room, under the damp, peeling ceiling, and away from the listening Namiases they allowed their love-making every latitude, and every sound. Which was how Saffarty came to believe – and then only through sound – that his body housed an extra man, a primitive stranger. Judith was as unafraid as she was abandoned; she embraced her nature as she embraced him, almost as if she believed this was her last chance. They brought bread, cheese and a coarse, rough wine, and kept to their room.

Once they went out, and listened to a street-singer and an accordionist playing and singing a new love-song, and they joined in the refrain, and sang, and their tears flowed publicly, and then, without words, left to return to their room and made love gently, sentimentally, as their time together came to an end.

Towards dawn Judith said dreamily, 'You're not twenty years old, Saffarty — '

'Why do you say that?'

'Because even a young man of no more than twenty could not be as virile as you.'

'What are you talking about?'

'That proves it. If you were older, you would know what I was talking about! Eight times in one day – *merde*! You don't know what that means!'

'All right. I'm not twenty. And you are not twenty. So what?'

'Tell me the truth, Saffarty. How old are you?'

'Fifteen.'

'A fifteen-year-old! My God! If I'd known that, I wouldn't have come near you. And I'd have missed all this. I would have gone to my grave never knowing — '

'How old are you, Judith?'

'Never mind.' She gave a wry sigh. 'Let me tell you something else, Saffarty. Never ask a woman her age, and you will be as successful with them as you will be with everything else.'

She sat up then and looked at him appraisingly, as if she were seeing him for the first and last time. 'You learn quickly,' she said, her voice soft and maternal.

And she took him in her arms and cradled him, and, soon, lost in her warm waters, he was saying, 'I love you, Judith. I love you. I love you. I will love you for ever.'

'Ah, Saffarty, Saffarty,' Judith sighed. 'You will say that to many, many women. You've got what they want. Because you've got what they know they should *not* want. I'm glad I'm too old for you . . . '

When Judith returned to Marseilles, Saffarty missed her intensely, his body still tingled with the lack of her – but he counted himself lucky to have known her at all. She left him with a constant inner smile, and the laughter came easily and often.

His grinning 'Bonjour, monsieur le Baron' persuaded even Monsieur Delange, the surly *patron* of the Hôtel Ouisseau, to move his lips into something that almost resembled a smile. Monsieur Delange was anxiously proud of his son Jacques, who was studying for the *baccalauréat*.

'It's his Greek,' he confided to Saffarty one day. 'It's not a Latin language, you see, and he breaks his teeth on it; and it's a barrier in the way of the university.'

'But Greek is the language of the gods,' Saffarty said seriously and, for once, without a laugh. He switched to Greek and, quoting his Greek teacher, said, 'Greek is the language of all civilised, eloquent men.'

'What's that? What are you saying?'

Saffarty translated.

'You speak Greek, then? You know Greek? Would you teach my son?'

Although Saffarty had been waiting for just such a request, he said, 'Unfortunately, I have my own studies to work at. Exams — '

'Just two lessons a week. For two francs an hour,' suggested Monsieur Delange, speaking slowly. 'It makes four francs a week. It's daylight robbery, but if it'll help Claude it's worth it!'

'Monsieur Delange! But who speaks of payment?' Saffarty protested.

'Well – of course – I mean. I expect to pay — '

'There is no need for money to change hands.'

'What do you mean? No need?'

'Permit me to explain. I will teach your son and, instead of your paying me, I will pay you thirty francs less each month.' He put his hand on Monsieur Delange's shoulder. 'If you don't pay me it will be less painful for you, no?' Then he laughed, and stamped his feet and slapped his thighs.

'I will take off twenty-eight francs.'

'It is a well-known fact, Monsieur Delange, that some months contain as many as five weeks.'

Monsieur Delange blinked doubtfully.

'Now it is only two francs a month that stand between your son and the university,' Saffarty went on smoothly. 'If we take four weeks to a month that is one franc thirty-three centimes a week, monsieur. And five weeks to a month gives one franc sixty-six centimes. Now if we divide, and then average — '

'Enough, enough. You make my head ache.'

'Thirty francs, then?'

'Robbery. Robbery.'

'If you think that, perhaps we should forget the whole thing,' Saffarty said, introducing a tone of finality into his voice. 'How can I be robbing you when you are paying me nothing? Not one *sou*?'

So Monsieur Delange capitulated, and the Greek lessons, originally to help pay his rent, began. But then Claude saw his opportunity, too, and introduced friends of his who needed extra tuition to Saffarty. Soon Saffarty had enough to live on and pay his tuition fees, just. And Claude? Well, he took his percentage, of course . . .

One day Saffarty was confronted with an unexpected problem. He had grown still further; he was six foot tall. His trousers were short. He could forgive himself for the trousers – after all, he had no full-length mirror – but he should have noticed his short sleeves. It was the Delange's son, his miserable pupil, Claude, who told him about the trousers.

'I was caught in the rain,' Saffarty lied, and shrugged. 'They must have shrunk.' Nothing would have induced him to reveal his true age. Now his savings would be ravaged, and he was so proud of the arrangement he had come to with Delange! Still, he had the money. He knew the expense was an essential capital outlay, but was depressed nonetheless.

He went to a second-hand stall at the flea market, but it was impossible to try anything on. He waited until the end of the day when the owner was ready to shut, and then, armed with a tape-measure and determination, he acquired a suit, larger than he needed, with room for growth. He felt good in this suit, because it made him look older, and because it was a fashionable three-piece. One day all his suits would be made to measure . . . Best of all, though, was the price. His sense of timing was no less accurate than his rapid arithmetic; because it was the end of the day he got thirty per cent off the asking price.

On his sixteenth birthday he received a card from Judith. She missed him. She wanted him to go to Marseilles. He was tempted; he just had the money for the fare. And the idea of travelling so far for a single weekend fascinated and appalled him. To think of what lay at the other end of the journey! Judith's body, Judith's breasts. Judith's . . . Yes, he would – he must – go. And very, very soon.

But then, after a fierce quarrel, he struck up a sudden friendship with Max Blum, a fellow student, and his life changed, and he did not go to Marseilles.

4

Max Blum did not come of an established family, as Saffarty had supposed. Indeed, he had no family in Paris – his own parents were still in Lodz, an industrial town in Poland. However, from his immaculate clothes and perfect grooming he certainly appeared to have come from an important family. Saffarty had never seen the likes of the cut of Max's pure silk shirts, or his woollen suits. His elegance set him apart from the other students. No matter when Saffarty saw him, he was always newly shaved and freshly dressed. His pale blonde hair gleamed and his wide, clever eyes sparkled. Though he was at least as tall as Saffarty he seemed to have been more delicately wrought. Watching the graceful movements of his long fingers, so much more slender than his own, Saffarty felt awkward.

Max was sure of himself. His was the powerful kind of confidence that is given to those who have always been served – the sort that lasts. Until his recent insolvency, his father had been as independent as he had been arrogant. Max had never forgotten those rare occasions his parents had been excluded from an important social gathering and his father's stock response had been, 'They didn't dare invite us!' He had inherited his father's fierce pride, and told no one that the business which had been his birthright was now in the hands of creditors.

Like Saffarty, Max had been fifteen when he had first come to Paris, two years earlier, in 1921. But unlike Saffarty he had not wanted to leave his parents or his native Poland. A brilliant student, he had passed his *Matura* with distinction, and but for the *numerus clausus* – closed numbers – which restricted the number of Jews at universities, it would not have been necessary for him to leave Poland, to study architecture at the Sorbonne.

Just as ambition had driven Saffarty from Salonika, so prejudice had driven Max from Poland. The pogroms, the organised massacres of Jews that were searching realities for Max, were distant rumours to Saffarty. To be a Jew, in Max's experience, was to be born a victim, and a guilty one at that. Unlike Max, Saffarty did not feel guilty because he was a Jew, but because he was a bad Jew.

A year after Max enrolled at the Sorbonne he received the news of his father's business failure, and his allowance had been stopped (his father did not tell him that his once haughty mother was now a dressmaker). Desperate for a job, he had taken the first that presented itself. Which was how he came to be working at the Ritz Hotel, and how he came to meet Colette, which was how he came to attend the Ecole Inter-Commercial.

Max seemed older than Saffarty; older, indeed, than most of the class. His age was hard to judge, though, especially when Saffarty considered his own successful disguise – after all he passed for twenty himself. Anyway, Max was at least twenty-three. He wore a hat instead of a beret and, what was more, he had several hats, and several suits. Saffarty concluded that he was obviously the son of a rich family, or if not rich then an established family. And yet with that strangely gutteral, but faintly Polish accent of his, just how established could his family be?

By this time, January 1925, Saffarty had been in Paris for over a year, and accents were easier to identify. But Max's country of origin was of no importance to Saffarty. No, it was his quick walk, and quicker, busier eyes that he found so arresting. Max seemed to be in a perpetual but clearly purposeful rush. His alert, busy grey eyes made him look clever as well as prosperous.

The quarrel developed when one of Max's books dropped at Saffarty's feet. Saffarty bent to retrieve it, saw the Hebrew lettering on the cover, and realised at once that it was a *siddur*, a prayer-book. Without thinking, he said automatically, '*Shmang Israel!*' He brought the book to his lips and kissed it.

Max snatched the book back and kissed it himself. 'You are mocking me,' he said angrily, 'mocking my religion.'

'What do you mean?'

'That proves it. If you were a Jew yourself,' he said, jabbing Saffarty in the chest as he spoke, 'you'd have said "*Shma Israel*" – not "*Shmang Israel*".'

'But I am a Jew,' Saffarty answered quietly. 'At least I was.'

'Where do you come from?'

Saffarty put his hand in his pocket, and grasped his precious key. 'I come from Macedonia,' he said.

'There are Jews in Macedonia?' Max asked, breaking into Yiddish to test him. 'I didn't know there were Jews there.'

'You didn't know that? You didn't know that in Salonika the port used to close on *shabbat*?' Saffarty answered, speaking German.

'That proves it. A Jew who can't speak Yiddish doesn't exist!'

'Open that *siddur* at any page you please. Test me!'

Max opened the book and thrust it at Saffarty. He listened, and, when Saffarty was halfway through the page, he said, 'I believe you. But you pronounce the Hebrew all wrong.' He put out his hand, and then drew it back. 'You said you *were* a Jew,' he said, suspicious. 'No one *was* a Jew.'

'I gave it up.'

'You gave it up?'

'Yes.'

'Impossible. Once a Jew, always a Jew! You must be ashamed of being a Jew.'

'My ancestor, Rabbi Joseph Ben Saffarty, taught the False Messiah!' Saffarty's furious scowl emphasised his squint. 'I am descended from the Jewish nobility.' He lowered his voice, and said sadly, 'But I no longer deserve to be a Jew.'

'I don't understand you. Something must be wrong with you. There's no such thing as Jewish nobility.' Max shook his head several times. 'Come on, I'll buy you a glass of wine, we'll talk about this.' He offered his hand. 'Peace?'

'Peace.'

They fell into step, and into excited conversation.

As soon as they were seated, before they had taken a sip of wine, Saffarty took out his ancient key. 'Have you ever seen one of these?' he asked gravely.

Max shrugged. 'No,' he said.

'It's more than four hundred years old, and it is the key to the house we left in Spain at the time of the Inquisition.' A brief look of contempt crossed his face, but he kept smiling. 'One of my ancestors was physician to King Ferdinand.'

'So what? My third cousin is also a doctor — '

'I am a Sephardic Jew — ' Saffarty stopped to correct himself. 'I mean I *was* a Sephardic Jew. But you are an Ashkenazic Jew. While my people were reading books, yours were still climbing trees!'

Seeing Max's bewildered, puzzled expression, Saffarty burst out laughing.

'What's so funny?' Max asked with a forced smile.

'You look just like a worried businessman,' Saffarty said quickly.

'But I am a businessman,' Max said indignantly. 'A shopkeeper without a shop, but a businessman. When the Cinéma Germaine is not showing a film, I sell socks and stockings in the foyer.'

'You've just got yourself a new customer,' Saffarty grinned.

'Come to the Avenue de Clichy tomorrow,' Max said.

Max left, and Saffarty stayed on at the Café. He was scarcely interested in buying himself a pair of socks. A shopkeeper without a shop meant little or no rent, which also meant that a man could become his own boss . . .

It was because of working at the Ritz Hotel that Max had met Colette, and because of Colette that he looked as he did – fit, well dressed, well fed and well cared for.

Worlds away from Poland, he tried to be worldly and nonchalant about the whole affair, but however often he told himself that Colette took care of his needs the way he took care of hers, his terror was undiminished. He was terrified her husband would find out – he would be beaten up, he would be killed . . . He still thought of the man as Monsieur Terblanche. Max was terrified even of the man's photograph. Monsieur Terblanche was at least fifty, but he was exceedingly muscular, and obviously knew how to use himself. He was tall – tall as a giant, Colette said. He told himself that the whole thing was something he had stumbled into, that it was not his fault; but that didn't help. He reminded himself that Colette had taken advantage of a young innocent naïf, but that did no good either. He was terrified; he was ashamed of her, too . . . .

It had been going on for six months. Just lately, he had begun to suspect that if he left her, she might confess it all to Monsieur Terblanche herself. She dropped one or two hints to the effect that no matter how faithless her husband had been, he would be forced to exact a terrible vengeance on his wife's young lover. She was beginning, she said, to feel nervous. So nervous that she might, herself, say the wrong thing.

If he had not been on his way to work on that wet and windy morning, and if Colette had not been wearing those flimsy high heels, he never would have met her in the first place. At the time, of course, he had been too bewildered, too stunned; and when he realised just what a stroke of bad luck had befallen him it was far too late.

Colette's heel had caught in one of those pavement ventilation grates, and she had fallen and all the contents of her straw basket had been scattered. How he wished now that he had not done the natural thing, which was to help her to her feet, and then pick up those carrots and potatoes, and even a chicken! No one else had stopped to help.

Shaken by the fall, she had asked him to help her to her apartment. It was not very far, only a few metres away. It had simply not occurred to him to refuse. She was very obviously a rich lady, and he had been brought up to be good-mannered. It began to rain. Colette took his arm – that, too, had seemed quite natural – and they had made their way to her apartment building.

They were both sodden when they reached her apartment. Colette's umbrella had buckled when she fell, and it would not open. She took him through her vast, marbled entrance hall, with the startling mirrored pool in the centre, and then to the kitchen. As soon as they had dispensed with the basket she said, 'What's your name?'

'Max Blum.'

'How old are you?'

'Seventeen.'

As if mystified, she repeated, 'Seventeen.'

He moved towards the door. 'It was a pleasure to be of service, madame,' he said.

'Wait, don't go. You're wet. You must dry off. Take your coat off.'

The imperious note in her voice made him obey. She took his coat from him, and draped it over a huge radiator. She flung her own coat over a chair. Though large, and glitteringly clean, it was a warm and comforting kitchen. A clock ticked. He stood awkwardly, not knowing what to do. The flutter of a bird in a huge cage caught his attention. 'Oh,' he said. 'You have a bird, madame. What sort of bird is that?'

'A toucan,' Colette said. 'It's name is Bijou – bird in a gilded cage, like me.'

'Madame?'

'You wouldn't understand. You're only a boy.' She began to leave the kitchen. 'Come with me. I'll light the fire and you'll soon dry off.'

Still obedient, still stunned, Max followed her. He might have been in the foyer of the Ritz – the room was so large. The fireplace was enormous, too, and filled with logs. Almost instantly, it seemed, a huge fire was roaring.

'Sit down, Max,' she said. 'You're shivering.' She shivered herself. 'A little cognac will warm us up nicely!'

Again, Max did as he was told. Casting a nervous look at the skins of wild animals that decorated the sofa, he sat down gingerly. He felt more and more uneasy. He was fascinated, and he was frightened – what if the woman set that fierce bird she called a toucan on him? She even had lamps in the shape of that bird. She was crazy, absolutely crazy. Anything could happen to him. He wished he hadn't helped her. Well, he would have a sip of the cognac, and then leave.

She presented him with a glass that reminded him of home and then seated herself beside him, among the animal skins. Nervous, he swallowed too much. His throat on fire, he fell into a fit of coughing.

Colette broke into a throaty giggle. 'Drink some more,' she said. 'You'll feel better. You'll feel wonderful.'

Max took another gulp.

'It's grand, isn't it? It will put hair on your chest, as they say.' She giggled again.

Max smiled weakly, and nodded.

'Tell me, Max,' she said, sounding breathless. 'Tell me what you think of me. You think I'm silly, no?' She thrust a long leg in his direction. 'Silly to wear these high heels, no?'

Max stared at the leg, and found it unexpectedly beautiful. Suddenly she withdrew it, and crossed it over her other leg. The flesh-coloured silk stockings made a rustling sound as she uncrossed and then stretched her legs towards the fire.

'You haven't answered me,' she said. 'That means you think I am very, very silly, no?'

Max's head seemed lighter, and strangely carefree. 'I think, madame,' he said, 'I think you have very long legs.' His voice sounded unrecognisable to him, as if it had come from a distant place. Somehow he didn't care.

'So you think I have long legs?'

'Yes. Long and beautiful legs.'

Colette moved closer to him. Her cherry-red mouth with its inverted heart-shaped upper lip moved closer, too. Her perfume swirled over him. Dimly aware that she was still wearing her hat, and afraid of catching her eye, he kept his eyes focused on her lips. He was no longer sure whether the breathing he could hear was hers or his. The space between them seemed as thin as an eggshell. Then Max did the strangest thing. He tugged at her close-fitting cloche, and removed it. Colette perceived that as a signal, and reacted as if he had assumed control. She crushed her mouth against his. That was when he let his tongue take over.

Soon she was clawing at his tie and shirt buttons. When they were all undone, she tackled his trouser buttons. Seconds later – except for her silk stockings and flesh-coloured garters – she was naked, and his last conscious thought – before his body took control of his mind – was that her flesh matched her stockings. And in another four seconds, for him anyway, it was all over.

She lay beneath him, quietly. The women he had been with before had never failed to wriggle out from under him at once. He listened to the logs crackle, listened to her breathing and fell asleep. Colette let him sleep for a while, and then stroked him awake. He felt her mouth against his ear. 'So you were not a virgin. Yes?' She did not wait for him to reply, but went on. 'You went with prostitutes before?' She took his silence for assent. 'Never mind, I will be better for you than prostitutes.'

All the while the stroking continued.

Suddenly he heaved away, and tugged at her garters with each hand. They heard the rip of her stockings as he tore them off. Then his hands flew to her breasts. Her movements were slow, almost leisurely, and her smile, without her lipstick, was wide and lively.

'I have a good body, you think?'

'You have a beautiful, beautiful body.'

Her smile widened further, her skin glistened and turned rosy. He squeezed, then pinched, her breasts, and tried to quicken. But she squeezed him tighter, and held him in place, and said only, 'Wait, Max, wait. It will be better if you wait.'

And it was better, unbearably better. She directed him all the way. Suddenly she cried, 'Now. Now. Faster. Faster.' His entire being rose with every lightning thrust, until it exploded, and he heard a strange cry, and knew that it had come from both of them. Then she disentangled herself, and lay quietly with her head on his shoulder. Over and over again, she said, 'Thank you. Thank you. Thank you, Max. Thank you.'

Still bewildered, yet very deeply pleased, Max felt as if he no longer knew who he was. He wondered what her name was. Suddenly, he was hungry. At the same moment she said, 'You are thinking you don't even know my name and your stomach is rumbling. Yes?'

That was when the first stirrings of terror began.

'My name is Colette,' she said. 'Colette Terblanche.' She rose from the couch and said, 'Wait. Don't move. I'll be back soon.'

She did not trouble to cover her nakedness and, stunned though he was, Max understood that it was because she knew she had a good body. Within seconds she had returned. She handed him a royal blue silk dressing gown. 'Put this on,' she said, 'and we'll eat.' She was wearing a dressing gown herself, he noticed. It was in the same salmon pink as the suit she had been wearing, and there was a fluffy, furry thing at her throat, and at her wrists, and even at her toes, on her slippers.

'Let's go back to the kitchen,' she said, giggling. 'We both deserve to eat!'

He saw his coat in the kitchen and remembered the laundry. He said at once, 'I'll lose my job.'

'Because you are late? I will phone your employer, and say that I am the doctor's nurse and that you have a high fever.'

He told her where he worked, and she went to the telephone, but not before she had laid out bread and salami. When she came back she said that she had told his employer that he would probably be away for a few days.

'Eat,' she said. 'I'll bring the mustard. And we must have some wine. Or perhaps, champagne?'

Max broke off some bread, and took a slice of cheese.

'You don't like salami?' she said.

'I don't eat pig.'

'I see. You are a Jew? Yes?'

'Yes.'

'Well, at least you are not a sailor!'

'Excuse me?'

'I was saying that you are a good-looking young man. There is a delicacy about you. A sort of elegance, I suppose. Your eyes are gleaming. They are grey, your eyes, but the grey of smoke, and not of steel.'

Max flushed with pleasure. 'You are a very pretty lady,' he said shyly.

She began to tell him about her life. She was certain he must have found her behaviour strange, to say the least. She could only agree with him. It was even stranger, probably, than he had supposed, because she had never before so much as thought of doing such a thing, of picking up a young man like that. Though, of course, he had picked her up off the pavement, hadn't he? Still, she was glad she had done it. And she was lucky, too, because he was a fine young man; she could tell he was a gentleman, really.

Not like her husband, who, she assured him, was no gentleman. He had such filthy habits, he was such a filthy man, her husband. Oh, he was a big shot in the insurance business, but Monsieur Terblanche – as she constantly referred to him – only bathed once every fifteen days. Not like Max, who was clean; she had noticed that at once, clean and fresh, gleamingly fresh. She could not bear her husband to touch her, and it seemed he couldn't bear her either. He probably had a mistress, but she didn't care. In fact, she was pleased. But a normal woman has normal needs, and she'd been starving, starving.

She went on and on, in a breathless, girlish voice. Once in a while the toucan cawed in its cage, as if in agreement, and from time to time Max nodded. Colette continued; she might, really, have been talking to herself. Max listened devoutly. Tears made white stripes in her rouged cheeks, and Max stopped her only once to ask, 'Where is Monsieur Terblanche today?'

He was in Canada, she said at once, again adding how much she hated to call him her husband. 'I must be boring you, no? Talking about myself. Tell me about you. Tell me, for a start, the month of your birth.'

'July.'

'July. In the year nineteen hundred and six?'

'Yes.'

'My son would have been your age exactly. You were not born on July the thirtieth by any chance?'

'July the thirty-first.'

'Good. At least I'm grateful for that.'

All Max's instincts warned him that now was the time to escape. But he lacked the courage and, besides, his other, baser instincts were more demanding.

Very quickly, and almost before he knew it, Colette took him over. She bought him clothes, and rented a studio – a *garçonnière* – for him, so that they could be private. And, of course, he gave up his job. It was thanks to Colette that he was now a student at the Ecole Inter-Commercial, and thanks to her that he had started selling socks and stockings in the foyers of empty cinemas. It was tough going, but he was, at last, beginning to acquire a small capital of his own.

He was terrified of Colette, terrified of Monsieur Terblanche, and terrified that his family in Poland might find out that he had turned into what he now knew to be a gigolo. This was the worst of all his terrors.

5

For Colette the past was as dead as her own darling mother was dead. She often dreamed of her mother, though a faded photograph was all she had, and almost all she knew of the young girl who had died giving birth to her in Detroit, Michigan. Max was ashamed of her because she was fourteen years older than he. Of course he did not know the exact age difference, but he was as ashamed of her as if she had been forty years older. He knew almost nothing about her, nothing of her past; certainly he had no idea she was not French. She dared not tell him she was the illegitimate daughter of a thirteen-year-old American girl. Still less could she face telling him that her grandmother – who had already raised a bastard daughter – had been compelled to raise a bastard grand-daughter as well.

When her grandmother discovered that at fourteen Colette, continuing the family tradition, was pregnant, she had had enough. Colette had to count herself lucky to be taken in by the sisters of the Mercy Mission. There she stubbornly refused to tell anyone that her step-grandfather – the one she called Pappy – was the father of her unborn child. That the child, a boy, survived only two days, seemed a fitting punishment. Like countless young victims before her, Colette blamed and hated herself for the disgrace. The nuns told her that the death of the baby was her just reward. She had called her son Paul. Two weeks later, still weak from the birth, she left the Mercy Mission hostel. She had answered an advertisement in the evening paper offering lodgings in return for domestic services. There she was employed by Madame Georgette. At first Madame Georgette was sympathetic – even motherly – and forbade her to do any sort of work for at least two months. One of the house rules was that, like Madame, all the girls had French names ending in 'ette'. Colette had shed her own name, Ellen, with gratitude. This way her step-grandfather would never find her. She was the youngest there, and while still recovering was taught the precise nature of what her work would be . . .

When it was discovered that she had left school at the age of eight to do most of the washing and ironing her grandmother took in, one of the girls took pity on her and taught her an enduring – and vastly different – skill.

She taught Colette how to read.

After she had been on the game for about eighteen months the shock and the fright left her, and the world-weary hopelessness set in. Around this time she met Dex Harvey, one of Madame Georgette's most flamboyant customers. Dex, a grain merchant, was about to travel to Europe. A man who seemed to need his nightly comforts, he took Colette along with him, borrowing her with the express understanding that, like a library book, she would be returned. He had a Miss Stephanie kit her out, as he put it, and Colette acquired a complete wardrobe that was as fine as it was fashionable. For one thing, the shop paid a commission on every item, and for another Miss Stephanie had excellent taste. At the end of it all Colette had gained at least seven years. She looked more like an elegant young woman in her early twenties than a child of sixteen. Her sad emerald-green eyes, her slow smile, and her pale clear complexion all combined to make her gravely beautiful. Her figure was perfect too, and she was undeniably intelligent. In short, as Madame Georgette liked to say, she had everything except luck.

Dex took her to Paris, to the Ritz Hotel, and during the three weeks they were together, he was not unkind, but spent several nights away from her as if she had slipped his mind, like an unimportant memory. When he did not show up for four consecutive days, she began to believe that he really had abandoned her. On the morning of the fifth day she was having coffee alone in the lounge when, aware of an elderly gentleman looking at her, she was overtaken by a fit of sobbing. She knew he was a fellow American because she had heard him talking. She stopped weeping only long enough to say out loud, 'What will become of me?'

The American took her under his protection, and six months later, when he left Paris and handed her on – by way of a bribe – to one of his customers, she knew better than to try to resist. She quickly learned to speak French, and very soon sounded – and looked – like *une vrai parisienne*. By this time she had lost all hope, just as surely as she had lost all self-respect when her step-grandfather had taken it from her.

For five years she was passed along from one man to the other, like a spare suitcase to be filled, used and discarded. Still, she managed to avoid walking the streets.

And then she was handed on to Guy Terblanche, obese and coarse, whose foul breath issued from thick lips and crooked teeth.

Life could have been worse, she told herself. After all, Guy Terblanche had now installed her in an apartment in the *huitième*, the best address in Paris, and if, with the help of three or four selected clients, she occasionally supplemented her allowance as a kept woman, she was still very far from being a woman of the streets, a *putain*.

One of the men was an Englishman, and when she was with him she spoke English, albeit with a French accent. But for that contact with her mother-tongue, she rarely thought of Detroit. However bleak, however lonely, life in Paris was infinitely better than the merciless poverty she had known in Detroit. Countless women would have changed places gladly with her, she consoled herself.

She lived for the day. There was no future to plan for; her step-grandfather had snatched that away from her long ago.

But all that changed when she met Max because she had *his* future to dream about and to plan for. It was as if his whole future had been given to her.

Max was not the first man but the first person she had ever really loved. She had told him that she was married, which was almost true. She had been with Terblanche for close on ten years. And the few men she still saw, although they insisted on paying, saw themselves as trusted friends. Of course Terblanche knew nothing about them. She was beginning to develop a small reputation for helping young girls. She used her contacts skilfully, and had already helped two of them find alternative respectable employment in shops.

Colette pressed the studded rubber rolling pin against her thighs. This was only one aspect of the daily regime of exercise on which she had embarked to improve and then keep her shape – that rounded, slender look that made her as agile as a snake. It had paid off, too. 'You're so slim and soft,' Max had said. However barbed, it was a compliment, and she treasured it. Satisfied with her thighs, she stood on her head and rested her toes against the mirrored wall. She had already taken her potion of slimming herbs. She counted to sixty, and then changed her position. Now she kept her head and shoulders on the carpeted floor, supported her hips with her hands and once more raised her legs. She looked up at the mirrored ceiling and rejoiced, because her body could easily have been mistaken for that of a young bride.

She had stopped dyeing her hair, and was delighted and surprised with the result. Once the sharp orange tint had gone, and her natural dark coppery shade was allowed to emerge, her appearance altered radically. Of course she had to tone down her make-up as well. The effect of all this was that she no longer looked tough and worn, but soft and fresh.

She decided that she looked exactly the way she felt, like a young and radiant bride.

And Max had done this for her. *Max!* Because until she had, quite literally, tripped and fallen into his life, she had been steadily rotting away. A drab life with only her toucan for company. She dropped her legs to the floor and lay back, giving herself over to the anticipation of her afternoon with Max, 'I fell into his life,' she told herself, over and over, 'and then he brought me back to life again.' For two years he had been her secret; a daily secret to begin with, now a twice-weekly secret. How she adored his smoky grey eyes, his strong chin, and his stronger keen and clean body. The *garçonnière* she had taken for him in Montmartre had a shower and the water was always hot enough, so Max took two and sometimes three showers a day. Colette was no longer ashamed of having taken a boy off the streets to become her lover. In any case, she was now convinced that she had fallen into *his* life . . .

So, she had taken a lover who was not only a boy, but a foreigner and a Jew. But she was now back in the world, she reasoned, living in the present instead of the past. And the present was Max. The future? Who cared about the future? It was like the past – it did not exist.

Correspondence between Saffarty and his family in Salonika was erratic. Saffarty wrote and told them about his progress at school, and his work as a tutor. His mother had never learned to write, and his father's penned letters in Ladino were written only when there was a momentous event such as Aaron Touro's marriage to his cousin, Sarica. Though Salonika, and the muddy streets, and the people were of little interest to him now, Saffarty smiled when he read that. That those people who had bought property soon after the fire were now

61

making huge profits was hardly his concern. It made him realise he had little wish to go back to Salonika ever again. The smell of fish made him ill. He believed that life was well behind him – just as he believed that his life in Paris was well beyond his parents. His father never mentioned the possibility of visiting Paris.

Which was as well, for Saffarty now saw them as primitive peasants, whose presence in Paris would have been embarrassing. Whenever he felt vaguely guilty about this, as he sometimes did, he made himself recall every detail of the injury his father had done to his eye. Yet no matter how much he despised his father, he was still deeply aware of the wisdom of the man's last words. *Never sell yourself. If your boss thinks you're good enough for him, you're good enough to be your own boss.*

There was no disputing the truth of that, and it was thanks to Max Blum that he could now begin to become his own boss.

It was obvious, the very first morning he called on Max at his little stall in the foyer of the Cinéma Germaine, that though he gave excellent value for money he was blind to the potential of his undertaking. He stood quietly behind his makeshift stall. He had told Saffarty that if only a quarter of his stock were to be sold he would be quite content. There were few customers, but Saffarty noticed three women handle the stockings lovingly and turn away regretfully. Neither he nor Max said anything, or made even the smallest effort to encourage them to buy.

That night, Saffarty could think of nothing but those three women. He recalled their sighs, and the way their work-worn hands had caressed the flesh-coloured silk stockings. *And they had left the stall without buying anything at all!*

Some instinct told him that the very touching of an item meant that it was already eighty per cent sold. The thought of these lost sales kept him awake. He already knew that the more you could sell, the more you could buy. And the more you bought the less you paid. Because quantity-buying meant discounts. And discounts meant greater profits. And Max, it seemed, could not see this. In any case, Max seemed abstracted, anxious. It was obvious that his heart was not in his business. Still, Max seemed to be loaded with cash, so perhaps Saffarty was misjudging him.

Whether he was right or wrong he was determined to do something about increasing these sales, for he had made up his mind that he and Max would become partners.

The next morning Saffarty skipped his classes at the Ecole Inter-Commercial and went, instead, to the Cinéma Germaine. It was cold and wet, and though he was counting every *sou* he allowed himself the luxury of a paper cone of roasted chestnuts. Then he bought his ticket, and waited in the empty foyer. The owner, the *patron* of the cinema, would not allow stall holders to open their stalls during the hours that a film was shown. Of course, if the *patron* could be induced to change his mind, he would have access to a ready-made supply of customers.

What about all those people who had already paid their good money to see the film? They would be in high spirits and ready to spend money on Saffarty's offer of undoubted bargains – two pairs of socks for forty centimes. Saffarty had already decided to reduce prices by ten centimes.

Word of mouth, he thought, word of mouth. Max would understand, would agree that a ten-centime reduction would pull in customers.

The foyer began to fill with people, but Saffarty turned his attention to the usherettes. They all wore uniform dresses of black crêpe, trimmed with white lace collars and cuffs. He watched the way they walked and listened to the way they talked. As soon as he decided which one he would approach he drew out his small change, and prepared an unusually large tip. He chose the smallest of the three, not only because she was the youngest, but because her collar and cuffs were the whitest.

She showed him to his seat, and when he gave her one franc – three times more than anything she had expected – and she said, 'Thank you, monsieur, thank you,' her accent told him that, like Judith, she too came from Marseilles. Good, he thought, a good omen. Besides, they would have something to talk about. He had no intention of seeing the film, and after about ten minutes he ambled out of the darkened cinema into the foyer. The usherette saw him, and asked timidly, 'Monsieur doesn't like the film?'

'I've seen it already. But I'd forgotten,' he said, with one of his mischievous laughs.

'You'd forgotten that you saw *Marquitta*?' she said, sounding amazed.

He knew she was thinking that he must be well off to forget the film he had paid eighty-five centimes to see. He said, 'Yes, but I see so many films.' He brought his chuckle into use, and did it so well that it produced a genuine smile.

'You are fortunate,' she said, smiling.

'Would you permit me to offer you a glass of wine at the Café Liberté, mademoiselle?'

'When?'

'If possible, now.' Again that chuckle.

'I will ask my colleagues if I can run off for a few minutes.'

As soon as they were seated in the cheerful, smoke-filled café, Saffarty said, 'May I ask mademoiselle from Marseilles to tell me her name?'

'Why, it's Mireille.'

'Just Mireille?'

'Yes, Mireille.'

'But, Mademoiselle Mireille, what is your family name?'

'Mourou.'

'That makes four M's, you know.'

'I don't understand.'

'Mademoiselle Mireille Mourou of Marseilles.'

This time she laughed, too. Her front tooth was crooked, but he thought she was still attractive. It reminded him of his eye.

'I'd like to know your name,' she said shyly. 'Unless, of course, you'd rather not tell me.'

'Saffarty. Everyone calls me Saffarty.'

'But that's a family name, surely.'

'I know that. But everyone calls me Saffarty.'

The waiter brought two glasses of wine. Saffarty said, 'I suppose I'll bore you if I tell you what beautiful yellow-brown eyes you have. I suppose everyone tells you that.'

She flushed, on cue, and he knew that his first impression of her had been correct. She came from Marseilles, where her father had worked in the docks, and her mother had taken in washing. She had come to Paris to seek her fortune; she had lost her hope but not her virtue, which was why she had ended up as an usherette. She was probably the third of a family of three daughters, two of whom were in a convent.

Ah, yes, he thought to himself, he had come a long way since he had put Salonika behind him. He always listened attentively to his landlord's wife, Madame Delange. Madame Delange criticised and scolded and denigrated her neighbours and even their distant families. And she made it her business to know all the sordid details of family skeletons. She had spoken of the usherettes who came from Marseilles.

And, yes, of course, he would mention to Madame Delange the possibility of scooping up a few bargains at the Cinéma Germaine – provided she got there early enough. Word of mouth, the best form of advertising . . . He would make her a special price, as a favour, even if it meant he would be losing on the deal. Madame Delange's boasting would be sure to bring the people in, and the losses would be turned into profits. And quickly, too.

With an effort, Saffarty recalled himself from his thoughts. 'Let me see your palm,' he said. 'I read palms, you know.'

Once again, she responded with delight. She believed him. 'I see ships,' he said seriously. 'And oil and blue overalls, and too much wine. One of your close relations works with ships, but is not a sailor. Am I right?'

'My father,' she whispered. 'You've been talking about my father. Both my parents are dead.'

'I'm sorry, Mireille,' he said, caressing her hand. 'I've seen you before, Mireille, but you didn't see me.'

'Where?'

'At the cinema. In the foyer. I own one of the stalls,' he said, lying casually. He changed the subject abruptly, and told her that he was still a student, but would soon have his commercial diploma.

'And then I suppose you'll get a wonderful job at a bank,' she said wistfully.

'*No!* I'll never work for anyone. *Never!*' he said violently. 'Now, talking about jobs, you'll lose yours if I don't take you back at once!'

Outside the café, an elderly woman accompanied by an accordionist was singing one of the newest songs. Her elbows protruded through the cloth of her coat. Her voice was sweet, though; it lifted with hope, and sounded almost girlish. Outside the cinema Saffarty shook hands with Mireille formally and wished her adieu. Mireille tried hard to hide her disappointment. 'Will we meet again?' she asked timidly. 'I'd like that.'

'But of course. Come to my stall tomorrow and bring your friends. I'll have special bargains. Tell them.'

There was no doubt about it, she would be there and she would bring friends.

Saffarty's predictions proved to be entirely accurate. Everything was sold, and Max was staggered. After they had counted their takings they went to the Café Pistou to celebrate. Max smoked cigarette after cigarette, and slapped his thighs with delight. Several glasses of rough red wine later, Saffarty said, 'Enough celebrating. Let's get down to basic business.'

'That's what we've been doing, Simonico. Counting profits. That's business.'

'See here, Max Blum,' Saffarty said in a hoarse whisper. 'We've been counting *your* profits, and *my* pittance of ten per cent!' He grabbed Max's wrist. 'And don't you ever dare call me Simonico again! D'you hear me?' His voice rose to a roar; in that smoky, steamy café it sounded a warning, like a fog horn.

'Hold on, Saffarty,' Max said, bewildered.

'Listen. For a ten per cent less reduction, you got a hundred per cent more sales. Think, you fool,' Saffarty continued fiercely. 'How did you get all those customers? Eh? I brought them, that's how. And I'll bring more of them; but we'll have to do a deal. Fifty per cent of the profit goes to me.' As if it were an afterthought, he added smoothly, 'And you'll still be making fifty per cent more than you were making on your own. Agreed?'

Max sighed. 'We'll see — ' he began.

'One more thing, Max,' Saffarty persisted. 'So you got my first name from the class register. But where did you hear that I was called Simonico?'

'From my rabbi,' Max said proudly. 'I told him I'd met you. I asked him if he knew there were any Jews in Macedonia. He laughed at me. Salonika is one of the most ancient and venerable Jewish communities in the world, he said. The rabbi wanted to know your name, and when I told him, he said it would be a good idea to call you Simonico. He said it would please you. It would remind you of your home, he said.'

'I don't want to be reminded of my home,' Saffarty replied angrily. 'My name is Saffarty!' He moved forward, and again grabbed Max's wrist. 'I told you. I've stopped being a Jew. Remember?'

'Yes, yes. I remember.'

'Don't forget it, Max,' Saffarty said, his voice frighteningly high. 'Don't forget it.'

'I won't forget it, I swear I won't.'

'Good man. Now we can celebrate. You'll see, Max, it will be caviar all the way. You'll see.'

For days – even weeks – after their celebration, Saffarty pondered his sudden flash of temper. It had taken him by surprise. At the same time, he could not help evaluating how much his outburst had won for him. He had not expected Max to collapse and cower, and give him his fifty per cent. Nor had he planned to test his own strength – far from it; it had clearly been too early for that sort of thing. Also, he knew that but for Max having called him Simonico he would not have become so enraged. Yet his temper had supplied him with a sudden, huge power. There was no doubt about it – it was a dangerously effective weapon.

Only that is, as long as it was under his control. To lose your temper is to lose control, and that would never do. It was a while before real understanding dawned. It was the noise of the rage, and not the rage itself, that had so effectively terrified Max. Accordingly, it was his voice, that ear-splitting loud drum of an instrument, that was, well, a weapon . . .

In time, both his voice and his laugh would become his hallmark, but Saffarty was not to know that then. He knew only that he was onto something – after all, had not the walls of Jericho succumbed to the piercing sound of a ram's horn?

Max was convinced that this strange Saffarty was the answer to all his prayers. While Saffarty congratulated himself on having acquired a free fifty per cent share, Max made the simple calculation that fifty per cent of five hundred was two and a half times more than one hundred per cent of one hundred. In other words, by dividing a larger profit into half he was making two and a half times more with Saffarty than without him. Saffarty's inspired salesmanship meant that Max had extra cash, more than he had ever earned before.

He decided to send it all to Poland. He went to his local *Havas* newsagent to buy the carbon paper that he used to wrap around the franc notes before he placed them in the envelope. This way the notes were protected and concealed from prying, thieving eyes. So far, all his envelopes had arrived safely.

It was while he was in the shop that his eye fell on the racing page of *Le Figaro*. Max had no interest in racing or, indeed, in any form of gambling whatsoever. But one of the horses was called the Prince of Macedonia, and the odds were thirty to one. Max had never heard of Macedonia until he had met Saffarty. A horse called the Prince of Macedonia was definitely a further sign from On High. For a few deliciously agonising moments Max debated placing the entire half of his unexpected extra cash on Prince of Macedonia.

No!

He was not a gambler. But he would indulge himself in a glass of wine – even though it was the middle of the morning. He sat back in his seat at the Café Liberté, and allowed himself to take in the warmth and the smoke, the noise and the laughter that men make. There were no women in the café.

A group of six men at the adjoining table were playing *poules* – drawing the names of the horses, each written on a separate piece of paper, from a hat. Then they would place their bets accordingly. Max watched idly. One of the men called out, '*Merde!* The Prince of Macedonia. No chance. This is a game for fools.'

Max made an instant decision. He would place his entire profit on the Prince of Macedonia. He asked the waiter what he thought of the horse.

'Not a chance. You'll be throwing your money away,' the waiter shrugged.

'Maybe I'll take the risk,' said Max. 'Where is the race track?'

'You really don't know much, do you?' the waiter said pityingly, before giving him directions to Longchamps.'

As soon as Max arrived at the racecourse he found himself in a different world. The excitement and tension was entirely new to him. The Prince of Macedonia was in the second race. His voice and his hands trembled when he handed over the cash.

The attendant sounded bored, and said only, 'Five hundred francs to win on the Prince of Macedonia.'

Max took his little ticket and kept it in a fist so tight that his nails pierced his palms. The man who had been standing behind him fell into step with him. 'You had a hot tip, heh?'

Max glared at him and walked faster. Everyone seemed to have binoculars. How would he know whether or not his horse won? His mouth was dry, but his palms sweated. For the first time it occurred to him that he might lose all his money. His mother had loathed gambling. Sometimes, on very special holidays, usually Hanukah, people would gather in her living room and play cards. He felt a terrible longing for his family, his mother especially. How he had shamed her with Colette! Truly, he had drenched his mother in blood . . . Suddenly, he heard the people about him shouting and cheering. Some sounded as if they were moaning. People stamped their feet, and called out the names of horses.

This strange sound, both harsh and shrill, frightened Max. Dimly he realised that the race must be on. He was just about to offer up a prayer when he heard someone shout, 'Prince Macedonia. *Merde!* Thirty to one! An outsider.' Had his horse won? Was that possible?

When the winner was announced Max ran all the way to the tote. He handed in his crumpled, sticky piece of paper, and received fifteen thousand francs. Suddenly he was stricken by anxiety. What if he should be robbed? Where could he keep the money? In his socks. He went to the men's lavatory, managed to find one with a functioning lock, and stuffed the notes into his socks. He ran all the way to the bus stop, and then ran all the way up the stairs until he reached his *garçonnière*. It was too late for the post office – he would have to wait until the morning to mail the money to his parents. He took off his socks, and began to count it. He counted it again and again, until he realised that he was weeping. He quickly replaced his socks, stuffed them with the money – and flung himself on his bed.

It was probably the first time in his life that he had let himself go. He wept for his months of fear and shame with Colette, and for his parents' bankruptcy in Lodz. He wept for his entire life; until now he had been too afraid even to cry. After a while he began to feel a sense almost of well-being, and knew that it was the money, the magical money that had, at last, permitted him the luxury of tears.

Exhausted, he fell into a deep and dreamless sleep. As soon as he awoke he thought of Saffarty. There was no doubt about it, this strange Jew who said he was no longer a Jew was his lucky talisman. Meanwhile, he would say nothing about the Prince of Macedonia. He had the feeling Saffarty would not approve, and he could not afford to antagonise him.

'We did well today, Mireille,' Saffarty said. 'Your friends brought their friends. They turned out to be good customers.' He pulled out a package. 'It's now two months since Max and I became partners. I'd like to make you a gift of these silk stockings.'

'There's no need,' Mireille said shyly. 'It was an honour to help you.' She made a move to touch Saffarty's arm, but plucked at the cloth of his jacket instead. 'I've made a *bouillabaisse* – a Marseilles speciality. I want to invite you to join me,' she said, speaking tentatively.

'Tonight?'

'Yes.'

'But I have to give a Greek lesson.'

'Later, perhaps?'

'But it will be too late. It will be after ten — '

'I could wait.' With a stuttering laugh, she added, 'The *bouillabaisse* would improve. The longer it cooks, the better.'

'Where do you live?

'Not far from you. Thirty Rue Robard — '

'How do you know where I live?'

'Max told me. Will you come after ten?'

'Thank you. I'd be honoured.'

It was hard to concentrate on Homer that night. Somehow, Saffarty got through the lesson and at last he was on his way to Mireille and a bowl of steaming *bouillabaisse*. He found himself ravenously hungry.

The rain came down hard, and as always Saffarty marvelled at the reflection of the bright neon lights on the cobbled streets – so different from the oriental Salonika. He was a Westerner now. From tomorrow he would have a capital of five thousand francs behind him.

An old crone carrying a basket of roses stopped him. 'A bunch of roses for your sweetheart, monsieur? Only fifty centimes.'

Normally he would have brushed her aside. But it might be nice to take Mireille some flowers, even though he had already given her a pair of silk stockings. He said, 'I'll give you thirty-five.'

'Forty,' the woman said.

'Done,' said Saffarty.

He felt his mood soar, and quickened his pace over the slippery cobbles.

Mireille was waiting at the front door when he arrived.

She led him up the steep, carpetless stairs to her room. As they made their way up the stairs, the smell of fish grew stronger. It reminded him of his father. His mood dropped, and he wished for a moment he had not agreed to come.

Her room was shabby but welcoming. A red and white gingham cloth was on the table, and a single candle already lit. A large wooden crucifix on a bright white wall was the only decoration. The room was warmed by a small gas coin heater. 'It's cosy,' he said, after he had taken off his coat.

'Thank you.' She turned away quickly and said, 'I must put these in water immediately.'

'Do you live alone?' Saffarty asked.

'No. My friend, Lorraine, shares with me. She's with her aunt tonight.' She made him sit down, and busied herself over her gas ring. The tips of her fingers were yellow, he noticed. She said, 'You're looking at my fingers, aren't you? I always add a little saffron at the very last moment.'

'As a matter of fact I *was* looking at your fingers.' Saffarty laughed then, and his mood lightened again. He watched her drop some fennel into the soup, and then she placed a round of toast in his bowl before spooning the soup over it. She carried the steaming bowls to the table, and then brought a large platter with four different kinds of fish. Langoustine, he noted. *Shellfish!* Well, he was no longer a Jew, and there was a first time for everything, and he supposed this was his first time for shellfish.

'I like these white walls of yours,' he said. 'I prefer them to wallpaper.'

'Oh, do you?' she said, pleased. 'I painted over the wallpaper myself.'

'You are an enterprising girl, Mireille,' Saffarty said, openly showing his admiration.

'I was so happy when you said you could come tonight. You see, it's my birthday,' Mireille said, pouring more wine.

He leaned across the table and kissed her on both cheeks. 'Congratulations,' he said. 'How old are you?' Suddenly he laughed. 'A very lovely girl I knew a long time ago – well, it seems long ago, now — ' He stopped for a moment, and then went on. 'Anyway, she told me never to ask a woman her age. Forgive me?'

'There's nothing to forgive,' she said gravely. 'I told you it was my birthday, didn't I? I'm twenty-one.'

'Well then, we both have something to celebrate. I've just acquired some extra capital. Tomorrow I shall invest it!'

'Congratulations, Saffarty!'

'Your nose is red. You have a cold, I think. But it looks pretty, your nose. And you are a wonderful cook!'

'Thank you.'

'Yes, Mireille, you have a pretty pink nose, and it matches your dress.'

Mireille laughed.

'That's better,' he said. 'You should laugh more often. There's only one thing not quite right in this room.'

'What?' she said anxiously.

'The electric light spoils the candlelight. You should switch it off.'

She jumped up at once. 'Certainly,' she said.

'That's better,' he said. 'That's much, much better.' He took her in his arms and began kissing her. He hated the slippery feel of her satin dress; the satin was too shiny and obviously cheap. It grated against his nails. He began undoing the press studs at the back of her dress. 'It's itchy, this material,' he whispered.

'Oh, Saffarty,' she said.

He kissed her more deeply, and soon his hands found her breasts, found her hard nipples. Gently, he began leading her toward the bed. Her breath was coming fast, and because she seemed about to swoon, he picked her up and carried her to the bed. Soon he had undressed her. 'What a beautiful body you have,' he murmured. 'So beautifully shaped. I didn't know, I had no idea it would be so beautiful. You go about in disguise, hiding your shape.' He was whispering now, and gaining her confidence. Within seconds he was nude himself. He picked her up again, pulled back the covers, placed her on the sheet, and then tenderly covered her with the blankets, before getting in beside her. The candlelight flickered and the gas heater hissed, and Saffarty, after one glance at the crucifix, began again to whisper about the shape of her body.

She received his kisses and his tongue, but made no move to touch his body. 'This is the first time for me, Saffarty,' she said softly.

'I know. I could tell. I'll be gentle.' He moved away, and said, 'Where do you keep your towels?' She pointed. 'In that cupboard,' she said.

'Wait a minute,' he said.

He fetched the towel and placed it underneath her. 'You'll be pleased about this later. It will save your sheets.'

He was as gentle as he had said he would be.

When it was over he said, 'You're disappointed, aren't you, Mireille? It will be better the second time, I promise. Go to sleep now, little one. I'll look after you.'

They lay quietly together, and whether he dozed or slept, she could not say. After about an hour or so, she turned toward him and kissed him deeply. They began to make love, very slowly at first, and then very urgently. 'Don't stop, don't stop, don't stop,' she whispered. And then, 'Now! Now! Now!' A cry escaped her, and it turned into sobs, and she put her face in his neck and weeping, said, 'I love you.'

Then they both slept.

It was not yet dawn when Saffarty awoke. He wanted to go to the lavatory, but didn't know where it was. Rain pounded the roof steadily, and pattered against the skylight. He tossed and turned, and finally got up and groped his way in the dark towards the window. As soon as he left the bed Mireille awoke.

'You can't sleep?' she asked anxiously.

'I just woke up. I need the lavatory.'

'I use the chamber pot under the bed,' she said, embarrassed.

'Do you mind if I use it too?'

'No.'

'I'm competing with the sound of the rain,' he said with a laugh. 'How do you like that, eh?'

'I love it, Saffarty. I love you.'

Saffarty returned to the bed. 'I was careless,' he said. 'And selfish. You could be pregnant?'

'No. It's the safe time. The rhythm method.'

'The rhythm method?' Saffarty repeated.

'Yes. A Catholic practice. You're not Catholic?'

'No.' He kissed her. 'If you're sure it's safe, I'd like to begin all over again.'

73

Afterwards they both decided it was too late to go to sleep again. The rain fell against the skylight, and they lay chatting quietly. She got up to make a cup of strong coffee for each of them.

When she returned, she said, 'What were you thinking of, Saffarty? While I was making the coffee I talked to you but you didn't seem to hear me.'

'I must have been thinking about my investment.'

'Just like my boss, Monsieur Feyard. He eats and sleeps investments. I'm going to stop being an usherette. I'm going to be his secretary.'

'He's a robber, your boss. Five hundred francs rent he charges us to use his foyer.'

'But he sells space, he says.'

'What else does he invest in, besides space?'

'Shares, that sort of thing.'

Saffarty wanted to know more about stocks and shares, and stockbrokers . . . He said, 'What sort of shares?'

'Monsieur Feyard says the cinema is not an art any more. It's become an industry.'

'So?' he said, keenly interested.

'So he's buying shares in a film company. He's a very clever man, my boss. He has an apartment on the Boulevard de France.' She shook her head wonderingly. 'He's always reading newspapers.'

'But I thought you said he never stops working — '

'He only reads the financial pages. He reads *Le Journal*, *L'Economiste Français*, *France Soir*. He says it's well known that some financial journalists take bribes from the Russians, and from the Germans!' She stopped speaking, and shook her head again. 'But I'm sure you know all this. I talk too much, don't I?'

'No, you don't talk too much,' Saffarty said firmly. 'What's more, you're a clever girl.'

The truth was that Saffarty did not read the newspapers. He had done no more than glance at the Delanges' papers. He had counted his centimes, and considered newspapers an unjustifiable extravagance. Nothing, however, would have induced him to reveal any of this to Mireille. Now he couldn't wait to buy them.

'Tell you what,' he said. 'Let's get up and go to the Vollard Bistro, and have some croissants while they're still hot. What do you say, eh?'

He began to get dressed. 'Will it be all right for me to walk downstairs with you?'

'That's no problem,' she said, sighing. 'A lot of the girls who live here make their living from men.'

'I see,' Saffarty said gruffly. 'Then you should move somewhere else.'

She warmed a pot of water for him on the little hot plate and then poured it into a large white pottery bowl. She had a large jug, and added some water to it. 'No shaving things, I suppose?' Saffarty said.

'Sorry.'

Just before they left the room, he glanced back toward the bed. The blood-stained towel told its own story.

'What time will your room-mate be back?' he asked.

Mireille had followed his glance, and understood. She said, 'She won't be back until this evening. I'll fix the bed later.' She moved toward him tentatively. 'I'm going to keep that towel for ever. I'll keep it for the rest of my life!'

As soon as Mireille returned to her room, after breakfast, she began attending to her chores. There was the bed to make, the chamber pot to empty, the towel to put away, and the dishes to wash. The room smelled of fish, but also of Saffarty. She did none of the things she had planned – she undressed instead. She unclipped the small mirror that hung inside her wardrobe and propped it against the wall. She wanted to study this body of hers that he had talked about even at breakfast. But, no matter at what angle, she could only see up to her waist. So she moved the mirror to her hot plate, and studied herself from the waist up. She thought the colour of her skin had changed – it seemed rosier, and felt softer. As for her shape – she had always seen herself as much too thin, in fact, skinny. But he said she was slim. Now, she conceded she could be slim. She took her firm hard breasts in her hands and she knew it was his hands that she still felt. She began to hum a love song.

Mireille had not expected to be enraptured by her own body, but Saffarty had done it for her. He had made her into a real woman at last. She hoped the rhythm method would work. Either way, she would have to ask her room-mate about other methods. Just the thought of Saffarty made her body throb. She wished she did not have a perpetual cold, and that her nose would stop being red and swollen. And for the thousandth time she wished she did not have a crooked tooth. She kept her lips closed, but smiled at herself; her teeth still tingled with the memory of his tongue . . .

Except for his squint, Saffarty was not so different from the man of her dreams. To begin with he was tall, and dark, and his shoulders were strong and powerful. But he was even more marvellous than her fantasies. There was a strength in him, a powerful strength that came, she believed, from being his own master. He had taken her and her body with such smooth ease, as if he had been showing and explaining her own body to her. Then he had taken over her body, and made it his own. She had given herself over to him, she realised, she belonged to him now and always would. Her soul felt lighter because it was no longer hers.

She supposed it was only because she had fallen in love with him that she even found his squint was attractive. Yet another usherette had remarked on it too, she remembered. They had giggled over it, because it seemed silly to think a crooked eye could make a man look so dangerously mysterious, like a Spanish bandit. Because his eyes were the colour of dark honey – a sort of topaz, really. He had said her eyes were yellow-brown, but her mirror showed her they were an ordinary light brown. She had noticed the usherettes quickly smooth their dresses, or their hair or do something to improve their appearance as soon as they recognised his laugh, even before they saw him. He had something, that strange *je ne sais quoi* – a kind of electricity that pulled them toward him, irresistibly, like moths to a light bulb. He always found something special to say to each one of them, and never failed to remember their names.

But he had chosen her.

She picked up the blood-stained towel, folded it neatly, and sat cradling it in her arms, rocking to and fro. She remembered the inept fumblings of other boys. But Saffarty was a *man*, and it was his manliness that made him so different. She had been determined she would not give herself until the urge was stronger than she was. Shortly before she left her home to take up domestic service her mother had taught her how to defend herself.

'If a bastard wants to start with you like you were a rabbit, you take his balls in both hands, and think of a rat you are squeezing to death.'

'How do you know about things like that, Maman?' Mireille had asked.

'Your father told me to tell you what to do. He told me to give you this message. All men are bastards!'

Mireille had been silent.

'Did you hear what I said?' her mother demanded.

'Yes, Maman.'

'Then my daughter, repeat what I just said.'

All men are bastards,' Mireille had repeated obediently.

But Saffarty was different, she decided. And she was a lucky girl. Both her parents had died of drink. Last night, Saffarty had taken no more than a single glass of wine . . .

For a long while she sat there, holding the towel, rocking gently in a kind of celebration. The power in him had left her powerless, and she liked that, and was glad she had waited for him. She had given her virginity up to him, and was proud of him for having taken it.

Colette let herself into Max's studio. As usual, she had brought a picnic lunch with her, and she laid out the crisp baguette and Max's favourite cheese, *Thom de Savoie*, with glazed duck, fat out-of-season strawberries and a bottle of red wine. She had washed the lettuce at home, and as she placed it in a bowl she smiled. Green vegetables were good for him; but she also had another of his favourites – a sweet and sour Polish cabbage salad. Then she checked herself in the mirror, and was frankly pleased with what she saw. Her softly flared *crêpe de chine* skirt of the new shorter length flattered her figure and showed it off to perfection. There was no need for her to polish the silver cigarette box; she had done that on Tuesday, and it still shone. Today was Friday. Tuesdays and Fridays were Max's days, and they were the axis of her life.

She heard his quick step, and at once rose to meet him.

'Max! You look wonderful — ' she said breathlessly. 'So handsome! I hope you're hungry.'

She saw his eyes go to her legs, and twirled in her new skirt. 'D'you like it, Max? It's new.'

'It suits you, Colette. Yes, I like it.'

'Come and eat. And tell me all about your studies. Six months and you'll have that diploma, no?'

'Six months.'

'And then you will be a banker.'

'A banker?'

'But of course. A banker. You see, little one, I've been in contact with Monsieur Pequy of the Banque de Commerce. He's an old friend of an acquaintance.'

'You told him about me?'

'Of course. I said you were the nephew of my dressmaker. I also told him you were at the Ecole Inter-Commercial. He knows the school. I told him how you'd worked and saved to finance your education — '

'And he said he had no place for an immigrant, I suppose?' Max said bitterly.

'I wish you wouldn't be such a pessimist — '

'Well, what did he say?'

'He wants references from your professors and he wants to meet you.'

'When?'

'A month before you have your diploma.' She leaned across the table and took his hand, and pressed it against her cheek. 'Are you pleased with me, little one?' she said.

It was only at some signal from her that they went to bed. Colette knew that he still wanted her. She also knew that he wished he didn't, but understood that there was something besides the money, and the clothes, the *garçonnière* and the general perks that made him want her. She knew that because of the way he made love to her. But he was ashamed, desperately ashamed, of his liaison with an older woman.

Though the bed was only a few steps away from the table, she made a sort of youthful skipping movement. Usually, she tore off her own clothes. Today, however, she sat at the edge of the bed, and said, 'These tiny buttons are so delicate. I'll need your help, little one.'

She saw his hands tremble as her pearls were undone. He turned away to attend to his own undressing. 'I want you to undress me,' she said. 'Please.'

'Why?' he asked, though he had already begun.

'Because it's good for you to wait a little — '

'But not too long,' he said. Suddenly he smiled, and her heart quickened with gratitude. She wanted to thank him for that smile, and had an insane impulse to drop to her knees. But she only said, 'You have a beautiful smile, little one.'

78

'And you are as slender as a snake, and your skin is as soft as — '

'As soft was what, Max? What?'

'As a silk stocking,' he said gruffly. 'Enough of this waiting. *Enough!*'

Not much later, he fell into an exhausted sleep. Colette loved watching him while he slept. He sleeps as greedily as he makes love, she thought. After a while she got up and sat naked at the table with the checked cloth, and delicately sipped some red wine. She listened to him breathe, each breath sounding like a sigh. For months, now, she had been struggling to find a way to help him overcome his shame of her. His mind thought of her as an old lady, but his body reacted to her as if she were a young girl. Once again, she assessed her newest idea. Then she stood up, took the high-heeled slippers from her shopping basket, and then tied a lacy maid's apron about her waist. She began collecting the plates noisily. He would wake, and her stubbornly youthful body would make him smile. She would join him in bed again, and they would wait awhile, and touch one another only, and then they would be able to talk.

But he slept heavily, and the clattering of dishes did not make him stir. Finally she dropped a plate.

'What's going on? What are you doing?'

'I'm sorry I woke you, little one.'

Then he smiled, as she had hoped he would. She approached the bed, kicked off her slippers, and got in beside him. Now there would be time to talk.

'It's quite fashionable, you know, for young men to have older mistresses,' Colette said, lying back, avoiding his eyes.

'That's what you think!'

'And you are naive. Just like a man,' she giggled flirtatiously. 'You wouldn't say no if Sarah Bernhardt asked you to put your shoes under her bed, would you?'

'Of course not.'

'See what I mean?' She went on to tell him about Coco Chanel, and her string of young lovers, and Valentino and his early affair, and the Prince of Wales and Peggy Guggenheim.

'But what's all that café society you're talking about got to do with me?' Max asked bitterly.

'You're not in Poland now,' Colette said sharply. 'You're in Paris. Even the Czarina, Catherine of Russia, had Lieutenant Pluto Zubof as a lover when she was sixty, and he was twenty-five.' She turned toward him and ruffled his thick black hair. 'But enough about me. You. Why don't you show me how young you are again . . . ?'

Colette walked home slowly. Once again she felt fully alive, and as conscious of the pale sun as she was of the flared softness of the *crêpe de chine* against her legs, of the shopping basket on her arm, of the elegance of her matching flared dove-grey jacket. She was aware, too, of the appreciative glances that men sent in her direction. Meanwhile her lover's traces were on her skin, and deep inside her throat, and nothing could dislodge that . . .

When Colette left Max lay back on the bed. That funny eye of Saffarty's would do an extra somersault when it saw just how much capital Max Blum was not only able but willing to invest. Selling brassières on a street – well, a stall in a cinema foyer was almost a street – seemed too daring. Saffarty was asking for trouble, they would be left with dead stock on their hands, and besides – who could tell? – they might even have to deal with the police. They had no licence. It was obvious that Saffarty had a good head for business, and although Max was doing well, and learning from Saffarty, he felt ill at ease with him. His discomfort had intensified when Monsieur Delange came to the cinema stall to buy some socks. 'Your partner Saffarty is a machine, not a man,' he had said. 'A man needs eyes at the back of his head to keep up with the crooked eye of that one!'

There was something ominous about the Greek. Max prayed, really prayed, that he would never find out about Colette. At the beginning he had half believed that Saffarty would help him escape her. Now the thought of his scorn was sickening.

Yet he could not get rid of the woman. It was sometimes impossible to deny that it was her flesh he wanted, and only her flesh. He had gone to bed with several other women since he had known her, but it had been mechanical and unexciting. There were times when the revulsion afterwards had been so great that he had been ill. And then the fear of having contracted a disease was almost as bad as the reality. Colette's shape, Colette's softness – the tricks that woman could do with those curves of hers . . . Just thinking of her, like this, he was in a full – and shameful – erection. It was proof enough that he was not a real gigolo.

Two months before his seventeenth birthday, by which time he had been in Paris for nearly two years, Saffarty had begun investing in newspapers, and was now an assiduous reader of the financial pages.

The result of all this was that he now had a stockbroker, and two weeks after he bought stock in the film company he sold half, and more than doubled his money. 'How much can I afford to lose?' and 'No one ever lost any money taking a profit,' were the two basic pillars of his thinking. In other words, by chance or instinct, he had developed his own business rules.

For the moment, though, he preferred dealing in his own merchandise because stocks and shares were abstracts, and could not be handled like a pair of socks. Besides, how could he trust those unknown directors who controlled his investment, and could do what they wished with his good money?

He was openly extravagant in his gratitude to Mireille for having introduced the financial pages to him. It was like learning a new language, and just as easy. He studied the barometers of business, the capital markets, dividend declarations and government finances. More than a new language, it was a new world.

Meanwhile, Mireille accepted his thanks with her own shy gratitude, and threw her entire soul into helping him with his newest dream. She saw it as a dream and he saw it as a project – without her inspiration it would have been neither. To think it had all come about a few weeks earlier, because of a broken chair! She had leaned back to answer the telephone for Monsieur Feyard when her chair had suddenly snapped. Feyard took a key from the collection in his locked drawer, and sent her to the dingy store-room at the front of the building, to the left of the foyer.

Mireille turned the key with difficulty, for the lock was rusted. The door opened on a stale, dark room – everything appeared to be covered in soot – and there was a strong stench of something rotting. The door slammed behind her, and she knew a moment of terror. Her hand flew to the matches she kept in her pocket – she had caught the smoking habit from Saffarty and quickly blessed him for it – and as she lit the match, she glimpsed a sliver of light coming from the wall. 'That light must be coming from a window,' she thought, and made her way towards it.

Yes, it was a window. And the room, though filthy and full of junk . . . She wasted five more matches as she explored it, then found the chair, and carried it up to Monsieur Feyard's office.

'What took you so long, my girl?' Monsieur Feyard grumbled.

'The room was dark, and, excuse me, monsieur, so filthy.'

'What do you expect from a store-room? I know the condition of the room.'

'I'm sorry, Monsieur Feyard, but it took me a little while to find the chair.'

Feyard grunted and Mireille flushed, but said nothing. He had forgotten to ask for the return of the key to the door . . . She prayed he would not remember. She wanted to show that room to Saffarty.

That night she told Saffarty about the room. 'It could be a shop,' she said quietly. 'It has a window.'

'I can't understand why I didn't notice it,' he said slowly. 'But, Mademoiselle Mireille from Marseilles, you're right.' His voice rose enthusiastically. 'You're absolutely right.'

'You could put your trestle tables up against the window, and sell through it.'

'True. I could also enlarge my range. The other day, when I was at the Sentier in the wholesalers' district, I met Aladeff – a shrewd old man who wholesales suspender belts, and the new, light brassières and garters. I talked to him. He laughed at me. Not suitable for the street, he said. No good for the hawkers. He deliberately insulted me. He who laughs last, laughs longest, I told myself. Now, we'll see what he says when I tell him I have a shop!'

'But you haven't seen it yet, Saffarty,' Mireille said timidly. 'I could be mistaken. And Monsieur Feyard might not let you use it.'

'Don't worry about that. Leave Monsieur Feyard to me. It's true I haven't seen it, but you and I will see it tonight.'

'There's one thing I didn't tell you,' Mireille said seriously. 'The room stinks. You'll have to hold your nose. I'm sorry about that, Saffarty.'

Saffarty did not answer. Instead, he let loose one of his loudest whooping laughs.

'What's so funny, Saffarty? What's the joke? I don't understand,'

Mireille said. She was embarrassed – his laugh even rang above the high clatter and chatter of the crowded bistro. They met there because Mireille's room-mate had the 'flu, and because Saffarty did not like to take her to his own room, under the watchful eyes of Monsieur Delange.

'You must not apologise for his filth as if it was your fault.' Saffarty stopped to take her hand. His thumb applied a gentle rhythmic pressure to her palm. 'And you look so worried.' Suddenly he said, 'Does the room stink of dead fish?'

'No.'

'Good. Not that I couldn't handle that, of course. So, the room's filthy *and* it stinks. A health hazard. Your boss could have the health authorities on his neck. A typhoid epidemic. Tell me, does the smell remind you of sewage?'

'Yes.'

'Good. You see, Mireille, there was something in *Le Monde* about typhoid a few days ago. I wonder how Monsieur Feyard will react when I offer him that bit of information?' He took her other hand and now held both of them in a tight grip in his fist. 'You were a clever girl to keep that key. A very, very clever girl.'

Oh! how she warmed to him, whenever he told her that she was a clever girl. Sometimes, while he was making love to her, he would whisper that magic phrase – *you're a clever girl*. There was nothing, then, that she would not have done for him. A few moments earlier when he laughed, he had sounded like a schoolboy. He may well have been a businessman, but he was still a student of course. She did not know his exact age. She knew only that under his commanding strength she felt as safe, and as protected, as a much-loved child.

Strolling back to the cinema, their arms tight about each other's waists, he stopped suddenly, and said, 'I think I could live in that room. That means that you and I could spend whole nights together. I have to leave the miserable Delanges, anyway. Tell me, tell me, what d'you say to that?'

Mireille could not trust herself to speak, and in answer, tightened her arm about his waist.

Saffarty thought long and hard about the manner in which he would conduct his negotiations. In the end he decided to invite

Monsieur Feyard to the Bergère Bar. Monsieur Feyard peered over his rimless glasses, and evaluated Saffarty's clothing. Then he raised his eyebrows, drooped his lips, and said, 'The Bergère, *hein*? Not the one on the Avenue Foch, certainly?'

'That's the one,' Saffarty said shortly. 'Shall we say at six o'clock tomorrow?' He dropped his voice confidingly. 'I assure you, Monsieur Feyard, that what I have to discuss is probably more in your interest than in mine!'

'Your young man has invited me to the Bergère Bar,' Monsieur Feyard reported to Mireille. 'Did he tell you about it?'

'No, Monsieur Feyard,' Mireille replied truthfully. 'No, he said nothing to me.'

'I see.' Monsieur Feyard gave an eloquent shrug.

'Did monsieur accept?' Mireille asked nervously.

'But of course. Why not?'

Saffarty, however, perceived the way in which his invitation had been accepted as an insult. 'Not the Bergère Bar on the Avenue Foch?' would have been bad enough, but with that condescending glance Feyard had added insult to injury. It was a look he knew too well – he'd seen it on his father's face often enough. The tongue has no bones, yet it can break bones . . .

Well, we'll see whose bones will be broken, Saffarty thought angrily.

The money Max had won at the races would have been more than enough to pay for the combined fares for his parents and his sister. He could and should, he knew, bring them all to Paris. But how would he be able to support all of them once they were there? How would they fit in? His father would force him to break off his association with Saffarty. Although his father had never heard of a Jew who was no longer a Jew, even if he was a strange kind of unknown Jew to begin with, he would see Saffarty as a living, walking, breathing offence against the faith. If Saffarty had been a member of his own family, he would have done his duty, and sat *shivah*, and said the prayers for the dead for Saffarty . . .

The thought of his pious father was enough to make Max feel confused and uneasy – and, worse still, guilty.

He and Saffarty had fallen into the habit of meeting two or more nights a week at the Café Pistou, and yet it took several glasses of strong red wine before Max's guilt lifted, and he allowed himself the luxury of enjoying Saffarty's crude jokes about their customers, and his coarse comments about Monsieur and Madame Delange. But it was only at the Café Pistou that Max felt anything approaching the open camaraderie of real friendship.

One night Max arrived at the restaurant a few minutes ahead of Saffarty. After much thought and several discussions with Colette he had decided to present Saffarty with an unusual gift – a black velvet eye-patch. He had been somewhat nervous about how to give it. 'Make it a joke,' Colette had suggested. 'Tell him that an Englishman with an eye-patch defeated Napoleon.'

Still, it was a delicate matter – Max wanted to help Saffarty without hurting him. Waiting for the right moment, he held the small package in his pocket. After at least an hour of nervous fiddling he pulled it from his pocket, impetuously unwrapped it himself, and handed it to Saffarty. 'Try it on,' he said gruffly.

Saffarty put it on at once, jumped up and crossed over to the bar, where he looked at himself in the mirror.

'It suits me,' he chuckled. 'What do you think, Pierre?' he asked the barman. He turned to Max, clapped him hard on the back and said, 'I should have worn it years ago.' He adjusted the fine strap and winked with his other eye. 'Thanks, Max!'

The eye-patch brought them closer. They spent more time together, flirted with girls, and talked about things other than business. There was no doubt it added both to Saffarty's good looks and to his confidence. There was a spring in his walk. The eye-patch attracted attention, which he thrived on. It was easy after that for Max to teach him how to go for quality. Unable to afford the best, they found the tailor who worked for the master tailor, and Saffarty had his first custom-made suit.

Several times Max came close to telling him about Colette, but each time his nerve failed him.

Once, Max felt relaxed enough to question lightly, 'If you have not eaten *trayf*, would you have given up being a Jew?'

'What difference does it make?' Saffarty rose suddenly and pushed his chair away from the table with a quick, violent movement, so that it screeched against the tiled flooring. 'Goodnight,' he said curtly.

Max stared after him. He realised he had been waiting for months to bring the subject up. He also realised that Saffarty acted as if the business had been his to start with, when in fact it was the other way round. Monsieur Delange had been right – he was a machine. He was also a clever machine . . . Max was determined not to be stupid enough to allow his sudden dislike of Saffarty to get the better of him.

Somehow, once Max got to the race track he forgot his troubles. Gambling, he had found, was a superb way of replacing lingering anxieties with others capable of instant resolution. Instant answers made for a simpler life; for an intense moment the pain of living was made exquisite, and therefore more bearable. Or so it seemed to Max when – against his will – he lifted the floorboards, grabbed two thousand francs, and set out for the race course.

He had three successive winners, and it was almost too much for him. Sweating, he put all his winnings on the fourth race, on number four, the favourite Belle Ciel, because he had met Colette on May 4th.

The man who had been standing beside him all day tried again to speak to him. Now he said, 'You've got good information, my friend. Three winners. Who d'you work for?'

'No one,' Max said shortly.

'How come you got three winners?'

Max shrugged but did not answer.

'I've been watching you,' the stranger persisted. 'I saw how much you put on the favourite. No one in his right mind takes such a risk unless he's in the know. Belle Ciel doesn't have a hope in hell!'

'How do you know that?'

'Everyone knows. That bastard of a jockey, Luc Soustelle, will come to a sorry end. That's one funeral I won't miss!' The man's breath stank of wine. 'Well, it's obvious you can afford to lose. I'm broke!'

Trembling, Max turned away. He censured himself for not owning binoculars. He took out his pencil and made frantic calculations on his racing card. Odds – he had scarcely considered the odds. What did it mean?

The stranger studied Max's scrawl of figures. 'You believe in luck, not skill, no?' The stranger clicked his tongue. 'Excuse me, monsieur, but you've got it all wrong — '

'The odds are nine to seven.'

'Correct. So, for your four thousand francs, if your horse wins – mind you I would lay odds myself that it won't — '

'Simply tell me what I stand to win,' Max interrupted nervously, loosening his tie. 'I know how much I'm losing!'

'Sure you do. You'll win something in the order of three thousand francs. You'll know your fate soon enough, monsieur.'

Max groaned aloud. The horses were at the starting box. No binoculars! He turned to the stranger. 'How much do you want for your binoculars?' he asked.

'Excuse me, monsieur?'

'I'll buy them. What do you want for them?' Max said, busying himself with a wad of notes.

'Five hundred francs,' the stranger said, quickly evaluating how much was in the wad in Max's hands.

Impatiently Max made the exchange. Now he was free to concentrate on the long, thrilling minute or less that would seal his fate. The roar of the crowd rose, but Max made no sound. His throat was dry. During the last few seconds came the shriek of a new name, Belle Ciel, and his heart raced, and then streaked along with his horse. The sound subsided. The stranger thumped his back. 'You won! You won!'

Dazed, Max sat down, his lips moved in a silent prayer. He wiped his face with his sleeve.

'*Merde!*' the stranger said. 'His horse comes in, and all he can do is cry.'

Max walked slowly to the *garçonnière*, barely aware of the heavy rain.

He prayed, and gave thanks. He began to make plans. With this and the money he'd already won he had enough to give him the upper hand. Saffarty was in for a shock. We'll see who gets the better of whom, he thought. Time would tell. Meanwhile he would say nothing.

While Max prayed in the rain, Saffarty was in the Café Rouge, telling Mireille about his meeting with Feyard.

'Your fat boss sat in the bar with his eyes rolling and his jowls shaking with astonishment. He couldn't stop himself from touching his own reflection in the shiny, black walls. The beige and the mauve didn't interest him, I suppose he couldn't see his own reflection in them, the fat peasant. He fingered the cloth of my suit, too, and then excused himself. He couldn't help himself, I could tell.'

The kind of explosive laughter that followed reminded Mireille of a schoolboy. Then he took both her hands in his tightest grip, and whispered. 'And when I ordered the latest cocktail, called Lady Mendl's Invention, he said, "What's that?" You should have seen the way the barman looked at him. *I* only knew it because I'd deliberately got there early enough to ask what the newest drink was. It tasted horrible – it's made of gin, grenadine and the white of an egg. He coughed and spluttered, but that didn't stop him having three more.'

Saffarty imitated Feyard's staccato coughing.

'But what did he say about the store-room? Did he agree?

'Of course he did.' Saffarty said, his voice cold and firm. 'I spent a fortune at the Bèrgere Bar, but it was a first-class investment. It brought our Monsieur Feyard down to size. He was on unfamiliar territory and he was lost, I tell you, lost!' He stopped for a moment and shook his head. 'I only had to raise my voice twice,' he went on, musing aloud. 'I'd expected to have a much harder time. I simply talked a little louder when I talked about typhoid and health inspectors.'

'But he can change his mind,' she said, almost whimpering. 'I'm sure he will — '

'That won't be possible,' he snapped.

'But — '

'I'm not a fool, Mireille. I wrote out the agreement, quickly, and then we got two waiters to witness it. Then we celebrated with champagne.'

When Mireille heard that, she had leaned across the table and kissed him full on the lips. A passing waiter said casually, 'Oh, what it is to be in love — '

But for Mireille his words were a benediction. Back in Marseilles, even her daydreams had been frugal. But she had allowed herself the luxury of a secret fantasy: one day she would marry a docker, who would rise to be a foreman, and then together they would have a grocery shop, or a café where his former fellow workers would be customers.

The newest love-songs suited Mireille perfectly. Their melody was with her constantly, like her heartbeat, because it was like her life, and her life was music, now. She was in a state of permanent surprise. Falling in love was altogether outside of her expectations. Of course she had expected to find a husband, a man whom she would love dutifully, and bear with bravely. Now, whatever she did – whether showing customers to their seat, or talking with her room-mate, or rushing to work, or scrubbing the filthy store-room, her body vibrated with the memory of Saffarty, of the promise of him. She rejoiced in her own flesh and it made her glow, and grow. She was twenty-one, and yet she could have sworn that in the three months since she'd known Saffarty, she'd grown taller.

Deep inside she felt exotic, sometimes even as exotic as Josephine Baker. Saffarty had done this for her. Fervently she stripped, scrubbed and scoured the store-room in an act of devotion, a ritual of gratitude.

Her earnest discussions with the *pharmacien* yielded remarkable results. The stench soon gave way to the safer pungency of antiseptics, the room gleamed. From time to time she would giggle to herself, or hum a song as she worked on her own. Saffarty was seeing wholesalers, inspecting other street markets, and she was doing this for him so that his weekend could be spent more profitably. Recalling Saffarty's account of his negotiation with Monsieur Feyard she would laugh out loud. He was a clever one, her Saffarty, sly as a fox.

Oh! He was going to go far, her Saffarty. She, too, had come a long, long way from being Mademoiselle Mireille from Marseilles. She was planning on making a velvet curtain. If she hadn't spotted the window, Saffarty would not have had his shop. She was only dimly aware of her raw and bleeding hands – her mind dreamed of curtains, but focused on the job in hand, the floorboards she was so energetically scrubbing – and so she did not hear Saffarty come into the room. He watched her silently, saw her grimace and look at her hands, shrug, and then return to her scrubbing.

In a flash he was kneeling beside her, 'What has mademoiselle from Marseilles done to her pretty hands?' he asked softly. 'Look, they're full of splinters.'

'It's nothing,' she said quickly. 'I'll attend to it later. I'll get them out with a needle.'

'A needle?' he said, alarmed.

'It's not so terrible. You use a large needle, sterilise it over a candle flame, and *voilà!* out come the splinters.'

'I'll do it for you.'

'It's not necessary.'

'I insist,' Saffarty said. 'Where's the needle?'

'I've only got a safety pin. But it will do.'

'Are you sure it's safe?'

'Yes, I'm sure.'

'Come into the light. You need a break, anyway.'

Mireille did as she was told. She sat on the floor, and rested her pale head against the wall. Now that she had stopped, fatigue set in and she felt faint. He seemed so sure of himself as he held the pin over the flame. He glanced at his watch, like a doctor, she thought. His eye patch made him look so – well, interesting. The flame illuminated his strong high cheekbones. Suddenly, she said, 'I love you, Saffarty.'

'Just a minute,' he said, withdrawing the pin from the flame. 'This will only take a minute.' He sat on the floor beside her. 'Two splinters in this hand, and one in the other.' She felt like a very cherished, very small girl. She doubted whether she had ever trusted anyone – even her mother – as much as she trusted this man. He worked deftly and gently, and two jagged splinters were quickly retrieved. The third was more deeply embedded. The probing went deeper, and though she cried out in pain, and tried to pull her hand away, he did not stop but pierced her skin still further.

When at last the splinter was excised, she gasped. Once more, she attempted to release her hand. But he held fast. 'It's not all out,' he said sternly.

'Enough,' Mireille begged. 'Leave it. Please, I beg you.'

'I always finish what I begin,' Saffarty said. He brought her palm close to his mouth and breathed on it. 'That will soothe it for you. It would be dangerous to leave that tiny bit in. You know I'm right.' He began once more to probe and to pierce. Mireille bit her lip and submitted. Saffarty would not give up, she knew. He did not like what he was doing, she was sure of that, but she had the feeling that he did not really care too much, either. He seemed unaffected. A sudden chill moved through her body. Just then, and with the lightest touch he moved his fingers over her head, scarcely touching her hair. 'You're a good girl, Mireille,' he said. 'I'm proud of you.'

Mireille's chill melted, and she nuzzled into his neck. They sat together quietly – Mireille wished it could be for ever – but after a while he moved restlessly and said, 'I found a place where I can get the suspender belts more cheaply. Only I'll have to buy in bulk.'

'But you've already bought too much as it is. You told me so yourself.'

'I know I did, because I was short of guts! But this way, you see, I'll get the stuff so cheaply I'll make two hundred per cent on each item. And if I sell every one I buy, that'll be ten thousand francs!'

'Ten thousand? But that's enough for an apartment!'

'Or a business,' Saffarty said, grinning.

'A business? Oh, yes. Of course, a real business.'

Saffarty stood up and paced the room. 'You've worked hard, Mireille; you've done wonders with this rat-hole.'

'What are you going to call it? Saffarty Marché?'

'You're thinking of Bon Marché again,' he said. 'No, my first shop will have no name. It'll be like an indoor-outdoor market, and people will come because there'll be bargains, and because they'll know I've got no overheads.' He flung his head back and clapped his hands.

'What does Max Blum say?'

'Max? I haven't told him yet. Why should I?'

'Isn't he your partner?'

'Max Blum is my partner, not my boss.'

They worked together for several hours, and only stopped when they agreed the room was now ready for painting. The walls were to be close to the mauve that Saffarty had noticed at the Bèrgere Bar. If the colour was unavailable he would mix the paint himself. They locked the door carefully. The shop was their secret. So far, Max knew nothing about it.

But then of course, they knew nothing about Max's winnings, either . . .

91

6

A week later Saffarty and Max arranged to meet at the Café Pistou. During the week they'd been unusually short with one another. Neither Saffarty nor Max realised that both were playing the same game; each believed he had successfully diverted the other from any sort of detailed discussion.

Saffarty wanted to do a deal with Max, and when the shop was finished he would be in a stronger position to lay down his terms and conditions.

The first condition was that Max would have to agree to pay half the conversion expenses, and the second was that he would have to pay key money. After all, shops were at a premium, and without him this would have been way beyond Max's reach. Saffarty planed to compromise over the expenses, but not over the key money. Saffarty and Monsieur Feyard had a written agreement – Max did not. Therefore, if Max refused he would have to find another stall and another partner.

Max had finally decided to tell Saffarty about his winnings but, unlike Saffarty, his decision was not strictly related to business. There were two things Max wanted from Saffarty: respect and envy.

'Our profits are up,' Saffarty began.

'That's all well and good,' Max said resentfully. 'But there's no cash in hand.'

'No cash in hand,' Saffarty repeated. 'What d'you mean?'

'I mean what I say. No capital. Nothing. Not a *sou*.'

'Are you trying to tell me that stock is not capital?' Saffarty said, his voice dangerously low.

'No, it's not. At least not as far as I'm concerned.' Suddenly Max called out, '*Garçon!* More wine!'

His newly boastful tone alerted Saffarty. 'Are you trying to tell me something, Max?'

Max merely smirked and said nothing.

'Don't tell me *you've* got capital!' Saffarty said scornfully.

'Perhaps.'

Saffarty's loud, vicious laugh cracked out like a machine gun.

The laugh drew its intended response from Max. 'I've got more capital, more cash, in my hands than you've ever dreamed of.' He drained the glass of wine that had just been set before him.

'How much?' Saffarty asked, quietly. 'Tell me how much.'

'Thirty thousand francs.'

'Thirty thousand francs?' Saffarty echoed. 'My God, that's a fortune. A fortune.' He spoke in an awed whisper.

'When I talk about capital, I know what I'm talking about.'

'Yes, you do, Max. You certainly do. And I'm glad you told me. Because, there's something I want to tell *you*. Or, rather, show you.'

He waved aside Max's protestations, as if they were so many bothersome flies, and all but marched him to the Cinéma Germaine.

Now, when he turned the key in the lock, it opened easily. The room sparkled, and the lacquered walls shone. A large tip to the doorman at the Bar Bergère had produced the name of the decorator. Saffarty, wearing his new suit, had called on the decorator to discuss designs for a private bar in the apartment he said he was about to buy. The ruse worked. The decorator showed him samples of several shades and Saffarty read the name of the manufacturer . . . He was no longer obliged to imitate the exact colour he wanted.

To the left of the room there was a small cubicle with mirrors for walls. To show Max the street from the window, Saffarty opened Mireille's mauve velvet curtains.

'A shop like this would cost you a hundred thousand francs. More, probably.'

'Nonsense,' Max said.

'Go and ask the *pharmacien*. Ask the butcher at the corner – of course that's a corner, so it costs more. Ask the shoemaker what he had to pay for his hovel.'

'Why are you telling me this?'

'Because this is our shop.'

Saffarty went on to outline his plans. He explained that at the beginning they would do this without a licence because it took years for permission to get a licence – neither of them were French citizens. And besides, the only way to get a licence was to buy an existing shop with a licence. And no one could call it a shop because it would not even have a name – there would be no name on the window. The room, as far as the authorities were concerned, was for Monsieur Feyard's new caretaker, Monsieur Saffarty. It was up to Max to choose whether or not he wanted to be a partner. Saffarty put his two conditions – the key money and the conversion expenses – and then added that Max could easily afford it. Incidentally, he added, Monsieur Feyard had agreed that every cinema customer who had the lucky seat number would have the chance of winning free stockings. All of which was free advertising.

'And by the way,' he concluded, 'Monsieur Feyard will get ten per cent of the profits.'

'On top of the rent, I suppose,' Max said thoughtfully.

'Instead of the rent. He believes in me. He knows we'll make more than his rent.' It was only then that he said, 'Well, Max Blum, how does it feel to be a merchant, huh?'

'What makes you think I'll agree? This premium of yours is robbery — '

'What's your money doing for you now?'

'Waiting for me to come and spend it.'

'It's earning interest, too, isn't it?'

'No.'

'Then your bank is robbing you. Thirty-five thousand francs at only five per cent would bring you seventeen hundred and fifty a year.'

'But it's not in a bank. I don't trust banks.' Max had always blamed his father's ruinous currency speculations on the banks.

In a flash Saffarty simultaneously devised and put forward a new proposition. He would borrow from Max, paying him a higher interest than the bank, and they could buy even more stock, and Max would then double his money. Saffarty now had a new wholesaler. Again and again he said, 'Bulk buying means cheaper prices which means higher profits.'

For all the two hours Saffarty tried to convince Max, they stood in the middle of the room like sentries on duty.

Suddenly Max said, 'How old are you, Saffarty? Come on, you've never told me.'

'How old do you think I am?'

'It's hard to tell. Because of your eye.'

'It was an accident, my eye,' Saffarty said truthfully. 'It happened fourteen years ago, when I was nine,' he lied smoothly. 'I'm twenty-three. How old are you?'

'Twenty-one.'

'A baby,' Saffarty laughed. 'You'd get four per cent at the most, from the bank. I'll give you five per cent.'

'How much will that come to?'

'On second thoughts I'll give you five thousand francs for the use of your money. For six months. That is thirty-three per cent interest.' He laid his hand on Max's shoulder. 'And you'll still get half our profits — '

'Thirty-three per cent? It's a deal!'

'*You* are robbing *me*,' Saffarty said. 'Fine partner you turned out to be.'

The most important trick Saffarty learned from that negotiation was the wisdom of telling at least half the truth. But Max's question about his age revived all sorts of memories, and that night, making love to Mireille, he thought of Judith, who had guessed his real age. It occurred to him that he'd stopped being a child when his father had almost blinded him. And he had abandoned youth when he came to Paris. He thought of the youth he'd missed, and he thought of the anxious, whining, pitiful, *older* Claude Delange. He felt no regrets. He thought of the way Claude was pampered and fed, nagged and cossetted, swamped and suffocated, and was glad that he had passed from childhood to manhood. Judith had turned him into a man; he'd never forget that. He had begun his life sooner than was usual, he supposed. Perhaps it gave him some kind of advantage, like the cyclist who started the race ahead of time. One thing was for sure, though. By beginning earlier, he had gained extra time, and lengthened his future. Time was on his side, he had plenty of it and he'd make it work for him – it was an extra profit, just as Max's interest was an extra profit. Perhaps, he sensed, by starting earlier he had unwittingly got hold of the most precious commodity of all, time, and he had got it free.

Only one thing troubled him now: Max was a compulsive gambler. He would have to watch him very carefully.

One night he woke Mireille to say, 'Max is a weakling.' He snapped on the light and kicked off the bedclothes. 'He's a weakling with a weakness. It's not good having a weak partner.'

'You're too hard on him,' Mireille said sleepily.

'I tell you, I don't like his gambling.'

'Come back to bed,' she murmured.

'I can't sleep. I can't get his gambling out of my mind.'

Mireille sighed. Naked, she got out of bed and went to him. She held him tightly, and pressed her body tight against his, and tighter still, until, standing on tiptoe, she pressed him into her, and when he cried out she led him back to bed. Not before she heard his deep, even breathing did she try to get to sleep herself. She rarely took a chance with the rhythm method – she was already worried about a previous risk, as it was.

In December 1926, Saffarty and Max were awarded their diplomas of proficiency from the Ecole Inter-Commercial. There was no real ceremony – the students merely lined up to shake the Director's hand, and to receive the rolled certificate tied with a red ribbon.

As far as Max was concerned his diploma only conferred a trade – it had none of the status of a profession, like the architectural career he had been forced to abandon.

Colette's boundless pride was both an embarrassment and an irritation. But then he was not to know how pitifully inadequate her own formal education had been.

Sending Max to the Ecole Inter-Commercial had made her no less proud than any mother who scrimped and saved to see her son become a doctor.

She had the certificate mounted on a gold border, and framed in gold. She looked on it as her proudest achievement.

In Max's opinion the frame was as excruciatingly vulgar as the mirrored pool in her hall. But for once he held his tongue and said nothing that would hurt her. At least, he told himself wryly, he still had enough grace left in him not to spoil things by showing her his true reaction.

The diploma meant nothing to Saffarty – it was already absolutely clear to him that he would never be required to present his qualifications. By way of celebration he sent five hundred francs to his parents. He also wrote and thanked them for having given him the opportunity to penetrate to the core of a balance sheet. 'One day when I buy a business, no one will be able to cheat me.' It was only as he wrote it that he realised he meant every word he had said.

Of what you hear believe nothing, and of what you see believe half.

It was certainly true of balance sheets, Saffarty thought, but decided against including it in his letter. He was doing a little business, he wrote, still buying and selling socks. He made no mention of his shop. His father would boast about it – others would come from Salonika to copy what he had done – and he was not yet successful enough to invite competition.

He finished his letter hurriedly and went to meet Max at the Bal Tabarin, where they were to go dancing. They had no classes to go to now, and occasionally used the time for their own amusement. Both had become fairly expert at the tango. Neither Mireille nor Colette were included – Saffarty had not yet learned of Colette's existence – and they enjoyed finding new and exciting dance partners. It was good harmless fun, they said. They both agreed that the buxom, blue-eyed Lucia was the finest dancer. They came to an agreement not to attempt to meet her anywhere but at the Bal Tabarin. But a strange sort of competitiveness over her developed between them, anyway, probably because she made it clear that she had only one passion in her life and that was dancing. This sort of indifference invited challenge, and each tried to spend a little more time with her on the dance floor than the other. It was light-hearted, and it was good, and it appeared to strengthen their friendship.

Mireille continued to work for Monsieur Feyard and, of course, to help Saffarty.

The boost in cinema attendance – sometimes customers were turned away – was ample testimony to the success of Saffarty's simple idea of a lucky, winning ticket number. As far as the public was concerned it was hardly a gamble; it simply meant the chance of getting something for nothing. As far as Saffarty was concerned, it was the best, and the cheapest, form of advertising.

For the three months following his graduation Saffarty was too busy to spare a thought for anything beside the day-to-day running of the shop – even his beloved phrase book was forgotten. Now that he – and frequently Mireille – lived in the shop, at the back, everyone knew about their affair.

Although she still worked for Monsieur Feyard, all her spare time was given over to helping Saffarty. She rose early every morning to go down to the basement, where there was a tap. Then she carried the bucket upstairs, poured some of the water into a second bucket, and boiled it on the hot-plate she had bought, so that he could wash and shave in comfort. His dark beard meant that it was not unusual for him to shave twice a day. She loved him for it – it was another proof of how manly he was, and how different from her unshaven, unkempt father . . .

Like all women in love she believed every other woman must find Saffarty as irresistible as she did. She welcomed the opportunity of performing the smallest, the most menial tasks as a way of demonstrating her gratitude to him for having chosen her. She helped serve customers and ran errands and it did not occur to her to ask for a salary. She continued to pay the rent on the lodgings she shared, and neither she nor Saffarty thought there was anything out of the way about that.

It did not, however, go unremarked by Max. And because Colette was old, and Mireille young, it made him seethe. One day he said jokingly to Mireille, 'You work so hard, we should pay you a salary.'

'Oh, no,' Mireille said, blushing. 'I'm only helping a little — '

'But you have your rent to pay, don't you?' he said quickly, taking her unawares. 'I'll speak to Saffarty about it.'

'Please, I beg you, Monsieur Max; I beg you not to say a word to him about this.'

She'd called him *Monsieur* Max – at least she respected him. 'Have it your own way, then. I'll say nothing.'

Meanwhile, because they were constantly replacing their stock, Max had no money in his pocket. The profits were there, but the trouble was it all went back into the shop. That was bad enough, but what made matters worse was that Saffarty behaved as if he was the boss. He thought nothing of butting in on a customer Max was serving, and he invariably persuaded the customer to buy three pairs of stockings instead of one. It was, to say the least, humiliating.

All of which was unforgivable. Saffarty was in debt to him, but had the nerve to act as if it were the other way round.

It was useless talking to Colette about his difficulties with Saffarty but he did so all the same. 'I sent you to the Ecole Inter-Commercial so that you could work at a bank,' she said. 'I went to so much trouble to arrange it for you.'

'And you told them I was your dressmaker's nephew,' Max said cuttingly. 'I haven't forgotten!'

'What else could I say?'

'I need some money now,' Max said, banging the table. 'But Saffarty says no! We have to buy more stock — '

'You'd have a regular salary if you worked at the bank — '

'But I'll have more if I hang on with Saffarty. I know that. But I've got nothing in my pocket *now*. Nothing to send to my family — '

'Colette will see what she can do,' she said. 'Perhaps Colette will have a surprise for you.' Then, as if she'd had a sudden inspiration, she added, 'I'll get rid of Bijou, my toucan. I'll sell him!' She picked up the delicate pink tulle brassière with ruched ribbon that Max had brought her. 'A present from my little one,' she said softly. 'We must see if it fits, mustn't we?'

Max sighed. The brassière was transparent, and her nipples under the veil looked firm and rosy and young. It was another of those signals he could not disobey. This time, when they made love, he was rough, almost brutal.

Later, while he was dressing, she said idly, 'How much will you be selling the brassières for?'

'Two francs.'

'Two francs!' Colette repeated.

'Is that too much?'

'It's a bargain. The ribbon's worth more! It's a bit out of fashion now, but I'd buy one myself.'

When they met, three days later, Colette gave him fifteen hundred francs. 'I sold Bijou,' she lied.

Now he could go to the races again. There his permanent, rumbling anxieties of Saffarty and Colette were replaced with the new and infinitely more exciting problems that he brought on himself. The man who had sold him the binoculars was called Albert Vionnet. They were now on first-name terms.

Albert's luck had changed, and he was teaching Max the game. He had already taught him to believe in luck.

Saffarty was a gambler of a different sort – he gambled on merchandise.

For weeks he had been telling his customers to be sure to come back on March 14th, because he would have special goods, at special prices. He had refused to specify the nature of his merchandise, saying only that there would be bargains that went even beyond his wildest dreams. And then he had laughed, and shaken his head in disbelief, and deepened the mystery. He expected to do well enough to clear his debt to Max; then they would come to a suitable agreement about dissolving their partnership.

It did not occur to Saffarty to keep to clothing. His simple criterion was value – he would have bargains, it made no difference whether they were kitchenware or clothing. The price was all-important. *Nothing would be sold for more than five francs.*

So he had bought brassières, and petticoats, and even two dozen ladies' pyjamas, all made of rayon. He had lacy fans and lacy suspender belts. He'd even got hold of a gross of jars of face cream and a huge supply of thermometers.

Convinced that people would buy anything – as long as it was a genuine bargain, and under five francs – Saffarty bought a quantity of army surplus aluminium buckets and scrubbing brushes.

The buckets were too much for Max.

'You're a gambler, Saffarty, the worst sort. You're gambling with *my* money,' he said angrily. 'No one will buy buckets. You're crazy.'

'It's a calculated risk.'

'It's a gamble.'

'Supposing I told you the supplier all but gave them to me because she needed the space? Would you say that was a gamble?'

'Of course not.'

'Well – pick one up. Go on, Monsieur Blum, pick one up and feel how heavy it is.'

'It weighs nothing. It's rubbish. You're buying *merde*, I tell you. *Merde!*'

'*Merde*, you say? Made in America. Lugged by the American Expeditionary Force all through Europe, and you say *merde!* D'you know what I paid for them?' Saffarty roared. 'No, you don't know what I paid. I'll tell you what I paid. Ten centimes.'

'I still say you're a gambler, Saffarty. People expect a heavy serviceable bucket, you know.'

'Ugh – what do *you* know, Blum? These are light and serviceable. If we sell them for two francs fifty centimes, we're making twenty-five times more than we paid. Two and a half thousand per cent!'

Saffarty knew that he bought at even better than the right price, and he knew why. It was because he had the most potent weapon of all – *cash*. Buying in quantity meant a substantial discount, and buying for cash meant an extra discount. And of course buying from under-capitalised factories, even buying surplus army materials, buying stock that other people were desperate to sell, brought the price down still further.

Still, he was not altogether immune to Max's frequent pessimistic talk, and he wavered between seeing his buying as a calculated risk and a gamble. During his many sleepless nights he would tell himself that *all he would lose would be profit* – at the very worst he would get his money back. His sleeplessness would disturb Mireille, and they would go over the stock, and his expenses, going so far as to take into account the interest he would have made if the money had been in the bank instead of in merchandise. The lost interest was counted as an expense.

And then, out of a need to drive the fear from his mind, he would make urgent love to her and finally, finally fall into an exhausted sleep. Mireille would stay awake, worrying; she grew thin and worn, and looked older than her years.

It was only a nameless room with a window on the street, not a real shop, but even so, in the final hectic days of checking and re-checking the merchandise in the cellar – how to fit it all in was a major problem – Saffarty took it all as if he were preparing for the opening of a huge, new store.

One Saturday morning, five months after he had graduated, Saffarty was ready. Nothing had prepared him for the hundreds who came.

The shop was so crowded, in fact, it was impossible to keep anything like an adequate check on thieves. 'With that eye of his you can't tell where he's looking,' Saffarty heard someone say. He laughed; he was too busy to feel hurt.

At that moment he saw Max carrying off one of the aluminium buckets. It was overflowing with their best bargains.

'Max,' he called out loudly, 'where the hell d'you think you're going with all that?'

'It's for some people I know.'

'Oh – customers?'

'No.'

'You mean it's for friends and relations. You're taking my bargains to give them to people who'll never come back, never spread the word about the shop. You can't do that!'

'I didn't come here to listen to quarrels,' a woman complained. 'I came to buy. How much are the buckets?'

'You can have that bucket for nothing, madame,' Saffarty shouted.

'Provided you fill it with bargains. A free bucket to everyone who buys enough to fill it!' He put his hand in the bucket Max was carrying, held up a brassière, and said, 'Bargains are for customers who are friends. Not for friends who are not customers!'

As several women made a rush for the buckets, Saffarty snatched the one Max was carrying. 'You're taking that to Lucia,' he accused. Max grabbed it back. Saffarty moved forward to retrieve it and then stopped. 'You didn't want me to buy these buckets in the first place,' he hissed angrily. 'I'm losing sales, talking to you.'

'You're not a man, Saffarty, you're a machine.'

But all Saffarty's energies were concentrated on his customers. He paid no attention to Max.

Afterwards, both Saffarty and Max believed that it was an aluminium bucket and a girl that had pulled them apart, and broken their partnership and their friendship. Max never went back to the Bal Tabarin again.

'It's all very well to be paid out,' Max said angrily to Colette. 'But Saffarty is ending up with *my* business!'

'But you're getting a fair price — '

'You're getting a fair price! You're getting a fair price!' Max said, mimicking her. 'Can't you think of anything else to say?'

'Who says you have to sell your share to him?' Colette asked thoughtfully. 'Where is it written that you have to sell to him? You don't have a legal document, do you?'

'No,' Max said slowly. He laughed mirthlessly. 'I think you might be on to something — '

The next day he called on Monsieur Feyard, who was not only receptive to his idea but almost excessively ready to cooperate. Saffarty would hardly wish to be in partnership with Feyard.

It all went according to plan. When Feyard went to inform Saffarty that he had bought out Max's interest, and was now his partner, Saffarty had no option but to offer him an immediate profit of twenty per cent if he would sell his share to him. He swore he would never forgive Max for having put him in such an intolerable situation, and never guessed that he had been outsmarted by a simple hoax.

Feyard had not laid out a single centime.

Saffarty wanted to be known as a man who drove a hard bargain but above all as a man to be trusted. Without that there could be nothing. Accordingly Monsieur Feyard received every last centime to which Saffarty had been fooled into believing he was entitled.

Monsieur Feyard was astute enough to admit to being surprised and delighted. 'This is ten times more than I ever expected,' he told Saffarty. 'I'm giving ten per cent to Mireille. It's the least I can do.'

'You're very generous,' Saffarty murmured. 'Very generous.'

'Mireille says she wants to work for you full time. I don't know what you pay her, but I'm sure she's worth double.'

'I'm ashamed to say I haven't paid her at all,' Saffarty muttered, embarrassed.

'You can't be serious. You've paid her nothing?'

'Nothing,' Saffarty said miserably.

'In that case, she thinks of herself as a wife.' Monsieur Feyard blew a perfect smoke ring and watched it thoughtfully. Then he said, 'Take my advice, young man. If you want her to think she's a wife, don't pay her.' He opened his hands and shrugged. 'If she's not going to become Madame Saffarty, and if you still want to keep her, then you'd better pay her very well.'

'I don't want to lose her,' Saffarty said softly. 'She said nothing to me – not a word – about working full time.'

'Who can understand women?' Monsieur Feyard sighed. 'They lay so many traps in so many ways, and then they hide them. If you ask me, you're about to be caught.'

'No, Monsieur Feyard, I think not. Once you've shown me not only the trap, but its shape — ' Saffarty paused, and went on. 'Now that I've been warned, I'd be a fool to be caught.'

'All men get caught in the end, Saffarty.' Monsieur Feyard sniggered. 'Good luck to you, my boy. At any rate she can't work for both of us, any longer. She looks ill, and she'll get worse, and I need a strong healthy girl who can work hard.'

'I understand,' Saffarty said, adding quickly, 'You've found a replacement?'

'Naturally — '

'Good.'

Predictably, Mireille said she didn't need a salary. 'I love you, Saffarty. You know that,' she whispered. 'The only thing you don't know is how much. I don't know that, either.' She tried to laugh and bit her lip against the tears. 'Too much to measure,' she said.

'I haven't been acting like a real businessman. Max taught me *that*. You're a fool, aren't you, if you don't learn from experience?'

'Yes.'

'Then it's settled. You'll get five hundred francs a month.'

'That's too much, Saffarty. It'll come off your profits. I know it will.'

'We'll just have to increase the turnover. And we will.'

Now that Max had left, and Mireille was on a salary, Saffarty felt peculiarly alone. True, he had not liked sharing the profits with Max, but the option of sharing losses had made for a perfect balance. It was a pity, as well as a waste, that he and Max had fallen out. The business could have done with Max's capital, too. They would have had a real shop by now, if Max had been with him. Max had gone without a salary too. Telling himself that regrets were pointless did little to help him overcome his sense of failure. He made no attempt to blame Max for the break. It was his fault; he had not troubled to understand that, besides profit, Max had wanted friendship.

His failure to understand that turned into an obsession to make up the sum that he had paid out. This necessitated all sorts of changes, including his dealings with the bank. And the problem of the licence remained. Saffarty was now compelled to apply for a licence and, in order to get a loan from the bank, set about finding a real shop.

'Rent makes other people rich,' he told Mireille. 'It's throwing money into their pockets.'

'One day you'll buy a shop,' Mireille said. 'You'll see, Saffarty! You'll buy a whole building.'

Saffarty now stocked dresses. Thanks to Mireille's nimble fingers, he was also able to offer free alterations. She was a perfect seamstress, and could well have opened her own shop. Indeed, some customers persuaded her to alter clothes they had bought elsewhere. Sometimes she worked through the night, while Saffarty slept. She never complained. She became still thinner, often sewing flesh from her fingers. Her hands were rough and bony like the rest of her body and Saffarty no longer found it comfortable to lie beside her.

7

Feyard's cooperation meant that when the partnership broke, Max had fifty thousand francs. His euphoria lasted a little over a week, and during that time he laid extravagant plans. He would send ten thousand francs to Poland and finally, finally, he would get rid of Colette. And what was more, he could lay bigger and more meaningful bets. He would become an important punter, a man to be reckoned with on the racecourse. However, as long as he belonged to the riff-raff, instead of the members' enclosure, he would be nothing.

Well, he had a friend now, Albert Vionnet. And if Albert had once been a member of the Longchamps he saw no reason why he couldn't be one, too.

He found Albert at the Café Gabin – an establishment that reeked of wine and sweat and gas. Max ordered a cup of coffee, mainly to overcome the fumes. He also ordered a bottle of wine for Albert.

'Connections,' Albert said with a long, shuddering sigh. 'It's who you know. It's not only a question of money; you need more than money to buy your way in. Club memberships are not for sale like a pair of socks, you know.'

'Nothing buys more than money. What are you talking about? No money buys nothing — '

'I already told you. It's connections, contacts. You need someone to propose you, and someone to second you.'

'Who proposed *you*, Albert?'

'The Comte de Fleur — '

'You paid him? How much did it cost you?' Max asked, excitedly.

'It cost nothing. He said it was an honour to propose one of the Vionnet family,' Albert said with a long, shuddering sigh. 'But all that's in the past. I don't want to be reminded of it.' He drained his glass in one long gulp. 'Forget it. To forget for ever – that would be a mercy.'

'What happened?' Max said, curiously.

'*I* happened,' Albert answered, maudlin tears spilling. '*I* happened.' He began to slur his words. 'Those binoculars I gave you. No! No – don't tell me you bought them,' Albert said, waving his arms. 'Only six pairs of those Zeiss binoculars were ever made. And I had to give mine away. Leave me alone. But order another bottle of wine, will you?'

Max threw some notes on the table, and got up to leave. Albert waited for him to reach the door and then called out, 'If you want to stay alive, stay away from the members' enclosure! They'll cut your balls off! I'm warning you!'

But Max did not heed Albert's warning. Albert had promised to teach him the game, and he was glad he had asked his advice, because he doubted whether Colette would have been very forthcoming. She disapproved of his racing . . .

Max did not ask for her help. Instead he instructed her, and she followed his orders with alacrity. Her husband was away in Canada again, so the introductions were performed at Colette's apartment, over a glass of champagne. Max was introduced as the newly arrived nephew of Count Poliatonski, who would be spending some months in Paris. His family wished him to be exposed to the kind of general educational improvement unique to that glittering, sophisticated city.

Colette's first invitation was to Maître Georges Leduc, the lawyer to the famous Hochschild family. Max arrived a half-hour before. Colette was waiting in the hall to meet him. He had not been in Colette's flat since he had worked in the laundry of the Ritz, and during those early bewildering days he had been too dazed to take in the detail of the hall. Now, as Colette welcomed him, he was frankly overwhelmed by what he saw. He tapped his highly shone shoes nervously against the gold mosaic floor, looked up at the angels floating on the ceiling, looked down and saw the angels reflected in the mirrored pond in the centre of the room. 'I didn't really notice all of this before,' he said, awed. He approached the pond and could not resist touching the water.

'Your mind was on other things, no?' Colette giggled.

'I didn't have a mind. I'd lost it,' Max said, dryly.

After that meeting with Maître Leduc, three more introductions to men of high standing followed, and at each meeting Max respectfully addressed Colette as 'Madame Terblanche', and she addressed him as 'young man', and the wheels were set in motion. Very soon he became a member.

Colette bought him three suits. But for one important difference they carried on as before, meeting Tuesdays and Fridays. The difference was that Max seemed happier than he had ever been. By now even the smell of the horses was part of the thrill of the gamble. He was charmed by the elegance of his surroundings – the clothes and perfumes of the women, the brilliant emerald of the race track, and even the colours of the jockeys' silks.

Once, after a stupendous win, he went so far as to buy Colette an extravagant and imaginative gift. It was a red and white bathing suit, by no less a designer than Jean Patou. It clung to Colette's body as if it had been moulded to it. 'You could be a mannequin, Colette,' Max said. 'Your body is perfect.'

She found herself unbearably moved by the gift; it told her how Max thought of her, how he valued her body. It was almost too good to be true. She found it hard to keep the tears from her voice. 'Thank you, little one,' she said, and added, unexpectedly, 'God bless you.'

He hugged her then. 'I need you,' he said gruffly. 'I need you, Colette!'

Max was aware that this was true. He was also aware that in some ways, he was afraid of her. Especially after she had shown him Bijou, her toucan. 'But you told me you had sold the bird,' he had said, aghast.

'No, I had him killed. My poor Bijou.'

'*What?*' he shrieked.

'And stuffed. My poor, sweet Bijou! But I took him to the best taxidermist in Paris.'

'Oh, my God. I'm looking at a *dead* bird! Why did you do it? How *could* you?'

'To teach you a lesson!' she said grimly.

'What lesson? What sort of lesson?'

She merely laughed.

'I don't understand you, Colette. I don't understand you at all.'

'Women have mysterious ways,' she whispered. 'If you've learned that, you will have learned not to be too demanding.'

And then Colette had broken their rule, and led him into her bedroom. After the first week of their affair she had decided that they would never make love in her apartment, and Max had been only too happy to go along with her. But now, in her bedroom, on the outsize brass bed, under a gold-lamé silk canopy, beside a large porcelain doll, the great fear in him could only be driven out by aggressive love-making. Colette responded with the violence that was in her, too. She scratched and pierced his back, and it was days before his wounds stopped burning. Weeping, she applied poultices and balms, with a mother's tenderness.

They did not meet at her apartment again, but the stuffed, dead toucan became something of a symbol in Max's life. He dreamed of the bird. Once he dreamed Colette had dispensed with him, too, and had him stuffed by the same taxidermist and placed on her bed alongside that outsize porcelain doll of hers.

Now more than ever desperate to get Colette out of his system and out of his life, he divided his time between three racecourses. He was in a state of permanent desperation. One day, he would be rid of Colette. He did not know how, he knew only that he would succeed and, when he knew that, his fear began to lessen. 'Happiness' – he said to Colette in bed – 'is excitement.'

'And I excite you, little one.'

'More than you know. But everything comes to an end.'

'We all have to die in the end, little one,' she said sadly.

A fit of shivering overtook her, and it was a long while before she could control it.

Longchamps continued to be Max's favourite racecourse. He was onto a winning streak, and he became more and more superstitious, forbidding Colette to wear green, and insisting that she put on her right shoe first.

Meanwhile, unbeknownst to him, he was acquiring the reputation of being a man in the know. In the easy camaraderie at the racecourse people asked his opinions and sought his advice. Soon the chic and fashionable women began to approach him, too. They found his modesty as appealing as his perfect manners. He always insisted, charmingly, that there were no guarantees in this racing game.

One of the more persistent – and innovative – of the elegant ladies was called Monique Dousset. She reminded him of Colette, so he was more than ordinarily wary of her. After the third race, when Max's horse had only just made it to the winning post in the last second, and he had continued shouting encouragement even after the horse had won, Monique Dousset handed him her card. 'But Monsieur Blum, your horse has won. Why do you still shout?'

'Excuse me, Madame Dousset,' he said, glancing at the card, 'but I shout from happiness.'

'Ah yes, I have heard you are a happy man.'

'And what else, may I ask, did you hear, madame?'

'Turn over my card, monsieur.'

Max turned the card, read, 'Albert Vionnet sends his greetings', and turned pale.

'And how, madame,' he asked, 'may I serve you?'

'My husband wants to meet you. He has – ah – a request to make of you. Could you join us for a drink at the address on the card? Say, tomorrow evening at six?'

'With pleasure, madame.'

Max thought quickly. He had not expected to get away with the story that he was the nephew of a Polish count. Not for long, anyway. The story had got him where he wanted to be, and if some of the truth had got out, it was too late to do any serious damage. Max now knew which side of the track was for him. He was going to become a breeder, and have a stable like the Baron de Rothschild. He had seen the Baron at Fouquet's bar and, of course, at the races. He admired everything about him, from his distinguished morning suit, gloves and top hat, to his slim grey moustache, thick black eyebrows and intelligent eyes.

As if reading his mind, Monique said, 'Didn't I see you at Fouquet's on Sunday?'

'Of course, I remember seeing you there. If I am not mistaken, you were wearing a Chanel tweed sports suit with a low leather belt?'

'No, Monsieur, you are not mistaken. But observation, of course, is part of your trade.'

'Really?' Max said stiffly.

'Now don't get offended, Monsieur Blum. We all know what you are.'

It was a veiled threat. She had made that clear, too. There was no alternative but to brazen it out.

'How do you know Albert Vionnet?' he asked politely.

'You mean he doesn't look my type, don't you?' Monique said quickly. 'Of course, you're a foreigner, so you can't be expected to know that Albert Vionnet was once a member of the famous two hundred families who ruled France.'

'I confess my ignorance; I did not know that.'

'You thought he was just a drunk?'

'I was not mistaken, madame. He *is* a drunk.'

'Tomorrow at six, then. *Au revoir* and *à bientôt*,' Monique said and, with a slight wave, she left.

Again, Max was faced with no alternative. He had to find Albert Vionnet and uncover what these Doussets were after. Above all, who they were.

He recalled having seen Vionnet and remembered, with a growing unease, that he had shunned him. He ought not to have done that, he realised now. He had the distinct feeling that Vionnet was exacting his price via these Doussets.

His instinct warned him that he was in deep trouble.

Forewarned is forearmed, he told himself.

He would have to make a tour of the seedier cafés and bistros. At the same time he marvelled how easily, and how comfortably, he had fitted into the world of luxury. He corrected himself. The truth was that though he did not feel comfortable among the chic, he preferred to be with them. He was not yet of them, of course, but with his sizable bank balance he was getting closer. The bank clerks now treated him with more respect.

Monique Dousset's mannish hairstyle, so close to her head, as severely uncompromising as her eyes, warned him that she was as heartless as she was shrewd. She reminded him of the terrifying chief laundress he had worked for at the Ritz.

As usual, his thoughts turned to Saffarty and above all to his fearlessness. Saffarty was afraid of nothing and no one.

At that moment a sudden insight flared. Max suddenly understood that of all the men in the world, the man he most wanted to emulate, the man he most wanted to *be*, was a man with a crooked eye.

He took a decision then. Even if he was not like Saffarty, he would try to be like him – daring, aggressive and unconcerned. Neither the Doussets nor Albert Vionnet would be able to detect the smallest glimmer of fear in him.

Max finally tracked Vionnet down in the sleazy, sour-smelling Bar

Lepic. His clothes were rumpled; he had clearly been in and out of bars and cafés for several hours. Max had no sooner seated himself on a stool beside Albert than three ladies of the night attached themselves to him.

'The nephew of the Polish count,' Albert snarled. 'Go away. You'll get nothing from this one,' he said to the women. 'Mean as cat's shit, this one. Go away. You're wasting your time. In any case, he's a thief! He stole my binoculars.'

'I bought them and I paid for them. You sold them to me.'

'Three thousand francs I paid, you got them for five hundred.'

The bar fell silent.

'Theft,' Albert said again. He held up his empty glass, and then cracked it against the counter. Now he held up the jagged glass.

Max felt the sweat run down his face like tears. His mouth tasted of salt and he couldn't speak.

'*Sale étranger*, dirty foreigner!' Albert said. He stood up, and Max realised that he was not drunk but stone cold sober.

'I came here to buy you a drink,' Max said quietly. And then he remembered Saffarty's laugh. He forced a loud, comradely laugh. 'Come on,' he said. 'Drinks are on me. Everyone! Drinks all round.'

'Yes, let him buy the drinks. He's paying with the money he stole from me. The drinks are on me.'

'Your health, Monsieur Vionnet,' the barman said.

Max breathed more easily, and the ugly moment passed. 'Come,' he said to Albert, 'we must have a private chat.' He steered Albert to a small table at the back of the bar. 'Tell me about your friends, the Doussets.'

'The Doussets? *Enfin*. So this is why you are here!'

'I think they want to do business with me,' Max said simply.

'*Merde!*' Albert exploded. 'What do they want?'

'A meeting. That's all I know so far,' Max said urgently. 'Monique Dousset told me she knew you. Other than that, I know nothing.'

'They want you to place a bet for them. They have some inside information and if they're seen placing the bet, the odds will change. Got it?'

'Yes.'

'Then you'll come and tell *me*. Got that? You'll pull me in on this.'

'Yes.'

'It will cost *you* nothing if you do. But if you don't — ' Albert paused menacingly, 'it will cost you your life. Got it?'

'Yes, I understand.' Max tried to reproduce Saffarty's laugh again, but it was a miserable failure.

'Don't take me for a fool, Max Blum,' Albert said rapidly, threateningly. 'Now that you know who I was!'

Max made no attempt to be anything but honest with Albert Vionnet, even though he was certain the Doussets were about to make a costly error.

Fifty thousand on Fume Hanibal would be fifty thousand down the drain. The horse had been injured as a foal, and had bad forelegs. He pointed to Fume Hanibal's weakness, but Albert merely said, 'Look closely at the statue of that magnificent horse at the main entrance of Longchamps. There you will see Gladiateur, the great and beautiful thoroughbred who even won the Derby, the famous British race. The statue shows you a horse of the essence of heavenly perfection, yet Gladiateur had weak forelegs.'

'When did Gladiateur win the Derby?' Max asked the question because he knew the answer.

'More than fifty years ago.'

'Things have changed. It's a long race. Now if it were a shorter — '

'*Merde!* Don't you know that Gladiateur won even though thugs captured his jockey, and then bled him, so that he would be too weak to do his job and perform up to his usual excellent standard the next day?'

'Who doesn't know that? It's an old story,' Max shrugged. 'I'll put on the fifty thousand francs for the Doussets, but not a centime for myself.'

'You will put on twenty-five hundred for me, then. Got it?'

When the race ended Max could have wept. Fume Hanibal came limping in, stone cold last. If only he had followed his instincts and not placed the bet, he could have kept the fifty thousand francs for himself. Or, better still, if only he had placed the fifty thousand on the horse of his choice, L'Emigrant, he would have picked up a cool two hundred and fifty thousand francs. It made him ill.

A month later, he again followed his instructions instead of his instincts, with the same bad result.

After that he began to think more clearly.

The next time, if there were to be a next time, he would follow his own counsel. No, he assured himself, he would not be stubborn – he would go according to the facts.

The facts. But he was becoming a little too selective about which facts were relevant and which were not. He cursed the day he had met the Doussets, because they had brought him bad luck. His bank balance had gone down, and the fact was that it could not be allowed to sink to zero and beyond.

He should have backed L'Emigrant. After all, he was an immigrant himself – he preferred horses with names he could relate to.

The one positive thing about having broken partnership with Max, Saffarty told himself over and over again, was that he no longer had to divide the profits. Though the business prospered beyond his wildest hopes, it would have reached even greater heights if he had a partner. He knew now why trust, that unbankable commodity, was priceless.

And now he was looking for a real shop. At first he had contemplated renting premises, and it was a while before he decided that he would have to buy both the shop and the premises. He did not like sinking capital into property, but could not bear the idea of contributing to a landlord what he could just as well contribute to himself.

The shop was to be called Saffarty's Window – La Fenêtre de Saffarty. Documents were being drawn up. The day before he was due to sign he began to flirt seriously with the idea of asking Max to come in with him. He went as far as calling on Max at his garçonnière, but the door-bell went unanswered.

He stopped at the Café Moulins and thought of asking for Max, but his pride forbade it. He ordered a large bowl of coffee and sat back to think. It was a bright café, and clean; even the bottles shone. The unexpected sound of his mother-tongue, Ladino, so rarely heard these days, made his heart lurch. Two women were talking in an accent slightly different from his own – from the island of Rhodes, he guessed. He eavesdropped shamelessly; the sounds drifted over and warmed him like sunshine. Suddenly he sat bolt upright. The woman was talking of selling up, selling everything, leaving Paris for ever to go to Divonne, where her daughter and her new grand-daughter lived. She had been trying to sell the business for six months, ever since her husband had died, but no one wanted a shop that specialised in pure lace. Now all she wanted was to rid herself of the property and enjoy her grand-daughter. Besides, her daughter and son-in-law had a restaurant, and they needed someone for the child, someone they could trust. Having delivered herself of her rapid monologue the woman took a sip of wine and said, reflectively, 'Trust is to life what clear air is to lungs.'

'Bravo, madame, bravo,' Saffarty called out in Ladino. Then, quoting an ancient proverb, he said, 'The child of my child is twice my child. And you, madame, you are the living proof of that most noble principle.'

The women responded as Saffarty had known they would – like two aged, maternal coquettes. '*Bonjour!* Join us, young man,' they trilled.

'My pleasure. But first I must beg your forgiveness for my bad manners in having eavesdropped, with such delight, to the sounds of my beloved mother-tongue.'

After an exchange of names he asked them about the old country, and enquired about the new grand-daughter, and said he was sure the child would enjoy the *salep*, the hot cinnamon drink he missed so much. He ordered a bottle of wine to celebrate their meeting, and soon turned the discussion towards his studies in commerce at the Ecole Inter-Commercial.

All the while Saffarty had been studying them as if they were balance sheets. It was clear that they were in credit and, if not wealthy, at least reasonably comfortable.

'What happened to your eye, Saffarty?' Madame Ravarino, the owner of the lace shop, asked, tenderly touching her own eye as she spoke.

'An accident.' Saffarty touched his own eye-patch.

'But you can see. I mean your vision — '

'No, madame, my vision is not affected. You are wearing Chanel blouses of last year, are you not?'

'I didn't mean to insult you. I only wanted to tell you that the great Professor Reincourt is an acquaintance of mine. You've heard of him, I'm sure.'

'Yes.' Max had told him of this man . . .

'He was the eye specialist for my poor husband,' Madame

Ravarino said kindly. 'He does not see new patients. But he would see you, Saffarty, if I asked him to — '

'I would be most grateful, madame.'

A week later Madame Ravarino and Saffarty met for the second time.

'Your reputation does honour to your parents, young Saffarty,' Madame Ravarino said in slow measured tones. 'I've made enquiries about you, you understand that — '

'But of course,' Saffarty said at once. 'I expected no less from you.'

'You are well known. You've done well. Even tourists come to your shop without a name!'

'I have been fortunate,' Saffarty said modestly.

'And shrewd. Good fortune shines seldom on fools, or hadn't you noticed?'

'I have noticed.'

'Then we may proceed to the point of our meeting. The trustworthy responsible buyer you have in mind for my little lace shop, the buyer who can pay cash in cash notes is none other than yourself, is that not so?'

Saffarty nodded and flushed, but said nothing.

'Ah, I see you not only have the grace to blush, but you are still young enough to do so.'

Saffarty judged silence to be his wisest move.

'Cash in notes, you say. Very interesting, that.'

'You would prefer a cheque, madame?'

'I did not say that, Saffarty.' Madame Ravarino attended to her gloves. 'No, cash in notes is more – shall we say – private?'

'I would say so, yes.'

'So we agree the first principle. But what you have not indicated, Saffarty, is the amount. This is important, the amount. You agree?'

'Certainly I agree, madame. And I will go further. I will even confess to some difficulty.'

'Difficulty?'

'Yes. Difficulty.' Saffarty paused, and sighed. 'You see, madame – it is not the shop I am buying. Lace is only a fraction of my business. Your enquiries must have confirmed that?'

'So — '

'It is the property I am buying. I may be over-committing

116

myself, madame, but after much thought I am prepared to take over your entire stock.'

'At cost price?'

'At a mutually agreed price, of course. But we will have no difficulty coming to terms over that, I'm sure.' Saffarty sighed again. 'The property, madame, is not quite of the standard I had anticipated. My misunderstanding, I'm sure.'

'But what did you expect?'

'Frankly, madame, I was disappointed, even saddened. You see, I expected a flat upstairs, a flat with plumbing and electricity, a flat where we could live.'

'I've heard about your living arrangements,' Madame Ravarino said frostily. 'I was going to discuss that with you later.'

'It is not pleasant living in a shop, I assure you.'

'I dare say.'

'As for the amount, madame, I suggest you tell me what you have in mind. I would dishonour not only my reputation but my family if I made an offer that you might consider insulting. Better no offer than an insulting offer.' Saffarty's ancient key, digging in his palm, gave him courage.

'I appreciate your candour. I had thought of fifty thousand for the shop, and twenty-five thousand for the stock.'

'I see,' Saffarty said calmly.

It was at least thirty-five per cent less than he had been ready to pay. 'That is a fair price for the property, but too high for the stock.'

'We can discuss that later.'

'Certainly, madame, I value your sense of justice.'

'So?'

'The price is fair. I won't even attempt to dispute that. The difficulty is that it is more than I can afford — '

'And how much can you afford?'

'Forty thousand. Please, madame, do not be angry. You said — '

'I know what I said,' Madame Ravarino said irritably. 'Cash is, of course, at a premium. I know that. I'm not a fool, you know.' She opened her handbag and took out a handkerchief. 'My poor husband will turn in his grave.' She patted her nose. From behind her handkerchief she added quickly, 'Forty-two and a half thousand and we have a deal.'

'And the stock?'

'You will pay me each quarter. I will ask only that you pay me what you receive. I trust you, Saffarty.'

'Trust is priceless, madame.' Saffarty shook his head. 'I learned that the hard way.' Then he leaned over and put out his hand. 'Madame Ravarino, you have yourself a deal.'

It was too good to be true. If he had not gone in search of Max, he and Madame Ravarino would never have met. He thought once more of contacting Max, but then remembered that the note he had left had gone unanswered.

'It's like preparing for a wedding feast,' Mireille said wearily.

'A wedding feast?' Saffarty said, abstracted. 'What wedding?'

'Not a real wedding. But the organisation, the planning for La Fenêtre de Saffarty.' Mireille lifted a length of shimmering lace and held it up to the light. 'It's all this wedding-gown lace, I suppose. It's so very beautiful — '

'Also very valuable,' Saffarty answered quickly. 'Madame Ravarino knew what she was doing when she told me I could pay her whatever I received for it. The stuff is worth a small fortune. It was a mistake not to have bought it outright.'

'And will you, Saffarty?' Mireille murmured. 'Will you pay her exactly what you sell it for?'

'But of course. I gave my word. She *trusts* me. D'you know what that means?'

'I only know that I trust you — '

'Yes, yes,' Saffarty said impatiently. 'Certainly, I'll tell Madame Ravarino the exact truth. But then I will add something to that — '

'How can you add to the truth?'

'You can add commission for the truth. I will tell her that I have entrusted her with my commission.'

'I'm proud of you, Saffarty.'

'La Fenêtre de Saffarty! I still can't believe it,' Saffarty said, racing outside to look, once again, at the temporary sign in white lettering on blue cardboard that had been erected that morning. He stared at the sign, and waved at Mireille. It was a Sunday afternoon and Montmartre was thronged with tourists, mainly British, who came to gape at the cafés patronised by the great artists, by Picasso and Braque and Lautrec and Léger. He looked up toward the Sacré

Coeur church, and let his eye linger on its white dome. A group of cheerful students were wending their way down the hill, laughing. For a long moment he envied them their light-hearted, carefree lives; he was probably younger than all of them, and fun had passed him by. Business was fun of a different sort. He looked at the sign with his name – La Fenêtre de Saffarty – and told himself that it was better than fun because it included the future. All the same, he thought, he and Mireille ought to have some fun of the carefree sort.

Suddenly one of the students called out in an obviously British accent, 'La Fenêtre de Saffarty. Let's go shopping, shall we?' The rest laughed. 'The shop is closed.' They spoke English. Saffarty understood nothing.

'Monsieur, can you handle some customers? May we come in?' one of them asked in perfect French.

'But with pleasure!' Saffarty said at once. He gave a light bow. 'Allow me to welcome you as my very first customers. My shop is not yet ready, as you can see — '

Mireille showed the laces, soft, gossamer and so luminous that the girls could not resist caressing them. They wore dreamy expressions, and Mireille guessed that they were dreaming of being brides, just as she was.

'You will bring me great good luck,' Saffarty said, jumping on the counter. 'In Paris we say that if the first customer is a tourist many more will follow. I propose to present each young lady with a white lace handkerchief.' He paused for a moment, and in English called out the first phrase that came to his mind, 'God save the King!'

Everyone laughed and clapped, and then one of them produced a bottle of champagne. Saffarty procured some glasses from a nearby café, and found himself laughing and talking with more abandon than he could ever remember.

Watching the students respond to Saffarty as to a shock of sudden energy, Mireille felt especially proud of belonging to him.

Though he had not been with English people before, he had been an Anglophile ever since the fire in Salonika when British soldiers had refused to take payment for their bread. She was well aware what this meant to him – it was a beacon of faith, a symbol of greatness, a kind of grandeur from another world. Now these students reminded her that only a few days before, his strong feelings about the British had led to a rare quarrel between them. It had happened on a day that Montmartre was filled with even more than the usual number of British tourists. Word had got round that they were unemployed English workers spending their dole money in France, taking advantage of sterling's inordinately high value over the collapsed franc. When the injustice of it all became too much for a concierge, she had wielded her broom and cried out, insultingly, 'Sales étrangers! Dirty foreigners. Go home!'

The cry was taken up by the crowd, and Mireille joined in, 'Sales étrangers!'

'Why are you saying that, Mireille? They bring *their* funds to *our* economy. Are you crazy?'

'They don't work. And they buy what we have for *deux fois rien* – twice times nothing!' Mireille replied sharply. 'It's this government . . . dirty foreigners!'

'But France – France welcomes foreigners. I am a foreigner. I am not French, but they allowed me to work here, and to live here. All I needed was an identity card.'

'Oh, Saffarty, Saffarty,' Mireille said miserably. 'I did not mean to insult you. Forgive me – it's just that — '

'Forget it, Mireille. Forget it.'

But she had neither forgotten nor forgiven herself.

She smiled bravely now as he vaulted over the counter, presented his handkerchiefs and then kissed the hand of each pretty girl.

'Isn't he thrilling? . . . They say Frenchmen make the best lovers . . . What he has, to use the current new phrase, darling, is called sex appeal . . . '

Mireille understood no English, but it never has been necessary to understand the language to know that women are flirting with your man. The movements of the hips, the lips, the hands, the eyes, and the pitch of the breath, the voice, and the laugh, belonged to a universal language. Besides, Saffarty's tall figure and eye-patch unfailingly drew attention, and a lingering glance.

When they left Saffarty said, 'Did you see, Mireille, mademoiselle from Marseilles, did you see how much they bought?'

'I did. And they will send you many more customers.'

'Enough work. This afternoon we are going dancing. And we are going to the Bal Tabarin. No. We are not going in the afternoon.

That's daytime. Tonight. Let me see, first to the Bal Tabarin, the Moulin Rouge, the Jockey, or all three?'

'But Saffarty, I have nothing to wear,' Mireille said nervously.

'But yes, you have,' he grinned. 'A surprise.' He disappeared behind the counter and returned carrying a large brown paper parcel.

'I thought that was some more lace,' she said softly.

He opened the package with a flourish. 'This is the coat, mademoiselle, and this is the dress.' The coat, made of a wool as fine as silk, was finished with a generous swirl of shiny black fox fur. The gleaming black waistless dress appeared to have been fashioned entirely out of silken fringes.

'But where — '

'Paris has just discovered the little black dress, mademoiselle,' Saffarty said, pretending to be a *vendeuse*. 'If you wish to try — '

'Saffarty! Where did you get — '

'Don't look so upset, Mireille. It spoils everything. I bought them from Madame Ravarino,' Saffarty laughed. 'Last year's models, I regret to say. The coat was lying on the chair in her salon; I fell in love with it. We were finalising things, and I told her I simply had to have that coat – for you, Mireille. She sold it to me at a very fair price, too, I'll say that for her. She couldn't wear anything, she said, if she knew someone had the eye on it.'

'The evil eye, you mean?' Mireille whispered.

'Something like that. Anyway, I got a bargain, I can tell you.'

It was one of those rare, unforgettable nights that even begin with a flash of brilliance. Mireille and Saffarty actually saw Josephine Baker in her famous brown Voisin car. The car had stopped under a neon sign bright enough to illuminate the snakeskin upholstery. The dancer's tight curls were plastered to her head with egg white. Beside her sat her white Esquima dog, and as the car pulled away Saffarty and Mireille caught a glimpse of the lipsticked kiss that Josephine Baker had placed on the top of its head.

'Our very own private cabaret,' Saffarty said. He put his arm about her waist and whispered, 'Please, Mireille, please, not a word about the cost tonight. Not one word.'

'But Saffarty — '

'For my sake, Mireille. Not one word.' He kissed her hand. 'You look spectacular. These clothes were made for you.'

They walked on, hand in hand. A smile, even a laugh, radiated from her eyes. He did not see that her happiness was so complete, and so burningly intense, that it was of the painful kind that sometimes makes the disillusioned turn away. Mireille seldom smiles these days, he thought. He felt her work-roughened hand and squeezed it. 'You work hard, Mireille,' he said admiringly.

'Thank you, Saffarty,' she said as if it were the highest praise. She said again, 'Thank you.'

Once they were in the Jockey Club they ordered gin fizzes. They stared at everyone and everything with undisguised curiosity. A woman no larger than a dwarf approached them and seated herself, saying, 'You don't mind if I sit down?' She had had too much to drink already, but ordered a gin fizz. She complimented Mireille on her dress and then raised her own dress to display the pattern of bruises and bites that had been rendered, she told them proudly, by her lover. Saffarty listened politely, but soon left her to dance with Mireille.

'She'll get the message,' he assured Mireille. 'She'll be gone when we get back to the table.'

The music, the aching sensuality of the blues, hit Saffarty with an unexpected force. Later, while they made love, he repeated over and over, 'We must do this more often. We must do this more often.' Just before he fell asleep, he said, 'We must get a wireless. *Tomorrow!*'

Sleepless, afraid to move lest she disturb him, Mireille lay stiff and still. This was the first time they had not talked about the business. So far her hopes for him had come true. He was going to be a rich and important man – that was as definite as the sound of his breathing. Only eight months ago she had told him that he would own not only a shop, but an entire building. She wondered whether he remembered that. She would remind him, the moment he woke up.

But when she told him he seemed not to remember. Almost desperate to revive his memory, she became unusually agitated. 'But you must remember, Saffarty? Surely you have not forgotten?'

'Of course I remember,' he said softly. 'You are a clever girl, Mireille.'

'And you, Saffarty,' Mireille answered with prayerful gratitude, 'you are a genius. And I – I am the first to have told you that, Saffarty.' She grasped both his hands, and bowed her head into them. 'One day everyone will know that you are a genius. But only you will know that I was the first to say so.'

'Nonsense,' he said roughly. 'Nonsensical women's talk. Not the talk of a clever girl.'

But for all his roughness, something in his voice told her that he was not entirely displeased with what she had said.

All the aluminium buckets had been sold. Saffarty retained one, and suspended it from the ceiling of La Fenêtre de Saffarty.

Meanwhile, he was desperate for a new source of supply. He even went into the question of importing them from the United States, but the price was prohibitive. He needed a product he could not only give away, gratis, but one that would induce his customers to buy more than they had intended. Aside from the lace, which he made certain to tell everyone was not his merchandise, nothing in La Fenêtre de Saffarty cost more than five francs. At the Cinéma Germaine his nameless shop continued to do well, staffed by a friend of Mireille's, an ex-usherette. He came to a deal with an accordionist, who now played the newest songs outside his shop. He also made the fullest use of a radio. He had always believed in word of mouth but, as he told himself over and over again, he had not expected his name to travel as far as England. He had obviously become included in the sightseeing lists as automatically as the Folies Bergères. He was even beginning to understand and to use more and more English phrases. The tourists seemed to like this – it made them giggle, and it made them spend.

No matter how busy he was, he always read Madame Ravarino's meticulously formal letters as soon as they arrived. The most recent one informed him that the great Doctor Riencourt had returned from the United States, and had done her the great honour of agreeing to examine Saffarty on Tuesday, the 14th, only two days away.

When he told Mireille she said, rather too casually, Saffarty thought, 'The fourteenth. That is the anniversary of our first night together. Do you remember?'

'I confess to a terrible lapse of memory, Mireille. But we will

123

celebrate. We will go to the Bal Tabarin – or perhaps, the Boeuf sur le Toit, and you will wear your — '

'Thank you, Saffarty,' Mireille said nervously. 'Thank you.'

The professor's surgery was on the Boulevard de Capucine. Saffarty arrived in good time for his consultation, so early that he decided to take a leisurely stroll down the avenue. It was a light April morning, and the chestnut trees were just in blossom. He was wearing a dove-grey suit and the cut and the feel of it was like a caress.

There was time for a quick coffee at the Café de la Paix, time, for once, to inspect the passing parade. He realised that he was missing the beauty of Paris, the beautiful women especially.

He watched people scatter and call out insults after a man who was running through the crowds on the pavement. The man wore a moss green hat which matched his magnificent tweed suit, and it was this that made Saffarty observe him with a keener interest. As he came nearer, Saffarty realised it was Max. He rose abruptly from his seat, spilling his coffee, and was just about to call out when Max's expression of naked desperation stopped him.

He sat down.

What was Max doing with that strange tram conductor's box dangling behind his back? Recognition dawned; it was a pair of binoculars, of course. Once a gambler, always a gambler.

Max was in trouble, that much was plain.

He pushed Max from his mind – it was time to present himself to the doctor.

8

Madame Delange had very mixed feelings about Saffarty. It was true that he had been an excellent teacher, and her son Claude was now at the university. She was grateful to him for that. Yet she was convinced that he had cheated them out of their rent. Her husband had not been similarly deceived – he had told her all along that in refusing to tutor Claude, Saffarty was using blackmail. Monsieur Delange had been ready to go along with Saffarty, and in the end it had paid off very well. '*C'est la guerre,*' he said.

Too well, Madame Delange thought. Her husband had been right, and she had been wrong, and the balance of their relationship had been altered in his favour.

A young man with a crooked eye had made her not only look – but feel – a fool.

What was worse was that Saffarty had acquired a disturbing importance in her life; she did not deceive herself that it was only his unbeatable bargains that lured her to La Fenêtre de Saffarty, again and again. No matter how busy he was, he would call out, 'Ah, Madame Delange, my most discerning customer!' And his laugh would resound through his shop. It lifted her spirits, she couldn't help it, and more than once she'd caught herself blushing. Saffarty's easy flattery was so different from the scared, respectful residents at her hotel – he made her feel special, and he made her laugh.

Today Madame Delange had decided not to go to La Fenêtre de Saffarty but then, as so often happened, she found herself removing the apron that protected her ample breasts, arranging her wispy grey hair, and even dabbing some of that deliciously expensive perfume that she could not forgive herself for having bought.

'*Eh bien,*' she said to herself, speaking out loud, 'I'll just have another look at that devil's lace. I'll go there before I go to the market – that way I won't waste the morning — '

When she arrived, Mireille was carefully counting a customer's change. She said abstractedly, 'He's gone to the doctor.'

'Is he ill? Is it serious?' Madame Delange asked anxiously.

Mireille, her eyes bright and feverish, looked up from the coins she was counting into her customer's palm. 'He's been waiting for this for years and years,' she said softly.

'What consultation?'

'It's with — '

Suddenly the customer said sharply, 'I gave you a hundred-franc note, mademoiselle. What are you trying to do – short-change me?'

'Are you not mistaken, madame? Was it not a fifty-franc note?'

'Now she's calling me a thief and a liar,' the customer shouted out to the shop in general. 'Give me back my money, and you can keep your socks!'

'I'm sorry, madame,' Mireille said miserably. 'By all that I hold holy, I could have sworn — '

Suddenly, she fell to the floor.

'She's fainted; the poor girl's fainted,' Madame Delange said, bending over Mireille. 'Move away, everyone. She needs air!'

'I'm taking back my hundred-franc note,' the customer said, stepping over Mireille and reaching into the till. 'And you're all witnesses to that. Understand?'

No one paid any attention to her, and muttering curses the woman left.

'She's coming round,' someone said. 'But she's gone deathly pale.'

Madame Delange took charge. 'I'll take her home,' she said firmly. 'Monsieur Saffarty used to live in our hotel. I know them well. So, if you'll all leave, I'll take her back with me at once. See – she's trying to sit up.'

'I can't leave the shop,' Mireille whispered.

'Nonsense, my girl.'

Too weak to protest, Mireille sat on the floor and rested her head against the counter. 'It's my head,' she said. 'It's bursting.'

'Give me the keys to the shop,' Madame Delange commanded.

Meekly, Mireille took the keys from inside her blouse.

'But what will Saffarty say about the shop being shut? How will he know what has happened?' Mireille asked rapidly, nervously.

'I'll leave a note on the door,' Madame Delange said grimly. 'I'd already thought of that!'

As soon as they had reached the hotel, Madame Delange said

firmly, 'You will lie on my bed. You look terribly pale. A vinegar compress is what you need for your head, mademoiselle.'

Mireille did not even try to argue. The room was spinning, and she seemed unable to control her trembling. At first she wept silently, and then gave up all attempts to stop the tears that had already wet the pillow.

Madame Delange took it all in with a single glance. 'It's not only your head, is it? It's your heart, no?'

Mireille did not reply.

'Another woman? They're all bastards, every last one of them,' Madame Delange said with shrill satisfaction.

Mireille shook her head.

Madame Delange removed the poultice from Mireille's forehead. 'You're in trouble, aren't you? How far along are you? Does he know?'

Mireille rolled over and hid her head in the pillow. Her body shook.

'Crying won't help you, my child. It's too late for tears,' Madame Delange said heavily. Sighing, she sat on the bed, stroked Mireille's wet hair and shook her head. 'Cry, my child, cry, it will do you good. You should sleep. What are you going to do? You will have to tell him, you know. He's a devil.'

Mireille turned to face Madame Delange. 'Please, madame,' she said forcefully, using all her strength, 'he is not a devil. You will see that for yourself.'

Madame Delange felt the newly familiar prickle of heat beginning to spread, and within moments her hair, like the skin under her breasts, was wet with the sweat of menopause. '*Ma pauvre petite*,' she murmured, 'we women are a cursed lot – our wombs punish us, and our men punish us.' She pushed out at her lower lip and blew air over her face. 'Men are bastards,' she said, her voice rising.

For several weeks her mother's warning, the warning Mireille had been made to repeat out loud – *all men are bastards* – had echoed through her brain. She could not endure the noise of Madame Delange's harsh voice a moment longer.

'I'll never forget your kindness to me, madame,' she said fervently. 'Never. But – forgive me – I need to be on my own bed now.'

Madame Delange scolded, then cajoled, and finally resorted to threats.

'I need to be alone with him when I tell him,' Mireille said fiercely. 'And *I* want to be the one to tell him. I want him to hear it from *me*!'

'Sleep then, *ma pauvre petite*,' Madame Delange said kindly. 'I will leave you to sleep.'

Madame Delange hurried back to La Fenêtre de Saffarty. No matter what that poor girl had said, she would be the one to break the bad news to Saffarty.

'Why are you standing outside the door of my shop, Madame Delange? You don't like my merchandise?'

'She fainted — '

'Excuse me?'

'Mireille – who else?' Madame Delange's arms waved wildly. 'She collapsed. It's the way you make her work! In her condition it's no surprise she fainted. It's bad enough that she's skin and bone — '

'What condition? Where is she?'

'Where do you think she's gone? Back to that stinking little cubicle of yours – that's where she's gone!'

'Thank you, madame. You will excuse me if I go to her now,' Saffarty said mildly.

Saffarty felt his mind catapult. *Her condition* – what did the disgusting old hag mean? He had just had the best news of his life. His eye could be corrected, surgically; and this old crone waved her arms like a scarecrow in the wind and spoiled everything.

The moment Saffarty entered their little room he said, 'I ran all the way, Madame Delange told me you fainted. How are you? A little better now?'

'What did Doctor Riencourt say?' Mireille asked keenly. 'Can he help?'

'Yes. He can. We'll talk about it later. You look pale, my love. Madame Delange says I make you work too hard, she's right — '

'But it's not that – it's got nothing to do with the work.'

'Your condition, Madame Delange said. What did she mean? She said I make a girl in your condition work too hard.'

'I wanted to tell you myself. I've tried everything,' Mireille said sadly. 'I've soaked nails and coins in water and swallowed the liquid. I've run up and down the stairs.' She paused briefly, and then continued tonelessly, 'I drank a whole bottle of gin and sat in Madame Feyard's hot tin bath. I've even tried rat poison.'

'Oh, my God,' Saffarty said, his voice hoarse. 'You're not saying that you are — '

'You can't bring yourself to say the word, can you? Yes, I'm saying I am pregnant.'

'I don't believe this,' Saffarty whispered. 'I don't believe this is happening to me.'

'Nor do I — '

'What are you going to do?'

'I don't know, Saffarty. That depends on you — '

'On me?'

'We've been together for more than a year, Saffarty. I was a virgin when I met you, and I thought, I hoped, I prayed – and I still think, and hope and pray that we'll be married.' She took his hand and placed it over her stomach.

Instantly, Saffarty withdrew his hand. Pacing the room, he said, 'Marriage? Me? Get married? Out of the question! D'you know what Doctor Riencourt told me today? He said it's because of my age – my *age*, d'you hear me – that I could have a successful operation. Because I'm still a boy, he said. I'm still growing — ' He covered his good eye with his hand. 'I only need to have a little muscle corrected, because I'm still growing. Until I have the operation I'm to keep my good eye covered.'

He drew his fists and approached the bed.

'*No! Saffarty, no!* For the love of — ' Mireille screamed.

He stood over her for a while, and then crashed his fists against their small wardrobe.

'A father! At my age!' he yelled. His breath came in rapid gasps. 'I'm still a boy, the doctor said — '

'How old are you, Saffarty?'

'Nineteen. I'll be twenty in November. Oh, my *God*,' Saffarty said, beginning to sob. 'What are we going to do?'

'You lied to me about your age,' Mireille said coldly. 'You lied. Why did you lie?'

'I had to lie. Would Max have even thought of making me a partner if he knew I was still a boy? Feyard would have thrown me out. You wouldn't have looked at a boy of seventeen, Mireille.'

Mireille did not answer, and for a long while neither of them spoke. At last she said, 'What more can I do?'

'We'll get help,' Saffarty answered. 'We'll get the best help. I can afford to pay. We'll get rid of it — '

'That is a sin for which I will go to hell — ' Mireille moaned, unconsciously repeating what her mother had once said.

'You tried to get rid of it yourself. You just told me. We'll get help.'

'I can kill myself, that's what I can do,' Mireille wept. 'I'm dead already.'

'Mireille, Mireille, don't talk like that!'

'You want me to murder our child. What's the difference if I murder myself as well?'

Saffarty hurled himself to the floor and pounded it with his head and hands, howling.

Desperate to stop this punishing sound, Mireille shouted, 'You're ruining your suit, Saffarty! And you'll get splinters in your hands like I did.' Then, as he rose from the floor, she said, 'I may not have known your age, Saffarty, but I do know you. You couldn't stomach the thought of spoiling your expensive suit. *I'm* ruined and *I'm* spoiled. You care more about your suit than you care about me — '

'Mireille, that's not true. Marriage is one thing, fatherhood another. Of course I care about you. I'll pay anything to get you out of trouble.' He knelt beside the bed, took her hand and kissed it. 'Remember how I took out your splinters? Remember how you trusted me? Trust me, Mireille. Trust me *now* — '

'Trust *you*? *Why*?'

'Because I am going to see Madame Ravarino. She is a very understanding woman. She'll know what to do.'

'What *is* it, little one? What is it?' Colette said, shaking Max awake. 'You'd only been asleep ten minutes and you were screaming.'

These days Max was desperate for sleep, yet afraid to close his eyes. The nightmares attacked at any time. Nor did a drunken stupor prevent them.

'I'm sick,' he said miserably. 'I think I've caught some disease.'

'It was your gambling. Now you're drinking. It's affected your liver — '

'My gambling has nothing to do with it. I'm ill. I've got a fever — '

Colette laid a cool hand on his forehead. 'You *are* warm. I'll sponge you down.'

'No,' Max cried urgently. 'Don't leave me. Stay in bed with me – I need to sleep, that's all.'

'Sleep, little one, sleep,' Colette crooned tenderly. 'Sleep will do you good.' She lay beside him and patted his back, and made soothing, hushing noises, and all but rocked him to sleep. He had grown so thin and gaunt. His cheekbones seemed about to pierce his skin, and his large slanting grey eyes, in which she had often fancied she drowned, now wore a haunted, hunted look. He had aged. He muttered in his sleep, and sighed.

It was clear to Colette that he was in financial trouble again. It was also clear that it brought him closer to her. He needed her, and came to her as a son comes to a mother for help . . . It was this gambling of his; she should not have helped him to become a member of Longchamps. Still, she did not regret it – his need for her was something akin to love. After all, he had not asked her for more money. He was too proud, she supposed. Or perhaps it was that he was too frightened?

Besides he'd bought her a large amethyst ring. She stared at it sightlessly, trying to guess precisely what it was that terrified him so much. He was desperate enough to do anything to stop this awful suffering of his.

'Tell me what the problem is,' she said when he awoke. 'I've helped you before, no?'

'I'm sick, can't you see that?' Max said wretchedly.

'I can see that something is making you sick. Is it money?'

'Is it money?' Max mocked. 'I wish I was dead.'

'So it *is* money. How much? Perhaps I can help.'

'You haven't got enough.'

'Do you want me to beg you to allow me to help you? How much, little one? Just tell me how much.'

'Thirty thousand francs.'

'Who are you in debt to?'

'I owe the moneylender fifty thousand. But I have to pay the thirty at once. Tomorrow night, in fact. They break knee-caps, you know. They warned me — '

'*Knee-caps! My God!* Why didn't you tell me? I'll find the money. It won't be easy, but I'll find it. But then you must stop gambling. You must!'

Max could not speak. He put his head between her breasts, and very soon she felt the trickle of his hot tears. She stroked his back, his buttocks, his thighs, and then he was driving inside her, driving with a force even greater than lust, driving his demons away. His tenderness after that made Colette's entire life worth while. And when he said, 'It's your skin, I love Colette. Your soft, translucent skin. Slender like a snake, you also wriggle like a snake.' He cast his eyes about the *garçonnière*. It was warm and cosy. Colette had added some colourful posters. It was a comfortable room, and in good taste. 'I'm a lucky man,' he said. 'You are my luck.'

Colette breathed his words in; even if what he was saying was true only for the moment, he *meant* what he said, meant every single word.

'I love you, little one,' Colette said. 'You mustn't worry about anything any more. I will look after you.'

She took off the amethyst ring and held it up to the early evening light. It was genuine; it had come from Cartier. She knew that because she had found the bill in his pocket.

At the same time that Colette was hoping to console Max, Saffarty was trying to explain to Mireille about Madame Chandler.

'Madame Chandler? Who is Madame Chandler?'

Plunging into explanations, Saffarty said that though Madame Chandler was a strange woman, she was a famous midwife, something of a saint, really. She had married an American sailor, and had even lived in America, but Mireille was not to worry about that, because Madame Chandler was as true a Frenchwoman as Mireille. Except she *did* have strange ideas. For example, she believed that men and women were equal, because she had lived in a place called Wyoming, and women there had had the right to vote since 1869. She had even voted for President Wilson and, as even Mireille had to admit, the French had reason to be grateful to the Americans. He wondered whom Mireille would have voted for in the last French election. Such a preposterous idea as a woman voting brought a smile to Mireille's lips. She almost laughed.

Emboldened by her smile, Saffarty went on to describe what this strange woman looked like. She was about sixty, he said, and large, so large, that each of her thighs looked like pillow-cases. She had blue eyes, he said, blue as violets, and she painted them with kohl so they looked even brighter. But she whitened her face with powder. Yet she dressed only in yellow. Everything in her apartment was yellow, all the furnishings, the walls, even the coffee cups and glasses.

She was not rich, certainly, but she was not poor either. In fact, she helped the poor.

The rich and famous who came to her were ready to pay anything; that was why she could name her price. But when a woman was too poor to pay she would give her services free.

'I didn't even try to bargain with her,' Saffarty said proudly. 'She asked for three thousand francs, and I said I'd give her three thousand francs.'

'*Money!*' Mireille said in a ragged whisper. 'Money, for murder. *She's a murderess.* But not me – Oh, no, not me! *I won't do it!*' She pulled the blankets over her head, and slid further down into the bed.

'What do you mean?' Saffarty shouted, snatching the covers away. 'Are you crazy? Have you gone insane?' He stood over her. 'What do you mean, you won't do it? Do you want to have an illegitimate child? If you do, you may be sure that I will never see you again!' He grabbed her nightgown, jerked her upward and heaved her out of the bed. 'I'll force some sense into you,' he said, shaking her frantically. His hands about her arms held her in a vice-like grip. He was in a fever of rage and hate. Her numb, unseeing, senseless stare added to his rage. Then he stopped shaking her, moved away, and with his left hand still holding her in a fierce grip he struck her face with the back of his right hand.

'Mireille, Mireille, why did you make me do this?' he said wildly. 'I'm sorry. I'm sorry. Lie down. Let me put a wet cloth on it. I'm so sorry, Mireille.'

Still numb, Mireille lay still and let him minister to her. She could fight no longer. All will and, it seemed, all life had drained out of her. She was going to murder her unborn child, and if she was lucky she would die, too. Her face stung but nothing mattered, nothing except giving in to the overwhelming lassitude and exhaustion.

After that, things moved swiftly. Mireille went to see Madame Chandler and allowed her to take over.

Madame Chandler was everything that Saffarty had said she was. Everything and more. The first thing she said was, 'You will get over this, *ma petite*, and you will get over *him*. He is too young to be a father, you know. That is why I agreed to help him.'

There was a sing-song tone to Madame Chandler's voice, and though she was big and heavy her movements were graceful. Mireille trusted her at once.

'He said he would never see me again, if I didn't,' Mireille confided. 'It's murdering my baby.'

'Few of the women who come to me have your scruples,' Madame Chandler said quietly. 'But abortion is *not* murder. It is only murder when the child is killed *after* it is born. Do you understand that?'

'It's a sin — ' Mireille said, her voice trembling.

'A sin. Is an act of mercy a sin?'

'But the Pope?'

'The Pope,' Madame Chandler repeated irritably. 'One day the Pope will change his ruling. There was a time when the Church was opposed to the use of any drug for the relief of pain for women in labour. Because the Church decreed that pain in labour was the Lord's just punishment for Eve's original sin. The Church has already changed that ruling, did you know that?'

Mireille shook her head.

'The Church will have to move with the times,' Madame Chandler continued. 'We live in a new world of the wireless, the telephone, a world of machines. And even the Church uses the wireless to broadcast prayers.' Madame Chandler went on more slowly, now showing her puzzlement. 'And yet, for what I do, the Church would not only send me to hell but to prison.'

'I won't say anything. I won't tell anyone,' Mireille said urgently.

'I know that, *ma petite*,' Madame Chandler said gently. 'Now, we will attend to your problem. Were you telling me the truth when you said you did not know how far pregnant you were?'

Mireille nodded miserably, and began an account of all her symptoms.

Madame Chandler listened, and then explained that many women bled all through their pregnancies; some bled lightly, some more heavily. She even knew of a woman who only realised she was pregnant when she went into labour. Still, she would be able to tell how far advanced Mireille was. An internal examination would reveal the size of the uterus, and the state of the cervix. 'Women should know more about their own bodies,' she said sternly. 'I will tell you exactly what I am doing – that way you will learn.'

She left Mireille little time for anticipation, and almost before she knew it, Mireille was lying on a bed listening to the sound of Madame Chandler scrubbing her hands. She accompanied her examination with a running commentary, only interrupting this to reassure Mireille it would not hurt for long, and that Mireille was being a good girl, a *very* good girl.

'Such a large, big, woman,' Mireille thought, 'and yet her touch is so gentle.'

When Madame Chandler had done, she removed her rubber gloves, and said briskly, 'It *is* late, but not too late. You are between sixteen and eighteen weeks. It would have been better if you had come to me sooner.' Seeing the look of terror in Mireille's eyes she said kindly, 'We will make it easier by injecting one of those very drugs that was forbidden by the Church.'

It was going to be more risky than Madame Chandler had thought. Mireille was no longer carrying an embryo, but a foetus. Accordingly, there was no alternative but to inject a saline solution that would cause the death of the foetus. The poor child would have to endure the long painful process of childbirth. She thought fleetingly of explaining this to Mireille, but discarded the idea. She said quietly, 'At this stage, it will take a little longer, for it has to come away.'

'But it hasn't quickened yet. It hasn't.'

'That's all to the good, then.' Madame Chandler was all too familiar with this response. Experience had taught her what she should not say. The poor girl did not know that the flicker of a flutter was quickening – it would take a second pregnancy to teach her that. '*Alors!* We will not begin until tomorrow. Tonight we will both rest. I will give you a good, strong cognac, and you *will* sleep. And then – after this is all over – you will begin a new life.'

When Madame Chandler awakened her the next morning, it was still dark. Madame's vast body was dressed in a sparkling white uniform that reached to the floor. Her hair had disappeared behind a stiff white cap. Mireille looked up at her, and felt safe. 'You are all in white, like an angel.'

'An angel of mercy,' Madame Chandler answered, smiling. 'First I will show you the room where I work. Then you will take a warm bath. Everything is ready.'

The room was all white, frighteningly, hygienically white. It had a certain smell Mireille had never encountered before. She shifted involuntarily. Hospitals must have this smell, she supposed. Madame Chandler had filled the tub. 'Wash yourself as thoroughly as if you were scrubbing the kitchen floor. And then put on this clean gown.'

Mireille did as she was told. A real bath was new to her – until now she had only showered. The warm soothing water was as comforting as a mother's embrace.

'I am going to tell you as much as I can as we go along,' Madame Chandler said when Mireille was lying on the clean bed.

Through the long night Madame Chandler had rehearsed the procedure she was going to use – a technique she had only used twice. The foetus could not be dislodged, or scraped away – it would have to be expelled by the uterus itself. 'Raise your knees, please, and open your legs,' she said firmly. 'Good girl.'

Mireille felt a warm metal instrument enter. It stayed still for a moment, and then it moved again, and when it stopped she was aware of a cranking which widened and stretched her. There was discomfort rather than pain. Then a second instrument entered, high and higher, a stiletto reaching up to her heart. She screamed, and quickly put her fist in her mouth. A gush of water spurted out and then the cruel thin dagger was removed.

'Has the bag of waters broken?' Mireille asked weakly.

'Yes. Now I'm injecting some extra water. This will not hurt. It is a narrow tube, attached to a syringe, but no wider than a cigarette. The fluid must enter slowly, very slowly.'

Mireille's lips moved in prayer. Her mind and her body seemed to be in different places.

For eight hours, every hour on the hour, Madame Chandler worked with the syringe. Mireille felt as if she had become a vessel of fluid – her terrible thirst made her drink gallons of water. Sometimes she thought she was drowning. 'It's the salt in the fluid,' Madame Chandler reassured her again and again. 'It will take time, but the contractions will begin. This I promise you.'

In the early evening Mireille said wearily, 'It's beginning. I felt it.'

'Good girl.' Madame Mireille placed her hand on Mireille's hardened stomach. 'It has begun.' Deftly, she removed the speculum and the tube.

The contractions grew fiercer, violent. Towards the end, fifteen

136

hours later, Madame Chandler held up an orange, rubber mask. 'It's ether, dangerous without an assistant.'

Mireille snatched it from her. 'I must have it!' she screamed. 'I must.'

Twenty minutes later, after one mighty push, it was out. 'What was it?' Mireille asked.

'A boy.'

'There's still more to come. And then we must wait for the placenta. Lie still, Mireille. Quite, quite still.' Madame Chandler massaged Mireille's stomach. Still the placenta did not emerge. Presently, she began kneading the stomach exactly as if she were kneading a lump of dough. 'Here we are.'

Madame Chandler dealt quickly and efficiently with the cord, removed the dead foetus and the rest of the mess, went to the bathroom and flushed it down the lavatory.

When she returned Mireille said, 'Long ago, in Marseilles, it was considered a blessing to be buried in the same grave as a stillborn baby. But my baby's grave is the sewer.' She bit her lip. 'I didn't want to lose him, you see. I was going to call him Simon — '

'You can't cry. It's hard, I know it's hard. You must sleep. But first you must have some hot consommé,' Madame Chandler said, stroking Mireille's forehead.

'How can I thank you?' Mireille said faintly.

Two days later Saffarty fetched her from Madame Chandler, and took her to stay with him in their little cubicle at the back of the nameless shop. This upset his plans – he had expected her to be cared for by her room-mate. 'You will take her back with *you*,' Madame Chandler had exploded when she learned of his plans. 'She's still asleep. You'll take her back to the place she calls her home. Either that, or I'll see that you get the thrashing of your life. Now, have you – or have you not – understood me?'

Saffarty agreed hastily.

But he slept on the floor.

It was four months before the Doussets approached Max for another bet.

It was to be on a superb horse, a champion called Apollinaire. Max had seen him perform, and his experience made him confident of placing the bet.

There was, however, one snag. Apollinaire's usual jockey was Raoul Vinci, and of late Vinci's reputation had been plummeting. He had been seen late at night in shady clubs with dubious actresses; it was said that he drank, heavily; it was even rumoured that he had resorted to drugs to make him fit for the race track. He was no longer, in Max's eyes, a serious jockey, and would constitute a considerable hazard to the horse's chances of winning if he were up on Apollinaire for the big race.

Two days before the race the horse's jockey had still been undecided.

A few days earlier, in the middle of the morning, Max had seen a man who looked like Raoul Vinci stagger out of a bar. Max had chased after him, only to find that he had the wrong man. He had streaked down the Boulevard de Capucine like a madman, and in his madness had even believed he had caught a glimpse of Saffarty. As if *he* would waste a moment idling over a cup of coffee!

He had been a fool to have fallen out with Saffarty. He missed his decisive enthusiasm, his infectious strength. Above all, he missed his advice – Saffarty would have been able to tell him what he should do.

Meanwhile, how could he put fifty thousand francs on a debauched jockey?

The beauty of that race track, the glamour of the people, even the power and the grace of the horses, had lost their allure for Max. He stared at them all with unseeing eyes, for his attention was focused only on the betting boxes, and on the decision he had not yet made. Max had at least made up his mind that if Raoul Vinci was the jockey, he would not place a single centime of the Doussets' seventy-five thousand francs on Apollinaire. That the Doussets had increased their bet at the very last moment from fifty to seventy-five thousand had added to Max's already overflowing anguish. Now they were nowhere to be seen. It was torture, nothing but torture.

There was Maximin, a handsome grey colt, an outsider with the magnificent legs of a purebred. Max had watched him in his first and only race, and although Maximin had not as much as been placed he was convinced that the horse had been pulled. *Maximin*. Could this be destiny, a message from the gods, a signal? Coincidence, perhaps, but a sign, surely? It depended on the jockey.

It all depended on the jockey.

The odds were fifty to one. Fifty thousand francs – that would equal two-and-a-half million francs. He multiplied it again, writing it all down laboriously, and felt his brain swell.

If he wanted to stay alive, he would have to give up this drug, this racing drug. He had told Colette he was quitting, and knew now that he had taken a decision as final as the official decision over which horse was the winner.

Maximin – the name was not only similar to his, but as close as dammit to maximum, and seventy-five thousand was his maximum bet so far.

So far, and for ever, he told himself.

Sometimes the jockeys were changed at the last minute. His decision had been narrowed down to two – Jean-Baptiste Barbe or Géraud Dinan. Either of these two up-and-coming jockeys would do.

Then, suddenly, it was final – Raoul Vinci was to ride Apollinaire.

Sweating now, Max decided to put all the money on Maximin, ridden by Géraud Dinan. By the time he placed his bet, he was unrecognisable. His hat, wet with sweat, was shapeless, his tie was undone, his hands shook, and he reeked of whisky.

He placed himself near the exit. He would watch from there. It was only when he was standing shivering in the high wind that he thought to ask himself exactly what he would do if his horse did not come in.

The race was on!

From the very outset Maximin gained on the field, storming his way past through the pack. On the last stretch Apollinaire blasted his way with the speed of an explosive. '*Maximin! Maximin!*' Max howled and, as if he'd heard him, Maximin streaked ahead and then, unbelievably, seconds before the winning post, he unseated his jockey and the crowd screamed as the riderless horse bolted through the winning post. Apollinaire was the winner. Max heard the cry that the jockey was killed, but only dimly. He was on his way out, running, streaking through the crowds as his horse had streaked through the field.

He hailed a taxi, and hurled himself inside it.

'Where to?' the taxi driver asked.

Max did not answer, because he did not hear.

'Where to?' the driver repeated.

Still no answer.

The driver studied Max briefly in his rear view mirror, and pulled up. 'Get out,' he shouted. 'Get out!'

'What's that?'

'*Merde!* You won't tell me where you want to go. I'm telling you to get out.'

'Thirty-five Avenue Foch.'

'Why couldn't you have said that in the first place?'

What was the use of saying that he didn't tell him because he didn't know where he was going? Max thought miserably. What was he going to do? The Doussets would send a hit man after him. He'd never escape. Never. Hide – but where could he hide? *Where?* Colette would save him . . . He'd confess everything to her. *Everything!*

She would give him the money, he was sure of that. He owed the Doussets three hundred thousand francs. Colette would help. Colette would save him. Overcome with relief, and above all with hope, his muscles relaxed. He stretched his legs, and looked down. It was only then that he saw the wet patch on his trousers. 'I've peed in my pants,' he said to himself. 'My God, I've actually peed in my pants.' He placed his binoculars over the stain, but they did not altogether cover it. The seat was wet, too.

He rang Colette's bell urgently. Oh God, she was out! She couldn't be! He pressed the bell harder, and heard its imperious ringing. At last he heard the sound of footsteps and then Colette called out, 'Who is it?'

'It's me. Max. Open up!'

'Max! What are you doing here? You know you can't come in — '

'Open the door,' Max yelled.

The door swung open.

'What is it? What's happened? You look like a ghost. Your trousers are wet,' Colette babbled.

Max didn't answer, but slammed the door shut. His eyes revolved wildly, and so it was a few seconds before they alighted on the bird on her shoulder. Bijou sat there as regally as if he were seated on a throne. Suddenly he knew that he was living a waking nightmare, and his last shred of control left him. 'You've been lying to me, Colette! Lying!'

140

Bijou shrieked.

'What's happened to you?' she wailed. 'What's the matter?'

'What's the matter?' Max repeated mockingly. 'What's the matter?' His voice was hoarse. 'You had the money all the time. First you told me Bijou died, and you had him stuffed, and now I see him alive and well and sitting like a king on your shoulder.' His hand flailed after the bird. 'Get him off,' he screamed. 'Get rid of him.'

'It's not Bijou. I bought another toucan,' she stammered. 'I'll get rid of him, Max,' she said, backing away.

'The hell with the bird,' he yelled. 'You've got to help me. The Doussets gave me seventy-five thousand francs to put on Apollinaire and I put it on Maximin.'

'I don't follow – what are you talking about?'

The reason Colette had taken so long to answer the door was because she was in the middle of creaming her face. She stood facing Max, her face pale and naked; the flaming colours of the toucan emphasised her pallid complexion.

The bird opened and shut its beak.

'I've got to give them back their money. Seventy-five thousand francs – Apollinaire was four to one, that makes three hundred thousand francs. You have to give it to me. You'll go to the bank tomorrow. I'll go with you.'

'Three hundred thousand francs. Are you crazy? I haven't got anything like it.'

'Liar,' he shrieked. 'Liar!'

'Little one. Please, please — '

'Liar!' Max roared. 'Lying whore! Why, I'll get rid of that bird,' he said, pushing her roughly. She was still walking backward. The bird opened its wings, but stayed like a sentinel on her shoulder. Senseless now with rage, half walking, half dancing, he advanced toward her, forcing her to continue backing away.

'Careful, Max, the pond, the pond,' she screamed, but at the same moment Max was wildly striking at the bird with his binoculars. Suddenly the bird alighted on his head. Claws ripped through his hat to his scalp as Colette fell back into the mirrored pool.

The toucan screeched.

He touched his head, and when he brought his hand down he saw that it was covered in blood. Then he looked into the pond.

Colette lay under the water, over the angels painted on the floor of the pond, her reflection projected in an infinity of mirrors

141

– her copper hair streaming, the apricot peignoir clinging, the water reddening. Paralysed, Max watched her blood spill into eternity.

The clatter of the bird's wings broke the terrible stillness and his paralysis. His single impulse was to escape. The bird began to caw again. He flung himself out of the flat and only stopped running when he saw an empty taxi.

This time he told the driver exactly where to go. He was going to La Fenêtre de Saffarty.

When Max saw that La Fenêtre de Saffarty was closed, he raced to the Cinéma Germaine.

'I can only sell what I would buy myself,' Saffarty was saying to a customer as Max entered the shop.

When he saw Max, and his bloodied head and wet trousers he excused himself immediately. 'What's wrong, Max? You look as if — '

'My life's in danger,' Max interrupted desperately. 'Where's Mireille? I've got to talk to you privately.'

'She's ill,' Saffarty said tersely. 'Never mind, I'll close the shop, anyway. We'll go to the Café Rouge.'

'No,' Max said wildly. 'I can't go anywhere. I can't be seen.'

'Wait, Mireille is in bed.'

'Where can we talk?'

'In the cellar. Go there now.'

Minutes later Saffarty joined him and gave him a clean handkerchief to replace the blood-soaked one he was holding to his head, and the story came flooding out. Max told him everything: how he had met Colette, how she had kept him, where she was now, and what he had done with the Doussets' money. Survival excluded shame.

'What do you think, Saffarty? What do you think I should do?'

'You must leave the country. Immediately!'

'I've got no money.'

'I know that. I'll help. You'll pay me back when you can.' Saffarty whistled through his teeth. 'Where do you have relations?'

'In Poland, of course.'

'That's the first place they'll look for you. Where else do you have relations?'

'South Africa.'

'Good. You will go there.'

'Saffarty – I — '

'Let me think, Max. Leave me alone to think,' Saffarty said. His hand swept over his forehead. 'I must clear my mind.'

Hatless and coatless, Saffarty went out again into the cold air. Facts and impressions crowded his mind. Regrets were pointless, he told himself, but how different things would have been, for both of them, if they had not killed their partnership with a senseless quarrel.

He walked briskly. A plan, or, rather plans, were rapidly being formed, and gaining coherence just as rapidly. Max Blum, *a gigolo*! Well, well, he thought, you live and you learn. It was childish of him, and he was naive and gullible not to have suspected it in the first place. As so often these days, he reminded himself of his true age.

Eighteen-and-a-half or not, he knew that he was shielding a criminal – a murderer! He could go to prison himself for harbouring Max; he saw no reason why he should bring his own house down upon himself.

It would mean the guillotine . . .

A gust of cold wind wafted the smell of roasting chestnuts to him. Stopping to buy a cone, standing beside the charcoal brazier he was reminded of Salonika. He moved away, absently popping the chestnuts into his mouth. But Salonika was as distant from him now as Africa or America. His mind leapt along his associations – Africa. South Africa, a different hemisphere, the Southern Hemisphere. He remembered his geography lessons – a different hemisphere meant a different season. It was summer there. Mireille was bloodless and grim. She had suffered. She needed a holiday, a sea voyage. He had the money and, as they say in Salonika, money wounds are not mortal . . .

A sea voyage for Mireille; now, what had made him think of that? He changed his direction, and slowly ambled toward the chestnut seller. Yes, yes, there it was – a poster – *Visit Egypt – 38 days luxurious travel, steamers de luxe, cabin steamers only eight thousand francs*. Egypt was at the top of Africa, but still it was Africa.

There was no time to lose. He hailed a taxi. Mireille had a passport – she had thought she might want to go to London – but that was before she had met him. She had seen great steamers at Marseilles, and had often told him how much she longed to board one, and sail away to a distant land.

'You've been hours, Saffarty. What took you so long?' Max rasped when he returned.

One look at Max's eyes told Saffarty that he had been crying. But he pretended not to have noticed.

'I have everything arranged, Max. You will take the train to Calais, and the ferry to Southampton. From there you will board the Union Castle for Cape Town. It will take seventeen days. And incidentally,' he continued, 'to avoid being recognised you will not be travelling alone.'

'I won't be alone? But surely you can't be — '

'No, I'm not,' Saffarty said smoothly. 'It is far more usual for a man and a women to travel together. Mireille will join you.'

'Mireille? Does she know about me? Have you told her?'

'Not yet. Leave that to me.' He laid his hand on Max's arm. 'Max, there is something I want to tell you. I want to tell you that trust is a priceless commodity. It was only long after you and I had broken up that I learned that. You see, Max, I trusted you. But I never said so.'

'But South Africa. That's in darkest Africa,' Mireille whimpered. 'Black people frighten me. I'm not going there.'

'I've bought your ticket. *Aller et retour* – an open ticket — '

'You can get your money back.'

'Mireille, just look at the brochure. Do me a favour, don't be a silly girl. You'll have the sun, and the sea. Look on it as a cruise. You can stay a few days in Durban, or Cape Town, and then come right back to Paris — '

He began opening the brochures.

'A swimming pool on deck,' he said, recounting what he saw on the pages. 'A fancy dress party . . . An orchestra . . . People dancing . . . What a magnificent ball gown . . . Now *that's* what I call a beautiful woman.'

'Show me. Let me see.'

'But you said you weren't interested.'

'Show me.'

'Only if you smile!'

Against her will, the beginnings of a smile glimmered. How she hated herself for the way she always, always gave in to him. She

144

had only to look at him and her will evaporated. The best thing she could do for herself would be to follow Madame Chandler's advice to go away, away as far as Africa. 'Go away,' Madame Chandler had counselled. 'Out of sight, out of mind.' Like a wizard, Saffarty had her under his spell.

She looked at the brochure, and then pushed it away abruptly. 'I can't go, Saffarty.'

'But you will recover your strength in the sun. You need a holiday.'

'I can't go on my own.'

'But you won't be alone.'

'Why?' she asked, her heart leaping. 'Why won't I be alone?'

'Max is going with you.'

'Max?'

Saffarty took her hand and kissed it. She wanted to withdraw it, but as usual she could not. 'Max is in bad trouble,' he said forcefully. 'He's lost every *sou*, everything he ever had. I've got to help him. His life is in danger.'

'You exaggerate.'

'No, Mireille, not this time.' Quickly he sketched a few, selected details, and though he did not mention Colette's fate, Mireille's eyes widened at the mention of his affair with an older woman.

'Let me think about it, Saffarty,' she said wearily. 'I'm too tired. I can't think.' She added plaintively, 'I'm still bleeding, and it hurts, Saffarty, it hurts. My breasts ache.' She fell into a fit of weeping, and Saffarty lay down beside her, and held her as if he loved her.

Once Mireille was safely asleep, Saffarty raced down the stairs to the cellar where Max waited for him in the lavatory. It was dank and cold and putrid down there, and Saffarty decided to risk moving to the deserted cinema. They talked quietly, urgently, and, now that the chips were down, found themselves in absolute agreement over every single issue. Saffarty would go out and buy the necessary clothes for Max; neither of them would go anywhere near the *garçonnière*. Saffarty would give him sufficient money – he would not need much, because he would be going to his relations. Max knew almost nothing about who his relations were. He remembered only that when he was a very small boy one of his uncles had gone to a place called Cape Town. Saffarty was surprised that the uncle had stayed in Cape Town. After all, the gold was in Johannesburg.

'The sun will cure you,' Madame Chandler said to Mireille, when she went for her check-up. 'Tears are the medicine of the heart, but too many tears drown the heart. Take this chance, *ma petite*. Leave this man. Besides, who knows what other young men you will meet on the voyage?'

'I'm still sore, madame,' Mireille answered. 'I don't wish to meet anyone else – ever!'

'Now, Mireille, almost every woman who has been through what you have speaks like that. But you are young, the gift of youth is still yours. Stay away for three months.'

'Will he miss me, do you think?' Mireille asked wistfully.

'Yes, he will miss you.' Madame Chandler sighed and fell silent. She wanted to tell Mireille so many things, but stifled them. What was the use of telling her that she was better off without this man who had never been a boy? This tall graceful man who, even with a crooked eye, would almost unthinkingly exploit his own power over women.

Mireille held her breath, and waited for Madame Chandler to pronounce. A church bell tolled in the distance. The yellow room was calm and as serene as the woman herself.

The silence spilled over the two women, spilled like hope, and Mireille felt that Madame Chandler was actually praying for her. She knew she would remember and take comfort from this moment for ever.

At last, Madame Chandler spoke. 'How can I even begin to comfort you, *ma petite?*' she said, her voice as melodious as the tolling church bell. 'Great love is a luxury given to very few women, you know. It has happened to me. Oh, you see me now, large and far from young, and it seems scarcely possible. It will be a long time before we meet again, and, since I am no longer young, we may never meet again.'

'Don't say that, madame. Please,' Mireille interrupted.

Madame Chandler raised her hand, and Mireille was silenced.

'And so I will be frank. Whatever life holds in store for you, you must not allow this tragic end to destroy the glory and the beauty that you knew. Believe it or not, my child, but you are one of the

146

lucky ones. I will tell you why. You found a man who found your secret core. It was good making love with his man, no? And, before him, you were a virgin, no? You were lucky because you found a man who knew that a woman's secret core is her skin – all her skin – not only the skin down below. Even her hair is part of that secret core. Most women do not know that, because they have not found a man who knows that. This is the truth of you and your man, isn't it?'

'Yes,' Mireille whispered, smiling in spite of herself. 'Yes.'

'When you walk in the streets you see people. People, animals, human beings. And every single one of them is the result of a man's sexual climax. Have you ever thought of that, *ma petite*? But how many of them are the result of the sexual climax of a woman? Few, *ma petite*, few. We women are not required to climax to reproduce. Understand? Somewhere, deep, deep in our souls we know this. But this luxury that you have known can stay with you, and shine in you, and pour strength through you, for ever. Yes, for ever! Even if you never, never experience it again. *Remembered ecstasy is ecstasy.* Remember this, and all the days of your life will be eased, purified . . . '

They talked of other things, and when Mireille was taking her leave, she said, 'I feel as if I've been to the confessional.'

'Perhaps, in a way, we both have.' Madame Chandler laid her hand on Mireille's hand. 'May God be with you,' she said.

Clothes, suitcases, money, even the new system of having traveller's cheques instead of cash – the following day Saffarty attended to all those details. His quick mind thought of everything. He bought new clothes for both Mireille and Max and even remembered a sun tan lotion.

It was odd buying sun tan oil on such a blustery day, so odd in fact that it forced Saffarty to pause for a moment and consider what he was doing. His sense of urgency had been so great that he had missed his breakfast of croissants and coffee. He stepped into a café. While he was waiting for his coffee he unwrapped the packet containing the bottle of sun tan oil. The flowers on the label reminded him of what Max had said about the water lilies at the bottom of Colette's pond. He hurried out to buy a newspaper, but nothing about Colette had been reported. It suddenly seemed important to have some details about the poor woman. On impulse, he telephoned her apartment.

'Would it be convenient to deliver the lamps madame ordered this afternoon?' he asked, improvising hastily.

'But no, monsieur. Madame is in the clinic – an accident you see — '

'I am sorry to hear that. I hope it was not serious?'

'Madame is out of danger. Good-day, monsieur.'

The phone clicked off.

Quickly, he telephoned Colette's apartment again, and disguising his voice asked for the name of the clinic she was at so that he could send her flowers. When he then got through to the clinic, a nurse told him that although Madame was out of danger, it would be best to wait a few days before delivering the basket of fruit.

His hands went cold.

There was no need for Max to escape.

Of course, if Max were to know this, he would decide not to leave France. For one thing, his life was not in danger of the guillotine, and for another he would want to be with Colette. Because even though Max had spoken of Colette as 'that old witch', it had been all too obvious that he had cared for her. But there was still the threat of the Doussets . . . It was Max's terror of *them* that had unhinged him in the first place, and got him into this fearful trouble. Surely the Doussets were reason enough for Max to skip France in a big, big hurry?

And what about Mireille? The plain truth was that it suited him to have her far, far away in South Africa.

Now that these emergency arrangements had been made it seemed as if there had never been any other alternative for her. He was too young to be a father, and he was too young to be tied down.

His head was spinning.

In a flash, it came to him that he would say nothing about his phone call to the clinic, now or ever. And even as he made his decision he knew it was irrevocable.

He went ahead with his plans and told Mireille that Max's gambling had brought him into the company of evil people who now threatened his life. She had heard of this sort of thing – it was not uncommon in Marseilles – and so she accepted it.

Later that afternoon Saffarty waited until they were at the Gare du Nord before handing over his last surprise, two Berlitz English phrase books. 'They speak English down there, in South Africa,' he said.

148

Just before they boarded the train, Max said urgently, 'Take these keys, Saffarty.'

'What keys?'

'To my *garçonnière*.'

'But it's hers.'

'No. The lease is in my name.'

'Who paid the rent?' Saffarty asked quickly. 'Did she pay the rent?'

'No. I did. She gave me the money. There's about two more years to go on the lease. It's fully paid.'

'It would be too dangerous.'

'Keep the keys, anyway.'

The whistle sounded. They began kissing, and hugging and crying.

Saffarty watched the train until it was out of sight. He tried to convince himself that he had been right to keep silent about Colette. Max had to escape from those gambling gangsters anyway – flee France. Mireille had tried to trap him into marriage. He needed a rest from her. He was relieved to see them go; at the same time, he felt acutely alone.

It suddenly struck him that the police might ask him about Max. He had the key to the *garçonnière*, and it could implicate him. With that thought in mind he strolled to one of the city's bridges, and dropped the key into the Seine. Long, long after the ripples had ceased, he was still watching the cruel, dark water, while across Paris bells pealed.

Part Three

9

It quickly became obvious to Saffarty that without Mireille he had lost not only his direction, but his balance. It seemed to him that his good eye, occluded by the eye-patch essential to his treatment, was symbolic of his life without Mireille, as if he had only one eye in every sense. Meanwhile, he waited for something that he could not identify. Though La Fenêtre de Saffarty absorbed all his waking moments, the nights were long, empty and often sleepless. He had twice sought the comfort of expensive women, and each time his loneliness was accentuated.

Besides, it was not easy, running the shop without her. He engaged two sales assistants, but his profits were falling. He caught one of them stealing and fired her.

Almost every day Madame Delange visited his shop. Sometimes she brought a friend with her, and sometimes not. She did not always buy, but she was a good customer and took care not to get in the way. Saffarty had grown used to her, and rather looked forward to her visits. The very day that he dismissed his sales assistant and Madame Delange offered her services, he accepted with gratitude. He saw at once how much her dignified authoritative bearing could add to the general ambience. It turned out to be an excellent decision; she had undeniable class and made a great show of deferring to his exceptional taste.

When Mireille's letter arrived, six weeks after it had been posted, the chestnut trees were already in blossom. He knew, then, what it was he had been waiting for, and read it again and again, until he had all but memorised every word.

Dearest Saffarty,

In three days' time we will land at Cape Town. We crossed the equator and learnt about the force of the sun.

I'll never know how I managed to leave Paris. I don't think I knew what I was doing – it was too soon after the worst time of my life. For the first few days I was too seasick to care about anything.

I am very worried about Max. I have had to force him to try to behave normally. A few French people asked me what was the matter with him and when I told him he almost went crazy with fear. In an effort to get him to behave normally I forced him to go to the Fancy Dress Ball, because everyone was going and it would have looked odd if he had stayed in his cabin. I went as Joan of Arc, and he went as the hangman. It was his idea and I went along with it because it was easy to make the costumes.

But then something terrible happened, and to cover it all up, I lied, and said that Max was drunk.

I still can't understand why Max reacted the way he did.

One of the passengers went to the Fancy Dress Ball as the famous British sailor, Captain Long John Silver – who had only one leg, and always wore a parrot on his shoulder. As soon as Max saw this Long John – a giant of a man – he went berserk, and started to shout something about the parrot being dangerous, and before anyone could stop him he knocked the parrot off that poor man's shoulder, and then there was going to be a terrible fight. I stopped it by saying that Max was more used to wine than whisky.

This ship is very grand, like a floating palace. No wonder it is called the *Windsor Castle*. I have not been inside the first class but even third class is real luxury.

I think about you all the time. My heart is so full, and so sad, and so sore. I ask myself, how can a broken heart also be full to bursting? I think of La Fenêtre de Saffarty, and I wonder, have you found a replacement for me? So many questions. My soul is full of questions. I ache to say so many things to you.

Madame C. told me that I would love you for ever.

I will finish this after we land.

Later

We were all up early. After seventeen days at sea, everyone was dying to see land. This is a part of Britain, so British and South African flags were waving in the wind . . . You always wanted to go to England.

So I saw the famous Table Mountain, covered with its famous

tablecloth cloud. I thought the cloud was like a baby's shawl. Why did you make me do it, Saffarty? *Why?*

My love always,
Your Mireille

Saffarty's immediate impulse was to tell her to get the first ship back to Paris. Halfway through his letter he realised that he did not have an address to write to. Max! He would write to her care of Max. But then he remembered: Max's relation was his mother's brother, and he knew neither his name nor his address. He had forgotten to ask.

He flung his writing pad and his new fountain pen across the room. The pen hit the wall, and as he watched the spreading black stain he cursed himself for having let her go. There was no point now, in even trying to sleep. He opened his Berlitz book of English phrases, and that was when his serious study of the English language began. He could not help noticing which English words had their roots in Greek, which in French, and, in spite of his black mood, his intellectual curiosity was aroused and the night passed quickly. The next morning he bought himself a textbook of English grammar. He did not doubt that he would have little difficulty in mastering this cold language.

Now, when the English-speaking tourists came, he practised his English. His humorous but obviously very real effort delighted his customers, and distinctly added to the friendly atmosphere. More and more, La Fenêtre was gaining the reputation of one of those little shops in Montmartre that one simply had to visit. In the small shop his high, rough laugh resounded. That June, when Paris was in high summer, Saffarty welcomed his first American tourists. He was able, by then, to distinguish between American and British accents.

Propped up in her hospital bed, her face white as the bandages swathing her head like a turban, Colette tried – and failed – to come to terms with the fact that Max had rushed out, leaving her for dead, or leaving her to drown. Anyone would have done more for a dog, she told herself. But not if he thought the dog would bite him. Max had been terrified. She carried on a long, interior debate, arguing that since he had done nothing to try to help her, she was well rid of him. She tried to convince herself that he was probably pleased

– as well as relieved – to be rid of her. At the same time she listened longingly and continuously for his footsteps. It was inconceivable that he had not even tried to find out what had happened to her. Surely he knew that she would protect him, come hell or high water? Everyone believed it had been an accident.

So many times, waiting and listening, she was sure she heard his footsteps in the corridor. She should never have deceived him into believing she was married to Guy Terblanche. Of course he could not possibly come to the hospital. It served her right. The irony of it all was, Guy had emigrated to Montreal . . .

The day before she was due to be discharged, Monique Dousset came to see her. Not that Monique troubled to introduce herself. Colette recognised her Chanel tweed suit as the one Max had described months ago.

'Where is he?' Monique demanded.

'I don't know,' Colette responded bleakly. 'I only wish I did.'

'He put you in here, didn't he?' Monique drew off her fawn kid gloves and sat down. 'Strange, I didn't think he was the type.' She studied her long scarlet nails. 'So he beat you up, did he?'

Colette covered her eyes with trembling hands, but said nothing.

Monique Dousset jerked herself out of her chair and stood beside the bed. She bent so low over Colette that her mouth was only two inches from Colette's nose. Her breath stank, making Colette shrink. 'I know you'll see him again,' she said menacingly. 'And when you do, tell him that Monique Dousset knows exactly what to do with men who beat women!'

Colette watched her flounce from the room.

Surely Max was waiting to make contact with her at home. She must warn him about Monique Dousset. She resolved to leave the hospital at once.

There, in her own bedroom, amongst her silver-topped scent bottles, she could no longer delay a face-to-face confrontation with herself.

She picked up her magnifying mirror.

Ever since she was about five years old the weary expression in her hurt eyes had made her seem older – and wiser – than her years. But now, only ten days after her near-fatal encounter with Max, it was not her suddenly aged sallow face but the look in her eyes that made her wince. There was no expression in them at all. Lifeless and unlit, they were like a camera; they saw, they registered, but showed nothing. As the day wore on, and she began to believe that he might have gone for ever, a dull uncomprehending numbness took over.

Again and again she forced herself to go over what had happened after she had fallen into the mirrored pool.

Moments after Max had vanished, panic-stricken by the sight of her at the bottom of the pond, she had been found by her maid, Marie, who had returned early from her day off. And if Marie's quarrel with her mother had not been more ferocious than usual, she would not have been coming up in the lift while Max was racing down the stairs. She had dragged Colette out of the pond and turned her over, screaming as she pounded her back frantically.

Everyone in the building had heard those piercing screams, and it was her good fortune that the doctor – who lived in the flat beneath – had been at home. Otherwise she would certainly not have lived. Everyone had assumed it was an accident, that she had caught her heel in her dressing gown and slipped. She said nothing to enlighten them.

A few days after she left the clinic she decided to cover the pool in the entrance hall. The workmen came and filled it in with sand. 'It could have been a shallow grave,' one of them murmured. Colette heard him. Max had left her to die in that grave, she thought. No, her inner argument raged on, he left her for dead . . .

But where was he now? What had become of him?

Yet she made no enquiries. In her heart of hearts she was convinced there was only one person who knew where Max was.

She wondered when she would summon enough courage to call on Saffarty.

The time finally came for Saffarty to have his eye surgery. As Professor Riencourt had expected, one of the tiny eye muscles had been pulled too hard during his first operation. Released, the muscle rapidly adjusted, and his eye was straightened. When it had all settled down, and he had an ordinary eye again, he experienced an inner exultation that was entirely new to him, as if with that straight eye he could aim his ambitions straight at the sky. Some would be bound to hit. His confidence soared. Now, when people stared at him as he made his jaunty way along the streets, he knew it was not his crooked eye they were looking at.

He wished Mireille could have seen him now. Max, too. Max was the one who had first made him a gift of a velvet eye-patch. It was no use thinking of them – they were in a new world now. It was all too obvious that they had no need of him.

The unexpected call of a travelling salesman was a major landmark in Saffarty's life; it proved that the business community regarded him as a man of substance, a man whose business was worth chasing. The salesman represented the illustrious house of Penzac Fabrics, an establishment Saffarty would not have dared enter, whose fabrics were in great demand. Until this time Saffarty's dealings had been with small wholesalers and struggling manufacturers. But news that Saffarty had sold Madame Ravarino's entire stock of lace had reached Penzac, who now wished him to carry some of their embroidered silks that had been fashioned after Chanel's so-called Russian phase three years earlier. The salesman, Monsieur Nette, readily admitted that these designs were somewhat out of date. 'But my dear Monsieur Saffarty, it has come to our ears that your gift of salesmanship is unique. We hear you can even sell something you don't own to someone who doesn't want it!'

'That is perhaps an exaggeration,' Saffarty said politely.

'I doubt it. But you are probably wondering why the house of Penzac would wish to sell to a customer so – uh – shall we say – different? – from our established outlets.'

'Not at all,' Saffarty said stiffly.

'We are interesting in exporting to Britain. And it seems that you have successfully attracted both the seriously wealthy and the importantly fashionable to La Fenêtre de Saffarty.'

'That is true,' Saffarty said, his tone no less smooth than that of Monsieur Nette. Actually, he had no idea who these British were.

'It has come to our attention that the Duchess of Maitland brought a quantity of lace from you. She let a select few in on her secret.' Monsieur Nette dipped his voice conspiratorially 'Now if she could also find Penzac silks at La Fenêtre de Saffarty — '

'Excuse me, Monsieur. Customers!' Saffarty said, seeing two fashionably dressed women enter the shop. 'You might like to see a selection of my ties while you wait.' Quickly, he opened a box for Monsieur Nette's inspection and left to attend to his customers. He welcomed the interruption. A duchess had been in his shop? Who would believe it? He thought fleetingly, but longingly, of Mireille. There was no one with whom he could share the news.

But by the time he returned to Monsieur Nette – having sold four of last year's bathing suits – he had developed his strategy. 'So many charming and beautiful ladies come here,' he said. 'I do not always remember who is who.'

Quick to take the hint, Monsieur Nette said, 'I have a photograph of the Duchess with me. I brought a copy of the British *Vogue* along.'

Saffarty studied the photograph carefully. A duchess! It seemed impossible. The woman looked anything but elegant or fashionable to him. In fact, she was downright dowdy.

Monsieur Nette watched him closely. 'Some British aristocrats have their own style of elegance,' he offered. 'High fashion is for the *nouveaux riches*, not for the blue bloods.'

'The colour of their money is the same as yours and mine,' Saffarty said, unleashing one of his roughest laughs.

Monsieur Nette found himself laughing with genuine amusement. Saffarty cut across his laugh. 'I will agree to carry your range. As you see, I am short of space.' He paused for a moment, and chuckled. 'Space is at a premium. If I enlarge my store it will lose something of its ambience. I'm not sure whether you understand the importance of atmosphere?'

'But certainly, I understand that very well.'

'Good. In that case you will understand that I cannot stock your range unless I have it on consignment. On a sale or return basis — '

'I don't see how we can do that and keep the price to your requirements.'

'You don't know my requirements,' Saffarty snapped. 'Sale or return. You tell me what your lowest possible price would be, and whatever I get over and above that, we'll split between us.'

'Come, come, Monsieur Saffarty. We — '

'Take it or leave it. I can live without you. You came to see me, didn't you?' Saffarty said, laughing again. 'I will be making space for a line you find difficult to sell. To do that I will have to deny some space to other proven, selling lines. You understand my problem?'

'But sale or return? It goes against our policy.'

'You are offering me your dud stock. Nothing rots on my

159

shelves!' Saffarty exclaimed, his voice rising. 'What right do you have to come here and waste my time? Who do you think you are? Even the Duchess of Maitland doesn't waste my time!' He felt himself warming to the sound of his own anger. 'I'm giving you the opportunity to make profits that will be higher and bigger than your wildest dreams. I'll sell the lot, within ten days, if I set my mind to it.' But his voice dropped. Now openly contemptuous, he went on, 'But you'd better talk to your boss. You haven't the authority to agree to my terms.'

'Certainly I have the authority,' Monsieur Nette said drawing himself to his fullest height.

'Well then, yes or no?'

'We'll treat this as an experiment.'

'Grand. We will do good business together,' Saffarty smiled.

'No wonder everyone says you will be a millionaire,' Monsieur Nette said slowly.

Saffarty laughed – this time to cover his confusion – and brought the transaction to a rapid conclusion.

Everyone says you will be a millionaire.

This chance remark, made by a complete stranger, became a major event in Saffarty's life. He turned the phrase over and over; like a catchy tune, his mind could not let it go. *Everyone says you will be a millionaire.* Who 'everyone' could be was of no real interest; it was the part about being a millionaire that was so endlessly fascinating to him. Because the possibility had not occurred to him, nor even, as he chuckled to himself, the possibility of the possibility.

He would simply have to prove that everyone was right. It was an intoxicating idea.

He began to look at his business from a different perspective. He reserved his judgements, but began to devise ways of accumulating capital with capital, ways of making money without having to depend on individual items sold to individual customers. At least he paid no rent. He already owned a property. All the same, he was careful to pay as much attention to his shops as if he had no other plans.

The first time Colette visited La Fenêtre de Saffarty, she managed to present herself as an ordinary customer. She made a fairly hasty purchase of a length of Penzac silk and left. Saffarty was there, and she caught a brief glimpse of him, but he was serving Americans and she didn't dare speak to him.

Every time she went she promised herself she would speak to him. But the small shop was always full, the air heavy with the scent of cigars and perfume, and the sounds of excited chatter or the notes of Swiss musical boxes. She never knew who or what she would meet there, so she continued to buy lengths of lace that she would never use. She was good at waiting; she would choose her moment well.

Saffarty's sales outstripped the House of Penzac's most optimistic projections. It seemed years since he had told those first customers of his, those young British students, that they would bring him luck, and even longer since Mireille had gone. In fact it was less than a year since La Fenêtre de Saffarty had opened, and only four months since Mireille and Max had left. By now Saffarty knew how to judge his customers, how to zoom in on those who were potentially serious spenders, and how to ignore those who were not. Several celebrities were now numbered among his clients – Jean Cocteau, Valentino, Gloria Swanson, and even Maurice Chevalier. Madame Delange was in her element.

Someone said that Charles Lindberg's spectacular flight to Paris that May had been something of a coup for Parisians, for Americans flocked to France. But the kind of Americans Saffarty was interested in were those for whom the annual summer in Europe was *de rigeur* – not the merely rich, but the mighty rich. So when his doorbell jingled to admit Mr and Mrs Courtney he had, in a sense, been waiting for them. The press had carried photographs of them disembarking from the luxury liner *Ile de France* at Le Havre. All the same, he had not dreamed that the likes of them, together with the illustrious Paris banker, Baron Rothson and his elegant, trend-setting wife, would ever cross his threshold.

Mr and Mrs Courtney spoke a slow and painfully accurate French. The two men expressed a polite, courtly interest in their wives' shopping. After a short while Mr Courtney turned to Saffarty and said, 'Do you speak German?'

161

Saffarty laughed. 'No, Monsieur. I regret not,' he lied. Mr Courtney asked him rather too casually, he thought.

Almost at the same moment Mr Courtney and Baron Rothson stepped away from their wives. Now Saffarty was on full alert. He attended to their wives and managed, without losing any of his charm, to eavesdrop on the conversation between the two men. 'A cable this morning,' Mr Courtney was saying in German. 'Radio Corporation of America is hot, very hot.'

'RCA? Why?'

'A discreet operation on the go. Shall we say, a shrewd operation?'

'What sort of participants are in?' Baron Rothson asked quickly. 'Without big names you can count me out — '

'Of course, I know that,' Mr Courtney said gruffly. 'I wouldn't waste your time, or mine, for that matter, otherwise. But I think you'll find they're an impressive lot. No less than Walter P. Chrysler, Charles Schwab – *the* steel man, Percy A. Rockefeller, John D's nephew, as you know. Would you like me to go on?'

'Men of great virtuosity, I'm sure,' Baron Rothson murmured.

'The aristocrats of America,' Mr Courtney agreed. 'Sell within seven days, and your important clients will turn into your dedicated clients.' He gave a cynical chuckle.

'What is the stock standing at now?'

'As of today, ninety. Next week, around one hundred and five, one hundred and ten — '

'Thank you, Mr Courtney. I appreciate the information. Perhaps we'll ask our good ladies to lunch without us?'

Ten minutes later Baron and Baroness Rothson and Mr and Mrs Courtney left the shop. About two minutes after that, so did Saffarty.

'Boulevard du Bourse,' Saffarty said to his Russian taxi driver.

'I don't know where that is — '

My luck, Saffarty thought, to get a refugee. 'Follow my directions,' he said, and moments later his patience snapped. He stopped the taxi and ran the rest of the way.

He was still panting when he stood in front of the stockbroker's receptionist.

'Monsieur Pasquier never sees anyone without an appointment.'

Saffarty turned on his heel and left. On the way out, he caught sight of his reflection in the glass doors. Even his eye-patch was awry. He stopped and straightened it thoughtfully. He didn't need this puny stockbroker. He had read about the leading but exclusive firm of Dumont et Cie in the financial pages. This time he would say he had an urgent message from Baron Rothson, of the Banque Rothson. What was more, he would insist on seeing no one but the senior partner, Monsieur Dumont himself.

His strategy worked like magic; undaunted, he was instantly ushered into the senior partner's ornate office. He knew he had nothing to fear – the truth was on his side, and he was going to tell Monsieur Dumont the whole truth.

Which turned out to be a simple but infinitely wise decision, for Monsieur Dumont was astute enough to be not only interested, but highly cooperative and exceptionally appreciative. According to Monsieur Dumont, though America was already prosperous, it was entering a new era of prosperity. He wished to show his appreciation. What better way than to allow Saffarty to buy his RCA stock on a cash margin? Saffarty needed therefore only advance ten per cent on his purchase; the rest was on credit. By the end of that week, with the franc at twenty-five fifty to the dollar, and RCA having risen from ninety to one hundred and nine, Saffarty had made himself a cool four hundred and ninety thousand francs.

It required all his discipline not to tell Monsieur Dumont that to equal that sort of profit he would have had to sell tens of thousands of metres of Penzac fabric.

He was, however, sorely tempted. For in all the world there was no one with whom he could share his triumph. He stroked and caressed his ancient key. Even Madame Ravarino had gone to Divonne. He longed for Mireille and, maddeningly enough, he missed Max too.

10

'Max, you've got to agree, Max. It *is* beautiful,' Mireille said, as they stood on the flat summit of Table Mountain.

It was autumn in this strange new hemisphere and spring in Paris. For five days, ever since they'd first landed and found rooms at the Purple Vines, a cheap boarding house, they had both been in a state of terror and panic. Max refused even to try to find his relations.

The very first morning on shore, at the ungodly hour of six-thirty, a large black 'houseboy' had unexpectedly awakened Mireille with the customary cup of milky tea. Max had heard her scream through the thin walls, and had raced in to protect her from the bewildered servant. There was so much to get used to. He had hated the tea as much as he hated the barbaric custom of serving it so early in the morning. He hated the country, and swore that the blacks smelled poisonous.

They were at the top of Table Mountain because Mireille had decided that they must, at least, get out and see the sights. The aerial railway was not yet completed, so they had climbed the three thousand or so metres to the long, flat summit. They heard the whistle of trains come up to them, and stared with distaste at the city of Cape Town laid out in white rectangular blocks, serenely beautiful, but intolerably different from Paris.

Mireille sat down under the icy shade of an overhanging rock. The struggle to the summit had exhausted her. Her breasts ached; they still felt swollen. She covered them with her hands and lay back. She felt giddy, as if she were falling down the mountain. She longed to go back to Paris, to Saffarty.

'Max, have you written to Saffarty yet?' she asked urgently.

But Max said nothing. He merely stared at the ocean below.

'*Max*!' Mireille said angrily. 'I'm talking to you!'

'What should I tell him?' Max said sorrowfully.

'You've got to go and find your uncle,' she said, returning yet again to the subject that had been preoccupying them. 'There are fifteen Abelmans in the phone book. You know, I phoned people called Cellier and du Plessis, because I thought they were French,' she continued sadly. 'Well they're not French, they're Afrikaans — '

'Who cares?'

'I phoned ten of them. Not one of them spoke French,' she said, sounding puzzled. 'But Solomon Abelman said he came from Lodz — '

'You phoned my relations? You dared to do a thing like that to me?'

'I had to, Max. How are you going to live?' Mireille shivered, but sweat ran down her forehead. 'I feel ill, Max,' she said miserably, weeping softly. 'I've been ill for so long – ever since – you know — '

'You've gone very pale,' he said, alarmed.

'It's that rat poison I took, I think. I told you about it.'

'I know. I'll have to get you to a doctor,' he said firmly. 'I'm going to help you down. Don't argue. *Don't!*' Loose stones, and even loose soil, slid perilously under his feet, but he knew he was drawing strength from her weakness. She looked deathly pale, he thought. He could feel the bones in her back. They made their way down, slowly and painfully, and as soon as they reached ground level Max picked her up and carried her all the way to the Purple Vines boarding house. He did not leave her room until the doctor arrived, and even then he stood, shivering, outside her door.

The doctor came out of her room, and shut the door gently. 'I thought I should speak to you, first,' he said to Max.

'Pardon, monsieur le docteur,' Max said helplessly. He looked searchingly at the doctor and then said quickly, 'Do you speak Yiddish?'

'Until I was ten that was the only language I could speak,' the doctor replied smilingly, in Yiddish. He held out his hand. 'Dr Abe Edelstein. *Shalom!*'

'Max Blum. Is she very, very ill? What's wrong with her?'

'Your wife is pregnant, Mr Blum. *Mazaltov!*'

'Pregnant?' Max whispered. '*Pregnant?*'

'About six months pregnant.'

'She's *not* my wife!'

'The baby doesn't know that.'

'I'm not the father,' Max said miserably. 'Let's go to my room. We can talk privately.'

He filled in all the relevant details, and when he had finished the doctor said slowly, 'She must have been carrying a twin. It happens rarely, but it does happen. One of them was aborted, the other not. It's too late to do anything now. She'll just have to have the baby.' The doctor shook his head. 'What's a nice boy like you doing in the middle of all this mess?'

'I'll explain that to you later,' Max said. 'Should we go in and tell her now?'

'*You* tell her,' Dr Edelstein said hastily. 'I'll look in on her after dinner.'

'You're not ill, Mireille. It's nothing serious. Mireille, I was so worried – so worried!' Max drew a rickety chair up to her bed. 'The doctor speaks Yiddish, you see — '

'What did the doctor say?'

'You must be calm, Mireille. I told you it's not serious. Your life is not in danger, Mireille!'

'What did he say?' Mireille interrupted. 'I want to know what he said.'

'You must have been carrying twins, Mireille. One of them is still — '

'*Oh, my God!*' Mireille's hands flew to her stomach. '*Oh, my dear, dear God!*' she repeated again and again. She shut her eyes.

Max patted her shoulder awkwardly.

Suddenly Mireille sat up. Her eyes wide and alive, she said, 'The Lord be praised. It wasn't a real murder. It wasn't. It wasn't a real murder.'

'What are you talking about?' Max said, his face ashen. 'Murder? What are you talking about, Colette?'

'It's me, Mireille. I'm not Colette,' Mireille smiled. 'I'm Mireille.'

'Of course. Of course, Mireille. Sorry.' *Colette . . . Murder . . . What was he saying? Mireille knew nothing of Colette's fate . . .* A terrible fit of trembling overtook him.

'Max. It will be all right, Max. Don't go to pieces, *please!*' The unexpected sound of her laughter filled the room. She seemed utterly changed. Her expression radiated serenity. 'God is good,' she said dreamily. 'If it's a girl, I will call her Theresa, after Marie-Thérèse, mother of Africa, and if it's a boy I'll call him — '

'I'll take care of you, Mireille,' Max interrupted. 'Or at least my

166

relatives will, when I find them. Did you keep the address of that Solomon Abelman?'

'Shouldn't you at least telephone first?'

'No, I'll go now,' he squared his shoulders visibly. 'I'll go at once.'

He left her to go to his room to change into a suit. When he was ready he checked his appearance in the mirror. This suit Saffarty had bought so hastily looked several times too large for him. Once more he straightened his back. True, he had done a terrible thing, but it had been an accident, and though he would never forgive himself, if he was to go on living he owed it to Mireille to make the best of things. Mireille's courage had been an inspiration to him. There she was, unmarried, expecting an illegitimate child, and still saying that God was good . . .

He saw that he had been sorry for himself.

He saw further. Here in this strange and sunny land, as new as it was promising, he had the chance to begin again. He would have to succeed. He would tolerate no other alternative.

Certain these were the wrong Abelmans, Max nevertheless made his way up the long oak-lined driveway to the huge white house. How was it possible that his relations lived in a mansion like this? The house was large and square and shining. Everything about it shone, from the sparkling white walls to the highly polished green steps leading up to the front door in which Max could see his reflection in the gleaming wood. He pressed the doorbell nervously. It rang loudly, and before long a black man, dressed in glaring whites and a scarlet sash, was saying 'Good afternoon, master.'

'I am looking for Mr Abelman,' Max said, using the words he'd been practising all the way.

'One moment, master.'

Max watched the servant glide away. He had no choice but to wait, he told himself. The worst thing that could happen to him was that they would throw him out. After all, how terrible was that? He'd been through much worse.

Soon a tall, bald and fairly plump man was saying 'Good afternoon. What can I do for you, young man?' Cigar scent drifted through the large cool hall.

Speaking Yiddish, Max answered nervously. 'I am Max Blum, the son of Jacob and Rachel Blum of Lodz.'

'Come in, come in at once,' Solomon Abelman boomed. '*Eva*. Eva! Come here. It's Max Blum, here. My sister Rachel's son is here.'

Max heard the high staccato sound of quick footsteps descending the stairs. 'Rachel's *son*? Why didn't he tell us?' the voice called out agitatedly. 'We should have gone to the docks to fetch him. Bring him in, he must be hungry.'

'That's my wife, Evie,' Solomon said. 'Do you speak a little English yet?'

'No.'

'Eva, he doesn't speak English yet,' Solomon said to his wife. 'We'll all speak Yiddish today, but only today. Afterwards, English only. Where are your bags?'

'Stop talking so much and bring him into the dining room.'

Soon Max was seated at the dining table and Eva Abelman, clucking about his weight, was urging him to eat. 'A bag of bones you are,' she said. 'The food on the ship! When my Solomon came here he was a bag of bones too. The Epsom salts, of course.'

'Epsom salts?'

'To avoid conscription. So he shouldn't look too healthy, on a diet of Epsom salts he went. But how is Solomon's beloved sister, your mother?'

'I haven't seen my parents for four years!'

'Four years? Why not? Where have you been? You haven't just come from Lodz?' the Abelmans said, talking over one another.

'Where are his suitcases?'

Solomon interrupted, shouting, 'I didn't see any suitcases, Evie.'

'At the boarding house, the Purple Vines.'

'Boarding house? Why a boarding house? I'll send Johannes, our driver, to fetch your things,' Solomon said, ringing the small crystal hand-bell.

'No. Please. I must go back to the boarding house.'

'Nonsense. Rubbish! You'll stay here. My own sister's son, my nephew in a boarding house! Whoever heard of such a thing?'

'I must go back there,' Max said obstinately.

'Rubbish,' Solomon shouted.

'Let him talk, Solomon. He must have a good reason, and for

168

such a good-looking boy, even though he's a bundle of bones, the reason must be a young lady — '

'You're right, Aunt Rachel. There *is* a young lady. But she is not *my* young lady. Let me explain.' Speaking barely above a whisper, Max told them everything he believed he could tell them. Except for Colette, about whom he made no mention, and Saffarty's name, which he instinctively abbreviated to 'Simonico', he held nothing back. They both listened carefully, but it was clear that Solomon left this sort of judgement to his wife.

'Whatever else he is, your friend Simonico is a good friend,' his aunt pronounced. 'You did right to escape from bad company, and gambling debts. But one problem is not yet solved; one question remains. You agree, Solomon?'

'You mean, will they come all the way here to look for him?'

'That is what I mean.'

'Did you tell your friend, Simonico, our name?' Solomon asked quietly.

Max shook his head. 'No,' he said.

'Good. You will be safe with us.'

'You did right to tell us about your past,' his aunt said solemnly. 'As my mother, may her soul rest in peace, always said, whatever you have to your discredit, be the first to tell it. Your secret will be safe with us.'

The weak winter sun had disappeared – the sun sets early in Africa, Max had been told. Though the room was far from dark Eva switched on the scaldingly bright chandelier. The silver teapot, the assortment of crimson jams, the white tablecloth, all seemed to be illuminated individually. His uncle sent for the schnapps, and when Max drank it, the hot, growing lump in his throat dissolved. Their welcome was open-hearted, yet absolute.

His aunt and uncle fell into reminiscences, and Max listened, with increasing wonder, to the beginnings that had led them to be the owners of a mansion with servants. Solomon was now in his twenty-sixth year in South Africa; he had arrived in 1901. Eva took over the telling of the story, and Solomon listened to her attentively, almost as if he were hearing it for the first time, and perhaps, in a way, he was . . .

It had been hard, and harder than hard. They had little English, and less money. Solomon had gone at once to Johannesburg, where all the gold was, and there he had found work repairing bedsteads. He had lived in what he now supposed would be called a slum, though he had been grateful enough to have a roof over his head. The place was known as Levy's Yard, because the simple single-storey building had been built around a courtyard where all the immigrant tenants could work: repair bicycles, be a blacksmith, generally do whatever they could to earn a crust. A gold mine, the Ferreira Deep Mine, was his neighbour on the one side, and a stable of half-starved dray horses on the other. Gold dust from one neighbour, and a stench of decaying horseflesh, a pestilence of attacking flies, on the other. It wasn't easy. And then, about eight months after he had arrived in Johannesburg, he had met and married Eva, who had only been there for two months. They had lived together in his poor room, but Eva cleaned it so well that anyone could have eaten off the floor, and she soon learned how to take care of the food that so easily turned sour in the hot sun.

Eva's brother had things a little easier in Cape Town, so when they were expecting their first child, Stanley – who was now studying to be a doctor in England – they decided it would be better to live with her brother David in his small cottage in Cape Town. David had been working for a furniture dealer, and he had been working with beds, so it was a natural partnership. And now, of course, they owned Adderley Furniture Mart. Two stores in Cape Town, and a new branch in Johannesburg. Eva still worked in the business.

'It's unusual for you to have found both of us at home on a Thursday afternoon,' Eva concluded. 'We're here because we had some private documents to go over.'

'I've been listening to you tell our story, Eva,' Solomon said gravely. 'And I've never been more ashamed of myself, and of you, too — '

'Ashamed, Solomon?' Eva said, aghast. 'What have I said?'

'We forgot our past – *I even forgot my own family*. How did it happen?' Solomon moaned, rocking back and forth.

'How could we remember? We had our own struggles, our own tragedies,' Evie said calmly, her wise eyes darkening. But for all her calm speech it was plain that Solomon had brought her attention to an unforgivable lapse in their traditional values. 'We needed to forget, Solomon,' she continued, with a sweeping gesture toward the glittering table. 'More than enough food, and more than enough sun melted the horrors, the pogroms and the poverty. When did *you* last think of the way *you* were hidden under the potatoes in the wagon, when you were escaping from the military?'

'I don't know, Eva. I just don't know.'

'But we came here and found paradise. South Africa belongs to the British Empire, and so we are under British protection, British justice, British democracy. We feel – ' she paused, and crossed both hands over her heart – 'we feel *safe*,' she concluded with a sigh of gratitude.

'Oh yes, thank God. We are safe,' Solomon said prayerfully.

'We will talk about this later, Solomon. Meanwhile, we are upsetting our nephew.' Then she turned to Max and said, 'The greatest pain is the one you can't tell others about.'

A sudden silence hung in the room. After a while Eva said passionately, 'God has sent you to us, Max Blum. We will make it up to your family; please God there is still time.' She rose from the table and placed her hand on her husband's shoulders. 'Max, you are with your own people now,' she said firmly.

'My sister Rachel's son,' Solomon sighed. 'I still think it must be a dream.'

Max tried to speak but failed.

'When the heart is full, the eyes overflow,' Eva said. And then, as if they had been given permission, all three wept openly.

'If it hadn't been for you, Mireille, I would never have found them!' Max began excitedly as soon as he returned to the Purple Vines. 'And they're going to help you, too, Mireille.'

'You told them about *me*?' Mireille wailed. 'You shouldn't have. They'll think badly of *you*, Max.'

'With these people one feels no shame, Mireille. They know about my debts, I told them everything about all that. But I didn't think they should know Saffarty's real name, so I said he was called "Simonico".'

'Why on earth did you do that?'

'I don't know. Anyway, don't forget – it's Simonico. Now, let me tell you the rest.' He told her how terrible they felt about his family, and went on and on about what a motherly woman his aunt was. 'Aunt Eva thinks she knows of an English family living over here who will take care of you, Mireille. Her dressmaker told her about them. She's going to ask the dressmaker tomorrow. They also know Dr Edelstein, he's a friend of theirs, can you believe it, Mireille? Listen to me. I've learnt some Afrikaans. *Alles sal reg kom!* Everything will be all right. Now, say it after me – say it! *Alles sal reg kom!*'

Mireille did as she was told, 'But what do they look like, these Abelmans?' she asked. 'You've told me where they live, and what they do. Now I want to know what these guardian angels look like.'

'My Uncle Solomon is – well, you couldn't exactly call him a good-looking man. He's got pale blue eyes that look as if they could easily pop out. He's bald, but I think his hair must have been red. He's not fat, not thin, not tall nor short. Aunt Eva looks like a mother looks – plump and motherly. What does it matter what they look like?'

'The fate of my baby is in their hands,' Mireille said breathlessly. 'They hold the keys to my whole life.' She began wringing her hands again.

'Have you written to Saffarty yet?'

'Of course.'

'You've told him about the baby?'

'No. I wrote before Dr Edelstein — '

'Are you going to tell him?'

'I don't know, Max. I simply do not know. One thing is sure, though. I won't tell him anything, nor will I ever write to him again, unless he replies to all the letters I have already written.' Her voice went hoarse, and she grabbed his lapels hysterically. 'Promise me you won't tell him either, Max. You've got to promise me.'

'You have my promise, Mireille. You must calm yourself. You do trust me, don't you?'

Mireille tilted her head back and raised her eyes to the ceiling. 'You are moving in with them tomorrow?'

'How do you know that?'

'Because of all the things you've told me about them — '

'They know about you. They also know that I won't let you down, Mireille. Listen, Mireille. I've had an idea. When their driver collects me in the morning, you'll come, too.'

'Thank you, Max. But no. You would create a very bad impression, and you can't afford that.'

Max tried to argue, but Mireille was adamant. Presently she said, 'It's tomorrow already. The driver will be here for you in less than three hours!'

From the moment the Abelmans' driver, Johannes, lifted his suitcase into the boot of their Packard, Max felt his life begin to change, to move. He was as conscious of it as if he was on a train that was pulling out of a station. His aunt and uncle were seated on the back seat and as he sat beside them, breathing the rich mixture of cigar, leather and his aunt's perfume, he knew that he had, quite literally, landed in a new world. A world where the sun shone even in winter.

'Well,' his uncle boomed in English. 'And how do you like our winter?'

'Yes. Good.' Max answered in English. He had learnt the names of the seasons from his phrase book.

'You must say, I like it very much,' his uncle said.

Aunt Eva was more exact. 'It is not winter. It is autumn,'she said.

'This is autumn. I like autumn, thank you,' Max said, speaking slowly.

'He has a French accent, I think,' Uncle Solomon said delightedly.

'Never mind his accent,' Aunt Eva interrupted. 'He wants to learn.' She turned to Max and pinched his cheek. 'You're doing well. You must not be frightened to make mistakes with your English.'

And so the lessons began, as relentless as they were merciless. Max had no choice in the matter; speech was as necessary as breath. Besides, as Uncle Solomon pointed out, 'You will be having it much easier than we did. After all, what did we know from an English teacher? At seven o'clock this morning your aunt was already on the phone, talking to an English teacher.'

That night, and every night except for Friday, he would spend two hours studying English with a teacher whose only other language was Afrikaans.

Shortly before they arrived at their store, the Adderley Furniture Mart, Uncle Solomon took out a large bundle of keys. 'I still like to open my shop for myself in the mornings,' he said proudly.

Reminded of Saffarty's strange, ancient key, Max's face darkened; but only momentarily, for he was soon striding behind his uncle into the large, cavernous warehouse. Both his aunt and his uncle showed him around, and made no attempt to conceal their pride. Electric stoves stood beside dining room suites and wardrobes. His uncle opened the doors of washing machines and refrigerators; he opened desk drawers. Lovingly he showed off the garden tools and the kitchen equipment, and proudly flung open bolts of curtaining and a roll of crimson carpet.

'Everything you see here is paid for! Not bad, huh, from bedsteads? Everything you see here is for the housewife. The most important person in the country is the housewife,' Max's aunt announced, first in Yiddish, and then in English. 'Remember that, Max, and you won't go far wrong!'

Max was introduced to several members of their staff, all of whom addressed his uncle as Mr A, and his aunt as Mrs A. Then his uncle took him to meet their chief accountant, and Max was immediately put to work checking invoices. 'Figures are the same in every language,' his uncle chuckled. Several times that day his uncle stopped by with an encouraging word, and Max instinctively called him Mr A. His uncle accepted that and later, at lunch in their large, austere office, so did his aunt. They discussed his salary. They had decided to pay him fifty pounds a month. Max swallowed hard, his Adam's apple working furiously. It was hard to speak. His aunt, obviously aware of his overflowing emotions, said, 'I have not forgotten that poor young woman you told me about.' She turned to her husband and said, 'She must be feeling so alone, so frightened. Solomon?'

'So you want to invite her to dinner, Eva? So invite her,' Uncle Solomon said kindly.

'My Solomon, I knew you'd say that,' she beamed. 'Phone her, Max. Tell her you'll go with the driver to fetch her.'

Once, and it must have been a very long time ago, the words, 'The Purple Vines' had been painted purple. Like the rest of the building, the sign was now faded and peeling. When Max and Mireille had arrived, Rebecca, a bare-footed black maid, had marched them into their rooms. Her dress, and even her apron, had perished over the breasts. Rebecca cleaned all twenty rooms, worked in the kitchen, and sometimes even managed to get to the telephone in time to answer it. Not surprisingly, the owner, Mrs Coetzee, wanted to get rid of the place.

They had heard about the Purple Vines from a taxi driver. It was as cheap as it was sleazy, and their rooms were filthy. The bare floorboards were sticky with grime.

Unused to servants, and unaware that she would be offending Rebecca, Mireille had immediately set about cleaning their rooms. She had used her phrase book to ask for cleaning materials, and had been compulsive about the cleanliness of the rooms ever since. After Max had left that morning she had scrubbed and polished with even more than her usual ferocity. She had offered to help in the kitchen, but with a look of incredulous contempt, and an exclamation of disgust – 'Ach! Are you mad?' – Mrs Coetzee had refused.

Now Mireille sat on the long wooden verandah trying to make sense of the amazing grace that had overtaken her life. Again and again, she told herself that this was God's will, God's gift, and that she would not, now, go to purgatory. She was not thinking so much as praying.

Lost in her own, intensely private world of prayers, she scarcely heard that she was being called.

Rebecca stood over her, and finally jabbed her arm. 'Telephone, Missus. Telephone!'

Mireille stared at her uncomprehendingly.

'*Telephone! Telephone!*' Rebecca repeated, shouting. 'Come.'

Mireille followed, as slowly, maddeningly slowly, Rebecca led the way to what posed as a reception desk, mumbling all the while. 'Cleans her own room herself. Makes trouble for me. Makes trouble for me with my missus.' Her voice rose. 'It's not my job to answer the phone. It's Willem's job!' Mireille, of course, understood nothing of this.

Dazed, she picked up the telephone and in a still greater daze heard that Max had not forgotten her. 'Yes, dinner with the Abelmans tonight.' Max laughed. 'Tonight. Thursday night!'

She put down the telephone. There and then, under Rebecca's disbelieving eyes, and in that sleazy public hallway, she fell to her knees, bowed her head, clasped her hands and gave thanks.

After that Thursday events moved too swiftly for either Max or Mireille to comprehend. They simply followed the tide and, propelled by a mixture of gratitude and disbelief, did as they were told. At the Adderley Furniture Mart Max addressed his aunt and uncle as Mr & Mrs A – at home, of course, he did not. A week or so later, Mireille found herself using the same form of address. She was a frequent guest at the Abelmans'.

Sometimes, when she felt the child quicken inside her, she would think, dreamily, that she would need larger dresses very soon. And yet, even if only vaguely, she was aware that somehow this strange and warm land, with its even stranger, warmer people, gave her courage, gave her strength. When she thought of Saffarty her mind turned more and more to Madame Chandler's words about Saffarty: *'Great love is a luxury given to too few women.'* Certainly she had loved Saffarty greatly. She loved him still, which was probably why she had tried, and failed, to hate him . . .

Already her life had acquired something of a secure routine. Every morning, at about eleven, the driver Johannes was at the boarding house to drive her to the Abelmans'. There she was served tea, and lunch, and later, when they all came home, she had dinner with them. She understood more English now, and understood also that the talk at the dinner table centred on the day's business. Her future was not discussed, but then she did not expect it to be. Besides, she felt protected by her pregnancy; it gave her a measure of hope, and a sense of serenity. In any case, she spent her long days on the verandah bent over textbooks of English grammar, the *Cape Times* and a French–English dictionary.

Still, she waited for the mail every day, even though she knew, by now, that mail from abroad was delivered only on Fridays. 'Nee, Missus!' Rebecca would say sullenly, impatiently, with a disapproving glare. 'No letters for you today.' Rebecca had caught her cleaning the skirtings of her room with a nail brush, and since then had been at pains to make her fury plain. 'Missus, you wasting my time, Missus. If I get your letter, I'll bring it to you,' she would say, her breasts quivering with rage under their frayed material.

Though the Purple Vines was the sort of cheap boarding house that attracted people who were down on their luck, Mireille and Max were their first overseas customers. Rebecca had not before come across a white woman who insisted on cleaning her own room. That would have been bad enough, but every morning Mireille hung her bed linen out of the window. Rebecca found this not only bizarre but insulting. She knew the white people complained that the dark people stank, and thought Mireille aired her bed linen to get rid of her smell.

It seemed to her that it made no difference to Mireille that although she was as dark as a black, she was not one of those kaffir blacks, but a coloured, a woman of mixed race, one of God's step-children as they had been called in South Africa. It did not occur to her that Mireille might be ignorant of those racial divisions that she had been born and bred to believe were as natural as disease to everyone everywhere in the world. Sure she was dark, but she was not a black. And even if Mireille could have explained that she rejoiced in the novelty of airing her linen in the sun and was not yet comfortable with domestics of any kind serving her, Rebecca would have said she was lying.

Mireille was not keeping to her proper place as a white woman, and Rebecca hated for her it and would make her pay dearly.

At first Mireille had found this hostile, black, perspiring woman frightening, and then the hospitable, friendly welcome shown by the Abelmans had made everything less painful, less frightening. Mireille mistakenly believed Rebecca despised her because she had guessed that she was an unmarried woman 'in trouble'.

If Mireille was certain that there could be no kinder people than the Abelmans on this earth, Eva Abelman was equally certain that she was not doing nearly enough for her. She felt badly about not taking Mireille into her home, not treating her as if she were one of the family. And yet, though she felt a distinct sense of responsibility for this poor young woman, she was also aware of the danger of her becoming too central to Max's life. After all, who knew what could happen, after the baby was born? And why should Max be saddled with another man's child? In any case, Max would do much better for himself with one of his own kind. And now that he had put on some flesh, and was no longer gaunt, he was, Eva thought, an unusually handsome young man, like a film star, like that Douglas Fairbanks. His slate-grey eyes were almost blue, and he had the sensitive, delicate expression of a musician.

Eva Abelman was not an indecisive woman. However, she had

been pondering how best to handle Mireille's future; and now it seemed that her original idea had been the best. Also, there was some urgency. Her daughter Ruth and her son-in-law Ben would soon be returning from Johannesburg, and she wanted the whole matter settled without any interference from them. Besides, before she knew it, her daughter Ruthie would have taken this poor pregnant girl into her own house. Ruthie was not the kind who would even begin to understand why it could be dangerous to put the temptation of a weak and pathetic young woman too close to her own husband.

On the other hand, if a good home could be found for Mireille all potential problems would be solved.

Which was where Mrs van Tonder, the dressmaker, came in.

That peculiar woman Mrs van Tonder had talked of had come to Eva's mind as soon as she'd heard about Mireille. Lady Rutherford would probably take Mireille in, as she had taken in that other girl.

Accordingly, Eva bought some suitable woollen materials, and arranged for Mrs van Tonder to come and sew for her.

On the appointed day Mrs van Tonder arrived, as planned, an hour ahead of Mireille. Over a cup of milky coffee, and Eva's special chocolate cake, she sat back, and waited for the flood of gossip to begin. The sewing machine stayed in its brown wooden box, for if there was one thing Mrs van Tonder enjoyed above all else it was gossip. Indeed she enjoyed it so much that not even a mouth full of pins could impede its flow.

Eventually Eva decided that enough time had elapsed for her to come to the point. 'You told me what happened to that – ' she paused, deliberately, dramatically, before going on – 'that unfortunate young woman who went to the Rutherford place. How is she getting on?'

'The luck of the Irish!' Mrs van Tonder said bitterly, 'Agh, man, Janet O'Brien's the best example of Irish luck that I've ever seen.'

'But Janet O'Brien has had such a hard time, hasn't she?' Eva prodded gently. 'If anyone deserved a little luck, she did. Pity, I don't remember all the details — '

Mrs van Tonder's eyes narrowed, but took on the gleam of the dedicated gossip. 'But you remember that she was – agh! man, excuse me, I don't like using the word – a prostitute?'

'Who could forget that?' Eva enquired mildly. 'It's those other details I've forgotten. How did she get in with the people at the Rutherford place?'

Mrs van Tonder put down her coffee cup, rearranged her black shawl, and settled herself comfortably. Eva listened with special attentiveness. While Mrs van Tonder's flat Afrikaans accent drawled on and on, Eva sorted out the essential facts. Janet O'Brien had answered an advertisement for an Irish domestic and then, when she had arrived, penniless, in South Africa, she had been told that her employers had been sent back to England. She had been met at the docks by a man who claimed to be their lawyer. He had taken her to his flat and then, when she'd had too much to drink, he had seduced her. Almost immediately she'd been forced on the streets. Until then Janet O'Brien had never known what the word pimp meant. As if that were not bad enough, this pimp had forced Janet to take on black men. It was this last which Mrs van Tonder could not condemn strongly enough. No white woman could be forgiven for that.

Lady Rutherford – a woman with crazy ideas – had read about the case in the local newspapers. Only the Lord himself knew how hard Mrs van Tonder had tried to make sense of Lady Rutherford's beliefs that if the prostitute went to prison the man should go too! It was mad, but then Lady Rutherford had herself been to prison in England. It was something to do with women having the right to vote. The result of all this was that Janet O'Brien had gone to work for the Rutherfords as a housekeeper. Mrs van Tonder had even been compelled to sew for her. Still, she needed the money, so what was she to do? Truly, there was no justice in this world. Because now Janet was going to marry the baker, Gerald Thompson; she was in the middle of making her a wedding dress, and a white one at that! Some people had all the luck.

It was time, Eva judged, to talk about Mireille. She said, 'Lady Rutherford sounds like an exceptionally charitable woman to me.'

'Yes, but she's crazy,' Mrs van Tonder said with a nasty laugh.

'I know of another deserving case,' Eva went on smoothly, slyly. 'A young French widow. She comes from Paris. I thought you might be able to — ' She stopped in mid-sentence, and added cunningly, 'Of course it's very, very confidential.'

'You can trust *me*!'

'Oh, I know that, Mrs van Tonder. I know I can trust you. It's just that I would feel terrible if her story got around — ' Eva lowered her voice. 'It's a tragic story, really it is. She married a sailor who used to beat her, and do – oh – the most terrible things to her, unmentionable things,' she lied, knowing that the surest way to engage Mrs van Tonder's sympathy was to stimulate her hatred of men.

'Unmentionable things?' Mrs van Tonder whispered, shivering. 'What sort of unmentionable things?'

'The poor girl ran away from him. He found her, of course, and then he — ' Eva stopped, making it clear that she could not go on.

'Raped her, I suppose,' Mrs van Tonder said sharply, showing that, unlike Eva, she was a woman of the world. 'Men! A man picks a helpless woman to prove his brutishness to other men!'

'The poor girl is left holding the baby. She – uh – she wouldn't do away with it, you see.'

The seamstress sighed and shook her head. Women survived men the way farmers survived locusts, she thought. 'What's she going to do now?' she clucked.

'She needs a job,' Eva said quickly. 'Perhaps Mrs van Tonder, you could help? I mean to say, you have the ear of the Rutherfords . . . '

'That's true,' she said. 'I'll talk to them.'

A comfortable silence flowed between the two women.

'What happened to the bugger?' Mrs van Tonder asked, curiously.

'Who?'

'Her husband. What happened to him?'

'Oh – her husband. Killed in a drunken brawl,' Eva said, hastily improvising yet again.

'Stroos God, justice for once!' Mrs van Tonder whispered, awed. 'Lady Rutherford will think so, too — '

Certain that the story Mrs van Tonder would tell of Mireille's life would more or less conform to her own account, Eva allowed the ensuing talk to wash over her. The woman could be relied upon to spread the word.

A sudden pitfall loomed. Mireille knew nothing about the husband who had been killed in a drunken brawl. Eva excused herself and went to telephone Max. Quickly, speaking Yiddish because this was an emergency, she told him what she had done, and then concluded, 'When Johannes goes to the boarding house to fetch Mireille you must go with him, and explain what I said about her. We can't afford two versions of the same story . . . '

Mireille accepted Eva Abelman's version of events the way she accepted everything else – unquestioningly, and with gratitude. She made no effort even to try to understand the direction her life had taken. Surrounded as she was by nothing but warmth and sympathy, her own sense of guilt and sin began slowly but surely to fade. Her look of radiant serenity deepened, making her almost beautiful. Her dark eyes softened, widened and seemed to turn to velvet.

She had more than absolved her sin, she was carrying Saffarty's baby. Had not Madame Chandler said, *Remembered ecstasy is ecstasy, remembered love is love?* But this child would be living proof, living love . . .

Eva's scheming could not have been more effective. Mrs van Tonder, filled with self-importance, arranged a meeting with Lord and Lady Rutherford, and astonishingly both the Rutherfords spoke French. Lord Rutherford spoke a schoolboy French, but Lady Rutherford, who had never been to school, had been educated at home by a French governess. The Rutherfords engaged her at once – she could not have come at a more convenient time – but, as they gravely told one another, they would have taken her in anyway, whether Janet O'Brien had been about to leave or not.

The Rutherfords were not afraid of paying for their principles. Indeed, they had already paid, exorbitantly. Or so everyone thought. The Rutherfords themselves thought they had got off almost too lightly. Thanks to Lady Rutherford's imprisonment as a suffragette, their family had banished them to the colonies. But the wilderness that both their families thought they deserved turned out to be a paradise, and they soon discovered they had been exiled to the fairest cape in all the world.

Their exile had begun ten years earlier, when they had taken over the vineyard. They had been there ever since.

From their graceful Dutch gabled mansion – snow-white in a land where it never snowed – however much they gazed downward into the valley below, or upward to the seemingly horizonless skies, they never got used to the heart-stopping beauty of their exile at Constantia.

For they had found not only beauty, but freedom – the freedom to pursue the interests that others found so reprehensible. Lord Rutherford was solidly engaged in the study of rodents, and Lady Rutherford in advancing the cause of women. She believed in, and needed, heroines. A disciple of Emmeline Pankhurst, and an admirer of Emily Hobhouse, she was the sort of woman who rises to every challenge, and to those of her own making even more enthusiastically. Lady Rutherford had taken it upon herself to make her own reparations for the crimes of British imperialism. After all, it was Emily Hobhouse who had exposed the high mortality rate of the Boer women and children held in camps during the Boer War. The Rutherfords' Home for Distressed Women now occupied much of her time.

Since the Rutherfords had many more important things than domestic trivia to attend to, they appointed a household administrator. Naturally they could not drop their living standards, and they saw no reason why they should not continue to live their lives in the same graceful and civilised way to which they had long been accustomed. Janet O'Brien was their household administrator, and Mireille would be her successor.

Even before Mireille moved in to take up what they called her appointment, the Rutherfords explained that since they had both decided to dedicate themselves to making the world a better place, they had also decided not to have any children.

'A small, but true, sacrifice,' Lady Rutherford had said crisply. 'We cannot accuse ourselves of being hypocritical.'

In the middle of June, six weeks after her arrival in Cape Town, Mireille went to live at the Rutherford Estate. Her bewilderment was matched only by the extravagance of her gratitude. Here, in this new world, it was mid-winter, but the skies were blue. Janet O'Brien and her future husband had agreed to stay on until the beginning of December, when Mireille's baby would be about two months old. Mireille's quarters consisted of a small sitting room, bright with chintzes, a bedroom and a bathroom.

The first night the luxury of it all kept her awake. The next night she discovered that her underwear had been washed and ironed for her, and that kept her awake too. During the day she wandered through the vineyards and the gardens, and her meals were served to her in the sitting room. They called it mid-winter and so, every day, at precisely five o'clock, one of the houseboys lit the fire in her sitting room. The Rutherfords expected only one thing from her in return – fluent English.

She decided that the best and the quickest way would be to do all her thinking in English. She began to dream in English. Her desire to please was in the realm of a logical imperative. She asked Janet

O'Brien to teach her to knit, and within a week had knitted three pairs of the canary yellow socks that Lord Rutherford always wore. Mireille found him utterly strange. She was sure something was wrong with his head. He tied his heavy brogues with string, wore black patent leather pumps at night, but dressed, day and night, in flamboyant colourful tweeds. She could not imagine him without his flowing beard; it seemed he had never been young. Sometimes, among the vineyards, or in the gardens, she would catch sight of him marching rapidly, but always with the same gnarled branch that served as a walking stick. She never saw him without his pack of golden spaniels. Unfailingly polite but distant, he would raise his cap to her. She was as frightened of him as she was of his wife. There was nothing strange about the way Lady Rutherford dressed – women also wore trousers in Paris – it was her high clipped voice and her long fierce jaw that frightened Mireille so.

She wondered what Saffarty would make of these strange people. Still no word came from him, and still she journeyed once a week to the Purple Vines boarding house to check the post. She had left her forwarding address, of course, but she doubted both Rebecca's willingness and her ability to send it on.

Though Mireille had found the steep climb from the tram-stop increasingly difficult to manage, she was unable to stop herself from making what she knew would be a last attempt before the baby was born. It was early September, and flowers were already in bloom. They said it was spring, and the baby rolled and kicked impatiently as if it knew – but as far as Mireille was concerned it was high summer.

She stood panting in the foul, airless hall of the Purple Vines boarding house, and rang the little hand-bell. Eventually Rebecca appeared.

'Missus,' she said without being asked, 'why you come all this way? You'll drop your baby, Missus. No letters for you, Missus.'

'Are you sure, Rebecca?' Mireille asked.

'You think I tell lies?' Rebecca said menacingly.

Mireille didn't answer. The baby moved violently, and she felt her belly harden. There was a long silence. After a while she said again, 'Are you absolutely sure there is not one letter for me?'

Rebecca shook her head, shrugged her shoulders and shuffled away.

Mireille's hands closed protectively over her huge, hard belly. Rebecca's hatred lingered in the hall. Suddenly she gave up all hope of hearing from Saffarty ever again. The baby lurched, and this time she felt her belly harden and then contract. Willing herself not to fall, she began the perilous descent to the tram-stop.

In the kitchen at the Purple Vines, Rebecca said idly, 'That child will come tonight. It will be bad — '

'Ja,' Mrs Coetzee mumbled.

'It's too big for her, that child.'

'You told her you took the letters to the post box?' Mrs Coetzee said abstractedly. 'Don't just stand there. I told you, I'm selling the place. Mr Botha is coming again. You didn't sweep the steps. Go quickly and sweep the steps.'

Rebecca picked up a broom and gazed at it. 'It's not my job,' she said defiantly. 'It's Willem's job.'

'Idiot! *Mamparra!*' Mrs Coetzee shrieked. 'Get out of my sight!'

Rebecca dropped the broom. 'It's not my job,' she said again. 'It's not my job to go to the post box. It's Willem's job!'

'What's that? Speak up, girl. Speak up!'

Rebecca took up her broom again. 'It will be very bad,' she said darkly. 'That child's too big for her. Her bones will crack.'

11

Saffarty was dismayed by Mireille's fifth letter; it was the way she ended it that was so unnerving. 'This will be my last letter, Saffarty dearest. If you do not answer me, Saffarty, my love, you will never hear from me again. But whatever happens, I will love you until I die.'

This was not the Mireille he knew – she had never been the uncompromising type. He had memorised her letters.

We have found Max's relations, and they are charming and generous. Max is waking to the sun; it is almost as if he has come home.

The sun shines, even when it rains. The salt wind sprays the city clean, like a white hemline for the Table Mountains. They say it is winter, but as I write this the sun is setting, and it is still scarlet. The sky is soft and high and yet I feel I could step into it. The nights, early, sudden nights, are without twilight. The low violet mountains are gaunt but not cruel. The Cape is made for lovers, Saffarty. My heart is cracked and leaking.

It is beautiful, my love, so beautiful that if you were here, it would be an earthly paradise.

Saffarty replied at once. In any case he had already written to her. He had received her last letter at the beginning of July; it was the end of September now, and there was still no word. When she had left for South Africa it had been spring, lilacs and horse-chestnut blossoms were everywhere, and now the chill autumn leaves were everywhere.

Still, he could not bring himself to regret the decision to have an abortion. 'We had an abortion together,' he told himself, 'instead of a child.' But how could he have taken on fatherhood? Sleepless and long, his nights, he consoled himself, were not wasted. He studied English and preferred his own company.

In Salonika, birthdays and wedding anniversaries generally went unremarked and uncelebrated by the Saffarty family. Anniversaries of deaths, however, were not only remembered but ritually honoured. For all that, as Saffarty's birthday for the year 1927 drew close he felt more and more alone.

His birthday was on November 10th, and as if in celebration his turnover at La Fenêtre de Saffarty reached a record level. And yet, though he was well satisfied, even pleased, he was less than elated. He locked the shop door thoughtfully, wondering what to do with the long, looming night ahead. It was already quite late, about ten o'clock, and, blown by a chill wind, the music and the false gaiety from the nearby permanent fair sounded mockingly loud in his ears. The Seine had turned to ice – it seemed incredible that Mireille and Max were in full sunshine. That is, if they were still in Africa . . . Only the day before he had received a short letter from Max, postmarked Johannesburg. It was a formal note of gratitude, and in it Max had enclosed one thousand dollars in full and final settlement of his debt. Yet Max had not registered the letter – it could easily have gone missing – which was not like Max at all. It was no oversight: Max did not want him to know where he was. There was no return address.

But why?

He realised he had been questioning this ever since he had received the money and the note. In a flash, the answer came to him. It was five months since he had heard from Mireille – Max must have taken up with her. For all he knew they were married!

And he could not blame either one of them.

Even so, he felt his guts tighten with loneliness and unexpected jealousy.

He walked slowly, caressing the key in his pocket. A whiff of toasting chestnuts made him stop and buy a cone. He realised that he did not know where he was going – he knew only that he could not spend another sleepless night alone. Standing beside the chestnut seller, in her usual place, was the woman with the wooden leg. Tonight, unusually, she greeted him. 'Evening, m'sieur,' she said.

Suddenly, overwhelmed with self-pity, Saffarty replied, 'Good evening.' He paid for his chestnuts and turned away.

Hidden in a doorway, Colette watched as the women called goodnight. Forcing herself to seize the moment she said, 'Happy birthday, monsieur.'

186

She was wearing fox furs and a close fitting hat with a light veil. He recognised her as one of his customers.

He bent low to kiss her hand. 'How do you know it's my birthday?'

'Max Blum told me.'

'I see.' He knew who she was at once. Instinctively he felt for his ancient key. He thought quickly. He might as well spend some time with her now and get it over. 'Would madame care to dine with me?'

'Why not?'

'Good. The Café de la Poste?'

He hooked her arm through his, and they fell into step, but did not speak.

They had hardly been seated at their table when she said, 'So you know who I am?'

Saffarty nodded. Then, discomfited by her empty eyes, he drew a deep breath, and was overtaken by a fit of coughing.

'So he must have believed I was dead,' Colette whispered.

A waiter came to take their orders, and Saffarty was saved from answering.

'Where is he?' Colette asked piteously. 'I've been counting on your knowing where he is.'

'Australia,' he said, improvising rapidly.

'Australia?'

'Australia. I think so.' He shook his head as if trying to remember. 'Maybe it was America. It began with an A. He left very suddenly.'

'The same day. Did he leave the same day?'

'Yes.' He placed his hand over hers. 'I'm very sorry, madame.' He paused for a moment, and went on in a rush, 'You are very beautiful, madame. He told me you were good-looking, but you are a beautiful woman.'

She ignored the compliment. 'Has he written to you?'

'Yes,' Saffarty answered truthfully, 'but there was no return address.' Sounding aggrieved, he added, 'I couldn't understand that.'

'But then you must know if it was Australia or America. The stamp would have told you.'

Saffarty shook his head regretfully.

'A. A.' she said impatiently. 'Could have been Africa.'

'I'd have remembered that,' he said, sounding definite. 'It's coming back to me. Australia. Isn't there a place there called Sydney?'

'Yes.'

'Then that's it. Of course. I remember now, Australia.'

Her lips trembled, and tears suddenly gushed down her cheeks. Saffarty handed her his handkerchief, which made her cry harder. 'You remind me of him,' she said when she regained herself. 'He had such perfect manners.'

'I know,' Saffarty said warmly, remembering that but for Max's influence he would never have carried a handkerchief. 'I have a great deal of admiration for Max.'

'He told you what happened?'

Saffarty nodded miserably.

'But it was an accident. He knew that, didn't he? He knew it was an accident?'

'He was terribly upset. Max was beside himself, I'd say.'

'Poor boy,' she said mournfully. 'How like him to take the guilt unto himself.' Fresh tears fell.

Hastily Saffarty refilled her glass with wine.

'I know what you are thinking,' she said, struggling for control. 'You're thinking that I must be mad. The man I adored left me to drown, or he left me for dead – same thing – so why don't I hate him for it?'

He made no answer.

'Oh, come on. Come on! Tell the truth.' She blew her nose loudly. 'You even think I should want revenge, don't you? He always said you were honest. You think I should hate him. You can't understand me, can you?'

'No,' he said simply. 'Not for the life of me can I understand you.'

'Good. That was a straightforward answer. Now we're getting places.' She smiled sadly. 'I'm different from what you thought, no?'

'Very different.'

'He told you I was old, of course? Thirty-one is not so old, you know. But to an eighteen-year-old, well; thirty-one is no different from forty-one, I suppose.' She played with her amethyst ring. Prisms of violet light glinted. 'He gave this ring to me; it's very old. I think it belonged to a Russian princess.'

'Max has impeccable taste,' Saffarty said smoothly.

'How old are you today? It's your birthday.'

'Nineteen,' he replied promptly, forgetting that not even Max had known his true age.

'I was sixteen when I came to Paris, you know.'

'Where did you come from?'

'America. From Detroit, Michigan. Max didn't know that. He thought I was French-born.'

'I thought I heard a slight accent. Did you come alone?'

'In a way, yes.' Suddenly, she was telling him the entire truth about the childhood she had never had, the youth that had ended even before it was begun, the step-grandfather who had snatched whatever small hope for affection she might have had.

There was no note of self-pity, nor any bitterness as she spoke – only a great sadness. Her hand, under the tight grip of his, felt small and infinitely vulnerable. 'You know more about me than Max ever knew,' she said.

'I am deeply honoured,' he said huskily.

'You are lonely, too?' she said questioningly.

He swallowed then, but said nothing. He felt almost tearful and bit his lip. He wished he had told Max that Colette had not been killed, and now he could not have told him even if he had wanted to. He did not have Max's address. There was a long silence. He simply could not speak. For the first time, the full enormity of what he had done to Max by not telling him that Colette was alive struck him. Still, it was just possible that Max would have fled anyway. After all, he had been in tremendous debt. But that was beside the point. He now saw that his silence had been the equivalent of a lie. And the result of that lie was that Max believed he was a murderer. Aware of her deep scrutiny, he fidgeted nervously.

At last she broke the silence. 'Tell me one more thing, and I will ask no more questions. Did he ask – in the letter he wrote to you – did he mention me?'

'No,' he murmured. 'I'm sorry.'

'Thank you for your honesty.' She sighed deeply. 'If you ever meet up with him again, I hope you will *not* tell him that I survived.'

In spite of himself, Saffarty raised his brows in astonishment.

'Because I love him, I have excused him. But he will never excuse himself. I will be on his conscience, burned into his soul for ever. He will have to endure living with the false belief that he is a murderer. Until the day he dies I will be the thorn in his heart.'

'And you say you love him!'

'I'd rather be a thorn than be forgotten.' She blew her nose again. 'Well, do I have your promise? My survival is our secret?'

'Of course.'

'Let's drink to that,' she said, raising her glass. 'The ways of women are mysterious, no?' She threw her head back. 'He told me about your eye. But the operation was highly successful, I see. You had an accident, no?'

He took the ancient key from his pocket, and showed it to her. Then he told her what he had told no one. He told her what his father had done to his eye.

'I believe I have made a friend tonight,' he said shyly. His mood changed abruptly, and he called out, 'Garçon! Garçon! More wine. More of the same. This is a celebration.' He turned to Colette. 'We must meet regularly,' he pronounced. 'Today is Thursday, and we must dine together every Thursday.'

Thus, out of her grief and his guilt, an undying friendship was born. For it would be that rare sort of deep, pure friendship between a man and a woman that is uncomplicated by sex.

That night Saffarty did not sleep, but he was not lonely. He was positively feverish with excitement. It was hard to reconcile the woman he had talked to with the image Max had given him. To be sure, she was older, as Max had said, but he would never be ashamed to be seen with her. In Saffarty's view she was chic and graceful, and commandingly lovely. She was the sort of woman men noticed; he had observed that for himself in the restaurant. He began to feel angry with Max for having run away like that, so heartlessly. And again he thought if Max and Mireille were not married, they were lovers. Max had not deserved a woman like Colette.

Meanwhile Colette's sad, wounded eyes reminded him of a hurt animal. He vowed he would do all he could to make it up to her. He had been terribly wrong not to tell Max that she was in hospital.

For her part, Colette found Saffarty very different from the way she had imagined him to be. For one thing he no longer had his crooked eye, and naturally that altered things. But what impressed her the most was that he was sure of himself, yet not arrogant. Doubtless he was as rough and as ruthless as Max had said he was, but that was of a piece with his unstoppable ambition. The last thing she expected was to feel sympathy for Saffarty, and but for her step-grandfather's damaging lessons in cruelty, she would not have understood how the force of the humiliation over the injury his father had done to his eye had penetrated his soul.

At the same time her heart went out to Max because she knew he had experienced nothing but love and affection in his family, and had not therefore even begun to understand Saffarty – you are suspicious of what you cannot understand. In any case, poor Max had been too young.

Colette and Saffarty fell into the habit of dining together every Thursday, and often over the weekend. One Sunday Colette offered to show him the *garçonnière*. Though they were both pleased he had not seen it before, he did not tell her that he had thrown the key into the Seine the night Max had left for South Africa. Colette told him that since she had been hospitalised she had only been to the *garçonnière* once and had realised immediately that Max had gone. She asked him rather shyly if he'd like to move in. At first he demurred.

But the next morning he realised that the spell of the place had been broken, and at once decided to move in. That same day he told the astonished, spluttering Monsieur Feyard that he was quitting the shop with no name, and transferred his remaining stock to La Fenêtre de Saffarty. Finally, when all that had been done, he took yet another decision – or perhaps it was a conclusion? He was no longer to wait, on the edge of his nerves, for a letter from Mireille.

Saffarty's spirits soared. For the first time he looked forward to his regular meeting with his banker, Monsieur Dumont, with real pleasure.

'Monsieur Saffarty, my congratulations,' Monsieur Dumont proclaimed with his sly smile. 'You are a man after my own heart, a man with a sixth sense.'

'I take that as a compliment,' Saffarty replied smoothly. 'But you exaggerate, surely? I can't think of any recent investment of mine that deserves so great an accolade — '

These days Saffarty was far from intimidated by either Monsieur Dumont or his lavishly furnished office. His desk, tooled in Moroccan leather, and his fine, silk Kashan oriental carpets were no longer awesome.

'I speak of the investment you did not make,' Monsieur Dumont murmured.

'Which one?' Saffarty said shortly.

'You did well not to heed my advice on the Tunisia investment,' Monsieur Dumont went on. 'The barley crop was destroyed by a plague of locusts. Might I ask you what it was that made you decline? After all, even for a relatively paltry investment you stood to make an enormous profit.'

'You don't have to be a genius to know that crops fail. Those who put their trust in human nature are as misguided as those who put their trust in nature. The soil is not a factory, you know.'

'But the soil was perfect. Everything was perfect,' Monsieur Dumont protested. 'The crop was perfect.'

'True enough. But the crop was defeated by nature. You asked me to invest in nature. I'm ready to make investments, as you know. I'm not above speculation, either. But nature is as unpredictable as it is cruel.' Saffarty leaned back, and drew heavily on his cigarette. 'To invest in nature is suicide — '

'An interesting philosophy. However, I can't say I agree. Think of the fortunes that have been made from the rubber plantations in Indo-China. The colonies are a great source of wealth for France — '

'On that score you and I are in entire agreement,' Saffarty said sagely. 'Now, those stocks in the Suez Canal . . . '

His business completed, Saffarty left Monsieur Dumont's office. It had been an altogether satisfactory encounter, not least because he now decided that nothing in the world would ever induce him to have a desk as vulgar as the one he had just seen.

Colette had made a substantial difference to his life. He had not been wrong about her – he had made a friend, one he knew he would keep for life. That his closest friend had been Max's mistress as well as a part-time whore did not strike him as odd, or even ironic, for he was his own man, and had enough self-confidence to know that Colette knew more, and could teach him more, than a hundred bankers. He was convinced that a deep understanding of human nature was the secret of successful business.

Colette, like all self-respecting Frenchwomen, was a skilled and accomplished needle-woman. At Saffarty's suggestion she began to wear trousers. She made them herself, and soon acquired an impressive collection. The new passion of the *haute couture* designers for pyjamas – known as tea pyjamas because they were worn by day and by night – was easily copied. Max had forbidden her to wear green, because it would bring bad luck. Now as an act of defiance, a step towards exorcism, she chose green frequently. Out of a cyclamen brocade and an emerald green satin, she fashioned a stunning ensemble of tea pyjamas. Saffarty's favourite among her outfits was made of black crêpe de chine, cleverly appliquéd with emerald velvet roses. Emerald, or shades of emerald, dominated her wardrobe – she wore streaming emerald scarves and fluttering fringes and she jewelled her sweaters and blouses with fake emeralds. Her clothes sparkled and moved and her features – as well as her expression – softened.

Colette and Saffarty were entirely frank and open with one another. On their seventh Thursday night at the Café de la Poste, she said quietly, 'You and I are more like an aunt and a nephew than a mother and a son.'

'Why do you say that?' he asked carefully. He scarcely remembered his aunt, and even his mother had become a distant blur.

'I don't know, *mon chou*. I've never been a mother, and I've never been an aunt.'

'So?'

'You are the only person in the whole world whom I trust, whom I respect.' She frowned deeply. 'Because I think we trust one another the way very close relations trust one another. Do you agree?'

'That we trust one another? Of course I agree,' he said feelingly.

'I've been thinking about this, *mon chou*. We have nothing to forgive one another for, which is a blessing.'

'Shall I call you Aunt Colette then?' he asked, attempting a light laugh.

'That wouldn't be right. It would sound false. It would spoil what we have.'

He thought of the way he had trusted Max. He would trust Colette with his life, yet he would never tell her about what he had done to Max . . . But it seemed as if Max had forgotten all about him. He said gruffly, 'I'm glad we talked about this.'

Colette's voice trembled. 'So am I, *mon chou*.' She leaned towards him and adjusted his tie.

'If you don't mind my saying so, Colette,' he grinned, 'you look like a dignified aunt tonight.'

'That's because I'm almost retired now. I only see one or two of my oldest customers,' she said shyly.

'That's the best news I've had.'

'I knew it would be.'

Suddenly, she offered him her hand. Their firm, formal handshake told them both that theirs was a deal for which no further negotiation would ever be required.

After that they chose more expensive and more fashionable restaurants. At Le Grand Ecart, and at the Boeuf sur le Toit – both cabarets named after Cocteau's works – they were an arresting couple. People talked and speculated about them, for they added a certain eccentric worldliness to the standardised sophistication. Once Colette commanded him to look at an astonishingly beautiful – as well as a glamorous – woman. 'See those crystal shoulder straps she's wearing? My dear Saffarty, they are the real thing pretending to be fakes. How do I know? Well, you know how I know . . . Her husband, the Baron de Falin, likes the lash – can't function without it, you know . . . '

It was wives of a certain kind that Colette despised, and she despised them much more than their husbands. For those wives were, she believed, the real harlots. They went to bed with men they loathed and wished dead. They were the real whores, whose only choice was obedience, whose only emotion for their men was hate. Yet they thought of themselves as slaves or martyrs, and denied that they, too, sold themselves. Few had enough self-respect even to set a price. Hypocrites, all of them hypocrites waiting for widowhood as the desert waits for rain. And they, those bourgeois moralists, had the nerve to believe that honest prostitutes were beneath contempt. She did not hate her customers.

'I'm a romantic Bohemian,' she would say loudly, and with a twinkle, causing spoons to hover in the silence. 'Not a hypocritical wife — '

She told him about several middle-class wives she knew who worked as part-time prostitutes. These were the wives who had her undying respect.

It was from Colette, too, that Saffarty learned about the *Guide Rose*, an annual directory of bordellos and the like. And of course, he owed his membership of the Maison Sphinx to her.

In later years Saffarty was to speak of the Maison Sphinx as *the* most important and influential club to which he had ever belonged. There he was introduced and mixed on equal terms with the rich and the powerful, the well-born poor, the professionals – engineers, lawyers and doctors. The Maison Sphinx was his university; it was where he gained his doctorate in self-confidence, a sort of social fearlessnesss mixed with charismatic charm that gave him the licence that contributed to his mystique – that rare licence that for ever after made it possible for him to make the most startlingly offensive remarks without ever giving offence.

Mines in Morocco, highways in Senegal and the Ivory Coast, railroads in Indo-China – the French Empire worked as well for Saffarty as it did for all those other investors and financiers in France who saw conscripted black labour in Africa as an excellent means of limiting risk. After all, even missionaries were keen on encouraging Western civilisation in darkest Africa.

'Only a financial fool would fail to take profit from the way economic development follows the cassock,' Monsieur Dumont proclaimed sagely, several weeks later, at their next meeting. 'The returns are enormous.'

'My investments are based on my faith in machinery,' Saffarty answered enthusiastically. 'And France has the best engineers in the world.'

'The Rothschilds built up the railroads of France, of course,' Monsieur Dumont offered.

'But not in the wilderness of Africa or Indo-China,' Saffarty snapped. 'There's been some unfavourable publicity about the forced labour. Some say it is slavery, you know. I'm speaking of the Ivory Coast, as you probably realise.'

'Think of the profits,' Monsieur Dumont continued aggressively. 'We are opening up their own country for them. So, of course, all major undertakings in the Ivory Coast are carried out – of necessity, you understand – with conscripted labour.'

'It is dangerous to rely on slave labour.'

'I can't say I go along with that,' Monsieur Dumont interrupted. 'Your portfolio has quadrupled — '

'Reason enough to get out of the colonial investments immediately,' Saffarty declared. 'Have you never wondered what makes a gambler different from an investor?' He did not w   for a reply, but went on, 'A gambler wins only because someone else loses. An investor does not need someone else to lose in order to win. I had a partner, once. He used to wait for others to lose.' His loudest and most infectious laugh exploded from him, and Monsieur Dumont found himself laughing, too. 'So I propose to move all my investments to America.' His voice switched to a tone of icy formality. 'They say the Stock Exchange is the barometer of a country. Well, then, the States is on the boil. It's booming. Besides, Monsieur Dumont, you are by now sufficiently well acquainted with my business philosophy to know that my faith is placed in real machines, not in the machine that is made up of forced human labour.'

'Idealistic talk,' Monsieur Dumont murmured.

'Perhaps, Monsieur Dumont. Perhaps. My kind of idealism is in the automobile industry, the steel industry, the radio industry.'

'Be that as it may, Monsieur Saffarty, but you will be breaking a fundamental rule of investment.'

'You have too many fundamental rules,' Saffarty said sarcastically. 'Which fundamental rule are you referring to?'

'We do not put all our eggs in one basket.'

'Are you seriously trying to tell me that the great continent of America is a single basket?' Saffarty said incredulously. 'America is at least twice the size of France. And you dare to call that omnipotent financial utopia a basket!' His voice rose as he deliberately gave full rein to his temper. 'It's 1928 and I'm moving into that market, lock, stock and barrel.'

On the morning of April 15th, 1928, Saffarty awoke with the feeling that there was something important about the day. Like a forgotten memory struggling to surface, the feeling nagged persistently all day. It was a Thursday, and he and Colette were meeting that night – there was nothing particularly special about that. It was while he was taking a long, luxurious bath and thinking, as he frequently did whenever he was in the bath, about Mireille, about the way she used to go down to the cellar to boil water for his shave, that he remembered. It was exactly one year since she and Max had left Paris.

No word from her; no word, since Max's repayment, from either of them. Mireille was no longer a part of his life; yet, though it galled him to admit it, he missed her. He longed to tell her about his business triumphs, as he longed to tell Max. The plain truth was that his business successes both in terms of La Fenêtre de Saffarty and of his investment portfolio, had surpassed his highest expectations. He sighed. He was now one of the more colourful landmarks of Montmartre, and nether Max nor Mireille knew anything about it. Still, he had Colette . . .

Clearly Colette had eased his loneliness. She was on his side, just as Mireille had been. He had the feeling that she would always be a part of his life, an honorary aunt, so to speak. She knew about Mireille though. 'You exiled Mireille,' she had said. 'You make people dissolve and vanish, like sugar in a cup.'

Colette always arrived at their rendezvous ahead of time, so he was not surprised to find her waiting for him at the Cintra Bar. However, even before he'd ordered his drink, she said, 'Saffarty, would you mind very much if we don't go to the Grand Ecart tonight?'

'Why not?' he said, alarmed. 'Are you ill or something?'

'I'm perfectly well, thank you,' she answered with one of her throatiest chuckles. 'It's just that tonight Pierre Benoit is giving a lecture on — '

'Don't tell me that Pierre Benoit – one of the greatest living French writers – is one of your customers!' Saffarty exploded.

'Hardly,' she said drily. 'He is, however, a friend of a former customer.'

'Who?' he interrupted, inquisitively.

'Never mind who. That is not interesting. It's what my – uh – friend told me about Benoit that is interesting. Benoit is a family friend of his. When Benoit visits his home, he pays more attention to my friend's children than to the other guests. Instead of holding forth in the *salon*, he goes to the nursery and reads to the children. He knows all the stories in their books off by heart. Imagine how impressed the children are!'

'My dear Colette, it will be my pleasure to escort you to hear your hero's lecture.'

Although Saffarty and Colette arrived thirty minutes early the lecture hall was already overflowing, and all the seats were taken. 'There's no room for us,' she wailed.

'Wait here. I'll see what I can do. Leave it to me,' he said at once.

Watching his purposeful stride, Colette knew she would have a seat. He was unfailingly successful with doormen, usherettes and head waiters. There would be an exchange of chuckles, and some cash, and he would have his way. A few moments later, she and Saffarty were comfortably seated in the third row.

Saffarty was certain that except for Colette and himself everyone else in the audience was a student. There was a thrum of excitement in the audience. He felt suddenly uneasy and out of place. It was a while before he identified what it was that had disturbed him so – he was among people of his own age, yet felt an oddity. If he had escaped being a premature father, he had not escaped being a premature adult, he thought. He sighed loudly.

Always sensitive to his moods, Colette asked, 'What's the matter, Saffarty? What's wrong?'

'Nothing's wrong,' he said shortly. 'This place is full of kids.'

'Still wet behind the ears,' she said, trying to make light of things.

'Excuse me,' someone interrupted. 'There seems to be some mistake with the ticket numbers.'

'Have my seat,' Saffarty said gruffly. 'I'll see you at the end of the lecture, Colette. I'll be at the back of the hall.'

He was glad of the excuse to leave. He hated being among these students, and did not really want to hear the lecture. He was making his way out – to a nearby bar – when he saw her.

He stopped.

His heart lurched.

He stayed.

Shamelessly, helplessly, Saffarty stared. Since she was surrounded, almost protected, by a group of students, he felt free to study her. The group laughed often, but gently, and from time to time he believed he could hear her speak. If he was right, if that voice did indeed belong to her, then it was the most beautiful voice he had ever heard. The girl was foreign, he was sure, and the voice was foreign, too. The lecture began, and the cluster round her fell away, leaving him a clearer view.

Her beret alone would have been enough to make her stand out. All the other students were in black berets – hers was white, probably, Saffarty thought, because it went with the peacock-blue and white striped blazer she was wearing. Her simple white pleated silk skirt, and soft beige silk blouse with a high collar, were both chic and gracious. But then, no matter what she wore, she would have been pretty enough – no, he amended, beautiful. Her beret all but covered her copper hair. Saffarty longed to take it off – how else could he know how long it was? Perhaps she had tucked it inside the beret.

He was at least a metre away from her, but even from that distance shafts of light sparkled from her dazzling, violet eyes. Her sharp, aristocratic cheekbones were set in the splendid oval of her face, so it was her nose, he decided, that saved her from having that high, heartless look. She was listening intently. Her mouth drooped, and a sudden sadness crossing her expression forced him to listen to what Benoit was saying.

Why, the man was being sharply critical of the British. It was clear that his book, *Châtelaine du Liban*, was a violent attack on Britain. How vicious this man was, he thought, how unjust, and above all how wrong.

The lecture ended and, once again, the students formed a tight cluster around her. Then she was being introduced to a new group – cards were being exchanged. Colette was waiting for him, he knew, but he could not tear himself away. In a sudden flash of inspiration he took out one of his visiting cards, folded it in half and handed it to her. 'Please feel free to call on me for anything at any time, mademoiselle,' he said. Then he turned away, and went to find Colette.

12

Edwina Wyndham opened her handbag, turned it upside down and shook the contents out on to her bed. She was searching for the folded visiting card that had been given to her. She had already glanced at it once; the man's name was no less strange than the man himself. She had difficulty, in any case, in remembering these foreign names. Ah, yes, there it was – Saffarty, La Fenêtre de Saffarty, 27 Rue Paradis, Paris. She looked at the card again. Saffarty; no Christian name. He had thrust the card into her hand and then, before she'd had time to take him in, turned on his heel and sped away.

Thank goodness she had not lost his card.

Edwina, the only child of the Catholic Sir William and Lady Wyndham, was in Paris to 'perfect her French'. Her mother, Alice, had waged a minor war to get her father to agree. Not that her father was against educating women, it was just that he had been against letting her loose in Paris. His wife had had a real education herself, and had graduated from Cambridge with a distinction in French. She had hoped that Edwina would go to Cambridge, but Edwina had insisted she was not enough of a bluestocking for that. She had a gift for languages, that was all, and, however high the academic standard at Cheltenham, excelling had been effortless.

It was purely because she was an only child, born long after her parents had given up all hope of having a family, that her mother had sent her to Paris. Not to have done so would have been entirely selfish, Lady Wyndham believed, for it would have been only too easy to take advantage of Edwina's loving nature. Besides, the girl needed to be with young people. Still, the truth was that it was no small sacrifice to be deprived of Edwina's company.

After exhaustive investigations a suitable chaperone had been found. Edwina now lived with the Count and Countess Thierny and her father was well satisfied that the Countess would permit no young man to climb the stairs to his daughter's bedroom. After she had been in Paris for three months her parents had come to visit her, and left with all their fears removed.

Meanwhile, Edwina found Paris and the Sorbonne exhilarating. She was intelligent and sensitive enough to be aware that there never was – and probably never would be – a more glorious time to be in Paris. Of course Paris was different for everyone, she knew. But in her Paris the sense of freedom, of optimism, bordered on sensuality. Everywhere her senses were assailed if not by the market of fresh fruits and vegetables then by the elegance of the women, to say nothing of the current exhibitions of Léger, Picasso and Braque, She was ready for every unimaginable experience, but something about her, her aura of innocence perhaps, protected her as securely as if she was encased behind a filigree of fine wire mesh. Yet she longed to feel vulnerable and exposed. This led her to spend her entire allowance until she was satisfied that she was as hard up as her fellow students. Then she would do crazy things, like choosing an egg and marking it with a pencilled cross, so that she could retrieve it later that day after her cheque had arrived. This way she felt like an authentic, hard-up student. It seemed you could not be one without the other.

If Edwina had not been in Paris nothing in the world would have persuaded her to call on a strange man. But, as she told herself, if you were in Paris you did that sort of thing. Because Paris meant freedom – the freedom to be whatever you wanted to be. After all, she had been given this year in Paris – 'your breathing year, darling', her mother had called it. Sometimes, walking through the leafy streets, she would hear the lilt of an accordionist, and then the romance of Paris would be almost too much for her. Now, as she made her high-heeled way through the narrow and winding streets of Montmartre toward La Fenêtre de Saffarty, her own daring excited her. What the girls of Cheltenham would think of her taking a chance with this strange man she could not quite imagine . . . Which only added to her sense of adventure.

The moment she entered his shop, Saffarty said, his voice hoarse, 'Welcome, a thousand welcomes.' He turned to his American customers and rapidly excused himself. 'Welcome, mademoiselle,' he said again, as he lowered his lips to her hand.

'Why did you fold your card?' Edwina asked, and then blushed. She had not meant to say anything like that.

'So that you would know who I was,' Saffarty shot back. His full-throated laugh drowned the sound of the Swiss musical boxes. 'Allow me to present you with one of these,' he said, picking up and winding a filigreed leather musical box.

'Oh, I couldn't possibly accept it. But thank you, anyway,' Edwina said, startled.

'You speak French with a beautiful British accent.'

'Thank you.'

'Will you have lunch with me?'

'Lunch? But it's too early for lunch.'

'I'd be honoured, mademoiselle, if you'd accept.'

'Thank you. I mean, yes.'

After a few hastily whispered words with Madame Delange, Saffarty took up his hat and they left.

'What sort of restaurant would you prefer?'

'Where there are no tourists.'

'Les Trois Tours, then. Renoir used to go there, you know. Excellent food, but rather too severe for tourists — '

'Renoir? Perfect,' Edwina said. 'Thank you.'

At eleven thirty in the morning the restaurant was empty. The waiter took their order and then gloomily informed them they would have a long wait. Then, because he sensed it would please her, Saffarty ordered a carafe, instead of a bottle, of red wine.

'Mademoiselle,' he said softly. 'Forgive my indelicacy – but I do not know your name.'

'Of course you don't,' Edwina said bluntly. 'We were not introduced.'

'Ah, I see. You'd rather not tell me your name?'

'It is Edwina Wyndham.'

'Edwina Wyndham,' Saffarty repeated. 'Do you have a brother? Delighted to meet you, Mademoiselle Wyndham.'

'Please call me Edwina. Why did you not print your Christian name on your card?'

'I've been known as Saffarty for four years – ever since I came to France, in fact. Besides, I don't like my name. I never use it.'

'I see. It's a secret?'

'No. It is Simon. But please call me Saffarty!'

They were interrupted by a waiter who handed over a brightly wrapped package. 'For you, Edwina,' Saffarty said.

'For me?'

She hesitated, but only very briefly. She removed the wrapping paper very carefully, lifted the lid off the gilt box, and took out a tiny enamelled piano. She held it up.

'Open the piano top,' Saffarty said.

Once again Edwina did as she was told. 'It's a music box,'

she exclaimed. 'But this is not the one I saw in your shop.'

'It was not for sale,' he said. 'It was mine. But it must have been made for you.'

Floating on their freely flowing conversation, they only realised how long they had been in the restaurant when their irritable waiter brought the bill. It was past four o'clock – they had been talking, non-stop, for almost five hours. When they were leaving Edwina said, 'D'you know, Saffarty, I've seen and heard many wonderful things in Paris, but I can honestly say that nothing has been as thrilling as this lunch.'

Edwina had planned on going to the Marie Laurençin exhibition. It seemed only natural for Saffarty to accompany her. He tried to buy one of the paintings that had captivated her but it was sold. Then they strolled through the Louvre. He walked her home, and arranged to meet her after her lecture the next day. When he told her that he would meet her outside the Sorbonne, that seemed only natural, too.

And so it continued for several weeks. Saffarty spent less and less time at La Fenêtre de Saffarty, and because her father frequently spent days away from his carpet mill, Edwina was unconcerned with how he managed to do this. He kept a watchful eye on the turnover, and while it was not growing it was not decreasing, either. They picnicked in the Bois de Boulogne, they went to the country, to the village of Barbizon, not too far from Paris, where Millet and Corot had worked. They went to the theatre, the opera, the cinema; always just the two of them and always with a sense of adventure.

Every day was a celebration. Both Saffarty and Edwina considered it something of a miracle that they had met at all. After all, they came from worlds so different they might each have inhabited separate planets. They talked and talked, and touched and touched, but, certain that she was still a virgin, Saffarty held himself in check. His desire increased with his control, for in one way at least his discipline was easily maintained – the ferocity with which he prized, valued and guarded her virginity was boundless.

This woman was a wife-woman.

And she would be his wife.

So he would wait until then.

Meanwhile he would protect her innocence.

About six weeks after their first meeting they returned to Les Trois Tours, the café where they had first lunched.

'I thought you said this was off the tourist track,' Edwina teased as the sound of high American voices forced them to speak louder.

'Americans,' Saffarty said triumphantly. 'I can tell the difference now.'

'Like the poor, the Americans are always with us — '

'Excuse me?' he said, bewildered.

'Just a bad English joke,' she giggled.

'You make French even more beautiful when you speak, Edwina. You make French sound as beautiful as you look, *chérie*,' Saffarty said. He lowered his lips to her hand and kept them there for a long while.

For some reason she was the only woman in the restaurant that evening, and the harsh, bawdy laughter made her feel distinctly uneasy, even frightened. The American voices grew louder and uglier, until it was impossible for her not to hear every word. 'Wouldn't mind giving her one . . . Looks like she's a great lay to me . . . Naw, too lady-like man, too lady-like . . . Too cold . . .

'I'd warm her up real quick . . . Red hair . . . wonder if it's red all over?'

It was too much for Edwina. 'I think we should leave,' she whispered. Her flushed cheeks, her flustered, anxious lips and her downcast gaze instantly alerted Saffarty to all he needed to know.

'Of course, *chérie*,' he said rising, immediately. He flung some money on the table. 'Let's go,' he said.

Ashamed, Edwina walked quickly and like countless women in that sort of difficulty, she lowered her eyes. As she drew alongside the table the laughter gained in brutality and all the men at the table leered at her. Suddenly, one of them called out the one French phrase he knew – the phrase that men often learned before they went to Paris as a sort of harmless joke. '*Voulez-vous couchez avec moi?*' Will you sleep with me?

The insult stopped Saffarty in his tracks; all his primitive male responses surfaced, and instantly turned into rage. One wild, violent, but accurate blow sent the man sprawling. Edwina screamed. The waiters rushed over, coming automatically to Saffarty's defence.

'Idiots! Get this young lady out of here at once!' The voice of undeniable authority came from a customer – an elderly woman who with her husband had just entered the restaurant.

The fighting stopped.

'Are you all right now, my dear?' the woman asked in English.

'Yes, thank you.'

In the ensuing flurry of apologies – 'We didn't know she was French, we didn't dream she would understand' – the foreigners left the restaurant. Saffarty and Edwina returned to their table.

'Oh, *chérie*,' he said, laying his hand over hers. 'I'm sorry. So very, very sorry.'

'You are so Latin,' she answered gravely.

Though she was still shaken, the fear had left her and her eyes sparkled. She had never come close to anything remotely resembling the raw, physical passion that Saffarty had just shown. Her skin under his hand burned, but then even his lightest touch did that. 'You are so Latin – so passionate,' she whispered. It was bewildering. He had touched her breasts, his mouth had explored her mouth, and she wanted more of him. She wanted all of him. Shamed by the depth of her accumulating desire, she bit her lip. *Why didn't he take her? Ravish her? It must be her fault*, was *something wrong with her?* Her senses ached with confusion. 'My father is arriving in Paris tomorrow,' she said irrelevantly, and to stop herself from saying anything else. 'A telegram came today.'

'I hope you will allow me to invite him to dinner.'

'I think not,' Edwina said anxiously. 'If he even thought I had a serious boyfriend he'd make me go home, I'm afraid.'

'I see,' he said thickly. 'And have you, *chérie*?'

'Have I?'

'Have you a serious boyfriend?'

'Oh, my darling. I do! I do!' She blushed at her own daring – this was the first time she had called him darling.

'How long will your father be here?'

'Two days.'

'Are you sure you don't want me to meet him?'

'Not yet, Saffarty.' Suddenly, as if the words were being wrenched out of her, she said, 'I've never seen where you live. Take me there, darling. Take me there tonight.'

'No,' Saffarty murmured. 'No, *chérie*. You know I want you, Edwina. You know I'm dying to make love to you. The first time must

205

be beautiful for you, beautiful and perfect. And we'll need the whole night into the morning, and we'll wake together in the same bed.'

'When?'

'Soon, *chérie*. Soon.'

Two days after her father had left Paris, Saffarty and Edwina were on their way to Medon, a small village near Chartres, about three hours from Paris. Edwina was studying Zola's works, and it was at Medon that Zola had fallen in love with the twenty-year-old girl, Jeanne, who helped his wife with the sewing and mending. Edwina had shown Saffarty the photograph Zola had taken of Jeanne as she sat sewing in the garden. When Saffarty met Edwina after her father had left, the first thing he said was, 'I've got the perfect alibi. We are going to Medon, and you will tell your insufferable chaperone of a landlady that you need to go there for your studies of Emile Zola.'

During her father's visit Saffarty had acquired a car. 'I'll buy this Citroen on one condition,' he had told the astonished car dealer. 'I'll give you two hours to teach me how to drive it.'

He had also arranged a meeting that was more like a consultation with Colette. Far from emphasising his own strength, Edwina's unmistakable fragility made him nervous. Of course Mireille had been a virgin, and if he had hurt her she had said nothing. But that did not really count; beside Edwina, Mireille's innocence seemed to have been counterfeit. He dreaded disappointing her, and was afraid of hurting her.

He explained all this to Colette. He wanted Edwina's eternal love, he told her, and so nothing less than perfection would do.

'If you want your Edwina's undying hatred, tell her that you came to see me about this. If not, keep your lips sealed,' Colette had warned. 'The first thing you must tell her is that in your eyes you and she are already man and wife. Then you will say that you and she will be formally married wherever and whenever she chooses.' She dropped her voice. 'But above all, teach her to glory in her own body. If you succeed, you will have given her the most priceless gift of all – the gift of her own skin.'

Five days in the country in mid-June, in mid-summer, away from everyone and everything, and to hell with his shop, and to hell with the world. They laughed all the way. He loved the car, he loved driving it, and he loved the girl beside him. Who, he asked himself, could ask for more? Who would dare?

They would have their honeymoon in advance of their marriage.

It was about five o'clock when they arrived at the Château Medon. The three-roomed suite he had booked – to protect Edwina's reputation he had made sure it would have two bedrooms – was on the ground floor. In the delicate salon, with the equally delicate Louis XIV furniture, the champagne he had ordered waited for them. 'To you,' Saffarty said, raising his glass. 'To my future bride, the future Madame Saffarty.'

'To my future husband,' Edwina answered bravely.

Through the long French windows the leafy light streamed into the room. She looked out over the golden mustard fields and clenched her fists. Saffarty said nothing, but quietly drew the shutters. Now the light softened into a gentle sprinkle in the room, and Edwina's luminous violet eyes met his, suddenly appearing sightless, as if they contained nothing but desire. He was terrified of hurting her, and terror paralysed him. She read his mind, and struck by a sudden instinct – it was she who would have to seduce him – she rose from her chair and seated herself on his lap. Then, with her arms tight about his neck, she pressed her lips hard against his and forced them open.

She stopped abruptly and stood up. 'Come, Saffarty. Come with me.' She took his hand and he followed her to the bedroom, to the large brass bed. Giving him a light push, she ordered, 'Lie down!' She untied his shoelaces, took off his shoes and then his socks, unbuckled his belt, unbuttoned his trousers, his underpants, removed them, and then, averting her eyes from his engorged and upright sex, she went to work on his shirt and tie. When he was naked, she tore off all her clothes, scattering buttons. Then she said, 'I am not afraid, and you must not be afraid, either.'

Light as the touch of an eyelash, his hands roamed her body, skimming but penetrating every nerve. The softest brush against her nipples, already hard and swollen, made her take a breast in her hand and offer it up to him. He took it, sucking deep, deep as if the source of all his oxygen came from there. She groaned, her body arching and twisting in readiness, but still his mouth clung to her breast. Her mouth felt dry and she heard herself swallow. But his fingers found her other, secret wetness and his exact, knowing movements made her understand that he was more familiar with her, down there, than she was. Concentrating on that troublesome berry, his rhythm quickened, and her body followed and matched his speed, until panting and shrieking through convulsion after convulsion she pushed his hand away. Spent, she lay back, though her entire body still shuddered.

'You are nearly ready, my darling. Nearly ready,' he said softly.

'Nearly ready?' she echoed.

'For the real thing, my darling. First you must recover. Your body was born for love; it will tell me when it is ready for more. It is exhausted now.'

After a while, first with his hands, and then with his tongue, he began to stroke her again. Now it was his tongue that probed every nerve everywhere, even there, even that hot, sticky mess, down, down deep inside her hot secret centre. A rash of shame came, but flashed past. His tongue stopped its probing, and in its place there was one finger, a second, and then a third. A scream. Searing pain. A spurt of liquid. 'It hurts less brutally, this way,' he whispered into her ear. 'It's all over now. I won't hurt you now.'

'Thank you. Thank you,' she said into his neck.

Tenderly, he stroked her hair to cherish her – if she would love her body she would love him more. Already she had lost her shyness. She was beginning to writhe. 'Are you ready?' he asked.

'Yes.'

'Wait one second,' Saffarty said, leaping from the bed and finding his trousers. 'You English call this a French letter,' he chuckled as he put it on. 'You are safe with me, my darling. No little Saffartys to worry about.'

He returned to her. 'Your skin is softer and smoother than silk,' he said, as slowly, slowly he entered her. 'Am I hurting you?'

'No, Saffarty. No!' she said urgently. 'Just go on. Please, please, go on,' she said, tightening her legs around his waist.

He struggled to hold back, but failed. Soon, too soon, she heard his strange, gull-like cry escape. 'I'm sorry, *chérie*. I couldn't wait for you. I couldn't. Next time I will.'

'I love you, Saffarty,' she said. 'You *are* my husband now.'

They fell asleep gently, and awoke starving. Room service sent them up a huge meal of *pâté de fois gras* and *coq au vin*. Halfway through their meal, they were back in bed again.

And so, for five gloriously long days, it continued. They went for walks and they made love, once in broad daylight with only the lacy mustard plants for cover. They laughed and laughed, and gloried in one another, and in the unfathomable mystery of chemical and other combinations that they were convinced they had not only fathomed but invented.

Five days later, on their way back to Paris, she asked, 'How, Saffarty, how did you know how to do it – so well?'

'To break you in, you mean?'

'Yes.'

'Love taught me. I should say, loving *you* taught me,' he said, remembering.

He did not take her back to her chaperone, but stopped to show her the apartment he had rented. In any case, it was several hours since they had left Medon, and therefore several hours since they had made love.

In three weeks' time, in mid-July, Edwina would be returning to England.

The day Saffarty returned to Paris, he telephoned Colette to invite her to dinner with Edwina. 'I've told her all about you,' he said excitedly, 'and she is dying to meet you.'

'So things went well, *mon chou*?'

'It was glory, sheer glory,' Saffarty said with conviction. He went on quickly, 'I hope you're free tomorrow night? I told her you were my adopted aunt.'

'You did? I'm flattered,' Colette laughed. 'If I am your aunt, we will dine at my home.'

Colette had long been waiting for this moment. With her habitual understanding and tact, she had contrived reasons for postponing their usual Thursday evenings until Saffarty actually told her that he wanted her to meet Edwina.

She replaced the receiver, and simultaneously began planning and revising the menu. Aware this would be one of the most important meetings of her life, she was more than a little apprehensive. What if Edwina turned out to be the possessive type, and wished to exclude everyone who was meaningful from her man's former life? That sort of thing was not uncommon.

What she would wear presented no problem; even as she was telling Saffarty they would dine at her home, she had already decided on her little black dress with masses of Chanel's gold costume jewellery. But the menu was another matter – it was a classic case of an embarrassment of choice. Because Colette knew she was equally talented in two areas, lovemaking and cooking, both of which had been entirely neglected since Max had gone. *C'est la vie*, she said to herself.

Since celebration was in the air, caviar and champagne before dinner would be in order. But the menu! After rejecting, including, then discarding several dishes she finally elected to go for her speciality, pale, hot chicken broth, followed by her *pièce de résistance*, boned duck stuffed with *foie gras* and *fois de canard* served on a silver dish garlanded with pineapple, onions tiny as pearls, small plums, strips of orange, egg fillets, cherries and a velvety prune jam. And, of course, a crisp green salad. The cheese, out of deference to Edwina, would be Stilton, while the dessert would be Saffarty's favourite – crème caramel, firm and smooth and golden, with lashings of her russet caramelised sauce. She would choose wines from the finest Rothschild *cuvées*, but with the crème caramel they had to have the exquisite Château Yquem.

Marie would serve. There would be no need for her to leave the table. But Marie would not answer the doorbell. She would be there, in the hall, ready to welcome Edwina herself.

Midway through her meticulous but joyful preparations it suddenly struck her she had never before cooked a meal for Saffarty. She remembered the very different kind of pleasure of cooking for Max. She sighed deeply. Cooking had become a mystical act of devotion, as much as a way of paying homage to his astonishing virility and his amazingly fine and sensitive good looks. She sighed again, shrugged and considered her pearl-like onions.

Fully ten minutes before they were expected, Colette was pacing the marble hall so nervously that she even forgot to avoid the area that had once been the mirrored pond. She glanced at her watch again – five more minutes to go. At that moment she heard Saffarty's laugh. They were early!

Edwina was a vision of radiance, and – with her trusting honest eyes – of such startlingly pure beauty that Colette could not stop herself from saying, 'But you're even more beautiful than he said you were!' And then, just as impulsively, she reached out to embrace her. A moment later Saffarty had both women tightly enfolded in his huge arms. It was some while before they broke apart.

Then they were in Colette's salon. After popping the cork perfectly, Saffarty poured the champagne into glasses delicate as gossamer.

Raising his glass, he said, 'To my bride.'

'To my husband,' Edwina replied.

They shared a long glance of profound intimacy.

Colette stared at them in wonderment. She had long been a premature adult, and had never experienced anything like the innocence of young, uncomplicated passion. But she was tasting it now, she knew. Just watching Saffarty, the essence of virility, and Edwina, the essence of fulfilled femininity. Together their obviously perfect erotic chemistry had struck a strange new chord deep within her own soul.

Tearing her eyes away from Saffarty's, Edwina said, 'If you are his honorary aunt, may I be your honorary niece?'

More champagne, more rejoicing.

Then to Colette's dinner, and a magically sensual experience of a different kind.

That night sleep came naturally to Colette. She knew it would, and for the first time in more years than she could remember she did not take her sleeping tablets.

When she awoke she was full of hope. It was clear to her that Edwina would always retain much of her happy childhood. And, for as long as she lived, she would place Saffarty's protection of her above all else, which was what he needed. Clearly, she was a young woman who had found the meaning of her life in Saffarty. Suddenly an old, forgotten saying darted into her mind. 'She that findeth her life shall lose it.' Frightened, Colette leapt off her bed and rushed to take a shower, hoping that the scalding water would wash her foreboding away.

She felt calmer when she came out. As soon as Edwina left for England, she would insist on speaking English to Saffarty.

Two days later Saffarty called on Monsieur Dumont.

'But you can't mean that you've sold me out?' Saffarty protested furiously. 'You can't be serious! Is this your idea of a joke?'

'But we could not reach you,' Monsieur Dumont said icily. 'You were incommunicado. The experience of this bank has shown that — '

'Who authorised you to sell?'

'You did.'

'I did?'

'Yours is a fiduciary account, Monsieur Saffarty. I need hardly remind you that it is the custom of this bank, as it is of all reputable — '

Once again, Saffarty interrupted brutally. 'A fiduciary account implies mutual trust, mutual respect, does it not?'

'Certainly.'

'Then how could you sell without my authority?'

'We have total autonomy over your account. You bought on margin. Your stocks fell.' Monsieur Dumont paused and shrugged. 'Need I remind you that you went into the American market against our advice? Hundreds – perhaps thousands – of people have been wiped out. There is talk of an impending depression. Of course, if you had not gone incommunicado, you could have covered your margin.' Wearily, and with much sighing, Monsieur Dumont handed him the *New York Times*.

'But this is in English,' Saffarty snapped. 'I don't read English.'

'In anticipation of that eventuality, we have had it translated,' Monsieur Dumont said.

Saffarty snatched the typed sheet of paper from Monsieur Dumont's hand. With growing incredulity he read:

June 13, 1928

Wall Street's bull market collapsed [yesterday] with a detonation heard around the world . . . Losses ranged from 23.5 points in active Stock Exchange issues to as much as 150 in stocks dealt over the counter . . . It was a day of tumultuous, excited market happenings, characterised by an evident effort on the part of the general public to get out of stocks at what they could get. Individual losses were staggering. Hundreds of small traders were wiped out . . .

The sales were countrywide. They flowed into the Stock Exchange not alone from New York brokerage houses but from every nook and cranny of the country . . .

When he had read it, he said coldly, 'I must ask you to let me have this *New York Times*. I must also ask you to let me study all my bank statements as well as those standard forms I signed.'

'By all means, Monsieur Saffarty, you can take the *New York Times*, and your statements. But I regret the standard forms you speak of may not leave this bank.'

'I am not aware that I asked to remove any papers. I am perfectly willing to study them here. Kindly send for them immediately.'

There was little point, Saffarty knew, in seeing these papers. Too late he understood now that he had been duped. What was worse was that his own gullibility, his own naïvety, was to blame. For he had based all his dealings on the false assumption that a fiduciary account implied mutual trust. The Banque Dumont et Cie, however, had put his investments in a fiduciary account because they had not trusted him enough to give him authority over his own funds.

Well, then, he had made a serious error of judgement. And it had cost him almost half his entire capital.

He studied the papers, and took detailed notes, and went so far as to copy out his fiduciary agreement word by word. When he had done, he stood up and said, 'Well, Monsieur Dumont, let's say I've exchanged money for experience.'

Saffarty planned on showing the *New York Times* to Edwina – he did not trust the translation the Banque Dumont et Cie had given him.

Not only had the bank lost nothing, it had made its usual profits from its usual bank charges and commissions. Saffarty's head reeled with rage. At least he was not in debt to the bank, he could be thankful for that. From one minute to the next four hundred thousand francs down the drain. Who would believe it?

Meanwhile, he still owned La Fenêtre de Saffarty. If it hadn't been for his aversion to paying rent he would not have bought the property from Madame Ravarino, and would have sunk more funds into the stock market. But he had been neglecting his shop.

Edwina's reaction helped to restore some of his faith in his own judgement.

He had decided to be entirely frank with her. She compared the bank's translation with the *New York Times*, and confirmed its accuracy. Then she said, 'You've been neglecting your business.'

'I know.'

'My fault.'

'Not at all.'

'I'm coming to the shop tomorrow, and every day until I leave.'

'Edwina, *chérie*, I wouldn't dream of — '

'Don't argue, with me. We'll double the turnover.' A ripple of laughter flowed through her body. 'Just think how it will improve my French,' she said.

Three weeks later they were at the Gare du Nord, the same station from which Mireille and Max had left.

'They say every parting is a little death,' Saffarty said.

'We could elope. But I don't want to do that to them. You know that, don't you?'

'Don't go, Edwina! Let's get married *now*. You can go to your parents one day later.'

'We've been through all that, darling. I *can't* do that to them,' Edwina wailed.

The train whistle blew. 'Listen, darling. I've fixed our wedding date for September the twentieth. Does that suit you?' She began to cry. 'Kiss me, Saffarty. Hold me.'

Then the doors slammed and the train pulled out and, like a true Frenchman, Saffarty wept unashamedly.

All the way back to his shop he thought how like Edwina it was to leave him with the security of a definite wedding date. Naturally enough, neither Edwina nor Saffarty knew that September 20th would also be the date of his daughter's first birthday.

13

On a bright spring day on September 20th, 1927, Mireille's baby was born. After leaving the Purple Vines, she had stumbled down the rocky path, not realising that her labour had already begun. Her mind was on Rebecca. On the tram the pain increased in intensity, and she groaned out loud. Then there was the long steep walk up the hill to the Rutherfords'. By the time she reached the house she was drenched in sweat.

Sarie, the servant who usually opened the door, let her in. 'The baby's coming,' Sarie called out excitedly. 'Lady Rutherford, come quick, milady. The baby's coming!'

In an instant Lady Rutherford was commanding, 'Call the driver! We'll take her to the Florence Nightingale Maternity Hospital.'

Suddenly Mireille sat down on the parquet floor. 'No time for the hospital, madam,' Sarie babbled. 'The child is coming — '

'She can't give birth in the front hall,' Lady Rutherford exploded. She looked up and saw Absalom, the driver. 'Phone Dr Edelstein,' she ordered.

'She can't walk up the stairs. I must boil water, quickly,' said Sarie, already on her way to the kitchen.

'Call Lizzie. Tell her to bring some towels. Some cushions. Blankets.' Lady Rutherford issued her commands calmly, making it clear that she was in control, and well able to rise to this emergency. She turned to Mireille. 'Dr Edelstein will be here soon.'

Minutes later Mireille was lying on a bed of towels and blankets. Lady Rutherford loosened the buttons around Mireille's neck and then gently withdrew her panties. Lady Rutherford's hands shook, her hair had come out of its chignon, and her upper lip was beaded with sweat.

'*Mon Dieu! Mon Dieu!*' Mireille screamed. '*Aides-moi! Mon Dieu! Aides-moi!*'

'I see the head,' Sarie said quietly. 'Push, Miss Mireille. Push hard. Come on, now – I've had kids myself. Push, push, *push* — '

With one long, final, animal howl, Mireille gave her last violent push, and the baby slithered out. 'It's a girl,' Lady Rutherford shouted triumphantly. 'A beautiful, perfect girl.'

Afterwards, when Mireille and her baby daughter were safely in bed, Dr Edelstein congratulated Lady Rutherford, Sarie and Lizzie. The birth had been exhilarating enough to make Lady Rutherford abandon all the usual conventions to the point where it seemed quite natural to be drinking champagne with her coloured servants. Her hair was still untidy, and her cheeks were scarlet; none of the servants had ever seen her in such an excited state. She raised her glass. 'To little Theresa,' she said passionately.

'I think, Lady Rutherford, we should drink a toast to you,' Dr Edelstein said gravely. 'To Lady Rutherford and the manner in which she conducted the emergency.'

Everyone agreed that there was absolutely no need for Mireille and the baby to go to the hospital. Sarie and Lizzie had given birth to fourteen children between them, and Sarie had been nanny to several newly born infants. Lady Rutherford was already breaking yet another rule – Sarie was going to sleep in Mireille's small sitting room.

Before leaving, Dr Edelstein went to examine Mireille. 'You're a brave girl,' he said. 'Is there anything I can do for you?'

'Yes, please,' Mireille whispered. 'Please telephone Max Blum.'

'Of course I will,' Dr Edelstein said soberly. 'I should have thought of that myself.'

That night anyone would have been forgiven for thinking that Lady Rutherford had been presented with an heir. All fourteen household servants and all the farm labourers joined together and celebrated. For about twenty minutes even the Rutherfords joined in. Then Lord Rutherford went to bed, and as usual his light was out by ten o'clock.

Lady Rutherford sat at her desk, trying to understand why she felt so elated. She also felt sad, which was confusing. After all, she told herself fiercely, nothing in the world was more commonplace than birth. Surely she could not be so stupid as to have regrets, now, when it was too late, that she had voluntarily renounced motherhood? Self-indulgent nonsense, she declared to herself. Undisciplined, illogical thinking was against her principles. Still, that baby girl was beautiful, miraculously beautiful. But to think of birth as a miracle was to believe that life itself was a miracle. Stuff and nonsense . . .

She left her desk, and went to bed. Towards dawn she awoke from a fitful sleep. Her first thought was that she had made a dreadful mistake; she ought not to have allowed the mother and child to stay at the Rutherford Estate. She corrected herself. She had not allowed, so much as encouraged, them to remain with her. Blithely, thoughtlessly, she had taken on this responsibility when she knew the servants were inclined to drink too much. What if anything went wrong? She sat up. She had permitted her emotions (emotions she had not known she possessed) to get the better of her. She was disgusted with herself.

The house, as usual at this hour, was silent, but the silence seemed ominous. She was being emotional again, she told herself scornfully. But she was unable to stop herself putting on her dressing gown, and going to Mireille's quarters, to make certain that everything was as it should be. She glanced at herself briefly in the mirror, gave an irrational exclamation, picked up her hairbrush and tidied her hair.

She made her way to Mireille's rooms. She half hoped the door would be closed, but it was open. The bed-side lamp had been left on. She stood at the threshold for a long moment, watching Mireille. She noted how long her hair had grown. The baby made some tiny movement, and in a rush of horror she realised that the room was far too silent. She moved at once to take a closer look at Mireille.

The girl was pale, deathly pale. There was a funny smell, too. Lady Rutherford sniffed. Suddenly she caught sight of the spreading red stain. Blood! The girl was bleeding – or had bled – to death. Then Lady Rutherford did what she had never done before. She screamed.

After that, all hell broke loose. Sarie awoke, Doctor Edelstein arrived in his pyjamas, and his diagnosis was immediate – post-partum haemorrhage. Before Lady Rutherford realised she was still in her nightgown, they were all in Dr Edelstein's car, speeding to the hospital.

At the hospital Lady Rutherford sat in the waiting room and wept silently. A nurse offered her tea, but she declined. The hospital seemed alive with sound, with movements. Doors opened and shut, bells buzzed, the phone rang, patients sighed and groaned.

Several hours later Dr Edelstein seated himself wearily beside her and said, 'We think she'll make it. We couldn't stop the bleeding. We had to do a total hysterectomy to save her life.'

Lady Rutherford said nothing; she could not trust herself to speak.

'The poor girl's lost her womb,' Dr Edelstein went on miserably. 'She'll never have more children — '

'Did you say she's not going to die?' Lady Rutherford interrupted.

'She's strong enough, and young enough to make a total recovery.'

'Then she's going to live,' Lady Rutherford said coldly. 'Nothing else counts.'

'Another hour like that and she would have died,' Dr Edelstein said authoritatively. 'Lady Rutherford, you saved her life!'

'Come now, Dr Edelstein. You operated, surely.'

'No, Lady Rutherford,' Dr Edelstein said, speaking very slowly. 'I do not exaggerate. You were almost too late as it was. If you — '

'Ifs and ands are pots and pans, Dr Edelstein,' Lady Rutherford said quickly and sternly. 'But I will have to be absolutely certain that she is entirely recovered before she leaves this hospital.'

Mireille was certain that the loss of a womb was a small price to pay for a perfect, healthy, beautiful girl. She called the baby Theresa after St Marie-Thérèse, the mother of Africa. She had sinned – she had murdered Theresa's twin, and the hysterectomy was her just punishment. She had feared that the baby might be born with a defective eye, like her father. But that she resembled Saffarty could not be doubted. Max thought so, too.

'But you must tell Saffarty,' Max said again.

'No.'

This row had continued over several days. Every time Max came to see her, in fact.

'But he's the father. He has the right to know the good news.'

'Bad news. You mean he has the right to know the bad news.' She fiddled with her blankets. 'I'm the mother,' she said carefully. 'I don't want any harm to come to my child. You understand that, don't you?' She did not wait for an answer, but sped on. 'Saffarty wouldn't see her as his child, he'd see her as his curse.'

'Mireille, please.'

'You know that's true, Max Blum,' Mireille burst out. 'So don't try to deny it. In all the world, only one person beside me

218

knows who her father is, and that person is you, Max Blum,' she said, beating her fists against the blankets. 'So help me, Max Blum, if you ever tell her who her father is, if you ever tell him who she is, even that he is a father, I'll kill you, I swear I will.'

'Why this Max Blum? What's wrong with Max? What's Max done to you?'

'It's important to me, Max. Nothing in the world is as important to me. Except, of course, that she keeps well and strong.' She looked at him searchingly. 'You are going to Johannesburg, Max. I owe you everything.' Her voice rose hysterically. 'I owe you my life. Without you – well, you know what I mean. I'll be grateful to you for ever. But — '

Max laid his hand on her hand. 'I swear I will keep your secret. No one will ever hear this from me.'

When the Abelmans remarked, as they often did, that Max was a changed man, they were not exaggerating. Everything about him had altered – from having learned English to learning how to swim. His body was muscular, his skin glowed, his tanned cheeks made his slate-grey eyes seem almost blue. The Abelmans looked at one another and smiled. 'He is blond, like an Adonis,' Eva said proudly. 'He's grown into a perfect specimen of a man.'

For a brief time after Max's aunt and uncle had taken him into their home the warmth of their welcome had, if not displaced, then softened the horror and pain of what he had done to Colette. But he had learned that guilt has a way of surfacing, at first slowly, later in floods.

I did not mean to do it – but I killed Colette . . . I am a murderer . . . It was with him always, at the edge of his brain, like a constant curse.

He hoped and prayed that, somehow, this move to Johannesburg would help him to forget . . .

He was moving permanently to Johannesburg, because his aunt and uncle had come to the conclusion that their new branch would do much better if it were in the hands of their nephew. 'It's not just because you're a relation,' Solomon had been at pains to point out. 'It's because you've proved how well qualified you are.'

The opportunity of proving his abilities had come about two

months earlier, when Max and his aunt and uncle had travelled to Johannesburg for a family wedding. The Abelmans had looked on their visit to Johannesburg as a way of doing several things at once. First they would inspect the Johannesburg branch of the Adderley Furniture Mart, then they would attend the wedding, and there was a good chance that Max would meet a suitable girl. Eva knew of several matches that had been made at wedding receptions. She had noticed how the combination of a party atmosphere and good will encouraged people to think of marriage.

The Abelmans were not wrong. Max met Fanny Golding.

The Abelmans spent more time visiting their relatives than they spent at the business. Max went to the store every day. Although he still felt insecure and inexperienced, a few small things had made him suspicious of the way in which the Johannesburg branch was being run.

Going over the most recent balance sheet Max found the low profit in relation to turnover puzzling. Furthermore the expenses appeared too high in relation to the turnover. And where were the receipts for these expenses? Further investigation revealed that wages had been paid for eight casual labourers, when only two such labourers could be accounted for. It was a clear case of fraud.

When his suspicions proved to be well founded, he gained not only his aunt's and uncle's gratitude, but their respect. Which was why, only six months after he had arrived in South Africa as an inexperienced newcomer, his aunt and uncle decided to make him the general manager of the Adderley Furniture Mart.

When Max had first arrived at Park Station, Johannesburg, Eva's cousin, Tilly Lazarus, and her husband were waiting for him.

All along the charcoal-grey station, with the exposed rails shining in the sun, were groups of people dressed in their best finery waiting to meet the train. The Lazaruses gave him a huge welcome and took him to their house, which they assured him would be his home. Once again Max found his emotions brimming over – the Lazaruses, instructed by Eva, had anticipated his every need. He was keen on swimming, so they arranged for him to become a member of the Wanderers Sports Club; he liked music, so they bought season tickets to the Johannesburg Symphony Orchestra.

He needed to meet more young people, so they threw several parties.

They did, however, fail to meet one of his needs. He wanted to pay for his board and lodging. 'Rent?' Tilly trilled, 'What rent? Don't insult us. Mervyn's room is empty. It'll be a pleasure to have it used again.'

Barney Lazarus owned his own factory, manufacturing floor and shoe polishes. Tilly had helped him in the beginning, but the house and the garden and the grandchildren and the servants now demanded all her attention. They lived a quiet family life, they said. They lived for their Friday nights and their Sundays, when all the family got together. They gave him the front door key, because 'a young man must be free to come and go', and he felt as at home with them as he had with the Abelmans.

But it was at the Adderley Furniture Mart that he felt more comfortable. The responsibility for controlling the stock, for the customers, for the staff, and the accounting drove all extraneous thoughts from his mind. He was only satisfied when every detail of every transaction was known to him.

Some of his customers bought on credit and the spectre of a bad debt was a constant source of anxiety to him. Gradually his new set of worries displaced his older worries. It seemed that putting a distance between himself and Mireille also helped to put a distance between himself and the past.

And then, of course, there was Fanny Golding.

Fanny with the lively brown eyes, the thick jet-black hair, and the quick mind. Fanny was secretary to the managing director of an insurance company. She liked her work and took it seriously. It was through Fanny that Max learned about loss of profit insurance in case of fire, a policy that not even Solomon Abelman had known about. And it was because of Fanny that he began to insist on his parents and his sister making the long journey to South Africa – the Abelmans had offered to pay. Neither of them could begin to understand why his parents were so resistant to the idea, though this brought them much closer. And Max (despite Fanny's constant hints) made no mention of marriage.

Which was hard for Fanny to understand. He kissed her and hugged her, and when they were out at the Bijou Cinema he always held her hand. He had never 'tried anything funny', which meant that he respected her, the same way his kissing, hugging, and hand-holding meant that he was fond of her.

Fanny and her parents were at a loss to understand Max's behaviour. After all, she had been 'going with him' for five months, and he still had not declared his intentions. When she came home from a date both her parents would be waiting for her, and the questioning, analysis and interpretation of Max's behaviour would begin. Far from resenting this, Fanny came to rely on it, for it took something away from the pain of not knowing how Max felt about her. She was fond of him; if he made her his wife she would adore him.

At nineteen Fanny was as shy, serious and dutiful a daughter as she was in all her relationships. It was considered only natural to want to marry and settle down; the fact that she confessed she was fond of Max did not signal any sort of departure from her usual reticence. There was nothing exceptional about her looks – she was young and slim and nubile – but any man who could not see that she would make a dedicated wife and devoted mother did not deserve to have her. What more could any man want? Besides, as all three agreed, she was spoiling her chances, missing opportunities to meet other young men.

Fanny was shy but she knew what she wanted. And she wanted Max. He was tall, and she enjoyed having to look up at him. His courtliness, his eager, secretive eyes, his fair hair and his glamorous French accent made him quite unlike any young man she had ever met before. He was still getting used to South Africa and the heat and the sandy suburban roads. After all, unlike her parents, who came from a *shetl*, a small village, Max was from Paris – an architectural paradise, he called it. Johannesburg was and would always be a mining town, he said, and nothing but a harsh and angular growth. It reminded him of a miner's helmet. Somehow this disdain of his set him apart and elevated him.

But Max would soon change, she was sure. He had already been in the country too long to escape its pull. Oh yes, Africa would not fail to get into his blood, and take mastery of it.

Thinking all these things as she sat on the edge of her mother's twin bed, Fanny's lips curved into a half-smile.

'Enjoy the film?' her mother asked.

'Not bad,' Fanny answered listlessly.

'We've come to a decision,' her mother said slowly.

'I'm going to talk to him!' her father burst out. 'Enough is enough, already.'

Fanny said nothing. She had wondered when they would do this.

'Something tells me something is holding him back,' her mother said firmly. 'He's making a living, he can support a wife. And you'll stay at your job until you're in the family way.'

'Your mother is right.'

'Max Blum is a frightened boy,' her mother said shaking her head sadly. 'Something terrible happened to him. It's like he's frightened of his past, of something in his past. He needs a wife – what that boy needs is a wife.'

'You are seeing Max tomorrow night, Fanny?'

'Yes, we're going to a concert.'

'He's fetching you?'

'Yes.'

'Well, concert or no concert, I'll talk to him when he comes — '

'But he's so looking forward to it. Stanislawki's playing Beethoven — '

'Your father is right, Fanella. He should have talked to Max a month ago.'

The following evening, when Max arrived to fetch Fanny, her father was waiting for him. 'Well, Max, so how's business?' her father asked genially enough.

'Can't complain, Mr Golding.'

'Good. Would you like a whisky?'

'No, thank you. The concert starts at — '

'I know about the concert, Max. But we must have a little talk,' Fanny's father said as he poured the whisky. 'She's a good girl, Fanny. She's very loyal, and a wonderful daughter — '

'I'm sure she is.'

'She'll make a wonderful wife. Just like her mother — ' Fanny's father broke off, and an uncomfortable silence invaded the room.

'I'm going to get to the point, Max. What are your intentions?'

'My intentions?' Max echoed.

'Towards my daughter.'

'I'm very fond of your daughter. I respect her — '

'That's not good enough,' Fanny's father snapped. 'Would you

223

like your daughter to be treated the way you're treating mine?' A mild man, Fanny's father seldom raised his voice. Now he shouted. 'What the hell's going on here?'

'I have been thinking of marrying Fanny,' Max began slowly. 'Only – only — '

'Only – what? What?'

'Only I didn't think,' Max said, improvising hastily, 'I didn't think she'd have me.'

'But, my boy, she'd be your wife tomorrow!' Fanny's father exclaimed, jumping up.

'Also, I don't think I can afford a wife. My parents. If we want to bring them out, I must support them.'

'We've got a small dowry for our daughter. It's not much; I haven't got my own business. But there's enough to help you with your expenses for your parents. I thought the Abelmans — '

'My aunt and uncle are more than willing to pay,' Max said stiffly. 'I'm not taking their charity.'

'Well, we'll work that out. Fanny's mother and I started with less than nothing.' Fanny's father got up to pour himself another whisky. 'You're turning me into a *shikkerer*, a drunkard, Max Blum.' He laughed. 'Have another.'

Max shook his head.

'I insist.' Fanny's father rarely took a drink. Now he drained the glass in one gulp. 'I'm going to call her,' he said, speaking quickly. 'I'm going to tell her you've asked me if you can marry her.'

'It will be an honour to be your son-in-law, Mr Golding.'

Fanny's father took one great leap towards Max and embraced him. 'Not Mr Golding; Poppa. Call me Poppa!' Half crying, he called out, 'Fanny, Esther, what are you doing? Bring the champagne from the ice-box!'

Blushing and trembling, with tears in her eyes, Fanny came in and stood beside Max. He took her hand and drew her closer, and brought his lips to hers. Fanny's mother kissed Max and then kissed Fanny; negotiations were over, and the engagement sealed.

The concert was forgotten, long-distance calls were placed to the Abelmans, and then all Fanny's relations – cousins, aunts and uncles – were telephoned. Fanny went to the kitchen and their Zulu maid, Lena, was told. Lena came in, clapped her hands, and half curtsied. 'I wish you luck, Master Max,' she beamed. 'Miss Fanny is a good girl. A good girl.'

They had forgotten in their joyous confusion to telephone the Lazaruses, with whom Max was living. Though it was late, just past nine o'clock – in Johannesburg most people went to bed early – the Lazaruses responded to the telephone call by getting up at once to go to the Goldings to proffer their congratulations – as they put it – in person. After all, Max had no close family of his own. At a time like this it was only right to let the boy have those who were almost his own rejoice with him.

Max believed he was doing the right thing. He did not delude himself that he had fallen in love, but then he had not expected to fall in love ever again. Through the eleven months of long, long nights he had come to the strange conclusion that he had both loved Colette and been in love with her.

Once his Uncle Solomon had told him, 'Not even God can change the past.' Now he managed to derive some comfort from it. Now, he told himself, he would have a new wife, and a new family, and a real new family meant a real new beginning.

Colette had loved him. He hoped she would have approved. She would have understood that he did not love Fanny. Beside an exotic, sophisticated Parisienne like Colette, Fanny was nothing. But as an ally Fanny would be as staunch as Colette had been.

He realised suddenly, and with deep gratitude, that Fanny's father had given him his greatest chance, not for happiness but for something greater; something that almost came close to peace.

In the eleven months since he had left Paris, he had not touched – nor even wanted to touch – a woman. With Fanny, his kissing and hand-holding had been partly affectionate, but mostly dutiful. He was without desire for Fanny because his desire had been lost in his guilt. It was not her fault. Realising this, he felt a sudden stirring of lust for his fiancée. Denying, and then obliterating his need for pleasure, had been one way of punishing himself – except that he would never be able to punish himself enough.

He was about to drift into sleep when he remembered Mireille. He must let her know that he was engaged to be married. He got up to write to her, but even as he did so, he knew he did not want her to come to his wedding.

. . . Please don't feel too bad if you are unable to come to my wedding. I am not sure when it will be, but I hardly think the beautiful little Theresa should be subjected to a journey of nearly a thousand miles . . .

Mireille read Max's letter carefully and was quick to take his hint. To set his mind at rest she replied immediately, saying how much she regreted that it would not be possible for her to be at his wedding. She had long sensed that something crucially important had been withheld from her. Her instincts warned her that it was in her best interests not to know what it was; this way no harm could come to anyone.

Theresa was now six months old. She gurgled and slept, and there was no doubt that the baby had transformed not only her mother's life, but also those of Lord and Lady Rutherford.

Though Mireille had regained her strength it had taken longer than she had expected. She took both a spiritual and a physical delight in her child; she adored Theresa's smell, and loving nothing better than holding the child's cheeks to her own. She regretted the loss of her womb because it had deprived her of the milk with which to breast-feed Theresa, but she was too grateful for Theresa to think of children that would never be born.

In many ways Lady Rutherford's way of life had changed even more profoundly than Mireille's. Previously, she had not only turned her back on all forms of organised religion, but actively despised what she called 'primitive ritualistic superstition'. Yet it was she who superintended all the arrangements for Theresa's christening in the large white Cathedral of the Cape. Further; after Mireille confessed that she was an unwed mother, Lady Rutherford went to the Registry of Births and bullied them into filling in forms, without the benefit of a death certificate, saying that Theresa's father was dead. Accordingly Theresa was registered as Marie-Theresa Emmeline Morou.

Lady Rutherford now took up the domestic arts she had found so loathsome. She smocked and embroidered dresses for Theresa and paid less and less attention to her charity committees. She frequently coaxed her husband away from his study to come and look at Theresa.

The household had never run so smoothly. Mireille had introduced French cooking to the kitchen, and it was taken for granted that she would no longer be expected to dine alone.

Lizzie, the cook, welcomed the opportunity to learn how to prepare *sole soufflée, navarin de mouton, coq au vin, pommes dauphinoise, champignons à greque*, and many other French dishes. Lord Rutherford no longer alarmed her. She got used to the dirty waistcoat he unfailingly wore to dinner, the way she got used to his fear of opening windows in the house (Lord Rutherford believed that fresh air, trapped indoors, trapped germs). Mireille's quarters, however, were in a separate wing, which meant the windows could be wide open, and so Lady Rutherford spent more and more of her time with her.

It was when a bacterial blight appeared that Mireille found herself dedicated to curing the vineyards. Lady Rutherford imported experts from France and Mireille followed their suggestions with a passion that bordered on fanaticism. She inspected every single cask herself, making sure that it was full, and so eliminated the development of a mould on the surface of the light wine.

She had learned to drive and was now able to go to Mass regularly. Lady Rutherford bought her a beautiful rosary made of real rubies. When Mireille read the note that accompanied the gift she wept. Lady Rutherford had written: For Mireille – the daughter I never had. May she always take care of my almost grand-daughter. E.

The flurry of activity that followed on Max's engagement extended as far as the small town of Lodz, Poland. His parents had finally agreed to emigrate to South Africa, and his wedding would therefore be a double celebration.

On July 1st, 1928, two weeks before the wedding, Max and Solomon and Eva were standing on the docks waiting.

Solomon was wringing his hands because it was drizzling and misty and dull, and he had hoped to welcome his sister in sunlight. All sorts of memories surfaced. He remembered the day after his sister's marriage, when she and her new husband had left Lithuania to settle in Poland. He remembered the day he had first heard of South Africa. News had reached Lodz that a Samuel Marks, who lived in Africa, had actually donated the unimaginably huge sum of five thousand *zlotys* for the restoration of a synagogue. He remembered his own voyage on the *Union Castle*, when the captain had graciously permitted the passengers the privilege of conforming to Jewish practices, which meant that they could slaughter as many sheep as they needed during their long passage. Tears came. He had not wanted to recall any of this. He wiped his eyes, and Max patted his shoulder, and Eva began to weep, too.

When at last they were all together again, their reunion was tearful yet restrained. Max's heart contracted as he saw how old and frail his parents looked; they were at least ten years younger than the Abelmans, but seemed twenty years older.

At the Abelmans' home a breakfast feast had been prepared of herrings and potatoes, and smoked salmon and cream cheese and bagels. When Max heard his father pronounce a blessing over the food he felt as if he had come home.

His parents spent a week in Cape Town, and then travelled to Johannesburg for the wedding. They would stay with the Lazaruses until their new flat was ready. Sol and Eva were paying for this flat, because they believed it was the least they could do. Max's parents met their future daughter-in-law and her parents, and because they were *landsleit* – compatriots who spoke Yiddish – they were like relatives; only their affluence was bewildering. 'All the same,' as Rachel Blum said to her sister-in-law, Eva, 'it is easier to get used to luxury than to poverty.'

More than a hundred guests came to the wedding. The ceremony took place in the great domed synagogue on Wolmarans Street, and, standing under the *chuppa* – the traditional wedding canopy – with both his parents beside him, Max believed that God had given him a second chance. The reception, a tea dance, was held at the Selbourne Hall, a small hall inside the City Hall building. The wedding put Fanny's father into debt, but he went gladly.

The wedding night showed Max how long he had deprived himself of sex, and how much he needed to make love. Fanny kissed him, but it was obvious that love-making was not something she expected – or thought she was expected – to enjoy. It was too soon to tell whether or not she would want to be taught, or even whether he would want to teach her.

Their honeymoon lasted only four days. After all, Max had already had time off to go down to Cape Town to meet his parents. They moved into their own small flat. Fanny continued to be a secretary, and at Adderley Furniture Mart the turnover increased steadily. Three months later, a day before Theresa's first birthday, Fanny told Max that she was pregnant.

It was then that Max said, for the first time, 'I love you Fanny.' And though Fanny held to her habitual reticence, the glow in her eyes told him that she knew he meant what he had said.

On Theresa's first birthday Mireille invited Eva Abelman to a small tea party. Remembering how chic Mireille had always looked, even when she was pregnant, Eva had carefully chosen to wear a navy and blue spotted silk dress. Eva rarely took time off from the Adderley Furniture Mart, and never went to tea parties, but she had accepted Mireille's invitation out of a mixture of curiosity and sympathy.

There was only one other guest, the Reverend Vincent, who had recently arrived from England to take up an appointment at St Mark's Mission. Lord and Lady Rutherford were there of course, and however hard Eva tried, her eyes returned again and again to Lord Rutherford's stained waistcoat. *Meshugge*, she murmured to herself, *meshugge* – crazy. Living with these people, it was no wonder Mireille looked the way she did.

She had let her brown hair grow long and wild, and it now glinted with golden flecks from so much time spent in the sun. She used no make-up at all. Her cream silk blouse had a soft bow at the throat, her beige trousers were decidedly masculine, and her tanned face gave her eyes a bright bronzed tint. Though she hardly conformed to Eva's notion of beauty, it was easy to tell how arrestingly she would stand out in a crowd.

It was obvious that Mireille adored her daughter; she seemed to swallow as Theresa swallowed, like a mother mouthing her child's lines in a school play. Eva was unusually silent, there was too much to take in. She had never been in such a large dining room – it reminded her of a school hall. The walls were covered in a deep ruby brocade and the chairs, tall as thrones, were upholstered in the same material. Though the windows were tightly shut the room was cool, probably, Eva thought, because of the marble hall. The table shone – there was no tablecloth, she noted with disgust – yet she had to admit that there was something beautiful about the way the highly polished wood reflected the china. Eva had a mirrored table-top in her own entrance hall but this, she decided, was much nicer. She thought

Lady Rutherford looked ill, but every time she turned to Theresa she was entirely altered by her smile. Lord Rutherford contributed little to the conversation. Apart from remarking that rodents were much misunderstood by society, he said nothing.

How could this young girl survive with people like this? How could any young girl stay sane? 'Have you made friends with young people, Mireille?' she asked gently.

'Oh, no, Mrs Abelman. I haven't really wanted to,' Mireille answered, smiling radiantly.

'You look so pretty, I thought you were going to tell me you'd met a nice young man,' Eva said coyly.

Lord Rutherford coughed.

'But I'm so happy and involved with Theresa and the farm,' Mireille said passionately.

'Your English is excellent, I must say,' Eva said.

'Mireille now speaks Afrikaans, too,' Lady Rutherford said proudly. 'I've been here for more than eleven years, and I can't speak a word.'

A waiter came in with glasses of champagne. Eva was just thinking – champagne at a tea-party? – when Lord Rutherford said, 'Mrs Abelman, we all want to drink a toast to you.' He coughed again. 'Without your intervention, Mireille and Theresa would not have been here to enrich all our lives.'

'Hear, hear,' Reverend Vincent called.

'I did nothing,' Eva said, embarrassed.

'I will never be able to thank you enough, and you will never know the depth of my gratitude to you, Mrs Abelman,' Mireille said quietly, though her voice shook with emotion. 'Without you, Mrs Abelman, I would not now be among the kindest people on earth. I give thanks to our Lord every single day. You restored my faith — ' She broke off for a moment. Tears streamed down her cheeks, but she continued bravely, 'I only hope I deserve such happiness as I have found here.'

'South Africa is God's own country,' Eva murmured.

'I brought Theresa into the world myself,' Lady Rutherford said proudly. 'I suppose you heard about that?'

Eva stayed longer than she had intended. She found, to her astonishment, that she could not easily remove herself from this company of these radiant people. Even Lord Rutherford – for all his dirty waistcoat – exuded calmness and serenity. There was something about this group, something almost sublime, Eva believed. For it had touched her too. She felt a profound contentment steal over her, and because she could not pull herself away, she stayed to watch Theresa being bathed.

Until Eva mentioned it, Mireille had not so much as noticed that she had no friends. She and Max wrote to one another intermittently, and there were young people among the coloured folk at the farm. She had helped the farm workers and the domestics to form their own choir and, much to everyone's amusement, was teaching them to sing 'Silent Night' in French, and 'God save our Gracious King' in English. This coming Christmas, the women and even the small girls would wear white lace veils, white dresses and white stockings and white *takis* or tennis shoes. The boys and the men would be an equal blaze of white. Now that she felt she belonged to the sea, the mountains and the vines, it seemed odd that she had been frightened by Rebecca. If she had known better, she would not have offended Rebecca by cleaning her own room. Shades of skin colour had been meaningless to her then, but that ignorance was well behind her now.

Yes, it was true that she had no friends, but, so far as Mireille could see, there was no hardship in that. She had never been less lonely in her life. She still thought of Saffarty, and often fantasised that the three of them – Saffarty, Theresa and she – were together . . . But there the fantasy stopped. Together, but where? Mireille could not contemplate living anywhere other than where she was now.

She thought, sometimes, that since she had lost her womb she had lost her sexuality. Whatever the reason, she had little sexual need of a man. Saffarty had been the only man in her life, and though she still dreamed of making love, it was always with him. She still remembered and cherished Madame Chandler's words – *remembered ecstasy is ecstasy*. Nor did she feel in the least deprived; instead, she felt blessed.

She loved all growing things; from the moment she heard that the huge, graceful oak trees had been grown from acorns planted 'for luck' by the early English settlers, she had become passionately interested in trees. Now she could even distinguish among the four types of yellow-woods. The Rutherfords had given her *carte blanche*, and she could now make as much of the Rutherford Estate as was suitable into a park of her own choosing.

Gradually she became a sort of unofficial assistant to the farm manager, and there was a tacit understanding that, when he left, the Rutherford Estate would be managed by a woman.

Most exciting of all, however, was her impending visit to France, where she was going to study at the Ecole du Vin. She had lost touch with Saffarty; she only hoped she would be strong enough to keep it that way.

Christmas came and went and then, before she knew it, it was March 1930, and her first-class passage was booked, her wardrobe prepared. She was ready to leave.

Two days before her departure Lady Rutherford fell ill. Mireille was with her when she collapsed with a heart attack. Mireille cancelled all her plans, and, although there was a roster of day and night nurses, was in constant attendance. Indeed the servants, and even Lord Rutherford, believed that she spent too much time with the sick woman and too little with Theresa.

Part Four

14

When Edwina left Paris and Saffarty to return to her parents, the church fête that was held annually in the grounds of her parents' home, Stanford Hall, was only five days away. Which, she concluded, was decidedly not the time to mention Saffarty to her parents. But no matter what they said or did, she was determined to marry him, on September 20th.

She had more or less planned a strategy. She was not going to show them a photograph of Saffarty, mainly because he looked so – well, so foreign. She would tell them that he had his own business; her father, a businessman himself, would not fail to be pleased about that. Of course her father was more of an industrialist than an ordinary businessman – his services to the carpet industry had earned him a knighthood. Still, he could not accuse Saffarty of opportunism; he had his own shop, and was obviously already doing very well. As for Saffarty's parents, there was little she could tell her parents about them. She realised he had rarely, if ever, mentioned his family.

Edwina's mother spoke reasonable French, her father none at all. Language was going to be a problem. She wondered how Saffarty was getting on with his English – she was certain he would have made great strides by now.

After the fête Edwina waited a further two days until the household had returned to normal. Then, over breakfast, she said, 'I've invited a friend to come and stay.'

'Lovely, darling,' her mother said at once. 'Do we know her?'

'I hardly think you do,' Edwina said, blushing. 'He's called Saffarty.'

'What sort of a name is that?' Sir William asked gruffly.

'He comes from Macedonia.'

'I see. He's Greek.'

'I don't know. He might have French nationality. He was born in Macedonia, though from his accent you would never guess it.'

'How long will he be staying, darling?' Lady Wyndham went on to answer her own question. 'A day or two, I suppose.'

'A month or more, I hope.'

'A *month*!' Sir William exploded.

'Don't you want to get to know your future son-in-law, Daddy?' Edwina said, blushing even more furiously.

'Son-in-law?' Sir William said incredulously. He turned to his wife. 'I told you no good would come of her time in Paris. I told you she'd get entangled with a foreigner.'

'William, do stop ranting, please!' Her unusually harsh voice shocked Sir William into doing as she said. Turning to Edwina, she said mildly, 'Do be fair, darling. You've taken us unawares. Now tell us everything you know about this young man of yours — ' Then, seeing the maid come in, she said, 'I think we'll adjourn to my sitting room.'

Once they were seated in her pale blue room, the only cosy room in the great house, Lady Wyndham said, somewhat reproachfully, 'You made no mention of this young man in your letters, darling.'

'I know that, mother,' Edwina said softly. 'I've never met anyone like him,' she began slowly. 'I suppose you'd like to know what he looks like?' Her parents nodded. 'He's tall, very tall, as tall as you, Daddy. He's got dark, thick, thick hair – he's olive skinned and not a sickly white. But, oh, mother! He is so handsome.' Her parents exchanged a glance. Now that this was over, she went on quickly, 'He's got his own business. As you would say, Daddy, he started from scratch, only eighteen months ago, and yet tourists from all over the world know about his shop!' She went on and she told them everything she thought they should know, including how they had met. When she had done, her parents exchanged another meaningful glance.

'How old is he?' Sir William asked.

Edwina blushed. 'I don't know,' she confessed. 'I never asked. Twenty-five or so?'

'I see,' Sir William said in a dangerously calm voice. 'You, Edwina, are only eighteen. Well, we'll talk about this again, I expect.'

'We can talk about it as often as you like, Daddy,' Edwina said, rising from her chair. 'But I am going to marry him.' Her voice dropped, almost as if she were thinking out loud. 'I think I'd die without him.' She paused for a moment, and then her voice rose. 'I will marry him – with or without your blessing. But I would much rather have your blessing, you know that. And, if you can only overcome your prejudice of foreigners, you will love him, too, Daddy!'

'You've always been a girl of some spirit, Edwina,' Sir William said thoughtfully. 'Just like your mother.'

Long before he reached La Fenêtre de Saffarty the acrid smell of a smouldering fire made him break into a run. Even as he ran, he relived – rather than remembered – that long-ago fire and the smell of it, as half of Salonika had burned to the ground. A crowd had gathered. With growing alarm, Saffarty pushed his way through. As he neared his shop, he saw that the area had been cordoned off. He was ignoring the barrier ribbon, when a gendarme stopped him. 'But he's one of the owners. He's the *patron* of La Fenêtre de Saffarty — ' someone shouted.

'Excuse me, Monsieur Saffarty,' the gendarme said. 'My condolences.'

'Let me though, please,' Saffarty answered.

'Of course, monsieur.'

Saffarty's entire building, as well as the two buildings on either side of it, had burned to the ground. An explosion of gas from the kitchen of the new restaurant being built next door to his shop had been responsible. 'You were lucky you were not living in the flat above your shop, monsieur,' the fireman continued. 'If you had been you would most certainly have been burned alive.'

One of his customers handed him a bottle of cognac. Dazed, Saffarty took a swig from it. Then, still clutching it, he stumbled into the charred ruin and found Madame Delange weeping silently. As soon as she saw Saffarty she broke into loud hysterical cries. He squatted down beside her, put his arms around and wept with her. Then he put the cognac bottle to her lips, and helped her to drink it.

'But he is so charming,' someone said. 'So kind.'

After a few moments he disentangled himself, and began once more to walk through the ruins, picking up charred bits of cloth and flinging them down again. People offered condolences, as if for a death, and though he responded politely he was too shocked to register who they were.

'He's shocked,' a woman said.

'Of course he's shocked,' said Colette who had just arrived. 'Wouldn't you be shocked? Come, Saffarty,' she said calmly. 'I'll take you home.'

At the *garçonnière* she made him a strong cup of coffee while he paced the room. From time to time, gesticulating wildly, he flung out curses and other phrases in Ladino, a language she had never heard before. She let him be, and made no attempt to stop him. Not a tear fell from his bright, wet eyes. 'I saw my own city burn, Colette!' The veins in his temple throbbed. 'I saw Salonika burn to the ground!'

'You've had a severe blow,' Colette said sadly. 'But you can make things worse, of course.'

'I can make things worse?'

'Nothing in life is so bad that it can't be made worse by how you take it.' She waited for that to sink in. Then, almost casually, she added, 'You are insured. Have you phoned your insurance company?'

As she had known it would, mention of the insurance company brought him to his senses. Wearily he got up off the floor and looked the number up in his diary. When he got through he explained, at first impatiently and then more calmly, who he was and what he wanted. Finally he was connected with the controller of his area.

Saffarty cut the controller's condolences short.

'Just one small moment, monsieur,' the controller said, 'while I check your file.'

'Certainly,' Saffarty answered.

'Excuse me, monsieur,' the controller said when he returned to the phone, 'there seems to be a small problem.'

'A small problem?' Saffarty echoed.

'Yes, monsieur. I regret to say so – but yes, there is a problem.'

'What is the problem?' Saffarty shouted.

'You did not renew your policy, monsieur. It is with regret that I must tell you that your policy lapsed. Monsieur, your policy expired.'

'I don't understand. Repeat what you have said — '

'You neglected to pay your premium. It should have been paid in April at the latest. It is now July. So, unfortunately, monsieur, your policy has expired. You are not covered by insurance. At least, not by our company.'

There was a long pause. Saffarty was speechless.

'Perhaps, monsieur, perhaps you are insured with another company?'

'No,' Saffarty said. 'No. I'm insured with you. Or I was insured with you.'

Shaking he turned to Colette. With icy calm he said, 'I forgot to renew my policy. My mind was on other things. So – I have only myself to blame, you see. I'll never forgive myself. Never!'

'I do see,' Colette answered calmly. 'I also see that it makes things worse.'

'I'm finished,' Saffarty exploded bitterly. 'I'm ruined. I've lost everything. If anyone in the world should have been extra vigilant about fire insurance it was me.' Almost spitting, he continued, 'For God's sake, Colette, I saw my own city burn to the ground!' Saffarty began to tear at his hair.

'Now listen to me, Saffarty, and listen well,' Colette said firmly. 'Be a man! Pull yourself together.' He stopped tearing his hair. 'Of course you had a blow. A severe blow. All I want to say to you again is this: nothing in life is so bad that it can't be made worse by how you take it. Didn't I make my own life worse? Didn't I?'

'Yes. *You* certainly did — '

'It's what we do with disaster that counts, Saffarty.'

'Oh my God, Edwina – what will I tell Edwina? I can't go to London now. That's out of the question.'

'You will go to London, and you will tell Edwina. And if Edwina can't take this, then she's not the girl for you — '

'I don't know how — '

Colette interrupted, 'If I know Edwina, and I believe I do, she will take it not only because she is the girl for you, but because you are the man for her!'

'I will phone her,' he said thoughtfully. 'I'll tell her what happened. Everything. Including the fire insurance.'

'She will not let you down.' Colette could not have made her own conviction more clear. 'Edwina would never let you down, any more than — '

'Any more than you would, Colette.'

'Telephone for you, Miss Edwina. A funny English – hard to understand,' Simpson, the butler, announced.

'Thank you, Simpson,' Edwina replied, going at once to the phone.

She listened carefully, and her face fell. 'You must come. Or else I will come to Paris.'

Then, sounding triumphant, she cried, 'I've told my parents all about you They know there's nothing they can do.'

Though the Banque Dumont had sold Saffarty out, he was not entirely penniless. Two hundred and fifty thousand francs remained. Almost nothing in terms of the profits he could have made, but much more than he had started out with.

'I will begin again,' he told Colette two days later. 'And do you know what? It will be easier, this time. And do you know why? Because I will not be alone. I will have a wife by my side!'

'That's better, Saffarty,' Colette exclaimed. 'Mark my words, you'll still be a millionaire. You can't keep a good man down.'

'Who knows?' he shrugged.

'I could help you, you know, Saffarty. Financially — '

'Thank you, Colette. But I'm not entirely destitute, and even if I was I'd never take charity.'

'It wouldn't be charity. But I've been waiting to tell you about something amazing that's happened. Read this, Saffarty, and tell me if you can believe it!' Her voice – something in the way she spoke – the excitement in her voice – made him snatch the letter from her. It was from the distinguished lawyer Maître Lambert, advising her that Monsieur Andrew Collingwood had bequeathed to her the sum of twenty thousand pounds sterling, which was approximately equivalent to five hundred thousand francs.

'Five hundred thousand francs!' Saffarty yelled. 'At your earliest convenience.'

'I received the money yesterday. The letter came on the day of the fire. I didn't open it. I was too upset. And then, when I read it, I wanted to be sure I wasn't going mad before I told you the news.'

'Who was Monsieur Andrew Collingwood?'

'An eighty-three-year-old Englishman. He never married. He liked the studded whip.'

'*Merde!*' Saffarty said.

'You're right, of course.' Colette leaned forward eagerly. 'You were sensitive enough not to try to reform me. Now I'm going to retire from the game completely.'

'That's the best news I've had in years,' Saffarty said. Suddenly, for the first time since the fire, he broke into that laugh of his. He snorted and chuckled, slapping his thighs. 'It took an eighty-three-year-old Englishman to reform you.'

'And five hundred thousand francs.'

'Why didn't I think of that?' Saffarty asked soberly.

'It never occurred to me either. In any case, I had enough. I didn't really need to work, you know.'

'*Merde!*' he said again.

'I would like to come to your wedding, Saffarty,' Colette said, as to the amazement of them both, she blushed. 'But if my presence would embarrass you, or if you are too ashamed — '

'Enough!' he burst out. 'Why should I be ashamed? I feel as if I've known you all my life.' He rubbed his eye. 'Edwina and I will be honoured to have you at our wedding. She's told her parents, you know.'

'You've told me that a thousand times.' Colette smiled. 'What about your parents, Saffarty? Have you told them?'

'No.'

'But you are going to tell them?'

'No.' He sighed. 'Later, perhaps.' He waved a hand dismissively, and Colette judged it wisest – for the moment – not to pry.

Though he was seventy-four, Sir William Wyndham's pride in his reputation as a tough, hard industrialist was undiminished. Indeed, more than one journalist had written of his lack of humanity. One had gone so far as to describe him as a carpet baron so intent on the modern desire for wealth and material progress that he would willingly smother all other traditional English values. Since Sir William believed that business was the backbone of the nation he was infuriated. However, both he and his wife managed to defuse that sort of comment with, as they put it, a 'traditional pinch of salt'. He was recognised as a keen negotiator, and as chairman of the Carpet Trades Association his skilful diplomacy with the Carpet Weavers Union had not only averted many a strike, but had also resulted in better wages and working conditions.

As far as he was concerned, Edwina had only entered the first round of negotiations. Like all experienced negotiators he knew that timing and information were vital. As of this moment, he knew nothing about the Greek in her life. Still, foreigner or not, Sir William would size him up. He had enough faith in his judgement of character to do that. He had not yet made an important mistake but there was always a first time. He would be – what was it these Frenchmen called it? – on the *qui vive*. Edwina was a girl of spirit, always had been, always would be.

It was not for nothing that Edwina was his daughter. She had learned a thing or two about negotiations herself. She therefore decided to make no mention of the disaster that had befallen Saffarty. But she had asked Saffarty to bring his insurance documents with him, for her father to see. He might even be able to help.

Saffarty was expected at Kidderminster station in about five hours. This Friday night, the night of Saffarty's arrival, there were no other guests. The Wyndhams still went in for fish on Friday nights, and their oyster suppers were famous. But it was late July, and, as there is no 'r' in July, they were dining on fresh lobster. They always ate in a dining room so vast it had two fireplaces, one at each end of the room. Lobster generally called for champagne. Tonight, however, the family drank more than usual, and there was much popping of corks and crunching of lobster.

Once or twice Edwina thought she heard the phone ring. 'Isn't that the phone?' she said.

'Edwina darling, your young man is on the train,' her mother said kindly.

'I'm sure it was the phone.'

'If it is the phone, it will be answered.'

But the phone had been ringing. Mrs Carson, concentrating on the soufflé they were expecting for their dessert, refused point blank to stop what she was doing. And then, when she completed her task, the ringing had stopped. 'People ought not to ring at meal times,' she clucked to herself. 'Sir William says it's not civilised; quite right.' And in any case the switchboard was far too complicated for her to manage. Simpson, the butler, was responsible for answering the telephone. But Simpson was in bed with a high fever. If she had remembered that while the phone was ringing, she would have made more of an effort to get to it sooner. She reminded herself to take Simpson his hot broth, or else she really would be in the soup. Mrs Carson smiled – getting into the soup over forgetting hot broth was her idea of a fine joke.

'I'm sorry, Mr Saffarty. There's still no reply from Sir William's residence,' the immigration officer said.

'But that's impossible!' Saffarty protested loudly. 'I can't understand it.'

'Nor can I.' The officer stood up. 'I'm afraid you'll have to come with me.'

Saffarty had no option but to comply. His difficulties had begun while, still on the ferry, he was going through the passport procedures. Speaking perfect French, the immigration officer had asked, 'How long will you be in England, sir?'

'One month.'

'I see. And how much money do you have with you?'

'Two hundred pounds.'

'May I see your wallet, sir?'

'Certainly.'

The officer searched his wallet carefully. He checked again. 'I'm sorry, sir. There does not appear to be any English money in this wallet at all.'

'Give it to me. There's two hundred pounds there,' Saffarty demanded. He snatched the wallet, and searched frantically. 'I've been robbed,' he shouted. 'Robbed!'

'Pick-pockets, I suppose,' the officer said sarcastically.

'I tell you I've been robbed.'

'Perhaps you put it somewhere else. In a pocket?'

'I know where I keep my money.'

'I'm sorry, sir, but we cannot permit your entry into this country for one month with no funds,' the officer said, tapping his teeth with his pen. 'Where were you intending to stay?'

'I have the address. It's in the wallet. Or it was in the wallet.' Once more Saffarty rifled his wallet. 'Here it is.' He handed over the Wyndhams' address. 'How could this have happened to me?'

'Sir William Wyndham. Good, I'll telephone him,' the officer said, sounding doubtful.

By that time it was seven o'clock and they were already in port. The officer led Saffarty to his office and attempted to telephone Sir William. 'I'm sorry, sir, but I cannot allow you into the country until I have spoken to Sir William. I'm afraid you'll have to spend the night with us. But there is no cause for alarm. When we've made contact with Sir William, you will be put on the train.'

He conducted Saffarty to a small room where several sailors in blue pullovers were playing cards. They tried to speak to him, but their Bradford accents were beyond him. Finally, when they offered him some food, he was able to make out the word 'sandwich'. So it was there, while he was in detention, that Saffarty had his second taste of English bread. And the bread was as soggy as it had been in Salonika. The sandwich was large, the bread was fresh, and it was filled with a slice of ham. Saffarty bit into it, and then opened it. One half of the ham was meat, the other white fat. Young, hungry and angry though he was he could not bring himself to swallow the slice of gleaming white fat. It was a little more than four years since he had first tasted pork, and renounced his faith, but it seemed a lifetime away. That this fatty meat had no religious connotations did not make it any the more appetising.

He could have wept. '*Be a man, Saffarty!*' Colette had said. The night was miserable and long and, Saffarty was convinced, inauspicious, most inauspicious.

Early the next morning, at about six o'clock, Saffarty overheard the immigration officer talking to Sir William. He found to his astonishment that he could understand every single word. Colette's English lesson . . . In less than twenty minutes he would be on the train, and in four hours he would be with Edwina. Nothing else mattered.

However much Sir William believed that business was the backbone of the nation, and however much he believed in the stiff upper lip, his strong beliefs had not turned him into a rigid unbending personality. When Saffarty did not turn up he and his wife did not leave Edwina to do her worrying alone. Instead, they shared her anxiety. Throughout the long night they waited with her for news, waited until seven o'clock the following morning.

They waited in the huge library Sir William was so proud of. The carpet, the curtains and all the chairs, and even the wall-length sofa, were all in a matching cobalt-blue velvet. The massive floor-to-ceiling bookshelves and the scent of cigars gave the room an atmosphere of calm and strength. From time to time they heard the click of Lady Wyndham fiddling with her pearls.

Edwina's dreadful anxiety for Saffarty had made her tell her parents much more about him than she had before. She told them about his laugh, gave more details of the way they had met, and about La Fenêtre de Saffarty, and finally discussed the disastrous fire and the lapsed insurance policy. Her parents reacted with immediate sympathy to Saffarty's disaster – twenty years earlier, the mill of one of Sir William's competitors had been destroyed by fire. Four hundred people had been laid off.

Sir William was particularly pleased to hear that Saffarty had a diploma from a commercial school, for he too had studied book-keeping when he was at King Charles I Grammar School. Her father's reminiscences about his beginnings helped the night to pass. Although Edwina had always known her father had founded Wyndham Carpets, she had not known that he had once been an employee. 'What did you think I did before I started the business?' her father asked. 'How do you think I got my training?' He did not wait for an answer, but went on, 'I had two jobs before I worked for myself. First, I was a stock clerk at Wells Carpet Factory, and then I got a job in the design department of Stainforths. Then I became a commission agent selling worsted yarns. Didn't need much capital, you see. Eventually, I accumulated enough capital to buy some second-hand machinery. But I wouldn't have risked it if I hadn't met Peter Bentwick.'

'Peter Bentwick?' Edwina repeated.

'Can't think why I've never told you about him. We were partners, you know, for nearly four years, until he vanished somewhere in Australia with his Australian wife. That was my worst time, I think. Bentwick was a loom engineer, you see.'

'One door closes, and another opens,' Edwina's mother said. 'Because that was when your father got hold of that vital patent.'

Edwina knew the story well, she'd heard it again and again, yet she listened as if she were hearing it for the first time. In some ways, it reminded her of Saffarty's beginnings. He had mentioned having had a partner.

'The patent for a new manufacturing process was developed

in America,' her mother continued dreamily. 'It was a machine that could make carpets – until then it took three people an entire working day to produce one and a half yards of Axminster carpet. The new power loom could process twenty to twenty-five yards of twenty-seven-inch carpet in a single day.'

'What happened to Peter Bentwick?' Edwina asked.

'I bought him out,' her father answered scornfully. 'His worst move was my best move. Soon after I bought him out, I bought Stanford Hall.' He looked around his beloved library. 'Stanford Hall must never be sold. Reggie Chilton must be turning in his grave. Chilton Manor is about to become a housing estate!'

When Neville, one of the footmen, came into the library to open the curtains, he was amazed to discover the Wyndham family had not gone to bed. 'Excuse me, sir, madam,' he said, retreating hurriedly.

'Neville, is Cook in the kitchen yet?' Lady Wyndham asked authoritatively.

'I believe so, m'lady.'

'Ask her to prepare breakfast now.'

It was while they were breakfasting on kipper and eggs that Sir William was called to the telephone. He returned to the dining room, told them what had happened to Saffarty, and concluded, 'Now, my dear Edwina. I will go to bed, and you, if you take my advice, will follow suit. Peele will drive you to the station at noon. I'll leave word for him to take the sports Rolls. I have the feeling your young man might like that.'

The following two months, during that unusually perfect summer of 1928, passed in a haze of glory for Saffarty. Edwina grew lovelier each day, and it truly was the case that every day 'she was more beautiful, and today she looked like tomorrow'. Sir William and Lady Wyndham experienced their own sense of glory, too. Sir William had immediately recognised Saffarty's business acumen – he liked to say that he had cottoned on to it before he and Saffarty had even met.

Two days after Saffarty had arrived, Sir William had shown him over the plant. He watched and appraised Saffarty's reactions, and knew at once that – in spite of Saffarty's lack of fluency with the English language – this was a young man who had been born with the instincts of a true entrepreneur. Saffarty's comments revealed both his innovative and administrative qualities. He showed Saffarty every aspect of the plant, from the dyeing of the yarn to the finished carpets in the showroom. Then, while they were having a quiet drink in Sir William's simple office, Saffarty – with rapid, frequent references to his dictionary – came out with suggestions for a few startling obvious improvements.

It would take only two mirrors, each one placed at an angle to the other, at the edge of a roll of carpeting, Saffarty explained, and then the reflection would give the customer a more accurate view of what the carpet, laid edge to edge, would look like. Sir William was so excited that he ordered two mirrors to be taken off the walls – so that Saffarty could demonstrate what he meant. 'It's a sea of carpeting!' Sir William exclaimed. 'The customer will get the effect wonderfully well.'

After that, Saffarty turned to the looms, and made a quick sketch to prove how much space was being wasted. Sir William liked the manner in which Saffarty made his suggestions as much as the suggestions themselves. It was clear that Saffarty could not help being fascinated by the mill, and that his spontaneous suggestions sprang from his spontaneous interest. Later that night, Sir William wondered if without his difficulty with English he would have seemed quite so modest. He thrust his reservations aside. What difference did it make? The young man was a born negotiator.

The next day, as if by unspoken agreement, Saffarty accompanied him to the mill again, and so it continued till the end of the week. Edwina and her mother accepted this routine, as if it had not been unexpected.

Until then Saffarty had never been in anything remotely resembling a real factory or mill. He quickly realised that those small establishments in Paris that called themselves factories were no more than glorified workrooms. Here at Wyndham Carpets the low but forbidding red-brick sheds, covering an area of twenty acres, reminded him of a series of giant tents. He consulted his ever-present dictionary and discovered that mill, plant and factory all meant the same thing. For Saffarty the entire process of turning raw greasy wool into carpeting was as exciting as the extraction of pure gold from the bowels of the earth.

But the distinctive smell of the piles of carpets – clean and cosy in his nostrils – gave out a peculiar element of unexpected sensuousness that was never to leave him. He could not quite identify the smell. Partly like newly cut hay, and partly like pencil shavings, it was predominantly the smell of luxury.

A huge staircase led from the main hall to the wing Saffarty was staying in. When he was first shown to his rooms, he thought he was being conducted to the third floor, the ceilings were so high. Saffarty remembered that the converted château they had stayed in had reminded Edwina of her parents' home. Stanford Hall was at least a hundred times larger than he had expected. The huge stone building with battlements was more like a castle than a mansion; in fact, his parents' house in Salonika could have fitted into the library with room to spare. But for several cleverly placed yellow awnings, the cold stone walls of the place would have been forbidding. He knew nothing of the elegance or the splendour of English country living, and so he did not know how rare the warmth and friendly atmosphere was. The house was always filled with flowers – Lady Wyndham's passion for roses was such that she and her five gardeners had succeeded in growing a new rose, now called the Wyndham rose.

Saffarty and Edwina maintained their celibate lives for four days. On the fourth day after Saffarty's arrival, Edwina decided to break their celibacy, and to visit Saffarty in his wing. If her parents, or the servants, knew what was going on, they turned a blind eye.

Two weeks later Sir William invited Saffarty to join him for a drink in his library. 'You're Greek Orthodox, are you?' he asked bluntly.

'I'm afraid I lost my faith, sir,' Saffarty answered ambiguously.

'I see.' Sir William paused for a moment, and said, 'We're going to church tomorrow. We rather hoped you would join us.'

'It would be a privilege, sir.'

'I'm not a man who likes to beat about the bush — '

'Excuse me?'

'Your English has improved so much that I forget the idiom is unknown to you,' Sir William said, smiling. 'What I mean is this – I'd like to get to the point. My daughter tells me you wish to marry her. But can you afford to keep her?'

'I made some bad investments,' Saffarty said, deciding to be absolutely frank. 'And we've discussed my negligence over the insurance policy. My entire capital is two hundred and fifty thousand francs, which is ten thousand pounds.'

'Ten thousand pounds,' Sir William chimed with him. 'Well, I think we could find a place for you at Wyndham Carpets.'

'Sir, I — '

'Don't interrupt until you've heard me out,' Sir William said fiercely. 'I know how you feel about being an employee; Edwina told me. They're my sentiments exactly.' He made a sweeping gesture. 'Edwina will inherit all this one day. Let's see how you get on with a boss. Give it one year and if it works out we'll come to some arrangement about an interest in the company for you. Are you ready to agree to that?'

'Sir, I'd like to talk to Edwina.'

'I thought you'd say that; I've talked to her myself. She thinks it's a smashing idea.' The old man suddenly looked his age. 'You've been honest with me, so I'll repay the compliment by being honest with you. My administrative department is not all I would wish it to be. Wyndham Carpets could do with some fresh, new blood. And, by God, I believe foreign blood is just what we need!'

'It is an honour to hear you speak like this, sir,' Saffarty said slowly.

'I speak not only as a father, but also as a businessman,' Sir William said gruffly. 'It won't be easy for you, Saffarty. Of course you'll always be a foreigner. And, round these parts, people are always suspicious of foreigners.'

It was clear that once the Wyndhams had consented to a foreign son-in-law, they would make even more effort to welcome him into their family than if he had been an Englishman. Saffarty decided to change his name to the way they pronounced it: Saffity. It was *much* more English. When he told them that his father's health would prevent both his parents from attending the wedding they were touchingly sympathetic. Naturally they were delighted that his parents would be represented by his French godmother, Colette Terblanche.

He showed no surprise the day his future father-in-law informed him that Father Rawlins expected him at confession as part of the marital instruction. Secure in the secrecy of the confessional, he said merely, 'I confess to nothing.' His marriage preparations therefore proceeded as planned.

As the wedding day drew nearer, Saffity found it more and more impossible each night to stay asleep. One early summer's morning he decided on a brisk walk through the estate.

As he drew close to the point where the lawns met the woodland the sound of a voice calling out, 'Fetch! Good boy, Tara, good boy!' made him stop in his tracks. There was a light mist. For a moment all was silent, then the dawn chorus of the birds was heard again. He made his way rapidly towards the same sound, 'Good boy! Good boy!' and saw at once that it was Myles Beecham, the Wyndhams' land agent who managed the estate. He lived on the Wyndhams' land, on what was called the home farm, in Swallow Grange, an ancient timber-framed farmhouse a good half-hour's walk from Stanford Hall. A thick-set, stocky man of about thirty-five with a slow smile and a pronounced limp, Myles was held in great affection by the Wyndham family. If it were not for a leg that had been badly fractured during the war he would have become a pilot. But he was the sort of man who could make a virtue out of a necessity, and so he went on to agricultural college, and became a dedicated professional land agent.

As Saffity started towards them, the dog gave a baying bark. At a sharp command from Myles, the dog fell silent at once.

'What a magnificent animal,' Saffity exclaimed. 'He's enormous.'

'Tara is an Irish wolfhound.'

'Ah – a wolf. I couldn't remember the English word for *loup*,' Saffity said with disarming candour.

'They say that wolfhounds are gentle as only giants can be and they are quite right,' Myles remarked. 'Here, watch this.' He turned to the dog. 'Tara! Fetch!' he commanded.

Tara bounded away, and to Saffity's great astonishment, set about digging a hole in the soft earth with great speed, until he retrieved the ball that had been buried there.

'How did Tara know the ball was there?'

'Let me tell you about Irish wolfhounds — ' Myles began.

Saffity listened attentively. He had never even come close to owning a dog.

Suddenly Saffity wanted a dog of his own, wanted one very, very much.

'Sir William's expecting me to breakfast. We've one or two things to discuss,' Myles said, sounding quietly pleased. 'I'll see you later.'

Two months later, on September 20th, 1928, Saffity and Edwina were married in the chapel at Stanford Hall. The reception also took place in Stanford Hall. Doors cunningly slotted into the panelling of the ballroom led into the dining room, where the same principle applied, except that the doors were fitted into the bookshelves. Once these doors were opened, the rooms were at least three times as large as a tennis court. There was more than enough space for the five hundred guests – many of whom were customers and business associates – and a full-scale orchestra.

Since everyone, including Edwina, seemed to take Saffity's altered name as a matter of course, he judged it wisest to do the same. In any case, he had always heard tell of the way names of immigrants were changed to fit in with their new country.

The notices in *The Times*, and the wedding invitations, all went out in the name of Saffity. He never would have accepted being called by his first name. He was still called Saffity, that was the important thing.

Edwina's satin wedding dress, with a scalloped hem, shorter at the knee, and gradually descending into a sweeping ermine-trimmed train, was considered by the guests if not by *Tatler* to be somewhat daring.

Tatler's description of the costume was euphoric. 'Made by Hartnell, it was a waterfall of shimmering jewelled satin . . . '

Colette was the bridegroom's sole guest, and if she recognised any of her former clients among the others, she gave no sign. Dressed entirely by Chanel, in beige wool trousers and jacket, a matching beige cloche with a delicate veil, a fox fur and pearls, she was according to *Tatler*, 'elegant, distinguished, and incontestibly French . . . '

Saffity and Edwina honeymooned at the Savoy. He barely knew London, and so they went to the theatre, and to Harrods, and to the Albert Hall. They were there for ten days, during which time he also visited several of Wyndham's largest customers. Every one of them gave him a substantial order. He was filled with exciting ideas for new designs.

It was tremendously fulfilling for Edwina to be not only Saffity's bride but his guide. His hunger for knowledge about London was as insatiable as it was informed, and it was for this reason that she left dining at the exclusive Café Royal, and a visit to Speakers' Corner to the last. Speakers' Corner would give him a close view of British democracy at work.

That Saturday night Saffity had chosen what she would wear and

251

later, standing before the full-length mirror in the cloakroom at the Café Royal, she readily admitted that he had been right – her black sequin coat cut like a man's dinner jacket was perfect. She returned to their table, and he rose at once and kissed her hand. He loved her boyish, shingled hairstyle, and the way she carried her long cigarette holder.

Suddenly, he heard her catch her breath. 'I can't believe my eyes. Look at that woman two tables away from us.'

Saffity turned and stared. The woman was wearing a black tulle dress decorated with puffs of beige feathers, and was cutting the feathers from the dress as calmly as if she were removing a cigarette from its holder.

'Why is she doing it?' Edwina whispered.

'Because a small, plump woman is wearing the same dress.'

'Where do you suppose she got the scissors?'

'From the waiter. He's placing the feathers on a tray.'

He was glancing absently at the waiter when something vaguely familiar made him study the man more closely. It was Samuel Touro! What was he doing in London? The last time Saffity had seen him was when he was taking his brother Aaron back to Marseilles, after that first fateful night they had arrived in Paris and eaten non-kosher food. He felt a mixture of discomfort and scorn – he did not wish for a confrontation with his past, and was contemptuous of Samuel Touro for being only a waiter.

But there was a new electricity in the atmosphere – the Prince of Wales and a group of his friends were being shown to the first banquette table on the right of the dance floor. As soon as the royal party was seated, Samuel Touro was in attendance.

'Oh, darling, must we go?' Edwina asked. 'The Prince of Wales — '

'I'd rather make love to my bride than look at him — '

'You are so — '

'Latin,' he said in unison with her – it was one of their private jokes.

At Speakers' Corner the next morning, Saffity succeeded in putting Samuel Touro from his mind. For even now, in 1928, the tradition of free speech continued. Listening to messages of political, social or religious salutation was like being at a carnival. Saffity and Edwina moved from one stand to another. A leaflet was thrust into his hands. He read it automatically and then, unconsciously mouthing the words, read it again. His lips tightened, his face whitened, and he began to crumple the paper.

'Let me read it,' Edwina said, taking the leaflet from him.

'It is well established, in spite of many shameful denials, that Jews practise the ritual murder of Christians in order to obtain fresh blood to mix in their ceremonial Passover bread.' Edwina skipped the next few paragraphs, and quickly read that, 'The writer of the leaflet, Arnold Leese, had been compelled to retire from practising as a veterinary surgeon because of the Jew method of kosher-killing . . . '

'This kosher-killing sounds pretty cruel to me,' Edwina said dismissively.

He snatched the leaflet from her hands and once again crumpled it.

He was no longer a Jew, but the leaflet frightened him even so. It made him feel as vulnerable as a child; even worse, it made him feel his true age, nineteen. Edwina believed he was twenty-two.

The very next day, when they returned to Kidderminster, Saffity decided to apply for British citizenship. When he received his new passport, his stated official age was twenty-two.

15

Although Max continued to fight shy of gambling after the tragic consequences of Longchamps, it was not possible to keep clear of risk. If he wanted to make a success as Branch Manager of the Adderley Furniture Mart, Johannesburg, he was compelled to risk extending credit to his customers. Max believed that the new hire purchase system was the surest way to attract new customers. His entire system of credit control was based on his own subjective judgement of whether or not he trusted the customer's honesty. If a customer delayed paying, he and Fanny would lie awake all night debating the merits and de-merits of the reasoning that had prompted Max to extend the credit in the first place. Again and again Fanny would reassure him that most people were honest and preferred to pay for the suite of furniture they had bought.

He took the risks, and paid for them with his digestive system. Both the profits and the turnover were higher than the Abelmans' most optimistic expectations. The only person who was not surprised was Fanny. Of course Max kept a rigid eye on the expenses; night after night he brought the invoices and accounts home to check through them with Fanny. He taught her to call out 'ninetaai' or 'sixtaai', instead of 'ninety' or 'sixty' – he wanted to be certain that he was not confusing 'ninety' with 'nineteen', or 'sixty' with 'sixteen'.

Sometimes, while in the midst of his calculations, he would remember Saffity's amazing agility with figures. Here he was in Africa, working with pounds, shillings and pence – British money – when it was Saffity and not he who had wanted to go to England. But his aunt had been right – this *was* a part of England.

His dedication to economy made him frugal and Fanny was his able and devoted assistant. Gradually, as his anxiety made his dependence on her more and more apparent, she became less and less reticent about expressing her point of view. It was while she was watching him split open three sides of a used envelope so that it could be used again that she said for the first time, 'It's not as if you're getting a share of the profits, Max. You're still only on a salary.'

The Abelmans gave me my chance. I'm honour bound to do the best for them,' Max answered fiercely.

When Doreen, the woman who worked as typist, telephonist, and sometimes even saleswoman, handed in her notice, it seemed only right for Fanny to resign from her own secretarial job and work for Max at a nominal salary.

The Abelmans gave him a free hand. 'I've got the utmost confidence in you,' his uncle said, never knowing that it was just this kind of statement that tied Max's stomach up in knots. What if he should fail his uncle? Fanny encouraged him to take advertisements in the local press. 'But the expense, Fanny. Think of the expense,' he moaned.

'It takes money to make money,' she replied implacably.

At lunchtimes Fanny would put on a hat and she and her mother, pretending to be ordinary housewives, would scour the competition. One day she discovered that L. David & Co. were selling nine- by twelve-foot Axminsters at twenty per cent less than Max. 'It's better than good value,' Mr David told her. 'It's the best value in Johannesburg. Why? Because who else but L. David would spend either the time or the money to take the boat and go halfway across the world to England to buy his carpets?'

That night, after a lengthy debate, Max and Fanny came to the conclusion that L. David must be buying more cheaply than Max. There was a handsome profit in carpeting as it was, but if Max could buy right, the profits would increase . . . The birth of the baby was imminent – Fanny would simply have to take some time off soon. They had already decided that the baby would come to work with her.

Like everything she did, Fanny gave birth to their son, Jeffrey, with a minimum of fuss. Two weeks later she and Jeffrey and the black nanny, Agnes, were at the Adderley Furniture Mart. That very day she said fiercely, 'You will have your own business, Max. You will be your own boss.'

'Don't talk like that, Fanny. It's disloyal to the Abelmans.'

'My first loyalty is to Jeff Blum. To your son. We must have a business for him.'

'And what will we do for capital?'

'We will make a plan,' Fanny said firmly. 'I already know what sort of business it will be.'

'Could you let me in on the secret?' Max asked sarcastically.

'The carpet business. When the Abelmans were here for Jeff's birth, I talked to them. Why do you think they're sending you to England on a buying trip?'

'So it's your fault,' Max said angrily. 'Have you thought of the responsibility of spending twenty thousand pounds? What if I buy dud lines? What if they don't sell?'

'You will not buy dud lines not only because you have very good taste, but because you know the market,' Fanny said fervently. 'Also, let me remind you once more that you are making the Abelmans, who are already very rich, much richer. And they know it!'

Fanny had hoped that the Abelmans would offer some material recognition to the new status and responsibilities that fatherhood had conferred on Max. After all, he had proved himself by behaving exactly as if he had a financial interest in their company. They had been astute enough to increase his salary even before the baby was born, and when it was known that Fanny was going to continue to help Max in the store they put her salary on a more business-like basis. The company was growing at the same rapid rate as Johannesburg.

It was already six years since Johannesburg had become the largest town in South Africa and the largest mining town in the whole world. Indeed in 1928, only the year before Jeff was born, Johannesburg had been officially proclaimed a city, with a population of almost four hundred thousand. Business was thriving and two new stores, Greatermans and the OK Bazaars, had opened that year. Adderley Furniture Mart now advertised the 'complete home furnishing scheme, from a lounge suite to a dustbin, at an inclusive price'. Johannesburg even had a traffic problem, and the great American pioneer, I. W. Schlesinger, presented the town with its first traffic light. When Fanny discovered that the OK Bazaars – only two years after it had opened its doors, it was already a legend – had been founded by a fiddler and a barber, it seemed a crying shame that Max still worked for a boss.

She kept up a relentless campaign to get Max his own business. Blocks of flats were going up all over the place, and several new suburbs were opening up. The famous Sir Arthur Conan Doyle toured the city and pronounced the new suburbs to be among the finest he had ever seen. Fanny watched the progress of Johannesburg with both eyes firmly fixed on the potential for home furnishing. Rumour had it that a thirteen-storey office building was about to be constructed. Several new office blocks had already been built, and when Fanny saw them she saw nothing but their potential for carpeting.

The news of the depression in America and in Europe was only news – Johannesburg, in 1930, was too distant to feel the full effect of such economic disaster. But in February of 1930, the depression suddenly became very relevant to Fanny. She had a hunch that the carpet factories must be looking for new customers, for they were experiencing difficulty in off-loading their stock. Max could therefore drive a hard bargain. It was not for nothing that Fanny was now reading the financial pages. It was in those pages that she learned about the British Commercial Attaché. She called on him, and that night she presented Max with a list of the most important carpet manufacturers in England, in a town called Kidderminster.

'Fanny has turned into a businesswoman,' Max said proudly to Mireille. 'She used to be so shy.'

'I know,' Mireille said. 'It's amazing how people change. Believe it or not, Max, but I've become very interested in the business side of the Rutherford Estate.'

Max was in Cape Town because he was about to board the *Warwick Castle* for England. It was April 1930, and he had not seen Mireille for six months. He had to admit that she had grown very beautiful. Her face was even more freckled now, and the sun had streaked her hair with gold. Still, if it was true that there were no men in her life, she scarcely seemed to be the worse off for it. She had learned to ride a horse, and all that riding through the farm had done wonders for her shape. These days she dressed in jodhpurs, and they suited her. She looked – and was – the essence of all that a fulfilled young woman should be.

Lady Rutherford was still bedridden, and Mireille still tended her with the same religious devotion; and it was this that gave her that expression of almost saintly serenity.

'Lady Rutherford made the great leap of faith,' Mireille said quietly. 'She is now a Catholic.'

'I see,' Max said.

'I don't think you do,' she said gently. 'You see, Max, her faith is what helps her stay alive.'

'I think *you* are what keeps her alive. What about your own life?'

'My life is more beautiful than you could possibly imagine.' She looked towards Table Mountain. 'Do you remember the day you helped me down the mountain?' she asked, and went on without waiting for a reply. 'That was the day I told you I'd found out where the Abelmans lived. I owe so much to you, Max, and to your relations.'

Theresa's coloured nanny, Sarie, brought the laughing child to join them. At eighteen months, Theresa's resemblance to Saffarty was so startling that it made Max jump. Her velvet, amber eyes were exactly the same as his. Even the intelligent, amused expression was the same. The child's laugh seemed as full-hearted as her father's.

'Yes, she does look like him,' Mireille said calmly.

'I've never seen a child resemble her father quite as much as Theresa.' Now Max looked away from Mireille toward Table Mountain. 'Yes, I remember that day on the mountain,' he said sadly. 'I remember many things.'

A silence fell between them. Even Theresa was quiet. It was not an uncomfortable silence but a measure of the deep, almost timeless bond between Max and Mireille, and a reflection of the terrible circumstances that had brought them together.

After a while, Max said, 'You should tell him. It's not right.'

'Don't you dare talk to me about right and wrong, Max Blum,' Mireille said passionately. 'He won't want her! Just imagine how Theresa would feel if she knew she had a father who had tried to murder her.'

'But Saffarty is — '

'Don't you dare mention his name to me, or to anyone else ever again,' Mireille said savagely. 'Listen to me, Max Blum. You have your secrets, and I have mine. We'll be good friends for ever, you and I, because each of us will keep the other's secret. I'll never let you down, and you will never let me down — '

'Mireille — ' Max began.

'No – let me go on, Max,' she continued fiercely. 'It's true that I have everything I could ever need. But it's also true that I need you, Max.' Her voice dropped to a whisper. 'You are my only link with . . . you are a part of me, Max. You swore you would never tell him. You are a father now yourself.' Now her voice rose from

258

a whisper to the high pitch of hysteria. 'I want you to swear on the head of your son that you will never, never, tell him.'

'You have my word, Mireille,' Max said, alarmed.

'That's not good enough. Tell me you swear on the life of your son — '

'I swear on Jeff's life that I will never tell him,' Max said quickly. 'In any case, how could I tell him? I don't even know where he is!'

'But this is not possible,' Max said in French. 'It can't be you!'

Exploding into laughter to cover his shock and confusion, Saffity shouted, 'Max Blum!' He rushed round from his desk and the next moment they were in a tight, emotional embrace. Moist-eyed, they kissed cheeks and clapped one another's backs.

Brian Anderson, one of the export salesmen, coughed ostentatiously.

'Mr Anderson, would you excuse us?' Saffity laughed. 'This is an unexpected reunion, as you can see. Ask Miss Kennedy not to disturb us for an hour, will you?' He turned to Max again and nudged him toward the cobalt-blue sofa at the end of his office. 'It's been a long time. How long has it been, Max?'

'Three years,' Max answered soberly. Suddenly, he jumped out of his seat. 'It's April the eighteenth – exactly four years to the day since we left Paris.' His eyes clouded over and he looked away.

'I've got rid of my eye-shield,' Saffity said quickly. 'How about that?'

This innocuous question forced Max not only to look into Saffity's eyes but to study them openly. He felt himself beginning to tremble. With a mammoth effort he controlled himself. Those amber eyes were Theresa's eyes. 'You had the operation?' He knew if Saffity asked just one question about Mireille he would have to tell him about Theresa. Forcing his voice to be steady, he said, 'I'm very pleased for you, Saffarty. It was obviously very successful.'

'You're still living in South Africa, Max?' Saffity asked, and then answered his own question. 'Of course you are. I was told about a South African carpet buyer — '

'What are you doing here? When did you get here?'

'I've been here three years. I married the boss's daughter,' he

259

laughed. 'Edwina.' He went back to his desk to fetch a silver-framed photograph. 'This is my wife,' he said proudly. 'Beautiful, isn't she? We met in Paris and I fell in love with her.'

'I'm married too,' Max said. 'We have a son. Jeff will be a year old next month. And you, Saffarty, do you have any children?' *Oh, God,* Max thought, praying to keep his mouth shut, *of course you have a daughter, Saffarty. She's called Theresa and she's the most perfectly beautiful child I've ever seen.*

'Not yet,' Saffity answered. 'Well, Max,' he said more briskly, 'it seems we're in the same sort of business again.' He hit his thighs and laughed and laughed until his mirth brought tears to his eyes.

Max joined in the laughter, and for a short while it was like old times, as if the separate tragedies of Colette and Mireille had never united them during those terrible hours before Saffarty had paid for Max to escape to South Africa.

'So you're in the carpet business, eh, Max? Is it your own business?'

'I'm not exactly in the carpet business. I'm with Adderley Furniture Mart, which is owned by my uncle and aunt. But we have a fairly large carpet department.'

'Yes. Of course you told me about these relations when — ' Saffity allowed a meaningful pause to drop. 'Do they have racing in South Africa?'

'Yes. They have racing in South Africa,' Max said firmly, 'but they've never had one penny out of me.'

'So you're cured, then. It seems going to Africa was a good move for you. Things are booming, I'm told. We've been developing our export market with as many colonial countries as will have us, but we haven't done well enough in Africa. Our agent down there is half asleep.'

'You should see the building that's going on in Johannesburg! The town's growing like weeds. And getting bigger all the time. It should be a lucrative and profitable market for you.'

'Pity you don't own your own business, Max. You should, you know. Well, if it comes to that, Wyndham Carpets doesn't belong to me, either. I get a share of the profits, and my father-in-law, Sir William Wyndham, has certainly given me a free hand in terms of modernising the plant, and design, and exports. Actually, we have a very large percentage of the export market.'

'There's a good profit in carpets,' Max said. 'And it's a nice, clean business to run, too. The profit margin is higher in carpets than in furniture. Carpets need less space than furniture. I've been enlarging our carpet department precisely for that reason.'

'Are there any businesses specialising only in carpets in Johannesburg?'

'People still go in for linoleum,' Max answered thoughtfully. 'No, nothing really worthwhile . . . '

'Why don't you do it?'

'It's a question of capital.'

'Wyndham Carpets could finance you. I'm thinking out loud, of course. I could send you stock on consignment. You won't have to lay out a penny yourself. You'll pay us when you get paid. Naturally, I'd want a share of your profits. But we can discuss all that.'

'That sounds interesting,' said Max eagerly. 'Fanny — she's my wife — has been nagging me to go out on my own.'

'I don't believe Wyndham Carpets has done much business on this sort of basis before,' Saffity said slowly, 'but I think they have faith in my judgement.'

The telephone rang. Saffity frowned and got up to answer it. 'Tell him I've got a new and potentially important customer. Ask him to forgive me, and fix another appointment for tomorrow afternoon, will you?' And he turned to Max and winked with his right eye, the eye that had once been crooked.

'You really are quite something, Saffarty,' Max grinned. 'Quite something.'

'Here, take a look at this,' Saffity said. 'My business card.'

It was a very simple white card, with cobalt-blue printing. Max read it quickly. S. Saffity, Director, Wyndham Carpets. 'You've changed your name,' he said.

'Only the spelling. They anglicised it, you see. But I'm still known only by my last name.'

'I've never forgotten how you felt about that.'

'I'm sure you haven't,' Saffity said smoothly. 'I take it you're staying at the Lincoln? We'll pick up your luggage, and you'll stay with us at Stanford Hall. We always put up our best customers at home. I'm going to show you over the mill.'

'The mill?' Max repeated.

'The factory,' Saffity explained. 'But before I do that there's one important thing you should know.'

'What's that?' Max asked, smiling.

'I was married in the chapel at Stanford Hall.'

'In church?' Max said, the smile leaving his lips. 'You got married in church?'

'I thought you'd find it – uh – surprising,' Saffity said mildly.

'Do they know what you are?'

'Was, Max, was. What I *was*,' Saffity said imperiously. 'And no, they don't.'

'Do your parents know you were married in church?'

'They don't even know that I'm married, my friend. And what they don't know can't hurt them. Come, I'll show you round.'

By the time Edwina and Saffity took Max to his guest suite it was close to midnight. When they left the plant, they had carried on talking about the business they would do together, stopping only to wash their hands before dinner. 'It's a tremendous opportunity for you, Max,' Saffity said again and again. 'Jump at it.'

Max, needless to say, was in entire agreement. Indeed his mind was reeling like one of those new calculating machines: ten thousand pounds' worth of stock on consignment, free of interest. And so Saffarty now called himself Saffity, just like people in Johannesburg who had changed from Wolfowitz to Wilton. It was done often enough, so who cared? It was of no importance. But the Imperial Preference Saffity had spoken of, if it became law and worked to their mutual benefit, was of major importance. 'The British Empire is great and noble, but it is also practical,' Saffity had said. Wholesale – bigger turnover, bigger profits . . . Neither he nor Fanny had thought of moving away from retail, but there were only two other wholesalers, Rosen and Kaufman, and they had upholstery materials as well. Adderley Furniture Mart already had a larger carpet selection than either of them . . .

All the same, no matter how preoccupied his brain was with business, Max thought Edwina was the most beautiful girl he had ever seen. Her fair, delicate complexion had a translucence about it that was almost unreal, as if it could not possibly be made of mere human flesh. But it was the way her clear, violet eyes softened every time she looked at Saffity that made Max's stomach lurch.

At the beginning, when Saffity had introduced him, both she and her mother had addressed him in French, but the conversation soon changed to English. They spoke of Edwina's interest in carpet design, which had begun when she had been redecorating the west wing of Stanford Hall in which she and Saffity lived. There was talk of her engaging young artists.

'Just wait till you see it,' Saffity said proudly. 'She has transformed the place.'

'She is talented,' Sir William said. 'We always knew she had a flair. But none of us expected her to become involved in the business. The two of them have created a new line of design that will take our sales through the roof.'

'Did you tell Max about Colette?' Edwina asked eagerly.

Max's wineglass fell from his hands. On the sparkling white tablecloth the spilt claret looked like a wound. He turned alarmingly white. 'Colette?' he whispered.

'It's the name Edwina gave our new range,' Saffity put in quickly. 'I wasn't keen on the name myself, but — '

'I have set my heart on it. I admire her writing so much, you see,' Edwina continued brightly. 'Please don't worry about the glass — '

Max's face shone with sweat. He mopped his brow. 'I'm so sorry about the glass and the tablecloth,' he muttered.

'Please ignore it,' said Edwina, placing a napkin over the stain and rearranging the cutlery.

'Hey, I didn't tell you about the disaster that overtook La Fenêtre de Saffarty, Max,' Saffity said, to make Max feel easier; and told him about the fire. 'Don't you ever make the same mistake and neglect an insurance policy — '

'They're robbers and thieves,' Max said angrily. 'Insurance companies give you an umbrella, and take it away when it rains.'

Slowly the colour returned to Max's cheeks.

'Are you feeling better, Mr Blum?' Lady Wyndham asked kindly.

'Thank you. Yes. It's been too much excitement for one day, I suppose.'

The guest suite was more like a large flat; it was certainly bigger than Max and Fanny's apartment. All four rooms – two bedrooms, a sitting room and a bathroom – were stamped with Edwina's bold and imaginative personality. Her attention to detail was obvious, but delightfully so. The huge bedroom that had been assigned to Max had a high vast four-poster bed whose apricot drapes matched the walls. The vaulted ceilings were painted in apricot, too, and the several vases of roses were in shades of orange, yellow and gold. Max glanced at the small needlework *prie-dieu* in the bathroom, and wondered for a moment what Mireille would have made of it.

But his mind reeled back to Colette. Had they been telling the truth? Was Colette the name of a new range? After all, they had not been expecting him. Or had they? Could Saffity have told Edwina why he left Paris? It was strange that no one had asked why he'd emigrated to South Africa . . . But if they did know, why would they do business with him, give him goods on consignment?

Should he have told Saffity about Theresa? Should he tell him now? Edwina was crazy about her husband. How would *she* feel about discovering that he had an illegitimate daughter called Theresa? If it was hard to keep silent about this, was it also wrong?

Saffity was lucky because he was heartless, he told himself. He had not as much as mentioned Mireille's name! As far as he was concerned, Mireille might never have existed . . . Yet his former partner was giving him the chance of a lifetime; the chance to run his own business, he scolded himself furiously. Why let past terrors, past tragedies, complicate things? Why couldn't he be like Saffity and bury the past? Saffity's parents did not even know that their son was married – he had exiled them from his past just as surely as he exiled them from his present.

The four-poster bed was so high that the little steps leading up to it were both functional and decorative. Once in bed Max lay back and, though he covered his eyes with his hands, could not rid himself of his last terrifying image of Colette lying at the bottom of that mirrored pool. When he opened his eyes he caught sight of the series of bird paintings on the opposite wall. Even from this distance the vivid painting of a toucan seemed alive.

He escaped to the sitting room, where Edwina's modern steel tubular furniture was uncomfortable but safe.

He fell into a fitful, unwilling sleep, and woke shivering in a pool of sweat. It would be safer to stand than to sit, he decided; that way there could be no danger of sleep. He stared unseeingly through the windows, and waited for the dawn to break. A sudden movement on the emerald lawns below forced him out of his daze. Two figures, each on a white stallion, were riding towards the fields. It was at least a minute before he realised that one was Saffity, the other Edwina. He watched them jump a few hedges. In a blur of disbelief Max decided on a cold shower.

The way Saffity fitted in with the family, he said to himself, would stun anyone. Even the frosty butler, Simpson, twinkled and smiled whenever Saffity talked to him. And Saffity's huge, graceful animal, an Irish wolfhound called Finbar that they told him had been their wedding gift from a man called Myles Beecham, was the most dignified and adoring dog Max had ever seen. The man led a charmed life; it was pointless, and destructive, to hate him for it. So what if it was he who had given Saffity his first chance at the stall in Feyard's cinema? One thing was for sure; Max was not going to bite the hand that would feed him. Fanny would agree.

That burning, spreading pain in his throat again. Hatred lasts longer than love, he thought bitterly, but then hatred is more easily concealed than love. If he and Saffity had stayed in partnership he would not have gone in for all that gambling, and Colette would not have . . . He could not bring himself to go further.

He would never stop hating Saffity, he knew that now, but he would make his hatred work for him, and against Saffity.

Any man who denied – and therefore betrayed – his Judaism, as Saffity had done, was a man to be despised.

He had been sorely tempted to tell him about Mireille and Theresa; it seemed unnatural for a man not to know he was a father. But if he had weakened, he would not only have betrayed Mireille but exposed what might turn out to be a powerful secret weapon.

Max hoped it would never be necessary but, yes, his knowledge of Saffity's illegitimate daughter could prove to be very useful. He was acutely aware of what Saffity knew about him, and his fear inflamed his hate.

Breakfast was a cheerful, sumptuous affair. A selection of kippers, bacon, sausages, haddock, eggs and mushrooms waited, on heated copper stands, under sparkling silver lids on the sideboard. Max was now quite used to large breakfasts; only the service was different from South Africa. The Abelmans also had a breakfast room and servants, but the style here was of a higher order altogether. For one thing, Sir William had his three spaniel dogs at his feet, and for another two maids remained in the breakfast room with them. Saffity had changed from his jodhpurs, but Edwina was still in hers. The Irish wolfhound lay on the floor between them.

Sir William was just rising from the table as Max sat down, but he paused to say to him, 'Saffity tells me he will be extending the African market.'

'We'll be going over the details of that this morning,' Saffity said smoothly. He turned to Max. 'Nigel Bryce, our solicitor, will be coming in to the office anyway. He'll draw up the appropriate agreement.'

Later that morning, Max met with Mr Bryce in Saffity's office. 'Have you thought of a name for your new company, Mr Blum?' Nigel Bryce asked.

'Certainly,' Max said with a smile. 'Trans-Empire Carpets Proprietary Ltd.'

'Good. Now our usual formula is to divide the shares into A shares and B shares. Of course, you and Mr Saffity will have equal shares in the company and an equal share, therefore, in the profits. The managing director will, I take it, be yourself, Mr Blum?'

Max nodded.

'Mr Saffity will be an alternative director.'

'But I won't draw director's fees,' Saffity said, unleashing his most convivial laugh. 'At least not until Trans-Empire Carpets is on its feet.'

'A shares and B shares?' Max said questioningly. 'Could you explain, Mr Bryce?'

'Since Mr Saffity is effectively advancing the finance, he will naturally have the A shares, the voting shares,' Nigel Bryce answered, the thick lenses of his horn-rimmed glasses magnifying his pale grey eyes. 'Strictly speaking, it's a mere formality. The profits will be divided equally, as I believe I've already mentioned. This is standard procedure for us.'

'Draw up a preliminary agreement, will you, Mr Bryce?' Saffity said authoritatively. 'I'd like Mr Blum to show it to his lawyer in South Africa.'

There had to be a catch in it, Max thought. But what could he do? He needed Saffity, and Nigel Bryce, and Wyndham Carpets far, far more than they needed him. He needed them so much, in fact, that he would have agreed to anything. He would not have the vote, but he would have half the company.

By the time he returned to South Africa, Max had called on several carpet wholesalers. He had a lot to learn, he knew, but the main thing was that he had been given a chance to start his own business.

His visit to the Mother Country had made him still more proud of what it meant to belong to the British Empire and its infinitely civilised traditions. The British names given to streets, towns, suburbs, golf clubs and so on made much more sense to him now. He was to tell Fanny that she had been right about him. For even Max Blum now understood that you can take a man out of Africa, but you cannot take Africa out of a man.

Max was in such a hurry to get to Johannesburg to discuss Saffity's proposals with Fanny and with a lawyer, that he went from the dock to the train without either telephoning or seeing Mireille. He decided to phone her from Johannesburg – he would tell her about Saffity then.

The next day he and Fanny were in Gerald Katz's law office. Gerald Katz was already something of a legend in Johannesburg – Katz and Kruger was a highly successful law practice and numbered important and respected mining magnates among its clients.

'But Gerald Katz must be very expensive,' Max had protested.

'You get what you pay for, Max,' Fanny said fiercely. 'And you need the best.'

'A shares and B shares. Voting and non-voting.' Gerald Katz reminded Max of a doctor giving a diagnosis and prescribing a treatment. 'It could be worse. Wyndham Carpets could have insisted on the fifty-one, forty-nine formula.' He took off his glasses and cleaned them. 'The voting shares will revert to non-voting if the company is sold. Fifty-one per cent would give them absolute control, of course. I recommend you go along with this proposal of Wyndham's. The day-to-day management decisions in the running of the company will be yours.'

Fanny let out her breath. 'I was hoping you'd say that, Mr Katz.'

'Gerald. Please call me Gerald,' the lawyer said with a dry laugh. 'Quite a partner you have here, Max.'

Max and Fanny resolved to say nothing to the Abelmans, or indeed to anyone, until he had found the right premises and arranged a further loan. Within two months he had daringly signed a two-year lease on a wholesale warehouse in Market Street. Max and Fanny walked through the city, inspecting it block by block. Similar businesses seemed to congregate close to one another. In Main Street, buildings and small shops had been torn down to make way for the garages that sprang up close to one another. The area was already known as Motor Town. Max had found the nerve to open Trans-Empire Carpets directly opposite his competitor, Rosen & Co.

Though his uncle and aunt were disappointed to lose his services as General Manager, they were generous enough to applaud his decision to 'start up on his own'. They made him an interest-free loan, and promised to put as much business his way as they could – provided the price was right.

Max's sleeplessness made him gaunt rather than delicate. He was in debt to the tune of fifteen thousand pounds. 'How can I sleep when Saffity has the A shares? The voting shares?' he grumbled to Fanny, his grey eyes encircled by heavy black rings.

'Count your blessings, Max. He's given us a chance!'

'I'll count my blessings when I get hold of the A shares.'

Jeff was almost two, and the day Trans-Empire Carpets opened its doors, in August 1930, Fanny told him that he could expect a new baby in January. The entire family was overjoyed. Max only hoped he could conceal his dismay. It was too soon to have another child, he thought – he was over-committed as it was. Two months later, when Fanny miscarried, he was astonished to find himself in tears.

But thanks to several important government contracts his business was doing well, so well that he ordered more carpets on consignment. Within a year he had a staff of six – four black men, a secretary and a salesman. He began to toy with the idea of buying from other suppliers. In Cape Town a new luxury hotel, the Colony, was being built. Determined to get the order for the carpeting, Max decided to travel to Cape Town. When he wrote to Mireille to tell her of his plans he received a reply by return of post. Lady Rutherford had died, and Mireille had important matters to discuss with him.

The Abelmans' driver Johannes was at the station to meet him. It had taken three men to replace Max, and privately the Abelmans agreed that they had slipped up – they ought to have offered him a share in the Adderley Furniture Mart. Still, he was their nephew and would therefore receive the best of their hospitality.

Later that afternoon, on the steep winding road down to Constantia to see Mireille, with the deep blue agapanthas still in full bloom, Max promised himself that one day he would own one of these lovely Dutch gabled houses. It was the first time since he'd left Paris that he had coveted something for its own sake, for the sake of its own beauty. It was good to be able to dream again, he thought. Dreaming had been beyond him.

Mireille and Theresa had ridden down the driveway of the Rutherford Estate and were waiting at the white gable gate to meet him. As usual Mireille was wearing her jodhpurs, and as usual he was struck by how beautiful life in South Africa had made her. What was unexpected was a similarity to Edwina – it had something to do with the upward tilt of their lips. But then, the next moment, he saw Theresa and the extraordinary, mysterious beauty of the child banished every other thought from his mind. Her shiny blue-black hair had grown longer; it flowed in tiny ringlets down her back, in stark contrast to her rosy complexion. And there were her laughing amber eyes, Saffity's eyes exactly. It was almost painful to look at her.

He had resolved to keep all references to Saffity down to the barest minimum, but the sight of the child undid his resolution, and as soon as they were seated in the lofty living room with the yellow-wood floors that overlooked the valley full of vines he began to tell Mireille about the consequences of his encounter at Wyndham Carpets. She called for Sarie to take Theresa away, and then listened with that grave expression of hers, and asked the question he had known she would – 'You didn't tell him about Theresa?'

'No.' He looked away. *But if he had asked after her just once I would have*, he thought. But he said, 'Mireille, I didn't even give him a hint.'

'Good. I'm glad.' Her lips trembled. 'I'm glad about his eye. Do you think he loves his wife?'

'He adores Edwina,' he replied at once and immediately regretted it. 'She looks like you, Mireille.'

'I'm pleased you told me all this, Max,' she said bravely. 'It has made it much easier for me to come to a decision. It is as if the Virgin Mary herself has sent you to give me the message.'

'What message?' he interrupted rudely.

'The message that Saffity is in love, and married to someone else.'

'Now I understand. I thought you hated him — '

'Of course I hate him. I will always hate him.' Her yellow eyes dimmed. 'Yes, I will always hate him as much as I will always love him.'

'But, Mireille — '

'Oh, don't ask me to be reasonable, Max. If anyone should know that love annihilates reason, you should, Max.'

'What do you mean by that?' he asked, alarmed.

'Remember the tormented state you were in after you had lost that woman in Paris?' she said gently. 'You never admitted you'd had a broken love affair, but I sensed it.'

He appeared to concentrate on the yellow-wood floors. He said nothing.

'Do you think I want to love Saffity?' she continued furiously. 'Do you think I haven't tried to stop loving him? How can you stop loving someone when you don't even know why you love him?' Her voice softened. 'I love his skin, I love his laugh, I love his animalism and I love his brain. He is beautiful to look at. Tell me, Max, does he still have such rosy cheeks?'

'But he let you down, Mireille!'

'The power of rejection; he has that, too.' She left her chair to pour herself a whisky. 'She deserves the best, Theresa, don't you think?'

'Of course.'

'Her mother has decided to become Lady Rutherford.'

'Lady Rutherford!' Max whistled through his teeth. 'Mireille, the other Lady Rutherford's hardly cold in her grave.'

'It seems months ago,' Mireille said quickly. 'She was ill for such a long time. But he loves me, you know, Max. He knows I don't love him. We will have separate bedrooms – Freddy expects nothing from me. Oh, of course I could have a physical relationship with a man, but I never want that again. He wants me to be his wife because he likes to watch me naked in my bath. I'm not embarrassing you, am I, Max? After all, you have lived in Paris. Yes, he likes to watch me naked in my bath, and if I agree to marry him he will build a bathroom out of the finest alabaster. He has no heirs, you see. If I marry him, he will make Theresa his heir. Even so, I hesitated. I suppose I thought that Saffity — '

Mireille broke off, exhausted, and for a long while neither of them spoke. She had talked urgently yet calmly, and she had talked as much to herself as she had to Max, as if she knew that if she explained her thinking to him she would explain it to herself.

'Of course you must marry him,' Max said with an air of finality. 'Theresa deserves nothing but the best.' He gestured toward the huge estate, and the golden vineyards, and could not help comparing it with Stanford Hall. The Cape seemed to have been created by nature itself, whereas Worcestershire seemed to have been made by man and the passage of time. He repeated, more aggressively, 'Theresa deserves nothing but the best.'

'The vine fascinates me,' she said softly, almost prayerfully. 'Do you remember that terribly run-down boarding house the taxi driver took us to when we first arrived?'

'Who could ever forget it?'

'It was called the Purple Vines. Doesn't that sound prophetic to you now?' She stopped to fling open the windows. 'We've started to harvest at night, you know. It's one way of keeping the grapes extra cool. The sun saps their fruit and their scent, too. Believe it or not, Max, you may be in the import business, but I'm in export. I've just exported my own sherry.'

'They grow grapes in greenhouses for fun in England,' he said stiffly. Saffity had shown him the greenhouses at Stanford Hall, where grapes and nectarines and strawberries and orchids were grown.

'Do they really grow grapes in greenhouses for fun?' she asked, keenly interested. 'Vineyards are becoming more and more scientific, so I shouldn't be surprised. The vine used to be a wild creeper.'

At that moment Theresa, chased by her nanny, Sarie, burst in, her shrill, excited laughter filling the room. She made a bee-line for Max, and hurled herself into his lap. He drew the shining child closer, and pressed his cheek against hers. Suddenly, Theresa jerked her face away from his, looked into his eyes and brought her face closer to his. The next second he felt the sharp nip of her small teeth. He yelped with pain and quickly lowered her to the floor.

Jumping out of her chair, Mireille said grimly, 'She bit you, didn't she?'

She grabbed Theresa's arm, almost pulling it out of its socket as she lifted the screaming child from the floor, then turned her over and spanked her hard.

'Stop it, Mireille,' Max shouted. 'You're hurting her!'

Although Mireille seemed not to hear him, she stopped. She thrust Theresa into Sarie's waiting arms, told her to take the child away and returned to her chair.

'She's just like her father,' Mireille said feverishly. 'Just when you think she's being nice and sweet, what does she do? She bites you.'

Still shocked, Max said, 'You're too strict with her.'

'Theresa is too strong willed. *Mon Dieu*, the child is not yet four years old.' Her face, her eyes – even her voice – had swollen. 'She's too headstrong for her own good. I'll tame her. You'll see!'

The following morning when he went to meet Mr Potter, the owner of the Colony Hotel, he took two bottles of white wine from the cellars of the Rutherford Estate, a gift from Mireille. Mr Potter was something of a connoisseur – he understood the value of a Château de Paulignac, 1910. Max got the order for the entire hotel. A few more orders like this and he would have to move to larger premises.

During the long overnight train journey back to Johannesburg, Max reflected that in just two months it would be four years since he and Mireille had arrived in South Africa. And now she was not only to become Lady Rutherford, but the châtelaine of a vineyard.

It was all too terrifyingly good to be true.

He cursed his pessimism. Why couldn't he be more like Saffity? He shook his head repeatedly. Saffity probably knew he was jealous of his fantastic style of living, of his wife, of his position at Wyndham Carpets. But he probably did not know that he was as jealous of Saffity's optimistic self-confidence as he was of his electrifying presence. His imposing bearing seemed to sweep people up in it like butterflies in a net. Everyone brightened in his presence, like sunflowers in the sun. His confidence in himself inspired the confidence of others. It was this, Max believed, that showed up all his own inadequacies. He hated him for this as much as he hated his own fear of what Saffity knew about him.

That night, during the Sabbath meal with Fanny and his parents, Max's mood suddenly lifted. He realised how relieved and glad he was to be home, back in his flat at Sylvan Court, far away from Mireille and their inevitable talk of Saffity. Reinforced by his family, he sat back to drink in the details of the evening.

The white cloth sparkled. The traditional plaited Sabbath loaf, baked by his mother, caught the candlelight and was a golden glow. He wanted to register and hoard it all, like a lone stranger temporarily sharing an evening's warmth. He was aware of Jeff's nanny, Annie's, nervous smiles as she removed the plates; he heard Martha the cook's clatter in the kitchen. They had two servants now – he corrected himself quickly – three, if he counted the houseboy who went with the rent, and did the heavy work.

Flushed with happiness, Fanny was still talking about the big order from the Colony Hotel. His father's eyes, brimming with pride, met his mother's and smiled. He watched his mother lean forward and tenderly brush the base of the silver candlesticks, chased with biblical scenes, which had been in her family for more than two hundred years.

'In Johnnesburg even the dust is made of gold.' His mother laughed. Fanny laughed with her.

'Did you hear that, Max?' Fanny called out. 'Poppa says even the dust is made of gold.'

'Those mine dumps give us plenty of headaches in the shop, I'll tell you that.' She turned back to her parents-in-law. 'If there's one thing I insist on at Trans-Empire Carpets it's cleanliness. But the dust that blows in from the mine dumps!'

Left to his own thoughts, Max concentrated on his parents, on how these two fragile, waning transplants, brought to this unlikely country, had taken root quickly with their heads held high to the bright light. Bronzed by the revitalising sun, they looked ten years younger. Six thousand feet above sea level, in the thin rarefied air of Johannesburg, his father's asthma had evaporated. True, most immigrants took to the country as favourably as they took to the climate, but he had expected his parents to be at least as frightened and repelled by the blacks as he had been.

In South Africa whites were officially classified as European, blacks as non-European. After Max had moved to Johannesburg it had taken some while before he realised how this official jargon had influenced him. Like any ordinary man of his time, Max believed European superiority to be as self-evident as it was unquestionable. And, in the wake of the victorious armies of the mighty British Empire the blacks had been taught to accept without question their own savage inferiority. In London and in Johannesburg the 'Native Question' was discussed as one of those timeless problems that only time would solve.

Fortunately, he and Fanny and their non-Europeans got along very well. His parents were very happy with their large, beaming, motherly 'girl' Violet. They also lived in Sylvan Court, but on the ground floor – just in case there was a problem with the lift. He listened to the happy hum of his parents chaffing with Fanny in English, rather than to what they were saying. Yiddish was Fanny's mother-tongue, his was Polish. No wonder his parents had found the designation – European and non-European – confusing. Since they came from Europe, they were far more European than the indigenous whites.

All the official signs stating 'Europeans only' meant superior facilities, just as 'non-Europeans only' indicated lesser ones. In common with many immigrants before them, they instantly found their status elevated; what could be more welcoming than that? Naturally, as Jews, they had been highly unwelcome in Poland, the country of their birth – it was the *numerus clausus*, the restricted numbers at university, that had forced Max to study architecture in Paris in the first place. But there was yet another bonus. As long as they were under the British Crown, they would be safe in the arms of the mightiest mother country in the world.

For a moment, Max shut his eyes. Why shouldn't they thrive? he asked himself, nervously. Why shouldn't they?

A sudden commotion in the kitchen hurled him from his thoughts. There was a loud wailing and clapping of hands.

'What's happening?' Max asked, leaving the table instantly. 'What's going on in there?'

'It's Violet,' his mother answered, following him at once. 'I recognise her voice.'

The moment they entered the kitchen, the wailing ceased.

'Ow, master, sorry master, sorry,' Annie said, her eyes downcast.

'What's wrong?' Max demanded.

'They arrest her husband, master,' Annie explained. 'He forget his pass. Another boy, he see it, he came to tell it to Violet.'

All four Blums were now standing in the kitchen.

'Pass laws, the bane of every housewife's life,' Fanny thought, clicking her tongue irritably.

Violet sat down on the floor, her head on her plump knees,

and though her whole body shook and heaved her sobs were muted.

'Which police station, Annie?' Max asked quietly.

A rapid exchange in Zulu followed and then Annie said, 'To the Fort. It's not far, master.'

'Ask her for her husband's name.'

'Absalom,' Max's father answered unhesitatingly.

'I'll just have to go to the police station,' Max sighed. 'Tell Violet not to worry.'

'Ow, master, thank you, master.' Violet raised her tear-swollen face, and cupping her hands in the traditional expression of Zulu gratitude, added, 'God bless you, master.'

Max was scarcely out of the kitchen when his father said, 'I'm going with you.'

'But it's *shabbat*! Why should you ride on *shabbat*?' Max protested.

'I *am* going with you,' his father persisted stubbornly. 'As it is written in the Talmud, you may violate the Sabbath to save a life,' he added defensively.

Max shrugged. His father was stretching the point, but there was no time to argue.

They drove to the Fort in a thoughtful silence. When they reached the police station, and Max turned off the ignition, speaking Yiddish instead of their customary Polish, his father said fervently, 'Absalom is a *mensch*. I know him.'

His father had chosen his words carefully. He had used the common term *mensch*, not in its most popular form which meant an honourable, decent person, but at its most exact, which meant human being.

'Leave it to me, Poppa,' Max answered. 'I know what you mean.'

They found Absalom having his fingerprints taken.

Max's polite – but authoritative – request for a private talk with the officer in charge was granted. Then, after a pleasant exchange of words and a five-pound note, Absalom was released.

Again they drove in silence, each locked in his own thoughts, Absalom in the back seat, worlds away from both of them.

In the basement garage of Sylvan Court, with the slightest bow of his head, Absalom looked them proudly in the eye and with great dignity said, 'I thank you for helping me.' His right hand moved fractionally forward. At once Max's father reached out to him, and his and Absalom's hands connected in a firm, long grip.

275

In his still halting English, he said, 'Violet waits for you by my son's house.'

Absalom left them then, to take the stairs. The lift was for Europeans only.

While Max was carefully locking his car, his father wondered out loud whether Trans-Empire Carpets could do with another driver. Max shook his head doubtfully. 'You should find a place for him,' Max's father said. 'You should take him. You won't find another man like Absalom in a hurry.'

'If that's what you want, Poppa, that's what I'll do.'

16

Saffity had fitted surprisingly well into Kidderminster; his lively laugh and his habit of hand-kissing had added colour to the town. His father-in-law, who had thought he'd have a particularly hard time as a foreigner, was delighted to have been wrong. His French accent made his near-perfect English intriguing, and people smiled when they talked about him.

'It would have been more difficult for you if you'd come from Scotland, say, or from Kent,' Sir William remarked one day. 'Then people would have identified the class you came from. As a foreigner, you're classless.'

'I know,' Saffity answered seriously. 'Edwina and I have talked about that.' He broke into a laugh. 'I'm a foreigner of no class,' he said.

'But classy, my boy, classy,' Sir William said staunchly.

The Wyndhams, in common with everyone who came into contact with the young couple, marvelled at them, at their genuinely exuberant happiness. It was generally agreed that it was Saffity's otherness that allowed his ardour for Edwina to be so transparently open that even her passion for him was exposed. Saffity took none of this for granted. He was well aware that the love of his beautiful young wife, and the loving kindness of her parents had done wonders for him. At the same time it made it possible for him to indulge his enthusiasm for Wyndham Carpets, and after three years his business acumen had already been proved by his remarkable results.

There were two grass courts in the grounds of Stanford Hall, and numerous stables and horses. He had learned to play tennis, and he had already learnt to ride, and he was astonishingly good at both. Sometimes he found the effortless ease of it all almost frightening.

The invitations to Edwina's twenty-first birthday party stipulated black tie and decorations. Sir William threw all his resources into organising a party of the lavish, no-expense-spared variety.

On the night of her party, Edwina was at her most radiant – her three-month pregnancy made her so. A cobalt-blue crêpe dress, trimmed with ermine, emphasised her still slender waist.

Saffity's skilfully cut tails made him look even taller than he was, and he was now six feet four inches tall. He believed he had stopped growing at last. He had turned twenty-one a couple of years before, but his new family had all believed that his twenty-first birthday was his twenty-fourth birthday. He had put it about that his passport gave an incorrect date of his birth, and had explained that away by saying, 'If the registry of births had not been destroyed in the great fire of Salonika, and if I had not been able to claim that I was three years younger than my real age, I would have been called up for military service. I would not have been allowed to leave Greece until much later.'

Edwina's birthday party was also a private celebration of Saffity's new status at Wyndham Carpets with a twenty-five per cent share in the company. Sir William stood beside Saffity and raised his champagne glass. 'To Saffity, who has become the son I never had,' he said emotionally.

'Just as long as that doesn't make you my brother, darling,' said Edwina, with a wicked twitch of her eyebrows.

Saffity kissed her on the lips. His father-in-law had got used to what he called 'Saffity's demonstrativeness' by now.

At that moment the lights of the ballroom were dimmed. Both orchestras played 'Happy Birthday'. Then, lighted by twenty-one candles, Edwina's birthday cake – an exact replica of the Morgan car her father had given her that morning – was carried in.

'The cake was your idea, wasn't it, darling?' Edwina said to Saffity when the fuss had died down.

Saffity winked with his right eye. Edwina knew how much it meant to him to be able to do this. She hugged him, and said, 'If I were to die now, I would die happy.'

It was at least three months since Saffity's suspicions about Peter Fisk, the chief accountant of Wyndham Carpets, had moved from blunt to sharp. The incredible thing was that but for his irritatingly meticulous book-keeping teacher at the Ecole Inter-Commercial, he would never have even begun to suspect Peter Fisk's sleight of hand.

Now, after a great deal of paperwork, Saffity had all the evidence and all the proof that he could possibly need. He had delayed telling Sir William, for the consequences that would undoubtedly have flowed from his revelations would have ruined Edwina's party.

They were lunching, the following day, in Sir William's office, off his treasured two-hundred-year-old cobalt-blue Royal Worcester china plates. Sir William always commented on them. For once Saffity failed to respond with his usual enthusiasm.

'You've got something on your mind, my son,' Sir William said firmly. 'Come on, out with it. A problem shared is a problem halved.'

'We do have a problem, sir,' Saffity said quietly. 'It's Peter Fisk, actually.'

'Peter Fisk?' Sir William's tone was incredulous.

'I know exactly how long Mr Peter Fisk has been with you, sir. Since eighteen eighty-eight – forty-three years, to be precise.'

'It's like you to do your homework, Saffity.'

Saffity drew out two sheets of paper covered in his neatly written figures.

'I regret having to bring this to your attention,' he said, 'but if you examine these figures you will see at once that it's a clear case of the purest – and the simplest – fraud.'

Sir William pushed his plate away and pored over the pages in silence. After a long while he said, 'Neat work. Diabolically neat work. What it comes down to is that we've been paying seven hundred and fifty pounds for one hundred quids' worth of yarn.'

'He's got away with it for the last seven years,' Saffity said fiercely. 'Seven years that we know of, that is.'

'Thank God we're not a public company,' said Sir William. 'At least there are no outside shareholders to raise hell.'

'What are you going to do, sir? Call in the police, I suppose?'

'I'd rather not.'

'But the man has been robbing you!'

'On the other hand Peter Fisk is, and always has been, more than an employee in my life. I've seen his children grow up. I know them all. His son, Colin, is probably one of the best shed foremen we've ever had.'

'Goddamn it, what the hell more did Peter Fisk want? You gave him a company house in one of the best parts of Kidderminster.'

Sir William shook his head.

'One hundred thousand pounds!' said Saffity. 'Where's the money gone? What the hell did he do with all that money?'

'The race track. I assume it must have gone on the horses. Peter always liked a flutter – we all knew that – but he can't have given one hundred thousand pounds to the bookies,' Sir William said, his face ashen. 'I almost wish you hadn't — ' He stopped.

'I know it's been a shock to you, sir. I dreaded telling you about it.'

'You did what you had to do.' Sir William patted Saffity's back awkwardly. He picked up his papers again. 'You see before you a bitterly disappointed old man, Saffity. It's an ugly business – too ugly for the police, I'm afraid.'

'But if you let him get away with it you will be letting down Wyndham Carpets,' Saffity said angrily.

'Peter won't be able to reimburse us, will he?'

'That's not the point. The man's a crook and must be punished.'

'I've been called tough and I've been called ruthless, but I've never been called cruel, Saffity. I'll confront Fisk with the evidence, and he and I will decide together what's to be done. For the moment, if you don't mind, I'll sleep on it.'

'Well, if you're going to let him off scot free — '

'I didn't say I would, did I?'

'Of what you hear believe nothing, and of what you see believe half,' Saffity mumbled.

'Where did you learn that?' Sir William demanded.

'In Macedonia.'

'Sounds a bit too harsh for my liking,' Sir William said shortly. 'Too cynical — '

The next day Sir William told Saffity that although he definitely would not be prosecuting, he would let Peter Fisk think that he was considering prosecution. 'Fourteen or fifteen thousand quid a year over seven years. You know, Saffity, I've taken greater losses than that in three months. A prosecution would do terrible things to the morale of everyone at Wyndham Carpets.'

Saffity shrugged. 'So you are going to let him get away with it.'

'Don't be ridiculous,' Sir William responded furiously. 'We'll get rid of Peter Fisk with the least delay, and with the most discretion. No one is to know about this. Is that clear?'

Two days later, while the family and Myles Beecham were at breakfast, Peter Fisk's son Colin burst in, shouting, 'He shot himself! My father went to the woods and shot himself. We've just found him.'

Saffity's hand was on Finbar's collar, restraining the growling wolfhound.

'Oh, my God,' Sir William moaned. 'Oh, my God.'

'You can't prosecute him now, can you?' Colin Fisk howled. 'This is his blood you're looking at. My father's blood,' he raged, pointing first at his blood-spattered shirt and then at Saffity. 'I can't look at you, you stinking, bloody snooping foreigner. I can't stand the sight of any of you. I'm getting out of here.'

Colin turned on his heel and rushed out. He had been in the breakfast room for a little more than a minute.

The moment Colin Fisk left the breakfast room Saffity turned to Edwina. Her face was taut and strained and the colour had left it. Lady Wyndham, anxious both for her daughter and for the child she was carrying, said briskly, 'Edwina, I think you should lie down.'

Obediently, though very obviously dazed, Edwina allowed herself to be led from the room.

Saffity rose to follow them.

'I'd leave them alone if I were you,' Sir William said sternly. 'Women's business.'

Saffity sat down again. '*Suicide!*' he began.

'I shan't be going to the mill today,' Sir William cut in roughly. 'However, if you don't want to be late for your meeting with Casson you'd better leave at once.'

Driving to the mill in Edwina's Morgan, Saffity admitted to himself that he had not considered the effect of his revelations on Fisk. His chief concern had been for the company. Still, he was not given to deceiving himself and readily acknowledged that he had also been certain exposing Fisk was yet another way of highlighting his own superior business sense. But for all his ruthless self-appraisal he was convinced that there had been no alternative – he would take the same course of action again.

He had been looking forward to his meeting with Casson for days, and it went as smoothly as he had hoped. Casson, the world's largest tailoring organisation, was expanding; a new, thickly carpeted store was being opened every week. He had managed to buy a large quantity of wool from a commodity speculator who was forced to sell at a loss, which meant that Wyndham Carpets was therefore well able to undercut the competition.

Although Saffity won the contract easily he felt none of the elation that usually accompanied his transactions. Instead, he was beset by self-doubt. Edwina's pale, taut face and his father-in-law's chilling manner troubled him deeply. He felt acutely aware that he was an outsider. On an impulse he went to seek the advice of Myles Beecham.

It was around mid-day when he drove up to Swallow Grange, where Myles lived and worked. Walking into the office, he found him seated behind a large untidy desk. Tara, lying at his feet, thumped his tail in welcome.

'What brings you here?' Myles asked mildly. 'Can I get you a drink? Whisky?'

'Thanks, that'd be fine. I'd like a word with you,' Saffity said quickly, stroking Tara absent-mindedly.

'By all means,' Myles responded with his habitual courtesy.

Though this was the first time that he and Myles had had a drink together, they had always got on well. Saffity's laugh, his friendliness and above all his eagerness to learn not only the English language but the English customs – especially those relating to class – had broken through the reserve that had at first seemed as tough as Myles' stocky, bony frame.

'Shocking tragedy,' Myles said, drawing in his lips.

'I know.' Saffity sighed and shook his head. After a while he said, 'I feel responsible.'

'When Sir William phoned, he told me you did what you had to do,' Myles said soberly. 'But, you know how it is, Saffity. Sir William sees himself as the head of the Wyndham Carpet family.'

Saffity was silent. He drank deeply, and wondered if he would ever get used to the bitter taste of whisky.

'I suppose you wish you'd kept your mouth shut,' Myles went on sympathetically.

Saffity nodded as if he agreed.

'Doing one's duty can be very unpleasant, I know,' Myles said. 'But you would have been less than honest if you'd kept quiet.'

Saffity put down his glass quickly. 'I'm glad I came to talk to you, Myles,' he said, sounding grateful. 'You've been a great help to me since I came to England.' After all, it was Myles who had suggested that he study Debrett and Burke's *Peerage* so that he could sort out and memorise the British aristocracy. He put out his hand, and shook hands firmly. 'I'll tell you what I'm going to do now, Myles, I'm going home to have lunch with my wife!'

Saffity drove home thinking he had both a friend and an ally.

By returning home impulsively, for lunch with the family, he had again struck the right note. Edwina received him rapturously. They all agreed over lunch that Sir William would have to pay his condolences to the Fisk family later that afternoon.

When Sir William arrived at the grieving Fisk household Mrs Fisk seemed scarcely surprised to see him. She was polite enough, but after a short while she made her excuses and left.

Although Sir William was justly famed as a brilliant negotiator, he was nevertheless forced to call on the sum of all his skills to persuade Colin Fisk that the exposure of his father's suicide would do no one any good, the Fisk family least of all.

Eventually Colin asked suspiciously, 'What's in it for you, and that foreign son-in-law of yours, if I go along with your idea of telling everyone my father's suicide was an accident?'

'You're quite right, of course,' Sir William replied frankly. 'There is something in it for me. It would get about that I'm a man of poor judgement, a man of misguided faith.'

'Misguided faith?' Colin echoed scornfully. 'What's religion got to do with all this, I'd like to know?'

'I am speaking of trust. I trusted your father as I trust myself. I believed he was a man of honour.'

'What are you going to do with Godfrey, then? The man who was in cahoots – I mean in partnership – with him? I'd like to know that. Prosecute him, too, will you?'

'I'd no intention of prosecuting your father. We've been through all that,' Sir William said wearily. 'Godfrey will have to go.' He paused significantly. 'Surely the fact that I am not prosecuting Godfrey is proof enough that I had no intention of prosecuting your father?'

'Have it your own way, Sir William,' Colin said abruptly. 'You may be the big boss, but you'll have to live with my father's death on your hands. You won't have that your own way, Sir William.'

'Wyndham Carpets will be closed on the day of the funeral.' Sir William's distress was very visible. 'I always had the greatest respect for your father, Colin – everyone did, you know.' He rose to leave and his shoulders, usually erect, drooped. He looked a shadow of himself.

No questions were asked. Everyone accepted that Peter Fisk had been killed in a tragic shooting accident. An air of gloom and sadness settled over Stanford Hall. Sir William stared unseeingly into space, and it was clear that he wished Fisk's fraud had never been exposed. Sometimes he could not quite meet Saffity's eye.

A week after Fisk's funeral Saffity and Edwina left – to get away from it all – for Paris. It was Lady Wyndham's idea. The light seemed to have gone out of Edwina, she was pale and tearful. Neither Edwina nor Saffity needed much persuading, and soon as they were on the train the heavy cloud began to lift. They had left Finbar with Myles.

They had planned on going to the theatre and to the ballet, but every night when the time came to dress they changed their minds, and dined alone in their suite at the Ritz. Edwina's belly had grown fuller and rounder and her breasts harder and whiter, yet translucent; her blue veins showed, as if through a veil. 'A real, ripe woman,' Saffity called her over and over again. Her changing shape filled both of them with the wildest desire. Every time they made love it was as if it was the first and last time, and they drank too much champagne, as if they knew this would be the last of their excesses. It was better than a second honeymoon, they said; more like an illicit love affair.

They bought exquisite baby robes, made of the finest cottons and as soft as a newborn baby's cheek. Hand-embroidered, with even the seams sewn by hand, so that not a single stitch would wrinkle the baby's skin. They shopped for shirts and ties, taking hours over every choice. They bought a pipe for Myles.

They hugged one another in the store.

Besides making love, the most delicious thing of all was speaking nothing but French with one another. English was no longer a strain for Saffity – he could barely remember when it had been – but French was a luxury.

They needed to be alone so much, that it was three days before they decided to let Colette know they were in Paris. When they were told she had left the day before for the country they were scarcely disappointed. They loved her, but they could not get enough of one another. They went to see what had become of La Fenêtre de Saffarty, and were dismayed to find that a small friendly hardware store had been erected in its place. 'You can't go back,' they said to one another, 'you can only go forward.' They were determined to move to their own home as soon as the baby was old enough.

The night Edwina and Saffity returned to Stanford Hall, Sir William announced at dinner, 'I'll not be lunching at Wyndham Carpets any longer. I'm going into semi-retirement. Not getting any younger, am I, Alice?'

'You don't look your age, William,' his wife protested. A silence fell over the table. It was a cold March night and at each end of the dining room a fire roared.

Saffity and Edwina exchanged a glance. Sir William looked every bit as old as his seventy-six years, if not older. The Fisk affair had definitely aged him.

'I'm a fortunate man,' Sir William continued. 'I can retire with a clear head and a peaceful heart. And it's all thanks to you, Edwina, for bringing Saffity into our family.'

'So that's why she chose me,' Saffity said, with his large wink. 'I always wondered.' He continued more seriously, 'I'll do my best, sir.'

'I've every confidence in you, my boy.'

In the three months that followed Sir William made a point of spending less and less time at Wyndham Carpets. At this late age he rediscovered gardening, and though it was a hot early summer he spent hours and hours in the greenhouses and in the rose gardens.

He applied himself to his new hobby with as much enthusiasm as he could muster.

One morning in late May Saffity woke to an inexplicable feeling of foreboding.

He stood at the window in his silk dressing gown and saw that it was one of those inexpressibly lovely English summer days. The sun was glinting off the dew on the lawns and hedges. The trees' rich foliage hung heavy and full in the stillness of the early morning air. Beyond the formal gardens the horses in the pasture, missing the exercise abandoned to Edwina's pregnancy, wheeled and pranced and then settled to nuzzling each other.

Saffity turned and observed his beautiful pregnant wife lying asleep in their bed, her arms outflung as if in search of him.

What more could a man want? Yet why this feeling of . . . of dread? Was it simply that he had *so much*, and could not bear the thought of losing it?

At breakfast the feeling persisted in the interstices of the normal desultory morning conversation. Edwina had grown lush in her pregnancy, and dreamy, and sat there in her peignoir, toying with her toast, smiling small secretive smiles as if she was privy to some mystery that no one else could know. Lady Wyndham would glance at her from time to time, fondly, and then turn back to her husband who was leafing through his post, commenting unfavourably on his correspondence.

'Ha!' he suddenly said. 'There's a new nursery over at Evesham. Might pop over there this afternoon and see if they've got anything interesting.'

'You just want another chance to drive the Morgan, don't you, Daddy? Never mind, we'll all go. Don't you think so, Mummy? You could do with an outing.'

'That would be lovely, darling, but don't you think you should rest?'

'Oh, I've had plenty of rest,' Edwina said, reaching languorously for Saffity's hand. 'You're not going to be late home tonight, are you, my love?' she asked, turning her liquid eyes on him.

They were his family. He carried that picture of them imprinted on his eyelids as he drove to the mill. His handsome family at breakfast, sunlight streaming in through the tall windows, dogs cluttering up the floor, the smells of coffee and polish and honeysuckle filling the air. His wife.

Towards tea-time, Edwina and her parents set off in the Morgan for the nursery.

The day had turned out as glorious and as eternally peaceful as only the English countryside can be. There was scarcely any traffic, which was not surprising, but the day was so tranquil that no one in the car expected any traffic at all. Choosing a little-used, wooded country lane, Sir William drove in a leisurely fashion. They came upon what appeared to be a field of wild violets.

'It can't be a real field of violets,' Edwina said, awed. 'It must be an illusion.'

'It's real, all right,' Sir William said, slowing down, and absently switching off the engine.

'Look out, William! Start the car!' Lady Wyndham called out urgently. 'It's a Wyndham van.'

Sir William had seen the van at the same moment. He turned the key but the car didn't start. 'Duck, Edwina! Duck!' he shouted. They were in an open car, and even if it had not stalled it would have made no difference. The gleaming, cobalt-blue van carrying a capacity load of Axminster carpets bore down on them, skidding hopelessly as it tried to pass.

Bad news travels fast.

'Where is she?' Saffity screamed, tearing his hair. 'Where is she?'

'At the mortuary, sir,' the policeman said.

'I want her home.'

'There has to be an autopsy, I'm afraid, sir.'

'Take me to her.'

'It's not advisable.'

'Take me to her!' Saffity roared. 'Are they all — ?'

'Yes. I'm sorry, sir. They are all dead.'

Miss Cobham, the secretary, and Desmond Turner, the General Manager, brought Saffity home to Stanford Hall. Myles Beecham took over, but Saffity was too crazed to be aware of that. Saffity made no attempt to control his monstrous raving grief. Myles telephoned Dr Gibbons who came and gave Saffity the appropriate knock-out injection for the circumstances. While the doctor was attending to Saffity, Myles fetched Edwina's address book, and telephoned Colette in Paris. She said she would be on the plane the next morning – the flight would take a little over three hours. The injection did not put Saffity to sleep, but it stopped his animal-like howling. Myles did not leave his side; he stayed unobtrusively in Saffity's room all night long. From time to time Saffity broke into weeping, and Myles, quiet, unobtrusive Myles, took Saffity in his bony arms and wept with him, and for him.

During a moment of quiet, several hours after she had arrived, Colette said, 'But shouldn't you at least tell your parents, Saffity? Perhaps they could comfort — '

'My parents,' Saffity interrupted rudely, almost spitting, 'don't even know I'm married. And if they had known, they would have sat *shivah* for me!'

'I don't understand you, Saffity,' Colette said sadly.

'*Shivah* is the prayer for the dead,' Saffity said bitterly. 'Because I married a girl who was not of their faith they would have regarded me as good as dead, and said the appropriate prayers for me. The dead me.' He stopped his pacing. 'Now do you understand, Colette? Do you?'

'Yes,' Colette whispered. 'I'm sorry. I'm so sorry.'

'We were going to call the baby Colette, you know, if it was a girl.'

Part Five

17

The accident sent the entire town of Kidderminster into mourning.

The competitors closed their mills.

Now, on that fine day, they came to the funeral service at Stanford Hall's small chapel, and spilled onto the lawns, and watered the lawns, people said, with their tears.

Saffity did not know how he got through the first week. He was only dimly aware of submitting to the care of Colette, and of Myles, neither of whom left him alone for a minute. They took it in shifts, and Colette marvelled at the way her English, so rarely used, came back to her. The wolfhound never left Saffity's side.

Two days after the funeral, Nigel Bryce, Sir William's lawyer, delivered the letter he had had in his safe-keeping.

'Your father-in-law left this with me,' Mr Bryce said stiffly. 'He asked me to give it to you, in person, in the event of his death. You and Edwina were, I believe, holidaying in Paris when it was written.'

'That was less than three months ago. D'you think he had some sort of premonition?'

'Ours not to reason why, Saffity,' Mr Bryce said formally.

'So I've been told,' Saffity replied dully. 'I'd like to read it at once, if you don't mind.'

'By all means. If you'll be good enough to sign this document of receipt, I'll leave you to it.'

Saffity signed hastily.

His hand trembled as he opened the letter carefully. He read it and closed his eyes. In a sudden rush of comfort it came to him that Sir William had regarded him as a true son. His father-in-law had not only heaped praises on his head, but had gone much further. He had bequeathed ten per cent of Wyndham Carpets to him. Since he already owned twenty-five per cent, this meant that his father-in-law had intended him to have a thirty-five per cent share – the largest single shareholding.

He read the letter again, very slowly, this time mouthing the words, as if to commit them to memory. Then he folded it carefully, kissed it, and handed it wordlessly to Myles who had been hovering anxiously at his side.

Myles looked at him questioningly.

Saffity nodded his head.

'You'd like me to read this, Saffity?'

Saffity nodded again.

'You're quite sure?'

'Read it aloud, Myles. Please. I would like you to read it.' His voice broke.

Myles sat down and read the letter and when he had done, he fumbled moist-eyed with his handkerchief. 'It is the finest tribute any man could have, Saffity. And you deserve every word of it.'

'Let prudence govern – but not tyrannise – your vaulting ambition,' Saffity said, quoting Sir William's words precisely. 'I'll need your help for that, Myles, won't I?'

At Saffity's desperate request Colette prolonged her stay indefinitely. She asked for an elocution teacher, and Myles made all the arrangements. Claire Ellis, who taught at the local school, came to give two-hour lessons. She proved an excellent student, and sometimes giggles were heard in the library. Everyone assumed that she and Saffity were related, and they saw no good reason to correct this.

Saffity moved into the guest suite that Max had stayed in, and which Edwina had redecorated so lovingly.

It was left to Colette to sort out the personal belongings of Sir William and Lady Wyndham. As far as Sir William's things were concerned, Simpson the butler proved invaluable. He knew of 'worthy cases' and Sir William's collection of pocket watches, studs and cuff links were catalogued and then locked away in the large safe that was used for some of the more precious silver.

The vicar's wife helped with Lady Wyndham's clothes – she saw that they were sent to a distant parish so that Saffity would not encounter anyone wearing them.

Colette returned to Paris briefly to sell up her apartment and most of her possessions. There was little that she wanted to ship to Stanford Hall. The few items that she did not sell she gave to

Madame Delange who now had the small shop of her own that she had always wanted.

For the moment, Stanford Hall was her home. Sometimes she would wake up early, and look out at the great stretches of lawn and try to understand how it was possible that she had come here from the slums of Detroit. Of course it would all end soon enough – Saffity would find himself a bride and she would have to move out of Stanford Hall . . .

In the cosy morning room, in the rocking chair she had made her own, working at her needle-point, she would often be joined by Saffity and Myles. Then Saffity's cigar smoke mingled with Myles' pipe, and Tara and Finbar lay quietly, and she would catch herself hoping that Saffity would never remarry. Then she would shake her head vigorously, and do her best to correct her hopes.

Two weeks after the accident, when Saffity returned to his office, he asked Myles to accompany him. For the first few days Myles merely sat on the cobalt-blue sofa with Tara at his feet, going over his own papers. But he was there whenever Saffity needed him. It turned out that Myles had not only learned a great deal about customers and suppliers, but that he knew everything there was to know about the workers. He appeared to have special knowledge about the women employees – it seemed he had made a special point of patronising those local pubs that the Wyndhams people supported.

Saffity found the quiet constancy of his presence both soothing and strengthening. He felt more confident when Myles was with him. It struck him that during the past terrible days he had in fact been depending on the opinions and judgements of a man who had no real connection with the factory.

Pretending a casual question, he asked, 'Did you always want to be a land agent, Myles? Or was it something you just drifted into?'

'I was going to be a pilot, but two leg injuries . . . '

'If you were offered an alternative occupation — ' Saffity began. He left his desk and joined Myles on the couch, and began again. 'Suppose I asked you if you could see yourself working here at Wyndham Carpets, how would you answer?'

'Well, it'd certainly be a bit of a change, old man,' Myles said promptly.

'But in principle? Would you be interested in principle?'

'I'm not quite sure in what capacity I could serve, Saffity.'

'As my personal assistant, to begin with,' Saffity said swiftly. 'And then, after a decent interval, as a director of Wyndham Carpets.' A brief, wry smile appeared. 'Sir William wasn't wrong to keep Wyndham Carpets as a private company.'

'You know, it would be quite a challenge — '

'At least think about it, Myles.'

' — and I'm at the kind of age where I could do with one of those.' Myles knocked out his pipe against the ashtray. 'You're on.'

Saffity began to discuss several key changes he thought were necessary. One of the lesser of these was the company solicitor, whom Saffity had long considered to be as incompetent as he was pompous.

'He's a violent man, Mr Bryce,' Myles informed him gravely. 'Beats up Mrs Bryce when he's had one too many. Likes the horses too, I'm told.'

'Another Peter Fisk,' Saffity said contemptuously.

'I wouldn't say that exactly — ' Myles frowned. 'But there are other solicitors, like Messrs Johnson and Neeme, who have an excellent reputation.'

'Who is better, Neeme or Johnson?'

'Neeme, I believe.'

'Arrange an appointment with Neeme, then. At Stanford Hall.'

'Very well.'

Industrial relations at Wyndham Carpets were both harmonious and efficient. Yet only one month after Saffity had assumed the chairmanship of the company he was shocked to learn that the loom operators were threatening to go out on an unofficial strike.

'Myles?' Saffity demanded of him. 'Why didn't you know about this?'

'I'm spending too much time in the office, with you. I did know there was a problem, but I didn't think it was quite so serious.'

'Well, what is it?'

'They say they're not being adequately protected from the anthrax.'

'The anthrax?'

'It's a disease, an infection of the skin that comes from imported wool. Sometimes it affects the lungs.'

'All our imported wools are disinfected at the port of entry. Is anyone seriously ill?'

'Mary Phillips had double pneumonia. But I don't think that it has anything to do with the anthrax.' Myles reddened. 'Actually, old man, the problem's got something to do with you. Some of them say they won't work for you — '

'Me? Why?' Saffity said astonished.

'I only know what Maggie Lane told me. It seems they blame you — '

'Blame me for the disease, you mean? For the anthrax?'

'I don't know quite how to say this, Saffity,' Myles said awkwardly. He stopped and went on rapidly. 'It's a totally irrational rumour. It seems they attach the blame for the accident to you; it's got about that you inherited one hundred per cent of Wyndham Carpets.'

Dangerously calm, Saffity said, 'Go on, Myles. Go on. Get to the point.'

'It's Peter Fisk's son, Colin. He says you tinkered with the car. He claims it's impossible for a Morgan to stall.' Myles averted his gaze, and stared at his shoes. 'Fisk's been to see the chief engineer at the works.'

'Fisk's been to see the engineer at the works?' Saffity echoed, incredulously.

Myles drew on his pipe. 'The rumour is that you are a murderer,' he said miserably.

Saffity believed that only two tactics were open to him – either to be conservative, and wait for the rumours to die down, or risk a frontal, public attack. He decided almost instantly that in this case attack was definitely the best means of defence, a conclusion he came to for two reasons, one emotional, the other rational. His honour had been insulted. Here, his oriental roots surfaced – anyone who did not defend his honour was a coward. It was as simple as that.

But apart from the matter of his honour, if he allowed the statement – 'there's no smoke without fire' – to go unchallenged, he would be doomed even before he began, and just as surely as if he had been proved guilty.

On June 14th, 1931, three days after Myles's shocking and dangerous findings, Saffity called an urgent extraordinary general meeting of everyone who worked at Wyndham Carpets. All departments of the mill were closed, but the workforce, from the directors to the cleaners, were free to make their own decision about whether or not they would attend. The notice that the meeting was to be held at two o'clock went out early on the same morning and by one o'clock almost the entire staff had assembled – including those who were off shift.

The hastily printed leaflets – blue printing on light blue paper – could not have been more direct:

> Mr. S. Wyndham-Saffity, who was recently appointed under tragic circumstances as chairman of Wyndham Carpets, wishes to address everyone who is willing to hear him.

Saffity expected a large turn-out. He hired the town hall and installed microphones, so that in the event of the hall being too small everyone would hear him. Myles' prediction that everyone would want to be in on the excitement proved correct – in many cases the Wyndham Carpet people were accompanied by husbands or wives who did not work for the company.

Saffity faced his audience alone. No one was on the stage with him. The four members of the executive board and Myles sat in the front row. He did not begin immediately, but stood on the stage, shuffling his papers, waiting for the restless crowd to settle.

'The poor man's gone white overnight,' someone whispered, and the whisper was taken up and carried along until it reached Myles, who nodded. True, his black hair had suddenly become streaked with grey but it certainly was an exaggeration to call it white. He looked older, by far, than his twenty-two years, but then he had long since effectively disguised his real age. His height, his bearing and his sad intense eyes, as well as some unidentifiable quality, gave him an appearance of distinction. Like a great actor, about to deliver a soliloquy, his mere silent presence was tangible.

He spoke hesitantly at first, the tinge of his French accent making his clear, deep voice profoundly moving.

'Ladies and gentlemen, I am here to introduce myself to those of you who do not know me.

'You all know the tragic circumstances under which I have assumed the leadership of Wyndham Carpets . . . ' He paused dramatically.

'My father-in-law always spoke of his family at Wyndham Carpets with the greatest affection and with the deepest respect. He began, as you all know, fifty-five years ago, as a yarn salesman. You will also know, too, how he secured the American patent and so revolutionised the carpet trade.

'Many of you were privileged to know him even then.

'I am a newcomer to the Wyndham Carpet family, as I am a newcomer to this great country of yours. Until one month ago, I was the happiest man, not only in the Wyndham Carpet family, but in the world. And let me assure every one of you that were it not that I wished to honour the memory of my darling wife, and her dear parents, I would not be standing before you today.

'Rumours and slanders about me have come to my ears, and this morning I received what is known as a poison-pen letter. I will return to this unfortunate and ugly matter in a moment, but before that, I would like to read you an extract of the letter Sir William wrote to me, less than three months before the terrible and tragic accident, and which he did not wish me to read until he had departed this life.'

He swallowed, ran his hands nervously through his hair, and went on to read the words he knew by heart.

'When, as a complete and utter stranger, and a true foreigner, you became part of the family, Wyndham Carpets was in a parlous state. Your new blood, your enthusiasm, your business acumen and, above all, your mighty ambition came to our rescue. You opened new markets and your aggressive original thinking stayed the depression from our threshold, saved Wyndham Carpets from chaos and kept the wolf from the doors of our faithful employees.

'As my son-in-law you are my logical successor. However, you deserve to succeed me on your own merit. I warned you that because you were a foreigner you would be at a disadvantage, but happily I was proved wrong. I must warn you again that, as my successor, you will experience difficulty of another kind. May God grant that you will overcome the jealousy of others.'

Folding the letter lovingly, Saffity paused again. The crowd began to murmur, and as the murmur mounted Saffity held up his hand and an instant hush fell.

'Now, I said I would return to those evil and dangerous rumours, and I will.'

Saffity swallowed hard.

'I have been told that some of you believe that I caused the accident that killed my darling wife, and both her parents.'

A gasp went up.

'Whoever believes I am guilty should accuse me to my face, not behind my back; he should accuse me publicly, here and now. Or take me to court, and lay a charge against me.'

Now he raised his voice, and as so often before sounded as if his own rage overwhelmed him. 'Or is my accuser – like all liars – too much of a coward to stand up and accuse me to my face? Is my accuser relying on the statement – there's no smoke without fire – to damn me?'

'You're a liar, Saffity!' Colin Fisk yelled. 'You say you come from a place called Macedonia. There is no Macedonia. Unless you count the Bible!'

'Macedonia is Greece. I was born in Greece and educated in France.'

A man who was on Colin Fisk's right tried to restrain him. 'Stop it, Colin! Forget it.'

'I'll say what I have to say,' Colin Fisk shouted. 'My father's dead because of you, Saffity! You as good as killed him!'

'I would have preferred not to have had to open up what happened to your father. I sympathise – and understand – your grief, Mr Fisk,' Saffity said, throwing his hands in the air. 'I only did my duty. I regret having had to perform that duty.'

'My father killed himself because of your duty!'

'Do you have any other accusations, Mr Fisk?' Saffity asked coldly.

'Go to hell, Saffity. God will punish you.' Colin Fisk turned on his heel, and rushed out of the hall alone.

A third voice shouted, 'I'd like to address this meeting. I'm Jack Grange, Secretary of the Works Committee, and I believe I'm empowered to speak for my committee. We would like to welcome you, Mr Saffity, and we want to assure you of our support. On behalf of the company I'd like to proffer our gratitude for everything Sir William said you had done for our company. I believe everyone will join me in commending your courage in having made all this public.'

'Hear, hear!' the crowd roared. 'Hear, hear!'

'Thank you, Mr Grange,' Saffity said gratefully. 'There will of course be a memorial service, but may I ask you all to rise for a minute of silence in memory of – ' Saffity's voice broke – 'of all of them . . . '

The general meeting was even more effective than Saffity had dared hope. The atmosphere at the mill changed dramatically, and he could detect nothing but goodwill towards him.

Saffity applied all his energies to a complete overhaul of the working conditions at the mill. He had not forgotten his shock at hearing about the anthrax, and was determined to make absolutely certain that every possible precaution would be taken against the relevant occupational diseases.

He cancelled Wyndham Carpets' fifty-fifth birthday party, which had been planned for November, only six months after the accident. Instead, every man and woman who had been with the company for twenty-five years or longer was given a present of twenty-five pounds, and those whose years with the company were fewer were given cash gifts on a descending scale.

It was then that people started to speak of Saffity as God's gentleman.

It was partly because Sir William had never wavered from the philosophy of the 'personal' touch – which really meant that his personal touch was a major article of faith in the paternalistic running of Wyndham Carpets – that his board of directors was largely a figurehead, and did little directing. The board was allowed to make suggestions, but all decision-taking was left to Sir William. Saffity therefore made a rapid study of the way in which the boards of the most successful companies were constituted. He learned quickly, and so recruited three powerful men from the City of London. He was badly in need of additional finance, and giving them seats on the board was the best way to get it.

A brief mention of the new appointments appeared in the *Financial Times*.

He brought a new sense of urgency to the business. Staring out of his office window at the mill, he said to Myles, 'We've got to bring in more money.' He made a sweeping gesture with his arms. 'The mill is too large, it needs streamlining. We could get rid of two sheds.' He strode to the window, and stared out at the workers streaming homeward. 'Of course it'd be much better to fill them with more work. More and more motor cars are being produced. Cars use carpet. I must get *those* contracts.'

From then on Saffity flung himself into the contract business – a new departure for Wyndham Carpets.

Chasing the order for a large Canadian hotel that had recently had a fire and was being refurbished, he went so far as to insert a revolutionary clause in the contract stipulating stiff financial penalties for failing to deliver on time. He won the contract only because he guaranteed delivery four weeks ahead of his competitors, which meant that only five weeks after Wyndham Carpets received the order no less than four tons of Axminster carpet were on the way to Canada.

Ruthlessly cutting back all expenses, he stopped all advertising. At the same time he hit on a new idea – if he could sell a range of standard-sized rugs to the Great Mail Order Company, it would provide both advertising and volume. Mail order catalogues were relatively new, and rugs had not so far been sold that way. Saffity's method was revolutionary and successful.

Then he became obsessed with getting the contract for Langham Castle. This time it was design, and not price that would be decisive. He remembered, from his Paris days, that Léger had also designed carpets. He commissioned a little-known artist to design, and so won that coveted contract as well.

He advanced Sir William's philosophy of the personal touch by creating the Wyndham Carpet Family Club. It was easy enough to donate ten of the two hundred acres on which Stanford Hall stood to Wyndham Carpets. Within eighteen months of the accident a club house, tennis courts, squash courts and a bowling green were ready for the official opening by the President of the Board of Trade.

Meanwhile, he continued to entertain important customers at Stanford Hall, and with Colette at his side his hospitality became something of a legend. Simpson's performance as butler had somehow acquired a continental flavour, and under Colette's instructions Mrs Carson, the cook, had widened her repertoire to include many French dishes.

Saffity was up at sunrise, riding, whatever the weather, with Finbar loping by his side. In the evenings he played squash at the Wyndham Family Club, not only to rid himself of some of his excessive energy, but to make his presence felt. By mid-1934, six years since he had first come to Wyndham Carpet, he had extended the acreage by an extra shed, and now employed four thousand people – fifteen hundred more than when he and Edwina were married. Everyone called him Saffity, and he counted this his greatest achievement, greater even than all the splendour that accompanied Prince George's royal visit to Wyndham Carpets in the autumn of 1934.

At the same time as the government imposed tariffs on imported carpets there was a boom in the building of houses, and Saffity was ready to meet the increased demand for carpets. He travelled to Australia, and to Canada, and opened warehouses in Sydney and in Montreal. There was no need to travel to South Africa – Trans-Empire Carpets was flourishing in Johannesburg, and it was a highly profitable outlet.

At least a year was to pass before Colette could begin to accept that not only was Stanford Hall a part of her life, but that the running of the place was now firmly in her hands.

The transition from her emergency visit upon the death of the Wyndhams to extended house-guest and then to châtelaine had been so gradual that she had scarcely realised how her role had changed. At the beginning there had been the matter of plumbing, which Myles had attended to, and which was one of the inevitable problems of a large Victorian country house. True, it was at her suggestion that bidets had been installed, but then the bathrooms were to be modernised anyway. Her first major intercession – or interference, as Simpson, Mrs Lynton the housekeeper and Mrs Carson the cook saw it – had been over a kitchen garden. The greenhouses grew grapes and gardenias and orchids, and at Easter special Easter lilies and lilacs, but there were no vegetables, not even an onion.

Her idea for a kitchen garden had been no grounds for complaint, but the way she went about it was the cause of grave concern. She failed to discuss her plans with anyone in the household but went directly to the head gardener, Mr Forbes. Even Simpson was 'put out'; it seemed that Colette didn't give a tinker's damn what anyone else might have thought of her idea.

Word of her indiscretion reached Myles Beecham, who explained to her that the correct form was to have mentioned it to Simpson, who would have told Mrs Lynton who would have told Mrs Carson. Simpson would have discussed it with Mr Forbes, and the kitchen garden would have gone ahead happily.

At the same time Myles had, with his customary tact, pointed out that if she insisted on going against the custom, and picking the roses herself, she should at least ask the head gardener's permission. In his gentle way he had suggested, 'You would be best advised, Madame Terblanche, to tell Mr Forbes which flowers you need and let him

301

arrange to have them brought into the house.' Like all keen students Colette had eagerly studied her mentor's teachings and soon became familiar with the protocol she was expected to follow.

Remembering the consternation the now flourishing kitchen garden had created, Colette smiled to herself. Besides onions and other vegetables, Colette had introduced herbs. An orchard had been planted, too.

Myles Beecham was coming to tea. It would be the third time that she and Myles would be having tea together on a Saturday afternoon. *Enfin*, at least her intuition had stopped her from making the smallest suggestion about what cakes should be offered with the way the English served their tea. No delicate, gossamer-thin French pastries such as *tarte au citron*. Instead she settled for Mrs Carson's fluffy scones, Stanford Hall's own raspberry jam, clotted cream and cucumber sandwiches. But she had learned fast and well, and in common with all zealous converts, she had a passionate need to be as competent as those who were born to luxury and privilege. Indeed, anyone watching her presiding over the small table covered with a white damask cloth on which sat a huge silver tea-kettle filled with boiling water, a spirit lamp underneath to keep the water piping hot, a silver tea pot and the silver tea caddy divided in the middle – one half for China tea, and the other for Indian – would have assumed she had been handling this ritual all her life.

Colette had learned rapidly that when it came to airing a problem, a cup of tea was most useful to a successful solution. Consequently, she waited until she poured a second cup before she broached the problem. 'Mrs Lynton and the cook are at loggerheads again,' she began.

Myles leaned forward to stroke Tara. He sighed. 'My word, not again.'

'I'm afraid so,' Colette answered thoughtfully, putting her elocution lessons to good effect. 'But I'm reluctant to bother Saffity with this. As it is he's working like a demon at Wyndham Carpets.'

'You can say that again,' Myles agreed fervently. 'He's working miracles.'

'We could do without Mrs Lynton, you know,' Colette said carefully. 'Thanks to your coaching, Myles, I think I'd know how to run the place.'

'I've no doubt.' He paused to pick up his pipe. 'D'you mind if I smoke this?'

'By all means, go ahead.' She waited in the comfortable silence until his pipe was lit to his satisfaction.

'My sympathies are with Mrs Carson,' she confided in a low voice. 'Mrs Lynton is too . . . too strict. With that bunch of keys at her waist, she reminds me of a wardress.'

'Of course you know how she began?'

'At the bottom — ' Colette answered briskly. She was about to add, 'like all of us', but stopped just in time. Myles Beecham had been to Harrow.

'She used to get up at six and scrub a half-mile-long corridor — '

'She still gets up at six.' Colette scowled. 'I wake at five, you know.' She smiled a vaguely flirtatious smile. 'To wake up at that time, in this glorious countryside, is pure heaven.'

Myles caught her eye and instantly looked away. He liked her but was not altogether comfortable with her scent and soft, feminine clothes. Colette had sensed this, and for a moment she wondered, as she so often did, about the women in his life. 'I wouldn't expect to be a paid housekeeper, of course,' she said defensively.

'Naturally not,' he said quickly. 'You'd be the châtelaine.'

'Until he remarries.'

'Until he remarries,' Myles agreed.

'He deserves to be happy, does he not?'

Although Colette had come to think of herself as a Frenchwoman it was never a case of *Mon Dieu, les anglais!* for her, probably because she admired the English so much that she could even be indulgent about their failings. If she was now the unmistakable but temporary châtelaine of Stanford Hall, she still knew her place as well as Simpson knew his. She was at Stanford Hall to ease Saffity's way, and to serve him with nothing less than the dogged devotion of a maiden aunt or perhaps, just perhaps, of a mother. If, at the same time, her own life took on a golden hue, she always likened herself to the full blooms that were daily harvested from the garden to fill the vases with their transient replaceable glory. She could be just as easily disposed of.

Meanwhile, she made the most of the new career that lay in her lap like a bouquet of full-blown peonies. Copying the lifestyle of other, authentic châtelaines, she discarded her habit of acquiring *couture* clothes, and found herself a local dressmaker who ran up the kind of frocks that she had observed were worn by those born to their station. She prevailed upon the vicar to hold services in Stanford Hall chapel one Sunday a month. She herself gave French lessons to the chauffeur's daughter.

Astute enough to look and dress somewhat older than her forty years, the dignity of her style earned her the kind of respect that makes for great confidence. She was aware, looking out through the gracious French windows, upon the acres of lake-like lawns, that in all the world only one person, Saffity, knew that she had once been frightened by grass and trees. But that time belonged, it now seemed, to another life in another century, when her first sight of a stretch of grass had been in the Bois de Boulogne.

So no bunch of keys was worn at her waist and she made certain never to use the servants' staircase.

But the linen room was now modelled on the one she had seen all those years ago at the Château Cologne, when she was about sixteen, shortly after she had arrived in Paris, and her American 'benefactor' had rented her out for a few weeks to the Viscomtess de Varenne. The linen-room shelves at Stanford Hall were now edged with lace.

That touch of lace had certainly been appreciated by Saffity. It had recalled La Fenêtre de Saffarty for him, as Colette had known it would.

In an otherwise perfect – if celibate – life, her chief anxiety was how the new woman who was bound to come into Saffity's life would accept her.

18

The management and staff of Wyndham Carpet Company regret to inform you of the tragic deaths on the 23rd of May, 1931, of Sir William and Lady Wyndham, and their daughter Edwina.

Mr Simon Saffity has been appointed chairman of the company.

Max Blum read and re-read the printed black-bordered card. It was September, only a few days before his and Fanny's third anniversary. He stared at the card, and then stared at the envelope. After several moments he understood that the under-stamped card had been sent by sea mail. It had taken four months to reach Johannesburg.

Lucky bastard, Max thought; he's probably inherited the whole caboodle! He tried to stop himself, but the thought would not go away. Who else, he thought bitterly, but Saffity had the power to bring out the very worst, the *unthinkable* worst, in him?

He had no idea how long he sat staring at the card, remembering Edwina's incomparable beauty, remembering the extraordinary happiness that had been so visible between the two of them. It was horribly cruel, and no matter how much he hated Saffity he felt unbearably sad for Edwina. He wondered how Saffity was taking it, and imagined him throwing himself into the business. After all, it was all his now, wasn't it?

So he was head of Wyndham Carpets, and a millionaire. Who had Saffity's luck?

The phone rang, but he merely stared at its reflection on his glass-topped desk. It stopped and rang again. The urgent sound of an unanswered phone made Fanny leave her customer to answer it.

'What's happened, Max? What's wrong?' she asked at once.

Wordlessly, he handed her the card. She read it quickly. 'I'll tell Mr Clark to look after Denny Furnishers, and I'll be right back,' she said.

She returned to Max's office at once. 'What a tragedy!' she exclaimed, sitting down. 'Still, it won't affect Trans-Empire Carpets.' She leaned over and stroked his hand. He said nothing. He took his hand away, folded his arms, laid them down on his square of blotting paper, put his head on his arms and wept openly.

Fanny sat silently for a while, and after a while got up to order a pot of strong tea. She had never seen Max behave like this before – he was not the sort of man who cried. She had heard him scream out during those terrible nightmares that woke both of them. Thank God it didn't happen so often any more. He had never disclosed the nature of the nightmares, though once he had mentioned something about a huge vulture-like bird. She had her own theories, of course, and had long suspected that Saffity was somehow involved.

She got up and stroked his back awkwardly. She knew how he felt about Saffity; they had talked about it often enough; and while she sympathised with his resentment over the voteless B shares, on the whole she was grateful to him. She suspected Max's relationship with Saffity to be more than a little one-sided, but she would not have dreamed of letting him know that.

Moses, the aged tea-boy, was taking too long with that tea, she thought, making a mental note to talk to him about it. Watching her husband cry gave her a strange feeling. True, he was not a happy man but he was a good husband, and a devoted father. Just thinking about her two boys, her son and her husband, brought a smile to her lips. Two and a half years old, Jeff was already swimming. They had taken lessons together, and had learned to dive together, and that had made Max almost happy. She had long suspected that something too terrible to talk about had happened to Max, and his uncontrollable weeping now confirmed her belief that Saffity was involved. On the other hand, who could blame him for not speaking about his past? No one here talked about life in the old country. Fanny believed that the immigrants transplanted themselves so effortlessly because in the welcoming, fertile, virgin soil of South Africa, people sank roots as easily as if they were geraniums.

The tea tray was brought in, and Fanny pulled herself out of her reverie.

'Have some tea, Max,' she said. 'Moses brought you a nice, strong cup of tea. It will do you good.'

She poured the tea and handed it to him. He drank it noisily.

'I think I'll take the afternoon off,' he said. 'I think I'll go home. I can't concentrate on anything now.'

'Let the driver take you then. I don't want you driving yourself. I'll call him for you.'

There was only one person Max wanted to talk to, and that was Mireille. He wanted to speak to her privately, from his own home, and not take the risk of his switchboard operator listening in. It made no difference to him that the girl couldn't understand French – perhaps she knew a few words, who could tell? In any case, he wanted to talk to Mireille for as long as he liked, and he did not want Fanny to hover over him as he spoke to her.

He dialled the trunk call operator, who put him through at once. 'Lady Rutherford, please,' he said, smiling at Mireille's new name. Mireille had become Lady Rutherford two months earlier.

'Lady Rutherford is in the cellars at the moment. Is that Master Max?'

'Yes, Sarie, it is Mr Blum.' Sarie was the coloured cook Mireille had engaged nearly two years ago.

'How are you, master? Nice to hear you.'

'Thank you, Sarie. I need to speak to Lady Rutherford urgently. Please ask her to telephone me at home. I'm not in my office.'

'Does she have your number at home, master? I'll go down to the cellar and call her for you — '

Max knew it would be only a matter of a few moments before his phone would ring. He was beginning to feel a fraction easier. Sarie's clear voice always sounded genuinely pleased to hear from him, and even the telephone connection with the tranquillity of Mireille's Rutherford Estate seemed to have a calming effect.

The phone rang just as quickly as he had predicted it would.

'What's happened, Max?' Mireille asked in French, speaking at her highest speed. 'Sarie said it was urgent.'

Max told her about the black-bordered card.

'When did it happen, Max? When was Edwina killed?' Mireille asked tonelessly.

'On the twenty-third of May.'

'That means Saffity's wife had already been dead for two months when I got married.' Mireille sighed into the telephone. 'I only agreed to get married because he was married,' she whispered.

'I can't hear you, Mireille. These trunk calls . . . Saffity's got no one, you know. He never told his family he was married. I thought, maybe, you would tell him about Theresa as an act of mercy.'

'*Mercy?*' Mireille hissed. 'Cruelty, you mean, surely? It's out of the question. I'll never tell him, and he must never know, and Theresa must never know.'

'Mireille, please — '

'Don't do this to me, Max,' Mireille said furiously. 'We've been through all this before. So Saffity is alone. Well, that has nothing to do with me.'

'Think it over, Mireille. Think it over, at least.'

'*You* think it over, Max!' Mireille yelled. 'I'm warning you, if you say one word about this, Max Blum, I'll destroy you. And that's not a threat, it's a promise.' She paused for a moment, and went on rapidly, 'I never wanted to say this to you, Max Blum, but I see I have no alternative.' Her voice dropped to a harsh whisper. 'Saffity told me about the trouble you had in Paris. He told me about your – your – difficulties – with a woman called Colette.'

'I see,' Max answered dully. His mind raced. What had Saffity told her? He would never know because he would never ask either of them . . . He said only, 'I thought we were friends, Mireille. I thought we would be friends for ever. I see I was mistaken.'

He slammed down the receiver, and loosened his tie. It was ten o'clock in the morning, an hour and a half since he had read the card. He drank rarely, but it seemed he was in need of a whisky. He was unlocking the liquor cabinet when the phone rang again. It was Fanny. 'Are you all right, Max?' she asked anxiously. 'You should take an aspirin and go to bed.'

'I'm going to,' Max answered mechanically. 'I'll phone you when I wake up.'

He was pouring his drink when the phone rang yet again. 'Max? Max, I'm sorry I spoke to you like that. I can't apologise enough. Please forgive me. Please tell me we're still friends?'

'I forgive you,' Max said miserably. What else could he do? he asked himself. How much did she know?

'Thank you, Max. Thank you.'

He heard her let out her breath.

'I'm like a vicious lioness protecting her cub,' Mireille said nervously, her words rushing. 'You see, Theresa is a very headstrong child. And I'm married now, Max. I'm *married*. And my *husband* believes Theresa's father died before she was born. But you know all this, Max.'

'Forget it, Mireille,' he said hastily. 'I'll never mention the subject again.' He made his voice sound cold and deliberate. 'This matter will not be discussed again.'

'Wait, wait, Max. I haven't told you the most important thing. He's going to adopt her. My daughter is going to be his daughter – *our* daughter.'

Max congratulated her, but his mind was on other matters. *What exactly did she know about him?* When he had replaced the receiver he poured the whisky back into the bottle, took a shower, and drove himself back to his office. A large warehouse in Commissioner Street was about to become vacant, and it had been offered to him. And even if it was only half as good as he had been told it was, it would still be too good to lose.

On a glittering autumn morning in May 1932, five years and one month after his arrival in South Africa, Max strolled towards the Law Courts. It was a momentous day – he was to become a South African citizen. He had expected to be part of a group, but it turned out to be a cold ceremony for one. A bored magistrate handed him a Bible, and told him to swear his allegiance to the King and Queen, the Empire and the Commonwealth. A document was thrust in front of him. He signed it, and was now a naturalised South African as well as a citizen of the United Kingdom and Colonies, and not even the chill of the bureaucrats diminished his pride in that.

He found his father waiting for him in the foyer. 'I'm glad you came, Poppa,' Max smiled. 'A lovely surprise.'

'I thought I'd be a *mensch*,' his father said. 'It's a big day for you, I know. So we'll walk back to the shop together. The exercise will do you good. You use Absalom too much.'

They stopped to watch a group of singing African labourers who were in the throes of sliding a heavy chunk of steel, moving it to the rhythm of the song. Their joyous harmony was led by a soloist, while the rest of the workers formed a chorus heaving the huge steel block in perfect rhythm.

A few whites who had gathered smiled their superiority.

'D'you know what they're singing, Max?' his father asked unexpectedly.

'Of course I don't know what they're singing,' Max answered impatiently.

'They sing against us whites, against the oppression of passes and permits — '

'Impossible!' Max laughed scornfully. 'Just listen to how happy they are. They're *singing*, aren't they?'

'Absalom told me. I persuaded him to translate the Sotho.'

'Let's get to the office,' Max said peevishly. 'Moses will give you a glass of hot lemon tea.'

'Moses was born here, but citizenship is forbidden to him. Yet foreigners like us . . . ' The old man hesitated, and then, clearly troubled, continued. 'It's like Poland,' he added sadly. 'The *numerus clausus*. Remember, you had to go to Paris because of the restricted numbers? Only here, it's the other way round. They're the majority, yet it's *numerus clausus* for them. I don't like it, Max.'

'It's such a proud day for me. Don't spoil it, Poppa.'

'You didn't like being restricted, did you, Max?' the old man persisted stubbornly. 'Absalom is a gentleman, a real *mensch*. He doesn't like it either.'

Certain his father was going senile, Max said decisively, 'You'll have some lemon tea and you'll feel better.'

During the next weeks and months Max came as close as was possible, for one of his anxious disposition and burden of guilt, to being happy. Trans-Empire Carpets moved into the vast single-storey warehouse of ten thousand square feet – all that space without a single pillar to occlude the customer's view. So much space required a vast stock, and the sheer quantity as much as the variety dazzled and impressed his customers.

Max's business prospered as Johannesburg prospered. At the end of that year, in December 1932, South Africa came off the gold standard. This meant that the selling price of gold – Johannesburg's staple – soared from four pounds five shillings to seven pounds an ounce. Share values rocketed and there was no shortage of money for carpets. Some called it wall-to-wall, others called it edge-to-edge – it made no difference. Carpeting had become a status symbol, and Trans-Empire Carpets had already overtaken its competitors.

The year 1933, in which General Smuts formed a coalition, and went ahead with legislation to protect white jobs from black competition, was also the year that Hitler came to power. There were fierce debates in Parliament about whether or not South Africa should remain neutral if there *were* to be a war. Dr Malan, who with his policy of *Swart Gevaar* – Black Peril – was to become Prime Minister three years after the war had ended, caused enormous distress to Max when he announced that the British Empire was finished at last.

Max and Fanny bought a large, square house in Lower Houghton, one of the new, fashionable suburbs. Max chose it because it reminded him of the Abelmans' house. It had no swimming pool, so they had one built.

Less than five years after he had opened his own business, Max had connections with a slew of new suppliers; carpet factories in Belgium, England and Holland now vied for his custom. Only one thing rankled, however, and that was what Saffity did with those profits that he chose not to remit to England. Saffity had become an ardent sponsor of the Summerville Church Choir, as well as of the music department of the Witwatersrand University, and from time to time he requested Max to send them substantial donations.

Everyone who knew her said that she was 'even better than a daughter' to her parents-in-law, and Fanny would have been the last person to disagree. It was true that she went out of her way to please, and that she was for ever devising ways of demonstrating the measure of her respect for them. She believed that the Blums were entitled to some kind of formal recognition, and it was with this in mind that she hit on the idea of having a small party to celebrate the fact that they were no longer tenants. Max was now the sole owner of the property to which he had moved his business nearly six years ago.

When the purchase documents were signed, in March 1935, Fanny planned the party for April. Even in spite of the mortgage she was overjoyed by Max's acquisition, not least because it meant that Saffity would therefore be forced to become Max's tenant. Not only that, but since he had a half share in Trans-Empire Carpets, the above-average rent the company would pay Max would go a long way towards paying off the mortgage. Fanny had never been able to plumb the depths of what she called Max's 'emotional attitude' toward Saffity. As soon as his name was mentioned, everything about her husband – from his posture to his mood – changed.

She was determined that one day she would get to the bottom of whatever it was.

Meanwhile to hell with Saffity, she decided to herself. Owning the property meant security; the rest was irrelevant. Max was doing well, and did not really require her help any longer, but the business was in her blood now and she could not imagine life without it. Besides, why should she? She loved the challenge of selling.

Max's parents were invaluable; they saw to the running of the house and were there when Jeff came home from school.

The party was an excellent way of honouring her parents-in-law, and it wouldn't do any harm to invite a few of their most important customers. Max's father Blum wanted to affix a *mezuzah* – a slender silver container, shaped like a fish, which holds the traditional prayer parchment – to the huge rolled metal door of Trans-Empire Carpets. By now, thanks to the large wooden counters and the bright lighting, all under Fanny's relentless efficient supervision, the business looked more like a shop than a warehouse. Indeed, Fanny and Max thought of it – and talked about it – as a shop.

The brief and simple ceremony to fix the *mezuzah* was held soon after six, when the shop was closed. When Isaac Blum recited the ancient blessing – 'Who has commanded us to fix the *mezuzah*' – tears streamed down his cheeks into his long grey beard. Then, when he lifted little Jeff, and placed the boy's fingers first to the *mezuzah* and then to his lips, there was scarcely a dry eye in the small assembly. Even Max, Fanny noted with pleasure, seemed moved. . . .

Suddenly Max raised his glass of sweet *kosher* wine. 'A toast to my wife,' he said proudly.

'A good wife is above rubies,' Isaac Blum intoned.

Fanny smiled. If Max was happy, she was happy. One day this business would be for Jeff, and as far as she was concerned the best wasn't good enough for Jeff.

The next morning Max flew into one of his rages. 'Saffity's done it to me again!' he fumed to Fanny. 'He's unloaded this dud stock of a pink background Axminster on me. I ordered blue, not bloody pink!'

As always when Max shouted Fanny rose to close the office door. 'I know you ordered blue, Max,' she said placatingly. 'Tell him you won't keep the pink unless he reduces the price. You can get a good discount, and I'm pretty sure Evans Furnishers will take the pink — '

'I'll send it back to him,' Max interrupted savagely, 'and he'll have to bear the shipping costs.'

'You'll do no such thing, Max,' Fanny said sharply. 'He probably knows you don't need to get goods on consignment from him any more. And he's still giving you the use of his money free of charge.'

'Of course he knows,' Max grunted. 'He sees the balance sheets, doesn't he?' A long, angry sigh escaped. 'The *devil*!'

Fanny said wearily, 'We're buying our stock from Holland, Belgium and Italy. We've got a staff of twenty-five now. We're the biggest wholesale carpet business in the whole of Africa. Can't you count your blessings, Max?'

'Saffity has still got the A shares.'

'So what?' Fanny said with an impatient flourish of her arms. 'You bought this property. His share of the rent pays your mortgage. You've had your own business for six years. Saffity gave you your chance. Just be careful how you handle him,' she said coldly. 'I've got a stake in this business too, you know.' She thumped the desk with her fist and walked out.

Max closed the ledger he had been attending to. Fanny was right, of course, but only up to a point. He buzzed his secretary and asked for the most recent letter from Saffity, and then told her he would call her when he was ready to dictate a reply. There was nothing unusual about the substance of the letter; it was Saffity's hand-written postscript that was so unsettling. Saffity had written, 'I'm learning to fly a plane – can you imagine, I'm almost a pilot?' Max shook his head wonderingly. 'Lucky bastard!' he said out loud.

Max buzzed his secretary again. 'Get me Hepworth's Sports on the line,' he said briskly. When he was put through he said, 'I've decided I will have that set of golf clubs after all . . . Yes, yes, I know it's your most expensive. Send it over and your cheque will be waiting for you.'

Saffity played golf, too. Max remembered having seen a photograph of him in full golfing gear. Max had played several rounds himself, and he had not been too bad at all. It had even crossed his mind that he and Saffity might have a round or two together when he went on his buying trip to England and Europe the following month. So now Saffity was

313

flying planes. He was unstoppable – and he had probably bought himself an aeroplane by now, Max thought enviously. He decided to go out and hit a few golf balls. His aim was sure – whenever his club connected with the ball, he imagined Saffity's head . . .

Max's mood shifted upward. One of the wonderful things about having his own business was that he could choose to take the occasional day off, though he rarely did so. After his round of golf he chose not to return to Trans-Empire Carpets but to go home. It was the middle of the afternoon. He hoped Jeff would be at home, too, and looked in his room. Through his half-opened bedroom door, he saw the boy standing with his back to a long mirror. Jeff's trousers were down, and Max saw his reflected blood-streaked buttocks.

'What happened, Jeff? What happened?' he shrieked. He lifted Jeff, laid him on the bed and began stripping his clothes. His back and his buttocks were covered in ugly scratches. 'Who did this to you?'

'The big boys.'

'Which big boys?'

'They told me to come to them, and then they threw me into the rose bushes. My trousers and my shirt got torn. I'm sorry, Dad.'

'To hell with your clothes. Which big boys did this?'

'It was Dirk. He's seven. And his friend. He was wearing my jersey. I knew it was my jersey because it was new, and when he was sitting at the desk in front of me in class, I turned it back and saw my name tag.'

'So you told him it was your jersey.'

'It was my jersey!' Jeff said angrily. 'What's a Yid, Dad?'

'A Yid? Why do you want to know what a Yid is?'

'Because when I told Dirk he was wearing my jersey, he said, "D'you know what you are? You're a bloody Yid. That's what you are." So I said I wasn't.'

'You are a Yid. You're a Jew.'

'I know I'm a Jew,' Jeff said, puzzled.

'Some people don't like Jews.'

'Why? Because they don't have Christmas stockings?'

'In a way.' Max laughed shortly. 'I didn't think it would happen here, in South Africa. I'll put you in the bath, and then I'll phone your mother to come home immediately.'

314

They were already in the bathroom. Max was pouring Dettol antiseptic into the bath, and thought that though the incident was disappointing, and even surprising, it was hardly shocking – it had always been like that, everywhere. It always would be.

Then Annie, the cook, called him urgently to the telephone. It was Fanny, telling him his father had had a heart attack, and was in an ambulance on his way to the hospital. Max left Jeff with Annie, and raced to the hospital.

Max was obliged to cancel his European buying trip; it took eight months for his father to die. About a week before the end came, his father read a newspaper report stating that Jews in Germany were forbidden either to sell dolls with Aryan features, or to use wax models with Aryan features in their showrooms or window displays. It was an insult to German womanhood.

Max's father's dying words were: 'Hitler should feel as I'm feeling now.'

Trans-Empire Carpets continued to prosper. Salesmen and agents vied with one another to get orders, and they came to Max's door all the way from America as well as Europe. It seemed it wasn't absolutely necessary for Max to go to Europe himself. Fanny, however, disagreed. She was keen on getting more exclusive lines, and was insistent that they laid in large stocks; war was imminent, and they would need the extra supplies before manufacturing ceased.

In March 1939, Fanny's sister in Lithuania wrote suggesting a reunion in London, in August of that year. Almost at once Fanny was overtaken by an obsessive longing to see her sister again. She nagged, cried, wheedled, shouted, sulked, and only stopped when she and Jeff were on their way to Cape Town, to board the *Windsor Castle* for England.

When Table Mountain disappeared from view she turned to Jeff and said, 'Your father came to this country on the same ship, you know. That was eleven years ago.'

'Before I was born,' Jeff said with satisfaction.

'Yes, my boy. Before you were born.' Fanny leaned down and

kissed his cheek. 'And you and I are going to meet Daddy's old friend – Mr Saffity.'

'I don't want to meet him!' Jeff said. 'I hate him.'

'But you don't know him. How can you hate someone you don't know?'

'If Daddy hates him, I hate him.'

Out of the mouths of babes, Fanny thought; but she said, 'Don't be silly. Your father likes Mr Saffity very much.'

Jeff was a tough and wiry little boy, and his aggressive determination more than made up for his smaller than average size. At school he was in the football and tennis A teams, and on the *Warwick Castle* he won races even when he was the youngest competitor. The last big event on board ship was the sixty-yard race and Jeff won a Swiss wristwatch. It was his proudest possession.

Nothing in England was as Fanny had expected it to be. Saffity was not at Wyndham Carpets. Fanny spoke to Myles, who asked after Max most cordially and told her that Saffity was in the Royal Air Force. Even amidst the confusion of pre-war preparations, and of her sister's insistence that they leave London at once for the safer seaside town of Bognor Regis, Myles' news was a bitter blow. At the same time Fanny felt a growing sense of fear, for although she had believed, for several months, that the war was imminent, she'd had no idea what 'imminent' really meant. True, she had been aware that many Afrikaners supported the Nazis; she had even witnessed a march of the Black Shirts in Johannesburg. And it would have been difficult to dismiss the tremendous Afrikaner resentment towards the six hundred German Jewish refugees who had escaped to South Africa on the *Stuttgart*, a ship specially chartered to beat the new restrictive South African Aliens Act.

None of this had really touched her, for it had nothing to do with her own secure, prosperous life in Johannesburg. South Africa was too far away to get even a glimpse of the big world. Now, she regretted the obstinacy that had made her leave her safe, distant and isolated haven of South Africa.

Ten days after they arrived in England, Germany invaded Poland. Three days after that, war was declared.

There was little joy in the reunion with her sister. It was

nineteen years since the two sisters had been together, and Sonja still saw Fanny as her 'young sister'. Fanny found the gas masks, her bossy sister, the terror of war and being without servants all equally hateful.

The sisters quarrelled bitterly and incessantly. Sonja insisted on going back to Lithuania.

Sonja was the stronger of the two. Finally Fanny gave in, and begged, 'At least let me take Geddie back to South Africa with me.'

'Leave my son, with you? Geddie?' Sonja shrieked. 'You've gone mad, Fanny, *mad*!'

'But you met those Polish Jewish refugees yourself, Sonja. They told you about the Gestapo!'

'*Pollaks*,' Sonja sniffed contemptuously. 'I'm a *Litvak*, and I'm going home to be with my husband. If they hadn't stopped the transfer of funds out of Lithuania, I wouldn't have to beg you for money for my fare!' Her voice dropped to a whisper. '*I'm* going mad without him. Can't you see that, Fanny? Can't you?'

Fanny stared at her once elegant sister and was forced to agree that she was, indeed, going mad. She had lost at least ten pounds in as many days, her face was gaunt and her sunken, restless, darting, imploring eyes forced Fanny to turn away. Suddenly Sonja grabbed Fanny by the lapels and yelled, 'You've got the money, Fanny. You've got to give me it. You've got to pay for those black-market tickets. You've got to!' She fell into a fit of weeping, and beat her chest. Fanny watched her, motionless, altogether unable to speak.

At last Sonja let go of Fanny's lapels. Now she sank to her knees and said, 'I want my husband, Fanny. I want to make love to my husband. Are you already such a dried-up old prune that you can't see that? What sort of husband have you got, anyway? Are you too frightened of him to give me the money?'

Fanny jerked her sister to her feet. 'Don't you worry about my husband!' she hissed, deeply hurt. 'Haven't you listened to a word I've said?' Visibly forcing herself to remain calm, she lowered her voice. 'The SS seized Jewish judges and lawyers and dragged them through the streets. For God's sake, Sonja, even *you* can't deny Kristallnacht – the night of the broken glass, when thousands of Jewish stores and synagogues had their windows smashed!'

'*Lies!*' Sonja shrieked. 'Germany is the most civilised, enlightened country in Europe. Lies, lies, lies! Stop lying to me!'

'But the Ministry of Education has banned all Jewish children from the schools,' Fanny continued urgently. 'They are going to have all Jews sterilised. They'll sterilise your Geddie!'

Sonja threw back her head and a burst of laughter tore from her throat. 'Now you've just proved that you are hysterical, Fanny,' she said witheringly. 'If I don't go back the Lithuanians – not the Germans – will arrest my husband – that was a condition of my departure!' She waved her hand dismissively. 'Of course we don't believe it.' She broke off. 'The money,' she moaned. 'Give me the money.'

'You can have the money,' Fanny said, deeply hurt. 'But you're forcing me to pay for your death passage. Have you no pity for me, Sonja?'

'God bless you, Fanny. I will bless you for ever.'

'All my instincts tell me I'll hate myself for ever!'

'Don't hate yourself, Fanny. The Germans have always been better to us than the Russians. It's the Russians, not the Germans, who call us Christ killers. It's the Russians, not the Germans, who have the pogroms. Or had you forgotten that?'

Four days later, on October 3rd, 1939, their reunion over, the four of them were at Victoria Station. Sonja looked calm and elegant in her fawn camel coat with its generous matching fox collar. Distraught and untidy, Fanny said, 'May God forgive me. I will never forgive myself.'

'You always were a pessimist, my dear,' Sonja said as she and Geddie boarded the train. 'You'll have to travel, too, you know. How safe do you think you'll be on the high seas yourself, Fanny? Haven't you heard of submarines, little sister?'

'I've heard of them,' Fanny said, managing a smile. '*Bon voyage*, Sonja. *Bon voyage*.'

The train started to pull out of the station. Suddenly Jeff streaked after it, and while he ran he unbuckled the wristwatch he had won on the *Windsor Castle*. He caught up with Geddie and handed it to him through the carriage window, shouting, 'It's a souvenir of me! I want you to have my watch.'

Fanny sobbed uncontrollably.

Jeff was ten years old, and much too wiry to be lifted bodily. Even so she picked him up, and though the cardboard boxes containing their gas masks got in the way, and the strings entangled, she kissed him wildly, saying, 'Why did you give him your watch, Jeff?' She repeated, 'Oh *why* did you give him your watch?'

'Because of the war.' Jeff struggled to get down. 'Because of the Gestapo.'

Even as Fanny and Jeff turned the key in the faded red door of the cottage at Bognor Regis they heard the telephone ringing. Fanny rushed to answer it.

'This is a radio call from South Africa,' the operator said.

'Yes. Yes. What is it?' Fanny said anxiously, her voice rising.

'A person to person call to Mrs Fanny Blum. Are you Mrs Blum?'

'Yes, yes.'

'Hold the line please. We're connecting you to the caller.'

Fanny's heart lurched. A phone call all the way from South Africa was unthinkable. Something terrible must have happened. She broke into a sweat.

'Fanny?' Max shouted.

'Are you all right, Max?' Fanny screamed. The line crackled.

'I want you and Jeff to get on a ship at once,' Max screamed back. He sounded hysterical. 'No matter what it costs. Get the money from Saffity's office. I don't care what it costs. D'you hear me?'

'It's terribly dangerous now,' Fanny answered.

'I can't hear you. This is costing a fortune. Get on a ship immediately!'

The operator cut in. 'Hurry up. This is the last private radio-call from South Africa to England.'

'I can't hear you, Max,' Fanny said desperately.

'Get on a ship,' Max shrieked.

The line went dead.

'We're going home, Jeff,' Fanny said. She began to cry.

At the Union Castle offices Fanny found crowds of people desperate to escape Britain, begging for tickets. She and Jeff had an open return ticket, which meant they had preference over the others, and would get their passage home. Several strangers stopped her, some offering as much as two thousand pounds for a single ticket.

Fanny got their tickets, sent a cable to Max, and prepared to leave.

She was nothing if not persistent. At the very last moment she telephoned Wyndham Carpets again. She was put through to Myles Beecham again. Suddenly, though it owed more to a need to save face than to pure business motives, she decided to place a large order.

'I doubt we'll be able to ship anything,' Myles said apologetically. 'The factory is not running normally.'

'I'll take whatever you can give me. You can ship whatever stock you like. Anything, that is, up to twenty-five thousand pounds' worth.'

'We'll do our best, Mrs Blum,' Myles said efficiently. 'You're a brave woman, Mrs Blum.' He hesitated briefly. 'I look forward to meeting you when all this is over. *Bon voyage.*'

Their dangerous, zig-zagging voyage home in convoy on the *Windsor Castle* was to take three or more weeks. Fanny and Jeff shared their cabin with six women. An emergency drill was held once every day, and three times daily Jeff watched the gun practice when wooden boxes with red flags were lowered into the sea as targets for the cannon.

Three days after they had been at sea the weather suddenly cleared. Now for the first time Jeff could see 204 Squadron's low-flying planes, their escort on this leg of their perilous journey. The huge Sunderlands reminded him of beautiful monsters from another world. But the Moths were smaller, and it was easier to imagine piloting one of them himself.

'Isn't Saffity a pilot, Mom?' he asked suddenly.

'I think so, darling.'

'Do you think he could be up there?' Jeff said, pointing to the sky.

'I hope not,' Fanny murmured.

Fanny was terrified they would be sunk by U-boats.

In the event they reached South Africa safely.

Max and Mireille – now a poised and confident Lady Rutherford – and Theresa were waiting for them at Cape Town docks. They spent the day at the Rutherford Estate, and it was there that Fanny found out that though conscription was not compulsory in South Africa, Max had attempted to enlist but had been rejected, on the grounds of his ulcer, as medically unfit for military service. Jeff and Theresa played happily together; they had never met before.

In the train on the way back to Johannesburg, Fanny said, 'I didn't meet your friend Saffity, after all. He was away, on government service, they said.'

'*He* hasn't got an ulcer,' Max said bitterly. 'The lucky bastard was already a pilot before the war. He's probably a wing commander in the RAF by now!'

'Conscription is compulsory in England,' Fanny replied tartly. 'I bet Saffity's in uniform in a safe desk job!'

'What do you know, Fanny?' Max said. 'Have you forgotten the photograph he sent us four years ago? The one beside a plane. He wrote on the back of it. *I not only fly her, but I own her too.* Surely you remember that, Fanny?'

Fanny remembered that photograph well, because she had studied it so carefully. It had been the first time she had been able to see what Saffity looked like. She had not expected him to be anything like as attractive as the tall, rugged white-haired young man who smiled so confidently into the camera. Max was good-looking of course, but beside Saffity his delicate, fine-boned looks seemed not so much sensitive as weak. She said irritably, 'Saffity, Saffity. Always Saffity. How could I forget Saffity? To think I wasn't even able to meet the man we've been talking about for more than eleven years!'

19

At the time of his first flying lesson, in April 1935, Saffity's flight instructor, Captain Mark Farquarson, rapidly concluded that he had nerves of steel and would therefore make an excellent pilot. Captain Farquarson was not to know that Saffity's hopelessness and the belief that he had nothing more to lose had left him without fear and almost nerveless. He knew only that after he'd heard a series of BBC broadcasts describing the procedure of becoming a pilot, he had decided to take up flying.

Saffity's first lesson was also his first flight – he had never been inside a plane before. It was Captain Farquarson's habit, as he warmed up the engine, to study his pupil. From his goggles to his windbreaker, there could be no denying that Saffity was certainly dressed for the part. The Captain had read the standard forms Saffity had completed, and knew that despite a mop of glistening white hair his pupil was no more than twenty-seven years old. He liked and respected Saffity's cold, almost professional interest in flying; it was in marked contrast to the shrill, nervous excitement he found in so many of the rich and fashionable young men who embraced flying the way they embraced any craze.

The captain and his pupil taxied down the runway and were preparing for take-off when two planes collided, and crashed. Instantly Captain Farquarson cut the engine, jumped out of the plane, and raced to the wreckage, but the pilots of both planes had been killed. After the fire engine and the ambulance had left, he said, 'I suppose you'd like to postpone the lesson?'

'What does the control station suggest?' Saffity asked calmly.

'I'll check with them.'

He talked to them through the headphones of the Tiger. 'They say it's OK.'

'Good,' Saffity said.

Two weeks later, during his fourth lesson, Saffity realised he had taken more naturally to flying an aeroplane than to riding a horse. Up in the sky, looking down through a filter of fine cloud at Edwina's beloved green England, the vision of the earth's eternity made him glad to be alive after all . . .

He had all the necessary credentials, and was only two days away from his first solo and his licence. As he came in to land from a lesson he saw a glittering new plane on the grass runway. Later he joined the people standing around it, stroking and touching its gleaming yellow wings. A strikingly attractive woman standing at some distance from the group caught his eye. She wore a grey flannel and gabardine trouser suit, with a white wool scarf and a white canvas helmet. Almost involuntarily he gave an approving smile. The woman smiled back, and Saffity walked over to her. 'That plane's a beauty,' Saffity said admiringly. 'Is she yours?'

'She certainly is,' the woman said in a slow Southern drawl that delighted him. 'How did you know?'

'Your elegant air of ownership gave you away,' he answered, and found to his astonishment that there was nothing forced about his laugh – he was laughing because he wanted to.

The woman laughed with him. 'I'm Brooke Cullen,' she said. 'I'm about to take her up. Like to join me?'

'Love to,' he said at once. 'I'm called Saffity.'

'Saffity who?'

'Just Saffity. Everyone calls me that.'

'Except me,' Brooke said slowly. 'I'll call you Saff.'

'Have it your own way,' he shrugged. 'When do we take off?'

'Right now.'

They climbed into the cockpit and the small group dispersed. When she put on her goggles she looked still more glamorous. For all that, he was more than a little nervous; but then, as he reminded himself, that was the whole idea. They took off and his spirits soared. He could tell at once that he was in the hands of a highly skilled pilot. After a while she said, shouting above the noise of the engine, 'Do you have your licence?'

'Not yet,' he grinned. 'Two days to go. How long have you been flying?'

'Long enough,' she said.

'How long have you had this plane?'

'It's brand new.'

'She's a beauty,' he said appreciatively.

'Isn't she?' she agreed. Suddenly she turned the de Havilland over, and they were flying upside down. His stomach felt it had been turned inside out. Shortly after that they landed.

Walking back to the clubhouse Brooke said, 'I guess you haven't done aerobatics before?'

'No,' Saffity said sharply. 'I've never gone in for stunts.'

'I'm sorry,' she said, contrite. 'I didn't mean to frighten you. You went green, you know.'

'Did I?' he chuckled. 'Good. That's the best news I've had in years. Will you join me for lunch at the clubhouse?'

'Thanks. I'd love to,' she said removing her helmet and releasing a great mass of jet-black hair.

When they were seated at a corner table under the wooden propeller on the ceiling, Brooke said, 'I guess you're the first man I ever met who was pleased to hear he'd turned green.'

'You obviously know the wrong men,' Saffity said drily. 'Are you a professional pilot?'

'Yes. I am a professional pilot.' She hesitated briefly, then continued, 'But if the fact that I don't earn my living by flying means that I'm not a professional, then I'm not a professional.'

'You're a professional,' Saffity said emphatically. 'You're wearing a ring. Are you married?'

'What is this – an inquisition?'

'It's nothing like an inquisition. It's getting down to basics,' he said bluntly. 'Are you married?' he asked again.

'More or less. Half and half,' Brooke replied, evasively.

'How half is half and half?' he asked seriously. 'Do you mean sixty-forty, or ninety-ten, or fifty-fifty?'

'That's a good question,' she drawled. 'You crystallised my thinking for me.' She passed her hand over her forehead. 'Zero.'

'So you are about to be an unmarried woman,' he said gently. He laid his hand over hers for a moment.

'Are you married, Saffity?'

'Yes,' he sighed deeply. 'That is, no. Edwina, my wife . . . Well, she died in an accident, four years ago.' It was clear that it was still difficult for him to speak about this.

'I'm very, very sorry, Saff.' She touched his cheek. 'Edwina was a lucky woman,' she said gravely, 'because you loved her, and because I'm sure she knew that.'

'What's your story?' he said kindly. 'Tell me why you are getting unmarried. Tell me why you said I had crystallised your thinking. I liked that phrase of yours.'

Brooke was a private person, not much given to revealing personal details. But something about Saffity's frank, direct approach pushed away the usual conventions and compelled her confidence. A sudden, graceful intimacy sprang between them. She drew a deep breath and began.

She told him that though she was not living with Edwin Meredith, they were not formally separated. She could not face up to a second failure, and she supposed that was why they had been drifting along. Her husband was a professor at London University, and he was more involved with his work than with his marriage; he was absent-minded to the point where he had hardly noticed that she'd moved out of their disgustingly primitive sixteenth-century cold-water flat. He lived in the sphere of the mind, he said, and was not really interested in creature comforts. So, when she checked into the Dorchester, he didn't seem to give a damn one way or the other. It was too bad that she was a bad picker. She had hoped she would have learned from an earlier mistake, but this was her second.

Still, she couldn't really blame herself for her first. She'd been a manicurist in her hometown, Atlanta, Georgia, and her first husband, Wayne Price, had been one of her clients. Wayne was a powerful man, a household name in the States, and though he was forty and she was twenty she had been so flattered by his attentions that she could not believe it when he asked her to marry him. Besides, she had loved him! He had been so courtly, and such a gentleman, and so respectful and considerate that it simply had not occurred to her that there could be anything wrong with him. Her voice trembled, but she went on to say that he had not been respectful so much as frightened. He could not touch a woman – a month after their marriage he had confessed everything. He could only love boys. He had begged her to keep it a secret, and in the end he had settled one million dollars on her.

'But you see, Saff, he needn't have paid me a dime. That was the worst of it. He thought he'd have to pay me. He never believed that I really, really loved him.'

Not long after the divorce, she had – as she put it – taken to the air, and back in 1929 she had been one of the twenty Flying Flappers who had competed in the Women's Air Derby. She had flown from Santa Monica to Cleveland, and when the competitors were not referred to as Flying Flappers they were called Petticoat Pilots, and the race was known as the Powder Puff Derby. It had been a glorious time, and it was the best thing she could have done. It had changed her life. One of the women pilots had told everyone that she found flying 'more thrilling than love for a man and far less dangerous', which was exactly how she had felt at that time.

Years later her flying had brought her to London, and she had met and married this professor, who, after six months of marriage on those rare occasions when he did make her feel like a woman, acted like he was doing her a favour. He'd actually had the nerve to say that when he made love to her he was giving her his blessing. 'You see, Saff,' Brooke concluded defensively, 'no self-respecting Southern gal could be expected to take that kind of insult for ever.'

'You're damn right,' he said fervently. 'You're a beautiful woman, Brooke, and a very desirable one. You've had bad luck, and you mustn't let it reflect on you as a woman.'

'You've let your food go cold,' Brooke said flatly. She picked up her fork. She did not want him to guess how much she had needed to hear a man tell her that she was desirable.

'You're living at the Dorchester now?' he asked.

'Yes.'

'That's a coincidence. So am I.'

'You live in London?'

'No. I live in Worcestershire, but I come up to London every now and then.' Saffity put down his napkin, and rose from his chair. 'Would you excuse me for a moment?' he said. 'I have to call my office.'

The secretary was delighted to be able to help him. Saffity augmented his generous tips with the personal touch; he never failed to ask after the health of the secretary's ailing mother. When he was put through to Myles he said, 'This is an emergency, old man.'

'What's wrong?'

'Hold on, Myles, it's the kind of emergency you'll approve of. Get me a suite at the Dorchester right away. Order champagne, flowers, fruit – the works. I'll leave it to you.'

'Colette will be pleased,' Myles said drily.

'Give her my love.'

When he returned to the table he said, 'Do you have your car with you, or would you like to drive back to London with me?'

326

'I do have my car,' she said softly. 'But I'd prefer to be driven by you.'

'I was hoping you'd say that.'

They were mostly silent on the drive back to London. After a while he said, 'So, my petticoat pilot, I can see why you questioned my use of the word professional.'

'I guess I'm a bit touchy about that,' she answered, sounding distressed.

'You're not wearing the standard pilot's gear.' Saffity grinned. 'And if you think it's not feminine enough for you, you're quite right.'

'Thanks.' She smiled. 'You look very masculine in yours, I must say.'

He touched the fur collar on his leather jacket, threw back his head and laughed his energetic laugh.

'You have a wonderful laugh,' she said.

Almost as if it had a will of its own, Saffity's left hand left the steering wheel and touched her wonderful hair. From then on – though the tension between them was as exquisite as it was excruciating – not a word was said.

When at last he pulled the Rolls up at the curved entrance of the Dorchester, he was pleased to note that the doorman sprang to the kind of attention that was reserved for especially welcome guests. At the same time, however, he seemed equally glad to see Brooke. They swept in and then both he and Brooke pretended not to notice the stares they provoked. They made an arresting, glamorous couple, and they knew it.

As soon as they were in his suite, and the door was closed, she looked out of the window and said, 'Well, Saff, I'm in your hands, I guess.'

'Not yet,' Saffity said gruffly. 'But you soon will be.'

He popped the champagne cork, poured two glasses, handed one to her, and said, 'To us.'

Brooke was still standing at the window. She had no sooner taken a sip, than he took the glass from her hand and placed it on the table. Then he lifted her bodily and carried her into the bedroom. 'You can't do that,' she protested. 'I'm too tall to be carried. No one's ever done that!'

'No one's ever been able to do that, you mean,' he laughed, flinging her on the bed.

'You're right,' she admitted.

'I don't know how I managed not to pull off the road,' he said hoarsely.

He began stripping off her clothes, and though she wanted to help him she could not quite bring herself to do so. She was no longer innocent but she was not an easy lay; because she was in a frenzy of desire she lay back and prolonged and savoured the waiting. Once she was naked he tore off his own clothes, and then, still standing beside the bed, he studied her nude body as thoroughly as if she were a balance sheet. She looked up at him, and into his lively, appreciative eyes; even his gaze was a sensuous experience. 'You have a perfect body,' he said. 'A beautiful body.'

And then, though she was lying on the covers, he flung them back, and a second later was beside her. He took her mouth inside his, and thrust it open, and it was more like an exchange of breath than a kiss. On and on he went, breathing her breath, making her breathe his, and all the while one hand supported her chin, while the other explored her throat, her shoulders, her firm high breasts, her curving belly, her thighs. His touch was light, tantalisingly light, and her nerves cried out for more, and she would have begged him to begin, but she was trapped inside his breath, and could not speak. It seemed an eternity, a wild, delicious eternity before he was inside her, striving after the same climactic moment. Their rhythm was as perfect as if they had been rehearsing for weeks. The great spasm arrived, simultaneously, for both of them.

Afterwards Brooke wept. 'Thank you, Saff.' She repeated, 'Thank you.'

'Don't say that,' Saffity said angrily. He added, more gently, 'Please don't say that, Brooke. Please don't *thank* me.'

'Your wife?' she whispered.

'Yes.' He took her hand. 'You're not the first woman since she died, you know. And yet – in the most important way – you are.'

'I think I understand,' she said slowly.

'You're a clever girl, Brooke. The other women were — '

'Professional women,' Brooke finished for him. 'No wonder you wanted to know whether I was a professional pilot,' she teased.

He put his hand over her left breast, and it felt like a hug. 'You're better than a professional woman,' he said firmly. 'Take it from one who knows.'

Then, as shameless as he had wanted her to be, she turned to him

328

and a moment later, making love again, they became co-conspirators, driving away the past, flying away from it, soaring in the present, with no thought for the future. They had known each other for only a few hours, but in that short space of time they knew they had become great friends, and this time their love-making was a passionate way of sealing their friendship. They fell asleep together, and woke together.

'Now I know why I took up flying,' Saffity murmured.

'Now *I* know why *I* took up flying,' Brooke echoed.

Brooke had come far – from manicurist to air ace, through endurance to enterprise – to appreciate what a rare happening an immediate, shared understanding could be. She felt confident that theirs was a man-woman understanding, and was certain that he knew this too. The most wonderful thing of all was how naturally they behaved with one another. He ordered dinner from room service, and she got up to go to the bathroom without feeling the need to cover herself with a sheet. When she returned to the bedroom she tripped over his trousers, and as she picked them up his ancient key dropped out of the pocket.

'What on earth is this? Where does it come from? An antique store?'

'It's been in our family for years. My father gave it to me before I left home.'

'It's beautiful,' she said, caressing the key. And then, disingenuously, 'When are you going back to Worcestershire?'

'I was going to go tomorrow. But I've changed my mind. The day after tomorrow probably.'

'I'm glad,' Brooke said simply.

Colette, delighted at the thought of someone new in Saffity's life, was confident that if she knew anything at all she knew and understood how men relate and react to women. After all, when she was a woman of the world her former professional services to men had been in the realm of their perceptions, expectations, hopes and fears of women as sexual creatures. She was confident, therefore, of her perception of Myles Beecham's feelings for her. His very awkwardness – sometimes he even stammered when he spoke to her – was in such marked contrast to his confident, authoritative manner with everyone else, including Saffity, that it gave him away. He wanted her, and it made him nervous as well as afraid.

Myles, for his part, could only hope that he had disguised what he believed to be his base feelings for her. Through long nights when the silence was broken only by the crackle of his pipe, or the movements of Tara, his thoughts would go to her, up at Stanford Hall, alone in her own bed. He had been both comfortable and content with his bachelorhood, but since Colette had come into his life, all that had changed. Even so, the thought of real, physical contact with her was still as alarming to him as it would have been with any woman.

Years before, he had been among the officers whom the glamorous actress, Clair Harpur, had visited in their hospital ward. He had fancied himself to be hopelessly – and eternally – in love with her. But this time, this woman Colette was the one he wanted to marry. 'I haven't got a hope in hell!' he would cry out loud, like a gong in the long night. 'Colette would never look at me!' Then he would have another whisky and smoke another pipe, but she had become as permanently fixed in his mind as the deeply etched laughter lines around his eyes.

For some months Saffity had been considering buying a town house in London. The day after he and Brooke met, they set off, as if they had been friends and lovers for years, to inspect the house in Eaton Place that he'd had his eye on. It was part of a deceased estate, and Saffity made no bones of the fact that because it was a bargain the house was more beautiful.

'People say I'd go anywhere to make five pounds,' he chuckled, 'and they're not far wrong.'

Brooke pronounced the house perfect. 'Bargain or no bargain,' she said.

At noon, an hour later, seated in the red and white drawing room – the luxurious furnishings were included in the price – the estate agent, a beaming Mr Combrook, brought over the relevant papers. There would be more documents to sign before ownership was transferred to him, but meanwhile to all intents and purposes the house – complete with housekeeper – was his.

'You're my idea of a decisive man,' Brooke said admiringly.

'Colette and Myles will be pleased, I can tell you. They've been nagging me to do this.'

'Who are they?'

'They live in Worcestershire. They're sort of family.'

'Don't you have any real family?'

'Not in England,' Saffity said with an air of finality. 'But you'll meet Colette and Myles, and you'll love them. And Finbar too. That's my dog.'

'I'm sure I will.' Brooke leaned forward and kissed him on the mouth. 'Let's spend the night here,' she said. 'I think I should get a change of clothes, don't you?'

So they drove back to the Dorchester, and arranged to meet at Eaton Place at five-thirty. She said she would go to Fortnum's to get a picnic supper for the two of them.

At Fortnum and Mason's, she quickly bought a selection of pâtés, a side of smoked salmon and some exotic French cheeses. She spent far more time choosing underwear. She was a tall, athletic woman, too tall, she had always believed, to be truly feminine. Yet her body was well proportioned, for her waist was slim, her hips curved, and her breasts, though small, were firm and high. She had always loved delicate lingerie and suddenly, at Fortnum's, she loved her body too. 'He's made me love my own body,' she said to herself, wonderingly, exultantly. She bought herself such quantities of underwear that the services of three saleswomen were required.

'Are you assembling your trousseau, madam?' one of the women asked.

'No,' Brooke said in her musical drawl. 'Well, I guess I mean yes.'

'You're American?'

'Now what made you think that?' she answered, smiling. 'Yes. I am American, and the man in my life is half French, half British. At least I think he is.' She frankly welcomed the opportunity to speak about Saff, as she called him. 'He's divine,' she went on. 'Handsome, as tall as I am, and probably the same age as I am, though his hair is white.'

Brooke's happiness overflowed and spilled onto everyone around her. When she left, an hour and a half later, a saleswoman accompanied her as far as the taxi – it would have been impossible for her to have carried all her packages without help. She had bought an assortment of nightgowns in black, red and ivory, all figure-hugging silks and satins, and chiffons, frothy with lace, with ribbon, with tiny bows and buttons. Some had halter necks and low backs, and of course they were all *décolleté*. Brooke smiled and blushed; she hoped to wear nothing at all most of the time. She had chosen lacy brassières and delicate knickers, and one or two lace-up corsets, and several silk and net suspender belts. She planned to drive Saff wild.

From Fortnum and Mason's to Asprey's. She kept the taxi waiting so that she wouldn't have to carry her packages. She had turned thirty the month before, and now that she had finally met a real man she had an irresistible urge to shower him with gifts. He was a man of such commanding elegance, too. She selected a pair of simple, even austerely designed cuff links, a single star sapphire set in a square of gold. She had got it bad, she had fallen hard, she told herself; it would last as long as it would last, and she would make the most of it. She had never met a man like Saffity, nor had she ever dreamed of knowing a lover like him . . .

Still, she would take only one of her lingerie packages with her to Eaton Place tonight. Meanwhile, there was just enough time to deposit her packages at the Dorchester, and to get her hair done.

Over the next two months Brooke moved more and more of her things to Eaton Place. She applied no pressure, however, and was always available. They went flying whenever Saffity was free and she advised him on which plane he should buy – the Moth that he would later photograph and send to Max. One morning after a particularly wild night she picked up the key and, perhaps too casually, asked, 'Saff? D'you think you could let me have your key just for today?'

'Why?'

'I — ' She stopped. 'Just for the day?'

'That's a hell of a thing to ask — '

'Only for today, Saff?' she wheedled. 'I want to feel very close to you the whole day long. I'll guard it with my love and my life, Saff. You know I will.'

'You'd better!'

A week later, she gave him a miniature gold replica of the key.

Her gift was a huge success. Saffity confessed he'd always feared something might happen to the bulky original; it could so easily have been lost or stolen. Now it was safely stored in a bank vault, and the miniature gold key was delicate and much easier to handle. 'Like you, Brooke,' he grinned. 'You look so athletic, but in bed you're as feminine as lace, aren't you?'

She treasured his compliments, and hoarded them the way she hoarded her time with him. They had been together, as she put it, for six months, and still she had not been invited to Stanford Hall. When he came up to London, once or twice a week, she stayed with him at Eaton Place. The rest of the time she was at the Dorchester. She had not yet met Colette or Myles, but she felt she knew them. It was obvious she was being excluded, as if she were a kept woman, from the rest of his life. But as far as she was concerned it was his life with her that counted; she could afford to wait. She did nothing so direct as to undertake the redecoration of Eaton Place. Instead, she went to Sotheby's and to Christie's and chose two paintings – a Léger and a Picasso.

His need to carry on as if they were having a clandestine, illicit love affair was in complete accord with her own mood, for even the most infinitesimal dilution of those hours when he seemed to belong to her was not to be contemplated. By now she was seeing lawyers, and a settlement of twenty-five thousand pounds had secured her husband's agreement to be the 'guilty party' in the divorce. Again, in case it would look as if she were pressuring him, she said nothing of this to Saffity.

But then that shocking news from Salonika came and he dropped out of Brooke's life for a whole month.

Saffity received three personal letters on the same day. The morning mail brought a letter from Max, who had included a photograph of his father caressing the *mezuzah* on the door of Trans-Empire Carpets. At that, he threw back his head and laughed.

The afternoon mail brought two letters from Salonika. Although one had been posted weeks ahead of the other, the two envelopes, each marked 'insufficient postage', arrived together.

One of them was, as usual, addressed in Greek. The other, thicker envelope was written in English. Saffity tore it open, and read the attached grey card, also written in English, with utter incredulity.

Dear Sir,

I be the nurse in our hospital attending your kind mother. There be inside this letter a second letter. This be your mother the letter she be herself writing in language Yiddish. I be understanding

Ladino. Your mother be translate her Yiddish into Ladino for me.
I be translate into Greek for you.

Your obedient servant,
Sister Maria Fetedes

Crazed with shock, Saffity smashed his hand against his forehead,
punched his intercom, and roared, 'No interruptions of any kind
whatsoever!' His hands shook. What the hell was going on? This
was some kind of dirty trick, he was sure. His mother was illiterate.
She couldn't write in any sort of language.

Thunderstruck, he turned at once to the Greek translation.

My son, my soul,

Now that I have finally found the courage to write to you in
my own mother tongue – Yiddish – you will know the truth, and
having asked for your forgiveness I will die in peace. Strange, no?
You probably think it should be the other way round.

I had hoped to see you once more before I die, but when
I learned that the British authorities did not have the power
to protect you in the country of your birth, for my own sake
I did not dare ask you to run the risk of being conscripted into
the Greek army.

On three occasions you half-heartedly suggested we visit you.
With the more than generous sums you gave us this would have
been possible. But even when you still lived in Paris I agreed
entirely with your father that it would be better for you, my
son, and better for us if we did not see what people like us
are not meant to see.

Now, too late, I believe we – and you – were wrong.

I made bad mistakes.

As you know, none of the women in our family can write. You
will understand in a moment why I hid my ability to write in any
language.

I concealed all my differences so that they would get used to
me, accept me, and forget what you have never known. When I
married your father I was the Ashkenazic widow of your father's
third cousin. I succeeded too well. In many, many ways, I myself
forgot what I had been. You will understand this, I fear perhaps
too well, my son?

I have been in this magnificent hospital for many days. Thanks to you, money is no problem. Take comfort – if you need it – from that, my son, my soul. I have learned much here about things past and things present.

Above all, I have learned that I guarded my secret too passionately, and too well. Certain that I could shield you from the contagious wound of my origins in a bandage of secrecy, I kept you at a safe, sterile distance.

When you were only nine, do you remember bringing me a patched bicycle tube, and telling me that though it was as good as new, it was like your life after the fire and would never be the same again? That was the day I knew for sure you would become an important man in the world. But I also knew that a price – no less than a sacrifice – would be extracted from me.

I almost told you the truth that day.

Then, when your father so brutally injured your eye, I thought you had suffered enough, and I vowed that I would never add my past sorrows to yours.

I know little about your present life.

I know that you now spell your name phonetically, as people who move to the West, I'm told, are inclined to do. I am pleased and proud but unsurprised that your textile company flourishes. That you also enjoy your work gives me much happiness. But you should enjoy your private life. You are twenty-eight years old, my son, my soul, and so handsome. You have two perfect eyes. What are you waiting for? I saw in the photograph that your hair is already silver. You inherit that from me. I went grey when I was in my early twenties.

Your father will never forgive me for telling you all this. At last I am at a place where that makes no difference to me. You are his son, but you are also my son. I am from Kiev in the Ukraine. My maiden name was Braudie, and there were rabbis in my family, too. I used to devour the works of Shalom Aleichem and Peretz.

I can only pray that you will try to forgive a mother who understood, too late, that she had sacrificed her son, and her soul not, as she had thought, on the altar of her love, but on the pyre of her superstition.

I already feel the pain and shock which my confession has brought to you. So I beg you not to mourn what might have been, and entreat you to embrace, with compassion, the gift of your life.

I will die with your name on my lips, blessing you.

Shattered now, his entire being a swirl of havoc, he turned to his mother's handwriting. Several of the Hebrew characters were unfamiliar to him, yet without any knowledge of Yiddish his German made it possible for him to interpret it for himself. She didn't even need to have it translated, he thought bitterly. At the absurd irony of this he broke down, laid his head on the desk and sobbed.

Then he snatched up the envelope from his father, and ripped it open. Written, in Ladino, two weeks after his mother's letter, it told him that she had died the day before. A primeval sound rose in his throat – he felt as if red-hot nails were piercing him. He stifled it, left his office abruptly, and drove to Heston Airport.

All the way there, and while he was in the air, he cursed his father's ignorance, and his stubborn refusal to install a telephone. Obviously it had not even occurred to him to send a telegram to inform him of his mother's illness or of her death. And if his mother had not believed her life was ending, he would never have known she was not an illiterate.

She had lied to him all his life.

She was not even Sephardic – she had been born in Kiev in the Ukraine – she was Ashkenazic, just like Max! He felt a fool. The injustice of it all overwhelmed him. His mother's self-inflicted purdah had been spawned out of her need to belong, to be like all the other women who could not write. She had erased her origins just as surely as she had erased the fact that she could read and write. Drenched in his past, he broke into a sweat. How he had always despised her for her illiteracy! He felt a wrenching regret, but little guilt. He remembered that she had only ever seen him with his straightened eye in photographs.

He made a perfect landing, and as he clambered out of the cockpit decided that for the present he wanted no close contact with anyone. He told Brooke and Colette that his mother had died, and asked them to bear with his need for solitude.

Night after night, as he paced his room, he railed against his father and raged against his mother. For the life of him, he could not begin to forgive her for her deception. He hated the puny, narrow-minded bigots like his father in the slums of his past who had ground her into concealing her literacy from them, and blamed and hated her just as much for keeping it from him.

Now – despite, or perhaps because of her instructions, he mourned her unlived life far more than he mourned her death.

He spent his long convulsive days and longer wrangling nights in endless quarrelling with his mother, berating her lack of faith in him. She should have *trusted* him. He had always known how to keep his mouth shut. Like a turbulent adolescent he found himself thinking that she should have trusted him enough to know he would never have told anyone.

Confessions have a merciless way of forcing confrontations. He had long believed he had purged his childhood from his system, but it had only been an incurable disease in long remission.

If she had trusted him, he would have respected her. Now he despised himself for having despised her. The price of her sacrifice had cost him the right to respect his own mother. She knew – even shared – his contempt for illiterates of the likes of the Aaron Touros of this world. The only woman who could read and write should have made her a queen among women, not a silent minion. Now, too late, he knew her deliberate silence had robbed him of his mother's tongue.

At a certain unidentifiable moment, when his feverish panic and raging despair began to ease a little, he finally drew some consolation from having been able to provide for her material comfort. One morning, combing his hair, he reminded himself that his mother had turned grey at an early age, too. He almost smiled.

The next moment he solved the mystery of the bicycle tube. Though he had no recollection of the conversation his mother had recounted, he realised that the patched tube had symbolised the way he had changed since he'd discovered – the night of the fire – that his powerful father was only a bullying coward. He gave a bitter laugh. All this dark, grievous time, except for sending his father a conventional condolence letter and an unnecessarily large cheque to cover any expenses he might now incur, he had scarcely wasted a thought on him.

It occurred to him then that until he met Max he had only heard the term Ashkenazi once, when his father had told him about his illustrious ancestors. As far as he was concerned he was neither Ashkenazim nor Sephardim, but half and half. Small wonder he was no longer a Jew.

337

Some days after that he lit upon another and far more profound similarity between him and his mother than grey hair. *Had he not also denied his origins?*

The obvious is easily drowned in a bleeding broken brain. His mother and he were the same. He forgave her at once, and having forgiven her, he could begin again. The scale of his passion was infinite.

It was then that he went impulsively to the Dorchester, hoping to find Brooke. He waited in the lobby. When she saw him she had both the sense and the sensitivity to behave as if nothing out of the ordinary had happened.

Their life together resumed its pattern; once again Brooke made their theatre bookings. Once, when he admired Whistler's sets for *Victoria Regina*, she bought him a Whistler. She put all her Southern womanhood at his disposal, and the way he took what she had to give was her finest reward. She would never be his first priority; that distinction belonged to Edwina and to his business. But she accepted that because it was enough – oh! it was enough! – to be included among his priorities. He was faithful to her, she was certain.

One night, over dinner, having seen Elizabeth Bergner give a profoundly memorable performance in *The Constant Mistress*, Saffity said unexpectedly, 'You are a lovely woman, Brooke.'

'Thanks, Saff.'

'I'm not being fair to you.' He fiddled with his cuff links.

'But, Saff — ' she interrupted.

'We've been together for more than a year, Brooke — '

Again she interrupted, and again he stopped her. 'I'm sorry, Brooke, but I can't begin to consider remarrying.' He broke off, and gazed into the distance. 'Edwina would have loved you.'

'Why, honey, you've just paid me the greatest compliment of my life!'

'But that's not good enough,' he said moodily. 'Compliments don't make a life.'

'*Yours* do, honey,' she said in her soft, musical drawl. 'Am I allowed to ask a direct question?'

'Certainly.'

'Are you breaking up with me?'

'I don't want to take advantage of you.'

'Will you answer my question directly? Please?'

'No,' he said stoutly. 'No, I do not want to break up with you.'

'Thank God,' she whispered. Then, making it clear that she was summoning up all her courage, she went on in a rush. 'You see, Saff, you *are* my life, and no matter what happens you always will be.' She bit her lip, and continued, 'I wouldn't marry you, even if you asked me!'

'Why not?'

'Because — ' she floundered. 'It's better this way.'

'You have such brave, beautiful eyes, Brooke. Let's go.'

On the way home they were silent. Brooke had never been one to squander her emotions in self-pity, yet she had no illusions about herself. She was not beautiful and her nose was too pronounced, it emphasised her small eyes. Yet when she was with Saffity she felt beautiful. Suddenly she wanted him to see her in *her* natural habitat, New York. How he would love it! Now, however, was not the right moment to broach the subject. Instead, she asked, 'Am I never going to get to meet Colette?'

As Colette poured Myles his usual cup of extra-strong tea, she asked, 'Did Saffity tell you Brooke would be coming down to Stanford Hall next weekend?' She did not wait for a reply but chattered on. 'I'm so pleased he's finally invited her. It's a good sign, I think.'

'A good sign?' Myles said, heaping his scone with Devonshire cream.

'It's four years since Edwina — ' Her voice trailed off.

'I know,' Myles said soberly.

'He says he's fond of her,' Colette began. 'They have an understanding, you know. She sympathises with his feelings for Edwina . . . ' Wrinkling her nose, she added some water to her tea. She had got used to everything about her English life except strong tea. 'Edwina was, and always will be, the only woman for him. I've seen him taking flowers to her grave.' She sighed.

'Some men fall in love once and once only,' Myles said moodily.

'But he needs to settle down again. He should have children — ' Her wise eyes clouded over. 'So what, if he's not crazily in love with Brooke? That mad kind of love – the kind he had for Edwina – happens only once to a man!'

'Mm,' Myles murmured, sipping his tea. 'Very true.'

Colette swung her gaze away from him. She liked him well enough, and was aware that it would take only the smallest encouragement from her for him to . . . But there she let the thought drop – she had never taken it further. But perhaps, just perhaps, if Saffity remarried . . . And yet if she had misinterpreted Myles' feelings for her, she could risk embarrassing or – even worse – shaming him. She dared not endanger their friendship.

Spring was at its most opulent that April weekend of 1936. The apple blossom lay laden on the branches, and though Brooke knew the Vale of Evesham was famous for its beauty it took her unawares, and left her breathless. For her part, Colette found Brooke even more beautiful than she had expected. There was never any doubt that Saffity would choose a lovely girl, but this Brooke was such an unusual combination of grace, dignity and warmth. And she had obviously planned things with great attention to detail – her soft tweeds and stout walking shoes were perfect for long walks in the woods. Even Finbar took to her.

Far and away more important than the way she looked, was the naked way she looked at Saffity. Once or twice Colette caught herself turning away from the awesome sight of those bright, burning eyes, spilling over with adoration. 'I have never seen a woman in love as Brooke is in love,' she murmured to Myles. 'It's a cruel fate when the other woman is in the grave.'

Edwina's portrait dominated the dining room. The soft colours did nothing to diminish the strength of Edwina's sensual, yet spiritual serenity. Brooke talked of her with easy affection, as if they had been friends. But for all that, she was sensitive to Saffity's moods, and Edwina's name did not sound crass on her lips . . .

The idyllic, perfect weekend drew to a close, marred only by talk of Hitler. 'The Air Age has come,' Saffity pronounced.

'We'll need the RAF,' Myles said definitely. 'This time the war in the air will be decisive.'

Colette shuddered. She steered the talk towards the garden.

Brooke's right moment came quite by chance, on December 11th, 1936, while they were listening to King Edward VIII's abdication speech. Saffity was far more shaken and disappointed than she had expected him to be. It made him nostalgic enough to tell her about that long-ago great fire of Salonika, about the way the British soldiers had offered to *give* them the bread. When he had done, she said, 'I've been thinking. I want to take you to America, Saff. More and more of you British are investing there, did you know that?'

'My father-in-law was keen on the States.'

'You must let me show you New York,' she said quickly, pressing her advantage. 'I want to be with you when you see the Empire State Building. I want to see you see it.'

A month later, in January 1937, Brooke and Saffity were on the *Queen Mary* on their way to New York. Saffity would take off three weeks only, he said. He could not afford to be away from Wyndham Carpets for longer than that.

As Brooke had predicted he fell in love with New York. The pace and excitement of the city filled him with awe and admiration. The results of President Roosevelt's Federal Building Project were everywhere to be seen, though he grumbled about the protective tariffs that were keeping his carpets out of New York. The skyline thrilled him; he felt like a real tourist. At El Morocco and the Stork Club the huge portions of food, like the garbage cans on the sidewalks overflowing with uneaten chicken legs in which cigarettes had been stubbed out, amazed and appalled him. Brooke took him to the Carnegie Hall, to the theatre and to Radio City Music Hall.

Business opportunities were as plentiful as they were irresistible. When one of Brooke's friends casually remarked that during the Great War forty per cent of the shells that were used were supplied by Du Pont, they bought stock in that company. He acquired a taste for Coca Cola, and on the strength of that alone they bought Coca Cola stock, too.

But even in America they heard, ever more distinctly, the rumblings of war.

Not long after they returned to London they went to an exhibition of gas masks, tried them on and found that they could breathe normally and speak clearly while they were wearing them. Saffity began to have meetings with informed politicians, and, because he had imported machinery from Germany, was soon included in Winston Churchill's personal intelligence network of industrial information.

They began to talk more and more about the war. Saffity frequently mentioned the Royal Air Force. In some ways, the turbulence of the world was something of a relief to Brooke. She was ashamed, as usual, but honest enough with herself, to admit that she was almost grateful that these uncertain times meant that Saffity was compelled to commit himself to his country, and not to her. That way, instead of being hurt by him, she could be proud of him.

Brooke was especially proud of the way Saffity had been unable to resist using his flying to advance the cause of Wyndham Carpets. Already, the sheer novelty of telling a customer that he would fly in with his samples had won several major contracts. They had planned to fly to Paris for just such a purpose.

It was a clear summer's day when they arrived at the unusually crowded Heston Airport. They were approaching the Moth aircraft they both loved with their usual sense of excitement when they were stopped.

'Sorry, sir. No flights out today,' a club official told them.

'Why not?' Saffity snapped. 'It's perfect weather.'

'I know it is, sir,' the official said gloomily. 'But our Prime Minister is flying in today.'

'Oh yes, of course he is,' Saffity said at once. 'I should have thought of that.' He turned to Brooke. 'I'll phone Paris and let them know we'll be there tomorrow. Then we'll have a drink, and see Mr Chamberlain face the press.'

So it was that Brooke and Saffity witnessed the historic moment when Mr Chamberlain waved a document bearing his and Hitler's signature, while he told the waiting world of the 'desire of our two peoples never to go to war again'.

'Perhaps there won't be war,' Brooke said placatingly. 'Perhaps Mr Chamberlain is right to try to avoid it.'

'Mr Chamberlain is buying Hitler still more time,' Saffity said scornfully.

Brooke waited until Poole's of Savile Row had tailored his Royal Air Force uniforms before she returned to America in 1938.

Convinced that nothing but death could separate her from Saffity, she threw everything she had into the British war effort, campaigning for the training – and use – of women pilots . . .

It was ironic, Saffity thought, that his need to live dangerously, recklessly and even irresponsibly had turned out to be the most useful, practical thing he had ever done. He had turned to the skies, out of a desperate attempt to dull his inner hopelessness and despair, so it was quite by chance that he had acquired the highly prized and much-needed skills of a pilot. Pilots in 1939 were thin on the ground and in the air, and a few months before war was declared he had written to Stanley Baldwin, a long-standing friend of the Wyndham family, asking him how he could put his pilot's licence to work. The reply had come almost by return of post, and very soon after that, in February 1939, Saffity was a wing commander in the Coastal Command of the Royal Air Force.

He took his beloved Moth with him, and flying it was some compensation for not having been posted to Bomber Command. Rather than protect merchant shipping, he would have preferred to have been on the offensive. He was shocked to discover that, at almost thirty, he was considered too old for Bomber Command. Based at Pembroke Dock, he made frequent visits to Stanford Hall, sometimes in his own Moth. It was only about a hundred and fifty miles away.

Once Saffity was in the Royal Air Force, Colette flew into a spate of restless activity. She had been through the Great War in Paris, and knew there would be shortages of men and food, so she set about bottling, pickling and planting. The gardeners had not yet been called up, but it would not be long. The orchard she had proposed was no longer a luxury. Already there was talk of rationing.

She had now been at Stanford Hall seven years, and even as she attended to the new and demanding details of her daily life, she began to feel dismayingly alone. For the first time in her life she felt lonely. She put it down to the terror of the coming war. She was tired, she told herself. She was sleeping badly. Soon she was having difficulty sleeping at all. It was during one of those long sleepless nights that it came to her that she was needlessly wasting her life in an empty bed. At the age of forty-eight she was shocked to discover that she still needed a man in her life. Or that, maybe, a particular man had made her want him.

It also came to her that she had been floating in an aura of purpose that came close to fulfilment. Saffity had been – and was – as vital to her as faith, the only man she had ever trusted. She amended this: he was the only human being she had ever been allowed to trust . . .

It was years since she had consciously thought of her step-grandfather, of his filthy, slimy assaults on her young innocent flesh. At once she rose from her bed, and paced the room. She had managed not to think of the men in her life. Even Max had become a distant memory. And however successfully she had persuaded herself that he had cared for her, he had still left her for dead at the bottom of the pool.

And yet, apart from the sense of maternal contentment inspired by Saffity and Stanford Hall, she was otherwise numb. Over the past two years or so, where she had been numb she now ached. And only recently had she identified that what she ached for was the sympathy of touch, Myles' touch.

She had known, privately, of his feelings for her; only now did she realise how much she had been encouraging him. She had been making all sorts of excuses to see him, to hear his slow voice, to watch the crinkling round his eyes as he smiled. Even the scent of his pipe had become delightful to her.

As well as sensual.

So where there had been a numb nothingness there was Myles.

But he would never make the first move. What was she to do? Had all her skills deserted her? Suddenly she clapped her hands with glee. *Voilà!* She knew what she must do. She would write to him. The English loved letters.

She composed herself and sat down at her Chippendale desk. She opened her fountain pen, and in the slow careful hand she had acquired along with her elocution lessons, wrote confidently:

Myles dearest,
    If what you are about to read embarrasses you, I ask your

understanding and your forgiveness. For too many years I have been too cowardly to face what I am now driven to write to you. It seems the smell of war has brought me the unexpected gift of the vast quantity of courage I needed if I am to be frank with myself, and with you.

Seven years ago, when I came to Stanford Hall, I did not know that I was in a state of deep, incurable grief. I grieved not only for the betrayed woman that I was then, but for the cruelty with which my childhood had been torn from me, even as it began. I am here now, because when Edwina died your compassion for Saffity led you to telephone me to come to him. The wildness of his grief for his dead bride took precedence over my grief for myself, and I threw myself into my new life at Stanford Hall, making it and Saffity overcrowd – and overgrow – my heart. Here, in this fertile valley, everything grew with lustrous opulence.

From the very beginning I turned to you for your help, and you never failed me. Your help, your guidance and your unstinting kindness flowed towards me. You made Stanford Hall and its customs comprehensible to me. Slowly and surely you made everything grow, everything verdant.

My heart has always been full of affection for you. I did not notice that affection grow into love. I should have known – you make everything grow.

To be loved by someone is as good – and perhaps better – than being in love. And, whether you allow it or not, I love you.

So, I repeat, if this letter embarrasses you, forgive me, and let us both pretend that it was never written. If not, then at dawn tomorrow morning, after you have had the night in which to think, you will find me waiting on that oak seat in the woods where you and Saffity so often meet.

At last the dawn breaks. Strange, that the war is coming, yet I am comforted by an inner peace. Because soon, soon you will read this, and I will be known to you.

Past shame, long past youth, but not past hope, I seal these pages with a trembling hand.

Colette

Long before the next dawn broke, with the sound of the crackling twigs loud in her ears, Colette made her apprehensive way towards the oak bench. Myles heard the twigs snap well in advance of seeing her, and though his injured leg did not allow him to run, he limped swiftly. They met and he took her hand. Together, as if supporting one another, their pace slow but in perfect timing, they reached the bench. They were no sooner seated than she placed her head on his shoulder, burrowing it into his neck. His arm cradled her shoulder. Their long shared silence fluttered over them, gentle as lace.

At last Myles murmured, 'I've been here since midnight.' With his free hand he took her clenched hands. 'Why did you wait so long?'

'I love your smell, Myles,' she answered into his neck. 'You smell so good.' Then she brought her mouth to his. 'I want to breathe you, Myles. Breathe you.'

It was one of those timeless kisses, full of hunger and need and longing. The kind that makes speech superfluous. When they finally broke apart they helped one another to their feet and, followed by Tara, walked to Myles' cottage.

When they came to Myles' bedroom, he gave a short command to Tara. 'Stay!'

He closed the door carefully and said, 'Am I allowed one question?'

'But of course.'

'Will you marry me?'

'Of course I will!' She gave him a dazzling smile and began to unknot his tie. She was grateful to the closed curtains and the dim flattering light, even though her feminine curves were still supple and firm. They shed their clothes quickly, as if to save themselves from suffocating. His body was more muscular than she had expected it to be, his upper arms especially. She could not press herself close enough, nor breathe enough of him, and he sensed that her longing equalled his, and then their twinned breathing, twinned moving dominated and obliterated all as their rushing inner worlds collided and merged.

At last, after a long silence, Colette said quietly, 'You are magic, Myles. Magic.'

Later that morning, he insisted on preparing her a huge breakfast of bacon and eggs in his large farmhouse kitchen.

'War or no war,' he said in his usual slow voice, 'I'd want us to marry as soon as possible.'

'Saffity will be here at the weekend — '

'We'll tell him then. But I'll see the vicar this afternoon,' Myles said decisively, buttering her toast with clean, precise strokes, as if he had been doing it for her for ever. Then he cut the toast into four strips, and handed her the plate.

He looked at her in wonder. Here was this woman, approaching fifty, wearing his faded navy-blue and maroon-striped dressing gown, with her deep copper hair untidy and almost wild, her usual dignity gone, but radiant and poised instead.

'Oh, Myles,' Colette said softly. 'You're mothering me. No one has ever done that for me before. I never had a mother; mine died giving birth to me.'

Myles left his seat and, standing close to her, took her head in his hands and rested it against his stomach for a while. Then cradling her in his arms he lifted her off her chair and carried her upstairs. 'I'll look after you for ever,' he murmured. 'You'll never be alone again.'

Soon they were breathing in rhythm, using their bodies to wipe out the past and celebrate the triumphant present.

That weekend Myles rather nervously invited Saffity to the farmhouse for a sherry. 'You may or may not have noticed this, Saffity, but I've ceased biting my nails.' He laughed discreetly. 'You suggested I should when we first met. You and Edwina used to tease me about it.'

'I remember, Myles,' Saffity said, his eyes darkening, as they always did when Edwina was mentioned.

Myles reddened. 'Well, I'm afraid my bachelor days are about to end,' he said abruptly.

'You're getting married, Myles? That's the best news I've had in years!' Saffity laughed loudly, rising to shake his hand. 'Congratulations! Fifty, aren't you?'

Myles nodded.

'Who is the lucky bride?'

Myles coughed. 'The lady is well known to you.' He coughed again. 'Colette has consented to become my wife.'

'*Colette!*' Saffity shrieked with delight. 'Colette? Well, I'll be *chocolat!*' he said, showing his huge surprise. 'You have made me a happy man, Myles, a very, very happy man. I think we'd better drink to it, don't you?'

347

Smiling – and Saffity could have sworn the man was still blushing – Myles poured two double whiskies. 'I was hoping you would be my best man.'

'But then who would give Colette away?' cried Saffity, laughing. 'Dammit, I can do both. But there's one condition,' he added. 'That you permit me to give you this house as a wedding gift.'

That night, Saffity and Colette met for a quiet drink. Myles, tactful as always, left them on their own in the library.

Colette positively glowed. 'So, this took you by surprise, *mon choux*,' she said quietly, her wise eyes shining.

'One of the happiest surprises of my life, Colette,' Saffity answered enthusiastically. 'My two best friends getting together like this. Well, it fills me with awe.' He leaned forward to take her hand. 'The two of you kept me alive. And sane. I know you don't want me to say this to you, but I must.' He stopped and closed his eyes. 'I could talk to you, and only you, about Edwina.'

'Myles and I have you in common, my dear. Our anxiety over you, and our love for you, brought us together, like a pair of doting parents, I suppose.' She looked out at the velvet lawns. 'And the war that will come at any moment . . . '

Saffity sighed, and shrugged sadly. A brief, comfortable silence fell.

'Myles is an utter snob,' he chuckled. 'But underneath all that stiffness there is a very kind man. Of course you know that. He'll be the most devoted husband.'

'Yes, I know,' she answered seriously. 'D'you know, he'd never really been with a woman before? He'd had a frightening, wounding experience when he was a young man, and after that he thought there was something wrong with him.'

'But I thought he liked the ladies?'

'He did. But he was too afraid of another failure.' She withdrew her hand. 'Myles doesn't know very much about me. About my past, I mean.'

'Why should he know? Give me one good reason.'

'You're right, as usual,' Colette smiled.

'You're still wearing the amethyst Max gave you, I see. Will you continue to wear it after you're married?' He flirted for an instant with the idea of telling her the truth about Max.

'I swore I would never part with this ring and I never will,' Colette answered emphatically.

'It is very beautiful,' Saffity said neutrally.

'What about *you*, Saffity? Why did you let Brooke get away?'

Saffity's laugh was as slight as it was bitter. 'You know I won't talk about that,' he said.

'But *I* will. You need love, you need warmth, you need affection. And what are you getting? An expensive commodity. As if an expensive fuck could ever be enough for you, or for any full-blooded man! And then what do you do afterwards? You go to Edwina's grave, and beg her forgiveness for having gone with a whore.' Tears dashed down her cheeks. 'Don't try and shut me up, Saffity. Who knows what I'm talking about better than I do? Sex is not a product, like a carpet!'

An angry exclamation, half-groan and half-whistle, escaped Saffity.

'You can make as many noises as you like, Saffity. But I'm right.'

He winked his right eye and laughed loudly, which deflected her as he had known it would.

'You must laugh more often, Saffity. It's been too long since I heard you laugh,' Colette said.

Three weeks later Saffity and his beloved Moth flew to Stanford Hall, and Colette became Mrs Myles Beecham. A woman close on fifty, with the glow of a young bride – really, it was positively embarrassing. Saffity teased her gently on the wedding day, for she was as nervous as any nubile bride.

The recent grey flecks in her hair only served to add to her timeless beauty, and her severely tailored blue silk suit, with its softening long-sleeved brocade waistcoat, made by the English couturier Hartnell, and not by a French fashion house, set off her well-proportioned figure to perfection. Even Myles had a new blue-grey suit, tailored in Savile Row. Saffity's RAF uniform gave him a dashing, glamorous look, and though the heavy whiff of fear of the coming war was with everyone in the chapel at Stanford Hall, it made the deep joy of the mature bridal couple even stronger – an affirmation of hope.

Before Myles, all the men in Colette's life had been either much older or much younger than she. If the consuming passion she felt for Max was, as she now believed, largely maternal, it was the kind

349

of emotional obsession she hoped never to experience again. Never! For she had not been comfortable or easy with Max.

The truth was that before Myles she had not known what feeling safe in the depths of intimacy could mean.

Until she came to Stanford Hall she had considered herself to be nothing more than a worthless creature for whom anything good was undeserved. Running Stanford Hall had presented her with a sense of purpose, of worth and even of importance. Myles had taken all that further; through the language of his ecstasy he had disclosed the very mystery of life. The nightmare of her childhood no longer hounded her – even if the war came suddenly, and she were killed just as suddenly, she would have been purged.

For his part Myles felt purged, too. Purged of the humiliating urges that – however ruthlessly controlled – had still made him feel uncivilised, and worse – unnatural. But now, with the language of her rapture, Colette taught him that sensuality was not sinful. He had accepted his celibacy as if he had no choice, much in the way he accepted being tone-deaf and therefore unable to carry a tune. Just as he had been silent when everyone else joined in the hymn singing so he had been abstinent. He had been fatalistic about it – until Colette. Now he had no regrets about having waited until he was fifty years old to discover sex, for his discovery had been through Colette.

Of what you hear believe nothing, and of what you see, believe half.

If only a fiftieth of what he heard was true, Saffity realised he would have to get his father out of Salonika. Despite all he felt, he *was* his father, after all. It would be quite a revenge to make him live out his days at Stanford Hall. Grinning to himself, Saffity had set about trying to make contact with the old man. Cable after cable went unanswered. Finally, after getting in touch with the synagogue, he elicited a response from them: 'Your father does not want to leave.'

Well then, he would go to Salonika himself and fetch the truculent old fool.

Only, now Saffity was in the Royal Air Force, he was no longer a free agent. His request to return to Greece was summarily rejected. It was the first time, since he had left home, that he had come up against an implacable authority against which he was as helpless as he had been as a small child in Salonika.

Like all grateful immigrants, his patriotism had assumed almost a religious strength. His King and his country commanded all his loyalty, and if this meant that he was forbidden to travel to Greece, then so be it. He was honoured to be of service to the country that had adopted him.

Then war was declared, and Saffity was in 204 Squadron. One of his first sorties during the period known as the phoney war was to escort as far as the Bay of Biscay a convoy en route to South Africa.

Shortly before he took off he phoned Myles.

After giving him the news that Wyndham Carpets had just produced its first lot of military blankets, Myles added, 'By the way, Max Blum's wife was in London. She telephoned.'

'In London?' Saffity repeated. 'Max must be mad to have — '

'She's on her way home,' Myles said quickly, following wartime instructions and deliberately not mentioning where she was going. 'She gave us an order. Said she'll take whatever we could give her. Up to twenty-five thousand pounds, she said.'

Saffity's sudden enthusiastic laugh reverberated in the small office. Myles smiled and held the phone away from his ear. Still laughing, Saffity hung up.

Later, while he was flying over the turbulent seas, it occurred to him he might be protecting Max's wife. He had never met her, and wondered briefly – and for the first time – what she was like.

Nine months later, in July 1940, just when Saffity had come to terms with being in Coastal Command, he was summoned to the Ministry of Economic Warfare. The Ministry informed him that his exceptional skills as an administrator, and his economic expertise as chairman of Wyndham Carpets, were being wasted in the RAF. When he protested, he was coldly advised that that was where he would serve the war effort best. At least he would be able to keep his RAF title – he was still Wing Commander Saffity.

The Ministry of Economic Warfare was in Berkeley Square and here, more than ever, Saffity's patience was put to the test. It was his first experience of the way constant in-fighting, and the petty back-biting of incessant political rivalries, delayed decisions.

Until Sir Hugh Dalton took over the Ministry of Economic Warfare it had been known as the Ministry of Wishful Thinking. He drew a certain wry pleasure from knowing it was Dalton who had suggested, in 1939, that incendiary bombs should be dropped on the Black Forest to teach the Germans, who were sentimental about their own trees, that war was not always pleasant and profitable and could not be fought entirely in other people's countries. But it seemed to Saffity that even Dalton, an Eton-educated Socialist, put his party before his country. He felt bitter.

It was partly out of frustration and partly out of boredom that he began buying blitzed properties. Also, he felt he was not working hard enough, his mind was not being stretched; it was here, in the Ministry, that he was being wasted, and it made him angry. Brooke was away in America, so he went to parties at Claridges, to the theatre, and sometimes he even made love to the same beautiful and aristocratic women he had known when he was in Coastal Command. But the gaiety left him flat.

Then on December 7th, 1941, Japan attacked Pearl Harbour, and the face of the war changed. Until that time, arrangements for vital military supplies in Britain were bogged down in intrigue as well as red tape, for America was not officially at war. In Washington, in January 1942, the business executive who was put in charge of streamlining the War Production Board declared, 'Debating societies are out'. Saffity heaved a sigh of relief. Things would begin to roll, now that a businessman was in control; armaments would at last be shipped through official channels. Even so, mistakes were made – for example, the wrong kind of engine oil was sent to Britain. Not long after that débâcle, Saffity was flown to Washington to negotiate and coordinate the supply of Sherman tanks to British forces.

Brooke, who was working on the establishment of the Women's Air Unit, joined him in Washington. He thought she looked wondrously sexy in her trim military uniform. In bed she was more spirited and more flamboyantly daring than she had ever been. Every night for eight nights she went all out to seduce him.

But for his insistent awareness of Brooke's dynamic new sensuality he would not have noticed that jewellery shop, still less gone in. As it was, the heavy gold bangles in the window reminded him of his first days in Paris and of his long-ago Judith. Impulsively, he went in and asked to see the bangles; he thought they'd make a good gift for Brooke.

While the salesman was unlocking the window, Saffity sat down. His eye was drawn to the small American flag displayed on the counter, beside which a neat brass plaque proclaimed: 'Samuel Tourou, jeweller'.

Could it be the same Samuel Tourou he had last seen waiting on table at the Café Royal when he and Edwina were on honeymoon?

The salesman laid the gold bangles on a black velvet pillow. 'Twenty-four-carat gold, sir,' he said.

Now, certain that the man was Samuel Tourou, Saffity was unable to resist bursting into Ladino. 'What sort of discount do you give for cash, Tourou?'

'But who?'

Saffity's reverberating laugh filled the shop. The crystal trembled. He took out his card and handed it over.

'*Simonico!*' Tourou exclaimed. 'A British officer.' He vaulted over the counter and hugged Saffity. 'I'm an American citizen now, you know. I had TB or I'd be in the military myself. Ah, I'm sorry; I heard you lost your mother. Your father is in Britain, I suppose?'

'My father is in Salonika.' When had he last said the words 'my father' out loud? 'I'm on my way to a meeting. But I would like the bracelets — '

'Have them at cost, OK?'

'It's a deal.'

As Saffity was leaving, he said, 'Tell me, did you ever work in London?'

'So it *was* you at the Café Royal — '

'I was with my wife, Edwina. It was our honeymoon. She was killed in a car crash.'

'I'm sorry,' Samuel said automatically. 'You know, I think the best thing that ever happened to us was that Aaron ate *traif* that night. You remember? He returned to Salonika the next day.'

'I remember.'

'I got so mad that night, I left Paris myself. Then I went to London, then I made up my mind to come to the States. Europe is no place for Jews right now.'

Saffity planned to give Brooke the bracelets the next day. That night was his second to last in Washington, and even though Brooke knew he had a crucial breakfast meeting at the Pentagon, at about four in the morning she began making love to him again.

Suddenly he heard himself saying out loud what he did not know he had been thinking. 'There is another man in your life, Brooke, isn't there?'

'But I love you, Saffity — '

'Cut the crap,' he said harshly. 'Is there or isn't there?'

'Yes.'

'He's asked you to marry him, hasn't he?' Without waiting for her to reply, he sped on. 'Well, you should do just that.'

She made a funny, sighing sound and he felt her shake her head against his shoulder and draw closer to him. He took her then, as he knew she wanted him to. A crude fit of violent jealousy struck him, and he lost himself and became rough, and though he knew he was hurting her he was out of control. He pinned her down, and pinched her breasts and made her cry out in pain.

Afterwards he asked savagely, 'What's his name?'

'Dwight Baker.'

'His rank?'

'Lieutenant-colonel.'

He got up to take a shower. When he returned, dressed, he thrust a package at her. 'You might as well show your lieutenant-colonel these,' he said. 'Gold bangles. I saw them yesterday. The first woman in my life used to wear exactly the same bangles. Wear them to your wedding!'

'Dwight — ' she began miserably.

'You're talking to the wrong man,' he said viciously. 'I'm Saffity, remember?'

Though it was only six in the morning he left the room, and went downstairs for coffee.

That night, when he came back, very late, she was gone. He told himself he was glad. She had left him the bracelets, and he was not surprised.

It was his last night in Washington, and it was too late to look for a woman. He took the gold bangles back to London and gave them to an Irish girl with a lilting voice. Afterwards, no matter how hard he tried, he could not remember her name.

Towards the end of that year, in November 1942, the famine in Greece brought him in on important meetings with the most senior directors of the Ministry. It was learned that Metaxas, the Greek Prime Minister, had commited suicide. How Saffity despised the country from which he had chosen to be a voluntary exile! When, in April 1943, entirely according to his predictions, the Commander of the Western Macedonian army negotiated an armistice and surrendered without government authorisation, Saffity's amazed and admiring superiors were not to know that he had based his official assessment on his personal understanding of the Greek talent for cowardice.

His father was now in German hands . . .

By this time he had learned to understand and to use the various power networks: those that were made up of merchant bankers, or City contacts and, of course, the old school tie. Though always on the fringe of these, he negotiated his passage through them, and with them, and his skill finally carried him all the way to an intimate lunch with King George II of Greece. Greece was starving, and the discussions at lunch were on the need for Britain to permit a shipment of wheat to Athens.

Saffity considered it both a blessing and a miracle to be in the presence of the King of Greece; *he would use the King to get his father out of Salonika* . . .

It turned out that the Greek government-in-exile was more preoccupied with Greece's post-war territorial claims than it was with resistance to the Germans. Saffity soon realised that his contact with the King was worthless. Still he did not give up. The British sabotage team who had cut the railway line from Salonika to Athens were instructed to find his father. Of course, as he bitterly told himself later, they were bound to fail, if only because Greek resistance was divided and fought amongst itself. His father fell between the warring factions and was forgotten.

In August 1943, Saffity learned that the last of nineteen train departures from Salonika to the death camps of Auschwitz had taken place.

Saffity believed he had done everything. He had overturned all the rocks of power, and in the end his efforts had been useless. He had taken his case all the way to the King of Greece, and it had got him nowhere. Serving in that pretentious, bureaucratic maze was driving him crazy.

He had served his country well in the Ministry, and was convinced that he had now earned the right to serve himself – he had a few scores to settle, with a few Germans. Action and straight combat was what he needed, and action was what he would get.

Max's letter did not help matters.

Saffity read it for the second time. That afternoon the windows had been blitzed out of his house at Eaton Place, and after he had inspected the damage his housekeeper, behaving as if nothing out of the ordinary had happened, handed him the letter. Strangely the letter, coming as it did all the way from South Africa, braving submarines and torpedoes, brought a dimension of normality into his war-torn drawing room. Max wrote regularly, and his letters, in one form or another, were a chronicle of complaints. His ulcer was troubling him; he was persevering with the new Hay diet. He still only opened the business once a month. No carpets were being manufactured, but fortunately he was still selling from his stock of hand-made Indian carpets. It made Saffity smile; Max was determined to show how scrupulous he was, for it was obvious he could easily have withheld this information . . .

When he came to Max's last paragraph, Saffity laughed out loud for the second time.

'Fanny and I were alarmed to read of the renewed bombing raids on London. We had been much comforted to know you had a more or less safe "desk" job, but it seems that as long as one is in the thick of things, no place is safe.'

So, he had a 'more or less safe "desk" job', did he? It was insulting, it was infuriating and, worst of all, it was true. It was the last straw. Max had unknowingly made up his mind for him. No matter what it would take to do it, Saffity was going to escape from all the pomp and vanity at the Ministry of Economic Warfare.

Part Six

20

'You speak French, don't you?' Group Captain Cecil Hayward asked Saffity. 'Isn't it your mother tongue?'

'That's how they pulled me out of the RAF,' Saffity answered drily. 'Any European waiter speaks at least four languages. I wish to Christ I didn't.'

'Actually, dear boy, your French could get you out of the Ministry of Economic Warfare, you know,' Cecil said seriously. 'Here, take a look at this,' he went on, handing what looked like a confidential memo to Saffity.

Saffity read quickly. 'Special Operations in France. French-speaking recruits essential . . . '

'They're taking me, *mon vieux*,' Cecil drawled. 'I'm off to Milton Hall for parachute training.'

'Could you spare me this?' Saffity asked thoughtfully.

'Just happen to have a spare one on me,' Cecil grinned. 'Don't see how they can refuse you this — '

It was January 1944, and Saffity had invited Cecil to lunch at the Connaught. They had become firm friends in those early, long-ago days in the RAF in 1938. Ruthlessly determined to get out of the Ministry, Saffity pulled every one of the numerous strings he now had at his disposal. His sense of timing was, as usual, excellent.

The outfit Cecil had spoken of was none other than the Special Force Headquarters, a new joint enterprise established by the American Office of Strategic Services and the British Special Operations Executive. Saffity would be one of the Company of Jedburghs – all volunteers – whose objective was to organise, coordinate and arm the French Resistance in France, the Maquis, in support of the coming Allied invasion. Their tactics – *surprise, mitraillage, évanouissement* – surprise, kill, vanish – suited Saffity's needs perfectly. His sense of personal guilt over the fate of his father gnawed away at him.

Six weeks later, in the middle of March 1944, he boarded the train at Paddington Station for Milton Hall, a huge Elizabethan mansion large enough to house two hundred and forty men, now converted into a commando training centre.

On the train, he was approached by an American captain. 'You going to Milton Hall?' he asked.

'I am.'

'Good.' The captain beamed. 'I'm Drew Wheatley. Glad to know you.'

'Saffity. I'm always called by my surname.'

'Great, I like people like that.' Drew smiled. Looking at Saffity's uniform, he said, 'I guess you've been in the bomber offensive over Germany?'

'No,' Saffity answered painfully. 'I was pulled out of the RAF Coastal Command in '41 to a desk job. I'm now a fully-fledged bureaucrat.'

'Is that right?' Drew said cheerfully. 'Bureaucrats are the same the world over, I guess. They tried to do me out of the extra money that goes with this job. In my book, money equals girls, and nobody does me out of them.' With which, he launched into a recital of adventures with the ladies. He was so different from the dour, serious Ministry officials with whom Saffity had been working that he warmed to him at once. Also, he smoked Gauloise cigarettes incessantly. Saffity was longing for a cigarette. 'You Brits have been short of things,' Drew said nonchalantly, handing over a packet.

They chatted amiably, and when they reached Milton Hall they felt as if they'd known one another for years. By this time Saffity knew Drew's background; he had been educated in France, and spoke French like a native. His weakness was women, and having, as he put it, 'fun'. Saffity could see why easily enough – he was tall, his blue eyes twinkled, and he was full of such expressive vitality that even his scalp moved when he talked.

He told Drew about Brooke. After all, she was a pilot in the American Air Force. Her letters had tailed off, and as he talked he realised she had pretty well faded from his thoughts and from his senses.

When they reached their destination the long driveway reminded Saffity of Stanford Hall. He was only about three-quarters of an hour from his own home, he thought wryly, but he might just as well have been on a different planet.

The training in para-military activities was as rough as it was thorough. Physical fitness was mandatory, and every day was punctuated by long cross-country endurance tests. The tranquil beauty of their surroundings, the sunken gardens, the golf course, and the meandering streams, added a certain surreal dimension to the practice of silent killing, the learning of Morse code, the firing of demolition charges, to say nothing of being dropped in training harnesses onto quiet, smooth lawns.

He learned how to live in the woods and the hills. He even learned how to kill and roast a sheep. It was arduous, there was no doubt about that; but for Saffity it was also therapeutic. Being at Milton Hall was very like being on leave from life.

At last he could believe, in the truest sense, that he was actively engaged in fighting a war. Here at Milton Hall he breathed the heady mix of tension and optimism.

On weekend passes Drew and he went up to London. Drew was determined to teach him what 'fun' meant, and Saffity proved a talented pupil. Weekends in hotel suites – girls and women, the adventure of the chase, of high living, of urgent free sex – kept Saffity too busy to think about buying up more derelict property. Life at the Ministry had been stultifying – Saffity was allergic to the qualities inherent in the Civil Service character – which was why he'd found a certain relief in attending to his own business interests, buying blitzed properties. Now, needless to say, there was no need to liven things up.

The Jedburghs were to be parachuted into France in teams of three, the threesomes to be formed on the grounds of 'personal affinity'. Within a month, Saffity and Drew had teamed up with Sergeant Emile, a French wireless operator who had fought with the Free French in Africa. Since every Jedburgh was a volunteer the morale was high, and the Maquis was in dire need of assistance from this newly formed, highly trained force and the weapons and ammunition they could bring.

Three days after D-Day, when Allied troops had landed in Normandy and the fiercest fighting was near Cherbourg, Saffity, Drew and Emile were in a converted Halifax bomber, in British-controlled skies, at two a.m. on the morning of June 9th, 1944, heading for Brittany.

Their aim was to bring arms and supplies to the Resistance, and help them form into fighting units in advance of the invading

American troops who were pushing south and west of the landing sites.

In what seemed like no time at all they were over the bonfires ringing the landing ground. Saffity's bowels contracted. How could the Germans possibly fail to see that blazing advertisement of an intended drop? He'd be gunned down even before he'd had a chance to begin . . .

Landed safely inside the ring of fires, and struggling to his feet, he suffered his second shock: the peasants who took away his parachute were quite drunk.

Around the field, packages of equipment were being separated from their parachutes and fires were being extinguished.

Saffity introduced himself to the tall, thin middle-aged man who seemed to be directing operations.

'Welcome,' the Maquis leader answered. 'My name is Gaston Mathieu. I expect you could do with some of this,' he said handing him a flask of brandy. 'You'll find it quite powerful, I believe.'

'No wonder your men are the worse for wear,' Saffity said, as the liquid burnt his throat.

'I thought I'd pee in my pants when I saw those bonfires,' Drew said nervously, looming up out of the dark. Emile joined them, and the Frenchmen exchanged quick handshakes.

Minutes later, several parachutes of armaments were dropped on the Halifax's second and final run, and they helped the men gather them and put them in the truck waiting under the trees.

'So you all three really do speak French,' Gaston said. 'That is a real surprise.'

'It is a good deal more than your men speak,' Saffity answered irritably. 'Breton isn't French, you know.'

The *maquisard* focused his shrewd gaze on Saffity. 'Your white hair is deceptive, *mon capitaine*. I thought they'd scraped the barrel and sent us a man from the geriatric brigade! *Allons en auto!*' The last of the fires was being put out, and the truck disappearing into the night, as he hustled them into a Citroën, reassured them that their packages were safe, and drove them to an old farmhouse, reached by a winding track. 'Tonight you sleep in real beds, with real sheets,' Gaston said before driving off again. He gave a Gallic shrug. 'After tomorrow – who knows? I'll see you in the morning.'

Over the previous six months arms and ammunition had been dropped in considerable quantities to the Resistance, with a high percentage of success. There were various groups ranging in size from fifty to as many as three thousand, fully armed and waiting to rise up, once the Allies had landed and were in sufficient control.

It was the job of Saffity's team to make sure those Resistance groups were properly armed, help them coordinate their activities, brief them on the progress of the invasion and pass on to them requests for particular acts of sabotage that came over the radio. They made contact with London twice a day.

None of this was made easier by the fact that the invasion was being fiercely contested less than eighty miles away. German units were constantly on the move either to support the front-line troops, to keep covering the Breton coast in case of further invasion or to reinforce their local posts and keep control of the countryside. Everyone in a uniform was jittery and trigger-happy.

This much Gaston told them over breakfast the next morning, served by the short, dark, monosyllabic farmer's widow, who was clearly keen to see them gone.

'No more the car,' he said. 'We move at night, by foot. The truck goes ahead at dusk. We go from place to place. I will tell you what they need, and you radio for supplies, yes?'

'No,' said Saffity. '*I* will tell you what you need, and what to do and when to move. When I see what you've got, and where you all are. You show me, you're the guide. But I'm in charge, OK?'

Gaston looked at him quizzically, then smiled. 'OK, you're the boss,' he said. 'Until it's our country again.'

Saffity grinned complicitly, and the other two laughed out loud.

That night, when they left – much to the relief of the farmer's widow – it was raining heavily. For three wet weeks they tramped through wheatfields, through byres, over undulating hills and down high-hedged lanes, along rocky, cliff-edged paths; Gaston in the lead, Saffity following with his burning eyes, Emile with his radio transceiver looming over his back, and Drew with his dreams of far-off frolics bringing up the rear.

In village after village – in farmyards, in chapels, in graveyards, in shuttered groceries shops, in cramped front rooms, and once in a reeking slaughterhouse – they met the *maquisards*, listened to their complaints, some justified, some not, and checked their ammunition and radioed in for supply drops which, in the event, proved so surprisingly forthcoming that Saffity began to be regarded with awe. Emile would tell them of the intimate progress of the war and Drew, having flitted like a shadow round the village as they talked, would come in and suggest inspired small acts of sabotage – such as blocking off the sewage pipe in a Gestapo HQ.

Mostly they slept in the barns of sympathetic farmers, during the daytime occasionally in church crypts, always being sent on their way, when they left in the evening, with a baguette and a sausage or two, and some local cheese.

By June 26th, when Cherbourg finally surrendered to the Allies, some thirty Resistance units in Brittany were organised, operational and under arms. Three trains had been derailed, ten German army vehicles had ceased to function, phone lines had twice been out of order for forty-eight hours at a time, two command posts had suffered collective food poisoning for a full three days, and Saffity's nerves were jagged from too many close escapes.

That night they slipped into the village of Maraban, where they were to meet in a church whose cellar housed a flourishing workshop where passports and papers were forged. Saffity, whose bag of equipment had been lost in the parachute drop, was wearing the same mildewed socks he'd been wearing the day he left England, and longing to remove them and scrounge another pair.

First, though, they were led to the cellar to see the operation. Over one table spread with papers hung a small, cracked mirror. Saffity, catching an unexpected glimpse of himself in it, saw that the beard on his gaunt, almost skeletal face, was grey too. It made him laugh; even in that tense, prickly atmosphere, he could not stop the wild joyous peals that shook his body. He laughed at the sound of his own laugh, and then laughed louder still, for he had not expected to hear the sound of genuine mirth ever again. There were about twenty war-used, war-scarred, war-drained people in that cellar, and every one of them, after a moment's pause, began to laugh with him.

Suddenly, high above the laughter, a raised female voice sliced through and shut it off. 'I know that laugh,' the voice cried furiously. 'Who is it?'

A terrible silence fell and instantly the group closed round him. One of their number, a large, sweating peasant, grabbed Saffity's arm and twisted it.

'What are you?' he spat. Saffity felt the foul spray on his face. 'Was that a *Boche* accent?' His arm was twisted again.

'*Merde!*' Drew called out angrily. 'This man is a British officer, and a volunteer!'

'An Englishman,' the sweating farmer snarled. 'Or a *Boche* pretending to be one?'

'I am Wing Commander Saffity of the Royal Air Force,' Saffity said coldly. 'And I'll thank you to take your hands — '

The same high voice interrupted, screaming hysterically, '*Mon Dieu! Saffarty! Saffarty!* It is you. But certainly, it *is* you!' The woman spoke in French, which was only to be expected; it was her use of the intimate *tu* that so shocked everyone. Saffity looked dazed. She covered him with embraces, wetting his cheeks with her tears. She turned to the group. 'His hair is as white as that of an old man, but he is only thirty-six years old.' Once again she faced the group. 'I knew him when I was a girl, in Paris. So you took my advice, Saffarty,' she said, pronouncing his name the old way. 'You had your eye operated on.'

'Judith!' Saffity exclaimed, recognising her at last. 'Forgive me, it's been too long.' She bore no physical resemblance to the girl he had known so long ago. If he remembered correctly she had been ten years older than he, which meant that she was at least forty-six now. She looked sixty or more.

She picked up his hand and kissed it. 'A British officer,' she said reverently. 'I knew you'd go far.'

'And you, Judith? Are you still a photographer?'

'Yes, Saffarty, I am still a photographer. I forge passports and documents. And I was married, but now I'm a widow.'

Saffity sensed the atmosphere change, and felt as much as saw their friendly expressions.

'They think I'm a fucking hero,' he said, in English, to Drew. 'I have the feeling this will be a highly successful operation.' Then,

365

raising his voice, he addressed the group. 'Forgive me for having reverted to English,' he said. 'But allow me to translate. I told my fellow officer here that if you think I'm a hero, I'm not. He agreed. It's *you* who are the heroes.'

Judith stood beside him, holding his hand. Now Saffity raised their interlocking hands above both their heads, and said simply, 'It is twenty years since last we met. We knew one another in Paris.'

Then with dramatic calm, he said quietly, 'The Boches murdered my father.' As he paused, he noticed Drew's head jerk back with surprise. 'You, all of you, have lost members of your families.' Abruptly, his voice struck a thunderous pitch. 'My friends, we will be avenged!'

There was an electric buzz in the group, and much emotion. He had hit the right note when he spoke of vengeance; every one of the twenty Resistance fighters gathered in that cellar had suffered at the hands of the Boches. Saffity was presented with a bottle of cognac and a pack of Gauloise cigarettes. The aura of hostility melted. Also, though he and Judith were both battle worn – and Judith obviously aged by the years as well as by the war – the sparkling tenderness between them made it very clear that they had once been lovers.

Saffity's bone-weariness left him, and he and Judith talked through the night.

She told him that her husband, Roland Legrand, had been the headmaster of the local school. He had been much loved, and was one of the first to join the Resistance. 'But it is because of me that he lost his life,' she said brokenly. 'Roland was denounced, but not for being a *maquisard*. *I* was his crime — '

'You were his crime?' Saffity repeated, puzzled.

'Roland was sheltering a Jew. Me. He, he was not a Jew.' She swallowed convulsively, her head moving to and fro, and her low, staccato voice was as beaten as she looked. 'Dumas sold him.'

'Sold him?' Saffity echoed.

'Yes, for two thousand francs only. It was a cut-price sale.'

'About twelve pounds,' Saffity interjected in spite of himself.

'Still the book-keeper, I see,' Judith said calmly. 'Yes, the Gestapo gave the traitor two thousand.'

'Where is this Dumas now? How do you know that's what he got?'

'Two thousand is the going rate for a Jew, now that they're so scarce.' She hesitated for a moment, and said abruptly, 'He hasn't been seen round here for months.'

'What does he look like?'

'What's the difference?'

'I'm in charge. Go on, describe him,' Saffity commanded authoritatively.

'Tall, thin, bald – what's left of his hair is black. His head is the shape of an outsize egg.'

'An egg?'

'You always did repeat things, didn't you?' Judith said with a feeble smile. 'Let's talk about happier times. Tell me about your life. Are you married?'

In July, as the British, American and Canadian forces moved south from Cherbourg, crossing the rivers Odon and Orne, taking St-Lô and striking for Caen, aiming to lay open Brittany to their west, the Jedburgh team stepped up their sabotage, ambushing supply vehicles and blowing up judiciously selected bridges – enough to make German communication difficult but not so many as to make Allied advance impossible. In this they were advised by radio from London.

They based themselves at Judith's church for a while and, finding daylight movement safer, commandeered bicycles for themselves. The toes on Saffity's left foot had become incredibly sore and painful; but he found that by careful application of his heel to the pedal he could both move as fast as the others and, for the most part, conceal his injury from them. Saffity and Drew cycled through the region and Gaston taught them where the best strawberries were to be found. Sometimes they even picked mushrooms, luscious *chanterelles* that Judith cooked for them.

The one thing they missed horribly was cigarettes. Emile even begged London for them, over the radio, but clearly nobody at that end was a nicotine addict. Even Gaston, to whom little seemed impossible, could find no stocks anywhere.

Although Gaston's formal reserve – as chilling as his eyes – rarely left him, he had gradually disclosed several details about himself. He was a lawyer, and one of the first to join the Maquis. Two years earlier both his parents and his young, crippled brother had been tortured and killed by the Germans. Now, his overwhelming hatred of the Nazis was the fuel that kept him going. There were half a million of these savages in France, he said. He spoke of them emotionlessly, tonelessly, as if he were trying to be above them.

After one particularly successful daylight mission, on their way back to Maraban, Saffity and Drew dismounted from their cycles and sat beside a stream. The rain had stopped and the fresh, sweet smell of the earth and the woods tempted them to have a swim. It was far too dangerous to do so of course, but it was pleasant and comforting to flirt with the idea.

At least Saffity could bathe his feet.

He dribbled them in the cool stream while Drew kept watch. 'Now, if we had some cigarettes,' Drew sighed, 'that would complete the picture.'

'Don't talk about it,' Saffity snapped.

Drew raised his binoculars. A short distance away in the valley below, he saw three Germans on motorcycles emerge from a wood and ride leisurely along the road.

'Move your ass, Saffity,' he said sharply. 'Let's go. Boches.' He was already running down the hill as he spoke, dropping behind a bush halfway down. Saffity followed and quickly caught up with him. 'Good, ringside seats,' he said approvingly. 'We see them, but they can't see us.'

By now it had become second nature to blend in with the vegetation.

'I bet they're loaded to the gills with cigarettes,' Drew said lazily.

Neither of them removed their eyes from their binoculars, holding them in their left hands. Their right hands were at the ready on their rifles.

'Are you thinking what I'm thinking?' Saffity said evenly.

'I guess so,' Drew said slyly. His scalp moved. 'We could have more fun taking twenty packs off them than — '

'Than *what*?' Saffity cut in coldly.

'I don't know. I couldn't give a damn,' Drew replied angrily. 'I'm dying for a cigarette. Want to hear something, Saff? I could kill for a cigarette.' He laughed wildly. 'How does that strike you, Saff?'

'Now's our chance,' Saffity said suddenly, his voice razor-sharp.

Their first shots, almost simultaneous, felled the two leading Germans. As the third wheeled, skidding desperately as he tried to turn, Drew carefully sighted and shot him between the shoulderblades. Quickly and in silence they searched the pockets of the three dead men. One of them didn't smoke; there were no cigarettes, only a blood-spattered photograph of a small blond boy and his blond mother.

Speedily, they pulled the bodies – a mess of bloodied meat – out of the sun, and hid them in the shade. Saffity quelled the urge to vomit. They manoeuvred the motor-bikes into a ditch. Climbing the hill again to where their bicycles were hidden, he thought they may have had their two packets of cigarettes, but it had been foolhardy and stupid. What's more, their headquarters would have to be moved.

Less than two hours later, their equipment, their armaments and the men and women of the Maquis had been moved to the Convent of Sacré Coeur.

Judith insisted on a final detail. 'You've become known, Saffity. They're hunting the old man, the man with the silver hair.' She went on implacably. 'So the old man will have red hair.'

'Dye my hair? Don't be ridiculous! Besides, how do they know about us?'

'You never see the hounds until it is too late,' she hissed. 'How do they know about you and Drew? Who knows? An idle boast, perhaps, from one of our own.' She shrugged eloquently. 'Don't press your luck. Just be grateful that Stefan managed to get hold of this bottle of henna.' Even as she spoke, she attended to his hair. She laughed quietly. 'It's as well there's no mirror,' she said brightly. Then, as if to distract him, she added, 'You know, I never did become a journalist, Saffarty. But I did learn shorthand.'

'Shorthand?' he echoed.

'You thought it was the greatest invention, shorthand. You persuaded me to learn it. But that was another time and in another world. I thought about you often, after that. Did you think of me?'

'You were my first woman, Judith.'

'So I was. Something of a privilege, as I recall. You were so strong, so virile, and so, so enthusiastic. I told you you'd be successful with women. Were you?'

'I loved my wife,' he said painfully. 'I love her still. Edwina knew about you, you know, Judith. We had no secrets, she and I. Except, perhaps — ' Saffity seemed to think again, and stop himself from going on.

'Except what?' Judith asked softly.

'She did not know that I was once a Jew.'

'Ah, how well I remember you telling me you had stopped being a

Jew — ' She shuddered. 'I knew even then that the world would teach you that even if you change the blood in your veins – and it is now possible to have a complete transfusion, Saffarty – that your new, anonymous blood would still be counted and registered as Jewish blood.'

'But I did stop. I have stopped.'

'If you are not a Jew, what are you?'

'A citizen of the world.'

'Has Hitler taught you nothing, then? What about your parents, your family?'

'My mother died of natural causes. My father is a lampshade. Auschwitz ash.'

'Jewish ash.'

'Ashes to ashes and dust to dust. What difference? If he had not been a Jew he would not be ash.'

'And you will escape that fate, Saffarty?'

'I will be ash, or I will be dust. It will make no difference then. Born a Jew, I was born with a congenital defect, like a squint, you could say. But that was cured and corrected.'

'But Hitler — ?'

'If I return to the faith I never had, that will be another victory for evil. And I will not allow that sub-human to dictate either my faith or my fate to me. If I am killed, it will be because I am a soldier, not because it was my special fate to have once been Jewish. A lapsed Catholic may be despised by his own, but not by the world. But it seems everyone despises a lapsed Jew.'

She laughed mirthlessly. 'I can't speak for everyone,' she said sadly. 'I am only Jewish myself.'

Now it was Saffity's turn to shrug.

'Well, you look like a fox, Saffarty. A red-headed fox.' All the while they had been talking, she had been working steadily on his thick hair. She picked up a clump of it, and pulled hard. 'Roland died because of my Jewish blood,' she said fiercely. 'You will not get away with it, Saffarty. You were born a Jew, you are a Jew and you will die a Jew.' She trimmed his bushy black eyebrows. 'You will agree with me one day,' she said bleakly.

At the end of the afternoon two days later, Judith, breathless and rain-sodden, rushed into the kitchen. 'The Boches are entering the village, hundreds of them. They're surrounding the Convent already.' Her voice trembled. 'You've got to get away, Saffarty. You, too, Drew. Emile's in the upper meadow, making his radio call.'

'Right, Judith,' said Saffity, grabbing his knapsack and his rifle. 'We'll all meet up at Belod as soon as we can; that's where we're headed anyway. See if you can intercept Emile before he comes back. You should be safe enough, anyway.' He kissed her quickly. 'Let's go!'

Saffity and Drew fled to the woods and lay up there until the German column moved on.

The Germans seemed to be getting more desperate by the day. Caen had fallen, and an Anglo-Canadian force was pressing south from there. The American General Dempsey was leading his soldiers in an irregular sweep through Brittany; the German column, passing through Maraban, were part of the Axis retreat westwards towards Brest.

In this confused state of affairs the countryside was particularly unsafe. Drew and Saffity kept to the woods as much as they could, crossing open ground with extreme caution, feeding on wild berries and potatoes dug out of the ground. They did not risk approaching farmhouses without Gaston to tell them where they would be safe. Saffity's foot had swelled ominously and was now giving him savage pain, which slowed their progress still further.

By the time they approached Belod, late one evening, they had, missing Emile – pray God he'd got there some other way – been out of radio contact with London for four days.

A kilometre outside the village they waited, listening by the side of the single lane that entered Belod. They were just about to stand up when there was a very audible clink of metal. Saffity crept forward, parted the bushes. A match flared and flickered. In its light he could see a figure sitting on the verge, hunched over a bicycle. Mending a puncture?

The man's hand slipped, he swore and sat back, and in the instant before the match went out Saffity saw a bald, egg-shaped head circled by black hair, and he knew who he was looking at – it was none other than Dumas, the *milicien* who had sold Judith's husband.

The man had his cycle over his knees. Saffity knew he must take advantage, and quickly.

He tore off his boots – no easy matter, for the mud held fast –

readied his revolver and, fearing that the sound of his own thudding heart must surely give him away, crept forward until he was standing over him. 'Monsieur Dumas, I presume,' he said pleasantly.

The man flung the cycle from his knees.

'Don't move,' Saffity said icily. 'Raise your hands above your head.'

'My name is not Dumas,' the man protested. 'I am Guy Ferraud.'

'Forgive me, my dear Monsieur Ferraud,' Saffity began. 'Keep your hands where they are.' He poked them with the butt of his revolver. Then he emitted the piercing bird-call he'd been taught at Milton Hall. Drew's answering call came. Saffity whistled again, the signal for Drew to join him.

'Well, then,' he said coldly. 'If you are Monsieur Ferraud you will not mind being arrested. In the event of a case of mistaken identity, you can sue me.'

The man stared at him unblinkingly. 'I demand to know by whose authority you are arresting me.'

'The authority of a British officer.

'And an American officer,' Drew said quietly. 'We can't let you Brits have all the fucking glory.'

'Allow me to present Monsieur Dumas, the murderer of Judith's husband,' said Saffity.

'I don't shake hands with murderers,' Drew said. 'I prefer this Gallic custom.' He spat in Dumas' face. Then he quickly frisked him. When he located handcuffs and a revolver, he said, '*Milicien! Merde!* Let's shoot him!'

'No,' Saffity said slowly. 'That is for Judith.'

'She won't be able to do it, she's too soft. Don't ask that of her.'

'But she must have the choice. She's earned it.'

Leaving Drew to guard him, Saffity limped quietly into the village and knocked softly at the side door of the priest's house, as he'd been told. Gaston opened it, smiled and led him to the front room, where Judith and a few others were gathered.

'We've got a new recruit,' Saffity said, as if he were announcing an unexpected guest.

'Why did you bring him here? Why should we trust him?' Judith said furiously.

'He says his name is Ferraud,' Saffity continued blandly. 'You won't have to feed him. He looks very well fed to me.'

Puzzled, Judith said, 'Where is he?'

'Drew's holding him. Beside a small pond, I believe,' he drawled.

'Holding him? Why?'

'For your permission, Judith. You might refuse him entry, you see,' he said slowly. He moved closer to her. When she was safe in his arms, in a low carrying voice just loud enough for everyone to hear he said, 'He's Dumas.'

'*Dumas!*' Judith gasped. The blood drained out of her face. If Saffity had not been holding her, she would have fallen.

'We must dispose of him at once,' Gaston ordered.

'I know that. But where?'

'In the woods. Follow me! I want everyone to witness this,' Gaston commanded.

Taking an oil lamp from the house, Saffity led them to the spot. A few feet away from Dumas, Judith said, 'Raise the lamp, Saffarty.'

A profound silence hung over the group; except for Saffity, everyone's eyes were trained on Dumas. For his part, he was mesmerised by Judith. The beaten look was gone, and an avid curiosity had taken its place. Her sallow cheeks were flushed, her lifeless eyes glowed again, and for these brief moments of what Saffity could only describe as total fulfilment, Judith was stunningly lovely . . .

Then she did a strange thing – she thrust her face so close to Dumas that her cheeks almost touched his, and tweaked his cheek. It reddened. 'He is made of flesh,' she said wonderingly. 'He *is* human, after all.'

'We must move,' Gaston insisted. He shifted the pick and shovel from his left to his right shoulder, and tied a gag over Dumas' mouth. 'Bullies are always cowards,' he said caustically.

Fifteen minutes into the woods they reached a clearing and Gaston ordered them to stop. He forced the pick and shovel on Dumas. 'Dig!' he commanded. 'It won't take long,' he told the group. 'This is one of our prepared graves.'

Dumas worked quietly; the soft, loosened earth seemed weightless.

When he'd done, Gaston ordered him to write his confession. 'You can confess with or without torture,' he said evenly. 'The decision is yours.'

'Pencil,' Dumas said hoarsely.

'Are you going to kill him, Judith?' Gaston asked pleasantly.

'No,' Judith said in ringing tones. 'I'll leave that to Wing

Commander Saffarty. My Jewish blood made me a widow. Saffarty's blood is different – he has the strong blood of a soldier.'

Dumas' confession was handed to her. 'Why did you sell him so cheaply?' she asked bitterly. 'I would have paid you so much more for his life than you got for his death.'

'Ready, Wing Commander Saffarty?' Gaston asked.

Dumas fell to his knees.

Gaston caught Saffity's eye, and cocked his head slightly. Saffity obeyed his unspoken order, and blasted the kneeling Dumas into the grave.

Judith insisted on waiting until the open wound of the grave had been covered.

By the beginning of August the military situation in eastern Brittany had become so confused that London, on their twice-daily radio contact, could no longer give specific targets with any confidence.

The remnants of the German Seventh Army to the west of Paris were in a quandary. From Paris to the mouth of the Seine on the coast only two bridges were still standing. The Paris bridges were still intact, but for a large army with heavy equipment it would be like retreating into a trap.

Consequently while individual towns – like Angers, on August 10th – fell to the Allies, the countryside was criss-crossed by columns from both sides, either in pursuit of each other or in flight.

Saffity's only instructions were to bring the Maquis out into the open to engage Germans where and when they could. Once more on bicycles, he, Emile and Drew went from village to village spreading the word.

One hot afternoon, leaving the tiny hamlet of Le Ponthou, they heard the familiar rumble of German tanks ahead, and in a well-practised routine swung their bicycles off the road and concealed themselves behind a hedge.

But wait, could those be American voices, GI voices?

'Drew, listen, Drew! They're Americans!' Saffity hissed.

'Shut up,' Drew snapped.

'They can't be more than thirty feet away. I tell you, they *are* American!'

Drew shot out of the ditch and rushed to the middle of the road. 'Hold your fire,' he yelled. 'I'm American. *American!*'

'Stand still with your arms over your head,' came the answer.

The three Jedburghs waited.

'Jesus!' the GI shouted when he reached them. 'Who the hell are you? You're covered in cow-shit!'

'We were parachuted in. We've been here for sixty days or so,' Drew answered.

Emile burst into voluble French. 'Who the hell is *he*?' the GI demanded, pointing towards Emile.

'A French officer on our team,' Drew said angrily.

'Do you have a medic?' Saffity interrupted weakly. 'Is there a medical officer with you?'

'Sure,' the GI said. 'Dr Parsons. We'll take you to him. What's the matter with you?'

The doctor was set up in a makeshift HQ in the next village, in a barn. Saffity's foot had gone through so many stages of agony it was now numb. That was what worried hm. He hadn't dared look at it for two days. When the doctor eased off his boot he said, 'Oh boy!' He poked around for a bit, cleaned things up, then said, 'Hold tight!' He reached for his antiseptic surgical spirits, splashed them on, pulled out a scalpel, and, without the help of a local anaesthetic, cut off Saffity's little toe.

Saffity bellowed with pain.

'You'll thank me for this,' the battle-worn doctor said crisply, staunching the wound. 'Throw those boots away and get some shoes.' Saffity said nothing, unable to speak. Tears of pain and rage streaked his cheeks. 'Here, hold this tight. This foot of yours is a mess; you're going to have to take the weight off it for a few days.' He handed him some bandages. 'Change the dressings twice a day.' He took a hip flask from his back pocket, wiped the neck with a clean towel, and said, 'Have some; you'll need it when I put the stitches in.'

The sweep of the American forces westwards and the eastern thrust towards Paris had created a sudden haven of peace in the area.

Saffity was taken to a small hotel, and for the next two days Gaston remained stalwartly at his bedside, bringing him the best of local food and drink which seemed to have appeared from nowhere. From time to time he would curse the American doctor, and call him by every known expletive. Saffity was in too much pain to argue. Every now and then Drew would look in, but he was, as he put it, having more fun with a gal named Françine than even he had dreamed possible. Emile had been altogether unnerved by having witnessed Dr Parsons' brutal surgery and was seldom sober.

On the third day Gaston brought Nellie Gérard, a young woman with some elementary nursing experience, to take care of Saffity. 'She is called Nellie. Like all good Bretons, she has a Welsh name,' he explained. 'You can trust her,' he told Saffity gravely. 'Nellie used to be a schoolteacher.'

'I'm not a schoolboy,' Saffity said with his old, infectious laugh. 'I don't know whether she can trust me.'

'You're getting better,' Gaston said shortly.

'Thanks to you, *mon vieux*,' he replied, taking the Frenchman's hand and shaking it. 'You've been more than a friend.'

Gaston gave one of his expressive shrugs, and left.

Saffity at first felt awkward being at the mercy of such a pretty young woman, but Nellie nursed his wound deftly and tenderly, and her pleasant chatter was as soothing as any salve.

Within four days, with the aid of a stick he felt strong enough to go on a short walk with her. They walked a little further next day, and Nellie later removed his stitches. The pain eased. In the miraculous, peaceful stillness, after the incessant noise of war, the world seemed fresh again. In the woods, in the rain, a strange sense of freedom overtook them. Coming back to the hotel one evening at dusk they found a bottle of champagne behind the bar and opened it; and after that it seemed only natural that they would share one another's bodies as well. They made love easily, freely and often that night, exploring each other's bodies as thoroughly and as diligently as if they were studying a map of enemy territory; as if every detail, every nuance, had to be understood and memorised.

The war had removed all restraint.

Three days later Saffity and Drew requisitioned the Peugeot sedan that had once belonged to the recently fled owner of the local whorehouse and drove all over the countryside. It was like a holiday.

Nellie, and Drew's girl, Françine, were old friends, and after Emile left to find his family in the South they became a foursome. They spent their time eating, drinking, sleeping and making love. They laughed a lot. Saffity took a boyish delight in spending the vast quantities of the phoney money he had been issued at Milton Hall. They were living for the moment only, denying the future as well as the past, obeying nothing but their own changing moods. On August 27th, two days after Paris had been liberated, Gaston, who was good at that sort of thing, procured a jeep – without a windscreen – for them, and the four of them set off for the capital.

Before their departure they painted an American flag on one side of the jeep and a British flag on the other. Then they lunched with Gaston and Judith. He'd brought them a feast – salami, cheese, olives, bread and a bottle of rough red wine. He assured them that the road they'd take was now under French control, but when they took their leave of him he smiled his sad, quiet smile.

Saffity promised to look for Judith's aunt and uncle, the Namiases, in Paris.

'I feel like a kid playing hooky,' Drew chuckled. 'It's a funny sort of freedom, with the Boches on the run.' His hand left the steering wheel and he patted his automatic. 'Wouldn't feel safe without this, though,' he said quietly. 'Or with these,' he went on pointing to the grenades in the door pocket.

'We could be going fishing,' Saffity said. 'It's a perfect day for fishing.' He hugged Nellie tight. 'Would you like to go fishing, Nellie?'

They passed through a small village, and some of the people in the crowded square threw flowers at them. Nellie broke into the *Marseillaise* and they all joined in. About five kilometres further on the hilly road was blocked by abandoned German trucks.

'We'll have to reverse and take a different route,' Saffity said.

'No, sir!' Drew said triumphantly. 'Not with this beaut of a jeep.' He pulled off the road, drove a short way through the fresh-smelling fields, and then joined the road again.

No one talked much after that. Saffity sat back and Nellie fell asleep with her head on his shoulder. Gently, so as not to disturb her, he removed the chain with his gold key from his pocket – the chain had broken and he no longer wore it around his neck – and quietly played with it. Gaston had called it a crucifix; perhaps, he thought, in a way it was. He could not think of anyone he respected more than that patriotic Frenchman with his melancholy clerical features, and his brown shirt made of parachute silk, but there was no one he liked more than Drew. He liked Drew's total lack of malice, his simple love of chasing girls, and the way he was looking forward to cashing in all that phony money of his so that he could get still more girls. Idly, Saffity wondered what Drew would do after the war.

Nellie stirred, awoke for a moment, and kissed him passionately. Then she fell asleep again. Oh, she was ardent and agile, this Nellie, yet she looked prim, even innocent. Suddenly Saffity realised he was happy with Nellie, and at the same moment he understood he'd been happy with Brooke, too. Nellie was so pretty, and so young. About twenty, he supposed. He would ask her later. It occurred to him how little they knew of one another. He was going to show Nellie, Drew and Françine the Paris he and Judith had known so long ago. Judith – it had been painful saying goodbye to her. She had done so much for him; she had helped him to be a good soldier. He wanted to tell her that.

Ah, well, he thought, it's war that's made it possible for me to feel real, primitive joy, again. Edwina, he believed, would understand . . . He sighed. Gaston had said that war was incurable, and he was probably right. Yet he could not recall when last – since Edwina's death – he had felt so at peace with himself.

He would get his hair cut in Paris, and get the henna out, somehow.

He had been fiddling with his key too much; it slipped off the broken chain, and fell to the floor of the jeep. Saffity bent to retrieve it, and that was the last thing he knew.

21

For months afterwards the memory of Jeff running after the train at Victoria Station continued to haunt Fanny. Sometimes her eyes would fill with tears. The Blitz dominated the news. 'You could still be in England,' Max said again and again. 'Just be grateful I forced you to come back when I did!'

'I am grateful, Max,' Fanny answered miserably.

Business was slow, which made it even harder for Fanny not to think about Sonja. She was always the first to look at the mail, but no letter ever came.

Six months after war had been declared, Trans-Empire Carpets was operating on a skeleton staff. All of their staff save one were in the army, volunteers. Max continued to pay their salaries as if they were still working. It eased his conscience and made him feel virtuous; though prevalent, the practice was far from universal. In any case, his business was sort of stock; so short, in fact, that he no longer went to the shop every day.

The twenty-five-thousand-pound order Fanny had so impetuously placed with Myles miraculously found its way to Johannesburg, and was worth its weight in gold. It had given them a tremendous advantage over the competitors. Even Max had to concede that it was a stroke of luck.

'There you are, Max, Saffity is lucky for you,' Fanny said triumphantly.

And then out of the blue came another stroke of luck. A huge shipment of Indian carpets on their way to England were diverted to South Africa. The British importers, the Bart Textile Company, were anxious to dispose of the carpets, so anxious they somehow sent their man, Mr Neville Parker, to South Africa. In London, a shipping company had advised Mr Parker that if one company could help him that company was Trans-Empire Carpets.

Mr Parker didn't even bother to travel to Johannesburg. He merely telephoned Max, introduced himself and said, 'I'm told you're the largest importer of carpets in Africa.'

'That's true,' Max said firmly, 'I am.'

'I have a shipment of two hundred thousand pounds of embossed Indian carpets lying in the bonded warehouse in Durban. They're all colours and sizes, ranging from two by four, to nine by twelve.'

'I'll take the lot,' Max said quickly. His hands shook. He had only gone to the shop because his secretary was ill. And he could not begin to imagine how he could raise two hundred thousand pounds . . .

'You'll take the lot?' Mr Parker repeated, sounding incredulous.

'Certainly,' Max said matter-of-factly. 'I'll take them all on consignment. That way, Mr Parker, you'll reduce your storage and insurance costs. It makes sense, doesn't it? Trans-Empire Carpets could dispose of the total shipment within six months.'

'I'll have to think — '

'We've done a vast amount of business on consignment. I can assure you that, for us, this is the normal course of business,' Max said a shade testily. 'But we will take ten-thousand-pound-bale lots at a time, for which we will pay on delivery. I suggest you telephone Barclays Bank to confirm our *bona fides*. Speak to Mr Fotheringham.'

Thirty minutes later the deal was concluded.

'It's a pleasure to do business with you, Mr Parker.' Max laughed, consciously imitating Saffity. He was elated when he put the phone down. He had done the deal of his life. He reached for one of his Havana cigars, a gift from a grateful customer. He tried the laugh out again, and was well satisfied.

He had no doubt that these carpets could command almost whatever price he asked for them; he would not sell them so much as allocate them. All consumer goods were scarce. True, the new price control regulations were in force, and there was a new excess profit tax, too; but all the same, it was the deal of a lifetime.

It was more out of a need to be occupied than out of an urge to do good that Fanny plunged herself into the war effort. She soon discovered that she was as talented an administrator as she was a saleswoman. Since few women were active company directors, her reputation as a businesswoman preceded her, and her tireless efficiency merely confirmed her reputation. Within months, she was chairwoman of the Transvaal Division of the Union of Jewish Women. She was not universally liked, but she was envied and respected.

She could no longer complain that she had too little to do. Max's mother now lived with them, which meant that with her mother-in-law's devoted maid, Violet, their household help now numbered ten. There was nothing unusual about that – most of her neighbours in Lower Houghton also had a houseboy, a cook, a waiter, a nanny, a washerwoman, and two to three gardeners. Fanny, unlike most of her neighbours, had never learned to drive, so they also had a driver, Absalom, who was her most trusted servant. Fanny was fussy about their uniforms, and insisted that they were changed twice a day.

When business was slow it was only logical to transfer Absalom from Trans-Empire Carpets to the Blum household. The fierce pride Max had encountered in the police station years earlier was undiminished. But there was besides an unflinching dignity, a certain aloofness, which, combined with his above-average English, made him the envy of all her friends.

From the very outset Absalom had made it clear that he ate neither the standard *mealie pap* – maize meal porridge – nor the standard inferior cuts of 'boys' meat'. Fanny had no choice but to comply, and placed standing orders with the butcher and the grocer. He also made it clear that domestic chores would not be among his duties. More than anything else, this made the rest of the servants defer to him.

For all that, he was as respectful as he was dignified. He showed little emotion. Fanny had only once seen an expression of rage cross his face, and that was shortly after he had joined the family, when he had angrily refused the tip that Jeff had proffered him. Fanny had even found herself apologising to him for that.

The tragedy in his own life had made him still more dignified. Three years earlier his son Paul had been killed in the township – stabbed to death by a gang of young *tsotsis*, delinquents. Broken with grief, Esther, his mother, refused food. Then, despite all Rachel Blum's sympathetic nursing and entreaties, she and her mother left Johannesburg and returned to their kraal in Zululand. Within a year the burden of living was removed from her. The

Blums tried to speak, or rather to appeal, to Absalom. But, with his usual pride, he made them understand they were interfering. 'It is our way,' he said.

As far as Fanny was concerned, Absalom was a rare gem of a servant. Things ran more smoothly with him around to settle all those incomprehensible tribal disputes that plagued so many white households.

On the first anniversary of the declaration of war their house became the venue for the annual fund-raising fête. The tombola stall netted twelve hundred pounds. People were extravagant, and wildly generous – the distant war and the mingling of military uniforms gave staid Johannesburg a carnival-like atmosphere. Max's new laugh boomed across the lawns in Beech Avenue.

Mireille and Theresa travelled from the Cape; the presence of Lady Rutherford would add enormously to Fanny's and Max's status. Mireille donated cases of wine from her estate, as well as several casks of brandy. After the fête the *Star* sent a reporter to interview her, and readers were delighted and proud to learn that authors such as Jane Austen, Longfellow and Baudelaire had written of the wines of Constantia. Though pleased to be remote from the outside world, many English-speaking South Africans still had a complex about being colonials. Few had travelled outside their country, and what Lady Rutherford told them about the history of their wines made them feel cosmopolitan.

Mireille could not help noticing Max's new laugh. 'You sound just like Saffity,' she said tonelessly.

Max's smile stiffened on his lips. 'Do I?' he said neutrally. He gestured towards Theresa. 'She looks more and more like him,' he said smoothly. 'She's very beautiful.'

'Don't mention his name,' Mireille said furiously.

'*I* didn't. *You* did,' Max replied, with the smallest measure of a taunt in his voice.

Fanny interrupted them. 'We've grossed two and a half thousand pounds,' she said exultantly. 'Theresa's looking lovely. How time flies! She'll be twelve in a few days, won't she?'

'She's a little woman, already,' Mireille said harshly. 'She's getting too big for her boots. I caught her wearing lipstick the other day, and had to punish her.'

Fanny drew back involuntarily. Mireille had sounded cruel – she preferred not to know what the punishment had been.

382

Fanny knew that war changed people and she didn't see why she shouldn't be changed, too. She went to a new hairdresser, Anita, in Plein Street.

'You've been doing your own hair, Mrs Blum,' Anita sniffed. It was a statement rather than a question.

'Yes.'

'We'll soon put that right,' she said smugly.

Fanny was delighted with the result of Anita's expertise; her hairstyle made her look not only fashionable, but affluent. She met Anita's blue but critical eyes in the mirror. 'You need to have your eyebrows plucked,' she pronounced. 'You have good, lively eyes, but they're hidden under a bush. You'll look younger, too, if you pluck them.'

'Could you do them for me?' Fanny asked at once.

Anita worked quickly and skilfully, but it was surprisingly painful all the same. Afterwards the area that had been plucked was red and inflamed. 'Don't worry,' Anita said airily. 'It'll fade before you get home.' She reached swiftly into her own handbag. 'You could do with some mascara,' she added calmly. 'Your make-up is terrible; it doesn't do you any justice at all.' She leaned Fanny's head against her soft breasts and worked quietly and efficiently. Fanny did as she was bid, and closed her eyes and tried not to worry. It would be easy enough, she told herself, to wash it all off. Anita thrust a hand-mirror at her. 'Look,' she said triumphantly.

Fanny looked and gasped. She was utterly transformed. She glowed; her sallow complexion appeared to have vanished. Her brown eyes had always been alert, but now they glittered. There was no doubt that Fanny's beetling brows had had the effect of dark glasses. Now that Anita had, so to speak, brought her eyes out into the light, they were luminous and soft. Her expression had changed, too. Where it had once seemed drooped in permanent disapproval, it was now open and expectant.

'You're a genius, Anita, that's all I can say. You're a genius,' Fanny said excitedly.

'What's happened to you?' Max asked when she got home. 'You look different.'

'I had a perm,' she answered shyly. 'Does it look nice?'

Max nodded.

Since he rarely seemed to notice what she looked like, Fanny took this as the highest praise.

She had further proof of Max's approval when they went to bed that night. His love-making was more ardent and considerate than it had been in years.

And he became altogether a little easier to live with. He was less objectionable about entertaining, and accordingly less objectionable to his guests. They were on the dinner-party circuit, where the men played poker and the women played rummy. They fell into the habit of keeping open house on Sundays, never knowing how many people would turn up. Fanny was a good organiser, everyone envied her perfect servants, and she took pleasure in being hostess. It was good for Jeff, too – there were always children about.

And the entertaining wasn't bad for business either – Max, Arnold Stern and Edgar Berman formed what they called a property syndicate. They combined their six initials, and called the company BEMSAS. Needless to say, it had nothing to do with Saffity. There were statutory restrictions on new building, so they bought existing, run-down properties. It was speculative, the three men told themselves, but what the hell; they could all afford the risk.

Of course the war was going on, but it was somewhere else, and the Blums saw no reason to discontinue their annual holidays to Durban in the winter, and to Muizenberg in the summer. The colonial Edward Hotel was still grand and still colonial, though now there were three sittings for every meal. Pirelli, the flamboyant maître d'hôtel, was coining money.

In July 1941 the Blums, for the second year running, were preparing to leave for Durban. Fanny was happy and confident about the trip – Absalom had driven them down last year, and she liked the idea of turning it into a tradition. The trunk of the car was loaded, her hair was safely tucked into the scarf and they were almost ready to leave. Jeff was twelve years old now, though he looked about fourteen. Like his father, he was dressed in khaki shorts, shirt, knee-length socks and sturdy brogues. One of his shoelaces was undone. He strolled over to the car, placed his foot on the open trunk, and called out, 'Absalom! Come here, Absalom! Tie my shoelace.'

'What did you say?' Max roared. 'What did I hear you say, Jeff?'

'I told Absalom to tie my shoelace,' Jeff answered sullenly.

'How d'you like that?' Max bellowed. 'You told Absalom to tie your shoelace!' His voice was dangerously high. 'He's a person, Jeff; Absalom is a grown man. How dare you talk like that to him? He's a man just like I am.' His head shook with rage. 'Get to your room,' he yelled. 'At once! Fanny! Fanny! Come here.'

When they were in Jeff's room, Max ordered him to take down his trousers.

He obeyed silently.

Max unbuckled his belt.

Then Jeff turned to his father and hissed, 'He's not a *man* like you are, Daddy. He's a native. And when you and Mommy go out at night, Absalom and Nanny get naked on your bed together — '

'*What?*' Max whispered. 'What did you say?'

'Put down that belt immediately, Max,' Fanny said icily. 'I want to hear what more Jeff has to say.'

'They're not people, they're kaffirs!' Jeff said scornfully. 'They don't use proper lavatory paper. They use scraps of newspaper. The weeding-women don't care who sees their tits when they feed their smelly babies. And they stink. You give them Lifebuoy soap and then you always say it's a waste!'

'What d'you mean, Nanny and Absalom get on my bed when I'm out?' Fanny asked, sounding horrified.

'First they get naked, then they laugh. Then — '

'Stop it, I've had enough,' Max thundered. He turned to Fanny. 'We're not leaving. I'm cancelling the trip.' Then he turned to Jeff. 'And you will stay in your room. Your mother and I will have to have a serious talk.'

There was no alternative; the nanny and the chauffeur would have to go. It was a pity, really it was, and it was damned inconvenient. It wasn't so bad about Nanny – Jeff was too big for a nursemaid, anyway. But Absalom; where on earth could they find another chauffeur with his unique qualities? He was as honest as he was devoted, as loyal as he was diligent. He had a dignified smile that made it easy for Fanny to ask him to drive her friends home on Sundays when it was supposed to be his day off.

But Fanny was adamant that they should go ahead with the holiday. They would delay leaving until the next day, so that things could be sorted out with the rest of the servants. They would travel by train, or else Max could drive. Fanny looked at her bed and shuddered. To think that Absalom and Nanny had . . . No, it didn't bear thinking about. She would buy new sheets, a new bed. She felt half inclined to buy a new house . . .

Meanwhile, there was no point in waiting. Max went downstairs to dismiss both Absalom and Nanny.

A short while later Nanny knocked on Fanny's door. Her dark complexion had turned a yellowish-grey, her usually sparkling eyes were mournful, and she was shaking and sweating. 'Ow, madam, I need the work. I've got three kids to support.'

Fanny shook her head and pursed her lips.

'Madam,' Nanny said softly. 'We could have gone to our own room, Absalom and I. But you told me never to leave Master Jeff when you were out.'

'Get out of this room,' Fanny said, her voice a high-pitched yowl. 'Get out of my sight at once! D'you hear me, at once!'

'Can I say goodbye to Master Jeff? I've been with him since he was born — '

'Don't you dare go near him!' Fanny answered fiercely. 'If you try to speak to him, I'll call the police!'

Max decided to drive to Durban himself. They tried to talk to Jeff, but he remained obstinately sullen.

Jeff hated his parents. He wasn't sure – and didn't care – which of them he hated most. He loved Nanny; she had been there since he could remember, in fact since he had been born. But he hated himself even more than he hated his parents. It was all his fault. He wanted to cry. He felt sick. He had loved being with Nanny and Absalom. Absalom had bought him thousands of those scented pink sweets his mother had forbidden him to eat. Nanny fried his eggs, and if he said they were not exactly right she would laugh and fry two more. It was all so unfair, so hard for him to understand. He remembered that long-ago day, long before the war, when his parents had been too busy to come to his Sports Day. He had won his race and collapsed afterwards in terrible pain. His teachers said it was nothing, but Nanny lifted him up, and she and Absalom drove him to the hospital. He had nearly lost his life, the doctors said; his appendix was about to rupture.

Where was Nanny now? What about her children? They had not even let him say goodbye to her.

But it was all his fault: he had said Absalom was not a person. Yet he had not told a lie. Kaffirs weren't real, full people. They were sort of half-people, unfinished, like half-complete. Perhaps one day, in about a hundred years, they would finish their growing, and turn white, and become real people. But Nanny and Absalom would be dead by then, so he would not see them when they became real people. He would be dead, too.

Suddenly, he said out loud, 'I wish I were dead.'

'What's that?' Fanny asked sharply.

'Nothing,' Jeff mumbled. 'I said nothing.'

He lay back and closed his eyes. He imagined himself on a train, his lips moving soundlessly in time with the rhythm of the wheels on the track. 'I-wish-I-were-dead, I-wish-I-were-dead, I-wish-I-were-dead.' It was like one of Nanny's lullabies and, like a lullaby, it sent him to sleep.

Many of their friends were at the Edward Hotel, and yet Fanny and Max were having anything but a good time. Jeff was icily respectful, and exasperatingly polite to the point of rudeness. He answered questions, his manners were impeccable, but it was obvious that his mind was fixated on the two servants.

'I wish you could have met the staff Saffity had at Stanford Hall,' Max said at breakfast one morning. 'They were real servants, I can tell you.'

'If I lived in England I'd also have real servants,' Fanny replied tartly. 'We're going to the beach today, Jeff. I bought you some calamine cream for your sunburn.'

'Thanks,' Jeff said.

'The Stern boy is going down to the beach as well.'

'I know,' Jeff said quietly. 'Mervyn told me.'

It was a perfect day, and the beach was crowded with soldiers on leave. Jeff and Mervyn bought 'twistie' ice-creams, rolled in red and blue cardboard strips that could be undone and twisted off as the ice-cream was eaten.

The strips reminded Jeff of his untied shoelace.

After a while he said, 'I'm boiling. Want to come for a swim, Merv?'

'He seems to be coming out of his mood,' Fanny remarked softly to Max.

'About time,' Max answered.

'Kids! They live in a different world,' Madge Stern said conversationally. The talk turned to the newest oddity on the beach, a visiting Indian in officer's uniform, whom everyone said was a prince.

'Wanna race in the water, Merv?' Jeff said.

'No. You always win.'

'I'm going in anyway'

'OK.'

Jeff swam out and out. Out through the high, foaming waves, to where the sea was calm, where he could float peacefully. He drifted on his back, watching the shore recede and recede. He swam out and farther out. But now that he was leaving the earth behind, he was beginning to feel a little less terrible. It didn't hurt so much now, it didn't really feel; because he was numb and growing steadily, peacefully more so. Yes, he would float away, float to a painless place, float to heaven where wishes come true, and where you could stop thinking, the way he was, at this very moment, stopping to think.

It was Mervyn who sounded the alarm. 'I've lost sight of Jeff,' he sobbed. 'He was floating on his back and then I couldn't see him!'

'Where's the lifeguard? Find the lifeguard!' Fanny commanded.

Everyone around them raced to the sea.

All four lifeguards went out. Not much later, though it seemed an eternity, they were forcing the water from Jeff's lungs.

'He's alive,' a lifeguard shouted. 'A few more minutes — '

Max and Fanny carried him back to the hotel and sent for the doctor.

Max was sobbing. 'He tried to take his own — '

'Shut up, Max. You're mad,' Fanny whispered.

It was all right now, she told herself. It was over. Everything was going to be all right.

When the Blums returned to Johannesburg, they tried to find Nanny and Absalom. But they had disappeared; the servants told them that Absalom was involved in a robbery, and was now in prison. They knew nothing about Nanny, except that she was a Tswana. 'But surely you know her surname?' Max asked, disgusted.

'She is a Tswana,' they replied, as if that ended the matter.

The Blums were not to know that, even if they had not been under dire threat, the servants' first loyalty was to Absalom and not to them. It was true that they had no idea where Absalom and Nanny had gone. But it was not true that Absalom was in prison. They were not lying so much as obeying Absalom's strict orders. Max even asked his lawyer, Gerald Katz, to make enquiries.

After that episode the house lost its charm and they decided to buy a new house, in huge grounds, in Hyde Park, a magnificent suburb on the white highlands on the northern borders of Johannesburg. Jeff could even keep a horse there, if he liked. They were also talking about buying a house in Muizenberg for his grandparents because the air was so good. These days his mother was always waiting for him when he came home from school. He was playing a lot of sport now – it was the football season – and when he was late on purpose, as he often was, it was because he knew it made her anxious.

The house in Hyde Park was called Oak Lodge, because oak trees lined the long, curving driveway. 'It's got real class,' Max said to Fanny. 'Saffity's drive is longer, of course, but this drive is very like his. It's even better, in a way, because it's paved in stone. His is made of sand.'

'Is that why you're buying the house?' she said, incredulous. 'Because it reminds you of Stanford Hall?'

'It happens to be a very good buy,' he said indignantly. 'D'you take me for a fool, Fanny?'

'Of course not, Max. You're right, it is a very good buy,' she said rapidly, nervously.

For although she had never let Max voice his fears about Jeff's near drowning, she was still haunted by it. She wanted to take Jeff away from those stinging memories of Nanny and Absalom; he was often rude to her, and the change would be good for them. The only disadvantage was that the house was out of town, in a peri-urban area, where there were no street lights. The African nights were so dark, and so very black, it was almost like being blind.

The move to Oak Lodge went smoothly and in July 1941 Fanny's father attached the *mezuzah* to the heavy oak door. Max missed his own father, but life had to go on, and the fact that his father was buried in the earth of this new country strengthened and tightened his roots.

Two months later the annual fund-raising fête was held there. Fanny had arranged for a funfair to be set up in the floodlit tennis court, and the grounds of Oak Lodge were so large that the zoo agreed to supply two elephants to give rides to the children. It went on well into the night. The Social and Personal page of the *Rand Daily Mail* carried a large photograph of the elegant and indefatigable Mrs Max Blum.

Fanny was gaining more and more social recognition; the Blums were no longer newcomers.

In December 1942, they took their summer holiday in the new home in Muizenberg where Fanny's parents and Max's mother, who got along well, were living. The Bermans and the Sterns had also bought houses in Muizenberg, so the three families continued their custom of spending their six-week holiday together.

Max was playing a game of poker on the beach when one of the servants told him that there was an urgent message to call Lady Rutherford immediately. Moments later he was on his way to Constantia. Mireille had been too distraught to talk properly on the telephone.

'Thank God you're here, Max,' she said, her voice trembling. 'You never let me down.' She gave him a glass of whisky and poured one for herself. She did not dilute hers with water.

'What's the trouble, Mireille?'

'It's Theresa,' Mireille answered. 'A spoilt and thankless child. My own daughter — '

'But what's happened?'

Mireille had become strangely beautiful. She still wore no make-up, but her deeply tanned face emphasised her gold-flecked hair and her bright angry eyes. She was still as slim and as muscular as a young girl.

'You think Theresa's all innocent and soft, don't you? Well, my eye she is!' Mireille said, spitting out the words as if they were grape pips. 'She's a whore and a harlot. My own daughter — '

'You don't know what you're saying, Mireille! Theresa's only fifteen.'

'That's right. She's a fifteen-year-old harlot. A *putain* at fifteen! Not bad, huh?'

'I'm not going to sit here and let you talk about your own daughter like that. It's been too strenuous for you, running this place. Calm yourself.'

'Calm myself?' Mireille said, her voice furiously out of control. 'You say that to me, when you fired two trusted servants simply because your son saw them making love! And if I told you that I saw, with my own eyes, my own daughter making love to Piet, the son of her nanny, Sarie, what would you say to that, hey, Max? What would you say to that?'

Sarie's son – Sarie, whom he always made a point of tipping lavishly? Sarie, the perfect smiling servant, who called him Master Max? The whole thing was incomprehensible to him. He stared blankly at Mireille.

After a long moment, Mireille said, 'Whisky, Max?'

He nodded.

'Yes, Max, that is what I saw yesterday afternoon. I went down to the cellars to check some temperatures.' She gave him his whisky, drained half her glass herself in one gulp and continued. 'I heard sounds – a sort of a moaning sound. So I took off my boots, and just followed the direction of the sound,' she said, her voice rising dangerously again. 'There's a part of the cellar where it's dark. I couldn't find the light switch. The sounds continued, reached a crescendo, and then stopped suddenly. So I waited. I thought perhaps it was my imagination.'

She crossed the room, ripped a photograph from its frame, and stared at it. 'I waited, Max, you see. I wanted to be sure I wasn't going mad. Then I heard a laugh – a woman's laugh. A soft, rippling, woman's laugh. Then I thought I heard whispering. I couldn't move. I suppose I already knew, but wouldn't face it. You can understand that, can't you, Max?'

Max nodded again. He lit a cigarette and was aware that he had been holding his breath.

'Then the laughing stopped, and I heard movement again. So I crept closer. Very quickly, the moaning began again. I couldn't bear it any longer, so I couldn't stop myself from rushing on to the back of the cellar.'

She began tearing Theresa's photograph, tearing it and tearing it until it fell about her in tiny squares of confetti. 'Yes, Max, I saw my own innocent daughter, her white, raised legs hugging his waist. He's coloured, Sarie's son, Piet, but he's dark' – Mireille's voice over the word 'dark' was like a gasp of pain – 'very, very dark.'

She fell into a flood of weeping. When it subsided Max said, 'What do you want me to do, Mireille?'

She wiped her eyes, and looked up at him. She said tonelessly, 'I'm not going to fire Sarie. Of course Piet was flogged. Sarie saw to that.' She continued in a satisfied tone, 'The foreman flogged him, put him in hospital.'

'Where is Theresa now?' Max interrupted.

'Locked in her room.'

'You've called the doctor to check?'

'To check if she got pregnant, like her mother, you mean?' she said bitterly. 'He was using a condom. It's been going on for weeks. Theresa insists she loves him, that she wants to marry him — '

'That's out of the question!' he broke in harshly.

'It certainly is out of the question,' she said furiously. '*You* got rid of your *servants*. *I'm* getting rid of my daughter!'

'You're getting rid of your daughter?' Max echoed disbelievingly.

'I'm sending her to live in a convent,' Mireille said triumphantly. 'The nuns will take care of her. She will expiate her sin.'

'No, Mireille, you can't do that,' Max said reasonably.

'She's got bad blood in her, Saffarty's blood,' Mireille said bitterly. 'She's always been too headstrong for her own good. I should have put her in the convent years ago.' She smiled suddenly. 'There's still time. You'll see, she'll reach a state of grace. The nuns will help her.' Her voice faded. 'They were lying on a flea-ridden blanket, you know, Max.'

Instead of driving home, Max went to look at Table Mountain, as if the sight of the mountain rising from the seas would ease his confused mind. He felt terribly aroused, and savagely ashamed of the way he felt. The tantalising thought of that dark boy with the beautiful, innocent Theresa on a flea-ridden blanket was too much for him. For a moment he imagined himself flogging the cheeky black bastard himself, and then, almost simultaneously, he imagined making love to Theresa.

He could no more control his thinking than his hard, heavy erection. He had felt nothing like this kind of burning, relentless desire since Colette.

He despised himself. He looked up again at Table Mountain and remembered the day, fifteen years earlier, when he and Mireille had struggled down the mountain together. That was the day she told him she had phoned the Abelmans, and that very same night they had learned that she was still pregnant.

And now he was entertaining thoughts of making love to that very child . . . Saffity's child. He had had too much to drink. He got out of the car and vomited.

It was late when he returned home, and everyone was waiting anxiously. 'I'm sick,' he said to forestall their questions. 'I had to stop the car. I must have got food poisoning or something. I don't know how I managed to drive home.'

The next day Fanny asked, 'What did Mireille want that was so urgent?'

'Oh, there are financial problems.'

'But Lord Rutherford was a millionaire!'

'Deceased estates always bring problems.'

'She's lucky to have your help, Max.'

That night, he made love to Fanny, pretending she was Theresa. By his very ardour Fanny knew that something strange had happened at the Rutherford Estate.

The next day he found himself driving back there. He glanced at himself in his rear-view mirror. He looked older than his thirty-eight years, but his deeply bronzed face made his blue eyes sky-bright. Though his hair was thinning, he was still good-looking. He had not warned Mireille of his visit; he did not want her to have the time to lock Theresa up again.

It was tea time, so he expected to find Mireille and Theresa on the long cool verandah. Instead, Sarie showed him to the living room. Mireille had filled the room with funereal white arum lilies. The shades were drawn and in that half-light, Theresa's white complexion was luminous. As she kissed him on both cheeks she gave a long shuddering sigh. She was wearing a simple white shirt and jodhpurs, and he was horribly conscious of her ripened body. The image of Piet making love to her was at the forefront of his mind. He was afraid it might show in the way he looked at her.

Mireille and Max were never at a loss for words, but today the silence was as heavy as it was threatening. Finally Mireille announced, 'Theresa's going to become a boarder at the Marymount convent.'

'Is that so?' Max said woodenly. 'Are you pleased, Theresa, my dear?'

'Yes,' Theresa said shortly.

'We all think Theresa needs a little more discipline in her life, don't we, Theresa?' Mireille said coldly.

'Discipline?' Theresa said defiantly, her eyes on the floor. 'Yes.'

'Discipline leads to purity,' her mother pronounced. 'Lilies are a symbol of purity, Max. Did you know that? Anyway, that is why we have filled the house with them. Because we believe in purity, don't we, Theresa?' She paused, and then intoned, 'Unto the pure all things are pure.'

The three of them had long since fallen into the habit of speaking French when they were together. Max broke into English.

'Perhaps I should leave you to get on with the scripture lesson,' he said icily, rising to leave.

'Oh, don't go, Uncle Max, please don't go yet,' Theresa cried anxiously.

He sat down at once. 'Will you be allowed to receive visitors during the term, Theresa?'

'Once a month,' Mireille said, answering for her daughter.

'But won't you be lonely, Theresa?' Max asked.

'No,' Theresa said with a terrible note of finality. 'I am already lonely.'

'That's enough, Theresa. Go to your room,' Mireille said furiously. 'Go at once.'

'I'm leaving myself,' Max said quickly. 'I'll come and say goodbye to you, Theresa. When does your new school term begin?'

'In thirteen days,' Theresa said bleakly.

Throughout the next week Max was tormented by Theresa's white, anguished face. He phoned Mireille several times, but nothing he said made the slightest impression on her. Finally he said, 'You're banishing your daughter, Mireille. Now, when she needs her mother more than ever, her mother is banishing her.'

'I know what I'm doing, Max. Don't interfere.'

Ten days later he telephoned a little earlier in the day. And as soon as Sarie told him that Mireille had gone into the city he drove to the Rutherford Estate, hoping to find Theresa on her own.

Sarie let him in. 'It's a terrible thing that has happened, Sarie,' he said sadly.

'My own son, Master Max. To do that to Miss Theresa! The foreman punished him, but God will punish him also.'

Max looked away. This woman had ordered the flogging of her own son . . . He didn't understand these black people; he never had and never would. He said, 'Miss Theresa is going away to boarding school now.'

'It will be better for her. Better for all of us, Master Max.' Sarie looked stooped and old. 'I don't know what I did to get a son like that. Stroos God, I don't. Miss Theresa's crying all the time. She says in God's eyes she's married. Did you ever hear a child talk like that?'

'You must tell no one about this, no one,' he said firmly. If a word of this got out, Mireille and everyone on the Rutherford Estate would be treated like lepers. He certainly did not want Fanny to know.

'I'll tell nobody, Master Max,' Sarie said, clapping her hands to her mouth in horror, as if the very thought of anyone knowing was even worse than what had happened. 'I'll call Miss Theresa now.' She clasped her hands together. 'I'll tell her you're on the stoep; she needs some fresh air.'

Max took the gift he had chosen so carefully out of his pocket and waited for her. He stood up as soon as she arrived and handed it to her at once. 'I brought you this,' he said awkwardly.

'Can I open it?' Theresa asked in her musical voice.

'Of course, my dear.'

She took out the gold crucifix necklace and held it up to the sun. When Max saw its reflection in her soft eyes he was compelled to look away.

'It's beautiful,' she said. 'Just beautiful. I'll wear it for ever.'

She seemed calmer now, he thought, as well as wiser. Her eyes were knowing, yet there was something mysterious, a sort of spiritual gravity that made her seem – well, innocent. Once again, he was confused.

'You know about Piet, don't you? I know you do,' Theresa said defiantly.

'Theresa — '

'It embarrasses you, doesn't it, Uncle Max?'

'Theresa, I — '

'And yet neither you nor my mother were born in this country. My mother is a devout Catholic. She knows that God created all men equally – but for her the only men are white men. The others are not men.'

This kind of talk was heresy, pure heresy. He murmured, 'You are only a little girl, Theresa. You're under age — '

'It doesn't matter. Nothing matters,' she said brokenly. 'He went to hospital, I don't know which. I don't know where he is!'

'You must work hard at school, Theresa. You're still a schoolgirl.'

'I'll never see him again. I know I won't,' she persisted recklessly. 'If only I was going to have a baby. I might have been – but he was too careful.'

'You mustn't talk like that!'

'You're shocked, Uncle Max. I'm sorry,' she said sadly. 'You know he was a sergeant? He'd been up north. He fought at El Alamein. He was even in Cairo. I wasn't the first white girl in his life. I wonder what will happen to him now?'

'Theresa,' Max said miserably. *'Please!'*

'I won't talk about it any more. It hurts you.'

'I'll come and see you at school,' he said wretchedly. 'Any time you need me just telephone. Promise?'

'I promise.'

When Max saw Theresa at the convent, about three months later, he found her still more changed. She seemed to have come to terms with herself, and was like any ordinary schoolgirl. The best thing of all, she said, was the praying. She was, she believed, closer to Jesus, and she felt especially close to the Virgin Mary. 'We have Mass at six-thirty every morning,' she said enthusiastically. 'And then we have breakfast. And after that we have assembly, and more prayers, and then at midday the Angelus rings and we can pray again. And then we have more prayers at six o'clock, and then prayers again in the dormitory, before lights out.' She turned her fever-bright eyes on Max; he had to force himself not to turn away. 'I feel like I'm living in a church,' she said gratefully. 'I'm beginning to feel I might be forgiven. I have taken a vow never to sin again. Never, never, never.'

'Does your mother know?'

'Yes. She's praying for me, too. She's pleased with me, because I had A's in every single subject.'

'Will you tell her I came to see you?'

'No.'

'Why not?'

'I don't know.' Theresa shook her head. 'I don't know.'

'Would you rather I didn't come to visit you?'

'I am so happy you came, Uncle Max. I hope you'll come again,' Theresa said fervently. 'My mother is still shocked. I pray that I'll be forgiven for the harm I did her. That's why — '

'That's why you don't want her to know I came, Theresa?' he said kindly. 'Don't worry. I won't tell her, either.'

The girl was still beautiful, Max thought, though her school uniform hid her curves. His fantasies about making love to her persisted, but mercifully he felt less threatened by them. In any case, it was impossible for him to understand Mireille, and he was beginning to dislike her. He had the strong suspicion that she would like nothing better than for her daughter to become a nun. Vows of chastity and the like were alien to him; it went against nature. It made no sense. Mireille wanted her daughter to become a nun, yet she herself was drinking too much. 'She's becoming a real *dronkie*!' Sarie had clucked. 'It's Lord Rutherford's fault for giving her baths of champagne.'

The whole thing was beyond him. But the irony of it all – or the miracle of it all – was that out of all this Fanny had become pregnant.

His fantasies about Theresa had made him more potent and it seemed, more fertile as well. Sometimes, he thought, good comes out of evil. But it was frightening, all the same, that his fantasies should switch from Mireille to her daughter. Saffarty's women . . .

As with everything else, Fanny took her pregnancy in her stride. If she wondered why Max had grown more ardent she asked no questions. She refused to allow her pregnancy to have any effect on her crowded schedule, and her reputation – as a woman of formidable organisational talents – soared. When Noël Coward performed at one of her fund-raising events she scored a major coup. When Sir Ernest Oppenheimer donated a diamond worth two thousand pounds to his wife's Caledonian Market Committee, Fanny prevailed upon Johannesburg's leading jewellers to do the same, albeit on a smaller scale. Lady Oppenheimer's committee had sold their raffle tickets for one shilling – Fanny charged five shillings and sold five thousand tickets, quite a talking point in Johannesburg. Fanny made little of it, however. After all, Lady Oppenheimer's committee had made the same amount with a fur coat. She was, she said, a pragmatist; she believed in getting things done efficiently, and with as little fuss as possible.

Indeed, on September 5th, 1943, when she and Max were returning by train to Johannesburg from an executive meeting in Durban, Fanny gave birth, one month ahead of time, to a baby daughter. Fortunately a doctor was on the train. Max panicked horribly, but Fanny calmly reminded him that she had seen Doctor Sol Fine, now a lieutenant-colonel, travelling in the next carriage to theirs. The birth was quick. When her labour began she looked down at the carpet on the floor of her first-class compartment, saw the initials SAR & H – South African Railways and Harbours – and there and then decided that if the baby was a girl she would call her Sarah.

In Germany the Nazis had ordered all Jewish men to add the name Israel, and all Jewish women the name Sarah, to their first name, thereby declaring their Jewish identity. But the Blums were acting out of choice, and to name their daughter Sarah was to celebrate that choice.

Needless to say the birth attracted enormous publicity. Almost every newspaper, the Afrikaans press included, ran features on Mrs Max Blum's courage. That she had even thought to call her daughter Sarah put her into an exalted order.

Hundreds of letters of congratulations poured in. Even Mrs Smuts, the Prime Minister's wife, wrote, and Fanny framed the letter. The public sent hand-knitted gifts and toys, and Fanny received several pairs of Kayser pure silk stockings. Both Max and Fanny were delighted as well as awed by the gifts they received.

Fanny and Max went to great lengths to ensure that the arrival of the new baby would not make Jeff feel displaced. The memory of that terrible day in Durban, when Jeff had almost drowned, was still strong. He was fifteen years old now, and though he regularly came first in class, and was the captain of the Under Sixteen cricket and soccer teams, it did not prove that their fears for his mental stability were groundless. Afraid of tempting fate, they never talked about it.

Though Oak Lodge was constantly filled with his friends, Jeff seemed to hold himself aloof. Fanny was aware of some deep resentment, but could not pinpoint it – she knew only that when she was alone with her son she felt uncomfortable.

And then, one crisp spring afternoon, after a highly successful game of poker, Max entered the large panelled hall where Jeff was waiting to surprise him with his newest pet.

His son had been given a dazzlingly bright parrot, which he was wearing on his shoulder.

All hell broke loose.

'Get it out!' Max yelled, waving his arms frantically. 'Get that bird out of here!'

The bird left his perch and alighted on Max's shoulder, exactly as Colette's Bijou had done so long ago.

Max roared and howled, trying to push the bird away, but its claws dug deeper, and would not loosen their hold.

It was only a matter of seconds before Jeff removed the bird, but in that short time Max lost himself completely. His single need was to escape. Terrifying sounds came out of him. He turned to run and, opening the front door, fell forward, cutting his head on the stone steps. The servants and Fanny rushed out and saw him lying there stunned and weeping.

A door slammed and Jeff reappeared, looking down at his father with a mixture of alarm and contempt. 'I locked the bird in a cupboard,' he said witheringly. 'You're quite safe!'

'What's happened? What's happening?' Fanny demanded.

'He's frightened of a bird.'

'Your father has cut his head,' Fanny said evenly. 'You'd better telephone Dr Goodman.'

Max's sobbing had dwindled to a whimper, but his body still shook. Fanny ordered two servants to carry him upstairs.

When the doctor came he put two sutures in Max's forehead, and gave him the standard knock-out injection. 'He'll sleep soundly, for at least twelve hours,' Dr Goodman told Fanny. 'Head wounds bleed horribly. It looks worse than it is.'

She drew up a chair and sat at Max's bedside.

Less than an hour later Max was awake again, and threshing about his bed. 'It's those nightmares, isn't it?' Fanny said sympathetically. 'It's to do with those nightmares of yours.'

'Leave me alone,' Max howled. 'Stop nagging. Get out of here!' He sat up suddenly. 'And shut the door behind you.'

Jeff was waiting for her. 'Is he all right?' he asked.

'I don't know,' Fanny answered truthfully.

'He's a coward,' Jeff said tonelessly.

'How dare you say a thing like that, Jeff?' Fanny hissed furiously. 'Do you know what happened to him in Poland?'

'No,' Jeff said sullenly. 'Do you?'

'You've got no heart, Jeff,' Fanny said sadly.

'A fat lot you can talk. Look what you did to Nanny and Absalom!'

'You're always throwing that in my face,' Fanny said wearily. 'I did try to find them.'

'Not all blacks live like they do here, in rags and tatters. It's different in other parts of the world.'

'Who told you that?' Fanny asked, shocked.

'My history teacher, Mr Weinstein. He says — '

'Don't tell me; I don't want to know what he says. Mr Weinstein is a Bolshevik, a communist!'

'So what? So am I,' Jeff said fervently. 'The Russians are saving the West.'

'Mr Weinstein again,' Fanny said angrily.

Max was in bed for a week. He never told Fanny what it was about the parrot that had upset him. Meanwhile, the bird was hidden in Abe the gardener's room. Fanny assured Max that it was gone.

On the day Max announced that he would get up and go downstairs, Fanny gave Abe a few shillings and instructed him to kill the parrot. 'When it's dead, call me!' she said imperiously. 'I want to see for myself. When I'm sure it's dead, you'll get more.'

A short while later she inspected the dead bird. Then she and Abe went to the compost heap and set the corpse alight. She watched until nothing but ashes remained. Then she gave Abe a third tip. 'Tell Master Jeff the bird escaped!' she ordered. 'No matter what he says, no matter how many questions he asks, you must say the bird escaped. Understand?'

'Yes, ma'am,' Abe answered quietly. 'You can trust me.'

Max's nightmares began again. Night after night his screams awoke Fanny. She did her best to settle him, and once went so far as to suggest a psychiatrist. She was amazed by Max's strength. Nothing she said or did made the slightest impact on his determination to keep his secret.

Fanny was contemptuous of people who learned to live with problems instead of actively doing their best to solve them. And, as she saw it, she had not yet done her best.

Mireille must know something about this . . .

When the summer holidays came round she went to call on her.

When Sarie let her in Fanny was at once struck by the gloom that had overtaken her, and the entire house. 'I'll tell madam you're here, Miss Fanny,' Sarie said anxiously.

'Are you well, Sarie?' Fanny asked pleasantly.

'Thank you, madam,' Sarie answered evasively. 'I'll tell madam you're here,' she repeated.

She left Fanny in the shuttered living room, and though it was arrayed in arum lilies Fanny was instantly aware that it had not been used for months. Lilies were everywhere, their heavy thick white flesh casting an eerie glow. She felt decidedly uncomfortable in the airless room; behind the shutters the windows were closed. She walked to the doorway, and stood there impatiently. She glanced at her watch. She would wait five minutes longer, she decided, surprised to find she was sweating.

She felt a sudden pressure against her shoulder and whirled round so fast that she almost lost her balance. 'Oh, Mireille, it's you,' she said nervously.

'Who else should it be?' Mireille said with one of her Gallic shrugs. 'Come in and sit down. Take the weight off your feet.'

Aware of the staccato sound of her high heels, Fanny followed her to the end of the huge room. As usual Mireille wore no make-up, but now her complexion was sallow and yellow, like her eyes. Her long brown hair was a wild tangle, and all the gold flecks had faded.

When they were seated, Mireille said, 'I've ordered tea for you.' Her cackle ricocheted across the room. 'Something stronger for myself, of course!'

Fanny noticed that she already had a glass in her hand. She said, 'What glorious lilies, Mireille.'

'Lilies are the symbol of purity,' she replied. 'If you can't have the real thing, at least you can have the symbol.'

'Purity?' Fanny asked, bewildered.

The tea and a drinks tray were brought in. Mireille poured herself a whisky and said, 'Help yourself, Fanny. You know about Theresa,' she went on hoarsely. 'Max must have told you.'

'Yes. He said she's at a boarding school,' Fanny said quickly. 'But she's at home now, for the school — '

'She certainly is not,' Mireille interrupted roughly.

'But it's the school holidays, surely?' Fanny said uncomfortably.

'I know why you came here. You came here to gloat.'

Fanny put down her cup of tea. 'Gloat? About what?' she asked reasonably.

'About Theresa. About my daughter and her affair with that kaffir!' Mireille cried, flinging her head from side to side.

'No, Mireille, you're mistaken. I have no idea what you are talking about,' Fanny said rapidly. 'I came to see you about Max. It's these nightmares. I thought you might help.' Her voice trailed off. Then, as if she could not stop herself, she burst out, 'It's brought on by a bird . . . By a bird, and by Saffity.'

Mireille jumped to her feet, and stood over her. The whisky fumes made Fanny gag. 'Never mention that man's name to me!'

she shouted. 'Never. I was right. You came here to gloat. To taunt me — ' She stopped and seemed to pull herself together. 'You must take some lilies with you when you go,' she said, dismissively, ringing the bell. Then she crossed to the doorway and called out, 'Sarie, come here! Sarie, bring some lilies for Miss Fanny. Bring them to the car. She's going now, so be quick. Be quick.'

Fanny had no option but to join Mireille in the doorway. 'Don't worry about the lilies, Mireille,' she said weakly. 'It's very kind of you, but not necessary. Really, not.'

'But I insist,' Mireille said forcefully. Then she added, 'I won't tell Max. Forget about it. I won't tell him.'

When Fanny reached her car the back seat was already loaded with lilies. Mireille must keep them cut and ready, like a florist, Fanny thought. She had never liked their heavy thick flesh and had no intention of taking them home with her. As soon as she could she stopped the car, and threw them into the veld. Besides, Max would have known that they had come from Mireille. She thought briefly of Theresa. Fanny had not been lying; other than saying that the poor girl was going away to school, Max had told her nothing. One thing was sure, though, she would no longer be able to count on Lady Rutherford's presence at her fête. The woman was nothing but a drunk.

Max was in the driveway waiting for her. 'Where have you been?' he called, waving a letter excitedly at her. 'There's another letter from Myles. Saffity was wounded, in France. And we didn't even know he was in France! It's January now, and Myles Beecham wrote in October. He said Saffity was on the critical list . . . '

22

For six weeks, from August 27th to October 14th, Saffity drifted in and out of consciousness. When he came to, he was at last able to register that it really was Colette at his bedside, and that she was not part of the strange nether world of dreams and hallucinations that had invaded his brain.

From Colette he learned that he had been taken to a field hospital and then transported to the Queen Victoria Hospital in East Grinstead, halfway between Brighton and London. Since Colette and Myles Beecham – as Saffity had stated clearly on all the relevant official forms – were his next of kin, they were immediately informed that he had been wounded. But it was thanks to Dr Archibald MacIndoe, the great plastic surgeon, who encouraged the families to be with his patients, that Colette had been able to be at Saffity's bedside for the past twenty-eight days.

Gently, she told Saffity what had happened: his left thigh had been badly broken and burned, but he would not lose his leg. 'There's a new drug now, Saffity. It's called penicillin. It's miraculous!' Then she told him he had been in an ambush, and if it had not been for the crudely painted British flag on the side of the jeep he might not have been found in time. He had been travelling over a hilly road, and when Drew lost control of the wheel the jeep had gone over a cliff. It was several hours before an American GI had spotted the bright colours of the flag.

'You are the only survivor, Saffity.'

Saffity said nothing. His right hand fumbled towards his neck until it found the gold key. He clasped it in his fist. After a while he said hoarsely, 'I had dropped it. I bent to pick it up. That's all I remember.'

'You were still clutching the key when they found you,' Colette whispered. 'That key saved your life. I had the chain repaired.'

'Tell me everything, Colette. I want to know it all.'

What they had pieced together was that he had been in an ambush – an ambush as cruel as it was simple, and yet so typical of the Boches. A taut thin wire had been strung across the road at a bend and the jeep had gone over the cliff. One of the mortars had exploded. Saffity had been flung clear.

The bones of his badly smashed and burned left thigh had been pinned together and his burnt flesh had been covered by a skin graft. Dr MacIndoe had taken a sheet of skin from his right thigh, diced it into postage-stamp-sized squares and grafted it to his left thigh.

Now that he knew all the facts he cooperated with his treatment but was otherwise silent. Colette visited him every day, and talked and gossiped, but Saffity merely stared, an awesomely knowing look in his eye. After a few days she dropped her pointless prattle and sat beside his bed, knitting.

The radio blared constantly. Men swathed in bandages lay in grotesque positions; immobilising skin flaps attached their legs to each other, their arms to their stomachs, their shoulders to their faces. As she knitted her interminable socks, Colette's eyes seldom left Saffity.

For four weeks Colette sat there, afraid that he had lost the will to live. She remembered how distraught he had been when his shop had burned down in Paris, how wild with grief when he had faced the tragic death of his young wife. Now there was just this dumb, tearless silence. Again and again she laid down her knitting, bent over him and whispered, 'Fight, Saffity! Fight back. Fight back . . . ' But it seemed there was no fight left in him. The vibrant, powerful, unbreakable man she had known was now broken and defeated.

If only Saffity would weep, she prayed. If only he would rant and rave. Anything would be better than this awful, dangerous silence . . .

It would take time, the doctors assured her. Time was all that was needed. He was still in a state of physical and mental shock; it was only natural for him to be severely depressed. Scrupulously, icily polite to the doctors and nurses, he remained inside his wall of silence. When Myles came to visit, Saffity nodded, and then turned away. Even when he told him of the wolfhound's death, hoping for expression of at least some emotion, there was no reaction at all. Myles abandoned his dignity and broke into tears, but Saffity was unmoved. He simply closed his eyes, which at least hid that horrible stare of his . . .

And then, early in the new year, at the beginning of 1945, a nurse tentatively proffered two letters that had recently been forwarded by Simpson from Stanford Hall. She expected Saffity to turn away from her, as usual, but instead he said, 'Read them to me.'

She opened the envelopes and two newspaper clippings fluttered to the floor.

'Show those to me,' Saffity said tersely.

The nurse paused; it was the first time in almost six months that Saffity had shown an interest in anything.

'Mr and Mrs Max Blum, standing outside the oak front door of their mock-Tudor mansion, Oak Lodge, in readiness for the opening of the all-day and all-night fête to be held in their grounds,' she read out loud.

'Is there a date on that? When was it taken?' Saffity asked.

'November nineteen forty-four.'

'Let me see the photograph. God, that's some house he's got there,' Saffity said with something like the old light in his eye. 'The business must be doing well.'

'The other cutting says the Blums have a daughter, called Sarah, because she was born on a train, South African Railways and Harbours. SARAH, you know, those letters make the name Sarah,' the nurse said hurriedly.

'Leave it to Blum,' Saffity said.

'Leave what to Blum?' she asked.

'Leave it to Max Blum,' he said again. 'There's a world war, there's all this' – he gestured toward the patients, the first indication he had given that he was even aware of them – 'there's all this carnage, and Blum gets away with it, stays safe, down there in South Africa, and what is more' – Saffity went on, his voice rising – 'he makes money and buys himself a palace!'

'Don't get excited, Saffity,' the nurse said nervously. 'You're getting too excited.'

'A shortage of goods and he gets hold of a shipment of hand-made Indian carpets,' he continued wildly. 'People are dying and starving and burning, and he makes a fortune.' By now tears were streaming down his face. The radio blared but people had stopped talking. Saffity had broken his silence. His voice was loud and, after such a long silence, his French accent was more acute. 'And Max Blum, a coward if ever I saw one, Max Blum makes money.'

By now he was half crying and half laughing. The nurses hovered by his bedside, but did nothing to try to stop him.

Over and over Saffity howled, 'Max Blum makes money. Max Blum makes money.'

His howl rose hysterically, and then suddenly changed to a laugh, a loud, runaway laugh. At last he began to quieten. 'It's ludicrous, ludicrous. So ludicrous that it's funny.'

Physically unable to turn his head into the pillow, Saffity covered his face with his hands and, at last, gave way and sobbed. It was Drew he wept for, Drew and his refreshing, exhilarating zest for life. Drew, whom he had wholeheartedly – and without reserve – trusted . . . The only friend who had been not only his equal, but in many ways his superior. It was Drew's simplicity that had put him way above everyone. His concern had always been with the immediate, with getting his danger money so that he could have more fun with women. Somehow his very openness about it meant that he was never resented. Instead, the women joined in with his expansive devil-may-care attitude, and grabbed the moment too, and so exacted all possible joy from it.

Far down in the low, wooden hut of Ward Three, one of East Grinstead's favourite long-term patients rang for his nurse.

'I want to know the name of the man who broke down,' the captain said to his nurse.

'His name is Saffity,' the nurse said. 'Wing Commander Saffity.'

'I thought I recognised his laugh.'

'You know him, then?'

'I know him all right,' the captain answered. 'Of course he won't recognise me now, with my new eyelids.' He went on, 'Come to that, he probably wouldn't have recognised me with my old eyelids.' A sudden grin lit up his face. 'Way back in nineteen thirty-one I emigrated to Canada. He's the reason I went. Turned out to be the best thing I ever did — '

'Go on,' the nurse said avidly. 'I want to hear all about it.'

'Some other time,' the patient said wearily. 'I'll tell you some other time. Right now, don't say anything to him. I don't know how he would feel about meeting me again. We parted badly, you see.' He sighed deeply. 'Mum's the word, OK?'

Tactfully the nurse withdrew and he lay back to think.

Captain Colin Fisk had recognised not only Saffity's laugh but his howl of anguish. Suddenly and without warning his hatred left him. For a moment he felt bereft, as if he had lost something integral to his psyche, something infinitely precious. And then, just as suddenly, he realised his hatred of Saffity had been consumed in his fight to stay alive.

He had hated Saffity for years, with the kind of hatred that had taken him out of his own country and out of the class system to Canada, where his station in life was not branded into his tongue as it had been in England. When he left Wyndham Carpets he had sought employment as a salesman at a firm of tailors in London, but had been told abruptly that with an accent like his he could not hope to serve their distinguished customers. In disgust and anger, he left England and worked his passage to Canada, with nothing but his hatred for Saffity to fuel his actions. In Canada he found that his accent was an asset; people said he 'talked good'.

By the time he joined the Royal Canadian Air Force he had been in Canada for seven years, and had risen to be manager of carpets and soft furnishings at the Longmans Department Store. He had a sixth sense for choosing the best selling designs in curtaining, as well as carpeting, and the manufacturers welcomed his advice. He was also the champion at his local squash club, and was as proud of that as he was of his position as manager.

Like Saffity, he had joined up even before war was declared but, unlike Saffity, he did not have a pilot's licence. His Air Force flying instructor reported that he was 'strong, alert, keen and intelligent – a natural'; within a year he had his pilot's wings and was Captain Fisk. In June 1943, on his way to bomb the Italian naval base at Spezia from a base in North Africa, his plane had crashed into the sea.

Nothing sorts a man out like surviving the elements, Colin thought now. He had been too close to death for too long, he supposed, to cherish his hatred. Through all his months of pain and suffering he had held on to the belief that he had come back from the dead.

He was now convinced that his path had been chosen for him. Things happened for a reason, and perhaps – just perhaps – he and Saffity had been destined to make their peace.

He hoped he could help Saffity. But it could be that it was not the right time now to make peace with Saffity, and never would be.

Slowly Saffity's cocoon of grief began to unravel. He liked nothing better than to talk to Colette about Drew, and when he did he could not help smiling.

He told her about Judith and Gaston, and ended by saying, 'You'll meet them and you'll love them.'

'Mmm,' she murmured absently.

She looked away. A long shuddering sigh escaped her.

'Have you had news of them?' Saffity asked at once.

She shook her head.

'Does that mean yes or no?'

'The Boches took terrible reprisals as they retreated. They burned whole villages — '

'They got Judith and Gaston?'

'I'm sorry, *mon choux*.'

Two days later, a nurse handed him a note from Colin Fisk. Colin had conducted a long interior debate with himself and had finally concluded that the kindest way to confront Saffity would be to leave the decision to him. Accordingly, he wrote:

Dear Wing Commander,

You and I are in the same ward.

Let me say at once that I'm offering you the hand of peace and of friendship.

Our last meeting was an unhappy one, and after all these years I readily admit that I was unfair to you. However, since both of us have appeared to have escaped the real thing, let us not go in for post-mortems.

I should be delighted to call on you – but should you not wish to renew our acquaintance, I will not hold it against you.

Very sincerely yours,
Colin Fisk, Cpt. (formerly of Wyndham Carpets)

Saffity read the note again quickly, and immediately called for his nurse. 'Please take down a message for me,' he said. 'It's for Captain Fisk. Have you got a pencil?'

The nurse nodded.

'My dear Colin,' Saffity dictated, 'if my bed could move, I'd be on my way! Come as soon as you can. Saffity.'

Even as Colin limped down the ward, he could see Saffity's outstretched hand.

'It was your laugh,' Colin grinned. 'I recognised your laugh. With my new eyelids and my new face, you wouldn't have recognised me, would you?'

'To be honest, no,' Saffity answered. 'But then you wouldn't have recognised me either. I'm old and grey, as you can see.'

Despite his good intentions Colin asked, 'And wiser?'

'Yes,' Saffity sighed. 'Much, much wiser. And so, I see, are you.'

'*If* you live, you learn.'

'I know,' Saffity smiled weakly. 'There was a time, only a few days ago, when I didn't want to learn any more. I thought I'd learned enough.'

'I know what you mean.'

'May I call you Colin?'

'Please do.'

'Thank you for your note, Colin. It was very – uh – generous of you.'

'No post-mortems.'

'No post-mortems,' Saffity agreed. 'D'you remember Myles Beecham, Sir William's land agent?'

'Yes, why?'

'The lady who's been visiting me every day – perhaps you've seen her? – is none other than Myles' wife.'

'You mean he got married? That old bachelor?'

'Colette is French.'

'That explains it,' Colin said dismissively. 'He never could resist their wine, either.'

Thanks to Colin, Saffity began to take a keen interest in everything that was happening at the hospital, which of course helped his own recovery. Colette brought photographs of the Wyndham Carpet Mills, which Saffity proudly showed to Colin. His mills now turned out blankets, and small parts for aircraft. The patients of Ward Three had little interest in the standard occupational therapy of basket weaving and wool mats that was on offer, and Wyndham Carpets set up a small factory in the hospital grounds, to provide one of the first Industrial Therapy Departments in Great Britain.

It was the devoted attention of Nurse Jane Lovett-Turner that finally revived Saffity's old *joie de vivre*. Jane was unusually skilled and competent and Saffity quickly realised that if not for the war she would never have gone in for nursing or, indeed, for any sort of gainful occupation. Her aristocratic accent, her bold bearing and her finely chiselled features gave her away at once. She was one of the band of young women who had joined 'for the duration' the Voluntary Aid Detachment, received basic training in first aid and nursing and then, much to her own and everyone else's surprise, had become genuinely interested in the work. She did not quite fit in with the other nurses, nor, as was clear to Saffity, did she wish to.

If she held herself aloof from her colleagues, she did nothing of the kind with her patients. Though she had only been on Ward Three for a few months, her efficiency, combined with an air of authority, had rapidly won respect from even the most testy men. Nursing in Ward Three was not for the faint-hearted, and several nurses whose qualifications and experience exceeded Jane's found that they were unequal to Dr MacIndoe's ward.

One day Saffity teasingly called her Lady Jane.

'How did you know that?' she snapped. 'Who told you?'

'Care to dine with me tonight, Lady Jane? I'm allowed to go on the town, you know.'

'If *you* think you're fit enough.'

Saffity gave an inner shrug. What the hell, he would give it a go. It was a long time since he'd wanted a woman's company.

At the beginning of May 1945, victory was only days away. Though like everyone else Saffity was euphoric, he had not expected to feel anything like the white-heat excitement that sparked across the table that night. Jane's cold, navy-blue eyes – a mixture of steel and passion that he found intriguing – softened in the candlelight. The perfect oval shape of her face was so irresistible that he put his hands to her chin and turned her face this way and that, as if he hoped to find a flaw. 'You are beautiful,' he pronounced hoarsely. 'Flawless as a blue-white diamond.'

'You exaggerate.'

411

'Surely you know me well enough to know I'm not given to exaggeration?' A sharp twinge in his leg made him wince.

'Are you in pain, Saffity?' Jane asked anxiously, laying her hands on his.

'No.'

Her hand still covered his, and her slightest touch burned.

'Excuse me,' he said abruptly.

She watched him as he limped determinedly away. He was still dependent on his crutches, yet the dignity and skill with which he used them added to his attractiveness. True, he looked much older than his thirty-eight years, but under that mop of gleaming white hair he was startlingly youthful. All his energy and dynamism were displayed in his expression, like medals on a chest. He knows he's attractive, she thought. They would be good together, she was certain; they were both special. It was the waiting that was so, well . . .

Saffity's reappearance interrupted her thoughts.

'Do you like blue-white diamonds?' he asked mildly.

'What a strange question.'

'Is it?' he murmured, seemingly absently. Then he said, 'I thought you'd answer me that way.'

'Did you?'

'I'm an impatient man. Are you an impatient woman?'

'Sometimes.' She hesitated briefly. 'I'm impatient for you.'

'I hoped you were. D'you know where I went?'

'When?'

'A moment ago.'

'You went to the lavatory.'

'Wrong.' He smiled delightedly. 'I had a word with John Sutherland, the proprietor of this hotel. And d'you know what he told me?'

'No.'

'He said he'd be delighted to let me have a room. And what's more he came up with a bottle of champagne.'

'Champagne?' Jane repeated, feeling silly.

'You do like champagne, don't you?'

'Yes.'

'Shall we go, then?'

'Yes.'

The room was plain and clean, the bed was turned back for the night and the champagne stood in the bucket.

'I'll undress you, Saffity,' Jane said.

'I'm glad you've seen all of me before,' he said frankly. 'Otherwise you might run away in horror.'

'Your leg's not so bad. I've seen much, much worse.'

'Your hands are shaking, Jane. Are you nervous?'

'No,' she said, tearing her clothes off. 'Impatient.'

They were still standing, so she led him to the bed.

'Don't let's wait,' she said urgently. 'Let's begin at once.'

They coupled crazily. Nine months of celibacy were undone in about nine seconds. Too spent to speak, Saffity said nothing for a while. Then, 'I was too quick.'

'I'm glad.'

'Why?'

'So that it will be better next time.' She stroked his cheek. 'Not yet. But soon, very soon.'

Quietly they lay, partly dozing and partly stroking, all tension gone for both of them and nothing, now, but blissful anticipation.

After a while she began again by kissing every single square of his patch-work thigh. He responded at once, but she forced him to delay. She set the pace and she set it deliciously, and he gave way to her, and the anticipation was like nothing he had ever known. His skin vibrated and hummed, and only when he was ready to scream, did she allow him to enter her. Still she set the pace, and he followed her rhythm until, sensing that she was reaching the thunderous moment, he imposed his own tempo, and it was only when he felt her body begin to convulse that he let his go.

She did something, then, that he had not expected. She went to sleep. He made no attempt to. Though Jane had nothing of Edwina's softness, she reminded him of her. He tried to identify what it was: of course, Jane's scent – underneath the antiseptic pungence there was the same lavender scent Edwina had used. He began to think he might even have fallen in love.

Well, it was good to be alive after all. It was his rage reaction to the Blums' South African press cuttings that had thrown him out of his secret, silent world. He supposed he should be grateful to Max Blum.

Towards dawn he woke her. She was supposed to be in her nurse's quarters, and he in Ward Three. 'I feel like a kid playing truant,' he said, with his old booming laugh. 'We'd better be getting back to school.'

'I don't want to go,' she said dreamily. 'I'll never want to go — '

Gratefully, Colette had returned to Stanford Hall as soon as it became clear that she was no longer needed at East Grinstead. The morning after his date with Jane, Saffity telephoned her, and told her that by fair means or foul she simply had to make sure that Nurse Jane Lovett-Turner's room was filled with flowers.

'You'll want a card, *mon chou*?' Colette asked.

'No card. Just hundreds of flowers – that's all.'

Saffity put down the receiver and chuckled. Jane hadn't come on duty yet, and he went off for his physiotherapy session.

When he returned to the ward, an embossed and particularly official-looking envelope stamped 'On His Majesty's Service' and 'Strictly Private and Confidential' was waiting for him. He opened the envelope slowly, and just as slowly read that he was to be awarded the Military Cross.

Saffity folded the embossed paper carefully, and put it back inside the envelope. His mind flew back to those British soldiers in Salonika who, all those years ago, had offered him bread. Now he, Saffity, was being offered the Military Cross. And it would be presented by the King of the very country he had vowed, when he was nine years old, to see for himself. Now he had not only seen that country, and become one of its citizens but had seen altogether too much.

Edwina and her parents would have been so proud, and as for his parents . . . But instantly, the way he always did, he banished them from his mind. Even so, he was unaware of the tears that rolled slowly down his face. Which was how Jane found him.

'What's the matter, Saffity?' she asked nervously.

'Nothing. Why?'

'You're crying.'

'Am I? I didn't know,' Saffity said, brushing his cheeks. Wordlessly he handed her the letter.

'I'm not supposed to read it,' she said. 'It says strictly private and confidential. Perhaps you were too upset to see that?'

'Read it.'

She read the letter quickly, and then said, 'But that's wonderful, Saffity! Congratulations!'

'I'm going to ask for a later Investiture.'

'Why? I know you're being discharged from the hospital on that day.'

'I have an even more important appointment on May the twenty-fifth. And I want to take you with me to the Investiture.'

'But what could possibly be more important?' Jane asked curiously.

'I have to go to a wedding.'

'A very close relation, I take it.'

'Yes, in a way. As a matter of fact, the wedding couldn't take place without me.'

'You're being very mysterious.'

'I'll tell you more about it tonight. Same time, same place? We'll meet at the hotel. And you're even more beautiful today than you were last night. Now, hadn't you better go and look after your patients?'

Saffity watched her as she walked away. She was tall and graceful and distinctly aristocratic.

When Jane met him at the hotel that night the first thing she said was, 'How did you get all these roses? Where did you get them?'

'Who said I sent them? There was no note.'

'Oh, Saffity, Saffity! Thank you.'

'I was wondering when you'd get round to saying thank you,' he teased.

The waitress poured two glasses from the champagne he had ordered.

'To you,' he said. 'To Lady Jane. To the future Mrs Saffity.'

'What did you say?' she said, spilling the champagne.

'You heard me. Now you know whose marriage is taking place on May the twenty-fifth.'

'Is this a proposal?' Jane asked, bewildered. 'Are you proposing to me?'

'I am. Do you accept?'

'Oh, Saffity, my darling, of course I accept. But I hardly know you. We hardly know each other.'

'That's not true. You've been my nurse. And last night I thought we'd got to know one another perfectly.'

'It was perfect. But — ' she paused, and then went on bravely, 'you haven't mentioned love.'

'I asked you to marry me, didn't I?' he answered.

Part Seven

23

Jane was counting Saffity's huge bouquet of roses, when without any warning at all, her mother's teaching – never marry beneath your station – suddenly entered her mind. It stayed with her, nagging like a catchy unwelcome jingle, and would not go away.

Then with sudden clarity she realised that the war had taught her that both her mother and her teachings were as hopelessly out of date as the Polish cavalry against the *Blitzkrieg*.

Merely thinking of the way her parents lived on past glory and boiled potatoes made her tremble with irritation. Boiled potatoes may have been an exaggeration, but it wasn't too far off the mark. Heirloom after heirloom had been sold; a tiara was all that remained, and they clung to that as if their title depended on it.

They fooled themselves that their secondhand lifestyle was as secret as their secondhand clothes.

Jane was determined that since there was no need to improve her pedigree – her father was descended from the Duchess of Dalkeith, from whom it was said she had inherited her extraordinary beauty – she could well afford to better herself. Her mind returned to the photographs of Stanford Hall. The place clearly deserved the aristocrat that had been lacking for too long.

She would fit Stanford Hall as perfectly as her blue-white diamond ring would fit her finger.

And if Saffity was a bit too rough, and a bit too Mediterranean in his ways she was more than ready to tame him.

Moments before Mr Churchill announced the end of the war on May 8th, 1945, Saffity gave Jane a large and flawless blue-white diamond engagement ring. They listened to the broadcast together. As Saffity and Jane heard the words, 'unconditional surrender' she felt a sudden chill; she had no intention of surrendering herself unconditionally to Saffity. She chided herself that she was thinking like a silly, love-struck schoolgirl, but she knew that Saffity was surrendering neither himself – nor his Edwina – to her. After all, he had told her about Edwina, and when he had explained that he simply could not face another religious ceremony he had gone as far as to confess that a part of him would always love and belong to Edwina. She had accepted that, because she refused to be jealous of a dead woman, and because there was no alternative.

Three months later, Saffity and Jane were married at the East Grinstead Register Office. Myles Beecham was best man, Colette was the other witness, and Simpson, Colin Fisk and Jane's parents, Lord and Lady Lovett-Turner, were the only guests. It was simple and it was good. Jane's suit – made of delphinium-blue silk, and tightly belted over the new lampshade-style peplum – emphasised her minute waist. If her matching hat with a chin strap was somewhat severe, it provided the perfect frame for her navy-blue eyes. Without the inevitable traumas that go hand in hand with the organisation of a large wedding it seemed likely that they would lead what everyone called a happy life. And the best and the quickest way to do that was to have children as soon as possible.

The matter of begetting children had already been taken well in hand.

Saffity's penchant for making plans was easily resumed. Ten minutes before the wedding lunch he put his latest plan into operation.

'The Captain and I need to go into conference,' he chuckled. 'Coming, Colin? We'll go to the bar.'

As their double whiskies were served he said, 'I've got a proposition to put to you.' He rested his hand lightly on Colin's shoulder.

'I'm going back to Longmans Department Store, Toronto, Canada,' Colin answered uncompromisingly.

'At least hear me out, man. What sensible man turns down an offer – an opportunity – before he even hears what it is?'

'Go ahead, then.'

'I wanted to talk to you about talent.'

'Talent? What's that got to do with the price of eggs?'

'Everything. It's *your* talent I'm talking about, Colin.'

'Come off it — '

'I'll get straight to the point. I've looked at the sketches you make when you're not even thinking, and I've come to the conclusion that you have the makings of the most successful – and the most brilliant – designer in the carpet industry.'

'You flatter me.'

'You've never thought of moving into design, have you?'

'Can't say I have.'

'I guessed as much,' Saffity's chuckle was more enthusiastic than ever. 'But I've never been afraid to act on my hunches, as you well know.' He paused at the reference to their past, to the meeting he had called to challenge and stop the rumours Colin had been spreading. 'I like to back my hunches with cash. I propose to make you Director of the design department, and to give you two and a half per cent of the overall profit after tax.'

'You can't be serious.'

'I've never been more serious in my life. Think about it. Let me know what you decide.'

'I think you're crazy, Saffity.'

'Think what it would do for the marketing of Wyndham Carpets! Two old enemies, one on crutches, forging ahead together. We're going to be the most powerful carpet mill in Europe.' Saffity stopped to drain the last of his glass. 'And I'll tell you this, design is going to become more and more important in our industry. Believe me, Colin, it'll be crucial.'

'But I've had no training.' He looked away. It was impossible to read his eyes behind the dark glasses that concealed the new eyelids. 'Cherish the past, adorn the present and create the future,' he murmured.

'Who said that?' Saffity asked, puzzled.

'It's an old designer's saying.'

'That's why we need you, Colin.' Saffity removed his hand from Colin's shoulder to his arm. 'I owe you a lot,' he said gruffly. 'Don't think I would have got out of that depression without you.'

During the next several months most of Saffity's plans went smoothly into action. Though neither of them knew it on their wedding day, Jane was already pregnant. Colin returned to Canada to fetch his wife, Dawn, and their small son, Michael. His designs were extraordinary, and Saffity quickly came to regard him as one of Wyndham Carpets' greatest assets.

421

Jane had been confident she would have an easy pregnancy, and when it was not she felt not so much anxious as humiliated. She was forced to surrender her will to her body, for there were times when her morning sickness persisted all day and, on occasion, at night too. The peaks of sensual ecstasy to which Saffity had once brought her were now a distant and even an irritating memory. She resented being ill; she resented everything, and everyone.

She had been too ill even to attend Saffity's Investiture, and when Colette was permitted to go in her stead Jane's resentment gathered momentum and turned to bitterness.

In a way, Saffity was pleased to have Colette and not Jane accompany him to Buckingham Palace. His and Colette's improbable backgrounds appealed to his sense of irony; they were the most unlikely pair, he was sure, ever to be invited to the Palace.

The war had changed him: Drew had taught him about fun. Jane had forgotten all about fun, but the baby would change that.

Saffity was surprisingly patient with Jane, and controlled his temper. She accused him of being too familiar with Simpson, who was 'only a servant'. She criticised the way he ate – like a peasant, she said. During the war, Colette had grown fruit and vegetables in the hothouses. Now her orchids bloomed again. One day Jane uprooted every single plant, and still Saffity held his rage. 'Women are not themselves when they're pregnant,' Colette told him.

He replaced the orchids.

Saffity hoped Jane's irrational behaviour was only temporary, but from time to time he had grave doubts. One evening he returned from London with dozens of red roses and laid them in their transparent cellophane wrapping over her knees. Jerking herself up in their lavish four-poster bed, she took the bouquet in her hands, reached for the nail scissors on her bedside table, slit the wrapping and rapidly proceeded to snip each rosebud silently and systematically until all of them had been reduced to confetti.

Saffity watched with a mixture of horror and fascination and said nothing.

'I don't like shop roses,' Jane said coldly, as if she'd done nothing out of the ordinary. 'Common things, shop roses.'

'I thought they were beautiful.'

'You have no taste. Shop roses are vulgar.'

Irritably she jabbed the bell to summon her maid. 'I'm tired,' she said to Saffity. 'Draw the curtains.'

Saffity left and allowed the maid to take over.

He engaged a new housekeeper, a Mrs Crispin, who had a married daughter herself. She knew how to mother Jane, and Jane's fifth and sixth months passed peacefully enough. She was still beautiful. The morning sickness meant that she carried no extra weight, and Saffity was content merely to look at her. She was carrying his heir; what else mattered?

Though Lord and Lady Lovett-Turner spent several weekends at Stanford Hall, they remained perfect strangers to Saffity, and, as far as he could make out, to their daughter as well. They would meet, by appointment, in the drawing room before dinner, and their conversation was stilted and unswervingly polite. Saffity had not yet visited their home, but gathered that they now lived in a cottage, and that most of their furniture had been sold. Sometimes he asked Jane for details about their lives, but beyond announcing that she 'didn't actually like them very much', she would say nothing. She knew that his parents were dead but, as she asked no questions about them, Saffity rightly concluded that she was not interested.

One night at dinner, when Jane was in her seventh month, she said, 'We're hoping to find someone like Nanny Bridgeland for the baby.'

'Nanny Bridgeland,' Jane's father echoed. 'I haven't thought of her since Joh — ' He stopped in mid-word.

'You were saying, Lord Lovett-Turner?' Saffity prodded curiously.

'Nanny Bridgeland was an excellent woman,' he said stonily, and changed the subject.

Later, when they were in bed, Saffity asked, 'Who was the John your father stopped himself from talking about?'

'My brother.'

'You have a brother?'

'Yes.'

'Why haven't you mentioned him?'

'We don't talk about him.'

'Where is he?'

'In Australia; the outback, actually.'

'Why is his name never mentioned?'

'He married a woman. She was called Helga.'

'Most men marry women,' Saffity chuckled.

'She was a German-Jewish refugee,' she said dismissively.

'What did you say?' he asked in a dangerously quiet voice.

423

'I said, a German-Jewish refugee.'

'I see.' He went on sarcastically, 'A crime, if ever there was one.'

'We couldn't forgive him for that,' she answered seriously.

Whether she ignored or failed to understand his sarcasm he could not tell.

'How did you feel about Helga?' he enquired mildly.

'Didn't like her, either.'

'Why? Because she was Jewish?'

'Should think that would be perfectly obvious,' she said, sounding bored. 'I think I felt the baby move.'

Lost in the thoughts that clanged and clashed in his brain, Saffity made no answer.

'Aren't you interested? I just told you the baby moved,' Jane said querulously.

'What is your brother's name?'

'I told you, John,' she answered irritably. 'Don't you want to feel it move?' She grabbed his hand and laid it on her stomach. Ever since Jane had become interested in love-making again, this was her way of signalling her wishes.

'My leg's in agony,' he said stiffly, withdrawing his hand. 'And now, if you'll excuse me, I'm going to take a hot bath. A very, very hot bath.'

He had given up his crutches but was still dependent on a cane. Now he forgot it, and hobbled hurriedly into the bathroom. He needed to think. He had made a mistake; he had married the wrong woman, and what was perhaps even worse she had married the wrong man. Inside her womb a half-Jewish child was moving. If she knew that she simply would not be able to stop herself from hating the child.

For the sake of his unborn baby, his own origins must never, never be revealed.

A month before the baby was expected Saffity came home to find Stanford Hall teeming with decorators.

'What's going on?' he asked pleasantly. 'The nursery is ready, isn't it?'

'I'm redecorating the rooms you keep locked.'

'You're not touching Edwina's apartment,' Saffity said loudly.

424

'We agreed to that before we were married.' He lowered his voice, and made an attempt at humour. 'A lady doesn't go back on her word, does she?'

'Mummy and Daddy are here,' Jane answered. 'Daddy wanted to talk to you about — '

'I know. He already has. He's selling your mother's diamond tiara. I'm buying it for you. It will stay in the family.'

'Daddy didn't tell me that,' Jane said distantly. 'He wanted to talk to you about my plans.' She placed her hands on her stomach protectively. 'I will not live with Edwina's ghost any longer.'

'Your father wants to talk to me about that?' he asked incredulously.

'Yes.'

'You're taking advantage of your condition,' he said, murderously calm. 'You shouldn't do that to me, you know. If you're in a decorating mood, why not your parents' rooms? They've become permanent fixtures here. But no decorator will set foot in Edwina's rooms, is that clear?'

'Very clear,' Jane said with a contemptuous sweep of her hands. 'You'll live to regret this, Saffity — '

He sighed. 'I think I'll take a shower,' he said calmly.

Under the soothing jets of water, Saffity tried to understand Jane's relationship with her parents. She had said often enough that she despised them, and yet they were living at Stanford Hall. But it was all temporary; he was convinced that things would change when the baby came.

During a violent snowstorm on February 6th, 1946, Saffity's daughter was born. When he held her in his arms, he wept unashamedly. For the first time since he left Salonika, almost twenty-three years before, he was touching and holding his own flesh and blood. He studied his daughter's nose carefully: there was nothing there to give him away, he noted with relief. But then his own nose had not let him down either. He wished, fleetingly, that he could call the child Ruth, after his mother, but knew better than to suggest it.

'What about calling her Edwina?' Jane said maliciously.

'Edwina?' Saffity snapped. 'That's out of the question. Are you out of your mind?'

'Just teasing, that's all,' Jane said sweetly. 'Jemima,' she announced. 'Her name is Jemima.'

'I don't like the name.'

'You'll learn to.'

He looked down at the baby in his arms.

'Jem,' he said to himself. 'She's a real jem. I'll call her Jem.' He said, emotionally, 'You do look radiant, Jane. Of course we'll call her Jemima.'

He said nothing about the nickname. She would have everything, this precious little bundle of his own flesh and blood. She was his daughter, and nothing in the world would ever be good enough for her.

'Colette's been like a mother to your Daddy,' Saffity said to the baby he held so confidently in his arms. 'And she and Myles will be the best god-parents in the world.'

'Are you suggesting that the Beechams will be my daughter's god-parents?'

'Of course.'

In answer, Jane jabbed the bell. A beaming nurse came at once, her veil flowing.

Saffity had gone out of his way to be especially charming and generous to the nurses, each of whom had been presented with a gift of perfume. The nurse flashed a smile at him.

'Take the baby back to the nursery, Nurse,' Jane said peremptorily. 'Her father has been overdoing things.'

The nurse's smile faded. But she did as she was told.

'I've invited Constance and Sebastian Hamilton to be her god-parents.'

'*That* hockey-playing girl guide — '

'How dare you?' Jane sat upright in her hospital bed. The room was oppressive – vases of roses were everywhere. Her cheeks reddened alarmingly. 'How *dare* you?' she repeated angrily. 'Who *are* the Beechams? My daughter has every right to be well connected, *whatever* her father may be!'

Clearly, this was not the moment to pursue the point, Saffity decided. He would opt for a compromise – Jem would have two sets of god-parents.

'We're giving her a party,' he said, looking at the floor and not at Jane. 'She's going to have the biggest party any newborn baby ever had. At Wyndham Carpets. Champagne and birthday cake — '

'And roast goose?' Jane smiled.

'Why not?'

'You're not planning on taking her to the party by any chance, are you?'

'I suppose not,' Saffity said reluctantly.

Myles and Colette arranged the party, and it was the talk of the town. Colin Fisk made the speech. Wyndham Carpets was still a long way from pre-war production levels, and yet after Colin had daringly commissioned a brilliant young abstract artist to design, two rival factories had tried to poach him for their design departments.

Meanwhile, Saffity did nothing with the properties he had acquired during the Blitz. He was an investor, not a developer. Licensing and building restrictions could not go on for ever, and he could afford to wait, just as he could, if the worst came to the worst, afford to lose. This, he was convinced, was the secret of good business – to sell when it suited him to sell, and never, never to be in the position of his father-in-law and the diamond tiara he'd been forced to sell.

The scarcity of office buildings meant that the government were compelled to requisition blocks of flats for office space. Saffity owned two such blocks and, though the rent barely covered his expenses, he was little troubled. His vision was strictly focused on using those properties as a collateral for raising finance, as assets against which he could borrow. Meanwhile he was still feeling his way, beginning to believe that a borrowing potential was as good, if not better, than money in the bank.

His training in accountancy in Paris provided him with one of his luckiest breaks. One of his prized customers, the venerable Mr Charles Hylton, of Hylton's Furniture Stores – a twelve-store chain – was unable to meet his commitments, and about to go bankrupt. Although Wyndham Carpets was one of the largest creditors, Saffity offered to help; but to do that he would, of course, have to examine the books of the company for himself. Charles Hylton accepted his offer gratefully, and accordingly Saffity met him at his office. A quick glance told him two things – firstly, the company was grossly mismanaged, and secondly, that all twelve shops were in properties owned by the company.

At his next meeting with Mr Hylton he said quietly, 'Who is doing your buying? You are over-stocked in carpets.'

'My son-in-law.'

'I thought something like that was going on.'

'What do you mean?'

'Your son-in-law has been paying our competitors fifteen per cent more for the same Wilton carpeting than he need have paid us.' He pitched his voice higher. 'And Hylton Furniture Stores have the nerve to pay back in full that very company that is overcharging them.' Now he whispered. 'Do you know why you're paying them and not me?'

'I did notice that,' Mr Hylton said weakly. 'But I don't know why we haven't paid you.'

'You mean you don't want to know why?'

'What's the use of knowing? I'll have to declare bankruptcy, anyway.' Mr Hylton covered his worn face with his hands. 'I lose my name, my reputation, everything I've ever worked for.'

'You could sell.'

'Who'd buy a bankrupt company? I'd get nothing for it.'

'Leave it with me,' Saffity said. 'I know of one or two possibilities.'

It was obvious that Mr Hylton's son-in-law was taking private bribes, but that was only marginally interesting. The idea of a ready-made outlet for Wyndham Carpets was tremendously appealing. And if the chain were properly managed, the properties would charge a proper rent. Two companies would be required to run Hylton Carpets, and one of them would be a property company Saffity himself would own. He did the deal quickly, and a grateful Mr Hylton preserved his name, his reputation and his sanity, but little else. He could have sold the properties to have paid his debts, but neither he nor his son-in-law were aware of the way present values had soared above the pre-war levels.

It was easy enough for Saffity to raise the finance; he merely negotiated a low-interest loan on the back of those valuable properties.

Saffity founded a new company, which he called Jem Securities. He now owned several properties, and it made sound economic sense to establish a new company to undertake their management. He had long since concluded that debt equals profit . . .

But a knack of turning losses into profits did not extend to his marriage which was beginning to look like a dead loss.

So far, like a diplomatic mother-in-law, Colette had pretended not to notice Jane's undisguised antipathy towards her. She waited until Jane and the baby had left the hospital before calling on her. Jane, however, had decided that she would only associate with Colette when she was compelled to – that is, at the odd business dinner. As soon as Colette had seen the baby – she was allowed the briefest glimpse – Jane began, 'I suppose you know Saffity over-ruled me about Jemima's god-parents?'

'Over-ruled?' Colette repeated weakly.

'In plain words I didn't want you and Myles.'

Colette made no answer.

'Best to be frank about these things, don't you think, Colette?' Dusting her hands of the scone she had just finished, she added, 'Of course Saffity told you?'

'He said nothing.'

'But the two of you are so close.'

'I don't think I understand . . . ' Colette's words trailed off.

'Well then, let me explain. We have nothing in common, Colette. We belong to different worlds. We see things differently.'

'We have Saffity — '

'I just said we see things differently. There are times when we will have to meet, of course.' She yawned elaborately, and went on. 'You're making this very awkward for me. Very well, if you insist on forcing me to be blunt, I will be. Except for official functions, when Saffity insists on having you, you are not welcome here.'

'I'm sorry you feel this way,' Colette said falteringly.

'Can't be helped, I suppose,' Jane said, sounding bored.

'But she was rude! Downright rude!' Myles expostulated when Colette told him about Jane's outburst. 'I'll have to see Saffity about this.'

'No, that is precisely what you must not do. That would be playing into her hands.'

He looked at her shrewdly. 'Go on, my dearest.'

'Because Saffity would confront her, and we might lose him altogether.'

'Nonsense! He's too strong to let anyone dictate to him.'

'Of course you're right about that. But you see, she would make life even more unpleasant for him — ' She gave one of the Gallic shrugs Myles had come to love. 'We'll just have to be diplomatic,' she said firmly.

Colette's tactic seemed to work. Saffity frequently dropped in on her for a drink, and their daily phone calls continued.

She was saddened, not defeated, by Jane.

In the grip of a rage more powerful than any Saffity could remember, as he sped up the long, graceful oak-lined drive at Stanford Hall, the impassive beauty of the trees seemed to mock him. The beauty and the peace of his home usually soothed him. But not today. He drove his Rolls himself – he had been too angry to wait for the chauffeur. When he reached the front door he flung himself out of the car, and with the help of his silver-topped cane, walked rapidly up to the front door. 'Where's Lady Jane?' he roared.

'In the greenhouse, sir.'

Nanny Bridgeland, Jane's old nanny, crossed the hallway, carrying Jem. For once, Saffity did not take his child in his arms, but turned on his heel and left.

Jane was tending the orchids.

Since Jem's birth her shape had rounded and ripened, making her cold dangerous eyes more challenging and still more seductive. The response stirring in his loins intensified his rage.

'How dare you tell my office to find other accommodation for the Blums? How dare you say that Stanford Hall is not an inn? That Wyndham customers are no longer welcome here?'

'Calm down, Saffity,' Jane said icily. 'You can easily put them up at the Finley Arms.'

'Are you mad?' he yelled, responding to his own rage, and growing angrier. 'It's an important part of the business, keeping our customers happy. You know that our major customers have always stayed here. It's a tradition.'

'Your Mr and Mrs Max Blum will not be staying here,' she said stonily.

'*You're* giving me orders! Are you crazy?' he said, smashing the greenhouse glass with his cane. 'This is *my* house. It's bad enough that your insufferable parents have moved in! Max Blum has stayed here once, and he will stay here again. And you will be gracious and you will be charming.'

'You're a thug, Saffity, a dirty, low-class thug,' she taunted. 'You can smash things, you can tear the place apart. You can even have Max Blum to stay,' she said, her eyes hard and motionless. 'But you can't make me gracious.' She clipped an orchid, and mashed it under her riding boot. 'Mr and Mrs Max Blum will feel how unwelcome they are.'

'You will pay for this, Jane,' Saffity said as he left.

He was already several paces away when she called out. 'I cancelled the Fisks.'

Saffity returned to the greenhouse. 'You did *what*?'

'I telephoned Dawn Fisk this morning and said tomorrow night's dinner was cancelled.'

'What's got into you, Jane?' Saffity said dully. 'Why are you doing this?'

Jane clipped another orchid. Holding the fleshy bloom up to the light she said, 'See this slight blemish? This is an inferior breed. And this,' she paused, snipping the petals viciously and efficiently, 'this is what I do to inferior breeds.' She paused dramatically. 'Is that clear?'

He limped away.

In his study he poured himself a large whisky and called Colin Fisk. 'Colin, are you tied up at the moment?'

'Not inextricably.'

'Could we have a quick drink at the Stainton Arms at about six?'

Colin and Saffity arrived at the same time. Observing Colin's tweed jacket and his pipe, Saffity reflected how much he had changed. He had an air of purposeful contentment about him, the air of a man sufficiently at peace with himself to welcome challenges as he welcomed life. 'I know what's what,' Colin liked to say – which was his way of stating that because he had survived against impossible odds, he had learned it all the hardest way, and was well worth listening to.

They talked shop for a while, and then Saffity asked quietly, 'Did Dawn tell you Jane phoned her this morning?'

'Yes.'

'Jane is not herself. The pregnancy and then the birth — '

'Have you considered a psychiatrist?'

431

Saffity did not answer immediately. How like Colin to be frank and forthright, he thought. And how fortunate that he did not even try to take shelter behind polite reticence.

'She wouldn't hear of it, Colin.' He looked down at his red carnation and fiddled with it. 'There is something wrong, seriously wrong with her. But I don't think a psychiatrist could help her come to terms with the fact that I'm not an earl!' He laid his hand on Colin's arm. 'I'm sorry she phoned Dawn — '

'You had nothing to do with it, Saffity,' Colin said staunchly. 'Dawn knows that, and I know it too.'

Suddenly hungry, Saffity ordered a sandwich. When it was brought to him, he took a large bite and broke into a gale of laughter.

Colin stared at him uncomprehendingly. The laughter continued. 'What's the joke?' he asked.

'It's the sandwich. It's the soggy bread,' Saffity spluttered. 'The soggy English bread!' He leaned towards Colin. 'When I was a very small boy I vowed I would somehow get to Britain. It was during the First World War, just after my town had burned to the ground. There was no bread. The French soldiers *sold* us bread, the British *gave* us bread. Can you understand what that means?'

'Yes, I think I can understand that,' Colin said evenly.

Driving home, Saffity knew he had been right to take Colin into his confidence. Colin was exceedingly valuable to Wyndham Carpets, yet Jane had seen fit to be rude to his wife. His mind turned to Jem. He whistled through his teeth. Some men were stuck with a good wife, and a bad marriage – he was stuck with a bad marriage and a bad wife. As always when he thought of Jane he thought of Jem. He had missed her bath time tonight. Divorce was out of the question.

He wished he had not mentioned the bread. The only bearing his life in Salonika had on his present life was his profound British patriotism.

24

In the spring of 1947, King George VI, his wife and his two daughters visited South Africa. Max and Fanny and Jeff were among the flag-waving crowds lining the streets waiting to welcome the Royal Family. As Max waved his Union Jack he was deeply – almost embarrassingly – moved. His lips moved in a silent prayer of gratitude to be part of the great British Empire.

Throughout that long Johannesburg summer a heatwave continued, all through to the fall. At Oak Lodge the sweating weeding-women struggled with the long lawns that had gone dry and yellow. A Xhosa baby sucked loudly at her mother's breast. On the way to the house Fanny passed the women and sighed. She hated the heat. She would have liked to have sat in the shade beside the pool – the bubbling sound of the mechanically filtered water always soothed her – but the house required her attention. The following day she and Max were flying to Europe on a buying mission. Meanwhile a few household chores still remained.

She viewed the prospect of being a house-guest at Stanford Hall at last with more than a little apprehension.

The projected trip demanded massive organisation and, like all perfectionists, Fanny attended to the finest details with military precision. Blessed – or perhaps, as she sometimes thought, cursed – with boundless energy and stamina, she welcomed the additional test of her administrative skills. Leave of absence from her various charities, eighteen servants in two houses, an assortment of animals, three ailing, elderly parents, food stores, clothing requirements and two children – to say nothing of the financial risks involved in this buying venture – meant that she was never seen without a list in her hands.

How she found time for everything no one ever knew. On top of it all, she was remarkably elegant. She had a dressmaker, of course, but where did she find time for all those fittings? The fact was that she'd had a tailor's dummy made of her own figure, and since, despite her well-known love of chocolates, her slim shape did not change, no fittings were required.

People spoke about her in tones of awe and reverence – her table was said to be the best in Johannesburg. On the days when she had one of her charity meetings she would leave the business for one or two hours, and then return to her station behind the wide, wooden counter, chocolates, cigarettes and tea at the ready, determined not to allow a single customer to go out of the door without having made a purchase.

By now she had customers throughout the length and breadth of South Africa, and they looked forward to seeing her; she had become a valued confidante. People trusted her judgement on family matters. She had been known to arrange special prices, to extend credit, and even, on occasion – when the circumstances were exceptional – to make an interest-free loan. Her customers rewarded her with their loyalty, and she asked no more than that.

'How do you do it?' people asked. 'How do you manage it all?'

'I'm an early riser,' she would answer.

Except for Jeff's room, everything had been checked. Fanny left this last, rather pleasurable chore to the Saturday afternoon before their departure for Europe. He was now a first-year medical student at the University of Cape Town, but because he'd be returning to Johannesburg for half-term she wanted to be sure his room was in perfect order. Max was out playing poker, so she could give his things her undivided attention.

She began with Jeff's sweaters. In his wardrobe she found several, rolled up and spattered in mud, though obviously unworn. She sighed. It was hard to understand this boy. He was an eighteen-year-old medical student, with nothing but A's, and yet he was obviously so embarrassed about letting his friends see how many new clothes he had he disguised their appearance. She smiled again. Medical student or not, at heart he was still only a small boy.

Still smiling, she took his desk chair so that she could reach into the high top shelf. A large leather book rather like a photograph album caught her eye. She carried it down, and opened it. It was not a photograph album, but a collection of letters.

Her discovery demanded absolute privacy.

She shut the cupboard door, replaced the desk chair and took the book to her bathroom. There she sat down to read.

The letters were from Theresa to Jeff. Her hands shook. She found several rough drafts of Jeff's letters, and some notes. Thank God the girl was in a convent, Fanny thought. She knew nothing about this friendship, nothing whatever . . . Fanny shuddered. The last time Max had spoken of Mireille he had said she was a helpless drunk – she was selling off bits and pieces of her farm. Fanny had no time for drunks, and she had never liked Mireille anyway. She always seemed to worsen Max's mood, and he was difficult enough to live with as it was.

Theresa's letters seemed harmless. She described spring, the beauties of nature, the immensity of the universe – and the purity of forgiveness. But now she was reading about Theresa's interview with the Dean of Medicine at Cape Town University.

Wait a moment, wait a moment, Fanny said to herself. Theresa was in a convent, but she was also a first-year medical student?

She laid the pages on her lap and shut her eyes.

No wonder Jeff had been so adamant in his refusal to go to the university in his home town.

They were obviously fellow-students.

Fanny felt dizzy, but resumed her reading.

Her eye fell on a paragraph in one of Jeff's letters. ' . . . When night falls, I think of Sister Theresa, of her soft footfalls, and while she says her prayers my heart tears, and I can't wait to be at her gate.'

It's a love-letter, Fanny said to herself, inwardly ranting. Good God, it's a poem as well!

She came to a page that had obviously been crumpled and smoothed out . . .

You urge forgiveness on me, Theresa, saying that to understand all is to forgive all. I agree. But I have failed to understand the nature of my cousin Geddie's massacre. Again and again, I have tried to understand that the SS released an asylum of lunatics, and then armed them with iron bars with which to murder the town of Kovno's Jews. Geddie was one of them.

Perhaps my Zionism will help me to forgive what I cannot understand?

Here the note ended. Fanny shut the file. She had read too much.

435

Forgiveness!

She had long ceased hoping to forgive herself for having paid for Sonja and Geddie to return from England to Lithuania, but it seemed she had compounded her guilt by having told Jeff the details of Geddie's fate. 'You'll do more harm than good if you tell Jeff,' Max had warned.

'Jeff must know what sort of world he is living in. It will make him work harder,' she had insisted stubbornly.

Now, too late, she realised Max had been right.

She shuffled into Jeff's room and replaced the file. She felt old and defeated, and so weary that she undressed and got into bed in the middle of the afternoon. She would have to think. Theresa may be a nun, but she would have to see that Jeff was transferred from the University of Cape Town. She shuddered violently. Theresa had had an affair with a kaffir! What could be worse for Jeff – than *that?*

But at this moment there was nothing she could do. She had to go on an aeroplane the next day.

'Mr and Mrs Blum?' the chauffeur said, taking Fanny's hand-luggage. 'I'm Giles, sir, Mr Saffity's chauffeur. The train was on time, I see. The car's just outside the station, madam.'

After making sure that they were seated at the back of the Rolls, he kept up a steady monologue on his wartime experience in Durban until he reached the Finley Arms in Droitwich, a town close to Kidderminster. Then he opened the door and announced, 'I'm sure you'll be very comfortable here.'

'Here?' Max echoed, confused. 'I thought we were expected at Stanford Hall.'

'I was surprised about that myself, sir, but I checked my instructions very carefully, sir. You'll be most comfortable here, I'm sure.'

'I'm sure we shall,' Fanny said, exchanging a glance with Max.

'As soon as you're settled, then, at six-thirty, I'm to pick you up and drive you to Stanford Hall, madam. The boss is expecting you for dinner.'

'We'll be ready,' Fanny said quickly.

They paid no attention to the flowers and fruit in their room.

'Well?' Fanny said.

'I can't understand it,' Max said. 'For the life of me I can't. Saffity always puts up his customers.'

'And you're his friend,' Fanny said thoughtfully. 'So at last I'm going to meet the unpredictable Mr Saffity.'

'Why unpredictable?'

'Because he always takes you by surprise, doesn't he?' Fanny said calmly. 'Anyway, it's a strange friendship. He's important enough that you hate him, yet he hardly knows you exist. He hasn't set eyes on you for sixteen years and he wasn't even at the station to meet you,' she ended scornfully.

'I'm not sorry to be staying here. I wasn't happy at Stanford Hall.'

'But you've been raving about it for years!'

'I know. But I wasn't comfortable there.' He moved towards the huge basket of fruit and opened the note. ' "Look forward to dining with you tonight," Saffity says.'

'It *is* a wonderful basket of fruit,' Fanny said to mollify him.

She unpacked their clothes and quickly changed into a dressing gown. She stood over his chair and pointed her finger at him. 'If you don't talk to Saffity about those A shares, I will,' she said.

'Don't you dare,' Max said warningly. 'And stop pointing your finger at me. What's come over you? You've always stopped me doing anything about those shares.'

'And I mustn't mention Mireille's name, either,' Fanny went on mockingly, as she walked toward the bathroom. 'I'm going to get ready. I want to look my best.'

Max had described the grounds and the driveway of Stanford Hall so many times that Fanny felt she would know it by heart. It was, however, far more beautiful than she had imagined. Saffity was waiting outside the front door to greet them, and immediately Fanny was uncomfortably aware of his silver-tipped cane. But even with his cane and his limp he was more attractive than she had expected. He was much taller, for one thing, and his gleaming white hair gave him a distinguished air. When she heard him laugh she realised whom Max had been imitating all these years. He led them into his study, and at once showed them a photograph of Jem.

'My daughter,' he said, smiling at the photograph. 'She's almost two. I was a slow starter, Max.'

'She's a beautiful child,' Fanny said dutifully.

'Isn't she? And she's clever, too. Worth waiting all these years to have your own flesh and blood, isn't it?'

'Oh, yes,' Fanny agreed.

Max thought of Theresa, and stared out at the lawns.

'My wife sends her regrets,' Saffity said. 'She is indisposed, unfortunately.'

'Nothing serious, I hope?' Fanny said politely, as Jane's parents entered the room.

'Allow me to present my parents-in-law,' Saffity said formally. 'Lord and Lady Lovett-Turner.'

To begin with, the dinner passed painfully, with several gaping silences. The dining room, however, as Fanny noted with more than a little satisfaction, had not changed. It was exactly as Max had described it.

It was only when Fanny began discussing medical schools that the conversation – though restricted to her and to Saffity – became livelier. For they were both agreed that Great Britain was the best country in which to study medicine. Saffity had powerful contacts at Oxford, and since Jeff was such an outstanding student he was sure he could arrange for the boy to be interviewed. Of course he would need letters from his professors and his teachers, and so on, and then, in due course, it would be arranged . . .

'As a matter of fact, my foundation – the Edwina Wyndham Foundation – is an important benefactor to Oxford University. So I don't anticipate any problems, do you? I should think they'd be delighted to have Jeff Blum, with his excellent academic credentials, among their number,' he concluded, letting loose one of his merriest laughs.

After Turkish coffee, served in the minute jewelled cups Saffity collected, Fanny said graciously, 'You'll forgive us if we leave. It's a long flight from Johannesburg to London.'

When they returned to the Finley Arms she said, 'I'm glad we're not staying there.'

'What made you change your mind?'

'Too many ghosts.' She shivered. 'Living ghosts, too. His parents-in-law — '

'What did you think of him?' Max interrupted.

'He's brilliant, he's amusing, he's ruthless and he's charming. I expected all that. But he is not a happy man, and that I didn't expect.'

'Why do you say that?'

'He went on and on about his daughter. As if he's trying, through her, to compensate — '

438

'Compensate? For what?'

'For a cold and heartless wife.' She picked up her hairbrush, and held it for a moment. 'But I don't think he cares too much about being unhappy. He's too interested in power.'

'You think you know everything, Fanny,' Max said irritably.

'Didn't you hear the way he spoke about Oxford? Besides,' she continued implacably, 'I overheard him on the telephone when I went to the ladies' room. He's buying the Saddler Building in New York.'

'You're not serious.'

'That's *his* business,' she said decisively. 'It's got nothing to do with us. I want to talk about something much more important. Tell me, Max, why are you so afraid of him?'

'You're talking rubbish.'

'No, I'm not. I know you, Max. You can't meet his eyes. Every time he looks at you, you look away. Why do you do that?' She grabbed his wrist. 'He's got something on you, hasn't he, Max? I saw what a fright you got when he mentioned Paris. Something happened in Paris. Something to do with Saffity and you and that bitch, Mireille.' She released his wrist. 'Who was Judith?'

'His first girlfriend.'

'Then Mireille was a girlfriend of his. I should have guessed.'

'Leave her out of this,' Max said sharply. 'And unless you're looking for big, big trouble, you'll make sure you don't mention her name.'

'You've told me that a thousand times. What's he got on you, Max?'

'Go to hell!'

Now that she had seen them together at last, she was certain Saffity had something on Max in which Mireille was somehow involved. Who knew what it could be? Some sort of blackmail? She had better not push him too far, she decided.

In any case, Fanny had another and infinitely more serious reason for caution. So serious, in truth, that she encouraged Max not to raise the question of the A shares with Saffity.

In all the world it was Saffity and only Saffity who could help her get Jeff into Oxford and away from Theresa. In any case, Oxford was way out of their reach; Fanny would never have dreamed of aiming that high. Saffity had not only found a way to her heart but, by merely dangling a promise, he had pierced it.

Saffity had given Max his chance in life, and now it looked as if he would do the same for Jeff, too.

'But how can you turn down an opportunity to go to Oxford, Jeff? How can you?' Fanny said, wringing her hands.

They were lunching at the Vineyards, one of the oldest restaurants at the Cape. As soon as they had returned from Europe Fanny had flown down, ostensibly to see their ailing parents. Her real reason was to talk to Jeff.

'I'm very happy here, Mom. Groot Schuur is one of the best hospitals.' He laid down his fork. 'What's got into you?'

'It's opportunity for my son, that's what. A glorious opportunity.'

'But *this* is where the opportunity is. Here, in South Africa,' Jeff said, his youthful enthusiasm blazing. 'There's a chance to change our society. It's changing already. There are people of every colour in my class. We don't *notice* colour. And I'm teaching illiterate blacks at night school, and you wouldn't believe how quickly they learn.'

'You're not eating,' Fanny said mechanically. 'You must eat.'

'I've made friends, here, Mom. Wonderful friends. Ex-servicemen, blacks, all sorts of interesting, intelligent — '

'Oh, I know about your *friends*,' Fanny said scathingly. 'I know all about them.'

'Such as? What are you getting at?'

'Such as that nun, Theresa!'

'Theresa? What's Theresa got to do with this? She's a positively brilliant student, the best in the class, if you must know. Everyone respects her, everyone! No one teases her for being a nun.' He added bitterly, 'No one except you, it seems.'

'We're talking about Oxford, Jeff. *Oxford!*'

'Look, Mom, if I go anywhere at all it will be to Palestine.'

'Palestine? What are you saying?'

'You know as well as I do.'

'I don't; I've no idea,' Fanny said, deathly pale.

'That's why you're turned pale, I suppose,' Jeff said softly. 'The Arab League is already training volunteers. Millions of Arabs against less than three-quarters of a million Jews. There's a group I'm involved in,' he said eagerly. 'But I may not be chosen.'

'Chosen? Oh, my God — '

'What about Geddie, and the millions of Geddies?'

Fanny said nothing. She wished now that she'd never mentioned Oxford.

'Look, Mom, if there is Partition, and if Palestine does become a Jewish state, and the Arabs do attack, who will defend it?'

Still Fanny said nothing.

'It will be up to the Jews,' he said fiercely. 'This time the Jews will determine their own fate. We will go to war, we will kill and we will be killed.' He turned away. Fanny thought his eyes were too bright. 'Geddie will not have died in vain,' he muttered. 'And if I die, I'll die fighting.'

Jeff was chosen, as Fanny knew he would be. Not content to rely on the normal procedures, he used every bit of influence he had. Thanks to Fanny's charitable activities, that was considerable. After several false alarms, once again in the early hours of the morning the Blums were at the tiny Palmietfontein Airport, just outside Johannesburg – the entire operation was very hush-hush – and Jeff, one of the chosen, was on his way to Palestine.

Just before he left he handed her an envelope, with red sealing-wax much in evidence. 'Open it,' he said quietly, 'if anything goes wrong.'

Fanny took the envelope and locked it in her private fireproof safe. It was a terrible time, made worse by the advancing illnesses of Max's mother and Fanny's father. She moved all three parents to Johannesburg, only to have two of them die within six weeks of one another.

Fanny was terrified. Things happened in threes . . .

Max went to pieces, and took to his bed. Fanny went to the business. It absorbed her mind, she said. It kept her occupied. Sometimes in the middle of a transaction she'd break into tears and then, after a quick apology, continue as if nothing was happening.

One day she received a letter from Saffity, enclosing details about Oxford. His PS infuriated her. 'Have not as yet received any of Jeff's academic documentation. It has gone astray, perhaps?' Saffity was trying to imply she had lied about Jeff's achievements. Frenziedly, she phoned his old school, his university, and asked for the relevant information. The edge to her voice, combined with her terse comment that Jeff was fighting for the state of Israel, brought replies by return of post.

Fanny sat down and wrote to Saffity, telling him that as a military man himself he would probably be interested to know that Jeff was a soldier, too. She enclosed the relevant documents, but beyond asking that he acknowledge receipt she made no comment on them.

In due course Saffity replied. It was an innocuous, colourless letter, saying that the matter of Oxford would be left in abeyance. Fanny shrugged. Meticulous as ever, she folded the letter back in the envelope and placed it in the safe beside Jeff's – the one she hoped and prayed she would never have to open.

Saffity gave Fanny's letter a cursory reading and handed it to his secretary for filing. These days he couldn't take his mind off his bid to acquire Charles Stores, a chain of ninety furniture outlets. Ever since he'd heard that housewives were resorting to bribing furniture salesmen to sell them a carpet, he'd been obsessed with the huge home furniture market that was waiting for Wyndham Carpets. Rationing had been abolished. Saffity was now convinced that two factors made up the oxygen of a business: finance, and the customer. The Jemsa Holdings and Trusts now owned and controlled several companies, most of which were financed on the strength of the assets he was buying. His uncanny gift of persuasion had convinced many a banker that a request from Saffity for a loan was an honour in itself.

If finance and the customer were the lifeblood of his business, then the business and Jem were his life blood. The business crowded Jane and her coldness out of his life and out of his mind. Lost in her world of horses, she was indifferent to him. She persisted in calling their daughter Jemima; he called her Jem. If he had not been satisfied that she loved the child, things would have been very different. Her icy beauty was at its zenith, and though he still responded to it, and liked to feast his eyes on her, his heart was unmoved. She might just as well have been a painting, like the Modigliani he had recently acquired.

He was lighting up a Havana cigar, his newest indulgence, when his secretary buzzed. 'Personal call for you, Mr Saffity. A Mrs Brooke Spellman.'

'Who?'

442

'Checked our cards, Mr Saffity. We've no reference on file,' the secretary clucked. 'She sounds like an American.'

'Put her on, put her on,' Saffity chuckled. 'It's my old friend Brooke.' As soon as he was connected he said, 'Brooke, where the hell are you?'

'Where the hell do you think? I'm at the Dorchester.'

'Splendid. What a wonderful surprise! What brings you here?'

'Business. I'm buying for my Contemporary Gift Store.'

'You're in business!'

'I sure am.' Brooke laughed. 'It seems to be taking off, too.'

'How is your husband – uh — '

'His name is Dwight,' Brooke said, sounding offended that he'd forgotten. After what he'd done to her in that hotel room in Washington, he should have remembered. To show him she knew the name of *his* wife, she went on, 'How is Jane? I'm longing to meet her.'

'We're coming up to London tomorrow. Should we all dine together, then? Say at eight?'

'Great. Where? Eaton Place?'

'Yes. Jane will be delighted.'

Saffity's mood lifted. He hadn't seen Brooke since that time in Washington, but they had kept up with each other's news by letter. He'd written to her from the hospital, wanting her to know that it was her gift of the gold key that had saved his life.

He decided to ring Jane at once. 'But I've a Hunt Committee,' she said. 'Don't you remember? I told you I wasn't coming up to London with you.'

Though he knew her Hunt Committee meetings were sacred, he said, 'Can't you get out of it just this once?'

'I'm sorry; I can't,' she said sounding unusually contrite. 'Pity, I wanted to meet Brooke.'

Saffity replaced the receiver. He could tell from her tone she really would like to meet Brooke. She still refused to entertain his customers, though. Ah well, he thought, he had probably always expected too much of her.

He returned to his balance sheets.

At the end of the afternoon he had his secretary telephone Brooke to ask her to meet him at the Dorchester. He did not want to receive Brooke and her husband at Eaton Place without Jane.

The next evening Saffity was, as usual, on time. Brooke and Dwight were not. He waited at one of the small tables in the

Dorchester Bar, and lit a cigar. About five minutes later Brooke joined him. He stood up at once. She kissed him on both cheeks and, still holding both his arms, stood back and openly appraised him.

'Same old Saff but with a cigar.'

'And a cane!' Saffity said grimly.

They sat down and then said together, 'Where's Jane?' 'Where's Dwight?' which made them laugh.

'So, it's just the two of us,' Brooke said thoughtfully.

'Just the two of us.'

They went into the dining room and, as if by mutual consent, got the ordering out of the way as quickly as possible.

'Well, Saff,' Brooke said in the drawl he loved. 'I sure didn't expect to be dining *à deux* with my ex-lover.'

'And you're disappointed?'

'Hardly. It's an unexpected break,' Brooke admitted. 'I made another bad mistake. Third time unlucky. A lush, this time; Dwight and I are splitting.' She tried to smile but failed. 'Thought I'd come clean.'

'You didn't deserve that, Brooke. I'm sorry,' Saffity said sympathetically.

'You win some and you lose some. I'm just a bad pitcher, I guess. I don't think I'll try again.' She leaned forward and touched Saffity's hand. 'Tell me about Lady Jane, and Jem. I want to hear everything.'

He told her that Jane was well, and still beautiful, and loved living in the country, and was an excellent horsewoman. He said that Jem was the love of his life, and the cleverest three-year-old in the world. 'You should have children, Brooke,' he said. 'Children are — ' He stopped.

'What were you going to say?'

'Children are roots,' Saffity answered seriously. 'In the end, there is no substitute for one's own flesh and blood.'

'I know, and I agree,' she replied sadly. 'I don't think I can have any. I hoped I would – when you and I were together — ' Her voice trailed off.

'I'm sorry your marriage didn't work out, Brooke.'

'Since we are *à deux*, I'm going to ask you something I never had the courage to ask before. May I?'

'Fire away.'

'Were you, that is, when we were together, did you give any thought to – I mean, would you have considered — '

'Marriage?'

'Yes.'

'There was the war,' Saffity said carefully. 'My best buddie Drew was killed. I was lonely – as lonely as when Edwina died. Or perhaps lonelier.' He hesitated, and went on. 'And then Jane was one of the nurses. Stunningly beautiful in her uniform, stunning. I always went for stunning women – that's why I went for you, Brooke.'

'Go on.'

'So we went out to dinner, and to bed, and three weeks later we were married.'

'So — '

'So what I'm trying to say is that I did not really consider marriage in advance, like a calculated risk. I hope you can understand. It was like parachuting. No, it was more like being in a fire, and jumping out of the window, and not thinking about what you'd break when you fell. You think you've got a chance to save your life, and instinctively you take it.'

'So you saved your life.'

'I think I saw her as my survival kit. It wasn't fair to her, of course it wasn't. But now we have Jem, and we both adore her.'

'Then you are happy, Saff?'

'Happiness,' he said caustically. 'What is happiness? A second-rate ambition? I don't know. Drew was happy, though. He always talked about having fun. He loved the girls – and he chased them, and chased fun, and he was happy. But I wanted something more than fun, I always did. I have tremendous fun with my business, and in that sense I suppose I am happy.'

'At this moment you could call me a happy woman,' Brooke said, raising her glass. 'I'd like to drink to you, the man who always makes me happy. I'm happy just being with you, Saff. I came to terms with that a long time ago.' She thrust her chin forward, and added defiantly, 'Jane should get her priorities right. She should look after you. A wife who doesn't take proper care of a man like you deserves the consequences.'

'Shall we go upstairs?'

'Need you ask?'

It was good being with Brooke again. Brooke was glamorous and shiny, her body muscular and strong, but nowhere nearly as beautiful as his lovely, galactic Jane. Except that Jane was not his . . .

Jane and her few carefully regulated emotions belonged to no one but herself. He entered Brooke, and knew that her whole soul welcomed him home, and in that moment he knew that Jane had no soul. Then his body and Brooke's body took him over, and he lost himself, and stopped thinking.

When their bodies had quietened down, and in that brief time of utter peace, Brooke said calmly, 'I love you, Saff. I love you enough for both of us, Saff.'

'Both of us?'

'I love you so completely that I can even bear your not loving me.' In measured, thoughtful tones she went on, 'I half believed I was half over you; so, to get over you completely, I got married.'

'You, at least, considered what you were about to do before you did it.'

'That's true. Except that I considered the wrong things, thought the wrong thoughts,' she said, running her hands through his thick white hair. 'Do you love her?' she asked unexpectedly.

'She doesn't need me,' he said. 'She doesn't seem to need anyone. She's unshockable.'

'You didn't answer my question, Saff.'

'I know that, genius,' he said. 'I don't know if I love her. She hasn't got a soul. Is it possible to love someone who has no soul?' he asked rhetorically.

'I envy her,' Brooke said. 'I envy her because — '

'Jane's unshockable,' Saffity continued, thinking out loud. 'Also unreachable. But she does love Jem.' He paused, and again said, 'She doesn't need me.'

'That sure is a challenge to a man like you,' Brooke said, the words rushing. 'Having to force a wife to need her own husband must be mighty exciting.'

She snuggled closer to him. Her fingers found the raised scars of his patchwork thigh. 'I guess everyone has a weak point, Saff,' she said slowly, 'and my weak point is you!' She spoke clearly and as calmly as if she was speaking of something over which she had no more control than the date of her birth. He understood this was her way of telling him she bore him no grudges. He felt relieved and immeasurably grateful. He drew her closer and they made love again, gently and leisurely, and the years slipped away, and all time receded.

In the morning he said, 'It's about time Jemsa Holdings and Trust had a head office in London. I've been running it from Wyndham Carpets.'

Brooke was silent.

He plunged on, 'I've been negotiating to take over another chain of ninety furniture stores.'

'What are you after, Saff? After all, Wyndham Carpets is in the big league. It's power you want, isn't it?'

'Yes, Brooke. Power. I like it.' He stopped to collect his thoughts. 'Power, for me, means having an impact on the way things are shaped. I have enough not to need to work ever again, so you're right, it's not money. Of course you understand that, Brooke; you had nothing once. Power is fun. And for a man like me there is no greater fun in the world than power. But only those of us who have been utterly powerless know how to get the fun out of power.' He shrugged.

'I'm with you, Saff. You're talking about the poor boy who watched his city burn down.'

'You know me, Brooke. You really know me,' he murmured. 'This key – your gift, Brooke, saved my life,' he added, fingering it. 'And you can help me make my life worthwhile.'

He took her in his arms and hugged her, and she felt his power, and knew she could be crushed.

25

Only eleven days after the birth of the state of Israel, shockingly and entirely unexpectedly, the South African government was defeated in the general election. English-speaking South Africa was in a turmoil of panic and despair.

So little was the country prepared for the change, that even the leader of the new government, the anti-British, pro-Nazi Dr Malan, admitted that his victory was a miracle. The new government, so long pregnant with its policy, gave birth to apartheid. The slogan became the reality. People talked of nothing else. Their beloved General Smuts, the man who was said to be one of the two great men of the Empire – the other being Churchill – had not only been defeated, but had lost his own seat.

'Smuts lost,' a friend said, 'because he should not have announced his *de facto* recognition of Israel on his birthday. It was only two days before the election. He should have waited until after the election!'

Fanny had clicked her tongue and said nothing. What could a small untrained army of about twenty thousand amateurs, with mainly home-made weapons, do against tanks, aircraft, and all the full equipment of the regular, real armies of the five Arab states?

'Come on, Fanny; you're a businesswoman, aren't you? In one week two hundred million pounds have already left the country — '

'So?'

'And people are talking of leaving. This apartheid business goes against the grain.'

It certainly went against Jeff's grain, Fanny thought miserably. Jeff had told her he didn't notice colour. 'They are not a different species,' he had said. 'Black blood is as red as white blood, you know.' Fanny shuddered . . . Blood, bleeding to death . . . Moaning inwardly, she shook her head. 'I've got my own troubles,' she said dismissively.

She could not decide whether it was a blessing or a curse that she could not be present at her son's military funeral, complete with gun salute, in Israel. His death was beyond her comprehension. Medical supplies of penicillin had been blocked in an ambushed convoy on the Burma Road to Jerusalem in July 1948, and it was lack of penicillin that had killed him. With it he would have survived his wounds, just as Saffity had. Somehow her mind fastened on this aspect of the tragedy; it tormented her. She believed now she had always known that Jeff would not make it. Weeks before she had received the news, when everyone else in Johannesburg had exultantly gone to the synagogue to give thanks for the declaration of the state of Israel, she had stayed at home. Even Max had roused himself from his bed to attend the moving service of thanksgiving at the Great Synagogue. That day, alone in her bedroom, she had done the unforgivable – gone down on her knees and prayed.

Her prayer was simple: not to have to open Jeff's envelope.

Two days after she received news of his death, Fanny over-rode Max's shocked protests and went to the office at Trans-Empire Carpets. Once there, she locked the office door and unlocked her private safe. She held the envelope in her hands for a long while, and then decided that this was not the place in which to read it. She reached for the telephone, booked a room and slowly made her way to the Carlton Hotel.

Moses, the tea-boy, stroked his grey beard and watched her stroll up the street. One of her saleswomen, Mrs Norton, returning from a customer, bumped into her. 'Mrs Blum, I'm so sorry,' she said, embarrassed.

Without altering her stride, Fanny thanked her politely. The saleswoman shook her head in confusion. Even at a moment as terrible as this, Mrs Blum retained her efficiency. Yet she was not as heartless as she looked; she had paid, out of her own pocket, for Mrs Norton's divorce lawyers.

Once in her room at the Carlton Hotel Fanny turned down the covers, took off her shoes, and climbed, fully clothed, between the sheets. Inside the envelope she found two others – one addressed to Mom and Dad, the other to Theresa. She hesitated, uncertain which she should open first. That one of them was distinctly not meant for her was irrelevant. Then, almost as if there had been no real choice, she opened Theresa's envelope and began to read.

Darling, darling Theresa,

I know you have begged me never again to address you as darling, but this letter is, in a way, sent from heaven. Pray for

449

my soul, my darling, though because my soul is your soul, it will be your soul that you are praying for.

Again and again I asked your forgiveness for my loving you. Graciously you granted it, yet I craved not your forgiveness but your love. Instead, after giving yourself to Piet, and then once and only once, gloriously once, to me, so that you could be certain of renouncing the evil of desire, you gave yourself to the Church. But it was not for love of me that you gave your body to me. It was an act of compassion. It was not an act of love.

My glorious moment, now more than two years ago, was your moment of hell. My lust made me take shameless advantage of your gentle and compassionate heart, but I meant it when I said I would kill myself if you did not let me make love to you. Now, when it is too late, I understand that I both blackmailed and raped you.

But my love is as undying as your purity is undying, and it was my love and my lust that became your sin. My love and my sin forced you into a convent.

You cannot imagine what a relief and what a blessing it is to say these things to you. Years and years ago you, only you, asked me if I had had any news of Nanny and Absalom. You and only you remembered, and cared. And I fell in love with you, and your milky skin, and your amber eyes, and your freckles and your soft breasts.

You, my darling, darling Theresa, you told me my cousin Geddie had died as a martyr. A perfect martyr, you said. Honour Geddie's martyrdom, you said. Go to Palestine for his sake, you said. Go, you finally said, so that there will be no more Geddies who will not have their own earthly home.

So I am going to the Holy Land, as you said I should, and if you are reading this, you will know that I am beyond destiny, beyond fate.

I want you to know that I am not afraid.

Yours, only yours, Theresa my love,
Jeff

Fanny had no idea how many times she read the letter, or how long she rolled about the bed, clutching her throat until it was bruised, beating her breasts, pulling out her hair, moaning and keening. Jeff was pitched where he said he was – beyond destiny, and beyond fate. He was dead. He really was dead. She could believe it now.

A crazed, evil *girl* was responsible for the death of her only son. Theresa's madness had driven him mad. It wasn't enough that she'd gone to bed, a fifteen-year-old girl, with a black – no, she'd had to have her poor, innocent, idealistic Jeff too. Theresa had played with Jeff, and fooled him, but she had not fooled his mother. She had distrusted Mireille even before she was a drunk, and she felt the same way about her daughter. Just like her mother, Theresa was a fake. True, she had become a nun, but that was only a temporary phase, a trick, a gimmick. She was sick, she was evil and she was disgusting.

Fanny's mind was in a frenzy; she did not know what to do, what to think. Certain she was going mad, she went into the bathroom, stood under the shower fully clothed and turned the cold tap to its fullest force. When she threw back her head and screamed the falling water flooded her throat. She turned off the tap, stepped out of the shower and threw herself on the bed.

She remembered the day at Durban beach when Jeff had swum too far out and almost drowned. She remembered his Sports Day, when Nanny and Absalom had driven him to the hospital. And of course she had never been able to forget the day he had told her about the servants' love-making on her own bed. She wrenched her mind back to Theresa. She had heard about the power and the pain of adolescent passion, but who, she asked herself, who takes that sort of thing seriously? Jeff must have thought he was living in a fairy tale. And then it came to her: the power of rejection is stronger than the power of love. Theresa had rejected her son. Nun or no nun, Theresa's rejection of him had sent him to his death.

She began to shiver violently. She forced herself to strip and went to the bathroom to dry herself. She found a towelling gown behind the door and put it on. Then she lay on the floor, and wept silently until she fell into a heavy, exhausted sleep.

It was not yet midnight when she awoke.

She stared at the envelope addressed to Mom and Dad. Still she did not open it. She caressed it and kissed it, then moved to a chair, studying Jeff's precise and distinctly legible handwriting. Finally she opened it, and read it quickly. It was not a long letter. He thanked his parents for their devotion and asked them not to grieve but to rejoice in the knowledge that *this* time a Jewish son had *chosen* to die for his heritage. He concluded with the request that his letter would be shown to Sarah when she was adult enough to understand.

Fanny realised she had barely thought of Sarah. She put on her still-wet clothes, called a taxi and went home.

When she returned to Oak Lodge she ignored everyone including the police, whom Max had called. She said cryptically that she had been out, thinking, and refused to account for her movements to anyone.

A month later the Blums received an unexpected visit from Mireille. 'I came as soon as I could,' she said.

'Jeff died a month ago,' Fanny said coldly.

'Theresa told me.'

'Theresa?' Fanny said sharply. 'Who told her?'

'They were good friends, Theresa and Jeff,' Mireille said mournfully. 'They were pen friends for years and years.'

'Do you have his letters, Mireille?' Fanny asked quickly.

'Letters? Why should I have Jeff's letters?' Mireille asked, puzzled.

Fanny's expression changed to acute distaste. Mireille's lovely shape had thickened and was now as coarse as her complexion, betrayed by raised wine-red veins that the carelessly applied make-up she had at last begun to use failed to conceal.

Aware of Fanny's dislike, Mireille turned to Max and reverted to French. 'Man proposes and God disposes,' she said sadly. 'And you have lost your only son. Such a handsome young man, like his father. He reminded me so much of you, Max, when we were young. How can I comfort you, my friend?' she said distractedly, beginning to weep.

Wordlessly Fanny handed her a whisky. She drank it noisily.

In a moment, Max, too, would begin to weep. It didn't take much to set him off, Fanny thought contemptuously; he seemed to have lost all sense of dignity. She hated him for it. Let him speak French with the mother of the girl who had sent his son to his death! But Max knew nothing of that, just as he knew nothing of Jeff's last letters.

'If both of you will excuse me,' Fanny said in a voice that sounded strident even to her own ears, 'I'm going to lie down. I have a headache.'

That night, because she could not face dining with Mireille, it was Fanny who was served dinner in bed. Unlike Max, she did not

452

waste her time staring at the ceiling. Instead she replied to a score of condolence letters. She waited for Max, and when he came stumbling in – he'd had too much to drink as she knew he would – she handed him Jeff's letter.

'Why've you only given it to me now, Fanny?'

'You were too upset. You were in no state ... It would have hurt you even more.'

Max read the letter out loud, and then said, 'You did right to keep this from me.' His eyes glistened. 'This letter is an historic document,' he said drunkenly. 'It will go down in history.'

Mireille stayed with the Blums for a week, and though it irked Fanny she had to admit that Max's spirits lifted. At least he got out of bed, and sat in the early spring sun. Fanny knew that, because the servants told her. She, of course, was back at Trans-Empire Carpets.

But the Blum servants knew better than to let her know that Jeff's death had inspired his father to make a final search for Absalom and Nanny. It suddenly became so overwhelmingly important that he told Violet, one of the oldest of his household staff, that he would give a big reward to anyone who could provide him with their whereabouts. Violet had been there when they had been dismissed; she had not asked questions then, and would not now. She was used to the incomprehensible ways of the whites.

Within four days she had not only found out where Absalom was, but had visited him at his house in Sophiatown. 'I'm sorry, master, but Nanny, she's dead. She died in childbirth. It was Absalom's child, a boy. They called him Jeffrey, master — '

Max swallowed hard. 'Has Absalom got a job?' he asked.

'He's working as a driver, master.'

'How old is the boy?'

'Seven years, master.'

'I want the boy to go to the best school. I'll pay. Don't tell the other servants. And I don't want madam to know. D'you hear me?'

'Yes, master, I hear you.'

When Max handed her a five-pound note she clapped her hands and, despite her huge girth, curtsied gracefully.

Max did not ask to meet Absalom; it was enough that he knew his surname. He opened an account at a building society in the name of Jeffrey Ndlovo and made an initial deposit of five hundred pounds, arranging for an annual standing order of one hundred and fifty pounds.

Absalom must have understood Max's need for secrecy, for his respectful letters of thanks were always delivered by Violet. Though Max was pleased with what he'd done – it suited his Talmudic perception of giving secretly – he was glad Fanny knew nothing about it. How could he expect her to understand something he scarcely understood himself?

And why had he not thought of bribing the servants years ago? That way he would have found Absalom, and Jeff might not have gone to Israel.

A month or so later, Fanny was at Cape Town University, waiting for Theresa outside a lecture theatre. The students looked so intolerably young, she thought angrily; Jeff should have been amongst them, or at Oxford. Those relentless tears again. She wiped her eyes, and stared unseeing at the untidy noticeboard. The boisterous sounds of young people bursting out of the door pulled her away from her reverie. She saw Theresa at once. Her long, flowing white nun's habit contrasted strongly with the grubby white laboratory coats the other students wore.

'Hullo, Theresa,' she said, hoping she sounded friendly.

'Aunt Fanny, how nice to see you!' Theresa said. 'What brings you here?'

'I wanted to see you. You have a lunch recess now, don't you?'

'Yes, I do. We could eat in the student canteen but it is rather noisy, I'm afraid.'

'I booked a table at the Mount Nelson. The car is waiting for us. Shall we go?'

Theresa was beautiful, serenely beautiful, Fanny thought. No wonder Jeff had written of her milky skin, her amber eyes and her freckles. But he had not mentioned the rosy hue of her cheeks, or the grace of her movement. The girl radiated calm and peace, and Fanny hated her for it. She had no right to those clear, soft, untroubled eyes that looked as though they had known neither sadness nor passion. Yet those innocent eyes were no less fraudulent, Fanny decided, than the rest of her.

In the restaurant, Fanny – certain that Theresa was being deliberately slow – ordered impatiently. Neither of them wanted a starter, and when their grilled fish, a succulent kingclip, arrived she summoned the head waiter and politely asked him to make sure that they would not be disturbed as they wanted to have a very private chat.

'I'm so sorry about Jeff,' Theresa began.

'Thank you,' Fanny said mechanically. 'His death is a grievous loss.'

'He was teaching at night school, you know.'

'I know.'

'Jeff lived like a saint, and he died like a saint,' Theresa said, her expression lit by ecstasy.

Observing Theresa's expression, a spasm of nausea made Fanny close her eyes. She thought bitterly: Theresa believes Jeff is her personal angel. But she said, 'I don't want a saint, I want a son.'

'But your son is a martyr. A true martyr,' Theresa said gently.

'A dead martyr, Theresa. I've got you to thank for that.'

'Excuse me?' Theresa said, bewildered. 'I don't quite follow — '

'Don't you?' Fanny asked, disbelievingly. '*You* made him a martyr. *You* made my son into a dead saint. *You* rejected him, but not before you used his body.'

'*Please*, Aunt Fanny, *please*,' Theresa said pleadingly.

Satisfied she had wiped the ecstasy off Theresa's face, Fanny went on, 'Oh, he loved your purity. It wasn't enough for you to reject him, so you made an innocent boy feel like a sinner, like you,' she said brokenly. 'It's all very well for you to sit here, now, pretending to be the soul of innocence and virtue, when all the time you're a fraud and a fake. Why couldn't you have been an ordinary girl?'

Fanny's face crumpled. She covered her mouth with her hand, her shoulders heaving with her dry sobs. Quickly she regained herself. 'Why couldn't you have been an ordinary girl?' she repeated. 'Normal, ordinary girls don't believe that sex is an evil that must be conquered. Normal girls know that sex is as natural as breathing.' Suddenly, almost in spite of herself, she laid her hand over Theresa's. 'Oh, I know you didn't mean him to die, Theresa. I know that. But if you had loved him, and not rejected him, he would not have gone to Palestine. He would still be alive.' Her voice dropped to a harsh whisper. 'You killed him. Your purity – your phoney purity – killed him.'

'I didn't know you knew about us,' Theresa said faintly. 'I beg you to forgive me.'

'Perhaps? One day? Who knows?' She added viciously, 'What about Piet? Has *he* forgiven you? Uncle Max told me about him.'

'Does Uncle Max know about Jeff and me?'

'Only that you were pen pals.'

'Are you going to tell him?'

'No. He's a finished man, as it is.'

'Aunt Fanny, I'm going to pray to the Virgin Mary that some time in the future you'll forgive me.'

Though neither of them had touched their food, Fanny called for the bill, and they left.

In an inner trance of grief and disbelief, Theresa carried on as if her inner being had not been shattered. She prayed for Fanny to forgive her, but knew that it was hopeless. If she could not forgive herself, how could she expect Fanny to? The sound of Fanny's dry sobs was with her constantly. Also, she had long been conscious of the hungry way Uncle Max looked at her. He wanted her. She had known that, the day he had given her the gold crucifix, and though she had been repelled by him her very repugnance had strangely produced a faint sexual stirring.

She could not quite bring herself to pray for a higher forgiveness. For she felt unworthy of God.

She could not eat and she could not sleep. Still she kept her torment and her guilt private; she had inflicted too much pain on others already. She attended her lectures and all the convent rituals dutifully, but the peace she had known was gone. She sang the hymns mechanically, but heard only Fanny's voice, Fanny's sobs. The awful thing was that she agreed with Fanny; she was not a normal girl. And yes, she was a fake. With Piet she had mistaken lust for love, and with Jeff she had mistaken love for lust. That was why she had not let Jeff make love to her again. She wept with shame and grief. She had not only squandered what she had been taught was the 'gift of virginity bestowed most richly upon women' but she had gloried in its loss. The pure beauty and pure glory in the Angelus bell, and in the choral music, had once made her faith soar, and taken her to a safer ecstasy. Now that same purity only emphasised her sin. Where she had faith, she now had guilt; it was guilt, not faith, that soared. Her pain was deserved. It was her comfort.

Fanny had forced her to face the truth of herself. For a long while she had been trying to deny doubt as she had denied her sensuality. But she could no longer deny that she had used her faith to lessen her sin, as if it were an aspirin to lessen pain.

She was no more innocent, now, than she ever would be again. Her virginity was lost and nothing, either in heaven or on earth, could ever restore it.

Her calling, her glorious sense of vocation, was fading. Though Theresa, of course, was unaware of it, she was reaching towards the same conclusion her father had come to so long ago, for very different reasons, when he had decided he no longer deserved to be a Jew.

For all her inner turmoil, the outer world was encroaching. General Smuts had lost the election, and at the university her fellow students spoke of the new regime as if they were all about to live under the Gestapo. Though forbidden by the convent to read novels, she read *Cry the Beloved Country*, which added to her doubts about her calling. She was beginning to want ordinary, physical human love, and beginning to feel less ashamed of it, too. When she understood that her unwavering ambition – to become a doctor – was the single hope that kept her going, she knew that her vocation lay outside the convent, and inside medicine.

But she had no money, and nothing in the world would have induced her to live with her mother or to ask for her help. After all, she had run away from her in the first place. In the end, she wrote to Max. She asked for help, and his advice. And when he responded by flying down to Cape Town she knew that her suspicions about him had been correct.

'You were too young, too immature to take that decision, to become a nun,' he said sorrowfully. 'There's no question about your not leaving.' He frowned suddenly. 'I don't know much about convents.' He sounded apologetic. 'Will it be difficult for you to leave?'

'I don't know whether I can afford to,' she said in a small voice.

'Leave that to me.'

'I'd hate my mother to know.'

'She won't.' He shook his head. 'We'll tell no one, not even Aunt Fanny.'

'I'll pay you back later, when I'm qualified.'

'Forget about that.'

'It's important to me, Uncle Max,' she said quietly. 'But I'd rather not stay here, in Cape Town, after I've left the convent. My mother — '

'I know. She's drinking too much. She's an alcoholic, I think.'

'So were her parents,' Theresa said sadly. 'But she refuses to admit it. That's why I'd prefer to be in Johannesburg, at Wits. I could live in the students' residence. It's a simple transfer — '

'Good girl, you've done your homework. I like that; it shows you're efficient.' He took out a piece of crumpled paper, made a few rough calculations with his blunt pencil, and said, 'I'm opening an account for you, in your name, at Barclays Bank. You'll have two thousand pounds capital, and a regular amount every month.'

'How can I thank you, Uncle Max?'

'By doing well.' He ran his eyes over her nun's habit. 'And by getting rid of that uniform,' he added crisply.

When she let it be known that her doubts had consolidated into a painful decision, and was finally released from her vows, she was sent on her way with mercy and prayers. And she knew that if she was not pure, she was at least honest.

Theresa's presence in Johannesburg lifted Max's mood; she was his personal responsibility, a responsibility he had undertaken gladly. She filled a void. According to their agreement Fanny was not told and their relationship was clandestine and therefore exciting. From time to time he would take her to lunch at one of the nearby student cafés, where there was little risk of seeing anyone he knew. She appeared to have adjusted, with the remarkable ease of the young, to what he called 'civvy life'. She wore no make-up, but her amber eyes sparkled. Her hair, shorn at the convent, had grown rapidly, and she now wore it in a single thick plait. They spoke French to one another, which unfailingly added to Max's sense of gallantry, and he always questioned her closely about her studies. She had become deeply interested in leprosy, she told him. She hoped to work at a leprosaurium when she qualified. Appalled, Max was wise enough not to attempt to dissuade her.

Though unaware of the cause, Fanny welcomed Max's return to what she called 'normal life'. He was still gloomy and morose, but then he always had been. At least he wasn't lying in bed under the covers all the time. He began to play poker again, but still insisted on token stakes only, and their lives became more bearable.

A year after the Nationalist Party came to power, in 1949, Fanny took Afrikaans lessons, and soon became fluent. She was not going to let a mere language stand in the way of government carpet contracts. She was also deeply involved in establishing several academic scholarships in Jeff's memory. Combined with her business activities, it gave her a sense of purpose. In a frantic attempt to obliterate thought, Fanny crammed her days to bursting point, and in time her overcrowded schedule became a habit which left little room for her daughter, Sarah. Fortunately, Sarah was a good and obedient child, who seldom got in her mother's way.

Besides the business, and the academic scholarships, Fanny chaired the fundraising committees for the Jeff Blum School for Handicapped Children. On the fifth anniversary of Jeff's death, in July 1952, the school was officially opened by the Mayor of Johannesburg. During those five years the Blums made three buying trips to England which, of course, included visits to Wyndham Carpets. Each time, Saffity was in America.

Saffity had decided to take a floor of offices in one of his buildings in the City to be his head office. Brooke gladly undertook the interior design of the place. So it was that his new offices were one of the first in the city to be influenced by the American style. Many eyebrows were raised; the City venerated its tradition of Victorian offices the way it venerated the monarchy. On the other hand, his offices still retained their sombre panelling, though silver inkwells gleamed on a modern chrome desk instead of a traditional wooden one. Brooke had gone further against tradition by adding the startling, tragic and timeless paintings of Rothko and Gottlieb, as well as Beliko's chrome lamps. She had, it seemed, an intuitive understanding of the City mentality; these artefacts showed that, though Saffity had been accepted by the

459

City, he was not trying to pass himself off as one of their number. He was a foreigner and therefore, as his first father-in-law had said, classless, but he was clearly not an imposter. It merely added to his style.

Brooke stayed on in London, toying with the idea of opening an art gallery. If she decided to commute between London and New York, the art gallery would be a means to an end. Whether he said so or not, Saffity needed her; as far as she was concerned, being needed by a man like Saffity was enough to make her feel not only privileged but blessed.

As he spent more and more time in London, and his reliance on Brooke increased, he realised that, filled as it was with Jem, Jane and his parents-in-law, Stanford Hall was an empty, lonely place. Absorbed with her horses, Jane seemed content enough. On very special occasions, such as dinners with the powerful and the influential, she would agree to act as hostess or guest. Saffity never allowed his ego to get in the way of his ambition, and while the convention whereby he and his wife were introduced – as Mr Saffity and Lady Jane Saffity – proclaimed his lesser birth, he was nevertheless the husband of an aristocrat.

When the state of Israel was declared, and he told Brooke about Jeff, he faced up to the fact that to all intents and purposes she was his wife. At that moment he decided to buy her the house on Eaton Place that was next door to his.

He replaced the simple two gold bangles he had flung at Brooke in Washington with new ones of exactly the same width and shape, but encrusted with diamonds. She wore them constantly.

One of the bonuses of living the double life, divided between Jane and Stanford Hall, and Brooke and Eaton Place, was that he now saw more of Colette and Myles. They spent a good deal of time in London; but best of all, Colette and Brooke were now firm friends. Brooke appeared to love Colette with the same intensity with which Jane hated her.

His days were hectic and triumphantly purposeful. He was on several powerful economic commissions and charity committees, where his reputation for generosity and the unexpectedly charming efficiency with which he worked made him something of a legend. Indeed, it was said that his laugh had forced a humorous response from the most gloomy of his associates.

In August 1951, almost three years after Brooke had entered his life again, Jane told him that she was pregnant. 'This *is* a surprise,' he said, trying to sound enthusiastic rather than shocked.

'Why?' asked Jane coldly. 'We do go to bed together. We still have the odd roll in the hay, don't we?'

Saffity let loose one of his laughs. 'Jem's five years old now. I'd given up hope.'

'Had you? It's years since you talked of having more children,' she said sweetly.

When Jane sounded sweet she was usually being mean. For the first time it occurred to him she might know about Brooke. His belief that she knew nothing about her was based on his certainty of her indifference to him. She never displayed the slightest curiosity in him or in his business.

'When?'

'In January,' Jane said. 'I'm just two months gone. I wanted to be absolutely sure before I told you.'

'Are you well?' he asked politely.

'Perfectly.'

'Good. Does Jem know?'

'Jemima will be told at the appropriate time.'

'I was thinking of spending January with you and Jem in St Moritz.'

'You'll have to go on your own, then.'

'I won't go at all,' Saffity said, freeing yet another laugh. 'I wouldn't dream of going to St Moritz without you.'

That night Saffity did not even try to sleep. Brooke would be hurt; devastated, in fact. How would he tell her? Had it not been for Jem, and his dreams of a knighthood, he would have done everything he could to get a divorce. He realised that without Brooke's deft and delicate understanding, and her tactful sympathy, his permanent balancing act would have long since collapsed.

He cursed himself not so much for his indecision in having failed to choose between the two women in his life, but for his decision to choose both.

For Jane's caustic reference to the odd roll in the hay had been all too accurate. To be sure, they only went to bed at her instigation, when she made one of her sudden, rare appearances in his bedroom wearing a sealskin coat, which she opened to disclose that she was wearing nothing else, and dropped to the floor. And

461

of course he responded, as much out of a need to keep the peace as out of desire. It was difficult not to respond – Jane was a beautiful woman, with a beautiful body, and silk-soft skin. Afterwards, more often than not, she would return without a word to the bedroom she had appropriated as her own. He reminded himself, yet again, that it was she who had left their bedroom.

What the hell, he had not been faithful to either of them. Yet he had been entirely faithful to Edwina.

Towards dawn, he reached a decision. He was in Brooke's hands. If she demanded that he give up Jane, and Jem, then he would do just that.

But Jane's announcement could not have come at a worse time. Saffity was in the midst of facing the kind of disappointment he thought he had put behind him all those years ago in Paris, when his banker had sold his shares without his permission. Then, he had misjudged not only his banker's character but, worse, his relationship with the man. Now he had made the same error with Sir Hugh Dalton, his former Minister at the Ministry of Economic Warfare. Suddenly, and without the courtesy of informing him, Sir Hugh had announced to the whole world that, as he intended to reduce the price of carpets, housewives should postpone their buying until then. In consequence Wyndham Carpets received scores of cancelled orders. One of the very few customers who informed him that no orders would be cancelled was Trans-Empire Carpets. Wyndham Carpets could weather this unnecessary storm, but major upheavals in his financial strategy would be required.

Six weeks went by before Saffity told Brooke about Jane's pregnancy. They were dining at the house he had bought her, the place where he now felt most at home. Brooke had turned into a master cook. She had discovered Saffity's latent weakness for Greek food and tonight she served a fragrant saffron rice pressed and folded in delicate vine leaves, baby marrows stuffed with veal, and spinach between tissue-thin sheets of pastry. She had also managed to import some jars of rose-petal jam which he said was almost as good as his mother's.

Saffity ate and laughed, and chewed as vigorously as he liked. Brooke amused him by telling him that the traditional tall white hats worn by the great French chefs originated in Greece when cooks in the Orthodox monasteries of the Middle Ages wore white hats because the monks wore black ones. She knew very little about his life in Greece except that it had been painful.

The velvet box containing the spectacular emerald and diamond necklace that had once been the Russian Princess Eugenia's was still in his trouser pocket. He ached to give it to her. He also hoped it would ameliorate the news that he had sired another child.

Over dessert, a *baclava* of honey and almonds and cinnamon she had prepared two days earlier, she said, 'Did you bring the photographs of Jem?'

Saffity took them out of his breast pocket.

'Isn't she beautiful?' he said.

'She looks like you, Saff,' Brooke said proudly. 'She's wearing the dress I chose, the velvet one with the sailor collar.'

'It is a beautiful dress,' he said softly.

'I just wish I could talk to her. Sometimes I dream she's sitting on my knee, do you know that? Anyway, at least I was able to see her, and real close, too, the day you took her to tea at the Ritz. Remember?'

'I remember,' he said, closing his eyes.

'I had the table next to you,' she continued dreamily, 'and we pretended we didn't know one another.' She became more animated. 'I guess we could have said we were neighbours. It would have been true!'

'Brooke, I've brought a little something for you. A surprise.' He took out the box and laid it on the table. 'It's unbelievable, but you're wearing exactly the right colour tonight. Go on, open it!'

She opened the box, and the delicately wrought necklace glittered in the candlelight.

'May I put it on for you?'

'Please. It's the most beautiful necklace I've ever seen. I don't deserve it.'

'You deserve it more than Princess Eugenia,' Saffity said dryly. 'It belonged to her, you know.'

'You shouldn't have — '

'I got a good deal,' Saffity laughed.

She stood up and he put it on, and together they went to the

463

mirror. She was wearing an emerald green jersey blouse, tapered blue and green velvet slacks and a lilac cummerbund, a Jacques Heim creation. 'It certainly is the right colour. You must have read my mind.' He laughed.

But his laugh trailed off. In the mirror Brooke saw his lips stiffen. She said, 'Something's worrying you, Saff, and it's not the business, I can tell. Come on, out with it!'

'How d'you know it's not the business?' he demanded.

'You're playing for time. I know you.'

'Let's go to bed.'

'I'd love to,' she said simply, leading him away from the mirror and into her softly lit drawing room filled with photographs of him. 'Only tell me.'

Saffity sat down and began to light a cigar. As usual, it appeared as if his entire mind was concentrating on making it draw perfectly. He puffed on it deeply, and said slowly, 'In January, Jane is going to have another baby.'

A silence fell.

'When did she tell you?'

'Six weeks ago,' he answered tonelessly.

'Why didn't you tell me then, Saff?'

'I couldn't bear to.'

Brooke nodded. 'You poor boy, what a horrible strain it must have been. I guess you thought I'd throw a real scene.'

'That, I must admit, never occurred to me. Jane throws scenes. You never do,' he said, sounding grateful.

'Are we going to carry on as before?'

Saffity had anticipated this question and gave his prepared answer. 'That depends on you,' he replied heavily. If she now insisted that he choose between Jane and herself, he would tell her that he had chosen her. Still hoping he could get away with keeping things the way they were, he held his breath as he waited for her to reply.

'You know what hurts me, Saff?' she asked, after a long while.

'What?' he said tonelessly, thinking: this is it, this is the ultimatum.

'That you thought you could soften the blow with this necklace. That you think so little of me; that you think I go in for bribes.'

'Oh, no, Brooke, no, you're wrong. I've been negotiating for that piece for weeks — '

'You're not a monogamous man, Saff,' she said sadly. 'Nor a

bigamous one either. You told me yourself that Camilla Wilson put her hand on your balls under the table at her dinner party — '

'So?'

'You didn't tell me you'd gone to bed with her. She very sweetly told me that herself.'

Brooke flung her head back, and then said, 'Let's go to bed!'

The next morning, as if nothing out of the ordinary had happened, she said, 'Now, that guest list for the British Legion dinner. I thought the American Ambassador would be rather pleased to meet your new Minister of Defence. Also, I met Lady Winnington recently, and we seemed to get on.'

'Godfrey Winnington!' Saffity exclaimed. 'Brooke, you're a genius. The Governor of the Bank of England – how do you do it? What would I do without you?'

From time to time Brooke gave large donations to the Disabled Veterans Society – this was the way she and Saffity managed to dine together in public. Since she now owned an art gallery, and represented the up-and-coming artist, Jake Piers-Anderson, whose works were concerned with war, her philanthropic connection with the British Legion, whose patron was a member of the Royal Family, seemed to be entirely fitting.

'And the Maharajah of Naipur would add a little colour, don't you agree?' she continued airily.

Saffity broke into genuine laughter. For Brooke, that sound was glorious and triumphant; she loved it and the man beyond all telling, and she was secure in her love for him.

Saffity did not love anyone except Jem.

But he needed Brooke.

He said, unexpectedly, 'You recall my dealings with the Starlight Company?'

'Sure. They were talking of taking over your chain.'

'We'll see who takes over who,' Saffity said, with a wink. 'Starlight has some assets in South Africa. I'm all for expanding. Export and expansion, that's what we need,' he went on thoughtfully. 'Will you come with me to South Africa, Brooke? I'm long overdue for a courtesy call on Trans-Empire Carpets.'

In answer, she rushed into his arms and rested her head against his strong, safe chest.

Above her head, out of sight, he scowled. He was asking for trouble . . . What if Brooke were to mention the Blums to Colette?

'We'll have three weeks together, my darling. I'm not going to include Colette and Myles.'

Against his chest, Brooke nodded her agreement.

'Say as little as you can about it, before we leave. And after we return, don't name any of the customers we meet.' He hugged her tighter. 'Have you got it? Are you with me?'

'Always.'

Every other Tuesday Colette and Brooke lunched at the Connaught. More than a habit, it was sacrosanct. They made a pact that, barring a major upset, nothing and no one would be allowed to intrude on their time together.

There was always so much to talk about. Then, when they left one another, each would remember something terribly important she had forgotten. They got on the telephone and laughed about it.

This Tuesday, as usual, several men and women in the restaurant let their eyes linger over them as they were shown to their table. In her plain white, flowing, circular-skirted dress, with its clinching black patent belt and her black cartwheel hat, Brooke was decidedly stunning, while Colette, in her immaculately cut tweeds and flattering, head-hugging hat, was decidedly chic.

Immediately they were seated they fell into animated conversation.

Each was interested in the other's work. When Saffity had set up his charitable foundation Colette had surprised everyone by offering to be its secretary. 'Unpaid, of course,' she had joked. 'Take me on trial, at least.' Both Myles and Saffity had agreed, though neither had expected her to be quite as efficient as she turned out to be. The Saffity Foundation supported several hospitals and schools and, thanks to Colette, was also heavily engaged in research in infertility. One of their doctors had recently published an important paper in the *Lancet*.

Discussing the research with Brooke, Colette concluded triumphantly, 'The Saffity Foundation could well be responsible for thousands of babies being born into the world!'

'I know of *one* baby expected in January,' Brooke answered attempting a weak smile.

'Yes, I know. Jane — '

'Jane,' Brooke echoed sadly.

'He needs you so much, Brooke!'

'I wonder?'

'You *know* he does!'

Brooke made no answer, but her eyes were suspiciously bright. She leaned over the table and took Colette's hand.

'I gave up trying to stop loving him too long ago.'

'You can never love a man like Saffity too much,' Colette said sadly. 'You can only love him more.'

'I know that.' Brooke's sigh turned into a groan. 'I guess I'm just one of those women who loves too much, anyway. Loving too much makes a woman like me greedy to love more. Oh, honey, what's the use?' she continued in her musical Southern drawl. 'When we took up together again I knew he was married, but I also knew that just being allowed to give my all, and then some, was a privilege.'

'You're better for him than — ' Colette broke off, and then went on hurriedly. 'What I mean is, *you* are good for him.'

'I know I want to be good for him,' Brooke said fervently, her expression alive with her passion, 'because he's my life.' Eyes glittering, she leaned closer towards Colette. 'There is no shortage of thinking time in my life. All the time he is with her, I think of nothing but him, of what he is to me.'

'He thinks you're a beautiful person. And he's right, of course.'

'Are you sure he said that? Exactly *that*?' Brooke asked urgently. 'When?'

'Many times,' Colette lied smoothly.

'Bless you for telling me that,' Brooke said happily. 'I'm lucky to have a friend like you.'

Early in September 1952 came Saffity's letter with the news that he was planning to visit South Africa in November. The Blums went into a flurry of activity. They redecorated the guest room, and Fanny flew down to Muizenberg to redecorate the entire house. Saffity would be sure to want to spend some time at the most glorious Cape in all the world. They would discuss business, too. For once and for all the question of those voteless B shares would be resolved. They planned a party for Saffity, their first real party since Jeff had died. Two orchestras were booked, and invitations to two hundred and fifty guests went out. There were no refusals.

A fortnight before Saffity was scheduled to arrive, Fanny and Max inspected the guest room and pronounced it perfect. New velvet hangers matched the new Wyndham cobalt-blue carpet; even the soap in the bathroom was as close to cobalt-blue as they could manage. They were both admiring the room when the newly installed telephone rang. Fanny answered it.

'Madame Fanny, it's Sarie, Miss Mireille's girl. I'm phoning you from Cape Town.' Sarie, Piet's mother, had been at the Rutherford Estate for more than thirty years, yet she still called herself a girl. Fanny held the phone away from her ear as Sarie's voice filled the room.

'What's the matter, Sarie?'

'It's Miss Mireille. There's been a fight. She's been fighting terrible with that man.'

'What man? What are you talking about?'

'Boss Michael. He's gone, Miss Fanny.'

'Where's your madam?'

'The ambulance take her to the hospital.' Sarie's voice broke. 'It's Boss Michael, he's taken all our madam's money. We got no wages, Miss Fanny.'

At that point Max grabbed the phone from Fanny. 'Have none of you been paid your wages?' he asked quietly.

Sarie sobbed into the phone.

'Try not to cry, Sarie. You'll all get paid. Why did Miss Mireille fight with Boss Michael? Is Boss Michael living in the house?'

'He's living in the house, Master Max. He take our madam's money. He sell everything, so they fight.'

'I'll take the aeroplane and come to Cape Town tomorrow, Sarie. Don't worry,' Max said, speaking deliberately simply.

He hung up.

'She's a drunk,' Fanny said contemptuously. 'Mireille's nothing but a drunk. What's all this about a man? Did you know she had a man?'

'No.'

'Mireille is Theresa's responsibility.'

'I know that. But Mireille and I go back a long way, as you well know. She's in trouble and I'm going to help her.'

'Who says you shouldn't?' Fanny said quickly. 'She sounds as if she's in big trouble to me. She must be at Groote Schuur Hospital. Isn't Theresa there?'

'How could Mireille have got through so much money?' Max asked, evading the question.

'Who knows? I thought she wasn't interested in men. I'll tell you one thing — '

'What?'

'This man Michael is younger than she is. She's probably been keeping him in a style to which he was not accustomed.'

'Mireille?' Max grunted. 'Never.'

'Older women go overboard for young men, you know.'

'I know,' Max said wretchedly. 'I know.'

He had not dreamed about Colette for years, but that night he woke screaming. Fanny spoke soothingly but asked no questions.

Mireille's face was bruised and swollen and her broken arm in plaster. She was in a drugged sleep. For a while Max stood at the bottom of her bed, staring disbelievingly at her, shaking his head.

A nurse came to check on her blood pressure and woke her. 'Mireille?' Max said gently.

Tears drizzled down Mireille's face. 'Who told you?' she asked.

'Sarie.'

'I've lost all my money,' she whimpered. 'It's gone. He took it all.'

'That's impossible,' Max said, drawing up a chair.

'I thought it was impossible, too,' Mireille wailed.

Over the next few hours the story emerged bit by bit.

Eighteen months ago she had met Michael Billingsworth in a bar. He was a handsome Englishman, on holiday at the Cape and interested in vineyards. He had mentioned a small vineyard in France, whose name Mireille recognised, and confided that it belonged to his uncle. She did not tell him, then, about the Rutherford Estate, but he invited her to join him at dinner, which was wonderful. He had impeccable manners. It was all harmless, she thought, but good; she had long forgotten how pleasant it could be to have dinner *á deux* with a man. There had been dancing at the restaurant, slow, cheek-to-cheek dancing. It was not in the least sensual, but comfortable. Comforting, too even though she'd been wearing the wrong sort of dress. They had quite a lot to drink but he held his liquor well, and when he offered to drive her home she accepted.

He drove very slowly, steering with one hand while his other hand held hers. He told her she had blazing tiger's eyes.

She had thought that without a womb she had no need of

love any more, but he promised to show her how wrong she was. And perhaps it was because she had been in a desert for so long, but whatever it was, he was a miracle in bed, a wonderful lover, as wonderful as Saffarty.

He was only twenty-five, with a powerful, beautiful body, and he knew so much about vineyards, he could easily put her farm right. It was a smaller vineyard by then; she had sold more than she had realised. Michael saw to everything.

At the beginning she spent her time making the best of herself, trying to make herself beautiful for him. She had masseurs and hairdressers coming to the estate. He was so kind and above all so helpful. But it was awkward, sometimes, waiting for her signature; it held things up. In the end she agreed that giving him her power of attorney made sound business sense. She simply signed a standard, printed form. She had assumed that if it had been a seriously important form she would have had to go to a lawyer. In any case, she felt safe with him. She trusted him. He was certain he would get the farm going again, and as soon as he had done that, he was going to take her to England, where they would stay at his parents' stately home, the house that was in his photographs.

After about nine months he began to get nasty and abusive, and she began to drink more and more, because of the humiliating way she now had to beg him to make love to her. This was not the first time he had beaten her up, only the first time he'd put her in hospital.

He took over the running of the house, and paid the servants – he had to, because she was drunk most of the time.

And then the day before yesterday – she could not be sure exactly when it was – she discovered the servants hadn't been paid for two months. Sarie made her phone the bank and they told her she was in overdraft. She did the first thing that came into her head: she hid his passport and then confronted him with what she knew. He went crazy. When he couldn't find his passport he beat its whereabouts out of her and then left.

Max knew the rest.

He had listened quietly, with mounting horror. He told her not to worry, and said he would see the bank manager, but he knew it was hopeless. It took him just a few moments to have his worst suspicions confirmed, that Mireille had dissipated everything. In the three years since he'd last visited Mireille, the Rutherford Estate of four hundred acres had shrunk to a shabby house and an overgrown garden. Only two devoted servants had remained, Sarie and Lizzie. Max paid them, and left them enough cash for at least two months' food. Then he undertook to pay Mireille's fees at a private nursing home. He told Sarie he'd be back in a month, by which time the important visitor he was expecting from overseas would have left.

Mireille was bankrupt. He wondered how Theresa would take it. She was writing her end-of-year exams; next year she would be only one year away from her final year at medical school. She had confided in him her ambitions for a high grade in pathology. Max decided it would be not only pointless but harmful to tell her about her mother now.

'So you're going to keep Mireille,' Fanny said furiously, four days later.

'From what the doctors tell me, it won't be for long.'

'Your friend will be here soon. Why can't he chip in?'

'Saffity?' Max exploded, horrified, 'Listen to me, Fanny! Don't mention any of this to him!'

'I don't see why not,' Fanny insisted stubbornly. She had been waiting too long to get to the bottom of Saffity and Mireille and Max, she was determined to extract the most from this moment. She added casually, 'For old times' sake, Saffity would be happy to help, I'm sure.'

'I'm warning you, Fanny, don't breathe a word of this to Saffity.'

'Why not?'

'He wouldn't like it.'

'So? I don't like the B shares.'

'Shut up, Fanny. Shut up!' Max said furiously. He dropped his voice dramatically. 'Shut up and *listen*! Do you want your husband to go to prison?'

'Don't talk rubbish.'

'You heard what I said. Answer me!'

His desperate tone made Fanny take him seriously. 'Are you mad? Of course I don't want my husband to go to prison!'

'In that case you won't antagonise Saffity.'

She clucked impatiently. 'But it's twenty-four years since Saffity helped you to come to South Africa. Twenty-four years, Max! Whatever you did, whatever he has on you, can't be such a crime you'd still go to prison twenty-four years later. You didn't commit a murder, you know.'

Max went white. 'You make me sick, Fanny,' he yelled. 'Leave the B shares to me. Do you understand that, Fanny? Leave the B shares to me!'

'I understand,' she answered quickly. To change the subject, she said, 'Do you think Saffity will bring his wife?'

Naturally enough, Fanny and Max were at Jan Smuts Airport to welcome Saffity. Hendrik Uys, a customer whom Fanny allowed to 'buy wholesale' was an important official at the airport, and he in turn alowed the Blums onto the tarmac to greet him. They had wanted Saffity to receive VIP treatment for a variety of reasons, not least to show him Max Blum had made quite a name for himself in Johannesburg.

This part of their meticulous planning went off successfully.

But they were quite unprepared for what followed.

First, Saffity calmly introduced them to Brooke, and, then, as if *that* hadn't been enough of a shock, he just as calmly declined their invitation to stay at Oak Lodge; two suites had been reserved for them at the Carlton Hotel. Worse ensued. The Blums had their Cadillac and driver, of course, but there was not enough room for the luggage, which had to be sent on by taxi. In Johannesburg anyway, no one who had any self-respect ever took a taxi. The Blums protested that there was more than enough room for everyone at Oak Lodge, but to no avail. However, Saffity assured them that he and his party would be delighted to dine with the Blums that night.

'You can never predict what that man will do,' Max said to Fanny as they left Saffity at the Carlton.

'I told you that five years ago,' Fanny snapped. 'He's got a nerve bringing his mistress with him. Who does he think we are?'

'That's probably why he's not staying with us,' Max said reasonably. 'Out of respect for you.' He shook his head wonderingly. 'Brooke is a good-looking woman, isn't she?'

Fanny shrugged. 'She's too skinny,' she said scathingly. 'Like a skeleton.'

Max stopped himself from saying that if perfectly proportioned figure was like a skeleton, it must be the sexiest looking skeleton he had ever seen. Saffity's women were always stunning – he certainly knew how to pick them.

The dinner went well – Saffity and Max seemed to laugh in unison. The two waiters, in their dazzling white and scarlet sashes, gave a magnificent performance, and even fulfilled Fanny's most stringent requirements. Every now and then Saffity said, 'Very impressive, Max. Very impressive. You've done well for yourself.'

Max glowed.

Later, over coffee and cigars, Saffity exclaimed over Sarah's photograph and talked about his Jem. Her photograph was shown around, and Fanny could not help noticing the pride and the tenderness in Brooke's voice whenever she spoke of the child.

'I suppose you'll soon be teaching her to fly,' Fanny said slyly to her.

'We don't go in for flying much any more, I guess,' Brooke answered faintly.

'Anyone can see how much you love her,' Fanny pressed on. 'You and she must be very good friends.'

'I'm crazy about the kid,' Brooke said warmly.

'I'm sure she's crazy about you, too.'

'She doesn't know who I am,' Brooke said sadly, with a brave smile. 'She – that is – we haven't met.'

'I see. I'm sorry, I was tactless. I'm sorry,' Fanny floundered.

'Don't apologise; it's an awkward situation. Like we say, it's one of those things. Saff and I were very close before he married Jane, and then I got remarried and divorced again.' Her brave smile returned. 'Saff's wife is expecting a baby in January.'

'Oh,' Fanny said, at a loss for words. The people *she* knew did not go in for this sort of thing.

'Saff's my whole life,' Brooke said simply.

There was a silence.

How right Saffity had been to warn her about Fanny, Brooke thought. 'Fanny's your original busybody,' Saffity had said. 'Don't mention Colette to her. I'd rather she didn't know my business. As a matter of fact, I'd prefer it if you didn't mention the Blums to Colette, either. I did not ask them to join us because I didn't want to share you.'

'I'm glad you told me, Saff,' she'd replied. 'I often talk about Colette.'

'That's one of the reasons I love you.'

'I hope you will all come to Trans-Empire Carpets with Saffity tomorrow morning,' Fanny said breaking the silence. 'We have wanted Saffity to see it for so long. Tomorrow night we're planning to take you to Ciro's night club. It has excellent food, and is magnificently decorated,' Fanny said, rólling her eyes. 'Pleated satin, oyster pink walls and ceiling. You'll think you're in Paris.'

'It's very kind of you, Fanny,' Brooke began, 'but — '

'No buts. It's all arranged.'

'I think Saff's dining with Sir Ernest Oppenheimer tomorrow night.' She bit her nails as she called out, 'Saff, are we seeing Sir Ernest tomorrow night?'

'We are,' Saffity answered and continued his conversation with Max.

'Do you know Sir Ernest?' Max asked astonished.

'We've done some business together. He's a nice chap. We usually see one another when he comes to London. Why?'

'I didn't know you knew him.'

'There's a lot you don't know about me, Max!' Saffity said, laughing.

A tiny shiver touched Fanny's spine. Saffity was way ahead of them, was mixing with the *crème de la crème* of Johannesburg, even though he was a stranger to the town. Yes, Saffity certainly was unpredictable. She had not as much as hinted, yet he had spontaneously given a huge donation to the Jeff Blum School for handicapped children. Now she leaned forward to listen to him, hanging on every word he said, charmed and moved by the warmth and good fellowship that radiated from him. She felt herself coming alive, felt her lips curve in a perpetual smile.

The Blums did not see as much of Saffity over the next few days as they had hoped. Of course he came to the shop, and told them again and again how vastly impressed he was. He had not expected it to be anything like as large. He was certain it was the biggest in Africa, and probably ranked among the largest carpet wholesalers in the world. Naturally Trans-Empire Carpets needed to have a varied selection, but he wished they hadn't helped put his Belgian, Italian and German competitors quite so firmly on the market. In exchange for a sizable order, Wyndham Carpets had one or two special lines to offer.

'It make me nervous seeing my competitors so well represented in the very company I helped found,' he concluded with a chuckle.

Fairly bursting with pride, Max found the courage to broach the subject of the voteless B shares.

'But you're doing so well,' Saffity answered mildly. 'Looms are running all over Europe because of you and Fanny. You don't want to rock the boat, do you?'

'No.'

'Good. My companies are expanding all the time.' He paused significantly. 'I can't give you the details yet, but I may be doing a deal over here — '

'Who with? Oppenheimer?'

'If I pull it off, I'll let you in. That's how I operate with my trusted friends.'

A moment earlier Max had been proud of himself; now he was not so sure. Even mentioning those B shares had been a mistake. After all, Saffity was a powerful industrialist, and he was only a merchant who also happened to own some property. Who knew what Fanny's nagging might cost him?

Two days later, on the morning of the party the Blums were giving, Saffity decided on a surprise visit to Max. Trans-Empire Carpets was in easy walking distance from the Carlton Hotel. It occurred to him – as he took in the shapely, tanned stockingless and obviously youthful legs just ahead that Max had certainly landed in the perfect climate.

Saffity always had a weakness for a woman's legs. If he had not been attending to those anonymous legs so carefully he might have been able to avoid the motorbike that knocked him down.

A crowd collected around him as he lay untidily on the pedestrian crossing. Beside him, his silver-tipped cane sparkled in the sunlight. 'He's dead, I think,' a passer-by said.

'He wasn't looking where he was going. He walked straight into the street,' the weeping motorcyclist said again and again.

'He's breathing, he's just unconscious. Call an ambulance.'

Moments later Saffity was lifted into the ambulance, and taken to the casualty ward of the Johannesburg General Hospital. The X-Ray of his head showed no brain damage, and the young intern's diagnosis of concussion was confirmed by the physician in charge.

'Find any identification?' the intern asked.

'We haven't a clue who he is,' the nurse said apologetically. 'He was wearing a gold chain with a gold key round his neck. We've already checked it, but found no engraving of his name.'

'We'll get an enquiry for him soon enough.'

'We may not, doctor. I don't think he lives here in Johannesburg. He was wearing a suit with a London label,' the nurse said eagerly.

'This isn't his first accident, that's for sure,' the doctor said blandly. 'He's been patched up before, by a highly competent plastic surgeon.' The doctor consulted his notes, scribbled an addition, and said, 'Call me when he comes round. Watch him carefully.'

About three-quarters of an hour later Saffity groaned and shortly afterwards began to mumble. The nurse listened carefully, and then called the doctor. 'He's talking in a foreign language,' she said.

'*Sales Boches*,' Saffity said. '*Encore! Sales Boches.*'

'*Encore*. That's French, isn't it?' the doctor said. 'Anyone here speak French?' he called out. 'What about the students? Ask one of the students.'

Several students were clustered around the senior physician, who was demonstrating a complicated case.

'Sorry to interrupt, sir,' the nurse said nervously. 'Dr Robson sent me to ask if anyone speaks French. That concussion case is speaking French.'

The senior physician sighed impatiently. 'I don't know who speaks French. All my students have been speaking rubbish.' He peered over his glasses. 'Do any of you speak French?'

'I do,' Theresa said. 'It's my mother-tongue.'

'Well, go along then,' the senior physician ordered. 'You're one of those on Professor Weiss' list to watch him operate, but you'll have to sacrifice that, I'm afraid. Stay with the patient as long as you have to.'

'*Parlez-vous français, monsieur?*' Theresa began.

Saffity suddenly burst into a lengthy tirade against the Germans who had killed his best friend, Drew, and then, just as suddenly, lapsed into Ladino – a language that was unintelligible to Theresa. This continued for almost an hour. Again and again Theresa asked his name and where he lived. Saffity seemed unable to register. Theresa decided to tell him where he was, and then to question him. She repeated several times, '*Vous êtes à Johannesburg, monsieur. Ou restez-vous à Johannesburg?*'

At last Saffity answered faintly, 'Johannesburg, Carlton.'

'*Vous êtes à l'Hôtel Carlton ici à Johannesburg, monsieur?*'

'*Mais oui,*' Saffity said feebly. 'Carlton.'

'He's staying at the Carlton Hotel,' Theresa said to the nurse. 'Is it OK if I go now? I'm on Prof Weiss' list.'

A nurse telephoned the hotel at once. Just as the manager was confirming that he did indeed have a guest with an amber and silver cane Saffity recovered full consciousness. He wanted to be discharged at once, but the doctors insisted he remain overnight for observation.

The Blums were compelled to go ahead with the party, but as far as they were concerned the evening was ruined. Fanny could have wept; she had not realised how keenly she had been looking forward to showing Saffity what sort of hostess she was.

A day later Saffity and Brooke were on the plane to London. As the plane took off he said, 'Jesus! I couldn't wait to get out of there!'

'But the Blums were so kind,' Brooke protested. 'Max really took me by surprise.' She added enthusiastically, 'I'd no idea he was so handsome. He's got such an intelligent, sensitive look; he reminds me of an artist.' She corrected herself, 'No, not an artist, more like a philosopher or a professor.'

'But he's losing his hair — '

'That makes you focus on his eyes. He's got slanting eyes. I guess he comes from one of those Slavic countries.'

'If you say so,' Saffity said irritably.

'Anyway it was real, warm Southern hospitality,' Brooke said, quickly changing the subject.

'I know what you mean,' Saffity responded. 'But the country gave me the creeps. Small time, small town – there are four times as many people in London as there are whites in South Africa. The blacks are locked up, so you can't count them.'

'Locked up?' Brooke interrupted.

'Crushed. Squashed. Locked up. Call it what you will. It's similar, but worse than where you come from in Atlanta, Georgia. The whites look on the blacks as a threat, I'll grant you that. But apartheid keeps them from competing. The blacks outnumber the whites of course, but they pay for their numbers by not being able to pit a fraction of their team against the competition. It's not even unfair competition – it's *no* competition. Where's the challenge in that? It's the able-bodied running against the disabled. No competition – just the right place for the likes of Max Blum.' He altered his tone from contempt to admiration. 'Still, I've got to admit he landed on his feet out there. He's made it. He let it slip that he owns the Trans-Empire Carpet building himself. I never suspected he was my landlord.'

'You mean you didn't know?' Brooke asked.

'No, I didn't know,' said Saffity, grinning. 'Protea Properties owns the building, and Max owns Protea Properties. Got it?' He whistled through his teeth in admiration. 'Without me Max Blum would be nowhere,' he continued. 'He owns the premises of our company, he doesn't tell me about that for years, and then he whines about his B shares.' He laughed suddenly. 'He's not cheating me. His balance sheets are impeccable. Wyndham Carpets makes a profit on the goods it sells him as well as on the goods he sells.' He shook his head. 'But Max certainly pulled the wool over my eyes.' He gave a broad wink. 'Well, he's stuck with his B shares, which means that he can't sell the company without my consent. And that's the main thing.'

'No, Saff, you're wrong,' Brooke interrupted forcefully. 'The main thing is that you weren't seriously injured when you were knocked down.'

'True,' he agreed. 'True.' He shut his eyes, and they were both silent for a while. Then he said dreamily, 'There was a girl in the hospital – a nurse, or a medical student – I'm not sure, I don't know what she was. There was something extraordinarily familiar about her.'

'Was she the one who spoke French?'

'Yes, that's right. She's the one who was telling me where I was.'

'I guess it was the language that was familiar.'

'I suppose so,' he said thoughtfully. 'I remember her better now. She had lovely eyes. Amber eyes.'

'Like yours, Saff,' Brooke said adoringly. 'You have lovely amber eyes.'

'So, Jane, you're telling me you're not pregnant, you only thought you were,' Saffity said suspiciously. 'You, a nurse, made a mistake like that?'

'It was not a mistake, it was a medical condition known as a phantom pregnancy,' Jane said imperiously. 'I missed three periods, my tummy was swollen and my breasts ached. Classic symptoms.'

Classic symptoms of a mean trick, Saffity thought. 'Phantom pregnancy, huh?'

'Why that should surprise you so much is beyond me, Saffity. We live with phantoms in this house, don't we? Your darling Edwina's phantom and I have lived together in this house for years. So don't try to patronise *me*!'

'There are forty-eight rooms in the house — '

'Her clothes are still in the cupboards. Her huge wooden rocking horse that she had when she was four years old is still there. You haven't been in those rooms for years!'

Two weeks had passed since Saffity had returned from South Africa, and he and Jane were sitting in his library, the only other part of the house he had refused to have redecorated. The angry sparks in Jane's eyes, and her bold superior manner, reminded him of the very first night he had taken her to dinner. She had always known about Edwina's place in his life – from the outset he had been at pains not to deceive her about that – but it did not make the fact of Edwina any easier for her to live with. Nor was this the first time Jane had brought Edwina, as his weakest point, into an argument. He said slowly, 'I've been thinking. You know so much about horses; has it never occurred to you to have a first-class racehorse? Does the name Blue Hugh mean anything to you?'

'Of course it does. Blue Hugh won the Derby.'

'But you must choose your own horse for yourself. Let me know when you've made up your mind.'

Jane's triumphant smile told him he had secured Edwina's apartment for at least two more years. He recalled the rose jam he had given Madame Namias the day after he arrived in Paris almost thirty years earlier.

When he told Brooke of the deal he'd done with Jane, she congratulated him. Neither Brooke nor Saffity denied that the phantom pregnancy had come as a relief to both of them. Still, far from bringing pressure for a divorce, Brooke joked, 'I'd rather be a mistress than a wife, Saff.' Then, more seriously, she added, 'We see each other when we want to. We're good friends, good neighbours and very good lovers.'

And perhaps inevitably, it was all too easy for Saffity to go along with her. Through her his life had struck the perfect balance.

When Saffity left Johannesburg, cutting his stay short, Max experienced an unexpected and confusing sense of loneliness. He had been drawn once again into a charmed circle of warmth and excitement, yet he had been firmly excluded from Saffity's important business associates, like the Oppenheimers. Obviously Max Blum was not good enough for Saffity's friends. His old, familiar feeling of impotence weighed heavily in his chest, and his ulcer began to give him hell again. Saffity had said nothing more about that mysterious South African deal of his. Max tried to convince himself that it would have been poor tactics to press for more details, but he knew that the truth was he had been too nervous, and too cowardly, to ask. Saffity had an uncannily accurate knack of unearthing and then highlighting his weaknesses, and Max hated him for it.

He and Saffity were more or less the same age, yet he felt he looked more like twenty years older. Theresa had often told him how distinguished he looked, now that his hair was thinning and beginning to go grey, but that was because she had never seen Saffity's mop that gleamed like burnished silver. Theresa! Max closed his eyes, as he always did when he thought of her. She was growing more and more beautiful; those oval, amber eyes of hers had become as soft and as tempting as honey. She was changing; no, she *had* changed. Had she become interested, at last, in men? It was only natural, yet he dreaded the inevitable the way he dreaded his own death . . .

He looked on his monthly lunches with Theresa almost as if he were on an illicit date with an ardent mistress. At the East India Restaurant, where they ate curry off plain china on a grubby white tablecloth, he told her about the Rutherford Estate. Her eyes turned from soft honey to hard amber. 'We'll have to sell everything, even the furniture, I'm afraid,' he concluded.

'Will there be anything left?'

'I'm working on it,' Max said vaguely. 'I've thought of buying what's left of the place myself. Your mother will have to go into liquidation, you see.'

'Will there be enough for her to stay on at the nursing home?'

'I don't think so.'

'I see,' Theresa said anxiously, fidgeting with the stethoscope that peeped out of the pocket of her white laboratory coat.

'Leave it to me, my dear.'

Theresa touched his hand briefly. 'Oh, Uncle Max,' she whispered, 'what would I do without you?'

'I knew you before you were born,' he said sadly. 'Leave everything to me. Now tell me about medical school.'

'Surgery,' she said at once. 'I've gone mad about surgery, there are such advances in surgical technique. And I was lucky enough to get on Professor Weiss' list.'

'Professor Weiss?'

'He's one of the greatest living surgeons. D'you know, surgeons come from all over the world just to observe him. I almost missed a session with him the other day. I nearly died.'

'You nearly died?' Max repeated. He loved her youthful exaggerations. But thank God she appeared to have got over her enthusiasm for leprosy. Meanwhile, his hand still burned from her light touch.

'You think I'm exaggerating, I know you do,' Theresa said, reading his mind. 'No one misses a session with Prof Weiss! But I had to be an interpreter for an accident patient who didn't speak English, only French. Anyway, I learned something important from that patient.'

'What did you learn that was so important?' Max said indulgently.

'Are you carrying any identification with you? If you were knocked down, would anyone know who you were?'

'Sometimes I have a business card — '

'But not always. Promise me you will never, never go without an easily recognisable form of identification. Go on, promise me!'

'I promise. Why? What happened?'

'No one knew who he was. No one had a clue. He was brought into the casualty ward and all he had with him was a walking stick. There was no name anywhere. He was wearing a neck chain with a gold key instead of a name tag.' She stopped abruptly. 'Are you all right, Uncle Max? You look pale.'

'I'm fine,' Max said with an effort. Saffity had shown him the gold key when he had told him how it had saved his life.

Theresa had seen Saffity, the man she did not know to be her own father . . .

He touched his head. Thoughts jammed about his brain. He remembered Saffity telling him about a beautiful student. 'I didn't know where I was, or who I was. My head ached,' Saffity had said. 'But I fancied that girl like crazy.'

'Anyway,' Theresa continued, 'the patient finally said he was staying at the Carlton, so I rushed off to watch Prof Weiss operate.' Now she was watching Max carefully. Suddenly she put her fingers firmly on his wrist, and took his pulse. 'It's very rapid, your pulse. I suppose I frightened you with all that talk about identification tags.' She released his wrist and said, 'Let's talk about other things.'

Max nodded, too dizzy to speak.

'I think you should go home to rest,' she said anxiously. 'Your face has gone white.'

'I do feel a bit dizzy,' he admitted.

She walked with him to his white Cadillac. 'No driver?' she asked.

'Not today,' he answered quickly. A driver would have spoiled the privacy. When he had a date with Theresa, he never took a driver.

'You look better now,' she pronounced. 'You remind me of Prof Weiss. He's also distinguished-looking. Much older than you of course, but the same sort of looks.'

Driving home, Max's mind was concentrated on the image of Theresa and Saffity meeting face to face in a hospital ward, in absolute ignorance of their unique blood-tie. The banal fact that a child can only be fathered by one man struck him suddenly, and as if for the first time.

At that moment he reached the traffic lights at the end of the wide and graciously curved Jan Smuts Avenue and only just managed to avoid running over a small barefoot Zulu picannin selling newspapers.

The screech of his own brakes shocked him out of his reverie. He pulled off the road and rested his head on the steering wheel. After a while he switched on the radio and drove home.

Two years later, on an early spring day in March 1954, Max stared hard at the white steps leading up to the main block of the University of the Witwatersrand. The wind blew the gold sands from the nearby mine dumps, and in sunlight the steps glinted with gold powder. His gaze was concentrated on the steps, partly because the gold dust symbolised his own undreamed of prosperity, and partly because his emotions threatened to run riot. Jeff should have been graduating as a doctor today. Instead it was Theresa's graduation day, and he had not been able to resist attending. Nor did he have the heart to let her down. After all, the poor kid had no one. Her mother was in a home, as lost to the world as she was to her daughter.

He had arrived early and was startled by Theresa's touch on his arm. 'I knew you'd be here, Uncle Max,' she said simply.

'Aunt Fanny couldn't make it. Something came up at the last minute,' he said apologetically.

'I didn't expect her,' she said frankly. 'I understand how she feels about Jeff.' She added softly, 'You too, Uncle Max.'

'Dr Theresa Rutherford,' Max answered. 'I'm proud to be here, and I'm proud of you. I had a shock this morning, but I doubt you can help.' He smiled sadly. 'I'm losing my hair. I caught a glimpse of the back of my head, and *voila!* I saw I was going bald.'

'Listen, old man,' she teased him, 'Professor Weiss will be here. I want you to meet him,' she said urgently. 'You know I want to specialise in surgery.'

They went into the hall, where Max took his seat among the parents and Theresa sat with the students. He watched the solemn procession of professors in their full academic regalia without really seeing it. As so often, when he was with Theresa, he thought of Saffity. Was it not a travesty, that Saffity was unaware of his own daughter's existence, especially at a moment like this?

At last her name was called. *Summa cum laude!* She had been too modest to tell him. He clapped crazily, and tears coursed down his cheeks.

'Your daughter?' the woman beside him beamed.

'No,' he said abruptly. He stopped clapping and wiped his eyes furiously. Considering the way he felt about her, thank God he was *not* her father.

Afterwards, at the garden party in the stifling hot marquee, Theresa seemed anxious. She introduced Max to her friends, and the parents of her friends, but her eyes roved restlessly, looking for the Professor.

Eventually, Max said, 'Don't worry if he's not here. We'll invite him to lunch, if you like, and I'll meet him then.'

'Professor Weiss never socialises,' Theresa said. 'When he's not with patients, or teaching, he's writing scientific papers. He's probably had more papers published than — '

'Is he married? Does he have a family?' Max interrupted rudely. She's in love with the man, he thought suddenly. He felt sick with jealousy and shame.

'Yes, he is married,' Theresa answered. 'Look, there he is. Can't you see him? There's a woman over there kissing his hand. Must be a grateful patient. Come on,' she said, grabbing Max's hand and pulling him. 'I'll take you to him.'

The Professor shook Max's hand. 'Theresa is a brilliant student,' he said warmly. He turned to her. 'Well, my dear, congratulations. Remember what Sir William Osler said?'

'Do the day's work well, and think not of the morrow,' Theresa recited at once.

To Max, Professor Weiss said, 'You will surely agree, Mr Blum, that Osler had the best formula for living.' And without waiting for a reply he ambled away. Max sized him up at once. He was at least sixty. Theresa couldn't possibly be in love with him, he was almost completely bald. Yet even in their brief exchange Max had heard a tender note in their voices.

'I wanted you to meet him for so long,' Theresa said softly. 'He's a genius, you know.' She handed Max a slice of cake. 'Ah, here are two chairs,' she said triumphantly. 'We can sit down. There's something I want to ask you. Now, Uncle Max, do you know anything about my real father?' she asked urgently.

Max dropped his plate.

'I've given you a shock, I'm sorry. It's just that my mother has always refused to discuss him. She used to go crazy if I mentioned it.' She gave a long shuddering sigh. 'Sarie told me — '

'When did you see Sarie?'

'I saw her at the Ridge Convalescent Home. She visits Mom, you know — ' her voice trailed off. 'Sarie told me I was born on the entrance hall floor. She told me my mother went to the Rutherford Estate to be a housekeeper. Is that true?'

'Quite true,' he answered steadily.

'But my father? My real father? Can you tell me anything about him? *Anything at all?*' she asked desperately. 'Lately, I've needed to know — ' She broke off. 'You see, Uncle Max, it might help me — '

Max was silent.

At last he said, 'I don't know anything.'

'Why did you take so long to say that?' she demanded.

'Because I wished there was something I could tell you,' he said simply.

At the end of that afternoon, as Theresa raced up the carpetless stairs to meet Fritz Weiss, she was still planning exactly how she would discuss Max Blum's medical condition with him.

'I'm worried about Max Blum,' she said, at once, and in her most professional tones. 'He had an irregular pulse, and vaso-constriction — '

'So, he was pale. Any sweating?' Fritz asked.

'No.'

'There's nothing to worry about. His pulse went crazy because you touched him. You drive men crazy, Theresa.'

He smiled his colluding smile. At the sight of it, as always, her heart lurched.

Then he kissed her, and she forgot all about Max.

Later, during the ten-minute sleep that Fritz insisted on taking she thought again how it was always like that, she forgot everything when she was with him. Though he lay asleep right beside her, she felt exactly the same as when she was not with him, that she had no meaning in his life. But her entire life was under his direction. The only advantage she could see in her insane love was that it spurred her on to study harder. Little else about her seemed to impress him.

The most personal thing he had ever said to her was that she drove men mad.

He kept her on a tightrope of confusion and uncertainty. For example, she never knew whether he would turn up for their rendezvous in bed, and when he did he was often late. Yet he had the gift of making her feel that when they were making love nothing else in the world mattered to either of them.

But when she was not with him, the difference in their ages made it impossible for her to understand him. So how could she even guess how he felt about her? On the other hand there was no uncertainty about how Max Blum felt, so the generation difference was hardly a telling factor.

It had all begun when she told him she had once been a nun. His immediate reaction had been utterly unpredictable, and entirely different from that of any man she had ever known. He had said, in a voice that managed to be musical and dispassionate at the same time, 'A long time ago I seduced a nun in a box at the Albert Hall. It was during Beethoven's Fifth. I remember it well.'

Not long after that, though to her constant bewilderment, she and Fritz became lovers. It made no difference whether his story about the Albert Hall was true or not. It was the coolness of his reaction to the fact that she had once been a nun that had seduced her. She told him that she and Sarie's son Piet had been lovers. 'Physical attraction and sexual chemistry are normal,' he had declared. 'And if colour is an element of chemistry, that is normal, too.'

He stirred, and immediately grabbed his watch from the bedside table. He leapt off the bed, saying, 'It's late.'

While they were dressing he said unexpectedly, 'I suppose you flirt a bit with old Blum sometimes?'

'Sometimes.'

'Good girl,' he said, buckling his watchstrap. 'It'll do him good.'

When he had gone, she decided a cold shower might help. It was because she'd begun to lose all hope of coming to her senses that she'd asked Max about her real father, hoping it might free her from a sick relationship with a father-substitute.

She dressed quickly, wondering how on earth Fritz had guessed she sometimes flirted with Max.

Though Max tried even harder to discipline his feelings about Theresa, he became even more involved. He managed not to probe about her relationship with Professor Weiss. When she told him, a year later, that she had completed her year of housemanship and was no longer working with the professor, he was not surprised. She had lost that haunted feverish look. Now she was thinking of specialising in children, she said. Meanwhile she planned to gain more experience in general medicine.

Over the next few years her interest in medicine seemed to follow the current doctor in her life. She introduced them all to

Max. Strangely he felt little jealousy, probably because they were so young. The professor was a year or two older than he was, and Max had found that intolerable.

Trans-Empire Carpets now employed three hundred people. It was the largest carpet wholesaler in Africa, and among the biggest in the world. Max and Fanny went on annual buying trips to America and to Europe. Sometimes they saw Saffity, sometimes they did not have the time to fit him into their crowded schedule.

These days, manufacturers in several countries accorded the Blums the kind of welcome reserved for their biggest and most important customers. The fact that Wyndham Carpets now bent over backwards to get their business, though satisfying, was of little consequence to Fanny – the right goods at the right price was all that mattered to her now. A terse memo had informed the Blums that, since his inclusion in the Queen's Honours List meant that he was now Sir Simon Saffity, the printed stationery of Trans-Empire Carpets should be adjusted accordingly. Fanny smiled; it was just the sort of signal she had been waiting for to establish an independent branch, and a separate business, in Cape Town. In no time at all Fama Carpets and Textiles, entirely outside Saffity's financial jurisdiction, was a coveted outlet for British, European and American exporters.

It was a good life on the whole and Max was convinced that emigrating to South Africa was the best thing that had ever happened to him. He was still contemptuous of colonials, though, and in 1960, when more than sixty blacks were shot in the back at Sharpeville for protesting against the hated pass laws and several of his friends left the country, his disgust at their lack of patriotism knew no bounds.

Among the South Africans whom Max considered to be disloyal was Theresa. He found her defection unforgivable, not only because it was unpatriotic, but because it was clear that she was using her mother's recent death to justify her decision to emigrate. They both knew alcoholic complications had turned Mireille into a zombie, just as they both knew that for the past three years Theresa had seen no point in having any contact with her at all.

As he saw it, Theresa was heartlessly taking the chicken run, and taking with her all the expertise that her country had put into her. The strength of his highly emotional patriotism weakened her hold over him. He simply lost patience. Finally, he was liberated from the tyranny of unrequited lust.

All the same Theresa and he embarked on a lengthy and detailed correspondence. Over the years they were to collect and carefully file their letters, even though they would seldom feel the need to re-read them. Geography had removed her physical presence, and though it was a distinct relief, he could not have contemplated having her vanish from his life altogether.

Property prices plummeted. Max went against Fanny, took advantage of the sudden bargains, and made several investments. After a break of more than thirty years, his gambling instinct was coming to the fore again; only this time, as he told himself with considerable satisfaction, he could afford to lose. Besides, Harry Oppenheimer had raised a loan of thirty million dollars, proving that despite Sharpeville, foreigners still had confidence in the South African economy.

His new freedom brought him the peace he had craved so long. Now, with his new-found security he could begin to devote himself to his daughter. True, he had neglected Sarah, but it was not too late to make it up to her, even if she was a far from devoted daughter. She was a stranger, and a hostile one at that. Hiding behind her thickly lensed spectacles, she had been as shy and as plain as a mouse. Then, as if by magic, her acne vanished. She fought and won a vicious battle with her contact lenses, and was now at war with her parents. She was seventeen and a social science student at the university which, as Max and Fanny agreed, was the best place for a girl to find a husband. After all, it was not as if she was studying for a real profession such as medicine or law.

They considered it fortunate that Sarah was not like Theresa. She told them that because she had a social conscience she would take a degree in social work, a qualification her parents considered to be as harmless as it was laughable. Unfortunately, they had no understanding of what a social conscience could mean.

26

Saffity, at forty-nine years old, had the unmistakable air of a leader. He had recently been knighted for his services to industry, and was now Sir Simon Saffity. His pure white hair, his elegantly tailored suits that sat so well on his tall, tapering body, made him at first glance an arresting, handsome figure of mature distinction. On closer inspection a surprisingly alert and youthful face was revealed, with an amused expression in the lively, amber eyes. Everyone deferred to him, and to his growing empire.

Everyone, that is, except for his cold and stubborn wife. Colette's talent for nurturing made up for Jane's indifferent mothering. He had come to believe that Jane's only interest in her daughter was in the standard of her horsemanship, but even this was secondary to her own and only passion for horses. Jane barely tolerated Colette, but since she had neither the time nor the patience to go shopping with a boring teenager, she grudgingly permitted Colette to take over. Frequently at dinner parties Jane would announce, 'My daughter bores me.' She seemed to think it chic.

In her own delicate way Colette steered Saffity's life to more peaceful waters. Her mothering of Brooke spared her many lonely days when he could not be with her. 'Jem deserves to know someone like Brooke, and vice versa,' Colette had suggested.

'That would be disrespectful to her mother, and I won't be a party to that!'

It was a recurring argument, but he had refused to relent.

Yet Colette had never as much as suggested divorce.

And then, when he least expected it, in October 1961, by which time his marriage had endured for sixteen years, Jane exploded.

Her explosion took the form of a command.

'You will *not* be cruising the Mediterranean for two weeks with Brooke Cullen on the *Jem II*,' she pronounced in a high, bold voice. She tossed her head, and her large, tear-shaped diamond earrings glittered, adding to the sparks of rage in her eyes. 'I will not stand for it. I tell you, *I will not*!'

She jerked her head again, and again her diamonds and eyes sparked in harmony. Whatever else, she was certainly beautiful, Saffity thought. He sighed deeply. Two years ago he had bought her those earrings at that great Dallas store Nieman-Marcus, during the Promote Britain fortnight.

In all these years Jane had never as much as alluded to his relationship with Brooke. For once, his silence had nothing to do with playing for time; he was altogether at a loss for words.

'The yacht is *my* territory,' Jane said icily. 'And Mrs Brooke Cullen is not welcome on it.'

'You're rocking the boat, Jane,' Saffity warned.

'I did not spend all those hours with the decorator arranging everything for Brooke Cullen's benefit.' She paused dramatically. 'You will cancel her and you will take me,' she said, imperiously as if she were talking to a stable boy.

Dangerously calm, he said, 'Just who the hell do you think you're talking to?'

'Oh, I know who I'm talking to all right,' she answered with a shrill, contemptuous laugh. 'I'm talking to an ill-mannered peasant who thinks he's an aristocrat because he bought himself a title. I thought you knew the rules. I must have been wrong.'

His cigar had gone out. He applied a match to it. His mind whirled. He could no longer remember when he had first assumed he and Jane had reached a tacit understanding that, even if the marriage was over, the family would endure. He had taken it for granted that she accepted Brooke the way he accepted her own stable of younger and younger men. Their attitudes owed much less to the new style of open marriage that was just becoming fashionable than to the belief that they were sophisticated. Jane was a perfect snob, whose belief in the aristocratic tradition of discreetly conducted affairs was absolute. She had nothing but contempt for those commoners, like her husband, whose titles were conferred rather than inhherited.

'Oh, that filthy cigar of yours again,' she cried impatiently. 'I said you will cancel Mrs Cullen, and that's my last word on the subject.'

He looked up from his cigar. 'And if I disagree?'

'You either cancel her or I divorce you.'

'An ultimatum?'

She stood up. With an air of finality she said, 'My last word.'

Saffity watched her glide gracefully from the room. She was elegant, he thought, and regal too. She carried herself superbly.

'By the way, Jane, those earrings are stunning.'

She stopped. Still with her back to him, she tore one earring off, hurled it at him and swept from the room.

She had chosen her timing well, he conceded. They had just given a particularly successful dinner party for the American Ambassador and it was past midnight. Afterwards he had gone, as usual, to his study when, quite without warning, she had appeared and sprung her bombshell.

He flung the remains of his cigar angrily across the room. It lay beside Jane's earring, which he picked up reluctantly, and placed in an envelope on which he wrote *Jane*. Never in a million years could he have predicted her behaviour. Goddamn it, six weeks earlier, on *Jem II*'s maiden voyage, she had done nothing but complain. As soon as the boat moved, she was seasick. She insisted they stay in port. Then, when he arranged a firework display for her, she said the sounds reminded her of the Blitz. She was like a dog in a manger: she didn't want the yacht, but she didn't want Brooke to have it either.

Still, divorce was a messy business. Until a few moments ago, he was certain that he and Jane had hit on the prefect formula for living. However imperfect, his family was effectively in unbroken working order. Jem was fifteen. Why divorce, then? Why break it all up? Brooke was content enough with the way their lives had welded into each other. It was she who had said, 'I'd rather be welded to you than wed to you.' Her intelligent compassion compensated for Jane's imperishable snobbery. And it was from Brooke's base that he had been able to give the fullest rein to his powers. Not for nothing had *Forbes Magazine* referred to him as 'The powerful tycoon, a giant among men who collects companies and art with equal infallibility'. Nor that several universities had invited him to deliver those major trend-setting economic lectures . . . In this general review he concluded that he had run the branches of his private life as successfully and as efficiently as he had run all his enterprises. It had been challenging, too. What was more, it had appeared to work for everyone.

But Jane's ultimatum amounted to a declaration of war. Of course she knew that, so she must have wanted war. His mind flew to the legal team he would assemble; Sir Archibald Harris QC was a brilliant barrister, and the best man to lead his team of lawyers. He hoped Jane had not got to him first.

He gave a moment's thought to the possibility of acceding to Jane's demand, and almost immediately dismissed it. To bend before an ultimatum went against his nature.

Saffity made no change in his plans; by the time he and Brooke boarded the *Jem II* he had already instructed his solicitors. His business schedule had been more frenetic than ever; Wyndham Carpets was in the throes of becoming a public company. And, as Chairman of the Trade and Exporting Commission, a governmental committee, his duties had demanded he waste more time and energy than even he could afford. For the very first time he was looking forward to a change of scene.

As skilled in the art of silence as he was in so much else, he decided to say nothing about Jane's ultimatum to Brooke.

The *Jem II* was, to say the least, opulent. The bathrooms of the main stateroom were panelled in lapis lazuli, the same hard blue as Jane's eyes, Saffity thought. She and her decorator had gone in for a lot of stone: black onyx lamps, green marble tables, red onyx bowls were everywhere. Wyndham Carpets in the famous cobalt blue, with the words 'Jem II' woven into them, almost succeeded in softening the harsh opulence.

After only three hours at sea Brooke confessd to a headache. This was so unlike her that Saffity immediately instructed the captain to make for the nearest port, Monte Carlo, and radio for a doctor.

He stayed on deck while Doctor Guillaume carefully conducted his examination. When the doctor had done he excused himself and joined Saffity.

'Some of her reflexes are slow,' the Doctor said gravely. 'She must have an X-ray of the head.'

'Is it serious, doctor?' Saffity asked.

'We cannot say,' Doctor Guillaume answered. 'Madame tells me she fell down some steps,' he added thoughtfully.

'She said nothing about that to me.'

'I also gained the impression that she had experienced some emotional upset. We never know with women, do we, monsieur?' Guillaume said genially. 'If you will excuse me, I will arrange for the ambulance.'

'An ambulance?'

'It is, I think, safer.'

'You will accompany us, doctor?'

'But of course, monsieur. Now, with your permission I would like to radio for a consultation with our esteemed neurologist, Dr Boulez.'

Saffity left him to go to Brooke. In the darkened, shuttered stateroom her pallor was luminous. Suddenly he was afraid. He said quietly, 'I didn't know you'd had a fall. Dr Guillaume is arranging for you to have X-rays. He asked me if you'd had an emotional upset. Have you?'

'Did he really ask you that?'

'Exactly that.'

'I would have told you if you had told me.' She whispered painfully, 'I was waiting for you to say something, Saff.'

'What are you talking about?'

Brooke opened her eyes briefly, then quickly shut them again. 'Jane came to see me,' she whispered.

'She'll pay for that!'

'She came on Monday. The day before we flew to Nice, I think. Yes, it was Monday.' She covered her head with her hands. 'The pain in my head began then.'

'Oh, Brooke, you should have told me.'

'I was waiting for the pain to stop.' She spoke nervously, rapidly. 'Jane said some — '

'Don't talk about it,' he said uncomfortably. 'You mustn't upset yourself now. We'll talk about it later.'

'My head hurts,' she whimpered piteously. She tried to smile. 'Jane threw a Giacometti at me. I dodged, so she missed. But I fell.' Her voice trailed away.

Saffity felt strangely powerless.

While she was undergoing a thorough investigation – first a head X-ray, then a lumbar puncture – Saffity was making frantic phone calls to London. Brooke had been admitted to the Monte Carlo Hospital at two o'clock, and three hours later his personal physician, Dr Christopher Keene, and the famed neurologist, Dr Jock Patterson, were on their way to Nice in a privately chartered jet.

'I get lawyers to check my lawyers, and accountants to check my accountants,' he said with disarming candour. 'Second opinions are a weakness of mine.' He placed his hand on Dr Guillaume's arm. 'I realise how much of your valuable time I'm taking, doctor. I expect both you and Dr Boulez to double your fees.'

The doctors were flown from Nice to Monte Carlo by helicopter, which saved fifteen minutes.

Fortunately, Dr Patterson spoke excellent French, so Saffity was not required to translate. He stayed with Brooke. She had been given something for the pain, but the invasive nature of the investigations appeared to have weakened her.

'Christopher Keene is already looking at your X-rays,' Saffity whispered. 'He's in Monte Carlo, and he brought a neurologist with him. You're in the best hands, Brooke. But I want you to fight back. You *must* fight back. The doctors will decide what is to be done, but you must fight back.'

From then on things moved very quickly. First, all the four doctors agreed the diagnosis of a subdural haematoma, a brain clot. The only treatment was cerebral surgery, and it was decided to operate at once.

'What are the risks of flying her to London?' Saffity asked crisply.

'There is a chance that the clot could burst,' Dr Patterson said uncompromisingly.

'But she flew here, and nothing happened. I'd rather we took her to London,' Saffity countered, as if there was no more to be said.

'We would all rather do that, of course,' Dr Patterson said. 'Unfortunately it is not possible. Travelling is out of the question.'

'But cerebral surgery is such a risky business,' Saffity said anxiously.

'We can only do our best. The brain is a mysterious place,' Dr Patterson said dispassionately.

'Who will operate?' Saffity asked rudely. 'You or Dr Boulez?'

'Dr Boulez has agreed to assist me,' Dr Patterson said smoothly.

'If it goes wrong, could it be fatal?' Saffity asked bravely.

'Even worse, Sir Simon: the patient could be left a vegetable.'

Automatically Saffity said, 'Please call me Saffity.'

'Be assured, Saffity, we will, all of us, do our best,' Dr Patterson said kindly. 'Are you a religious man?'

'No.'

'A pity. We could have done with your prayers.'

For three weeks Brooke's life hung in the balance. She developed an unidentifiable infection which made her temperature soar to dangerously high levels, and she was packed in ice.

'It happens frequently in these cases,' Dr Boulez said helplessly.

But Saffity was not interested in other cases. He had taken up residence in the hospital. Once again, Colette came to his rescue and joined him in Monte Carlo.

During the five weeks they were there, he made no business calls. He roared, and wept, and railed against the doctors, against Dr Patterson especially, who had returned to London. He flew in leading neurologists from all over the world. And then, when it became clear that Brooke would survive, it also became clear that she would be a vegetable.

Five weeks after the surgery Saffity had his way, and they flew Brooke back to England. He won his fight not to have her 'stowed away in a home' but a roster of nurses, indeed, a mini-hospital, was installed in the Beechams' household. Now, too late, Brooke was on Saffity's estate. Nothing but a small woodland was between Jane at Stanford Hall and Brooke at Swallow Grange.

And Jane was powerless. Since she had delivered her ultimatum he had not set foot in Stanford Hall.

Life goes on, Saffity told himself wearily. He had survived other hardships and he would survive this one, too. A new bitterness invaded and took possession of his soul. He and Brooke were both in their fifties now. He would find salvation in his work, the way he always did; for Brooke there was no salvation, no hope. But Saffity continued to fly in doctors, homeopaths and even faith healers. There was no way of knowing what she thought or felt, or even if she thought or felt.

For the first time since he had lost Edwina, Saffity put his personal life ahead of his business life. The rumours that the Wyndham Carpets flotation was likely to be heaavily over-subscribed neither excited nor disappointed him. His zest for the settling of old scores now took pre-eminence.

Accordingly he invited Jane to lunch at the Ritz where, the day before, he had entertained her father.

'Well, Jane,' he said, as he rose to kiss her on both cheeks, 'you're as lovely as ever.'

'And you're as courtly as ever,' she answered, sitting down and adjusting the black mink of her Saint Laurent jacket.

The waiter served the champagne and caviare that Saffity had ordered in advance. 'I've ordered your favourite menu,' Saffity announced, 'to save time.'

'I see. Efficient to the end,' Jane answered nastily.

'Not nearly as efficient as your lawyer, Julian Dowling,' he chuckled. 'That was an extremely terse communication for such – shall we say – unrealistically extravagant demands.'

'I'd hardly call my expectation to remain in my own house unrealistic.'

'Wouldn't you?' he smiled. 'I lunched with your father yesterday,' he added casually. 'Here at the Ritz. I must say, the old fellow was in fine form.'

'Oh, he had lunch with you, did he?'

'Didn't he tell you?'

'No.'

'That's odd. We talked about you. He rather welcomed the idea of being financially independent again. It's a terrible fate, he said, to have to take charity from one's own daughter.'

'So it is,' Jane said sharply. '*I'm* making sure I'll never be in that position.'

'Your father would love to have his own house once again, you know. You've hunted through the grounds of Hailsham Manor, haven't you?'

'Oh, you know I have,' she said impatiently.

'Beautiful place, isn't it? With a magnificent dower house.' Saffity paused. 'Your father thinks so, too. He and your mother would be more than delighted to live in it, he said.'

'Why don't you get to the point?'

'Your patience has become as thin as your lips,' he said bitingly. 'Your lips always were too thin. Now they're disappearing.' He shook his head. 'I've done a deal with your father. The dower house and four acres of Hailsham Manor will, by deed of covenant, go to him. And the Manor and the estate will go to you. Jem will come to me on alternative half-terms, her holidays to be divided equally between the two of us.'

'You should . put those terms and conditions to my lawyer, not to me.'

'Of course,' Saffity smiled nastily. 'But I thought it would be in your and my best interests to deal direct. I'll fight you all the way, Jane. I'll go to the highest court in the land, to the House of Lords if need be. But you will not get Stanford Hall. You will *not* get Edwina's house.'

'Do your worst, *Sir* Simon,' Jane said sarcastically. 'Stanford Hall is my home.'

'I can remember when you hated Stanford Hall,' Saffity said reasonably. 'But that's not important.' Once again he paused. 'I'll let that pass for the moment. There's something important you should know, something I am sure you would prefer your lawyers not to know. For your sake, and the sake of our daughter, I hope you will keep this – uh – delicate matter strictly between you and me.'

'I'm getting curiouser and curiouser.'

'I wouldn't be so flippant if I were you, Jane,' he snapped. 'You could be facing a charge of aggravated assault with intent to do grievous bodily harm, you know.'

'I can't think what you're talking about.'

'Brooke told me of your visit. She also told me about the Giacometti sculpture you threw. You know what has happened to her.' Saffity's voice had the rhythm and sound of gunshot. He grabbed her wrist and squeezed it hard. 'You injured her brain. She's a vegetable now.'

'The sculpture missed her. She was standing on the step leading into the sunken part of her drawing room, and she fell,' Jane said, speaking in clear, clipped tones. 'I did not touch her. She fell!'

'Brooke can't tell us what happened,' Saffity said bitterly. 'She can neither confirm nor deny what you say.'

Jane drew in her breath and swallowed hard.

Mercilessly Saffity continued, 'Your signed statement renouncing all claims to Stanford Hall will be all I require. I propose to do nothing else.'

'What else can you do?'

'Spread the word about the unsophisticated, savage Lady Jane flinging sculptures about. A juicy titbit for the gossip columnists, wouldn't you think?'

'You wouldn't do that,' Jane gasped. 'You wouldn't stoop so low.'

'It's easy for me, I am already low.' Saffity made no attempt to disguise the menace in his voice. 'I'd also sue for custody of Jem.'

'Blackmail.'

'You said that, I didn't. I'm negotiating a treaty with you, that's all. It's either a peace treaty or a declaration of war. Sue for peace and you'll have peace. Go to war – and I'll destroy you. The choice is yours.'

Saffity turned his energies and instincts to family matters with the same enthusiastic intensity he had once reserved for his business affairs.

As soon as he returned to his London office after his lunch with Jane he telephoned Jem's headmistress, whom he informed of the sad state of his marital affairs, and whose permission he sought to take Jem to lunch the next day. At the same time he made an appointment to discuss the matter with the headmistress.

'I'd like to try to minimise the emotional wound, the scars that inevitably follow divorce,' he confided. 'I know how many demands are made on your time, but I'd be exceedingly grateful if you would give me the benefit of your experience.'

The headmistress was no less helpful than Saffity had expected her to be; the Edwina Saffity Foundation was, after all, one of the school's major benefactors. Then he sent one of his secretaries to search for a first edition of Keats' poems. Jem would be sixteen in only three months, and she was passionate about the poet. She was also an excellent student. Already she had begun her 'A'-level course. In less than two years she would be at Oxford, and there was talk of a scholarship. But she was a shy girl, and sensitive, and he was anxious about her.

Then he telephoned his solicitor and instructed him to deliver to Jane the documents the legal team had spent all the previous night preparing, which he had scrutinised earlier that morning.

'You will, I take it, be delivering these documents yourself,' he said pointedly. He added smoothly, 'Might I suggest that also you inform Lord Lovett-Turner that the relevant documents are now in his daughter's possession?'

Whenever he saw Jem, Saffity's heart quickened. Brooke had always said she was his weakness, and she had been all too accurate. Jem was as brilliant as she was beautiful, and she was breathtakingly so. Her mother's eyes were a hard navy blue, but hers were soft violet and shy. She carried herself proudly, as if her long slender neck had been stretched into gracefulness by balancing books on her head. Her lean fluid movements reminded Saffity of Jane. Because her generous lips were like his, Jane had of course insisted they were thick.

He had decided to tell her the unvarnished truth, even if it meant that she would have to know about his involvement with Brooke.

When he had done, Jem said softly, 'But I always knew about you and Brooke.'

'You knew?'

'I saw you together.'

'Where?'

'Twice.' Jem blinked rapidly. 'Once at Asprey's. You were buying a silver frame together. The other time was outside Eaton Place. You were hugging her.'

'Jem . . . uh . . . Jem, I don't know what to say — '

'Colette explained things.'

'She didn't tell me!'

'I asked her not to. She said you needed more love than most because you give more love than most. She said she would have been nothing and no one without you. Did you know that she only learned to read when she was fourteen?'

But as he watched Jem's violet eyes darken, sadden and then gladden, he found himself talking, for the first time, of his own schooldays. He was telling her of the foot-stocks, the *sepos* that had been used to punish him so long ago.

'Where was this?' Jem asked curiously.

'In Macedonia.'

'I know that. But where in Macedonia?'

'Greece. Thessalonika.'

'Salonika,' Jem said brightly. 'It was originally called Therme, I think. And then it was renamed Thessalonika in honour of Alexander the Great's daughter. I didn't know you used to live there. Isn't that odd?'

'When I was nine years old, almost half your age, Jem, I watched the whole city burn down. My father and I were standing on a roof – he was paralysed — ' Saffity broke off suddenly.

'And then what happened?'

'I pulled him off. We jumped.'

'Foot-stocks,' Jem shuddered. 'How horrid for you.'

'It was a long time ago. I don't suppose it did me too much harm.' Saffity laughed lightly. 'I'm sorry about your mother and me.'

'I suppose you and Brooke would have got married if she hadn't fallen ill.'

'I don't know. That's a good question, Jem. Somehow, I don't think so.' Astonished, he heard his own voice break. 'Brooke always talked about you. I should not have kept her separate like that.'

'So why are you doing it now?' Jem interrupted.

'Doing what?'

'Divorcing. You can't marry Brooke, so why are you doing it?'

Nothing in the world would have induced him to tell Jem his response to her mother's ultimatum.

'Because *I've* changed,' he said wretchedly. 'I'm sorry about your mother; it's not very fair on her.'

'She'll manage,' Jem said coldly. 'Except for her horses, nothing really worries her.' Remembering their last shopping expedition and her mother's rudeness to the sales assistant – 'Are you the cleaner or do you help people buy things?' – her eyes darkened with embarrassment.

'Oh, Jem, you're such a good, kind girl,' Saffity said, making no attempt to conceal his tears. 'Perhaps too good for your own good.'

'No, I'm not,' Jem said firmly. 'I'm a realist, that's all.'

'Now, tell me, Jem, darling,' Saffity said with an almost flirtatious laugh. 'Tell me which French books you're reading for your 'A'-levels.'

'Racine – *Andromaque* — '

' "*Ah! je l'ai trop aimé pour ne le point haïr!*" ' Saffity burst out. ' "Oh, I have loved him too much to feel no hate for him." '

Softly yet dramatically Saffity continued the fluent recital. Jem watched him and listened, entranced. This side of her father was unknown to her. Occasionally, during the school holidays, he had helped with her French homework, and though he had followed her academic progress with interest he had exposed nothing of his own love of poetry.

Deeply moved, she said, 'That was beautiful, Daddy. Really beautiful.'

'You don't know me very well,' Saffity said, reading her mind. 'We don't know one another very well. My fault. I'm hoping to change that.'

Brooke died months later without ever waking up, as imperceptibly as day turns to dusk. Spring gave way to summer in the weeks following her cremation, and Saffity missed her savagely: her warmth, her generosity, her vitality. He remembered her wonderful physical presence and found her absence almost palpable. He sold her house in Eaton Place before he set foot in London again, and alarmed his City staff by having their offices redesigned in a bland new modern style so that he would not be confronted by Brooke's presence there too. He had had over ten years with her, the happiest of his life since Edwina, and he felt torn apart.

Part Eight

27

From then on Saffity began to arrange his life with almost mathematical precision, as if the only way he could live with himself was to ensure there would always be a shortage of time. He needed no more than three or four hours' sleep anyway. His reputation was by now as international as his business interests – bankers, industrialists and merchants courted him in America, in Canada, in Australia and South Africa. The value of his private holdings in Jemsa far outstripped Wyndham Carpets, and only his accountants knew what he was really worth.

Saffity did not set foot on the *Jem II* again. The yacht was sold; in its place he acquired a jet. He had added a permanent masseur to his staff who, together with Simpson, accompanied him on many of his travels. The masseur was also a gymnastic coach, and kept Saffity in remarkably good shape. Jane and he had the occasional civilised meeting to discuss Jem's holidays.

To assuage his grief he sought temporary amnesia in the arms of women who rapidly became as faceless as they were numberless. They were as luxurious, as standard, and as necessary as a VIP lounge in an airport. His requirements were simple: no under-age women, no married women. The services of a professional call girl were seldom required, though he was seen with models and starlets. Whoever they were, as far as he was concerned they were nameless.

Inevitably he mistook a model for a call girl, and left a fat envelope at her bedside. It was the third time he had been with that particular model and it was a particularly unfortunate mistake.

As if it had been a minor *faux pas*, he laughingly reported his mistake to Colette. She listened, smiled sadly and said, 'You are hiding your grief in arrogance, Saffity.' Laying her head on his arm she continued, 'I know it, and you know it, but the girl doesn't. You are making serious enemies. Don't say I didn't warn you!'

In the summer of 1963, Saffity invited Jane to lunch at the Connaught one Saturday. He badly wanted his daughter to attend the opening of his most ambitious American project, a shopping centre in Washington, but she was working for her 'A'-levels and he needed her mother's approval to remove her from the school.

'It's only for a few days – three in fact,' he said persuasively. 'And anyway she's going to walk through her exams.'

'Don't be too sure about that,' Jane said abruptly. 'Especially if that's what she said. Jemima's getting too big for her boots; you're spoiling her rotten. You're going to regret it.'

'Are you trying to imply that we should rob her of the opportunity to meet the President of the United States in case it will spoil her?' Saffity asked, genuinely incredulous.

'She's too young for that sort of thing,' she snapped. 'She's also too young to have Kupfurmann paint her portrait.'

'Annigoni painted yours, didn't he? He even managed to make you look as if you had generous lips,' he said scathingly. 'If you are considering withholding your consent about Washington — ' he paused dramatically, 'I'll go to the courts.'

'That is precisely why I am not withholding my consent,' she said sweetly. She crumbled her bread with her coarse, heavy hands, always a sign of her discontent, as he remembered well.

'So what's the catch?'

'If you're asking why I agreed to have lunch with you, I may as well tell you. Hailsham Manor's riddled with dry rot — '

'What's the bottom line?'

'I don't know yet,' Jane lied.

'I'll deal with it. Send me the account.' He shook his head with mock sorrow. 'Don't try this one again, Jane dear.'

'Just see that you keep Jemima away from your women,' she hissed. 'Or I'll see *you* in court. I will not have my daughter contaminated by your strumpets.'

Saffity unleashed one of his most genial laughs. He glanced at his watch. His mind was already on his next meeting. He was about to meet Jem and Colette to choose Jem's Washington wardrobe. They were most probably already at Hardy Amies.

He had been very careful not to let Jane know he was in London for the sole purpose of negotiating Jem's visit to Washington. The rest of the afternoon, spent shopping with Jem and Colette, was therefore a very special treat, and he looked forward to it with a childlike delight. Unusually, he had time to spare, and just as unusually, he decided to walk to Hardy Amies. He still limped, still carried a silver-tipped cane – more for effect than need – but, for all that, his walk was sprightly. As he made his way to Savile Row, he thought for the thousandth time that without Jem there would be no point to his life. She was also wondrously beautiful; having inherited her mother's porcelain-like skin. As he walked into Hardy Amies his heart was fairly bursting with pride.

28

Max was too late; Sarah was already a rebel. She'd dismissed and ignored her parents' intentions to see her safely married. University meant freedom. At the beginning freedom was defined by not having to dress to her mother's taste. Discarding conventional make-up, she rimmed her chestnut contact-lensed eyes with authentic Indian kohl. She set herself apart from her school friends who had also made it to the university. After she had left Roedean, the private school that imitated its British counterpart, so aptly described as 'hot God and cold cabbage', where she'd been compelled to walk like a lady, she rapidly shed the ladylike constraints and her ladylike friends.

By the end of her first year she was wearing sandals and blue jeans, and a man's wristwatch; a far cry from her mother's artificial world of first nights, and fashion, and business and charity committees. Though she and Fanny had never had much in common, Sarah had previously tried hard to adapt to her mother's ways and values, largely because she wanted to try, somehow, to make up to her for her brother Jeff's tragic death. But she'd realised that in her mother's eyes she would never be more than a substitute child, and a second-rate one at that.

She could already play the piano, and decided to learn how to play the guitar. It was a shock to discover there were no separate lavatories for blacks. Until then her only contact with them had been as servants. Now she was on terms of easy familiarity with blacks, Afrikaners, coloureds and Indians. She wanted to be a person rather than a lady, a serious student rather than the frivolous girl she was expected to be. She had gained four distinctions in her matriculation, and now set herself the highest academic standards. She lived at home, of course, for she had not yet acquired either the courage or the means to live anywhere else.

She gravitated towards student politics, not so much because she was interested in politics but because that was where she could meet the kind of people her parents were sure to disapprove of – students who were interested in poetry, art, the theatre and music. When she attended a non-violent demonstration on academic freedom, and the police used dogs to break up the meeting, she was more delighted than angry. No arrests were made, but it was an exhilarating experience all the same. It was the closest she'd ever come to anything like real danger. A little later, over coffee at the café across the road from the university, she began to laugh crazily. The black kohl streaked down her cheeks.

'You look like a clown,' Andries de Waal said. 'It's not so funny, you know. If you'd been black you would have been arrested.'

'I know,' Sarah said soberly. She stopped laughing and allowed her nervous tears to flow quietly.

Andries was a postgraduate fine arts student, who had already staged a successful exhibition of his sculptures and paintings. One of his works had depicted Jesus as a black man, provoking some controversy. Sarah had read about him everywhere. This was the first time he'd noticed her and she was overwhelmed. His gaunt face was pitted with the marks left behind by untreated acne. Her own acne had scarcely scarred her complexion, but she felt an instant sympathy for him all the same. His large Roman nose reminded her of one of his own sleek wood sculptures. A tight black sweater emphasised his tall, skinny torso. He was Sarah's idea of what a real artist should look like; she thought he was devastatingly attractive.

After a while she said bravely, 'So what if I had been arrested? This is still a democracy.'

'A democracy for whites,' Andries said scornfully.

'I saw your exhibition,' she said timidly. 'I'd love to see more of your work.'

'Let's go, then.'

'Where?'

'To my studio.'

He picked up his helmet and her guitar, and began to make his way out of the café. Sarah followed at once. She had the feeling she was walking in her own shadow. His motorbike, a gleaming Harley Davidson, was parked nearby. He unhooked a spare helmet, handed it and the guitar to her, and quickly mounted his bike. She climbed on behind and almost at once they were streaking down the long, gracefully winding Jan Smuts Avenue towards his studio. Sarah had never been on a motorbike and the combination of speed and balance was both terrifying and thrilling. At the same time she was intensely aware of her breasts pushing into his vertebrae. She felt almost cheated when he zoomed into a short, sandy driveway just off the road.

A youngish Zulu woman in slippers opened the front door even before they had dismounted.

'You're early today, Andries,' she laughed. 'Do you want tea? I baked some scones.'

'How's business?' Andries teased. 'This is — ' he turned to Sarah. 'I forgot your name.'

'Sarah.'

'This is Sarah. She wanted to see my studio. Sarah, this is Lily, the shebeen-queen of Parkwood. She runs an illegal beer hall.'

At that moment two glassy-eyed men stumbled past.

'Business is good, heh, Lily?' Andries said amiably.

'Hello, Sarah,' Lily answered casually. 'The scones are still hot. Do you want tea?'

'You look after your customers, Lily, we'll look after ourselves. OK?'

Lily's relaxed attitude — she had called her Sarah, not Miss Sarah — made Andries seem even more unconventional. Sarah followed him into the small house. It smelt of paint, of turpentine and wood-shavings. There was no hall. Andries had knocked down walls and installed fanlight windows, and though it was the smallest house she had ever been in, it was a large studio. He was currently working in charcoal, and several sketches of figures distorted with fear and grief were pinned to the walls. He explained that the week before he had passed a funeral lorry filled with blacks, all dressed in black. He had glimpsed an intolerably small coffin, and the result of what he had seen was now on his walls. As he talked, he gestured towards his work with his long graceful hands.

'Lily's scones are the best in the world,' he said, leading her to the kitchen. 'I'm starving, aren't you?'

'Does Lily work for you? Is she your cook?'

'I don't know who works for who round here. She's always busy with her *skokiaan* beer, and her shebeen.' He moved his hands angrily. 'I don't have a cook.'

'That may be,' Sarah answered thoughtfully, 'but that doesn't mean you haven't got a servant,' she ended triumphantly.

'How many servants do you have?'

'None.'

'Do you live with your parents?'

'Yes.'

'How many servants do they have?'

'I don't know,' Sarah answered truthfully.

'Where do you live?'

'Hyde Park.'

'Hyde Park, the Beverly Hills of South Africa? Beverly Hills-on-the-veld, people call it!' Andries snorted. 'The awful thing is I really do believe you don't know how many servants work for you.'

'Good,' she said, keeping her voice steady. 'Now you know I'm not a liar.' She added, 'You've got crumbs on your chin.'

He wiped his face with his hands and said, 'You don't get mad, you just get even?'

'Just like President Kennedy,' she countered coldly.

'Did you come here to spar with me or to get laid?' he asked gently.

He drew the kitchen blind and then, as casually as if he were taking a cup off the shelf, took her in his arms and kissed her thoroughly. Sarah found herself kissing him back, responding instead of submitting. She was already eighteen, but this was the first time her body was in control. Their tongues met and probed, and she was inside yet another new reality, and felt as if she were once again on his motorcycle, rushing speedily, dangerously, towards delicious extinction. Her knees began to buckle. He picked her up and carried her to his untidy double bed. Skilfully he undressed her, while she fumbled with his belt. As soon as they were both naked he said hoarsely, 'Are you ready?'

'More than ready,' she murmured, 'I'm dying.' She wrapped her legs around his slim waist, and took him into her hands, and guided him into her, and then, at the crucial moment, instead of tensing away, she arched her body yet closer to his. A short cry of pain escaped, and she was aware of the hot gush of blood, but her movements continued to keep pace with his, going from tentative, to certain, to frenzy until she felt a different warm fluid spurt against her stomach.

They lay quietly. After a while he asked, 'Why didn't you tell me you were a virgin?'

'I'm glad I waited for you, Andries,' she said.

He kissed her again, deeply, and turned away and fell sound asleep.

Listening to his rhythmic breathing, she suddenly realised that sleep was the last thing she wanted. She had often wondered how she would feel when she surrendered to a man; she had lost her virginity but not her senses. She was aware that his skin felt smooth, shimmeringly smooth, and soft. She had not expected anything like it. She was profoundly grateful she was no longer an outsider – that she, too, had been with a man. She had been raised to believe virginity equalled purity, yet faking it had come naturally to her. She trailed her fingers down the length of her body and contemplated the fullness of her breasts, the narrowness of her waist, the fullness of her thighs, then turned her attention to Andries' lean muscular body. It was covered in dark hair; she had not thought a skinny man would also be hairy. She slid her hand over his chest, ruffling his hair the wrong way. Very soon he was awake again, and almost at once began to make love to her again.

Afterwards he said, 'My God, Sarah, if I hadn't had proof you were a beginner I wouldn't have believed it!'

'Why not?'

'You're a natural, I suppose.' He slapped her thigh playfully. 'I'm taking a shower. Want to join me?'

'Love to.'

Later, when they were dressed and polishing off Lily's scones, he said, 'Is your father Max Blum?'

'Yes. Why?'

'I'm hoping to do a sculpture for one of his buildings. I'd like to meet him.'

'That's easily arranged. Only — ' She stopped suddenly.

'Only he'd better not know what his daughter's up to.' Andries laughed. 'His daughter had better go on the pill if she wants to see me again.'

'She will. She will,' Sarah said. 'When will I see you again?'

'Tomorrow?'

'Good.'

Sarah's life fell into a new routine, centred around Andries. From the very beginning he made it clear she was never to invade his space, never to show up uninvited. He was a serious artist, he said. He planned to go far, hs work was sacred, and he expected her to treat it the way she would treat anything that was holy. She was allowed to watch him work, though, and then she would speak when she was spoken to, or play

512

the guitar when she was invited to, and make love when he initiated it.

He was in his black and white phase, he told her; he did a series of her wearing nothing except her guitar. His work was abstract, and she would not therefore be recognised. Sometimes they would take time off, and smoke *dagga*, the very best kind of marijuana, that Lily cultivated so tenderly in his overgrown garden. 'You've never had real sex till you've had *dagga*, my *skat*,' he said. And it was true, just as it was true that he had called her *skat* – Afrikaans for 'darling'. It was only a word, yet it made her feel a little more secure.

Sometimes he would tease her about the number of servants there really were at Oak Lodge. 'Let's count again,' he would say with a wicked grin. 'We got to fifteen last time. There are six garden boys — '

'Gardeners,' Sarah interrupted fiercely. 'You don't have to call them boys.'

'OK. Gardeners. What are their names again?'

'Stop it.'

'Abe, Simon, Jos, Charles, Sixpence, and I've forgotten the sixth.'

'Philemon,' Sarah said stiffly. She changed the subject. 'I told my father about you.'

'About me or about my work?' he asked, his voice hard.

'About your work.'

'So that he won't know his little *skat* is screwing a Boer?'

'Naturally,' she answered. 'It's got nothing to do with him. Anyway, he said he has nothing to do with the decoration of the building, that's up to his managing architect. But he's going to put in a good word for you. He wants to meet you.'

'When?'

'He didn't say when. He left it to me,' she said proudly. 'When?'

'Tomorrow?'

'OK. You'll come for a drink.'

The next day Andries went to Oak Lodge. He took a portfolio of his work with him, called Max 'sir', was effusive about what a significant patron of the arts he could be, and managed to sell him one of his newest *Girl with Guitar* series for his office.

As soon as Andries left, Fanny said furiously, 'I'm not having that rubbish at the shop!'

'Who says it's for the shop?' Max asked mildly.

'But you said an office,' Fanny protested.

'It's for the property syndicate's headquarters.'

'Headquarters. Since when has there been a headquarters?' Fanny said suspiciously.

'Andries de Waal just gave me the idea,' Max said with a sudden smile. 'You know those buildings I bought eighteen months ago, after Sharpeville? I just had an offer on one of them, the Berry Office Centre. I turned it down. But we could do with some art in the foyer. We're putting the rents up; we might as well improve the place.'

'Just a minute, Dad,' Sarah asked, puzzled. 'Did I hear you say you bought property after Sharpeville?'

'One of my best decisions,' Max boasted. 'Your mother was against it —'

'Sixty-seven people were killed, one hundred and eighty-six wounded. What are you, a death merchant?'

'Have you gone mad, Sarah?' Max asked, his face white with rage. 'I had confidence in South Africa! I knew the economy would come right.' He clicked his tongue briefly. 'People panicked. They were giving their businesses away at rock-bottom prices. How else could I have taken over Anglo-Union Textiles? Do you know how many blankets we produce?' He crossed his cool panelled study to take a cigar from his humidor. 'Seriously, we ought to set up a headquarters. I've been running Anglo-Union Textiles and the property companies from Trans-Empire Carpets.'

'I can't believe this!' said Sarah, clapping her thighs in anger. 'You've got confidence in the economy. What about *the Africans, the majority*? But of course to you they are instruments, tools, machines, not people.'

'Stop it, Sarah!' Fanny said furiously. 'You are going too far.'

Throwing her mother a look of contempt, Sarah rushed on, 'Let me tell you they are not machines. I sit next to them in class, some have even made friends with me.' She mimicked, almost spitting, ' "Confidence in the economy," you say. We're not even part of your wonderful Empire any more!' she added, attacking his weak point. 'The very day that Verwoerd returned to South Africa after quitting the Commonwealth, Mandela was arrested. But you're white and privileged. Why should detention without trial, or a man like Mandela, mean anything to you?'

'Mandela *who*?' Fanny asked mockingly.

'I can't bear this!' Sarah said, storming out of the study.

'I told you she was difficult,' Fanny said primly.

'She's not difficult,' Max sighed. 'She's crazy! I didn't like that boy, Andries de Waal. That's why I bought his painting. D'you think he's — '

'No. He's not,' Fanny said, answering his unspoken question. 'Sarah's not yet interested in boys. You can tell that from the way she dresses. Well, I'd better go and see what the servants are up to,' she said resignedly.

Left alone, Max withdrew the folded back of a menu from his pocket. Flattening it thoughtfully, he studied the figures once again. The British Prime Minister Harold Macmillan's speech about the winds of change in Africa, the Sharpeville massacre, and the transfer of power from the Belgians to the Africans in the Congo had made Jaeger Mills, the Belgian textile company, decide to dispose of their South African operation, a factory making woollen and synthetic blankets. It was a huge enterprise, employing more than three thousand people. Max had arranged the finance – he would be stretching his resources – but it could be done. He could take over the company.

'Their boardroom is dull,' he said to himself. 'It could do with some art.' It was then that he knew he had taken the decision to go ahead and buy Jaeger Mills.

He turned to switch on his powerful radio. South Africa had left the Empire and was now a republic, but Max was still addicted to the BBC World News. Now it was no longer possible merely to switch on the local radio station and get the news from London; he was forced to tinker with the dial, not always successfully. He heard his beloved Big Ben chimes, but did not really hear the news. He was troubled by Sarah and that young man, Andries. He was a fine artist, but with the best will in the world his sixth sense told him that Andries was not to be trusted.

After that, Sarah's rebellion took the form of consistent rudeness to her parents and to their guests. She looked for opportunities to accuse them of exploiting black labour, of paying slave wages. But it was when she positively insulted one of her mother's most important customers that Fanny actually began to wish Sarah would leave home. She had the nerve to tell Sam Prosser, South Africa's leading industrialist, whose companies were valued in excess of two hundred million rand, that she hoped his workers would go on strike.

Sam Prosser could not have been more charmingly understanding. 'I see your daughter is a *kaffir-boetie*, a lover of blacks,' he pronounced. 'It's just a phase, she'll grow out of it.'

'She'd better,' Fanny said grimly. 'Meanwhile I can only apologise for her again.'

And then, as if she were not giving them enough trouble, Sarah bought herself a motorbike. Her parents tried everything to persuade her to give it up. They went from bullying to tears and even used poor Jeff's death. But she would not allow their pleading to defeat her. 'You're ruining our lives,' they said.

In a moment of private rage Fanny smashed Sarah's guitar, then, overcome with remorse and fear, quickly bought a replacement. The guitar had been in Sarah's room, so it was going to be difficult to explain away the accident. In the end she asked one of her maids, Violet, to take the blame. She remembered having had to do the same sort of thing years ago with that wretched toucan. Violet, naturally enough, cooperated.

'*Please* don't bow your head like that and clap your hands,' Sarah said when Violet apologised to her for having broken the guitar. 'Please don't. Can't you call me Sarah? Must you always call me Miss Sarah?'

'Ow, Miss Sarah,' Violet said, shaking her head. 'The madam, she was so upset.'

'It's only a guitar, Violet,' Sarah said helplessly.

'Ow, Miss Sarah! A guitar, it is very dear, very expensive.'

'Yes, it is. I know it is,' Sarah said, shamed. The price of that guitar was equal to two if not three months of Violet's salary. 'I don't know what's the matter with me,' she said tearfully.

'Miss Sarah should get married,' Violet clucked. 'Miss Sarah's eighteen years old now.'

'How old were you when your first child was born?' Sarah could never remember whether or not Violet was married.

'Fifteen years. It's getting late for you already, Miss Sarah.'

Two weeks later, when the lights snapped on at two-thirty in the morning, Sarah at first thought it was Violet bringing her in her early morning coffee. She realised very quickly that she was wrong. She screamed. Three balaclava'ed black men, silver axes glinting over their shoulders, advanced toward her. 'Shhh!' they said, with their hands over their mouths. 'Shhh! Shut up. Where's the gun? We want the gun.'

'We haven't got a gun,' Max said from the doorway. He and Fanny had raced to her room when they heard her scream.

'You're lying, man,' one of them said. He punched Max in the stomach.

'Get up,' another said to Sarah. 'Show us the safe.'

'What do you want?' Max asked quickly. 'You can have whatever you want.'

'The safe. Where is the safe?'

A fourth man entered the room. They were all shoeless, Sarah noticed dimly. They reminded her of gollywogs. The fourth man brandished a *sjambok*, a long whip as agile as a snake. Fanny recognised it at once; it belonged to their nightwatchman. 'Where did you get that *sjambok*?' she demanded. 'How dare you come in like this?'

The man answered by whipping her across her breasts.

'I'll show you the safe,' Max shouted. 'Don't hurt her. Take what you want, but don't hurt us.'

The gun can't be in the safe, Sarah thought. If it was in the safe, her father wouldn't have mentioned it. Suddenly her arms were thrust roughly behind her back, and she felt the rope bite into her skin as her wrists were bound. The same thing was done to her parents.

'Now, take us to the safe,' said the one who seemed to be the leader.

The three Blums were marched across the corridor to Max's dressing room where the safe was concealed behind his suits.

'There's not much there, I can tell you,' Max said nervously.

'Open it!'

Max's hands trembled, but he remembered the combination. The safe contained a hundred rand and a pair of nail scissors. One of the men grabbed the scissors and began to slash Fanny's upholstered walls. 'You even curtain your walls, you people,' he snarled. Then he turned to the telephone and cut the wire.

The Blums dared not exchange a glance; there were other phones in the house.

Satisfied that the phone was useless, the leader ordered, 'Get into bed! All of you! Now!'

'Don't touch them,' Max begged. 'Please.'

Suddenly Sarah said, 'I'm going to have a baby.' She turned to her father. 'I'm sorry, Dad,' she added. That blacks revered pregnant women was a well-known piece of folklore. 'I didn't want to tell you, yet.'

Max understood his daughter's deception, and went along with her. 'Who is the father?' he demanded pretending anger.

'Don't ask her that now, you fool!' Fanny said. Weeping, she turned to the leader. 'If you take the suitcases, you can fill them,' she sobbed. 'Take whatever you want.'

'We want the gun.'

'We have't got a gun.'

'We saw the master shooting the gun in the tennis court with the lights on. *Where is the gun? We want the gun!*'

'It didn't work well, so it went to be fixed,' Max lied. If he gave them the gun they would shoot him with it. 'It's at the gunshop now.'

Fanny winced as she watched her clothes being loaded into the suitcases. Her breasts burned. She looked down and saw blood on her nightgown. It was only then that she realised that her skin had been cut by the whip. She glanced at the clock, but remembered that she hadn't thought of looking at the time before. She had no idea how long they'd been there; it seemed an eternity.

At last the men were getting ready to leave. They were nervous, too. The three Blums were still cowering in the bed together.

'Where's your burglar alarm system, ma'am?' one of them asked.

'It doesn't work,' Fanny said.

'Where is it?'

'In my dressing room.'

Once more they heard the axe being wielded as the electrical equipment was slashed.

'We must get out of here,' the smallest one said. They began arguing with one another. What were they saying, Sarah wondered, in that black language of theirs? At the doorway the small man paused. 'I'm sorry, ma'am, that I had to do this to you. But my wife and children are starving. I can't get a pass, I can't get work!'

'*Dompas*,' Sarah said, using the African vernacular to show she was committed to their cause.

'*Dompas!*' he echoed incredulously. 'How do you know that word?' *Dompas* was the word for the pass, the hated symbol of slavery.

'Because I work for you people,' Sarah said quietly. '*Nkosi Sikele*,' she added. *Nkosi Sikele* – the opening words of the African national anthem . . .

Suddenly the room was empty.

They heard the lock turn at the entrance to the Blums' master-suite. 'They're leaving,' Max whispered. 'Will you be able to recognise any of them?'

'I'm bloody sure I will,' Fanny snapped.

'They've gone, Fanny, they've gone.'

Fanny was already leaping out of the bed. Only their wrists had been tied. The next moment she was kicking the floor to ceiling mirror in her dressing room. Blood spurted.

'Are you crazy?' Max screamed. 'Have you gone mad?'

'No,' Fanny yelled. 'I need the broken glass to cut the rope. Come, Sarah, I need you.' When Sarah joined her she said, 'Get a piece of glass between your two big toes. Try not to cut yourself. Good, you've done it. Now hold still while I cut the ropes around my wrists.'

Sarah worked rapidly.

'OK now,' she said. 'I'm free. I'll free you and Daddy.'

The moment Max was free he ripped out his handkerchief drawer and grabbed the gleaming revolver that lay behind it. Then he raced to the balcony and began firing, at the same time screaming for help. The servants' quarters were at least fifty yards away. He fired several more shots. 'Where's the night-watch?' he yelled.

'Drunk as usual,' Fanny answered.

Then they heard one of the servants call, 'Master, is that you, master? Are you calling me, master?'

'Charles?' Max shouted. 'Is that you, Charles?'

'No, it's me, master. It's me, Philemon.'

'Philemon! Come here quick! Call Violet. Phone the police. We've had the *skelms* here. Thieves!'

Minutes later the police arrived. Violet made tea for everyone. Details were given. 'You say you could recognise them?' Sergeant Pirrow said.

'I wouldn't even try to,' Sarah said scornfully. 'I'd do the same thing if I needed to get a pass to go to work. Wouldn't *you*?'

'She's hysterical,' Fanny said quickly. 'She doesn't know what she's saying.'

Sarah laughed derisively. 'I am not hysterical,' she said coldly. 'I know what I'm saying, and I mean every word.'

'Another self-righteous liberal,' Sergeant Pirrow sneered. 'She thinks she's superior because she's got a social conscience.' He pointed his finger warningly at Fanny. 'You'd better knock some sense into her head. Otherwise — '

'Otherwise?' Sarah cut in rudely.

'Big trouble,' Sergeant Pirrow drawled. 'Trouble with a capital T.'

During the following weeks the Blums grew seriously concerned for Sarah's sanity. She had almost been murdered, yet when all four blacks were captured by the police, she not only refused to identify them, but talked about whites having made fools of blacks *again*. After all, the blacks had believed them when they said there was no gun. Fanny and Max consulted a psychologist, who assured them that Sarah was quite sane; it was just that she had the social conscience of a liberal. He advised them to treat her gently – she was suffering from a delayed adolescence. The Blums were inclined to agree; it was certainly true that Sarah's real adolescent years had been tranquil. Too tranquil, as it now seemed.

Several weeks later, in October, when summer had just begun, Fanny received a phone call and then a visit from a woman she had never even heard of. The stranger said her name was Helen Swannepoel. Fanny only agreed to a meeting because the woman said it was a matter that concerned Sarah.

She listened carefully to what Helen had to say, and then immediately left Trans-Empire Carpets for her home. She could barely wait for Sarah to return from the university.

At last she heard the roar of Sarah's motorbike, followed by the front door slamming. She had instructed Violet to tell Sarah she wanted to see her.

'What's up? You're not usually home so early,' Sarah asked when she entered Fanny's chintz and copper morning room.

520

'Have some tea, Sarah,' Fanny answered. 'Tea with homemade scones. I'm told you like scones.'

'What's got into you?' Sarah said, sitting down at once. She unwound the tight elastic band that held her hair in place. It had grown – Andries said he liked wild streaming hair – and it now reached her waist.

'Does the name Helen Swannepoel mean anything to you?'

'No,' Sarah shot back. 'Should it?'

'Perhaps.'

'Why perhaps?'

'Because at this moment in time the name Sarah Blum appears to mean a great deal to Helen Swannepoel.'

'I don't know what you're talking about.'

'That doesn't surprise me. Andries de Waal appears to have kept her well out of your way.'

'I've never even heard of her.'

'She's pregnant, three months pregnant. And she was sweet enough to tell me that you and Andries have been lovers for four months. She came to see me at Trans-Empire Carpets.'

'Why?'

'Why did she come, you mean? She came to ask me to beg you to give him up. They've been going together for five years, she said.'

Sarah made a retching sound and fled from the room. Fanny ran after her, but was not quick enough; Sarah's motorbike was speeding down their winding, paved drive.

'You'll kill yourself! You're not wearing your helmet!' Fanny yelled helplessly.

When Sarah reached Andries' studio she jabbed the door-bell and banged his door-knocker. She heard the sound of laughter, and banged harder. Raw, painful sounds came from her throat.

'What do you want?' Andries said angrily, when he opened the door. 'What's the matter with you, *skat*? You look like a wild woman!'

Sarah pushed past him and then past Lily, who was shuffling out of the way in her usual bedroom slippers. Andries caught up with her and grabbed her arm. 'I told you only to come here when you're invited!' he hollered. 'You can't just come barging in!'

'Helen Swannepoel went to my mother's office this morning — '

'If you're looking for Helen, she's not here.'

'She's three months pregnant. She told my mother you're the father. Is that true, Andries?'

'What's it to you?'

'So she is pregnant by you?'

'That's what she says.'

'She's been going with you for five years.'

'Five years too long, if you ask me — '

'You're a low-down rat — '

'No one talks to me like that!'

'I do. You're a bastard and a rat. You're not *a* disease, Andries. You *are* disease.'

'You bitch! I never said I'd be faithful to you. D'you think you're such a great fuck that — '

'You are disease,' Sarah said again.

They were standing at the open front door. Andries lunged at her and slapped her on each cheek. She fell. 'Look at you!' he said icily. 'You look like a crazy madwoman!' He called out, 'Lily, come and see this madwoman with her wild, ratty hair — '

Sarah struggled to her feet, feeling dizzy. Her burning cheeks were already beginning to swell. Somehow she managed to get on her motorbike and ride through a mist of tears back to Oak Lodge.

As soon as she got home she made for the privacy of her bedroom, only to find her mother waiting for her.

'Leave me alone, Mom, *please*,' she begged, flinging herself on the bed.

A scandal was the last thing Fanny wanted. Johannesburg was a small town with a mentality to match. People would talk. Fanny had quickly realised her confrontation with Sarah had been quite the wrong way to handle things. Sarah would respond to kindness, and if it would take kindness at least to minimise the risk of a scandal then she would be kind. But she was furious with her daughter, furious because she had been forced to have an intimate conversation with a social inferior, and furious because her daughter was having an affair with a man who was Helen Swannepoel's equal.

'I'll go if you want me to, Sarah,' she said quietly, kneeling beside the bed, 'but I could help you.' She smoothed Sarah's hair, and then dropped a quick kiss on her cheek. 'It's hard for you, I know. But you'll get over this.'

'Oh, *Mommy*,' Sarah sobbed. 'I want to die.'

'I know you do,' Fanny said calmly. 'I don't blame you, either.' Then, still kneeling, she took Sarah in her arms and rocked her gently. 'Most girls have a big, passionate love affair that goes wrong,' she said softly. 'Cry, darling. Cry as much as you can. It will help you.'

After several minutes Sarah murmured, 'My face. My cheeks — '

'I know, darling. A hot poultice would help.'

'Thanks.'

Murder was in Fanny's heart, but she knew better than to give vent to her feelings. At one point Sarah asked, 'Does Dad know about — '

'He knows nothing.'

'Are you going to tell him?'

'That depends on you.'

'I'd hate him to know.'

'Then he won't.'

'I'd like to run away,' Sarah said bleakly.

'Then I'll take you away. We'll have a break, just the two of us.'

'You mean you'd take leave from Trans-Empire Carpets?'

'Of course, darling. This is an emergency.'

Four days later, Fanny and Sarah were on their way to Durban. It was October, and should be sunny. They would lie on the beach together, even if it was full of memories of the day Jeff had almost drowned.

Sarah's second-year exams were only six weeks away, so she took her books. But it was impossible to concentrate. It was two days before she realised she had been reading, and making no sense of, the same single paragraph in Piaget's *The Psychology of the Child*. She stopped trying, laid the book on the sand and gave her body, face-up, to the hot sun. Her cheeks were no longer swollen, but her entire body felt bruised and sore, as if her very intestines had been permanently scarred. She scarcely recognised the stranger in the mirror who now wore make-up, and had frown lines on her forehead. She had only recently turned nineteen, but looked hard, grim; the shape of her cheeks had sharpened.

She was filled with hate and despair, and it showed. She didn't care.

She was now utterly convinced that taking Andries unaware like that, and confronting him, had been a horrible mistake. She constantly relived those last terrible moments at his front door. Engrossed in her endless, constant interior debate, she was rubbing lotion and sand granules into her burnt shoulders when she heard, 'It's Sarah Blum, isn't it?'

She took off her sun glasses and peered at the young man squatting on the beach beside her. 'Dimitri Politis,' she said. 'Cleo's brother.' She sat up and flicked some sand off her shoulders. 'You recognised me?'

'What's so surprising about that?'

'Nothing, except that I hardly recognise myself. I've cut my hair.'

'What's a girl like you doing in Durban out of season? Besides reading Piaget, that is — '

'Looking for a husband,' she said flippantly. 'I'm looking for someone to marry me.'

'I'll marry you, if you like,' he said evenly. 'Meanwhile, would you care to go for a walk?'

His voice was neutral, but his eyes quickened assessingly. In her tight-fitting bikini her feminine contours were inviting. Her recently cut hair displayed the high dome of her forehead, and her oiled, sand-speckled body glittered in the sunlight. No doubt about it, he'd hit on a sexy piece. And a *hot* one too. He could sense the rage in her. He liked his women to be fiery.

Sarah threw a glance over her shoulder at her mother. Fanny appeared to have taken cover behind her newspaper, but the papers were too still for Sarah's liking. 'OK. Let's go for a walk,' she said.

They strolled along the firm, smooth sands on the edge of the sea. The beach was deserted, and the tide going out. From time to time she stopped and traced her big toe over the wet sand. Dimitri told her that he was taking a two-week holiday in Durban because he was on the threshold of his life; his father had bought him a partnership in a dental practice, and he was to start work as soon as he returned to Johannesburg.

Sarah listened, but thought of Andries. Dimitri was tall, like Andries, and skinny, too, but his short-sleeved shirt revealed hairless arms. His legs were hairless, too. If you liked the male-model kind, Dimitri was good looking, she supposed. But he was hardly her type.

She said irrelevantly, 'I had a brother once. His name was Jeff. He almost drowned here.'

'What happened to him?'

'He was killed in Israel.' She shrugged. 'I'm going in for a swim.'

'But it's out of bounds over here. The life-saver's beacon is — '

She ignored him and ran into the sea. He pulled off his shirt and plunged in after her. She was streaking ahead, fighting the waves, yet she was clearly not a strong swimmer. He caught up with her. 'You're too far out,' he called, 'it's dangerous.' She carried on. This was crazy, Dimitri thought. What was wrong with the girl? She was taking a terrible chance. Finally he caught her arm and began to tug her back. 'Are you trying to get us both drowned?' he shouted above the waves. She made no reply, but did not try to pull away. When they reached the beach she was shivering violently. He draped his shirt over her shoulders. 'What got into you?' he said.

'Nothing.'

An Indian ice-cream vendor went by and Dimitri bought two ice-cream cones. Sarah accepted hers listlessly. Then, as if trying to remember her manners, she said, 'Are you going into partnership with Doctor Cowley?'

'Yes. How did you know?'

'He's my dentist. He told me he was taking in a young partner.' She added, 'Your father owns the Apollo Café, doesn't he?'

'Yes.'

Sarah knew that café well. It was one of the many cafés owned by Greeks. They seemed to have a monopoly over this sort of business; it was really a shop that sold newspapers, magazines, fruit, vegetables, cigarettes and cool drinks. She and Andries often used to go there because it stayed open until ten at night. But Andries had objected when Mr Politis served him ahead of the queue of waiting blacks; there had been a quarrel, and they never went back. Sarah shuddered again. She said, 'Your father works long hours in that café, doesn't he?'

'His choice,' Dimitri said resentfully. 'He owns several buildings. He likes to be a martyr.'

Since Dimitri was also staying at the Edward Hotel, it was only natural he should join them at dinner. He insisted on ordering the wine, though, and Fanny had to admit to herself that he was civilised enough. After dinner, the two of them went off to the movies. Fanny approved; this kind of man was precisely the sort of diversion Sarah needed.

Fanny could not have guessed that the only reason Sarah had agreed to go out with Dimitri was because, his concave chest notwithstanding, his tall skinny frame reminded her of Andries, and it was possible to pretend she was with him.

The next day, unseasonably hot for October, they all sunbathed together. Dimitri seemed to follow her mood: when she picked up her book he picked up his, when she chose to talk he talked. Towards the end of the afternoon he suggested a ricksha ride. She agreed mainly because it was exactly the sort of thing Andries definitely would never have done – he loathed the way the tall, proud Zulus had been turned into carthorses. From the back of the ricksha she studied the powerful shiny black shoulders under the multi-coloured feathers of the ricksha head-dress. Andries had told her that ricksha boys were dead at thirty-five. Remembering this, she sighed resoundingly.

'Come here,' Dimitri said, patting the empty space on the seat beside him. 'Come closer.'

Sarah moved over reluctantly and Dimitri draped his arm over her shoulder. His touch was slightly repellent, but her body responded to the sensual rocking movement of the ricksha. The heat of the sun was like a mighty caress. Her nerves vibrated. She shut her eyes and laid her head on his shoulder. He kissed her closed lids; though flinching inwardly, she did not move away. But then, perversely, when he did not kiss her lips she felt both cheated and deprived.

Before dinner that night Sarah washed her hair and combed it carefully. She wore one of her new mini-dresses, made of white linen, with a beige waistcoat and high white boots. She was very tanned now, and glowed with health and youth.

Dimitri was a good dancer, Sarah had to give him that. He taught her the twist and her nerve-endings vibrated again. When the music slowed she thrust her pelvis against his, and before long he suggested they leave.

They walked back to the hotel with their arms around one another, slowly, as if to delay the moment. Sarah was looking for comfort, for release, and longing for Andries. They went to his room. Just before he entered her he asked, 'Are you OK?'

'I'm on the pill.'

'Good.'

Ah yes, she thought, as she received him, rocked with him, gathered speed, sprinted, and then raced for the finale, ah yes, this could be Andries, *this is Andries*! She heard herself cry out, *Andries! Andries!*

Locked in his own struggle, Dimitri seemed not to notice. Unlike Andries, however, he made no attempt to disengage immediately, but keeping her clasped to him he rolled her on her side and, still connected to her, fell asleep.

Sarah listened to his breathing. Her body registered his competence, which made her angrier with him. Just like Andries, he had not even said he loved her. She was determined to wrench the words out of Dimitri. She moved away from him, but he slept on. It occurred to her that before they made love she had not really looked at his body. Wondering whether he was hairless everywhere, she reached over and felt between his legs. No, he was not hairless, and even as she felt him he sprang into an erection. The power of her own hands made her smile in the dark. She would show him a thing or two that Andries had taught her.

She wriggled down and took him in her mouth. He struggled for a moment, then groaned and succumbed until he was quite spent. She smiled again in the darkness. But her smile quickly disappeared. For he regained himself more quickly than she had imagined he could, and very soon he was making love to her again. Only now he took his time, playing with her, forcing her to wait, tantalisingly, before allowing her to reach her netherworld.

Then, drenched in sweat, he said, 'I love you, Sarah.'

She smiled again.

'I'm going to marry you, you know, Sarah,' he went on quietly.

Her smile turned into a laugh.

'Laugh if you like,' he said crossly. 'But you will marry me, you'll see.'

Now that really would teach Andries a lesson, Sarah thought. She could think of no finer revenge. She began to feel victorious.

'I've got my exams,' she said unexpectedly.

'When do they finish? At the end of November?'

'Yes.'

'That's when we'll get married. The first week in December.'

'But you haven't even asked if I love you.'

'You don't,' he said flatly. 'But you will, you'll see. I'm a Greek, and Greeks know how to treat their women.'

The holiday ended, and they all flew back to Johannesburg on the same plane. Sarah said nothing to her mother about her resolve to marry Dimitri. They expected opposition from both sets of parents. In her case, defying her parents was an effective substitute for the emotion she did not feel for Dimitri. Certainly it was far, far better than being in love. She'd had more than enough of that with Andries . . .

Their parents' opposition, as expected, escalated into open warfare. There are plenty Greek girls, there are plenty Jewish boys . . . Dimitri and Sarah compared notes and, united in contempt for their predictable parents, they grew closer.

'Sarah hasn't been the same since that armed hold-up,' Max grumbled to Fanny. 'If it hadn't been for those kaffirs bursting in on us she wouldn't be marrying that Greek.'

'Come on, Max. You can't be serious.'

'I *am* serious. The way she refused to identify them. She wasn't normal after that, the shock affected her brain.'

Fanny shook her lacquered head. It was useless to argue with Max. Worse, it was boring . . . In any case her mind was on other things, like her breakfast meeting with the headmistress of the Jeff Blum School.

In the end their parents capitulated. They held a meeting. There would be no religious ceremony, of course, but the Blums would give a reception at their home. The invitations went out for December 20th, 1963.

528

29

When Saffity received the invitation to Sarah Blum's wedding, at first glance it merely irritated him, and he made a quick mental note to send a large cheque as a wedding gift. But then something in it compelled him to read the ornate script again, this time more carefully.

He did not bother to read any further than Odysseus Politis. It couldn't be! Was it possible this was the same Odysseus Politis who had written him that letter while he was in hospital recovering from the injury his father had done to his eye? Instinctively, his hand flew to the miniature gold key.

The boy Odysseus he had once known came flooding back. He remembered the time after their family's sudden departure when he had watched their garden run wild. He remembered the green shutters, and the olive trees, and felt again that childish envious admiration of Odysseus' own room.

He was getting maudlin, he told himself fiercely. Surely Max did not expect him to fly out to South Africa to attend his daughter's wedding? After all, he was fifty-six. So why the hell had Max sent him an invitation? To get a present, that's why! He wished again – not for the first time – that he had never met Max Blum. The man had always brought out the primitive worst in him. As he quickly wrote out his personal cheque, he thought that if it cost a thousand pounds to give Max a better idea just how rich he was, it would still be cheap.

Before long, the opposing factions reached a pre-wedding truce. The Blums and the Politises had the interests of their children in common and, as the wedding gifts began to arrive, both Odysseus and Max, now on first-name terms, were more than a little competitive over wedding gifts.

Saffity's gift was, of course, overwhelming, so overwhelming that it was a while before his name rang a bell with Odysseus. He was wolfing down some of Fanny's chocolate cake when he made the connection. His mouth full, he said, 'Simon Saffity? Do I know that name? Of course I do! But we pronounced it "Saffarty", in Salonika. I knew him when we were boys. He had a terrible accident to his eye. I never found out what happened to him; we left Salonika a long time ago.'

Fanny turned away. She could not bear people who talked with their mouths full.

'Does he come from Salonika, your Sir Simon Saffity?' Odysseus persisted.

'No,' Max answered too quickly. 'He's from Paris.'

Fanny snapped to attention.

'With a name like Saffarty? Impossible. That's not a French name, it's a well-known Sephardic Jewish name.'

Odysseus leaned forward over his bulging stomach. 'We were friends, you know. I often think about him,' he said sadly. 'I'll tell you exactly how old he is – he's three years younger than I am. Which means he's fifty-six. Am I right?'

'How old do you think Saffity is, Fanny?' Max asked, casually.

'Ageless, I'd say. He's had white hair ever since I've known him,' she answered brightly.

'Oh, well.' Odysseus laughed. 'Wherever he comes from, his kind of cheque is good enough for me!'

'It certainly is,' Fanny smiled.

She began to talk about the arrangements for a mock marble floor in the marquee.

The moment the Politises were out of the front door Fanny burst out, 'Why did you lie about Saffity? How do you know he wouldn't like to see Odysseus again? After all, they were childhood friends.'

'Saffity wants nothing to do with his past,' Max snarled. 'You know that, Fanny. Why can't you leave well alone. It's bad enough Sarah's marrying a Greek. Do you have to make it worse?'

Fanny sighed as she always did when Max was unreasonable. Still, she could not resist saying, 'He only gave a thousand pounds to show you how rich he is.' Turning to mount the stairs, she stopped suddenly. 'On second thoughts, he didn't have to give a personal cheque. It would have been perfectly legitimate for Wyndham Carpets to put it down to customer relations.'

'Who cares?' Max shrugged. 'It's better in Sarah's pocket than in his.'

That night Max dreamt of Colette. His screams awoke Fanny. Saffity, she thought sleepily; Saffity's the cause of his nightmares.

Though Saffity could not have cared less about the thousand pounds, he too had second thoughts about having written a personal cheque. It wasn't Max he'd wanted to impress but Odysseus Politis. Coming upon his name like that had unnerved him; it brought back so many unwelcome memories of Salonika. Too many, he thought moodily. Enough of the past.

Lighting a cigar, he stared thoughtfully through the smoke at Colette. The late afternoon sun fell gently through the drawing room windows onto her fine features. She was growing old, he realised with a pang. Her hair was grey. But she was fighting her anxiety over Myles with courage and cheerfulness. She wore an emerald-green linen trouser suit, and had tied a matching cashmere scarf into an extravagant bow. Her elegance almost made him smile.

Myles would be home in a couple of days – it had only been a small heart attack – and Saffity would miss his evenings with Colette. He thought ruefully of how he had relied on her over the years, how easy it would be to take her for granted. Myles, too; the shock of the news of his collapse had been severe. God knows what it must have been like for Colette to have found him. Still, if you thought of some of the other things she'd been through . . .

He should have told her about Max long ago. Impossible now, of course.

He glanced at the grandfather clock. Shouldn't Jem be home by now? He'd sent the chauffeur to pick her up from school on the last day of her last term, and left the mill early to be here to greet her. His features softened at the thought of her. His and Jane's divorce had actually seemed to do her a lot of good. From being a shy, rather nervous child, sensitive to the atmosphere between her parents, she coped with them far better separately than she had when they'd been together. She'd had to grow up fast, of course, but now she seemed as level-headed and direct as she was bright. She certainly knew what she wanted, and right now what she wanted was a degree in English Literature from Oxford University. Perhaps it wouldn't

531

be a bad thing if she did a little travelling first, saw something of Europe . . .

Colette, catching Saffity's glance at the clock, thought that it was nearly time to ring the cottage hospital and talk to Myles. He'd seemed so much better that morning; his ruddy complexion had returned, and his dry, laconic turn of phrase had had the nurses laughing. She felt a tightening in her chest at the thought of losing her beloved man. *Eh bien*; she'd have to serve him up a blander, more English diet from now on. And he'd seemed so extraordinarily strong, and fit . . . Shuddering inwardly, she forced her mind to focus on Saffity.

Pausing to check the stitches in her knitting, she observed him covertly. He's not getting any younger, she thought. Those lines under his eyes aren't all from laughter.

What he needed was a regular woman in his life. There was a restlessness about him. Much to the delight of the gossip columnists, his reputation as an inveterate womaniser had become well deserved. It was the sort of thing that was bad for a man; who knew better than she? The time for mourning Brooke was over.

The click of her needles began to irritate Saffity.

'Stop that knitting,' he said impatiently. 'You remind me of Madame Defarge.'

As she laid it aside they both heard the crunch of the car's tyres on the gravel, and a few moments later Jem came running in, straight into her father's arms.

'Ooh,' she said into his shoulder, 'thank God that's over.'

'Let me look at you,' he said, holding her at arm's length. She was still dressed in the school uniform of white blouse and grey skirt, and tendrils of raven-black hair escaped from her carelessly wrought ponytail, but the sparkle in her eyes and the flush in her cheeks were those of a girl on the confident threshold of her womanhood. 'Well, you don't *look* any older or wiser.'

She pouted, kissed him on both cheeks, then turned to Colette and hugged her.

'Poor Colette,' she murmured. 'How is Myles? How's my favourite uncle?'

'He's much better, darling, and he can't wait to see you,' said Colette, her eyes a little moist. 'Here,' she said taking Jem by the hand, 'Come and sit by me.' She patted the sofa by her side.

'What took you so long?' asked Saffity.

'Oh, I'm sorry, but we passed lots of people in the village, and I *had* to stop and chat, it's ages since I've seen them. I asked Michael up for a drink this evening,' she added, dropping her eyes. 'I hope that's all right.'

Saffity and Colette exchanged quick glances; at least some of Jem's sparkle could be explained by Michael Fisk, Colin's son, a brilliant young law student.

'Of course it is,' said Saffity. 'I'm always pleased to see Michael.'

'He's going to be up at Oxford with me. He's reading for his second law degree. Anyway, how are you two? It's lovely to be home.'

Colette squeezed her hand. 'It's lovely having you back, Jem. We become boring old sticks without you. Your father becomes positively grumpy.'

'Hmm,' he said. 'I don't know about that. I think I'm going to find you exhausting in long doses.'

'Nonsense, you find my company enormously stimulating. Think how often you came to visit me at school.'

'I only came to visit your red-haired French mistress, that Miss Whatsername. You were the excuse.'

Jem shouted with laughter.

'Then there's something very wrong with your pheromones, Daddy; she doesn't like men. But she'd go for Colette.'

'Then I hope you never bring your work home with you, my darling,' said Colette. 'I would feel most uncomfortable.'

'Take that ridiculous rubber band out of your hair, child,' said Saffity, struggling to regain his equilibrium.

'He *must* be getting old,' Jem said to Colette, obeying him and then picking up the knitting. 'Is this something for me?' When Colette nodded she stood up and held the half-finished jersey against her chest. 'Oh, it's going to be wonderful!'

The violet wool exactly matched Jem's eyes. Saffity was engulfed by such a rush of pride and love that he felt winded.

When the telephone rang Jem dropped the wool, said, 'That'll be for me, I bet,' and ran from the room.

Two minutes later Saffity looked up to see that she had noiselessly returned and was standing white-faced in the doorway, a look of childish panic in her eyes.

'Colette,' she said tremulously, 'it . . . it's the hospital. They want you to go in straight away.' Then she burst into tears.

Myles Beecham died as he had lived, quietly and courageously. Quietly, because the end came quickly, and courageously because he had faced up to the possibility of death and helped Colette to do the same. After his first mild heart attack he had gone to stay in the local cottage hospital. The doctors assured him the prognosis was good, but that indefinable sixth sense told him otherwise. He appeared to be completely recovered – there was no sign of any weakness and, as he told Colette, the best way to make the most of his moratorium was to let her know how very deeply happy she had made him. He was not sorry they had had no children, indeed he was pleased to have had to share her only with Saffity. He had always been reticent about his emotions, but now he poured his love into words because he knew she would treasure them as she had treasured him. Again and again he told her that he was the luckiest of men. His happiness with her had been a life of love surpassing all measure.

His moratorium ended seven days after it had begun, with a massive second heart attack. The service was held in the chapel at Stanford Hall, and he was buried close to Edwina and his beloved Wyndhams.

Saffity felt Myles' loss deeply, but Colette was inconsolable. She stayed on at the farmhouse, but she and Saffity dined together whenever he was at Stanford Hall.

30

Sarah had been married for a little more than a year and she could no longer deny that she had made a terrible mistake. But little Jeff was only four months old, and to have asked for a divorce would have been inhuman. Dimitri was not simply boring, he was disgusting. She had always found him faintly repellent; now she hated his touch. Taught by his fists, she had learnt not to refuse his greedy perversions.

Long since past the shame of admitting failure, she finally decided she would end the marriage when Jeff turned seven. Meanwhile, she would have no more children.

When Dimitri told her he was renting a separate dental surgery, for non-Europeans only, her blood boiled. He was opening a secondary suburban practice, and considering making it full time. There was plenty of profit in extractions, he said. The kaffirs only wanted their teeth pulled out.

When he took her to see the surgery she stared disbelievingly at the shabby dental equipment he had bought second-hand. The leather dental chair was peeling, and the strong smell of antiseptic was deceptive – far from sterile, the room was filthy. Driving home, to the charming Moorish-styled house Max had built for them, Dimitri said proudly, 'When I was a student, two years before I was allowed to do any clinical work, I practised using a syringe on the blacks at Baragwanath Hospital. The other students had to make do with an orange.'

'You mean you used people instead of fruit?' Sarah asked sarcastically.

'That's right.'

'Oh, God,' Sarah groaned.

'Are you trying to be funny?' Dimitri said menacingly.

'No, no,' she said fearfully. 'Of course not.'

The next day she went to see Andries. She had nothing more to lose. If he rejected her . . . well, she didn't dare think what she would do. Helen Swannepoel was out of his life, there never had been a baby, and if anyone understood, Andries would. At least he'd listen to her.

Andries not only listened to her, he made love to her. He kissed and soothed her bruised breasts. He said Dimitri ought to be prosecuted.

Driving home, she told herself she was a married woman having an affair. Thousands of women managed to stay married only because they had affairs.

She and Andries continued to meet frequently. Now, when it was too late or perhaps because it was too late – he told her he loved her. She was beginning to believe him. Some weeks later, when it was absolutely clear he understood her mind as well as he understood her body, she was altogether convinced that he did love her.

Speeding home one afternoon in the fast peacock-blue Alfa Romeo sports car her father had given her, she reflected once again on the divisions within her life. Free of make-up, free of all constraints, really, her soul as naked as her body, her proper life was with Andries. Yet it was her marriage to Dimitri that had forced Andries to come to terms with the fact that he loved her. This affair heightened everything. Moving into second gear, she felt utterly at one with the powerful engine. She felt everything more acutely these days.

It was young Jeff's birthday party the next day, and from the moment it began, and the mothers, babies, nannies and the grandparents started to arrive, Sarah observed it all with a sort of double vision – through her own and Andries' eyes. She imagined how he would react to the children seated around the extravagantly decorated birthday table, with their nannies standing behind them. Dianna Spronger's nanny constantly combed her flowing red hair. The young mothers, on this crisp, bright winter's day, draped mink coats over their shoulders. The birthday cake was a replica of the famous Blue Train; Andries would have hated it.

She knew he would have classified the party as yet another example of decadent white privilege. She needed to talk to him, and went to her bedroom to call him, but there was no reply.

The next day she went to see him.

She planned to tell him every last hateful detail about the party, but the words died on her lips. He was grim and white-lipped, his distinguished features sharp with anger. 'Dirk Wessels died yesterday,' he said flatly. 'At four o'clock in the afternoon.'

536

'I tried calling you,' Sarah whispered. 'I can't believe it. He was always laughing and joking — ' Her voice broke.

'Dirk found out he wasn't white.'

'He wasn't white?'

'He was coloured. He and Anna were going to elope, and Dirk needed documents.' Andries shook his head mournfully. 'He got them two days ago. That was when he found out he wasn't white. Anyway, he left a letter to the effect that he couldn't blame Anna for not wanting to marry him.' In his rage he hurled an ashtray against the wall. 'Anna's parents are under sedation. The thought that it might become public knowledge their daughter was in love with a coloured is too much for them.'

'But he was such a talented photographer. He was doing so well!'

'What difference does that make? According to the Race Classification Board, he was only part-white, therefore part-human.' Suddenly Andries broke into harsh sobs. 'Dirk was my *friend*.'

'For evil to succeed it is enough that good men do nothing,' Sarah said, quoting Edmund Burke. 'You taught me that, darling.'

Andries pulled his motorbike keys out of his pocket. 'I'm going back to the Wessels'. Lily is with them, helping with coffees and teas. You can't imagine the state they're in.'

Sarah followed him to his motorbike. 'They're going to cremate him,' Andries said. 'It's one way of avoiding a coloured grave in a coloured cemetery.'

After that they seemed to need one another more than ever; their afternoons stretched into whole days. They longed to spend a whole night together. Their love-making increased and intensified, and Sarah saw little of her small son. But since he was in the gentle, capable hands of his nanny, Georgina, she didn't feel too guilty. Georgina's off-duty Thursdays presented no problem for Violet, the cook – who used to work for Fanny – was delighted to mother Jeff the way she had once mothered Sarah.

Andries began to put her under pressure to take a decision. He wanted her to make his life her life. But he had become politically involved. His art, he told her earnestly, was now secondary to his idealism.

Sarah was aware of his year-long involvement with Resistance

Africa South – RAS – pronounced Race. It was a small group of fifteen, whose only political doctrine was that they were anti-racist, progressive liberals. They had extended their definition of passive resistance to include the destruction of inanimate objects such as electricity pylons and railway signal-boxes. They had nothing whatever in common with John Harris, who had been responsible for the explosion of a bomb at Johannesburg station. That explosion had cost lives. All the same, like all true libertarians they were, of course, opposed to the death penalty.

After swearing Sarah to secrecy, Andries told her that the group was composed of white activists – ten men and five women. They had limited the number to safeguard themselves against the risk of informers. RAS members kept a low profile, and were never seen at any political gatherings. The true identity of each member was known only to their leader, who was code-named Dunlop. Well-known brands such as Shell, Nestlé and Heinz were assigned to the rest.

'May I know your code, Andries?'

'Dunlop.'

'So you're the leader?'

'Yes.'

The decision Sarah eventually took boiled down to the fact that she could no longer continue with her fake marriage. In any case, the other members of the group were against the dishonesty Sarah's dual loyalties represented. They had taken a vote: she could join, but she and the dentist would have to split. Their ideology and her infidelity were incompatible.

She was given a two-month deadline. Meanwhile, even before she left Dimitri, she was code-named Lux and welcomed into the family group.

Sarah now knew what she was going to do; the problem was how to do it. She began to lose weight. Andries handled her, and her dilemma, with infinite tenderness. He understood her difficulties. He was sure that in the end she would find the courage to do what she had to do.

Their last debate on the subject was even longer than usual, and when she returned home the servants told her Dimitri was waiting for her in the bedroom.

'You're late, you bitch,' he yelled.

'I'm sorry, Dimitri.'

'Where have you been?'

'Shopping.'

'Where are the parcels, you lying bitch?'

'Please, Dimitri,' Sarah said starting to cry. 'Please don't call me a bitch.'

'What's the matter with you, anyway? You look like a ghost.'

Sarah flung herself on the bed and wept silently. Dimitri sat beside her and stroked her hair. 'Why don't you tell me what's worrying you? I'm your husband. I want to help you, you know. You should tell me. I'm sure I could help.'

'Could you?' Sarah said desperately.

'But I love you,' he said slyly. 'So I want to help you. You know I'd do anything for you. I want you to be happy.'

'You want me to be happy?' she repeated.

'Of course I do. What's the problem? Tell me the problem, and I'll do my best to help — '

Sarah told him.

When she finished there was a long silence while Dimitri stared out of the window. Then he said gently, 'You've just come from him, haven't you? Stand up, Sarah.'

'Stand up?' she echoed.

'Must you always repeat what I say, Sarah? Stand up. I want to look at you.'

Sarah stood up obediently.

'Come here,' he said kindly. 'Come to me.'

Almost sleep-walking, she moved towards him.

'How long has it been going on?'

'Since January.'

'Eight months?'

'Yes.'

Dimitri whipped both her cheeks with his open palm. When she dropped to the floor, he grabbed her hair and, using it to raise her head, systematically banged it on the floor. Suddenly he stopped. 'Too bad there's a carpet,' he grunted. He was panting. Too terrified to scream, Sarah revolved her eyes frantically. 'Stop acting!' Dimitri yelled. 'Stop doing that to your eyes!'

Quickly Sarah shut her eyes.

'I'm going to see that he gets the beating of his life, do you understand?' Dimitri hissed. 'I'll have the bastard's knee-caps broken. But first I'll finish with you!'

She heard her skirt tear, and as he ripped off the bikini panties he yelled, 'He's just fucked you. Now I'll fuck you! You'll have been with two men in one hour – just like a whore!'

He began banging her head again. For a minute or two everything went black. The next moment she heard the unmistakable roar of his car. He's gone to his parents, she thought. He's too much of a coward to touch Andries himself. He'll pay someone else to do it.

She crawled to the bell-push and pressed it three times. Violet answered to three rings, Georgina to one. Sarah had known Violet for as long as she could remember.

'Ow, Miss Sarah,' Violet said. 'Shame.'

'Violet, don't tell my parents, hey?' Sarah whispered. 'Run to the big house, and tell the driver to come quick. Where's my bag?' Violet handed it to her. 'Give him these keys. Tell him to start the car and then run back for me.'

'Ow, Miss Sarah!'

'Please, Violet,' Sarah whispered urgently. She took several rand from her purse. 'This is for you, Violet. Run now! *Run.*'

Despite her vast girth, Violet moved rapidly and gracefully. By the time she returned the driver had already started the car. Violet took in everything in a single glance with loud, sympathetic clucks and deep sniffs. The room was rife with Dimitri's scent, and she knew exactly what he had done. She lifted Sarah off the bed, carried her into the bathroom and crooning sorrowfully all the while, ran the bath and placed her in it.

'The water will be better for you, Miss Sarah,' she said grimly. Then she wrapped Sarah in a fluffy white towelling gown and helped her to the car.

That Violet knew she had been raped by her own husband subtracted something from the shame of it for Sarah. Violet, being black, understood such things in the way her mother never could.

'If no one is at the place you're taking me to, William,' Sarah said to the driver as they were speeding to Andries' house, 'we'll drive to the hospital.' Fumbling in her bag, she drew out another five-rand note. 'Don't tell my parents anything,' she said desperately.

At Andries' house she asked William to sound the hooter. He and Lily came out at once, and together they carried her inside.

The next day Andries and Sarah moved out of Andries' little house. Tony Kingsley, one of the members of RAS, a brilliant PhD student and the son of the chairman of one of Johannesburg's leading industrialists, offered to take them in. Andries and Sarah were confident that the Blums would have no influence over him.

Nevertheless they had to suffer endless visits, recriminations and threats from her parents, who were more concerned about her losing the custody of Jeff than about her beating. When Dimitri was awarded the intermediate custody of Jeff, Max and Fanny aligned themselves with him and were now solidly on his side.

By this time Andries and Sarah had been living together for six weeks. They were munching the grilled chicken they had bought at a roadside restaurant. This sort of unprepared eating was what Sarah loved – it was so different from those rigid, boring mealtimes.

Turning his attention to his sketchbook, Andries said, 'We've changed our minds. If your Alfa-Romeo is seen near the Chub Mine it will look suspicious. You pulled off like a real pro after we blew up those pylons.' He ripped a page from his sketchbook and tore it to shreds. 'But the Alfa's too great a risk.'

'Well, I have to say I told you so.' Sarah grinned.

'But we will need a very fast car.'

'I know.'

'We'll solve that problem somehow. If we succeed in paralysing just one gold mine,' Andries said, as he had said so many times, 'we'll put the fear of God into them.' His eyes clouded. 'I was brought up to despise the cruelty meted out to the Boers. My father talked about justice, justice and God-fearing men. And when I told him about Dirk Wessels, what did he say? He said, "The sins of the fathers are visited on the children. All God-fearing people know that," he said.'

It was nearing midnight, early in summer. Tony had given them the upstairs studio. The roof was made of cleverly designed glass; they could see out, but no one could see in. Sarah looked up at the distant stars and then down again at the sliver of a scar on her wrist. She and Andries knew everything there was to know about one another. They had explored one another's souls – indeed, she felt she knew more about his childhood than about her own. The scar had been put there by Andries. He had lightly slashed both their wrists, mingled their blood and pronounced them married. He was watching her. He went to her and began unbuttoning her blouse.

541

At that moment they heard the sound of a car door slamming. Waiting, hoping against hope that this would not be followed by the dread sound of a second door banging, Sarah hastily buttoned her blouse. A second car door banged loudly. Then came the sound of boots on the gravel, the imperious ring of the doorbell and the rap of the brass knocker against the door.

'We'll have to let them in,' Andries said bleakly.

'Yes.'

Sarah followed him down the stairs. They opened the door to admit two men in plain clothes, who waved documents at them. Soon other police arrived and began to search the house. Among other papers, they took the sketchbook Andries had been scribbling in only a few minutes earlier.

At the same time the Blum and Politis homes were raided. Fanny was indignant, but Max was as hospitable as he was cooperative. That was how he learned that Sarah was being detained at the Fort, a Johannesburg jail. She was being held under the provision known as one hundred and eighty days' detention without trial.

'My daughter's a little bit off her head,' Max confided to Detective Swart. 'It all started after we had that armed hold-up.'

'I'm very sorry for you, Mr Blum, very sorry.'

'Thank you.'

As soon as the police left, Fanny began to wail horribly.

'Shut up, Fanny,' Max said impatiently. 'I'm phoning Gerald Katz.'

'What's the good of a company lawyer now?'

'I'll get him over. He'll know the right sort of criminal lawyer for us.'

Gerald Katz lived less than five minutes away. In no time at all he was with them.

After telling him about Sarah, Max turned to Fanny and said, 'Leave us alone, please.'

'It's hard on a mother,' Gerald Katz said as Fanny left the room.

'Are you trying to tell me it's not hard on a father?' Max asked rhetorically. 'I want you to tell me all you know about Barry Ross.'

'That *shyster*!' Gerald Katz snorted.

'I just wanted to familiarise myself with some of the cases he's had a hand in,' Max said quickly. 'I seem to remember him getting Levin off with the customs and excise problem he had.'

'Barry Ross is less than scrupulous.'

'That's what I need.'

'True.'

'You see the trouble I'm in?'

'Indeed you are. Big trouble.'

'Does Ross's influence measure up to his reputation?'

'If you're asking me whether he uses what is euphemistically known as extra-legal methods – yes, he does.'

'Is he well in with the authorities?'

'If by authorities you mean the prison and criminal divisions, then, yes, he is well in with them.'

'I want you to get him for me, now.'

'I couldn't do that. Not at this hour. I've known you for something like forty years, Max. Surely you understand?'

'Then get him on the line. If you talk to him he'll be here in ten minutes.'

Gerald Katz made the call.

'I'll leave when he comes, of course,' the lawyer said unhappily.

'Please do.'

After Gerald Katz had made his hasty exit, Max told Barry Ross exactly what had just happened, and summarised the history of Sarah's marriage.

Ross raised his hand warningly. Very softly he said, 'Where is the bathroom?' He indicated with a gesture that Max should accompany him.

In the bathroom he turned the taps on full blast, and said, 'The place may be bugged already.'

'I don't care if you take me for the biggest ride of your life,' Max said rapidly, nervously. 'Money is no object. I want my daughter out of there.'

'It will take time as well as money, Mr Blum.'

'Can you do it?'

'I can only do my best.' Barry Ross chain-smoked. He lit another cigarette. 'I'll need cash, I'm afraid.'

'How much?'

'Fifty thousand rand, at least.'

'The Special Branch will be watching my bank balance like

hawks. The most I can give you in cash is ten thousand. I can give that to you immediately.'

'That's not nearly enough. This is not for my fee, you understand.'

'We'll make a plan. We can get money out through the company, later.'

'Why don't you ask your wife? In my experience wives usually have an emergency cache of funds.'

Max went to the foot of the stairs and shouted for Fanny. He met her halfway up, explained what was needed, and followed her. Almost at once he was back in his study. 'You were right, she had twenty. Added to my ten, that makes thirty. You can count it if you like – Fanny's never wrong about money.'

'Wives are particularly exact, I find,' Barry Ross said smoothly. 'There's no need for me to count it.' He paused. 'Should I get your daughter out, I'll need one of your contacts, someone with clout with the British authorities.' He grimaced. 'Someone who could respond in an emergency.'

Max shook his head negatively.

'You must have at least one contact,' he said sharply.

'Sir Simon Saffity?' Max said doubtfully.

'Are you sure Sir Simon would cooperate?' the lawyer asked urgently.

'Just ask your man to use the words, "La Fenêtre de Saffarty".'

Barry Ross noted phone numbers, and laboriously wrote, 'La Fenêtre de Saffarty'. 'But whatever you do,' he added, 'don't attempt to get in touch with him first.'

Two days later he reported that things couldn't be worse. Andries de Waal had turned state witness and, if his information was correct, Sarah would serve no less than ten years.

Terror had replaced time. Sarah felt distant from time; she had lost all sense of it. Her eyes throbbed. They had taken her watch away.

Actually, she had been in the Fort for four days. She lay on her side on the prison cot and tried to remember what she had told them. They could keep her there for as long as they liked, for ever if necessary. They had told her they could go on extending and extending the one hundred and eighty days. Her back ached. They'd kept her standing for whole days and whole nights. Her scalp burned, they'd pulled her hair out. She was confused and frightened. Her mind whirled in circles of chaos. They'd called her a Jewish whore, a whore of a mother, a disgrace to the word mother. Sometimes she didn't know whether she was sleeping or dreaming. When her name was called she jumped. They called her Politis.

On the fourth night one of the wardresses called her Sarah, and brought her hot tea. She wept with gratitude, and wept herself to sleep. Some time later the same wardress entered her cell and woke her. She sat on the bed and stroked her hair. She had thin eyebrows and thinner lips, Sarah noticed. She'd heard of lesbianism in prison and her skin crawled.

'I brought you something to eat. Tea and biscuits,' the wardress said.

'I can't eat.'

'You can and you will. Sit up.'

Sarah sat up obediently. 'How long have I been here?'

'This is your fourth night.'

'Only four nights! Oh my God!' Sarah moaned.

'Eat! I haven't got all night. I'll get into trouble myself for being here.'

'Why are you being so kind to me?'

'Try to sleep. You need your strength.'

Sarah couldn't sleep. She wished the woman had not been kind, it was too confusing. Only four days and four nights! She tried to calculate the hours and gave up. She was Lux, she wasn't Sarah. Had she told them her code name? What had she told them? Where was Andries? She would die here, she was sure. She would die soon. Soothed by images of her own funeral, she slept.

The next morning there were great weals all over her body. She showed them to a wardress. A doctor came and told her it was an allergy. She was given an anti-histamine injection. She slept the rest of the day away.

That night, at eleven o'clock, Sarah was woken by the same wardress. 'Get up! Get up!' the wardress hissed. 'You've got no time to lose.' The wardress pulled her off the bed. 'I can't switch off your light,' she complained.

'What?'

'Listen carefully. You are getting out of here.'

'Getting out?'

The wardress pulled out a bundle from under her dress. 'Listen to

545

me! You've got to change into this nurse's uniform. I'll help you.'

Quickly the wardress put the nurse's uniform over Sarah's head. 'Come on. come on. Pull it on. You've got to wear these black stockings, too. And the black shoes. Hurry! Hurry!'

While Sarah was dressing the wardress said, 'You've got to hit me hard over the arm with this truncheon!'

'What?'

'Very, very hard. Hard enough to break my arm.' She handed Sarah a standard nurse's cape – navy blue lined with red. 'Put that on now, and the cap. And listen to me.'

'I'm listening. I understand.'

'You have got to break my arm. With this truncheon, you hear me!' She thrust the truncheon into Sarah's arms. 'Wipe it with the cape. I don't want fingerprints.' She watched Sarah do as she said. 'Here's this thing – I don't know what it's called, but you must put it round your neck.' It was a stethoscope, and Sarah put it on. 'After you're broken my arm, you must walk out. If anyone stops you, just tell them that bloody traitor, Politis, was haemorrhaging. Say she started bleeding. Speak Afrikaans. But I don't think anyone will stop you. They're on a coffee break. Do you understand me?'

'Yes.'

'You must take your prison dress with you. A black Chev will be waiting for you right outside. Get in the front seat.'

The wardress lay on the floor of the cell. 'Now smash my arm,' she ordered.

'I don't think I can do it.'

'You'd better. I'm getting good money for this,' she said harshly. 'Quick, do you want to stay inside for ten years? I can't break my own arm. Bring the truncheon down hard, hey! You're weak. Come on! Pretend you are chopping wood! Slam the door shut. Take these keys.'

Sarah sighed. She brought the truncheon down, again and again, exactly as if she were chopping wood.

'Go now,' the wardress said. 'Be quick.'

She forced herself not to run.

The door of the waiting Chev was slightly ajar. Sarah jumped in and the car pulled off. The driver said nothing, but Sarah felt his tension. He snapped on the radio. She found the music deafeningly loud.

After several minutes she asked, 'Where are you taking me?'

'Swaziland. No passport barriers. From there you'll be flown to Botswana.'

'How long will it take us to get to Swaziland?'

'Four and a half to five hours, *if* we're lucky.'

'Who are you?'

'None of your business.'

Sarah stared into the black night. About two hours later, they heard the screams of sirens. 'Shit!' he fumed. 'It's the cops.' Without looking at her, he said, 'In case they ask you, my name is Eddie Khourie.'

He pulled to the side of the road and rolled down the window.

'You overshot the speed limit by — ' the officer began.

'I'm sorry, officer,' Eddie interrupted excitedly. 'I'm rushing the nurse to deliver my sister's child in Melville. She's in labour.'

'OK. Get moving then!'

'That was close,' Sarah said.

'Too close for my liking.'

'The casino at Manzini will be open. We've got to stop there and have breakfast.'

'Breakfast at the casino? I'd be too terrified to move out of the car.'

'Those are my orders. And you'll have to behave like a normal nurse.' He looked at her with distaste. Then he grinned nastily. He was getting five thousand rand for this courier job. Why the fuck should he care if she was a *kaffir-boetie*, a lover of blacks? Still, if they were caught, he'd be in deep shit. 'At Mbabane a chartered plane will be waiting to fly you to Botswana. A very sick patient needs you. Got it?'

'Yes.'

At three o'clock Eddie stopped the car. 'Go to the washroom and fix yourself up. I'll wait for you and then take you for breakfast.'

'What's the idea behind all this?' Sarah asked when she joined him.

'Would a fugitive have breakfast at a casino?'

'No.'

'That's the idea.'

Sarah's hand shook. As her teeth crunched the toast she thought of the wardress's arm. She wondered whether her escape had been detected yet. The ANC must have organised all this, she assumed.

Until now she had not known of any connection between RAS and the ANC.

They drove on to Mbabane in a brilliant sunrise. 'That's the airport,' Eddie said. 'It doesn't look like one, but it is. And that's your plane.' He made a sound that was almost a laugh. 'Five-thirty a.m. Smack on time!'

Minutes later Sarah was strapped inside the four-seater charter plane. 'Must be a mighty sick patient you have, nurse,' the pilot said.

Sarah nodded. The plane lifted. She had very little sense of geography, but knew that they were overflying South Africa. She could not get the wardress's arm out of her mind. Closing her eyes, she tried to sleep.

'Wake up, nurse,' the pilot called. 'We're about to land.'

The door of the plane was opened from the outside. As Sarah stepped onto the tarmac an educated voice said, 'Welcome to Botswana. Hugh Greaves.' He shook her hand formally.

Then Sarah was in a huge, luxuriously upholstered Mercedes. 'We're going to my home. I think you'll find it something of an oasis of civilisation in this wilderness.' He spoke in the high, rolling tones of a newsreader on the BBC. 'Have you been to Botswana before?'

Sarah shook her head. She looked out at the sunrise. When the Mercedes stopped outside an imposing mansion, she followed the man indoors.

'I'm sure you'd like to bathe and change. We have some fresh clothes for you.'

When she had bathed and changed, she studied herself in the mirror. Her frightened eyes were wide and staring; she looked ill, grey, at least ten years older. For the first time she noticed she had large bald patches. She wished she had a lipstick. The clothes – blouse, skirt, cardigan – were newly bought but cheap and ill-fitting.

On the bougainvillaea-covered verandah, Hugh Greaves presided over a sparkling silver tea service. 'Tea and croissants? Or coffee and croissants?' he asked genially. 'I have an excellent cook.' He smiled. 'You look much better.'

He held out a chair for her and she sat down. 'Well now, I expect you're more than a trifle confused,' he began. 'I'll fill you in on the details. The President of Botswana, Seretse Khama, is a close and valued friend of mine. He will shortly be in contact with President Kaunda of Zambia. He will, of course, inform Kaunda that you are yet another of apartheid's refugees.' He paused dramatically. 'Which will ensure you his personal protection.'

Sarah seemed not to have heard him. She said miserably, 'She forced me to break her arm! She made me do it!'

'Excuse me? I'm not sure I follow.'

'The wardress at the Fort. I smashed her arm with a truncheon.'

'I see,' he said politely, as if they were discussing a disagreeable play. 'It appears I've been somewhat remiss. Of course you know neither that I'm a lawyer, nor that I've been retained to arrange your safe conduct to London.'

'Then you've got to know something about Andries de Waal,' Sarah said excitedly. 'Can you tell me what's happened to him?'

Sighing flamboyantly, he cocked his head to one side. 'It grieves me to be the harbinger of bad news — '

'Bad news? About Andries?'

'Andries de Waal is in perfect health,' Hugh Greaves said dryly. 'He knows how to look after himself. The bad news is that he's turned into a state witness.'

'What does that mean?'

'It means he's cooperating with the police.' He paused as if looking for the right words. 'I'll be blunt, Sarah. He ratted on the lot of you. He betrayed you all and told the police everything.'

'I don't believe it — ' Sarah said bleakly.

'I can quite understand that. Meanwhile, you'd be well advised to keep your wits about you.'

The phone rang. Excusing himself, he went to answer it.

'There was a news flash about your escape on the SABC,' he announced. 'Shall we wend our way to the airport?' He pulled out her chair. 'Kaunda's crew should be ready for take-off.'

In the car, he said conversationally, 'Our last experience of this sort of thing in Botswana – when Goldreich and Wolpe made their famous escape – was not so happy. The South African security forces blew up that plane, and they had to wait for another. Happily, we learn from our experiences. Our plane is under armed guard. We are due to take off at nine-thirty and we should be in Zambia by noon.'

At Oak Lodge, Fanny and Max faced their furious interrogators. They made no attempt to disguise their confusion. They only knew

549

about Sarah's escape when Brigadier Reitz told them. They refused to believe she had broken the wardress's arm. Sarah may have gone off her head, they said, but she wouldn't hurt a fly.

It was six o'clock in the morning when the police had pounded on their door, and the interrogation had been going on for three hours. Brigadier Reitz suddenly lashed out at Max, '*Kaffir-boetie!* Paying out good money every year to Jeffrey Ndlovo!'

'Jeffrey *who*?' Fanny shrilled. 'What's he talking about, Max?'

'Come on, don't play the innocent little woman,' Brigadier Reitz said menacingly.

Embarrassed, Max quickly explained to his wife and the police how he had come to support the son of a servant they had dismissed so long ago. Then he begged to be allowed to send for their lawyer.

Gerald Katz arrived and protested loudly that if he'd been allowed to see the girl he might have been able to give them some information. Max and Fanny admitted they didn't know whether to be glad or sorry about Sarah's escape. She was their child and they would stand by her. That is, if she only gave them the chance to do so. Brigadier Reitz and his men left in disgust.

'Don't talk. The place is bugged,' Gerald Katz wrote on a piece of paper, so they launched into an agitated discussion about what could have happened to Sarah.

'Where is Barry Ross?' Max wrote.

'I'll get a call from London.' Gerald Katz shook his head and burned the paper. He gave a V for Victory sign and left.

'You should have told me about Absalom's son,' Fanny said reproachfully. 'I must say, they had a nerve calling their child Jeffrey!'

Now in London, in a suite at the Berkeley Hotel, Sarah tried to make sense of the last forty-eight hours. She was still feeling the after-effects of the massive injection of valium that had been given to her as she boarded the plane. The reality of Andries' betrayal had finally hit her. She had not been able to stop crying.

She recalled the rushing urgency with which her photograph had been taken and a Zambian passport issued. Everything seemed to have been happening to someone else. But the passport was there, on the coffee table. She picked it up. 'Sarah Blum – divorcee', she read.

Was she divorced already? As far as she was aware, the proceedings had only just been set in motion.

Her mother's words came back to her. Such ordinary words, such a boring cliché, she had thought. 'You've made your bed, you must lie in it.' Flushed with love, she had scoffed, 'You don't know the meaning of bed!'

But then who would have believed she would ever be a refugee and an exile? It was only when their British Airways flight was about to land that she had found the courage to ask Hugh Greaves if he thought she would be permited to return to South Africa to visit her son. 'Yes, if you are willing to serve ten or twenty years in prison. If not you will never be able to return to South Africa.' He had frowned. 'Doubtless the courts will appoint your son's father as his sole guardian. In the circumstances, it seems highly unlikely that Dr Politis will allow his son to travel to Europe to see his mother.'

Detective Swart had been right to call her a whore-mother. Sarah began crying again.

Hugh Greaves had the adjoining suite. He tapped on the door. When there was no response he shrugged and walked on. 'Oh, Lord,' he thought, 'she's carrying on.' He loathed weeping women.

Safely back in his own suite, he dialled again the number Barry Ross had given him. There had been no answer earlier.

'I'm afraid Sir Simon is not available,' a cool, high voice told him. 'This is his daughter, Jem. Can I help you?'

'This is something of an emergency, I fear,' Hugh Greaves answered. Then, speaking rapidly and clearly, he spelt out the details.

His conversation ended, and he replaced the receiver thoughtfully. Sarah needed a friend. Jem Saffity had been absolutely charming and almost immoderately helpful. When, more or less *en passant*, he had mentioned one hundred and eighty days' detention without trial, her response had been immediate. 'It sounds even worse than boarding school,' she said sympathetically. 'I understand exactly how she feels. I'll do all I can to help.'

He waited for a while, and then decided that the time had come to speak plainly. He poured a large cognac and took it to Sarah.

'Drink this!' he commanded.

Sarah looked up at him. Avoiding her swollen red eyes, he said, 'You'd better think about those who've risked themselves on your account.'

'I don't understand.'

'The wardress, for example. Have you spared a thought for her? Of course not. You're only thinking that your lover betrayed you.' He laughed derisively. 'You'd better grow up, my girl!'

She began to cry again. 'For God's sake, stop that,' he said, not unkindly. 'And concentrate on what I'm going to tell you.'

Satisfied that he had her attention, he went on. 'Fast cars, a chartered jet, a suite at the Berkeley, the cooperation of Kaunda, a wardress's broken arm . . . and then of course there's my fee. Who do you think is funding all this, Miss Blum?' he asked, sounding like a radio quizmaster.

'The ANC,' Sarah replied unhesitatingly.

'Ah! The ANC,' he repeated, rolling his eyes upward. 'You really believe the ANC would do all this for *you*?' he asked rhetorically. 'Why, you bungling, amateur liberal, the ANC couldn't even do this for Mandela!'

Sarah gave way and sobbed still louder.

Hugh strode over to her and shook her shoulders.

'Stop that noise!' he ordered. 'Stop it!'

When she had quietened he said, 'Firstly, the ANC possesses nothing like the funds required for this sort of enterprise. Secondly, an amateur revolutionary like you is hardly important enough to warrant luxury on every front. Do you understand that?'

Sarah nodded miserably.

'Good girl!' He clasped his hands. 'So who do you think is responsible for the funding?'

Sarah covered her face with her hands and shook her head mutely.

'Your parents,' he said scornfully. 'Your bourgeois parents!' His tone became friendlier. 'I telephoned the Saffitys a few moments ago. Does the name Jem Saffity mean anything to you?'

'Yes.'

'She sounds like a very understanding young woman. If you take my advice, Miss Blum, you'll make a friend of her.'

'Oh, Dad,' Jem called out as she heard her father's footsteps. 'I just put the phone down on Max Blum's lawyer.'

'Max Blum?' Saffity's hand went to his heart.

'He's an old friend, knew you in Paris,' Jem said, assuming that her father, who met so many people, had forgotten who Max Blum was. 'Anyway, his daughter's fallen foul of the South African authorities. She's looking for political asylum in this country. Of course I said we'd do all we could to help. So I'm going up to London to see her at the Berkeley.'

Jem's cheeks were flushed with excitement and her violet eyes sparkled. She was heartbreakingly beautiful, Saffity thought.

'What's her name?'

'Sarah.' Jem tossed her head impatiently. 'She escaped from prison!'

Max Blum's daughter? How dare Max presume like this? His mind instantly set to devising strategies to make certain Sarah's origins were kept from Colette.

He said mildly, 'You say you're driving up to London tonight, darling?'

'I told the lawyer I would.'

'I'll drive up with you,' he said at once.

'I was hoping you'd say something like that.'

He would need to have every detail of every fact. He was damned if he was going to allow Max Blum's idiotic daughter to spoil Colette's life for her. The anger rose in him. He coughed briefly.

Jem handled her car, an MG, with the same easy excellence with which she handled a horse. Saffity never ceased to marvel at her competence. She had a soft, fragile air, yet she took everything in her stride – including her mother. She switched on the radio and the sounds of Mahler's *Titan* took over, leaving them each to their own thoughts.

Jem had taken it for granted that her father would not only help but solve whatever problem might arise, the way he always did. When the parents of her friend, Melissa, had found it impossible to meet the school fees, he had assumed the bills immediately. Another friend's small sister had required urgent and expensive surgery in America, and here too her father had come to their aid. His generosity was matched only by his grace; he did nothing to make anyone feel beholden to him. He had mastered the art of giving.

They pulled up at a traffic light, and Jem caught sight of a motorist playing at being a conductor. 'He's listening to Mahler, too,' she said quietly.

Saffity nodded.

'Did you know Max Blum well?'

'Before you were born,' Saffity said soberly. The lights changed.

'Move on.' Directing the talk away from Max Blum, he continued smoothly. 'We shall have to be very discreet about this, you know. This girl, Sarah, may be a political fugitive, but there could well be people after her. It will all have to be very secret.'

At the Berkeley they were shown up to the suite Hugh Greaves had taken. Sarah was listless, cowed and apologetic. She apologised at once because she was wearing the hotel bath robe. She had no change of clothes with her, of course. As soon as the initial pleasantries were over, Saffity suggested that he and the lawyer talk while the two girls got to know one another. Obediently, Jem and Sarah went to the bedroom.

When the two men were alone Saffity said coldly, 'I would appreciate the facts.'

Equally coldly, the lawyer gave him a dry, legalistic account of what had happened.

Saffity uttered a short, contemptuous laugh. 'Nothing quite as irritating as a bungling amateur, is there?'

'Sir Simon, I couldn't agree more,' Hugh Greaves said, warming at once to Saffity.

'The bungling stops here,' Saffity announced, lowering his voice as if he were taking the lawyer into his confidence. 'This affair hardly reflects well on anyone, does it?'

'Frankly, Sir Simon, it could be extremely dangerous.'

'My thinking, exactly,' Saffity said. 'Clearly the girl will have to assume a new identity. What did you say her married name was?' he asked.

Here, in the shape of this stupid girl, was his past come physically and visibly to haunt him. 'Trust Max,' he thought furiously. 'Trust Max to use me again!'

'Her married name is Politis.'

'Her parents will have to be protected, even so. We cannot compromise their security.'

'I am not in direct communication with Mr and Mrs Blum, of course. However, on their behalf, I should like to express my gratitude to you.'

'Jem will take care of her,' Saffity said, managing to suppress a sigh. It really was too bad Jem had taken Hugh Greaves' telephone call; if she hadn't known about Sarah, he would have handled things altogether differently. But he was now forced to cooperate, for to go against Jem's compassionate nature would risk dangerous questioning.

Anticipating what he knew Jem would want to do, he called out, 'Jem, we're taking Sarah to Eaton Place!'

By breakfast time the next morning, it was apparent that Jem and Sarah had become friends. Although Jem was younger, she fussed over Sarah, mothering her. Sarah still looked helpless and defeated, but was more alert than she had been the night before. Taking all this in with a shrewd, sweeping glance, Saffity opened his negotiations.

He began by saying that he would take care of her entry into Britain. He loathed asking favours of his powerful friends, as Jem knew, but in Sarah's case he had no option. Indeed, he had made one or two calls in the early hours of the morning. After outlining the legal and other bureaucratic hurdles that would have to be overcome, he arrived at the issue that was crucially important to him.

'It has been made abundantly clear to me that there is no room whatsoever for any more amateurism — '

'*Daddy!*' Jem interrupted at once. '*Please.*'

'Sorry, Jem, No room for emotional outbursts, either. We're not playing games here, understand?' He consulted the small leather notepad he had laid on the table.

'This is a dangerous situation for *all* of us. No matter how much we may sympathise, Sarah remains a fugitive from justice. She does, nonetheless, have a duty to protect both her parents and herself. From what the lawyer told me – what was his name?' he asked.

'Hugh Greaves,' Sarah whispered.

'Right. Well, it seems that BOSS, the South African secret police, will be looking for her. If they find her, and tie her – er – elopement in with her parents, they will be in serious trouble, and could well face prison sentences. Equally, I have considerable business interests in South Africa, and if your disappearance, Sarah, was linked to me in any way I could be severely embarrassed, not least financially.'

Sarah gasped and Jem went a little pale.

'Not,' he added hastily, 'that that is of prime importance. The fact of the matter is,' he went on smoothly, 'that you are going to have to change your identity, Sarah. We must find you another surname, for a start. You must never respond to either "Blum" or "Politis" ever again. Do you understand?'

'Yes, of course,' said Sarah faintly.

'You must never mention your parents, or talk about your background,' he went on relentlessly. 'You are going to have to reinvent yourself. You must work on your accent. I will organise new papers for you – a passport and so on – but you must make yourself different. Jem will help you, won't you, darling?'

'Certainly I will,' said Jem with the beginnings of a smile.

'Well, you can start by taking this Australian girl shopping.'

'Australian?'

'The accent is similar. Yes, get her some clothes, get her hair done, put some healthy food inside her. Do whatever you like, but get it changed. Go to Mary Quant. I want her to look like a trendy, carefree young woman. Not like — ' He deliberately refrained from finishing.

'And afterwards I'll take her to Oxford with me tonight. I'll take care of Miss Adams.'

'Miss Adams?' he repeated sharply.

'She's Australian, isn't she?' It begins with an A, doesn't it?'

Which reminded Saffity of that long-ago moment when he lied to Colette about Max. An expression of irritation streaked across his face, but he turned it into a huge laugh, 'I see you're no amateur, Jem.'

Like an automaton, Sarah agreed to everything Jem suggested, beginning with a visit to Elizabeth Arden where she was given a facial and a massage. 'Your face is so swollen,' Jem said kindly.

There, with Jem standing at her side, she lay on the couch as if she were being examined by a doctor. All sorts of creams and unguents were applied, and a great deal of use was made of an ointment called 'Eight-hour cream'. At the end of it all her face and eye muscles no longer felt as if they were stretched to breaking point. There, among all these genteel pinks and greys that characterised the salon and its products, her transformation began. Although her skin may have felt less ragged, her mind was blank with bewilderment and shock. Jem, consulted excitedly about colours and concealers, insisted that Sarah would have to go to Vidal Sassoon for his new, short masculine haircut. The two young women left the softness of Arden's, for the seriously clinical ambience of Vidal Sassoon.

The result was astonishing.

Sarah scarcely recognised herself.

Her hair was not only short and shiny but, with her new

make-up, it gave her a cool, languid, sophisticated look she'd never known.

The stylist tilted a hand mirror behind her. 'See the nape of the neck.' he said patronisingly.

Sarah shut her eyes.

'What's got into her?' the stylist said in a stage-whisper. 'Having a nervous breakdown, is she?'

Jem dashed out and came back with a very large pair of sun-glasses. 'We wear them in the winter now,' she said triumphantly. Sarah's eyes – as well as her fright – were now fashionably concealed.

From there they went to Mary Quant for the brief mini-skirts that went so well with her hair, and waistcoats and culottes and even a cowboy-styled hat. Then to Harrods, and lacy, daisy tights, and jeans and silk blouses. Then to a photograph booth in her new outfit, for photos Saffity had asked for.

At last they were in Jem's car, driving to Oxford.

True to his intentions but not to his word, Saffity took care of the legalistic, bureaucratic side of things. Back in South Africa, the Department of the Interior were given certain stringent assurances in return for which an exit visa was granted. After all, the Prime Minister, Vorster, had once stated, 'If a fly is troubling you, you either swat it or let it out of the window.' Sarah, like others before her, had been let out of the window. There had been precedents – not a few young South Africans had been given a quiet asylum in Britain.

So the dogs had been called off her heels.

Saffity also called a high-placed friend he had made in the war and explained matters, and in a very short space of time she was a fully-fledged British citizen with, thanks to Wyndham Carpets' share in Trans-Empire Carpets, quite a sizeable bank account.

To protect himself he told neither Sarah nor Max what he had done.

All Sarah knew, as she stood in Jem's front room in her Oxford flat a week later, opening a package that contained a passport, driving licence and National Health card, was that she was a white British female aged twenty-two, born in London, height five foot six, parents deceased; that her name was Sarah Adams; and that her next of kin, as listed in the back of the passport, was Sir Simon Saffity.

Part Nine

31

In May 1967, six months after Sarah's escape, Max thought it safe enough to fly to England to see her. She came to his suite at the Dorchester and at once asked to see the home movies of her son he had brought with him. She had arranged in advance for the film projector.

When she asked him to run it through a second time, Max could no longer face her hungry eyes.

'It was a long trip. I think I'll lie down,' he said apologetically.

She nodded abstractedly.

He lay down and thought of Jem. He wondered again whether the gold Piaget watch he had brought her was a fitting gift for all she'd done for Sarah. Not that Jem's exceptional kindness could ever be paid for – it was beyond price, he knew.

Whenever he thought of Jem's many kindnesses to his daughter, his eyes misted over. He was still smarting from Saffity's aloof message that morning that in these delicate circumstances it would be unwise for them to meet. How fortunate that Jem had answered the telephone that day! The thought of what might have happened if she hadn't made Max shudder. She had found a flat for Sarah in Oxford, nursed her through her blackest despair and discovered her when she'd taken that overdose.

Was it all only six months ago? It seemed an eternity away. Nothing could have been better than Dimitri's coming remarriage, for little Jeff now more or less lived at Oak Lodge. Fanny spent more time with him than she spent at Trans-Empire Carpets. In Johannesburg the hue and cry had died down, and their friends and relations had been surprisingly sympathetic. Even the Politises had been unexpectedly civilised about the whole affair.

Small wonder that Sarah had commented anxiously on how much he had aged. What with screaming headlines like 'Desperate Detainee Shatters Wardress's Arm', and 'Tycoon's Daughter Escapes Detention', these past months had been fraught with anxiety and shame. But the sensational, embarrassing headlines and the police harassment were as nothing. What did he care about all the articles describing Sarah as a violent psychopath? They had got away with it.

About six weeks after her escape they issued a short statement to the effect that she was in a Swiss institution recovering from a nervous breakdown. It was credible enough; everyone believed she was mad anyway. Whether the British press had been silenced or were indifferent was unimportant. She was not in jail, he told himself again and again. They had got away with it.

Still, he had to admit that she was looking prettier than she had for a long time. She had filled out – become rather bosomy – but still had a haunted look. Again thanks to Jem, Sarah was to begin her first year at Oxford, studying medicine.

Lost in his own thoughts he did not hear her come in to his room. 'I can't thank you enough, Dad,' she said brokenly. 'I can't — '

She had been weeping.

He jumped off the bed and put his arms around her stiff and tense body, rocking her gently. She broke down then, and gave way to her grief.

'Cry, my darling, cry. You're entitled,' he murmured again and again. 'Your father loves you, and will always love you. Whatever you do, I'll always be behind you.'

After a while she grew calmer, and Max unashamedly dried his own tears. They ordered tea.

When they had each had their comforting cup of tea, she said, managing a grin, 'Great suit you're wearing, Dad.'

'Thanks,' he said with an answering grin. When Sarah was still a student the press had named him as one of the ten best-dressed men in Johannesburg; she had despised him for it. This was her way of apologising for that and for a lot else besides. 'You were — ' he began.

'Selfish,' she interrupted.

'Immature,' he corrected. 'Now you're older than your years.' To change the subject, he said, 'Jem doesn't seem at all like her father.'

'You've never liked him, have you?' she asked unexpectedly.

'Who?'

'Saffity.'

'I can't like every business associate. Thank God Jem answered the phone.'

'But it's more than that. He's not just another business associate.'

'Damn right, he *is* more than just a business associate. He's got a half interest in Trans-Empire Carpets, as well as the voting shares,' Max said bitterly.

'Oh, I know that, but — '

'You've never had a head for business, my love. Let's just say that Saffity never really played the game with me. The voting shares are of no importance to him, but he insists on holding them.'

'I've only really talked to him once,' she said anxiously. 'The day after I arrived here.' She bit her lip. 'But I don't remember much about him.'

'You're much better now, Sarah,' Max said hastily. He did not want to talk about that time. 'The best thing about Saffity's his daughter.'

During the ten days he was in England, Max did no business whatsoever. They went to museums and galleries and the theatre. One Saturday they actually saw two plays. She showed him Oxford and learnt for the first time he had been forced to abandon his architectural studies. Max rarely spoke about the past. And of course he took her shopping. A delicate pink evening gown that flowed like a sari from Zandra Rhodes, a polo-necked mini-dress from Cardin; and they both went mad about the peasant dresses in cheesecloth and lace from Laura Ashley. Sarah had thought he would turn up his nose at the masculine blue jeans but to her surprise he considered the Levis to be superbly cut.

His only disappointment was that Jem was away in Scotland with her fiancé, Michael Fisk.

'Is Michael's father on Wyndham's board?' Max asked.

'Do you know him?'

'Yes, we've met. He's a charming man.'

'Jem's amazing,' Sarah burst out. 'She's so serious about me. And she's been so kind. I don't know what I would have done without her.'

On their last day together he presented her with a first edition of William Osler's work.

'Osler?' Sarah said, astonished. 'How do you know about him?'

'Theresa talked about him.'

'D'you know, I can't remember ever having met her.'

'It was one of those things,' Max said unhappily.

'My mother?'

'Apparently she and Jeff used to . . . correspond.'

'And Mom knew?'

'It seems so. I didn't like to press it.'

'I don't blame you.'

When Max returned to South Africa, the first thing he did was to photocopy that long-ago letter Jeff had written from Israel. He had said it should be shown to Sarah when she was old enough. Well, she was certainly old enough now.

He sent it by registered mail. She wrote back saying it would always be her most treasured possession.

Three months later, in August 1967, Sarah was a bridesmaid at Jem's wedding to Michael Fisk. Like everyone else there, she thought Jem the most ethereal, radiant bride she had ever seen.

Jem and Michael had reluctantly conceded a conventionally styled wedding. Jem even agreed to wear her mother's diamond tiara, which – since Saffity had bought it from his impoverished father-in-law – was a source of considerable satisfaction to him.

Saffity had concealed his initial disappointment, but it had not been easy. Bearded like his father, though without the justification of a scarred, patched face, Michael was such a serious sort of chap.

Oxford had hardly been wasted on him; after a brilliant career there he was now making a name for himself as a barrister. But against Jem's iron determination to marry him, Saffity had been powerless. She had made her mind up years before, she said, and could wait no longer.

However, as he danced with his breathtakingly lovely daughter, in her ravishingly demure Hardy Amies wedding gown with its endless guipure lace train, none of his disappointment showed.

Colette was probably the only member of the congregation whose attention was focused not solely on the bride, but on her father as well. Saffity was fifty-nine now, but with his luxurious shock of snow-white hair and his intelligent eyes he was still strikingly handsome, and his tall, lean frame made him look several years younger. He had an undeniable dignity, yet it was a kind of animal-like power that commanded attention.

Then, at the reception, when Colette entered the spectacular marquee made of a cobalt-blue canvas with Jem and Michael's names woven discreetly into it, she was compelled, yet again, to admire Saffity's talent for extravagance. The walkway leading up to the marquee, depicting white, lacy alyssum bordered by grape hyacinths, cornflowers and bluebells, was like a magic carpet. Right down to the fully sprung dance floor, the design department of Wyndham Carpets had transformed it into a palatial ballroom.

If only Myles had lived to see the wedding, Colette thought sadly. But she must not allow anything to spoil this great day. Saffity had told her how, terse and tight-lipped, Jane had made no attempt to conceal her fury over Jem's choice of a husband. She considered Michael Fisk 'beneath contempt', and said she would do no more than lend her presence to the reception and her tiara to her daughter. Saffity's response to his disappointment had been typical of him; he had engaged extra gardeners and thrown his all into making his daughter's wedding an unforgettable event for everyone.

As he played the host, no one could have guessed that he and Jane had just had a furious row because she had heard Colette was to be in the receiving line.

Now Saffity was talking to Sarah. 'Well, my lovely, you look different from the last time we met. Changed your hairstyle again, have you?'

He lowered his lips to her hand. 'Jem's a lucky girl to have such a lovely bridesmaid. Have fun!'

She watched him glide away, then stop to chat with another group. Very soon she heard his deep, infectious laugh again. Then he moved on, pausing briefly to kiss the hand of a stunningly beautiful woman. Sarah marvelled at the way she carried herself. Her gold and mauve Damascus caftan flowed when she was stationary, swirled when she moved, and commanded the admiration of everyone.

Saffity beckoned her over, and introduced her. 'My dear, this is Madame Beecham.'

'And this is the most handsome father-of-the-bride in the world,' Colette said proudly, her eyes glittering.

'Madame Beecham is like a doting mother,' Saffity said to Sarah. But he kissed Colette's hand. 'Thank you, *mon choux*,' he said softly.

Then, turning to Sarah, he added in his confiding way, 'I want you to know you are talking to one of the most remarkable women in Europe. I'm not ashamed to admit Madame Beecham has been my survival ticket.'

Observing Colette glow, and feeling a sort of inner glow herself at having been singled out for what seemed to be confidential information, she wished she had not automatically tuned out of most of her parents' endless conversations about Saffity.

'Well, my lovely, I think you owe the father of the bride the honour of a dance.'

'I'd be honoured, Sir Simon.'

'None of this Sir Simon nonsense,' Saffity grumbled. 'Call me Saffity.'

'Saffity?'

'Saffity's been my name since I was eighteen.' He laughed loudly. 'If you are a good girl I might tell you about it one day. You're not the only one,' he added quietly, with a twinkle, 'who can change their name.'

He dances beautifully, she thought, so rhythmically that she followed him effortlessly. He stopped dancing, abruptly. 'Thank you, my lovely,' he said, his attention clearly elsewhere. 'Now I have to circulate. You're going up to Oxford, aren't you? I'll give you lunch one day if you like. I visit the place from time to time.'

'But will you know where to find me?'

'Of course I'll know where to find you,' Saffity said emphatically. 'You'll be at Somerville College.' He brushed her hand with his lips, turned on his heel and sped away.

Sarah had thought she was long past blushing. The blush spread, and she prickled as with a heat rash. She was not blushing because Saffity had kissed her hand, but because she realised she'd committed a serious gaffe. Of course Saffity knew which college she was at – he had talked to the Chancellor about her, which was why she had been accepted at Oxford. She doubted even he would have been able to fake academic qualifications. She was his protégée; no wonder he was going to keep his eye on her.

Oxford for Sarah was like a dream from which she never wanted to awake. Her small room overlooked a games field, lawns and hedges and had become the sort of haven Oak Lodge had never been. A few students expressed mild curiosity about her background, but it was easy to deflect their questions and turn the conversation to safer ground. Her studies seemed to take up most of her time anyway.

She had acquired a bicycle, and found to her surprise that the muscular exertion of riding was not only pleasurable, but therapeutic. Also, she liked the drizzle and the gloom – it meant that the promise of warmth and comfort was always present. Best of all, however, was that it was altogether unlike South Africa.

She had been determined not to risk being a moment late for her lunch date with Saffity. The invitation felt like a summons. She pedalled furiously, arriving ten minutes early, only to find him waiting.

'Am I late?' she asked anxiously. 'My watch — '

'No. I'm early.'

After they had ordered – Sarah followed his suggestions – he boomed, 'I suppose you know I'm to become a grandfather?' He didn't wait for an answer. 'I've persuaded young Mr and Mrs Fisk they need a country home to bring up children in. I found a place five miles from Stanford Hall and made them a late wedding present. There's not much acreage, but it's big enough. And very pretty, Georgian.'

'That sounds wonderful.'

'Do you know anything about architecture?'

'No.'

'That's what I thought,' Saffity said laughing. 'University life is different over here, I suppose?'

'Oh, it certainly is. It's — '

'A different kind of amateurism,' Saffity cut in. 'Can't interest these academics in industry. They're happy enough to take an industrialist's money, but trade and commerce are beneath them . . . ' he said, waving his hand dismissively.

'Jem thought so too — '

'You were a bit amateurish in the way you went about organising a revolution too, weren't you? But at least you were – *for* change, not *against* change. But change at Oxbridge, my lovely, is viewed with the same degree of enthusiasm as the plague.'

567

'But without tradition there'd be no civilisation to speak of — '

'And if I hadn't bucked tradition, I'd be nowhere. Not that I went in for idealism. Why, when I was your age — '

'What were you doing at my age?' Sarah asked, hoping to steer him away from her recent political past. She now believed her revolutionary aspirations had been stupidity verging on insanity, for which she was paying an extortionate price. Sometimes, feverish with longing for her baby, she would curse South Africa and everyone in it.

'How old are you, Sarah?'

'Twenty-two.' But he *knew*, she thought. It was on my passport.

'Twenty-two. Ah, my lovely, when I was twenty-two, I was madly, crazily in love, with the most beautiful girl in the whole world. I was in love with my own wife. We were married for three years when she was killed. Just like that . . . She and the baby we were expecting.' His body shook with a great sigh. 'Enough about me. Let's talk about you. You look too young to be the mother of a three-year-old!'

'He's not three. He's only two.' She hated herself for the way she was losing control. She bit her lip, but even so a sob escaped.

'You're crying,' he said, astonished. 'Why?'

She tried to speak, but no words came.

'It's the price of being an amateur, isn't it? That's really why you're crying, isn't it, my lovely?'

She nodded.

'You miss your child.' Saffity covered her hand with his, pressing it hard. 'That's only natural, my dear. It is cruel, parting a mother from her child. You are allowed your tears.'

'Thank you for saying that,' she said simply. 'It – it helps — '

'D'you have anyone to talk to?'

'Not about Jeff.'

'You should do more things, go out a bit. Do you like music?'

'Yes.'

'Tell you what,' Saffity said enthusiastically, 'I'll see you after my meeting with the Chancellor and take you up to London. We'll hear Leonard Bernstein conduct Mahler's Second Symphony. I have a box at the Festival Hall.' He pressed her hand again. 'It would do you good.'

'I'd like that very much. I like your carnation. Do you always wear one?'

He seemed not to have heard her. He went on, 'I'll pick you up at Somerville after my meeting. Bring a few things with you, we might as well spend the weekend in London.' He stopped to look at his pocket watch. 'You'll have Jem's room, of course.'

Later, at the Festival Hall, in the delicious hush that follows just after the musicians have tuned up their instruments, for the first time since her nightmare had begun Sarah felt she was not sorry to be alive. The Festival Hall's cold, geometric shape excited her. Saffity's guests, Sir Michael Prior, the banker, and his wife, Lady Selina, had gone out of their way to put her at her ease. They had been among the audience at the very first concert at the Festival Hall, they said, when Adrian Boult and Malcolm Sargent had conducted, and they talked about it with an enjoyment that was both touching and contagious. Saffity seemed quite content not to join in the conversation; his mind was obviously elsewhere. At one point Sarah noticed him jot a few figures on his programme.

The symphony began and she lost herself in it. Then, at a certain moment in the second movement, her emotions overwhelmed her. Though she managed not to sob out loud, tears dashed down her face, wetting her hands on her lap. This was a passage that Andries used to play on his guitar. Once again Saffity laid his hands firmly on hers. Eventually the passage ended and her tears ceased.

He made no comment, later, on what had happened. After the concert they dined at the Savoy Grill, and the range of his musical knowledge astonished her.

Too soon they were standing in the hall at Eaton Place.

'I think you'll find everything you need,' Saffity said. 'Mrs Butterworth will show you to your room. I'll be down in my study for a while, so if you'd like to join me in a nightcap later, you'll know where to find me.'

When she saw her guest suite, she gasped. She had never seen anything quite like the dazzling whites of Jem's room, and had not realised there were so many shades between white and cream. The brass four-poster bed and the heap of cushions were in the same delicate lace. Her eye caught the glitter of the finely engraved Venetian glass on the frame of a tiny white sofa, on which more lace cushions were piled. Potted camellias were everywhere.

The vibrant primary colours of an Alan Jones painting added to the pristine bridal freshness of the room.

She looked around for her suitcase, which the chauffeur had been instructed to deposit at Eaton Place after he'd dropped them at the Festival Hall. It was nowhere to be seen. She went down to ask Saffity if he knew what had happened to it.

'Mrs Butterworth must have put it in one of the cupboards when she unpacked,' he said.

'I didn't think of that.' She felt her cheeks redden.

'Would you like a glass of champagne, my lovely? I usually have some after a concert.'

'Thank you.'

They chatted easily. Once again she was amazed, this time about his understanding of architecture. It quickly emerged that he worked closely with several great architects.

'Architects may be artists and visionaries,' he laughed, 'but the realisation of their vision rests with vulgar businessmen. I don't seem to cause any great distress to American architects, though. They are much more realistic about vulgar businessmen over there!' Saffity went on to talk about his latest meeting with the prize-winning architect, Richard Sheppard, who had designed Churchill College at Cambridge.

'I know nothing about architecture,' Sarah admitted freely. 'But you make it all sound so fascinating.'

'You like to learn, don't you, my lovely?' he said companionably.

'Of course I like to learn. That's why Oxford — '

'How's your love-life?' he cut in.

'My love-life?'

'According to my sources it's not too good.'

'Your sources?'

'You have an awkward habit of repeating what I say. My sources are impeccable – I always listen to what women tell me.'

A silence fell. She stared at the red embers of the dying fire. Somewhere a grandfather clock chimed.

'Past my bedtime,' Saffity announced. 'It's midnight.'

'You are a very attractive man,' she said, the words rushing.

'You find me attractive, do you?' he chuckled. 'Well . . . '

Taking all her courage in both her hands – she thought she would die if he turned her down – she rose from her chair and walked toward him. She saw him uncross his legs, and took that as a signal that if she sat on his lap she would be welcome. She slid herself on his knees, put her arms around his neck and kissed him deeply. His response was all that she could have hoped for. His thrusting tongue seemed to find every crevice, it delayed and explored with a thoroughness previously unknown to her. At the same time he undid her bra so effortlessly she was only aware of her breasts hanging freely after they had been unleashed.

'Come to bed, my lovely,' he said. 'My room, I think.'

He led her up the stairs, limping rapidly, while, leaden-legged with desire, she stumbled to keep up with him. But even when she was between his neatly turned-back sheets, he made her wait while his tongue caressed her skin with the same intimate thoroughness with which it had tasted – and tested – her mouth. She thought he had invented a new eroticism for her.

'Please,' she begged. 'Please. Don't wait any longer. Don't hold back!'

Still, he made her wait. She opened her eyes and in the dim stream of light falling through the open dressing-room door saw that he was smiling. At that very moment he entered her, and her mind drifted away, and as spasm after spasm abolished thought she became a mass of shimmering sensation and it was only when she was reaching her final moment that he let himself go and joined her.

Before she knew it, she was asleep.

About two hours later he woke her and sent her to the guest room. She did as she was told. Feeling it would be a sacrilege to cover her body with anything at all she climbed naked into the bed. Saffity had turned her out of his bed, and yet – because she felt her very soul had been exalted – she was neither insulted nor hurt.

Early the next morning he carried her clothes into her room.

'You left these,' he said.

'Did I? What's the time?'

'Seven.'

He was wearing a sparkling white towelling robe. 'I thought I'd tell you my plans, my lovely,' he said speaking briskly. 'I'm tied up for the whole day, it can't be helped. But run along and do what you like. Go to the Tate, go to Harrods, get your hair done. Do things like that. Theatre tonight. How does that sound to you?'

'Wonderful.'

'Have you got everything you need? Money? I told your father I'd give you whatever you needed — ' He laughed wickedly. 'Though I hardly think he expected me to take care of *all* his daughter's needs.'

She took a long, leisurely bath, and marvelled that instead of feeling shame she felt blessed. The rest of the day passed in a haze of glorious anticipation of the night ahead. She managed to get a cancellation at Vidal Sassoon and had her hair set and re-styled. Then she saw Mr Charles, a make-up specialist, and had her face re-styled as well. Her eyebrows were plucked and arched and, suddenly enlarged, her chestnut eyes assumed a shining depth. She bought all sorts of cosmetics – cleansing lotions, body creams, scents, lipsticks, eye-shadows and mascara. Then she strolled through Harrods, got caught in the Saturday afternoon crush, and chose what she considered a naughty nightie. After that she went to the Tate Gallery, and on impulse bought a coffee-table publication of Francis Bacon's work for Saffity.

It was while she was in the taxi on her way to Eaton Place that she realised she had spent the first light-hearted, frivolous day of her entire adult life. You don't have to be in love to make love, she told herself. She understood why he had sent her out of his bed – he obviously preferred sophisticated, worldly women – women who were ready to go along with his need to remain uncommitted. So, if this was some sort of test, she'd scored an A.

At the same time she knew there was no escaping her griefs and her guilts – she was merely playing truant. Even so, it was exhilarating.

When she returned, flushed and laden with her packages, Saffity answered the door himself. He approved her hairstyle and took her into his study, demanding to see everything she had bought. She showed him the naughty nightie. He made her try it on and then, assuring her his housekeeper had gone out for the evening, made her take it off.

At once, they were on a leather couch, in front of a great log fire. For her it was like making love with all the intensity of practised lovers meeting again after an unendurably long absence.

Because, strangely, she felt neither naughty nor bad, as she had with Andries and Dimitri. Her body seemed to echo his. It even uttered sounds she had never heard before. It was a fabulous duet. There was no fight, no struggle – his older, carnal body felt light and spectacularly right. On and on her body went, following his whispered instructions, and at his orders to explore, a new cry tore out, and she knew she had found the kind of senselessness she had not known she had been looking for. It was perfect that he was an old man and her father's friend, more closely connected to her father than to her, and that marriage and commitment was out of the question. She could not recall ever having felt so safe before.

Under his expert musical touch, his curving fingers brushing like lips, all her inhibitions melted. She felt she had been chaste until this moment.

Sated, they lay quietly. There was no other light besides the fire, but the shining leather upholstery gleamed. The rain pattered pleasantly against the windows, and there was something absorbingly satisfying about the half-light, and the half-silence. He stroked her breasts, almost absently. Suddenly she said, 'But you've been circumcised! The first circumcised man I've ever been with!'

'You're very experienced,' Saffity said mockingly. 'How many men have you had?'

'Two,' she replied unhesitatingly. She corrected herself quickly. 'Three, *now*.'

'Do you know how much is spent in a single year in America on male circumcision? One hundred million dollars,' he laughed. 'So, my lovely, you've had three men. That's not enough, not nearly enough.'

'You're the best,' she said boldly. 'You're no amateur.'

'No substitute for experience, my lovely,' he said, jumping up. 'But we're too late for the second act.' He picked up the intercom and told the driver he would not be needed. 'Mrs Butterworth has probably laid out a cold supper for us. She generally does that on a Saturday night.'

'Good,' she said. 'I'm starving.'

Caviar in a tub of ice, smoked salmon with lemon wedges, and a green salad in a wooden bowl waited on the table; chilled champagne stood in a silver bucket. The heavy crystal glasses glittered, the silver sparkled, the china shone, and everything was reflected in the highly polished mahogany of a Georgian table.

Sarah took her seat beside him, and as she absently glanced downward and saw all these reflections she saw her own nudity reflected too. She had never felt more daring, more brazen or more elated. Dining in the nude with her father's friend was, in a way, more shocking than sleeping with him. She caught her breath.

'You're wondering what your father would make of all this, aren't you?'

'Not exactly.'

'Don't worry about it, he'll never know. Nor will anyone else, unless you tell them.'

'I hardly think that's likely!'

'Don't you? Young girls have the unnecessary habit of confiding in one another. On the other hand, if you're a woman of the world I believe you'll be sophisticated enough to keep private things private.'

'I won't tell Jem, if that's what's worrying you.'

He left the table and fetched a deep crimson dessert from the sideboard. 'Try this,' he chuckled, spooning it into her mouth. 'It's a speciality of the house.'

'It's delicious. What is it?'

'Summer pudding. It's made with bread and raspberries and currants and strawberries. We grow them in our greenhouses at Stanford Hall. It's very English.'

Looking down at the reflection of her breasts in the gleaming wood, she smiled.

'Fabulous tits,' he said softly. 'Fabulous. And since we're being so frank I'd like to tell you my considered opinion is that you are a fabulous fuck.'

'I take that as a compliment.'

'Believe me, my lovely, it *is* a compliment. But I don't want you to get any wrong ideas. There'll be no falling in love. I'm too old for you. I've been in love twice before, and now, at this stage of my life, it's the kind of complication I will not tolerate.'

'Yes, sir!'

'Don't be flippant. And by the way, stop picking your teeth with your thumbnail. It's uncouth. If you want to, we can have a great time together, but it will have to be on my terms.'

'Which are?' she asked, having shamefacedly removed her finger from her mouth.

'No falling in love. No dreams. No possessiveness. Jealous women drive me crazy . . . '

'I accept your terms, Saffity. But I have one condition to put to you.'

'What's that?'

'Absolute secrecy.'

'Agreed.'

'Then let's go to bed.'

The next morning she awoke early, and at once realised that she was still in Saffity's bed. She lay quietly and listened to his breathing. It had been a wild, wild night. She was aware of every stretched muscle – this fifty-nine-year-old man could certainly show much younger men a thing or two. She'd been thinking in naive stereotypes.

She turned to Saffity and woke him.

'I'm still here,' she whispered triumphantly. 'I'm still in your bed.'

'That's because it's Sunday,' he said, reaching for her again.

Later, he told her he had a lunch date, but that his chauffeur would drive her up to Oxford. 'We'll be in touch,' he said. 'We'll see each other very soon.'

On Easter Monday 1968, Jem gave birth to a daughter. She called her Diana Saffity Fisk. The baby was delivered at Jem's home by natural childbirth, and up to the final stages of labour both her husband and her father were at her side. Michael was with her when the baby was born.

The birth was far and away the most moving experience of Saffity's entire life; the baby was not ten minutes old when she was placed in his arms. His terror of dropping the infant rapidly gave way to an overwhelming emotion that was the closest he'd ever come to feeling in the presence of something holy. He tore his eyes away from the baby for a second and caught something of the rapturous atmosphere in Jem's sitting room. His eyes met Colette's though he quickly looked away, he could do nothing to stem his tears.

'You will be more philosophical about everything when you have a grandchild, *mon choux*. You will be calmer,' she had told him. A week later, when he saw the photographs Michael had taken during Jem's labour, he conceded she might have been right. He pored over the photographs for hours and hours, studying the rapt, awed expression on the faces of the obstetrician and the midwife contemplating the baby. After all, Saffity told himself, they had delivered thousands of babies; it was not as if this was a new experience for them. At the time, the constant clicking of Michael's camera had infuriated him.

Now he readily admitted his gratitude to the young, who really knew how to get the most out of everyday technology.

During the christening three months later, in the chapel at Stanford Hall in which he and Edwina, Jem and Michael had been married, Saffity was again overwhelmed by his emotions. Hugging Colin Fisk, it scarcely mattered to him that if Jem had a son it would be the Fisk name, not his, that would endure. He had a grand-daughter; and when the girl was twenty he would be eighty. Posing for photographs in the brilliant June sunshine Saffity thought, happy days, made altogether happier because Jem's mother was in Bermuda.

'Daddy, you must have a photograph with the godmother!' Jem called out. 'Come on, Sarah. You have to do your bit.'

Sarah moved toward Saffity and slid her arm awkwardly into his. As soon as the photograph was taken she unlatched her arm, looking for all the world like a young woman humouring an older man. Saffity congratulated her silently. She was truly extraordinarily gifted in the art of discretion.

They continued to meet frequently, if not regularly, and only when it was mutually convenient. Paradoxically, the fact that they had settled for convenience had added an unmistakable magic to their meetings. Their liaison suited them both – they were friendly confidants as well as lovers, and because there were no complicated strings to entangle them they trusted one another completely. He knew about her dates with other men, and she knew about his; fidelity had never intruded.

Still, it was fortunate Jem's house was currently over-run with builders; it meant Sarah could spend this weekend at Stanford Hall with impunity.

It was a little over a year since their liaison had begun, and perhaps it was because they had declared theirs to be an affair of convenience that their sense of freedom flourished. For example she had followed his suggestion and stopped wearing a bra, and then had no hesitation in telling him how her newly liberated breasts symbolised their relationship, to the point where they had grown larger so that now, as she cycled through Oxford, she was so pleasurably conscious of her jiggling tits that her nipples hardened; she had acquired an extra dimension of sensuality. All of which meant that her sexual need no longer embarrassed her as it had with Andries and Dimitri. 'Good, uncomplicated lust,' Saffity said happily when she told him.

The day after the christening Saffity and Colin met at the Stockton Arms for a private celebratory drink.

'We have a lot in common, Colin,' Saffity said soberly.

'I seem to recall a time when you and I had nothing except enmity in common,' Colin said dryly.

'Correction!' Saffity scowled ferociously. He spoke speedily, furiously, his words as staccato as rifle shots. 'It was one-sided. Your side. Why bring that up now?'

'To keep track, I suppose,' Colin grinned suddenly. 'Taking stock of life never did anyone any harm.' He looked around the pub affectionately. 'We've been coming here for more than twenty years — '

Meeting for a drink at the Stockton Arms was something of a tradition for the two men. It was there, twenty-two years earlier, that Saffity had apologised to Colin for Jane's appalling rudeness to his wife.

'Good thing Jane is in Barbados,' Saffity burst out.

'I've put out a few feelers about General Textiles,' Colin said briskly. 'I think we're onto something.' Five years earlier he had handed over the design department to a younger man and taken over as Marketing Director, when his predecessor had left to work in the States.

'Tell me more.' Colin only spoke like that when things were really interesting.

'The South African market is expanding. Of course, with your Max Blum's Trans-Empire Carpets as an outlet we can't really complain about our share of the market.' He tapped his pipe on the counter. 'We don't want to be greedy. Blum gets a hefty discount. The point is we would have a much greater share if we took over General Textiles. And if we wait long enough we'll get it for next to nothing.'

'Slater getting his fingers burnt out there too, is he?' Saffity said, shaking his head.

'Slater overestimated the poplin market,' Colin smiled. 'He didn't do his homework right. The timing is not quite right, for us – yet.'

For almost ten years, ever since General Textiles had been founded by Paul Slater, Saffity had been waiting for it to collapse. Quality was the byword of Wyndham Carpets, but the synthetic and far cheaper tufted carpets próduced by General Textiles, and sold directly to the consumer, had rapidly gained a thirty per cent share of the market. Fortunately the giant, ill-considered cotton mills Slater had opened in South Africa were now a serious drain on his carpet mills in Britain.

'We've got all the time in the world,' Saffity laughed. 'We waited for patterned carpets to come back into fashion, didn't we?' His laugh turned into one of his most conspiratorial laughs. 'We can wait. Then we'll take over Max Blum's outfit as well. Make him an offer he can't refuse.' He paused and laughed again, this time with real humour. 'Not that we'd have to make that kind of offer; half the shares in Blum's company belong to us. Of course, you know that.'

Colin nodded.

'But you may not know that our shares are the voting shares.'

Colin's neck jerked back in admiration. 'I did not know that, Saffity. But I should have guessed your share would be the vital one.'

While it was true that Sarah looked on Saffity as her closest friend, to whom she could disclose all her failings, there was one deep, darting heartache that she never mentioned. She had laughed, and joked, and done all the right things at Diana's christening, but her longing for her own child – now nearly three years old – made her want to rip her flesh from her bones. That night, when she and Saffity made love, in seeking to drive out her unquenchable longing she was insatiable.

Saffity, understandably, misunderstood. 'Don't go falling in love with me,' he said tenderly. 'That's not allowed.'

'You're even more vain and egocentric than I thought,' she replied savagely. 'Like all men, when you see lust in a woman you mistake it for love.'

'Touché,' Saffity said.

'You can say that again.'

Then, if she hadn't read those rave reviews and press reports about the exhibition of the South African painter and sculptor, Andries de Waal, at the Jeppe Art Gallery, she might have been able to keep her punishment silent. 'Bearded, with a look of restless intelligence in his eyes, the artist describes his work as an unvarnished look at man's inhumanity to man.'

By this time, in March 1970, Jem's baby was two and Jeff was nearly five. It was four years since she had seen or touched her son; and there was Andries, a man who had bought his freedom at the cost of betraying all his friends, giving interviews on the way his work symbolised man's inhumanity to man.

It was too much for Sarah. Weeping hysterically, she watched once more the latest movies of Jeff that her parents had sent her. She could never return to South Africa, and Dimitri would never allow Jeff to visit her. He had gone as far as to insist that her parents sign a legal document stating they would never request permission for Jeff to travel anywhere outside the borders of South Africa to see his mother.

How long she had been looking at the movies and the photographs, and listening to the tapes of Jeff's voice, she could not tell.

She was dimly aware of the doorbell ringing. The ring became more insistent and then the knocker rapped loudly. The sound of the knocker reminded her of the night she had been arrested. Nervously she ran to the window, looked out and saw Saffity's car. Immersed in Jeff, she had forgotten they were going to Cornwall together.

Wearily she went to let him in. He followed her into the sitting room where one of the films of Jeff was still running. Saffity took in and understood everything at once. He sat on the arm of her chair and said carefully, 'What are you going to do about it?'

'What can I do? Jeff doesn't even know who I am!'

'How long is it since you've seen him?'

'Four years.'

'That is a long time.'

'I can't go there, and he can't come here.'

'I know that. But let me think. There must be a way.'

'There is a way. I could go there, and go to prison and ruin his father's life, and Jeff would probably be allowed to visit me for half an hour twice a year!'

'Why have you never shared any of this with me before?'

'It's the only thing I couldn't talk to you about. I'm Sarah Adams, remember? *That*,' she said, jabbing her thumb at the screen, 'is Sarah Politis' child.'

'Have you had anything to eat?'

'I don't know.'

'I'll fix you something. Tea and toast?'

'What? You in a kitchen?'

'There's a lot you don't know about me.' He was already on his way to the kitchen when he called out, 'I'll think of something. We should have talked about this. But I'll think better when you have some food in your belly.'

When he returned she was still slumped in her chair. He put the tray down, and she heard him in the bathroom, opening and closing the cupboard. He came in carrying her hairbrush. After he had brushed her hair tenderly, he said, 'Eat.'

'Your carnation is not up to its usual standard,' she said dully.

He looked down at his lapel. 'It will do, there's nothing wrong with it. Come on, Sarah, at least one bite.'

'OK, OK.'

'Listen carefully. There are no passport barriers between South Africa and Swaziland. And between Swaziland and Mozambique the controls are nothing to speak of. In any case twenty-five pounds – something like fifty rand – would turn them from passport officials to a welcoming committee.'

'How do you know that? Are you sure?'

'I've done some business with the Swazi Minister of Trade and Development,' he said easily. 'You could fly to Lourenco Marques via Lisbon, drive the ninety miles to Swaziland, and your parents could bring the boy to see you. You owe it to yourself to see him. Talk to your old man about it.'

'I could ask him,' she said tonelessly. 'But I doubt —'

'Would it be better if I talked to Max?'

'Oh, no,' she said sourly. 'That would be counter-productive.' She gave a short, mocking laugh. 'He's full of himself at the moment. Saffity has given a college to Oxford, so Max Blum is giving a chair of architecture to Wits University.'

Saffity raised his brows, and then said quietly, 'I'll do all I can to help. You can count on me.'

Several months were to pass before Sarah could even begin to put Saffity's plan in operation. To have mentioned anything about it on the telephone or in a letter would have been disastrous. The Blums were in no doubt that their mail and their telephone were still under surveillance.

When her parents visited London the following year, she waited until they were having tea at the Ritz before broaching the subject of a possible reunion with Jeff in Lourenco Marques.

'I can guarantee one thing,' Fanny said, her voice high with anger. 'If Dimitri even suspects you're thinking of something like this, your father and I will never see Jeff again.'

'I only want to see him,' Sarah begged. 'I'm not abducting him.'

'We can't take the risk, Sarah,' Max said sadly.

'Have a cucumber sandwich,' Fanny said.

Stifling a scream, Sarah said quietly, 'Jeff is my son.'

'If you go on like this, we'll just have to go back to Johannesburg,' Fanny said.

'Then go back to Johannesburg!' she exploded, rising to her feet and storming out of the room.

The Blums were as good as their word; only a day later, they flew back to Johannesburg.

For months after that tea at the Ritz with his daughter, Max could not get her stricken eyes out of his mind. He was haunted by them. Whatever he did, wherever he went, he had the feeling that her eyes followed him.

When the property company, begun as an insignificant little syndicate formed by his poker-playing pals, sought and won a listing on the Johannesburg Stock Exchange, and was heavily over-subscribed, her eyes were there to haunt him. Leading bankers and lawyers sought his advice, but his greatest and certainly most unexpected accolade came when he was elected Businessman of the Year.

A seat on the board of the Transvaal Building Society only whetted his appetite for a seat on the board of Wyndham Carpets. He now had 4.8 per cent of the equity. He would have had more, but exchange control regulations meant it was difficult for him to transfer funds out of the country unless he had official permission from the Reserve Bank. These days, South African businessmen were investing abroad, companies were diversifying, and many of them were doing disproportionately well. Most interesting to Max was the fact that several important companies had successfully raised loans in France. He had taken the precaution of forming a separate company to buy shares; though of course, Wyndham Carpets shares remained his primary objective.

After several meetings with the Reserve Bank it began to seem likely that his application for funds to secure a twenty-five per cent equity in Wyndham Carpets would be granted.

A friend of his, Sam Ellis, had recently acquired a major share in a UK supermarket chain. His deal had been greatly assisted by his London firm of stockbrokers. 'You ought to consult with them before you get authorisation from the Reserve Bank,' he advised.

The following week Max was in London. Sarah met him at Heathrow and drove him to the City. Over dinner that evening she said quietly, 'Hugh Greaves was in London recently.'

'Hugh Greaves?' Max repeated.

'The lawyer who helped me escape. He's ready to help again. He'll see I get to Swaziland. I could meet Jeff there. According to Hugh the group of rondavels at Pig's Peak is almost indistinguishable from those in Kruger Park.' She paused to let her words sink in, before concluding, 'A small boy would hardly know which was which.'

Though Max did not capitulate immediately, he did discuss the plan with Fanny. Many months of delays and excuses followed, and finally, at the beginning of January 1971, Sarah was on a TAP flight to Lourenço Marques, attempting to predict how Jeff would react to her. So far she had passed all her Oxford intermediate exams with distinction, but her desperate need to see her son had robbed her of any sense of real satisfaction.

A suite had been reserved for her in Lourenço Marques, at the Polana Hotel, where she was to meet Hugh Greaves, who would take her to Swaziland. When she arrived, the ornate lofty rooms, the luxurious furnishings, and the exotic plants were as if she had stepped into the previous century, not in Africa but in Europe. But the veld beside the runway, the bright light of the hot summer sky, the earthy smell – all that was unmistakably Africa.

She bathed and changed into a linen dress. When the phone

rang she answered it quickly, trembling. It was Saffity. 'Just to let you know I'm thinking of you,' he said gruffly, and hung up.

Sarah smiled. He was a good, dear man, she thought. He had come to mean everything to her. Because he cherished his own freedom, he encouraged her to cherish hers. It was almost out of a need to please him that she had gone in for the odd casual sexual encounter. Once, while they were locked in one another's arms, she told him about one of her lovers' fumbling, bumbling inexperience, and they had rolled with laughter on the carpet.

Lately, though, the relentless knock of her biological clock had been deafening. Because she was broodingly longing for another baby, she longed for marriage. 'Anatomy *is* destiny,' she said out loud.

She checked herself in the mirror. Hugh Greaves would see that she had changed. She was twenty-seven, but looked older than thirty, and though she was not beautiful without the help of clothes, hairstyle and subtle make-up, men found her attractive.

There was a knock at the door. It was too early for Hugh Greaves, she thought. One of the maids?

Dishevelled and perspiring, her father stood there. 'I broke my neck to get here as soon as I could.' He strode past her and ripped off his jacket. 'I wanted to tell you in person. You can't trust the phones; they're bugged.' He turned to face her. 'I did my best but, well, against her obstinacy, my best wasn't good enough. It just wasn't — '

'Whose obstinacy?'

'Your mother's. She wouldn't let me bring Jeff,' he went on in a rush. 'She's terrified of losing him. She lives for him. She takes him to school herself and fetches him back. She invites his friends. Trans-Empire Carpets hardly exists for her any more. She's besotted with the child.'

'I won't be seeing Jeff?' Sarah asked dully. 'He's not in Swaziland?'

'She threatened to tell Dimitri. She won't give Jeff up; he needs her, she says. He's nearly six years old. She *is* his security. She has a point. Why should he have to face such an upheaval? What would happen to *him* if Dimitri refused to allow him to be with us? Have you thought of that? Dimitri has all the power.'

On and on he went. Sarah felt numb.

'Why don't you say something,' her father demanded suddenly, 'instead of sitting there like a dumb idiot?'

'She's taken over my son,' Sarah muttered.

'You gave him up, remember?'

'As if I could forget,' she said bitterly.

'I did my best, my love.'

'Thanks, Dad,' Sarah said brokenly. 'I appreciate all you did. All you do.' She bowed her head and folded her hands together as if she were praying. 'She's some mother, isn't she? She never liked me. She wanted another son, after Jeff was killed. Well, she's got another son now. She's got *my* son!'

She had to wait until the following day for the next flight to London.

She took her seat on the TAP flight, thinking that only forty-eight hours earlier she had probably been on the very same plane. For so long she had predicted the shape and the form of her reunion with Jeff; that there would be no reunion had simply not occurred to her.

Her mother had effectively sabotaged her.

She snapped her seat belt shut and closed her swollen eyes. Drained, and as empty of tears as she was of hope, she fell into an exhausted sleep.

'Excuse me.' The Portuguese air hostess was politely pressing her shoulder to wake her. 'May I see your ticket, please? I think you're in the wrong seat.'

Sarah looked up and glanced wearily at an obese, sweating young couple.

'Yes, the wrong seat. I'm sorry. May I take your things?'

Like a sleep-walker she moved to her correct seat. She attended to her seat belt automatically, but her trembling hands fumbled.

'Allow me,' the curly-haired man beside her said, as he hooked the metal clip into the socket.

'Thanks,' Sarah said curtly, making it clear she did not wish to talk.

The man shrugged and opened his briefcase.

Three hours later, when the meal was served, she waved the hostess away. The man beside her did the same, and continued correcting pages and pages of typescript. One of the pages slipped onto her lap, and as she handed it back to him part of its wording jumped out at her. 'The Cinchona Tree is the source of quinine, yet not long before the cause of malaria was discovered, there were many who chewed on its bark in the hope that it was therapeutic. Britain introduced the cinchona tree to India where malaria was endemic.'

In spite of her mood, Sarah was interested. 'Diseases of the Tropics' was one of her courses.

'You dropped these fascinating pages,' she smiled.

'I'm Franco Levin,' he said stiffly. 'I'm a doctor with the World Health Organisation.'

'Sorry I was rude to you before we took off,' Sarah said quickly. 'I'm Sarah Adams, and I'm a final-year medical student.'

'Which school?'

'Oxford.'

'Ah, your eminent Professor Silverstone is well known to me!'

They returned to his subject, and Franco communicated his knowledge easily and enthusiastically. He talked of the King of Swaziland, and of the Swazis, with affection. 'It really was the Switzerland of Africa,' he said. 'Have you ever been there?'

'No.' She said nothing about her own brief period in Swaziland during her horrendous escape, nor did she mention that at this very moment she was meant to be there, not on this plane.

While they were waiting in the baggage hall for their suitcases Sarah went to phone Saffity. When she told him what her mother had done, even he was at a loss for words. It emerged that he was tied up for the next few days. Overwhelmingly disappointed, she made her way to her luggage, reminding herself that if she had no rights to Saffity, she had no right to disappointment, either.

'Would you like to share a taxi into London with me?' Franco asked. 'You are going to London, aren't you?' he said, when Sarah did not answer.

'I suppose so . . . I came back much earlier than I'd planned . . . Where are you staying?'

'At the Cadogan Hotel.'

'I think I might have a few days in London myself. If they've got room for me, I'll stay there too.' She was a free agent, she thought grimly. Entirely free. She wasn't expected anywhere by anyone.

Four months later, trembling in her undergraduate gown, Sarah waited for the icy tinkle of the bell that would summon her to her final clinical exam. It was June, 1971, and summer had begun, but the weather was irrelevant. The bell sounded for Sarah, at last, and the next moment she was in the august presence of Professor Pepys, who was wearing the traditional flowing ermine-trimmed gown.

Sarah examined the patient, pronounced the diagnosis, and exactly fifteen minutes later it was all over.

She hurried away, cycling speedily and expertly to the Radcliffe Hotel where, in the cosy, panelled lounge, Saffity was waiting to give her tea. She hesitated in the doorway, looking for him, saw him catch sight of her, and in that brief moment caught him as he raised his newspaper and busied himself behind it. He really was anxious to know how it all went, she thought.

Saffity kissed her on both cheeks and held her chair out for her.

'How did it all go, my lovely?' he asked when they were seated.

'Better than I thought.' She leaned towards him and touched his carnation. 'I have you to thank,' she said shyly.

'My protégée,' he chuckled. 'One of my more successful protégées.'

'We've known each other for five years.'

'Four years and seven months.'

'And in all that time I've never left as much as a hairpin on your territory.' She poured the tea and handed it to him. She poured hers but left it.

'I ordered you scones,' he said quickly. 'I thought you'd be ravenous, my lovely. You're getting too thin.'

'Am I?' she said thoughtfully. 'I began to lose my appetite months ago.'

'Months ago? Why?'

'After Jem's son was born, I think,' she said crisply, 'and when I did not see Jeff.' She leaned towards him again. 'I want to have another baby. I'm close to thirty.'

'I thought we'd be talking about your career — '

'What else are we talking about?' she said nervously.

'I see.' He pushed his cup away.

A strained silence fell. After a while Saffity placed his hand on hers.

'Doctor Levin is a man of quality,' he said quietly. 'He's good husband material.'

'How like you to make it easy for me!'

'Have you shown him your worst side? Have you been difficult, capricious, ill-tempered and moody?'

'Yes, I have.' She smiled in spite of herself. 'I took the advice you gave me long ago — '

'Well, did he pass the test?' he interrupted gruffly.

586

'Yes. He turned up trumps.'

'Same advice I gave Jem before she married Michael. Didn't like him then, couldn't have a better son-in-law now.'

'I know.'

Saffity said mournfully, 'All that training. All that studying, and you're going to give it all up to wipe babies' bottoms. The state wastes its resources educating women.'

'I know you don't mean that,' she said gravely. Her nail fidgeted towards her teeth.

'How many times do I have to tell you not to pick your teeth?' he said severely. 'It's uncouth.'

Sarah bit her lip. 'I love you, Saffity,' she said shyly. 'I'm breaking the rules, I know, but I mean it.'

'I'm deeply touched,' he said. 'Deeply, deeply touched.' He paused for a moment, and said authoritatively, 'You have made the right decision, Sarah.' He flicked a non-existent crumb from his lapel. 'Jem is the only child I'm ever going to father. I have no need to produce any others.' He folded his newspaper. 'Besides, I'm sixty-three years old.'

It was forty-five years since he and Mireille had arrived at the Cape, but at last Max had acquired the sort of Dutch gabled farmstead he had vowed would be his one day. Of course he had not dreamed of owning anything remotely as lovely as this house, or the land with mountains behind, the ocean below and the cathedral-sized two-thousand-year-old tree that seemed to him to symbolise the eternity of the earth. Fanny had wanted to remove the old slave-bell, and his horror at that had led him to superintend the furnishing of the place himself. He filled it with ancient, golden Afrikaner furniture, removed all the shrubs that were not indigenous and stocked the land with every known specimen of the protea family. He brought in herds of deer, from the delicate springbok to the giant kudu. For his grandson's sake he allowed the swimming pool to remain. With the help of his inspired architect – the professor who held the chair of architecture Max had sponsored – the shimmering blue pool disappeared; the stone-lined pool that replaced it was less obtrusive. It was a perfect setting for his steel sculptures.

His stock of buck ran wild. Before landing the Lear jet on the private landing strip, the pilot was forced to buzz the deer, to warn them out of the way.

Max had found his place in Africa, and his place in the world. He gave it an Afrikaans name, *Hoop*, meaning hope.

Hoop was about to be featured in the *Architectural Digest*, and Max had already arranged to have a copy of the magazine sent to Saffity.

The thought of the look on Saffity's face when he found out that Max owned a stake in his company had become a major source of his re-charged energies. He was fully confident that 1972 was going to be his big, big, year. Nor was his confidence without foundation – a meeting with the President of the Banque Reugot was scheduled in Paris for October 9th.

Max had long ago since lost count of how many trips he had made to Europe in the past ten years. He liked to see Sarah, and he liked to escape from Fanny, who did not like to leave Jeff and so did not always accompany him. For the past five years he had had a regular arrangement with a buxom, laughing Frenchwoman called Germaine Poutierre.

The regularity of his correspondence with Theresa was another source of energy to him. She was now a research fellow at St John's Hospital in Milwaukee. One of the reasons he had set up his meeting with the Banque Reugot on October 9th was because Theresa was going to be among the delegates at the Paris International Symposium on Paediatric Cardiology. She loved America and she loved her work; the only thing she did not love was the shortage of research funds, which had obliged her to court several tycoons. Max had never quite forgiven her for having emigrated to America.

A meticulous organiser, Max was to meet Germaine in Paris on October 3rd, Theresa on the 8th, and his banker, Reugot, on the 9th. Five days before he was due in Paris he would be at the Randolph Hotel, in Oxford. He both dreaded and relished the thought of seeing Sarah again.

Two days before he was due to leave Johannesburg, she telephoned him. 'Daddy, don't forget to bring your black tie.'

'What for? I hate wearing a monkey suit, Sarah, you know that.'

'Saffity's giving a very special party, that's why. Even the Chancellor of the Exchequer will be there. Don't tell me you wouldn't like to meet him!'

'Of course I'd like to meet him.'

'He'll be wearing a black tie. The party is for Dr Franco Levin and it is on September 29th.'

It was purely coincidence that Saffity's party – at which Sarah's engagement to Dr Levin was to be announced – coincided with the week that he was on the cover of *Time* magazine. It was, however, just the right sort of crown for the ending of his affair with Sarah, he thought ironically. Besides, he found the idea of introducing the new fiancé of his long-standing mistress to her father, his oldest friend, rather amusing. In any case Max's presence would add to his sense of triumph. Because Max knew his true origins, he was the only person in the whole world who could measure his true achievement.

Endless trays of small squares of caviar and smoked salmon designed like chessboards, vintage champagne and orchids from the greenhouses at Stanford Hall gave the party a stylish, festive air. The guest list glittered with ambassadors, bankers, industrialists, leading politicians and media personalities. As Saffity welcomed them he could not help observing that no one of any importance had declined.

When Max arrived at Eaton Place Saffity greeted him affectionately, pressing each of his cheeks to his own.

'Congratulations!' Max responded quickly, both taken aback and flattered by Saffity's embrace. 'Congratulations, my old friend! What a success story!'

'And you, Max, are probably the only man in the world who knows when I first began to read the financial papers.' He laughed resoundingly. 'You remember our early days in Paris?'

'How could I forget?' Max murmured, discomfited, as always, by any reference to Paris.

'Let me present you to the Belgian Ambassador, Monsieur Boutikas.' Unable to resist a dig at the business Max gave his competitors, he added, 'The Ambassador will be glad to meet you. After all, you're a large importer of Belgian carpets!'

He introduced Max and swept away. A flicker of a grin crossed his face. Negotiations for the take-over bid for General Textiles was imminent. Trans-Empire Carpets would be next . . . At all costs, he wanted to avoid talking business with Max. For that matter, he did not want to talk to him about anything until he had introduced him to Franco Levin.

Max chatted quite amiably. The Ambassador was interested in Rhodesia, in sanction-busting particularly.

Feeling rather pleased with himself after the Ambassador had been whisked away to meet a Texan oil baron, Max made his way to the men's room. This was the first time he had been invited to Saffity's London house. Only a short while ago he would have been resentful about that; now, he was merely amused. He would have to be invited onto the board of Wyndham Carpets. That would be another first for Saffity.

Max was quite happy to talk to Jem; she'd been so good and kind to Sarah. Besides, she was stunningly beautiful. Several minutes later a tall, overbearing woman snatched her away, and he was on his own again. He'd had too much of Saffity's vintage champagne, and his need to go to the lavatory could no longer be delayed. The first one was being used, so he had no choice but to go upstairs in search of another.

Then, just as he was on the brink of opening a door that was three-quarters closed, he froze stock still.

There, right in front of his eyes, in what was obviously the ante-room to the master bedroom, a man was bending over the exposed succulent breast of a woman. The woman was his daughter and the man Saffity.

Saffity freed Sarah's breast, tucked it inside her dress and said, 'It's not easy to bid farewell to these tits, my lovely.'

At that point, a sound somewhere between a sob and a howl escaped. It was several seconds before Max realised it had come from his own throat. Obeying his instant and overpowering imperative to get away, he fled the house.

Moments later he was in a taxi, struggling to get his breath. When he arrived at the Dorchester Hotel, his pallor was so frighteningly pronounced that the porter asked, 'Are you all right, sir? Can I do anything for you?'

Max shook his head.

He was still shaking his head when he reached his suite. He was shivering, too. In his haste to escape he had left his coat at the party. Now there was no longer any need for self-control. Sobbing, he lurched to the bathroom. There he let himself go. The jumble of hate and disgrace, grief and disbelief, and the unforgivable, unmistakable lust in his own loins, made him vomit. No matter how long his hatred of Saffity had endured, at that moment he felt nothing short of murderous.

He rushed out of the bathroom and hurled himself on the bed. His daughter was a bitch and a whore – her mother had always been right about her. The telephone rang, but he did not answer it. He heard his door-bell ring but he did not answer that, either. It was only when he heard Sarah calling, 'Daddy, Daddy,' that he looked up and saw her with the same alarmed porter he had seen earlier.

'Leave me alone,' he whimpered. 'Get out.'

'Excuse us, please,' she said to the embarrassed porter. 'You look ill,' she said anxiously. 'Deathly pale.'

Max sat up and wiped his mouth furiously. 'You are a whore,' he said slowly and contemptuously. 'Your mother always *said* you were a first-class whore.'

'Because I've had an affair with Saffity?'

'You bitch! Get out!'

'I've never known why you hated him so much,' she said helplessly. 'You never told me.'

Max groaned loudly.

'Saffity helped me to stay sane,' Sarah went on as if she were talking to herself. 'It was all over between us, anyway. You need never have known about it, Daddy.' Her voice rose, and she went on defiantly. 'I have no regrets about my relationship with him. Except that I'm sorry you know about it. In all the whole world, it had to be you. No one else knows . . .'

She had been carrying his coat on her arm, and now laid it on a chair. Her voice sank to a whisper. 'Tonight I was going to introduce you to Dr Franco Levin, the man I'm going to marry. Actually, Saffity was going to introduce you to him; that's why he gave the party. He also helped Franco get one of the most coveted hospital consultancies in the country.'

At the doorway, she stopped long enough to say, 'So my mother still thinks I'm a bitch and a whore, does she? If you and she think that, then at least you've got the kind of daughter you deserve!'

With a mighty effort Max raised himself from the pillows. 'After all I've done for you!' he shrieked. 'It cost me tens and tens of thousands to get you out of that stinking jail. It would have been better if I'd left you to rot there!'

The next morning Max flew to Paris. One way or another, he would advance his meeting with the banker, Reugot. If not, there were other bankers.

He usually stayed at the Meurice, and did not at first take it in when he was told that every room was occupied. The concierge was obliged to repeat, '*Je regrette, monsieur, c'est complet.*' Paris was full, there were conventions, he explained wearily. 'But the concierge at the Ritz is a colleague of mine. Would you like me to try him?' he added.

Max hesitated, not, as the concierge thought, because he was calculating the size of the tip that would be required, but because he loathed the idea of the Ritz. If he had not been a menial laundry boy there he would never have met Colette; for that disturbing reason he had never stayed at – nor even entered – that hotel since.

What the hell, he had no choice. 'If you can get accommodation for me, I'll take it,' he said, peeling off a two-hundred-franc note.

Later, at the end of the afternoon, he managed to arrange what he called a 'preliminary meeting' with Reugot. The meeting went well enough, but understandably the bank needed a little time to study the matter. Just as well, he thought sourly; he had come to Paris sooner than he had intended. He was in no mood to see the buxom, accommodating Germaine, however. It was easily cancelled, and she would just as easily be mollified by the large traveller's cheque he sent her.

He was in two minds about cancelling his date with Theresa, and the next day telephoned her hotel to see if she was there. She was, and they arranged to meet that night. She said she would come to his hotel.

'You've changed,' he said almost accusingly, when they were seated at their table. 'What have you done to yourself?'

She had loosened her plait, and her long, gold-flecked hair now swirled below her shoulders. Her new fringe edged her brows, a perfect frame that made the most of her amber eyes, further pinpointing the distracting likeness to Saffity's.

'It's many years since we've seen one another,' she smiled gravely. 'Don't you like the way I look, Uncle Max?'

'You look lovely.'

'I look French, you mean. *Une vraie parisienne*, that's me. I've got a new look. It cost a bomb, but it was worth it.'

'I've known you for forty-four years,' he said emphatically. 'A long, long time. So I can't be fooled about your age. But you could easily fool anyone else.'

'How old do I look?'

'Thirty-four,' he said promptly and truthfully.

'As much as that?' she teased.

'Why did you want a new look?'

'Because I want a new life,' she said simply. 'I want to quit America; I'd like to try living in London. I'd love to get a consultancy at a hospital. And though I haven't got much hope, I'm going to try. Influence helps, of course. You have to know the big shots on hospital boards.'

Listening to her, Max was aware that, though her amber eyes were more vivid than ever, they had lost their hold on him. He was not exactly bored with her, but nor was he intrigued. She had been a heartless cock-teaser – he understood that now – and she had got away with it. Saffity would have known how to deal with the likes of her, he thought bitterly. Whatever woman Saffity wanted he got; Sarah was one of hundreds.

Sarah!

Forcing himself not to think of them, he said cruelly, 'I got your last letter, but there was no time to reply. So another lover jilted you, hey?'

'He didn't love me as I loved him,' she said wretchedly.

'Love? Men don't love, they only think they do,' Max snorted. He knew too well how many futile, yearning years he had wasted on her.

'I will never believe what you say, Uncle Max,' she said sharply.

'You will find a good man,' he said vaguely. 'You will get married, your children will let you down, and *then* you will believe me.'

'What's all that got to do with love?' she asked, bewildered. 'Anyway, it's too late for me. I'm too old to have a baby.'

'Yes, I suppose you are.' And then, to compound the cruelty, he added, 'You should have thought of all that before. What's the use of being a doctor if you can't think of the elementary things at the right time?'

593

On Thursday, Max realised he had been in Paris for three days without calling his office in Johannesburg. 'It just shows you,' he said out loud to himself as he reached for the telephone. 'It just shows you what kind of state my bitch of a daughter has got me into.'

He rang his office and then paced the room restlessly. The phone rang ten minutes later. It was Theresa. She just wanted to say hello, she said uncertainly. She wanted to know if he was quite well. Max was deliberately vague about when they would meet again.

He wanted to phone the Banque Reugot, but that would have exposed his anxiety to them. But if he stayed in his suite any longer, he might weaken. The best thing he could do would be to go out and buy all the newspapers he could lay his hands on, take them to Fouquet and read them there.

Shortly before lunch his restlessness overtook him again, and he returned to the hotel. He was on his way to the lift when the bellboy called after him. 'Monsieur Blum, Monsieur Max Blum?'

A distinguished, elegant old lady in the salon, who had taken to visiting Paris quite regularly, for sentimental reasons, since her husband's death – to do a little shopping, wander down the boulevards, glance at the fashions in the windows, in short to savour the air and ambience of the city she loved best in the world – cocked her head to one side, nodded to herself and crooked a finger at a waiter.

'Yes?' said Max to the bellboy.

'Call for you from South Africa. You can take the call in the *cabine*.'

If only it was the Banque Reugot, he grumbled to himself. He talked to Fanny briefly and irritably, and hung up.

The bellboy was waiting for him outside the call box. 'There's someone in the salon who wants to see you. Will you come with me, monsieur?'

Max took out a ten-franc note, gave it to the boy and followed him to the corner of the elaborate salon.

'Monsieur Max Blum, madame,' the bellboy said, and vanished.

'Yes, it is you,' a voice said. 'It is definitely you. I am enchanted to see you.'

Mesmerised, Max stared at the hand motioning him to approach. He knew that amethyst ring.

'You are Max Blum,' the voice went on relentlessly, 'and I used to be Colette Terblanche.'

Max fainted dead away.

The hotel staff sprang into their instant, tactful routine, and though Max recovered consciousness at once he was only dimly aware of being transported to his suite. 'No, no, he doesn't need a doctor,' the same voice said. 'He's just had a shock, that's all. Leave us, now. Go, leave us alone,' the voice continued imperiously.

Sitting stiffly in his chair, Max faced Colette on the sofa opposite.

'I thought I had killed you,' he said at last. Colette shook her head.

'I was sure you were dead. For forty-four years I have thought you were dead!'

'How terrible for you!'

'I thought I was a murderer — '

'How could I tell you I was alive? I had no idea where you were. Saffity thought you had gone to Australia.'

'*Saffity?* Did you say *Saffity?*'

'Don't you remember him? He used to be called Saffarty.'

'That's impossible. Of course you can't know him. There must be some mistake!' He flung himself out of the chair. 'Am I going mad?'

'When did you last see him?' Colette cut in.

'But just a few days ago! He gave a party for my daughter Sarah — '

'Sarah is *your* daughter?'

'You know her? You know Sarah?' He paced the room wildly. 'This doesn't make sense.'

'For the past forty years I've been living in a cottage in the grounds of Stanford Hall.'

'He knew you were alive! He knew it all this time,' Max said, bewildered. 'But not even Saffity could have been that cruel!'

Colette pulled her shawl tighter over her shoulders. 'He knew you'd left France, but he wasn't sure whether you had gone to Australia or America — '

'He *paid* for me to go to South Africa. He bought my boat ticket.' Max stopped pacing and fell on his knees beside her. 'For God's sake, tell me! What happened to you?'

They talked through the night. They talked over one another, and across one another, and at the same time as one another. They shouted and they whispered. It was a long while before they could begin to sort it all out.

595

Calmly and without a trace of malice, Colette told him what had happened when he left her at the bottom of the pond. Her maid, Marie, had found her, and sounded the alarm. She had been taken to the clinic. But from the very first she had understood that he had panicked. The Doussets had come looking for him. Then, when she had recovered enough, hoping for news of Max she had gone to see Saffity. He had been kind to her, and they had become friends, and from the very beginning she had looked upon him as a son. And he had been a good son, a wonderful son. Also a father. Because he'd given her a chance. She explained how she had met and married Myles – how both of them had doted on Saffity.

Max, in turn, told her how Saffity had given him his chance, first to go to South Africa, and then, when he had given him carpets on consignment, they had become partners again.

Dawn broke, and they ordered croissants and more strong coffee and continued talking. As they exchanged details of their lives, they allowed their emotions the fullest rein – from nostalgia to rage to friendship to tenderness, and even some humour. They laughed to think they had both believed thirty-one to be terribly old.

But throughout that night and the next morning they returned to the central question – why had Saffity done this to both of them? They each advanced theories. Colette believed he had wanted to keep things uncomplicated and it had long since grown too late for him to tell her the truth. Max was certain he had wanted to keep the upper hand, like an expert blackmailer. However painful it was, however disloyal it made her feel, Colette was compelled to agree that what he had done to Max was infinitely worse than what he had done to Colette. To let a man believe he was a murderer when you were absolutely certain he was not – that was evil. Now seventy-eight, Colette would have preferred never to have known Saffity's secret.

'But now that you do know, what will you do, Colette?'

'Wait.'

'But will you tell him?'

'I don't know. But if I do tell him I must first decide how I will tell him.' She sighed. 'I feel dizzy.'

'It is almost lunch-time, Colette. Let's both have a bath. We'll meet in the foyer, in an hour or so's time, and I'll take you to lunch at Maxim's.'

Her head felt dizzy but heavy. She bathed and dressed slowly, and made no attempt to make sense of the thousands of thoughts that crowded and jangled her brain.

During lunch, as she raised her spoon to her lips, the amethyst ring sparkled. 'You kept the ring,' he said in wonderment.

'I never took it off.' She rocked her hand, allowing it to catch the light. 'It's a very valuable piece, you know. You always did have superb taste.'

He told her about his nightmares, and about his son, Jeff. She promised she would come to South Africa one day.

'You know what Saffity's achieved. Now you must see what *I've* done in South Africa.'

'I remember the day you got your certificate from the Ecole Inter-Commercial.' Colette smiled.

'When I left you at the bottom of the pool I was absolutely certain you were dead,' Max said for the tenth time. 'You understand that, don't you?'

'But of course, I understood even then,' she said emphatically. 'Love is understanding, and forgivenesss. Love is *compassion*. I began to understand you more fully while I was still in hospital. It was an accident. People panic; you panicked, too. If you had not been a little hysterical to start with, you never would have left me like that, bleeding into that mirrored pool . . .

'Ah, *chérie*,' she continued sadly, 'I had always analysed your every expression, so you can imagine how closely I analysed your suffering that day.' Rearranging the folds of her shawl, she sighed. 'There was nothing you could do – you thought I was dead.'

'But I never forgave myself,' Max whispered.

She smiled then, and her worn, weary face was illuminated by tenderness. 'You know, Max, you did care for me. You didn't want to care. But I knew your lust had shamed you into not wanting to feel anything like affection for a woman who was so much older than you. The day you gave me this amethyst, I was certain I knew what you did not want me to know.' She sighed again. 'You were only a boy, Max. But mine was a woman's love. A mature woman's love.'

They left Maxim's, and made their way back to the Ritz. Colette, leaning on his arm, seemed as light as a feather. It was a bright autumn day, with a gentle wind. 'I always want to chase the autumn leaves,' she said breathlessly. 'I forget how old I am, you see.'

A sudden cough forced her to withdraw her arm from his. He

put his hand under her elbow to support her, but suddenly it wasn't enough. He held her desperately in his arms, a dead weight, her face inches from his, his eyes searching it for a message he could not read. Her eyes were closed, the lids fluttering like a small bird's wing. Her mouth worked and the breath flew out of her, carrying the words, '*Max, mon coeur* . . . '

He could bear to hold her up no longer; he was incapable of holding her. He laid her gently on the pavement and took a pace backwards. A *gendarme* blew his whistle. An ambulance was summoned. It all seemed to happen with great speed.

He gave details to officials: Sir Simon Saffity, Stanford Hall, Angleterre. No, he was just an old friend who had encountered her by chance. A close friend, yes. But not for years. She had a massive coronary, someone said. But it was so quick, he said – and after all that wasted time.

Two days later Colette's body was shipped back to England.

For the next two days Max took to his bed. He was feverish with his hatred of Saffity, and examined each insult he had inflicted on him over the years. And there was no doubt the affair with Sarah had been merely to taunt him.

'I was powerless,' he repeated inwardly, rubbing his forehead frenziedly. 'My God, the nightmares I had about Colette. The way I hated myself. Always, always the fear. I hated the fear as much as I hated him.'

What to do, what form his revenge should take, he had not yet decided.

On the third day he got up to go to his meeting with the Banque Reugot, which was all and more than he had hoped it would be. The finance would be forthcoming and, with the help of nominees, there was little doubt that within six months at the most Max would have seventeen per cent of the stake in Wyndham Carpets. 'We are not inexperienced in the art of the hostile take-over,' Monsieur Reugot assured him.

'Then it is fortunate, indeed, that we are on the same side,' Max joked.

He was determined that nothing would be revealed to Saffity until he was ready. When he had the stake, and when the timing was right to confront Saffity with that information, then and only then would he unveil what he knew.

The contemplation of what lay ahead made him euphoric. Colette had lived a good life, and had reached the age of seventy-eight. There was no point grieving over her now. He had been grieving for her all his life. The shock of Saffity's evil had surely killed her.

Though suddenly he would think, she was beautiful, but I didn't know it. Snippets of their long conversation came back to him.

'If only I had seen your loveliness instead of your age.'

Colette had given a delicious sigh. 'Ah, if youth knew and old age could,' she quoted. 'Did you ever fall in love, Max? You've talked about Saffity, and Sarah and your business, but you've had little to say about your wife.'

'Fanny is a good woman, and a good wife. But love — ?' he paused, as though he were both asking and answering a question that was new to him, and said, 'Love was not necessary.'

'But Max, you have had a great passion? You have fallen in love, surely?'

'Yes,' he said slowly. 'I fell in love, only I didn't know I was in love. *She* knew . . . And so she played with me, the way you play with a spinning top.'

'Who was she?'

'A sort of niece of mine.'

Some instinct stopped Max from saying more. He was the only person in the whole world who knew who Theresa was, and for good or ill he wanted it to stay that way.

His thoughts returned to business. The day Max Blum was on the board of Wyndham Carpets would be the day Saffity resigned as Chairman.

The morning of his departure to South Africa he breakfasted with Theresa. As usual, they talked about her medical career.

'I gave two papers at the symposium, Uncle Max,' she said proudly. 'I know you won't think I'm boasting when I say they were both well received.'

'Of course you're not boasting, Theresa,' he said expansively. 'If you can't tell me, who can you tell?'

'I still wish I could work in London,' she said wistfully.

'I believe I can help you there,' Max offered. He had been hoping she would raise the subject herself. 'I have some influence in London. It occurred to me that one of the trustees and benefactors of the Allditch Hospital is an old friend.'

'An old friend?'

To indicate that he did not want to be interrupted while he was thinking, he waved his hand impatiently.

A strained silence fell.

Meeting Colette had reawakened so many dormant memories. Max was now remembering the way Theresa had bitten him when she was a very little girl.

And Theresa had the distinct feeling that she was being studied and evaluated. Sensing the freshness of Max's hostility toward her, she had gone to considerable lengths to make sure she was correctly turned out for this breakfast meeting, and the appreciative glances of other men proved she had succeeded.

'I'll write to my friend,' Max said. 'And I'll give you a letter to take to him as well.' He signalled the waiter, and ordered some stationery. Opening his pen, he stared at her over his glasses. 'I believe Sir Simon Saffity would approve of you.' And then, as if he had other things on his mind, he sighed and said, 'He will see you, I'm sure. He likes high-achieving, goodlooking women, and I'll tell him you are both.' Sealing the envelope carefully, he added, 'By the way, don't ever tell him you are not Lord Rutherford's natural daughter. The man's a dreadful snob, so I'm mentioning your family background.' He handed her the envelope. 'You're probably a bit too old for him, Theresa. He goes for younger women as a rule — '

Sarah was not yet thirty.

Two days later Saffity re-read Max's letter, and let loose one of his loudest, bitterest laughs. He had not yet come close to accepting Colette's death; what the hell was Max trying to do? Max had written to him from Paris, and only ten minutes after he had received the letter the girl was on the phone. Convinced he had seen through Max's game – it was obvious the fool thought that the daughter of a lord could divert him from Sarah – he laughed again.

It meant nothing to him to invite Theresa Rutherford for a drink at Eaton Place. The door-bell rang, and he laughed yet again. Just as he'd predicted – the girl was early.

He stopped laughing when Theresa was shown into his study. The girl was not a girl but a real woman; and she was not only goodlooking – she was beautiful; she was alarmingly lovely. She reminded him of something mysterious and familiar – as known, and as unknown, as his own soul.

London, in May 1972, was a special place for Max. Everything had gone according to plan. From his suite at the Dorchester he looked out at the mass of daffodils in Hyde Park. In two days' time he would announce his seventeen per cent holding in Wyndham Carpets. He and Sarah were not yet reconciled, and he had not told her he was in London. That, too, was part of his plan.

The phone rang. It was hard, these days, to keep the cheerfulness out of his voice. 'Hullo,' he said enthusiastically.

'Hullo, Dad.'

'Sarah! Who told you I was here?'

'I needed to speak to you urgently, so I phoned South Africa. I had to call six thousand miles to find out you were here in London,' she said bitterly.

'What can be so urgent?' he said sarcastically.

'Is Saffity Jewish?'

'You call that urgent? That's urgent?' Max shouted, slamming down the phone.

Immediately it rang again.

Furious, Max counted six rings before answering.

'Little Saffity is dead,' Sarah said flatly. 'Saffity's grandson.'

'I'm very sorry to hear that.'

'Is Saffity Jewish?' Sarah went on implacably.

'So what if he is?' Max parried cruelly.

'Little Saffity died of an illness called Tay-Sach Disease. Ninety-seven per cent of all afflicted children are Jewish. That's why I want to know if Saffity is a Jew.'

Max remained silent. He felt deeply uneasy. No one deserved such a tragedy, not even Saffity.

'We haven't asked any of the grandparents yet, they're too distraught. That's why I'm asking you.'

'Yes,' Max said heavily. 'He is a Jew.'

'Thanks for the information, Dad.'

Shocked, Max slumped in his chair.

Sarah telephoned again to give him details of the funeral. The service was to be in the private chapel at Stanford Hall, she said. After pointing out that there was a piece about it in *The Times*, she told him that she thought he ought to attend.

Looking around the chapel, Max almost convinced himself that he was not merely a spectator come to gape at Saffity in his hour of grief. However, if he had stopped to think that Theresa might be in the congregation, nothing in the world would have got him there. The melancholy set to her face made her even more beautiful. Instantly he knew he could not face her. He decided to leave the chapel immediately, and was just about to slink away – when, with a sudden shock, he heard the opening chords of the haunting melody of the Kol Nidre prayer – the lament that has been intoned for centuries on the eve of the Day of Atonement. This was a church, not a synagogue. His head was uncovered. What was going on?

Now he could not help craning his neck to look at Saffity. Pale, his fists and teeth clenched, Saffity stared sightlessly ahead of him. No muscle moved, no nerve twitched. The flutter in the congregation turned to a gasp. Several people recognised the organ music and stirred uncomfortably. As the last note was sounded Max saw a tall, stately woman walk out. He wondered briefly who she was.

At last it was all over, and the monstrously tiny coffin disappeared from view.

Once again Max tried to leave, but when his own distraught daughter clung to him tightly and begged him to wait a little longer, he patted her hand and agreed.

Later, at the wake, while Max miserably balanced the cup of tea he could not drink, Sarah told him that Saffity's ex-wife had learned he had confirmed her grandson's genetic origins. It was she who had instructed the organist to play the Kol Nidre lament. She had told no one about it and had left the chapel as soon as the lament ended. Sarah went on to say that since each parent must carry the gene, the Fisks probably had some Jewish blood, too. But this had not yet been established.

Theresa came over to them. As Sarah kissed her on the cheek, Max averted his eyes. Theresa turned to him and said, 'I wrote to thank you for the introduction to Saffity, Uncle Max.'

'I know.'

'You didn't reply. That was very unlike you.' She moved closer to kiss his cheek and whispered, 'I really should have written to thank you for introducing me to the greatest love any woman could hope to experience.'

Disentangling himself he murmured, 'I must leave.'

At that moment Jem came up to him and took his hand. 'Thank you for coming,' she said bravely. 'I think my father would like to see you.' She had not let go of his hand and now led him gently towards Saffity's library. Then, just as gently, she withdrew.

Saffity was alone.

'I'm very sorry, Saffity,' Max said, meaning it. And then, before he could stop himself, he heard himself uttering the ancient phrase that was addressed to the bereaved. 'I wish you long life.'

'I must thank you, Max Blum,' Saffity said icily, in French. 'On the strength of your corroboration a theory became a fact.'

'What else could I do? Sarah asked me. I told her. The boy was already dead.'

'You knew it would do no good — ' Saffity clapped his hands together in rage and grief. His stricken face grew ugly with contempt. 'Yet you told her. Why? I know why. But I insist *you* tell me, Max Blum.'

Under the pressure of Saffity's arrogance Max's compassion evaporated. 'You just told me you know why I told her,' he countered.

'You can bet your fucking life I know why!' Saffity spat the words out. 'I was fucking your daughter, and you couldn't take it!'

Striking where he had always struck, on a raw burning nerve, Saffity was dead on target. But he had gone too far for Max. 'What I told Sarah was nothing more and nothing less than the truth,' he said coldly.

Compelled by the ring of unmistakable authority in Max's tone, Saffity's head jerked sideways.

He continued, 'I told myself that even if you deserve no mercy from me, your tragedy does. I decided that the news, the bad news – that I admit I had been looking forward to giving you – could wait until the customary week of mourning was over.'

'Spit it out, Max Blum. You've hated me for more than forty years. You never had the guts to do anything before, so why not have a go now, when I'm down?'

Throughout the entire exchange the two men had been standing.

'Sit down, Saffarty,' Max commanded, using the old pronunciation. 'What for?'

'I said, sit down.'

Saffity shrugged but sat.

Using his original name had produced the desired effect, Max noted.

He locked the door, and drew his own chair close.

Then, as if delivering a prepared statement, he said, 'Theresa Rutherford is your own daughter. She was born to Mireille Morou in 1927, on the twentieth of September. Mireille was carrying twins. Only one of them was aborted in Paris. The other was Theresa.'

A howl issued from Saffity's throat. He flung himself off his chair and rolled crazily on the carpet, his legs and arms flailing. One of his legs struck the low coffee table and several of the jewelled Turkish coffee cups were smashed. Minutes passed before the howling stopped.

Drawing himself to his knees, Saffity whispered, 'You introduced her to me?'

Max sat down. He had his answer ready.

'I met up with an old friend whom I believed to be long dead.' Max's voice shook. 'You blackmailed me for years and years, but that was nothing compared to what I suffered nearly every waking day, and yes, sometimes even in my sleep, because I believed I was a murderer.' He leapt out of his chair, and stood over Saffity . . . 'Yes, I spent a day and a night with Colette in Paris. No wonder she had a heart attack!'

Saffity dropped from his knees, and lay in a heap on the floor. At last he roused himself, looked up at Max and yelled, 'But Theresa was innocent!'

His shoulders heaved and he collapsed again.

'So was I,' Max whispered. 'I was also innocent.'

He moved toward Saffity, and gently tapped his sprawled body with the tip of his shoe.

Part Ten

32

The day after the funeral, and the shocking scene that followed, Max formally declared his seventeen per cent stake in Wyndham Carpets. Within two days his seat on the board was announced. Three days later he – and almost everyone else in the business world – read of Saffity's unexpected retirement.

In the brief statement Saffity issued later, he went out of his way to stress that after the excessively untimely death of his adored grandson, all his interests in the material world had entirely vanished. Accordingly, he was returning to the place of his birth, where he would remain for ever. He hoped, once again, to encounter the spiritual life that he had banished from his life when he was still a teenager. Above all, he hoped his need for utter solitude would be respected by everyone, including those closest to him.

When Max read that statement he was filled with admiration for the neat, honourable way in which Saffity had at once extricated himself from Theresa and protected her from the truth. But by then Max's revenge was already as stale and as putrefying as decaying cheese. He retreated to the Alps, taking a temporary refuge from the world. He had met and liked Sarah's fiancé, and though he had said he would do his best to be at their wedding he had been careful not to promise anything. There was no longer any point in being on the board of Wyndham Carpets, so he resigned.

High up in the snow, remote from everything he had known, Max was better able to endure the heavy guilt that had set in the moment the enormity of the injustice he had done Theresa penetrated his brain.

He sat on his high balcony in the sun and faced the snow-capped mountains, and the truth. Fanny telephoned him from Johannesburg.

He would have preferred not to have read about Saffity, but that would have meant ignoring every major magazine and most newspapers. A long article compared Saffity to that other Greek, Aristotle Onassis: 'Neither Greek was equipped with enough emotional stamina to cope with the death of an heir.' Suddenly Saffity, who had been so proud to be British, was a Greek. A lengthy correspondence on nationality ensued in *The Times*. Lady Jane, the former wife of the hermit tycoon, was a source of unending copy. Staring at Jane's photographs, at those cold blue eyes in that chiselled face, Max shivered.

He read that Saffity's grant of fifty million dollars from the immediate sale of two of his American assets to St John's Hospital, Portland, had carried a single proviso: the project was to be under the personal direction of Dr Theresa Rutherford.

Senseless though it was, he endlessly contemplated what his life might have been if it had not been so heavily weighed – and scaled down – by the guilt of the murderous crime he had thought he had committed. Entrenched in the vision of himself as a murderer, he had hated himself far more than he had ever hated Saffity.

But he had sacrificed Theresa . . .

He told himself he was convalescing from a long fever. Weeks went by, but still he was at war with himself. After he had been in the mountains for over six months, he knew he could not remain in there for ever. Still he could not bring himself to leave.

And then early in 1973 a strange letter, requesting not sympathy but help, came from Salonika.

Saffity sent his private jet for him. Still in the process of dismantling and liquidating his empire, he had not yet dispensed with his aircraft.

A hired car and chauffeur met Max at the airport. As they drove towards what he had been warned was Saffity's simple abode, Max was unaware of the landscape of rolling hills and the white-washed houses gleaming in the golden light.

You cannot argue with facts or change them, he told himself, and the awful fact was that since each had done the other a terrible wrong they were, at last, equal.

The car stopped beside a simple house and at once the door was opened for him. Max stepped out, murmuring his automatic thanks before he realised it was Saffity himself who had opened it. He caught his breath.

'Took you by surprise, huh?' he said, managing a pitifully feeble echo of his former laugh.

By way of a reply Max stretched out his hand. Saffity grasped it. For a while, each in the firm grip of the other, neither moved nor talked. Then, each spoke simultaneously – 'Max', 'Saffity' – they said.

'Come in. Welcome,' Saffity said softly. 'Or would you prefer to stay on the verandah?'

'The verandah would suit me just fine.'

'I rarely drink myself these days, but I got some drinks in for you. Would you like something different, an *ouzo*, perhaps?'

'I'll stick to whisky.'

There were no real servants about. The man who was sitting at the foot of the steps was obviously a bodyguard. Gesturing towards him, Saffity said, 'Costas only speaks Greek, so he can't eavesdrop.'

'That's good.'

'Thank you for coming,' Saffity said awkwardly. 'Your presence here is more than I deserve.'

'I think you and I have gone beyond apology.'

'Does that mean you've forgiven me, my friend?'

'It is easier to forgive another than oneself.'

'I have learned that, too.'

There was a long silence. At last Max said, 'So you've given up business, Saffity?'

'It's just as well I did. I had what the local doctors said was a coronary episode. In other words, a mild heart attack.'

'At our age these things happen. Are you satisfied with the doctors here?'

'Very. I feel stronger than I have for years. I have an excellent doctor who is treating me with rat poison. I thought it fitting.'

'You mean anti-coagulants to keep your blood thin — '

Over a lunch of bread and cheese, they went on to talk about the merits and demerits of anti-coagulation therapy. Saffity said a lot of nonsense was talked about cholesterol, and proceeded to explain why the therapy was viewed with so much healthy scepticism in some quarters. They were, of course, talking obliquely about Theresa, who was deeply engaged in debunking the cholesterol myth.

Suddenly Saffity said, 'We have more in common than I realised.'

'I know,' said Max, thinking they both loved the same woman. He had faced many truths as he looked out on the Swiss Alps, and the full truth of his feelings for Theresa was one.

'You remember my crooked eye?' Saffity asked suddenly. 'My

609

father did it to me. He struck me with this key.' He took the key from his pocket. Max knew it well. Rising from his chair, he continued, 'If it's not too hot for you, there's something I'd like to show you.'

'I'm not too hot.'

'I can't remember it ever being so hot in Salonika at this time of the year, but perhaps it was,' Saffity said abstractedly as they made their way through the small, unimaginative garden. 'It's supposed to be winter.'

Close to the boundary of his neighbour's garden, Saffity stopped and said, 'You must have wondered why I chose such a suburban bungalow.'

'For simplicity, I suppose.'

'This place does not have the virtue of simplicity,' Saffity returned, with a touch of his old scorn. 'It is merely mediocre.' He advanced a few paces. 'Yet I went to great lengths to acquire this place.' He dropped to his haunches and, squatting, traced the Hebrew lettering engraved into a marble paving stone. 'I bought it because of this stone. It was part of my grandfather's tombstone, once,' he said softly.

Max made a helpless gesture. He lowered himself beside Saffity and placed his hand on the marble.

'The Nazis appropriated our five-hundred-year-old Jewish cemetery and allowed the local Greek population to use the marble as a quarry. So the tombstones were used for things like building-blocks and walls. They even used them in latrines.'

Max shook his head sorrowfully.

'And, as you can see, they used them for paving.' He took his hand from the marble paving, and placed it on Max's shoulder. As he moved, the gold key he wore over his high-necked fisherman's sweater caught the sunlight and momentarily dazzled Max. 'Mostly the Hebrew lettering was removed, so I was exceptionally fortunate to find this one.' He went on, 'My own father has no tombstone, Max. You had the decency never to ask about him.' His voice sank. 'He was deported to Auschwitz. I tried to get him out. I tried everything I could, I even talked to the King of Greece. But for what? For nothing.'

'Oh Lord, do not inflict upon us all that we may be able to endure.' The ancient words sprang unbidden to Max's lips.

'A long time ago, Max, you made me prove I was a Jew. A Jew

never stops being a Jew, you said. You remember that, of course.'

'Yes,' Max sighed. 'I remember.'

'At the beginning, when I arrived in Paris, I believed I was unworthy of being a Jew. Much later I refused to allow anti-Semitism to force me to be a good Jew, a bad Jew or any kind of Jew.'

'You can no more refuse to be what you are, than you can be forced to be what you are not,' Max said gravely. 'A Jew is an essence, not a concept.'

Once more Saffity caressed the ancient lettering. 'Shortly before the war, I found out my mother was Ashkenazic — ' He threw up his hands. 'But that's another story,' he said sadly. 'I suppose Sarah told you Ashkenazic Jews make up ninety-seven per cent of all Tay-Sachs cases.' He gave a ghostly, crackling laugh. 'Sephardics fall within the same general population as the Fisks.'

'What can I say?' Max said helplessly. 'What can I say?'

They returned to the house in silence.

Later that evening Saffity thrust a piece of paper at Max. 'This is one of the few things I brought with me when I left England. A dentist in Brittany wants to erect a commemorative statue to the part my Jedburgh team played in the French Resistance.'

'Will you go?'

'I'm thinking about it. How long do you think you'll stay in Salonika?'

'About six days.'

'Good. Stay longer if you can.'

Over the next few days Max found that even the new, humbled Saffity still had the power to influence the mood of others. He threw away his sleeping pills.

On Thursday, his fourth day in Salonika, Saffity mentioned Sarah's happiness with Franco Levin, and her pregnancy, and that broke down some of the remaining barriers between them. Their talk grew easier. Occasionally Saffity would laugh, and though it sounded like an imitation of what it once had been, it was comforting to hear it again. It was while he was toasting figs in the hearth that he finally asked – and was told – about Mireille. Theresa's name never crossed their lips. Colette was not mentioned, either.

On Saturday morning, because he and Saffity were going to the synagogue together, Max awoke early. It was his last day in Salonika – he was leaving in the late afternoon.

The house was, as usual, calm. Shaved and dressed, Max went to the verandah. Everything was still. Gradually he became aware that the quiet was oppressive, even menacing. As he walked back into the house his footsteps sounded deafeningly loud. He stood outside Saffity's room and the silence was as palpable as a presence. Without stopping to knock he burst in.

At once he knew the reason for the stillness. Saffity's final serenity was the serenity of the dead.

Max moved silently to Saffity's death bed. Beside it a very large envelope was simply addressed 'Max'.

Taking the envelope, as he knew he was intended to, he left the room. He was amazed, as he opened it, to find his hands were quite steady.

The letter had been written in French.

Dear friend,

For the following two reasons Dr Hesperinedes will cooperate, and you will therefore experience no difficulty in instructing him to certify that my death was due to natural causes.

1) Previous history of cardiac disease.

2) Enclosed envelope with the required cash for the doctor.

I have taken the liberty of appointing you senior executor of my Will.

When it is read it will become clear that I was even richer than the wildest fantasies of the financial journalists.

Meanwhile, the following point is of particular relevance to you.

Dimitri Politis, your former son-in-law, is to receive the sum of one million pounds, payable anywhere in the world, on the sole condition that he signs over full guardianship and custody of his son to Sarah. (He will sign, Max, don't worry.)

However, the bequest appointing you as Director of the Saffity Historical Research Foundation may puzzle you. The following paragraph may explain.

For several reasons which I will not go into now, I developed an obsession to find those Nazis who were responsible for the deportation of the sixty thousand Salonikan Jews to Auschwitz. I engaged a Cambridge PhD history student to undertake further research. A well-known name kept cropping up. That name was Kurt Waldheim, who only a few months ago was elected Secretary-General of the United Nations. What good the confirmation of Waldheim's past will do is anyone's guess —

in my jaded view, it will be enough to make him President of Austria.

Jem's academic gift is considerable. However, the decision whether or not to involve herself in my foundation must be entirely hers.

You will find two wrapped packages in my bedside drawer. The smaller one contains the miniature gold key, and is for Jem. The other package contains the original key that has been in my family for more than four hundred years. It is for Theresa. The envelope contains the only letter I ever received from my mother. It is for my grand-daughter.

Finally, I ask that my ashes be taken to their rightful place, to Auschwitz, where they belong.

I thank you for coming to Salonika, Max Blum. You brought me more peace on earth than you know. It is enough to say that the manner of my leaving will be solely in your custody.

You alone will understand why I brought about my own finale.

You alone will understand what I mean when I say that though I am able to endure living without my soul I do not care to.

Farewell, old friend,
Saffity

Tears streamed down Max's cheeks. He wept not for his death, but for the way Saffity had honoured him.

No one could understand Max, but then, as his family agreed, he had always been a contrary man. He had hated Saffity all his life, yet when he died no one was more grief stricken.

When Saffity's ashes had finally settled, and Max began to compose himself, he drew some consolation from the fact that Jem never doubted her father had suffered a fatal heart attack.

But his greatest source of strength came from Sarah. They had a lot in common, having both been entangled with Saffity, and talked about him endlessly; and if their understanding of him was not as complete as they wished, they reached a deeper understanding of one another. When Sarah bore Franco Levin a fine male child, they named him after Max's father.

Almost a year later, in 1974, Max and Fanny emigrated to Britain. They liquidated all their business interests. Though their capital was blocked by the South African authorities, it seemed a small price to pay for being at the centre of a circle of family warmth of which Jem was an integral part.

Within five years of its inception the Theresa Rutherford Foundation, under Theresa's inspired leadership, had gained international recognition. Theresa's work brought her to London frequently, and though Max was never to feel at ease with her, the kind of sisterly affinity that had grown between Theresa and Jem lessened the pain of what he had done to her.

Epilogue

In 1986, Kurt Waldheim was elected President of Austria, and Saffity's prediction proved correct.

Even before he was elected, Waldheim's Nazi past, and his role in the forced deportation of the Jews of Salonika was exposed to the world. Ironically, in that same year the Conference of the Helsinki Accord on Human Rights was held in Vienna.

Not one of the thirty-five ministers from thirty-five governments who were in Vienna would agree to meet the President of Austria. As Jem said triumphantly to Max, 'There is no precedent in diplomatic history for that.'

Jem was looking more and more like Theresa, he thought. He was proud of her.

It occurred to him that though he and Saffity had played lifelong roles for which no one could ever be rehearsed, each had played his to the full. And if, on the swinging scales of passion, it was not he but Saffity who weighed in as both the theory and the legend, what did it matter? They had justified their existence, each of them.

Shirley Eskapa
The Seduction £2.99

How delicious it was to be seduced . . . and how dangerous.

The only remarkable thing about Emily Bradshaw was that she had written a book. Apart from that she was ordinary – married, with a young son and relatively happy.

A single phonecall from her American agent asking her to promote her book in the States marks the start of the seduction.

The transformation begins. Slowly at first – hair, clothes, make-up – and then faster, as Emily finds herself drawn into the world of limousines, photographers and first-class hotels. To her surprise she is excited by the pace and revels in a new assurance that comes with her burgeoning success.

But success has another side which includes the admiration of a glamorous lover, an obsessive gunman and a feeling that her husband and son are a long way away.

'Shirley Eskapa has written a frivolous and often funny story of an innocent abroad' THE DAILY TELEGRAPH

'A thoroughly entertaining, racy novel' COMPANY

'A biting account . . . thoughtful honesty' THE MAIL ON SUNDAY

'An acutely credible tale of life in the fast lane'
EASTERN DAILY PRESS

The Secret Keeper £2.99

Living in Geneva in the luxury world of golf clubs and banking executives, Pritchett Ward decides to leave his wife of twenty years to live with his German mistress – a younger woman many times more sexually exciting.

His wife returns to England leaving her son, ostensibly because he needs his father and will be company for the lover's own child, the delicate and asthmatic Jean-Pierre. The real reason is far more sinister – her son can spy for her and enable her to get her husband back.

Ominously, as Victor Hugo once said, no one keeps a secret so well as a child.

'Taut and clever . . . a chilly sketch of deadlier-than-the-male possessiveness' THE GUARDIAN

'Sophisticated and sharp-eyed . . . all the characters have a life and highly believable breath of their own.' COMPANY

'Had me shuddering with pleasure' THE NEW STATESMAN

Jennifer Bacia
Shadows of Power £3.99

Anthea James fought hard enough to escape the traumas and cruelties of her childhood. Fought hard enough to win the fame and fortune she enjoys as Australia's most glamorous television personality.

Now she stands on the brink of a political career that will fulfill her driving ambition – a quest for the power to free women from the tyranny of sexual oppression and prostitution.

For as humble Lenore Hamlyn, orphaned and taken into care in Sydney's most prosperous brothel in the early 1960s, she came to learn more about the darker side of human nature than anyone could ever know.

Except for one man. A man from her past. The only man she ever loved – and who now has the power to destroy her . . .

All Pan books are available at your local bookshop or newsagent, or can be ordered direct from the publisher. Indicate the number of copies required and fill in the form below.

Send to: **CS Department, Pan Books Ltd., P.O. Box 40, Basingstoke, Hants. RG21 2YT.**

or phone: 0256 469551 (Ansaphone), quoting title, author and Credit Card number.

Please enclose a remittance* to the value of the cover price plus: 60p for the first book plus 30p per copy for each additional book ordered to a maximum charge of £2.40 to cover postage and packing.

*Payment may be made in sterling by UK personal cheque, postal order, sterling draft or international money order, made payable to Pan Books Ltd.

Alternatively by Barclaycard/Access:

Card No. | | | | | | | | | | | | | | | | | | |

_____

Signature:

Applicable only in the UK and Republic of Ireland.

While every effort is made to keep prices low, it is sometimes necessary to increase prices at short notice. Pan Books reserve the right to show on covers and charge new retail prices which may differ from those advertised in the text or elsewhere.

NAME AND ADDRESS IN BLOCK LETTERS PLEASE:

....

Name————————————————————————

Address————————————————————————

_____

_____

_____

3/87

THE

MENNONITE ENCYCLOPEDIA

THE

Mennonite Encyclopedia

A Comprehensive Reference Work
on the
Anabaptist-Mennonite Movement

VOLUME II

D–H

Mennonite Publishing House, Scottdale, Pennsylvania
Mennonite Publication Office, Newton, Kansas
Mennonite Brethren Publishing House, Hillsboro, Kansas

1956

KEY TO SYMBOLS AND ABBREVIATIONS

A. Symbols Used for the North American Mennonite Bodies

Church of God in Christ, Mennonite (CGC)
Conservative (Amish) Mennonite (CAM)
Evangelical Mennonite Brethren (EMB)
Evangelical Mennonite Church (EMC)
Evangelical Mennonite (Kleine Gemeinde) (EMC, KG)
General Conference Mennonite Church (GCM)

Krimmer Mennonite Brethren (KMB)
Mennonite Brethren Church (MB)
Mennonite Brethren in Christ (MBC)
Mennonite Church (MC)
Old Order Amish Mennonite Church (OOA)
Old Order Mennonite Church (OOM)
United Missionary Church (UMC)

B. Geographical Abbreviations

States of the United States of America

Cal.	California
Col.	Colorado
Ill.	Illinois
Ind.	Indiana
Kan.	Kansas
Minn.	Minnesota
Mo.	Missouri
Neb.	Nebraska

N.D.	North Dakota
N.Y.	New York
Okla.	Oklahoma
Ore.	Oregon
Pa.	Pennsylvania
S.D.	South Dakota
Va.	Virginia

Countries

Can.	Canada
Ger.	Germany
Neth.	Netherlands
Par.	Paraguay
P.R.	Puerto Rico
Sw.	Switzerland

Provinces of Canada

Alta.	Alberta
B.C.	British Columbia
Man.	Manitoba
Ont.	Ontario
Sask.	Saskatchewan

Other

Co.	County
Twp.	Township

C. Bibliographical Symbols

ADB *Allgemeine Deutsche Biographie* 56v. (Leipzig, 1875-1912).

Beck, Geschichts-Bücher Josef Beck, *Die Geschichts-Bücher der Wiedertäufer in Oesterreich-Ungarn* (Vienna, 1883).

Bender, Two Centuries H. S. Bender, *Two Centuries of American Mennonite Literature, A Bibliography of Mennonitica Americana 1727-1928* (Goshen, 1929).

Bibliographie des Martyrologes F. Vander Haeghen, Th. Arnold, and R. Vanden Berghe, *Bibliographie des Martyrologes Protestants Néerlandais. II. Receuils* (The Hague, 1890).

Biogr. Wb. H. Visscher and L. A. van Langeraad, *Biographisch Woordenboek von Protestantsche Godgeleerden in Nederland,* A-L (I, Utrecht), later by J. P. de Bie and J. Loosjes (II, III, IV, V, and installment #29, The Hague) 1903- .

Blaupot t. C., Friesland Steven Blaupot ten Cate, *Geschiedenis der Doopsgezinden in Friesland* (Leeuwarden, 1839).

Blaupot t. C., Groningen . . . *Groningen, Overijssel en Oost-Friesland,* 2v. (Leeuwarden, 1842).

Blaupot t. C., Holland . . . *Holland, Zeeland, Utrecht en Gelderland,* 2v. (Amsterdam, 1847).

BRN S. Cramer and F. Pijper, *Bibliotheca Reformatoria Neerlandica,* 10v. (The Hague, 1903-14).

Catalogus Amst. *Catalogus der werken over de Doopsgezinden en hunne geschiedenis aanwezig in de bibliotheek der Vereenigde Doopsgezinde Gemeente te Amsterdam* (Amst., 1919).

DB *Doopsgezinde Bijdragen* (Amsterdam, 1861-1919).

DJ *Doopsgezind Jaarboekje* vv. 1-48 (Assen, et al., 1901-43, 1949-).

Friesen, Brüderschaft P. M. Friesen, *Die Alt-Evangelische Mennonitische Brüderschaft in Russland (1789-1910) im Rahmen der mennonitischen Gesamtgeschichte* (Halbstadt, 1911).

Gbl. *Gemeindeblatt der Mennoniten* vv. 1-85 (Sinsheim, later Karlsruhe, 1870-).

Gem.-Kal. *Mennonitischer Gemeinde-Kalender* (formerly *Christlicher Gemeinde-Kalender*) (various places, chiefly Kaiserslautern, Weierhof, Karlsruhe, 1892-).

Gesch.-Bl. *Mennonitische Geschichtsblätter. Herausgegeben vom Mennonitischen Geschichtsverein* (Frankfurt, later Karlsruhe, 1936-40, 1951-).

Grosheide, Bijdrage Greta Grosheide, *Bijdrage tot de geschiedenis der Anabaptisten in Amsterdam* (Hilversum, 1938).

Grosheide, Verhooren *Verhooren en Vonissen der Wederdoopers, betrokken bij de aanslagen op Amsterdam in 1534 en 1535,* in *Bijdragen en Mededeelingen van het Historisch Genootschap,* Vol. XLI (Amsterdam, 1920).

HRE Herzog-Hauck, *Realencyclopädie für Protestantische Theologie und Kirche,* 24v. (3.ed., Leipzig, 1896-1913).

Inv. Arch. Amst. J. G. de Hoop Scheffer, *Inventaris der Archiefstukken berustende bij de Vereenigde Doopsgezinde Gemeente te Amsterdam,* 2v. (Amsterdam, 1883-84).

Kühler, Geschiedenis I W. J. Kühler, *Geschiedenis der Nederlandsche Doopsgezinden in de Zestiende Eeuw* (Haarlem, 1932).

Kühler, Geschiedenis II,1 *Idem, Geschiedenis van de Doopsgezinden in Nederland II. 1600-1735 Eerste Helft* (Haarlem, 1940).

Kühler, Geschiedenis II,2 *Idem, Geschiedenis van de Doopsgezinden in Nederland: Gemeentelijk Leven 1650-1735* (Haarlem, 1950).

Loserth, Anabaptismus Johann Loserth, *Der Anabaptismus in Tirol* (Vienna, 1892).

Loserth, Communismus *Idem, Der Communismus der mährischen Wiedertäufer im 16. und 17. Jahrhundert: Beiträge zu ihrer Lehre, Geschichte und Verfassung (Archiv für österreichische Geschichte,* Vol. LXXXI, 1, 1895).

Mart. Mir. D(utch) Tileman Jansz van Braght, *Het Bloedigh Tooneel of Martelaers Spiegel der Doops-gesinde of Weereloose Christenen, Die om 't getuygenis van Jesus haren Salighmaker geleden hebben ende gedood zijn van Christi tijd af tot desen tijd toe. Den Tweeden Druk* (Amsterdam, 1685), Part II.

Mart. Mir. E(nglish) *Idem, The Bloody Theatre or Martyrs' Mirror of the Defenseless Christians Who Baptized Only upon Confession of Faith and Who Suffered and Died for the Testimony of Jesus Their Saviour . . . to the Year A.D. 1660* (Scottdale, Pa., 1951).

Mellink, Wederdopers A. F. Mellink, *De Wederdopers in de noordelijke Nederlanden 1531-1544* (Groningen, 1954).

Menn. Bl. *Mennonitische Blätter* vv. 1-88 (1854-1941), published variously at Danzig, Hamburg-Altona, and Elbing (W. Prussia).

MHB *Mennonite Historical Bulletin* (Scottdale, Pa.; 1940-   ).

Menn. Life *Mennonite Life* (North Newton, Kan., 1946-).

ML Christian Hege and Christian Neff, *Mennonitisches Lexikon,* 3v., A-R (Frankfurt and Weierhof, I, 1913; II, 1937; III, #31-36, 1938-42; #37-39 at Karlsruhe, 1951-54) *et seq.*

MQR *Mennonite Quarterly Review* (Goshen, Ind., 1927-).

Müller, Berner Täufer Ernst Müller, *Geschichte der Bernischen Täufer* (Frauenfeld, 1895).

Naamlijst *Naamlijst der tegenwoordig in dienst zijnde predikanten der Mennoniten in de vereenigde Nederlanden* (Amsterdam, 1731, 1743, 1755, 1757, 1766, 1769, 1775, 1780, 1782, 1784, 1786, 1787, 1789, 1791, 1793, 1802, 1804, 1806, 1808, 1810, 1815, 1829).

N.N.B.Wb. P. C. Molhuysen and P. J. Blok, *Nieuw Nederlandsch Biografisch Woordenboek* vv. 1-10 (Leiden, 1911-37).

Offer *Dit Boec wort genoemt: Het Offer des Herren, om het inhout van sommighe opgheofferde kinderen Godts . . .* (n.p., 1562, 1567, 1570, 1578, 1580, Amsterdam, 1590, n.p., 1591, Amsterdam, 1595, Harlingen, 1599). The 1570 edition is cited as reproduced in BRN II, 51-486, including *Een Lietboecxken, tracterende van den Offer des Heeren* (pp. 499-617).

Reimer, Familiennamen Gustav E. Reimer, *Die Familiennamen der westpreussischen Mennoniten* (Weierhof, 1940).

Rembert, Wiedertäufer Karl Rembert, *Die "Wiedertäufer" im Herzogtum Jülich* (Berlin, 1899).

RGG *Die Religion in Geschichte und Gegenwart* (2.ed., 5v., Tübingen, 1927-32).

Schijn-Maatschoen, Geschiedenis I Hermanus Schijn, *Geschiedenis dier Christenen, welke in de Vereenigde Nederlanden onder de Protestanten Mennoniten genaamd worden . . . , Tweede Druk op nieuws uit het Latyn vertaald, en vermeerdert door Gerardus Maatschoen* (Amsterdam, 1743).

Schijn-Maatschoen, Geschiedenis II, which is volume II of the preceding work, entitled *Uitvoeriger Verhandeling van de Geschiedenisse der Mennoniten* (Amsterdam, 1744).

Schijn-Maatschoen, Geschiedenis III, which is volume III of the preceding work, entitled *Aanhangzel Dienende tot den Vervolg of Derde Deel van de Geschiedenis der Mennoniten . . . in het welke noch Negentien Leeraars der Mennoniten . . . ,* by Maatschoen alone (Amsterdam, 1745).

TA Baden-Pfalz M. Krebs, *Quellen zur Geschichte der Täufer. IV. Band, Baden und Pfalz* (Gütersloh, 1951).

TA Bayern I Karl Schornbaum, *Quellen zur Geschichte der Wiedertäufer II. Band, Markgraftum Brandenburg (Bayern I. Abteilung)* (Leipzig, 1934).

TA Bayern II *Idem, Quellen zur Geschichte der Täufer, V. Band (Bayern, II. Abteilung)* (Gütersloh, 1951).

TA Hessen G. Franz, *Urkundliche Quellen zur hessischen Reformationsgeschichte. Vierter Band, Wiedertäuferakten 1527-1626* (Marburg, 1951).

TA Württemberg G. Bossert, *Quellen zur Geschichte der Täufer I. Band, Herzogtum Württemberg* (Leipzig, 1930).

TA Zürich L. von Muralt und W. Schmid, *Quellen zur Geschichte der Täufer in der Schweiz. Erster Band Zürich* (Zürich, 1952).

Verheyden, Brugge A. L. E. Verheyden, *Het Brugsche Martyrologium (12 October 1527-7 Augustus 1573)* (Brussels, n.d., [1944]).

Verheyden, Courtrai *Idem, Le Martyrologe Courtraisien et la Martyrologe Bruxellois* (Vilvorde, 1950).

Verheyden, Gent *Idem, Het Gentsche Martyrologium (1530-1595)* (Brugge, 1946).

Wackernagel, Kirchenlied Philipp Wackernagel, *Das deutsche Kirchenlied von der ältesten Zeit bis zu Anfang des XVII. Jahrhunderts, 5v.* (Leipzig, 1864-77).

Wackernagel, Lieder *Idem, Lieder der niederländischen Reformierten aus der Zeit der Verfolgung im 16. Jahrhundert* (Frankfurt, 1867).

Wiswedel, Bilder W. Wiswedel, *Bilder und Führergestalten aus dem Täufertum, 3v.* (Kassel, I, 1928; II, 1930; III, 1952).

Wolkan, Geschicht-Buch Rudolf Wolkan, *Geschicht-Buch der Hutterischen Brüder* (Macleod, Alta., and Vienna, 1923).

Wolkan, Lieder *Idem, Die Lieder der Wiedertäufer* (Berlin, 1903).

Zieglschmid, Chronik A. J. F. Zieglschmid, *Die älteste Chronik der Hutterischen Brüder: Ein Sprachdenkmal aus frühneuhochdeutscher Zeit* (Ithaca, 1943).

Zieglschmid, Klein-Geschichtsbuch *Idem, Das Klein-Geschichtsbuch der Hutterischen Brüder* (Philadelphia, 1947).

D. Other Symbols and Abbreviations

A.D.S. Algemene Doopsgezinde Societeit. **MCC** Mennonite Central Committee.

CPS Civilian Public Service. **KfK** Kommission für kirchliche Angelegenheiten (or Kirchenangelegenheiten).

q.v. "quod vide," "which see," is a cross-reference indicating that an article on the subject is to be found in the regular alphabetical order.

* signifies deceased. **†** indicates that an illustration will be found in the pictorial section at the end of the volume.

AML Amsterdam Mennonite Library

BeCL Bethel College Historical Library. **GCL** Goshen College Mennonite Historical Library.

MAPS AND ILLUSTRATIONS

The maps listed below will be found in the text next to the articles they serve. Illustrations are grouped at the end of each volume. For a complete list of illustrations in Volume II, see pp. 1 f. of pictorial supplement.

Alphabetical List of Maps, Volumes I—IV

KEY TO SYMBOLS FOR WRITERS IN VOLUME II

Albrecht, E. A., Fortuna, Mo.	E.A.A.	Dick, H. H., Salix, Iowa	H.H.Di.
Albright, Raymond W., Reading, Pa.	R.W.A.	Diener, D. Edward, Clarence, N.Y.	D.E.D.
Allebach, Clyde, Menahga, Minn.	C.A.	Dirks, Carl J., Halstead, Kan.	C.J.Di.
Amstutz-Tschirren, Oberbütschel, Sw.	A.-T.	*Dirksen, Joh., Siberia, Russia	J.D.
Andres, H. J., Newton, Kan.	H.J.A.	Dollinger, Robert, Weiden, Ger.	R.Do.
Baerg, J. G., Mountain Lake, Minn.	J.G.Ba.	*Driedger, A., Heubuden, Ger.	A.D.
Balzer, Gerhard, Fernheim, Par.	G.Ba.	Driedger, Johannes, Weierhof, Ger.	J.Dr.
Barkman, J. R., Henderson, Neb.	J.R.B.	Driedger, N. N., Leamington, Ont.	N.N.D.
*Bartsch, Franz (Russia)	F.B.	Dueck, A. H., N. Kildonan, Man.	A.H.D.
Basinger, Elmer, Summerfield, Ill.	E.B.	Dueck, H. H., County Line, B.C.	H.H.D.
Bates, Charles, Harrison, Mich.	Ch.B.	Dunn, John, Trenton, N.Y.	Jo.D.
Batten, Ernest, Wapato, Wash.	Er.B.	Dyck, A. J., Inman, Kan.	A.J.D.
Bauman, Harold, Orrville, O.	H.B.	Dyck, Arnold, Darlaten, Ger.	Ar.D.
Bauman, Howard S., Elmira, Ont.	H.S.Ba.	Dyck, Henry D., Plymouth, Wis.	H.D.D.
Bauman, I. W., Bluffton, O.	I.W.B.	Dyck, P. P., Rosemary, Alta.	P.P.D.
Beachey, Lewis M., Oakland, Md.	L.M.B.	Eash, Samuel T., Middlebury, Ind.	S.T.E.
Bender, H. S., Goshen, Ind.	H.S.B.	Eby, Martin C., Mohnton, Pa.	M.C.E.
Bender, Mrs. H. S., Goshen, Ind.	E.H.B.	Engbrecht, Marvin, Dolton, S.D.	M.E.
Bender, Nevin F., Greenwood, Del.	N.F.B.	Enns, Anna, Wadena, Sask.	A.En.
Bender, Wilfrid J., Tavistock, Ont.	W.J.B.	Enns, Elizabeth, Newton Siding, Man.	E.E.
Bennett, H. Ernest, Elkhart, Ind.	H.E.B.	Enns, F. F., Lena, Man.	F.F.E.
Berg, P. H., Hillsboro, Kan.	P.H.B.	Enns, J. H., Winnipeg, Man.	J.H.E.
*Bergmann, Cornelius, Jena, Ger.	C.B.	Enns, John J., Gruenthal, Man.	J.J.E.
*Binnerts, A. S., Haarlem, Neth.	A.S.B.	Ensz, John H., Reedley, Cal.	Jo.H.E.
Bixler, Annie, Dalton, O.	A.Bi.	Entz, Joh. P., Woolford, Alta.	J.P.E.
*Block, Th., Oberursel, Ger.	T.B.	*Epp, David H., Chortitza, Russia	D.H.E.
Boese, Curt D., Walton, Kan.	C.D.B.	*Epp, Dietrich H., Rosthern, Sask.	D.E.
Boese, J. A., Tyndall, S.D.	J.A.B.	Epp, G. G., Rosthern, Sask.	G.G.E.
Bohn, Ernest J., Pandora, O.	E.J.Bo.	Epp, H. D., Henderson, Neb.	H.D.E.
*Bossert, G., Sr., Stuttgart, Ger.	G.Bo.	Epp, H. F., Mountain Lake, Minn.	H.F.E.
*Bossert, G., Jr., Stuttgart, Ger.	G.Bos.	Epp, H. H., Wheatley, Ont.	H.H.E.
Bouman, Harold E., Springfield, O.	Ha.E.B.	Epp, J. H., Hepburn, Sask.	J.H.E.
Braun, A., Ibersheim, Ger.	A.B.	Epp, Justina D., Columbus, O.	J.D.E.
Braun, B. J., Dinuba, Cal.	B.J.B.	Erb, Allen H., Lebanon, Ore.	A.H.E.
*Braun, Peter, Oberursel, Ger.	P.Br.	Erb, Paul, Scottdale, Pa.	P.E.
Breetveld, A. R., Goes, Neth.	A.R.B.	Esch, Menno, Fairview, Mich.	M.Es.
Brenneman, T. H., Sarasota, Florida	T.H.B.	Ewert, Benjamin, Winnipeg, Man.	B.E.
Broer, A. L., Hilversum, Neth.	A.L.B.	Fast, Abraham, Emden, Ger.	Ab.F.
Brunk, Arthur S., South Boston, Va.	A.S.Br.	Fast, Alfred, Friesland, Par.	A.Fa.
Brunk, George R., Denbigh, Va.	G.R.B.	Fast, David H., Mountain Lake, Minn.	D.H.F.
Brunk, Harry A., Harrisonburg, Va.	H.A.B.	Fast, Eduard, Utrecht, Neth.	E.F.
Burgess, William K., Detroit, Mich.	W.K.B.	De Fehr, C. A., Winnipeg, Man.	C.A.DeF.
Burkholder, H. D., Dallas, Ore.	H.D.B.	Fellmann, Walter, Mönchzell, Ger.	W.F.
Buruma, Y. S., Nijmegen, Neth.	Y.S.B.	*Fluri, Adolf, Bern, Sw.	A.Fl.
*Busé, H. J., Hallum, Neth.	H.J.B.	Foth, Johannes, Friedelsheim, Ger.	J.F.
Byler, Raymond, Altha, Florida	R.B.	Foth, Robert, ————, Ger.	R.Foth
*ten Cate, E. M., Apeldoorn, Neth.	E.M.tC.	Francis, E. K., South Bend, Ind.	E.K.F.
Clemens, J. C., Lansdale, Pa.	J.C.C.	Fretz, Clarence, Harrisonburg, Va.	C.Y.F.
Conrad, Lloyd V., Wakarusa, Ind.	L.V.C.	*Fretz, J. C., Kitchener, Ont.	J.C.F.
Cook, Mrs. Lester, La Junta, Col.	L.C.	Fretz, J. Herbert, Freeman, S.D.	J.H.F.
Correll, Ernst H., Washington, D.C.	E.H.C.	Fretz, J. Winfield, N. Newton, Kan.	J.W.F.
Cressman, J. Boyd, Kitchener, Ont.	J.B.C.	Frey, Orlin F., Topeka, Ind.	O.F.F.
Crous, Ernst, Göttingen, Ger.	E.C.	*Fricke, Ed. J., Indianapolis, Ind.	E.J.F.
Decker, David, Olivet, S.D.	D.D.	Friedmann, Robert, Kalamazoo, Mich.	R.F.
*Deenik, M. L., Leeuwarden, Neth.	M.L.D.	Friesen, Arthur, Clinton, Okla.	A.F.
*Delden, J. van, Gronau, Ger.	J.vD.	Friesen, Isaac K., Conway, Kan.	I.K.F.
Derksen, I. A., Cavour, S.D.	I.A.D.	Friesen, J. J., Butterfield, Minn.	J.J.F.
Dester, Emil A., Deer Creek, Okla.	E.A.D.	Funk, Heinrich, Grigoryevka, Russia	H.F.
Dettweiler, Hermann, Munich, Ger.	H.D.	Gaeddert, Gustav R., N. Newton, Kan.	G.R.G.
Dettweiler, Reuben, Elmira, Ont.	R.D.	Galle, Christian, Weierhof, Ger.	C.G.
DeWind, Henry A., Whitewater, Wis.	DeWind	Garber, Henry F., Mount Joy, Pa.	H.F.G.

Miller, Mary, Hesston, Kan.	M.M.	Rilling, Mrs. Fred A., Hesston, Kan.	L.C.R.
Miller, Paul M., Goshen, Ind.	P.M.M.	*Risser, John D., Hagerstown, Md.	J.D.R.
Mulder, Abraham, Dordrecht, Neth.	Abr.M.	Rogalsky, J. P., Hillsboro, Kan.	J.P.R.
Müller, Ernst, Prehof, Ger.	E.M.	Rosenberger, Arthur S., Quakertown, Pa.	A.S.R.
Mumaw, Stanford, Dalton, O.	S.M.	Rouse, F. I., Kalamazoo, Mich.	F.I.R.
Muralt, L. von, Zürich, Sw.	L.v.M.	Roth, Willard, Wayland, Iowa	W.R.
Myers, Leidy, Danboro, Pa.	L.M.	Rupp, Charles L., Woodburn, Ind.	Ch.L.R.
Nauman, Norman W., Manheim, Pa.	N.W.N.	*Rupp, Jakob, Lemberg, Poland	J.Ru.
*Neff, Christian, Weierhof, Ger.	Neff	Sauder, Jerry H., Grabill, Ind.	J.H.S.
Neuenschwander, A. J., Wadsworth, O.	A.J.N.	Sawatzky, Victor, Pawnee Rock, Kan.	V.S.
Neufeld, H., Vancouver, B.C.	H.Ne.	Schellenberg, B. J., Winnipeg, Man.	B.J.S.
Neufeld, Heinrich T., Enid, Okla.	H.T.N.	Schellenberg, P. E., Reedley, Cal.	P.E.S.
Neufeld, I. G., Phoenix, Ariz.	I.G.N.	Schlichting, Emma, Akron, Pa.	E.Sch.
Neufeld, John J., Horndean, Man.	J.J.N.	Schmidt, Frank, Tampa, Kan.	Fr.S.
Neufeld, John T., Chicago, Ill.	J.T.N.	Schmidt, John F., N. Newton, Kan.	J.F.S.
Neufeld, Peter T., Inman, Kan.	P.T.N.	Schmidt, Nathaniel, Rich Hill, Mo.	Na.S.
*Newman, A. H., Macon, Georgia	A.H.N.	Schmucker, Tobe E., South Bend, Ind.	T.E.Sch.
Nichols, George M., Isabella, Okla.	G.M.N.	Schowalter, Otto, Hamburg, Ger.	O.S.
Nickel, J. W., Denver, Col.	J.W.N.	Schowalter, Paul, Weierhof, Ger.	P.S.
Nickel, Valentin E., Wymark, Sask.	V.E.N.	Schrag, David D., McPherson, Kan.	D.D.S.
Niepoth, Wilhelm, Crefeld, Ger.	W.N.	Schrag, Menno, Newton, Kan.	M.S.
Nightingale, De Lyon, Fort Cobb, Okla.	De.N.	Schroeter, A. A., Reedley, Cal.	A.A.Sch.
*Nijdam, C., Zeist, Neth.	C.N.	Schwemer, R., Frankfurt, Ger.	R.Sch.
*Oosterbaan, P., Hilversum, Neth.	P.O.	Sepp, A. A., Zaandam, Neth.	A.A.S.
Orendorff, Joseph, Flanagan, Ill.	J.O.	Shantz, Sidney S., Hanover, Ont.	S.S.S.
Osborne, Chester C., Hesston, Kan.	C.C.O.	Shelly, Andrew R., Chicago, Ill.	A.R.S.
Osborne, Herbert L., Fort Wayne, Ind.	H.L.O.	Showalter, Timothy, Broadway, Va.	T.S.
Oswald, Walter E., Goshen, Ind.	W.E.O.	Siemens, H. H., Gem, Alta.	H.H.S.
Pankratz, Jacob, Glenlea, Man.	J.P.	Sinclair, Frank, Exeland, Wis.	F.A.S.
Pannabecker, R. P., Goshen, Ind.	R.P.P.	Slee, J. C. van, Deventer, Neth.	J.C.vS.
Pannabecker, S. F., Chicago, Ill.	S.F.P.	Sluys. J. J. J. van, Texel, Neth.	J.J.J.vS.
Pasma, F. H., Hilversum, Neth.	F.H.P.	*Smissen, H. van der, Hamburg, Ger.	H.vdS.
*Pauls, H., Elbing, Ger.	H.Pa.	Smith, Albert, De Ridder, Louisiana	Al.S.
Peachey, Paul, Harrisonburg, Va.	P.P.	*Smith, C. Henry, Bluffton, O.	C.H.S.
Pearson, Bruce W., Flint, Mich.	B.W.P.	*Smith, J. B., Elida, O.	J.B.S.
Penner, A. A., Mountain Lake, Minn.	A.A.P.	Smith, Lena Mae, Newton, Kan.	L.M.S.
Penner, David, Sr., Grassy Lake, Alta.	D.P.,Sr.	Smith, Willard H., Goshen, Ind.	W.H.S.
Penner, Horst, Kirchheimbolanden, Ger.	H.P.	Smucker, Don. E., Chicago, Ill.	D.E.S.
Penner, John M., St. Anne, Man.	J.M.P.	Snyder, William T., Akron, Pa.	W.T.S.
Penner, Walter L., Dallas, Ore.	W.L.P.	*Sommer, Pierre, Grand Charmont, France	P.So.
Peters, A. H., Geary, Okla.	A.H.P.	Sperling, Homer, Kismet, Kan.	H.Sp.
Peters, George W., Fresno, Cal.	G.W.P.	Springer, N. P., Goshen, Ind.	N.P.S.
Peters, Gerhard M., Gotebo, Okla.	G.M.P.	Sprunger, Lyman W., Doland, S.D.	L.W.S.
Plett, C. F., Reedley, Cal.	C.F.P.	Stahl, Paul, Langham, Sask.	P.St.
Poetker, J. F., Lena, Man.	J.F.P.	*Stauffer, Ezra, Tofield, Alta.	E.S.
*Pohl, Matthias, Sembach, Ger.	M.P.	Steiner, E. G., Berne, Ind.	E.G.St.
Purdy, William J., Colborne, Ont.	W.J.P.	Stoll, Albert, Everton, Ark.	A.St.
Quiring, H. C., Henderson, Neb.	H.C.Q.	Stoltzfus, Grant, Harrisonburg, Va.	G.M.S.
Raber, F. B., Kansas City, Kan.	F.B.R.	Storms, Everek R., Kitchener, Ont.	E.R.S.
Redekop, J. F., N. Clearbrook, B.C.	J.F.R.	Stucky, Harley J., N. Newton, Kan.	H.J.S.
Redekopp, I. W., Winnipeg, Man.	I.W.R.	Swartzendruber, A. Lloyd, Kalona, Iowa	A.L.S.
Regehr, J., Wymark, Sask.	J.R.	Swartzendruber, D. L., Oakland, Md.	D.L.S.
Regehr, Jacob I., Main Centre, Sask.	J.I.R.	Swartzendruber, Elmer G., Wellman, Iowa	E.G.S.
Regier, G. B., Inola, Okla.	G.B.R.	Swartzendruber, L. L., Greenwood, Del.	L.L.S.
Regier, Walter H., Clinton, Okla.	W.H.R.	Teufel, Eberhard, Stuttgart-Fellbach, Ger.	E.T.
Regier, Wilbert A., Pratum, Ore.	W.A.R.	Thiessen, Martin D., Fritzmaurice, Sask.	M.D.T.
Reimer, David P., Giroux, Man.	D.P.R.	Tilitzky, C. G., Abbotsford, B.C.	C.G.T.
Reimer, Gustav E., Montevideo, Uruguay	G.R.	Toews, A. A., N. Clearbrook, B.C.	A.A.T.
Reist, H. F., Premont, Texas	H.F.R.	Toews, A. P., Dallas, Ore.	A.P.T.
Rembert, Karl, Crefeld, Ger.	K.R.	Toews, Dan, Lynden, Wash.	D.T.
Rempel, Alexander, Göttingen, Ger.	A.R.	Toews, H. P., Winnipeg, Man.	H.P.T.
Rempel, J. G., Saskatoon, Sask.	J.G.R.	Toews, Isaak J., Arnold, B.C.	I.J.T.
Rempel, N. A., E. Chilliwack, B.C.	N.A.R.	Toews, J. J., Kitchener, Ont.	J.J.T.
Ressler, C. L., Gladys, Va.	C.L.R.	Toews, John A., Winnipeg, Man.	Jo.A.T.
Rheinheimer, Floyd L., Milford, Ind.	F.L.R.	Toews, P. R., Hepburn, Sask.	P.R.T.
Rich, Mrs. Ronald, N. Newton, Kan.	E.S.R.	Torgerson, Lloyd, Olds, Alta.	L.T.

Troyer, Menno M., Conway, Kan.	M.M.T.	*Westra, H., Alkmaar, Neth.	H.W.
Tschetter, Paul G., Denver, Col.	P.G.T.	Widmer, Liesel, Bergzabern, Ger.	L.W.
Tschetter, Richard, Cordell, Okla.	R.T.	Wiebe, Alfred, Canton, Okla.	A.Wi.
*Uiterdijk, Menzo, Soestdijk, Neth.	M.U.	Wiebe, David V., Hillsboro, Kan.	D.V.W.
Umble, John S., Goshen, Ind.	J.S.U.	Wiebe, H. J., Leamington, Ont.	H.J.Wie.
Unruh, B. H., Karlsruhe, Ger.	B.H.U.	Wiens, David J., Fairview, Okla.	D.J.W.
Unruh, H. T., N. Newton, Kan.	H.T.U.	Wiens, H. E., Henderson, Neb.	H.E.W.
Unruh, J. D., Freeman, S.D.	J.D.U.	Wijnman, H. F., Amsterdam, Neth.	H.F.W.
Veen, O. L. van der, Amsterdam, Neth.	O.L.vdV.	Wiswedel, Wilhelm, Bayreuth, Ger.	W.W.
*Vis, P., Drachten, Neth.	P.V.	Woodring, A. G., Reading, Pa.	A.G.W.
Vogt, Albert F., Enid, Okla.	A.F.V.	Wray, F. J., Berea, Kentucky	F.J.W.
*Volkmar, Henri, Colmar, France	H.V.	Wyse, Lester A., Hartville, O.	L.A.W.
*Vos, K., Middelstum, Neth.	K.V.	Wyse, Olive G., Goshen, Ind.	O.G.W.
*Voth, H. R., Newton, Kan.	H.R.V.	*Yntema, J., Haarlem, Neth.	J.Y., J.IJ.
Wagler, Joel, Montgomery, Ind.	J.W.	Yoder, G. G., Hesston, Kan.	G.G.Y.
Wall, Bernhard, Fernheim, Par.	B.W.	Yoder, James D., Harrisonville, Mo.	J.D.Y.
Walter, Edwin F., Onida, S.D.	Ed.W.	Yoder, John Howard, Basel, Sw.	J.H.Y.
*Walter, Elias, Macleod, Alta.	E.Wa.	Yoder, Joseph J., Welda, Kan.	J.J.Y.
Waltner, Erland, N. Newton, Kan.	E.W.	Yoder, Paul E., Albany, Ore.	P.E.Y.
Warkentin, C. J., Herschel, Sask.	C.J.W.	Zehr, Harold, Rantoul, Ill.	H.Z.
Warkentin, G. P., Abbotsford, B.C.	G.P.W.	Zehr, Howard J., Fisher, Ill.	H.J.Z.
*Wartena, S. D. A., Hallum, Neth.	S.D.A.W.	Zijpp, N. van der, Rotterdam, Neth.	vdZ.
Weber, Aaron M., Mohnton, Pa.	A.M.W.	Zimmerman, E. E., Peoria, Ill.	E.E.Z.
Wedel, D. C., N. Newton, Kan.	D.C.W.	Zook, Ellrose D., Scottdale, Pa.	E.D.Z.
Wedel, Garman H., Moundridge, Kan.	G.H.W.		
Wedel, Ruben, Grulla, Texas	R.W.		

Corrections of Authors' Initials in Text

P. 62—article **Dillonvale** (Ohio), *for* A.B. *read* A.Bi.; p. 86—article **Doopsgezind Jaarboekje**, *for* A.Bi., vdZ. *read* A.S.B., vdZ.; p. 95—article **Doubs,** *for* P.S. *read* P.So.; p. 141—article **Echo-Verlag,** *for* A.B.D. *read* Ar.D.; p. 244—article **Erie County,** *for* E.D. *read* D.E.D.

Wenger, F. H., Moundridge, Kan.	F.H.W.
Wenger, Frank L., Aberdeen, Idaho	F.L.W.
Wenger, J. C., Goshen, Ind.	J.C.W.
Wenger, Michael N., Lititz, Pa.	M.N.W.
Wenger, S. S., Lancaster, Pa.	S.S.W.
Wertz, J., Bay Port, Mich.	J.We.

THE
MENNONITE ENCYCLOPEDIA

D

Dachau, a district of Upper Bavaria northwest of Munich, where Mennonites settled in considerable numbers from 1818 to the middle of the 19th century. Most of the families came from the Palatinate, and settled chiefly in the northwestern part of the Dachau district, founding the Eichstock (*q.v.*) congregation. Emigration to America and to other places decreased the size of the congregation, so that there are at present (1953) only a few families remaining. (*ML* I, 384.) E.M.

Dachselhofer, a distinguished family of Bern, Switzerland, who joined the Anabaptists. Some of the family emigrated to Moravia, and their capital, amounting to 9,000 pounds, was confiscated. (Müller, *Berner Täufer,* 98; *ML* I, 384.)

Dachser, Jakob (1486-1567), elder of the Augsburg Anabaptists in 1527. Though his work covered only a brief period, yet under his and Siegmund Salminger's (*q.v.*) leadership the congregation grew rapidly, reaching in a short time 1,100 members and including a large part of the population of the city.

He was born in Ingolstadt (chronicle of Clemens Jäger), served as a Catholic priest in Vienna, was compelled to flee because he had defended Luther's writings, whereupon he returned to Ingolstadt and in 1523 acquired his Master's degree there. He was arraigned before the court of the Duke of Bavaria for improper disputing and defending Lutheran ideas, and was cross-examined by several professors. The cross-examination revealed that he shared Luther's views on the Mass and fasting. On the duke's orders he was taken in chains to the bishop of Eichstätt, and after a period of imprisonment was expelled from the diocese. In 1526 he found refuge in Augsburg, earning his living by teaching. He was baptized here by Hans Hut (*q.v.*) in February 1527, and was appointed assistant head of the Augsburg Anabaptist congregation, and served with true devotion and increasing success. He baptized the preacher Hans Leopold (*q.v.*), who was martyred at Augsburg on April 25, 1528. The rapid growth of the congregation aroused the malice of the Lutheran clergy, who persuaded the council to suppress the Anabaptists. In the fall of 1527 numerous individual arrests were made, religious meetings forcibly broken up and the participants arrested. Dachser escaped capture, but not wishing to desert his congregation he presented himself to the mayor; he was so thoroughly convinced of the legality of his teachings and acts that he did not consider the possibility of danger in a Protestant city after an explanation of his position to the council. But on Aug. 25, 1527, five days after the Martyrs' Synod (*q.v.*), in which he had participated (Keller, *Staupitz,* 325), he was arrested. The Lutheran preachers Rhegius, Frosch, Agricola, and

Keller disputed long with Dachser and his fellow prisoners Hut, Gross, and Salminger, but were unable to make them forsake their convictions. To make them more amenable they were put into the dungeon. Voices were heard in the council recommending capital punishment. It was finally decided to leave them in prison until they recanted out of sheer physical exhaustion.

Dachser's wife Ottilie, who entered the service of Margrave George of Brandenburg soon after his arrest, interceded for his release. The margrave sponsored her petition before the council, but always received the reply that there was no possibility of release for Dachser unless he recanted. Ulrich Heckel, who later became a master of the weavers' guild, also presented petitions to the council, stating that before his arrest Dachser had served faithfully as a teacher in Augsburg, "whose equal will not soon be found; of this I have many honest witnesses at Augsburg among the rich and the poor." When "some of the Anabaptists asserted themselves, prophesied and held peculiar opinions he counseled against it; thus he acquired such disfavor among them that they wished to excommunicate him."

The council was relentless. Finally after confinement of more than three years Dachser yielded to the incessant entreaty of his wife and the persuasion of the clergymen Wolfgang Musculus and Bonifacius Wolfhart, who had been called from Strasbourg, and on May 16, 1531, five weeks after Salminger's recantation, he recanted. It was done in Latin on a weekday, at a time when few persons were present. Because of his "physical exhaustion and the need to earn a living" he requested permission to remain in the city. He would "seek his bread by industrious and faithful instruction of the children of the city in Christian discipline and doctrine as he had done before," and co-operate in the conversion of the Anabaptists. The council consented and appointed him as an assistant at St. Ulrich's Church.

Doubts on the part of the clergy concerning his dogmatic position prevented Dachser from obtaining a regular preaching appointment, though there was no cause for distrust. Dachser avoided the questions for which he had suffered so long, and occupied himself in a field that had thus far received little attention in the Protestant churches, namely, in verse for church singing. In this field he deserves more recognition than he has thus far been given. Even before his imprisonment he had as an Anabaptist preacher composed hymns and must therefore be considered one of the first evangelical poets and hymn writers.

His poems were very early circulated far beyond Anabaptist circles. While he was languishing in the dungeon, some of his songs were published in 1529 in the Augsburg hymnal, *Form und ordnung Gaystlicher Gesang und Psalmen,* and are among the best in the collection. The second edition, published in 1532, after his release, was the product of at least his co-operation, if not of his sole editorship. The foreword states that Dachser versified several psalms of David (Ps. 54, 103, 116, 138, 142, 143, published in Wackernagel). In the hymnal published in 1537 by Sigmund Salminger (*Der gantz Psalter, das ist alle Psalmen Davids, an der zal 150, . . .*), there are 42 psalms translated by Dachser into German for church singing; in addition there are several of his songs which had been published in the earlier collection.

In the following year at the request of many friends Dachser published the psalms with notes, titled *Der gantz psalter Davids nach ordnung und anzahl aller Psalmen.* Several psalms, he remarks in the foreword, which had been previously rewritten, including two by Martin Luther, he left unchanged except to correct them. The greatest significance of Dachser's hymnal lies in the fact that an appendix contains songs written by him for church holidays and ceremonies, making it the first practical Protestant hymnal. When the Augsburg clergy in 1555 published a *Gsangbüchlin* (new enlarged edition in 1557), not only all the psalms, but also the appendix of Dachser's book were included.

At this time Dachser was no longer in Augsburg. In August 1552 he and two other preachers (Johann Flinner and Johann Traber) were ordered by Charles V to leave the city, "because they spoke, acted, and practiced all sorts of things that might lead to sedition, revolt, and all mischief"; the fact that one of these preachers "had been an Anabaptist," would be sufficient reason for distrust (*Briefe und Akten zur Geschichte des 16. Jahrhunderts* III, 316). Dachser's wife was permitted to remain in Augsburg because of age and ill health; but the Bishop of Arras made the stipulation "that she practice nothing at all with anybody, and hold no meetings in her house." Dachser betook himself to Pfalz-Neuburg; he died in 1567 at the age of nearly 81. His name is in the Index of Venice (Reusch, *Der Index,* 231). According to Schottenloher, Dachser is the author of the anonymous publication, *Eine göttliche und gründliche Offenbarung von den wahrhaftigen Wiedertäufern, mit göttlicher Wahrheit anzeigt* (1527). This booklet was for a long time ascribed to Eitelhans Langenmantel (*q.v.*). It was printed by the clandestine Augsburg printer (*Winkeldrucker*) Philipp Ulhart, and was refuted by Urban Rhegius (*q.v.*) in *Notwendige Warnung wider den neuen Taufforden . . .* (1527). Dachser also published in Augsburg in 1526 a medieval mystical writing, *Aus was Grund die Lieb entspringt,* to which he wrote the preface. Copies of this booklet as well as Rhegius' *Notwendige Warnung* are in the Goshen College Library.

HEGE.

L. Keller, *Johann Staupitz . . .* (Leipzig, 1888); idem, "Salminger," HRE XXX, 270-72; C. Meyer and F. Roth in *Ztscht des hist. Vereins f. Schwaben u. Neuburg* I (1874) and XXVIII (1901); C. Prantl, *Gesch. d. Ludwig-Max.-Universität* I (Munich, 1872) 149; M. Radlkofer, "Jakob Dachser u. Sigmund Salminger," in *Beiträge zur bayerischen Kirchengesch.* VI (Erlangen, 1900) 1-29; F. Roth, *Augsburgs Ref.-Gesch.* (Munich, 1904); Wackernagel, *Kirchenlied* III, 701-7, where ten of Dachser's songs are given; A. Kamp, *Die Psalmendichtung Jakob Dachsers* (Greifswald, 1931); K. Schottenloher, *Philipp Ulhart, ein Augsburg Winkeldrucker und Helfershelfer der "Schwärmer" und "Wiedertäufer"* (1921) contains a section on Salminger, pp. 72-83; ML I, 93; Riezler, *Geschichte Bayerns* IV, 87; Druffel, *Bayrische Politik am Beginn der Reformationszeit* (1885) 643; V. A. Winter, *Gesch. der evangelischen Lehre in Bayern* I, 98 f.; ML I, 384-86.

Daele, van (van Daelle, van Dale, van Dalen), a family name rather common among the Flemish-Dutch Anabaptists and Mennonites. Four martyrs bearing this name were executed in Belgium: Lijntgen (Linken) van Dale (*q.v.*) and Heynderick van Dale (*q.v.*), both executed at Antwerp in 1562, and Guillaume van Dale (*q.v.*) and Maurissus van Dale (*q.v.*), both executed at Gent, in 1562 and 1573 respectively. In the early 17th century members of the van Daele family were numerous in Aardenburg and Cadzand in the Dutch province of Zeeland. They were engaged in farming, and some of them were deacons of the church. Bartholomeus van Daele (van Dale), a farmer, moved from Etichine near Oudenaerden in Flanders, Belgium, to Cadzand, where he became a preacher about 1629. This family name was also found in Rotterdam and Haarlem, Holland. In Haarlem some of the van Dale (van Dalen) family were deacons, while Anton van Dale (*q.v.*, 1638-1708) was a preacher there, as also was Mathys van Dalen (d. 1707), for whom his colleague D. Voorhelm held a funeral sermon, *Lyck-Reden* (Haarlem, 1707). Jacob Cornelisz van Dalen (*q.v.*, 1608-64) was a preacher in Amsterdam. It could not be determined whether the bearers of this name were related or not.   vDZ.

Dahlem, Valentin, one of the leading South German Mennonite preachers in the early 19th century, b. Dec. 26, 1754, at Erbesbüdesheim near Alzey. Before he was six years of age he lost his father. Under his stepfather Heinrich Borkholder, who settled in the principality of Nassau-Weilburg with other Mennonite families and in 1773 took over the court estate near Mosbach, he acquired an excellent agricultural education. He was an outstanding farm manager, and was one of the first to introduce scientific use of the soil in the Nassau region. After his marriage with Barbara Hüthwohl of Harxheim he leased the Koppensteiner estate at Wiesbaden and introduced scientific farming there, setting an example for the rural population. With amazement they saw that Dahlem planted potatoes, which were still unknown and were considered poisonous by many, sowed the "rank weed" clover and thus made use of fallow ground, but still always had the best crops.

Duke William offered Dahlem the Koppensteiner estate as a gift in recognition of his contribution to agriculture, but Dahlem was too modest to accept it. His services to agricultural science were also fully honored in a report by the Nassau ministers of State to the regent in June 1808, which states, "The grand theories of other countries are not found here; but in practice there is life and activity. Especially our Anabaptists set a good example—

neighbors of the Lower Palatinate—and in competition with them progress is made along every line. Cultivation of clover has been of benefit. Fallow land has been decreased, and animal husbandry is thriving."

By private study Dahlem acquired an amazing general education. He showed great proficiency in ancient languages, especially Latin and Greek; he could also use Hebrew fluently. When a Mennonite congregation was formed near Wiesbaden in 1790, Dahlem was chosen their preacher; he was well qualified for this office by his talents and his knowledge. At first the congregation met on the Borkholder farm at Mosbach, then in Steiner's Mill near Wiesbaden (today the house at 32 Walram Street) and in Massenheim. For a time Dahlem also served the church at Neuwied.

Dahlem's influence extended far beyond his own congregation. He devoted his energy to re-establishing strict discipline among the South German Mennonites; moral conditions were dubious in many places as a result of the Napoleonic war. With Peter Weber, the elder at Neuwied, he called a meeting of the leaders of the congregations on the left bank of the Rhine, which was held on June 5, 1803, at Ibersheim (q.v.) near Worms. The conference resolved no longer to tolerate sinful pleasures among the members and to stem the growing influence of fashion on dress.

The value his brethren in office placed on his capability is expressed in the resolution passed by this conference, appointing Dahlem to prepare a handbook for the use of ministers, especially beginners, in church services. Up to this time the South German churches had had no compilation of addresses and prayers for religious observances. Some preachers, of course, used a manuscript translation of the *Formular* of the Dutch Joannes Deknatel (q.v.), but it was not in general use. Dahlem worked out a manual which he presented at a second conference at Ibersheim on June 5, 1805. To this conference Dahlem had also invited the leaders of the churches in Baden and Württemberg. The manual was approved by all and was published two years later with the title, *Allgemeines und vollständiges Formularbuch für die gottesdienstlichen Handlungen, in denen Taufgesinnten, Evangelisch Mennoniten-Gemeinden benebst Gebetern zum Gebrauch auf alle vorkommenden Fälle beim öffentlichen Gottesdienst wie auch die Formen und Gebetern unsrer Brüder am Neckar* (Neuwied, 1807, 336 pp.). It was introduced in the Palatine and Hessian churches and served as a model for later manuals.

In his spare time Dahlem enjoyed writing poetry. "His verses," writes his great-grandson C. Spielmann (d. 1918) in Wiesbaden, "are simple but have good rhythmic form and thoughtful content, not to be classed with the rhymes of poetasters. He liked to write pastoral poems. It is a pity that his poetry has not been preserved. Spielmann published two of Dahlem's poems as specimens: "Vergiss mein nicht, du Gott voll Güte" and "Noch immer fand ich nicht die Ruh."

The church that he led so long split after his death, which occurred on Jan. 23, 1840. Apparently there had been neglect in ordaining young ministers. Individual members lost connections and moved away or joined other churches. Dahlem's descendants married members of the state church; their children did not adopt the Mennonite faith.

HEGE.

L. Spielmann, *Valentin Dahlem, Lebensbild eines nassauischen Mennonitenpredigers* (Wiesbaden, about 1912); W. Mannhardt, *Die Wehrfreiheit der Altpreussischen Mennoniten* (Danzig, 1863) 55; *Menn. Bl.*, 1895, 21, 36; 1914, 35-38, 43-45; Glasius, *Godgeleerd Nederl. Biogr. Wb.* I; *ML* I, 386 f.

Dakota Avenue United Missionary Church, Detroit, Mich., was organized in 1914 under the leadership of O. B. Snider. The first meetinghouse was built in 1916. In 1954 the congregation had 243 baptized members with William K. Burgess serving as pastor.

W.K.B.

Dale, Anton van, b. Nov. 8, 1638, at Haarlem (Holland), d. Nov. 18 or 28, 1708. Up to the age of 30 he was a merchant; then he studied medicine, received his doctor's degree, and became a physician. At the same time he studied classical languages, becoming a Latin scholar of importance. As physician in the civic charity hospital in Haarlem he won high recognition for his unselfish service. He was always cheerful and jovial, and liked to tell anecdotes combating superstition. For a time he was a Mennonite preacher, but because he wove too much Greek and Latin into his sermons, they found little acclaim; he therefore resigned his office. It is not quite clear in which congregation van Dale served, but presumably it was that of the Waterlanders. An anonymous letter written to Marten Schagen (found in *DB* 1863) indicates that van Dale was at first a member of the Flemish congregation of den Blok, but left this congregation about 1665 to join the Waterlanders. He wrote *Boere-praetje tusschen vijf Persoonen....Handelende of Galenus te recht voor een Hypocrijt is beschuldight ...* (1664); *Aanmerkingen over het Tractaatje van de heer J. Verryn* (Remonstrant preacher) *omtrent den waterdoop* (1685), *Verhandeling van de Oorspronk en Duuring van de Waterdoop* (1704); *Historie van 't Predik-ampt en het wapenvoeren* (1674 and 1704); *De Oudheid van 't Alleen spreken ...verdedigd* (1670), written against the Collegiants, which P. Langedult answered with *Het apostolisch oude gebruik vrij te spreken* (1672); *Dissertatio super Aristea de LXX Interpretibus. Additur historia Baptismorum* (1705); *De oraculis ethnicorum* (1683), and a translation, *Verhandeling van de Oude Orakelen der Heydenen* (1687), in which he explains that the oracles were merely priestly deception. This work was used by the wise Fontenelle and opposed by the German Möbius. An attack by two Jesuits caused him to publish the booklet anew with the title, *De Oraculis Veterum Ethnicorum* (1704). In addition to these he wrote *Dissertationes de Origine et Progressu Idololatriae et superstitione* (1691); *Dissertationibus ex antiquitatibus* (1702).

K.V.

᾿ *Inv. Arch. Amst.* II, **No.** 1189; *Biogr. Wb.* II, 345-51; Blaupot t. C., *Holland* I; *DB* 1863, 142; *Catalogus Amst.*, 128, 161, 174, 177, 178; *ML* I, 387.

Dalen, Jacob Cornelisz van, b. 1608 at Rotterdam, d. 1664, a noted Mennonite surgeon and preacher of the Waterlanders at Amsterdam, 1639-62. Operations he performed on facial abscesses are described and illustrated by C. E. Daniels in *Een Domine-Operateur in de zeventiende eeuw.* He became involved in a dispute with Reinier Wybrands and later with Joost Hendricks. He collaborated with Denys van der Schure in writing *Korte verthooninge van de onware beschuldingen* (1640), which was answered in the following year by Joost Hendricks. In 1652 he wrote *Oorciersel en Cieraet van de Godsalige vrouwen,* opposing fashion and championing very simple dress. In 1662 he wrote *Spiegel der Dischgenooten Christi* (repr. 1729) with an important foreword, a communion sermon which was reprinted in 1729 in G. Maatschoen's appendix to Schijn's *Gesch. der Mennoniten* (Amsterdam, 1745) 289-320. In addition to these he published *Betragtinge over het Onze Vader, Zes predikatiën over het Lijden van Jezus Christus,* and *Christelijke Betrachtingen. (Biogr. Wb.* II, 352 f.; *ML* I, 386.) **K.V.**

Dalen, Willem van, an Anabaptist martyr: see **Guillaume van Dale.**

Dallas, Ore., a town (pop. 5,000) in Polk County, in the northwestern part of the state. Mennonites have been living here for about 45 years. There are now in and around Dallas about 1,000 Mennonites, of whom about 300 live in town, and who belong to the M.B., E.M.B., and G.C.M. (Grace Mennonite Church) branches, each of which has a church in the town. Dallas also has a home for the aged, the Dallas Rest Home (capacity 26 guests), owned and operated by the M.B. Church. The leading industry of the town is a large lumber mill.   **W.L.P.**

Dallas Evangelical Mennonite Brethren Church, located in western Oregon, had a membership of 320 in 1954. The first E.M.B. settlers moved into the area in 1890, and in 1912 the first pastor was installed. The first church, built in the country in 1916, was moved to Dallas and enlarged in 1924. In 1922 the church was incorporated. In 1927 Mr. and Mrs. Lloyd Bartel were ordained as missionaries to China. Ministers who have served the congregation are Solomon S. Ediger, 1912-20; H. H. Dick, 1920-27; John J. Schmidt, 1927-28; J. H. Quiring, 1928-41; D. P. Schultz, 1941-47; A. C. Wall, 1947-48; A P. Toews, 1948-52; and Arno Wiebe, 1953- . The following missionaries were ordained for the foreign fields: Mary Quiring to China in 1946, Tina Friesen to Africa in 1951, Harvey Ratzlaff to Africa in 1949, Irene Claasen to Japan in 1951, Mr. and Mrs. Hugh Gookin to Venezuela in 1952, and Anna Fast to Africa in 1952.   **A.P.T.**

Dallas Mennonite Brethren Church, at the corner of Washington and Hayter streets in Dallas, Polk Co., Ore., is a member of the Pacific District Conference of the M.B. Church of North America. The church, an outgrowth of the North Dallas M.B. Church, which had started in 1905, was organized under the leadership of Abraham Buhler, on Dec. 21, 1919. In 1934 the first church was replaced by the present frame structure, which was remod-

eled in 1949. Its parsonage at 518 Hayter St. was procured in 1944.

On Jan. 7, 1923, the North Dallas M.B. Church membership was received into the Dallas church. With population increase in the Willamette Valley, the church membership increased. Some members who lived in Salem organized the West Salem Mennonite Brethren Church in 1941. The present membership (1954) in Dallas is 346, approximately half of whom are rural people.

Ministers who have served the church are D. A. Peters, G. G. Wiens, P. H. Berg, Abr. Buhler, P. E. Penner, Frank F. Friesen, Herman D. Wiebe, F. F. Wall, N. N. Hiebert, J. J. Toews, Henry Hooge, and the present minister, W. L. Penner. Mr. and Mrs. A. F. Kroeker of this church are serving as foreign missionaries.   **G.H.J.**

Dalmeny (Ebenezer) Mennonite Brethren Church, located approximately 20 miles northwest of Saskatoon, Sask., a member of the Canadian Conference of the M.B. Church, was organized on Feb. 28, 1902, with 15 brethren present. Abram Buhler came from Mountain Lake, Minn., to serve as the first leader. In October of the same year Jacob Lepp was chosen to the ministry and was installed as church leader in 1907; he served in this capacity until his retirement in 1941. He was replaced by Henry Baerg. George Dyck is the present pastor (1954), and the membership is 229. The first meetinghouse was built in 1902, but had to be enlarged in 1907, with the coming of more settlers. In 1945 the church was thoroughly remodeled to seat approximately 400.

The first M.B. missionaries to leave from the Canadian Conference for the M.B. foreign missions were Mr. and Mrs. Bergthold, the latter being a daughter of the Mandtlers of this congregation. Only one year later Mrs. Bergthold died in India. In February 1945 Emma Lepp, daughter of Jacob Lepp, left to serve in the same field.   **J.H.E.**

Dalmeny Evangelical Mennonite Brethren Church (Sask.): see **Langham** (North) E.M.B. Church.

Dalton, Ohio, is a village of nearly 1,000 located on U.S. Highway 30 in the heart of a rich farming and dairy community of Sugar Creek Twp., Wayne County. Mennonite pioneers from eastern Pennsylvania, such as the Martins, Eberlys, Horsts, and Buckwalters, settled on territory north of Dalton early in the 19th century, organizing the Martin's Church (MC). Many of their descendants still live there. The rolling territory southwest of Dalton was chosen by Swiss Mennonites who immigrated to this section as early as 1819. This prosperous Swiss community has since been known as Sonnenberg (*q.v.*). Within a ten-mile radius of Dalton are located nine Mennonite congregations with approximately 1,600 members and representing five different branches of the church.   **S.M.**

Dam, the name of a Dutch Mennonite family, from the 17th century found in Giethoorn (*q.v.*), where many of the members were deacons and (lay) preachers of the congregations both of Giethoorn-Noord and Giethoorn-Zuid. The last preachers of this name here were the brothers Harm Wichersz Dam and Albert Wichersz Dam, both serving in Giethoorn-Zuid 1809-25. Shortly after 1800, when a number of peat-diggers moved from Giethoorn to Tjalleberd (*q.v.*), province of Friesland, to break up the peatmoors around this town, there were among them many Mennonites, among them Harm Roelofs Dam, who, like many of his descendants, was a pillar of the Tjalleberd congregation, founded in 1817.

There have been a number of Mennonite ministers with this family name, whose relationship, if any, with the Giethoorn Dam family could not be determined. Kornelius Jansz Dam was a preacher at Dokkum 1710-*ca*.50. Two of his sons went into the ministry, Jelle Kornelis Dam serving at St-Annakerk and Oudebildtzijl 1739-54 (?), and Jan Kornelis Dam at Bolsward about 1735-38 and Workum 1738-82. In 1742 he married Grietje Keimpes Boothamer of Workum. Their son Keimpe Jansz Dam (d. April 24, 1810), educated at the Amsterdam Mennonite Seminary, served at Makkum 1771-73 and Rotterdam 1773-1810. vDZ.

Several issues of *Naamlijst; DB* 1864, 107, 114, 120; 1878, 27; 1905, 5 ff., 15 f., 25; *DJ* 1919, 66.

Damas, an Anabaptist leader of Hoorn, Dutch province of North Holland, a weaver by trade, who was listed with Jacob van Campen (*q.v.*) and Cornelis wt den Briel (*q.v.*) as one of the most prominent Anabaptists by Reynier Brunt, attorney-general of the Court of Holland, in a letter dated March 24, 1535 (*Inv. Arch. Amst.* I, No. 113). Damas baptized a Thomas Thomasz at Monnikendam (Grosheide, *Verhooren*, 127). He must also have been active in the province of Zeeland (*DB* 1917, 103). According to Vos (*ibid.*, 103-4), the man called David van Hoorn in the Confession of Obbe Philips (*BRN* VII, 132) was actually Damas, "David" being merely a slip of the pen. If this is the case, Damas was one of the 12 apostles sent out by Jan Matthijs (*q.v.*) to proclaim the imminent kingdom of God. After his activities of 1534-35 to spread the revolutionary ideas of Münsterite Anabaptism he disappeared and nothing more is known about him. (Mellink, *Wederdopers,* see Index.)
vDZ.

Damas Jacobsz, a native of Leiden, Dutch province of South Holland, a barber, one of the fanatical Anabaptists. He was probably a follower of David Joris (*q.v.*) and was beheaded at Delft, Holland, on Jan. 10, 1539 (not 1538 as G. Brandt, *Hist. der Ref.* I, 1677, 133, states). (*DB* 1917, 120, No. 113.) vDZ.

Dämberschitz, a village in Moravia southeast of Austerlitz, where the Hutterian Brethren set up a Bruderhof in 1550. In the disturbances of war several buildings, including the pottery, were burned down in September 1619, and in 1622 they had to flee from Dämberschitz losing all their possessions. They settled in Echtelnitz. (Beck, *Geschichts-Bücher,* 198, 374, 408, and 409; *ML* I, 387.)
HEGE.

Dame, Friedrich, pastor and provost at Rostock, author of the book *Abgedrungene Relatio dess Colloquii und was sonsten mit denen von Flensburg*

entwichenen Enthusiasten Niclaus Kuntzen und Hartwich Lohmann gehandelt, auch gründliche refutatio ihrer greulichen Schwärmerei . . . (Rostock, 1625, 152 pages), dedicated to the Count of Ahlefeld. The introduction contains a blunt warning against Schwenckfelders, Photians, and Anabaptists. The booklet would have some value for Anabaptist history if the assertion that Niclaus Kuntz of Husum "who studied in Amsterdam" was an Anabaptist were correct. But of this there is no possibility, judging by what is said about his faith. Perhaps he and Lohmann were Weigelians. (*ML* I, 387.) NEFF.

Damian, an Anabaptist martyr of Allgäu, executed at the stake at Ingolstadt in 1543. He was apparently a Hutterite. On the way to the site of execution he addressed the crowd in such a way that a student said, "One thing must be true. This man has either a devil or the spirit of God, since he knows so much when he is apparently a humble person." The judge was also conscience-stricken. (Wiswedel, *Bilder* II, 147; Beck, *Geschichts-Bücher,* 154; *Mart. Mir.* D 63, E 466; *ML* I, 388.) vDZ.

Damme, Elysabeth van (nee van Blenckvliet), a member of the Flemish Mennonite congregation of den Blok at Haarlem, Holland, who together with her husband Jaques van Damme founded the Zuiderhofje (an old people's home) there in 1640, and after the death of her husband contributed liberally to the orphanage of the Flemish congregation here. According to another tradition she was the founder of this (first Dutch Mennonite) orphanage. The remarkable "ordere van 't weeshuys van den Block," signed May 15, 1643, is found in the archives of the Haarlem congregation. vDZ.

De Weeshuizen der Doopsgezinden in Haarlem 1634-1934 (Haarlem, 1934) 11 f., 14.

Dammersfeld (Thankmarsfelde), once a Benedictine monastery, near Ballenstedt in the Harz, on which Prince Friedrich Albrecht settled a Swiss Mennonite family by the name of Sommer in 1787. They remained here until 1816, and were highly esteemed for their piety and economic capability. Very likely, they became homesick and returned to their Swiss mountains. (*Menn. Bl.,* 1859, 39; *ML* I, 388.)
NEFF.

Danforth Mennonite Church (MC), 2174 Danforth Ave., Toronto, Ont., now called Toronto Mennonite Church, was established in 1907. In 1954 it had 55 members, with Emerson McDowell serving as pastor. M.G.

Daniel Calvaerd (Kalvaert), an Anabaptist martyr, a native of Thielt in Flanders, Belgium, seized at Armentières, taken to Rijssel (Lille), France, and back to Armentières, where he was burned at the stake in 1564, exact date unknown. (*Mart. Mir.* D 301, E 666; *ML* II, 455.) vDZ.

Daniel van der Campt (or Vercampt, Verkampt), an Anabaptist martyr of Kortrijk (Courtrai), Belgium. He was a weaver and unmarried. After a cross-examination by the Inquisitor Pieter Titelman, the dean of Ronse, and by a certain Polet, he was burned in Kortrijk on Dec. 12, 1559. Van Braght, *Martyrs' Mirror,* relates that Daniel's mother, who was still a Catholic, was also examined and threatened with severe punishment, because she had hidden her son, knowing that he was a heretic. But she said that he was an honest young man and not a thief or a rascal and that she had hidden him for maternal love. She defended herself so well that she was set free. (*Mart. Mir.* D 201, E 582; Verheyden, *Courtrai-Bruxelles,* 34, No. 8.)   vdZ.

Daniel de Paeu (Pau, Pou), an Anabaptist martyr, a cobbler of Eeclo in Belgium, was burned at the stake at Gent, Belgium, on Dec. 29, 1568, together with Daniel van Vooren and Passchier Weyns (*q.v.*). In the first song of the supplement to the old *Liedtboecxken van den Offer des Heeren* (ed. 1578, BRN II, 649 ff.) the names of these three martyrs are also found. Particulars are lacking. (*Mart. Mir.* D 370, E 726; Verheyden, *Gent,* 50, No. 163; Daniel van Vooren is listed here No. 164; *ML* III, 332.)   vdZ.

Daniel van Vo(o)ren, an Anabaptist martyr, burned at the stake at Gent, Belgium, on Dec. 29, 1568. See **Daniel de Paeu.**

Dankels, Philipp von, a signatory to the agreement of the Anabaptist conference held in Strasbourg in 1555 (A. Brons, *Ursprung, Entwickelung und Schicksale der . . . Mennoniten,* Emden, 1912, 98), about whom nothing further is known. (*ML* I, 389.)   Neff.

Dannenberg, a former Mennonite congregation in Lithuania (*q.v.*). There are a number of documents and letters pertaining to the Dannenberg congregation in the Archives of the Amsterdam Mennonite Church (*Inv. Arch. Amst.* I, Nos. 1074-79, 1085, 1582-93; II, 2, Nos. 743, 755, 784). These letters show that this congregation in Prussian Lithuania belonged to the United High German, Frisian, and Flemish Mennonites. In May 1724 they were obliged to leave the country, but soon returned. In 1731 they numbered 47 families and asked the Amsterdam congregation for financial help, which was given. Their ministers were Hans Jantzen and Thies Ewerdt. Elder Jakob Denner of Altona arrived in November 1731 to spend the winter with the church at Dannenberg. On Feb. 22, 1732, by order of King Frederick William I of Prussia, they were expelled again. They had to leave Dannenberg before June 8 of this year. Most of them (with some other Mennonites) emigrated by ship, via Königsberg to Amsterdam, 110 souls in all. They were supplied with houses and land at Wageningen and on the island of Walcheren near Middelburg by the Dutch Mennonite Committee of Foreign Needs. This colonization proved to be a failure. (See *DB* 1905, 112-68; 1906, 93-138.) Beginning in September 1736 they gradually returned and settled in the environs of Danzig and Elbing. The exact relation of this congregation to the other Mennonite settlement (begun in 1714) and congregations is not clear. In any case it had only a short existence under the name Dannenberg.   vdZ.

Dantumawoude (shortened form *Damwoude*), a village in the Dutch province of Friesland, the seat of a Mennonite church, situated between Dokkum and Veenwouden. The time of the origin of the congregation is uncertain. Blaupot ten Cate places the date between 1580 and 1600. Practically nothing is known of its early history. The church records go back only to 1728. In 1767 the present church was erected; it was substantially enlarged in 1910. Until 1812 the congregation was served by lay ministers. The last of these was the well-known Uilke Reitses Dijkstra (1775-1823). Since that time the church has had trained ministers, the first of whom was Jan ter Borg, 1810-19. At this time a number of members of the Reformed Church were admitted into this congregation without rebaptism (*DB* 1882, 107).

The Mennonite Church of Dantumawoude is one of the most thriving rural churches in Holland. The Mennonite Bible studies and especially preaching services are attended also by people of other faiths. The church board manages the considerable capital of the church, assisted by an inspector. The congregation is a member of Ring Dantumawoude. The membership figures are as follows: 1695, about 150; 1838, 207; 1861, 277; 1898, 275; 1921, 270; 1954, 249. Ministers during the past half-century were U. J. Reinders, 1899-1916; F. H. Pasma, 1916-21; L. Bonga, 1921-26; J. IJntema, 1926-31; L. D. G. Knipscheer, 1931-35; H. H. Gaaikema, 1935-46; G. Kater, 1946-51; E. Daalder since 1951. The congregation has a Sunday school for children, a women's organization, a youth organization, and a club of catechumens, called *Menniste Bouwers.* (F. H. Pasma, *Onze Vermaning 1767-1917, Gedachtenisrede; ML* I, 389.)   F.H.P., vdZ.

Dantumawoude Ring, an association of Mennonite churches in the Dutch province of Friesland. After Ring Akkrum and Ring Bolsward were organized, the need for a similar federation in northeast Friesland became apparent. D. Plantinus, preacher of Holwerd and Blija, invited delegates from the church to meet at Dokkum on Aug. 6, 1850, to discuss and adopt a preliminary constitution which he had drafted. Representatives of nine congregations appeared: Surhuisterveen, Veenwoudsterwal, Dantumawoude, Ternaard, Holwerd-Blija, Oudebildtzijl, Hallum, and Ameland (Flemish and Waterlander) who formed a temporary union, "in order to support one another with regular preaching service in the event of sickness or a vacancy." The union was soon joined by the combined congregations of Rottevalle and Witveen. Dragten and Leeuwarden thanked Plantinus for the invitation; the latter promised to give as much service as possible to the Ring, but felt it did not need it itself. St. Anna-Parochie joined in 1872, and Berlikum in 1874.

On Sept. 6, 1855, the Ring began its work. Nes and Hollum on Ameland received special terms. In 1916 the congregation known as Kring Zwaagwesteinde, which does not have a preacher, was granted Ring service. The church at Dokkum, since it had more Mennonite members than Remonstrant, was received into the Ring in 1917 with full rights and obligations.

For a minister incapacitated by illness the service of the Ring lasts not more than a year, unless a majority of Ring members decide otherwise. For the widow or minor orphan of a deceased minister the service continues for six months. At present (1954) the Ring comprises 12 congregations: Ameland, St. Anna Parochie, Berlikum, Hallum, Holwerd, Oudebildtzijl, Rottevalle, Surhuisterveen, Ternaard, Veenwouden, and Zwaagwestcinde. (*ML* I, 389.) H.J.B.

Dantzig, Hans van, a Mennonite deacon at Amsterdam, concerning whose life little is known. Apparently he or his father was from Danzig. The following books, of which he is the author, have been preserved: *Een corte bekentenis van den eenighen Godt, vader, sone ende heyligen Gheest* (Alkmaar, 1605); *Een tafereelken ofte aenwijsinghe van eenighe schriften der Belofte Gods* (Haarlem, 1609); *Een vaderlijcke waerschouwinghe, gedaen aen sijne kinderen, daerin dat hij se vermaent tot een Godtsalich leven, waarachter opgesteld staat; een corte bekentenisse des gheloofs* (Haarlem, 1610); *Een vaderlijcke vermaninghe uyt den grooten schadt der heylige schrift* (Haarlem, n.d.). All of these treatises were reprinted in Amsterdam in 1714 (*Catalogus Amst.,* 227). Hans van Dantzig is the compiler of the Dutch hymnbook *Pruys Liedtboek* (*q.v.*). (*ML* I, 390.) J.L.

Dan(t)zigers or Dantziger Oude Vlamingen, a branch of Old Flemish Mennonites in the Netherlands: see **Flemish Mennonites.**

Danvers, Henry, "an English Anabaptist," who traced the origin of the Anabaptists to the Petrobrusians. This is reported by B. N. Krohn in his *Geschichte der fanatischen und enthusiastischen Wiedertäufer* (Leipzig, 1758) 13, note. Nothing further is known about him. (*ML* I, 390.) NEFF.

Danzig, a government district (*Regierungsbezirk*) of the province of West Prussia, before the partition in 1918 containing nearly one third of the Mennonites living in Germany, most of them in the triangle formed by Danzig (city), Elbing, and Marienburg. Whereas in the townships of Marienburg and rural Elbing the number of Mennonites decreased after World War I, it rose in the townships of Danzig-City, Danzig-Lowland, Danzig-Heights, and Elbing-City. Also in the township of Neustadt, particularly in Zoppot, more and more Mennonites settled.

Census figures show the following Mennonite populations in the various parts of the district:

	1861	1871	1880	1890	1900	1910
Elbing city	2075	405	535	477	591	606
Elbing rural	----	1491	1387	1329	1172	953
Marienburg	5343	5420	4999	5014	4928	4767
Danzig city	459	486	582	617	626	639
Danzig-Lowland				283	275	403
	544	428	397			
Danzig-Heights				72	87	138

	1861	1871	1880	1890	1900	1910
Dirschau				99	62	73
	52	69	65			
Stargard				13	20	29
Berent	12	1	1	11	6	1
Karthaus	----	----	3	7	5	5
Neustadt				13	88	161
	----	----	10			
Putzig				2	3	6
Totals	8485	8300	7979	7937	7863	7781

The district contained the following congregations up to the evacuation of all Germans under the Polish occupation: Fürstenwerder with 561 souls (in 1921), Heubuden 1,623, Ladekopp with Orlofferfelde 1,150, Tiegenhagen 823, and Thiensdorf-Markushof 1,083, Elbing-City 400, Elbing-Ellerwald 736, Rosenort 718, Danzig City 1,360, and Danzig-Lowland-Quadendorf 50. Parts of Fürstenwerder and Tiegenhagen also belonged to Danzig-Lowland.

From Jan. 20, 1920, to August 1939 the old district of Danzig was displaced in part by the Free City of Danzig, a politically independent state under the League of Nations. In 1939-45 it was called "Regierungsbezirk Danzig," and was part of the "Reichsgau Danzig-Westpreussen." With the conquest of Germany by the allied powers in 1945 and the reconstitution of Poland, the area was incorporated into the Polish governmental system, with the Polish name Gdansk.

In 1947 the Mennonite Central Committee established a relief program in the Danzig area, to which it had been directed by the Polish government, with headquarters in Tczew (Dirschau), conducting relief until the fall of 1948 when the Polish government in effect compelled the transfer of the work to Nasielsk near Warsaw. During the 1947-48 period many Mennonites were aided together with the general population. In 1947 there were still over 200 Mennonites in this region, nearly all of whom were permitted to go to Germany in 1947-49. A few individuals and one or two families of Mennonites have remained in the city or its environs. (*ML* I, 390.) HEGE, H.S.B.

Danzig, Free City of. The Treaty of Versailles (effective Jan. 20, 1920) placed the city of Danzig and its immediate vicinity (*ca.* 790 sq. mi.) under the protection of the League of Nations as an independent state, in an attempt to solve the conflict between the principle of self-determination (the city was German) and the need of Poland for a free port of access to the Baltic. From Nov. 7, 1920, the city had its own government with an elected senate of 21 senators and a president. It contained besides the city proper also the rural township of Danzig Heights, Danzig Lowland, and Elbing, the townships Neustadt and Marienburg, and the towns of Zoppot (pop. 15,000), Tiegenhof (3,000), and Neuteich (2,400). The total urban population was 225,000, the rural population 125,000. Of these, 220,000 were Protestants, 120,000 Catholics, 6,000 Mennonites, and 4,000 Jews.

Of the 120 delegates in the Volkstag in 1920, three

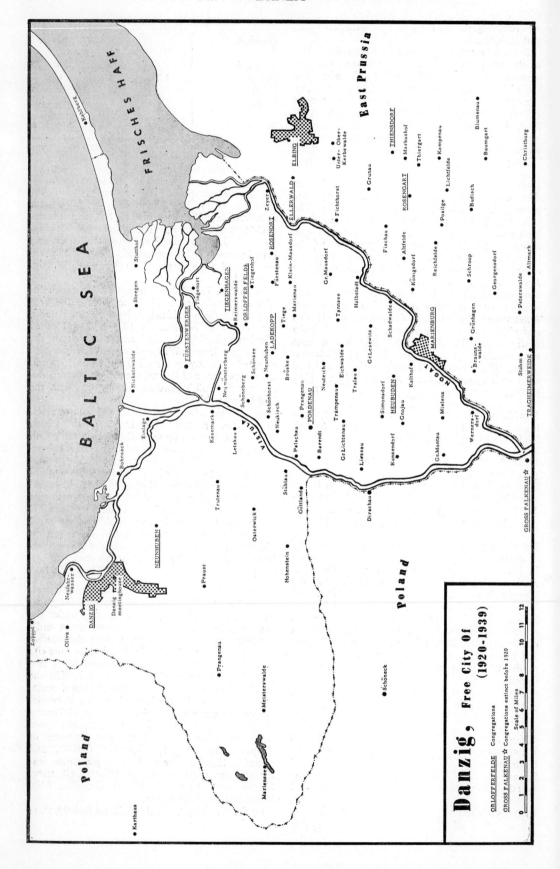

Danzig, Free City Of (1920-1939)

<u>ORLOFFERFELDE</u>   Congregations
<u>GROSS FALKENAU</u> ☆ Congregations extinct before 1920

Scale of Miles
0 1 2 3 4 5 6 7 8 9 10 11 12

were Mennonites. The constitution gave the Mennonites equal rights with other citizens, and in addition permitted them to substitute an affirmation for an oath. The Mennonites in the Free City belonged to the following congregations: Danzig, Fürstenwerder with its subsidiary Neunhuben, Ladekopp-Orlofferfelde, Tiegenhagen, Rosenort, and Heubuden. Heubuden was divided, only that part lying west of the Nogat belonging to the Free City.

The history of the territory was a turbulent one after the accession of Hitler to power in 1933. In 1934 Hitler arbitrarily denounced the German-Polish nonaggression treaty, and demanded the return of Danzig to Germany, which was naturally refused. From that time on, the Nazi party agitated and terrorized the population until by 1937 the Gestapo was in complete control of the city. Even a terrorized election of 1935 failed to secure the necessary two-thirds majority for the Nazis (they received only 57.3 per cent). In August 1939, by a coup d'etat, Forster declared himself head of the state, and shortly thereafter Hitler reincorporated Danzig into the Reich. The war with Poland was occasioned by this act, and was followed by World War II.

Danzig was first under the Teutonic Order, until 1454, when it voluntarily came under the protectorate of Poland 1454-1772. It joined the Hanseatic League in 1391, and under the Polish regime was to all intents an independent free city. In 1772 (fully only in 1793) it became Prussian, remaining so until 1920. It accepted the Reformation 1523-57. (*ML* I, 390.) H.G.M., H.S.B.

Danzig Mennonite Church, the largest city Mennonite church in East Germany, which had more than 1,100 baptized members in 1921. The late Danzig church was formed in 1808 from a union of the Old Flemish congregation (founded in 1569) and the Old Frisian congregation (founded about 1600).

The date of the coming of the first Mennonites to Danzig is not certain. Individual Anabaptists found their way here about 1530, especially from Holland. It is fairly certain that Menno Simons came to Danzig at least once, when he journeyed into the Baltic region and looked up his scattered brethren in and beyond Polish Prussia, and wherever possible organized them into congregations. In 1549 he wrote to the "children of God in Prussia," stating that he had been there that year. After Menno's death Dirk Philips came here again, and according to the tradition of the Danzig congregation was its first elder. He lived in Schottland near Danzig (Cramer, "Mennoniten," in *HRE,* 607) and worked with Hans Sikken several years—until 1567 or 1568—preaching and administering baptism and communion. Since during these very years Alba's reign of terror caused a greater influx of Dutch refugees to Danzig, they may have played a part in the formation of the congregation, which has existed in organized form since 1569. The list of elders and preachers is without a gap. The names of the founders are all Dutch— Hans van Amersfoort, Gijsbert de Veer (b. May 14, 1536, in Amsterdam), van Eyck, Beulke, van Buygen, van Almonde, Symons, van Dyck, Janzen, Maal

(Mahl), van Beuningen, van Berynghuysen, etc. Elder Leenaert Bouwens (*q.v.*), who visited Danzig in 1563-65, baptized only three persons here.

The divisions that had taken place in Holland were, of course, transferred to the new locality; thus a Flemish and a Frisian congregation existed here side by side. The points of difference were maintained for a long time in Prussia, sometimes more emphatically than in the mother country. Until 1786 it was customary to rebaptize members of the Frisian group who wished to join the larger Flemish group. The latter, the more important congregation, considering itself beyond question the real Danzig Mennonite Church, kept in live communication with the strictest wing of the Old Flemish (*q.v.*) in Holland, especially in Amsterdam, Haarlem, and Rotterdam. Its influence was so pronounced in Holland that a part of the Old Flemish there in the 17th century were called the "Old Danzig" group. That the Flemish congregations called themselves the "fine" is generally known; it is not so well known that they were also known as the "clear" (*Klare,* unambiguous), which gave rise to the term "Klarichen" or "Klärichen," in Low German "Klarken" or "Klerken" (*q.v.*). The Frisians, on the other hand, who were more liberal, were called the "coarse" (*Grobe*) or "worried" (*Bekümmerte*). Connections with Holland, by correspondence and by visits, remained intact as long as the Dutch language was used in church and home (1600-1750). The well-to-do Danzig congregation sent its young sons to Amsterdam to complete their education and learn a business, as well as to share youth instruction in the church and return to Danzig after receiving baptism. The Danzig baptismal registers of the 17th and 18th centuries nearly always contain an appendix of those who were baptized in Holland. In 1725, at the urgent request of the Old Flemish in Rotterdam and Amsterdam, Dirk Janssen, a Danzig preacher, was chosen by lot as elder to succeed Adriaan van Gameren, was ordained in Danzig, and was sent to Amsterdam. He left Danzig with his family on Dec. 7, 1725, and returned eight years later, serving as elder in Danzig with Isaac de Veer and then alone until his death on Nov. 25, 1750.

Evidence of these contacts between the Mennonites of Danzig and Amsterdam is found in a large number (more than 300) of documents in the Mennonite Archives of Amsterdam (see bibliography). Most of these are letters, received from or sent to Danzig. They are a rich source of information about conditions in the Danzig congregations, both Flemish and Frisian. They give information on such things as measures of the Danzig government against the Mennonites, hardships because of war, fire, and floods, the considerable sums received from the Dutch Mennonite Committee for Foreign Needs, and the spiritual conditions of the Danzig Mennonites. About 1730, when a quarrel arose between the Danzig Flemish congregation and its Elder Heinrich von Dühren (*q.v.*), two Dutch ministers, first Abraham Koenen and later Jacob Ouwejans, were sent to Danzig to settle the quarrel.

As shipping and trade between Holland and Danzig had already been active in the 14th and 15th centuries, the refugees from Holland did not flee into the unknown. At first, to be sure, the Lutheran clergy had induced the council to close its gates to them but the bishop of Cujavien, who had possessions near the city, received them in Schottland (today Altschottland), and gave them religious liberty and an opportunity to follow their trades. In the course of time the Polish kings granted them solemn letters of protection (W. Mannhardt, *Wehrfreiheit*) which of course did not prevent all oppression by self-centered officials or hostile clergymen, and especially by envious competing city guilds. Here as elsewhere the government took a friendly attitude toward the Mennonites on account of their civic virtues, and their industry and skill in trades and business; but the citizenry and the clergy opposed toleration. During the entire Polish period (until 1772) they suffered almost continually from hostility and arbitrary oppression, in many cases unabashed extortion by high-ranking persons. The notes (1667-92) of Elder Georg Hansen in the church archives cite numerous instances in which sometimes the elder or the ministers or individual members were summoned before the bishop's officer who had religious jurisdiction in the city on charges of false doctrine, Socinian connections, and the like. A more or less heavy fine was usually imposed. Fortunately the Mennonites were frequently defended from exploitation by the city council. But the council was not always able to protect them against attacks. From 1749 to 1762 a regulation was enforced by the small dealers in the city, prohibiting Mennonite merchants in the suburbs from selling anything but brandy (see **Alcohol**). This measure, added to the protection fee of 5,000 florins arbitrarily imposed on Mennonites living in or near the city (Jan. 14, 1750), impoverished a number of respected members. The fee was later reduced to 3,000 florins, then to 1,200.

In 1793, when Danzig passed into Prussian hands, much of the pressure was released. In 1800 the Mennonites were given the rights of citizenship, which permitted them to buy land without employing an agent. But this was also the beginning of their struggle to maintain their nonresistance, which lasted until 1867, and its aftereffects decades longer.

The Flemish group had its church before the Petershagen city gate, and the Frisian group before the Neugarten gate. In 1648 the Flemish purchased a lot in the city (title was not transferred to them until 1732) on which they built a church, and beside it the customary home for the poor, with room for about 30 persons. In 1734 the city was besieged by the Russians for two months, during which time the many Mennonites in the southern suburbs had to flee from their homes into the city proper. Church, poorhouse, and some private dwellings were destroyed. With aid from the Dutch and Prussian Mennonites and a legacy, the congregation was able to rebuild the church and the poor-home. Seventy years later, in 1805, the church was completely remodeled and an organ added against the wishes of an important minority. But in 1813, during a siege by the Russians, both were destroyed by fire.

The Frisian group, considerably smaller than the Flemish, also had a poorhouse beside their church, which was built in 1638 before the Neugarten gate. It was remodeled in 1788, but was destroyed in the French siege of 1806. After this event the two groups worshiped together and until 1813 used the Flemish church within the city limits. After the war this church was not rebuilt, for most of the members had meanwhile moved into the city. A suitable lot was bought in the city in 1816 and a poorhouse erected on it; then in spite of general impoverishment brought on by war and foreign occupation, the congregation proceeded to build the church, dedicating it on Sept. 12, 1819. Beside it they added a parsonage in 1884. The short street in front of the church was called "Mennonitenstrasse."

The Flemish group had from the beginning included the Mennonite settlers in the Danzig Werder. In 1768 this minority, finding the roads to the city church impassable, requested that occasional services be held among them; this was feasible, for two of the preachers lived in the Werder. In 1791 this group became independent of the city church, except that the elder of the city congregation had the oversight over them. Then in 1826, when the city group engaged a salaried elder, the Werder congregation broke away and became a subsidiary of the Fürstenwerder church. In 1844 they built a small church at Neunhuben (*q.v.*) and have since been known by that name.

At first the Danzig Mennonites used the Dutch language in their services and in private. By 1750, with a decline of contact with Holland, High German began to take its place in church and Plattdeutsch mixed with many a Dutch word for daily speech. After the death of Hans van Steen (*q.v.*), who spoke and wrote exclusively in Dutch, the change made more rapid progress. Dutch songbooks were in use in the congregations of Danzig until about 1780. Then a German hymnbook was introduced, in 1908 replaced by *Gesangbuch zur kirchlichen und häuslichen Erbauung* (Danzig, 1908).

Strict church discipline was one of the fundamental tenets of the Danzig Mennonites. But it was inevitable that as contacts with the world destroyed their isolation their simplicity of dress and life would gradually give way. Nevertheless, the church records tell us that even in the 19th century the church council opposed fashionable clothing, luxury, dancing, and cards. Disciplinary action in the case of moral lapses tended to become censoriousness, and church confession became a rather external affair.

It is difficult to determine the number of Mennonites in Danzig in the early days. The elders were reluctant to hand in names to the authorities, lest their number be found too great. Complete records of baptisms, marriages, and deaths have been preserved only from 1668 on. Very likely the membership was highest between 1690 and 1750. A list (probably incomplete) of Mennonite residents in Danzig in 1681, found in the city archives, names 180 families. In 1709 the plague carried away 160 adult members and 230 children of the Flemish church. Notwithstanding this the records of the next ten years show an annual average of 17 births, 20 candidates for baptism, and 16 marriages. In 1749 Hans van Steen enumerates 240 households, excluding rural homes. Statistics of the Frisian group are quite uncertain. When the two groups merged in 1808, the Frisian portion numbered 166 souls, the Flemish about 700. A membership list of January 1831 counts a total of 635; the membership apparently declined during the war and after principally by emigration to Russia, but also by rejection of mixed marriages and refusal to admit members of other faiths. In 1852 the number of baptized members had declined to 410. Not until 1867, when the church abandoned its practice of excluding those who married outside the church and admitted members of other faiths, did the membership begin to rise. In 1882 it reached 488 baptized members. After World War I it had climbed to 1,130 baptized members, some of whom had moved in from the country. The last statistics (1940) show 1,020 baptized members, 173 unbaptized children.

Among the 20 elders and 38 preachers in the Flemish group before 1808, there were several who merit special mention: Kryn Vermeulen (*q.v.*), who issued a fine edition of the Bible; Georg Hansen (*q.v.*), a simple craftsman who competently championed Mennonite rights, but who took a narrow-minded attitude toward the painter and elder Enoch Seemann (*q.v.*); Hans van Steen (*q.v.*), distinguished by his education and vigor, some of whose valuable historical notes have been preserved. In the 19th century Jakob Mannhardt (*q.v.*) in his long service, 1836-85, guided his church through the difficult transition from nonresistance to acceptance of military service, and was influential in drawing the Mennonites in all parts of Germany closer together by founding the *Mennonitische Blätter* (*q.v.*). Hans Momber (*q.v.*), a respected preacher and hymn writer, was influential in uniting the two factions in 1808.

H. G. Mannhardt, nephew of Jakob, had a long and influential career as preacher and elder 1879-1927. He wrote a history of the congregation, which was published in 1919. He was followed as pastor and elder by Erich Göttner, who was taken as a prisoner of war to Russia in World War II, since when no further news of him is known.

The last constitution was in use from 1886; the congregation was incorporated in 1887. The congregation was a member of the *Vereinigung* (*q.v.*) from the time of its organization in 1886, and was an active participant in its founding.

In addition to the lot on which the church, the parsonage, the cemetery, and the hospital built in 1902 were located, the congregation also owned two houses near by. The hospital contained the residence of the sexton and eight small apartments for aged individuals or couples, a chapel for instruction and meetings, and the church library and archives. The costs of the upkeep and management of this property were met by interest from investments and by voluntary contributions. The church property suffered some damage during World War II, and

during the hard winter of 1946 all the furniture and woodwork was torn out of the church building for fuel. The library and archives were in part plundered, and in part rescued and brought to the United States by American Mennonites who worked on cattle boats bringing relief cattle and horses to Poland via Danzig in 1945-46. In this way some church record books were saved and brought to the Bethel College Library.† (Vol. I)   H.G.M.

H. G. Mannhardt, *Die Danziger Mennonitengemeinde* (Danzig, 1919); H. Epp, "Die Westpreussischen Gemeinden von 1933 bis zum Untergang," *Der Mennonit* I (1948) 4-5, 20; Emil Händiges, "The Catastrophe of the West Prussian Mennonites," *Fourth Mennonite World Conference Proceedings* (Akron, Pa., 1948) 218-26; B. Ewert, "Four Centuries of Prussian Mennonites," *Menn. Life* III (April 1948) 10-18; *Catalogus Amst.*, 154 f., 334 f.; *Gemeinde-Ordnung der Vereinigten Mennoniten-Gemeinde zu Danzig vom Jahre 1841, revidirt im Jahre 1860* (Danzig, n.d.); *idem* (Danzig, 1925); *Inv. Arch. Amst.* I, Nos. 589, 1049, 1110, 1121-26, 1189, 1552-1745, *passim*, 1821, 1827-65; II, Nos. 2624-81, 2925-39; II, 2, Nos. 691-857, *passim*; W. J. Schreiber, *The Fate of the Prussian Mennonites* (Göttingen, 1955); *ML* I, 391-95.

Danzig Old Flemish Mennonites (Dantziger Oude Vlamingen), a branch of the Flemish (*q.v.*) Mennonites which arose shortly after 1630, when most Old Flemish Mennonites wished to merge with the (Young) Flemish. They were found in the Netherlands and in Prussia. In the Netherlands they sometimes were called *Huiskoopers* (*q.v.*), and in West Prussia *Clercken, Clarichen,* or *Klerkschen* (*q.v.*). In 1740 this group had congregations in the following towns: Haarlem (op de Smallegraft), Amsterdam (bij de kruikjes), Rotterdam (in de Lombardstraat), Blokzijl, Giethoorn (Noordzijde), Zuidveen (Oude Huis), and Oldemarkt; in former times this group had other congregations which died out before 1740, as Brielle, Oud-Beyerland, Landsmeer, and perhaps a number of other churches now unknown.

In Prussia the following churches belonged to the Danzig Old Flemish: Danzig (op het Schotland), Elbing, the Grosse Werder (later forming the four congregations of Rosenort, Tiegenhagen, Ladekopp, and Fürstenwerder), Heubuden, and Königsberg. There was some contact between these Prussian churches and the Dutch congregations; occasionally conferences of representatives were held, mostly at Danzig; Dutch elders of this group visited Prussia in order to hold baptism services and to ordain elders. And in 1725, when the elder of the Amsterdam congregation had died and no Dutch preacher was available for the eldership, Elder Dirk Janssen came from Danzig to Amsterdam and served this church for nearly eight years; then the Dutch preacher Isaac de Veer was appointed elder of the congregation of Amsterdam, and Janssen returned to Danzig. Most of these Danzig Old Flemish churches had only a small membership; that of Amsterdam, which was the largest of all, numbered in 1741 only 70 members. The Dutch congregations of this group all died out or merged with other Mennonite congregations during the 18th century. The Danzig Old Flemish congregation of Rotterdam died out shortly after 1750; that of Amsterdam merged with the Zonists (*q.v.*) in

1788, and that of Haarlem with the United Mennonites in 1789. The Danzig Old Flemish Mennonites were different from other conservative groups such as the Groningen Old Flemish in the practice of footwashing, not practicing it in connection with the communion services, but practicing it toward elders and members coming from other places (Rues, 19 f.). In 1743 they published their first printed confession: Pieter Boudewijns, *Onderwyzinge des Christelyken geloofs, volgens de Belydenis der Christenen, die men de Oude Vlaamsche Mennoniten noemt* . . . (printed at Haarlem, 1743).

vɒZ.

S. F. Rues, *Tegenwoordige Staet der Nederl. Doopsgezinden* (Amsterdam, 1745).

Danzig Refugees. The exact beginning of Mennonite history in the Vistula area in northern Europe cannot be determined, but it is known that by 1549 several congregations had been organized, for Menno Simons, who had worked among them, addressed them at that time as "the children of God in Prussia." Dirk Philips followed Menno as a worker among these churches and in the region of Danzig until 1568. These migrations may have taken place as early as 1529.

However, the larger migrations took place somewhat later following a special invitation extended by Simon and Hans von Loysen, owners of large undeveloped estates in the Lower Delta at Tiegenhof in 1562. Because of their experience in dikebuilding and in draining swamp areas the Dutch Mennonites were given a special invitation with the promise of liberal rights both religious and economic.

As the migrations continued, the settlements spread across the swamp lands of the wide Vistula and Nogat delta until prosperous communities and congregations had been established throughout the region of Marienburg, Schwetz, Graudenz, Culm, and Thorn. In succeeding generations these broadened out into surrounding territories.

For some two centuries the settlements enjoyed comparative liberty and freedom unhampered by restrictions until they became prosperous and influential. However, under the reign of Frederick William II (1786-97) the situation changed. Economic and religious restrictions were set up which made it clear that both state and church were determined to stop further growth of Mennonitism. In the midst of a period of anxiety and increasing distress came the invitation of Catherine II of Russia, inviting these people to come to her land, with an assurance of liberal privileges and opportunities. During the next half century almost half of the whole delta Mennonite population emigrated to Russia. This article confines itself to those who remained behind in the Vistula, especially in the Danzig area. Before World War II there were approximately 10,000 Mennonites living in the lower areas along the Vistula River. Two thirds of these lived in the territory of the Free City (State) of Danzig. The rest were in East Prussia and Poland. They were organized as the Conference of the East and West Prussian Mennonites. Preceding World

War I they had attained a high level of economic prosperity, although spiritually they suffered in the loss of some of the old Anabaptist principles. Following World War I the economic picture deteriorated until the rise of Hitler, under whom a short-lived period of prosperity again flourished.

In the summer of 1944 the tragic evacuation of the entire area began; the German army began to retreat before the onslaughts of the Russian army. By early fall thousands of refugees were fleeing from East Prussia. Many fled to Western Germany; others concentrated in the Free City of Danzig, hoping they would escape the terrors of war. Among these great masses were thousands of Mennonites leaving all their possessions in the hope of saving life itself. Most of the evacuation was completed by February 1945, but in the spring of 1948 there were still some 200 left in the Danzig area.

Those fleeing into Western Germany met with hardships and horrible experiences as they were overtaken by the Russian armies. Western Germany was already overcrowded with refugees and the coming of these additional groups only aggravated the situation. Here in this densely crowded area, living under most trying conditions, these brethren in the faith lived until resettlement plans could be formulated and successfully carried out. The United States and Canada were not ready to accept German nationals; Paraguay was looked upon with disfavor by the Prussian group. The danger of being moved back to the Russian Zone constantly faced them. Earnest efforts on the part of Gustav Reimer, Sr., on their behalf for settlement in France failed completely. So it was not until 1948, when some 450 Prussian Mennonites from the British Zone together with 300 Prussian Mennonites of the Danish internment camps arrived in Uruguay, that the doors began to open for new life.

Not all of the Mennonites of the Vistula area fled into Western Germany. Great masses fled into the area of Danzig, only to discover soon that even there they were not safe. With the retreat of the German army in the presence of the onrushing Russian tanks and artillery, Danzig, the beautiful homeland of Mennonites for over four hundred years, became a mass of flame. Countless thousands of helpless men, women, and children were herded upon ships by the German army and transported into safer regions. Great numbers went down into a watery grave in the flight; many leaped from flaming decks into the waters while others were burned to death, unable to escape. A remnant was saved and brought to the shores of Denmark, which was then occupied by Germany. The close of the war found this small nation of four million people with over 200,000 homeless, despised Germans upon its hands, confronted with great problems of housing, feeding, and clothing them. Of these, approximately 1,500 were of the Mennonite faith.

With the close of the war, when Denmark recovered her sovereignty, she attempted to solve the problems caused by having these refugees within her borders. Internment camps were established throughout the land, ranging in size from some 20,000 to a few hundred in population. At one time, approximately 40 camps were in existence, which were later consolidated. All were encircled with barbed-wire fences and posted with armed guards day and night to see that no one entered or left the camp without the proper papers. Thus these refugees became virtual prisoners of war. It was not until more than three years had elapsed that the last of these camps were finally closed and provisions had been made for the removal of these unfortunates into lands where they could begin life anew.

In the late fall of 1945 C. F. Klassen, returning from a three-month tour of Europe as special commissioner for displaced Mennonites, included in his report these 1,500 Mennonites in Denmark. Plans were formulated to aid these along with other refugees in Europe. It was not until late in the fall of 1946, however, that any work could actually be undertaken in their behalf. At that time Walter Gering and Elma Esau were sent as an MCC unit to work within the camps, with headquarters at Copenhagen. Their program was to be one of spiritual and material aid. Food was provided by the Danish government; however, clothing and shoes were distributed by the unit to Mennonites and non-Mennonites. Gering, as a minister, was to arrange for religious services and spiritual nurture of the Mennonites.

Mennonites were found scattered in the various camps—at one time in 34 different camps, often in very small groups. Attempts to bring these together into several camps were only partially successful. The MCC unit made its headquarters in Copenhagen, where the largest of the camps was located. From here they went out on regular tours of the country, visiting the various camps and distributing two shipments of clothing, totaling 25 tons and 4,000 pairs of shoes, among the refugees. The Danish government had agreed to this distribution under the condition that half of the goods be distributed by the camp officials to non-Mennonites. The other half could be distributed by MCC workers to the Mennonite internees. Elma Esau was in charge of the distributions while Gering arranged for and conducted Bible studies, worship services, and individual contacts of a spiritual nature. Bruno Ewert and Bruno Enns, elders from the Danzig area (Heubuden and Orlofferfelde) and fellow internees, were associated in the work of the MCC unit. Later Mr. and Mrs. P. S. Goertz, with Susie Peters, succeeded the first MCC workers.

While the problems of the work were such as are common to all refugees, yet the greatest one was that of instilling hope for the possibility of a new beginning. The total loss of all possessions including the loss of members of the family, the prolonged period of internment and the hardships of camp life, all contributed to create a spirit of hopelessness and despair. Together with this came the decision of MCC that while resettlement of these Danzig refugees was to be a part of the general program of resettlement, yet the first obligation should be that of providing for the Russian Mennonite refugees. The reason for this decision can be understood in the light of the danger in which the Russian Men-

nonites found themselves. However, this meant further delay for the Danzig Mennonite refugees, a delay which brought increased despair to them as they waited in uncertainty as to what their future held for them.

It was on Oct. 7, 1948, that the *Volendam* (*q.v.*) sailing from Bremerhaven carried with it 751 Prussian Mennonites (a small number were former Galicians, not Prussians), 284 coming directly from the Danish internment camps and the rest out of the British Zone in Germany. These were known as the Danziger Mennonites. They had been assigned to Paraguay, but the doors of Uruguay opened in a dramatic manner just as the refugees were about to embark. So it came about that the *Volendam* unloaded the 751 at Montevideo on Oct. 27, 1948, and the first group began the settlement of a new land. In October 1951 another group of 430 Mennonite refugees, largely from the Danzig group, landed to join the group which had come in 1948.

Since the granting of visas came unexpectedly for the original group in 1948 there was no time to make resettlement preparations in advance. The immigrants were housed in two camps, one at Colonia and the other at Arapey, where they were supported by the MCC until they found work or were settled on the land. In May 1949 the MCC with the help of a government loan purchased a land site known as "El Ombu" (*q.v.*), a tract including 2,962 acres on the main highway between Montevideo and Paysandu. In 1953 another large tract was purchased at Tres Bocas, 50 miles from El Ombu.

All this took time, as can be expected. In the meantime many of the immigrants secured work outside the camps and a number also succeeded in locating land themselves which they could rent with the possibility of purchase later. Gradually all those who were able to work left the camps.

The land at El Ombu was divided into 30 parcels, three families living on each parcel. Each of the three families was made responsible for the development of the land within its parcel and the payment of the debt against it. A co-operative was organized to transact the business of the colony. Some land was set aside for Mennonite couples who in later years will want to live with their own people. The development is along the line of diversified farming, the land being best suited for this.

While most of the families settled finally on the El Ombu colony tract, yet some who had found work of a permanent nature in the cities preferred to stay where they were. A goodly number of single girls found work doing housework in the city of Montevideo. For these and other Mennonites in the city, MCC opened a center which conducted sewing circles, Bible study, choir practice, and Sunday church services. Also a guest house was opened for Mennonites coming to the city on business.

W.G.

The door of emigration to Canada was opened for the Danzig refugees in 1951, and a total of over 200 emigrated to that country with the aid of the Canadian Mennonite Board of Colonization 1951-52.

The great majority of the Danzig refugees, however, have been resettled in Germany. Over a thousand, chiefly from the Denmark camps, were moved to the Palatinate-Hesse region, also to the region around Neuwied (Niederbieber, *q.v.*) in 1949. Others have since been resettled in small projects in Espelkamp (*q.v.*), Backnang (*q.v.*), Lübeck (*q.v.*), and Enkenbach (*q.v.*), where with the aid of the German government and the MCC new homes have been built. However, most of the refugees have taken care of themselves as best they can, locating in widely scattered areas through all four zones of Germany, with over 1,000 in the Russian Zone. These latter have the most difficult time.

Unfortunately the wide scattering has made it most difficult to provide pastoral oversight or to organize congregations in the new locations. Some are now attached to the older established congregations, but the following new congregations have been organized: Göttingen (1945), Bremen (1947), Bergisches Land (1948), Uelzen (1948), Kiel (1949), Lübeck (1950), together with the unorganized congregations of Nord-Schleswig, Holstein, and Westphalia. Three homes for the aged have been established, filled largely with Danzig refugees: Leutesdorf a. Rh. (1948), Enkenbach (Pfalz), and Pinneberg-Rellingen near Hamburg. These homes are operated by an association called *Mennonitisches Altersheim e.V.* (*q.v.*), organized in 1948. The old organization of the West Prussian conference has been reconstituted as *Aeltestenausschuss der Konferenz der west- und ostpreussischen Mennonitengemeinden,* and the *Vereinigung* has organized a relief program, *Hilfswerk der Vereinigung der Deutschen Mennonitengemeinden* (organized 1946). It is estimated that the total population of Danzig refugees remaining in Germany is about 7,000 including unbaptized children and adherents. Emigration had practically ceased by 1953, the situation having apparently stabilized. The prospects of retention of the scattered families and young people in the Mennonite fellowship are not good, since regular Mennonite worship and religious instruction are as yet insufficient; already numerous cases of transfer to the state church have been reported.

H.S.B.

E. Händiges, "The Catastrophe of the West Prussian Mennonites," *MQR* XXIV (1950) 124-29; Hermann Epp, "Die Westpreussischen Gemeinden von 1933 bis zum Untergang," *Der Mennonit* I (1948) 4-5, 20; B. Ewert, "Four Centuries of Prussian Mennonites," *Menn. Life* III (April 1948) 10-18; Lotte Heinritz, "Women's Odyssey," *ibid.,* 19-22; W. J. Schreiber, *The Fate of the Prussian Mennonites* (Göttingen, 1955).

Dariusleut (Dariusgroup), the name of the smallest of the three Hutterite kinship groups which make up the total Hutterite brotherhood in North America, the other two being the *Schmiedeleut* and the *Lehrerleut*. On Dec. 31, 1950, the Dariusleut had 29 colonies or Bruderhofs with a total population of 2,522—25 Bruderhofs in Alberta, and 4 in Montana. A complete list with census is given at the end of this article. The bishop (*Vorsteher*) in 1954 was John Wurz of Wilson Siding Colony, Lethbridge, Alberta.

The origin of the three groups took place as follows. Until 1857 the entire Hutterite brotherhood had only one bishop or president and had been living in noncommunal form for 32 years since 1842 in a separate village, Hutterthal, in the Molotschna settlement about 12 miles from Melitopol, Russia, near the Tashchenak estate of Johann Cornies. Elder George Waldner, ordained in 1846, desired to restore the communal form, but his endeavors led only to a division which frustrated his attempt. He made an actual attempt in 1857 at Hutterdorf near Orechov in Ekaterinoslav; it failed; he died shortly thereafter. Meanwhile three new Hutterite villages had been established: (1) Johannisruh (in 1853-57), 2½ miles from Hutterthal, (2) Neu-Hutterthal (in 1857), 80 miles northwest of Huttertal, (3) Dobritcha (location not clear). In Hutterdorf after Waldner's death three preachers were chosen. One of these, Michael Waldner, successfully established a communal Bruderhof in 1859 in one end of Hutterdorf village. A second preacher, Darius Walter, founded another Bruderhof in the other end of Hutterdorf in 1860. The third preacher finally joined the Walter group.

The two above Bruderhofs became in America in 1874-75 the mother Bruderhofs of two groups, Schmiedeleut and Dariusleut. Tendencies toward establishing a communal Bruderhof in Johannisruh in 1864 ff. failed to materialize. But in 1877 a few of the Johannisruh families, led by Jacob Wipf, one of the preachers there, left for South Dakota and established a third communal Bruderhof there. The remaining Hutterites from all the villages also emigrated to South Dakota, but did not establish Bruderhofs; they formed regular Mennonite congregations which ultimately all joined the General Conference Mennonite Church (the last in 1940).

The Michael Waldner group came to the United States in 1874 and settled Bon-Homme Colony near Yankton, S.D. With its descendants it has since been called the Schmiedeleut, since Waldner was a blacksmith (*Schmied*), Darius Walter's group also arrived in 1874, and in 1875 established the Wolf Creek Bruderhof, and have since been called the Dariusleut. In the 1880 census 137 souls were registered for this group. The third group, led by Preacher Jacob Wipf, left Johannisruh in 1877 and established the Old Elmspring Bruderhof near Parkston, S.D. They were called Lehrerleut, because Jacob Wipf was a teacher in Russia and also in South Dakota.

The differences between the three groups are very minor, such as the wearing of buttons by the men of the Lehrerleut in contrast to the hooks and eyes of the other two groups. There are no differences in faith or practice and no breach of fellowship, but most marriages are among members of the same kinship group, as are likewise business contacts and visiting. Recently a general conference of all three groups was held in Manitoba. The Schmiedeleut Bruderhofs are all in South Dakota (one in North Dakota) and Manitoba, the Dariusleut mostly in Alberta with four in Montana, the Lehrerleut mostly in Alberta with seven in Montana. Each group is completely separate in ecclesiastical organization (having its own Vorsteher or bishop, and preachers) as well as in economic matters. The Lehrerleut left the Old Elmspring Bruderhof in 1932.

In the last few decades, a few Hutterites left Dariusleut colonies to form dissident colonies. The split usually was based on personality differences between some of the adults, but as the years went by, the dissidents have shown a tendency for rapid assimilation. One such group near Lethbridge formally severed its ties with the Hutterite group, which excommunicated them, and joined the Mennonite Church, forming the Stirling (MC) congregation in the Alberta-Saskatchewan Conference with 23 baptized members (1954) and John Hofer as preacher. Another group of a few families at Felger Colony, near Lethbridge, also is not in good standing with the Hutterite Church, but no formal break has occurred. (Zieglschmid, *Klein-Geschichtsbuch*.)

H.S.B.

Census of Dariusleut Bruderhofs

Name of Colony	Address	Founded	pop. 1950	Head Preacher
Dariusleut Bruderhofs in Alberta				
Camrose	Camrose	1949	83	Paul Hofer
Cayley	Cayley	1937	80	Paul A. Walter
East Cardston	Cardston	1918	81	Jacob Hofer
Ewelme (Murphy)	Macleod	1928	69	Joseph Hofer
Ferry Bank	Ponoka	1949	75	Michael Wipf
Granum	Granum	1930	75	Martin R. Walters
Holt	Jarrow	1949	57	Peter S. Tschetter
Howl Ranch (Tschetter)	Irricana	1948	76	Jacob Tschetter
Husher (Rosebud)	Crossfield	1944	78	Christian Tschetter
Lakeside	Cranford	1935	91	Joseph K. Wipf
New Rosebud (Rosebud)	Beiseker	1926	65	Paul S. Stahl
New York	Maybutt	1924	110	Jacob Hofer
Pincher Creek	Pincher Creek	1926	85	Paul Gross
Pine Hill	Penhold	1948	86	Peter Hofer
Riverside	Glenwood	1933	86	Lorenz R. Tschetter
Rosebud	Redland	1918	187	George Hofer
Sandhill	Beiseker	1936	114	Jacob K. Wurz
Springvale	Rockyford	1918	77	Michael M. Wurz
Stahlville	Rockyford	1919	98	David R. Waldner
Stand Off	Macleod	1918	76	Jacob Walter
Thompson	Glenwood	1918	76	Paul J. Tschetter
West Raley	Cardston	1918	117	Christian C. Waldner
Willow Creek (Red Willow)	Stettler	1949	89	Jacob S. Stahl
Wilson Siding	Lethbridge	1918	140	John M. Wurz
Wolf Creek	Stirling	1924	76	Joshua E. Hofer
Dariusleut Bruderhofs in Montana				
Ayers Ranch	Grass Range	1945	54	John A. Stahl
Deerfield (Bank Ranch)	Danvers	1947	65	Paul Stahl
King Ranch	Lewistown	1935	61	Joseph Stahl
Spring Creek	Lewistown	1945	26	Paul Walter

Darlington Mennonite (GCM) Mission station among the Cheyenne (*q.v.*) and Arapahoe (*q.v.*) Indians. Darlington is a village near El Reno in central Oklahoma, once the center of the government agency for these tribes. The government built its first Indian schools here, and here several religious bodies began their mission work with these tribes. In 1880 S. S. Haury (*q.v.*) became the first teacher in the mission school opened at Darlington by the General Conference Mennonite Church. The government granted the station many material favors, such as the wood from the near-by forest, the use of the governmental sawmill, and 40 acres of good land. The mission home was opened in August 1881 and a school for 25 pupils in the same autumn. Instruction in the school was conducted in English, whereas work with the adults was done in the native languages of the Indians, at first through interpreters. Food, clothing, and other necessities were furnished by the government.

This encouraging beginning justified bright hopes for the future. But on Feb. 19, 1882, the beautiful new building burned down with practically all its contents. The only son of the Haurys and three Indian children suffocated in the smoke before they could be reached. In spite of the shock of the tragedy, a new brick building was put up before the close of the year, twice as large as the original building.

Since the station at Cantonment (*q.v.*) had been planned in the meantime and the Haurys were stationed there, the work at Darlington was assigned to the Schultzes, and six months later to the H. R. Voths, together with a staff of workers to care for the 50 pupils in the boarding school. Evangelization was carried on among the adult Indians in their camps. In 1889 Mrs. Voth died, and three years later the J. S. Krehbiels were put in charge of the station.

About this time the Indians began to move away to other places, and the school was taken over by the government. The church withdrew from the station, Voth transferring to the work with the Indians in Arizona (q.v.). No congregation was ever organized at Darlington. In 1889 the first baptism took place on one of the older girls in the school; another who was to have been baptized died the week before. Others were baptized at Halstead, where they had gone for further education. Many of the children and adults of this station died of tuberculosis, some of them in faith in the Lord Jesus, but too suddenly to be received into the church. Some of the Indians later joined other churches (ML I, 395 f.)   H.R.V.

Darmstadt, capital of Hesse, Germany, had a Mennonite congregation in 1910-35. Its members came from the Rhine Palatinate, Hesse, Baden, and Württemberg. Until the outbreak of World War I the church register listed 41 members who lived in Darmstadt or in Frankfurt and vicinity. The congregation was served by the Conference of South German Mennonites. The congregation now meets in Frankfurt (q.v.). (ML I, 395.)   HEGE.

Darney, the name given for a time (1933-41) in the *Gemeinde-Kalender* to the French Mennonite congregation living widely scattered in the region of which Epinal is the approximate center. Before 1933, and in the reissued *Gemeinde-Kalender,* the name is given as the Vosges (q.v.) congregation. The history of this congregation is given in *Christ Seul* for August 1930, 5-8. In recent years the congregation has been very small, 25-50 souls, and has met only once per month in the homes of the members.   VDZ.

Dartmouth Avenue United Missionary Church, located in Flint, Mich., was organized in 1936. In 1953 the congregation had 65 members, mostly factory workers. J. A. Bradley served as pastor.
                    B.W.P.

Dathenus (Daten, Dalten, Daets), **Petrus,** b. 1531 or 1532 at Mont-Cassel, near Hazebrouck, French Flanders, d. March 17, 1588, at Elbing, Prussia, a Calvinist theologian, who as chaplain of Elector Frederick the Pious, the first German prince to accept Calvinism, established this creed in the Palatinate. As a young man he entered the monastery of Yper, but soon fled to embrace Calvin's teaching. After a short residence in England (1553-55) he became preacher of the Flemish congregation at Frankfurt. Dathenus was frequently involved in disputes with the Lutheran clergy of the city. On April 23, 1561, the magistrate denied the Dutch further toleration, and Dathenus found refuge with Elector Frederick III of the Palatinate, who offered him and the 60 families exiled from Frankfurt the buildings of Gross-Frankental, the dissolved Augustinian monastery, and in 1566 or soon after made Dathenus his chaplain. Sijbolts, "De Doopsgezinden te Middelburg" in *DB* 1908, 1-64, says that Dathenus was largely responsible for the severe Calvinist persecution of the Mennonites (*Theol. Jahresbericht* 1909, 28, 391). But Sijbolts is wrong: Heidanus, not Dathenus, was responsible.

In his new position Dathenus soon came in contact with the Anabaptists who were seeking new converts through emissaries sent out from Moravia. The government had three traveling evangelists summarily thrown into prison and under this pressure tried to convert them. The charge that the government was persecuting the Anabaptists without first inquiring about their faith gave the elector some concern. He therefore summoned the Anabaptist preachers to a public disputation with the Reformed clergy to be held at Frankenthal (q.v.) on May 28, 1571. Dathenus was the chief spokesman for the Reformed church; his colleagues scarcely got a word in. Thomas Erastus, who had recently been a member of the Palatine church council and was opposed to this disputation, wrote to Heinrich Bullinger in Zürich: "Their spokesmen are uneducated, immature young men, who have never seen a meeting of this kind. The affair will come to a ridiculous end and will dishonor the Prince. But he will not let himself be dissuaded." Frederick hoped that the Anabaptists would be won to his church by instruction and become a valuable addition to it (K. Sudhoff, *C. Olevianus und Z. Ursinus,* Elberfeld, 1857, 319).

The Reformed theologians took Martin Bucer (q.v.) as their model. Some of the doctrinal points discussed were the same as those the Strasbourg reformer had considered 33 years before in Marburg with the Hessian Anabaptists. But what Bucer succeeded in doing in two days, viz., converting the Anabaptists to the state church, Dathenus could not do in 19 days with two sessions daily beginning at six o'clock in the morning and two o'clock in the afternoon. With dialectic skill he was able to help himself over the most difficult points and objections of his opponents. On many points they agreed. But he should not have expected these simple people to agree with his sophistry on other points. The Anabaptist preachers, who in their simple piety were unwilling to pick to pieces Bible passages that seemed clear to them, refused "to try to fathom those things which God alone had in His power." Hence his frequently very artificial expositions of Scripture and argumentation on unfathomable theological issues made little impression on them. The negotiations were doomed to failure.

In the following years Dathenus apparently made no Anabaptist contacts, for he is never mentioned in connection with them. Throughout his life Dathenus was a restless personality; he spent much time in traveling. In December 1566 he presided at the Antwerp (Belgium) synod. In 1572 he was again in the Netherlands and also later made many trips to Holland and Belgium. He also visited Switzerland. After the death of Frederick III, whose son was Lutheran, he again accepted a position as preacher in Frankenthal; but in 1578 he was presiding at the Reformed synod in Dordrecht,

Holland, and somewhat later in Gent, Belgium. Later on he became involved in a quarrel with William of Orange, perhaps because he felt that the prince was too tolerant of the Roman Catholics. In 1583 Dathenus was imprisoned for 50 days because of his attitude. Later Dathenus was in Schleswig-Holstein (Husum, and in 1585 Staden), where he also practiced medicine. During this period he apparently came somewhat under the influence of the Davidjorists. In 1587 he was in Danzig, and soon afterward in Elbing, where he practiced medicine until his death in 1588.

In 1566 Dathenus translated the Psalms from the French rhymed version by Clement Marot and Beza into Dutch. Dathenus' verse Psalms were adopted into the Reformed Church in Holland, and in spite of their shortcomings were used until 1773.

When the Mennonites of Holland in the early 17th century sang their *Schrijtuurlijke Liedekens* less and less, using the Psalms instead, they also used Dathenus' version. The Lamist congregation in Amsterdam used them until 1684, in Haarlem until 1713, and the Zonist congregation in Amsterdam until 1762, and many other congregations until well into the 18th century. HEGE.

Chr. Hege, *Die Täufer in der Kurpfalz* (Frankfurt, 1908); *Protocoll, das ist Alle Handlung des gesprechs zu Franckenthal . . .* (Heidelberg, 1571); *Biogr. Wb.* II, 383-401; *ML* I, 396.

Dau, a Mennonite family name of Frisian origin, appearing in the Frisian congregations in West Prussia, first mentioned in 1598 at Montau, 1601 at Orlofferfelde. In 1776, 13 families carried this name in West Prussia (without Danzig), and in 1935 (without Elbing) 30 persons. Outside Prussia the name is hardly known. G.R.

Dauphin County, Pa. When Lancaster County was formed in 1729, Peshtank and Derry townships took in most of the present Dauphin County, which was not organized until May 4, 1785. When the Lancaster-Harris Ferry Road was laid out in 1737, many Mennonites moved into this area, among them Andrew Hershey, Felix Landis, Jr., the Nissleys, Reesers, Mummas, and Stricklers. The Stauffer congregation existed as early as 1780. The present congregations in the county are Stauffer, Shope, Strickler, and Steelton, with a total membership of 278 (1954). Noah W. Risser and Clarence E. Lutz are the bishops in charge of these churches. In addition to the local ministry, the rural congregations early were served by ministers traveling to Juniata County and points west and southwest. I.D.L.

David van Hoorn, a Dutch Anabaptist leader: see **Damas of Hoorn.**

David Joris (*ca.* 1501-56), a Dutch Anabaptist, "in a single person prophet, apocalyptic, spiritualist, and mystic" (Kühn, 271), founder of the Davidjorists (*q.v.*). There are various versions of his name; besides David—named thus after the Jewish king, a role which his father George (hence Georgii or Joriszoon-Joris) is said to have played in the *Rederijkerskamer*—also Jan, after his maternal grandfather (Jan van Brugge was his pseudonym after 1544). The rank of his parents is debated. The city of his birth is given as Delft, Brugge, and Gent. Little is known of his youth. He is said to have been weak physically, and inclined to fanaticism. In glass painting he developed great skill, but by the death of his father he was compelled to support his mother as a merchant. In this calling he traveled from Antwerp through France and England. In 1524 he married in Delft and settled there. No particulars are known about his wife, Dirkgen Willems.

The Reformation made a deep impression on Joris. The earliest of his writings and hymns preserved to us are dated 1529; they reveal unusual Scriptural knowledge. Kühn says of Joris (p. 272): "There are probably few uneducated writers who have made more versatile use of the Bible." He was bold and open in his opposition to Catholic priests, and by 1528 had suffered various severe punishments (lashing, having tongue bored through, and banishment from Delft for three years).

During his exile Joris became acquainted with the Anabaptists of Holland, and was deeply moved by their martyrdom. After some hesitation he joined them, was baptized by Obbe Philips (at Delft, about September 1534), and ordained to the ministry. The songs he wrote in 1535 and 1536 reflect the excited mood of the harassed, fugitive Anabaptist (at Pentecost in 1535 he was in Strasbourg), but are very far removed from the revolutionary spirit of Münster; "he could not sanction attacking with the sword." He openly opposed Batenburg (*q.v.*). After the Münster catastrophe he tried vainly to unite the various factions at a conference convening at Bocholt, August 1536.

Soon afterward, inspired by the fanatical words of Anneken Jans (*q.v.*) and by fantastic visions, he began to consider himself a Spirit-anointed prophet, a third David. Borne by the utmost self-confidence, he preached deepest humility and self-denial; though living in rigid asceticism, he has been charged with moral lapses. A dangerous mysticism appeared in him, which could and did, at any rate among some of his followers, lead to antinomian, libertinistic views and moral errors.

Joris, supported by friends and relatives, now devoted himself entirely to the service of the Spirit. His followers had visions which centered around him. He established a large party of his own. In January 1539, the government took definite steps against him and his party. On Feb. 21, 1539, his mother was beheaded and his family fled from Delft. Until 1544 he stayed in various hiding places in Holland, East Friesland, and Belgium, everywhere in acute danger, and everywhere winning followers, most of them among the Batenburgers after the fall of their leader in 1538, and the Münsterites. With the moderate wing of the Anabaptists he met twice, at Oldenburg and at Strasbourg. But they were becoming suspicious of him and his doctrine, whereas his own followers glorified him more and more.

Success as well as resistance strengthened Joris' consciousness of his calling as a prophet and reformer of the whole world. In 1539 he sent a bold self-defense to the court of justice in Holland, and a prophetic writing to Philip of Hesse by his messenger, Jurriaen Ketel (q.v.), enclosing a letter to the emperor and the other estates. To Countess Anna of East Friesland-Oldenburg he sent a long defense, trying to reply to 25 charges, chiefly against his personal attitude and his expectations of the future, and closing with a long mystical confession of faith. It is also known that he wrote to Luther, warning him of his self-derived wisdom and reason.

Joris considered it a dead-letter faith to treat the Bible as the sole authority. Nothing definitive could be decided by the letter in religious disputes; it was necessary to look about for the "Son," to whom alone it is revealed, and who, as Joris is said to have written for the Regensburg Disputation in 1541, was to come from the Netherlands, whose type was Egypt. Whereas on the whole the Anabaptists held to the Scriptures as a principle, Joris rejected them and made a principle of mystical experience. "To the mystic Joris historical revelation was merely a matter of the senses; his religious experience lay outside it" (Kühn, 300).

In 1542, the year he published his principal work with the characteristic title: *'tWonderboeck, waer in dat van der Werldt aen ver sloten gheopenbaert is. Wie een der Ick (secht de Heere) senden sal, ontfanght in mynen Naem, die ontfanght my; wie my ontfanght, ontfanght den die my ghesonden heeft. Hoochghelovet moet hy syn, die als een Ambassatoer gesonden komt, in den Name des Heeren,* the difference between Joris and Menno Simons burst into a violent dispute. Menno had already in his *Fundamentboek* (1539) warned against the false prophet. Joris then attacked Menno in a fiery letter: "Gird on your sword, Menno Simons, . . . arm yourself with the most powerful Scriptural weapon! . . . Who advises you, Menno, to appear so boldly before the Lord, that you elevate yourself above all? Do say, dear man, what spirit or witness advises you to teach? Who has sent you? . . . I will show you (however firmly you may think you have it) that you do not know it, nor do you know what is truth and wisdom, except after the letter." Violently Joris attempted to make Menno recognize his divine mission; but Menno rejected "imaginations, rhetorical tricks, and other deceptions of the devil" which Joris substituted for the Gospel; he said Joris was correctly taken for the "anti-Christ, the man of sin, the son of perdition, a false prophet, murderer of souls, deceiver and falsifier of the divine truth and the commands of Christ." It was evidence of devilish pride and anti-Christian foolishness, that Joris "elevates his visions and dreams above the wisdom of the Holy Spirit, who has taught the apostles and prophets."

Without doubt Menno hit the crux of Joris' fateful error when he said, "Under the pretext of humility he promotes devilish defiance and under the name of perfection, chastity, and other virtues he promotes various vices and shameful deeds." Menno refused to carry the dispute any further.

Offended by Menno's sharp words, Joris protested in a leaflet which he tried to distribute among the Mennonites of East Friesland. For a long time Menno had difficulties with Davidjorists in his own camp; especially Blesdijk (q.v.) rose in defense of his future father-in-law, though he later deserted him.

After a violent debate between the Davidjorists and John a Lasco, the superintendent of the established church in East Friesland, principally on the subject of the authority of the new prophet, which a Lasco in spite of a tolerant nature would not grant, Joris secretly went to Basel in 1544 before the persecution against his group began in East Friesland and lived there with his family under the name of Jan van Brugge as a Reformed refugee, a wealthy and respected citizen.

Meanwhile he continued to influence his followers by innumerable letters to Holland, Belgium, Friesland, Holstein, Denmark, and other countries. His concealment he justified by the example of "Christ, who was likewise concealed in Egypt." He advised his followers against open confession; this course Menno and others called outright hypocrisy. But Joris outwardly held to the Reformed faith, lived in wealth and comfort, and at the same time preached to his followers to flee "false prophets and the wise and mighty in the world."

One remarkable feature of his teaching was his fight for unrestricted religious liberty. In Basel he wrote a petition to the Swiss cities on behalf of the "good and pious Servetus." He carried on a friendly correspondence with Schwenckfeld and Castellio, Calvin's famous opponent. On the other hand, at the end of his life he was on unfriendly terms with his own son-in-law, Blesdijk, who, formerly his warmest adherent, now became his most violent opponent.

Joris died on Aug. 25, 1556, and was buried with full honors in St. Leonard's church in Basel. But two and one-half years later quarrels within the Jorist party led to the discovery of his fraud. The family was summoned before the pastor and the magistrate; eleven men, relatives and friends, were taken to prison. A great number of books and letters, also a picture of Joris, were confiscated and given over to a learned commission for examination. The Jorist errors were compiled on the basis of Blesdijk's already published critique in eleven articles. His family claimed to know nothing of these doctrines, condemned them, and were released under certain conditions, including a public confession in church. But Joris' corpse and his books were publicly burned outside the city on May 13, 1559.

This execution, however, by no means eliminated the Davidjorists, who tried to refute Blesdijk and the Baslerites, and continued to challenge the official church and the theologians to bitter disputes. Examples are Coornhert's feud with the Davidjorists at the end of the 16th century and Ubbo Emmius's polemics against Huygelmumzoon (a pseudonym, perhaps identical with the anonymous opponent of Coornhert). In the 17th century the Davidjorists in Holstein became prominent; Moldenit and his son-in-law Jessenius wrote extensively against them. Gottfried Arnold, on the other hand, defended David Joris, and preserved extremely valuable source material in favor of the much calumniated man in his *Unparteiische Kirchen- und Ketzer-Historie.*

The numerous writings of Joris, especially in the Basel period, and the old literature about him, are compiled in van der Linde, who has evidence of 264 religious tracts. The older literature for and against Joris contains a long series of unresolved contradictions. G.H.

R. H. Bainton, *David Joris, Wiedertäufer und Kämpfer für Toleranz im 16. Jahrhundert (Arch. f. Ref.-Gesch., Texte und Untersuchungen, Ergänzungsband VI)* (Leipzig, 1937) is the definitive work which supersedes all others, supplements the Joris bibliography of van der Linde, brings Nippold's bibliography up-to-date, and prints 110 pages of Joris documents. An English condensation appears in Bainton's *The Travail of Religious Liberty* (Phila., 1951) 125-48; P. Burckhardt, *David Joris und seine Gemeinde in Basel* (reprint from *Basler Ztscht f. Gesch. u. Altertumskunde* XLVIII, 1949, 5-106) suspects Joris guilty of bigamy; Johannes Kühn, *Toleranz und Offenbarung* (Leipzig, 1923) 271-301; W. J. Kühler, *Geschiedenis* I; *Inv. Arch. Amst.* I, Nos. 3, 148, 203, 205, 208-10, 254, 269, 277, 309, 443, 767-70; Fr. Nippold, "David Joris, sein Leben, seine Lehre und seine Sekte," in *Ztscht f. d. hist. Theol.,* 1863 and 1864; Gottfried Arnold, *Unparteiische Kirchen- und Ketzerhistorie* (Frankfurt, 1699. B. XVI. C. XXI. 44 ff.); P. Burchhardt, *David Joris,* in *Basler Biographien* I, 1900; *Biogr. Wb.* IV, 575-82; *ML* II, 433-35.

Davidjorists, the followers of David Joris, must have been very numerous in the Netherlands. In 1539 a group of Davidjorist Anabaptists were put to death at Delft (*q.v.*), where David Joris himself had lived and been an elder. In this town followers of David Joris were still found in 1544 and even in 1596 traces of Davidjorism existed here. Elsewhere Davidjorism was also spread widely. In 1587 it was said that in the province of Overijssel the followers of David Joris were rapidly increasing (*DB* 1911, 40). They lasted until the 17th century (*Ned. Archief v. Kerkgeschiedenis* II, 1903, 272; *Biogr. Wb.* I, 310 f.).

Some martyrs, though included in van Braght's *Martyrs' Mirror,* were Davidjorists, for example, Anneken Jans (*q.v.*), executed in 1539, and Maria and Ursula van Beckum (*q.v.*), executed in 1544. In 1544 Jurriaen Ketel (*q.v.*), an ardent disciple of David Joris, who had edited his books, was put to death at Deventer. It seems that the Davidjorists were very active during this time, for in many records mention is made of their activity. In those records they are often called Davidjorists or Batenburgers, as for example the notorious Münsterite leader Cornelis Appelman (*q.v.*). (See *Inv. Arch. Amst.* I, No. 265.) The identification of Davidjorists with Batenburgers is, however, wrong. Davidjorists, like David Joris himself, were averse to violence; the Batenburgers were not. The principles of the Davidjorists were the same as those of their leader; they were not loyal to the strict principles of Christian discipleship, which often resulted in suffering and martyrdom, and avoided "the oppression and affliction because of the Word of the Lord." As Menno Simons summarizes, they tolerated dissembling with the world in order to live safely (Kühler, *Geschiedenis* I, 219-29). The accusation that they were as a group libertinists and guilty of sexual immorality has not been proved, though some Davidjorists confessed to horrible debauches (Brandt, *Historie der Reformatie,* 1677, 134), and though there are a few cases of conjugal disloyalty among the Davidjorists. (*Inv. Arch. Amst.* I, Nos. 264-65, 267, 271, 277, 310, 443.)

vDZ.

David van der Leyen (or Verleyen), an Anabaptist martyr, who was executed with Levina Ghyselius (*q.v.*) at Gent, Belgium, on Feb. 14, 1554, by burning at the stake. The first information we have about these two martyrs is found in the *Liedtboecxken van den Offer des Heeren* (1562) where they are celebrated in a song (No. 7) beginning: "Ghy Christen al te samen, bereyt u tot ten strijt" (You Christians all together, prepare for the conflict). It is also included by Wolkan. Another song about David and Levina is found in the *Nieu Liedtboecxken* (1562 and later editions): "Och Heere ic moet u claghen" (Oh Lord, I must complain to Thee), also found in Wackernagel. The later accounts including that of the *Martyrs' Mirror,* are prose adaptations of these songs. The *Liedtboecxken* song says that David was a young man who firmly confessed his faith and steadfastly suffered all vexations both of body and mind, and that after the fire had gone out, David was miraculously still alive.

Many members of the van der Leyen family at Gent were suspected of heresy and some of them died as martyrs: Tanneken (*q.v.*) on Aug. 27, 1555, at Antwerp; Franchois (*q.v.*) on April 28, 1558, at Gent; Laureys (*q.v.*) on Nov. 8, 1559, at Antwerp. According to an old chronicle of Gent David's father was also a Mennonite, but because he was dangerously ill, the count gave up further persecution. The noted von der Leyen (*q.v.*) family of Crefeld does not stem from the Flemish van der Leyens, as has sometimes been asserted. vDZ.

Offer, 531 ff., 235; *Mart. Mir.* D 160 ff., E 549; Wolkan, *Lieder,* 61; Wackernagel, *Lieder,* 132; Verheyden, *Gent,* 20-21, No. 41; *ML* II, 645 ff.

David Psalmen: see **Psalms.**

Daviess County (Ind.) Old Order Amish Mennonite Settlement, near Montgomery, began in 1868. Bishop Jacob Graber came from Allen Co., Ind., and the families of Isaac Yoder and Daniel Gingerich came from Wayne Co., Ohio. Deacon John Wagler, formerly from Germany, moved to Montgomery from Wellesley, Ont., and Jackson Knepp came from Hickory Co., Mo.

The first ministers in the church were Jacob Graber, bishop; John Graber, Peter Stoll, Joseph Gingerich, ministers; and John Wagler, deacon. Succeeding bishops who served were Joseph Wittmer, Peter Wagler, and Amos Yoder. The latter moved to Defiance County, Ohio, in 1943. In 1955 the settlement consisted of five church districts with two bishops serving, namely, Amos Wittmer and John L. Graber, and a membership of 400.

The Berea Mennonite Church (MC), organized in 1921, largely of Amish, had 230 members in 1955. Amos Weldy, a Mennonite deacon of Nappanee, Ind., was influential in organizing the congregation, and Edd Shrock serves as elder. In 1948 a group of the Old Order Amish Mennonites organized the Odon congregation of the "Beachy Amish" type and built a meetinghouse. Their ministers are Jacob Gingerich, William Yoder, and Ben Wagler; the 1955 membership was 165.   J.W.

Davis County, Iowa. Amish Mennonites settled in this southern Iowa county in 1854. In 1892 their one congregation, Pulaski (*q.v.*), became affiliated with the General Conference Mennonite Church. In 1955 it had 125 members.   M.G.

Davlekanovo, cultural and economic center of the former Mennonite settlement in the Russian province of Ufa, located between the Volga and the Ural Mountains on the Dyoma.

The first Mennonites settled near Davlekanovo about 1890, coming from South Russia and from Samara, the province adjoining Ufa. In 1893 there was already a small congregation in Gortchakovo (*q.v.*), which by 1914 had grown to several hundred members. At Berezovka (*q.v.*) another congregation was organized, which had a Mennonite school with a boarding house for poor children (*Armenschule*) and a large church in which general harvest festivals, song services, missionary meetings, etc., were held. More and more families settled alone or in small groups on separate farms (*Khutor*) around Davlekanovo at the beginning of the 20th century; others formed villages (Karanbash, Morozovka, Udryak, Golyshevo, etc.). Some of the isolated farms were the scene of violent attacks by robbers, who wiped out entire families.

About 1900 some Mennonite families settled in the Russian Tatar village of Davlekanovo, which was situated on the railroad. In a few years two fairly large congregations were organized here, one each of the Mennonite Church and the Mennonite Brethren. A seven-class Zentralschule for boys and girls developed under the leadership of Franz C. Thiessen and J. P. Perk into a nine-class secondary school, attended by about 200 Mennonite students, and in 20 years became a cultural center for the entire settlement around Davlekanovo.

Until the outbreak of World War I the colony enjoyed an extraordinary economic growth. Several large mills powered by steam or water power, business houses and warehouses, factories and shops were owned by Mennonites. Until the Revolution of 1917 half of the village bore a German and Mennonite character with its large school, church, and many beautiful homes surrounded by thriving gardens.

The war and the Revolution brought catastrophe to the prosperous Mennonite settlement. Repeatedly hordes of the "Reds" and the "Whites" flowed through the settlement, plundering and finally communizing the enterprises. In 1920 and the following year many villagers fell victim to starvation and typhus. In 1923-25 numerous families emigrated to the United States and Canada, while others were banished to North Russia or to Siberia. To avoid compulsory collectivization many fled in 1929 and reached Moscow, but the larger part of them were forcibly transported back to the East. Very few were able to return to Davlekanovo. Since the beginning of World War II (1939) there has been no word from the settlement.   G.H.

In addition to the Armenschule, founded by Jacob Martens, an evangelist, Karl Friedrichsen, a teacher in the Zentralschule, operated a small Bible School in 1923-26 (see **Mayak Bible School**). In 1926 the Mennonite population was 1,831, distributed over 19 "villages" and estates, farming nearly 30,000 acres of land. (See also **Davlekanovo** Mennonite Church. For the Davlekanovo M.B. Church, see **Gortchakovo** Mennonite Brethren Church.)   C.K.

Jacob Quiring, *Die Mundart von Chortitza in Südrussland* (Munich, 1928) 37; P. M. Friesen, *Brüderschaft,* 717; *Der Praktische Landwirt,* May, 1926, 2.

Davlekanovo Mennonite Bible School: see Mayak Bible School.

Davlekanovo Mennonite Church, Ufa, Russia, also called the "Ufimer" Church, was founded in 1898, and in 1905 had a membership of 153 with a total population of 401. The leading minister at that time was Gerhard Dyck, leader since 1902. Other ministers were Jakob Gerbrandt (*q.v.*) and F. F. Martens. The latter was ordained minister in 1909 and later as elder. Karl Friedrichsen (*q.v.*), who for a number of years operated the Davlekanovo Bible School (see **Mayak Bible School**), was also a minister of the congregation. (See also **Davlekanovo** Mennonite Settlement.)   C.K.

H. Dirks, *Statistik der Mennonitengemeinden in Russland Ende 1905* (Gnadenfeld, 1906) 38, 64.

Davlekanovo Mennonite Settlement, province of Ufa, Russia, near the Ural Mountains, was established near the station Davlekanovo on the Samara-Ufa railroad about 1894 by individual Mennonites who purchased large tracts of land and established large farms there. Although the settlement was not divided into the customary villages, groups of the landowners settled around the places named Karanbash, Golyshevo, Urtau-Tau, Gortchakovo, Berezovka, and Kulikovo. Some of the large estate owners were Tiessen, Reimer, Dyck, Martens, and Neufeld. Soon some Mennonites settled in and near the town of Davlekanovo and there established businesses such as agriculture machinery, a co-operative, and flour mills. Davlekanovo also had a Zentralschule and later a Bible school. In Berezovka was located a "school for the poor" (*Armenschule*), founded by Jacob Martens, an evangelist of the community. In 1926 the Mennonite population was 1,831, distributed over 19 "villages" and estates, farming nearly 30,000 acres of land (*Der Praktische Landwirt,* May 1926, p. 2). Little information is available pertaining to the beginning and the final phases of the settlement. (See also **Davlekanovo** Mennonite Church, **Gortchakovo** Mennonite Brethren Church, and **Mayak Bible School**.)   C.K.

Jacob Quiring, *Die Mundart von Chortitza in Südrussland* (Munich, 1928) 37; P. M. Friesen, *Brüderschaft,* 717.

Davlekanovo Zentralschule, Russian province of Ufa, opening in the fall of 1908, was founded by the brothers K. G. and G. G. Neufeld. The former took charge of the administration and was its first principal and one of its first two teachers, while G. G. Neufeld organized a society for its financial support. The Davlekanovo Zentralschule was a new type of secondary school among the Mennonites of Russia. Although its curriculum was similar to that of other Mennonite Zentralschulen, it differed from them in the composition of its student body. All the other Zentralschulen had only boys as students, and girls attended separate schools. Before 1870, to be sure, a few girls had been admitted to the Zentralschulen, but then the school authorities and the Committee for Public Welfare (*Fürsorgekomitee*) prohibited this practice. This was thus the first truly coeducational Zentralschule in the history of Mennonite education in Russia. After a few years of operation this type of school was not only approved by the parents of its immediate constituency, but schools in other parts of the country followed its example. The Davlekanovo Zentralschule had students, Mennonite and Lutheran, from several parts of Russia, but chiefly from the provinces of Ufa and Samara and from Siberia. It had the usual four-year course, to which a teachers' training course was added. Since this school also had an elementary school connected with it, the teaching staff usually consisted of 8 to 10 teachers. Among these teachers were F. C. Thiessen, D. P. Enns, G. J. Gaede, and Karl Friedrichsen. J. P. Rogalsky of the present (1953) Tabor College faculty was connected with this school from its very start until his departure to the United States in 1922. (Friesen, *Brüderschaft.*)   J.P.R.

Dax, Leonhard, a Hutterite preacher, a native of Munich, was a Catholic priest for 15 years, his last office being in Tschengels (Tirol). Attracted by the moral earnestness and loyalty of the Anabaptists, he joined them in 1558. He was present at the execution of Hans Mändl (*q.v.*). In Moravia, at Nemschitz near Prälitz, he was ordained to the ministry by the Hutterian Brethren in 1564, and in 1567 was sent to the Palatinate to visit the brethren there. Early in November he was arrested for his work of evangelization and detained through the winter with his wife and other Anabaptist men and women in the castle prison at Alzey. The Calvinist superintendent, probably Gerrit Dircks Versteghe (*q.v.*), cross-examined him repeatedly, and Dax defended his faith with skill, resisting all attempts to convert him to the Reformed faith. He boldly voiced his opposition to the use of force in matters of faith. He could not be moved by threats or bribes, and declared to the astonished superintendent, "I am ready not only to defend my faith and God's pious people with words, but also to suffer death for them." On Feb. 25, 1568, they were all released. Dax kept a record of his disputation with the city pastor of Alzey, manuscript copies of which are found in the libraries at Gran, Pressburg, Olmütz, and Budapest. An extract from it is printed in *Sammlung für die Geschichte, vornehmlich zur Kirchen- und Gelehrtengeschichte* (Nördlingen, 1779) 380-99. Dax died Aug. 4, 1574, at Dämberschitz (*q.v.*) in Moravia.

The account of the imprisonment of Dax as found in the Hutterite chronicle (Zieglschmid, *Chronik,* 424 f.) states that Dax also wrote several hymns. These have, however, not been found.   HEGE.

Beck, *Geschichts-Bücher,* 216, 265, 266; Chr. Hege, *Die Täufer in der Kurpfalz* (Frankfurt, 1908) 106-10; L. Müller, *Der Kommunismus der mährischen Wiedertäufer* (Leipzig, 1927) 117; John Horsch, *Kurzgefasste Gesch. der Menn.-Gem.* (Elkhart, 1890) 128; *ML* I, 397.

Dayton (Ohio) United Missionary Church began in 1896 as a mission appointment. After the flood of 1913, the church was established at its present location, East Fourth and McGee streets. In 1952 the congregation had 127 members, with Forest L. Huffman serving as pastor.   M.G.

Deacon, a direct derivative of the N.T. Greek word *diakonos* meaning minister or servant, used in Phil. 1:1, and I Tim. 3:8-13, where Paul states the qualifications for the office. Although Acts 6:2-5 does not use the title of deacon, it marks the beginning of the office of deacon in the early church. In later church history and modern Protestantism, particularly in the Anglican and other hierarchical churches, the office often became merely the lowest order of the clergy, whereas in the Anabaptist-Mennonite groups of both Swiss and Dutch origin the office was primarily one of caring for the poor and needy of the congregation and had to do largely with the material side. Hence the titles have been *Armendiener* or (Dutch) *Armendienaer* (minister to the poor), and *Almosenpfleger* (keeper of the alms). In Reformation times, however, both Lutheran and Reformed movements established the office of deacon as that of minister to the poor, the needy, and often the sick as well.

The early Anabaptist-Mennonite movement universally established the office of deacon as an important ordained office and thus created a threefold ministerial order; namely, bishop or elder, preacher or minister, and deacon. This threefold ministry has been maintained by all the groups in Europe except in Holland and Northwest Germany, as well as by the more conservative groups in America, particularly the Mennonite Church (MC), the Amish groups of all kinds, the conservative groups of Russian extraction, and the German-speaking groups of the General Conference. In the General Conference (GCM) English-speaking churches, the Mennonite Brethren of both English and German language usage, and the smaller groups such as Evangelical Mennonites, Evangelical Mennonite Brethren, and Krimmer Mennonite Brethren, the pattern of the one-pastor, one-order ministry is gradually being established. In Northwest Germany (Hamburg, Crefeld, Emden, etc.) the one-order ministry has long been established, and the deacon office dropped; but here in compensation the unordained office of *Vorsteher* (chairman of the congregation) has become very important.

The *Concept of Cologne* (1591) states: "Deacons shall be chosen according to the example of the Apostolic Church, to whom is to be assigned the care of the poor. They are to distribute to the poor the gifts received for this purpose, so that the giver shall remain unknown, as Christ teaches." Other Anabaptist-Mennonite confessions always mention and emphasize the office of deacon, down to modern times. For instance, the West Prussian Confession of 1895 says: "We also hold fast to the Apostolic arrangement according to which, along side of elders and preachers, deacons or alms-keepers (*Almosenpfleger*) are maintained in the church, who support the poor through the alms which are given by generous hearts, supply the wants of needy members, practice mercy with gladness, and otherwise lend a helping hand in the church in order that it may be well administered." The catechism (*Lehrbüchlein, 1878*) of the *Badischer Verband* makes similar statements about the deacon office and adds that he is to support the elders and preachers in their work and to share with them in the discipline (*Zucht und Ordnung*) of the church.

In the Netherlands the development of the deacon's office was as follows: The Waterlanders (*q.v.*) decided in 1568 (*DB 1877, 71*) that the preachers (*vermaner*) should also take care of the poor, but the deacons, if they should have the gift of speaking, should also preach, while the preachers should be chosen from among the deacons. Thus by 1568 the threefold ministry no longer existed in its strictest sense among the Waterlanders. In the 17th century it was not maintained by any of the Dutch Mennonites, except among the most conservative Jan Jacobs group (*q.v.*) and the Groningen and Danzig Old Flemish (*q.v.*), among whom it lasted until the middle of the 18th century. In both Lamist and Zonist congregations all members of the church board were called deacons (*diaken*), and the care of the poor has generally been a matter to be discussed and resolved by the entire church board, except in a few larger congregations like Haarlem and Amsterdam. Only in a limited number of congregations are the deacon's funds now separately administered; in most congregations there is only one treasury, from which all expenses of the church, such as the minister's salary, repair of the meetinghouse, etc., are paid, as well as the payments to the poor.

All American Mennonite groups officially maintain the office of deacon, though not every congregation actually has a deacon. Earlier all deacons were ordained, and served for life, the number of deacons varying with the size of the congregation. Now, in some cases, particularly in the General Conference (GCM) congregations, deacons are elected for short terms, and not ordained, and several (often three) serve together. The Central Conference (formerly Central Illinois), which merged with the General Conference in 1949, has always had only elected deacons, usually three in number.

The work of the deacon is much the same in all groups and includes (1) service to the poor and needy members, including usually the administration of the poor fund or alms monies, (2) assisting the bishop or pastor in the administration of the ordinances of baptism and communion (the deacon usually provides the bread and wine or grape juice), as well as providing the arrangements for footwashing, (3) assisting the bishop or pastor in visiting the sick and erring members, as well as helping to overcome or arbitrate difficulties between members, serving on the ministerial council of the congregation in matters of church activities and discipline, (4) reading the opening Scripture lesson and offering the opening prayer at the regular worship services, as may be directed by the minister in charge, and having charge of the entire service in the absence of the minister. Among the Old Order Amish as well as certain other groups of Amish background the deacon may preach on invitation, and frequently does, but in most groups he is not allowed to preach. In the eastern districts of the Mennonite (MC) Church, the deacon is often a very influential and weighty official, where it is commonly held that the bishop and deacon shall take care of church discipline, while the preachers only preach. In some congregations the deacon maintains the church membership record. In some groups the office of deacon is in a transition period and the older patterns are changing somewhat. (*ML I, 433.*) . Neff, H.S.B.

Deaconess, the office in the Christian Church committed to women for the alleviation of physical and spiritual need, especially in the care of the sick. It is of apostolic origin. In Rom. 16:1 we read: "I commend unto you Phebe our sister, which is a servant of the church which is at Cenchrea." It is possible that Phebe's service was a voluntary work of charity. But I Tim. 5:9, 10 shows that the early church chose women for church service: "Let not a widow be taken into the number under threescore years old, having been the wife of one man, well reported of for good works; if she have brought up children, if she have lodged strangers, if she have washed the saints' feet, if she have relieved the afflicted, if she have diligently followed every good work."

Among the Anabaptists the deaconess office was always based on the apostolic pattern. Elisabeth Dirks (*q.v.*), the martyr of Leeuwarden, was a deaconess (de Hoop Scheffer in *Menn. Bl.*, 1886, 74). The *Dordrecht Confession* of April 1632, Art. 9, Section 5 says, "Also that honorable old widows be ordained and chosen as servants, who besides the almoners, are to visit, comfort, and take care of the poor, the weak, the afflicted, and the needy, as also to visit, comfort, and take care of widows and orphans; and further to assist in taking care of any matters in the church that properly come within their sphere, according to their best ability."

In several Dutch Mennonite congregations the office of deaconess has been preserved from the beginning, e.g., at Sneek (*DB 1890, 112*; Th. Schäfer, *Weibliche Diakonie*, 289 ff.). In most congregations it continued until the middle of the 19th century. Barclay reports that the Amsterdam congregation had a deaconess and three deacons, all about 60 years old. "She visited the sick and the feeble, especially the women, and when necessary provided girls to stay with them and help them and if they were poor she furnished support given by those who could afford it, or reported it to the deacons, and she was obeyed as a mother in Israel and a servant of Jesus Christ." This institution influenced the Brownists, the Plymouth Brethren, and other English Independents, as well as the entire modern deaconess system. In the Amsterdam Mennonite Church there are five deaconesses, one of whom retires each year and is not eligible for reappointment for five years. They are appointed by the church board. In former times only married women or widows could be appointed to this office. In recent years two may be unmarried. The term "Mother-Deaconess" is still very commonly used. Similar arrangements exist in other Dutch Mennonite churches, as Haarlem and Utrecht. Among the deaconesses there are some who have had training for this vocation.

The German Mennonite churches also had the office of deaconess for a long time. Gerhard Roosen (*q.v.*), the noted preacher of the Hamburg-Altona Mennonite Church, wrote that his grandmother, Rischen Quins (d. 1626), was a deaconess in the congregation for many years during her widowhood; the last deaconess of the congregation was Mayken Govens (d. 1672), the widow of Hans Govens. In Danzig the office was maintained even later; the Flemish church almost always had a deaconess. The widow Magdalena von Kampen, who was appointed as deaconess in 1788 and served until her death (1810), was the last congregational deaconess among the Mennonites of Germany. The small size of the congregations in South Germany apparently made the office of deaconess unnecessary among them; wherever there is today an active deaconess service, it is patterned after the Fliedner institutions.

The idea frequently found in Mennonite circles that Fliedner (*q.v.*) became acquainted with the office of deaconess among the Dutch Mennonites and simply adopted it is false. When he visited the Amsterdam church to raise funds he became acquainted with a deaconess system that had nearly died out, and was thereby inspired to establish his deaconess system, which developed into a flourishing institution. He wrote, "There are in the Dutch Mennonite churches still some deaconesses who are chosen by the church board, work under it, and are engaged in the care of poor women. They visit the cottages of the poor, distribute the clothing given for that purpose, help the girls get positions as maids. Neither they nor the deacons receive a salary, and are members of the most respected families in the congregation, and therein subject themselves to great sacrifice of time, etc., with great willingness. This laudable primitively Christian institution should be imitated by other Protestant faiths." But Fliedner's creation was something quite different from the Biblical-Mennonite institution of deaconess. Not the single congregation, but in a sense all Protestantism became the bearer of this work of charity. He organized large associations and established "mother houses" to give a thorough training for this vocation. It was imitated on every hand, and everywhere new mother houses arose. In 1836 at Kaiserswerth, Fliedner founded the first modern deaconess home. In 1921 there were over 100 such homes, with about 20,000 deaconesses. These deaconess houses bear a denominational stamp. As a rule the sisters take communion in their own mother houses and re-main closely attached to them. The conditions set by the deaconess union at Herborn (district of Wiesbaden) with its seat at Berlin, are freer. Its purpose is to provide women without a vocation with vocational training and sure employment for life, thereby also promoting deaconess service. The only qualification for admission is membership in a Protestant church (*Menn. Bl.,* 1894, 60 ff.).

In Germany the Baden *Verband* instituted deaconess service among the Mennonites in 1904. While a Mennonite girl was in training in Kaiserswerth in 1894, the publisher of the *Gemeindeblatt,* Ulrich Hege, issued a suggestion that a Mennonite deaconess home be established. This suggestion was never carried out, and the sister in question went to America. Ten years later the matter was presented to the *Aeltestenrat* of the *Verband.* In March 1904 it was decided to look for a deaconess home that would be suitable for a Mennonite girl to receive training for the work. The deaconess homes in Strasbourg, Speyer, and Karlsruhe all made very favorable replies. The last of these was chosen, because there were already friendly relations between this house and the Mennonites of the *Verband* and because it was more centrally located. By 1918 six others had received their training there and then served in the hospital at Kochendorf, having lived for six years in Lautenbach near Neckarsulm. With Kochendorf as a center they served in all the South German Mennonite congregations, wherever they were called. They continued to return to the mother house in Karlsruhe when they were needed there and could be spared at home. Two sisters also helped with the nursing of wounded soldiers behind the front in World War I. The management of the work was in the hands of a committee of five brethren. Funds to carry on the work were contributed. No charge was made for nursing care, though the family served, if able to do so, made a contribution.

Since the Kochendorf hospital could not give the sisters a permanent home, the *Verband* in 1919 bought a house in Böckingen near Heilbronn as a home for retired sisters. But because of the great shortage in residences, only two sisters had been able to make their home there up to 1921. Later the deaconess work was transferred to the Bibelheim Thomashof near Karlsruhe. The Deaconess Committee still functions, although it has remained much restricted because of the small number of candidates.

In 1931 the Bavarian Mennonite relief organization *Christenpflicht* (*q.v.*), having received a house in Regensburg for the purpose of deaconess service, established a Mennonite deaconess work there with Sister Elise Hochstetler in charge, under the supervision of the Hensoltshöhe (Middle Franconia) mother house. Because of a lack of Mennonite candidates this work never developed.

The Mennonites of Russia founded a deaconess home of their own called Morija (*q.v.*) in Neu-Halbstadt in the Molotschna settlement in the Ukraine. It was a private undertaking and was built primarily with the funds furnished by Peter Schmidt of Steinbach. It was supported by voluntary contributions. It was opened on Dec. 3, 1909, for the purpose of training deaconesses and supporting them in sickness and old age. As long as they remained in the association they received their education free of charge and were provided with all other necessities (Friesen, *Brüderschaft, 659;* II, 96). By 1918, 89 sisters had been received. The Revolution brought them a time of suffering; the house was completely plundered. Nevertheless precisely in that time they were able to render a great service in the epidemics and other sicknesses accompanying the disturbances (record of the *Bundeskonferenz* held at Lichtenau on June 30 to July 2, 1918, p. 21).   NEFF.

Deaconess work among the Mennonites of America represents the continuation of a practice among the Mennonites of Russia and had its origin among the General Conference Mennonites in the United States with the work of David Goerz of Newton, Kan. He read a paper before the General Conference in South Dakota in 1890 in which he warmly advocated the deaconess work as a branch of home missions. In 1893, the General Conference in Ohio discussed the subject again, and the Board of Home Missions received instructions from the conference to further the cause. In 1898, the Bethesda Hospital was erected at Goessel, Kan., and in the next year the conference advised that if local conditions in any community within the conference became acute, the community should act as it seemed best. Bethesda Hospital assumed the responsibility of inaugurating deaconess work.

In 1900 Frieda Kaufman (*q.v.*) offered herself to Elder David Goerz as a candidate for the deaconess cause. He arranged to have her enter Bethel College for preparatory study. In 1901 Bethel College made the deaconess cause a part of its program, intending to establish or affiliate with a deaconess institution. In 1902 the Board of Directors of Bethel College made arrangements for deaconess candidates to continue their education for specific service at the interdenominational Deaconess Hospital in Cincinnati, Ohio, entering Frieda Kaufman as their first candidate. The following year Martha Richert enrolled in the same institution. In 1905 Catherine Voth was accepted as a candidate and also entered the Deaconess Hospital for a course in nursing. In the same year Ida Epp entered the Evangelical Deaconess Home and Hospital in St. Louis, Mo. Upon completing the two-year course in nursing, Martha Richert was ordained by Elder Peter Balzer as a parish deaconess in the Alexanderwohl church near Goessel. She served that community as well as the Bethesda Hospital until 1907 when she was married and, with her husband, Elder P. A. Penner, went as a missionary to India. Sister Frieda Kaufman, Sister Catherine Voth, and Sister Ida Epp were ordained when the Bethel Deaconess Hospital was dedicated June 11, 1908. They were the first three deaconesses of this mother house.

Since that time, 62 sisters have become members of the Bethel Deaconess sisterhood, 26 of whom are associated with the sisterhood at the present time. The deaconesses of this institution wear a special garb and are ordained by the church. Each sister has her place in the mother house, receives full maintenance, a monthly allowance, an annual vacation, and a vacation allowance. She is expected to remain loyal and faithful to her calling but does not take an oath of celibacy. Should a deaconess change her mind, believing it to be God's will that she serve in some other sphere apart from the sisterhood, she presents her resignation and receives an honorable discharge.

The Mennonite Deaconess Hospital in Beatrice, Neb., was dedicated July 16, 1911. Sister Elise Hirschler and Sister Maria Wedel, deaconesses of the Western District Conference, and Sister Katie Penner were the first deaconesses to serve here. Other deaconess candidates have furthered their education here and have been ordained by the Mennonite Church. Seven deaconesses serve in the Mennonite Deaconess Home and Hospital in Beatrice at present.

The Salem Home and Hospital in Hillsboro, Kan., was founded by the Krimmer Mennonite Brethren Conference in 1918. Several sisters had served as parish deaconesses prior to this but were transferred to the hospital when it was completed. A number of candidates entered for preparatory work and were ordained as deaconesses. They served in the hospital and in the home for aged. The school for both sisters and nurses has been discontinued. In the fall of 1937, the last two of the deaconesses active in the hospital left the work. Two sisters have continued in the Salem Home for the Aged at Hillsboro, Kan.

Not all deaconesses of the General Conference Mennonite churches are members of a sisterhood or serve in institutions. There are also a considerable number of congregational deaconesses without special training who do not wear a garb and who are elected rather than ordained. The Eighth Street Mennonite Church of Goshen, Ind., has three deaconesses with duties corresponding to those of a deacon. In the constitution adopted in 1947, their duties are stated as assisting the pastor in caring for the spiritual welfare of the church and the observance of the communion. The deacons and the deaconesses together with the pastor comprise the spiritual council of the church.

The appointment of deaconesses in the Mennonite Church (MC) varies considerably, although very few congregations have deaconesses. The purpose of female servants in the church has been one of good works and counseling rather than of exhortation in the church services. In certain areas, deaconesses are elected by the congregation, in others the church council gives a charge privately, and still in others the work of a deaconess is assumed without any official commission. Also the pledge of loyalty and helpfulness which is required of a deacon's or minister's wife at her husband's ordination has been regarded by some as a commission to the services of deaconess work. In no case is a congregational deaconess in this church given support. Her service is not regarded as a full-time occupation. There is no record of organized deaconess institutions in this Mennonite group. However, the Virginia Conference has had some deaconesses.   L.M.S.

Th. Fliedner, *Kollektenreise nach Holland* I (1831) 150 f.; Th. Schaefer, *Die Gesch. der weiblichen Diakonie* I (Stuttgart, 1879) 74, 86, 213; Rues, *Aufrichtige Nachrichten* . . . (Jena, 1743) 29; Schijn, *Historiae Mennonitarum* . . . (Amsterdam, 1729) 40; J. A. Stark, *Gesch. der Taufe und der Taufgesinnten* (1789) 412; Goerz, *Zur Diakonissensache, Ein Beitrag zur Kenntnis der weiblichen Diakonie mit besonderer Berücksichtigung der Stellung der Mennoniten zu derselben* (Newton, 1904); "The Deaconess and her Ministry," *Menn. Life*, January 1948; Frieda Kaufman, *Silver Anniversary Memorial* (1933); Edna Hunsperger, "The Deaconess Movement in the Mennonite Church," Sociology Seminar, 1948-49, Goshen College Historical Library; J. van der Smissen, "Bericht zur Feier der Diakoniearbeit des . . . Gemeindeverbands . . . zum 50 jährigen Jubiläum," in *Gbl. LXXXV* (July 1954) 69-71; *ML* I, 434.

Deaf, *Mary School for the,* at Tiege, Molotschna: see **Marientaubstummenschule.**

Dechtitz (Magyar, *Dejte*), a village in Hungary, where Hutterites expelled from Moravia settled in the 17th century. Their Bruderhof was ruined on Sept. 3, 1663, by Turkish troops; 35 inmates, mostly women, were carried away and some were killed. In the spring of 1664 the Bruderhof was ravaged by imperial troops, so that nothing was left to sustain life. In consequence of the continued molestation by soldiers in the summer and autumn they had to leave their desolate home. On Aug. 15 and 16, 1683, it was reduced to ashes by Turks and Tatars. Descendants of the Anabaptists who remained are still living in Dechtitz; they are Catholics. (Beck, *Geschichts-Bücher*, 427, 508, 517, and 541; *ML* I, 397.)   HEGE.

Deck, Ulrich, an Anabaptist of Waldshut, Germany: see **Teck, Ulrich.**

Decker (Dekker) is a Mennonite and Hutterite family name of Old Flemish background in West Prussia. It was first mentioned at Schönsee (Sosnovka) in 1695. From here it spread to Poland and Russia. The name is now found among American Mennonites of Polish and Hutterite background. The *Klein-Geschichtsbuch* (ed. Zieglschmid, 1947, 369) gives a brief account of how the Deckers joined the Hutterites. In 1783, two Hutterite brethren from Russia visited the Mennonites in Prussia, and were well received by Elder Gerhard Wiebe of Ellerwald (*q.v.*). From there they traveled along the Vistula to visit Abraham Nickel, deacon of the Schönsee Mennonite Church (now Poland). It was at this place that 15 Mennonites joined the Hutterite delegation to unite with their community at Vishenka, Russia. Among these 15 was Els Decker, a widow with five small children. The *Klein-Geschichtsbuch* mentions particularly Benjamin Decker as a member of a delegation to the authorities in Odessa, petitioning for more land (about 1842). When the Hutterian Brethren began their emigration to the United States in 1874, a Johann Decker is named among the first group to leave Russia. These people then settled in South Dakota, known there as the *Schmiedeleut* Hutterites. Today (1955) David Dekker, a grandson of Johann D., is the *Vorsteher* of the Tschetter Bruderhof, Mount Olivet, S.D., which is also the home of four other Dekker families (Michel, Paul, Jacob,

Joseph). Another Dekker family was among the pioneers of the Old Elmspring Colony (*q.v.*), founded by the *Lehrer-Leut* Hutterites. A Samuel Dekker is preacher at Rock Lake Colony, Alta.
                                                          R.F.

Deenik M.Lzn., Albertus Agathus, a Dutch Mennonite pastor, b. 1835 at Haarlem, d. 1903 at Veenwouden, Friesland. After finishing his studies at the Mennonite Seminary at Amsterdam, he served for nearly 40 years in the congregations of Ternaard (1860-81) and Stavoren-Molkwerum (1881-99). He had a weak constitution, which made it impossible for him to serve larger congregations; but though a minister of two small churches, he had some influence through his publications, which appeared in a number of Dutch periodicals. He was editor of a popular religious periodical, 1868-72, *De Nieuwe Richting in het Leven, bladen ter godsdienstige Volksontwikkeling*. From the beginning he was an ardent champion of Liberalism, with a tendency to radicalism. He translated publications of radical French and German theologians into the Dutch language: e.g., E. Renan's *Life of Jesus* (1863), and D. F. Strauss, *The Old and the New Faith* (n.d.). In addition to a number of theological books, he also translated a large number of German and English novels. (*De Zondagsbode,* XVI [1903] No. 50; *Biogr. Wb.* II, 404 f.)   vdZ.

Deenik, Marc Leonard, a Dutch Mennonite pastor, son of the former, b. at Ternaard, Friesland, Dec. 9, 1865, d. at Leeuwarden, Aug. 4, 1947, educated at Amsterdam (university and Mennonite seminary), served the congregations of Irnsum-Poppingawier in 1893-97, and Leeuwarden in 1897-1931. Like his father he was by principle a liberal; he played an important part among the Freemasons of the Netherlands. Among the Mennonites he was a very influential man, especially in the province of Friesland, where he was secretary of the *Friesche Doopsgezinde Sociëteit* (Mennonite Conference of Friesland) from 1899 to June 5, 1941. Through his thorough knowledge of Mennonites and his keen interest in Mennonite congregational life he was very helpful to many congregations in Friesland, especially the small ones, for whom he was a fatherly adviser. After he retired, he lived in Leeuwarden till his death.   vdZ.

Deep Creek (Va.) Mennonite Church (MC) is located near the village of Grossfield, in Norfolk County. The congregation is largely a result of recent colonization to this area. Land was purchased for a church in 1937, which was dedicated on Feb. 12, 1939. The congregation is a member of the Virginia Conference. In 1954 it had a membership of 102, with Eli Kramer as pastor. H.A.B.

Deep Run Mennonite Church (MC), the oldest Mennonite congregation in Bucks Co., Pa., is located near Bedminster and is affiliated with the Franconia Mennonite Conference. The original log building erected in 1746 was also used as a school until it was razed in 1842. One of the preachers, Samuel Godshalk, was an influential teacher and music instructor in this school. Deep Run has ever since had a strong group of choristers who have left their impress upon congregational singing. Later meeting-houses were erected at the same location in 1842, 1872, and 1949.

The first preacher and bishop at Deep Run was Abraham Swartz, who served over 50 years. Deep Run, being the oldest of the circuit of three Bucks County congregations, has always been the meeting place for the small conference (*Kleine Rath*) held each spring before the regular conference (*Grosse Rath*) held at Franconia. It has the distinction of being the only Mennonite Church in the Franconia Conference holding services every Sunday as early as 1847.

Sunday school was not organized until 1904. The German language was continued in services, although English had been introduced much earlier, until the death of John Leatherman in 1925. The Oberholtzer schism of 1847 took some 50 or 60 members, who organized a congregation bearing the same name (*q.v.*) and built a meetinghouse only a short distance from the old meetinghouse. In 1927 a number of members joined an independent group. Though in its earlier history the congregation suffered because of its slowness to change, more recently its leadership has encouraged youth and extension activities. The membership (1955) of 376 is served by pastors Wilson Overholt, Erwin Nace, and Abram Yothers. (J. C. Wenger, *Hist. of the Menn. of the Franconia Conf.*, Telford, Pa., 1937.)

Q.L.

Deep Run Mennonite Church (GCM) of the Eastern District Conference is located in Bedminster Twp., Bucks Co., Pa. At the time of the 1847 division in the Franconia Conference, a group at Deep Run withdrew from the old congregation in 1847 or 1848, but did not organize until May 14, 1849. Its charter, which fixes the official name of the congregation as the Mennonite Society of Deep Run and Plumstead, amended in 1913 and 1950, remains to the present day as the constitution of the congregation. Locally the congregation is known as the "New Mennonite" Church to distinguish it from the original Deep Run Mennonite (MC) Church. In the summer of 1849 the present brick meetinghouse was built near the meetinghouse of the original congregation. An addition was made to it in 1949.

Known ministers and their terms of service are: Martin Fretz, 1849-51; Joseph D. Rosenberger, ca. 1851-70; Enos F. Loux, ca. 1851-ca. 65; Jacob S. Moyer, 1871-83; Allen M. Fretz, 1883-1943; Russel Mast, 1940-45; Herbert Fretz, 1945-53; Claude Boyer, 1953- .

The present Sunday school was organized about 1876, and in 1892 a Christian Endeavor was organized. The membership in 1849 was about 60, in 1899 it was 140, and in 1954 it was 244. The common names today are Myers, Moyer, Mill, Fretz, Wasser, Wismer, Hunsberger, Charles, and Derstine.

J.H.F.

D. K. Cassel, *Hist. of the Mennonites* (Philadelphia, 1888); A. J. Fretz, *A Brief Hist. of the Old and New Menn. Congregation of Deep Run* (Bedminster, Pa., 1912); "History of the Deep Run Congregation," *1899 Menn. Yearbook and Almanac* (Quakertown, Pa., 1899);

Minute Book of the Congregation, 1848- ; J. C. Wenger, *Hist. of the Menn. of the Franconia Conf.* (Telford, Pa., 1937); J. H. Fretz, *History of the Deep Run Mennonite Congregation, Eastern Conference* (Bedminster, Pa., 1949).

Deer Creek (Okla.) Mennonite Church (GCM), a member of the Western District Conference. It was organized on Aug. 22, 1899, by Mennonite pioneers in the settlement of the Cherokee strip which was opened in 1893. The first settlers came from Halstead and Moundridge, Kan., and Donnellson, Iowa, and were mostly of South German background. Some of the common names are Stauffer, Dester, Krehbiel, Hohmann, Goebel, and Lichti.

The group first worshiped in a schoolhouse; it built its first church in 1902, and enlarged it in 1931. On Nov. 30, 1952, a new church was dedicated. The congregation was organized by Elder Wilhelm Galle and the first minister was Chr. H. Goebel, followed by M. S. Moyer, J. C. Peters, F. M. Moyer, J. Lichti, Richard Ratzlaff, Carl Landis, and W. G. Unrau (1954). In 1920 the congregation had a membership of 72 and in 1954, 128. Most of the 40 or more families live within a radius of five miles of town, and approximately 25 per cent live in town. (*ML* I, 390; *Menn. Weekly Review*, Jan. 1953, 4.)

E.A.D.

De Fehr: see De Veer.

Defenseless Mennonite Brethren: see **Evangelical Mennonite Brethren.**

Defenseless Mennonite Church: see **Evangelical Mennonite Church.**

Defiance County (Ohio) Old Order Amish Settlement, located near Hicksville and Mark Center, originated in March 1914, when 12 families of Sugarcreek, Ohio, moved in; their names were Schrock, Barkman, Mullet, Yoder, Miller, Coblentz, and Kurtz. The 1954 membership was 67. A congregation was organized in April 1914, and Bishop Moses A. Coblentz served as the only preacher for one year. Succeeding bishops were John Bontrager, David S. Bontreger, and (1954) Amos Yoder.

A Conservative Amish Mennonite congregation was organized by members leaving the Old Order Amish in 1922, led by Bishop John Bontrager and Deacon John F. Helmuth. Their number was increased by families from Allen Co., Ind. After four years the congregation was dissolved, and the members moved to other states.

In 1944 a "Beachy Amish" church was organized by members of the Old Order Amish congregation with the aid of Bishop David Burkholder of Nappanee, Ind. It was dissolved two years later, many of its members having moved to other states.

J.A.H.

De Kalb County, Ind., located on the Ohio line near the northeast corner of the state, was first settled in 1833 and organized in 1837, with a population of 1,000. Beginning at least as early as 1862 a small Mennonite settlement existed in the northern part of the county and the southern part of

Steuben County, to the north of De Kalb. In 1861 Anthony Freed moved to Steuben County from Pennsylvania after a brief stop in Stark Co., Ohio. His wife was Elizabeth Benner. In 1864, Peter Freed moved to De Kalb County with his son Henry from Virginia after stopping for several years in Columbiana Co., Ohio. Other families known to have lived there were Fretz, Myers, Brand, Bechtel, Beck, and Hunsberger. The congregation seems not to have built its meetinghouse, known as Pleasant Valley, until after 1869. In that year Daniel Brenneman preached the funeral sermon for Barbara Myer at the home of Jacob Brand. Ministers in the congregation at an early date were James Coyle and Eli Stofer, who usually preached in the English language. The latter was born in Columbiana Co., Ohio, and moved to De Kalb County in 1864. He was ordained to the ministry in 1871. Daniel Smith, who had been a deacon in Putnam Co., Ohio, was ordained a minister at Pleasant Valley. The meetinghouse and cemetery were located at Fairfield Center. Although the congregation never was large, at one time in the early '80's eight young people were baptized into the church. The congregation, being small, seems to have been unable to withstand the encroachment of worldliness. J. S. Coffman visited the congregation at numerous times, and at one time baptized a class of young people. Others would have united with the church but were unable to decide in favor of a plain church. Many of the descendants of the early Mennonites are now members of the United Brethren Church. A small Brethren in Christ congregation maintains a place of worship in the western part of the county. Some of the members of the Leo Mennonite congregation in Allen County live near Spencerville in the southern part of De Kalb County. In 1908 the congregation was still in existence, for in that year it asked the Indiana-Michigan Mennonite Conference, of which it was a member, for ministerial help. As late as 1913 students from Goshen College assisted in conducting services there.

J.S.U.

Deken, Agatha (Aagje), b. 1741 at Amstelveen near Amsterdam, d. 1804 at The Hague, a noted Dutch author of poems and fiction. Her parents, members of the Reformed Church, died when she was very young, and she was brought up in the Oranjeappel, the Collegiant orphanage in Amsterdam. In 1760 she united with the Collegiants, being baptized by immersion at Rijnsburg (*q.v.*). In 1769 she became a member of the Amsterdam Mennonite Lam en Toren congregation without rebaptism. In 1767 she left the orphanage to make her own living, and soon began to write religious verse and later short stories. In 1776 she met Elisabeth Bekker (1738-1804), the wife of the Reformed pastor A. Wolff, and became her very close friend. After Wolff's death the following year they lived together at Beverwijk near Haarlem, writing and publishing conjointly. They were warm friends in spite of fundamental differences in temperament, Elisabeth Bekker (or Betje Wolff, as she was usually called) being lighthearted and Aagje serious. Betje had already written some verse and a novel. Their best novels were *De His-*

torie van Sara Burgerhart (1782) and *Historie van den Heer Willem Leevend* (1784-85). Their novels, most of them written in the form of letters, describe the times in which they were living with a lively wit and gentle criticism. They were both opposed to the low moral standards of the time, as well as to the sterile formal orthodoxy of the Reformed Church; they were pious, but averse to bigotry; politically they were zealous Patriots (*q.v.*), filled with ideals of a better age which would be governed by a rationalistic, Christian morality. Aagje was warmly inclined to Mennonitism. She wrote to Adriaan Loosjes Pzn, the Mennonite minister at Haarlem (Jan. 22, 1802), "I should like to have the misinformed people informed that the Remonstrants and the Doopsgezinde are also good Christians," and "I want to help to increase the Doopsgezinde congregation, to whom I am dearly attached." In 1787, fearing the vengeance of the reactionary government for their anti-Orange Patriotism, they went into exile in France for ten years. In 1797 they returned to Holland and lived in The Hague. Their finances, never brilliant, were now rather bad, but they were aided by good friends, such as Pastor Loosjes. On Nov. 5, 1804, Betje Wolff died; eight days later Aagje followed in death and was buried in the same grave.

Besides the books they published jointly, there is a collection (not important) of devotional poems, *Stichtelijke gedichten van Maria Bosch en Agatha Deken* (Amsterdam, 1775), most of which was written by Aagje. She also contributed at least 74 hymns to the hymnal published by the Haarlem congregation in 1804. It is very probable that Betje Wolff wrote the major and best parts of the novels they wrote together; but Aagje must also have contributed some important passages.   H.F.W.J.

Of the abundant literature on these two authors we mention only G. Kalff, *Gesch. der Nederl. Letterkunde* VI (Groningen, 1910) 60-94, 326-32; J. Dyserinck, *Wolff en Deken* (De Gids IV, 1892); *N.N.B.Wb.* I, 696; *DB* 1865, 75; 1909, 100; N. van der Zijpp, "Wolff en Deken en de Doopsgezinden," in *Stemmen uit de Doopsgez. Broederschap*, November 1954; H. C. M. Ghijsen, *Dapper Vrouwenleven* (Assen, 1954).

Deken, Gaspard (de Decke), an Anabaptist martyr: see **Jasper, de Schoenmaker.**

Dekker (see also **Decker**), a family name frequently found among the Dutch Mennonites (not, however, exclusively Mennonite), especially those in the Zaan district (congregations of Zaandam, Koog-Zaandijk, Westzaan, and Wormerveer), who descended from Elder Jacob Dirksz (*q.v.*) of Wormerveer, while another branch was found in Rotterdam, where members of this family were deacons 1742-1883. They were nearly all merchants, mostly wood- or grain-dealers.

Jacob Dekker was a preacher at Den Helder 1742-47, Hendrik Dekker at Barsingerhorn about 1772-82. Adriaen Pietersz Dekker, a Mennonite of Amsterdam, played a part in the Collegiant (*q.v.*) movement. He was on the board of the Collegiant Oranjeappel orphanage, when this was founded in 1677. He wrote *Aanwyzing van de rechte gronden* (n.p., 1685). Samuel Johann Dekker, of Rotterdam, studied at the Amsterdam Mennonite Theological Seminary and served as a Mennonite pastor at Broek op Langendijk 1875-84, Monnikendam 1884-91, and Zutphen 1891-1901. His farewell sermon, at the same time a baptismal sermon, entitled *Christenbede*, was published at Assen (n.d.).

Of recent times mention should be made of Klaas Dekker (d. May 7, 1921), a merchant of Zaandam and deacon of the congregation of Zaandam-West, who first suggested the idea of the *Mennofonds* (*q.v.*), and Klaas Dekker Gzn (1850-1922), a wood-dealer at The Hague, who for many years was president of the church board of the congregation at The Hague and was one of the first promoters of the *Gemeentedag* (*q.v.*) movement.

The relationship of the different branches of this family could not in every case be determined. Another Dekker family, not related to the above Dekkers, lived on the island of Ameland; most of them were navigators. To this family belonged the (untrained) preacher Jan Douwes Dekker, who served about 1837, and the preacher Dieter Douwes Dekker (b. 1812 at Amsterdam, d. 1861 at Den Helder), who studied at the Amsterdam Seminary and served the congregations of Woudsend 1839-40, Beemster 1840-44, and Den Helder 1844-61. Eduard Douwes Dekker (1820-77) of Amsterdam, who under the pseudonym "Multatuli" wrote a number of well-known novels and plays, was also a member of the family. He, however, turned against the church, inclining to atheism.

It has been thought that the Dutch author Jeremias de Decker (Dekker) (b. 1609 at Breda, d. December 1666 at Amsterdam) was a Mennonite; but this has been denied by J. Geyl, who asserts that he was a Calvinist. At any rate, it has not yet been proved that he was a Mennonite. vDZ.

Zondagsbode XXXIV (1920-21) No. 28; *Brieven*, No. 14, October 1922; *DJ* 1840, 113; *N.N.B.Wb.* I, 691.

Deknatel, Jeme (or as he later called himself, Joannes), a Dutch Mennonite preacher, the author of widely used devotional books and the chief promoter of Pietism among the Dutch Mennonites and, through his writings, among the Mennonites of the Palatinate, b. Nov. 1, 1698, at Norden in East Friesland, d. Jan. 22, 1759, at Amsterdam. He was educated 1717-20 at the Remonstrant seminary at Amsterdam, where he studied under Jan le Clerc (Clericus) and Adriaan van Cattenburgh. When his father, a deacon at Norden, lost a large part of his property in a flood, his further education was sponsored by the church council of the Lamist congregation of Amsterdam.

On Dec. 12, 1720, Deknatel became assistant minister of the Amsterdam Lamist church with a salary of 300 guilders. Five years later, on Oct. 20, 1725, he was chosen as the fourth preacher of the congregation with a salary of 1,200 guilders. He preached his sermon of installation on Jan. 13, 1726, on I Tim. 4:16. His colleagues were Dominicus Eekens, Bartholomeus van Leuvenig, and Johannes Bremer (*q.v.*); in spite of differing views on the church, they worked together very well. Deknatel took an active part in the founding of the Amsterdam Mennonite Seminary (*q.v.*), and participated in the establishment of the fund for the support of inadequately paid ministers, which still bears his name (*Fonds van Deknatel*). He took a special interest in young Mennonite students of theology, caring for them like a father. This is attested by Marcus Arisz (*q.v.*) in his letters written to Deknatel's son Jan (*Menn. Bl.*, 1859, 12, 29).

In December 1734 Deknatel made the acquaintance of A. G. Spangenberg, the bishop of the Moravian Brethren, who was visiting Amsterdam, an event that was to be of lasting influence upon his character. Two years later he also met Count Zinzendorf, on the occasion of Zinzendorf's visit to Amsterdam from February to March 1736. A warm friendship developed between Deknatel and Zinzendorf and the Moravian Brethren. During Zinzendorf's visit of several weeks in Amsterdam in 1737 he celebrated communion in Deknatel's home. Deknatel alternated with the Reformed preachers in conducting services for the Moravian congregation and attended their conferences in Zeist where they had their center. He translated and published several hymns from the Moravian hymnal. His sons Jan and Jakob he sent to Germany to be educated at the schools of the Moravian Brethren at Lindheim and Marienborn in Wetterau. When he called them home, bad feelings arose between him and Zinzendorf. Deknatel united with the Moravian congregation organized in Amsterdam on Nov. 25, 1738, at the very outset, although he also remained loyal to his own brotherhood. In a letter to Leonard Dober (Dec. 30, 1749), he declared that he and his wife had been drawn closer to the Saviour through their contact with the Moravian Brethren and had rid themselves of much of their self-love and "self-made piety." But from 1751 on, he withdrew more and more from the Brethren. Deknatel thought that they should limit their activity to pastoral work, and not preach or set up a new church. A loan made by Deknatel to Zinzendorf, which Zinzendorf was unable to pay back, also disturbed their relationship. Nevertheless he remained on friendly terms with the Brethren, while at the same time he was warmly attached to his own brotherhood. "I have love for all men, and believe in a common Christian Church. Nevertheless I must testify that I bear my Mennonite brethren upon my heart and above all my own congregation, among whom I have been a member since my youth, and whose salvation (*Heil*) I seek to promote like my own." His fellowship with many outstanding men of God is attested by his extensive correspondence. In true brotherhood the Lutheran O. Martens wrote him from Copenhagen (March 12, 1737); David Nitschmann, the bishop of the Moravian Brethren, sent him letters from the Ronneburg castle (June 19, 1738) and from Pennsylvania (Jan. 3, 1741). Deknatel exchanged a number of letters with the Swabian pastor Friedrich Christoph Steinhofer in Ehningen near Tübingen, whom he had met at a conference in Zeist (*Menn. Bl.*, 1858), and also with L. Dober (Dec. 30, 1749). John Wesley was a guest in his home in 1738 and relates in his journal that he was received by Deknatel with Christian congeniality and heard one of Deknatel's sermons, which he liked so well that he took notes on it. Deknatel was at this time already a genuinely ecumenical Christian.

Deknatel's influence was great and lasting, extending far beyond the Dutch borders. Concerning his influence on the Palatine Mennonites, see **Weber, Peter.** Many of his writings were translated into German and were widely read. Some of his sermons were printed in America in the 19th century (*Acht Predigten . . . ,* Allentown, 1835; *Eine Reihe von Predigten . . . ,* Quakertown, 1883).

The Amsterdam archives contain letters written to Deknatel by the Hutterian Brethren of Sobotiste in Hungary (*Menn. Bl.,* 1894, 46). Mennonites of Switzerland traveled to Holland to visit the beloved and noted preacher. Until very recently his sermons were zealously read in Mennonite homes in the Palatinate. His catechism, *Anleitung zum Christlichen Glauben,* was long used by the Mennonites of South Germany. On March 7, 1757, Deknatel wrote an impressive letter to the Friedelsheim (Palatinate) congregation, which was published under the title, *Der Weg zur Seligkeit, geschrieben an die Gemeinde zu Friedelsheim (Menn. Bl.,* 1857, 56 ff.). Deknatel was attacked by the Dutch Reformed preacher G. Kulenkamp in *Aanmerkingen* (1740).

Among the Dutch Mennonites Deknatel occupied a unique place. He was a "Pietist among the Mennonites" (Leendertz), and in his experiential piety (*Bevindelijkheid*) he was quite different from the Lamist group to which he belonged, who were rather inclined toward rationalism. Nevertheless he was on good terms with his Amsterdam colleagues van Leuvenig and especially with Bremer, whose funeral address he delivered. He made many trips, holding revival meetings in many Dutch Mennonite churches. These were not always kindly received. The Mennonite church in Harlingen, of which Joannes Stinstra (*q.v.*) was the pastor, was denied him. In his house on the Leliegracht in Amsterdam he held regular Sunday evening devotional exercises, which were attended by many members of the Reformed Church, and which therefore caused some trouble in 1749.

Deknatel's writings are: *Klaag- en Troostdicht over . . . de zwaare Watervloeden in Oost-Vriesland* (Amsterdam, 1722); *Lijk-dicht op M. Oosterbaan* (1723); a foreword to the new edition of P. van Vloten's *Het Waare Bruiloftskleed . . .* (Amsterdam, 1726); *Lijk-dicht op H. Schijn* (Amsterdam, 1727); *Voorrede voor M. Symons, Bekenntenisse der Armen* (*q.v.*); an introductory poem for *Godts wonderen met zijne Kerke vertoont in een gedenkwaardig verhaal van meest Boheemische en Moravische Broeders . . .* (Amsterdam, 1735, 1738); *Evangelische Liederen* (translation of hymns from the Moravian hymnal with several of his own composition, Amsterdam, 1738, reprinted 1743, 1749), an introduction to Menno Simons' *Van de Rechtvaardigmakinge* (1737); *Aanleiding tot het Christelijk Geloove, Met de Woorden Gods; voornamelijk geschikt voor de Kinderen en Opwassende Jeugd* (Amsterdam, 1746, 1747, 1764); German transla-

tion, *Anleitung zum christlichen Glauben* (Amsterdam, 1756; Neuwied, 1790; Worms, 1829; Alzey, 1839); *Auf den allerseeligsten Heimgang meines lieben Sohnes Jacobus Deknatel* (1748), translated into the Dutch by Deknatel himself; *De Beede Christi aan zyne gekochte Zondaars* (sermon, 1754, Amsterdam); *De getrouwe Raad des Zaligmakers* (sermon, Amsterdam, 1755); *Menno Simons in't Kleine* (Amsterdam, 1753, 2d ed., 1758); German translation of the same, *Kurzer Auszug von Menno Simons Schriften* (Büdingen, 1758), reprinted (Königsberg, 1765) as *Auszug der merkwürdigsten Abhandlungen aus den Werken Menno Simons; Het Evangelium des Vredes* (Amsterdam, n.d.); *Het Oogmerk van Gods gerichten op aarde* (Amsterdam, 1756); *Acht Predigten über wichtige Materien* (Büdingen, 1757), a collection of sermons published previously as single Dutch prints, but not contained in the following collection of 12 sermons, and reprinted in America at Allentown in 1835, and in part at Quakertown in 1883; *Lijkrede . . . op Johannes Bremer* (1758); *Twaalf Predikatiën over Uitgeleezene Texten* (Amsterdam, 1758); *Naagelaten Predikatiën,* 2 vv. (Amsterdam, 1760 and 1763). Anonymously he wrote *De heilige en veilige weg des geloofs.* Deknatel is also the author of a service manual for ministers (*ML* I, 14), which appeared anonymously and is credited with being the basis for all later German Mennonite manuals of this type.†

NEFF, vDZ.

Inv. Arch. Amst. I, No. 773; W. J. Leendertz, "Joannes Deknatel, Een Pietist onder de Doopsgezinden," in *Geloof en Vrijheid* (1887); *Biogr. Wb.* II, 416-24; *Gem.-Kal.,* 1894; W. Lütjeharms, *Het philadelphisch-oecumenisch streven der Hernhutters in de Nederlanden* (Zeist, 1935) *passim;* R. Friedmann, *Mennonite Piety Through the Centuries* (Goshen, 1949); *Menn. Bl.,* 1860, 60; *ML* I, 398.

Delaware, a state on the Atlantic seaboard, first settled by the Dutch in 1631. It became a part of the grant made to William Penn in 1682 and remained under the governor of Pennsylvania until 1776. It has an area of 2,057 square miles and a population of 266,505. Pieter Cornelis Plockhoy (*q.v.*), a Dutch Mennonite, in 1662 planted a colony in Delaware, but it was destroyed by the English in 1694. The first permanent settlement of Mennonites was established in January 1914 near Greenwood. The Greenwood Conservative Mennonite Church (*q.v.*) now has a membership of 240 and supports a mission station in Wilmington. It established the Greenwood Mennonite School (*q.v.*) in 1928. Old Order Amish Mennonites moved into the state in 1915, locating west of Dover, in Kent County (*q.v.*). By 1952 they had five church districts with 282 members. In 1925 they established the Apple Grove Amish Mennonite School at Dover and in 1938 the Green Hill Amish Mennonite School at Cheswold. The Wesley Chapel Mennonite Mission (MC), established at Newark in 1950 under the Ohio and Eastern Conference, had 47 members in 1955.

M.G.

Delaware Mennonite Church (MC) of the Lancaster Conference is located in the Juniata Valley, a few miles north of Thompsontown, Juniata Co., Pa.

The congregation meets both in the Delaware meetinghouse and in Lost Creek under the bishop oversight of William W. Graybill, and Donald Lauver as assistant bishop. The ministers are W. Banks Weaver and Raymond Lauver. The membership (1954) is 75. The first meetinghouse was built in 1871. In 1953 a new one was built beside it. The older building is being used for a Christian day school.   I.D.L.

Delden, van, a Dutch Mennonite family, originally of Deventer, Dutch province of Overijssel, and in the 17th century residing at Deventer and Groningen, since the 19th century also in Gronau and Nordhorn, Germany, Jan van Delden, a Deventer merchant, having moved to Germany (see **Matheus van Delden**). Most of the van Delden family were merchants or manufacturers. In the 17th century nearly all members of this family belonged to the conservative group of Old Flemish Mennonites, and many of them did much for the church, a number serving the church as deacons. Mennonite preachers of this family were: Steven (Berents) van Delden (1672-1757), a rather wealthy merchant, who was minister of the Old Flemish congregation at Deventer from 1722 until his death (*DB* 1919, 82, 85-87, 97); Albertus van Delden (1748-1810), minister at Sneek, Oude Huis, 1773-97; Pieter van Delden (1763-1818), educated at the Amsterdam Mennonite seminary, minister at Winterswijk 1786-1800, lived at Almelo after his retirement; Mauritz Ernst van Delden (1818-72), educated at the Amsterdam Mennonite seminary, a minister at Franeker 1848-72 (*DB* 1873, 189). He wrote *Leerrede, uitgesproken bij gelegenheid der laatste godsdienstoefening in het oude kerkgebouw der Doopsgezinden te Franeker, 8 Mei 1864,* Franeker (n.d.).   vDZ.

V. Muthesius, *100 Jahre M. van Delden & Co.* (n.p., n.d.-Gronau, 1954); P. Moussault, *Das Geschlecht van Delden* (Haarlem, 1954).

Delden, Albertus van, Dutch Minister of Finance, b. Feb. 21, 1828, at Deventer, d. Nov. 7, 1898, a descendant of the above family. He never married, but lived with his unmarried sister.

He rendered outstanding service to his native city, his country, and the Mennonite brotherhood. From 1858 until his death he held high and honorable political office in provincial (Overijssel) and national legislative bodies, and finally the portfolio of Minister of Finance in the cabinet. His service to the Mennonite Church in Deventer was equally outstanding. In 1862 he became a member of the church council, and then its treasurer. For some years, when his political duties kept him away from home for long periods, he resigned this position, but after this obstacle was removed, he gave the church his devoted and untiring service as deacon and chairman.

He was a simple man who avoided all show and cared nothing for the applause of the world. He persistently followed the way he felt was right. With his money he was very generous. He fully deserved his place of honor in city, nation, and church. (*ML* I, 400.)   S.L.

Delden, Hendrick Wilhelm van, Dr. h.c. (1872-1950), a leading textile manufacturer of Germany, head of the largest cotton mill on the Continent (at Gronau, Westphalia), in 1938 president of the International Cotton Congress at Cairo, Egypt, b. Gronau, April 20, 1872, d. there Jan. 24, 1950, oldest of eight children of Gerrit and Engelbertha van Delden, older brother of Mathieu van Delden, was active in German Mennonite church organizations. For decades he was a member of the Gronau Mennonite church board and a member of the directors of the Vereinigung der Deutschen Mennonitengemeinden and served as treasurer of the Mennonitischer Geschichtsverein 1933-47.   H.S.B.

Delden, De Jonkvrouwen van, Anabaptist martyrs: see **Beckum, Maria van,** and **Beckum, Ursula van.**

Delden, Matheus (Mathieu) van, an important industrialist of Westphalia, Germany, b. May 26, 1828, in Nordhorn, d. Feb. 10, 1904, in Gronau. He was the son of Jan van Delden, a merchant of Deventer, who moved to Nordhorn in Hannover early in the 19th century. Matheus was the fourth of eleven children. At the age of 16 he attended the school of weaving at Elberfeld, and then learned the trade from the bottom of the ladder. His capabilities were such that he had no difficulty in finding the capital to set up his own weaving firm in Gronau in the 1860's, which went through the entire evolution from hand spinning and weaving (the latter done in the homes) down to completely modernized mechanized methods. In 1914 the factory employed 1,500 workers. He was still active in his business when his final illness overtook him and he died at the age of 76 years. Unfortunately he did not live to see the dedication of the Mennonite church in Gronau, in which he had a sincere interest, and for which he contributed a substantial sum. (*ML* I, 400.)   J.v.D.

Delegations: see **Mennonite Delegations.**

Delfshaven, a town in the Dutch province of South Holland, since the beginning of the 20th century a part of Rotterdam. During the rise of Anabaptism this movement had many adherents here. In 1550 the Anabaptists Quirijn and his brother Huig Jorisz of Delfshaven were beheaded at Delft. Leenaert Bouwens baptized 43 persons here between 1551 and 1565. Later there was a Mennonite congregation, probably very small, which met in a private house and of whose history little is known. The congregation, which it is thought belonged to the strict wing of Old Flemish Mennonites, united with that in near-by Rotterdam, *ca.* 1730.   vDZ.

Inv. Arch. Amst. I, 80, II, 2, 449-50; K. Vos, *Gesch. der Doopsgez. Gemeente te Rotterdam* (Rotterdam, 1907) 41.

Delft, a town in the Dutch province of South Holland with (1947) about 62,000 inhabitants (263 Mennonites). As early as 1534 there was live Anabaptist activity here. On March 27, 1534, the martyr Jan Evertsz (*q.v.*) of Middelburg, who had visited Delft shortly before, named nine persons at Delft who had been rebaptized, among them David Joris (*q.v.*) and his wife. In the fall of 1534 Obbe Philips (*q.v.*) visited Delft and ordained David Joris as an elder. Early in March 1535 and in December 1535 some Anabaptists were executed whose names are not known. Probably there was a congregation there at this time, which was deeply influenced by David Joris. In January 1539, 31 Anabaptists were put to death, including Maritgen, the mother of David Joris. All these persons were Davidjorists (*q.v.*). After this terrible execution some Anabaptists must have remained, though David Joris had left Delft. The Mennonite martyr Adriaen Cornelisz (*q.v.*), executed at Leiden in 1552, lived in Delft (*BRN* II, 205). And on Feb. 5, 1572, two Mennonites, Jan Hendriksen van Zwartewaal (*q.v.*) and Martin Jansen Korendrager (*q.v.*), who are both found in the *Martyrs' Mirror,* suffered martyrdom at Delft. Martin Jansen is definitely said to have been a citizen of this town. Leenaert Bouwens visited Delft several times in 1563-65 and baptized 30 persons here. Shortly after this there was a Mennonite congregation at Delft, which is said to have attracted some Reformed people. The Mennonites were opposed by the Reformed minister of Delft, Arent Cornelisz, who wrote two books against them: *Grondtlich bewijs ende onderricht wt der heyliger Schriftuyre dat het Godts wille ende bevel is, dat men de onmondiche kinderkens der Christenen doopen sal;* and *Wederlegginghe der voorneemste bewijsredenen.* From the records of the Reformed Church it appears that Niesgen Bruyne, the widow of Herman Schinkel and later the wife of Aelbrecht Heyndricksz, had reprinted the Mennonite *Offerboek* in 1578. This must have been the edition of *Het Offer des Heeren* of which until now the printer was unknown (edition No. 6, 1578 b; see *BRN* II, 11-12). In 1599 there existed at Delft a Frisian Mennonite congregation, of which Jan Woutersz was a preacher. Of this Frisian congregation nothing further is known; it may soon have united with the Flemish congregation, of which the origin is unknown but which existed in 1578, in which year Christiaen Adriaensz was an elder here. In 1626 the ministers of Delft, Michiel Jantz, Willem Theunisz, and Adriaen Jansz, signed the Confession of Outerman (*q.v.*). Representatives of this congregation attended the conferences of the Flemish at Haarlem in 1649 and other Flemish meetings. In 1664 they signed the *Verbond van Eenigheid* (*q.v.*) and joined the stricter wing of the Dutch Mennonites, the Zonists (*q.v.*).

In 1647 there was also a Waterlander congregation in Delft, of which five representatives were present at the general Waterlander conference at Amsterdam. The history of these three congregations is equally obscure; it is not clear when they were founded and only a few facts are given. Even the places where two of these congregations met are not known; the Waterlanders had a meetinghouse in the Huetersteeg. Since about 1630 the Flemish congregation had no minister of its own. For more than 50 years it was ministered to by preachers from other congregations, especially from Rotterdam (*buitenmannen*); it must have died out at the end of the 17th century. About 1680 the Waterlander congregation joined the Waterlander Sociëteit of South Holland and got a preacher of its own; how long this minister, C. de Wit Jzn, stayed here, is not known. The congregation, which during the 17th century was always very small and of which it is said in 1713 that it was nearly extinct (*DB* 1918, 69), must have disappeared soon after. At least it is not mentioned in the first *Naamlijst* (1731).

In April 1907 a number of Mennonites living at Delft founded a Kring (group). J. Dyserinck (*q.v.*), a retired minister of Rotterdam who was living at The Hague, conducted services once a month in the Remonstrant church; he also gave catechismal instruction and in the spring of 1909 held a baptismal service. The members of the Delft group were registered in the records of the Mennonite congregation of The Hague (*q.v.*). After the death of Pastor Dyserinck (1912), Pastor G. Wuite of The Hague took care of the Delft Mennonite group. In 1923 this group obtained its own minister, M. van der Vegte Jr. 1923-27, followed by Miss M. T. Gerritsma 1927-29, Miss J. H. van der Slooten 1929-32, and since 1934 until now Miss S. Goossen. In 1925 this group was organized as an independent Mennonite congregation. The membership, which numbered 98 in 1916, 115 in 1927, was 154 in 1954. The congregation has no church building of its own. Meetings are held in the Remonstrant church or in a rented hall. There is a Sunday school for children, a ladies' circle, and a youth group. vDZ.

H. J. Jaanus, *Hervormd Delft* . . . (Amsterdam, 1950); *Inv. Arch. Amst.* I, Nos. 80, 105, 108, 144, 146, 204, 216, 248, 297, 298, 443, 749, 812, 814, II, Nos. 1677-90; *DB* 1872, 67; 1892, 108, 124-26; 1896, 44; 1907, 78, 210; 1909, 187; 1917, 160-67; 1918, 69; Kühler, *Geschiedenis* I, *passim; ML* I, 401.

Delft, Minn., a village in the southwestern part of Cottonwood County. About 400 members of the Mennonite Brethren and General Conference Mennonite churches live within a radius of five miles of the town. The Carson Mennonite Brethren and the Immanuel Mennonite churches are located in the town. Mennonites settled in the community in 1880, and the town was founded in 1902. V.G.

Delpini, a Jesuit priest who was commissioned in September 1764 by Maria Theresa, Queen of Austria-Hungary, to convert the Anabaptists (Hutterites) living at Alwinc (*q.v.*) in the Hungarian province of Transylvania. With the help of the government and severe measures, such as confiscation of books, compulsory attendance at his sermons, threats, and imprisonment, he tried to make them forsake their faith. In the beginning he was not very successful, but after their preacher Joseph Kohr (or Gor) had been arrested and another preacher, Martin Roth (Ruth), had been forcibly "converted," others followed, threatened by imprisonment or tempted by the attractive promises of the government. A large number of them, however, fled to Russia or Turkey in order to keep the faith. In 1768 Delpini retired; his mission was finished; all but a few who suffered in prison had turned Catholic. Their descendants, many of whom are still living in those areas, are sometimes called Habaner (*q.v.*). (See also **Alwinc, Hungary, Hutterites.**) (*DB* 1910, 41, 69.)   vDZ.

Delsbergerthal, a Swiss Mennonite congregation north of Delémont: see **Lucelle.**

Delta Colony, Uruguay, the third Mennonite colony in Uruguay, located in southern Uruguay in Departamento San Jose, 60 miles northwest of Montevideo, and only 3 miles south of the principal Montevideo-Colonia highway, about 150 miles southwest of the two older Mennonite settlements, El Ombu and Gartental, is named Delta in remembrance of the Vistula Delta from which the settlers all originate. The site was selected after careful investigation and after all prospective settlers had registered agreement to the purchase, which was made on Feb. 18, 1955. The tract contained 1,462 hectares (*ca.* 3,600 acres), which was divided into farms of an average of 75 acres in size, and initially occupied by 40 families. The financial arrangements for the purchase called for a down payment of 250,000 Uruguay pesos, 100,000 of which were supplied by each family paying 2,500, and the remainder coming from North American friends. A mortgage was arranged through the government mortgage bank at 8 per cent interest. Delta Colony is independent of the other Mennonite settlements, with its own organization. The first officers of the colony were elected in 1955 as follows: Pres., Walter Sprunk; Sec., Wilhelm Regehr; Treas., Hans Warkentin; Committee members, Artur Schweitzer, Helmut Wiebe, Gerhard Willy Dueck, and Wilhelm Dueck.

All the settlers originally were refugees from the Danzig area and West Prussia, but came directly from the settlements of El Ombu, Il Pinar, Trinidad, Santa Rosa, Buschental, and Montevideo in Uruguay. The colony co-operative is called "Cooperativa Delta." To some extent the farmers are also operating independently on such products as milk, fruit, and vegetables. The principal farm product of the settlement is wheat, although some sunflowers, potatoes, and vegetables are grown. Slowly the colony will move into more dairying and more extensive production of fruit and vegetables. Marketing facilities are good because of the colony's location on the main road into Montevideo.

· The Delta church is a branch of the Montevideo church, but in time it is to become an independent church. At such time, Klaus Dueck is to assume eldership. Willi Jochem, formerly at El Ombu, is the present minister.   W.T.S.

Demak, a Chinese Mennonite congregation on the island of Java, Indonesia. Membership in 1949, 65. (*Jaarversl. Doopsgez. Zendingsvereniging 1949,* 17.)   vDZ.

Demolition of Dwellings. Among the suppressive measures taken by governments against the Anabaptists of the 16th century was the razing of houses in which the persecuted groups met for worship. The earliest records of such procedure come from the archbishopric of Salzburg, where ecclesiastical and secular authorities were combined in one person. Here Anabaptists were found as early as 1526. On Oct. 18, 1527, Matthäus Lang (*q.v.*), cardinal and

archbishop of Salzburg, issued a mandate against the Anabaptists in his realm, in which he forbade their meeting for worship. A few days later, on Oct. 27, a new mandate was passed, that extended the range of persons liable to the penalty. It says, "No one shall accept, lodge, feed, or give drink in his house to one of the brotherhood of Anabaptists, but get rid of him on penalty of having his house destroyed and the other announced penalties. Let every one guard against secret meetings, corner preaching and mobs" (Loserth, 37). Even those who announced such meetings were threatened in a further edict of April 18, 1528, with losing their homes (Loserth, 41). This threat was carried out in the case of two houses in which the Anabaptists had met. And on Nov. 6, 1527, six Anabaptists were locked into a house and burned to death in it (Loserth, 39).

The penalty of destruction of home was also applied in Lower Austria (*q.v.*), creating difficulties with the owners, who had no idea of the meetings being held in their houses; also in Tirol (see **Oberlehen**). In the Netherlands houses in which Anabaptists met were also torn down. This happened in Niedorp in 1535 (*Inv. Arch. Amst.* I, 101), and as late as about 1643 the meetinghouse at Visvliet, Groningen, was pulled down when the Mennonites began to hold meetings there. In view of such obstacles to meeting for mutual admonition and worship, there was often no other possibility of meeting than at night or in the open in outlying places.   HEGE.

J. Loserth, "Zur Gesch. der Wiedertäufer in Salzburg," in *Mitteilungen für Salzburger Landeskunde* VII (1912) 35-60; *ML* III, 248.

Denbigh, a village (pop. *ca.* 200) in the city of Warwick, Va. (formerly called Warwick County), in the southeastern part of the state. There are some 300 Mennonites living within shopping distance of Denbigh, all of the M.C. group. Most of these live in a settlement two miles southeast of Denbigh. Mennonites began to settle there around 1898. There are two Mennonite churches in the vicinity, a Christian day school, and a mission in the near-by city of Newport News, which is staffed with workers from the Warwick River congregation, it being the larger church with a membership of 300.   G.R.B.

Denison Civilian Public Service Camp No. 18, located one mile southwest of Denison, Iowa, was opened in August 1941 and closed in September 1946. A soil conservation camp under the Mennonite Central Committee, it had an enrollment of over 100 men, who were engaged chiefly in erosion control and emergency farm work. The campers were given credit for their help in saving Council Bluffs, Iowa, from destruction by the Missouri River flood of April 1943. During the school year 1944-45, a relief training school for campers who had volunteered for relief work was conducted at the camp. (M. Gingerich, *Service for Peace,* Akron, 1949.)   M.G.

Denk (Denck), **Hans** (*ca.* 1500-27), an outstanding leader of the South German Anabaptists, though of the spiritualist type, was born at Habach, near

Huglfing in Upper Bavaria; died of the plague in November 1527, at Basel, Switzerland. Denk stated in his confession of faith of Jan. 14, 1525: "I was taught the faith from my childhood by my parents." In 1517 he enrolled at the University of Ingolstadt, from which he received the Bachelor of Arts degree two years later. Later he attended the University of Basel. He was versed in Latin, Greek, and Hebrew, and was at home in the humanistic circles of the day. Although he may for a time have been a disciple of Erasmus, not much of the latter's influence on him is discernible. For a time he served as literary editor ("corrector") in the printery of the famous Cratander of Basel, later in that of Valentine Curio. At the latter he edited the last three volumes of a four-volume Greek grammar by Theodore Gaza. For some time in 1523 he also attended the lectures of Oecolampadius in Basel on the Prophet Isaiah, but was also not much influenced by Oecolampadius.

The real source of Denk's religious life and thought was in medieval mysticism as represented by *Deutsche Theologie* (q.v.), which Luther had reissued in 1518. He was also influenced by Thomas Müntzer's mysticism. Denk was burdened for the deepening of his own spirituality and that of the church.

At the age of 23 he was appointed rector of the St. Sebald School in Nürnberg, having been nominated for this position by Oecolampadius. By this time he was also married. Nürnberg was at that time torn between the Lutherans and those who were disappointed in the fruits of the Reformation; also some were returning to the Catholic Church. Denk was arraigned before the city authorities upon the tesimony of an "ungodly" painter, Sebald Beheim, who with several other painters was charged with unsound remarks about baptism and the communion, and who reported certain conversations with Denk which cast doubt upon Denk's doctrinal soundness. The result was that Denk was banished from the city, although he was not yet an Anabaptist.

Denk had by this time come to challenge the Lutheran doctrine of justification by faith which seemed to guarantee the standing of a believer with God regardless of the character of his life. Denk's whole emphasis was put instead on discipleship to Jesus. Indeed his motto was: "No one may truly know Christ except one who follows Him in life." Denk and the Lutheran Osiander were in sharp disagreement in spiritual matters. Osiander was, in fact, present at Denk's trial before his banishment from Nürnberg. At this trial the city council demanded a confession of faith from Denk, which he submitted in two installments, the first on Jan. 14, 1525, two weeks after his trial, and the second during the following week. In the former he made the following confession: "I, Johann Denk, confess that as far as my hereditary nature is concerned I am a poor soul, subject to every sickness of body and spirit. . . . For a time I prided myself as possessing faith, but I have finally become convinced that it was a false faith, because this faith did not overcome my spiritual poverty, my inclination to sin, my weaknesses and my sickness; on the contrary, the more I pol-

ished and adorned myself when I had such a nominal faith, the more severe became my spiritual sickness. . . . I do not venture to assert that I now have the faith which translates itself into life, although I see clearly that my unbelief cannot continue before God. Therefore I say: Yes, in the name of the Almighty God whom I fear from the bottom of my heart: Lord, I have the desire to believe; help me to come to faith. . . . When Christ the sun of righteousness arises in our hearts, then the darkness of unbelief is overcome for the first time. That has not yet taken place in me. . . . He who does not hearken to the revelation of God in his own breast (i.e., who does not receive illumination from God's Spirit) but undertakes of himself to give an exposition of the Scripture—which only the divine Spirit is able to do—makes of God's secrets which are contained in Scripture a desolate abomination, and misuses the grace which he has received from God." At the end of the confession Denk added: "All unbelief is sin; it is this which wrecks the righteousness of God by law. Only when the law has fulfilled its role, i.e., when self-seeking is conquered, does the Gospel find room in the heart. Faith comes by hearkening to the Gospel. Where there is faith, there is no sin; where there is no sin, there the righteousness of God dwells. The righteousness of God is God Himself; sin is that which is contrary to God. All believers were at one time unbelievers. To become believers they had to have their passions, their earthly man, die in the sense that it was no more they themselves who lived, as they had done when still in unbelief, but God lived in them through Christ; they no longer had their walk here on earth, but in heaven, as Paul says. All this I believe. May God break down my unbelief."

The second confession of Denk (submitted several days after the first) deals with baptism and communion. He distinguished between an outer and an inner baptism; the former is not necessary to salvation, while the latter is. Water baptism is of value only when it is performed as a covenant with God. The inner baptism is the one meant where it says, He that believeth and is baptized shall be saved. (The verdict of the Nürnberg clergy on Denk's confession is printed in Keller, *Johann von Staupitz*, 404-11.)

The magistracy of Nürnberg issued its verdict on Denk on Jan. 25, 1525. He was compelled under threat of imprisonment to swear never to come closer to the city than 10 miles the remainder of his life, and was thus banished from his wife and children, for whose support his property was appropriated. Denk swore the oath and left the city a deeply shaken man. Where he spent the next few months is not known.

In June 1525 Denk was staying at the home of an Anabaptist in St. Gall, where he attended also the Anabaptist meetings. It is said that his belief in universalism (*q.v.*) gave offense to the Anabaptists there.

From September 1525 until October 1526 Denk was in Augsburg in South Germany. He earned a living by teaching Latin and Greek to the children of two noblemen who took him into their homes.

Soon after his arrival he had to give account of himself because news of his banishment from Nürnberg
had reached Augsburg. Nevertheless he was not
banished.

Spiritually Augsburg was badly divided: Lutherans and Zwinglians were combating each other,
and there was also a Catholic minority. Moral conditions were bad. Yet there was apparently a small
group in the city, perhaps of Zwinglian inclination,
whose members lived a life of strict morality and
presumably formed the nucleus of the Anabaptist
congregation established in 1526 by Hubmaier (q.v.).
To this group Denk was attracted, and was baptized
by Hubmaier. After Hubmaier's departure for Nikolsburg in Moravia, Denk became the leader of the
Augsburg Anabaptists. He in turn won for the
brotherhood such men as Hans Hut (q.v.), and perhaps Siegmund Salminger (q.v.), Jakob Dachser
(q.v.), and Eitelhans Langenmantel (q.v.). It is estimated that about 1527 the Augsburg Anabaptist
congregation numbered 1,100 souls. (This number
has, however, not been substantiated.)

But Denk's stay in Augsburg was destined to
come to an end soon: Urban Rhegius (q.v.), the
reformer of the city, became his powerful opponent.
This led to a disputation between Denk and the
Lutheran clergy, to be followed by a second and
this time public disputation. But before this could
take place, the weary Denk left the city.

By November 1526 Denk was in Strasbourg.
Here he enjoyed the friendship of the Anabaptists.
But the presence of such an outstanding "heretic" as
Denk in Strasbourg was disconcerting to Capito
(q.v.) and Bucer (q.v.), the Protestant leaders of the
city. Once again Denk had to participate in a disputation, this time with Bucer. He was thereupon
expelled from Strasbourg and left the city in December 1526. Following brief residences in Bergzabern and Landau in the Palatinate—and another disputation at the latter city—he located briefly in
Worms, where he helped Haetzer (q.v.) finish the
translation of the Old Testament Prophets. They
were published in April 1527 at Worms, and are
therefore known as the "Wormser Propheten." They
were possibly used by Luther and the Swiss theologians in their German translations of the Bible.
Denk then visited Anabaptist congregations in South
Germany and Switzerland, and presided at the Martyrs' Synod (q.v.) in Augsburg on Aug. 20, 1527.
It was there decided to send Anabaptist preachers
and evangelists as emissaries to South Germany,
Switzerland, and Austria. Denk was in a group of
three commissioned "to comfort and teach" the
brethren in the Zürich and Basel areas of Switzerland.

In late September 1527, near the end of his life,
Denk arrived in Basel and found refuge in the home
of a friend. He was sick in body and spirit, weary
of conflict and persecution, longing for rest and
peace. He therefore wrote an appealing letter to
Oecolampadius, asking permission to stay in the
city (Comeniushefte 1898, 230-43; ML I, 409).
Oecolampadius seems to have taken a kindly attitude toward the sick Denk; he visited him repeatedly and engaged in many discussions with him. At

Oecolampadius' request Denk wrote a brief statement of his views, which Oecolampadius published
under the somewhat misleading title, Hans Denks
Widerruf (Recantation). In ten points Denk covered the following topics: Scripture, Christ's "payment," faith, free will, good works, separation and
sects, "ceremonies," "baptism, bread and cup of communion," and the oath. The whole thrust of Denk's
position is on the utter necessity of the inner life
with God; everything outward is secondary if not
useless. "Faith is obedience to God." Also, "God
sees the faith and the good works, is pleased by
them, and rewards them. Not that they have their
source in us, but that we do not receive the grace
which is offered us in vain. Everything comes from
one source, and that is a good one, namely from
the Word which was with God from the beginning
and in the last times became flesh. And happy is
the man who does not despise the gifts of God."
Denk confessed freely that he had erred in the past,
and still erred. He also expressed no particular objection to infant baptism, and promised never again
to baptize anyone. In reference to his own activity
in baptizing he remarked that the zeal of the Lord
had sent him out, and had again brought back his
understanding. It is evident that his mysticism, a
spirit foreign to the Swiss Brethren, had largely undermined his Anabaptist convictions—indeed he
fully approved of oaths in this same confession. It
was of the essence of authoritative Anabaptism to
insist on an open testimony and commitment with
baptism as its outward symbol. In agreeing to
abandon baptism, Denk abandoned Anabaptism in
a sense and approached the position of Schwenckfeld. But it is also true that Denk was now a
broken man, crushed by the harsh measures which
his religious opponents succeeded in having the
magistracy take against him, and his sensitive soul
was unable any longer to bear the load. At any rate,
Denk had now returned to his original mysticism.
He died of the plague in November 1527.

Denk has been accused by his enemies as well as
modern scholars such as Dunin-Borkowski of being
an anti-Trinitarian (see Anti-Trinitarianism). Modern Unitarian historians claim him as a spiritual ancestor, e.g., F. L. Weis and E. M. Wilbur, who
calls him "a pioneer of our movement." However,
the characterization of him by Schwindt as "a beginner of undogmatic Christianity" is more accurate. The final word has not been said on the matter of Denk's presumed anti-Trinitarianism and may
never be able to be said because of lack of evidence
in Denk's own writings.

Hans Denk is the author of the following items,
given in chronological order: (1) The Confession
of Faith of January 1525; (2) Wer die warheit
warlich lieb hat . . . (1525), a discussion of 40 paradoxes in the Bible. His conclusion is that only the
inner Word of God which comes through the Holy
Spirit is the authoritative, infallible guide. (3) Was
geredet sei, das die Schrift sagt, . . . (1526), a treatise
on the freedom of the will in the form of a dialogue
between the author and the reader. (4) Vom Gesatz
Gottes, Wie das Gesatz aufgehoben sei und doch
erfüllet werden muss (1526), a plea for genuine

holiness of life on the basis of Paul's ideas as expressed in Romans; man must strive to attain love for God and faith in God. (5) *Ordnung Gottes und der Creaturen Werk* (1526). This is one of Denk's most important works. It is principally a second treatise on the freedom of the will. In 12 chapters he discusses such questions as predestination, hell, heaven, the Trinity, idolatry in the pomp of the churches, and the peace of God. (6) *Von der waren Liebe* (1527), a sequel to the preceding work, deals with the love of God for man, as it is revealed in Jesus. The man who loves God has no need for institutions, which can blind his soul. This is Denk's masterpiece. It was reprinted at Elkhart, Ind., in 1888, edited by John Horsch, together with Hans Langenmantel's pamphlet on the Lord's Prayer, under the following title: *Von der wahren Liebe . . . . Auslegung des Vaterunser . . . . Zwei altevangelische Schriften aus dem Jahre 1527*. (7) *Hans Dencken Widerruf* (1528), which is a restatement of his original position and an abandonment of certain Anabaptist ideas, rather than a true recantation, given shortly before he died. (8) *Gespräch H. Dencks mit Joh. Bader über die Taufe*, which is preserved only in Bader's publication, *Brüderliche Warnung vor dem neuen abgöttischen Orden der Wiedertäufer* (1527), (9) *Micha, der Prophet, aus rechter hebräischer Sprache verdeutscht und wie den Denk auf diese letzte Zeit verglichen hab* (1532), a German version of Micah's prophecy. (10) *Etliche Hauptreden . . .*, also known by the title, *Wie Gott einig wäre . . . .* The former is the title in the appendix to the 1528 edition of the *Deutsche Theologie* (q.v.). (11) *Alle Propheten nach hebräischer Sprache verdeutscht von Ludwig Haetzer und J. Denk* (Worms, 1527).

Denk's contemporaries recognized his significance as a leader. Bader spoke of him as "the famous Hans Denk"; Bucer called him the "pope" of the Anabaptists; Rhegius called him their "abbot"; Haller spoke of him as their "Apollo"; Bullinger, as their "Rabbi"; and Vadian spoke of him as a highly talented youth. Yet it should be noted that Denk stood somewhat apart from the main theological stream of Anabaptism, and that he cannot be regarded as the spokesman of the group in those areas where he held to his peculiar emphases. His major contribution lay in the earnestness with which he contended for Christianity as discipleship, and in the beauty of his sincere Christian spirit. He is one of the few personalities of the 16th century who never indulged in controversy except with a heavy heart; not a trace of abusiveness or unfairness is to be found in his writings.

A critical edition of Denk's complete works, prepared by Walter Fellmann, appeared as *Quellen zur Geschichte der Täufer*, Vol. VI, Part II, in *Quellen und Forschungen zur Reformationsgeschichte*, Vol. XXIV (Gütersloh, 1956). Part I of this volume, published in 1955, was George Baring's exhaustive *Bibliographie* of Denk's writings.

NEFF, W.F.

Coba Boerlage, *Hans Denck* (Amsterdam, 1921); Alfred Coutts, *Hans Denck, 1495-1527: Humanist & Heretic* (Edinburgh, 1927); H. P. Gelbert, *Magister Joh. Baders Leben und Schriften* (Neustadt a.d.H., 1868); C. Ger-

bert, *Gesch. der Strassburger Sektenbewegung zur Zeit der Ref. 1524-1534* (Strasbourg, 1889); G. Haake, *Hans Denk, ein Vorläufer der neueren Theologie* (Norden, 1897); Wilhelm Heberle, "Johann Denk und die Ausbreitung seiner Lehre" *Theol. Studien u. Kritiken* (Tübingen, 1855) 817-90; idem, *Johann Denk und sein Büchlein vom Gesetz Gottes* (1851); A. Hege, "Hans Denk" (inaugural-diss., Tübingen, 1942); Chr. Hege, *Die Täufer in der Kurpfalz* (Frankfurt, 1908); A. Hegler, "Hans Denk," in *HRE* IV, 570-80; A. Hulshof, *Gesch. van de Doopsgezinden te Straatsburg van 1524 tot 1557* (Amsterdam, 1905); L. Keller, *Ein Apostel der Wiedertäufer* (Leipzig, 1882); idem, *Reformation*; idem, *Johann von Staupitz* (Leipzig, 1888); Tj. Kielstra, *Hans Denck*, No. 3 of the *Geschriftjes . . .* ; Th. Kolde, "Zum Prozess des Joh. Denk und der drei gottlosen Maler in Nürnberg," in *Kirchengeschichtliche Studien* (Leipzig, 1887); Th. Kolde, "Hans Denk und die gottlosen Maler in Nürnberg," in *Beiträge zur Kirchengesch.* VIII; H. Lüdemann, *Ref. und Täufertum in ihrem Verhältnis zum christlichen Prinzip* (1896); *Menn. Bl.*, 1883, 1886; *Monatshefte der Comeniusgesellschaft* I, 225; V, 286; VI, 77 ff., 139 ff.; VII, 230 ff.; VIII, 57; X, 173; XI, 145 ff.; G. E. Röhrich, *Essai sur la vie, des ecrits et la doctrine de l'anabaptiste Jean Denk* (Strasbourg, 1853); Ludwig Schwabe, "Ueber Hans Denk," in *Briegers Ztscht für Kirchengesch.* XII, 452-93; A. M. Schwindt, *Hans Denk, ein Vorkämpfer undogmatischen Christentums* (Schlüchtern, ca. 1922); Stieve, *Die Einführung der Ref. in der Reichsstadt Donauwörth, Sitzungsberichte der phil. hist. Klasse der Akademie zu München* (1884) 390; A. P. Evans, *An Episode in the Struggle for Religious Freedom; The Sectaries of Nuremberg 1524-1528* (New York, 1924); O. E. Vittali, *Die Theologie des Wiedertäufers Hans Denck* (Offenburg, 1932); F. L. Weis, *The Life, Teachings and Works of Johannes Denck* (Strasbourg, 1924; printed at Pawtucket, R.I., 1925), contains an attempted complete bibliography of Denk's writings with locations of extant copies; E. M. Wilbur, *A Hist. of Unitarianism: Socinianism and its Antecedents* (Cambridge, 1946); G. Baring, "Die Wormser Propheten," in *Arch. f. Ref.-Gesch.* (1934) 23-41 (with bibliography); E. Crous, "Zu den Bibelübersetzungen von Haetzer und Denk," in *Beiträge zur Geschichte der Mennoniten. Festgabe für D. Christian Neff* (Weierhof, 1938) 72-82; *ML* I, 401-14.

Denmark. Lutheran teaching found early entry into this country and soon became the established faith. But Anabaptism was unable to gain a foothold here. Melchior Hofmann was appointed as Lutheran preacher in the Nikolai Church in Kiel. But because he expressed views on the communion contrary to Lutheran doctrine, he was expelled from the country after the signing of the Peace of Flensburg in 1529. In the next year he joined the Anabaptist congregation in Strasbourg.

About the middle of the 16th century some Anabaptists expelled from the Netherlands came to Denmark, and since there were among them some skilled tapestry makers and goldsmiths and they were well behaved as a group, they were welcomed by private citizens at a number of places. But in 1554 King Christian III issued a warning to all clerical and government officials to be on their guard to prevent the infiltration of Anabaptists and ordered that every immigrant should be thoroughly questioned regarding his origin and religion. In the following year the order was repeated in sharpened form, to avoid the disturbances prevalent in Germany.

Thus most of the immigrant Anabaptists were expelled; they had, however, won some followers. Two clergymen who joined them were Christopher Michelsen of Odense, and Laurentius Hellissön, provost of Lundeherrad. They were censured by a

Lutheran bishop and warned by the "spiritual convent" in 1551. Nevertheless Hellissön baptized his grown son publicly at the beach near the Bridge of St. Anna. In 1557 they were arraigned in Copenhagen before a conference of bishops, professors of theology, and the King himself, and were declared guilty of the capital crime of *lese majesty*. The sentence was modified to life imprisonment, and they were incarcerated in Schonen and later in Soröe (Zeeland).

In 1562 King Frederick issued the "Lüneburg mandate," which again urged and commanded the Holstein authorities to exercise careful vigilance to prevent the coming of Anabaptists. Apparently some slipped in, for in 1569 he issued 25 articles, making it mandatory for all immigrants to answer very pointed questions and to be watched by the police for some time after their arrival.

After this there were no more Anabaptists in Denmark proper. In 1711, when the king of Denmark invited the Mennonites to settle in his country, they refused (*Inv. Arch. Amst.* I, Nos. 1324, 1331). (See also **Schleswig-Holstein.**)

In the spring of 1945 some 1,500 Mennonite refugees from East and West Prussia and Danzig were evacuated with some 200,000 German refugees from this region, to Denmark, by the German army and navy. At one time Mennonites were found in 34 different camps in Denmark where they remained for the most part until 1950. A small number went to Uruguay in 1948, and few to Canada, but most of them were finally allowed to enter Germany, a large part settling in the Palatinate. The Mennonite Central Committee served the refugees through a unit established in Copenhagen from December 1945 to January 1949. In 1947-48 the Mennonites were found chiefly in 9 camps as follows: Oxboel (near Vaarde), several hundred; Aalborg-Ost and Aalborg-West, 150-200; Grove (15 miles from Herning), 75-100; Rye (6 miles from Silkeborg), 100 or more; Frederikshavn, 18-25; Krudttarnsvej (near Copenhagen), 15-20; Dragoer (near Copenhagen), about 12; Gedhus (near Herning, 4 miles from Grove), about 20; Rom, a family of 5; and a group of 7 in an old people's home in Aalborg. For further information see **Danzig Refugees.**

The Danish historian, Fr. Hammerich, in his book, *Den Kristne Kirkes Historie* (1891), claims that Mennonites have been in Denmark since 1787. They supposedly came from North Germany and first settled near Frederikstad in Soenderjylland and Fredericia. They practiced immersion and called themselves "Mennonit Broederkirkens." The movement spread as far as Sweden. The first congregation in Copenhagen was established in 1871. It once had four meetinghouses, two in Sweden and two in Denmark, but lost them because of small numbers. A report by H. H. Janzen concerning contacts with this group in 1950, when it claimed 50 baptized members in Denmark, plus 25 in Sweden, 17 in Norway, and 3 in Finnland, appeared in *Mennonitische Rundschau* 73 (1950) Sept. 27, p. 3, and *Der Mennonit* IV (1951) 7. Later information indicated that this mysterious group really was not a genuine Mennonite group.   NEFF, H.S.B.

P. A. Andersen, "Die neuesten anabaptistischen Bewegungen in Dänemark," in *Ztscht f. d. hist. Theol.,* 1845, No. 2; W. Gering, "With Prussian Mennonites in Denmark," *Menn. Life* II (October 1947) 12-14; *ML* I, 388 f.

Denner, Balthasar, b. Nov. 15, 1685, at Hamburg, d. April 14, 1749, at Rostock, one of the most important portrait painters of his time. His father was Jakob Denner (*q.v.*), the well-known Dompelaar (*q.v.*) preacher of Hamburg-Altona; his mother was Katharine Wiebe. In 1710 Offenbach relates that among the important persons he visited in Hamburg was the Denner family; concerning Denner's parental home he remarks, "They [the Mennonites] in general all seem to be very fine and pious people." One of his best pupils was Dominicus van der Smissen, who married his sister Katharina.

Wichmann reports in his history of Altona that Balthasar Denner had to paint an annual portrait of Countess Reventlow in payment for the use of the church in which his father preached for the Dompelaars.   H.vDS.

Alfred Lichwark, *Das Bildnis in Hamburg,* I (Hamburg, 1898) 132-43; *Hamburger Künstlerlexikon;* Wichmann, *Gesch. Altonas* (Altona, 1865); *ADB* V, 54-57; *ML* I, 414.

Denner, Jakob (1659-1746), Mennonite-Dompelaar preacher of Altona near Hamburg, Germany, author of pietistic devotional books of wide circulation. His father was an elder of the "small" Mennonite church of Altona and a zealous champion of the Dompelaars or immersionists. In his youth Jakob learned the dyeing trade and studied mathematics and astronomy. He made long trips all over Europe. On Sept. 26, 1684, he was ordained minister of the Mennonite church in Altona, but he also preached in Lübeck (1687-94), Friedrichstadt (1694-98), and Danzig (1698-1702). Then he returned to Altona to preach for a time in the "large" Mennonite church, on the condition that he was not to preach any particularly Dompelaar doctrines. In 1708 Ernst Goverts, a wealthy Hamburg merchant, who was a deacon in the Mennonite church, helped him build a Dompelaar church. In 1732 Denner bought this church and requested the congregation to make contributions to pay for it.

Denner's strongly emotional sermons were widely acclaimed, and were attended by members of all Protestant groups. His delivery was called "gentle and sincere," and his personality "charming and pleasant." The nobility of Holstein and Denmark associated with him, and the later king of Sweden frequently attended his sermons. He never held the Lord's Supper in his congregation, and he performed the ceremonies of baptism and marriage only on his own children. Some of the orthodox Lutheran clergymen of Hamburg passionately opposed his activities (the new Pietism) and preached against him. (For an account of the open opposition in the Marienkirche, see **Schultze, Daniel Severin** and *Menn. Bl.,* 1880, 71 f.) His son Balthasar Denner (*q.v.*) was a well-known portrait painter, and his son-in-law Dominicus van der Smissen was likewise a painter. After Denner's death the Dompelaar congregation, declined, and the church was taken over by the Moravians.

Denner's writings exerted a tremendous influence in and beyond the Mennonite church, and did much to promote pietistic tendencies among the Mennonites. His extremely long and emotional printed sermons served both as devotional reading and as material to be read verbatim from the pulpit at Sunday services. He published two main sets of such sermons: (a) *Eenige Christelyke Uitbreidingen over verscheidene Schrijtuurlijke Texte* (Amsterdam and Danzig, 1706), containing 24 sermons on texts of the Old and New Testaments (at that time preaching in Hamburg and Danzig was still done in the Dutch language). Against this book Daniel S. Scultetus published his *Wohlgemeinte Warnung an die Evangelischen in Hamburg vor der Gemeinschaft des Gottesdienstes der Mennoniten* (Hamburg, 1706) (*Menn. Bl.*, 1880, 71). (b) The *Wysheid des Heeren* (Amsterdam and Danzig, 1707), containing some 50 sermons on the Gospels for every Sunday and holiday. Also against this book a violent attack was published by the Hamburg Lutheran pastor E. Neumeister (*Menn. Bl.*, 1880, 71). (c) Both these books were then republished in the same year as one volume under the title, *Eenvoudige predicatien . . .* (Amsterdam, 1707). A second edition of the combination book appeared in Hoorn, in 1771, entitled *LXXI Predicatien.*

In 1730 the first German edition of the complete sermon collection was published in Hamburg under the title, *Einfältige und christliche Betrachtungen . . .* ; Part I: *Erbauliche Betrachtungen über die Sonn- und Festtagsevangelia* (1,366 pages, the sermons of book b), and Part II: *Einfältige und christliche Betrachtungen über einige Texte des Alten und Neuen Testaments* (352 pages, the sermons of book a). It is a book of 1,718 pages quarto size. In spite of its bulk the book had a tremendous appeal to Christians of all types, there being no less than five German editions (besides the two Dutch ones), and one attempted English edition. The German editions are: 1730 and 1739, Hamburg; 1751, Königsberg; 1792, Frankenthal am Rhein; and 1860, Philadelphia. The English edition was planned in 1901, the translation was completed, the first proof sheets were published (for use in promotion), yet the undertaking eventually stopped due to lack of funds and subscribers. All posthumous editions contain besides the sermons of (a) and (b) also three sermons on the Lord's Prayer and a meditation on the nobility of the conscience. An engraved portrait of Denner is used as a frontispiece.

The story of the 1792 edition is particularly revealing. Two laymen in the Franconia (Pa.) Mennonite Conference, Johannes Herstein and Johannes Schmutz, undertook in that year the hardship of a voyage across the Atlantic to Germany for the sole purpose of procuring an edition of the big book for the brethren of their conference. When they returned they brought along and quickly sold no fewer than 500 copies of this work (Wenger, *Franconia,* 323). It demonstrates the strong pietistic interests and longings of the Mennonite church of that time and even later (1860, 1901). The book is still to be found in many Mennonite homes in the Palatinate, in Pennsylvania, and in the prairie states. NEFF, R.F.

C. B. Roosen, *Gesch. der Menn.-Gem. Hamburg-Altona* (Hamburg, 1886); R. Friedmann, *Menn. Piety Through the Centuries* (Goshen, 1949); J. C. Wenger, *Hist. of the Menn. of the Franconia Conf.* (Telford, Pa., 1938); *Menn. Bl.,* 1880, 71 f.; 1882, 29 f.; *ML* I, 414-15.

Denomination, a form of church organization in American church life, to be contrasted both to ecclesiastical institutionalism (state church type) and the brotherhood type of church life. In England with its established Anglican church, the analogous though mainly negative term is "Nonconformism"; in Germany likewise the *Freikirche* is distinguished from the *Landeskirche* or *Volkskirche,* the national church. In America, however, with its complete separation of state and church, a distinction of this kind has no clear meaning. All churches here are free churches and no church is "conformist." Hence a new kind of distinction has developed, based in the main on the type of church government, that is, on a sociological principle. The older distinction by Ernst Troeltsch (1912) between church and sect (*Kirche* and *Sekte*) seems no longer to hold true. To him the state church, in which everybody participates and of which everybody automatically becomes a member by infant baptism, no matter how much or little interest he later on takes in the work of the church, is the *Kirche;* its essential feature is its objective, institutional character. The Catholic Church is perhaps the best example of this type; yet also the Church of England, the Reformed Church in the Netherlands, and the Lutheran churches in Germany or Scandinavia are in a sense comparable to it. According to Troeltsch, everything else belongs to the "sect"-type of church organization, the term being used here in its best sense. The concept of a denomination was not yet fully developed by this outstanding sociologist of religion. As a specific type it was first studied by De Jong in 1938 ("The Denomination as the American Church Form"), and then in 1946, again by Joachim Wach (see Bibliography), who now clearly distinguishes between ecclesiastical church bodies, denominations, and sects. The ecclesiastical bodies all claim exclusiveness, authoritatively defined doctrines, sacraments and distinct orders. Under the denominational type Wach classifies the Congregationalists, the Baptists, the Disciples, and similar church bodies in which the local churches have more autonomy. For them the local congregation is the basic unit of the church; they are less bound by tradition, open to "liberal" reforms, are in brief "a voluntary society for carrying on the work of Christ . . . ." (Neve, 552.) The denomination shows the typical substitution of dignity of church office for spiritual charisma (grace). It evidences a weakening, both in authority (discipline) and inspiration. The "sect," finally, represents the morally rigid brotherhood type of church organization, the gathered church or believers' church, the Christian fellowship or a "Society of Friends" (as the Quakers call themselves). Among the sects, E. T. Clark distinguishes eschatological, charismatic, holiness, and communal groups.

The denomination is obviously the least demanding of the three groups, liberal in spirit and democratic in the sense of having no supreme central authority. Intellectuals flourish in this free atmosphere of the typical American denomination. Their "free" spirit shrinks from the rigid organization of the ecclesiastical bodies and from the rigid moral demands of the sectarians. Thus the denominational churches become seedbeds of "liberal Protestantism," gradually dissolving the original substance of the church. From this spring the ever-repeated yet not too successful revival movements. All of this is primarily true for the situation in the United States and Canada.

The implications of this analysis for the Mennonite Church here as elsewhere are quite obvious. Essentially Anabaptism and Mennonitism in its original form was a brotherhood church, the fellowship of committed disciples, with all the rigidity of such a group of conscious "nonconformists to the world." This was the type among them everywhere during the 16th century, and in Switzerland, Moravia, and Prussia even up to the 18th century. But in the Netherlands with its free and tolerant atmosphere and the absence of any oppression the shift to a denominational type (*Freikirche*) was soon achieved, hardly noticed at first, but completed in the 18th century. The same happened, perhaps slightly later, in Emden, Hamburg, Danzig, in the Rhineland (Crefeld), and in the 19th century also in the Palatinate. The church became well settled, and its prophetic tradition vanished, giving way to routine and tradition. The urbanization of the congregations helped in this process.

In America the situation was at first different. Though oppression was totally absent here, the brotherhood type survived among the Swiss-South German Mennonite immigrants to Pennsylvania because of their social isolation due to ethnic characteristics and the strongly conservative mind of the rural congregations. The same was true among the large rural congregations of Dutch-North German Mennonites in Prussia and Russia and their emigrant descendants in America, distinguished by their strong adherence to traditional Mennonite principles of separation, simplicity, and Biblicism during the 19th century, and in the American groups on into the 20th century. But almost inevitably in America, too, came the trend from the brotherhood type with all its implications to the denominational type, the adjustment to surrounding Protestantism. Evidences of this while subtle in some cases are nevertheless noticeable to some extent in all Mennonite groups, with the exception of the Old Order Amish, most Old Order Mennonites, and Old Colony Mennonites.

The most rapid shift has occurred in those groups which were formed in America by the schism of more liberal elements from the old-line conservative groups, and in those which, having broken away from their historical and traditional moorings, have come under the heavy influence of modern American Protestantism, either liberal or conservative.

The call "back to the forefathers" (Menno Simons, Conrad Grebel, Pilgram Marpeck, etc.) might be taken as an awakening toward a reverse movement, away from the denomination toward the gathered church of regenerated believers and disciples. Its success will depend exclusively upon a leadership with vision and dedication.

In conclusion it should be remarked that the same development toward the denominational type has occurred in most of the other "sectarian" groups of America. The Church of the Brethren is painfully aware of this "broken cup" (J. Ziegler). Also the Quakers with their principle of "birthright membership" are in full transition toward an established denomination with paid ministers instead of charismatic leaders. But it is true that responsible members of these groups are aware of this temptation and are trying to counteract it.   R.F.

E. Troeltsch, *The Social Teachings of the Christian Churches* (German, 1912; English at London, 1930); De Jong, "The Denomination as the American Church Form," in *Nieuw Theolog. Tijdschrift*, 1938, 347 ff.; Joachim Wach, *Church, Denomination, and Sect* (Evanston, 1946); J. L. Neve, *Churches and Sects of Christendom* (Burlington, 1940); E. Garber, "Cultural Adaptation in the Church of the Brethren," *Schwarzenau*, 1940, 17-61; J. Ziegler, *The Broken Cup, Three Generations of Dunkers* (Elgin, Ill., 1942); Richard Niebuhr, *The Social Sources of Denominationalism* (New York, 1929); S. F. Pannabecker, "The Development of the General Conference of the Mennonite Church of America" (Yale, 1944, unpublished dissertation); F. H. Littell, *The Anabaptist View of the Church, An Introduction to Sectarian Protestantism* (Amer. Society of Church History, 1952).

Denver, Col., a thriving city on the eastern edge of the Rocky Mountains, with its suburbs has a population of about a half million. The Mennonite (MC) Church has a congregation (see below) of 156 members in Denver under the leadership of Bishop E. M. Yost, the outgrowth of a mission. Maplecrest Turkey Farms, Inc., has attracted Mennonites to Denver. Mennonite nurses taking training in the Mennonite Hospital at La Junta, Col., have spent time in Denver during the final months of their training. A large group of I-W men has been serving in the Denver hospitals since 1950.   P.G.T.

Denver (Col.) **First** Mennonite Church (MC), 885 Delaware Street, is a member of the South Central Conference. The first services of the church were held on July 9, 1941, with P. A. Friesen in charge. The first communion service and the organization of the congregation took place on Dec. 22, 1941, with 25 charter members. The membership in 1949 was 100. On April 1, 1945, the work was taken over by E. M. Yost. On Jan. 5, 1947, the congregation voted to purchase the vacant lots on 9th and Delaware Street as the site for a new meetinghouse. The congregation has met in this new building for services since Dec. 12, 1948. In 1955 the membership was 156, with E. M. Yost as bishop and pastor. The Denver congregation has been host to a large group of I-W men working in the city.

V.L.G.

Denver (Pa.) Mennonite (MC) Meetinghouse. By deeds of 1878 and 1879 from the David Gockley and Brubaker farms, provisions were made for a union house and cemetery on the northeast corner of Denver, Lancaster Co., Pa. The building was first used by the Reformed, Lutherans, Brethren, and Mennonites. When the first two moved into the borough, the Reformed Mennonites and the M.C. Mennonites used this house. It was the only church used by both groups. The Reformed Mennonite membership has never been above 50. The Mennonite (MC) services were sponsored by John Bucher and the Hammer Creek ministers, but this membership has always been low. Recently all rights to the building were relinquished to the M.C. group. The Indiantown ministers conduct services there, with a Sunday-school average of 105. The membership in 1954 numbers 30. Amos S. Horst is the bishop in charge. I.D.L.

Denver (Col.) Unit No. 78 of Civilian Public Service was opened in January 1943, at the Colorado Psychopathic Hospital, and closed in March 1946. No. 78, under the Mennonite Central Committee, was one of the smaller mental hospital units. (M. Gingerich, *Service for Peace,* Akron, 1949.) M.G.

Derk Alles, elder of the Groningen Old Flemish: see **Alles, Derk.**

Derk Tasschemaker: see **Dirckgen Tasch.**

Derks, Alle, b. June 16, 1670, in Meeden, d. April 24, 1733 (*Inv. Arch. Amst.* I, No. 1094), the son of the Mennonite elder Derk Alles. In 1699 he was ordained a preacher of the Groningen Old Flemish by his father, and after his father's death he was ordained to the eldership by Jan Kriens. He took an active interest in aiding the Mennonite refugees from Switzerland. From Amsterdam, where the boats from Switzerland landed on Aug. 3, 1711, he conducted 126 persons to Groningen, and found homes for them in the city and vicinity. As a member of the Dutch Committee for Foreign Needs, he did much for the Mennonites expelled from Lithuania in 1724-26. Several times he was able to send them large amounts of money collected by the Groningen Old Flemish Mennonites in the Netherlands. In 1726 he forwarded to the preachers of the Culm district, whither a number of the Lithuanians had moved, 200 copies of the New Testament and many hymnbooks (*Inv. Arch. Amst.* I, No. 1575). Many letters and records written by or sent to Alle Derks, dealing with the needs of the Swiss and the Lithuanian-Prussian Mennonites, are found in the Archives of the Mennonite congregation at Amsterdam. In 1733 he visited the Groningen Old Flemish congregations in Prussia and Poland to administer baptism and communion, and to ordain elders. In 1713 he came in conflict with the government because he baptized a Reformed youth. All the police magistrates received the order to seize him and to close all meeting places of the Mennonites; but he remained fearlessly at his post. He published the new edition of the Biestkens Bible and wrote hymns. He edited the songbook, *Lusthof des gemoets* (Gro-

ningen, 1732), which was followed by an *Agterhofje.* This book was reprinted in 1736 with an appendix. K.V., vDZ.

Inv. Arch. Amst. I, No. 1368; Blaupot t. C., *Groningen* I, 130, 137, 143, 158, 183; II, 54; *DB* 1900, 5, 96 f.; *Bezoekreis van Hendrik Berends Hulshoff* (*Bijdragen en Meded. Hist. Genootschap* LIX, 1938, 33, 37, 41, 74); *ML* I, 415.

Derks, Jan, author of *Een Christelyke Proeve, of zijns zelfs onderzoekinge* (Deventer, 1717). This devotional treatise in the Dutch language is followed by Menno Simons' *Van de Geestelyke Verryzenisse* (Spiritual Resurrection); the volume closes with two hymns, *Twe gemoedsopwekkende liedekens,* by Jan Derks, about whom nothing further is known. vDZ.

Derstine (Thierstein, Dürstein, Dierstein, Durstine, Dirstine), a Swiss Mennonite family, in modern times found only in the Emmenthal district, canton of Bern, from which came J. R. Thierstein (1867-1941), educator and leader in the General Conference Mennonite Church. The family was in the Palatinate in the early 18th century (a Samuel Dierstein lived at Hasselbach in 1731), and is still to be found in Baden, e.g., in the Bretten congregation, and in northern Bavaria in the Trappstadt congregation.

The progenitor of the Derstines of eastern Pennsylvania was Michael Dierstein of the Palatinate who at 20 years of age arrived at Philadelphia on the ship *Samuel* Aug. 11, 1732 (Wenger, *Franconia History,* 21). A letter written to the Amsterdam Mennonites from Grumbach in the Palatinate described Michael Dierstein as unmarried. This letter was signed by the Mennonite ministers at Grumbach and stated that most of the 1732 emigrants either had money to pay their passage to America, or they were promised aid from Pennsylvania (Smith, *Mennonite Immigration,* 195 f.). Dierstein settled in what is now West Rockhill Twp., Bucks Co., Pa., less than a mile from where the Rockhill Mennonite meetinghouse now stands. He was a farmer, weaver, and miller. Dierstein became the first deacon of the Rockhill congregation not later than 1767, and died June 6, 1777. His son Isaac (1744-99) appears to have been deacon following his father; his grandson George (1770-1837) served as minister in the same congregation. Later descendants were John L. Derstine (1864-1932), deacon of the Deep Run congregation; Abraham Z. Derstine (1867-1942), minister of the Franconia congregation; Bishop Clayton F. Derstine (1891-), originally of Souderton, Pa., and now of Kitchener, Ont.; John Derstine Souder (1865-1942), local historian of Bucks Co., Pa. J.C.W.

Detmer, Alexander Heinrich (1852-1904), chief librarian at Münster in Westphalia, research scholar in history, who rendered valuable service to Mennonite history in a series of articles on the Anabaptist disorders in Münster. Of great importance is his publication of the source book by Hermann von Kerssenbroich, *Anabaptistici furoris Monasterium inclitam Westphaliae metropolim evertentis historica narratio* (in *Geschichtsquellen des Bistums*

Münster, 1899-1900). His extensive introduction to the book also appeared separately under the title, *Hermann von Kerssenbroichs Leben und Schriften* (Münster, 1900).

Other works in this field showing his thorough mastery of the material are (1) *Bilder aus den religiösen und sozialen Unruhen in Münster während des 16. Jahrhunderts* (Münster, 1903); (2) *Bernhard Rothmann, Kirchliche und soziale Wirren in Münster 1525-35;* (3) *Ueber die Auffassung von der Ehe und die Durchführung der Vielweiberei in Münster während der Täuferherrschaft;* (4) *Das Religionsgespräch zu Münster i.W. am 7. und 8. August 1533. Ein Beitrag zur Geschichte Bernhard Rothmanns und des sozialen Anabaptismus (Comeniushefte,* 1900, pp. 273-300).

Of his critical edition of the historical works of Hermann Hamelmann (*q.v.*) only the first two numbers appeared, 1902-5 (*Veröffentlichungen der historischen Kommission für Westfalen*). The book, *Zwei Schriften des Münsterischen Wiedertäufers Bernhard Rothmann,* edited by Detmer and Robert Krumbholtz, with an introduction on contemporary conditions, was published posthumously in Dordrecht, 1904. (*ML* I, 415.)   NEFF.

Detroit Lakes, Minn.: see **Lake Region** Mennonite Church.

Detroit (Mich.) Mennonite Brethren Church, now extinct, a small congregation established in 1923 as a Sunday school; for some time D. F. Strauss served them as minister. Later most of the families moved away and the church discontinued its meetings.
                                        H.E.W.

Detroit (Mich.) Mennonite Gospel Mission (MC), known locally as the Detroit Mennonite Church, located at 15559 Curtis Ave., was begun in 1926 by Mennonites who came to the city to secure employment. In 1927 the Indiana-Michigan Conference took over the work and built a small church. In 1930, it was transferred to the Mennonite Board of Missions and Charities. Over 100 persons have been baptized in the mission. The 1954 membership was 38. F. B. Raber was pastor 1930-50, J. F. Erb 1950-56, and C. Nevin Miller 1956- .   F.B.R.

Detweiler (Dettweiler, Dättwyler, Dettwiler), a Swiss Mennonite family name found widely in South Germany and in North America. The family is famous in South Germany for its agricultural achievements. The Dettweilers, who had followed Hans Reist (*q.v.*) in the division of 1693, settled first in Alsace. Elias Detweiler (b. 1735) was elder and preacher of the Schafbusch (*q.v.*) congregation. One branch of the family has been located in Bavaria since 1818. Elias, Jr., was the first elder and preacher of the Eichstock (*q.v.*) congregation near Munich. The family of Johannes Dettweiler (b.   1738), the brother of Elias, Sr., settled in Rhenish Hesse. J. N. Schwerz attributes the introduction of gypsum as fertilizer (*Düngergips*) in Palatine agriculture to Dettweiler.

Johannes Dettweiler's son Christian (1765-1838) was an unusually successful farmer and agricultural pioneer. He did much of his exceptionally fine work on the Wintersheim estate, Oppenheim district, in Rheinhessen. Christian Detweiler's brother Jakob (b. 1769) was a farmer in Kindenheim, birthplace of Christian. Christian's three sons, Johann, Peter, and Samuel, were also men of significance. Samuel became mayor of Wintersheim, and the office was still in the family in 1921. Peter's son Christian (1831-93), the oldest of the five children, made a contribution to scientific dairying in Hesse. Christian also introduced goats to Hesse, securing the best stock from Switzerland and founding the first Goat Association. Jean, the brother of Christian Dettweiler (1831-93), was a mayor, president of agricultural associations, and was especially active in the milk industry.

August Dettweiler (1839-1912) and his brother Heinrich (1840-1912) together managed a large estate, which had passed into the possession of the Dettweiler family in 1868. These Dettweiler brothers set an example of scientific farming, especially in the transition from extensive to intensive agriculture. Peter's third son, also named Peter (d. 1904), was a leader in German medical research, being himself a physician. Dr. Dettweiler was a pioneer in the successful treatment of pulmonary tuberculosis, demonstrating that it was possible to treat the disease in various climates and locations, rather than in just a few. He is called the "father of the therapeutic institutional movement (*Heilstättenbewegung*)." He was also an army doctor in the wars of 1864, 1866, and 1870.

Another Peter Detweiler (1856-1907) was a classical philologian and professor at the university of Giessen, later a prominent councilor in the Hessian government, and finally manager of the Freytag publishing house in Leipzig.

In America many Detweilers are found in the Franconia Conference in easternmost Pennsylvania north of Philadelphia, as well as in such other areas, as Ontario and Ohio, to which the Pennsylvania Mennonites emigrated. Among those who served in the ministry are Jacob Detweiler (1778-1858) of Ontario, Bishop Samuel D. Detweiler (1841-1917) of the Franconia Conference, Bishop Samuel H. Detweiler (1855-1923) of Kansas, and I. R. Detweiler (1873-1946), pioneer Mennonite missionary to India, as well as educator in America, for a time Acting President of Goshen College. William G. Detweiler (d. 1956) of Orrville, Ohio, was the radio preacher (MC) of "The Calvary Hour."
                                        E.H.C., J.C.W.

On the European Dettweilers see the article by Ernst Correll, together with the literary sources in his footnotes, *ML* I, 416-19; for the American Detweilers, see Daniel Kauffman, *Mennonite Cyclopedic Dictionary* (1937) 79 f.

Detweiler Mennonite Church (MC), located near Roseville, Ont., was one of the earlier thriving congregations of Waterloo County. Because of its decline through the loss of its young people and the lack of a resident minister, the congregation was taken over by the Rural Mission Board of Ontario in 1918, which had the old stone church repaired and arranged for regular services. For many years

J. W. Witmer was the minister in charge. Sunday morning services were conducted every second week until 1935, with little change in attendance. A series of meetings held in 1933 brought about an awakening, from which better interest dated. Lorne Schmidt was placed in charge in 1936 and served until 1938, when Moses Bowman of Kitchener was ordained for Detweiler's. The membership in 1954 was 20.   J.C.F.

L. J. Burkholder, *A Brief History of the Mennonites in Ontario* (Toronto, 1935).

Detweiler's Meetinghouse, Emmet Co., Mich., was listed as a Mennonite (MC) meeting place where services were held every two weeks in 1900. M.G.

Deunk, Machiel, is named by Wolkan, *Lieder,* 80, as the author of the martyr's hymn, "Mijn siele verheucht haer in den heer," following its acrostic. Nothing else is known about him. It is likely that his name was actually Michael Denk. (*ML* I, 419.)

Deutel, Jan Jansz, a bookseller and rhetorician in Hoorn, Holland, where he died before 1657. De Hoop Scheffer counts him among the Mennonites and has placed his writings under Mennonite authors in the catalog of the Amsterdam Mennonite library, but it has been impossible to determine this with certainty. Of his four works, Deutel himself published *Eenige Psalmen Davids en geestelyke liederen* (Hoorn, 1634) and *Huwelykx Weegh-Schael, waerin werdt overghewogen of 't huwelyck goed of quaet is* (Hoorn, 1641, reprinted 1662); the others, *Avontuerlycke ende gedenkwaerdige Gheschiedenissen* (Hoorn, 1666) and *Een cort tractaetje tegen de toovery* (Hoorn, 1670), were published after his death. In addition he prepared in 1644 an edition of the *Klein Hoornsch Liedboek* (*q.v.*), to which he added an appendix of four songs of his own composition, signed with his motto, "Voor al selfs."
                                                J.L.

Frederiks v. d. Branden, *Biogr. Wb. van Noord- en Zuid-Nederl. Letterkunde,* 200; *DB* 1887, 90 ff.; *Catalogus Amst.,* 216, 233, 273; *ML* I, 419.

Deutsch - englische Fortbildungsschule, Rosthern, Sask.: see **Rosthern Collegiate Institute.**

Deutsch-Kazun, a Mennonite village and congregation in Poland, located near Modlin below Warsaw on the left bank of the Vistula, was founded in 1776. Judging from the family names, the congregation seems to have been formed largely by emigrants from the churches at Culm and Graudenz (from Gruppe, Ewert, Kopper, Bartel; from Obernessau, Janz, Kerber, Balzer, Stobbe; from Grosswerder, Kliewer, Schröder, Penner). The old church, built in 1823, was torn down in 1891 because it was threatened by the floods of the Vistula. The new church, dedicated Oct. 30, 1892, was built with all the other buildings of the village behind a protective dam. In the years preceding World War I, the congregation numbered 548 souls, of whom 375 were baptized members. More than half lived in the village of Kazun. In 1940 the baptized membership was 260, with 144 unbaptized children.

A church record begun in 1834 indicates that the congregation was once much larger, for in 1846 there were 28 baptismal candidates and in 1851 even 38. Twenty to 25 were usual. In the 1860's a decline set in. The age of the candidates for baptism varied from 13 to 17. Deutsch-Kazun had 10 subsidiary congregations. All of them suffered in varying degrees from World War I. The church was destroyed in the war and rebuilt in 1924. For a year the entire membership was removed to the Deutsch-Wymysle congregation, 50 miles to the south.

In 1923 a Mennonite Brethren congregation was organized at Kazun subsidiary to the M.B. congregation at Deutsch-Wymysle.

The anti-German feeling in Poland after World War I, conditioned in part by Polish national feeling connected with the reconstruction of Poland as a national state, intensified by the rising tide of German nationalism accompanying the Hitler regime in Germany after 1933, plus the deliberate propagandizing by the National-Socialist movement's foreign section, made the situation of German enclaves like Deutsch-Kazun increasingly difficult. Added to this was the fact that most of the members of the congregation lived within the area of the ring of forts surrounding Warsaw, particularly the fortress Modlin. When therefore the German air force bombed Modlin in the early days of the German attack on Poland, September 1939, it was inevitable that the Kazun Mennonites should suffer. Five Mennonite homes were destroyed, and seven members were killed by an air attack Sept. 22, 1939. The Poles, naturally bitter because of the German attack, were brutally harsh toward the Germans in their midst. On Sept. 7, 1939, the elder of the church, Rudolf Bartel (ordained 1912), was shot by Polish soldiers, together with seven other members. All the remaining males of the congregation, 17-60 years of age, were interned in the Bereza-Katuska prison near Brest-Litovsk, soon to be released as the result of the German conquest of Poland. The reconquest of Poland by the Russian armies meant the liquidation of the congregation in 1945 by flight in part and by expulsion for those who remained. Wilhelm Schröder and Elder Leonard Ewert found their way into Germany. The fate of Peter Schröder and Eduard Schröder is unknown.
                                          W.K., H.S.B.

Menn. Bl., 1911, 92; 1916, 43, 61; Mannhardt, *Jahrbuch* 1883, 102; H. Wiebe, *Das Siedlungswerk niederländischer Mennoniten in Weichseltal* (Marburg an der Lahn, 1952); Erich Göttner, "Aeltester Rudolf Bartel, Deutsch-Kazun," *Gem.-Kal,* 1941, 89-93; *ML* I, 419.

Deutsch-Michalin: see **Michalin Settlement and Church.**

Deutsch-Nussdorf, a village in Hungary, where the Hutterian Brethren settled in 1548 and erected a Bruderhof; but ten years later they withdrew from it. (Beck, *Geschichts-Bücher,* 210; *ML* I, 419.)
                                              HEGE.

Deutsch-Wymysle (Poland). In 1762 Mennonite emigrants from the West Prussian congregations of Przechovka near Schwetz (*q.v.*), and of Montau-Gruppe (*q.v.*) near Graudenz made their way upstream into Poland and settled here in the province of Warsaw, district Gostynin, not far from the town of Gobin, and founded the Deutsch-Wymysle village and congregation. In 1764 a second group arrived from Przechovka. In 1818-20 and 1823-24 a further considerable influx came from Przechovka and the Brenkenhoffswalde - Franztal congregation (*q.v.*). Those who came in these last five years all joined the Deutsch-Wymysle congregation, although they settled for the most part in various villages in the adjacent German Vistula region, such as Piaski, Sordy, Korzykov, Vionczemin, Novosiadlo, Sviniary, Leonor Lyck, Piotrkovek, Lady, Arciechov, Januszev, and Sladov. Family names found among these immigrants were Balzer, Bartel, Block, Büller, Dirks, Dyck, Ediger, Ekkert, Frey, Funk, Geddert, Gerbrandt, Gertz, Görtz, Heier, Jantz, Kasper, Kliewer, Kraft, Kühn, Luther, Lyhrmann, Nachtigall, Nehring, Nickel, Pauls, Penner, Ratzlaff, Schmidt, Schröder, Unruh, Voth, Wedel, and Wilms.

The center of the Mennonite congregation of Deutsch-Wymysle was always located in the village of the same name until its dissolution on Jan. 18, 1945. A chapel and a school were built here between 1764 and 1770. Sometime between 1860 and 1864 the church burned down, destroying the original records of the congregation. It was soon rebuilt of tile with a tin roof. This meetinghouse was renovated after World War I, so that it looked quite new inside and out. The name of the original founder of the congregation is unknown to the writer; the names of some of the older elders were Wedel, Frey, Peter Buller, Benjamin Unruh, Jakob Voth, Johann Kliewer, and Johann Schmidt. Bernhard Voth served as deacon for 35 years, and was followed by Heinrich Unruh.

From time to time some families moved to Volhynia and South Russia. Since the 1870's many members of this congregation migrated to America, especially from the Vistula region. Up to that time the congregation had about 300 baptized members; after that the membership continued to decline. In 1883 many members transferred their membership to the Mennonite Brethren congregation, which was founded here through the influence of the Mennonite Brethren of Russia. Elder Jakob Voth died young. His successors, Johann Kliewer and Johann Schmidt, joined the Mennonite Brethren. Thereafter there was no further ordination of a Mennonite elder. The small remaining Mennonite congregation was served by the ministers Peter Kliewer, Peter Foth, and Jakob Foth. Only for baptism and communion services was it served by the elder of Deutsch-Kasun.

The first transfer of membership to the Mennonite Brethren occurred in 1883, when Heinrich Kliewer of Deutsch-Wymysle and Benjamin Schmidt of Arciechov joined that brotherhood and were rebaptized in Friedensfeld in South Russia. From that time on new members were won nearly every year by Elder Jakob Janz of Friedensfeld, and

preachers Nickel, H. Peters, and others of the Wymysle congregation were baptized in the Vistula and united with the Mennonite Brethren. Thus a subsidiary of the Mennonite Brethren congregation in Friedensfeld was established in Deutsch-Wymysle in 1884, which was led by Heinrich Kliewer until 1891.

On Nov. 6, 1891, Peter Ratzlaff was baptized by H. Peters and admitted into the Mennonite Brethren congregation. Ratzlaff was soon afterward chosen to the ministry and in 1893 to the eldership of the now independent Mennonite Brethren congregation in Deutsch-Wymysle. The first two persons Ratzlaff baptized were Johann Kliewer, the Mennonite elder, and Heinrich Wohlgemuth, on July 17, 1893. Kliewer was soon chosen as minister and coelder of the Mennonite Brethren congregation, and Wohlgemuth as deacon. In 1907 the last elder of the Mennonite congregation, Johann Schmidt, also united with the Mennonite Brethren and was likewise chosen to the ministry by them.

Peter Ratzlaff, Johann Kliewer, Heinrich Wohlgemuth, and Johann Schmidt served the Mennonite Brethren continuously until they were well advanced in years. The worship services of this congregation were held in the home of Heinrich Kliewer until 1894, and from that time until the end of 1914 in the home of Peter Ratzlaff. From that time until 1945 the services for all the Mennonites of the area were held in the Mennonite church; they were led by ministers of the Mennonite Brethren. By the grace of God the two congregations lived in peace and harmony throughout the 30 years.

By emigration to America the Mennonite Brethren also lost many members. At the close of 1914 their congregation had 86 baptized members. In 1920 there were 88. Between 1921 and 1938 new members were added by new converts; a total of 211 members was received during this time, giving the Mennonite Brethren a membership of 175. At the time of the dissolution of Deutsch-Wymysle the Mennonite Brethren membership stood at 157, and that of the Mennonite Church at about half that number.

Peter Ratzlaff died on Oct. 1, 1933. During his lifetime, perhaps between 1930 and 1932, a new elder and ministers were chosen by the congregation and ordained by Ratzlaff. These men were Leonhard Ratzlaff as elder, and Heinrich Wohlgemuth and Gustav Ratzlaff as preachers, and Erich Ratzlaff as deacon. Rudolf Witzke was chosen to lead the Sunday school. The Ratzlaffs chosen were all brothers, the sons of the deceased elder Peter Ratzlaff. Heinrich Wohlgemuth was the son of the deacon Heinrich Wohlgemuth, who died on July 18, 1930. Johann Kliewer died in Wymysle on Jan. 25, 1942. Johann Schmidt moved to Deutsch-Kasun at the end of 1930, where he had charge of the subsidiary Mennonite Brethren congregation, which was organized there in 1923. Other ministers there were Edmund Jantz and Rudolf Kliewer. Johann Schmidt died on Feb. 26, 1936. Of the men chosen to the ministry, Heinrich Wohlgemuth moved to Siemenkovo in the Siepr region in 1935 and joined the Baptists; he died there during the war. Edmund Jantz died in Poland after the collapse in 1946. Rudolf Kliewer was taken to Russia by the Russian army and is still missing. Leonhard Ratzlaff died of exhaustion on Aug. 12, 1946, in Frankfurt-on-the-Oder. Rudolf Witzke was taken to Russia, came back, and died in Stettin on his way to the West. Of the later ministers only Gustav Ratzlaff is still living (1951); he emigrated to Canada in 1948. The deacon Erich Ratzlaff is also in Canada.

Where are all the Deutsch-Wymysle Mennonites today? From May 15, 1947, until Dec. 31, 1950, the following members of the M.B. Church with their families have crossed the ocean:

	Members	Dependents	Total
to Canada	75	87	162
to Paraguay	18	32	52
to Uruguay	11	34	45
to Argentina	5	1	6
to Brazil		2	2
total	109	156	265

During the same period the following members of the Mennonite Church left for America:

	Members	Dependents	Total
Canada	26	20	46
Paraguay	14	10	24
Uruguay	4	8	12
Total Menn. Church	44	38	82
M.B. Church	109	156	265
Grand total	153	194	347

On Dec. 31, 1950, the following M.B. members were still in Europe:

	Members	Dependents	Total
in Germany	17	15	32
in Poland	2	6	8
missing	5	4	9

Of the Mennonite Church:

	Members	Dependents	Total
in Germany	15	21	36
missing	3	1	4

From the two congregations at Deutsch-Wymysle six young men were drafted into the Polish army before the outbreak of the war. All of them returned. Right after the outbreak of the war 15 more men (old and young) were taken away by the Poles. All of these also returned. Between October 1940 and the end of 1944, 77 young men were drafted into the German army. Fifteen of them fell on the battlefield, and eight are missing (two of them married men). The others returned. On Jan. 16, 1945, ten older men were drafted for defense. Of these, one died in a Polish prison camp, six returned, and three are missing.

After the collapse, Heinrich Foth, a teacher, was murdered in Gostynin by the Poles, and Franz Ratzlaff, a farmer, was so mistreated by the Poles on the unsuccessful flight to the West that he died on the day after his return to Deutsch-Wymysle.

Among those who emigrated from Deutsch-Wymysle to Fernheim, Paraguay, in 1930 was Friedrich Kliewer, who became a leader in the colony, returned to Germany to secure a doctor's degree in pedagogy, and then returned to Fernheim in 1940 to become the principal of the Fernheim high school until 1944. He is now a teacher at Witmarsum, Brazil. (*ML* I, 420.)   R. Foth.

Deutsche Theologie, a booklet written about 1500 by Berthold Pirstinger, Bishop of Chiemsee, Bavaria, and spiritual councilor at the court of the archbishop (not as is generally assumed, by a member of the Friends of God). It was written upon the request of the latter in the monastery of Raitenhaslach near Burghausen. It was the purpose of the booklet to counter the spread of antichurch doctrine, and also to inspire theological thinking among the clergy of Bavaria. It made so profound an impression on Luther when he read a manuscript copy in 1516 that he had it published in 1518 with the title *Eyn Deutsch Theologia, das ist ein edles Büchlein von rechtem Verstand, was Adam und Christus sey, und wie Adam in uns sterben und Christus erstehen soll* (Wittenberg). In the foreword he says, "With the exception of the Bible and St. Augustine no book has come to my attention from which I learned and shall learn more concerning the nature of God, Christ, man, and all things. . . . God grant that this book may become better known; then they will see that the German theologians are the best theologians." The book went through eleven reprints. Later on Luther, perhaps seeing in it a "source of fanaticism" (L. Keller in *Monatshefte der Comeniusgesellschaft,* 1902, 147), lost interest in it. A century later it was violently attacked by Lutheran dogmatists as "heresy." The interesting fact remains that the book was zealously distributed by nonchurch circles, such as the Anabaptists, Rosicrucians, Weigelians, and Pietists.

In 1528 it was published in the printing plant of Schöffer in Worms under the title *Theologia deutsch. Newlich mit grossem Fleiss corrigiert und gebessert. Etliche Hauptreden einem jeden schüler Christi wol zu studiren.* These "Hauptreden" were, as Ludwig Keller proves, written by Hans Denk (*q.v.*). Apparently Ludwig Haetzer sent them to Schöffer and thus brought about their inclusion in the book. It was a sort of debt of gratitude that he paid for his friend. The two writings were now to begin their course of building God's kingdom together. From now on in most editions of the *Deutsche Theologie,* of which more than 70 have been counted (*Comeniushefte,* 1902, 154), Hans Denk's additions have been included. Caspar Schwenkfeld and Sebastian Franck made it their concern to distribute the booklet. Gottfried Arnold speaks favorably of it in his *Kirchen- und Ketzer-Historie* (p. 735). Johann Arndt (*q.v.*) includes it at the end of his edition of *Deutsche Theologie* in 1597. Philip Jakob Spener adds it in his appendix to the six editions of Tauler's sermons.

The booklet can be properly understood only if one has read the author's *Onus ecclesiae* (The Burden of the Church) of 1524. Berthold holds fast to Roman Catholic doctrine. His principal source

for the doctrine is Augustine. In sharp but dignified terms he exposes the abuses of the new church,
but also sharply criticizes the ills of the old church.

The booklet contains 54 chapters. It proceeds
from Paul's statement in I Cor. 13:10, "When that
which is perfect is come, then that which is in part
shall be done away." The perfect is God; the creature, the imperfect, must destroy all personal identity and become one with God, to receive the true
nature. In Christ God has assumed human nature
and man has become divine through Him. This
must happen in each individual. As long as man
considers the creature and thereby divides humanity
into many identities, there is no glimpse into the
eternal and no crossing over into the Perfect, unless
man abandons sense and reason and forsakes himself. Then he achieves union with God and thus
enjoys the highest pleasure.

In the second part the idea of man's becoming
unified with God through obedience is further developed. Man is created for obedience. But Adam
did not remain in obedience; Christ on the other
hand accomplished perfect obedience. Our obedience must become like His; our old man must die,
the new one be born; this happens when one denies
himself and forsakes everything. Constant practice
is needed for this, lest spiritual pride and false liberty rise, which block the way to union with God.
The divine human being is much more possessed by
spiritual poverty and true humility. This can be
learned only of Christ. Only in following Him may
one experience that the true liberty, blessedness, and
union with God are one.

Jakob Horsch, Mennonite elder in Gelchsheim,
Bavaria, published a new edition of the *Deutsche
Theologie* in 1887, which was sold by Ulrich Hege
in Reihen (Baden) through the publishers of the
Gemeindeblatt (*Menn. Bl.,* 1887, 21, 71). It was
done at the urging of the elder's son John Horsch.
                                        NEFF, W.W.

Comeniushefte 1896, 44 ff. (article by F. Thudichum);
HRE XIX, 626 f.; Keller, *Reformation*; *Menn. Bl.,* 1885,
79, 87, 95; R. Mertz, *Entwicklungsgeschichte des Protes-
tantismus im Berchtesgader Land* (Berchtesgaden, 1933);
F. Selle, *Schicksalsbuch der evangelischen Kirche in
Oesterreich* (1928) 244-46; *ML* I, 421.

Deutsche Westen, Der, was published as a weekly
beginning February 1907, by Henry J. Martens,
with H. H. Fast as editor, and was printed by the
Mennonite Brethren Publishing House, McPherson,
Kan. It was a six-column publication, 15 x 22 in.
and carried mostly information and articles pertaining to the Mennonites in the prairie states and
provinces. In 1910, A. L. Schellenberg became the
proprietor and editor. Soon after this the paper
was discontinued.   C.K.

Deutsches Lehrer-Institut: see **German Teachers' Institute.**

Deutschhof, a Mennonite congregation in the Palatinate, Germany, which included until 1945 the following localities: Deutschhof and Kaplaneihof near
Bergzabern, Haftelhof between Bergzabern and Wissembourg, Geisberg and Schafbusch, one hour from
Wissembourg, and Niederrödern. The last three

are in Alsace, the others in the Palatinate. Since
1945 only the Palatinate communities belong to the
Deutschhof congregation. The origin of the church
goes back to 1716 when Johannes Krehbiel leased
the estate of the Baron of Hatzel at Niederrödern.
It later passed into the possession of Prince Max of
Zweibrücken, who leased it to Christian Dettweiler
(*q.v.*) in 1788, but during the French Revolution it
was confiscated and in 1794 sold at auction, when
Krehbiel's descendants acquired it. Today there is
only one Mennonite family living there.

In about 1720 we find Mennonites living on
Geisberg, a large estate also belonging to the Baron
of Hatzel, who apparently favored the Mennonites,
for he accepted them as renters of his estates while
the decree of Louis XIV of Sept. 12, 1712, banishing the Mennonites was still in force. The first Mennonites living here were Lehmann, Johannes Schowalter, and Daniel Hirschler. In the 1790's the
Hirschler family acquired possession of part of the
estate. At present all of it except a part of the castle
is Mennonite property. Five families occupy the
estate.

A quarter hour away is the Schafbusch, a leased
estate, which has been in Mennonite hands with few
interruptions since the beginning of the 18th century; since 1912 it has been Mennonite property.
The first renters were Peter Schowalter, Johannes
Müller, and Heinrich Schmitt. They seem to have
come at the same time as those at the Geisberg. At
any rate a preacher Johannes Borkholder of Schafbusch is mentioned in 1730. No doubt all the renters
immigrated from Switzerland (canton of Bern).
But it is not certain that they went directly to Niederrödern, Geisberg, and Schafbusch.

The Haftelhof was taken over by Mennonite renters about the middle of the 18th century, namely,
by Elias Dettweiler (*q.v.*) and Jakob (Christian)
Schowalter. The former, born in 1735 at Riedselz
near Wissembourg, as preacher and elder of the
congregation signed the Ibersheim resolutions in
1803. Since 1856 half of the estate has been in Mennonite possession.

Mennonites have been living on the Kaplaneihof
since the end of the 18th century. It belonged to
the elector Carl Theodore. He sold it in 1787 to
Joseph Schowalter of Klein-Bundenbach near Zweibrücken. The name is still represented there by
four families.

The Deutschhof came last into the congregation.
It was built in 1757. In 1794 it was auctioned by
the French government to Jakob Schowalter and
Jakob Schmitt of the Haftelhof, who were the first
Mennonites on the Deutschhof. In 1796 Jakob Lehmann was also living there. Seven Mennonite families occupy the estate at present.

Until 1848 the Schafbusch was the center of the
congregation. When the estate passed into non-
Mennonite hands, the services which had been held
in their own chapel were discontinued. In 1849 a
room was arranged for the purpose on the Geisberg. But the seat of the congregation was from
now on the Deutschhof, where a church had been
built in 1842. Since the late 1850's services have also
been held at the Haftelhof in a hall furnished for

the purpose. Services were also held from the beginning in Niederrödern in a private home; in 1875 a small church was built, which is now rarely used. Regular Sunday services were held in rotation on the Deutschhof, Haftelhof, and Geisberg until 1945.

The Deutschhof and Kaplaneihof maintained a school until 1860, when public school attendance was required. There has been a Sunday school since 1861. Each unit has its own cemetery, which is still used. Only Kaplaneihof buries its dead in the local cemetery.

The congregation belongs to the *Badischer Verband* and to the South German conference, and has been incorporated since 1892. The membership in 1941 was 115, plus 84 unbaptized children. It has never had a trained or salaried minister. The late missionary Hermann Schmitt of the Dutch Mennonite mission in Java, and pastors Otto Schowalter of Hamburg and Paul Schowalter of Weierhof stem from this congregation.

As a result of World War II the congregation has been divided. Geisberg and Schafbusch, lying on the Alsatian side of the border since 1945, form the Geisberg (*q.v.*) congregation. The Deutschhof church was burned down in the fighting of March 1945, and was rebuilt in October 1949. The present (1952) membership is 100, plus 22 unbaptized children. The ministers are Rudolf Hege (ord. 1921) and August Schowalter (ord. 1937).† (Vol. I) J.F.

P. Schowalter, "Eine Gemeinde erhält wieder ihr Gotteshaus," *Der Mennonit* (1949) 92-94; P. Hege, "Das kriegszerstörte Gotteshaus zu Geisberg wieder hergestellt," *ibid.*, 58 (both articles contain valuable historical material); *ML* I, 429 f.

De Veer (Defehr, De-Fehr, van der Veer, Devehr, Dever, Fehr, du Verre), a Mennonite family name in Holland (Claes Gysbertsz de Veer was a preacher of the Old Flemish congregation at Amsterdam in 1632-?) and in West Prussia, mainly at Danzig. Gysbert de Veer moved from Amsterdam to Danzig during the 16th century. In 1935, 17 persons of this name were counted in West Prussia (including Elbing). Leading members of the family include Isaac de Veer, elder of the Danzig "Flemish" congregation 1726-39; Jacob de Veer, 1774 minister, 1790-1807 elder of the same congregation, who edited a catechism in 1791 and helped to prepare the first High German songbook in 1780. Members of the family emigrated back to the Netherlands and also to Russia (Chortitza) and subsequently to Canada. Today the name is also represented in Mexico and Paraguay. C. A. De Fehr of Winnipeg, Man., is a lay leader in the M.B. Church. G.R.

Deventer, a city in the Dutch province of Overijssel, 1947 pop. 45,000, with 411 Mennonites, the seat of a Mennonite congregation. The Anabaptists made their first appearance here in the 1530's. The first phase of Anabaptism in this city was of a revolutionary character, under the direct influence of Münster and later of Batenburg (*q.v.*). The cry of the New Jerusalem in Münster appealed to the lowly as well as the upper classes, promising the baptized and the elect a happy life under the dominion of Christ. Hille van Renssen, a widow, Aleid ten Poorten and Lubbe van Wijnssen, as well as her brothers, the mayor Jacob van Wijnssen, and

Johan van Wijnssen de Jonge, W. Jurriaen, an apothecary, and several others went to Münster in 1533-34, and were baptized either in Deventer or in Münster. Upon their return to Deventer government authorities arrested them or banished them from the city. Jacob van Wijnssen and five other Anabaptists were beheaded on de Brink (a square) in February 1535, and Fenne, the wife of the notorious leader Jan van Geelen (*q.v.*), was drowned in April. Nevertheless the doctrine continued in secret, despite the repeated proclamations of the government, and after 1540 showed itself in the revolutionary following of Batenburg and later of the mystical David Joris (*q.v.*). Jurriaen Ketel (*q.v.*), the publisher of Joris' *Wonderboek*, was beheaded for this publication on Aug. 9, 1539, and the printer Dirk van Borne (*q.v.*) was arrested with Albert Paffraedt, who had printed several tracts by David Joris. They were released six months later when they had proved their faithfulness to the Catholic Church.

After this repression, Anabaptism was hardly felt in Deventer until about 1570, when religious strife was renewed and in March 1571, 12 peaceful Mennonites, six men and six women, were dragged from their homes by the Spanish soldiers and imprisoned, at times racked and finally beheaded or burned by the Inquisition. Most of them valiantly persisted in their faith (*Mart. Mir.* D 552 ff., E 885 ff.). When Deventer was freed from the Spanish yoke in 1578, the Mennonites again appeared there and held secret meetings, although this was forbidden by the magistrate. Their refusal to serve as armed guards gave rise to some brief difficulties in 1580. Quietly and little noticed by the world they continued to hold their meetings, living on a high moral plane, withdrawn from the world. Incited by intolerant Reformed preachers, the government forbade their meetings in 1619, 1620, 1623, 1628, 1652, 1663, and 1670. But these regulations were never seriously carried out. In 1651 the States-General passed a ruling in the *Naerder Unie* stating that though the Mennonites were among the groups excluded from the protection of the government, they were to be quietly tolerated. At that time they had in Deventer two congregations, one of the Old Flemish, which met in the home of their preacher Abraham Willemsz Cremer (*q.v.*), and one of High and United Flemish, who had Jan ten Cate as their preacher and met in the home of Ananias Willink. The Reformed found this toleration of the Mennonites offensive, and in 1669-70 tried to turn the government against them with charges of Socinianism, with the proposal that the Mennonites be required to answer 12 questions as a test. The result was that many polemics were printed, bringing new government prohibition of their meetings, which was, however, not seriously enforced.

For the free exercise of their religion they paid 3,000 Reichstaler in 1672-74, when Deventer was occupied by the armies of the Catholic bishops of Cologne and Münster. In 1690 they acquired release from civil defense by purchasing and presenting to the city two fire engines, which were operated throughout the 18th century by Mennonites, and which are now in the Deventer museum. They were several times refused admittance into the guilds, and were forbidden to perform marriages in their church (provision of 1670). But this was the last act of unfriendliness on the part of the government. In 1711 many Swiss Mennonite refugees were lodged in Deventer and later given homes.

The two congregations united in 1720, after several members had withdrawn and moved to Hoogezand (*q.v.*) in the province of Groningen on account of growing worldliness in the Deventer congregation. The congregation developed quietly. They made large gifts to their brethren in Poland, Lithuania, and Danzig, as well as to non-Mennonites, such as the Reformed refugees from Frankfurt in 1685. They sometimes also received large legacies. As late as 1662 they had to contribute such a legacy to the city for poor relief. In 1627, surprisingly, a deaconess was in charge of the care of the poor; this office was later given to a brother. Slight misunderstandings such as on the wearing of the periwig were settled on a friendly basis. The Old Flemish congregation had bought a church in the Korte Assenstraat in 1687, which was used until 1892. Baptism and communion were usually conducted by elders from Groningen. In 1761 the congregation called its first theologically educated minister; he was Hendrik Waerma. He was succeeded by Wybo Fijnje, 1774-76; Jacob Kuiper, 1775-1821; J. H. Halbertsma, 1821-56; H. ten Cate Hoedemaker, 1856-89; S. Lulofs, 1889-1902; A. H. van Drooge, 1902-39; and H. P. Tulner, 1939- . In 1797 the hitherto conservative congregation added an organ.

At present the congregation meets every Sunday in a beautiful church in the Penninckhoek on de Brink, which replaced the old church in 1891. It has never been large, but increased in membership in the 19th century. At the time of the union of the two congregations in 1720 there were about 40 members; in 1784, 37; 1840, 80; 1898, 255; 1950, 325. The congregation has very rich archives. It has a Sunday school for children, a missionary sewing circle, a young people's organization, and choir.

                                                    J.C.vS., vdZ.

Inv. Arch. Amst. I, Nos. 69, 84, 90, 246, 263, 267, 271, 278, 309, 318, 347 f.; II, Nos, 1261, 1691; *DB* 1870, 16 ff.; 1879, 3, 97; 1919, 1-109; *ML* I, 430.

Deventer, Hendrik van, an Anabaptist martyr: see **Hendrick Beverts.**

Deverakonda (India), a Mennonite Brethren mission station, is located 65 miles southeast of Hyderabad. Evangelistic work was begun in this area by J. H. Voth in 1913 and government sanction for a mission station was obtained in 1918. On the premises procured, the following main buildings have been erected: two residences for missionaries, church and school building, hostels for school boys and school girls, hospital, and Bible school quarters. Resident missionaries who have been stationed here for a longer period of time are the J. H. Voths, P. V. Balzers, J. A. Wiebes, Mary C. Wall, Helen L. Warkentin, and Rosella Toews. Among the activities of note on the station are the various church services, the work in the hospital, the conducting of a middle and primary boarding school, and of a

Bible School since 1946. The Deverakonda station field, which comprises an area of 1,200 square miles and has a population of 200,000, has many outstations and a total communicant church membership of 3,000.   J.H.L.

Devotional Covering: see **Prayer Veiling.**

Devotional Literature, *Anabaptist and Mennonite.* This term includes any religious book other than strictly doctrinal or theological works, intended to be used mainly for home devotion, that is, for meditation and prayer and also for uplift (edification). Books of this kind might further be used to strengthen the spirit in times of temptation and weakness, or to confirm one's own stand in an adverse situation, or to clarify one's faith by outline —confessions and catechisms. In short, all these books serve the practice of an inner rather than an external (ecclesiastical) devotion of an earnest believer; i.e., they support his "pious exercise of the mind," as it occasionally was termed. To this category of devotional literature belong prayer books, Bible stories, books for daily meditation, allegorical writings (e.g., the pilgrimage tot the eternal city); documents of particular experiences such as epistles, testimonies, diaries, and also chronicles, and so forth; hymnals; catechisms; and a host of small and large tracts of all kinds. Finally, also printed sermon collections must be counted among these books though often they were used not only for domestic but also for ecclesiastical purposes.

The English term "devotional literature" is wider than the corresponding German word *Erbauungsliteratur* (edificatory literature), which has a strong emotional tinge. The English word is more general, while *Erbauung* suggests a certain "pietistic" tendency. Thus Karl Holl's contention that a devotional literature did not come into full development until the time of Pietism (*q.v.*) during the second half of the 17th century, remains a controversial statement. Home devotion is as old as Christianity, and aids to it such as prayer books and books of meditation are not only well known during the Middle Ages but became a particularly popular literature with the coming of the Protestant Reformation. The *Hortulus Animae* (*Seelengärtlein,* pleasant garden of the soul) is a very old and tested type of such devotional literature, and there is no church in Christianity without printed prayer collections. The old prayer book by Habermann (1567), for instance, became a particularly well-liked manual in Lutheran Germany and soon found entrance also among Mennonite groups. It is, however, true that the entire character of home devotion changed with the centuries, and that with the rise of Pietism proper, the need for such printed aids vastly increased (books up to 2,000 pages became common) while the quality, the concreteness of the faith expressed, was clearly lowered.

Mennonites were no exception to this general trend. They produced devotional books as had their 16th-century Anabaptist forefathers. It must, however, be stressed that the entire Anabaptist-Mennonite devotional literature is rather small as compared with that of the dominant Protestant denominations (Lutheran and Reformed). The main devotional book of the Anabaptists and Mennonites was, and still is, the Bible; all the rest are but auxiliary to it. Mennonite devotional literature is almost completely devoid of books for daily meditation (they later borrowed them from the Pietists), of diaries (such as the Methodists cherish), of mystical journals (like those of the Quakers G. Fox, John Woolman, etc.), and of pious novels (like those by Jung-Stilling, *q.v.*, which were so much favored by the Mennonites later on). On the other hand, the writings of Menno Simons and Dirk Philips were in the deepest sense devotional literature. Though doctrinal, they were not systematically theological, like, e.g., Calvin's.

To secure an adequate understanding of Mennonite (and Anabaptist) devotional literature, one must organize the entire material into great periods according to the centuries which produced it. The 16th century (Anabaptist) was a time of concreteness and sternness in matters of faith, while the emotional element was given little attention. Confessions of faith, testimonies such as *Rechenschaften* and *Verantwortungen,* and martyrs' epistles including their background story, prevailed. The 17th century showed a decided change. The great spiritual upheaval, so to speak, was over, and denominations became more or less settled. Creedal orthodoxy and the adjunct systematic theology on the one side, emotional inwardness and subjectivity (the beginning of Pietism proper) on the other side, became typical for this century. Moreover, a rationalistic and ethical Christianity came more and more to the fore, likewise influencing the literature of devotion. The 18th century, finally, saw this Protestant emotionalism and subjectivism in full, even rampant flowering. The "confessional Christianity" of the beginning made room for an emotional, mystical, or ethical appreciation of the revealed truth. "Godliness" became the key word of the new piety and its literature. The individual was of greater importance than the brotherhood.

Devotional literature of the 16th century. Confessional writings (*Bekenntnisschriften*) stand first in this survey. Books like Menno Simons' *Foundation of Christian Doctrine* (1539) or Dirk Philips' *Enchiridion or Handbook* (1564) were widely read in Dutch as well as in German translation by the varied groups of Mennonites in the North and Anabaptists of South Germany. The distinction between devotional and doctrinal literature (*q.v.*) was not yet as sharply drawn as in the 17th century since even outspoken doctrinal books were not yet of a systematic theology type but rather of a testimonial character. The Hutterites, likewise, had a number of *Rechenschaften* and other confessional writings which show the same border quality (see **Riedemann, Walpot**). Next to this confessional reading material come the religious tracts which abounded in the great period of rising Anabaptism. Volumes V and VII of the *Bibliotheca Reformatoria Neerlandica* (1909-11) contain a fine collection of such tracts, all too little studied as yet, although the *Doopsgezinde Bijdragen* contain numerous studies of the earlier Dutch Mennonite literature.

Likewise Lydia Müller's *Glaubenszeugnisse oberdeutscher Taufgesinnter* (1938) contains tracts of this nature. J. C. Wenger has translated a number of such early tracts taken from a unique *Sammelband* (*MQR* 1945-47). A further category of 16th-century devotional literature is the epistles of the brethren, primarily the martyrs' epistles (see **Epistles,** Anabaptist). They represent the devotional reading proper among the Swiss and Hutterite Brethren. There was very little emotionalism and Pietism in them but rather the expression of a concrete and practical Christianity by which they lived. They exhort the addressees to remain steadfast in faith and to trust God's promise. Finally, the brethren loved to read and to hear about their great forerunners who suffered martyrdom for conscience' sake. Pamphlets like that which told the story of Michael Sattler (*q.v.*) or that which recorded Thomas von Imbroich's farewell circulated widely among all groups. Above all, the Hutterite great chronicle (*Gross-Geschichtsbuch*) is a living example of the chief interest of the Brethren. It was not only a historical record of the past, nor a mere reading for private edification, but a book intended to be studied and followed and abided by in its major truths. The codices of the Hutterites contain a great number of still another type of devotional reading not strictly deriving from their own kin. They accepted Hans Denk, Balthasar Hubmaier, Langenmantel, Salminger, and many more of the so-called "spiritual reformers" (*q.v.*) readily if their writings suited the general need. No study has yet been published regarding the immense scope of this handwritten devotional material.

Devotional literature of the 17th century. Now the picture changed to a large extent. The great tide of Anabaptism receded. In Holland and northern Germany Mennonites became an increasingly settled denomination of well-to-do middle-class people, while the rural Swiss Brethren barely maintained their existence in Switzerland or the Palatinate, lacking altogether major leaders. Formalism and Pietism could not create a devotional literature of any significance. The same was true of the Hutterites, although they had at least one outstanding man, the *Vorsteher* Andreas Ehrenpreis (d. 1665, *q.v.*), who gave new impulses to their weakened faith. His tract, *Ein Sendbrief . . . brüderliche Gemeinschaft, das höchste Gebot der Liebe betreffend* (1652), is one of the finest products of 17th-century Anabaptism (printed edition, Scottdale, 1920). The most outstanding type of religious literature of 17th-century Mennonitism is to be found in the martyr books (*q.v.*). Building upon the great first model, *Het Offer des Heeren* (1562), they were more and more developed in subsequent editions by different editors and their groups, culminating finally in the outstanding work of the 17th-century Mennonites, van Braght's *Martyrs' Mirror* (1660). The significance of this book for Mennonites is beyond discussion, yet in the present context it is a question not easily decided whether the book served primarily as a devotional reader for private edification according to the new piety, or rather as a book of examples to be emulated, such as the 16th-century pamphlets or the Hutterite Chronicle were intended to be. After all, the old spirit of the "suffering church" in a hostile world was by no means completely dead but lingered on through the centuries.

The question is not restricted to the *Martyrs' Mirror.* Ludwig Keller (*Joh. Staupitz . . .* , 395) observed that the old Anabaptist tracts and epistles which had completely disappeared in the later 16th century, suddenly experienced a revival around 1610-20. The writings of Denk, Salminger, Entfelder, Bünderlin, etc., now found new publishers and readers, and rarely did a single edition satisfy the demand. Apparently they were now read with new eyes; what once meant a confessional testimony now became an *Erbauungsschrift,* a book of edification, interpreted in the spirit of the new piety (namely, without the urge to follow such a concrete and often dangerous faith). The anonymously published collections of Anabaptistica, *Geistliches Blumengärtlein* (Amsterdam, 1680), and *Güldene Aepffel in Silbern Schalen* (Basel?, 1702), give ample evidence of this new predilection for Anabaptist literature made undynamic. Gottfried Arnold's great *Kirchen- und Ketzer-Historie* (1699), the outstanding link between Anabaptism and Pietism, then presented large excerpts from Anabaptist sources to its pious readers.

In the Netherlands the new type of undynamic devotional literature begins earlier than with Mennonites and Anabaptists anywhere else. Pieter Pietersz (*q.v.*) 1625 and J. P. Schabalie (*q.v.*) 1635 are among the first Mennonite authors who provided their church with devotional reading material of a new style. A very popular devotional "manual" was produced by T. T. van Sittert (*q.v.*) in 1664, called *Glaubensbekenntnis . . .* , following a Prussian Mennonite model of 1660. In Hamburg, Gerhard Roosen produced around the turn of the century a most popular catechism of the Mennonites, the *Christliches Gemüthsgespräch* (*q.v.*) 1702, together with other devotional reading material entitled *Unschuld und Gegenbericht,* 1702, pleading for the complete harmlessness of the Mennonite position.

The 17th century also saw the intrusion of a large amount of non-Mennonite literature into Mennonite homes, both in the Netherlands and in Germany. From Johannes Arndt's *Wahres Christentum* (1605) and *Paradiesgärtlein* (1612) to Gottfried Arnold's *Kirchen- und Ketzer-Historie* (1699), a long line of (Lutheran) devotional material became more and more the favorite reading with South German and Swiss Brethren. This type of literature then increased during the 18th century when Mennonites deviated still further from their original path, opening hearts and minds to this new kind of piety of the enjoyment of one's certain salvation after having overcome sin and reached a state of sanctification.

The late 17th and 18th centuries were characterized by a strange antagonism of rationalism (e.g., Socinianism, Arminianism, Collegiant groups) on the one side, and emotionalism (pietism, mysticism, quietism) on the other side, both replacing the

former simple but concrete Biblicism of the Brethren. The *Catalogus* of the Mennonite library at Amsterdam has a very large section on such *Stichtelijke lectuur* (edificatory reading), and one of the Mennonite historical libraries in the United States has considerable collections of non-Mennonite German devotional reading material collected from Mennonite homes, once eagerly read (as many signs indicate) but today completely unknown and ignored. Hardly any work of lasting significance was produced during this period by the Swiss or South Germans, with the exception of the *Ernsthafte Christenpflicht* (*q.v.*), the Palatinate prayer book of 1739. Apparently the genius of Anabaptism did not fit into this new piety, and the lack of such a tradition resulted in borrowing and adjustments to something which was essentially foreign. The great Lutheran prayer book by J. F. Starck, 1727, Madame Guyon's meditations, Carl Heinrich von Bogatzky's *Güldenes Schatzkästlein der Kinder Gottes,* 1718 (65th edition 1904), Jung-Stilling's mystical novels, and many more such books were now found in almost every Mennonite preacher's library, not to speak of the many bulky sermon collections, Mennonite and non-Mennonite. The most remarkable non-Mennonite book, however, adopted and assimilated into an everyday devotional book (of the Amish), is the *Geistliches Lustgärtlein* (originating around 1770), otherwise completely unnoticed in reference works and of uncertain background. It, too, is a kind of *Hortulus Animae,* with an extreme moralistic first part, the *Heilsame Anweisungen und Regeln eines gottseligen Lebens.* Sermon collections likewise increased in size and popularity. They were read from the pulpit but also used for home devotion. Joost Hendricxs, Tieleman van Braght, Willem Wynands, Joannes Deknatel, Jakob Denner, and many more Dutch preachers competed in this prolific production with non-Mennonite authors.

The 19th and 20th centuries of European Mennonite devotional production was rather insignificant. Ellenberger's *Bilder aus dem Pilgerleben* (1878-83) and Bernhard Harder's *Geistliche Lieder* (1888) might deserve mention (Ellenberger was a Palatinate preacher and Harder belonged to the Molotschna Mennonite Church in Russia). The main interest shifted more readily to historical studies of a pragmatic character.

Mennonites in the United States were not too creative either. Bishop Henry Funk's *Spiegel der Taufe* (1744) and *Restitution* (1763) are the only new books which came out of the 18th century, while Christian Burkholder's *Anrede an die Jugend* (1804) and A. Godshalk's *New Creature* (1838) remained for a long time the only new additions to the stock of books brought over from the old countries. Reprints of all these older books occurred in due time (mainly in Pennsylvania, later in Elkhart, Ind.), but the creative inspiration of a great past had died out completely, giving way to a traditional, often dry, formalism or to a new urge for historical appreciation of the things that once had filled the forefathers with so much faith and daring.

Surveying the entire field, certain generalizations are suggested by this array of books: while the piety of the great period of the 16th-century Anabaptists and Mennonites was dominated by the principle of the "fear of God" whose Word had to be obeyed, later periods softened this attitude, replacing it more and more by the principle of "godliness" (*Gottseligkeit*). The stern consciousness of obedience to God ("that He might be satisfied with us")—a challenge to the world—gradually changed into a mild enjoyment of the certainty that the faithful (or reborn) one is saved and now in God's grace. That is, the content of the new and individualistic piety was no longer "Anabaptist" in character. *Bekenntnis-Christentum* (confessional Christianity) has given way to a conventional Christianity, and the intimate brotherhood has changed into a conventicle of separate individuals. The devotional literature, however, may be regarded as the true mirror of all these transitions and as an indicator of the spiritual life of the church and its members.

Sources: Most of the material discussed can be found today in the Mennonite historical libraries where it found a deposit after it was no longer used by the English-speaking churches. In the present article neither hymnals (*q.v.*) nor catechisms (*q.v.*) are treated. The original devotional literature of the Mennonites in Russia (since 1789) seems to be rather small and secondary to non-Mennonite literature used. For that reason it was left untouched in this rapid survey; P. M. Friesen's comprehensive *Brüderschaft* gives little information in this field.

R.F.

R. Friedmann, *Menn. Piety Through the Centuries* (Goshen, 1949), Part II, deals with Mennonite devotional literature 1600-1800, covering Holland, Danzig, Hamburg-Altona, Swiss Brethren, and America, with separate treatments of Mennonite prayer books and non-Mennonite devotional literature used by Mennonites. As to the literature during the 16th century see in addition to the articles refered to above, R. Friedmann, "The Schleitheim Confession and Other Doctrinal Writings of the Swiss Brethren in a Hitherto Unknown Edition," *MQR* XVI (1942). J. C. Wenger has translated from this edition a number of tracts in the *MQR* 1947-48 and plans to continue. Lydia Müller's *Glaubenszeugnisse oberdeutscher Taufgesinnter*, 1938, and *BRN* V-VII (1909-11); Keller, *Reformation*, has thoroughly studied the little-known tracts, as have Rembert, Wappler, and Rufus M. Jones after him. W. Wiswedel's *Bilder und Führergestalten aus dem Täufertum* (Cassel, I, 1928; II, 1930; III, 1952) and many later essays also contain good material still to be studied. See also the informative article "Erbauungsliteratur" in *RGG*.

Deyevka: see **Orenburg Mennonite Settlement.**

Deyevka Mennonite Church, Orenburg settlement (*q.v.*), Russia, was a subsidiary of the Chortitza Mennonite Church in the Ukraine, founded in 1894. Abram Olfert of Kanzerovka was chosen as the first minister. The elder of Neu-Samara performed the functions of elder until Aug. 16, 1899, when Abram Penner of Nikolaevka was ordained to that office. After that time the congregation was independent, but remained in close contact with the mother church.

One of the outstanding ministers was the aged Jakob Rempel, who was always ready to encourage the downhearted and calm the impulsive. He stood firmly on the basis of the unity of all God's children. The democratic, fraternal attitude of the older ministers to the younger newly ordained ones was also a good influence in the congregation. Thus the church grew until 1907.

At that time discord over the location of the proposed Zentralschule arose between the elder with two or three ministers on one hand, and the remaining ministers on the other hand, which soon spread to the congregation. After about three years a large part of the membership demanded the withdrawal of Elder Penner from active service. He therefore retired, but kept the title of elder. Johann Bärgmann of Nikolaevka served the Deyevka congregation as elder about two years, until Heinrich Rempel was chosen to that office. Rempel served for about 12 years (1911-23?) until his death by tuberculosis. During this period came the revival through the agency of J. J. Peters.

On March 29, 1925, Isaak Krahn was chosen to the office of elder. He was a teacher by profession, and had served as minister since 1911, was very talented and strong of will. By that time the Red government was already a power to be reckoned with. Church organization became weaker and functioned with difficulty. Elder Krahn was strongly opposed to emigration. In 1930 he was banished to the Solovetski Islands in the White Sea for a period of ten years. It is thought that he survived the experience, but exact information is lacking.

Many of the members of the congregation went through similar experiences; some were released on certain conditions. Worship services ceased. Only pastoral care could be continued to a certain degree in secret. Dietrich Lepp of Deyevka was apparently an exception, for a letter of 1935 indicated that people were surprised that he was still performing full ministerial service (baptism and communion) for the congregation of Deyevka. But two years later he himself wrote that he had changed his address, but could not reveal the reason. He had been compelled to work very hard, and had broken two ribs by carrying a heavy load. As a consequence of this accident he died in 1939 at the age of 82.

Until 1926 the congregation at Deyevka had been served by about 25 ordained brethren. Three had come to the place as ordained ministers; the others were chosen there. Six were lost through death, three by moving away, and two by change of church membership. The congregation had a membership of about 1,300.

The relations between the Deyevka Mennonite Church and the Mennonite Brethren left much to be desired but gradually improved, especially during the Soviet rule.

P.P.D.

P. P. Dyck, *Orenburg am Ural* (Clearbrook, B.C., 1951) 60-66; *ML* I, 456.

Deyevka Zentralschule, Orenburg Mennonite settlement, Russia, was established in 1920, and continued for three years under a Russian principal named Korobov. I. P. Reimer served as second teacher in 1920-21, D. H. Koslovsky as second teacher in the last two years, and a Russian Svonov as the third teacher in the last year.   H.S.B.

P. Dyck, *Orenburg am Ural* (Clearbrook, B.C., 1951).

Deyl, Samuel van, Dutch Mennonite preacher of the Flemish branch. He was chosen preacher in a somewhat irregular way during a schism of the congregation at Utrecht on July 3, 1664. How long he served in Utrecht is not known, but in May 1666 he was named as a preacher of the Flemish congregation of Leiden. In May 1671 he left Leiden and moved to Amsterdam, where he served 1671-87. Together with Samuel Apostool (*q.v.*), the well-known Zonist elder of Amsterdam, he published a catechetical booklet, *Waerheydts-oeffeningh tot bevorderinge van kennis en godtsaligheydt* (Amsterdam, 1677).   vDZ.

Inv. Arch, Amst. I, No. 909; L. G. le Poole, *Bijdragen tot de kennis van ... de Doopsgez. te Leiden* (Leiden, 1905) 10, 30; *DB* 1916, 182; H. W. Meihuizen, *Galenus Abrahamsz* (Haarlem, 1954) 123.

Dhamtari, pop. 17,278, an important town in the Raipur District, Madhya Pradesh, India. It is headquarters for the Dhamtari Tahsil, a political division comparing approximately to a county in the United States. Its importance lies also in the fact that it is the terminus of a narrow-gauge railway line from Raipur, 50 miles to the north on the main Bombay-Calcutta line of the Bengal Nagpur railway. From here roads radiate to the south, east, and west, so that Dhamtari becomes the trading and shipping center for points 100 and more miles distant. Among the goods shipped from Dhamtari are forest products such as timber, shellac, morabulum nuts and biri (cigarette) leaves, along with rice, hides, and other farm produce.

Dhamtari is the headquarters of the Mennonite Church (MC) in India (successor to the American Mennonite Mission), established in 1899 and merged with the church organization in 1952. There is here a congregation of 558 members, worshiping in a large brick church. The Dhamtari Christian Academy, Dhamtari Christian Hospital, Samuel Burkhard Memorial Boys' Orphanage, and a nursing school are church-mission institutions located here.   J.D.G.

Dhamtari Christian Academy, an educational institution of the Mennonite Church (MC) in India (formerly the American Mennonite Mission), opened in 1931, consisting of high school, middle school, normal training, and primary practicing school departments; located in Dhamtari, Madhya Pradesh, India. It is coeducational with total enrollment of 595 in all departments, excluding practicing school. Of this total 462 are boys and 133 are girls. In addition 118 boys and 73 girls, total 191, are enrolled in the primary practicing school, making the grand total of pupils in all departments 786. Thirty-one teachers, 21 men, 10 women, make up the teaching staff. The following have served as principal since the beginning of the Academy: E. E. Miller, 1931-37; J. D. Graber, 1937-38; S. M. King, 1938-44; Wilbur Hostetler, 1944-46; J. N. Kaufman, 1946-47; S. M. King, 1947-53; J. W. Samida, 1953- . The Academy fits into the school plan of the

province as follows: years 1-4, primary; 5-8, middle; 9-11, high. Normal training is a two-year course corresponding to years 9 and 10, and graduates qualify for primary level teaching certificate.

The American Mennonite mission maintained primary schools and at least one middle and high school as well as a Bible school from the earliest years. In 1931 the Academy was organized combining the various schools into an integrated institution. The normal training department was closed in 1946 but reopened in 1951. The special year of Bible study was discontinued in 1946 and Bible classes are combined with the regular curricula in the various departments. The church co-operates with Bible schools and seminaries in other areas to provide special Christian worker training. (See **Mennonite Church in India**.)   J.D.G.

Dhamtari Medical Station of the American Mennonite Mission (MC) and the Mennonite Church in India is situated about a mile northwest of the city of Dhamtari, Madhya Pradesh, India. The buildings in Sundarganj, a suburb of Dhamtari, became too small to meet the need after the arrival of Dr. C. D. Esch in 1911. In 1912 the mission purchased the present site and built a medical dispensary and huts for patients. The medical missionary's bungalow was finished in 1913. The work of the medical station grew to such proportions that lines of wards for the hospitalized, an enlarged dispensary with laboratory, operating rooms, examination and dispensing rooms, and clinical facilities were added and an X-ray machine installed.

The poor are given rooms without charge, while wealthier patients are glad to pay for the service. In this ministry of healing religious teaching is given in daily devotional services with the sick, with an appeal to accept Christ as their Saviour. Christian literature is put at the disposal of patients and visitors. Prayer is always offered at the side of the patient on the operating table before operating.

During recent years the whole medical program of the mission was co-ordinated, so that all mission dispensaries are under the supervision of the medical missionaries. The medical station remained the medical center with station dispensaries as outposts, all to relieve the sick and to bring Christ to the people and the people to Christ.

The ministry of healing as a mission of pure love, usually without remuneration, has meant more to the Christian work in India than can be calculated. It has helped the Christians cast off their faith in witch doctors and medicine men. It has also given definite teaching on sanitation, the dangers of quackery and harmful drugs, the need for prompt and scientific treatment, and has offered sympathetic help for the ills of both mind and body.

      G.J.L.

Dialect, a local or provincial form of a major language differing from the standard or literary language. Dialects are usually sister languages of the ancestor of the modern standard form, which was at some point in history elevated to that status. Thus the basis of literary German (*Hochsprache* or *Schriftsprache*, popularly known as High German) is an elevation of the dialect or local forms used by Luther in his German translation of the Bible, giving its descendant its status as the accepted literary language of all German-speaking peoples. It is therefore difficult to draw a sharp distinction between a "dialect" and a "language." All the early Anabaptist literature is written in the particular dialect of the area which produced it. Many of these works are therefore valuable in the field of linguistics, an outstanding illustration being the Hutterite chronicles (*q.v.*), particularly in the Zieglschmid editions.

Among the dialects widely used by the Mennonites of Dutch and North German origins is Low German (*q.v.*) or Plattdeutsch. Mennonites took this dialect to Russia and from there to Canada, the prairie states, Mexico, and other countries in Latin America, where it is used in many homes today. (See also **Oosters.**)

The majority of American Mennonites living east of the Mississippi River until a generation ago used the Pennsylvania-German (*q.v.*) dialect. The Old Order Amish Mennonites use it almost exclusively in their family and social life, and to a certain extent in their church services. Eastern Pennsylvania Mennonites and other Mennonites of Amish background are generally familiar with this dialect, often referred to as the Pennsylvania Dutch. The dialect was brought to America by the immigrants from southwestern Germany, chiefly the Palatinate.

Mennonites in Switzerland have always used Swiss-German (*q.v.*) dialects and immigrants from that country have transplanted their mother tongue to Ohio, Indiana, and other states where they have settled. Today in the Swiss-German Mennonite communities of those states, the older generation has retained a limited knowledge of the language. An Alsatian German dialect is used by Mennonites in Alsace and immigrants from that area brought it to America, where it, however, unlike other Mennonite dialects in America, has almost completely disappeared. Other dialects spoken by Mennonites in Europe and transferred to America by immigrants include Galician (basically Palatine and Alsatian), Volhynian (a modification of Galician), and Hutterite (basically Carinthian). M.G.

Dialogus, *ofte 't Samenspraeck . . . Tracteerende het stuck van buytentrouwen, waerin verthoont wort de onvryheyt die een rechtgeloovige daerin heeft* . . . (Dialogue Dealing with the Question of Marriage Outside of the Congregation, in Which Is Shown the Lack of Liberty, Which a True Christian Has Concerning It). This treatise, found in the archives of the Mennonite congregation at Amsterdam (*Inv. Arch. Amst.* I, No. 635), is a manuscript of about 1590, containing 38 pages, in which the opponent and unknown author shows himself as an antagonist of the practice of marriage with a person who did not belong to the church, which the Waterlanders tolerated and which P. W. Bogaert (*q.v.*) had defended shortly before. Presumably this paper was intended to be printed, but no printed copy is known. vdZ.

Diamond Rock Mennonite Meetinghouse (MC) was formerly located near Cedar Hollow in Tredyffrin Twp., Chester Co., Pa. It was also known as "Beidler's" and "Chester Valley." The building was razed in 1927.

Jacob Beidler of Bucks County settled on a farm near Valley Forge about 1802. In 1835 he had an important part in building the Diamond Rock Meetinghouse about one-half mile west of his home. After his death in 1864 it appears that no services were held there until 1908, when an attempt was made to revive the work. Preaching services were alternated between the Lancaster and Franconia conferences, and a Sunday school was organized. In 1910 this work was transferred to Frazer, which resulted in the founding of the congregation at that place under the Lancaster Conference.

Israel Beidler, the son of the founder of Diamond Rock Meetinghouse, held preaching services alternately at Phoenixville and Diamond Rock under the direction of the Eastern District Conference (GCM) for some time after 1847. Q.L.

Diamond Street Mennonite Church (MC), 1814 Diamond St., Philadelphia, Pa., is a mission work among the Colored, begun July 1, 1935, at 191 West Dauphin St., and was known at first as the Mennonite Mission for the Colored. Sponsored by the Eastern Mennonite Board of Missions and Charities (MC), the work was transferred to Diamond Street in 1942. In 1954 Luke G. Stoltzfus was pastor and Emma Rudy and Alma Ruth, mission workers. A large number of Colored children were being reached through Bible teaching activities held in homes, open lots, and in the mission. The total baptized membership, including workers, was 19. C.Y.F.

C. Y. Fretz, "Mennonitism in Philadelphia," *CM*, August 1945; I. D. Landis, *The Missionary Movement Among Lancaster Conference Mennonites* (Scottdale, 1938) 46, 47.

Dick, Heinrich I. (1864-1928), son of Isaak and Margareta Dick, was born on Sept. 29, 1864, in Conteniusfeld, South Russia. In 1875 he came with his parents to North America and settled on a farm northwest of Mountain Lake, Minn. In his nineteenth year he was converted and was baptized by Elder Aron Wall. He was one of the founders of the Brudertaler Church at Mountain Lake in 1889. He was a Sunday-school teacher for 21 years and served in all the other offices in the church. In 1896 he was elected as deacon, on July 20, 1902, ordained as minister, and on July 18, 1906, as elder of the church. In 1918 he was compelled by poor health to resign his position as leader of the congregation, but continued to preach wherever he could.

In 1885 Dick was married to Mrs. Sarah Flaming. To this union were born six children, four of whom died in childhood. Their son Henry is a minister (ordained 1920) and is now field secretary of the Evangelical Mennonite Brethren. Their son John was a missionary in China for 14 years and died on an Indian mission field in Oklahoma. H.H.D.

Dick, Leopold, a jurist in the Imperial Court of Chancery in Speyer, died after 1562, was the author of a booklet of 84 pages in Latin against the Anabaptists, *Adversus impios Anabaptistarum errores,* *longe omnium pestillentissimos, Leopoldi Dickii LL. Doctoris, Sacri Romani imperialis Consistorii ab advocationibus et procuratoris, juditium, Roman. III. Omnes enim peccaverunt et egent gloria Dei. Hagenoae apud Johan. Sec. Anno MDXXX Mense Martio* (Hagenau, 1530). It presents in very diffuse form under the guise of great learning the Catholic doctrine of baptism, that its administration to infants at a very early age is necessary for their salvation because of original sin, and its repetition is blasphemy. As proof he offers besides the Bible, from which he makes special reference to circumcision, quotations from the Church Fathers and even refers to classical heathen authors. The booklet is of little factual value. Nor is its value increased by calling the Anabaptists all sorts of names and advocating the death penalty on the basis of the Old Testament and history in general. (*ML* I, 438.)   NEFF.

Dickson County, Tenn. In December 1894 the Benevolent Organization of Mennonites (MC) meeting in Chicago discussed the matter of sending a mission worker to Dickson County, where a number of Mennonites were living without a minister and under no conference. The organization voted to send A. J. Yoder to hold meetings in this county. A. I. Yoder (*q.v.*) was ordained in 1896 to serve the newly established congregation of 27 members but left the community in the summer of 1897.
                                                         M.G.

Dickson's Hill United Missionary Church, Stouffville, York Co., Ont., was organized in 1876 under the leadership of Abraham Raymer and J. H. Steckley. In 1948 the membership was 63, with Sidney S. Shantz serving as pastor.   S.S.S.

Didsbury, Alta., a town of some 1,200 located in Mountain View municipality, 48 miles north of Calgary. It was founded in 1894 by Jacob Y. Shantz (*q.v.*) and members of the Ontario Conference of the United Missionary Church. The Didsbury church, built in 1896, was the beginning of the Canadian Northwest Conference of the United Missionary Church, which was organized in 1907. Conference meets annually at Didsbury, as does also the annual camp meeting. Mountain View Bible College, now the oldest school in the United Missionary Church, was founded here in 1926. The local United Missionary Church is the largest denomination in the town. The West Zion (MC) Mennonite Church at Carstairs and the Bergthal Mennonite Church (GCM) with a Didsbury address are near by.   E.R.S.

M. Weber, "The Part Played by Immigrants from Waterloo County to the Didsbury, Alberta, Settlement in 1894," *Thirty-Eighth Annual Report of the Waterloo Historical Society* (Kitchener, 1950).

Didsbury United Missionary Church (MBC), the oldest, largest, and most prominent congregation of the United Missionary Church in the province of Alberta, was started in 1894 by members of the Ontario Conference (MBC), the first church being built in 1896. In 1952 there were 254 members. The pastor also has charge of an appointment at Davenport, ten miles southeast of Didsbury.

Another congregation meets at Mountain View, eight miles east of Didsbury, which dedicated a new church at Mountain View on April 12, 1953, under the leadership of the pastor, Amsey Frey.
                                                         E.R.S.

Diekirch, a town in Luxemburg, center of the Mennonite life in this country. The meetinghouse here was dedicated at Pentecost 1950. It is also used by the Protestant Church of Diekirch. (*Almanach Mennonite 1901-51,* 1950, 11; for further information, see **Luxemburg.**)   vDZ.

Dieleman Schneider, an Anabaptist martyr: see **Schneider, Dilman.**

Diemerstein, the ruins of a castle, a small forest settlement, and since 1925 a Christian convalescent and youth home in a narrow valley of the Palatine Forest near Frankenstein on the main highway to Kaiserslautern, Germany. The castle was built in the 12th century under Barbarossa by Dittmar and called Burg Ditmarstein. In the Reformation period it sheltered Ulrich von Hutten, the great humanistic foe of the papacy. In the 17th century it was reduced to a ruin.

Soon after the Thirty Years' War several Mennonite families settled in the dale of Diemerstein, who were members of the Fischbach (*q.v.*) congregation and later of the Sembach (*q.v.*) congregation. On July 9, 1687, Peter Küntzi of Buchholderberg (Switzerland) received the dilapidated mill in Diemerstein in hereditary lease from Countess Marie, who was a princess of the House of Orange. He and his family were specifically granted freedom of worship, "just as the people on the Fischbach estate have been doing." In the Diemerstein mill area a special building was put up for services, which stood until 1824. From 1782 on, baptismal services were also held here. In 1783 the cemetery still in existence in the valley was acquired. Previously Mennonites had to be buried in Fischbach; they could not, however, be carried on the highway, but had to be secretly carried through the valley and over the mountain.

In addition to the Küntzi (Kinzinger) family there were in Diemerstein in the 18th century also the Mennonite Steiner, Engel, and Strohm families, and later also Schnebele and Zürcher. On Feb. 2, 1811, Peter Eymann (*q.v.*), born in Lohmühle near Langmeil, came into possession of the tenure by marriage with Elisabeth Engel. He was for many years the mayor of Frankenstein and delegate of the district of Kaiserslautern-Kirchheimbolanden to the Bavarian parliament at Munich. His daughter married Christian Goebels, the son of Johannes Goebels of Hertlingshausen in 1847. Descendants of this family are still living in Diemerstein, Frankenstein, and Mannheim.

In 1925 a Protestant convalescent and youth home was established in Diemerstein, which acquired possession of the castle ruins and of the Mennonite mill. Since 1947 well-attended annual camps for Mennonite youth have been held at Diemerstein.
                                                         G.H.

Dienaarschap. In Holland in the early days the church board of Mennonite congregations was usually called the *Dienaarschap,* the members (elders, ministers, and deacons) of this board being called *dienaren* or *dienaers.* During the 18th century the terms disappeared, except in a very few congregations. The corresponding term in German West Prussia was *Lehrdienst;* in English the term "ministry" in several of the American Mennonite groups.   vDZ.

Diener am Wort (Minister of the Word), the term used by the Hutterites for their preachers; occasionally they were also called *Diener des Wortes* or *Diener im Wort,* sometimes *Diener am Evangelium.* The Chronicle speaks of them not infrequently also as *Diener des Wortes und Apostel.* The leader among them was called *Hirt* (shepherd or pastor) and bishop; he was at the same time the *Vorsteher* or head of the entire brotherhood who carried the heaviest burden and responsibilities both spiritual and temporal of his church.

The duties of an Anabaptist preacher were first defined in the famous *Schleitheim Confession* of 1527, Article five: "His office shall be to read, to admonish and to teach, to warn, to discipline, to ban in the church, to lead out in prayer for the advancement of all the brethren and sisters, to lift up the bread when it is to be broken, and in all things to see to the care of the body of Christ that it may be built up and developed" (*MQR* 1945, 250). The Hutterites accepted this confession, too, although as a final formulation of their creed and ordinances they considered only Peter Riedemann's great *Rechenschaft* of 1540 as binding. In this book one chapter deals exclusively with the "differences of ministries," and another with the "election" to these offices. The Hutterites, more strongly organized than most Anabaptist groups, clearly distinguished five different offices in their body: (1) Apostles, "who are sent out by God to go through the country and establish through the word and baptism the obedience of faith in His name." They are also called *Sendboten* or missioners, and must be ordained ministers. (2) Bishops and shepherds, who have the same duties "except that they remain in one place." (3) Helpers, "who serve along with the shepherds, exhorting and calling people to remain true." (4) Rulers or stewards (see **Diener der Notdurft**). (5) Elders, who like trustees consider "the good of the church together with the preacher, helping the latter to bear the burden."

In the election of preachers, the example of the choice of Matthias (Acts 1) was followed. After searching prayers "those who have been recognized through God's counsel to be suitable are presented to all. If there be many we wait to see which the Lord showeth us by the lot." The practice is still used not only by the Hutterites but also by some Mennonite groups. "None, however, is confirmed in his office except he be first proved and revealed to the church, and have the testimony of a good life, lest he fall into the snare of the wicked." If he has been found reliable, "his appointment to the office is confirmed before the church through the laying on of the elders' hands" (Rideman, *Account of Our Religion,* 80-82). The *Chronicle* of the Hutterites registers meticulously all elections, testings, and confirmations of their *Diener am Wort,* usually without comment. The number of these ministers must have been quite considerable though we have no exact figures. Each Bruderhof had at least one such *Diener* while others went out in the world as missioners. The fact that so many were ready to serve in this capacity, and to serve most successfully, presupposes a high standard of Bible knowledge and general education (see **Education, Hutterite**).

From the midst of all these men, one was chosen as bishop and *Vorsteher* (head) of the entire brotherhood or church. The *Chronicle* begins actually by listing all of these bishops from Jakob Hutter (d. 1536) to Johannes Rücker (d. 1687), 13 names in all, including Peter Riedemann, who strictly speaking, was not a bishop but was regarded by the Brethren as the spiritual coleader with the then ruling *Vorsteher.* Johannes Waldner (d. 1824), the author of the *Klein-Geschichtsbuch* (see **Chronicles, Hutterite**) and himself a bishop, follows in his work the same practice, listing not less than 22 bishops from Jakob Hutter to 1762; Zieglschmid, the editor (1947), adds five more names up to 1857, after which time no single *Vorsteher* has ever been elected. The bishop when elected is then presented to the entire brotherhood and ordained by the elders through the laying on of their hands.

A question of some significance was the livelihood of the *Diener am Wort.* Naturally they did not receive any compensation; on the other hand, in most cases their heavy work required abstention from manual labor. In a community organization such as that of the Hutterites this should not pose a major problem, and Riedemann has nothing to say on this point. In the *Chronicle,* however, we learn that this issue was thoroughly discussed with Swiss Brethren in the Rhineland before their joining the Moravian brotherhood. In 1556, Hänsel Schmid or Raiffer (*q.v.*), a most successful, later martyred Hutterite missioner, handed to the Swiss Brethren a written statement of Seven Articles (see **Brüderliche Vereinigung**), of which the fourth deals with *Der Diener Essen und Trinken und ihres Leibes Notdurft* ("Concerning the eating and drinking of the ministers and their bodily needs," Zieglschmid, *Chronik,* 363). It says that the brethren should prepare the food and offer it "with a ready heart" to the ministers; yet not more than the body requires. "Thus the God-fearing people keep their ministers in high esteem and consider them worthy of double honors and reward" (I Thess. 5:13; I Tim. 5:17).

The duties of the *Vorsteher* were of course heavier than those of the ministers in general. He carried on the elaborate correspondence of the brotherhood, mainly with the missioners abroad and with those who suffered in jails and bondship. He had to comfort all who were in tribulation and affliction; and some of the finest epistles (*Sendbriefe,* see **Epistles, Hutterite**) came on such occasions from the great bishops Hutter, Amon, Walpot, and others. The bishop had further to watch the observance of the inner discipline of the church (*Gemeinde*), and if necessary had to write down the essential regulations and ordinances of the brotherhood for a permanent standard. It was particularly the *Vorsteher* Andreas Ehrenpreis (*q.v.*), 1639-62, who excelled in this activity, collecting old orders and adding new ones to keep the brotherhood in good condition (see **Ordinances**). Zieglschmid printed some of them in the *Klein-Geschichtsbuch*, 519 ff. When a bishop feels his approaching end, he may recommend to his brethren a possible successor; more than once the *Chronicle* recorded such a moving farewell speech of a *Vorsteher*. It happened but once that the brotherhood had in effect two *Vorsteher* at once as mentioned above, when Lanzenstil and Riedemann directed the affairs of the church conjointly, even though the latter had not been ordained to the office of a bishop.

When a *Diener am Wort* had fulfilled his calling by outstanding service both at home and abroad, the Chronicle devoted elaborate words of praise and appreciation on the occasion of his death. "He was a faithful servant, he kept faithfully to the beliefs of the fathers, he taught not to practice vengeance, neither to help for war. He kept the right baptism and the true Lord's Supper . . . ." The highest regard, however, among all preachers was given to the *Sendboten,* the missioners or apostles who went out into the hazardous world to preach the renewal of hearts. As everyone knew, this was a task from which they most likely would never return. Thus their departure (*Aussendung*) was celebrated with greatest solemnity. On this occasion they would exhort the brethren at home to keep loyal to their faith, and they would ask for prayers of intercession on their behalf while away from home. Their adventures were eagerly followed by the brethren, as the detailed recordings in the Chronicle prove, taken mostly verbatim from their epistles sent home during their wanderings and perhaps from their jails and torture chambers. Hans Arbeiter was asked whether he was an apostle. "Yes," he answered, "this office has been bestowed upon me by God and the brotherhood that I may show the path of redemption to those who do not know it yet." In their great faith they were fearless and indomitable. "Faith cannot be simulated," says Veit Grünberger in 1573 to his judges; "we have to demonstrate and defend it." And Klaus Felbinger, a preacher not yet confirmed, said to his judges in 1560, "Where God opens to us a door there we go. We have committed ourselves altogether to God, and we are dedicated to go wherever He sends us, not worrying whatever suffering may come to us." They did not shirk martyrdom, in fact almost anticipated it as the consistent end of a true minister or servant of the Gospel. They knew that their example would be more effective than all preaching in the world. "Faith cannot be simulated." When, however, such an apostle returned home safely to Moravia, often after many years of absence, he was received with joy and grateful hearts, as is described many times in the Chronicle. It is obvious that these *Diener am Wort* represented the very backbone of the brotherhood, who kept it strong and in high spirits during periods of trial and hardship. This was true for the great century of the beginnings as well as for the period of the amazing

rejuvenation of the church in Transylvania in the 18th century, when new leaders and ministers revived the old spirit in the face of increased suffering and all the uncertainties of a new emigration.

The title *Diener am Wort* was used to some extent in non-Hutterite Anabaptist and later Mennonite groups for the preacher or minister of the Gospel, though apparently never as the regular and primary title for this office. Among the Dutch and their North German and West Prussian descendants *Leeraar* (*Lehrer*) was the most common title, although *Prediker, Predikant, Prediger* was also used. *Dienaar* was seldom used. In 1729 Abraham Alders was chosen as preacher in Goch; the record says he was *tot den dienst des woords verkoren.* In Switzerland and South Germany, while *Lehrer* was used somewhat, *Prediger* was the most common. The Amish came to use *Diener zum Buch* rather than *Diener am Wort.*   LOSERTH, R.F.

Loserth, *Communismus;* P. Rideman, *Account of Our Religion* (London, 1950); *ML* I, 438 ff.

Diener der Notdurft, the title used by the Hutterites for their elected and ordained managers or stewards of their Bruderhofs (*q.v.*) who took care of all temporal needs of the community of each colony. (The title was also used to some extent by the Swiss-South German Anabaptists for the deacon, *q.v.*). Since the Hutterites lived and still live by the principle of community of goods (*q.v.*), an elaborate organization of their establishments became necessary. It was based on the idea of Christian brotherhood, which means voluntary co-operation in all work, absence of "bossism" or paternalism, trusteeship, and acceptance of responsibilities for one another. For this organization to be efficient, it had to operate smoothly, economically, and above all cheerfully. At one place the Hutterite *Chronicle* compares these Bruderhofs with the work of the bees. In spite of all good will there was still much need for alertness against selfishness (*Eigennutz*), lust for domineering, and the tendency toward laziness. Much exhortation was needed.

From the very beginnings in the days of Jakob Hutter the main principles of such an organization were established: there were first the *Diener am Wort* (*q.v.*), who took care of the spiritual needs, and then the *Diener der Notdurft,* who were responsible for the smooth functioning of the Bruderhofs in all practical regards. Peter Riedemann states in his great *Rechenschaft* of 1540 the basic organization of the leadership in the chapter on "Differences of Ministries" (p. 82 of English edition): ". . . There are rulers (*Regierer*) who order and arrange the house or church (*Gemein*), putting each in his place that everything may go properly and well. They also see that the church is cared for in temporal distribution, and are also called ministers of temporal needs." The *Chronicle,* too, once describes in detail the functioning of the church (*Chronik,* 430 f.), and here again we learn something about this office of stewardship. The main source, however, for all further details is found in but one manuscript of 1640, containing a summary of all previous *Gemeinordnungen* (regulations or ordinances, *q.v.*) with added new material; its author is the *Vorsteher* Andreas Ehrenpreis (*q.v.*), who was eager to have his people stay strictly in the old tradition. Later *Ordnungen* of this kind were published by Zieglschmid in his edition of the *Klein-Geschichtsbuch* (1947), 519-65, but they are less elaborate than the one yet unpublished manuscript of Ehrenpreis (a transcript in the Goshen College Library). The following description is based exclusively on this document.

In general the *Diener der Notdurft* were active in four different functions or offices: (1) the most important office was that of *Haushälter*, general manager or steward of the house; (2) other brethren were *Einkäufer* (buyers); (3) again others were *Fürgestellte* or foremen of the different trades and shops; while (4) a last category, the *Meier*, were overseers or heads of the farms. Actually, still more subdivisions were named under the title *Diener der Notdurft;* for instance, there was the *Weinzierl*, who was the assistant to the *Haushälter* and in his absence his deputy; and then the *Kellner*, originally the manager of the vineyards and its revenues, later about the same as *Meier*, general steward. Another helper of the steward was the *Kastner*, originally the caretaker of the flour bins, and so on.

Each office had its distinct duties. (1) The *Haushälter* managed, so to speak, the Bruderhof on the top level. He took care of all material needs of the brethren and sisters, including even the clothing and bedding, he distributed all work and supervised it, and he was also in charge of the general demeanor and discipline of the group, mainly at work. For smooth functioning of the whole, the brethren had to submit to his orders and arrangements. He assigned each person to his place, be it workshop, farm, or home duty. He had to be the first up in the morning and the last to bed at night. He kept an eye on the fireplaces to prevent harm. The sick, the old, and the children were under his general care. He was responsible that everybody got what he needed, and yet that nothing be wasted. If any major purchase was due, a committee of elders and the chief steward made the decision. He had to watch the economy of the Bruderhof, to be careful in the administration of the money, and to keep an account of all transactions. From the craftsmen and shops he claimed revenues about every other week, and he watched also that they supplied the Bruderhof with all things needed. If one considers the rather large size of most of these Bruderhofs (200 to 500 persons), it becomes quite obvious that this office of *Haushälter* was a difficult and responsible one, and that he certainly was in need of an assistant (the *Weinzierl*). To fulfill these duties with tact and modesty a high standard of Christian character was needed, and only the best fitted were elected and ordained (after a time of probation) to this office. The flowering of the entire church depended, at least partly, upon his work, and thus he was in need of spiritual support by the bishop and the *Diener am Wort*.

(2) The *Einkäufer* or buyer was, so to speak, the liaison man with the "world" with which he had to deal. He, too, had to be careful with all his purchases, and "should not fall into the tricks of the traders, butchers, and Jews." When in doubt he was to ask the counsel of the elders. The funds which were entrusted to him he did not dare leave with the women but he might deposit them with the elders or the general steward.

(3) The *Fürgestellten* or foremen of the shops and the different trades (smiths, cloth makers, tanners, shoemakers, cutlers, etc.; see **Crafts**) took care of their particular business, bought whatever material they needed, and sold on the market whatever was not needed on the Bruderhof itself. The profits were handed over to the *Haushälter* and represented the major revenues of the entire closed economy. All the necessary regulations of the trades and crafts were discussed with these foremen.

(4) The *Meier* and *Kellner*, finally, were responsible for farm, orchard, vineyard, fields, barns, and cellars. These men were particularly appreciated by the noble lords as stewards on their estates. No more expert or reliable men could be found among the peasants. It was a position of trust which these men filled in accordance with their Christian conscience. They had to have their eyes at many places, watching for any fire hazard, and be on the alert regarding the upkeep of buildings, fences, and roads.

In view of the great number and size of the Bruderhofs the number of stewards must have been quite considerable. Beck's *Geschichts-Bücher* (pp. 193-95) records that in 1548 four *Diener am Wort* were elected and 14 *Diener der Notdurft;* two years later the text lists a total of 17 ministers and 31 stewards (p. 195). Without doubt this number increased during the next generation, the "Golden Era" of the brotherhood. Around 1600 decline set in, due to persecution and wars, and the stewards carried much of the responsibility for salvaging whatever was possible. Plundering made a sound economy next to impossible, yet the Bruderhofs survived somehow, and were estimated at the moment of complete abandonment in 1622 to be worth more than 364,000 Talers.

Naturally temptations were ever present, yet seemed to have become more noticeable in the later (17th century) period. Hence the repetition in the *Gemeindeordnungen* of exhortations and admonitions to these stewards. "If a *Haushälter* does not comply with the orders of the ministers it is no small wonder that the Lord withholds His blessings." Or we read about dubious manipulations with material and money which are strongly reprimanded and cut short. Yet this was the failing of only a few, within a group which could exist only if strong Christian principles governed its entire life. The fact that this particular type of community life did survive is proof that these principles were more dominant than the human failings which could be more or less successfully kept in check. (*ML* I, 438-40.)   LOSERTH, R.F.

Diener zum Buch, the title used by the Amish for preacher (*Prediger*) to distinguish from *Aeltester* or *völliger Diener* (bishop) and *Armendiener* (deacon). His sole duty was to preach from the Book (Bible).   H.S.B.

Diener-Versammlungen, the title generally given to a series of general conferences held annually (except 1877) by the Amish congregations of America from 1862 to 1878 for the purpose of reconciling certain differences in religious practice that had developed during this time among the different congregations because of their settlements being scattered and isolated throughout the north central states, and also because of the influx during the early part of the 19th century of Amish immigrants from Alsace and South Germany whose religious customs were somewhat different from those common among the Pennsylvania brethren, who had arrived in the 18th century.

Although meant primarily for the ministry, the conferences were open to the laity, and were largely attended by the local congregations where the sessions were held. For that reason, and because meetinghouses were not yet common, the sessions were often held in the large barns of local members.

The questions discussed throughout the various sessions indicate something of the specific differences between the congregations at the time, and also what was still regarded by the majority as orthodox and permissible in their religious and social practices and worthy of preservation.

At the first session held in Wayne Co., Ohio, in 1862, major consideration was given to the controversy over baptism which had troubled certain Pennsylvania brethren for some years. Shall baptism be administered in a flowing stream (creek or river) or in the house? This was the question on which seemingly there was no definite decision by the conference.

During the Civil War years the attitude toward war in all its phases was given repeated attention. Is participation in war Scriptural? It is permissible for a member to accept teamster service under military control? Is it permissible for a former member who has joined the army, been wounded, and now again rejoined the church, to receive a pension offered by the government? Can a member participate in the erection of a memorial monument to the soldiers? All these questions were answered in the negative.

All political activity, too, was either prohibited or discouraged. The holding of any public office, either judicial or under military supervision, which necessitated the use of force, attending political meetings and pole raisings, and even voting were discouraged as being unseemly for a nonresistant people. Unequal yoking with the world in business and social relations, too, was forbidden. Among the business contacts tabooed were holding bank stock and managing a store, post office, or express office. Levi Miller of Holmes Co., Ohio, in the initial session of 1862, listed among other threatening innovations that were objectionable to many—lightning rods, lotteries, likenesses (photographs), insurance, and big meetinghouses.

Meetinghouses, although coming into use among the western Amish churches, were a subject of controversy in the eastern states. To the question proposed in the 1863 session, held in Mifflin Co., Pa., Are meetinghouses Scriptural?, Jonathan Yoder of

Illinois, whose congregation had built a meetinghouse as early as 1854, replied he did not regard them unscriptural, and that it was much easier to maintain order during worship in a meetinghouse than in a home. John K. Yoder of Wayne Co., Ohio, stated that a meetinghouse was necessary in his congregation because the homes were too small to accommodate the large attendance. Jonathan Pitsche of Maryland added that he had no objection to meetinghouses if they were necessary, but too often they were not necessary, to which Abraham Pitsche of Mifflin County gave his assent, but added that he did not favor them in his own congregation. Shunning (*Meidung*), which ever since 1693 had been one of the distinctive doctrines of the Amish Mennonites both in Europe and America, but which was beginning to be questioned by some of the more progressive American Amish congregations by the time, was still upheld, though a certain degree of tolerance was recommended.

As for the dress question, which also played a large part in the life of the Amish, the old standards which still meant hooks and eyes, long hair, broadfall trousers, broad-brimmed hats, aprons, bonnets, and simply made clothes of a somber color, were evidently still taken for granted; for in spite of the contention of J. K. Yoder of Ohio, that non-conformity in dress (*Kleidertracht*) was one of the major causes of difference among the congregations at that time, the question did not loom large in the discussions, except in an occasional reference in the various sermons preached between the discussion periods, in which warnings were given against following worldly fashions, in worldly haircuts and fashionable clothes.

Perhaps one of the most far-reaching decisions made by the conference, judged by later results, was that made in 1872, in connection with a local controversy in the church of Joseph Stuckey (*q.v.*) in Illinois. Stuckey had in his congregation a member with rather radical views on religious questions, who in the course of a poem called "Die Frohe Botschaft" which he had written and distributed rather widely among the Amish congregations in Illinois expressed the view that God in His infinite love would not send any one into eternal punishment for his misdeeds, and that the only punishment the sinner suffered would be the results of his sin in this life. The committee appointed by the conference in 1872 to investigate this matter reported that when they asked Stuckey whether he regarded the author of this view as a brother, he replied in the affirmative, and that he had admitted him to the communion table. Upon receipt of this reply, the committee, made up of both easterners and westerners, withdrew fellowship from Stuckey and his congregation. Stuckey no longer attended the later conference sessions and his congregation later became the nucleus of the Central Conference of Mennonites.

Among the leading personalities in these conference meetings, judging from the part they took in the discussions, were J. K. Yoder of Wayne Co., Ohio, John P. King of Logan Co., Ohio, and Samuel Yoder of Pennsylvania, all three of whom frequently served as moderators (*Wortführer*) of the conference. Among others during the early sessions were Jonathan Yoder of Illinois, Joseph Stuckey of the same state, C. K. Beiler, Elias Riehl, J. K. Hartzler, and Shem Zook (a layman) of Pennsylvania, and Joseph Goldschmidt of Iowa. During later sessions among the leaders were Joseph Burcky, Christian Rupp, and John P. Schmitt of Illinois; C. K. Yoder of Ohio; Joseph Yoder, Jonathan Smucker, and Joseph Borntreger of Indiana; and Paul Herschberger, Sebastian Gerig, and Joseph Schlegel of Iowa.

The conference sessions came to an end largely, no doubt, because of lack of interest and failure to reach their original objective, i.e., reconciliation of the discordant elements. After this the course of Amish history followed three directions. The more conservative elements and such congregations as had never favored the conference movement retained all their old traditions and practices, and are today known as the Old Order Amish. The more liberal element, consisting of the congregation of Joseph Stuckey and several others, gradually discarded many of the old prohibitions, and for a time were called the Stuckey Amish, but later the Central Conference of Mennonites. Adopting a middle course were many of the more recent immigrant congregations in Illinois and Ohio, and some of the more liberal in Indiana who steered between the two extremes. These later formed themselves into district conferences, called themselves Amish Mennonites, but finally 1915-25 merged with the Mennonite churches, thus losing their name Amish, their three-century-old traditional Amish distinguishing doctrines and practices having been gradually dropped earlier. The conferences formed (with years of existence) were Indiana-Michigan A.M., 1888-1915, Western A.M., 1890-1920, Eastern A.M., 1893-1925. The last conference retained its name in the merged "Ohio Mennonite and Eastern A.M. Joint Conference" until 1954. A later emergence was the Conservative A.M. Conference, 1910-55, which is now the Conservative Mennonite (MC) Conference.

The proceedings of these *Diener-Versammlungen* were published annually, 1862-1865 and 1869, under the title, *Verhandlungen der Diener-Versammlung der Deutschen Täufer oder Amischen Mennoniten* (John Baer's Sons, Lancaster, 1862-65; 1869 at Chicago); then 1866-67 and 1870-78 (John F. Funk, Elkhart) under the title *Bericht der Verhandlungen der Diener-Versammlungen der Amischen Mennoniten- (Diener und) Brüderschaft.*

These annual Amish conferences were not the first such held in either Europe or America (see **Conference**). From old documents the following are known: 1809 in Lancaster Co., Pa. (minutes extant); 1826 in Ohio; 1830 in Somerset Co., Pa.; 1831 in Wayne Co., Ohio (minutes extant); 1837 in Somerset Co. (minutes extant). A conference of more conservative Amish leaders was held in Holmes Co., Ohio, in June 1865. The texts of the 1809, 1837, and 1865 records were translated in "Some Early American Amish Mennonite Disciplines," *MQR* VIII (1934) 90-98. The report of a European Amish conference of 1779, held at Essin-

gen near Landau in the Palatinate, was translated in "An Amish Church Discipline of 1779," *MQR* XI (1937) 163-68.   C.H.S., H.S.B.

J. A. Hostetler, "Amish Problems at Diener-Versammlungen," *Menn. Life* IV (October 1949) 34-38.

Dienstjarenfonds, a Mennonite fund in the Netherlands, founded in 1912 by a number of men in an effort to raise the salaries of the preachers which they considered too low, by granting a supplementary sum to those ministers who had served for ten years or more, and whose salaries were beneath a certain level. In 1917 the first payments to the ministers were made. In 1949 the *Dienstjarenfonds* was taken over by the *Algemene Doopsgezinde Sociëteit* (*q.v.*). Since then the contributions were increased and given to all ministers with ten or more years' service, the payment no longer limited by the income of the minister. (*DB* 1912, 203; 1918, 155; *DJ* 1919, 83-87.)   vdZ.

Diepenbroek, Coenraad van (d. Sept. 1, 1714), a Dutch Mennonite minister serving in the Waterlander-Flemish congregation of the Peuzelaarsteeg in Haarlem 1690-1714, was an advocate of the Lamist (*q.v.*) principles and a warm participant in the Collegiant (*q.v.*) movement. He succeeded in 1700 in settling a schism among these Collegiants, which had existed for many years between two groups. He often attended services at Rijnsburg, the Collegiant center, preaching and administering communion. Van Diepenbroek was also active in behalf of the persecuted Swiss Mennonites in 1710. He was a well-known preacher, who is said to have had a large attendance wherever he preached. In 1703 he was asked to dedicate the new meetinghouse at Krommenie (*q.v.*) after the old church had been devastated by fire. His sermon was published: *Predikaatsie . . . in de nieuw-gebouwde Vergaderplaats . . . te Krommenie* (Amsterdam, 1703). Other publications by Diepenbroek were *Redenvoering over de Hereniging der Twee Vergaderingen tot Rijnsburg,* 1700 (Haarlem, n.d.), and *Redenvoering op de Dank-dag over de Vrede,* 1713 (Haarlem, n.d.). The Mennonite Archives of Amsterdam contain seven manuscript volumes of his sermons (*Inv. Arch. Amst.* I, No. 715). J. L. S. preached his funeral sermon, *Treurgalm op het afsterven van Koenraad van Diepenbroek* (Haarlem, 1714). vdZ.

Biogr. Wb. II, 481 f.; J. C. van Slee, *De Rijnsburger Collegianten* (Haarlem, 1895) *passim,* see Index; *Catalogus Amst.,* 150, 165, 237, 243.

Dierick van der Hagen, an Anabaptist martyr, was beheaded at Antwerp, Belgium, in 1537 (exact date unknown); his head was put on a stake, and his corpse was burned. (Génard, *Antw. Arch.-Blad* VII, 434, XIV, 14-15, No. 160.)   vdZ.

Dierick (Dirk) Lambrechts (or Lambertsz), an Anabaptist martyr, originally from Voorthuizen near Deventer, Holland, a wool-weaver, was executed at Gent, Belgium, on April 12, 1563, by being burned at the stake. Van Braght (*Mart. Mir.*) only mentions the fact of the execution without giving the date. Dierick is also celebrated in a song found in the supplement to the *Liedtboecxken van den*

Offer des Heeren: "Alsmen schreef duyst vijfhondert jaar, ende twee ent sestich mede."　　　　v␡Z.

Offer, 651; *Mart. Mir.* D 300, E 666; Verheyden, *Gent*, 29, No. 95; Wolkan, *Lieder*, 69; *ML* II, 606.

Diericxken Roels, wife of Mathys Baseliers, an Anabaptist martyr, was executed by drowning at Antwerp, Belgium, on Nov. 19, 1573. During the trial she admitted that she had been rebaptized and had attended meetings of Mennonites, and also that Mennonite meetings had been held in her house. (Génard, *Antw. Arch.-Blad* XIII, 132, 133, 180; XIV, 92-93, No. 1041.)　　　　v␡Z.

Diesen, a hamlet near St. Avold in Lorraine, France, seat of an Amish Mennonite congregation since *ca.* 1840, known also under the name of *Boulay* (German, *Bolchen*), a small city situated 10 miles west of Diesen (see **Bolchen-Diesen,** *ML* I, 243). Originally meetings were held in homes; *ca.* 1870 there were 18 families whose homes served alternately as meeting places. Soon after 1870 all meetings were held in homes in Diesen, and in 1947 a chapel was built in the same village.

Family names in the congregations are Beck, Esch, Fonkennel, Guth, Hege, Hertzler, Nafziger, Oesch, Schertz, and Weisse. The first elder was Joseph Esch of Roupelstouden (ordained 1838, d. 1897); Nicolas Beck and Willy Hege were elders in 1954, assisted by Willy Nafziger and Joseph Oesch as preachers. Baptized membership in 1950 was 108. Meetings are held biweekly, entirely in German (except for slight use of French in young people's activities). The congregation is affiliated with the German-language Alsatian Conference.

In 1922 the congregation was divided, approximately half the members meeting on the farm St-Victor, under the leadership of Elder Pierre Esch, and known as Boulay or St-Victor. The two groups reunited in 1940.

A valuable description of the Mennonites living in the region of Diesen, dated 1850, is to be found in the archives of the Department de la Moselle, prepared as a result of an investigation ordered by the Minister of Education and Religious Affairs.

　　　　　　　　　　　　　　　　J.H.Y.

Dieteren, a small town in the Dutch province of Limburg, formerly belonging to the duchy of Jülich, about 1534 a center of Anabaptist activity. Jan Smeitgen (*q.v.*) and Lenart van Ysenbroek (*q.v.*) baptized here, the latter baptizing the martyrs Bartholomeus van den Berghe (*q.v.*) and his wife Mente Heynen (*q.v.*). After a short time the Anabaptist movement was entirely extinguished here.
　　　　　　　　　　　　　　　　v␡Z.

Rembert, *Wiedertäufer*, 84, 336, 395, 404, 421, 450; W. Bax, *Het Protestantisme in het Bisdom Luik en vooral te Maastricht* (The Hague, 1937) 37, 70, 72, 73, 93, 113, 114.

Dietrich, the German equivalent of the Dutch *Dirk* (*q.v.*).

Dietrich Nicolaus (*ML* I, 442) is identical with Claes Dirksz (*q.v.*).　　　　v␡Z.

Dietrich, Sebastian (or Bastl, 1553-1619), a Hutterite bishop and *Vorsteher* in Moravia. He was born in Markgröningen, Württemberg, and seems to have received a careful education. Somehow he was won for the Anabaptist way (we know that a copy of the great *Article Book, q.v.,* was found in his home), and in 1580 he went to Moravia to join the Hutterite brotherhood, much against his father's wishes. He was a barber-surgeon, but it is not known whether he learned this profession in his youth or only after he came in contact with some of the famous Hutterite barber-physicians such as G. Zobel or B. Goller, both of Nikolsburg. In any case, later Württemberg records call him "an excellent and widely renowned physician"; he certainly added to the high regard in which the Hutterite "barbers" were held among the Moravian nobility.

In 1587, Dietrich was elected *Diener am Wort* (*q.v.*), i.e., preacher, in Neumühl, Moravia, and three years later (1590) he was confirmed in this position by the elders and the entire church. From some records it may be assumed that he then lived in Altenmarkt, Moravia, where a large center of the Hutterites was situated. In 1600 he sent an authorized man to his home town to claim his paternal inheritance. The affair went on for years; his brother Konrad claimed the same inheritance, since Sebastian as an Anabaptist was considered as having no legal title to such claims. The records (in Bossert's *Quellen*) cover 13 years; eventually Konrad got one third of the amount, and Sebastian got nothing.

The "golden era" of the Hutterites had come to an end in 1592, when the rising Counter Reformation (*q.v.*), Turkish Wars, and oppression by feudal lords made life on the Bruderhofs increasingly hard. The brethren called the period 1592-1618 the "time of affliction." In 1604 they heard of Mennonites in East Prussia (around Elbing), and earnestly considered an emigration thither. Dietrich together with some other brethren was sent to Prussia, and an experimental Bruderhof was started there. It was, however, a failure (mainly due to the unfriendly attitude of the city magistrates of Elbing), and Dietrich and the others returned to Moravia.

In 1611 the outstanding *Vorsteher* Klaus Braidl (*q.v.*) died in Neumühl, Moravia, and Sebastian Dietrich was unanimously elected as his successor. For the next nine years (1611-19) he was then a most conscientious leader of the brotherhood during a difficult and trying time. His concern was above all the maintenance of the traditional ways of the Hutterites in all their strictness and austerity. In this he was fairly successful. From a later Hutterite codex (see **Ehrenpreis**) we learn of Dietrich's activities toward a more precise regulation both of life on the Bruderhofs in general and of the different trades in particular. In 1612 he laid down a sort of comprehensive program after having discussed it with the brethren in all details (see **Ordnungen**). These "ordinances" then were to be read to the entire brotherhood every year. Of special interest are the points which deal with the education of the young people. Youth was to be brought up in the fear of the Lord, and diligently read the epistles, hymns, and confessions of the brotherhood, so that they would be ready to give account if asked. They should practice faithfully penmanship, so that the children "of the world" would not receive better praise than those of the brotherhood. Children should not be pampered but hardened to endure work and hardship later on. The old regulations must be observed, and those in authority ought to set good examples. Should they know of some hidden "own money" they must report it so that it may be removed at once. Particular attention is paid to the newcomers. Anyone showing a spark of divine grace should be helped on. All property of the brotherhood is to be handled as a trust for which one is responsible to God. Let nothing be wasted, and all luxury done away with lest God think them rich and tax them unmercifully, Special care must be given to the sick, etc. All these points were read to the assembly for approval, and were also sent to those who were absent (this they called "visiting with the doctrine"). Dietrich made every effort to preserve the traditional principle of community of goods, and to do away with all bad customs which had been creeping in during the recent hard times.

Relations with those feudal lords who had been kind to the brotherhood during the Turkish invasion of 1605 were further cultivated, and the interests of the brethren were staunchly defended by the *Vorsteher*. The Bruderhof in Sobotiste (*q.v.*), Slovakia, was re-established in 1613, and the lords of that area gave Dietrich and two other elders a contract (*Hausbrief*) for this possession, stating rights and obligations, and granting religious freedom (text in Beck, *Geschichts-Bücher*, 364). When Dietrich felt that his end was approaching, he called the elders for a last address (text in the Great Chronicle). In return they assured him their appreciation of his loyal services for his flock, and that he had been a faithful shepherd. He died Dec. 8, 1619, and was succeeded as *Vorsteher* by Ulrich Jaussling.   LOSERTH, R.F.

Zieglschmid, *Chronik*; Loserth, *Communismus*; G. Bossert, in *Bl. f. Württemb. Kirchengesch.*, 1929, 38; idem, *Quellen z. Gesch. der Wiedertäufer I: Herzogtum Württemberg* (1931); L. Neubaur, "Mährische Brüder in Elbing," in *Ztscht f. Kirchengesch.* 1912, 447 f.; *ML* I, 442 f.

Dietrichstein, an old Austrian noble family, originally from Carinthia, which became quite influential during the 16th and 17th centuries, and played a decisive part in the oppression and final expulsion of the Austrian Anabaptists, mainly the Hutterites. Three generations of this family require attention: (1) Siegmund von Dietrichstein (1480-1533), governor of Styria, (2) his son Adam von Dietrichstein (1527-90), the first lord of Nikolsburg, Moravia, and as such overlord over the Hutterites on this estate. He had 12 children, of whom (3) Franz von Dietrichstein (1570-1636), cardinal and prince-bishop of Olmütz (Olomuce), Moravia, was the most outstanding. He was directly responsible for the total expulsion of the Hutterites from Moravia in 1622. His brother Siegmund von Dietrichstein was likewise instrumental in this painful process, a triumph of the Catholic Counter Reformation (*q.v.*), while Maximilian von Dietrichstein and Karl and Georg

were less active. Some of these brothers even sided with the Protestant opposition against the Habsburgs in 1619-20.

(1) Siegmund von Dietrichstein, a favorite of Emperor Maximilian I, became governor of Styria, 1515-33, in which capacity he quenched the peasant revolt of 1524, and ruthlessly carried out all the mandates of Ferdinand I against the Anabaptists in Styria (*q.v.*), thus retarding a forceful and popular Christian movement so that it never reached complete fruition. His Jesuit biographer Georg Dingenauer said: "He persecuted them not only in the cities but ferreted them out even in the forests where they had sought a hiding like wild animals." The hopeful small brotherhoods in places like Graz, Bruck, Leoben, etc., could not very long resist this pressure and soon died out, perhaps also due to a lack of strong leadership. In the chronicles of the Hutterites the name of Siegmund Dietrichstein does not appear at all.

(2) Adam von Dietrichstein, the favorite of Emperor Maximilian II. While some of his brothers turned Protestant, Adam remained a faithful Catholic, though leaning toward reforms and a broader interpretation of doctrines, like his sovereign Maximilian II. He filled high positions in the Habsburg realm (tutor of the later Emperor Rudolph II, ambassador to Spain, etc.), and in 1575 was enabled to purchase the Nikolsburg estate in Moravia (*q.v.*), formerly a possession of the Liechtensteins. As early as 1579 he called the Jesuits to Moravia to promote the Counter Reformation in this strongly Protestant country. The chronicles of the Hutterites, mentioning this fateful event (Zieglschmid, 505), call the Jesuits *das Bös Natterngezücht* (generation of vipers). The emperor and the pope, however, praised Adam for his zeal. Nevertheless, he knew the economic value of the Hutterites only too well, and in spite of several starts toward expulsion, he yet allowed them to continue as tenant farmers on his estate. He could not resolve this typical 16th-17th century conflict between religious zeal and personal interests as a manorial lord. He began also the collection of the rich library at Nikolsburg which was later looted by the Swedes (during the Thirty Years' War), and today can be found as the Queen Christiana collection of the Vatican Library at Rome.

Between 1590 and 1599 Nikolsburg was run by his son Maximilian von Dietrichstein, who is described by the *Chronicle* as amenable to negotiations with the Brethren, allowing them to stay on the estate.

(3) Franz von Dietrichstein (1570-1636), the eighth child of Adam, was destined to rise to a position second only to the emperor himself. He was the most aggressive champion of the growing Counter Reformation of the Catholic Church, and he was also the staunch supporter of the cause of the Habsburgs during the first phases of the great Thirty Years' War. At 27 he became priest, and at 29 he was made cardinal and at the same time bishop of Olmütz (Olomuce), then one of the richest and most influential dioceses of the Habsburg realm. His position was near to Emperor Rudolph II and

his successors Matthias and Ferdinand II, yet he found much opposition among the feudal nobility of Moravia which was predominantly both Czech and Protestant. (It was this nobility which protected the Hutterites through all the 90 or more years of their flowering in Moravia.) He arrived in Nikolsburg in 1599, and it may be said that from about then on very hard times set in for the Brethren: oppression by the Catholic powers, cardinal and emperor, which led to looting and final expulsion, and hardship by two wars, a Turkish invasion in 1605, and the beginnings of the Thirty Years' War, about 1619-22. The "Golden Age" of the brotherhood was over; the government, in need of money, tried to extort as much as it could from the Brethren, by means anything but just or decent. The Hutterite *Vorsteher* Hirzel (*q.v.*) was under false pretenses cheated into handing out to the cardinal all the money of the brotherhood. The number of Hutterite Bruderhofs gradually dwindled to about 24; many Brethren had died during these turbulent events, and many more had been forced to emigrate to near-by Slovakia. In 1620 the Catholic cause won a decisive victory at the Battle of the White Mountain near Prague over the new Protestant ruler of Bohemia. From now on the Catholic Counter Reformation threw off all restraint. Noble estates were confiscated both in Bohemia and Moravia (it was then that the Dietrichsteins acquired a fabulous wealth in estates and other riches), and Cardinal Franz von Dietrichstein was no longer willing "to tolerate the heretical sects" in his Moravian domain. Since Catholicism was to become the only religion of the realm, the persecution of the Brethren became "total." From 1622 to his death in 1636 the cardinal was governor of Moravia, and with the emperor's support became almost omnipotent over the array of opposing nobles. In September 1622, he ordered the complete expulsion of the Hutterites "within four weeks." All petitions, even to the emperor himself, were in vain. In spite of an early winter, and many sick and old people, no postponement was permitted. They had to go, leaving behind them houses and fields and goods worth more than 364,000 Talers, according to their own estimates (Zieglschmid, 756. The entire dramatic story of the expulsion and the cardinal's role in it is told in *ibid.,* 746-56). The nobles, however, seem to have felt that they could not go on without these highly efficient workers, and some Brethren, called by their former lords, actually came back from Slovakia the next year. The cardinal now intensified his endeavor, and sharper "patents" (mandates, orders) were issued in 1623, again in 1624, and even as late as 1628, making any returning Hutterite an outlaw. Though he knew only too well the economic harm to Moravia by these measures, Franz insisted on the religious uniformity of the country. For these activities the then victorious emperor made him a prince. To the Brethren, however, he was only a tool of the powers of this evil world. In the well-known Pribitzer hymn (*Lieder der Hutterischen Brüder,* 1914, 821-27) three stanzas (24-26) are devoted to the cardinal and his work.

All dringlich Bitten was unsonst,
Fanden auch weder Geld noch Gonst,
Der Cardinal der erste war (wor),
Ging anderen in solcher Tyranei zuvor.

But the final lines of the hymn sound hopeful again: God does not abandon His people, and He prepares a new place for them. It was not unknown to the cardinal either, that the lords in Slovakia, to his deep regret, showed more independence than those of Moravia. For another 130 years the Brethren found a refuge in this Hungarian land, until also the government and the Roman Church gained enough power to end this period of toleration.   R.F.

For (1) J. Loserth, *Die Reformation und Gegenreformation in den innerösterreichischen Ländern im 16. Jahrhundert* (1898); for (3) see particularly F. Hruby, *Die Wiedertäufer in Mähren* (Leipzig, 1935), where a wealth of archival material is digested, mainly the correspondence of the cardinal with the emperor. The Hutterite Chronicle, of course, is very elaborate on the entire period of the Cardinal: Zieglschmid, *Chronik* 597-760. In Beck, *Geschichts-Bücher,* the story of the expulsion is told 406-25 and 435. See also Loserth, in *Ztscht des dt. Vereins f. d. Gesch. Mährens u. Schlesiens* (Brno, 1917 and 1919), and his *Communismus.* There is a Latin history of the house of Dietrichstein written by the Jesuit Georg Dingenauer. Volume I appeared in 1621 in Olomuce; the entire work is preserved in manuscript form in the Vatican Library (*Bibliotheca Ottoboniana,* 827). Both Loserth and Hruby used this source extensively; *ML* I, 443.

Diets: see **Imperial Recesses.**

Dieuwertgen (Dieuwerken Jansdochter), an Anabaptist martyr, sentenced to die by being buried alive with a brother and two sisters after cruel torture at Leiden (Holland) on Aug. 21, 1552 (erroneously given as 1550 in the *Martyrs' Mirror*). When she was led to the site of execution she began to sing and then said, "Dear brethren, do not avenge me for this; for it is for the sake of the Lord." Her martyrdom is sung in the hymn, "Eylaes ick mach wel suchten," written by Adriaen Cornelisz (*q.v.*). (Wolkan, *Lieder* 63, 70; *Mart. Mir.* D 97, E 495; *Offer* 578, note 1; *ML* I, 448.)
                                                  NEFF, vDZ.

Dieuze, a town in the district of Chateau Salins, France, once the seat of a fairly large Mennonite congregation, which dissolved about the end of the 19th century. The congregation was a part of the Welschländer (*q.v.*) (Lorraine, *q.v.*) congregation. When Alsace-Lorraine was annexed to Germany in 1870 the new frontier divided the rather widely scattered congregation, but it continued to meet, using the German language. About 1893 due to border difficulties the congregation was finally officially divided, the French families joining the Nancy (*q.v.*) congregation, and the German families continuing to meet, sometime later joining the congregation of Morhange (*q.v.*) or Mörchingen. Emigration to America as well as farther westward in France, and a low birth rate, had already considerably reduced the size of the group. Only the names of a few elders have been preserved: Conrad Schweitzer (d. 1880), Christian Schweitzer (d. 1896), and Joseph Schweitzer (ordained 1891), the last elder, who joined the Morhange congregation. (*Christ Seul,* April 1931, 6-7.) H.S.B.

Diggers, a group of the Levellers, an important political party in the time of Cromwell in England (*q.v.*). Their name indicates their effort to convert idle land into a farm for the establishment of a colony of a religious communistic brotherhood. This is not the only aspect in which they resembled the Hutterian Brethren in Moravia (*q.v.*). The Diggers, or "True Levellers" as they also called themselves, were, with the entire group of Levellers, a part of the great Anabaptist movement that emanated from Central Europe. Like the Anabaptists, who were principally of the lower social strata, the Diggers were also landless, and again like them, they were concerned with religious and social renewal. It was in their manner of achieving this aim that they differed from the Anabaptists. (E. Troeltsch, *The Social Teachings of the Christian Churches,* N.Y., 1936; *ML* I, 448.) E.H.C.

Digna Jacops, wife of the sailor Peter Jacopssen, of Antwerp, an Anabaptist martyr, was drowned at Antwerp, Belgium, in the Schelde River on March 16, 1535. She left behind some goods, which was unusual, most martyrs of Antwerp being poor. (Génard, *Antw. Arch.-Blad* VII, 319, 366; XIV, 12-13, No. 138.) vDZ.

Digna Pieters, an Anabaptist martyr, a native of Dordrecht, Dutch province of South Holland, was put in a sack and drowned there on Nov. 23, 1555. She was accused of having been rebaptized and attending heretical (Mennonite) meetings. (*Mart. Mir.* D 162, E 551; *DB* 1862, 92 f.; *ML* I, 448; III, 371.) vDZ.

Dijk (Dijck), Aldert Sierks (1699-Dec. 6, 1779), was engaged as a preacher by the Old Flemish congregation at Groningen, Netherlands, on Aug. 16, 1733. Although he was not an elder, he was influential in the Groningen Sociëteit (conference). Especially at the conference of 1738 in Groningen he let himself be heard in the discussion on the elimination of the Mennonite divisions. He declared that it depended principally on a change of heart, without which externals were of no avail. He suggested that the elders should make an annual tour of all the congregations. In 1755 Dijk wrote the foreword to an Old Flemish Confession of Faith. He was generally loved for his piety of heart and his attitudes. He was the author of the following (all published in Groningen): *De heilbegerige Jongeling, Onderwesen in de nodigste vereischtens eens Dopelings* (1732); *Nutte Bybel-Oeffening over Gewigtige Waarheden en Toestanden des Christendoms* (1738); *Kleyne Catechismus ofte Beginsel van onderwyzing voor kinderen . . .* (1742); *Na-errinnering eener Redevoering over 't slot von den Bybel* (1744); *Het leven en sterven van een Christen door de genade Jesu en in de vereeniging met Hem . . .* (1744); *Sluit-reede, gedaan by het eyndigen der Algem. Vergaderinge der Doopsges. Sociëteit . . .* (1754); *Proeve eener Kleine catechistize Passi-school, . . .* (1759); *Catechetise behandeling over de geloofs-*

belydenis der Doopsgezinde, d'oude Vlamingen genaamt (1773). J.L.

DB 1879, 4; 1890, 108; Blaupot t. C., *Groningen* I, 137, 162, 195; *Biogr. Wb.* II, 678; *Catalogus Amst.,* 149, 232, 260; *Inv. Arch. Amst.* I, No. 962; *ML* I, 497.

Dijk (Dijck), Jan van, a Dutch Mennonite minister, serving the Zonist congregation at Amsterdam from 1664 until his death in 1678, author of *Noodtwendich Bericht tot Openinge der tegenwoordighe onlusten . . . in de Gemeente der Doopsgezinde . . . binnen Amsterdam* (Amsterdam, 1663), and *Antwoort op de Wederlegging van het Nootwendich Bericht . . .* (Amsterdam, 1664). In both booklets van Dijk shows himself as a champion of the views of the conservatives among the Flemish congregation of Amsterdam, usually called de Ouderen, and an ardent antagonist of Galenus Abrahamsz (*q.v.*) and his principles. The latter book was directed against a booklet by Pieter Balling, *Verdediging van de Regeering der Doopsgez. gemeente . . .* (Amsterdam, 1663), in which van Dijk's *Nootwendich Bericht* was opposed and the *Ouderen* had been accused of partiality, backwardness, and defamation. In 1665 van Dijk, about whose life nothing was available, signed the *Verbondt van Eenigheydt* (*q.v.*), an agreement of the conservatives, which stressed the outstanding confessions of faith. (*Biogr. Wb.* II, 681; *Catalogus Amst.,* 122, 123.) vDZ.

Dijkema, Fokke, b. 1877, at Leeuwarden, d. 1944, at Amsterdam, a Dutch Mennonite pastor serving the congregations of Winschoten 1901-5, Hilversum 1905-7, Rotterdam 1907-16, and Amsterdam 1916-42. His special field of study was the Old Testament and Hebrew; he published a few scholarly papers on Hebrew linguistic problems and Old Testament subjects in *Teyler's Theologisch Tijdschrift.* He was also a member of the board of the Dutch Bible Society and worked on the new Dutch version of the Bible. For a number of years he was a member of the board of the *ADS* (General Dutch Mennonite Conference). But his interest went out beyond the Mennonite brotherhood and he was a member of a large number of religious and charitable associations. For some time he was also a member of the board of the General (Dutch) Committee of Liberal Christianity; Dijkema was an adherent of liberal theology. He published many articles in the Mennonite weekly *De Zondagsbode* and a number of booklets including *Het Avondmaal* (Rotterdam, n.d., 1908), *De Ongeloovigen* (Amsterdam, n.d.), *Buitenkerklijke Stroomingen* (Amsterdam, n.d., 1933), and a historical study, *De Doopsgezinden in Amsterdam 1530-1930* (n.p., n.d.). vDZ.

Dijkstra, Uilke Reitses (1755-1823), was a farmer and preacher of the congregation of Dantumawoude, Dutch province of Friesland, 1781-1812. He was a very active and influential church leader, being the last *liefdeprediker* (untrained and unsalaried preacher) of this large congregation, and its only minister in 1803-11. Then Jan ter Borg, trained at the Amsterdam Mennonite Seminary, came to his assistance. J. Kuiper preached his funeral sermon, *Lijkrede op U. R. Dijkstra* (Leeuwarden, 1823). (*Naamlijst* 1829, 48.) vDZ.

Diller Mennonite Church (MC), located near New-ville, Cumberland Co., Pa., is a member of the Lancaster Conference. The Bowmansville Dillers moved near Newville in 1790. Their farmhouse was used as a meetinghouse until 1820, when the present church was built, which was enlarged in 1903. The 1954 membership and Sunday-school enrollment were 23 and 32 respectively. Walter Charlton and Earl Mosemann are serving as pastors.   I.D.L.

Diller, Michael (d. 1570), chaplain at the Palatine court, had originally been an Augustinian monk at Speyer and since 1530 prior of the monastery, but had to leave the city in 1548 on account of Protestant sympathies. He had been used by the city council to convert the Anabaptists (Medicus, 22). With the final establishment of the Reformation in the Palatinate, Elector Otto Heinrich appointed him as a member of the church council which was created in 1556. The tolerant elector tried to come to terms with the Anabaptists by peaceful methods. Hence the proposals of the church board express a more lenient attitude than was found in other regions at the time. Among other things they favored thorough indoctrination of the Anabaptists by the parsons of the state church, suppression of religious services outside the established church, and finally expulsion of persistent adherents to the Anabaptist brotherhood (Hege, 88-91). After the disputation at Pfeddersheim, in which Diller probably participated, the Anabaptist leaders and outside participants in the disputation were expelled.

A few weeks later Diller joined the conference of the leading Protestant theologians meeting at Worms, Sept. 11 to Oct. 7, 1557, in recommending to the German rulers the use of capital punishment against the Anabaptists. He signed the document published there in the same year, *Prozess, wie es soll gehalten werden mit den Wiedertäufern*, in which the idea that no one should be killed because of his faith is refuted by two Bible passages, Lev. 24 and Rom. 13 (Hege, 93-96 and *Menn. Bl.*, 1893, 108 ff.). It is very likely due to the efforts of chaplain Diller that the elector on Jan. 25, 1558, issued a stern edict against the Anabaptists, ordering "in accord with counsel we have received" that the leaders be punished in accord with imperial law; i.e., with death (see **Punishment of Anabaptists**). But the elector examined every case and in the remaining few months of his life he apparently signed no death sentences; for it is reported that he granted the Anabaptists domicile in his realm on condition that they conduct themselves quietly (Hege, 94-99). The extent of Diller's influence on the succeeding Elector Frederick III, who was at the beginning of his reign also strongly urged to persecute the Anabaptists, remains for investigation; likewise his co-operation in the suppression of the Anabaptists in the margravure of Baden-Durlach, where Margrave Karl II on June 1, 1556, issued the church order which had been drawn up with Diller's aid, and which is very similar to that of the Palatinate. Diller died in 1570.   HEGE.

Chr. Hege, *Die Täufer in der Kurpfalz* (Frankfurt, 1908); E. F. H. Medicus, *Gesch. der evangelischen Kirche der königl. bayr. Rheinpfalz* (supplement, Erlangen, 1865); *HRE* IV, 658; *ML* I, 448.

Dillon (Ill.) Mennonite Church (MC) was organized as a separate congregation under the Illinois Mennonite Conference in September 1952, after several years as a branch Sunday school sponsored by the Hopedale Mennonite congregation. Meetings are held in a building owned by the Methodist Episcopal Church in the unincorporated village of Dillon, about five miles southwest of Tremont. John V. Troyer was ordained as pastor when the congregation was organized, and still serves (1954), with a membership of 37.   N.P.S.

Dillonvale (Ohio) Mennonite Mission (MC), located in a coal-mining section near Steubenville, was started in September 1942, following a series of tent meetings sponsored by the Kidron Mennonite Church, which is still responsible for the work. Services are held every Sunday in the chapel of the two-and-a-half-story structure which was purchased in 1944 for that purpose. Evangelistic meetings and a summer Bible school are held every year. The membership in 1954 was 21, with Richard Hostetler as pastor.   A.B.

Dillsberg, a district near Heidelberg, Germany. The official register of Mennonites of 1759 names Muselmann and Bechtel in Langenzell, Horsch, Steiner, and Kaufmann in Mauer, Schellenberger and Brand in Angelloch, Neukomm in Schatthausen, a total of 78 persons of Swiss origin.

About 1800 Martin and David Kaufmann lived at Daisbach. In 1802 that region was added to Baden and the Mennonites were generally accepted as citizens. At that time the complaint of the Kaufmann brothers concerning the continued levying of defense fees (see **Nonresistance**) was referred to the constitutional committee of Mannheim for final decision; a general order of April 17, 1802, granted release from protection fees.   E.H.C.

Chr. Neff, "Quellen zur Gesch. der kurpfälzischen Menn." (ms); J. G. Widder, *Versuch einer vollständigen geog.-hist. Beschreibung der kurfürstlichen Pfalz* (Frankfurt, 1786-88); *ML* I, 449.

Dingentgen (Digna), a Dutch Anabaptist martyr, whose official name was Baudinken (Baudewijnken) Het; van Braght (*Mart. Mir.*) calls her Dingentgen van Hondschoote (Honschoten). She was originally from the region of St. Winnoxbergen, Flanders, was 30 years of age and unmarried. She was living in Hondschoote, Flanders, and had been baptized in this town by Paulus van Meenen (*q.v.*) in 1568. On Dec. 4, 1572 (*Mart. Mir.* gives no date), she was publicly burned at the stake on the *Vrijdagsmarkt* at Gent, Belgium, together with Martin van der Straten, Adriaen Rogiers, and Mattheus Bernaerts. (*Mart. Mir.* D 623, E 947; Verheyden, *Gent*, 59, No. 208; *ML* I, 449.)   vDZ.

Dinuba, Cal., is a town located about in the center of the state, in Tulare County, spreading over an area of slightly more than a section of land, with a population of 5,000, and a trade area of about 20,000. There are 1,000 to 1,200 Mennonites within the Dinuba shopping area, 10 to 15 per cent of whom live in Dinuba proper. The first Mennonite settlers came to the Dinuba area in 1904. In about 1908 the Krimmer Mennonite Brethren built their church five miles southwest of Dinuba. In 1938 a group of 250 Mennonite Brethren, former members of the Reedley Mennonite Brethren congregation, built a church in Dinuba, with a seating capacity of 1,000. Altogether there are 14 churches in Dinuba with a registered membership of 3,800. Dinuba is a clean, beautiful town, surrounded by a flourishing fruit-growing community in the heart of the prolific San Joaquin Valley. B.J.B.

Dinuba (Cal.) Mennonite Brethren Church had its beginning in Reedley, Cal., in April 1925, when a number of M.B. Church members organized as the South Reedley M.B. Church. A hall was procured and J. H. Richert served as the first pastor. The congregation was received as a church into the M.B. Pacific District Conference and continued to grow, numbering 163 members in 1926.

In 1937 the congregation built a large Sunday-school hall in Dinuba, in which it conducted all its services until 1939, when it built a large church with an auditorium seating over 1,000. The congregation has continued to increase and has at present (1954) a membership of 595. Most of these are farmers but some live in town and are engaged in business or as laborers.

The following ministers have served as pastors: J. H. Richert, John Berg, J. J. Hiebert, J. P. Siemens, and B. J. Braun, who is the present pastor. The congregation has a Sunday school, Christian Endeavor, Christian Fellowship, choir, and men's chorus. The Sunday morning service is broadcast. The church does extension work in other communities in which a number of young people are active. J.H.L.

Dinuba (Cal.) Mennonite (MC) Church (unorganized), now extinct. Members of the congregation located in this vicinity in 1906 and 1907. Sunday-school services were first held in the home of E. C. Weaver and then later in a schoolhouse in Dinuba. The conference records for 1911 reported a membership of 22; the maximum membership was 32. No minister was located here, and the members gradually moved away. (S. G. Shetler, *Church Hist. of the Pacific Coast Menn. Conf. Dist.*, Scottdale, 1921.) M.G.

Dirck: see also **Dirk.**

Dirck (Cuiper), an Anabaptist martyr beheaded at Leeuwarden, Dutch province of Friesland, on Dec. 20, 1551. He is said to have held a false opinion of the (Roman Catholic) Sacrament. This martyr is not identical with Dirc Cuper, who was one of the messengers of Jan Matthijs. vDZ.

Inv. Arch. Amst. I, No. 746; J. Reitsma, *Hondert jaren uit de Gesch. der Hervorming . . . in Friesland* (Leeuwarden, 1876) 41, 63.

Dirck, Cleynen (Dierick Jonckhans; Little Dirk in English edition of *Mart. Mir.*), an Anabaptist martyr, a native of Walderveen near Trier, Germany, was taken prisoner at Antwerp, Belgium.

He was examined three times and beheaded at the Steen prison at Antwerp, on July 21, 1558. His name is found in the song "Aenhoort Godt, hemelsche Vader" (Hear, O God, heavenly Father), in the *Liedtboecxken van den Offer des Heeren.* vDZ.

Offer, 565, No. 28; *Mart. Mir.* D 202, E 583; Génard, *Antw. Arch.-Blad* VIII, 447, 464; XIV, 24-25, No. 259; Wolkan, *Lieder*, 62-73; *ML* I, 449.

Dirc(k) Cuper (Cuiper, de Cuyper), an Anabaptist leader in the Netherlands during the first years of the movement. In December 1533 he was one of the twelve apostles sent out from Amsterdam by Jan Matthijsz van Haarlem (*q.v.*). With Bartel Boeckbinder (*q.v.*) Dirck came to Leeuwarden in Friesland, where they baptized and ordained as elders Obbe Philips (*q.v.*) and Hans Barbier (*q.v.*). Nothing more is known about his life. Reitsma erroneously identified him with the Dirck Cuiper who was beheaded at Leeuwarden in 1551. Karel Vos is probably right (*DB* 1917, 101) in stating that a man called Dirck Jacobsz de Cuyper, taken prisoner at Gouda, Dutch province of South Holland, and brought to The Hague on March 5, 1535, is identical with the Dirck Cuper who baptized Obbe Philips. vDZ.

J. Reitsma, *Hondert jaren uit de Geschiedenis der Hervorming en de Hervormde Kerk in Friesland* (Leeuwarden, 1876) 41; *DB* 1917, 98, 101.

Dirck Ewoltsz (Dirrick Eeuwoutssone), a fuller by trade, an Anabaptist martyr, who after having been tortured was beheaded at Haarlem, Dutch province of North Holland, on Nov. 7, 1536. Further particulars are lacking. vDZ.

Inv. Arch. Amst. I, No. 750; *DB* 1917, 153 (here 1537 is given as the year of execution); *Bijdr. en Mededeelingen Hist. Genootschap* XLI (Amsterdam, 1920) 205.

Dirck Houtstapeler, an Anabaptist martyr executed at Zwolle, Dutch province of Overijssel, in March 1534. He was one of the 3,000 Anabaptists who had sailed from Amsterdam to Bergklooster (*q.v.*) en route to Münster, and seems to have been a principal leader on this journey. He was the husband of the martyr Baef Claesdochter (*q.v.*). (Mellink, *Wederdopers*, 38 f.) vDZ.

Dirck Janssen (Dirck de Snijder), a glazier of Amsterdam, took part in the action of the Naaktlopers (*q.v.*); Anabaptists who ran naked along the streets in Amsterdam on Feb. 10, 1535), and was beheaded there Feb. 25, 1535. (Grosheide, *Verhooren*, 57-58.) vDZ.

Dirck Jansz, an Anabaptist martyr of Bocholt, was sentenced to be burned at the stake at Leiden, Holland, on Nov. 24, 1552, together with Heynric Dircsz (*q.v.*) and Adriaen Cornelisz (*q.v.*). These brethren, who steadfastly suffered martyrdom, are celebrated in a song found in the *Liedtboecxken van den Offer des Heeren:* "Ick magh wel droeflijck singen, in desen tijt van noot" (I must sing sadly in this time of distress). According to Karel Vos, *Leidsch Jaarboekje* 1918, 36 ff., Dirck Jansz is the author of a song which he composed while in prison, beginning "Waket doch op met grooten

vlijt" (Awake with zeal), found in the hymnbook
Een nieu Liedtboeck of 1562 and the following editions. (*Offer*, 526, 578 note; *Mart. Mir.* D 133, E
526; Wolkan, *Lieder*, 61.)   vdZ.

Dirck Jansz, an Anabaptist martyr, originally of
Borkelt near Münster, Westphalia, Germany, and
afterwards a citizen of Middelburg, Dutch province
of Zeeland, was tortured there, but refused to name
his brethren. He remained steadfast and maintained
his opinion, for which reason he was "punished"
by being strangled and burned at the stake. The
date of execution was likely Feb. 5, 1561.   vdZ.

K. R. Pekelharing, *Bijdr. voor de Gesch. der Hervorming in Zeeland, Arch. Zeeuwsch Genootschap* VI
(1866) 42, 43.

Dirck Maertenz, an Anabaptist martyr, a chair maker, beheaded at Haarlem, Dutch province of North
Holland, in 1535 together with Florys Ysbrantsz;
both men had been tortured two or three times. He
confessed that he had been rebaptized. Further information is lacking.   vdZ.

Inv. Arch. Amst. I, No. 750; *Bijdr. en Mededeelingen
Hist. Genootschap* XLI, 1920, 202, 203; *DB* 1917, 153.

Dirck Pietersz (alias Smuel or Simil), an Anabaptist martyr, a blacksmith by trade, living in Edam,
Dutch province of North Holland. He had been
baptized and held meetings in his house on the dike
near Edam. He was apprehended together with
Jacob de Geldersman (*q.v.*) on March 24, 1546, and
brought to Amsterdam by ship, where he was examined. Dirck Pietersz confessed that he thought
the Roman Catholic Church could not be the true
church, which was only to be found in the "meeting
of believers"; neither did he believe in purgatory.
He admitted that he had read in his house together
with others "the book of the Gospel." He did not
possess books of Menno Simons or David Joris, but
confessed that he had a Bible, a New Testament, and
a "booklet of the faith." (It is not clear what book
this was.) On May 5 both men were brought to The
Hague, where they were examined again. Dirck
was put on the rack on May 16, but remained
steadfast. He was sentenced to death on May 22.
The next day both Dirck and Jacob were brought
back to Amsterdam and burned at the stake on
May 24. The execution of Dirck must have been
very cruel, for it lasted for more than 24 hours. For
this reason the executioner received special remuneration. Dirck Pietersz while in prison wrote a letter (called *Testament*) to his wife, Wellemoet Claes,
and also a letter to all friends of the evangelical
truth. Both letters are found in the *Martyrs' Mirror*.
The account in the *Martyrs' Mirror* about Dirck
Pietersz is not quite correct. After having mentioned the martyrdom of Dirck Pietersz Smuel and
Jacob de Geldersman, van Braght inserts another
account of two martyrs Andries Smuel and Dirck
Pietersz, 1546 (without date). Here van Braght
must be in error; there is no further trace of a
martyr called Andries Smuel; Andries Smuel and
Dirck Pietersz must be the same.   vdZ.

Inv. Arch. Amst. I, No. 337, 745; *Mart. Mir.* D 75-80,
E 475-81; Grosheide, *Bijdrage*, 108-9, 303; *DB* 1887, 114-
15; 1899, 125.

Dirck de Schilder, an Anabaptist martyr, was executed on Oct. 8, 1558, at Antwerp, Belgium. It is not
known how he was put to death, whether by beheading or burning at the stake. He was probably beheaded, for in the song of the *Liedtboecxken
van den Offer des Heeren,* beginning "Aenhoort
Godt, hemelsche Vader" (Hear, O God, heavenly
Father), it is said that he had to kneel before the
executioner. His official name was Dirck Effeleer(s);
he was a native of Mechelen, Belgium, and a painter
by trade.   vdZ.

Offer, 565; *Mart. Mir.* D 202, E 583; Genard, *Antw.
Arch.-Blad* VIII, 450, 465; IX, 17; XIV, 24-25, No. 265;
ML I, 449.

Dirck van Wormer (Dirck Groede), a native of
Wormer, Dutch province of North Holland, had
tried to snatch the holy sacrament from the hands
of a priest during a procession at Wormer in the
spring of 1535. After this a fight arose, in which
some Anabaptists took an active part. Dirck had
bandaged a wounded Anabaptist and tended him
secretly. It is not clear if Dirck was an Anabaptist
himself or a Sacramentist (*q.v.*, a group who opposed the Roman Catholic doctrine of the holy
sacrament). (*Inv. Arch. Amst.* I, No. 83, 101; *DB*
1909, 15-16.)   vdZ.

Dirckgen Tasch (Dirck or Derk Tasschemaker),
originally from Amsterdam, a little known Anabaptist leader in the Netherlands in its earliest period.
In 1534 he was active in preaching and baptizing in
Leeuwarden and Emden. Later on he lived in Antwerp, where he died in late 1534 or early 1535. His
prophecy (summer of 1534) that after a darkness of
three days the Lord would give the city of Amsterdam to the Anabaptists without bloodshed, is evidence of his eschatological, but peaceful ideas. vdZ.

Grosheide, *Verhooren*, 48; *DB* 1917, 155, No. 57; Mellink, *Wederdopers*, 35, 69, 114 f.

Dirk Andriesz (Dierick Andriessen), an Anabaptist
martyr, beheaded at Zierikzee, Dutch province of
Zeeland, on Oct. 22, 1569. He was a native of
Oorschot in de Kempen, Belgium, and is said to
have been a Mennonite. By trade he may have been
an itinerant merchant or hawker, for his peddler's
pack was publicly sold (proceeds: two guilders and
six pennies).   vdZ.

Mart. Mir. D 424, E 774; K. R. Pekelharing, *Bijdr.
voor de Gesch. der Hervorming in Zeeland, Arch. Zeeuwsch Genootschap* VI, 1866, 82; *ML* I, 71.

Dirk Anoot, an Anabaptist martyr, a native of
Westvleteren, Flanders, Belgium, who was taken
prisoner with Willem de Zager and brought to
Yper (Ieper) in Flanders, where he was burned at
the stake in 1569, the exact date and further particulars being unknown. (*Mart. Mir.* D 406, E 758;
ML I, 74.)   O.H.

Dirk van Borne, a printer of Deventer, Dutch
province of Overijssel, had printed and published the
Groot Wonderboek by David Joris (*q.v.*). He was
seized July 1544; in January 1545 he was placed
under house arrest until August 1545, and even then
he was not allowed to leave the town. Dirk was not
a follower of David Joris; he was a Catholic and

defended himself by saying that he had not known that the book of David Joris which Jurriaen Ketel had given him for printing was a heretical book. (*Inv. Arch. Amst.* I, No. 309; *DB* 1919, 22-23.)

vDZ.

Dirk Gerritsz van den Busch, an Anabaptist martyr, a native of the hamlet of Bus or den Busch near Krommenie in Waterland, Dutch province of North Holland. The account by van Braght (*Mart. Mir.*) has been shown to be incorrect in calling him Jonker Dirk, which suggests that he was a nobleman. Dirk Gerritsz many have been called "jonkman," i.e., an unmarried man. Also the year in which van Braght places the execution, 1542, is wrong. It must have been 1534. On April 15 of that year three Anabaptists from Krommeniedijk were cruelly put to death at The Hague. Their names were Jan Dirksz Walen, Dirk Gerritsz, and Cornelis Luytgens (or Luytsz). They were seized at Bergklooster (*q.v.*) on the boats in which they had sailed from North Holland to go to Münster.

vDZ.

Mart. Mir. D 62, 13, E 464; J. G. de Hoop Scheffer, *Gesch. der Kerkhervorming in Nederland . . .* (Amsterdam, 1873) 567; *DB* 1896, 40; 1899, 125; 1917, 121 (No. 132) 170; Kühler, *Geschiedenis* I, 108.

Dirk Jansz: see **Cortenbosch, Dirk Jansz.**

Dirk Lamberts, an Anabaptist martyr: see **Dierick Lambrechts.**

Dirk Meeuwesz (Dirck Mieuwesz), an Anabaptist martyr, burned at the stake at Vlissingen (Flushing), Dutch province of Zeeland, on May 8, 1571, after he had been imprisoned for more than a year. Once he had the opportunity to escape from prison but he did not, because he did not want to get his jailer in trouble. He steadfastly suffered martyrdom. (*Mart. Mir.* D 537, E 872.)

vDZ.

Dirk van Nijmegen, an otherwise unknown Anabaptist leader in Holland, who was imprisoned at Amsterdam in 1534. (*Inv. Arch. Amst.* I, No. 67; *DB* 1917, 117, No. 67.)

vDZ.

Dirk Philips(z) (Filips) (1504-68), son of a Dutch priest. He became a Franciscan monk. As a man of good education he had a command of Latin and Greek, and also knew some Hebrew. It is doubtful that he wrote in French his booklet on the ban and avoidance, which he published in the French language. It is possible that he studied at a university. H. Schijn (*Hist. Menn. plenior deductio,* 1729, p. 186) calls him a learned man, more learned than Menno Simons. He was not acquainted with Luther's writings.

At the end of 1533 Dirk joined the Anabaptist brotherhood. He was baptized at Leeuwarden in Friesland, by Pieter Houtzager, and was soon afterward, presumably early in 1534, "upon the wish of the brethren" ordained an elder by the laying on of the hands of his own brother Obbe Philips (*q.v.*) at "Den Dam," i.e., Appingedam, in the Dutch province of Groningen. He was soon a leader; in 1537 he was named as one of the outstanding Anabaptist leaders; he took part in the most important

events of the following years, and nearly always was present at the conferences of the elders, as in Goch in 1547, where Adam Pastor (*q.v.*) was banned, and in 1554 in Wismar among the seven elders, who formulated an agreement on a number of contested points. Like Obbe and Menno he was an opponent of the Münsterite doctrines. Against Rothmann's *Restitution* (1534) he wrote his booklet, *Van de geestelijcke Restitution* (On the Spiritual Restitution).

At first Dirk worked in the Netherlands, then in East Friesland, Mecklenburg, Holstein, and Prussia. But he must have gone to the Netherlands on several occasions; about 1561 he baptized several persons in Utrecht and celebrated communion with about 20 brethren (*DB* 1903, 21 f.). We are told that the meeting lasted from four in the morning until seven in the evening; probably not because they needed so much time, but because they wanted to enter and leave the house under cover of darkness. Dirk is described on that occasion as "an old man, not very tall, with a gray beard and white hair." After 1550 his home was at Danzig, where a number of Dutch Mennonites had already located.

Dirk Philips is without doubt the leading theologian and dogmatician among the Dutch and North German Mennonites of that time. He is more systematic than Menno, though of course also more severe and one-sided. Like Menno he preached the doctrine of nonresistance, though there is not much in his writings on this subject. He shares Menno's conception of the Incarnation. Against Adam Pastor he upholds the doctrine of the Trinity. In opposition to his brother Obbe he always put much stress on the visible church, which should preserve itself from the world without spot or wrinkle. In the interest of protecting the brotherhood he demands a strict application of the ban and the subsequent avoidance. The open sinners shall be expelled from the congregation if they do not show genuine repentance; they are to be shunned in daily life, because the church of God, which consists of the elect, must be pure and holy. The bride of Christ dare not forsake her Bridegroom and yield herself to the world and the flesh.

In his book on the church he names seven ordinances of the church of God: pure doctrine, Scriptural use of the sacraments, washing the feet of the saints, separation (ban and avoidance), the command of love, obedience to the commands of Christ, suffering and persecution. On the whole it cannot be denied that there is in Dirk Philips' theology a certain moralism and legalism. He writes better than Menno, but he has less agreeableness, friendliness, and charm. He was a strict, indeed an obstinate person. This can best be seen in the disputes between him and Leenaert Bouwens (*q.v.*). Even considering that the question at issue concerns the pure church of Christ and that this ideal requires a measure of severity, nevertheless the sad consequences of this strict banning and partisanship are without question to be reckoned against the obstinate and proud elder, Dirk Philips. Already in 1565 Leenaert Bouwens had been suspended from his office. In 1567 Dirk journeyed from Danzig to

Emden. Then the division occurred: Dirk sided with the Flemish (*q.v.*), who at once banned the Frisians (*q.v.*), while the Frisians, whom Leenaert had joined, on their side banned the Flemish. Dirk was also banned (July 8, 1567), but did not let it trouble him, because he no longer considered Leenaert and the Frisians as members of the church of God. (Kühler, *Geschiedenis* I, 395-426.)

In the next year Dirk died at Het Falder near Emden, after he had completed his booklet on Christian marriage on March 7, 1568.

Although Dirk Philips surpassed the other elders in knowledge and was a good writer and an eloquent and influential man, he was nevertheless inferior to Menno Simons, with whom he had worked so many years and upon whom he exerted a certain influence in his later years when the severe banning took its course. It is unpleasant to note that Menno's name does not once occur in Dirk's writings. When in the first half of the 17th century the practice of the ban became more lenient among the Dutch and North German Mennonites, the interest in Dirk Philips also waned; his writings are held in high esteem by the Old Order Amish because they advocate the ban and avoidance.

Dirk Philips spread his views in numerous booklets. At the end of his life he collected his writings that had been published, several of which are still extant in their various editions, and published them in a single volume. This is the *Enchiridion oft Hantboecxken van de Christelijcke Leere,* . . . 1564. The "little" handbook (it contains almost 650 pages!) contains the following writings: Confession of Faith, Concerning the Incarnation, Concerning the True Knowledge of Jesus Christ, Apologia, the Call of the Preacher, Loving Admonition (on the ban), Concerning the True Knowledge of God, Exposition of the Tabernacle of Moses, Concerning the New Birth, Concerning Spiritual Restoration, Three Thorough Admonitions, Table of Contents.

In addition he wrote: *Verantwoordinghe ende Refutation op twee Sendtbrieven Sebastiani Franck* (printed in 1567, not extant, and 1619); *Cort doch grondtlick Verhael* (concerning the quarrels between the Flemish and Frisians, printed in 1567); *Van die Echt der Christenen* (printed in 1569, 1602, 1634, 1644, and perhaps other editions); and the tract left at his death on the ban and avoidance, which was translated from the French and printed in 1602.

Of the *Enchiridion* there are in the Dutch language editions of 1564, 1578, 1579, 1600, and 1627. A French edition of 1626 (in the same volume with some writings of Menno Simons and others), German editions in 1715 and Basel in 1802; Lancaster, 1811; Elkhart, 1872 (this and the following German editions include the writings on marriage and on the ban); Scottdale, 1917; English edition, Elkhart, 1910.

Two hymns from the pen of Dirk Philips have been preserved, and were adopted into the old Dutch hymnals of the Mennonites.

F. Pijper edited a complete edition of all the writings (including letters and hymns) of Dirk Philips (*BRN* X).†   vDZ.

Introduction to *BRN* X; *Inv. Arch. Amst.* I, No. 620; Schijn-Maatschoen, *Uitvoeriger Verhandeling van de Geschiedenisse der Mennoniten* II (Amsterdam, 1744) 325-85; K. Vos, *Menno Simons* (Leiden, 1914) see Index; *idem* in *Groningen Volksalmanak* 1916, 131 f.; 136-42; C. Krahn, *Menno Simons* (Karlsruhe, 1936) *passim*, see Index; *DB* 1864, 136; 1867, 59, 62 f.; 1873, 61; 1876, 26 ff., 38; 1881, 75; 1884, 2, 10, 15, 17, 20; 1887, 101 f.; 1893, 5, 12-14, 16, 50, 52-77, 88; 1894, 18-59 *passim*; 1903, 11, 21 f., 39, 41 f.; 1905, 106 ff.; *ML* III, 368.

Dirk Pietersz, an Anabaptist martyr mentioned in *Martyrs' Mirror* (D 75, E 476), is probably identical with Dirck Pietersz (Smuel) (*q.v.*).   vDZ.

Dirk Pietersz Krood, an Anabaptist martyr, a native of Wormer, Dutch province of North Holland, was executed at Enkhuizen, also in the province of North Holland. Particulars are lacking; even the year of execution is unknown. (*Mart. Mir.* D 61, E 464.)   vDZ.

Dirk Roloffszoon, an Anabaptist martyr of Zutphen, beheaded at Leeuwarden, Dutch province of Friesland, on Nov. 12, 1539, because he had been rebaptized and had "a bad opinion of the holy sacrament of the altar."   vDZ.

J. Reitsma, *Honderd jaren uit de Gesch. der Hervorming . . . in Friesland* (Leeuwarden, 1876) 63.

Dirk Vredricx (Vaertgen), an Anabaptist martyr of Krommeniedijk, Dutch province of North Holland, was sentenced to death and beheaded at Haarlem on March 26, 1534, together with six other Anabaptists, because they were rebaptized, had renounced the Roman Catholic doctrines and rebaptized many persons. Dirk is said to have been a preacher. (*Inv. Arch. Amst.* I, No. 745; *DB* 1917, 115, No. 55; *ibid.,* 151-52; 1918, 144; note 2.)   vDZ.

Dirk Wessels (van Wesel), an Anabaptist martyr, was one of a group of 12 Mennonites, among whom was also his wife Janneken, who were taken prisoner at Deventer (*q.v.*), Dutch province of Overijssel, during a hunt of "heretics" by Spanish soldiers. Some of this group forsook their faith for a while, but later repented, and all remained steadfast, though they were cruelly tortured. On May 24 they had a dispute with some monks. Between this day and June 16, 1571, Dirk was burned at the stake at Deventer together with Harmen de Wever (*q.v.*) and four women martyrs. Before he was put to death, he knelt for prayer, kissed Harmen and encouraged him by lifting up his hand to heaven; then he cheerfully went to the stake and was burned. (*Mart. Mir.* D 552 ff., E 885; *DB* 1919, 29, 35; *ML* I, 449.)   NEFF, vDZ.

Dirk Willemsz, an Anabaptist martyr, was born and lived at Asperen, Dutch province of South Holland. He was burned at the stake outside the town of Asperen on May 16, 1569. Van Braght (*Mart. Mir.*) relates the following story: Dirk managed to escape from prison; pursued by a guard or policeman he succeeded in saving his life by crossing a wide river covered with thin ice; the policeman following him on the ice fell in and was on the point of drowning. Then Dirk came back and saved the man, who was very grateful and would have let him go, but the burgomaster, coming along, ordered him to seize the heretic. So Dirk was brought back to prison and after some months died steadfastly. In the *Martyrs' Mirror* there is a fine etching of the rescue. (*Mart. Mir.* D 387, E 741.)   vdZ.

Dirks, Heinrich, a missionary, elder, evangelist, and writer, was born Aug. 17, 1842, at Gnadenfeld, Molotschna Mennonite settlement, Ukraine. His father was David Dirks from Brenkenhoffswalde, Germany, and belonged to the Gnadenfeld (*q.v.*) Mennonites of Russia who had been closely associated with the Moravian Brethren in Germany and stimulated a revival of missionary and cultural interests among the Mennonites of Russia. Heinrich Dirks graduated from the secondary *Vereinsschule* at the age of twenty-one. He was baptized by Elder August Lenzmann May 12, 1860.

Dirks was not only the first Mennonite of Russia to obtain a formal education abroad but also the first Mennonite of Russia to go out as a missionary to a foreign land. This happened in the days when revivals were sweeping through the Mennonite settlements renewing their religious and educational interests and also resulting in the founding of the Mennonite Brethren Church. Heinrich Dirks enrolled at the *Missionshaus* at Barmen, Germany, in 1862 and was graduated in 1866. During the following year he received private instruction in Amsterdam in the Javanese, Malayan, Dutch, and English languages. In 1867 he was ordained minister at Gnadenfeld and on Aug. 31, 1869, he was ordained missionary and elder by August Lenzmann. During the same year he married Agnes Schröder. After an impressive farewell from the Mission Board of Amsterdam they left the Netherlands on Nov. 24, sailing to the Dutch East Indies, where he opened a new Mennonite mission field at Pakanten, Sumatra, Jan. 10, 1871. On Aug. 6 he baptized the first three converts and within ten years he had baptized 125 converts from heathenism and Mohammedanism. Because of the education of his children he returned to Gnadenfeld in May 1881, and he was made elder of his home congregation. To the end of his life he was also a conference traveling evangelist and a promoter of missions. His wish to return to Sumatra to visit his son David, who succeeded him in mission work, was never fulfilled. He had already reserved passage for a trip in 1914 when he became ill. During his illness he was in Sumatra in thought almost constantly. He died on Feb. 8, 1915.

Dirks ranks among the men like Johann Cornies in his significance to the Mennonites of Russia. The chairman of the Dutch Mennonite Board of Missions wrote in his memory, "The fact that during the years a number of brethren and some sisters from Russia (a total of 13 not counting wives of missionaries) have joined our mission and the fact that the Mennonite congregations of Russia have supported the work of our mission in an increasing measure we owe above all to him" (*Zondagsbode,* May 16, 1915). In 1910 he was appointed a member of this Mission Board and attended the meeting in Amsterdam during that year. He traveled extensively in Germany, Holland, and America, in the interest of missions. In Russia he was the speaker at mission festivals which took place between Pentecost and the late fall from year to year at the various settlements, a tradition which he built up and which dated back to Moravian influence. At the *Bundeskonferenz* meetings and in the *Mennonitisches Jahrbuch* he gave his annual reports on the mission work. The financial reports of the Dutch Mennonite Mission Board indicate to what a degree they relied on the contributions solicited in Russia through his efforts.

Dirks was also a very active promoter of other conference activities. From 1903 to 1910 he edited the *Mennonitisches Jahrbuch,* which gradually became a conference publication and is today one of the most valuable sources of information on the Mennonites of Russia before World War I, dealing with settlements, congregations, education, missions, philanthropic institutions, including conference reports, etc. As a conference worker Dirks emphasized a warm, evangelical Christianity, and favored the establishment of a theological school and conference publications. In his numerous writings he not only pointed the way to an aggressive positive Christian witness at home and abroad but also lamented the disrupting forces at work through the "separatistic" efforts of the groups separating themselves from the main body of the Mennonites in his day. Many of his writings are devoted to this concern: to strengthen the congregations against all disrupting forces, whether of secular or religious nature.

Dirks was not only a very influential and popular speaker but also a gifted writer. Among his many booklets and articles we list the following: "Die Mennoniten in Russland," an annual survey started in 1903 in *Mennonitisches Jahrbuch* and continued until 1911; "Aus der Gnadenfelder Gemeindechronik," *ibid.,* 1908-12; "Die Mennonitische Aeussere Mission," *ibid.,* 1903-13; *Ist es recht, dass man sich noch einmal taufen lässt?* (Gnadenfeld, 1891); *Das Reich Gottes . . .* (Gnadenfeld, 1892); *Taufe, Gemeindebeschaffenheit und Abendmahl* (Gross-Tokmak, 1904); *Statistik der Mennonitengemeinden in Russland Ende 1905* (Gnadenfeld, 1906); *Adressbüchlein der Kirchenbuchführer der Mennonitengemeinden Russlands* (Berdyansk, 1913).   C.K.

Friesen, *Brüderschaft,* 552-59, 265-66; *Verslag der Doopsgezinde Vereeniging tot bevordering der Evangelieverbreiding,* 1865-1915; *DB* 1891, 32-41; 1893, 106-10; *Bundesbote-Kalender,* 1916, 28; *ML* I, 450.

Dirks, Kornelius, was ordained as minister of the Waldheim Mennonite Church in the Molotschna (*q.v.*) settlement in South Russia in 1876 and elder in 1877. When Mennonites of the Molotschna villages in the years after 1880 settled on the Kuban River he joined them and became the first elder of the Wohldemfürst - Alexandrodar Mennonite Church. Little is known about his life and activities. C.K.

Die Kubaner Ansiedlung (Steinbach, 1953) 37; H. Dirks, *Statistik . . .* (Gnadenfeld, 1906) 36.

Dirks Mennonite Church (CGC), located northeast of Halstead, Kan., is now the Grace Mennonite Church (*q.v.*), west of Halstead.   P.C.H.

Dirksen (Dircksen, Dirks, Duerksen, Derksen, Doerksen, Dercksen, Dyrksen, Dirssen, Dirck, Dircks, Derks), a Mennonite family name of Frisian origin, appearing in all West Prussian congregations; first mentioned in 1568 at Danzig and in 1605 at Gross Lubin. Most of the families in the Vistula Valley and their descendants adopted the form Dirks. In 1776, 42 families of this name were counted in West Prussia (without Danzig), and in 1935 (without Elbing) 62 persons. Members of the family emigrated to Russia and America. The name is now widely represented among all North and South American Mennonite groups having their origins in South Russia and Poland.

Some of the outstanding representatives of this name were Alle Derks (*q.v.*), Heinrich Dirks (*q.v.*), and David G. Dürksen (*q.v.*). (G. Conrad, *Gesch. der Familie Dirksen und der Adelsfamilie von Dirksen*, Görlitz, 1905.)   **G.R.**

Dirksz, Abraham: see **Bierens, Abraham D.**

Dirksz, Bastiaen, author of a Dutch Mennonite devotional writing and hymnbook: *Kleyn Boet-boecxken oft aenwijsinghe uyt de H. Schriftuere, hoe dat een Mensche hem behoort te schicken na den Raet des Heeren. Noch is hier achter by gevoeght de Pelgrimage des Christelicken Pelgrims. Hierna volgen noch sommighe Liedekens gemaeckt by den selfden* (Rotterdam, 1630). No further information about Dirksz was available.   **vDZ.**

Dirksz, Jacob (called Oom Jacob Dirksz), was an elder of the Frisian congregation of Wormerveer (*q.v.*), Dutch province of North Holland, 1648-89. During his leadership some troubles arose in the congregation of Wormerveer, because a part of the members turned to more liberal views. Oom Jacob, though maintaining the confessions and being more conservative than most of the members of his church, was much respected and succeeded in settling the quarrels. Jacob Dirksz wrote a number of books: *Eenige Predicatien tot Boete . . .* (1st ed., 1673; 2d ed., Amsterdam, 1697); *De Christelyke Huisvader* (Amsterdam, 1677); *Vijf Predicatien over eenige duistere . . . Schriftuurplaatzen* (Amsterdam-Hoorn, 1678); *Een Allegorisch-Historisch Verhaal van het . . . Koningryk van Salem,* with pictures by Jan Luyken (Amsterdam, 1683). He also composed some hymns, which were inserted in C. Stapel's *Lusthof der Zielen* (*q.v.*). Jacob Dirksz is the ancestor of the widespread Dekker (*q.v.*) family.   **vDZ.**

H. Schijn, *Uitvoeriger Verh. van de Gesch. der Mennoniten, . . .* (Amsterdam, 1744) 653-56; *Biogr. Wb.* II, 502-3.

Dirmstein, a district in the Palatinate, under the jurisdiction of Alzey (*q.v.*) until it was ceded to the bishopric of Worms. Mennonites were found here as early as 1588 and 1596. To the Dirmstein district belonged the villages of Obersülzen, Heppenheim auf der Wiese, Gerolsheim, Rodenbach, and Harxheim, where Swiss Mennonites settled after 1650. When the Anabaptist Concession of 1664 allowed them to settle, there were already 40 Mennonite households (172 persons) in the Dirmstein area; in

1680, 46 households (218 persons); in 1686, 57 households (number of persons not stated).

Economically, as rebuilders of the badly devastated regions of Alzey, the Swiss were highly esteemed. In 1667 the Count of Sayn-Wittgenstein advocated bringing in more Mennonites "from the lower countries." Nevertheless they received little favorable treatment. In 1658 the Mennonites appealed in vain for release from the fee (30 Talers) they were required to pay (see **Nonresistance**), even though there were many poor among them, and rebuilding the dilapidated farms required large amounts of money. In the 1680's their meetings were disturbed, contrary to the agreement in the renewed Concession. Orders were in fact issued forbidding their "too great attendance of meetings" (50 to 100 persons met every three or four weeks in a barn at Dirmstein), and expelling the preachers who came from the outside, principally from Mannheim (*q.v.*). The petitions of the Mennonites were finally granted to the extent of making religious activity a little easier.

This subdistrict is no longer listed in later documents, the Mennonites having left the villages largely because of war. In 1802 Dirmstein still had 33 Mennonites. The names of the Mennonites at Dirmstein were Baumer, Blos, Blum, Braun, Gassert, Grauwinkel, Hörstein, Jansen, Kramer, Linn, Michel, Schmidt, Schumacker.

The method of farming introduced by the Möllingers (*q.v.*) in Monsheim-Pfeddersheim spread to Dirmstein by 1800. Schwerz (*q.v.*), the noted agrarian reformer of the time, described conditions there, especially of the farm and distillery of the Jansons (*q.v.*).   **E.H.C.**

Chr. Neff, "Quellen zur Gesch. der Menn. in der Kurpfalz" (ms.); J. G. Widder, *Geogr. Beschreibung der Kurpfalz* (Leipzig, 1786-88); J. N. Schwerz, *Beobachtungen über den Ackerbau der Pfälzer* (Berlin, 1816) 188 ff.; Frey, *Geogr.-hist.-stat. Beschreibung des Rheinkreises, dermalen Pfalz* IV (Speyer, 1832); Chr. Hege, *Die Täufer in der Kurpfalz* (Frankfurt, 1908) 144, 154; *ML* I, 451.

Dirschau (Polish, *Tczew*), a city of some 25,000 pop. on the left bank of the Vistula some 20 miles south of Danzig, formerly Prussian, since 1920 Polish, was the seat of the headquarters of the MCC-MRC Polish relief unit 1947-48.   **H.S.B.**

Discipline, Book of (or *Rules and Discipline*), the body of rules and regulations governing the exercise of the authority of the church in the care and control of its members for the maintenance of purity of faith and life, the removal of offenses, and the general edification of the church, and including penalties for disobedience up to and including excommunication. All Catholic and Protestant denominations have such a body of rules and regulations, written or unwritten, and many of them specifically term the written form "the discipline" or "the book of discipline." For instance, the Presbyterian Church in the U.S.A. first adopted its present 30-page "book of discipline" in 1788. The Methodist Episcopal Church has a Book of Discipline of over 300 pages.

Printed disciplines either of congregations or conferences are found in all North American Mennonite branches. All the district conferences of the

Mennonite Church (MC) have a printed conference "discipline," which usually had its origin at the very beginning of the conference. The Eastern District Conference of the General Conference Mennonite Church published its *Ordnung* in 1848. The Evangelical Mennonites of Eastern Pennsylvania (now Mennonite Brethren in Christ) published its first *Doctrine of Faith and Church Discipline* in 1867 (tr. of *Glaubenslehre und Kirchenzucht-Ordnung* of 1866). In those groups which have congregational autonomy, the "disciplines" are usually congregational, sometimes stated in the form of constitutions or articles of faith; in others they are conference disciplines.

The content of the disciplines varies with the degrees of strictness in discipline. Usually a discipline specifies the various items of belief or conduct which are forbidden, states how disobedient members are to be dealt with, defines the duties of the church officials and the congregation with respect to discipline, and states the grounds for forfeiture and restoration of membership. H.S.B.

Discipline, Concept, Idea, and Practice of. The concept of discipline implies the adoption and maintenance by the group of standards of faith and life which are binding upon the individual members. It accordingly implies a certain doctrine of the church, namely (1) that the body of the church has authority over individual members, and (2) that the church needs clearly defined ideas of faith and conduct, which must be applied. Thus the church is not only a worshiping fellowship of believers or saints, but a body with a certain order as an essential part of its life. The concept of discipline implies that it is the duty of the church to maintain this order by the exercise of spiritual pressure as well as by the preaching of the Gospel and the proclamation of standards of righteousness and holy living. The spiritual pressure serves to impress upon the individual the serious nature of sin and transgression against the law of God and the standard of the Gospel as set forth in the standards of the church, warn him of dangers and harm to spiritual life resulting from such transgressions, and finally severs him from the fellowship of the body as unworthy of and dangerous to the body. The pressure may be exercised by the direct admonition of the bishop-elder, pastor, or deacon, or by the expression of the voice of the church in resolutions or votes, or by the ban and excommunication. Teaching and counseling of course usually precede and accompany such disciplinary pressures and are an aid. The purpose of all truly Scriptural discipline is the correction of errors and sins and the restoration of the offenders; discipline accordingly cannot be punitive, but must always be loving and redemptive.

Discipline and the maintenance of order was characteristic of the Anabaptist-Mennonite movement from the very beginning and in all areas, and continued to be so until in the late 19th century. By this time discipline was becoming lax in the more liberal Dutch and Northwest German groups and ultimately disappeared there. There has been a noticeable decline in certain other groups, also in North America. This decline of the principle of discipline is something different from the change of the content of discipline, which is also noticeable in most groups. In certain groups and times discipline has been very strict and rigid with the prescription of many and detailed rules governing conduct, costume, marriage, occupations, relation with the outside world, consumption of food and beverages, etc. Disputes over strictness, details of rules, or methods of enforcement have often occurred in Mennonite history and not seldom led to schisms both in congregations and in larger groups including an entire body. In fact most Mennonite schisms have been over matters of discipline.

Historically the bishop-elder has been the bearer of disciplinary power. When his prestige has been high, discipline has been vigorous and effective. The decline in the prestige and influence of this office has usually been the signal for a decline in discipline. Originally the congregation shared directly in the disciplinary function, its approval being required to make the disciplinary proposals or acts of the bishop effective. In later times (19th century in Russia, 20th century in Mennonite Church, MC, in Pennsylvania) the bishops acquired considerable freedom of disciplinary action either as individuals or as a body (e.g., Lancaster Conference Board of Bishops). Among the Old Order Amish it is still necessary to have the congregation approve the bishop's exercise of disciplinary power.

Severe or harsh exercise of disciplinary power by the bishop has often produced resentment and resistance among the membership and reduced the pastoral and preaching effectiveness of the bishop involved. At times the temptation to depend on personal pressure or authoritarian methods has resulted in a spiritually dangerous legalism and externalism. But Mennonite history has often proved that proper discipline, combined with good pastoral work and effective preaching, produces a wholesome church administration and leadership, which makes for a strong and vigorous church with high standards, in contrast to the church without discipline, when each "does that which is right in his own eyes."

The decision of the Anabaptists to withdraw from the state churches, both Catholic and Protestant, but particularly the Protestant, was in a certain sense the result of differing concepts concerning church discipline, which in turn were based on differing concepts of the church and the nature of Christianity. One of the most common charges by the Anabaptists was that the state churches tolerated sin among both members and clergy and did not attempt to maintain true holiness. The Lutheran churches did establish a certain amount of discipline, which gradually died out (excommunication was practically dead by the 17th century), and minor forms of discipline were displaced largely in the rationalistic period. The Calvinistic churches believed in discipline and practiced it much more than the Lutherans; in fact they considered true discipline as one of the marks of the true church. Even in Calvinism, however, discipline gradually died out. From the 18th century on, discipline was almost invisible in all Protestantism except the English Free

Churches and the North American denominations. The state churches had come to rely on preaching and religious instruction in the schools and on catechism. Methodism revived discipline and maintained it vigorously until the late 19th century.

The influence of the Anabaptist critique on the practice of discipline in the Reformation period is now recognized, though not fully studied. The best example is Hesse, Germany, where Bucer (*q.v.*) was called in by the authorities to aid in meeting the Anabaptist challenge and where the Ziegenhain *Kirchen-Ordnung* of 1538 was the direct result of a conscientious attempt to meet the Anabaptist critique. Adam Krafft, who was the court chaplain and Professor of Theology at the University of Marburg, and other leading clergymen had openly admitted the validity of the Anabaptist critique for some years and called for a stricter discipline as the best means to turn the Anabaptists (see **Hesse**). Bucer had been forced to face the Anabaptist challenge in Strasbourg from 1525 on, where the Anabaptist influence in a stricter discipline is admitted. Whether Calvin (*q.v.*) was influenced in his disciplinary concepts by Anabaptism, particularly during his Strasbourg period 1538-41 or even 1535-36 (he married Idelette de Bure, *q.v.*, the widow of an Anabaptist), is uncertain. Zwingli's introduction of discipline in Zürich was certainly motivated in part by the Anabaptist threat. The Bernese government struggled with the Anabaptists for three centuries and more than once admitted the prevalence of offensive sins and vices in the church, as the Anabaptists charged. In 1585, for instance, an official mandate declared, "This is the greatest reason that many God-fearing pious people forsake our church [to join the Brethren]."

This major difference between the state churches, for that matter the mass of nominal Christendom at all times, and the Anabaptist-Mennonite movement has always been present. But it is not only the latter who have called for and practiced discipline, but a long series of separatist groups from the very beginning of Christian history down to the present day. The requirement of discipline is in fact regarded by most students of church history and the sociology of religion as a characteristic of the "sect-type." For the Anabaptist-Mennonites at least it has been a mark of the true New Testament Church. (See **Ban, Excommunication.**)   H.S.B.

Disputations (colloquia, religious debates), discussions on matters of doctrine, with the purpose of eliminating differences within a group, throwing light on differences between various religious groups, and bringing victory to one side in the argument. Discussions of this kind have been known from the very early days of Christianity, but they were not of great influence in preserving the unity of the church until the time of the Councils, at which religious debates constituted a part of the arranged program. The presupposition was that the church was in possession of the absolute truth, that deviations were due to erroneous thinking on the part of the differing side, and that absolute truth would be restored by the revelation and condemnation of the error.

From the point of view of theological history these debates took place against a background of medieval views and concepts. Thinking does not yet have as its goal understanding through reason, but rather understanding through revelation. The word is still accompanied by mystical conceptions and a bondage to the medieval manner of thought is still noticeable in the leaders. The masses likewise were still more held by the medieval attitudes and frequently gave these disputations a significance approaching direct revelation from God. For this reason the leaders of the parties in the disputes often laid great value on publicity.

The disputations took place publicly and privately, before the assembled populace with noted speakers and theologians, or in the narrower circle of scholars and leaders. Public debates cut deeply into the life and thinking of all classes of society, since each side wanted to win the masses to decide in its favor. Thus the colloquia in the course of time became discussions with "party political" purposes designed to win popular support, which were hardly able to produce a change of opinion in the opposing party. Every utterance of either side was turned into a weapon against it, so that in medieval times the church frequently refused to sponsor such debates.

When the Reformation had progressed to the point where differences between the various parties were clearly defined and there was no possibility of union or arbitration of differences, the ruling princes of the most democratic regions (Switzerland, Holland, South German states) tried by means of public disputations to compromise divergent views among the representatives on certain definite doctrines, and to present them for decision to the populace, which thought in accord with "natural law," and thus hoped with more or less compulsion to eliminate debatable and disturbing questions from the relations of individuals to the church as a whole and to the state. For instance, the invitation to the disputation of Frankenthal in 1571 gives as its aim the lessening of the lamentable division then prevailing.

Besides the religious debates of a public and general nature there was also an enormous number of dialogs between the heretics and the pastors of the church, which were exploited as propaganda by means of broadsides. They had their influence upon the people, who were very deeply disquieted and were therefore actively interested in religious and political thought; but their benefit to the larger parties was merely incidental.

We shall consider here only those disputations that deal with the Anabaptists. Of the three great Protestant churches only the Reformed arranged public disputations with the Anabaptists and Mennonites, and usually at government initiation; there were none with the Lutherans. Public debates between Catholics and Anabaptists were completely out of the question; only individual cross-examinations by inquisitors in the various prisons are reported by van Braght in the *Martyrs' Mirror*.

In August 1525 the first debate between the Anabaptists and Oecolampadius took place in Basel.

No formal decision was reached at the conclusion of this debate. Nor was the second disputation, June 10, 1527, sponsored by the government.

In Austerlitz (Moravia) a debate took place between the Anabaptists and the Reformed, at which it was decided that children should take part in the communion service. Conditions in Moravia were very similar to those in Switzerland.

At the great disputation of 1528 in Bern, which was to give impetus to the introduction of the Reformation, some Anabaptists were present, but they were held under arrest until the close of the disputation, lest their appearance disrupt the existing unity against Rome. They were invited to a private discussion with the clergy on Jan. 17 (*ML* I, 282). "Completely convinced of their error" they were banished from city and canton. George Blaurock and Hans Pfistermeyer of Aarau were the Anabaptist leaders.

In Zürich as well, there was no want of attempts to bridge the differences. On Jan. 17 and March 20, 1525, disputations were held with the Anabaptist leaders, dealing chiefly with the question of infant baptism, without any yielding by the Anabaptists. Zwingli met their just demands to the extent that he introduced the Protestant communion service in place of the Catholic mass, as well as a new baptismal formula. Even though he remained far behind the actual demands of the radical Anabaptists, this concession, which was not even a concession to him, deprived the radicals of some of their basis for opposition. Of greater significance for both parties was the debate that took place Nov. 6-8, 1525.

1. The November disputation at Zürich was arranged under the influence of the peasant unrest. It was attended by Zwingli, Leo Jud, and the Anabaptist leaders, Grebel and Manz. Hubmaier did not appear, contrary to his promise to be there. Four special supervisors were appointed to see that the debate took an orderly course: the abbot of Cappel, the steward of Küssnacht, Dr. Sebastian Hofmeister, pastor of Schaffhausen, and Dr. Joachim Watt, mayor of St. Gall. A great crowd appeared. The proceedings were held in the cathedral, since the council chamber proved too small. The theses formulated in Zwingli's *Taufbüchlein* were used as the basis of the discussions. In spite of the deficient discipline of the Anabaptists in their speaking, the victory was not an easy one for the Zwinglians. The arguments pro and con are given in Zwingli's book, *Ueber Dr. Balthasar Hubmaiers Taufbüchlein.* The disputation took its course without positive results, because the Anabaptists could not be deflected from their views. After this debate severe measures were passed against the Anabaptists.

The disputation of Dec. 20-22, 1530, at St. Gall was an interlude, in which the Reformed sought clarification on the demands made by the Anabaptists, especially the church ban. At the Städtetag (Sept. 27, 1530) Oecolampadius made the proposal that the ban be introduced, but this was rejected by Zwingli.

2. The disputation in Zofingen (Bern), July 1-9, 1532, was attended by the pastors B. Haller of Bern, Caspar Megander, Sebastian Hofmeister of Schaffhausen, and Sulzer of Basel. Among the 23 Anabaptists present were Hans Hotz, Simon Lautz, Christian Brügger, and Linggi (whom Haller described as *homo doctus, eloquens et mirus hypocrita, ad imponenedum aptissimus,* in a letter to Bullinger, July 25, 1532). The report (protocol) was edited by both sides. It constitutes one of the earliest doctrinal statements for many Anabaptist congregations of Switzerland and South Germany. The basis of the disputation was the first article, "The love of God and one's neighbor is an overriding principle in all discussions in this debate." The question as to whether the call of the Anabaptists was a divine one received a negative answer from the Reformed side. The Anabaptists required a church composed of members who had been converted to repentance and a reform of life. The discussion on the ban develops into the query, whether one man is competent to judge concerning the salvation of another and ends on the point of faith in good works, as a criterion. In reply to the question on the "call of the preachers, whether they are of God and who should send them out," the Anabaptists held to appointment by the congregation as the only Scripturally valid one and refused all material pay, i.e., all salary from the "possessions of idols," the Catholic endowed funds. The discussion ended with the question of baptism. Exile from the canton and a mandate against the Anabaptists were the tangible results of this debate.

3. The Bern disputation of March 11-17, 1538, was arranged at the request of the Anabaptists of the canton of Bern who sought an opportunity to explain their faith and doctrine. It is one of the most important disputations ever held and of great value in documenting the doctrines of the Swiss Brethren. The minutes were not published but have been preserved in three copies in the Bern Cantonal Archives. Many Reformed pastors from all parts of the canton were present; their chief speakers were the three Bern preachers, Dr. Sebastian Meier, Peter Kunz, and Erasmus Ritter, also Simon Sulzer of Basel, and Johannes Relligkan, although 20 speakers took part. The apostate Anabaptists, Andreas Rappenstein of Rohrbach and Hans Pfistermeier of Aarau, were present by request. Forty-one Anabaptists were present, five being from outside the canton. Their chief speakers were Hans Hotz of Grüningen, Mathis Wiser of Bremgarten, Wälti Gerber of Röthenbach, Lorentz Aeberli and Hans Haslibacher of Sumiswald, and Christian Brügger of Rohrbach. Seven articles were set up for the discussion, which was to be "based on the New and Old Testaments which were to be the authority": (1) the Old and New Testaments (their relative value and authority); (2) the ministry (its proper calling and mission, and which side has the true calling?); (3) the church (which side has the true church, and is it to be sinless?); (4) infant baptism (is it Christian?); (5) the oath (can a Christian take an honest, true oath?); (6) the state (can a Christian serve as an official?); (7) the ban (how ought it to be used, and which side uses it correctly?). Four presidents were appointed to represent the council, two from

each house, who not only presided but determined the outcome. If the Anabaptists hoped to secure toleration they must have been disappointed. The conclusion was that the Anabaptists were heretics, not to be tolerated in the canton. The five foreigners, as well as any Bern citizens previously expelled, had to leave at once, while those who were condemned for the first time were given a short time to wind up their affairs and leave. And disobedience to the decrees, or return to the canton by the exiles, would result in an immediate death sentence. Only one Anabaptist recanted. Three of the Anabaptist speakers were later executed: Aeberli in 1539, Gerber in 1566, and Hans Haslibacher in 1571 (J. Matthijssen, "The Bern Disputation of 1538," *MQR* XXII, 19-33).

4. In 1540-50 the disputations already had a political character. The attempts of some Anabaptists to emigrate to Moravia led to other disputations, in order to retain the Anabaptists and their economic value in the country. This was especially the case in South Germany, where Calvinistic tendencies had found entry, which made contacts with the Anabaptists easier. It was hoped that "the poor, misled people" could be won for the church, i.e., for the nation. The more open-minded theologians sought points of contact. This must be considered as the reason for calling the disputation of Pfeddersheim shortly before the disputation of Worms, by Otto Heinrich of the Palatinate (August 1557). Marbach, the more liberal theologian of Strasbourg, conducted the debate; 19 heads of Anabaptist congregations were also present. Subjects for discussion were all the debated questions (baptism, government, oath, leaving the state church, etc.). The state church declared itself the victor and demanded that the other side, "convinced of its error," give up its views. A mandate against the Anabaptists settled the matter; the leaders were expelled from the country. The disputation in Worms (September-October 1557) found the Catholic and Lutheran clergy united in their condemnation of "all the sects and mobs of the Anabaptists," upon penalty of death.

5. The minutes of the Frankenthal disputation of May 28-June 19, 1571, for the various views of the Swiss, German, and Dutch Anabaptists furnish by far the most important document of the period. It was instituted by Elector Frederick III with the purpose of uniting the Reformed and the Anabaptists. All Anabaptists, of whatever branch, were promised safe conduct. It was a larger version of the disputation of Pfeddersheim (Hege, *Die Täufer in der Kurpfalz,* 112-35). To avoid all misunderstandings, the program for each day was presented and reviewed in advance. Representatives of the Palatine church were G. Verstegus, Peter Dathenus, Eng. Faber, P. Colonius, Fr. Mosellanus, Xylander, Martin Neander, C. Eubuleus, and G. Gebinger. The Anabaptists were represented by 15 persons. The speakers of the Swiss Brethren were Hans Büchel, Rauf, and Ranich; Peter Walpot, Peter Hutt, and Leonhard Summer were the Hutterian Brethren speakers. According to Wolkan (*Lieder*) there were also Mennonites among them, though

they cannot be identified. Nor did the Hutterites speak officially; indeed, they refused to speak when challenged to do so by Dathenus.

Thirteen points were presented to the Anabaptists to be answered. The first question, whether the Scriptures of the Old Testament were equally valid with those of the New Testament, they answered by saying that they gave the preference to the New Testament, but without rejecting the Old. To the second question, whether Father, Son, and Holy Spirit were one being and three persons, they answered yes. The third question was purely theological: whether Christ received His physical being from the physical substance of the Virgin Mary or elsewhere. The Brethren gave an ambiguous answer. They admitted that Christ was conceived of the Holy Spirit and born of the Virgin, but they declined to discuss "what or how much He received from the Virgin Mary." The fourth question concerned "whether children are conceived or born in original sin and are therefore by nature the children of wrath and deserving of eternal death." The Brethren admitted that children were sinful, but they declined to say anything about their damnation. On this point the Swiss Brethren differed from the Hutterian Brethren. The formulation of the question by the Palatinate clergy was based on this difference. The Swiss Brethren were also at variance with the Mennonites in asserting that all men must die for their own sin and not because of Adam's disobedience. To the fifth question, "whether the believers of the Old Testament are one church with the believers of the New Testament, and one people of God," the Swiss Brethren replied that the people of the Old Testament were governed by the law, the others by the liberty of the Gospel, and that the former would also receive forgiveness of their sin. The fifth question carried the additional point, whether a Christian could accept government office; this the Anabaptists answered negatively, but expressly denied having asserted that the government serves the devil, and said they considered the government to be a "servant of God, which will reward each justly." The sixth question treated the question whether salvation comes by grace through faith, or whether it could be partly earned by good works. The Brethren agreed with the Reformed that the ground of our salvation is absolute obedience to Jesus Christ. The seventh article discussed the question whether the essence of this flesh will be resurrected or whether another body will be created by God. The Reformed insisted that the substance of this flesh will be resurrected, whereas the Brethren believed that this body will be dissolved and that the risen body will be a glorified one. The eighth article discussed the harsh regulations of the Dutch Mennonites on the ban and the divorce of the unbelieving spouse, whereas the Swiss Brethren consented to divorce only on the grounds of unfaithfulness. The ninth question, whether Christians may buy and own property without violating brotherly love, had reference to the Hutterian Brethren, for whom Walpot replied that none of them wished to discuss this question. The Swiss

Brethren condemned only the misuse of possessions and superfluous possessions by some in the face of the poverty of others. The tenth question dealt for the second time with the government, the eleventh with the oath, the twelfth with baptism and infant baptism, the thirteenth with communion, which the Brethren interpreted as an outward symbol in memory of the suffering and death of Christ.

6. The disputation of Emden in 1578 was occasioned by the imprisonment of an Anabaptist preacher for holding forbidden meetings. When he declared himself willing to discuss his faith with the Reformed, he was released. Other political questions became involved. Mennonite leaders from Holland were called to Emden to heal the breaches between the parties. Leaders of the Flemish, Frisians, and Waterlanders were present (Blaupot t. C., *Groningen* II, 88 f.), even Dirk Philips came. The Reformed were represented by laymembers and preachers (Menso Alting, *q.v.,* Mellesius of Huite, Frito Ryords of Oldersum, and others). Alting had already published a book against the Anabaptists. The Anabaptists were represented by Pieter van Ceulen, Brixius Gerritsz, Busschaert, Paulus de Bakker, Christiaen Arends, and Jan van Ophoorn. The disputation lasted from Feb. 27 to May 17, 1578, with 124 sessions. The minutes were immediately recorded and signed by the secretaries and the participants. The public was admitted by Duke John, contrary to the original intention. Many citizens attended.

Fourteen points were agreed upon for the Emden debate: (1) the Trinity and its essential unity; (2) the creation of man; (3) the fall, original sin, and freedom of the will; (4) Christ, His true deity and humanity, and whether He was born of the substance of Mary; (5) justification, sanctification, and regeneration; (6) good works; (7) the church and membership therein; (8) the call of the preachers and ministers; (9) baptism and infant baptism; (10) communion; (11) the ban; (12) government; (13) the oath; (14) the resurrection of the body.

The representatives of the Anabaptists were all simple men who insisted on Luther's translation of the Bible as the foundation of their arguments. Only of Brixius was it said (reported by Emmius) that he was "somewhat unusual in this sect, well-versed in the ancient languages and the liberal arts." Of Pieter van Ceulen one of the chairmen said that he would argue them all out of the church, if he had the education of his opponents. Questions and illustrations were generally taken from real life. Herein Pieter van Ceulen occasionally embarrassed his opponents. The course of the disputation produced less ill nature than might have been expected. Pieter van Ceulen's questions: should a preacher in time of revolution on the basis of his office and not on orders of the government assume governmental power? Does the call of a minister give him the inherent right to cause his brethren and sisters to sentence Mennonites to death, so that these are burned to death? could be answered by the opposition only with a provisional yes. Alting postulated a different concept of the church, which transferred government authority to the church (*Gemeinde*)

and permitted the persecution of heretics. The outcome was not a definite success for the Anabaptists. They were afraid of the consequences and also refrained from joining in the conclusions. The minutes were accepted by the Anabaptists with only slight objections (*Protokol van Emden: U. Emmius, Vita Mensonis Altingii*).

7. The disputation of Leeuwarden in the Dutch province of Friesland was held Aug. 16-Nov. 17, 1596, between Ruardus Acronius (*q.v.*) and Pieter van Ceulen. The chairmen were Douwe van Sytzama, Aede van Eysinga, Rombertus Ulenborgh, mayor of Leeuwarden, and Dr. Pieter Jansz, a sheriff. Pieter van Ceulen was supported by Dirck Doedesz, a fellow citizen. The disputation was conducted in question and answer, in statement and refutation. Sessions took place every morning and afternoon. The occasion for the disputation was Mennonite agitation on behalf of their teaching, to which Ruardus had replied with a polemic pamphlet, which was to be answered by Isbrandt Isbrandtsen, "preacher of a part of the Anabaptists," and Jelmer Symonsz, who however declined to do so. Pieter van Ceulen, "a preacher of the other part" of the Mennonites, then wrote a reply in 1595. The chairman knew the results of the Frankenthal and Emden disputations. The disputation was held in the Galileër Reformed Church.

The subjects for discussion included eleven articles: (1) the equality of the Old and the New Testaments; (2) the Trinity, the unity of the Divine Being and threefoldness of the persons; (3) the true humanity of Christ and the union of the two natures in Him and its significance for our salvation; (4) the covenants of divine grace; (5) baptism as the seal of God's grace; (6) the ability of man to do good works, or his incapacity to do them since the fall; (7) Ruardus' charge that the Mennonites turn the Christian ban and church discipline into dangerous and disgraceful tyranny; (8) the written and oral oath; (9) the government and whether a Christian may hold government office; (10) nonresistance and the use of arms; (11) the fact that the Anabaptists consider only themselves as the true church of God; also the believers of the Old and New Testaments, the office of preaching, the effectiveness of the Word of God is not dependent on the person who preaches it. The minutes, with a long preface, were published at Franeker in 1597 by Gillis van den Rade.

A number of other minor disputations were held to bridge the gap between groups, or to expose the opposition, especially in the Netherlands (van der Zijpp, 137-39). They played a part in the total picture of the Reformation. The disputations also furnish evidence that under the cover of current and religious questions all the important events and movements of social and individual life were given expression. Anyone who does not allow superficial appearances to confuse him will find the questions anchored in the economic, social, intellectual, religious, and political conditions. Religious disputation is merely the form, not the exclusive content. These were the times of social and political revolutions, the release of the individual from the bondage imposed by the church and the social conditions established by the church. This release was sought in the only means the church had developed in which right and wrong in the field of religion could be recognized. There was a search for formulations, necessarily conditioned by the new state of affairs. The disputations are indicative of the nature of contemporary organized groups and their new ideals and goals.   C.B., H.S.B.

N. van der Zijpp, *Geschiedenis der Doopsgezinden in Nederland* (Arnhem, 1952) 137-39; *ML* I, 451-56.

Dissenters or *Nonconformists* (*q.v.*), the designation of all religious groups not belonging to the Church of England, such as the Independents (*q.v.*), Baptists (*q.v.*), Methodists (*q.v.*), Quakers (*q.v.*), etc. The Act of Toleration of 1689 granted such groups conditional toleration. Equal rights with members of the established state church were not granted them until 150 years later. In the Netherlands the Dissenters, including the Mennonites and Remonstrants, were conditionally tolerated like the Roman Catholics after 1584; in 1651 a new law was enacted limiting toleration of Dissenters and Catholics to those places only where they had been worshiping before; establishing congregations and building churches in new places was prohibited. In 1796 toleration was replaced by full recognition, the Dissenters and Catholics receiving the same rights as the Reformed State Church. (*ML* I, 456.)

NEFF, VDZ.

District Superintendent, an office in the United Missionary Church, known in the earlier period of its history as Presiding Elder, has been an important office from the beginning. The District Superintendent presides over the annual conference of his area, and is recognized as the pastoral head of the ministers of the area which he serves. He also presides over quarterly conferences and conducts communion services with the various churches. He serves as chairman of the stationing committee in the annual assignment of the ministers to the various pastorates. For the quadrennial General Conference the chairman is elected from the District Superintendents of the several conferences.   J.A.H.

Divorce has not been permitted among the Anabaptists and Mennonites from the earliest times except for the cause of adultery, in accordance with the Biblical standard as found in Matt. 19:9, although separation (either legal or privately arranged) has been and is generally allowed.

In a tract entitled *Concerning Divorce* written by one of the first Swiss Brethren in 1527, possibly by Michael Sattler, appears the earliest known Anabaptist treatment of the subject. The main points in this tract stress: (1) the permanence of the marriage bond; (2) the supremacy of one's obligation to Christ over obligation to the marriage partner; (3) the only ground for divorce is adultery; (4) to marry one guilty of fornication is itself fornication; (5) the innocent party to a divorce is not forbidden to remarry, and is by implication permitted to do so. Except for the fifth point, regarding which there has been some ambiguity and occasional divergence

within the brotherhood, this tract can be thought of as summarizing quite well the position of the Mennonite church regarding divorce throughout her entire history.

Menno Simons also clarifies the Anabaptist position on divorce, referring directly to the words of Christ and of the Apostle Paul. He reiterates the theme of adultery being the only acceptable ground for divorce. "And also, that the bond of undefiled, honorable matrimony is so unchangeably bound in the kingdom and government of Christ that neither a man nor a woman can forsake one the other, and take another, understand rightly what Christ says, except it be for fornication, Matt. 19:9. And Paul also holds the same doctrine, that they shall be bound to each other, and that they are to live in union; that the man has not power over his own body, nor the woman over hers, I Cor. 7:4" (*Works,* 247). The Wismar Resolutions of 1554 (*q.v.*), (as quoted in *ML* I, 530) say: "Adultery on the part of one member breaks the marriage relationship. However, the responsible party may return to re-establish the relationship provided he (or she) gives evidence of due repentance and a changed life. In cases of deliberate adultery, the innocent party may be free to remarry after consulting with the congregation." The position taken by the Hutterian Brethren (also quoted *loc. cit.*) was ". . . that nothing can break the marriage bond except adultery. In cases where a man is married to an unbelieving woman, and she desires to live with him, he may not divorce her (nor vice versa). If the unbelieving husband threatens her faith or hinders the training of the children in the faith, she may divorce her husband, but must not remarry so long as that man is living."

There has been some discussion in the earlier literature regarding the bearing of the ban and excommunication on divorce. However, the position was invariably that the ban is of itself not sufficient grounds for divorce, but only adultery, as stated by Christ in Matt. 19:9 (see Menno Simons, *op. cit.,* 241-68; Part II, 123-37).

The predominant approach to the problem of divorce among the Mennonites has been direct and positive rather than indirect and negative. It has consisted chiefly of stressing the obligations of marriage, and an emphasis on the permanency of the marriage bond. This is evidenced not only by the dearth of literature on divorce, but also by the fact that neither the Dordrecht Confession (*q.v.*) nor the Cornelis Ris Confession (*q.v.*) directly treats divorce. However, both confessions put great stress on the importance of marriage, insisting that it be "in the Lord," and that it should never be entered into lightly or unadvisedly.

More recent literature on the question of divorce among the Mennonites is rather rare. Only occasionally does an article or editorial appear in one or another of the official publications of the various Mennonite bodies. Such as do appear are primarily of a hortative nature, and follow quite closely the theme expressed above (e.g., *The Gospel Witness,* Oct. 31, 1906, 482; *Herald of Truth,* Dec. 26, 1907, 482; *The Mennonite,* Dec. 10, 1946, 2).

That this theme still represents the official and general position of all branches of the church can hardly be doubted. But that the standard has not always been upheld is also quite evident. The Doctrine and Conduct Committee of the General Conference Mennonite Church through A. Warkentin and Jacob D. Goering recently made a survey of divorce and remarriage within the congregations of this branch of the church in the United States only. These statistics would seem to indicate that approximately one marriage in thirty ended in divorce in this group in 1940-45. The accuracy of the statistics may be doubted, and the validity of the survey questioned because it covered abnormal war years. Whether or not these divorces were all caused by adultery is impossible to say, on account of the nature of the survey and the responses obtained. However, it is an unmistakable indication of the beginning breakdown of the high marriage standards heretofore prevailing.

In a paper read by J. Winfield Fretz before the Mennonite Cultural Problems Conference held at Grantham, Pa., in June 1951, it was pointed out that one of the crucial problems facing the Mennonite church is whether or not to grant membership in the church to converts who have been divorced before their conversion. To accept them threatens the stability of the brotherhood because of the scarred and broken personalities and families often involved. Yet the church feels the call to evangelize all men, to call them to repentance and into the fellowship of the believers regardless of past sins. This paper also corroborated the impression made by the earlier survey, namely, that the divorce evil is becoming an increasing problem in the congregations. Industrialization, urbanization, and evil social influences of modern society tend to have a disintegrative effect on Mennonite families and communities in some areas. Those Mennonite groups which have undertaken a vigorous program of evangelistic outreach in the city mission and rural mission work are facing increasing pressure in the matter of accepting candidates for membership who have been previously divorced and remarried, since the number of such cases in the general American population is relatively high. J. C. Wenger's study shows that before 1900 the Mennonite Church (MC) tolerated the acceptance of divorced and remarried persons into membership, at least in some sections such as Virginia, Ohio, and Indiana, but that after that date the position became stricter, no such persons being admitted to membership. The current practice on this point in various North American groups is as follows: M.C., M.B., C.G.C., O.O.A., C.A.M., and E.M.(K.G.) groups do not accept divorced and remarried persons into membership. E.M.B. and U.M.C. do accept such persons. The practice in the G.C.M. group varies, since there is local autonomy, but many congregations do accept such persons into membership.

In Europe the Dutch, Northwest German, West Prussian, and Palatinate-Hesse groups have for some time accepted divorced and remarried persons into membership, and have permitted divorce to members, although the cases have been rare, and the last-named group permits divorce only on the ground of adultery. The Badischer Verband until World War II did not permit divorce except for adultery nor receive divorced and remarried persons, but now permits reception of the innocent party in such cases, with remarriage allowed. Swiss and French Mennonites maintain a position similar to that of the Badischer Verband. J.D.G.

The Complete Works of Menno Simon (Elkhart, 1871); J. C. Wenger, *Dealing Redemptively with Those Involved in Divorce and Remarriage Problems* (Goshen, 1954); *ML* I, 529 f.

Divorce from Unbelievers among 16th-century Anabaptists presents a special historical case. In the first half of the 16th century at least, members of the church were allowed, and in some cases expected, to break marriages with spouses who refused to accept the Anabaptist faith, but whether this was only separation or a full divorce is not altogether clear from the records. Nor is it clear whether remarriage was allowed in such cases—probably not. The evidence, not fully collected as yet, includes the following items: (1) The tract of 1527, *Concerning Divorce,* cited in the preceding article, **Divorce,** states clearly that the union of a believer with Christ is more precious than an earthly marriage to an unbeliever; therefore if such conflicts arise, the obligation of the believer is to do the will of God and separate from the unbeliever. (2) A Thuringian Anabaptist, Heinz Kraut, on Dec. 6, 1535, testified at a hearing under Melanchthon's chairmanship, that when a man is not in agreement with his wife regarding the Word of God "the marriage no longer exists between them" (Wappler, 142). As a result of this hearing Prince John of Saxony issued a mandate against the Anabaptists on April 10, 1536, prepared by Melanchthon, which listed among the prevalent beliefs of the Anabaptists that "an Anabaptist may leave his non-Anabaptist spouse." The full statement of the mandate is as follows: "If in a marriage the one person is orthodox in faith and the other married person is not orthodox, such a marriage is prostitution, and the orthodox person may forsake the other, solely because of his faith, and marry another." Melanchthon included similar charges in his *Verlegung etlicher unchristlicher Artickel welche die Wiedertäufer vorgeben* (Wittenberg, 1536?). The case of Melchior Rinck (*q.v.*), who justified his separation from his non-Anabaptist spouse in 1531, is a complicated one (Wappler, 149-52), but no remarriage was considered.

(3) A more elaborate statement on divorcing non-Anabaptist spouses is found in the fifth of the *Five Articles* of the Hutterites of 1547 (see **Article Book**), written probably by Peter Walpot (Zieglschmid, *Chronik,* 308-16, also in Beck, *Geschichts-Bücher,* 215 note). The Scriptural foundation is, as usual, I Cor. 7. "Nothing can break the marriage bond but adultery. Where, however, a brother has an unbelieving wife, and she agrees to live with him, he may not divorce her (nor vice versa). But where she is endangered in her faith or is hindered by the unbelieving husband in the training of her children in the true faith, she may divorce her husband, but must remain unmarried as long as her husband lives.

If the unbelieving one departs, let him depart. 'A brother or sister is not under bondage in such cases,' says Paul, as if he would say: The union with God weighs a thousand times more than the union of marriage between men." (This sentence is often repeated in Hutterite documents.) . . . "We greatly dislike it that one part should forsake the other one, and we would advise nobody to do so without great earnestness; we would rather wish that the other (the unbelieving) part commit himself unto the Lord, so that both would follow Him in faith. Since, however, faith is not given to every man, so each part must do what he understands and what is given to him, and leave the other as he is" (see also Friedmann, 212 and footnote 3; see also **Mixed Marriage**).

The Wismar resolutions of 1554, which were adopted by a conference of Dutch and North German elders including Menno Simons, speak (in Point 5) concerning divorce of an unbeliever from a believer as follows: "If an unbelieving [spouse] desires to divorce on account of the faith [of the partner], the [believing spouse] shall remain honorable without marrying [again]. However, if the apostate partner remarries or enters into immorality, then [the believing spouse] may also remarry, but only with permission of the elder and the congregations. This does not grant permission to a church member to divorce an unbelieving spouse, but recognizes the divorce as valid."

Dirk Philips (*Enchiridion,* 358) argues from the Old Testament, i.e., the Law (Lev. 19) and the case of Ezra (Ezra 10:11, 12), who broke mixed marriages that had been contracted between Israelites and the heathen, that a mixed marriage between believers and unbelievers cannot stand, although he does not specifically authorize divorce on this ground. "In view of the fact that such unclean matrimonial alliances and mixed marriages between the children of God and unbelievers could not stand under the imperfect dispensation of the Law, how could it stand before God and His church under the perfect dispensation of the Christian age of the Gospel? Let everyone meditate upon and consider this matter." Philips' tract *Christian Matrimony* forbids marriage with unbelievers under penalty of excommunication, but does not authorize divorce if the one party becomes a believer, while the other one remains in unbelief.

By the 1570's the Anabaptist position in Germany was fully clear on the matter of not allowing divorce of non-Anabaptist spouses. In the Frankenthal disputation of 1571 the eighth question for discussion was "whether the ban and unbelief break marriage" (*Ob der Bann und Unglaub die Ehe scheiden*). Rauff, an Anabaptist leader, answered as follows: "We believe that nothing may divorce a marriage except adultery. But if the unbeliever wants to divorce because of the faith, I would let him divorce as Paul says in I Corinthians 7. But we believe that the cause of the divorce should not be found in the Christian" (*Protocoll,* 550). The Confession of the Swiss Brethren in Hesse of 1578 states an identical position in an article entitled "Concerning Divorce": "We believe and confess, that man and woman who

have by the divine foreordination, destiny and joining in marriage become one flesh, may not be divorced by ban, belief or unbelief, anger, quarreling, hardness of heart, but only by adultery" (Sippel, 32).

The somewhat different position of the Hutterite group remained unchanged, however, and is not affected by the above statements from middle and south Germany.   R.F.

P. Wappler, *Die Täuferbewegung in Thüringen von 1526-1584* (Jena, 1913); *Protocoll, Das ist, Alle Handlung des gesprechs zu Franckenthal* (Heidelberg, 1571); Th. Sippel, ed., "The Confession of the Swiss Brethren in Hesse, 1578," *MQR* XXIII (1944) 22-34; R. Friedmann, "Eine dogmatische Hauptschrift der Hutterischen Täufergemeinschaften in Mähren," in *Archiv für Ref.-Gesch.* XXVIII (1931); J. Oyer, "The Writings of Melanchthon Against the Anabaptists," *MQR* XXVI (1952) 259-79; *TA Hessen; BRN* VII, 52; D. Philips, *Enchiridion* (Elkhart, 1910) 358; *ML* I, 529 f.

Dixmuiden, a city in West Flanders in Belgium with about 6,000 inhabitants, where there was a small Anabaptist church in the 16th century. On March 4, 1581, a conference of Dutch Mennonite Waterlanders, meeting at Amsterdam, decided to elect a preacher at Dixmuiden. (*DB* 1877, 80; *ML* I, 456.)   NEFF.

Dmitrovka: see **Neu-Schönwiese** and **Arkadak.**

Dneprovka, a Mennonite village in the Ukraine: see **Kronsweide.**

Dnepropetrovsk: see **Ekaterinoslav.**

Dobbert was pastor of the Evangelical Lutheran Church of Prishib near the Molotschna settlement at the time of the activities of Eduard Wüst (*q.v.*) and the founding of the Mennonite Brethren Church. P. M. Friesen (*Brüderschaft,* 171-73, 324-30) reprints statements along these lines. He sympathized strongly with Wüst's zeal for Christ and in his report about the events which led to the founding of the Mennonite Brethren Church he takes a mediating position with strong sympathies toward the new group.   C.K.

Dobrovka was a Mennonite village of the Orenburg (*q.v.*) settlement, volost of Kipchakskaya, post office Deyevka in Russia, founded in 1908 by settlers from Chortitza, South Russia. (*ML* I, 456.)

Dobrovlany near Stry, Galicia, Poland, was a large estate bought by Peter Müller (*q.v.*) and Daniel Rupp (*q.v.*) in 1869. In 1871 several Mennonite families, mostly from Einsiedel (*q.v.*), bought half of this estate from Peter Müller and founded the Dobrovlany daughter settlement. It became the center of a small congregation, which had its own chapel and (1888) a membership of 41. For a while the two elders, Heinrich Brubacher and Daniel Rupp, lived here.   C.K.

H. Mannhardt, *Jahrbuch,* 1888, 78; *Menn. Bl.,* 1878, 8; P. Bachmann, *Menn. in Kleinpolen* (Lemberg, 1934) 274-77; *ML* I, 456.

Dock, Christopher, the "pious schoolmaster of the Skippack," was born in Germany (place unknown), and came to America about 1714. By 1718 Dock was teaching a subscription elementary school among the Mennonites of the Skippack settlement north of Germantown, Pa. His teaching career, probably begun in Germany, now continued for ten years at Skippack, until he gave up teaching for farming in 1728. In 1735 he bought 100 acres near Salfordville, and probably lived there the rest of his life. Soon after giving up the Skippack school, Dock says he felt the "smiting hand of God" calling him back to the teaching profession. He taught four summers in the (Mennonite) school at Germantown. Finally in 1738, after an interval of ten years of farming, Dock resumed full-time teaching at Skippack and Salford, and continued teaching until his death in 1771.

Christopher Dock's life and work is best known by reading his essay, *School-Management (Schul-Ordnung)*, written in 1750, but not published until 20 years later. One of his pupils, Christopher Saur, Jr., of Germantown published the first two editions in 1770. This work reveals the gentle and loving character of Dock as a teacher and his successful methods of instruction. Printed in the German language, it found its way into many Pennsylvania-German homes and must have had a profound influence on those who taught the German schools of his day. Teaching was a divine calling; pupils were given individualized instruction; character and godliness were the chief objectives in Dock's school.

Christopher Dock was one of the selected contributors to Christopher Saur's *Geistliches Magazien* (1764-73). Among the articles he contributed were "A Hundred Necessary Rules for Children's Conduct," and "A Hundred Rules for Children," both of which reveal the interesting customs and practices among the Germans of colonial times.

Not only was Dock a successful teacher of the 3 R's, but he also made a real contribution in teaching art. Dock's specialty was *Fractur-Schriften,* or beautifully illuminated manuscripts. These consisted of Scripture texts or mottoes artistically penned in colored inks. It is said that Dock had 25 of them on the walls of his schoolroom. He used some of them as copy forms (*Vorschriften*) for his pupils. Others were given to pupils as rewards for excellent work. Some of Dock's originals have been preserved in the Historical Society of Pennsylvania and in the Schwenkfelder Library of Pennsburg, Pa. Dock's influence can also be seen in collections containing the work of his pupils. Teachers of the 19th century continued the practice of this art and used Dock's ideas for the encouragement of pupil effort.

Dock also wrote at least seven hymns. Five of these hymns found their way into the earliest American Mennonite hymnal, *Kleine Geistliche Harfe* (1803), and were retained in later editions. It is quite possible that Dock's emphasis on teaching hymns in the schools and his very probable able service as chorister in the Salford and Skippack churches were largely responsible for the unusual interest in singing among the Mennonite congregations of Montgomery County.

Dock was not only a good teacher of academic subjects, but also an effective character builder and teacher of religion. His education was "Christian" education, with perfect integration of the sacred with the secular. He used religious materials such as the New Testament and the hymnal in his regular classes, he opened every school day with worship, making religion a natural experience for the children, and infused his entire teaching with a warm, sincere piety. Furthermore his religion was not superficial and external, but essential, and was the firm foundation for a genuinely effective program of character building. Narrow sectarianism and theological dogmatism were entirely absent; a devout and wholehearted following of Christ was his great concern.

Dock's burial place is unknown, but tradition gives us a very plausible account of his death. It was his custom to remain at school after dismissal of the children to pray for each of his pupils in turn. One evening in the autumn of 1771 he did not return home at the usual time. He was found on his knees in the schoolroom, but his spirit had gone.

A memorial stone in honor of Christopher Dock was erected in 1915 by the Montgomery County Historical Society in the cemetery of the Lower Skippack Mennonite Church. It bears this inscription: "Here Christopher Dock, who in 1750 wrote the earliest American essay on Pedagogy, taught school, and here in 1771, he died on his knees in prayer."† (Vol. I). Q.L.

Primary Sources and Collections: Abraham H. Cassel Collection of *Fractur-Schriften* listed as "Dock's Manuscripts," Pennsylvania Historical Library, contains art manuscripts and merit cards of Dock, so marked by Cassel; Samuel W. Pennypacker Collection, Schwenkfelder Historical Library, Pennsburg, Pa., contains several of Dock's manuscripts and merit cards, so marked by Pennypacker; Christopher Dock, *Eine Einfältige und gründlich abgefasste Schul-Ordnung,* . . . (Christopher Saur, Germantown, 1770). A facsimile of the first edition is in Brumbaugh's *Life and Works of Christopher Dock;* Hymns (five of Dock's hymns have been definitely authenticated through their publication by Christopher Saur); "Copia einer Schrifft welche der Schulmeister, Christopher Dock, an seine noch lebende Schüler zur Lehr und Vermahnung aus Liebe geschrieben hat," *Geistliches Magazien* I, No. 33 (1764, Germantown, Christopher Saur); "Hundert Noethige Sitten-Regeln für Kinder," *Geistliches Magazien* I (No. 40); "Hundert Christliche Lebens-Regeln für Kinder," *ibid.* I (No. 41); "Zwei erbauliche Lieder," *ibid.* II (No. 15); M. G. Brumbaugh, *The Life and Works of Christopher Dock* (Philadelphia, 1908); J. E. Hartzler, *Education Among the Mennonites of America* (Danvers, Ill., 1925); Q. Leatherman, "Christopher Dock, Mennonite Schoolmaster, 1718-71," *MQR* XVI (1942) 32-44; H. S. Bender, "Christopher Dock," *German-American Review* XI (1945) 4-6; K. Massanari, "The Contribution of Christopher Dock to Contemporary Christian Teaching," *MQR* XXV (1951) 100-15. The material in the *Magazien* from Dock was reproduced in facsimile by M. G. Brumbaugh in his biography, with a translation. S. W. Pennypacker translated the *Hundert Noethige Sitten-Regeln* and one of the hymns, in his *Historical and Biographical Sketches* (Philadelphia, 1883); *ML* I, 456.

Doctrinal Writings of the Anabaptists. During the 16th century Anabaptism did not make a real distinction between doctrinal and devotional writings (*q.v.*). The doctrinal writings are not of a formal theological type but rather of a confessional character, stressing in the main the difference of Anabaptist viewpoints from those of the large churches of the Reformation. No Anabaptist ever felt the need for an elaborate system of theology, not even those who had the necessary education. Whether by Menno Simons or Pilgram Marpeck, Dirk Philips, or Peter Riedemann, all these books and tracts were at once confessional (doctrinal), devotional, and also polemical, but they were never scholarly and academic like many of the books by Luther, Calvin, or Zwingli. One source collection of such tracts is rightly called *Glaubenszeugnisse oberdeutscher Taufgesinnter* (by Lydia Müller, 1938). All Anabaptist writings were such testimonies of faith.

The amount of these writings must once have been rather large, though a complete list of them does not exist as yet, and a systematic study has never been undertaken. Lydia Müller's publication is perhaps the best collection yet published, though incomplete and too much abridged. The book presents South German and Hutterite material, taken from Hutterite manuscript books, our richest source. The contents of this book are as follows: Jörg Hauck (*Anfang eines christlichen Lebens*), Hans Hut (*Vom Geheimnis der Taufe, Ein christlicher Unterricht . . .*), Michael Sattler (*Artikel und Handlung;* for the famous Schleitheim Confession see below), Leonhard Schiemer (5 tracts, particularly profound writings of 1526-7, deserving special attention), Hans Schlaffer (*Ein kurzer Unterricht zum Anfang eines rechten christlichen Lebens,* like Schiemer very early and extremely penetrating), Eitelhans Langenmantel (*Vom Nachtmahl Christi*), Jörg Zaunring (*Eine kurze Anzeigung vom Abendmahl Christi*), Jakob Hutter (various epistles), Ulrich Stadler (next to Riedemann or Walpot the ablest doctrinal writers of the Hutterites; four tracts are published in excerpts), Peter Walpot (*Die fünf Artikel des grössten Streites,* 1547?) (see **Article Book,** a major work of the Hutterites), Antoni Erdfordter (*Urlaubsbrief*), *Brüderliche Vereinigung mit dem Brüdern am Rheinstrom* (1558), and *Anschlag und Fürwenden* (Hutterite, about 1560, by Walpot), etc. For volume II were scheduled: Peter Riedemann (*Rechenschaft unseres Glaubens, q.v.,* 1545, the greatest doctrinal and confessional book of the Hutterites), Andreas Ehrenpreis (*Ein Sendbrief brüderliche Gemeinschaft betreffend, q.v.,* 1652, a book of 200 pages), but the volume was not published until 1955. In brief, Riedemann and Walpot are shown as the two main authors of doctrinal books among the Hutterites. The compilation list is, of course, in no way complete. Many of the outstanding *Verantwortungen* (testimonies) are not mentioned though we have prints of most of them, e.g., by Claus Felbinger, Veith Grünberger, Hans Mändl, etc. (see **Verantwortungen**). Worth mentioning is also one tract by the Philipite brethren, *Concerning a True Soldier of Christ (q.v.)* by Hans Haffner, 1535.

The Schleitheim Articles of 1527, called *Brüderliche Vereinigung etlicher Kinder Gottes, sieben Artikel betreffend,* drawn up, most likely, by Michael Sattler (English tr. *MQR.* XIX, 1945, 242 ff.), must be considered the earliest doctrinal writing of the Swiss or South German Brethren. It was, according to F. Blanke, "a genuine confession of faith, intended to erect a dam against the intrusion of heretical views into the brotherhood" (*MQR* XVI, 1942, 85 f.). A number of similar doctrinal writings of the South German "Swiss" Brethren were discovered in a *Sammelband* in the Goshen College library, and translated by Wenger (*MQR,* 1945-47); authors and dates are undisclosed, but the style points to an early origin (*Von der Genugtuung Christi, Von der Ehescheidung, Zweierlei Gehorsam, Von der Hörung falscher Propheten, von bösen Vorstehern,* discussed in *MQR* XVI, 1942, 82 ff.). In Switzerland itself no Anabaptist literature of any kind could develop, though the brotherhood lived there, in spite of severe oppression, up to the great expulsion early in the 18th century and even later. Only disputations (*Religionsgespräche*) afford an insight into the doctrinal thinking of the Swiss Brethren, such as the meetings at Bern, Basel, and Zofingen (see **Disputations;** also *MQR* XXII, 1948, 19 ff.).

South German Brethren have produced at least one outstanding writer, Pilgram Marpeck (*q.v.*), whose great *Verantwortung* (1542) is a prime source, although it, too, is more polemical than systematic in its outline. There are also Marpeck's *Testamentserläuterung,* his *Vermahnung,* his Strasbourg Confession, and a concordance, *Gestern und Heute.* These writings were also used by Brethren in Grisons, Switzerland. The "Swiss" Brethren in the Rhine Valley (around and below Cologne) had as their outstanding teacher Thomas von Imbroich (*q.v.*), martyred 1558, whose *Confessio oder Glaubensbekenntnis* became extremely popular among other groups, spread by way of printed pamphlets (see **Epistles, Anabaptist, non-Hutterite**). As late as 1692, the Swiss authorities complained about this book found among the Anabaptists around Bern (Müller, *Berner Täufer,* 104). Likewise, all American editions of the *Ausbund* (since 1742) contain in an appendix this particular *Confession.* (For other writings of that region see **Epistles, Anabaptist, non-Hutterite,** also **Güldene Aepffel.**)

The Dutch brethren were much more fortunate than the Swiss Anabaptists in having in Menno Simons and Dirk Philips leaders who were also capable of formulating their new faith in a number of doctrinal writings of lasting effect. Menno Simons' *Fundament des christelijcken Leers (q.v.)* (in a translation of 1575) was widely read also among the Brethren in South Germany, particularly Württemberg (Bossert, *Quellen*). Dirk Philips' *Enchiridion (q.v.)* should not be forgotten. North German and East Prussian Mennonites were served mainly by their brethren in the Netherlands. The Altona (Hamburg) congregations were partly served by Jan de Buyser's *Christelijck Huys-Boeck* (1643) (*q.v.*), later by G. Roosen's (*q.v.*) writings (*Christliches Gemüthsgespräch,* and *Unschuld und Gegenbericht,* 1702).

The Prussian church had its first *Glaubensbekenntnis* in 1660, which became a standard work through the centuries. Far more elaborate and theologically refined were the writings by George Hansen (*q.v.*), namely, his *Glaubensbericht an die*

Jugend (1671, much used also among the Mennonites in Russia), *Confession of Faith* (1678), and *Fundamentbuch* (1696). Mennonites continued to produce confessions and catechisms, and also some doctrinal writings.

The printed records of the various disputations (*q.v.*), such as Zofingen (1532), Frankenthal (1571), and Emden (1587), contain much doctrinal material.

A few general remarks might well conclude this survey. Because of the exposed nature of the Anabaptists in a hostile world, all these early tracts have a polemical strain: Stadler's tracts are written like a discussion, "Rede und Antwort"; Marpeck's great book alternates "Rede und Gegenrede," and Walpot's Article Book is presented "punkt und argumentweis." There is always an undertone of defense in them, either against the world or against wavering or "heretical" brethren (as, e.g., the Schleitheim Articles have in mind). All these tracts do not present any formal theology but only statements of faith beginning somewhat like "Wir bekennen . . . ." Argumentation is achieved in the main by ample quotations from the Bible; a strict, sometimes even dry, Biblicism is the rule; yet there is no lack of genuine spiritual interpretation, as in the earlier writings of men like Schlaffer, Schiemer, Hans Hut, and Riedemann. Academic scholarship is rejected everywhere; simplicity (*Einfalt*) in thought and speech is the accepted standard, even though the popular allegorical (*figürliche*) interpretation of Bible texts is often refined and occasionally very rationalistic. The Christianity of these tracts is concrete and genuine. Baptism and the Lord's Supper stand in the foreground of all doctrinal interests while the question of salvation seems to be secondary to the life dedication of a man. The Trinity is accepted and defended, though not stressed. The eschatological element, though not altogether absent, remains in the background. The practical implications matter most, even in the most "theological" tracts of the 16th century. The 17th and 18th centuries show distinct changes toward formalism and a slackening of concreteness; but even then there is little likeness to the systematic theology of the state churches. Mennonitism is, after all, not a theological church but one which seeks to express faith in life.

Although the 17th and later centuries produced practically no doctrinal writings among the Mennonites in other European countries, the Netherlands produced a large number of such writings in the post-Anabaptist period and on down into the 19th century, when outstanding theologians, such as Sytse Hoekstra (*q.v.*), were productive. (See articles on respective authors; also **Devotional Literature**; **Catechisms**; **Confessions of Faith**.)

No specialized study is known dealing with the entire field. On the Hutterites, see R. Friedmann, "Eine dogmatische Hauptschrift, . . ." in *Archiv f. Ref.-Gesch.* XXVIII and XXIX (1931-32), with extensive discussions in general; other material in the *MQR*, 1942-48, particularly J. C. Wenger's translations of Anabaptist doctrinal tracts (Jan. and Oct. 1947; Jan. and July 1948). On Marpeck, see the special Marpeck issue of the *MQR* XII (July 1938), specifically J. C. Wenger, "Life and Work of Pilgram Marpeck," *MQR* XII (July 1938) 137-66; *idem*, "Pilgram Marpeck's Confession of Faith Composed at Strasbourg . . . ," *op. cit.*, 167-202; *idem*, "Theology of Pilgram Marpeck," *op. cit.* (Oct. 1938) 205-56; Franklin H. Littell, *The Anabaptist View of the Church* (Philadelphia, 1952).

Doctrine and Conduct Committee is a unique committee in the General Conference Mennonite Church, for it is not a standing committee, and must be completely re-elected at every session of the General Conference. This close control of the committee by the conference reflects something of the controversial issues under which it arose in the early twenties.

The principal issue giving rise to the committee was the traditional testimony against secret orders. Particularly vigorous leadership was given when the late P. R. Schroeder was secretary of the committee. From 1929 to 1933 the committee sent out 22,000 anti-secrecy leaflets featuring the conference anti-secrecy resolution and Article 12 of the Constitution, the longest single item in the doctrinal area.

Meanwhile, the committee began to broaden its work to include other questions such as the oath, the nature of baptism, the nature of the church and modernistic theological tendencies. Another trend in the church was the growing disinclination to enter into distinctly disciplinary problems and the development of a broadly educational approach to controversial issues in the conference.

In recent years the committee has continued to have a conservative orientation. But it has worked closely with the fundamental purposes of the conference in a wide range of educational activity, including the following: reprinting of the Ris confession, a statistical and descriptive study of divorce trends in the conference, a study of stewardship, preliminary studies of Christianity and communism, church discipline, universalism, as well as the production of an over-all book on the theology of the conference.

At the conference held at Freeman, S.D., in 1950 the Doctrine and Conduct Committee was absorbed by the Board of Education and Publication, and placed in a subcommittee on Education in Church, Home and Community. This was part of a major reorganization of the conference structure.   D.E.S.

Doetinchem, a town in the Dutch province of Gelderland, where in 1903 a *Doopsgezinde Kring* (group of Mennonites) was founded, in charge of S. D. A. Wartena, pastor of Zutphen (*q.v.*). Services were regularly held and catechismal instruction was given; on July 12, 1903, a baptismal service took place here (*DB* 1903, 187). But a few years later this group had dissolved. A new group organized on Oct. 22, 1947, and was called *Kring Doetinchem en omgeving*. The group started with 29 members (34 in 1954). It meets one evening a month for discussion, and co-operates with the *Nederlandse Protestanten-Bond* (association of liberal Christians) in organizing church services. Miss J. M. Eelman, the Mennonite minister of Winterswijk, is now in charge of this group.   vDZ.

Dohn, Hans, an Anabaptist martyr, who was burned at the stake under Elector August of Saxony. In the records of his trial is found the version of the

Lord's Prayer peculiar to the Thuringian Anabaptists, "Give us the eternal heavenly Bread." This version is attested in other records also.

P. Wappler, *Die Täuferbewegung in Thüringen von 1526-1584* (Jena, 1913) 503-5; 518-21.

Dohner Mennonite Church (MC), located near Annville, Lebanon Co., Pa., is a member of the Lancaster Mennonite Conference. Bishop Frederick Kauffman gave land for a meetinghouse in 1768 two miles north of Annville. In 1851 when friction developed with the United Brethren, Bishop Jacob Dohner moved a mile east and built the present 24 x 36 ft. brick church. Membership and Sunday-school enrollment in 1954 were 29 and 45 respectively. Simon Bucher is bishop, Robert Miller preacher.   I.D.L.

Dokkum, a town (pop. 5,600) in the Dutch province of Friesland. An Anabaptist congregation must have originated here between 1551 and 1557. Leenaert Bouwens (*q.v.*) baptized at least 453 persons here, and in 1562 the Reformed congregation, which was also meeting secretly, requested the Reformed congregation at Emden to send them an ordained man, because the Mennonites were winning so many of the people that they comprised most of the inhabitants of Dokkum. In the early 17th century Dokkum had at least three Mennonite congregations, one of Waterlanders, one of High Germans (Blaupot t. C., *Friesland,* 169), and one of Jan Jacobsgezinden (*q.v.*). By 1695 the Waterlanders and High Germans had been united for some time and numbered about 180 members; the Jan Jacobsgezinden had disappeared by 1786.

The liberal spirit of the time was shown in a proposal by the Remonstrants in 1796 that all the Christian bodies in the Netherlands unite in a single Christian church. The proposal was rejected nearly everywhere. The Frisian Sociëteit also decided not to enter the proposed union, because adult baptism, the distinguishing mark of the Mennonites, would be dropped. But the Mennonite congregation of Dokkum thought otherwise about it. After the departure of Matthijs Siegenbeek they were without a minister, as was also the Remonstrant congregation, and consequently obeyed the summons. Although they numbered 70 or 80 members and the Remonstrants only 13, it was decided that the local united congregation should be attached to both creeds, but especially to that of the Remonstrants, since they had issued the invitation. The annual support of 550 florins which the Remonstrants received from their brotherhood, was to accrue to the united congregation.

On May 10, 1798, the union was completed, confirmed by the signature of 30-34 members of the Mennonite congregation, and six of the Remonstrants. Article 4 stipulated that it would be the duty of the pastor to baptize adults as well as infants; this was an obstacle to the union with the Frisian Sociëteit. After tedious correspondence it was decided at the Sociëteit meeting of June 6, 1800, that the Mennonite congregation had ceased to exist. Members who were unable to make the concessions necessary to the union became members of the Dantumawoude (*q.v.*) congregation. The united congregation meets in the old Mennonite church, which was completely renovated in 1852.

At first the congregation had difficulty in finding a preacher, although they asked many groups to help them. The Mennonite preachers refused because they objected to Article 4. In 1799, however, Karel Ayelts, the Reformed preacher at Laren and Blaricum, accepted the call, and since that time 3 Reformed and 10 Remonstrant preachers have served. In 1826-27, during an illness of Ayelts, the Mennonite pastor at Dantumawoude occasionally preached for the group. Since 1827 the congregation has had only non-Mennonite preachers. B. ten Bruggencate, the Mennonite minister at Baard, who received a call to this congregation in 1865, refused it. In that year there were some difficulties, resulting from the mixed character of the congregation. Since then its course has been smooth. In 1865 this United Christian Church of Dokkum was admitted to Ring Dantumawoude (*q.v.*); sometime later it withdrew, but was reinstated in 1917. In 1810 the congregation had 69 members (193 souls), and in 1951, 122 members (200 souls). In the census of 1910, 88 persons at Dokkum said they were Remonstrants, and 75, Mennonites; in 1947 there were 53 Remonstrants and 187 Mennonites.   J.L.

Scheltema en van Wijk, *Een poging tot verbroedering der Protestantsche Christenen en haar verwezenlijking in de Vereenigde christelijke gemeente te Dokkum* (Amsterdam, 1874); Tideman, *De Remonstrantische Broederschap* 368-72; Blaupot t. C., *Friesland,* 88, 91, 157, 169, 224, 231, 367; DB 1865, 159-60; 1890, 16-17; 1893, 1 ff.; 1903, 81; *Inv. Arch. Amst.* I, 1, No. 607; II, Nos. 1692 f.; ML I, 457.

Dokkumburg (Dokkenburg), **Sjoerd Pietersz van,** a Dutch Mennonite minister, originally of Friesland, who served the congregation of Berlikum until 1731, Heerenveen and Knijpe 1731-35, where his work was fruitful, but his salary very small, Enkhuizen and Venhuizen 1735-51, Koog en Zaandijk from 1751 until his death between 1775 and 1779. He was an ardent defender of the conservative Mennonite principles. He wrote: *Eenige Artykelen van de Leere der Waarheid, die naar de Godsaligheid is . . .* (Haarlem, 1743), *De Gebeden van Jezus Christus . . .* (Haarlem, 1745), and a long poem in the Frisian language for the dedication of the Mennonite church at Buitenpost (1742). This poem is found in A. Wynalda, *Davids Liefde tot Gods huis* (Amsterdam, 1743). (*Biogr. Wb.* II, 523; *Catalogus Amst.,* 262.)   vDZ.

Dokkumburg (Dokkenburg), **Pieter van,** a son of S. P. van Dokkumburg (above), born on Jan. 22, 1737, at Venhuizen, d. May 2, 1811, at Koog aan de Zaan, was a Mennonite minister. He served the congregations of Oudesluis, 1758-63; Twisk, 1763-70; and Koog-Zaandijk, 1770-1811. He trained a large number of young men for the ministry, for (like his father) he followed the principles of the Zonists (*q.v.*) and opposed the (Lamist) Amsterdam Theological Seminary. He wrote: *Verhandelingen over wysgerige onderwerpen; De Wederleggende Godgeleerdheid; Het Stelzel van de Godgeleerdheid,* all of which are found in manuscript in the Amsterdam Mennonite Library. These treatises may have been composed for his theological students. (*Biogr. Wb.* II, 523; *Naamlijst* 1808, 75; 1815, 80 f.; *Catalogus Amst.*, 221.) vDZ.

Dolinovka, the name of several Mennonite villages in Russia: see **Adelsheim, Münsterberg,** and **Orenburg.**

Dolinsk: see **Kronstal.**

Dolinskoye, a village of the Neu-Samara (*q.v.*) Mennonite settlement in Russia, district of Buzuluk, volost Yemurau-Tabynsk, post office Pleshanovsk, founded in 1890. (*ML* I, 458.)

Dolton (Turner Co., S.D.) United Missionary Church was organized in 1924. In 1948 a community church building was used for a meetinghouse for the 26 members, with Marvin Engbrecht as pastor. M.E.

Dominicus, an Anabaptist martyr, who was burned at the stake with two preachers, Thomas and Balthasar, in Brno, Czechoslovakia, in 1528. When they were about to be sentenced they warned the Council against shedding innocent blood. One of the Councilmen replied that he was doing a service to God in condemning them to death. (*Mart. Mir.* D 18, E 428; Zieglschmid, *Chronik,* 63; Beck, *Geschichts-Bücher,* 65; *ML* I, 458.)

Dominicus Abels "van der Vecht," a goldsmith of Utrecht, was a preacher and bishop of the Anabaptists, called "bishop of Gooiland," preached in the Gooi near Amsterdam, baptized members in Amsterdam, and was beheaded there March 30, 1534. He was a man of great eloquence, and was one of the principal leaders on the journey from Amsterdam to Münster in March 1534. After his death his wife Janneken joined the revolutionary Batenburgers (*q.v.*). vDZ.

Inv. Arch. Amst. I, No. 265; *DB* 1917, 113, No. 34; de Hoop Scheffer, *Geschiedenis der Kerkhervorming . . . tot 1531* (Amsterdam, 1873) 463; Mellink, *Wederdopers, passim,* see Index.

Dompelaars, a Dutch word meaning "immersionists" or "Dunkers," the name of a small branch of the Mennonite Church at Hamburg-Altona (*q.v.*), which led to a division of the congregation in 1648. The name indicates Dutch origin. It has been assumed that the Collegiant (*q.v.*) brotherhood, which had been formed in Holland in 1619 and which required and practiced immersion, was transplanted to Hamburg, with momentous consequences to the Mennonite congregation there. But it is more likely that Abraham de Vosz, who had apparently been a Baptist in Colchester, England, and who joined the Flemish Mennonites in Hamburg, caused the division. He won two preachers and fifteen laymen to his side, who now demanded the practice of immersion and footwashing before communion; communion services should be held at night with unleavened bread. In 1628 the Mennonite church board of Hamburg explained the difficulties which had arisen in the congregation concerning baptism by immersion in a 13-page letter to the Flemish congregation "bij 't Lam" at Amsterdam (*Inv. Arch. Amst.* I, No. 567.) Most of the congregation, led by Gerrit Roosen, opposed this innovation. From 1648 on the two parties held separate services in the Mennonite church. After a violent quarrel the Dompelaars were forced out and thus the formal division ensued in 1650 which lasted 100 years.

In 1661 Bastiaan van Weenigem (*q.v.*), on a visit to the Mennonite church at Hamburg-Altona, preached a sermon against the Dompelaars. When he returned to Hamburg two years later the Dompelaar preacher handed him a document which he was to refute. This he did in nine letters which he published with the title, *Maniere van Doop,* in 1666. It was answered by Joan Arents (probably the Dompelaar preacher) in 1668 in *Eindelycke verklaringe der gedoopte Christenen* with an "Appendix by Antoony de Grijs." Thereupon van Weenigem published *Antidotum ofte Tegengift* in 1669.

The first church of the Dompelaars at Altona was a small, dark building below street-level, on Reichengasse. Baptism was administered in a pond at Barmbek near Wandsbek. On Nov. 5, 1670, they secured permission from Christian V of Denmark to hold religious services. Noted separatists like Jakob Taube and Christian Hohburg (*q.v.*) preached here for a while. On April 28, 1708, they were given permission to build a church; it was erected almost altogether by money given by the merchant Ernst Goverts. Here the last Dompelaar preacher, Jakob Denner (*q.v.*), preached. When he died (1746) the Altona Dompelaar congregation became extinct. The church, which belonged to Denner's heirs, was later used by the Moravians.

The Crefeld Mennonites also had a Dompelaar movement, but it was without any great significance, though the Crefeld Dompelaars were described in the records of the Cleve Synod (1717-20) as "particularly dangerous." In 1700-30 adherents of the "noble mystical enthusiasm," represented by men like Ernst Christoph Hochmann (*q.v.*) and J. Dippel, were deeply stirred by the question of the baptism of believers by immersion. In 1714 six men of the Reformed congregation in Solingen, who had close contacts with the Crefeld Dompelaars, were baptized by them in the Wupper, and after three years in the prison at Düsseldorf were subsequently condemned to life imprisonment in Jülich where they spent three additional years at hard labor, until they were released Nov. 20, 1720, at the intercession of the General States of Holland. They were also visited by Mennonites from Crefeld, among them Hubert Rahr (of whom Goebel records that as a zealous Mennonite, a friend of Tersteegen, he publicly reproved the Reformed preacher Pull in Crefeld for several harsh statements after the funeral sermon for George Heshus), Jahn van Jurath, Jan Crous (from 1716 to 1724 preacher of the Mennonite church at Crefeld), Wilhelm von der Leyen, and Gosen Goyen (*q.v.*), a Mennonite preacher who had himself been immersed in the Rhine in 1724. J. Crous was Goyen's opponent on the question of baptism. In a sermon on April 5, 1716, he advocated baptism by pouring.

In 1719 a part of the Crefeld Dompelaars and other like-minded persons in the county of Wittgenstein (Schwarzenau)—about 200, led by Christopher Seebach—emigrated to America, where they have since been known as Dunkers. In Ephrata (*q.v.*), Pa., they founded a monastic brotherhood with complete community of goods and work, which in 1739 consisted of 60 unmarried persons. About the same time as in Crefeld some difficulties concerning immersion (*dompeldoop*) arose in the Dutch Mennonite congregation of Leeuwarden. Here in 1714 the deacons favoring immersion were in the majority. In 1715 a baptistery for immersion was installed in the church. But the opponents of immersion having appealed to the city magistrates, the baptistery disappeared in 1720 (*DB* 1874, 63 ff.). This immersion movement at Leeuwarden may have come from pietistic influence from Germany. In a few other Dutch congregations, as Amsterdam, Leiden, Rotterdam, Schiedam, and Surhuisterveen, as a result of Collegiant principles, baptism was sometimes performed by immersion during the 17th and early 18th centuries (see **Immersion** and **Baptism**).   NEFF, vDZ.

J. A. Bolten, *Hist. Kirchen-Nachrichten von der Stadt Altona* I (1790); B. C. Roosen, *Gerhard Roosen* (Hamburg, 1854); M. Goebel, *Gesch. des christlichen Lebens in der rhein.-westfäl. Kirche* III (Coblenz, 234); H. Renkewitz, *Hochmann von Hohenau* (Breslau, 1935); Fr. Nieper, *Die ersten deutschen Auswanderer aus Krefeld nach Pennsylvanien* (Neukirchen, 1940); M. G. Brumbaugh, *A Hist. of the German Baptist Brethren in Europe and America* (2d ed., Elgin, 1907); *ML* I, 458.

Donatists, a brotherhood in the church which at the beginning of the fourth century caused a serious division in the Christian Church, until it was forcibly suppressed 100 years later. The initial cause was personal rivalry between bishops; but soon important fundamental differences rose, founded in the newly established relationship between church and state instituted by Constantine, and the ensuing increasing secularization of the Christian Church.

The Donatists, named after their bishop, Donatus the Great (316-46), wished the church to be a holy community; they required moral purity of their members, and especially of their bishops. They taught the following tenets: no one may spend what he does not have; no one shall impart purity who is himself not pure; a bishop or clergyman living in sin cannot effectively administer the sacraments. The church that tolerates in its clergy the "deadly sins" is unclean and spotted, and must be renounced. Their own brotherhood they considered the "pure bride of Christ"; anyone joining them from the Catholic Church must submit to rebaptism. In the Numidian church they grew to great strength. At a disputation at Carthage (A.D. 411) 279 Donatist bishops were assembled. The state, whose right to be concerned with spiritual matters they denied, broke their power by suppressing them; small remnants maintained themselves up to the time of Islam. In the struggle against them Augustine took a leading part, and summoned the might of the state against them. They can hardly be considered representatives within the Catholic Church of the Protestant doctrine of salvation. Among the Mennonites the Donatistic view that the church should be without spot or wrinkle (Eph. 5:27) and that

bishops and preachers should be "pure" has found wide application.   NEFF.

W. Thümmel, *Zur Beurteilung des Donatismus* (Halle, 1893); A. Harnack, *Gesch. der altchristlichen Literatur* I (Leipzig, 1893) 744 ff.; W. Freud, *The Donatist Church* (Oxford, 1952); *ML* I, 459.

Donaumoos (Danube Moor), the site of the first Mennonite settlement in Bavaria (1802). It was a moor southwest of Neuburg on the Danube considered dangerous to man and beast. It was not until the reign of Karl Theodore in 1777 that any attempt was made to cultivate this infertile district. But in spite of the duke's desire to develop it in the interest of his own finances, the project failed.

Under Max Joseph (1799), however, who acted on the advice of experts, a more advantageous settlement of the Donaumoos was begun. He was interested first of all in acquiring the right kind of people to achieve this end, and therefore found it necessary to break into the hitherto jealously guarded Catholic unity of the Bavarian state. Thus the area of Bavaria proper was also made accessible to the Mennonites, and especially to them, in addition to the Palatinate, which had just been acquired by the Bavarian monarch. The elector was no doubt familiar with the reputation of the Mennonites in agriculture, and his agricultural director Kling (*q.v.*) was a native of the Palatinate. About 120 Mennonite families came to the moors of the Danube (and also the Schleissheim and Rosenheim moors) upon the invitation issued by the elector on March 6 and 12, 1802. Among these the first eight families were given waste forest land in Grünau, later called Maxweiler (*q.v.*). Kling expressly states that he selected a Mennonite of Grünau to be a member of the Agricultural Society composed of expert farmers. In this society agricultural reforms were to be discussed which had long been the practices of the Mennonites of the Palatinate. Mennonite farming techniques were to become a measure of the arability of the Donaumoos. The permission to settle at Rosing states, "The Mennonites are known to be not only very industrious, but also have the best understanding in the economic management of field and house, hence hereby an experiment could be made to determine to what extent the moor could be developed with the settlement of more families."

The settlers were to be granted the tax- and rent-free use of the land for ten years, and were given substantial subsidies for their buildings, and also temporary freedom from military service. The first eight families were first lodged in the hunting lodge Grünau. By the end of two years they had built four houses, and the colony showed every sign of becoming a thriving settlement. That it ultimately failed was not the fault of the colonists. On the 30 Tagwerk allotted to each they made astounding progress. Their religious unity was an important factor in their achievement. Elder Heinrich Zeiset of Willenbach, Württemberg, ordained the first preacher of the settlement in 1803.

The official records also reveal the untiring efforts of the settlers to set up their own schools. In 1807 they were already presenting an urgent petition to the government for permission to erect a church and school. Again and again their petition was rejected with excuses of all kinds. Finally, on Dec. 9, 1832, they were able to dedicate a church and school built by the labor of their own hands. (The opinion that King Ludwig drew the plan for the building is false. On the contrary, negotiations were needed to induce the king to grant a sum of 684 guilders in 1833 to defray building costs; it is also true that he made the final choice from among the various plans presented to him.) Not until 1850 was the "extremely defective corner school," as it was designated officially, supplied with a trained teacher. Meanwhile the Mennonites had supplied their own teachers. Among them were Johann Dahlem and "the aged Dester," and also a 16-year-old youth. Considering that their economic circumstances were becoming more and more difficult, this was indeed a notable achievement.

By the middle of the 1850's unfavorable economic conditions induced the Mennonite settlers to leave for other settlements, e.g., Eichstock near Dachau. In 1854-55 most of them left Bavaria for America. This was the end of the first Mennonite settlement in south Bavaria. Maxweiler, as a settlement of *Knöpfler,* i.e., Mennonites rather than Amish, became the center of that first migration into the Swabia-Neuburg-Bavaria region, which spread further to Münster, Mittelstetten, Illdorf, Heinrichsheim, Marienheim, Langlohe, and Doseshof. Little is known of these Mennonite localities after the great emigration, nor what happened to the settlers at Giglberg, Gietlholz, Hardt, Kreut, Dittenfeld, Seehof, Furthof, Probfeld, who were Amish. Maxweiler was later occupied by members of the Reformed Church. Since that time (and since the disbanding of the Eichstock, *q.v.,* settlement) the Mennonites in Bavaria live on single farms rather than in colonies. E.H.C.

D. Müller, "Entstehung der Kolonie Maxweiler," *Menn. Bl.,* 1885, 34, 48; Fr. X. Wismüller, *Gesch. der Moorkultur in Bayern* (Munich, 1909); E. H. Correll, "Mennonitische Moorbauern," *Gem.-Kal.,* 1922; R. Ringenberg, *Familienbuch der Menn.-Gem. Eichstock* (Munich, 1942); *ML* I, 459-61.

Donauwörth, a district of Swabia and Neuburg, Bavaria. At the beginning of the 19th century Alsatian Amish Mennonites settled here, all of whom except a few families have moved away. Since the 1890's Mennonites, mostly from the Neckar region of Baden, have settled here as leaseholders or owners of farms. The following farms in Donauwörth were occupied by Mennonites in 1921: Bartelstock, Bäldleschweige, Ellgau, Hellmaringen, Herrlehof, Hygstetten, Markt, and Urfahrhof. They were at first a part of the Ingolstadt (*q.v.*) congregation. But as they became more widely scattered they found it increasingly difficult to assemble there, and in 1914 formed their own congregation with its center at Donauwörth. In 1928 the congregation (67 souls) was renamed as the Augsburg (*q.v.*) congregation, having moved its place of meeting to Augsburg. (*ML* I, 461.) E.H.C.

Donauwörth, a town in Swabia, Bavaria, Germany, with a population of 4,800, at the time of the Reformation a free imperial city, to which the Reformation found early entry, so that the Protestant population soon predominated, and in which Anabaptists also found adherents. In 1527 Hans Denk (*q.v.*) is said to have lived here for a while after he had completed his translation of the Prophets; information is scanty. The bloody persecutions setting in on every hand made further growth very difficult.

The only extant information on the presence of Anabaptists in Donauwörth is found in the official records of the persecutions. Most of them fled to Moravia, where they were for a time unmolested. But when persecution broke out there in 1535, many hoped to find refuge in the home town. Their return was made extremely difficult, for the dukes Wilhelm and Ludwig had the border strictly guarded to prevent the entry of any Moravian Anabaptists. On May 19, 1535, a group of seven men, five women, and three children trying to return were arrested at Passau and put into the castle dungeon. Of these, Georg Lang, from a farm at Atzersweilen on the Swabian-Franconian border, had been baptized at Donauwörth by Adam Stock; and Adam Schlegel had baptized Hans Hultzhoder of Kupferzell, Amalie, the wife of Hans of Atzersweilen, Kunigunde, the wife of Dittrich of Heilbronn, and Katharina, the wife of Hans Haffner of Riblingen. On Sept. 24, 1535, the leader (*Vorsteher*) Hans Betz (*q.v.*) of Eger was seized, who had been baptized in 1530 above Donauwörth by Georg Haffner. According to the statements of court officials, the prisoners openly admitted belonging to the Anabaptist brotherhood (Wolkan, *Lieder* 29 and 21), and in spite of torture remained steadfast, comforting their persecuted brethren in a series of hymns which they and their fellow prisoners in Passau composed, thus laying the foundation for the *Ausbund* (*q.v.*), which was used for centuries by the Mennonites of South Germany and America and is still used by the Old Order Amish. Hans Betz, who wrote 12 hymns, died in prison in 1537; most of the others died after three years in the dungeon (V. A. Winter, *Gesch. der bayerischen Wiedertäufer,* Munich, 1809, 35; *ML* I, 461). HEGE.

Donauwörth, Bavaria, a Mennonite congregation 1912-28. Since 1900 Mennonites from Baden have purchased and leased land near the city. In 1912 they organized a congregation which met monthly in a rented hall in Donauwörth, had a membership of 42 adults and 36 children, and belonged to the *Verband* (*q.v.*). With the congregations at Munich, Regensburg, Ingolstadt, and Eichstock, it also belonged to the South Bavarian conference, which had been meeting quarterly since 1920. The elder was Daniel Lichti of Ellgau. In 1928 the congregation was reorganized and moved its meeting place to Augsburg. (*ML* I, 461.) HEGE.

Dondi, a mission station (MC), located in Madhya Pradesh, India. The village of Dondi is situated 52 miles southwest of Dhamtari on an arterial highway which is extended through the western part of the Indian state of Kanker. At the close of 1927, as a result of negotiations during the year, the mission received word from the Rani Sahib (Queen) of the Dondi-Lohara Zemindari that she had granted a permanent lease for the occupancy of four acres of land in the village of Dondi on condition that medical work be carried on in addition to other mission interests. The land transfer was made without cost. The land is free of rent. An annual government tax must be paid.

A. C. Brunk was appointed the manager of the Dondi mission station and plans were started at once for the construction of living quarters for Christian workers, a medical dispensary, and the missionaries' bungalow.

In the Dondi district are found all classes of people from the most primitive aborigines to the different castes and classes of farmers and trades-people. This mission evangelistic station with its corps of Christian workers and its outstation Kusum Kasa is well located and organized for the witness of the grace of God among a spiritually needy people. In 1954 there were 27 members in the Dondi congregation, with O. P. Lal as pastor.   G.J.L.

Donnellson is located in Lee Co., Ia., in the southeastern corner of the state. In 1940 it had a population of 518. The early Mennonites of this county came from Bavaria, Germany, more than 100 years ago. There are approximately 85 Mennonite families in this locality, most of them living north and northwest of Donnellson, and 25 living in the town. The Zion (*q.v.*) Mennonite Church (GCM) of Donnellson is the only Mennonite church now located in Lee County. (M. Gingerich, *The Mennonites in Iowa,* Iowa City, 1939; *ML* I, 462.) E.B.

Donner, Hans, an Anabaptist martyr of Austria. All that is known of him is the little information concerning his death in the chronicles of the Hutterites. From the phrase "aus Wels" it is assumed that he was probably in contact with the older group of Upper Austrian Anabaptists. In the summer of 1535 he offered comfort to his brother-in-faith Wilhelm Griesbacher (*q.v.*) who was about to be executed. From Upper Austria he went to Carinthia and worked in St. Veit, where active life was evident in connection with church reform. It is known that "heretical" books were offered for sale here. On Oct. 20, 1537, Hans Knyssler, the district clerk, reported to King Ferdinand that he had confiscated the wares of some booksellers and had the sellers put in chains. Perhaps this was the occasion of Donner's arrest, for the records say that "he lay in prison on Wednesday after Christmas of 1537, with his brother Hans Seydel of Murau." Both were sentenced to death and beheaded. From prison Donner wrote a moving letter to his "dearly beloved brethren and sisters." He and his companion did not forsake the truth "as long as their eyes were open and breath was in their nostrils." Two other manuscripts from his hand have been preserved. Donner is the author of the hymn, "Ich dank dir, lieber Herr, mein Gott, in dieser Not, du kannst uns helfen," printed in *Lieder der Hutterischen Brüder* (Scottdale, 1914) 83.   LOSERTH.

Beck, *Geschichts-Bücher,* 141 f.; idem, *Ein Beitrag zur Gesch. der Wiedertäufer in Kärnten* (Klagenfurt, 1867); Wolkan, *Lieder,* 172; J. Loserth, "The Anabaptists in Carinthia," *MQR* XXI (1947) 238; *ML* I, 462.

Donner, Heinrich, an elder of the Mennonite congregation at Orlofferfelde in the district of Marienburg, West Prussia, 1772-1804, b. 1735 at Danzig, d. 1804. With his parents he moved to Tiegenhof and became a farmer. He was descended from an old Frisian family. His great-grandparents were Daniel Donner and Elisabeth Roosen of Hamburg; his grandfather was Johann Donner, preacher of the Frisian congregation of Danzig. Heinrich Donner was one of the leading elders in West Prussia in the closing decades of the 18th century. He lived first at Schönsee, then at Orlofferfelde. In this latter congregation discord arose between Donner and his coelder Hans Siebert (or Siewertsz) of Thiensdorf, which resulted in a schism and the building of a new meetinghouse in Markushof (*q.v.*). (*Inv. Arch. Amst.* II, Nos. 856 f.) He read extensively and wrote much, rendering valuable service by keeping notes and collecting documents on the history of his church in Prussia. In 1778, with Gerhard Wiebe (*q.v.*), he published a catechism which was later known as the Elbing-Waldeck Catechism. In 1783 he published a brief report on the Hutterian Brethren, titled *Kurzer Bericht von den Taufgesinnten Christen, welche die Huttersche Brüder genannt werden,* based on an account given him by Joseph Müller, a Hutterite preacher of Moravia, who was visiting the Mennonites in West Prussia. This report was reprinted in *Menn. Gemeindeblatt* (VII, 1876, No. 6, 44 f.; No. 7, 53 f.). Other publications from his pen include *Unterricht von der heiligen Wasser-Taufe* (n.p., 1792, reprinted Tiegenhof, 1906), and *Abendmahlsandachten, Gebete, und Lieder* (Marienwerder, n.d.). (*ML* I, 463.)   H.G.M.

Donner, Johann (1771-1830), son and successor of Heinrich Donner (*q.v.*) as elder of the Orlofferfelde Mennonite Church, West Prussia, 1804-30, equaled his father in importance to the Mennonite churches in Prussia, possessed an education quite unusual among the rural population of the time, knew the Bible from memory so that he could locate any passage at once, wrote much in the interest of his fellow believers, was their spokesman in five different deputations sent to Berlin to present the Mennonite cause to the king or the cabinet. He continued the chronicle his father had begun. By his warm, pious, upright personality he contributed to the elimination of friction between the Frisian and Flemish churches in West Prussia. He was born in Schönsee in 1771, owned a farm in Beyershorst, and died there in 1830. His valuable autobiography is published in the *Gemeinde-Kalender* for 1932, pp. 74-103. (*ML* I, 463.)   H.G.M.

Donnersberg, the highest mountain (2,320 ft.) of the Haardt Mountains of the Palatinate, was once the seat of the worship of Thor (Thunder), hence the name. Until the early years of the 20th century there was on it a "Mennonite farm" (*Mennonitenhof*).

The first Mennonite family to live here was the Eymann family. In 1755 Michael Krehbiel, a great-grandson of the Peter Krehbiel who was the first Mennonite to settle on the Weierhof (1682) after expulsion from the canton of Bern in Switzerland, leased it as a hereditary possession from the reigning prince. It contained nearly 200 acres of arable land and meadow. The farm remained in the hands of the Krehbiel family for 100 years, the grandson of the original purchaser dividing it with his brother-in-law Jakob Danner.

During the Palatine Revolt of 1849 against the rejection of the constitution adopted by the Frankfurt Parliament (*q.v.*), the peace of the Mennonite farm was also broken (see A. Krehbiel, "Im Jahre 1849 auf dem Donnersberg," in *Nordpfälz. Gesch.-Blätter,* 1908, No. 7).

Since the lease of the farm carried with it also certain rights to the use of other pasture and forest lands, the government tried by various means to reclaim possession of the farm for the hunting and wood rights attached to it, about the middle of the 19th century. Finally, after lengthy litigation the Krehbiel and Danner families were compelled to sell it to the state in 1854 for the sum of 24,000 florins, and settle on land near by.   NEFF.

Mont Tonnerre was also the name given by the French, who occupied the Palatinate from the time of the French Revolution until 1814, to a government district with its center at Mainz, extending far beyond the present district called Palatinate. In 1811 Ferdinand Bodmann, the divisional superintendent of the prefecture at Mainz, in an annual report to be found in the archives at Speyer, characterized the Palatine Mennonites as "being occupied solely with that which concerns their faith and their personal affairs, indifferent to political events, the consequences of which do not extend to them, reminiscent of the patriarchal life of olden times." The description of eight pages, characterizing the Mennonites of the Donnersberg Department, i.e., of the entire region of the Palatinate, is of interest as being the first official document that openly presents the religious and moral customs of the Mennonites as noninjurious to church and state. Hitherto such judgments had been expressed at most only in the secret official records, and then acted upon with the old prejudice. "Simple clothing and simpler manners" were to this writer the marks that distinguished the Mennonites from Catholics and Protestants. His interest in their civil rights is evident in the opening description of the Mennonites: "Industriously and soberly they carry on their agriculture and cattle raising with fortunate results. Agriculture in our department owes much to this sect." Bodmann estimated their number as 2,200 individuals, having increased by 850 in nine years. "The craze for emigration, which has not left the Mennonites untouched," is given as a reason why they were not still more numerous. In the department they were living chiefly in Speyer, in the cantons of Bechtheim, Kirchheimbolanden, Mainz, and a few in the Zweibrücken district.

Strangely, the Amish of the district are called "Anabaptists." They differed from the Mennonites (says the Bodmann account) in that they let their beards grow. Both the Anabaptists and the Mennonites are described as peaceful and moral; their legal difficulties were arbitrated by the elders, and their conduct was influenced by church discipline. "Tale-bearing and cursing are rare among them. They do not swear. . . . Their clothing and their homes are as simple as their customs and their manner of life. . . . Prosperity and cleanliness, but nowhere does one find signs of show or extravagance. They support the needy without regard for creed." Then he described the conscientiousness with which the Mennonites obey the law. War they do not consider permissible; but this religious opinion yields to the mighty law and they subject themselves to military conscription as obediently as other citizens. In order to reconcile their civil duty as much as possible with their faith, they have requested the emperor to grant them the favor of serving preferably with the transportation corps of the army.   E.H.C.

J. Ellenberger, *Bilder aus dem Pilgerleben* III (n.p., 1883) 88 ff.; *Nordpfälz. Gesch.-Blätter* III, 1906; *ML* I, 463-65.

Donorodjo, a leper colony in the territory of the former Dutch Mennonite mission on the island of Java, Indonesia. The founding of Donorodjo was made possible by the gift of Queen Wilhelmina of the Netherlands, who used money given to her by the Javanese population in honor of the birth of her daughter Juliana (1909), to build an infirmary for lepers. The buildings were erected in a forest near the coast and on April 30, 1916, the infirmary was opened by Dr. H. Bervoets (*q.v.*). It was administered by the Dutch Mennonite Mission Society. In course of time the leper colony was much enlarged and many buildings were erected; a small church was built in 1923, a larger church in 1935 (Church of the Resurrection). The physicians in charge were H. Bervoets and K. P. C. A. Gramberg; the nurse was W. Steinmetz; the administrators R. W. de Clercq, Chr. van Rhijn, P. J. Bouwer and their wives. In 1936 the number of lepers was 200, 160 men and 40 women. One hundred and ten of them were Mohammedans, 90 Christians. Missionary N. Thiessen (*q.v.*) was the leader of the Christian leper population. He was ably assisted by Kandar, a native Christian, a leper who bore his cross with a strong faith. The colony achieved a certain prosperity both financially and spiritually. Here the lepers, outcasts from their own island society, found a quiet place where they could live (also as married couples if they wanted to) and work, and where they were cared for. In 1940 the number of lepers reached about 300.

In March 1942 when the Japanese occupied Java, the fanatical Mohammedans began the "holy war" against the Christians. Donorodjo was partly destroyed; the medical instruments and medicines were all destroyed. F. C. Heusdens, a Reformed missionary who had taken over the administration of the colony after the departure of Bouwer, was put to death by stoning because he refused to become a Mohammedan. During the Japanese occupation, March 1942-August 1945, the colony was somewhat restored. In 1948 the government of the new Indonesian Republic also took some care of the colony.† (Vol. I)   vᴅZ.

Donorodjo, 20 jaar arbeid onder de Melaatschen (1936); (Abr. Mulder), *Uit verleden en heden van de Doopsgezinde Zending* (1947); *Verslagen van het Doopsgezind Zendingsveld op Java over de jaren 1940-47; Jaarverslagen 1945-49.*

Donskoye, a village of the Neu-Samara Mennonite settlement in Russia, located in the district Buzuluk, volost of Yemurau-Tabynsk, founded in 1898.

Doopsgezind, official name of the Mennonites in the Netherlands, by which they have been registered since 1796, and also the name which they gave themselves. The name is very old. Prince William of Orange wrote in 1578 a letter to the city government of Middelburg (*q.v.*), Dutch province of Zeeland, in behalf of a group of "citizens, called Doopsgesint" (*DJ* 1930, 128). From this expression it is not quite clear whether the Mennonites also called themselves *Doopsgezind,* or that they were merely called so by the outside world, but in a letter written by the Middelburg congregation to the magistrates of the city and also in a petition by this congregation to the Prince of Orange in 1582, they use the word in the same way: *die men noempt Doopsghesinde* (*DJ* 1930, 133, 137). At any rate this name was much more agreeable to them than "Anabaptist" and *Wederdoper.* The name *Doopsgesinde,* says T. J. van Braght in the foreword of the *Martyrs' Mirror,* was not assumed by them by preference, but by necessity, because their proper name rather should be *Christgesinden, Apostelgesinden,* or *Evangelischgesinden.* Mennonites in Holland soon began to call themselves *Doopsgezinden;* the Waterlanders used this term as early as 1580, the Young Frisians about 1600, and the Flemish shortly after 1620. Hence it is not quite correct for van Braght (*Mart. Mir.* 1660, introduction) to say that the name had "only lately come into use" (Eng. ed., 1950, 16). In the 17th and 18th centuries the more conservative groups (Old Flemish, Janjacobsgezinden, and also Zonists) preferred the name Mennonites, while the more progressive group of the Waterlanders and later on the Lamists called themselves almost exclusively *Doopsgezinden,* because they did not like to be named for an earthly creature, desiring to be only followers of Christ, while they rejected the name "Mennonite" particularly for the reason that they on the whole did not agree with the doctrines of Menno Simons. Still some conservatives also used the name of *Doopsgezind:* T. J. van Braght calls his book on martyrs the *Martyrs' Mirror* of the *Doops-gesinde* Christians (1660), and the Dutch Zonist minister and historian G. Maatschoen (*q.v.*), editor of Schijn's *Historiae Mennonitarum,* writes in his Dutch translation (*Geschiedenisse dier Christenen . . . ,* Amsterdam, 1743, 97) that the name *Doopsgezinden* is right and well chosen.

Since about 1800 in the Netherlands the name *Mennonieten* or *Men(n)isten* has been replaced by *Doopsgezinden,* though until now in the province of Friesland, and here and there elsewhere, in common parlance the word *Menist* is often used. The derivation and meaning of the word *Doopsgezind* is not clear. It is composed of two words, *doops* (genitive of *doop,* baptism) and *gezind,* i.e., inclined to, or minded. Some authors are of the opinion that the word means "inclined to (the true Biblical) baptism (on confession of faith)" e.g., Galenus Abrahamsz (*Verdediging der Christenen, die Doopsgezinde genaamd worden,* Amsterdam, 1699, 28 f.). This explanation is more nearly correct than the opinion of G. J. van Rijswijk (*Leerredenen* II, Amsterdam, 1825, 55), who suggests that they were called *Doopsgezind* because of rejection of (infant) baptism.

The German word *Taufgesinnt,* used in Switzerland and Germany to indicate the Mennonites and so used by themselves, is the exact equivalent of the Dutch word *Doopsgezind,* and was taken over from the Dutch Mennonites.   vᴅZ.

S. Muller, "De oorsprong en beteekenis der benamingen van Mennoniten en Doopsgezinden," *DJ* 1837, 39-52; *DB* 1861, 32-50; *ML* I, 465.

Doopsgezind Emeritaatfonds: see **Algemeen Doopsgezind Emeritaatfonds.**

Doopsgezind Emigrantenbureau: see **Hollandsch Doopsgezind Emigrantenbureau.**

Doopsgezind Jaarboekje, a yearbook published by the Dutch Mennonites since 1902. In contrast to the more scholarly *Doopsgezinde Bijdragen* (*q.v.*) it presents a more popular type of reading matter of interest to the Mennonites of Holland. For every Sunday and holiday it has a devotional paragraph, followed by the biographical sketch of some person of note in the Mennonite world. Besides this it contains poetry and prose of stimulating and instructional nature and articles on current affairs. Its founder and first editor was A. Binnerts Sz. in Haarlem. Binnerts was the editor 1902-26. He was followed by J. Wuite, 1927-31, and S. H. N. Gorter, 1932-43. The *Jaarboekje* appeared annually 1902-43, when it had to cease publication by order of the German occupation authorities. Since 1949 it has been published by the *Algemene Doopsgezinde Sociëteit,* edited by L. D. G. Knipscheer and D. Richards. (*ML* I, 465.)   A.Bi., vᴅZ.

Doopsgezind Kinderhuis Oud-Wulven, a Dutch Mennonite children's home, managed by the *Stichting voor Bizondere Noden* (Foundation for Special Needs). It provides a home for normal children (ages 5-13) from families that for moral or other reasons are unfit to care for them. The home Oud-Wulven, which is located near Houten, a few miles south of Utrecht, was opened on Sept. 16, 1947, and is conducted by Mrs. de Zeeuw, wife of the present secretary of the *Algemene Doopsgezinde Sociëteit.* In January 1953, 29 children were sheltered here.   vᴅZ.

Doopsgezind Pensioenverhogingsfonds, a Dutch Mennonite fund, founded in 1929 to increase the pensions of retired ministers by giving a supplementary payment. These allowances were first paid in 1930. In 1948, after the *Pensioenfonds van de ADS* (*q.v.*) was founded in 1946, and the matters of pensions entirely reorganized, the original

Pensioenverhogingsfonds was included with other funds in the general *Pensioenfond*.   vDZ.

Doopsgezinde Bijdragen, a yearbook published by the Mennonites of the Netherlands 1861-1919. In 1837 S. Muller (*q.v.*) published his *Jaarboekje voor Doopsgezinde Gemeenten in de Nederlanden* in Amsterdam. It was to be a continuation of the *Naamlijst* (*q.v.*), which ceased publication in 1829 —to furnish a list of ministers and congregations in the Netherlands. Muller added two sections to this list of names, one headed *Kerknieuws* (Church News), and the other *Doopsgezinde Mengelingen* (Mennonite Miscellany). Three issues of this significant yearbook appeared (1837, 1840, and 1850). Four years later D. S. Gorter (*q.v.*) published his *Godsdienstige lectuur voor Doopsgezinden*, also in three issues (1854, 1856, and 1858).

A need for such a publication concerning major events and information on church affairs had been established. Three years later (1861) the ministers D. Harting in Enkhuizen and P. Cool in Harlingen sought to meet this need by publishing the *Doopsgezinde Bijdragen* (Mennonite Contributions). They sent a circular to the Mennonite congregations stating the purpose of the new periodical; viz., "to cultivate and strengthen the spirit of brotherly communion among the Dutch Mennonites by means of historical information on the life and work of our forefathers, fraternal discussion of church affairs and concerns which can exert an influence on the welfare of our brotherhood, and finally collecting such reports from one another to promote acquaintance with one another and interest in the present status of the brotherhood."

The project soon grew beyond its original plan, becoming the most important periodical of the Dutch Mennonites. It gave reports not only on changes in ministerial charges and other events in the congregations, but also presented important scholarly articles on all sorts of questions from history and current affairs, so that the periodical has become a mine of information for the research scholar and is thereby of permanent value.

It was originally printed by Frederik Muller in Amsterdam; 1868-70 by H. Kuipers in Leeuwarden; 1872-80 by G. L. Funke, Amsterdam, and H. Kuipers in Leeuwarden; and 1881-1919 by E. J. Brill at Leiden. In 1866 and 1871 and 1913-15 it did not appear. In 1870 J. G. de Hoop Scheffer became the editor. After his death in 1893, it was edited by S. Cramer 1894-1912. In consequence of certain difficulties no further issue appeared until 1916, when W. J. Kühler took it over. The final issue appeared in 1919, when the project was discontinued. An exhaustive index of the first 50 volumes (1861-1910) was prepared by K. Vos and was published in 1912.

The *DB*, an annual volume of small format with a scholarly content of 110-190 pages, is the first Mennonite scholarly periodical to be published in any country, has the longest record of publication, and is one of the most valuable sources of printed information on the Dutch Mennonites. (*ML* I, 465.)   NEFF.

Doopsgezinde Bundel, a Dutch Mennonite hymnbook. From the middle of the 16th century until 1940 a large number of Dutch Mennonite hymnbooks were published (see **Hymnology**). In 1900 there were still 15 or 16 different hymnals in use in the Dutch congregations, most of them using two to five different books; in 1940, 13 different editions were still being used, though the *Leidse Bundel* (*q.v.*) and the two *Protestantenbondbundels* predominated. For many years it had been felt desirable to have a single songbook for the entire Dutch Mennonite brotherhood. In 1936 the church boards of the Amsterdam and Haarlem congregations co-operated with the *Vereniging voor Gemeentedagen*, which was also planning to compile a new hymnal for their Elspeet and other conferences. In 1937 the *Nederlandsche Protestanten-Bond* (*q.v.*) also appointed a committee to make a new hymnal, and this committee then joined the two Mennonite groups in composing a hymnbook for the use of all the groups. This book was ready in 1943, but was not used in the congregations until 1945. The book contains 250 hymns. Special attention was given to restoring the music for the hymns to its original form by removing extraneous additions.

This hymnal is used by a large number of Dutch Protestant churches, Mennonites, Remonstrants, Lutherans, *Vrije Gemeente* (Free Church of Amsterdam), and *Vrijzinnig Hervormden* (Liberal Reformed churches), besides the departments of the *Nederlandsche Protestanten-Bond*.

For many Mennonites, however, the book in this form was not quite satisfactory. For this reason 50 favorite hymns from former Mennonite songbooks were inserted. Some hymns suited to particular Mennonite services like baptism were also given place. So the *Doopsgezinde Bundel*, edited by the Algemene Doopsgezinde Sociëteit (*q.v.*) (preface of 1944), consists of 300 hymns. It is now in use in nearly all Mennonite churches of the Netherlands, the old hymnbooks all having been abandoned. Only the congregations of Ameland, Blokzijl, and Ouddorp did not adopt the *Doopsgezinde Bundel*, but retained the old Reformed songbooks.   vDZ.

Doopsgezinde Jeugdraad (Dutch Mennonite Youth Council) was founded in 1946 after World War II by the *ADS* (General Conference of Dutch Mennonites) on the initiative of C. Nijdam, at that time moderator of the *ADS*, for the purpose of co-ordinating and promoting all work for and by Mennonite youth. The council has a board composed of representatives of several youth activities. The affiliated groups are the *Doopsgezinde Jongeren-Bond* (*q.v.*) (Dutch Mennonite Youth Union), ages 18-25. *Menniste Bouwers Federatie* (Federation of Dutch Mennonite Builders), ages 8-18, *Elfregi* (*q.v.*) (Mennonite Boy Scouts), ages 8-25, and West-Hill Sunday school for ages 4-12. The Youth Council has its office in the Amsterdam Singel Church. Special attention is given to training leaders for the different branches of youth work, and to this end a periodical is published entitled *Koers* (Course), *Leidersblad voor Doopsgezinde Jeugdwerk.*

The Dutch Mennonite youth is represented by the *Jeugdraad* in the Ecumenical Youth Council, in the *Nederlandse Jeugdgemeenschap* (Dutch Youth Association), and also for the purpose of broadcasts for youth. Each year a number of meetings are held. To promote the West-Hill Sunday-school work and to train its leaders an instructor has been employed who visits Mennonite congregations in rotation. The Youth Council also contacts Mennonite students of the seven Dutch universities. The work of the *Jeugdraad* is subsidized by the *ADS*, in the board of which the *Jeugdraad* has a representative with consultative voice.   H.W.

Doopsgezinde Jongeren-Bond, Friese: see **Friese Doopsgezinde Jongeren-Bond (F.D.J.B.),**

Doopsgezinde Jongerenbond (Dutch Mennonite Youth Union), usually abbreviated *DJB.* After the *Vereeniging voor Gemeentedagen van Doopsgezinden* (*q.v.*) had been founded in 1917 it soon took care of the young members of the church, for whom special *Jonge-Leden-dagen* (Young members' meetings) were organized. In the course of time in many a congregation a *Jongerenkring* (youth circle) arose, and to promote mutual contact between those circles a general youth secretariat was founded, of which Gerrit Honig of Zaandam soon became the life and soul. In 1924, when the *Friese Doopsgezinde Jongeren Bond* (Frisian Mennonite Youth Union) was founded in Friesland, the young members of the church all over the country wanted to have a central organization, of which all young Mennonites would be members. This general Union was founded in 1926. Among the founders were Gerrit Honig, mentioned before, and the (now) Mennonite minister, Miss Aafke Leistra, then living at Grouw. During the first years the Youth Union was conducted by the *Vereeniging voor Gemeentedagen,* but on April 9, 1928, it became an independent association. All young Mennonites from 18 to 35 years and also sympathizing non-Mennonites can be members (in many congregations, however, only those from 18 to about 25 are engaged in the youth circles). From 1928 on the *DJB* was not a kind of organization conducted by church leaders, as it is often the case in other countries, but a self-conducted movement; it has a board of about ten members, being all representatives of the youth circles of all parts of the Netherlands.

First secretary of the *DJB* was Gerrit Honig. P. Vis, then minister of the congregation of Arnhem, who had also been a founder of the Frisian Youth Union, was the first president of the *DJB.* It is not exactly known how large the membership was when the *DJB* was founded. It might have been about 600, spread over 39 congregational youth groups. On Jan. 1, 1939, the membership numbered about 1,500 (in 78 groups); it reached its peak in 1944 with 2,250 members, spread over 94 groups. Since then it has decreased. Now (1953) there are about 1,200 members in 75 groups. In 1932 the *DJB* and the Frisian Youth Union merged.

In the course of time many activities were promoted. The most outstanding activity is the yearly general youth meeting, held in June in the brotherhood home at Elspeet (*q.v.*). Here sometimes 250 young men and women assembled. In former years the meeting was so large that two general meetings had to be held, one in June, the other in August, both at Elspeet. Besides these general meetings, provincial youth meetings are held in Friesland, Groningen, North Holland, etc. During the last years the interest in these meetings, also in the Elspeet meetings, is somewhat decreasing. The *DJB* also organizes youth camps: in 1954 three camps were held in Holland, and seven in Germany and Austria (total number of participants, 300). In 1937 the Union arranged a trip to the Mennonites of Danzig, Prussia, and Poland. The next years' trips were made to England and to the Alsatian Mennonites.

For a number of years the announcements of the *DJB* were published in the *Brieven* (*q.v.*) of the *Vereeniging voor Gemeentedagen,* but in 1935 they acquired their own monthly *De Hoeksteen* (the cornerstone), which still exists. In 1946 the *DJB* published the *Menno-Bundel,* an informational booklet of 80 pages.   vdZ.

Onze eerste tien jaren, tenth anniversary booklet of the *Vereeniging voor Gemeentedagen* (Wolvega, 1927) 37-41; *Menno-Bundel,* 1946; *Brieven,* 1921-35; *De Hoeksteen* (1935-).

Doopsgezinde Kalender is a devotional calendar with a page for each day, and usually also in book form (diary), in the Dutch language, edited by a special committee. This calendar, the first issue of which appeared 1937 (during the years 1943-46 the calendar could not be published), is sometimes also called *Zendingskalender* or *Broederschapskalender.* (See **Abreisskalender.**)   vdZ.

Doopsgezinde Liederen, a Dutch Mennonite hymnbook, usually called *Nieuwe Haarlemsche Bundel.* It was composed by a committee of the congregation of Haarlem and for the use of this congregation. This hymnbook, printed at Amsterdam 1895, contains 108 songs collected from older hymnbooks. It was also used in a few other congregations, viz., Apeldoorn, Beemster, The Hague, and Warns. (*DB* 1896, 132-34, *Catalogus Amst.,* 330.)   vdZ.

Doopsgezinde Vereeniging tot bevordering van den Predikdienst *in Zuid-Westelijk Friesland:* see **Bolsward, Ring.**

Doopsgezinde Vereniging *tot Verbreiding des Evangelies in de Nederlandsche Overzeesche Bezittingen:* see **Dutch Mennonite Mission Association.**

Doopsgezinde Vredesgroep (Dutch Mennonite Peace Group). This group is a postwar continuation of the *Arbeidsgroep* (*q.v.*) *van Doopsgezinden tegen de Krijgsdienst,* which was a Dutch Mennonite anti-militaristic association, founded in 1922, which during the war co-operated with Quakers and other nonresistant groups to relieve the needs of the war times: help to Jews, to enable them to leave the Netherlands secretly, and later in sending food to the Jewish concentration camp at Westerbork, where the German Nazis had confined a large number of Jews (each week 700 packets of 10 lbs. were sent); to the population of Rotterdam after the severe German bombardment of May 14, 1940; in 1943-44, when food became scarce, by moving children out of the larger cities of the Western Netherlands to the country; and helping the *onderduikers*, i.e., persons who were in hiding because of the Gestapo, etc.

After the war, on Aug. 31 and Sept. 1-2, 1945, the *Vredesgroep* was founded during a peace meeting in the Elspeet Brotherhood Home (*q.v.*). The aims of the Peace Group are as follows: In loyal obedience to the Lord Jesus Christ they wish to give a testimony to the world by acknowledging Christ's command of love even to enemies, and the obligation of Biblical nonresistance; to strengthen the peace convictions in Mennonite congregations; to give spiritual and material help to those who are in trouble in consequence of their nonresistance, and especially to those who refuse military service for the sake of Christ; to contribute to a form of service of love, substituting for military service, like the Civilian Public Service (*q.v.*) of the Mennonites in the United States; they are willing to co-operate with other nonresistant organizations.

An important support for conscientious objectors is the *Doopsgezind Vredes-Bureau* (Mennonite Peace Office), founded by the Peace Group in 1946 (leaders: T. O. Hylkema and C. P. Inja), which gives assistance and instruction to all who wish to refuse military service, or who as conscientious objectors are in trouble. The number of C.O.'s to whom assistance was rendered from September 1946 to Jan. 1, 1953, totaled 700 (Mennonites 250, other Christian denominations 283, no church 167). Besides this, relief work was taken up "in the name of Christ." Supported by the whole Mennonite brotherhood, food was sent to Vienna, Austria, 1947-50, and from then to Emden, East Friesland. This relief work was largely stimulated by the example of the Mennonite Central Committee (*q.v.*) which had much impressed the Dutch Mennonites. The members of the Peace Group felt much allied to the American Mennonites, both groups holding the principles of nonresistance. By this positive principle the Dutch Mennonite Peace Group has much influence in similar non-Mennonite organizations.

The membership of the Peace Group, when founded in 1946, numbered 50; in May 1947 it had increased to 250; on Jan. 1, 1953, the membership was 607. Besides this there are about 100 *belangstellende leden* (sympathizing members, who do not agree on all points with the constitution of the group). Among the members there are 40 ministers (32 per cent of all Dutch Mennonite ministers).

C.P.I.

Doopsgezinde Vredesbureau: see **Doopsgezinde Vredesgroep.**

Doopsgezinde Weezenvereeniging: see **Haarlemsche Vereeniging.**

Doopsgezinde Zendingsvereeniging: see **Dutch Mennonite Mission Association.**

Dooregeest, Engel Arendszoon van, was born Dec. 26, 1645, at Dooregeest, a polder near Uitgeest, Dutch province of North Holland, and at the age of about 30 was ordained Mennonite minister at De Rijp, serving there until his death on Aug. 16, 1706. At the same time he seems to have been a physician. He belonged to the more orthodox Zonists, but in his book *Onderwijzinge in de Christelyke Leere na de Belijdenissen der Doopsgezinden* (Amsterdam, 1692) he differs from Menno's position with regard to original sin, ban, and communion, nor does he consider footwashing a sign of the covenant.

When Prof. Spanheim of the university of Leiden accused him of various heresies in his book *Selectarum de religione Controversiarum elenchus* (1687), Dooregeest showed himself a real champion of Mennonitism in his reply, *Brief aan den Heere Fredericus Spanhemius* (Amsterdam, 1694), which was translated into German in 1694, and in its third edition in 1700 was combined with a *Brief aen den Eerw. Heer Hermanus Schyn, Leeraar der Doopsgezinden* (Amsterdam, 1700) in order to defend the good name of the Mennonites the better. In it he opposes Galenus Abrahamsz de Haan (*q.v.*), who, as he thought, had deviated rather far from the old doctrines in his *Korte Grondstellingen.*

When the Frisian preacher Jan Klaasz van Grouw seemed in his writings to have unitarian and socinian views, Dooregeest again came to the defense of the ancient orthodox doctrine with his *Verantwoordinge Voor de Leere der Doopsgezinden* (Amsterdam, 1704); he likewise made an attack on the Reformed preacher at De Rijp in his *Verdeediging van de Leere der Doopsgezinden, tot Wederlegginge van de twee Tractaaten, tegen dezelve uitgegeeven door Henricus Schevenhuisen, Predikant der Gereformeerden tot Rijp* (Amsterdam, 1705).

The conference of the Zonist Sociëteit in June 1697 commissioned him together with Herman Schijn and Pieter Beets to draw up a *Kort Onderwijs des Christelijke Geloofs, . . . geschickt na de Belijdenissen der Doopsgezinden* (Amsterdam, 1697); its fifth reprint was issued in 1740. It is evident that van Dooregeest, though not formally educated, was a man of understanding, intelligence, and was highly respected. Though a Waterlander, who usually were more liberal, and serving a Waterlander congregation, he was an ardent adherent of the conservative Zonist (*q.v.*) principles. He was a coauthor of the booklet *Grondtsteen van Vreede en Verdraegsaemheyt* (1674), which invited the congregations to join the Zonist Conference. He was often the moderator of the Zonist Conference meetings. In 1684-85, when efforts were made to reunite the separated groups of Zonists and Lamists, van Dooregeest was one of the representatives of the Zonist branch.

With C. A. Posjager, the minister of the neighboring Noordeinde van Graft, he also wrote *De Ryper Zeepostil, bestaande in XXII Predicatien, toegepast op de Zeevaart* (Amsterdam, 1699), to which he added a brief account of the rise of Holland, a description of Waterland (a district of the Dutch province of North Holland) and the origin of fishing for herring and whales. He also wrote a foreword for a new edition (1686) of the *Belijdenis des Christelyken Geloofs* by Hans de Ries and Lubbert Gerritsz.   J.L.

Schijn-Maatschoen, *Uitvoeriger Verhandeling van de Geschiedenisse der Mennoniten* II (Amsterdam, 1744) 157 ff., 548-73; *Inv. Arch. Amst.* I, Nos. 903-26; *Biogr. Wb.* II, 548-50; *N.N.B.Wb.* I, 518; Blaupot t. C., *Holland* I, 293-96; *DB* 1897, 87; 1898, 60, 78-99 *passim;* 1917, 40-46; H. W. Meihuizen, *Galenus Abrahamsz* (Haarlem, 1954) *passim,* see Index; *ML* I, 466.

Do(o)reslaer, Abraham à, a Dutch Reformed preacher, coauthor with Austro-Sylvius of the only scholarly work comparing the doctrines of the Calvinists with those of the Mennonites, entitled, *Grondige en klare Vertooninghe van het onderscheijdt in de voornaemste hooftstucken der Christelijcker Religie, tusschen De Gereformeerde ende de Weder-dooperen,* . . . (Enkhuizen, 1637, 2d printing 1649). The book contains many quotations from extremely rare or now nonexistent books. The 1626 synod at Alkmaar commissioned Petrus Jakobus Austro-Sylvius (*q.v.*) to write this work, considering it necessary because of the confession of faith published by Jacques Outerman (*q.v.*), a Mennonite preacher, in 1626. At the synod of 1627 Austro-Sylvius was already looking for help, and Dooreslaer was appointed to the task. Dooreslaer was the pastor at Oude Niedorp in 1602, and at Enkhuizen in 1605. In addition to several sermons, Dooreslaer also made a new translation of the Bible with explanations (Amsterdam, 1614), a forerunner of the *Statenvertaling* (*q.v.*). He must therefore have been one of the most learned of the Calvinist theologians. After the outline of statements and counter statements had been approved by the synod committee (Antonides and Sibema), the two authors proceeded to work out the comparison. The book is divided into 24 chapters and contains no less than 856 pages (in two columns) with an exhaustive index. Dooreslaer died at Enkhuizen March 19, 1655. His three sons, Samuel, Isaac, and David, also became Reformed preachers. (*Biogr. Wb.* II, 557-60; *ML* I, 466.)   K.V.

Doornaert, Hans, was a weaver at Gent, Belgium, and a preacher of the Mennonite congregation there, who fled to Haarlem, Dutch province of North Holland, with many others of his faith. Here he also served as a preacher (*Vermaner*) of the Waterlander Mennonites, opening and closing each meeting by asking the congregation to pray silently. Since this was permitted only to regularly appointed preachers of the congregation, Jakob Jansz Scheedemaker (*q.v.*) opposed him vigorously, while others considered it proper and defended Doornaert, inasmuch as he could do it in a more edifying manner than they were accustomed to hear. In 1587 a conference was held at Haarlem on this question, at which delegates from Amsterdam, Alkmaar, and several congregations in Waterland also appeared. Nothing was accomplished, and a division of the Waterlanders was averted only by the tact of Dirk Volkertsz Coornhert (*q.v.*). (Blaupot t. C., *Holland* I, 123, 124; *DB* 1877, 81; 1897,

93 ff.; Kühler, *Geschiedenis* I, 368-71; *ML* I, 466.)
                                              J.L.

Doornbosch, Bernardus, was preacher of the Frisian Mennonites of Wormerveer, Dutch province of North Holland in 1764-80. In 1780 there was some disagreement between him and his congregation, so he resigned. He is supposed to have gone over to the Reformed Church, but this is not certain. Doornbosch is the author of *Godgeleerde en Zedekundige proeven* (Zutphen, 1784). From 1759 to 1764 he collected a large number of sermons preached by Mennonite and Remonstrant ministers. This curious manuscript, entitled *Thesaurus Theologicus* (10 volumes), is now found in the Amsterdam Mennonite Library. This library also contains another manuscript by Doornbosch, called *De Christenleeraar* . . . , a collection of extracts from theological and ethical studies and sermons. (*Biogr. Wb.* II, 552; *Inv. Arch. Amst.* I, No. 1748; *Catalogus Amst.,* 246.)   vDZ.

Doornik (Tournay), a town (pop. 32,500) in Belgium, where in the 16th century were found many adherents of the Reformation. The first victim of persecution was a former Augustinian monk, Hendrik van Westfalen, who was burned here on July 13, 1528. The total number of martyrs in this town was 227, only 30 of whom are listed in Mennonite or Reformed martyrbooks. Most of them were followers of Calvin, Calvinism being very strong in this town. In 1568 at least 92 Calvinists were put to death, and in the next year another 53.

There were six Mennonite martyrs of Doornik: Adriaen van Hee, Joos Meeuwesz, Willem the Hatmaker, Egbert the Hatmaker, Goossen the Hatmaker, and Lambert van Doornik, all in 1558. They were seized without resistance when a meeting was surprised in the forest of Obignies near Doornik. They were first brought to Doornik. Five of them were from abroad; only one was a native of Doornik. The trial was conducted at Bergen (Mons); after they had all remained steadfast and were sentenced to death, they were brought back to Obignies, where the execution took place; all six were burned at the stake in 1558, exact date unknown.

These six men may have been baptized by Leenaert Bouwens (*q.v.*). According to his list this elder baptized 11 persons at Doornik in 1554-56 and 20 in 1557-61. The Inquisitor Pieter Titelman (*q.v.*) wrote in a letter, that in 1561 there was still a Mennonite congregation in Doornik. Of this congregation nothing further is known.   vDZ.

A. Hocquet, *Tournai et le Tournaisis au XVIe Siecle, au point de vue politique et social* (Brussels, 1906); J. Meyhoffer, *Le Martyrologe protestant des Pays-Bas, 1523-1597* (Brussels, 1907); F. Besson, *Edits de Charles-Quint* (Buenos Aires, n.d.) 12.

Doornik, Jan van, an Anabaptist martyr: see **Jan Poote.**

Doornkaat (Dorencate, Doorenkaate, or ten Doornkaat), a Mennonite family, which is found from the beginning of the 17th century in the district of Twenthe, Dutch province of Overijssel, where Hendrick Dorencate (d. 1755) became a preacher of the

Old Flemish congregation of Hengelo (*q.v.*) in 1729, in which Hendrik Engbertsz Doorencate was a preacher 1735-*ca*.79. In later times this family lived especially in the Dutch province of Groningen and in East Friesland, Germany (see also **Coolman**).

vDZ.

Doornkaat Koolman, Jan ten, b. Oct. 1, 1815, at Norden, East Friesland, Germany, part owner of the Doornkaat distillery, which his father, who came from Holland in 1806, founded in Norden. Anna Brons (*q.v.*) was the only child of his father's first marriage. Jan was the oldest son of the second marriage, to Jeikelina Kool. He and his brother Fiepko made a thriving business of the distillery. For his native city and his country Jan ten Doornkaat Koolman performed meritorious services. In 1848 he was elected president of the civic assembly; this was the beginning of a long and honorable career of political service in both elective and appointive positions in local and national government.

In addition to all this professional and political activity, he also found time and energy to follow his scholarly inclinations. Though he had no formal academic training, his work in several areas won the recognition of scholars. Evidence of his versatile interests is found in his book, *Die Unendlichkeit der Welt, Eine Naturbetrachtung* (Norden, 1866, 2d ed.). An imperishable gift to his home country is his three-volume dictionary of the Frisian language, 1862-65. In the Norden Mennonite Church he held the office of elder for many years. C.A.L.

Biography in *Jahrbuch der Gesellschaft für bildende Kunst und vaterländische Altertümer von Emden* II, 399 ff.; *Deutsches Geschlechterbuch* (published by B. Koerner) XXIII; *Ostfriesisches Geschlechterbuch* (1913); *ML* I, 467.

Doornkaat Koolman, Jan ten, b. Nov. 12, 1850, d. Nov. 29, 1913, nephew of the above, president of the board of directors of the Doornkaat distillery and brewery, from 1883 to 1896 president of the civic assembly, 1896 senator, 1895 city councilor. In the Mennonite church of his home town of Norden, he served for many years as deacon, and after 1909 as senior deacon. In his leisure he studied the treasures in the archives of Norden and the Mennonite church of Norden and the community. In 1903 he published *Kurze Mitteilungen aus der Geschichte der Mennoniten-Gemeinden in Ostfriesland im allgemeinen und aus der Nordener Gemeinde im besonderen bis zum Jahre 1797*. In 1904 appeared *Mitteilungen aus der Geschichte der Mennoniten-Gemeinde zu Norden im 19. Jahrhundert*. In addition he published *Mitteilungen aus der Vergangenheit Nordens*, two volumes (1908 and 1909).

J.tD.K.

Deutsches Geschlechterbuch (published by B. Koerner) XXIII; *Ostfriesisches Geschlechterbuch* I (1913); *ML* I, 467.

Doornkaat Koolman, ten, Mennonite family: see **Coolman** family.

Doove Barend: see **Barend Dirksz.**

Dordrecht, a city in the Dutch province of South Holland (pop. 68,000 in 1947). In the 16th century there was a large Mennonite congregation here. Early Anabaptism, however, had no great number of adherents here, although Bartholomeus Boeckbinder (*q.v.*) and Willem de Cuyper (*q.v.*) preached here as early as 1533-34. Of great blessing was the activity of Elder Leenaert Bouwens (*q.v.*), who baptized 6 persons here in 1557-61 and no less than 44 in 1563-65. About this time the congregation was greatly increased by immigrants from Flanders, as is indicated by the family names. Yet the congregation was severely persecuted. The *Martyrs' Mirror* names as martyrs here: Digna Pieters, 1555; Joris Wippe, burgomaster of Meenen, Belgium, 1558; ten persons in 1569; Jan Woutersz van Cuyck, an artist, 1572. When Calvinism prevailed, the Synod of Dordrecht in 1574 passed a sharp resolution against the Mennonites.

Among the important Mennonites of Dordrecht were the historiographer Matthijs van Balen (*q.v.*), the painter and poet Samuel van Hoogstraten (*q.v.*), and the artistic Houbraken family. The congregation once had many well-to-do members. In 1655 it made a donation of 300 florins for the victims of persecution in Savoy. Of the elders the following are known: Gerrit van Bylaer (d. Oct. 12, 1617), Hendrik Terwe (d. Oct. 2, 1625), Mees Ghijsbrechts (d. June 19, 1648), Bartholomeus van Stein, and Tieleman Jansz van Braght (*q.v.*, d. Oct. 8, 1664); in the 18th century, Bartholomeus de Groot and Abraham Verduin (*q.v.*). One of their preachers was a Menno Simons, who resigned on Jan. 19, 1653. A statement in the *Doopsgezinde Bijdragen* (1862, p. 104) seems to indicate that the elders Cornelis van Braght and Abraham Ferrier were appointed to that office by the government in 1689 and 1691 respectively. The last preacher was Adam van Moerbeek, 1749-93. After that the Rotterdam preachers occasionally served the Dordrecht congregation.

In the 17th century the church, which belonged to the Flemish branch, was at its zenith. It was here that the Dordrecht Confession of 1632 was drawn up by Adriaen Cornelisz. Van Braght, the noted author of the *Martyrs' Mirror*, and Bastiaan van Weenigem of Rotterdam were the leaders of the conservative wing in opposition to the liberal views of Galenus Abrahamsz de Haan (*q.v.*), and the principal authors of the Zonist *Verbond van Eenigheid*.

In 1624 the congregation built a church on Lange Breedstraat, and in 1643 enlarged it. The Calvinists in 1664 persuaded the authorities to forbid the building of a little gate to the church. On Sept. 17, 1683, the Mennonites asked the city authorities for a new church location, apparently in vain.

During the 18th century the congregation decreased steadily. In 1732 there were 80 members left, in 1742, 40. After 1793 they had no pastor, and their church was used for other purposes, e.g., for meetings of the Dutch Missionary Association. About 1840 a certain Karsdorp exploited this state of affairs; he prevented any Mennonites who moved into the city from joining the church; and when he alone was left he sold the church and had the government grant him the capital. For ten years the Rotterdam Church was involved in litigation to secure these funds, but lost. The lower chamber passed a resolution acknowledging that the government director was in error in giving Karsdorp the funds, but could not make it retroactive.

When the membership had again increased to 60 in 1895, the congregation was reorganized (Dec. 13, 1895). A church council was chosen. Johannes Dyserinck (*q.v.*), a minister in Rotterdam, was *consulent* and gave religious instruction. On Jan. 12, 1896, the first sermon was delivered to the new congregation. In 1897 they built a church on Lenghenstraat, and dedicated it on Jan. 9, 1897, with a sermon by Dyserinck. On Oct. 15, 1899, they called a preacher of their own and the government, to atone for the error made earlier, gave them an annual subsidy of 200 florins. For preaching services they were united with Breda (*q.v.*) from 1899 to 1945. The ministers were A. J. van Loghum Slaterus, 1899-1908; W. Koekebakker, 1908-45; Abraham Mulder since 1946. The membership in 1898 was 74; in 1926, 180; in 1953, 148. The congregation has a Sunday school, Bible courses, women's circle, and many youth activities.

K.V., vdZ.

Inv. Arch. Amst. I, Nos. 569, 583-85, 588, 591, 1180, 1185, 1284; II, Nos. 1694-1712; IIa, Nos. 39-42; *DB* 1862, 88-114; 1867, 156 f.; 1868, 145 ff.; 1869, 125-28; 1896, 207-8; 1897, 256; 1898, 242; Mellink, *Wederdopers*, 228-31; *ML* I, 467-68.

Dordrecht Confession of Faith. Written in the first draft by Adriaan Cornelisz, elder of the Flemish Mennonite congregation in the Dutch city of Dordrecht, this confession of faith, containing 18 articles, was adopted April 21, 1632, and signed by 51 Flemish and Frisian Mennonite preachers as a basis of union. The official (Dutch) title reads: *Voorstellinghe van de principale articulen onses algemeynen Christelijcken Geloofs, ghelijck de selve in onse Gemeynte doorgaens geleert ende beleeft worden.* On Feb. 4, 1660, six preachers and seven deacons from Alsace, in a meeting held at Ohnenheim in Rappoltstein, adopted the Dordrecht Confession "as our own." Later it was adopted by the Mennonites in the Palatinate and North Germany; the Swiss Mennonites never accepted it, perhaps because it teaches shunning (Article 17) which only the Swiss Amish practiced, not the Swiss Mennonites. Probably through the influence of the Dutch Mennonites of Germantown, Pa., the Mennonites of southeastern Pennsylvania, of the Franconia and Lancaster conferences (MC) adopted the Dordrecht Confession in 1725. The more conservative Mennonite bodies in America, including the Mennonite Church (MC), now recognize it as their official articles of faith, but its personal acceptance is not required either for baptism or ordination. Historically this symbol has been much used as an instrument of catechetical instruction in preparation for baptism.

The Eighteen Articles of Dordrecht teach the basic doctrines of the Christian faith: God is viewed as "eternal, almighty, and incomprehensible" and as existing in three Persons, "Father, Son, and the Holy Ghost." God created the first man Adam in His own image, gave him Eve as a companion, and from these two spring all the people of earth (Art. I). The original pair fell into sin by transgressing the divine command and became so estranged from God as to be utterly lost had not God "interposed in their behalf and made provision for their restoration" (Art. II). Even while Adam and Eve were still in the Garden of Eden God promised to give His Son as their Saviour, a divine promise in which they hoped, as did all the pious patriarchs, "expecting that He . . . would at His coming again redeem and deliver the fallen race from their sins . . ." (Art. III). In the fullness of time Jesus was born, the long-awaited Saviour: the Word became flesh, having been conceived by the Holy Spirit in the Virgin Mary. "But how or in what manner this worthy body was prepared . . . we content ourselves with the declaration which the worthy evangelists have given." Jesus died for all men, purchasing redemption for the entire race, for He "tasted death for every man" (Art. IV). Before His ascension Jesus established His New Testament with His followers, which Testament contains all that men need for the Christian life if they accept and obey it (Art. V). The first step in beginning the Christian life is "repentance and amendment of life" (Art. VI). Those who in penitence become Christian believers, those who "through faith, the new birth and renewal of the Holy Ghost have become united with God," are to be baptized with water in the name of the Holy Trinity to the burying of their sins, for their incorporation into the communion of the saints, and as a pledge of faithful discipleship, "to observe all things whatsoever the Son of God taught . . . His followers to do" (Art. VII). Those who have repented, become true believers and been baptized, constitute the church of Christ, the body which He redeemed by His blood and which He will preserve and protect until the end of the world. The true church is known by her evangelical faith, Christian love, godly manner of life, and observance of the "true ordinances of Christ" (Art. VIII). The Lord has appointed that the congregations of His church should be provided with elders, pastors, deacons and deaconesses, so that the Lord's ordinances, baptism and supper, might be administered, "the body of Christ may be edified, and the Lord's vineyard and church be preserved in its growth and structure" (Art. IX). The Lord's Supper is to be observed as a memorial of our redemption in Christ's blood and as a reminder of our duty to love one another and to maintain the unity of the church (Art. X). Believers shall also wash the feet of their fellow Christians as a token of humble service, "but yet more particularly as a sign to remind us of the true washing —the washing and purification of the soul in the blood of Christ" (Art. XI). Marriage is instituted of God and shall be entered into only with those who are members of the same Christian fellowship, who have received "the same baptism" and who belong to "the same church" (Art. XII). God has established the civil government for the punishment of the wicked and the protection of the good, and Christians shall recognize rulers as ministers of God, rendering honor to them, paying taxes and praying for them (Art. XIII). Christians shall follow only the law of love, manifesting to enemies the same spirit of love and forgiveness as did Jesus, being Biblical nonresistants in suffering and abuse. They shall pray for their enemies, "comfort and feed them," and seek their welfare and salvation: all this in obedience to the express teaching of Christ (Art. XIV). Christians shall make only a solemn affirmation of the truth; they shall not swear any oaths whatever: this also in obedience to the explicit instruction of Christ (Art. XV). When a member of the church reverts to a life of sin and loses out as a Christian, it is necessary for the church to excommunicate such an apostate, for his amendment and "not for (his) destruction": the purpose being to purge the church of such "leaven," to preserve the good name of the church, and "that he may again be convinced of the error of his ways, and brought to repentance" (Art. XVI). Excommunicated apostates are to be "avoided" or shunned; all social fellowship with them must be broken, even in eating and drinking. Nevertheless "such moderation . . . (shall) be used that such shunning and reproof may not be conducive to his ruin but serviceable to his amendment. . . . We must not treat such offenders as enemies, but exhort them as brethren . . . to bring them to a knowledge of their sins and to repentance" (Art. XVII). On the Day of Judgment all men will be resurrected from the dead and appear before Christ where the saved will be severed from the lost, the righteous to enter into the unspeakable joys of eternal life, and the wicked to be damned to "eternal, hellish torments" (Art. XVIII).

The language of the Dordrecht Confession is simple and direct, not literary or philosophical in character; it abounds in Scriptural quotations, and follows the general emphases of evangelical Protestant thought except that it teaches the baptism of believers only, the washing of the saints' feet, earnest church discipline, the shunning of the excommunicated, the nonswearing of oaths, marriage within the same church, strict nonresistance, and in general places more emphasis on true Christianity involving being Christian and obeying Christ rather than merely holding to a correct system of doctrine.

A number of documents pertaining to the origin and adoption of the Dordrecht Confession of Faith are found in the Amsterdam Mennonite Archives (*Inv. Arch. Amst.* I, Nos. 569, 583-92). The confession was printed as early as 1633 (*Confessie ende Vredehandelinghe tot Dordrecht anno 1632,* Haarlem, 1633), and was reprinted in Dutch at least three times, but only one copy of the 1633 edition is extant. A reprint is found in the introduction to the first part of T. J. van Braght's *Martyrs' Mirror* (Amsterdam, 1660; also Dutch *Martyrs' Mirror* of 1685 and the German and English translations). Shortly after this it was printed together with other confessions, in *Algemeene Belydenissen* (Amsterdam, 1665, reprints 1700, 1739). The oldest German translation, by Tieleman Tielen van Sittert, appeared at Amsterdam in 1664, entitled *Christliches Glaubensbekenntnus* (reprints in Europe at Amsterdam, 1691; n.p., 1686, 1711, 1742; Basel, 1822; Zweibrücken, 1854;

Mümpelgart, 1855; Regensburg, 1876). A French translation, entitled *Confession de Foi Chrétienne, des Chrétiens sans défense, connus surtout dans les Pais-bas sous le Nom des Mennonites,* appeared in 1771 (n.p.) reprinted in 1862 (n.p.). There are numerous editions in English. The oldest, *The Christian Confession of the Faith of the Harmless Christians, in the Netherlands Known by the Name of Mennonists,* was printed at Amsterdam in 1712 at the request of the Pennsylvania churches. It was reprinted in Philadelphia, Pa. (1727), New Market, Va. (1810), Niagara, Ont. (1811), Doylestown, Pa. (1844), West Chester, Pa. (1835), Skippackville, Pa. (1836), Elkhart, Ind. (1890, 1895, 1900, 1906, 1914, 1917, 1925, and in numerous combinations). See also S. F. Coffman, ed., *Mennonite Confession of Faith . . . with reference texts printed in full . . .* (Scottdale, 1930) and *idem,* ed., *Mennonite Church Polity, A Statement of Practices in Church Government together with Mennonite Confession of Faith . . .* (Scottdale, 1944). See also **Confessions of Faith** (*ME* I, 682 f.).† (Vol. I) J.C.W.

ML I, 468; text of Dordrecht Confession in Wenger, *The Doctrines of the Mennonites* (Scottdale, 1952) 78-86.

Dorfbrunner, Leonhard, one of the most successful of the evangelists of the South German Anabaptists in the Reformation period. All that is known of him is based on the statements of various persons he baptized when they were subjected to torture after his death. At his trial in 1528 he confessed that he had been ordained as a priest in Bamberg in 1524, and had received his title of imperial knight from a chapter of that order in Weissenburg in Middle Franconia (Nicoladoni, 205). His was a gifted and notable personality.

He joined the Anabaptists in the spring of 1527; he was baptized in Styria (Upper Austria) by Hans Hut (*q.v.*) and at once named as an evangelist and sent out with three others, Jerome Hermann (*q.v.*) of Mansee, Leonhard Schiemer (*q.v.*), and Jakob Portner, who was still the chaplain in the castle at Styria. Dorfbrunner went in the direction of Salzburg and Munich, participated in the Martyr Synod in Augsburg, which was led by Hans Denk (*q.v.*), on Aug. 20, 1527, and was here appointed to do evangelistic work in Austria with Hänslin Mittermeier of Ingolstadt, especially in the city of Linz, where after the destruction of the Styrian church a new congregation had formed, which became the center of Anabaptism in the region of the Ens. But Dorfbrunner apparently did not reach his destination; if he did, he was there only a few days. There is no mention of his work in Linz.

From the end of September he worked in Augsburg, the Anabaptist congregation there having been robbed of its leaders at the instigation of the Lutheran clergy between Aug. 25 and Sept. 19, 1527, when Jakob Dachser, Hans Hut, Jakob Gross, Siegmund Salminger, and many other members were arrested. Disregarding the risks, Dorfbrunner took charge of the church and very soon won new adherents, performing the first baptism before the end of September. By the end of the year he had baptized about 100 persons in Augsburg (*q.v.*)

alone, the majority of whom remained true to their faith in spite of pressure by the authorities; there were among them a number of women who were seized at the Easter service in 1528 and cruelly mistreated, as Elisabeth Hegenmiller, whose tongue was cut out, and Anna Benedikt, whose cheeks were burned through on order of the council and who was then expelled from the city. In January 1528 Dorfbrunner apparently wished to visit the congregation at Linz; he was seized at Passau and died at the stake. Dorfbrunner must be considered one of the most successful pioneers of the Anabaptist movement in South Germany and Austria. In the very brief period of his ministry he is reported to have baptized about 3,000 converts. Hege.

F. Roth, *Augsburgs Ref.-Gesch.* (Munich, 1901) 234-62; *idem,* "Zur Gesch. der Wiedertäufer in Oberschwaben," in *Ztsch d. hist. Vereins für Schwaben und Neuburg,* 1900, 15-27, and 1901, 7-115; A. Nicoladoni, *Johannes Bünderlin von Linz* (Berlin, 1893) 205-7; ML I, 469.

Dörksen, Jakob Johann, a Mennonite Brethren elder, born in Rudnerweide, Molotschna, South Russia, June 18, 1853. In his sixteenth year he moved to Rosenort where he was baptized a year later. In 1873 he was married to Aganetha Rempel of Rosenort. In 1885 they emigrated to Memrik and settled in the village of Nordheim. Here he was ordained to the ministry on Sept. 8, 1885, for the Mennonite Brethren congregation at Kotlyarevka, and served until 1905, when he was called to Terek, where he was ordained to the office of elder by Elder Hermann A. Neufeld. In 1912 he moved back to Memrik, where he died Aug. 29, 1930. Mrs. F. I.

Dornseiffen, Hoite Godert, a Dutch Mennonite minister, b. Jan. 25, 1841, at Heerenveen, Dutch province of Friesland, d. Jan. 3, 1922, at Heerenveen. On Nov. 3, 1867, he preached his first sermon for the congregation of Terhorne in Friesland, where he lived and worked until his retirement in 1902.

In giving religious instruction to the children of 14 to 16 years, he noticed that many of them, the children of bargemen, could not read or write. He gave his attention to this problem. He established a fund to teach the bargemen's children in his own community, and beginning in 1882 he and his brother-in-law, H. Rutgers, extended the service to all of Friesland. There is now a permanent fund, supported by an annual government grant and many private donations. This example has been followed by the entire country. For thirty-five years Dornseiffen worked with pleasure and devotion, until his death in April 1918. The cross of the Knights of Orange-Nassau, which the queen bestowed upon him on the occasion of her visit to Friesland in 1905, is a worthy recognition of his services. In the School Fund he had erected a permanent monument to himself. (*ML* I, 469.)
E.M. tC.

Dornum, Ulrich von, of the castle of Oldersum (*q.v.*) near Emden, Friesland, Germany, was an aggressive promoter of the Reformation, supporting Edzard I (*q.v.*) and Enno I (*q.v.*). His estate became a refuge for a wide range of persecuted reformers, such as Karlstadt (*q.v.*), who was given the privilege of publicly proclaiming his views from the pulpit, Melchior Rinck, and Menno Simons. Ulrich von Dornum was first influenced by Luther, but through Karlstadt he turned to the Swiss and Strasbourg reformers with Anabaptist leanings. He was in touch with Erasmus and Capito, and Sebastian Franck wrote a letter to his followers. Ulrich personally wrote a report on a disputation at Oldersum between Dr. Laurenz, a Jacobite of Groningen, and Jürgen Aportanus, an evangelical minister of Emden, East Friesland, which was published in Wittenberg (1523; sec. ed. Groningen, 1614; German translation by Ohling, 1955).

To what degree Menno and his followers were protected through the intervention of Ulrich von Dornum, as tradition records, cannot be fully ascertained because of lack of sources. Dr. Ohling states that he was "close to the Anabaptist movement but did not join it publicly as his descendants did." Ulrich von Dornum (b. *ca.* 1465) died in 1536, the year during which Menno Simons came to Oldersum for the first time. It is possible that the two met. Ulrich's daughter Essa married the Anabaptist Johan Gerdsema (Gersema), and the youngest is also said to have married an Anabaptist. C.K.

Ohling, "Aus den Anfängen der Reformation. Ein Brief des Sebastian Franck . . . an die Oldersumer Gemeinde," *Ostfriesland,* 1954, 111-15; C. A. Cornelius, *Der Antheil Ostfrieslands an der Reformation* (Münster, 1852) 6-11, 27-33; E. Meiners, *Oostvrieschlandts kerkelyke Geschiedenisse* I (Groningen, 1738) 15-19, 25, 166 f.; K. Vos, *Menno Simons* (Leiden, 1914) 71, 322; *Groningsche Volksalmanak* 1919, 139 f.; Gerhard Ohling, *Junker Ulrich von Dornum* (Aurich, 1955); ML I, 617.

Dorothea Pieters, a Dutch Anabaptist martyr of Dordrecht, was drowned April 25, 1534, together with Marytgen Huig Cranen (*q.v.*). The place of execution probably is The Hague. Dorothea had joined a group of Anabaptists who were planning to go to Münster (*q.v.*), but were arrested at Bergklooster (*q.v.*). (*Inv. Arch. Amst.* I, No. 745; Mellink, *Wederdopers,* 191 f., 229.) vdZ.

Dorrance (Kan.) Mennonite Brethren Church, located in Russel County, a member of the Southern District Conference, was organized on Oct. 24, 1913, with 30 members, under the leadership of the elders John Foth and M. M. Just. The first meetinghouse was built in 1913 and dedicated Oct. 26, 1913. By 1924 the membership had grown to 63. In later years, however, some moved away, so that the 1950 membership was down to 32. The first minister was Peter Wiens. Others have been J. B. Reh, Hermann P. Dyck, Elmo Warkentine, and E. C. Ollenburger. In 1954 the membership was 52, with G. Warkentin as pastor. P.C.H.

Dorsch, Jörg, of Wiebelsheim, an Anabaptist at whose home on June 11, 1528, about eleven Anabaptists of Munich and Augsburg met with a clothnapper from Upper Bavaria who preached to them. When they no longer felt safe there, Dorsch took them to a place of concealment in the Wiebelsheim woods, where they preached for people who came to them from Hohenegg and Windsheim. He was captured in the latter half of 1530 in Creglingen, and declared that he had never heard that the Anabaptists were opposed to government or had their wives in common.   NEFF.

J. Jörg, *Deutschland in der Revolutionsperiode von 1522-1526* (Freiburg, 1851); Wiswedel, *Bilder* II, 33; *ML* I, 470.

Dorsten, Trijntje van, an Anabaptist martyr: see **Trijntje Dirks.**

Dosie: see **Jacques D'Auchy.**

Dosser, Balthasar, an Anabaptist martyr of Lüsen (*q.v.*) in Tirol, who was described as a "particularly dangerous rabble-rouser," executed at Innsbruck in 1552. (*ML* II, 702; Zieglschmid, *Chronik,* 156, note 2.)

Doubs, a department in eastern France on the Swiss border. It was formed from the province of Franche Comté. In 1816 most of the county of Montbéliard was added to it, which was ceded by Prince Eugene of Württemberg to France in 1796. Count Leopold Eberhard of Montbéliard and Württemberg had accepted Mennonite refugees from Switzerland and Alsace in the first half of the 18th century as renters on his numerous farms. Until the present there has been sporadic immigration. In the southwest part of Doubs, which was not a part of the county of Montbéliard, the intolerance of the French kings prevented any Mennonite settlement.

Their proximity to the Swiss border and ties of relationship enabled the Mennonites here to keep the German language for a long time in the French environment. In religious respects they also had the advantage of living among a Lutheran population. The French language was not used in religious services until the 20th century.

Mennonites in the department of the Doubs formed the two congregations of Montbéliard (*q.v.*) and Seigne (*q.v.*). At the beginning of the present century the latter had decreased to a few families because members moved away, some into Switzerland and Alsace (see **Courgenay**). Montbéliard is thus today the only Mennonite church in the department of Doubs. (*ML* I, 470.)   P.S.

Doucher, Susanna (Ducher), a member of the Augsburg (*q.v.*) Anabaptist congregation, wife of the Augsburg sculptor Adolf Doucher (Bode in *Jahrbuch der pr. Kunstsammlungen,* 1887, No. 1; "Zur Augsburger Kunstgesch.," in *Ztscht des hist. Vereins für Schwaben und Neuburg,* 1887, 95). She and her sister Maxencia Wisinger were baptized by a preacher named Thomas (probably Thomas Waldhausen) in the house of the lacemaker Huber. In their house in the Easter week of 1528 during the absence of her husband the last large meeting was held before the violent suppression of the Augsburg Anabaptists. This meeting was surprised, and the council had all those present who could not escape, eighty-eight persons, arrested. Whereas in Augsburg those who permitted Anabaptist meetings to be held in their homes had their cheeks burned through with irons, Susanna Doucher as an expectant mother escaped this inhuman treatment, but was expelled from the city. What became of her is not known.   HEGE.

F. Roth, "Zur Gesch. der Wiedertäufer in Oberschwaben: III, Der Höhepunkt der wiedert. Bewegung in Augsburg und ihr Niedergang im Jahre 1528," in *Ztscht des historischen Vereins für Schwaben und Neuburg,* 1901, 44 and 52; *ML* I, 470 f.

Douglas-Moultrie counties, Ill., Amish Mennonite settlement is located in the east-central part of the state. The first Amish residents, coming from Pennsylvania, settled in the community in 1865. Additional settlers, coming from Iowa, Ohio, and perhaps other states, increased the size of the church so that it was divided into two districts in 1888. By 1952 the Old Order Amish of the community were divided into eight church districts, which had a membership of 702. In addition a Conservative Amish Mennonite congregation, organized in 1945, had 45 members in 1952. The Mennonite Church in Arthur, begun in 1936 by dissatisfied members of the Old Order church, had 230 members in 1952. (See **Arthur, Arthur** Amish Mennonite Church, **Arthur** Conservative Mennonite Church, **Arthur** Mennonite Church, and **Arthur** Old Order Amish Mennonite Community.)   M.G.

Douwe Eeuwouts, a Dutch Anabaptist martyr, the father of five small children, was seized at Leeuwarden on Jan. 3, 1570 (van Braght, *Martyrs' Mirror,* has erroneously 1571), and put into a dungeon. He steadfastly confessed his faith before the bishop who examined him repeatedly under torture. After months in a dungeon he joyfully suffered death by drowning on Oct. 12, 1571. When he was led to the execution place he sang a hymn, "Ic arm Schaepken aen groen heyde, waer sal ic henen gaen." This sentence was passed by a clergyman, the Catholic bishop of Leeuwarden, rather than by a secular judge as was customary. Douwe is the author of a song beginning, "Ich mach wel droevich singen in desen ellendigen tijt." It is found in an extremely rare booklet, *Sommige Belijdingen . . . van Reytse Aysesz* (*ca.* 1577), a copy of which is found in the Library of the Society for Dutch Letters at Leiden.
                                                  NEFF, VDZ.

Mart. Mir. D 560, E 893; Blaupot t. C., *Friesland,* 81; *Bibliographie* I, 20; *ML* I, 507.

Douwe Schoenmaker (Shoemaker), a Dutch Anabaptist leader. Of his activity nothing is known but the fact that at Witmarsum, Friesland, he baptized Griet, the wife of Rein Edes, who was a sister of Menno Simons' wife. Douwe was a Münsterite (*q.v.*), and Griet, troubled because she had been baptized by a revolutionary preacher, asked first Menno Simons and then Leenaert Bouwens to baptize her again. But both these elders refused to do so. (*BRN* VII, 236; K. Vos, *Menno Simons,* Leiden, 1914, 5, 42, 190; *DB* 1917, 119, No. 102.)   VDZ.

Douwen, Wiebe Jans van, b. April 9, 1846, in Dokkum (*q.v.*), Dutch province of Friesland, d. Aug. 20, 1912, at The Hague. He was a student at the Mennonite seminary and the university in Amsterdam, 1865-71, and was a man of thorough scholarship. He was pastor of the congregations at Borne, 1871-74; De Rijp, 1874-87; Bolsward, 1887-92; and Almelo, 1892-1911. He was the author of the important work, *Socinianen en Doopsgezinden, Doops-*

gezinde Historien uit de Jaren 1589-1626 (Leiden, 1898). He also translated a work written in the sixth century by John Bishop of Ephesus, on the life of oriental saints of the monophystic sects from Syrian into Latin. It was published by the Royal Academy of Sciences in Holland in 1889. (*Biogr. Wb.* II, 571-73; *Catalogus Amst.*, 109; *DB* 1912, 215-17; *DJ* 1922, 21-29, with portrait; *ML* I, 471.)

NEFF.

Douwes, Cornelis, a preacher of the Mennonite congregation (Jan Jacobsz group) on the Dutch island of Terschelling (*q.v.*) in the first decades of the 18th century. His grandson with the same name (b. 1712 at Terschelling, d. 1773 at Amsterdam) was director of the *Algemeen Zeemanscollegie* (School of Navigation) at Amsterdam. He was a man of great learning whose arithmetical theories in the field of nautical science were generally adopted and operative until the 19th century.

vDZ.

E. Crone, *Cornelis Douwes* (Amsterdam, 1941); *Inv. Arch. Amst.* II, No. 361.

Douwes Dekker: see **Dekker.**

Dowie, John Alexander (1847-1907), once a Congregational minister, born at Edinburgh, Scotland, pastor in Australia to 1878, who established the International Divine Healing Association at Melbourne in 1882, but moved to the United States in 1888. In 1893 he transferred to Chicago, in 1896 established the Christian Catholic Apostolic Church in Zion, and in 1901 founded Zion City on the shore of Lake Michigan, 42 miles north of Chicago. Here he enjoyed immense power and influence, both through his professed "healing miracles" and his magnetic personality, and received large gifts from his followers. Unfortunately a number of Mennonites from central Illinois, including some of considerable wealth, were drawn into the ranks of his followers. He was deposed from his office as "general overseer" in 1905 and died in 1907.　　H.S.B.

R. Harlan, *John Alexander Dowie and the Christian Catholic Apostolic Church of Zion* (Evansville, Wis., 1906).

Downey Civilian Public Service Camp No. 67 was a soil conservation camp under the Mennonite Central Committee, located near Downey, in southeastern Idaho. The camp was opened in November 1942, when Camp Henry was transferred to Downey, and closed in February 1946. The work consisted primarily of the construction and improvement of irrigation systems and of emergency farm labor. Several side camps were operated by No. 67.

M.G.

Doyer, a Dutch Mennonite family of Zwolle, province of Overijssel. They are said to stem from thatchers, who immigrated from France. The first member of this family found in the Netherlands was Antoni Doyer, b. about 1580 and d. before 1642 in Zwolle, who was a member of the Mennonite Church. His son Anthoni (1614-56) was married to Saartje Crane, a daughter of Assuerus Crane, a Flemish Mennonite immigrant who may have been related to the great Dutch poet Joost van den Von-

del, whose mother (Mennonite) was also called Sara Kranen.

His descendants at first were *rietmakers,* i.e., they were thatchers or worked in reeds or cane. In the course of time they became businessmen (linen, wood, tea), while a number of them in the 18th and 19th centuries were distillers, well-to-do stock dealers, or bankers. In the 19th and 20th centuries some were state-officials.

A number of the Doyer family have gone into the ministry. First of all was Assuerus Doyer (*q.v.*), son of the linen merchant Antoni Doyer. Two sons of Assuerus were also Mennonite ministers, Matthys, b. at Crefeld 1790, d. at Velp 1859, who served the congregation of den Hoorn on the island of Texel 1824-48, and Abraham, b. Zwolle 1794, d. Amsterdam 1851, serving successively at Joure 1818-23, Nijmegen 1823-28, and Amsterdam 1828-51.

Anthony Doyer, b. Amsterdam 1787, d. Leiden 1853, who was a son of the distiller Thomas Doyer (brother of Pastor Assuerus Doyer mentioned before) and Sara Fijnje (sister of Pastor Wybo Fijnje, *q.v.*), served the churches of Nijmegen 1810-18 and Leiden 1818-53.

A descendant of this family too is Miss Sara Elisabeth Doyer, b. Zuidbroek, 1897, pastor of the churches of Wageningen 1923-26, Rottevale 1926-43, Warga 1943-46, and since 1946 serving at Witmarsum-Pingjum-Makkum. Many members of this family also served as deacons at Zwolle, Leiden, Amsterdam, and other congregations. (*Ned. Patriciaat* XXX, 1944, 36-38; *DB passim,* see Index.)

vDZ.

Doyer, Assuerus, the son of Antoni Doyer and Tanneken Schimmelpenning, b. Dec. 13, 1758, at Zwolle, studied at the Mennonite seminary in Amsterdam 1778-83, then at the university of Halle, taking his doctor's degree under Prof. Wolff. After a period in Zwolle he studied under Prof. Hesselink at Amsterdam. In 1787 he was called to Cleve as pastor and in the following year to Crefeld. In 1793 he resigned and lived with his father-in-law Matthijs van Maurik on a small estate near Crefeld. In 1794 the Zwolle congregation asked him to assist their sick pastor Thomas Menalda and in 1799 he became Menalda's successor. In 1833 he sought to retire, but the church gave him an assistant, Lambertus ten Cate Coster, with whom he worked until 1836. He was an opponent of religious liberalism, which was prevalent at that time in Holland, and maintained active contact with the revival movement known as the *Reveil* (*q.v.*). He died on March 21, 1838, trusting, as he confessed, not in the perishable good that he had done, but in the mercy of his Saviour and Redeemer.

Doyer was characterized by great zeal, purity, and eagerness to learn, and occupied himself all his life in a study of the Bible. For many years he was vice-president of the board of directors of the Mennonite seminary in Amsterdam. In 1787 he married Katharina van Maurik (d. 1804) and in 1805 Magdalena Teune (d. 1836). The following books came from his pen: *Specimen philosophicum de duello* (Halle, 1786); *Leerrede ter aanprijzing van de Koepok-inenting* (Zwolle, 1808); *Brieven over de aanbidding van Jezus Christus* (Zwolle, 1911); *Hulde aan Joannes Chrysostomus* (Zwolle, 1815); *Twee Leerredenen over het lijden van onzen Heiland* (Zwolle, 1817); *Leerrede ter viering van het derde eeuwfeest der Hervorming* (Zwolle, 1817); *Invallende gedachten* (Zwolle, 1825); *Vraagboek over de Wet der Tien geboden, het Gebed des Heeren en de Twaalf Artikelen des geloofs* (Zwolle, 1825); *Bijdrage ter instandhouding en bevordering van godsdienstige plechtigheden bij de Gemeenten der Doopsgezinden* (Zwolle, 1825); *Redevoering ter aanprijzing van het begraven der lijken buiten de steden* (Zwolle, 1826); *Vertaling en uitlegging van den Eersten brief van den Apostel Petrus* (Zwolle, 1827); *Vertaling van den Eersten brief van den Apostel Johannes, met Aanmerkingen* (Zwolle, 1829); *Schriftuurlijk Vraagboek voor kinderen* (Zwolle, 1831); *Verhandeling over den zelfmoord* (*Vaderlandsche Letteroefeningen*, 1827).

J.L.

Blaupot t. C., *Groningen* I, 175-78; *idem, Holland* II, 129; *DB* 1897, 169; 1900, 115; 1901, 24, 25; *Biogr. Wb.* II, 576-78; *ML* I, 471.

Doyer, Thomas, a Dutch Mennonite missionary, b. 1823 at Zwolle, the son of the Mennonite minister Assuerus Doyer (*q.v.*), first studied architecture. In England his contacts with the Wesleyan Church and his work in Sunday school inspired him for missions. In 1854 he was accepted by the Dutch Mennonite Mission Board for training. In December 1857 he sailed for Java. Here he founded a new mission field at West Java, at Pijaminka, district of Batavia, which through the warm faith and the great love of this very capable missionary soon promised abundant fruit. But in August 1861 Doyer fell ill because of too much exertion and hardship. He died Nov. 21, 1861, on the ocean en route to the Netherlands. Doyer was unmarried. (*Jaarverslagen Dg. Zendingsvereniging* from 1854 to 1862; *ML* I, 471.)

vDZ.

Doylestown. A town of 5,000 in southeastern Pennsylvania and county seat of Bucks County; originally it was known as Doyle's Tavern, but by the time of the Revolutionary War, Doyle's Town. The Mennonite Church known as Doylestown is located a mile northwest of the city and has a membership of 260. The first building, made of logs, was erected about 1775, displaced by stone in 1808, enlarged in 1840, razed in 1900 and replaced by a new stone structure. The Mennonite settlement lies west and northwest of the city, but a considerable number of Mennonites also live in the city itself. There are a number of Mennonites operating stores in Doylestown, as well as a cabinet shop and building firms (building contractors). The church building stands in what is now Doylestown Township, but prior to 1818 this plot was a part of New Britain Township and the congregation was then known as New Britain rather than Doylestown. (J. C. Wenger, *Hist. of the Menn. of the Franconia Conf.,* Telford, Pa., 1938, 192-99.)

J.C.W.

Doylestown Mennonite Church, located northwest of Doylestown, Pa., is affiliated with the Franconia Conference (MC). Land for the building was bought in 1772, and the first building, a log structure, was erected about three or four years later. This log church building was displaced by a stone structure in 1808, which in turn was enlarged in 1840. In 1900 this enlarged stone building was razed and in its place the present building was erected. Prior to 1806 the services were conducted by the ministers in the Deep Run-"Perkasie" (Blooming Glen) - "New Britain" (Doylestown) circuit, but in 1806 a resident minister was ordained, John Kephart, a Revolutionary War soldier who had married a Mennonite girl and joined the congregation. He was followed by the following ministers: Jacob Kulp (who moved to Ohio in 1831), Abraham Godshalk, John K. Gross, David L. Gehman, Bishop A. O. Histand, Mahlon Gross, Bishop Joseph L. Gross, and Silas Graybill. The membership of the congregation (1954) is 260. The congregation has been one of the more progressive bodies in the Franconia Conference, having inaugurated evening services in 1906, sewing circle work in 1908, Bible instruction meetings (Bible conferences) in 1909, Sunday-school meetings in 1914, and young people's Bible meetings in 1915. The congregation also established an outpost known as Trevose Heights. (J. C. Wenger, *Hist. of the Menn. of the Franconia Conf.,* Telford, Pa., 192-99.)

J.C.W.

Dragass, a former Mennonite village near Gross-Lubin, Schwetz district, on the left shore of the Vistula in Polish Prussia. Here Dutch Mennonites settled in the 17th or even 16th century. (F. Szper, *Nederl. Nederzettingen in West-Pruisen gedurende den Poolschen tijd,* Enkhuizen, 1913, 134-35.) vDZ.

Drachten en Ureterp, a Mennonite congregation in the eastern part of the Dutch province of Friesland, about 15 miles southeast of Leeuwarden and 14 miles northeast of Heerenveen. The congregation, which formerly belonged to the Groningen Old Flemish Mennonites, was apparently founded in the first part of the 17th century, when Drachten arose as a peat-cutting center. After the peat had been removed, the soil was suited to farming. The earliest account of a Mennonite congregation here is of 1645, though the congregation may have been older. In February 1645 a meeting was held in the home of Jan Wibbes, a shoemaker. From the beginning the congregation was closely connected with the Mennonites of near-by Ureterp (*q.v.*), who were farmers, and Ureterp should perhaps be considered as the oldest kernel of the congregation. As Drachten grew, more Mennonites moved to Drachten, and about 1690 a meetinghouse was built at Drachten. The membership then (1695) was 82.

Of its history little is known. Its members were mostly peat-diggers, farmers, and a few sailors, who were absent from their home town from about February to November. For this reason, as in other towns of Friesland, where sailors formed a considerable part of the membership, like Grouw, Joure, and Warns, baptism and communion services were formerly not held just before Easter, as is common in Dutch congregations, but at the end of January or the first Sunday of February. It is not quite clear whether Drachten and Ureterp were two more or less independent congregations or only one. Since the beginning of the 18th century the name of the congregation has been "Drachten en Ureterp." It developed peacefully; in 1695 it joined the Mennonite conference of Friesland (Friesche Sociëteit), founded in that year. It soon became more progressive in church practices, abandoning the old Flemish practices like footwashing and silent prayer. In 1708 a small group of conservative members, wishing to maintain the old principles and practices, separated from the main body; this group, the membership of which in 1710 was only 14, was dissolved in 1787.

The main congregation grew steadily both in membership and spiritual strength. This was due in large part to the apt leadership of its lay preachers, including Albert Sybolts (1690-ca. 1745), his son Sybolt Alberts (1718-67), his grandson Albert Sybolts, Jr. (1744-79), and Sybolt (1780-1809) and Tjalling Arends (1789-1805). The descendants of Tjeerd Arends, a brother of Sybolt and Tjalling, are still numerous in the congregation (see **Arends** family).

In 1790 the old meetinghouse at Drachten was replaced by the present church; an organ was acquired in 1857. Until 1808 the congregation was served by untrained preachers. Then it obtained a minister who had been educated at the Mennonite Seminary of Amsterdam, viz., Jan Plantinus, 1809-50. He was followed by F. Born 1850-54, H. A. van Gelder 1855-58, G. ten Cate 1858-83, S. F. van der Ploeg 1884-87, H. van Cleeff 1888-89, A. van der Wissel 1890-1903, J. Wuite 1904-12, M. van der Vegte, Jr., 1913-19, P. Vis 1920-26, M. A. Hijlkema 1926-35, J. E. Tuininga 1936-39, G. J. W. den Herder 1939-42, J. W. Sipkema 1942-47, and G. de Groot 1948-54. The membership numbered 82 in 1695, 142 in 1809, 265 in 1861, 220 in 1900, 223 in 1954.

Church activities include a Sunday school for children, *Menniste Bouwers* (youth group), young members' circle, ladies' circle, men's circle, Bible circle, ladies' choir; church services for youth in cooperation with the Reformed Church are regularly held in the Mennonite Church.   P.V., vDZ.

G. ten Cate, *Geschiedkundig overzicht van de Doopsgezinde gemeente te Drachten en Ureterp* (Drachten, 1890); *Inv. Arch. Amst.* II, 2, No. 43; Blaupot t. C., *Friesland,* 160, 168, 188, 223, 247, 254; *idem, Groningen,* 128, 142; *DJ* 1840, 43; *DB* 1861, 132 f.; 1879, 2, 91; 1891, 111; 1894, 98; 1900, 93; *ML* I, 471 f.

Drechsel, Thomas, one of the "Zwickau Prophets," who at the beginning of the Reformation attracted much attention and were mistakenly called Anabaptists in many of the older histories. Little is known of Drechsel's life. When Nikolaus Storch (*q.v.*), who was to be given a hearing with 15 of his group at Zwickau, Dec. 16 and 17, 1521, before the assembled clergy and other dignitaries because of erroneous opinions on marriage and baptism, left the city before the hearing took place and betook himself to Wittenberg, Thomas Drechsel and Marcus Stübner joined him. At Wittenberg they talked to Philip Melanchthon (*q.v.*) on Dec. 27, and told him that at Zwickau several persons had been im-

prisoned on account of their views on the baptism of children. Their arguments proving the unscripturalness of infant baptism made a deep impression on Melanchthon, a young professor of theology; neither he nor his colleague Nikolaus Amsdorf (*q.v.*) was able to answer their argument based on Mark 16:16. Stübner said that in the light of some wonderful conversations with God, he would preach only what God commanded. On that very day (Dec. 27) Melanchthon wrote to Elector Frederick of Saxony concerning this visit and events in Zwickau, expressing a concern that God's Spirit should not be suppressed and, on the other hand, that Satan should not take them unawares.

Amsdorf, who did not feel capable of replying to the visitors from Zwickau, avoided meeting them, but on Dec. 28 also wrote a letter to the elector, suggesting that they be countered only with reasonable and Scriptural arguments, for rebellion and revolt might follow violent suppression. Meanwhile the Zwickau men sought adherents in the city, Storch relating his wonderful visions and dreams in the homes of the craftsmen, Stübner dealing more with the students and professors, and Drechsel remaining somewhat in the background. Stübner made a lasting impression on Martin Cellarius (*q.v.*), who at the time did not share the views of the other theologians on baptism.

The elector and Martin Luther, who had at once been informed of the presence of these men, were more reserved in judgment. To Luther the divine conversations of which they boasted seemed somewhat dubious. But he was also impressed by their objections to infant baptism, and now took pains to defend it anew, thereby developing further his view that through the work of the Holy Spirit faith is created which accepts the grace of baptism; faith is infused into the child. Let anyone who disagrees prove the opposite.

When Luther came to Wittenberg Drechsel paid him a visit. Luther was very short with him and warned him against playing with God's name. Drechsel left with an angry threat that in six weeks Wittenberg would perish, exclaiming, "Whoever does not say what Luther wishes must be a fool!"

Nothing is known of Drechsel's further activity. There is no evidence that he acted on his doubts concerning infant baptism. Neither he nor his companions Storch and Stübner were baptized on the confession of their faith, nor did they baptize others thus. Hence the Zwickau Prophets cannot be called representatives of Anabaptism. (P. Wappler, *Thomas Münzer und die Zwickauer Propheten,* Zwikkau, 1908; *ML* I, 472 f.)   HEGE.

Dreherthalerhof, a large estate, once the location of a settlement of Huguenots and Mennonites, today a hamlet with about 300 inhabitants near Otterberg (*q.v.*) in the government district of Kaiserslautern (*q.v.*), has an interesting connection with the Mennonites of Crefeld and of the Palatinate. The Heydweiller family, which later became prominent in the Crefeld Mennonite Church, settled at Otterberg in 1579 as religious refugees from Antwerp. Duke Johann Casimir, who again made Calvinism the state religion, settled about 100 families here, most of whom were weavers. Extensive commerce reaching Holland and England made them prosperous. In agricultural lines their contribution consisted in introducing clover seed into the Palatinate, and deep plowing with an iron plowshare.

The descendants of the refugee Heydweiller also excelled in agriculture, but were more prominent as cloth merchants. His great-grandson Johann Heinrich H. (1657-1724) was a wool-weaver, merchant, and master glassmaker, and in 1697 erected a factory of his own on the Dreherthalerhof, which had been in the family as a hereditary lease since 1579. Franz Heinrich Heydweiller (1720-95) moved to Crefeld (*q.v.*), married Sibilla von der Leyen (1740), and built an independent knitting mill for the manufacture of silk stockings. In 1770 his brother Johann Valentin Heydweiller (b. 1734) followed him to Crefeld and also engaged in the manufacture of silk materials, businesses which contributed to the growth of Crefeld.

The Dreherthalerhof with more than 2,000 acres of land was then devoted to agriculture. Johann Jacob Heydweiller, the youngest brother of those who went to Crefeld, died in 1772 as the last of the family. The Palatine Mennonite census list of 1773 lists a family of seven, named Höfli (Höfle, Hefli), as living on the Dreherthalerhof. For his progressive methods Hans Höfli received several public awards in the 1770's from the *Kurpfälzisch physikalisch-ökonomische Gesellschaft.*   E.H.C.

E. Correll, "Die ersten Heydweiller in Krefeld . . . ," in *Die Heimat, Mitteilungen des Vereins f. Heimatkunde in Crefeld* II (1922) 75-77; Chr. Neff, "Beziehungen zwischen der Krefelder und den Pfälzer Mennonitengemeinden," in *Beiträge zur Gesch. rheinischer Mennoniten* (Weierhof, 1939; No. 2 of the *Schriftenreihe*); Gerhard von Beckerath, "Die wirtschaftliche Bedeutung der Krefelder Menn. . . . im 17. u. 18. Jahrhundert"* (Diss. Bonn, 1951); *ML I,* 473 f.

Dreiborn, former district in the Rhine Province of Prussia, where the Anabaptists found adherents in the 16th century. The von Harff family in Burg Dreiborn have in their possession court documents on the Anabaptists in the district of Dreiborn (41. "*Akten betr. die Wiedertäufer und Reformierten in der Herrschaft Dreiborn, 16. und 17. Jahrhundert, I, No. LXIX*"), which have not yet been examined (see *Uebersicht über den Inhalt der kleineren Archive der Rheinprovinz* III, Bonn, 1909, 13). (*ML I,* 474.)   HEGE.

Dreier, Hans, a Swiss Anabaptist martyr, a cabinetmaker, was drowned in Bern on July 8, 1529, with Hans Hausmann (*q.v.*) and Heinrich Seiler. At his cross-examination he confessed that he would adhere to his baptism; a Christian may be a member of government, but not for long; the oath is forbidden; he knew nothing about community of goods; a Christian will not let others suffer want, etc.   NEFF.

Müller, *Berner Täufer;* Th. de Quervain, *Kirchliche und soziale Zustände in Bern nach Einführung der Ref.* (Bern, 1905) 151; *ML I,* 477.

Drekwagen, de (garbage wagon or street sweeper's cart), a name give by Leenaert Bouwens (*q.v.*) to the Waterlander group of the Dutch Mennonites, because they admitted into the membership of their congregations even those persons who were banned by the other Mennonites, and also because they accepted members of other Mennonite branches without rebaptizing them. (*BRN* VII, 55, 465, 523 f.)   vDZ.

Drenthe, a province of the Netherlands (population 272,000). In the Reformation period Drenthe was passed by. Only at the border, as at Koevorden, there were some Anabaptists about 1540. After the Reformed faith had become the established faith in the 17th century, we find some Mennonites in the border towns of Havelte and Roderwolde. At the former place there is record of them until 1659, though there was no organized congregation. At Roderwolde there was a small congregation, which had a preacher and its own church in 1639. In 1657 the Synod of Drenthe complained that there were several unbaptized children there. The congregation probably died out soon afterward. It was located in the territory of the castle of Nienoord belonging to the Ewsum family, several of whom were Mennonites. In the 19th century two churches were established in Drenthe, Assen (*q.v.*) and Meppel (*q.v.*). In Emmen (*q.v.*), Hoogeveen (*q.v.*), and Roden (*q.v.*) there are Mennonite groups, and other Mennonites live scattered through the province. The number of Mennonites (souls) in Drenthe was 286 in 1859, 641 in 1899, 933 in 1947.   K.V.

Joosting-Knappert, *Schetsen uit de kerkelijke geschiedenis van Drenthe* (1916); Reitsma, *Acta der prov. en part. Synoden* VIII (Groningen, 1899) 94, 97-98, 111; *ML I,* 478.

Dress *(Costume).* Distinctive religious costumes have been worn by custom or by requirement by many and varied groups in Christian history; for example, by religious and monastic orders (monks and nuns), clergy of various ranks, and Salvation Army workers. Special garments have been prescribed for certain important religious occasions such as baptism, confirmation, weddings, and funerals. However, none of these has been directly based on the Scriptures and none has had any bearing or influence on Mennonite distinctive costume or dress regulations.

It is difficult at times to determine, either in Europe or America, whether what seems to have been (and may still be) a distinctive Mennonite item of costume is the result of deliberate choice on religious grounds established and maintained by action of the church, or is purely a sociological phenomenon such as the retention of older forms of costume because of resistance to change. Much of the peculiarly Mennonite costume and clothing regulation is probably of the latter character. For most Mennonites, with the exception of Holland and the North German city congregations, have been rural, and rural people have been notorious for their resistance to change, particularly in earlier times before modern urban culture penetrated rural areas, as well as in current pockets of cultural isolation. Religious sanctions have, of course, often been imposed to maintain earlier costume forms, and at times even Biblical sanctions by specific verses have been claimed, sometimes with a faulty exegesis or application of quite irrelevant passages (e.g., "boots" from the German of Eph. 6:15, "an den Beinen gestiefelt," or the beard requirement from Lev. 19:27, "[not] mar the corners of thy beard," etc.). Actually, the customs or traditions originated first, to be reinforced later by church sanctions. In the most conservative American groups (Old Order Amish and Old Colony Mennonites) most of the clothing regulations have never been written out or specified. The power of custom suffices.

On the other hand, the doctrine of separation from the world, and the strong sense of the actual separation of the small group from the larger general society has worked powerfully (1) to produce distinctive nonworldly costume, and (2) to restrain the group from following the changes of costume and fashion in "the world" about them. This, reinforced by the instinctive spirit of withdrawal, humility, and even inferiority resulting from persecution, besides a very real poverty in many cases, and a strong teaching against pride and for simplicity, has often furnished deep religious motivation for distinctive (though not necessarily uniform) costume. Distinctive and plain garb has been characteristic of many earnest Christian groups past and present, not only of Mennonites, and many such have resisted the changing fashions of the society in which they lived, which fashions were often not only extreme or unhealthful, but also immodest or expensive. Designers and manufacturers of fashionable costume have themselves stated that fashions are deliberately changed to increase sales, and have even been designed to emphasize sex.

The strongly patriarchal character of the more conservative Mennonite groups may also contribute to the emphasis upon controlled costume. The elders and ministers may have such a strong sense of domination as shepherds over their flocks that they consciously or unconsciously seek for outward signs of submission which are most readily furnished by uniform, conservative, distinctive items of costume and drab and dark colors. The emphasis upon submission as one of the chief virtues desired in members may well be an index to the psychology of costume in such a patriarchal or near-patriarchal type of church life.

Another principle affecting some Mennonite costume has been that of sex distinction in attire. (Deut. 22:5, "The woman shall not wear that which pertaineth unto a man, neither shall a man put on a woman's garment.") Although society in general has observed sex distinction in clothing, yet Mennonites have often been more conservative than the rest of society on this point, particularly in recent times when many women are wearing slacks or shorts.

In America plainness of attire was long characteristic of numerous "sects" in Eastern Pennsylvania and adjacent areas, who were often grouped together as "the plain people." This category, which once included Quakers, Moravians, Schwenckfelders, and Brethren or Dunkards as well, now includes only Mennonites, Amish, and Brethren in Christ.

It seems probable that the Quaker costume imported from England in the 17th century, when the Quakers were the governing class in Pennsylvania, and when they were a nonresistant, strict-living, nonworldly group, had considerable influence on the costume of the other "plain sects," who were all of German origin, and were all both nonresistant and strict-living. The later gradual but complete loss of plain attire by some of the "plain" people, and dilution in the practice by others, may be due in part to a loss of the sense of "separation from the world" accompanying cultural and religious assimilation. Sometimes the process of accommodation to prevailing styles was aided by the introduction of cheap factory-made clothing and the loss of the practice of weaving and clothing construction at home. On the other hand, the concomitant loss of distinctive doctrines such as nonresistance along with the loss of distinctive costume (nonconformity in dress) may point to spiritual decline or change as a significant factor in the change of costume.

Every item of men's and women's clothing has been involved at some time in Mennonite history, or in some Mennonite group, in the matter of a distinctive Mennonite costume, either as prohibited or prescribed in one form or pattern or another. A mere enumeration results in an enormous list. For most of these, special articles will be found in this Encyclopedia. Only a few summary notes can be given here. Some of the costume prescriptions have been purely traditional or customary and unwritten, while others have been put into specific rules by congregations or conferences. Disciplinary action has usually followed violation of the regulations, whether written or not. On the other hand, slow changes have usually modified the traditional practices or rules without direct action.

The following is a summary list of costume traditions or regulations which have been applied at one time or another in history in one or another Mennonite group or area. This list is probably not exhaustive and refers primarily to practices among the most conservative North American groups such as Old Order Amish and Old Colony groups, but also in part to the large Mennonite Church (MC) group and related groups, as well as to the more conservative Russian Mennonite groups in Canada and Mexico. Details of costume prescriptions among the earlier European Mennonites, particularly in Holland and Switzerland, have not been available. *Headdress:* for women, kerchiefs or bonnets have been required, and hats forbidden or a specific type of broad beaver or straw hat required; for men requirements have been black hats, broad brim, without crease in crown, or with a flat crown, or caps instead of hats. *Hairdressing:* for women, bobbed hair has been forbidden, a center part required; for men, short cut hair has been forbidden. *Overcoats:* for women coats have been taboo in favor of shawls, or only half-length coats allowed; for men, long overcoats with capes have been required. *Pants:* for men knee breeches or broadfall type (sailor type) have been required. *Dresses:* a prescribed cut (cape dress) has been required, and unfigured cloth of solid color with full-length sleeves, and the dress quite long. *Aprons* have been required for women, or for wives of ministers alone. *Coats for men:* collarless, divided tail or frock coat have been required. *Fasteners:* for men and women buttons have been forbidden, hooks and eyes required for men, pins for women. *Corsets* have been forbidden. *Stockings for women:* silk forbidden, black color required, anklets forbidden. *Neckties* for men forbidden, or required to be bow ties instead of four-in-hand. *Suspenders* for men have been forbidden in whole or in part. *Shoes:* buckle, lace, and button shoes have been required or forbidden, boots required for preachers. *Shrouds:* white has been required. *Wedding dress:* floor length and white color have been forbidden. *Color:* bright or light colors have been forbidden for all items of costume from hats to shoes, both men and women, and black or gray required. *Clothing material:* silk has been forbidden, and home-woven cloth required. *Homemade clothes* have been required rather than "store" clothes.

Interestingly often the minister (and his wife) has been required (by custom or regulation) to be more conservative than the group as a whole, as a result of which, unintentionally, a distinctive clerical garb has developed in a brotherhood which has strictly opposed clericalism. Sometimes this has meant for the minister a long black frock coat, in other cases a clerical coat much like the state church Protestant or Roman Catholic attire. Sometimes (in Europe, in Holland and North Germany) ministers and members of church boards are required to wear high hats and frock coats to church services. Sometimes boots have been required. Among certain conservative Manitoba groups the preacher is even required to continue to wear the coat he was ordained in.

Wedding costumes have often been fixed. Among the most conservative Manitoba groups brides must wear black. In some groups the floor-length wedding gown is forbidden. In some groups (e.g., Franconia Conference, M.C.) the dead must still be buried in white shrouds, while black mourning garments are forbidden.

In the Old Testament only priests were required to wear a religious costume, although Jewish men were required to wear garments with a fringe or tassel of blue as a reminder that they belonged to the Lord (Num. 15:37-40). The New Testament does not prescribe any form of garb or external dress symbol for Christians. But it gives a number of warnings against external adornment such as worldly styles of hairdressing, and the wearing of gold, pearls, and costly clothing (I Tim. 2:9, 10; I Pet. 3:3, 4), and it indicates that Christian women are not to shear off their hair which was given them by God for a "covering" (I Cor. 11:6, 15). It gives a few hints as to how not to dress, and warns about undue concern for providing food and clothing (in Matt. 5 a situation of poverty).

Anabaptist Costume. Many, though not all, of the early Anabaptists were drawn from the common people and evidently continued to wear the conventional clothing of the common people. There is no evidence to show that the early Anabaptists created any uniform garb for the members of the church. Neither the ministers nor the laity wore any distinguishable attire, as numerous incidents in the *Martyrs' Mirror* indicate. The Concept of Cologne of 1591 (*q.v.*) states that it is impossible to prescribe for each individual what he shall wear, but requires simplicity of attire. The Anabaptists took seriously the principle of simplicity of life and the avoidance of the ostentation, display, and luxury of the rich. Menno Simons made a vigorous protest against conformity to the world in attire (*Complete Works* I, 144), but did not demand a special garb for the brotherhood.

In the course of time the Anabaptists became recognizable at sight by their refusal to carry any kind of arms, and by their plainness of dress: no jewelry, lace, etc., were worn. This plainness tended to develop into a sort of standard garb. For as new modes of dress appeared the Anabaptists clung to the older forms, sometimes adapting them over the years, and refusing to keep up with the ever-changing styles— which T. J. van Braght likened to the changes of the phases of the moon (*Mart. Mir.* E 10). Consequently the Anabaptists early began to make some specific regulations on clothing. For instance, the Strasbourg Discipline (*q.v.*) of 1568 included the following: "Tailors and seamstresses shall hold to the plain and simple style and shall make nothing at all for pride's sake. Brethren and sisters shall stay by the present form of our regulation concerning apparel and make nothing for pride's sake" (*MQR* I, 1927, 65). This confirms the testimony of Johannes Kessler (*q.v.*) concerning the Swiss Brethren in 1525: "They shun costly clothing, and despise expensive food and drink, clothe themselves with coarse cloth, (and) cover their heads with broad felt hats. Their entire manner of life is completely humble. They bear no weapon, neither sword nor dagger, but only a short breadknife . . ." (*Sabbata,* 147 f.). Sebastian Franck (*q.v.*), perhaps in irony, wrote that the Anabaptists had a ruling on how many pleats the apron must have. By 1600 there were instances in South Germany of Anabaptists being recognized by their clothing (Bossert, . . . *Württemberg* I, 691, 741, 806, 881). But the Swiss and South German Mennonites never seem to have developed any specific religious garb; they remained simple Christians avoiding the luxury and ostentation of the rich. When Jakob Amann (*q.v.*) attempted to introduce avoidance (*q.v.*) and stricter clothing regulations into the church, he caused the division of 1693, after which his followers (the Amish) practiced extensive regulation of attire, maintaining until the present, in America, specific rules about headdress, hooks and eyes (instead of buttons), cut and color for coats and dresses, homemade instead of factory-made clothing, etc.

European Mennonite Costume. The Dutch Mennonites, even more than the Swiss, did not adopt a special religious garb. When Dutch believers were apprehended it was not by means of identifiable peculiar clothing. As early as 1550 a Dutch Mennonite martyr told the bystanders at his execution that if he could name 20 fellow believers in the surrounding crowd, he would not do so: this would indicate that they wore no specific garb. In 1572 a brother pressed his way through a crowd to encourage a man who was to be martyred, and then merged again with the crowd before the authorities could seize him: this again points to the fact that the Mennonites of Holland at that time wore no distinctive garb. This was even true of the preachers, for in 1565 a minister and part of his congregation were caught by the authorities: the officers could not tell which one was the minister, so the latter voluntarily stepped forward and confessed his identity (these illustrations are taken from van Braght's *Martyrs' Mirror;* documentation in Wenger, *Attire,* 22).

By the late 17th century Heinrich Ludolf Bentheim could still say of the Dutch Mennonites: "Above all, they insist on modesty in respect to clothing" (Horsch, *Mennonites,* 251), though he also states that some of the Amsterdam Mennonites were beginning to wear wigs and other worldly articles. That there was some clothing regulation among the Dutch Mennonites in the 18th century is evident from the testimony of S. F. Rues, who visited the Netherlands specifically to study the Mennonites there, and whose *Aufrichtige Nachrichten* (*Sincere Reports*) about them was published in 1743. Rues divided the Dutch Mennonites of that day into two general classes—the stricter groups, which he called "Fine," and the more lenient and tolerant groups, which he called "Coarse." The former prescribed the cut of men's coats and women's dresses, required that clothing be black, prohibited the use of shoelaces or buttons, and required the men to wear beards. On the whole, the stricter rules were followed more closely by the country congregations than in the cities (see summary in Smith, 211-15). Rues also reports (48) a bishop pushing back the cap on the head of a woman candidate for baptism.

In the course of time, such dress regulations were discontinued by the Dutch Mennonites, although the Balk congregation retained some of them until the middle of the 19th century (*ML* I, 113). Although the rural congregations generally dress more plainly and simply than do those of urban character, no prescribed garb remains among any European Mennonites.

The history of the costume requirements and traditions in Northwest Germany (Emden, Hamburg), Danzig, and West and East Prussia, was much like that of Holland, since these groups had not only largely Dutch antecedents but also continuing cultural and religious ties with the Dutch Mennonites. The Mennonites who emigrated from the Danzig area to South Russia in turn continued the traditions of their homeland. As rural people the latter remained quite conservative in their costume, and retained much of the simplicity of earlier times. Until the 20th century somber colors and conservative cut characterized the costume of both men and women, and the women wore only kerchiefs on the head, or a special dark hood. No uniform costume was required although the power of tradition tended toward uniformity and resulted in an apparent uniform simplicity. The remoteness of the Russian Mennonite settlements from the major metropolitan centers of culture and commerce reduced the influence of changing fashions considerably.

The Mennonites of South Germany, Switzerland, and France, being largely rural and conservative, long retained the emphasis on simplicity in costume which characterized their earlier Anabaptist forebears, but in recent generations have adapted themselves generally to prevailing styles, though with a certain conservatism. No uniform dress regulations were ever developed, although the women, especially in Baden, wore a black fascinator-type veil instead of hats, both for general public wear and church wear until into the early 20th century.

American Mennonite Costume. It is reported that in 1727 "a large number of Germans, peculiar in their dress . . ." had settled on the Pequea, a Lancaster County stream (Rupp, 194). But in what the peculiarities consisted is not made clear. The earliest known description of the costume of the 18th-century Mennonite immigrants to Pennsylvania (from the Palatinate), written by Redmond Conyngham in 1830 ("History of the Mennonites and Aymenists," ms.), but seemingly based upon earlier contemporary newspaper reports, whose authenticity cannot be checked, reads as follows: "The long beards of the men and the short petticoats of the females just covering the knee . . . . The men wore long red caps on their heads; the women had neither bonnets, hats, nor caps, but merely a string passing around the head to keep the hair from the face. The dress both of the female and the male was domestic, quite plain, and of coarse material, after an old fashion of their own." I. D. Rupp, a reliable historian of Lancaster Co., Pa., says of the Mennonites in 1844, "They are distinguished above all others for their plainness of dress." L. J. Heatwole (b. 1852), a Mennonite bishop and historian in Virginia, describes the Mennonite costume of that area in earlier days (*Christian Monitor,* 1922, 592-93) as follows: "The early habits and customs of dress among pioneer Mennonites in Virginia were strictly in keeping with separation from the popular styles of their time. It is known that the men held to the universal color of drab for all their clothing. . . . The breeches however barely reached to the knees. . . . The women wore the plain bodice, from which draped the linsey gown in comfortable folds to the feet, while the arms and shoulders were covered with a woolen home-made kerchief. The head was usually covered with a kerchief of home-made linen that was drawn close about the neck with corners tied under the chin."

It is evident that the American Mennonites of the colonial period (and on into the 19th century) dressed plainly, but there is no evidence that they then had a special uniform cut of coat for the men, or a peculiar form of headdress or costume for the women. Their difference from "the world" consisted of regulations proscribing luxuries and articles worn for display, such as lace collars, etc. Morgan Edwards (*Baptists,* 95) claimed in 1770 that the Mennonites were so strict in dress regulations that some had been expelled for wearing buckle shoes or outside coat pockets, but it is impossible to evaluate his report for accuracy. Since they lived in close proximity to the Quakers, who at this time had a distinctive garb for men and women which was very similar to that in time adopted by the Mennonites, it is quite possible that the Mennonites were influenced by them.

When long trousers for men came into general use, some of the older men, especially the ministers, clung to the old-fashioned knee breeches. The last minister of the Franconia Conference (MC) known to wear them died in 1834 (Wenger, *Franconia,* 286). Eventually all Pennsylvania Mennonites adopted long trousers, but they did not all adopt the modern sack coat with its short tail and lapels; the preachers and some of the laymen retained the use of the colonial plain-collared coat without turn-down collar or lapels, and the ministers of the Mennonite Church (MC) in the Franconia, Lancaster, and Washington-Franklin conferences still wear the frock-tailed colonial coat.

Mennonite (MC) women in the Eastern United States and (some areas) elsewhere also wear a bonnet which used to be called a Quaker bonnet, the name being an indication of its probable origin. (The Pennsylvania Quakers adopted the bonnet around the year 1800; see Gummère, *passim.*) They also commonly wear what is called a "cape" over the shoulders, an article of dress which is probably an adaptation from the shawls which were current in the early decades of the 19th century. In the (MC) areas west of Pennsylvania fewer men wear the "plain coat," and the bonnet is no longer universally worn; in some areas only the older women cling to its use. But the members as a whole oppose the use of jewelry, insist on simplicity of attire, avoid the use of cosmetics, etc. The women generally wear their hair long. Furthermore, in worship the women wear a veil or cap, basing this on I Cor. 11:2-16. In this group and related conservative groups the wedding ring is forbidden.

The position and practice of the Old Order Mennonites and of the Conservative A.M. Church is similar to that of the Mennonite Church (MC), although generally more conservative and more uniform.

The Old Order Amish and the Hutterian Brethren require beards (*q.v.*) of the men, a definite garb by both men and women, the use of hooks and eyes in place of buttons, the worship veil for the women, etc. In the East Amish men wear a flat, black, very broad-brimmed hat. The Hutterite women wear a black polka-dot kerchief as a worship veil, which they also wear at all times. The Old Order Amish women wear a white cap for a prayer veiling, which they also have their daughters wear from infancy, and wear shawls instead of coats, a holdover from the earlier universal women's costume.

The Church of God in Christ, Mennonite, requires the beard for men, not as a symbol of nonconformity (they have no garb), but because they believe this requirement to be a part of the permanent law of God. The women wear a black kerchief head-covering during worship.

The Evangelical Mennonites of Canada (Kleine Gemeinde) have no special garb, but stress general simplicity of dress, and the women wear a black kerchief head-covering during worship.

Other Mennonite bodies such as the General Conference Mennonite Church, the Evangelical Mennonite Brethren, the Evangelical Mennonite Church, the Mennonite Brethren, and the United Missionary Church, have been traditionally conservative in dress and opposed to outward display in clothing, but in recent decades in America have tended more and more to follow the general conventions of society so that nonconformity in attire has largely become a dead letter; the members of these groups are not particularly distinguishable from non-Mennonites by their appearance. In these groups there are no specific church regulations proscribing the use of jewelry, requiring a worship veil, or forbidding the cutting of women's hair, and wedding rings are commonly worn.

The Old Colony, Sommerfelder, Rudnerweide, Bergtal, and Chortitz Mennonites of Manitoba and elsewhere are conservative groups in which the older traditions are strong, but in which there is little interpretation of cultural patterns in terms of specific Biblical teachings. The dress of members of the Old Colony, Sommerfelder, or Chortitz groups as worn to church services has the appearance somewhat of a prescribed uniform garb; the Chortitz men, for example, wear hooks and eyes. Some of the groups, Sommerfelder and Rudnerweide, e.g., now permit the wearing of the wedding ring. Short hair for women would be frowned on in all these groups though it would not be made a test of membership in most of them. In many of the groups (such as Old Colony, Sommerfelder, and Chortitz) it is traditional for the women to wear a black kerchief (head shawl) during worship, but the average member would not associate this with any Biblical teaching on the veilng of women.

A review of the history of costume in the Mennonite congregations of Europe and America reveals that among the original Anabaptists and the stricter bodies of Mennonites in later centuries there was a strong sense of estrangement from "the world" which resulted in a deliberate nonconformity to the generally accepted cultural patterns of current society. This involved the rejection of jewelry and anything worn for the display of wealth. In the course of time, especially among the Dutch Mennonites, this crystallized more or less into a garb in the stricter Mennonite groups. Eventually, however, much of the internal vigor of the European groups tended to disappear and the process of cultural accommodation continued until the whole concept of nonconformity to the world disappeared entirely and with it went usually not only nonconformity in dress but the practice of rejection of military service (*q.v.*) as well. In America the same processes have been at work, but some groups have withdrawn in reaction and settled into a formalism which tends to be devoid of spirituality; in these groups there is apt to be a feeling of contentment in being different in dress, etc., whether or not there is any inner spiritual life, evangelistic outreach, or program of missions and relief service to the needy of the world. Other groups have allowed the process of cultural accommodation to go on with little or no resistance, sincerely believing that Christianity does not consist in outward forms, but they have often tended to underestimate the power of the forces in contemporary society to mold the members of the brotherhood into the same types of character, belief, and practice, as are current in America in general. This has resulted in a loss of sense of unique mission as well as the partial surrender of basic Mennonite doctrines such as nonresistance. Groups of the first type, which lean toward formalism, have been labeled as "conservatives," and those of the second type, which tend to become more like American Protestants than the Mennonites have historically been, have been called "progressives." This leaves a third type (of which the largest group is the M.C.), the "moderates" (Smith, 744-46). These "moderates" constitute about two thirds of the entire Mennonite population of the Americas. They are attempting, though not always successfully, to maintain a vigorous inner sense of mission, and a voluntary simplicity of life which is applied even to their external appearance as described above. In this respect the "moderates" are seeking to have more of the type of spirituality which characterized their Anabaptist spiritual forebears with a truly Biblical separation unto God with its consequent nonconformity to the evil world about them, interpreting this nonconformity to apply to all areas of life. The progressives have a similar concern for spirituality, but do not usually apply the principle of nonconformity to the dress area. Neither of these two groups today attempts to maintain a uniform garb, except in so far as the Eastern wing of the moderate group still strictly requires a uniform garb for women, though not consistently for men.

The special ministerial garb which is today uniformly required in the Mennonite (MC) Church and the Conservative Amish in the 19th and 20th centuries, has no antecedent in earlier Mennonite-Anabaptist history. It is probably a survival from earlier practice when all male members wore the distinctive garb. The origin of the special ministerial garb among the Old Colony Mennonites is obscure, but the garb has become stiffly fixed in tradition, ministers wearing a special coat and boots to the services. There is no connection between any of the special types of American Mennonite ministerial garb and the clerical garb of Roman priests or high-church Protestant clergymen of various denominations. Nor have Mennonite ministers anywhere in the world ever worn a gown in the pulpit, except in Danzig, where some of the pastors wore the clerical gown with the white neckbands; Jacob Mannhardt wore a special square cap (*biretta*). In certain North German churches (e.g., Hamburg, Emden, Danzig, Crefeld) and commonly in Dutch churches, the ministers wore (and in part still wear) special high black hats, gloves, and frock coat to the Sunday services.   J.C.W.

Karl Baehr, "Secularization Among the Mennonites of Elkhart County, Indiana," *MQR* XVI (July 1942) 131-60; G. Bossert, *TA I. Württemberg* (Leipzig, 1930) 691, 741, 806, 881; J. Horsch, *Mennonites in Europe* (Scottdale, 1950) 251, 350, 368; ibid., *Worldly Con-*

formity in Dress (Scottdale, 1926); Amelia Gummere, *The Quaker, A Study in Costume* (Philadelphia, 1901); *Johannes Kesslers Sabbata* (St. Gallen, 1902) 147 f.; E. Jane Miller, "The Origin, Development, and Trends of the Dress of the Plain People of Lancaster County, Pennsylvania" (M.S. Thesis, illustrated, Cornell University, 1943); I. Daniel Rupp, *History of Lancaster County* (Lancaster, 1844) 194; *Complete Works of Menno Simons* (Elkhart, 1871) I, 21, 72, 97, 118, 175, 178, 185, 202, *et passim;* C. Henry Smith, *The Story of the Mennonites* (Newton, 1950) 744-46; *Mart. Mir.* (1950) 466, 495, 688, 789, 819, 841, 848, 898, 1001, 1061; John M. Vincent, *Costume and Conduct in the Laws of Basel, Bern and Zurich, 1370-1800* (The Johns Hopkins Press, 1935) 19, 60, 85; J. C. Wenger, *Christianity and Dress* (Scottdale, 1943); idem., *Historical and Biblical Position of the Menn. Church on Attire* (Scottdale, 1944); idem, *Separated unto God* (Scottdale, 1952) 139-51, 313-31; idem, *Hist. of the Menn. of the Franconia Conference* (Telford, 1938); I. D. Rupp, *An Original History of the Religious Denominations . . . United States* (Philadelphia, 1944); Morgan Edwards, *Materials Toward a History of the American Baptists* (Philadelphia, 1770).

Driedger (Driediger, Drüdger, Dridger, Driger), a Mennonite family name in the rural Flemish congregations of West Prussia, numbering 7 families in 1776 and 105 persons in 1935. Members of the family emigrated to Russia and subsequently to America. Jacob N. Driediger and Nic. N. Driediger are Mennonite (GCM) ministers in Ontario. Among those bearing the family name were Peter Driedger (1831-1921), minister of the Heubuden congregation, main editor of a two-volume collection of sermons, and originator of the Heubuden church library; and Abraham Driedger (1868-1945), son of the former, influential in conference activities, promoter of church music and historical research, who revised the West Prussian *Choralbuch* for its second edition, and wrote "Die Entwicklung des Gemeindegesanges in unseren westpreussischen Gemeinden" (*Menn. Bl.,* 1931, 30-32), and the article **Heubuden** and others in *Mennonitisches Lexikon.*   G.R.

G. H. Reimer, "Beiträge zur Stammtafel der Familie Driedger," in *Schriftenreihe des Menn. Geschichtsvereins* (Weierhof) III, 121-32.

Driscoll Mennonite Church, located in Burleigh Co., N.D., had a membership in 1911 of 19 and a Sunday-school enrollment of 40. Particulars are lacking and the conference connection unknown.

Dronrijp, a village in the Dutch province of Friesland, where Leenaert Bouwens (*q.v.*) 1568-82 baptized eight persons. There was never a congregation at Dronrijp; the newly baptized persons may have joined the congregation of near-by Blessum.
                                    vdZ.

Drooge, Alexander Hubertus van, a Dutch Mennonite pastor, b. Oct. 4, 1872, at Bakkeveen, Friesland, where his father was a schoolteacher, d. June 22, 1942, at Warga, Friesland, where he lived after retiring. He was educated at the university of Amsterdam and the Amsterdam Mennonite Theological Seminary and served two congregations: Holwerd-Blija, 1897-98; and Deventer, 1898-1939. He was a very serious and modest man, with a warm heart for his congregations. From 1934 to 1939 he was president of the *Algemene Doopsgezinde Sociëteit* (General Conference of the Dutch Mennonites).

In this capacity he preached the closing sermon of the Third World Conference at Witmarsum, Friesland, on July 3, 1936 (*Der allgemeine Kongress der Mennoniten,* Karlsruhe, n.d., 18-20, 168, 173-83). He also served for a number of years as president of the Elspeet Doopsgezind Broederschapshuis. He was also active in general liberal Protestantism: in 1911-21 he was a member of the board of the *Nederlandsche Protestantenbond* and 1920-21 its president. He was especially interested in religious education; for the Mennonites of Holland he projected a booklet for baptismal candidates. (*DJ* 1943, 18-35, with portrait.)   vpZ.

Drug, a Mennonite church (MC) in India: see **Durg.**

Dry River Union Church was located one mile northwest of Lily, in Ashby District, Rockingham Co., Va. It was originally sponsored by the Methodist Episcopal, German Baptist, and Mennonite (MC) denominations. After the old early 19th century log building was destroyed by fire on Sept. 22, 1912, the church was rebuilt the same year under the auspices of the United Brethren, Methodist, and Mennonite churches. The Mennonites held their last service here in the 1930's. In 1942 the trustees sold the building. Two unkept graveyards separated by the main highway are all that remain.   H.A.B.

Dublin (Pa.) Union Church was built in 1869 by the combined effort of Lutherans, Reformed, and Mennonites (MC). The church, now known as St. Luke's, is used alternately by Lutheran and Reformed groups. Mennonites have never conducted services here, although many of the present members are of Mennonite background.   Q.L.

Dubnitz, a market town with (1900) about 1,800 Slavic inhabitants near Trentchin in Hungary, center of the former Trentchin government, where Hutterian Brethren, expelled from Stigonitz (*q.v.*) in Moravia in 1622, found refuge. The feudal lord, Count Kaspar Illéshazi, permitted them to establish a Bruderhof a half hour below Trentchin on the Soblahof (*q.v.*), which they, however, had to abandon in 1688 on account of continued plundering. (*ML* I, 479.)   HEGE.

Dubovka: see **Eichenfeld.**

Dubrovna, a town in the Russian province of Mogilev, the stopping place for the winter for the first Mennonites coming from Danzig in 1788 on their way to South Russia. Two hundred and twenty-eight families were cared for here by the Russian government during the winter of 1788-89 through Baron von Staal. The delegate Jakob Höppner was with the group but there was no elder or minister to care for the spiritual needs. It was here that the first attempts were made to elect a spiritual leader with the help of the mother congregations in Danzig.

Early in the spring of 1789 Höppner and the delegates went on to Kremenchug on the Dnieper in the Poltava region to make arrangements for their settlement. Here they met Potemkin, who informed them that the land promised them near Berislav (*q.v.*) in the province of Kherson was not available and that they should proceed to the area where the Chortitza River flows into the Dnieper. Four weeks after the arrival of the delegates the total Dubrovna group arrived in Kremenchug by wagon and by barges on the Dnieper, and from Kremenchug proceeded to Chortitza (*q.v.*) for settlement. (D. H. Epp, *Chortitzer Mennoniten,* Rosenthal bei Chortitz, 1889.)   C.K.

Duchess Mennonite Church (MC), approximately 120 miles east of Calgary, Alta., is a member of the Alberta-Saskatchewan Conference. Duchess is located in a prosperous irrigation district. The first Mennonite to settle in the Duchess district was S. B. Ramer, who came in 1915. J. H. Brubaker and family came in 1916, others following later. In April 1917 the congregation was organized by Bishop N. B. Stauffer. Services were held in the schoolhouse in Duchess until 1923. A church was dedicated March 9, 1924. The Duchess congregation, while of Pennsylvania origin, nevertheless has members from various other places, including some from Duchess itself.

In 1948 the church was enlarged. Its membership in 1954 was 100. Ordained men who have served the congregation are J. S. Ramer, H. B. Ramer, C. J. Ramer, Paul Martin, Chris Snyder, Eli Kauffman, David Ramer, and Marlin Brubaker. Prominent family names in the congregation are Ramer, Martin, Brubaker, Burkholder, Friesen, and Torkelson. In 1954 the bishop was Clarence Ramer, the ministers H. B. Ramer and Paul Martin. E.S.

Dück (Dick), **David J.,** large estate owner and benefactor, b. June 29, 1860, at Rosenhof (Brodsky), Melitopol district, South Russia; attended the Gnadenfeld Zentralschule, became a member of the Petershagen Mennonite Church, married Katharina Schmidt Oct. 27, 1887, and lived at Steinbach until 1894, at which time he took over the large estate "Apanlee," on which he lived until his death on Oct. 16, 1919. The net income of this estate amounted at times to 100,000 rubles. Dück was above all a model farmer who greatly improved the breed of cattle and horses among the Mennonites. He emphasized the significance of rural life and was opposed to the tendencies toward capitalistic speculation in industry. In 1904-10 he was president of the Mennonite forestry service camps (*q.v.*) in Russia, looking after the spiritual, cultural, and economic welfare of the young men in alternative service. He was one of the founders and benefactors of the Alexanderkrone Zentralschule (*q.v.*) and the Halbstadt Kommerzschule (*q.v.*), and member of the boards of these schools. He was the benefactor of most of the Mennonite welfare organizations and institutions.

Dück also sponsored teachers' and Bible conferences, which were held at the estate Apanlee, Steinbach, and Yushanlee and were attended by all Mennonite groups of the various settlements. He was a founder of a Mennonite tract society, of which he was the chairman 1904-14, which distributed tracts in the Russian and German languages. When he was imprisoned during the Revolution friends solicited seven thousand signatures among the neighboring

Russian population requesting his release, evidence of his popularity with the peasants. On Oct. 16, 1919, he and his wife were killed by armed bandits who came to rob them of their possessions. C.K.

A. A. Töws, *Mennonitische Märtyrer* (North Clearbrook, 1949) II, 369 ff.

Dück, Gerhard Gerhard (1863-1949), a Russian Mennonite minister, was born Sept. 9, 1863, in Schönau, a Mennonite village in South Russia, the oldest son of Gerhard Gerhard Dück (1835-73), a tailor, and Anna Kliewer Dück (1840-82). He attended the Zentralschule in Orloff for four years, and then taught the village school in Fürstenwerder. The date and place of his baptism are not known. He married Justina Penner (b. Feb. 19, 1866), and became the teacher in Schardau, where their only child, Elizabeth, was born (Sept. 2, 1891). In 1894 they moved to Zagradovka. He taught a village school in Nikolaifeld until 1898. Then the family moved to Ufa and took up farming. On June 30, 1902, he was ordained to the ministry by Johann Schartner of Alexanderwohl. In 1910 he resigned from this office, sold his farm, and in 1911 moved to Slavgorod, in the Barnaul settlement in Siberia. His wife died there in the same year. In the following year he married Helena Toews (b. Dec. 26, 1883), a deaconess in Bethania (*q.v.*). This marriage was blessed with three sons and two daughters, all of whom are still in Russia. In 1923 Dück and his wife moved to the home of their daughter Elizabeth in Goloshevo, Ufa, and in 1924 they went on to Blumstein in South Russia. Though his daughter Elizabeth and his brother and sister succeeded in emigrating to Canada, he was unable to do so on account of eye trouble. For a number of years they lived in a Russian village in Samara. On Feb. 27, 1949, nearly deaf and blind, he died. E.E.

Dueck, John D. (1856-1918), a son of John and Agatha (Dück) Dueck, was born on Aug. 3, 1856, at Muntau, Russia. His mother died when he was 18 weeks old. His father then married Margaretha Reimer. He was reared in Russia, where he received a fair education. Immigrating to America in 1875, he settled near Steinbach, Man. He married Margaretha Hiebert on Oct. 7, 1877. Nine sons and six daughters were born to them. He was converted in his early years, and baptized on Dec. 25, 1881, joining the Church of God in Christ, Mennonite (*q.v.*). He was ordained to the ministry on Jan. 6, 1884. Soon after the ordination he moved to Gretna, Man., to serve a small congregation. In 1887 he moved to Hillsboro, Kan., and served the Alexanderfeld congregation until his death. Much of his time was spent in serving the church at large. In the early years he was appointed to serve different churches which did not have a residing minister, and was called to Oklahoma, Missouri, Ohio, Michigan, and Manitoba for special services. He possessed a very amiable character. In his preaching he was emotional and blessed with an exceptional ability to unfold the love of God. He served as associate manager of the *Botschafter der Wahrheit* (*q.v.*) from the time it was founded in 1897 until 1900, when he became the editor and in that capacity

served another 12 years. At the age of 61 years he died in his home near Hillsboro, Kan., and was interred in the Alexanderfeld cemetery. P.G.H.

Duerksen, John F. (1863-1932), a pioneer educator in the Mennonite Brethren Church of North America, was born in Alexanderthal, Molotschna Mennonite settlement, South Russia, July 25, 1863, the oldest of the seven children of Jacob J. and Katharina Funk Duerksen. After receiving an elementary education in the village, John attended the Zentralschule at Gnadenfeld and the teacher-training school at Neu-Halbstadt. Then he entered the teaching profession and taught in the Mennonite schools for three years.

At the age of 15 he was converted and on April 30, 1879, joined the M.B. Church. He early felt called to definite Christian service and at the age of 21 dedicated himself for such service.

In 1887 he emigrated to America and came to his parents in Kansas, who had preceded him three years earlier. Here he taught school near Lehigh, Kan., 1887-90, and in a Mennonite *Vereinsschule* near Buhler, Kan., 1890-99.

In 1899 the Mennonite Brethren Conference decided to affiliate with the Brethren College at McPherson, Kan., and to establish a department of its own in that institution. John F. Duerksen was principal of this educational effort for six years, during which he was instrumental in training many of the early leaders of the M.B. Church. When this German department school at McPherson was discontinued in 1905, the Duerksen family moved to Corn, Okla., where he established the Corn Academy and Bible School, serving as its principal for 11 years. He was ordained to the ministry in 1919, and served as assistant pastor of the Corn M.B. Church for 16 years in addition to his work in education.

Duerksen was a very active conference worker, serving repeatedly on the secretarial staff and was the secretary of the General Conference, 1919-21. He was editor of the Sunday-school quarterly of the M.B. Church for many years.

Duerksen married Katharina Warkentin on Jan. 9, 1890. To this union seven children were born. After the death of his first wife, he married Mrs. Gertrude Warkentin on Sept. 24, 1924. He died May 1, 1932, and was interred in the Corn M.B. cemetery. J.H.L.

Dühren, a village in the Sinsheim area of the Heidelberg district in Baden, Germany, where a Mennonite church came into being in the second half of the 17th century. The founders were refugees from the Swiss canton of Bern. In spite of the Palatine decree of tolerance of 1664, the religious activities of the Mennonites were still subject to arbitrary Palatine officials. This often led to conflict between the government and the noblemen on whose estates the Swiss exiles were settled. A register of 53 Mennonites arrested at a meeting in Steinfurt in 1662 includes the names of Rudolf Hagi and Martin Maylin of Dühren.

The refugees arrived in a pitiable state; e.g., in Dühren the family of the forty-year-old Ulrich

Widmer with three children aged three years to six weeks. To alleviate their dire poverty the Dutch Mennonites gave them brotherly aid in 1672. The adjacent farms were already in Mennonite hands. On the Birkenauerhof were Ulrich Rieck, the widow Magdalena Neglee, and B. Mengel (*Arch. Amst.*, No. 1196). The earliest list of members extant is dated 1731 (Müller, *Berner Täufer*, 210) and includes 13 families. Only two of the names, Bletscher and Sauter, on the list are still found in the congregation. Some families emigrated to America, while others moved in from neighboring churches. In 1858 most of the members dissolved their connections with the Mennonite *Badischer Verband* and became followers of Michael Hahn (*q.v.*), but without leaving the Mennonite Church. In 1921 the congregation numbered 37 souls, living in seven towns, and most of them farming. They held their services three times a month in Dühren and in the neighboring Ursenbacherhof (called Bleihof), hence was called Ursenbacherhof-Dühren. It appeared for the last time in 1941 in the directory of the *Gemeinde-Kalender* with a membership of 50 plus 7 unbaptized children. In 1945 the group joined the Sinsheim (*q.v.*) Mennonite congregation. (*ML* I, 485.)   HEGE.

Dühren (von Dühren, von Düren, von Dihren, Dieren), **van,** one of the oldest of the Dutch Mennonite families who immigrated into Prussia. Most of the van Dührens lived in Danzig and were numerous in the Mennonite congregation there; formerly there were also some in Königsberg and Elbing. Hendrik van Dühren served as elder of the Frisian church on Neugarten in Danzig, 1676-94; his oldest son Albrecht succeeded him until 1696, and after his untimely death the younger son Hendrik (or Heinrich) served, 1701-46. During the eldership of this Hendrik van Dühren a number of difficulties arose in the congregation, mostly caused, or at least aggravated, by his obstinacy and extreme conservatism. In 1739 he refused to ordain Johan Donner, who had been chosen as elder. Finally two elders from Holland, Abraham Koenen (*q.v.*) and Jacob Ouwejans (*q.v.*), in 1740-41 succeeded in settling the quarrels. (*Inv. Arch. Amst.* I, Nos. 1624, 1628; II, Nos. 2637-75; II, 2, Nos. 742, 751.) Other members of the family have served as preachers (e.g., Isaac van Dühren, *q.v.*) and on the council. The name did not spread beyond Berlin and Prussia. Heinrich van Dühren (d. 1945) was president of the Berlin Mennonite Church and a judge in the Prussian courts. (*ML* I, 485.)   H.G.M., vDZ.

Dühren, Isaac van, b. 1725, a Mennonite dyer and weaver in Danzig, served as preacher from 1775 until his death in 1800. In 1782 he wrote a book, *Geschichte der Märtyrer oder kurze historische Nachricht von den Verfolgungen der Mennonisten* (Königsberg, 1787). The book has three chapters: (*a*) *Verfolgung der Mennonisten von den Catholiken;* (*b*) *id. von den Lutheranern;* (*c*) *id. von den Reformirten,* which is followed by a supplement *Von der Kindertaufe.* The first part (*a*) is taken from van Braght, *Martyrs' Mirror,* and gives information on 102 Dutch martyrs; the sources of

(*b*) and (*c*) are J. Mathesius *5e Predigt vom Leben Lutheri;* Gottfried Arnold (*q.v.*), *Unparteiische Kirchen- und Ketzerhistorie;* Gerber, *Historie der Wiedergebohrenen;* Crespin's (*q.v.*) martyrbook, and others. The book by van Dühren, which contains 169 pages, was printed without the name of the author, but a copy belonging to the Amsterdam Mennonite Library (*Catalogus Amst.*, 16) contains a note that Isaac van Dühren, minister of the congregation of the Frisian Mennonites at Neugarten near Danzig, is the author. The book was reprinted in 1863 at Stuttgart (*Bibliographie,* 259-60) and at Winnipeg in 1939. Concerning his development and inner life see his correspondence with Elder Cornelius Regehr in Heubuden (reprinted in *Menn. Bl.,* 1885, 3 and 14 ff.).   H.G.M., vDZ.

E. Crous, "Vom Pietismus bei den altpreussischen Mennoniten im Rahmen ihrer Gesamtgeschichte 1722-1945," *Menn. Gesch.-Bl.* XI (1954) 9-11; *ML* I, 485.

Duisburg, a city in the Ruhr district, Rhine Province, Germany. There is evidence of some participation of Duisburgers in the Münsterite affair and its sequels 1534-38. No actual peaceful Anabaptist congregation was ever established in Duisburg in the 16th century, although as late as 1560 Duke Wilhelm of Cleve called the noted Catholic scholar George Cassander to Duisburg to convert the Anabaptists there. There may have been some continuing traces of Anabaptism in Duisburg throughout the 17th century, but it was apparently not until the 18th century that a regular Mennonite congregation existed. When there was no minister, the baptisms were apparently conducted in the Crefeld Church, whose church book records the names of 17 persons from Duisburg baptized. Risler (*Menn. Geschichtsbl.,* 1951) reports 20 families definitely identifiable as Mennonites in the early 18th century. Most of these were refugees from persecution elsewhere. Evidence shows that there was at this time considerable interconnection between Duisburg and Crefeld, Cleve, Goch, and Emmerich, the other Mennonite congregations along the Lower Rhine.

The first evidence of an organized congregation is the record in the church book of the Mennonite congregation at Goch, under date of Oct. 14, 1706, that Christian Kray was a preacher of the Duisburg Mennonite congregation.

According to the *Naamlijst* of 1731, which calls this town Doesburg, there was here a Mennonite congregation, which had no minister at that time but was served by the minister of Crefeld. In the *Naamlijst* of 1743 two preachers of Duisburg are mentioned, Johan Pryer and Gerhard Decker. In the *Naamlijst* of 1755 no mention is made of this congregation; the congregation must have died out between 1743 and 1755. In 1726 the widow of Pieter Andriessen of Duisburg requested financial support from the Amsterdam congregation. vDZ.

W. Risler, "Mennoniten in Duisburg," *Menn. Geschichtsbl.* VIII (1951) 2-18; *Inv. Arch. Amst.* I, No. 1446.

Dukhobors (Wrestlers with the Spirit), a Russian "Protestant" sect, probably an outgrowth of a dissident Khlysty group, which derived its peculiar doctrines from a number of sources, including heterodox Protestantism, Freemasonry, and Khlysty teaching. The sect arose in the village of Okhochee about 1755 and in the Russian province of Kharkov, and shortly thereafter in 1785 received its present name from the archbishop of Ekaterinoslav. In 1802 they were deported to the province of Taurida, where they adopted semi-communism. They were located as next neighbors to the Mennonites in the Molotschna colony in nine villages. In 1841 under pressure they settled further east in Transcaucasia, when they numbered about 4,000. In 1886 the group split. One part, under Peter Verigin's leadership, was much influenced by Count Leo Tolstoy and adopted complete nonresistance as well as rejection of private property.

In 1898-99 the Verigin group of 7,400 migrated to western Canada with the strong financial aid of Count Tolstoy. Their anarchistic views and practices have resulted in frequent and prolonged conflicts with the Canadian state. Only with great difficulty and gradually have they arrived at a *modus vivendi* with the state. The total of about 17,000 have broken up into several parties, one of whom, the moderate independent Dukhobors, has drawn near to the United Church in Canada. Another group has continued to follow its anarchistic and communistic practices and has come into frequent conflict with the authorities. Those Dukhobors who remained in Russia survived in a few places and are now affiliated with the Pentecostal Christians.

The Dukhobors are unitarian and pantheistic in theology, denying a personal transcendental deity. They attach very little importance to the Bible, and claim that their only source of doctrine is the living tradition of the sect, supposedly originally derived from Christ Himself.

The superficial similarity in a few points to the Anabaptists, Mennonites, or Quakers, has led some to assert a genetic connection with these groups, though without any proof at all. There is no ground whatsoever for the confusion which has occasionally arisen in the popular mind, both in Europe and America, with the Mennonites. The only contact with Mennonites was the period 1802-41 when they lived in the Molotschna, where Johann Cornies (*q.v.*) rendered them considerable assistance.   H.S.B.

Serge Bolshakoff, *Russian Nonconformity* (Philadelphia, 1920); J. F. C. Wright, *Slaya Bohu, The Story of the Dukhobors* (New York, 1940); D. H. Epp, *Johann Cornies* (Ekaterinoslav and Berdyansk, 1909) 171-83, "Die Duchoborzen"; P. Jansen, *Memoirs of Peter Jansen* (Beatrice 1921) 85 ff.; ML I, 479-84.

Dülken in the Brüggen district of the duchy of Jülich had some Anabaptists in the first half of the 17th century, whose names are listed in the registers of 1638 and 1652. Among them was the father of Jan Floh, who came to Crefeld (*q.v.*) from Gladbach in 1694. They had been expelled in 1652. (State archives of Düsseldorf, *Jülich-Berg* II, 252.)   W.N.

Dülmen, a town located southwest of the city of Münster in Westphalia, Germany, in which Bernhard Rothmann introduced the Reformation in 1533. On Sept. 8, 1533, Bishop Franz of Waldeck had two preachers of this movement arrested. That the Anabaptist movement had also gained a foothold here and that a group survived after the collapse of the movement in Münster is indicated by the fact that even at the beginning of the 17th century, after the severe activity of the Counter Reformation, at least one Anabaptist is reported to have resided here.
    C.K.

Fr. Brune, *Der Kampf um eine evangelische Kirche im Münsterland 1520-1802* (Witten, 1953) 43 f., 132.

Dulmen, Trijntje Janssen van, an Anabaptist martyr: see **Trijntje Janssen.**

Duma. Long before the socialist movement, and then parallel with it, there were movements in Russia whose objective was a democratic free state. But not until the 20th century did the absolutism of the czars yield to the pressure of all strata of Russian society, and then only to a very limited degree, when (in 1905) Russia established a popular, although weak representation in government. Until the March Revolution of 1917 four Dumas tried, in the face of tremendous difficulties and handicaps, to undertake legislation.

The Mennonites had, of course, no representatives in the Duma elected specifically by them; nevertheless there were two Mennonite representatives who had their interest at heart and defended them. They were the landowners Abraham Bergmann (*q.v.*) of the province of Ekaterinoslav and Peter Schröder of the Crimea. The former was a member of both the third and fourth Dumas, the latter only of the last. Bergmann belonged to the Octobrist Party, whose aim it was to bring into actuality the October Manifesto (1905) granting a constitution, but which again and again turned to a reactionary course. Schröder was a member of the Cadets Party. Both representatives worked only in committees and used their influence especially in working out a liberal solution to religious freedom preparatory to passing a law on the question. Bergmann became a tragic victim of the Revolution of 1917.

In the elections for the new national assembly of 1917, the Mennonites tried hard to elect a representative, combining with the other German elements for this purpose, but failed in spite of their hard campaigning in the summer of 1917. (*ML* I, 485 f.)
    B.H.U.

Duncanus, Martinus (or Maerten Dunck), of Wormer, b. *ca.* 1506 at Kempen near Crefeld, a Catholic priest, who lived in the focus of the Anabaptist movement in Waterland in Holland in 1535. At least 57 persons in his village were persecuted, of whom 32 had taken part in the procession to Münster. He was one of the first Catholic opponents of Menno Simons. His book, *Anabaptisticae haereseos confutatio* (1549 at Antwerp), is one of the most violent ever published against the Dutch Anabaptists. He gave it to the city of Amsterdam and received as a gift from the mayors of the city the sum of 22.80 guilders (12 "Caroli-daalders"). As inquisitor of several persons baptized by Gillis van Aken (*q.v.*) he earned 5.70 florins in the same year. Later Duncanus was priest at Delft, deacon at The Hague, and from 1572-78 priest at Amsterdam. He died in Amersfoort in 1593. It is probable that he gave Simon Walrave information on a number of items mentioned in Walrave's *Successio Anabaptistica* (1603). In addition Duncanus wrote a less significant book, *Van die Kinderdoop* (Antwerp, 1593). When Amsterdam joined the party of William of Orange, Duncanus was one of the persons expelled from the city.   K.V.

F. Rütter, *Martin Donk (Dunkanus) 1505-1590* (Münster, 1906); *Ztscht für Kirchengesch.* XXVIII (1907) 240; K. Vos, *Menno Simons* (Leiden, 1914) 304-5; *DB* 1865, 115-16; *ML* I, 486.

Dunin-Borkowski, Stanislaus von (1864-1934), an Austrian Jesuit scholar, who made a very thorough scholarly research of the anti-Trinitarian writings of the 16th century prior to the coming of Socinianism. In this research he included also several Anabaptist writers (above all Pilgram Marpeck) whom he falsely classified as anti-Trinitarians. Since his scholarship is of the first rank, his studies have added to the confusion of the concept of the Anabaptists. He published (*a*) *Quellenstudien zur Vorgeschichte der Unitarier des 16. Jahrhunderts,* in *75 Jahre Stella Matutina* (Feldkirch, Austria, 1931, 91-138) (*b*) *Untersuchungen zum Schrifttum der Unitarier vor Faustus Sozzini, ibid*. II (1931) 103-47 (on Pilgram Marpeck 110-12); (*c*) "Die Gruppierung der Anti-Trinitarier des 16. Jahrhunderts," in *Scholastik* VII (Bonn, 1932), dealing also with Adam Pastor (*q.v.*) and other Unitarians with Anabaptist leanings. Dunin-Borkowski's findings were extensively used by E. M. Wilbur, *A History of Unitarianism* (Harvard Press, 1946), and by Roland H. Bainton, "The Left Wing of the Reformation," *Journal of Religion* XXI (1941), where these early Anti-Trinitarians were misleadingly called Anabaptists. John C. Wenger in his study, "The Theology of Pilgram Marpeck," *MQR* XII (1938) 214-16, convincingly refutes the contentions of Dunin-Borkowski of Marpeck's alleged anti-Trinitarian leanings. R. Friedmann, "The Encounter of Anabaptists and Mennonites with Anti-Trinitarianism." *MQR* XXII (1948) 139 ff. (particularly 146), likewise analyzes the material, arriving at a more clear-cut ideological distinction. (For details see **Anti-Trinitarianism.**)   R.F.

Dunkard, Dunker. This name, popularly used throughout the 19th century and into the 20th for the denomination now called Church of the Brethren (*q.v.*), is a corruption of Dunker, English for *Tunker*, a German word meaning "Dipper" or "Immerser," referring to the mode of baptism practiced by the group. The name is still used today by two minor conservative bodies deriving from the original body namely, Old Order Dunkards (*q.v.*), and Dunkard Brethren. The name Tunker (*q.v.*), once the official name for the Brethren in Christ in Ontario, has no doubt a common origin, since this group adopted immersion from the Church of the Brethren at the time of the former's founding in Pennsylvania in the 1770's. However, "Dunkard" has never correctly been used as a name for this group.   H.S.B.

Dunnville Mennonite Church (OOM), located in Haldimand Co., Ont., had a membership of 18 in 1911. Particulars are lacking.

Durango (area 48,000 sq. mi., pop. 484,000 in 1940) is a state of northern Mexico directly to the south of the state of Chihuahua. The climate is generally dry and healthful and the rainfall very light in the eastern part. There are no rivers of any size in the state. The principal industry of the state is mining, although extensive cattle ranges are found on the higher elevations. The capital city is Durango (pop. 33,412 in 1940), which is located in the picturesque Guadiana Valley about 6,200 feet above sea level. It is an important mining and commercial center and is famous for the great mountain of iron that lies northwest of the city. Its manufacturing establishments include cotton and woolen mills, glass works, iron foundries, tanneries, flour mills, sugar refineries, and tobacco factories. It was founded in 1563.

An Old Colony Mennonite settlement with a population of 3,000 is located about 75 miles northwest of the city of Durango. (See **Patos.**)   J.W.F.

Durango Mennonite Settlement was established in the state of that name in Mexico some 75 miles northwest of the city of Durango in 1924 by Old Colony Mennonites (*q.v.*) coming mostly from the Hague (Sask.) Mennonite settlement. Johann P. Wall (*q.v.*) and B. Goertzen, delegates who investigated Mexico for possible settlement, were instrumental in choosing this site instead of the one in the vicinity of Cuauhtemoc, Chihuahua. Thirty-five thousand acres of land were purchased through the mediation of Arturo J. Braniff from Juan L. Losoya for $7 per acre, on which 17 villages were established. In the years following additional land was bought as it was needed for landless families.

The settlement has its own elder, Peter P. Wiens, a civic leader called *Oberschulze* (*q.v.*), and other organizations characteristic of the Old Colony Mennonites. The economic development of the Durango settlement has been similar to that of the others in Mexico. During the last years they have experienced a setback because of the severe drought. In 1925 the population was 946, in 1949 it was 2,861, and in 1953 the total was 3,281. (See also **Old Colony Mennonites** and **Mexico.**)   C.K.

Durdenitz (now Turnitz), a locality east of Lundenburg in Moravia, where the Hutterian Brethren erected a Bruderhof in the 16th century, which burned down when ignited by a neighboring house. (Beck, *Geschichts-Bücher,* 269; *ML* I, 486.)
                      HEGE.

Durg (English, *Drug*), a Mennonite (MC) congregation in Madhya Pradesh (formerly Central Provinces), India. It is situated on the Bengal-Nagpur railway 25 miles west-southwest of Raipur and about 50 miles northwest of Dhamtari. The center consists of a bungalow for the missionaries and living quarters for the Christian workers, and a well-constructed chapel.

Durg was founded by Methodist Episcopal missionaries before 1900, but because of their enforced retrenchment after World War I they asked the American Mennonite Mission to take over the Durg field, comprising about 2,000 square miles with a population of about 350,000. The members of the

Christian community living in the town and adjacent villages were formerly Methodist, but soon after the work was taken over in 1935, they were reorganized into a Mennonite church.

In this area, because of the intense evangelistic program of the missionaries and their Indian workers, Hindus have accepted Christ and many more were open to the Gospel, although they were opposed by organized non-Christian forces. The congregation in 1954 numbered 157 members, besides about 50 children. J. Haider was the pastor. G.J.L.

Durgerdam, a small town near Amsterdam, in the Dutch province of North Holland, an Anabaptist center as early as 1534. Shortly after there must have been a congregation, of which the martyr Willem Jansz (*q.v.*), executed at Amsterdam on March 12, 1569, was a member. Leenaert Bouwens (*q.v.*) had baptized 11 persons here about 1565. Later the congregation joined the Waterlander Conference in North Holland. In 1675 the membership numbered 100. In 1687 the church burned down, but was rebuilt soon after. Continuously during the 18th century there was no minister and the membership decreased rapidly. In 1727, 1733, and 1736 the small congregation generously contributed to the Dutch Committee of Foreign Needs to help the Prussian Mennonites. In 1817 the congregation was dissolved; an amount of 6,000 guilders which was the property of the church was turned over to the Waterlander (Rijper) Sociëteit.   vDZ.

Inv. Arch. Amst. I, No. 1180, II, No. 1713; Blaupot t. C., *Holland* I, 24, 252, 355; II, 92, 231; *DJ* 1942, 40; *Naamlijst* 1815, 107; *DB* 1872, 64; 1918, 50; *ML* I, 193.

Durgerdam, Willem Jansz van, an Anabaptist martyr: see **Willem Jansz.**

Durham, Kan., a village of about 200 in Marion County, the center of a Mennonite community of over 400 members, who belong to the four Mennonite churches (GCM, MB, EMB, and Church of God in Christ Mennonite) in the vicinity. (*ML* I, 493.)   P.G.H.

Durham (Kan.) Church of God in Christ Mennonite Church: see **Logan** Church of God in Christ Church.

Durham Mennonite Brethren Church, now extinct, located six miles northwest of Durham, Marion Co., Kan., a member of the Southern District M.B. Conference, was organized on Dec. 29, 1906, by a few families who had remained there after an unsuccessful attempt in 1885-90 to establish a church, known as the "Mennonite Brethren Group North of Lehigh." Jacob Kliewer and Henry Bergthold had served the earlier congregation as ministers. Because of poor soil and high land prices, the group broke up. The remaining families elected John A. Nickel as leader, who was succeeded by Abraham Pankratz at the time of the organization as a church in 1906. New families moved in and the membership of the church in 1911 was approximately 34. In 1934 the church was discontinued when members continued to move to neighboring Mennonite Brethren communities and to Texas and Oklahoma.

I.G.N.

Durieu (Du Rieu): see **Adriaen Olieux.**

Dürkheim, Bad, a town (pop. *ca.* 8,000) in the Palatinate, Germany, until the French Revolution the residence of the counts of Leiningen-Hardenburg. Since the end of the Thirty Years' War Mennonites have been living in this region. A report by Michael Frey (*Versuch einer geogr.-hist.-stat. Beschreibung des königlichen bayerischen Rheinkreises dermalen Pfalz,* Part IV, Speyer, 1837) states that there were in the canton of Dürkheim in 1801, 159 Mennonites; in 1823, 284; and in 1834, 198. They lived in Dürkheim, Dackenheim, Erpolzheim, Freinsheim, Friedelsheim, St. Grethen, Röhrig, Hausen, Seebach, Herxheim, Leistadt, Ungstein-Pfeffingen, and Wachenheim. Emigration to America has been the principal cause of the decline in the Mennonite population (1922) to 74 souls: 48 in Friedelsheim, one in Gönnheim, 9 in Erpolzheim, 2 in Freinsheim, 11 in Dackenheim, and 3 in Dürkheim. All belong to the Friedelsheim (*q.v.*) congregation.

On Oct. 15, 1949, the Mennonite Central Committee (*q.v.*) opened a Children's Home in the city, to provide relief for 40 undernourished children sent by public welfare organizations of cities of the region. Each group of children stays for three months to rebuild their health, and is then replaced by another similar group. The home was still operated in 1955, but with some government support. (*ML* I, 493.)   J.F.

Dürksen, David Gerhard (1850-1910), an elder of the Mennonite Brethren Church in the Crimea. Not much is known of his childhood and early youth, except that he grew up in a Mennonite (not Mennonite Brethren) home. He did not have the opportunity for educational advancement in his youth; but since he was not interested in becoming a farmer, he studied independently to prepare himself for the teaching profession. He taught first in the village school of Margenau. By his use of modern methods of instruction, his excellent discipline, and his friendly relations with the pupils and their parents he set an example to his younger colleagues, who looked up to him as their leader.

Before long the Margenau Mennonite Church chose him as minister. About this time he underwent a deep spiritual experience, as a result of which his preaching differed from the customary sermon in content and manner. Instead of reading aloud to his congregation for an hour or more from the yellowed pages of the sermons used by the previous generations, he spoke freely and directly to his audience, reviving the religious life of the congregation and leading many to conversion. Though his innovations also evoked some hostility, he was one of the most sought-after speakers for special services and conferences among all the Mennonites of South Russia.

His type of piety brought him in close contact with the Rückenau Mennonite Brethren congregation; he felt at home in this circle. His desire to live only in accord with the Word of God, to build the church on the apostolic pattern, and the warm fraternal love he found in Rückenau must have influenced his decision to leave the Margenau congregation and unite with the Rückenau M.B. Church. At first there was some tension between the Mennonite Brethren and the Mennonites in consequence of this step, but his conciliatory manner and his obvious devotion and spiritual depth soon overcame this tension, and he was again invited to preach in Mennonite pulpits.

For a time Dürksen tried to do justice to both his teaching and preaching offices, but soon gave up his beloved school to devote himself entirely to preaching. He was appointed as traveling evangelist by the General Conference of the Mennonite Brethren Church, serving in this capacity with outstanding success. He preached in nearly all of the Mennonite churches in both European and Asiatic Russia, in many M.B. churches of America, and also in West Prussia. He also took part on one occasion in the Blankenburg Alliance Conference (*q.v.*) at Blankenburg, Germany.

Dürksen was also an able writer. Unfortunately most of his powerful addresses were never put in writing, but whenever he found time he wrote for the *Zionsbote* (*q.v.*) and the *Abreisskalender* (*q.v.*), as well as other periodicals.

Dürksen's most successful field of service lay perhaps in his work on the Crimean Mennonite school board, of which he became a member soon after his ordination as elder. His wide experience and understanding of human nature did much to raise the standards of Mennonite education. The Zentralschule in Spat and Karassan and the Crimea Mennonite girls' school were the result of his influence.

Dürksen was ordained elder of the Spat M.B. Church (*q.v.*) in 1899. His duties as elder in the Crimea restricted his evangelistic tours more and more. The rise of Alliance groups, who sought to introduce open communion in the M.B. congregations, led to bitter struggles in the entire Mennonite Brethren group, which were at times waged by carnal methods. Dürksen was at first pacific, but gradually espoused the side of the proponents of closed communion, adopting also the violent methods used by both sides. In addition, he made a very unfortunate second marriage, which blighted the rest of his life, so that his rugged physical frame broke under the strain. After an illness of nine months he died, mourned by Mennonites of all branches, including those who had been his severest critics. (*ML* I, 493-95.)† J.K.

Durlach, a city near Karlsruhe, Baden, Germany, where an Anabaptist congregation was formed in the first years of the movement, which succeeded in maintaining itself for decades in spite of the severest persecution. It belonged to the branch known as Philipites, after their preacher Philip Plener (*q.v.*), who worked as an evangelist in this region in 1527-28 (Chr. Hege, *Die Täufer in der Kurpfalz,* Frankfurt, 1908, p. 60). Severe persecution by Margrave Philip (d. 1533), who in a mandate of Dec. 15, 1527, ordered the extermination of the Anabaptists, caused many to emigrate. Some must also have given their lives for their faith. The chronicles state that there were 12 executions in 1531.

Under Philip's successor Ernst (d. 1552), the progenitor of the Baden-Durlach line, the Anabaptists had more freedom. In the region of Jöhlingen two or three hundred sometimes met for worship. Some of the Anabaptists who had fled to Moravia a few years earlier wished to return to Durlach when persecution broke out in Moravia in 1535 and were seized en route at Passau on Sept. 15, 1535. Among them was Hans Steubner of Durlach, who had been baptized by Konrad Lemlin and whose wife Anna had been baptized by Hans Kellner at Haidlitzen (probably Heidelsheim near Bruchsal) (Wolkan, *Lieder,* 30). A later trial reveals that in 1543 Michael Jungmann was sheltered in Durlach, and Margarete, Bernhard Bierer's widow of Pfaffenheim, had moved there. In Königsbach, which at that time belonged to the Imperial Knights, there were also some Anabaptists, for whom Hans Schoch preached about 1555 (G. Bossert, *Ztscht für die Gesch. des Oberrheins,* 1905, 86). The Anabaptists around Maulbronn also found asylum here; Eberhard von Venningen received Hans Braunsbacher of Rudersberg in 1574 when he no longer felt safe in Freudenstein (Bossert, Supplements of *Staats-Anzeiger für Württemberg,* 1895, 271).

Under Margrave Karl II, 1553-77, who was only 24 when he assumed government, the Lutheran theologians called Jakob Andreae (*q.v.*) and Michael Diller (*q.v.*) from Württemberg and the Palatinate to introduce the Reformation. These men took a position at Worms in 1557 favoring ruthless extermination of the Anabaptists by means of dungeon and death, and very likely used their influence to root them out. The fact that from now on for over 150 years nothing more is heard about Anabaptists in the region leaves no doubt as to the success of their cruel effort.

Not until the beginning of the 18th century was the brotherhood tolerated in the country. Then the Mennonites exiled from Switzerland found refuge in the margravure of Baden-Durlach as well as the adjacent regions. Centers of the Durlach settlement were Hohenwettersbach and Königsbach. Toward the end of the 19th century several families moved into Durlach; other Mennonites were already living on leased farms near by, and together in 1901 they organized a congregation in Durlach, which the Mennonites in Karlsruhe as well as the Thomashof have also joined. The census of December 1910 showed 81 Mennonites living in the Durlach area; of these, 43 lived in Durlach (including 7 on the Lamprechtshof and 8 on the Rittnerthof), 33 in Königsbach (5 on the Johannistalerhof), and 8 in Hohenwettersbach. In 1954 the congregation had 109 members and 22 unbaptized children. The elders were Chr. Schnebele, Joh. Hodel, Martin Funck, Heinrich Bachmann; preachers were Heinrich Schneider, Theo Glück, Rudolf Bletscher. Durlach is now incorporated in the municipality of Karlsruhe. Its population is 18,000. (*ML* I, 495 f.) HEGE.

Durr, John N. (1853-1934), the son of Jacob J. and Annie Johnson Durr, was born near Masontown, Fayette Co., Pa., Sept. 3, 1853, the fourth child in a family of six children. In the spring of 1855 the family moved across the Monongahela River into Greene County. On Feb. 17, 1876, he married Malissa Jane Steele of Masontown, who transferred her church membership from the Methodist Church to the Mennonite Church, in which church she remained active until her death, March 18, 1889. To this marriage were born six daughters: Annie Frances, Sara Elizabeth, Mary Magdalene, Hannah Malissa, Katie Mae, Laura Jane. These six daughters were married to two bishops, three ministers, and a deacon. The family moved back to Fayette County about 1880. In August 1898 he moved from Masontown to Martinsburg, Pa. On Sept. 22, 1898, he married Mary Susan Caufman of Chambersburg, Pa. One son, who died in infancy, was born to this marriage. His second wife died Jan. 1, 1929. On Dec. 30, 1931, he married Sarah B. Gsell Leidig at Lake Charles, La., where they lived until her death in 1932. From 1932 until his death he lived with his daughter Hannah (Mrs. N. E. Miller) of Springs, Pa.

Durr was baptized Nov. 18, 1871, and became a member of the Masontown Mennonite Church. His conversion took place at a series of revival meetings held at the Huston Schoolhouse by the Methodists during the fall of 1870. Following a three-week series of meetings in January 1872 he was ordained to the ministry (MC) on Feb. 5, 1872, by John F. Funk and Daniel Brenneman. On Nov. 26, 1873, he was ordained by lot to the office of bishop by Jacob N. Brubacher. He is the youngest ever ordained to these two offices (aged 19 and 20) in the Mennonite Church (MC) as far as records show.

John N. Durr served as bishop in the Mennonite Church from the time of his ordination until his death, a period of 61 years. During this time he served for various lengths of time as bishop of the following churches: Masontown, Rockton, Scottdale, Schellsburg, Altoona, Martinsburg (Morrison's Cove). His longest term was at Martinsburg, 1899-1931. He assisted in the organization of the Southwestern Pennsylvania Mennonite Conference and was elected as its first moderator, serving 1876-98. In the district conference he served on the following committees: Bible conference, missions, Sunday-school conference. He served as vice-president of the district conference mission board and was its representative on the local board of the Altoona Mennonite Mission 1918-34.

He served as representative from the Southwestern Pennsylvania District Conference on the General Conference Committee and was elected as moderator of this committee from its first meeting in 1896 and served also as moderator of the preliminary General Conference held in 1897.

He died Nov. 17, 1934, at Springs, and was buried in the Martinsburg Mennonite cemetery.   E.D.Z.

Dürr, Martin, an Anabaptist of Augsburg, concerning whom nothing is known except that he wrote hymn No. 49 in the *Ausbund,* "O Herre Gott, in meiner Not, Kläglich ich zu Dir ruffe." (Wolkan, *Lieder,* 146; Wackernagel, *Das deutsche Kirchenlied* V, 1101; *ML* I, 496.)   NEFF.

Dürsrüttilied, an Anabaptist hymn containing 21 quatrains, describes the seizure of a congregation of Anabaptists with their preacher, Uli Baumgartner, on the Dürsrütti in the Emmental (*q.v.*), Switzerland, in 1659. Most of the prisoners were, after prolonged imprisonment, taken to Holland. The song is found in Müller, *Berner Täufer,* 123-25. (*ML* I, 496.)   NEFF.

Dusentschuer, Johann, a Münsterite Anabaptist, a goldsmith from Warendorf, Westphalia, Germany, played a significant role in the attempt to establish a "New Jerusalem" in Münster. Zurhorn reports "that he limped on one leg and when he came to Münster he was at first considered a fool, but soon the fool became a prophet." According to Brune he sent out 27 apostles to preach repentance and he himself is supposed to have proclaimed and anointed Jan von Leiden king of the "New Jerusalem." In October 1534, Dusentschuer was in a group that came to the city of Soest and preached repentance on the streets. They entered the city hall stating that the king of Zion had sent them to preach the Gospel of peace and repentance in Soest. When the burgomaster did not receive them, Dusentschuer threw his coat and a "peace penny" to his feet saying, "Since you are not willing to accept the peace, we are turning to the common people to reveal the will of the Father to them. Your blood be upon your head." They proceeded to the market preaching the same message. After their arrest, the Soest record reports, they stated that infant baptism was vain, that Christ had no human flesh, that the Lord's flesh and blood were not present in the Lord's Supper, and that they had all goods in common. On Oct. 21, 1543, they were beheaded.   C.K.

Rembert, *Wiedertäufer,* 308-10; Fr. Brune, *Der Kampf um eine evangelische Kirche im Münsterland 1520-1802* (Witten, 1953) 39-40; L. Keller, *Geschichte der Wiedertäufer und ihres Reiches zu Münster* (Münster, 1880) 168, 322.

Düsseldorf, a government district in the Rhine Province of Prussia, includes the former duchy of Cleve (*q.v.*) as well as parts of the duchies of Jülich (*q.v.*) and Berg, where the Anabaptist movement attained considerable strength in the 16th century. Large congregations maintained themselves in Gladbach and Cleve; the former died out in the 17th century, and the latter in the 19th, although there have always been several Mennonite families living in Cleve. Mennonites expelled from adjacent territories and towns gathered in Crefeld (*q.v.*) in the 17th century. They laid the foundation for the velvet and silk industry there, which soon acquired a leading position in Germany. Crefeld was the only modern Mennonite congregation in this district. When many Danzig refugees located in this area, a congregation of this group, called Bergisches Land (*q.v.*), was organized in 1948, and had a membership in 1952 of *ca.* 250 including children. Most of the members live in the district of Cologne. (*ML* I, 496.)   HEGE.

Dutch East Indies: see **Indonesia.**

Dutch Mennonite Emigrant Relief Office: see **Hollandsch Doopsgezind Emigranten Bureau.**

Dutch Mennonite Mission Association (*Doopsgezinde Vereniging tot Evangelieverbreiding,* previously called *Doopsgezinde Vereeniging tot Verbreiding des Evangelies in de Nederlandsche Overzeesche Bezittingen,* i.e., Mennonite Association for the Spread of the Gospel in the Dutch Colonies), founded Oct. 21, 1847, as a separate organization, preceded however by the Dutch Section of the (English) Baptist Missionary Society 1821-47, whose officers (and most members) were Mennonites and took the initiative in setting up the new Mennonite missionary organization. Samuel Muller of the Mennonite seminary was the first president, having been president of the previous Dutch Section, whose entire treasury balance (8,000 guilders) was transferred to the new organization. An attempt (1849) to make the new organization a section of the Dutch Missionary Society of Rotterdam (founded 1797) failed because of the refusal of the Society to permit the nonpractice of infant baptism by the future Mennonite missionaries. This was a fortunate decision in that it permitted the Dutch Mennonites to enlist the support and co-operation of foreign Mennonites (German, Swiss, Russian) which would otherwise have been impossible, and which proved to be so very essential. The Missionary Association, because of the small interest in the congregations which was further hindered by the growth of modernism among the Dutch Mennonites, was from the beginning a private association, with a self-perpetuating board of directors. Besides the contributions of the Dutch Mennonites gifts were soon received from abroad, first from certain Mennonite congregations in Germany—Norden, and Neuwied, followed by Friedrichstadt, Heubuden, and Danzig, then Liebenau and Gnadenfeld in Russia (1854), and later by congregations in the Palatinate. Some contributions were received from the United States, especially from the General Conference Mennonites. (Kaufmann, 49, 67, 73, 98, 103-4, 165.) Associate members were later appointed to represent the German and Russian Mennonites who were supporting the work. Then in 1951 a larger European Mennonite Mission Committee was formed to co-ordinate the missionary interests of the various national mission committees (German, French, and Swiss), particularly with a view to the support of the work of the Dutch Association in Java and New Guinea, but the actual administration has always remained fully in the hands of the Dutch organization.

The first mission field to be opened was Java (*q.v.*), with P. Jansz (1820-1904, *q.v.*) going out in 1851 (first baptism of 5 converts in 1854) as a teacher. A second and third worker were also sent out with secular occupations, H. C. Klinkert (*q.v.*) in 1856 and Thomas Doyer (*q.v.*) in 1857. The first worker to go out as a formally (government-) approved missionary was N. Schuurmans in 1863. The four first missionaries were Dutch, but after the appointment of P. A. Jansz in 1878 (son of P. Jansz) no other missionaries were sent out from Holland to Java, the next three being Russian Mennonites. After World War I two South-German and one Swiss Mennonite (statistics as to wives were not available) plus two single women missionaries,

daughters of a Russian Mennonite missionary, were the only missionaries sent out from Europe. The formal mission work came to an end in 1940 when the mission congregations were organized as an independent Javanese Mennonite Church. The Chinese Mennonite Church in Java, though arising out of contacts with the Dutch missionaries, was always independent. Since it was very difficult to find a way to spread the Gospel among the Mohammedan Javanese, who by strong religious and social traditions (*adat*) were very dependent on the *dessah* (village) communities (in 1877 the number of converts was only 77), P. Jansz suggested (1864) that special agricultural colonies be established, where Christians could live together and make their own communities; but it was not before 1879, that P. A. Jansz, the son of P. Jansz, carried out this idea and founded the colony Margoredjo (Way to Happiness), which was followed by other colonies; this proved to be a success; about 1925 the number of Christians was 4,000. Special attention too was given to medical help and several hospitals and clinics were erected.

The second mission field, Sumatra (*q.v.*), was opened by Heinrich Dirks (*q.v.*) in 1871. In 1928 it was turned over to the German *Rheinische Mission* at Barmen. All the missionaries (7 men) in Sumatra were Russian Mennonites. The third mission field, called Inanwatan in Dutch New Guinea (*q.v.*), was opened in 1950 with the sending out of a Dutch missionary couple, followed by a second couple from Holland in 1953. At the same time, a Dutch missionary (with wife) was sent as Bible teacher to serve in the Javanese Mennonite Bible School, followed by a second Dutch teacher in 1953.

Numerous contacts were established between the Dutch Missionary Association and the United States Mennonites, particularly of the General Conference group, beginning as early as 1868, and in 1921 J. M. Leendertz visited North America in the interests of the Dutch mission work whose financial state was very precarious. Plans to send American workers (e.g., S. S. Haury, *q.v.*, in 1888) and to have an American board take over the Sumatra work (1921 ff.) did not materialize.

After World War II interest in the missionary enterprise increased considerably among the Dutch Mennonites, though the hope to make the Missionary Association an official work of the entire Dutch Mennonite Church failed to be realized. The visit of the president of the Javanese Church to Holland (and other European countries) in 1952 in connection with the Mennonite World Conference in Basel had a strong beneficial effect upon the missionary interest and support.

Annual reports (*Verslag van den Staat en de Verrigtingen der Doopsgezinde Vereeniging tot Bevordering der Evangelieverbreiding,* etc.) have been published in Dutch (1848-   ) and in German (*Bericht über den Stand und die Thätigkeit der Taufgesinnten Gesellschaft zur Beförderung der Ausbreitung des Evangeliums*) for most of these years. A monthly periodical, *Evangelie-verbreiding,* has been published since Aug. 20, 1949. A centennial booklet was published in 1948, *Uit Verleden en heden van de Doopsgezinde Zending, Jubileum-Uitgave van de Doopsgezinde Zendings-Vereniging 1847-1947.*   H.S.B.

A. Mulder, "A Century of Mennonite Missions," *Menn. Life* III (1948) 12-15; W. F. Golterman, *Waarom Zending* (n.p., 1952); E. Kaufman, *The Development of the Missionary and Philanthropic Interest among the Mennonites of North America* (Berne, 1931).

Duttweiler, a region in the Neustadt district of the Palatinate, Germany. In 1716 three Mennonite families, Janzen, Berdoldt, and Egli, were living there. When in 1724 a register was made of the Palatine Mennonites "in what state of nutrition and wealth" they were, only two families are named: the wealthy Abr. Egli, hereditary leaseholder of the monastic estate of St. Lamprecht, and the "poor" family of Ulrich Burkhart, who had taken over Bergtholdt's farm. The list of Mennonites of 1738 names only Abr. Eichli; that of 1743 lists three families—Jac. Egel, Joh. Lichti, and Egel's widow; in 1759 two families, Joh. Lichti and Isaac Bergthold; in 1768 the same; in 1778 a total of nine Mennonites, presumably two families. In 1832 only four Mennonites are named. (Chr. Neff, "Quellen zur Gesch. der Menn. in der Kurpfalz," manuscript; *ML* I, 496 f.)   E.H.C.

Dyck (Dueck, Dück, Dick, Dieck, von Dyck, van Dyck, von Dick, van den Dyck), a Mennonite family of Dutch descent in the Flemish congregations of West Prussia, first mentioned in 1592. 119 families of this name were listed in West Prussia (without Danzig) in 1776, 492 persons in 1910, 385 persons (with Elbing) in 1935. Members of these families moved to Russia and America. Among the better-known European members of the family were Gerhard Dück or Dyck, elder of the Chortitza congregation from 1855, delegate to St. Petersburg 1871; Jacob Dieck or von Dieck, first elder of the Heubuden (West Prussia) congregation, 1728-48; and Jacob Dyck, elder of the Chortitza congregation, whose pastoral letters written in 1846-47 were published in 1900 by the *Mennonitische Rundschau* and separately. American members of the family include the following number of ministers: 21 M.B., 4 Kleine Gemeinde, 2 E.M.B., 24 G.C.M., 7 Old Colony, and 6 in Paraguay.   G.R.

Dyck, David, was an elder and pioneer leader of the Mennonite Brethren Church, born at Chortitza, South Russia, Jan. 25, 1846. His educational opportunities were limited; yet he procured a remarkably wide range of knowledge through independent study. In September 1867 he married Helena Rempel. To them 15 children were born. In the spring of 1873 he was converted and joined the M.B. Church. He immediately had a strong desire to enter Christian service and became active as a colporteur.

In 1876 he emigrated to America, coming first to Marion Co., Kan. In 1877 he went to the new Mennonite Brethren settlement of Woodson Co., Kan., where he lived seven years. Here he was soon elected minister and a little later elder of the church. He attended Rochester Theological Seminary for a **short** time. In 1884 he took charge of the church at Lehigh, Kan., where he ministered six years, and was ordained elder in 1890. In 1892 he went to Kirk, Col., where he served as elder of the M.B. Church for three years.

When the Mennonite Brethren Church began to develop in Manitoba, the conference appointed Dyck to take charge of the work at Winkler. During his ministry of eleven years a strong congregation developed. As new settlements were made in Saskatchewan, Dyck moved there and continued a very active ministry in the churches of Borden, Bruderfeld, and Waldheim. He was also much interested in mission work in the Russian settlements of that vicinity, helping at the stations Petrofka and Eagle Creek.

David Dyck was a most active worker and leader of the M.B. Conference. The early yearbooks mention him 17 times as engaged in itinerant evangelism. For many years he served on the Board of Foreign Missions. He was the first moderator of the Canadian District Conference and filled this office for 13 years. After a fruitful ministry of 53 years, he died at Waldheim, Sask., Jan. 6, 1933, and was buried at the Bruderfeld cemetery.   J.H.L.

Dyck, Gerhard G., was born in the Chortitza community of South Russia, either in Rosenthal or in Nieder-Chortitz, on June 4, 1809, chosen to the ministry in 1848, and to the office of elder March 29, 1855. He was ordained by Jakob Braun of Bergthal (Mariupol). He died May 11, 1887. He resigned from his duties in 1885 on account of the infirmities of old age. His term of service saw the Crimean War, the Mennonite alternative civilian public service, economic and religious growth, development of the school system, and the establishment of several daughter colonies. Since daughter colonies were under the care of the elder of the mother settlement, the intervening distance caused some difficulty, in view of the difficulties of traveling in those days in Russia.

When compulsory military service threatened the Mennonites of Russia, he was one of the delegates who made several trips (1871, Feb. 26, 1873, and autumn 1873) to St. Petersburg to request permission to have Mennonite young men perform some alternative service; this was a strenuous task for the aged elder.   B.J.S.

Dyck, Isaak, elder of Chortitza Mennonite Church, son of Elder Gerhard Dyck (*q.v.*), b. Dec. 9, 1847, Chortitza, Russia, d. in the same place, Aug. 24, 1929. He attended elementary and secondary schools at Chortitza, married Margaretha Hamm (June 28, 1870), taught at Fürstenland settlement 1873-76, and was called into the ministry in 1876. From 1882 to 1888 he was minister and leader of the Anadol Forestry Camp (*q.v.*) where Mennonite boys did their alternative service. In 1888 he returned to Chortitza where he was elected elder in 1896 to succeed H. Epp (*q.v.*). He was a minister for 53 years and an elder for 26 years. He served several times as president of the Allgemeine Bundeskonferenz. His motto was *Bete und arbeite.*

For many years Dyck was the president of the committee which maintained and supervised forestry camps and president of the board of the Chortitza Zentralschule and Mädchenschule. Repeatedly he was delegated to negotiate with the government of St. Petersburg regarding the Mennonites. His sound judgment and vision usually assured him success. During the Revolution and civil war following World War I, he felt that a younger person should shoulder the task and responsibilities. Thus he ordained and introduced Peter Neufeld (q.v.) as his successor in the office of elder in 1922. His wife followed him in death in 1931. Mrs. J. P. Klassen of Bluffton, Ohio, Mrs. Franz Epp of Hanley, Sask., and Mrs. Peter Klassen of Hanley, Sask., are daughters of the Dycks. Gerhard Dyck, a son, was a minister at Hague, Sask. The other children have died or remained in Russia.† C.K.

A. Töws, *Mennonitische Märtyrer* (Abbotsford, 1949) 380 ff.

Dyck (Dyk), **Jakob,** was elder of the Chortitza Mennonite Church in Russia. He was born in Neuendorf, June 5, 1779, and chosen elder in 1812. In 1851 Fr. Wiens was chosen as coelder but he died in 1853 without having served in the office. Jakob Dyck died Oct. 18, 1854.

His pastoral letters written in Neuosterwick to Isaak Penner, a teacher in Rosengart (dated 1846-47), bear eloquent testimony to his faithfulness as a shepherd. He states: "The repentant sinner receives the justification of Jesus through grace without the merit of works (Rom. 3:24). A thorough conversion must be followed by a life that demonstrates who dwells within us" (Friesen, 104). "Without Him I am a doomed sinner, who errs and falls but whatever good I want and do is done through my Lord Jesus" (Friesen, 106). Friesen refers to these letters as crowning evidence that spiritual life was not extinct in the Mennonite congregations at that time and that this should be kept in mind when the origin of the M.B. Church of Chortitza is considered. B.J.S.

D. H. Epp, *Die Chortitzer Mennoniten* (Odessa, 1889) 104 ff.; Friesen, *Brüderschaft*, 102-6, 700; *Menn. Auslese* (A. Dyck), No. 1, pp. 7-9.

Dyck, Jakob, was elder of the Chortitza Mennonite Church, South Russia. He was born Nov. 29, 1813, chosen to the ministry in 1844 (probably on June 1), ordained elder in 1854, and died March 5, 1855. B.J.S.

Dyck, Jakob J., b. Dec. 7, 1890, in the Crimea, South Russia, to Jacob J. and Sara (Reimer) Dyck, who owned a large ranch. He was the fifth in a family of nine children. He completed his secondary education in the Crimea and then went to Ilmenau, Germany, to study engineering, and worked for some time as an engineer in Berlin. Just before World War I he returned to Russia and in 1914 entered the medical service (*Sanitätsdienst*) in Moscow. On Aug. 26, 1916, he was married to Tina Fehderau of Neu-Halbstadt. To this union one son was born, who died in infancy.

Jacob J. Dyck was converted at the age of 17 under the preaching of Johann Warns, and was received into the Mennonite Brethren Church at Rückenau, Molotschna. Immediately he manifested a special interest in the salvation of his fellow men, and distinguished himself by his leadership in fostering Christian organizations among the men during the war. Upon his release from the medical service he devoted his talents to evangelism in tent-missions, preaching the Gospel and traveling from village to village with his colaborers until he and his party were seized while conducting evangelistic meetings by Machno bandits in the village of Eichenfeld, Yazekovo settlement, and murdered on Oct. 26, 1919. The former Mrs. Jakob J. Dyck now lives in Kitchener, Ont. (1950). A.A.T.

A. A. Töws, *Mennonitische Märtyrer* (Abbotsford, B.C., 1949) 130-34; A. Kroeker, *Bilder aus Soviet-Russland* (Hillsboro, 1922) 18-19.

Dyck, Johannes Dietrich, b. Dec. 5, 1826, in Poppau, West Prussia; d. Nov. 11, 1898, in Fresenheim, Am Trakt, Samara, Russia. At the age of 12 he was apprenticed to a grocery and dry-goods merchant. In 1844 he was baptized and received into the Ellerwald (W. Prussia) Mennonite Church by Elder Jacob Kroeker. He continued in the grocery business at Marienburg and Caldove until 1847. In August 1848 he left for the United States, promising his fiancee, Helene Janzen of Gross Lesewitz, that he would return in two or three years. Upon arrival in America he spent the first year in Chicago and in Wisconsin, from where he went to the gold mines of California early in 1850. On his return trip to the East, probably in 1853, he was attacked by Indians and lost all his possessions, whereupon he returned to the gold mines. In 1858 he came back to Prussia, and was married to Helene Janzen. Because her relatives had moved to Russia and because of increasing militarization, they left for Russia in 1859, settling at Fresenheim. He soon proved to be a successful farmer. In 1865 he was elected Oberschulze (mayor) of the Trakt settlement, which office he held for 18 years. He was active in many community affairs and strongly promoted the interests of the settlements. For this leadership he received two medals from the Russian government, engraved "For Faithful Service," and the third time a ribbon bearing the inscription "For Service to the Czar and the Fatherland." C.J.D.

The diaries of Johannes Dietrich Dyck, 2 vols. of 400 pages each; Johannes J. Dyck, "Einiges aus einem Lebenslauf," *Der Herold*, Oct. 14, 1937, and Oct. 21, 1937; Cornelius J. Dyck, "In the California Gold Rush," *Menn. Life* XI (January 1956) 25-28; see also *Menn. Life* XI (April 1956) 88.

Dyck, Peter (1821-85), the first elder of the Zion Mennonite Church of Elbing, Kan., was born in Klein Montau, near Marienburg, West Prussia, on April 3, 1821. On July 12, 1849, he was married to Agathe Entz. They had five children, Catharine, Agathe, Peter, Johannes, and David. Peter Dyck served the Ladekopp Mennonite Church in West Prussia as minister until his emigration in 1876. In May 1869 he and four other men visited friends and relatives in Russia. In 1870 various interested families and churches commissioned him to visit Russia again, this time to determine the possibilities of settlement there. He was accompanied by Wilhelm Ewert of Thorn and Abraham Regier. Peter Dyck again visited the various settlements and went to much trouble to study the farming possibilities. He apparently preferred South Russia as a future location for the Prussian Mennonites, and he even entered into negotiations with government to this effect. It is of interest to note that Cornelius Janzen (*q.v.*) strongly urged him to investigate America before deciding in favor of Russia. In 1876 Peter Dyck and his family came to Kansas with many other Prussian Mennonites, and settled several miles south of Peabody, Kan. He served the Emmaus church as minister until 1883, at which time he was instrumental in organizing the Zion Mennonite Church at Elbing. He was one of 14 charter members. In May 1881 he left Peabody for a visit to his former home in Prussia, in July went on to Russia, returning to Kansas in September 1881.

The record clearly indicated that Dyck loved the ministry and worked hard to be a good shepherd. He had keen insight and good interest in many things. His records reveal minute descriptions of churches, farming methods, and spiritual conditions as he found them in Russia and elsewhere during his travels. He was respected and loved as a community and church leader.   C.J.P.

Dyck, Wilhelm I., an elder in the M.B. Church, b. Feb. 4, 1854, at Rosental, South Russia. Upon the early death of his parents he was brought up by Gerhard Krahn of Neuenburg. He completed the Zentralschule at Chortitza. He was drawn into public work and served as secretary treasurer in the municipal office with such ability that he was decorated by the czar with a medal for meritorious service. He was known as always showing sympathy with the oppressed and needy, deciding for what he thought right and equitable. Soon he came to be used as mediator between the church and the then generally suspicious Russian government. Together with Elder D. Schellenberg he obtained full legal recognition for the M.B. Church in Russia.

Elder Dyck also prospered in a material way, becoming owner and director of a large milling concern; but neither business nor municipal duties ever kept him from manifesting a deep interest in the work of the church and the salvation of souls. In 1890 he gave up his municipal duties and devoted himself largely to the ministry, pioneering in many areas, including travel to Poland, Siberia, Bulgaria, Turkestan, the Terek, and Orenburg, ministering also to the native Russians, which was contrary to the wish of the ruling powers.

He was married to Maria M. Ridiger in 1877, who died in 1896. About a year after, he was married to Emilie Petker. In 1907 he visited the churches in America, but returned to his native Russia, where he was ordained elder in 1914.

World War I together with the Russian Revolution cost him the loss of his business and all his property, including his home. He emigrated to Canada in 1924, where he continued his spiritual ministry until shortly before his death in 1931.   C.A.DeF.

Dyserinck (also Dyselinck), a Dutch Mennonite family, originally from Flanders, Belgium. Cornelis

Dyserinck, b. at Brugge, Belgium, in 1608, left the Roman Catholic Church and emigrated to Aardenburg (*q.v.*), Dutch province of Zeeland, in 1637; in 1639 he was baptized here (*DB* 1877, 7-8) and was a strong pillar of the congregation until his death, April 30, 1688. He was a deacon for many years, and after 1681 he seems also to have been a preacher (*DB* 1884, 40). After the middle of the 18th century the Dyserinck family moved from Aardenburg to Haarlem, where they were engaged in several kinds of business and industry. During the 18th century a wing of this family was living at Middelburg.

A prominent member of this family was Hendrik Dyserinck, b. 1811 at Haarlem, d. 1906, who after a successful military career became a Dutch state Minister of the Navy, 1888-91 (*N.N.B.Wb.* IV, 550-51). He was a brother of the Mennonite minister Johannes Dyserinck (*q.v.*). (*Ned. Patriciaat* II, 1911, 116-21.)   vDZ.

Dyserinck, Johannes, a Dutch Mennonite minister, b. March 12, 1835, at Haarlem, d. Sept. 26, 1912, was at first a painter, but then decided to devote himself to study, studied at Amsterdam and Leiden, especially under the professors Hoekstra, de Hoop Scheffer, and Kuenen. His first call to preach came from Helder and Huisduinen in 1861. At the request of the Minister of War, L. G. Brocx, he composed a volume of *Godsdienstige Overdenkingen en Gebeden* (Devotional Meditations and Prayers) for use in religious services on board warships. In September 1879 he accepted the pastorate of Vlissingen, remaining there until July 1884, when he transferred to Rotterdam. He remained here until his retirement in December 1901. Until May 1912 he lived at The Hague, then moved to Baarn, where he died on Sept. 26, 1912.

Dyserinck was the most versatile of the Dutch Mennonites of the 19th century, without doubt publishing more books than any other. As a distinguished scholar of Hebrew he made a new translation of the Psalms, which won him an honorary doctor's title, and translations of some Apocryphal and Talmudic writings. Well at home in the fine arts, on which he wrote several studies, he showed that Rembrandt's "Night Watch" was disfigured in that pieces of canvas were cut off. In literature and history few surpassed him in learning; he wrote comprehensive biographies of several novelists and poets (Beets, Bellamy, Bosboom Toussaint, Wolff and Deken, Haverschmidt, Winkler Prins are among them). Among his articles in periodical literature, mention should be made of "Het gebed voor de zitting van de gemeenteraad van Amsterdam" (1887) and "Het vraagstuk der onsterfelijkheid" (1901). In addition, he wrote a collection of sermons, *Laatste Godsdienstige Overdenkingen* (1908). On Mennonite history he published two treatises of particular importance in the *Gids:* "De Vrijstelling van den eed voor de Doopsgezinden" (1882) and "De Weerloosheid volgens de Doopsgezinden" (1890). He was awarded many honors. The king bestowed on him the Order of the Lion.

The university of Leiden conferred an honorary doctor's degree upon him. In addition he was a member of a number of learned societies.

Of his other writings several deserve mention: (1) *Waarop moet volgens Paulus, de Christen zijn hoop der zaligheid bouwen?* (Helder, 1864); (2) *Verscheidenheden* (Haarlem, 1867); (3) *De Spreuken van Jezus, den zoon van Sirach* (translation from the Hebrew, Haarlem, 1870); (4) *Vrede zij in uwe vesting. Een toepasselijk woord ter wijding van het tweede eeuwfeest van Aardenburgs verdediging, 1672* (with pictures of the Mennonites, A.M. van Eeghen and H. van Eeghen, Haarlem, 1872); (5) *Bloemlezing uit de Spreuken van Jezus Sirach* (1872); (6) *Sparsa. Verzameling van verstrooide opstellen en kleine geschriften* (Amsterdam, 1882);

(7) *Stillen in den lande* (The Hague, 1895); (8) *Het recht der waarheid tegenover den Staat. Bijdrage tot de eedsvraag* (Amsterdam, 1902).

K.V.

DB passim, especially 1912, 217-20; *Levensberichten v.d. Maatsch. v. Ned. Lett.* 1912-13, 1-6; *De Zondagsbode* 1912, 194, 195; *Biogr. Wb.* II, 687-91; *ML* I, 497.

Dyurmen (Schottenruh), a Mennonite village in Crimea, district of Perekop, volost of Bohemka, founded in 1876, contained 1,600 acres and in 1920 had a population of 120. (*ML* I, 456.)

Dzhaga-Shaich-Eli, a Mennonite village on the Crimean peninsula, Feodosiya district, founded in 1886, which had in 1913 a population of 95 on an area of 3,000 acres.

E

Eagle Grove, Iowa, the post-office address of an Amish Mennonite community (1893-1910), now extinct, in Wright County (*q.v.*). Correspondence in the church papers from this congregation came generally from Eagle Grove or Clarion.　M.G.

Eash: see **Esch** family.

East Aldergrove Mennonite Brethren Church, located near Abbotsford, British Columbia, was organized on June 13, 1947, by a group of 34 families because the North Abbotsford church, to which they belonged, was overcrowded. At that time the membership was 100; by 1953 it had increased to 207. Its leader in 1953 was George P. Warkentin, who had served from the beginning.　G.P.W.

East Bend Mennonite Church (MC), located near Fisher, Champaign Co., Ill., was largely developed in the "east bend" of the Sangamon River by settlers from Dillon Creek, Goodfield, Hopedale, and other Amish Mennonite communities in Illinois. The first Amish Mennonite settler in Champaign County was Charles Stormer, who came in 1882. Other early settlers were August Ingold (1883), Jacob Heiser (1887), Andrew Birky (1888), and Peter Zehr (1889). Sunday school was begun in the Dixon schoolhouse near by in the spring of 1889, and the next year a congregation was organized under the leadership of Peter Zehr, which for a time rented the Houstonville Methodist church. In 1895 the East Bend congregation dedicated a new frame church. In 1907 this building was wrecked by a tornado and was replaced by a larger frame church, 40 x 60 ft., seating 300, which was remodeled in 1919. In 1948 a new brick church, 50 x 80 ft., seating 750, was built adjoining the old structure, now in brick veneer.

The ministers who have served this congregation are Peter Zehr 1889- (ordained bishop in 1893), Daniel Grieser 1890-1923, Joseph Baecher 1893-1931, George Gingerich 1893-1907, Samuel S. Zehr (a deacon who preached when an English sermon was required) 1906- , Joseph A. Heiser 1917-52 (ordained bishop in 1921), Harold Zehr 1931- , Dr. George Troyer (retired missionary) 1937-44, Howard Zehr 1953- , bishop and pastor.

The East Bend congregation has through its Christian Workers' Band sponsored a number of extension projects. In 1936 services were begun in the home of a member living in Arthur. In 1940 this work was organized as an independent congregation with 59 members, and an extension Sunday school was opened in Dewey. Ivan Birkey served the Dewey group as acting pastor for a number of years. In April 1946 the A.M.E. Colored Church was reopened by the East Bend congregation, and services are held there each Sunday afternoon. In 1948 the East Bend congregation began to sponsor services at Lake City, Ill., and Harold Oyer, a minister of the Morton congregation, was asked to move to that community to serve it. The East Bend

congregation was a member of the Western District Amish Mennonite Conference, which merged in 1921 with the Illinois Conference of the Mennonite Church. In 1951 a group of about 130 left the East Bend Church and formed the Gibson City Bible Church, with J. A. Heiser as pastor. The 1954 membership of East Bend was 350.　H.Z.

H. F. Weber, *Centennial Hist. of the Menn. of Illinois 1829-1929* (Scottdale, 1931); E. W. Heiser, *Sixty Years with East Bend 1889-1949* (Fisher, 1949).

East Brewton, Escambia Co., Ala., is a mission center (MC) established by the Itinerant Evangelizing Committee of the Lancaster Conference. John R. Lehman was ordained for this work in 1944, J. Wilbur Martin in 1945, and Elam B. Hollinger in 1947. The work was started by short-term social service workers from the north in numerous summer Bible schools and in evangelism in Alabama and Florida. In 1954 Edgar S. Denlinger was in charge of the congregation of eight members.
　　　　　　　　　　　　　　　　　　I.D.L.

East Cardston Hutterite Bruderhof near Cardston, Alberta, was founded in 1918 by members of the Hopson (Mont.) Bruderhof. Their preachers are David Hofer, chosen by the Jamesville (S.D.) Bruderhof in 1911, and Joseph Hofer and Jakob Hofer, chosen in East Cardston in 1927 and 1933. In 1947 the Bruderhof numbered 76 souls with 28 baptized members.　D.D.

East Chestnut Street Mennonite Church (MC), a member of the Lancaster Conference, is located at East Chestnut and Sherman streets, Lancaster, Pa. The first meetinghouse was built on this site in 1879, services having previously been held in a rented building on Charlotte Street. This meetinghouse was replaced in 1906 by the present larger brick church. The trustees of the first meetinghouse, members of adjoining country churches, took their turns in caring for the afternoon services. A Sunday school was opened in 1894 with Benjamin F. Herr and David Lantz as superintendents. On Dec. 11, 1904, John H. Mosemann was ordained to the ministry, and in 1926 to the office of bishop. On June 30, 1907, David H. Mosemann was ordained to the ministry. For years the church has been a young people's center every second Sunday night. Numerous all-day meetings are also held here. The ministers in 1955 were Noah G. Good, Jacob E. Brubaker, and Mylin Shenk. Services are held twice each Sunday, with a Sunday school, a summer Bible school, and a weekday Bible school each fall.

The congregation has been directly or indirectly the mother of a number of mission congregations in and near the city of Lancaster, among them being Vine Street (*q.v.*), North End, Rossmere, South Christian Street, Laurel and Freemont Streets, Lyndon. It has also suffered many losses by withdrawals. A considerable number of the present Calvary Bible Church (independent) come from East Chestnut Street, while a block of members leaving in

1952 organized the Neffsville Mennonite Church under the Ohio and Eastern Mennonite Conference. Earlier a number had left to share in the organization of the Monterey Mennonite Church under the same conference, near Bird-in-Hand, Pa. As a result of these vicissitudes, the congregation has declined severely in membership (1955, 200). I.D.L.

East Chilliwack (B.C.) *Bible School* (MB) was established Oct. 20, 1947, with 56 students and G. Thielmann as principal, by the East Chilliwack M.B. Church, which had purchased a former store building for this purpose. At first a 5-month school with a 3-year curriculum, it was changed in 1955 to an 8-month school with a 2-year curriculum. By 1955 a total of 303 students had attended the school. G. Thielmann was still serving as principal in 1955-56, with 33 students enrolled. H.S.B.

G. Thielmann, "East Chilliwack Bibelschule," *Konferenz-Jugendblatt* XI (1955) Nov.-Dec., 17 f.

East Chilliwack (B.C.) Mennonite Brethren Church, a member of the Canadian Conference, was organized on Jan. 6, 1945, under the leadership of N. A. Rempel, with a membership of 82. The services were held in a newly built Sunday-school house. Because of the influx of Mennonites, this place was soon overfilled and a second group, the Chilliwack M.B. Church, was organized in the city. The 1953 membership of East Chilliwack was 236; the leader was Gerhard Thielmann. There were in addition seven ordained ministers in the congregation. N.A.R.

East Chilliwack (B.C.) United Mennonite Church (GCM), formerly known as the Westheimer Mennonite Church of Chilliwack, located 3½ miles southeast of Chilliwack, was organized in 1945, the first members having arrived in the previous year. In 1947-48 a school was remodeled to serve as a church. The 1953 membership of 162 has its background largely in the Russian Mennonite immigrations since the 1920's. Abram J. Peters was the minister in 1953. C.G.T.

East Fairview Mennonite Church (MC), northeast of Chappell, Deuel Co., Neb., since 1953 called the Chappell Mennonite Church, was founded by families who had previously moved from Holmes Co., Ohio, to Seward Co., Neb. In 1883 Abraham Stutzman, who had in the previous year filed claim to a homestead in that section, settled here together with five other families. Sunday school was held from the beginning. In 1890 a meetinghouse was built 6 miles northeast of Chappell and a church organized. N. C. Roth was ordained to the ministry by Joseph Birky of Tiskilwa, Ill. The membership in 1954 was 63, about 75 per cent of whom live either in Chappell or in Julesburg, Col., 15 miles distant. The ministers in 1954 were John Roth and Fred Gingerich. The congregation is a member of the Iowa-Nebraska Conference. F.Gɪ.

East Fairview Mennonite Church (MC), located west of Milford, Seward Co., Neb., is a member of the Iowa-Nebraska Conference. The first communion service was held in 1875, with eleven members,

and the first meetinghouse was built in 1878 and dedicated with a membership of 50. The 1954 membership was 440. Bishops who served this congregation were Joseph Schlegel, N. E. Roth, P. R. Kennel, and J. E. Zimmerman; ministers were P. P. Hershberger, Joseph Gasho, Joseph Rediger, Jacob Stauffer, William Schlegel, and George S. Miller. In 1954 the ministers were Ammon Miller and Oliver Roth, with W. R. Eicher serving as bishop. A.M.M.

East Friesland (*Ostfriesland*), Germany, made a principality on April 22, 1654, became Prussian in 1744, Dutch 1807, French 1810, a part of Hannover in 1815, and Prussian again in 1866. The government seat is located at Aurich. East Friesland has played a significant role in the history of the Anabaptist-Mennonite movement in Northwest Europe.

The East Frisian historian Eggerick Beningha reports in his *Chronyk* (p. 652) that Anabaptists appeared in East Friesland in 1528 for the first time. This statement has been repeated many times, but specific information about who these Anabaptists were and where they appeared is lacking. Count Enno wrote to Philip of Hesse in 1530 that there had been unbaptized children in East Friesland for five years (Cornelius, *Anteil Ostfrieslands,* p. 20), and *Gründlicher warhafftiger Bericht* (p. 21) speaks of followers of Müntzer who found refuge in East Friesland. On Jan. 19, 1530, before Melchior Hofmann baptized in Emden, the counts Enno and Johann published the Edict of Speyer banning all Anabaptists from their territory. The first *Kirchenordnung* presented in 1529 strongly emphasized infant baptism.

As long as specific information as to sources, contents, and proponents of these views is lacking, it is questionable whether they can be called Anabaptist. Warnings against Anabaptism may simply be an echo from Wittenberg or may refer to views held by Carlstadt, who indeed had followers in East Friesland. There is no record available to prove that believers' baptism was practiced in East Friesland prior to the coming of Melchior Hofmann from Strasbourg in 1530, where he had joined the Anabaptists. Everything preceding this must be considered as premonitory of coming Anabaptism. On the other hand, Melchior Hofmann did not bring much that was new to East Friesland and the Low Countries except the seal of the Covenant, believers' baptism.

The success of Hofmann and the rapid spread of the early Anabaptist movement in East Friesland, its survival and later cultural contribution are due to factors unique to the country and its Reformatory movement in general. Culturally and politically it had close ties with the provinces of the Low Countries, particularly Groningen. The Brethren of the Common Life and Humanism (Georg Aportanus, Johann Wessel Gansfoort, Wilhelm Gnapheus) also paved the way for the Reformation. Friesland was ready to accept the light coming from Wittenberg, was in touch with Strasbourg and Zürich, and developed a Sacramentist movement similar to that in Holland, but was in all matters quite independent in accordance with the Frisian national characteristic. The chief promoters of the Reformation here were

Edzard I (*q.v.*, 1491-1528), Ulrich van Dornum (*q.v.*), and Hicco van Oldersum. Aportanus of Zwolle, the tutor of Edzard's three sons, publicly preached "the new Gospel" in the Grosse Kirche of Emden, and Ulrich van Dornum sponsored a Catholic-Evangelical disputation at Oldersum in 1526, sheltered Carlstadt and Melchior Hofmann in 1529 (both dedicated books to him and he had his printed in Wittenberg), and was in touch with Sebastian Franck. This indicates somewhat the scope and nature of the original Reformatory movement in East Friesland. One of the most significant factors, however, of the later development was the great influx of Dutch refugees in the days of the Inquisition. Among them was Hinne Rode, who introduced the Reformation in Norden. Until the death of Edzard I the Reformatory movement of East Friesland showed little of the characteristics of "Lutheranism" and "Zwinglianism," but was rather of a Sacramentist nature, to Luther's great disgust. It was in this atmosphere that Carlstadt, Hofmann, and Franck found a hearing. In these crucial days young Enno II (leaning toward Lutheranism) saw the Spiritualist-Sacramentist forces come to the foreground which likely caused him to publish the Edict of Speyer on Jan. 19, 1530. On March 25, 1530, he reported to Philip of Hesse that his ministers held Sacramentist views and denied its sacramental character; some advocated baptism at the age of 33, not having had their children baptized for the last five years (Cornelius, 58).

Thus when Melchior Hofmann (*q.v.*) appeared in East Friesland in May 1530, this time coming as an Anabaptist evangelist, he found the soil well prepared. Contrary to his first visit he could now appear publicly. Even the doors of the Grosse Kirche of Emden were opened to him and he is said to have baptized some 300 persons there, both "burgher and peasant, lord and servant." This bold act can be explained only by the assumption that he had followers in leading circles, including the ministry (Kochs, *Reformation* III, 74). That Count Enno was moved to tears by Hofmann's deliberations is likely a fable. Whether Hofmann voluntarily left East Friesland or was compelled to do so is not definitely known; in any event he went to Strasbourg in October, unfortunately leaving no able leader behind.

This was the origin not only of the Anabaptist movement in East Friesland but in Northwest Europe in general. From here it spread in all directions and to this place Anabaptist refugees returned for protection in spite of mandates issued against them. Although they did not achieve numbers and strength to compete successfully with the Lutherans and Zwinglians, they greatly benefited from the rivalry between them. From Emden Jan Volkertszoon Trypmaker took the message to the Low Countries. Thousands of Anabaptist refugees from Antwerp to Friesland, among whom were Menno Simons, Dirk Philips, Leenaert Bouwens, and Hans de Ries, and even extreme mystics like David Joris and Hendrik Niclaes, found a haven there.

In 1534-35 Enno II issued warnings against the Melchiorites, which apparently had little effect. After his death his widow, Anna of Oldenburg (1540-62), called on John a Lasco to complete the Reformation and organize the church. Under pressure of the imperial government Anna issued decrees against the Anabaptists which through the mediation of a Lasco were applied primarily against David Joris and his following. With Menno Simons he had a public discussion in January 1544, hoping to win him. During the same year Menno left East Friesland and the following year Countess Anna stated that those "Mennisten" who were not willing to accept the instruction of her ministers were to leave the country.

The extent of the movement during the 16th century can be estimated to some degree by the number of individuals baptized by Leenaert Bouwens, who kept a record for the years 1551-82, which lists over 600 persons baptized in East Friesland, over 400 of whom were living in Emden and vicinity. It is likely that many of them were the second generation of refugees from the Netherlands. If the other elders mentioned were only partly as successful, the total number of Anabaptists of East Friesland during the 16th century could easily have been several thousand. The fact that the ministers and church councils of the Reformation churches were so alarmed about the spread of the Mennonites is also an indication that they must have been numerous. In addition to those baptized in Friesland the Dutch Anabaptists continued to pour in throughout the 16th century. It is interesting to note that there was little change in the location of the Mennonites during the 16th century as found in Leenaert Bouwens' list of baptismal candidates and those lists compiled by the government to solicit payment (*Schutzgeld*) during the 17th century. They were living in Leer, along the Ems River, in Emden, in the Greetmer Amt between Emden and Norden, and in Norden and the rural area north of it. It is likely that their services as experts in draining the land were appreciated and for generations they were welcome renters on the estates of the nobility. Thus the Mennonites were mostly located in the western part of East Friesland including the area of Aurich. However, at least one settlement of Mennonites was already located in the east on the estates of Freitag at Gödens near Neustadt in the days of Leenaert Bouwens, where he baptized 20 persons.

Today there is hardly a Mennonite located on a farm. Not only are they mostly urban, but their number has shrunk considerably (the total, including children, is about 500). No scholarly research has been made about the socio-economic changes and contributions of the East Friesland Mennonites similar to those of Hamburg and Crefeld, with the exception of the part played by the Mennonites in the linen industry of Leer. It can be assumed that the constant pressure, restrictions, and high payments (*Schutzgeld*) which were extracted from them for centuries and the decrease in vigor and vision within their ranks caused many to escape the stigma by joining the Reformed and Lutheran churches to acquire equality and full citizenship. The cultural and economic contributions of a number of prosperous families in Emden, Norden, and Leer were outstanding and have been sketched by Abram Fast (*Die Kulturleistungen*).

The manifold divisions among the Mennonites of the Low Countries during the 16th century were also transplanted to East Friesland, including the Flemish, the Old Flemish (Ukowallists), the Frisians, and the Waterlanders. During the 17th century the lists referred to above, however, speak only of two groups—the Mennonites and the Ukowallists. Some of the significant Anabaptist meetings of elders during the 16th century, at which far-reaching decisions were made, were held at Emden. In 1547 nearly all elders of the Low Countries met there to discuss matters pertaining to discipline, and in 1568 the Waterlanders met there to draw up 16 articles pertaining to their congregations and ministers. In 1578 the Flemish and Frisians met at Emden to discuss matters pertaining to a pending union. Nikolaas Biestkens van Diest, the well-known Mennonite publisher, here produced Bibles, New Testaments, and the songbook *Het Offer des Heeren,* through which he greatly helped to spread the movement. Some of the numerous disputations between the Anabaptists and the churches of the Reformation took place in East Friesland. In 1544 Menno and a Lasco held their discussion in Emden. In 1556 there was a similar discussion between the Mennonites and their opponents at Norden and in 1578 the better known disputation of Feb. 27-May 17 took place at Emden. In addition to John a Lasco (*q.v.*), Gellius Faber (*q.v.*), Marten Micron (*q.v.*), Menso Alting (*q.v.*), all of whom tried to "win" the Mennonites, although not so vehemently as Luther and his co-workers, there were the following less known representatives: Georg Aportanus (Emden), Hermanus Aquilomontanus (Oldersum) (whose letters to Heinrich Bullinger throw significant light on the early development of the Anabaptist movement and have not yet been made use of), Johann Oldeguil (Emden), Gerhardus Nikolai (*q.v.,* Norden), and Bernhardus Buwo (*q.v.,* Eilsum). Nikolai translated Bullinger's *Adversus anabaptistas* and Buwo published a *Dialogus . . .* (1563) against the Anabaptists, which is, considering the age, exceptionally tolerant. Ubbo Emmius (*q.v.*) wrote against David Joris. The Reformers of Bremen and Lüneburg, i.e., Bugenhagen and Luther and their followers, and the Strasbourg Reformers, i.e., Bucer and Capito, as well as Zwingli, not to speak of the Catholic and imperial forces, tried to shape or influence the future of the Reformation in East Friesland. Had it not been for Edzard I, who refused to follow the example of many Reformation-minded rulers of his day, i.e., to reform his country from above (*cujus regio, ejus religio*), and who let the Reformation take its own course in East Friesland by giving it gentle and wise direction, its fate would have been different. Because of this independent attitude East Friesland became the haven of the greatest variety of factions who had fled from many places because of their convictions. Even a survivor of the Münsterite kingdom, Hermann Krechting (*q.v.*), became a respected citizen in Neustadt-Gödens.

The question as to what percentage of the Reformation-minded forces and the Anabaptists came from the Low Countries and other places has not been investigated. Neither is it known to what an extent East Friesland served as a temporary shelter whence they proceeded to other places. That this was the case is established. Many Anabaptists must have returned to the Netherlands after the Catholic authorities had been overthrown. Others had already gone east to Schleswig-Holstein, among them Menno, and to the Vistula region. How long this process continued and the relationship between the homeland and the daughter settlements has not been studied. The culture and language, particularly in worship, in the "church of strangers" remained Dutch until the middle of the 19th century. However, little was published after the 16th century. The congregations obtained their ministers from Holland and were members of the various Dutch Mennonite organizations, including the A.D.S., of which they are still members. Since World War I the remaining congregations—Emden, Leer, and Norden—are being served by one German minister. Among the outstanding leaders of the early days were Menno Simons, Dirk Philips, Leenaert Bouwens, Hans de Ries, and Uko Walles, and many others resided and worked here for longer or shorter periods. A list of elders and preachers of the Old Flemish wing from 1640 to 1750 (*DB* 1879, 7-8) names 7 for Emden, 5 for Leer, 7 for Neustadt-Gödens, 3 for Norden, and 1 for Oldersum. The Oldersum congregation must have died out soon after this report; the Neustadt-Gödens congregation was discontinued during the 19th century.

The successors of Edzard I, with the exception of Anna van Oldenburg (*q.v.*), 1540-62, did not all follow the example of their great ancestor regarding the Reformation and basic principles of tolerance. Edzard II (*q.v.*), 1562-99, under whom the Emden Disputation of 1578 took place, and Enno III (*q.v.*), 1599-1625, issued severe edicts against the Mennonites. Rudolf Christian, 1625-28, issued a *Schutzbrief* (guarantee of protection) for the Mennonites on May 26, 1626, granting them limited religious freedom for the payment of a certain amount per family, thereby setting the pattern for his successors until East Friesland became Prussian in 1744. At this time the Mennonite church at Emden was exempted from all special payments. Step by step the congregations had to struggle to gain full liberty and equality as citizens and congregations, a status which was not fully attained until the Revolution of 1918. The German constitution of 1919 made provision for complete equality. Meanwhile the principle of nonresistance, not the refusal to swear an oath, had been given up.

Not only did the government extract large sums annually under the pretext of granting an "intolerable" religious group a letter of protection, which was usually issued to "Jews, Mennonites, and Ukowallists," but also the ministers, particularly of the Lutheran church at Norden, joined in the extortion by demanding of the Mennonites taxes for the upkeep of their churches and fees for services such as funerals which they did not conduct. Weary of this situation, the Mennonites of Norden petitioned the government in 1821-22 to be admitted to take part in the public affairs of the city and the country, particularly in view of the fact that though they constituted only 4 per cent of the population, they contributed one eighth of the revenue of the city. This was achieved only through a long struggle. Not until 1892 were they exempted from paying contributions to the state church. (A detailed account of the struggle with the state is to be found in the article "Ostfriesland," ML III, 319-21.)

In modern times (since 1700) there have been only four Mennonite congregations in East Friesland: Emden, Leer, and Norden, which are still in existence, and Neustadt-Goedens, which died out about the mid-19th century (in 1840 it had 10 members). The membership of the three surviving congregations has been recorded as follows: 1888 total 298 (Emden 81, Leer 52, Norden 165); 1940 total 300 (Emden 200, Leer 20, Norden 80); 1954 total 373 (Emden 218, Leer 40, Norden 115). The 1954 figures include some Danzig area refugees. (For additional information on East Friesland see the articles **Aurich, Emden, Leer, Neustadt-Goedens, Norden, Oldersum, Menno Simons, Melchior Hofmann.**)   C.K.

J. P. Müller, *Die Mennoniten in Ostfriesland* I (Emden, 1887); II (*Jahrb.* IV, Emden); idem, "Oorzaken van de vestiging der Doopsgezinden in Oostfriesland," *DB* 1881, 64-77; E. Meiners, *Oostvrieschlandts kerkelyke Geschiedenisse* I and II (Groningen, 1738-39); E. Beninga, *Volledige Chronyk van Oostfrieslant* (Emden, 1723); Ubbo Emmius, *Rerum Frisicarum historia* (1616); H. Reimers, *Ostfriesland bis zum Aussterben seines Fürstenhauses* (Bremen, 1925); C. A. Cornelius, *Der Anteil Ostfrieslands an der Reformation bis zum Jahr 1535* (Münster, 1852); Hagedorn, *Ostfrieslands Handel und Schiffahrt im 16. Jahrhundert* (Berlin, 1910); idem, *Ostfr. Handel und Schiffahrt vom Ausgang des 16. Jh.* (Berlin, 1912); E. Kochs, "Die Anfänge der ostfr. Reformation," in *Jahrb. d. Ges. f. bild. Kunst u. vaterl. Altertümer zu Emden* XIX, 109-273 and XX, 1-125; H. Reimers, *Die Gestaltung der Ref. in Ostfr.* (Aurich, 1917); H. Garrelts, *Die Ref. Ostfr. nach der Darstellung der Lutheraner . . .* (Aurich, 1925); J. ten Doornkaat Koolman, *Kurze Mitteilungen aus d. Gesch. d. Menn.-Gem. in Ostfr. . . . u. d. Norder Gem. . . .* (Norden, 1903); idem, *Mitteilungen aus d. Gesch. d. Menn.-Gem. zu Norden im 19. Jh.* (Norden, 1904); Blaupot t. C., *Groningen, Overijssel en Oost-Friesland* I and II (1842); K. Vos, "De dooplijst van Leenaert Bouwens," *Bijdr. en Mededeel. v. h. Hist. Gen.* XXXVI (1915) 39 ff.; W. I. Leendertz, *Melchior Hoffman* (Haarlem, 1883); C. Krahn, *Menno Simons* (Karlsruhe, 1936); H. Dalton, *Johannes a Lasco* (Utrecht, 1885); Ohling, "Aus den Anfängen der Reformation. Ein Brief des Seb. Franck . . . an die Oldersumer Gemeinde," *Ostfriesland* (Norden, 1954) 111 ff.; W. Hollweg, "Bernhard Buwo . . . ," *Jahrb. d. Ges. f. bild. Kunst u. vaterl. Altertümer zu Emden* XXX (1953) 71 ff.; E. Esselborn, "Die Leinenweberei in Leer," *Jahrb. d. Ges. f. bild. Kunst . . . zu Emden* XXV (1937) 91 ff.; XXVI (1938) 95 ff.; XXVII (1939) 106 ff.; A. Fast, *Die Kulturleistungen der Mennoniten in Ostfriesland* (n.p., 1947); *ML* III, 319-21.

East Goshen Mennonite Church (MC), 2600 East Lincoln Ave., Goshen, Ind., was organized Dec. 6, 1947, and was admitted to the Indiana-Michigan Mennonite Conference on June 2, 1948. A new brick meetinghouse was dedicated Oct. 17, 1949. The congregation began in 1946 as an extension Sunday school of the Goshen College Young People's Christian Association. Its membership in 1954 was 180. The bishop-pastor was Paul M. Miller and the minister Ray Keim.   P.M.M.

East Gwillimbury Mennonite Brethren in Christ Church, Ravenshoe, Ont., now extinct, was served by W. H. Yates in 1948.

East Holbrook Mennonite Church (MC), located near Cheraw, Col., originated when the Mennonites living there met to worship with other denominations in a school building. Eventually, the Mennonites were responsible for most of the services. In 1904 they built a church with John M. Nunemaker as the charter pastor. This building burned down in 1907, and was replaced with the present building.

In 1954 this congregation had 134 members. Richard Birky was the bishop, Aaron Leatherman the minister, and Bert Snyder deacon. The congregation is a member of the South Central Conference. It co-operates with the La Junta congregation in holding quarterly singing programs and annual Sunday-school workers' conferences.   L.C.

East India Company. Under this name there arose in the 17th century several enterprises with special privileges from various European governments for trade with the East Indies. The oldest and most important of these trading companies were founded by the English and the Dutch. The English East India Company received a charter on Dec. 31, 1600, from Queen Elizabeth. The Dutch East India Company was formed in 1602 through the union of several companies founded after 1595. Their field was principally the East Indian islands. In a short time this company became dominant there. In it there were Mennonites at first; but they withdrew when the company became involved in conquest and violence (Cramer, 611).

The council of Bern hoped that it might be able to use the Dutch East India Company in its suppression of the Mennonites. The expulsions previously carried out had not shown the desired results, since the exiles could not take their families with them and therefore frequently returned. By taking them to a distant island the council hoped to make a return impossible. On May 17, 1699, it therefore applied to the company in Amsterdam with the request to take the Mennonites to the East Indies. The Amsterdam company, however, did not comply (Müller, 253).   HEGE.

A. Brons, *Ursprung, Entwicklung und Schicksale der . . . Mennoniten* (Emden, 1912) 195-206; S. Cramer, "Mennoniten," in *HRE* (1902); Müller, *Berner Täufer; ML* III, 321.

East Jordan United Missionary Church, Charlevoix Co., Mich., in 1953 had 35 members, with E. W. Thompson as pastor.

East Petersburg (Pa.) Mennonite Church (MC) is a member of the Lancaster Conference. From 1831 this congregation had a meetinghouse in East Petersburg on the site of the present Brethren church. It was an old log house that had formerly been a union church-schoolhouse, probably built in pre-Revolution days. The membership at that date was but 12-15, although numerous Mennonite families had settled in this area. But by 1867 the group was sufficiently large to build a brick church 40 x 60 ft. on the present location on the north edge of the village; and by 1896 the present church became necessary. This has since been enlarged and remodeled. David B. Huber and Benjamin F. Charles were the first Sunday-school superintendents (1893). In 1954 the membership was 450. The deacon is Wallace M. Hottenstein and the ministers are Frank N. Kreider, his son Irvin Kreider, and James B. Siegrist.

I.D.L.

East Prussia. (1) *The Anabaptists in the Early Years of the Reformation.* East Prussia consists for the most part of the eastern part of the former land of the Teutonic Knights, as it existed for several centuries as the duchy of Prussia, whereas West or Polish Prussia was separated from the Teutonic Knight state in 1466 and assigned to the Polish crown. The last grand master of the Teutonic Order, Albrecht von Hohenzollern, secularized the remainder of the Teutonic Order lands in 1525 and made of them a hereditary duchy under the loose sovereignty of Poland. Thereupon the pope excommunicated him and Charles V outlawed him.

Although Duke Albrecht's decision can be traced to the influence of Luther, in the first years of his reign he was not unfavorable to the separatist religious groups, being influenced by the mighty Baron Frederick of Heydeck. Because of an initial scarcity of Protestant pastors in the duchy, Heydeck traveled to Silesia, came in contact with Caspar Schwenckfeld here, and brought clergymen of his stripe to Prussia. The duke himself engaged in religious correspondence with Schwenckfeld in 1527-28. It was the followers of Schwenckfeld in Prussia who were in the first decade of the Reformation called Anabaptists by the Lutheran clergy. Between Schwenckfeld and the Lutheran bishop Paulus Speratus a colloquium took place in the presence of the duke and Heydeck on Dec. 29 and 30, 1531. In 1532, upon inquiry by the duke, Luther demanded the expulsion of all the Sacramentist (Reformed) and Anabaptist elements out of the duchy. In the early years of Albrecht's rule, some of the most important men, even some of his councilors, were Anabaptists or akin to them. In 1536 Christian Entfelder (*q.v.*), a native of Carinthia, who was probably a preacher in the Moravian Anabaptist brotherhood 1526-27, became a ducal councilor, and in the next ten years was very influential at the court in Königsberg. Of him Speratus wrote to Poliander in 1539: "Entfelder is exceedingly cunning; he writes nothing on the sacraments but as a Sacramentist and as an Anabaptist"; and to a friend in Wittenberg in 1542: "I nominate Entfelder, formerly the antistes in Moravia."

In July 1541 the Dutch Humanist William Gnapheus became a ducal councilor, though it was known of him that he was "not ill informed and learned in the Scripture," but otherwise "somewhat attached to the Anabaptist or other fanatical sects." He held occasional theological lectures in the recently established University of Königsberg. On Feb. 22, 1542, Gerhard Westerburg of Cologne, known as an Anabaptist in Frankfurt, became a ducal councilor. Polyphem, the court librarian, and Pyrsus, the Dutch physician, held views similar to those of the above and were closely associated with them. To what extent they openly espoused their views is an open question. But their influence on the court was so great that the Lutheran bishop did not venture to oppose them publicly.

It is easily understood that under such circumstances Mennonite refugees would seek asylum in Prussia, especially in view of the close trade connections between the two countries. To Polish Prussia they could not yet go, since the Polish king had in 1526 had a large number of Danzig citizens executed because they were too ardently Protestant, and also since the incoming ships were carefully examined for heretics.

In the Prussian duchy, however, the first Dutch settlers came in 1527, locating in its western tip, in the Oberland that had been devastated by the Reuter war (1519-25). They were assigned to the desolate villages of Bardeyn (*q.v.*), Thierbach, Schmauch, Liebenau, Plehmen, and Robitten, with an area of about 9,000 acres. The first settlers were not Anabaptists, but by 15 years later these lands were almost exclusively occupied by Mennonites. The land-complex on which these Mennonites settled became the nucleus of the entire Mennonite settlement in East Germany. Refugees continued to come from the Netherlands to Bardeyn (*q.v.*) and the neighboring villages, while others of the settlers left; there was a constant fluctuation.

The theological position of the Dutch in the duchy reflected the first decades of the Reformation in the Netherlands. Until the early 1530's the immigrants were almost all Sacramentists (forerunners of the Anabaptists and also of the Zwinglians), who differed radically from Luther in their interpretation of the communion. After the middle 1530's following the appearance of Melchior Hofmann in the Netherlands, the Protestants in the Prussian lowlands were more and more of the Anabaptist persuasion.

The violence of the Münster episode (1534-35) and the attack by radical Anabaptists on the city hall in Amsterdam (1535) fanned the persecution mania of the Dutch and German authorities to the uttermost. But not only the revolutionary Anabaptists, but also the great mass of quiet Anabaptists who had nothing to do with violence, were persecuted with fire and sword. In this period therefore faraway Prussia, whose ruler was himself an imperial outlaw, in whose land the imperial laws against the Anabaptists were no longer valid, seemed a final place of refuge to the harassed souls.

In early 1535 a company of some 200 Moravian Anabaptist refugees came to Marienwerder by way of Thorn and Graudenz. A disputation with them revealed their "error," and they were banished. Nevertheless a part of them remained, protected by the mighty Baron of Heydeck.

After 1534 nearly every boat brought persecuted Anabaptists from the Netherlands to the shores of Prussia, especially to the Polish part. In the early summer of 1536 the estate Robitten near Bardeyn was given out to Johann Solius, an Anabaptist and a follower of Melchior Hofmann, but at the end of the year he left the estate and went to Danzig. There was a flow of Anabaptists into Danzig and to the rest of West Prussia (*q.v.*), although it cannot be determined which were the revolutionary type and which were peaceful Anabaptists.

(2) *Peaceful Anabaptists in the Duchy.* Soon after

Menno Simons came upon the scene, the entire Anabaptist movement (including that part in Prussia) took quieter channels. The Dutch refugees now sought not only a temporary place of refuge in the Oberland, but were obviously settling there permanently. Therefore a second area of about 4,500 acres about six miles north of Prussian Holland was given them in 1539, giving their total settlement about 30 square miles. In 1538-39 a number of families were negotiating in Königsberg concerning these lands. It is significant that Christian Entfelder conducted the negotiations for the government. The spokesman of the Dutch was Herman Sachs, who was known to have been an Anabaptist before he left the Netherlands. The village of Schönberg with 1,800 acres of land was to be occupied first by them; later Judendorf and Greulsberg were to follow. In religious matters they were to obey their local diocese. They were released from compulsory state labor. All mention of military service was omitted from this treaty in contrast to those made with the Sacramentist Dutch immigrants of 1527-29. Very likely the Anabaptist settlers wished to have these passages eliminated, especially in order to distinguish them from the Münsterite group.

The Dutch settlers were punctual in meeting their financial obligations, but in church relationships they soon aroused the ill will of Bishop Speratus. A letter of complaint written by the local parson in 1542 made it clear that the Dutch did not give weight to either the sacrament of the altar or that of baptism, that they did not go to the Lutheran churches in general, and acted contrary to the Prussian church regulations. Until then they had had a preacher, the letter went on: on Sunday they met with his widow, who read to them from the Bible, though they were forbidden to have a preacher of their own and "to preach secretly." All these facts show that these people were quiet Anabaptists.

Suddenly these conditions came to an end; a church inspection was made by the duke with his bishops and councilors in early 1543. It was ascertained that the Dutch immigrants did not adhere to the Prussian church discipline in matters of communion and baptism. They were thereupon ordered to place persons with "pure doctrine" on their farms and leave by Pentecost. Most of them were loyal to their faith. A small minority promised to obey the Prussian church constitution in order to be able to remain. But Bishop Speratus kept a watchful eye on these, for the same heresy again became evident, so that the bishop had to threaten them with expulsion in 1550.

This first Anabaptist settlement in East Prussia was given a mortal blow by the order of expulsion of 1543, though some isolated new settlements were still made. In 1557 Tonnies Florissen owned the village of Schönberg as mayor. He was the only one paying taxes until 1561, although he had his property together with the other Mennonites in the Danzig Werder. Schönberg was temporarily held as a land reserve until the areas in the Tiegenhof district (see **West Prussia**) were opened to the Mennonites for settlement in 1562. Now the 30 square miles in the Oberland were no longer needed; they

had already been given up in large part with their woods and hills, having been little suited to the Dutch mode of agriculture.

The Dutch colonists who settled on the city estates of Königsberg, especially in Rossgarten after the middle of the 1520's, fared exactly like those in the Oberland. Although they had a strong support in their fellow countrymen at court, the majority of the Dutch had to leave Königsberg for religious reasons. For in Königsberg-Rossgarten there was also a church inspection, which revealed the same deviations from Lutheran doctrine with respect to communion and baptism.

The Oberland Anabaptists we find again among the settlers who were placed on the flooded lands of the Danzig lowlands in 1547. The Anabaptists of Königsberg may also to a large extent have gone to Danzig or Elbing; this would explain the sudden increase in the number of Anabaptists in these cities in the next few years.

The Anabaptists who moved from the duchy to the Danzig Werder and to Polish Prussia in 1543 belonged for the most part to the group later called Mennonites; for there is no mention of any other wing after this time in Prussia. Menno Simons himself visited the Anabaptists here in 1549.

In spite of the various decrees of expulsion, the Mennonites were able to maintain themselves in Königsberg (*q.v.*) even after 1543. In 1579 they presented to the ruler a statement of their chief doctrines and a petition for permission to settle freely in the duchy. The reply was negative, because they "first of all regarded the sacrament of infant baptism quite offensively and mockingly." By May they were to leave the country. Church and school inspections continued to show that "all kinds of rabble and sects, especially the Anabaptists, had settled in the duchy." This is also shown by the continued issuing of decrees of expulsion. In 1669 they received some recognition; the Mennonites were permitted to come to the country on business, but not to settle permanently in either town or rural areas; when their business was finished they had to return to their home towns. Nevertheless some Mennonites acquired property at this time, although no congregation was formed.

(3) *The Mennonite Congregations of East Prussia as Daughter Colonies of West Prussia.* Pietism and Rationalism broke wide gaps into the dogmatism of the Lutheran Church in the 17th and 18th centuries. The tolerance extended to the Reformed and Catholics for a century was now also applied to the Mennonites. When Frederick I of Prussia in 1710 tried with all the means at his disposal to settle Swiss Mennonite refugees—without success, to be sure—in the towns of East Prussia in Lithuania which had been depopulated by the plague, a new era began for Mennonite history in East Prussia.

The efforts of the West Prussian Mennonites at settlement in East Prussia in the 18th century concentrate on two points. The first Mennonite craftsmen and merchants to settle in Königsberg with the permission of the authorities came in 1716. One of their specialties was the distillation of a certain whiskey "in the Danzig manner." They brought trades to Königsberg which had existed there only in a primitive state or not at all. In 1722 a small but prosperous congregation was organized, with members from Danzig and Elbing, and a few of Dutch birth. In 1735 the young congregation numbered 22 families, and later under Frederick the Great 35 families. Though they were small in number in 1769, they built a church, and two alms-houses with facilities for six families.

The second region in which West Prussian Mennonites settled after 1713 is the delta mouth of the Memel and its left tributary, the Gilge. Here they found a colonization site that suited their way of farming better than the woods and hills of Preussisch-Holland. Most of them came from the Graudenz and Culm lowlands along the Vistula, and formed a congregation of the Frisian branch. Some of the names of the colonists have been handed down from 1722, names at that time found almost exclusively in the Frisian congregations in West Prussia: Albrecht, Barthel, Becker, Eckert, Frantzen, Funck, Harms, Heinrichsen, Jansen, Kettler, Lorentz, Penner, Quapp, Quiring, Rhode, Schröder, Siebert, Sperling, Schmidt, and Weitgraf.

The colonizing contracts of this group show a tendency similar to that of their compatriots who had been shut out from the Oberland 200 years before. They were guaranteed freedom of religion and of trade, were permitted to elect their own mayor, divide the land among themselves without anyone else, and the division was to be "as binding as if they had been done in court." They accepted a piece of land, and paid a large price for it in order to arrange everything according to their own wishes. They wanted to build up their religious, political, and economic life according to their own ideas, at a time when almost everything was determined by an absolute ruler.

The Memel lowland with its excellent meadows gave the Mennonites almost the same living conditions as did West Prussia. Their knowledge of cattle raising and of butter and cheese manufacture assured them a decided advantage over the native peasants. In 1723 they were supplying the market in Königsberg nearly 400 tons of "Mennonite" cheese, which was known all over East Germany as Tilsit cheese. But in the next year they were expelled from the Memel lowlands; this attempt at colonization was ended. Frederick William would not tolerate in his country any who would not be soldiers. Only the Mennonite merchants in Königsberg who were indispensable because of their contributions to the taxes, were permitted to stay.

When Frederick the Great came to the throne in 1740 with his principle of toleration, he issued a declaration that guaranteed tolerance to the Mennonites as to all other subjects; the way was now opened to them to make new settlements along the Memel. The Lithuanian congregation (q.v.) then came into being, which had in 1772 a membership of over 200 souls, and in 1890 with its 743 souls within the government district of Gumbinnen (q.v.) reached its highest point. In 1891 it acquired the rights of incorporation. In its final period before its dissolution in 1945, it is worth noting that in the 1920's this congregation, called Memelniederung (q.v.), engaged a theologically trained pastor, but in 1931 returned to the lay ministry. A peculiarity of this congregation was the use of the liturgy of the Lutheran Church. In 1940 the congregation still had a membership of 450 souls. Both this congregation and the smaller Königsberg congregation were completely wiped out by the Russian conquest in 1944-45. Numerous survivors however reached West Germany and are now scattered throughout the country.   H.P.

M. Beheim-Schwarzbach, *Hohenzollernsche Kolonisation* (Leipzig, 1874); A. Brons, *Ursprung, Entwicklung und Schicksale der . . . Mennoniten* (Amsterdam, 1912); C. T. Cosack, *Paulus Speratus* (Braunschweig, 1861); B. M. Ch. Hartknoch, *Preussische Kirchenhistorie* (Frankfurt and Leipzig, 1886); E. Keyser, *Die Niederlande und das Weichselland* (*Dtsch. Archiv f. Landesu. Volksforschung* VI, Leipzig, 1942); H. G. Mannhardt, *Die Danziger Mennonitengemeinde, Ihre Entstehung und ihre Geschichte von 1569-1919* (Danzig, 1919); W. Mannhardt, *Die Wehrfreiheit der Altpreussischen Mennoniten* (Marienburg, 1863); H. Penner, *Ansiedlung mennonitischer Niederländer im Weichselmündungsgebiet von der Mitte des 16. Jh. bis zum Beginn der Preussischen Zeit* (*Schriftenreihe des Menn. Gesch.-Ver.*, No. 3, Weierhof, 1940); E. Randt, *Die Mennoniten in Ostpreussen und Litauen bis zum Jahre 1772* (Königsberg, 1912); B. Schumacher, *Niederländ. Ansiedlungen im Herzogtum Preussen zur Zeit Herzog Albrechts (1525-1568)* (Leipzig, 1903); B. H. Unruh, *Kolonisatorische Berührungen zwischen den Mennoniten und den Siedlern anderer Konfessionen im Weichselgebiet und in der Neumark* (*Dtsch. Arch. f. Landes- und Volksforschung* IV, 1940); H. Wiebe, *Das Siedlungswerk niederländ. Mennoniten im Weichseltal zwischen Fordon und Weissenberg bis zum Ausgang des 18. Jh.* (Marburg, 1952); Horst Penner, "The Anabaptists and Mennonites of East Prussia," *MQR* XXII (1948) 212-25; J. Gingerich, "Die Mennonitengemeinde Königsberg und ihr Ende," *Der Mennonit* II (1949) 21 f.; E. Wermke, *Bibliographie der Geschichte von Ost- und Westpreussen für die Jahre 1939-1951* (Marburg, 1953); *ML* III, 322-25; the Mennonite archives at Amsterdam contain a large number of documents concerning the East Prussian Mennonites, especially from the early 18th century.

East Reserve, Man. "Reserve" was the name given to a contiguous tract of land set aside by the Canadian government for a certain number of years for exclusive occupation by a homogeneous group of settlers, to be divided according to their own plans. Two different reserves were provided for the immigrant Mennonites from Russia. One, the East Reserve, was identical with the land grant of seven (later raised to eight) townships (each six miles square) offered to the Mennonite delegates from Russia in 1873, and coextensive with the present Municipality of Hanover, which lies just east of the Red River, its northern boundary being about 20 miles southeast of Winnipeg, its southernmost boundary about 20 miles north of the United States border. Its total acreage is 185,000 or 290 sq. mi. The West Reserve was established three years later, and made about two and one-half times as large as the East Reserve. Its boundaries were changed several times but corresponded roughly with those of the present Municipality of Rhineland and portions of adjoining municipalities, lying just west of the Red River, including 17 townships (612 sq. mi.). The names are still locally used to indicate the two major Mennonite settlements in Manitoba, although the old grants cover only the nucleus of the two

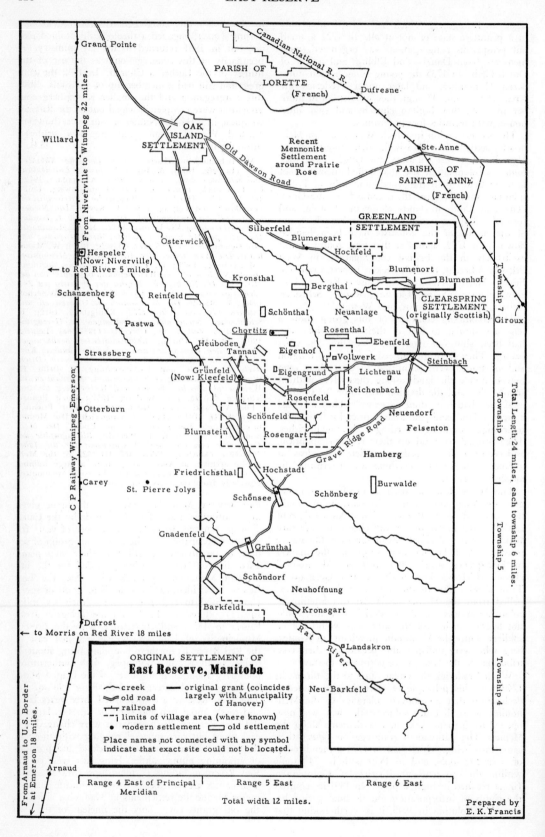

ORIGINAL SETTLEMENT OF
East Reserve, Manitoba

⌇ creek   ▬ original grant (coincides
largely with Municipality
☇ old road   of Hanover)
┬┬ railroad
┆┄┆ limits of village area (where known)
• modern settlement   ▭ old settlement

Place names not connected with any symbol
indicate that exact site could not be located.

Prepared by
E. K. Francis

areas of present-day Mennonite concentration in Manitoba. They represent the two largest compact Mennonite settlements in Canada (or the United States), and manifest many unique characteristics.

The East Reserve had never been meant to accommodate all intended Mennonite immigrants from Russia, at that time still estimated as 40,000 in number. Doubts as to the desirability of the area offered to them by the government had already arisen in the minds of the delegates of the land search committee of 1873, so that they, before returning to Russia to report, had requested the privilege of selecting, at a later date, some other portion of the country under the same conditions under which the original grant was made. When the first rather dry year (1874) was followed by several unusually wet seasons, it became quite clear that the East Reserve not only had a shallow stony soil texture in many parts, but suffered also from excessive moisture. As late as 1941 only 45 per cent (75,000 acres) of the land was improved, in contrast to the Rhineland Municipality of the West Reserve where 96 per cent (220,000 acres) was improved.

While all other early settlers came from woodlands and consequently sought the wooded hills further west, Mennonites had been adjusted in Russia to life in the open steppes and preferred the open prairies. They knew how to strike living water from level ground, how to build comfortable huts, and how to heat them, too, without a stick of wood; they also knew how to plant shelter belts for protection against the icy winds of the northern plains. Moreover, the open-field system of farming which they practiced, unknown among other settlers, did not require any wood for fences at a time when barbed wire had not yet been made available to provide cheap enclosures for the scattered farmsteads of the West. Thus the West Reserve, laid out between Emerson and Mountain City, at a depth of 18 miles north of the United States boundary, was really the first permanent agricultural settlement ever established in the open prairies of Western Canada without direct access to a major body or current of water. It also turned out to be some of the best farm land in the whole province of Manitoba. When this area was finally set aside "for the exclusive use of Mennonites from Russia" by Order-in-Council of April 25, 1876, the two Reserves together included 25 townships of over 500,000 acres, that is, about 6 per cent of the total area of Manitoba up to 1881.

The colonists who settled the East Reserve were composed of two groups: (1) the smaller Kleine Gemeinde group (some 35 families out of an original 100 who had left Russia, 30 families being diverted to Jansen, Neb., en route, and 30 families refusing to settle on the wet land of the East Reserve and locating instead near Morris, just west of the Red River in what was called the Scratching River Colony), a schism of the Molotschna settlement in 1812, which had left the Molotschna in 1865-66 to settle in the Borozenko settlement and in part in Fürstenland, near the more conservative Mennonite Church groups which had settled in these areas from the Chortitza settlement (often called the Old Colony); and (2) the much larger (507 families) Berg-thal group, which had left the Chortitza settlement in 1836-52 to found the Bergthal settlement (and which was accordingly Old Colony). The Bergthal settlement had consisted of 540 families living in five villages of the Bergthal volost, all but 34 families (who stayed in the Old Country) of which joined in the mass migration to North America. Of the total number of migrants, 453 families moved to Manitoba and settled in the East Reserve in 1874-79, while 53 families went to Mountain Lake, Minn. The Bergthal group in the East Reserve was joined by 45 families from the Chortitza settlement in Russia, and 9 families from Puchtin. From this group a gradual drift of a considerable number of families to the West Reserve set in early, which by 1887 composed almost half (220 families) of the total Bergthal group (246 families remaining in the East Reserve). The West Reserve was settled first by the "Fürstenland" group, from the Fürstenland settlement in Russia which had been established in 1869 by settlers from the Chortitza settlement and was almost as large as the Bergthal settlement, and also "Old Colony." This group emigrated en masse to Manitoba and occupied much of the West Reserve in 1875-79, forming a compact settlement. The rest of the West Reserve settlement was composed of the Bergthal transfer mentioned above.

The Kleine Gemeinde group in the East Reserve settled in five villages in the northern part of the East Reserve, viz., Blumenhof, Blumenort, Grünfeld-Kleefeld, Steinbach, and Rosenfeld. The 24 villages permanently established in the East Reserve by the Bergthal group were Osterwick, Hochfeld, Reinfeld, Chortitza, Schönthal, Kronsthal, Bergthal, Rosen-thal, Ebenfeld, Schönfeld, Rosengart, Blumstein, Schönsee, Burwalde, Kronsgart, Hochstadt, Grün-thal, Gnadenfeld, Friedrichsthal, Hochstadt, Reichenbach, Barkfeld, Neubarkfeld, and Tannau, in addition to part villages and those which were soon abandoned such as Pastwa.

The founding of colonies such as the East Reserve was nothing new to the Mennonites. To their minds, a Reserve in Manitoba was in no way different from a daughter-colony in Russia or elsewhere in the world. Accordingly, they simply followed a pattern which they considered to be the reflection of their own sacred traditions, although in reality it was largely a result of the master plan provided by the Russian Colonial Law. This pattern included (1) village habitat, (2) open-field system, (3) separation between church and civil government, (4) autonomy both on a village and regional level, corresponding to village commune and district *volost* in Russia, and (5) a series of subsidiary institutes such as school, *Waisenamt* (*q.v.*), and fire insurance.

The settlement pattern of the Mennonite village in the East Reserve, as it had been in Russia, was that of the northeast German colonial *Gewanndorf* characterized by a combination of line village with open-field economy. Each holding included a *Hauskörgl* (message, toft) along the village street and one strip in each of the "Gewanne" (open fields) into which the total area belonging to the village was divided. The toft provided space for house and farm buildings, barnyard, flower and vegetable garden, an orchard, and a small piece of plowland to be used for bulkier crops for home consumption, such as potatoes or cabbage. The fields were larger areas of plowland selected in such a way that the value of all land in each field, as determined by distance, soil quality, moisture, etc., was uniform, providing an equitable share in the available arable land of each villager. The size and number of fields varied greatly according to local conditions. The remaining village territory was set aside for utilization as woodland, hayland, and pasture. As the name open-field system indicates, there were no enclosures because all livestock belonging to individual villagers was pastured in common under the care of a herdsman, and in this way prevented from wandering about and damaging the crops. Moreover, after harvest the arable fields themselves were used for stubble pasture. Each homesteader was entitled to send out a definite number of animals with the village herd and to take a fixed amount of hay and wood from the common lands. Additional rights in these common lands and services were sometimes granted to either villagers or outsiders; in this case the rent or other payments collected were added to the income of the commune. This village system was ultimately abandoned in Manitoba, being finally discontinued in the East Reserve in 1909.

The open-field system is closely associated with the practice of crop rotation. A four-crop rotation with summer fallow (called *Schwarzbrache*) had been introduced by Johann Cornies among the Mennonites in Russia, and was brought by them to Canada where fallowing was particularly important in order to preserve moisture in the soil. As a rule, *Flurzwang* is an obvious concomitant of the open-field system, whereby all the owners of individual strips in a given field are compelled to plant the same crop or fallow at the same time. Since headlands and roads were usually kept at a minimum to facilitate weed control and save valuable plowland, all farmers had to agree upon a rigid rhythm in their operations so as to give each one access to his property in season. This frequently required the close cooperation of several farmers or even of the whole village, particularly during harvest when time was at a premium.

The village organization briefly described above may be called the solidaristic type of settlement. For it presupposes and fosters strong social coherence, intensive interaction on a face-to-face level, readiness to co-operate and offer mutual aid, and a common value system which leaves few alternatives in one's everyday conduct, and which is enforced by strict social controls based on both inner and external sanctions. In fact, it would appear that it cannot be made to work adequately unless these sanctions have a distinctly religious connotation. For whenever hedonistic and other secular values become dominant, undermining the inner consistency of the total system of constituent group norms perceived in a religious context, the solidaristic type of rural community organization soon tends to collapse, yielding to characteristically individualistic forms of social and economic behavior.

Such was the settlement pattern which the Men-

nonites intended to reproduce faithfully in Canada's West. Yet, allowance had to be made for the essentially individualistic property system embodied in the Dominion Lands Act. According to it, legal title to land could not be vested in whole village communes as had been the case in Prussia or in Russia, but had to be acquired by each homesteader individually. Moreover, the unit of land measurements was a regular square, nowhere following the natural topography of the country. Planning after the traditional pattern was further restricted through the withdrawal of four sections in every township, sections 8 and 26 being reserved for sale by the Hudson's Bay Company, while sections 11 and 29 were set aside for sale by the Provincial Government for the support of schools.

Accordingly, in selecting the sites of future villages, the Mennonite pioneers had to do some careful surveying and figuring so as to fit the precise number of prospective villagers to the available surrounding area, measured in terms of quarter-sections to be taken up by each of them. They also had to consider the quality of the land, access to water and wood, the location of the village site in relation to its area of land, and its adequacy for building purposes. Once this problem in geometry was solved, however, the individual claims for homesteads were entered haphazardly, for legal ownership in any particular quarter-section had no real significance when the land was finally divided and laid out in common fields with individual strips in each of them, in common pastures, and so on.

While this method of land division, which was actually contrary to the intentions of the Canadian land laws, was made possible by the special concessions granted to the Mennonites by the Dominion Government, it rested on an entirely voluntary basis. Whoever claimed, or would claim in the future, full possession of the particular quarter-section legally entered under his name, could in no way be prevented from doing so. Unlike in Russia, the law of the country did not support the open-field system, so that its institution and maintenance depended entirely on the strength of inner sanctions and social controls among the group itself. Although in the beginning the wishes of most group members favored the establishment of compact villages, there were even then a few who preferred to settle individually on their own pieces of land.

A second adjustment was indicated by the topography of the country. Since this was different in the two Reserves, certain definite variations in the overall settlement pattern resulted. According to the earliest survey maps the East Reserve looked like this: In the northwestern corner there was rolling prairie land interspersed with marshy patches, willow brush, and undergrowth. To the east, part of a big swamp, most of which lay outside the Reserve, made a dent into otherwise open land. Next to it there was more shrub and bush. In the center of the Reserve only the environs of the present town of Steinbach were marked "clear prairie" or at least "prairie with bluffs of poplar and tamarack." From there a high gravel ridge ran southwest to the present site of Grünfeld, and a small ridge just north of it. Most of the center was broken land marked on the maps as poplar, willow, tamarack, slough, burnt stumps, granite stones, gravel, and lots of weeds as a whole; though drainage seems to have been better here than in townships to the south where numerous sloughs are shown on the maps.

In the beginning, village sites were obviously chosen in natural clearings or on high land. The two gravel ridges alone gave rise to six or seven villages. Several sites chosen in a dry season had to be abandoned afterwards when the water level rose again. The villages founded in wooded land were inevitably strung along the banks of a river or creek; in these cases the village street followed the characteristic slant of the country from southeast to northwest. In open country, however, the rows of houses were parallel to section lines, usually running east and west as a protection against the north winds.

Although the location of some villages was changed in the course of time, while many others have disappeared altogether, an inspection of mounds marking basements and foundations, together with accounts gathered from old-timers, have made it possible to reconstruct the exact location of most of them. In 1877, when population density in the East Reserve was higher than at any other time before 1900, 38 villages were in existence. Five of them, on better soil and larger than the average, were occupied by the Kleine Gemeinde people, while all the others belonged to the Bergthal group. Not all the places mentioned, however, were fully organized village communes. Some were either small hamlets (Schanzenburg, Pastwa, Strassberg, Heuboden, Tannau, Eigengrund, Eigenhof, Ebenfeld, Vollwerk, Lichtenau, and Landskron), or incomplete villages planned to accommodate large numbers of later immigrants who never arrived. Most of the settlements laid out in the early years in township 7-4 East, and east and south of the gravel ridge, either on wet or on poor soil, were soon abandoned when better land west of the Red River became available, causing a partial exodus from the East Reserve (Pastwa, Strassberg, Neuendorf, Felsenton, Hamberg, Schönberg, Schönhorst, and Neuhorst, somewhat later also Burwalde). On the other hand, a few new hamlets and villages were founded in later years in areas left unoccupied during the first period of settlement (Blumengart, Silberfeld, and Neubarkfeld, a daughter colony of Barkfeld).

The further history of the East Reserve will be told in the article Manitoba. It will suffice to report only a few points here. The Kleine Gemeinde group suffered a serious schism in 1881, when the elder and over a third of the members withdrew to join the Church of God in Christ (Holdeman) Mennonites. By 1885 also almost half of the Bergthal families had transferred to the West Reserve, and a full separation between the two groups occurred in that year. The East Reserve Bergthal Church then changed its name to Chortitz Mennonite Church to demonstrate its full disapproval of the other group. Thus since 1885 there have been three basic groups in the East Reserve: Chortitz, Kleine Gemeinde, and Holdeman group. In 1944 these groups had respectively the following population—3,223, 1,365, 957, while three

newly established congregations of the General Conference Mennonites had 1,101. There were also two smaller Mennonite Brethren churches established in 1927-29, and one Evangelical Mennonite Brethren church established about 1900. In 1954 the baptized membership of these groups in the East Reserve (and closely adjacent territory) was as follows: Chortitz 1,480; Kleine Gemeinde 1,248; Holdeman 1,012; General Conference 900(?); Mennonite Brethren 427; E.M.B. 312, a total of 5,379.

Emigration from the East Reserve had established or contributed to the following new settlements: Holdeman group to Swalwell, Alberta; Kleine Gemeinde to Chihuahua State in Mexico; Chortitz to the Paraguayan Chaco (815 persons and 13 families). Practically none of the Chortitz group went to Mexico.   E.K.F., H.S.B.

C. Henry Smith, *The Coming of the Russian Mennonites* (Berne, 1927); E. K. Francis, *In Search of Utopia: The Mennonites in Manitoba* (Altona, Man., 1955).

East Swamp Mennonite Church (GCM) of the Eastern District Conference is located in Milford Twp., Bucks Co., Pa. In 1771 the Swamp congregation built a schoolhouse about a mile east of its meetinghouse. It is not known whether this school was also destroyed by fire and a second log house was built which served the double purpose of school and meetinghouse. In 1850 the present brick meetinghouse was erected; in late years it has been greatly enlarged and altered. From the earliest days East Swamp and West Swamp were one congregation. In 1847 under the leadership of their minister John Oberholtzer, both meetinghouses and all but a few members joined the new conference. In 1877, because of increased growth, East Swamp became a separate congregation, and in 1921 it chose its own minister.

Known ministers and their terms of service are: Michael Musselman 1773 (?)-90, Jacob Nold 1794-1817, Samuel Musselman 1808-47, Christian Bliem 1814-31, Christian Zetty 1817-43, Jacob Hiestand 1832-42, John H. Oberholtzer 1842-88, William N. Shelly 1847-58, Levi O. Shimmel 1858-69, Andrew B. Shelly 1864-1904, Harvey Gottshall 1901-13, Harvey Shelly and Victor Boyer supplied during 1914, Harvey G. Allebach 1915-21, Victor Boyer, Joseph Hagenbush, Reed Landes, Grover Soldner, and Freeman Swartz supplied 1921-25, Howard G. Nyce 1925-29, William Rivelle supplied 1929-30, William S. Gottshall 1930-39, Harold Burkholder 1938-45, Abraham H. Schultz 1945- .

The Sunday school was organized in 1866 or earlier, and in 1911 a Christian Endeavor was organized. The membership in 1864 was 79, in 1902 it was 119, and in 1953 it was 196. The common names today are Landis, Auckland, Bleam, Barndt, Shelly, Schaeffer, and Hallman.   J.H.F.

J. C. Wenger, *History of the Mennonites of the Franconia Conference* (Telford, Pa., 1937); "History of the Swamp Congregations," in *Menn. Yearbook and Almanac* (Quakertown, 1918).

East Union Conservative Amish Mennonite Church is located approximately seven miles east of Wooster, Ohio, a short distance north of U.S. Highway 30.

It was first listed in the *Mennonite Yearbook* in 1948 under "Pleasant View and East Union" and was listed as a separate congregation for the first time in the 1950 yearbook. In 1953 the congregation had 87 members, who were served by the ministers Paul Kandel and Mose Swartzendruber.

M.G.

East Union Mennonite Church (MC), located three miles north of Kalona, Johnson Co., Iowa, was organized in 1884 under the leadership of Christian Warey, having come out of the large Old Order Amish settlement in this locality. It first met for worship at the Prairie Dale schoolhouse, 1½ miles west of the present location, and was known as the Union Church. Christian Warey was ordained bishop the following year, with Jacob B. Yoder as deacon. Others who have served as deacon, minister, or bishop are A. J. Yoder, Jacob J. Schwartzendruber, Jacob S. Yoder, Fred Gingerich, S. C. Yoder, A. C. Brenneman, Harold Brenneman, and Edward Shettler.

The East Union congregation was a member of the Western A.M. Conference until the merger of 1921 and since then has been a member of the Iowa-Nebraska Conference. The present church was built in 1922, and is the largest Mennonite church of its branch west of the Mississippi. The ministers in 1955 were D. J. Fisher, bishop; A. Lloyd Swartzendruber, assistant bishop; J. John J. Miller, minister; and Henry H. Miller, deacon; the membership was 565.

A.L.S.

East White Oak Mennonite Church, unaffiliated, located in McLean Co., Ill., 7½ miles southeast of Carlock, was organized in 1892 with Peter Schantz as pastor, and a church was built in the same year. Emanuel Troyer was ordained as assistant pastor in 1899, and later succeeded Schantz as bishop or elder of the church, which he served until 1928. R. J. Zehr was then called to serve as pastor. The church was a member of the Central Conference of Mennonites from its beginning until 1934, at which time it severed its relation with the conference and has since operated as an independent organization. In 1934 the membership was 260.

R.L.H.

East Zorra Amish Mennonite Church, located near Tavistock in East Zorra Twp., Oxford Co., Ont., is a member of the Ontario A.M. Conference. The East Zorra congregation was organized about 1837 as an offshoot from the Wilmot congregation and was joined by other families from Pennsylvania and Europe. Services were held in private homes until 1883, when the 16th Line meetinghouse was built. Preaching was conducted every Sunday since 1883. In 1903 a Sunday school was organized and this was alternated with the preaching services. Since 1933 both Sunday school and preaching services have been held every Sunday. The church has had young people's meeting since 1920. All services were in the German language until 1932. Singing schools were held frequently. In 1925 the church was enlarged to accommodate nearly 800 persons. In 1935 an Evangelical church four miles southeast was bought **and** remodeled to seat 200 persons. It is now known

as the Cassel church. In 1942 a building in Tavistock was also rented to provide for the overflow. This building was used until July 1950, when a new church was built on the west outskirts of Tavistock, which is known as the Tavistock church. It seats around 350. In 1951 the East Zorra church was removed and a new and large building with basement and gallery was built, seating about 900. In December 1932 the first four-week winter Bible school was held here. It met every year until 1941, when it was closed through the war years, reopening in 1947 in Tavistock, and two years later was again held at the East Zorra church, where it has been held ever since. Since 1940 summer Bible school has been held at East Zorra, and since 1950 in Tavistock. The membership of 230 in 1890 had increased to 910 by 1953. (For a list of ministers who have served these congregations see L. J. Burkholder's history.) The following were the ministers in 1954: bishops Daniel Jutzi, Henry Jantzi; ministers Daniel Wagler, Menno Kipfer, Joel Swartzentruber, and David Swartzentruber; deacons Andrew Zehr and Daniel Zehr.

W.J.B.

L. J. Burkholder, *A Brief History of the Mennonites in Ontario* (Toronto, 1935).

Eastern Amish Mennonite Conference, one of three (the others Indiana-Michigan A.M., and Western A.M.) conferences (MC) organized among the more progressive Amish Mennonite congregations after the Amish Mennonite General Conferences (*Diener-Versammlungen*) of 1862-78 had been discontinued. The Eastern A.M. Conference, covering the territory east of Indiana, actually Ohio and Pennsylvania, was organized in 1893 and held its last session in May 1927. The formal merger with the Ohio Mennonite Conference to form the Ohio Mennonite and Eastern A.M. Joint Conference took place on Dec. 9, 1927. In 1927 it had 19 organized congregations (several had more than one meetinghouse) with a baptized membership of 5,187. Ten of these were in Ohio (Fulton County at three places, Oak Grove and South Union at West Liberty, Walnut Creek and Martin's Creek in Holmes County, Oak Grove and Orrville in Wayne County, Beech in Stark County, Plain View in Portage County, East Orwell in Ashtabula County) and nine in Pennsylvania (Conestoga and Millwood-Maple Grove in Lancaster County; Allensville and Belleville in Mifflin County with near-by Mattawana; Maple Grove in the west at New Wilmington; Westover, Md.; and the small congregations at Oyster Point, Va., and Long Green, Md.) The conference customarily met annually the last week in May. It contained an unusual number of large and strong congregations with many able leaders both in the conference and in general church work. Among these were John S. Mast (1861-1951) of Morgantown, Pa.; S. E. Allgyer (1859-1953) and A. I. Yoder (1866-1932) of West Liberty, Ohio; E. B. Stoltzfus (1860-1942) of Aurora, Ohio; E. L. Frey (1856-1942) of Wauseon, Ohio; J. S. Gerig (1866-) and C. Z. Yoder (1845-1939) of Smithville, Ohio; O. N. Johns (1889-) of Louisville, Ohio; I. W. Royer (1873-) of Orrville, Ohio, and Aaron Mast (1880-) of Belleville, Pa. H.S.B.

Report of the Eastern Amish Mennonite Conference. Constitution and Appendix 1893-1911 (Sugarcreek, Ohio, 1911); *Report . . . 1912-1919* (Sugarcreek, 1920); *Report . . . 1920-1924* (Scottdale, 1924); *Report . . . 1926* (West Liberty, 1926).

Eastern District Conference *of the General Conference Mennonite Church.* During the second quarter of the 19th century great changes entered into American religious life. A resurgence of revivalism and evangelical fervor broke through widespread deadness in many denominations. Throughout the country, home and foreign mission boards, tract and temperance societies, church colleges and seminaries, religious literature and periodicals, and Sunday schools were founded.

The Mennonites of the Franconia Conference (MC) in southeastern Pennsylvania, in spite of their attempted isolation, also felt the impact of this new religious environment, with its new visions of opportunity and responsibility. Locally the Pennsylvania Public School Law of 1834, with its emphasis on the English language and American cultural patterns, had a profound, though quiet, influence upon traditionally minded German Mennonites, especially those of the younger generation.

In the 1840's some of the younger ministers of the Franconia Conference, including John H. Oberholtzer of Swamp, and Abraham Hunsicker of Skippack, manifested a more progressive spirit in church matters. Oberholtzer, a gifted schoolteacher and skilled locksmith, became a fervent preacher and student of the Scriptures. He organized children's meetings, printed a catechism, preached in other denominations, and refused to wear the regulation minister's coat. Because of this latter act, he and several like-minded ministers were excluded from the conference meeting in 1844. In seeking to be reinstated soon after, Oberholtzer became deeply impressed with the lack of proper procedure in conference. With no secretary, no minutes, no business nor voting procedure, irregularities were bound to occur in the applications of the old, unwritten church rules.

In the spring of 1847 Oberholtzer, encouraged by Abraham Hunsicker, drafted a conference constitution, which was unofficially accepted by a like-minded group of 16 ministers and deacons. On the following day at the spring conference Oberholtzer appeared, dressed in a regulation coat, to present his constitution, but was denied the opportunity to read it. The constitution was later printed and distributed among the ministers. At the fall conference the sponsors again appeared, asking for a committee to study the constitution. In the end, however, the conference adopted a vigorous resolution excommunicating all signers of the constitution unless they renounced it; if they did so they again would be received in love. That such controversy could occur between sincere brethren is indeed lamentable, especially since the issues involved concerned not the major doctrines of the church but rather new methods of promoting and preserving the old Gospel.

On Oct. 28, 1847, three weeks after the decision of the conference, the signers of the new constitution met at the Skippack meetinghouse to consider their future course. After due consideration of the conference resolution favoring the "old evangelical order," they decided that such would be conscientiously impossible. Thereupon, they adopted the new constitution, and the name, "The East Pennsylvania Conference of the Mennonite Church." This Skippack meeting marks the official founding of the present Eastern District Conference.

Those who attended this historic meeting were John Hunsicker, William Landis, John H. Oberholtzer, Abraham Hunsicker, Christian Clemmer, and Joseph Schantz, as ministers, and William Gottschall, John Detweiler, Henry B. Shelly, Jacob Benner, and Samuel Kaufman, as deacons. These men represented the entire congregations of West Swamp, East Swamp, Flatland, Skippack, Schwenksville, Upper Milford, Germantown, and Bertolet's; and elements of the congregations of Worcester, Providence, Rockhill, Saucon, Springfield, Boyertown, and Hereford. The Deep Run congregation was not represented at this meeting because the division there was purely a laymen's movement. Some of the signers were absent from this meeting. All in all, the new conference started with 8 ministers, 11 deacons, and 16 congregations, totaling about 500 members, or one fourth of the Franconia Conference. Of the 70 ministers and deacons in the Franconia Conference at that time, 16 withdrew including John Hunsicker, the senior bishop of the conference, one of the five bishops functioning at that time.

John H. Oberholtzer's constitution adopted by the new conference reveals that the aims of this group were not radical, but substantially followed traditional Mennonite doctrine and polity. The method and approach, however, were new. The early activities of the East Pennsylvania Conference verified this progressively traditional policy. The traditional forms of worship and vigorous discipline were continued alongside of such innovations as children's meetings and Sunday schools in the 50's, a conference Sunday-school union in 1876, a religious periodical, the *Religiöser Botschafter,* in 1852, the inward calling of ministers, ministerial support, pulpit fellowship with other denominations, and limited open communion.

A survey of the beginnings of religious groups in church history frequently reveals that the greater the birth pangs, the greater will be the growing pains. The East Pennsylvania Conference was no exception; its growing pains were severe. In 1851, the Hunsickers (John and Abraham) were excommunicated for advocating tolerance toward secret societies and more liberal interpretation of open communion than conference was willing to accept. In the middle 50's, the emotional religion and revivalism of the Methodist style began to penetrate the northern congregations in the form of prayer meetings. Matters came to a climax in 1858 when William N. Shelly, William Gehman, and five other ministers withdrew and formed the Evangelical Mennonite Conference (*q.v.*), one of the groups which later formed the Mennonite Brethren in Christ. The third and last controversy centered at Skippack over footwashing. This congregation, demanding the literal interpretation of this rite, and refusing to agree with the conference's spiritual interpretation, seceded in 1859 to become an independent congregation (called popularly the Johnson Mennonite Church, because the leader and most of the ministers after him had that name). The first two of these controversies reveal that conference was unwilling to accept either a weakened liberalism or a radical revivalism, though in so rejecting them it lost both the educated Hunsickers and men of evangelistic fervor. The last controversy, on the other hand, reveals the liberal spirit of conference as opposed to the more literal spirit of the minority, though again the fellowship of a strong congregation was lost to the young and struggling conference.

Following the organization of the East Pennsylvania Conference, John H. Oberholtzer vigorously championed a greater unification of Mennonites all over America. The East Pennsylvania Conference was also much interested in this movement, and in 1860 delegated Oberholtzer and Enos Loux to go to a church unification meeting at West Point, Iowa. At that historic meeting with Oberholtzer in charge, the General Conference was organized to include the East Pennsylvania congregations and the Iowa congregations. In a short time the congregations of like-minded brethren in Canada, Ohio, and Illinois joined this unification movement.

Publication activities continued through the years. Minutes, catechisms, reports, Sunday-school literature, and other papers were printed by conference at Milford Square. The *Religiöser Botschafter* became *Das Christliche Volksblatt* in 1856 and the *Friedensbote* in 1867, which in 1882 was merged with a western paper to become the G.C.M. German periodical, *Der Christliche Bundesbote*, now *Der Bote*. In 1885, N. B. Grubb and Allen M. Fretz, with the approval of conference, founded *The Mennonite*, which became the General Conference English periodical. In 1895, conference published the first *Mennonite Yearbook and Almanac*, which later became the official conference yearbook. The Conference has always had an active home mission program. Congregations organized by the Conference were Wadsworth, Ohio, in 1852; and in Pennsylvania Bowmansville in 1852, First Philadelphia in 1865, Souderton in 1893, Pottstown in 1895, Quakertown in 1899, Allentown in 1903, Perkasie in 1905, Lansdale in 1929, and Lancaster in 1946. During the last 50 years a group of congregations and missions have been added in central Pennsylvania (Fairfield, Richfield, Roaring Spring, etc.) and Stirling Avenue at Kitchener, Ont.

In the 1890's, Christian Endeavor societies were organized in many of the congregations, and were soon after followed by the organization of a conference Young People's Union. In 1928 a young people's retreat was organized, which since 1941 has been held at Men-O-Lan Retreat Grounds near Finland, Pa., owned and operated by the conference. In 1896 a home for the aged was begun at Frederick, Pa. A brotherhood organization for laymen was organized in 1918. An orphanage society and a women's organization have been active for many years. In many of these ventures the Eastern District Conference pioneered among American Mennonites.

According to the constitution, the Conference is made up of congregations which "taking the Sacred Scripture of the Old and New Testament as the only and infallible rule of faith and life, hold fast to the doctrine of salvation by grace through faith in the Lord Jesus Christ, and in their teaching and practice adhere to the Mennonite principles of administering baptism only on confession of faith, avoiding the use of all oaths, a life of meekness, peace, and Biblical inoffensiveness, and the practice of a Scriptural church discipline to the end of separating from the communion of believers the unrepentant and incorrigible transgressors against the laws of God."

Most of the controversial activities and methods early promoted by the Eastern District Conference are now accepted by the great body of Mennonites. The Eastern District Conference still differs from more conservative Mennonites in such things as the absence of detailed church rules, the absence of a prescribed religious garb, the use of a trained and supported ministry, a wider denominational fellowship, and open communion.

The 100th anniversary of the Eastern District Conference was observed in the historic Lower Skippack meetinghouse, with appropriate meetings on Oct. 26-28, 1947. The first issue of a conference periodical, *The Messenger*, was published at that time.

In 1956 the conference had 4,558 members in 28 congregations, with 25 active ministers and 52 deacons.   J.H.F.

S. F. Pannabecker, "Development of the General Conference of the Mennonite Church of N. A. in the American Environment" (ms., unpublished Yale doctoral dissertation, 1944); *Gesch. der Trennung in 1847 und 1848 der Menn. in Ost-Pennsylvanien* (broadside, 1863), which was used as a basis for John Oberholtzer's testimony in the Boyertown court trial of 1883 (for an English translation see the *Mennonite*, Nov. 2, 1922, p. 2); *Supreme Court of Pennsylvania Eastern District—January Term, 1883. Appeal . . . Paper Book of Appellants* (Reading, 1883); the *Messenger* I (Oct. 1947); J. H. Oberholtzer, *Der Wahre Character von J. H. Oberholtzer* (Milford Square, 1860); idem, *Ordnung der Mennonitischen Gemeinschaft* (1847); F. H. Swartz, "The Origin and Development of Our Conference," *Messenger*, October 1947, January 1948, and April 1948; J. C. Wenger, *History of the Mennonites of the Franconia Conference* (Telford, Pa., 1937); P. R. Shelly, *Religious Education and Mennonite Piety Among the Mennonites of Southeastern Pennsylvania 1870-1943* (Newton, 1952).

Eastern District Conference Brotherhood (GCM), probably the first laymen's organization among American Mennonites, was organized Aug. 11, 1918, at the Zion Mennonite meetinghouse, Souderton, Pa. This movement was first suggested in an address delivered by Maxwell H. Kratz at a Sunday-school convention in Perkasie in 1917. The purpose of this Brotherhood was "getting our men better acquainted with each other, keeping them more keenly interested in the various phases of the work of our church, fostering a stronger loyalty to its principles, and to have them stand together in Christian service."

The Brotherhood has done much pioneering work in fostering service and stewardship among the conference men. In 1919-23 the Brotherhood raised $41,663 for World War I relief, especially among the distressed Mennonites in Crefeld (Germany) and Russia, to be sent with clothing, etc., through the Mennonite Central Committee organized in 1920. Maxwell Kratz was a prime mover in both organizations. In 1924 and a few years after, over $1,000 was raised by the Brotherhood for the purchase of Mennonite historical items from the Pennypacker collection, for the Schwenkfelder Historical Library in Pennsburg, Pa. During the late twenties and early thirties several thousand dollars was given for the relief of Russian Mennonite refugees in Canada and South America. In 1921 pioneering work was started on pensions and salary standards for ministers in the conference.

The Brotherhood has done much for the fellowship and spiritual life of the men in the conference. Among the institutions it has fostered are rallies and deputation groups; an annual Labor Day Bible conference, held at Camp Men-O-Lan since 1946 with outstanding results; and an annual choral festival of 300 voices since 1951. The education of young ministers among South American Mennonites has been a late project.

The Brotherhood is made up of members from most of the conference congregations. However, local Brotherhood "chapters" hold monthly meetings at Lansdale, Denver, East Swamp (Bethany, Flatland, Springfield, West Swamp), and Kitchener. Early leaders in the Brotherhood were Maxwell H. Kratz, F. K. Moyer, and Seward M. Rosenberger.

J.H.F.

N. K. Berky, "History of the Brotherhood of the Eastern District Conference," The Mennonite, March 14 and 21, 1944; "Brotherhood Briefs," in The Messenger of the Eastern District Conference, quarterly.

Eastern Mennonite Board of Missions and Charities (MC) was organized in 1914 (incorporated 1916) to serve the missionary interests of the Lancaster Mennonite Conference. The organized interest in missions as such in the Lancaster district had its beginning about 1893. In the Paradise district of Lancaster Conference the first meeting to promote mission work was held on Sept. 15, 1893, by a group who called themselves Home Mission Advocates. In spite of opposition, they met regularly afterwards. The third regular meeting, held at Paradise on Nov. 14, 1895, was a very stirring occasion, at which strong opinions were expressed for and against the movement. It was learned here that official church leaders would not object to Sunday-school work. This then became the open door for the movement, and the group changed its name to Sunday School Mission, and for the next 22 years held regular quarterly meetings. Sunday schools were opened at several rural points in the county, beginning at Welsh Mountain. Work in Lancaster city soon followed, and by 1899 a city mission work was opened in Philadelphia.

The Sunday School Mission group became the pioneers of the mission activities now sponsored by Lancaster Conference. John H. Mellinger (1858-

1952), at whose home the first meeting had been held, was chairman all through the 22 years of the Sunday School Mission, became the first chairman of the new board and continued until 1934, when he asked to be relieved after 41 years of leadership. To a large extent he molded the mission trends of the conference. J. A. Ressler, who later became one of the first two missionaries to India for the Mennonite Church (MC), was also a member of that group.

On June 8, 1914, a meeting was called by the secretary of the Lancaster Conference to organize a mission board, which was named Eastern Mennonite Board of Missions and Charities. Since then the Board's work has become extensive and varied. It operated the Welsh Mountain Samaritan Home for the Aged. It has shared generously in past years in the war relief programs in Europe and in the migrations of European refugees to Paraguay, Canada, and the United States. It sponsors 67 home missions, including such cities as New York, N.Y.; Reading and Philadelphia, Pa.; Washington, D.C.; Brewton, Ala., and Tampa, Fla., and including 9 Negro missions and 3 centers for Jewish evangelism. In 1934 it opened foreign work in Tanganyika Territory, Africa. By 1953 there were 39 missionaries on furlough and on this field, and native membership was about 950 with about 600 additional catechumens. In 1948 approval of the Ethiopian government was received to open work in that country, and the first missionaries were soon on the field, with a total of 35 workers by 1953. In 1950 work was begun in Honduras, with five workers in 1953. A work was started in Luxembourg in 1951, with four workers in 1953. In 1953 work was opened in Italian Somaliland with four workers. The Board also sponsors work in Israel (started 1953) jointly with the Mission Board at Elkhart. A total of 87 foreign workers was serving under the Board in 1953. A system of voluntary short-term services was set up in 1948 to provide opportunities for the young people of the church. In 1953 the total income of the Board for all purposes was $390,000.

This Board co-operates with the Mennonite Board of Missions and Charities at Elkhart, Ind., in the program sponsored by that Board in its various home and foreign missions. The Eastern Board officers in 1954 were as follows: Henry F. Garber, president; H. Raymond Charles, vice-president; Orie O. Miller, secretary; Paul Graybill, assistant secretary; and Ira Buckwalter, treasurer. The Board supports the work of the Mennonite Central Committee and has had a representative on it from the beginning in 1920.

Beginning with April 15, 1924, the Board has published its own organ, the *Missionary Messenger,* since May 15, 1925, a monthly, usually 16 pages, which is a rich source of material on the history and work of the Board. Beginning with 1952 it has published a comprehensive annual report; previously for many years the annual financial report was published. A mimeographed *Newsletter* has been issued regularly beginning with 1952.   H.F.G.

I. D. Landis, *The Missionary Movement Among Lancaster Conference Mennonites* (Scottdale, 1937).

Eastern Mennonite College. In the second decade of the 20th century, a number of Virginia Mennonite (MC) leaders believed there should be a church school in the East. It was observed that a great many Mennonite young people who attended the local high schools were being lost to the church. It was to prevent this loss and to establish a school that would promote the cause of the Mennonite Church, that steps were taken to organize a church school in the East. It was difficult to find a permanent location for the school. Warwick County and Alexandria, Va., were considered as possible locations in 1914 and 1915, but these were rejected because they were off center from the total Mennonite population in the East. The Assembly Park, a 16-acre forest area, 1½ miles northwest of Harrisonburg, with a large, three-story frame building which had been previously used as an industrial school, was chosen as the location, since it was located near the border between the Middle and the Northern districts of the Virginia Conference. This property was purchased in 1916, and used until the winter of 1920, when the college was moved to its permanent location on the hill west of the Assembly Park. The first building on the new site was a large (50 x 120 ft.) three-story tile stucco building providing classrooms, dormitories, dining hall and kitchen, and administration offices. In 1926 a south annex was constructed providing additional dormitories on the third and fourth floors, a new chapel on the first floor, and a science laboratory and dining room in the basement. With the exception of the gymnasium, no further major building enterprise was undertaken for more than a decade. In 1938 Vesper Heights Observatory was constructed as a class project. Its development has attracted wide attention.

In 1940 building operations were begun again on a large scale. The new north annex provided for science laboratories in the basement, a library on the entire first floor, and an infirmary on the second and third floors. The old frame building in the Assembly Park was razed and some of the material used in the construction of an industrial arts building. The largest unit of construction in the early 1940's was the auditorium with a seating capacity of 1,500. An assembly room in the basement provided accommodations for 500.

During World War II and several years following, building operations were practically at a standstill except for emergency building. In 1949 the board of trustees decided to undertake building again on a larger scale. Work was begun on the largest single building unit in the history of the school—the women's dormitory, which accommodates 250 persons and includes a larger kitchen and dining room as well as additional classrooms; it was completed in 1953.

The building program has not been the most important phase of life at Eastern Mennonite College. Curriculums have been added and expanded; accreditment has been sought and attained. Work of college grade was offered first in 1920. In the following years, two and three years of college work were offered. In 1930 the College was accredited by the state as a standard junior college. Two years

later the College received state approval for a two-year teacher's training course leading to a normal professional certificate. A Bible course of college grade has been offered from almost the first. The course has been expanded along with the general college work, so that in 1937, a four-year Bible course leading to the Th.B. degree was offered. A four-year liberal arts college program was initiated in 1945. The Virginia State Board of Education in 1947 gave Eastern Mennonite College the rating of a standard four-year college with permission to grant the A.B., B.S., B.S. in Education, B.R.E., and Th.B. (6-yr.) degrees.

The college now (1955) offers the following curriculums: Bachelor of Arts, Bachelor of Science, Premedical Course, Bachelor of Science in Home Economics, Bachelor of Arts in Secondary Education, Bachelor of Science in Secondary Education, Bachelor of Science in Elementary Education, and Bachelor of Science in Nursing; in the Bible School, the Christian Workers' Course, Junior College Bible Course, Bachelor of Religious Education, and Bachelor of Theology.

These increased offerings and accreditment by the State Board has meant much from the standpoint of enrollment. In the 1930's the enrollment was around 50 students; by 1952 it had increased to 260, almost exclusively members of the Mennonite Church (MC). The College also operates a strong high-school division with about 200 students. In 1955-56 the total enrollment was 623, with 381 in the college, and 242 in the high school.

By 1955-56 the College was staffed by 41 teaching faculty members. Six of this number have the doctor's degree, or its equivalent, and two are candidates.

A large variety of extracurricular activities is provided. The Christian service activities are under the direction of a Director of Christian Service and the Young People's Christian Association. This provides an outlet of expression for the religious emphasis in all departments of training. The college is characterized by a strong religious atmosphere and a conservative viewpoint. It aims to train youth for service in the church and has for its motto "Thy Word Is Truth."

The school is owned and operated by the Virginia Mennonite Conference through a board of 17 trustees elected for a three-year term by the conference. In addition there is a Religious Welfare Committee of four elected by the conference. (*ML* I, 498 f.)†

H.A.B.

Eastern Mennonite College Bulletin, first issued in May 1922 as the *Eastern Mennonite School Bulletin,* is the official organ of Eastern Mennonite College, now published monthly by the board of trustees to inform friends of the college about the work of the school. It includes annual reports of the administrative officers and special numbers dealing with current developments and needs. The annual catalog constitutes one number. H.A.B.

Eastern Mennonite College Journal was first published in January 1923 as the *Eastern School Journal.* In January 1924 the name was changed to *The Eastern Mennonite School Journal.* It was edited by members of the faculty until 1929, when student editors took over the work. Historically an important number of the paper was the enlarged pictorial commencement number. In the spring of 1949 it was decided to make the commencement number a separate publication. The name of the paper was changed to *The Eastern Mennonite College Journal* in April 1948. In June 1956 it was discontinued. It was published monthly during the school year, 30 pages in size. **H.A.B.**

Eastern Mennonite College High School (called Academy until 1927) from the beginning has been a very important division of instruction at Eastern Mennonite College. The first year of high school was given during the first regular school year 1917-18, with a full high-school course offered the second year. There were seven graduates in 1919 and five in 1920, which was the smallest class in the history of the school. The enrollment continued to grow until there was a graduating class of more than 80, although it has declined somewhat in recent years, due to the organization of church high schools in other places in the East such as Lancaster Mennonite School. The high school, while a part of the total institution, is under its own director.

The curriculum has been enriched by the addition of a wide range of electives including art, bookkeeping, typewriting, German, oral expression, chemistry, home economics, youth guidance, and physics, as well as additional courses in history and mathematics. Seventeen units, including two units of Bible work, have been required for graduation from the first.

An effort is being made to retain the values of the high-school course in spite of an increased enrollment and emphasis in the college department of the school. Separate meetings in various types of activities have been provided for the two groups. The Young People's Christian Association has been reorganized to give high-school students more responsibility in the form of leadership and committee work. The high-school enrollment in 1954-55 was 224. **H.A.B.**

Eastern Mennonite Convalescent Home, an institution established by the Franconia Mennonite Conference (MC) in 1942. A board of seven brethren from the churches in the Franconia Conference District were appointed by the bishops to serve as trustees. A charter for the institution was granted Dec. 14, 1942. The buildings are beautifully located on Highway 309 near Hatfield, Pa., with accommodations for 16 patients. In the rear of the main buildings is a separate building, the first floor of which is used for a laundry and garage and the second floor for the workers' rooms when they are not on duty.

Although established for the care of members of the Mennonite Church, a majority of the guests have been non-Mennonites. Sunday school is held every Sunday morning and a worship service every two weeks. A midweek song service is held every two weeks. Devotions are conducted every morning. The nurses read the Scripture once every week to those who are unable to read. M. K. Kerr and his wife serve at the present time (1953) as steward and matron. **J.W.K.**

Eastern Mennonite Home, Souderton, Pa., a home for the aged in the Franconia Conference (MC) though not officially under conference control. On Oct. 7, 1915, the building of a home at Souderton was approved by the conference. Among the promoters were Andrew S. Mack, William M. Moyer, Henry Krupp, John S. Nice, Garret S. Nice, Joseph Bechtel, and W. R. Moyer. The home was opened for service on May 17, 1917. In 1921 an annex was built. The total cost of buildings and furnishings amounted to $100,000. The main building is 37 x 144 ft., an annex 36 x 96 ft., and one 36 x 36 ft., with 88 single beds and 13 double beds. The institution is supported by contributions and is free of debt. The officers in 1954 were Henry Delp, president; Oliver Nyce, vice-president; Norman Moyer, secretary; and John S. Nice, treasurer. The capacity of the Home is 84 inmates.† **J.C.C.**

Easton (Pa.) Mennonite Brethren in Christ Church, 28 members in 1911, had 53 members in 1953, with D. E. Thomann as pastor.

Ebbe Pieterszoon, a Mennonite elder at Harlingen in the Dutch province of Friesland, whose lack of ability and lust for power were the chief cause of the division between the Frisians and the Flemish (1566-68). At the conference at Harlingen in 1555, where Menno was compelled by Dirk Philips and Leenaert Bouwens to side with the proponents of the strict ban, he was present as a preacher. Soon afterward he was ordained elder against Menno's wishes (see Menno's letters, *Complete Works* II, 232, where the typographical error "Lebe" stands). In 1561 or 1562 Leenaert Bouwens was deposed by a conference at Emden. Ebbe also helped to bring this about, although he soon repented it. The consequence was that baptism stopped in Friesland. Bouwens lived close to Harlingen, but did not wish to baptize, and Ebbe was incompetent or perhaps too fearful of persecution to undertake the traveling. When Ebbe disregarded the requests for help brought by Laurens Verniers and Jeroen Tinnegieter, representatives of the Flemish who had settled in Friesland, the Flemish decided to ordain Tinnegieter as preacher. Since this was done without asking Ebbe's advice, he felt that his authority as an elder had been violated. He brought this complaint before the preachers, and in the discussion of this quarrel the division grew deeper and deeper until it led to the great division (see **Flemish Mennonites**), causing many thousands of Mennonites to join the Reformed Church in disgust. **K.V.**

The account of this dissension is told by de Hoop Scheffer, *DB* 1893; new facts have been presented in the *Zondagsbode*, Aug. 16 and 23, 1914; see also Kühler, *Geschiedenis* I, 398, 400-18; *ML* I, 500.

Ebbink, Hinrich, identical with Hendrik van Vreden (*q.v.*).

Ebenezer Evangelical Mennonite Brethren Church, in Henderson, York Co., Neb., had a membership of 93 in 1954. It was organized as a congregation on Nov. 5, 1882, with Elder Isaac Peters (*q.v.*) as its first leader. Its first services were held in a school-house. A little later a church was built one mile south of the present village of Henderson. In 1915 the church was moved to Henderson and remodeled. A parsonage was built in 1934. The Sunday school was organized in 1883, the Christian Endeavor on Feb. 16, 1908, and a church choir in 1915. This congregation was one of the two (the other was Mountain Lake, Minn.) founding congregations of the E.M.B. group. Johann P. Epp was one of the leading ministers, following Isaac Peters. He served as minister 1883-1917, four years of this term as elder. In 1953 F. G. Thomas was pastor.† H.C.Q.

Ebenezer Krimmer Mennonite Brethren Church, Doland, S.D., was organized in 1919 by seven families under the leadership of Jacob J. Hofer. The first services were held in the Irving church, located ten miles south and five miles west of Doland. In 1923 a church building near Bloomfield was moved to the present Ebenezer location, which is eight miles south and four miles west of Doland. This building was remodeled in 1949 to obtain a seating capacity of 250.

A few years after the church was organized, Mathias Kleinsasser came into the community and assisted Jacob J. Hofer, each giving a 15-minute sermon. Since Hofer's death in 1929, the church has been served by Jake P. Glanzer, David J. S. Mendel, and Paul H. Glanzer, who came to Doland in September 1946. In 1955 the membership was 105.

P.H.G.

Ebenezer Mennonite Brethren in Christ Church, now known as the Bethlehem (*q.v.*) M.B.C. Church.

Ebenezer Mennonite Brethren Church, now extinct, located four miles east of Buhler, Reno Co., Kan., had its beginning in 1878, when a number of families from Russia settled in the community, with Franz Ediger and Peter Wall as leaders. In 1879 Elder Abraham Schellenberg organized this group as a church; he served as elder until 1906. Their first building, erected in 1880, was of earthen brick, 30 x 50 ft., and was replaced by a frame church in 1900. Other ministers who have served this congregation are Elder Henry Adrian, Franz Ediger, Peter Wall, and Gerhard Franz. In 1921 this congregation united as a body with the Mennonite Brethren Church of Buhler, after having been the mother church of other congregations in Reno, McPherson, and Harvey counties in Kansas.

J.J.T.

Ebenezer Mennonite Church (GCM), located two miles east of Bluffton, Ohio, is a member of the Middle District Conference. This congregation forms one of the two centers of the original Swiss community between Bluffton and Pandora. A meetinghouse was built near the site of the present building in 1846, enlarged in 1883, and again in 1928. After Pandora in 1904, and Bluffton in 1918 had organized separate congregations, Ebenezer and St. Johns remained united as one congregation under the ministry of William Gotschall, the last of the ministers to serve the united Swiss community. In 1923 this union was dissolved, and Elmer Neuen-

schwander became the first minister of the separate congregation. The 1953 membership was 507, with Howard T. Landes as pastor.   C.H.S.

Ebenezer Mennonite Church (GCM), a member of the Western District Conference, located three miles east and one-half mile north of Gotebo, Okla., was organized in 1903. The first church building, seating approximately 130, is still in use. The 1953 membership was 67.   G.M.P.

Ebenezer Mennonite Church (GCM) was organized near Fitzmaurice, Sask., on Aug. 4, 1946, under the leadership of Martin D. Thiessen and A. P. Loewen. The congregation is a member of the Conference of Mennonites in Canada. In 1953 there were 27 members, with Martin D. Thiessen as minister.

M.D.T.

Ebenezer Mennonite Church (MC), located four miles northeast of South Boston, Halifax Co., Va., is a member of the Virginia Mennonite Conference. The church was organized in 1904 under the leadership of Henry H. Good, the first pastor, with 20 charter members. The 1953 membership was 37, all rural people. They worshiped in a union church until 1931, when a brick church with a seating capacity of 150 was built; it was dedicated in 1932. Otis B. Snead is the present minister in charge (1954).   A.S.Br.

Ebenezer United Missionary Church, a rural congregation of the Ontario Conference, located seven miles east of Stayner. The original church was destroyed by fire in 1947. The present church, built under the leadership of W. E. Prosser, was dedicated Aug. 29, 1948. The church had 35 members in 1954.

E.R.S.

Ebenfeld, a Mennonite settlement in the province of Ekaterinoslav, South Russia, which in 1926 had three villages with 5,700 acres of land and a population of 187.

Der praktische Landwirt (1926) No. 5, p. 2; *ML* I, 70.

Ebenfeld Mennonite Brethren Church, southeast of Hillsboro, Marion Co., Kan., had its beginning in 1875, several M.B. families from Russia having settled in this community in 1874. Another party of 75 families settled here in 1876. The meetings were at first held in the East Gnadenau schoolhouse and in the earliest M.B. Conference yearbooks this congregation was called Gnadenau. It is the first organized M.B. congregation in North America.

The church grew rapidly and in 1888 had a membership of 253. Since then it has retained about this number and in 1953 had 250 members. At times the congregation declined through the moving away of many young families to new settlements, particularly to Oklahoma. It again increased remarkably through large revivals. The church has had three noted revivals: 1892, when 50 members were added; in 1907, 67; and in 1937, 59 members. The Steinreich M.B. Church, 10 miles to the east, was until Oct. 29, 1946, an affiliated branch of the Ebenfeld Church.

In 1883 the congregation built its first church, which was replaced by a larger church in 1904. This building was destroyed by fire in December 1924, but was at once replaced by the present church.

The ministerial or pastoral leadership has been as follows: Peter Eckert 1875-82, Abraham Cornelsen, Sr., 1882-84, Elder Johann Foth 1884-1915, J. K. Hiebert 1915-33, G. W. Lohrenz 1933-45, J. G. Baerg 1945-50, J. J. Gerbrandt 1950-52, and Allen Fast 1952- . The following ordained ministers have also served the church for a greater length of time: Wm. Hergert, D. D. Claassen, Theodor Freuchting, Cornelius Hiebert, Abraham Cornelsen, Jr., Cornelius Nickel, Johann Harder, H. W. Lohrenz, P. C. Hiebert, Christian Seibel, J. W. Lohrenz, and P. P. Hiebert.

The church has always been known for its missionary zeal and for many years conducted an annual spring mission festival. The following missionaries have come from this congregation: A. J. Becker and Katharina Penner to the Comanche Indians in Oklahoma; Katharina Lohrenz, Anna Hanneman, and J. H. Lohrenz to India; and Clara Lohrenz Buschman to Africa. J.G.Ba.

Ebenfeld Mennonite Church (GCM), Montezuma, Kan., a member of the Western District Conference, was organized Aug. 8, 1920, by H. J. Dyck. Abe A. Schmidt, one of the charter members, was elected pastor and served the church intermittently for about 15 years. The membership in 1955 was 21, with Joseph W. Goossen as minister. H.Sp.

Ebenfeld Mennonite Church (GCM), located near Herschel, Sask., was organized in April 1925, by Mennonite immigrant families who had come to this area from southern Russia in 1923 and 1925 and by other families who soon joined them. The congregation had 34 charter members under the leadership of Elder Jacob B. Wiens and Gerhard Wiens. In 1926 the congregation joined the Canadian conference and in 1927 built a church 2½ miles north of Herschel on Highway 31. Besides this church, the congregation of 268 members (1953) has three other churches—at Fiske, Glidden, and Superb. Following the death of J. B. Wiens in 1939, J. J. Thiessen served the church until 1943, when C. J. Warkentin was elected and ordained elder. He is assisted by five associate ministers who serve without remuneration.

The Glidden-Kindersly group (Russian immigrants of 1927-29) joined the Ebenfeld congregation in 1953. (*Der Bote,* Aug. 26, 1953, p. 5.) C.J.W.

Ebenflur ("Prairie") Mennonite Church (GCM), now extinct, in Hamilton Co., Kan., was founded in 1907 with about 40 members and Peter Heidebrecht as minister. On account of unfavorable climatic and economic conditions this rural settlement project failed, and most of the members gradually moved away, including finally the preacher and deacon. The small neighboring Mennonite Brethren congregation suffered the same fate. (*ML* I, 500 f.) H.R.V.

Eberli (Aeberli), **Lorenz** (Lenz), an Anabaptist martyr of Grünau in Emmental, Switzerland, was executed June 3, 1539, at Bern (*Mart. Mir.,* German 1780, 812; E 1130). This martyr is not found in the Dutch edition (1685). vDZ.

S. Geiser, *Die Taufgesinnten-Gemeinden* (Karlsruhe, 1931) 179, 182, 201.

Eberli (Aeberli), **Melchior,** a staunch Anabaptist of Sumiswald in the Emmental, Switzerland, nephew of the preceding martyr Lorenz Eberli, successfully withstood severe torture in January 1569 at Bern. vDZ.

S. Geiser, *Die Taufgesinnten-Gemeinden* (Karlsruhe, 1931) 200 f.

Ebersole (Ebersol, Eversole, Eversull, Aebersold, Ebersohl), a Swiss family name found frequently in the Mennonite Church (MC) of North America, especially in Lancaster Co., Pa., and in Illinois. Among the Ebersohl immigrants of the 18th century were Abraham (1727); Johannes, Peter, and Jost (1739); Carl (1753); and Jacob (1763). The Lancaster Conference (MC) has had several deacons by the name of Ebersole, seven or more ministers, and bishops Peter Ebersole (1791-1870) and John G. Ebersole (1849-1934). Lancaster Conference currently has a minister and a deacon named Ebersole, and Ohio and Eastern Mennonite Conference has Bishop Allen Ebersole. Among the first ministers in the Partridge, Ill., congregation (now Metamora) was Andrew Ebersole. Frank S. Ebersole (GCM) (1875-), former business manager of Goshen College (to 1912), served as mayor of Goshen, Ind., 1943-48. J.C.W.

Charles E. Ebersol, *The Ebersol Families in America—1727-1937* (Lansing, Mich., 1937).

Eby (Ebi, Ebie, Uebi, Aby, Aebi, Eaby, Ebee), name of a large and influential Swiss family in Mennonite history. Some historians of the family claim that their ancestral family belonged to the Italian Waldenses and fled north to the Swiss canton of Zürich in the 16th century. In any case it is in Zürich that the name appears first in Mennonite history, Jacob Eby being ordained bishop there in 1683. His son Theodorus Eby (1663-1730) migrated to the Palatinate in 1704 and to Lancaster Co., Pa., in 1715, where he settled at Mill Creek. His grandson Christian (d. 1807) became a deacon in the Hammer Creek congregation, and two great-grandsons were prominent bishops in Lancaster County and in Ontario—Peter Eby (*q.v.,* 1765-1843) and his younger brother Benjamin Eby (*q.v.,* 1785-1863) respectively. (Theodorus Eby also had a nephew Peter Eby who came to America in 1720. Theodorus had another nephew in Bern, Switzerland, a cousin of the 1720 immigrant, named Andrew Eby. Andrew's son Nicholas emigrated to America in 1753 and settled in Wisconsin; he was a Lutheran. Andrew Eby had another son Christian who settled in Alsace where he reared a family.) The descendants of Theodorus Eby are located mostly in eastern Pennsylvania, especially Lancaster County, and in Ontario. The Lancaster Mennonite Conference (MC) had five ordained men named Eby in 1953. Special mention should be made of Bishop Isaac Eby (1834-1910) of the Lancaster Conference, and of Preacher Solomon Eby (*q.v.*, 1834-1931) of Ontario who was one of the leaders whose followers merged with other groups to form the Mennonite Brethren in Christ (now U.M.C.). Another immigrant to Pennsylvania was Matthias Eby (d. 1893), who in 1853, shortly after arriving in Pennsylvania from Germany, located at Freeport, Ill. In 1856 he was ordained as a minister, later as a bishop, in which office he served until 1878 when he retired because of age. Swiss Mennonite history records the banishment from Trachselwald of a Preacher Durss Aebi, 1670.   J.C.W.

Ezra Eby, *A . . . History of the Eby Family* (Berlin, Ont., 1889); Jacob Eby, *A Brief Record of the Ebys* (Lancaster, 1923).

Eby, Benjamin (1785-1853), pioneer Mennonite (MC) bishop in Ontario, the eleventh child of Christian Eby and his wife Catharine Bricker, was born in the old homestead on Hammer Creek, Warwick Twp., Lancaster Co., Pa., May 2, 1785. On Feb. 25, 1807, he married Mary Brubacher. That spring he and his wife emigrated to Waterloo Co., Ont., arriving at what was later Berlin (now Kitchener) on June 21. On Nov. 27, 1809, he was ordained a minister of the Mennonite Church (MC) and on Oct. 11, 1812, was ordained as bishop. In 1813 his dream of a meetinghouse was realized with the erection of a log structure of modest dimensions, the first building erected solely for religious worship in Waterloo County. The congregation had not fewer than 150 members. Possibly as early as 1815 Benjamin Eby built a frame annex to the log church, with a movable partition between it and the main building. This annex served as a schoolhouse of which he himself was for many years the teacher. At the same time he carried on his farming. His farm was lot 2 of the Beasley Tract, comprising a large part of the East Ward of the modern city of Kitchener. To Benjamin Eby were born eleven children. In August 1834, his wife died of cholera. Some time after her death he married the widow of Abraham Erb, the founder of Waterloo. On June 28, 1853, Eby died.

To sketch the life of Benjamin Eby is to consider the man, his work, his interests, and his influence. As a farmer he seems to have been successful. At least he was generous with his money, as the record of the very few of his financial transactions which have come down to us would indicate. In 1816, when the church purchased an acre of land to add to its holdings, he donated an additional three quarters of an acre. All this is now part of the property of First Mennonite Church of Kitchener. Between 1825 and 1830 two men, John Hoffman and Samuel Bowers, wanted to establish a furniture factory. Appealing in vain to various sources for land, they came finally to Bishop Eby, who readily made land available to them. This too was a gift. The third transaction was in connection with the founding, in 1835, of the first newspaper in inner Canada, the *Canada Museum*, by Henry W. Peterson. Benjamin Eby not only encouraged this enterprise by word but purchased two shares of stock at $40.00 each, a larg-

er risk than anyone else, apart from Mr. Peterson, was willing or able to take. Again, in 1836, he donated $16.00 toward the building of a cemetery wall, the next highest gift being $4.00. Relatively small as those sums are today they were important in those pioneer days. Judged in relation to his times and his contemporaries all these transactions establish Benjamin Eby as a substantial farmer in his community. Of him as a preacher only a few comments have come down. H. W. Peterson, publisher and Lutheran lay preacher, says in his diary: "Stayed all night at Benjamin Eby's, went with him and his family to the meeting or church. He prayed and preached well. He is a good man." An anonymous writer in the Berlin *Daily Telegraph* for May 19, 1906, says: "His sermons were full of good sense, very intelligible, lying parallel with the understanding of attentive hearers." A tradition has it that there were invariably tears in his eyes when he entered the pulpit on a Sabbath morning. For many years, from 1818-19 to the early 1840's, he was also the community schoolmaster. In this period he wrote two spelling or reading books, *Neues Buchstabir- und Lesebuch* (1839) and *Fibel* (1843). He also wrote a work on Mennonite faith and history entitled: *Kurzgefasste Kirchen-geschichte und Glaubenslehre der Taufgesinnten Christen oder Mennoniten* (1841). He was most likely the compiler of the *Gemeinschaftliche Liedersammlung* (Berlin, 1836), which was long used in Ontario. Thus he was farmer, teacher, preacher, and author. As might be expected, his interests went beyond his own community. He corresponded with European Mennonites and published some of the letters received in *Briefe an die Mennonisten Gemeine in Ober Canada* (1840) and *Zweyter Brief aus Dänemark* (1841).

The physical man must be noted briefly. There was a tradition that he was frail. *Aus 'em Bennie gebts ka Bauer, er muss Schulmester werre.* (Bennie will never make a farmer, he must become a schoolteacher.) Yet he made two journeys to Canada on horseback through the wilderness, hewed for himself a home, prospered substantially, and was unusually active in church and community affairs. One of his coats, seen by the present writer, would indicate him to have been a man about five feet, six inches tall, and weighing possibly 150 lbs.

Up to 1833 the Waterloo County settlement was known as "Ben Eby's" or "Ebytown," thus establishing Eby as the leading citizen of his community. With the arrival of increasing numbers of German non-Mennonites, the name was changed in 1833 to Berlin. That he had both a keen sense of civic and denominational responsibility the record of his influence and activities bears eloquent testimony. In his account of Benjamin Eby's funeral, written for the July 7, 1855, issue of the Guelph *Advertiser*, H. S. Peterson calls him "an Israelite in whom there was no guile, and that he was sincerely pious, humble, exemplary, practical, and non-sectarian, and eminently successful in his day and generation." The anonymous friend in the *Daily Telegraph* (Berlin, Ont., May 19, 1906) says: "He was a person of unblemished character. Naturally of a sweet and gentle disposition, friendly and obliging, always ready to serve his friends in any way that he could by his interest and authority. This he did freely and generously, not proud or haughty, but serious in giving good counsel, and greatly esteemed for his integrity by all ranks and denominations. All very much desired his company and wholesome conversations."

Eby's *Kurzgefasste Kirchengeschichte* of 1841 had many reprints: Lancaster 1853; Elkhart 1868, 1879, 1901; Kitchener 1919. His *Neues Buchstabir- und Lesebuch* of 1839 was also often reprinted: Berlin, Ont., 1842, 1847; Elkhart 1869, 1871, 1882, 1896, 1909.   J.B.C.

J. Boyd Cressman, "Bishop Benjamin Eby," *29th Annual Report of the Waterloo Historical Society* (Kitchener, 1941); *ML* I, 501.

Eby, Christian (1734-1807), grandson of pioneer Theodorus Eby, son of Christian (1698-1756), settled on his father's Hammer Creek homestead in Lancaster Co., Pa., and in 1760 married Catharine Bricker, daughter of Peter Bricker and aunt of Samuel Bricker of Ontario. They reared a family of ten children, including Peter (*q.v.*), the venerable bishop of Pequea; Benjamin (*q.v.*), bishop, schoolteacher, and molder of the Ontario colony; and Hans, the philanthropist who saved Ontario for the Mennonites. He was a large man of athletic type, wore a long beard, and possessed unusual health and vigor until his death. He was a very successful miller and extensive farmer. His home was known for its hospitality. Destitute Revolutionary War soldiers at his home and at the Brickerville church found in him a Good Samaritan. His home was one of the eight used for church services in the district before the building of the first Hammer Creek meetinghouse (MC) in 1819. He is the first known deacon in the district. He was buried on the hill overlooking his home.   I.D.L.

Eby, Heinrich, a printing establishment, at Berlin (now Kitchener), Waterloo Co., Ont. On March 4, 1835, a proposal to establish a printing press in Berlin was drawn and opened to signature by those willing to contribute to the subsidizing of the enterprise. Thursday, Aug. 27, 1835, the first fruits of the enterprise appeared in the form of the first number of a weekly newspaper entitled *Canada Museum und Allgemeine Zeitung.* The printer's name is given as Heinrich Wilhelm Peterson. The list of subscribers to the enterprise includes a large number of Mennonites, prominent among them being Benjamin Eby and Heinrich Eby, the latter of whom soon (1840) issued publications over his own name as printer. Apparently Eby took over the Peterson press at that time. Benjamin Eby was the bishop, 1812-54, and spiritual and cultural leader of the large Mennonite settlement in this region. Heinrich Eby (1820-55), one of his sons, published in addition to other literature the following Mennonite books at Berlin: *Briefe an die Mennonisten Gemeine in Ober Canada* (1840); *Kurzgefasste Kirchengeschichte und Glaubenslehre der Taufgesinnten-Christen oder Mennoniten* (1841); *Die Gemeinschaftliche Liedersammlung* (1841, 1849); *Zweyter*

Brief aus Dänemark an die Mennonisten Gemeine in Çanada (1841); *ABC- Buchstabir- und Lesebuch* (1842, 1847); *Geistliches Sendschreiben des Christlichen Lehrers und Predigers Heinrich Nissly* (1842); *Fibel zu den ersten Lese-Uebungen* (1843); *Kleiner Katechismus* (1845); *Glaube und Lehre von der Taufe der Mennoniten in Deutschland* (1845); *Die Ernsthafte Christenpflicht* (1845). In 1852 a Mennonite book appeared at Berlin under the imprint of Peter Eby, Heinrich Eby's younger brother, but in 1857 the hymnbook *Gemeinschaftliche Liedersammlung* appeared at Kitchener under the imprint of Boedecker und Stuebing. Peter Eby apparently took over the Heinrich Eby press until he moved to New York State in 1856. This is the short history (1840-56) of the only Mennonite printing establishment ever operated in Ontario. It appears that Peter Eby left the Mennonite Church, if indeed he ever belonged to it.   H.S.B.

Eby, Isaac, who with Jacob N. Brubacher shared the leadership of the Lancaster Conference (MC) at the turn of the 20th century, was born Jan. 26, 1834, in Salisbury Twp., Lancaster Co., Pa., the son of Peter Eby and grandson of Bishop Peter Eby. He died June 19, 1910. He was survived by eleven children, eight born to his first wife, Mary Mellinger, and three to his second wife, Lizzie K. Lehman.

Isaac Eby joined the Mennonite Church (MC) during his twenty-sixth year, and on Nov. 9, 1876, he was ordained by lot to the ministry. Two years later he was ordained bishop in the Pequea district where his grandfather had been a leader in the early 19th century. Isaac Eby was one of the first leaders of the Lancaster Conference to preach in the English language.

Bishop Eby was an eloquent speaker, forthright in his preaching and devoted to the spiritual welfare of the church. He was a pioneer in the Sunday-school movement in the Lancaster Conference. His greatest contribution to the church was the impetus which he gave to the newly developed interest in mission work. His influence extended beyond the confines of his own conference in that he worked sympathetically and co-operatively with other contemporary leaders in the church, such as John F. Funk and John S. Coffman, both of Indiana.

S.S.W.

Eby, Peter (1765-1843), b. Oct. 14, 1765, north of Lititz, along the Hammer Creek in Lancaster Co., Pa., was the son of Christian and Catharine Bricker Eby, and the third child in a family of twelve. The father was the first known deacon in the Hammer Creek (MC) district. The fourth child was Hans, whose influence helped decide the fate of the Waterloo, Ont., colony. The eleventh child was Bishop Benjamin of Ontario. Of Peter's boyhood and youth we have no record.

Peter's great-grandfather Theodorus, son of Bishop Jakob Eby, was born in Switzerland in 1663. In 1704 he emigrated to the Palatinate, and in 1715 to America, settling in Earl Twp., Lancaster Co., Pa. In 1735 his son Christian and wife, Elizabeth Meyer, settled on a 236-acre tract on Hammer Creek. In

1754 they built the large house in which their son Christian, Peter's father, reared his family. In this house regular meetings were held. It is still occupied and in good condition (1948). The barn Peter's father built is also still in use. In 1750 Peter's grandfather built a mill which the family operated until 1790, when Peter's father built a new one further downstream, which mill was rebuilt in 1850 and is operating in good condition to date. Peter's father freely furnished supplies for wounded soldiers quartered at Zion Church of near-by Brickerville.

Such a heritage and environment was the school of the youth who became "the great bishop of Pequea," who, according to Ellis and Evans, "was a positive man of clear native mind, a natural orator, and though making no pretense to a thorough scholastic training, commanded, both in temporal and spiritual matters, the deference of his brethren." Of him J. F. Funk wrote, "The doctrines of Peter Eby were sound Mennonite doctrines. He was a most remarkable man." Harris says his preaching was extemporaneous, eloquent, and very effective, appealing to reason, not emotion; and also that in the councils of the church his decisions were impartial and just.

In July 1788 Peter married Margaretha, daughter of John Hess, of Hess's congregation, Warwick Township, and in 1791 they moved to the Mt. Patton farm in Salisbury Township, near Gap, their home for the rest of their lives. They had nine children and to date their descendants number well over 2,000, many of whom have been valuable assets to the church and society.

No record exists of the date of Peter's baptism, nor the exact date of his ordination as minister or bishop. Present sources of information indicate his ordination as minister about 1800, and as bishop of the Pequea district (MC) about 1804, in which office he served until his death. Under Peter's bishopric the church grew from a few scattered families to strong congregations. In 1806 Paradise meetinghouse was built, Hershey's school and meetinghouse in 1814 and a new meetinghouse in 1837, and in 1841 Old Road. Peter also shepherded the church through the War of 1812, and the troubled times of the organization of the Reformed Mennonite Church by John Herr. He was a member of the Lancaster bishop board and in 1831 became moderator of the Lancaster Conference.

Peter's labors, however, were not confined to Pequea. Tradition says he journeyed to Canada to ordain Benjamin Eby minister in 1809, and bishop in 1812. He ministered to the congregations of Susquehanna Valley, Southwestern Pennsylvania, Maryland, and on some occasions, Virginia. He also made social visits to the Franconia Conference area. In 1840 Christian Herr, Peter's personal choice, was ordained bishop as his assistant and successor, a unique event in the Lancaster Conference, and a tribute to the stature of Peter in the eyes of his brethren.

Peter Eby died April 6, 1843, in his seventy-eighth year, and was buried in the old cemetery at Hershey's Church. He left no writings or books, but his ministry made an impression that still lives a century later.   M.C.E.

Ezra Eby, *A Biographical History of the Eby Family* (Berlin, 1889) 1-26; Ellis and Evans, *History of Lancaster County* (1883) 338, 339, 620; Ira D. Landis, "Bishop Peter Eby of Pequea," *MQR* XIV (1940) 41-51; "The Correspondence of Martin Mellinger," translated and edited by H. S. Bender, *MQR* V (1931).

Eby, Solomon (1834-1931), a founder of the Mennonite Brethren in Christ Church (now U.M.C.), the son of Benjamin and Elizabeth (Cressman) Eby. He was born May 15, 1834, in Waterloo Co., Ont., was raised on the farm, and attended public school. On June 17, 1855, he married Catharine Shantz, to whom were born 12 children. He moved to Port Elgin, Ont.

In 1858 he was ordained to the ministry in the Mennonite Church, and served in that capacity for 14 years. According to his testimony, he was not converted until eleven years after his ordination (1869, Port Elgin, Ont.). Following his conversion he became a zealous advocate for a definite religious experience. Eventually he was expelled from the Mennonite Church, and in 1874 he and Daniel Brenneman of Indiana organized the Reformed Mennonites, a group that later became a part of the Mennonite Brethren in Christ Church (now the United Missionary Church).

For various terms totaling 18 years Eby was presiding elder in the Ontario Conference, and for 14 years he served as pastor, holding pastorates at Breslau, Elmwood, New Dundee, Markham, and Kitchener circuits. He was a member of the first six general conferences, and was chairman of the first one (Zionsville, Pa., 1885). Eby retired from active work in 1906. A few years later he became interested in the Pentecostal movement, and in 1912 he transferred his membership to that organization. He died in 1931.†   E.R.S.

Echo, Das, originally *Lehigh Echo,* was started in 1897 as a four-page German weekly Mennonite newspaper, edited, published, and printed by Jacob J. Wiebe, Lehigh, Kan. It carried news, information, and publicity of interest to the Mennonites of the prairie states. The last issue of this weekly found in the Bethel College Historical Library is dated Jan. 1, 1909. It is likely that *Das Echo* was discontinued soon afterwards.   C.K.

Echo-Verlag (*Echo Publishers*) was founded in Winnipeg, Man., on July 3, 1944, by former students of the Chortitza Zentralschule (opened in 1842) who emigrated from Russia to Canada after 1923, to commemorate the centenary of that school. The object of the organization was to collect and publish historical material dealing with the history of the Mennonites with special consideration of their settlements in Russia. Its publications appear with the subtitle "Historische Schriftenreihe," Echo-Verlag. The Verlag is a purely Mennonite, nonprofit undertaking, without denominational or other obligations. All work in connection with it is honorary. The Verlag owns no printing press and no other property. At its head is the president who was elected at the organization meeting. He is assisted by a council of five members, including the secretary, all appointed by him. The secretary is also the business manager, and in his hands rests the responsibility for all the work undertaken.

Since its organization Dietrich H. Epp of Rosthern, Sask., has been president, and Arnold Dyck of Steinbach, secretary, the latter serving as executive officer. The following books have been published, all in German: C. P. Toews, *Die Tereker Ansiedlung* (The Terek Settlement), 1945; David H. Epp, *Johann Cornies*, 1946, reprint of 1909 edition; A. Loewen and A. Friesen, *Die Flucht über den Amur* (Flight Across the Amur), 1946; G. Lohrenz, *Sagradowka*, 1947; F. Bartsch, *Unser Auszug nach Mittelasien* (Our Emigration to Central Asia; a new edition with a closing chapter by Alexander Rempel), 1948, reprint of 1907 edition; *Am Trakt*, 1948, a condensed translation from the Russian with a supplement by J. J. Dyck; H. Görz, *Die Molotschnaer Ansiedlung*, 1950-51; David H. Epp, *Heinrich Heese*, and Nikolai Regehr, *Johann Philipp Wiebe* (one volume), with the further title: *Zwei Vordermänner des südrussländischen Mennonitentums*, 1952; *Die Kubaner Ansiedlung*, 1953; H. Goerz, *Memrik*, 1954; and H. Sawatzky, *Templer mennonitischer Herkunft*, 1955.   A.B.D.

Echsel (Excel, Exern), **Wilhelm**, a cobbler of St. Gall (or Wallis?), Switzerland, was baptized by Fridli-Ab-Iberg and was one of the first Anabaptists at Zürich. He was one of the group that were arrested, but escaped from prison on April 5, 1526. At a hearing on April 19 (Egli, *Actensammlung*, 308, No. 691) he explained exactly how the flight had been accomplished. Under the torture of the rack he confessed that he had never baptized or preached and therefore requested that he be permitted to return home. On pain of death by drowning if he returned, he was expelled from the canton. He then became an active member of the congregation at Strasbourg. Subjected to a trial there, he said that he had been baptized at Zürich because the Bible teaches first faith, then baptism, and that when the Anabaptists met, they warned one another of sin and shame. He left Strasbourg to evade a disputation with the clergy, and arrived at Augsburg at Christmas 1527. At the Easter meeting there in 1528 (see **Augsburg**, also **Doucher**) he was among those captured and tried. Here he recanted and was expelled (Roth, *Ref.-Gesch.*, 222, 258). Nothing is known of the rest of his life. Neff supposed him to be a native of the Swiss canton of Wallis; but A. Hulshof states that he was from St. Gall. The Zürich documents (von Muralt-Schmid) call him *uss Wallis*.   NEFF, vDZ.

F. Roth, "Der Höhepunkt der wiedertäuferischen Bewegung in Augsburg," *Ztscht des hist. Vereins für Schwaben und Neuburg*, 1901; idem, *Augsburgs Ref.-Gesch.* I (Munich, 1901); A. Hulshof, *Geschiedenis van de Doopsgezinden te Straatsburg* (Amsterdam, 1905) 18; von Muralt and Schmid, *Quellen zur Gesch. der Täufer in der Schweiz* I: *Zürich* (Zürich, 1952); *ML* I, 501.

Eck, Johann (1486-1543), the disputatious, immoderately violent opponent of Luther. He became a friend of Hubmaier, his student at the University of Freiburg i. Br. When Hubmaier won his master's degree, Eck delivered the Latin laudatory oration. When Eck was transferred to Ingolstadt as professor of theology Hubmaier entered the university there. In Waldshut Hubmaier challenged his old teacher to a disputation; Eck ignored it. Among the numerous polemics written by Eck the following are of interest in the history of the Anabaptists:

(1) *Ein Sendbrieve an ein frum Eidgenossenschaft betreffende die Ketzerische disputation Frantz Kolben, des ausgeloffen Münchs und B. Hallers, des verlogenen Predikanten des hochwürdigen sacrament des altars* (Ingolstadt, 1528); (2) *Articulos 404 ad disputationes Lipsicum, Baden et Bernen attinentes partim vero scriptis pacem ecclesiae perturbantium extractos . . . offert se disputatorum* (Ingolstadt, 1530), in which he attacks Hubmaier and his *Schlussreden* (Calvary, 46). His letter to Duke George of Saxony, Nov. 26, 1527, must also be mentioned (Seidemann, 150).

In the 404 articles Eck proposed for the disputation of Ingolstadt in 1536, he intentionally throws Zwingli, Luther, and the Anabaptists together indiscriminately, and derives the Anabaptists ("who deny the Deity of Christ") from Luther.   NEFF.

Verzeichniss seltener und werthvoller Werke, S. Calvary Antiquariat (Berlin, 1870) 46; J. K. Seidemann, *Thomas Münzer* (Leipzig, 1842); *ML* I, 501.

Eckart, Ulrich, a member of the Anabaptist congregation at Augsburg, a grinder, was chained in a dungeon at Augsburg in September 1527 for his faith, and on Oct. 18 expelled with Eitelhans Langenmantel, Endres Widholz, Gall Vischer, Laux Vischer, Peter Schleppach, and Hans Kissling. In addition he had to pay a fine which was contributed to the city alms fund. Nothing is known of his further activity.   HEGE.

Fr. Roth, "Zur Gesch. der Wiedertäufer in Oberschwaben," in *Ztscht des hist. Vereins für Schwaben* XXVIII (1901) 2; *ML* I, 502.

Eckerhof, an estate an hour east of Wiesloch in Baden, Germany, was in the 18th century the seat of a Mennonite congregation. (Müller, *Berner Täufer*, 210; *ML* I, 502.)

Eckhart, Johannes ("Meister Eckhart"), was one of the greatest of the medieval German mystics. He was born about 1260, perhaps at Cologne, joined the order of the Dominicans, and held many high offices. He died in 1327 during his trial on charges of heresy before the Court of Inquisition at Cologne, which ended in 1329 in the condemnation of 28 propositions contained in his sermons.

The roots of Eckhart's mysticism are found in Neo-Platonism. There is evident in his doctrines a strong dependence on Thomas Aquinas, whom he, however, surpasses in that he strives to transform into knowledge the deep and powerful feeling of his piety without reserve.

His mystical-theological ideas may be summarized as follows:

God is the supreme Being. He is the One and Only, the one true and good existence. As the source of all things He is beyond comprehension—negative or positive. Any statements about God are always inadequate and a robbery of God. Therefore Eckhart could say that in God there is neither good nor better nor best. He who says that God is good is just as wrong as he who says the sun is black. God's existence and essence coincide completely; thought and being are identical with Him.

In this essence of God, the "denatured" nature of God is to be distinguished from His "natured nature," which is the revelation of His triune being in relation to the universe. The concept of Trinity is, however, not to be here understood in a dogmatic sense, since Eckhart completely transforms and interweaves it with a mystical pantheism. The Father eternally begets the Son (the Word) and in Him ideas. In the fact that God recognized Himself in the Logos, He Himself lives in the Son and this love of the Father to the Son "is the Holy Spirit." In the Logos God brings forth all things. "All things are God Himself," and "God is all things."

Every creature is a phenomenon of God and bears in itself "a record of divine nature." This is especially true of reasoning creation, i.e., man, who bears within himself the "divine spark." In him Eckhart recognizes the "reversal point (*Umkehrpunkt*) of the world process." In his innermost being man yearns to become fully one with God. In order that this may take place, all the striving of the soul must be directed toward turning from all creature, from sin, the world, indeed from himself. To become rich in God man must become poor in the creature. "If anyone wants to come into the origin (*Grund*) of God, into His greatest, then he must first come into his own origin, into his least." But then man rises to God, and is so-to-speak deified (genuinely Neo-Platonic); the circle closes, for "Being is the Father, unity the Son, and goodness is the Holy Spirit. Now the Holy Spirit takes the soul that is sanctified in the Purest and the Highest, and bears them into His origin, that is the Son, and the Son bears them at once into His origin, that is the Father, into the source, into the inheritance, in which the Son has His being." This "parting" from the manifoldness of the external world is man's highest task. To be sure, he should occupy himself in this world; but above all outward deeds, above the righteousness by works of the sense is the "inner work," purity of mind, "poverty of the soul and its return to the divine source."

Until 1886 only the German writings of Eckhart were known—mostly sermons, tracts, and sayings; since that time Denifle has discovered a long list of Latin writings by Eckhart and has translated excerpts. Eckhart's importance rests, however, on his German works, for it was his striving to impart "the innermost and truest truth" not as the privilege of an exclusive circle, but for all the people. It was especially in "simple piety" but that he felt himself understood, and so, as Windelband says, he "transposed the most delicate formulations of concepts into a German form with linguistic forcefulness of a genius." Thereby Eckhart burst the narrow bonds of medieval scholasticism and through his stress on the new birth he becomes the forerunner of a new understanding of Christianity. Not only Luther and the other reformers profited from it, but also the extra-church circles, especially the Anabaptists.

Eckhart became the representative of a specifically German theology, the head and center of a numerous circle of disciples, and as Ludwig Keller (163) correctly says, the "originator of impulses, from which all the parties that in later centuries grew out of the Waldenses, have been more or less touched."

It is very probable that Hubmaier, Haetzer, and especially Hans Denk, at least indirectly, were strongly influenced by Eckhart and German mysticism in general. This is seen in their doctrine of the freedom of the will, in their slight interest in the dogma of the Trinity, and, especially in the case of Denk, in his teaching on regeneration. There is a conspicuous relationship between Eckhart and Denk in style of writing and the entire complex of ideas. Where Eckhart speaks of "the impoverishment of the creature" and of "poverty of the soul" as a condition for entry into God, Denk uses very similar expressions when he says that we "must therefore become so spiritually poor that we feel we must of ourselves perish." Similarity is again seen in the expressions with which on the one hand Eckhart describes the divine birth in the depths of the soul and on the other hand Denk describes the new birth of the elect of God.

But however related in language, style, and manner of expression, Eckhart and Denk may be, their agreement is of a merely formal nature. Factually there are very deep differences. In Eckhart the concept of God is philosophically abstract and mixed with pantheistic mysticism; in Denk it is real and concrete. In Eckhart Christ appears essentially only as the Logos, and, in so far as he reflects on the Incarnation at all, it is only as an example (Loofs, 629); in Denk Christ is the "Lord and Prince" of salvation. In Eckhart the new birth is an act of deification, almost in a Neo-Platonic ascetic sense; in Denk the new birth is preceded by a moral collapse, a "sitting in the abyss of hell"; it is the needle's eye "through which immense camels must slip and yet cannot do it," until God helps them, and the eye of the needle becomes for them a narrow door to life. In Eckhart moral obligations of a practical nature retreat quietistically; in Denk they are developed into full activity in the service of God for the world. In Eckhart, all is in its essence asceticism, ecstasy, mysticism; in Denk it becomes discipleship of Christ and a listening to the revelation of God in Christ, which finds its resolution in the "inner word," which, to be sure, has a counterpart in Eckhart's "divine spark."

The effects of Eckhart's mysticism are later to be found in Jakob Böhme (1575-1624), G. W. Friedrich Hegel (1770-1831), and Schleiermacher (1768-1834). Also in Gerhard Tersteegen's (1697-1769) hymns there are echoes of Eckhart, without, however, the danger of falling prey to pantheism, which is inherent in Eckhart's system.   E.H.

C. Schmidt, "Eckhart" in *HRE* IV, 26 ff.; Fr. Loofs, *Dogmengeschichte* (4th ed., Halle, 1906), Section 71: "Die Laienfrömmigkeit und die Mystik als Wegbereiter einer Reduktion der publica doctrina auf die Sphäre der Heilslehre"; W. Windelband, *Lehrbuch der Geschichte der Philosophie* (4th ed., Tübingen, 1907) 279 ff.; **Ad.** Wuttke, *Handbuch der christlichen Sittenlehre* I (3rd ed., Leipzig, 1874) 142 f.; L. Keller, *Reformation; Meister Eckhart, A Modern Translation* by R. B. Blakney (N.Y., 1941); R. M. Jones, *The Flowering of Mysticism* (N.Y., 1939); *ML* I, 502 f.

Ecole Biblique Européenne: see **Europäische Mennonitische Bibelschule.**

Economic History *of the Hutterian Brethren.* Although material is abundant, a comprehensive study of this topic has never been made; but it would be of value to consult those studies which are named at the end of this article.

The details of the economic activities of the Hutterian Brethren changed greatly according to the degree of freedom experienced, but the underlying principles and general patterns were fairly uniformly held ever since the beginnings under Jacob Hutter in 1533. The climax of Hutterite life and their most complete carrying out of their communal principles fall in the "Good" and "Golden" periods, 1554-92, mainly during the reign of the more lenient emperor Maximilian II (1564-76, see **Hapsburg**). We are fortunate to possess a fairly graphic picture of the communal life at that time, called *Beschreibung der Gemein Wohlstand (Geschicht-Buch,* ed. Wolkan, 331-38; ed. Zieglschmid, 430-40), inserted into their Chronicle at the year 1569. Here the details of their social organization are described. We learn how a Christian community of goods was observed, how obedience and honor were given to the authorities of the world, how missions were established (*Aussendung*), also how *Diener des Wortes* (*q.v.*) and *Diener der Notdurft* (*q.v.*) were properly elected, etc. In short, the chronicler assures us, "We supported ourselves with all manner of occupations" (*man nähret sich mit allerlei Handwerk*), and in addition served also the manorial lords in many ways. No member of the community was allowed to be idle. "It was like a big clockwork where one wheel drives the other, promotes, helps, and makes the whole clock function." Still more graphic is another simile offered by the Chronicles: such a Bruderhof (*q.v.*) is somewhat like a big beehive where all the busy bees work together to a common end, the one doing this and the other that, not for their own needs but for the good of all. This simile very characteristically hints at the essentially anti-individualistic attitude of the brotherhood. It was understood by all that hard physical labor for the common good (production) was expected of all, while at the same time consumption was restricted according to the principle of frugality as was befitting for a life of discipline and Christian obedience. Large-scale production and restrained consumption necessarily led to economic success or wealth of some sort, which almost inescapably led to jealousy and slander on the part of the surrounding population (see **Fischer, Christoph A.**). The repute of the wealth of the Brethren (in their best time they numbered about 15,000 baptized members) spread as far as to the Emperor's court in Vienna; everyone knew or claimed to know that they bury "great treasures" to hide them from the authorities. Most likely that was true to a certain extent, but should be understood as an act of prudence (in absence of a banking system) in anticipation of times of hardship and persecution. During the period of the Turkish Wars (1605-6) and again during the early years of the Thirty Years' War (1718-22) almost all their savings were confiscated by the government. Yet one generation later Grimmelshausen (*q.v.*) reports again of their considerable wealth in equipment, livestock, and all the rest in their new Bruderhofs in Slovakia. (Zieglschmid concluded that this was in Mannheim (*q.v.*) rather than in Slovakia.) We know from Max Weber's sociological analysis that this situation is typical of all "ascetic Protestantism" or "inner-worldly asceticism," such as can also be observed in Puritanism or later Pietism. Grimmelshausen reports that he saw the craftsmen-brethren at work in their shops "as if they had hired themselves out for pay." Since no one could go about without contributing his share to the common weal, doing it with greatest conscience and discipline, the net result was a rational establishment of great efficiency, something otherwise completely unknown in Europe in the 16th and early 17th centuries, where the factory system had not yet been established. It might be helpful to stress here that there was absolutely no motivation for such organization from the profit angle, since the basic economic philosophy of the Brethren was that of stewardship of all earthly possessions (Correll, Chapter 2), requiring a dedicated care for and optimal organization of all work along certain previously laid out rational plans. In this regard Hutterite communism is truly unique in the entire history of Christian sectarianism.

As to the social status of the Hutterian Brethren one cannot call them either peasants or craftsmen, and it would be misleading to derive their basic Christian convictions from their social background. Theirs was neither a peasant's Christianity nor a craftsman's Christianity (see Dedic, Peachy, also Friedmann, *MQR* 1946, 153 f.). Anyone who joined the brotherhood had to learn a craft or had to accept his particular assignment, often very different from his former background. That belongs to the pattern of "ascetic Protestantism" with its prevailing rational order and subsequent tendency toward saving (*asketischer Sparzwang*). All money earned was considered as part of the working capital (*Betriebskapital*), and not as wealth, and its management was entrusted to the bishop (*Vorsteher*), to the manager (*Diener der Notdurft*), and sometimes to the buyers (*Einkäufer*). In many regards the entire economic organization and pattern was not unlike that of the medieval monastery, with the one difference that for the Hutterites married life was not only favored but almost required.

The education of the growing generation of the Bruderhof tended to make these young people fit into this accepted pattern: industriousness, care, uttermost honesty, frugality, solidity of work, and reliability were the main virtues stressed in their economic pursuits, likewise selflessness and concern wherever required. Luxury was out of the question, it was simply not valued, hence no longer desired.

All crafts were strictly regulated, and these regulations, not unlike medieval guild-regulations, were ever and again read before the assembled groups (see **Crafts,** also **Gemeindeordnungen**).

The economic activities of the Brethren may best be divided into two distinct areas: (*a*) those within the Bruderhofs, including such activities as the pottery kilns and the bathhouses, and (*b*) those performed outside, on the estates of manorial lords or even in some cities (where occasionally Brethrensurgeons were found to be active).

(*a*) On the Bruderhof we may again distinguish between the farm activities proper, the care for food, shelter, and clothing (in this regard the Hutterites of today continue these practices as of old: see Bertha Clark's study), and the different crafts which brought in some needed cash for farm enlargement and the paying of taxes. As far as the farms were concerned, we meet here again the rationality of a large-scale enterprise. Nothing was wasted; everything was carefully used. For instance, hides came from the slaughterhouse to the tannery, and from there to the harness makers, cobblers, pouch makers, etc. Wool was sent to the women who spun it and then sent it on to the weavers or cloth makers and thence to the tailors. Since cooking was done for the entire Bruderhof (150 to 200 adults plus all the children) utmost economy was possible and practiced. *Diener der Notdurft* (*q.v.*), without ever having learned modern techniques of shop organization, soon developed an admirable tradition of efficiency, on the farm level supported also by the *Weinzierl*, the foreman or work clerk who supervised all agricultural labor.

As to the crafts, it is truly amazing how these Brethren developed skills otherwise nearly unknown in these early centuries of modern times. Besides, their pottery ware (now called *Habaner faiences:* see **Ceramics**) reveals a taste for the shapely and aesthetically appealing which made them stand out in this craft and true competitors of the Italian (later also Dutch) fayence or majolica ware. In the main this particular craft was developed primarily for cash sale and not so much for Bruderhof needs. The research of F. Hruby shows how much the nobles appreciated these products. Another cash product of high quality was the knives and cutlery wares of finest steel, again somewhat unique in the 16th century. Both crafts continued to be practiced among the *Habaner* (*q.v., apostate descendants of the Hutterites*) in Slovakia until after World War I, although among the Brethren in Transylvania, Russia, and later America this skill died out completely. Hruby tells of additional skills of the Hutterites otherwise little practiced in their days: thus we hear of an artistic clock sold for 170 talers to an Austrian archduke, and another one sold to Cardinal Dietrichstein (*q.v.*). Famous were also the Hutterite carriages, which were much in demand among the Moravian nobility. Likewise much appreciated were their new-fashioned iron bedframes. In short, the nobles knew only too well why it was advantageous to protect these industrious Brethren and why they ignored as far as possible the repeated persecution orders from the Viennese government or from the counter-reformatory clergy.

A unique activity of the brethren was also their bathhouses and their barber-surgeons and physicians (see Sommer and Friedmann). They worked for a high standard of hygiene and health among the Brethren, and likewise attracted many lords and their families from the surrounding areas. Christoph A. Fischer (*q.v.*) was most enraged about this fact. "Every Saturday their bathhouses are filled with Christians [Catholics]," he writes, "and not only the ordinary man but also the lords run to them if they need any drug, as if the Anabaptists were the only ones who understand this art." All these facts explain why the Brethren thrived even after 1592 (the end of the "Golden Age" period) when the Counter Reformation (*q.v.*) set in with full force and wars raged over the country (Turk invasion).

(*b*) Not less important were the economic activities of the Hutterites outside their Bruderhofs. There were two motives for it: the Brethren needed additional cash (all earnings of individual workers were pooled in a common purse), and even more the Brethren needed the favor of their noble manorial lords, whom they were willing to serve in many capacities, thus demonstrating their indispensability. This latter point was one of the strongest arguments for toleration in Moravia. Manifold were the services of the "hired-out" brethren: they were managers of the farms (*Meier*), vineyards (*Winzer*), wineries (*Kellner*), mills (*Müller*), sawmills, etc. There was hardly any noble estate in Southern Moravia and adjacent Slovakia which did not have one or several brethren in its service. Due to their excellent preparation and moral qualities, these men quickly gained the utmost confidence of the lords and the respect of those who worked under them. This is incidentally also true after 1622, the fateful year of "complete" expulsion from Moravia. There was practically no one who could take their place, and in spite of increasingly sharp mandates we find Brethren working on manorial estates in Moravia as late as 1630, and occasionally even 1640.

Not less significant was the service of the Brethren in the field of surgery and medical care; time and again we hear of Brethren doctors employed by the one or other lord (Cardinal Dietrichstein, the head of the Counter Reformation in Moravia, always called a Hutterite for such service), or in some resort places such as the mineral springs of Trenchin in Slovakia. We do not know exactly the inside story of these services to the "world" and their economic implications, but the motives of service and gaining favorable public opinion seem to have prevailed also in this field.

Very interesting are Hruby's studies concerning the financial situation of the Brethren, their cash reserves, and the way they were taxed and finally deprived of all their savings (capital). Around 1570 (Golden Age) the Brethren had to pay a 2 per cent tax of all house-assessed valuation for the needs of Moravia (about 10 guilders or florins per house). Besides this they also had to pay a poll tax (*Kopfsteuer*) and a tax on home-brewed beer. The house tax steadily increased; in 1600 it was already 100 fl. per house and in 1608-10 even as high as 160 fl. The government was always in need of money for military purposes; since the Brethren refused to pay war taxes, the amounts were simply requisitioned in the form of cattle, horses, or casks of wine. (Wolkan, *Geschicht-Buch,* 309 [to 1579] and 428 [to 1589.]) In 1602-5, during the Turkish invasion which did also so much harm to the Bruderhofs, the need of the Hapsburgs for more money grew immensely. In 1602 the government requisitioned 7,000 guilders, and in 1604 the emperor asked for a "loan" of 20,000 guilders, which, however, was never attained. The request for money became more and more urgent as the great catastrophe of the Thirty Years' War approached. Cardinal Dietrichstein and imperial messengers exerted unbelievable pressure upon the Brethren to extort all the money possible. In 1621, finally, the authorities prevailed upon the *Vorsteher* Rudolf Hirzel to divulge the hiding place of their money. A total of 30,000 fl. thus fell into the hands of the Cardinal and Emperor Ferdinand II (Hruby, 91; *Geschicht-Buch,* ed. Wolkan, 576-88, ed. Zieglschmid, 766-80). The story of this confiscation is one of the most exciting in the long history of the Brethren. The *Chronicle* admits, however, that there was still some money left (which Hirzel did not know), buried somewhere in the fields. Hruby estimates that prior to 1619 the Brethren might have possessed around 60,000 fl., but he calculates that this sum was by no means exorbitant as it represents the working capital of a community of about 15,000 Brethren, or about 5 fl. per member. Eventually, in 1622, the Brethren had to leave Moravia altogether, leaving behind practically everything, 24 Bruderhofs with their entire inventory of grain, wine, 200 head of cattle, 150 horses, 655 pigs and hogs, all furniture and kitchen utensils, woolen material, linen, tools, and all shop equipment. Ignoring the value of the houses, gardens, fields, and meadows, the Brethren estimated the value thus lost at at least 364,000 talers (*Geschicht-Buch,* ed. Wolkan, 570-71).

In spite of this very tangible loss and the ever-increasing fury of war (with plundering, etc.), the Brethren were able to start to rebuild their communal life in near-by Slovakia, where about one generation later Grimmelshausen found them prosperous again and well organized (under the last great *Vorsteher* Ehrenpreis, *q.v.*). The 18th century, then, saw a decline of both the religious and the communal life of the Brethren and the enforced conversion of most Brethren to Catholicism (see **Habaner**). (The total decline of the Habaner came after World War I in the new state of Czecho-Slovakia.)

In Transylvania the Bruderhofs were never as flourishing as those in the Moravian and Slovakian area. Then, around 1760, came the great exodus from the Hapsburg empire into Walachia and Russia, and now the Brethren became exclusively farmers. Although they were still sober and industrious, their previous well-being was gone, and thus also their remarkable skills and crafts.

In 1874-78 the Brethren settled in the United States, partly with money borrowed from the Rappites (*q.v.,* New Harmony people). Miss Clark, who reports on the Hutterite colonies in 1924, gives a description as if visiting 16th-century Bruderhofs in Moravia. The only difference is that now the *Diener der Notdurft* or *Haushalter* is called "boss." He handles all money, he has the keys to all storage rooms, and he organizes the work plan of the entire community. Under him we find the foremen of the farm, mill, carpentry, forge, bootery, etc. Money is only used in contacts with the "world." Needless to say that since there is no private possession, nothing can be bequeathed to one's children (save, perhaps, some handwritten old books). All savings are used to buy more land or machinery. Every Bruderhof is supposed to be self-supporting, although loans are known between the colonies. Crafts are no longer practiced except for the immediate needs of the colony. Today the Brethren accept farm machinery and thus their economy has become fairly thrifty again. Idleness is practically unknown, but so is also haste and rush. To avoid monotony, all work rotates among the Brethren within a certain time. In spite of their peaceful attitude it yet happens now and then that neighboring groups oppose their extension and their land buying (Saskatchewan); the old suspicion and jealousies, which prevailed so long in Moravia, have not yet completely died out. (See **Bruderhof, Community of Goods, Diener der Notdurft**.) R.F.

Wolkan, *Geschicht-Buch;* Zieglschmid, *Aelteste Chronik;* Loserth, *Communismus;* L. Müller, *Der Kommunismus der Mähr. Wiedertäufer* (Leipzig, 1928); F. Hruby, *Die Wiedertäufer in Mähren* (Leipzig, 1935, the most important source for Hutterite economic history); Bertha W. Clark, "The Hutterian Communities," in *Journ. of Pol. Economy* (Chicago, 1924); *The Hutterites and Saskatchewan, a study of inter-group relations* (Regina, 1953); P. Dedic, "Social Background of the Austrian Anabaptists," *MQR* XIII (1939) 5-20; J. L. Sommer, "Hutt. Medicine and Physicians," *MQR* XXVII (1953) 111-27; R. Friedmann, "Hutt. Physicians and Barber-Surgeons," *MQR* XXVII (1953) 129-236; E. Correll, *Das Schweizerische Täufer-Mennonitentum* (Tübingen, 1924); Max Weber, *Protestant Ethics and the Spirit of Capitalism* (German 1905, English 1930); P. Peachey, "Social Background . . . of the Swiss Anabaptists," *MQR* XXVIII (1945) 102-27; *ML* II, 105 ff.

Edam, a town in the Dutch province of North Holland (pop. about 11,000), famous for its cheese. Anabaptism reached Edam very early. On May 22, 1546, two martyrs from Edam, Andries and Dirk Pieters Smul (*q.v.*), with Jacob de Gelderman (*q.v.*) of Harderwijk, who was attending Anabaptist services in Edam, were executed at the stake. A letter written by the martyr Thys Joriaensz (*q.v.*) of Rarop in 1569 to his friends in Edam has been preserved (*Mart. Mir.* D 485, E 823). It is also known that Leenaert Bouwens (*q.v.*) baptized 21 persons between 1551 and 1578 in Edam.

For a long time there were two Mennonite churches in Edam, a Frisian and a Waterlander. The Frisian group had their church on the Halig; the present Mennonite church is on the same street. The Waterland church stood less than 50 paces away, at the corner of Groote Kerkstraat and Molensteeg. Little is known of the latter group;

there were presumably only six members left when they joined the Frisians in December 1742. The united congregation was attached to the Waterlander (Rijper) Sociëteit, the Frisian Sociëteit in North Holland, and the Zonist Sociëteit.

For communion, baptism, and marriage, they were often assisted by ministers from neighboring towns.

Until 1760 the congregation had only lay preachers, usually three. From 1760 to 1803 they were rarely without a preacher. In case of need Jan Nieuwenhuisen, the pastor of Monnikendam, served, receiving two guilders each time. Jakob Rienksz, Jr., who was called as preacher on Dec. 22, 1771, had to submit to an examination on April 8, 1772, given by Cornelis Ris (*q.v.*) of Hoorn and Jan Slot and Pieter Groot of Middelie. Until 1803 each minister had to promise to preach and instruct the children in the Zonist doctrine. At that time they were no longer able to support a preacher, and were served every two weeks by the ministers of Monnikendam, Middelie, and Axwijk; later on only the Monnikendam minister came, but on Feb. 27, 1859, R. de Vries asked to be excused from this service. Then Ring Noord-Holland and the Algemene Doopsgezinde Sociëteit supplied them with preachers until September 1862, when, after a period of about 60 years, the congregation was again able to support itself.

Since that time the following ministers have served: Aemilius W. Wybrands 1862-70, I. J. le Cosquino de Bussy 1870-72, C. R. van Dokkum 1873-77, C. N. Wybrands 1878-81, P. K. Bijl 1881-86, A. Sipkema 1888-1912, P. A. Vis 1912-18, A. A. Sepp 1918-26, Miss A. Leistra 1927-44, J. Maarse 1947-51, and S. L. Verheus since 1952. Since 1935 the Edam congregation has united with Monnikendam for preaching services. The minister lives in Edam. In 1900 the congregation adopted the *Leidsche Bundel* (*q.v.*) as its hymnal, and replaced it in 1946 with the new *Doopsgezinde Bundel*. The membership, 60 in 1726, dropped to 20 in 1834, but has since then steadily increased: 26 in 1847, 80 in 1900, 111 in 1950. The congregation has an active Sunday school for children and a women's organization. A.A.S., vDZ.

Inv. Arch. Amst. I, Nos. 20, 334, 337 f., 1136, 1164; II, 1715; C. N. Wybrands, "Anteekeningen uit de geschiedenis der Doopsgezinde Gemeente te Edam," in *DB* 1887, 113-31; *ML* I, 503 f.

Eden (Kan.) Church of God in Christ Mennonite Church, formerly known as the Burns (*ME* I, 478) church. The congregation sold its meetinghouse in the town of Burns sometime after 1950, and built a new meetinghouse two or three miles south of the town, at which time it changed its name to Eden. In 1955 the membership was 174, with Norman M. Eicher, Dennis Smith, and A. Koehn as ministers.

Eden High School, Virgil, Ont., had its origin in an evening Bible school in the M.B. Church at Virgil in 1938, which developed into a day Bible school in 1943, and was then taken over by the newly organized Virgil Bible Society and located in 1944 on a 10-acre estate bought by the Society for this purpose.

In 1945 a high school was added, which required the erection in 1947 of a separate high school building. In 1948 the school, now called Eden Bible and High School, was transferred to the Ontario M.B. Conference. In 1955 Eden had 6 teachers and 186 students, 122 of whom come from M.B. homes, most of the others from G.C.M. homes. Forty of the students come from more distant communities such as Kitchener, Leamington, and Detroit and live in the school dormitory. The first principal of the high school was H. B. Thiessen, who was succeeded in 1950 by the present principal, D. H. Neumann. In 1955 the Bible school department was transferred to the Kitchener M.B. Church, and "Bible School" was dropped from the name.   H.S.B.

H. H. Dueck, "The Eden High School," *Konferenz-Jugendblatt* XI (1955) Sept.-Oct., 9 f.

Eden Mennonite Church (GCM), located west of Moundridge, Kan., was organized in 1895 as the Hoffnungsfeld-Eden Mennonite Church; this was changed in 1924 to the present name. The congregation joined the Western District Conference in 1895 and the General Conference Mennonite Church in 1896. The first church was erected in 1898, replaced in 1924 by the present building, which was remodeled in 1949. Ministers who have served the church are Peter M. Krehbiel, Peter Stucky, C. J. Goering, Phil Wedel, and Walter Gering, the latter serving as elder 1937-50. C. J. Goering served as elder 1901-37. The congregation is of Swiss background, having immigrated to the present location in 1874 from Volhynia (*q.v.*), Russia, where they were a part of four main communities formed by settlers from France, the Palatinate, and Switzerland. The most common names are Goering, Kaufman, Krehbiel, Schrag, Stucky, Waltner, Wedel, and Zerger. The membership in 1955 was 777. Peter J. Dyck accepted the call as pastor of the church in 1950.   W.G.

Eden Mennonite Church (GCM), located at Inola, Rogers Co., Okla., a member of the Western District Conference since 1915, was organized on Nov. 12, 1914, with 27 members under the leader W. J. Ewert. The first meetinghouse, a frame structure, was destroyed by fire in 1918, and was replaced by a new frame building with a seating capacity of 175, dedicated on May 2, 1920. Ministers who have served the congregation are Herman P. Jantzen, Sol. Mouttet, G. B. Regier, and Homer Sperling. The membership in 1955 was 147.   G.B.R.

Eden Mennonite Church (GCM), a member of the Eastern District Conference, is located in Schwenksville, Montgomery Co., Pa. Previous to 1818 Mennonites in the vicinity worshiped every four weeks in a building also used as a school, located on the present Keely Church grounds, which was also used by the Reformed and Lutherans; it is possible that the building was a Lutheran-Reformed union church. In 1818 the Mennonites organized a congregation here, choosing William Gottschall (1784-1875) as their deacon, and built their own meetinghouse of stone just outside Schwenksville. In the summer of 1851 a new brick meetinghouse replaced the old one. In 1894 the third and present church was built across the valley on the edge of the town. Previous to 1894 the congregation was known as "Gottshall's," or less frequently as "Ziegler's" or "Mine Hill."

Before 1818 Skippack and Germantown ministers supplied the pulpit, and from 1818 to 1847 Franconia conference ministers supplied the pulpit. In the Oberholtzer division of 1847 Deacon Gottschall and the entire congregation withdrew and joined the new Eastern District Conference. The first resident minister was Moses H. Gottshall, ordained preacher in 1847, and bishop (elder) in 1850. Ministers and their terms of service are: Moses H. Gottshall 1847-88, Samuel H. Longaker 1868-70, N. B. Grubb 1872-82, William H. Gottshall 1884-1905, J. W. Schantz 1907-17, Reed Landis supplied 1917, William H. Grubb 1917-21, Freeman H. Swartz 1921- .

The Sunday school was organized in 1867. The membership in 1847 was 30; in 1908 it was 209, and in 1953 it was 275. The common names today are Clemens, Wood, Alderfer, Kolb, Markley, Nyce, Moyer, Bergey, Hunsicker, and Gottshall. J.H.F.

D. K. Cassel, *History of the Menn.* (Philadelphia, 1888); "History of the Eden Congregation," *1919 Mennonite Yearbook and Almanac* (Quakertown, 1919); J. C. Wenger, *History of the Menn. of the Franconia Conf.* (Telford, Pa., 1937).

Eder, Georg (1523-86), a Catholic jurist and humanist, one of the radical champions of the Counter Reformation (*q.v.*) in Austria and Bavaria during the second half of the 16th century. He was six times the "rector" of the University of Vienna, and rose high in the Austrian bureaucracy. His radical fight against all Protestant parties of the Reformation, but above all against the Lutherans, began at the time when the rather lenient Emperor Maximilian II (see **Hapsburg**) came to power (1564). He opposed the idea of conciliation with the Protestants, and worked for their total destruction. Since the emperor did not favor this line, Eder came into repeated conflicts with the government. Henceforth he leaned more heavily toward Duke Albrecht V of Bavaria (*q.v.*), the actual prime mover of the South German Counter Reformation. His correspondence with the duke (published in 1904) reveals most impressively the spirit of that entire movement, which gained momentum also in Austria after the death of Maximilian in 1576.

Of the many polemical writings of Eder two are of greater significance to us, the *Evangelische Inquisition,* published 1573 by the Jesuit press of Dillingen, Bavaria (second edition at Ingolstadt in 1580), and the somewhat more restrained *Malleus Haereticorum* (*Hammer of the Heretics*). In both books Eder tries to justify himself for writing about such a subject in spite of being a jurist. Yet, he declares, he is writing not as a theologian but as a politician who is concerned with the general condition of the country both civic and religious. Church life has deteriorated, he laments, and all obedience to the authorities has nearly vanished, even in Vienna, the seat of the government, in spite of apparent faithfulness externally.

The *Evangelische Inquisition* is dedicated to two Hapsburg archdukes and was presented personally to the emperor. Nevertheless the imperial government reprimanded him for his attacks on the Lutherans, tried to confiscate all copies available, and forbade him to write further concerning such religious subjects. Since the emperor died only three years later (1576), this order was of little effect, and the book was soon republished (1580). A second volume was also planned but never published, perhaps due to the death of the author in 1586.

The title of this book runs as follows: *Evangelische Inquisition wahrer und falscher Religion, wider das gemeine unchristliche Klaggeschrei, dass schier niemand mehr wissen könnt wie oder was er glauben soll* (500 pages). Part I describes "the present condition of the churches and the general unchristian polemic" (*Klaggeschrei*), including also a *Ketzertanz* of 48 tables or charts. Part II discusses more of the heretical clamor "concerning the false repute of the new-fangled Gospel." Of all the Protestant groups the Anabaptists receive Eder's most acid attacks. In the "Fourth Table" (pp. 57-160) he enumerates not less than 38 different Anabaptist sects, mainly in Moravia (Erhard later repeats this list, enlarging it to 40 names), rather arbitrarily and without solid factual knowledge. Concerning the origin of Anabaptism, Eder claims that it derives somehow from Luther and his teachings. Most of what Eder writes is hearsay; mingled with a few correct statements is much fancy. In general the book is intended to be a defense of Catholicism against charges by the Lutherans.

Also the *Malleus Haereticorum* at many places mentions the Anabaptists, whose teachings and institutions are allegedly nothing but repetitions of errors revealed as such long before by the Roman Church. One of his sources here is Luther's well-known *Brief an zwei Pfarrherrn* of 1528, a tract likewise known to have little factual information. Yet in general this work is less vitriolic than the *Evangelische Inquisition.*

Both books were of great influence upon Christoph Erhard (*q.v.*), the parish priest of Nikolsburg, Moravia, who continued the fight against both Lutherans and Anabaptists in his area, with about the same arguments. He, too, makes Luther responsible for the rise of Anabaptism, but is somewhat better informed than Eder. Very little is known about Eder's influence and success in the great fight he undertook. (See **Counter Reformation.**) LOSERTH, R.F.

ADB V, 642; *ML* I, 504 f.; Eder's correspondence was published by Schrauf in Vienna in 1904; *ML* I, 504 f.

Eder (Oeder), **Marx** (Markus), an Anabaptist martyr concerning whose life only the story of his martyrdom is known, as it is succinctly given in the chronicles of the Hutterites. He was a wagoner by trade. He was seized at Mörenbach in Bavaria, Germany, on April 24, 1605, together with Hans Polzinger, a tailor, probably on their way to Moravia. On the following morning they were put into prison at Ried, where they remained 15 weeks, while Jesuits from Oettingen vainly tried to convert them. Twice they were asked while on the rack who had sheltered them and where they were going, but they revealed nothing. Then the authorities in Burghausen issued an order to behead and then to burn them. This was done at Ried on Aug. 5, 1605. Eder requested the executioner first to behead his companion, and when this was done, said to all the people, "God be praised. My brother has stood the test!" The government was apparently hopeful to the last moment that one or both would be converted, for the executioner had been instructed not to take the life of either if he recanted. Their martyrdom is sung in the hymn beginning, "Hört, hört, und merkt ihr Gottes Kind, die ihr Liebhaber Gottes sind."   LOSERTH.

Lieder der Hutterischen Brüder (Scottdale, 1914) 812; Beck, *Geschichts-Bücher;* Wiswedel, *Bilder* II, 163 f.; *Mart. Mir.* D 803, E 1103; *ML* I, 505.

Edgeley is a "country corners" on No. 7 highway in Vaughan Township about 12 miles north of Toronto, Ont. It is within a quarter of a mile of the oldest Mennonite church now standing in Ontario (1824) usually known as the Schmitt (*q.v.*) Mennonite Church. A few miles south of Edgeley on the township line between Vaughan and York the Mennonite Brethren in Christ conducted Sunday school and worship in a small country church for a number of years, but the congregation is now extinct.   J.C.F.

Ediger (Edger, Oedger), a Mennonite family name in West Prussia, appearing in the Frisian congregations of the Vistula Valley. Ten families were counted in 1776, and 40 persons in 1935. Members of this family also migrated to Russia (Molotschna) and subsequently to America. Bearers of this name in Russia were Alexander Ediger (*q.v.*), Heinrich A. Ediger (*q.v.*), and Salomon Ediger (*q.v.*). Jacob B. Ediger was a missionary to the Cheyenne Indians in Oklahoma. Other North American representatives include ministers (GCM) Peter Ediger, Fresno, Cal., and Jacob H. Ediger, Inman, Kan., and Elmer Ediger (GCM), executive secretary of the Board of Christian Service, Newton, Kan.   G.R.

Ediger, Alexander, an outstanding Mennonite leader during the revolutionary years in Russia, was born in 1893 in the seaport city of Berdyansk where his father, Heinrich A. Ediger, was a bank manager and owner of a printing establishment. After graduating from the local Gymnasium, Alexander studied history and philology at the University of St. Petersburg for four years. After graduation he returned to South Russia and in 1919 married Kathie Dyck, the daughter of a formerly wealthy landowner. Meanwhile the Bolshevik Revolution had reached the south of Russia and the newly married couple escaped on an icebreaker to the Crimea, where conditions were more peaceful at the time.

For several years Ediger supported his young family by teaching at the Gymnasium in a suburb of Simferopol, the largest city of the Crimea. In 1922 he was chosen minister by his home congregation at Berdyansk, and in 1923 he received a call as teacher and preacher to the village of Liebenau,

belonging to the Schönsee congregation in the Molotschna settlement. But as a minister he soon had to give up teaching and from then on devoted all his time and energy to his duties as preacher and elder, to which latter office he was ordained in 1925 by David H. Epp. Ediger was an earnest Christian, a man of remarkable ability, of a very friendly and amiable disposition, and of great devotion to his work. He was also a good public speaker and an outstanding musician. Not only was he a master of the piano, but he also composed music and was the leading choir director in the Molotschna.

From the very beginning Ediger brought new life to the Schönsee congregation, which soon spread to other congregations of the Molotschna. In 1925 he became the chairman of the KfK (*Kommission für Kirchliche Angelegenheiten*) and as such had to represent the Mennonite Church before the Communist government, an exceedingly difficult task at that time. His duties led him frequently to Kharkov and Moscow, where his reception by the government officials usually was far from friendly.

In 1925 Ediger also became the editor of *Unser Blatt* (*q.v.*), the only Mennonite publication under Bolshevik rule. This, too, was a very difficult and dangerous undertaking in those days. From the very beginning of its existence the little magazine was censored very strictly and after three years it had to be discontinued.

When religious persecution broke out, Ediger was one of the first to be arrested. In 1933 he was sent to a prison camp at Murmansk, on the shores of the White Sea in the Far North of Russia. After two and a half years he was released and returned home, only to be arrested again and sent with his wife to Eastern Siberia. Mrs. Ediger was sent back to South Russia in 1938 and has heard nothing of her husband since. The Edigers had two children, a daughter Dagmar, born 1922, and a son Harry, born 1926. Mrs. Ediger escaped from Russia during World War II and is now in Canada (1955), but she had to leave her children in Russia.†   H.G.

A. Töws, *Mennonitische Märtyrer* (Winnipeg, 1949) 73-78.

Ediger, Heinrich Abram, b. Nov. 6, 1858, at Gnadenfeld, Molotschna, Russia, d. June 23, 1943, Karlsruhe, Germany, publisher, editor, banker, and burgomaster of Berdyansk, South Russia, was the son of Abram Ediger, whose father, Salomon Peter Ediger, had come from Prussia to the Molotschna in 1819. Abram Ediger taught at Rosenhof, Melitopol district, 1861-67, then moved to Berdyansk to start a business. The young Heinrich received his training under David Görz. He was graduated from the Gnadenfeld Zentralschule, taught for a number of years, and established a print shop and bookstore in Berdyansk, where he became a leading businessman and for a number of years the burgomaster. He was also coeditor of *Der Botschafter* (*q.v.*) and active in the Mennonite brotherhood of Russia. Ediger had three sons with a university training, Theodor, a historian, Harry, a lawyer, Alexander (*q.v.*), the elder of the Schönsee Mennonite Church. After the Russian Revolution Ediger came to Germany and lived at Karlsruhe until his death. He published an article, "Meine Schulzeit bei Lehrer Heinrich Franz" (*Bote*, Nos. 20-25, 1930), and a book, *Erinnerungen aus meinem Leben* (Karlsruhe, 1927). B.H.U.

Ediger, Salomon Salomon, a preacher and teacher of the Mennonite Church in Russia, was born Nov. 14, 1876, in Gnadenfeld, South Russia, the son of Salomon and Susanna Mierau Ediger. He attended school in Gnadenfeld, and later taught in the elementary school there for several years, then studied theology at the Predigerschule in Basel. The director of the school was Wilhelm Arnold, a student of Tobias Beck, and the instructors in theology were Johannes von Huene, the father of the noted Tübingen professor; Hermann Gottsched, an authority on Kierkegaard; Samuel Preiswerk; and a certain Schlitter. A number of talented and stimulating fellow students also contributed to Ediger's development into the personality he was later to become. For many years Ediger taught religion and German in the Zentralschule at Ohrloff, succeeding Kornelius B. Unruh. His wife was a daughter of Heinrich Dirks (*q.v.*) of Gnadenfeld, a missionary; she died in 1924.

When religious instruction was prohibited in the Zentralschule, Ediger taught German and other subjects, and in order to be able to continue his work in the school, he gave up his ministerial status; but since he was unable to join the atheistic league, he was deprived of his position. To support his family, he accepted a position as instructor in the culture of silk in the collectives. But in 1934 he was arrested and sentenced to five years of exile. He returned to Melitopol in 1939 in broken health, and died on Nov. 16, 1940.

In August 1917 Ediger preached the opening sermon of the Allgemeiner Mennonitischer Kongress, a sermon that the delegates at that meeting will never forget. He was a Christian in whom there was no guile!—In August 1941, when the German army was about to enter the Melitopol district, his children were sent into exile. Their subsequent fate is unknown. B.H.U.

Education, Hutterite. Among the various Anabaptist groups of the 16th century, perhaps none had so much opportunity for a systematic Christian upbringing of the youth as the Hutterites, who on their large collective Bruderhofs (*q.v.*) in Moravia could organize and systematically take care of the entire education from the nursery school to kindergarten and through the grades. Education beyond that was expressly declined as nonconducive to the fear of God—the highest goal of all Anabaptist education. That Hutterite education had a very high standard can still be seen from all their handwritten books, done with excellent penmanship, good spelling, skillful style, and as for contents, with excellent Bible knowledge and often deft arguments—things not so commonly found among people of the 16th and 17th centuries.

The organization and spirit of Hutterite education is known through a number of preserved documents. The earliest perhaps is the *Handbüchel wider den Prozess* . . . of 1558-9 (see **Bedenken**), which in its section XII contains an *Ordnung und Brauch wie man es in der Gemein mit den Kindern hält* (A Regulation Concerning the Upbringing of Children in the Brotherhood). Here we read for instance, "That our children are dear to our heart before God according to truth, and a precious concern, to this God would testify for us on the Day of Judgment." Most likely this document was written by Peter Walpot (*q.v.*), later bishop of the brotherhood, from whom we also have an *Address to the Schoolmasters*, Nov. 5, 1568 (*MQR* 1931, 241-44), and a *School Discipline* ("*Schulordnung*") of 1578 (*ibid.*, 1931, 232-40). Also of 1578, we have further the report of a sympathetic observer, Stephan Gerlach, later professor at Tübingen (Bossert, *Quellen*, 1106-7). There exists also a catechism or *Kinderbericht*, used in Hutterite schools, of which two versions became known, of 1586 and of 1620 (*Arch. f. Ref.-Gesch.*, 1940, 44-60). It gives the impression that it was written by Peter Riedemann (*q.v.*, d. 1556), the author of the great *Rechenschaft*, with which it shows much similarity. There is among the Hutterite manuscripts a third brief *Kinderbericht* which deals extensively with the ordinance of baptism and communion. The use of the *Kinderbericht* in child training accounts for the fact that the Hutterite prisoners always had a ready answer to the court questioner when on trial and also for the fact that they so often agreed word for word with each other.

Each Bruderhof had two types of schools within its organization: the "Little School," a nursery and "Kindergarten" (age 2-6), in operation three centuries before the modern European Kindergarten was developed, and the "Big School," i.e., the grades (age 6-12). The latter was actually more than a mere school, and may be compared to a children's home where they lived and were taken care of practically throughout the year, in conformity with the Hutterite principle of community living. The two documents by Peter Walpot (above) laid down the principles which should guide the entire upbringing, and which were to be obeyed by the schoolmasters, the schoolmothers, and their assistants (*Kindsdirn*). "Let each schoolmaster," Walpot declared, "deal with the children by day and night as though they were his own, so that each one may be able to give an account before God . . ." (*MQR* 1931, 240). The spirit which permeates the school regulation of 1578 is that of a free and cheerful discipline in love and the fear of God, peaceful in spirit. To be dutiful and peaceful is conducive to good discipline. One cannot take too much care of the children, and the adults should always be mindful of setting a good example, since the children watch them and learn from their behavior. Walpot takes great care to instruct the teachers how to handle difficult cases. The use of a rod may sometimes be necessary, but great discretion and discernment should be exercised therein, for often a child can be better trained and corrected by kind words whereas harshness would be altogether in vain. The exercise of discipline of children requires the fear of God on the part of the teachers and high sense of responsibility. Children should be trained to accept punishment willingly, and care should be taken that they do not become self-willed. But above all they should be trained to love the Lord and to be diligent in prayer.

Great care was also taken of cleanliness and healthful living—in an age when those hygienic principles were by no means generally accepted. Even small details are regulated and enjoined, about eating, washing, sleeping, the children's clothing, and then above all the separation of the sick and the special handling of their laundry. The major emphasis, however, is laid on the right spirit and the ever alert responsibility of those in whose care the children are entrusted, so that the honor of God may always be promoted.

Basically these principles have been preserved fairly unchanged among the Hutterites up to the present day, though documents of later times are lacking. Bertha W. Clark, who visited the Brethren in South Dakota in 1923, describes the Hutterite system of education in the Bon-Homme Bruderhof, showing that in spite of certain necessary adaptations to American ways the spirit of the upbringing of the youth is by and large the same as of old. It is true that in the grade schools the legally prescribed curriculums have to be taught (if possible by Hutterite teachers—though the teachers are usually non-Hutterite, since Hutterites do not meet the educational requirements of the state for teaching), but the nursery and kindergarten is still today "really Hutterian."   R.F.

"A Hutterite School Discipline of 1578 and Peter Scherer's Address of 1568 to the Schoolmasters" (translated by H. S. Bender) *MQR* V (1931) 231-44; W. Wiswedel, "Das Schulwesen der Hutterischen Brüder in Mähren," *Arch. f. Ref.-Gesch.* XIV (1940) 38-60 (contains the catechism in toto); Loserth, *Communismus*, 278-85; *idem*, "Aus dem Liederschatz der mährischen Wiedertäufer," *Ztscht des Deutschen Ver. f. d. Gesch. v. Mähren und Schlesien*, 1925 (discusses hymns with a pedagogical content); St. Gerlach's report of 1578 in *TA* I (*Württemberg*) 1106 f.; the *Handbüchlein* of 1558-59 is discussed by Friedmann, in *Arch. f. Ref.-Gesch.*, 1931, 105 and 111; in the same study further references to the Hutterite system of education, 107 and 108 and notes; Bertha W. Clark, "The Hutterian Communities, I," *The Journal of Pol. Economy* (Chicago) June 1924, 372 f.; *ML* II, 717.

Education, Mennonite. Mennonites originated during the 16th century, more or less simultaneously in Holland, Germany, and Switzerland; since then they have migrated from these countries to France, Russia, Canada, United States, Mexico, Paraguay, Brazil, Uruguay, and Argentina. Living under the differing political, economic, and social orders of 12 national cultures, they have naturally not developed a common educational system that is peculiar to the whole body. Only in Russia, where the Mennonites colonized in a retarded civilization, did they develop an extensive educational system of their own designing. In the United States, where the national life was progressive and democratic, they have found a separate school system less necessary. Hence Mennonite education must be studied separately in each country where Mennonites have established themselves.

1. *Holland.* The Mennonites in Holland have not lived in closed communities as their brethren have done, more or less, in other countries. Being largely an urban people engaged in business and the professions, they have become an integral part of the national life of the Netherlands, closely identified with their country's economic activities, social order, and educational institutions.

With one exception (Haarlem) there have never been any Mennonite schools of any level in Holland, elementary, secondary, or college. Children from Mennonite homes attend the schools established by various other organized church bodies or by secular agencies. Dutch Mennonites by principle believe that this is better than to have separate Mennonite schools. Only the Haarlem congregation has operated Mennonite parochial schools. There have been two such schools. The first was opened in 1782 at the Groot Heiligland, in order to give a good education to the children of poor members, and closed in September 1952, since there were then only a few children in the inner city. The second was opened on Ripperdastraat on May 1, 1893, for the same purpose, and was still operating in 1954.

In 1811 the Algemeene Doopsgezinde Sociëteit (*q.v.*), the "General Conference" of all the Mennonite churches in Holland, was established, mainly for the purpose of assuming the joint responsibility for the Theological Seminary at Amsterdam, which the church at Amsterdam had operated in 1680-1706 and continuously after 1735. This school represents the only educational activity of the Mennonites in Holland except for the two Haarlem elementary schools.

2. *Germany.* Like their brethren in Holland, the Mennonites in Germany have not established their own school system. During the period of persecution followed by various imposed economic, religious, and educational restrictions, the Mennonites promoted no institutions which would encourage greater opposition. A careful study of the literature pertaining to Mennonite life in Germany reveals but few references to educational activities. Sometimes in communities where the population was solidly Mennonite or in communities where a sufficient number of Mennonite children were available, the local minister organized a school in the church. The Mennonite Church of Hamburg-Altona had such a school in the 18th century. The congregation at Deutschhof, Palatinate, also had such a school. For longer or shorter periods some elementary schools were operated by Mennonites in Eastern Germany (Brenkenhoffswalde before 1834), Galicia, and Bavaria (Bildhausen, 1838 ff.).

However, one Mennonite secondary school was established. Through the efforts of Michael Löwenberg, a Mennonite minister of the Weierhof congregation in the Palatinate, the Realanstalt am Donnersberg (*q.v.*), later named the Weierhof Real- und Erziehungs-Anstalt, was formally opened on Dec. 2, 1867. The school, a secondary boarding school, grew immediately in students and financial gifts from numerous Mennonite churches. The original purpose, to add a full Biblical seminary for the training of Mennonite ministers, however, was not realized. All efforts by Löwenberg to secure the conference sanction and acceptance of the school failed. The school became a very successful private boys' high school, but though always operated by a Mennonite board of directors, and always having religious instruction by the Weierhof Mennonite pastor, it never had more than a handful of Mennonite students. It was taken over in the Hitler government for a Nazi training school. In 1945 the French army and in 1952 the American army took over the buildings for the use of occupation forces. In 1952 the trustees of the Weierhof school established a boys' dormitory (Schülerheim) at the nearby (2½ miles) Kirchheimbolanden Gymnasium for Mennonite students attending the Gymnasium.

3. *Switzerland.* The Mennonites in Switzerland have maintained a small number of German elementary schools in the Jura district during the past 150 years, since the Mennonite communities there are German cultural islands surrounded by French culture. The elementary schools operating at the present time (seven in 1954) comply with all the educational requirements provided by Swiss law. In 1949 the Basel Bible School (*Europäische Mennonitische Bibelschule, q.v.*) was established in Basel, sponsored by the Swiss, Alsatian, French, and South German Mennonites.

4. *France.* During the past 250 years of residence in France the Mennonites there have remained in touch with their brethren in Switzerland and South Germany and have shared their religious and cultural heritage with them. They have, however, become fully integrated into French life and have never had any schools of their own; Isaac Rich conducted a private school at Exincourt (*q.v.*) in 1869-76.

5. *Russia.* For the first 100 years on the steppes of South Russia, beginning with the Chortitza settlement in 1789, the Mennonites enjoyed almost complete political, religious, and educational autonomy. Left free of governmental regulations and restrictions, they developed an educational system whose underlying philosophy was determined by the ideals of their leaders. (See **Education Among the Mennonites of Russia.**)

Probably the most original and interesting contribution to Mennonite education was the development of secondary schools called *Zentralschulen.* These schools were either established by organized educational associations or by wealthy individuals. Although a few Zentralschulen were coeducational, most of the secondary schools were for boys. Both Halbstadt and Chortitza established high schools for girls.

Since the Mennonites in Russia established and supervised their own schools, they were able to offer religious instruction at the elementary and secondary level without maintaining separate Bible schools for that purpose. No liberal arts colleges were ever established. Advanced training was obtained at various universities of Europe.

By 1943 the Russian Mennonites had either been scattered, exiled, or moved to other lands. For 156 years they had lived in the steppes of the Ukraine. Today a splendid Mennonite educational system lies in complete ruin behind the iron curtain.

6. *United States.* The educational activities of the Mennonites in the United States are varied and an adequate description of them becomes quite complex. They began with the first settlement in Germantown in 1683 and have continued, more or less, to the present time. The student of Mennonite education must recognize the fact that these educational activities are carried on by a number of the different Mennonite branches independently of each other. The Amish, for instance, operate a number of elementary schools, but they are opposed to secondary and collegiate training. The Mennonites (MC) on the other hand maintain some schools at all levels: elementary, secondary, and college. The Church of God in Christ, Mennonite has never established any educational institutions. The Mennonite Brethren Church has one college, one Bible College, but no high schools in the United States; however, it has several high schools and one Bible College in Canada; but it has no elementary schools. The General Conference group has a similar situation in Canada, but has several high schools and three colleges in the United States. The North American pattern is indeed varied, intricate, and to the outsider confusing.

When the Mennonites from the various countries of Europe settled in the vast spaces of the New World, they were anxious to preserve both their religion and their German language. To achieve these two aims they established many elementary schools (*q.v.*). But, in the course of time, conflicts arose between the public school systems controlled by the various states in which Mennonites had settled and the Mennonite parochial schools, which have never been wholly dissolved.

A strong interest in Christian education manifested by the Mennonites in the United States has motivated the establishment and the operation of many schools. This interest has not only been continuous but is very definitely increasing. If the Mennonites in the United States were more united doctrinally, and if they were more concentrated into compact communities, they could maintain an educational system comparable to that conducted by other churches, such as the Lutherans or Catholics.

Since 1938 there has been a very decided increase in the number of church-controlled elementary schools (*q.v.*), commonly called Christian day schools, among the Mennonites in the eastern half of the United States. These schools, thus far, are sponsored only by the Mennonite (MC) churches and the Amish.

The ever-increasing stream of America's youth into high schools during the last quarter century has swept the Mennonite boys and girls into the movement. Although in many communities Mennonite parents encourage high-school attendance, there are those who oppose secondary education as administered by the state. This opposition has been responsible for the establishment of 15 (1954) Mennonite high schools (*q.v.*), and the number is increasing. These schools strive to offer a standard secondary education in a Christian atmosphere. The curriculum, for each, is prescribed in part by the state in which it operates, but the environment is determined by the sponsors of the schools.

There are at present eight Mennonite Liberal Arts colleges (q.v.) in the United States. Two of these offer only a two-year course and therefore are classified as junior colleges. All of them are comparatively young. The oldest, Bethel College (in Kansas), was organized in 1893 and the most recent, Bethel College (in Indiana), was established in 1947. In addition there are three Bible colleges offering three- to four-year programs above high school.

Of the sixteen Mennonite bodies in the United States, only five have been instrumental in bringing the eleven colleges into existence. These five branches constitute about 75 per cent of the total Mennonite population in the United States. Some of the other eleven smaller branches are strongly opposed to higher education, while others co-operate with the larger branches.

The development of colleges among the North American Mennonites has been fraught with many difficulties. The two main opposing factors have been a fear of higher education and the enormous cost of the establishing and operating of a college. Most of the active colleges represent second attempts. Bethel College (Kansas) emerged out of Halstead Seminary, Goshen College was preceded by Elkhart Institute, Bluffton College represents a reorganized Central College. Several other colleges functioned for brief periods and then failed, never to be reorganized. Inexperienced leadership, biased opposition, lack of financial support, and an unwillingness among the various branches to co-operate with each other were some of the main contributing causes of difficulties and failures.

The rise of Bible institutes and theological seminaries among the Mennonites in the United States is of recent origin. These schools have experienced considerable encouragement and support. The establishment of these schools expresses a trend toward a more educated leadership in all phases of Christian work. There are now three graduate seminaries (q.v.) (G.C.M. in Chicago, M.C. at Goshen, M.B. at Fresno), with strong Bible departments granting degrees at four other colleges, and three Bible Colleges which are in effect lower grade seminaries.

7. *Canada.* Education among the Mennonites in Canada has become increasingly more active during the past several decades. During the school year 1947-48 they operated 22 Bible schools, 11 high schools, and 2 Bible colleges. Of particular significance is the decided trend toward the establishment and operation of Mennonite private high schools.

Undoubtedly the most serious conflict between Mennonites and the state in modern times took place in Manitoba over the school question in connection with the outbreak of World War I, which resulted in wholesale emigration of the opposing groups to Mexico and Paraguay. The attempt to secularize and nationalize schools operated by these conservative churches with the requirement that the schools be conducted in the English language was the chief cause of the conflict. (See **Old Colony Mennonites**.)

8. *Mexico.* When the more conservative Mennonites of Canada realized that they could not continue instructing their children as they had done for generations, about 5,000 left their Canadian farms to till the soil on the semiarid plains of Chihuahua, Mexico. With educational freedom assured by the Mexican government, the colonists re-established their own traditional elementary schools which the Canadian government had labeled inadequate.

In 1935, hardly a decade after the establishment of their settlements on Mexican soil, there came from that government the unexpected order to close all Mennonite schools. The Mexican officials who came to carry out the order contended that the Mennonite schools were being conducted in an unlawful manner and that they would have to conform to the school laws of the land. As a result of several petitions to governmental authorities the Mennonites were permitted to resume their school activities.

The Mennonites in Mexico represent an ultraconservative wing of the Mennonite Church. They have migrated twice to escape the nationalization of their schools. Their educational philosophy is rather simple. Every child must learn to read the Bible in the German language. His education is completed with a few sacred hymns and the catechism. Such traditional courses as science, history, literature, geography, and government are not included in the curriculum.

9. *South America.* The Mennonites in Paraguay, Uruguay, Brazil, and Argentina are newcomers to these South American republics. Except for a small group from Canada, they came from war-torn Europe, poor and homeless. They are beginning a new life in a strange environment. Among their number are well-trained teachers, ministers, and craftsmen. Because of the prevailing poverty and the hard conditions of pioneer life, their schools are still somewhat primitive, though constantly improving. Elementary schools have been opened in all the villages in the Paraguay colonies and several secondary schools have been established in the various colony centers. In Brazil the pre-World War II Mennonite elementary German schools were closed by a government order which required the language of instruction to be Portuguese and the teachers to be native-born Brazilians. In 1954 a Mennonite high school (Zentralschule) was established near Curitiba.

One Mennonite village school was in operation in Uruguay in 1953. No such schools are contemplated by the small number of Mennonite immigrants in Argentina.

General Characteristics of Mennonite Education. Certain experiences in the history of the Mennonites have resulted in traditions and attitudes that explain the peculiar emphases in Mennonite education.

1. *German Language.* The determination to maintain and perpetuate German as a language of instruction and church worship has resulted in conflicts between Mennonites and the state in certain lands, such as Russia, Canada, Mexico, and Brazil. In 1870, for instance, the Russian government began

a program of nationalization of all German schools within the land. When the Mennonites, who had operated their own independent school system for nearly a century, began to feel the effects of state control, they protested. They feared the results of compulsory use of Russian as the language of instruction, but ultimately submitted and discovered that they could still keep the German language as their cultural language. The process of assimilation has practically completed the shift from German to English among most of the Mennonites in the United States. But in Canada, Mexico, Switzerland, Brazil, and Paraguay, the language problem is still a source of difficulty.

2. Due to the divisions in the Mennonite brotherhood, no conjoint or integrated educational program for the entire group has been planned or can well be planned.

3. *Mennonitism and Education.* An increasing awareness is growing in the minds of the leaders that an educational system at all levels will have to be operated if Mennonitism is to be preserved and perpetuated. In Western Europe, where the Mennonites have not established their own schools, substantial changes have been made in the traditional Mennonite faith, including the abandonment of some major original principles; whereas in Russia and North America where church schools have been established on a wide though varying scale, the changes have not been so damaging to the original heritage and faith. The past 50 years has seen a great growth in Mennonite educational activities in both the United States and Canada. In the last two decades one can almost speak of an educational renaissance. In order to preserve their youth for the Mennonite faith and prepare workers for the growing program of the church, new schools have been established, programs of the church enlarged, financial investment increased, and standards raised. The Mennonite schools of North America are now playing a very important role in the church; they will undoubtedly be increasingly important. In fact we can no longer conceive of the church without its schools. In 1951-52 a total of 5,704 Mennonite seminary, college, high-school, and Bible school students of all branches were in attendance at Mennonite schools in the United States and Canada. In 1953-54 in the elementary schools of the Mennonite Church (MC) alone (no other statistics available) an additional 3,500 pupils were in attendance. Reckoning those not reported, one can assume 10,000 young Mennonites attending Mennonite schools of all levels in 1953-54. (See **Education Among the Mennonites in Russia; Elementary Education.**)

M.S.H.

W. Leendertz, "Higher Education Among Mennonites in Europe," *Proceedings of the Fourth Mennonite World Conference, Aug. 3-10, 1948* (Akron, Pa., 1950) 270-75; Ed. G. Kaufman, "The Liberal Arts College in the Life of the Mennonite Church of America," *loc. cit.,* 276-87; S. Hertzler, "Attendance at Mennonite Schools and Colleges," annually in *MQR* since 1928; P. Erb, "Mennonite Colleges and the Mennonite Heritage," *MQR* XVI (1942) 23-27; L. Froese, *Das pädagogische Kultursystem der mennonitischen Siedlungsgruppe in Russland* (Göttingen Univ. dissertation, 1949, ms.); J. E. Hartzler, *Education Among the Mennonites of America* (Danvers, 1925); M. S. Harder, "The Origin, Philosophy, and Development of Education Among the Mennonites" (dissertation, University of Southern California, 1949); E. K. Francis, "The Mennonite School Problem in Manitoba," *MQR* XXVII (1953) 204-36; *idem, In Search of Utopia* (Altona, Man., 1955).

Education Among the Mennonites in Russia. One of the rights granted the Mennonites by the Russian government at their immigration was the management of their own school system. From 1789 to 1881 Russian authorities concerned themselves little with the Mennonite schools. The Mennonites had brought with them from West Prussia (*q.v.*) the conviction that it is the duty of parents to provide for the elementary instruction of their children, and they tried to fulfill this obligation. Even though because of poverty they could not at once build schools, they nevertheless saw to it that their children received instruction. In the very first years, because of lack of space and teachers, it is possible that two villages united here and there to maintain a school; but as a rule each village had its own school from the very beginning. This was the practice of the Russian Mennonites always and everywhere, in the first mother settlements, Chortitza and Molotschna, and later in the many daughter colonies in Caucasia, Central Asia, in northeastern Russia, in Siberia, in Canada, and in recent times in the latest settlements in Mexico, Brazil, and Paraguay.

The educational system of a country or people is to a large extent dependent on its economic situation and material prosperity. Higher culture can develop only where there is energy left over and above the requirements for existence. In the early days in Russia the educational system was primitive. Not until the 1870's, after various internal difficulties had been solved and the Mennonites had become prosperous through better agricultural methods and the introduction of winter wheat, did the schools receive a strong forward impetus; but by World War I they had reached a high state of development.

(1) *The Elementary Schools.* The first schools were, like the time and circumstances, extremely primitive in teacher preparation, equipment, and methods. The first teachers were farmers who managed the schools in winter in addition to their farms, or craftsmen who carried on their trades besides teaching the children. Too often the schoolroom also served as a shop. It also occurred in the early period that young journeymen learning a trade, non-Mennonites, were engaged as teachers. As late as the 1820's there were still some Lutheran teachers in the Molotschna settlement. But on the whole the Mennonites tried to have only Mennonite teachers. And later, especially during the most intensive program of Russianization (1890-1905), the Mennonites always and sometimes successfully protested the engagement of a non-Mennonite teacher. The problem was simplified by the fact that the villages paid their own teachers.

Instruction consisted of reading, writing, arithmetic, and religion. Much emphasis was placed on memorization (the Ten Commandments, hymns, etc.), on illuminated writing and penmanship; arithmetic was also thoroughly drilled, though quite mechanically.

German was the language of instruction. The Russian language was not generally taught until it became a compulsory subject in 1866 at the demand of the Fürsorge-Komitee (*q.v.*), though some progressive teachers were giving instruction in Russian as early as the 1830's. In the 1890's Russian became the obligatory language of instruction for all subjects but German and religion, and remained so until the end of organized Mennonite life in Russia, about 1925.

The supervision of the schools was by law the responsibility of the elders and preachers. But in practice leadership in the educational field was always in the hands of outstanding teachers or other laymen in the community. In the early period the schools were usually the concern of the civil government of the Mennonites. Thus a school regulation (*Schulverordnung*) was issued on Jan. 26, 1808, in the Molotschna, in the third year of the existence of the colony, which was to regulate school conditions in the villages. There was at that time no central organ to direct the educational system.

This was changed in 1843 when the Fürsorge-Komitee placed the management of the Mennonite schools in the hands of the Agricultural Association (*q.v.*), which was founded in 1831. At its head was Johann Cornies (*q.v.*). To the association with its extended authorization and to the first two chairmen, Johann Cornies and Philipp Wiebe, the Mennonite schools owe a great deal. The old, narrow schoolrooms were replaced by spacious, bright ones; a new general school regulation was passed to improve the relationship between the teacher and the community. The choice and examination of teachers was carefully supervised by the Association, and the inspection of teachers was more rigorously organized. Teaching was improved by rules concerning methods and the treatment of school children as well as by a unified curriculum. Compulsory attendance was more strictly enforced. General and local teachers' conventions were held.

Later the authority of the Agricultural Association was limited to its special agricultural task. At the instigation of a group of teachers the Molotschna Mennonite School Board (*Molotschnaer Mennoniten-Schulrat, q.v.*) was organized, and was without hesitancy approved by the Fürsorge-Komitee. This board was for 50 years (1869-1920) the leader and protector of the Mennonite educational system. Under its well-informed leadership the schools made a long stride forward. Especially in the first 25 years of its existence was the school board very effective, due to the untiring efforts of such men as Andreas Voth, Johann Klatt, Peter Heese, Abr. Görz, and Heinrich Unruh.

The Molotschna board worked out a new program for the village and secondary schools (Zentralschulen), which was approved by the national authorities in 1876, and which won state rights for the Mennonite schools, a matter of particular importance for the performance of the alternative service. In Halbstadt and in Chortitza special two-year teacher-training schools (*Lehrerseminar*) were established. The system of teacher conventions was also reorganized, making them a source of inspiration and

training. The other Mennonite settlements also appointed school boards similar to the one in the Molotschna.

In 1881 the situation was radically changed, when the educational system was put under the national department of education. To the Russian school authorities the Mennonite school boards were unwelcome; but they were permitted to function for a number of years, though with decreasing authority. But in the 1890's the program of Russianization was so rigorously carried out, especially by the department of education, that the Mennonite school boards had to struggle for the very existence of these schools and for their own existence as a board, until finally they were no longer able to function at all.

The year 1905 brought a slight though only temporary relaxing of the situation. But the teachers still had the right to form associations, and they did this. These teachers' associations then assumed various functions of the former school boards, such as conventions, organization of general vocational courses, working out of syllabi and curricula, choice of textbooks and equipment, etc.

All the Mennonite schools were church schools. Religion had always been one of the principal subjects of instruction, and until the 1870's the Bible was a reader in the elementary schools. The students were at that time divided into three groups: *Fibler* (lower grade), *Testamentler* (middle grade), and *Bibler* (upper grade). The school deputation (Elder A. Görz, school board member A. Voth, and secondary school teachers H. Franz and H. Lenzmann) which was sent to St. Petersburg in 1876 on the matter of the new national program for the schools made the Mennonite position on this question very clear: "Both the village and secondary schools and also the teachers' seminary must have absolutely the character of church schools, and only if they are confirmed as such do they fulfill their purpose, since in these schools not only our teachers, who must also be the religious instructors of our children, but also our preachers and pastors must be trained. All schools under us must be so definitely founded on the Mennonite confession that the students can acquire a religious training that will qualify them to assume the office of a preacher or elder, for according to our organization and the Holy Scripture, these officials must be chosen from among the people" (A. Görz, 16).

The religious character of the Mennonite schools was then recognized by the Russian authorities, and was preserved even after the schools were placed under the national ministry of education in 1881; for this law contained the reservation that the religious and spiritual training of any group should be under the direction of the clergy of that group, and that the curriculum should provide enough time to preserve the principles and native tongue of the group. One third of the total time, or about thirty hours per week or ten hours of class instruction, were considered adequate. This plan was maintained until the Revolution in 1917. The ten hours were equally divided between religion and German. The five hours thus devoted to religious instruction must be considered generous. In the Zentralschulen a course in church history was added, and in the teacher-training school also Mennonite history, dogmatics, Christian ethics, etc. Instruction in German and religion were not under Russian supervision, but under the Mennonite ministerial body or the Mennonite school board.

Fresh motivation was received from Germany and Switzerland again and again, first through young teachers who came from there, such as Tobias Voth (immigrated in 1821), Heinrich Heese (1827), Heinrich Franz I (1834), Fr. W. Lange (1837), and David Hausknecht; and later, about 1870, by young people who were sent to Germany and Switzerland for advanced education. Some of the first to go abroad to study were Heinrich Franz II, Kornelius Unruh, and P. M. Friesen, and many others followed. At first they went to Barmen and later to Basel. In the 1880's the Russian influence became predominant, and many a teacher made personal contacts with the leading Russian pedagogues, such as Ushinski, Baron Korff, Baranov, and Yevtuzovsky, whose works were also eagerly read. But about 1900, probably in consequence of compulsory Russianization, the German influence again became predominant. In the last 15 years before World War I hardly any major German school reform idea was unknown in the Mennonite schools in Russia, be it Kerschensteiner with his idea of the *Arbeitsschule,* or E. Linde with his pedagogy of the personality, H. Scharrelmann with his "heartfelt (*herzhaft*) instruction," or Freud with his investigations in experimental psychology; they were all industriously and thoroughly read and found imitators with more or less skill among the Mennonite teachers.

Relations with the Moravian Brethren (Herrnhuter) also are worthy of note. Tobias Voth, the first teacher of the Orloff Zentralschule (1822-29), carried on a correspondence with them. When Andreas Voth as the president of the Molotschna school board opened the first girls' school (*Mädchenschule*) in Halbstadt in 1874, he called as the first teacher a young Herrnhut woman, Sophie Schlenker of Königsfelden, of whom P. M. Friesen says that all of his pedagogical ideas came from the Herrnhuters (through her). When Peter Braun, the teacher of the Halbstadt Zentralschule and later president of the normal school (*Lehrerseminar*), spent the summer of 1912 in Germany, he went to Niesky for a a week in order to become acquainted with the Moravian Brethren school system.

(2) *Secondary Schools.* One of the problems of the Mennonites of Russia was that of finding teachers for their schools. In the early period all the teachers were self-taught men, and even later not a few were of this type. Some of these were Johann Peters of Neuendorf, Johann Bräul of Rudnerweide, Peter Siemens of Münsterberg, Peter Holzrichter of Rosenort, Johann Bräul of Orloff, and David Dürksen of Margenau. Also the two elders who were teachers, Abr. Görz and Heinrich Unruh, who were also many years later successful members of the school board, were purely self-taught men.

Another way of preparing teachers was by the method of apprentice teachers, which also produced many a competent schoolman. Boys who felt a desire for teaching as a vocation went into an apprenticeship with approved teachers, in winter serving as their assistants and in summer taking courses in educational theory under these teachers. In this way Peter Siemens prepared many a young man for the teachers' examination.

These methods, which were feasible only for a few individuals, could not satisfy the need. The need of a higher school for this purpose soon became apparent. As early as 1820 the Christian School Association (*Christlicher Schulverein, q.v.*) was formed in Orloff, which opened the Orloff *Vereinsschule* in 1822 to prepare teachers for the elementary schools, where the native language should be taught besides German. The soul of this association was Johann Cornies. The first teachers in the school were Tobias Voth 1822-29, and Heinrich Heese 1829-42, both of whom had received training in Germany.

In 1835 at the request of the Fürsorge-Komitee a district school was founded to prepare young men for service in the colony offices, which required a knowledge of the Russian language. In 1838 the private school in Steinbach was opened. In Gnadenfeld a *Bruderschule* was established. In 1842 Chortitza also acquired such a *Fortbildungsschule.*

All of these secondary schools, which were later commonly known as Zentralschulen, had to contend with all sorts of obstacles for a long time. The necessary understanding and interest were lacking among the settlers in general, and for many years there were very few students in these secondary schools. They were conspicuously not at all touched by the reforms introduced into the village schools by the Agricultural Association. P. M. Friesen says that until 1870 the Mennonite school authorities were unable to comprehend why two teachers should or could be employed at the same school at the same time! And so these schools usually had only one teacher, and instruction in the Russian language was usually rather weak. Nor did they prove to be teacher-training institutions, even though a number of successful teachers came from them.

The Zentralschulen finally achieved their proper organization as "general educational schools" under the administration by the school boards. The program worked out by the school board and approved by the ministry of education was planned for four years (for ages 13 or 14 to 17 or 18), and was adapted to the program of the Russian city schools. There were two classes, each of two years. In 1884 a school was opened in the Molotschna with three classes of one year each instead of the two classes with two years each. This type of school was also introduced by the daughter colonies of the Molotschna. But in 1912, when the city schools were converted into "higher elementary schools," with a four-year program, the Zentralschulen of the Molotschna type also went back to the four-class system. The Zentralschulen of Chortitza and the Chortitza daughter colonies always had the four-year course.

In the beginning the language of instruction was German, but by the middle 1880's Russian was the language of instruction for all courses but German and religion.

After the reform the Zentralschulen soon gained in importance in the public life and sympathy. They acquired a good reputation, and the enrollment increased year by year. Especially the Orloff Zentralschule (*q.v.*) under Kornelius Unruh 1873-1905, and Johann Bräul 1905-17, and the Chortitza Zentralschule (*q.v.*) under Abr. Neufeld 1890-1905 enjoyed an excellent reputation.

The four freedoms of 1905—speech, the press, meetings, and associations—stimulated a growing social consciousness in all classes of the Russian people. Among the Mennonites it found expression, first of all, in the building of new schools. In the decade 1905-14 twice as many secondary schools were opened as in the century before, and throughout the settlements as far as Siberia.

After the Zentralschulen were no longer thought of as teacher-training institutions, which they really had never been, special schools had to be created for this purpose. In 1878 a two-year pedagogical course was added to the Zentralschule in Halbstadt, Molotschna, with a practice school. In 1890 such courses were created in the Chortitza school, and increased to three years in 1911. For admission, graduation from a Zentralschule was required.

These two institutions thereafter furnished the teaching staff for most of the Mennonite schools throughout Russia. It is to their credit that the teachers they produced maintained the closest contact with Mennonite society, faith, and life, and at the same time gave thorough teaching in the Russian language and literature. But it was not until 1917 that the Russian school authorities permitted these schools to become independent, full teacher-training schools.

When the pedagogical courses were opened, another lack in the Mennonite school system became apparent. Not all the graduates of the Zentralschule wanted to become farmers or teachers. Of those interested in higher education only a small fraction were able to attend a university in a foreign country; and those who wanted to attend a Russian university first had to attend a Russian Gymnasium (or Realschule). This route was expensive and difficult, because the Zentralschulen were not integrated into the Russian pattern. In addition many parents were very reluctant to send their young sons into a Russian city, where they were exposed to all sorts of danger and might easily be harmed in soul or body. How could this handicap be removed? The simplest and surest way was to open a Realschule in a Mennonite center.

In 1908 a Mennonite Realschule was opened in Halbstadt, which continued the work of the Zentralschulen. But since this school was hard to maintain under the direction of the ministry of education, it was after a year changed into a four-year business college (Kommerzschule) because the ministry of commerce permitted its schools a greater degree of independence. Graduates of the Zentralschulen were admitted to the fourth or fifth class of the business college without examination. In order to provide a corresponding education for girls, the Halbstadt Mädchenschule (*q.v.*) (girls' school) was gradually developed into a full eight-year girls' Gymnasium.

This was the final status of the Mennonite attempt at education in Russia, a closed school system (elementary school, Zentralschule, teachers' training school or business college or girls' Gymnasium), which admitted to the Russian universities.

During World War I Mennonite schools were not greatly affected. Teachers' associations were abolished, but the schools remained in operation, and the German language was not prohibited.

After the February Revolution of 1917 new hopes inspired the peoples of Russia. The Mennonite school boards were reorganized, the teachers' associations were reconstituted, and it was commonly believed that a time of new growth and joyous work had dawned.

But this was not to be the case. For three years the civil war raged, ending in October 1920 with the Soviet government in control in all of Russia. Thereby a hoarfrost fell on the thriving school system of the settlements, and destroyed it. All schools came under state control, and the Mennonite schools soon lost their Mennonite character and influence. After 1920 there were some schools which used the German language, but no Mennonite schools. There was a brief revival of the old school system during the German occupation of the Ukraine in 1941-43.

(3) *Statistics.* (*a*) *Elementary Schools.* With a total population of about 110,000, the Mennonites of Russia had about 450 elementary schools in 1920 (village and farm schools) with about 16,000 pupils. The elementary schools had a seven-year course, but it happened frequently that a child dropped out after six or even five years of school. But it is not likely that a mentally normal child of Mennonite parents remained illiterate. All the elementary schools were coeducational. Most of them (about 350) had only one teacher. The maximum number of pupils assigned to a single teacher was set at 60, but such instances were rare. Most schools with 50 pupils had 2 teachers. There were a total of 85 two-room schools, 9 three-room, and 5 four-room elementary schools.

Five of the elementary schools were town or city schools: Berdyansk, Melitopol, Ekaterinoslav, Davlekanovo, and Slavgorod; two were charity schools: Berezovka near Davlekanovo, and Halbstadt; and one for orphans at Grossweide. In addition there was a five-room school for the deaf in Tiege with about 50 pupils.

There were about 570 Mennonite teachers in these schools, about 70 being women.

(*b*) *Secondary Schools.* As a continuation of the elementary schools, the Zentralschulen were founded. There were ultimately 25 of these. In 1920 the Zentralschulen were almost without exception four-year schools and adapted to the Russian "higher elementary schools" in their curriculum. Of these Zentralschulen 19 were boys' schools, 4 were girls' schools, and 2 were coeducational (two schools were called *Handelsschulen*—business schools). In addition there were two schools (*Ministerialschulen*), in Köppental and Alexandertal on the Volga, sponsored by the Department of Education. These latter schools had the same rights as the Zentralschule, but were on a different plane. The total number of pupils in the Zentralschulen was about 2,000, with a teaching staff of about 100 teachers.

The most advanced schools were (1) the two teacher-training schools (Halbstadt and Chortitza), each with a three-year course, which trained the elementary teachers and were considered continuations of the Zentralschulen. In normal times each of these schools had an enrollment of about 60 students. (2) An eight-year business school for boys, located in Halbstadt, whose graduates were admitted to the state university. In normal times its enrollment was about 300. (3) An eight-year girls' Gymnasium, also in Halbstadt, with the complete curriculum of the state gymnasium; its enrollment was about 150.

In all of these schools, with the exception of the school for the deaf (where for technical reasons only German was taught), the German and Russian language and literature were taught in equal amount. The school of commerce had as an additional requirement a choice of either French or English.

(c) *The Teaching Staff.* About 15 per cent of the elementary teachers had no certificate, being only students at the Zentralschulen or self-taught. These teachers usually worked in the new schools opening year by year in new settlements and large estates. Of the remaining 85 per cent about one half had a regular pedagogical education from Halbstadt or Chortitza. The others were students at Zentralschulen or self-taught to the extent that they were able to earn the state teachers' diploma.

The teaching staff in the Zentralschulen was composed of (a) those who had graduated from Russian teachers' institutes, (b) those who had a secondary-school education and had a corresponding teacher's certificate, (c) those who after a few years of teaching in an elementary school passed an examination for one or more subjects qualifying them to teach in Zentralschulen.

The religious instructors of the Zentralschulen were commonly elementary schoolteachers who had attended some institution or university in a foreign country; for German they had as a rule a teacher's certificate.

The average salary of the elementary teachers, often paid in kind, was perhaps 500 roubles annually with lodging. Zentralschule teachers received an annual salary of perhaps 1,200 roubles, also with rooms. (At that time a rouble was equivalent to 50 cents.)

All the schools, with the exception of the two *Ministerialschulen* (Samara) which were supported by the district (Zemstvo), were built and maintained by the Mennonite communities, but were under state supervision.

A late attempt to establish a theological school was frustrated by the chaotic conditions after the Revolution. Four Bible schools were established: Friedensfeld (1907-10), and in the period 1923-26 Davlekanovo, Tchongrav, and Orenburg.   P.Br.

P. Braun, "Der Molotschnaer Mennonitische Schulrat" (ms.); Friesen, *Brüderschaft;* Abr. Görz, *Die Schulen in den Mennoniten-Kolonien* (Berdyansk, 1882); A. Neufeld, *Die Chortitzer Zentralschule* (Berdyansk, 1893, a cut of the Halbstadt Zentralschule); D. P. Enns, "Die Mennonitischen Schulen in Russland," in *Menn. Jahrbuch,* 1950; Peter Braun, "Educational System of the Mennonite Colonies in South Russia," *MQR* III (1929) 168-82; Leonhard Froese, "Das pädagogische Kultursystem der mennonitischen Siedlungsgruppe in Russland" (unpublished doctoral dissertation, Göttingen, 1949); M. S. Harder, "The Origin, Philosophy, and Development of Education Among the Mennonites" (unpublished doctoral dissertation, University of Southern California, 1949).

Educational News, a four-page 8 x 12-inch periodical, published monthly by Dr. H. A. Mumaw in the interests of his Elkhart Normal School and Business Institute from 1896 to at least 1899.   H.S.B.

Educational Committee of the Mennonite Brethren Conference, the controlling agency in the operation of Tabor College since 1933, succeeding the Tabor College Corporation (M.B. and K.M.B.) which had built and operated the school for 25 years but felt itself unable to continue. At a special meeting on Sept. 18, 1933, the Corporation offered the school to the conferences supporting it, proposing an educational committee to be charged with the responsibility of effecting a new organization of Tabor College and continuing the operation of the school in accordance with the spirit and teaching of the conferences. At the M.B. General Conference Oct. 24, 1933, the proposal was accepted and an Educational Committee of nine members, two from each of the Canadian, Pacific, and Central districts and three from the Southern District, elected by the delegates from the district conferences and approved by the General Conference, was organized.

The organization and duties of the Educational Committee were defined in the constitution adopted by the Fortieth Convention of the Conference of the M.B. Church of North America in Reedley, Cal., Nov. 25, 1936, which provided for a membership of five elected so that each of the four district conferences would have representation. The Committee was authorized to approve all courses of study and other activities of the school, to prepare the budget for each ensuing three-year term and recommend ways and means for securing the contributions required by the budget for Conference action, and to appoint and discharge faculty members and other workers. In November 1945, by amendment to the constitution at the conference in Dinuba, Cal., the membership was changed from five to six members with the stipulation that each of the district conferences be represented and that three members be elected at each regular convention of the Conference to serve a term of six years. In July 1951 at the convention of the Mennonite Brethren Conference at Winkler, Man., the membership of the Educational Committee was enlarged to include nine members of the M.B. conference by the addition of three supernumerary members.

In 1945 the Krimmer M.B. Conference was invited to share in the work of the school. In November 1945 this conference voted to accept Tabor College as the official conference school and obligated itself to voluntary offerings, deputation work, and representation on the Educational Committee. Its official participation in the Educational Committee began on Jan. 17, 1946.   P.E.S.

Edzard I, Count of East Friesland (1492-1528), acquainted himself with the contents of the Bible and the writings of Luther, which led him to favor the Reformation of the church in 1519. He was in touch with Luther, had his sons educated by Aportanus, who favored Zwingli, and let the Reformation of East Friesland take its course, tolerating not only Lutheran and Zwinglian influences but also Catholic clergy and extreme spiritualists, who paved the way for the coming of Carlstadt and Melchior Hofmann. Although he died before Anabaptism was fully established in East Friesland, and although his sons did not share their father's tolerance, the variety of Protestant refugees who found asylum in East Friesland, and the attitude toward them established by Edzard I, made it possible that soon after his death (1530) Emden in East Friesland became the cradle of Anabaptism in northwest Europe.   C.K.

J. P. Müller, *Die Mennoniten in Ostfriesland* (Emden, 1887); E. Kochs, "Die Anfänge der ostfriesischen Reformation" (II), *Jahrbuch der Gesellsch. f. b. K. u. vaterl. Altertümer zu Emden* XIX (1916-18) 173-273; H. Reimers, *Die Gestaltung der Reformation in Ostfriesland* (Aurich, 1917) 6 ff.; *ML* I, 505.

Edzard II, Count of East Friesland, Germany, 1562-99, a grandson of Edzard I, was a violent opponent of the Mennonites. On Aug. 9, 1568, he issued orders to the city council of Emden to confiscate the property of Mennonites who had fled as well as of those who remained, and to expel them from the city; half of the proceeds was to go to the city and half to the count. There was apparently no haste in complying. On July 14 the magistrate of Emden had received a warning from the count to watch the Mennonites closely. Edzard promised the Emden clergy prompt help in reply to their petition of Jan. 6, 1577, which complained "that the Anabaptists not only increase daily, and not only occupy the best houses . . . and form associations for big business and carry on trade, but are also so bold as to hold public conventicles of their . . . false doctrine in large numbers, preach, and let themselves be seen." Meanwhile the Emden magistrate was to forbid all preaching, public or private, and prevent their gathering. In February 1578 Edzard wrote to Emden that Menso Alting had reported that about 1,000 Mennonites would soon be coming from the Netherlands to settle in Emden; they should not be permitted to do so. And finally on Aug. 13, 1582, he issued an edict forbidding his subjects to sell or rent houses or lands to a Mennonite. But apparently this sharp mandate was not very carefully obeyed.   NEFF.

J. P. Müller, *Die Mennoniten in Ostfriesland* . . . (Emden, 1887) 30-33; *ML* I, 505 f.

Edzardi (*Glaneus Jodocus*) (1595-1667), pastor of St. Michael's Church in Hamburg, wrote the following books against the Mennonites: (1) *Notwehr der Kindertaufe, welche die Wiedertäufer den Kindern wehren, den Mündigen zweifelhaft machen und eine gefährliche Wiedertäuferei einrichten in zwei Teilen, darin unsere Beweistümer vor die Kindertaufe wider sie verteidigt, ihre aber widerlegt werden. Mit einer ausführlichen Vorrede von der wiedertäuferischen Sekt aus ihren eigenen Büchern verfasst* (Hamburg, 1636). (2) *Geistliches Bade-Tuch, den neuen wiedertäuferischen Tauchern, welche nach des falsch genannten Pontani und des-*

selben Vermehrers Jacob Mehrnings Lehre von der Besprengung oder Begiessung in der einmalig empfangen Taufe nicht vergnüget eine neue Wiedertaufe in den tiefen Strömen oder Fischteichen durch Ein- oder Untertauchen vorhaben, entgegengesetzt. Zwei Predigten am Fest der Hl. Dreieinigkeit und Johannistag dargestellt (Hamburg, 1651).

The contents of the former is indicated by the detailed title; the latter opposes the Dompelaars (*q.v.*), under the motto of Matt. 23:24, "Ye blind guides, which strain at a gnat and swallow a camel," which he applies to Mehrning and nearly all of the Mennonites, "because they quarrel bitterly about unimportant ceremonies, and neglect the most necessary and most comforting articles of faith." This (says he) is especially true of immersion, which creates a dangerous offense, for it disquiets simple souls concerning their baptism by pouring or sprinkling. The latter is of course Scriptural; Christ was baptized in the Jordan by pouring. Although immersion occurred in the warm Orient, nevertheless, then as now, baptism by sprinkling or pouring is equally valid. This he expounds at great length with illustrations from the Bible.   NEFF.

Schröder, *Lexikon der Hamburger Schriftsteller; ML* II, 506.

Ee, a village in the Dutch province of Friesland, where Leenaert Bouwens (*q.v.*) baptized 33 persons in 1568-82. This rather large number indicates that there was very likely a Mennonite congregation at Ee. Yet nothing is known of the existence of such a congregation. The Mennonites may have joined the near-by Anjum (*q.v.*) congregation.   vDZ.

Eebe Wytses-Volk, a branch of Dutch Mennonites found in the province of Friesland about 1665. It must have been a small group. Of its origin, special principles, and end nothing is known. (*DB* 1877, 126.)   vDZ.

Eeghem (Eeghen), **Adriaan van,** a member of the large van Eeghen family (*q.v.*), b. June 14, 1631, at Cortemarck, Flanders, d. May 24, 1709, at Middelburg. As a boy he was a Catholic priest's attendant at Mass. Adriaan went to Haarlem, Holland, to learn weaving, and was baptized into the Flemish Mennonite congregation there on March 17, 1652. In 1653 he settled in Middelburg, Dutch province of Zeeland, and began to preach there on March 21, 1655. He opened a book business, learned Latin, Greek, and Hebrew, became a competent theologian, and wrote the first Mennonite systematic theology, *De Christelijke Godgeleerdheid,* printed posthumously in 1711. In 1658 he debated with the Quaker Frijkes Emble after the sermon in Vlissingen.

Joost Isenbaart, the elder of Middelburg, on Dec. 3, 1659, accused his colleagues Adriaan van Eeghem and Pieter Baart of unorthodoxy on the Incarnation and the Trinity. When Baart moved to Vlissingen in 1663, three new preachers were chosen, one of them being Thomas van Eeghem, Adriaan's nephew (d. July 28, 1693). Soon afterward the Galenist dissension broke out in Zeeland. Isenbaart now brought suit against his colleagues. Adriaan was summoned before the magistrate. In the presence of Thomas van Eeghem, he declared that he believed in the eternity of Christ, that Adam's sin was not only for himself and Christ's death was not only for Himself. He refused to sign the 12 Utrecht Articles (*q.v.*). This was followed by a debate with Samuel Apostool (*q.v.*) of Amsterdam. The government forbade him to preach any longer until he promised not to preach contrary to the 12 questions (Dec. 19, 1655). Isenbaart died in 1673. In 1701 Adriaan was attacked by the Reformed preacher on account of his book, *De Wet der Nature*.

For his preaching Adriaan received nothing but a rent-free home. He refused a call to Rotterdam. He continued his service into his advanced old age, and preached a sermon one week before his death at the age of nearly 78. He was married three times: to Janneke Willems 1656-78, Martijntje Goudesebois 1680-84, and Petronella Haijs 1702 until his death. He had no children. He wrote several books, which were published at Middelburg by Michiel van Hoekke: *Verhandelinge van de stemmelijke gebeden in de vergaderinge der geloovigen* (1685), in which he showed himself to be a determined opponent of "silent prayer"; *Catechismus ofte onderwyzinge in de Kristelijke Godsdienst* (1687), reprinted in 1715; *Korte Catechismus* (1691); *Verhandelinge van de Wet der Nature* (1701). This last book had an appendix: an answer to several questions; notes on the first 18 verses of the Gospel of John; may those who are not members of the church come to communion? (He answered it negatively.) This book was reprinted in 1731 by Gerardus de Wind, who had previously edited and published a manuscript left by Adriaan: *De Christelijke Godgeleerdheid* (1711). It has about 650 pages, and is divided into five books: the Scriptures, God's name, qualities and works, God's covenant with Abraham and his descendants, the new covenant, and the Christian church or the congregation of the new covenant. Gerardus de Wind also wrote a funeral sermon on Adriaan's death.

K.V.

C. P. van Eeghen, Jr., *Adriaan van Eeghem, Doopsgezinde leeraar te Middelburg* (Amsterdam, 1886); Schijn-Maatschoen, 40-48; *Inv. Arch. Amst.* I, No. 452; *Biogr. Wb.* II, 700 f.; *DB* 1898, 56-60; *Catalogus Amst.*, 155, 158; *ML* I, 506 f.

Eeghen, van (van Eeghen, Eeghem, Eegen, Egen, Egene, Hegen), a Dutch Mennonite family, numerous members of which, usually merchants or bankers, have been important members of the church both by their generosity and their loyalty, often serving it as deacons or even as ministers. Many wealthy members of this family have rendered valuable service to the Dutch nation, and especially the city of Amsterdam, by their charity, their promotion of public welfare, and their cultural and artistic contributions.

The ancestor of this van Eeghen family was *Adriaen van Eeghen,* of whom nothing is known but the name. His son was Christiaen, b. *ca.* 1565, d. *ca.* 1660. They lived and died at Cortemerck (Kortemerk), some miles south of Brugge in Flanders, Belgium. The name van Eeghen is derived

from a farm called 't Eeghem near Cortemerck, which they leased. Both Adriaen and Christiaen seem to have been Catholic, as were also Christiaen's children in their youth.

One of Christiaen's sons, *Christiaen de Oude,* b. *ca.* 1595 at Cortemerck, left the Catholic Church and emigrated to Aardenburg, Dutch province of Zeeland, about 1632 as a cloth-merchant. Here he joined the Mennonite Church and became a prominent lay member of the congregation; in 1665 he promoted the building of a church (*DB* 1877, 10-11), and in 1657-62 he negotiated with the city government concerning exemption from military service on payment of a head tax (*DB* 1879, 32-34). He died at Aardenburg in 1669.

Adriaen van Eeghem, also a son of Christiaen van Eeghen and a brother of Christiaen de Oude, moved from Cortemerck to Aardenburg about 1645, where he joined the Mennonite Church; his son was *Adriaan van Eeghem* (*q.v.*), a well-known Mennonite minister of Middelburg.

Christiaen's youngest son, *Thomas van Eeghen de Oude,* a linen-trader, also left Flanders and resided in Middelburg, capital of the Dutch province of Zeeland, where he became a citizen in 1646, and died in 1657. His son Thomas van Eeghen de Jonge, b. at Cortemerck (year unknown), lived at Aardenburg 1654-62, where he was a deacon of the congregation; from 1662 until his death in 1693 he served as a preacher of the church of Middelburg. He was married to Leuntje van Daele.

Jacob van Eeghen, the son of Christiaen de Oude, b. at Cortemerck 1631, emigrated with his parents to Aardenburg. He became very influential in the Mennonite congregation; he married Tanneken Hebberecht (1635-61), a sister of Gillis Hebberecht (*q.v.*), the preacher of the church of Aardenburg, of which Jacob van Eeghen was a deacon 1657-59. In 1662 he moved to Amsterdam, where his descendants are now found. Shortly before his settling at Amsterdam, he was married to Maria Bocxhoorn (1637-84), a granddaughter of Leonhard (Leenaerdt) Clock (*q.v.*). Through this marriage he became one of the well-to-do Mennonite merchants of Haarlem (linen bleachers) and Amsterdam (trade to Baltic ports and Spain). Jacob van Eeghen also was a merchant (especially linen, but also linseed, salt, and wines). His business was very prosperous and he became wealthy, though he had to send large amounts to his son-in-law at Aardenburg, who had suffered from war and other calamities. Jacob van Eeghen is to be considered the forerunner of the later *Handelshuis van Eeghen.* He died in 1697, while visiting Aardenburg.

Of the Amsterdam branch of the van Eeghen family, founded by the above Jacob van Eeghen whose members all belonged to the moderate Flemish Lamist congregation, these should be mentioned:

Christiaan van Eeghen, grandson of Jacob, b. 1700 at Amsterdam, d. there 1747, a well-to-do merchant and shipowner. He extended his business to the islands of the Caribbean Sea (tobacco, cacao beans, pelts and furs from America). He was married to Cornelia Cornelje (1695-1749). Twice he served the congregation of Amsterdam as deacon. He is said to have been a kind and very generous man. He published (translated from the English) *De konst der Vergenoegtheit* (Amsterdam, 1728), by an unknown author.

His grandson *Christiaan van Eeghen*, b. 1757 at Amsterdam, d. there 1798, married to Catharina Fock (1762-1807), who also served the congregation as a deacon, and associated with his brother Pieter van Eeghen in founding the *Handelshuis* (trading company) *P. en C. van Eeghen* in 1778, later called *Van Eeghen en Co.* The brothers were much interested in the American trade after this country had declared itself independent in 1776. They not only shipped all kinds of goods in large quantities to and from the States, but also the van Eeghen banking house, *Huis of Negocie,* procured loans for the new country, first in 1782. They also, together with other Dutch bankers, bought a large area of land in the state of New York, south and west of Lake Ontario. Projects were made to build a city here, to be called Nieuw-Amsterdam, but the city arose much later and was then called Buffalo. Christiaan van Eeghen became the director of the company founded to administer the land, soon called Holland Land Company. In this time P. and C. van Eeghen collected a large collection of books, pamphlets, maps, and caricatures concerning America, most of them now being in the Library of the University of Amsterdam. Soon after, during the war between England and France, business was very difficult and subject to great dangers and losses, and the assets and also the revenues decreased rapidly after 1796. Nevertheless Christiaan van Eeghen, who was a pious man, found time for his congregation, his family (five children), his hobbies (history and art), and his home country. He was a moderate Patriot (*q.v.*). In 1795 he became a member of the Financial Committee of the city of Amsterdam. After a short illness he died on May 9, 1798, only 40 years old.

Jacob van Eeghen (grandson of the foregoing), b. at Amsterdam 1818, d. there 1834, left behind a number of sensitive poems, some of which were published in 1835, entitled *Keuze uit nagelaten gedichtjens . . .* (*N.N.B.Wb.* I, 790).

Christiaan Pieter van Eeghen, b. 1816 at Amsterdam, d. there 1889, was a partner of the *Handelshuis van Eeghen* 1839-89. Business was very slow in the post-Napoleonic era; in nearly all branches of trade there was a recession which was not restored until 1839. The *Nederlandsche Handelmaatschappij* (Dutch Trading Company), founded in 1824 by the king and supported by the government, did much harm to private companies like the *Handelshuis van Eeghen.* So young Christiaan Pieter had a hard time of it, but proved to be a good businessman. For this reason he was later appointed a member of the board of directors of the Dutch National Bank (1859) and in 1864 president of this board. He is known for his philanthropy and the promotion of public health by stimulating the building of better homes for workmen in his home city, and also for the founding of the Vondelpark, still a large recreation center of Amsterdam. He contributed liberally to many needy causes and many

Christian institutions. He was also interested in the fine arts. On his instigation and with his financial aid the van der Hoop-Museum (now Rijksmuseum) was thoroughly improved and many old pictures restored. He founded the *Koninklijk Oudheidkundig Genootschap* (Royal Dutch Antiquarian Association). He is of special interest for church history and Mennonite history for his inclination to Christian revivalism (*Réveil, q.v.*). Most of the outstanding revivalists in the Netherlands, like Heldring, Beets, and van der Goot, a Mennonite minister of Amsterdam, were his personal friends, whom he received in his stately house. He was very active too in missions, being a member of the board of the Dutch Mennonite Mission Society from the beginning (1847). He also served the church as a deacon (1845-51). He was extremely averse to religious modernism, and watched the growing liberalism in his home church with grief and uneasiness. In 1842 he was married to Catharina Huidekooper, daughter of the (Mennonite) mayor of Amsterdam. "Christiaan Pieter van Eeghen was one of the greatest of all in his family" (Rogge, 342; *N.N.B.Wb.* I, 789).

Hendrik van Eeghen, b. at Amsterdam 1831, d. there 1893, a partner in the *Handelshuis van Eeghen* and president of the Dutch National Bank 1884-93, served the congregation of Amsterdam as deacon 1857-61 and was treasurer of the A.D.S. from 1869 until his death in 1893.

Pieter van Eeghen (son of the foregoing Christiaan Pieter, and like his father a partner in the same *Handelshuis van Eeghen* 1872-1907), b. Amsterdam 1844, d. 1907 at Cortemerck near Nijmegen, was a member of the city council of Amsterdam 1878-99 and of the provincial government of North Holland 1877-1907. Like his father he was a patron of the arts. He was the founder of the Stedelijk Museum (city art gallery of Amsterdam), and for more than 25 years was president of the *Oudheidkundig Genootschap,* established by his father. But in addition to contributing his affection, his time and his money, he was also active in writing. He published *Jan Luyken en zijn bloedverwanten* (Amsterdam, 1889), and, together with J. Ph. van der Kellen, *Het leven en het werk van Jan en Casper Luyken* (2 vv., Amsterdam, 1905), a magnificent book containing the biography and description of the etchings and drawings of Jan Luyken (*q.v.*), illustrator of the *Martyrs' Mirror,* and his son Caspar. He published *Jan Minnaerts,* a very interesting study of the relief of the poor among the Mennonites (in *DB* 1907).

In 1872 Pieter van Eeghen married Maria de Clercq, of an old Mennonite family. He had great love for the church. Three times he served the congregation of Amsterdam as a deacon. From 1881 to 1907 he was member of the executive board of the A.D.S., serving as treasurer 1892-1907 (*N.N.B. Wb.* I, 790-91; *DB* 1907, 195-204, with portrait).

Samuel Pieter van Eeghen, b. 1853 at Zeist, d. 1934 at Amsterdam, associate in the *Handelshuis van Eeghen* 1880-1934, member of the provincial government of North Holland, a member (1893) then president (1904) of the Amsterdam Chamber of

Commerce, also served the congregation of Amsterdam as deacon (1878-84).

Christiaan Pieter van Eeghen, Jr., a son of Christiaan Pieter (see above), b. 1853 at Amsterdam, d. 1917 at Oosterbeek, studied theology at the university of Utrecht and the Amsterdam Mennonite seminary, served as pastor in the congregations of Medemblik 1882-83 and Aardenburg 1883-92. Then he resigned and moved to Amsterdam. Here in 1892-1912 he served as pastor of a group of Mennonites who were meeting separately and had founded a Sunday school, because they did not agree with the general (liberal) trend of the congregation. In 1912 the group returned to the church, considering the preaching in the church to be sufficiently orthodox (*DB* 1912, 224). C. P. van Eeghen, Jr., published a historical study on his ancestor: *Adriaen van Eeghem, Doopsgezind leeraar te Middelburg* (Amsterdam, 1886); and a collection of sermons, including his *Afscheidsrede* at Aardenburg (Amsterdam, 1892). He was one of the editors (with J. W. van Stuyvenberg, J. Loosjes, and others) of *De kleine Medewerker,* later called *Doopsgezind Maandblad voor uit- en inwendige zending.* For a number of years he was on the board of the Dutch Mission Society. In 1886 he was married to E. W. A. van Helden (1861-1915). They had no children.

Christiaan Pieter van Eeghen, the son of Pieter, b. Feb. 10, 1880, at Amsterdam, married in 1906 to Henriette Heldring, studied law at the university of Amsterdam, was a partner in the *Handelshuis van Eeghen* 1908-24, director of the Dutch-Indian Trading Bank (later called National Trading Bank) from 1924, a member of the Amsterdam Chamber of Commerce 1921-52, and its president 1945-52.

He served the congregation of Amsterdam as a deacon 1907-11, 1917-21, 1927-31; was a member of the board of the A.D.S. 1920-51, member of the executive committee 1932-51, member of the board of directors of the Amsterdam Mennonite Seminary 1927-32, and its president 1932-51.

Peter Hendriks, later also called Pieter van E(e)gen (also de Eegen, or van E(e)ger), d. 1770 at Nijmegen, Dutch province of Gelderland, a (unsalaried) preacher of the Nijmegen congregation 1717-70 (*Naamlijst,* and *Inv. Arch. Amst.* II, No. 2154), did not belong to this van Eeghen family.

vDZ.

Ned. Patriciaat II (1911) 121-28; X (1919) 96-105; F. K. van Lennep, *Verzameling van Oorkonden, betrekking hebbende op het geslacht van Eeghen in Nederland* (Amsterdam, 1918); J. Rogge, *Het Handelshuis van Eeghen* (Amsterdam, 1948); DJ 1837, 96 ff.; DB 1864, 2; 1865, 175; 1873, 46; 1876, 112; 1877, 9 ff., 11 f., 14, 18, 22; 1879, 18, 33, 35 f., 38, 47 ff.; 1881, 12; 1883, 11, 22, 56; 1884, 37 f., 42, 63, 123; 1889, 108; 1897, 85 ff.; 1898, 56 f., 73; 1901, 123; 1907, 145, 195 ff.; 1919, 224.

Eeke (Eecke, Eken), **Cornelis van,** a Dutch poet who was living at Amsterdam about 1700, published *Vale Mundo, ofte Noodinge tot de Broederschap Christi* (Amsterdam, 1684); a new rhymed version of the Psalms, entitled *De koninklyke Harpliederen, op nieuws in rym . . . uitgebreid* (Amsterdam, 1698); *Krommenie verbrand Ao 1702 den 22 July en uyt zijn assche herboud, en de vergader-* *plaats der Doopsgezinde de eerste maal geopend Ao 1703 den 17 May op Hemelvaartsdag* (Amsterdam, 1703), and *Lyk-digten ter gedagtenis van Dr Galenus Abrahamsz* (Amsterdam, n.d.—1709). Van Eeke, a mediocre poet, was a Collegiant, and a member of the Amsterdam Lamist congregation, a warm admirer of the Mennonite preacher Galenus Abrahamsz (*q.v.*).

vDZ.

N.N.B.Wb. X, 251 f.; C. B. Hylkema, *Reformateurs* (Haarlem, 1900, 1902) see Index; *Inv. Arch. Amst.* II, 2036.

Eekens (Ekens), **Dominicus,** b. 1682 at Dokkum, Dutch province of Friesland, d. July 11, 1732, at Amsterdam, a Dutch Mennonite minister, was trained 1699-1705 for the ministry by the Amsterdam preacher Galenus Abrahamsz (*q.v.*), and served the congregation of Amsterdam in 1710-13 as preacher and from 1713 until his death as an elder. He is said to have been a very modest man, whose sincere messages were of great blessing to the congregation. He did not leave behind any publications. He was married to Margaretha de Flines, of an old Flemish family. His colleague B. van Leuvenig delivered his funeral sermon, *Lykrede op Dominicus Eekens,* published at Amsterdam in 1732. (*Inv. Arch. Amst.* II, No. 686.)

vDZ.

Eelke (Fouckensz, Foekes), an Anabaptist martyr, a preacher though he was not yet baptized, was captured with a fellow believer named Fye (*q.v.*) at Boorn (Oldeboorn in the Dutch province of Friesland) and beheaded at Leeuwarden in 1549 three weeks before Easter. A hymn was written on their death which begins, "Nae u belooft, O goede Heer, wilt troost van bouen senden" (According to Thy promise, gracious Lord, Thou wilt send comfort from above), and published in *Het Offer des Heeren.* (*Offer,* 430-36; *Mart. Mir.* D 84, E 484; Wolkan, *Lieder,* 68; *ML* I, 507.)

NEFF, vDZ.

Eenighe gheestelijcke liedekens, *gemaeckt aen verscheyden personen,* a Dutch hymnbook, containing 46 songs written by Jan Jacobsz (*q.v.*). They were collected by Harmen Harmensz and edited by Pieter Willemsz, who wrote an introduction and also a conclusion and the end of the book, bearing the date 1613. The front page states that the book was published in 1612 by Nicolaas Biestkens at Amsterdam. The poetical quality of the songs is mediocre, though they were much liked by the congregations of the Janjacobs group, most of them using these hymns until the middle of the 18th century.

vDZ.

J. Loosjes, "Jan Jacobs en de Jan-Jacobsgezinden," in *Nederl. Archief voor Kerkgesch.,* No. 3 (The Hague, 1914) 16-22.

Eenighe nieuwe gheestelijcke liedekens, *gemaeckt door verscheyden personen,* a Dutch hymnbook published in Amsterdam in 1612 (though the last page of the book bears the date 1613). It is a sequel to *Eenighe gheestelijcke Liedekens* by Jan Jacobsz (*q.v.*). It was edited by Pieter Willemsz, and contains 36 songs, most written by Pieter Willemsz himself. Like the songbook of Jan Jacobsz it is poetically of poor quality. It was used by the Janjacobs group.

vDZ.

Eenigheid (Unity), the old Dutch expression for the Lord's Supper, and *Eenigheid houden* (to celebrate the Lord's Supper), both to indicate the unity with the Lord Christ and to express the union of the members of the church as members of the body of Christ (I Cor. 12:12). vDZ.

Eenigheydt, Verbondt van: see Verbondt van Eenigheydt.

Eenkes, Rippert, like his father Eenke was a preacher of the Waterlander Mennonite congregation of Workum, Dutch province of Friesland. About 1600 he became an elder (*Leeraar tot den vollen dienst*). He had considerable influence in Friesland and also preached in Haarlem, in the province of Groningen, in Emden, and even in Danzig. He often had trouble with his coelders; in 1618-20 he was suspended from his office. Hans de Ries (*q.v.*), the leading elder of the Dutch Waterlanders, attended and was apparently the moderator of the meeting held at Workum on Aug. 14, 1618, in which Rippert was suspended. An account of these quarrels is found in *DB* 1903; the Amsterdam Archives contain a large number of letters about this conflict. About 1605-6 Rippert was involved in a conflict with Joannes Biltius, Reformed pastor of Workum. Biltius (*q.v.*) debated with Rippert in the Mennonite meetinghouse in 1605. Thereupon Rippert had to hand in a written account of his principles to the magistracy of Workum; this account was handed in by Rippert in November 1606, not to the magistrate of Workum, but to the States of Friesland at Leeuwarden. Biltius answered with a very detailed refutation. It is not clear whether Rippert wrote an answer to this writing or not. The theme of this conflict was the question of the Scripturalness of infant baptism. The conflict seems not to have led to bad consequences for Rippert, since he was still serving after 1620. It is unknown how long he carried on his activities. He was still living in 1627, for in that year he published, as a contribution toward the settlement of the conflict which had arisen among the Waterlanders in Amsterdam concerning Nittert Obbesz (*q.v.*), a booklet entitled *Derthien Artijckelen, ghestelt door Rippert Eenkes ende sijne mede-hulpers . . . Nittert Obbes voor-gheleyt . . .* (n.p., 1627). vDZ.

DB 1873, 90-102; 1903, 57-77; *Inv. Arch. Amst.* I, Nos. 526, 529; II, Nos. 1193, 2925, 2931, 2932, 2936; II, 2, Nos. 652-57, 661-65, 667-70.

Eenrum: see Mensingeweer.

Egbert (de Hoedemaecker), an Anabaptist martyr, a hatter. He was taken prisoner at a meeting near Doornik (*q.v.*) in Belgium, first brought to Doornik and then to Bergen (Mons), where he was tried. He was executed by burning at the stake at Obignies near Doornik in 1558 (exact date unknown) with five other brethren. All remained steadfast. (*Mart. Mir.* D 203, E 584; *ML* I, 502.) vDZ.

Egelhaaf, Gottlob (1848-1934), rector of the Karls-gymnasium in Stuttgart. In his *Deutsche Geschichte im 16. Jahrhundert bis zum Augsburger Religionsfrieden* (2 vv., Stuttgart, 1889, 1892) he discusses the Anabaptists, but presents nothing new, dwelling principally on events in Zwickau and Münster, and on Wullenweber. The work is based on Cornelius (*q.v.*), Egli (*q.v.*), and Keller (*q.v.*), as far as they were available at the time.

Egen, Bastian, an Anabaptist martyr, of Ulbach, Württemberg, Germany, was executed at Esslingen (*q.v.*) in 1530.

Egg, on the Bregenzer Ach in the Vorarlberg (between Bregenz and Au), where the last executions of Anabaptists took place in the Holy Roman Empire. On May 24, 1618, on the eve of the Thirty Years' War, Jost Wilhelm, who had joined the Hutterian Brethren, was beheaded on account of his faith; and on Aug. 8, 1618, Christine Brünnerin, a poor widow, suffered the same fate, because she was planning to join the Hutterian Brethren and to go to Moravia. (*ML* I, 507 f.) HEGE.

Egge, Oom, an elder of the Waterlanders in the Dutch province of North Holland, of whom nothing is known but a conflict with Elder Gillis van Aken in 1555. (*DB* 1876, 23-24; Kühler, *Geschiedenis* I, 314.) vDZ.

Egges, Lubbert, b. 1706 or 1707, d. April 11, 1770, who in 1739 became preacher of the congregation at Uithuizen and in 1755 was chosen elder of the Groningen Old Flemish conference. In this capacity he faithfully visited the churches, as his careful notes show. His daughter Eltje dedicated an interesting epitaph to him (*DB* 1879, 69 f.). His "Aanteekeningen van eene rondreize" was published in *DJ* 1840, 33-52. (*ML* I, 508.) K.V.

Eggiwyl, a village in the canton of Bern, Switzerland, in the 17th century the seat of an Anabaptist congregation of 40 members. They were to be put into the prison in Bern and from there sent out of Switzerland. The village community refused to permit this, and had to send 12 of their most well-to-do men as hostages to Bern, to be kept there at the expense of the village until the order from Bern was obeyed. On Oct. 16, 1671, the Reformed pastor of the village was able to report that the Anabaptists had left of their own accord. They probably settled in Alsace or in the Palatinate, Germany. (Müller, *Berner Täufer,* 338 ff.; *ML* I, 508.) NEFF.

Eghels, Janneken, an Anabaptist martyr: see Janneken van Aken.

Eghels, Maeyken, an Anabaptist martyr: see Mariken van Meenen.

Eglauch, Caspar, elder and chronicler of the Hutterian Brethren in Slovakia, was born 1609 in Württemberg, and died 1693 at Lewär (Velké Levary), Slovakia. By trade he was a shoemaker. Apparently he joined the brotherhood at an early age. In 1647 he was chosen *Diener der Wortes* (preacher), and was confirmed one year later. As an old man of 79, he became *Vorsteher* or bishop of the entire brotherhood in 1688, serving in this capacity for five years. His time was a most trying period for the Brethren: repeated Turkish attacks deprived the Brethren of their homes, and the rising Counter Reformation (*q.v.*) in Slovakia tried to convert them to Catholicism and to compel them to have their children baptized. Some complied, but most of the Brethren remained true to their convictions, willing rather to emigrate than to obey such orders (Beck, 555). The institution of community of goods (*q.v.*) likewise became strained and in places was given up altogether (1685-95). In these difficult times Eglauch governed the brotherhood with power, industry, intelligence, and great earnestness, as stated in the *Väterlied* (*Lieder, 877*). He insisted upon the preservation of the community of goods as far as he was able to. As a chronicler of the brotherhood, we know Eglauch from the one manuscript codex which he wrote, a "Chronicle" covering the period 1647-82, now in the University Library of Budapest (Beck, cod. XXIII). Eglauch's successor as elder was Tobias Bersch (*q.v.*). HEGE.

Beck, *Geschichts-Bücher;* Zieglschmid, *Klein-Geschichtsbuch; Die Lieder der Hutterischen Brüder* (Scottdale, 1914); *ML* I, 508.

Egle, Christian R. (1858-1926), for many years pastor and elder of the Salem Defenseless Mennonite Church near Gridley, Livingston Co., Ill., was the son of Amish Mennonite parents, Christian and Maria (Rediger) Egle. Born in Württemberg, Germany, he came to America in 1874 to avoid military service. Although he had been baptized at the age of 15 in the Amish Mennonite church at Zweibrücken, Palatinate, Germany, he experienced a religious awakening in 1878 while attending the revival meetings conducted by Henry Egly (*q.v.*), founder of the Defenseless Mennonite Church. In June 1879 he was rebaptized and joined the Defenseless congregation at Gridley, Ill. In June 1883 he was elected by ballot to the ministry of his congregation and ten years later was ordained elder. After the death of Joseph Rediger, the elder of Salem, Egle was chosen as the Salem elder, a position he held until his death. In December 1891 he was married to Bena Augermeier. Egle was editor of the *Heils-Bote* (*q.v.*) throughout its entire history (1898-1917). For several years he also printed the publication. M.G.

"Biography of Christian R. Egle," *Zion's Tidings,* March 15, 1938, 11; Ruth Litwiller and Viola Gerig, *History of the Salem Evangelical Mennonite Church* (Flanagan, Ill., 1951).

Egli (Egly, Egle), a Mennonite family name, prominent in America and appearing in the *Martyrs' Mirror.* Rudolf Egli of Switzerland was imprisoned for his faith in 1635. Jacob Egli died a martyr's death in a Zürich prison in 1639. In 1660 Rudolph Egli signed the Dordrecht Confession of Faith as a minister representing Kühnenheim in Alsace. The Palatine Mennonite census list of 1717 has an Abraham Egli in Branchweilerhof and the 1743 list a Jakob Egly in the Duttweiler congregation.

Among the Amish members of the family emigrating to America in the 19th century were Henry Egly (*q.v.*), founder of the Defenseless Mennonite Church, and Christian R. Egle (*q.v.*), leader in the Defenseless Mennonite Conference. The Egli family has been prominent in Illinois Mennonite circles but has also been represented in Indiana, Iowa, and Ontario. Merlyn Egle is a minister of the Evangelical Mennonite Church, living in Chicago. M.G.

Egli (Egly), **Adelheyt** (Adelheid), the wife of Felix Landis (*q.v.*), was imprisoned at Oetenbach, canton of Zürich, Switzerland, in 1642 and repeatedly harshly treated. After four years in prison, she escaped, but found her house stripped by the authorities, who had confiscated the 5,000 guilders, and put her children out among strangers. (*Mart. Mir.* D 821, E 1120.) vDZ.

Egli, Emil (1848-1908), a Swiss church historian. He studied theology, was ordained in 1870, and served in several villages of the canton of Zürich. In his student days he was deeply interested in historical studies. In 1873 appeared his important work, *Die Schlacht bei Cappell 1531;* in 1879, *Die Züricher Wiedertäufer zur Reformationszeit,* a brief product of his *Aktensammlung zur Geschichte der Züricher Reformation in den Jahren 1519-1532,* which he published (1879) with the support of Zürich and offers an uncommonly rich source on the early history of the Anabaptist movement. In 1887 followed a smaller volume, *Die St. Galler Täufer.*

H. S. Burrage calls Egli the first research student to find a new point of view for judging the Anabaptists. His penetrating study of the documents and his understanding of the social movements of the Reformation period and of the specifically Swiss nature of this movement caused him to deviate from the traditional condemnation of the Anabaptists. He recognized it as a popular movement and understood its connection with individual more or less visionary leaders and was able to do justice to their intentions. Even the mass psychotic epidemics of the St. Gall Anabaptists he treated objectively. The interpretation of history in the light of related and connected events, and the personal attitude of the Anabaptists to their religious concepts were his norm.

Egli occupied himself principally with the Reformation in Switzerland. In 1879 he began his work at the university of Zürich as lecturer in church history, and in 1892 he was made a full professor. In addition to a series of shorter works he published *Heinrich Bullingers Diarium des Jahres 1504-1574* in the second volume of the *Quellen zur schweizerischen Reformationsgeschichte,* which he founded. After 1897 he published a semiannual periodical, *Zwingliana,* and after 1899 two volumes of *Analecta Reformatorica* (documents and treatises on the history of Zwingli and his times; also biographies of Bibliander, Ceporin, Johannes Bullinger). In 1902 he provided for a new edition of the Kessler's *Sabbata* (a publication of the historical association of St. Gall). With G. Finsler (Basel) he began the publication of the new edition of Zwingli's works (*Zwingli's Werke,* Leipzig, 1905 ff., in *Corpus Reformatorum*).

Egli was a conscientious scholar, who understood the correct approach to the Reformation period and thereby acquired a many-faceted historical sense. (*ML* I, 508 f.) C.B.

Egli, Jakob, an Anabaptist of Grüningen in the Swiss canton of Zürich, who was seized in 1639 and held in chains for 70 weeks in the convent dungeon at Oethenbach, which caused his death. His farm was rented for an annual fee of 500 guilders, which were put into the state treasury. (*Mart. Mir.* D 814, E 1113; *ML* I, 509.) NEFF.

Egli, Rudolf, was imprisoned with Uhli Schmied and Hans Müller in the Rathaus of Zürich in 1635, escaped, and was recaptured in 1637; his house was destroyed. His wife, Martha Lindingerin, was brutally compelled to betray where the alms fund of the congregation was hidden, which was in Rudolf Egli's care, and which amounted to 2,000 talers. (*Mart. Mir.* D 814, E 1109 f.; *ML* I, 509.) NEFF.

Egly, Henry (1824-90), founder of the Defenseless Mennonite Church (now Evangelical Mennonites), was born in Baden, Germany, the son of Abraham and Magdalena (Reber) Egly. In 1839 he with his father settled in Butler Co., Ohio, where he was baptized at the age of 17 and became a member of the Amish Mennonite Church.

In 1849 Egly was married to Katherine, daughter of Joseph Goldsmith (*q.v.*), bishop of the Amish Church in Lee County, Iowa. After two years of residence in Butler County, the Eglys moved to Adams Co., Ind., where they lived the rest of their lives. They were the parents of 6 sons and 2 daughters. Egly was ordained a deacon of his church in 1850 and a preacher in 1854. Previous to the time of the 1854 ordination, while he was suffering from a prolonged illness, he experienced a spiritual rededication and was restored to health. Thereafter he stressed the importance of an experimental knowledge of conversion and regeneration and the necessity of care in receiving members into the church. Following his ordination to the office of bishop of his congregation in January 1858, he continued his emphasis upon the necessity of a vital religious experience and won approximately one half of his church to an acceptance of his emphasis. After he had been asked to resign his pastorate by a number of his members, he organized his followers into a separate congregation in 1866. The movement spread to other Amish communities and in later years Egly spent much time in organizing and visiting these congregations.

Egly was a dynamic speaker and a radiant personality. His constant emphasis was placed upon the necessity of Bible study and the possibility of obtaining assurance of salvation. His death occurred on June 23, 1890, and he was buried in the cemetery near his church at Geneva, Ind. (See **Evangelical** Mennonite Church.) M.G.

D. N. and K. E. Claudon, *Life of Bishop Henry Egly* (Valparaiso, Ind., 1947?).

Ehrenberg, Richard (1857-1921), national economist, and professor of political sciences at the University of Rostock, made a valuable study of the commercial history of Hamburg-Altona. In it he gives the first extensive account of the development of the Mennonite settlement there. J. G. Büsch (1728-1800), also an economist, had previously stressed the cultural importance of the Dutch Mennonites in Hamburg-Altona, especially pointing out their contributions to shipping (*Versuch einer Geschichte der Hamburgischen Handlung,* 1797). Ehrenberg and other research scholars inspired by him continued this study. The economic development of prominent Mennonite families in Altona, and their immediate influence on the unusually early attainment of liberty of economic pursuits, is put into the framework of German economic history. The result of his investigations is summarized under the title, *Altona unter Schauenburgischer Herrschaft* (Altona, 1891-93), published and most of it written by Ehrenberg with the support of the Royal *Kommerzkollegium,* of which he was secretary 1888-97. Especially No. 4, *Gewerbefreiheit und Zunftzwang in Ottensen und Altona, 1543-1640,* is of interest in this connection, in which "Anfänge einer Grossindustrie" (founded by Mennonites) gives much information. In No. VI, pp. 90-97, P. Piper discusses "Die Reformierten und die Mennoniten Altonas," based on B. C. Roosen's *Geschichte der Mennonitengemeinde zu Hamburg und Altona* (1886). Other pertinent works by Ehrenberg are "Hamburgs Handel und Schifffahrt vor 200 Jahren" (1892), in *Hamburg vor 200 Jahren,* and *Altonas topographische Entwicklung* (Altona, 1894). A complete survey of Ehrenberg's works is contained in the *Archiv für exakte Wirtschaftsforschung* (Thünenarchiv) (which he founded and published until his death), Vol. IV, No. 4, pp. 462 ff. (Jena, 1922). (*ML* I, 530.) E.H.C.

Ehrenfeld, near Blyszczyvody, Galicia (then Austrian, now Polish), was a Mennonite settlement established in 1864 through the efforts of the real estate dealer (*Güterhändler*) Peter Müller and his brother Elder Johann Müller, who bought 3,080 acres of land in Blyszczyvody, four miles east of Zolkiev. The Alte Hof estate was taken over by Johann Müller, while the following settled close together forming the village of Ehrenfeld: Heinrich Müller (b. 1842), Johann Linscheid (b. 1806), Jakob Brubacher (b. 1814), Heinrich Brubacher (b. 1846), Peter Ewy (b. 1841), Jakob Rupp (b. 1833), Jakob Schmidt (b. 1841), Johann Schmidt (b. 1843), Johann Ewy (b. 1828), Daniel Müller (b. 1834), Heinrich Müller (b. 1845), Jakob Hubin (b. 1841), Michael Ewy (b. 1839), and Jakob Müller (b. 1834). Of these 15 Mennonite families of Ehrenfeld 12 went to America in 1882 and after, forming a part of the Galician Mennonite groups in Minnesota and Kansas. In 1934 only one Mennonite family was living in Ehrenfeld. (Peter Bachmann, *Mennoniten in Kleinpolen,* 250-55.) C.K.

Ehrenfried, Joseph, was born in Mainz, Hesse-Darmstadt, Germany, Dec. 25, 1783, of Catholic parents. Coming to America in 1802, he taught in western Lancaster Co., Pa. Soon thereafter he was translator and bookkeeper in Albright's Printery in Lancaster. On Aug. 9, 1808, he and William Hamilton published the first issue of the *Volksfreund.* In 1817 they sold the paper to John Baer's. For 20 years Ehrenfried remained with the latter firm as editor, translator, and compositor. In this period he published at Lancaster several Mennonite books in German: (1) the *Enchiridion* of Dirk Philips (1811), the first American edition; (2) the German *Martyrs' Mirror* (1814) in a beautifully printed and bound (full polished calf) edition, which according to J. F. Funk caused Ehrenfried's bankruptcy; (3) the *Ausbund* (1815). He made two trips to his homeland around 1837, returning to Harrisburg, Pa., to publish *Vaterlands Wächter*. He published the *Friedensbote* and *Lecha County Anzeiger* 1812-21 in Allentown. Either alone or in partnership he published at least ten other books in German between 1810 and 1820. From 1845 to 1860 he was Register of Wills in Lancaster. In religion he was a Swedenborgian. He died in Lancaster, March 6, 1862.   I.D.L.

Ehrenpreis, Andreas (1589-1662), Hutterite bishop (*Vorsteher*); the last outstanding leader of the brotherhood, during a period of decline aggressively active in a restoration of the old spirit. Born on a Bruderhof in Moravia, he was a miller by profession. In 1621, still in Moravia, he was elected *Diener am Wort* (preacher), and was confirmed in this office two years later in Sobotiste, Slovakia, where the brethren had immigrated after their tragic expulsion from Moravia. For the rest of his life Ehrenpreis remained at this place. In 1639 he was elected bishop, and it was in this capacity that he developed his richest activities during the remaining 23 years of his life. Four days before his death he gave a farewell address to the elders (*Chronik*, 868-70) which shows all the nobility of his character and the deep faith which motivated him throughout his life.

His was a life of dedication to his brotherhood and its unspoiled testimony. Things were not at all easy: the Thirty Years' War was raging (until 1648), economic misery was rampant, and an epidemic took a heavy toll in 1645. Even worse was the inner spiritual decay. The great period of the beginning had long since passed, moral slackening was observable everywhere, and the exacting standards of a life in community of goods as the Hutterites understood it were no longer obeyed. Poverty and insecurity prompted many a member to think of laying aside some money, or to take refuge to arms if there be need for "self-defense." One hears also about clandestine luxuries here and there; in short the old plain ways of committed people had tangibly deteriorated, and no one seemed to know how to stop this trend. Ehrenpreis now set to work to do just this, reviving the old rules and regulations, and writing epistles and tracts to guide and train his people, in this reminding one sometimes of Jakob Hutter and his work. The earliest document of Ehrenpreis's activity seems to be an address to the brethren in 1633, contained in the *Klein-Geschichtsbuch* (ed. 1947, 168-72, Engl. translation *MQR* XXV, 1951, 116-27 with commentaries). Though no name is given, there can be little doubt that it was Ehrenpreis who had summoned the brotherhood to follow again the principle of nonresistance, which in a recent event had been so badly scuttled.

On Oct. 4, 1639, Ehrenpreis was unanimously elected bishop, and from now on he intensified his attacks against the internal evils, and led his flock with such spiritual vigor that the brotherhood could survive for more than another century. Two kinds of activities may be distinguished in his work: (*a*) his insistence upon a stricter discipline of life as laid down in old and new *Gemeindeordnungen* (regulations, ordinances), and (*b*) a spiritual and moral revival as can be found for instance in his challenging *Sendbrief* of 1652 and his many other epistles.

(*a*) Of his renowned *Gemeindeordnungen* we know two completely different sets: the first one is contained in a Hutterite codex of 1640 (now in Esztergom, Hungary; a transcript in the Goshen College Library). A few excerpts were printed by Beck in the *Geschichts-Bücher*, 478-79, and 485-87. The other, of 1651, was for the first time made known in the appendix of the *Klein-Geschichtsbuch* (1947, 519-32). The former collected all earlier regulations (41 all told), beginning with a *Schuster-Ordnung* of 1561, and then added Ehrenpreis's own injunctions and ordinances, not even forgetting one for the preachers. From this work we gain an excellent insight into the organized life of the Hutterite community. These regulations not only helped the brethren to make their community run smoothly and efficiently, but they were also a continued reminder toward stricter discipline, the very core of a nonconformist life. In a regulation for the barber-surgeons (dated 1654) much is said in order to make this profession as outstanding as was to be expected from people who had such a reputation in matters of medical care (Beck, *ibid.*, 485 ff.). With great concern Ehrenpreis noticed certain laxities in the administration of buying and selling, and he warned his brethren that no one must own or put aside money or do anything in the execution of his duties contrary to Christian principles. Community of goods should be strictly observed and kept unspoiled as in the earliest days. Not even books should be considered private property, and nothing could be bequeathed to one's kin. Very detailed are the regulations for the *Haushälter* (stewards of the Bruderhof) and their assistants, the *Weinzierl* (see *Diener der Notdurft*), since so much depended upon their devoted performance. In the 1651 regulations the brethren and sisters are reminded of the old principle of a plain life of labor, worship, and communion. Elaborate dresses and food are proscribed. And yet, in spite of all its inherent austerity this document is permeated by a Christian spirit of great humility and kindness. A footnote in the *Klein-Geschichtsbuch* says that this regulation was reread to the Brethren eight times during the next decade to keep its points alive in their minds.

(*b*) Ehrenpreis's spiritual leadership may best be learned from his great *Sendbrief an alle diejenigen so sich rühmen ... dass sie ein abgesondertes Volk von der Welt sein wollen, ... Brüderliche Gemeinschaft, das höchste Gebot der Liebe betreffend* (1652), one of the few Hutterite writings which were printed in their time. In 1920 the Hutterites in America had it reprinted (at Scottdale) as a small book of about 190 pages. It contains (1-154)

Ehrenpreis's tract, and then (155-90) the *Brüder-liche Vereinigung* of 1556 (*q.v.*), appended by Ehrenpreis as information for his brethren concerning the principles upon which the brotherhood was founded. The *Sendbrief* makes a very strong case for community of goods, quoting among others also the beautiful parable of the grain and the grape which have to give up their individuality to make bread and wine (used at the Lord's Table). In like manner men have to give up their individuality in order to become real brothers (again at the Lord's Table). This *Sendbrief* is certainly no theological tract, and yet it is one of the strongest and finest products of the Hutterite spirit concerning "brotherly communion, the highest commandment of love."

Then there are his epistles. Some of them, like the three of 1650-54 to (later Unitarian) Daniel Zwicker, show an astounding theological alertness, confirming Loserth's statement "that his training was quite adequate to discuss theological questions with university graduates." But the epistles which he wrote as a shepherd of his church breathe a still more genuine Anabaptist spirit. They are letters of concern, they admonish his brethren to watch their life and conduct, to bring up their children in the right spirit, and to be on the alert in all dealings with the "world." All this is said in great modesty and without any paternalism. But it has authority in it. Two of these letters, sent to the Brethren in Transylvania, were incorporated into the *Chronik* (831-37, 847-56). Then there is an epistle dealing with an unpleasant affair in Slovakia where a small group of Brethren tried to introduce an element of fanaticism (1645); this epistle is called *Antwort und Widerlegung der irrigen . . . Meinung Benjamin Kengels und seines Anhanges* (Wolkan, *Geschicht-Buch*, 631, note 1, where a brief summary is given).

There are two more tracts from Ehrenpreis's hand: (1) *Kurze Widerlegung des grossen Streites von Christo, dem Sohn Gottes, wie er von Christoph Osterrod in seinem . . . Büchel samt seinem Anhang als polnische Brüder oder Arianer schimpflich und nachteilig verkleinert wird* (Sobotiste, 1654; see *MQR* XXII, 1948, 161). It is a polemical pamphlet against the Unitarians (against Dr. Zwicker who most likely gave the book of 1591 to Ehrenpreis), and a strong plea for the idea of Trinity. (The only extant copy is to be found with the Brethren in Canada.)

(2) *Die Fünf Artikeln des grössten Streites zwischen uns und der Welt* (several codices in Esztergom). This is Ehrenpreis's own version or edition of the "great article book" (*q.v.*) of 1547, originally written most likely by Peter Walpot. Though the title is identical with the one in the *Chronik* (269 ff.), the text is different, a kind of paraphrase of the original, made by Ehrenpreis for his people to teach them the fundamentals of their specific Anabaptist position. The book might be compared with the *Brüderliche Vereinigung* of 1556 (appended to the *Sendbrief*) although it is much more elaborate than the latter. At the bottom, however, the idea was always the same: renewal of the old spirit of Anabaptism and training of the Brethren in the

things which were central, so that they could endure trials and temptations and remain a living witness to the idea of genuine discipleship.

A brief list of Ehrenpreis's writings follows: *Gemeinde-Ordnungen* 1640; *Gemeinde-Ordnung* 1651 (Zieglschmid, *Chronik*, 519-32); his speech of 1633 concerning nonresistance (*MQR*, 1951); *Ein Sendbrief . . . brüderliche Gemeinschaft, das höchste Gebot der Liebe betreffend*, 1652 (reprint Scottdale, 1920); *Die fünf Artikeln des grössten Streites zwichen uns und der Welt* (a revision of the tract of 1547); *Kurze Widerlegung des grossen Streites von Christo*, 1654 (against the Unitarians, copy in Canada); *Antwort und Widerlegung der irrigen Meinung des Benjamin Kengels . . .* , 1645; three epistles to Dr. Daniel Zwicker, 1650-54, on theological matters; two epistles to the Brethren in Alwinz, Transylvania, of 1642 and 1649 (Zieglschmid, 831 ff., 847 ff.); his farewell address of 1662 (*ibid.*, 868 ff.); several hymns (*Lieder der Hutterischen Brüder* 1914, 13, 55, 639, 851, 854, 857, and two more not yet printed). LOSERTH, R.F.

Loserth, *Communismus* (particularly elaborate on *Gemeindeordnungen*, 251 ff.); R. Friedmann, "Eine dogmatische Hauptschrift . . . ," in *Archiv für Ref.-Gesch.*, 1931, 86 and 96 (concerning the *Fünf Artikel*); idem, "The Epistles of the Hutterian Brethren," *MQR* XX (1946) 169 (concerning the parable of bread and wine); idem, "Encounter of Anabaptists and Mennonites with Anti-Trinitarianism," *MQR* XXII (1948) 139-62; idem, "An Ordinance of 1633 Concerning Nonresistance," *MQR* XXV (1951) 116-27; Zieglschmid, *Chronik*; Beck, *Geschichts-Bücher*; Wolkan, *Geschicht-Buch*; ML I, 530-32.

Eibenschitz (German for *Evancice* or *Wancice*), a town situated on the Iglau, in the Brno district of Moravia, population 5,000, mostly Czech. In the 1420's the Hussite doctrine won numerous adherents and prospered here. During the Reformation the Protestants shared the town church with the Utraquists, the former using the smaller part, the latter the larger. In the outskirts of the city some Swiss Protestants had a church and a school; the Swiss Brethren (*q.v.*) had their meetinghouse in a lane in a suburb. There were also some Schwenckfeldians in the town. The Hutterian Brethren, however, held their services in the neighboring village of Alexovitz (known also as Olekovitz and Alecotz). When the Brethren of Alexovitz are mentioned in the chronicles, those living in Evancice are also meant.

In Evancice and probably also Alexovitz the Hutterites settled about 1527 and 1528 (Beck, 68); the baronial Lipa family received them kindly. In Alexovitz they had a Bruderhof (Beck, 393) with deacons (352) and preachers (352). The Swiss Brethren had their center in a suburb of Evancice (152). Although the people of Evancice were absolved of blame in the revolt against Ferdinand II, the non-Catholic inhabitants were so severely oppressed that the Hutterites of Alexovitz preferred to move to Alwinc (*q.v.*) in Transylvania (396); those who did not leave voluntarily were expelled in 1622, and joined the colonies in Transylvania. There they had ordained Konrad Hirzl as preacher on Aug. 6, 1621; in the following year he voluntarily resigned.

Through the withdrawal of these capable people and, of course, also through the devastation of the Thirty Years' War Evancice fell into a decline from which it never fully recovered.   LOSERTH.

Beck, *Geschichts-Bücher*; Gregor Wolny, *Die Markgrafschaft Mähren* III (2d ed.) 335-41; *ML* I, 532 f.

Eichacher (or Eicher), **Konrad,** one of the first Anabaptists to die as a martyr in Bern, Switzerland, was a native of Steffisberg. He was seized in 1529 because of his faith; but after his trial, begun on Oct. 18, he was released, for he said that he had erred. On Dec. 30 he was arrested again and after a long cross-examination was drowned on Feb. 21, 1530. The execution apparently attracted much attention, for the *Ratsmanual* of Dec. 31, 1534, contains a statement that the council regretted Eichacher's execution. Nevertheless in the next six years 20 additional executions, 158 imprisonments, and 109 expulsions were imposed on the Anabaptists in Bern. The records of Eichacher's trial were published by Adolf Fluri (*Berner Heim*, 1896, Nos. 37-38), authenticating the execution, which had already been related in the *Martyrs' Mirror*.   HEGE.

Th. Quervain, *Kirchliche und soziale Zustände in Bern unmittelbar nach der Einführung der Reformation* (Bern, 1906) 123 ff.; *Mart. Mir.* E 1129; *ML* I, 533.

Eichen, Christoph von der (Christoph Rudolf of Oberdorla), an Anabaptist of Thuringia, was won to the Anabaptist movement by the Anabaptist apostle Alexander at Easter 1533. In May of that year he was arrested with six other Anabaptists (Ludwig Spon, Martin Dippart, Hans Rinkleben, Heinrich Hutter, Hans Breuning, and Lorenz Möller) at Mühlhausen. They were imprisoned 21 weeks at Treffurt and Mühlhausen. Elector John and Duke George of Saxony, who had jurisdiction over the imperial city of Mühlhausen alternately with Landgrave Philip of Hesse after the revolution (1525), demanded that they be punished with death in accord with the imperial mandates. But Philip (*q.v.*) refused his consent. He sent Balthasar Raidt, the pastor of Hersfeld, to talk to them, and Raidt succeeded in making them recant. They were released in November 1533, and were required to give an oath that if they backslid they would sell their possessions within two weeks and permanently leave the district.

Soon they were again working for the Anabaptist cause, though they had not yet been baptized. Christoph von der Eichen refused to let the priest give his dying father supreme unction, and is said to have spoken disparagingly of it. He was therefore returned to prison. Duke George insisted that he be punished by death for depreciating the sacrament. But he was released with the other prisoners in 1535.

On June 15 and 26, 1545, Christoph was re-examined. He had not yet been baptized, but confessed that he definitely held Anabaptist views. Thereupon the council ordered him to leave the city with his family and never to return on penalty of death.

On Dec. 11, 1562, John issued the command to arrest Christoph von der Eichen as the head of the Thuringian Anabaptists as soon as he was seen on electoral territory. But he managed to elude them for two years. On Sept. 12, 15, and 19, 1564, he was subjected to a trial with eleven other Anabaptists. Because he declared positively that he held Anabaptist views he was to be expelled, but refused to accept the sentence. The magistracy at Leipzig, asked for an opinion, recommended that Anabaptists be given further instruction by the clergy, and if they persisted in their error they should be punished with death by fire, in accord with the imperial decrees. They were therefore questioned again on Nov. 28, 1564, and Jan. 17, 1565. After another short period in prison they promised to do better and were released.

After their release they began anew to propagate Anabaptist doctrine. In the middle of July 1565 Eichen was again seized and imprisoned at Mühlhausen. In a few weeks he was released upon a promise to leave Mühlhausen forever. But he remained in Oberdorla and continued to hold meetings. When Franciscus Strauss, the Superintendent of Langensalza, was about to carry out the sentence of expulsion, Eichen wrote him a sharp letter and posted it on the Rathaus door on June 5, 1571. A councilor on his way to church saw the act, tore down the letter, and had the perpetrator arrested. But now the patience of the authorities was exhausted. Very likely Eichen suffered a martyr's death in July 1571.   NEFF.

P. Wappler, *Die Täuferbewegung in Thüringen 1526-1584* (Jena, 1912) 98 ff.; *ML* I, 533.

Eichenfeld (Dubovka) was a village of the Yazykovo Mennonite settlement (*q.v.*), Chortitza, Russia, founded in 1869. In 1913 the village had a population of 307 and about 5,000 acres of land. During the Russian Revolution and the Civil War the village was completely destroyed. In October 1919, 79 men and 3 women were murdered in a single night. The rest of the population fled.   C.K.

H. Toews, *Eichenfeld-Dubovka, ein Tatsachenbericht aus der Tragödie des Deutschtums in der Ukraine* (Karlsruhe, n.d.); *ML* I, 479.

Eicher (Eichert, Eichler, Eycher), a Bernese Mennonite family name which appears in the *Martyrs' Mirror*. In 1529 Konrad Eicher of Steffisberg was executed for his Anabaptist faith at Bern, Switzerland. In the latter part of the 17th century the Eicher family was represented in the Thun area of the canton of Bern. Eicher was among the family names represented in the Bernese migration to Alsace in 1671-1711, and occurs in the Montbéliard, France, list of 1759. Among the Palatine Mennonites of 1685 was Ulrich Eicher of Osthoven bei Wachenheim. A 1706 list of Mennonite families living in Mannheim, Germany, included the name Eycher, while a 1738 census names Christian Eicher of Mossbach. The 1759 Palatinate Mennonite census list names Jacob Eichler of Erbesbüdesheim. The 1936 *Adressbuch* of Mennonite families in South Germany lists 12 Eichers in 3 congregations.

In 1754 Johannes Eicher and Christian Eicher were among 27 Mennonites landing in America. In the 18th century the Eichers were represented among the Amish Mennonites of Ontario. In 1848 five Eicher brothers, Martin, Christian, Daniel, Benjamin (*q.v.*), and John, the sons of Johann and Margaret (Conrad) Eicher of Pulversheim, Alsace, migrated to Wayne Co., Ohio, and then later settled in Henry and Washington counties, Iowa, in the early 1850's. Benjamin was the founder of the Eicher Emmanuel Mennonite Church (*q.v.*) of Washington Co., Iowa. Their descendants live principally in Iowa and Nebraska. Among them is William R. Eicher, bishop of the West Fairview Mennonite Church (MC), Beaver Crossing, Neb.

M.G.

M. Gingerich, *The Mennonites in Iowa* (Iowa City, 1939).

Eicher, Benjamin, a Mennonite (GCM) bishop of the congregation near Noble, Washington Co., Iowa, was born in Alsace, March 10, 1832. In 1849 he came to America and located in Wayne Co., Ohio. Four years later he moved to Washington Co., Iowa, where he lived the remainder of his life. He was married to Lydia Sommer in 1855. One of his children was Congressman and Judge E. C. Eicher (*q.v.*). In 1862 Eicher was ordained minister of the newly organized Amish congregation in Washington County. On Oct. 28, 1866, he was ordained bishop by Bishop Joseph Stuckey of Illinois. Although Eicher had served as a secretary of the Amish conference (*Diener-Versammlung*) in 1866, by the time of the conference in Iowa in 1874 it was clear that he and his church were no longer in harmony with the Amish conference and so after that meeting his congregation followed an independent course. Finally in 1892 the Eicher congregation, known since 1937 as the Eicher Emmanuel Mennonite Church, became a member of the Middle District Mennonite Conference (GCM) and in the following year a member of the General Conference Mennonite Church. Eicher at once was elected a member of the Foreign Mission Board, although his death on Dec. 7, 1893, cut short his period of service on that board.

Living on a farm, Eicher engaged in farming and threshing. He also taught school for about 15 years. At one time he was urged to become county superintendent of schools but he refused to become a candidate for the position. In 1890 his name was before the Democratic Convention as a candidate for Congress, "but by his express direction to his friends it was withdrawn, otherwise he would have been nominated and elected." ("Biography of Benjamin Eicher," *Mennonite Year Book and Almanac for 1896*.)

Eicher was a man of striking personality whose mind was keen and penetrating. He was a student all his life and kept pace with the progress of scientific and religious thought. Although he had pronounced convictions, he was charitable toward those who disagreed with him. His biographer declared, "There was behind all his acts and utterances, great or small, an intense earnestness, a force of conviction, a moral courage, and an inflexible will—and all gave distinct character to the man . . ." (*Mennonite Year Book and Almanac for 1896*). M.G.

Eicher, Edward Clayton, was born at Noble, Iowa, Dec. 16, 1878, and died in Washington, D.C., Nov. 30, 1944. A son of Bishop Benjamin Eicher, founder of the Eicher Emmanuel Mennonite Church of Noble, Iowa, he was raised in the Mennonite faith and died a member of the congregation (GCM). He was married to Hazel Mount of Washington, Iowa, in 1908. Graduating from the University of Chicago in 1904, he continued his study of law in that institution. He was admitted to the Iowa Bar in 1906. From 1907 to 1909 he was cashier and assistant registrar of the University of Chicago. During the years 1919-33 he was a member of the law firm of Livingston and Eicher, Washington, Iowa. Elected to Congress in 1932, he was twice re-elected to that position. In December 1938 he resigned his position in Congress to become a member of the Securities and Exchange Commission. Appointed chairman of the Commission in April 1941, he served in that capacity for almost a year. In 1942 he was appointed Chief Justice of the District Court for the District of Columbia. At the time of his death he was presiding at the 119-day mass sedition trial of 30 defendants charged with conspiring with Nazi Germany to undermine the loyalty of members of the armed forces of the United States. His fair conduct of the trial won the praise of newspaper reporters. A Democrat and a liberal in politics, he supported the reform measures of President Franklin D. Roosevelt. (*Who's Who Among the Mennonites,* 1943, North Newton, Kan.)

M.G.

Eicher Emmanuel Mennonite Church (GCM), located in Washington Co., Iowa, was organized in 1862. Previous to its organization the congregation had been in charge of Joseph Goldsmith (*q.v.*), the bishop of the near-by Henry County church, and was also served by preachers Joseph Wittrig and Christian Bechler. Meetings were held in private homes until 1868, when the first church, called the Noble Church, was built northwest of Noble. This meetinghouse was replaced in 1895 by a more modern building. A third church, built in 1911 on the same site, is now in use. The first preacher and bishop after the 1862 organization was Benjamin Eicher (*q.v.*).

After its separation from the Amish Mennonite Conference in 1874, the Eicher Church, as it came to be called, with about 50 members, followed an independent course for a number of years. In 1892 it joined the Middle District Conference (GCM) and in 1893 the General Conference Mennonite Church.

Those who have served as pastors of the Eicher Church are Benjamin Eicher, H. G. Allebach, P. E. Stucky, S. M. Musselman, L. L. Miller, P. K. Regier, H. J. Schrag, A. H. Miller, D. E. Welty, H. D. Metzker, Walter H. Regier, Leander Fast, and H. L. Metzker. In 1953 approximately half of the congregation of 179 withdrew from the Mennonite Church to establish the Fern Cliff Free Evangelical Church under the leadership of Leander Fast. In 1955 the membership was 112, with H. E. Nunemaker as pastor. W.H.R.

M. Gingerich, *The Mennonites in Iowa* (Iowa City, 1939); *ML* I, 564.

Eicher, Konrad, an Anabaptist martyr: see **Eichacher.**

Eichstock, a Mennonite congregation northwest of Dachau (*q.v.*) in Upper Bavaria, Germany, which was founded in 1818 by Mennonites from the Palatinate, Baden, Alsace, and Donaumoos (*q.v.*). In the first 25 years about 35 families settled on farms and in small villages in the wooded region of Eichstock; often from two to six families lived at one place, as in Eichstock, Hammerhof, Thann, Schwaig, and Singern, which were at that time almost exclusively Mennonite settlements. All of these families owned their land. Since they came from regions which were farther advanced, they were able to be a progressive influence on the peasants of the Dachau region. The principal reason for settling here was probably the fact that land was cheaper than in the Palatinate or Baden.

Religious services were held alternately in Eichstock and Hammerhof in the homes of members until the church was built. There was some difference of opinion as to where it should be erected; the government of Upper Bavaria decided in favor of Eichstock because of its burial site, and granted the concession on Jan. 18, 1841 (Records of the B.K.M. No. 25, 606). The funds were raised by the members.

Thus the church had its wished-for meetinghouse, in which they could worship undisturbed. Economically the families were also prosperous. But a certain restlessness took possession of many families; in the years 1844-56, 22 families emigrated to America, most of them to Iowa (*q.v.*); six families returned to the Palatinate. The church decreased rapidly, but until the end of the 19th century a considerable number remained. Then still other families left, chiefly for economic causes, so that by 1922 the little church was nearly deserted; only three Mennonite families were left.

The following preachers have served the congregation: Johannes Strohm 1821-47, Franz Krämer 1821-24, Jakob Seitz 1825-39, Jakob Haury 1825-39, Elias Dettweiler 1839-45 and 1854-55, David Ruth 1839- (emigrated to America), Jakob Krehbiel 1845- (emigrated), Johannes Stiess 1845-48, Georg Zeiset (1844 until he emigrated), Christian Dettweiler 1851-55 (emigrated), Ulrich Hirschler 1854- ?, Johannes Berger 1855- ?, Jakob Dester 1861- ?, Jakob Schowalter 1861- ?, 1856, 62-64; Hauser (no dates), Jakob Ellenberger (called to Friedelsheim in 1881), Michael Landes 1881-87, Johannes Hirschler 1887-99, Daniel Bähr 1889-1905, Emanuel Landes of the Ingolstadt congregation 1905-54; Hermann Schmutz 1954- .

At present (1954) meetings are held monthly at Eichstock. In addition, the young people of Munich as well as those of the Regensburg and Ingolstadt congregations hold youth conferences here, for the church is very beautifully located. On the Sundays when there is no service in the church, the families gather in various homes for Bible study. The congregation belongs to the *Vereinigung* and is incorporated. The membership in 1954 was 20.

H.D., Em.L.

C. Krahn, "Zur Auswanderung der Mennoniten von Maxweiler und Eichstock," *Gesch.-Bl.*, December 1938, 81; Chr. Hege, "Der Kirchenbau zu Eichstock bei Dachau," *ibid.*, December 1937, 57-60; Ed. G. Kaufman, *The Development of the Missionary . . . Interest Among the Mennonites* (Berne, 1931) 37; R. Ringenberg, *Familienbuch der Mennonitengemeinde Eichstock (Schriften des Bayerischen Landesvereins für Familienkunde*, No. 18); *Menn. Bl.* III (1856) 62-64; IX (1862) 32; *ML* I, 534.

Eiderstedt, a peninsular district (pop. 29,720) in southwest Schleswig-Holstein, Germany. Because of lively trade between Eiderstedt and Holland, many Dutch religious refugees, including Davidjorists and Mennonites, found their way to Eiderstedt. As early as 1557 a ducal rescript deals with them. In 1566 five of them were expelled, and in 1588, after futile negotiations, six more. Article II of the Eiderstedt *Landrecht* (1572, printed in 1573, 1591, 1737, 1794) concerns the Anabaptists, as does also point 6 of the oath imposed upon the Lutheran clergy of Eiderstedt in 1574. The fear of a repetition of the Münster episode, and the envy of the wealth of many of the refugees, played a part in the attitude of the authorities and also in the accusations brought by the people. Some opposition and questioning of the Mennonites and Davidjorists followed in 1596, 1597, 1602, and 1604. Now the Mennonites had an able representative and advocate in Johann Clausen Codt (Coodt), called Rollwagen, who was familiar with the Scriptures and who rendered valuable service in building the dikes by introducing the wheelbarrow. In 1607-8 a succession of negotiations, cross-examinations, and disputations took place. Even the use of the new Lutheran cemetery in Tönning was not granted until the Mennonites sent a petition to the duke. On the other hand, the duke ordered them to have their infants baptized, upon penalty of expulsion. But it was not enforced; the Mennonites even brought their own preachers from Holland. In 1614 began a new series of complaints, replies, arrests, and cross-examinations. Finally the duke decided that the Mennonites might stay in the country, but must conduct themselves quietly. In 1623 the newly founded Friedrichstadt (*q.v.*) was opened to them, where they alone were to conduct all religious services for the entire region. Many Mennonites went there; they were freed from the oath, military service, and the obligation to fill public office. In 1642 a Davidjorist trial took place. But for the Mennonites a confirmation, declaration, extension of their privileges was issued in 1645; in 1663 followed a prohibition against making proselytes among the Lutherans.

In the 18th century there were still Mennonites in Eiderstedt, who were generally respected for their quiet industry. In Koldenbüttel and Tetenbüll they were buying so many farms that in 1763 they were required to pay an additional levy to Lutheran preachers and teachers, so that there should be no great loss of income to them. In 1784 a mandate was issued that they must register the birth of their children not only with their preacher in Friedrichstadt, but to keep school and tax records in order, also with the Lutheran preacher of the town, and in 1787 more detailed orders were given concerning their school tax. But then their number declined.

In 1834 there were only four; in 1880, when there were only nine who were not Lutherans or Catholics, there were probably no Mennonites. E.C.

Reimer Hansen's articles in *Schriften des Vereins für schleswig-holsteinische Kirchengesch.* (second series) I and II (Kiel, 1897-1903); A. Niemann, *Handbuch der schleswig-holsteinischen Landeskunde: Topographischer Teil* I (Hamburg, 1799) 264, and bibliography cited there; also bibliography of "Friedrichstadt"; H. N. A. Jensen, *Versuch einer kirchlichen Statistik des Herzogtums Schleswig* (Flensburg, 1840); J. M. Michler, *Kirchliche Statistik der evangelisch-lutherischen Kirche . . .* I (Kiel, 1886); *Inv. Arch. Amst.* II, 2, No. 863; *ML* I, 546 f.

Eifel, a plateau in the Prussian Rhine Province between the Mosel, Rhine, and Roer rivers, was probably even before the Reformation a center of those groups who opposed the worldliness of the Catholic Church and who are now, following the example of Ludwig Keller (*q.v.*), usually known as the old evangelical brotherhoods. This would account for the letter written in 1531 by Sebastian Franck "to several in the Eifel at the request of Johann Beckestein" (Rembert, 226-28). Later on the Anabaptist movement must also have found a wide following here. In the 16th century there were many Anabaptists in and around Monschau and in the Schleiden area. Thomas and Zillis worked here as ᵃapostles. The Anabaptists were sorely oppressed. One of the martyrs in 1552 was Maria of Monschau (Montjoie) (*q.v.;* see also hymn No. 25 in the *Ausbund*). At the Strasbourg conference of 1557 there were delegates representing about 50 churches "from the Eyfelt to Moravia." Daniel Notemann built a hammer for "red copper" in Pleushütte near Einruhr, but settled in the Neuwied congregation. In 1711 there was still a congregation in the Eifel highlands, which met in Einruhr. In the course of the 18th century several Mennonites of Einruhr were baptized at Crefeld. The last member there was Daniel Becker, who died in 1886.

In 1922 there were living in the Eifel region (between Trier and Andernach) about 14 families, some of whom came from the Palatinate about 1827 and settled on leased farms. There were Mennonites in Eischeidhof near Daun, Jägershof near Trier, Jakobstal near Andernach, Kalbergerhof near Trier, Kaltschick near Bassenheim, Leyerhof near Königsfeld, Lissem near Bitburg, Mayen, Pönterhof near Andernach, Spangdalem near Wittlich, and Unkel. The Mennonites in the eastern part of the Eifel belonged to the Neuwied congregation, and those in the western part formed a congregation with the Mennonites of Luxembourg, who are descendants of Eifel Mennonites. They held their meetings in the homes of the members.　　　　NEFF, W.N.

Rembert, *Wiedertäufer;* Ottius, *Annales anabaptistici* (Basel, 1672); State archives at Düsseldorf, *Jülich-Berg* II, 254; III, 980; *Monatshefte für Rheinische Kirchengeschichte,* 1914, 21 ff.; 1917, 161 ff.; W. Scheibler, *Geschichte der evangelischen Gemeinde Monschau* (Aachen, 1919) 12-34, especially the chapter "Die Wiedertäufer im Monschauer Land"; *ML* I, 547.

Eigenheim Mennonite Church (GCM), located six miles west of Rosthern, Sask., a member of the Canadian Conference, was organized in 1894 as a subsidiary of the Rosenort Church of Saskatchewan by members of that church who settled in the Eigenheim area at that time. The congregation built a church in 1896. It became an independent congregation in 1929. In 1954 the congregation had 245 members with G. G. Epp as elder and H. T. Klaassen as minister.

The congregation has German services, 14 Sunday-school classes, 2 ladies' aid societies, a large choir, and Friday evening catechism and Bible classes through the winter months. Jacob Klaassen (d. 1948) and Johann Dueck have also served the congregation as ministers.　　　　G.G.E.

Eigenhof, a village near the post office of Gretna, Man., where is located one of the 10 churches of the Rudnerweide Mennonites (*q.v.*).　　　　H.H.H.

Eight Square Mennonite Church (OOM), located near Wooster, Wayne Co., Ohio, is a member of the Ohio and Indiana Conference of Old Order Mennonites (commonly called the Martin or Brubaker group). The congregation began in 1907 as a division from the Chester Mennonite Church, Wisler protesting the use of some modern inventions, chiefly the telephone, and English preaching. The congregation still rejects many inventions and uses the horse and buggy for transportation. They retain the original name for the church in the community, which comes from an octagon-shaped schoolhouse built on the same lot as the church. The group worships on alternate Sundays in the same building as that used by the Chester Mennonite Church. The membership, five in 1953, has been steadily declining. Ministers who have served the group are Peter Imhoff and Daniel Martin, who both withdrew from the Wisler group in 1907, but Martin rejoined the Wisler adherents in 1940, and William Brubaker, the present minister (1954).

　　　　H.B.

Eighth Street Mennonite Church (GCM), located in Goshen, Ind., is a member of the Central Conference of Mennonites and of the General Conference Mennonite Church. Organized in 1913 with a congregation of 15 members (formerly of the Silver Street Church, *q.v.*), which met in a remodeled dwelling, the congregation numbered 298 in 1953 and meets in a substantial brick building erected in 1920. The group is largely urban, of diverse geographical background. The minister since 1946 has been Robert W. Hartzler. The church carries on an active program with regular meetings of Sunday school, young people's organization, six women's organizations, weekly morning and evening services, a choir, and other activities. The observance of footwashing is optional; an organ is used in worship; discipline is practiced to a limited extent.

　　　　R.W.H.

Eiman: see **Eymann** family.

Eindhoven, an important industrial town in the Dutch province of North Brabant (1947 pop. 137,000, with 367 Mennonites), is seat of a Mennonite congregation. There must have been some Mennonites here in 1570-77, but we know no particulars. Then the traces disappear, and Mennonites are not found here for centuries. On Oct. 10, 1928, the Mennonites who were employed in the city, especially in the noted Philips factories, united to found a Mennonite fellowship (*Kring*), which organized as a congregation on Nov. 27, 1936. In 1936-42 the congregation was served by S. M. A. Daalder, pastor of Heerlen in South Limburg. Since 1942 the congregation has had its own resident minister: H. Wethmar 1942-46, and J. W. Sipkema 1947- , both serving also the congregation of Breda (*q.v.*). The young congregation of Eindhoven, which is very active, built a beautiful church, dedicated on Sept. 30, 1951. The membership numbered about 104 when the congregation was founded in 1936. In 1956 it numbered 205. There is a women's circle and a youth group. (*DJ* 1952, 51-54.)   vdZ.

Eine Mutter, a novel by Peter G. Epp (*q.v.*), b. 1888 in Russia, professor at Bluffton College, 1924-34; Ohio State University, 1934-54. *Eine Mutter* presents a panoramic view of a span of over 80 years of the history of the Mennonite settlements in Russia, as seen through the eyes of the narrator of the story, the mother of the title. As the reader follows with her the life, the character, and the fortunes of her parents, her half brothers and sisters, her full brothers and sisters, her nephews and nieces, her children, grandchildren, and great-grandchildren, he receives an intimate picture of Mennonite life over the vast expanses of Russia. The span begins in the early period of settled, well-established patterns in the nearly self-contained Mennonite settlements in the Ukraine, and describes the upheaval of the first emigration to America in 1873-85, the development of new settlements for the landless, the increasing interest in industrial life and education, the first great war, the terrible consequences of the Revolution, the famine, and the second emigration (in the 1920's) to Canada.

The book lacks the technical form of the novel. It is a tale, told as an old woman might naturally tell it in reminiscing. The story has so compelling a tone of realism and truth that it is quite safe to assume that the material is basically factual or autobiographical. To a large extent its charm lies in that tone, which might have been lost if the author had tried to shape it into some specific artistic form. The simplicity of the style gives the story a luminous, poetic quality in keeping with the personality of the extraordinary mother. Her deeply religious interpretation of life is as unifying as any plot or other artistic design could have been.

Eine Mutter is a thoroughly Mennonite story, which deserves to be translated to make it accessible to American Mennonites.   E.H.B.

Warkentin and Gingerich, *Who's Who Among the Mennonites* (North Newton, 1943); *MQR* V (July 1931) 225 f.; XXI (April 1947) 111-13.

Einfältige und Christliche Betrachtungen *über die Jährlichen und Heiligen Evangelia, durch Gottes Gnade in öffentlicher Versammlung in Altona mündlich vorgetragen durch einen Liebhaber der allgemeinen Wahrheit unsers Herrn Jesu Christi, Und unter währender Predigt von einem Christlichen Zuhörer aus dem Holländischen ins Hoch-*

teutsche versetzt; Sodann durch einen andern Freund zu des Nächsten Erbauung zum Druck befördert, im Jahre 1730. Nebst einem Anhange unterschiedener Texte, sowohl aus dem Alten als Neuen Testamente. This popular collection of sermons by Jacob Denner (*q.v.*, 1659-1746), the influential Mennonite-Dompelaar preacher of Hamburg-Altona 1684-1746, leader of the immersionist schism of the Altona Church (with periods of absence at Lübeck 1687-1694, Friedrichstadt 1694-98, and Danzig 1698-1702), according to the title page translated from the Dutch, appeared in Hamburg (?) in 1730 in a quarto volume of two sections of 1,366 pp. and 352 pp. respectively. The former contained 60 sermons for the Sundays and festival days of the church year; the second contained 24 sermons on selected Old and New Testament texts. The title page of the second part is identical with that of the first part except that instead of "über die Jährlichen und Heiligen Evangelia" the phrase "über einige Texte, sowohl aus dem Alten als Neuen Testament" is used. The popularity of Denner's sermons is indicated by the reprints. In 1739 it was reprinted entire at Hamburg with a double title page, the new 1739 title page being placed in front of the old one of 1730. The second part has only the old title page. This may not be a new edition, but merely a rebinding with a new title page, namely, *Jacob Denners Erbauliche Betrachtungen.* The Amsterdam Mennonite Library has a copy of an almost identical 1739 edition at "Dantzig." It differs from the 1739 Hamburg edition by having separate pagination and a new title page for each of the two parts, and a third part of 40 pages at the end, with its own title page, containing three more sermons. The title page reads: *Drey Geistreiche Predigten über das Heilige Vater Unser; gehalten, unter dem Beystande des Geistes der Gnaden und des Gebets, von einem der von Herzen wünscht zu seyn ein Anbeter im Geist und Wahrheit.* All three title pages carry the date 1739. In 1751 it was again reprinted (at Hamburg?) under the title *Jacob Denners Christlich- und Erbauliche Betrachtungen* (Pt. I, pp. 1-1144; Pt. II, pp. 1145-56, with the three additional sermons, pp. 1457-58, also *Der Adel des Gewissens*, pp. 1487-1502, and *Nachricht von den Lebens-Umständen Herrn Jacob Denners,* 3 pp. in Preface). This edition was reprinted at Frankental in 1792 for American use (*Neue, auf Kosten Johannes Herrstein und Johannes Schmutz gemachte Auflage, welcher die Betrachtung vom Adel des Gewissens, und eine Nachricht von den Lebens-Umständen des seligen Herrn Denners beygefüget worden.*), and again in 1860 at Philadelphia, Pa. As late as 1901 an English translation was planned, and a prospectus issued at Doylestown, Pa., but it was never published.

Two earlier Dutch collections of Denner's sermons appeared in 1706 and 1707 under the following titles: *De wysheit des Heeren, vertoont door eenvoudige Predicatien, In het uitbreiden van de gebruikelijke Sondaagse als ook eenige Feest-daagse Evangelien. Onder Gods genade gedaan en beschreven door Imant Die van herten verlangt ende wenst een getrouw Dienstknegt des Heeren Jesu te sijn ende blijven.* (Amsterdam, and Danzig, 1707), 60 sermons with 2 more in a supplement; and *Eenige uitbreidingen; over verscheidene Schriftuerlijke Texten soo wel uyt het Oude als Nieuwe Verbondt, 17* sermons. Under new title pages but with identical content both volumes were published at Hoorn in 1771. The two volumes were printed and bound together in one book without volume number but with separate pagination and title pages, the former with 746 pp., the latter with 202 pp.

The 1730 German edition described at the beginning of this article is almost identical in content with the Dutch book of 1706-7. The first part contains 60 sermons, the same as those in the 1707 and 1771 Dutch editions, but omits the two supplementary ones of the Dutch editions. The second part contains 24 sermons, 2 of which are taken from the supplement of Part I of the Dutch editions, 9 are taken from Part II of the Dutch editions, and 14 new ones are added (thus 8 from Part II of the Dutch edition were discarded). The volume is, however, not a direct translation of the Dutch book; it claims that the sermons were translated from the Dutch into German while they were being preached.

Denner's sermons, thoroughly evangelical, Biblical, and experiential (pietistic) in emphasis, were very popular, attended by people of all denominations, including the nobility of Holstein and near-by Denmark, as well as the later King Adolph Frederick of Sweden. A Lutheran pastor, Erdmann Neumeister, attacked Denner's book of sermons in a polemical pamphlet, *Anmerkungen über Jakob Denners Postille* (Hamburg, 1731).   H.S.B.

Einlage (Kitchkas) was one of the largest Mennonite villages of the Chortitza settlement (*q.v.*) on the right bank of the Dniepr, province of Ekaterinoslav, Ukraine, established in 1789 by Prussian Mennonites, who named the new village after the one some had come from. Soon after the settlement a flood of the Dniepr River made it necessary to transplant the village to a higher level. Again in 1927 the whole village was moved because of the Dneprostroi power dam which put the village level under water.

Before World War I the village had a population of some 1,500 and about 7,500 acres of land. Because of the favorable location of the village, business and industry, in addition to agriculture, became essential activities of Einlage. Steam-driven mills, factories, and businesses were established and some of the Mennonites became well-to-do. During 1902-7 the second small Katherine Railroad was built through Einlage, greatly promoting industry and business. At that time one of the largest arch-span supported bridges of the world was built here across the Dniepr River; it was destroyed in the two world wars.

One of the earliest industries was the wagon factory of Heinrich Unger, active during the first half of the 18th century. His son Abram was the first Mennonite to construct spring wagons. Abram's son, A. A. Unger, enlarged the factory considerably. Johann Friesen established a factory which produced the first grain reaper among the Mennonites (possibly the first in the Ukraine) in 1879. The firm

Koop and Co. bought and enlarged the Friesen factory, producing motors, machinery for steel roller flour mills, etc. The early Dutch windmills were replaced by the large flour mills owned by Heinrich Unger, Kornelius Martens, and others. Einlage also had lumber yards and carpenter shops and a number of business enterprises.

When in 1910 the centennial of the Einlage school was commemorated, the school was housed in its fourth building, which had four large classrooms, a library, and four teachers. By 1927, 42 teachers had taught school in Einlage. In addition to the general Mennonite-supported and controlled school, Einlage had a private school during the middle of the century which was taught first by David Hausknecht (1838) and continued by Heinrich Heese (*q.v.*) (1846-68). Among the other outstanding teachers of Einlage were Gerhard Loewen and J. D. Rempel. The Revolution changed the Mennonite school completely and when Einlage was resettled (1927) it became a state school. Although the teachers remained predominantly Mennonite, the school soon became a tool of the Soviet state in promoting Communism. During the German occupation (1941-43) the school was resumed by Mennonites.

The Mennonite congregation of Einlage met for a long time in the school and was a part of the Chortitza Mennonite Church (*q.v.*), without an elder of its own. In 1900 a modern brick church was built in Einlage at the cost of 16,852 rubles, which was torn down in 1929 by the Soviets. Einlage was the center of the beginning and spread of the Mennonite Brethren of the Chortitza settlement. The Einlage Mennonite Brethren Church (*q.v.*) started in 1860 and erected a church building in 1904. Some of the industrialists of Einlage were members of this church and generous supporters of the cause. Not far from Einlage at the beautiful spot where the Dniepr River divided to form the Chortitza island owned by Mennonites, there was the Mennonite Sanatorium Alexandrabad (*q.v.*) and the Bethania Mental Hospital (*q.v.*).

During and immediately following the Revolution of 1917 Einlage suffered severely. Many battles raged here between the Russians and Germans during both world wars, as well as during the Revolution. Many of the inhabitants succumbed to epidemics. A total of 100 persons died thus in 1919-20, besides many who were murdered. In 1921, 56 persons died of starvation (figures according to J. D. Rempel). When American help reached the village, rehabilitation and reconstruction began.

In 1926 the Soviet government decided to raise the water level of the Dniepr by building a power dam to make it navigable and to produce electricity. This necessitated the removal of Einlage in 1927. The new Einlage had 27 Mennonite and 16 Russian farmers each receiving about 45 acres of land. The construction of the power dam and the Soviet philosophy determined the course of the new village considerably. Up to 40,000 laborers were drawn to this project and settled near Einlage; this resulted in the development of a number of industries. Soon Einlage was forced to farm its land collectively, producing grains and fruit and raising vegetables, hogs, and dairy products, which found a ready market in the vicinity.

The exile of Einlage Mennonites to the Far North or Siberia came to a climax on July 30, 1938, when two trucks of men were taken away, of whose destination no one ever heard. By 1941 a total of 245 Mennonites had been sent to forced labor camps. When the German army invaded the Ukraine, the Soviet authorities managed to evacuate only 23 persons eastward. During the brief time of occupation the former Mennonite way of life was somewhat restored. Einlage was taken by the Germans on Aug. 18, 1941, and was abandoned early in October 1943. On Sept. 29, 1941, 997 Einlage Mennonite laborers were evacuated by the Germans by train, arriving in Danzig on Oct. 9. Twelve hundred and thirty-five Einlage farmers followed on wagons, making the total population evacuated to Germany 2,232. From here many were sent into industries at Zoppot near Danzig, Dresden, and other places. Automatically they were made German subjects and the young men forced into the army. During the final stages of the war many perished in the bombing of Dresden. After the German collapse most of the Einlage Mennonites were forcibly repatriated by the Soviets and sent to Asiatic Russia. Those that succeeded in remaining in Germany finally reached Canada and Paraguay.   C.K.

J. D. Rempel, "Einlage," ms. in Bethel College Historical Library; K. Stumpp, *Bericht über das Gebiet Chortitza . . .* (Berlin, 1943); *ML* I, 547.

Einlage Mennonite Brethren Church in the village of Einlage, Chortitza settlement, Ukraine, Russia, was organized on March 11, 1862, when 18 persons were baptized, and within a few months reached a membership of 91. Abraham Unger (*q.v.*) and Heinrich Neufeld were the first ministers elected, and Unger was the first elder (served 1862-76) elected, to be followed by Aaron Lepp as the second elder (served 1876-1903). For the first two years the Einlage group suffered considerably from repressive measures by the existing Mennonite leadership, and sent Gerhard Wieler as a delegate to St. Petersburg for help. By 1864 the right of existence of the new M.B. group both in Chortitza and in the Molotschna had been granted by both the Mennonite Church and the Russian government, and progress was easier. However, internal troubles caused much difficulty, chiefly due to the radicalism of Gerhard Wieler. The unruly elements did so much damage that Unger lost control and resigned, while the erring members were expelled or reconciled through the intermediation of the Molotschna M.B. leaders. Unger later regained his leadership and the church prospered. Einlage and Andreasfeld became the two leading M.B. centers in Chortitza, with Einlage in earlier years the larger congregation. Out of a total of 600 M.B. members in Russia in 1872, 188 were at Einlage. By 1885 Einlage had six branch congregations and was still the largest M.B. church in Russia.

In 1873 the Einlage Church, while under pressure of officials who challenged them to prove their Mennonite status, hurriedly prepared a Confession of Faith. This was printed in 1876. Since it was written at a time when the church stood in a close relationship with the Baptists, it contained much from their Confession; and since the attitude toward the existing Mennonite Church was then somewhat estranged, it included several harsh expressions about the church. This confession of faith, therefore, later proved to be an embarrassment rather than a help and was not fully acceptable to the Einlage Church and still less to other M.B. congregations (quoted from Lohrenz, p. 40 f.).

The relationship with the Baptist Church was a problem which concerned the M.B. Church in general and the Einlage congregation in particular for a number of years. While August Liebig lived in Andreasfeld and did a good deal of preaching in the various congregations, the relationship between the two churches was intimate and friendly. Later Eduard Leppke, a former Baptist from Prussia, joined the M.B. Church and soon became an influential traveling evangelist. Leppke, together with some brethren of a kindred mind, took an estranged attitude toward their neighboring Baptists and influenced the M.B. Church in this way. After several years a more consistent and more brotherly relationship between the two churches evolved, so that each recognized and respected the autonomy of the other.

The Einlage Church continued to be the leader of the Chortitza M.B. group throughout the 19th century, although this group declined relatively in importance in the entire M.B. Church. Gerhard P. Regehr was elder from 1903 on; and Preacher Johann Siemens, who lived here, carried on an extensive and effective itinerant ministry. Other significant preachers were Dietrich Klassen, Peter Peters, and Cornelius Fehr. Several of the branch churches became independent in 1885-1914, such as those in the villages of Petrovka, Vassilevka, Elenovka, and Barvenkovo.†   P.H.B.

Friesen, *Brüderschaft*; J. H. Lohrenz, *The Mennonite Brethren Church* (Hillsboro, 1950).

Einruhr in the Eifel, Germany, the seat of a Mennonite congregation in the 18th century, of which there are no particulars. (See also **Eifel**.)   vdZ.

Einsiedel, a village 18 miles south of Lemberg in Galicia, formerly a Mennonite settlement and the seat of a Mennonite congregation, was organized in 1786 after Joseph II of Austria had invited German settlers to Galicia. The settlement was named after Count von Einsiedel. The original settlement consisted of 20 farms of about 33, 41, or 50 acres of land each. The village was located on a hill on both sides of a wide street in a very regular pattern. Eighteen of the farms were given over to Mennonites, of whom three settler families were Amish, the other two to families (Schmalenberger and Schweitzer) related to them. They soon built a school (1816), which also served as a church and was for a century the chief meeting place of the Galician Mennonites. In 1786 Jakob Müller, Jr., was elder of this congregation, and Jacob Müller, Sr., was preacher. In 1799 Johann Müller succeeded to the eldership.

At the turn of the century half of the Mennonite settlers went on to Russia to the region of Dubno, Volhynia. In order to secure permission to emigrate the families had to turn their farms over to other families just as they had received them, and repay all the expenses of the government in their behalf, namely 4 guilders per person for traveling expenses and approximately 50 guilders for maintenance which they had received in Galicia before their farms were given them. In 1790, 1859, and 1860 the congregation received financial support from Holland (*Inv. Arch. Amst.* II, Nos. 2685-88). The following families remained in Einsiedel: Hubin (also von Howen or Huwen), Müller, Brubacher, Kintzi, Linscheid, Rupp, Merk, and Klein. Gradually other families from the two neighboring villages moved in, namely, Bachmann, Bergtholdt, and Ewy.

In 1860 Johannes van der Smissen signed his name as minister of the congregation of "Einsiedel and Horozanna" in a letter he wrote to Amsterdam. There were 13 Mennonite families living in Einsiedel at that time, most of them leasing or purchasing larger estates through the efforts of Peter Müller (*q.v.*). Some emigrated to America in the 1880's. In 1892 there was only one Mennonite family left in Einsiedel. The name Einsiedel was transplanted to America and was used by the Hanston (Kan.) Mennonite (GCM) Church until 1952.

H.Pa.

Peter Bachmann, *Mennoniten in Kleinpolen* (Lemberg, 1934) 133-56; Kaindl, *Gesch. der Deutschen in den Karpathenländern* III (Gotha, 1911); Church records of Einsiedel; *Inv. Arch. Amst.* II, Nos. 2685-88; *ML* I, 547 f.

Einsiedel Mennonite Church (GCM): see **Hanston** Mennonite Church.

Eisfart, Hans, an Anabaptist martyr of Hausbreitenbach on the Werra, Germany, was executed with his wife at Eisenach in 1532 at the order of Elector John of Saxony because they refused to have their children baptized and joined the Anabaptists.

NEFF.

P. Wappler, *Die Stellung Kursachsens und des Landgrafen Philipp von Hessen zur Täuferbewegung* (Münster, 1910) 36; *ML* I, 548.

Ekaterinoslav (now Dnepropetrovsk), a province (Russian, *oblast*) of the Ukraine, USSR, crossed by the Dnieper River, founded in 1786, named after Catherine II, changed to Dnepropetrovsk in 1917. Ekaterinoslav is bordered on the north by Poltava, on the east by Kharkov, on the south by Taurida, and on the west by Kherson. In 1946 it had an area of 12,590 sq. mi. (size of all Holland) with an estimated population of 2,200,000. The capital city by the same name as the province had in 1939 a population of 500,000.

The Mennonites settled first in this province in 1789, establishing the Chortitza (*q.v.*) settlement with 18 villages. Daughter settlements which originated in this province were as follows: Bergtal (1836), 5 villages; Tchernoglas (1860), 1 village; Borozenko (*q.v.*, 1865), 7 villages; Brazol (1868), 4 villages; Yazykovo (1869), 8 villages; Neplyuevka (1870), 2 villages; Baratov (1872), 2 villages;

Schlachtin (1874), 2 villages; Neu-Rosengart (1878), 2 villages; Wiesenfeld (1880), 1 village; Memrik (1885), 10 villages; Miloradovka (1889), 2 villages; Ignatyevo (1889), 7 villages; Borissovo (1892), 3 villages. Before World War I the Mennonite population of the province was 30,000, distributed over 74 villages and some large estates. Including both the village settlements and the large estates, they owned a total of 761,400 acres. Next to the province of Taurida, Ekaterinoslav had the largest Mennonite population in Russia. The center of government, education, and industry for the Mennonites was Chortitza. Alexandrovsk (today Zaporozhe) also became an industrial center.

Most of the Mennonites who came to Canada after World War II came from the province of Ekaterinoslav, since the Soviets did not succeed in evacuating the settlements from west of the Dnieper River to the east when the German Army invaded the Ukraine in 1941. (For information on the Mennonites of this province under the Soviets, see **Chortitza, Ukraine, Russia,** and the individual settlements listed above.)   C.K.

Die Mennoniten-Gemeinden in Russland . . . 1914 bis 1920 (Heilbronn, 1921); Jacob Quiring, *Die Mundart von Chortitza in Südrussland* (Munich, 1928).

Ekaterinoslav (now Dnepropetrovsk), pop. 500,000, the capital of the province of the name in South Russia, on the right bank of the Dniepr, founded in 1787. It was the largest city in the vicinity of the Chortitza Mennonite settlement, about 50 miles south, which was founded in 1789, and served as the business center for the Mennonites. In 1805 the Mennonite Heinrich Thiessen family was operating a vinegar distillery and later a steam mill in Ekaterinoslav. At about the same time, or perhaps a little later, came Heinrich Cornies and David Schröder, and then Heinrich Töws and Jakob Epp. The initial period of the Mennonite congregation ended with the coming of young Abraham Hamm and Heinrich Heese II, a son of the teacher Heinrich Heese (*q.v.*), who was sent here as a student, and married into the H. Thiessen family. In 1889 there were in the city 9 Mennonite families with about 50 souls. Ten years later there were 31 families with 158 souls. The rapidly growing milling industry, in which nearly all were engaged, kept drawing others from the settlements. At that time the following firms were in the business: J. H. Thiessen, Johann Töws, the Heese Brothers, and the Fast Brothers. The Mennonite group in the city was again augmented in 1919-21, when many large estate owners sought protection from anarchist attacks there.

At first the Mennonite services were held in a private home on alternate Sundays. For official services, such as baptism, communion, etc., they called on the elder of Kronsgarten, a Mennonite village about 40 miles distant. In October 1889 they called their first minister, D. H. Epp of Rosental, who also served as a teacher in their school until 1912. He was followed by Johann Klassen, who had until then been the teacher of religion at the Chortitza Zentralschule, and in 1918 for a short period by Jakob Rempel, who was later ordained as an elder, until anarchy completely destroyed the once thriving Mennonite community.

In 1851 the Mennonites opened a German elementary school, especially for their own children, which developed into a larger school with three teachers, and was also attended by Russian students and foreigners as a school preparatory to the Russian secondary school. In 1910 the congregation built a new school with an apartment for a teacher or minister; in it church services were also held. The war breaking out in 1914 prevented the church they had planned from being built.

In its prime the Ekaterinoslav Mennonite Church had a beneficial influence on outside circles. To meet the needs of the large number of Mennonite students who came to the city to study in the Russian secondary schools there, it organized various activities with this definite objective. By means of family connections, choral groups, lectures, amateur presentations, and a large library of German books they sought to keep the young people together, away from the disintegrating influence of the metropolis. In addition to Sunday services, religious instruction was given all age groups.

The first work preliminary to the establishment of Bethania (q.v.), the hospital for the mentally ill, was done here, as also for the founding of the Chortitza girls' school. There were always experienced men here, who were willing and able to aid the brethren in the colony in matters relating to government institutions, banking, or church business. There was, for instance, Johann Thiessen, with all his wealth a humble Christian, always ready to help wherever the need arose, an anonymous benefactor of the poor; Heinrich Heese in his position on the board of directors of the city branch of the federal bank and many private banks; Jakob Heese, a young attorney, who devoted himself to youth work, serving many years as an excellent choral director; Heinrich Töws, in whose large, beautiful home all youth festivities were held; Jakob Esau, long a practicing physician in the Chortitza villages, then head and owner of an eye clinic in the city. Finally engineer Johann Esau must be named, who remained faithfully at his responsible post, first as assistant to the mayor, then as mayor, when none of the Russians would allow themselves to be elected because of political disturbances. Under his leadership and his energetic support, a series of welfare institutions was inaugurated in the city: a great new water system was laid, a streetcar line built, and several excellent girls' schools erected. When ingratitude and envy made it impossible for him to serve any longer, even his enemies had to recognize his incorruptible fidelity. After the Russian Revolution in 1917 the Mennonite community of Ekaterinoslav never regained the significance and strength of the former years. The large enterprises were confiscated and the Mennonites scattered. Although Mennonite students attended schools and others lived here, the community life and congregation gradually disintegrated. (See also **Ukraine, Russia.**) (*ML* II, 402.)

D.E.

Ekelo: see **Eckelo.**

El Ombu Mennonite settlement and congregation in Uruguay, *ca.* 185 miles north of Montevideo, on the main highway to Paysandu (65 miles away), the town of Young (pop. 5,000) being the nearest market, founded in 1950 with the aid of the Mennonite Central Committee by Mennonite refugees from Danzig and West Prussia, most of whom had been in refugee camps in Denmark since their flight from Danzig in January 1945. El Ombu (the name refers to a shade tree) is actually the name of a 25,000-acre estate, 3,000 acres of which were bought at a price of $100,000 and occupied April 17, 1950. About half of the 750 Mennonites who arrived in Uruguay Oct. 7, 1948, on the *Volendam* settled here, a total of 80 families and 12 single persons. (In April 1951, about 400 persons in 100 family units were living in El Ombu, 10 of whom had previously belonged to two congregations in Poland, Deutsch-Kazun and Wymysle.) In September 1950 the El Ombu co-operative ("Flor del Rio Negro") was organized, to which every settler (head of a family) belongs. The El Ombu congregation was organized on March 10, 1952, with the following ministerial organization: elder, Ernst Regehr, formerly elder (1934) of Rosenort; preachers, Gustav L. Reimer (1931 Heubuden), Heinrich Wall (1934 Fürstenwerder), Alfred Hinz (1935 Orlofferfelde), Otto Jochem (1941 Fürstenwerder), Reinhard Fast (1952 El Ombu); deacons, Johannes Wiebe (1933 Heubuden), Heinz Dyck (1952 El Ombu). The crops in El Ombu are wheat, corn, flax, sunflowers, and peanuts. Milk, butter, and fruit are also in production. An orange orchard of about 100 acres with 11,000 bearing trees was on the tract when bought. El Ombu is the oldest Mennonite settlement in Uruguay and to date the center of Mennonite life there.

H.S.B.

W. Dück, "Neue Heimat in Uruguay, Die Mennonitensiedlung El Ombu," *Gem.-Kal.* 1952, 56-65; H. Wall, "Drei Jahre in Uruguay," *Menn. Gesch.-Bl.* IX (March 1952) 18-26; J. E. Reimer, "Von Danzig nach Uruguay," *Menn. Life* IV (1948) 12-14.

El Trebol, the third settlement effort by Mennonite refugees who fled from Russia and landed in Mexico. El Trebol was located in the state of Durango on a tract of land east of the Old Colony Mennonite village of Grünfeld. Twenty-four families moved from Irapuato (q.v.) after that effort failed. These families, not all of one branch of Mennonites, struggled for three or four years to eke out an existence but finally gave up. Some of the families moved to Cuauhtemoc in the state of Chihuahua, others moved to Canada, and one or two married into the Old Colony group. Today all evidence of a former settlement has disappeared.

C.K.

Elahuizen, a hamlet in the Dutch province of Friesland, where Leenaert Bouwens (q.v.) baptized 14 persons in 1551-54. Yet there is no evidence that a congregation ever existed in this town. Likely the people baptized by Bouwens joined the congregation—now extinct—of Legemeer (q.v.).

vDZ.

Elbert Pieter Sinckes, an Anabaptist martyr, was beheaded at Alkmaar, Dutch province of North Holland, Feb. 1, 1536, because (1) he had been rebaptized, (2) he had taken part in the journey to Münster, being taken prisoner at Bergklooster (*q.v.*), and (3) he had not prevented Dirk Krood (Dirk of Wormer, *q.v.*) from taking the holy sacrament from the hands of a priest at Wormer. vᴅZ.

Inv. Arch. Amst. I, No. 748, 3; G. Boomkamp, *Alkmaar en deszelfs Geschiedenissen* (Alkmaar, 1747) 84.

Elbing, a city in West Prussia (pop. 85,000), was until after World War I the seat of two Mennonite congregations. As early as 1531 Anabaptists are said to have lived in Elbing, and since about the middle of the 16th century Mennonites had lived in Elbing and vicinity. The city had suffered so severely in the war between Poland and Prussia (1519-21) that the government made serious efforts to attract capable colonists. They gladly accepted the Mennonite refugees fleeing religious persecution in Holland, and gave them charge of managing the farms in the vicinity. In the city proper they were at first not tolerated. In 1550 the council announced to the Mennonites a royal decree that they must leave the city within two weeks. But the expulsion was not rigorously carried out. Nor was the order of expulsion issued by the Polish King Sigismund in 1556 taken very seriously by the city authorities. Their services seem to have been especially required to clear the land in the Ellerwald, which was apportioned to the ruling families of the city in 1565. In 1571 Sebastian Neogeorgius, the pastor of St. Mary's, declaimed against tolerating them on the Ellerwald estates and induced the council to issue an order that the "foreigners" were to leave the region of the city by Easter of 1572. The terminus was extended to autumn, "until the Mennonites have harvested their grain," and then again to Jan. 6, 1575; then the order was completely forgotten (Mannhardt, *Wehrfreiheit,* 71). The Mennonites stayed on the country estates and are said even to have won Lutheran fellow citizens to their faith.

Soon after this they began to settle in the city of Elbing again. In 1585 Jost van Kampen and Hans van Keulen were granted citizenship and the permission to engage in the silk trade, which had not yet been introduced into the city (Mannhardt, *Danzig,* 49), and in 1610 several other Mennonites were accepted as citizens; by 1612 there were 16 Mennonite families living in the city. Difficulties were placed in the way of their residence in the city by the decree of Sigismund III in 1653 requiring the oath of citizenship. But they continued to be tolerated and were not molested by any demands running counter to their conscience. In giving the oath of citizenship with "yea" and "nay," they were required to place the hand on the breast; for freedom from military service they paid a special tax —the regulations of 1660 required one Polish guilder (Carstenn, p. 35), whether they were natives or foreigners, and only in a few insignificant matters in trade and commerce did the council give the Lutherans any advantage (Mannhardt, *Danzig,* 72).

In the meantime a Mennonite congregation had formed in Elbing. The first church was built in 1590 on land owned by Jost van Kampen, Kurze Hinterstrasse 8, now Wilhelmsstrasse. It served the congregation until 1900, when a new, larger building was erected on Berlinerstrasse 20, which was used by the Elbing-Ellerwald congregation until 1945. This congregation had a second church in Ellerwald, a village near Elbing, which was dedicated by Elder Gerhard Wiebe on Oct. 5, 1783, together with a school which was opened by permission of the king of Prussia (*Naamlijst* 1787, 63). The city and country groups have from the beginning formed the single congregation of Elbing-Ellerwald, with a jointly chosen elder, preachers, and deacons. This is demonstrable back as far as 1606. An old record says, "In 1606 Henrich von dem Bosche served the union in Elbing." In 1610 the council complained to Sigismund III that "the Mennonites among themselves, without the foreknowledge of the government, granted divorces (i.e., proclaimed the avoidance of a spouse), married one another and divided inheritance, whereupon a royal rescript was issued on June 27, 1611, forbidding these independent rites on penalty of a fine of 100 Hungarian guilders. In 1648 Dirk v. Haegen, in 1674 Zacharias Janssen, Hermann Fock, and Anton Momber are called preachers. Then the office of elder appears to have been vacant for a considerable time.

There are letters in the Mennonite archives at Amsterdam that show that the Elbing Mennonites in the early 18th century suffered severely from flooding caused by broken dikes and from crop failures. They received substantial aid from the Dutch Mennonite Committee on Foreign Needs (*Inv. Arch. Amst.* I, Nos. 1569, 1579, 1652, 1658). In 1726 many Mennonites from Lithuania came into Elbing, but most of them went elsewhere after a short time (*Inv. Arch. Amst.* I, Nos. 1578-79, 1692). This was an Old Flemish Mennonite congregation. From 1727 a complete succession of elders can be followed. On Jan. 12 of this year, Hermann Janson, who came to Elbing from Holland in 1690, was ordained elder by Dirk Siemens from the Grossen Werder. He was followed by Zacharias Schröter 1745-70 (d. 1771), Antony Wölcky 1770-78, Gerhard Wiebe 1778-98, Peter Dick of Ellerwald 1798-1807, whose ordination caused a brief division between the city and country groups. The former was dissatisfied with his election and chose Antony Wölke, who served as elder of the city church from 1788 until his death in 1804. In that year the groups reunited. Peter Dick was succeeded by Jakob Kröker from Ellerwald 1808-46, Johann Andreas (*q.v.*) of Nogattau 1846-69, who emigrated to America because he could not reconcile his conscience with the duty of military service on the basis of the royal order of cabinet of March 3, 1868. Andreas was followed in the office of elder by Johann Mierau of Elbing 1870-78, Abraham Dick of Ellerwald 1879-86, Wilhelm Dückmann 1890-97, and Rudolf Wieler of Kraffohlsdorf, later living in Elbing 1898-1923, and Emil Händiges 1923-45.

On Jan. 1, 1920, the congregation numbered 736 souls (male 346, female 390, baptized 572, unbaptized 104, married 276, unmarried 399, widowed 61). Church books were kept since 1825. The church was incorporated in 1897. Until 1904 the Mennonites buried their dead in the Lutheran cemeteries of the city, but the Protestant clergy were frequently intolerant toward the burial rites. Therefore in 1904 the Mennonites purchased a tract of land near the city and furnished it with a mortuary. Services were held in the city church every Sunday and in the Ellerwald church once a month. The church was served by a lay ministry until recently. Only the elder received any financial compensation for performing the functions of his office. Most of the members were farmers or merchants; few had trades; a number lived on their private means. The church was a member of the *Vereinigung* (*q.v.*). Church discipline was exercised in cases of gross sin.

From this congregation of Elbing-Ellerwald came a second Mennonite congregation in Elbing, known as the Elbing Mennonite Church. In the middle of the 19th century a number of the members of Elbing-Ellerwald felt the need for a trained minister. For the city people, many of whom were educated, the country preachers no longer sufficed, and the instruction of youth left much to be desired, as the emphasis was placed on the recitation of memorized answers to the regular questions. The city young people were in danger of being lost to the church.

It was therefore decided to engage as preacher Carl Harder (*q.v.*), a young Königsberg Mennonite who had just completed his theological studies at the University of Halle. But Harder was chosen preacher by his home congregation and ordained there in 1845. He occasionally preached at Elbing. But when the Königsberg church received as a member a man expelled by the Rosenort church, and by the conference at Neuteich July 15, 1847, was consequently cut off from fellowship by the other West Prussian churches, the board of the Elbing-Ellerwald church forbade Harder to preach in the Mennonite church in Elbing. Harder then held his services at first in a private hall, then (1850-51) in Lutheran Heilig-Geistkirche. When all negotiations with the board of Elbing-Ellerwald failed, several Elbing Mennonites built a second church in the Reiferbahnstrasse, which was dedicated Aug. 1, 1852. The new congregation, which became a subsidiary of the Königsberg church, was joined at once by 24 families. Harder preached to the congregation, which chose its own board, every two weeks. In 1857, when Harder was chosen by the Neuwied church to take the place of de Veer as preacher, the preachers of the Danzig church, J. Mannhardt and van Kampen, alternately served the Elbing congregation for a time.

After van Kampen's death in 1868 the connections with Elbing came to an end. Elbing now had to make its own arrangements, and called Carl Harder of Neuwied, who moved into Elbing at Easter 1869. From that time on services were held every Sunday in the Mennonite church on the Reiferbahn. The Mennonite minister taught the courses in religion in the Elbing schools. Mennonite children were thus no longer compelled to attend religious instruction given by members of the state church; this was true of no other city in Germany. In 1882 the church had a membership of 298 souls, of whom 197 lived in Elbing and the immediate vicinity. Harder died in 1898. The congregation chose Adolf Siebert to take his place; he was installed on Aug. 14, 1898. In 1922 the congregation had a total of 450 souls. In 1940 it had a membership of 113 baptized members and 11 unbaptized children. Aron Mäkelborger was ordained as pastor and elder in 1938, but was called into military service in 1940 and never returned. Both congregations in Elbing were wiped out in January 1945 by the flight before the advance of the Russian army. In 1947, when the MCC relief program was established in the Danzig-Marienburg-Elbing area, one remaining family of members of the Elbing-Ellerwald congregation was found. H. S. Bender baptized their two daughters in the spring of 1948. Some relief supplies were distributed in Elbing (Polish Elblag) by MCC workers, but a child-feeding program was cut short by the Polish government. The fate of the former Elbing ministers is as follows: Elder Händiges was called to serve as pastor at Monsheim, Rheinhessen, where he served until his retirement in 1954, and Preacher Jakob Friesen of the same congregation died in a camp in Denmark in 1945; Adolf Siebert of Elbing (*Stadt*), d. Jan. 26, 1945, on the flight westward.† E.H.

W. Mannhardt, *Die Wehrfreiheit der Altpreussischen Mennoniten* (Marienburg, 1863); E. Carstenn, "Elbings Verfassung zu Ausgang der polnischen Zeit," in *Ztsch des westpr. Gesch.-Ver.*, No. 52 (Danzig, 1910); H. G. Mannhardt, *Die Danziger Mennoniten-Gemeinde* (1919); L. Neubaur, "Mährische [Hutterite] Brüder in Elbing," in *Ztscht für Kirchengesch.* XXXIII (1912) 447-55; *Kurzgefasste Geschichte der Elbinger Mennonitengemeinde* (Elbing, 1883); *Inv. Arch. Amst.* I, Nos. 1022-23, 1231, 1347, 1569, 1571, 1575, 1578-79, 1652-54, 1668, 1689, 1692, 1695-96; II, 2, Nos. 698-99, 701, 746, 749, 752, 755, 776, 792, 844; *DB* 1886, 5; 1887, 49; *ML* I, 549 f.

Elbing, a village in Butler Co., Kan., 12 miles east of Newton, so named because the first members of the Zion Mennonite Church (GCM) here, organized in 1883, came from the area near Elbing, West Prussia, Germany. The 1953 membership of 143, however, included Mennonites from almost every background. The Berean Academy (*q.v.*), a four-year high school, operated by the Berean Christian Laymen's Association, an organization of Mennonite laymen, is located at the edge of the village. The Gnadenberg Mennonite Church (GCM), located about four miles southwest of Elbing, in 1953 had a membership of approximately 185. (*ML* I, 550.)

L.A.J.

Elbingscher Werder: see **Marienburger Werder.**

Elbow Mennonite Brethren Church, now extinct, located at Elbow, Sask., was organized in 1927 by immigrants from Russia who had settled there on farm land. The membership soon rose to some 70 or 80, but declined on account of lack of rainfall to about 12. Frank Wiens led the congregation for many years, but moved away in 1945. The church was no longer listed in the 1948 M.B. Year Book.

P.C.H.

Elconius, Hermannus (Herman Eelkes), b. at Harlingen, Dutch province of Friesland, d. there after 1607, was the last Roman Catholic priest at Harlingen before the Reformation; about 1580 he left the Catholic Church and in 1581 became a Reformed minister at Utrecht, and from 1589 at Harlingen. Here he came into conflict with the Reformed Synod; in 1602 he left the Reformed church and joined the Mennonites at Harlingen. In 1605 he is reported to have been their preacher. Nothing further is known about this remarkable man. (*N.N.B.Wb.* I, 798; *DB* 1911, 45-48.)   vdZ.

Elder (German, *Aeltester;* Dutch, *Oudste*) is the name for the highest and most responsible office of the Mennonite ministry in a large number of Mennonite congregations and conferences. The origin of the word goes back to the Biblical times and is mentioned in Acts 14:23; I Tim. 5:17, etc. The New Testament equivalent is presbyter or bishop. In the early Anabaptist usage, the terms elder (*Aeltester, Oudste*), *Leeraar,* and bishop (*q.v.*) were used interchangeably. Gradually, however, the term *Oudste* or *Aeltester* became predominant until the usage of "bishop" disappeared in Europe with the possible exception of the Hutterites. At present, wherever this office is referred to in Europe, it is either *Aeltester, Pastor,* or *Dominee.* In America, however, large groups, particularly those of Pennsylvania-German background, use the term bishop only. This article will deal mostly with the office and function of the elder. (Regarding the office and the function of a bishop, see the article **Bishop.**)

It was a principle of the Anabaptists to have their congregations function in a democratic way in contrast to the large state churches, which had a somewhat episcopal form of church government, operating usually from the top down. It would, however, be misleading to assume that the early Anabaptists were able to develop and maintain a thoroughly congregational type of church government. This was impossible because of the very severe and lasting persecution under which the congregations originated and existed. In many instances, the congregations could only survive through strong leadership, which was either delegated or assumed. In principle, and also in practice compared to the state churches, the Anabaptist congregations were democratic. However, the above-mentioned emergency conditions necessitated and were conducive to the development of strong leadership. Capito (*q.v.*), in a letter of July 31, 1528, to Zwingli, says, "There are among them 'principes' and leaders, whom they themselves call 'Vorsteher.'"

The office of a minister was twofold; some ministers were ordained to preach only (*Diener am Wort*—servant of the Word, *Dienaar, Vermaner Prediger*). The elders or bishops (*Oudste, Leeraar*) were authorized to perform all functions (*voller Dienst*—full service) of the church. In addition to this, of course, there were also deacons (*Armendiener*—servants of the poor).

The Emden *Protocol* (1579) treats in detail the call and function of elders and ministers of the 16-century Anabaptists of Northwest Europe. Pieter van Ceulen states: "Bishops and preachers (*Dienar-*

en) are chosen by the congregations under God's guidance by a majority of the vote with fasting and prayer unto the Lord. Such ministers are ordained by the laying on of hands of the elders" (p. 229b). And again this is emphasized when Brixius Gerrits says "that the entire congregation must meet to elect elders or preachers" (*Leeraers ofte Dienaren,* 239a). The *Protocol* and *Het beginsel en voortganck der geschillen* refer to the elders as *Leeraar, Oudste,* and *Biscop.* The *Protocol* uses all of these terms, while *Het beginsel* consistently uses *Leeraar* only. The latter uses *Dienaer* and *Vermaender* for preacher. These usages are also found in "Oude Gemeente verordeningen" by de Hoop Scheffer (*DB* 1877).

Thus in the early days the Anabaptists of Northwest Europe spoke of their elders interchangeably as *Oudste, Leeraar,* and *Biscop.* Such functions as the administration of baptism and the Lord's Supper and the ordination of church officers could be performed only by holders of this office. They are also referred to as *Leeraer in den vollen dienst* (*Het beginsel,* p. 16). The *Dienaar* (servant, minister) or *Vermaner* (admonisher) held an office which entitled the holder to preaching only, mostly in his own congregation, while the elders were traveling extensively in the various congregations of their respective districts. An unusual example of the extensive work of such an elder is found in the list of persons who were baptized by Leenaert Bouwens, extending from Meenen to Emden.

In the beginning the number of elders was small. Those who were to practice the "full ministry" (*voller Dienst*) were usually selected from among preachers and were then ordained as elders or bishops by laying on of hands (Krahn, *Menno Simons,* 147). This ordination entitled the elder not only to preach and assume leadership in the congregation, but also to baptize, administer the Lord's Supper, and ordain preachers and elders, and exercise discipline, which functions the common preacher could not fulfill.

The early Anabaptist ministers quite often had to defend their calling in their disputes with Catholic, Lutheran, and the Reformed ministers, who, more or less, claimed that their call was based on the Apostolic Succession (*q.v.*) and denied that the Anabaptist elders and ministers had a proper calling. (See Emden *Protocol,* "Van de Verkiesinge ende Beroepinge der Predicanten ofte Dienaers," pp. 229-45.) This concerned the Anabaptist leaders very little. Since they did not find a "true apostolic church" anywhere, and since the Bible demanded it, they felt not only authorized but compelled to establish a congregation. Elders and preachers were not working in their own authority, but had received their calling from a congregation or directly from God. Menno Simons says, "Ministers of the Sacred Word are to be called in an orderly manner, either by the Lord Himself or through the God-fearing" (*Works* II, 342a). The Wismar Agreements (1554), however, state clearly that no one has the right to preach without being called by a congregation or ordained by an elder (*BRN* VII, 53).

The elders, and particularly the preachers, did not receive a fixed salary, partly because the early

Anabaptists were opposed to the practices along these lines prevailing in the state church. The prevalent corruption and lack of integrity, religious convictions, and sincerity they linked to the practice of hiring and paying the ministry for its services. A voluntary church membership and a voluntary ministry with personal conviction and high moral integrity was the aim. This, however, did not mean that the elder was not to receive support and aid out of "the hand of the God-fearing disciples," so that the elder could take care of his spiritual duties (Menno's *Works* II, 31 ff., 341). In the Emden *Protocol* Brixius Gerrits states, "To the question whether a congregation should support the minister it has called in a Christian way, we say yes. But we do not know whether they [apostles] had a fixed income" (p. 233b).

Rues states (*Aufrichtige Nachrichten,* 27-30) that during the early 18th century the conservative groups of the Netherlands still adhered to the practices of the early days. The elder specially ordained for these functions was the only minister to baptize, administer the Lord's Supper, and ordain ministers. He was always the chairman of the church council and took the initiative in matters pertaining to the congregation. The conservative groups were, in principle, opposed to a specially trained ministry, basing their argument partly on statements of the early Anabaptists, while the more progressive Mennonites of Holland soon realized the necessity of a specially trained leadership. The latter probably found as much justification in the writings of the early Anabaptists as the former. Although the early Anabaptist leaders strongly denounced the misuse of learning among the theologically trained ministers of the state churches, they hardly ever said anything against training as such. On the contrary, they made full use of it (Krahn, *Menno Simons,* 109 ff.).

Among the Waterlanders the distinction between the elders (*Oudste, Leeraar*) and preachers (*Dienaar, Vermaner*) soon disappeared. In Rotterdam this distinction was given up in 1687, when the elder died and the three remaining ministers were authorized to perform all functions on equal terms (Kühler III, II). Among the Groningen Old Flemish, where the old practice was adhered to longest, the elders were also known as *Opzieners* or *Commissarissen* (Blaupot t. C., *Groningen,* 132 ff.). The more progressive urban Mennonite congregations of Holland soon felt the need for a trained ministry, which they remedied by electing physicians or other educated members of the congregations into the ministry and eldership. These, in turn, promoted the establishment of a seminary for the training of ministers (see **Amsterdam Mennonite Seminary**). With this change, the office of elder was considerably altered. Formerly the elder served several congregations, having a number of coministers as assistants. Congregations then chose the elder from among the preachers, who usually had been chosen out of the congregation. With the special theological training of young men interested in serving as ministers, the whole system was gradually altered and finally disappeared. The minister did not necessarily stay for life. Soon there was only one minister in each congregation, ordained at once as both preacher and elder and performing all functions in the congregation.

This new system, started as an accommodation to the need of the day, spread from Holland to the neighboring German congregations, such as Crefeld, Emden, Hamburg-Altona, and Danzig, and finally to the Palatinate. Needless to say there was often a difference of opinion regarding this new system, which sometimes caused splits in congregations (Danzig, Elbing). There was usually the intellectual urban wing urging the calling of a specially prepared minister, and a conservative rural population opposing this change. However, the unwillingness, and sometimes inability, of lay ministers to cope with the multiple and complex problems and responsibilities of urban congregations compelled congregations to accept this change. In Holland the majority of congregations accepted this change during the 18th century, while the neighboring German Mennonite congregations inaugurated it during the 19th century, often calling on trained Dutch Mennonite ministers. The Danzig Mennonite congregation elected Jacob van der Smissen in 1826 as its first theologically trained preacher, but he did not become the elder of the congregation. Later Elbing followed. However, most of the rural Prussian Mennonite congregations retained the traditional system to the end of their existence (1945). Preachers and particularly elders were usually of the well-to-do class with a fairly good education, who could afford to devote a considerable part of their time to their congregational duties. The elders were organized like those of the Verband (*q.v.*) group in South Germany in a council of elders (*Aeltestenrat, q.v.*). The elders and preachers together constituted the *Lehrdienst* or ministerial body.

With the above change, the title of the ministers also underwent a change. In Holland, the word for elder (*Oudste*) was changed to the title in general use in the state church, *Dominee* (abbreviated *Ds.*). The North German and Prussian elders with a theological training, serving the congregations on a salaried basis, are usually referred to as *Pastor,* but also as *Aeltester.*

The Mennonite congregations of Poland never came to the point where the old practice regarding elders and preachers was affected. In Russia the matter of eldership caused considerable difficulties when the Chortitza (*q.v.*) settlement was established. No elders had joined the immigrants and the one appointed by letter by the home congregation in Prussia was not fully accepted. After the initial difficulties had been ironed out by visiting elders from Prussia, the traditional elder-minister practice functioned without great change into the 20th century. The elders and ministers were organized in a *Kirchenkonvent,* the equivalent of the *Lehrdienst* in West Prussia.

With the raising of the educational level and the introduction of secondary schools among the Russion Mennonites during the middle of the past century, the demand for specially trained preachers and elders increased. It gradually became the practice to elect preachers from the ranks of the teachers, who sometimes combined the two professions. Thus at the turn of the century most of the elders had secondary school training. With the interest in mission work and the training of missionaries in foreign theological schools came also the demand for the establishment of a theological school, and when this did not materialize, the training of some ministers and evangelists in Swiss and German Bible Schools and theological seminaries came about. Although there was a trend away from the older system in which the elder had charge of a number of other congregations and ministers in addition to his own, a radical change did not take place. Theologically trained and conference-appointed traveling evangelists received some remuneration, as did also some elders, but the system of the unsalaried ministry in general prevailed. On the whole, the development in this matter was about the same among all groups of Mennonites in Russia. The tradition and practice regarding elders and preachers among the Mennonite Brethren congregations was more or less the same.

In Russia, in accordance with an old Flemish regulation, only the elders, not the preachers, were ordained by the laying on of hands; this practice continued in some of the Flemish congregations until 1900.

The Mennonite immigrant congregations of Prussian, Polish, and Russian background of the prairie states (U.S.A.) and provinces (Canada) maintained the traditional office of an elder who was assisted by preachers and was possibly in charge of a number of congregations. For many years lay preachers were elected from the midst of the congregation. Gradually, with the advancement of secondary education and the felt need for an English-speaking, theologically trained ministry, the practice in the United States has been completely changed, very much after the pattern introduced in the Netherlands. This applies especially to the General Conference Mennonite congregations and the Mennonite Brethren. Most of their congregations are now served by men who voluntarily chose the work of a minister by majoring in Bible in college or attending a theological seminary or Bible school, and who have received a call from a congregation to serve full time on a contract basis. Most of these ministers are ordained at one and the same time as preachers and elders and thus perform all functions. Occasionally, in the process of changing, some of the old lay preachers also continue to preach. Thus, each congregation is served by a preacher-elder who performs all functions and can resign and accept the call of another congregation. This change is almost complete in all congregations of the above-mentioned background in the United States.

In Canada, where the more conservative element settled during the 1870's and where the more recent Mennonite immigrants from Russia are predominant, the old system still prevails, although it is apparent that a change is coming. Elders of the Rosenort Mennonite Church, the Blumenort Mennonite Church, the Bergtal Mennonite Church, the Schönwiese Mennonite Church, and others still have charge of several congregations, assisted by a number of preachers, and are the only ones who administer baptism and the Lord's Supper and ordain ministers. However, in the Mennonite Brethren Church, where the office of elder has been completely dropped and the office of elected "leader" substituted, and the recently established General Conference congregations, particularly in the cities, the minister is often in charge of one congregation only, and in some instances, has no assistant ministers. With the demand for college and seminary trained, English-speaking preaching ministers, the usual change will likely take place soon. In the more conservative groups, such as the Old Colony Mennonites (Canada, Mexico), Sommerfelder (Canada, Mexico, Paraguay), and the recent immigrants from Russia and Prussia to South America, the old system of eldership will likely prevail for some time to come.

With the change from the German language to the English, the title *Aeltester,* which was the only form in use, has been translated "elder," although Canadian groups, particularly when dealing with the public and government, use the Anglican title "bishop." However, generally speaking, the title "elder" will probably disappear since the commonly used title, "The Reverend," in its abbreviated form "Rev.," is becoming predominant. When referring to the office of the minister-elect without the personal name, "minister" is the generally accepted term. "Preacher" is not used as a title preceding the name, as is common among the conservative groups of Pennsylvania-German background. An exception in using "Preacher" as a title is the Church of God in Christ, Mennonite.

The older method of electing an elder (and preacher) among the Dutch, Prussian, and Russian groups prior to the modern change was usually by majority vote. In some instances, however, the lot may have been used (Krahn, 144). References to it are extremely rare and the only known present practice is by vote. When at present a minister is to be called, the congregation has a committee to nominate candidates, one of whom is elected by a majority vote, possibly after the congregation has had occasion to become acquainted with the candidate.

The office of elder, both in the earlier times (16th-18th centuries) in Holland and North Germany and in the 19th-20th centuries in Russia, developed great prestige and considerable power. At times certain elders exercised this power in arbitrary and domineering ways, in effect "ruling over" their congregations or districts. In Holland such exercise of authority was a major factor in many of the schisms of the 16th and 17th centuries. In Russia the village type of settlement, the dominant religious concern, and the prestige of the elder tended to the development of a type of hierarchial theocracy in which at times the elders practically controlled both the civil and ecclesiastical life of the community. The village Schulze or mayor seldom acted in cultural matters without the counsel of the elder, and almost never acted against this counsel when it was received. However, there were men like Johann Cornies who successfully steered their own course, with the backing, to be sure, of the Russian governmental authorities. The Prussian and Russian Mennonite society was essentially patriarchal (as was generally the case in the Swiss-South German type also), in which the elder incorporated in his person in a sense both the familial and the ecclesiastical authority. This tradition is continued among the conservative Old Colony Mennonites of Canada, Mexico, and Paraguay. The common Dutch and Low German title *Oom* (*Ohm;* i.e., Uncle) as applied to the elder symbolized and carries much of this feeling of high regard for the church authority. C.K.

I.H.V.P.N., *Het Beginsel en voortganck der geschillen . . .* (Amsterdam, 1658); *Protocol Das is, Alle handelinge des Gesprecks tot Embden . . .* (Emden, 1579) 229-45; J. G. de Hoop Scheffer, "Oude Gemeenteverordeningen," *DB* 1877; S. F. Rues, *Tegenwoordige staet der Doopsgezinden of Mennoniten . . .* (Amsterdam, 1745); *idem, Aufrichtige Nachrichten von dem gegenwärtigen Zustand der Mennoniten* Jena 1743); S. Hoekstra, Bz., *Beginselen en leer der oude Doopsgezinden . . .* (Amsterdam, 1863) 236-40; Friesen, *Brüderschaft,* 33 ff., 728 ff., 762 ff.; K. Vos, "De keuze tot Doopsgezind Bisschop," *Nederl. Arch. voor Kerkgesch.* XVI (1921); W. J. Kühler, *Geschiedenis* III, part 2; Cornelius Krahn, *Menno Simons* (Karlsruhe, 1936) 143 ff.; N. van der Zijpp, *Geschiedenis der Doopsgezinden in Nederland* (Arnhem, 1952) 126 ff.; Blaupot t. C., *Groningen; ML* I, 39 f.

Eldert (Aeldert) **Gerritsz,** born at Velthuysen, near Zwolle, Dutch province of Overijssel, a revolutionary Anabaptist, a follower of Jan van Batenburg (*q.v.*), was charged with belonging to corrupt sects and having robbed many Catholic churches. He was beheaded at Utrecht (Netherlands) on July 21, 1544. (*Berigten Historisch Genootschap* IV, 2, 1851, 146.) vDZ.

Eldorado Community Church, located 15 miles southwest of Henderson, Neb., was organized as an M.B. congregation in 1903. Before that the members met with the Sutton M.B. Church. John Deines had the leadership of this group for many years, and M.B. ministers from Henderson assisted in pastoral duties. In recent years Eli Cook served the congregation as pastor. The Eldorado congregation has not been listed in the M.B. conference reports since 1950. H.E.W.

Elementary Education, a term commonly used in America for the training given to children during the first eight years of their attendance at school. The term is in contrast to secondary education, which refers to the work in grades 9-12 inclusive.

A. *Europe.* During the early days of Anabaptism in Switzerland and Holland conditions were not favorable for the establishment of church or parochial schools. In the days of persecution such institutions would not have been permitted. Lacking relatively permanent and closely knit communities the Anabaptists of these areas would have found it difficult to establish their own schools. The Hutterites, on the other hand, living in colonies, were able to establish their own schools, which they did as early as 1533. School attendance was compulsory and their schools were good enough to attract non-Hutterite children. M. S. Harder explains, "The Hutterite schools were divided into three departments. The first accepted the children when they were one-and-a-half years old. It was like a Kindergarten in modern education. It was concerned chiefly with the physical care of the children. The

little children were taught to speak, and received their first instruction in religion and social living. At the age of 5 or 6 the children entered the next department, not unlike an elementary school. Here they were under the supervision of a schoolmaster who taught them how to read and write. The religious training was greatly emphasized. Prayers, the catechism, and religious hymns occupied the center of the curriculum. . . . The children remained in this department until they were old enough to learn to work."

After the persecution of the Dutch Mennonites ended, they became absorbed in the urban life of their country, not living in closed communities. They sent their children both to secular schools and to church schools maintained by other Christian groups. Only in Haarlem did they have their own institutions, where they owned and supported two elementary schools, one of which was still in existence in 1954, both of which however were essentially schools for poor children and not conceived as parochial church schools.

After the Swiss government organized its national school system, the Mennonites organized elementary schools in their homes to comply with the new law. During the last half of the 19th century there were at least 20 such schools among the Mennonites in the Jura Mountains. When the financial burden of these schools became almost too heavy for the Mennonites to bear, they were given state financial aid. The Chaux d'Abel elementary school was the first to be granted equal status with other state schools and therefore to be declared eligible for state aid. A few years later, in 1899, the Mont-Tramelan school was granted similar recognition. In 1949 there were seven one-teacher Mennonite schools in Switzerland, offering nine grades of work, and all complying with the educational requirements of Swiss law. The schools at Chaux d'Abel, Montbautier, and Perceux have their own buildings. The Moron and Jeangisboden schools are held in churches and the Mont-Tramelan and the Perceux schools meet in private homes.

In Germany the Realanstalt am Donnersberg, later known as the Weierhof Real- und Erziehungs-Anstalt, a private secondary boarding school founded by Michael Löwenberg, and patronized by Mennonites, was opened in 1867. A ruling of the Bavarian state compelled it to operate on the elementary level from 1878 to 1884. In 1869 an elementary school was opened in the French village of Etupes for the Mennonite children of this area. Later the school was moved to an estate near the village of Exincourt (*q.v.*), where it was operated successfully for seven years. The Mennonites of Altona operated an elementary school in 1723-95 with interruptions (Dollinger, 169 f.). The Mennonites of Neustadt-Goedens, East Friesland, maintained an elementary school for some time in conjunction with the Reformed (archives at Aurich). The Deutschhof, Palatinate, congregation also operated its own elementary school for a time.

When the Mennonites moved to South Russia in 1789 ff., they soon established their own elementary schools, although during the first 50 years they were inadequate because of the poverty of the colonies. In 1820 a movement to improve elementary education was begun in the Molotschna Mennonite colony by planning for secondary schools to train teachers. Such a school was the Ohrloff Zentralschule opened in 1822. Johann Cornies as leader of the Agricultural Union in these Mennonite settlements brought about changes in the educational standards which greatly improved the quality of their elementary schools in the years following 1843. By 1910, the number of elementary schools in the Mennonite villages had grown to 400, taught by 500 teachers, mostly men. After 1880 the Mennonite educational system increasingly came under the control of the state. Following the Bolshevik Revolution, the Mennonites lost their control over their schools, which then were used to destroy rather than to maintain Mennonite ideals, and their educational autonomy which had lasted a century was completely destroyed.

B. *America.* In colonial Pennsylvania, the Mennonites established schools in their communities, although these were not parochial but rather private subscription schools. It was a common practice of the Mennonites to use their churches for school purposes. Sometimes their school was built on the same grounds as the church. J. E. Hartzler mentions more than a dozen Mennonite churches of eastern Pennsylvania prior to 1800 that were used as buildings for elementary schools. Silas Hertzler states that by 1776 at least 16 schools were being conducted by the Mennonites of Pennsylvania. The noted Mennonite schoolteacher Christopher Dock (*q.v.*) taught two such schools in Eastern Pennsylvania, at Skippack and at Salford, in the first half of the 18th century. His *Schulordnung* (1770) was a pioneer book on pedagogy in colonial America. During the second half of the 18th century the public school system replaced the private schools in that state, but not without opposition from the Mennonites and other sectarian groups who wished to maintain the former system.

By the last half of the 19th century the Pennsylvania Mennonites and their daughter colonies to the west had accepted the public school system and were no longer maintaining private schools. Later immigrants, however, such as those who came to Lee County, Iowa, from Germany, established their own school in 1853. The subjects taught in the seven-month term included the catechism, singing, reading, writing, arithmetic, geography, and nature study. Instruction was given in both English and German. At one time there were three of these parochial schools in Lee County and one in Washington County. One of these was continued until shortly before World War I.

Another pioneering experiment in elementary parochial education was launched by the Amish in Iowa when they organized the German School Association of the Old Order Amish (*q.v.*) in 1890. Although their schools placed much emphasis upon learning German and the catechism, several of the elementary subjects were taught both in the summer and in the winter terms.

When the Mennonites from Russia settled on the western plains in the 1870's they established the kind of elementary schools that they had been accustomed to in Europe. This was possible because there were well-trained teachers among the immigrants. Their first schoolhouse in Kansas was a sod house in Gnadenau, in which Johann Harder taught during the winter of 1874-75. Besides teaching the usual elementary subjects, these early instructors taught German, Bible history, and the Mennonite catechism. Although the public schools soon began to offer competition to their church elementary schools, their numbers increased down to the time of World War I. In the 1898 meeting of the Western District Conference (GCM), it was reported that their committee on education had received reports from 42 schools. There were seven others from which reports were not received. In the conference of 1915 it was reported that questionnaires had been sent to 60 schools in the district. The demand for trained teachers led to the development of preparatory schools and eventually colleges among the General Conference Mennonites. The German Teachers' Association (*q.v.*) and the German Teachers' Institute were outgrowths of this educational program. The 1903 Institute, for example, had an attendance of 57. Eventually the competition of the public schools and the dropping of the German language brought about the abandonment of the system of private elementary schools, so that by 1954 only a very few remained.

Soon after most of the General Conference Mennonite elementary schools had been discontinued, the Mennonite Church (MC) and the Conservative Amish Mennonites launched a program of building elementary schools. The first of these was the Mennonite Private School, started at Dover, Del., in 1925. From there the movement spread to Pennsylvania (1938), Virginia (1941), Ohio (1944), Arkansas (1944), Tennessee (1944), Idaho (1945), Florida (1946), New York (1948), Oregon (1948), Arizona (1949), Illinois (1950), Indiana (1950), and Michigan (1953). In the school year 1955-56 there were 86 of these elementary schools, in which nearly 5,000 children were enrolled in the first eight grades. The disappearance of the isolation which Mennonite communities had earlier enjoyed, the tendency of public schools to become completely secular, the realization that certain standards, such as nonresistance and nonconformity to the patterns of a worldly society, were endangered by the public schools, and in some instances a reactionary approach that tried to stop all changes, were in part responsible for this vigorous new movement that was still advancing in 1954.

When Pennsylvania Mennonites migrated to Ontario in the early 19th century, they took the private school pattern with them. Benjamin Eby, leader and bishop in the early Waterloo County settlement, not only taught such a school but wrote his own *Neues Buchstabir- und Lesebuch,* first published in 1839 and often reprinted, also a *Fibel.*

One of the chief reasons why Mennonites from Russia settled in Manitoba in 1874 ff. was that here they were granted complete school autonomy, a privilege which they enjoyed without interruption until 1883. During those years they established their own German private elementary schools, supported by village taxes. They regarded these schools as the "nursery of Christianity" and guarded their privileges zealously. Although at first these Mennonite schools were as good as or better than the public schools of the province, in time they became stagnant because of the growing shortage of well-trained teachers. Progressive elements in the settlements wanted the better schools which public tax money could afford. As a result the school problem became a most serious one in the Mennonite settlements, producing not only intragroup conflict but also conflicts with the provincial regulations designed not only to improve the quality of education but also to impose an English-Canadian culture upon the Mennonites. In the end the Mennonites lost their battle and those conservative groups, the Old Colony Mennonites, who refused to surrender, retreated to Mexico and Paraguay, where they were privileged to establish their own elementary school system. In 1922-24 some 5,000 Manitoba Mennonites settled in Mexico and in 1926-27 some 1,700 in Paraguay. Some of them, however, solved their problem for the time being by moving into Canada's Far North, where public schools have not been organized, and where they are again allowed to carry on their own elementary schools.

The thousands of Mennonite refugees from communist Russia who also settled in Paraguay after World War I and again after World War II have established their own schools. Twelve thousand Mennonites in Paraguay were living in 138 villages in 1950. In these villages 2,330 Mennonite children were enrolled in 94 elementary schools. In 1951 the Mennonites in Brazil had at least one elementary school and in 1950 the Mennonite refugees recently settled in Uruguay had one such school. (See **Education Among the Mennonites** in Russia.)

M.G.

M. S. Harder, "The Origin, Philosophy, and Development of Education Among the Mennonites" (unpublished doctoral dissertation, University of Southern California, 1949); H. P. Peters, *History and Development of Education Among the Mennonites in Kansas* (Hillsboro, 1925); J. E. Hartzler, *Education Among the Mennonites of America* (Danvers, Ill., 1925); J. W. Fretz, *Pilgrims in Paraguay* (Scottdale, 1953); E. K. Francis, *Tradition and Progress Among the Mennonites in Manitoba* (reprint from *MQR* XXIV, October 1950); idem, *The Mennonite School Problem in Manitoba 1874-1919* (reprint from *MQR* XXVII, July 1953); S. Hertzler, "Mennonite Parochial Schools: Why Established and What They Have Achieved," *Proceedings of the Seventh Annual Conference on Mennonite Cultural Problems* (North Newton. 1949); M. Harder, "Disadvantages of the Parochial System," *op. cit.;* L. Froese, "Das pädagogische Kultursystem der mennonitischen Siedlungsgruppe in Russland" (unpublished doctoral dissertation, University of Göttingen, 1949); R. Dollinger, *Geschichte der Mennoniten in Schleswig-Holstein . . .* (Neumünster i. H., 1930).

Elenchus (*Refutation*). Two Latin polemics against the Anabaptists appeared in the 16th century with this Greek word in the title: Zwingli's *In catabaptistarum strophas elenchus* (Zürich, 1527), and Hendrik Anthonieszoon van der Linden's (Antonides, *q.v.*) *Elenchus Anabaptisticus* (1576).

Eleutherobios, Stoffel and **Leonhard,** two 16th-century humanists from Upper Austria (Linz and Wels), whose real name "Freisleben" they translated according to the humanistic fashion of the day into Greek ("Eleutheros" means "frei," i.e., "free"; "bios" means "Leben," i.e., "life"). They belonged to the circle around Bünderlin (*q.v.*), with interests both in the Anabaptist way of life and the world of the "spiritual reformers" (like Hans Denck and Sebastian Franck). They were active in the 1520's. Later they drifted into other directions, mainly Catholic. Their influence upon Anabaptist thinking can be traced in many Anabaptist tracts, mainly where humanist scholarship was needed (church history).

1. *Christoph (Stoffel) Freisleben* in the records sometimes called the "schoolmaster of Wels." He had some humanistic education, most likely at the University of Vienna, was then a follower of Erasmus, and also had some correspondence with the latter. In his religious life he went through all stages: Catholic, Lutheran, Zwinglian, Anabaptist, and again Catholic. In Austrian court records of the 1520's (Nicoladoni, 208) we hear that he was "the beginner and leader" of an Anabaptist group in Wels, Upper Austria, and that also his wife, son, and daughter belonged to this brotherhood. It is most likely that he was won by Hans Hut, who in 1527 was most active all over Upper Austria, and who had also baptized his brother Leonhard (Nicoladoni, 31-33). He now began an intensive activity himself between Linz, Wels, and Passau. Around the turn of 1527-28 Stoffel left his home, perhaps together with Bünderlin, and went to Bavaria and beyond. In 1528 he had a book of his printed in Strasbourg, entitled *Vom wahrhafften Tauff Joannis, Christi und der Apostlen/ Wann und wie der Kindertauff angefangen und eingerissen hat/ Item wie alle Widerreden der Widerchristen wider den Tauff sollen verantwortet werden./* (15 leaves, 4°). (A copy of the 1528 edition may be found in a *Sammelband* of the University of Utrecht; a copy of the second edition of 1550 is found in the Amsterdam Mennonite Library.) It was a book much read among the Anabaptists, supplying them with good arguments, both historical and otherwise, against infant baptism, in this respect almost equaling Hubmaier's tracts on the same subject (excerpts in Rembert, 469-71). Thomas of Imbroich (*q.v.*) quotes it and in handwritten form we find it in no less than five Hutterite codices. A careful study proves that it was of definite Anabaptist character. The fact that another print was necessary in 1550 (when its author no longer cared for his earlier work) shows its continuing popularity among the brethren.

In 1530, Stoffel had found his way back to the Catholic Church; he taught the school of St. Mauritius in Augsburg. Later he returned to Vienna, where he became a syndicus of the University, and in 1547 an official of the bishop of Vienna, said to have been the very soul of the latter's government.

2. *Leonhard (Linhart) Freisleben,* his brother, in the records sometimes called "the schoolmaster of Linz." Like his brother he must have had some

humanistic education (Vienna?); in 1524 he published a German translation of Bugenhagen's (*q.v.*) Latin booklet, *Was und welches die Sünde sei in den Heiligen Geist . . . die nicht vergeben wird, . . .* (Nicoladoni, 13-14). Three years later he also joined the Anabaptists. He admitted later on that Hans Hut (*q.v.*) had baptized him and his wife at Hut's lodging in Linz, in 1527. Soon hereafter we find him in Regensburg, now baptizing and preaching in genuine Anabaptist fashion. On Nov. 15, 1527, he, his wife, and his sister stood before the Regensburg authorities and made a full confession. Afterwards he was expelled from that "Free City," but his later fate is not known. Most likely he followed the steps of his brother.　　　NEFF, R.F.

G. Bossert, Sr., "Zwei Linzer Reformations-Schriftsteller," *Jahrbuch der Gesellsch. f.d. Gesch. des Protestantismus in Österreich.*, 1900, 131 ff.; Rembert, *Wiedertäufer*, 469 ff.; A. Nicoladoni, *Johannes Bünderlin von Linz und die oberösterreichischen Täufergemeinden 1525-1531* (Berlin, 1893); K. Schornbaum, TA V: *Bayern*, Part II ("Regensburg," ed. by L. Theobald); R. Friedmann in *Arch. f. Ref.-Gesch.*, 1931, 238 f.; U. Bergfried, *Verantwortung als theologisches Problem im Täufertum des 16. Jahrhunderts* (Wuppertal-Elberfeld, 1938); *ML* I, 551.

Elfregi, a Dutch youth association founded Dec. 27, 1929, at Zaandam, Dutch province of North Holland, composed of the Mennonite catechumens of the whole Zaan district. A clubhouse at Zaandam was obtained in 1931; besides this, church services for the youth were organized in September 1932 and meetings were held in the Broederschapshuizen (*q.v.*, brotherhood homes) of Elspeet and Schoorl. In 1945 the association was reorganized, becoming a Mennonite scout organization, which now has sections at Zaandam-Wormerveer, Haarlem, Amsterdam, and Groningen. The name Elfregi symbolizes the contacts of the three Mennonite brotherhood homes and camping centers which existed when the Association was founded, Elfregi being formed of the first syllables of Elspeet, Fredeshiem, and Giethoorn. The total membership in 1954 numbered about 400.　　　VDZ.

D. J. C. *"Elfregi" Zaanstreek 10 Jaar* (Zaandam, 1939).

Elgersma, Franciscus (1625-1712), Dutch Reformed minister of Oudkerk 1650, Leeuwarden 1652, Oudeschoot 1661, and Grouw after 1669. He was an ardent opponent of the Mennonites, whom he attacked both orally and in writings. In 1683 he charged Foecke Floris (*q.v.*), the Mennonite preacher of Surhuisterveen who had preached in Grouw, with the heresy of Socinianism (*q.v.*); when the States of Friesland did not take action against Foecke, Elgersma published a book dedicated to the States of Friesland, *Rechtzinnige Leere van het Sacrament des H. Doops . . . teegen Socinianen, Papisten, Mennisten en andere Dwaalgeesten* (Leeuwarden, 1685) and *Kanker der Sociniaansche Ketterye* (Leeuwarden, 1688). Foecke answered his antagonist by *Beschermingh der Waerheyt Godts, of Schriftuyrlijcke Verantwoording* (Leeuwarden, 1687). Thereupon Elgersma published *Seedige Verhandeling van de hooge Verborgentheit der H. Drieeenigheid* (Leeuwarden, 1689). Then Elgersma was attacked by the anonymously published (the author

was probably C. Stapel, *q.v.*) *Klaar vertoog, Dienende tot Wederlegginge van de ongefondeerde Beschuldigingen door Franc. Elgersma . . . tot last van Foeke Floris en andere Christenen, die hy Socinianen noemd* (1689, n.p.). Meanwhile Foecke was arrested at Leeuwarden (1687), and banished from the province of Friesland (1688), but Elgersma, not satisfied that his enemy had been expelled, continued to warn about him and his pernicious doctrines in a Reformed Synod of 1689. (*Biogr. Wb.* II, 719-20; *DB* 1887, 50-69; *ML* I, 551.)　　　VDZ.

Elhorst, Hendrik Jan, b. Oct. 29, 1861, at Wisch in the Dutch province of Gelderland, the oldest son of W. F. G. L. Elhorst and Jacomijntje van der Ploeg, who belonged to an old family of Mennonite ministers; d. March 20, 1924, at Amsterdam. He attended the Gymnasium at Deventer and studied at the university and the Mennonite seminary in Amsterdam 1880-86, became a ministerial candidate in 1886, and served as minister in Irnsum (Friesland) 1887-88, Arnhem 1888-98, The Hague 1898-1900, and Haarlem 1900-6. He then accepted a position as professor of Hebrew and other Semitic languages, Old Testament exegesis, and Hebrew literature in the University of Amsterdam 1906-24. He received the degree of Doctor of Theology from the University of Amsterdam (1891) and an honorary degree from St. Andrew's University (1911), was a member and editor of the Teyler Theological Association, and was one of the founders and editors of *Teylers Theologisch Tijdschrift.*

Of his publications the following should be mentioned: *De Profetie van Micha* (1899), and *Israel in het licht der jongste onderzoekingen* (1906). He also wrote articles for Dutch and foreign periodicals. (*DJ* 1925, 21-32, with portrait; *ML* I, 551 f.)　　　M.L.D.

Elida, Ohio, is a town of 550 inhabitants seven miles northwest of Lima in Allen County. The first Mennonite church in the vicinity was organized in 1841. There are now three Mennonite (MC) congregations in this area, with a combined membership of approximately 450. The Central church is located in Elida, the Salem church three miles northeast of Elida, and the Pike church three miles west of Elida.　　　J.B.S.

Elim Bible School was established in 1929 in Gretna, Man., to meet an urgent need of the Bergthal and Blumenort Mennonite churches of southern Manitoba. The school functioned for two years. It was again opened in 1936. In 1940 it was moved to Altona and a board of directors was elected of eight conference (GCM) churches and one independent. It is a member of the Evangelical Teacher Training Association, and stresses an evangelical teaching along Mennonite principles. In 1953-54 there were five teachers on the staff, A. A. Teichroeb serving as principal, and the enrollment was 107. The Bible school plant consists of a modern four-room school with separate dormitory facilities for girls, boys, a principal's residence, and a teachers' residence.　　　H.J.G.

Elim Gospel Beach, a beautiful retreat ground and summer resort, including 260 acres of ground and 60 acres of water located at the north end of Lac Pelletier, about 26 miles southwest of Swift Current, Sask. The beach is owned and operated by the Mennonite Youth Society (GCM) of Saskatchewan, with the head office at Rosthern, Sask. Elim Gospel Beach offers a quiet place for rest, spiritual worship through retreats, Gospel services, and missionary and Sunday-school conventions. It has an auditorium, restaurant, refreshment booth, and cabins.   J.P.L.

Elim Mennonite Brethren Church, located at Kelstern, Sask., a member of the Herbert District Conference, was organized in 1910 under the leadership of Peter Penner, in whose home the church meetings were held at first. From 1911 to 1918 worship services were held in the newly built Queen Centre school. In 1918 the congregation built its own meetinghouse. The 1955 membership was 54. Following Penner, the leaders were Jacob Mueller, Gustav Ewert, Paul Koop, Jacob J. Knelson, Abram J. Redekopp, John G. Redekopp, and (1955) J. H. Kehler.
                                             J.I.R.

Elim Mennonite Church (GCM), located at Gruenthal, Man., composed largely of Mennonite immigrants from Russia in 1923-26, was organized on Feb. 27, 1927. The members live in the villages of the Old Colony Mennonites who emigrated to Mexico. The central church is located in Gruenthal. There are three additional places of worship. In 1955 the congregation had 250 members and was served by Elder J. J. Enns, two ministers, Abraham H. Froese and Heinrich A. Warkentin, and two deacons, Abraham Driedger and Jacob Woelke. There are two Sunday-school classes, a youth organization, and two sewing circles.   J.J.E.

Elisabeth, an Anabaptist martyr, executed at Leeuwarden in 1549: see **Elisabeth Dirks.**

Elisabeth, an Anabaptist martyr, executed at Gent in 1551: see **Lysbeth Piersins.**

Elisabeth, wife of Michael Matschilder, was in prison at Vienna, Austria, together with her husband 1546-49. On paying a fine they then were released. (*Mart. Mir.* D 73, E 474.)   vDZ.

Elisabeth Berents, an Anabaptist martyr: see **Betken van Gent.**

Elisabeth (Elysabeth) **Bruyne,** an Anabaptist martyr, wife of Janne de Snydere, was burned at the stake at Brussels on May 5, 1571, together with her husband. Their six children were baptized in the cathedral of St. Gudule at Brussels by a Catholic priest the very day the parents were executed. (Verheyden, *Courtrai-Bruxelles,* 102, No. 155.)   vDZ.

Elisabeth Christiaens, an Anabaptist martyr: see **Lysken Smits.**

Elisabeth (Lijsbeth or Lijsken) **Dirks,** an Anabaptist martyr, perhaps the first Mennonite deaconess (*q.v.*), was drowned on May 27 (not March, as van

Braght erroneously states), 1549, at Leeuwarden, Dutch province of Friesland. As a child she had been taken to Tienge, a convent near Leer in East Friesland, Germany. At the age of 12 she was profoundly impressed when she heard that a heretic had been burned for repudiating the sacraments. She managed to get a Bible and as she read it she became more and more doubtful of the doctrines of the Catholic Church. She was later imprisoned for a year on a suspicion of heresy, but on the petition of the nuns she was released and kept under constant supervision, until she fled disguised as a milkmaid. She went to an Anabaptist home in Leer, and joined the brotherhood there. Later she was in Leeuwarden, in the home of an Anabaptist woman by the name of Hadewijk (Hadewych, *q.v.*), the widow of a man who had had to beat the drum at the execution of Sikke Frerichs (*q.v.*) to prevent his addressing the crowd. Because he expressed his horror at the execution and his sympathy for the martyr, whom he had known as a friend, he had to flee and was never heard of again. The two women lived together quietly. Elisabeth apparently was much with Menno Simons, for she was mistaken by her captors to be his wife. On Jan. 15, 1549, the women were arrested. Hadewijk escaped and lived to an advanced age in Emden. Elisabeth was cross-examined and gave a moving testimony of her faith. In spite of terrible torture she neither recanted nor betrayed the names of the brethren. A song was written on her death beginning "Twas een maechdeken van teder leden Elisabeth dat was haren naem." It has 21 stanzas and is found in the *Het Offer des Heeren* (1562), and also in the *Ausbund,* No. 13. She is said to have composed a song, which was included in *Sommige Stichtelycke Liedekens* (Hoorn, 1618), but this song has as yet not been identified.   NEFF.

A. Brons, *Ursprung, Entwickelung und Schicksale der . . . Mennoniten* (Emden, 1912) 89; Blaupot t. C., *Holland* II, 211; Wolkan, *Lieder.* 65; K. Vos, *Menno Simons* (Leiden, 1914) 5, 250, 332 f.; *Offer,* 91-97; *Mart. Mir.* D 81 f., 156 ff., E 481 f., 546; *ML* I, 449 f.

Elisabeth (Betken) **Huevels,** an Anabaptist martyr: see **Betken, Doof.**

Elisabethtal, a village of the Molotschna settlement in the Ukraine, volost of Gnadenfeld, province of Taurida. It was founded in 1823, had about 5,000 acres of land, and in 1913 a population of 436. The elementary school was attended by 52 children. The inhabitants were members of the Pordenau Mennonite Church (*q.v.*), who with the Flemish branch opposed the merger of the Flemish and Frisians in the 1820's as well as any other innovation (such as the Ohrloff Zentralschule and the Bible Society). Concerning the fate of the village and the congregation under the Soviet government, see **Molotschna Settlement, Collectivization, Concentration Camps.** (*ML* I, 552.)   C.B.

Elizabethtown, a borough of 5,000 in northwestern Lancaster Co., Pa., was laid out by Barnabas Hughes in 1753 and named in honor of his wife, Elizabeth. The Harrisburg-Lancaster Pike, built in 1805, passed through the town, thus bringing the stage coaches and the six-horse Conestoga wagons. With Lancaster, Harrisburg, and Lebanon 18 miles away, the town was a prosperous trading center. A variety of industries, the State Crippled Children's Home to the north, and also the Elizabethtown (Church of the Brethren) College on the east side, make it a prominent, prosperous, and clean town for retired Mennonite farmers. The Elizabethtown (MC) Church was established here in 1905, with 223 members in 1953, and there are five other old established congregations in the vicinity, viz., Good's, Bossler's, Risser's, Strickler's, and Stauffer's, in addition to several mission stations, with a total of *ca.* 900 members more.   I.D.L.

Elizabethtown Mennonite Church (MC), located in western Lancaster Co., Pa., is a member of the Lancaster Conference. In 1905 a meetinghouse was built in town, where a number of retired Mennonite farmers had settled. A revival meeting followed with 125 confessions. A young people's Bible meeting was organized in 1911. The congregation in 1955 numbered 225. Noah W. Risser and Clarence E. Lutz were bishops, John W. Hess and Walter D. Keener, Jr., the ministers, and Walter D. Keener deacon.   I.D.L.

Elk Run Brethren Church, located on the Leaksville Road four miles southwest of Luray, Page Co., Va., was a preaching point once a month for the Mennonites (MC) during the last half of the 19th century.   H.A.B.

Elkhart, Ind. (pop. 35,000), a leading commercial and railroad center in northwest Elkhart County, 100 miles east of Chicago, founded in 1832, seat of the Prairie Street Mennonite Church, the oldest city congregation of the Mennonite Church (MC), established in 1871 (two daughter churches have since been established in the city, in addition to two U.M.C. congregations). Elkhart achieved importance as a strong center of life and activity for the Mennonite Church (MC), first through the establishment here of the Mennonite Publishing Company (*q.v.*) by John F. Funk in 1867, which was the publishing center for the M.C. until 1908, then through the establishment of the headquarters office of the Mennonite Board of Missions and Charities in 1892. From here the first foreign missionaries of the church were sent out in 1898 (to India), and here the first church school was established in 1894 as Elkhart Institute, which was moved to Goshen in 1903 to become Goshen College. Elkhart is also the seat of the Bethel Publishing Company and Bookstore, the publishing agency of the United Missionary Church.   H.S.B.

Elkhart County, Ind., the center county in the northern tier of Indiana counties on the Michigan border, is the seat of one of the largest concentrations of Mennonite and Amish populations east of the Mississippi. The total of 43 organized congregations with nearly 8,800 members is distributed as follows: M.C., 17 churches with 4,200 members; U.M.C., 10 churches with 1,400; O.O.A., 7 churches with 600; G.C.M., 3 with 700; C.A.M., 2 with 425;

O.O.M., 2 with 250; A.M., 2 with 250. Expansion into Lagrange County on the east and St. Joseph County on the west has added 28 additional churches, to make a total of 71 with 11,000 members (1953). Two large O.O. Amish settlements with a total of 2,300 members are included in the above figures, the larger being that east of Goshen and reaching well into Lagrange County with 1,600 members in 23 congregations.

The first Mennonite settlers came from eastern Ohio in 1845, locating west of Goshen in the Yellow Creek district. The first Amish contingent arrived in 1841, locating east of Goshen in Clinton Township.

The county has been the scene of several schisms: (1) the Old Order (Wisler) Mennonite of 1871 west of Goshen; (2) the Brenneman (UMC) of 1874 in the same area; (3) the Progressive Amish *vs.* Old Order Amish, east of Goshen about 1860-65; (4) the Central Conference group in 1892 at Silver Street; (5) the similar schism in 1924 at Nappanee, Middlebury, Topeka, and Goshen; (6) the Burkholder Amish in 1948.

The county since 1894 has been the seat of Elkhart Institute-Goshen College and of the Mennonite Board of Missions and Charities (MC) since 1892. It has always been a strong center of Mennonite life and influence.   H.S.B.

A. E. Weaver, *A Standard History of Elkhart County, Indiana* (2 vv., Chicago, 1916).

Elkhart Institute (1894-1903), the forerunner of Goshen College, was a secondary school established at Elkhart, Ind., by an unofficial group of laymen and ministers to offer educational opportunities to the young people of the Mennonite Church (MC). During the first year, Aug. 21, 1894, to June 4, 1895, it was a small proprietary school owned and operated by Dr. H. A. Mumaw, a Mennonite physician with a strong interest in education, and conducted in the G. A. R. Hall in downtown Elkhart. The enrollment was small, chiefly of short-term students (10-20 weeks) securing training in commercial subjects and a review of elementary school subjects for prospective teachers' examinations, although the high-sounding name, Elkhart Institute of Art, Science, and Industry, promised much more.

The real history of the school began with the transfer of the school from proprietary to corporate ownership on May 16, 1895, when the Elkhart Institute Association (*q.v.*) was incorporated to take over the school and continued to operate it at Elkhart to 1903, then in Goshen as Goshen College to 1906, when it turned over the school to the newly organized official church agency, the Mennonite Board of Education.

After a period of weakness (1895-98), during which the principals (four of them in succession), much of the small staff, and most of the small student body were non-Mennonite and the program of the school was poorly defined, N. E. Byers, B.A., a Mennonite from Sterling, Ill., became the principal. Byers reorganized the school, established it on a sound academic basis, and led its development into a junior college (1903) and finally a senior college (1908). J. S. Hartzler, a preacher of Topeka, Ind., was the other strong figure in the school, along with the president of the board, preacher-evangelist J. S. Coffman. Lewis Kulp, treasurer of the board, early business manager and financial supporter, was a strong asset. C. Henry Smith, who came in as teacher the same year as Byers (1898), was an important faculty member. Other important teachers were D. S. Gerig (1900-3), E. J. Zook (1901-3), J. W. Yoder (1900-2), and W. K. Jacobs (1899-1903).

The academic program included Latin-Scientific (College Preparatory), Seminary (3-year course), Commercial, Bible, and Normal curriculums, plus a summer school from the beginning and a special Bible Term (six weeks in the winter beginning in 1898). The teachers in the Bible Term were S. G. Shetler, Daniel Kauffman, J. S. Coffman, A. D. Wenger, and George R. Brunk. The student body grew more rapidly beginning about 1900, reaching a peak of 245 in 1902-3, including the Summer Session and Special Bible Term (Academic 134, Commercial 59, Bible 52). A total of 73 certificates of graduation were issued: 23 commercial, 6 Bible, 12 Normal, and 32 Latin-Scientific and Seminary. The Latin-Scientific course actually included about the equivalent of first year college. A considerable number of the Latin-Scientific and Normal graduates went on to advanced college, university, and professional study to become leaders in various fields (1900, S. F. Gingerich; 1901, I. R. Detweiler, F. S. Ebersole, C. E. Bender, J. M. Kurtz, John Umble; 1902, W. B. Christophel, G. J. Lapp, A. B. Rutt, O. C. Yoder, D. B. Zook; 1903, S. T. Miller). Among the outstanding Bible graduates were A. J. Steiner and I. W. Royer of 1900, Mrs. J. A. Ressler (Lina Zook) of 1901, and I. R. Detweiler of 1902. An Alumni Association was organized in 1901 (now the Goshen College A.A.) composed of all those who completed a course of two years or longer.

The first and only building of the Institute was dedicated Feb. 22, 1896, located on South Prairie Street almost opposite the Mennonite meetinghouse. The school had no other campus than the lot on which the building stood. The need for space for expansion led to the search for a new location which culminated in the move to Goshen in 1903 as the result of an attractive financial offer, with the condition that the name become Goshen College.

From 1898 on the school had an active student life with a strong religious and Mennonite emphasis, and many of the student activities and organizations (Y.P.C.A. and literary societies, for instance) which played such a vital role in the later Goshen College were established in the old Institute.

The Elkhart Institute pioneered in a great movement of education in the Mennonite Church (MC) which has now become a powerful force in the life of the denomination with three colleges, ten high schools, a theological seminary, and two schools of nursing. It had to face much opposition and misunderstanding, since the great majority of the church was opposed to it, although the two local Indiana-Michigan Conferences (Mennonite and Amish) and the General Conference endorsed it in the period 1898-1902. Those who fought the battle for education in these early days, board members, faculty and staff, and students, deserve much credit. Chief among them, without whom the enterprise would probably not have succeeded, were J. S. Coffman, N. E. Byers, and J. S. Hartzler. H.S.B.

Elkhart Institute Memorial, published by the Elkhart Institute Alumni Association (Goshen, Ind., 1903); *Catalogue of the Elkhart Institute,* at Elkhart annually 1896-1903 except 1897; *The Institute Monthly* (Elkhart, beginning October 1898, becoming *The Goshen College Record* in 1903); *Fiftieth Anniversary of Goshen College 1895-1945,* published by the Faculty of Goshen College (Goshen, 1945); John Umble, *History of Goshen College* (Goshen, 1954); J. E. Hartzler, *Education Among the Mennonites of America* (Danvers, Ill., 1925); *Golden Anniversary Alumni Directory of Goshen College* (includes the Elkhart Institute directory also) (Goshen, Ind., 1951); C. Henry Smith, *The Education of a Mennonite Country Boy* (mimeographed, Bluffton, 1943); *idem,* "A Pioneer Educator—N. E. Byers," *Menn. Life* III (1948) 44-46; N. E. Byers, "The Times in Which I Lived," *Menn. Life* VII (1952) 77-81.

Elkhart Institute Association, a stock company incorporated in the state of Indiana May 16, 1895, with 15 original stockholders, for the purpose of owning and operating a Mennonite school in the city of Elkhart, Ind., specifically to take over the Elkhart Institute from its owner, Dr. H. A. Mumaw. The original capital stock was $10,000, later raised to $25,000. The Association elected a board of directors of nine members which carried on the work of the Association. The first president was Dr. H. A. Mumaw, the secretary A. C. Kolb. J. S. Coffman was the president from 1896 to his death in 1899, followed by M. S. Wambold 1899-1902, and John Blosser, 1902-6. J. S. Hartzler was secretary 1896-1906, and Lewis Kulp treasurer 1898-1904. In 1901 the board of directors was enlarged from 9 to 25, selected from the various conference districts of the Mennonite Church throughout the United States and Canada; previously the membership had been largely local of Elkhart and Northern Indiana. In 1903 the Association moved the school to Goshen, renaming it Goshen College, although the corporate name remained unchanged. In 1906 the Association turned over all its assets to the Mennonite Board of Education, organized in that year as the official educational corporation of the Mennonite Church (MC), although the Association was not legally dissolved until Oct. 16, 1911. Thus what had originally been a local self-appointed group of interested persons in northern Indiana developed finally into a nation-wide official church board. The men of the Association were the pioneers who for eleven years carried the burden and opened the way for Goshen College with its highly significant contribution in educational leadership and service to the Mennonite Church (MC). H.S.B.

Elkhart-Lagrange County (Ind.) *Old Order Amish Settlement,* now (1955) consisting of 24 districts with a membership of *ca.* 1,850, was founded in 1841 by settlers from Somerset Co., Pa., and Holmes Co., Ohio, who settled first in Clinton Township about 5 miles east of Goshen, then in Newberry Township in Lagrange County, about 15 miles farther east. The first preacher was Joseph Miller, one of the very

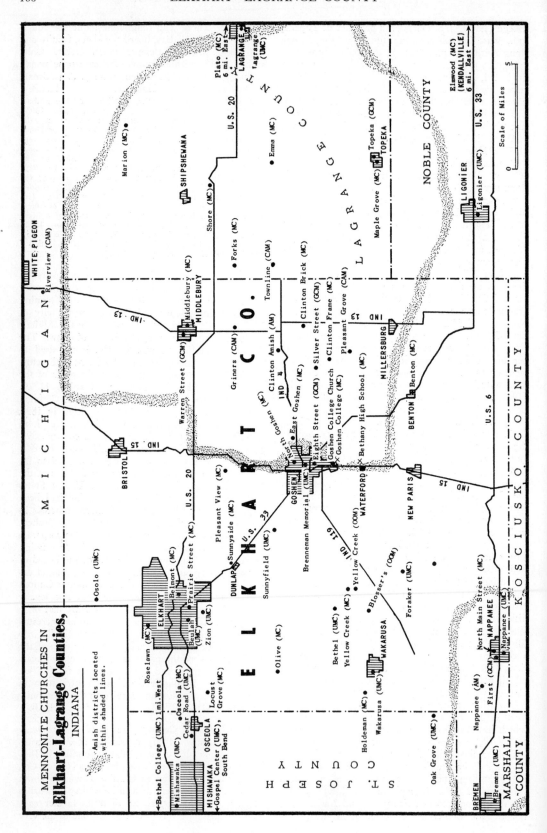

first settlers, who was ordained bishop in 1848. The second preacher was Isaac Schmucker from Holmes Co., Ohio, who arrived the same year and was ordained as the first Amish bishop in Indiana (1843). The settlement has spread eastward until it now occupies an almost solid block 12 x 25 miles. In the early 1860's a split occurred between the Old Order and the more progressive elements. The latter group began to build meetinghouses and ultimately formed a part of the Indiana-Michigan Amish Mennonite Conference, 1888-1915, organized chiefly in the Clinton Frame and the Forks congregations. About 1855 another Amish group from Fairfield Co., Ohio, settled near Topeka (Maple Grove congregation), joining the progressive conference group.

In the 1890's another group broke off, forming the Griner Conservative Amish Mennonite group. In 1945 still another group broke off to form the Burkholder Amish Mennonite group. Today the descendants of the original Amish settlement constitute a total of at least 4,000 members in the area east of Goshen, of whom about 1,600 have remained true to the Old Order pattern, maintaining rigidly the older forms of worship, costume, and home life. They still use the Pennsylvania-German dialect, and rigidly reject modern conveniences such as automobiles, telephones, gasoline engines, and electricity. Next to the Holmes County (Ohio) and the smaller Lancaster County (Pa.) areas, it is the largest Old Order Amish settlement in North America.

The smaller Amish settlement around Nappanee, some 25-30 miles southwest of the Clinton settlement, has a different origin and has had little connection with the latter. H.S.B.

H. Borntreger, *Eine Geschichte der ersten Ansiedlung der Amischen Mennoniten und die Gründung ihrer ersten Gemeinde im Staate Indiana* (Elkhart, 1907).

Elkton Mennonite Church (GCM), now extinct, located in Hickory Co., Mo., was established in 1868 by settlers from Berne, Ind., and a few from Wayne Co., Ohio. It participated in the sessions of the General Conference Mennonite Church in 1884, 1887, and 1890, but had died out by 1896. The leader of the settlement was the preacher P. S. Lehman from Berne, who continued to serve to the end, when he moved back to Berne in 1896. Some of the congregation moved to the Bethel Church in Morgan Co., Mo., others back to Berne. By 1910 practically no Mennonites were left in the settlement. M.G.

H. P. Krehbiel, *History of the General Conference of the Mennonite Church of North America* (2 vv., Canton and Newton, 1898, 1938); D. Gratz, *Bernese Anabaptists* (Scottdale, 1953) 164 f.

Elkton (Mich.) United Missionary Church had a membership of 24 in 1952, with R. Dettwiler as pastor.

Elle Nannincxs Smit, an Anabaptist martyr of Winkel, Dutch province of North Holland, was sentenced to death by the Court of Holland and beheaded on Dec. 22, 1540. He was apparently baptized in February 1534; he had taken part in the journey to Münster and was seized at Bergklooster (*q.v.*). He did not ask for pardon, but remained steadfast. (*Inv. Arch. Amst.* I, Nos. 234, 744, 745.) vDZ.

Ellenberger, a Swiss Mennonite refugee family living in the Palatinate as early as 1717. In that year Michael Ellenberger lived at Gönnheim and Hans Ellenberger at Branchweilerhof. In 1738 a Christian Ellenberger lived at Obersülzen. Christian Neff's *Mennonitisches Adressbuch* of 1936 listed Ellenbergers as members of the Friedelsheim congregation. Jakob Ellenberger (*q.v.,* 1800-79) was a well-known minister of the Friedelsheim, Germany, Mennonite Church. His nephew Jakob Ellenberger (*q.v.,* 1831-1901) served as minister in the Mennonite churches of Ibersheim, Eichstock, and Friedelsheim. Albrecht Ellenberger arrived in America Sept. 9, 1749, with a large number of Mennonite and Amish immigrants. Jacob Ellenberger, a cabinetmaker from Bavaria, settled in the Lee Co., Iowa, Mennonite community in 1847. Two years later he was chosen preacher by the Lee County church, although there is no proof he ever served in the office. A Mennonite Elder Henry Ellenberger, father of Jacob, moved into the community in 1850, where he served the church many years. The family is still represented in the Lee County Mennonite settlement. Adolf Ellenberger was the last minister of the Friedrichstadt Mennonite Church, Schleswig-Holstein; he emigrated to the United States, settling near Los Angeles, Cal. M.G.

M. Gingerich, *The Mennonites in Iowa* (Iowa City, 1939).

Ellenberger, Jakob, minister of the Mennonite congregation at Friedelsheim, Germany, b. Oct. 18, 1800, at Gönnheim, Palatinate, d. Feb. 8, 1879, attended the pietistic school in Beuggen, Baden, 1824-29, taught the Mennonite children at Friedelsheim after passing his examination at the normal school at Kaiserslautern, was chosen preacher in 1832 and ordained at a conference at Weierhof by J. Molenaar of Crefeld, and served the Friedelsheim congregation with great blessing until his death. He helped to formulate the Palatine catechism, the *Formularbuch,* and the hymnal of 1832 and 1854. In addition he compiled the book of tunes (see **Choral Books**), and sponsored the development of singing in his church by organizing a men's choir. Both Jakob Ellenberger of Friedelsheim and Heinrich Ellenberger, preacher at Eppstein, received subsidies from the Amsterdam congregation. NEFF.

Jakob Ellenberger (Frankfurt, 1879); *Inv. Arch. Amst.* I, Nos. 1545 f., 1549; II, 2742-45; *ML* I, 552.

Ellenberger, Jakob, nephew of the preceding, b. Aug. 2, 1831, at Gönnheim, Palatinate, Germany, d. Feb. 5, 1901, at Friedelsheim, became a bookbinder in Dürkheim (1853), entered the missionary training school at Basel in 1867, was unanimously chosen as preacher by the congregation at Ibersheim, but resigned in 1871. In 1872 he served the congregation at Eichstock, Bavaria, and from 1881 to the end of his life he worked with great success at Friedelsheim. His outstanding contributions are three volumes of *Bilder aus dem Pilgerleben* (1878,

1880, and 1883) and the *Christlicher Gemeinde-Kalender* (1892), which was founded at his instigation. (*Gem.-Kal.*, 1902, 76 ff.; *ML* I, 552.)

NEFF.

Ellert (Ellart) **Jans,** an Anabaptist martyr, a tailor of Woerden, Dutch province of South Holland, baptized by Gillis van Aken (*q.v.*), was executed by burning at the stake with five men and two women of the same faith at Amsterdam on March 20, 1549. He could have taken part in a successful escape, but declined because he had a wooden leg. He cheerfully went to the place of execution and talked to his cousin Jan Jans whom he met on the way, so that all that heard were amazed. Through the iron bars of his prison he handed his cousin his will, and admonished him to join the brotherhood of the cross. His cousin did so. His martyrdom is sung in the hymn which begins, "Tis nu schier al vervult ons broeders getal," in *Veelderhande Liedekens* (1566 and succeeding editions).   NEFF, vDZ.

F. C. Wieder, *Schriftuurlijke Liedekens* (The Hague, 1900) 193; Grosheide, *Bijdrage*, 155 f., 308; *Mart. Mir.* D 82-84, E 483 f.; *ML* I, 552; II, 390.

Ellerwald, West Prussia: see **Elbing.**†

Ellice Township, Perth Co., Ont. Meetings (MC) were held here in a Mennonite home as early as 1854.   J.C.F.

Elm Creek (Man.) Mennonite Brethren Church, located a few miles northeast of the town by that name, was organized in 1929 with 20 charter members and H. J. Wiebe as first pastor. In 1954 it had a new up-to-date meetinghouse, with 183 members and J. G. Wiens as pastor, and J. J. Funk as assistant pastor.   H.NE.

Elm River Hutterite Bruderhof (Schmiedeleut), one mile west of Newton, Man., was founded in 1934 by Preacher Zacharias Hofer and ten families from the Rosedale Bruderhof near Elie, Man. They bought land and built houses and barns. Zacharias Hofer, who was born in Russia, died in 1936. In 1935 David Hofer was chosen minister. In 1947 the Bruderhof numbered 153 souls.   D.D.

Elmira, Ont., a town of 2,800, is located in the northern part of Waterloo County about 12 miles north of Kitchener. Approximately 2,200 Mennonites live within shopping distance of the town. The various branches of Mennonites in the community are Old Order Mennonites, 60 per cent; Mennonites (MC), 35 per cent; and the Dave Martin group, 5 per cent. Elmira is centrally located in this Mennonite settlement, which also extends into Wellington County. Approximately 10 per cent of the Mennonites live in town or in the villages in the community. Mennonites have lived in the community since the early 1800's. The Elmira Mennonite (MC) Church (256 members in 1953) was established in the town in 1924. The Old Order Mennonite church at the edge of town has a total of over 400 members in two divided groups.   H.S.Ba.

Elmira Old Order Mennonite Church, formerly known as the West Woolwich Mennonite Church, is located at the western limits of the town of Elmira, in Woolwich Twp., Waterloo Co., Ont. Two acres were donated for church purposes about 1853 by Christian Schneider and a frame church was erected, which is still standing. A large cemetery adjoins the church. Two additions have been built to the church. The church, which seats 500, is often filled to capacity. In 1939 the church was divided. Since that time both groups have held regular church services in the building. One group drives horses; the other uses cars. Each group has a baptized membership of at least 200. The Elmira Mennonite (MC) group uses the old cemetery conjointly with the O.O. groups.

The first minister here was Peter Martin and the first deacon William Hembling. Other ministers were David B. Martin, Amos Gingrich, Jesse Bauman, Edward G. Martin, Amsey Martin, and George Brubacher.   I.G.M.

Elmira Mennonite Church (MC), in Elmira, Woolwich Twp., Waterloo Co., Ont., a member of the Ontario Conference, was organized on Aug. 31, 1924, with Oliver D. Snider as minister. Deacons of the congregation include Reuben Dettwiler, 1929-34, and Aaron B. Martin, ordained in 1935. O. D. Snider was ordained bishop in 1936. Simeon W. Hurst of this congregation, who was ordained to the ministry in 1940, is now serving in Tanganyika, Africa. Others who were ordained within the congregation are Howard S. Bauman in 1945 and Osiah W. Horst in 1946 for the pastorate of the Latschar congregation. A number of members of the Elmira Church became charter members of the recently organized Bethel and Hawkesville congregations. In 1954 the membership was 264, with Howard S. Bauman as pastor.   H.S.BA.

Elmspring (Tanny) Hutterite Bruderhof (Lehrerleut) established in 1929 near Warner, Alberta. In 1950 it had a population of 177, with Michael Entz serving as leading preacher.

Elmspring (S.D.) Hutterite Bruderhof was established in 1877 on the James River at Alexandria near Parkston, S.D., 65 miles northwest of Yankton, by 13 Hutterite families from Johannisruh, Ukraine, Russia, led by Jacob Wipf, a teacher and preacher. This was the last of the three original Hutterite colonies to be established in North America and is the one which with its descendant colonies or Bruderhofs has been called the "Lehrerleut," one of the three Hutterite subgroups. The development of daughter colonies was as follows: (1) in 1892 Rockfort Bruderhof, 6 miles north of Elmspring; (2) in 1900 New Elmspring, 3 miles southwest of Elmspring; (3) in 1910 Milford Bruderhof in Beadle County, 80 miles north of Elmspring. Due to persecution experienced during World War I a considerable number of families removed to Alberta in 1918, establishing there five Bruderhofs, viz., Milford (Raymond County) and Rockfort, Elmspring, and New Elmspring (all three in Magrath County), and Big Bend in Woolford County. In South

Dakota, Milford and New Elmspring were closed, while Elmspring and Rockfort continued but in affiliation with the Schmiedeleut (*q.v.*). In 1955 the Lehrerleut had 30 Bruderhofs, 19 in Alberta, 8 in Montana, and 3 in Saskatchewan, with a total population of *ca.* 3,000 souls.

Joseph Hofer and Michael Hofer, the two Hutterite conscientious objectors who died in Alcatraz prison during World War I as a result of brutal treatment by the military prison officials, came from the Elmspring group.   J.P.E., H.S.B.

Elmwood, a village in Grey Co., Ont., on the county line between Bruce and Grey, about six miles north of Hanover, was a location in which Mennonites (MC) were to be found from before 1870, when ministers from Waterloo County were sent to Brant Township every eight weeks to conduct services which alternated in the homes of Mennonite families living there. Before 1875 these families were losing members to the United Brethren Church. In 1875, when the Mennonite Brethren in Christ were organized in Ontario, Elmwood became one of their earliest places of worship. It was the village into which the retired farmers moved when they left the farms in that community. The M.B.C.'s first worshiped in private homes in the village and then in the U.B. Church. As the U.B. group lost out and the M.B.C.'s grew in strength, the U.B. church building was taken over by the M.B.C. group, whose work continued well into the present century. Then as Mennonite young people were attracted away from their homes, the M.B.C. membership decreased, until only a few members remained. In 1948 the church building was sold. This work was not far from the Mennonite settlements near Lake Huron—Brant Township, Hanover, and Port Elgin and Culross townships. From Elmwood many M.B.C. ministers, missionaries, and pioneers went to Alberta in the early 20th century.   J.C.F.

Elmwood Mennonite Brethren Church, 155 Kelvin St., Winnipeg, Man., formerly North End Mennonite Brethren Church, 621 College Ave., Winnipeg, originated in 1907, when several brethren from Winkler, Man., under the guidance of the late John Warkentin, opened a mission in Winnipeg. In 1913 the Northern District Conference took over the mission, which by now had developed into a mission church. The membership in 1913 numbered 33; by 1926 it had risen to 60. In that year the membership doubled through immigration from Russia; in 1936 the membership was 550.

The first church was constructed in 1929. Originally the whole congregation met for worship at this North End meetinghouse, but the increase of membership and the housing and rental conditions made it expedient for the congregation to assemble at three different localities, North End, South End, and North Kildonan, where later on church buildings were either purchased or built. Besides these three groups in Winnipeg, the church at that time had affiliated rural branches in Springstein, Marquette, McAuley, Foxwarren, and Moosehorn-Ashern.

The larger groups gradually developed into independent churches. In 1936 the South End group was organized with a membership of 110, and in 1942 the Springstein group with a membership of 50. Until 1937 the city missionary was also entrusted with the leadership of the church. Since that year the congregation has had its leading minister, while the city missionary has been solely engaged in city mission work.

Because of need for more room and a more central location, the church voted on Nov. 22, 1953, to sell the church building on 621 College Avenue and build a new church at 155 Kelvin Street in the district called Elmwood, the name to be changed accordingly to "Elmwood Mennonite Brethren Church." The new meetinghouse seats approximately 1,100 persons, and has an educational building adjacent to it. The present (1955) membership stands at 420 with 13 ordained ministers and 4 deacons, with I. W. Redekopp serving as pastor.†
                                                  I.W.R.

Elmwood Mennonite Brethren in Christ Church, now extinct, in Grey Co., Ont., had a membership of 82 in 1911.   M.G.

Eloisten, followers of Eloy Pruystinck (*q.v.*).

Eloy (Loy, Lodewijk) **Pruystinck,** Anabaptist leader, by trade a slater, who was taken prisoner at Antwerp, Belgium, in July 1544, and after recanting was burned at the stake on Oct. 23, 1544. He had many followers, called *Eloisten* or *Loisten,* not only in Antwerp, but also in Amsterdam and other towns. It is possible, though the matter is not clear, that he was a follower of David Joris (*q.v.*).   vDZ.

Inv. Arch. Amst. I, Nos. 275-76, 290, 292, 294, 295, 306; *DB* 1917, 143; Rembert, *Wiedertäufer,* 168, Note 2, 175.

Else, wife of Gysbrecht van Baeck: see **Lostadt, Else van.**

Elsge(n) of Wesel, an Anabaptist martyr, was drowned at Alkmaar, Dutch province of North Holland, on June 17, 1539, together with two other women, for having been rebaptized. Particulars are lacking. Mellink supposes her to have been a follower of David Joris (*q.v.*).   vDZ.

Mellink, *Wederdopers,* 173; *DB* 1909, 22 f.; *Inv. Arch. Amst.* I, No. 748, 4.

Elsgen Heynderic Schenckelberghsdochter, of Clever Ham (near Cleve, Germany?), an Anabaptist martyr, was put into a sack and drowned on Jan. 23, 1539, at Delft, Dutch province of South Holland, because she had been rebaptized. Three other women were executed with her. She was probably a follower of David Joris (*q.v.*). (*Inv. Arch. Amst.* I, No. 749.)   vDZ.

Elsken (Elsgen), wife of Joriaen Ketel (*q.v.*), was beheaded at Utrecht in the Netherlands on July 18, 1539, because she had been rebaptized.   vDZ.

Inv. Arch. Amst. I, Nos. 209, 212; *Berigten Historisch Genootschap Utrecht* IV, 2, 1851, 139; *DB* 1919, 21.

Elspeet, a village (pop. 1,500) in the Veluwe district, Dutch province of Gelderland. Two miles south of this village on a fine wooded plot are found the buildings of the Doopsgezind Broederschapshuis Elspeet (Elspeet Mennonite Brotherhood House). Its first simple building was opened on June 1, 1925. In course of time more buildings were added; in 1928 a chapel (capacity 200) was dedicated. During World War II the buildings, all built of timber on concrete foundations, were severely damaged; they have been restored. Besides camping grounds for youth, there are 72 rooms (about 200 beds). The Broederschapshuis Elspeet, followed by other such houses elsewhere, was built to lodge the meetings of the *Vereeniging voor Gemeentedagen* (*q.v.*) and its several subdivisions, and also for the youth conferences. In 1936 the Mennonite World Conference met here. It is also used as a recreation center, led by a Mennonite minister as a *pater familias*, where Mennonites and non-Mennonites may spend their holidays in a Christian atmosphere for moderate price. It is opened each year from about May until September. The first president of the Board of Management was J. Koekebakker, followed by A. H. van Drooge (*q.v.*) and C. Nijdam (*q.v.*). In 1953 the president was N. van der Zijpp. Mrs. M. Bennema-Feenstra (*q.v.*) was treasurer for nearly 25 years.

vDZ.

Brieven van de Ver. voor Gemeentedagen VIII, No. 6 (June 1925) 4-10; *ibid.*, XI, No. 6 (June 1928) 2-5; *DJ* 1951, 27-35.

Elspeetsche Vereeniging: see **Broederschapswerk, Gemeenschap voor Doopsgezind.**

Elten, von, a prominent old Mennonite family in Crefeld, which is still flourishing there. Their progenitor, Gottschalk Dietrichs, was born in Cologne *ca.* 1580. In 1609 he purchased the estate "auf der Deusz" in München-Gladbach-Eicken, and was a wholesale dealer in yarn and linen. His son was Jan Gottschalks (*q.v.*) auf der Deusz. Jan's son Gottschalk Jansen von Elten lived later on in Rheydt, was expelled in 1694, and in the same year acquired citizenship in Crefeld. The second son of Gottschalk Dietrichs, Dietrich Gottschalks, went to Haarlem when the Mennonites were expelled from Gladbach, but in 1664 he moved to the Merxhof in Rheydt-Bonnenbroich, and was therefore called Dietrich Gottschalks Merx, and at least after 1681, also von Elten. His son Gottschalk Dietrichs von Elten or Merx bought the Kütges estate in Rheydt-Geneicken in 1684. Expelled in 1694, he betook himself to Wesel, but acquired Crefeld citizenship in 1697. He died April 18, 1707, in Wesel. In Rheydt the family has also continued the linen business. In 1694 all the Mennonites in and around Rheydt were suddenly arrested by Palatine commissars of the duchy of Jülich, taken to Jüchen and Pfaffendorf, and all their goods confiscated. Among the 40 persons seized, the two von Eltens were especially threatened; but in spite of threats of imprisonment and execution they could not be moved to recant. After days of misery the "heretics" were released upon payment of 8,000 Reichstaler in addition to 800 Reichstaler to cover the cost, which was raised by brethren in Crefeld and Holland (*Inv. Arch. Amst.* I, No. 1427).

Most of the families then, like the von Eltens, moved to Crefeld, where a place of refuge had been opened under the house of Orange for the persecuted, and laid the foundation for the prosperity of the city. The Mennonite congregation now felt itself strong enough to build an adequate church (1695); on Jan. 19, 1696, the first wedding was performed in it. William III of England, who belonged to the house of Orange, and the minister of the States-General furthermore induced the Palatine Elector to restore the confiscated and partly wasted Mennonite estates in 1697; the exiles were also permitted to offer their houses and other goods for sale. The proceeds made it possible for them to share in the extension (the first extension) of the city.

Concerning their expulsion, the Mennonites of Rheydt had a record made in Crefeld in 1696 by the notary Hermann Marthens in the presence of the mayors, Johannes Reiners and Johannes Bruckmann (as witnesses), which describes their sufferings. It was printed verbatim 107 years later in Crefeld with the title, *Instrumentum Publicum wegen desjenigen, was bei denen Churfl. Pfaltzischen Herren Commissarien gegen die Protestante Menoniste zu Rheydt in Anno 1694 in facta vorgenohmen und sich zugetragen* (24 pp.).

In the family chronicle, which has been carefully compiled by Friedrich von Elten (b. 1835), with the family trees of most of the older Crefeld Mennonite families, to whom the von Eltens are related, as the op den Graaf, Scheuten, von der Leyen, Jentges, von Beckerath, Cornelius Floh, van Dulken families, the reason for the persecution in Rheydt is also stated (according to an oral tradition from the 18th century): "The origin of this persecution I heard from a reliable source as follows: the flourishing linen business of the Mennonites there was coveted by the Reformed. The Mennonites gave money to the lord of Rheydt for protection and freedom from military service. The Reformed therefore had to render more guard and military service; therefore they sued their lord. The Mennonites would not contribute to the cost of the suit. All of this embittered the Reformed to such an extent that they besought the Palatine elector, their feudal lord, to persecute the Mennonites, as can be seen from their petition full of lies."

The von Elten family has successfully shared in the thriving linen and silk industry in Crefeld. Most of the branches of the family still adhere to the faith of their fathers, and several members are always active in the consistory of the Crefeld Mennonite Church.

In Rotterdam there have also been members of this family. Antony Godtschalck was before 1632 a preacher of the High German Mennonites in Rotterdam. The minister of the Flemish congregation here in 1672-85, Adam van Reed (Rheydt?), was married to his daughter Marytje Antheunis Godtschalck. Her brother Wouter Antoni van Elten was preacher of the same congregation, 1680-83. In the year 1683 he moved to Amsterdam, where he died Nov. 11, 1689.

Jan Godtschalcx, also called J. G. van Elten (*q.v.*), a weaver who moved from Gladbach to the Dutch town of Nijmegen in 1655, and Dierick Godtschalck, also a weaver, who migrated from the territory of Jülich to Nijmegen in 1657, obviously belonged to a collateral branch of this von Elten family.

Jakob Gottschalk (*q.v.*), elder of the German-town congregation, whose Mennonite ancestors lived first in Gladbach and then in Goch, from where Jakob Gottschalk emigrated to Pennsylvania in 1701, though he and his family did not bear the name of von Elten, may have been members of the same family (*MQR* I, 1949, 35-47).   K.R., W.N.

H. Keussen, *Gesch. der Stadt und Herrlichkeit Crefeld* (Crefeld, 1865) 179 f.; L. Schmitz, *Gesch. der Herrlichkeit Rheydt* (1887) 142; Rembert, *Wiedertäufer*, 158, 530 ff.; W. Niepoth, "Beiträge zur Forschung über menn. Familiennamen," in *Die Heimat* (Crefeld, 1935) 117 ff.; *DB* 1874, 1 ff.; 1875, 68 ff.; K. Vos, *Gesch. der Doopsgez. Gemeente te Rotterdam* (Rotterdam, 1907) 42; *ML* I, 563.

Elten, Jan Godtschalks van (Jan Godtschalcx), rendered invaluable service to the Mennonite congregation at Nijmegen, in the Dutch province of Gelderland, which arose about 1635. In consequence of the decree of expulsion of Dec. 30, 1652, he had emigrated from Gladbach in the Jülich region with his family in 1654, and on April 11, 1655, became a citizen of Nijmegen. He was a weaver. On July 11, 1656, he was ordained deacon by Jan ter Mehr of Crefeld. For a period of more than 40 years he served by reading sermons to the congregation, and especially by his management of the church capital, so that it contributed much to the thriving growth of the congregation.   NEFF.

P. C. G. Guyot, *Bijdrage tot de Gesch. der Doopsgezinden te Nijmegen* (Nijmegen, 1845) 61; *DB* 1874, 1 ff., and 1875, 68 ff.; *ML* I, 563.

Elton (Pa.) Mennonite Church (MC), a small congregation listed in the *Mennonite Yearbook and Directory* 1906-1908 with 24 members, Alexander Weaver, preacher, and D. S. Yoder, deacon, but by 1912 apparently incorporated with the neighboring Weaver congregation.   H.S.B.

Elze Quirijnsdochter, a revolutionary Anabaptist, who together with her husband Harman Henricxszn and others was taken prisoner at Amsterdam on July 18, 1540. Before this time she had been in Antwerp, Belgium. She was drowned on March 28, 1541, at Amsterdam. This group likely were followers of Batenburg (*q.v.*). During the trial she revealed that she had been taken *in't verbont* (into the union) of the Anabaptists by Cornelis van Schiltwolt, an otherwise unknown leader; she became a member not by baptism, but merely by laying on of hands. (Grosheide, *Bijdrage,* 145-46, 308.)   vDZ.

Emancipation, a legal term denoting the release of a child of the family from the father's control. Whereas the word kept its legal meaning until very recent times, it had already by 1700 become a political catchword and remained thus in many kinds of connections. At times it means release from oppressing injustices or prejudices that hinder progress. After religion, especially the Christian religion,

had in the course of history become closely connected with temporal government, it is proper to regard the Anabaptism of Central Europe as the first great attempt to emancipate religious life from the guardianship of the state. In England it was primarily the Anabaptist spirit in the Independent movement that carried on this emancipation struggle with great political consequences (see **England**). In that country there was also the further phenomenon that later furnished the typical case for a narrowed concept of "emancipation." The adherents of the Catholic faith were subject to oppression that the nation sought to justify. The Catholics had actually been disfranchised. Emancipation proceeded very slowly for them. The struggle for the emancipation of the Catholics in England is one of the most disturbed epochs of Parliament. The "Emancipation Acts" (Peel) of 1829 became the foundation of the legal recognition of the Catholics, though even today they do not enjoy complete freedom.

The political position of the Anabaptists or Mennonites in Central Europe was similar. Besides them, only the Jews occupied this status of differentiation. The omission of the Anabaptists from the several religious peace treaties of the 16th and 17th centuries was followed by a legal depreciation of the Mennonites. This was evident in various ways in the different political units. The most serious in its effect was the law of recession or *ius retractus* (*q.v.*) in the Palatinate, that could become a tool for the injury of the Mennonites by any person of another faith. The exclusion of Mennonites from public office was at first not thought of as oppression, since taking such offices conflicted with their old religious principles. But as these were gradually modified and the Mennonites were willing to assume such office, the prohibitive laws still blocked them. These restrictions were usually based on the principle of nonresistance (*q.v.*) and the rejection of the oath (*q.v.*). Likewise in the rise of constitutional government both the active and passive franchise of the Mennonites was questioned.

In the Netherlands, after the Calvinists had obtained the majority (about 1570), the Mennonites and other dissenters, as well as Catholics and Jews, had the political status of only "tolerated citizens." It was not till 1795 that they obtained full citizenship.

It must be stressed that the Mennonites never engaged in a public struggle for their political emancipation. To the extent that such a struggle existed, it was stirred up by the outside and compelled the Mennonites to defend themselves. On the contrary, the Mennonite achievements in economic lines and their advancement of the common good brought them recognition. From this consideration they were also led into politics. In this field several of their great men, such as Hermann von Beckerath (*q.v.*), who once warmly defended the political rights of the dissidents and the Jews, by their own character proved the harmlessness of the Mennonites for the state and made the greatest contribution to the emancipation of their coreligionists. (*ML* I, 564 f.)   E.H.C.

Emblems. An emblem is a device, sign, or article associated with a person or truth; in Catholic piety, e.g., a carpenter's square is associated with Joseph; an eagle with the evangelist John and with Augustine. In Mennonitism the term has most frequently been used in connection with the bread and cup of the Lord's Supper, the expression most commonly being the "sacred emblems." In the Anabaptist-Mennonite tradition the bread and wine are symbols only, the doctrines of transubstantiation and consubstantiation being alike rejected.

In modern times the Mennonite Central Committee (q.v.) emblem has become familiar in Mennonite circles and in relief work—a circle within which is a cross with two clasped hands superimposed over it, along each side heads of grain, and over the cross a dove, together with the words, "In the Name of Christ." This symbol of peace, love, and service represents the concern to minister to mankind in the name of Christ and in response to His love which moves His children and disciples.

In the Netherlands youth groups like *Menniste Bouwers* (q.v.) have emblems; on the Dutch hymnbook of 1945, appear the symbols of Lamb and Sun (emblems of the former separated groups of Lamists and Zonists). The Mennonite congregation of Aardenburg (q.v.) has a seal which shows a lamb.

J.C.W.

Emden, a seaport city (1950 pop. 36,762) of Lower Saxony, West Germany, on the Dutch border, largest city of East Friesland, the seat of a Mennonite congregation ever since early Reformation times. In the summer of 1530 Melchior Hofmann (q.v.) came to the city and united the Sacramentist elements that had been fleeing to Emden from the Netherlands. He must also have had some following among the Reformed clergy of the city, for he baptized about 300 persons in the *Geerkammer* (vestibule) of the Grosse Kirche. This bold deed attracted a great deal of attention. The authorities of the city and the province, both civic and clerical, prepared for energetic resistance. Hofmann left the city and went to Strasbourg (z. Linden, 256).

Before he left he installed Jan Volkerts Trypmaker (q.v.) to take his place. Trypmaker continued the work in the city and also sent out missioners. Two weeks before Christmas 1530 he baptized the martyr Sicke Freerks (Vos, 24), but soon had to leave the city because of increasingly severe measures against the Anabaptists. Exactly a year later he was martyred at Amsterdam. But the brotherhood in Emden continued. On May 12, 1534, Count Enno (q.v.) wrote a letter to the Emden authorities, urging a close watch on the Anabaptists, and ordering that they be arrested wherever found. Also Enno's stern mandates of 1535 and 1537 prove the presence of Anabaptists. Especially Dirk Philips (q.v.) must have worked here with considerable success. At Enno's death in 1540 their number was greater than before. His widow, Countess Anna (q.v.), gave them protection and toleration.

Menno Simons took advantage of this toleration to make a brief visit to Emden. During 1536-42 he spent some time in the near-by village of Oldersum.

Johann a Lasco, the reformer of Emden, invited him to a debate, which was held with Anna's consent in the church of the Franciscan monastery in Emden, Jan. 28-31, 1544, before a large audience. Present were also the Reformed clergymen Gellius Faber and Hermann Brassius. The debate dealt with the Incarnation, infant baptism, original sin, sanctification, and the true calling of preachers. Both sides claimed the victory. A regrettable literary feud developed between Menno and a Lasco.

Menno soon had to leave the city. At the insistence of Charles V, Anna passed a mandate ordering all the adherents of a sect, especially the Anabaptists, to leave the city and province at once. A Lasco succeeded in having it limited to the Davidjorists (q.v.). Nevertheless Menno left and went to Cologne. His followers, the quiet Anabaptists, were unmolested. To be sure, to comply with the emperor's demand, the countess issued another severe edict on April 6, 1549, but it was not vigorously applied.

In 1547 a momentous meeting of the Anabaptist leaders was held in Emden. Menno Simons, Dirk Philips, Frans de Kuiper, Adam Pastor, Hendrik van Vreden, Antonius of Cologne, and Gillis van Aken debated the important doctrines of the Incarnation, infant baptism, and avoidance in marriage. Frans de Kuiper and Adam Pastor sharply opposed Menno and his friends, and finally left the brotherhood. Once more, in 1549, Menno was in the city to discuss matters with his opponents (Vos, 91, note 4).

Two years later, in 1551, Menno ordained Leenaert Bouwens (q.v.) as elder in Emden. Bouwens lived in 't Falder (q.v.), a neighboring village. In 1551-54 he baptized 51 persons in Emden (City) and in 1556-82 another 360. Through his extreme severity on the question of the ban, he brought great trouble upon the brotherhood. When Zwaantje Rutgers, a pious woman of Emden (Vos, 132) of blameless conduct, did not want to give up companionship with her husband, who had been placed in the ban, Bouwens banned her. The others disagreed with this procedure. Letter after letter of complaint reached Menno; he wrote a conciliatory letter to Emden, urging peace.

The three-day colloquy to which the Reformed challenged the Mennonites in 1556 was held in Norden (Blaupot t. C., *Friesland,* 120). It dealt chiefly with the Incarnation.

In a letter of April 8, 1562, the Mennonite congregation at Dokkum requested Emden to assist them in obtaining a preacher. The request was presumably granted.

In 1567 Dirk Philips came from Danzig to Emden. Here he wrote a reply to Hoyte Renix and four letters to Jan Willems and Lubbert Gerritsz, the elders at Hoorn, summoning them to Emden to talk with them. When they did not comply, he commanded them in the fifth letter to "stand still" in their office until it could be determined whether they were guilty or innocent. In the same vein he wrote to the Hoorn congregation. When the congregation replied that they would not let their elder go to Emden, but that he should come to Hoorn, he sent a sixth letter to Jan Willems and Lubbert Gerritsz, demanding more positively than before that they lay down their office, threatening to put them out of the brotherhood if they refused to come. Hoyte Renix had obeyed the demand, but in return demanded that Dirk Philips come to Bolsward to prove his charges. When this did not happen, his congregation exonerated him, and he felt justified in resuming his office. Then four representatives of the churches in North Holland and five from Friesland came to Emden to settle the dispute. After being urged six times, Dirk Philips agreed to come to a border city in Holland to deal with his opponents and bring the matter to a decision. Meanwhile a meeting of the preachers in North Holland had been held, from which Jan Willems, Lubbert Gerritsz, Pieter Willems, and Bogaert and Hoyte Renix were sent to Emden. They met with the nine brethren on their return to Holland in Appingedam and decided to go to Emden together, in order to clear the matter there. But Dirk Philips did not wish to deal "with the crowd" and ordered only Jan Willems and Lubbert Gerritsz to come to him; they did not comply, whereupon Dirk Philips put them and their friends in the ban on July 10, 1567.

This led to a division in the Emden congregation into a Flemish and a Frisian group. The two parties at first opposed each other radically. There was absolutely no communion between them. The most sacred ties of family were broken by strife. Anyone who wished to join the other party had to be rebaptized. All attempts to unify them failed. On April 2 and May 22, 1578, a mutual offer of peace was made (*DB* 1893, 81), but it failed. The elder of the Flemish congregation at Emden about 1569 was Jan van Ophoorn. He was austere and implacable, and is reported to have banned the entire congregation except himself and his wife (*BRN* VII, 69 f.).

On Jan. 17, 1568, a meeting of Waterlander preachers was held at Emden, at which 21 points were agreed upon. It was the first meeting of this kind in this branch of the brotherhood. Points 1-7 deal with the elders and their work in the churches, 8-15 with preachers and deacons, and 16-20 with the bearing of arms, working for the churches, and marriage outside the brotherhood, and point 21 was an appendix on the regulation against lending money on interest (*DB* 67-75).

External pressure was added to internal strife. On Jan. 9, 1577, the mayor and the city council wrote a complaint to Edzard II (*q.v.*), saying that the Mennonites were doing a thriving business in the city, and that they were holding their meetings openly (Müller, 29). Edzard replied that all such preaching and meetings should be strictly forbidden. In February 1578 he wrote that Menso Alting had informed him that about 1,000 Anabaptists were coming from Holland, and that they should not be permitted to settle in Emden.

This warning was also occasioned by the large number of Mennonites from the outside gathered for the disputation of Emden from Feb. 25 to May 17, 1578, between the Reformed and the Mennonites. The leaders of the Flemish, Frisian, and Waterlander Mennonites from the Netherlands and Friesland were there. In 124 sessions they discussed 14 points of doctrine. It was peaceful in character, but did not lead to any practical results. An extensive report of the debate was published at Emden in 1579 with the title *Protocol. Dat is, Alle handelinge des Gesprecks tot Embden*. (See **Emden Disputation**.)

In the next year, April 3, 1579, seven representatives and preachers of the congregations at Rijp, Purmerend, Amsterdam, and Rotterdam gathered in Emden; a consequence of this meeting was the union of the Emden congregation with the Waterlander wing of North Holland (*DB* 1877, 79; Blaupot t. C., *Groningen* I, 264-70). Under the influence of Hans de Ries (*q.v.*) an agreement was drawn up which breathes the spirit of true Christian generosity and brotherly love (Brons, 121). The assumption that Hans de Ries was the elder at Emden at that time is probably an error. He was there only temporarily, and did not serve as elder of the Emden congregation until 1592-98. The church had experienced a great influx of Waterlander Dutch refugees, and de Ries gave it valuable assistance in making the adjustment (*DB* 1863, 115).

Further growth of the congregation at Emden was prevented by severe repressive measures on the part of the government; the center of the Mennonites in East Friesland was shifted to Norden. Count Enno III (1599-1625) issued an edict on Nov. 21, 1612, prohibiting the Mennonites from exercising their religion in the open, and a mandate of Nov. 20, 1630, set a fine of 5,000 talers on any Mennonite worship services. For eight years the Mennonites remained quiet. Many may have left the city in the meantime. As usual, the prohibition ended in extortion. For a payment of 12,000 talers on Aug. 22, 1622, Enno granted the 400 Mennonites living in his realm the right of private worship services for a promised period of ten years. When this sum was not paid he issued a new edict on Sept. 25 depriving the Mennonites of all rights and protection.

His successor, Rudolph Christian 1625-28, finally gave the Mennonites a letter of protection, which became the basis for all future terms (*Mitteilungen der Gemeinde Norden*, 1914, 150 f.). But this was not the end of oppression. Again and again these rights were violated, until an additional payment was made. Rudolph Christian's successor, Ulrich II 1628-48, revoked all liberties granted the Mennonites on March 10, 1641. After further extortion they were restored by Enno Ludwig, 1651-60, in May 1658; but in 1666 Christine Charlotte, regent for the minor Christian Eberhard, forbade Mennonite worship. On Sept. 18, 1666, the Mennonites were summoned to give an account of their teaching, and two days later a fine of 30 gold guilders was set for Mennonite religious services. After lengthy negotiations the Old Flemish group received the desired letter of protection for the sum of 400 talers on Dec. 7, 1666, and the Waterlander group on April 2, 1667.

The Old Flemish or Uckowallists (*q.v.*; they were often called Mennonites, whereas the Waterlander group had since 1579 adopted the name *Doopsgezinde*) were a branch of Mennonites named after Ucko Walles (*q.v.*), who came to East Friesland from Groningen in 1637, from where he had been

expelled, and is said to have lived in a village between Emden and Norden. He returned to Holland, was expelled again, and rented the land of
the former monastery of Sielmönken in East Friesland until shortly before his death. He was the
strictest of all the Mennonites, adhering to footwashing and a severe interpretation of the ban. A
register of Mennonites in Emden and vicinity (Emderland) in 1644 shows 12 families belonging to
this group. For a long time they met "outside the
old New Gate," in the house (Wilhelmstrasse 11)
now known as the "Uckenvermaning." Members
of this Uckowallist congregation or Groningen Old
Flemish congregation lived in Emden, Emderland
(*q.v.*), and Norden (*q.v.*). This congregation in
1710 had a total of 65 men (the number of women
is not given). In that year a friendly division took
place, and henceforth there were two congregations—one at Norden, and one of Emden and Emderland. The Emden-Emderland congregation had
65 members in 1733, 70 in 1746, 44 in 1754, and in
1767 Emden had only 7 (Emderland apparently became independent between these dates). In 1739
the Uckowallist congregation acquired a new
church. The preachers then were Myndert Waerma,
Lourens Warners (from 1721), Pieter Popkes (from
1731). They were followed by Hendrik Waerma
1741-60. By 1767 it had been without a preacher
for several years. On March 9 of that year it merged
with the Waterlander congregation, sometimes also
called the United Flemish and Waterlander congregation, or even United Frisian and Waterlander
congregation. It is not clear whether the entire
Flemish congregation adopted the strict convictions
of Ucko Walles, or whether a part of this congre
gation acted independently and then later, perhaps
soon after 1665, united with the Waterlander-Frisian
congregation.

A strange division occurred on Oct. 22, 1692, in
the Waterlander congregation. Jehring relates the
following account: A preacher, Mindelt van der
Stork, moved from Groningen to Emden "for business reasons." In preaching he had a silent prayer
before the sermon and an audible one at its close.
Soon he offered both of the prayers audibly. When
the preacher in charge grew weak, van der Stork
was requested to take his place for a small compensation, on condition that he offer the opening prayer
silently again. He did not consent and the church
council yielded the point. All this had taken place
without the knowledge of the congregation, "which
alone had the right to negotiate in such affairs." A
meeting was held after the church service to ask
the preacher why he had done this. He explained
the situation and persisted in his view. The consequence was a split. The dissenters were called
the "silent ones." The division lasted 40 years. In
1732 the group that had sided with the preacher
joined the "silent" wing, sold its church, and gave
all of its capital to the "silent" branch, which met
"in the warehouse."

For 37 years more the congregation continued to
meet here. Then they purchased a house on
Hofstrasse and remodeled it into a church. The
total cost amounted to 6,174 guilders, which the
members obligated themselves and their children
to pay according to a rate depending on income. In
1776 the church was free of debt. The new church
was used for the first time on Jan. 26, 1770.

On Dec. 25, 1717, a flood devastated Emden,
filling the church chamber with four feet of water.
All the church records, which had been kept since
1582, were soaked and had to be replaced.

In 1739 the Mennonites were required to present
to the government a record of births and marriages.
Both groups entered their marriages on the same
register.

In 1744 Prussia took possession of East Friesland.
The Emden congregation was released from all special fees (the exact date is unknown) and no longer
needed a letter of protection; it could now develop
undisturbed. Its membership, however, remained
small, declining no doubt through emigration. But
at the same time its members were faithful and
united, as is shown, for instance, by the numerous
bequests and gifts made to the brotherhood.

For a long time church discipline was exercised
earnestly and carefully. Thus on Jan. 19, 1643, the
ministers of the congregation summoned a married
couple to the church rooms and notified them that
their conduct had created some offense in the congregation and that they had not kept their marriage vows. Thereupon they shook hands and
promised to live as was fitting. Then the ministers
prayed with them, asking that God might preserve
them in evangelical discipline. On Jan. 24, 1772,
a chorister (*Vorsänger*) was excommunicated for
some misdemeanors and had to give up his apartment in the church buildings.

The Emden Waterlander congregation joined the
Zonist Sociëteit in 1674 as soon as it was organized.
All of the Emden ministers belonged to it; until
most recent times they had all come from Holland.
Some of them had studied in the Lamist Seminary
and to some extent represented the more liberal
point of view of this brotherhood. In 1702 Cornelius van Huyzen (*q.v.*) was confirmed in the
ministry, and on July 28, 1709, he delivered a sermon in Altona on John 17:3, which resulted in his
noted book, *Historische Verhandeling van de opkomst en voortgang, mitgaders de Godgeleerdheijd
der Doopsgezinde Christenen* (Emden, 1712). In
1739 Cornelius van Campen became the preacher of
the congregation. He was followed by Sjoerds
Sijtses Hoekstra, who delivered his initial sermon
on Nov. 17, 1757. For 30 years, until his death on
Aug. 17, 1789, he faithfully performed the duties of
the ministry. Under his leadership a new translation
of the Psalms was introduced as a hymnal. On Oct.
10, 1771, he began to conduct Thursday evening
meetings from November to February, for an increase of 25 guilders in his annual salary. These
meetings were discontinued after 13 years because
of lack of interest. From April to September, beginning in 1784, the regular Sunday services were
held in the forenoon, and in winter in the afternoon. The duty of the chorister (*Vorsänger*) was
defined thus: the first song was to be Psalm 37:1;
then Psalms 1, 25, and 116 were to be sung; Romans
16 was then to be read. Relations with the Reformed

Church were friendly. For the celebration of peace observed by the Reformed Church in 1779 the Emden Mennonite congregation made a considerable contribution.

After Hoekstra's death the Emden pulpit was vacant for three years. Four deacons, Tobias Bouman, Pieter Onne Brouwer, Jan Tobias van Oterendorp, and Ysaak Bouman, took care of the congregation during this time. A list of voluntary annual contributions begun at this time showed the amount of 356 florins. Then a contract for a preacher was drawn up (the contract is found in *ML* I, page 568 f., footnotes).

Of six proposed candidates, Wynald Ewertzoon, the preacher at Blokzijl, was chosen on Dec. 25, 1790; he refused the position even after a second offer with an increase of 1,000 florins in salary. The position was rejected also by the following preachers: Jansen of Campen, Hoekstra of Utrecht, and Rahusen of Altona. In 1792 Jan de Bleijker, a ministerial candidate of Utrecht, was chosen; he accepted, and on June 24, 1792, in the presence of the magistrate and numerous visitors from the city, he was inducted into his office by Hoekstra of Utrecht. But the hope of the Emden church now to have a capable preacher for an extended time was not to be realized, for in May of the following year de Bleijker was called to Helder and left Emden in spite of an offer of 100 additional florins and the omission of winter evening sermons.

His place was filled by Konrad Bavink, the minister of the Groningen congregation, who was installed by Pieter Beets (*q.v.*) in May 1795. In 1808, after eleven years of faithful service, he accepted a call to Nijmegen. Again the congregation was left for some years without a minister. Again a series of preachers refused the call to Emden: M. Martens of Holwerd, who preached for a while, ministerial candidate Plantinus, A. R. Vink of Winterswijk, Jan van Hulst of Norden, J. Goverts of Rijsdijk, J. van Hulst of Cleve. The congregation was in need of a competent minister, especially since the Reformed Church had some good ministers who attracted members of the Emden Mennonite Church. Finally, in March 1811, the congregation acquired a preacher—Hendrik van Someren Greve, who served for 15 years, until his death in 1826.

The congregation grew slowly. Whereas it had 74 souls in 1808, it had increased to 86 by 1814 (23 men, 18 women, 24 young men, and 21 young women). In 1834 the membership was 51. In 1860 it was 62, with a total of 106 souls. The levies for the support of the poor were high. The congregation spent almost 700 florins for members in need of support, and so for this reason it very definitely rejected the suggestion to assume the obligation to furnish money to young men of military age to pay for substitutes (May 28, 1816). Equally definite was the position of the congregation on the question of the oath in a statement handed to the magistrate of the city of Emden on Jan. 6, 1822, which says, "The church council, after taking the voice of the congregation on this matter and finding it in agreement with its own, considers the swearing of any oath in conflict with its principles, and therefore

unpermissible and this on the basis of the requirements of Jesus Christ as found in Matthew 5:36-37, and James 5:12, at the same time supporting its position with the doctrine of various church fathers and honorable men after the time of Christ and on the general regard with which this opinion has been recognized by all governments here as well as in other countries through all ages. It must also be added that the upright, earnest declaration of the truth or promise of conscientious faithfulness, with the words 'Yea' and 'Nay'—the arbitrary misuse of which we consider equally punishable with perjury and thereby offer the state adequate security—is considered as completely satisfactory for the decision of important debated questions, as well as in the assumption of public office here (at least under French and Dutch authorities) as well as in neighboring Holland."

Also under Greve's successor, L. van Hulst of Norden, who was initiated on Jan. 10, 1827, in the Emden congregation, the congregation vigorously defended its legal position as well as its religious point of view. On Nov. 17, 1828, the congregation presented a petition to the magistrate of the city of Emden for an increase in the subsidy to the preacher's salary equal to that of the preachers of the other creeds, especially since all the creeds were considered equal and the Mennonites enjoyed equal rights with the others. This petition says:

"We take the liberty here to remark that we believe we have so much the more right to an equating also on this point because

"(1) We have no special educational institutions as have the other congregations of the city which draw contributions from the city treasury for their support and the pay of the schoolteachers.

"(2) Even though our congregation is not so large with respect to the number of persons as the Reformed and the Lutheran Church of the city, nevertheless, certain members of our congregation can make substantial contributions to the city taxes. A number of us have quite extensive communications as merchants. A number own important city real estate. These are conditions which are too well known here to require any extensive presentation so that we relatively pay just as much to the city expenses as other churches.

"(3) The endowment fund of our congregation is very small. The truly small salary of our minister of annually 700 Dutch florins, cannot even be met from the revenue of our endowment. The church members must make considerable contribution from their private funds for this purpose and in addition make further private contributions for the upkeep of the church building and to cover the support of impoverished church members."

The magistrate replied on Nov. 27 that he "could neither grant this petition himself nor recommend it to a higher office, since the constitution of the city of Emden in paragraphs 5, 27, 55, 57, and 58 by no means grants the Mennonite congregation equal rights with the three principal Christian confessions." In the reply of Dec. 4 the congregation insisted on its right and referred to a royal rescript of July 27, 1822, which expressly stated: "It shall be permitted to well-qualified members of the East Frisian Mennonite congregations to enter into public office to the extent that they can be admitted to administrative positions of the city (if they upon entering this service submit themselves to those regulations which the A.G.O. wishes to have observed with respect to the performance of oaths in affairs of private law), and that members of the Mennonite brotherhood shall in the future participate in the rights granted to all citizens of the principal creeds, with respect to their appearing in the meetings of the citizens and in active voting."

The church council of this congregation had obviously, with all the openness and the decisiveness with which it presented its position to the magistrate, already adapted itself to the circumstances of the established church. The council made a demand for support by the state equal to that which the ministers of the state church drew, whereas, as a matter of principle, the Mennonite brotherhood rejected all state aid. The same is evident in further negotiations with the magistrate of the city and with the government of the country.

An inquiry of the magistrate concerning the celebration of the third centennial of the signing of the Augsburg Confession was given the answer that they did not want to participate in the celebration. When the consistorium of the state church in Aurich asked for a statement of the differentiating tenets of faith, the East Frisian Mennonite congregations made a unanimous reply. The Emden congregation sent its document off in February 1831, which expressed itself briefly and definitely:

"1. That we have no creedal books like other religious parties, but only have the Bible as our *regulam fidei* (rule of faith).

"2. That on the whole we differ from other Protestants only on two points of doctrine; namely, with respect to baptism and with respect to the oath.

"To be sure, the idea that Christ had forbidden war service was formerly accepted and vigorously defended by all the Mennonites, and this may still be the case with some few individuals. In general, meanwhile, a thorough exegesis and free investigation has long since convinced the Mennonites that this their former position is by no means tenable. Our brethren in Holland have already for several decades and we in the last years clearly enough shown that we have given up this opinion and no longer differ from other Protestants therein." In this writing the principle of nonresistance was abandoned and the principle of brotherhood was not stressed.

A long-drawn-out struggle developed with the authorities in the matter of the political rights of the Mennonites of East Friesland. It was fought out together by the congregations of Emden, Leer, and Norden. In 1831 they presented a petition to the meeting of the estates in Aurich, asking for a change in the requirement that a deputy must be a member of one of the "three confessions."

In January 1832 a lengthy document composed by a jurist (Brückner) was sent to the government with the petition "that paragraph 30 of the constitution of the state be authentically declared to mean that we as members of the Evangelical Anabaptist brotherhood in East Friesland enjoy absolutely equal civic and political rights with the members of the Protestant and Catholic churches."

When the answer was long in coming they sought further legal counsel, and on March 2, 1848, they decided to send delegates, together with Norden and Leer, to Aurich to present this case. All in vain. In 1857 Consul Bernhard Brons was chosen as the delegate of the town of Emden to the second chamber, but he was rejected by the government because the Mennonites were not one of the recognized churches. It was agreed at a conference in Emden, that for the time being they would take no further steps of this sort until they had more favorable prospects with the government.

In 1863 a deputation was sent to the king, who was staying on the island of Norderney for his health. It was apparently successful. Soon afterward, on Sept. 18, 1863, the Norden congregation received upon its request of Aug. 10 of that year the very important government decision that it should be counted among those churches which had been explicitly accepted by the state (details in *ML* I, 570 f.).

The matter was, however, settled only on paper. When a member of the Mennonite congregation of Norden was elected to participate in the extraordinary session of the provincial states in November 1863 and admission was refused him as a Mennonite, the representatives of the three East Frisian Mennonite congregations met in Emden on April 15, 1864, and decided to present a petition to the assembly of the estates at Hanover; this was sent on April 25. The petition requested that the new constitution about to be drawn up should make a clear statement that members of the Mennonite churches were admittted to complete political equality with the other recognized Christian churches in the country. This petition was not successful. It was finally the government of Prussia that granted the Frisian Mennonites full civic equality. In 1866 East Friesland, which was under Dutch dominion 1807-10, and French 1810-13, again became a part of Prussia. On Sept. 7, 1900, the decisions of the Hanover government were set aside by the governor at Aurich, and the Mennonites were urged to secure the right of incorporation according to the Prussian law of June 12, 1874, relating to the Mennonites. This they did on Oct. 23, 1901. But civic equality did not give the Mennonites religious equality. When their preacher, Dr. J. P. Müller, in a dispute with the magistrate of the city insisted on his right as a clergyman, it was pointed out to him that as a Mennonite preacher he was not one of the clergy in the intention of the regulation of Sept. 23, 1867, and that the Mennonites could not claim complete equality with the Lutheran, Reformed, and United churches. Higher instances confirmed this decision. It was not until the great revolution of 1918 and the new German constitution of Aug. 11, 1919, that the Mennonites of Germany received full religious equality, with the rights of a public religious society.

Another law, unsought to be sure, secured to

the Mennonites of East Friesland their membership in the Prussian state. When East Friesland was from Nov. 17, 1813, to Dec. 15, 1815, in Prussian hands, the Emden congregation in co-operation with Leer and Norden (without informing Norden of this step) asked for release from military service, obligating themselves not only to pay the customary protection fee, but also to show themselves grateful in other ways financially. Already on Dec. 17, 1815, Frederick William decreed that the East Prussian Mennonites, like other Prussian Mennonites, be released from military duty. The total sum of 46,060 talers was set, of which the Emden congregation was to pay 14,950 talers. In response to a petition the total sum was, however, reduced to 15,000 talers. But the East Frisian Mennonites were not to enjoy this release from military service for very long. Even before the end of 1815 they became citizens of Hanover. They made a special appeal for consideration and finally achieved an offer of release from military duties if they would pay the sum of 100 talers for each member of the congregation that was subject to military duty, whether he was rich or poor (July 15, 1817). The Emden congregation refused this offer, whereas Norden collected a sum for the purpose. On May 23, 1821, the special position of the Mennonites on the matter of military service was legally removed and henceforth they were treated like any other citizens. Then when East Friesland became Prussian again this question once more became acute. It was agreed at a meeting in Emden on Oct. 17, 1867, not to present a special petition to the government and to make no use of any exceptional status.

In the execution of the written and oral negotiations Deacon Ysaak Brons was outstandingly active. From Jan. 6, 1832, to Sept. 22, 1875, in addition to his business, political, and charitable activities, he managed his office in the congregation with unusual faithfulness, circumspection, and vigor, giving five pastors a most understanding support.

Laurens van Hulst served the congregation for 23 years, 1827-50. He provided for the use of an organ, the introduction of a new songbook, for the repair of the church, the new pews, which were now rented out for the first time (1834), founded a branch of the Dutch Society for the Common Welfare, and founded a nature study association, which still exists. In recognition of his services the congregation raised his salary from 800 to 1,200 Dutch guilders and in the last years gave him an honorary sum annually of 100 talers. In 1850 he resigned to become one of the directors of the Teyler (*q.v.*) Association at Haarlem. With great sorrow they saw him leave the congregation.

Next L. E. Halbertsma of Ternaard was chosen as preacher; he was initiated on Nov. 10, 1850, by Leendertz, the pastor of Leer. On Oct. 26, 1854, he died. His widow was granted a pension of 200 talers. The Algemeene Doopsgezinde Sociëteit of Holland gave the congregation a considerable contribution.

The next minister was L. T. Goteling Vinnis of Stadskanaal. After a trial sermon he was unanimous-

ly chosen on May 27, 1855. The congregation offered him an annual salary of 1,500 florins. He succeeded in stirring up and preserving an active spiritual life in the congregation. With the Dutch congregations he maintained active connections. Repeatedly the Emden congregation had the opportunity of aiding younger or even older Dutch congregations in building churches or parsonages. Also with the preachers of the congregations in Norden and Leer he maintained close connections and instigated a regular exchange of ministers with them. He required young baptismal candidates to make a written confession of faith to the church council. In the benevolent institutions of the city of Emden the congregation participated in an outstanding degree, as for instance in building a hospital or establishing an educational board. Vinnis also provided for the purchase of a new parsonage and for equipping the church with gas lights. Upon the request of several church members that he occasionally preach in German he held the first German sermon on Jan. 1, 1860. The congregational endowment was considerably increased by the substantial sum of the "Boumannsfonds." On account of unpleasant domestic circumstances Vinnis had to resign, and on Oct. 3, 1869, he preached a moving farewell sermon on Rom. 3:28.

His successor was S. Cramer, the minister of Zijldijk, Tjeenk Willink of Tjalleberd having rejected the offered position. On Sept. 25, 1870, Cramer was initiated by Leendertz of Leer, but already on Aug. 15, 1874, he accepted a call to Enschede in Holland.

Then J. P. Müller, preacher of Zwartsluis, was chosen. He was also introduced into his office by Leendertz and held his initial sermon on Nov. 17, 1874. Soon the wish became predominant that the preaching be done in German for the most part. The record book was carried on in Dutch until 1889, likewise the baptismal instruction. By 1889 the German language was the only one in use. Also a German hymnal was introduced. A plan to adopt a songbook of their own in common with the other East Frisian Mennonite congregations was not accepted on account of the cost; but on Oct. 1, 1876, the Emden congregation adopted the *Gesangbuch für die Reformierten Gemeinden Ostfrieslands.*

The women of the Emden congregation (women have voted in the church since 1826) presented a petition for the establishment of an endowment for the education of ministers in the German language. It will probably not be an error to assume that Anna Brons (*q.v.*) was the instigator of this move. She revealed a deep interest in the Mennonite brotherhood in Germany and it may be ascribed to her and to her oldest son, Bernhard Brons, who served as deacon of the congregation from Sept. 22, 1875, to his death June 8, 1911, that the Emden congregation supported all the spiritual and communal efforts of the German Mennonites most warmly. Thus she participated in the founding of the *Vereinigung der Mennoniten-Gemeinden im Westen Deutschlands* (which had only the one meeting at Friedelsheim in 1874), the Mennonite

Central Relief Treasury in the Palatinate, and above all, the *Vereinigung der Mennoniten-Gemeinden im Deutschen Reich* at Berlin in 1886.

The Emden congregation also promoted actively the rising research in Mennonite history. Mrs. Brons in 1884 published the first history of the Mennonites in the German language (*Ursprung, Entwickelung, und Schicksale der . . . Mennoniten*); Pastor Müller published the results of his research in the state archives of Aurich in his book, *Die Mennoniten in Ostfriesland vom 16. bis zum 18. Jahrhundert*. His congregation supported him substantially in this undertaking. Also the publication of the Mannhardt *Jahrbuch* in 1888 and the research of C. A. Cornelius (*q.v.*), Nippold (*q.v.*), and Ludwig Keller (*q.v.*), as well as the *Comeniusgesellschaft* founded by Keller were received with great interest. A congregational library was established. On Oct. 18, 1898, when Müller resigned on account of advanced age, J. G. Appeldoorn of Gorredijk was chosen as his successor. He served for 18 years, and then accepted a call as professor at the Mennonite Seminary at Amsterdam. In 1918 A. Fast, a German-Russian, was chosen pastor, who has continued to the present, 1956. In 1921 the congregation had a membership of 80 and 10 children.

World War I and its consequences struck a severe blow at the outward existence of the Emden congregation. The income from former endowments was wiped out in the inflation of 1923, as was also the capital of many members. As a result of losses on the field of battle and especially because of emigration of many younger members in search of better opportunities to make a living, the membership dropped sharply to 30 adults and 4 children. But there was enough spiritual strength left to give the impulse for a new growth, by means of two important decisions of the church council at the instigation of the new pastor in 1918.

First, the three congregations of East Friesland, Emden, Leer, and Norden, as well as the small Gronau congregation, formed an experimental union. All four of these congregations had hitherto been served by Dutch ministers, all of whom retired because of age during these years. In 1941 the union was strengthened by three agreements: one between Emden and Leer, stipulating that the church capital of Leer be transferred to Emden in case the Leer membership should decline below a certain point. Second, a similar agreement was drawn up between Emden and Norden. Since the capital of Emden had already been assigned to the *Vereinigung,* that of the other two congregations is now also assigned to it. Third, an agreement was drawn up between all four congregations to support the common pastor on a specified ratio. This was, of course, an emergency measure, which reduced the number of regular services and also the amount of time available for baptismal instruction. But these drawbacks were more than compensated for in the increased participation in all church functions.

The second decision was, after consultation with other congregations, the removal of the restriction practiced in all European Mennonite churches with the exception of Holland, limiting the membership to old Mennonite families. This custom, originating in the earlier lack of legal status, which of course contradicted the principle of baptism upon confession of faith, and which promoted a clannish spirit, was to be dropped. The result of this decision was that more and more children of other creeds came to the instruction classes and were received by baptism into the Mennonite congregation. In 1925, 70 families, in most cases the parents of the children, requested admission. Also the congregations of Gronau, Norden, and Leer received members from other confessions. In Emden the membership including children rose to 200 in 1933, and in 1934 was able to enlarge the church and improve the residences of the pastor and the sexton. The "Mennonitentag," when the world conference met at Amsterdam in 1936, held a service at Emden. The congregation was in a thriving condition. Plans were being made to employ a second pastor for the Northwest German churches.

Then came World War II, with its 80 per cent destruction of Emden. The church, the parsonage, and all the homes and businesses of the members were annihilated. The Mennonite library, with its very valuable Bibles and hymnbooks of former centuries, and also the archives with 39 large record books bound in pigskin burned at Sögel, where they had been put for safe keeping.

In the following severe years of hunger, the completely impoverished members received food and clothing through the relief work of the American and Canadian Mennonites (MCC). The Dutch Mennonites also contributed relief goods. Services were held in a barracks in the cemetery. But this was not yet the end of this, the oldest Mennonite congregation, in which Menno Simons himself worked. Since it was not feasible to build a church in the ruined city, it was decided to build a congregational house with a chapel and a residence for the pastor on the second floor. One half of the required sum was furnished by the four participating congregations, one third by American and Canadian congregations, and the rest as a loan from a bank. On Sept. 13, 1953, the house was dedicated. The membership in 1954 was 218 baptized members. The pastor was still Abraham Fast.

The Emden congregation has been a member of the Vereinigung der Deutschen Mennonitengemeinden from its founding in 1886. It was also a member of the Dutch A.D.S. from its founding in 1811, and from 1829 of the Dutch Groningen Sociëteit, which had been founded in 1826, and also of a number of charitable funds. (For a complete bibliography, see **East Friesland**.) NEFF, AB.F.

A. Brons, *Ursprung, Entwickelung und Schicksale der altevangelischen . . . Mennoniten* (Emden, 1912); C. A. Cornelius, *Der Anteil Ostfrieslands an der Reformation bis zum Jahre 1535* (Münster, 1852); A. Fast, *Die Kulturleistungen der Mennoniten in Ostfriesland und Münsterland* (n.p., 1947); F. O. zur Linden, *Melchior Hofmann* (Haarlem, 1883); J. P. Müller, *Die Mennoniten in Ostfriesland vom 16. bis zum 18. Jahrhundert* (Emden, 1887); J. C. Jehring, *Gründliche Historia* (Jena, 1720); Jan ten Doornkaat-Koolman, *Kurze Mitteilungen aus der Geschichte der Mennoniten-Gemeinden in allgemeinen und der Norder Gemeinde im besonderen bis zum Jahre 1797* (Norden, 1903); idem, *Mitteilungen aus der Geschichte der Mennoniten-Gemeinde Norden im*

19. Jahrhundert (Norden, 1904); K. Vos, *Menno Simons* (Leyden, 1914); *Inv. Arch. Amst.* I, Nos. 249, 254, 260, 465, 474, 484, 487 f., 490, 540, 594, 597; II, Nos. 2689-99; II, 2, No. 681; *DB* 1861, 176 f.; 1877, 79; 1879, 7, 78; 1893, 13, 15, 59, 89 f., 81; 1898, 61 f.; *ML* I, 565-73.

Emden Disputation. The protocol book of the Dutch Reformed Church of Emden has an entry dated Jan. 20, 1577, stating that some of the ministers were to go to Count Edzard II to ask him to issue a mandate to restrain the Anabaptists from preaching (*leren en predigenn*). Should they not be willing to defend their faith their meetings should be prohibited. Then it is added that Willem de Visscher should first be spoken to "as a brother," asking him whether the above plan was advisable. A later entry states that the brethren had spoken to him on Jan. 30. On Feb. 20, 1577, Menso Alting, Jasper Celos, and Luppe Sikkes proposed to the Drost of Emden a disputation with the Mennonite leaders. Although the protocol book does not further mention this event, what followed is known through other sources. The protocol book does, however, reveal that among the Reformed clergy and church council there had been during the preceding years a concern and jealousy regarding the spread of the Anabaptists.

Early in 1578 numerous Mennonite elders met in Emden, a fact which did not remain unnoticed (*Protocol . . . des Gesprecks,* 378b). In the preface to the Protocol Count Johann of East Friesland, reviewing the factors that had led to the disputation, stated that it had always been the concern of the government to keep the land free of "errors" and "sects." It attempted to achieve this by securing good and qualified ministers for the congregations and by issuing mandates forbidding the introduction of sects by severe penalties. In spite of all efforts, he continued, the Anabaptists had increased in numbers and therefore his government was thinking of other means "to maintain the pure evangelical teaching" (ija, iija). In February 1578 Edzard wrote that Menso Alting made a statement from the pulpit of the Grosse Kirche indicating that about a "thousand Anabaptists were coming to Emden from Holland and other places to live there" (Müller, 32 f.).

In addition to this an Anabaptist leader was apprehended who declared himself willing to discuss matters of faith with the Reformed ministers. Not able to "condemn anyone without a hearing," the government granted the request of the Reformed ministers to combat the Anabaptists with "decent means" (*met behoorlijke middelen weyren*) and to arrange for a disputation. The Waterlanders and the Frisians did not accept the invitation, while the Flemish not only accepted it in a response of Feb. 23, but also suggested Feb. 27 as the first day of the disputation (*Protocol,* iijb, iiija). The disputation was first held in a private home (Klunderberg), but soon was transferred to the Gasthaus Church and opened to the public.

From Feb. 25 to May 17, 1578, the debate continued, through 124 sessions, at eight in the morning after a prayer, and at two in the afternoon. The Reformed debaters were the preachers Menso Alting and Johannes Petrejus of Emden, Wicherus Mellesius of Hinthe, Feyto Rumerdi of Oldersum, and Johannes Nicasius of Borssum. The Flemish speak-

ers were the preachers Hans Busschaert, Peeter van Ceulen, Paulus Backer, Christiaan Arends, Jan van Ophoorn (of Emden), and Brixius Gerritsz. The chief speakers were Alting, Petrejus, Peeter van Ceulen, and Busschaert. Of the Flemish only Brixius knew the classical languages.

The following served as chairman: Ocko Vriesen, Helmerus Diurken, Onno Tyabbren, Henricus Geerdes, and H. Paulinus. The speeches were taken down by the imperial notary, Dominicus Julius, and on the Flemish side by Carel van Gent. The records were then read aloud and signed by the chairmen, speakers, and recorders. In 1658 a book appeared written by J. H. V. P. N., entitled *Beginsel . . . der geschillen* (1910 reprinted in *BRN* VII), in which (page 67) the author calls himself "their secretary." But this was not Carel van Gent; for he later became a Reformed preacher. There was a second Mennonite scribe at the debate, Abel van Oosterwolde, as is seen on page 380 of the record, where an unofficial record is mentioned.

Certainly the following Mennonites were present: Hans van Deutekom, Willem Jansen, Gerritt Tincken, Beno Dolinck, Hans Krop, Hermann von Manschlacht, Hans de Clerck, Gerhard Rebbers, Hans de Boser (son of the martyr Maeyken Boosers, *q.v.*), Johann von Arssum, Frans Moltmaker, Antonius Tingieter, and Ariaen Berents. But the second secretary is not one of these, but presumably Cornelis Jansz (*q.v.*), the compass maker, who was later preacher at Middelburg. The following points were debated: (1) That God, the Father, Son, and Holy Ghost are three independent and differentiated persons, and yet one eternal true God and one divine Being; (2) Concerning the creation of man; (3) Concerning the fall of man and the ruin that has resulted, as original sin and the loss of freedom of the will; (4) Concerning Christ, that is, that Jesus Christ, true God and man in a single person, received His humanity from the substance of His mother Mary; (5) Concerning justification and sanctification or second birth of human beings; (6) Concerning good works; (7) Concerning the Church of God, and by what means one may confess it; (8) Concerning the election and call of preachers; (9) Concerning baptism and whether infants of the covenant shall be baptized; (10) Concerning communion; (11) Concerning the proper use and misuse of the ban; (12) Concerning the oath and the meaning of Matthew 5; (13) Concerning the resurrection of the flesh.

The debate was carried on in the spirit of Christian love. According to J. H. V. P. N. it was fortunate that Peeter van Ceulen was present, for Busschaert, who was actually the most important Flemish preacher, was sometimes embarrassed for an answer. Of Peeter van Ceulen the chairman said: "I tell you, Peeter, if you had the training we have, you would dispute all of us out of this church" (*BRN* VII, 548 f.).

The original record as it was taken down by Dominicus Julius and Carel van Gent has been preserved in the archives of the *Gesellschaft für bildende Kunst und vaterländische Altertümer* at Emden, and a microfilm copy has been obtained by the General Conference (GCM) Historical Committee (Newton, Kan.). A careful study of this record, comparing it with the printed copy, would reveal whether and to what extent changes have been made. The Protocol book of the church council of the Reformed Church of Emden, dating back to 1557, preserved in the archives of the Grosse Kirche (microfilm copy with G.C.M. Historical Committee), contains valuable information regarding the relationship of the two groups in Emden.

The recordings of the disputation were first published in the Saxon language (literary language of that area) under the title *Protocol. Dath is, alle handelinge des gesprecks tho Emden in Oistfrieszlandt mit den Wedderdöperen, de sick Flaminge nomen, geholden* . . . (Embden, G. Goebens, 1579). Printed by the same printer and during the same year appeared also a Dutch translation of the *Protocol* done by Dominicus Julius under the title *Protocol. Dat is, Alle handelinge des Gesprecks tot Embden in Oostvrieslant met den Wederdooperen, die hen Vlamingen noemen, gehouden* . . . . Of this edition a reprint appeared at Leiden in 1616. Copies of all three editions are found in the Mennonite libraries of Amsterdam, Bethel, and Goshen.

Before the *Protocol* was published the Mennonite participants expected a biased slant and published a *Voorlooper,* a warning, entitled *Een Christelicke ende voorloopende Waerschouwinge,* written by a "lover of divine truth" (*Liefhebber der Godtlijcker waerheyt*), whose identity is unknown. This pamphlet was added to the *Protocol* with a brief introduction and a refutation point by point (pp. 375-84). The Mennonite representative makes numerous accusations to the effect that his group was not treated fairly. The refutation and the preface to the *Protocol* by Count Johann make it obvious that the Mennonites were not treated as equals and that the disputation was not a brotherly conference, but that it was a means to defeat the movement in East Friesland.   C.K.

J. P. Müller, *Die Mennoniten in Ostfriesland vom 16. bis zum 18. Jahrhundert* (Emden, 1887); *ML I, 573.*

Emderland: see **Emsiger-Land.**

EMEK (Europäisches Mennonitisches Evangelisations-Komitee) was organized in August 1952 as the central mission committee of the Mennonites in Europe representing the four countries of Holland, Germany, Switzerland, and France. A preliminary meeting was held at Elspeet, Holland, in 1950. The committee meets annually in the four countries in rotation. Meetings have been held in Germany (1953), Switzerland (1954), and France (1955). The committee promotes the mission cause among the Mennonites, particularly the support of the work of the Dutch Mennonite Board in Indonesia and New Guinea, but it does not administer any work itself. It is composed of 11 members appointed as follows: (1) four by the Dutch Mennonite Mission Board; (2) three by the German Mennonite Mission Committee; (3) two by the Swiss Mennonite Mission Committee; (4) two by the French Mennonite Mission Committee. The chairman and treasurer of the Dutch Mennonite Mission Board (Doopsgezinde Vereniging tot Evangelieverbreiding) are ex officio the chairman and treasurer of EMEK, and together with a vice-chairman and secretary chosen annually by EMEK constitute the executive committee.

H.S.B.

Emels, Anna, an Anabaptist martyr: see **Anneken vanden Hove.**

Emergency Relief Board of the General Conference Mennonite Church was organized as a standing body of the General Conference in 1899 under the name of Emergency Relief Commission. The immediate occasion was a famine in India. This Commission had been preceded by the Mennonite Board of Guardians (*q.v.*) formed on behalf of the Mennonites then planning to migrate to the United States and Canada from Russia. After contributing $7,000 and 800 bushels of corn for relief in India in 1900, the Emergency Relief Commission continued to function as a relief agency among members of local churches in the conference.

At its regular session in 1920, the General Conference authorized the Emergency Relief Commission to give aid to the needy Mennonite brethren in Russia and to send a representative to that country to investigate the conditions and to help in relief work; it further authorized the commission to unite its relief efforts with those of the all-Mennonite organization then in the process of formation, the Mennonite Central Committee, with which it has continued its affiliation by the regular election of two members.

In 1933 the Emergency Relief Commission was recognized by the General Conference as a permanent board known as the Board of Emergency Relief, consisting of five members. Since 1938 the Emergency Relief Board has co-operated with MCC in its war relief and rehabilitation program, in the Civilian Public Service program, and other projects. In addition its work included relief to needy members of local Mennonite churches of the conference, co-operation with the home and the foreign mission boards in relief projects in the mission fields, and co-operation with other boards and organizations in various conference projects. In 1950 the board was merged with the Board of Christian Service (*q.v.*) by action of the General Conference of that year.   I.W.B.

Emeritaatsfonds (Fund for Pensions of Retired Ministers). Since the ministers of Dutch Mennonite congregations give full time to their ministry, provisions have been made to grant them a reasonable yearly pension when they retire at the age of 65. These funds serve at the same time as *Invaliditeitfondsen,* i.e., they provide for those who have to leave the ministry before they have reached the age of 65, because of bad health. There are now (1953) four of these superannuation funds in the Netherlands: *Friesch Emeritaatsfonds,* founded in 1845, *Zaansch Emeritaatsfonds* since 1848 (see **Algemeen Emeritaatsfonds**), *Groningsch Emeritaatsfonds* since 1917, and *Pensioenfonds der A.D.S.* (*q.v.*) since 1940.   vDZ.

Emigranten-Bureau: see **Hollandsch Doopsgezind Emigranten-Bureau.**

Emma Mennonite Church (MC), 5 miles north of Topeka, Lagrange Co., Ind., was organized in 1901, with 40 charter members formerly belonging to the Shore and Forks congregations. The church is a member of the Indiana-Michigan Conference. The first minister was O. S. Hostetler and the first deacon Menno J. Yoder, both ordained Oct. 15, 1902. Hostetler has served as bishop since 1923, and Yoder as minister since 1923. On June 29, 1924, Amos O. Hostetler was ordained to serve as deacon and on Sept. 3, 1944, he was ordained minister. On April 1, 1945, Ivan Miller was ordained deacon and March 1954, bishop. The membership in 1953 was 205. A new church was built in the Plato community 5 miles east of Lagrange, where a number of the present members have located and organized a separate congregation.   A.O.H.

Emmanuel Bible College, Kitchener, Ont., is operated by the Ontario Conference of the United Missionary Church for the purpose of training young people for service in the church. The school was founded in 1940 with Ward M. Shantz as the first principal. In 1953 Shantz became president and Lyness L. Wark was elected principal. To date there have been 140 graduates, many of whom are ministers and missionaries, serving in five countries. The enrollment for 1954 was 108, of whom 44 were registered in the day classes and 64 in the evening classes. The college offers courses in theology, missions, and Christian education, but does not require graduation from a high school for entrance.   E.R.S.

Emmanuel Church of God in Christ Mennonite Church, organized in 1936, is situated six miles south and a half mile west of Fredonia, Wilson Co., Kan. The present building with a capacity for 108 persons was purchased in 1938. Jesse H. Jantz and Lee Schultz were the ministers in 1955, with a membership of 65.   J.J.

Emmanuel Church of God in Christ Mennonite Church, located one mile south of Rich Hill, Bates Co., Mo., was organized in 1923. The first worship services were held in homes and schools. In 1942 a church was built with a seating capacity of 120, with Henry Dirks as the leading minister. In 1945 J. J. Esau was ordained as minister and Nathan Schmidt as deacon. The 1955 membership was 90, with Harvey Yost and Henry Dirks as ministers.   N.SA.

Emmanuel Krimmer Mennonite Brethren Church, now extinct, located 20 miles northeast of Garden City, Finney Co., Kan., came into being when settlers from various churches, especially from Janzen, Neb., came there in 1918, with Elder J. K. Ens as leader. In 1926 the membership had reached 80 and the Sunday-school enrollment 110. A public school and later a church basement served for a meeting place. The church was disbanded in 1936 when the majority of its members moved to other localities.

Other ministers who served the congregation are I. M. Friesen and J. J. Voth.   C.F.P.

Emmanuel Krimmer Mennonite Brethren Church, now extinct, located 4½ miles northwest of Chasely, N.D., was organized on July 3, 1921, under the leadership of Paul F. Gross, who served as first pastor. In 1927 the membership was 34. The new church was built and was dedicated on Pentecost 1920. A German parochial school was carried on for some time. The church died out in 1932. D. M. Hofer served the church with special meetings, at baptisms, and in the organization and dedication of the church. Samuel J. R. Hofer served as pastor about ten years.   C.F.P.

Emmanuel Krimmer Mennonite Brethren Church, Langham, Sask., had its beginning in 1901 when a few members moved in from South Dakota. A. Stahl served as the first pastor, when the church was organized and a meetinghouse was built in the summer of 1917. The baptized membership in 1955 was 50, all of whom were rural people, and the pastor was Paul Stahl. The meetinghouse is located 11½ miles southeast of Langham.   P. St.

Emmanuel Krimmer Mennonite Brethren Church, located 6 miles straight east of Onida, Sully Co., S.D., was organized on Oct. 10, 1920, with 28 members, under the leadership of David J. S. Mendel, who served it as pastor up to the fall of 1934. In the spring of 1940 Edwin F. Walter accepted the call as pastor of the church. Its 1955 membership was 99, with E. L. Hofer as pastor.   Ed.W.

Emmanuel Mennonite Church (GCM), sometimes known as Homestead, now extinct, located five miles southwest of Aberdeen, Idaho, a member of the Pacific District Conference, was organized April 22, 1912, under the leadership of Jacob Hege, who served as the first pastor. The membership at the time the church was disbanded (December 1930) was approximately 75, consisting almost entirely of rural people. Other ministers who served the church were Leonard Dirks and John Toews.   F.L.W.

Emmanuel Mennonite Church (unaffiliated), located in Meade Co., Kan., 5 miles south and 4 miles east of the city of Meade, was organized April 30, 1944, as an independent church, with 124 charter members, under the leadership of Henry R. Harms, who served as its first pastor, as a direct result of the dissolution of the Kleine Gemeinde congregation at Meade. One of the two church buildings formerly used by this group has been enlarged to seat about 350, and is now being used by the Emmanuel Mennonite Church. In the winter of 1952-53 the congregation built a new parsonage near the church. Samuel H. Epp, the present pastor, successor to H. R. Harms, serves an average congregation of 230, the membership to date (1954) being 210. The deacons assisting the pastor are George J. Rempel and Peter L. Classen.   S.H.E.

Emmanuel Mennonite Church (GCM), until 1931 known as the Canton Church, located six miles north and one-half west of Moundridge, McPherson Co., Kan., a member of the Western District Conference, was organized in 1875 by Mennonites from Poland.

The Christian Endeavor Society was organized on May 8, 1908. The women's mission society was organized in 1941. A new church was dedicated on June 14, 1942. The membership in 1955 was 87, with Garman H. Wedel serving as their pastor.

G.H.W.

Emmanuel Mennonite Church (GCM) near Pratum, Marion Co., Ore., formerly called Waldo Hill's Mennonite Church or Emmanuel's Mennonite Church was organized May 25, 1890, although the first building was not built until 1904. The present building was remodeled in 1940. The 1955 membership was 232, with Frank S. Harder serving as pastor. (*ML* I, 564.)   W.A.R.

Emmanuel Mennonite Church (GCM), located near Denver, Lancaster Co., Pa., was organized in 1939 with 22 members under the leadership of the present pastor Elmer D. Hess. The congregation united with the Eastern District Conference in 1940 and the General Conference Mennonite Church in 1941. Its membership was 55 in 1953.   E.D.H.

Emmanuel Mennonite Church (GCM), located 13 miles south and one mile west of Doland, Spink Co., S.D., a member of the Northern District Conference, was organized in 1921 with 36 members under the leadership of J. W. Kleinsasser, the first pastor. The 1953 membership was 89, and all were rural people. The original frame meetinghouse, erected in 1922 and seating 180, was still in use in 1954. Ministers who have served the congregation are J. W. Kleinsasser, Jacob A. Friesen, missionary Elmer Dick, who served two months as interim pastor, Frank Loewen, Lyman W. Sprunger, and the present pastor, Paul Quenzer.   L.W.S.

Emmatal Fortbildungsschule was established as a Kansas Conference Mennonite (GCM) secondary school in 1882 and occupied an empty school of the Emmatal school district, Marion County. H. H. Ewert (*q.v.*) was the teacher. After the first year the school was transferred to Halstead where it was known as the Halstead Seminary (*q.v.*), and in 1893 to Newton to continue as Bethel College (*q.v.*). The Emmatal Fortbildungsschule, also called a "Zentralschule," was the first attempt of the Mennonites of the prairie states and provinces to introduce secondary education.   C.K.

P. J. Wedel, "Beginning of Secondary Education in Kansas," *Menn. Life* III (October 1948) 14 ff.

Emmaus (Pa.) Mennonite Brethren in Christ Church, 28 members in 1911, had 156 members in 1953, with W. W. Hartman as pastor.

Emmaus Mennonite Church (GCM), located 1½ miles north and 2½ miles east of Whitewater, Butler Co., Kan., a member of the Western District Conference, had its origin with the arrival of West Prussian immigrants in 1876. Family heads included

Abraham, Dietrich, and Eduard Claassen, Johann Dyck, Johann and Bernhard Harder, Heinrich Penner, and Gerhard Regier. These were joined in the following year by the Leonhard and Abraham Sudermann families coming from South Russia. Leonhard Sudermann served as the first elder (1877). He was assisted by his brother Abraham Sudermann and Peter Dyck as ministers. The former later affiliated with the First Mennonite Church of Newton, and the latter with the Zion Mennonite Church of Elbing. Succeeding ministers and elders were Eduard Claassen, minister 1884-1902, and elder 1900-2; Gustav Harder, minister 1884-1923, and elder 1902-23; Johann P. Andres, minister 1893-1905; Heinrich M. Wiebe, minister 1902-5; Bernhard W. Harder, minister 1902-39, and elder 1923-39; Henry Thiessen, minister 1908 (installed in 1911) -39; Bernhard Wiebe, minister 1910-21; John C. Kaufman, minister and elder 1939-47; Walter H. Dyck, pastor 1948-54; and L. R. Amstutz 1955- .

The first meetinghouse was erected in 1878 with a seating capacity of 200; the second in 1908, seating 400; and the third in 1929, seating 800, which was still in use in 1953. A parsonage was built in 1950. The membership continues predominantly rural. Weekday parochial schools and catechetical instruction have been provided from the early years. Until 1908 the hymnal used at worship services was one without notes brought from Germany. Until 1929 four brethren had taken turns in leading congregational singing. At present a song leader (see **Chorister**) is elected annually.

The first deacons were elected in 1917. These together with the ministers constituted the church board. A church constitution was adopted in 1923. Communion is observed three times per year. Footwashing has not been observed. Morning worship services still include a kneeling prayer and ten minutes of song and meditation in the German language. The first missionaries to go out from the membership were Alfred Wiebe and wife, who went to the American Indians in Montana in 1911. Members have shown an active interest in the Berean Academy, Elbing, Kan. The membership in 1955 was 379.   W.H.D.

In Commemoration of Seventy-Five Years in America (Whitewater, Kans., 1952); J. W. Fretz, "A Tree at Whitewater," *Menn. Life* V (April 1950) 11-15; L. Sudermann, *Eine Deputationsreise von Russland nach America* (Elkhart, 1897); *ML* I, 576 f.

Emmaus Mennonite Church (GCM), located in the area of Swift Current, a city of about 9,000 in southwestern Saskatchewan, a wheat-growing area, is a member of the Conference of Mennonites of Canada. The congregation has (1954) seven church buildings, the largest of which, with a seating capacity of 250, is in Swift Current.

In 1913 the Home Mission Board of the Canadian Conference began to serve the scattered families living in the area and in 1914 the first 12 candidates were baptized. During the following years this group was served by Elder Johann Gerbrandt, Drake, Sask.; Gerhard Buhler, Herbert, Sask.; Peter J. Epp, Eigenheim, Sask.; and Elder Benjamin

Ewert. After World War I, a number of families from Russia settled here. As a result a congregation was organized June 16, 1928, and Isaac H. Wiens was ordained as the first minister, although Benjamin Ewert served for some time longer as elder.

The first meetinghouse was built in 1916 near Neville. The other six churches have been built with aid from the General Conference Home Mission Board since 1937. The membership in 1954 was 371, about half urban and half rural.

The congregation has Sunday schools, Christian Endeavor groups, women's mission groups, prayer meetings, and choirs. The German language is used for some morning services and the English in Sunday schools and in some morning and all evening services. The ministers in 1954 were Werner Zacharias, David Quiring, Wilhelm Zacharias, Cornelius P. Kehler, Jacob J. M. Friesen, and Valentine E. Nickel, who was ordained as elder Oct. 31, 1948.

V.E.N.

Emmen, a rapidly growing town (1947 pop. 55,500, with 175 Mennonites) in the Dutch province of Drenthe. In 1879 there were about 100 Mennonites here, most of whom seem to have joined the Baptist Church which arose here at this time (*DB* 1894, 85). In 1939 the Mennonites living here, having held occasional meetings in the preceding years, organized a Mennonite fellowship (*Kring*). About 30 members joined. From 1942 the group met in a school building, then once a month in a room of the Reformed Church, and now (1956) in a rented hall. The membership in 1956 is 35; there is a Sunday school for the children (39 children). J. Meerburg Snarenberg, pastor of the Zwolle congregation, is in charge of this group.   vdZ.

Emmenholz, Zuchwil district, in the Swiss canton of Solothurn, in the angle where the Emme flows into the Aare. In 1899 Christian Gerber leased a large farm here and converted it into a model agricultural project. By industry and capability father and son won recognition and were elected on community and school boards.

Always interested in the welfare of the Mennonite Church and led by the wish to keep his family true to it, Christian Gerber furnished a hall with chairs and an organ as a place of worship. He thereby established in Emmenholz a new subsidiary of the Kleintal (*q.v.*) congregation. He put the hall also at the disposal of the Evangelical Society in which he was active; meetings were held here twice a month, alternately led by Mennonite preachers (Jura and Emmental) and evangelists of the Society. Communion is observed four times annually. Since 1910 there has been a Sunday school. In 1922 the congregation numbered 15 baptized members and 27 children. In 1953, Elder Abraham Gerber of Brestenberg was the local minister in charge. Since 1946 the meetings of the Mennonites of the Solothurn district are no longer held in Emmenholz, but in the home of Elder Abraham Gerber in Brestenberg near Riedholz, where 8-10 families assemble. A Mennonite preacher serves on the

first Sunday of the month, and a preacher from the Evangelical Society on the third Sunday. Emmenholz (Brestenberg) has never been an independent congregation. (*ML* I, 577.)   A.T., S.G.

Emmental, a district in the Swiss canton of Bern, where Anabaptism gained a following in the Reformation era, and in spite of very severe persecution has maintained itself up to the present. The narrower Emmental (Emme Valley) is made up of the two townships, Signau (the upper valley) and Trachselwald (the lower valley), together with the adjacent Konolfingen and Burgdorf. The meadows of the upper part of the Emmental extend to the Lower Alps. Mt. Napf rises to a height of 4,670 ft. Here is the home of the famed Emmental cheese. In the lower regions farming and fruit-growing predominate. In the narrower Emmental there are only a few towns of any size, of which Langnau, with its population of 8,600, is most important. In general it is an extensive region of individual farms. Besides the church and school there are few buildings to mark a center. The brooks have cut deep, narrow furrows in the meadows. Thickly sprinkled over the landscape are the trim homesteads. This form of landscape and of settlement produces in the inhabitants a strong self-reliance and a consequent weakening of group or community consciousness. Their independence of thought has frequently been demonstrated to both state and church. To this territory we add the flatter land of Aarwangen and Traubrunnen (the Oberaargau). This extended Emmental embraces a considerable part of the canton of Bern, approximately 450 sq. miles with 160,000 inhabitants.

What is said in the article **Bern** (*q.v.*) about the Anabaptist movement applies in especial degree to the Emmental. Here Anabaptism arose and spread very quickly. Although the movement spread throughout the canton, nevertheless the Emmental was specifically an Anabaptist region. This may be due in part to the fact that it is adjacent to the cantons Aargau, Lucerne, and Solothurn, where the Anabaptists were likewise more numerous during the 16th century. The canton of Basel (*q.v.*) also extends to within five miles of Wangen and Aarwangen. Thus missionary Anabaptists always reached this region first to strengthen the brotherhood, and were then all too frequently seized and finally also executed.

Since the history of Emmental has already been discussed in **Bern,** the present discussion will center especially on those places where Anabaptists are mentioned in documents (see the map). The first dealings of the council of Bern with the Anabaptists (Oct. 22, 1525, and Jan. 13, 1526; see *R.A.* Nos. 746 and 801) lead in the direction of Aargau (*q.v.*), which was at that time largely under Bernese jurisdiction (until 1798). On March 7 and 12, and April 27, 1526, dispatches were sent to the magistrate of Wangen (*R.A.* Nos. 839, 843, 876), which mention secret meetings, clandestine preaching (*Winkelpredigen*) and preaching in the tavern, and order the magistrate to banish these preachers if they will not desist. It is not certain that these acts deal with

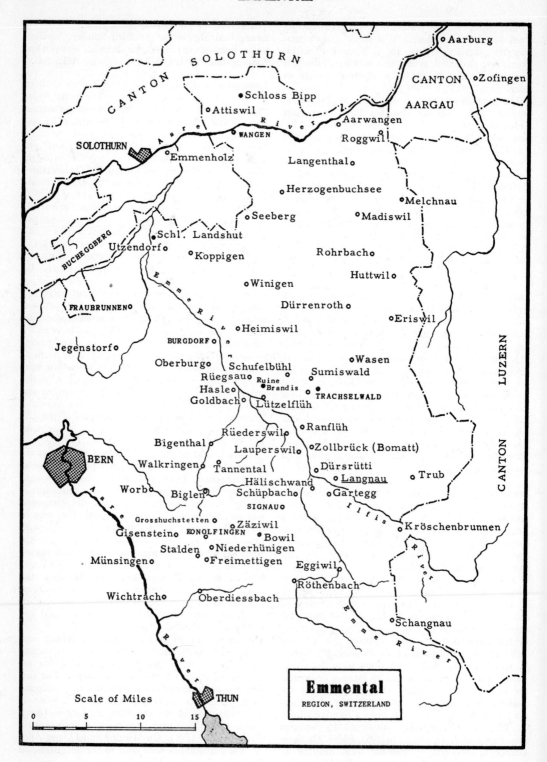

SOLOTHURN

•Aarburg

CANTON

•Zofingen

CANTON AARGAU

•Schloss Bipp

∘Attiswil

•Aarwangen

•Roggwil

WANGEN

SOLOTHURN

∘Emmenholz

Langenthal∘

•Herzogenbuchsee

•Melchnau

•Seeberg

•Madiswil

BUCHEGGBERG

•Schl. Landshut

Utzendorf∘

∘Koppigen

Rohrbach∘

Huttwil∘

∘Winigen

FRAUBRUNNEN∘

Dürrenroth∘

∘Eriswil

LUZERN

Jegenstorf∘

•Heimiswil

BURGDORF∘

Oberburg∘

Schufelbühl

•Wasen

Rüegsau∘

Sumiswald

Hasle∘

Ruine Brandis

Goldbach∘

Lützelflüh

TRACHSELWALD

•Ranflüh

CANTON

Rüederswil∘

Bigenthal∘

Lauperswil∘

Zollbrück (Bomatt)

Walkringen∘

Tannental

Dürsrütti

•Trub

Worb∘

Biglen∘

Hälischwand

Schüpbach∘

Langnau

Gartegg

SIGNAU∘

Grosshuchstetten

Kröschenbrunnen

Gisenstein∘

KONOLFINGEN

Zäziwil

Stalden

Niederhünigen

•Bowil

Münsingen∘

Freimettigen

Eggiwil∘

Röthenbach

Wichtrach∘

Oberdiessbach

Schangnau∘

BERN

Aare River

Emme River

Ilfis

River

Emme River

Scale of Miles

0   5   10   15

THUN

Emmental

REGION, SWITZERLAND

Anabaptist preaching. But in later dispatches the preaching of the Anabaptists is often referred to as "corner preaching" and "tavern preaching" (*R.A.* Nos. 2721 and 3058). A similar case occurs in a dispatch of May 8, 1527, in which two men of Lower Huttwil are to answer for talking about the sacrament and are released (*R.A.* No. 1202).

On Sept. 6, 1527, in an order to the communes, the Anabaptists are mentioned, which indicates that the movement was widespread. Measures are passed to "eradicate these weeds." The banished outsiders who return are to be "drowned without mercy," likewise their leaders and "masters." On Jan. 7, 1528, a command is issued to keep Anabaptists imprisoned until the conclusion of the approaching disputation (*R.A.* No. 1456). On Jan. 10, 1528, Jegenstorf receives instructions concerning the imprisonment of Anabaptists (*R.A.* No. 1459). On Jan. 22, 1528, a dispatch is issued to city and canton, which deals only with Anabaptists, with the "earnest and urgent command" to watch carefully and closely all Anabaptists, whether "foreign or native" (*R.A.* No. 1481). On Feb. 23, 1528, an order is given to the communes concerning the Reformation: Anabaptists are not to be tolerated anywhere, neither in city nor canton; they are to be captured and sent to Bern (*R.A.* No. 1534). Strangely there is now a gap in the succession of notices about the Anabaptists, from Feb. 23, 1528, to Oct. 7, 1529 (*R.A.* Nos. 1534-2557). On Oct. 7, 1529, an order is issued to the magistrate of Wangen, to send the "peasants and pastors" of Rohrbach and Madiswil to him, the "Disputatz thöuffer" (disputation Anabaptists) (*R.A.* No. 2557). On Oct. 14, 1527, and 28, 1529, orders go to the same magistrate concerning the Anabaptists in his territory. The towns Wangen, Rohrbach, and Huttwil are named (*R.A.* Nos. 2564, 2565, 2584, and 2585).

Upon receipt of information that the Anabaptists of Basel were planning a missionary campaign in Bernese and Solothurn territory, Bern issued orders to the districts of Attiswil, Bipp, Wangen, Aarwangen, and Landshut (as also Seeland and Aargau) to guard carefully against the Anabaptists, in order that "such weeds be exterminated" (*R.A.* No. 2693). This appeal was not without purpose; on Feb. 1, 1530, the magistrate of Bipp is to "guard the Anabaptists well and give information." Feb. 2, 1530, Bern reports to Solothurn about the Anabaptist movement in Wangen, Aarwangen, and Bipp (*R.A.* No. 2716). Feb. 7, 1530, Röthenbach appears, and Feb. 18 Oberdiessbach (Diessbach) in the same affair (*R.A.* Nos. 2721 and 2728). On the same day instructions are issued to the magistrate of Landshut, to inform himself actually and secretly by day and night concerning the Anabaptists in Utzenstorf (*R.A.* No. 2728).

On Feb. 18, 1530, Bern reports to Basel that in the district of Bipp four Anabaptists have been captured, and on May 18 Bern issues a warning to Solothurn on account of the Anabaptists. In the district of Solothurn the persecuted and banished Anabaptists of Emmental often found refuge and temporary asylum (in Bucheggberg, Lüsslingen, Aetigen, Kriegstetten). In a rather lengthy, undated dispatch of the close of 1530, all deans are ordered, each in his own chapter, to give faithful warning against the "seditious sect of the Anabaptists." Now the Council is occupied with "Uli Flückinger" and "Osswalden" of Huttwil.

The severe mandate of July 31, 1531, to city and canton demands the "abolition and extermination" of the Anabaptists. Proof of the seriousness of the Council's intention are the numerous edicts and directives to officials; for example, Aug. 31 to Trachselwald and Signau, Sept. 6 to city and canton, Oct. 10 to Burgdorf, Huttwil, Wangen, Aarwangen, and Trachselwald, Nov. 21 again to Burgdorf. The captured Anabaptists are taken to Bern and tried; but their names are rarely given. For example, there are Anabaptists brought in from Aarwangen, Huttwil, Trachselwald, Signau, Burgdorf, and Rohrbach. The pastor of Dürrenroth complains that the Anabaptists are preaching and attacking his teaching. An Anabaptist teacher has been preaching at Sumiswald, and intends to preach in the market place of Huttwil. In Sumiswald and vicinity the Anabaptists have created "general confusion." The priest is removed and replaced by another, who "is to preach at Sumiswald, Dürrenroth, and Eriswil, to try to bring the churches back to their old custom." In prison in Bern are mentioned Christian Brügger of Rohrbach and Hans Riff, called Kaderli of Madiswil. The magistrates of Wangen, Aarwangen, Bipp, Trachselwald, Sumiswald, and Huttwil receive a reprimanding order to obey orders at once. In 1533 orders are issued to Aarwangen (to bring an Anabaptist to Bern with his father), to Trachselwald (concerning Miescher, a tailor at Dürrenroth), to Burgdorf (to keep the Anabaptists in prison until further notice or punish Miescher's wife and child), to Brandis (to send prisoners to Bern), to Signau (to come to Bern for instructions or to release Klaus Schumacher and the Müller of Gunten from fines), and to Melchnau, Sumiswald, Wangen, Aarwangen (to capture Anabaptists en route; and imprison leaders of the rabble and fine those who keep them in their homes). The pastor of Sumiswald is removed because of scandalous speech against the Anabaptists. At the close of the year the "Küfferli" is brought in, which is of significance to the people of Emmental. In 1534 directives are issued to Aarwangen, Trachselwald, Trub, Burgdorf, Brandis, Sumiswald, Oberburg, Signau, Wangen, and Heimiswil.

Several Anabaptists recant; thus in Rüegsau, Oberburg, Zäziwil, and Bigental. Others join the Anabaptists, and backsliders return to them; thus in Trachselwald and Grosshöchstetten. The Anabaptist Grete Wyss of Höchstetten is released on account of sickness. Peter Hofer of Biglen must appear before court because he "murmured" in church when the pastor said "the Anabaptists disregard the government." The number of steadfast (Anabaptists) increases, the measures of the government fail. In 1535 directives are issued to Wangen, Aarwangen, Bipp, Brandis, Trachselwald, Signau, Sumiswald "where Anabaptists are living."

On Jan. 30, 19 persons at an Anabaptist meeting, all from Emmental, appear before the council, among them Stucki, Vögeli, Blum, Tierstein, Bürki, Lienhart, Gfeller, Baumann, Künzi, Jenni. As new towns of their origin are named Konolfingen, Gisenstein, Niederhünigen, Stalden, Freimettigen. Two days later four appear from Rüegsau and Lützelflüh and seven from Signau (Wyss, Bürki, Salzmann, etc.), then from Höchstetten, Dürrenroth, Sumiswald, Biglen. From Huttwil comes bitter complaint that in Rüegsau there are unbaptized children, and in Madiswil the constable has helped the Anabaptists to hide. In Sumiswald the people warn the Anabaptists when they are in danger.

At the Anabaptist disputation of March 1538 (see **Disputation**) Emmental Anabaptists were present from Eggiwil, Signau, Grosshöchstetten, Walkringen, Schufelbühl, Sumiswald, Burgdorf, Niederhuttwil, Rohrbach, Madiswil, and Winigen. According to magistrates' reports there were Anabaptists also in the districts of Sumiswald, Bipp, Trachselwald, and Signau. In 1551 it is found that "the strip of land from Münsingen over Höchstetten throughout the Emmental has experienced a significant increase in the number of Anabaptists and the regulations are to be more strictly observed." In the districts of Signau, Trachselwald, and Brandis an open letter must be read from the pulpits, proclaiming that those who do not desist are to be punished in body and possessions, likewise those who shelter them. In 1585 the statement is made that all previous efforts have failed, and that the number of Anabaptists has rather increased. The pastors of Langnau often took pains to try to teach the Anabaptists in a friendly manner. In 1620 the pastor of Langnau receives the names of 17 Anabaptists in the vicinity (Mühlibach, Dürsrütti, Scheidegg, Brügglen, Gartegg, Frittenbach), among them names like Baumgartner, Probst, Friedrich, Bichsel, Ruch, Studer, Jost, Dählenbach, Reber, Krähenbühl, Röhtlisberger, Gerber.

In 1640 directives are issued to Aarwangen, Signau, and Brandis, in 1644 to all officials where Anabaptists are living. Teachers (preachers), "agitators and seducers" are to be sent in, especially Uli Zaugg, Uli Nüwhus, and Christen Stauffer. In 1654 the preacher of Eggiwil in reply to a request names 40 Anabaptists in his district. In 1658 a record of Anabaptists is demanded of the chapters (deanships) Burgdorf and Langenthal. In 1660 an order from the Council is again sent to Langenthal. A record mentions eleven Anabaptists in the penitentiary, of whom eight are from the Emmental, one from Lauperswil, and one from Koppigen. In 1669 the Anabaptist teachers Christian Güngerich and Hans Burkhalter escape in Bern. In 1670 an interdict is issued to Konolfingen against "harboring and visiting" Anabaptists. In particular they are to try to seize the Anabaptist teachers Durss Aebi and Hans Haldimann. The preacher of Lauperswil holds a discussion with the Anabaptists there.

On May 3, 1671, the magistrate of Signau receives orders to seize the Anabaptists of district Eggiwil, and to deliver them to the orphanage. Somewhat later 12 of the wealthiest persons in the district are sent to Bern as hostages until the Anabaptists would be delivered to Bern or move away. The hostages were to be kept at their own expense. This measure proved "effective in several places."

In 1692, 28 known Anabaptists are staying in Langnau; the populace is very favorable to them and does not want to hear them preached against. In 1693 a division occurs (see **Jakob Ammann**). The Emmental Anabaptists stay with the more lenient group led by Hans Reist. In the same year directives concerning Anabaptists are issued to the districts of Landshut, Burgdorf, Brandis, Trachselwald, Signau.

Further places appearing in Anabaptist history are Herzogenbuchsee (Niklaus Häberle of Buchsee, in prison in 1710), Ranflüh (Peter Geissbühler has given six "High German Anabaptist Testaments" to the bookbinder for binding), Goldbach (the forbidden Froschauer Bible to be demanded of Hans Reber), Wasen (Ulrich Scheidegger and Hans Wysser, smith, are on trial), Worb (Trini Bigler, a simple poor soul of 52 years), Wichtrach (Daniel Loris's wife), Hasli (Jakob Schüppach in der Träyen).

The names and places of persons executed in Bern 1529-71 point predominantly to the Emmental, especially to Sumiswald, Lützelflüh, Rüderswil, Rüegsau, Signau, Hasli, Röthenbach, Schüpbach, and Tannental.

In 1670 the chapter (deanery) Burgdorf complains to the Council: "The number of these sectarians increases daily; for instance nine members of the little Reformed Church at Schangnau have withdrawn this year. The half-Anabaptists, who differ in that they still attend our services at will, are so numerous that it is to be feared that in some places there are more of them than of ours." Ernst Müller remarks correctly: "The surmise of the pastors that the 'half Anabaptists' (q.v.) might in several places constitute the majority of the congregation, explains the renewed zeal of church and secular authorities, and shows again how independent the Emmental always was toward church and government."

At that period the movement in the Emmental reached its greatest following. In the following period persecution took a severer turn. Fluri states: "The almost unceasing persecution of the Bernese Anabaptists occasionally burst out with the violence of a volcanic eruption, . . . it never stopped, not even in the years of pestilence 1667-69, and in 1670 took on the form of actual hunts." The persecuted Anabaptists often fled to Lucerne territory, as for instance Daniel Grimm and Hans Brechbühl at Willisau. The Anabaptist hunts frequently led to the violation of district and cantonal boundaries. Especially long-drawn-out proceedings followed a hunt near Kröschenbrunnen, in which Anabaptists entered Lucerne territory. The sound folk-will of Emmental expressed itself forcibly against the Anabaptist hunts. In Sumiswald a crowd of 60-70 persons released the Anabaptists and severely beat the hunters (1714).

Naturally the perpetrators of this deed whose names were known were punished. "Bendicht Widmer, the schoolmaster, took part, is removed from his position for a half year to Brassu in the district of Romanmostier," Uli Loosli in Trachselwald receives 24 hours of imprisonment because of "improper conduct" toward the Anabaptist hunters when his sister was seized by them. The canon Hans Schöni of Sumiswald ventures to defend the Anabaptists; he receives 24 hours of imprisonment. Anabaptists are warned by "horns, cries, and similar signs."

If we compare the present congregation at Emmental (*q.v.*) with the complaint of the Burgdorf chapter in 1670, it is evident that Anabaptism was greatly weakened by continued persecution. This is, however, not due to any extensive recantation, but to the numerous voluntary removals from the canton, the frequent banishment, and above all to the extensive emigration. True to their faith, the Anabaptists sacrificed their kin and homeland, went out into the unknown, depending on God and the help of the Brethren.

The canton of Solothurn (*q.v.*) probably served as nearest refuge for shorter or longer sojourn. Then the blue mountains of the Jura (*q.v.*) beckoned, where in the district of the more tolerant bishops of Basel numerous Emmental Anabaptist families found shelter and work. Beyond these mountains France became an asylum for the refugees. In the Jura and in France even today the majority of Anabaptist families are of Emmental origin (Mathiot).

In the 16th century Moravia (*q.v.*) was also for a time the goal of fleeing Swiss Anabaptists. The migration was at times unusually great (for example in 1585-86). Bern attacked the problem of emigration several times and tried to prevent it. Names like Gerber, Schenk, Hofer, Baumann, Amsler, and Born prove that Emmental had a part in this emigration.

A far more important goal for emigrants in the 17th and 18th centuries was the Palatinate (*q.v.*) with the adjoining country (Hege, 178). Already in 1527 an immigration takes place here from Switzerland, and only from Swiss Anabaptists did the movement in the Palatinate make any considerable gains (Hege, 7). It is also significant that the Moravian Anabaptists called their brethren in the Palatinate Swiss Brethren. The greatest emigration, chiefly from Bern, took place in 1671—about 700 persons, large and small, impoverished (record in Müller, 200-94). Most of the names given indicate Emmental as their home. Emigration continued for many years. Lists of heads of households in the Palatinate congregations in the years 1731 and 1732 name for the most part Bernese names, and those chiefly from the Emmental (Müller, 209-12; *Menn. Jugendwarte* II, 1921-22, 10). The present-day Mennonites in South Germany probably derive for the most part from the Emmental.

A further goal of emigration was Holland. Sympathetically and continuously the Dutch Mennonites concerned themselves for their harassed brethren,

with financial support and petitions to their persecutors. They did their best in word and deed to ease the lot of their persecuted brethren. Some Swiss Brethren settled in Jülich and Berg in 1653. Driven out by the Jesuits, others fled to the Netherlands. On Sept. 10, 1660, eleven exiles left Bernese territory, of whom eight were from Emmental. Jakob Schlappach of Oberdiessbach, Ulrich Baumgartner of Langnau, Hans Zaugg of Signau, Peter Frider of Biglen, and Matthys Kaufmann, stopped at Koppigen. Later other Anabaptists attached themselves to this first small emigration to Holland. Benedicht Baumgartner (see **Dürsrüttilied**) and Christen Christen returned and were again incarcerated. In 1711 came the great emigration of about 346 persons (Müller, 307, 313). On the Emmental boat the overseers were Hans Bürki, Christen Gäumann, and Jakob Rechener. This ship to be sure did not harbor only refugees from the Emmental (e.g., from Bolligen, Stettlen, Rüeggisberg); on the other hand there were on the "Oberländer" boat, the "Thuner" boat, and the "Neuenburger" boat many persons of Emmental descent, so that Emmental here again furnished the greatest number of immigrants. Many returned because of homesickness and others settled in the Palatinate.

A new haven for emigrants was Prussia. Bern and Prussia negotiated. Prussia offered favorable terms and the investigation commission, headed by Benedikt Brechbill, brought back a good report. But the Swiss Brethren disregarded this goal. In greater numbers they settled in Neuchâtel (*q.v.*) which was at that time Prussian.

The greatest territory for emigration was, however, America. In 1699 the Bernese government intended to banish the Anabaptists to the East Indies, but this plan had to be abandoned. Instead in 1710 more than 50 persons were to be banished to America. The exiling took place, but the Dutch managed to bring it about that the plan of the "gracious patrician lords" of Bern ended in favor of the Brethren. A large number of the exiles had to be left behind in Mannheim, because of sickness, and the rest were freed in Holland. The Mennonites who from this time on emigrated from South Germany to America are probably almost all of Emmental origin. These numerous emigrations in the 18th and 19th centuries had serious consequences at home. In the Jura several congregations died out.

Love of home and kin induced many emigrants and exiles to return, where they were again persecuted, imprisoned, and exiled. With their intense love of home these Emmental exiles must have suffered severely from homesickness. (See the deeply emotional poem "Peter Krehbiel's Abschied aus der Schweiz," 1671, in *Gem.-Kal.,* 1911, 46.)

The Bernese government made an effort to exile the Brethren as penniless as possible and keep their resources in the country. Numerous communities had Brethren estates to manage, as Roggwil, Seeberg, Huttwil, Dürrenroth, Sumiswald, Eriswil, Heimiswil, Trachselwald, Lützelflüh, Rüegsau, Rüederswil, Walkringen, Münsingen, Wichtrach, Oberdriessbach, Grosshöchstetten, Hasli, Lauperswil,

Langnau, Trub, Eggiwil, Röthenbach, Schangnau. These lands were used for church and school purposes. From the income from the Anabaptist land, Lützelflüh paid its church musician and repaired the church tower. Sumiswald and Langnau returned some of the income to the descendants of the original owners; Langnau finally restored the land to its rightful heirs.

From about 1720 there was some lessening of persecution, although even until the middle of the 19th century harsh measures were taken by the cantonal government against the Mennonites. In 1743 the Anabaptist Commission (*Täuferkammer, q.v.*) was disbanded, and the "Anabaptist-hunters" disappeared from the country.

A new cause of emigration from the Emmental lay in the conflicts concerning military service. In 1737 it was decided that Mennonites who refused military service were to be sent to work in the silver mines. In 1745 those who failed to appear were charged with fines, and in 1780 they were threatened with banishment from the territory of Bern. The plan of 1786 to compel each Mennonite liable to military service to work a month per year in harvesting the crops of the poor was never carried out.

Through the influence of ideas of the French Revolution (*q.v.*) conditions improved greatly for the Emmental Mennonites. In 1798 they obtained formal recognition and toleration, but soon again a number of restrictions were made. In 1810 four leaders of the Emmental congregation, Niklaus Gerber, Christen Gerber, Ulrich Kipfer, and Christen Brand, made an appeal to the Bernese government, recalling the rights granted them in 1798. But about the same time the Langnau parish ordered a compulsory baptism of all who had not been baptized since the French Revolution, and in 1811 some 27 young Mennonites were brought to the state church by the local police and baptized by the minister Stephani. In 1823 the Mennonites had to hand over lists of all members, in order to enable the magistrates to determine whether proselytes were being made among the members of the state church. This system continued for several years in the Signau district of Emmental until as late as 1850.

After the formal toleration of 1798 the question of military services remained critical for more than a century. In 1815 the Mennonites of the canton of Bern were freed from military service on condition that they send a person as a substitute, or pay a special fee. From 1835 exemption from military service was granted on paying a special tax. In 1874 the matter was settled by a federal act for all Swiss citizens (see **Military Service**).

Notwithstanding these conditions only a few Emmental Mennonites emigrated after 1798. In January 1852 a number of them left, most of them settling in Adams Co., Ind., where they founded the town of Berne. Among them there were two Emmental ministers, Matthias Strahm and Ulrich Kipfer.

When we consider the difficult terrain, the complicated district and cantonal boundaries, the frequent visits of outside Anabaptists, the amazing love of home of the Emmental inhabitants, the almost unmatched steadfastness in faith, and the generally favorably-minded populace, then we understand why the century-long persistent attempts at annihilation on the part of Bern were unsuccessful against the Anabaptists of this region. Anabaptism had from the very beginning struck such deep roots that it outlived all the storms of persecution. Of course the numerous exilings and emigrations broke off some powerful limbs. But these branches have taken fresh root in other places and thus have helped to spread Anabaptism. The Emmental is the original home of many Mennonites in the Jura, France, Hesse, Bavaria, Baden, Württemberg, Galicia, and the Netherlands, as well as the American Mennonites who came from these places, and is thus the source of numerous Mennonite congregations in Europe and America.

There are no stone monuments to the suffering of the Brethren in the Emmental. But the recently discovered Anabaptist history speaks insistently of it. The books of local folklore say little about it. Ernst Marti created a literary monument in his novel, *Zwei Häuser, zwei Welten* (Two Houses, Two Worlds) (Frauenfeld, 1911). A living token is the still extant "Old Evangelical (Ana)baptist Church of Emmental" in Langnau.†   A.-T.

Aktensammlung zur Geschichte der Berner Reformation 1521-1532 (R.A.) ed. R. Steck und G. Tobler (Bern, 1918-22); Müller, *Berner Täufer;* A. Fluri, *Beiträge zur Geschichte der bernischen Täufer* (Bern, 1912); Th. de Quervain, *Kirchliche und soziale Zustände in Bern unmittelbar nach der Einführung der Reformation* (1906); E. Serck, "Der Kanton Bern," in *Land und Volk* (Zürich, 1916); C. Mathiot, *Recherches historiques sur les Anabaptistes* (Belfort, 1922); Chr. Hege, *Die Täufer in der Kurpfalz* (Frankfurt, 1908); D. Gratz, *Bernese Anabaptists* (Scottdale, 1952); M. G. de Boer, "Vom Thunersee zum Sappemeer," in *Berner Ztscht für Gesch. und Heimatkunde* (1947); S. Geiser, *Die Taufgesinnten-Gemeinden* (Karlsruhe, n.d.); ML I, 577-83.

Emmental Mennonite Church in the Swiss canton of Bern (*q.v.*) is the oldest of the Mennonite churches existing in Switzerland, and probably the oldest anywhere. It originated in 1530. Its history is a story of suffering without equal (see **Bern** and **Emmental**). Only after 320 years did the severely tried congregation, which remained steadfast, receive full liberty of conscience. This occurred through the Bernese cantonal constitution of 1846 and the Swiss federal constitution of 1848. Now its religious life could develop undisturbed. Meetings were held in the various homes; for example, in Bädertschen, in Zollbrück, in Frittenbach, in Stock, in Raingut, in Hälenschwane, in Bowil, in Kurzenberg, and other places. Outstanding men of God, like Ulrich Steiner (1806-77, commonly called "Steiner Ulli," preacher 1825, elder 1835) and Ulrich Habegger in Bädertschen, Ulrich Kipfer in Raingut, Johann Gerber in Stock (1838-1918, commonly called "Stockhannes," preacher 1875, elder soon after), Christian Wüthrich in Lihnen, and others, led the congregation.

In 1882 a monthly periodical called the *Zionspilger* (*q.v.*) was founded by Samuel Bähler and others, which has continued to be published by the Emmental congregation, for a number of years jointly with the Free Church.

By about 1800 the consequences of the old Ammann-Reist schism had entirely disappeared. But soon after, a new schism arose in the Emmental congregation. Samuel Fröhlich (*q.v.*), a member of the Reformed Church who had been compelled to break off his theological studies at the University of Zürich because of his revivalistic principles and his aversion to infant baptism, and Georg Steiger, an adherent of Fröhlich's, introduced some pietistic and revivalistic ideas among the members of the Emmental Mennonite Church about 1832; finally many of the members, including the preachers Christen Baumgartner and Christen Gerber, were rebaptized by Steiger, left the Mennonite church, and with a number of Fröhlichianer who had been members of the Reformed Church in 1835 founded the "Neutäufer" (see **Apostolic Christian Church**). The ministerial body (*Dienerkonferenz*) of the Mennonites, who were now sometimes known as "Alttäufer," excommunicated Baumgartner and Gerber, who had withdrawn from the congregation. The Emmental church was greatly weakened by the loss of so many members, but soon recovered.

On Oct. 21, 1888, a meetinghouse built in Kehr near Langnau with a residence for the pastor, financed by a building association, was dedicated (*Menn. Bl.*, 1888, 132). In 1898 it was decided to build another meetinghouse at Aebnit near Bowil. Also in Bomatt near Zollbrück the congregation has its own church with an apartment. Meetings are also held in Rüederswil, Rüttimatt near Aeschau, Gartegg, Hälenschwand, Gohl, Fahrn near Lauperswil. On April 3, 1898, the congregation elected a "board of nine members for the conduct of congregational affairs. Elders and ministers of the church have the right to vote and to take part in the council." The board was chosen because "new fields of work kept opening, greatly increasing the work of the ministers; in order to relieve this burden somewhat and to distribute the work through the entire congregation, and in order to rouse and preserve the interest of individual members in welfare of the whole congregation. For this reason the separate districts of the congregation are to be given the highest possible consideration in the choice of members of the board." This was done. The first board was composed of Peter Kipfer in Raingut, Ulrich Salzmann in Langnau, Friedrich Stettler in Langnau, Hans Luginbühl in Aebnit near Bowil, Ulrich Steiner in Rüttimatt near Aeschau, Hans Lutki in Brügglen, Hans Mosemann in Hälenschwand, Ulrich Wittwer in Rüederswil, and Ernst Spengler in Langnau. On Dec. 24, 1899, the new statutes of the "Altevangelische Taufgesinnten-Gemeinde Emmental, located in Langnau," were accepted; thereby the congregation acquired corporation rights. As organs of the church they name (1) the members' meeting; (2) the board of directors; (3) elders, preachers, and deacons. At a members' meeting on Jan. 7, 1903, women were given the right to vote. The chief occupation is farming; but other occupations are also represented.

For religious life the congregational statutes give the following directive: "Furtherance of the religious and moral life of the members. Exercise, conduct, and promotion of the worship services of the old-evangelical confession, the acquisition of suitable buildings; support and care of the poor and sick within and without the congregation, support and promotion of charitable work in home and foreign missions." Religious life is very active, church attendance and Christian unity are gratifying. Variety is given the religious services through annual celebrations, missionary meetings, song services, and services held in the woods. Since 1898 communion is observed on the second Sunday of every month. Discipline is exercised from exhortation to exclusion from the church. Members are received upon request through the believers' baptism. If it is requested, immersion may be used. The idea of admitting believers who have shown their affection for the church without believers' baptism is often presented and opposed.

Instruction of youth lasts two years; here the catechism of the Badischer Verband is used. Sunday schools receive full attention and are conducted with non-Mennonites. The number of children in the Sunday schools is over 600. Boys' clubs, girls' clubs, and song clubs are very active. Love feasts (*Agapen*) and teas are held.

Bible courses (formerly always conducted by Jakob Hege, the traveling evangelist of the Mennonites of Baden) and "evangelization weeks" are conducted regularly in the various places. The latter are usually led by brethren from the outside (from the Jura churches, from Chrischona, from the Evangelical Association or the Free Church).

In the care of the sick the church took the lead in the Langnau community. Much is done for the poor, for home missions, and particularly for the China Alliance Mission.

Religious life is in the charge of the elders, ministers, and deacons. These offices are considered important, responsible positions. Usually the ministers preach trial sermons before they are ordained. Preachers and deacons are chosen from the laity; elders from the ranks of preachers and deacons. In 1900 three ministers were chosen by lot; since then they are chosen by the vote, usually by ballot, of the congregation. The elders from 1920 were John Kipfer, Fritz Gerber, and Fritz Mosimann. The membership in 1922 was 286.

In addition to the services held in the three meetinghouses (weekly at Kehr near Langnau, monthly at Aebnit near Bowil and at Bomatt near Zollbrück), monthly meetings are held (1955) at the following places: Fahrn (Rüderswil), Moosbad (Emmenmatt), Hauetershaus in der Gohl, Erlenbach (Signau), Gartegg (Langnau), Häleschwand near Schüpbach (Signau), Margelhof near Hellbühl (Luzern). The meetinghouse at Kehr was much enlarged in 1947. Hans Rüfenacht, the present (1955) pastor, graduate of St. Chrischona, was called to be preacher at Kehr in 1943 and ordained elder in 1944, also serving as editor of the weekly *Zionspilger,* published by the congregation, as successor to Elder Johann Kipfer (*q.v.*). In 1955 the congregation had about 350-400 baptized members.

In 1947 the Emmental congregation officially

joined the State Church of the Canton of Bern, without surrendering either its membership in the Swiss Mennonite Conference or its congregational autonomy. Although this connection has made little or no change in the life of the congregation except to free it from taxes, it was deeply opposed by the rest of the Swiss Mennonite congregations, who feared its impact.

In 1937 the Emmental congregation adopted as its confession of faith a doctrinal statement prepared by its elder, Johann Kipfer, *Glaubensbekenntnis der Altevangelisch Taufgesinnten-Gemeinde im Emmental*. Kipfer sought to have the other Swiss Mennonite congregations adopt the confession but they refused when he declined to revise the articles which appeared to tolerate infant baptism.   A.-T., S.G.

S. Geiser, *Die Taufgesinnten-Gemeinden* (Karlsruhe, 1931); *ML* I, 583 f.

Emmerich, a city (pop. 16,300) in the Prussian Rhine province, six miles from the Dutch border, in which there was a small Mennonite congregation for almost four centuries, going back to 1534. The radical Münsterites presumably also had a following in Emmerich. Bernhard Peters in 1574 printed here a book on polygamy for the "king" Johann Wilmsen, who had his headquarters in Wesel and was executed in Dinslaken in 1580. Nothing is known about the early history of the peaceful Anabaptists. From 1663 to 1717 Hendrik van Voorst preached there. During that time, in 1672, Emmerich was occupied by the French for a short period, who attempted to catholicize the town. To convert the Mennonites they sent Dr. Formantijn (*q.v.*) from Paris; but van Voorst's superior knowledge of Scripture blocked the attempt (*DB* 1873, 58). On Dec. 1, 1676, the magistrate of Emmerich granted freedom from taxation for a church they were planning. They purchased a large lot on Steinstrasse and on it built a church and parsonage. In the 17th century a number of members of the prominent Block and Leeuw families in this congregation emigrated to Amsterdam and Haarlem, Holland. Hendrik van Voorst was succeeded by Abraham Fortgens. During a later pulpit vacancy Cornelis van Braght preached here occasionally. From 1742 on, the congregation was served by Dutch-speaking ministers, mostly trained at the Amsterdam Mennonite Seminary: Klaas de Vries 1742-44, Hermanus Jaarsma 1744-83, Joannes Stijl 1786-89, Matthias Hesseling 1788-98, Anthoni de Vries 1798-1817, J. Kuiper 1819-20. In 1820-49 the congregation was served by H. W. van der Ploeg, the pastor of Goch. The last preachers were P. W. van Zutphen 1850-73 and D. Lodeesen 1873-83. The church was then served by preachers of the neighboring Mennonite churches, Nijmegen, Zutphen, and Winterswijk. In 1740 there was a baptized membership of 65. In 1825 there was no church board and only a few members. By 1836 the membership had declined to 18, 1870 to 16, 1898 to 7, and 1912 to 5. For more than a century the congregation was financially supported by the Amsterdam congregation.   NEFF, vDZ.

F. Nippold, "Zur Ref.-Gesch. der Stadt Emmerich," in *Monatshefte für rheinische Kirchengesch.* III (1909) 289-300; *ibid.* IX (1915) 19-24; *Inv. Arch. Amst.* I, Nos. 1164, 1424; II, 315, 2571, 2581, 2700-41; II, 2, 860-62; *DJ* 1850, 64; *DB* 1873, 58-73; 1895, 183; 1898, 242; 1912, 242; *Menn. Bl.*, 1887, 80; 1915, 36; M. Goebel, *Gesch. des Christlichen Lebens in der rhein.-westf. Kirche* (Coblence, 1849) I, 208 ff.; *Naamlijst* 1829, 70; *ML* I, 584.

Emmittsburg (Md.) Mennonite Church (MC), now extinct, located 10 miles southwest of Gettysburg, Pa., had services every six weeks during the 1880's and earlier. The congregation was under the care of the Mummasburg ministers, Daniel Shenk, bishop; Martin Wisler, preacher, and John Boyer, deacon. Information concerning the exact place of worship, period of continuance, and who were served is lacking.   I.D.L.

Emmius, Ubbo (1547-1625), a Frisian historiographer, professor of history and rector of the University of Groningen, Netherlands, whose most important work, *Rerum frisicarum historia* (1596-1615), is a valuable source for Mennonite history. He was a violent opponent of David Joris (*q.v.*), concerning whose life and family relationships he gives important information in *Ein grundtlick Bericht Van der Lere und dem Geist des Ertzketters David Joris . . .* (1597, Dutch edition, Middelburg, 1599). In 1600 a refutation of the book appeared in *Wederlegginghe, vande grove onbeschaemde vnde tastelicke Logenen van Vbbo Emmen . . . tegen het leven vnde leere van Dauid Iorissoon*, written by Andreas Huygelmumzoon (Bernardus Kirchen). Emmius prepared a detailed answer (442 pages) which he had translated from the "Saxensche sprake" (East Frisian literary language in which the first book against Joris appeared) into the Dutch language and published in 1603 under the title *Den David-Jorischen Gheest in Leven ende Leere, breeder ende wijdtloopigher ontdect en grondlicken verklaert, tegens den vermomden schaemtloosen D. Andreas Huygelmumzoon* (The Hague). According to Emmius, Huygelmumzoon was Bernardus Kirchen, a physician and son-in-law of David Joris. Emmius seems to have restricted his opposition to David Joris and his followers. Although he must have had contacts with the Mennonites he does not seem to have written against them. He himself, a native of Norden, East Friesland, where he became rector of the school, had to leave his country because as Reformed he was opposed by the Lutherans of the city.   C.K.

E. Meiners, *Oostvrieschlandts Kerkelyke Geschiedenisse . . .* (Groningen, 1738) 267 ff.; J. J. Boer, *Ubbo Emmius en Oost-Friesland* (Groningen, 1926); *ML* I, 584.

Empens, Gillis, was the author of a book published in 1627, now lost, concerning events in 1555, "how Menno joined with five brethren." Several citations in Dooreslaer (*q.v.*) lead to the supposition that this is a valuable historical work, especially on the Flemish between 1568 and 1627. It would therefore be of great value if this book could be found. (*ML* I, 584.)   K.V.

Emsiger-Land (Emderland), located between Reiderland and Broekmer-Land at the mouth of the Ems River, East Friesland, Germany (the region between Emden and Greetsiel, *q.v.*), was a government district at the time of the Reformation under Edzard I. Later this territory between Emden and Greetsiel was divided into Emden Amt, Pewsum Amt, and Greetmer Amt. During the Reformation this was the area in which the largest number of Anabaptists of East Friesland were located. Melchior Hofmann began his work in Emden and Leenaert Bouwens baptized more than 450 persons in this area, most of whom were living in Emden and 't Falder, a suburb. That the Mennonites were soon located all over the rural area can be seen from the lists of names of persons who paid a protection fee to the government during the 17th and 18th centuries. These lists have been preserved in the archives of Emden and Aurich and been partly published by Müller. Mennonites were located in and around the following places as renters of farms, farm hands, etc.: Suurhusen, Osterhusen, Canum, Canhusen, Wirdum, Eilsum, Jennelt, Hösingwehr, Schoonorth, Greetsiel, Pilsum, Manslagt, Grothusen, Upleward, etc. Uko Walles, for example, for many years rented the estate of Sielmönken, a former monastery.

Emsiger-Land is sometimes also referred to as "Emderland." Blaupot ten Cate (*Groningen* I, 225 f.) reports that there were two (Groningen) Old Flemish congregations in this area in 1715, one in Emden and the other in Hösingwehr, the latter usually known as the Emderland congregation. In 1746 the congregation at Emden had 70 members and in 1762 there were only "five or six brothers" left, while the one at Hösingwehr was a little larger. Today there are hardly any Mennonites located in the villages north of Emden. Whether they all moved to the cities or gradually joined the Reformed and Lutheran churches is not known. The spread of the Mennonites in the rural area of Emsiger-Land and East Friesland in general, the number of congregations found here and their gradual disintegration has not been studied. (See also **East Friesland.**)

C.K.

H. Reimers, *Ostfriesland bis zum Aussterben seines Fürstenhauses* (Bremen, 1925), see "Karte II" and "Karte III" in appendices; *Heimatkarte von Ostfriesland* (Oldenburg); J. P. Müller, *Die Mennoniten in Ostfriesland* . . . (Emden, 1887) 207-26.

Enchiridion Oft Hantboecxken *van de Christelijcke Leere ende Religion, in corte somma begrepen, ten dienste van alle Liefhebbers der waerheit wt der Heyliger Schrift ghemaect, nv nieus gecorrigeert ende vermeerdert Door D.P.* . . . *Ghedruckt int Jaer ons Heeren M.D. LXIII.* The *Enchiridion* (Handbook) by Dirk Philips (*q.v.*) is a collection of writings which had previously appeared separately. Dirk Philips himself prepared this edition, which was published in 1564 and contains eleven writings and five letters. The following writings were systematically (not chronologically) arranged with a detailed index: "Confession of Our Faith," "The Incarnation of Christ," "The True Knowledge of Jesus Christ," "An *Apologia,* or a Response," "About the Calling of Preachers and Teachers," "Admonitions About How to Deal with Those Who Are Committing Carnal Deeds," "About the True Knowledge of God," "An Explanation of the Tabernacle . . . ," "Concerning Regeneration and the New Creature," "Concerning the Spiritual Restitution," "Concerning the Church of God . . . ."

Like the *Fundament-Boek (Foundation Book)* of Menno Simons, this was to be a guide or handbook for the Christian to furnish him with basic doctrinal and ethical instructions in a day of distress and persecution. Dirk presents basic Christian convictions with some characteristics of Anabaptism such as the separation of the church from the world, strict church discipline, practical and fruitful Christian living, regarding the Dutch Anabaptist view on the incarnation of Christ, etc. Although he reveals a good knowledge of the Bible, deep Christian convictions, some knowledge of Latin, Greek, and Hebrew, he scarcely quotes writers of the past or the days of the Reformation, not even his co-worker Menno Simons. Luther, Sebastian Franck, and Erasmus are each referred to once. The many reprints of the *Enchiridion,* however, prove that it filled a great need and fulfilled its intended purpose of being a guide for the Christian. F. Pijper, who made a special study of Dirk Philips and prepared and edited all his writings, which appeared as Vol. X of the *Bibliotheca Reformatoria Neerlandica,* says, "What the *Loci communes* of Melanchthon was for the Lutherans, the Confession of Beza for the French Protestants, and the *Leken wechwyser* for the Dutch Reformed, the *Enchiridion* was for the Mennonites" (*BRN* X, 4).

The first edition of the *Enchiridion* of 1564 (of which there are at least two copies extant, at Amsterdam and at Goshen), was reprinted with no change in 1578, 1579, 1600, and 1627. The last contains also Dirk Philips' response to two letters of Sebastian Franck, who, as a spiritualist, minimized the significance of a visible church, which view is criticized and corrected by Dirk Philips. The only known French edition of the *Enchiridion* appeared in a volume with the writings of Menno Simons and others and was published in 1626. The first German edition, edited by C. J. Conert and printed at Haarlem, Holland, in 1715, the above-mentioned response to Franck's letters at the beginning. The next edition (Basel, 1802) places these letters in the back of the book and also "Von der Ehe des Christen . . ." and "Schrift und Handlung von dem Evangelischen Bann . . . ." The first two American German editions (Lancaster, 1811; Neu-Berlin, 1851) do not contain the latter two writings, while the Elkhart edition of 1872 and the Scottdale edition of 1917 included them. The first English edition, translated by A. B. Kolb, appeared in Elkhart in 1910. The final Dutch edition of the *Enchiridion* and the other writings of Dirk Philips, with a scholarly introduction and annotations by F. Pijper, appeared in Vol. X of *BRN.* Five previously unpublished letters and two songs were added. According to Vos (*Menno Simons,* p. 330) a writing concerning avoidance, to be found in the Mennonite Archives in Amsterdam, is missing in this edition. For the various editions of separate writings of Dirk Philips, see *Catalogus Amst.,* pp. 92-96.† C.K.

Enckus, Willem: see **Willem de Cleermaker.**

Endress, an Anabaptist of Solm, Hesse, Germany, whom Philip of Hesse vainly tried to release after a nine-year imprisonment. (*Archiv für hess. Gesch. und Altertumskunde* X, 1864, 371 ff.)

Engagement, the term most commonly used among North American Mennonites for betrothal (*q.v.*).

Engel (Engle, Angle), a Swiss family name represented in Europe and America by a number of Mennonite families. One of the significant members for Mennonite history was Ulrich Engel, who emigrated from the Canton of Basel to Pennsylvania in 1754. His son Jacob (Yokeli) (*q.v.*) became the chief founder of the Brethren in Christ (River Brethren). Another immigrant, Paul Engel, was in Germantown, Pa., before 1698, and is believed to have been a Mennonite. As early as the 17th century (after 1664) the name Engel appears among the Mennonites in the Palatinate; in the 18th century there were four branches of the Engel family in Sembach, descended from four sons of the first Engel settler's son and his wife, who was a Würtz. In 1936 there was still one Engel left in the Sembach congregation. In the 18th century there was a minister named Klaus Engel at Montreux near Belfort in Alsace.

As early as 1831 an Alsatian named John Engel settled near Metamora, Ill., and he was in turn followed two years later by Bishop Christian Engel, his father, who had been ordained in Europe, whereupon the Partridge congregation (now Metamora) was organized. Christian died in 1838, but in 1835 his son Joseph Engel (d. 1852), also ordained a bishop in Europe, located in Illinois and served the Partridge congregation. Christian and Joseph Engel were respectively the first and second Amish Mennonite bishops west of Ohio. The Brethren in Christ Church has had a large number of bishops, ministers, and deacons by the name of Engel or Engle.   J.C.W.

Morris M. Engle, *The Engle History and Family Records* . . . (Hummelstown, Pa., n.d.).

Engel Cornelisz of Bergen, Dutch province of North Holland, was beheaded at The Hague on May 11, 1534, because he had joined the Anabaptists. He was in the group seized at Bergklooster (*q.v.*) en route to Münster. No particulars are known. (*Inv. Arch. Amst.* I, Nos. 744, 745.)   vdZ.

Engel, Jacob (Yokeli), a founder of the Brethren in Christ (River Brethren), born in Switzerland Nov. 5, 1753, son of Ulrich and Anna Brechbill Engel, emigrated with his parents to America the next year, arriving at Philadelphia Oct. 1, 1754, and settling in Donegal Twp., Lancaster Co., Pa., not far from Marietta and the Susquehanna River. Ulrich died about 1764 and his wife a few years later. Young Jacob was placed under the guardianship of Jacob Schock, whose daughter Veronica (1750-1816) he married on May 3, 1773. He was apprenticed to a weaver at 14. About the same time he is said to have joined his mother's church, Mennonite.

According to a number of Engel descendants, Jacob experienced a spiritual awakening at 18 but was not baptized until about 1778 when he and a man named Witmer are said to have immersed

each other in a river, pledging secrecy as to who performed the first baptism. But another seven years passed before Jacob ventured to baptize any converts; it was in 1785 when he is said to have immersed eleven persons, after which the group met in a second story room in Jacob's house for a love feast and the communion service. The group soon chose Jacob as its first overseer or bishop. He had an active ministry. Besides being a weaver he is also said to have taught "English and German in a country schoolhouse near Stackstown." He died Feb. 10, 1832. His body was first interred on the homestead near Stackstown but was later removed to the East Donegal Cemetery of the Reichs Church near Marietta. Many of his descendants have been active in the church he founded.   J.C.W.

A. W. Climenhaga, *History of the Brethren in Christ Church* (Nappanee, 1942); Morris M. Engle, *The Engle History* . . . (Hummelstown, n.d.).

Engelbert Dircxsoen, a citizen of Haarlem, Dutch province of North Holland, and a weaver, was beheaded there about 1534, because he confessed, while being tortured, that he had been rebaptized. Further information is lacking.   vdZ.

Inv. Arch. Amst. I, No. 750; *DB* 1917, 153; *Bijdr. en Mededeelingen Hist. Genootschap Utrecht* XLI (1920) 202-3; Mellink, *Wederdopers,* 179.

Engelen, Cornelis van, b. about 1722 at Utrecht, d. 1793 at Leiden, a Dutch Mennonite pastor. He studied philosophy at the University of Utrecht, where he obtained his doctor's degree in 1745. Then he studied theology at the Amsterdam Mennonite Seminary 1747-49. In 1749-58 he served the congregation of Harlingen, Dutch province of Friesland, as a pastor. In 1758 he resigned because of bad health, but in 1764 he again became an active minister, serving the small congregation of Huizen, Dutch province of North Holland until 1769. Then he retired again and lived at Leiden until his death, devoting himself to the study of philosophy and literature. He was editor of several scholarly and popular philosophical reviews like *De Philosooph, De Denker,* and *De Rhapsodist,* and contributed to the many cultural periodicals (*Spectatoriale Geschriften*) of his age.

In 1767 he founded the *Maatschappij tot behoudenis der verdronkenen,* now *Maatschappij tot redding van drenkelingen* (Society for Rescuing of Drowning Persons), through which thousands of lives have been saved. Van Engelen, who indisputably was more interested in cultural matters than theological problems, was a typical and influential representative of 18th-century Dutch Mennonitism.   vdZ.

Inv. Arch. Amst. II, Nos. 1902, 1997; *Biogr. Wb.* II, 735; Chr. Sepp, *Johannes Stinstra en zijn tijd* II (Amsterdam, 1865) 150 ff., 278 f.; *DB* 1867, 106; 1868, 70, 100, 106; 1912, 106.

Engeltje Hermansdochter, of Benschop, Dutch province of Utrecht, was one of a group of Anabaptists which was apprehended at Bergklooster (*q.v.*) en route to Münster. She was drowned, likely in The Hague, on Aug. 27 or 28, 1534. Details were not available. (*Inv. Arch. Amst.* I, Nos. 744, 745; Mellink, *Wederdopers,* 233.)   vdZ.

Engen, Fred, played an important role in 1919-29 in the original settlement of the Manitoba Old Colony Mennonites in Paraguay. Having been a millionaire, but having lost his fortune, he entered the service of Gen. Samuel McRoberts of New York (Corporacion Paraguaya) in connection with the latter's land interests in South America, about the same time that the Manitoba Mennonites made contacts with McRoberts. It was he who called McRoberts' attention to the Chaco, making explorations there in 1919, and thus he is probably chiefly responsible for the selection of this area for Mennonite settlement. He worked for the Corporacion Paraguaya, mostly in the Chaco, until his death in 1929. In his memory the Chaco station at Km. 145 on the Casado railway was named Fred Engen.

H.S.B.

England. The name "Anabaptist" in England first occurs in references to the movement on the Continent by that name. As early as 1526 a list of proscribed books included a tract by Zwingli against the Anabaptists. In 1528 and later Erasmus and Sir Thomas More corresponded about the "Anabaptistarum haeresis." William Barlow, in the pamphlet *Lutheran faccyons* (1531), described at length the movement in Switzerland and Germany as "the thyrde faccyon" of the Reformation. More, in the second part of the *Confutation* (1533), accused William Tyndale of becoming party to "those abominable heresies . . . the Anabaptists have added." Beginning about 1535 the name was also given to both foreign and native adherents of the movement present in England. Henceforth "Anabaptist" became a common pejorative of the English Reformation and throughout the 16th and 17th centuries was used with specific as well as generic connotations. Almost invariably the Latin form was employed, while the vernacular "rebaptizer" (German, "Wiedertäufer"; Dutch, "Wederdooper") retained the sense it had in patristic literature (see **Anabaptism**).

The first Anabaptists in England, according to various polemical treatments written in the 17th century and later, came from Holland subsequent to the seditious uprising at Amsterdam on May 10, 1535 (*A Short History of the Anabaptists,* 1642, 48). The source of this information is Lambertus Hortensius, a Dutch ecclesiastic and chronicler, who lived contemporary with the events and whose *Tumultuum Anabaptisticarum* was first printed at Basel in 1548, but he nowhere holds that these Anabaptists were the original ones in England. The 25 Dutch Anabaptists arrested and brought to trial at St. Paul's on May 25, 1535, 14 of whom were condemned and burned at London and other English towns on June 4, 1535, may have been members of the party mentioned by Hortensius. Anabaptists were present in England before 1535. During the fall or early winter of 1534 Anabaptist ministers ("leraers") from England were at Amsterdam. Anneken Jans, a devout Dutch Anabaptist and later a martyr, with her husband Arent Jansz fled to England from Den Briel in Holland in the summer of 1534. Six English and two Flemish persons who held Anabaptist views were arrested in connection

with the importation and distribution of "the booke of Anabaptist confession" sometime in 1532-34. They had a place of meeting in London, and their leader was a certain Fleming named Bastian, described as "the bishop & reder of the Anabaptists." (Reference to a 1534 proclamation against the Anabaptists, which is sometimes found in secondary sources, is due to the misdating of a 1538 proclamation in David Wilkins' *Concilia.*) The relationship between Anabaptists and Lollards during the early Reformation in England is obscure. The spiritualistic character of Lollardy provided a fertile soil for the Dutch-Flemish variety of Anabaptism, and it may be said, at least in a generic sense, that "new Anabaptist was but old Lollard writ Dutch" (E. G. Rupp). Nevertheless, in the 1530's Anabaptism supplanted Lollardy in name as well as in doctrine and became the left wing of the English Reformation.

Apart from the missionary intentions of a Bastian and his associates, the great number of Anabaptists who reached England were Dutch and Flemish refugees escaping from the severe persecution of the Hapsburg rulers in their homeland. This escape was facilitated by the flourishing commerce across the North Sea as a result of the textile trade. Many of the Anabaptists settled in London and port towns on the east coast, including Hull, where their foreign character and nonparticipation in English life made it possible for them to retain their religious beliefs. For reasons of trade and diplomacy these foreign communities were often exempt from English laws, but when they began to influence the native population drastic action was taken against them. Although Henry VIII repudiated papal authority by the Act of Supremacy (1534) he endeavored to keep the English church orthodox in doctrine and practice in the Roman sense. His treatment of the Anabaptists was mild compared with Hapsburg policy, but, as R. W. Dixon observes, "there were more Anabaptists burned by Henry the Eighth than Lollards in the whole of the previous century."

The Anabaptists from the Netherlands came to England for the most part in two waves: in 1535-36 as a result of the persecution which followed the rise and fall of seditious Anabaptism at Münster; in 1567-73 when the Duke of Alva was in the Low Countries and sought to exterminate them along with other Reformation parties, particularly in the southern Netherlands. In July 1535, shortly after the Münster debacle, the agents of Thomas Cromwell passed word on to London that many Anabaptists were fleeing across the North Sea. One of the leaders who escaped to England was Jan Mathijsz van Middelburg, an important figure in the early movement. In spite of the prevailing severe persecution, the leaders of radical Anabaptism held a conference at Bocholt in Westphalia during the summer of 1536. An Englishman named "Henry" is reported to have borne the expenses of this meeting in order to bring about some unity in the movement, especially in behalf of peaceful practices. Jan Mathijsz van Middelburg represented the English Anabaptists at Bocholt, and with others took a stand against the seditious Münsterites and Batenburgers. The attitude in England in 1536-37 appears to have been lenient, but a change occurred in the fall of 1538. In September of this year Henry VIII received a warning about the "Anabaptist pest" from Philipp of Hesse and John Frederick of Saxony in Germany. Their communication, composed by Melanchthon, was prompted by an Anabaptist letter seized in Hesse which revealed that Anabaptists in Germany were in touch with members of the movement in England, and that the latter, among other activities, had published a book on the doctrine of the incarnation. Possibly as a result of this letter, on Oct. 1 Henry VIII issued a commission to Archbishop Cranmer "to search for and examine Anabaptists . . . and destroy all books of that detestable sect." In November 1538 two proclamations went out against Anabaptists: the first prohibited the printing, importation, and possession of their books, and the second ordered all rebaptized persons to leave the realm. There are records of some Anabaptists who recanted; three, however, were executed. One of these was the leader, Jan Mathijsz van Middelburg; he was burned at Smithfield on Nov. 29, 1538. On the same day Peter Franke and his wife, Flemish Anabaptists, were burned, the husband at Colchester and the wife at Smithfield. In the controversial literature of the time Franke is described as a "godly and perfect" young man, whose piety and steadfastness converted many at Colchester. It was in December 1538 that Anneken Jans and her traveling companion, Christiana Michiel Barents, were taken while on a journey from England to Delft. They were drowned on Jan. 7, 1539, at Rotterdam. Christiana and her husband, originally from Louvain in Brabant, were like Anneken and her husband, Anabaptist refugees in England. At her trial Christiana referred to Lijnken, another Anabaptist from Louvain, who had died in England. On Feb. 26, 1539, Henry VIII issued a proclamation of pardon to all heretics in England except those from abroad. This appears to indicate that a considerable number of English subjects were affected by the new beliefs and that persecution had done more to spread than to counteract them. (The account in *Mart. Mir.* E 450, concerning the execution at Delft of 31 Anabaptist refugees from England, who had fled in the winter of 1538-39, is the result of faulty reading of the original documents. These Anabaptist martyrs were residents at Delft and were arrested and condemned upon information given by Anneken Jans, who had come from England. Van Braght had taken the incident from P. J. Twisck's earlier martyr book. See K. Vos, "De Delftsche martelaren van 1538 en 1539 ontward," *DB* 1917, 160-67.) In the Six Articles Act of July 1539 the aging king reaffirmed a strict advocacy of the mass and other cardinal tenets of Catholicism. Among the score or more persons executed in 1540-46 for violation of this Act several were condemned as Anabaptists. Two of these were Maundeveld, "a French groom of the Queen," and Collins, an Englishman, who died at the stake in April or May 1540. Another account mentions the burning of two Flemish Anabaptists in June 1540. Because the offending charge was a wrong view of the sacrament, distinction between Sacramentarians and Anabaptists is difficult. In

July 1540 Henry VIII again offered his people a general pardon, but Anabaptists of all kinds were excepted. The pardon listed the specific heresies of the Anabaptists, among which were: baptism is for adults and not for infants, refusal to "beare office or rule in the Commen Welth," nonswearing of oaths, "that Christe toke no bodily substance of our blessed lady," and "that all things be common."

The government of Edward VI, 1547-53, while promoting a Reformation on the continental pattern and in close co-operation with the leaders at Zürich and Geneva, continued the suppression of the Anabaptists. In January 1550, as in the previous reign, a commission was issued to Cranmer to search out and examine Anabaptists. On the whole, however, the reign was characterized by more leniency and efforts to meet the Anabaptist influence on positive and ideological grounds. License to establish a congregation for foreigners at London was granted, the king recorded in his journal, for "the avoyding of al sectes of Anabaptistes and such like." Archbishop Cranmer was particularly forbearing in his treatment of the Anabaptists, and he yielded to the use of violence only when heavy pressure was brought to bear upon him by the King's Council. Cranmer's leniency became so flagrant during the latter part of Edward's reign that John Hooper and John Knox, both stanch supporters of the Reformed party, were called in by the government to combat the Anabaptist menace in London and Kent. Cranmer was active, however, in seeking to convert Anabaptists by methods of persuasion. In April 1549 he and other church officials debated with a party of Anabaptists in St. Paul's at London. As a result three gave up their views; one of the members who persisted was Joan (Jane) Boucher, who, in spite of Cranmer's continued efforts to win her, was burned at the stake on May 2, 1550. Joan was a lady of some social standing in London, probably of noble blood, and appeared to have some influence in court circles. The particular view to which she tenaciously held was the Melchiorite doctrine that Christ in His incarnation took no substance of Mary's body. In June 1549 Cranmer won Michael Tombe, a tailor of London, from his Anabaptist views. In the spring of 1549 John Hooper complained to Bullinger how "Anabaptists flock to the place [where he gave lectures in London] and give me much trouble with their opinions respecting the incarnation of the Lord." In June of the following year he said that the counties of Kent and Sussex were "troubled with the frenzy of the Anabaptists more than any other part of the kingdom." During Edward's reign four pamphlets by Bullinger and one by Calvin against the Anabaptists were translated into English. They were published as follows: H. Bullinger, *An Holsome Antidotus or counterpoysen* (1548); J. Calvin, *A short instruction for to arme all good Christian people* (1549); H. Bullinger, *A treatise or sermon . . . concernyng magistrates* (1549); H. Bullinger, *A moste sure and strong defence of the baptisme of children* (1551); H. Bullinger, *A most necessary & frutefull Dialogue* (1551). Jean Veron, a French Reformed minister, prebend at Worcester, was an active opponent of the Anabaptists. He translated many of the Bullinger tracts and added long prefaces to them. During Elizabeth's reign he had a controversy with Robert Cooche, an Anabaptist, and wrote two pamphlets in defense of election. William Turner, "doctor of physick" and dean of Wells, also engaged Cooche in debate, especially on the doctrines of original sin and infant baptism. Turner's pamphlet, *A preseruatiue or triacle* (1551), is a reply to Cooche on the first of these questions. The book by John Knox, *An answer to a great number of blasphemous cauillations written by an Anabaptist,* first published at Geneva in 1560 and later at London in 1591, is a lengthy rejoinder to a controversial work from the pen of Cooche which is no longer extant. John Hooper wrote *A Lesson of the Incarnation of Christe,* a tract against the Anabaptist view of the doctrine; it went through at least three editions during 1549-50. Thomas Cole, who at one time had Anabaptist leanings, wrote *A godly and frutefull sermon . . . againste dyuers erronious opinions of the Anabaptistes and others* (1553). Probably more influential than Cooche as a leader among English Anabaptists was Henry Hart, who, we are told, was among the Kentish sectaries who "were the first that made separation from the reformed church of England." Hart was the author of two tracts of admonition, *A Godly newe short treatyse* (1548), and *A Godlie exhortation* (1549).

While in the reign of Henry VIII the Anabaptist movement had grown in secret, in Edward's reign it came out into the open. The movement had its inception at the time the Melchiorite wing was dominant in the Netherlands and hence the English phase was characterized by spiritualistic tendencies. The names of some leaders are known; there is evidence of secret meetings and congregations among native Anabaptists in Sussex and Kent; Anabaptist leaders debated both privately and publicly, orally and in writing, with the ecclesiastics of Edward's reign; yet a large part of what one finds designated as Anabaptism pertains to views held or promulgated by persons who never separated from the national church. The principal doctrinal views considered Anabaptist during the early English Reformation were believers' baptism; the freedom of the will; intentional sin after conversion is unpardonable, and Christ in the incarnation took no substance from the flesh of Mary. These are the identical issues controverted by Martin Bucer against Melchior Hofmann at the Strasbourg disputation of 1533, and are views which characterized the Melchiorite phase of Anabaptism in the Netherlands and elsewhere. That much of English Anabaptism in this early period was nonseparatist may be due to Lollard precedents as well as to the spiritualistic strain of the Anabaptists who came to England. It may have had more separatist manifestations than we are able to discover today, but from the evidence available it is clear that it did not become an organized movement of gathered churches comparable to the Swiss Brethren and the Mennonites on the Continent. Not until Elizabeth's reign and the period of the early Stuarts were the separatist bodies to be formed, and then more from the spiritual ferment within the national church than from a direct lineal descent from the Anabaptists of Edward's reign.

The separatist development of Anabaptism in England may have been cut short by the Marian persecution. During the reign of Mary, 1553-58, the persecution of Anabaptists can scarcely be distinguished from that of Protestants in general. Since the greater percentage of the martyrs came from eastern counties and from the artisan classes, some historians assume that up to as high as 80 per cent may have been professing or fellow-traveling Anabaptists. Records do not exist to examine this question more precisely. John Foxe, in *The Acts and Monuments* (1563), the chief source of information, is not specific enough to enable one to identify Anabaptists. The persons in Foxe, for example, who were indicated as lay ministers, were no doubt Anabaptists. Apart from Foxe it is known that two Anabaptist ministers, Henry Hart and Humphrey Middleton, were imprisoned in Mary's reign. Middleton died as a martyr in July 1555. Hart and other Anabaptists in prison had running debates, evidently in writing, with prisoners in other parts of the prison. John Bradford, prebendary at St. Paul's and a martyr in January 1555, devoted much time in the last months of his confinement to an attempt to convert Hart to Reformed views regarding election. Hart's circle, to which Bradford was warmly attached, included a number of ministers from the counties of Kent and Essex.

When Elizabeth ascended the throne in 1558 she soon came into conflict with both native and foreign Anabaptists. Bishop Jewel, writing to Peter Martyr in November 1560, reported: "We found at the beginning of the reign of Elizabeth a large and inauspicious crop of Arians, anabaptists, and other pests, which I know not how, but as mushrooms spring up in the night and in darkness, so these spring up in that darkness and unhappy night of the Marian times." In 1559 Bishop Parker told Bullinger that the realm was full of Anabaptists and other heretics. In 1560 Elizabeth issued a decree ordering Anabaptists to conform or leave the country upon pain of imprisonment and confiscation of goods. The decree specifically mentioned "the Anabaptists and such Hereticks, which had flocked to the Coast-Towns of England from the parts beyond the Seas, under colour of shunning Persecution." An ecclesiastical commission was appointed to make registers and bring to trial all those who were tainted with the Anabaptist heresy. With the coming of Alva into the Netherlands and the institution of a policy of inquisition and persecution, thousands fled across the North Sea to England. The commission was slow in proceeding, but in 1562, Grindal, then Bishop of London, pushed the case of Adrian van Haemstede, a Flemish minister of the foreign Dutch Reformed congregation (Austin Friars), on a charge of encouraging Anabaptism by recognizing "the Anabaptists as his brethren and as weak members of Christ," to whom eternal life was also granted. When van Haemstede refused to recant he was excommunicated in 1562 and banished from England by royal decree. That there were Anabaptists

among the Dutch and Flemish refugees is also af-
firmed by the Queen's proclamation of 1568, which
states that they met in secret conventicles and had
influenced the English populace. A later regulation
ordered that investigation be made among both
foreigners and native subjects who had adopted of
the heretical principles of the Anabaptists. Refusal
to conform meant leaving the country within 20
days. Richard Heath, as well as other historians,
considers the secret conventicles of this period to
be the germ cells of the Baptist Church.

In 1575 a number of incidents occurred pertaining
to the arrest, trial, and persecution of Dutch Anabaptists in England. At London and Ely meetings
were discovered by the authorities. Van Braght devotes 16 pages (*Mart. Mir.* E 1008-24) to accounts
and letters concerning the experiences of the London
group (not all details agree). On April 3, Easter
Day, about 20 persons were apprehended at a gathering "beyond the Aldgate." In May they were
cross-examined by the Bishop of London, with three
preachers from the Austin Friars church serving as
interpreters, on four points: the incarnation, infant
baptism, the oath, and the office of the magistrate.
Under threat and exposure to public disgrace some
of the group recanted. One account states that 14
women were banished from the city and one youth
was "scourged behind a cart." Some were released
under bail and two escaped from prison. Two of
the group, Jan Piers Wagemaker (also called Jan
Pietersz) and Hendrick Terwoort, were burned at
Smithfield on July 22, "in great terror, weeping and
crying," according to one account. Members of the
Austin Friars church, as well as the martyrologist
John Foxe, interceded before the Queen and her
Council in behalf of the imprisoned men, and Foxe
obtained a reprieve to stay the execution for a month.
Van Braght published a letter from the prisoners to
Foxe, in which they reject his admonition to recant,
and a confession of faith in which they elucidate
their stand on the four points raised in their trial
before the Bishop of London. A martyr ballad,
"The Two Friends," is extant, and depicts in detail
the death of Wagemaker and Terwoort. Van Braght
also recorded the case of Hans Bret, apparently an
English Anabaptist living at Antwerp, who was
burned at the stake there in 1577 (*Mart. Mir.* D
1037-54). Bret wrote a letter to his brother in England who "had not yet come to the knowledge of the
truth," and during the cross-examination replied that
he himself had been in England. When asked, "What
sort of people were those put to death (in England)?"
he replied, "I believe they were Menno's."

About 1580 Anabaptism in England entered a new
chapter. As a movement it was embraced and succeeded by the Separatist movement of the Brownists
and Barrowists, culminating in the formation of the
Congregationalist and Baptist denominations in the
17th century. Burrage has shown how congregations
of Separatists formed at scattered places in England
in 1588-1641, but the movement found its principal
centers in the areas where Anabaptism had been
strongest, in London and in the southeast and
middle-east counties. The earliest leaders, Robert
Browne and Robert Harrison, organized a congregation at Norwich in 1580 which fled to Middelburg
in the Netherlands during the following year. Separatism in London found its leaders in Henry Barrow, John Greenwood, and John Penry, all three
martyrs by 1593. The same year the congregation
migrated to Amsterdam with Francis Johnson as
pastor. It is to these origins that the Congregationalists owe the inception of their church. A Separatist congregation on the same pattern formed at
Gainsborough about 1606, of which John Smyth was
one of the pastors. In 1608 this group escaped to
Holland and organized two congregations there, one
under Smyth at Amsterdam, the other at Leyden
with John Robinson as pastor. To the Smyth congregation, which accepted adult baptism as a result
of contact with Dutch Mennonites, the General Baptists owe their origin, especially to the segment
which Thomas Helwys and John Murton led back
to England in 1612. A number of members from
Robinson's church were among the Pilgrim Fathers
when they sailed for the new world in 1620.

All of the Separatist groups were at various times
labeled "Anabaptist" by their enemies, as the prolific anti-Anabaptist literature of the first half of
the 17th century testifies. It is necessary to distinguish between the generic and the specific use of
"Anabaptist" during this period as well as in the
16th century. Robert Bailie, for example, wrote a
work against all left-wing groups, entitled *Anabaptism, the True Fountaine of Independency, Antin-
omy, Brownisme, Familisme, and the most of the
other Errours* (1647). Bailie succeeds to his own
satisfaction in finding certain doctrinal similarities
and historical connections among these groups which
justify, for him, placing them all in one family. Actually, he followed a precedent common in his own
time and earlier of using the term "Anabaptist" to
label all kinds of nonconformity. "Anabaptist" became synonymous with "heresy" or "fanaticism."
In the 16th century the term was used to refer to
contemporary Pelagians ("free-willers"), to An-
tinomians, to Familists, and to other groups which
had no relationship to the historic Anabaptist movement. Archbishop Whitgift accused T. Cartwright
of being an Anabaptist. In the 17th century the term
sometimes refers to Socinians, Ranters, Quakers, and
other groups, as well as to the Independents and
Baptists. This indiscriminate usage calls for great
caution and discernment on the part of anyone making use of English Anabaptist sources. "Anabaptist"
however did also have a specific use. In the 16th
century it meant the English wing of the Dutch
movement begun by Melchior Hofmann, as the
official records assume. In the 17th century, from
the 1630's onward, it was applied specifically to the
Baptists, although it never lost its connotation of
"fanaticism" or "enthusiasm." The name "Baptist"
was first used in 1641. The literature on the Anabaptists, together with the subject of baptism, is
enormous in quantity throughout the 17th century
in England. Henry Martyn Dexter, whose bibliography, *Collections toward a Bibliography of the First
two Generations of the Baptist Controversy in England,* is not complete, lists no less than 401 separate
works published from 1618 to 1700.

The connections between Anabaptism and Separatism do not submit to exact statement. It has been pointed out that the strongholds of both movements were located in the same geographical areas. As for historical connections, the most plausible were those between Robert Browne and Anabaptists in London and Norwich, but conclusive evidence has never been presented. It is on theological and spiritual grounds that the evidence is more convincing. The Separatist doctrine of the church and to a certain extent its attitude toward the state are characteristically Anabaptist. Both groups believed in a visible church of true believers, and that the civil magistrate had no authority in ecclesiastical matters. The biographer of Henry Barrow, F. J. Powicke, has pointed out that he was an Anabaptist in every respect except in regard to the concept and practice of adult baptism, yet Barrow strenuously denied any connection with the Anabaptists. One may not overlook the strong Calvinistic spirit and position of the Separatist movement, owing to the influence of Thomas Cartwright and others at Cambridge where most of its leaders were educated. Only in the case of Smyth and his colleagues was there a departure from the predestination doctrines, with the result that the General Baptists became Arminian in their theology. It is possible that this was a result of their sojourn in Holland. But the Anabaptists in England in the 16th century contended strongly for the doctrine of free will and were frequently labeled Pelagian.

Relationships between Anabaptism and Quakerism have also not been clearly established. Quakerism, which arose about 1644 around the prophetic and missionary leadership of George Fox, was in many respects more akin to historic Anabaptism than any of the segments within Separatism, especially in regard to the doctrine and practice of nonresistance. The English historian, G. P. Gooch, states that a large number of "Baptists" went over to the Quaker movement during the Puritan Revolution when no stand was taken by their leaders against participation in Cromwell's army.

The presence of Anabaptism in England is reflected in the confessional literature of both the Anglican and Presbyterian churches. The earliest formularies, the *Ten Articles* (1536) and *The Bishop's Book* (1537), as well as *The King's Book* (1543), name the Anabaptists and oppose their view of baptism. In a much more inclusive way the views of the Anabaptists are rejected in the *Forty-Two Articles* of 1553. E. J. Bicknell observes that, although the Anabaptists are mentioned but twice (in regard to original sin and the community of goods), they are opposed in at least half of the articles. The Articles "are a double-edged weapon" designed to smite medieval teaching and abuses on the one hand, but "even more keenly the teaching of the Anabaptists" on the other hand (*The Thirty-Nine Articles,* London, 1955, pp. 11-12). This Edwardian confession is reflected in the better-known *Thirty-Nine Articles,* first agreed upon in 1562 although in general the latter reflect a greater latitude of opinion. Article 38 states that "the riches and goods of Christians are not common . . . as certain Anabaptists do falsely boast," while Anabaptist

views on war, the oath, and the magistracy are reflected in other articles. The Westminster Confession (Presbyterian) of 1647 also opposes several Anabapist doctrines, and the Scottish confession of 1560, in article 23, rejects "the error of Anabaptists who deny baptism to appertain to children."

English literature, particularly of the 16th and 17th centuries, also bears evidence of the Anabaptist movement in England. The name "Anabaptist" does not occur anywhere in Shakespeare (1564-1616), although "Brownist" does, but at least one Elizabethan scholar, J. F. Danby, has suggested Anabaptism as one of the sources of Shakespeare's equalitarian ideas, especially in *King Lear*. In Edmund Spenser's (*ca.* 1552-99) *The Faerie Queene,* the virtuous Artegall debates with and destroys the "mighty Gyant" of communistic Anabaptism. The allegorical encounter is related in 26 stanzas (Book V, Canto II, stanzas xxix-liv). Some commentators see here in Spenser "a mind which was at once conservative, aristocratic, and influenced by Calvinistic theology," opposing "the general restlessness of the times and growth of democratic ideals." At any rate, the subject was of current interest to Spenser's readers, and contemporary pamphleteers such as Robert Crowley (d. 1588) kept it fermenting in the public mind. Thomas Nashe (1567-1601), in contrast to the decorous Spenser, relates in a racy manner the story of the Anabaptists at Frankenhausen and Münster in *The Unfortunate Traveller* (1594). Although he confuses the two events, he appears to follow Sleidanus faithfully enough to arrive at the traditional interpretation. Nashe is interested chiefly in telling a story, but he does betray a sympathy with the victims, the account of which no doubt reminded him and his readers of the current executions in London. Nashe's polemical tracts also contain references to Anabaptists, and John Greenwood and other Barrowist leaders are often mentioned.

The 17th-century literature relating to Anabaptism, as already indicated, is enormous in quantity. Most of the upwards of 400 pamphlets and books are of primary interest from a theological point of view, but some have literary merit, such as those by John Taylor, Thomas Hooker, and Richard Baxter, to mention only a few. One finds references to Anabaptists in both Milton and Bunyan, but more important is their spiritual affinity to the Anabaptist way of life, a discovery which has led more than one Baptist historian to adopt them into the brotherhood. In more secular literature, especially in the drama, one finds a satirical and even farcical treatment of the Anabaptists and their views. This can be seen already in the comedy of the Jacobean satirists, where with topical Puritanism it becomes a special object of ridicule. One sees a similar treatment in the "character," a type of literature which was exceptionally popular in the 17th century. In the early collections of "characters," such as those of Overbury and Earle, where the type is treated in a short, concise essay in imitation of the classic models of Theophrastus, the Anabaptist and Brownist do not occur. But in the later imitations, particularly those of Francis Wortley and Samuel Butler, there is a riotous castigation of the sects in both prose and verse. One of Butler's rhyming "characters," in the manner of *Hudibras,* begins as follows:

Among these rank rebellious Weeds,
The Anabaptist next succeeds;
These Saints derive their way of fooling
From Sutor, Humor, Knipperdoling,
Hut, Hetzer, Hofman, and a Crew
Of frantick Fools, the Lord knows who . . . .

Satirical references to Anabaptists appeared also in the 18th century, chiefly in the drama and the periodical essay, but soon declined. The name "Baptist" replaced the older label, which remained, however, as a term to denote religious fanaticism or "enthusiasm."

If one surveys the results of current research regarding Anabaptism in England one might make the following observations. For the 16th century we have available only scanty information concerning a movement which for the most part was an underground one. What is known comes chiefly from the sources which sought to suppress it. How deeply and extensively the movement penetrated into English life, who its leaders were, where its congregations were located, what its literature was, and how its theology was taught and practiced—these are all questions concerning which we know very little. In the absence of such detailed information possibly the best way to estimate the scope of the movement and the importance of its achievement is to note its impact on the times. This can only be hinted at here, and a few tentative conclusions stated. One way to view it is to hold that, as a distinct movement, Anabaptism came to an end about 1580 when its message and genius gained acceptance and was linked with other elements in the Separatist movement, and that it probably reached its highest peak of life and activity during the reigns of Edward VI and Mary (1547-58). It is also possible to view the movement as one which was effectively crushed and whose spiritual potency was suppressed until it was granted a better opportunity to develop within the Separatist groups of the 17th century. Whichever view one may adopt, it is clear that the Anabaptist views of the church and state were embraced by the Separatists. One may not claim that Anabaptism was the exclusive source of these insights, but the evidence is overwhelming that it was a major influence. Ernest A. Payne quotes H. N. Brailsford as saying in 1948, "The English Puritan Left can be understood only when we realise that it drew much of its inspiration directly from the Swiss, German, and Dutch Anabaptists." The influence of Anabaptism on Independency and the later Congregational movement can be traced especially on the form of church government and on the character of church worship and life. Much more radical was its influence on the movement which bore the name "Anabaptist" the longest, the General Baptists, who were the closest English counterpart to the main-line Anabaptists on the Continent (Mennonites, Täufer). In another sense, however, especially in reference to the practice of nonresistance and a radical nonconformity, the purest expression of the Anabaptist spirit is to be sought in Quakerism, which dates from the year 1644. Thus we see that Anabaptism in

England was no spiritual backwater, not merely a fanaticism held by Dutch refugees whose influence on English Protestantism was only peripheral, but that it deposited a ferment of religious ideas which were finally absorbed into both English and American church and secular history.   I.B.H.

Bibliographies: W. T. Whitley, *A Baptist Bibliography* (London, 1916) 2 vv.; J. H. Bloom, *English Tracts and Printed Sheets, 1473-1640* (London, 1922-23) 2 vv.; A. W. Pollard and C. R. Redgrave, *A Short-Title Catalogue . . . 1475-1640* (London, 1926); H. M. Dexter, *The Congregationalism of the Last Three Hundred Years, as Seen in Its Literature . . .* (New York, 1880); C. R. Gillett, editor, *Catalogue of the McAlpin Collection . . . in the Union Theol. Seminary Library* (New York, 1927-29) 4 vv.

Primary source materials: *Calendars of State Papers,* including the Letters and Papers of Henry VIII and the Domestic Series of the Reigns of Edward VI, Mary, and Elizabeth; the sources for ecclesiastical Reformation history are found in the 55 vv. of the *Parker Society Publications;* John Strype, *Annals of the Reformation and Establishment of Religion . . . during Queen Elizabeth's Happy Reign* (Oxford, 1824) 4 vv.; John Stow, *The Annales of England* (London, 1605); Charles Wriothesley, *A Chronicle of England during the Reigns of the Tudors* (London, 1875-77) 2 vv., in the Camden Society Publications.

Secondary sources: G. Weber, *Geschichte der akatholischen Kirchen und Sekten in Grossbritannien* (Leipzig, 1845); B. C. Roosen, "Anfänge der Gemeinden der Taufgesinnten in England," *Menn. Bl.,* 1856-73 ff.; R. Heath, six essays on the Anabaptists in the *Contemporary Review,* 1891-97, of which the following three relate to England: "The Anabaptists and Their English Descendants," *C.R.,* 1891, 399-406; "The Archetype of the *Pilgrim's Progress," C.R.,* 1896, 542-58; "The Archetype of the Holy War," C.R., 1897, 105-18; G. P. Gooch, *English Democratic Ideas in the 17th Century* (Cambridge, 1927); R. Barclay, *The Inner Life of the Religious Societies of the Commonwealth* (London, 1876); J. G. Burn, *History of French, Walloon, Dutch . . . Refugees in England from Henry VIII to the Revocation of the Edict of Nantes* (London, 1846); C. Eden Quainton, "The Anabaptists in England During the Commonwealth, 1648-1654," *MQR* VI (1932) 30-42. The three 20th-century books on Anabaptism by English authors all have chapters entitled "Anabaptism in England": E. B. Bax, *Rise and Fall of the Anabaptists* (London, 1903) 332-83; E. C. Pike, *The Story of the Anabaptists* (London, 1904) 55-72; R. J. Smithson, *The Anabaptists* (London, 1935) 192-204. The exhaustive English treatment is that by Champlin Burrage, *The Early English Dissenters in the Light of Recent Research* (1550-1641) 2 vv. (London, 1912). Carl Heath (son of R. Heath), *Social and Religious Heretics in Five Centuries* (London, 1936), has a chapter on "The Anabaptist Movement" pp. 62-101), which treats the English phase on pp. 89-96. R. Barclay's *Inner Life* treats the English Anabaptists briefly in Chapter I, but is of great value on the 17th-century developments, particularly as to relations with the Dutch Mennonites of Holland. W. K. Jordan, *The Development of Religious Toleration in England, From the Beginning of the English Reformation to the Death of Queen Elizabeth* (London, 1932). The letters regarding Pieter Tasch are in the *Corpus Reformatorum* III, 578-83. Of the older Baptist histories, the one by Edward Bean Underhill found in "An Historical Introduction" in the first two volumes (*A Martyrology of the Churches of Christ,* I and II) of the Hanserd Knollys Society Publications, I (London, 1850) pp. cxxii-cxxviii, II (London, 1853) pp. xliv-lxxvi, is especially valuable for the 16th century. Ernest A. Payne, *The Baptist Movement in the Reformation and Onwards* (London, 1947); idem, *The Anabaptists of the 16th Century and Their Influence in the Modern World* (London, 1949); idem, *The Free Church Tradition in the Life of England,* 3rd revised ed. (London, 1951).

A partial list of Anabaptist references in English literature is as follows: Edmund Spenser, "The Faerie Queene" in *The Works of Edmund Spenser, A Variorum Edition* (Baltimore, 1936) vol. V; F. M. Padelford,

"Spenser's Arraignment of the Anabaptists" in *Journal of English and Germanic Philology* XII (1913) 434-48; the best ed. of Nashe is R. B. McKerrow, *Works of Thomas Nash* (London, 1902-10) 6 vv., fully indexed; *Works of John Taylor the Water Poet*, Vol. VII of the Spenser Society Publications, 1870; Sir Francis Wortley, *Characters and Elegies* (London, 1648); Samuel Butler, *Characters and Passages from Note-Books* (Cambridge, 1908) edited by A. R. Waller; Irvin B. Horst, "The Anabaptists in English Literature, A Research Note," *MQR* XXIX, 2 (July 1955) 232-39; *ML* I, 584-91.

Englewood (Montgomery Co., Ohio) United Missionary Church was organized in 1890. The membership (1955) is 60, mostly urban, with J. E. Seeker as pastor. **J.A.S.**

English Language. All the Mennonite immigrants to North America, except a very few from France in the late 19th century, were German-speaking when they came, and accordingly established their worship in the German language. The English edition of the Dordrecht Confession (*q.v.*), published in 1712 in Amsterdam and in 1727 at Philadelphia by the Pennsylvania Mennonites, is no exception to this, for it was published for the sake of the English-speaking public of the region in which they settled. German hymnbooks, prayer books, catechisms, and devotional books were used exclusively until well into the 19th century. In the Mennonite congregations and groups established before the 1874-80 immigration from Russia the definite change-over from German to English did not begin until the last quarter of the 19th century. The change came first in Virginia, where the Dordrecht Confession in English was published in 1810, and the first English Mennonite hymnbook in 1847, the latter antedating the next one, published at Elkhart in 1880, by 33 years. The small Reformed Mennonite group also issued an English hymnbook in 1847 at Lancaster and apparently shifted early into English; Herr's first book appeared in an English translation as early as 1816. The first English church paper was the *Herald of Truth* (MC) at Chicago (1864), later Elkhart, but the German counterpart, *Herold der Wahrheit*, continued publication until 1902. The next English church organ was the *Gospel Banner* (MBC) 1878, followed by the *Mennonite* (GCM) 1885. The *Words of Cheer* (MC), a children's Sunday-school paper, appeared only in English, beginning in 1876.

The first English catechism edition was that of 1849, published by the Oberholtzer (GCM) group, but not reprinted until 1874 (Elkhart, MC). The popular *Gemüthsgespräch* did not come out in English until 1857 at Lancaster. Both of these catechisms are still being printed in German. The prayer book *Ernsthafte Christenpflicht* has never been translated into English. English editions of other European Mennonite works appeared as follows: *Martyrs' Mirror* 1837 at Lancaster, 1886 at Elkhart; Dordrecht Confession 1811 at Niagara, Ont., 1814 at Doylestown, Pa.; Schabalie's *Wandering Soul* 1834 at Carlisle, Pa.; Menno Simons' *Foundation Book* (John Herr edition) 1835 at Lancaster; Menno's *Complete Works* 1881 at Elkhart. All of these had prior German editions in America. The first original book or pamphlet publication in

English was A. Gottschall's *Description of the New Creature* of 1838, which appeared simultaneously in both languages at Doylestown. The next such work was an English edition of Heinrich Funk's *Spiegel der Taufe* in Virginia in 1851, reprinted in 1853 at Skippack, Pa. The Lancaster meeting calendar appeared in English as early as 1854. Only scattered English pamphlets appeared before 1880. In that year John F. Funk began the publication of Sunday-school helps in English (also German); the Sunday school no doubt contributed greatly to the use of English. The real change to English came with authors who wrote only in that language, the first of these being Daniel Kauffman (MC), with his first book in 1898, *A Manual of Bible Doctrines*. J. S. Coffman, then president of the Elkhart Institute board, stated in his dedication address for the Institute building at Elkhart in 1896: "Here we are at an epoch that marks a transition period in our beloved brotherhood. It is really a final crossing over a large body of our people, the way having been gradually prepared, from the German language into the language of the country." The turn of the century was the pivot of the language change, although the use of German tapered off gradually. In many congregations some German preaching continued until World War I. In the transition period 1875-1900 preachers were often ordained specifically to preach English alongside of the regular German preaching of the older ministers. German Sunday-school classes have persisted longer particularly in those congregations with an Amish background. The *Church and S.S. Hymnal* (MC) of 1902 had a German appendix, and a special edition of the *Church Hymnal, Mennonite,* of 1927, with a German appendix, was prepared for the Franconia Conference, where the use of German has persisted longer than in any other section of the Mennonite Church (MC). The priority of German in the General Conference Mennonite Church in the third quarter of the 19th century is evidenced by the fact that the Wadsworth School (*q.v.*) for the training of ministers (1868-78), in existence six years before the Russian immigration, imported its chief teacher from Germany and conducted all its work in German.

In the communities established by the immigrants from Russia 1874-80 the change to the English language came a generation later. World War I forced the change in many places because of the severe stigma placed upon the German language; even the label "pro-German" and "traitors" was tagged on its users. In some communities the use of German in public was even forbidden. Some congregations hastily shifted to English for their main worship services. By 1920-25 the change was relatively complete in the United States except for the Old Order Amish and Hutterites. The Mennonite Brethren in Christ used English primarily from the beginning in 1874, although some German was also used, as is evident from the fact that their organ, the *Gospel Banner,* had a German edition 1880-95, and a few disciplines were printed in German in the early days.

In Canada the matter is quite different. To this

day all the Russian immigrant communities maintain German as the primary language in church life, both in worship and in official conference proceedings. The arrival of 20,000 immigrants from Russia in 1922-25, and 7,000 again in 1948-52, has further fastened the German and delayed the change to English. The only exception to the above is the Church of God in Christ, Mennonite, which has moved far into English. There is scarcely a congregation in any other group of Russian background, except the Bethel Mission (GCM) in Winnipeg, and certain of the Kleine Gemeinde (EM), which uses English in its main worship service in 1954. The two Bible Colleges in Winnipeg still use German as the major language of instruction. The fear, however, of the loss of German has led to the organization of a special intergroup Mennonite organization in Manitoba for the retention of the German language, a sign that the forces working for the change to English are more powerful than appears on the surface. The Mennonite Church (MC) in Canada has followed the pattern of that group in the U.S.A.

The difficulties for a religious group in a language transition are many and complicated. The older generation has real difficulty in providing religious literature with its own emphasis in the new language. It is difficult to man schools in what is a foreign language. For a time the use of the former or mother language is almost inevitable. Deep feeling of reality and loyalty attach to old vocabularies, and the prestige of the older generation is at stake, so that there is danger of real loss of religious values.

On the other hand the German-English problem has been the cause of serious damage to the Mennonite brotherhood in North America. Many young people have been alienated from the church because of the delay in the change, while others who have remained in the church have often been denied adequate spiritual resources in their own working language, whether in worship and preaching or in available literature. Also the retention of the German language in an English-speaking culture without any real attachment to a German culture has at times led to group and personal impoverishment both culturally and spiritually. The worst forms of this impoverishment have occurred in those groups which have not had adequate German schools of their own, such as the Old Order Amish and other Pennsylvania-Dutch-speaking groups, but also the Old Colony Mennonites with their inadequate elementary German schools and no literary production. The continued exclusive use of dialect in the home, whether Pennsylvania-Dutch or Low German, has been a further handicap. Finally the barrier of a different language has seriously inhibited evangelism and outreach, has at times alienated the group from the national culture, and has intensified the phenomena of ingrowth and inferiority feeling. The struggle over the introduction of English has also contributed to schismatic tendencies at times, particularly in the mid-19th century in such cases as the Old Order Amish and Old Order Mennonite divisions. For a further discussion of the general question of language matters see **Language Problems**.

H.S.B.

Enid, Okla., is a city (pop. 36,000) in the state's wheat belt, built on an economy of agriculture, petroleum, and industry. Enid's trade territory, extending especially to the west and north, covers Mennonite communities with 15 separate congregations: 8 G.C.M., 5 M.B., and 2 Church of God in Christ, Mennonite, their membership totaling more than 2,000. The city has many churches, including 3 Mennonite churches: 1 M.B., and 2 G.C.M., Bethel and Grace. More Mennonites continue to move to Enid. Some come to retire and others to make a living. A number of Mennonite students generally attend Philips University, a church-related college of more than 1,000 students.   H.T.N.

Enid Bible School and Academy (*Enid Bibel- und Akademie-Schule*), Enid, Okla., was founded in 1921 by the local Mennonite Brethren and administered by a committee of five. The emphasis of the school was on Bible and German. In 1925 a school building was erected and in 1938 the school was discontinued. Among its teachers were P. E. Nikkel and A. J. Dick.   C.K.

Enid (Okla.) **Country** Mennonite Brethren Church: see **North Enid** M.B. Church.

Enid (Okla.) Mennonite Brethren Church, sometimes known as the Enid City Church, was organized in 1925 under the direction of the Home Mission Committee of the M.B. Southern District Conference. P. C. Grunau shepherded this congregation for 18 years. Services were at first held in a mission building at 300 East Maple. When this proved to be too small, a church building was purchased at Sixth and East Broadway in 1926. The 1955 membership was 189. Abraham Wiens, A. A. Steinle, A. F. Vogt, and Menno Flaming have served the church as deacons. Lando Hiebert and Jack Adrian served the church recently as pastors. The pastor in 1955 was C. E. Fast. Besides these the following have assisted in the ministry: H. P. Dyck, J. E. Schmidt, H. H. Bartel, and A. P. Koop.   A.F.V.

Enkenbach, Palatinate, Germany, a small village about six miles northeast of Kaiserslautern, the location of a new Mennonite Home for the Aged, *Friedenshort* (*q.v.*), established in 1949, and a resettlement project for Mennonite refugees from Danzig and West Prussia. The Enkenbach settlement, begun in 1953, was planned to provide for 60 refugee families in apartment houses each containing 4 four-room dwellings. Each refugee family received a government loan for 80 per cent of the cost. Since the refugees did not have any capital at all for the remaining 20 per cent, the MCC furnishes the equivalent through the free labor of young American Mennonite conscientious objectors, who assisted in building the houses as their alternative service to meet the requirements of the United States law for a two-year term of work (I-W service). The MCC unit which performed this work in Germany is called PAX. Fifteen PAX boys began to work at Enkenbach in the summer of 1953. The PAX service constitutes a testimony of Christian love in sacrificial service "in the Name of Christ" and for peace. The administration of the Enkenbach resettlement project is in the hands of a German Mennonite organization setup for this purpose known as *Mennonitische Siedlungshilfe e.V.,* with headquarters at Ludwigshafen, Richard Hertzler, director. It was planned to build a meetinghouse with PAX help and organize a congregation.

In recent years numerous large Mennonite meetings with up to 1,000 participants have been held in Enkenbach, using the facilities of the Home for the Aged.† H.S.B.

Enkhuizen, a town in the Dutch province of North Holland, formerly on the Zuiderzee (pop. 10,000), has since the middle of the 16th century been the seat of a Mennonite congregation. Leenaert Bouwens (*q.v.*) baptized 36 persons here. During the days of the persecution the government was favorably inclined to them. When the mayor Sievert Meinertszoon Bokgeest was informed (1558) that the Mennonites were holding secret meetings, which the government was obliged to prevent, he sent them warning, so that they could escape arrest. The magistrate likewise showed no great interest in persecuting them. Van Braght's *Martyrs' Mirror* lists the following martyrs executed in Enkhuizen: Dirk Pietersz Krood, Pieter Trijnes, Claes Roders, and Pieter Claes Jansz. The year of the execution is not known. None of them were citizens of Enkhuizen. Whereas the membership was large in the 16th century, it declined sharply according to the report of the Reformed preacher Bogerman in 1603. The division into various factions had a deterrent influence.

Little is known concerning the history of the various congregations. There were at least two Mennonite congregations in Enkhuizen. The larger of these belonged to the Waterlander branch; the other, which was always small and in 1733 had only 22 members, belonged to the Groningen Old Flemish. The Waterlander congregation sent a representative to the conference of this branch meeting at Amsterdam in 1647. In 1760 difficulties with the magistrates arose in the ordination of Reinhard Rahusen (*q.v.*) and in 1765 in the ordination of Hendrik van Gelder, since the mayors of the city claimed the right of confirming the ordination. The church council did not yield, and both ordinations proceeded without disturbance. In 1765 the union between the (Groningen) Old Flemish and the Waterlander congregations took place, the small congregation in near-by Venhuizen (*q.v.*) having merged with the Waterlander congregation of Enkhuizen in 1735. Evidence of a willingness to sacrifice is shown in the contributions of this congregation to the relief fund for foreign needs: 117 guilders in 1727; 112 in 1733; 203 in 1736. From 1840 until his retirement in 1888, the pastor was D. Harting (*q.v.*), a man of great learning, especially in the Greek. He was the founder of the *Doopsgezinde Bijdragen.* During his pastorship in 1860, the church, parsonage, and custodians' residence were restored. From 1888 to 1900 this church was united with Medemblik. From 1901 to 1907 the minister was H. Bakels (*q.v.*). He was followed by S. Spaans

1907-17, F. F. Milatz 1918-29; after a vacant pulpit for four years, the congregation joined with Hoorn (*q.v.*) to provide ministerial care (1933).

In 1847 the membership was 40 (90 souls). At present (1953) it numbers 112 baptized members. The congregation has a youth club and a choir.
K.V., vDZ.

Blaupot t. C., *Holland* I and II, *passim; Inv. Arch. Amst.* I, Nos. 88, 708, 1149, 1164, 1180; II, Nos. 1716 f.; *DB* 1879, 6; 1883, 72; 1889, 134; 1907, 169; *ML* I, 591 f.

Enno I, Count of East Friesland, 1528-40, the son of Edzard I (*q.v.*), at first attempted to direct the Reformation into Lutheran channels in his realm. Unpleasant experiences with Lutheran clergy and a letter from Prince Philip of Hesse deterred him. External wars kept his attention from religious matters. His measures against the Anabaptists were not adequately enforced. On Jan. 19, 1530, he and his brother Johann issued an edict sternly ordering the Anabaptists to leave the realm before Shrovetide on penalty of loss of life and goods. But nothing happened; Melchior Hofmann could venture to preach in the vestibule (*Geerkammer*) of the Emden church and publicly baptize several hundred adherents. But Obbe Philips' statement that Enno was favorably inclined toward Hofmann's doctrine and had been moved to tears in a conversation with him is surely erroneous. On May 12, 1534, Enno sent a letter to Emden, urging that a close watch be kept on the Anabaptists and that definite steps be taken against them. In 1535 he issued a stern edict against them, not only commanding the baptism of infants, but also threatening to punish rebaptism with severe penalties. Nevertheless the Anabaptist movement grew rapidly in his reign. When he died, his widow Anna (*q.v.*) of Oldenburg took over the government. She favored the Anabaptists, and only imperial pressure induced her to expel them. NEFF.

J. P. Müller, *Die Mennoniten in Ostfriesland . . .* (Emden, 1887); *ML* I, 592.

Enno III, Count of East Friesland, 1599-1625, though not favorable to the Mennonites, apparently did not institute proceedings against them until 1612, when the complaints of the Protestant clergy in the city of Norden caused him to do so. On Nov. 23, 1612, he issued an order to the bailiff of Norden to keep close watch on the Mennonites and to require a list of the houses where they lived and where they held their meetings, and who their pastor was. Apparently little was done, for the Protestant preachers complained again, and on Nov. 20, 1613, a second order was issued to the bailiff: with several councilors he should break up a Mennonite meeting where a wedding was to be performed and arrest the preacher. This he did, and four days later received a letter of praise from the count, which also instructed him to release the preacher (bishop) with the warning that if, contrary to the mandates, he continued to hold their meetings, a fine of 5,000 talers would be required of them and the house in which they met would be confiscated. This decree was to be announced in the pulpits and posted in the customary places.

For eight years the Mennonites were unmolested.

On New Year's Eve in 1621 an order was issued to the mayor and council of Norden to make a list of all Mennonites and all others who did not adhere to the Reformed or Lutheran creed and send it to the count. The last decree Enno III issued against the Mennonites, Sept. 25, 1622, was unusually harsh. No matter what complaints any Mennonite made, he was not to receive justice; anyone making a complaint against them was to have it speedily satisfied. Both audience and preacher were to be arrested if they continued to hold their meetings. Any laxity in enforcement would meet with the count's disfavor. But this mandate, like the others, was little or not at all enforced.   NEFF.

J. P. Müller, *Die Mennoniten in Ostfriesland* . . . (Emden, 1887); *ML* I, 592.

Enno Ludwig, Count of East Friesland 1647-60, was elevated to the rank of prince April 22, 1654. In 1654 he sent a letter to the emperor protesting against his confusing the Mennonites with revolutionary Anabaptists, and to the imperial court he vouched for their loyalty as subjects and their love of order and peace. Nevertheless he obstinately refused to grant them full recognition in his realm. Using his elevation of rank as a pretext he denied them their former protection. It was without doubt a question of money with him; he hoped to extort from them the 6,000 talers of debt his predecessor had made with the Mennonites. They declared themselves ready to pay the sum if he would release them from the annual protection fee for a definite period, and from the obligation to render the oath by raising their fingers; they requested instead the "Mennonite oath," as it had been granted them by Count Ulrich II (*q.v.*). The negotiations dragged on until 1658.

On March 9, 1658, a new letter of protection was prepared for the Mennonites. It recognized the separation of the Uckowallists (*q.v.*) from the Mennonites, who were known as "Flemish, Frisians, and Huiskoopers" (*q.v.*). This differentiation is made in all the later letters of protection, the last of which was issued by King Frederick II. Only the latter group received this letter. It ruled that the Mennonites were to hold their services quietly, but without interference, and that visiting preachers might instruct them in God's Word. This was a definite step forward. The very poor were excused from paying the protection fee, and those without capital should pay "according to our findings." The Mennonites were obligated to report marriages to the local pastor, but the fee was to be determined alone by those to be married. Of great importance is the order to the military authorities at Norden, Leer, and Aurich, forbidding them to draft Mennonites or punish them for refusing to serve. Finally the Mennonites were specifically told that the additional tax required at this time should never again be levied against them or their descendants. At the same time instructions were issued to the courts that the Mennonites—not the Uckowallists—should use an expressly stated formula in place of the oath.

On May 29, 1658, a letter of protection was also given to the Uckowallists. Its content was almost identical with that granted to the Mennonites, except that the Uckowallists were not required to be married in the church or be registered in the church books. They were thus treated more like an independent brotherhood. This favorable treatment, the reason for which is not known, was, however, of short duration.   NEFF.

J. P. Müller, *Die Mennoniten in Ostfriesland* . . . (Emden, 1887); *ML* I, 593.

Enns, a town in Upper Austria, on the Enns near its junction with the Danube. In the late 1520's it was one of the Anabaptist centers of Austria. (*ML* I, 639, 255.)

Enns (Entz, Ensz, Enss, Ens, Enz, Enten), a Mennonite name in the rural Flemish congregations of West Prussia. Fifty-eight families of this name were counted in 1776, 275 persons in 1910, and 197 persons in 1935. Members of this family migrated to Russia and America. In South Russia they mostly adopted the form Enns. Mennonite ministers carrying the family name are now located in Kansas, California, Arkansas, Alberta, British Columbia, Manitoba, Saskatchewan, and Ontario. Important members of the family included Abraham Ensz, son of a Heubuden farmer, with rationalistic and socialistic tendencies, who offered subscriptions in 1873 for a book on his grandfather (*Das Vermächtniss des Mennoniten-Aeltesten Abraham Regier in Gurken-Heubuden. Ein Beitrag zur Klärung und Versöhnung der Mennoniten-Gemeinden unter sich und mit anderen Confessionen*) which, however, never appeared (see *Menn. Friedensbote,* June 1, 1873). Jakob Enns (*q.v.*) was the first elder of the Flemish congregation in the Molotschna settlement in South Russia, 1805-18. Cornelius Enten (Entz) was a preacher of the Old Flemish congregation of the Gross-Werder, Berwaldsche Quartier, after 1800. Gerhard Enns (Entz) was one of the first preachers of the Old Flemish congregation of Chortitza (*q.v.*), serving 1794-*ca.* 1820. Daniel P. Enns (*q.v.*) served as secretary-treasurer of the Canadian Mennonite Board of Colonization. John E. Entz (b. 1875) served 1917-46 as pastor of the First Mennonite Church, Newton, Kan. J. H. Enns (b. 1889) has been serving as elder of the Schönwiese Mennonite Church, Winnipeg, since 1939.   G.R.

Enns, Daniel Peter, the son of Peter and Katharina Toews Enns, was born at Wasserreich, Don Province, Russia, July 17, 1877, and emigrated to Canada in July 1924, where he died June 4, 1946. He was married to Katharina Janzen, May 6, 1907, at Gnadenfeld, Taurida, Russia. To them were born three children: Alice, Anna, and Theodore. He attended the teacher-training school at Halbstadt, Taurida, 1894-96, and the Commercial Institute at St. Petersburg, 1911-13. He obtained his high-school teacher's certificate at Simferopol in 1907 and his commercial teacher's degree at St. Petersburg in 1913. He was baptized in 1897 at the Mennonite Church in Halbstadt, and was elected to the ministry in the Alexanderkrone congregation in 1916, but did not accept the office.

He served in the following offices: chairman, Mennonite Teacher's District Conference, Schönau, Taurida, Russia, 1896-1906; chairman, Mennonite Teacher's Conference, Davlekanovo, Ufa, Russia, 1909-11; chairman, Electoral District, Alexanderkrone, 1917; member Molotschna Teachers' Association, 1917-19; member Molotschna Mennonite Board of Education, 1917-19; member Central Bureau, All Russian Mennonite Organization, 1919; chairman, Sanitation District Committee, Seven Villages, 1922; chairman, Ontario Mennonite Immigrant Committee, 1924; member Central Mennonite Immigrant Committee of Canada, 1925-34, and secretary 1925-27; secretary, Board of Directors, German-English Academy at Rosthern, Sask., 1931-36; and chairman, German Cultural Society, Rosthern, 1933-36.

He was a teacher in Mennonite schools in Russia for 28 years; founder of *Landwirtschaftliche Schule* at Gnadenfeld in 1922; member of the original *Studienkommission* (Commission for the study of possibilities for mass emigration); at Rosthern accountant of the Canadian Mennonite Board of Colonization 1924-26 and secretary-treasurer of the same, 1926-46.

During his years of residence in Russia he held the following positions as teacher: elementary school teacher, Schönau, Molotschna, 1896-1906; high-school teacher, Spat, Crimea, 1906-9; high-school teacher, Davlekanovo, Ufa, 1909-11; private teacher-student St. Petersburg, 1911-13; commercial school teacher, Alexanderkrone, Molotschna, 1913-22; principal-inspector, Commercial School, Alexanderkrone, 1920-22; high-school teacher, Gnadenfeld, Molotschna, 1922-23; principal Agro. School, high school, and elementary school, Gnadenfeld, 1923-24. A.En.

J. G. Rempel, "D. P. Enns," in *Der Bote*, Sept. 27, 1950.

Enns, Franz F., a minister of the Terek (*q.v.*) Mennonite congregation, was born in Alexandertal, Molotschna, South Russia, on Oct. 25, 1871, the son of Franz F. and Elisabeth Franz Enns. He was baptized in Gnadenfeld in 1891 and married Anna Dürksen of Alexandertal on May 27, 1893. Six children were born to them. One of the two sons is Dr. G. F. Enns of Chilliwack, B.C.

He was one of the pioneers of the newly opened Terek settlement and was elected a minister of the Mennonite congregation there in 1903. In 1906 he was ordained elder. After the flight from the Terek in 1918 he served as elder of the Mennonite church in the Memrik settlement, 1920-23, and at Suvorovskaya, 1923-25. He moved back to Memrik (village of Waldeck) in 1925, and emigrated with his family to Canada in 1926, arriving at Winkler, Man., in May. In July Franz Enns took over the work of itinerating minister for the Board of Home Missions (GCM). He remained in this work until incapacitated by ill health early in 1939.

In November 1926 Franz Enns with his family and sons-in-law moved to a farm near Lena, Man., where he organized the newly settled immigrants as the Whitewater Mennonite Church, of which he was elder until 1938. In 1931, in order to be better able to follow his ministerial duties, he left the farm and moved to a small home in the town of White-

water, close to daily mail and railroad services. He died in Winnipeg on March 2, 1940. During the years in Canada he did an invaluable work in looking up and serving the immigrants who had settled in scattered groups and families far from organized congregations throughout Manitoba.

F.F.E.

Enns, Jakob, the first elder of the Flemish congregation in the Molotschna settlement, South Russia. He was probably one of the small group of immigrants from Neuenhuben near Danzig who settled in Russia on Aug. 23, 1804. He had been made preacher in Prussia, and was ordained an elder in Russia in 1805 and served as such until 1818. P. M. Friesen describes him as a man of great zeal but without spiritual life. As a result of his violent character serious strife arose concerning civil punishment and inadequate church discipline, which finally led to division and the organization of the Kleine Gemeinde (*q.v.*). (Friesen, *Brüderschaft,* 74 f., 106 ff.; *ML* I, 593.) A.B.

Ens, Gerhard (1864-1952), is usually considered the founder of the town of Rosthern, Sask. (in 1892). In 1905-13 he was a member of the Legislative Assembly of Saskatchewan. For many years he also was an immigration agent of the Canadian government. As such he made a number of trips to Mennonite settlements in the United States and successfully enlisted settlers for the Canadian West from Minnesota, the Dakotas, Nebraska, and Kansas. He also went to Russia to promote Mennonite immigration to Canada. Though he joined the Church of the New Jerusalem (Swedenborgian), thus breaking with Mennonitism congregationally, traditionally he remained a part of the Mennonite community. As a descendant of the Russian Mennonites he was deeply concerned with the fate of these Mennonites after World War I, when revolution and famine struck. When the great immigration of Mennonites from Russia to Canada in the early 1920's was about to begin there was an Order-in-Council in Ottawa forbidding all Mennonite immigration to Canada as a result of the nonresistant stand taken by the Mennonites of Canada during World War I. Through his influence in political circles in Ottawa and his friendly relations with such leaders as W. L. Mackenzie-King, Gerhard Ens was instrumental in helping to remove these seemingly insurmountable obstacles. J.G.R.

Ens, Maria, daughter of the Dutch Mennonite pastor Hendrik Ens, b. Feb. 6, 1882, at Gorredijk, d. Aug. 21, 1936, at Deventer, Holland. She was teacher of German at Deventer, but in the secretaryship of the *Vereniging voor Gemeentedagen* (*q.v.*) she found her real lifework. From June 1923 to June 1936 she gave much time and devotion to the stimulation of this spiritual movement with its many activities. In 1932 she initiated conferences for unemployed at the Elspeet Brotherhood Home, which have proved to be of blessing for a large number of men and women. Miss Ens was very active also in lending assistance to the Mennonite emigrants from Russia to North and South America, especially in 1931, when she organized a large collection of clothing for the Russian Mennonites, whom she visited repeatedly in their temporary camps at Prenzlau and Mölln, Germany. (*DJ* 1937, 34-38 with portrait; see also *Brieven,* 1923-36 *passim.*)

voZ.

Enschede, a town in the district of Twenthe, Dutch province of Overijssel. This industrial town (textiles, ironworks) with its rapidly growing population (12,000 in 1910; 102,000 with 809 Mennonites in 1947) is the seat of a Mennonite congregation, of whose origin and history not much is known, because in 1862 the archives were destroyed with the church by fire.

The idea that the Mennonite congregation was founded about 1530 by Waldensian weavers, who had moved from Flanders to Twenthe (J. Beets, *Aanteekeningen* in *Inv. Arch. Amst.* I, No. 757), has been proved to be false. Probably it was founded by Mennonite immigrants from Westphalia. It really arose some decades after most of the congregations in the Netherlands had been founded; nothing is known of it before 1580. The most prominent families in this congregation, all of Westphalian descent—van Lochem, Blijdenstein (*q.v.*), Paschen, Stenvers (i.e., Steinfurters), were among the founders of the present large textile industry in Enschede. In 1620 some well-to-do members of the Burgsteinfurt congregation in Westphalia settled in Enschede, among them Hendrick Gerritsz and Everwijn Franken. For a long time meetings were held in a private house, the membership being very small. In 1698, when Isaac Paschen was a preacher, a room in the van Lochem house was enlarged and adapted for church meetings; it was not until 1769 that a church was built, dedicated on Dec. 17 of this year with a sermon held by the minister Cornelis de Vries, which was published: *Inwijdingsreden over de tempels* . . . (Amsterdam, 1769). In 1786 an organ was placed in this church.

In the second half of the 17th century and the 18th century the congregation belonged to the conservative Zonist wing of the Dutch Mennonites. By the end of the 18th century much had changed. The prominent members were Patriots (*q.v.*) and were politically liberal. In 1795 the Mennonites in the Netherlands were recognized on an equal basis with the Reformed. Jacob H. Floh (*q.v.*), minister of the congregation, became (in 1796) a delegate of Twenthe to the lower house of the States-General, as was Jan B. Blijdenstein, a member of the congregation. In 1810 this Jan Blijdenstein was appointed burgomaster of Enschede.

The first trained minister here was Cornelis de Vries, mentioned above, 1763-71. He gave his considerable library of Mennonite and other books to the congregation (Blaupot t. C., *Groningen* I, 222). This library also perished with the church, when a fire devastated a large part of the city on May 7, 1862. The church, which was completely destroyed, was rebuilt on the same spot and dedicated May 2, 1864. This building was enlarged in 1952.

Among the ministers of this congregation was S. Cramer (*q.v.*), later professor at the University and

the Mennonite Seminary of Amsterdam; he served at Enschede 1872-85 and was followed by C. N. Wybrands 1886-98, P. B. Westerdijk 1899-1912, E. Pekema 1912-42, S. M. A. Daalder 1942-45, and since 1945 J. P. Keuning. From 1864 to 1923 the congregation of Gronau, Germany, was a branch of Enschede, served by its preachers. As to the number of baptized members, the following figures were available: 1698, about 60; 1771, 83; 1781, 55; 1840, 65; 1864, 94; 1900, 180; 1916, about 300; 1930, 479; 1940, 520; 1953, 600. The congregation has a Sunday school for children, two women's circles, a youth group, and a choir.

voZ.

G. Heeringa *et al., Uit het Verleden der Doopsg. in Twenthe* (Borne, n.d.) *passim;* Blaupot t. C., *Groningen* I and II; *DB* 1864, 182-83; *Inv. Arch. Amst.* I, No. 1164; II, Nos. 1718-20; *ML* I, 593-94.

Ensisheim, a town (pop. 3,212) in Upper Alsace, Gebwiller district, was in the 16th century the seat of the Austrian government in Alsace, which ruthlessly stamped out the Anabaptist movement. Six hundred Anabaptists are said (by Sebastian Franck) to have been executed here.

Eberhard Hofmann, the city clerk of Ensisheim, participated in the trial of Michael Sattler (*q.v.*) in Rottenburg, Württemberg, Germany, and with his venomously hostile attitude contributed to the injustice of the trial. (See **Basel** and **Alsace.**) NEFF.

Von Muralt and Schmidt, *Quellen zur Gesch. der Täufer in der Schweiz* I (Zürich, 1952) 251; C. A. Cornelius, *Gesch. des Münsterischen Aufruhrs* II (Leipzig, 1860) 57; W. Beemelmans, *Die Verfassung und Verwaltung der Stadt Ensisheim im 16. Jahrhundert* (Strasbourg, 1908); L. Spach, *Description du Departement du Bas-Rhin* I, 178; *ML* I, 594.

Entfelder (Endtfelder), **Christian,** a pupil of Hans Denk (*q.v.*), a friend of Hubmaier (*q.v.*), probably the preacher of an Anabaptist congregation in Eibenschitz (*q.v.*) in 1526-27. Having been expelled from Eibenschitz, he came to Strasbourg in 1529, after which nothing more is heard of him until 1544, when he was at Königsberg, Prussia, in a position of some influence in the Prussian court. Probably he was one of those intellectuals who were for a time close to the Anabaptists, and then broke the connections with them, either from fear of suffering or inner dissatisfaction, and then spent their lives alone in various positions. He wrote the following three books:

(1) *Von den manigfaltigen im glauben zerspaltungen, dise jar entstanden. In sonderheit von der Taufspaltung unn jrem urtail. Ain bedacht* (Strasbourg, 1530).

(2) *Von warer Gottseligkeyt wie der mensch allhie in diser zeyt dartzu kommen mag, ain kurtze (aber gar nutzliche) betrachtung. Apocal. 14. Fürchtend Gott und gebt jme die eer* (Strasbourg, 1530).

(3) *Von Gottes vnnd Christi Jesu vnnseres Herren erkändtnuss, ain bedacht, Allen schülern des hailigen gaysts weiter zu bedencken aufgezaichnet, mit freyem vrthayl* (1533).

All three books were also printed by Philipp Ulhart (*q.v.*) at Augsburg about 1530 (Schottenloher).

The first book, "a dark and confused" (Veesenmeyer, 312) writing, falls into two parts; in the first he seeks to discover the source of religious division; in the second he takes up the dispute on baptism and communion. The content of the first part he treats in five statements, as follows:

(1) That many people think they have what has not been given them, and presume to give what they do not have; this is a source of great error.

(2) That many pretend to be learned and attend the true Master's school very little, from which follows that divine and human art are confused, divine and human word are not distinguished, and many concern themselves with more things than are committed to them, and this is a source of much error.

(3) That nobody believes that he does not have what he after all really has, and that nobody sincerely seeks or desires that without which he cannot be saved; this is a cause of many divisions.

(4) He who could properly judge divisions causes none, but creates unity in the midst of division.

(5) As the understanding zeal nourishes the spirit and consumes the flesh, likewise the zeal without understanding consumes unity and nourishes all divisions wherein the spirit disappears and the flesh struggles with the creature.

In this book Entfelder attacks the dead letter of the law. He speaks very unclearly about the voice of God and of men. The treatise on baptism he wrote upon the request of some Anabaptists, from whom he seems to have detached himself. He says it is a divine counsel, Christian command, and elementary ceremony. *Von den manigfaltigen im glauben zerspaltungen* was translated into Dutch by Petrus Serrarius, and under the title *Bedenckinge over de veelderley Scheuringen ende Dwalingen* added as an appendix to Serrarius' book, *De Vertredinge des Heyligen Stadts* (Amsterdam, 1659). It had some influence in Dutch Collegiant (*q.v.*) circles.

The second booklet (17 pages) deals with generally mystical ideas. Blessedness is nothing but a rest in which the Spirit of God works in man through Christ, to rid him of all creature including himself, so that he hears only what God speaks to him. Man can acquire this rest by the rebirth, in which Christ is formed in him. It takes place in six stages. Only then is man able to take his outer senses captive and to activate his inner senses in the power of Him who indwells him, so that he performs perfectly that which God commands him. His faith puts him into this position, as is illustrated in Abraham and Peter. It is a matter of not only accepting the Word outwardly, but of making it one's own with a complete loss of himself. Because man does not want to lose himself, he can never come to rest. . . . It is very reprehensible that one wishes to pay for Christ with mere words. Man will not find rest until he is one with God. Then the true Sabbath dawns with peace, joy, love, 'gentleness, comfort, and all pleasure. . . . But such unity cannot take place unless man tolerates the will of his God, which has been revealed to him in Christ Jesus, the first fruits of all. . . . To take up one's cross (without the cross it cannot take place, the servant is not above the Master), with Christ

committed to a simple, poor life, as the seed grain must first die, grow and become fruitful, be threshed out and crushed in true submission, then one becomes the true food from God the heavenly Father. . . . The one who so sincerely loves us can be recognized only through the suffering of His Son through the Holy Spirit. . . . If one comes to Him like the prodigal son one learns to love Him ardently; one finds in Him peace, rest, salvation, and all sufficiency, so that one disregards the whole world and without Him is so poor that one would not wish to be poorer even if the whole world were ours; "for here is nought but love and love, the peace of the Lord Jesus Christ in the rest of the Holy Spirit, in whom man may cry with the joy of the free princely spirit: who shall separate us from the love of God? shall tribulation or peril, persecution, hunger, thirst, danger, want, or the sword: I am certain that neither death nor life, angels, principalities nor powers, neither the present nor the future nor height nor depth nor any other creature shall be able to separate us from the love of God, which is in Christ Jesus our Lord. And this is true blessedness, to which may God, the heavenly Father, help us with grace. Watch, pray, be sober, for ye know neither the day nor the hour." This booklet was republished by Friedrich Nicolai, Lessing's friend, in 1781.

The third book contains an obscure treatise on the nature of the Trinity, which we follow with difficulty. In the foreword the author assures us that only love to the truth has moved him to publish this work and to add his mite to the removal of aberrations on the doctrine of the person of Jesus Christ, without any pretension of infallibility and with the solemn conviction that he would be very sorry if he should cause offense to anyone with this writing. He makes three assertions, on the basis of which he deals with the questions:

(1) How the one God from the single reason of His love, has in threefold power, known as the three Persons, revealed Himself.

(2) How the manifold human beings are reminded of the revealed knowledge of God by means of manifold causes and oppositions.

(3) Concerning the knowledge of the true Mediator, concluded with the introduction of several afore-mentioned things (Veesenmeyer, 321-28, where is found the letter written in March 1544 by Entfelder to Johann a Lasco, *q.v.*). Krollmann (p. 247) says that Entfelder returned to the service of Duke Albrecht of Prussia. NEFF.

A. Hegler, *Geist und Schrift bei Sebastian Franck* (Freiburg, 1892); Calvary, *Verzeichnis seltener und wertvoller Bücher* (Berlin, 1870) 47; L. Keller, *Reformation und die älteren Reformparteien* (Leipzig, 1885) 433, 470; idem, *Johann von Staupitz* (Leipzig, 1885) 213, 360, 380, 394; Veesenmeyer in Gabler's *Neuestes theologisches Journal* IV, No. 4 (Nürnberg, 1800); K. Schottenloher, *Philipp Ulhart, Ein Augsburger Winkeldrucker und Helfershelfer der "Schwärmer" und "Wiedertäufer"* (München and Freising, 1921) 85, 89; Krollmann, "Die Entwicklung der preussischen Landeskirche im 16. Jahrhundert," in *Monatshefte der Comeniusgesellschaft* XVIII (1909); *ML* I, 594 f.

Enthusiasts, a term little used in modern English or German, though much used in both English and

German, in the 16th-18th centuries, with a meaning similar to though not quite so intense as "fanatics" or "zealots." In German the more common term is *Schwärmer* or *Verzückte*. The third edition of the *HRE* titles its article on the subject *Verzückung, Enthusiasmus, Schwärmerei*. The latest book making much use of the term is that by the Roman Catholic Oxford don R. A. Knox, *Enthusiasm, A Chapter in the History of Religion with Special Reference to the XVII and XVIII Centuries* (Oxford, 1950).

Knox includes in his survey the following groups: Montanists, Donatists, Joachim of Fiore, Albigenses, Waldenses, Anabaptists, Hendrik Niclaes and the Familists, George Fox and the Quakers, Jansenists, Quietists, Moravians, and John Wesley and the Methodists. He labels the symptoms of enthusiasm as "ascetic legalism, millenarianism, antinomianism, ecstasy." In the Elizabethan Age the term "Enthusiasts" became almost a technical term as used by leaders of the Church of England in referring first to Anabaptists and then to Puritans. At times the term seems almost to mean any group of sectarians who depart from the historic church; i.e., who generate sufficient conviction and courage (=enthusiasm?) to break away from the main line of historic Christendom as expressed in the state churches, whether Catholic or Protestants, and to make a fresh start. The assumption behind the term is that such breakaways are due to an overemphasis on immediate guidance by the Holy Spirit or an "inner light," a relaxing of normal controls and restraints, permitting either excessive emotionalism or undue self-exaltation to overbalance common sense and respect for history and tradition. Knox even calls enthusiasm an "ultra-supernaturalism."

The term and concept of Schwärmer and Schwärmertum as used chiefly by the Lutheran theologians and historians from Luther on down to the present day, best translated by "fanatics," has proved more serviceable than "enthusiasts," and is a far more dynamic term in church historiography. Conservative modern Lutherans are still very conscious of the Schwärmer, both historically and currently, and of opposition to them—far more than is Anglo-Saxon Christendom. The difference may be due to the fact that the ideals of the free churches, who are in a sense the spiritual heirs of the Schwärmer (Anabaptists) of the Reformation time, are now dominant in the Christendom of the United States, and very influential in English Christendom in general, whereas the Lutheran countries have never developed vigorous or large free churches (although Anglo-Saxon importations like the Baptists and Methodists have become significant). The Lutheran state churches, having remained dominant in the Christendom of their countries, have continued throughout their history in effect to view all divergent (sectarian) movements, from the Anabaptists on down, as dangerous and inexcusable aberrations and threats to the life of "*the* church." One of the weapons in their fight against these groups has been the derogatory designation of Schwärmer. The term carries both the sense of "sectarian" and somewhat of "fanatical" and "unbalanced." It is the

product of a sincere state-church mind, which has difficulty in conceding the validity of the free church concept. The typical Lutheran sees, perhaps correctly, not just isolated individuals or groups of Schwärmer but a whole front of opposition, another type of Christianity, of which the Anabaptists were the leading exponents in Reformation times. In this understanding, the Anabaptists-Mennonites and their historians would in effect agree, with reversed evaluation, however. They would rate the Anabaptist front as nearer to the true intent of Christ and the New Testament than the state church type. Such historians, and of course modern Mennonites, would not agree to classify the extremist and fringe groups or cults of today such as, for instance, the Jehovah's Witnesses, in the same category with the Anabaptists at all. Thus in reality the Anabaptist-Mennonite and free churchman will take a position on the concept of Enthusiast-Schwärmer diametrically opposed to that held by the Lutheran state church side. For him the term is intolerable as applied to the main line of his own and related groups through history. The early Anabaptists rejected and resented the term as it was applied to them by the Reformers. Their spiritual descendants can do no less.

The use and prevalence of the term "Schwärmer" (Enthusiast) has a varying value through the centuries. From Luther and Melanchthon to Gottfried Arnold (1666-1714) it was an accepted term, most commonly a term of contempt applied to the Anabaptists and similar heretics. Beginning with Gottfried Arnold a change gradually came in, particularly among the more advanced and liberal thinkers; the heretics of the Reformation were now held to be the true Christians and forerunners of Pietism and the Enlightenment. Through the 18th and 19th centuries this view was held alongside of the older view. The continental liberals of the 19th-20th centuries interpreted the Reformation Schwärmer to be the pioneers and forerunners of the modern religious spirit and gave them much recognition in the development of modern toleration and freedom of conscience. Alfred Hegler of Tübingen with his book *Geist und Schrift bei Sebastian Franck* (1893) was the brilliant beginner, and Ernst Troeltsch with his *Soziallehren* (1912) was the climax of this trend, followed by Walther Köhler (d. 1942), with many other historians in agreement. In Anglo-Saxondom it was Rufus Jones (d. 1950) with his *Spiritual Reformers* (1905) and other writings. Karl Holl, however, the noted Berlin scholar, reversed the trend to some extent with his brilliant and powerful essay, *Luther und die Schwärmer* (1922), reviving the older evaluation. Since then a still undecided battle has in effect been raging in modern Lutheran scholarship. The evangelical trend, coupled with the Luther renaissance, in general glorifying Luther, has largely taken Luther's position against the Schwärmer. The most recent publication of this view has been *Heft 6* of *Schriften des Theologischen Konvents Augsburgischen Bekenntnisses* (Berlin, 1952) containing the following three essays: W. Maurer, "Luther und die Schwärmer"; H. Wendland, "Gesetz und Geist des Schwärmertums bei Paulus"; and F. Schumann, "Schwärmerei als gegenwärtige

Versuchung der Kirche." These essays were papers read at the sixth meeting of the *Theologischer Konvent Augsburgischen Bekenntnisses* in Fulda, Germany, March 25-28, 1952. The report of the discussion at the meeting as published in the same *Heft* clearly indicates the position taken toward the Schwärmer by the group attending the session. A few extracts (in translation) will suffice to indicate it. "How is the phenomenon Schwärmertum to be conceived? Is it not a significant symptom, that although it professes to depend on the Word of God, actually it delivers the *dynamis* of the Word to the devil? The Schwärmer contend that man, as pious man, remains free before God. Here the essence of Anabaptism must be sought. The approach of God to man in the incarnation is for the Schwärmer the stumbling block (*skandalon*). The Schwärmer uproots the word of God not in the form of rejection but acceptance; therefore Schwärmertum is the most pious and deceptive (*verlogenste*) form of self-assertion before God." These and similar astonishing assertions are quite in the spirit of Luther's attack on the Schwärmer (Anabaptists). It is true the report does not identify the Anabaptists as specifically mentioned in the discussion, and claims that the writers are concerned about the general theory of Schwärmertum, not concrete cases, but the implications are there, and the first essay was on the Anabaptists.

Fritz Heyer's *Der Kirchenbegriff der Schwärmer* (Leipzig, 1939) is written in the same general spirit of Lutheran evaluation of all Anabaptism as a dangerous "Schwärmertum." Christian Neff's reply to Heyer should be noted in his review in *Mennonitische Geschichtsblätter* V (1940) 48-52. A far more objective and valuable discussion is Karl Steck's *Luther und die Schwärmer* (Zollikon-Zürich, 1955), No. 44 of *Theologische Studien herausgegeben von Karl Barth*. An adequate historical and theological valid answer to this age-old concept of Anabaptist-Enthusiast-Schwärmertum has not yet been rendered. It cannot be done by modern Mennonites who follow either the liberal or the Lutheran position, or who have no clear historical knowledge or a Biblical Anabaptist-Mennonite theological line of their own. Meanwhile the misconception of the Anabaptist-Mennonites as Schwärmer-Enthusiasts persists in far too many circles and requires correction. Anabaptism is a sober, Biblical, realistic theology of regeneration and discipleship, subject to the Word, constitutive of a true New Testament church, and not "Enthusiasm." H.S.B.

Entz, Johann, was chosen preacher of the Hutterian Brethren, July 24, 1892, and confirmed by Elder Peter Hofer on May 30, 1897. A 1916 list of Hutterite preachers names him as the leader of the Old Elmspring colony in South Dakota. D.D.

Ephrata, Pa., a borough (pop. 7,000) in Lancaster County, 12 miles northeast of Lancaster, the site of the famous Ephrata Cloister (*q.v.*). At these cloisters was located a Seventh-day Baptist colony, claiming a thousand acres, famous for mills and the printing press, where the German *Martyrs' Mirror* (1748 imprint) and 42 other books were printed.

It developed first through the industry and prominence of the Cloister group, and then later their decline added materially to the growth of the town. It is a business center for a large Mennonite community. The Ephrata Mennonite (MC) congregation (*q.v.*) of 362 worships in the town. The principal Mennonite Central Committee clothing center is also located here. I.D.L.

Ephrata Cloister, established by the Seventh-day Baptists at Ephrata, Lancaster Co., Pa., a group which separated from the Dunkards (Church of the Brethren) in 1735, headed by Johann Conrad Beissel. They were a mystical group who organized a communal life, separating the sexes and binding themselves to a simple life, in effect establishing a Protestant monastery. Rudolph Naegle, a Groffdale (Lancaster County) Mennonite preacher, and other Mennonites with names of Landis, Lang, Meylin, Graff, Weber, Greybill, Funk, Eicher, Hildebrand, Hoehn, and Martin joined them. Soon the group owned all lands within a radius of three or four miles, farmed the lands of Cocalico, and built an industrial center with a gristmill, sawmill, paper mill, oil mill, and fulling mill, a tannery, and weaving and pottery factories. They were musicians, teachers, did excellent *fraktur* work and embroidery, painted on walls and canvas, were spinners, quilters, and makers of household remedies, sulphur matches, and waxed paper. They established one of the earliest German printing establishments in the New World in 1745.

As friends of mercy Ephrata cared for soldiers after Braddock's defeat and the Battle of Brandywine. The Mennonite preacher John Baer and his wife, who had come to help in the care of soldiers who were sick with typhus, died with the 150 soldier victims of the disease. With the best press and the only good paper in America they produced 43 books, the largest of which was the German *Martyrs' Mirror* (in 1748) for American Mennonites. Their Ludwig Hacker had a Sunday school here 40 years before Robert Raikes's in England. Peter Miller, the talented prior 1743-96, founded the Ephrata Classical Academy, translated the *Martyrs' Mirror* from Dutch to German, and translated the Declaration of Independence into seven languages. In 1789 he interceded for the First Amendment to the Constitution of the United States which guarantees religious liberty, and freed a Tory, his worst enemy, walking barefooted to West Chester via Valley Forge, to appeal to General Washington. The State of Pennsylvania has established the Ephrata Cloister as a shrine, and is restoring all buildings to their original form.

The Ephrata Cloister press was of much service to the early Pennsylvania Mennonites, particularly in the first half of the 18th century. The following Mennonite books were printed here: 1745 *Güldene Aepffel;* 1745 *Das Andenken einiger heiligen Märtyrer;* 1745 (also 1770, 1785) *Die Ernsthafte Christenpflicht;* 1748-51 *Märtyrer-Spiegel;* 1769 (also 1770) *Christliches Gemüthsgespräch;* 1787 *Das Ganz Neue Testament* (Froschauer). The translation service of Peter Miller for the *Märtyrer-Spiegel* was of very great value. This tremendous folio volume of 1,482 pages in fine calf binding was an extraordinary achievement in those pioneer days in a frontier wilderness village. It was the largest book published in the American colonies before the Revolutionary War.† I.D.L.

J. F. Sachse, *The German Sectarians of Pennsylvania 1708-1742, A Critical and Legendary History of the Ephrata Cloister and the Dunkers* 2 vv. (Philadelphia, 1899, 1900); *ML* I, 595 f.

Ephrata Mennonite Christian Day School was opened one mile northeast of Ephrata, Pa., in September 1946, to provide a more Biblical emphasis than was possible in the public schools. With the very substantial help of those interested, including several Mennonite groups beyond the borders of the sponsoring congregations, a two-room building was constructed. The 1953-54 enrollment was 97, including one year of high school, with Michael N. Wenger serving as principal and Gideon S. Eberly and Anna Ruth Hess completing the faculty.
M.N.W.

Ephrata (Pa.) Mennonite Church (MC), Lancaster County, is a member of the Lancaster Mennonite Conference. After the city of Ephrata became a center for Mennonite families from the Metzler and Hammer Creek districts of Lancaster County, a meetinghouse was built on West Fulton Street in 1901. The above-named districts supplied bishop and ministerial oversight until Amos S. Horst was ordained to the ministry in 1918. The 1901 building was the location of the Winter Bible School of Lancaster Conference, 1939-43. It now serves as a clothing center for the Mennonite Central Committee. On May 6, 1937, a large new meetinghouse on Sunset Avenue was dedicated. In 1953 the bishops were Amos S. Horst and Mahlon Zimmerman; the ministers were Eugene Landis and J. Elvin Martin; and the deacon was Elam S. Stoner. The 1953 membership was 383. I.D.L.

Epistles, Anabaptist. (A) *Hutterite*. These are among the most unusual literary documents of Anabaptism, in type, style, and spirit reminiscent of the epistles of the New Testament. Though single epistles by other Anabaptist groups have been preserved (see section B), we know of no other group which so systematically collected all of their epistles and made them available to the brotherhood. In their totality the epistles represent one of the richest sources for our understanding of the Anabaptists, and a moving testimony of the courage, strength, and genuineness of their faith. No other group of Anabaptists has produced such an amazing amount of devotional literature as have the Hutterites, who enjoyed writing and copying their literature almost up to recent times. European archives and libraries as well as the colonies of the Brethren in the United States and Canada hold an astonishing number of handwritten devotional and other books. Joseph Beck (*Geschichts-Bücher, q.v.*) describes a great number of these European codices (as does also Lydia Müller, *Glaubenszeugnisse* . . . , 1938) which once belonged to Hutterite colonies in Slovakia but

were confiscated, mainly by Jesuits during the 18th century and stored away (Beck, 563-642). About 300 such codices are known but many more must once have existed which were lost in times of persecution and wandering, or were destroyed by fire or plunder. They represent a complete Hutterite devotional library which was, to be sure, never printed and was hardly known to the outside world until rather recent times. In these books (*Sammelbände*) are found also all the epistles to be discussed in this article.

Moravia was the main center of Hutterite activities during the 16th century. Here were their large Bruderhofs with a *Vorsteher* or elder at the helm, and here were also their scriptoria (*Schreibstuben*) where all the incoming and outgoing epistles were collected and copied. The Brethren developed an extraordinary literary activity: the largest of these codices comprises 700 to 800 leaves quarto (of solid, strong paper), written in excellent penmanship, and beautifully bound in leather with clasps. The number of epistles known is likewise amazing; 400 to 500 have been counted. But it is fairly safe to say that once the number must have been still greater. Many of these epistles are of unusual length, covering in print occasionally as much as 20 pages folio size. Only about one fifth of all derive from the 17th century; all the rest belong to the great era of the 16th century; the time of writing stretches from 1527 to 1662.

Apparently most of the brethren were passionate letter writers; their strong inner life and their complete devotion to their new way found no better expression than in such epistles. Their topics were brotherhood, community of goods, a working faith in God and Christ, martyrdom as the inevitable lot of an earnest Christian, victory over flesh and world, absolute certainty in their way of resignation and nonconformity, love to everyone. Theological speculations were rare and less popular since they lack the actuality of a given situation. All these letters were read and reread by the Brethren, who thus learned the genius of their own tradition as well as the right behavior of earnest Christians living like sheep among wolves. It was their sacred legacy.

The epistles may be classified into different types: missionary letters to and from those who were working for God in all countries of German tongue, martyr letters to and from those who were in prison or just about to give the highest testimony of their faith, letters of admonition and encouragement, and finally also a few personal letters to friends, and so on. The elders or the entire community also sent many letters to the Brethren abroad.

About 80 personal letter writers have been counted, half of whom died sooner or later as martyrs. Some of these writers were very prolific, in some cases writing as many as 20 or more letters to the church at home, while others wrote just one or two letters in a long while but then often very long ones. Not all writers were leaders, ministers, or other functionaries. Often simple and very humble brethren produced true gems of epistolary literature. Many of these letter writers name Tirol as their home country. Four of them (of the earliest period) had formerly been Catholic priests. Only one writer is known to have been a schoolmaster; others were millers, blacksmiths, cabinetmakers, etc. About one third of all the epistles have no individual author; they are, as so many other documents of the Anabaptists, anonymous.

Most prominent of all these letters are those written in prison and dungeon (about 130 in number). It was the very joy of the Brethren who suffered for conscience' sake to write home to the community as a whole. The consciousness of belonging to the brotherhood gave them strength, firmness, and courage to stand all of these unbelievable hardships and tortures. Only 30 of all letters studied are addressed to the "marital sister," i.e., wife, containing farewell greetings and exhortations to remain steadfast in their faith. Perhaps not all letters of this sort were filed in the scriptorium, though that is not likely in a group as closely knit as this. One epistle which has become particularly well known, even famous, is the long letter which Jakob Hutter, the great first leader, wrote to the governor of Moravia on behalf of the entire brotherhood when this group was about to be expelled from Moravia in 1535. This letter has been reprinted seven times in different connections, and has been used as a major source. More than 200 epistles have a collective address (e.g., "To the brethren on the Rhine," or "To the brethren wherever they are," etc.). In some epistles an imprisoned brother comforts his comrade in bonds who lies in a nearby prison (*Trostbrief an einen mitgefangenen Bruder*). Many epistles were written by the elder or *Vorsteher* of the community to the distant workers for God in tribulations and need. It was particularly during the "Golden Era" in Moravia (1565-78), the period of the elder Peter Walpot (*q.v.*), that a great number of missioners (*Sendboten*) went out into many lands. Hence many epistles arrived and were answered by busy writing-hands.

The high standard of most of these epistles is truly amazing; simple tradesmen and husbandmen wrote letters of great perfection in expression and effectiveness. In the Hutterite colonies they learned reading and writing and of course the spiritual foundations of their life. They also studied the writings of those who lived and suffered before them. Equipped in this way, they were eager to write under any situation. In jail and dungeon they somehow procured paper, ink, and quill, and there were always messenger-brethren for the contact back and forth with Moravia. At home all letters were carefully preserved, copied, collected in separate codices, and also inserted into the text of the Great Chronicle (*Geschicht-Buch*) which was so carefully carried on through the centuries. One fifth of the entire Chronicle consists of such inserted epistles, while the great part of the text is made up of excerpts from such records. It was the real life of the Brethren which was thus mirrored in these writings.

Only the epistles of the New Testament offer an adequate comparison to this unique literature which has the same spirit and in many cases even the same style as the apostolic models. Their genuineness and immediacy make them outstanding. It was, of course, inevitable that occasionally stereotyped forms crept in. But most of the letters written in prison—and they are the majority—in face of a supreme test, show a spontaneity of expression not too often met in religious literature. Distress and tribulation, but at the same time hope and trust in God, thus became verbal; likewise the assurance to have lived up to God's commands. There was no room for great excitement. Simplicity is combined with deep spirituality, and an emotional warmth with healthy restraint and dignity in expression. Occasionally a folksy note comes to the fore, but surprisingly it is not the rule. The Pauline style is often imitated as the Brethren felt a kinship to the spirit and life of the early apostles. Sometimes a natural rudeness and wittiness shows up, which enhance the attractiveness of these letters. An example from 1568 might illustrate this side. A brother in prison reports of his conversations with a Catholic priest who wants to persuade him to give up his way, "Then I spoke, 'Since you want to derive infant baptism from circumcision which so obviously is straight against infant baptism, I must speak about it. Now, you tell me: did Abraham invent circumcision by himself?' Upon which he said, 'It was ordered to him by God.' Then I answered, 'Then wait until infant baptism will be ordered to you by God.' Then he said, 'You are a rude straw-cutter and do not understand the Scriptures, and yet you want to teach me; you should rather believe me and follow me; I am a highly learned man and well versed in many languages.' Upon which I said, 'A long time ago there was not one swine-herd all around Rome who would not have known Latin since it was a common language then, as ancient history clearly makes out. Nowadays it is a secular art and not at all divine piety or discipline.' "

Freshness of style, and always a witness to their faith make these epistles stimulating reading. True, there were not many new ideas to be propagated, since Anabaptism is a simple Biblical faith. Yet there is almost in every line of this literature a concreteness and existentiality of a faith which was less meditated than lived out. That explains why there is no unctiousness in their speech and no empty talk. As one brother wrote in 1561, "For that reason, beloved brethren, accept my little writing in love and good spirit, not as a work of the pen or the ink, but as truth and living word. All that I have taught you I am set to seal with my blood through the grace of God. . . . My letter is not in pleasant words of human wisdom but in the testimony of the Spirit and of power (*in der Beweisung des Geistes und der Kraft*)."

There is little wonder that these human documents were so highly esteemed; they were studied and copied and represent the source of strength for everyone in the colony. Here the Brethren learned the right demeanor in facing the world, and the right spirit of suffering. This reading gave them strength in the martyrdom which threatened them in almost every corner of the country. All that explains why these epistle-codices became such a precious heritage and why they were preserved and carried along throughout all the long history and wandering of the brethren.

Published letters: Geschicht-Buch (q.v.) in its several editions (1883, 1923, 1943); A. Zieglschmid, "Unpublished 16th Century Letters of the Hutterite Brethren," MQR XV (1941) 5-25, 118-40 (German); R. Friedmann, "An Old Anabaptist Letter of Peter Walpot (1571)," MQR XIX (1945) 27-40 (English); Lydia Müller, Glaubenszeugnisse oberdeutscher Taufgesinnter (Leipzig, 1938, passim); G. Bossert, TA (Württemberg) has all the epistles by Paul Glock, 1563-69, pp. 1049-1102. This is the most extensive printed collection of epistles coming from a single brother. Hans Georg Fischer published Hutter's letters with a biography in 1956. Robert Friedmann is editing a volume of Hutterite letters for publication in 1957.　　　　　R.F.

R. Friedmann, "The Epistles of the Hutterian Brethren, 1530-1650, A Study in Anabaptist Literature," MQR II (1946) 147-77 (a revision of the author's study, "Die Briefe der österreichischen Täufer," in Archiv für Ref.-Gesch. XXVI, 1929); H. G. Fischer, Jakob Huter, Leben, Frömmigkeit, Briefe (Newton, 1956).

(B) Non-Hutterite. The Hutterites were not the only passionate letter writers; it seems as if such activities were particularly appealing to all Anabaptists, who thus testified to their faith, expressing their uncompromising stand, and above all leaving a legacy for those who came after them. These letters were in most cases written by martyrs who wanted to send a last farewell to their beloved ones or to the entire group, together with some admonitions and exhortations to keep loyal to the faith. In the same way as the great Hutterite Chronicle was built upon such epistles (either inserted or else used as main sources for the narrative), so were also all the martyrbooks, which originated in the Netherlands and found their climax in van Braght's great Martyrs' Mirror of 1660 (q.v.). Even a superficial perusal of this book will demonstrate this fact; nearly half of its second part is made up of such letters written by martyrs in many lands in prison, on the eve of their execution, and addressed to wife, husband, child, or the brethren wherever they were. No special study has yet been undertaken in this direction, but the similarity in spirit, form, and style with the Hutterite letters is striking. Only in one point is a significant difference observable; while the Hutterites have not one single letter written by a woman (though they had female martyrs), van Braght presents a great number of epistles written by women who were about to face the supreme sacrifice. J. C. Wenger (Glimpses, 177-78) prints the translation of such a most moving letter by Janneken von Munstdorp to her child, which was born in prison and now had to be abandoned (1573). This is a real gem of Anabaptist epistolary literature. Other great letters were written by Anneken of Rotterdam 1538, and many other women who were ready to seal their faith by martyrdom and death.

The sources of van Braght or the earlier martyrbooks are little known. No central office existed in the Netherlands or in the Lower Rhine district as was the case with the Hutterites in Moravia, and no central body could take care of these precious legacies. And yet they were preserved. The Amsterdam Mennonite Library has the original of a letter written by the martyr Maeyken Wens, who was executed at Antwerp on Oct. 6, 1573. This letter is written on the back of a letter which her husband had written to her while she was in prison. This is the only autograph letter of a Dutch martyr that has been preserved. It was later included in the Dutch martyrbooks, including van Braght's Martyrs' Mirror. It was, most likely, done by way of small printed pamphlets (Flugschriften) published soon after the tragic event and circulated among fellow believers. Today several libraries in America and Europe hold collections of such pamphlets (q.v.). These anonymous booklets, containing epistles together with introductions of admonition and exhortation, must once have been very popular. Large collections (Sammelbände) of later centuries impressively demonstrate this fact. The oldest printed copy of a letter by a Dutch martyr seems to be one written by Anneken Jans, who was executed in 1539 at Rotterdam, published in the very year of her execution with a song, also written by Anneken. Beginning about 1577 a large number of booklets containing letters by Dutch martyrs appeared. They were published (at first anonymously) by Gillis Rooman at Haarlem, Nicolaas Biestkens at Amsterdam, and others. The following volumes are known: letters of Jacob de Keersmaecker 1577, Hendrick Alewijnsz 1577, Thys Joriaensz 1577, Joost Verkindert 1577, Reytse Ayseszoon n.d., Jan Woutersz van Cuyck 1579, Christiaen Rijcen (Christiaen de Rijcke) 1582, and Joose de Tollenaer 1599. Of some of these volumes there may have been older editions; some of them have been reprinted. A considerable collection of letters was already published in the oldest martyrbook, the Dutch Offer des Heeren (q.v.) of 1562, of which a number of reprints have appeared of each successive enlarged edition. The most outstanding of these collections is Güldene Aepffel in Silbern Schalen (q.v.), most likely of Swiss origin, published 1702 and 1742 in Europe and 1745 in Pennsylvania. It contains altogether 24 epistles: (1) First the Sendbrief an die Gemeinde zu Horb (1527) by Michael Sattler (q.v.). In this case the source, a pamphlet with all the Sattler material, published right after his execution, is known and found in Mennonite libraries. (2) Eight epistles by Thomas Imbroich (q.v., executed 1558), including his famous Confessio, sent to his wife and the brethren. In this case also we know the pamphlet serving as a source (see MQR XVI, 1942, 99-107). (3) Two epistles by Soetge van der Houte (q.v., martyred 1560), one a Sendbrief an ihre Brüder und Schwestern und auch Kinder, and one a testament (legacy) to her children. (4) Eleven epistles by Michael Servaes (q.v., died 1563), called Sendbriefe welche er vor und in *seinem Gefängnis zu Köln an seine Verwandten nach dem Geist und Fleisch geschrieben.* (5) Two epistles from prison by Konrad Koch (*q.v.*), who died as a martyr in 1565. Of the Houte, Servaes, and Koch epistles we do not know the original sources; yet there is little doubt that printed booklets existed also in these cases. As to the contents of these epistles and their skillful form of expression the same can be said as of the Hutterite letters: they are certainly superior documents.

It is surprising that one more such pamphlet of the 18th century has preserved almost the same spirit and form. That is the *Sendbrief von einem Liebhaber Gottes Worts* (*q.v.*), written by an unknown brother in the darkness of prison in Bern, Switzerland, about 1715, and published most likely in Basel as an anonymous tract (copies in Mennonite historical libraries). This brother sends his admonitions to his "fellow members of the household of faith" as a call to steadfastness and loyalty and as a reminder to stay in the true fear of God, which befits earnest believers. It has 40 pages in print, and strikingly continues the old tradition of Anabaptist epistles.

Many more such epistles have been found in archives where trial records are stored away. The great *Täuferakten* publication in Germany (Bossert, Schornbaum) contains a number of such epistles though all too often in excerpts only. More such source publications are scheduled and will no doubt increase our knowledge of Anabaptist letter writing. But one particular letter still deserves our special attention because of its historical significance. That is Conrad Grebel's famous writing to Thomas Müntzer, from Zürich, Sept. 5, 1524 (see Bender, *Conrad Grebel*). Strictly speaking this is not yet an Anabaptist letter since Grebel was at that time not yet baptized on confession of faith. Still it might be called the very first Anabaptist statement in existence. It is not a martyr's epistle, but a friendly admonition together with a brief exposition of the new Anabaptist faith and attitude toward life. As such it does not quite fall into the scope of the present article, but represents rather an introduction to this entire field.

In July 1955, a remarkable find of Anabaptist epistles was made in the Bürgerbibliothek in Bern, Switzerland, where a bound manuscript volume of 42 letters and documents of 1527-61 was found. The letters are largely by Pilgram Marpeck and his associates, collected by Jörg Malèr in a volume together with a few other documents, to which he gave the title *Kunstbuch*.   R.F.

R. Friedmann, *Mennonite Piety Through the Centuries* (Goshen, 1949); H. S. Bender, "New Discoveries of Important Sixteenth Century Anabaptist Codices," *MQR* XXX (1956) 72-77; H. S. Bender, *Conrad Grebel* (Goshen, 1950).

Epp (Eppe, Ep, Epps), a Mennonite family name in the Old Flemish congregations of West Prussia, mainly rural, mentioned (Danzig Archives) in 1584. In 1586 an Epp, born at Losendorff, Dutch province of Groningen, lived at Langgarten near Danzig. Forty-six families were counted in 1776 (without Danzig), 131 persons in 1910, and 121 persons in

1935. Members of the family emigrated to Russia and America. They are numerous in Kansas, Nebraska, and Canada.

In the Dutch *Naamlijst* the name Epp is first found among the ministers in 1766, Peter Epp (*q.v.*, 1725-89) and Cornelis Epp being preachers of the Flemish congregation of Danzig. Peter served from 1758 as a preacher and became elder in 1779, serving until about 1790; Cornelius was a preacher until at least 1810. Hendrick Epp was a preacher of the Old Flemish congregation of the Grosse Werder in the Bärwalde district of West Prussia 1765-ca. 80. Leading later members of the family include David Epp (*q.v.*), elder of the Chortitza (Russia) Flemish congregation 1793-1802, one of the delegates to St. Petersburg 1798-1800, who obtained the *Gnadenprivilegium* from the Czar; Bernhard Epp (*q.v.*, 1854-1926), elder of the Lichtenau congregation; David Epp (*q.v.*) and his son David Epp, author of *Geistliche Lieder* (Marienburg, 1841); Claasz Epp, Jr. (*q.v.*, d. 1913), chiliastic leader of the ill-fated migration to Central Asia; Heinrich Epp (*q.v.*, 1827-96), a teacher and elder of the Chortitza Zentralschule; Heinrich H. Epp (*q.v.*, b. 1873), a son of the above, a teacher in the same school; David H. Epp (*q.v.*, 1861-1934), also a son of Heinrich Epp, a teacher at various schools and elder of the Chortitza Mennonite Church; Dietrich Heinrich Epp (*q.v.*, 1875-1955), editor of the *Bote* 1924-55; Abraham P. Epp (*q.v.*, 1871-1941), minister in the M.B. Church at Fairview, Okla.; Jacob B. Epp (1874-1945), a missionary to the Hopi Indians, and his son Theodore H. Epp (b. 1907), who conducts the outstanding radio program, "Back to the Bible Hour"; Peter G. Epp (*q.v.*, 1888-1955), professor at Bluffton College and the University of Ohio; Gerhard G. Epp (b. 1895), minister at Rosthern, Sask.; Johann P. Epp (1854-1917), long-time minister and for years elder of the church at Henderson, Neb.; John H. Epp (b. 1877), long-time pastor of the Hillsboro (Kan.) Mennonite church; Peter P. Epp (b. 1861), long-time minister of the M.B. Church at Henderson, Neb.; Kornelius P. Epp (*q.v.*, 1863-1944), leading minister of the E.M.B. Church at Henderson, Neb.   G.R.

Epp, Abraham P., minister of the Mennonite Brethren Church, was born at Evanecke, South Russia, Nov. 19, 1871, the seventh of the ten children of Peter and Katharina Klassen Epp. In 1876 the family emigrated to America, settling on a farm near Hillsboro, Kan., where Abraham grew up and joined the M.B. Church in 1891. In 1893 he took a homestead on the Cherokee Strip, southeast of what is today Fairview, Okla., and established his home, marrying Carolina Bekker on Dec. 27, 1894. They had a family of three children. He was very active in the South Fairview M.B. Church from its very beginning, serving as Sunday-school superintendent and deacon for many years. In 1925 the congregation elected him to the ministry, and for some time he was its pastor. In 1928 he retired and moved to Fairview.

Abraham Epp was an active worker in the Southern District Conference and served as its treasurer in 1924-39. He died at his home in Fairview on Oct. 8, 1941, and was buried in the South Fairview M.B. Cemetery.   J.H.L.

Epp, Bernhard (1854-1926), elder of the Lichtenau-Petershagen congregation, Molotschna, Russia, was born in 1854 at Rosenort, Molotschna. In 1875 he married Anna Wiens; their family consisted of 13 children. In 1889 Epp was elected minister and 1908 elder of his congregation. Although he had only an elementary education, he served with wisdom and devotion through all the troubled years of the War and the Revolution. During his years of service he preached 641 times at funerals and 271 times at weddings, not to speak of the many Sunday services he conducted. He instructed and baptized around 1,200 persons. He died at Lindenau, Molotschna, in 1926.   H.G.

Epp, Claasz, Jr., was born in Fürstenwerder (q.v.) in West Prussia. His father, Claasz Epp, was the mayor of this village and played a prominent role in the last (1853 f.) Mennonite emigration from Prussia to Russia; he was deputized to lead it, and authorized by the government of Russia to supervise it. He traveled over the country to select a site for settlement, and was one of the first who emigrated in 1853. In the founding and laying out of Hahnsau, the first and oldest Mennonite colony in the Volga region, he took a leading part, and settled here with four sons, of whom Claasz Epp, Jr., was (probably) the oldest.

Like his father, Claasz had a pronounced gift for leadership and was in many respects an attractive personality, although at times he showed ruthless severity. But at first he did not succeed in acquiring a leading position. In agriculture he was successful. When he emigrated to Central Asia he owned, in addition to his land in Hahnsau, three farms in the village of Orlov.

In the 1870's Claasz Epp began to stress in private circles the imminent end of the age, the return of Christ, and the particular calling of the Mennonites, to whom God had promised an open door (Rev. 3:8-10), in order to prepare a place of refuge (Rev. 12:14) for the other believers in the Christian church fleeing the Tribulation. When the Russian Mennonites faced the decision of their government (1870) to cancel the special privileges of the Mennonites, including military exemption, and most of them considered emigration to America in the West, Epp proclaimed that deliverance would be found in the East, an idea not original with him but coming from Jung-Stilling and others.

In his booklet published in 1877, *Die entsiegelte Weissagung des Propheten Daniel und die Deutung der Offenbarung Johannis,* which appeared in three editions and was distributed free at his own expense, in which he incorporated the ideas of Jung-Stilling, Ernst Mühes, and Peter Christoph Clöter, Epp ventured to set dates so definitely that he could not help becoming discredited. Here a new epoch opened for Claas Epp: lacking the humility necessary to admit his error, but rather trying to retain his adherents by a series of new interpretations, he became a false leader instead of merely a man in error. He claimed for instance that his own little flock of followers was the "Philadelphia" church of the Revelation, before which the open door was set. Finally in 1880, at the close of the period of transition to the new regime in Russia when compulsory alternative service was to be inaugurated he led a small group from the Trakt settlement on one of the most visionary and tragic adventures in all Mennonite history, an exodus to the wild, unknown, barren land of Turkestan in the heart of a Mohammedan population to meet the Lord and inaugurate the Millennium. Another group led by Elder Peters of the Molotschna undertook a similar move at the same time. The result was the establishment of the Mennonite settlement at Aulie Ata (q.v.) in Turkestan. In Aulie Ata the group divided, most remaining under the saner leadership of Elder Peters, while Epp took a smaller group in 1881 farther on, first to Bokhara, and finally to Ak-Mechet in the Khanate of Khiva, where they settled in 1882.

Epp's fanaticism grew constantly, guided by dreams and visions. He now claimed to be one of the two witnesses to the ushering in of the Lord's appearance on earth. A fellow minister, excommunicated by him, now became the Red Dragon of Revelation, whose expulsion was celebrated annually by the church. Soon Epp was to meet Elijah in the skies and with him ascend to heaven bodily. The time was actually set for the event, and the faithful gathered to bid Epp farewell as he stood behind an altar dressed in ascension robes. The day set for Christ's appearance was March 8, 1889, later changed to 1891. The climax came when Epp claimed to be the Son of Christ, the fourth person of the Trinity.

By this time most of Epp's followers, disillusioned, had left him, but a handful remained steadfast almost to the end. Finally the remnant excommunicated Epp. He died Feb. 3, 1913. (See **Asiatic Russia**.)
                                                       F.B.

Franz Bartsch, *Unser Auszug nach Mittelasien* (Halbstadt, 1907); Claasz Epp, *Die entsiegelte Weissagung des Propheten Daniel und die Deutung der Offenbarung Johannis* (n.p., 1877); idem, . . . *der Offenbarung Jesu Christi* (Alt-Tschau bei Neusalz a.O., 1877); C. Henry Smith, *The Story of the Mennonites* (3rd ed., Newton, 1950) 455-62; *DB* 1887, 15 f.; *ML* I, 596.

Epp, David, immigrated in August 1789 from Danzig to Russia (*Menn. Bl.,* 1856, 20), was chosen as elder in 1793, and ordained in the following year by C. Warkentin, who had come from Prussia for the purpose of ordaining him. He was sent with Gerhard Willms to St. Petersburg, June 29, 1798, and after waiting there over two years procured the charter of privileges from Emperor Paul I on Sept. 6, 1800. He died Sept. 29, 1802. (Friesen, *Brüderschaft,* 98, 700; *ML* I, 596.)   NEFF.

Epp, David (1779-1863), brother of Claas Epp, Sr. and minister of the Heubuden congregation 1817-62. He was very influential in the first decades of his ministry, successfully promoting mission interests. He emigrated from Prussia to Russia in 1862. G.R.

Franz Isaak, *Die Molotschnaer Mennoniten* (Halbstadt, 1908) 95 ff.

Epp, David, according to the *Katalog der Kirchenbibliothek der Mennonitengemeinde zu Danzig* (Danzig, 1869), was the son of the Heubuden (West Prussia) preacher D. Epp (? David Epp, *q.v.*, preacher 1817-62), and author of *Geistliche Lieder. Herausgegeben nach dem Tode des Verfassers* (Marienburg, 1841). Only copy known was in the Danzig library.   H.S.B.

Epp, David Heinrich, the son of Heinrich Epp (*q.v.*), teacher, minister, and writer, copublisher of the *Botschafter* (*q.v.*), b. May 30 (Old Calendar), 1861, in Chortitza, South Russia, taught at Osterwick and Rosental 1878-99. In 1886 he was chosen minister of the Chortitza Mennonite congregation, and in 1899 accepted a call to the Ekaterinoslav congregation. At the same time he taught in the elementary school at that place and also gave religious instruction in the local business college. In 1912 he moved to Berdyansk and devoted all his time to the *Botschafter* and to church work. For many years he served as chairman of the *Kommission für kirchliche Angelegenheiten* (KfK, *q.v.*), which was organized in 1910 to represent the Mennonites in dealing with the government. In this office he performed a very valuable service. He made repeated trips to the capital and secured more favorable conditions which made it possible for the *Allgemeine Mennonitische Bundeskonferenz* to continue to meet.

In 1914 at the outbreak of World War I the *Botschafter*, like all other German periodicals, was compelled to cease publication. He was thus deprived of his livelihood, and he became impoverished. In 1923 the Lichtenau Mennonite congregation (Taurida) invited him to serve as chief minister to re-establish the torn congregation. With clear vision, great skill, and much charity, he succeeded in this undertaking. In 1927 he was called to his home congregation of Chortitza and served it as elder until 1931 with marked blessing, in spite of the most unfavorable conditions imaginable, for the Communists hindered his every step. As one without any legal rights, as were all the preachers, he was so heavily taxed that neither he nor the congregation was able to raise the funds. He therefore resigned in 1931. He nevertheless continued his pastoral care privately, and was able to strengthen and revive many an oppressed heart in that difficult time. He died in 1934. D. H. Epp was the last ordained elder of the Chortitza Mennonite Church.

Through his pastoral care of the mentally disturbed in the insane asylum at Ekaterinoslav, he became aware of the need for a Mennonite mental hospital to give better spiritual and physical care to patients in the brotherhood. By means of energetic appeals and propaganda in the *Botschafter*, lectures and pamphlets, he succeeded in interesting the congregations in the idea, and thus Bethania (*q.v.*) came into being, which was supported by all the Mennonites of Russia. He also saw the need of a better education for girls and became a cofounder of the Chortitza Mädchenschule (Girls' School).

As an author David Epp also accomplished much. He wrote of himself, "My inmost feeling urged me to serve wider circles with a pen in my hand." By private study he acquired a good knowledge of Mennonite history, and as the first fruits of this study he published in 1889 (for the centennial celebration of the founding of the Chortitza colony) *Die Chortitzer Mennoniten*. In 1896 he wrote *Kurze Erklärungen und Erläuterungen zum Katechismus. . . .* This book was intended for the "young men and women who are preparing for baptism, that it may be a good friend to them, in which they may be able to find inspiration and instruction, to bring to the sacred act a consecrated heart." The book was well received, and was published in a second edition in 1898. The third edition (1941) appeared after his death at Rosthern, Sask. In 1909 appeared his valuable biography, *J. Cornies, Züge aus seinem Leben und Wirken*, the second edition of which was published in 1949 at Rosthern. In 1910 appeared his centennial booklet, *Die Memriker Ansiedlung*.

Before the founding of the *Botschafter*, David Epp was an active contributor to the *Mennonitische Blätter*, and also to the *Odessaer Zeitung*. Many of his articles appeared in the *Mennonitisches Jahrbuch* (H. Dirks) and in *Unser Blatt*. In the last years of his life he sent many contributions to the *Bote* (*q.v.*) of Rosthern. (*ML* I, 597.)†   D.E.

Epp, Dietrich H. (1875-1955), an outstanding educator, publisher-editor, and civic leader of the Mennonite Church in Russia and Canada, was born March 29, 1875, Chortitza, Russia, the son of Heinrich Epp (*q.v.*), educator and minister of Chortitza. On June 27, 1898, he married Marie Thiessen, who died in May 1906. On July 27, 1909, he married her sister, Malvine, who died March 4, 1942. They adopted John Heese as their child.

Epp attended the elementary school, the Zentralschule and the Normal School of Chortitza (1881-92), and the Teachers' Institute of St. Petersburg (1892-95). From 1895 to 1923 he taught at the Chortitza Zentralschule and Normal School, serving also as director during the last four years. He organized the Chortitza Public Library and functioned as its director in 1902-14. He was the secretary of the Chortitza Life Insurance Company (*Sterbekasse*) 1901-10, and of the Chortitza Mädchenschule 1906-23.

In 1923 Epp went from Russia to Rosthern, Sask., where he established a print shop the same year. He founded *Der Bote* (*q.v.*), and served as its editor continuously from its beginning in 1923 until his death in 1955. He also published and edited the *Saskatchewan Valley News* and numerous books in the interest of the Canadian Mennonite constituency. He served as chairman of the Central Mennonite Immigration Committee (*q.v.*) 1923-34, on the Board of Directors of Rosthern Junior College, and as member of the Canadian Mennonite Board of Colonization. In 1944, when the *Echo-Verlag* (*q.v.*) was founded by former students of the Chortitza Zentralschule, he was elected chairman of this organization. D. H. Epp made a significant contribution to the cultural life of the Mennonites of Russia

and Canada. He died on March 31, 1955, at Rosthern. (*Der Bote,* March 30, 1955, pp. 3-7; April 13,
1955, pp. 1-2.)†   C.K.

Epp, Heinrich, b. Dec. 18, 1827, at Chortitza,
province of Ekaterinoslav, d. April 11, 1896. In
1854 he taught a school with seven children in
Neu-Petersdorf. Two years later he taught in the
Mennonite private school in Ekaterinoslav. In 1858
he was called to the Zentralschule to succeed Heinrich Franz, and served there 19 years. During this
period, which D. A. Neufeld (*q.v.*) calls a "new
bright period," the school made an appreciable
growth. The church likewise had complete confidence in him.

When the Mennonites were alarmed by the introduction of general military duty and sent a
delegation to St. Petersburg to be released, Heinrich
Epp was one of the delegates, and was the spokesman in St. Petersburg. Repeatedly he visited St.
Petersburg to represent the Mennonites in this matter.

The confidence of the church was also shown
in the fact that in 1864 they called him to preach
to the Chortitza congregation. For 13 years he
energetically and successfully filled his double vocation. For seven and one-half years he was chairman of the board of the Zentralschule. But because
his office of preaching for the Chortitza church demanded more and more of his energy, he resigned
his teaching position and devoted all his time to
his church. In 1885, when Elder Gerhard Dyck
resigned his office on account of his advanced age,
Epp was elected by a large majority. He accepted
the office reluctantly. "Will I be able to lead the
church aright? Will it be built up by me?" he
asked. But then he faced the congregation with the
text, "Here am I. Thou hast called me!" (I Sam.
3:8). His service, lasting until his death, was attended with great blessing.   A.B.

Friesen, *Brüderschaft*, 730; H. Epp, *Heinrich Epp,
Kirchenältester der Menn.-Gem. zu Chortitza* (Leipzig,
1897); *ML* I, 597.

Epp, Heinrich D., the tenth child of Dietrich and
Katharina Siemens Epp, was born Jan. 26, 1861, in
Novopodolsk, South Russia, where his father was
for about 48 years the superintendent of the "Jewish colonies" (see **Judenplan**). The family belonged
to the Mennonite Church of Chortitza. Heinrich D.
Epp attended the elementary school of his native
village and then the school at Burwalde, where his
teacher was Peter Penner. Then he attended the
Zentralschule in Chortitza, and upon completing
his study in 1878 he was appointed to teach in
Peter Penner's school in Burwalde. In 1880 he
moved to Michaelsburg in Fürstenlande, Taurida,
and taught the village school there for 15 years. In
1883 he married Sarah Redekop. This marriage was
blessed with five sons. On Oct. 30, 1886, he was
ordained to the ministry by his uncle, Heinrich
Epp, the elder of the Chortitza congregation.

In 1895 Heinrich D. Epp was made principal of
the school in Burwalde (Chortitza volost), and also
served as preacher. In 1906 he was called to teach

religion and German in the Nikolaipol Zentralschule.
He retired in 1921, having been a teacher for 43
years.

On Dec. 5, 1920, he was ordained as an elder of
the Nikolaipol Mennonite Church (*q.v.*) by Isaak
Dyck, the elder of the Chortitza church, and served
in this capacity until 1935, when the church was
confiscated by the Russian communistic authorities;
Heinrich D. Epp then moved to Adelsheim (Nikolaipol volost), where he died on June 18, 1941, at the
age of 80 years.   H.H.E.

Epp, Heinrich H., the son of Elder Heinrich Epp
(*q.v.*), was born in 1873 in Chortitza, a village in
South Russia. Upon completion of the Zentralschule
he attended the Gymnasium in Ekaterinoslav for
two years, and completed the work for his A.B. degree in history and philology at the University of
Moscow in 1900. He then became a teacher in the
Chortitza Zentralschule (*q.v.*) and devoted his entire life and work to it. In 1905, when A. A. Neufeld withdrew, he became the principal of the school
and gave instruction in the field of education in the
teacher-training program operated in connection
with the Zentralschule. These courses were taught
much better here than in the corresponding Russian
schools, for Epp kept himself informed on the new
pedagogical currents. He equipped the Zentralschule
library, which had been begun by Neufeld, with all
the newer books. He stimulated in his students a
desire for further education, thus producing a stream
of ambitious young teachers for the Mennonite elementary schools. He used to say that good elementary schools were of greater value than good secondary schools or universities. He therefore declined
the proposal made to him by some prominent persons to establish an intermediate school. His ideal
was a three-year normal school in addition to the
Zentralschule to offer all the courses of value to
elementary teachers. Thanks to his efforts, such a
school was opened in 1913. But the curriculum he
had planned was reduced by the government, since
it surpassed that of the government-operated schools.
After the Revolution, persistent unrest made it impossible to introduce these courses.

As chairman of the Chortitza Teacher's Association Epp conducted the monthly and annual meetings; his influence was the more deeply felt since
most of the teachers had once been his students. He
was appointed inspector of the final examinations of
the elementary schools, thus acquiring direct influence on their instruction. And since he was also
chairman of the committee in charge of the final
examination of the Zentralschule, he was able to
unify the system from the elementary schools
through the Zentralschule and the educational
courses.

In 1920, when the new government tried to remodel the Russian educational system on the Western plan, the Russian teachers were frustrated. But
Epp, aware of Western currents, was able to lecture
at home and in other German colonies and to reconstruct his curriculum along the new lines. The com-
missariat for elementary education recognized Epp's
contribution and gave him the title of "professor,"

which was ordinarily reserved for teachers at the universities, with a suitable salary.

Epp participated in all movements for the common welfare. Like his father, he was authorized by the Chortitza Mennonites to represent their causes to the governments. In 1919 he resigned from the leadership of the school and representation to the government in favor of his younger brother and colleague, Dietrich H. Epp (q.v.). But he remained as a teacher and the soul of the institution. When the Soviet government approached him with the question: Do you believe in God? and he replied affirmatively, he had to withdraw from the school in 1929. After 29 years of devoted and fruitful service, he left this Mennonite school, which was then fitted into the communistic pattern.

In 1925 Epp's students and colleagues celebrated the 25th anniversary of his successful work. His wish and hope to spend the closing years of his life in peace was not to be fulfilled. In the mass evacuation of intellectuals from the Ukraine in 1937, Heinrich Epp was also arrested and without benefit of trial sent away. Since these exiles were not permitted contact with their families, nothing more has been heard of him.   D.E.

Epp, Johann P., oldest son of Peter and Barbara Isaak Epp, was born July 20, 1854, at Pastva in the Molotschna settlement of South Russia. With his parents and their four other children, he emigrated to America in 1875, settling near Henderson, Neb. Here he lived the remainder of his life on a farm, excepting the last four years, when he resided in Henderson.

He was married to Kornelia Franz, Feb. 1, 1877. To this union were born two daughters and five sons, one daughter dying in infancy. All his children were active in church work and all prosperous farmers. His son John has served for many years as minister and elder.

Johann P. Epp was a charter member of the Ebenezer (q.v.) Mennonite Church (EMB) at Henderson. He served about 34 years as minister, including 4 years as elder of the church. For about 15 years he served as secretary of the Evangelical Mennonite Brethren Mission Board, and 2 years as conference chairman. He died Jan. 25, 1917, at his home in Henderson, and was buried in the Ebenezer Mennonite cemetery near this town.   H.F.E.

Epp, Kornelius P., b. Oct. 28, 1863, at Pastva in the Molotschna settlement, South Russia, the seventh child of Peter and Barbara Isaak Epp. With his parents and the rest of the family he came to America in 1875, settling near Henderson, Neb., in which community he lived the rest of his life. His education he received at Pastva and a private Bible school in America. He taught in an elementary Bible school near Henderson.

He married Aganetha Schierling Nov. 26, 1886. To this union were born two daughters and three sons. He farmed for many years. He was a charter member of the Ebenezer (q.v.) Mennonite Church (EMB), and served for many years as Sunday-school superintendent and as chorister. In 1895 he was

chosen as deacon, and in 1917-31 he was the leading minister of the church. He had a great interest in missions and served for about 14 years on the Board of Home and Foreign Missions of the E.M.B. Conference, the greater part of the time as treasurer and the remainder as secretary. He died April 30, 1944, and is buried in the Ebenezer Mennonite cemetery.   H.F.E.

Epp, Peter, Elder of the Flemish Mennonite congregation in Danzig 1779-89. He was born Jan. 23, 1725, lived as a farmer in Neunhuben near Danzig, was chosen as deacon April 3, 1757, as minister Feb. 5, 1758, and as elder Sept. 26, 1779. He went through the difficult period of the transfer of West Prussia from Polish to Prussian sovereignty, when the Danzig congregation was for a while divided between the two realms. In this period the emigration to Russia also began, in which Epp took an active part. He died in the midst of preparations for a trip to South Russia, Nov. 12, 1789. H.G.M.

H. G. Mannhardt, *Die Danziger Mennonitengemeinde, ihre Entstehung und ihre Geschichte von 1569 bis 1919* (Danzig, 1919) 122, and 127 ff.; *ML* I, 597.

Epp, Peter (1862-1922), Elder of the Pordenau Mennonite Church, Molotschna, Russia, was born in 1862 at Prangenau, Molotschna, and married Sara Klassen in 1885. His family consisted of seven children. One son, Jacob Epp, at present is minister and leader of the Mennonite Brethren congregation at Steinbach, Man. Epp received his elementary education at his native village, then attended the Zentralschule at Gnadenfeld. In 1893 he became minister and in 1910 was ordained elder of the Pordenau church. From the very beginning he did pioneer work in his congregation, which when he took charge of it was backward in many ways. In its life and worship many forms and customs dominated which had outlived their usefulness and kept religious life at a standstill. Epp changed all this gradually and brought a new spirit into the congregation. He also reorganized the singing in his church and for the first time introduced choir singing. Epp died in 1922 during the great typhoid epidemic after exposure to the disease when visiting the many sick and dying of his congregation.   H.G.

Epp, Peter G. (1888-1954), Mennonite author and teacher, was born Aug. 13, 1888, at Petershagen in the Molotschna settlement in South Russia, the fifth of the seven children of Gerhard and Elisabeth (Fast) Epp. He was married twice. His first wife was Helene Matthies, whom he married in 1912; they had two sons. On June 6, 1926, he married Justina Dyck; they had one son. Epp was educated at the Teachers' Institute at Halbstadt, Russia, the Predigerschule (1906-8) at Basel, Switzerland, the University of Heidelberg (1908 ff.), Germany, and received his Ph.D. at the University of Basel (1912). After this he taught at the Barvenkovo School of Commerce, Russia (1912-18), and the Teachers' Institute at Halbstadt, Russia (1918-24).

In 1924 Epp immigrated to the United States; he lived at Bluffton, Ohio, serving on the faculty of

Bluffton College until 1934. In that year he joined the faculty of the Ohio State University at Columbus, Ohio, teaching German and Russian. In 1946 he became ill with tuberculosis, after which he never completely regained his health, though he still taught some courses. He died on Jan. 9, 1954, and is buried in Union Cemetery, Columbus.

Peter Epp was an outstanding Mennonite author. His published works were *Die Erlösung, Eine Mutter* (*q.v.*), *Johanna,* and *Das Geisslein.* His largest work, "An der Molotschna," a manuscript, on which he made some entries four days before his death, is being prepared for publication by his wife. Other manuscripts, "Eros Multiformis" and "De Homine," have been accepted by the University of Basel for safekeeping until the year 2000.   J.D.E.

Who's Who Among the Mennonites (North Newton, 1943).

Epp Mennonite Church, Rosthern, Sask., appears in H. P. Krehbiel's *Mennonite Churches of North America* (Newton, 1911) as an unaffiliated congregation of 60 members, with Cornelius Epp as pastor.

Eppenhof, a former Mennonite family, now extinct. Members of this family came from Burgsteinfurt (*q.v.*) in Westphalia, Germany, to Enschede, Dutch province of Overijssel, and especially to Winterswijk, Dutch province of Gelderland, where this family was found in the 17th century. Harmen Eppenhof, b. about 1620, d. 1693, and married to Henrica Willink (1614-81), was the last unsalaried and untrained minister of the Winterswijk congregation. In the 17th and 18th centuries members of this family are also found in Amsterdam, where some of them were deacons of the Lamist congregation. Laurens Hendriksz Eppenhof, formerly also a deacon and a Collegiant (*q.v.*), wrote two booklets against Galenus Abrahamsz: *Nieuwe Jaars-geschenck, of Twalef Bedencklijcke Vragen* (Amsterdam, 1682) and *Sesen-dertigh Grontstellingen aangaande de Reformatie der Protestanten* (n.p., 1697).   vdZ.

P. Beets, *Stam-boek der Willingen* (Deventer, 1767); H. W. Meihuizen, *Galenus Abrahamsz* (Haarlem, 1954).

Eppstein, a village near Frankenthal in the Palatinate, Germany, in which Anabaptism found entry in its earliest period. Anabaptists living here perhaps belonged to the congregation at Lambsheim (*q.v.*), who signed the Concept of Cologne in May 1591 (Hege, 152). Their leader, Heinrich Gramm, belonged to a Mennonite family that lived in Eppstein through the upheavals of the Thirty Years' War, until the end of the 19th century. It is assumed that Anabaptists from Eppstein also took part in the Frankenthal (*q.v.*) disputation in 1571. And when the Palatine church council at Heidelberg reported July 4, 1603, that the number of Mennonites in the vicinity of Ruchheim had increased to 300, those of Eppstein may have been included.

But it is not until after the Thirty Years' War that there is definite information concerning the presence of Mennonites in Eppstein. The barons of Hundheim, to whom the village belonged, apparently received Mennonite refugees from Switzerland and protected them. In the register of Mennonites in the Palatinate (*Karlsruher Generallandesarchiv-Akten*) the place is mentioned first in 1685; a Peter Kintzi was living there. At the close of 1699 two families had settled there, and had to pay a protection fee. In the following years they were probably excused from the payment of this fee through the intervention of the von Hundheims, for they are not mentioned in the lists until 1752, when 14 families were recorded as having been accepted by the barons von Hundheim. Their names are as follows: Heinrich Pletscher with a family of 6; Christian Kaegy, 7; Heinrich Rohr(er), 6; Christian Jotter, 6; Johannes Hertzler, 4; Jakob Blickensdörfer, 5; Christian Stauffer, 5; Christian Neukumet, 7; Christian Hirschberger (Hirschler?), 7; Jost Krehbiel, 7; Christian Göbels, 6; Jakob Rohrer's widow, 6; Neukumet's widow, 3; and Christian Kaegy, 3. In the register of 1759 the following are listed: Christian Göbels, Christian Stauffer, Christian Kaegy, Jakob Heer, Jakob and Heinrich Rohr's widow, Samuel Kaegy, Christian Jotter, Jakob Hirschberger, Jakob Jotter, Johannes Hertzler, Johannes Blum, Jost Krehbiel. In 1773, 12 families with 33 sons are briefly mentioned. In near-by Lambsheim the 1717 list mentions Bernhard Schowalter, Friedrich Steiner, Emanuel Balzel; in 1738, Christian Hirschberger, a weaver, and Jakob Eschelmann, widower and day laborer with many children. In Flomersheim, only a few minutes from Eppstein, the 1738 list mentions Johannes Steiner and Jakob Baer, and in 1752 Heinrich Becker. In Oggersheim there are in 1717 Hans Weber; in 1742, Jost Jotter, Michael Bechtel, and Valentin Schmutz, all of whom no doubt belonged to the Eppstein congregation.

Nearly all of these families came from the Emmental (*q.v.*), Switzerland, as their names show. They formed a single congregation with the Mennonites in Friesenheim (*q.v.*) and Ruchheim (*q.v.*). The preachers in 1732 were Christian Neukomm, Melchior Everlein, Hans Jakob Hiestand, deacon of Friesenheim, and Ludwig Gross of Ruchheim. Elders of the Friesenheim-Eppstein congregation were Ulrich Hirschler 1738-68, and Johannes Möllinger 1768-80. In 1779, when Eppstein built a church, it chose as its elder Johannes Stauffer, after which Möllinger was elder only of Friesenheim. The center of church activity was Eppstein; but services were held in all three villages. In 1734 the congregation began an alms book, which was continued until the middle of the 19th century. When this record was begun, Jakob Rohrer took over the alms fund in place of Benedikt Balzel (*Menn. Bl.,* 1879, 51).

In 1777 the Eppstein congregation purchased a plot of land for a cemetery from Johannes Blüm and Ludwig Strub. Services were at first held in various private homes, then regularly in the home of Elder Christian Stauffer. According to a notation in the alms book he was paid eight guilders in 1779 for the use of a room for two years for their meetings. In that year they built a small church with room for 120 persons, probably on the cemetery plot; it was dedicated on Sept. 5, 1779 (*Inv. Arch. Amst.* I, 1545). On each side of the entry a vestibule was built, one to be used for meetings of the preachers, the other for funeral purposes. Both were later sacrificed for space in the auditorium. Instead of a pulpit there was a plain table; there were no seats for the preachers. In 1828 and again in 1914 the church was enlarged.

The Ibersheim resolutions of 1803 were signed by Heinrich Rohrer as preacher of the Eppstein church. He was followed by Heinrich Jotter, who died in 1824. Heinrich Ellenberger, a tailor from Gönnheim, took his place, and was the first preacher in Eppstein to receive remuneration. He also served the Friesenheim congregation until he emigrated to America in 1850. During the next four years Jakob Ellenberger (q.v.) looked after the church. In 1854 the congregations of Eppstein and Friesenheim chose the one-armed Christian Krehbiel of Wartenburg as their preacher. He had completed his theological studies at Erlangen, and was ordained in 1855. But he soon emigrated to America, too, where he died in 1878. Then Eppstein and Friesenheim were served by Heinrich Neufeld, the preacher of the Ibersheim church; since that time the three congregations have joined in supporting a preacher. When Neufeld took over the office of preaching in Friedrichstadt a.d.E., Jakob Ellenberger, nephew of the above Ellenberger, took his place for a short time. Hinrich van der Smissen preached for them in 1872-82, Thomas Löwenberg 1883-1917, E. Händiges 1917-23, Erich Göttner 1923-27, Abraham Braun 1928- , Daniel Habegger, assistant pastor, 1953-   .

According to Frey's statistics there were in 1802, 68 Mennonites in Eppstein, 7 in Flomersheim; in 1834, 117 in Eppstein, 11 in Flomersheim, 4 in Heuchelheim, 2 in Lambsheim, and 2 in Hessheim. In 1953 the church numbered ca. 120 souls. The church is a member of the *Vereinigung*, the Palatine-Hessian Conference, and the Conference of the South German Mennonites. The Palatine-Hessian Conference has met repeatedly at Eppstein.

The Eppstein congregation was repeatedly assisted by the Dutch Mennonites (Committee for Foreign Needs). In 1714 some Swiss refugee settlers received aid. In 1781 they asked and obtained assistance because they had to pay a double poll tax to the "lord of Eppstein," and had built a new church. In 1828-43 they again received gifts from the Amsterdam congregation.   NEFF.

Chr. Hege, *Die Täufer in der Kurpfalz* (Frankfurt, 1908); *Inv. Arch. Amst.* I, Nos. 1441, 1445, 1545 f., 1549; II, 2742-45; *ML* I, 597-99.

Erasmus, Desiderius, b. 1466 at Rotterdam, Holland, d. 1536 at Freiburg, Germany, known as Erasmus of Rotterdam, the greatest humanist of the 16th century, was the son of a priest, Rogerius Gerardus. Erasmus attended the public school at Gouda, and continued his education at Deventer. In 1487 he became an Augustinian canon in the monastery of St. Gregory's at Steyn. He was ordained to the priesthood in 1495. He was released from the intolerable restrictions of monastic life by Henri Bergen, bishop of Cambrai, who made him his secretary, and aided him in his further studies and travels. In the succeeding years he found a number of generous patrons.

In 1500 appeared the first edition of his *Adagia*, a collection of short sayings with witty interpretations. He lived in a number of different countries, but was apparently happiest in England. Here, in the home of Sir Thomas More, he wrote his *Encomium Moriae* (In Praise of Folly) (1526), which was translated into many languages. He was involved in disputes with many scholars in Europe on various aspects of intellectual and academic liberty as opposed to the stereotyped practice of the day. He remained Catholic, though his sympathies were at least equally on the Protestant side. He wrote a vast amount; the most significant of his works were his theological studies and commentaries.

The services rendered by Erasmus for the Reformation are very great. (1) In his work to improve the scholarly editions of the Greek and Latin New Testament he laid the foundation for the Bible translations of the Reformation. (2) His merciless mockery of stupidity undermined for a large part of the laity the authority of the clergy. It was due to his idea that I John 5:7 (the text on the Trinity) was spurious, that this verse was omitted from the older Anabaptist translations and was enclosed in parentheses in the later Biestkens Bible (q.v.).

Furthermore, F. Pijper has demonstrated that the great difference between the Lutheran Reformation and the early Dutch Reformation was due to the influence of the writings of Erasmus on the Dutch clergy. This fact is sufficient to understand that the Dutch Anabaptists were deeply influenced by Erasmus, an influence that is evident in two respects: (1) The large number of citations from Erasmus found in the works of Menno Simons, shows his thorough acquaintance with the works of Erasmus. This is also true of the writings of Adam Pastor and Dirk Philips, who may have been somewhat influenced by him. (2) The Dutch Anabaptists of the 16th century were in the great majority of cases believers in the freedom of the will as defended by Erasmus against Luther.

It is not very likely that the Dutch Anabaptists derived their principle of nonresistance from the treatise on war by Erasmus, entitled *Dulce Bellum inexpertis*, of 1525, for Erasmus' ideas are more humanistic and negative, those of the Anabaptists more Biblical and positive. Besides, the Dutch translation of the treatise from the original Latin did not appear before 1560.   K.V., vDZ.

German Anabaptism also shows no small degree of influence by Erasmus, especially among the leaders on the Lower Rhine. Campanus (q.v.) and Thomas von Imbroich (q.v.) often quote him in their writings and speak of him in terms of great appreciation. On baptism and communion, the Trinity, and freedom of the will Erasmus offered so much that was in accord with Anabaptist teaching, that he was suspected not only of promoting their cause, but even of being one of them (Rembert, 26). In designating the Bible as the sole source of Christian truth, in promoting the use of the Bible in the vernacular, in stressing that "Christianity is essentially a life of discipleship of Christ," he expressed common Anabaptist demands. His *Enchiridion militis christiani* (1502), "a fine devotional book of the educated world," in which he promoted a Christianity interpreted by the Sermon on the Mount, was read in Anabaptist circles, especially after it was available in a Dutch translation (about 1550). The extent of Erasmus' influence on Hans Denk is still to be investigated. Some personal contact while they were both living in Basel can be assumed. But their agreement on points of doctrine is probably caused by the common source of their concepts, viz., German Mysticism. Erasmus' *Dulce bellum inexpertis* (War Is Sweet to Those Who Have Not Experienced It) of 1525 and other pamphlets in which he showed the evils and the misery of war and satirized those who glorified warfare may also have influenced the Anabaptists and Mennonites to strengthen their peace principles. H. S. Bender has discussed Erasmus as a possible source for the pacifism of the early Swiss Brethren, particularly Conrad Grebel in Zürich, in his Grebel biography (201 ff.) but concludes that the Erasmian pacifism was humanitarian whereas that of Grebel and his associates was Biblical. He says, "Between the opportunism of an Erasmus who would be willing to let a ruler decide whether a war was just or not, and the absolutism of a Grebel who would dare to say that 'among believing Christians killing is done away with altogether' there is a world of difference. It is unthinkable that Grebel derived his deep conviction on this point from his humanist background."

Erasmus' judgment of Anabaptism is worthy of note. Though he sharply rejects and condemns their consistency, he also notes their pious conduct which sets them apart. They are to be commended above others for the blamelessness of their lives (Rembert, 566). In 1534 he also wrote to Guido Morillon, "The Anabaptists have flooded the Low Countries just as the frogs and locusts flooded Egypt, a mad generation, doomed to die. They slipped in under the appearance of piety, but their end will be public robbery. And what is like a miracle, although they teach absurdities, not to say impossibilities, and although they spread unlovely things, the populace is attracted as if by a fateful mood or rather the impulse of an evil spirit in this sect" (Erasmus, *Op.* III, 1186). In their spirit of sacrifice unto death and their faithfulness to conviction the Anabaptists far surpassed the learned but vacillating scholar. Walther Köhler said significantly: "The Anabaptists were closer to Erasmus than to Luther, but they popularized and hence spiritualized him" (*Flugschriften* II, No. 3).

The degree of influence of humanism upon the early Anabaptists or even the very rise of Anabaptism and its theology is still debated. Recently Köhler and others have pressed strongly their belief that Anabaptism owes much to humanism, and particularly to Erasmus. At the same time Köhler stresses, and rightly so, their essential Biblicism, and it is evident that many Anabaptists came directly out of Lutheran and Zwinglian circles. In Zürich the first Anabaptists were all Zwinglians, not Erasmians. The difficulty in answering the question is due in part to the variation among those outwardly belonging to the movement in the earlier days. If one makes the very necessary discrimination between spiritualists and Anabaptists and assigns such as Denk and Campanus to the fringes rather than to the heart of Anabaptism, the answer becomes easier; the Anabaptists were far more Biblical-evangelical than humanistic. Nevertheless the question is not yet fully cleared up; the final answer is still to be given and awaits a more thorough study of Anabaptist theology.   NEFF, H.S.B.

J. Huizinga, *Erasmus* (New York, 1924); Preserved Smith, *Erasmus: A Study of His Life, Ideals, and Place in History* (N.Y. and London, 1923); P. S. Allen, *The Age of Erasmus* (Oxford, 1914); J. Lindeboom, *Erasmus, onderzoek naar zijn theologie en zijn godsdienstig gemoedsbestaan* (Leiden, 1909); *DB* 1912, 2; 1916, 141; Kühler, *Geschiedenis* I, 14, 40-42; H. W. Meihuizen, *Galenus Abrahamsz* (Haarlem, 1954) *passim;* R. Kreider, "Anabaptism and Humanism," *MQR* XXVI (April 1952); W. Köhler, *Desiderius Erasmus* (Berlin, 1917); *ML* I, 599-601; H. S. Bender, *Conrad Grebel* (Goshen, 1950).

Erb, a Mennonite family name first represented in America by Nicholas Erb (1679-1740), who came to Lancaster Co., Pa., from the Emmental, Switzerland, via the Palatinate, Germany, before 1722, and settled on the Cocalico Creek in Warwick Township. He was a Mennonite pioneer farmer and is buried on the present Garman farm, his home. His family included John, Nicholas, Christian, Jacob, and Magdalena (Johns). Of Christian's line, Abraham founded Waterloo, Ont., John built the mills at the center of Preston, Ont., and Christian Erb and his sister Susanna, wife of Jacob Brubacher, with Jacob, Daniel, and Peter, gave the impetus to establish the Mennonite church in Kitchener. John Erb in Cumberland Co., Pa., donated land for Erb's church three miles east of Carlisle (*q.v.*). This John was the father of John (1840-1913), a preacher of Strickler's church, Dauphin Co., Pa. Jacob Erb (1804-83), the tenth bishop of the United Brethren Church, was reared in a Mennonite home. Tillman M. Erb (1865-1929), bishop of the Pennsylvania church, Hesston, Kan., and his sons Bishop Allen Erb of Lebanon, Ore., and Paul Erb, editor of the *Gospel Herald,* and Paul's son, Delbert Erb, Mennonite missionary to Argentina, are part of the numerous Nicholas progeny. Bishop J. Frederick Erb of the Detroit, Mich., Mennonite Church comes from this line. There is also an Amish Erb line chiefly located in Waterloo Co., Ont.   I.D.L.

Erb, Tillman M., only son of Jacob B. and Leah Miller Erb, was born Nov. 3, 1865, near Mt. Joy, Lancaster Co., Pa. He was descended from a Swiss-German family who had immigrated in the early 18th century. On Nov. 18, 1886, he was married to Lizzie Ann Hess at Ephrata, Pa. Four sons and seven daughters were born to them, two dying in childhood. Allen, the oldest son, became a minister and bishop in the Mennonite Church (MC) and is active in the hospital work of the church. Paul, the second son, also a minister, has taught at Hesston and Goshen colleges and became editor of the *Gospel Herald* in 1944. Erb's formal education was interrupted after one year of high school. He and his wife joined the Pennsylvania Mennonite Church (MC) near Newton, Kan., on July 31, 1887. He was ordained minister in 1893 and bishop in 1898. He was at various times moderator of the district conference. He was for many years a member of the

Mennonite Board of Education and business manager of Hesston College and Bible School 1908-29. He helped to establish missions in Kansas City and Wichita. His residences were Mt. Joy, 1865-85; Newton, 1885-89, 1894-95, 1900-10; Hesston, 1889-94, 1910-24; Harper, Kan., 1895-1900. He was a businessman (creamery) and farmer (dairy) in addition to engaging in church and school work. As a community builder he served on the city councils in Harper and Hesston. His chief contribution was as an organizer of churches and institutions, particularly as the chief promoter of a church school in the West. He was severely burned in 1912, which was the indirect cause of his death on Jan. 25, 1929. He is buried in the Pennsylvania Cemetery, Harvey Co., Kan.† P.E.

Erb Mennonite Church (MC), now extinct, was located in Cumberland Co., Pa. John Erb, David Martin, Benjamin Ebersole, and others had moved into the Cumberland Valley, 10 miles west of Slate Hill and 3 miles east of Carlisle. In 1834 John Erb was ordained to the ministry, and the following year he donated ground for the erection of a meetinghouse. This was transferred in 1843 to Abraham Hertzler and Jacob Nissley as trustees, and therefore it is also called "Hertzler." This building and Herr's, six miles south, provided worship facilities for years in these communities. The cemetery remains, but the building has been razed. The bishop oversight was supplied from Lancaster Mennonite Conference, of which this congregation was always a member. I.D.L.

Erb Mennonite Church (MC) in the Lancaster Mennonite Conference, midway between Manheim and Lititz, Lancaster Co., Pa. Previous to its organization about 1794, it was a part of the Rapho Township congregation. The first meetinghouse was built in 1794. At that time the minister and probably bishop of the congregation was Peter Lehman of Rapho Township. The 1955 membership was 243. The bishops were Henry E. Lutz and Homer D. Bomberger; ministers, Joseph A. Boll and Joseph W. Boll; deacon, Harold G. Holdeman. N.W.N.

Erb Street Mennonite Church (MC), located in Waterloo, Ont., a member of the Ontario Conference, was organized by settlers who came from Pennsylvania in 1810-25—David Eby, Jonas Bingeman, and Samuel Schantz. The meetinghouse was built about two miles west of Waterloo and was known as the David Eby Church. In 1902 a new church was built in town, which was rebuilt and enlarged in 1950. Among the earlier leaders were the ministers Elias Schneider, Jonas Snider, and Noah Hunsberger, and the deacons Abram Hunsberger and Noah Weber. In more recent years the leaders have been Newton Weber, Jesse B. Martin, and Clare Shantz. It was within the Waterloo congregation that the first evangelistic meetings were held in private homes, about 1885. In 1886 a Sunday school was held in a schoolhouse, and later in the David Eby Church. Also in 1890 "Edification meetings" began in private homes. Foreign missionaries

from the congregation were L. S. Weber and his wife, and Edna Good, in South America. The present minister and bishop of the congregation is Jesse B. Martin, and the membership is 281. J.B.M.

L. J. Burkholder, *A Brief History of the Mennonites in Ontario* (Toronto, 1935).

Erbe, Fritz, an Anabaptist of Thuringia, who suffered a tedious martyrdom in chains with steadfast loyalty. He owned a large farm in Herda, a village in the Eisenach district. Early in October 1531 he was arrested because he had been baptized on his faith, and taken to Eisenach. At the end of January 1532 he was released by Philip of Hesse, perhaps as a result of recanting (Wappler, 210). When he took the Anabaptist Margarethe Koch, *die alte Garköchin*, into his house and refused to have his child baptized on the ground that baptism would not benefit it as long as it could not desire it, he was again arrested in January 1533. John Frederick, the elector of Saxony, insisted that he be put to death, basing his verdict on an opinion of the Wittenberg theologians and jurists recommending death by the sword for rebaptized persons. But Philip, who had joint jurisdiction over Hausbreitenbach, to which Herda belonged, did not give his consent. He hesitated to execute a man for his faith, since faith is a gift of God; and if it is an erring faith it is accepted out of ignorance, not malice. He favored expulsion from the country. A long correspondence between the two rulers followed, as well as lengthy negotiations with courts and officials.

Meanwhile Fritz Erbe lay in his dungeon in a remote tower of the city wall. His friends and the Anabaptists were moved by deep sympathy and honored him as a martyr. In the depth of night they came to him to talk to him and to give and receive strength of faith. Two visitors were seized and executed in November 1537. In 1539 three other Anabaptist visitors were arrested; after cruel torture they recanted and were released. When people approached the tower by day and requested to be imprisoned with Erbe, he was taken to a tower in the Wartburg. His unhappy lot stirred the sympathy of the bailiff, Eberhard von Tann. Though Tann was a decided opponent of the Anabaptists he brought it about that an attempt was made to convert Erbe. To this end Erbe was taken to the monastery in Eisenach and kept there in chains for four weeks (1541). His long imprisonment ruined his health, but his spirit remained firm. At the close of the fruitless attempt at conversion he was returned to a back tower in the Wartburg. On June 8, 1544, lightning struck there, setting the tower afire. Erbe's cries of alarm summoned the men of the castle and the town to extinguish the flames. After an imprisonment of 16 consecutive years, the sorely tried martyr was released by merciful death in 1548. He was buried in the Wartburg near the chapel of St. Elisabeth. NEFF.

P. Wappler, *Die Stellung Kursachsens und des Landgrafen Philipp von Hessen zur Täuferbewegung* (Münster, 1910); *idem, Die Täuferbewegung in Thüringen von 1526-1584* (Jena, 1913); Wiswedel, *Bilder* I, 84; ML I, 601.

Erbe, Peter, an Anabaptist martyr in western Thuringia, Germany, who was executed in 1548 on order of Elector John Frederick of Saxony (*q.v.*).

P. Wappler, *Inquisition und Ketzerprozesse in Zwickau* (Leipzig, 1908) 90.

Erbesbüdesheim, a village in Rhenish Hesse near Alzey, where there was a Mennonite church in the 18th century, since 1829 the Uffhofen (*q.v.*) congregation. The *Martyrs' Mirror* reports that in 1529, 350 Anabaptists were put to death at Alzey (Hege, 53 ff.); this figure is questioned by Krebs. About 1550 Hutterites settled in the region of Kreuznach (*q.v.*) and Sprendlingen (*q.v.*), near Erbesbüdesheim (Hege, 80). In 1568 there were still some Anabaptists in prison at Alzey, who received a letter of consolation from Peter Walpot (*q.v.*) in Moravia (Hege, 110). The congregation at Kreuznach is listed among the signatures of the Concept of Cologne (Rembert, 618). A list compiled at the end of 1610 counts 41 families in the region of Kreuznach, whose farms were confiscated because they were Anabaptists. Apparently during the next 30 or 40 years the congregation became extinct. The villages are unfortunately not named. After the Thirty Years' War (1618-48) this region was one of the first to receive Mennonite refugees from Switzerland.

In 1738 Mennonites are mentioned for the first time in the official lists drawn up in the Palatinate (*Karlsruher Generallandesarchiv*); seven families were living near Erbesbüdesheim on the von Rohan and Laroche estates, where they were received during the reign of Karl Ludwig (*Karlsruher Akten, Rechtsverhältnisse*). They were Jost (elder and younger) and Christian Eicher, Oswald Neff, Ulrich Leonhard, Hans Jakob Boxler, and Anna Andres, widow. Evidently the families living at Kriegsfeld, Michael Lichte and the widows of Michael Andres and Christian Fischer, also belonged to the Erbesbüdesheim congregation. The list of 1743 names a Johannes Schowalter family, and those of 1752 and 1753 the families of Valentine Dahlem (1749), at Nack (the castle) Jakob Stauffer and Christian Eymann (1751), at Schniftenbergerhof Jakob Heer (1747), and in 1759 a Jakob Neukumet family.

In the Dutch *Naamlijsten* (first mentioned in 1766, when the congregation is called Rheingrafenstein-Erbesbüdesheim-Weierhof) the following elders and preachers are listed for Erbesbüdesheim: Elder, Ulrich Ellenberger, 1743-67; Johannes Möllinger; Christian Stauffer; Christian Göbel; Heinrich Plätscher; Jakob Gally (Galle), preacher 1762, elder 1767; Jacob Heer (no dates); David Hüthwohl, 1769-86; Christian Eicher, preacher 1786, elder 1798; and Jacob Galle, 1801-?

At first they held their services in the Nack castle, later at the Erbesbüdesheim castle. Until 1748 this congregation and the Weierhof (*q.v.*) congregation had the same preacher and a common alms fund. In the second half of the 18th century the Erbesbüdesheim congregation met at the Schniftenbergerhof. It is listed by this name in the records of the Ibersheim conference of 1803, which were signed by Christian Eicher for this church. When the Schniftenbergerhof was leased to a Protestant in 1824,

Eicher offered the Mennonites the use of his house for their meetings. In 1829 the seat of the congregation was moved to Uffhofen (*q.v.*). At present there are no Mennonites in Nack and Erbesbüdesheim.   NEFF, vDZ.

Chr. Hege, *Die Täufer in der Kurpfalz* (Frankfurt, 1908); Rembert, *Wiedertäufer; Mart. Mir.* D 29, E 437; Johann Risser in *Menn. Blätter*, 1855, 51; Manfred Krebs, "Beiträge zur Geschichte der Wiedertäufer am Oberrhein. I. Zum ältesten kurpfälzischen Wiedertäuferprozess 1527-1529," in *Ztscht für die Gesch. des Oberrheins*, n.s., Vol. 44 (Karlsruhe, 1931) 566-76; *ML* I, 601.

Erbkam, Wilhelm Heinrich (1810-84), professor of theology at the University of Königsberg, author of *Geschichte der protestantischen Sekten im Zeitalter der Reformation* (Hamburg and Gotha, 1848), a book that "is a valuable contribution to the history of the Reformation, based on most thorough study" (*HRE* V, 449). Later research has, of course, overtaken it. Its value lies in the author's laudable attempt to present an independent, objective account, rare among Protestant theologians, of the history of the Anabaptists. He found the roots of this great movement in Christian Mysticism, and to it he devoted a lengthy study, which presents much that is noteworthy. In this connection he presented at great length Carlstadt, Sebastian Franck, and Caspar Schwenckfeld as representatives of Christian Mysticism, and in the second part of his book a brief summary of Anabaptist history. He exploited the sources available to him; but since he approached them with a bias, and, for example, regarded Bullinger's statements as unassailable truth, and furthermore since many sources now available were unknown to him, he was unable to present a true picture of Anabaptist history. Hans Denk he handled with a few words; Michael Sattler he did not even mention. His book has a purely antiquarian value for Anabaptist history. (*ML* I, 602.)   NEFF.

Erbpacht: see **Leasehold, hereditary.**

Erbrecht: see **Inheritance, right of.**

Erfordter, Antoni, was the most outstanding of the Anabaptists in Carinthia. Nothing is known of his youth, nor how or when he was won to the Anabaptist movement. In 1538 he was in Klagenfurt, where he owned a house. There he wrote his *Urlaubsbrief,* viz., a severe sermon against the immorality and lack of faith of his contemporaries, especially the rich and those clergymen "who practice idolatry and lie on cushions." He aims his blows at the followers of the pope as well as those of Luther, and in plainness of language he surpasses even Luther. His censure is meant for a clergy that praises the Law of God with lofty words, but never in the least translates it into action; for rulers and subjects "who know the rascality of the clergy, and yet roar with them." They all continue to sin against God's mercy "and remain in their old shoes." King Ferdinand fares very badly, "who persecute Christ in His members. Today your mandates are proclaimed that one may no longer speak, write, nor sing the name of Jesus." Concerning governments he says, "If they are no good, how can the subjects be good?" The gentlemen on the council and court fare equally badly.

It is a type of eloquence that the common man understood. It is not different from the speeches of the Estates in the Carinthian diets. Klagenfurt had an unusually bad reputation: "A pigeon could carry all the Christians away on its back," he wrote. Erfordter then attacked the superstitions of the time, citing some striking examples which offer a good picture of moral conditions. In such company he did not care to live. He adhered to the Anabaptists Donner (*q.v.*) and Brandl. Thrown into prison for this he was "so violently threatened by his ruffian jailors to wall him up alive, that he was compelled to call the confession of faith of the two men of God a sect and a seduction." This declaration now grieved him, and so "he wanted to retract it now, and loudly confess that the teaching of these men is the real truth." To his fellow citizens he said, "Do not be surprised that there are here in Klagenfurt, Villach, St. Veit, and Völkermarkt, indeed perhaps in all Carinthia scarcely one or two pious Christians to be found; and there you have the reason for my departure from you."

Erfordter went to Moravia and was there ordained as a preacher (*Diener des Wortes*). When the Anabaptist meeting at Steinabrunn, Lower Austria, December 1539, was surprised and 136 members taken prisoner to the castle at Falkenstein, he wrote them (in 1540) an epistle and a moving poem of consolation. "Would to God," he wrote, "that I could serve you and die for you."

Erfordter was one of the best poets among the Brethren. He is the author of several fine songs, which praise the deeds of the Hutterite martyrs and describe the sorrows of the prisoners. The song "Ach Gott, wem soll ichs klagen?" pictures their suffering under constant persecution. His most famous song is "Ich armes Brüderlein klag mich sehr," which describes his own distress. It was written at the time when he bade farewell to his wife and his people in Klagenfurt. Two other songs should also be mentioned. "Susanne war in Aengsten gross," and "Wol auf, wol auf, von hinnen, im Kampf, ihr Brüder wert."

Erfordter died in 1541 on the Bruderhof either of Pausram or of Schackwitz (near Austerlitz), where the largest Hutterite settlements were located. His songs are published in *Die Lieder der Hutterischen Brüder* (Scottdale, 1914) 107-15, and Wolkan, *Lieder*, 173-78 and 248.　　　　　　　LOSERTH.

J. Loserth, "The Anabaptists in Carinthia in the 16th Century," MQR XXI (1947) 235-47; the *Urlaubsbrief* is printed in extenso in J. v. Beck, "Ein Beitrag zur Geschichte der Wiedertäufer in Kärnten," *Archiv des Hist. Vereins f. Kärnten* XI (1867) and in excerpts in L. Müller, *Glaubenszeugnisse der oberdeutschen Taufgesinnten* (1938) 258-62; an English translation of large parts of this letter is found in Loserth's article in MQR, *loc. cit.*; ML I, 605 f.

Erhard, Christoph, an Austrian Catholic theologian of the second half of the 16th century, aggressive champion of the Counter Reformation (*q.v.*), and polemical writer against the Hutterites. Around 1582-83 Adam von Dietrichstein (*q.v.*) called him to Nikolsburg, Moravia (*q.v.*), as parish priest with the special assignment to promote the recatholization of this noble estate and by all means to suppress the Anabaptist "heresy" of that area. For the next six years he worked vigorously in this direction, after which he was called to Salzburg to become a counselor of the archbishop. While in Nikolsburg he naturally came into closest contact also with the Hutterites. Since they resisted his attempts toward conversion to Catholicism, he had nothing but contempt for them, pouring his vitriolic invectives against them into his books. It is these books which attract our interest to this otherwise not very important man.

Four titles have become known: (1) *Zwelff wichtige und starcke Ursachen Hansen Jedelshausers von Ulm seines Handwercks ein Nadler, Warumb er mit seinem ehelichen Weib und vier Kindern von den Widertauffern, so man Hutterische Brüder nennt, sey abgetretten* (Ingolstadt, 1587; allegedly Erhard was only the editor of this small pamphlet and wrote the preface); (2) *Gründliche kurtz verfaste Historia von Münsterischen Widertauffern: und wie die Hutterischen Brüder so auch billich Widertauffer genent werden* (Munich, 1589. The title page has an interesting woodcut showing a Hutterite house with a Hutterite man, woman, and child in front. Copy in Goshen College Library); (3) *Catholische Brief(e) und Sendschreiben, darinnen vermeldet wie es eine Beschaffenheit um das Religionswesen in der Herrschaft Nikolsburg in Mähren, sampt angedrucktem Gespräch* (Ingolstadt, 1586); (4) *Salus ex inimicis. Goliaths Schwerdt. Augenscheinliche Erweysung, was wir Catholische unnd alte Christen für klare unnd kräfftige Argumenta und Zeugnussen haben. . . . Mit angehängten Ursachen, warumb all jetzt schwebende Sectierer und Ketzer, als da seynd Zwinglianer . . . und Widertauffer, ihrer Communion halben, von den Catholischen gestraffet werden* (Ingolstadt, 1586, copy in the Amsterdam Mennonite Library). Of these only the second-named book is of any significance for Anabaptist studies. The first book, claiming to be a genuine recantation and confession of a former Anabaptist who had turned Catholic, hardly deserves more than passing mention. It abounds in stark lies in order to bring the Hutterites into disrepute (for instance, it is claimed that Jakob Hutter was executed for adultery). The *Gründliche Kurz Verfasste Historia* of 1589, a book of about 130 pages, is more important as a polemical pamphlet, as one learns from it some of the material which the opponents used to incite hatred against the Brethren. It is a very poor performance in this regard, and outdoes in untruth the first-named pamphlet. There is no vice which "after the example of the Münsterites" could not also be found with the Hutterites. They have the same goal as the Münsterites and commit the same horrible deeds. They are drunkards and brawlers, thieves and adulterers; they are arrogant and puffed up, even insolent. Hutter is an ignorant ass, a robber and rebel, etc. The *Chronicle* he calls a book of lies. He also quotes the "new song" of Johann Eysvogel (*q.v.*) of Cologne (1583), in which the fraud of the Anabaptists is "unmasked." The book ends with a warning against these "miserable confused heretics."

The third book (1586) is more or less a boasting about Erhard's great achievements in Nikolsburg, formerly a stronghold of heretics and now again Catholic. It is a eulogy of the Dietrichsteins who have promoted this new movement of the Roman Church. Actually he had little reason to boast about his work. It was not until 1619-22 that the Hutterites had to leave the place and the Counter Reformation could record a full victory. The polemics of Erhard, however, were soon taken up by another Catholic priest, the bellicose Christoph A. Fischer (*q.v.*) of the same area, whose attacks were much more subtle and matter-of-fact than those of the *Gründliche Historia*. But all these pamphlets brought about much hardship for the Brethren, hard pressed and slandered as they were already.

LOSERTH, R.F.

These pamphlets were used as source materials by V. A. Winter, for his historical work, *Geschichte der bayrischen Wiedertäufer im 16. Jahrhundert* (Munich, 1809), as he notes on page 126; J. Loserth, *Communismus; ML* I, 606.

Erie County in western New York, located at the eastern end of Lake Erie. Mennonites live chiefly in the northeastern part. Approximately 400 Mennonites in the county represent three branches, Mennonites (MC) constituting about one half, Conservative Amish Mennonites about 45 per cent, and Reformed Mennonites about 5 per cent of the total. The Mennonite settlement extends north into Niagara County, and east into Genesee County. The first Mennonite settlers arrived here from eastern Pennsylvania in the early part of the 19th century, but their descendants became inactive in their relation to the Mennonite church in the last part of that century and the first part of the 20th. Another settlement made between 1920 and 1930 represents the present M.C. and C.A.M. churches. (See **Clarence**.)

D.E.D.

Eriksz, Jan, was for a certain time a leader of the Dutch Waterlander Mennonites in Friesland, but left this group in 1613. Nothing more is known about him. (*DB* 1876, 37.)

vDZ.

Erisman Mennonite Church (MC) formerly met in a meetinghouse built in 1798 on lands of Abraham Erisman in Rapho Township on the Mt. Joy-Manheim Road, in Lancaster Co., Pa. In 1891 the present brick church was built. The congregation of 214 (1953), belonging to the Lancaster Mennonite Conference, is a conservative growing fellowship which still bears the impress of the work of Bishop Jacob N. Brubacher (d. 1913). In 1953 Henry E. Lutz and Homer D. Bomberger were the bishops, Martin G. Metzler and John S. Eby the ministers, and Harvey E. Metzler the deacon. Missionaries Elam and Grace Metzler Stauffer in Africa and the Elam Hollingers in Alabama are from this congregation.

I.D.L.

Ernest (German, *Ernst*) (1497-1546), Duke of Brunswick-Lüneburg in 1521-46, called "the Confessor." He introduced Lutheranism into his realm (1527). When he was asked by Philip of Hesse for an opinion on the punishment of Anabaptists, he sent one drawn up by Urban Rhegius in 1536 with the remark that a more detailed statement would require exact information on the activities of the Anabaptists; this he lacked, as the movement had not found entry into his realm.

NEFF.

K. W. H. Hochhuth, in *Ztscht f. d. Hist. Theologie*, 1858, 566 ff.; *ML* I, 608.

Ernfart, Klaus, the mine superintendent of Ellrich (Thuringia), an Anabaptist martyr *ca.* 1536 concerning whom nothing else is known.

P. Wappler, *Die Stellung Kursachsens und des Landgrafen Philip von Hessen zur Täuferbewegung* (Münster, 1910); *ML* I, 608.

Ernsthafte Christenpflicht, the first complete and self-contained German prayer book for Mennonites, most likely of Palatine origin. In general, Mennonites practiced free, extemporaneous prayer at church and at home. Soon after 1600, however, Dutch Mennonites seem to have felt a need also for printed prayers, mainly for home devotions, and a few short collections of such prayers were published. Yet it was not until the early 18th century that the "Swiss" Mennonites in South Germany (Palatinate) took the decisive step of producing a complete prayer book of their own, a modest but independent publication of far-reaching influence. Its full title (first edition) is *Die Ernsthaffte Christenpflicht, Darinnen Schöne Geistliche Gebäter, Darmit sich fromme Christen-Herzen zu allen Zeiten und in allen Nöhten trösten können. Gedruckt im Jar 1739, Zu finden in Kayserslautern bei dem Buchbinder* (only known copy in Goshen College Library). It is a small book of 323 pages of prayers, with appended index and the "Haslibacher-Lied" (*q.v.*). It contains a total of 36 prayers; namely, 2 prayers for every day, 5 prayers in temptation and anxiety, and 29 "general" prayers. Later 19th-century editions increased the number of prayers to 50, including also prayers for church services and other occasions, thus changing the character of the book. The book went through many editions; Europe saw 13 editions between 1739 and 1852, printed in Kaiserslautern, Saarburg, Zweybrücken, Herborn in Nassau, Reinach, Basel (Mechel pub., *q.v.*), Regensburg; in America 32 editions, all in the German language, were produced between 1745 and 1955. The oldest American edition was printed at the Ephrata Cloister, Pa. (*q.v.*), surprisingly as early as six years after the first (known) European edition. The book is still today in demand by the Amish congregations (last edition was produced for the Amish in Lancaster Co., Pa.), who have preserved their German worship. The book has never been translated and hence came into disuse when the congregations shifted to the English. Today most Mennonites are completely ignorant of the existence of any prayer book of Mennonite origin.

As is the case with nearly all prayer books in existence, this one represents but a compilation of older models, Mennonite and non-Mennonite, partly rephrased and extended, and partly simply copied from other prayer books. It is an attractive task to trace all these models and forerunners, and to study their gradual changes. The main Mennonite source seems to have been a collection of 18 prayers by the well-known hymn writer Leenaerdt Clock (*q.v.*), first published as a "formulary" in Holland in 1625. It was later reprinted by T. T. van Sittert (*q.v.*) in his church manual, *Glaubensbekenntnis,* etc., 1664, in a German translation. This rather modest collection (*Formulier etlicher Gebete*) unexpectedly became the prayer model of the Mennonites for centuries to come, much changed, of course, in form and spirit during this period of borrowing. In Switzerland one particularly extensive "general" prayer of this *Formulier* became strangely popular and was twice printed previous to the *Christenpflicht* though in paraphrased form (Reist, *q.v.,* *Sendbrief, q.v.*). The *Christenpflicht* then brings still another version of this same prayer, adjusted to the new needs and conditions, and also breaks it up into 16 shorter prayer passages, *in vielen Anliegen und Nöten zu sprechen,* amplifying the different paragraphs of the former prayer, without, however, adding any new thought. Worth noticing is an ever-recurring passage in all these prayers on behalf of "those goodhearted people who love us and do good unto us and prove mercy with food and drink . . . but who have little strength to come into the obedience of God." It alludes to the "Half-Anabaptists" (*q.v.*) in Switzerland who were sympathizers with the Brethren, yet never joined the brotherhood.

Among the non-Mennonite sources of the *Christenpflicht,* two major prayer collections could be identified from which prayers were lifted verbatim without any change: Johannes Arndt's *Paradies-Gärtlein* (1612), from which three prayers were taken, and Caspar Schwenckfeld's *Deutsches Passional,* 1539 (many anonymous editions since), from which at least five prayers were adopted, of course, without knowing that they come from a man who in his lifetime had opposed their Anabaptist forefathers. In fairness it must be said that it had always been the usage in producing new prayer books to borrow from older models. That was true with Cranmer's *Book of Common Prayers* in England, and it was also true with Schwenckfeld or Arndt or with the Dutch Reformed prayer book which Clock might have used as a model for his short *Formulier.* In spite of all these transfers, however, the *Ernsthafte Christenpflicht* should be viewed as a completely new and original work, produced by and for Mennonites in the Palatinate. It was originally intended for private devotion only, not for use in church services (as the later editions might suggest). Its spirit, to be sure, is rather remote from that of the great beginning, it being nearer to the spirit of Arndt (or even of Schwenckfeld) than to that of the *Ausbund* or of Menno Simons. It most likely contributed to shaping the new, 18th-century pattern of Mennonite piety which came so close to that

of the German pietists. (See **Prayer and Prayerbooks.**)† R.F.

R. Friedmann, *Mennonite Piety Through the Centuries* (Goshen, 1949) 189-95 (contains a detailed account of the contents and character of all the prayers); *ML* I, 608.

Ernstige Aenporringhe tot Gemeenschap der Heyligen, a Dutch Mennonite pamphlet, which appeared after the Frisian and High German Mennonites in Holland had resolved to unite. It is a peaceful and moderate writing, condemning discord and schism among the brethren, and first published in Amsterdam in 1630 together with Jan Cents' confession, which was to be the basis of the union of the Frisian and High German groups in 1639. Some extracts of it were reprinted together with other documents by Geleyn Jansz at Vlissingen in 1666. (H. W. Meihuizen, *Galenus Abrahamsz,* Haarlem, 1954.) vDZ.

Ernstweiler, a village near Zweibrücken in the Palatinate, Germany, where a Mennonite congregation has been meeting since about 1770, which had its origin about 1680. It was formerly called the *Gemeinde bei Zweibrücken.* Its members are descendants of refugees from the canton of Bern in Switzerland who settled in Alsace and the Palatinate at the end of the 17th century and the beginning of the 18th, whence they gradually made their way to the duchy of Zweibrücken. They lived scattered on farms and mills or singly in villages as renters or owners of farms. At first they met in rotation on the Heidelbingerhof, Ernstweilerhof, Kahlenbergerhof, Freishauserhof, Hornbacherhof, Neuhof, and Kirchheimerhof. Early preachers were Johannes Schöny 1749, Johannes Lehmann 1745, Johann Schmidt 1755, Peter Böhn 1757, Joseph Schnebele 1762, Christian Lehmann 1813 (elder 1819), Jakob Schnebele 1829. The Ibersheim resolutions of 1803 were signed for the "congregation near Zweibrücken" by Ulrich Lehmann. Other later preachers were Jakob Finger of Bamsterhof, Christian Lehmann, Jr., of Waldhausen, Joseph Dahlem of Hunackerhof, Weber of Hornbacherhof, Böhr of Unterhof. In 1843 the congregation built a church in Ernstweiler. In 1876 the Ernstweiler congregation united with Kühbörncheshof (*q.v.*) and Neudorferhof (*q.v.*) in maintaining a preacher. They were served 1876-79 by S. Blickensdörfer of the Kohlhof, a teacher at the school at Weierhof (*q.v.*), and previously a student at the missionary school in Basel (*Menn. Bl.,* 1877, 15), the first trained and salaried minister. When he was called to Sembach (*q.v.*) his place was filled by A. Hirschler of Kaiserslautern (*q.v.*), who served 50 years 1880-1930. He was followed by A. Harder 1931-35, and H. Scheffler 1935-37. In 1898 the church was incorporated. In 1923 the congregation numbered about 140 souls. In 1937 it was merged with Ixheim (*q.v.*) to form the Zweibrücken (*q.v.*) congregation. At that time it had 114 baptized members. NEFF.

H. Scheffler, "Vereinigung Ixheim-Ernstweiler," in *Gem.-Kal.* 1939, 71-81; *ML* I, 608.

Erntefeld, a bimonthly 8-page (at the beginning) periodical 6 x 8 in., started by the Mennonite Brethren missionaries at Nalgonda, India, in 1900, not published after 1914-15, had 1,550 readers. Its editor was the missionary Abraham Friesen, and it was printed by the Raduga firm at Halbstadt, Russia. (Friesen, *Brüderschaft*, 565, 672.) C.K.

Erpolzheim, a village in the Rhenish Palatinate, Germany, near Bad Dürkheim, the seat of a Mennonite church which has always been closely connected with Friedelsheim (*q.v.*). Its existence before the Thirty Years' War is probable, for on Oct. 20, 1600, the Reformed Church Council at Heidelberg reported to the elector that "in the vicinity of Erpolzheim the Anabaptists hold their night meetings" (Hege, 163). Since Erpolzheim belonged to the county of Hardenburg, the Mennonites living there were not listed in the registers required by the Palatine government. Only once was there an incidental reference in the records of the Karlsruhe *Generallandesarchiv,* stating that a Mennonite by the name of Nikolaus Zerger lived in Erpolzheim about 1689, whose Mennonite maid Anna Marie joined the Reformed Church. In 1732 a deacon of the Friedelsheim church was a Hans Berger, who lived at Erpolzheim (Müller, 211). In the Lutheran and Reformed registers of deaths the following Mennonite names occur (1753-97): Johannes Ummel (d. 1764), Berger, Herbach, Rothen, Ellenberger, Neff, Latscha, Eicher, Bergtholdt, Herstein, Schnebel, Lichti, Wissler, Pletscher, Kinzinger, Zercher, Gut. In a commissary's list to the French army (1795-96) are found these names: Johannes and Heinrich Bergtholdt, Johannes and Peter Pletscher, Nikolaus and Georg Hodel, Johannes Latscha's widow, Jakob Schnebele's widow, and Heinrich Berger's widow. According to a later war-debt list the following lived at Erpolzheim in 1807: Peter Pletscher, Jakob Schnebele's widow, Jakob Schnebele's children from his first marriage, Johannes Latscha's widow, Philip Hodel, Katharina Hodelin, Heinrich Ummel, Jakob and Heinrich Bergtholdt, Heinrich Berger's widow, and Christian Hirstein.

The church seems to have been strongest in the second half of the 18th century, perhaps even surpassing Friedelsheim. According to Frey there were in Erpolzheim in 1802, 40 Mennonites, in 1834 only 10; perhaps many had emigrated to America. In 1923 two families, Becker and Bergtholdt, were living there. In 1954 there were resident in Erpolzheim 20 members of the Friedelsheim congregation, 11 of whom were refugees from the Danzig area.

According to the Dutch *Naamlijsten* the elders and ministers of the Erpolzheim-Friedelsheim congregation (first mentioned in 1766) were as follows: elders—Abraham Ellenberger, 1738-76(?); Abraham Ellenberger, Jr., 1776-?; Jacob Näff, Heinrich Wiesler, and Heinrich Pletscher, all 1790-?; preachers—Abraham Ellenberger, 1738 (then made elder); Peter Becker, 1752-76; Johannes Strohm, 1757 (d. 1780); Abraham Ellenberger, Jr., 1761-76 (then made elder); Heinrich Wiesler, 1762-90 (then made elder); Heinrich Pletscher, 1782-90 (then made elder); Heinrich Krämer, 1785 (1790).

In 1756 a member by the name of Johannes Ummel built a little hall with a chamber over his winepress and put it at the disposal of the congregation.

After his death, however, his sons closed its doors to them. In 1788 the farm again came into the possession of a Mennonite preacher, Johann Heinrich Wissler, who sold the hall to the congregation for 400 guilders. It was entered in the *Grundbuch* as the property of the Friedelsheim congregation in 1902. During the summer months six or seven meetings are held here, which are attended by the Mennonites at Erpolzheim, Freinsheim, and Dackenheim, who are members of Friedelsheim.
J.F., vDZ.

Chr. Hege, *Die Täufer in der Kurpfalz* (Frankfurt, 1908); Müller, *Berner Täufer;* Frey, *Historisch-statist. Beschreibung des . . . Rheinkreises;* ML I, 608 f.

Ertzwiller, Fredrik van, a preacher of the High German congregation of Haarlem, Holland, and later a preacher of the united congregation of High Germans, Frisians, and Waterlanders (*Bevredigde Broederschap, q.v.*) at Haarlem, who together with other preachers suspended Leenaerdt Clock (*q.v.*) in September 1613 from his office, because he had disturbed the church by leaving the Bevredigde Broederschap. (*Inv. Arch. Amst.* I, 542.) vDZ.

Esau, a Mennonite family name appearing in the rural Old Flemish congregations of West Prussia, first mentioned in 1617 at Tiegenhof. In 1662 a Jacob Esous was a deacon of the Danzig Flemish Mennonite (Huiskopers) congregation at Rotterdam, Holland. In 1776, 16 families of this name were counted in West Prussia, and in 1935, 86 persons. Members of this family emigrated to Russia and America. Peter Esau seems to have been the first preacher of this family, serving the Grosse Werder congregation 1765-*ca*.81. Abraham Esau (1799-1885) was for 48 years an active preacher in the Tiegenhagen congregation in West Prussia, during 29 of which he served as elder. Abraham Esau was rector of the University of Jena in 1931-34; Johann J. Esau (1859-1940) was a Mennonite engineer in the Ukraine, and Jacob Esau was a Mennonite physician in Chortitza before 1900. (*ML* I, 609.) NEFF, G.R.

Esch (Eash, Esh, Oesch), a family name represented among European and American Mennonites. John Horsch lists Oesch among the names of Swiss Mennonite refugees in the Palatinate after 1664, who later came to Pennsylvania. Christian Neff's *Mennonitisches Adressbuch* of 1936 lists an Oesch family in the Augsburg Mennonite Church and three Esch families in the Ernstweiler Mennonite Church. Franz Crous's list of Mennonites (1940) in South Germany has four families bearing the name Esch and ten the name Oesch. The family is prominent in the Luxembourg congregation; Joseph Oesch, who was serving as bishop in 1953, died on July 15, 1954.

C. Z. Mast reports that 100 families bearing the name Esch are mostly farmers in Lancaster Co., Pa. The immigrant ancestor of this family, Jacob Esch, landed in Philadelphia in 1751. Among his sons was Jacob Eash, Amish bishop who died in 1850. The family history of Jacob Eash names 2,946 of his descendants, many of whom are Amish, living principally in Pennsylvania, Ohio, Indiana, and Iowa.

Near the time that Jacob Esch, Sr., came to America, James Esch also emigrated from Europe to eastern Pennsylvania. Among his descendants was Christian D. Esch (*q.v.*), Mennonite bishop and missionary doctor to India. Menno Esch, Mennonite bishop at Mio, Mich., is a member of this family.

Daniel Kauffman is the authority for the statement that John Oesch (1792-1850) was a native of Bavaria, who settled in Waterloo Co., Ont., where he was ordained preacher in 1829 and five years later bishop. In 1953 ten ordained men in various Mennonite conferences bore the name Esch or one of its variants. **M.G.**

L. T. Eash, *Descendants of Bishop Jacob Eash* (Middlebury, Ind., 1934); C. Z. Mast, *Annals of the Conestoga Valley* (Elverson, Pa., 1942).

Esch, Christian David (1883-1931), pioneer Mennonite doctor to India, was born near Wellman, Iowa, the eleventh child of David and Fannie (Kanagy) Esch. Soon after uniting with the Mennonite Church (MC), he felt the call to missionary service and therefore decided to obtain an education. After completing his high-school work and two years of college at Goshen College, he entered medical school, receiving his M.D. degree from Bennett Medical College in Chicago in 1910. While living in Chicago he was active in the work of the Mennonite Home Mission.

In 1908 he was married to Mina Brubaker, with whom he sailed for India in 1910, arriving in the Central Provinces in November. In March 1911 he was ordained to the ministry. Returning to America on his first furlough in 1917, the World War forced a four-year stay, during which time he practiced medicine in Hesston, Kan., and received his A.B. at Goshen College. In March 1924 Esch was ordained bishop for the India field. During his second term in India his work was principally among the lepers, in recognition of which the governor of the Central Provinces bestowed upon him the Kaiser-I-Hind silver medal. Returning on their second furlough in 1928, they made their home in West Liberty, Ohio. After 15 months in America, they returned to the mission field, where Dr. Esch took charge of the mission hospital in Dhamtari. He died on Feb. 21, 1931, leaving his widow and six children. **M.G.**

J. N. Kaufman, "Christian David Esch," *CM*, June 1931, 173, 174; M. W. Gerber, "Biography of Doctor Christian David Esch," *YCC*, Aug. 15, 1937, 678-80; Clara B. Esch, "Christian David Esch," *MHB*, July 1947, 1-2.

Eschatology, literally the doctrine of the last things, i.e., of the end, also called the doctrine of the future, but in its fullest sense the teaching about the Christian hope or the outcome of history and God's program. Individual eschatology deals with the destiny of the individual, including death and eternal destiny (resurrection, judgment, immortality, heaven, hell). General eschatology deals with the destiny of the race and the universe, i.e., with the outcome of human history and the end of the world, including all the items involved in individual eschatology. The particular question of the future millennial kingdom, though involved in general escha-

tology, is treated under the article **Chiliasm.** The doctrine of ultimate universal salvation will be treated under the article **Universalism.**

In general Anabaptists and Mennonites have taken the position of classic evangelical Christianity and have no distinct eschatology different from that of evangelical Protestantism. This position as held by all the groups in North America and the conservative groups in Europe is well set forth in Article XVIII of the Dordrecht Confession (1632) as follows: "Regarding the resurrection of the dead, we confess with the mouth, and believe with the heart, that according to the Scriptures—all men who shall have died or 'fallen asleep,' will—through the incomprehensible power of God—at the day of judgment be 'raised up' and made alive; and that these, together with all those who then remain alive, and who shall be 'changed in a moment, in the twinkling of an eye, at the last trump,' shall 'appear before the judgment seat of Christ,' where the good shall be separated from the evil, and where 'everyone shall receive the things done in his body, according to that he hath done, whether it be good or bad'; and that the good or pious shall then further, as the blessed of their Father, be received by Christ into eternal life, where they shall receive that joy which 'eye hath not seen, nor ear heard, nor hath entered into the heart of man.' Yea, where they shall reign and triumph with Christ forever and ever.

"And that on the contrary, the wicked or impious shall, as the accursed of God, be cast into 'outer darkness'; yea, into eternal, hellish torments; 'where their worm dieth not, and the fire is not quenched'; and where—according to Holy Scripture—they can expect no comfort nor redemption throughout eternity.

"May the Lord through His grace make us all fit and worthy, that no such calamity may befall any of us; but that we may be diligent, and so take heed to ourselves, that we may be found of Him in peace, without spot, and blameless. Amen."

A distinctive feature of early Anabaptism was the martyr theology, i.e., its philosophy of history, according to which the great battle being fought between God and His enemies is best observed in the struggle between the prophets and martyrs of the Old Covenant, then in Christ and His cross and resurrection, finally in the martyrs of the Christian church beginning with apostolic times. The Anabaptist martyrs, they believed, have joined in this great struggle and will, with the help of God, win the victory not only for themselves as individual heroes of faith, but as co-warriors with Christ. This conflict means suffering, and accordingly the doctrine of the suffering church is vital in Anabaptist theology. But the victory will come through suffering, and suffering is accordingly a testimony to the martyr that he is a part of the true church and a true child of God. This is the hope of the Anabaptist, a sure and confident hope in ultimate victory in union with Christ, in spite of and even because of present suffering. The enemy may seem temporarily to have the upper hand but this is but for the moment. In this vision of the course of history the Anabaptist sees the great state churches, both Catholic and Protestant, lined up with the enemy. Are they not persecuting the true church of Christ? But nothing can withstand the power of the suffering church; the mighty power of its faith, its ability to absorb all the wicked onslaughts of the enemy and to bear the suffering without yielding, is itself a power which the enemy cannot conquer. This magnificent interpretation of the history of the church and the unquenchable vision of a victorious outcome is repeatedly testified to in the writings of Menno Simons and others, in the martyr testimonies in the *Ausbund* and in the *Offer des Heeren* as well as in the *Martyrs' Mirror* and elsewhere.

Anneken of Rotterdam said to her judges in 1539 (*Offer*), "I tread the path of the prophets, the way of the martyrs and apostles." Balthasar Hubmaier (d. 1527) used as his great motto a statement which implies the entire cross-centered theology of history of the Anabaptists: "The divine truth cannot be killed, and although it may for some time let itself be scourged, crowned (with thorns), crucified, and laid in the grave, it will nevertheless rise up again victorious on the third day and reign and triumph in eternity." One of the hymns of the *Ausbund* says, "The bride, like the bridegroom, must enter through suffering into joy," making suffering a way station on the road to glory. The cross, says Stauffer (*Anabaptist Theology of Martyrdom*), is for the Anabaptists always both the sign of victory established by God once for all, and the law which comes true in the lives of the faithful over and over again; it is the deed by which God made a new start, and the form by which He will consummate His work. Menno Simons' great work, *The Cross of Christ,* concludes with a vision of the coming glory of the martyrs founded on the victorious sayings of the Book of Revelation.

The Anabaptist-Mennonite emphasis on the overcoming power of a martyr faith and belief in an ultimate victory for Christ and His cause (although with the strong emphasis on discipleship and holy living) and the reaction against any type of revolutionary Chiliasm led in the course of time to a minimum emphasis on the doctrine of the second coming of Christ as having little practical relation to present-day living. In some circles the doctrine also developed that the individual could not be sure of ultimate salvation but could only live in hope. This denial of the doctrine of assurance persists today particularly in the radically conservative and traditional groups such as the Old Order Amish and Old Colony Mennonites. It is in radical contrast to the joyful assurance of the early Anabaptists, including the martyrs, for whom such a doctrine would be inconceivable.

The doctrine of universalism, namely, that all men shall ultimately be saved, including the idea of a second chance for the wicked dead in hell, considered in orthodox Christendom as heresy, has occasionally though rarely found adherents among Mennonites, although it has usually been formally repudiated when it has raised its head.

Under modern outside influences particularly since 1900, chiliastic views such as premillennialism and even dispensationalism have won considerable acceptance in nearly all Mennonite groups in North America except the radically conservative groups such as the Old Order Amish, Old Order Mennonites, Old Colony Mennonites, and Church of God in Christ Mennonite. The Mennonite Brethren Church, the United Missionary Church, and such smaller groups as the Evangelical Mennonites (United States), the E.M.B. and the K.M.B. groups, have become almost completely premillennial. In the two largest groups, the Mennonite Church (MC) and the General Conference Church, the millennialists are still a minority group, though rather large in some areas (see **Chiliasm**).

When the Dutch and Northwest German Mennonites generally adopted the liberal theological point of view in the late 19th century, they abandoned the belief in the bodily resurrection, a literal judgment, and a literal second return of Christ, though retaining belief in immortality. Along with this change went a general acceptance of the optimistic evolutionary view of history which was characteristic of 19th-20th century prewar liberalism. The hope of the world and the church was seen in the achievements of man. The shocking experience of World Wars I and II, together with the powerful growth of atheistic communism, has rendered this hope vain; hence with the resurgence of evangelicalism in Dutch Mennonitism there has also come a revival of evangelical eschatology with an evangelical hope. Since creedal or doctrinal positions have no longer been defined by Dutch Mennonites since the 18th century, it is impossible to state a general eschatological position for the group as a whole.

The revolutionary Münsterites (1534-35), a fringe group under the leadership of Jan Matthys and Jan of Leiden, carried the apocalyptical eschatology of Melchior Hofmann (he began his radical teaching about 1530) much further than Hofmann did, adding to it the concept of actually establishing the kingdom of God by human action. This fantastic concept they carried through, creating a legal kingdom or state patterned on Old Testament concepts, which was destroyed by the military action of the Bishop of Münster. The actual happenings in the kingdom of Münster were a mixture of radical eschatology, social revolutionary ideas, and the personal misconduct of "king" Jan of Leiden. Because of the difficulty of assessing the latter's sincerity and distinguishing the eschatological and purely social-revolutionary elements, it is difficult to draw a clear picture of the Münsterite eschatology, which in any case stood by itself outside the main stream of Anabaptist thought. (See **Münster**.)   H.S.B.

E. Stauffer, "The Anabaptist Theology of Martyrdom," *MQR* (1945) 179-214, a translation of "Täufertum und Märtyrertheologie," *Ztscht f. Kirchengesch.* LII (1953) 545-98; H. W. Meihuizen, "De verwachting van de wederkomende Christus en het rijk Gods bij de oude Doopsgezinden," *Stemmen uit de Doopsgezinde Broederschap* III (1954) No. 2, 42-50; I. D. Landis, *The Faith of Our Fathers on Eschatology* (Lititz, Pa., 1946); C. K. Lehman, *The Fulfillment of Prophecy* (Scottdale, 1950); *Prophecy Conference: Report of Conference Held at Elkhart, Ind., April 3-5, 1952* (Scottdale, 1953).

Eschelbronn near Dillsberg (*q.v.*), in the former Palatine region of Heidelberg (*q.v.*), has been at least since 1717 the home of Swiss Mennonites, lease-holders on the estates of Baron von Feltz. It is not certain whether the name Bamberger found in the Mennonite list of 1717 belongs there or in the Jewish list drawn up at the same time. The same list names the Muselmann family, and the list of 1724 also the Pletscher family. A table of inhabitants, buildings, and farms in the Palatinate, 1790, designates two Mennonite families, presumably Pletscher and Muselmann (Records of the Palatinate, Generallandesarchiv at Karlsruhe). (*ML* I, 609.)

E.H.C.

Escondido Mennonite Brethren Church, now extinct, known also as Bethania Mennonite Brethren Church, was located one mile from Escondido, San Diego Co., Cal., and was a member of the Pacific District Mennonite Brethren Conference. Founded by Elder Abraham Schellenberg of Buhler, Kan., who moved there in 1907, it had a membership in 1910 of approximately 100. Families began to move away after 1917 when heavy frost for two years in succession destroyed the citrus fruit crops. Most of the members left for places farther north, Shafter, Wasco, and Reedley. The church building was sold in 1921 for $535.00; a small group of members remaining there received financial and spiritual support from the conference until about 1929. I.G.N.

Escondido Mennonite Church (GCM), now extinct, located in Escondido, San Diego Co., Cal., was a member of the Pacific District Conference. The first meetinghouse was dedicated Oct. 29, 1911, with M. M. Horsch of Upland, Cal., officiating. The congregation was organized in the spring of 1912 under the leadership of J. S. Hirschler, also of Upland, with 19 charter members. Shortly after its organization a number of Mennonite families moved away and the attendance began to decrease. In 1930 the Sunday school was discontinued and worship services were held once a month. The congregation was finally dissolved in 1934. The ministers who served the congregation are Herman Janzen, H. H. Adrian, and H. D. Voth. H.D.B.

Espelkamp-Mittwald is a new city located 60 miles south of Bremen, Germany, built for East German refugees after World War II on the site of a former German munitions dump and poison gas factory. The area, formerly thickly wooded, covers about two square miles and contained at the close of the war about 120 barracks and warehouses of various sizes. These buildings were all earmarked for destruction by the British army of occupation, but were saved for transformation into residences and factories by the intervention of Birger Forell, a Swedish Lutheran pastor. The project was begun by the German Evangelical *Hilfswerk,* but later conjoint responsibility was also assumed by the state of Nordrhein-Westfalen. Late in 1948 the Mennonite Central Committee opened a semipermanent international voluntary service camp to aid the poorer refugees in establishing their homes. Considerable religious activity grew up around this camp, which activity was later taken over by the Conservative Amish

Mennonite mission board. In recognition for their services the city invited a number of German Mennonite refugees to settle there, and with MCC help about 30 families (120 souls) had become established by late 1953. Elder Albert Bartel has pastoral oversight of the new congregation. At the same date Espelkamp had a total population of 5,500, with a number of small industries such as furniture factories and a textile mill. P.P.

Emily Brunk, *Espelkamp* (Frankfurt, 1951); M. Harder, " 'Die Mennoniten' at Espelkamp," *Menn. Life* VII (1952) 109-10.

Eshleman (Eshelman, Aeschleman, Aeschliman, Aeschiman, Ashliman, Eschelmann), a Swiss family name found among the Mennonites (MC) of Lancaster Conference and the areas to which they have migrated, especially Maryland and Ontario, and also among the Alsatian Amish. Among the Eshleman immigrants to Pennsylvania were Daniel (before 1718), John (1731), Ulrich (1750), and Frank (latter 18th century). The name appears in Swiss history, Langnau district, 1550. The Swiss canton of Bern was struggling with the Mennonites in the early 18th century: some were sent to the galleys, and Preacher Michael Aeschlimann, 81, was sentenced to lifelong imprisonment; also imprisoned was Kaspar Aeschlimann of Rüegsau. In 1764 two Emmental Mennonite couples named Aeschlimann went to the Jura and were there married by Mennonite ministers, whereupon the Swiss authorities sought to declare the marriages null and void. In 1753 a Christian Eschelmann was living at Ibersheim in the Palatinate. The name Aschliman is common also among the 19th-century Alsatian Amish Mennonites of Fulton Co., Ohio. Among the ordained men have been Bishop Peter Eshleman (1798-1876) of the Miller district, Washington Co., Md., and his son Deacon Peter Eshleman (1834-1917) who served in the same district for about 40 years. Three Africa missionaries of the Lancaster Conference are named Eshleman (1953), and two deacons are serving in the home conference district. A minister named Eshleman is also serving in Virginia. J.C.W.

H. Frank Eshleman, *Historic Background and Annals of the Swiss and German Pioneer Settlers of South-eastern Pennsylvania* (Lancaster, 1917) 240.

Essex County, Ont., is located in the southwestern corner of Ontario in the southernmost part of Canada. The Mennonites live along the southern border of the county and are grouped around the towns of Wheatley, Leamington, Kingsville, and Harrow, along the shores of Lake Erie. A number of Mennonite families can also be found in the border city of Windsor. All the Mennonites came from Russia after World War I, the first settlers arriving in 1925. At present there is a total Mennonite population of 1,600 in the county, of whom approximately 1,300 belong to the General Conference Mennonite Church and the remainder to the Mennonite Brethren. The Essex County United Mennonite Church (GCM) with churches at Harrow and Leamington had 860 members in 1953 and the Leamington M.B. Church had 118 members in the same year. The General Conference Mennonites have recently completed the

construction of their own high school and have named it the United Mennonite Collegiate Institute.
N.N.D.

Essex County United Mennonite Church (GCM), Oak St., Leamington, Ont. Leamington (pop. 6,951) is located 35 miles southeast of Windsor. The church consists exclusively of immigrants from Russia mostly during 1923-30; in fact, all the Mennonites near Leamington are immigrants from Russia, and belong either to the General Conference Mennonite Church or to the Mennonite Brethren. The first 15 families came from the vicinity of Waterloo as farm hands and share farmers. In the course of time other families came from all parts of Ontario and the western provinces of Canada.

The first ministers chosen from the congregation, J. D. Janzen and N. H. Schmidt, were ordained by Elder J. H. Janzen. Services were held every Sunday, at first in private homes, and later in rented halls. In the first years church life was very difficult to maintain because of the general poverty and the distances to the center.

From 1925 to 1929 all the General Conference Mennonites in Ontario who had come from Russia were united by Elder Jacob H. Janzen into a single organization, called at first the General Refugee Church in Ontario (*Allgemeine Flüchtlingsgemeinde in Ontario*), but later (Aug. 15, 1926) changed to United Mennonite Church in Ontario. Waterloo was the center. Because of steady growth and the great distance between groups of the members, the body was divided on Jan. 20, 1929, into three independent congregations, of which the Essex County United Mennonite Church is one, with its center at Leamington.

In 1929 the church had 303 baptized members. Until 1933, J. H. Janzen, Waterloo, administered baptism and communion, and contributed much to the general courses for ministers. In the autumn of 1932 the congregation chose N. N. Driedger as elder from among the ministers, and ordained him on May 20, 1933. He was still serving in 1955. In 1933 a church was built, and in 1948 an annex was added.

Most of the members are farmers. Only a few live in town. Low German is usually spoken at home. In 1955 the church had grown to 930 baptized members.
N.N.D.

Essingen, a village (pop. 1,500) three miles northeast of Landau in the Palatinate, Germany, in the late 18th century the center of an Amish Mennonite congregation, descendants of refugees from Switzerland, who lived in the neighborhood of Landau. Elder Hans Nafziger (*q.v.*) was a leading personality. Two Amish Mennonite conferences were held in Essingen, attended by ministers of the congregations at Montbéliard, Alsace, Breisgau, Lorraine, Palatinate, Nassau-Weilburg, and Waldeck. At the first of these conferences, held on May 1, 1759, 13 congregations were represented; at the second, Nov. 22, 1779, there were 19. An *Ordnungsbrief* (*q.v.*) was drawn up at each meeting, both of which have been preserved. In 1809 Essingen contributed 10 doubloons to the traveling expenses of the Mennonite delegates sent to interview Napoleon on behalf of exemption from military service. Nothing more is heard of the Essingen congregation. Toward the end of the 19th century and early in the 20th there was a small congregation at St. Johann near Albersweiler (somewhat to the south of Landau). Its last elder, Jakob Hege of Mörlheim (east of Landau), died in 1911. After his death Matthias Pohl, the minister of the Sembach congregation, held services in Landau; later the ministers of the Deutschhof-Geisberg congregation performed this service. But this group was not Amish, but Mennonite, and had nothing to do with the Essingen Amish congregation.

The few Amish families which continued to live in the Essingen neighborhood after the dissolution of the Amish congregation maintained connection with the Amish congregation across the Alsatian border near Wissembourg, called Lembach (*q.v.*) or Froensburg, later Fleckensteinerhof. After the meetings at the latter place ceased in 1929, the remaining Amish families in the neighborhood affiliated with the Deutschhof-Geisberg (*q.v.*) congregation, which held occasional meetings in Landau.

The Essingen congregation was called the "Pfälzer Obere Gemeinde" in the signatures to the 1759 *Ordnungsbrief,* when the following ministers signed: Jörg Holi, Christen Nafziger, Christen Imhof, Jakob Holli, Hans Nafziger. In the 1779 *Ordnungsbrief* the signature of the congregation appears as "Essingen," with the following ministers signing: Hans Nafziger, Christen Nafziger, Christen Erismann, Jakob Ullmann. In the Lutheran church book for Essingen for the years 1730-61 deaths in the following Mennonite families are reported: Hans and Michel von Huben, Ulrich, Johannes, and Peter Nafziger, and Valentin Güngerich. From the evidence in the Karlsruhe Landesarchiv, the following families belonged to the Essingen congregation *ca.* 1780: Christian Bürky and Johannes and Christian Ehresmann (all three living on the Mechtersheimerhof), the Ullmann and Gingerich families on the Pfalzhof (Breitwieserhof), Christian Nafziger of Geilweilerhof, and certain unnamed families in Mühlhofen (Pfalz-Zweibrücken) and in Essingen (estate of Baron von Dalberg). Somewhat later the Schönbeck and Wagler families appear here.   P.So., P.S.

P. Schowalter, "Die Essinger Konferenzen 1759 und 1779. Ein Beitrag zur Geschichte der amischen Mennoniten," *Gesch. Bl.* III (1938) 49-55; H. S. Bender, "An Amish Church Discipline of 1779," *MQR* XI (1937) 163-68; Ernst Correll, "The Value of Family History for Mennonite History: With Illustrations from Nafziger Family Material," *MQR* II (1928) 66-79, 151-54, 198-204; Müller, *Berner Täufer; MQR* I (1928) 71, 198 ff.; III (1930) 140 ff.

Esslingen, a city (pop. 70,000) of Württemberg, situated on the Neckar, six miles east of Stuttgart, from 1209 to 1802 a free imperial city, in which Anabaptism early found many adherents, with some protection from the nobility. The name has survived in the "Wiedertäufer-Klinge," a forest ravine where they were accustomed to assemble. As early as 1527 there was an Anabaptist congregation here, which prepared the ground for the introduction of the Reformation (see **Ambrosius Blaurer**), but also suffered severe persecution. Its leaders were the knifesmith Hans Krafft (*q.v.*) of Augsburg, and the cobbler Felix Pfudler of Esslingen, Zuberhans (*q.v.*) of Hegensberg, Stephan Böhmerle, and others. The number of members soon increased to 100. Esslingen was at this time a place of refuge for the Anabaptists; Hans Leupold (Hege, 45), Leonhard Eleutherobius (Freisleben), and others spent some time here. Several of the Anabaptists imprisoned in the dungeon at Passau stated that they had been baptized at Esslingen, that Lienhard Wenig, a vinedresser, was their elder, and other prominent Anabaptists were Martin Arnold and Paul Frank of Hainbach (Nicoladoni, 188 ff.). Expelled early in 1528, they emigrated to Reutlingen under the leadership of the guild master Leonhard Lutz (Hege, 45). Stephan Böhmerle returned, and was executed on Oct. 5, 1529, as the first martyr of Esslingen.

The city council of Esslingen had issued a warning, Nov. 10, 1527, against the "deceitful seduction of Anabaptism," but did not take steps of suppression until the Austrian government at Stuttgart reminded the councilors of its presence in the city. Many men and women were arrested and by torture compelled to make confessions as follows: their faith they based alone on the Scriptures; faith must precede baptism; communion is a commemoration of the death of Christ; bearing arms is forbidden, nor may one do battle against one's enemy, be he Jew or Turk; peace and unity must be preserved; and it is a duty to obey all reasonable commands of the government. If several said that all who refused baptism should be killed as heathen, and that they were awaiting the coming of aid from Moravia where there were many of their faith, it is clear that either their statements were misunderstood or were extorted by torture, for there can be no thought of murder in connection with the Hutterian Brethren (Pfaff, 473). Nevertheless it may be correct that some required community of goods and asserted that Christ was not God, but a prophet and a sinless man, like any other; for all who do God's will are His sons. The contemporary chronicler, Dyonisius Dreytwein (b. about 1500 in Esslingen), makes an interesting statement at the conclusion of a comparison of the different creeds, "Therefore the Anabaptists are still the best and most pious; they do not swear, they do not practice usury, they do not drink to excess, as thou, miserable crowd" (p. 97).

Six of the arrested Anabaptists recanted and were released with a fine of 10 to 30 pounds; the others were banished. Stephan Böhmerle, who returned, was beheaded on Oct. 5, 1529. In 1530 Joachim Fleiner (*q.v.*) and Ludwig Lichtenstein met the same fate, as well as Bastian Egen and Jakob Schneider of Uhlbach.

When, in 1531, the Reformation was carried out in Esslingen, a more lenient attitude was taken toward the Anabaptists. Ambrosius Blaurer, the Swabian reformer who arrived in Esslingen in 1531, won most of the Anabaptists by the earnestness of his preaching and by personal contacts. But when he left in the following year a bitter quarrel which broke out among the clergy caused the Anabaptists to leave the church again. They also took offense at the manner of life of many members and the lack of church discipline which Blaurer had introduced at their instigation. Thus the serious-minded returned to the Anabaptists, and new repressive measures were initiated by the clergy. The *Zuchtordnung* of 1532 provided that anyone who rejected infant baptism and was rebaptized, should be admonished by the preachers, and if he did not desist from his error he should be imprisoned, and if he still persisted, expelled. On Feb. 4, 1532, the Anabaptists were summoned to the Rathaus, to be cross-examined by the clergy. Oddly, they confessed that they held the doctrine of the sleep of the soul (*q.v.*) (Pfaff, 47). In February 1533 a new examination was ordered, at which three Anabaptists were compelled to recant publicly. Following an opinion given by the Esslingen clergy, all meetings of the Anabaptists were forbidden. But the order was not enforced.

On April 5, 1534, an Anabaptist meeting in the region of Esslingen was surprised, which was attended chiefly by Anabaptists from Württemberg. A list of persons who had harbored Anabaptists was found and sent to Stuttgart. In the following year Anabaptists again appeared in Esslingen. On Aug. 23, 1535, Duke Ulrich of Württemberg wrote to the Esslingen authorities, urging them to suppress the "false doctrine of the Anabaptists." But nothing was done. In 1541 the clergy of Esslingen complained that for years the Anabaptists in the small parishes had so corrupted the populace that few acknowledged the pastors as the true preachers. On June 29, 1544, the council of Esslingen commanded the parishes to show more respect for the clergy, and arrested three men and women on a suspicion of Anabaptism. At their trial they said that the taking of interest is wrong; no one is condemned for original sin; infant baptism is useless; preaching is an aid to salvation if it is rightly done; but because it is not, it bears no fruit and reforms nobody. Veit Bechtold said Christ was true man and God, born of Mary, but crafty arguing about it should be avoided. They were dismissed with a serious warning.

In 1551 several Anabaptists of Hainbach were again arrested for holding meetings contrary to the order of the council. One of them, Gerhard Feygenbutz, declared that faith must precede baptism; he could not swear, but would otherwise conduct himself like any other citizen and do twice as much as one. They were dismissed with the warning that if they did not desist from their error their goods would be confiscated.

Duke Christoph of Württemberg in 1558 requested that the Esslingen authorities watch the Anabaptists, who were meeting in the outskirts of the city, and in 1560 he wrote them that the sectarians were meeting in a forest between Hainbach and Rüdern; this mischief should be stopped. An investigation revealed that the Anabaptists were particularly numerous and were increasing in Möhringen. After some lenient measures the council issued a sharp decree against Möhringen and Vaihingen, warning all of the ungodly error of Anabaptism, and threatening any who sheltered them with confiscation of property, corporal punishment, and exile.

On June 6, 1562, 28 Anabaptists, most of them from Württemberg, were seized in a ravine at Katzenbühl not far from Hainbach, where they had frequently assembled. When they obstinately refused to recant they were expelled from the region of the city. Again in 1564 several Anabaptists were banished. In 1567 Jakob Andreae (*q.v.*) preached eight sermons against the Anabaptists, which he published in 1568, and which influenced the governments again and again to proceed against the Anabaptists. Repeatedly the dukes of Württemberg, Ludwig and Friedrich, accused the council of Esslingen of tolerating Anabaptists. In 1598 several Anabaptists were again arrested. Some of them said they held their meetings in the woods near Stetten, and one of them justified their meetings on the grounds that the apostles had also done so. Most of them recanted, and the rest were banished. In 1609 Duke John Frederick warned the council of Esslingen of Anabaptists who had reputedly come to Hainbach and were trying to win converts. The council, however, replied that in the last three or four years, since Walter Lichtenstein had left Hainbach, there were no Anabaptists there. Nothing is known of their presence there since that date.   HEGE.

K. Pfaff, *Gesch. der Stadt Esslingen* (Esslingen, 1840); Gayler, *Historische Denkwürdigkeiten von Reutlingen* (1846); D. Dreytwein, *Esslinger Chronik* (published in the *Bibliothek des Literarischen Vereins zu Stuttgart*, vol. 221, Tübingen, 1901); Chr. Hege, *Die Täufer in der Kurpfalz* (Frankfurt, 1908); A. Nicoladoni, *Johannes Bünderlin* . . . (Berlin, 1893); Salzmann-Haffner, *Gesch. der Esslinger Wiedertäufer* (Esslingen, 1932); J. Rauscher, *Württ. Ref.-Gesch.* (1934); ML I, 609-11.

Esslinger, Georg, was Landprocurator of the Duke of Württemberg about 1600. His office included the collection of taxes from the Mennonites of the duchy. In 1608 he was accused of fraudulently appropriating 50,000 guilders of the *Täufergut* (a fund made up of income from the sale of Anabaptist property). The trial, which was held at Stuttgart, ended with Esslinger's dismissal from office and punishment. During the trial he had misrepresented the Mennonites as being disloyal subjects. (Bossert, *TA: Württemberg,* 1444 and Index.)   vDZ.

Esslinger, Wolfgang, one of the seven martyrs who were put to death Dec. 7, 1529 (not 1531, as stated in the *Martyrs' Mirror*), at Schwäbish-Gmünd (*q.v.*). In this city, at that time a free city, the Anabaptist preacher Martin Zehentmayer (*q.v.*), also called Martin der Maler, from Bavaria, formed a congregation which in 1529 had over 100 members, but was ruthlessly nipped in the bud.

In February 1529 the council had Zehentmayer and 40 adherents, 19 of them women and girls, thrown into prison; Esslinger shared this fate. The council made an effort to have them renounce their faith, but with little success. The prisoners seem to have been encouraged to steadfastness; for in various regulations "all women, girls, and children" were forbidden to go to the towers, to sing or to read there or talk to the prisoners. The captives suffered willingly.

Meanwhile a bitter conflict had arisen between the mayor Egen and a part of the council concerning their power and authority, which the mayor managed to decide in his own favor by calling in outside force. At the expense of the Swabian League (*q.v.*) he demanded that 250 soldiers be sent to him immediately on the ground that he feared an insurrection on the occasion of the approaching execution of the Anabaptists, considering their great following in the city. His request was granted. After the arrival of the troops and the notorious imperial provost Berthold Aichele (*q.v.*), who was accompanied by two executioners, legal proceedings were at once opened against the Anabaptist prisoners; the councilors did not all agree with this procedure but had to yield to force.

In order not to heighten the excitement of the citizenry who were worried about the life of the prisoners who had already languished in prison 42 weeks, they apparently tried the nonresidents first, among them Wolfgang Esslinger. The council promised them liberty if they renounced their faith. When this failed to move them, seven of them, including Wolfgang Esslinger, Zehentmayer, a woman, and a youth of sixteen, were sentenced to death. When the mayor read the verdict Esslinger called out to him, "Just as you are judging today, God will also judge you when you appear before His face; God will recognize you. Leave your sins and unrighteousness and repent, then God will not hold it against you." The sentence roused general horror and was carried out Dec. 7, 1529, on an open place before the city. On the site of execution in the presence of the executioners another attempt was made to make them recant, but, as the council later reported, the spectators, especially the women, called out encouraging words to the victims. After a short prayer they all went to their death completely unafraid.

The steadfastness of the martyrs made a deep impression on the Anabaptists and was celebrated in several hymns; one of the songs written by the victims in prison, "Aus tiefer Not schrein wir zu dir," of which each one composed a stanza, was widely distributed. The songs are found in *Die Lieder der Hutterischen Brüder* (Scottdale, 1914) 48-59.

HEGE.

Mart. Mir. D 32, E 439; Emil Wagner, "Die Reichsstadt Schwäbish-Gmünd in den Jahren 1526-1530," in *Württembergische Vierteljahrshefte für Landesgeschichte,* 1881, 81 ff.; Wolkan, *Lieder,* 17-21; ML I, 611 f.

Esztergom (German, *Gran*), a city (pop. 22,000) on the Danube in Hungary, 25 miles northwest of Budapest, seat of the Catholic archbishop and primate of Hungary. In the library of the primate many valuable codices (manuscript books) of Hutterite origin are kept, once confiscated from the Brethren. When around 1757 the last great persecution of the Anabaptists (Hutterites) set in under the Empress Maria Theresa, which eventually ended in a complete liquidation of the brotherhoods in Slovakia and with their forced conversion to Catholicism (see **Habaner**), government orders were issued that all of their handwritten books and their (non-Catholic) Bibles were to be confiscated and handed over to the ecclesiastical authorities (mostly to the Jesuits). Such large-scale confiscations of books (raids) took place in 1757-63, and again in

1782-84. Joseph Beck (*q.v.*) collected all of the relevant material (orders, reports, etc.) from Hungarian and Slovakian archives and published it in the appendix of his *Geschichts-Bücher,* pp. 578-634. From these excerpts we also learn that many books were successfully hidden by the Brethren before the coming of the officers. On the other hand a good number of books were not preserved but were simply burned as "heresy" by some parish priests (*Arch. f. Ref.-Gesch.*).

Some 30 codices were kept in the former Jesuit College of Bratislava (Pressburg), now the library of the chapter of the Canons of the Cathedral. Another set of 27 codices was sent to the primate in Esztergom, where these books are still well preserved in the primatial library. Ten more codices came somehow into the library of the University of Budapest, and many more were scattered in various libraries. All in all much more than 100 such codices must have been taken away. The hidden ones came to light almost a century later, and a few even found their way back to the Brethren in America.

The Hutterite collection in Esztergom comprises 5 chronicles (*Denkbüchel, Geschichtsbüchel*), 3 epistle books, 5 hymnbooks (*Liederbüchel*), 12 codices with religious tracts and ordinances, and 2 more books with miscellaneous contents. The chronicles usually run from the beginnings (around 1525) up to 1620, 1668, and even 1694; the epistle books were written in 1574, 1581, and 1601; the hymnals originated in 1637, 1650, etc. Among the 12 codices with a varied content is found a beautiful copy of Riedemann's *Rechenschaft* (*q.v.*) in a small-sized codex of 1614; Andreas Ehrenpreis's great *Sendbrief* of 1652 (very likely the original ms., Cod. No. III, 137); then three codices with the great "Article Book" (*q.v.*) of 1602, 1655, and 1679; and one codex (No. III, 198) with the famous *Gemeindeordnungen* (regulations and ordinances) by Ehrenpreis (*q.v.*), around 1640. Other codices contain most carefully written epistles (from Jakob Hutter up to Andreas Ehrenpreis), a variety of doctrinal tracts, Bible concordances, catechisms, and an "Apocalipsis" (written 1593), and the apocryphal "Testament of the Twelve Patriarchs." One codex contains nothing but the writings of Sebastian Franck (written 1597), and one codex of 1657, called *Weinbüchel,* instructs "how to treat wine when spoiled."

All of these books are beautifully bound in embossed leather, often showing the year and ownership, and locked by brass clasps. They average 300 leaves (some have up to 600), most are octavo size, and are carefully written (occasionally in black and red) on heavy paper. In the introduction to his *Geschichts-Bücher* (XXIII-XXXIII) Beck lists in detail all the codices he used, briefly summarizing their contents. However, the library of Esztergom has many more such books than are listed by Beck, and a complete catalog is still needed. Transcripts of almost all this material are kept in the provincial archives of Brno, Czechoslovakia, known as the "Beck Collection" (see **Beck, Joseph von**).

A description of these books is also found in R. Wolkan, *Die Hutterer* (Vienna, 1918), and in R. Friedmann, "Die Briefe der österreichischen Wieder-

täufer," in *Archiv f. Ref.-Gesch.* XXVI (1929) 40 f. and 166 f. (*ML* II, 156 f.) R.F.

E.T.E.B.O.N. (Eigen Tabak en bollen om niet), a fraternity (corps) of the students of the Mennonite Seminary at Amsterdam, formerly connected with the fraternities of the University of Amsterdam, was founded on May 7, 1814. The association song is the Latin *Patriam Canimus.* Its colors are red, white, and blue—the colors of the Netherlands. Nearly all the ministers of the Dutch Mennonite churches were members of this corps as students. The records of its meetings are written in verse. Admission is bound with certain mysterious ceremonies. Formerly a pilgrimage was made every two years to Hotel de Grebbe at Rhenen on the Rhine. The 25th, 50th, 75th, 80th, 100th, 125th, and 140th anniversaries were celebrated, and *Gedenkschriften* were published on a number of these occasions. At the end of World War I (*ca.* 1918) the E.T.E.B.O.N. broke its connection with the student fraternities, and has lost much of its importance. (*DJ* 1914, 59-68; 1953, 17 f.; *ML* I, 612.) K.V.

Eternal Security, the doctrine that Christians can never apostatize after coming to faith, in Calvinism known as "perseverance of the saints," as a special term was used by Walter Scott (Plymouth Brethren) as early as 1913 (Holness, 186). Under a section heading, "The Eternal Security of the Sheep," he writes, "Can my sins separate me from Christ or break the bond of eternal life? Impossible!" Elsewhere he states, "Eternal life therefore cannot be lost: It is absolutely secure" (Holness, 110). L. S. Chafer, whose Gospel ministry extends back to 1900, does not know when the term came into use; the significance which he attaches to this doctrine is shown by the 100-page treatment given to it in his vast *Systematic Theology.* "Those chosen of God and saved by grace are, of necessity," he holds, "preserved unto the realization of the design of God. . . . The Scriptures could not . . . do other than declare the Christian's security without reservation or complication" (*Systematic Theology* III, 268).

By eternal security of the believer, H. A. Ironside declares, "we mean that once a poor sinner has been regenerated by the Word and the Spirit of God, . . . it is absolutely impossible that that man should ever again be a lost soul" (*Eternal Security,* 6). Other leading advocates of this teaching during the past 50 years have been H. C. Trumbull, C. I. Scofield, and A. W. Pink. Chief among Scriptures alleged in its support are John 5:24; 6:23; 10:27-29; Rom. 8:32-39; I Cor. 3:15; Phil. 1:6; II Tim. 1:12; I Pet. 1:3-5; I John 5:13.

The influence of this teaching upon the Mennonites has not been negligible. While European Mennonites have barely been touched, the teaching has gained some adherents among Mennonite groups in America. In the Mennonite Brethren Church of North America the doctrine had little chance in the past to be generally accepted, but gaining a foothold in 1910-20 the doctrine has more recently had a greater influence with young ministers and students. In general, however, the M.B. group rejects the teaching. In the General Conference Mennonite

Church this doctrine does not represent its established tradition. Since its appearance about 1930, however, sizable groups of adherents are now found in a small percentage of congregations. In the Mennonite Church (MC) this teaching has made small progress excepting in one conference where a private estimate guesses that 25 per cent of the members and 40 per cent of the ministers hold to it.

The teaching is clearly exotic to Mennonite faith, its chief sources in North America being "Fundamentalist" Bible schools and Bible institutes, a few colleges and seminaries, and some independent Bible teachers and periodicals.

While the term "Eternal Security" had its origin early in the 20th century, the idea of unconditional election is as old as Augustine. Sharpened in the hands of Gottshalk of the 9th century the doctrine was strenuously advocated by Zwingli and developed into a logical system by Calvin. Against this predestinarian background with all its implications the Swiss Brethren and Dutch Mennonites had to work. Pilgram Marpeck called predestination a blasphemous doctrine (Horsch, *MQR*, 145), and says that we know of no knowledge of Christ or clarity of claim to eternal life, apart from keeping His commandments and teachings (Wenger, *MQR*, 236). Only by remaining in Christ is one His disciple, and only so does he have a God, says Marpeck.

The Swiss Brethren recognized the possibility of apostasy, of Satan's disturbing the minds of believers in the simplicity of faith (Wenger, *MQR*, 236). They held just as firmly to Christian assurance. "We know, thank God, of the freedom in and through Christ . . ." (Marpeck, 239). "His Holy Spirit . . . will guide us until the end" (Marpeck, 239). Conrad Grebel held that if the believer continues to live in this new life and resolutely separates himself from sin, he may be sure of salvation (Bender, 131). Menno Simons speaks of Zwingli's statement that the sinner is not responsible for his evil deeds as "an abomination above all abominations" (*Opera*, 311a; *Works* II, 294b, quoted by John Horsch, *op. cit.*, 146). That the Swiss Brethren and early Mennonites sensed a responsibility for the spiritual well-being of the membership lest they fall by the way and be lost. That he himself does not believe this Zwinglian doctrine is witnessed by the rigid discipline he exercised and executed in the measures of the ban and avoidance. Obedience of discipleship was held to be necessary for assurance.

The *Eighteen Articles of Faith* drawn up by Mennonite (MC) General Conference in 1921 seek to meet Eternal Security teaching in two of its articles. Article VII, of Assurance, reads: "We believe that it is the privilege of all believers to know that they have passed from death unto life; that God is able to keep them from falling, but that the obedience of faith is essential to the maintenance of one's salvation and growth in grace." Part of Article XIV, of Apostasy, reads: "We believe that the latter days will be characterized by general lawlessness and departure from the faith; . . . that on the part of the church there will be a falling away and 'the love of many shall wax cold.'"

The Bible lays a real foundation for absolute assurance based on God's love (John 3:16; Rom. 8:35-39), His omnipotent keeping power (John 10:38, 39; Jude 24, 25), His eternal purpose and foreordination (Rom. 8:28-30; Eph. 1:4), the efficacy of Christ's sacrifice (Rom. 3:24, 25; Gal. 1:4; 2:20; Eph. 1:7; Heb. 9:11-14; I Pet. 1:18, 19), the saving power of His resurrection (Rom. 4:25; 5:10; I Cor. 15:20-22), His intercession at the right hand of the Father (John 17; Rom. 8:34; Heb. 7:24, 25; I John 2:1), the testimony of the Holy Spirit (Rom. 8:16), the sealing of the Holy Spirit (II Cor. 1:21, 22; Eph. 1:13, 14; 4:30), the present experience of eternal life (John 3:36; I John 5:13), and the sufficiency of His grace (II Cor. 12:9).

In equally clear language believers are admonished to faithfulness (Matt. 24:24-51; 25:21-30; Rom. 1:17; Rev. 2:10) and warned against apostasy (Mark 24:11-13; I Tim. 4:1; II Pet. 2:2). The entire Epistle to the Galatians is directed to Christians who were removing from Him who called them unto a different Gospel (1:6; 5:4) and enjoins a return to faith in Christ. In like manner the practical purpose of the Epistle to the Hebrews is the re-entrenchment of faith. The lengthy cumulative warnings pointed up in such unequivocal statements as in 2:1; 3:6, 12, 14; 4:11, 14; 6:4-6; 10:26-31; and 12:25 can be understood only in terms of the possibility of final apostasy of those who had once been regenerated. In similar strain the warnings to the Seven Churches of Asia must be understood in the light of the doubtful issue of the conditional clause, "Except thou repent," of Rev. 2:5, 22 (see also 3:3).

The divine purpose of God to save us does not invalidate genuine human responsibility of faithfulness and obedience. The matchless benediction of Jude 24, 25 is not incompatible with the awful warning of Heb. 10:26-31. (See **Free Will**.)

C.K.L.

A. Holness, *Selections from Our Fifty Years Written Ministry* (London, 1913); L. S. Chafer, *Systematic Theology III* (Dallas, 1947); H. A. Ironside, *The Eternal Security of the Believer* (New York, 1934); John Horsch, "The Faith of the Swiss Brethren," *MQR* V (1931) 145; J. C. Wenger, "The Theology of Pilgram Marpeck," *MQR* XII (1938); H. S. Bender, "Conrad Grebel's Theology," *MQR* XII (1938) 131.

Etliche schöne Christliche Geseng *wie sie in der Gefengkniss zu Passaw im Schloss von dem Schweitzer Brüdern durch Gottes gnad geticht vnd gesungen worden,* a collection of 52 hymns published in 1564 (n.p.). It was published in a second edition in 1583 with the title, *Etliche sehr schone Christliche Gesenge, wie dieselbigen zu Passaw, von den Schweitzerbrüdern, in der Gefengnuss im Schloss, durch Gottes gnad gedicht vnd gesungen worden.* This edition was combined as part two with a first part bearing the title *Ausbund Etlicher schöner Christlicher Geseng, wie die in der Gefengnuss zu Passaw im Schloss von den Schweitzern und auch von andern rechtgläubigen Christen hin und her gedicht worden.* A 1622 reprint is identical with the 1583 edition. The next undated edition (17th century) is the first to combine the two parts into an integrated whole. The Goshen College Library has copies of all the above editions except the one of 1622, the 1564 copy being a unicum. Two hymns of the first edition (1564) were omitted in the second, viz., No. III, Lobt den Herren ir Heyden all, and No. XVII, Wir schreyen zu dir Herre Gott. The second edition (1583) added one hymn, viz., No. LIII, O Herr nit stoltz ist mein hertz doch. Thus the first edition had 52 hymns, and the second 51. Most of the hymns are anonymous; but 12 of them, signed with the initials "H.B.," were written by Hans Betz (as Wolkan proved, not Hans Büchel as Wackernagel surmised). (Wolkan, *Lieder,* 26-43, 118-20; see **Ausbund.**)   **H.S.B.**

Ettingerbrunn, former name of Busau-Aktatchi (*q.v.*).

Ettingerbrunn Mennonite Church: see **Busau** Mennonite Church.

Etupes: see **Exincourt.**

Eugene Mennonite Church (MC), now extinct, was located approximately 11 miles west of Eugene, Ore., in the 1890's. It was founded by Amish families who came to the Eugene area from Hubbard, where they had settled about 1887. During the early years two Sunday schools were organized in this region, the one about 6 miles west of Eugene having at one time an attendance of approximately 50. Several years later the church was built and Peter Mishler was ordained bishop. Following his death, his brother J. D. Mishler was ordained bishop in 1895. Because of church difficulties and because land in other Oregon communities was preferred, the families moved away and by 1950 only one remained in the neighborhood. The church was sold and the money was used for the construction of the Hopewell Mennonite Church, near Hubbard, which was built in 1901-2.   **M.G.**
S. G. Shetler, *Church History of the Pacific Coast Mennonite Conference District* (Scottdale, 1931?).

Eureka, Ill., a town of 1,500 inhabitants, the county seat of Woodford County. It is the home of Eureka College, a school of the Christian denomination, and of the Mennonite (MC) Home for the Aged. Between Eureka and Roanoke, some miles to the northeast, is located the Roanoke (*q.v.*) Mennonite Church (MC). A few miles north of Eureka is the Metamora (*q.v.*) Mennonite Church (MC). The village claims to be the "Pumpkin Center of the World."   **C.H.S.**

Europäische Mennonitische Bibelschule (*Ecole Biblique Européenne*), opened at Arnold Böcklinstrasse 11, Basel, Switzerland, at that time the MCC European headquarters office, was founded on the initiative of Harold S. Bender on March 20, 1950. Members of the school board at the founding were: Hans Nussbaumer, France; Christian Schnebele, Germany; Pierre Widmer, France; Samuel Gerber, Switzerland; C. F. Klassen, Canada-Germany; and the current MCC director of Europe. Later it was decided to elect on the school board two representatives from each of the supporting conferences. These conferences are the Pfälzisch-Hessische Conference, Gemeindeverband, Swiss Conference, Alsatian Conference, and the French Conference. The president of the board since its beginning has been Hans Nuss-

baumer, Schweighof, France. Samuel Gerber of Les Reussilles, Switzerland, was director of this school 1950-52, Cornelius Wall of Mountain Lake, Minn., since 1952. The MCC helped in many respects to start and operate this school. Since students from all over Europe attend the school, courses are conducted in French and German. There were *ca.* 60 students in 1955. Originally the term of the Bible school was 4 weeks; in 1955 it was extended to 10 weeks. It is hoped to extend the term to 12 weeks in the winter, and add a short summer term. The school was moved to Starenstrasse 41 in Basel in 1953, when the MCC headquarters was moved to that address. The purpose of the school is to acquaint young people with the Word of God and to train them as Sunday-school teachers, youth workers, and for other church service. (See **Basel,** *ME* I, 245 f.)†   **L.W.**

Europe. It must be said at the outset that in spite of basic unity on all major points of faith and life (barring the revolutionary and radical fringe elements) the Anabaptist-Mennonite movement in Europe has never been a fully unified movement or church. Politic-cultural and language barriers, among other things, have prevented this. Apart from a very small French movement in French Flanders and an elusive English movement, the Anabaptist movement was wholly Teutonic, but composed of two German-speaking parts and one Dutch-speaking part: (1) the Swiss-South German founded in 1525, (2) the Hutterite group in Moravia founded in 1528, essentially the communistic wing of the first group, and (3) the Dutch-speaking Dutch-North German-West Prussian group, begun in 1530. (There was also for a time a Middle German-Middle Rhine branch of the Swiss-South German group, but this did not survive the first half-century.) The rapid spread of the movement is most remarkable. Beginning in January 1525 in Zürich, by 1535 the entire Teutonic block of Western Europe had been covered. An approximate circumference line would run Chur, Gratz, Brno, Königsberg, Leeuwarden, Ypres, Strasbourg, Basel, Chur.

This article will trace the general history of the above three groups from an over-all European perspective, leaving the detailed story for the national articles—**Austria, Belgium, England, France, Germany, Moravia, Netherlands, Poland, Russia, Switzerland,** and for other articles on provinces and regions. The following outline will be used:

1. 1525-1648, *General Anabaptist History and Group Interrelations;*
2. 1648-1918, *General Mennonite History, Group Interrelations, Inner-European Migrations, Emigration to North America, Developments in Theology and Piety;*
3. 1918-56, *Post-World War I Developments and Current Situation.*

1. *1525-1648, General Anabaptist History and Group Interrelations.* From the beginning Anabaptism was a proscribed movement, with the imperial mandate of 1529 (Speyer) calling for universal extermination. Apart from early transient and partial

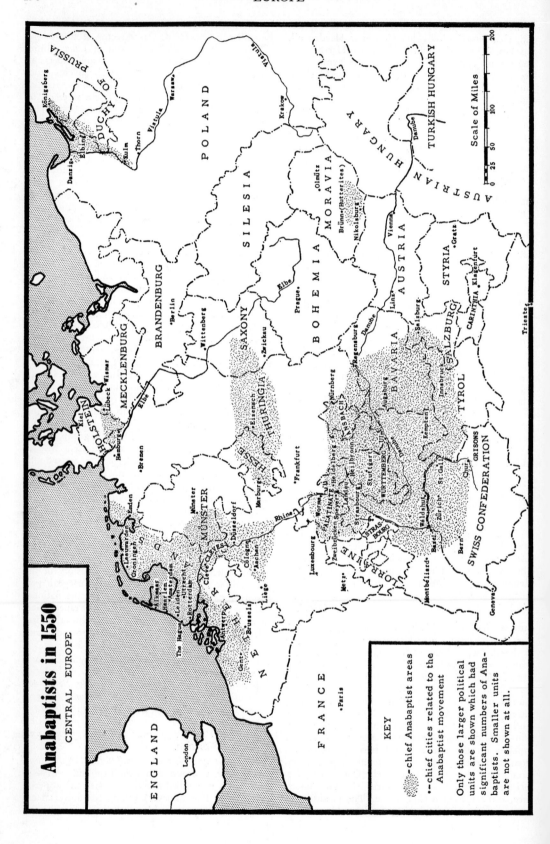

Anabaptists in 1550
CENTRAL EUROPE

KEY

- chief Anabaptist areas

• chief cities related to the Anabaptist movement

Only those larger political units are shown which had significant numbers of Anabaptists. Smaller units are not shown at all.

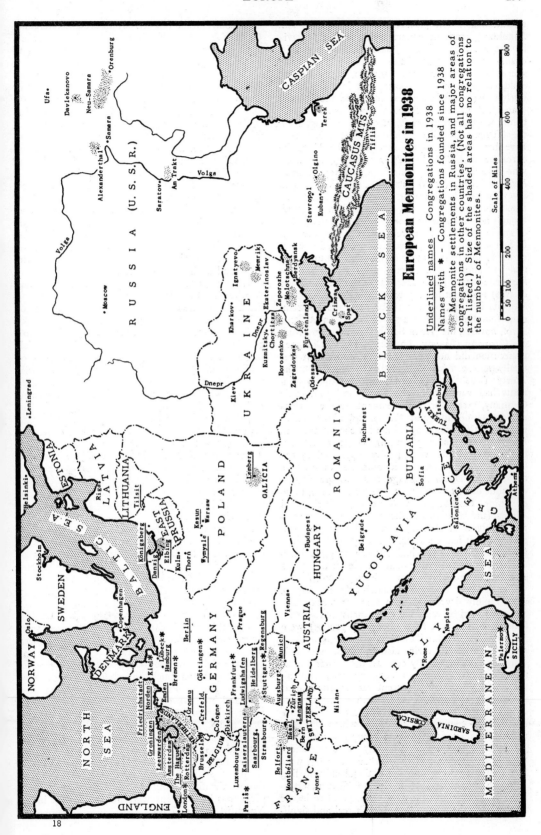

European Mennonites in 1938

Underlined names – Congregations in 1938
Names with ✳ – Congregations founded since 1938
Mennonite settlements in Russia, and major areas of congregations in other countries. (Not all congregations are listed.) Size of the shaded areas has no relation to the number of Mennonites.

toleration at a few places such as Strasbourg and Nikolsburg, and the general toleration in Moravia by the nobility until the Jesuit reaction began its deadly work (1592), to be an Anabaptist was to be a criminal subject to arrest, torture, imprisonment, exile, confiscation of property, and in most larger territories (except Hesse) execution. In the first ten years, 1525-35, several thousand were executed, and before the last execution (Zürich, Switzerland, 1614, the Netherlands 1574, Belgium 1594) there must have been at least 5,000 martyrs. The Hutterite chronicle as of 1540 lists 2,147 brothers and sisters who gave their life for their faith, and van Braght's *Martyrs' Mirror* (1660) lists 2,500. The MENNONITE ENCYCLOPEDIA has name articles for over 2,000 martyrs. Toleration came first in Holland, about 1572, though not complete at once, and by 1600 the period of severe persecution was really past in that country. In Switzerland severe persecution continued (canton of Bern) until the middle of the 18th century, and real toleration did not come until 1815. For the Hutterites heavy persecution (after the initial decade or two) really set in only with their expulsion from Moravia in 1592, but continued until the last remnant found refuge in Russia in 1770. In Austria, Tirol, Bavaria, the rest of South Germany, and Middle Germany (Saxony, Thuringia, Hesse, Cologne) persecution did not cease until the movement was totally destroyed (*ca.* 1580-1600). By the time of the Thirty Years' War (1618-48) all Anabaptist remnants had vanished in the South and in Middle Germany, except for small remnants in the cantons of Bern (Emmental and Thun) and Zürich (Horgen) and the struggling Hutterite communities in Hungary. The once promising Westphalian Anabaptist communities were finally suppressed by the Counter Reformation. On the other hand the movement in the Dutch language area was growing at that time almost everywhere: the Netherlands, Lower Rhine, East Friesland, Schleswig-Holstein, and Altona (the latter two settlements founded by refugee immigration 1600-50) except in Catholic Flanders where it had been wiped out by 1630, and in a few areas where it still had a severe struggle. Likewise the important settlements in the Vistula Delta area (Danzig-Elbing, Culm-Thorn, Königsberg), which had been founded by Dutch refugees 1535-60, were rapidly developing into a major block. The Swiss, Hutterites, and West Prussians (except the Danzig, Elbing, and Königsberg city groups) were all rural and destined to remain so almost exclusively throughout their history, including their daughter settlements. By contrast the Lower Rhine, most Northwest German congregations, and all the Dutch Mennonites (except certain rural areas in Groningen, Friesland, and North Holland) were solidly urban, already manifesting some of the industrial and commercial enterprise which was later to be so characteristic of these groups. Only in the Netherlands, because of relatively early toleration, their large number, and their urban character, were Mennonites entering into the national cultural life, although this came also in Crefeld, Emden, Hamburg, and Danzig in the next century. Here in the Netherlands the Mennonites made a real and signif-

icant contribution (1600-1700) in art and literature (Golden Age) as well as in medicine; they also were often leaders in trade and banking, navigation, and whale fishing.

During this period the three major groups listed earlier remained relatively distinct, with little intergroup contact. The Hutterites viewed the Swiss, Dutch, and Prussians as lacking true Christian principles in not adopting the communal way of life, and at times indulged in vigorous polemics against them, although on at least one occasion (Frankenthal, 1571) they joined with the Swiss in a disputation against the state church leaders. The language barrier kept the Swiss-South Germans and Dutch apart. Menno Simons was not translated into German until 1575, and then only the *Foundation-Book*. A "short Menno" appeared in 1754, but Menno's complete works were never translated in Europe. Dirk Philips was translated into German in part in 1611, but no other Dutch Mennonite writings at all until the next period.

An attempt to draw the Swiss and Dutch closer together in the mid-16th century was frustrated by the intransigence of the Dutch (Wismar articles of 1554 and Menno's writings against Zylis and Lemke of 1559) on the two points of shunning and Menno's peculiar doctrine of the Incarnation, neither of which the Swiss could accept (Strasbourg conferences of 1555 and 1557). The Dutch actually put the Swiss under the ban about this time. Only a century later (1660 ff.) when the severe need of the persecuted Swiss touched the brotherly love of the Dutch, and the latter had somewhat relaxed their severity, did the situation change. There was a High German group (Swiss-South German refugees and influence in the region of Cologne) who came into closer fellowship with certain Dutch elements and actually joined in several Dutch "unity" confessions of faith (Concept of Cologne in 1591, High German confession of Jan Cents, *q.v.,* in 1630, Dordrecht Confession in 1632).

During this period the relations of the Dutch with the North German and Vistula congregations were very close. The latter were composed largely of refugees from the Netherlands (Friesland) and Flanders, and maintained the Dutch language in family and church life (first German preaching in Hamburg 1786, in Danzig 1760's, and first German publication a 1660 confession of faith at Danzig). During this period and for another hundred years Amsterdam remained the mother of the eastern churches in more ways than one.

At the end of this period the distribution of Mennonite population (including children) might have been as follows: the Netherlands (including East Friesland and Lower Rhine) 140,000; Switzerland 1,000; Schleswig Holstein-Hamburg 1,500; Vistula Delta and Königsberg 5,000; Hutterites 5,000; a total of over 150,000. Without unbaptized children the baptized members hardly exceeded 75,000. (No list of congregations, ministers, or members is available at all before the Dutch *Naamlijst* of 1731, and no thorough statistics until the late 19th century. Congregations in Germany were not on this list in the *Naamlijst* before 1766.)

During this period the original Anabaptist heritage of faith and life was maintained relatively intact. There was a loss of the sense of mission and consequent development of introversion, but the original concept of the church as a brotherhood of believers separated from the world and maintained pure by discipline was staunchly maintained, together with nonconformity to the world, nonresistance, nonswearing of oaths, simplicity of costume and manner of life. Theologically the only minor changes were those due to Socinian and Collegiant influences in the Netherlands. The serious major divisions (1565-80) in the Netherlands and in the North German and Vistula congregations persisted, particularly the Flemish and Frisian (the Waterlander in Holland only). Mennonite literature flourished in the Netherlands, but nowhere else. Hans de Ries, P. J. Twisck, Lubbert Gerritsz, and J. P. Schabalje ranked with the best in Dutch Christian literature, and the Mennonite Biestkens Bible had reached a peak of popularity with over 100 editions of the whole Bible or New Testament in 1560-1648. The Swiss had their *Ausbund* hymnbook and Froschauer Bible (not originally Mennonite) reprints, but little else. The Hutterites had their extraordinary manuscript chronicles, epistles, theological treatises, and confessions, but only two printed books, Riedemann's *Rechenschaft* of 1545 and Ehrenpreis' *Sendbrief* of 1652.

2. *Developments 1648-1918.* This period witnessed a series of migrations of prime significance. From 1650 to 1750 a considerable number of Swiss (from Zürich and Bern) migrated to Alsace, the Palatinate, and Baden, and after 1709 to Pennsylvania (joined by numerous Palatine immigrants), with a smaller contingent settling in Groningen in Holland, and another group transferring from inner Bern to the Jura territory and Basel. Emigration from the Netherlands ceased altogether, except for the tiny group of 1853 from Balk to Indiana, which is now extinct. There are no Dutch Mennonite colonies; in fact the Dutch Mennonite population declined so greatly (to 30,000 by 1800) as to forebode extinction. A few of Dutch extraction came to Pennsylvania 1683-1710 from the Lower Rhine region and Hamburg. A small group of Palatines and Alsatians also settled in Galicia 1780 ff.

But the major migration was from the overcrowded, restricted Vistula Delta region, whence in 1788-1840 some 10,000 souls went to the Ukraine (a few in 1853 to Samara) to establish the great Mennonite body in Russia, which by 1914 had reached 100,000 souls with some 30 distinct settlements, including the Caucasus, Crimea, Volga area, Orenburg, and Ufa, Western Siberia, and Turkestan. This growth was in spite of the loss of one third of the Russian Mennonite population (18,000) by emigration to the prairie states and provinces of the United States and Canada in 1873-80. Smaller settlements of Vistula Mennonites had also been made in inner Poland (near Warsaw) and Volhynia (both Russian after the Congress of Vienna in 1815).

Another notable migration was the post-Napoleonic (1817-50) emigration of several thousand Swiss, Alsatian, and South German (also some Galician and Hessian) Mennonites to the North Central States (western Pennsylvania, Ohio, Indiana, Illinois), Iowa, and Ontario.

In this period there were two serious divisions with permanent consequences. The first was the Amish schism of 1693-97, which permanently split the Swiss-South German group in half, and which is still perpetuated in North America though now fully overcome in Europe. The second was the Mennonite Brethren schism in the Ukraine in 1860 ff., which ultimately won about one fourth of the Russian Mennonites (25,000 souls in Russia by 1914) and has been perpetuated in North and South America. The smaller divisions include the immersionist Dompelaers in Hamburg 1648, extinct by 1676; the Kleine Gemeinde in the Ukraine in 1812, with its sub-schism of 1862 the Krimmer Mennonite Brethren, both perpetuated exclusively in North America as very small groups; the further small Russian divisions, now practically all extinct, the Jerusalemsfreunde (1866), the Apostolic Brethren (*Brotbrecher*) (1890), Allianzgemeinde (1905); and the Hahnische Mennonites in Baden in 1868, still existing there in three small congregations. Also to be noted is the Neu-Täufer division of 1835 in the Emmental (half from the Reformed Church, also called Fröhlichianer after their leader Samuel Fröhlich) existing today in moderate numbers both in central Europe (Switzerland and South Germany), where they are called *Evangelische Taufgesinnte*, and in the central United States, where they are called Apostolic Christians. The older Dutch divisions were completely healed, together with the newer division of Lamists vs. Zonists (1664-1801), in the A.D.S. (General Mennonite Conference) of 1811, although the Flemish-Frisian division persisted in superficial form in West Prussia and Russia until into the 20th century.

The first century of this period was marked by the closest relations that have ever developed between the Dutch and Swiss-South German groups. The severe persecution by the Bernese government brought vigorous though ineffective political intervention by the Dutch Mennonites, while the physical suffering of the Swiss and the Palatines in this time brought generous financial aid from the Dutch for a very long period of time (1650-1750) through the noted Commission for Foreign Needs. This commission helped also in emigration, assisting some Swiss to settle permanently in Groningen (1710 ff.), where they have been completely assimilated, and many more Swiss and Palatines to emigrate to Pennsylvania 1710-50. A similar attempt to resettle Tilsit-Memel Mennonites in Holland (1732) miscarried.

During this first century of the period also the relations between the Netherlands, North Germany, and West Prussia remained close, even down to Napoleonic times, with considerable translation of Dutch Mennonite literature into German (confessions, catechism, sermons), as well as the maintenance of the Dutch language in preaching until late in the 18th century. Later with the rise of nationalism, particularly in Germany with the rise of Prussia and the formation of the German Empire in 1870, international relationships among European

Mennonites declined noticeably, except between the West Prussians and the Russians and the Dutch and Northwest Germans. Alsace-Lorraine being a part of Germany 1870-1918, the French Mennonites were badly divided during this time, but the Alsatian Mennonites at the same time were strongly oriented toward the South Germans, especially the Baden group. The growing sense of German unity in turn finally overcame the century-old distance between the Northwest Germans, the West Prussians, and the South Germans, though slowly. The *Mennonitische Blätter,* founded in 1854 as an all-German periodical, the first Mennonite church paper in Europe and the only one for another generation (*Gemeindeblatt,* Baden 1870; *Zondagsbode,* Netherlands 1887; *Zionspilger,* Switzerland 1882; *Mennonitisches Gemeindeblatt,* Galicia 1912; *Botschafter,* Russia 1905-14; *Unser Blatt,* Russia 1922-26; *Friedensstimme,* a private venture in Russia, 1905). The attempted Vereinigung of Mennonite Churches in Germany (1886-   ) was only partly successful, since most of the West Prussians, all of the Badischer Verband, and part of the Palatinate-Hesse churches stayed outside.

A serious twofold block to closer fellowship between the Dutch Mennonites and the remaining Mennonites of Europe during this period was the differing theological and ecclesiastical development as between the Netherlands and the rest of Europe. Liberal theology came into the Dutch churches in the second half of the 19th century and by 1870 had nearly completely captured Dutch Mennonitism, together with East Friesland and Crefeld. Along with this came the surrender of nonresistance and nonconformity rather completely, as well as a complete shift from a lay ministry to a trained and salaried ministry (this latter change had begun already in 1735 with the founding of the seminary at Amsterdam). Everywhere else in Europe, except in the German city churches where liberalism also made inroads in the 20th century, the chief new influence was pietistic. The West Prussian, South German, Swiss, French, and Russian churches either remained traditional and relatively inert, or became pietistic (especially Hamburg, Palatinate, Baden). These groups also retained nonresistance longer (Germans fully to 1870 and partly to 1914, Russians to the end, Swiss partly to the present time, French not after 1815), also a degree of nonconformity combined with a rural culture, and (except in the German city churches and the Palatinate) kept the lay ministry. Pietism also found an echo in the Netherlands in the 18th century (J. Deknatel of Amsterdam) and later a similar influence, the *Reveil* (Isaac da Costa of Amsterdam) in the 19th century.

At the same time, in the course of the 19th and 20th centuries all the European Mennonite groups (the Swiss last, and the Russians scarcely at all since they developed their own German-Mennonite culture) became increasingly nationalized and assimilated into their national life and culture, losing largely their sense of separation and acquiring a political interest. Particularly was this the case in the urban groups. Ernst Crous has vividly described this process in Germany in his essay, "How the Men-

nonites of Germany Grew to Be a Part of the Nation." No Dutch Mennonite would have thought of writing such a comparable essay for the Netherlands, because that assimilation had taken place two centuries earlier and the Dutch Mennonites occupied in a sense an elite status in Holland. And in Russia the Mennonites were proud to have remained distinct from the Slavic culture of the nation as an autonomous German-Mennonite culture group; those Russian Mennonites who became interested in a rapprochement with the Russian culture were usually under suspicion and often criticized.

It is remarkable that only the Russian Mennonites developed their own church educational program (they in a sense had to, of course, to survive). The Dutch vigorously object to church schools even today, and have never developed a full school of any sort, not even a full theological faculty. The attempt at a German Mennonite high school at Weierhof in the Palatinate (1805 ff.), while educationally successful was a relative failure as a church school because of the small Mennonite patronage. A weak and late attempt in West Prussia died in birth, although there had been some elementary schools in certain West Prussian communities in the 17th-19th centuries. The German-speaking Jura Mennonites, living as a German-language island in a French culture area, have maintained a series of Mennonite elementary schools for a century, latterly with state financial aid.

The 19th century was marked also by a noteworthy development of the regional conference system, Switzerland 1780, Dutch A.D.S. 1811, West Prussia 1830, Baden 1848, Palatinate-Hessen 1870, South German 1884, Mennonite Brethren in Russia 1876, Mennonite Church in Russia 1880, Alsace 1905, French-speaking 1905. While the autonomy of the local congregation was largely retained (except in the Badischer Verband where the conference had complete centralized control over the local churches) the conference inevitably began to influence the local churches toward more uniformity and more alertness and activity.

A noteworthy development in the 19th century was the rise of foreign mission interest, although home missions and evangelism remained either totally undeveloped or quite rudimentary. Through Baptist influence the foreign mission cause came to be supported in the Palatinate (1820 ff.), in Holland (1830 ff.), and in West Prussia (1830 ff.). When the Dutch Mennonite mission board was organized in 1847 (work in Java began in 1851) it found considerable support in West Prussia and Hamburg, also some in the Palatinate, and in South Russia whence it drew much of its support and most of its few missionaries until 1914.

Except for the Netherlands there was a remarkable paucity of Mennonite literature in Europe throughout this period. This might be expected from the largely uneducated and rural groups such as Switzerland, France, Baden, and West Prussia. Even in the German city churches with their trained ministers little was produced, except in Hamburg and Emden. The same is true for the Palatinate. Even in Russia the literary output was noticeably small down to the very last. Perhaps the Mennonites were too much assimilated to other thinking, some to Pietism, some (the trained clergy) to the current liberal or orthodox theology of the main trends in European life. In some cases of course the constituency was too small to support the publication of literature. In Russia preoccupation with the problem of colonization no doubt played a role. Dutch Mennonites published relatively much all through this period. Four major Mennonite areas developed their own hymnbooks, confessions, and catechisms: Holland, West Prussia, Russia, and South Germany, but no church publishing house ever developed among the Mennonites of Russia. Mennonite population remained relatively static in Germany, France, and Switzerland during the 19th and 20th centuries, doubled in the Netherlands 1815-1918, and multiplied tenfold in Russia.

3. *1918-56; Developments since World War I.* The two serious world wars (1914-18 and 1940-45), together with the rise of Communism in Russia, have had decisive effects on Mennonitism in Europe. The repeated German attacks on France in 1870, 1914, and 1940 seriously alienated the French and Swiss Mennonites from the Germans, though brotherly good will has in part overcome this. The rise and temporary rule of Nazism (1933-45) together with the German attack on the Netherlands caused even more serious alienation between the Dutch and the Germans. World War I between Germany and Russia brought a serious strain on the German-oriented Mennonites in Russia. The defeat of Germany in 1918 returned Alsace to France but ruptured the growing fellowship of Alsatians and Germans. The defeat of Germany in 1945 resulted in the destruction of the age-old Mennonite settlements in inner Poland and Galicia, also making the condition of the German-speaking Mennonites in Russia almost intolerable. About 35,000 Russian Mennonites, mostly of the Chortitza settlement, were able to escape in 1943-45 with the retreating German army and some 12,000 were ultimately resettled in Paraguay and Canada, the rest being recaptured and returned forcibly to Russia.

However, the most important development in this period was the practical destruction of Mennonitism in Russia as a consequence of the Russian Revolution and the establishment of atheistic communism as the ruling force in Soviet Russia. The Mennonites did not revolt by force against this development, but being unable spiritually to accept it, they resisted communization. This made them *de facto* enemies of the Communist state, and Stalin's measures to liquidate the peasant resistance to collectivization in 1927-34 hit the Mennonites very hard. Had it not been for the decision of some 21,000 to emigrate to Canada (1922-25), partly because of the great famine and disorder of 1918-20, and the escape of some 4,000 in 1929-30, the losses would have been still greater. Statistics are impossible, but it is clear that most of the Mennonite settlements in Russia no longer exist, at least with any large number of Mennonite families. Mennonite church life became practically extinct in that land by 1935, although there was sufficient private and family religion left to make pos-

sible a brief reinstitution of church life in the Ukraine in 1941-43, especially in Chortitza during the German occupation. The Siberian settlements suffered the least, and there was actually a new settlement established on the Manchurian Amur border 1926-30, which, however, was almost extinguished, largely by mass flight, in 1930-31.

Noteworthy developments have taken place in inter-Mennonite relations since 1918. One is the Mennonite World Conference, held in Basel in 1925, Danzig in 1930, Amsterdam in 1936, Goshen and Newton (United States) in 1948, Basel again in 1952. Another was the great relief work in the Russian famine (1920-22) largely by the American Mennonites, but also in part by Dutch Mennonites. (German Mennonites cared for several hundred who were stranded for a time in Germany, e.g., at Lechfeld, *q.v.*, and in Mecklenburg.) A third was the extensive relief work of the American Mennonites (MCC) in Western Europe, including all Mennonite areas except Russia, 1945- .

Finally mention must be made of the highly significant migrations of Russian Mennonites to Canada (1) in 1922-25 and 1930, and (2) 1947-52 which have vitally affected Canadian Mennonitism, and the similar substantial Russian settlements in 1930-32 in Brazil and Paraguay, also in 1947-50 in Paraguay again. The last movement of migration was of small groups of Danzig-West Prussian Mennonites to Uruguay 1950-52 and a few to Canada.

One of the historic tragedies of Mennonite history, though not as extensive as the tribulation and suppression in Russia, was the total destruction of the 400-year-old Mennonite community in West Prussia-Danzig in 1945 as a result of the German defeat by Russia and the Polish reoccupation of the Vistula Delta (Russia taking over the Königsberg corner). About three fourths (9,000) of the West Prussians survived as refugees and are now relocated as follows: 1,000 in Uruguay, 300 in Canada, 8,000 in West Germany, with a rather compact block of about 1,000 in the Palatinate.

A theological trend worth noting since 1910 is the substantial decline of liberalism in Holland and Northwest Germany during this period, paralleling the decline of liberalism in European Protestantism in general, and the resurgence of an evangelical theological emphasis.

The present distribution of Mennonite baptized membership in Europe is as follows: Netherlands 41,000, Germany 8,000, France 3,000, Switzerland 1,500, total (without Russia) 53,500. (*ML* I, 614 f.)

H.S.B.

European Mennonite Evangelization Committee: see **EMEK.**

Eusebius of Caesarea (266-340) was bishop of Caesarea in Palestine, one of the leading men at the Council of Nicea and the favorite theologian of Constantine the Great, conspicuous for his great learning. His fame rests on his *Ecclesiastical History* from the apostolic times to A.D. 324. Today it is our chief source for the early church, being very comprehensive and beyond doubt reliable. Eusebius lived through the last (and worst) persecution of the Christians under Emperor Diocletian (around 300). This experience prompted him to collect the stories not only of the martyrs of his time but of all Christian martyrs since the beginning. This "Collection of Martyrdoms" was then extensively used in his great church history which was leading up just to the time of the Council of Nicea (which to most left-wing Christian groups later meant the turning point, the downfall of the Christian Church). It is most likely that it was these records of martyrdom which so strongly appealed to the Anabaptists who read in them a confirmation of their own way, the way of the "suffering church." That might account for the fact that Eusebius' church history is so frequently used as a reference in Anabaptist tracts. This is particularly true for Hutterite devotional, doctrinal, and church historical tracts found in their numerous codices. Eusebius' great popularity among Anabaptists can be inferred from the hymn (*Lieder der Hutterischen Brüder*, pp. 669-75) entitled, "Ein schönes Lied von den Aposteln und Heiligen Märtyrern, aus Eusebius auf das Kürzeste gezogen und gesangsweis verfasst" (1567, not 1570 as in the *Liederbuch*). This hymn has 57 stanzas and was possibly composed by one Christoph Scheffmann, who wrote several hymns of this kind.

The question as to where the Brethren got their knowledge of Eusebius is not yet solved. Humanists, of course, and Catholic scholars, knew the book as it was written in Latin. But among the Anabaptists very few ever mastered this language (a few converted priests in the earliest period, also Thomas of Imbroich, and a few more) and they hardly translated the book for their group. The main source then seems to have been the various works by Sebastian Franck (e.g., his *Chronica,* 1531) which were widely read among the Hutterian Brethren and represent the link between Anabaptism and Humanism. Balthasar Hubmaier may also have been instrumental, since he was very learned and widely read. Finally one might assume that pamphlets circulated among the Brethren with excerpts from Eusebius in translation, edited by free-lance scholars of the early 16th century who sympathized with nonconformist movements. Hutterite codices contain many historical references (even an entire sermon by John Chrysostom of the 4th century) which all point to such little-noticed sources of popular education.

R.F.

R. Friedmann, "Eine dogmatische Hauptschrift . . . ," in *Arch. für Ref.-Gesch.* XXVIII (1931) 233-40.

Eussestal (Eysestal), a parish of Germersheim, Baden, Germany, the location of the Eussestal monastery. Here and on the estates of Breitwieserhof, Hilspach, Stadtwies, Laubenwald, Oberbergerwies, and Lautertal, Swiss Mennonites had settled by the 1720's. A 1720 directory of Schafsweiden mentions the name Wohlgemuth. In 1724 the Germersheim lists name "four poor Anabaptists, who are temporary renters." One, named Bauer, was the monastery miller. In the course of the 18th century these names occur:

Schneider, Zuber, Herzler, Müller, Gingerich, Christmann, Eschelberger, and Draxel (records of the Palatinate, *Generallandesarchiv* at Karlsruhe). (*ML* I, 615.)   E.H.C.

Eva Pieters, widow of Gheeraert Listync, an Anabaptist martyr, was born in Alkmaar, Dutch province of North Holland; she was baptized in Münster in Westphalia while the city was besieged by the bishop's army. When the city was taken on July 25, 1535, she succeeded in escaping to the Netherlands, where she was taken prisoner, but saved her life by renouncing her faith. She then went to Belgium and joined the Anabaptist congregation at Brugge (*q.v.*). Since there were no traces of Münsterism in this congregation, it may be assumed that she had given up all Münsterite ideas. When she was seized she remained steadfast and loyally sacrificed her body for the sake of Christ. On Aug. 20, 1538, she was burned at the stake in Brugge together with Josyne Schricx (*q.v.*). (Verheyden, *Brugge,* 32, No. 6.)   vDZ.

Evangel United Missionary Church, Kitchener, Ont., was organized in October 1949, and dedicated its meetinghouse on Sept. 24, 1950; it had a membership of 31 in 1951.

Evangelical Mennonite, the official organ of the Conference of Evangelical Mennonites. Its first number was dated July 15, 1953. It replaces *Zion's Tidings* and *Gospel Tidings.* It is a monthly periodical of 24 pages, 9 x 12 in., published at Berne, Ind. Its purpose is to promote the cause of the Conference of Evangelical Mennonites. The Commission on Promotion is responsible for its publishing. In 1954 E. G. Steiner was the editor, C. A. Classen associate editor, and E. E. Zimmerman executive manager. It had a circulation of approximately 2,200.   E.G.St.

Evangelical Mennonite Brethren. The Evangelical Mennonite Brethren Conference was organized Oct. 14, 1889, under the name Conference of United Mennonite Brethren in North America, the first session being held at Mountain Lake, Minn. Later this name was changed to Defenseless Mennonite Brethren of Christ in North America. In 1937 the present name was adopted. For a time many of the congregations used the name "Brudertaler," probably under the influence of the Mountain Lake founding church, and the Conference was popularly called the "Brudertaler" Conference. The Ebenezer Church at Henderson, Neb. (separating from the Bethesda Church), under the leadership of Elder Isaac Peters, and the Brudertaler Church at Mountain Lake, led by Elder Aaron Wall, were the first churches organized. Wall's following was about one third of the Mountain Lake Mennonite community; the other part organized to form two churches, Bergfeld and Bethel. The churches from which Peters and Wall separated later joined the General Conference Mennonite Church. The ground given by Peters and Wall for separation was the need of (1) the new birth and changed life as a requirement for baptism and church membership; (2) a separated walk as

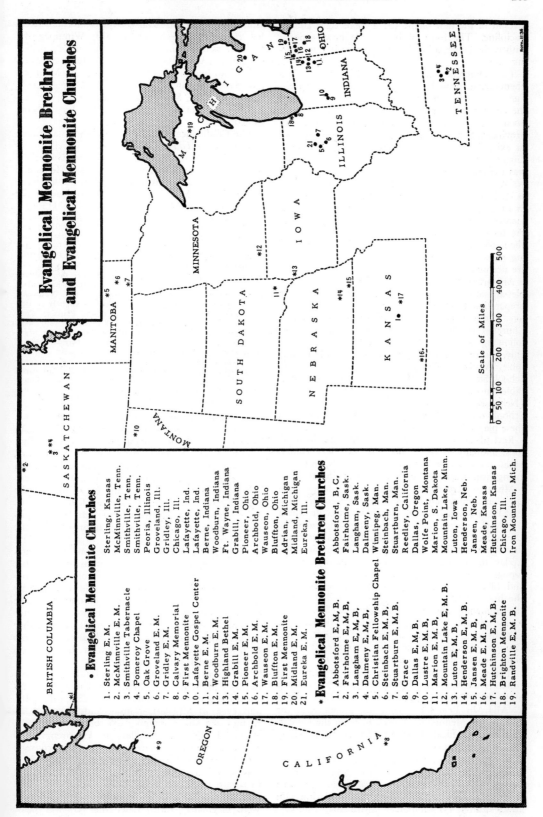

Evangelical Mennonite Brethren and Evangelical Mennonite Churches

● **Evangelical Mennonite Churches**

1. Sterling E. M. — Sterling, Kansas
2. McMinnville E. M. — McMinnville, Tenn.
3. Smithville Tabernacle — Smithville, Tenn.
4. Pomeroy Chapel — Smithville, Tenn.
5. Oak Grove — Peoria, Illinois
6. Groveland E. M. — Groveland, Ill.
7. Gridley E. M. — Gridley, Ill.
8. Calvary Memorial — Chicago, Ill.
9. First Mennonite — Lafayette, Ind.
10. Lafayette Gospel Center — Lafayette, Ind.
11. Berne E. M. — Berne, Indiana
12. Woodburn E. M. — Woodburn, Indiana
13. Highland Bethel — Ft. Wayne, Indiana
14. Grabill E. M. — Grabill, Indiana
15. Pioneer E. M. — Pioneer, Ohio
16. Archbold E. M. — Archbold, Ohio
17. Wauseon E. M. — Wauseon, Ohio
18. Bluffton E. M. — Bluffton, Ohio
19. First Mennonite — Adrian, Michigan
20. Midland E. M. — Midland, Michigan
21. Eureka E. M. — Eureka, Ill.

* **Evangelical Mennonite Brethren Churches**

1. Abbotsford E. M. B. — Abbotsford, B. C.
2. Fairholme E. M. B. — Fairholme, Sask.
3. Langham E. M. B. — Langham, Sask.
4. Dalmeny E. M. B. — Dalmeny, Sask.
5. Christian Fellowship Chapel — Winnipeg, Man.
6. Steinbach E. M. B. — Steinbach, Man.
7. Stuartburn E. M. B. — Stuartburn, Man.
8. Grace — Reedley, California
9. Dallas E. M. B. — Dallas, Oregon
10. Lustre E. M. B. — Wolfe Point, Montana
11. Marion E. M. B. — Marion, S. Dakota
12. Mountain Lake E. M. B. — Mountain Lake, Minn.
13. Luton E. M. B. — Luton, Iowa
14. Henderson E. M. B. — Henderson, Neb.
15. Jansen E. M. B. — Jansen, Neb.
16. Meade E. M. B. — Meade, Kansas
17. Hutchinson E. M. B. — Hutchinson, Kansas
18. Brighton Mennonite — Chicago, Ill.
19. Randville E. M. B. — Iron Mountain, Mich.

Scale of Miles

0 50 100 200 300 400 500

a result of the new birth; (3) a more rigid church discipline. The form of baptism is now optional with each congregation, though earlier it was pouring only.

The Conference, although at no time attaining a phenomenal growth, can report steady progress. Families moving into new settlement areas became the charter members of newly organized churches. Soon a dozen churches dotted several states and provinces. Some of these churches have since ceased to exist, largely because of repeated crop failures during periods of continued drought. G. P. Schultz was the outstanding evangelist. H. P. Schultz, John N. Wall, and John R. Dick served the Conference as chairmen more than any other. The Conference in 1954 numbers 21 organized churches with a total membership of 2,309, and 3 mission stations not as yet member churches with a total attendance of about 65. There are 64 ordained ministers, including missionaries (men) and educators, and 12 men are licensed to preach.

An increasing number of Conference young people are attending schools of higher education in preparation to serve as missionaries, ministers, doctors, nurses, educators, and in other lay professions. Churches of the Conference co-operate with the following schools: Dalmeny (Sask.) Bible Academy, Lustre (Mont.) Bible Academy, Meade (Kan.) Bible Academy, Mountain Lake (Minn.) Bible School, Steinbach (Man.) Bible Academy, and Grace Bible Institute, Omaha (Neb.). The Henderson (Neb.) Bible School and the Dallas (Ore.) Bible School, once operated by the E.M.B. churches at these places, have been discontinued.

Revival and evangelistic meetings are held almost annually in all of the churches. Bible conferences, Bible camps, vacation Bible schools, and child evangelism are encouraged in all constituent areas.

Missions were encouraged from the inception of the Conference. The P. A. Friesens were the first E.M.B. missionaries to India (1906), serving under the M.C. Board; the G. T. Thiessens went to China in 1914; and the A. F. Wienses were the first home missionaries, going to Chicago in 1906. Today the conference has 60 missionaries on the foreign fields, 9 on extended furlough or retired, and 10 candidates. About 45 missionaries serve on the home fields. The Conference is affiliated with the following mission organizations: China Mennonite Mission Society, Congo Inland Mission, Gospel Missionary Union, and the Far Eastern Gospel Crusade. Missionaries are also channeled through eight nonaffiliated mission organizations.

The E.M.B. Conference is affiliated with and supports the Mennonite Central Committee (MCC) and the National Association of Evangelicals (NAE). In 1953 the Conference joined with the Evangelical Mennonite Church to form the Conference of Evangelical Mennonites (q.v.), but retaining its own conference organization also.

In 1953 the Conference consisted of the following congregations (with membership): Nebraska—Henderson 96, Jansen 70; Kansas—Meade 266; Minnesota—Mountain Lake 256; South Dakota—Marion 115; Iowa—Luton 43; Montana—Lustre 100; Illinois—

Chicago 77; Oregon—Dallas 313; California—Reedley 20; Manitoba—Steinbach 310, Winnipeg 42; Saskatchewan—Dalmeny 183, Langham ?; British Columbia—Abbotsford 103. The Conference was divided into five districts in fellowship: (1) Manitoba and Saskatchewan, (2) Montana and Oregon, (3) Mountain Lake, Marion, and Chicago, (4) Nebraska, (5) Alberta, but this system has been discontinued.

The Conference published its own journal, *Evangelisationsbote* (*q.v.*) 1910-53, after 1934 called *Gospel Tidings*. Since the affiliation of the Evangelical Mennonite Church and the Evangelical Mennonite Brethren in 1953, this paper and the conference paper of the E.M.C. have been combined under the name *The Evangelical Mennonite*.   H.F.E.

G. S. Rempel, *A Historical Sketch of the Churches of the Evangelical Mennonite Brethren* [1889-1939] (printed in both English and German: *Die Konferenz der Evangelischen Mennonitenbrüder*, Rosthern, 1939); *Annual Report, Progress Number 1953*, *The Evangelical Mennonite Brethren* (Mountain Lake, 1953), and previous annual reports called before 1950 *Year Book of the Evangelical Mennonite Brethren*; *Glaubens-Bekenntnis der Mennoniten in York und Hamilton Co., Nebraska, Nord Amerika* (Elkhart, 1899), actually a slightly revised (by Isaac Peters) form of the G. Wiebe Prussian Confession of 1792, and reprinted at Elkhart in 1907 with the change in the title of *Glaubens-Bekenntnis der Mennoniten in Nebraska und Kansas, Nord-Amerika*, found both times with *Katechismus oder Kurze und einfache Unterweisung . . .* , was apparently not a conference publication. But in 1923 an official publication appeared containing the Constitution and Discipline and a newly prepared Confession of Faith. The cumulated conference reports 1901-38 were published in a booklet in 1938.

Evangelical Mennonite Church, before 1948 known as the Defenseless Mennonite Church of North America and earlier popularly called the "Egli Amish," was conceived about 1864 in Adams Co., Ind. Henry Egly, since 1858 a bishop of the Amish congregation near Berne, claimed to have experienced regeneration of heart, and began to urge the necessity of a definite experience of regeneration. He charged his group with formalism, lack of spiritual vitality and depth, looseness in maintaining the old customs, especially in regard to dress, and rebaptized those who had not experienced regeneration at the time of their first baptism in order that their baptism could be the answer of a good conscience toward God. No sooner had Bishop Egly made the announcement of his position than the congregation was divided, about half claiming they had had a personal experience of salvation either before baptism or after. These became adherents to Bishop Egly's teaching, and with these in 1866 he organized his own church.

The contention that arose under Bishop Egly's ministry in Adams Co., Ind., spread to certain Amish congregations in Fulton Co., Ohio, Gridley, Ill., and even to Missouri, Kansas, and Nebraska, although the main centers have been Berne, Ind., Archbold, Ohio, and Gridley, Ill. He strengthened his cause in all these places and won many converts who later became leaders in the conference when it was organized. The early teaching was very strict in regard to discipline and dress. The prayer head covering (a black three-cornered veil) and bonnet were originally worn. Later the veil was made larger and longer and eventually was discarded for the costume of the general populace. The men commonly wore beards but did not practice wearing the collarless coat and did not wear ties in the early days. In place of this a sort of black kerchief was worn around the neck. The modern tie was, however, adopted later, although some of the older ministers never wore it. Wearing of ornamental jewelry was banned, as was the use of tobacco and strong drink. The holy kiss was in favor but gradually was dropped by the laity, being practiced only in the reception of members and among ministers. This is no longer practiced except that where the rite of footwashing is observed the two washing each other's feet exchange the token. At first the group was quite exclusive, lived independently of other religious organizations, and was conservative in its relations with other people. In the early years they had no musical instruments, but had singing schools; but finally organs were permitted and now piano and other instrumental music are considered an integral part of the worship service.

The church services were conducted with singing and testimony for all the members and preaching by the minister, or by the deacons in the absence of the ministers, and sometimes in their presence. There were also special prayer and testimony meetings. At first German was spoken but later English was introduced and part of the service was in German and part in English. There were usually two services on Sunday, morning and afternoon. The early church had a kitchen and dining room attached so that members could stay all day, families taking turns in providing the meal, which consisted of bread and butter with syrup or apple butter and coffee.

The first Sunday schools were started in 1870-74 and were conducted in schoolhouses. These schools were independent of the church, since they met considerable opposition. Their purpose was not fully understood and they did not last long. In 1880 the first official Sunday school was held in the meetinghouse and was generally accepted. During the first few years the classes were conducted in German. *Jubeltöne* was the songbook used, and the Bible was the textbook. The smaller children used a special German A-B-C book and the next classes *Hübner's Biblische Geschichten,* both of which were published by the Mennonite Publishing Company of Elkhart, Ind. Children were taught to memorize verses of the Bible; later Sunday-school quarterlies of the Mennonite Publishing House of Scottdale, Pa., were used and some are still used. Services are now all in English.

The church membership was gained by preaching repentance and the forgiveness of sins as a personal, definite experience. This was expressed in general or special meetings by the convert rising to his feet sometimes during the sermon and asking the church for their prayers, asking forgiveness of parents and friends, making wrongs right, and holding on in prayer until he received through faith in Christ's atoning blood the evidence that his sins were forgiven. Later opportunity was given at the close of the message for those wishing to be saved

to raise their hands for prayer and also come forward and kneel at an altar. Conversions were confined to the immediate families but as years passed the spirit of evangelism reached outside the immediate Mennonite fold. Yearly, and sometimes oftener, special evangelistic services are now conducted to reach not only the Mennonites but also those in the community who have no church home and are in need of salvation.

The first annual conference was held in 1883 although incorporation did not take place till 1908. This conference was confined to the discussion of the various doctrines of the church and transacted no business. Bishop Henry Egly was in charge. Others taking active part in the discussions were C. R. Egle, Peter Hochstettler, Detsch, Christian King, S. Leip, Joseph Rediger, Daniel Rupp, and Christian Zimmerman. Topics included Sinners and Unrighteousness, Justification, Repentance, Atonement, Baptism, Immersion, Adoption, Footwashing, Marriage of a Child of God, Oaths, and Nonresistance. It was another decade before another conference was held, but since 1895 there has been a yearly conference with routine business. Each local church was represented by one delegate for each 25 members. Since 1948 each local church has been represented by one delegate for each 35 members.

The church began missionary work in 1896 when the conference supported Matilda Kohm in Africa. Interest in this venture was stimulated by Joseph Rediger, elder in the Salem Church, Gridley, Ill. She went out under the Christian Missionary Alliance Board to the Lower Congo just north of Boma. After her first furlough, on her return to the field in 1900 she took with her Alma Doering, and both worked under the Swedish Missionary Society in territory between the Congo and the Kasai. Missionary interest multiplied until finally the Congo Inland Mission Board was organized (1912) in cooperation with the Central Conference of the Mennonite Church, and in later years has expanded its operations to include two other Mennonite conference representatives on its Board, with a total of 74 active missionaries on the field and 8 who are on the retired list. Also in 1949 missionary efforts were extended by the church to the Dominican Republic, where there are now 7 workers.

In 1898 the Salem Orphanage near Flanagan, Ill., was founded by Daniel R. King and his wife, a childless aged couple, members of the Defenseless Mennonite Church, when they gave their farm of 100 acres, two miles south of Flanagan, for the cause. A charter was granted Dec. 22, 1896, the name "Salem Orphanage" legally adopted, and a Constitution and Bylaws framed by the first six trustees. Since then the Board of Directors has been chosen by the Conference. In 1905 Henry Broad of Flanagan also willed his farm of 160 acres, which lies within one mile of the Home. The churches of the Conference give monthly offerings for its maintenance. The name was changed to "Salem Children's Home" in 1945.

In 1897 the annual conference resolved to publish a paper in the interest of the Conference and orphanage under the name *Heils-Bote.* Its English companion was begun about the same time under the name *Zion's Call,* with D. N. Claudon as editor. This was published by the Salem Orphanage until a Conference resolution in 1913 made it the official organ of the Defenseless Mennonites. Later on Sept. 1, 1921, the paper became a combination of *Zion's Call* and *Good Tidings* and was published under the name *Zion's Tidings.* Since the merger of the E.M.B. and E.M.C. conferences the paper now represents both of these groups and is called *The Evangelical Mennonite.*

In the last decade of the 19th century a group under the leadership of J. A. Ramseyer insisted upon immersion as the only mode of baptism and taught the infilling of the Holy Spirit to be an experience separate from regeneration, and became exceedingly zealous to do missionary work. As this was not generally accepted by the church, a split occurred, the Ramseyer group leaving in 1898 to form the Missionary Church Association (*q.v.*). In the 1940's attempts were made to reunite the two groups, but without success. Finally in 1953 a successful merger was made with the Evangelical Mennonite Brethren (*q.v.*) to form the Evangelical Mennonite Conference (*q.v.*). In 1954 the Evangelical Mennonite Church consisted of 19 congregations with a total of 2,103 baptized members as follows: Ohio—Archbold 437, Wauseon 184, Pioneer 41, Bluffton 62; Indiana—Berne 263, Woodburn 163, Grabill 144, Lafayette 70, Ft. Wayne 71; Illinois—Gridley 224, Groveland 153, Chicago 39; Kansas—Sterling 142; Tennessee—McMinnville 17, Smithville 18, Pomeroy 17, Sparta 3; Michigan—Adrian 34, Midland 21.   E.E.R.

Church Manual of the Defenseless Mennonite Church, Confession of Faith, Rules and Discipline, Revised and Adopted . . . Aug. 30, 1917, and again . . . Aug. 1936 (Berne, 1937); *Discipline of the Evangelical Mennonite Church,* revised and adopted . . . Aug. 13, 1947 (replacing manuals of 1917, 1951) (n.p., 1949); annual report of the Conference 1883-1953; Harry F. Weber, *Centennial History of the Mennonites of Illinois* (Goshen, 1931); C. Henry Smith, *The Mennonites of America* (Newton, 1950).

Evangelical Mennonite Church is the new name adopted in 1952 by the Kleine Gemeinde Mennonite Church of Canada. For the history of this group see **Kleine Gemeinde.**

Evangelical Mennonite Conference, properly "The Conference of Evangelical Mennonites," a joint conference of the Evangelical Mennonite Church (*q.v.*) and the Evangelical Mennonite Brethren Church (*q.v.*), was formed June 14, 1953. It does not constitute a true merger, since each conference maintains its own separate identity and name and internal organization. The new joint conference has its own committees, publishes an official monthly organ *The Evangelical Mennonite* (first number July 1953) and annual *Conference of Evangelical Mennonites Calendar.* Organizationally it has an Executive Board, an executive secretary appointed by the Board, and four commissions as follows: Commission on Missions, Commission on Education, Commission on Promotion, Commission on Departments. An equal number of representatives of the two sub-

sidiary conferences are appointed for a term of three years on the above. The conference meets triennially.   H.S.B.

Evangelical Mennonites (Gehman group), 1857-79, one of the constituent groups which entered into the formation of the Mennonite Brethren in Christ-United Missionary Church. It arose as a schism in the Eastern Pennsylvania (GCM) Oberholtzer group, beginning initially in the Upper Milford congregation and centering in the person of Preacher William Gehman (1827-1918), who became the leader of the New Evangelical group. Gehman, ordained in 1849, began holding private prayer meetings in 1853 (with conference approval), which in 1856 were forbidden by the bishop of the conference. In the 1857 spring conference a vote was taken on the question and all those voting against the bishop's decision were expelled, 24 persons in number. The expelled group built a new meetinghouse at Upper Milford and on Sept. 24, 1858, organized the Evangelical Mennonite Conference with two elders, William N. Schelly and William Gehman, two preachers, David Henning and Henry Diehl, and three deacons. In 1876, when the conference first published its confession of faith and discipline, there were four elders, David Henning and Eusebius Hershey having been added, six preachers, Abel Strawn, J. L. Romig, John Musselman, and Abraham Kauffman having been added, and three deacons. In 1879 at the time of the merger there were nine congregations, nine ministers, and six deacons. After Upper Milford the next organized congregations were Coopersburg and Quakertown. The Evangelical Mennonites were strictly evangelistic and practiced a warmer, more emotional type of piety than the other Mennonites of that time. They definitely represent the entrance of a Methodistic type of piety, activity, and church organization into the Mennonite brotherhood in America. As early as 1876 they had an official missionary society, whose constitution was published in the book of discipline. This was essentially a home mission society, and did not operate foreign missions even though the constitution included foreign missions in its name. Eusebius Hershey of this group, the first American Mennonite foreign missionary, waited long to be sent by the church, but finally, in 1890, went out independently to Nigeria at the age of 67, dying there a year later.   H.S.B.

J. A. Huffman, *History of the Mennonite Brethren in Christ Church* (New Carlisle, 1920); *Doctrine of Faith and Church Discipline of the Evangelical Mennonite Society of East Pennsylvania* (Skippackville, 1867); C. Henry Smith, *The Story of the Mennonites* (3rd ed., Newton, 1950).

Evangelical Society of the Canton of Bern (*Evangelische Gesellschaft des Kantons Bern*), organized in 1831, in the circles of Heimberger Brethren (Oberland Brethren) and the pietists of the city of Bern, Switzerland. Its object is to revive spiritual life in the Reformed Church. The official organ of the Association is *Brosamen, Evangelisches Volksblatt.* It maintains a school of evangelism in Bern, an office, and a bookstore.

The society has connections with the Mennonite congregations of the canton of Bern (*Alt-Taufgesinnte, Alttäufer*). A number of Mennonites are members of the main conference of the society. It often serves the Mennonite churches with evangelists (in evangelization weeks, holidays, etc.). On the other hand, Mennonites also serve at the conferences of the society. In Emmenholz (*q.v.*) in the canton of Solothurn, a part of the Kleintal congregation, Mennonite preachers and evangelists alternate in conducting the services. In Chaux d' Abel (*q.v.*) connections have been maintained since 1868, and in Kleintal (*q.v.*) since 1881. **A. -T.**

W. Hadorn, *Gesch. des Pietismus in den Schweizerischen Reformierten Kirchen* (Constance, 1901); annual reports of the Evangelical Society; ML I, 615.

Evangelical United Brethren Church. This denomination was formed in November 1946 through the merging of the former Church of the United Brethren in Christ and the Evangelical Church. These denominations were born almost simultaneously and developed side by side through 150 years before this union.

The Church of the United Brethren in Christ resulted from the efforts of Philip William Otterbein (*q.v.*), then pastor of the Second Reformed Church in Baltimore, and Martin Boehm, a Mennonite bishop living in southern Lancaster Co., Pa. Otterbein, imbued with the Reformed pietistic spirit which he inherited during his student days at Herborn, was so favorably impressed by a sermon preached by Boehm at Long's barn, near Neffsville, Pa., about 1767, that he threw his arms about Boehm's neck and said, "We are brethren!" whence the name "United Brethren." For a long generation, Otterbein, Boehm, and other pastors with similar pietistic and evangelistic inclinations continued their work in their respective denominations. By 1800 the work was sufficiently distinct to warrant the calling of the first general conference, at which time Otterbein and Boehm were named bishops. The first rules and order were printed in 1815.

This denomination stressed the observance of "footwashing" during the earlier years of its history and permitted the practice of baptism by immersion, though prescribing no one form. Through differences of opinion about the constitution of the church, a small faction left the denomination in May 1885 to form the Church of the United Brethren (Old Constitution), which continues as a small denomination to the present.

The Evangelical Church was founded by Jacob Albright (*q.v.*) in 1800 in eastern Pennsylvania. Upon his death in 1808, his associate, George Miller, drafted the first *Discipline* (rules and order) of the denomination, which was printed in 1809. The first general conference of the denomination met at Linfield, Pa., in 1816 and established a printing press at New Berlin, Pa.

A division in the denomination gave birth to the United Evangelical Church in 1894. Most of the clergy and members of this denomination were reunited with the Evangelical Church in October 1922; a small group continues to the present as the Evangelical Congregational Church.

Both constituent groups of the present denomination have been closely related to the Mennonite and other Anabaptist groups. Baptism by immersion was permitted, occasionally members wore "plain" clothes or partially "plain" clothes, while the observance of footwashing had practically disappeared at the infrequent observances of the "lovefeast."

The Evangelical Church was significant to the Mennonites as it, more than any other movement, mediated the revivalist spirit and methods of the Methodists to the Germans in Mennonite communities. Many Mennonites were drawn into the movement while others reacted against it.

The Evangelical United Brethren Church in 1954 was sponsoring seven colleges and three theological seminaries, one of which is located in Reutlingen, Germany, where the Evangelical Church established in 1850. Missionary work is being supported in Europe, China, Japan, the Philippines, Africa, Puerto Rico, and Peru. The official weekly paper is the *Telescope-Messenger,* and a similar organ for young people is called the *Builders*. The 1954 membership was almost 800,000. **R.W.A.**

A. W. Drury, *History of the Church of the United Brethren in Christ* (Dayton, 1924); R. W. Albright, *A History of the Evangelical Church* (Harrisburg, 1942; rev. ed., 1945); R. S. Wilson, *Jacob Albright, The Evangelical Pioneer* (Myerstown, 1940).

Evangelical United Mennonite Publication Society, Goshen, Ind., appears in 1880 as the publisher of *The Doctrines and Discipline of the Evangelical United Mennonites,* and in 1881 as the publisher of *A Choice Collection of Hymns.* The Mennonite Brethren in Christ Publication Society, Berlin, Ont., appears as the publisher of the *Doctrines and Discipline of the Mennonite Brethren in Christ* in 1888 and again in 1897. By 1903, however, the Bethel Publishing Company appears as the publisher of M.B.C. books. It appears, although this is not confirmed by J. A. Huffman's *History of the Mennonite Brethren Church* (New Carlisle, 1920), that the first two names refer to the official denominational publishing agency of this group, which, though continuous, changed its name. The annual conference of 1879 had established a church printing plant and appointed a publishing committee. The printing plant was first located in Goshen, then in 1885 in Berlin, Ont. The Bethel Publishing Company was, however, a private venture of J. A. Huffman, which became a denominational agency in 1918. **H.S.B.**

Evangelical United Mennonites, 1879-83, formed October 1879 by a merger of the Evangelical Mennonites (Gehman group 1856-79) of Pennsylvania, and the United Mennonites (Indiana, Ohio, Michigan, and Ontario, 1875-79), a transition group which became the Mennonite Brethren in Christ in 1883 by the addition of the Swank (Ohio) faction of the Brethren in Christ (1861-83). At the time of the union in 1879, the group had some 40 ministers and 18 congregations, organized into 3 district conferences, Ontario, Pennsylvania, and Indiana-Ohio-Michigan. The discipline of the United Mennonites (slightly revised) was adopted for the merged group.

The presiding elders of the three conferences during this period were as follows: Pennsylvania—William Gehman 1880-91; Ontario—Solomon Eby 1875-86; Indiana-Ohio-Michigan—Daniel Brenneman 1879-80, 1881-82, 1883-84. By 1883 the group had 58 ministers, 37 churches (and 76 preaching places), and 2,076 members. H.S.B.

J. A. Huffman, *History of the Mennonite Brethren in Christ Church* (New Carlisle, 1926); *The Doctrines and Discipline of the Evangelical United Mennonites of Canada and the United States* (Goshen, 1880); German edition of the above, 1880.

Evangelisationsbote (*Gospel Tidings* since 1943) was first published in January 1910 as a four-page German monthly organ of the Evangelical Mennonite Brethren Conference. Its purpose is to serve as a tie between the conference churches, to further and to unify their joint efforts in evangelism, missions, charity, youth work, and spiritual edification. From 1921 on for 30 years it was issued twice monthly. In 1943 the name was changed to *Gospel Tidings.* For the first 28 years the language was almost exclusively German, then the English portion increased until January 1951, when the German was dropped. For four years (1947-50) the regular issues consisted of eight pages. From 1951 it was published monthly with from 16 to 20 pages, when it had about 900 subscribers. From January to June 1953 *Gospel Tidings* has been published jointly with the *Zion's Tidings,* official organ of the E.M.C., in 24-page monthly issues, size 9 x 12 in., and printed in Berne, Ind. The last issue was June 15, 1953, after which it was succeeded by *The Evangelical Mennonite,* organ of the Conference of Evangelical Mennonites, the affiliation of the E.M.B. Conference and the Evangelical Mennonite Conference.

Since the conference did not have its own publishing house and did not employ a full-time editor, there were frequent changes in the journal; there were 13 editors and 8 printing places in the 42 years of its existence.

Of special interest are the 25th Jubilee issue of May 15, 1936, and the Historic Review number of Aug. 1, 1948. H.F.E.

Evangelische Mennoniten-Brüderschaft (see **Allianz-Gemeinden**), a Mennonite congregation of South Russia, which was organized May 16, 1905, at Yushanlee in the Molotschna settlement. It arose from the desire to have fellowship only with truly believing members of the church. (Friesen, *Brüderschaft,* 722-24; *ML* I, 615.) NEFF.

Evangelische Mennoniten-Gemeinden was the name of a number of Mennonite congregations in Russia, of which the Molotschnaer Evangelische Mennonitenbrüderschaft (*q.v.*), founded in 1905, and Altonauer Evangelische Mennonitengemeinde (*q.v.*), founded in 1907, were most significant. The popular name for these congregations was Allianz-Gemeinden (*q.v.*). P. M. Friesen, as indicated in the title of his book, *Alt-Evangelische Mennonitische Brüderschaft,* and expressed throughout it, was one of the chief promoters of the concern which caused the founding of these congregations. He himself was for a time the leader of the Evangelische Men-

nonitische Brüderschaft at Sevastopol. His book contains much information regarding the basic philosophy of the movement.

As a member of the Mennonite Brethren Church he was disappointed, and with him others, in the course which his church followed. Raising the question as to whether the promising beginning had been fulfilled particularly regarding John 17:21, he concluded that the concept of the fellowship of the saints was too closely identified with being a member of the Mennonite Brethren Church (375 ff.). Although basically in agreement with the Mennonite Brethren principles, he strongly advocated an *Allianz,* a fellowship of all children of God particularly within the Mennonite brotherhood in daily life and also around the Lord's table. The segregation type of *Allianz* as promoted by the Darbystic Bible School of Berlin (later Wiedenest) was too narrow for him. He strongly promoted an inter-Mennonite fellowship, simultaneously stressing Mennonite principles and tradition and the evangelical warmth of Pietism. Contrary to Mennonite Brethren practices he went so far as to recognize baptism by sprinkling or pouring (156 ff.) and stated that the Evangelische Mennoniten-Gemeinden "have found a way out for those who do not wish to be rebaptized and at the same time are not satisfied with the practices of the Mennonite Church [in Russia]. The Mennonite Brethren Church has [justly] lost the monopoly in the realm of being the 'church of believers'" (footnote 723).

There were also others who were not fully satisfied with the spiritual life and practices of the Mennonite Brethren and the Mennonite Church in Russia. The leadership of this group could be counted among the better educated. In a way this development among the Mennonites in Russia was duplicated among the Mennonites of the prairie states in America when in Henderson, Neb., and Mountain Lake, Minn., separate congregations were organized which later became known as the Evangelical Mennonite Brethren (*q.v.*). Although there was no direct connection between these two groups there was similarity not only in name but also in practice and emphasis. The Evangelische Mennoniten-Gemeinden have never had a large following, but have exerted a beneficial influence not only through their congregations, but also through groups of sympathizers, particularly regarding the relationship between the Mennonite and the Mennonite Brethren churches and their weaknesses. Members of the group that came to Canada after World War I organized originally as separate congregations and joined the Mennonite Brethren Church, while those going to Brazil joined the General Conference Mennonite Church, and only those of Paraguay have remained an independent group. C.K.

Friesen, *Brüderschaft,* 722-27, particularly footnotes, 168-89, 256 ff., 376 ff.; G. Lohrenz, *Sagradowka* (1945) 75 f., 80.

Evangelische Stimmen, the title of a collection of sermons "for all Sundays and holidays. Published in co-operation with several Mennonite preachers by Johannes Molenaar" (*q.v.*). The first volume, published at Leipzig in 1844, contains six sermons: (1)

an Advent sermon by Molenaar on Matt. 21:1-9; (2) for the second Advent Sunday by Jakob Mannhardt (*q.v.*) of Danzig on Mark 1:14, 15; (3) for the third Sunday of the Epiphany by Isaak Molenaar of Crefeld on Matt. 8:1-13; (4) for the fifth Sunday of the Epiphany by Jakob Ellenberger (*q.v.*) of Friedelsheim on Matt. 11:28-30; (5) for the first Sunday of the Trinity by J. de Liefde of Zutphen, Holland, on Acts 2:47; (6) and for the twenty-third Sunday of the Trinity by Johann Gottfried Lübkes of Neuwied on Phil. 3:17-21. Further volumes were presumably not published. (*ML* I, 616.)   NEFF.

Evangelische Botschafter, Der, a 16-page monthly Mennonite periodical, 10 x 12 in., of which only one issue (2,500 copies), dated July 1, 1836, was published, edited by Heinrich Bertholet (1796-1853), printed by C. A. Pulte at Skippack, Pa. Bertholet, a preacher in the Mennonite (MC) congregation at Skippack, Franconia Conference, states the purpose of his paper under the following description of contents (translated):

"*Der Evangelische Botschafter* shall consist of two parts, the first of religious and the second of agricultural reading matter.

"In the first part special attention will be given to (*a*) consideration of divine subjects generally; (*b*) explanations and expositions of separate passages from the Bible, the Book of all wisdom; (*c*) information concerning the condition of the Mennonite congregations; (*d*) information concerning the condition of other religious bodies; (*e*) record of all marriages and deaths occurring in all Mennonite congregations so far as the information can be obtained.

"In the second part attention will be given to (*a*) articles of general interest in industrial pursuits; (*b*) articles on farm and garden work; (*c*) information relating to inventions and improvements along industrial lines in general and concerning farm and garden in particular; (*d*) information from the best authorities on the cultivation of the vine, silk, and tobacco; (*e*) miscellaneous subjects."

No reason is known for the discontinuance of the paper. This was the first attempt at a Mennonite periodical anywhere in the world. The first successful journal was John H. Oberholtzer's *Religiöser Botschafter* (GCM), established in 1852 at Milford Square, Pa., not far from Skippack, which has been continued under other names and publishers to the present. Since it used part of the name, it might in spirit be considered the successor to Bertholet's paper.

H.S.B.

Evangelism, "spreading the Gospel," the outreach of the Christian Church to win unbelievers. For the outreach expressed in foreign missions and city missions see the relevant articles. Evangelism is to be distinguished from revivalism (*q.v.*), which refers to reviving indifferent or spiritually weakened members of the church, though in popular language in North America the term "revival" is often used indiscriminately to refer to evangelistic outreach as well. This latter confusion is due in part to the fact that at times evangelistic and revival efforts are combined in the same meeting or series of meetings in a congregation or community, and the joint effort called "revival." The problem of terminology is further confused by the fact that many American Mennonite congregations in various branches have come to have an annual series of meetings of a week or two in length, to serve both of the above purposes, and also to secure conversions of their own children. The common name given to such a series of meetings is "revival meetings," although "evangelistic services" is also not infrequently used, and at times the terms are used interchangeably to refer to the same thing. Usually a preacher is called in from the outside to conduct the meetings; he is almost always called "the evangelist," not "the revivalist," although his work may be, by nature of the local conditions, far more revivalistic than evangelistic. Some congregations try to have their Sunday evening services of an evangelistic nature, including the preaching of an evangelistic sermon. In some congregations evangelistic appeals (by which is meant appeals for unconverted persons to accept Christ as their personal Saviour) are made in the regular Sunday morning services. Personal work by individuals who seek to win others to Christ in personal conversation is often called personal evangelism. The term is used also for literature evangelism or tract evangelism, and radio evangelism. Visitation evangelism is used for house to house solicitation of commitments to Christ and church membership. Thus the term "evangelism" is used today for many and varied procedures, and can be used for any attempt to win men to Christ and church membership.

The Anabaptists were originally intensely evangelistic. Their only hope of expansion was by this method. Since they controlled no political units as the Reformers did, they had to win others. However, the main reason for their strong evangelistic program, as F. H. Littell has clearly shown, was their acceptance of the Great Commission of Christ as their action program. K. S. Latourette has pointed out that the Anabaptists were the only group in the Reformation period to carry out the Great Commission, and that the Free Churches have always been in the forefront of missionary and evangelistic action. The Reformers were not evangelistic (in the strict sense), partly because they adopted the principle of the territorial state church, and the principle that the ruler determines the religion of his people. Thus they were immobilized by political boundaries and the state church concept, whereas the Anabaptists had full mobility.

The records are full of accounts of the vigorous itinerant evangelism of the early Anabaptists. The Hutterian Brethren in particular had a magnificent record, sending their missionaries all over Germany, Austria, and Switzerland, often two by two, throughout the 16th century and later. The scaffold and the stake, indeed all scenes of execution, became evangelistic platforms. The evangelistic appeal of the death of the martyr and accompanying testimonies was so attractive that at some places the authorities forbade public executions, conducting them in private to avoid the undesired effects. Many individual evangelists could be named. One of the outstanding evangelists of Holland besides Menno Simons was Leenaert Bouwens (d. 1582), who baptized 10,378 persons in many different places from Meenen to Danzig, according to his diary. The Reformers could not understand men who left their families to engage in itinerant evangelism, as many Anabaptist missioners did, and vehemently condemned them for it.

Gradually, however, the persecutors won the upper hand. By countless imprisonments and executions the Anabaptist movement was throttled, and in many regions extinguished; the evangelistic fires died down. Those who were once flaming evangels and courageous missioners now became the *Stillen im Lande,* happy to be permitted merely to exist. In some areas the rulers permitted and even invited the Mennonite (Anabaptist) refugees to settle in their lands, with the distinct understanding that they were not to proselyte, that is, not to evangelize their neighbors. They were often not allowed to give public evidence of their presence as a religious group. They were forbidden to hold public services or to have church buildings, or if the latter were allowed, they were not to appear like religious edifices and could not have bells. In some places it was illegal for outsiders to join them. In 1780 Bishop J. Nafziger of Essingen in the Palatinate was fined 500 florins and exiled from the Palatinate because he dared to receive into his congregation two children of Mennonite parentage who wanted to return to the faith of their fathers after having been reared as Catholics.

By the mid-17th century the spirit of evangelism was completely extinguished in all Mennonite groups. It remained so everywhere until late in the 19th century, and still remains extinct in such groups in North America as the Old Order Amish, the Old Order Mennonites, and the Old Colony Mennonites. There has been little of the evangelistic spirit or outreach activity among Mennonites anywhere in Europe in modern times, although there are some evidences of it today in France, Switzerland, and a few places in South Germany. In Holland, as also in Crefeld and Emden (Northwest Germany), there have been many transfers in recent decades from the state church to the Mennonite churches, largely cases of persons of a liberal theological position seeking more congenial religious fellowship in the Mennonite brotherhood. This transfer movement can scarcely be called evangelism, however, since it is passive reception of transfers rather than aggressive solicitation of the individuals.

The institution of *Reiseprediger (q.v.,* itinerant minister), which came into the South German groups about 75 years ago and somewhat later into France, West Prussia, and Russia (both M.B. and G.C.) and recently into Switzerland, has not been a case of evangelism, since the *Reiseprediger* is in effect an itinerant pastor, visiting scattered families and seeking to provide spiritual help to members of the church, particularly those in danger of falling away. However, some of the *Reiseprediger,* as well as some local pastors, having secured training at St. Chrischona (Basel, Switzerland) or certain other Bible schools in Germany, France, and Switzerland which fostered an evangelistic spirit, brought with them something of the spirit and practice of evangelism into their Mennonite congregations. Several of them, such as Christian Schnebele and Ulrich Hirschler of South Germany, have actually served as evangelists in such non-Mennonite organizations as the Tent Mission (*Zeltmission*) and the Pilgermission. Some congregations, such as Montbéliard in France and Ingolstadt in Bavaria, have conducted evangelistic services to reach their neighbors. In German-speaking areas such meetings are called *Evangelisation.* Recently J. B. Muller of Toul and Pierre Widmer of Montbéliard served as evangelists for the American Mennonite mission in Belgium.

According to Neff (*ML* I, 616), the outstanding South German evangelists, Elias Schrenk (d. 1911) and Jakob Vetter (d. 1919), as well as others, found entrance into Mennonite congregations in Switzerland, Württemberg, and the Palatinate. Vetter, in particular, exerted considerable influence.

In Russia German Baptists and Pietists (Eduard Wüst), Moravian Brethren, and English Plymouth Brethren of the evangelistic type about the middle of the 19th century visited certain Mennonite areas and scattered the seed of the evangelistic spirit there. B. Harder (*q.v.*) of Halbstadt was the most outstanding pulpit speaker and evangelist of the Mennonite Church in Russia. Jakob Quiring (Samara, died in New York) was also an outstanding evangelist in his younger years. The Mennonite Brethren arose (1860) to a large extent as the result of the Wüst revival and naturally perpetuated it more than did the main body of Russian Mennonites. The first recorded evangelistic outreach by a Mennonite among the Russian people was that by Johann J. Wieler (1839?-89) of the Mennonite Brethren, who had a thorough knowledge of both the Russian and German languages and served as a teacher in the Halbstadt Zentralschule 1879-83. Upon leaving the school he became a *Reiseprediger* and worked much among the Russians. As a result he was banished from Russia and went to Rumania, where he engaged in evangelistic work, establishing a congregation and where he lost his life accidentally in 1889 at the age of 50. Another early worker among the Russians was a certain Kalweit, also M.B., the grandfather of the Adolf Reimer mentioned in the next lines.

About 1906 a young M.B. schoolteacher, Adolf Reimer, dedicated himself completely to evangelism among the Russian people. He worked intensively throughout Russia, including St. Petersburg, until his death of typhus in 1924, reaching even the circles of the pietistic nobility in St. Petersburg. He edited a Russian *Abreisskalender* (block devotional calendar), which had extensive circulation. A. H. Unruh, founder of the Bible school at Tchongrav (Crimea) and later for many years a teacher in the M.B. Bible College in Winnipeg, did evangelistic work among the Russian people before 1914 and was at one time on this account imprisoned together with G. Froese, his lay co-worker. The Mennonite Brethren Conference began a public mission work among the Russians about 1905, which soon had to be stopped because of opposition by the government.

But regular support of evangelistic efforts among the Russians was continued privately by financial support of native Russian evangelists, a somewhat dangerous procedure. The treasurer of this secret fund was J. P. Isaak. The M.B. publishing house "Raduga" at Halbstadt promoted evangelistic effort among the Russians by the publication of evangelistic and devotional literature in the Russian language, particularly in connection with the Russian preacher Prokhanov of the Russian Evangelical group.

The Mariental M.B. Church in Alt-Samara developed direct evangelistic work among the native Russian population of its environment beginning about 1914, first in the Russian village of Koshki, where a meetinghouse was secured. Jakob Hein was a regular worker living in the village from 1917 until his death in 1921. There were converts, but the work was given up when no further regular workers could be provided. In 1920 work was begun among the Mordvins with good results. In 1924 work was begun among the Russian population in the cities of Samara and Simbirsk with excellent results. Both the above mission efforts were in operation in 1925, according to a report published in *Unser Blatt* in December of that year.

A notable chapter in Russian Mennonite evangelism is the mission to the pagan Ostyaks in (Khants) Siberia along the Ob River in a territory beginning about 300 miles north of Tomsk. Johann J. Peters of Orenburg, a graduate of a Bible school (J. Warns) in Berlin, began the work independently in loose connection with Karl Benzien. In the spring of 1928, ten years later, it was still in operation. In the intervening period Peters was joined by other volunteer workers, most of whom settled among the Ostyaks as families and supported themselves, although there was also support from the churches. Most of the workers came from the Slavgorod settlement in Siberia. Numerous reports in *Unser Blatt* 1925-28 show that there were converts and that Christian communities were established. (See **Ob Mission.**)

Mention should also be made of the brief activity of the Tent Evangelism work in Russia under the leadership of Jakob J. Dyck (1890-1919). Dyck, a former student in Berlin (J. Warns), while in Moscow serving as an army Red Cross worker (*Sanitäter*) joined a Christian Soldiers' Association (mostly Mennonites) in 1917, which was active in personal evangelistic work in the city. The association purchased a tent, and a number of members, among them Dyck, started tent evangelism among the native population in Central Russia. In June 1919, 24 men and women, most of them Mennonites, were consecrated to the work of tent evangelism in the Rückenau (Molotschna) M e n n o n i t e Brethren Church. The headquarters for the work was established at Panyutino about six miles from Losovaya. Shortly thereafter Dyck and four associates, who were conducting evangelistic meetings in Dubovka-Eichenfeld, were murdered in the attack on the village by the Machno bandits.

Jakob Kroeker (1872-1948), one of the ablest preachers produced by the Russian Mennonites (M.B. group), trained in the Baptist Seminary in Hamburg, became a *Reiseprediger,* traveling far and wide, cofounder of Raduga, friend of the pietistic nobility in St. Petersburg, influenced much by the German evangelist Baedeker and associates, moved to Germany in 1910, was cofounder with Pastor Jack of the mission for evangelization of Russians living in Germany and still more in Russia proper, known as *Licht dem Osten* (Wernigerode a.H.). This organization did a great work among the Russians by training and sending out workers, publishing a Bible concordance in Russian, as well as other religious literature, distribution of Russian Bibles, etc. *Licht im Osten* had many supporters among the Russian and German Mennonites, and occasional Mennonite workers, such as Jakob Dyck, continued (1954) in the service of the organization.

Two factors have contributed to inhibit the development of evangelism among the Mennonites of Europe: (1) the tradition of withdrawal and introversion plus a certain amount, no doubt, of inferiority feeling, the *Stillen im Lande* attitude, and (2) the general immobility and static condition of European religious attitudes. Because of the deeply set cultural patterns, the feeling in Europe is widespread that one is born into a religious group and ought not to change, and ought not to be solicited to change, even though the religious connections may be very tenuous and remote. Most of the population, up to 95-98 per cent, has actually been baptized into some religious confessional group. In line with this, particularly in Germany, Mennonites are inclined to look askance upon inquirers, and to discourage them from entering the Mennonite fellowship. Many such inquirers, most of them certainly sincere, approached Mennonite pastors during the time of the great postwar Mennonite relief work in Germany (1946-54) with its accompanying widespread favorable publicity, some being attracted also by the peace testimony of the relief workers. An alert evangelistic spirit might have led at least to the establishment of a number of evangelistic centers and possibly the creation of new local Mennonite fellowships. American Mennonites hesitated to step in but considered the possibility seriously when they saw that the German Mennonites for one reason or another did not move. Some contacts were actually established by MCC workers, especially with student and youth groups, such as at the University of Mainz and at the MCC centers at Frankfurt, Vienna, Salzburg, Berlin, and the Espelkamp reconstruction unit. In some places, such as Vienna, direct invitations and encouragement were given by local Protestant leaders for the establishment of permanent Mennonite work. Several representatives of the M.B. group were sent to Europe, particularly to Germany and Austria, on evangelistic preaching missions. M.B. churches have been established at Neuwied and Linz.

The Conservative Amish Mennonites have established a work at Espelkamp. In 1954 the Swiss Mennonite Conference, with an MCC subsidy, took over the opening established by the MCC in Vienna. Mennonite (MC) evangelistic centers have been established in Brussels and Paris, with the co-operation of the French-speaking Mennonites (a French-American advisory committee has been created), as well as in London and at Esch, Luxembourg. Incidentally, and almost by chance, a small work (MC) has been begun at Palermo, Sicily. Plans had been considered for opening a Mennonite work in Poland as a follow-up to relief work there, but the expulsion of the Mennonite workers in May 1950 by the government negated these hopes. The full import of the evangelistic impact of the testimony of the Mennonite relief work in Europe 1946-56 (and continuing) remains to be seen.

The Mennonite immigrants to America at all stages and locations before the coming of the Russian Mennonites 1873 ff. brought with them the *Stillen im Lande* spirit, happy simply to find freedom and peace. They devoted themselves vigorously and successfully to carving homes out of the wilderness and establishing traditional Mennonite congregations, but they undertook no evangelistic work among the American Indians (as did the Moravians, for instance) and did not share in the various religious awakenings and revivals from the Great Awakening of 1734-44 on down, even rejecting these influences and at times expelling those who accepted the new methods and new piety. Witness Bishop Martin Boehm of Lancaster Co., Pa., who was expelled in 1770 to become a cofounder with Otterbein of the new United Brethren Church in 1803. (W. W. Sweet's assertion in his *Revivalism in America* that the Great Awakening of 1734, which began in New Jersey, was sparked by Mennonites along with Theodore Frelinghuysen and Gilbert Tennent, is incomprehensible and without documentary proof.) The small group of German Pietists led by Alexander Mack, who came to Pennsylvania in 1719-22 (now called Church of the Brethren), by contrast to the Mennonites, was aggressively evangelistic, and as a result increased rapidly in membership, even winning many Mennonites.

The spirit of evangelism finally penetrated the older Mennonites east of the Mississippi in the 1880's and following, coming from the outside—largely through the aggressive work of the American Sunday School Union and the frontier evangelism of the Methodists, Baptists, United Brethren, and similar groups, with whom they often came into close contact. The evangelistic revivalism of Charles G. Finney (beginning in 1837) and more especially of D. L. Moody, 1870-1900, and his successors, had probably still greater influence. But the old inhibitions were still powerful. The tensions stirred up by the new spirit led to the schism of the Evangelical Mennonites (*q.v.*) in 1858 in Pennsylvania and the Menonite Brethren in Christ (*q.v.*) in 1874-75 in Indiana (Daniel Brenneman, *q.v.*), in Ontario 1870 ff. (Solomon Eby, *q.v.*), and elsewhere. Meanwhile, in the old church (MC) the ferment grew, and J. S. Coffman (*q.v.*) introduced the spirit and method of evangelism (also revivalism) 1879 ff. He was followed by others. A Mennonite (MC) Evangelizing Committee (*q.v.*) was organized at Elkhart, Ind., in 1882, followed by a Mennonite Evangelizing and Benevolent Board (*q.v.*) in 1892, the forerunner of the Mission Board of 1905. City missions (*q.v.*), beginning with Chicago in 1893, were a definite fruit of the new spirit. Evangelism was definitely established and recognized as a church function and responsibility by 1910 and came into its own in overwhelming force after World War II. At present this group (MC) has over 250 evangelistic mission outposts, plus additional mission Sunday schools, many in the immediate vicinity of the base congregations, others in faraway Vermont, Alabama, northern Minnesota, northern Michigan, northern Alberta, northern Ontario, and Kentucky. A similar outreach has developed in Negro missions, Jewish missions, radio evangelism, colonization evangelism, and a large tract distribution program. The effectiveness of these extensive efforts remains to be seen, but they are a testimony to a widespread and powerful interest in evangelistic outreach, indicating that the group has fully accepted the evangelistic responsibility and discarded the *Stillen im Lande* spirit. The sense of mission that was lost for almost three centuries has returned.

Similar developments, though not so extensive, have taken place in other North American Mennonite groups. In some groups persistence in maintaining the German language has continued to be a severe practical block, as well as an internal inhibition to evangelistic advance. Distinctive patterns of Mennonite behavior and custom have often interfered with evangelistic effectiveness, at times to the great frustration of those in the front line of evangelistic effort. Actual net gains of outside converts have often been small.

A striking exception to the above pattern has been the Mennonite Brethren in Christ—United Missionary Church. Founded (1874-83) by leaders with a strong evangelistic emphasis, such as Daniel Brenneman, Solomon Eby, and William Gehman (*q.v.*), this group has grown largely by evangelism among non-Mennonites in all areas. This is notably true of its Michigan Conference, which today has 2,000 members, won almost wholly in non-Mennonite territory. One of the outstanding early evangelists was Eusebius Hershey (*q.v.*, 1823-91) of Pennsylvania, who spent 43 years in evangelistic work mostly among non-Mennonites in eastern United States and Canada before going abroad as the first foreign missionary (1890) from any Mennonite group in the United States. Another was Andrew Good (*q.v.*, 1838-1918), who traveled over 200,000 miles preaching in nearly every state in the Union, also making 20 trips to Ontario. The first evangelist in Ontario was Noah Detwiler, who spent 12 years in evangelistic work in Ontario besides working in Pennsylvania and Kansas. Numerous men have served as full-time or part-time evangelists for periods of 20-40 years. The evangelistic work of this denomination has up to recent times far exceeded that of any other Mennonite group. It was the first group in North America to operate a city mission, opening its Grand Rapids, Mich., mission in 1884. All the group's city missions, over 100, were founded as evangelistic centers and have been used to build up churches from the non-Mennonite sources. A major method of evangelism used by the M.B.C.-U.M.C. group is the "camp meeting," a method taken over from the

Methodists. The first such meeting was held in 1880, and every district conference of the church has sponsored such a meeting annually for many years. Of the two goals of these meetings, revival and evangelism, the latter has always been the predominant one. A high percentage of the members of any typical congregation would be found to have been converted at a camp meeting.

Part of the Mennonite groups who came from Russia to the United States 1873 ff. brought with them an awakened mission and evangelistic interest, resulting from their support of the Dutch Mennonite mission work in Java, as well as influences from Moravian, Baptist, and pietistic sources. This, fortified in America in the case of the General Conference group by an awakened spirit in the Oberholtzer group, the urge of the immigrant groups from the Palatinate, and the Wadsworth school, led to a strong work in 1880 ff. among the American Indians in Oklahoma and Arizona (later in Montana) by the G.C.M. group, and by the M.B. group among the American Indians, certain Volga Russian immigrant groups in the Dakota region and elsewhere, and among the Mexicans in Texas. It did not produce a corresponding outreach in city missions or rural missions in either group. Of the smaller groups the Evangelical Mennonites, the Evangelical Mennonite Brethren, and the Krimmer Mennonite Brethren have shown a strong evangelistic spirit. The Missionary Church Association (q.v.) which branched off from the Defenseless Mennonites in 1898 has been very strongly evangelistic from the start and has grown very largely by evangelism among out-group persons. After World War I, evangelistic work among the Mexicans living in the United States developed, with the Mennonite Church (MC) working in Chicago, Colorado, and Texas, the Mennonite Brethren group in Texas, and the Church of God in Christ Mennonites in Mexico and in New Mexico. The latter group also began work among the Indians in Arizona and also in Alberta.

With the evangelistic emphasis, especially in the M.B.C. and M.C. groups, a class of workers arose known as "evangelists." This consisted largely of preachers or pastors who gave much of their time to evangelistic meetings in Mennonite congregations. But few of these became full professional evangelists giving all their time to such work as was customary in other larger churches except in the Mennonite Brethren in Christ group. After World War II mass evangelism developed in the M.C. group, Geo. R. Brunk, Jr. (q.v.), Howard Hammer, and Myron Augsburger outstanding in this work. This type of work is marked by the use of large tents holding 2,000-6,000 persons, and extended community-wide campaigns of 3-6 weeks in a location. It remains to be seen whether this type of work is more a revival effort among Mennonites, or a real evangelistic outreach to unbelievers. So far (1956) it has remained largely the former.

With the development of the evangelistic spirit and activity has often come, particularly in North America, a change in type of piety in the direction of a warmer, more expressive, more verbalized spirituality, and an emphasis upon crisis conversion, together with some change in theological emphasis in the direction of more attention upon conversion and status, rather than ethics and discipleship. These subtle changes have as yet not been fully studied nor evaluated. Influences of other kinds have also come to bear upon Mennonites of various groups, from the same sources that have brought evangelistic influences, often from the Bible institutes and Bible schools where numerous Mennonites have secured training, and which are usually quite evangelistic. This influence includes not only new methods of church work and a considerable emotionalism, but also such doctrines as eternal security, second work of grace, and millennialism. Thus the movement for evangelistic activization has been accompanied by significant side-effects and related changes. In the major groups, and some of the minor ones as well, these changes have produced a significantly different Mennonitism.

A recent development is "Child Evangelism," an outside movement which has won considerable support in certain areas. This movement attempts evangelistic methods similar to those used with adults on children as low as 3-4 years of age, regularly on all children below 8, claiming that they are lost sinners and must be regenerated before any Christian nurture can be given. Its theology is strongly Calvinistic; its basic theory denies the age-old Mennonite doctrine that all children are saved by Christ's atonement before the age of accountability and that conversion cannot take place before that age is reached, which is normally the age of puberty. A strong reaction is, however, developing against this movement as its theological errors and psychological and educational faults are uncovered. Acceptance of the basic thesis and method of this movement would destroy the very foundation of the Mennonite concept of adult baptism, a responsible believers' church, and discipleship.   H.S.B.

J. Umble, "Race Prejudice an Obstacle to Evangelism in the Mennonite Church," *Goshen College Record Review Supplement* (Sept. 1926) 29-132; idem, "John S. Coffman as an Evangelist," *MQR* XXIII (1949) 123-46; F. H. Littell, "Anabaptist Theology of Missions," *MQR* XXI (1947) 5-17; idem, *The Anabaptist View of the Church* (1952), particularly Chap. V, "The Great Commission," 94-112; J. Hostetler, "The Impact of Contemporary Mennonite Evangelistic Outreach on the Larger Society," *MQR* XXVII (1953) 305-30; *Die Gemeinde Christi und ihr Auftrag, Vorträge und Verhandlungen der Fünften Mennonitischen Weltkonferenz* (Karlsruhe, 1953), particularly pp. 145-85, including J. R. Mumaw, "Wie treiben wir Mission und Evangelisation?"; J. A. Hostetler, *The Sociology of Mennonite Evangelism* (Scottdale, 1954).

Evangeliums Panier. This was the German issue of the *Gospel Banner* and was first published by the United Mennonite Church (now the United Missionary Church) at Goshen, Ind., in January 1879 with Daniel Brenneman as editor, 1879-82. Succeeding editors were Timothy Brenneman, November 1882 to April 1885; Joseph Bingeman, April to October 1885; J. B. Detweiler, 1885-88; and H. S. Hallman, 1888-95(?).

After a year as an 8-page monthly publication, 10½ x 13½ in., it was enlarged to a semimonthly, 10½ x 15½ in., in January 1880, and further increased in

1885 to 16 pages, 8¾ x 11½ in. In 1880 the publishing of the paper was transferred from Indiana to Berlin (now Kitchener), Ont. In 1893, however, with the decline of the use of the German language in the church, it was reduced to eight pages, and was finally discontinued in 1895 (?).   E.R.S.

Eveleens, a Dutch Mennonite family, found at Aalsmeer (q.v.), North Holland, since about 1600, whose numerous members through more than three centuries belonged to the Mennonite church, and of whom a large number are still found among the Mennonites of the Aalsmeer congregation, where the name is very common. Dirk Eveleens was a preacher and elder of the Oude vermaning (Old Frisian congregation) on the Uiterweg, until this congregation merged in 1866 with the Zijdweg congregation.
                                                      vdZ.

Everling (Eberling, Eberlin, Everlin, Everlinck), **Jakob,** an elder in the Obersülzen (q.v.) church in the Palatinate, who lived in the second half of the 17th century and was deeply concerned for the oppressed circumstances of his brethren.

On Nov. 2, 1671, he informed Hans Vlamingh (q.v.) at Amsterdam of the arrival of a number of Swiss Mennonite emigrants to the Palatinate (Inv. Arch. Amst. I, No. 1405). On Jan. 4, 1672, he wrote another letter to the Amsterdam congregation, with further information about the refugees settling in Obersülzen (ibid., No. 1248). Thereupon the Dutch Mennonite Committee for Foreign Needs sent a large sum of money to support these immigrants, and later another sum (11,000 guilders), which was distributed by Everling and others. They gave their report in a letter (ibid., No. 1198) signed by Jacob Everling, Johann Krämer, Valentin Huthwol, and Heinrich Kosel. This letter (undated, 1695 or 1696) shows that Everling, of whom nothing more is known, was still living at that date. In a letter of May 16, 1672 (Inv. Arch. Amst. I, No. 1417), he wrote that he could not recognize the Dutch Mennonites as brethren because they admitted marriages with nonmembers of the church. Furthermore he declared himself satisfied by their letter which had informed him that they were Biblical in the doctrine of satisfaction, and that they did not admit to the communion persons who had not been baptized.
                                                 NEFF, vdZ.

Mart. Mir. D does not list him; E 1125-27 gives extracts of his letters; Müller, Berner Täufer, 195; ML I, 616.

Evert Aerts of Utrecht, a maker of knives, executed as an Anabaptist on May 14, 1535, at Amsterdam, along with nine others. He was one of the revolutionary group who joined Jan van Geelen (q.v.) to attack the city of Amsterdam (May 10-11, 1535). (Grosheide, Verhooren, 62 f.)   vdZ.

Evert Hendricks (Naeldenverkooper) was a native of Warendorf, Westphalia, Germany. This Anabaptist martyr, who was a clothmaker, was apprehended in Amsterdam. He confessed that he had been rebaptized about 1565 at Veere, Dutch province of Zeeland. He had traveled widely in his business, disseminating his Anabaptist opinions. In Emden he had bought some Mennonite books, to sell them elsewhere. Among those books were the Offerboek, by which must have been meant the Offer des Heeren (q.v.), and a small Gospel-book and a Concordance. He also confessed that he had been married in Middelburg, Dutch province of Zeeland, according to Mennonite customs (op der Mennonieten maniere). This means that a Mennonite minister had performed his marriage in a meeting of the congregation. He also admitted that a Mennonite meeting had been held in his house at Amsterdam two months previously (March or April 1572). On June 20, 1572, he was sentenced to death, but the execution for some reason or other was delayed until Sept. 3, 1572, when he was burned at the stake with Sander Woutersz (q.v.) at Amsterdam. Evert and Sander were the last victims of persecution in Amsterdam. (Grosheide, Bijdrage, 184-85, 308; Mart. Mir. D 620, E 944; ML I, 616.)   vdZ.

Evert Jans, a cobbler of Coesfeld in the district of Münster, Westphalia, Germany, who was living in Amsterdam, was one of the first Anabaptists of the Netherlands. He was arrested in Amsterdam and on Dec. 5, 1531, beheaded at The Hague together with nine other Anabaptists, including Jan Volkertsz Trypmaker (q.v.). They all renounced their faith and for this reason were not included in the Dutch martyrbooks. (Grosheide, Bijdrage, 50, 302; DB 1917, 159.)   vdZ.

Evert Nouts, a Dutch Anabaptist taken prisoner at Rotterdam in February 1558 together with some other members of the congregation. During his trial on Feb. 28 he confessed that he had been baptized more than three years ago at Antwerp, Belgium, by Gillis van Aken (q.v.) and that he had lived at Rotterdam for about three months. He was about 27 years of age. He was sentenced to death on March 28, 1558, with four other Mennonites. On the day set for the execution, when the victims had been brought up to the scaffold and one of them, Jan Hendricks (q.v.), had already been strangled, an insurrection arose among the spectators. During this riot the victims, including Evert Nouts, were liberated by the insurgents. Nothing further is known about him. (Mart. Mir. D 191-94, E 574-77; DB 1905, 172; ML III, 277.)   vdZ.

Everts, Dirk, separated from the Waterlander Toren congregation at Amsterdam in 1616 with a number of adherents to form the congregation of the "Afgedeelden" (q.v.), which apparently shortly after 1630 joined the United Frisian and High German group at Amsterdam. (Inv. Arch. Amst. I, Nos. 1201-3.)
                                                      vdZ.

Evertsz, Jan, a preacher of the United Mennonite congregation at Haarlem, Holland, meeting at den Blok on the Klein Heiligland. In 1670, when this congregation was divided into a Lamist (q.v.) and a more conservative Zonist (q.v.) group, Evertsz joined the latter. In 1680 a schism arose in this Zonist group between Jan Evertsz and Thomas Snep (*q.v.*). In 1685 Thomas Snep left the Zonist group with the majority of the members, leaving behind a small number, of whom Jan Evertsz was the leader. Evertsz, who is said in his youth to have been a Catholic, was very conservative, and a violent antagonist of marriages outside of the congregation, and of audible prayer, which he rejected as an undesirable innovation. In 1658 he published *Kort en bondig Bewijs, dat Dr Galenus Abrahamsz ende David Spruyt hebben een verkeert en verleydelijck Verstant, . . .* (n.p.). (*DB* 1863, 137, 144-51.)

vdZ.

Ewert (Ewertz, Ewerts, Evert, Ebert, Efert), a Mennonite family name of Frisian-Dutch descent, frequently found in West Prussia. This name is a patronymic of Evert (Dutch Christian name) and may formerly have been Everts or Ewerts. In West Prussia the members of this family all belonged to the more progressive Frisian or Waterlander wing. It was first mentioned at Danzig in 1572, and Montau in 1605. Thies Evert (Ewert) was a preacher of the congregation of Dannenberg (*q.v.*), Lithuania, at the time when this church was expelled from Lithuania; most of them moved to the vicinity of Elbing in West Prussia (1731). (*Inv. Arch. Amst.* I, No. 1583.)

Gillis (Gils) Evert (Ewert) was a minister of the Dannenberg congregation; he migrated to the Netherlands in 1732 and was aided by the Dutch Mennonite Committee of Foreign Needs to a farm on the island of Walcheren, Zeeland (*Inv. Arch. Amst.* I, Nos. 2095-96). He gave much trouble to the Committee, and the Amsterdam Archives contain a large number of his letters, full of complaints and reproaches (*Inv. Arch. Amst.* I; the most important are Nos. 2041, 2043, 2045, 2129, 2137, 2180, 2192, 2209-10). In 1739 he went back to Prussia, and with the financial aid of the Dutch Committee obtained a small farm there (*ibid.*, No. 1675) and served the (Frisian) congregation of the Kleine Werder in the territory of Elbing until at least 1755.

The Dutch *Naamlijst* 1743-1802 names a number of members of this family who served as preachers in several Prussian churches. Hans Ewert was an elder of the Frisian (also called Waterlander) congregation of *Schwyngrube in de Stuumsche Needering* 1755-76 (?), later Tragheimerweide. Other preachers of this family who served the same congregation were Gillis Ewert (d. about 1760), Jacob Ewert serving 1776-1800, also as elder, and another Jacob Ewert from 1795. Andries (Andreas) Ewert is mentioned as a preacher of the Waterlander Lithuanian congregation about 1750.

Members of this family migrated to Poland, Russia (Molotschna settlement) and America. Among the better-known members of the family were Elder Wilhelm Ewert (*q.v.*), a delegate to America in 1873 and an emigration leader; Gerhard Ewert of Gross Lunau, Prussia, author of *Sieben Betrachtungen des andächtigen Pilgers auf dem Wege gen Zion* (Graudenz, 1843, 130 pp.); Henry H. Ewert (*q.v.*), son of Wilhelm, educator in Manitoba; Wm. J. Ewert (*q.v.*), elder of the Brudertal Mennonite Church; Benjamin Ewert, leader in the General Conference of Mennonites in Canada, and Bruno Ewert, the last elder of the Heubuden congregation in West Prussia and later minister in the Montevideo, Uruguay, congregation, and Jacob G. Ewert (*q.v.*) of Hillsboro, Kan.   G.R., vdZ.

Ewert, Henry H., a Mennonite (GCM) minister and educator, b. April 12, 1855, at Nessau near Thorn, West Prussia, the oldest of 12 children born to Wilhelm and Anna Janz Ewert. In the spring of 1874 he with his parents migrated to Kansas, settling near Hillsboro. On Aug. 20, 1882, he married Lizzie K. Baer of Summerfield, Ill., and after her death Mrs. Katie Kruse (nee Krehbiel) in 1926.

Ewert received his elementary and intermediate education at Thorn. In Kansas he attended the state normal school at Emporia 1878-79. Later he studied at the Des Moines Institute, Des Moines, Iowa, and took a two-year theology course at Marthasville, Mo.

Soon after arriving in Kansas and obtaining the necessary preparation, Ewert taught school for a few years in his home district. In 1882 he became teacher and principal of a Mennonite parochial school at Alexanderwohl, Kan. In 1883 this school, sponsored by the Kansas Mennonite Conference, was transferred to Halstead, Kan., to be continued as a conference school, under the name of Mennonite Seminary. Here H. H. Ewert continued to be teacher and principal for nine years (1883-91). In 1884 he was ordained as conference minister and preached in different churches. He organized the Kansas Sunday School Convention.

In 1891 H. H. Ewert came, upon invitation, to Manitoba, to take over the schoolwork here among the Mennonites of this province. Here he was appointed school inspector of Mennonite schools by the government and engaged as teacher and principal of the newly established parochial Mennonite school at Gretna, Man., which was at first named Gretna Normal School, then Mennonite Educational Institute, and later changed to Mennonite Collegiate Institute. In the latter capacity he was active 43 years. He died on Dec. 29, 1934, at the age of nearly 80 years, and was interred in Gretna.

H. H. Ewert was deeply interested in educational and religious matters, in church and conference undertakings among Mennonites in Manitoba and also at large, including Sunday schools, teachers' conventions, church conferences, and other benevolent organizations and establishments. He was organizer of the General Conference of Mennonites in Canada.

H. H. Ewert did not publish any books but wrote many articles for publication in Mennonite church papers, and some pamphlets. Among the pamphlets may especially be mentioned an address given by him under the auspices of the Historical and Scientific Society of Manitoba in Winnipeg in 1932, on the topic, "The Mennonites," which has been published in both English and German. He also edited a monthly German church paper, *Der Mitarbeiter* (*q.v.*), for 28 years.†   B.E.

Ewert, Jacob G., was born Nov. 24, 1874, in Markoviziane, Poland. His father, Gerhard J. Ewert, emigrated to Kansas with his family in 1882, and was one of the 39 charter members of the First Mennonite Church in Hillsboro when this was organized in 1885. He lived there the rest of his life.

Due to financial difficulties Jacob Ewert was unable to get a well-rounded formal education, but being apparently of more than average talent and certainly a man of will power he got his teacher's certificate and taught in the Kansas public schools, intermittently studying at Bethel College. It was here in 1897 that rheumatism struck him, paralyzing him to such an extent that only an arm and a shoulder remained free to move. He even had to be fed through a tube. He thus spent over 26 years in bed, cared for by his brother David (1878-1924), himself also an invalid. However, Jacob Ewert continued his studies in bed, gaining a fair reading knowledge of several modern European languages as well as Hebrew, Latin, and Greek, which he taught to students of Tabor College who came to him for instruction. He also made a contribution to Wenig's *Wörterbuch,* a dictionary published in Germany.

He was also active in journalism, coediting for several years the German monthly *Vorwärts,* published in Hillsboro, writing the column "Gegenwärtige Aussichten." He was much in sympathy with the socialistic views of the times and wrote among other pamphlets one entitled *Christentum und Sozialismus.*

Being an ardent pacifist, it became his work to advise many young men drafted into the country's services during World War I. In the interests of pacifism he also translated the correspondence between Count Leo Tolstoy and the American pacifist Adin Ballou, published by Lewis G. Wilson in *Arena.*

Due to the active interest he took in prohibition, he was elected secretary of the Prohibition Movement in Kansas, which position he held for several years. In the interests of this movement he wrote *Die Bibel und die Enthaltsamkeitslehre,* published by the *Christliche Mässigkeitsverein* (Berne, Ind.).

Possibly his greatest efforts went into the relief work in Europe, especially Russia, after World War I. He wrote untiringly in the various Mennonite papers in its interests, and considerable sums of money were entrusted to him to help feed the hungry abroad. The records show some $89,000 passing through his books. He died March 16, 1923. (*Vorwärts-Kalender,* 1925, Hillsboro, Kan.; *ML* I, 617.)　　　　　　　　　　　　　　NEFF, J.W.N.

Ewert, Peter, a member of the Kicin (*q.v.,* Poland) Mennonite Church, was instrumental in taking the congregation into the Baptist Church. Johann Penner, a Mennonite at Adamov who had joined the Baptists, visited his relatives at Kicin in 1855 and spread Baptist ideas among members of the Mennonite congregation. In July 1860, G. F. Alf (*q.v.*), the Baptist evangelist of Poland, visited Kicin and conducted meetings at the home of Peter Ewert. Ewert and others were baptized by immersion, and Johann Penner ordained Ewert as minister. Thus the Kicin Mennonite Church merged with the local Baptists, mostly of Lutheran background.

Soon some difficulty arose on the principle of nonresistance, which was unknown to the Baptists, but which the Mennonites wanted to maintain, and on the practice of footwashing and baptism. Peter Ewert carried on a lively correspondence regarding these questions with Alf (*q.v.*) and with Mennonite Brethren in Russia (Friesen, 244). According to Kupsch, Ewert and Penner with the Mennonite-Baptists went their own way for a while, but finally merged with the Baptists again. "Ewert recognized his error, repented and came back to the Baptists, and became a missionary. Penner also returned to the Baptists in 1863."　　　　　　　　　　　　C.K.

Friesen, *Brüderschaft,* 244 f.; E. Kupsch, *Gesch. der Baptisten in Polen* (1932) 59-66; J. F. Harms, *Geschichte der Menn. Brüdergemeinde* (Hillsboro, 1924?) 69; *ML* I, 617.

Ewert, Wilhelm, a Mennonite elder and leader, b. Feb. 23, 1829, at Stronske, Thorn, Prussia, d. June 21, 1887, near Hillsboro, Kan., was the youngest son of Peter and Maria Ewert. He attended a secondary school in Thorn, and learned carpentry. On May 30, 1854, he married Anna Janz, a daughter of Cornelius and Sarah Janz. Of the 13 children, only 6 outlived their father.

In 1843 Ewert was baptized by Elder David Adrian of the Ober-Nessau Mennonite Church (*q.v.*), which elected him as minister in 1860 and as elder in 1868. When the West Prussian Mennonites were in danger of losing their principle of nonresistance because of the compromise accepted by most of the West Prussians following the order of cabinet of 1867, he was active in finding a country which would honor their convictions. In 1870 he and Peter Dyck visited Russia to investigate settlement possibilities. When they saw that the Mennonites in Russia were confronted by the same problem, they directed their attention to America. Again Ewert was one of the delegates who investigated the prairie states and provinces.

In the spring of 1874 Ewert and his family and a few families of his congregation settled in Marion Co., Kan., joining with a group of Mennonites from Russia to found the Brudertal Mennonite Church (*q.v.*) the same year. Ewert was the first elder. He at once became active in community and conference activities and was one of the great promoters of elementary and secondary education, and particularly of Bethel College. He was always generous in aiding needy individuals and groups financially and spiritually. He was succeeded as elder by his son William J. Ewert (*q.v.*). Another son, H. H. Ewert (*q.v.*), was the well-known teacher of Halstead Seminary and Gretna Collegiate Institute.　　　　　　　　　　　　　　　　　C.K.

D. Goerz, "Wilhelm Ewert," *Christlicher Bundesbote,* July 15, 1887; Ewert Collection, Bethel College Historical Library.

Ewert, William J., second son of Elder Wilhelm Ewert and Maria Thiart, was born May 22, 1856, in West Prussia. He died April 5, 1928, in Kansas. He was married to Ernstine Dirks Sept. 6, 1889. To them were born seven children. He received his education in Prussia. In 1874 at the age of 18 he came with his parents from Prussia, settled in Marion Co., Kan., and became a member of the Brudertal Mennonite Church of that locality, of which he was elected a minister. On Nov. 22, 1891, he was elected elder (bishop) of this church, and ordained to this position Jan. 24, 1892, which position he kept to the time of his death. Besides being a farmer, he was also interested and employed in publication and conference work, in which he acted as secretary.   B.E.

Ewsum, Christoffer van, b. 1523, d. April 9, 1583, a nobleman of a wealthy and influential family of Groningen, Netherlands, who had extensive landholdings there. Through his marriage to Margaretha, a daughter of Ulrich van Dornum, of Oldersum, East Friesland (which could not have taken place in 1536 as stated *ML* I, 617, but is known to have occurred by 1551), he not only acquired additional properties but also a unique spiritual heritage. Ulrich van Dornum (*q.v.*) was a stanch promoter of the Reformation with special connections with men like Karlstadt. Even Melchior Hofmann and Menno Simons are thought to have found refuge on his estates. A younger daughter married a follower of Menno **Simons.**

Christoffer van Ewsum lived in the Asingaburg near Baflo and also had possessions in Middelstum, where the family castle was located. Here Menno Simons must occasionally have found shelter. On May 15, 1551, the chancellor of Gelderland reported to the imperial representative at Groningen that Menno Simons was staying with Christoffer van Ewsum. Van Ewsum himself was expelled from Groningen by Alba. When the ban was repeated on Jan. 10, 1570, he was referred to as a "Mennonist." A Reformed relative of Margaretha and her sister left some inheritance for them, provided they would "purge" themselves of "heresy."

This does, however, not justify the assumption that Christoffer van Ewsum and his wife were full-fledged followers of Menno Simons or Anabaptists. Van Ewsum was also a supporter of the Reformed Church at Emden, a friend of Johann a Lasco, and a "benefactor and protector of pious refugees" (Reformed). He had a large library, which was used by the well-known historian, Hermann Hamelmann. In a statement of August 1569 he said that he had lived in East Friesland during the last 17 years, having possessions at Emden and Jennelt. To what an extent the Mennonites had a protector in him here is not known.   C.K.

DB 1906, 35; 1916, 107; 1917, 125; *Groningsche Volksalmanak* 1919, 112; 1921, 25; F. Ritter, "Eine ostfriesische Lutherreliquie. Der Jennelter Junker Christof van Ewsum," *Jahrb. d. Ges. f. bild. Kunst u. vaterl. Altert.,* XX (Emden, 1920) 126-44; *ML* I, 617.

Excommunication, Procedure and Grounds. The doctrine and theory of discipline behind the practice of excommunication is discussed in the articles **Ban** and **Discipline;** here only the procedure and grounds will be treated. (The corresponding German term is *Ausschluss aus der Gemeinde.*)

Excommunication is here taken to mean the exclusion of the offender from all church fellowship. In the Catholic churches, both Roman and Greek, excommunication has been maintained uninterruptedly, administered by the bishop (or the pope or papal legate). The grounds and procedure are specified in the canon law, but the bishop is authorized to exercise his judgment in cases not covered by the law. The chief grounds are heresy, i.e., deviation from the dogma of the church, and any persistent defiance of the authority of the church or disobedience of its regulations. In medieval and later times the state was expected to and did join in the punishment of the offender by civil penalties, including the death penalty for heresy and blasphemy. The Reformers continued excommunication in a modified form, including the participation of the state in punishment. Gradually, however, the practice died out in the Protestant state churches and by the 17th century was practically extinct, except in certain Calvinistic countries, particularly in Scotland, and in colonial America. Today excommunication is almost unknown among the major Protestant bodies, except for cases of bold heresy by the clergy in certain groups such as the Episcopal Church and the Presbyterian Church, which have had some noted heresy trials in the 20th century. In such cases the decision is made by regularly constituted church courts and according to church law. The smaller and stricter Protestant churches in America have largely retained excommunication as a major aspect of discipline.

Excommunication was practiced from the very beginning by Anabaptists and Mennonites, and has been retained down to the present time in all groups which have retained discipline, which includes all but the Dutch Mennonites and Northwest German city churches. The power of excommunication has generally resided in the office of bishop or elder acting in the name of the congregation. The exercise of the power was customarily subject to an approving vote of the congregation, as it still is among the Mennonite Brethren and the Amish. The bishop, in consultation with the ministry of his congregation, presented the case to the congregation, stating the offense, and after an approving vote, pronounced the formula of excommunication. In some Mennonite (MC) churches more recently the bishop has the authority to excommunicate without a vote of the congregation. In some groups (e.g., G.C.M.) the decision as to excommunication (like admission to membership) is made by the church council or some representative group rather than by the pastor or responsible leader of the church. Restoration of the excommunicated member was and is possible usually only after a lapse of time upon repentance and confession. In the stricter groups, e.g., the Mennonite Church (MC) and the Amish, excommunicated members are received back into membership "from their knees," that is, they kneel to make confession and renew their vows, and are then given the right hand of fellowship and asked to rise just as in the case of baptism. Often a lapse of time, such as a month, is required before restoration.

The grounds for excommunication have always included both heretical doctrine and misconduct. The latter has included not only gross and flagrant sin but also disobedience to the regulations of the church, including a variety of points depending upon the character of the congregational or conference regulations. At various times and places the following have been (and still are) grounds: immorality in any form, theft, lying, etc., drinking of alcoholic beverages or drunkenness, smoking tobacco, attendance at theaters (including motion pictures), gambling and card playing, military service and training, unethical economic practices including taking advantage of bankruptcy laws, wearing of jewelry and fashionable attire, violation of the requirements of uniform costume, etc. An earlier universal ground was intermarriage with "outsiders," often even with those of other Mennonite branches; it is still the rule in a number of the more conservative groups, even in the Bergthal district of the Canadian G.C.M. Conference which excommunicates for marriage to any non-G.C.M. member. The rigid groups, such as Amish and the Old Colony Mennonites, have excommunicated for the use of modern inventions and conveniences, such as automobiles, electricity and electrical appliances, telephones, floor carpets, wall pictures, photography, etc. At times excommunication has been applied to schismatic leaders and even whole groups, and the threat of excommunication has been used to maintain control and to ward off incipient schisms or the appeals of internal or outside leaders for followers. In some cases bishops or elders, abusing their power, have high-handedly excommunicated personal enemies or have excommunicated for very minor infractions of rules or personal interpretations of them. More than one schism, especially in Holland in earlier times, has been wholly or partially caused by such actions. Occasionally assertions have been made to the effect that the early Anabaptists or Mennonites tolerated freedom of doctrine. This is clearly contradicted by the actual excommunications for heresy.

An excommunication formula developed, probably by tradition, which ultimately was printed in the ministers' manuals, or handed down in manuscript form as among the Amish. A typical formula is that printed in the *Allgemeines und vollständiges Formularbuch* (Neuwied, 1807) which was often reprinted: (Translated) "Since by your sinful life you have grieved God, given offense to the church, and made yourself unworthy to be a member of the church, therefore we excommunicate you herewith in the name of God, and by the authority of Christ's Word and commandment, according to Matt. 18 and the teaching of Paul in I Cor. 5, from our church, until you return, feel penitence and sorrow for your sin, ask God and the church for forgiveness, and lead a renewed life; to which may the Lord Jesus grant you grace, light, and understanding." The common rule was that the offender was to be admonished or visited before the excommunication could take place, but that in case of gross and flagrant publicly known sin, this prior admonition was not necessary.

In recent years excommunications are not so frequent, since it is now common to permit an offender to withdraw before excommunication, in which case the bishop or elder merely announces the withdrawal, or it is recorded in the church book without announcement. A painless type of excommunication is the practice of some congregations of dropping from the church rolls those who fail to pay their church dues for a period of time, or discontinue participation in the church activities, or cease attendance at the services. In some places members who have been disciplined by the "small ban," i.e., "setting back" from communion, may be continued as noncommunicant members for a long time, even until death. In others such noncommunicant members are carried only for a few years and then either quietly or publicly dropped. In a few Mennonite (MC) conferences deliberate abstention from the communion service three or more successive times is a ground for severance of membership.

A few historic cases of excommunication are worthy of note. In 1547 Dirk Philips, with Menno Simons' agreement, excommunicated Elder Adam Pastor at Goch because of his unitarian theology. In 1549 Menno Simons excommunicated Elder Frans Cuiper for pro-Catholic leanings. In 1552 he excommunicated Elder Gillis van Aken for adultery, restoring him in 1554 on confession. In 1560 he excommunicated Zylis and Lemke, two leaders of the High German churches, and, with the support of the Dutch leaders and churches, all the High German leaders, for not agreeing to the strict practice of avoidance including marital avoidance, as decided at the Wismar Conference. This marked a permanent division between Menno's followers and the South German and Swiss Brethren. In the course of the numerous factional disputes and schisms among the Dutch Mennonites 1560-1650, excommunication (including mutual excommunication of entire groups) was resorted to more than once. The same thing occurred in the Amish schism in Switzerland and Alsace in 1693, when Jakob Ammann excommunicated all those who refused to join him in the strict practice of avoidance, and the Reist party in turn excommunicated the Amish party. In America similar occasions can be reported. In 1777 the excommunication of Bishop Christian Funk by the Franconia Conference for supporting the colonial side of the Revolutionary War led to the Funkite schism. In the schism of the Brenneman group in Indiana in 1874, Daniel Brenneman was excommunicated by the conference (MC). Other similar cases have occurred in the MC group in more recent times.

The formation in 1847-48 of the new Oberholtzer group (first stage of the General Conference Mennonite groups), as well as its own early history, contains four striking cases of group excommunication. At the 1847 fall meeting of the Franconia Conference (MC) the Oberholtzer faction of 16 ministers including the moderator of the conference were expelled from the conference for having subscribed to an unsanctioned new constitution. Soon thereafter the chairman of the new conference and another minister, Abraham and Henry Hunsicker, were expelled together with their following for opposing the conference ruling of prohibition of membership in secret orders. In 1858 the new conference expelled Preacher William Gehman and 22 others for persisting in holding special prayer meetings contrary to a conference decision. In 1861 it expelled Preacher Henry Johnson of Lower Skippack, who took with him most of the congregation. The Hunsicker faction died out, but the Gehman faction developed into the Evangelical Mennonites (*q.v.*), the oldest unit of the later M.B.C. Conference, still in vigorous existence with about 5,000 members. The "Johnson" Mennonites have continued as an independent group.

In 1697 the Danzig Elder Georg Hansen excommunicated the Mennonite artist Enoch Seeman, Sr., for painting portraits in violation of the Second Commandment, and would not reinstate him until he promised to paint only landscapes and decorations.

In later years, when the pressure to participate in military service became greater, numerous cases of excommunication of those who departed from the nonresistant faith are reported in Holland as well as in the Danzig area. In 1793 a Texel (Holland) Mennonite was excommunicated for serving on a naval vessel. W. Mannhardt, speaking of the practice of the West Prussian churches, says (in his *Wehrfreiheit der Altpreussischen Mennoniten,* 1863), "From earliest times in all the Prussian churches the acceptance of military service has been counted as a sin requiring excommunication, . . . by which the offender drops out (*ausscheidet*) from the church. Earlier when certain members had been forcibly taken into the army and served in a war, they were forgiven and restored to membership upon repentance. Later, when military service was followed by continuing obligations in the reserve corps, the excommunication was made irreversible." When an Elbing Mennonite who had served in the 1815 campaign against Napoleon tried in 1816 to force the church to receive him again by an appeal to the King, which the elders resisted, the case was taken to court (*Kammergericht*) in Berlin, which in 1818 freed the elders of all charges, stating that in the light of their age-old principles the Mennonites had a right to such excommunications. Military service is no longer a ground for excommunication anywhere among European Mennonites and not in most American congregations of the General Conference Mennonites, the Evangelical Mennonites, the Evangelical Mennonite Brethren, and possibly a few others. However, in the Mennonite Church (MC) and related groups, the Old Order Amish and Old Order Mennonites, the conservative groups in Canada, and the Mennonite Brethren Church in Canada it still is. In most cases the forfeiture of membership is automatic. The Canadian M.B. Conference took action in 1948 more clearly defining its position by requiring excommunication for participation in combatant service but not for service in an unarmed medical corps. In the M.C. group in World War II some 1200 men lost their membership, some 500 of whom were reinstated later.

The land-commissioners Jacob Höppner and Johann Bartsch, who located the Chortitza colony in the Ukraine (founded 1788-89), were excommunicated from the Flemish church at Chortitza because of bitter feeling about their work. Bartsch was reinstated later, but Höppner became a member of the Frisian branch of the church. Johann Wiebe, elder in Chortitza, attempted to deter Claas Reimer from organizing the schismatic Kleine Gemeinde in 1812 by threat of excommunication and unfrocking. The elders of the Mennonite Church in the Molotschna and Chortitza colonies in 1860 excommunicated the 18 founders of the Mennonite Brethren group, even though the latter had already formally withdrawn from the old church. In the confusion of the early days of the M.B. group (1860-65) a number of cases of excommunication, even of leaders, occurred, some by radical elements. Among these cases were J. Reimer, B. Bekker, and C. Schmidt. H.S.B.

Exeland Mennonite Church (MC) began as a rural mission project in the area a few miles southeast of the town of Exeland, Wis. In 1949 services were held in the basement of the church under construction. The completed church was dedicated on May 9, 1954, on which date the congregation was organized as a member of the North Central District. The membership was 25, with Wallace Kauffman as pastor. F.A.S.

Exeter Civilian Public Service Unit No. 117 was opened at Exeter School, Lafayette, Rhode Island, Nov. 9, 1943, and closed in August 1949. The 20 men of the unit, under the direction of the Mennonite Central Committee, performed various services in this institution, which cared for mentally defective boys. M.G.

M. Gingerich, *Service for Peace* (Akron, 1949) 239.

Exile (Banishment), a punishment which in former times could be applied to citizens if they tried to assert their religious independence and left the state churches. Thus the third article of the fourth Lateran Council of 1215 (Roman Catholic) obligated the temporal authorities to expel all subjects who had deviated from the Catholic faith.

During the Reformation this punishment was inflicted upon the Anabaptists in nearly all the Protestant countries, whereas death was the corresponding penalty in Catholic regions. The exiles were usually bound by oath not to return to the country; if they broke their oath, their return was considered a crime and was severely punished. Questions of faith were then no longer considered, and judgment followed on the basis of disobedience of the temporal authorities. Since the Anabaptists held the oath to be incompatible with the teachings of Jesus, and since they were aware of no criminal deed, they did not grant the state the right to banish them, referring to the verse of Scripture, "The earth is the Lord's" (Bossert, 315). The authorities, however, forcibly took them over the border if they refused to go voluntarily. Corporal punishment was not infrequently added to exile. In some countries they were whipped, in others branded on the cheek.

But in the neighboring country after their expulsion they were not safe either, for the authorities always notified these countries of the expulsion and demanded that they also banish the victim (Strickler, 336, 586). Hence if some returned to their homes, it was not always due to a fault of theirs.

Exile was the first penalty visited upon the Anabaptists, having been applied at Zürich in the very week of the inception of the movement. After Zwingli's first disputation with the advocates of adult baptism on Jan. 17, 1525, the council of the city ordered all the nonresident Anabaptists to leave the canton. On Jan. 19 the council issued a mandate making it compulsory to have all unbaptized infants baptized; "He who will not do this shall get out of the city, jurisdiction, and canton of my lords with wife and child, goods and possessions, or await what will happen to him." On March 11, 1525, it was decided that anyone who received adult baptism should be expelled with his family. Later on both Zürich and Bern confiscated the property of the exile. In Switzerland Mennonites continued to be banished on religious grounds until within the 18th century, particularly in the cantons of Bern and Zürich.

The history of Anabaptist banishment is particularly noteworthy in Bern where this punishment was applied even more rigorously than in Zürich. After the foreign Anabaptists had been expelled at the introduction of the Reformation into Bern (1527-28), the council issued a mandate on July 22, 1531, ordering that Anabaptists should first be submerged under water and then ejected from the canton; if they returned they should be drowned. The mandate of July 31 repeated this order. Following the great disputation at Bern (q.v.) of March 11-17, 1538, the foreign Anabaptists were told that they were to leave the canton immediately. Native Anabaptists were told that they would be conducted over the border by the police and in case of return they were to be executed with the sword unless they recanted. This was the procedure followed during the next decades. Innumerable persons, regardless of sex or age, were thus driven from their homes. An official opinion of the clergy (1585) recommended that especially the leaders of the Anabaptists be banished from the country and sent to the galleys. Others who were not leaders, but obstinate persons, were to be expelled. In the mandate of Sept. 3, 1585, it was accordingly ordered that the stiff-necked Anabaptists were to be taken to the border in chains. The mandate of 1597 added the threat of death in case of return and declared the property of exiled persons confiscate to the state (see Täufergut). The mandate of Dec. 26, 1644, decreed that returning Anabaptists should be publicly whipped. Thus the Bernese government in the course of time tried various means of force to induce the Anabaptists to return "to the right way." When all these measures proved fruitless, and they still wanted at any cost to get rid of the "damned sect," the authorities proceeded to expel all the Anabaptists held in prison in the penitentiary. The exiles had to sign the following *Verbannungs-Revers*: "I, the undersigned, herewith confess that after I on account of my adopted aforesaid Anabaptist doctrine had been for a time detained by our high Christian government in their penitentiary or orphanage in Bern, and had been admonished on the subject to withdraw from the doctrine, but I can and will not desist from my assumed opinion . . . I have fallen more and more into the punishment and disfavor of my high govern-

ment in consideration of my adopted doctrine, which is exactly contrary to the government mandate. And that I now therefore am to avoid their city and canton and depart. Therefore I herewith vow and promise to accept such banishment from now on when I am to be conducted over the border, and avoid the city and canton and the borders altogether, and henceforth to have no contact by oral or secret or public communication with its citizens in any way, on the aforesaid doctrine. With this further declaration that I shall and will not in any form let myself be seen or enter into their lands and territories, but if contrary to expectations, I do not keep this my promise but act contrary to it, it shall be regarded as if I had broken a properly sworn oath and that therefore a high government without further ado act in accord with the law and the content of the publicly read mandate, and as it is customary to judge such persons by law, shall I the false teacher be judged, by virtue of this letter, which I herewith in this matter sign with my own hand." On Jan. 20, 1663, the chancellery of Bern announced that most of the banished Anabaptists were again at home. A mandate of Sept. 8, 1670, ordered the expulsion to begin again, "to clear these intolerable people out of the land." Those who returned should be branded with a hot iron. (Concerning the fate of one of these exiles see **Heinrich Funk**.) The ejection of the Swiss Brethren is one of the most inglorious chapters in the history of the Bernese state.

In Protestant Germany banishment was early used against the Anabaptists. In Saxony the Protestant pastors engaged in the general church inspection in 1527 were directed to warn "all those who held to an error in faith, whether on the sacrament of the body and blood of Christ, baptism," or any other doctrine, to leave the country at once; if they returned they would be severely punished. If laymen refused to desist from their error they should be ordered to sell their possessions and leave the country within a certain time (Sehling, 142 ff.). Banishment was also applied in Hesse, and in the imperial cities of Strasbourg, Augsburg, Nürnberg, Lindau, and others.

In Württemberg the theologians, in the opinion they drew up on the penalizing of the Anabaptists at the request of Duke Ulrich upon his return in 1535, reported that the "fine appearance of the life" of the Anabaptists caused many members of the church to join them. These poor people would not do this out of malice, but out of pure simplicity of mind and the good zeal which they have to God; on the other hand they see "with us and the great multitude of ours unfortunately very wild, bold, and wicked living." One should have patience with the Anabaptists and not inflict the death penalty on them. The dangerous leaders should not be expelled into other countries, for they would thus spread their doctrines into neighboring regions, but be kept in prison on meager fare, which "might serve to their correction and conversion by the grace of God." But other Anabaptists, who are not so skillful "in seducing," should if admonition, prison, and public humiliation do not avail, be banished (Bossert, 53 f.). The duke issued orders to confiscate the property of all unmarried Anabaptist exiles. He who is banished without oath and returns shall receive either corporal or capital punishment; he who is banished under oath, shall receive both corporal and capital punishment (Bossert, 60). But capital punishment was never inflicted. When the councilors explained that banishing the Anabaptists from one country to another merely spread their doctrine, Duke Ulrich gave the order on Dec. 15, 1544, to have the preachers instruct the prisoners and persuade them to recant; at the next diet he would suggest a conference to decide "how to deal with such wrong and stubborn people" (Bossert, 101). His successor, Duke Christoph, also issued a mandate on June 25, 1558, ordering the proscription of dissenters (Bossert, 171). In 1614 an Anabaptist from Dettingen was refused permission to stay in the country unless he "abstained from his error" (Bossert, 854).

Under Catholic jurisdiction exile was the exception. In the Palatinate it was adopted after executions had reached their height (Beck, *Geschichts-Bücher,* 32). In Bohemia the estates raised a protest against the execution of Anabaptists in 1529, in effect calling for other punishments such as exile.

In Moravia the Landtag at Znaim consented to the banishment of Anabaptists in 1535. A large number of fugitives were captured in neighboring lands, especially in the bishopric of Passau (*q.v.*). The repeated demands of Ferdinand that the Moravian estates expel them (in 1540, 1546, and 1550) indicate that numerous Anabaptists were still being protected by the more benevolent barons or hiding in subterranean passages (see **Lochy**). Martial developments occupied the king's attention, pushing the persecution of Anabaptists into the background. Later it revived. In 1563, when Ferdinand sent his son Maximilian to Moravia, the estates requested Maximilian to influence his father to permit the Anabaptists to stay, in view of the labor shortage, since there were among them "neat and artistic craftsmen in all fields," who had done not a little work in Moravia. Maximilian answered evasively, but did nothing against the Anabaptists. But when he assumed the government, and Pope Pius V threatened to depose him if he permitted Protestantism free exercise of religion, he ordered the expulsion of the Hutterites by the end of the year at the Landtag in Brno in 1567; if they returned they faced death. The estates protested that exile was impossible, for the Anabaptists "would not want to leave. And they would not know whither to go; they would rather be killed than expelled." In reply to the request of the estates that the king inform them what steps to take if the Hutterites refused to go, he king said he would consider the problem. But there was no further word, nor did the problem come up for discussion at any future Landtag (Hruby, 21 ff.).

When in a humaner era the death penalty for deviation of religious ideas was no longer possible, it was gradually replaced by exile, which was in its turn gradually abandoned too. In France a mandate of Louis XIV, Aug. 13, 1712, decreed that Mennonites must leave the country, but it was only partially enforced. The last major exile of Anabaptists on religious grounds was the expulsion of the Hutterian Brethren from Transylvania when police conducted them to the Polish border and left them to their fate in the mountains, under penalty of death if they returned, because they had refused to become Catholic (see **Kuhr, Joseph**). However, as late as 1780, Bishop Johannes Nafziger of Essingen in the Palatinate was sentenced to be exiled from the Palatinate because he had baptized two former Amish Mennonite orphan girls who had been reared in a Catholic orphanage.

In the Netherlands there were during the rise of Anabaptism (about 1532) a few cases where Anabaptists were banned from a city. In 1535-50, those were usually banished who attended Anabaptist meetings, but confessed that they had not been rebaptized, and did not agree with the Anabaptist principles. After persecution was over and the Reformed Church established, there were only a few individual cases of exile; for example, Hans de Ries (*q.v.*), who was banished from Middelburg in 1578 (*q.v.*), Ucko Walles (*q.v.*), who had to leave the province of Groningen in 1637, and Foecke Floris (*q.v.*), who in 1683 was banished from the province of Friesland.

HEGE, S.G.

E. Egli, *Die Züricher Wiedertäufer* (Zürich, 1878); J. C. Füsslin, *Beiträge zur Kirchen- und Reformationsgeschichte des Schweizerlandes I* (Zürich, 1741); Müller, *Berner Täufer;* S. Geiser, *Die Taufgesinnten-Gemeinden* (Karlsruhe, 1931); G. Bossert, *TA: Württemberg;* E. Correll, "The Value of Family History for Mennonite History Illustrated from Nafziger Family Material of the Eighteenth Century," *MQR* II (1928) 66-79, gives the Johannes Nafziger story; J. Strickler, *Aktensammlung zur schweizerischen Ref.-Gesch.* I (1878); E. Sehling, *Die evangelischen Kirchenordnungen des 16. Jahrhunderts I* (Leipzig, 1902); Beck, *Geschichts-Bücher;* Fr. Hruby, "Die Wiedertäufer in Mähren," in *Archiv f. Ref.-Gesch.* XXX (1933); *ML* II, 610-12.

Exincourt, a village near Montbéliard, France, where a Mennonite school enjoyed a brief but active existence. Isaac Rich, who had received his education at Wadsworth (*q.v.*), founded it to provide religious instruction for the Mennonite children of the vicinity who had to attend Catholic schools. Gradually, however, the care of orphaned and neglected children became its more important task. They were accepted regardless of creed and supported without charge or for a small sum contributed by friends until they reached the age of 14 years. At first the school was located at Etupes, a village 15 minutes from Exincourt; then Rich leased the stately manor house in Exincourt and transferred the school into it.

Through the energetic interest of the founder, who frequently attended the conferences of the Hessian-Palatine Mennonites to promote his cause, the school received generous financial support from the Mennonites of France and South Germany, though it was not accepted as a charge of the general conference. The school flourished. Six years after its modest beginning it supported 40 children and had an annual expenditure of 12,000 francs. Then there was a sudden collapse. On the night of June 28, 1876, Rich was suddenly arrested on account of moral lapses and was sentenced for life to

New Caledonia, where he died penitent on May 6, 1878. (*Gbl.* and *Menn. Bl.,* 1870-76; *DB* 1872, 111-16; *ML* I, 622.)   NEFF.

Extract Ende Seeckere Antwoort *van der Switser broederen, ofte hoochduytschen also genoemt, overgegeven aan de Arrianen in Polen betreffende het punct der menschwerdinghe, ende godtheydt Jesu Christij. Gescreven met gemeender vergaderinghe der olsten ende dienaren wt vele landen binnen Straetsborgh,* a pamphlet of 13 manuscript pages, found in the Amsterdam Mennonite Library. This confession on the Incarnation of Christ as believed by the Swiss Mennonites was published in *Handelinge der Ver-eenigde Vlaemse en Duytse Doopsgesinde Gemeynten* (Vlissingen, 1666), pp. 74-81. The conference mentioned in the title was held at Strasbourg in 1592. The "Arrianen" mentioned in the book were the Polish Socinians.   vDZ.

Eyckenplancken (Oak Planks), nickname for Mennonites of the Netherlands, presumably because of their steadfastness or perhaps for their simplicity in manners and dress. The expression is found in a writing of Franciscus Lansbergen (*q.v.*), *Van de vremde ende onschriftmatighe maniere der Wederdoopscher Leeraren heymelycke gebeden, . . .* (Rotterdam, 1596). Which group or denomination of the Mennonites was meant is not clear. (*DB* 1897, 79.)   vDZ.

Eyebrow (Sask.) Mennonite Brethren, which belongs to the Herbert District Conference, was organized in 1927, with approximately a dozen members. A number of families left for British Columbia; hence there has been no increase in the membership. The founder and leader was John Heinrichs (still serving in 1953) and the 1953 membership was 16.   J.I.R.

Eyebrow-Tugaske Mennonite Church (GCM), located about 50 miles northeast of Moose Jaw, Sask., and 6 miles west of Eyebrow, was established in 1926 by settlers from Russia. In 1929 this church became a member of the Canadian Conference, but the first meetinghouse was not built until 1946. The first minister was Johann Martens. In 1953 there were two ministers: David Bueckert, leader, and Gerhard Fedrau, with a membership of 50.

J.G.R.

Eylert, Ruhlemann Friedrich (1770-1850), Lutheran bishop and court chaplain at Potsdam, Prussia, spiritual counselor of Frederick William III of Prussia. He gives the Mennonites friendly treatment in his book, *Charakterzüge und historische Fragmente aus dem Leben des Königs von Preussen Friedrich Wilhelm III. Gesammelt nach eigenen Beobachtungen und herausgegeben von R. Fr. Eylert* (Magdeburg, 1844). Unfortunately the partly imaginary tale of the Mennonite youth who took part in the Wars of Liberation (1813-15) and was consequently excommunicated for violation of the principle of nonresistance furnished the material for Wildenbruch's (*q.v.*) drama *Der Menonit.* (See **Literature**; *Menn. Bl.,* 1884, 17-20; *ML* I, 623.)   NEFF.

Eymann (Eiman, Eyman), a Bernese Mennonite family which migrated to Alsace, France, in 1671-1711. Three Eymann families are named by Ernst Müller (*Berner Täufer*) in his list of Mennonite families in the Palatinate, Germany, in 1672. The census of 1940 by Franz Crous lists 87 Eymanns in South German congregations, 23 of whom were members of the Weierhof congregation, 28 of the Monsheim congregation, and 31 of the Sembach congregation. Peter Eymann (*q.v.*) was a South German Mennonite active in political affairs, being elected to the provincial diet at Munich in 1848. Mennonites from Bavaria established a settlement in Ashland Co., Ohio, in the 1830's. Living in this settlement was Jacob Eyman, who in 1851 with his family moved to Lee Co., Iowa. Among the Amish and Mennonite immigrants arriving in America on Sept. 9, 1749, was Jacob Eiman. The Eiman family was already represented in the Ontario Amish Mennonite community in the late 1830's. Representatives of the Eiman family now live principally in Iowa, while members of the Eyman branch have lived in Ohio, Indiana, and Michigan.   M.G.

Eymann, Peter (1788-1855), a South German Mennonite who entered political life and was at the same time active as a leader in his congregation. He was born Nov. 13, 1788, at the Lohmühle tanning mill in the community (*Gemeinde*) of Langmeil in the Rhenish Palatinate; died at his mill in Diemerstein on March 14, 1855. In 1833 he was elected mayor of Frankenstein, and with one brief exception, held this office until his death 22 years later. In spite of a limited education he was quite successful in this office. Politically he favored a republican government. In 1848, the year of the revolution, he was elected as a delegate from the district of Kaiserslautern-Kirchheimbolanden to the Bavarian diet at Munich. He was the first German Mennonite to hold this position. The diet convened in January 1849. On May 15 the republic was proclaimed in the Palatinate, and on May 29 the diet at Munich was dissolved. Eymann went home a sick and broken man following this. Prussian troops restored order in the Palatinate.

Eymann served after 1816 as an assistant minister of the Mennonite congregation at Sembach, but avoided this work as much as possible. As a result of his earnest efforts the first salaried minister was installed at Sembach. (*ML* I, 623.)   M.P.

Eysenburg, Johann, one of Melchior Hofmann's 16 prophets, who was persuaded by Martin Bucer to join the Reformed Church and was then used by him with Peter Tasch (*q.v.*) to try to persuade the Anabaptists, and especially Hofmann, to come into the church. On May 5, 1539, they had their first interview with Hofmann, which lasted six hours. Four others of five hours each were held before May 26; but they were not successful. On May 22, 1539, the Strasbourg authorities sent a letter to the Speyer council, requesting them to receive the two to convert the Anabaptists at Speyer.   NEFF.

F. O. zur Linden, *Melchior Hofmann, ein Prophet der Wiedertäufer* (Haarlem, 1885) 396-400; *ML* I, 623.

Eyssen, Pieter, a Dutch preacher of the Flemish Mennonite congregation of Amsterdam, chosen July 28, 1664, and an ardent antagonist of Galenus Abrahamsz (*q.v.*), the prominent leader of this church. When the congregation was divided by the schism of the *Lammerenkrijg* (*q.v.*) into a more liberal Lamist (*q.v.*) congregation (Galenus Abrahamsz) and a more conservative Zonist congregation (Samuel Apostool, *q.v.*), Eyssen joined the latter, serving as a preacher until 1670. In this year, together with his copreacher Isaac van Vreede and a number of members, he left the Zonist congregation because of a conflict and founded a new congregation called *De kleine Zon,* which however returned to the Zonist mother church in 1679. Eyssen died in 1681.   vDZ.

Inv. Arch. Amst. II, Nos. 1273, 1393, 1404; H. W. Meihuizen, *Galenus Abrahamsz* (Haarlem, 1954).

Eysvogel, Johann, of Cologne, supposedly a former member of the Hutterite brotherhood who returned to Catholicism in the 1580's, and to justify this step wrote a slanderous pamphlet against his erstwhile coreligionists. He called it *Ein Ander schön neues Lied darin der Betrug und arglistige Art der Hutterischen Wiedertäufer wahrhaftig und eigentlich vor Augen gestellt wird. Allen gutherzigen frommen Christen zur notwendigen Erinnerung und getreuen Warnung gemacht und in Druck gegeben durch Johann Eysvogel von Cöln, gewesten Hutterischen Wiedertäufer Bruder zu Austerlitz in Mähren . . .* 1581 (written in form of a popular song). It is a booklet very similar in type and spirit to that of Hans Jedelshauser (*q.v.*) of the same year, which was published by Christoph Erhard (*q.v.*). Whether the publication of Eysvogel's pamphlet had the same connection is not known, but Erhard reprints this poem in his *Gründliche . . . Historia* (1589), pp. 35-38.

It contains, so to speak, all the arsenal of hostile arguments against the Hutterites which ever were launched against them. Eysvogel attacks the educational system of the Brethren (*q.v.*), their community of goods (*q.v.*), their somewhat unusual marriage system, and their legendary wealth (see **Economic History of the Hutterites**). He says they buy up all crops in Moravia so that no one else may have them; they spoil all the trades and rob people with the prices they charge for their products. In short, they chase after money and drive prices higher and higher. In their dress they show a studied modesty but wear only the very best of materials. They act puffed up like noblemen, have the best farms and the best horses, on which they ride around in the manner of the lords.

> *Das Brot tun sie abschneiden*
> *Dem Armen wohl vor dem Maul.*

Worst of all (in Eysvogel's opinion) is the fact that they pay for all their purchases with cash, and thus dominate markets and fairs. (Incidentally, this is a reproach which occasionally may be heard even today, mainly in Canada.) They are wealthy but hide their treasures from the world, etc. The argument of tense economic competition by these large-scale Hutterite enterprises is repeated time and again, and

becomes the standard polemical slogan in all subsequent attacks on the Brethren.

Small as the pamphlet was (and who can say whether it was original or merely fabricated as in the Jedelshauser case), its arguments had a major influence upon another representative of the growing Austrian Counter Reformation (*q.v.*), Christoph A. Fischer (*q.v.*), who repeated them almost verbatim about 20 years later. Also the government in Vienna availed itself of the same arguments in its ill-famed General Mandate (edict) of 1601, reprinted by Fischer.   LOSERTH, R.F.

Loserth, *Communismus,* 58-61; Rembert, *Wiedertäufer* 505; *ML* I, 623, 646.

Eyte (Ayte), a former Dutch Mennonite family living in the Zaan district near Amsterdam, of which a number of members were preachers. Pieter Pietersz belonged to the Waterlander denomination. Having preached in the congregation of *Menniste buurt* near Zijpe and returning by boat to Zaandam, on Nov. 10, 1664, he was fatally struck by the falling mast when his boat collided with another boat. His three sons, Gerrit Pietersz Eyte (1656-1728), Dirk Pietersz Eyte (1663-1736), and Pieter Pietersz Eyte (1664-1744), all served as preachers of the Nieuwe Huys united Flemish and Waterlander congregation at Zaandam in 1680-1728, 1692-1736 (?), and 1692-1744, respectively.   vDZ.

S. Lootsma, *Friesch Doopsgezinde Gemeente West-Zaandam, Het Nieuwe Huys.* (Zaandam, 1937) 31, 57, 58, 103, 186, 191, 222-28.

Ezinge, a village in the Dutch province of Groningen, where Leenaert Bouwens (*q.v.*) baptized 20 or 25 persons in 1561-63. This number suggests that a Mennonite congregation may have existed here; but since there are no traces of such a congregation, we must assume that the newly baptized joined a congregation in the neighborhood, presumably Oldehove (*q.v.*).   vDZ.

Ezra (Esdras), **Fourth Book,** also called *Second Ezra,* a pseudepigraphical book of semi-canonical dignity; in the Latin Vulgate Bible it stands at the end of the entire book, after the New Testament, although it definitely belongs to the class of Jewish Pseudepigrapha of the inter-testamental period. The latter are books published after the conclusion of the Biblical canon under the alleged authorship of some Old Testament writers, such as Ezra. The book is actually one of the numerous late Jewish apocalypses couched in such terms that this literature could become acceptable also to the rabbinic Judaism of the period after the destruction of the temple in Jerusalem by the Romans in A.D. 70. Thus it is assumed that the *Fourth Ezra* was written around A.D. 100 by a Jew who tried to comfort his coreligionists and to make them hope for a glorious future, that is, salvation under the expected "Son of Man" or Messiah. The influence of the school of the great teacher Shammai is noticeable.

The book became exceedingly popular in the early church, and soon was expanded. Chapters 3-14 are original, while chapters 1 and 2 (sometimes called *Ezra V*) and 15 and 16 (also called *Ezra VI*) are

Christian additions of the second century after Christ. The Vulgate has all 16 chapters. The Church Fathers often used the book, and thus also the Reformers. Luther knew it well, and Leo Jud, the collaborator with Zwingli in Zürich, translated it from the printed Vulgate.

The numbering of the Ezra books is somewhat intricate: the Vulgate counts four such books, including Ezra, Nehemiah, and (as No. III) a sort of summary of both plus Chronicles, so that the apocalypse becomes the fourth book of that name. In modern Protestant scholarship and editions our book is called "Second Ezra," since here only the original Ezra and our book are counted.

The Anabaptists seemed to have been rather fond of the book: Michael Sattler quotes a lengthy section from it (2:34-37) in his well-known letter to the congregation at Horb (1527). Peter Riedemann in his *Rechenschaft* of 1540 refers to it at many places but strangely enough used texts only from chapters 3:4-24 and 7:20-56.

The Mennonites of Northern Germany also seem to have been rather fond of Ezra in earlier days. Georg Hansen (*q.v.*) quotes Ezra IV in his *Glaubensbericht für die Jugend*, 1671, using chapters 7 and 8 (Friedmann, 131), and Gerhard Roosen quotes it in his *Christliches Gemütsgespräch* (*q.v.*) (1702), in the section "Concerning the Fall of the Human Race," question 65. Here we read the rather famous passage: "Oh thou Adam, what hast thou done! For though it was thou that sinned, thou art not fallen alone but we all that come of thee" (Ezra IV, 7.48) (Friedmann, 145). It is not unlikely that more such references would be found if a thorough study were made.

One should not forget that the Anabaptists were rather fond of both the apocryphal literature (*Apocrypha, q.v.*), such as Jesus Sirach or the *Gospel According to Nicodemus,* and the pseudepigraphic books, which include, besides Ezra IV, the very popular *Testament of the Twelve Patriarchs,* with its "wisdom"-emphasis.

The Ezra IV book teaches that but few will be saved either through divine compassion or through good works (whence the Catholic doctrine of meritorious works). It is a genuine apocalypse: Rome is called "Edom," the author has visions like Daniel (of the Son of Man, of an Eagle, etc.), and he describes the signs preceding the end of the world. Chapters 1 and 2 comfort Christians because the days of distress are near, but there is also hope for the glory envisioned. The book knows the doctrines of original sin (see above 7:48)—otherwise foreign to Judaism—, and the consequent suffering of all men. But, while Paul teaches release from sin for all who believe, Ezra IV still remains within the framework of Jewish nationalism, both in suffering and in its expectations.

Chapter 2 (the "Christian" supplement) promises that "the Shepherd is nigh at hand. Be ready for the reward of the Kingdom. . . . I asked the angel: Sir, what are these? and He answered: . . . those who have put off mortal clothing and put on the immortal, and have confessed the name of God. Now they are being crowned and have received palms. . . . And He [A Youth of great brightness] is the Son of God whom they have confessed in the world. Then I began greatly to commend those who stood so staunchly for the name of the Lord." (This is Sattler's text, somewhat abbreviated.)   R.F.

R. H. Charles, *Religious Development Between the Old and the New Testaments* (London, 1934) 249-52; R. Friedmann, *Mennonite Piety Through the Centuries* (Goshen, 1949). The Sattler "text" may also be found in *MQR* XXVIII (1954) 20.

Ezumaburen and **Ezumazijl,** hamlets in the Dutch province of Friesland. Leenaert Bouwens baptized 7 persons in Ezumaburen in 1563 and 25 in 1568-82; and in this latter period he baptized 7 persons in near-by Ezumazijl. There was, however, no Mennonite congregation here. The Mennonites living here were no doubt members of some neighboring congregation, perhaps Anjum (*q.v.*) or Dokkum (*q.v.*).   vdZ.

F

Faber de Bouma, Gellius (Jelle Smit), was a Catholic priest at Jelsum near Leeuwarden, Friesland, who left his home community at the same time as Menno Simons in 1536, but joined the Reformed Church and became a minister at Norden and in 1538 at Emden. In 1544 he took part in the disputation between Menno Simons and á Lasco (Jan. 21-31). He died on June 2, 1564.

In 1552 Gellius Faber published a booklet of 78 pages presumably in reply to an Anabaptist writing of 1550. The Faber book (no longer in existence) had the title, *Eine Antwert Gellij Fabri dener des hilligen wordes binnen Emden op einen bitter hönischen breeff der Wedderdöper* . . . (Magdeburg). Menno Simons, who felt that not only his co-workers but he himself had been unjustly attacked, wrote a response in which he closely followed the outline of Faber's booklet. Menno defends the calling of the Anabaptist ministers, their baptism, the Lord's Supper, the ban, their view regarding the church, and the Incarnation. The book was entitled *Een Klare beantwoordinge, over een Schrift Gellii Fabri* . . . and appeared in 1554 very likely in an Anabaptist print shop in Lübeck. In this, the longest book that Menno produced, can be found his "Conversion" or the "Renunciation of the Church of Rome," which he presented in connection with his defense of the calling of the Anabaptist ministers. This account is both very important biographical information and a jewel of Menno's writings and has been reprinted many times. **C.K.**

K. Vos, *Menno Simons* (Leiden, 1914) 108 ff.; C. Krahn, *Menno Simons* (Karlsruhe, 1936) 77 ff.; Menno Simons, *Complete Works* II (Elkhart, 1871) 1-105; J. G. de Hoop Scheffer, *Geschiedenis der Kerkhervorming in Nederland* (Amsterdam, 1873) 59, 60, 488; *Biogr. Wb.* I, 542-44; *ML* I, 623.

Faber, Engelbert (d. 1580), born near Cologne, Germany, was ordained as minister in P. Dathenus' refugee church of Frankfurt in 1561, was a Reformed minister at Wolfsheim near Alzey in the Palatinate, in the Lower Rhine region, and in the Netherlands. In a letter to H. Bullinger dated April 23, 1562, at Alzey, he said concerning his contacts with the Anabaptists along the Lower Rhine, it "was a bitter thought that he could not present his word in an appropriate manner while these simpletons accept Anabaptist heresies in masses, and yet he could not be silent." He reported that he had now found a copy of the book by Bernhard Buwo (*q.v.*), *Een frundtlyke thosamensprekinge* . . . (1556, in Low Saxon; in 1557 a Dutch edition appeared), directed against the Mennonites, which he had translated into German, asking Bullinger whether he found it appropriate to have it published. Bullinger's reply must have been favorable. In 1563 in Heidelberg his book entitled *Dialogus: Das ist, Ein gespräch zweyer Personen, von dem Tauff der jungen Kinder* . . . appeared. He was a participant in the Frankenthal (*q.v.*) disputation of 1571. In 1575 he became a pastor in Gau-Odernheim, and in 1580 he died at Venlo on the Maas. **C.K.**

W. Hollweg, "Bernhard Buwo, ein ostfriesischer Theologe aus dem Reformationsjahrhundert," *Jahrb. d. Ges. f. bild. Kunst u. vaterl. Altertümer zu Emden* XXX (1953) 71 ff.; Rembert, *Wiedertäufer; ML* I, 626.

Faber, Johann (*Heigerlin*) (1478-1541), the son of a blacksmith. He studied law and theology at the universities of Tübingen and Freiburg i. Br. It appears to be an ancient misconception that he was a Dominican. He was more or less closely associated with outstanding leaders like Erasmus (*q.v.*), Vadian (*q.v.*), and Zwingli (*q.v.*). Faber advocated church reform, but only to the extent that it might remove abuses in the Catholic Church. His complete break with the Reformation occurred in Rome, whither he had gone in the fall of 1521, presumably to interest the pope in his work against Luther: *Opus adversus nova quaedam et a christiana religione prorsus aliena dogmata Martini Lutheri* (Rome, 1523). Luther had his young friend Justus Jonas write the reply; he did it with wit and humor (*Adversus J. Fabrum . . . Justi Jonas . . . defensio. Item M. Lutheri ad eundem Jonam Epistola*, 1523).

In Germany Faber engaged in an untiring struggle against the reformers, in writing, in preaching, and in dealing with authorities and rulers. His feud with Zwingli followed. He says that he attended the Zürich disputation of Jan. 29, 1523, as a counselor. Faber then wrote his popular booklet, *Ain warlich underrichtung, wie es zu Zürich ergangen,* to which Zwingli countered with his friends' highly spiced *Das Gyrenrupfen.*

Faber was employed by Duke Ferdinand (*q.v.*) in many offices, chiefly at diets and disputations. In 1528 he was in Vienna to prepare a German translation of the Bible to replace Luther's. His attempts to win Erasmus of Rotterdam (*q.v.*) for the declining University of Vienna and his former friend Melanchthon back into the Catholic Church failed.

In 1528-30 he did his most permanent work against the Reformation. His first effort was to suppress the growing Anabaptist movement in Moravia and Austria. When Balthasar Hubmaier (*q.v.*) lay in prison in Greizenstein (Kreuzenstein), afflicted by sickness and discouraged, he requested an interview with Faber, who had once been his friend. Ferdinand gave his consent.

The interview took place in the last days of 1527, lasting until after midnight on the first day. They discussed the proper interpretation of the Bible, tradition, and infant baptism. On the second day they began at 6:00 A.M. and discussed communion, the intercession of the saints, and purgatory, and Faber gave Hubmaier his booklet against Zwingli on the adoration of the saints. On the next day they discussed faith and good works, the satisfaction of Christ, Christian liberty, freedom of the will, the worship of Mary, the end of time, repentance and confession, fasting, the teachings of Luther and Zwingli and the councils.

The interview with Hubmaier was published at Leipzig in 1528 under the title, *Doctoris Joannis*

Fabri, adversus Doctorem Balthasarum Pacimonta-num Anabaptistarum Nostri saeculi, Primum au-thorem, orthodoxae Fidei Catholicae Defensio. It was reprinted at Leipzig in 1537 in Faber's *Opuscula* under the following title: *Disputatio episcopi Vien-nensis* (which he was not yet) *Joannis Fabri de praecipuis rebus orthodoxae religionis adversus Bal-thasarum Pacimontanum Anabaptistam.* Copies of both works are in the Goshen College Library. A copy of the 1537 folio volume of sermons, containing the sermons against the Anabaptists, also is in the Goshen College Library. A copy of the 1528 work is in the Bethel College Library.

At the conclusion of the talks Hubmaier declared his intention to present his confession of faith to Ferdinand. He wrote a booklet which Faber called *Liber Retractationum,* thanking the king for sending Faber to him, and saying that Faber had been kind to him. Although Hubmaier declared himself wil-ling to yield on every point except baptism and com-munion, which he would leave to the decision of the council, there could be no thought of saving his life. These two points were actually the most important of all, and Hubmaier's former political attitude in Waldshut was also reckoned against him. He died at the stake in Vienna, March 10, 1528.

On the following day a polemic sheet of nine pages, entitled *Ursach warumb der Widertauffer Patron und erster Anfenger Doctor Balthasar Hueb-mayr zu Wien auf den zehnten Martii Anno 1528 verbrennet sey* (Landshut, 1528), was published by Faber with a dedication to the Duke of Saxony. Faber said he had not written these things because Hubmaier's death gave him pleasure; he had faith-fully warned him in prison and in all Christian humility dealt with him, as is seen in Hubmaier's letter; but because it might be said in some places that he had not received justice and was, like John Hus, a martyr in God's sight, he (Faber) testified to the truth.

On April 24, 1528, he dedicated his next work, *Sermones doctoris Joannis Fabri . . . adversus Ana-baptists* (printed in *Opuscula,* Leipzig, 1537), to the bishop of Olmütz (Olomouc). On his journey to Moravia with the king he so pitied these poor mis-led people that he preached these sermons at Znaim; since the Moravians did not understand German he had them translated into Latin. There are six sermons; here, as also in the *Ursach,* he names Hub-maier as the originator of Anabaptist doctrine, and calls the Anabaptists "water bathers."

As a reward for his zeal in persecuting the Ana-baptists he asked the Innsbruck government and King Ferdinand to acquit his brother of the debt of 200 guilders. In 1530 he was made Bishop of Vienna. In 1529 he attended the Diet of Speyer as the repre-sentative of the Bishop of Constance, and at the Diet in Augsburg in 1530 he was a coauthor of the refu-tation of the Confession of Augsburg and of the *Confessio Tetrapolitana.*

In the following years Faber was preocccupied with the work of his episcopate, which he carried on along three lines: (1) He sought to preserve Catholic doctrine by resisting all innovations; he set a good example to his frequently uncouth clergy,

taking part in the religious instruction in his dio-cese by many sermons and writings, and providing capable pastors. (2) He attended the diets of the empire even in the last years of his life. In 1536 Faber wrote a valuable description of church condi-tions in Germany with advice on the attitude to be taken. (3) His work for the University of Vienna was outstanding. He wrote an extraordinary num-ber of sermons, doctrinal works, and polemics in German and Latin. Not all of them have been printed. The sermons and other theological works he published in folio volumes (Cologne, 1537-41), to which Johannes Cochlaeus (*q.v.*) added a supple-mentary volume (Leipzig, 1537). One of his oldest tracts, *Declamationes divinae de humanae vitae miseria* (Augsburg, 1520), takes a very pessimistic view of human life. Most of his writings are polem-ics, as his *Malleus haereticorum* (Cologne, 1527), the tracts against the Picards and Hussites, and *De actis ac mandatis imperatorum et regum . . . adversus haereses et earundem autores liber unus* (Leipzig, 1538), and against the reformers, Luther, Zwingli, Oecolampadius, Bullinger, Schwenckfeld, Hubmaier, and Denk. During his lifetime Faber collected a library of 3,800 volumes, unusual for that time, most of which is now in the Hofbibliothek in Vienna.

Faber died after a long illness, May 20, 1541, and is buried in the cathedral of Vienna. (See **Hub-maier.**)   NEFF, LOSERTH.

Faber's polemic of March 1528 on Hubmaier's death is found in the Munich Staatsbibliothek (4 H. ref. 735); K. Schottenloher, *Die Landshuter Buchdrucker des 16. Jahrhunderts* (Mainz, 1930) 50; excerpts were printed with comments in B. F. Hummel, *Neue Bibliothek von seltenen Büchern* I (1775) 218; see also J. O. Pr. Fabri, *Doctoris Johannis Fabri adversus Doctorem Balthasarum Pacimontanum* (Leipzig, 1528) ML I, 624 f.; II, 361.

Faber (Fabri), **Johannes** (1504—after 1557), of Heil-bronn, Germany, a Dominican and polemic-ascetic author, canon at Augsburg, author of the book *Christenliche undtterweisung an die Widertauffer von dem Tauff der Jungen Kindlein. Und von der Gaistlichen und weltlichen Oberkait an die Wider-tauffer* (Ingolstadt, 1550), which violently attacks the Anabaptists. He also wrote the pamphlet: *Von dem Ayd Schwören. Auch von der Wiedertauffer Marter. Und woher es entspringe, dass sie also fröh-lich und getröst die pein des Tods leiden. Und von der Gemeinschaft der Wiedertäufer* (Augsburg, 1550), in which he involuntarily gives them great praise when he says, "Whence does it come that the Anabaptists so joyfully and confidently suffer the pain of death? They dance and jump into the flames, see the flashing sword without dismay, speak and preach to the spectators with laughing mouth; they sing psalms and hymns until their soul departs, they die with joy, as if they were in a merry com-pany, remain strong, confident and steadfast until their death. Persisting defiantly in their intention, they also defy all pain and torture." Faber explains this phenomenon as the work of hell's dragon. Cop-ies of the 1550 booklets are in GCL.   NEFF.

R. Friedmann, "Eine dogmatische Hauptschrift der hutterischen Täufer in Mähren" (*ARG* 1932, 14); Cal-vary confuses this Faber with the Viennese Bishop Jo-hannes Faber; Wiswedel, *Bilder* II, 70; Beck, *Geschichts-Bücher,* p. XX; *ML* I, 624.

Fabricius, Jakob (1560-1640), a Protestant clergyman in Schleswig, Germany, held a public disputation with the Mennonites of Eiderstedt (*q.v.*), Sept. 13-15, 1608, which brought him "much honor." NEFF.

Schröder, *Lexikon der Hamburger Schriftsteller;* ML I, 626.

Fabricius, Johannes (*Montanus*), a Reformed divine, b. 1527 at Bergheim in Alsace, a nephew of Leo Jud, who was Zwingli's co-worker, was made pastor in Chur (*q.v.*) in 1557. Here he attacked the Swiss Brethren, who held their meetings in the home of a local citizen. In 1560 he disputed with one of the Swiss Brethren before the city council and in the following year he arranged a colloquy with the Swiss Brethren, in which he was announced as victor (Schiess, *Bullingers Korrespondenz mit den Graubündnern* II, 33). On the other hand, his attempts to convert an imprisoned Anabaptist failed (see **Grisons**). (*ML* III, 162.) HEGE.

Fabricius, Theodor (Dietrich Smit) (1501-70), a Lutheran theologian, studied theology and Hebrew at the universities of Cologne and Wittenberg. He returned to Cologne in 1527 to teach Hebrew, but had to flee from the city before the end of the year because he had sided with Clarenbach (*q.v.*) and Fliesteden (*q.v.*). He fled to the duchy of Jülich, and was there received in noble families and associated with the "Wassenberg preachers (*Predikanten*)," especially Campanus (*q.v.*) and Klopreis (*q.v.*). It was probably Fabricius who freed Klopreis from prison in Cologne on New Year's night 1529 and took him to Wassenberg, where Klopreis was ordained in the house of the bailiff.

In 1533 Fabricius was in Kassel. In November Philip of Hesse (*q.v.*) sent him with Johannes Lening, the pastor at Melsungen, to Münster to promote the Protestant cause. Day after day he spoke in St. Lambert's Church. At the same time Fabricius was commissioned to define Luther's doctrine as over against that of the Anabaptists; the document was drawn up by Fabricius and Dr. Westermann of Lippstadt. On Nov. 15 they reported that they had reached an agreement with Bernhardt Rothmann (*q.v.*) on all points but infant baptism. In his sermon on the following day Fabricius stated that there was disagreement only in the matter of the proper time for baptism, and this was a minor issue on which difference of opinion was admissible. But in the end the unification failed and the Hessian clergymen returned home. But Fabricius remained at his post in spite of hopeless prospects until he was expelled in 1534. In November Philip sent him back to Münster to negotiate with the Anabaptists for peace. This mission also ended in failure.

Once more Fabricius was used by Philip to convert imprisoned Anabaptists. In August 1538, when he was pastor at Allendorf, he and Noviomagus, a professor at the University of Marburg, repeatedly cross-examined the Anabaptists held at Wolkersdorf, and tried to lead them from their faith, but without success. When Fabricius protested against Philip's dual marriage, he lost his freedom and his possessions. He returned to Wittenberg, where he took

his degree under Luther May 29, 1544. In 1570 he died as superintendent at Zerbst. NEFF.

C. A. Cornelius, *Die Münsterischen Humanisten und ihr Verhältnis zur Reformation* (Münster, 1851) 26 ff.; L. Keller, *Gesch. der Wiedertäufer und ihres Reiches zu Münster* (Münster, 1880), supplement; Rembert, *Wiedertäufer*, 310; Th. Vollbehr, "Zur Gesch. der Münster'schen Unruhen," in *Arch. des German. Museums* II (1889) 97-103, where Vollbehr offers evidence against the assumption by Cornelius that Fabricius was the main source or even the author of the work published under the name of Heinrich Dorpius, *Wahrhaftige Historie* (1536); *ML* I, 626 f.

Faes Dirks, an Anabaptist martyr, a chairmaker of Gouda in the Dutch province of South Holland, was received into the Mennonite Church by baptism in 1569, at the age of 30. On April 7, 1570, he was seized, on May 27 "tyrannically tortured," and three days later burned at the stake in Gouda. Van Braght gives the records of three trials he was subjected to. He confessed his faith frankly and steadfastly. On the rack he named several fellow believers, who had been baptized with him and were now in the city. He had been baptized in an attic in Rotterdam. The death sentence, which is given verbatim, gives a shocking insight into the cruel mind of the Catholic Church of the time. The populace was evidently horrified by his execution, for when the city was conquered by William of Orange, they took the bones of the martyr from the place of execution and placed them with those of his cruel judge, a priest. (*Mart. Mir.* D 508 f., E 846 f.; *ML* I, 450.) NEFF.

Fagel, Caspar (1634-88), a Dutch statesman, studied law at the University of Utrecht 1648-53, practiced law in The Hague, then became clerk of the States-General of the Netherlands 1670-72 and finally grand pensionary (secretary) of this body. He was a member of the Reformed Church, and a champion of religious tolerance, especially on political grounds. The intercession of Fagel with the Dutch Stadholder Prince William of Orange brought about the release of Foeke Floris (*q.v.*), a Mennonite preacher at Oostzaan, from persecution for "heresy." On Nov. 1, 1688, the Mennonite Lamist congregation at Amsterdam and a number of churches in the neighborhood of Amsterdam sent a letter of thanks to Fagel, because he had declared that he would maintain absolute freedom of conscience wherever he could. (*Inv. Arch. Amst.* I, No. 455; *N.N.B.Wb.* III, 382.) vDZ.

Fagel, Francois, a Dutch statesman, nephew of the above and like him a defender of religious toleration, who did much for the Mennonites in Europe. He was born at The Hague in 1659, died there in 1746. In 1690-1744 he was clerk of the Dutch States-General. François Fagel threw himself into the cause of the oppressed Mennonites in the Palatinate, Switzerland, and Prussia. At the insistence of the Dutch Mennonites, especially the congregations of Amsterdam and Rotterdam, and in accord with the resolutions of the States-General, Fagel, who warmly promoted this intercession, induced Prince William of Orange to write a letter to Elector Johann Wilhelm of the Palatinate in 1694, and again in 1697 in favor of the Mennonites living there, who were suffering many hardships. On March 15, 1710, Fagel in the name of the States-General made a strong protest (*Inv. Arch. Amst.* I, No. 1758) to the republic of Bern, Switzerland, in behalf of the persecuted Mennonites, many of whom had been thrown into prison and others sold to Venice and elsewhere to serve on the galleys (*q.v.*). It was Fagel who proudly declared that the Mennonites, who were being forcibly shipped by the Bern government to the English colony of Carolina in America in 1710, would be set free when passing the Dutch border (which indeed happened), because this country did not allow suppression or persecution for the sake of religion (*Inv. Arch. Amst.* I, Nos. 1763, 1768). And when the King of Prussia, Frederick William I, adopted harsh measures against the Lithuanian Mennonites in 1732, it was again Fagel who, at the request of a number of Mennonite congregations in Holland, moved the States-General to instruct the Dutch ambassador in Berlin to make a strong protest against this persecution. The Mennonite archives at Amsterdam contain a large number of letters exchanged between Fagel and the Dutch ambassador in Switzerland, Johann Ludwig Runckel (*q.v.*), who by order and at the expense of the Dutch States was active in the cause of emigration of the Swiss Brethren. Of special interest is a document of March 22, 1710 (*Inv. Arch. Amst.* I, No. 1764), which states that the Dutch Committee of Foreign Needs thanked François Fagel for promoting the intercession for the Mennonites of Bern. It was Fagel too, who in 1720 successfully intervened with the Duke of Jülich on behalf of Wilhelm Grahe (*q.v.*) and other Dompelaars (*q.v.*), who had been imprisoned. (*N.N.B.Wb.* III, 382; *DB* 1861, 80; 1909, 136-37, 146, note 1.)

vdZ.

Fair Grove (Mich.) Mennonite Church (MC) was listed as a member of the Ontario Mennonite Conference at least as early as 1907, when it had 11 members. As early as 1905 the name of Daniel Lehman appeared under the Fair Grove address, among the Michigan ministers. Although the church is listed for 1913-16, the membership and the minister are no longer given by the *Mennonite Yearbook and Directory*. (*ML* I, 627.)   M.G.

Fairbanks (Tex.) Church of God in Christ Mennonite Church, now extinct, was organized in 1897 with 30 members by Henry A. Koehn. Peter A. Friesen and John Schlabach also served as pastors. This congregation was dissolved by 1906, although a few members remained longer. The Galveston flood of 1899, which destroyed their crops, contributed to the dissolution.   I.K.F.

Fairfield County, Ohio (county seat, Lancaster), formed in the east central part of the state by governor's proclamation in 1800, was the home of a large Mennonite congregation southeast of Bremen during the first half of the 19th century. The first settlers came from Montgomery and Lancaster counties in Pennsylvania after a short sojourn in Rockingham Co., Va., and a still briefer stay in Greene Co., Pa. The first Mennonites settled southeast of

Bremen in the first decade of the 19th century. In the early years German-speaking pietistic groups like the Dunkards and Evangelicals made serious inroads on the membership. The lure of better farming opportunities along the Ohio-Erie Canal a few miles to the west and of cheaper land in northwestern Ohio further depleted the membership. The Civil War hysteria led many young men of Mennonite families to volunteer for military service. Entire congregations of other faiths in this county are now composed of descendants of former Mennonites. Mennonite emigrants from Fairfield County forsook their rugged hillside farms to form congregations in Franklin, Allen, Putnam, and Logan counties in Ohio. Those in Franklin and Logan are now extinct. After the emigrations and defections of the mid-century, the two congregations, one at Pleasant Hill near Bremen and the other at Turkey Run, south of the border in Perry County, suffered from poor leadership and a conservative spirit that opposed English preaching and Sunday school. The Pleasant Hill meetinghouse was abandoned and sold and the one at Turkey Run nearly suffered the same fate but has enjoyed a mild revival during recent years, having 36 members in 1955. Fairfield County was the early home of bishops John M. and George Brenneman and of Elder Daniel Brenneman, founder of the Mennonite Brethren in Christ Church. Other prominent names in the congregation were Blosser, Culp, Funk, Stalter, Stemen, and Sherrick.

An Amish congregation flourished in Fairfield County not far from Colfax during the middle decades of the 19th century. Members of the congregation, in search of cheaper land, moved to Logan and Champaign counties, Ohio, during the middle of the century; others moved farther west to Noble Co., Ind., near Topeka, and to Johnson Co., Iowa, where they helped to found a flourishing congregation. The last minister, Jonathan Zook, moved to Holmes Co., Ohio. Prominent names in the congregation were Bontrager, Gingerich, Guengerich, Hartzler, Miller, Kempf, Plank, and Stutzman.   J.S.U.

Fairfield Amish Mennonite Church, an independent congregation not under the Conservative Amish Mennonite Conference, located in Bureau County, near Tampico, Ill., was organized in Shelby Co., Ill., with 42 members under the leadership of Levi C. Hostetler in 1933, and was moved to Henry County in 1938 and to Bureau County in 1944. In 1953 there were 144 members.   H. Ho.

Fairfield Bethel Mennonite Church (GCM), in Beadle Co., S.D., 11 miles north and 2 miles west of Huron, a member of the Northern District, was organized on July 13, 1927, under the leadership of Elder P. P. Tschetter. The congregation had 53 members in 1955, with Wm. H. Dahlenburg serving as minister.   I.A.D.

Fairfield Mennonite Church (GCM), located in Adams Co., Pa., was formed in 1925 by a schism in the Mennonite (MC) congregation at Mummasburg, Pa., because of the question of insurance.

Those carrying insurance, contrary to the regulations of the Lancaster Conference, to which the congregation belonged, organized the Fairfield Church with A. W. Geigley as pastor, and with 40 charter members. In 1955 it had 68 members, with Lamont Woelk serving as pastor. The congregation remained independent until 1941, when it joined the Eastern District Conference (GCM).

A.W.G.

Fairmount Mennonite Brethren in Christ Church, now extinct. In 1883 Mennonites from Henry Co., Iowa, located south of Fairmount, Prairie Co., Ark., and organized a Mennonite Brethren in Christ church, with John Krupp of Iowa serving as the first minister. Christian Bechler was an influential member of the congregation and many of the meetings were held in his home. The congregation had approximately 50 members in 1891 but was discontinued in 1899.

M.G.

Fairview, Mich., is an unincorporated village (pop. *ca.* 150) in Oscoda County, in the north central part of the state. The village is the center of a farming area, largely surrounded by forests, settled by Mennonites in 1900-12. The Mennonite congregation (MC) of over 400 persons is the only church body located near Fairview. A small General Conference Mennonite congregation is located at Comins, a village five miles north of Fairview. Despite the handicaps of geographic isolation, poor soil, and a rigorous climate, the community has developed into one of the strongest congregations of the Indiana-Michigan Conference District. J.H.KA.

J. Howard Kauffman, "The Mennonite Community at Fairview, Michigan," *MQR*, October 1947.

Fairview, Okla., is a village of 2,400 inhabitants in the north central part of Major County. Approximately 600 adult Mennonites live within shopping distance of the village. Mennonites settled in the county in 1894 and now have four churches in the area. They are members of the Mennonite Brethren, Church of God in Christ Mennonite, General Conference Mennonites, and Church of God (Penner's). J.J.M.

Fairview (Okla.) Church of God (*Gemeinde Gottes*) is a branch of the Apostolische Brüdergemeinde (*q.v.*), which was originated in Russia by Hermann Peters, in close connection with the origin of the Mennonite Brethren. Only a few families of this group came to America in the great migration of the 1870's. Among these was Peter Gaede (*q.v.*), who came to Hillsboro, Kan., from the Kuban Mennonite settlement, where he originally was a member of the Mennonite Brethren. Because of disagreements in the Kuban he started a new group in co-operation with Jaeckel brothers. Through their zeal and missionary activities, the group found followers among Mennonites and non-Mennonites.

After Gaede's arrival in Kansas he organized near Hillsboro a group consisting mostly of former Mennonite Brethren and Volga Germans, which became known as the "Gaede Church." However, Gaede soon was won to the Seventh-Day Adventists, taking with him a number of his members. Most of the remaining members moved to Oklahoma near Fairview and Orienta, where a Church of God was organized. A. B. Penner, son of Bernhard Penner, was ordained minister Dec. 21, 1898, by Heinrich Peters, brother of Hermann Peters, the founder of the Church of God in Russia. Heinrich Peters was a leader of another small congregation of this group at Mt. Lake, Minn. A. B. Penner died in 1937, having ordained his son Aron A. Penner as his successor on April 4, 1926.

The meetinghouse of the Fairview group, erected around 1914, was originally located near Orienta. In 1952 a church was erected in the town of Fairview. The group consists of some 20 members and those that fellowship with them. Its minister visits smaller groups and families affiliated with his church at other places in Kansas and Canada. The small group has had some great losses in membership. After Gaede left the church near Hillsboro, Abraham Loewen was its leader until he too joined the Seventh-Day Adventists. D. K. Esau left the group in Oklahoma with a number of families and moved to Alberta.

The group emphasizes conversion, baptism by immersion, nonconformity, church discipline, footwashing, head covering for women, wearing of beards for men, the holy kiss, the greeting "Peace be unto you" instead of the regular greetings, and traditional Mennonite practices. The worship services are mostly in German. Sunday school is held on Sunday afternoon, and evening worship on Sunday. Common names in the group are Penner, Koop, Flemming, and Unruh. The North American families of this group were formerly in contact with their mother church in Siberia, the Crimea, and Kuban. The present minister is Aron A. Penner. C.K.

D. P. Gaede, *History of the Gaede Family* (1952); *Die Kubaner Ansiedlung* (Steinbach, Man., 1953).

Fairview Church of God in Christ Mennonite Church, organized in 1895, is situated four miles southeast of Fairview, Major Co., Okla. Worship services were held in the homes until 1901 when a church was built, which was enlarged in 1920, and again in 1944, so that it now seats 350. The 1953 membership was 235, in the charge of George M. Nichols, assisted by Dan Smith, Fred Penner, Sam W. Koehn, and Elmer Boehs. Weekly Sunday morning and evening worship services, Sunday school, and midweek meetings are being held.

G.M.N.

Fairview City Mennonite Brethren Church, formerly North Fairview M.B. Church, a member of the Southern District Conference, is located in the city of Fairview (pop. 3,000), Major Co., Okla. In 1893, when the Cherokee Strip was opened for homesteading, a number of Mennonite Brethren families, who had previously settled in Kansas, filed claims. The group, which in 1900 had about 100 baptized members, met under the leadership of Jacob Kliewer and William Hergert. To accommodate families living at a distance two churches were erected in 1895, one four miles south and one four miles north of Fairview. In 1896 Jacob Kliewer was ordained leader of the North Fairview group. Members of both

20

churches met for union services and communion once a month until 1900, when each group began to meet independently. When the congregation decided to build its new church in the city, membership rose from 106 in 1947 to 217 in 1949, most of the increase coming from the South Fairview Church. The new church, with a seating capacity of approximately 400, was dedicated May 7, 1950. On Sept. 1, 1951, David J. Wiens was installed as pastor of the Fairview Church. The membership at that time was about 260. On Oct. 7, 1951, the entire membership (135) of the Süd-Hoffnungsfeld Church was received into the fellowship of the Fairview City M.B. Church. The membership in 1954 was 415.   D.J.W.

Fairview Conservative Amish Mennonite Church is a part of the Upper Deer Creek-Fairview congregation, located 4 miles north and 2 miles east of Kalona, Iowa. To serve members living in this area a meetinghouse 42 x 60 ft. was built in 1936. Ministers serving this congregation are Elmer G. Swartzendruber, bishop; Albert S. Miller, Jacob J. Miller, and Morris Swartzendruber, ministers; and Noah S. Miller, deacon. The 1954 membership of the congregation was 470. (See **Upper Deer Creek**.)
                                              E.G.S.

Fairview Mennonite Church (MC), located in the village of Fairview, Oscoda Co., northeastern Michigan, a member of the Indiana-Michigan Mennonite Conference, was organized with 35 members on Feb. 2, 1904. Eli A. Bontrager was the first pastor. In 1953 the church had a membership of 391, under the leadership of Bishop Harvey Handrich. Other ministers who have served the congregation are Menno Esch, N. Z. Yoder, L. A. Kauffman, Moses S. Steiner, and Floyd Yoder; the deacon in 1953 was Otis J. Bontrager. Menno Esch served as bishop 1909-52.   M.Es.

J. H. Kauffman, "Mennonite Community at Fairview, Michigan," *MQR* XXI (October 1947) 252-74.

Fairview Mennonite Church (MC), a rural congregation near Minot, Ward Co., N.D. A group of 22 members organized a congregation, having ordained I. S. Mast, one of their number, to the ministry in March 1903 in the Kishacoquillas Valley of Pennsylvania. They arrived in Surrey, N.D., on April 2, 1903, built the church, and dedicated it on Thanksgiving Day of 1905. In 1908 the first church conference was held and I. S. Mast was ordained bishop. In 1911, 12 members withdrew and joined the Nazarenes. In 1914 L. S. Glick was ordained a minister and served until 1930. The congregation has sponsored two mission Sunday schools. L. A. Kauffman served as pastor 1930-45. In 1931 R. E. Myers was ordained deacon and served until 1939. In 1942 Floyd Kauffman was ordained minister and S. K. Zook deacon; both are still serving the congregation. In 1944 Floyd Kauffman was ordained bishop. The congregation has besides the regular meetings a quarterly Sunday-school meeting, and a summer Bible school. The membership in 1955 was 52.   F.E.K.

Fairview Mennonite Church (MC), located 6 miles southeast of Albany, Ore., a member of the Pacific Coast Conference, was organized in 1895 with 12 members. Church services were held in a Dunkard church building approximately 8 miles southeast of Albany until 1911, when the meetinghouse was built at the present location. Jacob Roth served the congregation as first minister and as bishop until 1903. Christian R. Gerig, who came to this community from Iowa, was ordained bishop in 1904 and served until 1930. Since May 1938 Nick M. Birky has served the congregation as bishop. In 1954 the ministers were Henry Gerig and Ivan Headings, and the deacon was Verle Nofziger; the membership was 372. The congregation was a member of the Amish Conference until the Amish and Mennonite Church Conferences were united into the Pacific Coast Conference. Immigration from midwestern states has been an important factor in the growth of the church.   A.L.

S. G. Shetler, *Church History of Pacific Coast Mennonite Conference District* (Scottdale, 1931) 13-15.

Fairview Mennonite Home, Preston, Ont., a home for the aged, owned and operated by the Mennonite (MC) Conference of Ontario, was dedicated on Feb. 10, 1956, with John A. Cressman as superintendent. It has a capacity of 92 beds, 75 for guests and 17 for staff. A bed-patient wing provides facilities to care for 20 chronically ill or convalescent patients. It is the successor to the former Braeside Home (*q.v.*) at Preston.   H.S.B.

Fairview Old Order Mennonite Church, located in Lebanon Co., Pa., was started in 1915, when a group who had settled experimentally in Osceola Co., Iowa, came to Lebanon County. They worshiped in a schoolhouse, and John A. Weaver of the Pike Mennonite Church, Hinkletown, Pa., preached the first sermon. In 1917 they entered larger quarters two miles north of Myerstown. On Jan. 1, 1928, most of this group joined the Old Order Mennonites, with Moses Horning as bishop. Since the price of land in Lancaster County was very high, the O.O.M. (Martinites) congregation in Lebanon County increased in numbers. Beginning in January 1938 they rented the Royer Brethren Church, and in the summer of 1943 built a commodious brick meetinghouse two miles south of Myerstown. Milo Lehman was ordained to the ministry on June 1, 1944, and Aaron Horning on Dec. 1, 1954. Joseph Hostetter had the bishop charge. The membership in 1954 was 250.
                                              I.D.L.

Fairview Street Mennonite Mission (MC), Reading, Pa., grew out of a need for more room at the Twelfth Street Mission. A small number of families who had been attending the Mennonite services at the Twelfth Street Mission moved to the southeast end of Reading. Since there was no church of any denomination in the immediate area, and many children wanted to attend Sunday school, a dwelling was rented for that purpose in 1932.

The Fairview Street Mission was opened under J. B. Gehman, who was then in charge of the mission work in Reading with its center at Twelfth and Windsor streets.

After the work had grown a few years preaching services and congregational life were established. The double house in which the Sunday school had been held was bought and renovated. It now has a roomy chapel in the first floor, Sunday-school rooms, and living quarters for mission workers. Luke L. Horst, minister, his family, and two workers, Elsie Gehman and Ireta Gassman, have been living here and assisting regularly at all three of the missions in Reading.

The Sunday school is the largest regular activity, usually about 125. The summer Bible school has the largest attendance, usually reaching 200.

N.G.

Faith Memorial Mennonite Church (GCM) of Filer, Idaho, a member of the Pacific District Conference, was organized on March 6, 1955, with 19 members. A church with a seating capacity of 140 is in process of building, based on a former Dutch Reformed church. The minister (1956) is W. Harley King.

W.H.K.

Faith Mennonite Church (GCM) is located 1 mile west and 3½ miles south of Greensburg, Kiowa Co., Kan. After conducting Sunday school and church services in a schoolhouse for about two years under the leadership of Dennis Smith, the congregation organized in 1948 with 18 charter members and joined the Western District Conference. Curt D. Boese, the first resident pastor, began his full-time service on Sept. 1, 1950. A frame church with full basement was built and dedicated on July 27, 1952. In 1955 the membership was 35, with Vernon Lohrentz as pastor.

C.D.B.

Fak (Fack), a Dutch Mennonite family, originally from Flanders. From about 1630 they are found in Vlissingen, Dutch province of Zeeland, while at the end of the 17th century some members also lived at Rotterdam, where Hieronymus Fack was a deacon of the Waterlander congregation.

vDZ.

K. F. van Lennep, *Oorkondenboek van Eeghen* (Amsterdam, 1918) see Index; K. Vos, *De Doopsgezinden te Rotterdam* (Rotterdam, 1907) 47.

Fälber, Leonhard (erroneously called *Föller*), an Anabaptist leader who was known by various names. It is probable that the names Lenaert van Ysenbroeck, Leonhard of Eschenbroich (Rembert, 450; *DB* 1909, 117 f.), Leenaert van Maastricht (Hochhuth, 638), Leonhard (Lenhart) von Fritzlar (Lenz, 321), Leonhard in Geldern (Bouterwek, 56, 78), and Leenaert Unusels (*q.v., DB* 1909, 117 f.) designate the same person. Krohn (338) erroneously identifies him with Leonhard Jost of Strasbourg.

Leonhard Fälber was a native of Brackel (Brachelen), a village in the duchy of Jülich, Germany, where he left his wife behind. He was "of small stature and wore a black coat." As an apostle of the Anabaptists he was especially active in Hesse. In the duchy of Jülich in 1536-41 he baptized at Dieteren, Born, Sittard, and Dremmen. In Brackel he organized a congregation. One of his most prominent converts was Johannes Kesselflicker (*q.v.*) in 1541. He was probably a man of some education. "He liked to speak," says Noviomagus, "of the power of the living Word that leads a man from the evil to the good and completely renews him. His sermons reveal dialectic skill and rhetorical rhythm; quite moderate in form, he did not, however, conceal his contempt for the established church and its dead word, which nowhere put an end to the sinful and contaminated life of its adherents" (Wappler, 72).

In 1536 he was seized with about 30 other Anabaptists at a meeting in an abandoned church near Gmünden on the Wohra in the district of Kassel and put into prison at Wolkersdorf and then at Marburg, where they were for a while lightly confined. They could leave their prison for weeks and preach in the community. Repeated attempts were made to change their views. The chancellor Feige had already despaired of any success and when an interview on Oct. 15, 1538, again ended in failure, he expressed the opinion "that Fälber, if he had an opportunity, would conduct himself like the Münsterite king." Bucer (*q.v.*) was more successful when he disputed with them on Oct. 30 and Nov. 1. Hochhuth (638-42) presents the conversation between Fälber and Bucer verbatim. On Dec. 9, 1538, they presented to the Landgrave a document prepared by Peter Tasch (*q.v.*), and signed by Fälber and eight companions, entitled "Bekenntnis oder Antwort etlicher Fragstücke oder Artikeln der gefangenen Täufer oder anderer im Lande zu Hessen." It is not a true recantation, but rather an essentially modified confession of their faith; Bucer and the Hessian clergy were not entirely satisfied with it, but nevertheless were willing to pardon them and receive them into the church (Hochhuth, 612-26). Their position on separation, the oath, and attitude toward government they surrendered. Concerning infant baptism they said they would not condemn those who baptized their children, because they thought such baptism was based on the Scripture, but neither could they yet recognize it as God's plan.

Leonhard Fälber apparently joined the Protestant Church with the others. Nothing more is heard of him.

NEFF.

P. Wappler, *Die Stellung Kursachsens und des Landgrafen Philipp von Hessen zur Täuferbewegung* (Münster, 1910); Rembert, *Wiedertäufer*, 450; B. U. Krohn, *Gesch. der fanatischen und enthusiastischen Wiedertäufer vornehmlich in Niederdeutschland* (Leipzig, 1758); K. W. H. Hochhuth, "Mitteilungen aus der protestantischen Sektengesch." in *Niedners Ztscht fur die hist. Theol.*, 1858, 538 ff.; Max Lenz, *Briefwechsel Philipps von Hessen mit Butzer* I (Leipzig, 1880) 318 ff.; K. W. Bouterwek, *Zur Gesch. und Literatur der Wiedertäufer* (Bonn, 1864); G. Franz, *TA: Hessen* (see Index); *DB* 1909, 117 ff.; 1917, 119, No. 106; *ML* I, 627.

Falder (Het), usually called 't Falder, now a part of Emden, Germany, consisted during the 16th century of the two villages, Gross- and Klein-Falder. By 1557 it was outwardly a unit with Emden and in 1574 Edzard II incorporated it with Emden. Anabaptists were found here from 1529, and Dirk Philips died here in 1568. Of the more than 600 individuals baptized by Leenaert Bouwens in 1551-82 in East Friesland, 320 are listed under 't Falder and only some 90 in Emden (1551-54, 42; 1554-56, 67;

1557-61, 27; 1563-65, 184). It is likely that in the two villages the Anabaptists enjoyed greater toleration. There was no congregation here; the members belonged to the congregations of Emden (*q.v.*) and Emderland (*q.v.*). Much of their activity no doubt took place in this part of the town of Emden (*q.v.*). Even today old Emden citizens point out a place where the Mennonite *Vermaning* (meetinghouse) was located. 't Falder was not as severely damaged as the interior of the city in World War II. This section of the town is clearly visible from the balcony of the present Mennonite church.   C.K.

Blaupot t. C., *Groningen, Overijssel en Oost-Friesland* I, 51, 111 f.; K. Vos, "Dooplijst van Leenaert Bouwens," *Bijdr. en Mededeel. van h. Hist. Genootschap* XXXVI (1915) 65.

Falfurrias, Texas, is a town (pop. 5,000) in Brooks County in the southern part of the state. Mennonites have lived in the area for 22 years. In 1954, 59 Mennonites, belonging to the M.C. and M.B. groups, lived within shopping distance to the north and northwest of the town.   H.F.R.

Falk, Jakob, an Anabaptist martyr of Gossau in the district of Grüningen, canton of Zürich, Switzerland, one of the most zealous and faithful followers of Conrad Grebel. He was imprisoned in 1525 at Appenzell with Heini Reimann. On a Sunday of May 1526 they took part in a meeting in the Herrliberg forest between Rubikon and Wetzikon, which was surprised and broken up by the magistrate (*Amtmann*) Berger. They told Berger fearlessly that they had been baptized and had baptized others, although they knew it was punishable by death to do so, and intended to continue. The magistrate and the Zürich council now expected the Grüningen authorities to inflict capital punishment on them in accord with the mandate of the Zürich council issued on March 7. The authorities refused to do this, on the basis of an ancient privilege granted by Austria. The dispute was referred to the courts in Bern. The matter was not decided until 1528, when it was placed in the hands of the Zürich council. After an imprisonment of more than 18 months because they "remained obstinate"—Falk declared that he would continue to baptize, strengthened only by the Son of God, who would never leave him—they were sentenced to death and drowned at Zürich at 1:00 on the afternoon of Sept. 5, 1528. This was the second Anabaptist execution in Zürich. His brother Hans Falk, a tanner, was also a zealous Anabaptist, with whom Berger also had much trouble.   NEFF.

E. Egli, *Die Züricher Wiedertäufer* (Zürich, 1878) 51, 58, 81f.; Füsslin, *Beiträge* . . . IV, 87; L. von Muralt and W. Schmid, *Quellen zur Gesch. der Täufer in der Schweiz* (Zürich, 1952) *passim* (see Index); H. S. Burrage, *A History of the Anabaptists in Switzerland* (Philadelphia, 1881) 167, 177, 191; *ML* I, 628. Either Jacob or Hans Falk may have furnished the inspiration for the principal character of the Anabaptist drama *Brüder in Christo* (Zürich, 1947) by Cäsar von Arx, named Diethelm Falk.

Falkenau, a Mennonite church in West Prussia, Germany, which was organized on Feb. 14, 1885, but soon died out.

Mannhardt, *Jahrbuch* 1888, p. 13; *Menn. Bl.*, 1900, 29; *ML* I, 628.

Falkenstein, a market village in Lower Austria, southeast of Nikolsburg, acquired special interest in Mennonite history through the surprise on Steinabrunn (*q.v.*), where the Anabaptists were seized and taken to the Falkenstein castle in chains. The castle is now in ruins. In the vicinity there were many Anabaptists, according to the books of Christoph Andreas Fischer (*q.v.*). About 1550 the priest Niklas Woisch reported to the authorities that four or five of his predecessors had had to deal with Anabaptists. He himself is reported to have joined them. At any rate, all that Fischer relates about affairs in Veldsberg applies also to Falkenstein.   LOSERTH.

Beck, *Geschichts-Bücher*, 144; *Topographie von Niederösterreich* III, 8-25; L. Müller, *Glaubenszeugnisse oberdeutscher Taufgesinnter* (Leipzig, 1938) 190-205 contains the *Rechenschaft* of the 150 Anabaptist prisoners; *ML* I, 87, 628.

Falkenstein was the name of the first Mennonite settlement of Galicia, Poland. It was established in 1784 by seven Mennonite families from Falkenstein in the Palatinate, Germany. The families were Michael Bachmann, Christian Ewy, Daniel Ewy, Peter Krehbiel, Josef Mündlein, Johannes Schrag and his son Jakob Schrag. Johannes Schrag, Peter Krehbiel, and Josef Mündlein with others left Galicia in 1796, joined the Hutterites at Vishenka, Chernigov, Russia, whence they went to Volhynia and became the progenitors of the Swiss-Volhynian Mennonites of Kansas and Dakota.

The village of Falkenstein was settled in the shape of a cross. It consisted of 36 homesteads, of which 29 were settled by German Lutherans and the seven in the western part of the village by Mennonites. This settlement project was sponsored by the Austrian government, which paid a part of the transportation and prescribed the building plans, each farmer receiving 35 acres of land.

Descendants of the Bachmanns, the Ewys, and other settlers emigrated to America in 1882. In 1934 only two of the original Mennonite farms were still owned by Mennonites and there were altogether five farms owned by Mennonites in Falkenstein. (See **Galicia, Poland.**)   C.K.

P. Bachmann, *Mennoniten in Kleinpolen* (Lemberg, 1934) 127-33.

Falling Spring: see **Springs,** Pa.

Falling Spring Reformed Mennonite Church, near Chambersburg, Franklin Co., Pa., had a membership of 14 in 1948. The first members were baptized in 1841 and the first meetinghouse, on the Falling Spring road, was built in 1847. The present edifice was constructed in 1903.   J.L.K.

Falls Mennonite Church (MC), now extinct, was located in Niagara Co., N.Y., near Sanborn village about 10 miles east of Niagara Falls. According to D. K. Cassel, Hans Witmer and Abraham Witmer came here from Lancaster about 1810. David Habecker (1791-1889), who came from Pennsylvania in 1832 and was ordained in 1834, was the only minister. A meetinghouse on his property came into use soon after settlement. J. Treichler (d. 1897) was the first deacon. This congregation never was strong.

Regular communion services continued until 1870, and preaching appointments were recorded until 1884. With Jacob Krehbiel active in the neighboring Clarence community for the General Conference group and the inactivity of the aged Habecker, the scattered members lost interest in the Falls congregation. On the flyleaf of Habecker's Bible is found the statement that he had read it more than 50 times. He studied it with the aid of a Greek lexicon.

J.C.F.

D. K. Cassel, *Geschichte der Mennoniten* (Philadelphia, 1890) 221.

Familien Freund, Der, a 4-page weekly newspaper published at Milford Square, Bucks Co., Pa. In 1905 it was in its 39th year and published by D. G. Stauffer. It was not a denominational or religious journal, though read by many Mennonites. H.S.B.

Familien-Kalender, an annual Mennonite (MC) almanac, published 1870-1940, at Elkhart 1870-1908 by the Mennonite Publishing Company (1870-75 by J. F. Funk and Brother), and at Scottdale 1909-40 by the Mennonite Publishing House. It paralleled the *Family Almanac* (*q.v.*), containing the same almanac calculations (prepared by L. J. Heatwole of Dale Enterprise, Va., for many years) and a directory of Mennonite ordained men (1909-40). The literary and historical miscellany was different in the two annuals. John Horsch was the editor 1909-40. The earlier issues had 36 pages, the later ones 64, always including a small amount of advertising. H.S.B.

Familists, the members of the "Family of Love," a brotherhood founded about 1540 by Hendrik Niclaes (*q.v.*). It had a pantheistic mystic character. The leadership lay in the hands of a bishop, assisted by 12 elders and 4 classes of priests. The priests were required to give up all personal property, and lay members to tithe. The brotherhood found adherents in Holland, where they are last mentioned in 1649, and especially in England, where it existed until the end of the 17th century. They were often associated in the popular mind with the Anabaptists. Even Samuel Cramer called them "without doubt, real Anabaptists" (*BRN* VII, 286). But they had nothing in common but their discipline and their demand for a "holy" church. "It is a peculiar mixture of spiritualistic mysticism, Catholic hierarchy, and the Anabaptist brotherhood ideal, together with a strong emphasis on the perfection and oneness with God of the original creation which is to be reestablished" (Troeltsch). NEFF.

E. Troeltsch, *The Social Teachings of the Christian Churches* (N.Y., 1931); F. Nippold, "Heinrich Niclaes und das Haus der Liebe" in *Ztscht für hist. Theol.* 1862, 323-402 and 473-563; J. Lindeboom, *Stiefkinderen van het Christendom* (The Hague, 1929) 201-9; *ML* I, 632.

Family. The Mennonite concept of the family is closely related to other Protestant groups, although there are some differences. An early characteristic among the peaceful Anabaptists along these lines was the emphasis on a union of heart and mind and a common loyalty to God. This emphasis on the devotion to a common cause, ideal, and community,

transcending the personal preferences, was an outstanding feature of early Anabaptist family life. Only if this is realized can other characteristics be understood. The individual who entered into a covenant with God and joined the church of believers owed his first and supreme allegiance to God. For this reason marriages outside this covenant (church) were not desirable nor permissible. If a member of the church transgressed and was consequently banned, the marriage partner within the church was expected to conform to the regulations and standards of the congregation to the point of "shunning" the marriage partner outside the fold. The body of Christ and its members and their well-being were considered primary, and personal matters, even in family life, secondary. For this reason a member of the church severed his relationship by marrying outside the church. In many instances this was even the case when a person from a conservative group married into a more tolerant branch of Mennonites. All this is in line with Roland H. Bainton's observation regarding the characteristics of marriage and family life during the days before the Reformation and also afterwards. The Middle Ages emphasized the sacramental nature of marriage and family life. Love and companionship were not prerequisites for marriage. In a more "romantic age" love was emphasized, although not necessarily as a prerequisite for marriage. It was during the Reformation and particularly among the Anabaptists that a third stage came about. This was the idea that it is essential that marriage partners have the same ideals and thus become life companions.

Attention must also be called to a much advertised and exaggerated development among the Münsterite Anabaptists (1534 f.) pertaining to marriage and family life. Although originally the Anabaptists and Münsterites were strictly monogamic with high ethical ideals based on the covenant idea, through Jan van Leiden's example and the introduction of the Old Testament pattern for an Anabaptist kingdom at Münster polygamy was introduced, partly to take care of the women whose husbands had been killed during the siege of the city. This occurrence on the periphery of Anabaptism during the 16th century has been exploited by the opponents of the movement and used to "prove" a lack of ethical conduct in all Anabaptists. With the fall of Münster this development came to a close without finding imitation anywhere in Mennonite history.

Literature and illustrations emphasize a strong family life among Mennonites. It is true it was patriarchal in the early days (see picture by Aurèle Robert, "The Anabaptist or the Bernese Farm," Lausanne, Switzerland). The basis for an integrated harmonious and strong family life lies in the emphasis on common ideals for which families and groups were willing to sacrifice property and homes and even their lives, migrating from country to country. Hardships experienced in isolation not only tied the members of one family closer together, but also united groups of families. Living in closely knit small groups in isolation and practicing nonconformity to the world over longer periods of time not only emphasized and strengthened family relationships, but also caused marriage among relatives. Although there seems to have been strong opposition to this practice and conferences have been held to discuss this matter (*ML* I, 516), the practice could hardly be avoided as long as Mennonites were opposed to outside marriages and lived in small isolated communities. Gustav E. Reimer, who studied five Mennonite congregations in America, mostly of Prussian background, has shown that marriage among first and second cousins has been quite common among Mennonites, particularly of rural groups. He found that in the Whitewater Mennonite community of 93 young men, 15 were related to less than half of all the girls in the community, 24 to more than half, and 6 to more than three fourths. Fifty-three boys were related to 44 girls. However, Reimer suggests that there probably have not been more consanguine marriages among Mennonites than among other similar rural groups. He also comes to the conclusion that the results of consanguinous marriages in the number of defective offspring do not seem to be greater than in families where the marriage partners are not related. Such marriage tends to double in children certain traits common to both partners, both desirable and undesirable. It seems, however, that some of the children with weaknesses tend to remain unmarried and that endogamic marriages cause the group to withdraw from society and that the chances for successful outside contacts are weakened.

The practices of proposing for marriage among Mennonites were in harmony with earlier concepts of marriage and family life and differ considerably from our day. Among the Swiss Anabaptists and their conservative descendents (Amish), the practice was based literally on Genesis 24. The deacon (*q.v.*) or *Steckelmann* (*q.v.*) among the Swiss and the deacon or *Umbitter* (*q.v.*) among the Prussian Mennonites were entrusted by the family of the young man with the task of presenting the proposal to the chosen girl's parents. After this initial contact he himself came to the home of the girl of his choice. D. Chodowiecky's "The Mennonite Marriage Proposal" and Cornelis Troost's illustrations to Asselijn's *Jan Klaasz* (Mauritshuis, The Hague) have featured this event. This practice was also observed among the early Anabaptists of the Netherlands. The Wismar Articles of 1554 define the views and practices along these lines. It was stated that children should not marry secretly, should consult their parents before taking steps along these lines, but that they should be given an opportunity to make their own decisions (Brons, 99). This was again stressed in the Twelve Articles of the Frisian Mennonites which were presented annually to the congregations in 1639-1716, stating that young people should not marry without the consent of the parents, that boys and girls should not associate too freely, that the approaching marriage should be properly announced, and that weddings should not be too elaborate, but "in the fear of the Lord and according to the example of Tobit" (Brons, 130). In 1765 regret was expressed in the Danzig congregation that the good old practice of having the *Umbit-*

ter present the proposal was gradually being given up (*ML* I, 516).

The engagement was announced from the pulpit, after which the young couple visited day after day with relatives of the community. The marriage usually took place two weeks after the announcement of the engagement, to which occasion not only all relatives, but often the whole community was invited. The weddings were plain but all guests were served a regular full meal, and friends and relatives from a distance stayed for a number of meals.

For a long time the Mennonite ministers had to struggle to obtain permission to marry their own church members and to have the officials recognize such a marriage. In Germany the last barriers were not removed until 1918. In the Netherlands this was achieved at an earlier date. In Russia and in America Mennonites never confronted any problems along these lines.

The Mennonite family has been traditionally large. In Russia the population doubled within a generation (25 years), which is still the case among the Old Colony Mennonites in Mexico. In 1926 the Manitoba Mennonite settlement in Mexico had a total population of 3,340, and in 1949 it had increased to 7,706, which indicates that it did not even take twenty-five years to double their number. Similar increases can be found in conservative isolated rural Mennonite settlements. In Galicia the increase was 30 per thousand annually and among the Hutterites it was 45.9 per thousand in 1946-50, which is almost double the national rate (24.2). Reimer found that the average number of children of the Mennonite community of Whitewater, Kan., was 7.45 in 1876-84; 6.11 in 1885-1900; 6.21 in 1901-10; 7.11 in 1911-18; and 3.5 in 1919-24. The average for the Amish of Elkhart Co., Ind., was about 8 and for the Hutterites about 10. The age of marriage for men at Whitewater was 28.2 and for girls 22.85 in 1885-1900; for men 28.16 and for girls 22.74 in 1901-10; and for men 28.65 and 23.78 for girls in 1911-18. Statistics for the Mennonites of Prussian background in Nebraska were similar. The age of marriage among the Amish and Hutterites is lower. These statistics also correspond somewhat with those available regarding the Mennonites of Russia. From 1890 to 1910 the average number of children per family was seven; and in 1911-25 there was a gradual decrease to an average of five, which was mostly due to the impact of World War I, the Revolution, and other outside factors. By the time of the outbreak of World War II there was only one child per family. The main reason for this decrease was that most of the young men had been exiled (Stumpp, *Tafel* K.).

One of the striking observations regarding the old-fashioned Mennonite family of the Prusso-Russian background is that widowers would usually remarry soon after the death of a spouse. In this case they would quite often marry a much younger girl instead of a widow. Records prove that this observation is not an exception but a rule. As an example we mention Bernhard Harder (*q.v.*), whose wife died on Oct. 13, 1878, and who remarried on

Feb. 13, 1879. This was comparatively a "long" period of mourning. Schmiedehaus reports that among the Old Colony Mennonites remarriage after a few weeks is common. (See also **Birth Rate** and **Marriage**.)   C.K.

Some of the best descriptions of the Mennonite family and home of Prusso-Russian background can be found in Peter Epp, *Eine Mutter* (Bluffton, Ohio, 1932); Arnold Dyck, *Verloren in der Steppe* (Steinbach, Man., 1944-48); L. Froese, the chapter "Familie und Kleinkind" in *Das pädagogische Kultursystem der Mennonitischen Siedlungsgruppe in Russland* (Göttingen, 1949); Walter Schmiedehaus, "Mennonite Life in Mexico," *Menn. Life* (April 1947). The most detailed study of this subject was made by Ernst Correll in the article "Ehe," *ML* I, 509-26, which contains the most complete bibliography. K. Stumpp, *Bericht über das Gebiet Chortitza im Generalbezirk Dnjepropetrowsk* (Berlin, 1943); A. Brons, *Ursprung- . . . der . . . Mennoniten* (Amsterdam, 1912); Gustav E. Reimer, "Socio-biological Aspects of the Development of Five Mennonite Congregations in Kansas and Nebraska" (unpublished manuscript, Bethel College, North Newton, 1949); Adolf Ehrt, *Das Mennonitentum in Russland* (Berlin, 1932).

Family *in Mennonite History and Life in America.* Any attempt to describe the nature and significance of the family in Mennonite life and thought is unfortunately handicapped by a number of limiting factors. The more important of these limitations are:

(1) The paucity of sociological studies of Mennonites in general, and the Mennonite family in particular; (2) the highly subjective nature of many of the references to aspects of family life found in the existing literature on Mennonites; (3) the lack of adequate descriptive materials on the Mennonite family before the present century, with which present-day family patterns may be compared; (4) the marked differences in religious beliefs and cultural traits in the area of family life found between the various branches of Mennonites today.

In the last decade a few pioneer studies of an objective, scientific nature have been made of specific Mennonite groups. Notable among these studies, which give some attention to family organization, are (1) Walter Kollmorgen's cultural anthropological study of the Old Order Amish of Lancaster Co., Pa.; (2) an exhaustive study of the Hutterite colonies of the United States and Canada by a research team headed by Professor Joseph W. Eaton of Wayne University; (3) the study of the Mennonites in Paraguay by J. W. Fretz; (4) John A. Hostetler's studies on the Amish, particularly in Mifflin Co., Pa.; (5) extensive research on Mennonite settlements in Mantitoba by E. K. Francis; and (6) the Mennonite family census conducted in 1950 by the Mennonite Research Foundation.

It should also be noted that several Mennonite church historians have included brief but helpful descriptions of Mennonite family traits in their historical works. These include John C. Wenger's history of Franconia Mennonites, Melvin Gingerich's study of the Mennonites of Iowa, and John Umble's study of the Amish Mennonites of Union Co., Pa. Limited studies of family size, marriage, and birth and death rates have been made on Mennonite groups in a few local areas. It is obvious that the foregoing isolated, though valuable, studies of Mennonite life can present at best only a fragmentary picture of family organization among Mennonites as a whole. A more complete analysis of the Mennonite family must await additional years of painstaking research by qualified scholars both within and without the Mennonite faith.

The fourth limiting factor mentioned above refers to the cultural variations between existing Mennonite bodies. Although there is general subscription to the central doctrines of Anabaptist-Mennonite faith by all Mennonite branches, the practical applications of these doctrines vary markedly. At one end of the cultural continuum are the very rural, conservative Amish and Hutterite bodies with their many distinguishing overt cultural traits. At the other end of the continuum are the most "progressive" or "liberal" bodies, such as the General Conference Mennonites and the Mennonite Brethren in Christ, whose overt cultural traits are not so easily distinguishable from the dominant American cultural pattern.

Cultural variation among Mennonite bodies is clearly reflected in family traits and organization. Courtship patterns, marriage ceremonies, authority patterns, family size, attitudes toward divorce, attitudes toward birth control, and other aspects of the family vary considerably between Mennonite bodies. For that reason, generalizations about the "Mennonite family" are frequently difficult and sometimes impossible. Frequent reference must be made to specific groups, and differences noted between them.

Because of the limited nature of information available, this article deals almost entirely with five American groups: Old Order Amish, Hutterian Brethren, General Conference Mennonites, Mennonites of Paraguay, and the Mennonite Church (MC). The omission of other Mennonite groups is due solely to lack of materials.

As in all cultures, the family is the primary social institution among Mennonites. In the Mennonite culture, however, the family has been especially significant. This is true in part because the Mennonites fortify the family institution with a literal interpretation of the Scriptures, and in part because in the more than four hundred years of their history they have been largely agrarian. Mennonite culture patterns have frequently been forged in frontier settlement conditions, such as in Russia, United States, Canada, Mexico, and Paraguay. The rigors of pioneering have always made great demands on the institution of the family.

Mennonites believe in the words of God when He said concerning Adam, "It is not good for man to be alone" (Gen. 2:18). Considerable social pressure is normally exerted against the bachelor and "old maid." With regard to size of family Mennonites tend to accept literally God's command to Noah, "Be fruitful, and multiply, and replenish the earth" (Gen. 9:1).

The Mennonite family is strictly monogamous. Marriage is regarded as a sacred union to be consummated only "in the Lord" and to be sustained "until death do us part." Divorce occurs very rarely, and is strictly taboo except for reason of adultery as permitted in Matthew 19:9. Among the Amish, divorce, desertion, or separation does not exist. Any party to such a marriage dissolution would become the object of severe social disapproval. This is slightly less true in certain sections of the most liberal Mennonite bodies, where not only has an occasional divorce occurred, but where there have been a few instances of the remarriage of divorced persons, such persons at the same time retaining church membership. A 1952 study of 52 mission stations maintained by the Mennonite Church (MC) revealed that six persons on membership rolls were divorced. In rare cases a divorcee may be found on the roll of an established congregation in the Mennonite Church (MC). The remarriage of a divorced church member would not be permitted in any Amish or Mennonite (MC) congregation. Only one divorce and two separations have occurred among the Hutterites since their settlement in the United States over 70 years ago.

Courtship and mate selection practices vary considerably along the conservative-liberal Mennonite continuum. Amish young people begin to "run around" at about 16 or 17 years of age. Dating is carried on more secretly than openly, and its purpose is solely to find a mate. The American pattern of extensive "casual dating" (that is, dating different persons without intent to court), carried on very openly and with a great amount of romantic sentimentality, is simply not found among the Amish. Amish young men and women have frequent opportunities for mingling, but "pairing off" takes place largely at the close of an evening social event, and couples rarely appear in public together until near the time of the wedding.

In the less conservative Mennonite branches, the conventional American dating and courtship practices prevail. A considerable amount of casual dating takes place. After a period of from several months to several years of "going steady," the successful courtship eventuates in engagement. Traditionally among American Mennonites and Amish Mennonites engagements have not been announced (see (Courtship)), but this custom is changing.

Among the Mennonites of South America "young people may fraternize informally at times of church gatherings such as weddings, funerals, and religious holidays, but the idea of a young man or woman dating many different individuals is as unfamiliar to the young people in the colonies as it was to our grandparents" (Fretz, chapter IV).

In the Mennonite colonies of South America it is customary for the minister to announce engagements at the close of a Sunday morning worship service. Among the Amish, engagements are not announced, but "publishing the banns" is required. Publishing the banns is also customary among the Hutterites and, in general, among most European Mennonites, including those who have immigrated from Europe in recent decades. The practice is found also among some conservative congregations in the M.C. group. However, in most present-day M.C., G.C.M., and related branches, the custom has been dropped.

Data from the M.C. family census (1950) show that for M.C. males first marriages have occurred at the average age of 24.8 years. The corresponding average for females was 23.3 years. The median age at marriage for Mennonite women was 21.7 years. For all persons married for the first time in the United States in 1950 the median age at marriage was 20.3 for women and 22.8 for men. The median age at marriage in 1950 for Hutterite marriages was 23.5 for men and 22.0 for women. For the Amish, Hostetler reports that "on the average, girls marry at 22 and boys at about 24. The normal age for marriage ranges from 18 to 26." These data suggest that Mennonites tend to marry at slightly older ages than the United States population as a whole, and that the age span between husband and wife is somewhat less. Eaton and Mayer discovered that the age at marriage has been increasing among Hutterites. For the United States, age at marriage has been decreasing. Trend data are not yet available for other Mennonite groups.

Data on marriage rates are available only for the Hutterites. Eaton and Mayer discovered that Hutterites have a very high marriage rate. By the age of 45 less than 2 per cent of all Hutterites remain unmarried. For the United States as a whole, 8 per cent of men and 7 per cent of women had not married by the age of 45, a rate which is high compared to other countries.

In many congregations (MC) known to the writer the number of unmarried women of marriageable age is considerably larger than the number of unmarried men of marriageable age. It is probable that greater numbers of young men than of young women leave the church, causing an excess of unmarried women. An investigation should be made as to whether this may be a general pattern for Mennonites, and if so, how it may affect the female marriage rate.

Available data indicate that Mennonites (MC) have larger families than is true for the United States as a whole. The average completed family in the United States today has 3.1 children. The average completed Hutterite family has 10.4 children. For Paraguayan Mennonites the figure is 8.4 children. In a Pennsylvania Amish community the average completed Amish family was found to have 7-8 children. The family census study indicated that completed M.C. families have 4.9 children. The data also indicate that there is a direct relation between Mennonite conservatism and large families. Of four Mennonite groups studied in Elkhart Co., Ind., the G.C.M. had the smallest families, and the Amish the largest. Since urban families in general have fewer children than farm families, the rurality of the conservative groups no doubt is a major factor in the larger family size. Birth control practice may partially explain variations in family size. Hutterite and Amish families shun all methods of birth control, whereas the more educated and urbanized Mennonite families frequently practice birth control. The more liberal groups do not oppose such practice.

As is usual in rural societies, the Mennonite family is the basic unit in other social institutions of the community. Parents seldom attend functions without their children. Only among the more urbanized, progressive families in recent times has "baby sitting" become more common. The entire family normally attends church services, weddings, funerals, picnics, and other social events as a unit. It is customary to bring infants to church as soon as they are old enough to be taken anywhere, not infrequently as young as six weeks.

The home also tends to be the center of social and religious events. Among the "house Amish," who have no meetinghouses, church services and all other events take place in the homes of the members. Among most Mennonite groups, family reunions, neighborhood get-togethers, and young people's social and literary events usually take place in homes. Among the more urbanized Mennonite congregations, however, such events tend to be scheduled outside the home either in church or community facilities.

Religion plays an important role in the Mennonite family. Grace at meals (usually audible, sometimes silent) is universal, and probably the most overt religious activity in the home. In addition, many homes have some type of family worship. In some cases family worship is perfunctorily routine with little variety or imagination. The extreme of this is where the father daily reads a passage of Scripture and leads in prayer. In other cases considerable variation in programing, in participation of all members of the family, and in the use of music is to be found. Church conference resolutions frequently call attention to the need for stronger and more extensive family worship programs in Mennonite families. Ministers periodically exhort parents to establish "family altars." Nevertheless statistics gathered through the Sunday schools in 1952 indicate that only about 30 per cent of M.C. families have some form of family worship.

Other religious traits found in Mennonite homes include religious wall mottoes, religious literature, and collections of sacred music on records. The latter item, however, would not appear in Amish homes.

More significant than material traits is the role that religion plays in the inner life of the family members. The Spirit of God, when manifest in the lives of family members, yields the fruits of the Spirit: love, joy, peace, long-suffering, gentleness, goodness, faith, meekness, and temperance. It is by such spiritual qualities that the highest and noblest in human relationships is achieved, in the family as elsewhere. Mennonites have perhaps succeeded in manifesting these spiritual qualities in their interpersonal relationships to a greater extent than the bulk of the human race. This is not to overlook the fact, however, that some Mennonite families seriously lack these qualities, and give evidence of maladjustment, either between mates or between parents and children, or both. In marriages which are basically unhappy, the mates tend to endure each other, working out some type of accommodation rather than dissolve the marriage.

The recognition of family frictions has led the more progressive Mennonite churches to give attention to family life education. Through sermons, Sunday schools, Sunday evening services, and special conferences and institutes increasing attention is being given to the social, psychological, and spiritual factors which affect the success of family living. In 1952 the M.C. Commission for Christian Education prepared a series of popularly written booklets on courtship and family relations. Careful studies should be made of discipline methods, authoritarian controls, and other aspects of parent-child interaction in Mennonite families to discover their effect on the personality development of Mennonite youth.

With respect to authority, Mennonite families are patriarchal. The degree of authority exercised by the head of the family varies considerably among the Mennonite branches, and between families within a given branch. Patriarchal forms are most strongly evidenced among the conservative Amish and Hutterite groups. Traditional forms stemming from European culture of centuries ago have been fairly well preserved to this day among these groups. On the other hand, the M.C. in the United States and Canada, and particularly certain sections of the G.C.M., have assimilated many of the equalitarian, democratic, and individualistic values and ideals of the dominant American culture. Mennonites of recent immigration from Europe to Canada, Mexico, and South America reflect the more authoritarian patterns of Old World patriarchal family life.

Among the Mennonites of North America it should be noted that the process of assimilation is bringing about some notable changes in family organization. Among the more "modernized" Mennonite families the husband is likely to share much of the decision-making process with his wife and children. Family devotions may be on a more democratic basis. The wife has in some cases come to share in the management of family finances. She is likely to share with her husband in property ownership. She may have a joint bank account with him. She may assume more leadership in the church and community than was formerly thought correct. Sex differentiation tends to disappear in the seating arrangement in church. The wife, and even the mother, has in some cases taken a job outside the home and thus shares with her husband in the "breadwinning" process. The Amish mother, writes Hostetler, would be horrified by the thought of working outside the home and at the same time trying to raise a family. The Amish husband is still occasionally seen walking ahead of, rather than beside his wife. On festive occasions among the Amish the men are always served before the children and women. The women are expected to "keep silence in the churches" (I Cor. 14:34).

Concerning Paraguayan Mennonites, Fretz relates: "A North American visitor is likely to be impressed with the way the woman of the house plays the role of servant. In the writer's many home calls, the woman was seldom present during the visit, and in most instances, where the visit took place over mealtime, only the husband and guest were seated at the table. The wife generally served the food, but only in a few instances did she take part in the conversation."

Discipline in Mennonite and Amish homes is generally strict, and children are carefully taught to obey their parents and the rulings of the church. It appears that discipline may on some occasions be too strongly administered, resulting in the arresting of healthy personality development, and in the rejection of the authority of both the parent and the church he represents. On the other hand, there are instances where it appears that discipline is administered too lightly, or, what may even be worse, without consistency.

With respect to mate selection, Mennonites are endogamous. Here again the pattern varies from one group to another. For the Amish, "Be ye not unequally yoked together with unbelievers" (II Cor. 6:14) is literally interpreted as "Do not marry a person who is not Amish." M.C. district conferences have often declared that Mennonites should marry only "in the faith," implying within the Mennonite faith. Although basically endogamous, the more culturally liberal groups frown less on the intermarriage of a Mennonite with a member of some other Protestant (especially evangelical) denomination. Nevertheless in the liberal groups there is considerable teaching on the inadvisability of intermarriage. The research findings of Terman, Burgess Cottrell, and other family sociologists are cited in defense of this position. Furthermore it is always hoped that a person marrying outside the Mennonite faith will bring his mate into the Mennonite fold rather than vice versa.

In Mennonite culture the "kinship system" also operates. Grandparents, grandchildren, aunts, uncles, nephews, nieces, cousins, and in-laws are apparently more significant in the lives of Mennonites than in American society at large. This is no doubt partly due to rurality, but is also a result of familistic idealism together with rather highly developed in-group feelings. Much visiting of relatives is carried on. This, of course, diminishes where urban families settle some distance from the home community.

Among Amish congregations church services have been traditionally held only on alternate Sundays. This allowed the intervening Sundays to be used for visiting relatives. Visiting is, of course, very informal, often without benefit of prior invitation. Among the more assimilated Mennonites social etiquette would normally call for at least some advance notice that a family was coming for a meal, or to stay overnight. In most cases a formal invitation would necessarily precede such a visit.

Among the Amish, where familism is very strong, a modification of the "extended family system" may be found. In such a system grandparents, their children, and their grandchildren live together in one household, as for example in traditional China. It is customary for an Amish couple to remain on the farm as long as they live. If financially possible, the couple will obtain farms for the older sons when they marry. A younger son normally will remain on the home farm after he is married, continuing to live with the parents. Instead of all living in the same house, however, a "grossdawdy" house is constructed next to (and often attached to) the main farmhouse. The grandparents and any unmarried daughters occupy this smaller house, while the son's expanding family occupies the main house. The son gradually takes over complete responsibility for the farm.

In Hutterite society, an even stronger familistic system prevails. Over one hundred Hutterite colonies are located in South Dakota, Montana, Alberta, and Manitoba. Organized along communal lines, each colony consists of from 50 to 150 persons of all ages who are for the most part interrelated. The single family unit is, however, strong and clearly defined despite the fact that all property is held in common, all families work together under one management, and live and eat together in one location.

The aged in the Mennonite culture have an unusually secure position compared to aged persons in urban American culture. This is especially true in the Amish and Hutterite groups. The communal system of the Hutterites and the "extended family" relationships among the Amish provide the aged with a life guarantee of care and protection. The aged patriarch retains a role of counselor, if not direct manager, in the affairs of his kinship group. Thus he retains considerable social status in relation to others, a condition usually denied the urban resident, who is frequently forced to retire at an arbitrary age, thus losing the sense of usefulness and responsibility so important to human happiness.

No Amish or Hutterite aged person would be left to a government agency for care as a public ward. It is regarded as not only a disgrace, but also a sin for any child to allow his parents' needs to go unmet.

The same interest and concern shown for the aged also is evidenced in relation to all other defective or dependent persons, such as the physically handicapped and the mentally deficient and deranged. Medical care is normally sought when needed. However, the reluctance of these groups to submit their dependent members to the care of some outside agency has in a few cases resulted in a family's attempting to provide necessary care which they were incapable of giving. Especially among the Amish there prevail a number of superstitious practices and "home remedies" which have on occasion served to deny a family member the necessary physical or mental health care which modern medical and psychiatric practice is able to provide.

Among the other Mennonite branches the aged and dependent family members are also well cared for. As one goes in the direction of the more liberal groups among Mennonite bodies, there is increasing readiness to seek the aid of public and private health and welfare institutions. The inroads of urbanism and secularism weaken the familistic system, and the security of dependent persons is proportionately reduced. There are, however, few Mennonites who become wards of a government agency.

In conclusion it should be noted that the Mennonite family is not static but dynamic. It is true that among the Old Order Amish and Hutterite groups social change is occurring very slowly. Traditional family forms tend to persevere in spite of the unusually dynamic nature of the surrounding American environment. Even the modern inventions of the telephone, the radio, electricity, and modern household appliances have been resisted by the Old Order Amish group, thus offsetting the extensive social and economic changes which such inventions normally precipitate in the family.

The more progressive Mennonite branches have generally welcomed the new inventions which science has offered. While enjoying the conveniences and leisure which these inventions afford, they at the same time are subjected to subtle and fundamental changes, some of which tend toward family disintegration rather than integration. Perhaps no single invention has made a greater impact upon family life than the automobile. The automobile has shortened the time-distance to the hospital, the doctor, the market, the church, and distant relatives. At the same time it has multiplied the potentialities for breaking down the associational pattern of the family unit. Possibly the greatest threat to Mennonite family stability today is the increasing number and complexity of the activities which draw members out of the family into the community institutions and activities round about. Family recreation, for example, which once was about the only type of recreation available, now is maintained only at the price of concerted effort and planning. Even family worship suffers from the blows of irregular and activity-packed time-schedules. The lines of communication between Mennonites and the surrounding increasingly urbanized, secularized, and individualized culture pattern have been multiplied in number and intensity.

Time alone will reveal whether the strong Mennonite familism will withstand the disintegrating forces which increasingly face it. Shall additional Mennonite groups, bent on preserving their familistic culture, cut the lines of communication with surrounding cultures by migrating to the remote areas of the world's remaining frontiers? Or will the sturdy religious and moral convictions of past generations continue to meet the challenges of today? In past generations, Mennonite family stability has been protected partly by compact settlement in geographically and socially isolated rural communities. As this pattern gives way, increasing spiritual resources and a greater awareness of the issues at stake will be needed to meet the challenge of modern urbanization, individualism, and secularization.

J.H.Ka.

J. W. Eaton and A. J. Mayer, *Man's Capacity to Reproduce: The Demography of a Unique Population* (Glencoe, Ill., 1954); E. K. Francis, "The Mennonite Commonwealth in Russia, 1789-1914: A Sociological Interpretation," *MQR* XXV (July 1951) 173-82; *idem, In Search of Utopia* (Altona, 1955); J. W. Fretz, *Pilgrims in Paraguay* (Scottdale, 1952) Chapter IV; *idem*, "Sociological Aspects of Divorce Among Mennonites," *Proceedings of the Eighth Conference on Mennonite Cultural Problems* (1951) 132-38; M. Gingerich, *The Mennonites in Iowa* (Iowa City, 1939) Chapter XXII; H. Good, "A Study of Mennonite Family Trends in Elkhart County, Indiana," *Proceedings of the Sixth Annual Conference on Mennonite Cultural Problems* (1947) 41-46; J. A. Hostetler, *Amish Life* (Scottdale, 1952); W. Kollmorgen, *The Culture of a Contemporary Community: The Old Order Amish of Lancaster County, Pa.* (*Rural Life Studies No. 4,* U.S. Department of Agriculture, September 1942); R. L. Mast, "How Can Mennonite Educational Institutions Combat the Disintegrating Forces Which Threaten Family Life?" *Proceedings of the Ninth Conference on Mennonite Educational and Cultural Problems* (1953) 13-18; I. G. Neufeld, "The Life Cycle of Mennonite Families in Marion County, Kansas," *Proceedings of the Sixth Annual Conference on Mennonite Cultural Problems* (1947) 47-57; *Proceedings of the Fifth Annual Conference on Mennonite Cultural Prob-

lems (1946) includes seven papers on the Hutterites; J. Umble, "The Amish Mennonites of Union County, Pennsylvania," *MQR* VII (January 1933) 71-96; J. C. Wenger, *History of the Mennonites of the Franconia Conference* (Telford, Pa., 1937) Chapter III.

Family Almanac, first published in 1870 by John F. Funk & Bro., Elkhart, Ind., was issued annually from 1870 to 1908. Since 1909 it has been published annually by the Mennonite Publishing House, Scottdale, Pa. The issues of 1902-12 inclusive were combined with the *Mennonite Yearbook and Directory.* Almanac calculations were made by Lawrence J. Ibach 1870-79, L. J. Heatwole 1880-1933, J. T. Sparkman 1934, Hart Wright 1935-55. Edited by Daniel Kauffman 1909-22, John L. Horst 1923-42, Ellrose D. Zook 1943-55. The 1949 issue, with 69 pages and a circulation of 7,000, contained the calendar, almanac calculations, religious articles, general information for the home, and a ministerial directory of the Mennonite Church (MC) and other Mennonite bodies. It was discontinued with the 1955 issue. E.D.Z.

Family History. The study of family history and genealogy, though an ancient and widespread enterprise in western culture, did not become a significant matter among Mennonites until the 20th century. It has had very little vogue in Switzerland, France, or Russia, and little more in Germany, though considerably more in Holland, but has grown to considerable proportions in North America, especially among the descendants of the early Pennsylvania Mennonite and Amish immigrants. The earliest known Mennonite family histories published in Europe are the following published in Holland: Teyler van der Hulst, *Stamboek der Teyler's of Geslachtsregister der nakomelingen van Thomas Teyler en Trijntje van de Kerkhoven van 1562-1728* (Haarlem, 1728?); P. B.(eets), *Stam-boek der Willingen of geslachtregister der nakomelingen van Jan Willink en Judith Busschers 1591 tot 1767* (Deventer, 1767). The first-known Mennonite family history published in America was *The Genealogical Register of the Male and Female Descendants of John Jacob Schnebele now Snively* (Chambersburg, 1858). For a complete listing of all known published Mennonite family histories see **Genealogy.**

In addition to genealogies family history has produced many interesting narratives of pioneer experiences and travels, as well as accounts of customs and practices, and religious and moral behavior. These materials, including other family records and genealogical data, have considerable value for general historical study, and also for specific Mennonite history. The often serious lack of group and congregational records coupled with a meager historical sense in the past seriously handicap the student of Mennonite history, theology, and piety. At times family history materials furnish important or even unique clues and traces, or major illumination. Some published genealogies contain significant historical materials in the introductory chapters.

The Mennonitischer Geschichtsverein of Germany has a section for Family History led by Kurt Kauenhoven. H.S.B.

Ernst Correll, "The Value of Family History for Mennonite History, with illustrations from Nafziger Family Materials," *MQR* II (1928) 66-79, 151-54, 198-204; K.

Kauenhoven, "Mennonitische Familienforschung," *Menn. Jahrbuch* 1951, 28-33; *ML* I, 631.

Family Reunions, social gatherings of descendants of a common ancestor, usually lasting a half day, including an outdoor semireligious program and a picnic meal and often held in a public park, have been rather common among American Mennonites since the beginning of the 20th century. Sometimes the gatherings are small, but at times they develop into enormous meetings of 1,000 to 2,000 persons, and partake more of the nature of a clan gathering than a family meeting. The small reunions commonly meet annually, the larger ones every five years. Among the notably large family reunions of essentially Mennonite character (though with very many non-Mennonite participants) have been the two Stauffer reunions of Waterloo Co., Ont., and Lancaster Co., Pa., the Landis reunions of Lancaster Co. and Bucks Co., Pa., the Burkholder reunion held at Hershey, Pa., the Birky family reunion with meetings alternating between central Illinois; Manson, Iowa; and Kouts, Ind., and the Bender reunion of New Hamburg, Ont.

In Europe, where they are called "Familientag," family reunions have not been widely observed, although the strong development of family history studies in the Nazi period in Germany led to the establishment of a number of family organizations, called "Sippenverband," such as the Kauenhowen and Zimmerman organizations, which held occasional reunion meetings. The German meetings have been rather gatherings of specialists in family history, whereas the American reunions have been primarily for social fellowship and have emphasized appreciation and emulation of the religious and moral virtues of the ancestors. Both groups, however, have often subsidized research in family history as well as the preparation and publication of genealogies or even of family periodicals, such as *Mitteilungen des Sippenverbandes der Danziger Mennoniten-Familien* and *Der Berg; Sippen-Zeitung der Sippe van Bergen, van Bargen.* (See **Family History.**)

The American family reunions often flourish during the second and third and even fourth generation of descendants, to die out gradually as the sense of connection with the first ancestor fades out. The large reunions, often based on a common ancestor of 100-250 years back, usually flourish so long as a few older historians and genealogists with much leisure and some money carry the load of organization and promotion. H.S.B.

Famine Relief, as distinct from emergency disaster relief or war sufferers' relief or general relief, has engaged the Mennonite action in three countries: India, China, and Russia.

India. Because of overpopulation and frequent floods and droughts resulting in full or partial crop failures, both India and China have had almost chronic famine conditions for centuries, with occasional extraordinarily extensive famines. The great famine of 1896-97 led to an extensive relief project by the Mennonite Church (MC) in 1897. The Home and Foreign Relief Commission (*q.v.*) was organized, with headquarters at Elkhart, Ind. A shipload (mostly Mennonite) of corn and beans was sent to Calcutta in early 1897, and George Lambert of Elkhart was sent to India to supervise distribution of this food and given approximately $20,000 in cash for further purchases and services on the spot. He did most of his work through local missions along the central line from Calcutta to Bombay. The establishment of the Mennonite (MC) Mission in the Central Provinces in India in 1899 was a direct result of this relief project, and one of the first mission institutions was an orphanage to care for famine orphans.

In 1899 the General Conference Mennonite Church organized the Emergency Relief Committee which in 1900 sent out David Goerz to India on a mission similar to Lambert's, with some 8,000 bushels of corn and several thousand dollars in cash. The G.C.M. India Mission was started later in the same year and benefited directly from the Goerz relief project, receiving some of the relief funds for distribution.

Both the above India missions continued famine relief at intervals throughout their history. In 1919-22 for instance the M.C. mission received over $56,000 for famine relief.

The serious Bengal famines of 1941-42 and later led to the organization of the Mennonite Relief Committee of India (MRCI, *q.v.*) on which all the Mennonite missions in India were represented. This committee had oversight of the relief work carried on by the MCC in India in the sending of both supplies and workers. The chief famine relief was in 1942-44. The MRCI was still in existence in 1954.

China. In China the recurring famines were due more to the great floods along the valleys of the main rivers; hence only those Mennonite missions directly in these areas did famine relief work. However, the G.C.M. mission transmitted famine relief money to the China Relief Commission in 1921-23 and leased two missionaries to this opening for relief work in the Yellow River flood area.

Russia. The great famine of 1919-20 led to extensive famine relief work (1) by the American Relief Administration (ARA—Herbert Hoover) (*q.v.*), which received a $40,000,000 appropriation for this purpose from the U.S. Congress, and (2) by North American Mennonites, as well as on a smaller scale (3) by the Dutch Mennonites. M. B. Fast and W. P. Neufeld took food and clothing to the Mennonites in Siberia in 1919, and the Mennonite Central Committee (MCC), organized in July 1920 specifically for this purpose, in 1920-23 administered relief in food, clothing, and medical supplies to the value of about $1,250,000 in addition to 25 tractor-plow outfits. (See **American Mennonite Relief, AMR.**) Some 60,000 Mennonites (and 15,000 others) received direct famine relief from the AMR. The Dutch Mennonites organized, also specifically for famine relief in Russia, the General Commission for Foreign Needs (*Algemene Commissie voor Buitenlandsche Nooden*) in November 1920. Their first supplies reached Russia in early 1922. They worked chiefly in the Molotschna and raised a total of about 400,000 guilders ($160,000) and also contributed seed grain and agricultural implements.

(For a fuller account of Mennonite relief activities see **Relief Work.**)   H.S.B.

G. Lambert, *India, The Horror-stricken Empire* (Elkhart, 1898); M. B. Fast, *Geschichtlicher Bericht, wie die Mennoniten Nordamerikas ihren armen Glaubensgenossen in Russland jetzt und früher geholfen haben. Meine Reise nach Sibirien und zurück* (Reedley, 1919); D. Woelinga, "Nood van en hulp van de Mennisten van Russland 1920-21," *DJ* 1922, 64-93; F. C. Fleischer, "Ons Hulpwerk in Ockraine en de Krim," *DJ* 1923, 43-78; G. A. Peters, *Die Hungersnot* (n.p., 1923); D. M. Hofer, *Die Hungersnot in Russland* (Chicago, 1924); P. C. Hiebert and O. O. Miller, *Feeding the Hungry, Russia Famine 1919-25* (Scottdale, 1929); Ed. G. Kaufman, *Development of the Missionary and Philanthropic Interest Among the Mennonites of North America* (Berne, 1931); H. P. Krehbiel, *History of the General Conference of the Mennonite Church of North America II* (Newton, 1938); M. C. Lehman, *The History and Principles of Mennonite Relief Work, an Introduction* (Akron, 1945); J. D. Unruh, *In the Name of Christ, A History of the Mennonite Central Committee and Its Service 1920-1951* (Scottdale, 1952).

Färber (Ferber), **Kaspar,** one of the first Anabaptists in Augsburg (*q.v.*), Germany. He came from Tirol, Austria; he was already a member of the brotherhood when he came to the city. He was in close contact with the South German Anabaptists, especially with Hans Denk (*q.v.*), who was expelled from Nürnberg on Jan. 21, 1525. Hans Hut (*q.v.*), who was everywhere enthusiastically received as a popular preacher, was won to the Anabaptist group by Denk and Färber at Pentecost in 1526.   HEGE.

W. Neuser, *Hans Hut* (Berlin, 1913) 26; F. Roth, *Augsburgs Ref.-Gesch.* (Munich, 1901) 225; Chr. Meyer, "Die Anfänge des Wiedertäufertums in Augsburg," in *Ztscht des hist. Vereins für Schwaben und Neuburg,* 1874, 224 f.; *ML* I, 632.

Far East: see map and pertinent countries.

Farel, Guillaume (1489-1565), the ardent friend and co-worker of Calvin (*q.v.*). He was an unusually energetic pioneer in the Reformation in France, and was particularly enthusiastic in introducing it in Geneva, Switzerland, persuading Calvin to settle there, co-operated in Neuchâtel, and in Metz, France. At first his position was close to that of the Anabaptists; he agreed with them on adult baptism, but was unwilling to forbid infant baptism (letter of Sept. 7, 1527). Zwingli's ideas concerning the Zürich Anabaptists apparently influenced him, but he still defended the Anabaptists against unjust accusations. Later he accepted Calvin's views and took the same position as he against them.   NEFF.

A. J. Herminjard, *Correspondance des réformateurs dans les pays de la langue française* II (1868) 18, 48, 164; F. Bevan, *W. Farel* (London, 1883); *Guillame Farel 1489-1565* (Neuchatel, 1930); *ML* I, 314-16, 632.

Farkenschin (Hungarian, Farkashida), a village an hour and a half from Trnava (Tyrnau), Czechoslovakia, which at the time of the expulsion of the Hutterian Brethren from Moravia belonged to Count Thurzo, who leased them a farm and a mill (1622). Four years later they suffered serious damage from marauding troops, and in 1627 they lost their leader, Uhl Müller, through death. After the devastation of the Thirty Years' War came the Turkish invasions. In 1663 the house was "completely burned down after suffering much larceny and plundering, and as the chronicles relate, our people were lost in the prolonged warfare, so that very few of the Farkaschin people remain; most of them died in continued flight. Thus we lost the house at Farkaschin, including people and possessions." (Beck, *Geschichts-Bücher,* 410, 431, 433, 506; *ML* I, 632.)   LOSERTH.

Farm Machinery used by the Mennonites is usually the same as that used in their surrounding communities. Certain conditions have caused some exceptions. As pioneers in less civilized countries, the Mennonites found frequently that no farm machinery was available or that which was available was inferior in quality to what they had been used to in the country they came from. Thus they were compelled to continue making traditional and creating new machinery for the land they were tilling. This has been the case particularly in Russia, where they had an exceptional opportunity to invent and develop the agricultural machinery they needed. To some extent, this is again the case in Paraguay.

When the Mennonites settled in the steppes of the Ukraine at the end of the 18th century, they found only nomadic neighbors and possibly a few Russian peasants tilling the soil with wooden plows and harvesting their crops with a sickle and flail. They soon found the machinery they had brought with them inadequate for the large-scale farming in the Ukraine. Markets for better agricultural machinery were hardly accessible to them. Thus they were compelled to repair and replace their old machinery in their own smithshops, some of which gradually developed into factories for producing machinery more suitable and practical in the new environment.

One of the first implements thus invented was a multiple-share plow known as the "bukker," which appeared on the market before 1850 (Rempel, 248). The first bukkers were made with three or four plowshares. Later five-, six-, and seven-share bukkers became common. The single-share plow with the furrow of about 10 inches in width was, in many cases, replaced by a bukker plowing up to 36 inches and more. Later, about 1880 (Rempel, 251), this bukker was developed into a drill-bukker, a broadcast sower with a seeding box placed on the top of the plow dropping the seed into the open furrow.

The second advance enabling the Mennonites to farm on a much larger scale was the reaper which became known as the "lobogreika" (this Russian word means "brow-sweater"), invented and manufactured by Peter H. Lepp, Chortitza, during the sixties. The lobogreika spread very rapidly in the Mennonite settlements during the seventies and eighties, enabling two men, one as driver and another throwing off the grain in sheaves, to reap from 15 to 18 acres a day, whereas formerly they had reaped only 5 acres by hand. Because of the rapid spread of the lobogreika among the Russian population, this reaper was manufactured by a great number of Mennonite factories such as Koop, Hildebrandt, Neufeld, Klassen, Niebuhr, and Franz and Schröder. It was even produced by the International Harvester Company in Russia. With the coming of the binders at the beginning of the 20th century, the lobogreika was gradually replaced in Mennonite communities, and some Mennonite manufacturers changed to the production of binders. The

SIBERIA-U.S.S.R.

INNER MONGOLIA

MANCHURIA

Chotzeshan, Chahar (KMB)

Vladivostok

HOKKAIDO

6

Peiping

KOREA

JAPAN

CHINA

Kaichow (GCM)

Taegu (MCC)

Tokyo (MCC)

Paoki (GCM)

Kaifeng (GCM)

China Menn. Miss. Society

Osaka

5

Shuanshipu (MB)

Chengtu (GCM)

Hochwan (MC)

Chungking

Shanghai

4

INDIA

Shanghang (MB)

BURMA

Canton

Hongkong

Hualien (MCC)

FORMOSA

SIAM

SOUTH VIETNAM

PHILIPPINES

Saigon (MCC)

KEY

1. Malay and Chinese Mennonite Church Area, Java
2. Former Dutch Mennonite Mission Area, Sumatra
3. Dutch Mennonite Mission Area, Inanwatan, New Guinea
4. General Conference Mission Area, Japan
5. Mennonite Brethren Mission Area, Japan
6. Mennonite Church (MC) Mission Area, Japan

MCC: indicates relief work carried on in 1956 by the Mennonite Central Committee.

Underline: Centers of former Mennonite missions in China.

Singapore

Natal

SUMATRA

2

BORNEO

Inanwatan

3

NEW GUINEA (DUTCH)

Jakarta

JAVA

1

AUSTRALIA

MENNONITES IN THE
Far East

Scale of Miles

0   150   300   600   900   1200

first binder produced by Mennonites in Russia came from the factory of A. J. Koop in 1914. However, World War I and the following revolution and nationalization of all factories prevented the development and large-scale manufacturing of the binder among the Mennonites.

A number of Mennonite manufacturers also produced the "Colonist" single-furrow plow, which found wide acceptance beyond the Mennonite communities. However, the German "Sack" and "Eckert" plows furnished a strong competition. Harrows, wagons, cultivators, drills, winnowers, corn shredders, chaff cutters, weeders, rakes, threshing machines, fanning mills, oil engines, etc., were invented, patented, and produced by Mennonite manufacturers, as well as by non-Mennonite Germans in Russia.

Although the tilling and harvesting machinery had been improved by the end of the century and was manufactured in large quantities, threshing was still primitive. The Mennonites were using a horse-drawn stone roller, running it over the grain on the threshing floor. These threshing stones, with grooves cut lengthwise along the outside, were transplanted to the prairie states and provinces and used in pioneer days (the threshing stone is the emblem of Bethel College). By the end of the century, they were gradually being replaced in Russia by horse-power threshers or, on the larger estates, by motor and steam threshers of English and German make. Mennonite manufacturers produced threshing machines on a large scale, not only for their own communities, but also for the Russian population.

Various types of wagons were produced in Russia since the middle of the past century. The common wagon with steel axles and a wooden box used on the farm became popular far beyond the Mennonite settlements. Spring wagons produced in Mennonite factories were also used by almost all Mennonite farmers. Some of these wagons found their way to the prairie states and provinces of North America, but were soon discarded. One is found in the Tabor College museum, Hillsboro, Kan.

In quality the Mennonite agricultural machinery was far above most of the Russian-produced implements. Some of the larger factories, employing 300 and more workers, were Hildebrandt and Sons, A. J. Koop, Lepp and Wallmann, J. G. Niebuhr, Franz and Schröder, and J. M. Janzen. In addition to these, a great number of small factories and shops could be found in most of the Mennonite settlements. The eight larger Mennonite factories alone produced nearly one tenth of the total Russian output of agricultural machinery, with a total output of 3,162,632 rubles with 1744 workers in 1911. The largest factories were located in Chortitza, Alexandrovsk, and in some of the Molotschna villages. (See also **Industry, Agriculture in Russia**, and **Business in Russia**.)   C.K.

D. Rempel, "The Mennonite Colonies in New Russia" (doctoral dissertation, Stanford University, Cal., 1933); A. Ehrt, *Das Mennoniten in Russland* (Berlin, 1932); C. Krahn, "Agriculture among the Mennonites of Russia," "Mennonite Industry in Russia," Jakob Niebuhr, "Jakob G. Niebuhr Fabriken," *Menn. Life* X (January 1955) 14-30.

Farm Trainees. The year 1950 marked the inception of the Mennonite Central Committee European Trainee Program, and in the five years of its existence 123 young men and women between the ages of 18 and 25 have been brought into the United States for a one-year training period. They have come from Germany, the Netherlands, France, Switzerland, Luxembourg, and Japan. The program is officially approved by the Department of State, Washington, D.C., as a program for "practical training in industry, medicine, agriculture, or some other field of knowledge or skill" and in the specific interests of promoting better understanding between the peoples of the various countries represented and in the general interests of international exchange of knowledge and skills in these various fields. It is regarded as an important bridge-building project between the Mennonites of various lands, whereby they may strengthen each other and their faith.

Counselors located in each community assist in locating suitable Mennonite sponsors for the placement of the trainees and stand by with counsel to the trainees or sponsor as needed during the training period. Each trainee is placed with two sponsors, for six months each, in entirely different communities, to gain the widest possible contact and experience both occupationally and in the Mennonite church and community life. A midyear conference of the trainees gives them opportunity to evaluate the program and experiences, exchange ideas, discuss problems, and draw challenge from God's Word.

The program is financed through monthly payments by the sponsors to cover ocean and inland transportation, medical expenses, and overhead. In addition to maintenance, each trainee receives from his sponsor a nominal allowance as spending money.

W.T.S.

Farming and Settlement. The Anabaptist-Mennonite movement in the Low Countries and Northwest Germany has from the beginning been predominantly urban in character, and has its strongest roots in the artisan and merchant classes. Only in the Dutch provinces of Friesland and Groningen was it predominantly rural. The Dutch Mennonites were therefore not typically farmers and have accordingly had no particular contribution to make in agriculture, although the Frisian Mennonite farmers have long been a sturdy and significant part of Dutch Mennonitism. By contrast the strong urban and artisan character of the earliest Anabaptists in Switzerland, Austria, and South and Middle Germany was soon displaced (by 1540 at the latest) by a strongly rural peasant type. In the area of East and West Prussia, except for the city congregations of Danzig, Elbing, and Königsberg, the Anabaptist-Mennonites were exclusively farmers from the beginning. Here they were, however, not peasants but occupants of larger farm units in the Vistula and Nogat delta lowlands which they made arable by skillful drainage operations, and which they were therefore allowed to purchase at a minimum price. The Hutterites were strongly agricultural, although their completely self-contained communal Bruderhofs included much more than farming in their economies.

Thus the Mennonites of history, in all places but Holland and Northwest Germany, have been farmers, and have almost universally produced outstanding achievements in agriculture. The following articles in this Encyclopedia are designed to give thorough surveys of Mennonite farming in the various areas in which Mennonites have established permanent sizable rural settlements: **Agriculture Among the Mennonites of Russia, Farming Among 'the Mennonites in France, Farming . . . in North America, Farming . . . in Germany, Farming . . . in Switzerland, Farming . . . in West and East Prussia; see also Migration.**

The notable achievements of Mennonite farmers in the Palatinate and Baden-Württemberg gave them a reputation which made them eagerly sought after as renters and managers of the larger estates in South and Middle Germany, Alsace, and Switzerland. Toleration and protection by the noble landowners, and even by the rulers, often against the bitter opposition of the local state church clergy, was their reward. The grant of exemption from military service was often based upon the exceptional contribution of the farmer Mennonites to the community and to the country.

The widespread settlement of the Mennonites on such estates in South Germany, often widely scattered from one another, on the one hand lifted them above the village peasant class and aided in their cultural and religious isolation from the surrounding world, while on the other hand making an organized active congregational life very difficult and throwing much weight on family religion. It also made land ownership almost impossible, since large farms or estates were seldom available for sale because of the laws of primogeniture and entailment of inheritance, even after the early restrictive laws forbidding the ownership of land by Mennonites had been annulled, and the law of *jus retractus* (*q.v.*) abolished.

A noteworthy development among many of these South German Mennonites was the tradition that Mennonites ought not to own land, but, as strangers and pilgrims on the earth, should remain only renters. Among the few exceptions to the almost universal practice of renting have been the small Mennonite villages in the Palatinate and adjacent regions such as Weierhof, Ibersheim, Deutschhof, Branchweilerhof, Geisberg, and Kaplaneihof, where, by various fortunate opportunities, groups of 2 to 20 Mennonite families have been able to purchase large estates and divide the land among themselves in small or medium size farmsteads of 20 to 75 acres. In Alsace and Bavaria more outright purchase of farms both large and small has been possible.

In the Vistula Delta area the farm lands were early secured in full ownership by the Mennonite occupants, usually in relatively large farmsteads, so that the Mennonite settlers here were neither peasants nor villagers for the most part, and in some cases became very large-scale master farmers. However, here the Mennonites, as nowhere else in Europe except in Russia, could settle in relatively compact blocks, with but a relatively small intermixture of non-Mennonites, since the land had been previously unoccupied. Here also the Mennonites were economically and culturally on a considerably higher level than their neighbors, and received toleration and special privileges from the landowners and the rulers because of their economic contribution. The special privilege grants (called *Privilegium*) issued by the Polish kings are noteworthy.

The Mennonites in Russia constitute an extraordinary segment of Mennonite history in so far as their manner of settlement and agricultural achievements are concerned. It is not correct, as has been at times assumed, that special concessions were made to Mennonites to secure their settlement in Russia. The privileges of civil and cultural autonomy, freedom from military service, free land (160 acres per family unit), etc., were available to all German settlers coming to Russia, although it is true that a special *privilegium* was granted to the Mennonites by the decree of the Czar Paul in 1800. The opportunity in Russia to settle in large tracts or colonies was of unusual significance, not only at the beginning (1789-1820), but later on in the purchase of large tracts for "daughter" settlements. All these large settlements were in effect "colonies," i.e., cultural and religious islands in the vast Slavic empire. This Mennonite colonization in Russia is of fascinating interest from many points of view. Not the least interesting is the village type of settlement, which was almost exclusively the only type, except for a certain number of large estates owned by very wealthy Mennonite landowners. It was, however, not chosen by the Mennonites, who had seldom lived in villages in Prussia, but was ordered by the Russian government for purposes of governmental and social control and administration. This method of settlement, in colonies and villages, guaranteed cultural and religious isolation from the much lower Slavic environment, and thus protected the Mennonites from "the world" in a certain sense. At the same time it contributed largely to the development of a "culture Mennonitism," in which the Mennonites came to think of themselves at times, and to be thought of by others, as a racial and culture group rather than a religious group, and in which ultimately a considerable proportion of the population never even became members of the church. Thus the believers' church concept of the Anabaptist originators of the Mennonite church was gravely impaired. The consequences of this development have continued to pursue and plague the Mennonites who left Russia between the two world wars and who settled in Paraguay (and in part in Brazil) again in closed colonies and villages with cultural and civic autonomy and exemption from military service, as it had done earlier to some extent in Manitoba (and Mexico). Here again the problem of racial and cultural Mennonitism has been serious, with one third to more than one half of the population in some settlements not members of the church but counting themselves as Mennonites and claiming Mennonite privileges. The method of colonization and the cultural autonomy has, however, also here helped to protect the settlers from the corrosive effects of the much lower type Latin-American environment. The serious religious plight of most of the Mennonites (now almost 700) who left Paraguay to settle in scattered locations in urban Argentina, particularly in Buenos Aires, is a instructive comparison.

The relative isolation of the Mennonite settlers in Russia (and to some extent later in Manitoba, Mexico, and South America) contributed, along with other important factors, to their loss of a sense of religious mission, and a certain overemphasis on economic and cultural rather than religious achievements. There was, however, a considerable recovery from this in the later decades.

The Mennonite settlement in the United States was of an entirely different character. Since the settlers here for the first two centuries (1683-1873) came from Switzerland, South Germany, and Alsace, where there was no Mennonite village settlement and no cultural differentiation from the surrounding population, and since usually no large group settlement was possible in Pennsylvania, individual farmsteads were the prevailing settlement pattern (except Germantown, which was settled by urban weavers, not farmers), although in most cases settlement was made in fairly compact communities. Thus the early settlements, such as Franconia and Lancaster, though strongly and compactly Mennonite, had no autonomy, civil or cultural, and no isolation, and enjoyed no special Mennonite privileges granted by the government which were not available to all. The exemption from military service available in colonial Pennsylvania, and later in other colonies and states, was a constitutional privilege available to all conscientious objectors, such as the Quakers, Moravians, etc. The Mennonites were here again almost exclusively farmers, and highly successful. Their agricultural contributions in Eastern Pennsylvania have been widely recognized.

When the large movement of Russian Mennonites of 1874-80 to the prairie states of the United States and Manitoba took place, the Russian Mennonites sought at first to reproduce their European type of settlement and autonomy in their new homes. This was impossible in the United States, both because the federal and state governments would never have countenanced any autonomous political groups, and because the interspersal of railroad reserved sections of land (most land secured by the Mennonites in Kansas and Nebraska was purchased from the large railroad companies such as the Santa Fe and Burlington roads) made really exclusive Mennonite settlements on a universal basis impossible. This did not interfere, however, with large compact rural settlements similar to those in Eastern Pennsylvania of 100-200 years earlier. The few initial village settlements were soon abandoned. The Manitoba Mennonites by contrast did secure large compact blocks of land (East and West Reserves) and did establish closed and relatively autonomous colonies with the village type settlement, and with special privileges granted by the government. All this, however, after a generation or more ultimately had to be surrendered.

The earlier Manitoba pattern of settlement was reproduced by the emigrant groups from here who settled in Mexico in 1921 ff. and in Paraguay 1926 ff.

In both cases the full Russian pattern was reproduced, with an extraordinary *privilegium*. The very serious effects upon the cultural and religious life of the Old Colony groups in Manitoba, Saskatchewan, Mexico, and Paraguay are striking illustrations of the dangers of such a type of exclusive colony-type rural settlement and life, when long-continued isolation from the main stream of culture of the host land, and poor leadership, results in extreme introversion, regression, and degeneration. Even the agricultural effectiveness of such a group begins to decline, since the cultural isolation and extreme conservatism prevents acquisition or use of new and progressive methods, impoverishes education and personality, weakens health by poor nutrition and bad health practices, increases superstition, destroys individual initiative, and prevents any development of a sense of religious mission. Even their relatively better agricultural achievements, compared to those of the (very poor) neighbors, are bought at too heavy a price in body, soul, and spirit.

By and large, however, it can be safely asserted that the reputation of Mennonite farmers as good farmers, whether Swiss, French, Russian, American, or Paraguayan, is justified. The readiness, or even eagerness, of the governments of Canada, Paraguay, and Brazil to secure and admit them has been rewarded. The Mennonites' economic value continues to outweigh their minor threat to the unity and military strength of their host countries.

What has been the secret of Mennonite farming effectiveness? Certainly not book learning. Well could the noted Jung-Stilling, professor of agriculture at the University of Heidelberg a century and a half ago, advise his students to go to the farm of David Möllinger, the master farmer of the Palatinate, where they could learn more and better than their professor could teach them. There was reason for Klopfenstein's almanac of Belfort (1819 ff.) to call itself *The Anabaptist or the Farmer by Experience.* Mennonites have seldom studied farming in the schools, except in recent decades and in small numbers. Nor was it unusual Mennonite wealth which permitted large purchases of equipment and labor. Ernst Correll has sought the answer in part in their religiously based culture, and in part in the necessity resulting from persecution and the fight for survival. Frugality, simplicity, avoidance of dissipation of mind and body through indulgence in drinking and immorality, belief in the Christian virtue of work, large and well-integrated families, freedom from tradition because of their break with the state-church culture system, determination to make good agriculturally and thus countervail the condemnation of society, all of these no doubt played a role. Some of these Anabaptist-Mennonite virtues were no doubt intensified by good German traits, which were aided and carried by the German language and culture in which Mennonites had been immersed before they settled in foreign culture areas, and which they took with them. German culture-historians have long claimed Mennonite farmers and colonizers as a prize illustration of the German cultural contribution to the world, and rightly so. But they thereby overlook the fact that Mennonites have usually been and largely still are not essentially Germans but Christians with a uniquely determined ethical and cultural behavior pattern and a religio-centered group solidarity.   H.S.B.

Ernst Correll, *Das schweizerische Täufermennoniten-tum, Ein soziologischer Bericht* (Tübingen, 1925); *idem,* "The Sociological and Economic Significance of the Mennonites as a Culture Group," *MQR* XVI (1942) 161-66; A. Ehrt, *Das Mennonitentum in Russland* (Langensalza, 1932).

Farming *Among Mennonites in France.* Until the present century, the Mennonite congregations of France have been exclusively agricultural. None of the urban congregations dating from the Reformation survived into modern times, with the result that the character of today's Mennonite society has been determined almost exclusively by successive immigrations of farmers, weavers, and millers from Switzerland.

Mennonites seem to have introduced some new drainage methods into the region of Ste-Marie-aux-Mines, according to the writer of *"Promenades Helvetiques, Alsaciennes"* (*q.v.* under article **Alsace**). Since in this mountainous area subsoil or tile drainage is out of the question, the reference is probably to the system, still in general use, of draining hillside pasture land by means of small surface ditches cut in the sod. The historical sources from other areas mention no special farming methods, but testify to a general reputation for honesty and hard work, and to a tendency to raise more livestock than other farmers.

This reputation for honesty permitted Mennonites to obtain leases on the best farms, which belonged generally to the nobility. The nobles would even rent to the lower bidder, if a Mennonite, because of their confidence in his industry and honesty. The Mennonites thus attained a favored position in comparison with the local peasant population, whose holdings were less profitable to farm. This privileged position, supported as it was by the unpopular nobility, led to a general dislike of Mennonites in some of these areas where they were most numerous (Montbéliard, Ste-Marie).

The industry and prosperity of Mennonites led in turn to a popular tradition according to which they had special gifts or farming secrets. This reputation led one Jacques Klopfenstein to publish at Belfort, beginning in 1812, a farmer's almanac entitled *The Anabaptist or the Experienced Farmer* (*L'Anabaptiste ou le Cultivateur par Expérience*). Of Klopfenstein nothing is known, though he was certainly of Mennonite origin. The idea of an almanac profiting from the Anabaptist reputation was followed by other publishers in Montbéliard and Nancy, although it is doubtful that Mennonites actually contributed anything to the editing.

The general pattern of Mennonite agriculture in history shows a steady rise in social and economic standing. Beginning on unwanted lands a refuge from persecution, Mennonite farmers came to hold, first as tenants and then sometimes as owners, some of the best land, especially those farms which being isolated from the villages, gave more social and religious freedom and more incentive for individual enterprise.

Mennonites (counting only those families which maintain some degree of church connection) now operate perhaps 300 farms in Eastern France, of which one fourth are in southern Alsace, one fourth in the Belfort-Montbéliard area, and the remainder scattered farther north and west, especially in Lorraine (see maps, incl. map in *Menn. Life,* July, 1952). The average size of Mennonite farms in the Territoire de Belfort, the only area where figures have been worked out, is about 50 acres, compared to an over-all average of 17 acres (it is to be borne in mind that many of the non-Mennonites whose holdings contribute to this low average combine their farming with factory work). This relationship may be assumed to hold as well in other parts of France, with the exact figures varying considerably with regional differences. In southern Alsace, where 52 per cent of all farms are smaller than 12 acres, the comparison would be still more striking. The average size of the Mennonite farms would further rise, to a degree incommensurate with the general pattern, in those areas where an especially large estate is operated by a Mennonite (Schweighof near Altkirch, Schopenwihr near Colmar, Schafbusch near Wissembourg, l'Epina near Verdun, Votrombois near Revigny, the Kennel farm at Ligny-en-Barrois).

On the other hand the percentage of Mennonites who own their own farms is noticeably lower than among non-Mennonites. Historically this has its origin in the period of persecution, when the changing political climate forced Mennonites to remain mobile and invest in livestock rather than land. After persecution ceased, a sort of conscientious scruple against buying land persisted until a generation ago, growing out of the "stranger and pilgrim" attitude with which the New Testament itself regards worldly security. This greater mobility was one of the factors which facilitated the 19th-century migrations of Amish Mennonites to America. There are however also material reasons for not acquiring farms. The larger estates, which Mennonites tended to seek out, belonged to noble or bourgeois families who had, and still have, little intention of selling, but who are happy to have their land farmed, if possible by the same family for several generations, by Mennonites. In addition, modern price and tax relationships make it more profitable for the tenant farmer on a large farm to invest in machinery than to attempt to acquire land.

Contrary to the pattern in some pioneer countries, Mennonites could not seek out the most fertile lands when arriving in France. The most fertile areas, Kochersberg in Alsace, and Xantois and Vermois in Lorraine, have practically no Mennonites, because the fertility had encouraged, before the arrival of Mennonites, the formation of a village-centered peasant-ownership structure which left no room for newcomers.

Parallel to the rise in economic and social standing of Mennonites, there can be observed a sloughing-off tendency resulting in the reabsorption of certain elements by village society and the mass (Catholic) Church. Mennonites unable to obtain larger farms, for reasons of land scarcity or limited management capacity, migrated to America, moved into areas where there was no organized congregation, or else gradually abandoned their Mennonite relationships, often through mixed marriage, in favor of integration in the surrounding society, in such a way as to maintain the pattern according to which Mennonites farm some of the best land and most of the isolated farms.

Except for woodcutting around Normanvillars, and flour-milling in a few Alsatian families, Mennonites generally carry on the same type of diversified agriculture as their neighbors. In modern times they have been among the first to adopt machinery, new crops, and scientific methods. Some are authorized to produce seed grains under government control or to test new varieties on an experimental basis.

Current crops in Alsace and the Montbéliard-Belfort area are wheat, oats, barley, corn (chiefly for green fodder and ensilage, the growing season barely permitting the grain to ripen), forage beets, potatoes, tobacco (in the plains around Colmar), rape (for oil), hay, and orchard fruits. Livestock is also diversified, with dairying (multipurpose cattle also fattened for beef), hogs, poultry, and rabbits. In Lorraine, where the soil does not permit use of the more demanding crops, farms are larger but devoted more largely to grazing of sheep or cattle and to small grains.   J.H.Y.

"De Mennonieten in Frankrijk" (unpublished thesis, C. Wegener Sleeswijk and A. Doornbosch, Amsterdam, 1951); E. Correll, "Master Farmers of France," *Menn. Life,* April 1952, 61; A. J. M. de Pezay, *Les Soireés Helvetiennes, Alsaciennes, et Fran-Comtoises* (Amsterdam and Paris, 1772); Alfred Michiels, *Les Anabaptistes des Vosges* (Paris, 1860).

Farming *Among the Mennonites in the Netherlands.* The first Anabaptists in the Netherlands were found both in the country and in the cities (Groningen, Leeuwarden, Hoorn, Alkmaar, Amsterdam, Leiden, Middelburg, etc.). Later on we find Mennonites in the cities and small towns engaged in business, as well as in the country. Mennonite farmers are found particularly in the provinces of Groningen, Friesland, and North Holland, and many of them have been promoters both of new methods in agriculture and of cattle-raising. The Mennonite farmers of the Netherlands never founded special Mennonite agricultural associations as they did in other countries, because the Dutch villages do not consist of Mennonites only (as, e.g., in Russia) and because most farmers do not live together in villages, but often have their farm buildings (*boerderijen*) on their own land. Special mention should be made of the flower-growers of Aalsmeer (*q.v.*) near Amsterdam. Here the world-renowned nurseries that export roses and other flowers all over the world have for many generations been to a great extent owned or run by Mennonites; e.g., Eveleens, Hilverda, and Keessen.   vDZ.

Farming *Among the Mennonites in North America.* Nowhere in the world has rural life changed more rapidly and more drastically than in the United States. These radical changes are commonly referred to as the revolution in rural life. The changes have not been confined to technological areas, such as the tractor replacing the horse; the automobile, the buggy; and electricity replacing kerosene. The changes have altered the general structure. They have affected birth and death rates, population shifts, cultural patterns, and have even significantly altered religious and social values. American Mennonites, who have so predominantly an agricultural heritage, have been visibly affected by this revolution in American agriculture. With the exception of the Old Order Amish and the Old Colony Mennonites, North American Mennonites have, in principle, completely accepted the technological and scientific methods of farming. Only economic limitations seem to have prevented them from using the latest scientific methods and modern mechanisms. At a slower rate and somewhat less obvious, the impact of the agricultural revolution has been felt on the religious and social values and the cultural patterns of the Mennonites.

There are several factors in the history of Mennonites which explain their devotion to agriculture. Because of persecution many became pioneers in agriculture. Due to their emphasis on the virtues of thrift, diligence, frugality, and humility, they, in the course of time, learned to earn a living on the poorest soils where persecution often drove them. They learned to drain swamps, to improve the fertility of poor soil, and experiment with new ways of farming until, in the course of centuries, they developed both skills and a reputation as expert farmers. These aspects of the Mennonite heritage developed in them a deep-seated tradition as farmers. This tradition, plus their desire to perpetuate themselves as a peculiar people, resulted in church regulations which often prohibited residence in towns and cities and encouraged the pursuit of farming as a vocation or occupation closely related to farming. While the old prohibitions have been lifted everywhere with the exception of the most conservative American Mennonite groups, farming is still predominantly preferred as the occupation, about 80 per cent of the largest group being farmers. Thus we find American Mennonites scattered over the states and provinces of North America in compact settlements in the best farm lands. Many of these agricultural areas were developed out of raw prairie lands and others were improved after purchasing them from earlier settlers who had abandoned them in search of richer soils or other occupations. The largest numbers of Mennonites are found today in the states of Pennsylvania, Ohio, Indiana, and Kansas with smaller distributions in 29 other states. Others are scattered in Canada throughout the provinces of Ontario, Manitoba, Saskatchewan, Alberta, and British Columbia. In both Canada and the United States, the Mennonite settlements followed the general pattern of a westward movement, from Ontario to British Columbia in Canada, and from Pennsylvania to the Pacific Coast in the United States.

Mennonites have made a number of significant contributions to American agriculture. Perhaps the most outstanding contribution is the general one of having developed prosperous agricultural communities composed of a large number of individually owned family-farm size units. If the key to a stable civilization is the stable family, Mennonites have contributed significantly because of their large families and their well-organized community life centered around the church. A more specific contribution of the American Mennonite group is the introduction, cultivation, and processing of hard winter Red Turkey wheat, which was brought from Russia to the plains states especially centered in Kansas and Oklahoma in 1874. This contribution has been widely recognized as a distinctive gift of the Mennonites and has been accepted as the one factor making Kansas the "bread basket" of America. It is not without significance that the Mennonites who migrated from Russia to America in the 1870's were successful wheat growers in Southern Russia, having produced as much as one-half million bushels of wheat as early as 1855. The hard winter wheat, introduced in the late 19th century, has now been generally accepted as the most preferable wheat for milling purposes. From it have been developed a number of other varieties of wheat.

A second significant contribution of the American Mennonites stems from the Swiss Mennonites. It is the method of farming by means of a systematic rotation of crops. By this means it is possible to preserve soil fertility by means of natural processes. The rotation consists of a three-, four-, or five-crop cycle. The cycle may begin with a legume crop such as clover or alfalfa, followed by corn, oats, and wheat. This natural method of maintaining fertility is also supplemented by the use of domestic and commercialized fertilizers. Common barnyard manure has long been considered by Mennonite farmers as a highly valuable soil builder. Perception of its value was one incentive to a cattle-feeding program which, in turn, produced additional quantities of manure and provided meat supplies and dairy products, both marketable, cash commodities. Pennsylvania Mennonites showed a preference for locating on limestone soils. They earlier discovered the profitable use of burnt lime as a valuable fertilizer. Today commercial brands of fertilizers are used in addition to lime and manure. Thus Mennonites have had a reputation of being good farmers because they preserved the productive capacity of their soils for centuries on end. This is one reason why farms have been kept in single families for as many as six or seven generations. The improvements of the fathers are handed on to the sons generation after generation.

A significant Mennonite contribution is the practice of various forms of mutual aid. This is a rural virtue, formerly very widely practiced, and today still common in Mennonite agricultural areas. It is especially dramatized in the Amish communities where insurance is taboo and where, if destruction to buildings is incurred as a result of accident, the whole community, consisting of as many as several hundred people, will rally to the festive occasion of reconstructing the destroyed buildings. Thus Amish farmers experience the cheapest possible type of insurance and yet the best because it is a volun-

tary assistance. In less conservative groups there are numerous mutual aid societies for the rendering of various functions. Within the United States and Canada there are at least 60 Mennonite mutual insurance societies, most of them covering risks incurred from fire and storms. These are all based on a simple assessment plan of mutually sharing the costs of the losses. Much informal mutual aid is still practiced in farming communities where farmers exchange work, share machinery, plow or harvest fields for neighbors who are incapacitated, and in some cases, even extend financial assistance.

An interesting contradiction among American Mennonite agricultural practices is the custom of raising tobacco. American Mennonites generally have come to discourage the use of tobacco. Nevertheless, among the Amish and some Mennonite groups in eastern Pennsylvania, large quantities of tobacco are still grown. The county of Lancaster in Pennsylvania is among the most highly productive farming areas in the entire country, and it is in this county that more Mennonites reside than in any other in America. In recent decades, this county has been the leading tobacco producer in the country and Mennonites and Amish are among the largest producers in that county. This is explained in part by the highly profitable nature of the crop and because it provides work during the winter months for the farm family. Many young farmers get their start by sharecropping several acres of tobacco in order to put up a cash reserve.

The following significant trends may be noted in Mennonite agricultural communities. Mennonite farmers have been generally prosperous. They have adopted the latest methods of farming, but interestingly, very few Mennonite farmers have had formal training in agricultural schools or colleges. Their skills have been acquired through home training and practice. Increasing numbers of Mennonites have joined farmers' co-operative organizations for the purpose of benefiting through corporate action in producing, buying, and marketing of their crops and necessities. There has been a trend in the more populated sections toward a declining size in farms and a more intensive agriculture characterized by specialization in farming, although preserving a large element of self-sufficiency and family-type enterprise. In the prairie states especially, there has been a noticeable trend in the direction of larger farms and operating units. This is accounted for in large measure by the increasing acreages that can be operated by modern machinery and by the high capitalization which must be offset by a greater volume of production. In some areas, there is a noticeable concentration of wealth in the hands of a few with the development of a landless or renter class of those who cannot establish themselves on farms of their own.

A peculiar problem confronting many Mennonite farmers is the question of co-operating with the government in various agricultural practices. The traditional opposition to participating in government is still contended for in theory but with the United States government becoming increasingly a welfare state, it is more difficult to maintain this sharp line of separation. Such governmental agencies as the Agricultural Adjustment Act, with its subsidy payments for reduced crop acreages, have found most Mennonite farmers co-operating. Many have borrowed money through the Farm Commodity Administration and the Commodity Credit Corporation. Participation in the federal crop insurance and Rural Electrification Administration programs, has further involved Mennonite farmers with aspects of a government program. Amish farmers who have resisted mechanization and electrification and have frequently refused AAA subsidies, have maintained a clearer witness than other Mennonites in this respect. Even many of them have accepted some parts of the government program. It appears that Mennonites would continue to co-operate rather than withdraw from government co-operation.

Since about 1930, there has been a growing self-consciousness among American Mennonite farmers. From colonial days until the recent past, Mennonites have taken farming very much for granted. Even during the heavy population shift from rural to urban areas in the late 19th and early 20th centuries, Mennonites resisted the trend although they were by no means unaffected by it. During this urbanward shift, farming came to be looked upon as among the less preferred occupations. Urban people, including the most lowly laboring men, tended to feel higher in social rank than the farmer. In the course of time, farmers came to sense this stigma and developed something of an inferiority complex. This general feeling was accompanied by difficult and unpredictable economic circumstances. Since 1940, about the beginning of World War II, the economic lot of the farmer has improved and so has his social rank. At the same time there has been a new effort to interpret the values of the rural community to rural people. Newly established magazines such as *Mennonite Life* and *Christian Living* along with articles in church organs and independent journals such as the *Mennonite Weekly Review,* have done much to interpret agriculture in a new light to urban and rural Mennonites alike. It is probable that the future will see American Mennonites clinging strongly to the land and maintaining their age-old tradition as agriculturalists.

J.W.F.

Ira D. Landis, "Mennonite Agriculture in Colonial Lancaster Co., Pa.," *MQR* XIX (October 1945) 254-72.

Farming *Among the Mennonites in South Germany.* The Thirty Years' War (1618-48) devastated large areas of South Germany and decimated the population especially in rural areas. For this reason a number of the many territorial rulers were willing to admit and to tolerate the Mennonite farmers, who were being expelled from Switzerland. This was particularly the case with Charles Louis (*q.v.*), the Palatine Elector, whose domains at the time embraced large parts of the present Palatinate, but also extended to the other side of the Rhine, including Mannheim, Heidelberg, and even Sinsheim on the Elsenz. In 1672 about 359 persons were counted left of the Rhine, and 160 families right of the Rhine, who were registered as Anabaptists from Switzerland (Müller).

At this time the land was commonly cultivated on the traditional "Dreifelderwirtschaft"; i.e., in a sequence of three years the farmers in one part of a given area had to sow winter grain, those in another part summer crops, and those in the third part leave their land uncultivated, thus creating a pasture for the cattle of the area, which were cared for as a single herd by a village herder. This method of farming, however, checked the development of better methods of cultivation.

After the first great immigration of 1671, many of these Swiss refugee families, usually without financial assets, were assigned to smaller farms or estates (*Höfe*) for a term of usually 6-9 years (known as "Temporalbeständer"). But in a short time their industry, integrity, and their skill earned them such a good reputation that from 1680 they were permitted to lease larger estates without a time limit and with the right to pass such leases on to their heirs (known as "Erbbeständer"). These farms were usually outside the village land and were not subject to the rule regarding the common pasturing of cattle, but were under the control of the *Hofkammer* of the feudal lords. Thus these farmers had more freedom to experiment and develop newer methods.

Since the Mennonites had always practiced hospitality and their religious services were held in their homes, and they were thus separated voluntarily as well as by compulsion from the rest of the population, the knowledge acquired by one of them soon became their common possession and practice.

After the unfavorable consequences of the French War of Succession (1689-97) had been overcome, a marked difference became evident between the fields of the "Mennists" and the other lands. Following a fundamental rule of farming, viz., no feed, no cattle; no cattle, no manure; no manure, no crop, the Mennonite farmers, seeking new methods of raising cattle fodder, found them in the cultivation of new varieties of clover, which permitted them to feed the cattle in the barns even in summer. The agricultural authorities of that time ascribed the introduction of Esparsette (Esper) to the Mennonites and Waldenses (?). To what extent they were responsible for the introduction of Lucerne can not be determined; but this "everlasting blue clover" soon found entry into all Mennonite establishments. The first experiments with mineral fertilizers were made at this time by scattering ground gypsum over the clover fields. The results far exceeded expectations. The careful handling of manure, the preservation of the liquid manure, which were traditional practices brought from Switzerland, played an important part. The liquid manure keg (*Jauchefass*) is popularly attributed to the practical sense of the Mennonite farmers.

The culture of potatoes, tried experimentally by a Mennonite of Mannheim, was quickly adopted on Mennonite farms. These potatoes, not yet accepted for human consumption, were used commercially for the manufacture of brandy; this produced as a by-product an excellent feed for fattening cattle. Also the first cultivation of mangels is attributed to the Mennonites of the Palatinate; these beets were at first also used for distilled liquor products. Thus one advance led to another, finally producing a completely new method of farming and bringing it to a high fruition on exemplary farms. Where previously there was only one skinny cow with a poor udder there were now three fat cows with high milk production or three fat steers.

Outstanding leaders in the progress of South German agriculture were David Möllinger (*q.v.*, 1709-87) of Monsheim, Johannes Dettweiler (b. 1738) of Kindenheim, his son Christian (1765-1838) of Wintersheim, Valentin Dahlem (1754-1840) of the Koppensteinerhof near Wiesbaden, and David Kägy (1767-1846) of Offstein. They were considered the best farmers of their time, and were cited as models by specialists and by the government authorities. Thus the reputation of the model Mennonite farms spread into wider and wider circles, and they were called into more and more distant areas, and even into foreign countries. Thus the Mennonites moving into remote parts were motivated both by economic and religious concerns.

In 1785 there were 250 Mennonites in the area of Usingen in Hesse-Nassau. In 1784 there were 28 Mennonite families among the settlers called into Galicia (*q.v.*) by Emperor Joseph II. In 1802 eight Mennonites families, upon the wish of their leaselord, settled in Donaumoos (*q.v.*) in Bavaria (*q.v.*). They were soon followed by others, especially from Alsace, but also from Baden and Württemberg, who later settled in various parts of Bavaria. Beginning with the French Revolution, which extended the French border to the Rhine, the sociological development on the two sides of the Rhine no longer followed a uniform pattern. The French expelled all the feudal lords on the left (west) bank of the Rhine and introduced the French civil law. The former estates of the rulers and lords, as well as those of the monasteries, were sooner or later transferred to the possession of the renters and divided. On the right (east) of the Rhine conditions generally remained as they had been, unchanged. Even though the "Erbbestand" farms were replaced by "Pacht" (lease) farms, with few exceptions due to local conditions the leasing of large farms remained the dominant form of Mennonite farming, many families remaining for decades or even a century on the same farms. With the beginning of the 20th century begins the transfer of large leased estates into Mennonite possession.

Even though since the middle of the 19th century the Mennonite farms have no longer been so sharply differentiated from those of non-Mennonites, the Mennonite farms are on the whole still considered the best managed and exemplary. No exposition of the German Agricultural Association passes without giving a prize or award to a Mennonite for achievements in the culture of plants or animals.

Outstanding for plant cultivation today are Hauter of Dreihof, Stauffer of Obersülzen (Palatinate), Hege of Hohebuch (Württemberg), Lichti of Herrlehof (Bavaria). As animal breeders there are Hauter of Herschweiler-Pettersheim, Stalter of Heckenaschbacherhof, Guth of Heyerhof (Palatinate), Hege of Hohebuch, Schneider of Eckhof (Württemberg). In leading positions in the German Agricultural Association are Dr. h.c. Hans Hege of Hohebuch and Dr. Erich Musselmann of Helmeringen (Bavaria).

C.G.

Müller, *Berner Täufer;* E. H. Correll, *Das Schweizerische Täufermennonitentum* (Tübingen, 1925); Fritz Hege, "Beruf und Berufung des Mennonitischen Landwirts," *Menn. Jahrbuch,* 1954, 19.

Farming *Among the Mennonites in Switzerland.* The Swiss Anabaptist-Mennonites have always been almost exclusively farmers, in spite of the fact that the first stages of the movement in Zürich and Basel included many from other classes such as clergymen and artisans. By 1540, however, the urban phase of the movement was largely past and the survival of Anabaptism was the work largely of peasant farmers in the outlying rural areas, especially in the Emmental. A deep suspicion of all forms of trade and business and urban activity marked the later history of the movement down to modern times. Practically all of the modern Mennonites living in Switzerland descend from the original Emmental Swiss Brethren, who lived to a large extent on individual small farms in the region of Langnau.

Most of the Mennonites living in the Emmental and later in the Jura (*q.v.*) in Switzerland were primarily engaged in dairying and cattle breeding or horse breeding. They made a virtue out of necessity and became extraordinarily successful in these lines; otherwise they could not have survived. Wherever these Swiss Mennonite farmers went later on, as they emigrated into Alsace, the Palatinate, Pennsylvania, or elsewhere, they took with them and maintained their exceptional abilities as farmers. They developed new methods of fertilizing through the conservation and use of animal manure, and also in the use of water for meadows. They were known everywhere as the best farmers.

The Jura Mennonites, living on the 3,000-foot plateau of the Jura Mountains in northeastern Switzerland since 1700 as immigrants from the Emmental and Thun, had to succeed under exceptionally difficult conditions. The land of the Jura is stony and poor in water resources, as well as naturally infertile, but the experienced Mennonite farmers from the Emmental and neighboring territory succeeded in making farming here profitable through their extraordinary industry and rational methods of farming. Here they were compelled to devote themselves exclusively to dairying and cattle breeding, since their chief resource was the cheaper land. Here they developed also an exceptionally fine-flavored cheese called the "Jura" cheese, which found a good market as long as the Mennonites produced it. Until about 1900 the Jura Mennonites also engaged in weaving. Their half-linen clothes and bed linens, which furnished most of their own consumption of these items, were of good quality.

Since 1900 cattle and horse breeding has enjoyed an unusual vogue among the Jura Mennonites. They breed the Simmental cow and the Freiberg horse.

The modern Mennonite farmer in the Emmental has one of the most fruitful soils of all Switzerland to cultivate, although the soil is often so hilly that it cannot be cultivated with the usual machines, and the land which they own is in the foothills of the Alps, where there are many deep valleys. The exceptionally fine grass in the Emmental is one of the reasons for the world-famous Emmental cheese which is produced here. The Emmental Mennonites largely own their farms, which are usually small in acreage, whereas the Jura Mennonites long had to rent their farms and still are not universally owners of their land.

The Mennonite farmers in the neighborhood of Basel (*q.v.*), immigrants since 1780 from the Jura or from Alsace, live mostly on larger rented estates. Since the soil is fruitful and not so hilly as in the Emmental the farming of this region is largely mixed and very different from the other Mennonite areas. The Basel farmers, however, are just as outstanding in skill as those of the other two regions. Before 1890 no Mennonites in Switzerland owned their own farms.

The natural increase of Mennonite population in recent decades, together with the increase in land values and the limited number of farms available, has forced many young Swiss Mennonites into the cities and towns. This is particularly true in Basel and in the Jura watch-making areas, such as Tramelan and Chaux-de-Fonds. This is bound to have a significant effect on the future of Swiss Mennonitism, which hitherto has been almost exclusively rural.   S.G.

Müller, *Berner Täufer;* E. H. Correll, *Das Schweizerische Täufermennonitentum* (Tübingen, 1925); S. Geiser, *Die Taufgesinnten-Gemeinden* (Karlsruhe, 1931); A. J. Amstutz, "Kurze Geschichte des Jura," *Gem.-Kal., 1924,* 63-76; *idem,* "Alttäufer (Mennoniten) im Berner Jura," *Gem.-Kal., 1924,* 77-83; Samuel Gerber, "Swiss and French Mennonites Today," *Menn. Life* VI (July 1951) 58.

Farming *Among the Mennonites in West Prussia and East Prussia.* Mennonites practiced agriculture for over 400 years in West and East Prussia, most of their families being farmers throughout the entire period of their occupancy 1534-1945. In West Prussia their historic location was in the lowlands of the Vistula Delta; in East Prussia it was in the lowlands of the Memel River near Tilsit, where they first settled in 1713. The chief and extraordinary agricultural achievements of the Mennonite farmers lie in the field of land-drainage. It was only their proved ability to make arable the land lying below sea level that secured the privilege of settlement in the Vistula Delta for the Dutch Mennonite refugees of 1534 and later, since the political sovereignty of the area at that time was in the hands of a strongly clerical and intolerant Poland.

The Teutonic Knights Order had, to be sure, built the great Vistula dikes and drainage establishments, but the skill of the century-old Dutch drainage techniques was necessary to drain completely the shallow lagoons and swamps of the Vistula Delta, much of which lay as much as six feet below sea level. Furthermore, after the disappearance of the Order there was no strong authority which understood how to operate for the common good. The drainage arrangements which had been built were scattered widely over the area. As a consequence the great breaks in the dikes in 1540 and 1545

inundated the whole territory of the Danzig Werder for years, reducing it to a watery waste which gradually became overgrown with reeds and rushes, since it lay below sea level. The Master of the Order, Konrad von Jungingen, stated in one of his documents regarding the inhabitants of the village of Petershagen near Tiegenhof, "They have only watery land and boundary dikes."

In 1547-50 the drainage of this entire low territory was begun in all three sectors of the Vistula Delta on a forty-mile front, from Drausensee through the Ellerwald area and the Gross-Werder to the gates of Danzig. It was a gigantic undertaking. The landowners of this territory, namely, the Polish king, the Catholic Church, the cities of Danzig and Elbing, and the Polish barons, leased blocks of land ranging in size from 250 to 2,500 acres to Mennonite leasing associations. These associations constituted at one and the same time village communities and drainage companies, and were obligated to pay the landowners a joint rent as well as to assume responsibility for the draining of the land. It is clear from the surviving drainage arrangements that the boundaries of the individual leaseholds were chosen with consideration of the natural elevations of the land which would make possible satisfactory diking, as well as in consideration of the possible channels for discharge of the water. The land area of each of the associations had to be diked off against the inroads of water from the outside, and accordingly the associations had to join each other in arrangements to dike in the channels for the discharge water. Then a windmill was erected at the lowest place in the land area at the outlet channel, which then was constantly worked to lower the water level of the polder which it served. Side channels then had to be dug out to make possible the steady flow of water to the windmill, since the drop in the land level was very gentle. These side channels were so arranged that the smallest parcels of land were from about 2½ to 7½ acres in size. These individual tracts then had to be so leveled off that there would be a slight drop in the surface. Water furrows were then marked at right angles to the plow furrows to make possible the rapid discharge of rain water, since the land in any case also suffered under a high ground water level. The land also had to be cleared of all bushes and grass. All this hand labor became a very severe burden to the families of the settlers, who seldom possessed any capital. An extraordinary skill was required to avoid unnecessary work in the erection of each drainage polder as well as in other drainage work if this enormous job was to be made possible for the weak labor resources available. In addition to all this there was swamp fever. It is reported that 80 per cent of the first settlers died from it.

This first and most difficult drainage work took three to four generations. The first fruit of the drainage was meadows and pastures with excellent grass. Since the drainage channels with their low dikes carried water which stood considerably higher than the surrounding land there was great danger in rainy seasons or snow thaws that the north wind would blow and drive the water of the Baltic back into the land and through the channels into the rear areas so high that the windmills would not dare to pump the water out of the polders, since in that case the dikes would have been immediately flooded. Consequently the polders were often flooded, and this was tolerable only for meadows and pastures.

The grassy pastures called for a very intelligent handling of the cattle to be pastured. The Prussian Mennonites therefore took up dairying. By careful breeding they were able to develop a high quality milk-producing cow which was popularly called the "Milk Boat." Until modern times it was proverbial among the cattle dealers of Germany to say, "The best milch cow of Germany grows around Neuteich," the settlement area of the West Prussian Mennonites. The Dutch Mennonite immigrants brought with them from Holland the knowledge and skills essential to the conquest of the pasture land and the successful improvement of milk production and the utilization of the milk. For this purpose they developed flat funnellike earthenware containers with a large surface area which aided the rise of the cream. They also developed churns and the art of cheese making. The very good Werder cheese was a special Mennonite product. The Mennonites of the Memel district also developed a special cheese even in the first years of their settlement there, of which they annually delivered tons to the markets in Königsberg and Tilsit. This "Tilsit cheese" became a famous product which found a market all over Germany and which has retained its reputation to the present day.

But the Mennonites of the Vistula Delta settled not only in areas which lay below sea level but also in swampy areas which lay above sea level but had poor drainage because of lack of discharge channels. In such areas they also succeeded in draining considerable areas of land through development of controlled discharge channels. On such land wheat and rape could be planted, in addition to the raising of dairy cattle. This combination of grain raising and cattle raising give the Mennonite farmers a considerable advantage above their other neighbors in the delta since they were able to use a considerable amount of animal manure at a time when artificial fertilizers were not yet available.

While the men achieved extraordinary results through their drainage work, the milking and conversion of the milk into other dairy products was the extraordinary achievement of the Mennonite women in comparison to the other farm women of the area. These achievements, due to the great industry of the Mennonites, were well known, as may be seen from the statement of the administrator of Marienburg at the 1676 Landtag when he said, "One can easily detect where a lazy drunken peasant or an industrious and sober Mennonite lives."

In the building of the barns and houses in the farms below sea level care had to be taken to locate the building area above high water. Since the earth necessary to build these elevated locations was scarce it had to be hauled in from considerable distances. For this reason the farmyards were small. This explains also why in small farms, up to possibly 45 acres, the dwelling house, stables, and

barn were built together in a row under one common thatched roof, called "Reihenhof." In the case of larger farms this "row" would soon get too long and waste too much land for the approach. Consequently, an "angle" farmyard was developed, in which the dwelling house and stable were built in one row but the barn of approximately equal length was built on at a right angle. The farmyard was then located inside the angle. The exit road led around the barn and served at one and the same time as the rear exit from the barn and as the exit for the manure pile, which was located on the opposite side of the stable. When the farm exceeded 125 acres in size a cross-shaped farmstead was constructed. Here the barn was built crosswise to the stable and on both sides of it. By this manner of construction the shortest cut was achieved for the route to haul the hay and straw from the barn to the stable. This corresponds in a large degree to the recommended method of construction of a farmstead in our day.

It is noteworthy that the agricultural settlements of the Mennonites in West Prussia through the centuries remained intact longest in those areas where a systematic drainage of the land was an absolute necessity. The necessary communal task of drainage required a sense of community which was natural to the Mennonites. Furthermore, the originally unfruitful lands which they occupied were freed from many of the taxes and levies which other lands had to carry.

On the other hand, the Mennonites resisted with all their strength the labor which was required of them on the dikes and for the villages which had been established by the teutonic Order. Personal serfdom to other persons was an abomination to them, and they sought with every means at their command to keep their young people out of the low type of life which was common among the hired farm laborers, both men and women, of the larger peasant farmers in the villages.

A noteworthy characteristic of the Mennonite farms in Prussia was the well-ordered garden. Until the very end of the Mennonite settlements one could always determine where a Mennonite lived from the state of the garden.

With the development of the steam engine a change came into the drainage procedures in the Vistula Delta. The more powerful pumps of the steam engine were able to do so much better work than the windmill, and the circular pump was able to lift the water so much higher than the millwheel, that the smaller polders could readily be combined and the water level lowered still further.

The further development of motor power through the use of the big diesel motor, as well as the increasing interest of the state in aiding the agricultural development of its people, led to a still further consolidation of the drainage units and to a deeper drop in the ground water level. As a result the whole area of the Gross-Werder was finally consolidated into two great drainage areas lying on both sides of the Schwente. One of these areas lay along the Elbing Vistula and the other at the "Jungfersche Lake." They were protected by dams from flooding from the side of the Baltic. The last areas where there was swamp fever then disappeared, and wheat and sugar beets could be raised everywhere. This final consummation of the drainage work of the Mennonites was only achieved during World War II.

Because of the general rise in the standard of living and the consequent demand for meat in the second half of the century it became necessary to substitute a heavier, more meaty type of milch cow for the earlier purely milch (Werder) cow. This development was inaugurated by the Mennonite Cornelius Jansson of Tiege, who imported in 1852 a high-quality breeding bull of the black-and-white East Frisian type of Dutch origin. For the same reason the Mennonite Gerhard Wiebe of Gross-Lesewitz introduced breeding stock of the Holstein Wilstermarsch race. This East Frisian type with its greater milk production won out in the competition and led to the establishment of the West Prussian Registered Cattle Association. West Prussian Mennonites remained the leaders in this successful breeding association, both on the breeding side and the marketing side. The Mennonite Gustav Friesen of Klein-Lichtenau three times won the gold medal (1936-39) for the best milk production of any herd in the territory. His best herd production for one year was an average of 13,860 pounds of milk with 4 per cent butter fat per cow. The last president of the association was Ernst Penner of Liessau. Chairman of the cattle co-operative of Danzig-West Prussia, with an annual turnover of $9,000,000 in beef cattle and $1,000,000 in milk cattle, was Johann Driedger of Heubuden.

As a result of the expansion of the acreage of the Mennonite farmers in West Prussia following the lowering of the ground water level and the cancellation of the restrictive regulations against Mennonites, the creative activity of the Mennonites in the area of agriculture was considerably increased. The Mennonite Epp of Quadendorf produced a type of wheat in the second half of the 19th century which found wide distribution in West Prussia far beyond purely Mennonite farmers under the name "Quadendorf Epp Wheat." The Mennonite Ernst Wiens of Damerau achieved the highest ranking in 1930 in the money value per acre of the product of all the agriculture operations of similar character in the entire German national area. This was a result of his careful handling of his land. The biggest sugar beet producer in the Vistula Delta in 1944 was the above-named Mennonite Penner of Liessau, who harvested 30,000 dozen sugar beets.

The three top executives of the Dike Associations in the Vistula Delta who had the responsibility for the maintenance of all the river dikes and the supervision of the whole drainage process were always Mennonites on the basis of a free election, although the Mennonites did not have either by number or by area the majority. J.Dr.

Horst Penner, *Ansiedlung mennonitischer Niederländer im Weichselmündungsgebiet von der Mitte des 16. Jahrhunderts bis zum Beginn der preussischen Zeit* (Weierhof, 1940); idem, "Die westpreussischen Mennoniten im Wandel der Zeit," in *Menn. Gesch.-Bl.* VII (1950); H. Wiebe, *Das Siedlungswerk niederländischer Mennoniten im Weichseltal* (Marburg, 1952); F. Szper, *Nederlandsche Nederzettingen in West-Pruizen gedurende den Poolschen tijd* (Enkhuizen, 1913).

Farmsum, a town in the Dutch province of Groningen, where Leenaert Bouwens (*q.v.*) baptized 10 persons in 1554-82. Nothing is known, however, of a congregation here. The newly-baptized probably joined neighboring churches. vdZ.

Farnhurst (Del.) Civilian Public Service Unit No. 58 was officially opened in Nov. 1942, although 25 C.P.S. men had arrived there a month earlier. The unit employed by the Delaware State Hospital performed a variety of skilled and unskilled tasks in this mental institution, including work in occupational therapy and physiotherapy. The unit was closed in Oct. 1946. M.G.

M. Gingerich, *Service for Peace* (Akron, Pa., 1949) 219.

Farwendel, an Anabaptist elder at Kreuznach, Germany (according to the chronicles of the Hutterian Brethren a preacher in the Anabaptist congregation at Neustadt). In 1556 a violent dispute arose between him and Theobald, the elder at Worms, "concerning original sin and concerning the sin of the soul and the sin of the flesh." About 1500 brethren at Worms sided with Farwendel. Theobald apparently violently upbraided him. Two preachers were deposed. Presumably this quarrel was laid before the large conference in Strasbourg in 1557, where 50 elders wrote a letter to Menno Simons (*DB* 1894, 45).

In 1564 Farwendel was held as a prisoner in the tower at Oggersheim near Worms, where he defended his faith before the official preachers. Since he was subjected to many temptations, he summoned Klaus Braidl (*q.v.*), a missionary of the Hutterian Brethren, to strengthen him in the faith. After his release in 1565 he moved to Moravia with his family, and with other members of his former congregation in the Palatinate he joined the brotherhood there. K.V., HEGE.

Chr. Hege, *Die Täufer in der Kurpfalz* (Frankfurt, 1908) 79-82; Beck, *Geschichts-Bücher*, 236-39; W. Köhler, *Brüderliche Vereinigung* (1908) 20; *ML* I, 632.

Fasser, Georg, an Anabaptist martyr, a preacher of the Hutterian Brethren, who with his wife belonged to Jakob Hutter's (*q.v.*) inner circle and after Hutter's death was closely associated with Leonhard Sailer (Lanzenstiel, *q.v.*). He was a native of Kitzbühel, Tirol, Austria. Nothing is known of his earlier life. His name is listed in the table of Anabaptists who escaped from Tirol and whose property was confiscated.

The statement in this list, that "Georg Fasser has no possessions," must refer to real estate. For in connection with the dissension between Jakob Hutter and Siegmund Schützinger in 1533 it is known that Fasser put all his possessions (beds, chests, etc.) into the common room; his wife, who tried to reserve some money for her children, was severely reproved and expelled from the brotherhood, but was later reinstated, as Hutter expressly states in his letter of November 1533.

Valentin Luckner (*Urgicht,* Oct. 6, 1533) reports that Georg Fasser conducted a service in the woods behind Michelsburg; 20 or 30 persons were present, among them the notable Anabaptist names of Hans Amon and Onophrius Griesinger.

Fasser was also a friend of Hieronymus Käls, who sent him greetings from prison. In 1533 he stayed in Moravia and watched the disagreement between Hutter on one hand and Philip and Gabriel on the other, and Hutter's ultimate success in creating order in the brotherhood. In the next two years he experienced the bitter persecution of the Anabaptists in Tirol and in Moravia; this did not, however, deter him in carrying out his mission as an apostle.

In 1536 he accompanied Lanzenstiel to Austerlitz in Moravia. In Neudorf, Austria, they found several sisters and other good persons; in the tavern, however, "an immoral crowd." They found another inn, and people from the tavern followed them with violent derision. "As far as we were concerned, the matter was easy; but when they began to blaspheme we were moved with zeal to call their attention to their rascality."

The two were then captured and on the following day taken to Mödling (south of Vienna) and tried under torture. To Hans Amon they wrote, "We gave testimony to the truth in such a manner that they were all shocked and answered not a word." In the prison they lay "with ungodly and shameful people, whose company was very repulsive."

From May 8 to June 9 they sent at least six letters to Amon, to which he replied with comforting expressions. From the first letter we learn that "a dear brother from Vienna" was with them. The second letter expresses their desire to hear the worst concerning their fate and to depart from this world. With the fourth letter Lanzenstiel sends Amon Jakob Hutter's washcloth, apparently a keepsake from Hutter, concerning whose end Amon had told the prisoners. The fifth letter they thought would be their last, for the judges and council were threatening them with torture if they did not recant. The next letter says if they had not mentioned that Hieronymus Käls and his companions were their brethren they would have been released. An important personage had been with them and told them they must renounce certain articles if they wanted to be free. On May 25 a rich merchant's wife had visited them and described Hutter's death to them.

The news of the capture of two such proved brethren as Lanzenstiel and Fasser filled the brotherhood with dismay, since they had recently been deprived of their most capable leaders. Therefore Amon wrote them four letters expressing his concern, and urging them to "fight bravely to the end, for our beloved Jakob (Hutter) and Hieronymus (Käls) are waiting with the elect." His second letter was disconsolate, for he had received no word from the Puster Valley. In the fourth he admonished them to be faithful and think of dear Jakob who was true through all the torture. Fasser's Ursula had recently fallen asleep and had entered into her eternal rest.

After Fasser and Lanzenstiel had been in prison almost a year and were prepared for death they were mysteriously released. They went first to Trasenhofen in Lower Austria near the Moravian border.

Fasser at once gathered a congregation at Peckstall in Austria. But he was betrayed by a man pretending to seek instruction and he was imprisoned again. The chronicles give two conflicting accounts of his death. According to one he was killed with the sword after severe torture in 1537; according to the other he was burned at the stake in 1538. His converts joined the brotherhood in Moravia.

Loserth.

J. Loserth, *Der Anabaptismus in Tirol* I (Vienna, 1892); *ML* I, 633 f.

Fasser, Jörg (Vasser). A second person with this name, not identical with the above, for he came from Schwaz in Tirol not Kitzbühel, and having been a monk he was able to read and write, whereas the above could not. After leaving the monastery he was a technician in the mine at Schwaz. In the brotherhood he distinguished himself through his great zeal; this is indicated by the names "Jörg Tauffer" and "Principaltäufer" given him in the Tirol court records. A poster issued by the government against him April 2, 1528, describes him as a tall young man, with black beard and full face. Fasser was seized soon after, but escaped and made his way to Stams into the Petersberg district, then to Telfs and over the mountain toward Seefeld, leaving distinct traces of his work. All the efforts of the government to seize him were unavailing. He arrived safely in Moravia with his wife. Nothing more is heard of him. (*ML* I, 634.)   Loserth.

Fast (Feste, Faast, Vast), a Mennonite family name in the rural Flemish congregations of West Prussia, rarely also in the Danzig Flemish and the Montau Frisian congregations. It was first mentioned 1582 at Wotzlaff, where an Arendt Feste appears in the record. The first appearance of the name Fast in a church record was at Danzig in 1669. According to records there were nine bearers of the name in 1727, all of whom had Dutch given names. The name was represented in such congregations as Ladekopp, Fürstenwerder, Heubuden, Elbing, and Danzig. Thirty-three families of this name were counted in 1776, 157 persons in 1910, 108 persons in 1935. Members of the family also migrated to Russia and America. Among the prominent leaders of this family were Daniel Fast, an elder of the M.B. Church in the Kuban 1877-1902; Gerhard Fast, a minister of the Heubuden congregation in 1903-32, leading in conference activities after World War I; Bernhard Fast (*q.v.*), an elder of the Orloff (Molotschna) congregation, and Martin B. Fast (*q.v.*), former editor of the *Mennonitische Rundschau,* last in California.

Ten M.B. ministers living in Kansas, Oklahoma, California, Manitoba, and British Columbia carry the name Fast. Four ministers in the E.M.B. Conference, and four among the G.C. Mennonites have this family name (1953). The Mountain Lake, Minn., telephone directory for 1949 listed 24 Fasts. Eleven Fasts served in Civilian Public Service. Well known is Henry A. Fast, Bethel College professor and vice-chairman of the Mennonite Central Committee; also Aganetha Fast, a missionary to China.

G.R.

Fast, Bernhard, was born in Prussia, ordained minister in Russia in 1814, ordained elder Jan. 13, 1821, died 1860. Fast succeeded Jacob Enns as elder of the large Flemish Ohrloff Mennonite Church (*q.v.*) and became a very significant progressive leader of the newly established Molotschna Mennonite settlement. He was a supporter of Johann Cornies' endeavors, of the Ohrloff Vereinsschule, and of more progressive measures in promoting the Gospel and co-operating with other Protestant groups. Because of his progressive views he soon encountered opposition which led to a split within the congregation.

Some of the reasons for the division were: (1) some objection to Fast's decision to be ordained by a Flemish elder; (2) Fast had admitted a non-Mennonite missionary, Moritz, to the Lord's Supper in his congregation; (3) he promoted the work of a Russian Bible Society, a branch of which was organized in the Molotschna Mennonite settlement; (4) he supported the Ohrloff Vereinsschule; and (5) he favored the observance of the holidays according to the calendar in use in Russia.

Four of his co-ministers led in the opposition which culminated in the split of the congregation, leaving Fast only one fourth of the members (150 families). Jakob Warkentin was ordained elder of the conservative wing on Aug. 3, 1824. This congregation became known as the Lichtenau Mennonite Church (*q.v.*). The objectives which Fast promoted became generally accepted after one or two generations. It was unfortunate that circumstances in his day caused friction and division, but it was fortunate that he stood for a cause which paved the way for better education and a more meaningful practical Christianity.   NEFF, C.K.

This episode of the Molotschna Mennonites has been dealt with at some length by various writers: Friesen, *Brüderschaft,* 77, 84, 113-19, 197, 305; Franz Isaak, *Die Molotschnaer Mennoniten* (Halbstadt, 1908) 91-123; H. Goerz, *Die Molotschnaer Ansiedlung* (Steinbach, 1950) 58-60. Isaak and Friesen relate sources and express somewhat colored opinions; most objective is Goerz. The article in *ML* I, 634, was based on Friesen.

Fast, Bernhard J., Mennonite teacher and minister, b. July 23, 1857, Halbstadt, Russia, d. Oct. 17, 1917, in the Terek Mennonite settlement. Fast was a teacher for 27 years, and minister 10 years; he served as minister and leader of the Azov Forestry Service Camp for 5 years. He lived in village No. 7 of the Terek settlement and was killed by nomadic tribesmen.   C.K.

A. A. Töws, *Mennonitische Märtyrer* II (North Clearbrook, B.C., 1954) 189 ff.; C. P. Toews, *Die Tereker Ansiedlung* (Steinbach, Man., 1945) 22, 51 f.

Fast, Daniel, b. 1826 at Halbstadt in the Molotschna, Ukraine (Russia), d. at Wohldemfürst in the Kuban, in 1843 became village schoolteacher at Tiegenhagen and in 1862 at Blumenort, where he joined the Mennonite Brethren in 1864. Soon afterward he emigrated to the Kuban. Here he was ordained as preacher Jan. 14, 1870, traveling evangelist May 14, 1872, with an annual compensation of 200 roubles, and as elder May 5, 1877. Through his moderate, intelligent, and genuinely pious and sober attitude he exerted a wholesome influence on the young

Mennonite Brethren wing and worked with great blessing until 1902, when he retired because of his age and ill health. (Friesen, *Brüderschaft; ML* I, 634.)   NEFF.

Fast, Heinrich, a Mennonite (EMB) minister, born Aug. 23, 1849, in Gertuamalee, South Russia, the oldest of the five children of Johann and Sara Peters Fast. In July 1875 the family (with the exception of one sister) immigrated to Minnesota, settling on a farm six miles northwest of Mountain Lake. In 1876 Heinrich Fast married Maria Hamm (also from South Russia). They were the parents of ten children, six of whom lived to become adults, two of the sons, John and George, becoming deacons in the church. In 1910 he retired from farming.

Fast was also a minister for about 25 years in the Brudertaler Mennonite Church north of Mountain Lake, and also served as traveling evangelist (*Reiseprediger*) for about five years. He died on Feb. 27, 1930, having passed the age of 80 years, and was buried in the cemetery near the Brudertaler church.   D.H.F.

Fast, Hermann, b. April 27, 1860, at Gnadenfeld, Molotschna, Russia, and died March 22, 1935, at Petrovka, Sask., was the thirteenth of fourteen children of Isaak Fast, who had come to Russia from the Marienburger Werder, Prussia. For four years he attended the Ohrloff Vereinsschule and received catechetical instruction under Elder Bernhard Harder. After this he returned to Gnadenfeld where he graduated, after three years, from the Zentralschule. In 1878-79 he taught school at Rudnerweide. The next year while teaching a Lutheran school at Berdyansk he experienced a conversion, after which he attended the Bible school of St. Chrischona near Basel for three years.

After his return to Russia in 1883, he taught for two years at the Musterschule of Halbstadt. In 1885 he went to Feodosiya, Crimea, where he preached in a Lutheran church and studied the Russian language. Here Countess Schonnenlov of St. Petersburg invited him to become the tutor of her grandson, which position he held from 1886 to 1894. On June 22, 1887, in the Baptist Chapel at Riga, he was married to Elizabeth Garinovitch, a Greek Catholic who had been a private tutor at Halbstadt while Fast was teaching there.

In 1892-93 he accompanied two English Quakers, Joseph Neive and John Bellow, to the Caucasus to visit exiled Evangelicals, serving as an interpreter. Because of this and other religious activities he was watched by the Russian police. In 1895 Fast and his wife, together with the widow of the poet N. A. Nekrassov, settled on an estate near Simferopol, Crimea, and lived there until 1897. Since the police were watching him here also, he accepted the invitation of F. W. Baedeker to go to Rumania, where he taught a private school in Constanta and served as a minister of a German Baptist church in Dobruya. In 1901 he went to Canada and settled in Petrovka, a Dukhobor village north of the Saskatchewan River. Here he and his wife continued their religious work among the Russians, carrying on farming, and teaching for a time in the Quaker-built school of Petrovka, preaching, serving as postmaster, etc. He also represented the British and Foreign Bible Society, traveling in various provinces of Canada. Elizabeth Fast died on Feb. 27, 1915. Of their five children, two sons died and three daughters are living, Maria Novikoff (Toronto, Ont.), Olga Good (Eugene, Ore.), and Constance Reusser (Deer Creek, Okla.).

Elder David Toews said at the funeral of Hermann Fast, "He served the Dukhobor village as organizer, counselor, and minister to the welfare of their souls. He was a true child of God, not bound to a denomination but in all races and tongues found brothers and sisters."

In Petersburg, Russia, Fast was a member of the Baptist Church, but in Canada he was a member of the Waldheim (Sask.) Mennonite Brethren Church. During the last years of his life he lived at Perdue, Sask.   C.K.

Hermann Fast, "Autobiographie" (unpublished); Sophie Fritschi, *Biographie von Hermann Fast* (Zürich, 1949).

Fast, Isaak, b. 1847 at Gnadenfeld, Molotschna, Russia, was a leader and elder of a group of Mennonites which separated from the main body and established a new church known as the Alexandrodar Mennonite Church of *Jerusalemsfreunde* (*q.v.*) in the Kuban region in 1868. When a controversy arose during the sixties regarding the Bruderschule of Gnadenfeld, Molotschna, Isaak Fast joined the brothers Johann and Friedrich Lange (*q.v.*), who had been influenced by the chiliast Christian Hoffmann (*q.v.*) of Württemberg. All the petitions and correspondence in this case reprinted by Franz Isaak in *Die Molotschnaer Mennoniten* (207-59), bear the signature of Isaak Fast. Fast became a minister of the group in 1884, and elder in 1902. He also taught the school at Alexandrodar. At the Molotschna he had been a teacher of the Ohrloff Vereinsschule and in Russian schools. Little is known about his life and later activities. (Friesen, *Brüderschaft,* 456, 728; *ML* I, 26.)   C.K.

Fast, Isaak P., father of Hermann Fast (*q.v.*) and Abraham Fast of Jerusalem, was born April 4, 1815, son of Peter Fast of Neumünsterberg, Danzig, where he received his elementary and secondary training—the latter in the school of Lange (*q.v.*) at Rodloffer-hufen—after which he taught school. On Aug. 10, 1836, he left Prussia and went to Gnadenfeld, Ukraine, where he married Elisabeth Dück and taught school in various Mennonite communities and opened a bookstore. A booklet containing a preface by Hermann Fast, the autobiography of Isaak P. Fast, and a sermon preached by Heinrich Dirks at his funeral was published by A. J. Fast (Winnipeg, 1932) under the title *Züge aus meinem Leben.*   C.K.

Fast, Isaak P., the son of the well-known teacher Peter Fast of Tashchenak-Friedensfeld, South Russia, was born on Feb. 4, 1856, and died November 1908. Among the pioneers of the Memrik settlement in the district of Bachmut, which was purchased by the Molotschna settlement for its landless families in 1885, there were 28 members of the M.B. Church of Rückenau. One of these was Isaak P. Fast, who settled here with his wife and family. In the fall of 1885 Fast was ordained to the ministry to lead the young church (affiliated with Rückenau). On Sept. 11, 1900, the church became independent and on this occasion Fast was ordained as an elder. Under his leadership the Memrik (Kotlyarevo) M.B. Church grew, reaching a membership of 350 by May 1902.
A.H.D.

Fast, Johann, a Mennonite missionary, b. Jan. 23, 1861, at Ohrloff in the Molotschna, Russia, the son of Gerhard Fast. He attended the Zentralschule at Ohrloff and the Teacher's College at Berdyansk. After teaching in the Crimea for a time, he attended Chrischona Bible School near Basel for two years and entered the Dutch Mennonite mission of Java in 1888. In 1890 he married Jakoba A.M. Jansz, the daughter of missionary Pieter Jansz. They had five children, two boys and three girls. The oldest, Johann, became a medical missionary of the Neukirchen mission 1928-36, after which time he had a private practice. He died in a Japanese camp at Tjimahi, Java, on Jan. 4, 1945.

The missionary Johann Fast returned to Russia in 1898 for a furlough and spent another term, 1901-09, on the mission field, and then returned to Russia because of poor health. Here he promoted missions, taught Bible in the Zentralschule of Spat, Crimea, and after the Revolution worked in a dairy. In 1920 he returned to Java via Holland as a missionary at Kaju Apu until 1928, after which he lived in retirement at Salatiga, and died Oct. 15, 1941.   E.F.

Fast, Johann J., a nephew of Daniel Fast (*q.v.*), was born in South Russia in 1834, and through reading and independent study he became a well-informed and powerful minister in the M.B. Church of Russia.

Five sons and one daughter reached maturity: Johann, Peter, Bernhard, Isaak, and Justina stayed in Russia, most of them perishing behind the Iron Curtain, while Daniel came to Canada in 1904, entered the teaching profession, and now lives in Vancouver, B.C.

Johann J. Fast began with a prosperous lumber business, but when this was destroyed by fire, he gave himself more and more to the ministry of the Gospel. Although he lived in several villages of the Molotschna, he settled in Rückenau, close to the church, where he worked in close fellowship with the renowned M.B. Bible expositor, J. W. Reimer. In his preaching Fast was not particularly dramatic but the fervency of his spirit and the excellent testimony of the purity of his life gave his presentation of the Gospel a dynamic impact. He made a particular contribution in the work of house-visitation and personal contacts with neighbors and friends, and thus led many to the saving knowledge of Christ. He died in Rückenau in August 1898, his last admonition being, "Brethren, cover up and forget." (*ML* I, 635.)   NEFF, J.J.T.

Fast, Martin B., K.M.B. author and editor, was born Jan. 6, 1858, at Tiegerweide, South Russia, the son of Peter and Aganetha Barkmann Fast. Here Martin attended elementary school. At 19 years of age he joined the Mennonite Church at Rückenau. With his parents he came to America in 1877 and settled near Jansen, Jefferson Co., Neb., where he was converted, baptized, and received into the fellowship of the Krimmer Mennonite Brethren Church, May 23, 1880. He married Elizabeth Thiessen of Jansen on Feb. 24, 1884. In 1887 he became a United States citizen. He served as editor of the *Rundschau* (*q.v.*), Elkhart, Ind. (later Scottdale, Pa.), 1903-10, and as the first editor of *Der Wahrheitsfreund* (*q.v.*), Chicago, Ill., 1915-17. In 1908 he made a trip to Russia, visiting relatives and friends in the Molotschna settlement and elsewhere. In June 1919 he made a trip to Siberia with clothing and money for the relief of the poor, and later sent many food drafts for Russian relief. In 1929-33 he served the Krimmer Mennonite Brethren Conference as chairman of the Board of Foreign Missions; and for some time he was secretary of the Mennonite Aid on the west coast. He died March 15, 1949, at Reedley, Cal., following a brief illness, at the age of 91 years, and was buried in the Zion K.M.B. cemetery, Dinuba, Cal.

Fast was correspondent to various German papers, and wrote numerous booklets, including *Mitteilungen von etlichen der Groszen unter den Mennoniten in Russland und in America* (1935); *Meine Gedichte vom Jahre 1880 bis jetzt* (1943); *Reisebericht und kurze Geschichte der Mennoniten* (1909); *Geschichtlicher Bericht wie die Mennoniten Nordamerikas ihren armen Glaubensgenossen in Russland jetzt und früher geholfen haben* (1919).   C.F.P.

Fast, Peter P. (brother of Hermann Fast?), graduated from Ohrloff Zentralschule and teacher-training course at Halbstadt, taught elementary school at Rudnerweide, graduated from the University of Moscow, and taught for a number of years at the Halbstadt Zentralschule and the Gymnasium of Feodosiya. In 1909 he succeeded A. A. Neufeld as the director of the Realschule of Berdyansk, and he taught there until the end of his life.   C.K.

H. Görz, *Die Molotschnaer Ansiedlung* (Steinbach, 1950) 163-64.

Fasting. Did the Mennonites ever have the practice of fasting, as for example the Roman Catholics? It is not very probable that they did; nothing is found about fasting in the writings of their leaders such as Menno Simons and Dirk Philips, though they occasionally insisted on sober eating and drinking, as did also Galenus Abrahamsz, the well-known preacher of Amsterdam, at the close of the 17th century.

But there was a three-day fast in the Anabaptist congregation of Amsterdam in 1534, ordered by "the prophets and preachers of the church." This curious fact is found in the Confession of Jannetgen Thijsdochter on Jan. 23, 1535 (published by Grosheide, *Verhooren,* 180). In 1754 among the Groninger Old Flemish, after eight preachers had finished their preaching tour of all the congregations (see **Cremer, Lubbert Jansz**) a day of general fasting and prayer was proclaimed by the elders before a new elder was chosen.

That fasting was practiced by the Mennonites in colonial Pennsylvania is shown by references in a notebook of Hans Tschantz, one of the earliest (serving *ca.* 1717-45) bishops of the Lancaster County Mennonite settlement in what is now the Strasburg and Willow Street congregations. He refers to two fast days, one in the spring and one in the fall. It is probable that these fasts were observed in connection with the communion services. The observance of such fasts, usually the breakfast on Saturday before communion, was continued into the 20th century in the Lancaster Conference, and has only recently fully died out. It was longest observed by the bishops.

A similar observance of fasts before communion is still fully maintained by many Old Order Amish communities. Although the exact day for the observance has varied, it has always been limited to a breakfast fast. Most commonly the fast has come on the Sunday before communion Sunday, when the preparatory service or "inquiry" meeting is held. The morning of Good Friday is also observed as a fast. Some churches of Amish background have fasted the Friday or Saturday morning before the communion Sunday.

P. M. Friesen (*Brüderschaft,* 82) reports that the Gnadenfeld-Alexanderwohl (Molotschna) joint confession of faith, first drafted in 1787 by Jacob Wedell of Przechowka near Schwetz, contained a statement regarding a "right evangelical fasting according to the teaching of the Holy Scriptures."   vDZ.

Faukelius, Hermann, b. about 1560 at Brugge, Belgium, studied theology at the universities of Gent and Leiden. In 1585 he was made preacher of the secret Reformed congregation in Cologne, and June 27, 1599, at Middelburg, Dutch province of Zeeland. He refused a call to Amsterdam. In Zeeland he was a zealous member of the synod and energetically attacked the Mennonites and Remonstrants. In 1617 he published a new Dutch translation of the New Testament. He was a delegate to the national synod in Dordrecht (1618-19). In addition he was a member of the committee on the affairs of the church in the East Indies. He was one of the translators of the well-known "state translation" of the Bible. He died May 9, 1625, at Middelburg. He incurred the disfavor of the Mennonites with the publication of his book, *Babel dat is verwerringhe der wederdooperen onder malkanderen, over meest alle stukken der christelycke leere. Met een kort verhael van de oorspronk, verbreidinghe, menigerley verdeelinghen ende scheuringhe derselven van malkanderen* (1621). It was reprinted later. Two Mennonite preachers wrote a reply to it. Claes Claesz (*q.v.*) published *Bekenntenisse van de voornaemste stucken des Christelyken geloofs en der Leere* (1624), and Anthoni Roscius (*q.v.*) wrote *Babel, d. i. Verwerringe der Kinderdooperen onder malcanderen* (1626). Faukelius' *Babel* is a libel; but as the author used several books that have been lost or are very rare, it contains some historical accounts that are not without value. He could not refrain from relating some offensive facts that, though greatly exaggerated, contain a germ of truth.   K.V.

Biogr. Wb. III, 14-23; Kühler, *Geschiedenis* II, 46 f., 68, 76-78, 177; *DB* 1883, 7 ff.; 1897, 115 f.,; *ML* I, 635.

Fauquier County (Va.) Old Order Amish congregation was organized in October 1945 under the leadership of William A., Simon, and Rudy Byler. The first settlers moved there from Delaware and were joined by others from Pennsylvania, Ohio, and Iowa. The settlement is located 45 miles south of Washington, D.C., near Warrenton, Va. In 1953 the 55 members were led by Bishop Daniel Nissley.　　M.G.

Faustendorf, formerly a Mennonite congregation in Baden, Germany, now called Adelsheim (q.v.).

Fayette County (Ill.) Old Order Amish community, now extinct, was located near Brownstown and Vandalia in 1894-1906. The community at its largest consisted of about 25 families. John A. Miller was the first minister, and he was joined by Mose Yoder of Howard Co., Ind. Sam Bender was ordained minister and bishop of the church. Joe Bontrager, who lived in the community for about two years, also assisted in preaching.

Probably because of internal difficulties the Amish began to scatter, and by 1906 the settlement was completely gone. Many returned to Iowa, others went to Douglas County, and to Oklahoma and Mississippi. There remains a small cemetery of 14 graves five miles northwest of Brownstown.

J.A.H.

Fayette County, Pa., Mennonite churches. There are no official church records known to be in existence for the first one hundred years of the Mennonite settlement in northern Fayette Co., Pa. Land was acquired in this western Pennsylvania county by four Mennonite families in 1789-91. The first minister and bishop was Abraham Stauffer, who came from Lancaster Co., Pa., and in 1790 purchased 278 acres of land in Tyrone Twp., Fayette County. Early settlers came from Lancaster County and Washington Co., Md.

Tradition states that the first meetinghouse, about one mile west of Pennsville, was erected before 1800. Rebuilt in 1852, it served almost continuously until membership dwindled and after 1903 it was no longer used. Throughout most of its existence the congregation held biweekly meetings. It alternated with the Stonerville meetinghouse (q.v.) five miles across Jacobs Creek in Westmoreland County. The Pennsville meetinghouse (q.v.) and burying ground became property of the Scottdale congregation (formerly Stonerville and Pennsville) which in 1903 authorized the disposal of the property. Throughout its existence the Pennsville membership was one with the Stonerville congregation and the combined memberships numbered at most 200.

After 1850 a decline set in and by another 50 years the combined membership at the two meetinghouses had declined to 20 persons or less. However, later years witnessed a growth and revival in the Scottdale (q.v.) congregation as it became the congregational center of the church's publishing plant. Aaron Loucks played a leading role in this work.

It is believed that the Masontown Mennonite (MC) Church (q.v.) in southern Fayette Co., Pa., was the second oldest Mennonite congregation west of the Alleghenies. Settlers came from eastern Pennsylvania before 1800 and perhaps as early as 1790. They were the Longeneckers, Johnsons, Bixlers, Fretzes, Honsakers, Saylors, and Leckrones.

What is thought to have been the first Mennonite Sunday school in the United States was held here in 1842 when Bishop Nicholas Johnson began teaching the Bible to children of this church. In 1872 John F. Funk and Daniel Brenneman held revival meetings for four weeks. These meetings were among the first, if not the first, revival meetings in the Mennonite Church. J. N. Durr (q.v.) was an important leader in the congregation for many years. The 1954 membership of the congregation was 112.

In 1951 the Kingview Mennonite (MC) Church (q.v.) was built in East Scottdale in Fayette County, the outgrowth of extension work that began in this territory in 1906.　　G.M.S.

Feddriks, Douwe, van Molqueren, a Dutch Mennonite minister of whose life little is known. He may have been a native of the little town of Molkwerum (q.v.) in Friesland, as his name indicates. At the end of the 17th century he was minister of *het kleine hoopke* (the small group) at Harlingen, Dutch province of Friesland, which had separated about 1696 from the main body of the Flemish congregation in this town. Later on he was preacher at Emden, East Friesland. He was extremely conservative and a champion of the authority of the Mennonite confessions. He is especially known for his writings. In 1698 he published *Der Mennoniten Leere of onderwijsinge voor de Doopsgezinde Christenheid; waarin de leerstucken van hunne belydenis . . . aan den dag gebragt worden en met de Schriftuur verrijkt . . .* (Amsterdam). After Galenus Abrahamsz (q.v.) had published his *Korte Grondstellingen* (1699) Feddriks, who thought Galenus was introducing the heresy of Socinianism (q.v.), was instructed by the Zonist (q.v.) Sociëteit, meeting on May 1-12, 1700, to draw up a refutation; accordingly he published *Mennonitisch Ondersoek op de Korte Grondstellingen, Die van Dr. Galenus opgestelt zijn . . .* (Amsterdam, 1700). Now Feddriks was attacked by Jan Klaasz van Grouw (q.v.), who published *De leer der Doopsgezinden verdedigd . . .* (Amsterdam, 1702). Thereupon Feddriks answered by his book *De Rechtsinnigheyd van de Leer der Mennoniten opgestelt . . . tegen de vreemd gemaakte misduydingen van Jan Klaassen van Grouw . . .* (Amsterdam, 1703). Feddriks' writings and his opposition to the Socinian doctrines were highly appreciated not only by Zonist Mennonites like L. Bidloo, H. Schijn, and E. A. van Dooregeest, but also by the Reformed in the Netherlands. Feddriks left behind an unpublished manuscript, "Harmonie of Overeenstemminge der vier Evangelisten."

vdZ.

DB 1878, 83, 96, 97; *Biogr. Wb.* III, 26-27; Schijn-Maatschoen, *Geschiedenis* II, 606-10; H. W. Meihuizen, *Galenus Abrahamsz* (Haarlem, 1954) see Index; *ML* I, 637.

Federal Council *of the Churches of Christ in America,* an official federation of the national bodies of most of the larger and some of the small evangelical Protestant churches of the United States, designed "to manifest the essential oneness of the Christian churches of America in Jesus Christ as their divine Lord and Saviour." The General Conference Mennonite Church joined the Federal Council in 1908, the year it was organized. With the war in 1914, growing militarism caused opp᷉sition to affiliation, which led to Mennonite withdrawal in 1917. However, at that time the majority report of the investigating committee of the General Conference actually favored continuing the relationship. Since that time the alienation from the Federal Council has been more complete, particularly in view of extensive attacks upon it by American fundamentalists. During World War II the Mennonite Central Committee had functional relationships to the Federal Council committee on conscientious objectors, and sent representatives to several meetings sponsored by the Council's Commission on International Good Will and Justice. In 1950 the Federal Council was merged with several other interdenominational bodies to form the National Council of the Churches of Christ in America. D.E.S.

Feenstra, an old Mennonite family of Friesland in the Netherlands, which has produced a number of preachers. The oldest of these was Wepke Feenstra, preacher at Franeker 1773-79. His son Thys became mayor of Leeuwarden; another son of Wepke Feenstra, Pieter Wepkes Feenstra, b. 1792 at Franeker, d. Aug. 23, 1858, at Sneek, was called in 1792 to Holwerd, and from 1797 until his retirement in May 1842 he was the pastor at Sneek, where he dedicated a new church on April 10, 1842. He published a sermon for the day of thanksgiving and prayer, Feb. 22, 1809. Under his leadership the union of the two branches in Sneek took place. One of his daughters was married to J. Kuiper, pastor of the IJlst congregation, another to the notary Kuiper of Bolsward. A son of the latter was Taco Kuiper (*q.v.*), a Mennonite minister of Amsterdam, the father of A. K. Kuiper (*q.v.*), also a preacher of Amsterdam, and of K. Kuiper (d. 1922), professor of Greek language and culture. A third daughter was married to P. H. Veen (*q.v.*), minister at Bovenknijpe, whose grandson became the pastor of Monnikendam, also P. H. Veen, and whose daughter married J. Oosterbaan, a Mennonite minister of Makkum, whose son became preacher at Hilversum. (*Biogr. Wb.* III, 28 f.; *Inv. Arch. Amst.* I, No. 731.)

Pieter Wepkes had three sons, two of whom, Wepke and Pieter Feenstra, should be mentioned. Wepke, a physician in Holwerd, was the father of Pieter Wepkes Feenstra, b. 1831, preacher at Dantumawoude 1854-70, at Leeuwarden 1870-97, d. 1919 at Rolde, father-in-law of J. Wuite, minister at Leyden. He wrote the ceremonial address for the bicentennial of the founding of the Friesche Doopsgezinde Sociëteit (*DB* 1895). Pieter was also prison chaplain at Leeuwarden and active in the *Maatschappij tot Nut van 't Algemeen* (*DJ* 1921, 19-28).

Pieter Feenstra, b. in 1800, was pastor of the Mennonite congregation at Sappemeer 1824-30, at Leer 1830-37, and again at Sappemeer-Hoogezand 1837-71,

father of Pieter Feenstra, Jr. (*q.v.*). He was one of the founders of the Groninger and Oostfriesche Sociëteit, and died in retirement on Jan. 5, 1886. (*ML* I, 635.) K.V.

Feenstra, Pieter, Jr., son of Pieter Feenstra, the Mennonite pastor at Sappemeer, b. there Oct. 18, 1850, d. Aug. 16, 1936, married A. M. C. Tjeenk Willink (d. 1920), studied at the Athenaeum and the Mennonite seminary in Amsterdam, and became a candidate for the ministry in 1872. Introduced by his father, he delivered his first sermon on March 16, 1873, at Witmarsum and Pingjum. In 1881-91 he served as minister at Nijmegen, and from that time until his retirement on Jan. 30, 1916, at Amsterdam. He died in Amsterdam, Aug. 16, 1936.

Feenstra was one of the leading Dutch Mennonite preachers in the 20th century. To his influence many congregations owe their institutions for the strengthening of the brotherhood. In Witmarsum he dedicated a new church in December 1877. On the site of the "Menno Simons church" he had a monument of Menno unveiled, for which many contributions came in from the churches. A memorial booklet was issued of this celebration (later reprinted in the publication of the *Doopsgezinden in de Verstrooiing,* No. 37). Feenstra's study on Menno Simons, published in his *Pro Sancto* (Haarlem, 1899), was one of the best characterizations of Menno published to that time. In the field of religious instruction he rendered meritorious service in publishing two handbooks, one in co-operation with the Mennonite minister J. Sepp, and one with J. H. Boeke (1898). He also published his memories of J. G. de Hoop Scheffer (*q.v.*) and a biography of A. Loosjes (in the Biographies of the Society for Dutch Literature). Outside Mennonite circles he was chairman of the Dutch Protestant union and was active in the Association of Modern (Liberal) Theologians, in which he gave addresses in 1895 and 1898.

He was coeditor of Teyler's *Theologisch Tijdschrift,* in which he published a number of papers, among them a thorough study on *De godsdienst en de Fransche revolutie* (edited as a book at Haarlem, 1926). He was one of the six members of Teyler's Godgeleerd Genootschap (Theological Association), and held other positions of honor.

When the *Zondagsbode* (*q.v.*) was on the point of expiring at the close of its seventh year, he revived it and conducted it with notable success 1894-1916, writing many articles of all kinds for it. As curator of the Mennonite seminary in Amsterdam he became acquainted with practically all the students who became preachers after 1891. He was presented with the gavel as honorary chairman in 1914 at the centennial of the E.T.E.B.O.N. (*q.v.*) (students' association of the Mennonite Seminary).

From 1890 to 1935 he was a member of the Board of the A.D.S. (*q.v.*) and several times he served as its president. In 1923 he effected an important modification of the rules of the A.D.S. (Dutch Mennonite general conference). (*De Zondagsbode,* Aug. 23, 1936; *DJ* 1937, 17-24 with portrait; *ML* I, 635-37.)

K.V., vdZ.

Fehr, Kornelius A., an elder of the M.B. Church, born Sept. 24, 1846, in Alt-Kronsweide, Molotschna settlement, Ukraine, the oldest son of Abram Fehr. He received only an elementary school training, but through diligent study, wide reading, and participation in courses for ministers he acquired a good knowledge of the Scriptures as well as of life in general. His marriage to Margaretha Koslowsky was childless, but they adopted an orphan girl. As a young man Fehr joined the M.B. Church, in which he soon began to serve in various capacities: choir leader, Sunday-school superintendent, and deacon. Up to 1901 the Fehr family remained in the Ukraine (Morozovo), where he was also known as a progressive and prosperous farmer. In the spring of 1901 Fehr and his family moved to Orenburg, in northeast Russia. Here he was ordained as elder of the M.B. Church for the Orenburg district on July 17, 1901, by Abram Martens of Neu-Samara. His charge included the Kamenka, Klubnikovo, and Karaguy congregations. With great faithfulness and self-denial he served his church from 1901 to 1917. He was also a member of the school board for the Pretoria Zentralschule, which served the Orenburg settlement, and of the Foreign Mission Board. He was a man of vision and determination, and did much for the material and spiritual progress of the Orenburg colony in its pioneer years. In the last days of December 1919 both Fehr and his wife became the victims of a postwar epidemic only 28 hours apart. Fehr willed one third of his estate to foreign missions. I.J.T.

Feisser, Johannes Elias, b. 1805 at Winsum, d. 1865 at Nieuwe Pekela, both in the Dutch province of Groningen, studied literature and theology at the University of Groningen, received his Th.D. degree in 1828 and became a Reformed pastor, serving Lekkum 1821-31, Winschoten 1831-33, and Franeker 1833-38. In 1838 he resigned because of bad health. In the same year he "experienced a new conversion." In 1839 he again went into the ministry, serving the Reformed Church of Gasselter Nijveen. In 1843 he was involved in a conflict with the Church Board because he required Scriptural discipline against offenders and because he refused to baptize children, having come to the conviction that infant baptism is unscriptural. He now was dismissed. He then came in contact with J. G. Oncken (*q.v.*), the father of the German Baptist movement at Hamburg, and was won over to the Baptists (*q.v.*). He was baptized in a canal near his house by Köbner, one of Oncken's assistants, together with six of his former Reformed members. This incident marked the founding of the first Baptist congregation in the Netherlands (*Gemeente van Gedoopte Christenen*). In 1849 he moved to Nieuwe Pekela. Here he also founded a Baptist congregation which thrived under his pastorate, attracting also a small number of Mennonite families who joined the Baptists. Feisser published a number of edificatory writings and the history of the founding of the first Baptist congregation in the Netherlands. vDZ.

G. A. Wumkes, *Opkomst en vestiging van het Baptisme in Nederland* (1912) *passim; N.N.B.Wb.* II, 441-44.

Felbinger, Jeremias, frequently erroneously listed as a Mennonite by older historians, b. at Brieg in Silesia, was a Socinian (after 1642) educator and writer who spent the last years of his life in poverty in Amsterdam. He was for a time rector of a school at Köslin in Pomerania, and later an educator in Helmstadt, Bernstadt, Greifswald, and Wratislav in Poland. For a time he lived at Strasswitz near Danzig as a member of the Socinian congregation there. His only common doctrine with the Mennonites was his rejection of the oath. His most noteworthy writing was the *Christliches Handbüchlein* (1661), published in Dutch at Rotterdam (1675) as the *Christelyke Handboeksken.* (*ML* I, 637 f.)

NEFF.

Felbinger, Klaus (also called Schlosser, meaning "Locksmith," after his trade), an outstanding Hutterite martyr, died in 1560 in Landshut, Bavaria, Germany. We know nothing of his origin and earlier life. The Hutterite chronicles give his name for the first time when he was chosen *Diener des Worts* (preacher) in Moravia in 1558. Soon afterwards he was sent out as a missionary to Bavaria, most likely his native country, together with a brother. But in 1560 the two men were seized near Neumarkt in Lower Bavaria, and soon thereafter brought in chains to Landshut, a well-known fortress and castle. Here they were kept in the dungeon for over ten weeks. The Catholic clergy vainly tried all means of persuasion to make him recant. Then he was racked to the point where even the executioner pleaded for him. But Felbinger still remained firm in his faith. From prison he sent two extensive epistles (*Sendbriefe*) home to the brotherhood in Moravia, in which he gives a detailed report of his many debates with the clergy and other officials, and from these documents we learn his extraordinary knowledge of the Bible and his skill in defending his position. His opponents were obviously amazed. Two learned clergymen came expressly from Munich to convert him, but it was to no avail. Their rational theology was one thing, his living faith in Christ and His commandments another. At the end we read in one of his epistles the following episode: "You cannot convince me," said Felbinger to his inquisitors, "for you do not stand in the Truth, and therefore I intend to stay in the simplicity of Christ." To this the chancellor answered, "I do not think that you are so simple. [Note that the word 'simplicity' is here used in a double meaning. Felbinger means plainness, absence of sophistication, while his opponent thinks of ignorance.] I think there is not one in a hundred who could defend himself as well as you do. For I do not think of you as a fanatic (*Schwärmer*) as are found everywhere and have no reason for their beliefs." To this Felbinger added, "God made him admit this, a comfort for me" (Loserth, 309-10; *Chronik,* 402). Felbinger had also drawn up a brief tract, his Confession of Faith (or *Rechenschaft*) which he submitted to the lords of Landshut. But they were not willing to deal leniently with sectarians. The mandates were applied, and on July 19, 1560, he was beheaded in Landshut, together with his brother-companion.

His confession as well as his epistles circulated widely among the brethren and did not fail to strengthen them in their faith. When the Hutterite brother Veit Grünberger (*q.v.*) was examined in Salzburg in 1573, he had this to say: "They may do with us as they wish. We will bear it with endurance, for I have carefully read the *Rechenschaft* of Claus Felbinger and of Hans Mändel, more than once, so that I know that our faith is well founded in God's Scriptures."

We have from Felbinger these two epistles: (*a*) *Sendbrief an Leonhard Sailer,* 1560 (published by Loserth, "Zur Geschichte der Wiedertäufer in Mähren," *Ztscht f. Allg. Gesch.* I, 1884, 451-54); (*b*) *Ein Sendbrief Klaus Felbingers geschrieben aus seiner Gefenknus an die Gemein Gottes in Mähren im 1560. Jahr* (published by Loserth in "Der Communismus der mährischen Wiedertäufer," *Arch. f. österr. Gesch.* LXXXI, 1894, 292-310). This epistle contains the details of his debates, and is strongly dogmatic. There exists also his confession, *Abgeschrift des Glaubens welchen ich, Klaus Felbinger, zu Landshut den Herrn daselbst für mich und statt meines mitgefangenen Bruders zugestellt habe* (this is his *Rechenschaft oder Verantwortung*). This document has not yet been published but exists in several Hutterite codices.

Felbinger is also the author of five well-known hymns, four of which are published in the *Liederbuch der Hutterischen Brüder* (Scottdale, 1914) 647-49, and (out of place) 441-46. The fifth hymn is known only from European codices. R.F.

Wolkan, *Geschicht-Buch; Mart. Mir.* D 274, E 643 (van Braght must have known both the Hutterite chronicle and also the *Sendbrief,* since he gives excerpts from both); Loserth, *Communismus;* Wolkan, *Lieder,* 228-29, V. A. Winter, *Geschichte der bayrischen Wiedertäufer im 16. Jahrhundert* (Münich, 1809, still valuable); *ML* I, 142, 637.

Feldthaler, Michael: see **Veltthaler.**

Felger (Alberta) Hutterite Bruderhof of 25 souls (1951) near Lethbridge, Alberta, was founded in 1928. D.D.

Felger (Mont.) Hutterite Bruderhof was founded in 1946 by Paul Walter, preacher of the Felger Bruderhof near Lethbridge, Alberta. It numbered 18 souls in 1947. D.D.

Felistis Jans (official name *Felistis Resincx*), a Dutch Anabaptist martyr, originally from Vreeden in the Münsterland, Germany, but living for eleven years in Amsterdam, where she was arrested in 1552 with many others. Obviously she was an elderly woman. During the trial she admitted that she had lodged some Anabaptists in her house and attended Anabaptist meetings, where she had heard Gillis van Aken preach. She repudiated the Roman Catholic doctrine of the Mass, and related that she had learned to read two or three years ago, "in order to know the truth." She had also taught other persons. Remaining steadfast even in cruel torture on Jan. 2, 1553, she was sentenced to death with confiscation of her goods. On Jan. 16, 1553, she was burned at the stake at Amsterdam. vDZ.

Mart. Mir. D 148, E 539; *Inv. Arch. Amst.* I, No. 371; Grosheide, *Bijdrage,* 161-62, 309; *ML* III, —.

Fellmann (Fellman), a Mennonite family of Swiss origin, now numerous in the South German Mennonite congregations. Concerning the family in Switzerland no particulars are as yet known. The Palatine lists of Mennonites in the archives at Karlsruhe first name a Fellmann in 1717; Melchior Fellmann, living in Bruchhausen near Heidelberg, and a Jakob Fellmann in Rohrhof near Heidelberg. The Mennonite archives of Amsterdam contain a family list of 1731, which gives the same information (but says Rohrhof near Mannheim). The Fellmanns are named as preachers of the Mennonite congregation of Bruchhausen. At this place there was also a Hans Fellmann, a member of the congregation at Eckerhof near Wiesloch. The later Mennonite lists of the Baden archives of 1738, 1743, 1752, and 1759 contain additional references to Fellmann families in this area. The *Mennonitisches Adressbuch* of 1936 (Karlsruhe) gives a complete oversight of the modern status of the family (residence, vocation, members of families), which is found principally in Baden, Württemberg, and Bavaria. Walter Fellmann is a retired minister who served the Monsheim congregation. W.F.

Felsenthal, a large Mennonite estate on the Molotschna River in South Russia, founded in 1820 by David Reimer, the father of Jakob R. Reimer (*q.v.*). It took its name from the granite ridges that follow the valley, through which flows a stream fed by a perpetual spring. Felsenthal was known for its orchards and nurseries, which sold trees everywhere. For a time this estate was the center of a mystical group which engaged in a life of contemplation. They were incorrectly called Quakers. The name "Gichtelianer" describes them better. (Friesen, *Brüderschaft,* 132; *ML* I, 638.) NEFF.

Femmetgen Egberts, an Anabaptist martyr. She was captured at Hoorn in the Dutch province of North Holland with three brothers and a sister and, remaining steadfast, was drowned with them on June 7, 1535. (*Mart. Mir.* D 36 f., E 443; *ML* I, 507.) NEFF.

Fenneken, a Dutch Anabaptist martyr, wife of the revolutionary leader Jan van Geelen (*q.v.*), was drowned in the IJssel River at Deventer, province of Overijssel, on April 17, 1535 (not Feb. 6 as is stated *DB* 1917, 114). She had been baptized by Jacob van Antwerpen (*q.v.*) and remained in Deventer, while her husband went to Münster. (*DB* 1917, 114; 1919, 10-11.) vDZ.

Fennema, a Dutch Mennonite family, living at Sneek, Friesland, one of whom was Enno ten Cate Fennema (1849-1929), a notary public at Sneek and a pillar of the Mennonite congregation in this town; he was also a member of the First Chamber of the Dutch States-General. In 1898, when the law for compulsory military service was passed in the Netherlands, abolishing the system of substitution which has since 1796 made it possible for the Mennonites (and others) to avoid military service, Fennema voted against this law, because many Mennonites still had objections to military service. (*DB* 1898, 130 ff.) vDZ.

Ferdinand I (1503-64), Archduke of Austria, with residence in Vienna (after 1521), after 1526 also King of Hungary and King of Bohemia (by inheritance), and after the abdication of his brother, Emperor Charles V in 1556, Holy Roman Emperor 1556-64. He had been brought up as a staunch Catholic, and vigorously defended his church in the great struggle of his time. And yet he could not stem the rising tide of Lutheranism, either in Germany or in his own domain (*Erblande*) of the two Austrias, Tirol, Styria, Carinthia, etc. Eventually he had to tolerate it *de facto,* particularly in view of the ever threatening danger of Turkish invasion which made the help of the Protestant estates indispensable. The Peace of Augsburg of 1555 with its formula "whose region his religion" (*cuius regio eius religio*) would have entitled him to re-Catholicize all his domain, yet political circumstances prevented him all his life from carrying out this plan. Thus Austria remained predominantly Protestant until well toward the end of the century.

With so much the more vigor Ferdinand fought the Anabaptists, who were being denounced as archheretics by Catholics and Protestants alike. A great number of mandates (*q.v.*) were promulgated by Ferdinand against "sectarians and heretics." The first one, dated Aug. 20, 1527, was particularly harsh against the Anabaptists because of "their misuse of the tender *corpus Christi*" and their custom of "renewed baptism." With this mandate a ruthless persecution set in, in which Ferdinand took a personal lead. One of his first victims was Balthasar Hubmaier (*q.v.*); the baron Leonhard von Liechtenstein was asked to deliver this man from his refuge in Nikolsburg. He was condemned, however, officially not because of his Anabaptist faith but rather because of his connections (remote though they were) with the Peasants' War of 1525 in Waldshut. On March 10, 1528, he was burned at the stake in Vienna. In 1527-28 a number of trials against Anabaptists were carried out in Upper Austria (Steyr with six executions, Freistadt, Enns, also Gmunden and Wels); but in view of the tremendous spread of Anabaptism everywhere from Tirol to Moravia, this method appeared to Ferdinand to be too slow and ineffective. He therefore appointed the nobleman Dietrich von Hartitsch as special "Profos" (commissioner) against all Anabaptists with authority to proceed against them the short way. Von Hartitsch was active particularly in Lower Austria, where within a short time Anabaptism became nearly extinct. Persecutions were ordered in all areas under Ferdinand's jurisdiction, even in the outlying Hapsburg districts (*Vorlande*) of Alsace, Breisgau, and Württemberg. Everywhere special commissions were set up to make any further spread of Anabaptism practically impossible. The stakes (pyres) burned everywhere; according to one source, in the Inn Valley in Tirol alone no fewer than 1,000 Anabaptists were burned between 1527 and 1530. In Linz (Upper Austria), for a short period a center of the Brethren under the vigorous leadership of Wolfgang Brandhuber (*q.v.*), 70 Brethren were put to death in one procedure, including the afore-mentioned "bishop" Brandhuber (1529). In Bruck on the Mur

River (Styria) nine brethren were beheaded and three sisters drowned in 1528.

The mandate of the Imperial Diet of Speyer in 1529 against the Anabaptists, ordering death by fire for all heretics throughout the Holy Roman Empire, intensified these persecutions still further and gave them a legal basis. Ferdinand published the corresponding mandate for his domain on May 10, 1529. It is amazing to what minute details Ferdinand himself devoted his attention in this matter. When, for instance, he learned that some noblemen in Lower Austria employed simple "Anabaptists" as farm hands during the season of haymaking, he sent strong reprimands to these lords and ordered them to stop this practice at once. The correspondence with the provincial government of Tirol in Innsbruck is very detailed as to the proper procedures against the Anabaptists. No mercy of any sort was permitted, and leniency by local judges (many had been quite in sympathy with these earnest Christians) was strongly disapproved, even in cases where members of the lower nobility were involved (see **Freyberg, Helene**).

The events of Münster 1534-35 prompted even more intensified persecutions. Now Ferdinand had the "argument" that such revolutionary dangers must be prevented by any means; once Anabaptists were in power they would certainly act this (Münsterite) way, all denials of imprisoned Brethren notwithstanding. Tirol had been the very center of Anabaptist activities at that time, and here persecutions were the most ruthless. Eradication of this "heresy" seemed at first nearly hopeless, all the more so since the Brethren were supported by sympathizers in all the remote mountain valleys. In 1528 the two outstanding leaders, Leonhard Schiemer (*q.v.*) and Hans Schlaffer (*q.v.*), were put to death (see **Inn Valley**). But soon Jakob Hutter (*q.v.*) was to fill the gap, tireless in working for his new faith. As life in Tirol had become so precarious, Hutter began to lead an exodus to Moravia, then the only country in Central Europe where freedom of religion was practiced by the nobles. Here in Moravia (part of the Kingdom of Bohemia) the power of Ferdinand was rather restricted, and Ferdinand's mandates were but very little obeyed. The medieval independence of proud feudal lords still lingered on, giving the Anabaptists the unique chance of a safe refuge. To Ferdinand it was a point of particular grief. In 1535 he gained a temporary success, and for a short time the Brethren were driven out of their places. Some sought refuge in near-by Slovakia; others returned to Germany (see **Philippites**). But soon the former privileges were restored, in spite of Ferdinand's sharp mandates of 1545, 1548, and 1554, requiring the expulsion of the Brethren. More peaceful development now became possible in Moravia, and for the Brethren began their "Golden Age" (*ca.* 1550-90).

Elsewhere, however, in the Austrian domain Anabaptism slowly died out by the middle of the 16th century, due mainly to Ferdinand's tireless activities and detailed attention in this direction. Only now and then do we learn of new victims of persecution, such as, e.g., the migrating **Brethren** from Kaufbeuren, Bavaria, to Moravia in 1545, who were intercepted in Vienna and soon executed there.

In 1551 the Jesuits, champions of the now rising Counter-Reformation (*q.v.*), arrived in Vienna; soon thereafter they came also to Prague, Innsbruck, and other places in the Hapsburg realm. However, new conflicts with the papacy (Paul IV) prevented any radical acts by Ferdinand. Thus Lutheranism was still rather strong in Austria at the time of the death of Ferdinand I. Though he had tried hard to create a stronger central government in Vienna, the time was not yet ripe to overcome the particularism of the feudal lords or the relative independence of the thriving cities. (See **Rechtsprechung**, *ML* IV, in press.)   G.M., R.F.

Loserth, *Communismus; idem, Der Anabaptismus in Tirol* (Vienna, 1892 and 1893); W. Wiswedel, "Kurze Charakteristik etlicher Herrscher Oesterreichs hinsichtlich ihrer Stellung zum Täufertum," in *Der Sendbote* (Cleveland, 1937) No. 19; Zieglschmid, *Klein-Geschichtsbuch* 63 note and 119 f. note, with bibliography; *ML* I, 638-41 (with good bibliography).

Ferdinand II (1578-1637), grandson of Ferdinand I (*q.v.*), Holy Roman Emperor 1619-37 during the first part of the Thirty Years' War. It is his sad reputation to have almost completely destroyed Protestantism (Lutheranism) in Austria. Educated by the Jesuits of Ingolstadt (see **Jesuits**,), he soon became the very symbol of the inexorable Counter-Reformation (*q.v.*). Prior to his becoming emperor, he had already begun this trend as ruler of "Inner-Austria" (i.e., Styria, Carinthia, Carniola), with mandates of 1598 ff. With the tremendous victory of the Imperial army over the Protestants at the Weissenberg, outside Prague) on Nov. 8, 1620, the fate of all non-Catholics in the Hapsburg realm was sealed. While up to this point the "Kingdom of Bohemia" (part of that realm) still could enjoy a certain (though restricted) liberty of religion, this old privilege was now wiped out altogether, and no opposition by the Protestant nobility was any longer even remotely possible. Thousands of Lutheran nobles, city people, and peasants emigrated to other parts of Germany, thus seriously injuring the economy of Bohemia and Moravia.

In Moravia (*q.v.*), the erstwhile refuge of the Hutterites and other sectarian groups, the activities of Cardinal Franz von Dietrichstein (*q.v.*) had made it harder and harder for the Brethren to carry on, and the number of Bruderhofs was reduced every year after the turn of the century (1600). Only a shift to near-by Slovakia could save the remnants of the Brethren. But now the imperial edicts of Sept. 8 and 17, 1622, made even a precarious foothold in Moravia impossible. All Hutterites without exception were expelled; it was the end of a period of 90 years of sojourn in this country. All their property was lost (valued at more than 300,000 florins), and no Protestant lord could extend any help. (For bibliography see **Ferdinand I.**)   G.M.

Ferdinand III: see **Hapsburg.**

Fernheim Agricultural Co-operative (*Sociedad Civil Cooperativa Colonizadora Fernheim*), located in Colony Fernheim in the Paraguayan Chaco, was of-

ficially organized on Nov. 20, 1944, in Filadelfia, Colony Fernheim, in the presence of all village administrators and the colony leader as well as representatives of Paraguayan courts, with a total membership of 311. It sold 10,000 shares valued at 25 guaranies, thus having a total operating capital of 250,000 guaranies, the shares being paid out of net proceeds of the co-operative. Its operating capital on Dec. 31, 1949, was 525,000 guaranies and its 1949 turnover 1,920,721.77 guaranies. Of the yearly earnings, 10 per cent are paid into the reserve fund and 10 per cent into the social security fund, which monies are used for the support of the old and ill in the colony as also to cover school deficits and other colony undertakings of this nature. The co-operative was organized for the purpose of facilitating all buying and selling for its members and also to establish and operate small basic industries within the colony such as sawmill, oil press, woodwork shops, cotton ginning, creamery, and extraction of essential oils. Also it manages the colony cattle herds and arranges all land purchase transactions. Among its primary difficulties have been the long distances to markets with inadequate roads and the instability of markets. Like the other Mennonite colony co-operatives in Paraguay it is legally recognized by Paraguayan Law No. 13, 635 of 1942 and its managers are responsible to the colony administration. Its first president was Bernhard J. Wall and its present one (1954) is Heinrich Dürksen.

The 1944 co-operative organization is the lineal descendant of the earlier Fernheim Co-operative which was established in 1931, in the second year of the colony's history. All the other Mennonite colonies in Paraguay also have co-operatives founded as follows: Menno 1936; Friesland 1942, reorganized 1947; Neuland, Volendam, Sommerfeld, Bergthal, 1947 and 1948.   C.J.D.

Fernheim Colony, located in the Paraguayan Chaco, South America, was founded on April 26, 1930. The first group of Mennonites having fled from Russia to Germany were given temporary refuge by the German government largely because of the intervention of B. H. Unruh of Karlsruhe, Germany, and upon the promise that they would not stay in Germany. The entire group hoped to move on to Canada, but that country refused to admit them. Consequently the Mennonite Central Committee at its meeting held on Jan. 25, 1930, decided to assist this group in resettling in the Paraguayan Chaco. Plans were made accordingly, and 374 families (1,853 souls) prepared to leave. A smaller group went to Brazil. The first group left camp Mölln (*q.v.*) in Germany for Paraguay on March 15, 1930, followed by seven other groups in the following order: Group 1, 61 families under Johann Funk; Group 2, 68 families under Gerhard Schartner; Group 3, 67 families under Nicolai Siemens; Group 4, 69 families under Abram Klassen; Group 5, 5 families under Gerhard Isaak; Group 6, 14 families under David Thielmann; Group 7, 10 families under Heinrich Willms; Group 8, 80 families under Jakob Siemens. Travel and financial arrangements were made by the German government and the MCC.

Friends and German Protestant churches helped to equip the Mennonites before their departure and much household equipment and tools and clothing were collected under the slogan *Brüder in Not*. The MCC purchased agricultural implements, and other equipment for them.

In Paraguay the MCC had made arrangements with the Corporacion Paraguaya for the sale of land by that company to the immigrants. On April 11, 1930, the first group arrived at Puerto Casado and immediately went on to the interior where their land lay. At the railhead, Station Fred Engen, they were met by the Canadian Mennonites already living in the Chaco since 1926, and taken to the colony site. Temporary shelter was provided by tents. Whereas that entire movement was permitted to enter Paraguay on the basis of Law 514 of July 26, 1921, which gave the original *Privilegium* to the Canadian Mennonite group, a delegation from the colony arranged for an amplification of this law to include this new group known as "Colony Fernheim," which was granted under Decree No. 43,561 of May 4, 1932, and which also included the benefits of Law 914 of Aug. 29, 1927, passed to permit the entry of other Pacifist groups to the Chaco. According to the privilege of self-government, the colony was first administered by the leaders of the first three groups, Franz Heinrichs later being elected the first administrator (*Oberschulze*). Each village has its Schulze and his assistants (Zehntmänner). Fernheim has had six administrators to the present: Franz Heinrichs, David Löwen, Jakob Siemens, Julius Legiehn, Bernhard Wall, and Heinrich Dürksen. Elections are held annually, and all colony citizens are allowed to vote. The colony has its own registrar's office, insurance and pension bureau.

Three weeks after the arrival the initial land surveys were completed and lots were drawn for the village sites, as also for the individual farm sites within each village. Fernheim colony today has 20 villages besides Filadelfia: Schönbrunn, Schönwiese, Friedensfeld, Friedensruh, Rosenort, Landskron, Wüstenfelde, Kleefeld, Blumental, Lichtfelde, Gnadenheim, Waldesruh, Wiesenfeld, Blumenort, Karlsruhe, Schönau, Auhagen, Orloff, Hohenau, and Grünfeld. Originally each family was allotted 96 acres, increased in 1937 to 240 acres per family, and in 1946 the total colony land holdings averaged 432 acres per family. The first steps of the immigrants were house construction and securing a water supply. Some houses were built temporarily, small and primitive, while others were at once built more permanently, usually 23 x 13 ft., of adobe brick and thatched roof. Today burned brick is usually used, with galvanized or aluminum roofing. The houses are frequently built facing north or northwest for better ventilation from the frequent northeast winds. Glass windows have only begun to appear in recent years. The water situation was and remains one of the gravest problems of the settlement. During the first months only one well was available, and because of the water scarcity, a boy was at times stationed at the bottom of the well to dip the trickling water with a cup and gradually fill the bucket.

Digging of wells is dangerous because of the sandy nature of the subsoil. By Jan. 1, 1935, the colony had dug 198 wells, of which 124 had sweet water and 75 salt water. On Jan. 1, 1950, the colony had a total of 255 wells, of which two thirds are sweet wells, turning bitter if excessively used. In addition to the original severe water shortage, the poor transportation facilities resulted in irregular supply of essential foods. This, together with the unaccustomed climate, environment, and food, led to the outbreak of a typhoid epidemic shortly after their arrival in the Chaco, which claimed 65 lives in a few weeks' time, mainly in the villages of Friedensruh, Schönwiese, and Schönbrunn. Hollowed bottle trees (*palo boracho*) served as coffins.

Many reverses were also experienced in the cultivation of their field crops. Being unaccustomed to a tropical climate and wishing to retain their farming methods of Russia, many suffered severely in the early years. A group of 140 families, feeling that they had little future in the colony, left in August 1937 and settled in East Paraguay, near Rosario, calling their new colony Friesland. After several futile attempts the growing of such crops as wheat and potatoes was abandoned, replaced by sorgo (kafir), sweet potatoes, Paraguayan beans, peanuts, and mandioca (manioc). These furnished their household necessities and provided for the stock and also an occasional surplus for the market. The staple cash crop was and is cotton. In 1950 the total cultivated colony acreage was 6,636 acres. The Indian is the chief source of labor for the cotton crop, but because of increase in acreage and influx of new immigrants to the adjoining colony Neuland, the labor problem is annually becoming more acute. Limited mechanization is now being tried. The watermelon thrives especially well in the Chaco, a single melon sometimes weighing up to 30 pounds. In the two decades 1930-50 the colony has had 11 good crops, 5 average crops, and 4 crop failures. Annual rainfall over a period of 15 years, 1934-48, averaged 28.3 inches. Especially trying are the winter sand storms which usually make their appearance during the months of June to September, being strong north winds from the *matto grosso* of Brazil.

To provide essential equipment for farm and home small basic industries were established, beginning with wagonmaking in 1931, until today there are several blacksmith shops, a furniture shop, a tinsmith shop, and more recently such industries as a cotton gin, oil press, creamery, and essential oil extraction plants, all of which add considerably to the colony and individual family income. The long-hoped-for etablishing of a spinning and weaving plant has not yet been realized. Further industrial development is hampered by the very inadequate transportation system. All freight must still be hauled 66 miles by wagon or truck to the railhead, then 88 miles by rail to Puerto Casado, where it is reloaded onto river transportation for Asuncion. However, the colony has a good airstrip at Filadelfia, and weekly plane service makes passenger travel considerably easier. Both it and the colony-Asuncion radio communication system have developed in recent years and continue to improve. A direct all-weather road from Asuncion to Filadelfia is under construction with U. S. Point IV aid.

The colony hospital, located at Filadelfia, serves as medical and surgical center for all Chaco Mennonites and consists of 42 beds in a two-story adobe brick building. Doctors have changed frequently, coming from Asuncion, the United States, and more recently from Germany. In 1953 the first native physician, Wilhelm Käthler, returned from a full medical training in the United States to begin practice in the colony. All illness except rare cases and serious eye defects can be treated here. A five-room house for the mentally ill has also been built in Filadelfia, but is proving inadequate, and plans are being made to increase its facilities. A dentist provides all dental care required, including aid to many non-colony individuals.

All Fernheim children must attend the local village school for six years. If they wish to continue their education, they may attend the Zentralschule (secondary school), which offers an additional four-year course of study. Those wishing to become teachers or enter other higher professions can attend the Pedagogical Institute (*Pädagogisches Institut*) for an additional two years, making it possible to receive a total of 12 years of schooling in the colony itself, not including Bible school. While other colonies also have their secondary schools, the pedagogical school serves all Paraguayan Mennonite settlements and provides their teachers.

There are three groups within the colony today: the Mennonite Brethren with 567 members, the Mennonite Church (GCM) with 350 members, and the Evangelical Mennonite Brethren, also known as the Allianzgemeinde, with 171 members. The work of these churches is co-ordinated through the interchurch committee known as the *Komitee für kirchliche Angelegenheiten* (KfK, *q.v.*). On Jan. 1, 1955, the population of the colony was 2,491 persons. In 1954 there were 14 deaths and 78 births.   C.J.D.

A. L. Elwood, *Paraguay—Its Cultural Heritage, Social Conditions, and Educational Problems* (New York, 1931); J. W. Fretz, *Pilgrims in Paraguay* (Scottdale, 1953); C. Kempski, *La Agricultura en el Chaco Paraguayo* (Buenos Aires, 1948); Fritz Kliewer, *Die deutsche Volksgruppe in Paraguay* (Hamburg, 1941); Annemarie Krause, *Mennonite Settlement in the Paraguayan Chaco* (Chicago, 1952); W. Quiring, *Deutsche erschliessen den Chaco* (Karlsruhe, 1936); idem, *Russlanddeutsche suchen eine Heimat* (Karlsruhe, 1938); W. Smith, *Paraguayan Interlude* (Scottdale, 1950); H. S. Bender, "With the Mennonite Refugee Colonies in Brazil and Paraguay —A Personal Narrative," *MQR* XIII (January 1939) 59-70; H. A. Fast, "Mennonites in Paraguay," *Menn. Life*, January 1946, 36-39; W. Hiebert, "Mennonite Education in the Gran Chaco," *Menn. Life*, October 1947, 28-32; Fritz Kliewer, "The Mennonites of Paraguay," *MQR* XI (January 1937) 92-97; W. Quiring, "The Colonization of the German Mennonites from Russia in the Paraguayan Chaco," *MQR* VII (April 1934) 62-72; G. H. Fadenrecht, "Mennonite Migration to Paraguay" (M.A. thesis, University of Kansas, 1947); S. C. Yoder, *For Conscience Sake* (Scottdale, 1945).

Fernheim Bible Institute, Filadelfia, Chaco, Paraguay, was opened in March 1956, with the assistance of the Mennonite Brethren Board of General Welfare of North America, with a faculty of six, G. H. Sukkau of Yarrow, B.C., serving as principal. Its purpose is to train ministers, mission workers, and Sunday-school workers for witness and service in South America, primarily for the Mennonite Brethren Church.   H.S.B.

Fernheim Evangelical Mennonite Brethren Church, located in Colony Fernheim in the Paraguayan Chaco, was organized on Oct. 5, 1930, with 44 members, under the leadership of Nicolaus Wiebe. Its statutes, with slight modifications, were those of the Krimmer Evangelical Mennonite Brethren Church of Russia, from where a large number of its members came in 1930-31. The work of the church is carried on in complete co-operation with the G.C.M. and M.B. groups in the colony. In 1942 an adobe brick church with a seating capacity of 300 was built in the village of Waldesruh; it was remodeled in 1949. The membership of the congregation in 1953 was 171, under the leadership of Abram Harder and his assistant Johann Käthler, both of whom have rendered valuable service as leaders of the KfK (*q.v.*), the interchurch organization. In addition nine other ministers and two deacons also serve the congregation. Worship services are held twice monthly for members only, and on the remaining Sundays with the other groups. Communion and footwashing are observed on the first Sunday of each month. Youth work and choir work are carried on regularly. The entire church actively supports the Indian Mennonite missions in the Chaco.
B.W.

Fernheim Mennonite Brethren Church, located in the Paraguayan Chaco, South America, was organized on June 9, 1930, by a group of immigrants from Russia under the leadership of Isaak Jakob Braun of Barnaul, South Russia, as the Paraguayan Mennonite Brethren Church. It consisted of 50-60 members. It was joined later that year by two other immigrant groups from Russia, and because of poor roads and communications the entire Mennonite Brethren Church was divided into two groups on April 7, 1931; the group settling to the west under the leadership of Gerhard Isaak of the Crimea, Russia, being called the "Schönwieser Lokale," and the group settling to the east under the leadership of Isaak Jakob Braun being called the "Lichtfelder Lokale." Upon the arrival of another group of immigrants from Russia via Harbin, China, in 1932, a third group was formed under the leadership of Johann Schellenberg, Ignatyevo, Russia, and was called the "Orloffer Lokale." The name in each instance was that of the village in which meetings were held. In 1932-44 these three groups were co-ordinated under the leadership of Isaak Braun, then Gerhard Isaak, and later Gerhard Balzer. In 1947 the Schönwieser Lokale and the Lichtfelder Lokale were united as the Filadelfia Mennonite Brethren Church, with a total membership of 400. A brick church was built in 1945 in Filadelfia with a seating capacity of 350. In 1950 another church was built with a seating capacity of 1,000. Because of difficulties in communication the Orloffer Lokale has remained separate and in 1953 had a membership of 140. In 1948 both the Filadelfia Mennonite Brethren Church and the Orloffer Lokale became members of the South American District Conference and thereby members of the General Conference of the Mennonite Brethren of North America. The ministers of the congregations receive partial financial support. Most of the members live on farms, or farm from Filadelfia. Sunday schools and young people's work are carried on regularly. While the regular church services are attended also by members of the G.C.M. and E.M.B. groups, the first Sunday of each month is set aside for worship of the M.B. group alone. In church men and women are seated separately, the men remaining seated until the women have left the church. The church has no musical instrument. The total membership (1955) is 567.   G.B.

Fernheim Mennonite Church (GCM), located in Colony Fernheim in the Paraguayan Chaco, was organized at a meeting of 30 members immigrating from Russia, in Trebol, Chaco, on June 22, 1930. Johann Bergmann, formerly of Siberia, Russia, called the meeting and was elected as the spiritual leader of the new church, with Johann Teichgraef and Heinrich Unruh (not ordained) as assistant ministers. Jakob Boschmann was elected deacon. Coming from various scattered Mennonite churches in Russia, with their own separate customs, many former members failed to find satisfaction in the new church; even four ministers left to join the Evangelical Mennonite Brethren. After this difficult and trying period, the new church in Fernheim grew, happy in the new-found freedom after their experience of Communist oppression and persecution. Since 1947 the church has been a member of the General Conference Mennonite Church. In 1950 a church was built in Filadelfia with a seating capacity of 500 and a full basement. All church meetings are held in co-operation with the M.B. and E.M.B. groups with the exception of the special services for members only on the first Sunday of every month. Saturday evening meetings known as *Wochenschluss* are held regularly. Footwashing is not practiced. Youth work, choir work, and ladies' aid circles are carried on regularly and the Chaco Indian missions are actively supported. The membership in 1953 was 350, under the leadership of Jakob Isaak.   J.I.

Fernheim Zentralschule. The Mennonites in Paraguay have a public school system based on six years of elementary and four years of high school. The Fernheim Zentralschule was organized in 1931 in the village of Schönwiese (No. 7) and was taught by Wilhelm Klassen, Julius Legiehn, and Fritz Kliewer. In 1936 this school was moved to Filadelfia, which is the center of the Fernheim Colony. In 1940 there was added to its curriculum a pedagogical course of two years to train public school teachers for the colony.

In its beginning the school drew much support from Germany in the way of literature and supplies. After World War II much aid for the school came from North America through the Mennonite Central Committee in the way of supplies, money, and teachers. In 1947 the building of a much larger and better school building was begun.

The Zentralschule offers a four-year high-school course and two years of teacher training. Courses are prescribed and patterned largely after the European system and method. Although the school is independent of the Paraguayan governmental school system, it does follow certain government stipulations such as the teaching of several Spanish subjects and the observance of the Paraguayan holidays.

The immediate purpose of the school is to train leaders for the colony, especially in the field of education, industry, and religion.

Its facilities include the above-mentioned new building, plus dormitories for both girls and boys, a kitchen, and three teacherages. The school is owned and operated by the colony. The enrollment increased from 28 in 1945 to 180 in 1950, and the number of teachers employed increased from 3 in 1945 to 8 in 1950. C. C. Peters of Abbotsford, British Columbia, was principal in 1947-52. Two teachers were sent to Switzerland for training in 1952-55. In 1955 Peter Wiens was appointed director. W.D.H.

Fernland Mennonite Church (MC), located near Germfask, Schoolcraft Co., Mich., began as a mission station under the Indiana-Michigan Mennonite District Mission Board. In the spring of 1938 it was organized into a congregation with Chester C. Osborne serving as pastor. He resigned in October 1947, and Bruce Handrich was ordained and continues as pastor. The membership (1955) is 24. This is the first Mennonite church to be established in the Upper Peninsula of Michigan.   C.C.O.

Ferrara: see Italy.

Ferrière (La), a village in the Courtelary district of the canton of Bern, Switzerland, near the French border. In 1870-93 an Amish congregation existed here, which at first held its meetings in the homes of the members. The lack of space was a severe handicap. When David Ummel-Stähli of La Chaux d'Abel in La Ferrière bought a farm for his son-in-law Menzi, he had a room furnished for the use of the congregation. Meetings were held here every two weeks. The membership numbered about 45. The elders were Ummel-Stähli (1797-1896) and David Gerber of Torneret near Le Locle (1838-1921), who emigrated to America.

Through emigration to America the congregation was so greatly reduced in numbers that the few remaining members united with the small congregation at La Chaux d'Abel (*q.v.*). After this merger the chapel was built in Aux Bulles in 1894. The congregation kept no records. (Mannhardt, *Jahrbuch* 1888, 40; Müller, *Berner Täufer*, 234; *ML* I, 642.)
                                                    A.-T.

Ferry Bank, a Hutterite Bruderhof, established in 1949 near Ponoka, Alberta. It had a population of 75 in 1950.   M.G.

Ferwerd, a town in the Dutch province of Friesland, where Leenaert Bouwens (*q.v.*) baptized 65 persons in 1568-82. Blaupot ten Cate (*Friesland*, 306) supposes that this large number proves the existence of a congregation at that time, but nothing is known of such a congregation, and it is more likely that the newly baptized joined churches in the neighborhood.   vDZ.

Fest, Ludwig. The little that is known of this martyr is found in the Hutterite chronicles and a few documents in the archives of Tirol. He was a native of Pinnegg, and in the days when the Tirolese authorities were searching for Jakob Hutter with all the means at their disposal, Fest was trying to win converts in the mines around Schwaz in the Inn Valley. Here he was captured and taken to Schwaz. Several attempts were made to convert him to the Catholic Church, and because he was adamant he was sentenced to death and beheaded July 3, 1533. In prison he wrote a letter (still extant) to the church at Rattenberg on the Inn, Austria, which admonishes "that we should not be selfish, for greed is the root and the origin of evil," and which names several persons who are better known in the annals of the suffering of the Brethren; since he names Marpeck's wife, it is likely that he belonged to the circle of Pilgram Marpeck (*q.v.*).   LOSERTH.

Beck, *Geschichts-Bücher*, 107; J. Loserth, *Der Anabaptismus in Tirol* (Vienna, 1892) 83; *Mart. Mir.* D 34, E 441; his letter is found in *MQR* XV (1941) 23-25; Zieglschmid, *Chronik*, 104; *ML* I, 642.

Feyerer (*Feirer*), **Hans,** an Anabaptist martyr, whom the chronicles name as a preacher (*Diener des Worts*). He was probably active in Munich, Germany, and vicinity after Georg Wagner's execution (Feb. 8, 1527). He was baptized by Leonhard Dorfbrunner. In Bavaria the Anabaptist movement was extensive at that time, but was soon severely suppressed by Dukes Wilhelm and Ludwig. On Nov. 15, 1527, they issued a decree from Munich ordering that all Anabaptists be seized and punished as criminals by death and confiscation of property. Many fled. Several Munich families went to Augsburg, which was at that time the center of the Anabaptist movement in South Germany. Anyone who was suspected of Anabaptist ideas was arrested. All the prisons in the entire country were filled with Anabaptists; it was especially bad in the Falkenturm in Munich, from which no Anabaptist was released without punishment (Winter, 35).

Feyerer was also arrested and apparently subjected to several cross-examinations and finally sentenced to death and burned at the stake at Munich with five companions as "obstinate Anabaptists" on Jan. 28, 1528. Three days later his wife and the wives of two other martyrs of this group, also remaining true to their faith, were in mercy first drowned and then burned. Evidently the authorities had dealt with them in hope of leading them back to the Catholic Church. The chronicler Sender writes that they were "much more obstinate than their husbands."   HEGE.

Beck, *Geschichts-Bücher*, 24; Sender, *Augsburger Chronik* (1894) 188; *Mart. Mir.* D 18, E 428; V. A. Winter, *Gesch. der bayrischen Wiedertäufer im 16. Jahrhundert* (Munich, 1809): *ML* I, 642 f.

Fichter, Konrad (*Füechter, Kuntz*), an Anabaptist martyr, executed for his faith at Sterzing in the Adige Valley, Tirol, Austria, in 1532. He was treasurer of the Hutterian brotherhood, and evidently influential. In 1532 he was taken prisoner while working in Tirol. The Chronicles relate that he was so severely racked that the hangman thought he would "break."

From prison he wrote two epistles. One contains consolations and greetings to Jakob Hutter, Hans Amon, and his wife, as well as the request to support him with prayers in his coming struggle. The other one is written to the earnest believers in the Adige Valley in South Tirol (*q.v.*), which seems to indicate that this was his chief field of labor. This epistle is particularly remarkable for its folkloristic or popular slant and the vigor of its expression. It has been published in full (*MQR* XV, 1941, 16-23) by A. J. F. Zieglschmid, with a plate showing a facsimile of the beginning of this epistle in one of the codices.

Repeated attempts by the clergy to convert Fichter failed, and therefore he was put to death. He is reputedly the author of the hymn, "Als man mit dem Kreuze ging."   LOSERTH.

J. Loserth, *Der Anabaptismus in Tirol* (Vienna, 1892) 508; R. Friedmann, "The Epistles of the Hutterite Brethren," *MQR* XX (1946) 164 f., with excerpts of one of these epistles in translation, *Mart. Mir.* D 34, E 441; *ML* I, 643.

Fieguth (Figut, Fiegeth, Fiut, Viegut), a Mennonite family name in rural Flemish congregations of West Prussia, first mentioned 1656 at Pasewark. Only one family of this name was listed in 1776, 120 persons in 1910, 112 persons in 1935. A few members of this family also migrated to Russia and America (Paso Robles, Cal.).   G.R.

Stammbaum der Familie Fieguth, ed. Abraham Fieguth (Marienburg, 1938).

Figken, Benedikt (1625-93), a Protestant clergyman in Danzig, the author of a peculiar book, *Historia Fanaticorum oder eine vollkommene Relation und Wissenschaft von den alten Anabaptisten und newen Quäkern*, with a *Zugabe was mit etzlichen Quäkern hiesiges Ortes . . . passiert ist* (Danzig, 1664; second ed., 1701). It is the translation of an English book by R. Blome, *The Fanatic History or an Exact Relation and Account of the Old Anabaptists and New Quakers* (London, 1660), the first 65 pages of which are a reprint of an anonymous booklet published in London in 1642, *A Short History of the Anabaptists of High and Low Germany*. This book presents utter nonsense as historical truth; it relates with relish and in great detail the abominations of Münster; it does not mention Menno Simons, and barely touches Melchior Hofmann's work. It tells terrible but contradictory stories about the Mennonites in Amsterdam and Switzerland. It is incomprehensible that all of this could be printed, and it is regrettable that the book is cited and used as an authentic source. (*ML* I, 643.)   NEFF.

Fije (Feije Bauckezoon), an Anabaptist martyr, was seized with Eelken (*q.v.*) three weeks before Easter 1549 at Oldeboorn, Dutch province of Friesland. During his trial he confessed that he had attended many secret meetings, at which he heard the Scriptures explained by "lay persons." Before the judge they were both greatly excited, kissed each other, and danced for joy in being permitted to suffer martyrdom; in this they were an exception to most of the martyrs. They were in the same prison as the noted martyr Elisabeth. Fije was first (June 7, 1549) sentenced to death by beheading, but "persisting in his unbelief," the sentence was increased in severity, and he was executed on that very day by burning at the stake. At his execution Fije refused the bread and wine offered him, saying he had food prepared for him in heaven. Fije was burned, Eelken was beheaded on June 7, 1549, at Leeuwarden, in the presence of some monks. To the spectators he cried out, "Weep not for me, but for your sins." A hymn was written on his martyrdom, "Nae u belooft, o goede Heer" (According to Thy promise, O good Lord. (*Offer,* 430-36; *Mart. Mir.* D 84 f., E 484; Wolkan, *Lieder,* 68; *ML* I, 643.)

K.V.

Fije Danen, an Anabaptist martyr of Amsterdam, a native of Loenen, Dutch province of Utrecht. She had lived for many years in Woerden, Dutch province of South Holland, and had been (re)baptized by Gerrit van Benschop (*q.v.*) in his own house at Benschop near Woerden. In March 1534 she had joined the group which sailed from Amsterdam to Hasselt, en route to Münster in Westphalia. With a large number of other Anabaptists she was arrested at Bergklooster (*q.v.*), but escaped or was set free. Back in Amsterdam, she took part in the meetings of the Anabaptists and had contacts with many Anabaptist leaders. She often brought letters or messages to Jacob van Campen (*q.v.*), bishop of the congregation at Amsterdam; at the time van Campen was wanted by the police (March 2, 1535) and had hidden, Fije daily brought him food. She was arrested in May 1535 and because she refused to recant, she was sentenced to death on July 10, 1535, and on that very day executed at Amsterdam by being hanged and strangled, which was an unusual execution for women. Her few goods were confiscated.   vDZ.

S. F. Grosheide, *Verhooren,* 99, 105-8, 109; Mellink, *Wederdopers,* 96, 126-30, 135, 147.

Fijne Mennisten (in Germany *Feine Mennonisten,* Strict Mennonites), the designation of those Mennonites in the 18th and 19th centuries in Holland and West Prussia (*Inv. Arch. Amst.* II, 2, No. 767) who in opposition to the *Grove Mennisten* (Common Mennonites, such as Lamists and Zonists, *q.v.*) conservatively maintained the strict old doctrines and practices of Mennonitism like avoidance (shunning), footwashing, old-fashioned clothing, and arrangement of meetinghouses and liturgy. S. F. Rues states that there were *Fijnen* and still *Alderfijnsten* (Most Strict Ones). A hundred years or more ago the name was very common, but now it has completely disappeared.   NEFF, vDZ.

S. F. Rues, *Tegenwoordige Staet der Doopsgezinden* (Amsterdam, 1745) 8-13; *ML* I, 637.

Fijne, Passchier de (1588-1667), born at Leiden, Holland, whither his parents had fled from French

Flanders to escape persecution, was at first a weaver, then studied theology, and in 1611 became a Reformed pastor at Jaarsveld; in 1619 he was dismissed because of his Remonstrant (*q.v.*) opinions. Until 1633 he mostly traveled about in Holland, and from 1633 until his death he was a Remonstrant minister at Haarlem. De Fijne published a large number of pamphlets, some of which deal with the Mennonites. He defended them against the vilification of Petrus Bontemps (*q.v.*), but found fault with the fact that so many Mennonites sympathized with the Rijnsburg Collegiants (*q.v.*).   vDZ.

Biogr. Wb. V, 507 ff.; *N.N.B.Wb.* VI, 530 ff.; *Catalogus Amst.,* 122, 160, 200-2.

Fijnje, Wybo, b. Jan. 24, 1750, at Zwolle, studied at the Amsterdam Mennonite Seminary 1766-67, and then at the University of Leiden, where he obtained his Ph.D. in 1774. He was a son of Jan Wybes Fijnje of Harlingen (and Johanna Seije), who studied at the Amsterdam Mennonite Seminary in 1739-45, served for a while at Zwolle and 1751-ca. 63 at Haarlem. Wybo Fijnje was for a time pastor of the Mennonite congregation at Deventer, but resigned in order to devote himself to political science. He was editor of the *Delftsche Courant* and was compelled to flee in 1787 on account of his "Patriot" opinions. After the revolution of 1795 he was made director of affairs in the government of the Dutch East Indies. In 1798 he had to flee again. When he returned to The Hague he was seized but was released upon the intercession of the French ambassador. He died in Amsterdam on Oct. 2, 1809. He is the author of the following works: *Beknopt tydrekenkundig overzicht der algemeene geschiedenis* (1783) and *Theoriae systematis universi* (1774). His son H. F. Fijnje van Salverda (1796-1889) was chief inspector of the water office and planned the reclamation of the Haarlem Lake.   K.V., vDZ.

Biogr. Wb. III, 157 f.; *Inv. Arch. Amst.* II, No. 1691; 2458 f.; *DB* 1919, 94 f.; *ML* I, 644.

Fijt Pilgrims (Veit Pelgrims, Fitus to Pilgrams), an Anabaptist martyr, who was brutally tortured at Gladbach in the duchy of Jülich, Germany, in 1532 (1537?), when he steadfastly confessed his faith, and was then burned at the stake. (*Mart. Mir.* D 33, E 440; Rembert, *Wiedertäufer,* 15, 437; *ML* III, 375.)

Fijts, Simon: see **Simon Fijts.**

Filadelfia, a town located in the Colony Fernheim of the Paraguayan Chaco, was founded in 1931. Upon arrival of the Fernheim Colony group in 1930 they decided to concentrate their common undertakings, such as hospital, schools, industry, and printing press, at one site centrally located, from where the colony would also be administered. In July 1931 a committee was appointed to determine the geographical center of the colony, and on Aug. 26, 1931, a camp was selected as the future site of the town. A site about 2½ x 2¼ miles (4 x 3.85 kilometers) was staked off for this purpose. A study commission recommended that the town plan be drawn in four circles, the first of which would contain 240 building lots, the second 300, the third 440, and the fourth 530, totaling 1,510 building lots of 1.8

acres (three-quarters hectare) each. Because of the help of European and North American brotherhoods to make the settlement possible, and because it was to be the center of all co-operative undertakings, it was decided to call the town Filadelfia, meaning "brotherly love." The names of the principal streets are Asuncion Street, Bender Street, Cemetery Street, Lengua Street, Miller Street, Menno Street, Market Street, Russia Street, Main Street, and Unruh Street. The first four families to settle in the new town by 1932 were Gerhard Isaak, administrator of the hospital; David Neufeld, warehouse manager; Johann Funk, warehouse bookkeeper; Peter Boldt, cafe owner. The first school was opened in 1934. Filadelfia today is the center of the Chaco settlements—Menno, Neuland, and Fernheim, as well as being Fernheim's administrative center, with industries such as a cotton gin, oil expeller, furniture plant, creamery, essential oil extract plant, blacksmith shop, printing press where the biweekly paper *Menno-Blatt* is published, airport, hospital, dentist, telephone switchboard, all of which serve not only Fernheim but all Chaco Mennonites. It has one Mennonite Brethren church and one Mennonite church; one co-operative and two private stores; two public schools and one high school and normal school; the Chulupi Indian mission and the Chaco MCC workers' home. Because of its greater conveniences as electric light, nearness to shopping center, and others, many retired farmers are moving to Filadelfia. Its population in 1950 was 546; in 1954 it was about 700.

C.J.D.

W. Quiring, *Deutsche erschliessen den Chaco* (Karlsruhe, n.d., 1936?); F. Kliewer, *Die deutsche Volksgruppe in Paraguay* (Hamburg, 1941); A. Krause, *Mennonite Settlement in the Paraguayan Chaco* (Chicago, 1952) 122-28; J. W. Fretz, *Pilgrims in Paraguay* (Scottdale, 1953).

Filadelfia Experimental Farm, five miles north of the town of Filadelfia, the capital of the Fernheim Colony (*q.v.*), Paraguay, was established in August 1946 as a result of the joint efforts of the Mennonite Central Committee and the Fernheim Colony. Menno Klassen from Gretna, Man., was sent to Paraguay to establish this work. Significant progress has been made. The buildings erected include a large ranch-style house, a combination laboratory, office, workshop, and seed storage building. In 1952 there were five full-time workers engaged on the farm. The chief objectives are experimentation with seeds and soils, production of seeds of grasses, vegetables, and farm crops, and nursery stock, the setting up of demonstration units, and a general program of agricultural extension and information service. Since agriculture had not been carried on in the Chaco prior to the coming of the Mennonites nothing was known as to the best types of crops to grow, the long-time characteristics of the growing season, the rainfall, and the general climatic conditions. Chaco farmers had neither time nor money to carry on the experimentation needed.

The experimental farm has made valuable contributions to farming in the area by growing seedlings so that farmers may eventually produce their own fuel and timber supply. Experiments have also been carried on with green manure crops which are needed to fertilize depleted soils. By means of contact with the United States Government personnel in Paraguay (STICA) helpful information has been secured about crops, trees, and seeds best adapted to the Paraguayan climate. Assistance has also been received in fighting pests that damage crops. Pamphlets are often translated into German for the colonists' use. The experimental farm was at first not enthusiastically supported by the colonists but during its short life it has proved its worth and farmers are increasingly coming to recognize how valuable an aid it is to intelligent farming and successful colonization.

J.W.F.

Filer, Idaho, a town (pop. 1,400) in Twin Falls County on a branch of the Union Pacific in south central Idaho. The Mennonites (MC), of whom there were 101 members in the community in 1954, first located here in 1912. In 1914 they organized a congregation and in 1915 built a church in Filer. The United Missionary Church (MBC) located here about five years earlier.

S.H.

Filer Mennonite Church (MC), located at 115 Fifth St., Filer, Idaho, a member of the Pacific Coast Conference, was organized on Jan. 31, 1914, with 22 charter members, and with David Hilty as bishop, Samuel Honderich as minister, and Chris Snyder as deacon. In 1955 the membership was 106. The first church was dedicated on Sept. 19, 1915, enlarged in 1953. The 1954 ministerial body was E. S. Garber, bishop; Samuel Honderich and Louis Landis, ministers; Joe E. Slatter, deacon. The General Conference Mennonites organized a congregation here in 1955 with 19 members.

S.H.

S. G. Shetler, *Church History of the Pacific Coast Mennonite Conference* (Scottdale, 1931).

Filer (Twin Falls Co., Idaho) United Missionary Church was organized Feb. 16, 1905. In 1949 the membership was 69 and David Johnson served as pastor. He was followed by A. B. Neufeld, who served for three years, and was succeeded by T. J. Sparr. In 1955 J. K. Myer was assigned the pastorate.

D.J.

Filips Bostijn was a preacher of the Mennonite congregation at Antwerp. In 1566 he came to Friesland with other elders and preachers from Flanders, to mediate in the problems that had arisen there between the Frisians and the Mennonites who had immigrated to Friesland from Flanders.

vDZ.

K. Vos, "De Doopsgezinden te Antwerpen in de zestiende Eeuw," in *Bulletin ... d' Hist. de Belgique* LXXXIV (Brussels, 1920) 363, 376; *DB* 1893, 35, note 2.

Filips, Dirk: see **Dirk Philips.**

Filips, Lucas, a preacher of the Old Flemish Mennonite Church at Haarlem, Dutch province of North Holland, in the early 17th century, quarreled with his copreacher Vincent de Hondt (*q.v.*) about the practice of banning and shunning. De Hondt was of the opinion that a young brother of the church, who he thought had acted improperly with his fiancée, should be banned from the congregation. Filips, however, considered the ban too serious a punishment. Thereupon de Hondt banned not only

the young man but Filips as well with all who
shared his view. The adherents of Filips were called
Lucas-Filipsvolk or *Borstentasters*. The separation,
which took place in 1620, lasted only for a few
years. Then the Lucas-Filipsvolk and the de-Hondt-
volk reunited. (*DB* 1863, 135; *Inv. Arch. Amst.* II,
2, No. 58.)   vdZ.

Filips, Obbe: see **Obbe Philips.**

Fill (or Vill), a village near Neumarkt in the Adige
Valley of Tirol, Austria. In the late 1520's Benedikt
von Bruneck, a former lay priest, was active here
in the Anabaptist cause. As a priest he had protested
against the execution of heretics, and was called to
account and promised to desist. But the courage,
piety, and conduct of the Anabaptists won him
completely. It was he who held Blaurock's congregation together after the latter's death and served
it by preaching and baptizing in Fill and Tramin.
The Hutterite chronicles list eight Anabaptists seized
in Fill in 1529. They were Wolfgang of Moos near
Deutsch-Nofen; Thoman im Wald near Aldain;
Georg Frick of Wirtsburg; Mang Karger of Füssen;
Christina Tollinger of Penon, a widow; Barbara of
Thiers, the wife of Hans Portzen; Agatha Kampner
(*q.v.*) of Breitenberg, and her sister Elisabeth. They
were taken to the castle and examined on the rack.
They revealed that Wolfgang von Moos had been
baptized in August 1528 with two companions by
Michael Kürschner, who was later executed at the
stake in Gufidaun. Thoman im Waldt was bap-
tized by Blaurock, and Georg Frick by Benedikt,
Elisabeth Kampner and Christian Tollinger by
Blaurock, Barbara of Thiers by Benedikt, and Agatha
Kampner in Switzerland near St. Gall by Tepich.
They all remained steadfast and were executed.

                                              LOSERTH.

Beck, *Geschichts-Bücher,* 64 ff.; J. Loserth, *Der Anabaptismus in Tirol* I (Vienna, 1892) 61; *ML* I, 644.

Finger, Jakob, Mennonite lawyer and statesman, b.
Jan. 13, 1825, at Monsheim, Hesse, Germany, d. Jan.
31, 1904, at Darmstadt as retired Hessian Minister
of State. When he was a child in the public school
in Monsheim, his teachers and especially his pastor,
Leonhard Weydmann, recognized his talents, the
latter taking the boy along to Crefeld when he took
over the pulpit there. Here the boy received thorough instruction in the classical languages.

But already in the next year he was called home
on account of the serious illness of his father. Since
he was now too far advanced for the village school
at Worms he was sent at the age of 12 to the
Gymnasium at Worms. At this time it was very
unusual for the children of South German Mennonites to receive academic training. At the age of
16, he was admitted to the University of Giessen to
study law, and a year later he went to the University
of Heidelberg, where he became the friend of B. C.
Roosen (*q.v.*), who was a student of theology, and
who later became pastor of the Hamburg-Altona
Mennonite Church. Finger was tempted to study
theology rather than law, but finally remained with
the course he had begun. After another year at
Giessen he passed his first juristic examination with

honor, and continued his study at the University
of Berlin until 1846.

Finger's first position was with the court at Alzey.
Here he became engaged to the daughter of the
state's attorney. Then for a time he was assistant
judge in the court at Oppenheim. In 1855 he began
to practice law in Alzey. From 1862 to 1865 he was
a member of the lower chamber of Hesse. In 1872
he was called to Darmstadt into the ministry of
justice, and had charge of the reorganization of the
department of justice. From 1884 to 1898 he was
Minister of Justice and rendered his country outstanding service. In 1898 he retired.

Until his death Finger remained a faithful member of the Mennonite Church of Monsheim, coming
regularly for communion and remaining a faithful
supporter. For the Mennonite Church in Hesse he
acquired a legal status unique in South Germany.

His brother Christian Finger (1830-1907), a farmer and miller at Kriegsheim near Monsheim, was
from 1896 to 1905 a member of the curatorium of
the *Vereinigung der deutschen Mennoniten-Gemeinden* and from 1885 to 1907 on the board of his local
congregation. (*ML* I, 644 f.)   NEFF.

Fink, Anthonius Ruardus, d. Oct. 27, 1834, at Winterswijk, a Dutch Mennonite minister who had
previously been a Lutheran pastor at Pekela and at
Kampen. In 1795 he resigned and became a bookseller at Leeuwarden, since he was a Patriot (*q.v.*)
and deeply interested in politics. He soon became
a representative of the Frisian people in the legislature, and thereupon a judge in the Court of Friesland. Being somewhat disappointed in his political
ideals, he left the magistracy to enter the ministry
again. This time he served a Mennonite congregation, having been introduced by his fellow Patriot
and friend Abraham Staal, the Mennonite minister
of Leeuwarden. He was baptized on Oct. 10, 1802,
at IJlst and for a short period he served the IJlst
congregation as assistant pastor; in 1802-34 he served
the congregation of Winterswijk.   vdZ.

Finland Mennonite Church (MC), located in Milford Twp., Bucks Co., Pa., is the result of mission
effort of near-by congregations. Visitation and
cottage meetings held in the community finally led
to the organization of a Sunday school on May 17,
1931, and the monthly church services beginning
on Nov. 1, 1931. Claude Shisler served as mission
superintendent from March 12, 1933, to Nov. 22,
1938, when he was ordained as pastor of the growing congregation. The mission was first housed in
a store building in the village of Finland. The
present building was erected in 1939. The congregation was organized in 1940. The membership in
1953 was 101.   Q.L.

Firdale Mennonite Church (MC), now extinct, near
Airlie, in southern Polk Co., southwest of Salem,
Ore., was organized under the Pacific Coast Mennonite Conference. Mennonite families moved into
the area in the fall of 1913. Their first religious
service was held in October 1914, with an attendance
of 35. Soon after this, the group began meeting at
the Berry schoolhouse, where they met until the

church was disbanded. The congregation was listed as a rural mission station of the Pacific Coast Conference from October 1914 until its organization as a church in December 1915, when the name Firdale was chosen. In 1916 G. D. Shenk was ordained minister of the church. At one time the membership reached 68, but poor soil conditions caused the members to move away. The last service was held in September 1924.   M.G.

S. G. Shetler, *Church History of the Pacific Coast Menn. Conference District* (Scottdale, 1932?) 32-4.

Fire and Storm Aid, an organization of the Reformed Mennonite Church of the United States and Canada, was organized on Jan. 6, 1924. It covers assessable property of seven million dollars. Their rate is $1.50 per thousand for houses, $4.50 for barns, and $6.50 for "hazardous risks." The assessment of $31,000 is made only every two or three years, when the general fund gets down to $5,000. The annual loss on houses is one fifth of the total, the other two categories being equally divided. Frank E. Eshelman is the secretary. Its headquarters is at Lancaster, Pa.   I.D.L.

First Names. In the areas and brotherhoods which did not follow the custom of having names given by godparents, the parents gave their children the first names of their own parents (the children's grandparents). This was the case with the Reformed on the Lower Rhine and quite particularly with the Mennonites. For example, they named their oldest son after one grandfather, the oldest daughter after the other grandmother. For the second son and the second daughter they reversed this procedure. With the following children names of the nearest relatives were used in succession and when these were exhausted Biblical names. It remained this way until the Enlightenment slowly put an end to this loyal custom. This custom for the assignment of names was called the *Leitnamensitte* by Heinrich Müllers, a former archivist in Rheydt; from this method of naming he developed a method of research which makes it possible to determine with some assurance the name of the grandfather from the name of the grandson. Since the church records of the Mennonite congregations of the Lower Rhine only rarely give the names of the parents of the bridal couple this method of the *Leitnamensitte* gives a safe means for the investigation of Mennonite families.
                                    W.N.

First Mennonite Church (GCM) of Butterfield, Minn., formerly known as Bergthal Church, located four miles north of the town of Butterfield, was organized in 1878 under the sponsorship of what is today the First Mennonite Church of Mountain Lake. The members of this group had been affiliated with the Bergthal (*q.v.*) congregation of the Bergthal Mennonite settlement in South Russia, whose elder was Gerhard Wiebe. Elder Wiebe and his whole congregation migrated to America in 1874. Wiebe and the majority of his people chose Manitoba as their future home, but a smaller group, settling in the vicinity of Butterfield, constituted the Bergthal

Church, today known as the First Mennonite Church.

During the early years services were conducted in the homes. Elder Neufeld and his co-ministers David Loewen, Johann Schultz, Gerhard Fast, Peter Voth, and Cornelius Enns served the two parishes of the one congregation at Mountain Lake and near Butterfield. A meetinghouse was built in 1882 and remodeled in 1942. In 1892 David Harder was elected to the ministry, and in 1900 Jacob Stoesz. Both served the congregation for many years, Jacob Stoesz as elder 1919-30. When Elder Stoesz laid down his work there came a succession of leaders chosen from the outside: John Warkentin, Sam Quiring, Victor Sawatzky, M. M. Lehman, and R. A. Heinrichs. At present, May 1956, the congregation is without a pastor; its membership in 1955 was 95. The congregation is a member of the Northern District Conference.   J.J.F.

Fischart, Johann (*ca.* 1546-90), a German author of Alsace, wrote *Bewärung und Erklärung des Uralten gemeynen Sprüchworts: Die Gelehrten die Verkehrten: Etwan vor vielen Jaren (in massen solchs ohn disz art zureimen bezeugen) von eim guthertzigen Wargelehrten etlicher massen aussgelegt. Nun aber bei heutigem vnauffhörlichen vnd vnabwehrlichen einreissen der Verkehrung der Letz vn Falsch gelehrten/ durch ein Warheitlieber Gerngelehrten/ auff ein Newes durchgangen vnd angelegt. Darbey neben andern nötigen Erinnerungen vnd Lehren/ auch dise daran hangende Fragen begriffen. Ob man jemands zum Glauben zwingen soll/ vn ob durch Schwert/ brand/ bann/ zang/ strang/ vnd zwang in der Religion ein einigkeit sei zustifften. Item/ was zwischen Welt vnd Christenheyt/ vnd deren beider Oberkeit/ sei für ein vnderscheyd. Anno M. D. LXXXIIII.* The frequently combined edition is based on two originally independent rhymed poems opposing suppression of religious freedom, "Die Gelehrten die Verkehrten" and "Vom Glaubenszwang," which Wilhelm Scherer in his introduction to the reprint attributed to the Anabaptists. Hauffen, however, has shown that they were probably written in 1531 by Sebastian Franck in Strasbourg.   E.C.

A. Hauffen, "Johann Fischart," in *Schriften des wissenschaftlichen Instituts der Elsass-Lothringer im Reich* (Berlin and Leipzig, 1921-22), which gives the rather extensive older literature; the *Deutsche Bibliothek* IX (Leipzig, 1866) Part II, contains a reprint of the *Bewärung; ML* I, 645.

Fischbach, a village near Hochspeyer in the Palatinate, Germany, where in the 17th and 18th centuries there was a small Mennonite congregation, the members of which lived in Fischbach, Münchhof, Diemerstein, Frankenstein, and Enkenbach. There were Mennonites here before 1687, for a contract of lease dated July 9, 1687, by which a Mennonite named Peter Küntzi of Buchholderberg, Switzerland, acquired from the Countess Palatine Marie bei Rhein the delapidated mill of Diemerstein, and which states that he and his family were permitted to exercise their faith, "just as the people on the *Hof* have hitherto practiced."

In 1732 the congregation in the village of Fischbach and vicinity numbered 35 families. The preachers were Johann Würtz and Johann Neff, with Hans Langenacker as deacon. They assembled in a building that later became a school and also in the Diemerstein mill, where there was a small building for that purpose, which was torn down in 1842. A Mennonite cemetery still in existence was begun in Diemerstein in 1783. "Previously the corpses of the Mennonites of Diemerstein were taken to Fischbach; they could, however, not be carried on the highway, but had to be quietly carried through the Diemerstein valley across the mountain."

Toward the end of the 18th century the Fischbach congregation merged with Sembach (*q.v.*). The last preacher of the Fischbach congregation, Christian Schnebele, elder (*völliger Diener*) 1782-98, preached occasionally in Sembach. The congregation slowly declined on account of agricultural reverses, and loss of members by moving to other congregations, emigration to America, and mixed marriages. The combined congregation long kept the name "Fischbach-Sembach." G.H.

Church Record book of the Sembach church, p. 269; Müller, *Berner Täufer*, 212; *Menn. Bl.*, 1855, 53; *ML* I, 645.

Fischer, Christoph Andreas (1560- after 1610), a Jesuit priest, one of the most aggressive opponents of the Hutterite Brethren in Moravia around 1600. He was born in Glatz, Silesia, was educated as a cleric at the Jesuit colleges of Vienna and Rome, where he seems to have received also his theological doctorate. In the 1590's he returned to Vienna and soon after became the parish priest of Feldsberg, Lower Austria, near the Moravian border. He was one of the many fighters in the great Catholic Counter Reformation (*q.v.*) in Austria, and should be grouped together with Georg Eder (*q.v.*), Christoph Erhard (*q.v.*), and the Jesuit Cardaneus, the father confessor and biographer of Cardinal Franz von Dietrichstein (*q.v.*), all of whom fought relentlessly both the Lutherans and the Anabaptists. Their program allowed no further compromise (as in the days of Maximilian II) but aimed at complete elimination of all non-Catholics. That the relative tolerance of the Moravian nobles toward the Hutterites and their economic activities was to these men a real "scandal" can be easily seen; they tried to oppose it with every possible means. In many regards Fischer was more dangerous than Eder or Erhard because he did not confine his polemics to the religious field, but attacked the Brethren above all from an economic angle, appealing to the jealousy of the surrounding population and denouncing the economic prosperity of Hutterite large-scale farming and crafts. It seems, however, that the manorial lords of southern Moravia, knowing their own advantage, protected the Brethren and were fairly immune to the invectives of Fischer.

Although Fischer must have known the Brethren from personal contact, he yet was also familiar with the polemical writings of his forerunners; he quotes Eysvogel's (*q.v.*) *Lied* and repeats his arguments in detail.

Four books or pamphlets are known from his pen: (1) *Von der Wiedertauffer verfluchtem Ursprung, gottlosen Lehre, und derselben gründliche Widerlegung. Nach welcher gefragt wird, ob die Wiedertauffer im Lande zu leiden sein oder nicht . . . 1603, gedruckt zu Bruck an der Teya*. It was dedicated to the lord Karl von Liechtenstein (a family once much in sympathy with the Anabaptists). In its first part Fischer describes the "heretical doctrines and vices" of the Brethren; he knows surprisingly much of the (manuscript) literature of the Brethren which must have circulated then among the neighboring population. Often he also quotes Peter Riedemann's *Rechenschaft* (*q.v.*). In its second part he exhorts the Viennese authorities to wipe out and exterminate these Brethren without mercy, else they would spoil all good "Christians."

To this pamphlet the Hutterite *Vorsteher* (bishop) Claus Braidl (*q.v.*), a man of strong and upright character, answered with a pamphlet, *Ein Widerlegung und warhafte Verantwortung der alten, grausamsten, abscheulichen . . . Gotteslesterung, Schmach und unwarhafftigen Beschuldigungen so Christoph Andreas Fischer . . . über uns Brüder erdacht* (n.p., 1604), defending the Brethren as well as he could against all these calumnies.

(2) Fischer replied with another booklet, *Antwort auf die Widerlegung, so Clauss Breutel, der Wiedertauffer König oder Oberste sampt seinen Spiessgesellen hat getan . . . Gedruckt im Kloster Bruck an der Teya, Anno 1604* (156 pages). As text he uses Prov. 26:5, "Answer a fool according to his folly, lest he be wise in his own conceit." In the main it contains but a repetition of number 1. It is necessary, he says, to forbid them all their farms, sheep runs, mills, etc. The nobles should not use their women as wet nurses for "Christian children lest they get all false ideas with their milk." In this book Fischer also reprints the great mandate (*General Mandat*) of the government of Emperor Rudolphus II of 1601 which ordered the expulsion of all Brethren from Austria within three months. The mandate also claims (with Eysvogel), and Fischer repeats it, that the Brethren snatch away profit and food from the artisans and the entire "Christian" citizenry of the country.

(3) The next book was dedicated to the lord Maximilian von Dietrichstein (*q.v.*), otherwise known in the Hutterite Chronicle as being rather in sympathy with the Brethren. It has the inciting title, *Der Hutterischen Wiedertauffer Taubenkobel, in welchem all ihr Mist, Kot und Unflat . . . zu finden, auch des grossen Taubers, des Jakob Huters Leben . . . angehängt. Durch Chr. A. Fischer, Gedruckt zu Ingolstadt . . . Anno 1607* (67 pages). The title page has a woodcut illustrating this simile that the Bruderhofs are like dovecotes where the brethren deposit all their refuse. Like doves they fly in and out (see illustration). These Bruderhofs are found in the finest places of the country. Again complete expulsion of the Brethren is demanded.

(4) The climax and worst type of this Brethren-baiting is the last pamphlet, entitled: *54 erhebliche Ursachen warum die Wiedertauffer nicht sein im Lande zu leiden. Gedruckt zu Ingolstadt . . . Anno*

1607 (54 Strong Arguments Why the Anabaptists Should Not Be Allowed to Live in This Country) (130 pages). The title page has the same woodcut as number 3: the symbolic dovecote. Its text is Ex. 22:18, "Thou shalt not permit a sorcerer to live" (the Bible has "witch" or sorceress). Among the many arguments he mentions also the fact that "the nobles run to the Brethren bathhouses and use their barbers and physicians, and also their drugs, as if no one else knew that art." Fischer claims that the Brethren taught contempt for the authorities. "They steal your religion and call you pagans and infidels." He closes about this way: "Do not allow your country to fall into the disrepute of being a den of murderers because of the presence of these murderers, adulterers, and renegade monks."

A vindication of the Brethren in the face of these slanders is hardly necessary; the article **Economic History of the Hutterites** provides some of the factual background of this hostile propaganda. At first Fischer's fight was not very successful since the lords wanted to keep these industrious people on their estates; even Cardinal Franz von Dietrichstein (*q.v.*), the very head of the Counter Reformation in Moravia, kept the Brethren around Nikolsburg, at least for the next decade.

Fischer, however, seems to have moved away from this area, for already in 1607 he is in Ingolstadt, Bavaria, a famous Jesuit center, involved in a "colloquy" with William Laud, the later Anglican archbishop (d. 1645), who published this debate in English. No further information about Fischer is available.   LOSERTH, R.F.

Loserth, *Communismus*, 62-66; *ML* I, 646-48; pamphlets number 2, 3, and 4 are in Goshen College Library, number 1 in Bethel College Library.

Fischer, Gall, a member of the Augsburg (*q.v.*) Anabaptist congregation, and after Huber's defection a deacon with Hans Kiessling. He was a weaver, and had already reached an advanced age when he joined the congregation. He was baptized by Siegmund Salminger (*q.v.*), but was soon thereafter captured. Because he recanted he was not executed, but with four others, including Eitelhans Langenmantel, was expelled from the city Oct. 18, 1527. But he remained a member of the congregation after his expulsion, and in February 1528 he and Augustin Bader (*q.v.*) were sent to visit the newly formed congregation in Kaufbeuren (*q.v.*). On Saturday before Easter, April 11, about 40 persons met to worship in his house in Augsburg in his absence. On the next day the council struck the congregation an annihilating blow. They surprised them at a meeting in the home of the sculptor Doucher (*q.v.*) and seized 88 members, some of whom were executed and some after torture expelled from the city. Four women, in whose homes meetings had been held, had their cheeks burned through with hot irons; one of these was probably Elisabeth, Gall Fischer's wife.

Gall was likely wandering about in Swabia with Augustin Bader as a fugitive. The experiences of their dearest friends who were tortured and even killed, as for instance the leader of the Kaufbeuren congregation who had been chosen under their supervision and who was beheaded June 13, 1528, with 5 men who would not recant, and 30 men and 5 women who were either branded or whipped out of the city, all of whom Gall Fischer had baptized, weighed heavily upon the two men and confused them. On the basis of visions and dreams they proclaimed the imminence of the judgment and the establishment of God's kingdom on earth. Their contacts with the Anabaptists, who rejected these new ideas, were entirely lost. At Lautern near Ulm, where they had found shelter in a barn, Fischer claimed to have received a great vision (see **Bader, Augustin**), upon which Bader furnished himself with royal insignia. The purchase of these objects aroused suspicion and on Jan. 16, 1530, led to the arrest of the entire group of five men, three women, and eight children. The government feared revolution, and though the fears were proved groundless, Fischer was taken to Nürtingen and subjected to questioning on the rack. He maintained his loyalty to Bader throughout, and was executed about March 26, 1530, at Nürtingen.   HEGE.

G. Bossert, "Augustin Bader von Augsburg," in *Archiv für Ref.-Gesch.* X (1913) 117 ff.; F. Roth, "Zur Gesch. der Wiedertäufer in Oberschwaben," in *Ztscht des hist. Vereins für Schwaben und Neuburg* XXVIII (Augsburg, 1902) 31 ff.; K. Alt, *Wiedertäufer in und aus Kaufbeuren* (Kempten, 1930); K. Schornbaum, *TA: Bayern* II; G. Bossert, *TA: Württemberg*, 930-34, 953-55; *ML* I, 648.

Fischer, Michael, an Anabaptist martyr. His death sentence, pronounced on Aug. 7, 1587, in Ingolstadt, states that he had joined the Anabaptists about 20 years previously and persuaded others to do so. During his imprisonment of 12 weeks the Jesuits tried in vain to lead him back into the Catholic Church. An account of the execution as given by an eyewitness and found in the Hutterian chronicles relates that as soon as the sentence was pronounced he was at once led to the site of execution, accompanied by a Jesuit and another monk, who were still trying to convert him. At the place of execution they held a crucifix before his eyes and bade him look at it. Fischer shook his head and told the executioner to proceed, for he wished to die loyal to his faith; he knelt, motionless and unafraid. The executioner was so dismayed by this exhibition of courage that he did not behead him correctly, and had to be led back into the city with a firm supporting hand.

Fischer's martyrdom is sung in an anonymous hymn beginning "Mich ursacht euch zu singen." It is found in two manuscripts in Pressburg, one in Gran, and one in Budapest, and also in *Die Lieder der Hutterischen Brüder*, p. 785 f.   LOSERTH.

Die Lieder der Hutterischen Bruder (Scottdale, 1914); Wolkan, *Lieder*, 235; Beck, *Geschichts-Bücher*, 299 f.; *Mart. Mir.* D 756, E 1062, where he is called Michael Vischer; *ML* I, 648 f.

Fischer, Volkmar, an Anabaptist peasant of Rohrborn, a village in the district of Erfurt, Hesse, Germany, baptized by Hans Römer (*q.v.*), apparently took part in an attack on Erfurt, escaped all persecution, arrived at Basel, where he stayed in the home of Michael Schürer, a tailor from Freiburg. Here he renounced all ideas of revolution and joined the quiet Anabaptists. He left for Bohemia six weeks later, and was imprisoned in Prague for a while.

For about a year he was a distiller of whiskey at Kaaden on the Eger, and then worked as a day laborer in various villages in the Erz Mountains. On Nov. 1, 1534, he was arrested by the council of Erfurt and probably executed the following March.

NEFF.

P. Wappler, *Die Täuferbewegung in Thüringen von 1526-1584* (Jena, 1913) 41 ff.; *ML* I, 649.

Fisher, Ill., a town (pop. 800) located in east central Illinois in Champaign County, about 20 miles northwest of Champaign-Urbana, and serves the fertile agricultural area near by. The Mennonite settlement began in 1883, when a few Mennonites came from Tazewell Co., Ill., to the northwest corner of Champaign County. In 1954 the Mennonite population is located for the most part north, east, and west of the town. Over half of the membership of some 500 live within shopping distance of Fisher; of this number nearly 100 actually live in town. The Mennonite population of the town has been increasing steadily during the past decade. The Mennonites in this area are served by the East Bend Mennonite Church (MC), located two miles north and one mile east of Fisher.   K.L.M.

Fisherville (Pa.) Mennonite Church (MC), now extinct. On Aug. 9, 1874, the first services were held in a new meetinghouse 3 miles north of Halifax in Dauphin County, 28 miles north of Harrisburg. Slate Hill and Strickler ministers were in charge. With exclusively German preaching, the young people were lost by 1900 and the house was sold. In 1928 eight members from Virginia located here and church privileges were granted them from Slate Hill in an abandoned schoolhouse. By 1930 the group had scattered and services were discontinued.

I.D.L.

Flag Run Conservative Amish Mennonites: see **Beachy.**

Flamingh, Hans: see **Vlamingh, Hans.**

Flanagan, Ill., is located in Livingston County, in the north central part of the state, and has a population of 680. Three branches of Mennonites live in the vicinity of Flanagan, all of Amish background: the Evangelical Mennonites, Salem Mennonite Church; Mennonites (MC), Waldo Mennonite Church; and Central Conference Mennonites, Flanagan Mennonite Church. The settlements are southeast, south, and southwest of Flanagan. Mennonites have lived in this area since 1859 and at that time were known as Amish Mennonites. At present approximately 90 Mennonites live in Flanagan, and practically all in the general area live within shopping distance of the village.

In 1898 the Salem Orphanage, now known as the Salem Children's Home, was founded two miles southeast of Flanagan by the Salem Mennonite Church and continues to be supported by the Defenseless Mennonites, now the Evangelical Mennonite Church.   J.O.

Flanagan Mennonite Church (GCM), a member of the Central District Conference (formerly known as Central Conference of Mennonites), located about two miles southwest of Flanagan, Ill., began as a Sunday school for Amish residents in the vicinity. In 1878 the congregation was organized with Christian Rediger as its pastor. Four years later a church was built. Succeeding ministers and/or bishops were Stephen Stahley 1885-1916, Joseph Zehr 1890-1934, Emanuel Ulrich 1918-   . A full schedule of regular Sunday services is carried on. In 1954 the membership was 79.   R.L.H.

Flanders (Dutch, *Vlaanderen*), once a county extending along the coast of the Low Countries, covering the present Belgian provinces of East Flanders and West Flanders and (in the 16th century) the area of the French departement of Nord from Dunkirk to Lille (Rijssel). In the southern part of Flanders the French language predominated; but in by far the larger area Dutch was spoken. It is strange that this part of Belgium is now strictly Catholic, whereas in the Middle Ages it was a center of all sorts of faiths and in the 16th century there were at first many Anabaptist congregations, followed by still more numerous Reformed congregations.

It may be that Bakhuizen van den Brink is right in saying that the origin of Anabaptism here is not to be found in Melchiorite influence as is the movement in Holland and Friesland, nor in the Swiss Brethren influence, but in the remnants of Waldensian groups which existed here in concealment. Bakhuizen may also be right in believing that about 1565 great numbers of Anabaptists joined the Reformed Church. Fruin calls attention to the astonishing fact that in consequence of the hatred of the working classes against the immoral clergy and of the economic conditions of the populace, they were led into a very destructive iconoclasm, only to unite in droves under the banner of the suppressors of the Reformation. On the other hand, the courage of hundreds of martyrs shines gloriously, and there is no area in western Europe where the soil was so thoroughly watered by the blood of the heroes of faith and where execution stakes were so frequently set up; and hundreds of Flemish fled to Holland, Friesland, Groningen, East Friesland, Twente, the Rhine Province, and England.

A number of these refugees apparently settled in the north in 1555-66, before the breaking of the images and the arrival of Alba. They were of great importance for the northern congregations. They produced a number of families of ministers, and were of great influence in introducing an element of trade into our churches of sailors and peasants. Van Braght's *Martyrs' Mirror* lists nearly 400 Anabaptist martyrs from Flanders, and since that time research in the archives by Edouard de Coussemaker and especially A. L. E. Verheyden (*Martyrologia* of Brugge, Gent, etc.) has brought many more to light. Not all the archives of Flanders have been investigated, and some are no longer in existence, such as the important archives of Ieper, which were destroyed in World War I in 1916.

The beginning of Anabaptism in Flanders, especially in the great trade centers of Gent, Brugge, Kortrijk (Courtrai), Meenen, and Ieper, is best explained as being slumbering remnants of former religious anti-Catholic movements and as the result of the cosmopolitan population of these cities, their extensive but dwindling industry and their international trade with the shipping connected with this trade, creating here a fertile soil for reformatory efforts and easy entry for new ideas.

It is, however, remarkable that among the Flemish weavers in the Middle Ages there were many adherents of religious brotherhoods, and that Anabaptism found its following chiefly among the workers in the textile industries; and also in the disinclination of the city authorities to persecute religious faiths, since it would be injurious to international trade. It was actually the servants of the rulers that led the persecution, supported principally by the monasteries, whose members, however immorally they might be living, were willing to furnish inquisitors, such as the abhorrent Brother Cornelis Adriaansz of Brugge. The adherents of the new ideas were very likely the descendants of the party of Klauwaarts, whose freedom-loving views conflicted with those of the party of Leliaart. Behind our heroes of faith rises the shadow of the great man of the people, Jacob van Artevelde.

Henri Pirenne in his history of Belgium (III, 404 ff.) has drawn a sad picture of the moral decline of the clergy of the time. Their education and scholarship was as slight as their sins were great. The tie with the church, which was actually hated by the populace, became so loose that it was quite easily broken by the reading of a reformatory writing that was secretly printed in Antwerp. Here we have the center of religious enlightenment through literary means. But, above all, the new doctrine was propagated both openly and privately by itinerant preachers, who proclaimed the new faith in small gatherings held here and there in a granary or a basement, as well as in larger concourses in remote woods, and occasionally, like the martyr Gillis van Aken (q.v.), preached on the street or the market place following the example of the preaching monks. From foreign countries came dealers and seamen and related in the inns what was believed in other lands.

The first Anabaptist victims in Flanders were Willem Mulaer, who was beheaded in Gent on July 15, 1535, and Arendt de Jagher and Jan van Gentbrugge, who were beheaded four days later. The first proclamation against the Anabaptists was posted at Antwerp on Feb. 12, 1535. This was the time of the disturbances in Münster. The authorities everywhere now saw in Anabaptism only a revolutionary movement dangerous to the security of the state. From now on, it was threatened with severe punishment, viz., the stakes for men and drowning for women, while those who sheltered its adherents or promoted their work were banished; the death penalty was set for holding meetings. Münsterite preachers such as Jan van Geelen and Jacob van Herwerden moved through Flanders preaching their doctrine. But it may be assumed that the number of their followers was rather small in comparison with that of the northern areas, and that there was little desire here to institute the New Jerusalem with the sword. But here too, as is seen in the accounts

of Hans van Overdam (q.v.), who died as a martyr at Gent, they originally called themselves *Bondgenooten* (q.v.). The notorious Jan van Batenburg (q.v.) was arrested at Artois in 1537; in his confession made in the castle of Vilvoorden, he betrayed a number of names, among them some from the south.

Presumably at about this same time the preacher Wouter van Stoelwijk (q.v.) was arrested and in 1541 after many years of imprisonment executed as a martyr. His writing, which is found in the *Martyrs' Mirror,* is both inspiring and dogmatically sound. But there had already been other similar movements in Flanders. The David Jorists had a number of followers. There were also some followers of Hendrik Nicolai (Familists), members of the "House of Love." The secrecy practiced by both groups blocks the inquiry into their numbers. Nevertheless it is certain that they were favored. The "sermons" of Brother Cornelis reveal that there were some in Brugge, and that the unitarian ideas of Adam Pastor, on account of which he was banned by Menno and Dirk Philips, found an echo in Flanders, as, e.g., in the case of the martyr Herman van Vlekwijk (q.v.). This has been proved by Hans Alenson (q.v.) (BRN VII, 196).

The doctrine of the Incarnation as adopted by Menno from Melchior Hofmann was not shared by all the Belgian Anabaptists. It is, for example, rather strange that the publishers of the Haarlem *Offerboek* for this reason omitted a part of a letter by Claes de Praet (q.v.). Also Jacob van de Wege, who was burned at the stake at Gent in 1573, held a different view. He had a brother Hans, who had died at the stake three years before. They were nephews of Claes, the colleague of the notorious Inquisitor Pieter Titelman, deacon of Ronse (Renaix), their home.

Another characteristic doctrine found among the Anabaptists was the "sleep of the soul" (q.v.), i.e., the human soul is in a state of sleep until the final judgment. A surgeon of Rijssel (Lille) was drowned at Metz in 1538 on account of this heresy. Several other Flemish Anabaptists have been discussed by K. Vos in the *Theologisch Tijdschrift* of 1918, viz., Jacob de Rore or Keersgieter, a preacher at Brugge (d. 1569), Hans de Vette (Gent) and Hans van der Maes at Warneton near Ieper (both d. 1559), and Hendrik Verstralen at Rupelmonde (d. 1571), who said, "That we may go to our chambers (graves) with peace and calm and await the coming of the Lord, who will awaken us below the ground." But most of the martyrs believed that they would at once inherit heaven.

Presumably most of the martyrs died without possessions. Confiscation rarely produced any goods. Only rarely is there a statement regarding making property secure. It seems that those who had means succeeded in fleeing. Only in 1567 are five rich men of Rijssel (Lille) mentioned, who were sentenced at Antwerp. The nobility as well as the wealthy risked grave losses when they opposed the government. Nor should it be forgotten that this religious movement arose at a time of decreasing prosperity and declining industry, in which the coming of the kingdom of Christ upon a new earth was expected for half a century, and that its adherents were found for the most part among those who were dissatisfied with their lot on earth.

Furthermore, it seems that in only two periods (1534-35 and 1566) did any great number of the laboring class join the movement for a time, but only a few of these became members, and these gave an adequate account of their transfer. They were able to read the Bible and the reformatory writings, they composed good letters, and their confessions of faith were well considered. There were also some writers of songs among them. A number were able to give pointed replies to the inquisitor. Actually, the brotherhood made lofty demands of its members. Baptism was imparted only to those whose confession of faith and conduct were considered worthy.

The trials also show that the meetings were attended by 20 persons at the most; this was the usual number found by the authorities when they surprised a meeting. And only a few persons were baptized at a time. The prisoners on the rack were never able to give more than a few names, which suggests that the congregations were not large. But the members must have had unusual financial resources, for in no other way could the large number of published writings be explained. It must also be considered that in the Frisian vs. Flemish disputes one of the causes for friction was the costly clothing of the Flemish, and that one reason why Leenaert Bouwens was removed from his office of elder was that he drank too much wine.

The organization of the congregations was also different from that of the north, partly because of difference in national characteristics, and partly because they had other preachers. Menno and Dirk Philips were never in Flanders; nevertheless they were no doubt very highly regarded here. The Flemish congregations were more independent. Whereas in the north only the elder could perform the rite of baptism, in the south it was frequently performed by men who were not yet ordained as elders.

The strict adherents of the ban and shunning did not live in Flanders. On the contrary, there were many here who favored milder views. Still, they did not want to be too lenient. The martyr Christian Rijcen (burned at the stake at Hondschoote in 1588), formerly a preacher in Leyden, had to resign from his office for that reason.

The following preachers and leaders served in Flanders: Leenaert Bouwens, who baptized about 350 persons in Flanders in 1554-82, Joachim Vermeeren, Joost Verbeeck, Herman de Timmerman, Hans Busschaert de Wever, Gillis van Aken, Jan van Ophoorn, Jan van de Walle, Gillis Bernaerts, Michiel Bernaerts, Adriaan du Rieu, Hendrik van Arnhem, Paulus van Meenen, Hans Symons of Rijssel, Olivier Willems, Gillis de Hevile, and Filips Bostijn (all of these are discussed by K. Vos, *De Doopsgezinden te Antwerpen in de 16. eeuw*). Additional names are Joos de Tollenaar, Hendrik van Rosevelt, Martin van der Straten, Wouter van Stoelwijk, Christiaen Rijcen, Jacob de Rore, Hartman Sybrands, and Christoffel van Leuvene.

Without doubt Gent (*q.v.*) had the largest congregation. Other congregations that produced martyrs were: Aire, Armentières, Bailleul (Belle), Brugge, Cassel, Comines, Dixmuiden, Halewijn (Halluin), Hondschoote, Ieper, Kortrijk (Courtrai), Meenen, Messines, Middelburg, Nieppe (Nijpkerke), Oostende, Oudenaarde, Pamele, Rijssel, Rupelmonde, Thielt, Vinderhoute, Waastene (Warneton), Wervik, and Wynoksbergen. Anabaptists were also living at Harelebeeke, Ronse, Rousselare, Steenwerk, and Swevegem.

The last Anabaptist martyr of Flanders was Michiel de Cleercq (*q.v.*), executed at Gent in 1592. Thereafter the Mennonites in Flanders died out or emigrated. Until about 1630 Mennonite congregations were found in the neighborhood of Gent, at Lovendeghem (*q.v.*) and Zomerghem (*q.v.*). At this time many Mennonites fled to the Netherlands, especially to Aardenburg (*q.v.*). Others went to the Rhine Province of Germany. Among the Mennonite families in the Netherlands of Flemish descent (in large part they have died out) are the Anselmus, Apostool, de Block, Beheydt, Boekenoogen, van de(n) Boogaert, Calvaert, Claeys, de Clercq, Coppens, Couwenhoven (Kauenhoven), Cranen (Craen), van Daele (Dalen, Daalen), Dobbelaere, Dyserinck, van Eeghen, Fack, de la Faille, de Forest, de Fremery, Goudeseboys, Gryspeert, de Haan, van Halmael, Hartsen, van Outryve (Hauteryve), d' Hoye (de Hoeye), van Houcke, Hebberecht, de Heere, Hennebo, Huygaert, van de(n) Kerckhove(n), van der Meersch, Mehoude, Messchaert, Mulier, de Neufville, de Pla, Plovyer, le Poole, des Rameaus, Roose(n), de Sitter (de Suttere), van (der) Sluys, van der Smissen, van de Steenkiste, Ta(c)k, Verhamme, de Wale (de Wael), de Wolff.   K.V., vdZ.

A. L. E. Verheyden, "Introduction to the History of the Mennonites in Flanders," *MQR* XXI (April 1947) 51-63; *idem, Brugge; idem, Gent; idem, Courtrai-Bruxelles; idem, Le Protestantisme à Nieuport au XVIe siècle* (Brussels, 1951); *idem,* "History of the Mennonites in Flanders," to be published in 1957 at Scottdale; K. Vos, *De Doopsgezinden te Antwerpen in de zestiende eeuw* (Brussels, 1920); *ML* I, 649-52.

Flatland Mennonite Church (GCM) of the Eastern District Conference is located in Richland Twp., Bucks Co., Pa. In 1837 Mennonites of the Swamp and Springfield congregations living in this community built a small stone meetinghouse, which with subsequent interior changes, remains to the present day. In the early days the congregation sometimes was known as "Tohickon," the name of the near-by stream. In 1847 most of the congregation followed Jacob Benner out of the Franconia (MC) Conference into the new conference, while George Landis and perhaps a few others remained with the old conference and went elsewhere. In 1857 a portion of the congregation left the conference and with William N. Shelly joined the Evangelical Mennonites (*q.v.*), later known as the Mennonite Brethren in Christ.

Known ministers and their terms of service are as follows: George Landis 1837-47, John H. Oberholtzer *ca.* 1842-70, W. N. Shelly *ca.* 1847-57, L. O. Shimmel (?) *ca.* 1858-69, A. B. Shelly 1864-1913, Harvey W. Shelly 1914-18, Harvey G. Allebach 1919-21, Peter E. Frantz 1922-25, Seward M. Rosenberger 1925-29, Arthur S. Rosenberger 1930-34, A. J. Neuenschwander 1934-49, William Denlinger 1949- .

A Sunday school was begun perhaps as early as 1853, although it was not continuous. The present Sunday school was organized in 1886. The membership just before 1847 is reported to have been about 50; in 1864 it was 30; in 1908 it was 44, and in 1954 it was 61. The common names today are Frei, Ahlum, Fluck, Kilmer, and Yeakel.   J.H.F.

"Flatland Mennonite Church," *1899 Mennonite Yearbook and Almanac* (Quakertown); "Building the Flatland Meetinghouse," *1938 Yearbook of the General Conf.* (Berne); J. C. Wenger, *Hist. of the Menn. of the Franconia Conf.* (Telford, 1937).

Fleckenstein, a small Mennonite congregation in the Lower Alsace, near the German border, not far from Wissembourg, now extinct, which held its meetings on the Fleckensteinerhof until 1929. (See also **Essingen** and **Lembach**.)

Fleetwood Mennonite Brethren in Christ Church, located in Berks Co., Pa., was organized about 1875. In 1954 the congregation had 138 members, with T. D. Gehret serving as pastor. In 1868 a church was built here by the United Mennonites.   J.B.H.

Fleiner, Joachim, an Anabaptist martyr, of a respected family in Esslingen, Württemberg, the young son of a guildmaster, was probably baptized in 1528 by Wilhelm Reublin or Christoph Freisleben (Eleutherobion). In September 1528 Augustin Bader (*q.v.*) of Augsburg invited him to a meeting of his followers at Schönberg near Gerodseck, at which baptism, ban, and communion were to be discussed. Fleiner, impressed with Bader's knowledge of Scripture, accepted, but was repelled by Bader's ideas of grandeur and returned to Esslingen the next day. He was prominent among the Anabaptists here, baptizing others.

At the end of 1529 he was arrested. No fewer than 14 learned men tried to convert him. His relatives, brothers, and sister begged him with tears to renounce his faith. He replied that he would renounce evil, but do good. At his trial he denied that the Anabaptists wanted all property to be held in common. It was good not to swear, but one might swear or refuse to do it. In all temporal matters they wanted to obey the commands of the government unless they were contrary to God's commands. No one should offend another; therefore it is not right to bear arms.

On Feb. 21, 1530, Fleiner was taken to the place of execution with Ludwig Lichtenstein. On the way he sang, "Aus tiefer Not schrei ich zu dir," and asked the pardon of all as he also pardoned all. Then he looked up and said, "Father, into Thy hands I commend my spirit," made a cross with his right foot, and knelt. The executioner again asked him to recant, pointing to the body of Lichtenstein, who had already been executed. He replied, "I shall not die today, I shall be with God," and amid the general weeping he continued to speak. His courage deeply impressed the people.   G.Bo.

A. Diehl, ed., *Dreytweins Esslinger Chronik* (Tübingen, 1901) 104 ff.; K. Pfaff, *Gesch. der Reichsstadt Esslingen* (Esslingen, 1840) 476; Keim, *Reformationsblätter der Reichsstadt Esslingen*, 1860, p. 31; *Arch. für Ref.-Gesch.* XI, 115 ff. (ev. 35 und 36); G. Bossert, *TA* I: *Württemberg* (Leipzig, 1930) 963, 966; J. Rauscher, *Württemb. Ref.-Gesch.* (1934) 85; *ML* I, 652.

Fleischer, Frederik Cornelis, b. 1863 at Amsterdam, d. 1929 at Beekbergen, at first a teacher, then a Dutch Mennonite pastor, serving Broek op Langendijk 1896-1902, Makkum 1902-9, and Winterswijk 1909-24. He is known for his interest in social work and as the founder of a Dutch Association for public hygiene, called *Het Groene Kruis* (The Green Cross), in 1900, of which he was the president, serving until his death. Its purpose is to promote public health by fighting tuberculosis, by training nurses and maternity nurses, by giving material help during illness, etc. This undertaking of Pastor Fleischer, who planned the organization for the benefit of all the Dutch people, has proved to be very successful. The work, which at first was done from the Mennonite parsonages of Makkum and Winterswijk, has spread all over the country. In 1919 an office was established in Utrecht, and the *Groene Kruis* was subsidized by the government. Besides this work Fleischer also served as secretary of the Dutch General Committee of Foreign Needs from July 1, 1921, until his death. He energetically organized the Dutch Mennonite aid for the suffering Russian brethren, whom he visited in the Ukraine in 1922 (see **Fonds voor Buitenlandsche Nooden**). Fleischer published a booklet on *Menno Simons* (Amsterdam, 1892); *Bloesemknoppen* (sermons) (Broek op Langendijk, 1902); *Die Taufgesinnten in den Niederlanden* (n.p., 1904); *De Doopsgezinden* (Baarn, 1909); *De Doopsgezinde Gemeente te Winterswijk* (Winterswijk, 1911); a number of sermons and some articles in the *Doopsgezind Jaarboekje* on the activities of the Committee of Foreign Needs (*DJ* 1923, 43-78; 1924, 61-78). From 1896 to 1910 he was the author of the yearly statistical surveys in the *Doopsgezinde Bijdragen*. Besides this he published a large number of articles in the *Zondagsbode* and in various Dutch non-Mennonite daily and weekly papers.

In 1908, while visiting the Unitarian Conference at Boston, Mass., he also visited some Mennonite congregations in America, e.g., in Philadelphia. His son Willem Isaak Fleischer is also a Mennonite pastor, serving Terschelling 1930-33, Balk and Woudsend 1933-42, Steenwijk and Meppel 1942-46, Meppel 1946-49, and Groningen since 1949.

A.G.v.H., vDZ.

DB 1908, 200; *DJ* 1931, 21-29 with portrait; *Catalogus Amst.*, 13, 43, 91, 318; *ML* I, 653.

Flemish Mennonites (Dutch, *Vlamingen* or *Vlaamschen*) was the name of a branch of Mennonites that originated in 1566 in opposition to the Frisians (*q.v.*). The conflict and hence the division arose after many Mennonites, in order to escape from the most oppressive persecution, had emigrated or fled from Belgium, and especially from Flanders (hence they were usually called Flemings or Flemish), to the Netherlands. Many of them settled in the Dutch province of Friesland. Here the four congregations of Harlingen, Franeker, Leeuwarden, and Dokkum formed a union in 1560 on the basis of 19 articles on various questions of congregational life. The union was known as the *Ordinantie der vier steden.* Among other things they stipulated that a preacher chosen for one of the congregations should also serve the other three, and that all matters of discord arising in one should be settled by the preachers of all four churches. The care of the poor was also provided for in common. By this arrangement the autonomy of the individual congregation, a fundamental principle of the brotherhood, was abrogated, and this gave rise to the fateful division between the Frisian and Flemish members.

The Flemish had come to these four cities too. The difference of background soon led to all manner of disagreement. The Frisians were offended by the Flemish way of living and dressing, and the latter resented the greater stores of linen and household goods possessed by the Frisians, and accused them of siding more with the world, whereas they (the Flemish) had proved their world-denying faith in persecution. It was stated in this way: the Flemish are worldly in respect to their dress, the Frisians in their homes.

In Franeker (*q.v.*) Jeroen Tinnegieter, a refugee from Henegouwen (Hainaut), Belgium, was chosen preacher. This choice seemed questionable to Harlingen. With the aid of preachers from outside (Hoyte Renix, Nette Lipkes, and Hans Bouwens Busschaert) the difficulty was settled; but a sting remained. Tinnegieter was hostile to the union of the four cities, seeing in it—probably correctly—the real cause of his having been rejected. At a meeting of the brotherhood he declared that the Franeker congregation was leaving the union. A part of the congregation, which had not been heard, protested this move. The two sections held separate church services. This marked the beginning of the baneful division, which soon reached Harlingen also. The designations Frisian and Flemish were already current.

All efforts to reunite them were futile. Again preachers from outside were asked to aid; this time they were Jan Willemsz (*q.v.*) and Lubbert Gerritsz (*q.v.*), both of Hoorn. They succeeded on Dec. 19, 1566, in effecting a compromise and both groups agreed on four specific points. But the general discussion at Harlingen on Feb. 1, 1567, did not lead to harmony; and the unyielding attitude of Dirk Philips (*q.v.*), who had been called to arbitrate and traveled to Emden with two other delegates from Danzig, made the schism permanent. The Flemish pronounced the ban upon all the Frisians (June 1567). Anyone marrying into the other party was subject to the ban; any member of one party wishing to join the other had to be rebaptized. Dirk Philips took the part of the Flemish, whereas Leenaert Bouwens joined the Frisians. Not only in Friesland, but all over the Netherlands the churches became involved and divided, and in most towns there were henceforth found both a Flemish and a Frisian congregation. The congregation of Zierikzee (*q.v.*) in Zeeland, which refused to decide either for the Flemish or for the Frisians, but which wished to remain neutral, was banned both by the Flemish and the Frisians.

The name "Flemish" is not geographic; it does not mean that its members came from Flanders, nor does "Frisian" mean that its members live in Friesland, or are natives of this province. Flemish and Frisian have become party names. The Frisians were in the majority in North Holland and Friesland, while in Groningen and Overijssel the Flemish were more numerous.

Once again in 1568 an attempt was made to reconcile the divisions. The congregations at Blokzijl, Giethoorn, and Steenwijk, who had as yet not been involved in the strife, investigated the matter and sided with the Flemish, presented their view in a statement of Jan. 3, 1569, called the *Stichtsche groote presentatie,* and after useless negotiations they broke off fraternal relations with all the Frisian congregations (there were more than 50 of them) on April 2, 1569. This step made the rupture final. Neither the Humstervrede (*q.v., peace of Humsterland,* 1574) nor the negotiations at Hoorn (1574) and Emden (April 2 and May 22, 1578), nor the discussion at Haarlem (1582), or the confession of guilt by the Frisian and Flemish preachers (1589), could bridge the gulf and bring about a union. In the Netherlands it took 200 years to wipe out the last signs of the division. (An account of the Flemish division and its course is found in *DB* 1893, 1-90.)

Twenty years after the Flemish-Frisian schism a new division arose in the main Flemish body. In Franeker, Friesland, the elder of the Flemish congregation, Thomas Byntgens (*q.v.*), bought a house; because Thomas's purchase seems not to have been above reproach a quarrel arose in 1586 and the Franeker Flemish congregation was divided into two groups, that of Byntgens, soon called *Huiskoopers* (*q.v.*) (Housebuyers), and a group led by the deacon Jacob Keest (*q.v.*), called *Contra-Huiskoopers.* Attempts were made by the Flemish congregations of Amsterdam, Haarlem, and Hoorn to reconcile the two groups, but in vain, and soon the whole Flemish body was divided in two parties: *Huiskoopers, Thomas Byntgens-volk,* or as they were mostly called, *Oude Vlamingen* (Old Flemish), while the others were called *Contra-Huiskoopers, Jacob-Keestvolk, Zachte* (mild) *Vlamingen,* or simply *Vlamingen* (Flemish). (Concerning this quarrel see *Inv. Arch. Amst.* I, No. 479; 558 III; *DB* 1912, 49-60.)

It seems somewhat ridiculous and even sad, that the buying of a house could divide the Mennonites, but this was only the outer motive. The point of the quarrel was rather a different conception of the church among the Flemish, whether the church should be conceived as strictly separated from the world, as a church without spot or wrinkle or not (Kühler, *Geschiedenis* I, 430-31). The (mild) Flemish were less conservative than the Old Flemish, and more moderate in banning and shunning. There were also a few local schisms; viz., among the Old Flemish at Haarlem and Danzig in 1598 the *Vermeulensvolk* (*q.v.*) or *Bankrottiers;* in Haarlem and Amsterdam in 1620 the *Borstentasters* (*q.v.*) or *Vincent de Hondtvolk.* The Flemish congregation at Haarlem was divided in 1685 into two congregations, the *Thomas-Snepvolk* (*q.v.*) and the *Jan-Evertszvolk* (*q.v.*).

Shortly after 1600 many among the (mild) Flemish realized that those pitiful and unprofitable divisions among the Mennonites must be ended. Some of them made contacts with the *Bevredigde Broederschap* (*q.v.*), a group of United High German, Waterlander, and (Young) Frisian Mennonites. At Harlingen (*q.v.*), Friesland, the Flemish congregation merged with the Frisians about 1610. This was much censured by many other Flemish congregations, especially those of the province of Groningen, who banned the Harlingen peacemakers (*Inv. Arch. Amst.* I, Nos. 522, 523, 539, 557, 558 V, 561, 564, 570).

In 1626 the four preachers of the Lamist Flemish church at Amsterdam, who already had previously defended the Harlingen group against the ire of the Groningen churches, made an attempt to unite all Dutch Mennonites, except the Waterlanders (*q.v.*) who were excluded. For this purpose they sent an invitation to peace, attended with a confession of faith, the well-known *Olijftack* (*q.v.*), which was printed in 1629 (*Inv. Arch. Amst.* I, No. 565). The result was disappointing; the Old Frisians and their leader P. J. Twisck (*q.v.*) repudiated such a "monstrous" alliance (*Inv. Arch. Amst.* I, No. 566, 568). The Flemish churches in Groningen too warned against a union with High Germans and Frisians (*Inv. Arch. Amst.* I, Nos. 564-65). But in Amsterdam after negotiations which lasted for a number of years a union was accomplished in 1639 between the Flemish congregation and that of united Frisians and High Germans (Kühler, *Geschiedenis* II, 184-200).

In the meanwhile the *Olijftack* had scored a great success at Dordrecht in 1632, by uniting the Flemish and most Old Flemish congregations on the basis of the confession of Adriaan Cornelisz (Dordrecht Confession) (*Inv. Arch. Amst.* I, Nos. 583-92, 595-98; Kühler, *Geschiedenis* II, 195-96). Only two groups of the Flemish did not join this general union: first a large number of congregations in the province of Groningen and elsewhere in the country, which from the beginning had protested against the *Olijftack,* and now separated from the main body (about 1637). They are called Groningen Old Flemish (*q.v.*) or after one of their most influential leaders Uckowallists (*q.v.*) (*Inv. Arch. Amst.* I, Nos. 557, 562-64, 571, 575-77, 600, 605 f., 934; II, Nos. 1413-20). The other group which did not agree and remained separated comprised a number of conservative Old Flemish churches, who were then called *Huiskoopers,* or "Dantziger (Danziger) Old Flemish" (*q.v.*). Thus the Groningen and Danziger Old Flemish remained independent of the union.

After the Old and Mild Flemish had united in 1632 and merged with the Frisian-High German group in 1639, the Waterlanders applied for admission to this large body of Dutch Mennonites in 1647.

But the conference of Flemish leaders at Haarlem in 1649 refused this, and the Waterlanders remained excluded. Since in the *Lammerenkrijg* (*q.v.,* War of the Lambs) new party-names of *Galenisten* and *Apostoolsen* came forth, soon called *Lamisten* and *Zonisten,* the name "Flemish Mennonites" disappeared in Holland. Only the Groningen and Danziger Old Flemish, mentioned before, maintained the name until the 19th century.

The Flemish-Frisian schism, begun at Franeker, Friesland, in 1566, was not limited to the Netherlands. In Flanders too the church was divided; especially in the congregation of Antwerp there were found both Flemish and Frisian followers. But in general the matter was less of an issue in Belgium, for nearly all the congregations belonged to the Flemish party.

In Prussia also the church had its schism, and here and later in Russia the split lasted much longer than in the Netherlands. In Prussia too the names of Flemish and Frisian do not refer to the origin of the members of a congregation from Friesland or from Flanders, but are also merely names of the parties.

The Flemish congregations in Prussia were Danzig (meeting outside of the Neugarten gate, formerly *op het Schotland*), Heubuden, Ladekopp, Rosenort, Tiegenhagen, Fürstenwerder and Elbing-Ellerwald, Wintersdorf and Kleinsee, Culmsche Niederung (Schönsee), and Königsberg. Of this group the congregations of Wintersdorf and Kleinsee-Jeziorka belonged to the Groningen Old Flemish; Königsberg probably belonged to the Danziger Old Flemish. Frisian congregations (later also called Waterlanders) in Prussia were Danzig (Petershagen gate), Orlofferfelde, Thiensdorf, Markushof, Montau-Gruppe, Schönsee, Stuhmsche Niederung (Tragheimerweide), Memelniederung, and Obernessau.

Variant practices in the observance of communion and baptism still show slight remains of the division. In the Flemish congregations the preachers read their sermons while seated (*Menn. Bl.* 1912, 5), whereas in the Frisian congregations the sermons were not read. In the Flemish group the baptismal candidate had to name two character witnesses, whose names were read from the pulpit; they baptized by pouring, and the Frisians by sprinkling. In the communion ceremony the Flemish preacher distributed the bread to the members, who remained seated; in the Frisian congregations the members filed past the elder, who put the bread on the handkerchief of the member (*DB* 1886, 21). In Friedrichstadt the unification occurred in 1698, in Danzig not until 1808 (Mannhardt, 89, 104). In West Prussia the preachers and elders of the two groups held annual conferences together beginning in 1772. The first instance of reception into the other group without rebaptism occurred in 1768. Since the great Flemish conference at Petershagen on Feb. 9, 1778, where the question was discussed, but blocked by the Flemish, intermarriage between the two groups was quietly accepted.

Concerning the relationship in Russia, Friesen (*Brüderschaft,* 44) says that in accordance with an old Flemish regulation, only the elders, not the preachers, were ordained by the laying on of hands; this practice continued in some Flemish congregations until 1900. At the time of the original settlement in Russia (1789) the opposition between the two groups was still so sharp that the Flemish organized themselves into the Chortitza congregation and the Frisians into the Kronsweide congregation, and maintained strict separation between the two. The Dutch Mennonites made an appeal in a letter dated May 10, 1788, to the new settlers to unify: not until decades later did this happen, and then only gradually. (See **Friesische Mennoniten**, *ML* II, 8 f.)   NEFF, veZ.

H. G. Mannhardt, *Die Danziger Mennonitengemeinde* (Danzig, 1919); Friesen, *Brüderschaft;* Kühler, *Geschiedenis* I and II; J. G. de Hoop Scheffer, "Het verbond der vier steden," *DB* 1893, 1-90; *ML* I, 649.

Flensburg, a city (pop. 50,000) in the Prussian province of Schleswig-Holstein, Germany, in which a colloquy with Melchior Hofmann took place on April 8, 1529.   NEFF.

B. U. Krohn, *Gesch. der fanatischen und enthusiastischen Wiedertäufer vornehmlich in Niederdeutschland* (Leipzig, 1758) 149 ff., gives the official records of the debate as published by Bugenhagen; F. O. zur Linden, *Melchior Hofmann* (Haarlem, 1885) 134 ff.; *ML* I, 654.

Fliedner, Theodor, b. Jan. 21, 1800, at Eppstein in Taunus, Germany, d. Oct. 4, 1864, in Kaiserswerth, the founder of deaconess (*q.v.*) work in the Protestant Church. He received the idea on a money-raising visit to Amsterdam, where the Mennonites had deaconesses in their church work. In his book *Collektenreise in Holland und England* 1831 he devotes a chapter to the Mennonites under the title, "Mennoniten oder Taufgesinnte, grobe und feine Taufgesinnte." His detailed description, given with thorough knowledge and acute judgment, is still of value. In it he describes the character of the Dutch Mennonites, their customs, and their life, their church organizations, and their benevolent institutions, even though his verdict is somewhat colored by his orthodoxy.   NEFF.

G. Fliedner, *Theodor Fliedner, Leben und Wirken* (2 vols., Kaiserswerth, 1908, 1910); *ML* I, 654.

Fliesteden, Peter of, a Protestant martyr, who died with Adolf Clarenbach (*q.v.*) at the stake in Cologne, Germany, Sept. 28, 1529. It is not clear whether or not he was an Anabaptist. He was born in Fliesteden in Jülich. In December 1527 he went to Cologne. During the celebration of the Mass in the cathedral he kept his head covered and was otherwise disrespectful toward this "idolatry," and was therefore arrested and so terribly tortured that the executioners pitied him. But neither the rack nor a two-year imprisonment in the dungeon altered his views. He remained true to his convictions and endured his martyrdom with admirable courage. (Rembert, *Wiedertäufer,* 114 ff.; *ML* I, 654.)
                                    NEFF.

Flinck, Govert, a Mennonite artist, b. Jan. 25, 1615, at Cleve, Germany, d. Feb. 4, 1660, at Amsterdam. His parents wanted to educate him for the textile trade, but his employer discharged him because he

was always drawing. The Mennonite preacher and painter Lambert Jacobsz (*q.v.*) at Leeuwarden convinced his parents that artists were not necessarily frivolous; they then permitted him to follow his bent. After his apprenticeship with Jacobsz he went to Amsterdam with Jacob Backer (*q.v.*), and there became Rembrandt's pupil. He soon gained fame and wealth, and painted many portraits for mayors and princes. His chief work was in portraits, religious scenes, and genre paintings. In the museums of Munich, Dresden ("David Presenting the Letter to Uriah"), Berlin, and Paris, as well as The Hague, and Amsterdam ("Isaac Blesses Jacob"; "Amsterdam Sharpshooters Celebrating the Peace of Westphalia"; "Joost van den Vondel," *q.v.*) his best-known works are found. He also painted the portrait of Gozen Centen, the property of the Amsterdam Mennonite Church, but loaned to the national museum at Amsterdam.   K.V.

H. Dattenberg, "Die Beziehungen von G. Flinck zu seiner Heimatstadt Cleve," in *Die Heimat,* Krefeld, XIX (1940) 69-71; W. Martin, *Rembrandt en zijn tijd* (3d ed., Amsterdam, 1944) 115-19 and notes 148-55 on p. 506; *ML* I, 654.

Flines, de, a Dutch Mennonite family, originally from Flanders, from where they emigrated to the Netherlands because of their faith. In the 17th century they are found in Middelburg, Amsterdam, Haarlem, and Leiden, as members of the Waterlander (Amsterdam, Haarlem) or the Flemish branch (Middelburg, Leiden). Especially at Amsterdam, where they now have died out, they were very numerous in the 17th century and related by marriage with a number of other Mennonite families like Willink and Leeuw. Some of them were deacons of the Amsterdam Toren Waterlander congregation—Gillbert de Flines 1625-48, Gijsbert Philips 1649-54 and 1660-71, and Sibrand after 1663, while Jaspar de Flines was a deacon of the united Lamist and Toren congregation 1674-79 and 1680-85.
                                    vdZ.

Flint Conservative Amish Mennonite Mission, located at 2124 East Williamson Ave., Flint, Mich., was organized in 1928, by the Conservative Amish Mennonite Conference. The mission had 24 members in 1953. Both the meetinghouse and the residence were built in 1929. Noah Swartzendruber was ordained in 1929 to be superintendent of the mission. He was followed by Edwin Albrecht, Andrew Jantzi, and Jesse L. Yoder, who was appointed superintendent in 1948. During World War II, many Civilian Public Service men in dairy service in Michigan worshiped at the Flint Mission.
                                    J.We.

Flint-Dartmouth (Mich.) United Missionary Church had a membership of 65 in 1953, with J. A. Bradley serving as minister.   M.G.

Flint-Hamilton Avenue (Mich.) United Missionary Church had a membership of 87 in 1953, with G. N. Bridges serving as minister.   M.G.

Flintstone Mennonite Mission (MC) is located near Flintstone, Md., 12 miles east of Cumberland on U.S. Route 40. The first services were held in private homes about 1925, but with the exception of a few years have since been held in a Brethren church near by. The work is in charge of the district mission board of Washington Co., Md., and Franklin Co., Pa., Mennonite Conference. The 1953 membership was six. In 1954 a meetinghouse was built for the group by the Mennonites of Washington Co., Md. **J.D.R.**

Floh, a Mennonite family of Crefeld, of importance for its mercantile business. Derich Derichsen Floh was living in Dülken in 1638 and built a house there, and then, having been expelled from Dülken, he came to Crefeld. The line of his son Paul died out soon after 1800. Derich's son Johann lived in Gladbach after his marriage (about 1650). He was expelled from that town in 1654; from 1669 to at least 1680 he was living in the Rheydt house (see **Bylandt**). In 1687 he was granted permission to return to Gladbach (see **München-Gladbach**) if he would introduce "Haarlem bleach" there. But in 1694 he had to leave again, and in that year he became a citizen of Crefeld. He was the most important linen dealer of his time along the Lower Rhine. His descendants continued the linen trade and weaving until they changed to velvet and silk in the 19th century and became very wealthy. The line became extinct soon after 1900 with the unmarried children of the linen manufacturer and councilor Peter Floh. In the 17th and 18th centuries there were in the Amsterdam Mennonite Lamist congregation a number of members of the du Flo family; this family, which is of Flemish descent, may be related to the Floh family of Crefeld. **W.N., vDZ.**

Floh, Jacob Hendrik, a Dutch Mennonite preacher and author, b. 1758 at Crefeld, Germany, the son of Johannes Floh and Arnolda Albertine Mauritz. He is probably the Hendrik Floh who was baptized at Cleve in 1776. He studied at the Mennonite Seminary in Amsterdam 1777-83, was called as preacher to Nijmegen in 1783, but moved to Enschede in the same year, and remained there until 1829, with the exception of a few years devoted to politics. He died in Enschede on March 25, 1830. He was an ardent Patriot (*q.v.*) and took an enthusiastic part in the events leading up to the revolution of 1795. In 1796 he was elected to the States-General of Holland, and was for a time secretary of the first chamber of the body representing the "Batavian Republic." He was a member of the committee of popular representatives that planned the separation of church and state. Then he returned to the pulpit. In 1800 he was also made school inspector of the province of Overijssel, and later secretary of the provincial board of education.

He wrote: *Vertrouwelijke gesprekken over verlichting, vrijheid en gelijkheid,* 1795; *Onderrigtingen, raadgevingen en wenken voor . . . schoolonderwijzers,* 1808; *Handleiding tot het oprigten en in stand houden van . . . industrieschoolen,* 1813; *Volksgeluk zonder volksdeugd onbestaanbaar,* 1822. He won several contests put on by learned societies. In addition he wrote: *Proeve eener beredeneerde verklaaringe der geschiedenissen van's Heilands ver-* *zoekinge in de woestijne,* 1790; and *Iets over bedestonden,* 1817. In the States-General meeting on Aug. 23, 1796, he advocated granting the rights of citizenship to the Jews. On this question several polemics were published by E. Kist and others; Floh was defended by J. Brouwer of the Mennonite Church at Leeuwarden. (*Biogr. Wb.* III, 65-69; *Inv. Arch. Amst.* II, 1718-20; *Naamlijst* 1829, 41; *ML* I, 654.) **K.V.**

Floodwood Bible Chapel (EMB), located in the town of Floodwood about 60 miles west of Duluth, Minn., was organized in 1934 at Meadowlands, 10 miles northeast of Floodwood, with 24 charter members under the leadership of C. H. Funk, who was their first pastor. They met for worship in an old store building until 1939, when they rented the Methodist church in Floodwood, a frame structure 22 x 40 ft. In 1945 with the help of the conference they purchased the church and also the parsonage about 3½ blocks from the church. The membership in 1953 was 34 and the average attendance was 61. The following have served as pastors: C. H. Funk, Ferdinand Thiessen, Gustave Schroeder, E. E. Peters, and A. F. Lutke, the pastor in 1953. **H.H.Di.**

Floradale Mennonite Church (MC), located about 16 miles north of Kitchener, Ont., is affiliated with the Ontario Conference. The first Mennonite services in the community were held in 1857. Various places of worship were used before an Evangelical church was purchased in 1868, which was used until 1899 when a division took place and the Old Order Mennonites obtained the building. After worshiping in the homes and in the village Evangelical Church, in 1896 the congregation constructed a building one-half mile north of the village. This was used until 1936 when a new church was built in Floradale. Sixty-four members recently transferred their membership to two newly organized Mennonite congregations in the vicinity; the 1953 membership was 136. Rufus Jutzi was the minister and Ivan Gingrich and Simeon Weaver the deacons. **R.D.**

Florida, a peninsula in the extreme southeastern part of the United States, is increasingly becoming a favorite winter resort because of its attractive climate. Mennonites and Amish, largely from Indiana, Ohio, and Pennsylvania, first came to Florida in the 1920's, most of them going to Sarasota County, located over halfway down the peninsula on the west coast. The number of permanent settlers was very small and the combined total with the winter visitors never exceeded 300 until 1945. Old Order Amish, Conservative Amish Mennonites, and Mennonites (MC) all held union services in various schools and other temporary meeting places. By 1944 the M.C. group of permanent residents was large enough to organize a congregation. A new church building was dedicated in February 1946. In that same year a large bakery was bought to provide a meeting place for Old Order Amish, Conservative Amish Mennonites, and those Mennonites who cared to continue meeting with them. Thus two permanent places of worship were established about six miles apart, each being about three miles from the business district of the city. The winter of 1944-45 brought a great increase of winter visitors. Since that time there has been a steady increase in the number of permanent settlers and a phenomenal growth in the number of Mennonite tourists. The establishment of a congregation and the new church building seem to be an added attraction for permanent settlers as well as for tourists. An increasing number of Mennonites own their own winter homes in Sarasota which are unoccupied during the summer. During January and February 1949, about 1,200 persons were in attendance at Sunday morning services in the two meeting places. Attendance during the summer months at the two places combined in 1948 averaged something over 100. A mission operated by the Lancaster Mennonite Conference (MC) was established at Tampa on the west coast in 1927. In 1955 there were a total of nine organized Mennonite congregations in Florida; five at Sarasota (belonging to four conferences: Lancaster, Virginia, Ohio and Eastern, and Conservative Mennonite), with a total of 248 permanent members, and a colored mission with 10 baptized members, two in Tampa and vicinity with 43 members, belonging to the Lancaster Conference, four additional Lancaster Conference missions with 23 members, and a newly founded Conservative Mennonite mission-colonized congregation at Blountstown, 50 miles west of Tallahassee. The total baptized Mennonite membership in Florida in 1955 was thus approximately 350.

T.H.B.

Florimont, a French village on the Swiss border, about 12 miles southeast of Belfort, the center of a Mennonite congregation. In the villages and on the farms in the vicinity of Florimont a number of Mennonite families are living, some of them on Swiss soil. Nothing is known of the origin of the congregation, but since Florimont belonged to Alsace (q.v.), its history is a part of Alsatian history. The family names indicate Bernese origin.

In 1780 a report was made to the magistrate of Alsace, which stated that most of the Mennonite families around Belfort had long been there; they were farmers or linen weavers; the former were tenants on the large estates; they were preferred as farmers, for they raised larger crops and paid their rent more regularly. The weavers quietly pursued their trade in remote houses. There were 12 families of them living in the forest of Normanvillars, which belonged to Florimont. If the government should find it necessary to reduce the number they might begin with these, for the farmers were more needed. Until the end of the 19th century there were linen weavers among them; now they are all engaged in agriculture, with some fishing, for the forests abound in small lakes.

Until the middle of the 19th century their meetings were held in the homes of members. In 1849 a church (Chapelle des Fermes, or des Bois) was built and a cemetery laid out. Twice the church was destroyed by fire—in 1904 by arson and again in World War I. In 1921 it was rededicated, and serv-

ices are held in it every two weeks. Since 1880 the services have been conducted in French.

Like all the French congregations, Florimont is Amish. In 1871 Elder Peter Klopfenstein opposed footwashing, thereby causing some tension in Alsace. A conference was called Feb. 19, 1876, to be held in Basel-Binningen, in which an unequivocal position was taken against Klopfenstein. But footwashing was not reinstated in Florimont. The congregation is thus somewhat isolated. It long resisted all attempts to secure co-operation between the several congregations. At present, however, there is increasing co-operation with the French-speaking congregations. In 1953 the baptized membership was about 160, with 60 children. In 1954 the church was enlarged to accommodate the growing congregation. The elders in 1955 were Joseph Freidinger, Joni Geiser, and Henri Zaugg; the ministers were René and Armand Klopfenstein and René Yoder. Chief family names are Klopfenstein, Riche, Roth, Zaugg, Graber, Yoder, Kaufmann, Amstutz, Boegli, Widmer, Bourquin, Choffat, Geiser, Schnegg, Zbinden. (See **Normanvillars.**)

P.So.

D. Gratz, *Bernese Anabaptists* (Scottdale, 1953) 89-95; P. Sommer, "Assemblée de Florimont," *Christ Seul,* June 1930, 9 f.; *ML* I, 655.

Floris, Foecke (*ca. 1650-ca. 1700*), was a blacksmith and a Mennonite preacher at Surhuisterveen in the Dutch province of Friesland. On April 16, 1683, Franciscus Elgersma (*q.v.*), a Reformed preacher of Grouw, charged him openly with Socinianism, and wrote *Rechtzinnige leer van het sacrament des hl. Doops* (Leeuwarden, 1685). Foecke replied with *Beschermingh der waerheyt Godts* (Leeuwarden, 1687). Elgersma again brought his accusations before the Leeuwarden Reformed Synod and with their approval wrote the following booklets: *Seedige verhandeling van de hooge verborgentheit der hl. Drieëenheid* and *Kanker der Sociniaansche ketterij* (Leeuwarden, 1688). An anonymous friend now entered into the dispute, defending Foecke with a pamphlet: *Klaar vertoog, Dienende tot wederlegginge van de ongefondeerde beschuldigen* (1689).

Meanwhile the Reformed Synod of Harlingen had taken the affair in hand. Both parties were summoned to appear before it. By a decision of Nov. 18, 1687, they condemned Foecke's book, ordered all copies to be burned, and forbade him to preach on penalty of five years' penitentiary. Soon afterward he was arrested and brought to Leeuwarden; but he found so much sympathy that over 2,000 persons came to visit him. Eight weeks later he was banished and went to Oost-Saandam (Zaandam in the province of North Holland) where he again began to preach. In 1688 the Synod of North Holland decided to bring their charges before the bailiff of Kennemerland. Then the persecuted man presented an appeal to Prince William, which had been drawn up by Galenus Abrahamsz de Haan (*q.v.*). The prince gave orders to let the matter rest until more information could be gathered (this letter with the signature of the prince is found in *Arch. Amst.* I, 456). Hence the synod of 1690 was unable to proceed further. Representatives of the synod were given audience by the prince in two successive years, and both times received a noncommittal answer. Then the bailiff of Kennemerland came to the rescue of the synod and forbade Foecke to preach in August 1692.

Nevertheless he resumed his preaching in March 1693. Apparently his influence declined from this point, at least the complaints ended. But his following in Grouw did not disappear. In Jan Klaassen (q.v.) he had a worthy successor. Foecke's writings reveal that he was not a full-fledged Socinian, but that he was on the other hand not entirely free of unorthodox views. He wrote also *Leerregel der Bibels, Eenige vorbeelden onzer loffelyke vaderen*, and *Een Hemelsch ABC* (Haarlem, 1690), and *Afdeeling der H. Bibelwetten* (Amsterdam, 1696).

K.V.

S. D. van Veen, "Foecke Floris," in *DB* 1887, 49-85; S. Blaupot t. C., *Holland* 229; *N.N.B.Wb.* III, 71-73; *ML* I, 655.

Floris Ysbrantsz, an Anabaptist martyr, beheaded in 1535 (exact date unknown) at Haarlem, Dutch province of North Holland. Under torture he admitted that he had received (re)baptism. vpZ.

Bijdr. en Mededelingen Hist. Genootschap Utrecht XLI (Amsterdam, 1920) 202-3; *Inv. Arch. Amst.* I, No. 750; *DB* 1917, 153.

Flugschriften: see **Pamphlets.**

Fluri, Adolf, b. Feb. 15, 1865, at Tramelan, J.B., Switzerland, d. 1930 in Bern, teacher of French in the Muristalden Training School at Bern, Switzerland, who rendered notable service in research on Anabaptist history and aided in the amplification of Ernst Müller's (q.v.) noted book on the Bernese Anabaptists (1895) with respect to their cultural history. In the center of Fluri's later work was the question of the history of the Bible and its distribution in the field of the Swiss Reformation. The first Bible printers in Zürich at that time, the Froschauers (q.v.), belonged to the religiously radical circles. Fluri's investigations on the Bible brought him in direct contact with Anabaptist history through the phenomenon peculiar to them of having their own editions of the Bible. (*Täufertestamente*). He was the first to make a thorough study of this one phase of Anabaptist history. Previously he had already confirmed and added to the *Martyrs' Mirror* ("Täuferhinrichtungen in Bern im 16. Jahrhundert," in *Berner Heim*, 1896, Nos. 35 ff.). In 1903 he received the honorary doctor's degree from the University of Bern.

Most of Fluri's published material is found in *Blätter für Bernische Geschichte, Kunst und Altertumskunde*. Some of the more important articles are "Bern und die Froschauerbibel mit besonderer Berücksichtigung der sogenannten Täufertestamente" (XII, 342; XIII, 263 ff.), and "Das Täufertestament von 1687" (XIX, 1 ff.). His earlier writings from this journal also appeared in a separate reprint volume under the title, *Beiträge zur Geschichte der bernischen Täufer* (Bern, 1912), including "Der Märtyrerspiegel," "Das Waisenhaus als Täufergefängnis," a valuable example of Bernese persecution in the 1670's, "Das Wiedertäufermandat

vom 9. August 1659" with commentary, and "Die Lötscher von Latterbach" (later changed to Latscha), in which the typical Anabaptist family is excellently characterized. *Die Beziehungen Berns zu den Buchdruckern in Basel, Zürich und Genf, 1476-1536* (Bern, 1913) includes a discussion of the Anabaptist colloquy (*Täufergespräch*) of 1531 and that of 1532 at Zofingen. He wrote the article "Froschauer Bibeln und Testamente" for the MENNONITISCHES LEXIKON (*ML* II, 15), which has been translated and published in this ENCYCLOPEDIA (II, q.v.). A valuable feature of Fluri's work is his thorough bibliographical notation, which presents otherwise unobtainable material. (*ML* I, 658.) E.H.C.

Foam Lake (Sask.) Mennonite Brethren Church, a member of the Canadian Conference of the M.B. Church, was organized in 1938 with 30 members. Until 1945, when a new church was built, the services were conducted in a community hall. Its 1953 membership was 17. Its leaders have been Nick Janz, David Thiessen, Henry Regehr, P. P. Penner, and the present leader Gerhard Petkau. J.H.E.

Fock, an old Mennonite family which has held an influential position among the Dutch Mennonites, has produced outstanding leaders in economics and politics up to the most recent times. In the 18th century its members were among the wealthiest merchants and freighters of Holland. Abraham Fock of Danzig (1695-1759) settled in Amsterdam as a merchant, acquired citizenship in 1723, and became a deacon in the Mennonite church in 1725. From his third marriage with Katharina Fortgens a son Abraham (1732-96) was born, who married Cornelia de Clercq. His son Jakob Fock, b. April 15, 1770, d. Nov. 21, 1835, who was a member of the firm Jakob de Clercq, married Johanna de Bondt. He was a deacon 1797-1803 and 1810-14, and after the Wars of Liberation was made financial adviser to the King of the Netherlands. He was influential in establishing the Bank of Holland, and became its first managing director. He was also the moving spirit in the union between the Lamist and Zonist branches in 1801. His sister Geertruida Margaretha (married to P. Bel) was a deaconess (1804-9).

Jacob's son, Abraham Fock, b. Aug. 2, 1793, d. Sept. 24, 1858, married to Alida Johanna van Heekeren, was also director of the Bank of Holland, a deacon 1820-24 and 1830-34, besides serving as executive officer of the North and South Holland Widows' Fund. Also his three sons, Jakob, Justus Hendrik, and Cornelis, filled important posts in church and in civil life. Jakob, b. May 16, 1817, d. Dec. 9, 1891, married Cecilia Dorothea de Kock, and later her sister Sarah Adriana Dorothea, a close friend of J. G. de Hoop Scheffer (q.v.), and with him set up a fund for the improvement of the salaries of Mennonite preachers. His daughter Cecilia Dorothea (married to J. P. Portielje) was also a deaconess. He was also a director of the Bank of Holland. Justus Hendrik, b. 1826, d. 1911, was a merchant and deacon (1858-62). Cornelis, b. Nov. 29, 1828, d. May 9, 1910, married to Maria Anna Uyttenhoven, was mayor of Vreeland, Wijk-bij-Duurstede, Haarlem and Amsterdam (1866), Minister of the Interior (1868-71), a member of the second chamber, royal commissioner in South Holland (1872-1900), and chief curator of the University of Leyden. Around 1880 he spent much energy in organizing a Mennonite congregation in The Hague, and became its first deacon. Mention should be made of some of his children: Alida Johanna Jakoba, married to J. W. C. Tellegen, mayor of Amsterdam, Cornelis Fock, b. 1871, Rear Admiral and commandant of Den Helder, and Dirk Fock (*q.v.*).   K.V.

D. G. van Epen, *Nederlands Patriciaat* VIII (1917) 148-53; *DB* 1898, 2, 29-31, 36; *ML* I, 658 f.

Fock, Dirk, a Dutch Mennonite lawyer and statesman, b. at Wijk-bij-Duurstede, June 19, 1858, married W. C. C. Doffegnies, earned his degree of LL.D. and Ph.D. at the University of Leiden. He practiced law in Semarang (Java), and served as consul for Austria-Hungary in Batavia. In 1898 he returned to the Netherlands and settled in Rotterdam as adviser on East Indian affairs. Here he was a deacon of the Mennonite congregation. In 1901 he was elected to the local council and the legislature of the province of South Holland. In 1901 he was elected to the Second Chamber of the States-General. In 1905-8 he was Colonial Minister, and 1908-11 governor of Surinam. After his return he was chosen to represent Haarlem in the Second Chamber (1913) and in 1917-20 he was its chairman. In addition he was chairman of the society for the promotion of music. He traveled through China, Japan, and America, and visited Tunisia and Algeria. Many articles from his pen were published in important journals. In 1921-26 he was Governor General of the Dutch East Indies; during his governorship the Indian population acquired greater influence on public affairs than it had had before. On his return to the Netherlands he was elected a member of the First Chamber, 1929-35. In 1928 he was appointed Minister of State, an honorary position without rights or duties. He died at The Hague on Oct. 18, 1941. (*ML* I, 659.)   K.V., vdZ.

Focsen (Foksen, not Focpen as it is sometimes written), **Adriaen Antheunis,** a schoolteacher, one of the Anabaptist *Naaktloopers* (*q.v.*, people who went naked through the streets for religious reasons) at Amsterdam, and was sentenced to death by beheading on Feb. 25, 1535. (Grosheide, *Verhooren*, 57-58; *DB* 1917, 117, No. 63.)   vdZ.

Folk Meetinghouse, built in 1878 in Somerset Co., Pa., former name of the Springs Mennonite Church (*q.v.*).   M.G.

Fonda Mennonite Mission (GCM) station located 8½ miles west and 5 miles north of Canton, Dewey Co., Okla. Work among the Cheyenne Indians in this district was begun by Rodolphe Petter under the Board of Foreign Missions of the General Conference in 1907 as an outstation from Cantonment. From 1913 to 1916 H. Albert Claassen was in charge of Cantonment and Fonda; 1916-21 Fonda was a separate station in charge of H. T. Neufeld. It was supplied from Cantonment by G. A. Linscheid 1921-

38, Benno Toews 1938-40, and from Canton by Arthur Friesen 1940-47, and Alfred Wiebe 1947- . The total number baptized up to 1954 was 332. In 1954 there were 156 members, which included those living around Seiling, Cantonment, Longdale, and Fonda.   A.Wi.

Fondament, *ofte de principaelste liedekens over de poincten des Christelijcken Geloofs* (Haarlem, 1633), is a Dutch Mennonite songbook, of which, however, no copy has been found as yet (*DJ* 1837, 64).
vdZ.

Fonds tot Ondersteuning *van Weduwen en Weezen van Doopsgezinde Predikanten in de Provincien Noord- en Zuid-Holland* (Relief Fund for the Widows and Orphans of Mennonite Ministers in the Provinces of North and South Holland), usually called *Noordhollands Weduwenfonds,* founded at Amsterdam on April 8, 1794. This is the oldest fund of its kind in the Netherlands. The initiative in its founding was taken in 1789 by Ragger Bos, preacher of the Noordeinde van Graft (*q.v.*) congregation, and the question was discussed at the meetings of the Rijper Sociëteit (*q.v.*) in 1791 and 1792. The Fund is supported by contributions made by the member congregations and ministers. In 1844 the Fund, which still is active, was opened to ministers in other provinces of the Netherlands.
vdZ.

Inv. Arch. Amst. I, Nos. 967-85; Blaupot t. C., *Holland* II, 69-70; L. G. le Poole, *Bijdrage tot ... het kerk. Leven onder de Doopsgez. te Leiden* (Leiden, 1905) 244-49.

Fonds tot verhooging *van Doopsgezinde Leeraars tractementen* (Fund for the Raising of the Salaries of Mennonite Ministers) was founded in 1911 and administered by the treasurers of the A.D.S. (Dutch General Mennonite Conference). In the province of Friesland a *Verhogingsfonds* was founded in 1919 by the Friesche Sociëteit (Conference of Mennonite Congregations of Friesland) in order to raise the salaries of the ministers.   vdZ.

Fonds voor Buitenlandsche Nooden (Dutch Relief Fund for Foreign Needs), a substantial relief undertaking of the Dutch Mennonites for the aid of persecuted and suffering foreign brethren. The history of this important fund has not yet been written. The archives of the Mennonite Church in Amsterdam contains several hundred documents, the description of which occupies about 300 printed pages. A few of these were described by A. van Gulik (*DB* 1905, 1906, and 1908), and de Hoop Scheffer wrote an account (*DB* 1869) of the relations between the Fund and Pennsylvania.

The sufferings of the Mennonites in the 17th century in Switzerland, the Palatinate, Poland, and Prussia, usually caused by persecution by the state, induced the Dutch Mennonites to raise collections, e.g., in 1660 for Danzig, 1662 for Poland, 1665 for Moravia, 1672 for Switzerland, 1674 and 1678 for the Palatinate. A persecution of the Palatine brethren in 1690, which was repeated in 1694, was the occasion for taking up two collections by the entire

Amsterdam Mennonite Church, in which 52,279 florins was raised.

In 1709, when the severe persecution in Bern began, the Amsterdam Mennonites invited delegates to meet in a conference in Amsterdam on Feb. 24, 1710. There were delegates from Rotterdam, Leiden, Haarlem, Gouda, Alkmaar, Hoorn, Enkhuizen, Monnikendam, Zaandam, Koog-Zaandijk, Wormerveer, Krommenie, Wormer, Jisp, de Rijp, Graft, and Harlingen. Resolutions were passed: (1) that the Amsterdam representatives (Willem van Maurik, Jan Willink, Abraham Fries, Frans van Aken, Herman Schijn, Jacob Vorsterman, Cornelis Beets), with the support of the Rotterdam delegation (Hendrik Toren and Jan Suderman), Haarlem, Gouda, Hoorn, Alkmaar, Dordrecht, and Monnikendam present a petition to the States-General requesting aid to the Swiss Brethren through diplomatic channels; (2) that the Amsterdam congregation should bear the chief responsibility for the negotiations. But Amsterdam's ensuing attitude gave rise to some dissension, since the delegates of Rotterdam, Leiden, and Haarlem thought the conference had decided that these three congregations were to work together with the Amsterdam representatives. At a second meeting held on Nov. 5, 1710, this disunity was eliminated by the conciliatory talks by Steven Cremer of Deventer. Amsterdam was given the authority to act. If anything unusual should arise, two representatives of the Haarlem, Leiden, Rotterdam, and Zaandam congregations were to be called. In the following year two Frisians were called (Hans Douwens, Sieuwerd Edens) together with Steven Cremer.

Fifty thousand florins was at once collected, letters were sent to Switzerland with intervention made by the mayors of the cities, and correspondence carried on with Runckel (q.v.), the Dutch ambassador in Switzerland. To ensure good management of the funds, the congregations were divided into seven classes:

1. Amsterdam (Lamist), Beverwijk, Emmerich, Middelburg, Vlissingen, Enschede, Cadzand, Zierikzee, Brouwershaven, Rees, Zutphen, Deventer (Flemish), Almelo, and Ameland.

2. Amsterdam (Zon), Hamburg, Zwolle, Uithoorn, Dordrecht, Goes, Brielle, Aardenburg, Kampen, Aalsmeer, Harlingen (Flemish), Blokzijl, Hazerswoude, Zoetermeer, Emden.

3. Alkmaar, Hoorn, Enkhuizen, Medemblik, Monnikendam, Edam, Purmerend, de Rijp, Graft, Westzaan, Koog-Zaandijk, Zaandam-Oost, Zaandam-West, Wormerveer, Uitgeest, Krommeniedijk, Knollendam, Durgerdam, Ilp, Graftdijk, Barsingerhorn, Niedorp, den Hoorn, Burg, Vlieland, Terschelling.

4. All the Frisians in North and South Holland.

5. Haarlem, Leiden, Rotterdam, Schiedam.

6. Harlingen, Leeuwarden, Hindelopen, and Groningen Old Flemish.

7. Deventer, Old Groningen (Danzig Old Flemish), and Jan-Jacobsvolk.

On Aug. 2, 1711, four boats with 400 refugees from Basel arrived at Utrecht. From Amsterdam as headquarters they were sent out to Deventer, Groningen, Hoogezand, Kampen, and Sappemeer. In 1713 another troop of refugees arrived.

In 1714, 10,000 florins was raised for Polish Prussia, and in 1715 and 1717 about 12,000 florins. But since this money was soon spent, it was decided in 1726 to take a general collection for the purpose of establishing a permanent fund. The occasion for this decision was the oppression of 1714 in Polish Prussia, causing many to emigrate to Lithuania, who by 1724 had been compelled to flee again in order to avoid military service. Some fled to Elbing and Thorn in Polish Prussia. In addition there were new complaints from the Palatinate. The general collection of 1727 amounted to over 30,000 florins, that of 1733, 64,000 florins, and 1736, 51,000 florins. In 1734 the Dutch congregations which had not yet contributed raised over 1,000 florins. In a half century more than 270,000 florins were contributed by the Dutch congregations for relief of foreign distress.

The Fund supported many brethren in other lands and saved them from starvation, and enabled three dozen Prussian Mennonites to emigrate to Pennsylvania in 1731, and helped numerous Swiss and Palatine brethren to come to the Netherlands. A twofold colonization of Prussians on Walcheren, an island in Zeeland in 1732, and at Wageningen failed through the inadaptability of the settlers, depleting the Fund by about 50,000 florins. It was therefore decided in 1744 not to assist persons who of their own free choice wished to settle elsewhere, but to give aid only to those who were banished from a country for the sake of their faith, or were impoverished through war, flood, fire, etc.

When the persecution in foreign countries ceased, the Fund ceased to operate. The last meeting was held in 1758. Eleven representatives from Amsterdam were appointed as managers of the Fund. Since for nearly a half century there had been no use for the money, Amsterdam decided to liquidate the Fund. In its name a circular letter was sent to the congregations by P. Lugt and B. de Bosche in March 1803. After voluminous correspondence, about 27½ per cent of the contributions made in earlier years was returned to the congregations in 1803. The sum amounted to about 40,000 florins. (ML I, 659-61.) K.V.

After World War I the situation of the Mennonites in Russia had become very critical; much suffering was caused by the Revolution and civil war. In 1919 the American Mennonites organized shipments of food and clothing and other relief. In Germany the *Mennonitische Hilfskasse* had begun to function. Soon the Dutch Mennonites too became aware of the situation of their Russian brethren through publications in the Mennonite press of America and through letters written by Benjamin H. Unruh (q.v.). The congregations in Holland were informed by the booklet by T. O. Hylkema, *De Geschiedenis van de Doopsgezinde gemeenten in Rusland in de oorlogs- en revolutiejaren 1914-20* (Steenwijk, 1920), and by reports in the Dutch Mennonite weekly, *De Zondagsbode*. On Nov. 7, 1920, a Dutch relief committee was founded, which was named the *Algemeene Commissie voor Buitenlandsche Nooden* on Dec. 8, 1920. The first executive board consisted of Pastor A. Binnertsz Sz of Haarlem, Pres.; D. Woelinga of Vlissingen, Sec.-Treas.; and Pastor T. O. Hylkema of Giethoorn; in March 1921 J. W. van der Vlugt of Haarlem became the treasurer, and in October 1921, Pastor F. C. Fleischer (*q.v.*) secretary. Contacts were made with the MCC, the German *Mennonitische Flüchtlingsfürsorge,* the Quakers in England, and soon also with the Dutch Red Cross. Jacob Koekebakker, then pastor of Middelburg, Zeeland, succeeded in penetrating into Russia and reaching Moscow on Sept. 13, 1921.

In the meantime money had been collected in the Netherlands. Between October and December 1920, the sum of 5,383 Dutch guilders was collected, and in 1921 nearly 22,000 guilders. When relief work ended in February 1924, a total of 239,991 guilders had been collected, besides clothing sent to Russia. In October 1922 a total of 1,576,180 kilograms of food and clothing was shipped from the Netherlands to Sevastopol and distributed among the Mennonites. With the Mennonite committee a number of other organizations co-operated: the Dutch Red Cross contributed 10,000 guilders. F. C. Fleischer visited Ukraine in the spring of 1922 and organized the relief. R. J. C. Willink of Haarlem had charge of the work in Russia, staying there in 1922-23. In the summer of 1922 a children's home was founded at Ohrloff, under the special care of the youth group of Amsterdam. Relief ended in the summer of 1923, when it was no longer possible to get into Russia.

Then another activity was laid upon the Dutch Mennonites. Many Russian Mennonites escaping from Russia came to Holland, hoping to go to America. Many of them stayed for some months in Dutch Mennonite homes. Then in June 1924 the *Hollandsch Doopsgezind Emigranten Bureau* (*q.v.,* Dutch Mennonite Board of Emigration) was founded to aid the Russian refugees in obtaining transportation to the New World. The Board of Emigration was founded by the Mennonite Church of Rotterdam in co-operation with the *Algemeene Commissie voor Buitenlandsche Nooden.* After World War II the *Algemeene Commissie* was replaced (1948) by the *Stichting voor Bijzondere Noden in de Doopsgezinde Broederschap,* which raised funds for relief in Germany and Austria.

vDZ.

W. J. Kühler, "Dutch Mennonite Relief Work in the Seventeenth and Eighteenth Centuries," *MQR* XVII (1943) 87-94; Hiebert and Miller, *Feeding the Hungry; Russian Famine 1919-25* (Scottdale, 1929); archives of the committee, *DJ* 1922, 71, 78-93; 1923, 43-78; 1924, 61-78; A. P. van de Water, "Relief Work in Holland," *Proceedings of the Fourth Menn. World Conf.* (Akron, 1950).

Fontanus, Johannes (1545-1615), an important Reformed preacher and zealous Calvinist, who served at Neuhausen near Worms, Germany, and from 1578 on at Arnhem, Dutch province of Gelderland. Here he opposed the Mennonites and induced the council to take steps to suppress them (March 23, 1591, and regulation of 1596) and forbid their meetings (Nov. 1, 1607, and Aug. 21, 1608). (*DB* 1863, 48 ff.; *ML* I, 661.)   NEFF.

Fontein, a Dutch Mennonite family, which according to a family tradition (which is probably erroneous), had emigrated about 1520 from French Flanders to Friesland (see Blaupot t. C., *Friesland,* 178, note) and lived at Harlingen (*q.v.*) in Friesland; here Jurjen Scheltes Fontein and his son Schelte Jurjens were both burgomaster. It could not be decided whether these two men belonged to the Mennonite Church, but probably they did. Claes Jurjens Fontein, b. 1616 at Harlingen, d. there 1670, a deacon in the church and the son of Schelte, was a sheriff of the city of Harlingen and later its tax collector and steward. Claes's son was Reyner Claesen Fontein, b. 1654 at Harlingen, d. there 1727. He was a well-to-do merchant and owner of a salt work. Besides this he served his home church (Flemish and Waterlander congregation) as a preacher. He was among the founders (1695) of the Friesche Sociëteit (Conference of Friesland). The address delivered by Reyner Claesen in 1719 at Leeuwarden to make peace between the proponents and opponents of baptism by immersion in the Mennonite congregation of Leeuwarden is found in Blaupot t. C., *Friesland,* 319-20. Reyner Claesen was rather liberal, an adherent of Collegiant (*q.v.*) principles (*DB* 1878, 79-86, 90-91). Reyner Claesen Fontein had no sons; his daughter Auckje was married to Dirk Pietersz (1686-1737), a member of the congregation, sheriff of Harlingen, and a saltmaker. This Dirk Pietersz adopted his wife's family name. One of their children was Pieter Fontein (*q.v.*), Mennonite minister of Rotterdam and Amsterdam; another son of Dirk Pietersz was Claes Dirksz Fontein, d. 1787, who was a deacon of the congregation of Harlingen and treasurer of the Friesche Sociëteit 1771-87. His son Feddrik Fontein ab Andla, b. 1736 at Harlingen, d. there 1765, was a physician at Harlingen. Claes Dirksz was married to Grietje Feddriks van Deersum, who was a collateral descendant of the Frisian Andela family (mentioned as early as 1300) and who inherited the stately country-seat of Andla State at Ried near Franeker. She was a daughter of Feddrik Anskes van Deersum, who had been a copreacher of Reyner Claesen Fontein, the grandfather of her husband.

A great-grandson of Dirk Pietersz was Freerk Dirksz Fontein (1777-1843), a merchant or wholesale dealer like most members of this family, living at his country house Salverd near Franeker; he was renowned for his beautiful collections of rare books, engravings, and valuable manuscripts and honored for his studies in history and genealogy by being appointed (1829) member of the *Maatschappij der Nederlandsche Letterkunde* (Association for Dutch Literature) (*N.N.B.Wb.* VI, 518). The Fontein family was related by marriage with other Mennonite families of Harlingen like Braam, Dreyer, Hannema, Huidekoper, Oosterbaan, Stinstra. A lateral branch of this family is found in Franeker, where some Fonteins also served as deacons. vDZ.

Vorsterman van Oyen, *Stam- en Wapenboek* III (Groningen, 1890) 399-406.

Fontein, Pieter, b. 1708 at Harlingen, Dutch province of Friesland, d. Aug. 7, 1788, at Amsterdam, studied theology at the University of Franeker and the Athenaeum and the Remonstrant seminary in

Amsterdam and in 1732 was called as pastor to the United Mennonite Church in Rotterdam. Here he created some trouble in the congregation by his declaration that he did not like the expression *weerloose Doopsgezinden* (nonresistant Mennonites). From 1739 until 1748 he served the Lamist congregation in Amsterdam and then retired to devote his full time to the study of literature. He was a highly respected scholar in Latin and Greek literature and published a number of books in this field. He bequeathed his extensive library to the Amsterdam church; it forms a part of the theological library which the church maintains for the use of students in the Mennonite seminary. In addition he bequeathed 4,000 guilders to the library. He was married to Jozina Stol (d. 1746). K.V.

Inv. Arch. Amst. I, Nos. 2325-26; II, No. 616; Chr. Sepp, *Johannes Stinstra en zijn tijd* I (Amsterdam, 1865) 17, 174-76; II (1866) 258; *DJ* 1840, 113; 1850, 136; *Biogr. Wb.* III, 94-96; K. Vos, *De Doopsgez. te Rotterdam* (1907) 30; *ML* I, 661.

Fonteyn, Thomas, of Haarlem, Dutch province of North Holland, in the first half of the 17th century printed a number of Mennonite books and hymnals, including Soetjen Gerrits, *Een geestelijck Liedtboecxken* (1632) and *Geestelijck Bloem-Hofken* (1637); *Wtganck: ofte Bekeeringhe van Menno Symons . . .* (1633). (*ML* I, 662.) K.V., vdZ.

Fonteyne des Levens, De, is a Dutch devotional book, containing a large number of Scriptural passages, which according to K. Vos (*ML* I, 662) is of Anabaptist origin. There are known three editions of it, printed at Delft, 1533; Steenwijk, 1580; and at Rotterdam, 1619. The third edition, which is found in the Amsterdam Mennonite Library, contains two engravings (*Catalogus Amst.*, 97). It was much used among the Mennonites. Adriaen Carbout and Adriaen Piersen are said (1547) to have traveled on the island of South Beveland, Dutch province of Zeeland, with rucksacks, containing a few tools for the repair of old shoes, but in which were also hidden Bibles, *Fonteynkens des Levens,* and similar books. (*Archief Zeeuwsch Gennotschap* VI, 1886, 38.) vdZ.

Footwashing, also called the "washing of the saints' feet," is observed as an ordinance by most Mennonites in the world today. It is customarily based on the express command and example of Jesus, who washed His disciples' feet at the Last Supper (John 13:1-17), and on the statement by Paul (I Tim. 5:9, 10) that having washed the saints' feet was a qualification for a widow's acceptance into the church widows' group. Rarely has the Old Testament practice of washing the feet of visitors as an act of hospitality toward strangers (Gen. 18:4; 19:2; 24:32; 43:24; Judg. 19:21; I Sam. 25:40, 41) been used to support the practice, except in the early days in Holland, when the practice in some groups was limited to washing the feet of visiting elders and ministers or even of laymen as a sign of affectionate recognition. The most common practice has been and still is to observe the ordinance immediately following the communion service. In the Franconia Conference (MC), where the ordinance was long

out of practice, it is observed at the preparatory service on the day preceding communion. Since most congregations that observe it today celebrate the communion twice a year, in the spring and fall, footwashing also comes twice a year.

The most common mode of the observance is as follows: After the communion service is completed, one of the ministers or deacons reads and comments on John 13:1-17. Basins, usually small wooden or metal tubs, with warm water and towels have meanwhile been provided in sufficient quantity to permit a fairly rapid observance. These are placed, either in the front of the church or in the "amen" corners, and in the "ante-rooms," or in some cases in the rows between the benches. The sexes then wash (more properly rinse or lightly touch with water) feet separately in pairs, concluding with the greeting of the holy kiss and a "God bless you." In some localities towels are furnished in the form of short aprons to be tied by cords around the waist, in presumed imitation of Jesus "girding himself," though most commonly ordinary towels are used. In some congregations the practice is not pair-washing but row-washing, in which case each person washes the feet of his right-hand neighbor in turn in a continuous chain (United Missionary Church, some G.C.M. congregations). In the Church of God in Christ Mennonite group the ministers wash each other's feet first, and then wash the feet of all the brethren in turn, the ministers' wives doing the same for the sisters.

Although the interpretation of the ordinance may vary, it is always held to be symbolical of a spiritual lesson, and is never considered to have any religious value *per se,* or to be a "good work." The most common interpretation is that it teaches humility and equality. Often the lesson of service is included along with the other meanings. In some instances it has been and is observed as a symbol of the daily sanctification which is needed by the Christian as he comes into contact with sin and temptation.

Among the North American Mennonite groups the observance varies. The following groups practice it universally, following the communion service: Mennonite Church (MC), Conservative Mennonite Church, Old Order Amish, Evangelical Mennonites, Evangelical Mennonites (Kleine Gemeinde), Reformed Mennonites, Mennonite Brethren in Christ, United Missionary Church, Krimmer Mennonite Brethren, Church of God in Christ Mennonites. The Mennonite Brethren formerly universally observed the ordinance, but now in the United States the number is 85-90 per cent of the congregations, while in Canada only a minority do so. Among the General Conference Mennonites only a small minority of the congregations practice footwashing, depending upon the background of each congregation. A study by S. F. Pannabecker in 1929 showed that of 107 G.C.M. congregations in the United States, 23 encouraged it. Of the 23, the Western District had 10, the Northern District 8. Since then the number has decreased. An official conference study in 1943 showed that then 9 congregations made it obligatory, while 14 encouraged it. The Evangelical Mennonite Brethren, who formerly practiced it universally, have almost completely dropped it. The

Lower Skippack Mennonite Church (Johnson Mennonite) withdrew from the Eastern District Conference (GCM) in 1861 because it observed footwashing, while the conference refused to make it mandatory. The Evangelical Mennonites and the Mennonite Brethren in Fernheim Colony, Paraguay, also practice footwashing.

It is customary in the Mennonite Church (MC) and related groups to have a collection for the alms fund or charity fund in connection with the footwashing service. Usually the contributions are placed in the collection plate by the members individually upon completion of the footwashing ceremony.

The History of the Ordinance: Pre-Reformation Times. In the time of Jesus it was customary for the host to make provision for the washing of the feet of guests (Luke 7:44-46), but without religious significance. Jesus gave the rite religious significance and told His disciples, "Ye also ought to wash one another's feet. For I have given you an example, that ye should do as I have done to you" (John 13:14, 15). Paul's report in I Cor. 11 concerning the observance of the communion does not mention footwashing, but this is no absolute proof that it was not practiced in Corinth. The widows' washing of "the saints' feet" (I Tim. 5:10) is clearly a rite performed only for church members, but no indication is given of when or how often it was to be done. Apparently the widows had a special office or function in the church which included this duty. The implication is that they washed the feet of others, possibly visiting brethren and sisters, rather than practicing a universal mutual ordinance.

Tertullian (145-220) of North Africa in his *De Corona* is the first Church Father to indicate that footwashing was practiced in his time, but he gives no clue as to by whom or how. Ambrose of Milan (340-97) states that it was not the practice of the Roman Church, but endorses it as a symbol of sanctification. Augustine mentions it as being rejected by some. Knight (p. 816) says flatly that footwashing always remained "a purely local peculiarity, introduced at an early date into some parts of the Catholic Church, but never universal." Among the monks in particular, the hospitality custom of footwashing was widely practiced, and often in the name of Christ, but not as a universal ordinance of the church. For the monks the observance was often intended to express humility. St. Benedict's *Rule* (A.D. 529) for the Benedictine Order prescribed hospitality footwashing in addition to a communal footwashing for humility.

The ordinance of footwashing persisted down through the Middle Ages, with varied interpretations and applications, more prevalent in the East than in the West. The Roman Church finally observed the practice only as a part of the liturgical festivities of the Holy Week (Maundy Thursday), not as a sacrament, while the Greek Church recognized it as a sacrament, but seldom practiced it. When practiced outside the monastery, it was gradually taken away from the laity and made a pompous ceremony for state officials and clergy. It was frequently observed at coronations of kings and emperors, and installation of popes and archbishops. As late as the 18th century it was a common feature of Maundy Thursday in European Courts, and there are references to it in Bavaria and Austria as late as 1912. Monastic footwashing is still practiced in both Roman and Greek churches.

The Albigenses and Waldenses, two medieval sects which arose in Southern France in the 11th and 12th centuries, apparently observed footwashing as a religious rite. The Albigenses observed it following the communion service. Among the Waldenses it was the custom to wash the feet of visiting ministers, but there is no evidence of the practice of the ordinance by the members. The Bohemian Brethren or Hussites also practiced it, at least in the 16th century. The ordinance was not introduced into the new Reformation state churches, but it was adopted by the Anabaptists.

Anabaptist-Mennonite Practice. From the beginning (1525-35) some Anabaptists practiced footwashing, but it was not universal. It was most common in Holland and the related or descendant groups in Northwest Germany, West and East Prussia, and Russia. It was not practiced by the Swiss Brethren or Hutterites, nor by the 16th-century Anabaptists in South and Central Germany, with rare exceptions. Hubmaier (d. 1528) practiced footwashing at least once in his early (1525) Anabaptist congregation at Waldshut, but does not mention the ordinance in any of his writings. Sebastian Franck in 1531 (*Chronica*) mentions the practice as observed among some of the Swiss Brethren. William Gay claims (in an unpublished M.A. thesis of 1947 at Columbia University), though without giving documentary proof, "Among the various Anabaptist sects which sprang up all over Western Europe early in the 16th century, . . . footwashing as a sacramental act of communal humility was practiced almost universally at one time or another. The rite fitted in well with their tendency toward communalism, their Biblical fundamentalism, and their emphasis on self-effacing equalitarianism among the members. Often the ceremony was done in connection with a 'complete' observance of the Last Supper, with the *agape* and the communion itself following mutual footwashing, segregated according to sex."

If the practice was prevalent at the beginning in Switzerland and South Germany (and there is no proof of this), it must have died out very soon. There is no mention of it in the Schleitheim Confession (1527) or the Peter Riedemann Hutterite confession (1545) or in any other known source except in the writings of Pilgram Marpeck (*ca.* 1495-1556). Marpeck's great book of *ca.* 1542 (*Verantwortung*) makes repeated mention of footwashing as a Christian ordinance on a par with other ordinances. The first edition of the *Ausbund* (n.p., 1564) contains a hymn of 25 stanzas (No. 42 in the 1742 first American edition, pp. 692-700) for use at the observance of the ordinance, still used by the Old Order Amish.

Wappler (*Thüringen,* 128) reports a case of footwashing observed among the Thuringian Anabaptists in 1535 (see also **Halberstadt**). The leader of a group conducted a communion service, before which he washed the feet of all the 16 participants and greeted them with a kiss. Bullinger claims there was a group called "Apostolic" Anabaptists who practiced footwashing. This is possibly the ultimate source of a statement by E. Daniel Colberg which names an "apostolic" Anabaptist sect, "also called footwashers, who had as their ancestor Matth. Servatus" (Servaes?). Colberg adds, "modern Anabaptists are almost all footwashers as Joh. Hoornbeek has shown from their writings," probably meaning the Mennonites in North Germany and Holland.

Menno Simons (1496-1561) mentions the practice twice in his *Complete Writings,* but only as a hospitable practice and not as a church ordinance. However, his colleague, Dirk Philips (1504-68), gives detailed teaching on footwashing as an ordinance in his *Enchiridion* of 1564 (English edition, Elkhart, 1910, pp. 388-90). His treatment reveals careful and serious thought and exhorts vigorously to its practice. There is nothing like this treatment in any other 16th-century Anabaptist writing. It was practiced in general by the Dutch Mennonites in the 16th and early 17th centuries.

The first direct evidence that footwashing was practiced as a general ordinance in Holland is found at the time of the division of the Danziger Old Flemish *ca.* 1635 from the Groningen Old Flemish. The Groningen group required the observance in connection with the communion service, while the Danzigers required it only for visiting elders who came from other districts to administer baptism and communion. For these the ordinance was to be observed in the house in which they were guests.

Out of the 19 confessions of faith produced by European Anabaptists and Mennonites from 1527 to 1874, 12 speak of the ordinance of footwashing as a Christian practice, while 9 omit it altogether. The first one to mention it (Dutch Waterlander Confession of 1577) indicates that it is to be done for visitors from a distance, particularly refugees, but is not prescribed as a church ordinance for a worship service. The same is true for the *Concept of Cologne* (1591), the Twisck 33 Articles of about 1615, and the George Hansen Flemish Confession of 1678 (Danzig area). All the other seven which mention it (Olive Branch of 1627 in Holland, Dordrecht 18 Articles of 1632, Jan Centsen of 1630 in Holland, the first Prussian confession of 1660, the Prussian confession of G. Wiebe of 1792, and the confession adopted in Russia in 1874 by the Mennonite Brethren) treat it as a general ordinance of the church. The Cornelis Ris' Dutch Confession of 1773 does not mention it, probably because it was already dying out in Holland. The widely used Elbing-Waldeck catechism of 1778 includes it, as does the Russian Mennonite catechism of 1870.

The Alsatian congregations which adopted the Dordrecht Confession in 1660 were probably the channel for the adoption of the same confession with its footwashing article by the Amish schismatic group which originated 1693-97 in Switzerland. The Amish have ever since been fully committed to footwashing and in fact were distinguished from the other Mennonites of Switzerland, France, the Palatinate, and South Germany by it, since the latter did not practice it. The Northwest German Mennonites,

being closely related to the Dutch Mennonites, followed them both in the observance earlier and in discarding it in the 18th and 19th centuries.

The decline of the practice among the European Mennonites who had earlier practiced it had set in by the 17th century in Holland. N. van der Zijpp supplies the following account of the history of the practice in Holland.

"While in course of time the practice among the Waterlanders soon fell into decline—it is not mentioned in the ordinances of the Waterlander churches of 1581—it was maintained for some time, though not after 1640, by the Frisian, Flemish, and High German congregations. (In the Hamburg congregation under Dutch influence the question arose in 1628 whether footwashing should be maintained or not; see *Inv. Arch. Amst.* I, 576.) But among the conservative Old Flemish and Old Frisians in the 17th century it was again more earnestly practiced. Among them, and also among the Jan Jacobsgezinden and other *Fijne Mennisten* (*q.v.*), it became a church practice observed in connection with the Lord's Supper. So it was still in 1741, when Simon F. Rues visited several Dutch churches among the Groningen Old Flemish (Rues, 53 f.). (A pictorial illustration of footwashing as practiced in the Groningen Old Flemish congregation of Zaandam is found in Schijn's *Geschiedenis* of 1743.)

"In this same way footwashing was performed 'publicly in the meeting,' as Rues says, among the Old Frisians and also among the Swiss Mennonites who had immigrated to Holland about 1711. The Swiss in Holland practiced it until 1805. Most Old Frisians had abandoned it by 1770, and most Groningen Old Flemish by 1800, though in some of their congregations it was performed until 1815.

"Among the Danzig Old Flemish Mennonites (*q.v.*) footwashing was not practiced in the meetinghouse in connection with the Lord's Supper, but in the older hospitable form, i.e., to a visiting preacher or elder. The ceremony was performed at his arrival, or in the evening, the host washing the guest's feet in the room in which the guest lodged. It was also done to new members who had come from other places (Rues, 19). The practice was continued among this group until about 1780, when the last Danziger Old Flemish congregation died out. In the 19th century footwashing in the old form (to visiting elders) was performed only in four Dutch congregations: Giethoorn, Ameland, Aalsmeer, and Balk. Since 1854 no footwashing has been practiced in Holland."

Footwashing died out among the French and South German Mennonites of Amish background much more slowly than elsewhere. The last observance in Luxembourg was in 1939. There are still five congregations in France which practice it: Birkenhof, Diesen, Haute-Marne, Meuse, and Montbeliard.

Clarence Hiebert (S.T.B. Thesis, Biblical Seminary, 1954) comments upon the decline of footwashing in Europe as folows: "The decline of this practice was due largely to secularization and compromising influences in the church. Along with the loss of this practice European Mennonitism has gradually lost almost all beliefs that were once distinctive to them. In America, footwashing was rigidly observed by most Mennonite groups, the form and mode being more uniform than it ever was in Europe." Hiebert speculates further as to the causes for the decline, suggesting five reasons.

"1. The ridiculing of the peculiar beliefs of the Mennonites and their emphasis on the 'fringe doctrines' rather than the cardinal beliefs stimulated them to question some of their literalistic practices. Many abandoned this practice as a result of re-examination of their beliefs, in favor of the more cardinal emphases.

"2. The literal interpretation of the Johannine footwashing narrative had never been satisfactory to all. The spiritual concept came to be emphasized as being sufficient without the external act.

"3. The influence of the larger denominations upon the Mennonites played no little part in bringing about compromises in their traditional beliefs. This was especially true in Holland, where the Reformed and the Mennonite churches often united.

"4. The liberal tendencies which began in the 18th century, especially through the Mennonite Seminary in Amsterdam, were influential in changing the entire church.

"5. Because the more conservative element was constantly emigrating in the 19th century from Germany and France in search of religious freedom, the liberalizing tendencies gained the upper hand.

"Other reasons could be listed, but these are the cardinal factors and suggest the trend of European Mennonitism."

Russia. Here, according to P. M. Friesen (*Brüderschaft,* 40, 82), the Flemish group observed the ordinance in connection with the communion, while the stricter of the Frisians practiced the observance in the home of the minister when a guest minister arrived. Specifically the Gnadenfeld and Alexanderwohl congregations were among those that observed the ordinance at communion. Among Bernhard Harder's (1832-84) poems, published in 1888 at Hamburg as *Geistliche Lieder,* was one written to be sung at the footwashing service. Its dominant emphasis is that of cleansing from "sin which collects like dust" in men's souls. All the schismatic groups in Russia, Kleine Gemeinde (1812), Mennonite Brethren (1860), and Krimmer M.B. (1869), continued the practice. The observance was brought to North America by all these groups and the Mennonite congregations as well which had practiced it there. The Swiss-Alsatian Amish in Volhynia also brought the practice with them.

North America. The first documentary evidence of the observance of footwashing in North America is found in a document of *ca.* 1775 relating to the Martin Boehm case, in which the leaders of the Lancaster Conference specifically refer to the ordinance of footwashing as commanded by Christ to show humility. John Herr, the founder of the Reformed Mennonite Church in 1812, describes the Lancaster Mennonite group as having declined greatly and states, "The washing of feet, if not rejected, was at least practically omitted for many years" (Funk, 13). By contrast Funk (p. 114) quotes a letter of an aged member in 1878 who specifically recalled that Bishop Jacob Hostetler's (bishop 1831-65) charge to the bishops he ordained included the administration of footwashing. The Lancaster Conference hymnal, *Unpartheyisches Gesangbuch* (1804), contained one hymn (p. 117) to be used during footwashing, and the first English Mennonite hymnal, *A Collection of Psalms, Hymns and Spiritual Songs* (Mountain Valley, Va., 1847), contained three (pp. 288-91). A pamphlet published in 1859 at Berlin, Ont., written by Ulrich Steiner (?), was devoted exclusively to footwashing (*Fusswaschung und Deutung derselben*).

The strange deviation in the Franconia Conference from this general practice of the Mennonite Church is unexplainable. The Dordrecht Confession, first printed in English in 1712 for the Germantown group, and adopted in 1725 by a conference of all the congregations in America at that time (printed at Philadelphia in 1727), has a specific and strict article on footwashing. Yet J. C. Wenger reports, "It appears that until a generation or so ago what is now the Skippack bishop district was the only one which observed Feet-Washing" (*Franconia,* 34). This is supported by the fact that the Franconia Conference hymnal *Die Kleine Geistliche Harfe* (1803), in contrast to the Lancaster hymnal, had no footwashing hymn. Only gradually did the observance spread after 1900, particularly when Henry S. Bower, a preacher, and the noted bishop Andrew Mack put his influence behind it. "As late as 1917," says Wenger (p. 105), the conference admonished the ministers "to teach the subject of footwashing more earnestly, so that it may be more generally observed." But there are some facts on the other side. The letter of Andreas Ziegler *et al.* to Holland in 1773, written on behalf of the Franconia Conference, inquires "whether you keep up the observance of footwashing" (*Franconia,* 401), thus implying the observance in Franconia at that time.

It is interesting to note that the Oberholtzer group, which broke away from the Franconia Conference in 1847, according to Hiebert, for a time after their initial organization continued the practice of footwashing in connection with the communion service. In 1851, four years later, they decided the observance should not be compulsory, and in 1853 it was made an optional practice with complete freedom in the local congregation. Finally, in 1855 it was no longer recognized as a church ceremony. A spiritual interpretation of the passage (John 13) was agreed upon at the 1859 conference. The Lower Skippack congregation, which intended to continue the observance of the ordinance, thus came into conflict with the conference. Henry G. Johnson, the bishop, was declared out of order by the conference in 1859, and formally excommunicated in 1861, taking most of the congregation with him. Lower Skippack has continued as an independent congregation to this day. J. C. Wenger (*Franconia,* 360) suggests that the conference may have originally adopted footwashing to meet the demands of Johnson who was a strong advocate of it, but without any connection with a general practice by the body as a whole.

Footwashing has been introduced into the foreign mission fields of the American Mennonite groups in accord with the constituency.

The following other North American denominations are among those which still observe footwashing as a standard ordinance: Church of the Brethren, Brethren Church, Grace Brethren Church, Brethren in Christ, and a number of minor Baptist bodies. The Moravian Brethren practiced it until 1818 when it was discontinued by act of the Moravian Synod.

There is no uniformity in the writing of the term "footwashing." Five other forms often used are: foot washing, foot-washing, feetwashing, feet washing, and feet-washing. The initial letters "F" and "W" are sometimes also written in captials.

Much of the material of this article has been drawn (and sometimes directly quoted) from Clarence Hiebert's thorough unpublished S.T.B. thesis of 1954 at the Biblical Seminary in New York, entitled "The History of the Ordinance of Feet-Washing in the Mennonite Churches with a Survey of the Pre-Reformation Evidences of This Practice." Daniel Graber's unpublished paper (1952) at the Mennonite Biblical Seminary in Chicago, entitled "The History of the Ordinance of Feet-Washing as Observed by the Mennonites," was also of service. The items in the following bibliography were all (with one exception) taken from the very extensive bibliographical section of Hiebert's paper. H.S.B.

Books. P. Bergstrasser, *Baptism and Feetwashing* (Phila., 1896); George R. Brunk, *Ready Scriptural Reasons* (Scottdale, 1926); E. Daniel Colberg, *Das Platonisch-Hermetische Christentum* (Leipzig, 1710); A. W. Dale, *The Synod of Elvira and Christian Life in the Fourth Century* (London, 1882); "Foot-washing" in McClintock and Strong's *Cyclopedia of Biblical, Theological and Ecclesiastical Literature* (N.Y., 1891); J. F. Funk, *The Mennonite Church and Her Accusers* (Elkhart, 1878); William Gay, "The Origin and Historical Practice of Foot-Washing as a Religious Rite in the Christian Church" (unpublished M.A. thesis at Columbia University under the Faculty of the Union Theological Seminary in N.Y., 1947); John Horsch, *Mennonites in Europe* (Scottdale, 1942); Daniel Kauffman, *Doctrines of the Bible* (Scottdale, 1949); G. A. F. Knight, "Feetwashing," *Encyclopedia of Religion and Ethics V* (N.Y., 1912) 814-23; D. W. Kurtz, "Washing of Feet," *International Standard Bible Encyclopedia V* (Chicago, 1915); A. Malvy, "Lavement des Pieds," *Dictionnaire de Theologie Catholique IX* (Paris, 1926) cols. 16-36; Alexander Mack, Appendix to *The Refuted Anabaptist* (Ephrata, 1788); S. F. Pannabecker, "The Development of the General Conference of the Mennonite Church of North America in the American Environment" (unpublished Ph.D dissertation at Yale University, 1914); S. F. Rues, *Tegenwoordige Staet* (Amsterdam 1745); H. Schijn, *Geschiedenis dier Christenen welke . . . Mennoniten genaamd worden I* (Amsterdam, 1743); George Smoker, "Permanent Principles Implicit in the Ancient Christian Rite of Feetwashing," unpublished S.T.B. thesis at the Biblical Seminary in New York (1940); Herbert Thurston, "Washing of Feet and Hands," *Catholic Encyclopedia XV* (N.Y., 1913); Johann Ursinus, *Historisch- und Theologischer Bericht vom Unterschied der Religionen Heutiges Tags auf Erden und Welches der Waare Allein-Seligmachende Glaube Sey* (Nürnberg, 1663); J. C. Wenger, *History of the Mennonites of the Franconia Conference* (Telford, Pa., 1938); C. F. Yoder, *God's Means of Grace* (Elgin, 1908).

Periodicals, Articles, and Pamphlets. B. W. Bacon, "The Sacrament of Footwashing," *Expository Times* XLIII (1931-32) 218-21; E. J. Berkey, "Is Feet-Washing a Command" (tract, Scottdale, *ca.* 1905); *Feet-washing* (tract, Scottdale, *ca.* 1910); S. F. Coffman, "Christian Ordinances: Feet Washing," "*Christian Monitor* XLIV

(Scottdale, 1952) 206-7, 240-41, 245, 276-77; Walter Fleming, "The Religious and Hospitable Rite of Feet Washing," *Sewanee Review* (January 1908); Jacob H. Janzen, *Fusswaschung und Abendmahl* (Winnipeg, n.d.); U.[lrich] S.[teiner], *Fusswaschung und Deutung derselben* (Berlin, Ont., 1859); *ML* II, 22-24.

Foppe Ones, b. Oct. 22, 1626, at Ameland, an island in the Dutch province of Friesland, was baptized at Ballum by the elder Teunis Abes, was chosen as preacher on Jan. 24, 1665, and ordained as elder on Jan. 13, 1664, by Cornelis Jansen and Teunis Abes, d. Jan. 27, 1696. His son One Foppes, b. Oct. 4, 1658, was ordained preacher of the Flemish congregation on Jan. 4, 1704. In about 1670 a group of Mennonites separated from the Jan Jacobsz wing of the Flemish in Ameland and organized the Foppe Ones congregation. The library at Amsterdam has in manuscript a "spiritual song" by Cornelis Hiddes on the subject. This division existed until the beginning of the 19th century. It was also known as the Lausoms branch and had churches in Nes and Ballum. In 1804 it had only 99 members, and decided to unite with the Jan Jacobsz group, which numbered 432 members. K.V.

J. Loosjes, "Jan Jacobsz en de Jan-Jacobsgezinden," in *Ned. Arch. voor Kerkgesch.* XI (1914) 216-18; *DB* 1889, 11 ff., 18 f.; 1890, 26 ff.; *ML* I, 662.

Foraker (Ind.) United Missionary Church originated in 1890 when revivals were conducted in the Swoveland Schoolhouse, in Union Township, by such leaders in the Indiana Conference as Daniel Brenneman and Andrew Good. A few years later, when the new village of Foraker was formed a mile and a half away with its post office and railway station, a church was built there, and a congregation organized in 1920. The total membership reported in 1952 was 73, with Jesse A. Beery serving as pastor. J. A. Hu.

Foreign Mission Board of the General Conference Mennonite Church. One of the main reasons for the organization of the General Conference in 1860 was to give opportunity for expression of the growing interest in missions. Even before the organization of this conference various groups were interested in the Dutch Mennonite missions in Java and Sumatra. At the first meeting of the conference two mission treasuries were created, and at the third meeting of the conference another was added, so that the western, central, and eastern groups each had their own treasurer.

At the fourth session of the conference in 1868, the Central Mission Society of the United Mennonites of America was created and instructed to support the work of the Dutch Mennonites in Java, but also to educate young American Mennonite men in preparation for conference mission work. At the sixth session of the General Conference, 1872, the above society was dissolved and a Foreign Mission Board composed of five members was created. In 1878 the various mission treasuries were consolidated.

In order to prepare ministers and missionaries the conference established the Wadsworth school, which opened its doors in 1868. One of the students, Samuel S. Haury, decided to enter mission service and in 1871 applied to the Mennonite Mission Society at Amsterdam. In 1872 the conference decided to support Haury while in school and asked that he put himself under the direction of the conference Mission Board. This he did, and in 1875 after completing his studies at the Barmen Mission School in Germany, he returned to America to be ordained as the first conference missionary.

The first field considered was Java and Sumatra; however, since no satisfactory basis of co-operation with the Amsterdam Society presented itself, Haury was asked to visit the churches and look for a field among the American Indians or elsewhere. Several Indian tribes were visited and Quaker missionaries among them were consulted. In 1879 Haury, accompanied by J. B. Baer, visited Alaska and conferred with Presbyterian missionaries there. After a second visit to various Indians, accompanied by three board members, Haury finally began mission work in 1880 among the Arapahoe tribe at Darlington, Indian Territory.

In 1884 work was begun among the Cheyenne tribe. In 1891 Rodolphe Petter arrived on the field and in time became an internationally recognized philologist, reducing the Cheyenne language to writing, building a dictionary, and translating the Bible and other books into Cheyenne. In 1893 work among the Hopi tribe was begun. Much of H. R. Voth's Hopi material was later published with profuse illustrations in eleven volumes by the Stanley McCormick Hopi Expedition, Field Columbian Museum, and much of his Hopi collection was placed on permanent exhibition in some 20 large cases in the Field Museum, Chicago. Nearly 90 persons have served as missionaries in some capacity among the Indians. During the first decade only about 20 converts were won. The total number baptized among the three tribes in Oklahoma, Arizona, and Montana since the beginning is about 800.

The work in India began in 1899 when David Goerz arrived with relief supplies and instructions to look for a mission field. The pioneer missionaries, P. A. Penner and J. F. Kroeker and their wives, came in 1900. The field is in the former Central Provinces, an area of about 8,000 square miles with a population of about 1,200,000. In 1950 there were 15 organized congregations in the India field with a membership of over 3,500, some 25 schools with about 1,300 pupils, 2 orphanages with a capacity of 80 each, a widows' home, 2 hospitals and 6 dispensaries with some 13,000 new and some 10,000 return patients per year, and a recognized leper asylum with a capacity of 500, in which more than 3,400 lepers have been cared for. Some 230 native workers were being employed and more than 40 missionaries had given some service on 5 stations: Champa, Janjgir, Mauhaudi, Korba, and Jagdeeshpur.

The work in China was begun by Mr. and Mrs. H. J. Brown in 1909 and taken over by the Foreign Mission Board in 1914. The field was in southern Hopei province, about 40 by 100 miles, with a population of over 2,200,000. In 1940 there were 40 preaching places, 24 congregations, 125 native workers, and a church membership of about 2,300, 2 high schools, 60 grade schools with an enrollment of over 2,300, a hospital, 2 dispensaries with over 3,500 patients and over 52,000 registered treatments per year. About 30 missionaries have given some service in this field. With the Japanese invasion and the coming of the Communists the work was seriously hindered. In 1950 Chinese Christians were carrying on as best they could while the few remaining missionaries moved to the interior to open a new field in Szechwan, where the work was just beginning. But shortly all missionaries were compelled to leave the field.

For a number of years the Foreign Mission Board has co-operated with the Congo Inland Mission (q.v.) in Africa. In 1947 work was started in Colombia, South America, mainly with untainted leper children. Eight workers are there at present.

Much credit for the high standard of work by the Foreign Mission Board belongs to J. W. Kliewer and P. H. Richert, who for many years served as president and secretary respectively of the board. Kliewer was president of the board from 1908 to 1930. In about 1916 the board published *A Manual for Missionaries* covering various aspects of the subject. Regarding educational qualifications it states: "It is regarded as essential that a missionary have a good college education and at least some work in a good theological seminary or other graduate school." In more recent years this standard has not been adhered to. For the fiscal year 1949-50 the budget of the board was $255,000. Over 200 missionaries have rendered service under the Mission Board and in 1950 there were about 97 active in the five fields mentioned above.

In 1950 the General Conference session merged the Foreign Mission Board and the Home Mission Board into a Board of Missions of 12 members.

E.G.K.

Ed. G. Kaufman, *The Development of the Missionary and Philanthropic Interest Among the Mennonites of North America* (Berne, 1931).

Foreign Missions Committee of the Conference of the Krimmer Mennonite Brethren Church (headquarters at Hillsboro, Kan.) was chartered on Oct. 5, 1901, as the Missionary Board of the Krimmer M.B. Church. The original charter was signed by John Esau, Cornelius Thiessen, Peter A. Wiebe, John J. Friesen, and David E. Harder. Out of this developed gradually the Foreign Missions Committee with a missions emphasis, now composed of nine members elected for three-year periods, three being elected every year. The purpose of the organization as stated in the charter is "to carry on Home and Foreign Mission work in the preaching of the Gospel and advancing education and to secure and administer the funds necessary thereto." The committee is responsible to the conference and its current annual budget is $48,000. Thirty-three missionaries are supported at present on 5 continents and in 12 countries. The first station was opened among the Negroes at Elk Park, N.C., in 1901. The same year H. C. Bartel went to the Shantung and Honan Provinces of China and soon organized the China Mennonite Mission Society (q.v.). The committee is not exclusive but sends missionaries to fields under other boards where it has no work of its own. Reports are found in the yearbooks of the K.M.B. Conference, *Der Wahrheitsfreund* (now extinct), and *The Christian Witness,* the present church organ. C.F.P.

Forestry Service (*Forsteidienst*), the alternative service rendered in lieu of military duty by the Russian Mennonites. In 1874 universal conscription was introduced in Russia. The proposal to pass such a measure, which was announced in 1870, was a cause of great concern to the Mennonites, who at all costs wanted to remain true to their principle of nonresistance, a privilege promised them when they immigrated. They sent deputation after deputation to St. Petersburg to secure release from military duty. When this effort seemed to be futile, the great emigration of Russian Mennonites ensued.

But the authorities, who had learned to appreciate the Mennonites as competent farmers and as an important cultural asset, did not want to lose the contributions this group was making to the cultivation of the land. The government therefore proposed to the Mennonites a system of release from military service by service (1) in the shops of the Navy Department; (2) in fire companies, or (3) in mobile companies in the Forestry Department. Service in the medical corps, which had been considered by the government committees, was rejected by the Mennonites on the grounds that in time of war the medical corps was directly involved in the war effort. The third of the proposed systems was accepted. The Mennonites now planned to keep their young men together in large groups in order to provide pastoral care for them and to keep them from foreign influence. They accordingly sent a deputation to St. Petersburg with a petition to allow them to render their alternative service in fixed forestry companies under civilian government authority, and as much as possible in the neighborhood of a Mennonite settlement.

In June 1880, after lengthy negotiations, Councillor Bark informed the Mennonite elders of the decision: Mennonite young men under military obligations would be employed in the forests of South Russia; but the Mennonites were to assume the expense of building the barracks and also provide for the food and clothing of the companies. In return the government would pay each young man in service 20 kopeks per working day. On Sept. 19, 1880, the plan became obligatory for all the Mennonites of Russia. Six barracks were to be built within three years. In the spring of 1881 the first young men were drafted into forestry service. Soon two additional barracks were built and in the course of time the "Phylloxera" company was added.

All matters of the forestry service were regulated on the Mennonite side by the "Delegate Meeting for Forestry Service Affairs." Its executive officer was called the "Forestry President" or simply "President." It was his duty to settle all questions with the government, to provide for the welfare of the men in service, and to be in charge of the economic affairs of the companies. Each company had an "Oekonom-Prediger," who was usually known as

"Papa" by the men in service; he had charge of the material care of the companies and the pastoral care.

The assignment and supervision of the jobs was taken care of by government officials. Each forestry unit had a forester with the rank of captain, and an assistant, usually with the rank of lieutenant. From the ranks of the men in service an "elder" was chosen with the rank of a noncommissioned officer, and several corporals. Usually these persons were appointed by the forester after suggestion by the departing elder; but sometimes they were also elected by majority vote, and then proposed to the forester for appointment. Neither the elder nor the corporals received from the men in service any military salute or other military honor. The elder had the duty of assigning and supervising the jobs of the company and preserving discipline in the barracks. Every evening he had to give a report to the forester or his assistant on the work done; the corporals supervised the smaller subdivisions and jobs of the company.

The object of these forestry units was to plant forests on a large scale in the steppes of South Russia, to lay out nurseries, and to raise model orchards. Every year many improved trees both for fruit and for forests were given free of charge to the Russians living in the neighborhood to create in them a desire to plant orchards and woods.

The work of the Phylloxera units, which served principally in Crimea and were active only six months in the year (whereas the other companies received only a few weeks or at most three months of vacation in winter), consisted in finding and exterminating the aphid Phylloxera in the vineyards. The men in service were not called soldiers, but in the records were designated as "obligatory workers." Detailed annual reports of the forestry service were published in German and Russian, e.g., *Jahresbericht des Bevollmächtigten der Mennonitengemeinden in Russland in Sachen der Unterhaltung der Forstkommandos im Jahre 1907.* A.B.

In 1917 a change was made in the management of forestry service in so far as they concerned the Mennonites. During World War I about 14,000 Mennonites had been mobilized, about half of whom were engaged in forestry service. These 7,000 forestry workers were scattered into all parts of Russia, in larger and small groups.

During the Revolution and the movement for freedom that initially accompanied it there was also enthusiastic and extensive activity in organization in these groups. This circumstance, as well as the fact that providing for the men in service had been made difficult by the rise in the cost of living and the scattered state of the units, led to the appointment by the meeting of the delegates of the Mennonite congregations, together with the delegates of the men in service, held at Halbstadt in August 1917 of a committee for the management of forestry matters, with the shortened name "Iksume" (Executive committee of the delegate meeting of the Mennonite congregations). The first chairman of the committee was the former president. The committee provided for the preservation of the economic and legal interests of the men in service, which had become very difficult in the impoverished state of affairs in the throes of the revolution; it had become necessary to

24

draft and harness all the forces on which the committee had its historical basis. A further task of the committee was to keep an account with regard to the care of clothing and traveling of the various forestry committees and the individuals still in service after demobilization in 1918.

In consequence of the unstable political conditions in 1918-19 any orderly operation of the forestry service became impossible. When business operation of the units, which was in some places quite profitable, was threatened, the Mennonites proceeded to liquidate the forestry units, without, however, wanting to give up the forestry service as such as a matter of principle. For the purpose of this liquidation committee members were now and then delegated, who succeeded, often at the danger of their life, in disposing advantageously of the stock of cattle, products, equipment, and materials; only in a few minor cases had the forestry services already been plundered by the surrounding population. Thus the forestry service was abandoned and not resumed. **T.B.**

Friesen, *Brüderschaft;* Abr. Görz, *Ein Beitrag zur Geschichte des Forstdienstes der Mennoniten in Russland* (Gross-Tokmak, 1907); Jacob Sudermann, "Origin of Mennonite State Service in Russia 1870-80," *MQR* XVII (1943) 23-46; F. C. Peters, "Non-Combatant Service Then and Now," *Menn. Life* X (1955) 31-35; *ML II,* 663-65.

Forest Hills (Mich.) United Missionary Church had 23 members in 1953. M. J. Jones was pastor. M.G.

Forks Mennonite Church (MC), located six miles southeast of Middlebury, in Newbury Twp., Lagrange Co., Ind., is a member of the Indiana-Michigan Conference. The first Amish settlers came to Elkhart and Lagrange counties in 1841-42. A group broke away from the Amish in 1854 to form the Amish Mennonite Forks Church. Christian Plank and Christian Miller were the first ministers. The first known bishop was Jonas Troyer. D. J. Johns then retained oversight until D. D. Miller was ordained bishop in 1906. Miller, who died in 1955, was ordained deacon in 1890, minister in 1891, and bishop in 1906, all three times by D. J. Johns. In 1953 Earley C. Bontrager was the bishop, Donald E. Yoder the minister, and Malvin P. Miller the deacon; the 1953 membership was 213. The first church, built in 1864, was replaced in 1893 by a larger structure, which was remodeled in 1915. In 1927 the house was destroyed by fire but was soon replaced. Missionaries from this congregation include Dr. and Mrs. W. B. Page, Ernest E. and Ruth Miller, S. Jay and Ida Hostetler, Wilbur and Velma Hostetler, and Amsa and Nona Kauffman. Forks was also the home congregation of Orie O. Miller, executive secretary of the Mennonite Central Committee. **F.L.R.**

A. Augsburger, "History of the Forks Congregation," *MHB* IV (Sept. 1943) No. 3, and (Dec. 1943) No. 4.

Formantin (*Formantijn*), **Femundus**, a Catholic priest, professor at the University of Paris, received the commission from Louis XIV of France to gather information on the Anabaptists in his newly conquered lands. Peter Valkenier, a Dutch resident of Frankfurt, Germany, gives a detailed report in his book, *Das verwirrte Europa.*

Formantin first went to England to investigate the life and doctrine of the Quakers. On the basis of his report they were forbidden on penalty of death and confiscation of their goods, to remain in France on account of "their unreasonable doctrine and offensive living." On July 16, 1672, he came to Emmerich (*q.v.*), where he inquired of the bookdealer Cornelius van Beughem whether there were Mennonites living in Emmerich, and asked him to arrange a conversation with them. On the next day he met with Hendrik van Voorst (*q.v.*), the Mennonite preacher, and after Formantin had expressed his astonishment at the simple dress of the Mennonite preacher, they discussed original sin, baptism, grace, the Trinity, the Incarnation, communion, power of government, marriage and divorce, punishment of heretics, prayer to the saints, the oath, etc. The professor was amazed to find an ordinary citizen who looked after his business daily, and had yet acquired so thorough a knowledge of Scripture that he could answer the learned professor on every point, citing chapter and verse. He assured van Voorst that he would give the king so favorable a report that the Mennonites would everywhere receive complete freedom of worship, and would publish his report to all the world in print; he added that he had found the life and doctrine of the Mennonites more edifying than the Catholic, and called all who had defamed them with the king slanderers.

Formantin of course did not keep this promise. Upon the bookdealer's question what the non-Catholics could expect of the king, he replied that the king would grant freedom of religion to Lutherans and Reformed, but that in less than two years the Mennonites would be subjected like all other heretics to special fees, then perhaps persecuted and their possessions confiscated unless they adopted Catholicism. Louis' reign here was too brief to carry out this plan. (*DB* 1868, 32; 1873, 58 ff.; *ML* I, 662.) **NEFF.**

Formula of Concord (*Formula Concordiae*), one of the symbolic books of the Lutheran Church, the purpose of which was to heal the schisms that had arisen in the church since Luther's death and to restore pure Lutheran doctrine. The formula of unity worked out in 1576 at a convention of theologians at Torgau by Jacob Andreae of Tübingen, Martin Chemnitz of Brunswick, David Chyträus of Rostock, Andreas Musculus of Frankfurt a.d. Oder, and several theologians of Saxony, was not found satisfactory, and was therefore revised in March 1577, at the Bergen monastery near Magdeburg. But this new version called the *Formula Concordiae* was not approved by all the Lutheran churches either.

The Formula of Concord comprises 12 articles. The last chapter deals with "other gangs and sects, who have never confessed themselves to the Augsburg Confession." This chapter is included to prevent the suspicion that such groups were tolerated. Among them were the Anabaptists, Schwenckfelders, Arians, and Anti-trinitarians.

Concerning the Anabaptists the Concordia states: "The Anabaptists are divided into many groups, of which one defends much error, another little; on the whole, however, they teach such doctrine as cannot be tolerated in the churches, by the police, or in temporal government," and the suspicion is aroused that all branches without distinction hold the enumerated tenets.

The articles are divided into three groups. In addition to several doctrinal points, the Anabaptist views on government and economics are condemned, in agreement with article 16 of the Augsburg Confession.

The erroneous tenets of the Anabaptists are listed as follows in the *Formula of Concord:*

Intolerable Articles on the Church

(1) That Christ did not receive His body and blood from the Virgin Mary, but brought it with Him from heaven.

(2) That Christ is not true God, but merely has more gifts of the Holy Spirit than other holy persons.

(3) That our justification before God does not rest alone on the merit of Christ, but on the renewal, and thus on our own piety, in which we walk. Which is in large part on one's own, peculiar, self-chosen spirituality, and is fundamentally nothing but a new monasticism.

(4) That unbaptized children are before God not sinners, but righteous and innocent, which are saved in their innocence, because they have not yet reached accountability, without baptism (which, according to their assumption, they do not need). They thus reject the entire doctrine of original sin and what is attached to it.

(5) That children should not be baptized until they come to understanding and can confess their faith themselves.

(6) That the children of Christians are holy and children of God even without baptism, for the reason that they are born of Christian parents; and for this reason they do not regard nor promote infant baptism, contrary to the express word of God's promise, which includes only those who keep His covenant and do not despise it, Gen. 17.

(7) That the church in which sinners are still found is not a true church.

(8) That one should hear no sermon or attend any temple in which Papist Mass has been held or read.

(9) That one should have nothing to do with preachers who preach the Gospel in accord with the Augsburg Confession and reprove the preaching and error of the Anabaptists; one should neither serve them nor work for them, but flee and avoid them as perverters of God's Word.

Intolerable Articles Concerning the Police

(1) That the government is not a God-pleasing position in the New Testament.

(2) That a Christian cannot with a good conscience fill or officiate in a government office.

(3) That a Christian cannot with a good conscience use a function of government in occasional matters against the wicked, nor may its subjects call upon its power received from God, for safety and protection.

(4) That a Christian cannot with good conscience swear an oath nor offer allegiance to the ruling prince by means of an oath.

Intolerable Articles on Economics

(1) That a Christian with good conscience cannot keep or own any property, but is obliged to give it to the brotherhood.

(2) That a Christian cannot with a good conscience be an innkeeper, merchant, or knifesmith.

(3) That married persons must for the sake of their faith separate from one another, and one leave the other and marry another who is of the same faith.

These articles were compiled by the provost Jakob Andreae (*q.v.*), who preached 33 sermons in Esslingen in 1566-67 against "Papists, Schwenckfelders, and Anabaptists," which included eight against the Anabaptists. For the most part they refer to the Hutterian Brethren (*q.v.*), who had no brotherhoods in Germany, but were doing successful missionary work there. From their confession of faith, Peter Riedemann's (*q.v.*) *Rechenschaft unserer Religion, Lehre und Glaubens,* he quotes entire passages and tries to refute them: infant baptism (p. 28), community of goods (p. 160), oath (p. 141), church officials (p. 75), hearing sermons in the temples (p. 51), Christian and government (p. 101), magistracy (p. 129), merchants (p. 157), knifesmiths or armorsmiths (p. 156), and inns (p. 159). These sermons were printed in 1568, in a second edition in 1575, and enlarged with six additional sermons in 1753.

The views expressed by Andreae in these sermons were concentrated in the *Swabian Concordia* of 1574, from which they were put almost verbatim into the *Formula of Concord.* Only a few sentences were added. One on Calvin at the request of the theologians of Brunswick and Wolfenbüttel in session at Riddagshausen read: "The error of Calvin, that the children of baptized Christian believers are in the covenant of grace and are saved even before they receive baptism, and that they are baptized only because baptism in them signifies and seals the salvation they have beforehand, for such error minimizes the doctrine of original sin." The others were those on the Incarnation.

The *Formula of Concord* was widely used. It was adopted in Saxony, Brandenburg, the Palatinate, in 20 duchies, 24 counties, and 35 imperial cities. It was rejected by Anhalt, Brunswick-Wolfenbüttel, Denmark, Hesse, Holstein, Pfalz-Zweibrücken, Pomerania, Sweden, and a number of cities and counties (Bremen, Frankfurt, Magdeburg, Nürnberg, etc.). Though it failed to become a unifying formula for the Lutheran church, it formed the foundation for church doctrine from that time on in the sections that accepted it.   HEGE.

Jacob Andreae, *Dreyunddreissig Predigen, Von den fürnembsten Spaltungen in der Christlichen Religion,* IV; *Wider die Lehr der Widerteuffer* (Tübingen, 1568) 1-172; Fr. H. R. Frank, *Die Theologie der Concordienformel* IV (Erlangen, 1865) 345-91; F. H. Heppe, *Gesch. des deutschen Protestantismus* III (1857); J. Loserth, *Quellen und Forschungen zur Gesch. der oberdeutschen Taufgesinnten im 16. Jahrhundert* (Vienna, 1929); J. T. Müller, *Die symbolischen Bücher der evangelisch-*

lutherischen Kirche (Gütersloh, 1890) 558-60, 727 f.; Peter Riedemann, *Rechenschaft unserer Religion, Lehre und Glaubens* (*ca.* 1545); *ML* II, 543 f.

Formularies (German, *Formularbücher, Agende*): see **Ministers' Manuals.**

Forrer, Joh. Rud. Philipp (b. 1598), the Reformed pastor in Langnau in the Emmental (*q.v.*), Switzerland, who debated with the Mennonites in 1621, soon after taking the pastorate. His notes on the colloquia were published by Emil Blösch (*q.v.*) in the *Archiv des historischen Vereins des Kantons Bern* XII (1889) 282-307. In 1629 Forrer was made dean at Aarburg, and in 1652 at Burgdorf in the Emmental. (*ML* I, 663.)   HEGE.

Forsteidienst: see **Forestry Service.**

Forsterhof: see **Ueberlingen.**

Fort Collins (Col.) Civilian Public Service Camp Number 33 was opened in June 1942 and closed in October 1946. A soil conservation service camp operated by the Mennonite Central Committee, it was located nine miles north and two west of Fort Collins. The work consisted of emergency farm labor, construction on the Greeley dam, forest fire suppression, building irrigation ditches and outlet boxes, tile drainage, surveying, land leveling, and soil analysis. Some of the men worked in the agronomy section of the Colorado Experiment Station and others were stationed at the Buckingham permanent side camp, about 70 miles east of Fort Collins. In 1946 a cooking school to train camp cooks was held at the Fort Collins camp. Its camp paper was known as the *Poudre Canon News,* later changed to *Rising Tide.* In 1945 the men of the camp published a 64-page yearbook entitled *Service for Peace.*   M.G.

M. Gingerich, *Service for Peace* (Akron, Pa., 1949) 122.

Fort Vermilion, Alberta, a village and trading post located about 600 miles northwest of Edmonton. In 1934 a few families of Old Colony Mennonites moved from Saskatchewan to this location in search of new colonization opportunities, and in 1937 they were followed by settlers from Mexico. In 1954 the Old Colony Mennonites in the vicinity numbered about 814 souls, one third of whom were dissatisfied colonists from Mexico. Their neighbors were few and were mostly Indians and half-breeds. There were three meetinghouses: Rosenfeld, Blumenort, and Rhineland. The bishop in charge was William Wiebe. Although the growing season is extremely short and equipment is very limited, farming has been the chief means of livelihood. The settlement is extremely isolated from the main stream of society, and the inhabitants hold very tenaciously to the customs of the fathers.   J.A.H.

J. A. Hostetler, "Pioneering in the Land of the Midnight Sun," *Menn. Life* III (April 1948); Martha B. Nafziger, "We Serve in the Land of the Midnight Sun," *Youth's Christian Companion* (Nov. 7 and 14, 1954).

Fort Wayne, Ind., the second-largest city (pop. 120,000) in the state, located in Allen County. "Mad Anthony" Wayne built a stockade fort here in 1795. The first permanent settlement at Fort Wayne was made in 1815. For a long time Fort Wayne was a fur-trading center.

The Mennonites (MC) opened a Sunday school in Fort Wayne in 1903, and erected a building for worship in 1905. The present church was built in 1915. The city has become the seat of the headquarters of the Missionary Church Association (*q.v.*) and is the location of the Fort Wayne Bible College operated by this group, as well as a strong congregation. There is also an Evangelical Mennonite church in the city.   J.C.W.

Fort Wayne (Ind.) First Mennonite Church (MC) began as a mission upon the authorization of the Ohio Mennonite Conference in 1902, after the repeated requests of John B. Federspiel and wife, Mennonite residents of the city. M. S. Steiner was appointed to open the work, which began at 1921 South Hauna Street, in 1903. In 1904 the mission was moved to 2237 Oliver Street and from there to St. Mary's Avenue. Two years later a church was constructed at 1209 St. Mary's Avenue. In 1915 the present chapel was built on the adjoining lot. The following pastors have been in charge of the work at Fort Wayne: J. F. Bressler 1903-5, Ben B. King 1905-30, Frank Martin 1930-34, Newton Weber 1934-41, Allen Ebersole 1941-52, Rudy Bontrager 1952- . Others have served for shorter periods of time. In the early 1920's the Fort Wayne Mission became an organized self-governing congregation, but with limited support from the mission board, which was continued until September 1953, when the congregation became entirely independent of the mission board. The membership in 1955 was 136.   M.G.

B. B. King, "Our Mission Work at Ft. Wayne, Indiana," *YCC,* Sept. 27, 1925, 1, 2; Esther Sevits, "History of the Fort Wayne Mission," *MHB,* January 1947, 1, 4.

Fortbildungsschule: see **Preparatory Schools.**

Fortgens, a Mennonite family, first living at Emmerich, Germany, from where a number of members migrated to Amsterdam, among them Jacob (?) Fortgens, father of the well-known Zonist preacher Michiel Fortgens (*q.v.*). Abraham Fortgens was a Mennonite deacon of Emmerich about 1690. His son Isack, b. 1685 at Emmerich, d. *ca.* 1751 at Amsterdam, moved to Amsterdam and served the Zonist congregation as a deacon 1715-20 and 1728-35; Catherina, daughter of Isack, in 1731 married Abraham Fock (*q.v.*), a Mennonite emigrant from Danzig. Some members of this family joined the Zonist congregation and are often found as deacons until the end of the 18th century; others joined the Amsterdam Lamist congregation.   vDZ

Fortgens, Michiel, b. Jan. 13, 1663, d. Aug. 18, 1695, became a preacher of the Zonist (*q.v.*) congregation in Amsterdam at the age of 20, and served until death snatched him out of an effective ministry at the age of 33. Fortgens was an ardent defender of the conservative Zonist principles. He served as secretary of meetings held in 1684 and 1685 to unite the two congregations *bij 't Lam* and *van den Zon* at Amsterdam; his report *Verhael der Onderhandelingen . . .* was published at Amsterdam in 1685.

On this question he also wrote *Een Brief aan N. N. rakende de laatste onderhandeling . . .* (Amsterdam, 1692). Especially in this last-mentioned booklet he proves himself to be an orthodox Mennonite, averse to the unlimited tolerance he found among the Lamists, and convinced that the church needs a concise confession.

He was a very good preacher; his sermons were Biblical, simple, not marred by quibbles or redundant display of learning, and spoken with persuasive power. His published sermons were much read by the Reformed also.

Hermann Schijn (*q.v.*) delivered the funeral sermon, which was published with the title, *Zalige Nagedagtenis ter gelegentheid van het Zalig, dog voor de Gemeente ontydig ontslaapen van Michael Fortgens, veel geachten en getrouwen Leeraar der Doopsgezinden te Amsterdam, onder het zedig verklaaren, en toepassen van Davids Leeven, en Sterven uit Hand der Apost. 13 v. 36 plegtig gehouden op den 11. September 1695* (Amsterdam, 1695). His friend Pieter Beets (*q.v.*), minister of Hoorn, also delivered (at Hoorn) a funeral sermon: *Het bereidwillig sterven, gesien in de zalige verhuisinge van wijlen Michiel Fortgens* (published at Hoorn, 1695).

After Fortgens' death three collections of his sermons were published: (1) *XLII Predicatien over uitgeleze Texten des Ouden en Nieuwen Testaments gedaan door Michael Fortgens, in zyn Leeven Leeraar der Weereloze en Doopsgezinde Christenen te Amsterdam. Deeze Tweede Druck vermeerderd met Drie uitgeleezene Predicatien van denzelven Auteur. Gedrukt te Hoorn 1719.* The first edition was published by Schijn in 1696. (2) *Tyd en Feest-Predicatie over uitgeleze Texten des Ouden en Nieuwen Testaments. De Tweede Druck vermeerderd met 7 Predicatien over Ps. XXVII* (Amsterdam, 1722). The first edition is undated. (3) *Predicatien over de twee eerste Capittels van den eersten Brief van Petrus, den Uijttogt van Abraham uit zyn Vaderland en de Opofferinge van zynen Eenigen Zone Isaac, beneffens de overdragt, of Vergelykinge derzelve in de Offerhande van Jesus Christus, onzen Heere.* This collection, published by H. Schijn in 1711, contains 33 sermons on the first two chapters of the first epistle of Peter, three on Heb. 11:8-10, and four on Gen. 22:1-14; new editions came out in 1729 and 1738. At 16 Fortgens had published a Latin devotional poem, *De pace et Tranquilitate Animi Carmen heroicum* (Amsterdam, 1679). A picture of Fortgens is found in Schijn-Maatschoen.

NEFF, vDZ.

Schijn-Maatschoen, *Geschiedenis* II, 83, 658-62, 668; *Catalogus Amst.*, 132, 234, 241; *Biogr. Wb.* III, 96-98; *ML* I, 665.

Fortschritt was a four-page monthly published at Newton, Kan., and edited by David Goerz to promote the Mennonite Mutual Fire Insurance of North America (*q.v.:* now Midland Mutual Fire Insurance). The paper contained information of interest to Mennonites in the prairie states. The first issue appeared probably in December 1886, since the only available issue, that of June 1887, is No. 6 of Vol. I, in which it is stated that it was a monthly publica-

tion. When publication was discontinued is unknown. C.K.

Fortuna, Mo., a village (pop. 200) in Moniteau County in central Missouri. Approximately 60 Mennonite families live in a settlement a few miles southeast of Fortuna. In this Mennonite community are two churches, Bethel (GCM), and Mount Zion (MC). The first Mennonite settlers came to Moniteau County in 1866. This settlement has remained almost entirely rural with only an occasional family retiring to live in a near-by town or village. The address of the Bethel Mennonite Church is Fortuna, but the address of the Mt. Zion Mennonite Church and of most of the 60 families is Versailles, and most of these are located in Morgan County. E.A.A.

Fortuyn, Symon Jansz, composed a Mennonite hymnbook entitled *Geestelijck Liedtboeck genaemt de Basuyn,* with 694 pages. It was published after his death by the printer Jacob Aertsz Calom at Amsterdam, with an introduction by P. J. Twisck. Apparently Fortuyn, about whom no further information was available, belonged to the Old Frisian branch. vDZ.

Foth (Voth, Voet) is a common name among the Mennonites of Prussian background. Jacob Foht (Foth) was elder of the Deutsch-Wymysle Mennonite Church, Poland, ordained in 1875 (*Namens-Verzeichniss,* Danzig, 1881, p. 67). Heinrich Foth was elder of the Ober-Nessau Mennonite Church of Prussia, succeeding David Dirks (*Menn. Bl.,* 1892, p. 99, and **Obernessau,** ML III, 285). Johann Foth (*q.v.,* d. 1932) was a prominent elder of the Mennonite Brethren Church at Hillsboro, Kan. Johannes Foth has been pastor since 1904 of the Friedelsheim, Palatinate, congregation near Ludwigshafen, Germany. Hans Voet (*q.v.*) (Foth) was a preacher of the Groningen Old Flemish in Lithuania and at Schönsee, West Prussia. (See also **Vogt.**) C.K.

Foth, Johann, elder of the Mennonite Brethren Church, was born in West Prussia, Aug. 20, 1844. When he was a child, his parents moved to the Mennonite settlement on the Don River in Russia. Here Johann was baptized in 1872, joining the M.B. Church. He married Carolina Janzen on Jan. 6, 1871. To this union 13 children were born. A man of rare ability with the gift of leadership, Foth was soon elected to the ministry, in which he served in Russia until 1883.

In 1883 the family emigrated to America, establishing a farm home in the community of the Ebenfeld M.B. Church southeast of Hillsboro, Kan. Here he at once became active as a minister, was elected to its leadership in 1884 and ordained elder in 1885. He served in this position until 1916. During his ministry the church grew into one of the strongest congregations of the M.B. Conference.

Elder Foth was very active in the M.B. Conference, doing much itineration for many years. He served on the Foreign Mission Board for a long time. When the Conference was subdivided into district conferences in 1909, Elder Foth became the first moderator of the Southern District Conference, a position to which he was elected a number of times.

He died Dec. 11, 1932, and was interred in the Ebenfeld M.B. cemetery southeast of Hillsboro.

J.H.L.

Foundation, *A, and Plain Instruction of the Saving Doctrine of Our Lord Jesus Christ;* Dutch: *Dat Fundament des Christelycken leers op dat alder corste geschreuen* (n.p., 1539) is the most important, though not the first book of Menno Simons, comparable in significance to the *Enchiridion* (1564) of Dirk Philips.

After addressing himself in his preface to the "pious government and all people," he expresses the confidence that they will find his writings in accordance with the Scriptures. He treats "The Time of Grace," "True Repentance," "Concerning Faith," "The Apostolic Baptism," "The Lord's Supper," "Separation from the World," "The True Ministers," and concludes with an appeal to the government, the scholars, the common people, the heretics, and the bride of Christ. The *Foundation-Book* was one of the most important instruments for gathering the true, peaceful, and Biblical Dutch Anabaptists—after the Münster catastrophe—into a body of believers, a church of Christ, which soon became known as Mennonites. In simple language he presents the basic doctrines and ethical standards based on the New Testament to a bewildered, seeking group, who found in the book the guide they needed and were looking for.

Only a few copies of the first edition have survived. They can be found in the Mennonite Library of Amsterdam (two copies); the University Library of Amsterdam; Royal Library of The Hague; British Museum, London; Municipal Library, Hamburg. In 1616 a new edition of the 1539 *Foundation-Book* appeared under the title *Dat Fundament der Christlycken leere. Door Menno Simons op dat alder correckste geschreven/ ende wtghegheven/ Anno M.D.XXXIX. Ende nu nae het alder outste exemplaer wederom herdruckt/ Anno 1616.* The earlier assumption that this edition was published by the Frisian Reformed Synod is hardly tenable. It must have been published by followers of Menno Simons rather than opponents. Copies of the edition can be found in the Mennonite Library, Amsterdam; C. P. van Eeghen Jr. private library, Amsterdam; University Library of Leiden; Colgate-Rochester Theological Seminary, Rochester, N.Y.; Union Theological Seminary, New York; Goshen College Library; and Schwenckfelder Library, Pennsburg, Pa.

The first writing of the *Foundation Book* was in a dialect with an "Oosters coloring," that is, Menno adapted his Dutch to the new environment of the provinces of Groningen and East Friesland where he had found temporary shelter (see **Oosters Coloring and Dialect**). About 1554 an edition followed in the Oosters dialect, which was linguistically even more adapted to the environment in which Menno was now living. Menno refers to this book as the *Fondament-Boeksken (Opera,* 1681, p. 235). It bore the title *Ein Fundament vnd klare Anwisinge, van de heylsame vnd Godtsellyghe Leere Jesu Christi, vth Godes woort mit gueder corte veruatet, und wederumme mit grooter vlyte auerghelesen vnde ghebetert.* This edition was printed by B. L. around

1554, very likely in Lübeck or Wüstenfelde, where Menno had a place of refuge. Menno was probably busy preparing a larger collection of his writings when he died in 1561. In 1562 the *Foundation-Book* appeared in a somewhat revised Dutch edition, considerably enlarged, under the following title: *Een Fondament ende clare aenwijsinghe van de salichmakende Leere Jesu Christi, wt Gods Woort int corte begrepen, ouergeset wt dat Oosters, in dese onse Nederlantsche sprake.* The following books had been added: "Concerning the True Christian Faith," "Concerning Regeneration or the New Creature," "A Consolation Regarding Suffering, the Cross, and the Persecution of the Saints," "Meditation on the Twenty-Fifth Psalm," "Concerning the Spiritual Resurrection," "Concerning Excommunication, Ban, and Avoidance," ". . . How Pious Parents Should Train Their Children. . . ." It is this combined edition of the *Foundation-Book,* reprinted repeatedly in Dutch (1565, 1567, 1579, 1583, and 1613), which found its way into the complete works of Menno Simons (1600, 1646, and 1681), and was translated into German, appearing first in 1575. All German editions in Europe (also the von Riesen edition of Danzig) and the various American editions are based on the 1562 Dutch edition which appeared after the death of Menno Simons. Only slight variations are noticeable.

European German editions include an undated reprint of the 1575 edition and one of 1834-35, published by Peter von Riesen primarily for distribution in Russia, but printed in Danzig(?). Six American German editions appeared in 1794 (reprint of the 1575 edition), 1835, 1849, 1851, 1853, and 1876. All English editions (1835, 1863, 1869) were published for the Herrites (Reformed Mennonites), who emphasized their loyalty to Menno Simons, and contain a preface by Johann Herr.

No other Mennonite author has ever written a book which found such an immediate widespread acceptance and so specifically met a need as the *Foundation-Book* of Menno Simons. It was one of the most significant factors in gathering "the sheep without a shepherd" and giving a Scriptural basis and much courage to a group of believers and thus preventing their disintegration. (See also **Menno Simons.**)

C.K.

ML II, 17, 84-86; C. Krahn, "Menno Simons' *Fundament-boek* of 1539-1540," *MQR* XIII (October 1939) 221-32; *idem, Menno Simons* (Karlsruhe, 1936) 52-55; K. Vos, *Menno Simons* (Leiden, 1914) 272, 296.

Fox Valley Mennonite Brethren Church, now extinct, a rural congregation located about 100 miles northwest of Swift Current, Sask., was founded in 1913-14 and had 50-60 members. A number of members moved to Medicine Hat, Alberta, and others to Woodrow, Sask. The church was dissolved in the early 1920's.

P.C.H.

Fox(e), John (1516-87), an English Protestant scholar, who was compelled to flee from England because of his faith, and after a brief stay in Antwerp, Frankfurt, and Strasbourg settled in Basel, Switzerland. Later he returned to England and died there in 1587, having lived a very active life. While he lived in Norwich (*q.v.*) he may have had contacts with the Anabaptist circles there. He interceded with Queen Elizabeth of England for the lives of the Anabaptists (Barclay, 25).

Fox's great *Book of Martyrs,* which became the model of all later martyrologies and was immensely popular with the English masses, appeared in English (Latin edition at Basel in 1559) first in 1563, then in 1570, 1576, 1583, etc., under the title *Actes and Monuments of the Latter and Perillous Dayes, Touching Matters of the Church . . . from the year one thousand. . . .* A good modern edition is that edited by W. B. Forbush, *Fox's Book of Martyrs* (Chicago, 1926). A German edition appeared at Philadelphia in 1831 under the title, *Allgemeine Geschichte des Christlichen Marterthums . . . .* It includes a lengthy section (pp. 748-934 out of a total of 971 pp.) on the "History and Doctrine of the Mennonites" (pp. 748-85), and one on "Persecutions of the Mennonites" (785-934). The latter is taken from the *Martyrs' Mirror,* but neither its editor, nor the author of the historical section is identified. It was almost certainly I. D. Rupp of Lancaster, Pa., who translated several Mennonite books into English, including the *Martyrs' Mirror* (Lancaster, 1837), the *Works of Menno Simons* (Elkhart, 1871), the *Wandering Soul* (Carlisle, 1833), and Menno Simons' *Foundation* (Lancaster, 1835). The title page of the 1837 English *Martyrs' Mirror* names Rupp as the author of *Der Maertyrer Geschichte,* which is no doubt an abbreviated title for the Fox book. Rupp used the writings of Deknatel (*q.v.*) and Abraham Hunsinger (*q.v.*), in addition to the *Martyrs' Mirror,* on the historical sections, which actually constitute the first treatment of the history and doctrines of the Mennonites published in America. The only original contribution is the material (not very extensive) on the American Mennonites, which has been completely overlooked. H.S.B.

R. Barclay, *The Inner Life of the Religious Societies of the Commonwealth* (London, 1877) 25; *DB* 1899, 113; *ML* I, 665-67.

France. Throughout the late Middle Ages France was the major center of "pre-evangelical" heretical movements; these movements, parallel in certain of their aims and principles, of whose relations with one another and with Anabaptism so little is known, from Martin of Tours to the Waldenses, embodied in varying degrees the concern for Scriptural reformation which the Anabaptists were later to apply consistently. Since, however, the debate on the relation of these movements to Anabaptism has not yet been closed, their history does not fall within the scope of this article.

The greatest centralization of royal and ecclesiastical authority in France prevented any real beginning of Anabaptism in the 16th century. Protestants themselves being a persecuted minority, the issues on which focused the break between Zwingli and the Anabaptists never came to the same degree of clarity in the French-speaking Reformation. Flanders (*q.v.*) and Alsace (*q.v.*) were both centers of Anabaptism, but were at that time not part of France, and little if anything of the original 16th-century movement existed in either of these two provinces at the time of their acquisition by France.

During and after the Thirty Years' War (1618-48), at the end of which Alsace became French, the movement of Mennonites into Alsace from Switzerland became important. Some went on to the Palatinate, and others remained to reclaim lands laid waste by the wars. They settled both on the plains around Colmar, where on Feb. 4, 1660, a group of elders and ministers adopted the Dordrecht Confession of 1632, and in the valley of Sainte-Marie-aux-Mines (Markirch), where they were given citizenship and exemption from military service, against payment of a special tax. Although already in this area by 1640, they seem to have come in force especially after 1670, when a new wave of persecution broke over the Bernese Mennonites.

It is in this latter area (Markirch) that we encounter in 1696 the name of Jakob Ammann, who represented a newly arrived group of Swiss Mennonites before the Prevost of the valley with the aim of reminding the government of the privileges previously granted concerning military service. The Amish division in France seems probably to have grown from the triangular tension between the newer elements of the Markirch settlement, its parent congregations in the canton of Bern, and the older congregations of the Alsatian Rhine plain, which alone are known to have adopted the Dordrecht Confession, whose eleventh and twelfth articles do not represent Swiss Mennonite tradition. The final result of this division was that all surviving (1954) congregations in France, with the exceptions of Geisberg and Florimont, and including Binningen-Holee and Courgenay-Lucelle across the Swiss border, are of the Amish branch.

For some time Mennonites in Alsace enjoyed relative liberty, being able to avoid the requirements of military service and the oath. Gradually, however, their nonconformist position, their privileges, and their general prosperity attracted the ill will of their neighbors and of the Church, and with the tightening of France's hold in Alsace there came also, in February of 1712, the order to expel all Anabaptists from Alsace, since—so ran the argument—the Peace of Westphalia (1648) had promised religious freedom only to Calvinists and Lutherans. Migration began in all directions; east and especially north into Germany, south into the principality of Montbéliard, and west through the Vosges Mountains into Lorraine. Lorraine was at that time independent under a Polish duke, and Montbéliard belonged to Württemberg and thus to Austria. The movement into Lorraine was chiefly infiltration, profiting from the relative isolation of the mountainous headlands of the Muerthe and Sarre basins. The movement to Montbéliard was, on the other hand, massive and intentionally encouraged by Count Léopold Eberhard, who sought honest farmers to manage the lands which he had acquired from his people by oppressive means. Though the state church in Montbéliard was Lutheran, this tolerance on the part of the count was purely commercial and had no basis in his Protestantism or in any ideas of religious liberty. Mennonites had no right to meet openly for worship, to intermarry with the local Lutheran population, or to acquire new members.

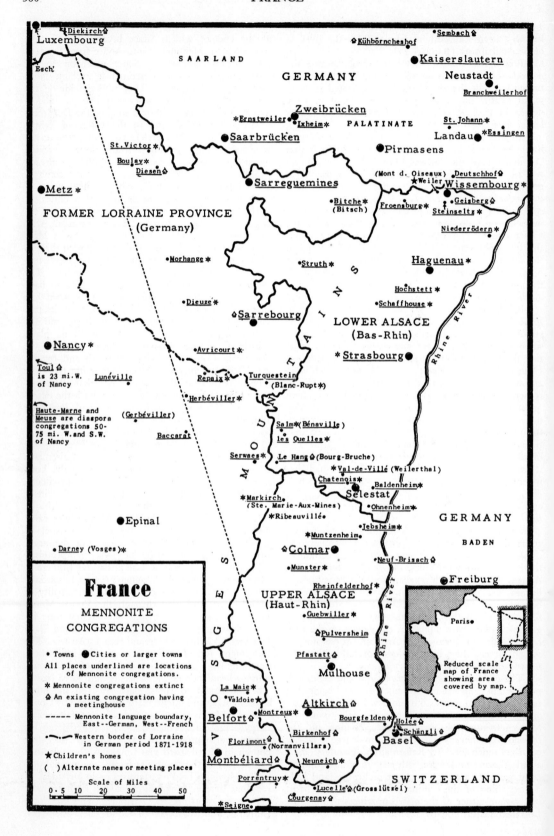

Luxembourg
Diekirch
Esch'
SAARLAND
GERMANY
Sembach
Kühbörncheshof
Kaiserslautern
Neustadt
Branchweilerhof
Zweibrücken
Ernstweiler
Ixheim
PALATINATE
St. Johann
Landau
Essingen
Saarbrücken
Pirmasens
St. Victor
Boulay
Diesen
Sarreguemines
(Mont d. Oiseaux)
Deutschhof
Weiler
Wissembourg
Metz
FORMER LORRAINE PROVINCE
(Germany)
Bitche
(Bitsch)
Froensburg
Geisberg
Steinseltz
Niederrödern
Morhange
Struth
Haguenau
Hochstett
Schaffhouse
Dieuze
Sarrebourg
LOWER ALSACE
(Bas-Rhin)
Nancy
Avricourt
Strasbourg
Toul
is 23 mi. W.
of Nancy
Lunéville
Repaix
Turquestein
(Blanc-Rupt)
Herbéviller
Haute-Marne and
Meuse are diaspora
congregations 50-
75 mi. W. and S.W.
of Nancy
(Gerbéviller)
Baccarat
Salm
(Bénaville)
les Quelles
Serwaes
Le Hang
(Bourg-Bruche)
Val-de-Ville (Weilerthal)
Chatenois
Baldenheim
Markirch
(Ste. Marie-Aux-Mines)
Selestat
Ohnenheim
Ribeauvillé
Iebsheim
Epinal
Muntzenheim
Darney (Vosges)
Colmar
GERMANY
BADEN
Munster
Neuf-Brisach
Freiburg
Rheinfelderhof
UPPER ALSACE
(Haut-Rhin)
Paris
Guebwiller
Pulversheim
Reduced scale
map of France
showing area
covered by map.
Pfastatt
Mulhouse
La Maie
Valdoie
Altkirch
Belfort
Montreux
Bourgfelden
Holee
Schänzli
Montbéliard
Birkenhof
(Normanvillars)
Basel
Florimont
Neuneich
Porrentruy
SWITZERLAND
Seigne
Courgenay
Lucelle (Grosslützel)

France

MENNONITE
CONGREGATIONS

• Towns ● Cities or larger towns
All places underlined are locations
   of Mennonite congregations.
✳ Mennonite congregations extinct
⌂ An existing congregation having
   a meetinghouse
----- Mennonite language boundary,
   East--German, West--French
•—• Western border of Lorraine
   in German period 1871-1918
★ Children's homes
( ) Alternate names or meeting places

Scale of Miles
0 · 5 10   20   30   40   50

Their status as a "foreign body" being thus underlined, and their presence in the region being a result of Leopold Eberhard's confiscation of private lands, Mennonites were naturally not popular among the natives of the principality. Whereas the count continued to invite the Mennonites, even sending representatives to Bern to ask them to come, both the neighboring provinces, such as Burgundy, and the local populations remained opposed to the "Swiss." Only with the Revolution of 1789 ff. did Montbéliard become a part of France. The first effect of "Liberty, Equality, Fraternity" for the Mennonites was not religious liberty, but rather the opportunity given the local populations, through local revolutionary committees, to express their accumulated resentments. Both the loyalty oath and obligatory militia service became means of applying pressure. (There even attempts in both Montbéliard and the Haut-Rhin to forbid the wearing of beards in the name of equality.) Fortunately, the higher revolutionary authorities were more understanding than the local hotheads, and the right to perform alternative service with the supply or hospital troops was generally granted, as was apparently the right to replace the oath by a pledge sealed with a handshake. Their critics raised the question whether such people could be considered as citizens. On this point the departmental government of Doubs (Montbéliard) appealed to the National Assembly, and the Comité du Salut Publique, apparently in response to this request, though not answering the question, confirmed on Aug. 19, 1793, the right to noncombatant service. Napoleon, institutionalizing the principle of military service, allowed no exceptions for reasons of belief, in spite of delegations sent by the Mennonites of Montbéliard, Alsace, and Lorraine, but apparently continued to permit assignment to noncombatant units. Also the Mennonites' objections to the oath were honored, and as early as 1810 the French supreme court (*Cour de Cassation*) accepted a simple promise as alternative.

Very little is known as yet of Mennonites in the entire period 1712-1870 outside of the principality of Montbéliard, except for the joint project just mentioned of sending a delegation to Napoleon (see **Alsace**). A few generalizations may nevertheless be hazarded. (1) Parallel to the movement to Montbéliard, a smaller group of Amish from Markirch settled in the south of the Sundgau (present congregations of Birkenhof and Holee). (2) In the latter half of the 18th century a fresh Swiss (non-Amish) settlement was formed in the wooded area of Normanvillars (present congregation of Florimont—see Gratz article, *MQR*, April 1952). (3) The expulsion from Alsace, ordered in 1712, was never fully carried out. The Count Palatine of Birkenfeld, on whose territory of Ribeaupierre the Ste-Marie-aux-Mines settlement was located, and who had lost 70 families and thereby a third of his income, requested from Louis XV and finally received in 1728 the authorization to tolerate those who remained, on condition that they should not increase in numbers. Those who did remain were frequently annoyed but never driven out. (4) The infiltration into Lorraine from the Vosges but also from the Palatin-

ate continued uneventfully, reaching Nancy by 1850 and Bar-le-Duc and Chaumont by the end of the century. Widely scattered, the Mennonites of Lorraine had great difficulty in maintaining any sort of church life, and held on largely through the force of tradition, family links, and continuing relations with the stronger centers at Montbéliard and in Germany beyond Zweibrücken. Meetings were monthly or even less frequent; congregational leaders were devoted but frequently lacking in vision and occasionally even illiterate. Sermons and prayers were read or repeated by rote (see Pierre Sommer's reminiscences in *Almanach Mennonite du Cinquantenaire,* 1951). (5) From all these areas migration to America continued intermittently through the entire period from 1820 to 1900, making up the major part of the Amish settlements from western Pennsylvania to Iowa. The increasing difficulty of obtaining assignment with the noncombatant service, and perhaps also a dissatisfaction even with the noncombatant privilege, was one of the continuing reasons for emigration, with the result that by the end of the 19th century there was no longer any objection raised against full military service by Mennonites remaining in France.

The annexation of Alsace and a part of Lorraine by Germany in 1871 cut off both the weak congregations of Lorraine and the strong center of Montbéliard from their brethren in German-speaking territory. The next quarter-century was the transition to the French language in both home and church, but not without difficulties which weakened the hold of traditional religion on the younger generations. In the 1890's young people who knew only French were obliged to memorize in German the 18 articles of the Dordrecht Confession, and to pronounce in German the formula, "My desire is . . . ," whose original intent was to guarantee the principle of baptism on confession of faith, but which could mean no more to them than if it had been in Latin. This language problem, coupled with the wide dispersion of Mennonite families, the end of discrimination against them, the growth of French nationalism and centralism, continuing emigration, and mixed marriages, led to the disappearance of a number of congregations between the Alsatian border and the Moselle (Blanc Rupt, Bitscherland, "Welschland," Dieuze, Morhange, Nancy, Herbéviller, Repaix, Vosges, "Lothringer"; see articles on these congregations). This evolution has continued up to the present, taking in as well most of the congregations of the Vosges (Ste-Marie-aux-Mines, Chatenois, Quelles, Bénaville, Salm, Senones, Struth, of which only the reconstituted congregation of the Hang remains). The general spiritual tone of Mennonitism in France and Alsace was at its lowest point toward the end of the 19th century.

Beginning around 1900 several factors combined to initiate a degree of renewal. (1) The Alsatian churches began to hold regular conferences and entered into contact with the Conference of South German Mennonites. After the return of Alsace-Lorraine to France (1918) the Alsatian conference united the German-speaking Mennonites in France (see **Association des Eglises** and **Conference of Mennonites in**

France). (2) A new immigration of Swiss Mennonites into Upper Alsace brought fresh leadership into the Alsace-Lorraine Conference, and led to the formation of two new (chiefly Swiss) congregations (see **Pfastatt** and **Altkirch**). This brought the end of conservatism in matters of dress as well as the observance of footwashing, although the latter still survives in five French congregations. (3) Outside influences, such as the Salvation Army, and revivalists like Ruben Saillens in France, St. Chrischona, and, later, Pentecostalism in Alsace, brought both renewal of spiritual concern and a certain lack of respect for peculiarly Mennonite traditions. Surprisingly, the Pentecostal influence produced more interest in nonresistance and in a critical attitude toward nationalism than did the types of spirituality more favored by Mennonite leadership. (4) A revitalization of the Mennonite heritage, involving a renewed interest in personal spiritual life, in missions, in Mennonite history, in international Mennonite contacts, and in nonresistance, was undertaken by Pierre Sommer (*q.v.,* minister of the Repaix congregation, later at Montbéliard) and Valentin Pelsy of Sarrebourg. Their efforts brought into being the French-language conference (*q.v.*) beginning in 1906, a ministers' manual, and the supported post of a traveling pastor to visit scattered families. This development expanded further after World War II to bring about the naming of a second traveling pastor (under the German-language conference), and the formation of a mission committee, a youth commission, and a charitable organization (*Association Fraternelle Mennonite, q.v.*), all of which serve both language groups. *Christ Seul* began its appearance as a monthly journal in 1907.

The Amish origin of the French Mennonites is now scarcely visible, though only a generation ago there remained a conscious conservatism in matters of dress. Only the congregations of Diesen, Haute-Marne, Meuse, Birkenhof, and Montbéliard have retained the practice of footwashing. Each congregation is autonomous, choosing its own ministers and elder (or elders—Montbéliard had four elders in 1954). The conferences have a purely consultative character. The ministers and elders of both conference groups have been meeting conjointly semiannually in Valdoie since 1951 for study and discussion, but this meeting has no administrative authority. The Dordrecht Confession is still the official expression of belief and its study (and in some cases memorization) a prerequisite to baptism, though Articles XIV, XVI, and XVII are no longer literally applied. Most congregations meet biweekly. Sunday schools (for unbaptized children) are the exception, but their importance is rapidly growing. Children of Mennonite families are generally baptized by aspersion at 14-15 years; adhesion of members of non-Mennonite ancestry is rare.

Mennonite Central Committee work in France began in February 1940 as an extension of the work in Spain, and continued under the direction of Ernest Bennett, J. N. Byler, and Henry Buller until Jan. 26, 1943, when the remaining workers, Lois Gunden and Henry Buller, were interned by the Germans. The work was first of all directed toward Spanish

refugees at Cerbére on the Spanish border, and grew also to include child-feeding programs, such as the one at Lyons. The child work was carried on through the war during the absence of MCC workers by Augustin Coma, a Spanish refugee, and Roger Georges, a French citizen, partly with funds left by MCC and partly with subsidies from French government welfare agencies. Work was again begun in early 1945, both with children's homes and with more general food and clothing distributions. By the end of the year 14 MCC workers were directing at least seven children's homes besides the clothing distribution. In 1946 contact was for the first time established with the French Mennonites, and late in the same year a reconstruction unit was established in Wissembourg, Alsace. Increasing contacts with French Mennonites led to the formation of a Youth Commission in the French churches (1948), the beginning of summer Bible camps (1949), the foundation of the *Association Fraternelle Mennonite* (*q.v.,* 1950), and the purchase of two properties for the continuation of the MCC's children's work in collaboration with the French at Valdoie near Belfort and at Mont des Oiseaux near Wissembourg. The Mennonite Church (MC) began a mission in Paris in 1953.

Congregations now existing in France are Altkirch, Belfort, Birkenhof, Colmar, Diesen, Florimont, Geisberg, Le Hang, Haute-Marne, Lunéville-Baccarat, Meuse, Montbéliard, Neuf-Brisach, Pfastatt, Pulversheim, Sarrebourg, and Toul. (See articles on all these congregations as well as the extinct ones listed earlier.) A monthly meeting has begun in Paris in 1954, but as yet without congregational organization. Mennonites in France are mostly engaged in agricultural pursuits, although a movement toward all levels of urban employment has been marked in the last half-century. (See **Farming** and **Business.** For more detailed local history see the provincial articles **Alsace** and **Lorraine.**) J.H.Y.

Les Soirees Helvetiennes, Alsaciennes, et Fran-Comtoises (Amsterdam and Paris, 1772); Alfred Michiels, *Les Anabaptistes des Vosges* (Paris, 1860); Ch. Mathiot, *Recherches historiques sur les Anabaptistes de l' ancienne Principaute de Montbéliard, d' Alsace et des regions voisines* (Belfort, 1922); V. Pelsy and P. Sommer, *Précis d'Histoire des Eglises Mennonites* (Montbéliard, 1914 and reprint 1937); *ML* I, 681-85.

Franchijne van der Borcht, an Anabaptist martyr: see **Fransken de Vroedvrouw.**

Franchois Ferijn, a Mennonite preacher who was active in Flanders, Belgium, about 1565, but about whom nothing else is known. (Verheyden, "Mennisme in Vlaanderen," Ms.)

Franchois van der Leyen, an Anabaptist martyr, was burned at the stake at Gent, Belgium, on April 28, 1558. This martyr, by trade a dealer in old clothes, was a member of the van der Leyen family (*q.v.*), many of whom died as martyrs. (Verheyden, *Gent,* 24, No. 55.) vDZ.

Franchoys de Corte, an Anabaptist martyr, a clothmaker, b. in Brugge, Belgium, was arrested at Antwerp, and because he "persisted in his rebaptism" was sentenced to death and executed by secret drowning at the Steen castle at Antwerp on July 24, 1561. His furniture and other goods had been confiscated and publicly sold before his death on June 23, 1561. (*Antw. Arch.-Blad* IX, 124, 133, 138; XIV, 30-31, No. 342.) vdZ.

Franciscans, a Roman Catholic order of begging friars (*Ordo Minoritum*) founded by Francis of Assisi (d. 1226). The principle of apostolic poverty was carried into the later Middle Ages with a reforming effect by the stricter party, the Observants. It was especially effective through the creation of the Tertiary order, which formed a transition to the laity, in addition to the first order and the order of St. Clara, and which supported these orders. Occasionally there was some fanaticism in connection with the prophecies of Joachim of Fiore and some opposition to the papacy.

In his "Prolegomena zu einer Geschichte des Pietismus" (*Ztscht für Kirchengesch.*, II, 29), Albrecht Ritschl interprets the Anabaptist movement as a revival of the reformation of St. Francis, produced by jealousy toward Luther and Zwingli, proceeding from the Tertians, particularly the Observants. The supposition of a direct descent of the Anabaptists from the Tertians has been rejected by research, and even by Ritschl himself in his *Geschichte des Pietismus*. On the other hand, the assumption of a certain connection between the Anabaptists and the late medieval—indeed strongly Franciscan—piety has found some acceptance. E.C.

A. Ritschl, *Gesch. des Pietismus* I (Bonn, 1880) 30; *Ztscht für Kirchengesch.* II (Gotha, 1878) 29; *Theologische Zeitung* V (1880) Col. 311 (Weizsäcker); *ibid.* VIII (1883) 369 (Kolde); *ML* I, 686.

Franciscus von der Sach (della Sega), an Anabaptist martyr: see Sach, Franciscus von der.

Franck, Caspar (*Casparus Francius Ortrandus*) (1543-84), the son of strict Lutheran parents. While he was serving as chaplain at the court of Duke Ladislaus of Haag in Upper Bavaria, Germany, he experienced the first Counter Reformation decrees of Albrecht V of Bavaria, and in 1568 he entered the Catholic Church at Ingolstadt, remaining there as Professor of the Holy Scriptures at the university. His epitaph lauds him as a defender of the Catholic faith and church. Among his numerous polemics, his *Catalogus Haereticorum* (Ingolstadt, 1576) lists the names of all the opponents of the Catholic Church. Luther, Melanchthon, and other Protestant leaders are treated at length. Briefly but not incorrectly he names the Anabaptist leaders, Hans Denk, Balthasar Hubmaier, Ludwig Haetzer, and Melchior Hofmann. The sections on the Hutterites and Anabaptists present utter nonsense. The Batenburgers and Davidjorists are also touched. The book is of very little historical significance. (Wetzer and Welte, *Kirchenlexikon*, 1885; *ML* I, 668.) Neff.

Franck, Sebastian (1499-1543), the great German chronicler and popular historiographer of the 16th century, b. in 1499 in Donauwörth, Bavaria, d. in 1542 or 1543 at Basel, Switzerland, studied at the universities of Ingolstadt and Heidelberg, held a cure

in the bishopric of Augsburg, in 1526 became a priest in Buchenbach near Schwabach, and in 1527 Protestant pastor in Gustenfelden near Nürnberg. Here in 1528, he translated and edited Andreas Althamer's (*q.v.*) *Diallage,* a book attacking Hans Denk and the "fanatics."

In this work Franck reveals himself as a strict Lutheran; but his complaints against the abuse of the Bible and the doctrine of grace already indicate the beginnings of his later position. This position becomes clearer in his next work, *Von dem gräulichen Laster der Trunkenheit.* Here he is still entirely a Lutheran; but he censures the unchristian life of the clergy and demands the introduction of the ban (*q.v.*). Mere preaching does not suffice. "We cannot be raised from our pillows, one preaches always to flocks of geese and blue ducks without any fruit, . . . because it yields milk, wool, and money. Alas, we are not only filled with wine, but full of the spirit of deception, error, and ignorance. Open vices should be censured, by the preachers with word and ban, by the princes with the law and the sword. For because the ban is not exercised, I know nothing to say of a Gospel or of a spiritual church" (Erbkam, 357, note; Hegler, 27).

In 1528 Franck resigned his position in Gustenfelden. He may have been compelled to do this on account of his attitude toward the Anabaptists, who were still numerous in and around Nürnberg. This is the surmise of Martin Frecht (Hegler in *HRE*). He went first to Nürnberg and on March 17, 1528, married Ottilie Behaim, probably the sister of the "ungodly" painters, Bartholomew and Sebald Behaim, whom Hans Denk calls his friends. It is almost certain that he came in contact with Anabaptists here, but there is no evidence for Ludwig Keller's assertion (*Comeniushefte*, 1900, 322) that he became a personal friend of Hans Denk.

In Nürnberg Sebastian Franck experienced a complete transformation. The theologian became an author, the Lutheran a Spiritualist, the churchman an individualist who felt at home in no religious organization but wished to establish an invisible, spiritual church. He expressed himself to that effect in the conclusion of his book *Die Türkenchronik,* written in Nürnberg in 1530. In this book he discussed the "10 or 12 nations or sects of Christendom," and called attention to the fact that "besides the three faiths which now have a great following, viz., the Lutheran, Zwinglian, and Anabaptist, the fourth is already arising, that seeks to clear away all outward ceremonies, the sacraments, and also the ban and to establish an invisible church, gathered in the unity of the Spirit among all peoples, and governed without external means by God's eternal invisible Word" (Hegler, *HRE*). These are ideas encountered in many a person of the time who was spiritually akin to the Anabaptists or in some connection with them, such as Campanus (*q.v.*), Bünderlin (*q.v.*), Schwenckfeld (*q.v.*), and Servetus (*q.v.*).

In the fall of 1529 he went to Strasbourg and there became acquainted with Schwenckfeld, Servetus, and Bünderlin, as he wrote in a letter to Campanus on Feb. 4, 1531 (Hegler, 50 ff.; Nicoladoni, 124;

ML I, 320). In this letter he called Bünderlin a "learned and wonderfully pious man, dead to the world." He wrote that he desired with all his heart also to be baptized with the baptism with which Bünderlin had been baptized; faith could not be learned out of a book or from a human being, however holy he might be, but it is learned from God and implanted by Him in the school of the Lord under the cross. He admitted that he did not know whether or not Bünderlin was his brother in the faith, but was sure that Bünderlin was much more learned and God-fearing than he, "wretched man" that he was (Hegler, 52 and 264 ff.). This letter is found in Schellhorn, 114, and in *Amoenitates.*

In Strasbourg Franck very probably also became acquainted with Melchior Hofmann (*q.v.*) (Krohn, 208). Catrou's (*q.v.*) opinion (*Histoire* III, 237), which is based on Meshovius (*q.v.*), that Hofmann won Franck to his group, is wrong; for Franck, in his *Paradoxa* (145), expressly attacked Hofmann's doctrine of the Incarnation. The two men were of such opposite positions—only in their mysticism are they somewhat related—that any closer kinship is hardly thinkable, even though they shared the common lot of expulsion from Strasbourg.

Franck was expelled from Strasbourg on Dec. 30, 1531, with his family. The occasion for the ban was the publication of his *Chronica, Zeytbuch and geschychtbibel* (*q.v.*), his first major work, which he completed and published in Strasbourg in 1531, and which became a very widely read book. It was probably his most significant work, and was published in various editions. In Anabaptist circles it was also cherished and much read and used. Menno Simons took more quotations from it than from any other author (Vos, 262). He "believed in him as in an oracle" (Vos, 40). It is possible that Menno acquired his knowledge of the ancient writers chiefly from this book, as Duncanus (*q.v.*) charged in 1549. His idea of the imminent end of the world and return of Christ seems to have been influenced by it. It also contains valuable source material on the Anabaptists.

This book aroused everywhere a most painful excitement, because all existing religious groups felt themselves deeply wounded and criticized; all thought they had the truth, but no one, said Franck, had it. The author met with bitter hostility and entered a period of deep suffering. Erasmus (*q.v.*) was also offended because he had been ranked among the heretics; he lodged a complaint with the council in Strasbourg, perhaps under the influence of Bucer, and brought it about that the matter was investigated, Franck arrested, and the *Chronica* confiscated. Franck was then released and expelled from the city, and the sale of his books was forbidden.

From Strasbourg he went to Kehl; in the spring of 1532 he addressed a petition to the Strasbourg Council to permit his return and the publication of the *Weltbuch,* which was to appear as a fourth part of the *Chronica;* both requests were refused. From Kehl he went to Esslingen and made a poor living as a soapmaker. In the summer of 1533 he attended the weekly markets in Ulm with his wares. This aroused in him the wish to live in the city. He was given permission. He had expressly promised not

to seek any church office "in these dangerous times"; he did not want to deprive others of their living. "What I have received from the Lord I want to share in writing with the people of God and not bury it."

At Ulm he entered the printery of Hans Warnier in the summer of 1534 and there published his *Paradoxa* (280 statements about God and the world), and his translation into German of Erasmus' *Encomion Moriae,* with the addition of three tracts which he named the *Kronbüchlein;* one of these deals with the vanity of all human arts and sciences, the second with the tree of the knowledge of good and evil, and the third with the praise of the foolish divine Word and the difference between the inner Word and the outer Word. Most significant are the *Paradoxa,* in which he developed most clearly his doctrinal system, if one may call it by this term. In 1534 also appeared his *Weltbuch,* a description of the countries and peoples, their customs, religions, and institutions in four parts; the last deals with the newly discovered America; the conclusion is a presentation of the various doctrinal ideas on earth.

In Ulm too Franck was severely attacked. Martin Frecht, the Protestant clergyman in Ulm, proved to be his most violent opponent. Philip of Hesse demanded his expulsion from Ulm as an "Anabaptist and revolutionary." Franck was to be expelled from the city on March 3, 1535. He protested against this since this constituted a violation of law; as a citizen of the city—he had been granted citizenship on Oct. 28, 1534—he could not be expelled without a hearing. He was not guilty of sedition, nor was he a heretic or Anabaptist, but had instead converted a number of Anabaptists. In his *Deklaration* he defended himself against Frecht's charges, also expressing himself on the subject of community of goods. For more than two years he was now left in peace in return for the promise not to write anything against the clergy nor to publish anything written by himself or by anyone else without censorship. In the meanwhile he had established his own print shop and bookstore. But he was able to publish in his own shop only a few smaller writings, such as the 613 Commands and Prohibitions of the Jews, and a revision of a Latin booklet by Sebastian Münster, and the satirical poem "St. Pfennings Lobgesang." The larger works he had to have printed elsewhere, since he could not secure permission to print them in Ulm. Thus on March 15, 1538, his *Guldin Arch* appeared in Augsburg, and in August 1538 his German chronicle *Germaniae Chronicon* appeared in Frankfurt a.M. In the former he discussed the principal points of the Christian faith with citations from the Bible and the church fathers as well as from heathen poets and thinkers. In the foreword he sharply accused the theologians for writing long commentaries and quarreling about sacraments, while they let practical Christian living in faith perish. For genuine pious Christians it was sufficient to know the Apostolic Confession of Faith and the Ten Commandments. By this publication his opponents were newly aroused against him; they finally had him and Schwenckfeld banished from Ulm, on Jan. 8, 1539.

On Jan. 10 Sebastian Franck with his wife and five children, aged 7 years to two months, arrived at Basel, Switzerland, where he entered the book printing business of Nikolaus Brylinger. In Basel he wrote his noted letter to the "Christians in Lower Germany" upon the request of a certain Johann von Beckenstein of Oldersum (*q.v.*) (Rembert, 226, who thought the letter was sent to the Bohemian Brethren in the Eifel, *q.v.*, area). Since Menno Simons stayed there a while in 1537 (Vos, 64), it can be assumed that this letter was meant for the Anabaptist brotherhood. The letter admonishes his dear brethren, who are like sheep in the midst of wolves, to seek Christ and the kingdom of God not outwardly but within themselves, and warns them against sectarianism and separatism. "Consider as dear people all who tolerate you in your faith and conscience and are willing to admit you as God-fearing citizens beside themselves; show them so much the more kindness, in order to win them through your innocence, love, faithfulness, and upright conduct without the preaching of the Word of God, even if they preach Christ and nevertheless walk in error and seek, worship, and vainly teach God with a mistaken zeal. From open and ungodly sinners, adulterers, liars, and usurers, do not separate yourselves in any other respect than from their ungodly life; do not partake of this if Christ is dear to you. . . . In brief, seek Christ not here or there, and do not mistakenly think that He is more with us than with you. He is no respecter of persons; we are all equally dear to Him. He is equally close to every nation even if they are outwardly called heathen, Jews, Turks, or Christians. Anyone who lives right and well, let him be to you a true brother, flesh and blood in Christ. It must be thus, Christ's sheep must lie among the wolves to the end of the world, as Luke 21 clearly shows. I have written this much about this as a favor to Johann Beckenstein and also at the request of other persons, for in general I do not like to write my faith abroad. Nor do I desire to have a special sect or following in the world. Let no one believe anything out of love to me which his heart of nature does not help him to accept. For here nothing can be counted according to the blessings of other people; but if you dig you will surely find. The servant of all of you in the Lord, Sebastian Franck at Basel."

Rembert published this letter in a Low German version and Hegler mentioned the Latin original, which is located in Königsberg.

In his last years Franck produced a number of writings of varying length. In 1540 his collection of proverbs appeared at Frankfurt, from which Lessing published extracts in 1857 in his *Collectanea* (*Comeniushefte*, 1901, 193). His *Kriegsbüchlein der Friedens* attacks the chaplains of the princes who defend warfare; his *Handbüchlein* collects briefly the main points of Christian doctrine. His *Verbütschiert Buch* is a concordance of the Bible which especially deals with the contradictions in it. In his exposition of Psalm 64 he sharply lashes the attitude of the scribes who drive away as heretics the true followers of Christ by misusing the Scriptures. His Latin paraphrase of the *Theologia Deutsch* (*q.v.*) (a tran-

script made in the 16th century is found in the Mennonite Library in Amsterdam; *Comeniushefte*, 1902, 86) was never printed. For the sake of completeness mention should also be made of the following additional writings: *Klagschrift oder Suplication der armen Dürftigen in England an den König daselbst gestellt wider die reichen, geistlichen Bettler* (1529); *Eine künstlich höfliche Deklamation und heftiger Wortkampf, Kant und Hader dreier Brüder vor Gericht. Nämlich eines Säufers, Hurers und Spielers. Von Philippo Beroaldo in Latein gestellt, verdeutscht von Seb. Franck* (Nürnberg, 1531); *Von Ankunft der Messe und der Wandelung des Brots und Weins im hochwürdigen Sakrament des Altars. Eine Disputation Seb. Francks mit Antwort Joh. Cochlei auf 88 Artikel aus der neuen Chronica* (1533); *Von der achtfältigen Belagerung und erschröcklichen Zerstörung der not-festen Stadt Jerusalem* (Frankfurt, 1532); *Wie man beten und psallieren soll* (this is the first hymn in the *Ausbund*, *q.v.*); *Dass Gott das einig ein und höchstes Gut sei* (1534); *Cornelius Aggrippas Lob des Esels. Verdeutscht von Seb. Franck; Von der Hoffnung und der Liebe Gottes; Sieben Weise in Griechenland, berühmt. Samt der hochverständigen, erleuchteten Personen, Philosophen und Gelehrten Leben. Von der Babylonischen Gefängnis der Juden bis auf Christum. Schöne nützliche Historien.* He also wrote three devotional tracts: *Von dem Reiche Christi; Von der Welt, des Teufels Reich;* and *Von der Gemeinschaft der Heiligen,* which were not printed until after his death.

Franck's point of view is most significantly expressed in the song in which he rejects the four contemporary religious groups, the Catholic, the Lutheran, the Zwinglian, and the Anabaptist, which has the title, "Von der zwieträchtigen Kirche, deren jede die andere verhasset und verdammet" (Wackernagel, *Kirchenlied* III, 817). The first stanza begins with the words, "Ich will und mag nicht Bäptisch sein," stanza 2, "Ich will und mag nicht Lutherisch sein," stanza 3, "Ich will und mag nicht Zwinglisch sein," and stanza 4, "Kein Wiedertäufer will ich sein." The fourth stanza is as follows:

Kein Wiedertäufer will ich sein,
Ihr Grund is klein,
steet auf dem Wassertauffen;
Die andern Secten schreckens ab,
da kein Gotts gab,
drumb in bsonder Kirchen lauffen.
   Leiden drob nott,
Welt hass unnd Todtt;
desshalb ohn spott
neher bey Gott
dan ander all drey hauffen.

Sebastian Franck was a sharp observer, an intelligent judge, a brilliant popular author, and a courageous historian animated by an unpartisan love of truth. He had at his disposal a widely inclusive knowledge. Almost every movement of his time is reflected in his writings. How well he knows how to reveal the wrongs of his time and to illuminate the weaknesses of the leading men and their doctrinal systems! He holds firmly to the Christian faith in God; but it takes on a tinge of the pantheism of ancient heathen philosophy. He has excellent statements about the value and nature of the Scriptures, about their importance and significance, but he does not accept them as a sole platform; for him the Word of God is implanted in all human beings and is effective in all believers, i.e., those who let it take effect in them. For this reason he does not really understand Biblicistic Anabaptism.

And yet Franck is very close to the Anabaptists. This has been strikingly shown by Walther Köhler in his article in *RGG*. Among the Anabaptists he had friends and admirers who "praise and highly value him" (Arnold, 284). Elsewhere he was attacked and rejected. Melanchthon, Bucer, and other theologians at the convention at Schmalkalden on March 5, 1540, uttered their verdict of damnation upon him because he separated from the church, despised the Bible and the office of preaching, and spread the satanic doctrine that all churches were alike. In 1545 Luther, in his foreword to the discussion on marriage, utters a very harsh judgment upon Sebastian Franck, one of the noblest and most open spirits of the time, saying, "He had not wanted to write anything about such people, because he too deeply despised him; he was a slanderer, and the devil's own and favorite mouthpiece. . . . In so far as I can judge by the smell of my nose, he is a fanatic or spiritualist who likes nothing but spirit, spirit, and who thinks nothing of Word, sacrament, and the office of preaching. . . . He has wandered through all filth and suffocated in his own filth" (Arnold, *loc. cit.*).

For Anabaptism Sebastian Franck is of lasting importance. This importance can be summarized in the following points: (1) he had personal connections with the movement and many of its leaders; (2) for this reason his evaluation of them which he gives in his writings has a special value and forms a principal authentic source of information for their earliest history and doctrine; (3) he is their advocate and warmest defender against false accusations; (4) by means of his writings he had considerable influence on them; (5) he was himself influenced by them and based on their teaching his world-wide free concept of a practical Christianity which is based on inner experience and which activates itself in love. "He never tires of proclaiming the right of the individual in matters of faith, on the wrongness of all force, the responsibility of the individual, which can be taken from him by no brotherhood and no tradition." These are ideas found in Anabaptism, which were not universally recognized and valued until our time. Upon his own time Franck had little influence. In Germany he was soon forgotten, but in the Netherlands and in England his writings continued to live and bear fruit. NEFF.

Concerning the extent of Sebastian Franck's influence on the Anabaptists and the Dutch Reformation movement there is difference of opinion. Karel Vos thought that "Menno Simons believed in him as an oracle" (p. 40); whereas Christian Sepp claimed that the Dutch Anabaptists considered Franck an opponent (*Geschiedkundige Nasporinge* I, 163 f.). There is no doubt that the Anabaptists appreciated Franck's sympathetic and objective attitude and treat-

ment of their views, and that they had much in common with him. (Menno Simons made many quotations in his booklets from Franck's works.) On the other hand, it is obvious that they did not share his noncommittal views regarding the church and certain doctrines. Dirk Philips took occasion to write against him. It was undoubtedly due to Franck's influence that Obbe Philips (*q.v.*), Dirk's brother, left the Anabaptists about 1540 because they laid so much stress on a visible church, while Obbe like Franck was a spiritualist who did not believe that one church, e.g., the Anabaptist Church, was the true church of God (*BRN* VII, 122). Hans de Ries (*q.v.*), another Dutch leader, influenced by Coornhert (*q.v.*), who has been called the "Sebastian Franck of the Netherlands," also, at least for a while, came under the influence of Franck. In the 17th century the Lamist Mennonites and particularly their leader Galenus Abrahamsz (*q.v.*) held many of Franck's views, which were at this time common property among the Collegiants (*q.v.*).

The letter (see above) which Franck wrote to Johan von Bekesteyn no doubt influenced the Mennonites. Dirk Philips reported that some elders and brethren gave him this letter and also the one Franck had written to Campanus, with the request that he respond to them. This he did by writing *A Response and Refutation of the Two Letters by Sebastian Franck According to the Word of God Briefly Composed by D. P.* (*Een verantwoordinghe ende Refutation op twee Sendtbrieven Sebastiani Franck, cortelijck uyt die heylighe Schrift vervaet D.P.* [*BRN* X, 473]).

This, however, does not mean that the Anabaptists and particularly the Dutch did not rely heavily on Franck's writings. On the contrary, this proves that some of the leaders thought that their followers were depending too heavily on him.

The identity of Johan von Bekesteyn is also an unanswered question. Bekesteyn made it a point to visit Franck and upon his request Franck wrote the letter addressed to the "Christians in Lower Germany." This letter has been published in its original Latin form (Hegler, *Beiträge*) and in a Dutch-Low German translation by Rembert (p. 226), and most recently by Ohling in a modern High German translation (*Ostfreesland*, 1954, 114). The Dutch-Low-German edition was evidently first published in 1564, at which time Pieter de Zuttere edited the two letters of Franck to Campanus and von Bekesteyn. It was evidently this edition which was handed to Dirk Philips for a response.

Some scholars think that von Bekesteyn was an Anabaptist, although no definite record seems to confirm this. He was a refugee from the Netherlands who found shelter in Oldersum (*q.v.*), East Friesland, where many Dutch refugees were located. He was a friend of William Gnapheus and Entfelder. That he was a full-fledged Anabaptist is unlikely, mainly for the following reason. On his way to South Germany he was in touch with the reformers of Strasbourg, viz., Capito, Bucer, etc., and sent the two letters to Felix Rex Polyphemus, a reformer in Prussia and friend of Paul Speratus, including letters by Bullinger and Calvin. This span of friends and spiritual interests definitely goes beyond that of an average Anabaptist of the 16th century. Until there is more evidence it must be assumed that von Bekesteyn was a Dutch Sacramentist who found refuge in East Friesland and associated and sympathized with leaders and views of the Sacramentists, Reformed, and Left Wing Anabaptists. A closer check of all records should indicate the church to which he belonged in East Friesland. C.K., vdZ.

Arch. f. Gesch. d. Phil. V, 389-400; Hase, Seb. Franck von Wörd, der Schwarmgeist (Leipzig, 1869); Alfred Hegler, Geist und Schrift bei Sebastian Franck (Freiburg, 1892); idem, "Sebastian Franck," HRE VI (1899) 142-50; idem, Beiträge zur Geschichte der Mystik in der Reformationszeit (Berlin, 1906); K. Rembert, Wiedertäufer; Hermann Oncken, "Sebastian Franck als Historiker," Historische Ztscht, n.s. XLVI (1899) 385-435; J. H. Maronier, Het Inwendig Woord (Amsterdam, 1890); A. Reimann, "Sebastian Franck als Geschichtsphilosoph." (Comenius-Schriften zur Geistesgeschichte I), Geisteskultur und Volksbildung (Berlin, 1920); W. Köhler, "Sebastian Franck," RGG II (1928) cols. 649-50; Chr. Sepp, Geschiedkundige Nasporingen I (Leiden, 1872) 158 ff.; E. Seeberg, Gottfried Arnold, die Wissenschaft und die Mystik seiner Zeit (Meerane, 1923); Rufus M. Jones, Spiritual Reformers; Will-Erich Peuckert, Sebastian Franck, ein deutscher Sucher (Munich, 1943); Eberhard Teufel, "Landräumig," Sebastian Franck, ein Wanderer an Donau, Rhein und Neckar (Neustadt an der Aisch, 1954); idem, Theologische Rundschau XII (1940) 99-129; idem, Luther und Luthertum im Urteil Sebastian Francks (Tübingen, 1922); Walter Nigg, "Sebastian Franck," Das Buch der Ketzer (Zürich, 1949) 382; K. Vos, Menno Simons, 1496-1561 (Leiden, 1914); Hans Franck, Sebastian. Gottsucher-Roman (Gütersloh, 1949); Kuno Räber, Studien zur Geschichtsbibel Sebastian Francks (Basel, 1952); J. Lindeboom, Een Franc-tireur der Reformatie. Sebastian Franck (Arnhem, 1952); Cornelius Krahn, Menno Simons (1496-1561) (Karlsruhe, 1936); Bruno Becker, "Nederlandsche Vertalingen van Sebastiaan Franck's Geschriften," Nederlandsch Archief voor Kerkgeschiedenis (1928) 149-60; Gerhard Ohling, "Aus den Anfängen der Reformation. Ein Brief des Sebastian Franck aus Donauwörth an die Oldersumer Gemeinde," Ostfreesland (1954) 111-15; De geschriften van Dirk Philipsz, BRN X (The Hague, 1914); H. W. Meihuizen, Galenus Abrahamsz (Haarlem, 1954) 44 f., 58, 82, 134 f.; ML I, 668-74, with exhaustive bibliography.

Francois van Ludick (i.e., Liege in Belgium), also called François Bepen, an Anabaptist martyr, a former halberdier who was converted and baptized at Maastricht (q.v.), Dutch province of Limburg, by Henric Rol (q.v.). When arrested, he recanted, and was therefore executed by beheading instead of being burned at the stake. The execution took place at Maastricht on Feb. 13, 1535. His confession gives interesting information concerning the Maastricht congregation in this time. vdZ.

W. Bax, Het Protestantisme in het Bisdom Luik I (The Hague, 1937) 122.

Franconia, Pa., is a small village located in the center of Franconia Twp., Montgomery Co., Pa. It was called Franconia Square until 1849. It is in the heart of a prosperous farming community inhabited largely by Mennonites. The Mennonite Church (MC) is located one-half mile west of the village. The German settlers probably brought the name from the duchy of Franconia. Q.L.

Franconia Mennonite Aid Plan for Fire Insurance. As early as 1883 the Franconia (MC) Conference took action to encourage taking offerings to cover losses by fire. In 1896 a systematic attempt was made to organize a Mennonite aid plan, but it met with the disapproval of conference. In the meantime losses were not covered by offerings, and members held insurance in nonreligious fire insurance companies. In May 1935 the conference approved such an organization, and appointed a committee of four to study the proposal and draw up bylaws. A state charter was granted on Dec. 2, 1936. The board of directors is composed of one member from each congregation. The 1954 organization is as follows: Ezra Myers, Doylestown, president; Ernest R. Clemens, Lansdale, secretary; and Henry A. Bishop, Blooming Glen, treasurer. In 1954 the Aid Plan listed 1,200 members and $11,000,000. J.C.C.

Franconia Mennonite Board of Missions and Charities. The Franconia Conference (MC) decided on May 3, 1917, to organize a mission board. Members of the conference had already been serving in the Philadelphia Mission, which was started by the Lancaster Conference Sunday School Mission, now the Eastern Mennonite Board of Missions and Charities. Joseph Bechtel served as superintendent from the beginning until his death in 1928. The conference in May 1908 had decided to aid in the purchase of the Howard Street property in Philadelphia. It was decided that each congregation should have one member on the board.

The first officers of the organized board were Allen A. Freed, president, Isaac F. Detwiler, vice-president, William D. Roth, secretary, and Garret S. Nice, treasurer. A charter was secured in July 1918. The first conference mission station was opened at Norristown on April 6, 1919, and others followed in rapid succession; by 1954 there were 17 stations in the district, and a mission in Cuba (1954). J.C.C.

J. C. Wenger, The History of the Mennonites of the Franconia Conference (Telford, 1937).

Franconia Mennonite Church (MC), located near Franconia, Montgomery Co., Pa., the largest congregation in the Franconia Mennonite Conference, had a membership of 800 in 1953. The earliest building, probably a log house erected before 1748, served for both school and church services. This building was replaced by a stone structure in 1833 which was enlarged in 1866 and razed in 1892. The present building, built in 1892 and enlarged in 1917, seats over 1,000 people. Since 1769 Franconia has served as the meeting place for the semiannual sessions of the Franconia Mennonite Conference.

Among the outstanding leaders of Franconia were bishops Henry Funk (d. 1760), his son Christian Funk (1731-1811), Jacob Gottschalk (1769-1845), Josiah Clemmer (1827-1905), A. G. Clemmer (1867-1939), and preachers Henry Nice (1804-83) and Michael Moyer (1836-1912). The first minister to preach in English, Menno B. Souder, ordained in 1914, was still serving the congregation in 1953.

The Franconia Almsbook (1767-   ) is a valuable record signed by the ordained men of Franconia and four other congregations in the Franconia Conference District. (See J. C. Wenger, "Alms Book of the Franconia Mennonite Church 1767-1836," MQR X, 1936, 161-72.)

The Sunday school at first served as a medium for teaching the German language. In 1871 or 1872 such a school was founded by Preacher Henry Nice. Sessions were held in the near-by schoolhouse during summer. By 1876 it became a Sunday afternoon school and was held in the meetinghouse. By 1918 it became an all year Sunday school.

Church services are held every two weeks Sunday mornings, and Sunday-school sessions are held in the afternoon. On the alternate Sunday when there are no services, Sunday school convenes in the morning. Evening services every four weeks were begun in 1938. The ministers in 1953 were Menno B. Sauder, E. D. Derstine, with Arthur Ruth serving as bishop from the outside.   Q.L.

Franconia Mennonite Conference (MC), with the Lancaster Conference the oldest conference of the Mennonites in North America, the congregations of which are located mostly in Montgomery and Bucks counties in southeastern Pennsylvania, with scattered congregations historically in Philadelphia, Chester, Berks, Lehigh, and Northampton counties. Until 1936 it was called "Eastern Pennsylvania Conference" in the *Mennonite Yearbook and Directory*. The town of Souderton, 30 miles north of Philadelphia, lies close to the geographical center of the present cluster of congregations comprising the Franconia Conference. The name Franconia came to be applied to the Conference because for the last two centuries the semiannual ministers' meetings have been held in the meetinghouse of the Franconia congregation, which building is located in Franconia Twp., Montgomery Co., near the village of Franconia, about two miles southwest of Souderton. The township seems to have been named in honor of the Germantown pioneer, Francis Daniel Pastorius, who had been born at Sommerhausen near Würzburg, Lower Franconia, Germany.

The origins of the Franconia Conference are connected with the settlement of the Mennonites at Germantown (*q.v.*) near Philadelphia in 1683. The early Mennonite settlers of Germantown represented four distinct groups: (1) those from Crefeld who arrived in 1683 ff. and bore such names as Lensen, Op den Graeff, van Bebber, Telner, Umstat, Jansen, Neuss, Tyson, Sellen, and Hosters, William Rittenhouse (*q.v.*), first Mennonite minister in America, H. Kasselberg, and Jacob Godshalk (*q.v.*), the first American Mennonite bishop: these last three families came from the Lower Rhine; (2) a group of families from the Hamburg-Altona congregation represented by such names as Karsdorp, van Sinteren, and Klassen; and (3) a group of Palatine families named Kolb, Kassel, Bowman, and Graf; (4) a father and son named Keyser from Amsterdam. Most of the original Mennonite settlers of Germantown were therefore of Dutch ethnic origin with the exception of the Palatines who were Swiss. An early account, written by Jacob Godshalk, says that when the Palatine Mennonites arrived at Germantown in 1707 they stood aloof from the rest of the Mennonites in Germantown for a year, but as soon as the two groups merged the church chose three deacons, and shortly thereafter two preachers, one of whom was the Palatine Martin Kolb. In the long run it was Palatine Mennonites of Swiss extraction

who constituted by far the bulk of the membership of the Franconia Conference. Probably 95 per cent of the present members bear such German (mostly Swiss German) names as Alderfer, Allebach, Bechtel, Bergey, Clemens, Clemmer, Derstine, Detweiler, Fretz, Funk, Gehman, Gross, Hunsberger, Hunsiker, Kolb, Landis, Lederach, Meyer and Moyer, Mininger, Overholt and Oberholtzer, Ruth, Schantz, Souder, Stauffer, Swartley, and Yoder.

The Skippack outpost of the Germantown colony was established at least by 1709 (the name may have come from Schüpbach near Signau in Switzerland), and the new daughter colony soon outgrew its mother. In rapid succession new settlements were made in Chester County, in the valley of the Schuylkill River, and on up in the Manatawny section of what is now Berks County, and at numerous points in Montgomery and Bucks counties. Log meetinghouses, usually used for school purposes as well, were quickly erected at various points beginning with Germantown in 1708. By 1840 the Franconia Conference consisted of about 22 congregations, served by 5 bishops, 40 preachers, and 25 deacons; in Montgomery County, Skippack, Towamencin, Worcester, Salford, Franconia, Plain, and Providence; in Bucks County, Rockhill, Lexington, Blooming Glen, Deep Run, Doylestown, Springfield, East Swamp, West Swamp, and Flatland; in Chester County, Vincent and Coventry; in Berks County, Boyertown and Hereford; and in Lehigh County, Saucon and Upper Milford.

No date is known for the formal organization of the conference, if indeed there ever was a formal organization. The semiannual meetings of the ministry likely began spontaneously and met irregularly at first. Christian Funk (*q.v.*), early Franconia bishop, wrote in 1809, when the semiannual meetings of the ministers were already well established, of similar meetings in the 1760's: it is likely that they had been started by 1750 or earlier. Down to the present generation these meetings remained strictly business sessions, led by the bishops, presided over by the senior bishop in years of service, without formal addresses except the individual messages of the bishops on the issues facing the churches. No official secretary was appointed to keep minutes until 1909, when J. C. Clemens was chosen, who served until 1950.

The Franconia Mennonites have always stood strictly for the doctrine of nonresistance, although some of their young men served in the Civil War and either united with the church for the first time after their release from the army or were reinstated as members after excommunication. It is traditional to adopt a statement at the close of each ministers' meeting that this conference "still desires to continue in the simple and nonresistant faith of Christ." In general it may be said that historically the Franconia Mennonites represented a rather tolerant type of Mennonitism: this is evident in a letter written by three Franconia bishops in 1773 in which they state, "With regard to our confession of faith, our forefathers have taken the articles adopted . . . 1632 at Dordrecht in Holland, and outside of these we have held to no human regulations, but have taught simply those of the Holy Scriptures and what may further God's honor and man's happiness." The same letter reports that the congregations were growing numerically, that they were enjoying "unlimited freedom in both civil and religious affairs," that they had never been compelled to bear arms, that they were not asked to swear oaths, that those marrying outside the brotherhood were placed under church censure until reinstatement following "expiation" (acknowledgment of error to the congregation). They said they had the writings of Menno Simons, van Braght's *Martyrs' Mirror,* the *Güldene Aepfel* (Anabaptist confessions, martyrologies, prayers, and hymns), and the sermons and writings of such Mennonite leaders as Joost Hendricks, Willem Wynands, Jacob Denner, "and many others."

It appears that the Franconia Mennonites have also long been interested in good music, for on the occasion of the effort of the Franconia and Lancaster Mennonites to issue a common hymnbook soon after 1800, the project had to be abandoned because when the representatives of both groups came together for the necessary committee work, the Franconia brethren had already selected "enough hymns for a complete hymnbook," and they further wished to include "a number of Psalms and notes." The outcome was that they issued their own hymnal at Germantown, *Kleine Geistliche Harfe* (1803), reprinted a half-dozen times between 1811 and 1904. The Lancaster deacon in whose home the committee meeting had been held reported that "the Skippack brethren . . . have a large and strong church, as well as a large district, and are well trained in singing." At the time of the committee meeting they already had 3,000 subscriptions for the purchase of the proposed hymnal.

Like the Mennonites of Switzerland, and in contrast with the Lancaster Mennonites who on this point resembled the more conservative Dutch Mennonite groups, the Franconia Mennonites seem not to have generally observed footwashing (*q.v.*) as a church ceremony until the era 1875-1925, during which time it was gradually introduced, but not in connection with the Lord's Supper; it is now observed in all the congregations at the "Preparatory Service," held on the Saturday before (Sunday) communion service. The latter was always observed only annually until the present generation, again in conformity with ancient Swiss Mennonite practice, but in contrast with Lancaster where it was observed semiannually.

Prior to 1900 no "evangelistic" meetings were ever held. Catechetical instruction was given to the young people who applied for membership in the brotherhood. In recent years at least this instruction was based largely on the "Shorter Catechism" of 35 Questions and Answers, and on the Eighteen Articles of the Dordrecht Confession of Faith (*q.v.*). Not only were evangelistic meetings shunned as an emotional phenomenon unworthy of those who believed in a life of separation from the world and of commitment to Christ, but the giving of personal "testimonies" of the assurance of salvation and of God's dealings with the individual testifying was regarded as an evidence of spiritual pride: it seldom

if ever occurred in the church life of the Franconia Mennonites for the first two and a half centuries of their life in America (from 1683).

As to costume the Franconia Mennonites resisted the following after new fashions and fads in clothing, but eventually adopted what became conventional attire with some exceptions; i.e., they resisted for a long time long trousers, shoes with laces, the wearing of coats rather than shawls by women in cold weather, etc. The exceptions relate mostly to the continued wearing of the colonial frock coat by ordained ministers, the wearing of a "plain" coat (without lapels) by some of the lay brethren (but the coat is of conventional length), the wearing of "cape" dresses by some of the women, and the adoption and maintenance of the plain Quaker bonnet by many women during the 19th and 20th centuries. In the plainer congregations of the conference, especially in Montgomery County, the bonnet was apparently universally worn since early in the 19th century. But in a number of the Bucks and Berks County congregations some of the women wore some sort of hat during much of the 19th and early 20th centuries. In a number of the Bucks County meetinghouses the women's anterooms were equipped with shelves on which small boxes were kept for the storing of the "devotional coverings" or worship veils. The women then wore their bonnet or hat to the meetinghouse, took it off, put on the veil which they kept at the meetinghouse, and entered the service. In 1905 Hartzler and Kauffman reported in their *Mennonite Church History* the partial nonobservance of footwashing in the Franconia congregations, and also that "in a few of the congregations . . . the sisters wear hats instead of bonnets." Mennonite leaders from Montgomery County strongly protested against the worldliness of some of the Bucks County churches, and such non-Franconia leaders as Daniel Kauffman and S. G. Shetler were imported for a strong indoctrination in essential Mennonite doctrines and practices. The result was the complete adoption of the bonnet as compulsory headdress about 1912. During the last 50 years there has been a growing emphasis on the continuous, daily wearing of the "devotional covering" by all women members of the church.

Two divisions have occurred in the Franconia Conference; the first was led by Bishop Christian Funk (*q.v.*) in 1778 over the issue of recognizing the American government before the issue was decided by the American winning of the War of Independence: Funk favored the American side, while the other bishops felt that nonresistant Mennonites should not recognize a rebellion. The Funkite group built four small church buildings, and worshiped in a few others, but they never prospered, and disintegrated by 1850. The division of 1847 was led by a vigorous and able minister, John H. Oberholtzer (*q.v.*), who favored more progressive attitudes, a milder discipline, a more tolerant and cooperative attitude toward other denominations, etc. In this division 16 ordained men withdrew, including the senior bishop who had been the conference moderator, leaving about 54 ordained men in the Franconia Conference. The new group claimed six meetinghouses (Upper Milford, Schwenksville, Skippack, East Swamp, West Swamp, and Flatland), worshiped on alternate Sundays from the Franconia Mennonites at seven other points (Saucon, Springfield, Providence, Worcester, Hereford, Boyertown, and Rockhill), and at once erected a new church building at Deep Run. Those who withdrew probably constituted a fourth of all the members of the Franconia Conference in 1847, possibly 500 members. In 1860 Oberholtzer helped to organize what is now the General Conference Mennonite Church (*q.v.*). His 1847 group now constitutes the Eastern District (*q.v.*) of that body. The two conferences in 1954 were almost equal in membership: Franconia, 5,372; Eastern District, 4,525. In 1950 a small independent group withdrew to form the Calvary Mennonite Church, with 170 members in 1954.

Among the modern developments in the Franconia Conference should be mentioned the adoption of a constitution by the conference (1947); the acceptance of Sunday schools around 1900, and young people's meetings and "revival" meetings two to four decades later; a vigorous program of establishing mission stations in southeastern Pennsylvania, Long Island, and Vermont; the establishment of both primary schools (1945) and a high school (1954), the first by an association of patrons, the latter by the conference; the erection of the large home for the aged, Eastern Mennonite Home (1916); the establishment of Eastern Mennonite Convalescent Home (1942); a closer working with the Mennonite General Conference (MC) to whose General Council it sends an official delegate; and in common with many other areas of the church, considerable difficulty in attempting to take a vigorous stand against any breakdown of historic Mennonite principles, and against any cultural changes which are regarded as being a threat to a Christian simplicity and to a genuine spiritual nonconformity to the world, without falling into the danger of legalism and without occasioning new secessions from the group. The Franconia Conference has shown a stronger resistance to the entrance of Chiliasm than any other district conference (MC) and in fact forbids it. Harold S. Bender has correctly observed that "Franconia has also preserved in its customs and traditions more nearly the ancient Mennonite forms of worship, doctrine, and church government than any other American district" (*Franconia History*, p. vii).

The present congregations of the Franconia Conference may be divided into two categories: about 17 established and historic Mennonite congregations with a total membership of over 4,500, and a larger number of mission stations with a total membership of close to 800. There are 9 bishops serving in 4 districts, about 60 ministers, and about 30 deacons.

J.C.W.

J. C. Wenger, *History of the Mennonites of the Franconia Conference* (Telford, 1937); W. Hunsberger, *The Franconia Mennonites and War* (1951); *Doctrinal Statement, Constitution and Discipline of the Franconia Mennonite Conference, 1725-1947* (Franconia, 1947).

Franconia Mennonite Historical Society, originally called the Historical Society of the Franconia Conference District (MC), was organized in October 1930 at the Plain Mennonite Church, Lansdale, Pa., with John D. Souder as president and Samuel R. Swartley as secretary. In 1952 the officers were Quintus Leatherman, president, David K. Allebach, vice-president, Herbert Derstine, secretary, and Ernest R. Clemens, treasurer. The Franconia Mennonite Historical Library, established in 1950 and located in Souderton, contains the archives, books, and papers of the society.

The meetings of the society are held annually in the various churches of the conference district. Programs consist of addresses on local history of the churches and general Mennonite church history. The purpose of the society is to stimulate interest in the study of the historical background of the Mennonite Church and its bearing upon our church life today.

In 1935, through the inspiration of the president of the society, John D. Souder, the collection of sources for a Franconia conference church history was begun. John C. Wenger was selected as the writer, and by 1937 the work, *History of the Mennonites of the Franconia Conference,* was completed and was published by the society.　　　　Q.L.

Francyntgen, an Anabaptist martyr who was burned at the stake with her niece Grietgen and Maeyken Doornaerts in 1556 at Belle (Bailleul) in Flanders. At the stake Maeyken said, "This is the hour for which I have greatly longed." (*Mart. Mir.* D 166, E 553; *ML* I, 674.)　　　　NEFF.

Francyntgen (*Francyntgen Meulenaers,* wife of Andries Viblarre, or Andries de Molenaar), an Anabaptist martyr who was arrested with many other Mennonites in Brugge, Belgium, on Nov. 10, 1561, while they were attending a meeting outside the town. They all remained steadfast and were burned at the stake at Brugge. Five of them were executed on Dec. 10, 1561, among them Andries, the husband of Francyntgen, and on the next day Francyntgen with the five others was put to death. Their martyrdom is celebrated in a hymn, "Genade ende Vrede moet godvresende sijn," found in the old Dutch songbook, *Veelderhande Liedekens* of 1569, and in Wackernagel, *Lieder*. The records of van Braght (*Mart. Mir.*) are somewhat inexact as to these martyrs. (*Mart. Mir.* D 288; E 655; Wackernagel, *Lieder,* 130; Verheyden, *Brugge,* 50, No. 41.)

vDZ.

Franeker, an old town in the Dutch province of Friesland, about 10 miles west of the Frisian capital Leeuwarden, pop. (1947) 9,050, 211 Mennonites, is the seat of a Mennonite congregation, which has had a varied and interesting history. Of its oldest history there are only a few bits of information from direct sources; of the rich archives of the Franeker congregations not much has been saved; the membership list begins with 1722; the children's book dates a few years later; the earliest minutes of the church board date only to 1800.

There must have been Anabaptists here from the earliest times: an edict of March 9, 1535, orders that owners of land and houses are forbidden to lease them to Anabaptists, and if this had happened those

Anabaptists should be driven out; and in a second edit of July 7, 1537, the magistrate of Franeker is charged to exercise close supervision on "Lutherans, Sacramentists (*q.v.*) and Anabaptists." But the city government seems to have been rather tolerant, for there are no martyrs from this town.

In the second half of the 16th century, when the Mennonites were organized into a congregation, they must have been very numerous. For the year 1560 they are estimated at about 620 members (1,300 souls). The number of members had largely increased, especially by the activity of Elder Leenaert Bouwens (*q.v.*), who baptized at Franeker 16 persons in 1551-54; 45 in 1554-56; 37 in 1557-61; 381 in 1563-65; and 360 in 1568-82; total, 839. But in this period Franeker played a not very admirable, though important role in Mennonite history. First of all in 1555 or 1556 a group of more progressive members, who were averse to strict banning and shunning and disappointed by the fact that Menno Simons at a conference in near-by Harlingen agreed with Leenaert Bouwens and the stricter wing of Mennonites, separated from the main body. Their leader was Hendrik Naeldeman (*q.v.*), and their adherents in other congregations were at first called *Franekeraars;* later on they were usually called Waterlanders (*q.v.*).

After ten years it was again in Franeker that a new quarrel arose. From Flanders many Mennonites had fled to the Netherlands and a number of them had settled in Franeker; in the Mennonite congregation, the Flemish at first were accorded a brotherly welcome, but soon both Flemish and native Frisians mutually considered one another as much deviated from the old Mennonite plain style of living, the Frisians looking upon the less plain dress and manners of the Flemish as worldly, and the Flemish regarding the care the Frisians bestowed upon their houses and furniture as a great evil. In the congregation the Frisians outnumbered the Flemish. (In 1566 there were only 30 brethren from Flanders.) Then it happened that Leenaert Bouwens, because of a fault he had committed, was suspended from his service of elder (1565), and Ebbe Pietersz, elder at Harlingen, was also unable to travel about the churches. So the Franeker congregation decided to choose a preacher. The Flemish succeeded in having Jeroen Tinnegieter, a Flemish immigrant, chosen as a preacher. But he was not accepted by the Frisians. This was the origin of the Flemish-Frisian schism, which divided (1567) the Mennonites throughout the Netherlands, and even in West Prussia (see **Flemish Mennonites**).

Twenty years later, in 1586, Franeker was the scene of a new schism. Thomas Byntgens (*q.v.*), elder of the Flemish congregation, bought a house intended for a meetinghouse, but when it became clear that the deal had not been above reproach, a quarrel arose in the congregation. By this Huiskooper (*q.v.*) dispute the Flemish church was divided into Huiskoopers or Old Flemish Mennonites and Contra-Huiskoopers or (Mild) Flemish. The leader of the Huiskoopers was Thomas Byntgens, and leader of the other party was the deacon Jacob Keest (*q.v.*). This conflict too was not limited to Franeker only; nearly all the Flemish congregations were divided.

So after the Huiskooper dispute there were at Franeker at least four congregations: (*a*) Waterlanders, (*b*) Frisians, (*c*) Huiskoopers (Old Flemish), (*d*) Flemish. At the beginning of the 17th century there must have existed here at least three more congregations: (*e*) Jan Jacobsgezinden (*q.v.*), (*f*) a congregation of unknown type, presumably a separated Frisian church, maybe of Pieter-Jeltjesvolk (*q.v.*). Finally mention is made of the existence of (*g*) a High German congregation in 1614, which still existed in 1640, in which year it was involved in a quarrel.

But little is known of these congregations because of lack of documents. Of the Jan-Jacobsgezinden we know that Elder Joris Jacobsz baptized 29 persons here in 1640-44. Soon the membership decreased. In the 18th century it had strong contacts with the Jan-Jacobsgezinden at neighboring Menaldum (*q.v.*). Wybe Jans (d. 1778) was its last preacher, from 1729 on. In 1762 it merged with the only other then existing congregation; it then numbered 13 brethren, the number of sisters being unknown. About most of the other Franeker congregations there is still less information. The Waterlanders (*a*) sent a representative to the Waterlander conference held at Amsterdam in 1647. About 1670 this congregation must have united with one of the other churches. The Huiskoopers or Old Flemish (*b*), of whom Jelle Daniel Keest was a preacher in 1640 and Agge Classen in 1648, had their meetinghouse, called "het Valkje," in the Schoolsteeg.

In 1663 there were three Mennonite congregations in Franeker, one, of which Jouke Wybes was a preacher (membership 30), a second, of which Watse Watses was a preacher (membership 50), and a third, of which Isbrant Japiks (or Jacobs) was a preacher (membership 41). The membership of those three churches had in one century decreased from 620 to 121. (In a census of the town of Franeker of 1667 there are found, however, 107 Mennonite family names; names of non-taxpayers—wives, minors, and poor people not being included in this number. If the total number of Mennonites of the census list is true, the membership must have been much more than the 121 mentioned in 1663.) These three churches, which are said to have met in het Valkje, in the Eerste Noord, and in the Tweede Noord, are not easy to identify; the one meeting in het Valkje was that of the Huiskoopers (*c*), of which either Isbrant Japiks or Watse Watses was the preacher. Jouke Wybes was preacher of the Waterlanders (*a*), for he was in 1647 in Amsterdam as a representative. The third congregation must have been that of Jan Jacobsgezinden (*c*).

In 1695 at the founding of the Conference of Mennonite Churches in the province of Friesland (see **Friese Sociëteit**), there were only two congregations at Franeker, one called Old Flemish (the Jan-Jacobsgezinden) and the other called the United Flemish-Frisian-Waterlander and High German congregation, later usually called Flemish and Waterlander church, or simply United congregation. This united church, whose membership numbered 216 in

1695 (this number must be a mistake; it must have been lower), joined the Conference of Mennonite congregations in Friesland. Paulus Tiesma and Tiepke Abbema, both members of it, were members of the first board of the conference. From now the information is more frequent and clearer. In 1711 the United congregation, which held its meetings in the old church on the Tweede Noord, requested permission to rebuild the meetinghouse, but the States of Friesland refused. Preachers of this congregation were Melle Takema 1721-ca. 50, and Ate Sierds of Poppingewier (d. Aug. 20, 1770) 1720-65. In 1760 the meetinghouse was enlarged and on July 22, 1762, the Jan-Jacobsgezinden merged with this congregation. Shortly before, on July 1, 1766, the congregation of near-by Tjummarum had also united with it. Until this time the congregations had been served by untrained ministers. In 1765 Franeker wished to call an educated minister, for whom the church board obtained a yearly subsidy from the Lamist congregation at Amsterdam, and on July 29, 1765, Jan Lippens, a ministerial candidate who had finished his study at the Amsterdam Mennonite Theological Seminary, preached his induction sermon at Franeker. He stayed here only one year, receiving a call to the Amsterdam congregation in December 1766. Wopko Molenaar, his successor, served here 1767-70, then moved to Crefeld. Pieter Stinstra (b. 1743 at Franeker), nephew of Joannes Stinstra) (q.v.), minister of Harlingen, served his native church 1770-1800. Whether Wepke Tyssen Feenstra (d. 1779), who in the Naamlijst of 1775 is listed as having been a preacher at Franeker since 1773, but who is not mentioned in the following Naamlijsten, served this church as a minister or not, cannot be determined. Stinstra was followed by Bern. Cremer 1801-11, Klaas J. Overbeek 1812-47, Matthys E. van Delden 1848-72, H. Boetje 1873-79, C. J. Bakker 1879-99, M. Honigh 1900-32, G. J. W. den Herder 1933-39, C. C. de Maar 1940-46, A. J. de Kam 1947-50, and G. Kater since 1951.

On May 29, 1863, a new church on the Voorstraat was dedicated; the old characteristic meetinghouse, which is now used by the Baptists, was then sold. The Voorstraat church of 1863 is still in use; the organ was renovated in 1899.

In 1899 Miss Sytske Stinstra, a member of the congregation, bequeathed her stately house to the church (now parsonage) and willed in addition a considerable amount of money, which is managed by the church board as the Stinstra Fund.

During the last quarter of the 19th and the first part of the 20th centuries (preachers Boetje, Bakker, and Honigh) the congregation turned to a rather radical modernism (theological liberalism). Even the Lord's Supper was not observed here from 1915 to 1934.

The membership, which is said to have been 212 in 1695, was about 90 in 1796, 49 in 1812, 95 in 1838, 114 in 1861, 128 in 1900, and 140 in 1953, of whom 90 live in the city of Franeker and 50 in neighboring towns and on farms in the neighborhood. Church activities are a Sunday school for

children, youth group called "Hendrik Naeldeman," ladies' circle, choir.

The city of Franeker was the seat of a university from 1585 to 1842. At first there was no contact between the Mennonites and the university, the Mennonites having lay preachers (untrained ministers) and being averse to scholarly theology, and the professors of the university, who were all Calvinists, regarding the Mennonites more or less as heretics, like Prof. Henricus Antonides (q.v.), who in 1585 orated against the Mennonites and their "false doctrines." But in the 18th century many Mennonites studied at the Franeker University, especially medicine. From about 1730, 25 young men attended the theological lectures of this university before finishing their study at the Amsterdam Mennonite Seminary, among whom were a number of outstanding Mennonite ministers, such as Klaas de Vries, Heere Oosterbaan, Hoito Tichelaar, Pieter Stinstra, Pieter Feenstra, and Jan ter Borg. vDZ.

Inv. Arch. Amst. I, Nos. 477, 479, 557, 558-III; II, Nos. 1721-35; *DB* 1864, 163; 1879, 2, 89; 1893, 1-90 (*passim*); 1900, 225; Blaupot t. C., *Friesland*, 67, 88, 91, 104, 133, 157, 169, 188, 191, 220, 224, 246, 247, 254; Kühler. *Geschiedenis* I and II, *passim;* M. E. van Delden, *Leerrede, uitgesproken bij gelegenheid der laatste godsdienstoefening in het oude kerkgebouw* (Franeker, n.d., 1863); *ML* I, 674 f.

Franekeraars (or *Franekers*), the name of a group of Dutch Mennonites who about 1556 followed Hendrik Naeldeman (q.v.) of Franeker, also called *Scheedemakers* (q.v.). They were a progressive group among the Dutch Mennonites and soon merged with the Waterlanders (q.v.). (*BRN* VII, 55; *DB* 1876, 21.)   vDZ.

Franke, Ottilie, an Anabaptist martyr who was drowned with nine others in the Unstrut near Mühlhausen in Thüringia, Germany, Nov. 8, 1537.
                                                                NEFF.

P. Wappler, *Die Täuferbewegung in Thüringen von 1526-1584* (Jena, 1913) 162; *ML* I, 675.

Franke, Peter, an Anabaptist leader and preacher in Flanders and England, burned at the stake with his wife and Jan Mathijsz van Middelburg in Smithfield (London) on Nov. 29, 1538. He is probably identical with Pieter de Bontwerkere (Peter the Furrier), who led Pauwels Vermaete (q.v.), a Flemish preacher and martyr, to the Anabaptist faith.

Franke is included with the English Reformers in a Catholic satirical poem, "A Genealogye of Heresye," written by John Huntington about 1540:

> Next after him (i.e., John Lambert)
> Came in a limb
> Of Antichrist
> An Anabaptist
> One Peter Franke
> Which said full rank
> That Christ and God
> Take not manhood
> Of Mary the Virgin
> Which was without sin.

John Bale in *A Mysterye of Inyquyte* (1542), which is a refutation of Huntington's verses, declares that

Franke's life was pious, for his death was "godly and perfect." His "patient suffering" was instrumental in converting some at Colchester from "papism into true repentance, whereas nothing before could convert them." "For in his death confessed he the Lord Jesus Christ to be his only saviour and redeemer, which is the true seal of the servant of God." Although the Melchiorite view of the Incarnation was prevalent among Anabaptists in England, Bale claims Franke "died in no such wicked opinion as many have credibly reported" (fols. 53r—57r).   I.B.H.

Chronicon ab anno 1189 ad 1556 in the *Monumenta Franciscanae, The Rolls Series* (1858) 202; John Bale, *A Mysterye of Inyquyte* (1542) fols. 53 recto—57 recto. Verheyden, *Brugge*, 45; *Letters and Papers, Foreign and Domestic of the Reign of Henry VIII*, Vol. XIII/2, p. 374.

Franken (Francken, Vranken), a Mennonite family, originally from Burgsteinfurt, Germany. (1) *Everwijn Franken* migrated about 1620 from Burgsteinfurt to Enschede, Dutch province of Overijssel. (2) *Jan Franken*, b. at Burgsteinfurt 1659, d. Enschede in 1764 at the age of nearly 105 years. He was precentor (chorister) of the Enschede congregation, and in 1684 married Hendrikje Willink. They had no children. (3) *Everwijn Francken,* grandson of (1) Everwijn, dates of birth and death unknown, was married to Anneken van Lochem of Enschede. He was a Mennonite preacher at Zutphen about 1690 until his death (*DB* 1881, 46 ff.). (4) *Isaäk Franken,* son of the foregoing (3) Everwijn, b. about 1680 at Zutphen, d. 1738 at Utrecht, was trained 1699-1705 by Galenus Abrahamsz (*q.v.*) of Amsterdam and served the congregation of Cleve 1707-13 and Utrecht 1713-38. While at Cleve he was active on behalf of a number of Swiss Brethren who were being transported to America in 1710, and who were released in Nijmegen, Holland, and traveled to the Palatinate via Cleve (Huizinga, 26; Müller, 272 f.). (5) *Jan Franken,* youngest son of (3) Everwijn, years of birth and death unknown and of whom it is not clear whether he was trained by his father (see *Inv. Arch. Amst.* II, Nos. 2396 ff.), or studied at the Remonstrant Seminary at Amsterdam, succeeded his father as a preacher in Zutphen, where he served (year of beginning unknown) until 1731. In this year he was suspended because of misconduct. By the intercession of the church board of Amsterdam he was again admitted to the pulpit but suspended anew in 1734. In 1735 he received a call to the small congregation of Nieuwvliet in Cadzandt (*q.v.*), where he served until 1753. (*DB* 1881, 48; 1889, 114-15; *Inv. Arch. Amst.* II, Nos. 2400-10; 1662-74.) (6) *Jan Franken,* b. Oct. 23, 1726, at Leiden, d. there (year unknown). He was a son of Matthijs Franken, a beer brewer, who served the Mennonite congregation between 1684 and 1722, eight periods as a deacon; his sons Matthijs and Pieter were also deacons. Jan Franken studied at the University of Leiden and 1748-51 at the Amsterdam Mennonite Seminary. Then he served as minister at Zwolle (1751-56) and Harlingen (1756-63). Evidently he was a man of troublesome character, quick-tempered, and resentful. Disharmony arose on an unimportant matter between him on one side and the church board of Harlingen and his copreacher Johannes Stinstra (*q.v.*) on the other; he moved to Leiden and devoted himself to his father's brewery. (*Inv. Arch. Amst.* II, Nos. 2460 f.; *DB* 1868, 70, 77.)   vDZ.

J. Huizinga, *Stamboek van Samuel Peter en Barbara Fry* (Groningen, 1890); Müller, *Berner Täufer*; Chr. Sepp, *Johannes Stinstra en zijn tijd* II (Amsterdam, 1861); L. G. le Poole, *Bijdr. tot . . . het kerk. Leven van de Doopsgez. te Leiden* (Leiden, 1905) see Index.

Frankenthal Disputation. This disputation held in Frankenthal, Palatinate, Germany, in 1571 is the most important of the disputations of the 16th century arranged by representatives of the state churches with South German Anabaptists. In the range of subjects discussed and the duration of the dispute it exceeds all others. The published report records all the details.

The initial instigation came from the Palatine elector Frederick III (*q.v.*). He was the first German prince to embrace Calvinism and he tried to lead his people into the same fold. In general the change from the Lutheran and Catholic creeds to the Reformed was accomplished in a short time under government pressure. On the other hand, all attempts to win the numerous Anabaptists scattered over the land met with failure, on account of Anabaptist insistence on founding their faith solely on the Bible and rejection of government regulation of matters of faith. Economic pressure was equally unavailing, for they preferred prison and exile to disloyalty to their faith.

To Frederick III it was a matter of importance to win the pious Anabaptists to his creed, that they might have a reviving influence on the state church. When severity failed to bring about the desired union, he tried to achieve it by peaceful negotiation. Like his predecessor Otto Heinrich, who had the leading Lutheran theologians of South Germany debate with the Anabaptists at Pfeddersheim in 1557, Frederick decided to have the questions at issue publicly debated, assuming that the Anabaptist preachers would accept the proofs offered by his theologians. He therefore arranged for the public disputation on May 28, 1571, in Frankenthal, at which all Anabaptist preachers would be permitted to express themselves freely. He promised them safe conduct 14 days before and after the dispute, and free board and lodging for its duration. Foreigners were invited and prisoners could take part on condition that they refrained from preaching and baptizing.

In spite of the assurance that no risk of life and liberty was involved, very few came to take part, for they knew that any Anabaptist who openly stated his faith would be subject to new oppression at the expiration of the stated period. This fear was justified, for the elector, who on April 10 issued the proclamation for the debate, signed the death sentence of Sylvan in Heidelberg for religious nonconformity. Participants from other countries where the Anabaptists were not tolerated would by attending the debate draw the attention of the authorities, thus running a grave risk.

From the Anabaptist congregations 15 participants arrived, including preachers from Moravia and the South German imperial cities. Most of them were Swiss; two of them, Peter Walpot and Leonhard Summer, were Hutterian delegates. Dutch Mennonites were also reputedly present, but they did not announce themselves as such. The Hutterian Brethren took little part in the discussions. The Palatine representatives were also very reserved. The chief speaker was Diebold Winter from the imperial city of Weissenburg in Alsace, who had attended the Pfeddersheim disputation and after the opening at Frankenthal made a speech in the name of his brethren, expressing thanks for the privilege of talking from the Word of God with the theologians of the Palatinate; they were willing to change their views if convinced of error; they were concerned only with the glory of God and their salvation. In addition Hans Büchel (q.v.) of Mur, a noted writer of hymns, took an active part in the discussions. Rauff Bisch (q.v.) was chosen to represent the Palatine preachers. Others present from the Palatinate were Claus Simmerer of Siebeldingen near Landau, Hans Rannich of Dossenheim near Heidelberg, Hans Greiker of Heppenheim auf der Wiese near Worms, Peter Hutt of Kleinbockenheim near Frankenthal, and Anstadt Habermann of Heinsheim. In addition there were Jost Meyer of Rauensperg, Felix Frederer of Hofheim, Hans Sattler of Andernach, Philipp Jösslin of Heilbronn, and Peter Walter of Schlettstadt.

Rannich and Simmerer were brought from prison to Frankenthal. They were cross-examined repeatedly beforehand in order to use their statements at the public discussion, where somewhat different interpretations might be given by their brethren. They were, for instance, questioned on their conception of the nature of the human body after the resurrection, which question was also presented by the theologians at the public debate. The Anabaptist preachers were not learned, but they knew the Bible well. They were therefore convinced of the Scripturalness of their doctrine and were not confused by the clever sophistical arguments of their eloquent opponents. Rauff Bisch expressed his surprise to Dathenus, the chaplain, at the captious questions.

For 19 days, from May 28 to June 19, 1571, the disputation continued. On every day except Sunday two sessions were held, which began at six in the morning and two in the afternoon. The elector attended the opening session and kept himself informed on the progress of the discussions.

The following 13 points were presented to the Anabaptists:

(1) Concerning the Holy Scriptures. Whether the Old Testament is as valid to the Christian as the New; i.e., whether the principal doctrines of faith and life can and must be proved from the Old Testament as well as the New.

(2) Concerning God. Whether the Father, Son, and Holy Spirit are a single divine Being, yet in three distinct Persons.

(3) Concerning Christ. Whether Christ received the nature of His flesh from the substance of the flesh of the Virgin Mary or elsewhere.

(4) Concerning original sin. Whether children are conceived and born in sin and are therefore by nature the children of wrath, worthy of eternal death.

(5) Concerning the churches. Whether believers in the Old Testament are with the believers in the New Testament a single church and people of God.

(6) Concerning justification. Whether the perfect obedience of Christ accepted in true faith is the one and only sufficient atonement for our sins and the reason for our eternal salvation, or whether we are saved partly through faith in Christ and partly through bearing the cross and good works.

(7) Concerning the resurrection of the body. Whether the essence of this body will rise on the last day, or whether another will be created by God.

(8) Concerning marriage. Whether the ban and unbelief dissolve a marriage.

(9) Concerning community of goods. Whether Christians may buy and own property without transgressing against Christian love.

(10) Concerning government. Whether a Christian may be a ruler and punish the wicked with the sword.

(11) Concerning the oath. Whether Christians may render a proper oath in the name of God, i.e., to call on God as a witness to the truth.

(12) Concerning baptism. Whether the children of Christians should be baptized.

(13) Concerning communion. Whether the communion is merely an empty symbol and an admonition to patience and love, or also a powerful seal of the blessed fellowship which all believers have with Christ unto eternal life.

The answers of the Anabaptist preachers to these questions are briefly stated in the article **Disputations**. For the most part they were the same doctrinal points which Martin Bucer (q.v.) discussed with the Hessian Anabaptists. But in addition questions were asked which cannot be unambiguously answered from the Scriptures; Rauff Bisch finally remarked, "It almost seems to us that you are asking questions that are over our heads; for we know nothing else to say about them than what the texts simply say." What these men, versed in the Bible, could not grasp they did not try to fathom; they did not deviate from this principle. They therefore withheld their opinion when Dathenus expounded his views on the most mysterious matters.

Although there was agreement on a number of questions, nevertheless the captious argumentation of the chaplain on unfathomable matters roused the objection of the simple Biblicist Anabaptists. Thus Frederick III failed in 37 discussions to secure what Philip of Hesse had obtained 33 years earlier in two days through Bucer's attitude of moderation. "We do not want," said Rauff Bisch in his concluding speech, "to burden our consciences with several articles which we cannot believe with a good conscience, but only as we hope to answer to God, and as we do not know any better way, to remain on this position."

In a report that the chairman read aloud at the end of the disputation, the elector's disappointment was expressed in the failure of his "gracious and paternal benevolent intentions." But he still did not give up the hope that the Anabaptists might be won to the church, and promised, if they did so, that he would protect and help them, and restore anything that had been taken from them.

But even these promises could not change them. Only one of their leaders, presumably one of the prisoners, showed an inclination to agree with the State Church, except on the question of baptism. It is not stated whether he did so. The others were not moved from their opinion and finally said that even if they agreed in doctrine, the wicked living of those who called themselves orthodox would not agree with theirs.

The elector then forbade the Anabaptists to teach in his realm, "in order not to confuse our subjects." The preachers were regarded as insurrectionists and violators of electoral commands, and after another attempt to convert them, were banished.

The protocol was published three months after the disputation closed in a 710-page book, and reprinted in 1573, both times at Heidelberg. In 1571 a Dutch translation was also published, arranged by Caspar Heidanus, the Reformed preacher at Frankenthal. The Palatine clergy used the book as a basis for attempts at conversion. Copies of all three editions are in the Goshen College Library. Hege.

Protocoll, Das ist Alle handlung des gesprechs zu Franckenthal inn der Churfürstlichen Pfaltz, mit denen so man Widertäuffer nennet (Heidelberg, 1571); Chr. Hege, *Die Täufer in der Kurpfalz* (Frankfurt, 1908); *Monatschrift des Frankentaler Altertums-Vereins,* May 1903, 18; "Religions-Gespräch zu Frankental mit den Wiedertäufern 1571," in *Thesaurus Picturarum der Grossherzoglichen Hofbibliothek in Darmstadt,* 96-102 (describes the disputation. The elector at first presided in person. Names of other chairmen follow, with the names of the Reformed and Anabaptist debaters. The 13 articles are stated, and the threatened severe measures); *Ztscht für die Gesch. des Ober-Rheins* LXIX, n.F. 29, 1914; *Menn. Bl.,* 1882, 75; A. W. Bronsfeld, *Gespreek met de Doopsgezinden te Frankendal 1571* (Harderwijk, 1871); *ML* I, 675-77.

Frankfort, Hutterite Bruderhof of the Dariusleut group (1904-18), now abandoned, located on the James River, nine miles south of the town of Frankfort, S.D., a daughter of the original Wolf Creek colony. The site was purchased by members of the Wolf Creek Bruderhof in 1904. By 1918 the settlement consisted of 20 families. The participation of the United States in World War I created some difficulties for them with respect to their nonresistant position, and they decided to migrate to Canada, where their young men would be excused from military service. On May 20, 1918, they purchased 4,000 acres 18 miles southeast of Macleod, Alberta, and established the Stand-Off Colony. Other Hutterites in South Dakota followed their example and acquired land near Stand-Off, so that by 1923 nine Bruderhofs were established in a radius of 40 miles. Thus the Frankfort colony led the emigration and was the pioneer Hutterite colony in Canada. The Frankfort colony initiated the publication of the *Lieder der Hutterischen Brüder* (Scottdale, 1914), a collection of hymns hitherto found only in manuscript form, copied from originals now preserved in various archives of Austria and Hungary. In this

Bruderhof was also found the original manuscript of the great Hutterite *Geschicht-Buch,* which was generally believed to have been lost, and which was then used by Prof. Wolkan (*q.v.*) in editing the *Geschicht-Buch* (published in the Stand-Off Colony in 1923), and which was published in a letter-perfect edition by Prof. Zieglschmid in 1943. Elias Walter (*q.v.*) was the elder of the Wolf Creek-Frankfort-Stand-Off Bruderhof from 1903 to 1928, and the outstanding leader of the entire Hutterite brotherhood in North America. (*ML* I, 677 f.) E.Wa.

Frankfurt Land Company, a German land company composed of Lutheran Pietists who hoped to locate in Pennsylvania, whose agent, Francis Daniel Pastorius, arrived in Philadelphia Aug. 20, 1683, and who was helpful to the Crefeld party which arrived at Philadelphia on Oct. 6 of that year. On Oct. 25 the 13 family heads of the Crefeld group met in the dugout home of Pastorius and drew lots for their respective parcels of land. Practically none of the Frankfurt Land Company ever settled in Pennsylvania. The Company is remembered principally because of the good services of Pastorius, their agent, in behalf of the Crefelders, some of whom became the charter members of the first permanent Mennonite settlement and congregation in America.

J.C.W.

Frankfurt am Main, a city (1950 pop. 523,923) in the Prussian province of Hessen-Nassau, Germany, until 1866 a free city, one of the few cities of South Germany in which the Anabaptist movement did not take root, though it seems to have found brief entry in the person of Dr. Westerburg, who was influential in bringing the Reformation into the city, and who at that time was in sympathy with the Anabaptist movement, later being for a short time a member. Shortly before his arrival in Frankfurt in early October 1524, he sought to make contacts with the "Brethren" in Zürich, who three months later, Jan. 25, 1525, performed the first adult baptism. The Swiss Brethren, however, grew distrustful when they learned that he was maintaining connections with the revolutionary masses, and thus their ways parted (Rembert, 39).

The Protestant movement in Frankfurt, having lost the support of the defeated imperial knights, was threatened with collapse. Westerburg saved the cause, and helped to give it permanence in the city (Steitz, 95). But because the council considered him the leader of the revolt in Frankfurt he was banished May 17, 1525.

The position of the Lutheran preachers was now so secure that the council was entirely on their side and suppressed any religious groups they did not like. Especially the Anabaptists felt their power. Available facts on the subject are few. A day laborer who had preached Anabaptist doctrine in Bornheim was expelled (Dechent, 125). There is evidence that the Anabaptist movement had reached some proportions, for at the instigation of the preachers Bernhard Algesheimer (Johann von Hohenstein) and Dionysius Melander the council issued an edict on March 23, 1528, forbidding the citizens to lodge

Anabaptists (Jung, 116). This measure effectively suppressed the movement here; the law passed by the Diet of Speyer on April 23, 1529 (see **Punishment**), actively supported the measures of the council.

This imperial law which imposed the death penalty on rebaptism also occupied the Reichstag at Frankfurt in 1531. The ruthlessness which resulted from this law shocked the citizenry; hence Brandenburg and Nürnberg on June 6, 1531, proposed changes in the law. But the majority favored the retention of the law as it was (Winkelmann II, 49 f.). The estates hoped to subdue the general excitement by admitting in a decree in 1531 that the edict of Speyer had been passed "somewhat too quickly," and by giving the deed another name, explaining that "such persons are punished not for their faith, but for their offense." Milder punishments should be applied only in exceptional cases, when the interpretation of the regulations was not clear. In such cases the council could request the opinion of learned theologians and other honorable persons and perhaps render a more lenient verdict (Neudecker, 188). The law itself was not altered. It was still in force at the opening of the Thirty Years' War (*q.v.*).

In 1704, when Mennonites expelled from Switzerland wanted to settle in Frankfurt, they were refused after giving a statement of their faith. At Frankfurt the plan for the settling of Germantown (*q.v.*) was originated, which was carried out by Crefeld Mennonites. (See **Frankfurt Land Company.**)

The census reports state that in 1858 there were two Mennonites in Frankfurt; in 1880, eight; in 1885, twenty-nine; in 1890, seventeen; in 1895, twenty-four; in 1900, twenty-three; in 1905, thirty; and in 1925, twenty-five.

On May 16, 1897, the traveling preacher (*Reiseprediger*) G. van der Smissen conducted the first services of the Mennonite congregation in the city. Since 1913 the ministers of the South German Conference have been serving here. Services are now (1956) held every two weeks in the MCC center, Eysseneckstrasse 54. In 1952 the number of baptized members was 125. The congregation was organized in 1948, and though it is independent of conference affiliation, Richard Wagner, an elder in the Badischer Verband (*q.v.*), serves as elder and pastor.

Frankfurt has been the seat of the MCC administrative headquarters since 1950, and since 1952 for all Europe. HEGE.

H. Dechent, *Kirchengesch. von Frankfurt a.M. seit der Ref.* (Leipzig and Frankfurt, 1913); R. Jung, *Frankfurter Chroniken und annalistische Aufzeichnungen der Ref.-Zeit* (Frankfurt, 1888); C. G. Neudecker, *Urkunden aus der Ref.-Zeit* (Kassel, 1836); Rembert, *Wiedertäufer;* G. E. Steitz, "Dr. Gerhard Westerburg," in *Arch. für Frankfurts Gesch. und Kunst,* n.S., 1872; Otto Winkelmann, *Politische Korrespondenz der Stadt Strassburg im Zeitalter der Reformation* (1887); ML I, 678.

Frankfurt Parliament, the German constitutional assembly which met at Frankfurt a.M., Germany, on May 18, 1848, to May 30, 1849, is of interest to Mennonites because two Mennonites, Isaak Brons (*q.v.*) of Emden and Hermann von Beckerath (*q.v.*) of Crefeld, were elected members of the parliament. Brons took no part in the public debates, although he served on two committees (Navy and Economics), but von Beckerath, an able and experienced statesman, took a leading part in the debates and on Aug. 4, 1848, accepted the cabinet post of Minister of Finance. Von Beckerath was a firm monarchist and a strongly patriotic Prussian.

Of particular interest is von Beckerath's strange opposition to the proposal for exemption of conscientious objectors from military service, which he as a Mennonite might well have made himself, but which was actually introduced by a non-Mennonite though intended specifically to serve the Mennonites as the only religious conscientious objector group in Germany. The following extract from this address on this subject not only indicates clearly that von Beckerath had surrendered the historic Mennonite nonresistant position, but that he was fully committed to the typical Prussian military point of view. "I do not deny that the proposals issue from a well-intentioned human point of view; but, Gentlemen, they are based on political concepts which no longer exist. It must be remembered that since no universal military duty existed in Prussia at the time when the Mennonites received the right to withdraw from military service and as a compensation had to accept certain restrictions on their citizenship rights, the Mennonite privilege did not constitute an infraction of the right of other citizens. But when in 1808 in Prussia every able-bodied man was obligated to military service the Mennonite exemption constituted an abnormality, and now that a free state is to be established whose strength rests upon the equality of its citizens in rights and duties, such a special privilege becomes utterly untenable. As the previous speaker, Mr. Martens, has stated, the Mennonites in Rhenish Prussia with few exceptions render military service without question, and refusal of military service is in no sense considered as an integral part of Mennonite doctrine. It is certain that in other parts of Germany the heightened appreciation of the state will result in the performance there [by Mennonites] of this first duty of the citizen. But even if here and there this should not be the case, and individual conscientious objectors might arise, this would be a condition which it would be impossible to take into account in the establishment of the basic constitutional provisions. . . . I declare that it is contrary to the welfare of the Fatherland to provide for any exception in the fulfillment of citizenship duties, no matter on what ground."

This did not settle the question of Mennonite exemption from military service. On Sept. 14, 1848, the West Prussian Mennonite congregations submitted a petition to the Parliament on which they protested against the views expressed by von Beckerath, without, however, achieving any positive results for their position in the final formulation of the constitutional provisions. However, the Mennonite privileges were maintained in Prussia even after the adoption of the new constitution. It was not until the federal law of Nov. 9, 1867, was passed that the exemption was lost. Even then the Order-in-Cabinet (*Kabinettsordre*) of March 3, 1868, granted the Mennonites the privilege of noncombatant service.

It is interesting to note that the historian C. A. Cornelius, who was also a member of the Frankfurt Parliament, decided during the sessions to write his *Geschichte des Münsterischen Aufruhrs*.

R. Sch., H.S.B.

Franz Wigard, *Stenographische Berichte der Verhandlungen der deutschen konstituierenden Nationalversammlung* (Frankfurt a.M., 1848, 1849); Richard Schwemer, *Geschichte der Freien Stadt Frankfurt a.M.* III, 1 (Frankfurt, 1915); Heinrich Laube, *Das erste deutsche Parlament*, rev. ed. (Leipzig, 1910); W. Mannhardt, *Die Wehrfreiheit der Altpreussischen Mennoniten* (Berlin, 1863); *ML* I, 678-84.

Franklin Center, Iowa, now known as Franklin, is a village in Lee County, southeastern Iowa, near which the first Mennonite settlers in Iowa lived. The first Mennonite congregation in Iowa (now extinct) was located east of the present village; its church was dedicated in 1850. In 1868 it was replaced by a church built in the village by the Mennonite immigrants from Bavaria and the Palatinate who lived near by. M.G.

Franklin County, Ohio, organized in 1803, was the home of two Mennonite (MC) congregations during the middle and later years of the 19th century, the Jacob Bowman Church (*q.v.*) near Canal Winchester and the Stemen Church (*q.v.*) near Pickerington on the border between Fairfield and Franklin counties. The burial ground of both congregations was near Canal Winchester. The founders had moved from near-by Fairfield and Perry counties to improve their economic status after the opening of the canal from Portsmouth to Cleveland. John M. Brenneman, a miller, moved near Canal Winchester from Fairfield in 1848 and was ordained bishop here in 1849 but moved again to Allen County in 1855. The stress of the Civil War period further reduced the membership. In the later years poorly qualified leadership, protracted retention of the German worship service, and the lure of the more spirited religious activities in the U.B. and M.E. churches drew the Mennonite young people away from the simple faith and worship of their fathers. Some became prosperous farmers and businessmen. In a final effort to perpetuate the Mennonite faith Benoni Stemen, a wealthy Mennonite farmer and stock raiser, built for himself and the families of his four sons and three daughters a Mennonite meetinghouse near Pickerington, but could not stem the decline. When the church building fell into disuse after his death, the benches were moved to the Turkey Run Church in Perry County south of Bremen. J.S.U.

Franklin County, Pa., is located near the center of Pennsylvania's southern border. Its shape is roughly triangular with its base resting on the famous Mason and Dixon's line. The Mennonites (M.C. and Reformed Mennonites) have never been grouped in a close colony, but are scattered among the Scotch-Irish throughout much of the area. The membership of the Reformed Mennonites is small; in 1954 the M.C. group had 821 members organized into 8 congregations. They are members of the Washington Co., Md.-Franklin Co., Pa., Mennonite Conference. The Reformed branch has one bishop, one minister, and one deacon.

According to an article on the Mennonites by John B. Kauffman in a history of Franklin County published in 1887 a few Mennonites found their way to the county as early as 1735. The largest influx occurred in 1790-1800. The first church was erected in 1810. The congregations were never large, and in 1878 one bishop and five ministers served five small congregations. (*ML* I, 681.) J.I.L.

Franklin Mennonite Church (GCM), now extinct, was built in the village of Franklin Center, Iowa, by Mennonites from Lee Co., Iowa, in 1868. They had previously worshiped in the near-by Zion and West Point churches. The members were German immigrants and the congregation early became a member of the General Conference. John S. Hirschler served as elder 1872-84. Services were discontinued perhaps in the late eighties, after most of the members had moved to Kansas and other places. M.G.

Franklin (Neb.) United Missionary Church had 27 members in 1949 with Kenneth Baker serving as pastor. M.G.

Frans van Bolsweert (Bolsward), an Anabaptist martyr: see **Frans Dammasz.**

Frans Claesz, an Anabaptist martyr, a native of Hallum, Dutch province of Friesland, was beheaded at the Frisian capital Leeuwarden on Feb. 8, 1539, with four others, because he had been rebaptized, and had "a bad opinion of the Holy Sacrament and the constitution of the Holy (Roman Catholic) Church." (*Inv. Arch. Amst.* I, No. 746; *DB* 1910, 123 f.; *ML* I, 359.) vDZ.

Frans de Cuyper (Frans Kuiper, Frans Reines) was an elder of the Dutch Anabaptists, ordained by Menno Simons in 1542; but in 1554 he recanted and returned to the Roman Catholic Church. He had preached and taught especially in the Dutch province of Friesland. vDZ.

BRN VII, 3, 50 f., 86; K. Vos, *Menno Simons* (Leiden, 1914) 91 ff. *et passim*.

Frans Dammasz (Frans van Bolsward, or Francis of Bolsweert), an Anabaptist martyr, was burned at the stake, March 28, 1545, at Leeuwarden, Dutch province of Friesland, having been seized because of his refusal to give an oath. In prison he wrote the song, "Wel hem die in Gods vreeze staat" (Blessed the man, who is God-fearing), which is included in the Dutch hymnbook *Veelderhande Liedekens* of 1569 and many other Dutch songbooks, and Wackernagel, *Lieder*, 97. This song, translated into German, "Wol dem der in Gottes Forchten steht," is also found in the old Anabaptist German hymnbook, *Ein schön Gesängbüchlein Geistlicher Lieder* (*q.v.*). At his execution his flesh had miraculously refused to burn, according to the song, "Verhuecht u Gods kinder alletijt," in *Het Offer des Heeren*.

K.V., vDZ.

Offer, 505-9; *Mart. Mir.* D 71, E 472; Wolkan, *Lieder*, 60, 79, 98; *ML* I, 244.

Frans Dirksz Quintijn (Frans of Wormer), a revolutionary Anabaptist, who at a meeting at Wormer in the Dutch province of North Holland had unfolded the plan to take the city of Alkmaar (q.v.) by force of arms; but when he arrived at Alkmaar to prepare the attack, he was taken prisoner on Jan. 24, 1535, together with his wife Brechte Adams and four others. On Feb. 1 he was burned at the stake. In the sentence no mention is made of the planned attack. Frans was sentenced to death because he had been rebaptized and had also rebaptized others. (*Inv. Arch. Amst.* I, No. 159; *DB* 1909, 17-20.)

vdZ.

Frans (Franchoys) van Elstland(t) (Frans van Meenen), an Anabaptist martyr of Belgium, a mason, was baptized on the confession of his faith, was seized Oct. 9, 1561, and burned at the stake on Oct. 21 of that year at "Arien in Walschvlaenderen" (van Braght), thought to be Aire, Belgium. (*Mart. Mir.* D 286, E 654; *ML* I, 563.) NEFF, vdZ.

Frans Frederycxzoon *in de Trompe,* a native of Arnhem, Dutch province of Gelderland, living in Amsterdam, who by order of Hendrik Goedbeleid (q.v.) slyly obtained possession of the key of the Amsterdam town hall and so partook in the Anabaptist assault at Amsterdam May 10-11, 1535. Being arrested after the attack had miscarried, he was tried several times and after torture sentenced to death on June 1 and beheaded.

His revelations are very valuable in reconstructing the views and intentions of the revolutionary Anabaptists. That Frans had been rebaptized himself is not evident from the records. (Grosheide, *Verhooren,* 76-83; Mellink, *Wederdopers,* 131, 137-39, 145.)

vdZ.

Frans Jansz, a sheriff of the North Holland town of Alkmaar from about 1528, was a Sacramentist (q.v.). By trade he was a glazier. In 1533 he is found among the Anabaptists, attending Anabaptist meetings at Limmen, near Alkmaar, where Geeryt *mitten baerde* and Aeffgen Lystyncx (q.v.) preached; he also held meetings in his own house at Alkmaar, where the question was discussed, whether they should go to Münster (q.v.) (*DB* 1909, 7, 11, 12, 14).

At the same time, there was another Anabaptist Frans Jansz living at Alkmaar, who was a ship's carpenter, and who must be distinguished from the above. This Frans Jansz the carpenter, who had previously lived at Krommeniedijk, took part in the journey to Münster in March 1534, was arrested at Bergklooster (q.v.), brought to Haarlem, renounced his faith, and was set free on Sept. 18, 1534, upon payment of a fine (*DB* 1909, 14-15).

He may have been identical with Frans Jansz the locksmith, born at Alkmaar, who was a follower of the Anabaptist revolutionary leader Jan van Batenburg. If this is the case, he must have changed his trade after his imprisonment at Haarlem and rejoined the Anabaptists of the Batenburg group. Frans

Jansz the locksmith was arrested at Utrecht in 1541. He had been rebaptized about 1534 and was charged with having broken into the prison of Leiden and liberating some Anabaptist prisoners, and also robbing some Catholic churches. He was sentenced to death together with his wife Aeff Peters (q.v.) and hanged at Utrecht on April 2, 1541 (*Inv. Arch. Amst.* I, No. 283; *DB* 1909, 21-22, 25).

Another person of this name, Frans Jansz Mickers, also living at Alkmaar, who presumably was also a follower of Batenburg, was put to death at Alkmaar on April 16, 1540, together with his mother Stijntgen, Jan Mickers' widow, and his sister Geertje (or Guertje) Jansdochter (*DB* 1909, 21, 24). vdZ.

Frans (Franchoys) Jorissen, an Anabaptist martyr, was burned at the stake at Antwerp, Belgium, on July 17, 1553. He was born at Geertsberge in Flanders and was a journeyman-bricklayer by trade. (*Antw. Arch.-Blad* VIII, 421, 423; XIV, 20-21, No. 224.)

vdZ.

Frans (Francoys) van Leuvene, an Anabaptist martyr, b. at Gent, Belgium, a weaver, was put to death at Gent with three others, "not on account of any misdeed, but only because they, according to the command of the eternal God, had separated from this corrupt world, which lies in inhuman wickedness, and sought, according to their weak ability, to follow Christ in the regeneration." Frans had been baptized at Gent in 1569, and was executed on July 28, 1573, on the Vrijdagsmarkt, together with Jacob van der Wege, Hendrick Bauwens, and Calleken Meere. During the execution the sympathy of the spectators for the four victims, who were prevented by gags from speaking to them, was so great that incidents could not be prevented. (*DB* 1899, 67; *Mart. Mir.* D 647 f., E 968; Verheyden, *Gent,* 63, No. 225; *ML* II, 643.) NEFF, vdZ.

Frans Pieters of Leiden, Dutch province of South Holland, an Anabaptist martyr, was sentenced to death by fire on May 11, 1534 (executed at Amsterdam ?). He had taken part in the journey to Münster in March 1534, and had been arrested at Bergklooster (q.v.). (*Inv. Arch. Amst.* I, Nos. 744, 745; *DB* 1917, 121, No. 142.) vdZ.

Frans Pietersz, a Dutch Anabaptist martyr of Groningen, a joiner, was beheaded at Delft, province of South Holland, with 10 others, because of having been rebaptized. He was likely a follower of David Joris (q.v.). (*Inv. Arch. Amst.* I, No. 749; *DB* 1899, 158-60; 1917, 160-67.) vdZ.

Frans Reines Kuiper: see Frans de Cuyper.

Frans Reynertszoon of Birdaard, Dutch province of Friesland, an Anabaptist martyr, who was sentenced to death at Leeuwarden, Friesland, on April 10, 1535, because he had been (re)baptized. (K. Vos, *Menno Simons,* Leiden, 1914, 228.) vdZ.

Frans Snyder (Clothmaker), an Anabaptist martyr of Leeuwarden, Dutch province of Friesland, was beheaded there on Feb. 8, 1539, with 10 others. Particulars are lacking.   vDZ.

Inv. Arch. Amst. I, No. 746; J. Reitsma, *Honderd jaren Kerkherv. in Friesland* (Leeuwarden, 1876) 63.

Frans (Francoys) **de Swarte,** an Anabaptist martyr of Belle (Bailleul), French Flanders, was burned at the stake at Hondschote, Flanders, Belgium, on March 23, 1562. He obviously belonged to the Anabaptist de Swarte (*q.v.*) family, many members of which were executed about the same time. (*Mart. Mir.* D 298, E 663.)   vDZ.

Frans Swertveger (Sweerdtveger), a cloth shearer, whose official name was Frans Deens or Doos, an Anabaptist martyr, was put to death in Antwerp on Aug. 27, 1555, with three brethren, Hans Borduerwercker, Jan Drooghscheerder, and Pieter with the lame foot, after a valiant confession of his faith. Their names are celebrated in the song, "Aenhoort, Godt, hemelsche Vader" (Hear, O God, heavenly Father), which is found in the *Liedtboecxken van den Offer des Heeren* (1563) No. 16. Frans's property was confiscated.   vDZ.

Offer, 564; *Mart. Mir.* D 161, E 550; *Antw. Arch.-Blad* VIII, 426, 428, 468; XIV, 20 f., No. 227; Wolkan, *Lieder,* 63, 72.

Frans Tibau (Thybault), an Anabaptist martyr, originally from Ieper, Flanders, was beheaded at Antwerp, Belgium, on July 7, 1558. The secret execution took place during the night in the Steen prison. Frans had been baptized only one year before. His name is also found in a song, "Aenhoort, Godt, hemelsche Vader" (Hear, O God, heavenly Father), found in the *Liedtboecxken van den Offer des Heeren* (1563) No. 16.   vDZ.

Offer, 565; *Mart. Mir.* D 201, E 583; *Antw. Arch.-Blad* VIII, 447, 464; XIV, 24-25, No. 258; Wolkan, *Lieder,* 63, 72.

Frans Willemsz, one of the first Anabaptists in the Netherlands, who was executed at The Hague on Dec. 5, 1531, with 8 or 9 others, one of whom was Jan Volkertsz Trijpmaker (*q.v.*). All of them recanted and for this reason were not listed in the martyrbooks. K. Vos, who studied the sentence pronounced on these victims, did not find Frans Willemsz, who is, however, listed by Grosheide. The answer to this puzzle is that Frans Willemsz and Vranck Wimsz (Willemsz), both mentioned by Grosheide, are probably the same person. (*DB* 1917, 159; Grosheide, *Bijdrage,* 50, 302.)   vDZ.

Frans van Wormer, an Anabaptist martyr: see **Frans Dirksz Quintijn.**

Fransken de Vroedvrouw (midwife), an Anabaptist martyr, whose official name was Franchyne van der Borcht. She was born at Lier, Belgium, and put to death because she had been (re)baptized, and refused to recant. She frankly confessed her faith and baptism and "did not respect her infant baptism." The execution took place secretly by drowning in a tub within the Steen castle at Antwerp, on March 19, 1559, together with Pleuntgen van der Goes and Naentken Leerverkoopster. Her name is found in a hymn, "Aenhoort, Godt, hemelsche Vader" (Hear, O God, heavenly Father), in the *Liedtboecxken van den Offer des Heeren* (Hymn 16, No. 43).   vDZ.

BRN II, 566; *Mart. Mir.* D 244, E 618; *Antw. Arch.-Blad* VIII, 460, 472; XIV, 26-27, No. 282; Wolkan, *Lieder,* 63, 72.

Fransoois (Fransoys) **de Timmerman** (in van Braght, *Mart. Mir.,* called François), an Anabaptist martyr living at Meenen (Menin) in Flanders and arrested there with five others, who were all sentenced to death and executed by being burned at the stake at Kortrijk (Courtrai) in Flanders, Belgium, on April 30, 1569. Fransoois had been (re)-baptized in 1562 or 1563. The other five were Jan Wattier, Pieter den Ouden (or Oudeghodt), Jan van Raes, Wouter Denijs, and Kalleken, the widow of the martyr Anpleunis vanden Berghe (*q.v.*). They all remained loyal to their faith. Their goods were confiscated. (*Mart. Mir.* D 408, E 759; Verheyden, *Courtrai-Bruxelles,* 39, No. 24.)   vDZ.

Frantz, Gabriel, a preacher of the Frisian (also called Waterlander) congregation of the Culmsche Niederung (or Schönsee), Poland, in 1725-50, wrote a number of letters to the Dutch Mennonite Committee of Foreign Needs at Amsterdam, asking their financial help in obtaining from the Catholic bishop of Culm the permission to live in peace and freedom in his territory. In reply, the Dutch Mennonites repeatedly sent him money. (*Inv. Arch. Amst.* I, Nos. 1088, 1597, 1600 f., 1604, 1641 f.; II, 2, No. 780.)   vDZ.

Franz (Frantz, Franzen, Fransen, Franssen, Frantzon), a Mennonite family name in West Prussia, mainly appearing in Frisian congregations. The name was first mentioned 1578 at Montau, 1595 at Scharfenberg. The majority, those living in the Vistula Valley and their descendants, adopted the forms Franz and Frantz. Members of the family moved to Poland, Russia (Molotschna), and subsequently to America. Gysbert Franssen was an elder of the Danzig Flemish congregation 1588-1602. Heinrich Franz (*q.v.*) was a prominent teacher. In 1954 the name was represented by four Mennonite Brethren ministers in Kansas and five General Conference Mennonite ministers in Alberta, Ontario, Oregon, and Kansas. The Franz Farm Shop on the Bethel College campus was named in honor of Julius Franz. In Civilian Public Service, those named Franz or Frantz numbered 22. Rufus Franz served as a CPS camp director. L. J. Franz is president of Tabor College.   G.R.

Franz, Heinrich, an outstanding teacher among the Mennonites of Russia, and with Tobias Voth and Heinrich Heese a cofounder of their school system. He was born Oct. 6, 1812, in West Prussia, died May 27, 1889, at Neu-Halbstadt, Taurida. For three years he attended the Vereinsschule headed by F. W. Lange (*q.v.*) at Rodlofferhufen, near Marienburg; in 1832 he passed the Prussian teachers' examinations, became a tutor in his home town, then a teacher at the Brenkenhoffswalde (*q.v.*) school. After his emigration to Russia in 1832 he was for a short time a private teacher at Felsental, and 1835-44 he taught in the Gnadenfeld village school. His abundant determination is attested by the fact that in order to learn the Russian language he served for two years as supervisor in the boarding-school of the Ekaterinoslav Gymnasium. As a teacher in the Chortitza Zentralschule 1846-58 his influence was felt throughout the settlements in his teaching, in his influence on their school system, in the statutes he worked out for the Chortitza Mennonite schools and the schools in general. His deficient knowledge of Russian made him less effective in this field than his predecessor Heinrich Heese; but in German and arithmetic (including elementary algebra and geometry) he did outstanding work. With his "150 tables" in arithmetic and their key Franz dominated the instruction in arithmetic for a half century, as he dominated religious music in the home, school, and church with his *Choralbuch* of 1860 with notes.

Franz's most lasting influence lay in the strength of his personality and his Draconian severity in school. These traits also brought him into conflict with influential persons and with the Chortitza authorities, and he was consequently obliged to resign in 1858. He, of course, had enthusiastic supporters, but also outspoken opponents among his pupils. He again turned to private instruction in Gnadenfeld and on the Rosenhof at Brodsky, owned by Jacob Dick. In 1880 he resigned, having devoted 50 years to teaching. He settled in Neu-Halbstadt, where he gave a few hours' instruction in religion in the secondary school for girls, and in 1888 he edited and published the poems of Bernhard Harder, the popular preacher of the Russian Mennonite brotherhood. His memory survives today, and he is spoken of simply as "der alte Franz." (Friesen, *Brüderschaft,* 584 ff.; *ML* I, 685 f.)

B.H.U.

Franz, Johann Friedrich, Reformed clergyman at Lichtenberg in the canton of St. Gall, Switzerland, in 1824 at Mogelsberg in the same canton, author of the book, *Die schwärmerischen Greuelszenen der St. Galler Wiedertäufer zu Anfang der Reformation . . . aus den Original-Handschriften Joh. Kesslers* (Ebnat, 1824). Franz was induced by libertinistic movements to produce this book, which follows Kessler closely, and which has been superseded by recent research. The material he presents apart from Kessler is inferior; as his sources he mentions Vadian, Zwingli, Ottius, etc. In support of his anti-Anabaptist prejudice he adds "Blicke auf das Leben einiger Widertäufer," and in conclusion he reprints the "Abschid der Stette Zürich, Bern und St. Gallen von wegen der Wiedergetauften," of Sept. 7, 1527. (*ML* I, 686.)

NEFF.

Franz Weber, an otherwise unknown Anabaptist leader, who is said in 1550 to have baptized in Dremmen, district of Heinsberg in the duchy of Jülich.

vDZ.

W. Bax, *Het Protestantisme in het Bisdom Luik* I (The Hague, 1937) 306; Otto R. Redlich: *Jülich-Bergische Kirchenpolitik* (Publikationen der Gesellschaft für rheinische Geschichtskunde XXVIII), II, 1 (Bonn, 1911) 312 f.

Franzfeld (*Varvarovka*) was a village of the Yazekovo Mennonite settlement (*q.v.*) near Chortitza, Russia, established in 1869. In 1918 the village had a hundred farms and 5,500 acres of land. After the collectivization the village had 3,436 acres of land. In 1914 the population was 466 and in 1941, 630. Eleven persons were murdered in 1919 and 85 were exiled in 1929-41. During the German invasion 36 persons were evacuated eastward. When the Germans retreated the village population was taken along. Some were later repatriated by the Red army and others found their way to America.   C.K.

K. Stumpp, *Bericht über das Gebiet Chortitza* (Berlin, 1943).

Franztal in der Neumark, Germany, where there were Mennonites from 1765 to 1834 who formed the Brenkenhoffswalde-Franztal congregation (see **Brenkenhoffswalde**).

Fraser Valley, B.C., directly north of the Canadian border and almost parallel to it, since 1928 has attracted approximately 12,000 Mennonites from the Prairie provinces. From Rosedale to Vancouver, an important Pacific ocean port, a distance of 74 miles, the valley is up to six miles wide. The fertile soil, an abundant rainfall, and the mild climate, as well as the opportunity to settle in close-knit communities, have been the chief causes of the westward migration of the Mennonites, most of whom had come to Canada from Russia during the 1920's. The chief Mennonite population centers from east to west are Chilliwack, Sardis-Greendale, Yarrow, Abbotsford-Clearbrook, and the Greater Vancouver area. Scattered through the valley are 24 churches; 12 M.B., with 76 ministers and 4,129 baptized members; 10 G.C.M., with 31 ministers and 1,736 members, and one church each of the E.M.B. and C.G.C.

While an increasingly large number of Mennonites in the valley go into small business, most of them are engaged in dairying, poultry, or small fruit raising, particularly raspberries and strawberries. Yarrow, the oldest settlement, an unincorporated village of 2,000, has 27 Mennonite business establishments, such as berry processing plants (4), grocery stores (3), dry goods (3), box factory, sawmill. The Abbotsford-Clearbrook area on both sides of the trans-Canada highway is rapidly developing into a Mennonite shopping district. Mennonite co-operatives organized during the depression in Yarrow, Sardis, and Abbotsford provided much of the needed credit to the early settlers. Inexperienced management and better transportation facilities to near-by larger shopping centers have all but killed the co-operative movement. With the exception of a cold storage plant at Greendale, the remaining four co-operatives are berry processing plants. Jacob C. Krause of Yarrow, A. A. Rempel and Jacob Schroeder of Greendale, and John J. Rempel of Abbotsford, were among the outstanding early leaders in the co-operative movement. A postwar slump in the berry market, together with the devastating flood during the summer of 1948, which inundated the Greendale Mission settlements, produced a major economic crisis. Only one Mennonite, however, lost his life when the dikes of the Fraser River broke,

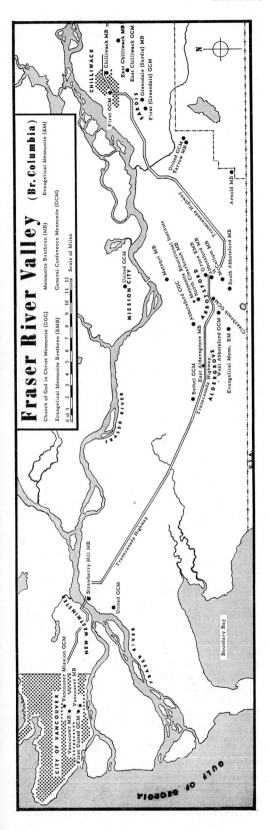

Fraser River Valley (Br. Columbia)

Church of God in Christ Mennonite (CGC)   Mennonite Brethren (MB)   Evangelical Mennonite (EM)
Evangelical Mennonite Brethren (EMB)   General Conference Mennonite (GCM)

covering the settlements with up to eight feet of water. Total bankruptcy of hundreds of Mennonite farmers was prevented by the generous and far-reaching assistance given by the Canadian government and the Red Cross.

The concentration of the Mennonite population in a relatively small area has been conducive to the development of parochial schools. General interest in education is shown by the fact that during 1953 a total of 828 young people from M.B. churches attended high schools, Bible schools, colleges, and universities. Interest in retaining the German language is attested by the attendance of 617 children from M.B. homes at German classes conducted on Saturdays. Two Mennonite high schools in 1953-54 had a total enrollment of 476 students, while the four Bible schools enrolled 137 students. The oldest and most successful of the high schools, the Mennonite Educational Institute at Abbotsford, was founded in 1944, and is supported by six M.B. (and one G.C.M.) churches. Under the leadership of I. J. Dyck as principal the enrollment has grown from 43 to 385 students. The Sharon Mennonite High School at Yarrow, founded in 1951, is supported by the parents of the local M.B. church and has an enrollment of 91 students. Because of economic difficulties and disunity among the four M.B. churches operating it, an earlier Mennonite high school, founded at Yarrow in 1945, had to close its doors four years later. The local public school authorities have acquired its elaborate school plant, which is now used as a junior high school. For similar reasons the Mennonite high school at Greendale, supported by General Conference churches, had to close in 1948, having operated only two years.

There are two old people's homes in the valley, one privately owned in Yarrow, and one operated by G.C.M. churches in Abbotsford. Although there are no Mennonite hospitals, for many years a Mennonite hospital insurance society has assisted its members in defraying their medical and hospital expenses. Thirteen Mennonite physicians and dentists, and numerous Mennonite graduate nurses, provide medical services.

Politically, Fraser Valley Mennonites became conscious of their combined voting power when in 1940 the Mennonite block of votes elected a Liberal member of Parliament for the first time in many years. Thirteen years later, in 1953, this same member of the federal house was defeated by the same Mennonites who in the intervening years had been affected by the socialistic theories of the C.C.F. (Canadian Commonwealth Federation) and the Social Credit Party, and elected socialistic representatives to both the provincial and the federal legislatures. In Vancouver a Mennonite (Regehr) was elected on the C.C.F. party ticket to the Federal House of Commons at Ottawa, although no generally recognized Mennonite political leader has as yet arisen.

The strongest bond, and practically the only one, uniting all branches of Mennonites in the Fraser Valley in a common program is the Provincial Mennonite Relief Committee of British Columbia, which under various names has functioned since 1928. It has become the official spokesman in matters of immigration of displaced persons, citizenship, settlement of landless families, care of mental patients and the indigent. Since 1945, more than $961,000 has passed through its treasury, and 3,000 persons have been assisted to migrate to Canada. A. A. Wiens of Yarrow has been secretary-treasurer of the committee since 1945.

The very tense feeling between Mennonites and other Fraser Valley residents, which reached its climax during World War II, and which was based on social and economic factors, has subsided. The press, local and provincial government officials, as well as the general public, have learned to appreciate Mennonite industry and integrity.   I.G.N.

Frazer Mennonite Church (MC) of the Lancaster Mennonite Conference is an outgrowth of Diamond Rock in an early Amish settlement two miles north of Malvern, Chester Co., Pa. The Weaverland Missions Committee in 1908-9 revived this work, and in 1917-18 a frame church was built along the Lincoln Highway, west of Malvern. The 1955 membership, many of non-Mennonite extraction, was 115; Mahlon Witmer had the bishop oversight, Marcus Swanenberg, Milton G. Brackbill, and C. Ralph Malin were the ministers, and Irvin J. King the deacon.   I.D.L.

Freckenhorst, near Warendorf, Westphalia, Germany, was a *Stift* (ecclesiastical territory) in which the Reformation was introduced by Agnes, Countess of Limburg-Styrum in 1527. Niesert publishes sources which indicate that the countess at least harbored strong Anabaptist leanings. She offered persecuted Anabaptists a refuge and protected them. Dirick Schomeker stated during this trial in 1546 (Niesert, 343 f.) that among her servants were the Fischer, Schluter, Koch families and others who were followers of David Joris and that Agnes would employ only members of this group.

During the church inspection program of the Counter Reformation there were still some Anabaptists found in Freckenhorst (1612). In a complaint of 1625 the Vicar General of Münster stated that there were still some Anabaptists living in the *Stift* of Freckenhorst. He named Jörgen Danielsz and Jobst Nickel and asked the government to have them removed (Niesert, 410).   C.K.

Fr. Brune, *Der Kampf um eine evangelische Kirche im Münsterland 1520-1802* (Witten, 1953) 41-122; J. Niessert, *Münsterische Urkundensammlung* I (Coesfeld, 1826).

Frederick, the name of several princes of the house of Oldenburg, which reigned in Denmark and Schleswig-Holstein (now Germany). Those of interest here are the following:

Frederick I (b. 1471), the second son of Christian I of Denmark, in 1490 duke of half the duchies, in 1523 after the overthrow of his nephew Christian II sole duke and at the same time king of Denmark. Even though at his coronation he had to promise to preserve the old church, he soon issued an edict of tolerance (presumably in 1524), probably under the influence of his son Christian, who had attended the 1521 Diet of Worms, and in 1527 appointed Melchior Hofmann (*q.v.*) as chaplain in Kiel. But Hofmann's fantastic apocalyptic writings, his sermons, and his sharp attacks upon his opponents as well as the Wittenberg group caused grave offense; thereupon Frederick gave his consent to the great colloquium in Flensburg, April 8, 1529. Although Hofmann's ideas had not actually been refuted, he was expelled from the country; but he was permitted to choose the time most favorable to him, and was assured of the safety of his person and property. Frederick did not oppose the spread of the Reformation in his realm.

Frederick II, the grandson of Frederick I, king of Denmark 1559-88. Dutch emigrants, including Mennonites, Davidjorists, and Sacramentists, repeatedly came to Holstein, Schleswig, and Denmark. At the urging of the clergy the king took steps to prevent their growth; in 1558 against Johann Knijpmark and his companions in Krempe, and Sept. 20, 1569, by an edict of 25 articles which were to be signed by foreigners before they were given permission to settle to prevent perversion of doctrine and schism. In 1574 Frederick ordered the provost Johann Vorstius at Itzehoe to examine all the Dutch residents of the Wilstermarsch, as they were suspected of Davidjorism. A preacher Andreas had to surrender his books and promised to reform, and was therefore permitted to keep his property.

Frederick II, Duke of Gottorp 1586-87, son of Duke Adolf, grandson of Frederick I. The region of Eiderstedt (principal town Tönning), where many Dutch had settled and become prosperous, belonged to his realm. Among these were many Mennonites and Davidjorists. On Feb. 21, 1587, Frederick issued an order that the Dutch immigrants must present a statement of their religious views before being admitted, and that the clergy from the pulpits warn the people to "beware of false prophets," and enjoin upon them not to sell land to suspicious persons.

Frederick III, Duke of Gottorp 1616-59, continued the moderate toleration his father Johann Adolf had shown the Mennonites. Dutch immigrants founded the city of Friedrichstadt at the conjunction of the Treene and the Eider in 1621; Remonstrants were among the leaders of the undertaking, and it is owing to them that the Mennonites in the city were also granted complete religious liberty. Those living in other towns were permitted to come to Friedrichstadt to worship, but were to avoid private conventicles. He was less tolerant toward the Davidjorists in Eiderstedt. At the request of the Lutheran provost Johannes Moldenit at Tönning he ordered the search of homes for Davidjorist books in 1635. He supported Moldenit in the long-drawn-out trial against the Davidjorists. Though he was not as severe as their accusers wished, he nevertheless demanded that they sign a confession renouncing their heresies; a quantity of Davidjorist books were publicly burned, the defense of their doctrine and possession of Davidjorist books strictly forbidden. But all hostility toward those who had "purified" themselves by confession was also forbidden.

Frederick III, King of Denmark 1648-70, in 1664 elevated Altona to the rank of a city. He granted the Mennonites the privileges they had formerly enjoyed under the counts of Schauenburg, as his father had also done. R.H.

R. Hansen, "Der David-Joristen-Prozess in Tönning 1642," in *Schriften des Vereins für schleswig-holsteinische Kirchengesch.* I, No. 5 (Kiel, 1900) 31-115, 175-237, 344-99; also "Wiedertäufer in Eiderstedt," *op. cit.*, II; *ML* I, 713.

Frederick I, King of Prussia 1701-13, who in 1688 as Frederick III, Elector of Brandenburg and Duke of Prussia, took the side of the Mennonites in the matter of admitting the severely persecuted Swiss Mennonites. Frederick offered these exiles refuge in his East Prussian realm, especially in the Lithuanian marshes near Tilsit, with a promise of complete freedom from military service and toleration of their principles. He co-operated fully with the Dutch government, which was also deeply interested in these victims of persecution.

On May 3, 1710, Frederick instructed his ambassador in Bern to work for greater toleration of the Mennonites. If this should not be agreeable to the canton, he was determined to "establish them in his realm." He also communicated with the Mennonite churches in The Hague, Amsterdam, and Hamburg-Altona, which were also in active sympathy with the oppressed Swiss.

On Sept. 26, 1710, the Swiss government granted the following concessions: (1) The Mennonites were to be permitted to withdraw without hindrance and to dispose of their property upon payment of a 10 per cent emigration fee and with loss of citizenship (the provision also contained a threat of the execution by sword of any who returned). (2) Bern would expedite them to its border at its own expense and feed and lodge the poor as far as Frankfurt. (3) A delegation to the king was not feasible. Only after all the Mennonites had left the country would they be permitted to deal with the king.

Then with the aid of the Mennonites of Amsterdam, Hamburg, and Danzig, a number of the exiles were settled in Lithuania. The king naturally expected a larger number of settlers than actually came, for he had personally secured for all the refugees the necessary passes through the intervening countries. But most of the exiles went to Holland, and a few families went to Pennsylvania.

The Mennonites who settled in Lithuania in 1711, after three delegates had previously looked over the land and found it very fertile, were received there by General von Dönhof and by the Königsberg legal councilor von Reuter in the name of the king. These men were commissioned to promote the settlement in every way possible.

From Polish territory, especially around Elbing and Culm, the king drew a number of Mennonite families to Lithuania with the guarantee of complete military freedom. But he died before the negotiations were completed, Feb. 25, 1713.

H.G.M.

E. Randt, *Die Mennoniten in Ostpreussen und Litauen bis 1772* (Königsberg, 1912); *ML* II, 1.

Frederick II (known as *Frederick the Great*), King of Prussia 1740-86. This enlightened and farsighted monarch established the principle that participation in civil rights and privileges should not depend on religious creed. He thereby laid the foundation for a toleration of the small Mennonite groups in his realm which was very different from that based on the arbitrary whims of an individual ruler; from this time on they were no longer to be dependent on the mercy of the king, but were expressly permitted to live in Prussia.

On May 31, 1740, he ascended the throne, and on Aug. 14 he rescinded a harsh order which his predecessor, Frederick William I (*q.v.*), had passed against the Mennonites Feb. 22, 1732, and declared that all Mennonites who wished to settle in Prussia should again be received and be tolerated in the cities and in the country like any other self-supporting citizens if they paid the usual fees and conducted themselves properly. Through his ambassadors he had this declaration read in Polish Prussia (West Prussia) and even in the Netherlands and invited Mennonites from both places to settle in any part of his domain. To the Mennonites living in Königsberg he granted citizenship in 1744; and in 1745, when East Friesland became a part of his realm he confirmed all their former privileges and rights to the Mennonites in that area.

When the large West Prussian congregations with their strong peasant population came under his rule in 1772 after the first partition of Poland, he also took a friendly attitude toward them. In the Elbing district, which had been leased by Prussia since 1698, General von Gesler, who had been appointed by Frederick William I, tried in 1746 to compel young Mennonites to take military service. The Mennonites presented a complaint to the king, who then commanded the general to desist (Mannhardt, *Gem.-Kal.* 1902).

On Sept. 13, 1772, Frederick took possession of West Prussia and thus became the ruler of the Mennonites, who until this time had been subjects of the King of Poland. On Sept. 27, on the occasion of the homage at Marienburg, representatives of the 13,000 Mennonites in West Prussia presented a petition to the king requesting the continuance of their privileges. In reply Frederick issued a resolution to the Ministry of War and Crown Lands in Marienwerder, Oct. 6, 1772, that the Mennonites under his protection were not to be discriminated against. For release from military service they were to pay a fee of 5,000 talers, which was to be raised annually by the Mennonites of East and West Prussia for the support of the military school at Culm. The order states explicitly that this sum was not to be considered a payment for religious freedom, but a sum for recruiting, in return for release from military duty.

To be sure, in the following years the king felt it necessary to restrict the acquisition of land by the Mennonites, "lest the cantons suffer too severely therefrom"; but he decided on each case individually, and was so lenient that the Mennonites acquired 296 new parcels of land 1781-83.

To assure the Mennonites a firm basis for their future rights and privileges he issued on March 27, 1780, the *Gnadenprivilegium,* guaranteeing them permanent freedom from military service, as well as the unmolested enjoyment of religious freedom and protection in the practice of their trades in accord with the laws of the country.   H.G.M.

W. Mannhardt, *Die Wehrfreiheit der Altpreussischen Mennoniten* (Marienburg, 1863); H. G. Mannhardt, "Die Mennoniten unter den preussischen Königen," *Gem.-Kal.* 1902; *ML* II, 1 f.

Frederick, Duke of Württemberg, Germany, 1593-1608, a son of the half brother of Duke Ulrich (*q.v.*), a gifted and competent ruler, who, however, was always like a stranger among the Swabians. He freed Württemberg from Austria, and worked toward a union of Protestant rulers even at the risk of conflicts with Catholic rulers. He sought to improve the welfare of his subjects, and settled Lutheran exiles from Styria for whom he founded Freudenstadt.

By creed Frederick was strictly Lutheran, opposed to both Calvinism and Catholicism. But he lacked moral and religious seriousness. The numerous Anabaptists in his country interested him only in connection with the practice of confiscating their land for the benefit of his coffers. He was in perpetual need of funds. In 1594-95 there was complaint in the Diet concerning the curtailment of the inheritance of the children and other heirs of the Anabaptists because of the confiscation of their property. In 1600 and 1606 Frederick demanded official reports on the number of Anabaptists emigrating to Moravia. The measures against them became increasingly severe, since his councilor Enzlin persuaded him that the royal coffers were being seriously injured by the previous handling of Anabaptist property and its extremely low selling price. Then the land procurator Esslinger was commissioned to examine the matter and see to the rapid sale of these lands (officially still treated as orphans' property). Payment for the land, which had hitherto been done little by little, was now to be made as soon as possible; this created difficulties in years of poor crops, and threatened to estrange still further the people from the duke and the church. When in 1608 Frederick died, the complaint concerning the handling of Anabaptist properties ceased altogether, which from now on came under separate management. But when the Austrian government occupied the country (after the Battle of Nördlingen), all these funds from Anabaptist properties were confiscated again.   G.Bos.

C. F. Sattler, *Gesch. des Herzogtums Württemberg unter d. Regierung d. Herzogen V* (Ulm, 1772); Paul F. Stälin, "Das Rechtsverhältnis der religiösen Gemeinschaften und der fremden Religionsverwandten in Württemberg nach seiner geschichtlichen Entwicklung," in *Württembergische Jahrbücher*, 1868, 151-312; *ML* II, 2 f.

Frederick, the name of a number of Electors Palatine and lords of the Upper Palatinate, of the Palatine branch of the Wittelsbach family who in the 16th and 17th centuries influenced the course of Mennonite development: *Frederick II,* 1544-56; *Frederick III,* 1559-76; *Frederick IV,* 1583-1610; *Frederick V,* 1610-23 (d. 1632).

Frederick II, after a frivolous youth, assumed the reign rather late in life and until his death remained an easygoing man of the world. He was as little able to come to a decision on the great questions of the day as to establish himself politically. He found the more or less excitable citizens of the Palatinate, made up of various elements, in ferment; besides the faithful adherents of the old church there were Lutherans, Zwinglians, and also Anabaptists, especially around Neustadt and Kirrweiler, in the district of Lauterburg and around Stromberg. Jobst Kinthis of Freinsheim, with his *Christliches und trosthaftiges Gesprächbüchlein* (*q.v.*), *so mit etlichen der Wiedertäuffer öbristen Rabonen oder Vorsteher gehalten* (1553), sought to convince his ruler from the Lutheran point of view, that the Anabaptist doctrines, especially adult baptism, were unscriptural. Among the "Anabaptists" he includes men that have not the least connection with them. "Most of them speak disparagingly of the government and show it no honor. All pretend to be the elect and the just. The Michael Sattlers are the most pious." Just how much this booklet influenced Frederick is not known. At any rate, many lost their goods and were expelled. But this was mild treatment compared with the ruthless edict of the Diet of Speyer in 1529, passed unanimously by the Catholic and Protestant estates against the Anabaptists. At the Diet of Augsburg in 1555 the Catholic majority, in disregard of the emperor and the pope, granted equal rights to Lutheranism. The elector had vainly demanded freedom of worship for all classes and freedom of conscience for all subjects. His nephew Ottheinrich (*q.v.*) established the Lutheran Reformation in the Palatinate, on the whole considerate of the Catholics, the Zwinglians, and also, in spite of severe mandates, of the Anabaptists. The Heidelberg line expired with him.

From the rough Hunsrück Frederick III of the Simmern line came to the throne. He was a serious person, not always free of harsh traits and not always entirely honest; in conducting a state this may be difficult or impossible. In opposition to his father he had embraced Lutheranism; then, in opposition to nearly all his subjects, repelled by some degeneration in Lutheranism, he had come to the conclusion that Calvin had penetrated most deeply into the thought of the Holy Scriptures. Heidelberg now became the German stronghold of the Reformed Church; the Heidelberg Catechism became the most popular expression of Reformed doctrine. With the determination peculiar to Calvinism the elector took action against other faiths. Like so many genuinely pious Catholic and Protestant rulers of that time he felt responsible to God for the orthodoxy and salvation of his subjects. Many Palatines remained true to the old church, and were not molested as long as they did not carry out its worship. Many Lutheran pastors gave up their positions, refusing to renounce their faith. As Calvin had Servetus (*q.v.*) taken to the stakes for denial of the Trinity, so also the Inspector Silvanus of Ladenburg was executed on the public market place in Heidelberg for the same error. On April 11, 1571, the elector signed the death sentence, and on April 10 he had invited the Anabaptists to a disputation in Frankenthal (*q.v.*). He had hitherto been unwilling to enforce the stern imperial laws against them, for he thought them only poor, simple, good, but misled people. Now their elders and preachers were to express themselves openly, have safe conduct for two weeks before and after the disputation, and free lodging. In every city and village the invitation was publicly posted and twice read from the pulpits. Only 15 participants appeared. Nevertheless Frederick appeared at the opening in person and had the daily report brought to him in Heidelberg. When he saw his well-intended attempt to win them to the state church and bring about a unity of faith in his realm end in failure in spite of his efforts, he was conceivably wrought up. Bitterly he complained about the "bad fellows." He forbade them to preach or baptize and threatened severe penalties. At a synod in 1573 they were classed with magicians and sorcerers. In his will he again emphatically said, "Our children shall not be permitted to become eight, nine, or ten years old . . . and then be baptized." But he did not expel the Anabaptists. The Elector had wished to enforce the severe church discipline of Geneva on his light-hearted, wine-loving subjects, and had met in part active resistance, and in part dull apathy. Perhaps he did not, after all, overlook the fact that the Anabaptists, in spite of their false doctrines, lived more in accord with his demands of Christian living than many a Reformed congregation.

His oldest son and successor, Ludwig, became a Lutheran; the state religion also again became Lutheran. Many preachers, refusing to make the change, were dismissed. Under Ludwig's brother Johann Kasimir and Ludwig's son Frederick IV the Reformed Church was reinstated, and the Lutheran preachers and teachers experienced the same fate as the Reformed had previously met. But the people for the most part accepted the change apathetically, as they did a change in the weather (a Heidelberg poet's observation). But does spiritual violence of this type not leave its traces on the character of a people? Most of the populace remained Lutheran in mind (as did the Catholics) in spite of the Reformed order of service, says M. Ritter.

Frederick IV was a good-natured, indolent, insignificant prince, but had capable advisers. In 1608 they brought about a union of the Protestant imperial estates against the growing Catholic party, which with the aid of other nations, principally France, aimed to break the might of the Catholic imperial house. On both sides preparations were made for a war which was to determine whether Catholicism or Protestantism was to predominate in Germany, a concern which had long since ceased to be a purely religious one, but involved matters of money and temporal power. In the Palatinate conscription was begun. Very likely the Anabaptists refused to take any part in military drills. Is this perhaps the reason for the sterner attitude now taken against them? Until then there had been hesitation. The emperor and the Diet wanted Anabaptism completely eradicated. But the increasing and spreading dissolution of the empire was of benefit to the Anabaptists as to the Protestants in general. Many princes and imperial cities simply ignored the imperial edicts and the resolutions of the Diet, refusing to expel persons who were useful to their

realms for their industry and skill, and who often won the sympathy of their fellow men and even of the minor officials through their honesty. The Palatinate was interspersed with the territory of other temporal and spiritual rulers, with whom exiled Anabaptists frequently found hospitable reception. Was the Palatinate to drive industrious, obedient citizens into the realm of the counts of Leiningen, Falkenstein, and Nassau, or the bishops of Worms and Speyer? It seems at times that the rulers had no intention of enforcing the severe edicts they passed at the insistence of their chaplains and church councilors. Many officials simply did not carry them out. When the officer of Bretten was to expel an Anabaptist in 1576 on the basis of an earlier regulation of Frederick III, he stated that he was unable to find the regulation.

But the sterner measures now undertaken in the Palatinate were perhaps passed for the same reason as those in the canton of Bern several decades later, when Bern, threatened by Louis XIV, increased its military strength and would not tolerate the steady increase in the number of its nonresistant citizens. It may thus have been not so much a concern for the spiritual welfare of the subjects and the religious unity of the state, as a concern for the security of the government that compelled so many of the quietest and most industrious citizens to choose between abandoning faith or home. Yet there are no records in the archives to confirm this assumption. Parsons and church councils merely report that the Anabaptists mocked at the citizens who presented themselves for military drill. The reported utterances of the Anabaptists indicate that they had taken on many of the characteristics of their neighbors. They sound very different from those 50 years before. According to the records of the inspector Titus Wittich in Dirmstein their leaders declared, "We have our own preachers who are much better than you. We are surprised that you are so greatly and so vainly concerned with us and incite the government against us, which would otherwise not take any steps against us, and has no right or authority to do so. We are a group in ourselves and in short, here we are, here is body and life. We do not wish to be advanced, much less to dispute, and least of all to make converts." The Anabaptists of Grosskarlbach, Weisenheim am Sand, and Hessheim assured him that all talking would be in vain, even if 12,000 dozen theologians would try to persuade them to enter the state church. At any rate the number of Anabaptists in the Palatinate was greatly reduced, owing in part to emigration to Moravia and in part to the dying out of some families.

Frederick V, son of Frederick IV, married Elizabeth, the niece of the unfortunate Mary Stuart. This connection with England was intended to strengthen the Protestant cause in Germany. She was received in the Palatinate with great pomp and grand display and exuberant merrymaking, while the clouds gathered in the southeast of the empire, from which the terrible storm of the Thirty Years' War of religion was discharged, and in which the "Winter King" lost his crown and his domains. In this war, which brought incomparable suffering upon the German people, especially those in the Palatinate, the last remnants of the Anabaptists in the Palatinate were nearly or perhaps entirely wiped out. E.G.

(For bibliography, see end of article in *ML* I, 714-17.)

Frederick (Pa.) Mennonite Home for the Aged: see **Mennonite Home** for the Aged, Frederick, Pa.

Frederick William I (known as the Soldier King), King of Prussia 1713-40. What Prussia owes this economical and stern ruler lives on in history. Toward the Mennonites he was at first benevolent, but later became rather ungracious. Like his fathers he had promised them freedom of worship, their own church buildings, release from conscription even for their servants, and even in 1721 he again issued an invitation to the Mennonite families living in Polish Prussia along the Vistula to settle in his domain. But his partiality toward the "Potsdam guards," for which he needed tall men, led him into injustice. His recruiting agents, who did not hesitate to use force when they saw strong young men six feet in height, also came to East Prussia, and during the night of Sept. 14, 1723, they dragged a number of young Mennonites off to Königsberg, and tried to make them consent to accept military service by starving them. The Mennonite congregation complained to the king, and the perpetrators of the violent deed were punished. Yet the king was not willing to release all these tall men. He had the six stateliest brought to Potsdam and put under severe discipline. But when all threats and mistreatment failed to weaken the young men in their refusal to take service, he dismissed them, but kept a personal grudge against the Mennonites, who had told him they would emigrate if their freedom from conscription was not granted.

In his first flush of anger he ordered all the Mennonites to leave the country, and some families actually returned to Polish Prussia (see **Dannenberg**). Only in Königsberg and near Tilsit did some Mennonites remain, protected by the civil authorities for their capability. Again on Feb. 22, 1732, the king issued an order that all Mennonites leave the country within three months. However, the Royal Ministry of War and Crown Lands declared that the tax funds would be appreciably lowered by this measure, for the Mennonites contributed to the royal treasury both as industrialists and as farmers. In addition, these people had been lured into the country precisely by the promise of freedom from military service, and their numbers were so small that their refusal to do this service could not injure the state in any way. Frederick William rescinded his order of banishment on the condition that they establish weaving mills.

In another part of his realm, at Crefeld, Frederick William I throughout his reign showed the same kind attitude toward the Mennonites. In 1721 he granted them a *Privilegium* permitting the practice of nonresistance in return for a fee, and in 1738 he even paid them a rather cordial visit.

H.G.M.

W. Mannhardt, *Die Wehrfreiheit der Altpreussischen Mennoniten* (Marienburg, 1863) appendix, p. LXX; *ML*

II, 3; *Beiträge zur Geschichte der rheinischen Mennoniten (Schriftenreihe des Mennonitischen Geschichtsvereins*, No. 2, Weierhof, 1939) 38-45, 56 f.

Frederick William II, King of Prussia 1786-97, the successor of Frederick II (*q.v.*), was as benevolent toward the Mennonites as his great-uncle. He recognized the significance of the work which these economical, sober, and industrious people accomplished in the crafts and in agriculture, and was therefore not opposed to their spread in West Prussia. But he was at the same time unable to evade the fear of his officials that if too much land passed into Mennonite hands there might be difficulty in raising replacements for the army. In the Marienburg region the complaint was also made that the rapid increase in Mennonite ownership of land jeopardized the Lutheran Church. The king therefore decided to regulate matters concerning the Mennonites by a specific law. Thus the "Edict concerning future regulation of Mennonite life in all the royal provinces with the exception of Silesia" came into being July 30, 1789. It consists of 14 paragraphs; it confirms their liberty of conscience including nonresistance, but it also restricts their acquisition of land, sets a fee to be paid to the Lutheran Church by Mennonite landowners, and specifies the official attitude toward persons of other creeds who join the Mennonites. Because this edict made it difficult for young Mennonites to acquire new land, the emigration of West Prussian Mennonites to the steppes of South Russia began in 1789. During his reign the Danzig Mennonites came under Prussian rule. H.G.M.

Reiswitz and Wadzek, *Beiträge zur Kenntnis der Mennonitengemeinden* (Berlin, 1821); H. G. Mannhardt, *Die Danziger Mennonitengemeinde, ihre Entstehung und ihre Geschichte von 1569-1919* (Danzig, 1919); W. Mannhardt, *Die Wehrfreiheit der Altpreussischen Mennoniten* (Marienburg, 1863); *ML* II, 3 f.

Frederick William III, King of Prussia 1797-1840, was one of the most peaceable of the rulers of Prussia, and for that reason friendly toward the Mennonites. But under his reign Prussia became involved in the most serious wars. Hence the Mennonites of Prussia not only shared the suffering of the entire country, but also had to struggle to preserve their nonresistance. More than once when this principle was threatened the king personally defended them. Nor did he overlook their voluntary offer of money and provisions to the utmost of their capacity, as well as their service in nursing care. In 1827 he issued the special law of March 11, legally freeing the Mennonites from the obligation to swear an oath. H.G.M.

W. Mannhardt, *Die Wehrfreiheit der Altpreussischen Mennoniten* (Marienburg, 1863); *ML* II, 4.

Frederick William IV, King of Prussia 1840-61, at his ascension to the throne assured the Mennonites that he would continue the protection they had enjoyed under his predecessors. But after 1848, when a constitution was passed, he could no longer decide these matters alone. It was a basic idea in the new constitution that as far as possible differences in creed should neither limit civil rights nor carry exemption from civil duties. The release of the

Mennonites from military duty could not be permanently retained in a state that required universal military service. Frederick William and his cabinet were, however, able to guarantee this freedom once more in 1852, but only by assuring the house of representatives that a law governing Mennonite affairs would soon be presented. But this did not take place under his reign. Fifteen years of uncertainty and unrest passed for the Mennonites, until under William I (*q.v.*) their former freedom from military duty was rescinded by the Reichstag in 1867. (*ML* II, 4.) H.G.M.

Frederik Maartens (Frederick Maertsz), an Anabaptist martyr, residing at Hoorn, Dutch province of North Holland. He had taken part in the journey from Amsterdam to Bergklooster (*q.v.*) en route to Münster in March 1534. Because he refused to recant he was beheaded (place unknown, but likely Amsterdam) on May 11, 1534. (*Inv. Arch. Amst.* I, Nos. 744, 745; Mellink, *Wederdopers,* 165.)

vDZ.

Fredeshiem (House of Peace), a Dutch Mennonite brotherhood home (Broederschapshuis) in a lovely wooded spot about three miles east of Steenwijk (*q.v.*), province of Overijssel. It was built in 1929 and is used as a recreation center, convalescent home, and a quiet place for all who want rest. Sometimes conferences are also held here, e.g., by the Dutch Mennonite Peace Group. It is open throughout the year and has a capacity of about one hundred guests. It is managed by a committee of five members.

vDZ.

Free Will, Anabaptist Position. The question of freedom of will is concerned with the relationship between God's sovereignty and the exercise of will by men. In particular it raises the question whether or not men have sufficient freedom to affect the course of history or to do that which will bear upon their ultimate salvation or damnation. This issue, which had come to a head early in the fifth century in the Augustinian-Pelagian controversy, was revived in the 16th century when the Protestant reformers espoused the Augustinian viewpoint. Erasmus of Rotterdam, Sebastian Franck, the Anabaptists, and certain other dissenters generally rejected the Augustinian position, but they did not go to the opposite extreme of asserting complete human freedom. They recognized that God controls the possibilities within which the events of history take place and the ultimate goal toward which history is moving. These men held that within certain limits God had granted free will, and that each person may at least either accept or reject divine grace offered to all. Anabaptists and those closely associated with them, however, held varying opinions as to the precise degree of freedom enjoyed by men. Nor did the Anabaptists agree entirely with the position of Erasmus.

Among the earliest Anabaptists to be concerned with the problem was Balthasar Hubmaier, who wrote two small pamphlets on the subject (*Von der Freyhait des Willens,* and *Das ander Biechlen von der Freywilligkeit des Menschens,* both published at Nikolsburg in 1527). He distinguished between God's "secret will" (plenary power) and His "revealed will," by which He has mercy on men. According to Hubmaier, God's "revealed will" is composed of an "attracting will" which offers grace and mercy to all, and a "repelling will," or will of judgment and punishment, by which He leaves in blindness and evil those who refuse His grace. With respect to the nature of man, Hubmaier held that originally Adam had been completely free to choose good or evil and that through disobedience Adam had lost this freedom for himself and his descendants. The body became corrupt and sinful; the soul lost its freedom of choice; and the spirit became the helpless prisoner of the body. Through God's grace, however, if the soul receives it, man's freedom is imperfectly restored. Hubmaier understood God's grace to mean that God awakens the soul by His Word, leads it by His Son, and enlightens it by the Holy Ghost. Hubmaier made it clear, however, that such freedom as man possesses in no way conflicts with the sovereignty of God over history. Man may propose, but his will is effective in actual events only to the extent that God wills or permits.

Hubmaier's contemporary, Hans Denk (*q.v.*), held a similar point of view. Denk also recognized the omnipotence of God and believed that a divine plan of salvation, coexistent with human freedom, would be fulfilled. Denk thought that man was created primarily to fulfill God's desire for voluntary obedience as opposed to the blind obedience of "a log or a stone." God forces no one. "For the sake of human free will, He must permit sin." Like Hubmaier, Denk believed that only the flesh was corrupted by Adam's fall and that the spirit was made the prisoner of the flesh. Sin, according to Denk, is a kind of sickness. If a man would recover, he must surrender himself to God; only then can the spirit within him dominate the unwilling flesh. Only then is man able to keep the law of love in obedience to God. Thus Denk found the highest fulfillment of human free will in self-surrender to God (see **Gelassenheit**).

Although the Swiss Brethren were more concerned with practical Christianity than dogmatic theology, the idea of human free will appears now and then in the hymns in the *Ausbund* (1564, 1583, and later). Rewards and punishments are genuine, the result of voluntary obedience or disobedience. The hymn "Merket auf ihr Menschenkinder" states that God has no pleasure in the destruction of sinners and that He desires repentance; yet He will not leave unpunished the sins of those who refuse to serve Him. The same thought is contained in the hymn "Gross Unbill thut mich zwingen," in which the Biblical examples of the punishment of evil serve as a warning to the "ungodly." In the Last Judgment, "what one sows now, the same shall he reap, be it evil or good."

The South German Anabaptist view of free will is probably best represented by Pilgram Marpeck, who, unlike Hubmaier and Denk, accepted the Augustinian premise of the total depravity of man.

Marpeck therefore stressed the atonement of Christ to a greater extent than did Hubmaier, but at the same time he accepted in substance Hubmaier's doctrine of God's attracting and repelling will. Marpeck's Biblical literalism, however, would not permit him to ignore such passages as Romans 8 and 9. He found a solution by subjecting God's foreordination to His prescience, not the reverse. Marpeck also pointed out that God's eternal condemnation must not be confused with manifestations of His wrath in this world, where innocent and guilty may suffer alike. Thus the ultimate destiny of each is still determined by his free choice, even though God may know in advance what that choice will be.

In many respects the Hutterite elder Peter Riedemann was in agreement with Marpeck. With respect to the total depravity of man, the necessity of God's intervention in Jesus Christ, and the consequences of resisting the proffered grace, the views of the two men appear essentially the same. Riedemann, however, placed greater emphasis upon the sovereignty of God over history, and stressed the view that disobedience to God does not establish human independence, but makes the culprit a slave of Satan. Riedemann also stressed the necessity of surrendering oneself completely to God in order that God's grace may operate. Man's actual deeds are immediately determined by the master he serves. Thus Riedemann reduced the scope of human freedom to the choice between obedience to God and the service of Satan, but the responsibility for this choice rests squarely upon man.

In the Netherlands, Menno Simons and his followers continually stressed the responsibility which men and nations must bear for their own misdeeds. Although Menno saw a cosmic struggle between the attempts of Satan to lead men astray on the one hand and God's redeeming love and mercy on the other, he believed that each person might choose whether to follow the enticements of Satan or to obey the commands of God. The course of history is fixed, but the will of the individual is free. Menno's writings are filled with examples of the punishment of those who permitted themselves to be beguiled by Satan and refused to heed the warnings and promises of God.

In the debate with Reformed preachers at Emden in 1578, two Mennonite representatives, Peter of Cologne and Brixius Gerritts, claimed that God's promise of salvation extends to all men who have not forfeited it by their own direct and actual sins, that is, by willful disobedience. In support of their position Peter and Brixius cited Gen. 4:7 and 6:3. These arguments were repeated in substance in the debate at Leeuwarden in 1596; and the Mennonite confessions of faith of 1600 and 1630 take the same position. This must not be confused, however, with a Pelagian denial of the corruption of human nature. Only because of God's pardon and through divine grace, not from any human merit, are men permitted to exercise free will. But this grace can be rejected; hence men are responsible for their own destruction. Mennonite confessions of 1627 and 1632 imply such limited freedom, although they do not deal directly with the question.

The author of the confession of 1600, like Marpeck, used the semi-Pelagian device of ascribing divine predestination to divine prescience in order to reconcile God's foreordination with human free will.

The erstwhile Anabaptist David Joris attributed even greater importance to the freedom of the human will. Joris recognized no independent existence to the freedom of the human will. Joris recognized no independent existence of Satan; the devil is simply the sinful flesh, the temporal corrupt being, which, when it dominates the human will, introduces evil into the world. Thus the betrayal of man was self-betrayal. But God, through the example and power of Christ, has broken the power of the flesh. For salvation to be effective, however, man must take the initiative. He must first repent in order to be renewed through God's grace. Joris reconciled human freedom with God's sovereignty by recognizing that the consequences of man's disobedience spring from God's law, and that God withholds His hands for the time being.

The revolutionary branch of Anabaptism, on the other hand, follows more closely the familiar interpretations. Melchior Hofmann, like Marpeck, declared that man had completely fallen and could be saved only by God's grace. Yet grace, according to Hofmann, makes salvation possible; God does not force one to receive it. Like Denk, Hofmann emphasized God's desire for a "voluntary sacrifice," a "willing bride" for His Son Jesus Christ.

Bernhard Rothmann of Münster pictured the history of the world as a continual abuse of free will by human beings. God created man for righteousness; He gave him a knowledge of right and wrong; but man chooses whether or not he will obey. The way of obedience is open to all, for God wishes all men to be saved; but each man chooses the way he shall go. The emphasis upon human responsibility for the failure to obey God is increased in Rothmann's later works by attributing disobedience to human wisdom, reason, and levity instead of the enticements of the devil. Rothmann, as other Anabaptists, retained the sovereignty of God by placing human freedom within limits set by God. Like Hubmaier, he distinguishes between the will and the deed. With respect to predestination, Rothmann at one point based God's foreordination on His foreknowledge. At another point Rothmann reverted to the Lutheran device of the paradox beyond human wisdom to unravel. At another time he fell back, in substance, upon Hubmaier's explanation of God's will. In any case, Rothmann and his coreligionists at Münster called men to "repentance" and preached the imminent doom of those who refused the last chance which God would offer them.

Two Mennonite discussions of free will in the 17th century deserve to be mentioned. Jan de Buyser's *Christelijck Huis-boeck* of 1643 contains a long chapter on this subject by Vincent de Hondt. Georg Hansen, a noted elder in Danzig (d. 1703), also discussed it in his book of 1671, *Ein Glaubens-Bericht* (Friedmann, *Mennonite Piety,* 131 f.).

In general, Anabaptist concern with the problem of free will appears to have been motivated by three considerations. In the first place, God is righteous;

therefore, He can in no way be responsible for evil. Secondly, without free will there can be no real repentance, which for Anabaptists was an indispensable element in entering the Christian life. Thirdly, without free will there can be no real commitment to discipleship.   F.J.W.

F. J. Wray, "History in the Eyes of the Sixteenth Century Anabaptists" (unpublished Ph.D. dissertation, Yale University, 1953); W. O. Lewis and G. D. Davidson, "The Writings of Balthasar Hubmaier" (typed ms., Library of William Jewell College, Liberty, Mo.); L. Keller, *Ein Apostel der Wiedertäufer* (Leipzig, 1882); G. Haake, *Hans Denck* (Norden, 1897); J. Heberle, "Johann Denck und sein Büchlein vom Gesetz," *Theologische Studien und Kritiken XXIV* (1851) 121-94; J. C. Wenger, "The Theology of Pilgram Marpeck," *MQR XII* (1938) 137 ff.; (Marpeck), *Vermanung* (n.p., 1542); P. Rideman, *Account of Our Religion, Doctrine and Faith* (London, 1950); *Complete Writings of Menno Simons* (Scottdale, 1955); van Braght, *Martyrs' Mirror;* David Joris, *'T Wonder-Boeck* (n.p., 1542); F. O. zur Linden, *Melchior Hofmann* (Haarlem, 1885); Carl Sachsse, *Balthasar Hubmaier als Theologe* (Berlin, 1914); R. Friedmann, *Mennonite Piety Through the Centuries* (Goshen, 1949).

Freedom of Conscience: see **Religious Liberty.**

Freeland Seminary, located near Collegeville, Pa., 27 miles northwest of Philadelphia, was established in 1848 by Abraham Hunsicker (1793-1872), who had been ordained as a minister of the Skippack Mennonite Church in January 1847. In October 1847 he with John Oberholtzer left the Mennonite Church (MC, Franconia Conference) to organize the Eastern Conference of Mennonites. When Abraham Hunsicker was elected as minister "he felt more than ever before the need of a provision for more and better knowledge and resolved before God to found a school that should afford to others means of obtaining that of which he was deprived." Therefore in 1848 he purchased 10 acres of land, erected a building, and established Freeland Seminary. The school opened Nov. 7, 1848, with an enrollment of three, which grew to 79 during the year. The curriculum included the first two years of college. Henry A. Hunsicker, his son, who was the principal, stated, "The school flourished beyond expectation, though it received small patronage from the Mennonites whom it hoped to benefit." Among those who attended the school were John F. Funk (*q.v.*) and Warren Bean, later a bishop in the Franconia Conference. On Jan. 1, 1850, Henry A. Hunsicker was ordained as minister by the Eastern Conference of Mennonites (GCM).

The Hunsickers and some of their followers pursued a more liberal policy than the Eastern Conference. The differences became so great that by 1851 Abraham Hunsicker, his son Henry A., and others were expelled from the group. In 1854 they established the Trinity Christian Society (*q.v.*), an undenominational congregation. Gradually this group disintegrated, which ultimately affected Freeland Seminary.

After 17 years Freeland Seminary was leased to A. H. Fetterolf, and in 1869 a group of men organized a corporation and purchased the school, which then became known as Ursinus College. This corporation primarily served the Reformed Church. During the first 20 years of the existence of Freeland

Seminary more than 3,000 young men received their education here.

Abraham Hunsicker was also the founder of "the Pennsylvania Female College."   C.K.

Henry A. Hunsicker, *A Genealogical History of the Hunsicker Family* (Philadelphia, 1911); M. S. Harder, "The Origin, Philosophy, and Development of Education Among the Mennonites" (Dissertation, University of Southern California, 1949) 274; J. C. Wenger, *History of the Mennonites of the Franconia Conference* (Telford, Pa., 1937); J. E. Hartzler, *Education Among the Mennonites of America* (Danvers, 1925) 128-29.

Freeman, S.D., a town (pop. 1,000) located in the southeastern part of the state, in Hutchinson County. The town itself is not solidly Mennonite, nor was the site originally platted by a Mennonite. However, the Mennonite influence is by now a predominant one. The population of the Mennonite churches within the immediate shopping district of Freeman approaches 2,000. Perhaps around one fifth of these live in town.

Five General Conference Mennonite churches lie within and to the east (Swiss) and west (Hutterite) of the town. A Mennonite Brethren and an Evangelical Mennonite Brethren church are located north and northeast of Freeman in a predominantly Low German district; the Krimmer Mennonite Brethren have a church northwest of town. These latter three, along with two other General Conference churches, lie at least partly within the shopping area of Marion (15 miles from Freeman). The earliest Mennonite settlement in the Freeman area dates back to 1873-74.

The Mennonite constituency of Freeman supports and controls a home for the aged, a junior college, and an academy. It also gives considerable support and patronage to a community hospital.

The Freeman community is perhaps unique in the fact that four different Mennonite conferences co-operate in maintaining institutions and commuity activities which are distinctively Mennonite in character.   H.H.G.

Freeman Junior College, a Mennonite school in Freeman, S.D., had its inception in the "South Dakota Mennonite College" which came into being in response to a feeling among the Russian Mennonite settlers in Dakota in the 1870's that the German language should be maintained and that there should be some Biblical instruction. This feeling came with particular force to Frederick C. Ortman during the winter of 1894-95 while he was visiting the various Mennonite communities in Kansas, where he noted the good influence of Bethel College, particularly in training Mennonites to teach in the elementary schools.

Ortman took his burden of a Mennonite school to Elder Christian Kaufman in the winter of 1899-1900. Out of this meeting followed a series of meetings to which representatives came from the various Mennonite churches in the community. The idea of a Mennonite school became more popular with each meeting. At the fourth general meeting it was decided that since Freeman was very nearly in the center of the community the school should be built there. At the fifth meeting, held on Dec. 10, 1900, a board of directors was elected and on the

14th of the same month a charter was obtained from the State of South Dakota.

The task of raising money was then begun. Construction on the first building, a frame structure costing $7,000, was begun in 1902. It was completed in time for school to begin in the fall of 1903. The dedication services were held on Oct. 25, 1903. This building served for all instructional purposes until the completion of the new administration building in 1926 at a cost of more than $60,000. In the meantime two dormitories had been erected, one in 1906 at a cost of $6,000 and a second in 1915, costing $4,500. In 1923 the auditorium-gymnasium was erected at a cost of approximately $7,500. After the erection of the new administration building in 1926, two additional buildings were placed on the nine-acre campus. One was a men's dormitory built out of army barracks, with two apartments for faculty members. The other was the imposing new auditorium-gymnasium completed in 1950 at an estimated value of $125,000. It was named Pioneer Hall in honor of the settlers who first came to Dakota in 1874 from southern Russia. The men's dormitory was valued at $16,000. In addition to the nine-acre campus with its seven buildings the college in 1950 had two farms and a small endowment fund. Total fixed assets as per annual statement of July 31, 1953, were listed at $334,547.01.

When the school opened in 1903 the course of study did not comprise much more than the common school subjects, except for German. Even beginners were admitted during the first year. However, new courses were added as the school developed. In 1911 the Teacher Training Course was recognized by the State Department of Public Instruction. In 1922 the Academy was fully accredited. The following year the first year of college work was offered. By 1927 the University of South Dakota accredited the full Junior College course. In 1950 the school offered (1) a Junior College course; (2) a One- and Two-Year Teacher Training course; (3) an Academy course; (4) Bible courses; (5) special courses in Agriculture, Commerce, Farm Shop, and Home Making; (6) and work by correspondence. The Associate in Arts degree was being conferred in Bible, Teacher Training, Commerce, and Liberal Arts. In the earlier years all of the Bible classes and many of the other subjects were conducted in German. But as the use of German declined in the homes, it was gradually less used as a language of instruction, so that by 1914 only some of the Bible courses were given in German. Since that time German has been only an elective modern language course.

The institution is not under the direct management of the Mennonite Church but operates under a board of trustees of nine members elected from a corporation consisting largely of members of the various Mennonite churches of South Dakota and surrounding states. Anyone who contributes $25 to the school becomes a member of the corporation, and each $100 contribution constitutes a vote; no one, however, can ever cast more than 10 votes at a corporation meeting—five of his own and five by proxy. The name of the school has changed twice since it was incorporated—to Freeman College, and since 1939, to Freeman Junior College.

While established primarily for the benefit of the young people of the Mennonite faith, emphasizing the simple life, industry, the sanctity of the home, freedom of conscience, and Christian love as the guiding principle in all situations of life, the benefits and privileges of the college have been heartily extended to young people of other denominations. The Board of Trustees has adopted the Statement of Doctrine of the General Conference Mennonites.

Hundreds of young people who have graduated from the various courses through the years have become active workers in the community life of Freeman as well as in other communities. In its first 50 years the leadership of the school changed quite frequently. The following have served as president or acting president: H. A. Bachman 1903-4, 1908-12; John R. Thierstein 1904-8; Benjamin J. Kaufman 1912-13; Eddison Mosiman 1913-17; A. J. Regier 1917-21, 1922-27; P. F. Quiring 1921-22, 1927-28; P. R. Schroeder 1928-31; John D. Unruh 1931-35, 1936-38, 1939-48; B. P. Waltner 1935-36, 1938-39; Edmund J. Miller 1948-51; and Ronald von Riesen 1951- . The total enrollment in 1954-55 was 158, of which 46 were in college and 112 in high school. (*ML* I, 694 f.)   J.D.U.

Freeman Junior College Bulletin has been published (bimonthly at first) since 1914, by Freeman Junior College and Academy. Each (monthly) issue now contains eight pages, 6 by 8½ in. Its purpose is to inform the constituency and alumni of the aspirations, needs, and accomplishments of the school. It was published in German until 1924, but is now published in English, edited by Marie J. Waldner. It has a circulation of about 5,500.   H.H.G.

Freeport Mennonite Church (MC), located about 7½ miles northeast of Freeport, Stephenson Co., Ill., is a member of the Illinois Conference, and in 1954 had a membership of 170. It was organized about 1845 by Mennonite settlers from Ontario. The first building was constructed about 1863, and to meet the increasing membership was enlarged about 1888, and again in 1912 and in 1943. The first Sunday school was organized in 1878, the young people's meetings in 1890, and the sewing circle in 1910. The congregation through its history has ordained three deacons, ten ministers, and three bishops. In 1954 Richard Yordy was pastor and bishop.

                                                           H.J.Z.

Freeriks (Freerks), **Jakob,** a preacher of the Mennonite congregation of Harlingen, Dutch province of Friesland, who together with his copreacher Ebbe Pieters (*q.v.*) was the leader of the Frisian group at Harlingen in the Flemish-Frisian controversy of 1566. Jacob Freerks' attempt to restore peace (September 1566) was not successful. Particulars about Jacob Freerks' life were not available. (*DB* 1893, 22, 26-34, 36.)   vDZ.

Freiburg, Anna von, an Anabaptist martyr, who was drowned at Freiburg (most likely in Switzerland) in 1529. The *Martyrs' Mirror* prints a prayer by her.

The *Ausbund* prints a hymn attributed to her (No. 36), "Ewiger Vater vom Himmelreich, Ich ruf zu dir gar inniglich," which is also found in Wackernagel's *Kirchenlied* (III, 487), but which actually, according to Hutterite sources, was written by Ursula Helriglin, who was imprisoned at St. Petersberg in Tirol 1538-43. NEFF.

Beck, *Geschichts-Bücher*, 157; Wolkan, *Lieder*, 178; Wolkan, *Geschicht-Buch*, 194; Wackernagel, *Kirchenlied* III, 487; *Mart. Mir.* D 26, E 434; *ML* I, 696.

Freie Zeuge, the temporary (1918-21) name of the *Zionspilger* (*q.v.*), the weekly periodical published by the Emmental Mennonite Church since 1882. Because of the financial difficulties experienced by the paper during World War I, and after the "Freie Gemeinde," to which many of the subscribers to the *Zionspilger* belonged, was considering establishing its own weekly journal, a joint publication by the two groups was undertaken. Beginning with the issue of Jan. 6, 1918, and ceasing with the issue of June 27, 1921, the name of the paper became *Der Freie Zeuge, vormals Zionspilger, Ein Wochenblatt für christliche Gemeinschaften und Familien.* No change in content was to be made. Editors were Johann Kipfer for the Mennonites, for the Freie Gemeinde W. Mili of Bern. Beginning with the number for July 3, 1921, the name was changed back to *Zionspilger,* although the paper continued for a time longer as a joint publication with the same two editors. Until May 12, 1940, there were always two editors, one for the Freie Gemeinde. With that number only Johann Kipfer appeared as editor.

H.S.B.

Freisleben, Christoph and **Leonhard:** see **Eleutherobios.**

Freischütz, a Hutterite Bruderhof: see **Sobotiste.**

Freistadt, a city in Upper Austria. Concerning the Anabaptist congregation in this city we have relatively more information than about many other places of Austria, mainly because of its well-kept city archives with the many Anabaptist records. The origin of the congregation is not known but it seems unlikely that it was founded by Hans Hut (*q.v.*), even though this Anabaptist apostle was temporarily active also in Freistadt in June 1527, baptizing several citizens there. It is more likely that the congregation goes back to Hans Schlaffer (*q.v.*), who in 1526 was staying in the near-by castle of Weinberg, which then belonged to the Baron of Zelking. An indication of Schlaffer's influence is the tract *Am anfang ains cristlichen lebens,* which upon the personal command of King Ferdinand was deposited together with the confessions of six Anabaptists who had been imprisoned in Freistadt Aug. 12, 1527. This tract is divided into two parts: the first part is an enlargement of the earlier tract by Hans Schlaffer, *Bericht und leer eines recht christlichen lebens* (Müller, 94 ff.), which in turn is dependent on Hans Hut's pamphlet, *Vom geheimnus der tauff* (Müller, 12 ff.). The second part is an independent new piece. This tract, as found in the archives of Freistadt, was signed by six Anabaptists, Jörg Schoferl, Heinrich Panreiter, Hans Egkhart, Hans Tischler, Paul Goldschmid, and Wolfgang Pirchenfelder (Tuchscherer; see Nicoladoni, 250 ff.). These six men confessed in their statement that they had received the "sign" (of rebirth), baptism, but they denied having heard teachings concerning baptism from any human being, neither from Hans Hut, nor from Luther nor from Zwingli, as the imperial mandate asserted. They rather claimed to have depended alone on the testimony of the Scriptures. King Ferdinand agreed on Oct. 25, 1527, that Master Wolfgang Künigl, who at that time was occupied with the cross-examination of Anabaptists in the city of Steyr (also in Upper Austria), should function as prosecutor also in Freistadt. Thus Künigl went to this city in the middle of November, and the examination was set for Nov. 27, 1527. Jörg Schoferl apparently recanted at once. When the "punishment of Horb and Rottenburg" (see **ML** II, 347) was imposed upon him, he asked for moderation of this severe stipulation; there is no record, however, that this request was granted. The trial was then interrupted, but resumed in February 1528. It ended with the recantation of all the imprisoned Anabaptists, who now had to make a public "church penitence" on a certain Sunday.

In addition to these six men there were other Anabaptists in the city at that time. We hear of meetings and also of a "terrible, offensive, and revolutionary booklet" of these Anabaptists (Nicoladoni, 269). The magistrate arrested three more men and two women in May 1528, while other Anabaptists fled to some other places. Apparently no death sentence was pronounced at that time. All the records indicate that the sympathies of the council were on the side of the accused. An inner revulsion against imposing the severe penalties decreed by the authorities in Vienna is noticeable in the writings of the mayor of Freistadt. The willingness of the council to protect its fellow citizens is also shown by the trial (dragged out over several years) of the imperial "gate-keeper" Gilg Kurtz, to whom King Ferdinand had assigned as a gift the house and fortune of the Anabaptist Thomas Tanzer, who had fled from Freistadt. By 1530 the Anabaptist movement in Freistadt seems to have been extinguished; the city later became almost entirely Lutheran. LOSERTH, G.M.

While the city archives apparently show no records whatever concerning death sentences against Anabaptists, the chronicles of the Hutterites quite definitely state that martyrdom was by no means unknown in or around this city. The great "Catalogue of Martyrs" (Beck, 280; Wolkan, 182; Zieglschmid, 232), inserted in the *Geschicht-Buch* at the year 1542, lists for "Freynstat" not less than ten victims of ruthless persecution. Likewise the Codex "Kremser" (in Beck listed as codex "N"), formerly of Bratislava, expressly mentions three martyrs at this place: Hans Weinberger from Freistadt, Madlen Frelich from the city of Enns, and another Madlen from Steyr (all in Upper Austria). No execution date is given. R.F.

Beck, *Geschichts-Bücher;* Wolkan, *Geschicht-Buch;* Zieglschmid, *Chronik;* A. Nicoladoni, *Johannes Bünderlin* (Berlin, 1893); L. Müller, *Glaubenszeugnisse oberdeutscher Taufgesinnter* (Leipzig, 1938); *ML* I, 699 f.

Freitäufer, a designation for those persons in the era of the Reformation who neither championed nor rejected infant baptism, asserting that the Holy Scriptures neither forbade nor commanded the baptism of infants. The name was first used by Bishop Aug. Marius of Brod to refer to Oecolampadius, the local reformer, who at first did not take a clear position on the question. The term was not widely used in the literature of the 16th century.   HEGE.

U. Heberle, "Johann Denk und die Ausbreitung seiner Lehre," in *Theol. Stud. u. Krit.,* 1855, 885; *ML* I, 700 f.

French Revolution, the designation of the movement which after a long process of preparation, both political and philosophical, broke out on the night of Aug. 4, 1789, with the removal of all feudal privileges by the National Convention in Paris. The results of this Revolution are ineradicable.

Occasionally in the history of ideas connections are assumed between the intellectual forerunners of the French Revolution, especially Voltaire (*q.v.*) and Rousseau, and Anabaptists, or between some political phenomena and former Anabaptist demands. The "Declaration of Human and Civil Rights" (1789) expresses the fundamental principle of religious freedom, which is undisputably of Anabaptist origin, and which by remarkable routes, including the Anglo-American constitutional concept, finally achieved universal significance. But these are usually somewhat violent interpretations, and aside from the contradiction to fundamental Anabaptist faith which the excesses of the Revolution revealed, are based on exaggerated and ill-considered comparisons. Even the concept of a direct connection between the French Revolution and the ideas of the sword-bearing revolutionary Anabaptist movement (Münster) is untenable, unless all revolutionary activism is to be forced into one historical line.

But the effects of the French Revolution on the Mennonites were very real, and not only on those under French jurisdiction but everywhere else in Europe, in the Netherlands, Germany, and Switzerland. Although on the eastern border of France (Alsace, *q.v.*) even revolutionaries like Robespierre protected the Mennonite principle of nonresistance, soon afterward the Napoleonic wars led to the abrogation of this protection. Thus the Mennonite confession was suppressed in one of its most essential aspects. In conspicuous contrast to this was the granting of substantial legal privileges as a result of the Revolution to the Mennonites of the German Rhine region. This latter implied an increasing recognition of the Mennonite faith (with the exception of nonresistance) and concerned their private rights (see **Ius retractus**), especially the regulation of their marriages (see **Marriage**). The process of equalization instigated by the Revolution finally removed the last traces of the old heresy laws, and had an emancipating effect within the Mennonite congregations themselves.

In Switzerland toleration for the Mennonites, which finally came in 1815, was also the result primarily of the French Revolution. The "Helvetic Revolution" of 1798 in Switzerland, which changed the Swiss confederation (*Eidgenossenschaft*) into a federal republic, was the result largely of the diplomatic-military action of France together with the Swiss revolutionary party. In 1799 the New Helvetic Republic passed an act of toleration granting religious liberty to every faith, and permitting those who had been banished on religious grounds to return. This act ended active persecution but did not give the Mennonites full equality with the state church, particularly in matters of baptism and marriage. Finally in 1815 the Bernese Mennonites were granted complete religious toleration with full rights of citizenship.

Another consequence of the Revolution was the end of the rule of the Prince Bishop of Basel in the Jura territory. This was initiated with the invasion of the French troops in 1798, and completed with the action of the Congress of Vienna in 1815, incorporating the Basel Bishopric with the Canton of Bern.   E.H.C.

S. Geiser, *Die Taufgesinnten-Gemeinden* (Karlsruhe, 1931); *ML* I, 686.

Netherlands. Under the influence of the principles of the French Revolution the dominant position and the rights of the Reformed Church in the Netherlands were abrogated; since 1796 there has been no state church in this country, and all citizens have equal rights. The dissenters (Mennonites, Remonstrants, Roman Catholics, Jews) were thereafter permitted to hold civil offices, and marriage by civil authorities became compulsory, the church ceremony being permitted only after the civil ceremony had been performed in the town halls. Most Dutch Mennonites were much pleased by the improvement in their social and political status, the more so since the principle of nonresistance was not attacked; it was now possible to avoid compulsory military service by engaging a substitute. In the Netherlands a number of Mennonites eagerly watched developments after 1789. Most of them, but not all, were enthusiastic about the "human and civil rights," for which they had been prepared during the last quarter of the 18th century by a growing liberalism in their congregations, a tendency toward natural religion, and the readings of French and especially English philosophical writings. Besides this, the fact that in this country they were still only tolerated often drove them into the arms of the Patriots (*q.v.*) against the oligarchy of the Reformed governors of the country. Hence they were among the first to dance around the "trees of liberty" enthusiastically erected when the French army came to the Netherlands; among them were those Mennonites who in former wars had left the country as "Patriots" to save their lives.   vDZ.

N. van der Zijpp, *Geschiedenis der Doopsgezinden in Nederland* (Arnhem, 1952) 188-90.

French-Speaking Mennonites. Very early there were French-speaking Anabaptists. In the south of Flanders and in South Brabant there were in the first half of the 16th century many Anabaptist congregations. Severe persecution drove a mass of refugees north; some fled eastward where their traces are found in Metz, Strasbourg, and Geneva.

Among the martyrs many French names are found, such as Jacques d'Auchy, Adriaen Olieux,

Charlo de Walle, Claudine le Vettre, Daniel Calvaert, and Guillaume of Rebais (Roubaix). Many French Mennonites came shortly after 1600 as refugees to the Netherlands, with such family names as de la Faille, de Fremery, Hennebo, de Neufville. In Hamburg there was a Francois Noe. In Leiden (*q.v.*), Dutch province of South Holland, there seems to have been a congregation of Walloons in the early 17th century; in Haarlem (*q.v.*) sermons were also preached in the French language (*DJ* 1840, 65).

The Flemish who fled to Strasbourg, not feeling quite at home with their German-speaking brethren, lost some of their number to Calvin's French congregation. Among them was Calvin's wife, Idelette van Buren (*q.v.*), the widow of the Anabaptist Jean Stordeur.

In later periods, chiefly 1700-50, the German-speaking Swiss Mennonites in their flight-like migrations frequently came in touch with French language and people. Many Swiss refugees settled in the French-speaking parts of Switzerland (Jura) and Alsace-Lorraine and with varying success maintained their German. In the Jura (*q.v.*) German-language schools have helped to maintain the German, and only in the towns has French come in.

At the present time the French congregations of Hang and (half of) Saarburg, and the Swiss of Pruntrut, Courgenay, Kleintal, Sonnenberg, Cortébert, Chaux d' Abel, and Les Bulles, and Le Locle-Brussels, though located in the French-speaking regions, have retained the German, although Les Bulles is rapidly becoming French. In former Alsace-Lorraine German has been maintained, but in Montbéliard and in inner France (*q.v.*) the Mennonites have become exclusively French-speaking in the last 50 years.

New French-speaking congregations have been established at Brussels (1953) and Paris (1955) through the work of American Mennonite (MC) missionaries.

Maintaining the German language in a French environment is less difficult for the Mennonites in the canton of Bern, Switzerland, for the cantonal government favors the German; they were able to set up their own schools and appoint their own teachers. In the canton of Neuchâtel, on the other hand, French influence was stronger; here the cantonal government did not support the Mennonite use of German.

The originally German-speaking congregations in France were in a very difficult position. They were too weak and scattered to maintain their own schools. They tried faithfully to teach their children German, though they themselves were unable to read or write it properly; the teachers they found were not much better qualified. Teaching materials were also lacking. Often the old family Froschauer Bible (*q.v.*) with its antiquated text, served as the only reader. More fortunate children were sent to Alsatian relatives. The Franco-Prussian War (1870 f.) was the turning point in the use of the French language. Those parts of the French-speaking churches that became politically German received German schools; but those who remained French found it difficult to maintain connections with those in Alsace. By the end of the century they were using the French exclusively. In the meantime, however, great damage had been done by their tenacious clinging to the German language. Many members no longer understood the German sermons, and many learned their Dordrecht Confession in German by memory without understanding a word of it. In consequence many young people lost interest and became worldly. The language difference finally led also to a division of the congregations in France into (1) the Conference of French-speaking Mennonites (*q.v.*) and (2) the Conference of Mennonites of Alsace (*q.v.*). In recent years the French-speaking Mennonites have gone far toward overcoming the ill effects of the language transition.

German family names have in many cases been adapted to the French. Some were simply translated; Kaufmann became Marchand, and Schweitzer, Suisse; but most changed their spelling to approximate the original; Bächer became Bacher or Pécheur; von Känel became Fonkennel or Kennel; von Gunten became Fongond; Schrag became Gérard; Balzer, Pelsy; Krähenbühl, Krépille; Luginbühl, Lugbull, etc.

The French Mennonite writings are not numerous. There are several translations of the Dordrecht Confession, and one of the Zweibrücken Catechism, to which a collection of prayers and several hymns was appended. This booklet was called *Confession de foi chrétienne des Chrétiens sans défense* and was published in 1771 (without name of place), Nancy 1862, Baccarat 1898, and Montbéliard 1922; to the last a brief Mennonite history was added. The first edition of the Dordrecht Confession and the translations by Virgile de Las are very rare. From 1907 to 1914 a monthly church paper, *Christ Seul,* was published, which printed a *Formulaire pour les différentes cérémonies du culte* (1922) and *Précis d' histoire des Eglises mennonites* (1914), and then published them separately, the latter being reprinted in 1937. It was resumed 1927-41, and 1945- .

A number of classic Mennonite writings by Menno Simons and Dirk Philips have been translated into French; in 1626 (n.p.) a translation of Dirk Philips *Enchiridion* by Virgile had appeared, followed by some tracts by Menno Simons: *Enchiridion ou Manuel de la Religion Christienne, avec plusieurs autres traitez touchant la doctrine Euangelique faites par Menno Simonis et autres Autheurs.* It also contains the story of the martyrdom of Jacques d'Auchy and three writings of Matthias Jurien (Thijs Jorriaensz), Henri Alevin (Hendrik Alewijnsz), and Jaques le Chandelier (Jacob Keersgieter). A French translation of Obbe Philips' booklet *Bekentennisse* was published under the title *Obbe Philippe Recognaissance . . .* (Leyden, 1595). In 1711 a French book appeared, *Confession de foi Christienne* (*q.v.*), containing the Dordrecht Confession, translated from the German into the French, a number of hymns and prayers, and a sermon. There was also a French edition of the Jan Cents Confession of 1630, *Brieve Confession de Foy* (*q.v.,* 1684, n.p.); of Galenus Abrahamsz' *Apologie* there is a French edition *Apologie pour les Protestants qui croyent qu' on ne doit baptizer que ceux qui sont venus a un age* de raison, followed by (same author) Articles contenant les fondements de la Doctrine des Protestants, qui croyent . . . (Amsterdam, 1704). A separate edition (Leiden, 1685) of the Jan Luyken etchings used in van Braght's Martyrs' Mirror, with French captions, was likely not intended for French-speaking Mennonites, but for the art-loving public in France and elsewhere. It carried the title, Theatre des Martyrs. P.So., vDZ.

The most important French works on the Mennonites are the following: Guy de Bres, La racine, Source et fondement des Anabaptistes ou Rebaptisez de nostre temps (1645); Histoire des Anabaptistes (Paris, 1695); Histoire des Anabaptistes (Amsterdam, 1699); Catrou, Histoire des Anabaptistes (Paris, 1706); Beck, "Les Mennonites" (Dissertation, Strasbourg, 1835); Brumder, "Sur les causes qui ont adouci les moeurs des Anabaptistes" (Dissertation, Strasbourg, 1836); G. E. Röhrich, Essai sur la vie, les écrits et la doctrine de l'Anabaptiste Jean Denk (Strasbourg, 1853); M. Th. de Bussierre, Les Anabaptistes (Paris, 1853); F. Bastian, Essai sur la vie et les écrits de Menno Simons (Dissertation, Strasbourg, 1857); L. Hauth, Les Anabaptistes à Strasbourg au temps de la Reformation (Dissertation, Strasbourg, 1860); A. Michiels, Les Anabaptistes des Vosges (Paris, 1860); Ph. A. Grandidier, "Les Anabaptistes d' Alsace," in Revue d' Alsace, 1867; A. Weill, Histoire de la guerre des Anabaptistes (Paris, 1874); C. A. Ramseier, Histoire des Baptistes (Paris, 1897); Ch. Mathiot, Recherches historiques sur les Anabaptistes de l'ancienne principauté de Montbéliard (Belfort, 1922); there are in addition many articles in magazines, yearbooks, and encyclopedias, one of which is Annuaire statistique du department du Mont tonnerre pour l'an 1810; Christ Seul, 1910, Nos. 4, 5, and 6; also Gem.-Kal. 1916, 122-26: Almanach du Cinquantenaire (Montbéliard, 1950); recent issues of Christ Seul, especially the December numbers, 1951-55; ML I, 687 f.

Frensburg (Elsassfrensburg), about 12 miles from Wissembourg in Alsace, formerly the seat of a Mennonite congregation of Swiss descent. About 1760 Christian Naftziger was the elder, and Peter Güngerich and Michael Schantz preachers. After the death of Naftziger (about 1782) Michael Schantz became elder, who was still serving in 1802. vDZ.

Frerichs, Geert Elias, a Dutch Mennonite pastor, b. Nov. 24, 1836, at Rake, East Friesland, Germany, d. Dec. 22, 1906, at Helpman, near Groningen in the Netherlands, was at first a sailor. At the age of 14 he intended to go into mission work, but afterwards decided on the ministry. He was trained by Jan Pol, Mennonite minister of Norden, East Friesland, and at the Amsterdam Mennonite Theological Seminary. Becoming a ministerial candidate in 1861, he served the following Dutch congregations: Hoorn on the island of Texel 1861-63, Warns 1863-78, Nes on the island of Ameland 1878-84, Oudebildtzijl 1884-90, and Borne 1890-1901, in which year he resigned. He was well versed in Mennonite history and published a number of papers; in DB 1874 the history of the congregation of Warns, in DB 1905 a paper on "Menno's taal" (the language Menno Simons used), and in DB 1906 on Menno Simons' residence in the first years after he had left the Roman Catholic Church. Frerichs' manual for catechetical instruction, entitled De godsdienst in het menschenhart en in de menschenwereld, was formerly much used (1st ed., St-Anna-Parochie, 1890; 2d ed., 1899). The 3d edition of this manual was published 1905 in four separate booklets: (1) Waarom

zijn wij godsdienstig? (2) Waarom zijn wij Christen? (3) Waarom zijn wij Protestant? (4) Waarom zijn wij Doopsgezind?

Other publications apart from a large number of articles in the Dutch Mennonite weekly De Zondagsbode, were: Leer van den Christelijken Godsdienst (St-Anna-Parochie, 1885); Vragen ter voorbereiding van het Lidmaatschap in de Doopsgezinde gemeente (St-Anna-Parochie, 1886, 1891, 1901; Vroege Vroomheid (St-Anna-Parochie, 1886, repr. 1888, 1893); De beteekenis van Menno Simons voor onze Broederschap (Amsterdam, 1893).

Pastor Frerichs introduced the use of private communion cups instead of the general cup in Borne in 1896.

His son J. G. Frerichs, b. 1880 at Nes, Ameland, was the Mennonite minister at Ternaard 1906-14, Staveren-Molkwerum 1914-21, Aardenburg 1921-27, Zaandam-Oost 1927-32, and Haarlem 1932-46. In 1946 he retired. K.V., vDZ.

Biogr. Wb. III, 129-30; DB 1907, 186-88; DJ 1908, 21-30 with portrait of Geert Elias Frerichs; ML I, 701.

Frericks (Frederiksen), **Jan,** a member of the Flemish congregation of Deventer, Dutch province of Overijssel, who was much interested in the troubles which the Swiss Brethren had in their country. The Amsterdam Mennonite Library contains a letter by him, dated Jan. 6, 1708, and addressed to Herman Schijn at Amsterdam (Inv. Arch. Amst. I, No. 1254a), in which he gives details about the situation and troubles of the Mennonites in Bern. In March 1710, when a number of Swiss Brethren, who had been expelled and were on their enforced transport to America, were to pass through the Netherlands, Frericks contacted the Dutch States-General and the ambassadors of Switzerland and England in The Hague, and undoubtedly it was largely due to Frericks that the Swiss Mennonites were set free on April 6, when their ship arrived at Nijmegen (q.v.), Holland. Information about Frericks' intervention is found in "Aanteekeningen over de vervolgingen in Zwitserland," by Hendrik Toren, a manuscript in the Amsterdam Mennonite Library (Inv. Arch. Amst. I, 1009; see also I, Nos. 1329, 1870, 1904). Of Jan Frericks himself no further information was available. He was well versed in the French, German, and English languages. He was unmarried and evidently a merchant. vDZ.

J. Huizinga, Stamboek . . . van Samuel Peter and Barbara Fry (Groningen, 1890) 23, 24, 40, 69.

Freriks (Freerks), **Sicke,** a Dutch Anabaptist martyr: see **Sicke Freerks.**

Fresenburg, an estate in Holstein near Oldesloe between Hamburg and Lübeck, Germany, which was in the possession of the van Ahlefeldt family in 1526-1641. Bartholomäus van Ahlefeldt (q.v.), who had learned to know the persecuted Anabaptists, granted them refuge on his Fresenburg estate from 1543 on. In 1554 an Anabaptist printer from Lübeck was examined in Oldesloe where he had planned to continue his trade. From here he proceeded to the Fresenburg estate where van Ahlefeldt had a house built for him to be used as print shop. It is likely that it was at this time that Menno Simons left Wismar and proceeded to Fresenburg, which increasingly became a refuge for Anabaptists. Although King Christian III of Denmark did his utmost to have van Ahlefeldt remove the Anabaptist refugees from his estate, he remained their protector. Here the books of Menno Simons were printed from that time on.

In the days of Menno Simons and after there was very likely a large settlement and congregation here. Gerrit Roosen, whose grandmother knew Menno Simons, reports about conditions at that time. Anabaptists from surrounding communities such as Oldesloe came here to worship. Although mandates against the Anabaptists were issued by King Christian III in 1555 and by his brother in 1557, the group was protected by their benefactor. There is a story that Menno Simons' printer was taken prisoner and was freed by van Ahlefeldt by force. During the Thirty Years' War the settlement was destroyed and many of the Mennonites moved to Altona (q.v.) and Glückstadt (q.v.). In 1656 King Frederick III and also Duke Frederick III (each of whom ruled a part of the district) issued a mandate against the few remaining families, who were finally granted permission to stay. This was the last mention of Mennonites in the Fresenburg area.

In 1902 a monument was erected by the German Mennonites on the place where, according to popular tradition, Menno Simons was buried in 1561 on the Mennoberg. A bronze plate shows Menno holding the Bible in his hands. Not far from this site, the house in which Menno Simons' writings supposedly were printed and the linden tree which he is supposed to have planted in front of it still stand. After World War II the monument was moved near the linden tree and house. C.K.

R. Dollinger, *Geschichte der Mennoniten in Schleswig-Holstein, Hamburg und Lübeck* (Neumünster, 1930) 129-32; G. Roosen, *Unschuld und Gegen-Bericht* (Hamburg, 1702); E. F. Goverts, "Das adelige Gut Fresenburg und die Mennoniten," *Ztscht der Zentralstelle für Niedersächsische Familiengesch.* (Hamburg, 1925) Heft 3-5; H.v.d. Smissen, *Mennostein und Mennolinde zu Fresenburg* (1922); C. Krahn, *Menno Simons* (Karlsruhe, 1936) 80, 85-88; *ML* I, 701.

Fresno, a city (pop. 100,000) in the San Joaquin Valley, Fresno County, central California. Fresno is in the raisin industry area and is surrounded by rich farm lands producing not only a variety of fruits but also cotton, grain, and dairy products. Almost 5,000 Mennonites live in the area extending from Fresno south through Reedley and Dinuba. In 1940 the Mennonite Brethren organized a church in Fresno, in 1944 the Pacific Bible Institute (q.v.), and in 1955 the M.B. Biblical Seminary. The Mennonite Community Church (GCM) was organized in Fresno in 1953. G.W.P.

A. R. Shelly, "Fresno in the Heart of Raisin Country," *MWR,* May 13, 1954.

Fresno County, Cal., in the geographical center of the state, lies in the center of California's great interior San Joaquin Valley. It contains 5,950 square miles and has a population of 300,000. The raisin center of the world, it is the nation's largest grower of grapes, figs, and cotton. It also produces citrus fruits, grain, alfalfa, dairy products, livestock, melons, vegetables, poultry, petroleum, and lumber. The first Mennonite settlers arrived in the county in 1904. Approximately 2,300 adult Mennonites now (1954) live in the south central part of the county, 70 per cent of whom are Mennonite Brethren, 28 per cent General Conference Mennonites, and the remainder Evangelical Mennonite Brethren and Krimmer Mennonite Brethren. Five churches serve these groups. The Pacific Bible Institute (q.v.), operated by the Mennonite Brethren, is located in the city of Fresno. The Mennonite Home for the Aged (q.v.), located within the county in Reedley, is owned by the Mennonite Brethren. Jo.H.E.

Fresno Mennonite Brethren Church, also known as the Bethany Mennonite Brethren Church, located at the corner of Orchard and Olive streets, Fresno, Cal., had its beginning in 1920 when several M.B. families began to hold services. The church was organized in June 1942 with 34 members.

After renting a hall for services a number of years, the congregation purchased a building site in 1946 and erected a spacious church building which was greatly enlarged in 1954. Since the M.B. Pacific District Conference opened a Bible Institute in Fresno in 1944, this congregation has grown rapidly. The congregation has provided a church home for students and has in turn also greatly benefited through the services rendered by instructors and students of the Institute. The 1955 membership was 402, with Dan Friesen as pastor. Others who have served as pastors or assistants are J. D. Hofer, Sam Wiens, S. W. Goossen, Henry G. Wiens, Arthur Willems, and A. P. Koop. J.H.L.

Fresno (Cal.) Mennonite Community Church (GCM) began as a General Conference Mennonite Church Fellowship in May 1953 with a group of 40. Peter Ediger became the pastor of the church in 1954. A church has been built a short distance beyond the eastern boundary of the city. A.R.S.

Fretz (Frätz, Fraetz), the name of a Mennonite family in the Palatinate, Germany, in the 18th century, likely of Swiss origin. A Markus Frätz was a deacon at Ziehmerhof in the Upper Palatinate in 1731. Three years later a Christian Fraetz arrived in America. Most of the families bearing the Fretz name in the Mennonite Church today live in the Franconia Conference area and in Ontario, and are largely descended from two brothers, John and Christian Fretz, who immigrated from near Mannheim in the Palatinate to Deep Run in Bucks Co., Pa., between 1710 and 1720. The former's son John Fretz (1730-1826) removed to Ontario in 1800, where he was ordained a deacon in the Moyer congregation at Vineland in 1801. A number of ministers and deacons named Fretz have served in the Franconia and Ontario conferences (MC). Perhaps the most influential and vigorous minister bearing the name was the Eastern District (GCM) minister, Allen M. Fretz (1853-1943), ordained as preacher at Deep Run in 1883, and elder in 1892. Clarence Y. Fretz of the Franconia area served for a number of years as minister of the Norris Square Mennonite Church in Philadelphia, and is currently a missionary in Luxembourg, serving under the Eastern Mennonite Board of Missions and Charities (MC). A. J. Fretz has written at least ten family histories of Mennonite families such as Fretz, Funck, Kratz, Meyer, Nash, Oberholtzer, Rosenberger, Swartley, Stauffer, and Wismer. J. Winfield Fretz has for some time been a professor at Bethel College. J. Herbert Fretz is a pastor (GCM) at Freeman, S.D. J. C. Fretz (d. 1956), of Kitchener, Ont., was a historian of the Ontario Mennonites.   J.C.W.

Fretz, Allen M. (1853-1943), a Mennonite (GCM) minister of Pennsylvania, was born in Tinicum Twp., Bucks Co., Pa., the oldest of the eight children of Ely and Mary Meyers Fretz, and the sixth generation from the immigrant John Fretz, who settled in Bedminster Township about 1720. He grew up on the old Fretz homestead at Bedminster, and early showed an intense interest in books besides the work on the farm. His father therefore sent him to the new Mennonite school at Wadsworth, Ohio, when he reached the age of 16. In 1871 he attended normal schools in Pennsylvania, and at the age of 19 began his career of teaching. In 1880 he married Sarah Leatherman, who died in 1882. In 1885 he married Anna Rittenhouse of Campden, Ont. They were the parents of six children, two of whom are deacons—Jacob R. Fretz at the Lansdale Mennonite Church (GCM), and Ely R. Fretz at the Deep Run Mennonite Church (GCM). Anna died in 1923, and in 1925 Allen M. Fretz married Amanda Fretz.

On Oct. 13, 1883, Fretz was ordained to the ministry, in which office he served for nearly 60 years. In addition to his home congregation he served as follows: Souderton 1893-1910, Allentown 1910-12, Pottstown 1909-10, Bowmansville 1917-27, Springfield 1913-38, Perkasie 1918-42, and Lansdale 1928-29. He was secretary of the Eastern District Conference 1913-27, and one of the founders of the *Mennonite* (q.v.), and was active on various Eastern District and General Conference committees. He died on April 26, 1943. "He was the embodiment of Christian humility, the personification of love in action. Throughout his life he demonstrated the beauty of simplicity in word, in deed, and in thought. Many lives were enriched, many hearts warmed by his gracious teaching and preaching ministry" (J. Winfield Fretz).   J.H.F.

"*Allen M. Fretz," 1938 Yearbook of the General Conference* (Berne, 1938); J. W. Fretz, "A Memorial," *1944 Yearbook of the General Conference* (Newton, 1944).

Frey (Frei, Fry), a Swiss Mennonite family apparently originating in the lower Aargau of the canton of Bern. In the latter 17th century the name was represented among the Anabaptists of the Oberland area of the canton. A 1717 Palatinate census list of Mennonite families of Bernese origins names a Hans Martin Frey and a Johannes Frey. In 1731 Hans Frei was a member of the Streigenberg congregation of the Upper Palatinate. By 1759 the name was found among the Mennonites of the Montbéliard area. A list of Mennonite families in South Germany published in 1940 named one Frei of the Sinsheim congregation.

In 1717 a Johannes Frey landed in America. In the colonial period the Frey family was represented not only in the Skippack community of eastern Pennsylvania, but was also found in the Mennonite settlement in Virginia at least as early as 1730. Later the family was represented in Ontario, Franklin Co., Pa., Ohio, Indiana, and Illinois. Jacob Frey, who migrated from France to America in 1839, settled in Fulton Co., Ohio, where numerous descendants live. Eli L. Frey (q.v.), Amish Mennonite bishop, and J. C. Frey, Amish Mennonite deacon, both of Fulton County, were prominent church leaders who were descendants of Jacob Frey. P. L. Frey, son of E. L. Frey, and Bishop E. B. Frey, son of J. C. Frey, are Mennonite ministers in Fulton County. Frey also appears among the Prusso-Russian Mennonites. Gustav Frey was an active educator and pastor (GCM) in Kansas and California.   M.G.

Frey, Claus, a fanatical Anabaptist of Rottenburg, Württemberg, Germany, a furrier by trade, who in 1525 fled to Windsheim, a town of Bavaria, to avoid the persecution which had set in at Rottenburg. His wife and eight children, who refused to follow him, he deserted in utter poverty, and with pious words persuaded Elsbeth Pfersfelder (q.v.) to accompany him. The Anabaptist congregation excommunicated him for his conduct. Upon arrival at Strasbourg, Alsace, the pair were also refused admittance into Melchior Hofmann's congregation (Gerbert, 154). The Strasbourg council condemned him to death by drowning on the charge of adultery. But Thudichum (*Reformation,* 620) has shown that this execution was a legal error, for his wife's refusal to follow was in Protestant lands a ground for divorce. Furthermore, death was by no means the general penalty for adultery. The Strasbourg council inflicted it because Frey was inconvenient to them, and because he was reported to be an Anabaptist, though both he and the Anabaptists denied this claim. Capito (*Ein wunderbar Geschicht und ernste warnung Gottes . . . ,* 1534) relates the affair, trying to show the consequence of depreciating the clergy (appointed by the council), and adds the remarkable sentence, "That the Anabaptists are so willing to die for their faith is simply the work of the devil"—the exact opposite of his words of 1528.

It is possible that the reason for the council's rejection of Elsbeth Pfersfelder's request to be likewise punished by death was a vague disquiet as to the justice of Claus Frey's execution. Thudichum, as a professor of jurisprudence, was in a position to judge impartially on the evidence. The council used this case against the Anabaptists.   E.T., Neff.

E. F. H. Medicus, *Gesch. der evangelischen Kirche in Bayern* (Erlangen, 1863) 52; *Ztschr. für d. hist. Theol.,* 1860, 66 ff.; F. O. zur Linden, *Melchior Hofmann* (Haarlem, 1885) 315 ff.; Fr. Thudichum, *Gesch. der deutschen Ref. 1525-1537* (Leipzig, 1909) 620; C. Gerbert, *Gesch. der Strassburger Sektenbewegung* (Strasbourg, 1889); ML I, 702; III, 359.

Frey, Elias (Eli) **L.** (1856-1942), a leading Ohio Mennonite (MC) bishop in the first half of the 19th century, bishop of the Fulton County Amish Mennonite district under the Ohio and Eastern A.M.

Conference 1908-42, descended from an old Montbéliard (France) family, his father having immigrated from there in 1839, settling in Fulton County near Pettisville in 1844. He was baptized in 1880, ordained deacon in 1884. He married Anna Short, was the father of 11 children, one of whom, Philemon, is now a minister in his father's congregation. He was an able speaker and administrator, a rare combination of conservative and progressive attitudes, served as moderator of the Eastern A.M. Conference several times and as moderator of the Mennonite General Conference 1917-19, was a member of the Peace Problems Committee 1919-37 and its chairman 1925-35, and a member and officer of the Mennonite Relief Commission. H.S.B.

Freyberg, Helene von, a baroness, one of the few members of the Tyrolean lesser nobility of the 16th century who turned Anabaptist. She was born at the castle of Münichau near Kitzbühel (*q.v.*), Tirol (*q.v.*), Austria, and was married to Onufrius von Freyberg, Lord of Hohenaschau in Bavaria. She had three sons. About 1528 she came into contact with Anabaptists; the town of Kitzbühel was well known as a strong center of that movement. Apparently Helene was then also baptized into the new faith. As she had inherited the castle of Münichau, she gave asylum there to numberless Anabaptists who fled the harsh measures of the provincial government in Innsbruck (see **Tirol**). Both King Ferdinand (*q.v.*) and Duke Wilhelm of Bavaria (*q.v.*) soon learned of the activities of this noble lady, and Ferdinand ordered expressly that "if she does not recant she has to be brought before the judges." About 1530, when the situation became very critical, she decided to flee, bequeathing her castle to her sons. Apparently she went to Constance on Lake Constance (*q.v.*), another well-known place in Anabaptist history. Early in 1532, Ambrosius Blaurer (*q.v.*) warned his brother Thomas (*q.v.*) that Helene was in town and was known as a great admirer of Pilgram Marpeck (*q.v.*). In November of the same year she was finally expelled from this city and her possessions were confiscated. Thomas Blaurer in a letter to his brother expressed great satisfaction about this fact. It is claimed that in 1534 she agreed to recant, but the details are uncertain. In any case the contact with the Brethren continued and her life did not become much easier.

Next we hear of Helene in Augsburg (*q.v.*), again a big rallying point of the Brethren. (It is said that at that time the brotherhood in that city numbered about 1,100 members.) But Helene did not find rest in this city either. In April 1535, she was arrested, laid in chains overnight, cross-examined and finally banished. It appears that she then returned to Tirol. Of her married life nothing further is recorded; the husband died in 1538, and the sons supported the mother. In 1539 her sons petitioned the city council of Augsburg to permit her to reside in that city, and to it she now returned.

A letter Caspar Schwenckfeld (*q.v.*) wrote to Helene on May 27, 1543, gives the information that through her brother-in-law Jörg Ludwig von Freyberg she had given Schwenckfeld a copy of Pilgram

Marpeck's printed *Vermahnung* (*q.v.*), for which Schwenckfeld thanked her now. He said that he had made a short summary of the book for casual readers, and he sent her a copy that she might forward it to Pilgram. He regretted that Pilgram could not come himself to his present place (home of Jörg von Freyberg) that they could have a full and free discussion of their problem. This letter is the last record. Her end is not known. R.F.

W. Wiswedel, "Freifrau Helene von Freyberg, eine adelige Täuferin," *Ztscht f. Bayrische Kirchengesch.*, 1941, 46 ff.; M. Krebs, *Badische Täuferakten* (1951) with further reference to the Blaurer correspondence; Fr. Roth, *Augsburger Ref.-Gesch.* II (1904) 410, 426-28; *Corpus Schwenckfeldianorum* VIII (1927) 616-18 (with brief biography; erroneously the "book" is here named *Verantwortung*, Marpeck's polemical work against Schwenckfeld, to which Schwenckfeld would not have answered so mildly; only the *Vermahnung* was printed), *ML* II, 502-4.

Frick, Georg, an Anabaptist martyr of Wirtsburg in Tirol, Austria, a tailor, was seized in 1529 in Fill (*q.v.*) near Neumarkt in the Adige Valley, Blaurock's last field of labor. His confession of faith made Nov. 16, 1529, before the court states that he was baptized by the former lay priest Benedikt of Bruneck, and that he was unwilling to renounce his faith. He was therefore executed with seven other Anabaptists—three men and four women. HEGE.

Beck, *Geschichts-Bücher*, 89; Wolkan, *Geschicht-Buch*; Mart. Mir. D (not found), E 435; *ML* I, 702.

Frick (Fricken), Heinrich, a well-to-do and notable citizen of Zürich, Switzerland, who had been converted and become a Mennonite, in 1625 refused to serve as the military standard-bearer because it was contrary to his conscience. This refusal caused a new persecution at Zürich. Frick was imprisoned (1641) and so severely treated that he consented to attend the Reformed Church, and was released. But soon he repented, and "went back to Zürich, . . . to be confined, . . . which was done." In the meantime his two large farms and a considerable amount of money were confiscated. Then he was released, "but again apprehended, out of which bonds he escaped," and "wandered about in misery and poverty." Later Frick was allowed to emigrate to the Palatinate, Germany. vDZ.

Mart. Mir. E 1119; this information is not found in *Mart. Mir.* D; it is inserted in the German edition of 1780, p. 804.

Frick (Frijk), Leonhard, an Anabaptist martyr concerning whom nothing is known except the little that is given in the records of the capture and death of his companion Hans Schlaffer (*q.v.*). They were seized Dec. 5 or 6, 1527, by the Schwaz-Freundsberg magistrate Sigmund Kapeller. It is not known whether he, like Schlaffer, was subjected to torture; it is merely known that at his trial he declared that he would not renounce his faith nor betray his brethren. Sentence was passed on both, Jan. 20, 1528, to be carried out on Feb. 10. They were executed by the sword at Schwaz, Tirol, Austria. LOSERTH.

Beck, *Geschichts-Bücher* 60-73; J. Loserth, *Der Anabaptismus in Tirol* I (Vienna, 1892) 35 f.; Wolkan, *Geschicht-Buch*, 45; *Mart. Mir.* D 14, E 425; *ML* I, 703.

Fricke, Fredrick C. (1867-1947), an elder and editor of the Church of God in Christ, Mennonite, was born April 14, 1867, near Hannover, Germany, the eldest son of Fredrick and Wilhelmina Fricke. When he was two years old the family immigrated to America and settled near Lansburg, Mich., where he grew up. He was brought up in the Lutheran faith. At the age of 15 he felt that he was a lost sinner; after much prayer and searching the Scriptures, he received light that he must be born again. He was baptized upon confession in June 1882, by Elder John Holdeman into the Church of God in Christ, Mennonite. He married Leah B. Litwiller on Dec. 10, 1890. Five sons and five daughters were born to them. Two of their sons, Harvey and Sam, were ordained to the ministry.

Fredrick Fricke was ordained to the ministry on Oct. 31, 1893, by Elder Holdeman, serving in this office for nearly 54 years. He traveled extensively as an evangelist and as an elder for many years. He was a faithful witness and a wise counselor, whose advice was sought by young and old. By his efforts Sunday schools were introduced into many congregations. He served as moderator of the conference for many years. His editorial articles in the *Messenger of Truth* (*q.v.*), which he edited for 36 years, and other doctrinal writings were permeated with Scripture. He was one of the early and most successful evangelists of the church. He died at the age of 80 years, and was buried in the Greenwood cemetery near Middleton, Mich. His home address was Ithaca, Mich.   E.J.F.

Fridli ab Iberg, a native of Schwyz, Switzerland, who had joined the Anabaptist movement and moved to Zürich in 1525. Here he baptized Wilhelm of Wallis and was in prison with Manz, Grebel, and Ockenfusz. Especially Hans Ockenfusz had a great influence upon him. Fridli was released from prison on April 4, 1526, but banished from the territory of Zürich. Concerning further activity nothing is known. On Nov. 27, 1526, his relatives in Schwyz addressed a remarkable letter to the magistrate of Zürich, writing that he "no longer would give any evidence of his former Anabaptist views," and asking permission for him to live in the city and canton of Zürich. He had thus apparently given up the Anabaptist faith.   vDZ.

Von Muralt-Schmid, *Quellen zur Gesch. der Täufer in der Schweiz* (Zürich, 1952) 177-79, 193, 211-12.

Friedelsheim, a village near Bad Durkheim in the Palatinate, Germany, the seat of a Mennonite congregation since the earliest period. Its beginning is closely connected with the Friedelsheim castle, which was built in 1418. In the Thirty Years' War it was conquered and burned with the village Friedelsheim, and the remains were completely burned in 1689. Elector John William leased the village with the estate belonging to it in 1698 to his chancellor Francis Melchior von Wieser, who began to rebuild the castle. His son Francis Joseph completed the building and used it as his residence. During the French Revolution the castle was burned by the French on May 4, 1794. In 1800 Duke

Francis Joseph, the son of Count Frederick, had a new residence built, which is now the parsonage; together with the chapel close by, it is popularly called "die Burg."

When the Mennonites came to Friedelsheim cannot be definitely ascertained. The first certain information concerning their presence is found in a rental contract of 1682, in which Elector Charles Louis leased his Friedelsheim estate, about 1,000 acres, together with the dwelling houses and farm buildings of the Mönchhof, now called the "Mennonitenhof," to Christian Herschi, Ulrich Weydmann, Jose Erbsal, and Hans Burgholder. But it is probably safe to assume that Mennonites had been living here before 1682 and that they had likewise been renters of the electoral estate; for the contract states: "As the same has been held by the renters before them." Very likely soon after the Thirty Years' War some of the refugee emigrants from Switzerland who came to the Palatinate settled in Friedelsheim. Religiously they were tolerated. "They shall have no public or secret meetings or conventicles attended by others than those living on the estate, . . . much less draw or mislead our other subjects and people to them." According to this it may be assumed that a congregation had already been formed, especially since in addition to these four families, the Mennonites Ulrich Wilemi and Christian Hummel are named around 1685.

In 1698 the castle and estate passed into the possession of the Baron von Wieser. In 1715 he issued a new rental contract. Of the original lessees only Christian Herschi was still here. In addition the document was signed by Hans Rüsser, Benz Ebersohl, Christ Ehlenberger, Hans Schneider, and Hans Schanz. Even though the clause concerning religious meetings was inserted in the new contract, it seems not to have been enforced. By 1732 the villages of Gönnheim, Erpolzheim, and Wachenheim were already a part of this congregation, which at that time numbered 40 families. The preachers were Hans Schanz of Gönnheim and Hans Jakob Schneider (of Friedelsheim?); the deacons were Christian Herschi and Hans Berber, the former for Friedelsheim, the latter for Erpolzheim (*q.v.*). (Details concerning these renters may be found in *ML* I, 704, footnote.)

Some information concerning members living outside is found in the reports which the electoral government required from time to time on the numbers, names, and financial circumstances of the Anabaptists. Not more than 200 families were to be admitted to the Palatinate and each family was to pay its protection fee of 6 florins, and these lists were to serve as checks. But they are not always complete.

In 1749 there was again a change in the contract. The document states: "Since all of my lessees have in part died, and in part emigrated, I have found it necessary to take other renters, having the names Daniel Brennemann, Johannes Risser (Hans Rüsser), Abraham Risser (Rüsser), Johannes Strohm, Jakob Lichty (Lichte), Johannes Leysi (Lysy), and Ulrich Wittmer." Religious freedom for the renters had been somewhat extended; they were permitted to hold meetings together with the foreigners in the neighborhood quietly on the condition that one of those living there should annually contribute a pound of wax to his chapel, and their funerals were to be conducted without music or the use of the church bells. The Mennonites had indeed acquired "a little spot for hereditary burial" (*Gem.-Kal.* 1909, 55 ff.). How long this little cemetery was used is not known, but it may have been discontinued after the French Revolution, which brought to the Mennonites social and religious liberty.

The Mennonites had their own meetinghouse very early; in 1779 a new one was built, because, as a document says, "the meetinghouse is quite dilapidated." Outwardly it had to look like an ordinary peasant home with a chimney. Indeed, the date and the inscription which had been carved in the stone over the entry had to be completely covered with mortar. During this time the Wieser property was sold to citizens of Friedelsheim. Most of it was acquired by former Mennonite renters. In 1803 the castle estate with gardens, buildings, and remains of walls was sold to several Mennonites, who occupied it together until 1808, and then divided it among themselves. Abram Leisy took over the "Burg." His son Abraham sold the property in 1820; the congregation bought it in 1836, for a sum of 4,000 florins, to be used for a church and parsonage. At considerable cost a building still extant, with a cellar under it, was rebuilt into a spacious chapel, which was dedicated Oct. 4, 1848. The expenses for the purchase and building were largely covered by substantial assistance from other congregations; also Protestant citizens made considerable contributions.

The Mennonites of Friedelsheim kept up their own school, very likely from the very early time. About 1814 the teacher was a certain Stübner. In 1824-27 the Mennonite children attended the village school, but in 1827 the congregation called Jacob Ellenberger (*q.v.*); in 1829 the school received public recognition. After this it was subject with the village school to inspection by the state and by the Protestant Church. In 1869 Ellenberger was compelled to resign because of old age, and since that time the Mennonite children have been attending the village school, though they receive their religious instruction from their own pastor.

In 1830 Ellenberger was also chosen as preacher and thereby the change was made in this congregation from a lay ministry to a professional ministry. Another preacher, who served with and before Ellenberger, 1825-32, was Johannes Risser, a zealous and gifted man who also held missionary meetings. In 1832 he emigrated to America. He was preceded in the ministry by Abraham Ellenberger, Sr., 1765-99 (Erpolzheim), Abraham Ellenberger, Jr., 1765-82 (probably Gönnheim), Johannes Strohm 1765-82 (Friedelsheim), Heinrich Wissler 1765-93 (Erpolzheim), Peter Becker 1765-93 (Erpolzheim), Peter Weber about 1769 (Seebach), Heinrich Krämer 1786-89 (Seebach), Heinrich Pletscher 1790-1816 (Friedelsheim), Jakob Neff 1791-1811 (Hardenburg), Heinrich Ellenberger 1812-24 (Friedelsheim), who moved to Eppstein and served as minister of that congregation until he emigrated to America in 1850.

The Erpolzheim congregation was very closely associated with the Friedelsheim congregation, so that the two actually formed a single congregation. Among its members were also the Mennonites of the surrounding villages—in addition to Gönnheim and Wachenheim, also Dürkheim (*q.v.*), Seebach, Hausen, Hardenburg, Grethen, Ungstein-Pfeffingen, Leistadt, Herxheim, and Freinsheim. In 1843 the Mennonites living in Dackenheim also united with this congregation. According to Frey there were in the area in 1834 a total of 198 Mennonites, 99 of them living in Friedelsheim. Between 1803 and 1824 the congregation of Assenheim (*q.v.*) also merged with this congregation. It is not known when the Gronau or Alsheim Mennonites joined this congregation, but it was probably at the beginning of the 19th century. Mennonites had been living there since very early times (for particulars see *ML* I, 705, footnotes).

In 1833 the Kohlhof (*q.v.*) congregation near Schifferstadt merged with the Friedelsheim congregation, though it has kept its identity to a certain extent and takes part only in matters pertaining to the pastorate. In 1861 a closer union was made financially through the establishment of a "Menno Fund" in commemoration of the quadricentennial of Menno Simons' death, to provide for their common needs, in which the Mennonites of Kohlhof and Friedelsheim both took an active part. This foundation has rendered a good service to weak congregations and had grown to 30,000 marks before the inflation of 1923. With 1857 the Branchweilerhof congregation (*q.v.*) was also served once a month. But this connection was only a personal one with the minister Jacob Ellenberger. In 1879 Jacob Ellenberger died after a very active life as a minister and teacher. His nephew Jacob Ellenberger II (*q.v.*), who succeeded him in office in 1881, wrote his obituary under the title, *Jakob Ellenberger, Lehrer und Prediger der Mennonitengemeinde Friedelsheim. Ein Lebensbild, dargestellt auf Grund seines handschriftlichen Nachlasses. Mit einem Anhang einiger seiner Gedichte* (Frankfurt, 1879). As a poet he is also represented in the hymnal of the South German Mennonites by hymn No. 226.

Jacob Ellenberger II served the congregation from 1881 until his death in 1901. His successor, Gustav Stauffer, died in May 1903, after having taken over responsibility for the congregation only in November 1902. In 1904 Johannes Foth became the minister of the congregation. He was still serving in 1954, when he observed his 50th anniversary as pastor.

In 1881 the congregation established a library, which in 1924 contained 241 volumes. The congregation belongs to the Vereinigung (*q.v.*), the Mennonite Hilfskasse (*q.v.*), and to the Conference of the South German Mennonites (*q.v.*).

The conference met in Friedelsheim on May 7, 1826, and Sept. 12, 1826, and also the Palatine-Hessian ministers' conference on May 28, 1874; May 24, 1884; May 30, 1894; May 11, 1905; May 6, 1914. The conference of 1874 was important in that the first attempt was made here to unite with the Vereinigung, although the results were negative.

Since 1891 the congregation has been incorporated. It was once quite numerous, but in the course and urgency of the times it has lost many members. The families which were especially strong in the earlier periods saw too little chance for making a living here and emigrated to America. This was chiefly the case in 1824-55, when about 160 persons from the congregation emigrated. Many of the Leisys, Schowalters, Rissers, and other families now living in Kansas, Oklahoma, and other states came originally from Friedelsheim. In 1952 the membership (without Kohlhof with 65 souls) was 135 (including unbaptized children), who were living rather widely scattered in 16 villages and towns. Some Mennonites from the Danzig area have joined the communities and congregations.   J.F.

F. Braun, "Nineteenth Century Emigrants from the Mennonite Congregation of Friedelsheim in the Palatinate," *MQR* XXX (1956) 133-54; Müller, *Berner Täufer*, 211; *ML* I, 703-6.

Friedenreich, Lorenz (1718-94), came from Switzerland to Neuwied, Germany, in 1743, became minister of the Mennonite congregation there in 1755, elder from 1758 until his death, did much to improve the lot of his brethren in Switzerland and the Palatinate. He was the intermediary in establishing connections with Holland, Danzig, and Hamburg-Altona through an extensive correspondence, and repeatedly visited the directors of the Amsterdam Committee on Foreign Needs on behalf of his Swiss and Palatine brethren. This remarkable man, who during the summer of 1774 received Goethe, Lavater, and Basedow in his home, must have had considerable education. By trade he was a *Gürtler,* i.e., he made shoe buckles and other objects of brass. His son Heinrich (1747-97) was also a preacher in the same congregation 1788-97, and his grandson Abraham (1785-1864) was a *Vorsteher,* as was also Abraham's son Theodor (1822-1909).   NEFF, vDZ.

Müller, *Berner Täufer,* 47; W. Mannhardt, *Die Wehrfreiheit der Altpreussischen Mennoniten* (Marienburg, 1863) 54; *Inv. Arch. Amst.* I, Nos. 1543, 1544; *Beiträge zur Gesch. rheinischer Mennoniten* (No. 2 in *Schriftenreihe des Menn. Geschichtsvereins,* Weierhof, 1939) 145 f., 149; *Goethe's Rheinreise mit Lavater und Basedow im Sommer 1774* (Zürich, 1923) 119; *Menn. Bl.* LXXVII, 107 f.; *ML* I, 706.

Friedensau Mennonite Church (GCM), now extinct, was located in Noble Co., Okla., six miles southeast of Perry. In 1911 it had 23 members with C. E. Hirschler and P. Perry serving as ministers.   M.G.

Friedensberg Mennonite Church (GCM), a member of the Northern District Conference, is located 65 miles southwest of Freeman, S.D., in Bon Homme County, and 8 miles southwest of Avon. The ancestors of the present membership left Prussia in 1798 under the leadership of Peter (Hans) Schmidt, and settled in Waldheim, a Mennonite village in Russian Poland, in 1838; in 1848 they organized Heinrichsdorf, Volhynia. In August 1874 the greater part left for New York, proceeding in September to Yankton, S.D. Seven families homesteaded late in 1874 and the remaining 35 families followed early in 1875. A new church was dedicated early in 1878. On Sept. 5, 1878, Benjamin P. Schmidt was or-

dained as elder by S. F. Sprunger. Later the church was under the leadership of D. A. Schultz assisted by Henry U. Schmidt. Beginning in 1941, the church has been under the leadership of Edward Duerksen. In 1953 the church had 91 members with Emil Krahn serving as pastor. Many members have been called into the ministry and foreign missions.   J.A.B.

Friedensfeld (*Miropol*), a Mennonite village with 5,400 acres of land in the province and district of Ekaterinoslav in South Russia, 30 miles from Nikopol, was founded by 1867 by members of the Kleine Gemeinde of the Molotschna settlement. Three families of settlers were Mennonite Brethren. In 1869 two other Mennonite Brethren families moved in; since the Kleine Gemeinde congregation was in the process of dissolution, all the remaining inhabitants of the village joined the Mennonite Brethren. Friedensfeld was at first a subsidiary of the Molotschna M.B. Church, but in 1875 it was organized as an independent congregation with 45 members. Friedensfeld from the beginning gave much thought to its school system, and especially to clubs devoted to youth welfare, to music, and to singing. Several Baptist families were admitted into the village. Its fate since the Revolution and World War II is no doubt similar to that of other Molotschna (*q.v.*) villages. (*ML* I, 713.)   A.B.

Friedensfeld Mennonite Church (GCM), a member of the Western District Conference, is located four miles north and four miles east of Turpin, Okla. In 1903 Mennonite families began to settle in Beaver County, where free land was offered to homesteaders. By 1907 a number of families had moved to the Turpin community. The Home Mission Committee of the Western District Conference took an interest in the group, and in 1907 under the leadership of H. R. Voth organized a church with 19 charter members. The first meetinghouse was built in 1908, which was replaced in 1940 by a larger church. The membership in 1953 was approximately 100; the pastor was Levi H. Koehn.   L.H.K.

Friedensheim Mennonite Brethren Church, located 16 miles north of Main Centre, Sask., was organized as a congregation of the Mennonite Brethren Conference in 1929. The community began in 1925 when five families established their homes at Beechy, Sask. The membership rose to 75, but in the thirties it decreased. John Wiens was the organizer and the leader of the group for 18 years, until he moved to Herbert, Sask. His successor was Jacob Wiens. Other preachers were John D. Hiebert and Jacob Schellenberg. The deacons were Abr. H. Dück and Friedrich Mielke. In 1944 a new church was completed four miles southeast of Beechy, which was moved into Beechy in 1953. The membership in 1953 was 26, with Jacob Wiens as leader.   J.R.

Friedensstimme, a German-language periodical, the organ of the Mennonite Brethren in Russia, founded in 1903 by Jakob and Abraham Kröker, who at that time lived in Spat (Crimea). Because there seemed to be no prospect of obtaining permission to publish the paper in the neighborhood, they had it printed the first three years in Berlin. Under these circumstances the paper could not thrive. In January 1906 permission was obtained to publish it under censorship in Halbstadt, province of Taurida; the editors had moved there in 1904. At first the paper appeared semimonthly, then 1906-8 weekly, and after 1908 twice a week. In March 1913 the subscription list reached its highest point, 5,800. The printers were the book concern *Raduga* (*q.v.*) in Halbstadt. Its program included inspiration, edification, exegesis, home and foreign missions, education at home and in school (for many years it was the organ of the Molotschna Mennonite teachers' association), politics, news from the Mennonite settlements; discussions of local questions, general welfare (housekeeping, farming, hygiene, etc.), entertainment, and advertising. At the outbreak of World War I it was discontinued. (*ML* I, 713.)

Friedenstal Mennonite Church (GCM), located at Tampa, Kan., a member of the Western District Conference, was organized in September 1899 with 33 charter members, immigrants from Poland. Until 1902 it was known as the North Lehigh Mennonite Church. The first church building was built and dedicated in 1907 and remodeled in 1944. Ministers who have served the congregation are Daniel Schmidt, Andrew Ewert, Johann Gerbrandt, Peter Balzer, Wilhelm Ewert, Henry Schmidt, John H. Epp, Walter H. Regier, and Harvey Jantz. Two missionaries have gone out from this congregation, namely, Mable (Wedel) Suderman to Arizona and Selma Unruh to Africa. The congregation has always practiced footwashing with the Lord's Supper. In 1955 the membership was 123. FR.S.

Friedensthal Mennonite Church (GCM), now extinct, located at Gotebo, Harrison Co., Okla., was organized in 1903 by J. J. Kliewer and in 1911 attained its largest membership with 75 members. In 1912 John J. Kliewer and some 44 members of the congregation went to Carlsbad, N.M. In 1913-20 P. R. Voth served as elder of the Friedensthal group. In 1921 the congregation seems to have dissolved, with the remaining members joining the Ebenezer Mennonite Church at Gotebo. It was an active congregation having regular Sunday services, Christian Endeavor, prayer meetings, and other activities.
J.F.S.

Friedrichsen, Karl, was born in the Crimea, graduated from a Zentralschule and the Bible school of St. Chrischona near Basel, Switzerland, was principal of the Karassan Zentralschule, Crimea, and member of the Busau Mennonite Church, where he also served as a minister after 1905. He was ordained May 31, 1911. In 1913-22 he was instructor of religion at the Davlekanovo Zentralschule at Ufa. After his resignation he founded the Davlekanovo Bible School (*q.v.*), which, however, had to be closed soon because of religious persecution. The last years of his life he spent at Zaporozhe, Ukraine, with his daughter. Occasionally he served the Mennonites of Einlage as minister (1935-36). When his daughter

Marianne was exiled in 1941, he had already passed away after a long illness. C.K.

A. A. Töws, *Mennonitische Märtyrer* (Abbotsford, 1949) 164 f.

Friedrichsen, Peter, b. July 10, 1866, at Tashchenak, Ukraine, baptized June 3, 1884, Saribash, Crimea, married Sarah Martins April 25, 1891, was ordained as minister of the Busau Mennonite Church (*q.v.*), Crimea, by Elder Heinrich Martins on May 15, 1903, was ordained elder of this same congregation May 7, 1906, by Elder Abr. Friesen of the Karassan Mennonite Church. After the death of his first wife, he married the widow Maria Fast on Aug. 23, 1920.

In addition to his work as a minister and elder, Friedrichsen was also a farmer and held other public positions. He lived in the village Busau-Aktachi, Crimea. Friedrichsen was a fearless preacher of the Gospel, free of legalism. He preached a total of 2,015 sermons. He died July 16, 1926 (see *Unser Blatt* II, 148-49). C.K.

Friedrichsgraben, a district in the Lubianer Niederung, West Prussia, Germany, where Mennonites lived about 1740. They soon left this region because of repeated floods, which made living and farming there impossible. Of their activity the "Mennonitendamm" still bears evidence. vDZ.

Herbert Wiebe, *Das Siedlungswerk niederl. Mennoniten im Weichseltal* (Marburg a.d. Lahn, 1952) 44.

Friedrichstadt, a city (pop. 3,600) on the Eider River in Schleswig-Holstein, Germany, founded in 1619 by Dutch Remonstrants with the consent of Duke Frederick III (*q.v.*) of Gottorp, and laid out in the Dutch pattern. By its grant of religious liberty it became an asylum for all who were persecuted for their faith. The Mennonites received a charter on Feb. 13, 1623, which permitted them to settle there and carry on their trades; but at the same time it required them to live quietly and not to cause offense either "privately or publicly" to annoy anyone in religious matters. All the Mennonites living in Friedrichstadt and in the Eiderstedt (*q.v.*) area were freed from the oath and from military duty.

This far-reaching charter was confirmed on Feb. 17, 1657, again on Nov. 25, 1695, and by all the succeeding dukes and kings, finally by Christian VIII. In no other part of Germany did the Mennonites enjoy such extensive rights and privileges. The congregation had the rights of incorporation; their preachers enjoyed state recognition, freedom from communal taxation (which was not rescinded until April 14, 1869), and permission to wear their special garb.

In the earliest period there were in Friedrichstadt three Mennonite congregations: (1) the High German (merged in 1653 with the Flemish); (2) the Flemish; (3) the Frisian. On May 12, 1639, a short-lived union was formed between the churches at Hamburg, Glückstadt, and Friedrichstadt. Though the union did not last, there was always a friendly relationship and close connection between these three churches.

The Flemish and Frisian congregations merged on April 16, 1698; the Frisian congregation then had

70 members. It held its services in the rear of the "Alte Münze" which one of their members had purchased in 1652. Neither group was now willing to forsake its place of meeting. The lot decided in favor of the Frisians; but because their building was not very suitable, the congregation in 1708 bought the "Alte Münze" (picture in *Menn. Bl.,* 1904, 46). On May 29, 1708, the first service was held in the remodeled building, which still serves the congregation. In 1839 a thorough remodeling was begun which was completed in 1884. In 1850 it suffered extensive damage in the bombardment of the city; the organ purchased in 1847 was also struck.

The Friedrichstadt congregation in 1703 had 178 communicant members. One hundred years later it had only 36. An attempt made by South German Mennonite families to settle in the city apparently failed. On Oct. 13, 1693, 12 families came from the Upper Palatinate; but on April 9, 1698, most of them returned to South Germany and the rest emigrated to America. Only two families remained in the city, one named Strickler from Ibersheim, and one Egly, probably also from there. Neither exists at present.

The great decline in the congregation is explained in part by the ruling brought about by the Lutheran clergy after the death of Duke Frederick III, that no Lutheran was permitted to join the Mennonites; if the latter permitted it, they would be deprived of all their privileges. No Mennonite could marry a Lutheran without a dispensation and the payment of a fee, and then only on the condition that the children be christened as Lutherans. (In 1823 Preacher Jakob van der Smissen succeeded in having this law abrogated in the city; therefore the rural Mennonites saw to it that their children were born in the city in order to be able to claim this privilege for them.) Again, the ruling that Mennonite services could be held only in the city had a deterrent effect on the development of the congregation, for many rural members were unable to attend the city services for long periods. Still worse was the fact that the services were conducted in the Dutch language, which was used only rarely in the country. The "black death" in 1713 snatched away 52 members. Visits of Dutch and Hamburg preachers like Bastian von Weenigem, Gerrit Roosen, P. Beets, and especially Jakob Denner aided in sustaining church life. When they no longer came the congregation declined perceptibly.

The church had a capital of 100,000 marks, which was managed by two elders, of whom one had charge of the ministerial fund, the other of the poor fund. Later the two funds were united into one. The church record was begun in 1763. The church was always interested in the common welfare of the brotherhood, and assisted wherever there was need among the members. The Swiss, Palatine, and Polish Prussian Mennonites were aided by them. In 1850, when the city and vicinity were badly damaged by a flood, the congregation was aided by the Dutch Mennonites. Menso Draaisma was the first trained preacher. He studied at the Amsterdam Mennonite Seminary and served in Friedrichstadt 1746-84. He

was followed by Sybrand Martens 1784-1816, Jakob Mannhardt (*q.v.*) 1828-36, J. C. van der Smissen (*q.v.*) 1838-68, H. Neufeld (*q.v.*) 1869-99, and Samuel Blickensdörfer 1899-1920. Besides them, outstanding service was given by Deacon Jan Jelle Schütt (leader 1805-55) and his son Jelle Jansen Schütt (b. 1802, deacon 1836-86); and Christian Grosskreutz (deacon-treasurer 30 years, d. Jan. 19, 1899). The membership in 1898 was 34, with only two catechumens; in 1919 it was about 45, with 25 children; and in 1952, 29, with 13 children. The congregation was served in 1953 by Albert Goertz of Grünhorst, who had pastoral charge of a number of Mennonite congregations in the area.

NEFF.

R. Dollinger, *Gesch. der Menn. in Schleswig-Holstein, Hamburg und Lübeck* (Neumünster, 1930); *Menn. Bl.,* 1854, 48; 1856, 11; 1858, 35 ff.; *DB* 1891, 93; *Comenius-hefte,* 1901, 34 ff.; *Inv. Arch. Amst.* I, 578, 1003, 1180; II, 2754-58, 2789; *ML* II, 4 f.

Friedt, Heinrich, d. 1761, from about 1710 a preacher of the congregation of Obersülzen (*q.v.*), Germany, who had some contacts with the Amsterdam Committee of Foreign Needs. (*Inv. Arch. Amst.* I, Nos. 1258, 1491, 1522, 1525, 1527.) vDZ.

Friend of Truth, a 16-page monthly, was published at 1216 Diversey Parkway, Chicago, Ill., by Joseph W. Tschetter (KMB), editor, sole publisher and printer of the paper. It was begun in September 1934, and discontinued in April 1939. It appeared in 8½ x 11½ inch size and reached a circulation of approximately 1,200. The paper contained articles on missions, reports, a children's page, sermon suggestions, and other items of general interest. It was an English counterpart of the *Wahrheitsfreund,* which Tschetter had previously published in cooperation with D. M. Hofer. C.F.P.

Fries, Abraham Jacobs (years of birth and death unknown), a son of Jacob Fries (de Vries) and Maria van Heyningen, was a member of the Lamist Mennonite congregation of Amsterdam and belonged to a family of which many members served the Amsterdam church as deacons. Fries was four times a deacon (1677-82, 1687-92, 1697-1702, 1707-12). He is of special interest as a member of the Dutch Committee of Foreign Needs, serving from 1680 to 1714 as its secretary. He wrote and received a number of letters which are found in the Amsterdam Mennonite archives and which not only bear witness of his activity, but are of great importance to the history of Mennonites in the Palatinate, Switzerland, Poland, and Prussia. vDZ.

Fries(ch) Studiefonds, a fund of the *Friesche Sociëteit* (Conference of Friesland), founded in 1859 after the Sociëteit had resolved not to appoint any more ministerial candidates, but to support young Frisian Mennonites studying at the Amsterdam Mennonite Seminary, or preparing for the Seminary by studying in a secondary school. During the first 60 years of its existence more than 30 ministerial students received assistance. (*ML* II, 9.) vDZ.

Friesche Doopsgezinde Predikanten Vereeniging (Mennonite Ministers' Conference in Friesland).

From 1847 to 1926 the Mennonite ministers in the Dutch province of Friesland held their (unofficial) meetings twice a year, in the spring at Leeuwarden and in the fall at Sneek, discussing problems of special Mennonite interest and hearing scholarly theological addresses given by one of the ministers. The Friesche Vereeniging was dissolved in 1926, when a general Dutch Ministers' Conference was founded (see **A.N.D.P.V.**). vdZ.

Fries(ch)e Sociëteit: see **Friesland, Sociëteit van** *Doopsgezinde Gemeenten in.*

Friesche Sociëteit in Noord-Holland: see **Noordhollandsche Sociëteit.**

Friese Doopsgezinde Jongeren Bond (*Mennonite Youth Association in Friesland*). After World War I there was a spiritual revival among the Dutch Mennonites, especially among the young people. They wanted to judge and discuss the problems of Christianity in their own way, critical of former times, enthusiastic as to the future. In the Dutch province of Friesland this revival was rather strong: in 1921 youth groups had been founded in the Frisian congregations of St-Anna-Parochie, Bolsward, Heerenveen, Leeuwarden, and Veenwouden. The first *Jongerendag* (youth meeting, age 18-35) was held at Veenwouden on Sept. 21, 1921. Since then youth meetings have been held annually in the province. They have a large attendance, sometimes more than 300 young Mennonites being present.

On Feb. 4, 1924, the *Friese Doopsgezinde Jongeren Bond* was founded at Leeuwarden. It acts as the top organization of all youth groups; gradually the number of associated groups rose to 40. The total membership of affiliated circles numbered 180 in 1924, 430 in 1934, 360 in 1953.

At the outset a large number of church boards and ministers stood rather skeptical or even negative toward this movement, but other ministers promoted it from the very beginning: C. Nijdam, W. H. toe Water, P. Vis, J. IJntema. The relation to the general Dutch Mennonite Youth Association, founded in 1928 (see **Doopsgezinde Jongerenbond**), was at first somewhat troubled and co-operation was somewhat difficult, but in 1932 the difficulties were entirely cleared away, and there is now a feeling of unity. Besides the yearly youth meetings, the F.D.J.B. organized instructional meetings (*kaderbijeenkomsten*), mostly held at Fredeshiem (*q.v.*) and *Samen Een* at Giethoorn (*q.v.*). The F.D.J.B. has a *bondslied* (group song) written and set to music by Pastor L. Bonga of Leeuwarden. Many particulars about the founding and the early history of the F.D.J.B. are found in the program of the 13th youth meeting, jubilee meeting 1924-34 held at Grouw on May 27, 1934. vdZ.

Friesen, German for Frisian Mennonites (*q.v.*).

Friesen (Friese, Friessen, Fresen), a Mennonite family name in West Prussia, appearing in the rural Flemish congregations and in the Frisian congrega-

tions of the Vistula delta. Evidently in the 19th century, it was sometimes contracted from the family name "van Riesen." It was first mentioned in 1547 at Reichenberg. Fifty-nine families of this name were counted in 1776, 140 persons in 1910, and 121 persons in 1935 (without Elbing.) Abraham Friesen, a brother of Peter von Riesen, was an elder of the Kleine Gemeinde; Abraham Friesen was a missionary to India; Johann Friesen was an elder of the Kleine Gemeinde; P. M. Friesen (*q.v.*) was an outstanding Mennonite historian.

Friesen families came to America in the migration from Russia in the 1870's and also after World Wars I and II. In 1953 there were 39 Mennonite ordained Friesens in Canada, 12 in the United States, 13 in Latin America, and 3 in Africa and India. Manitoba had the largest number with a total of 24, and among the Mennonite branches the General Conference Mennonites had the largest number, with at least 19. No less than 10 Mennonite groups were represented in this list of 67 ministers. The Morris, Man., telephone directory listed 29 Friesens in 1949; Mountain Lake, Minn., 12; Hillsboro, Kan., 16; Inman, Kan., 21; and Reedley, Cal., 22. The family was scattered through South Dakota, Nebraska, Oklahoma, as well as in the above states. In the United States 41 Friesens served in Civilian Public Service (*q.v.*) during World War I. Peter A. Friesen was for many years a missionary in India (MC). *Who's Who* (Menn.) lists 16 Friesens. G.R.

Friesen, Abraham, an elder of the Kleine Gemeinde, of Ohrloff, Molotschna, who was elected to succeed Klaas Reimer as elder on April 3, 1838. Bernhard Fast of the Ohrloff Mennonite Church, having been requested to ordain him, discussed the matter with his coelders, Peter Wedel, Wilhelm Lange, Benjamin Ratzlaff, and Abraham Friesen. Since Friesen was not willing to agree to certain conditions—such as not accepting members from other congregations without a church letter—for his ordination as elder, he assumed the elder's functions without the usual ordination. When the elders were reluctant to recognize Abraham Friesen as an elder of the Kleine Gemeinde, Johann Cornies had him decreed an elder in 1843 by the Board of Guardians (*Fürsorgeamt*) at Odessa. Abraham Friesen must have been a better educated leader than his predecessor, Klaas Reimer (*q.v.*). Numerous (handwritten) writings by him have been preserved and can be found in homes of the members of the Kleine Gemeinde and in the Bethel College Historical Library. The booklet, *Eine einfache Erklärung über einige Glaubenssätze der sogenannten Kleinen Gemeine* (Danzig, 1845), written by a "Faithful servant," has under the conclusion the initials "A. F.," which very likely stand for Abraham Friesen. This booklet also contains the correspondence with Elder Bernhard Fast. Friesen died July 1, 1849. (*ML* II, 5.) C.K.

Friesen, Abraham, a cominister of Elder Johann Friesen of the Kleine Gemeinde in Russia, was excommunicated by Friesen in 1868 because of differences of opinion. On May 4, 1869, his following elected him as their elder. He was ordained by Johann Harder, the elder of the Blumstein Mennonite Church. In the immigration to America in 1874, the Abraham Friesen group settled in Jansen, Neb., while the other group under the leadership of Elder Peter Toews, elected to the ministry in 1869, went to Manitoba (*Menn. Life* VI, July 1951, 18). C.K.

Friesen, Abraham (1859-1919), a Mennonite Brethren missionary, was born May 15, 1859, at Niederchortitza, South Russia, the second son of Johann and Margaret Wieler Friesen. He grew up and attended school in the village of Einlage. Abraham was converted at an early age and became a member of the Mennonite Brethren Church of Einlage. His abilities soon became evident and he was his father's right-hand man in his large flour mill and farm machinery factory. In his early twenties he married Mary Martens. No children were born to this union.

In 1885 Abraham and Mary Friesen volunteered for service in a foreign field. That same autumn found the Friesens in Hamburg, Germany, at the German Baptist Seminary, where Friesen studied for four years. Due to regulations of the Russian government an independent mission of the Mennonite Brethren Church was an impossibility and therefore Friesen worked out a co-operative basis with the American Baptist Mission Union and he himself opened the first mission of the Mennonite Brethren Church to the Telugus of South India.

He and his wife arrived in Secunderabad on Dec. 5, and stayed with the Baptist missionaries to study the Telugu language. Finally on Oct. 25, 1890, they were ready to open the work at the Nalgonda mission station. Nalgonda comprises the southeastern section of the former Hyderabad Native State.

Friesen's ministry proved successful from the very beginning, and on Jan. 4, 1891, he organized the first church with 129 members. Some evangelistic work had been done in this section prior to the Friesens' coming to Nalgonda. Due to the rapid growth of membership, the Nalgonda church was subdivided and in June 1891 three independent churches were established. From the very beginning the missionary established the principle of self-support and the dependence of the pastor upon the native church.

During his furlough in 1898-99 he visited the Mennonite Brethren churches in the United States and Canada with several workers, and also visited the headquarters of the Baptist Mission Union at Boston, Mass. (now at New York), to strengthen the bond of co-operation. Finally in August 1904 Friesen met with Dr. Barbour of the Baptist Union in Stockholm, Sweden, to lay down definite rules to guide in the association of the American Baptist Mission Union and the Mennonite Brethren Church of Russia.

After a most effective ministry of almost 20 years the Friesens returned to Russia in 1908 and settled in Rückenau, Molotschna. He became the guiding spirit in the foreign mission enterprise of the Mennonite Brethren Church of Russia. In 1914 Friesen went to India once more to help in the great work,

returning to Russia in 1915 to experience all the tragedies of World War I and the Revolution. He died in 1919.

Friesen was the author of two books: *Kardu, das Hindumädchen,* and *Morgenstern auf finstrer Nacht.* He also served as editor of the mission periodical, *Das Erntefeld,* published in Russia in the German language. G.W.P.

G. W. Peters, *The Growth of Foreign Missions in the Mennonite Brethren Church* (Hillsboro, 1952); *ML* II, 5.

Friesen, Abram A. (1885-1948), was a prominent member of a study commission of four men sent to America by the South Russian Mennonites in 1920 to investigate immigration prospects in either North or South America and also to obtain assistance from American Mennonites for the oppressed Mennonites in Russia. When the other members of this commission returned to Europe, Friesen stayed at Rosthern, Sask., since Elder David Toews (*q.v.*) was located here. Friesen then helped to prepare for the great immigration movement, and in particular was instrumental in eliminating the restrictions in Ottawa against the immigration of Mennonites into Canada. He was for some years (1922-26) business manager of the Canadian Mennonite Board of Colonization in Rosthern. In 1926 he withdrew to follow his private activities.

A. A. Friesen was born in 1885 in the village of Schönau in the Molotschna settlement of South Russia. He attended the Zentralschule in Halbstadt, taking also the special course in pedagogy, then went on to the Gymnasium in Ekaterinoslav and the University of Odessa. He then took a position as instructor in the then newly established School of Commerce in Halbstadt. For ten years he worked fruitfully in the position, until he came to America. In 1948 he died at Rabbit Lake, Sask. J.G.R.

J. H. Janzen, "Erinnerungen an A. A. Friesen und David Toews," in *Menn. Jahrbuch,* 1950.

Friesen, David, the leader or *Oberschulze* of the Molotschna settlement, Ukraine, South Russia, in 1848-65, the time of the struggle of the landless Mennonites of the settlement for recognition of their demands and for acquisition of land. Through their organization (see **Landlosen-Kommission**) and the support of the government they finally achieved their aim. David Friesen was a strong supporter of the landholding class, opposing the distribution of the surplus land among the landless. C.K.

H. Görz, *Die Molotschnaer Ansiedlung* (Steinbach, 1950) 110-18; Franz Isaak, *Die Molotschnaer Mennoniten* (Halbstadt, 1908) 27-87.

Friesen (Ladenmacher), **Georg,** an Anabaptist martyr, a cabinetmaker by trade, was arrested in 1562 at Cologne, Germany, with Wilhelm von Keppel (*q.v.*), a former priest, now an Anabaptist preacher. An attempt was made to convince them of the rightness of infant baptism. The magistrate of Cologne offered Friesen money and his maid as a wife if he would recant. But he replied, "Your servant maid, riches, or money cannot take me to God; but I have chosen something better, for which I hope to strive." Favorable offers were also made to Wilhelm, but in vain. Both were taken on the Rhine by boat, and they bade each other farewell with "a holy kiss of love." After Friesen was drowned the executioner told Wilhelm he wanted to take him to the shore to behead him. Wilhelm then indicated he was willing to recant. So when they reached the shore he was released, and banished from the city and region. Van Braght records a brief letter written by Friesen in prison during the night before his execution. It contains earnest fraternal admonitions to faithfulness and endurance. Their capture and the execution of Friesen was commemorated in the song beginning "Zu singen will ich heben an," written by Wilhelm von Keppel, which is correct only in so far as it refers to Friesen. Georg Friesen is also the author of a song that begins, "Ich verkündt euch niewe Mare." (*Mart. Mir.* D 295, E 661; *Ausbund,* 22; Wolkan, *Lieder,* 101; *ML* II, 6.)   NEFF.

Friesen, Isaac P. (1873-1952), Mennonite (GCM) evangelist, minister, and poet, came as a two-year-old boy with his parents from Russia to Canada, and spent most of his life in Rosthern, Sask., the center of the large Rosenort Mennonite congregation. With the revivalistic character of his preaching he led most of the ministers of this large congregation, and in fact those far beyond his own church, in this type of work. With his fluent speech and the dominant emotionalism in his sermons, he held and inspired his audiences. His poems, two volumes entitled *Im Dienste des Meisters* (In the Service of the Master), were and are extensively read. When in the fall of 1910 Isaac P. Friesen made a journey to Palestine, a dream of his life became a reality. His account of this journey is found in *Meine Reise nach Palästina* (My Journey to Palestine) (*Winnipeg,* n.d.). Before he entered the ministry Isaac P. Friesen had been a well-to-do businessman in the town of Rosthern, and during his ministry he liberally supported various Mennonite missionary undertakings, such as the Old Folks' Home in Rosthern, the Children's Home on the Mennonite Youth Farm near Rosthern, and other missionary and welfare projects.
                                                        J.G.R.

Friesen, Johann Isaak (1860-1941), born Jan. 15, 1860, in the Molotschna settlement in South Russia, the oldest of the six children of Abram Friesen. In 1874 the family came to America and settled in Manitoba. Through a serious accident he was led to conversion at the age of 19, and was baptized as a member of the Kleine Gemeinde on Aug. 3, 1879. In 1880 he married Helena Penner. They lived in the village of Blumenort, and had eight children. In 1892 they moved to Steinbach, Man., where he became a partner in a milling business, remaining in the business for 26 years. He was known to be very punctual in his office work or any other obligation. After the death of his first wife in 1917 he married Mrs. Abram K. Friesen (d. 1939) at Meade, Kan., and lived there until 1940, when he returned to Steinbach. He died here on Jan. 22, 1941, at the age of 81 years. He was interested in Mennonite history and was very gifted in tracing back various relationships, for over a century. He traced his own ancestry back to Abraham von Riesen (1756-1810),

who emigrated from Prussia to Russia, where the name was changed to Friesen.   A.R.

Friesen, Johann J., an elder in the Old Colony Mennonite Church of Manitoba. He served in the village of Neuenburg, but later migrated to Mexico in 1923 with his people and died there.   H.H.H.

Friesen, Peter Martin (1849-1914), minister, educator, and Mennonite historian of South Russia, was born at Sparrau, Ukraine, died in 1914. After graduating from the Zentralschule in Halbstadt he studied in Switzerland and later in Odessa and Moscow, where he mastered Russian. At the age of 16 he joined the young Mennonite Brethren Church (1866). As a young man he lost his faith under the influences of rationalism, but by God's grace returned to his faith in Christ, and remained faithful to the end. In 1884 he was ordained as an M.B. minister. In 1902 he wrote the Confession of Faith of the M.B. Church. He had acquired a good theological education.

In 1873-86 Friesen served in the Zentralschule in Halbstadt, enjoying great popularity as teacher and 1880-86 as principal. Thanks to his efforts, the first teacher training institute among the Mennonites of Russia was opened there in 1878. After leaving the teaching profession in 1886 he spent most of his time in non-Mennonite communities in the Kuban (1886-88), Odessa, and Moscow. After a serious illness and long convalescence he moved to Sevastopol, where for 13 years he served a Russian evangelical church; and his home was the meeting place for Mennonite students. He served here also as a private tutor. Friesen, however, never lost his love and loyalty to his people. On a number of occasions, because of his command of Russian, he acted as their representative before the Russian Government, fearlessly defending their civil as well as their religious interests. The results of his work on this problem he published in a pamphlet entitled *Konfession oder Sekte?* Friesen became widely known as a philanthropist and defender of the weak and oppressed, especially during the pogroms against the Jews, and the persecution of the Russian Stundists. His greatest lifework, however, on which he spent 25 years, is the *Die Alt-Evangelische Mennonitische Brüderschaft in Russland* (1789-1910) *im Rahmen der mennonitischen Gesamtgeschichte* (Halbstadt, Taurida, 1911) (*q.v.*). It contains a valuable collection of documents which serves as a source book for much historical research. Friesen finally went to Moscow, where his home became a center for the young Mennonites studying there. His last years he spent in Tiege on the Molotschna; they were saddened by almost total blindness.

He was a gifted and fiery speaker, but not a popular one; his sermons often went over the heads of most of the people. In castigating evil he could be very sharp; he was in general courageous and unafraid. At conferences too he occasionally spoke with vigor. As a preacher he sought to reduce the tensions and bring about co-operation between the Mennonites and Mennonite Brethren, who were sharply opposed to each other in the second half of the century.

As a member of the Mennonite Brethren Church Friesen was disappointed, and with him others, in the course which his church followed. Raising the question whether the promising beginning had been fulfilled, particularly regarding John 17:21, he concluded that the concept of the fellowship of the saints was too closely identified with being a member of the Mennonite Brethren Church. Although basically in agreement with the Mennonite Brethren principles, he strongly advocated an *Allianz,* i.e., a fellowship of all children of God, particularly within the Mennonite brotherhood, in daily life and also around the Lord's table. The segregation type of *Allianz* as promoted by the Darbystic Bible School of Berlin (later Wiedenest) was too narrow for him. He strongly promoted an inter-Mennonite fellowship, simultaneously stressing Mennonite principles and tradition and the evangelical warmth of Pietism. Contrary to Mennonite Brethren practices he went so far as to recognize baptism by sprinkling or pouring (156 ff.) and stated that the *Evangelische Mennoniten-Gemeinden* "have found a way out for those who do not wish to be rebaptized and at the same time are not satisfied with the practices of the Mennonite Church [in Russia]. The Mennonite Brethren Church [justly] lost the monopoly in the realm of being the 'church of believers'" (footnote 723).†

H.P.T., C.K.

P. Braun, "Peter Martinovitch Friesen," *Menn. Life* III, October 1948, 8; F. C. Thiessen, "My Recollections of P. M. Friesen," *loc. cit.,* 9 f.; *ML* II, 6.

Friesenheim, formerly a village in the Palatinate, Germany, now incorporated into Ludwigshafen, has since the beginning of the 18th century been the seat of a Mennonite congregation, which is today called the Ludwigshafen-Friesenheim congregation. At first the Mennonites living in the adjacent villages of Ruchheim, Oppau, Hemshof, Gräfenau, Petersau, Scharrau belonged to this congregation.

The membership has remained constant in spite of several emigrations to America: in 1820 there were 103 members; in 1825, 109; 1834, 120; 1923, 130. In 1784 the congregation suffered severely in a flood; the same fate (*Heimatsblätter für Ludwigshafen a. Rh.,* 1915, No. 5) befell them in 1824 and 1882-83 because of a broken dam (*Heimatsblätter,* 1915, Nos. 6 and 7; also *Menn. Bl.,* 1883, 8 and 15).

Originally Hemshof and Gräfenau belonged to the Mannheim congregation (*q.v.*). It is not known when they joined Friesenheim. It was perhaps the work of Heinrich Ellenberger, who was the first minister to serve the Eppstein and Friesenheim congregations for a salary. These two churches seem to have long been united (Müller, *Berner Täufer,* 211). The Ibersheim resolutions of 1803 are signed by Johannes Möllinger, minister of Ruchheim, for the "Ruchheim (*q.v.*) and Friesenheim congregation." At first meetings were held in private homes. On June 21, 1807, the Friesenheim Mennonites acquired the right to share the Protestant church building in the village for the sum of 400 guilders. The document was signed for the Mennonites by Johannes Möllinger of Ruchheim and Christian Schowalter of Hemshof. When the building was remodeled

in 1902, this contract, unique in German Mennonite history, was dissolved for the payment of a nominal sum. The Ludwigshafen-Friesenheim congregation, which was incorporated in 1891 under this name, built a small church on Kurze Strasse 12 in Ludwigshafen, which was dedicated Sept. 6, 1903. Here the conference of the South German Mennonites meets whenever a session is held in Ludwigshafen. Ulrich Hirschler was elder of the Friesenheim-Eppstein congregation 1738-68; Johannes Möllinger, preacher 1754, elder 1768 to at least 1793. Other ministers in the 18th century (found in *Naamlijst*) were Christian Stauffer, Christian Gebel, Heinrich Plätscher, Christian Schmutz from 1762, Johannes Krehbiel from 1771, Johannes Deutsch from 1774, and Jacob Hackmann from 1774.

The first salaried minister of the congregation was Heinrich Ellenberger (see **Eppstein**). From 1850 to 1854 Johannes Risser (*q.v.*) of Sembach preached for the orphaned congregation. Then Christian Krehbiel of Wartenberg, who had studied at Erlangen, was made preacher. After his emigration the Frisenheim congregation together with Eppstein joined Ibersheim, whose preacher, Heinrich Neufeld, preached for the united congregation. Neufeld served until 1869; J. Ellenberger II 1869-71; H. van der Smissen 1872-82; Thomas Löwenberg 1883-1917; Emil Händiges 1917-23; Erich Göttner 1923-27; A. Braun 1928- .   NEFF.

Naamlijsten van de Professoren en Predikanten . . . 1766 ff.; *Inv. Arch. Amst.* I, No. 1541; *ML* II, 6.

Friesenov, a Mennonite settlement in West Siberia, which embraced about 5,400 acres, was situated 18 miles from Petropavlovsk and 4 miles from Tokushi, the railroad station. This estate was settled in 1901 by eleven families; it was laid out in individual farms rather than in the customary village pattern. The villa of the former owner was rebuilt into a school, which was also used for church services. (*ML* II, 7.)   A.B.

Friesenov and **Gorkoye** Mennonite Brethren Churches. Many Mennonite settlements arose along the great Siberian railway at the beginning of the 20th century. One of the earliest of these was that at Tchunayevka, west of the Irtish River, near Omsk, which was founded in 1899. In 1901 the village Friesenov (*q.v.*) near Petropavlovsk was settled. Among the first to settle here were Peter Friesen of Rückenau, and Heinrich Reimer of Margenau of the Molotschna settlement, whose farewell service was held in the Mennonite Brethren Church in Rückenau on March 18, 1901. In the new settlement, which was situated north of the stations of Tokushi and Assanovo and east of the town of Petropavlovsk, the Mennonite Brethren united into a congregation, whose leader was Isaak Braun. When Braun moved to Barnaul as that settlement was founded, David Janzen was chosen to lead the congregation and held that position until his death, Jan. 18, 1922. There were also other ministers, some of the later ones being Johann Barkmann, Johann Abr. Janzen, and Jakob Franz.

In 1903 two new villages were established near Gorkoye. These were Margenau and Putchkovo.

They were made on leased land, which was, however, later purchased. Here the Mennonite Brethren organized a congregation under the leadership of Jakob Friesen of Margenau. On June 19, 1907, Jakob Fr. Hübert of Margenau and Peter Fast of Putchkovo were ordained as ministers and Heinrich Martens of Putchkovo as deacon. Officiating at this service were the elders Jakob G. Wiens of Tchunayevka, Hermann A. Neufeld of Ignatyevka, and Jakob Janz of Friedensfeld, of South Russia. Thereupon Jakob Fr. Hübert had charge of the congregation. In that year a meetinghouse was built and dedicated on Oct. 7, 1907.

When Elder Jakob G. Wiens of Tchunayevka faced the question of moving to the Pavlodar settlement, Jakob Fr. Hübert was ordained elder by Jakob G. Wiens on June 4, 1913 (Old Calendar) in the presence of missionary Cornelius Unruh. Until 1929 Jakob Fr. Hübert then served all the Mennonite Brethren congregations along the Siberian railway. In that year he was among the refugees before the gates of Moscow, and succeeded in escaping with his family (with the exception of a son) to Germany and then to Brazil. There too he served as a Mennonite Brethren elder as long as his health permitted, and is now living near Curitiba in retirement. The remaining members at Margenau continued to hold their meetings, but it is not known how long.

After 1903 the following villages were settled in the region of Gorkoye: Nikolaifeld, Ivanovka, Alexanderkron (Mirolyubovka), Alexandrovka (where the Mennonites built a church); and near the Kuyan-Bar station the village of Korneyevka was settled. All the Mennonite Brethren in these villages belonged to the Margenau congregation. In 1907 a settlement consisting of several villages was made north of the town of Issil Kul; in Friedensruh a Mennonite Brethren church was dedicated on Sept. 26, 1910, as a subsidiary of Margenau. Its ministers were Heinrich Barg (leader) and Abraham Hildebrandt, and later also Aron Warkentin and Johann Sperling. Hildebrandt was arrested by the Communists during the Revolution in 1920. He died of typhus in the prison at Omsk on May 1, 1920. Heinrich Barg died in April 1915. (*ML* II, 7.)

H.J.WIE.

Friesland, a province in the North of the Netherlands (area 1,431 sq. miles, 1949 pop. 464,450; 13,328 Mennonites or nearly 3 per cent). In Friesland there are no big cities: the largest are the capital, Leeuwarden (pop. 77,000) and Sneek (pop. 19,000). There is not much industry in Friesland, farming being its principal means of support. The center of the province is below sea level, protected from the water and divided into polders by dikes; in this part there are still a number of lakes. In the summer Sneek and Grouw are centers of aquatic sports. The southeast part of the province is the less fertile. Very few Mennonites live here. In the north agriculture predominates (potatoes, especially seed potatoes for export, wheat, flax; intensive gardening in the Bildt district). The west and southwest part is excusively used for dairy farming and cattle breed-

ing. Cattle breeding is at a high level; most cows, of the black-and-white Frisian breed, are registered. Cows and bulls are exported to all parts of the world. The Leeuwarden Friday cattle market is one of the largest of Europe (highest sale 10,000 head). Of great importance is the production of milk (770,000 tons per annum); hence there is a considerable export of butter. There are 98 dairy processing plants, most of them large; 78 of them are co-operative enterprises. Since 1932, when the Zuiderzee (now IJsselmeer) was closed in by a dike, the fishing industry, formerly of importance at Staveren, Makkum, and other seacoast towns, has largely declined. To the province of Friesland also belong the North Sea islands of Schiermonnikoog, Ameland, and Terschelling.

Friesland has its own language, quite different from the Dutch and closely related to Old English. The Frisian language is still the common language in Friesland, at least in the country. In church services, however, the Dutch language is generally used, but services in the Frisian language are occasionally held. There is a Frisian translation of the Bible.

Mennonites in Friesland. There are (1954) 46 Mennonite congregations in Friesland and 9 fellowship groups (*Kring*) in towns where there is no organized Mennonite church. All congregations are organized into one conference, the *Sociëteit van Doopsgezinde Gemeenten in Friesland*. The youth groups of the several congregations are organized in the *Friese Doopsgezinde Jongerenbond* (F.D.J.B., *q.v.*) and the Ladies' Circles also in a general confederation, meeting regularly at Leeuwarden. For the practical purpose of assisting each other in cases of pulpit vacancy, the congregations are organized into three groups of district conferences called *Ring* (*q.v.*), viz., Dantumawoude, Akkrum, and Bolsward.

History. As to Anabaptism and Mennonitism Friesland occupies a prominent place among the Dutch provinces. Anabaptism was found here as early as 1530 and nowhere in the Netherlands was Mennonitism as deeply rooted in the population as here. About 1530 a circle of peaceful Melchiorites arose at Leeuwarden, probably through the preaching of Melchior Hofmann. In 1531 Sicke Freerks (*q.v.*), a tailor, was beheaded in Leeuwarden. It was this martyrdom that caused Menno Simons, who was a priest at Witmarsum, a village near Leeuwarden, to become interested in a study of the question of infant baptism, which doctrine he consequently rejected as un-Biblical. Here, too, Münsterite Anabaptism caused some confusion; Jan van Geelen distributed the noted booklet *Van der Wraeke,* and as a result a group of revolutionary Anabaptists in the spring of 1535 seized the Oldekloster (*q.v.*) near Bolsward. A week later it was retaken by the Stadholder of Friesland. In this disturbance a brother of Menno Simons lost his life. About 50 prisoners were taken and executed at Leeuwarden.

Menno then wrote his booklet *Against the Blasphemy of Jan van Leiden,* and in January 1536 withdrew from the Catholic Church. The leader of the Anabaptists at that time was Obbe Philips in Leeuwarden. Early in 1537 he ordained Menno, who

KEY
Canals
Railroads
Larger towns
Places of
Mennonite congregations
underlined.

PROVINCE OF
Friesland
NETHERLANDS

IJSSEL LAKE
(former Zuider Sea)

Northeast
Polder

was then living in a quiet village in Groningen, as elder. Menno for some time traveled about
Friesland, preaching and baptizing, but fled to Germany with Obbe Philips when the authorities put a
price upon his head. Another preacher, Frans de
Kuiper, was arrested at Leeuwarden, but was released upon recanting and betraying a number of his
brethren. By 1575 about 50 Anabaptists had been
seized and executed, of the many who lived here.
Soon after 1550 the influx of Anabaptist refugees
from Flanders, where severe persecution had set in,
to the Netherlands began. Some of these refugees
settled in Friesland. Most of these new members
were baptized by Leenaert Bouwens (*q.v.*), who
fearlessly made repeated journeys through Friesland.
It was about this time, after Menno Simons had
sided with the strict party of Dirk Philips and Leen-

aert Bouwens at the conference in Harlingen in 1555,
that the four important congregations, Leeuwarden,
Dokkum, Sneek, and Harlingen, formed a union,
and chose Ebbe Pieters of Harlingen as their elder.
Pieters was, however, unable to travel over the province to administer baptism, and since Menno Simons
had died and Leenaert Bouwens had been suspended
from his office as elder, baptism was for a while not
performed. Thereupon the Flemish in 1565 chose
Jeroen Tinnegiteter as their preacher.

This led to great disunity, because Ebbe was so ambitious to secure this election, and the brotherhood
throughout the country was divided into two parties,
the Flemish (*q.v.*) and the Frisians (*q.v.*). About
1588 a new conflict arose among the Flemish over
the purchase of a house that was to serve as a church,
causing a division into Huiskopers (*q.v.*) or Old

Flemish, and Contra-Huiskopers (*q.v.*). The Frisians also divided into the "Hard" and "Soft" Frisians. Besides these divisions, further schisms resulted in the groups known as the Waterlanders, Jan-Jacobsgezinden, Pieter-Jeltjesvolk, and others. The consequence was that in the small villages there were usually two or more congregations side by side. But most of these groups were reunited in the course of the 17th century. The last union took place at Oldeboorn in the 19th century.

After the period of persecution was past, the Mennonites of Friesland, as indeed in all of the Netherlands, were scarcely tolerated. Nevertheless with few exceptions the situation of the Mennonites in Friesland was generally satisfactory, especially after the close of the 17th century. In return for a contribution (compulsory, to be sure) of 1,032,943 guilders in 1672-76 for the equipment of the Frisian navy flotilla, they were officially released from the oath and military service. For the benefit of their orphanages and their care of the poor they were excused from taxes on flour, meat, beer, and peat. By 1673 the Mennonites of Friesland had been given certain political rights, such as joining with the Reformed citizens in electing the representatives in the regional Frisian government, and were called "Lovers of the true Reformed Religion." Nevertheless there was not yet real toleration; even in the following century the edict (*placaat*) against the Socinians, Quakers, and Dompelaars (1662) was still in force, and in the first decades of the 18th century the Mennonites were often opposed on the basis of this regulation. In 1683 the preacher Foecke Floris (*q.v.*) was expelled from the province; in 1719 Jan Thomas (*q.v.*), a preacher at Heerenveen, was suspended from his ministry by the government of Friesland, and upon the request of the Reformed Synod in 1722 the government passed an edict compelling all Mennonite preachers to sign a formulary of faith prescribed by the Reformed Church. Since all of the 150 Mennonite preachers of the time with the exception of one (Meint Cuyper of Grouw) refused to sign, all the Mennonite churches were closed; and a month later the requirement was withdrawn. In 1738 two Mennonite preachers of Heerenveen were dismissed from their office (see **Pieke Tjommes**), and Joannes Stinstra (*q.v.*), preacher at Harlingen and chairman of the Frisian Sociëteit, was forbidden to preach 1742-57. Not until 1795 were the Mennonites given equal rights with the Reformed.

The violent quarrels at the end of the 16th century resulted in a large number of Mennonites uniting with the Reformed Church. The War of Liberation against the Spanish also contributed to this transfer of membership. Most of the Mennonites, with the exception of the cities in the north and west, were living along the seacoast and the canals. In the southeast the congregations were less numerous. The institution of the lay (untrained) ministry in the congregations also had an adverse effect on the numerical growth.

In the second half of the 17th century the Dutch Mennonites were split into the Zonists (*q.v.*) and the Lamists (*q.v.*) through the influence of the liberal Galenus Abrahamsz (*q.v.*) and the more liberal

Socinians. But this division was less serious in Friesland, where a provincial conference was organized in 1695, the *Sociëteit van Doopsgezinde Gemeenten in Friesland,* which was a great blessing throughout the 18th century—the age of decline, in which Friesland lost no fewer than 22 congregations—in its striving to hold the church together as much as possible and to aid the poorer congregations in supporting a preacher. The Sociëteit organized a fund for the support of ministers, a fund for retired ministers, and a fund for the support of widows of ministers, to which all the congregations of Friesland belong. A fund for the increase of ministerial salaries was founded in 1865, and a fund (*Studiefonds*) for the education of ministers in 1857.

A new "golden age" came when after the French occupation the A.D.S. was established and gradually led to the employment of trained ministers in all the congregations. In the second half of this century nearly all the congregations acquired modernist preachers. Not until recent decades was this situation changed to some extent, a number of congregations in Friesland now having called young, more orthodox ministers. Bovenknijpe (*q.v.*) in Friesland was the first Dutch congregation to engage a woman as minister: in 1911 Miss Annie Mankes, now Mrs. A. Mankes-Zernika, accepted this office. The congregation at Dokkum (*q.v.*) has for 150 years been united with the Remonstrant congregation, but it is nevertheless a member of the Mennonite Ring.

The membership of the Mennonite congregations in Friesland has dropped appreciably since the 17th century, particularly in relation to the population increase. In 1666 there were 4,856 baptized male members, indicating a probable total of 20,000 souls, or 22 per cent of the total population. In 1838 there were 12,870 souls, or about 5 per cent, and in 1949, 13,328, or 3 per cent.

In the 19th century a number of new congregations arose: Appelscha, which was soon dissolved, and the following congregations which are still in existence; St-Anna-Parochie, Koudum, Ternaard, Tjalleberd, and Wolvega. In the 20th century Zwaagwesteinde was added, as well as the fellowship groups (Kring): Bergum, Giekerk, Kollum-Buitenpost, Langweer, Oosterwolde, Oranjewoud, Stiens, Twijzel-Eestrum, and Vrouwenparochie.

The following list gives a survey of the distribution of the baptized members in the various congregations in Friesland:

	1883	1885	1923	1956
Akkrum	321	408	370	181
Ameland[1]	320	290	225	197
Anna-Parochie, Sint	----	65	170	133
Baard	86	115	90	51
Balk	35	91	72	85
Berlikum	12	72	89	151
Bolsward	157	216	208	120
Bovenknijpe	123	231	145	94
Dantumawoude	207	263	305	244
Drachten-Ureterp	183	278	220	212
Franeker	95	116[2]	175	120
Gorredijk-Lippen-				
huizen	118	195	150	155
Grouw	275	433	345	206

Hallum	20	40	125	155
Harlingen	272	514	400	351
Heerenveen	144	286	229	209
Hindeloopen	57	32	65	48
Holwerd-Blija	165	268	140	92
IJlst	135	104	75	84
Irnsum	87	112	135	102
Itens	65	112	100	98
Joure	200	358	350	230
Koudum	----	35	40	26
Leeuwarden	270	782	1350	1020
Makkum	90	97	78	48
Molkwerum[3]	20	29	47	----
Oldeboorn[4]	288	521	338	182
Oude Bildtzijl	34	71	125	143
Poppingawier	----	80	65	45
Rottevalle-Witween	72	112	128	142
Sneek	310	444	460	465
Staveren	25	47	68	56
Surhuisterveen	68	70	105	134
Terhorne	119	135	100	85
Ternaard	----	66	80	101
Terschelling	131[5]	154[6]	140[7]	144
Tjalleberd	104	132	115	103
Veenwouden	36	83	155	195
Warga	159	192	166	91
Warns	108	131	106	110
Witmarsum-Pingjum	50	85	70	54
Wolvega	----	61	80	101
Workum	74	81	105	94
Woudsend	34	32	38	34
Zwaagwesteinde	3	?	75	88
	5072	8039	8217	6779

[1] The congregations of Ballum, Hollum, and Nes.
[2] In 1895.
[3] Merged with Warns in 19—.
[4] Divided into two congregations in 1838.
[5] In 1847.
[6] In 1897.
[7] Until 1942 Terschelling belonged to the province of North Holland. K.V., vDZ.

Blaupot t. C., *Geschiedenis der Doopsgezinden in Friesland* (Leeuwarden, 1837); H. J. Busé, *De verdwenen Doopsgezinde Gemeenten in Friesland* (reprint from *De Frije Fries* XXII); F. H. Pasma, *De Friese Doopsgezinde Gemeenten in de laatste halve eeuw* (n.p., n.d., 1947); Kühler, *Geschiedenis* I and II, *passim;* N. van der Zijpp, *Geschiedenis der Doopsgezinden in Nederland* (Arnhem, 1952) *passim; ML* II, 9-12; detailed information is found in the articles on individual congregations.

Friesland Agricultural Co-operative (*Cooperativa Agricola de Friesland*), located in the Friesland settlement in Alto Paraguay, near the port of Rosario, was organized July 5, 1941, with 38 members, in order to provide for adequate and economical purchase of necessities and profitable sale of colony produce; to establish basic industries to provide for the needs of the settlers; to prevent the settlers from purchasing their requirements outside the colony, thereby weakening its financial stability. Its original capital was 200,000 pesos, and in 1950, 62,540 guaranies. Shares are valued at 20 guaranies, since 1947 payable in cash and obligatory for each colony member, the shares of the Cooperativa being automatical-

ly sold with the land at any time. David Wieler, leader (*Oberschulze*) of the colony, is also president of the Cooperativa, which is under the direct supervision of the colony administration. Special difficulties are encountered because of poor transportation facilities, lack of reliable markets, and the instability of the Paraguayan guarani. Its 1949 turnover was 185,000 guaranies, and in 1950, 458,000 guaranies, the increase being due in part to inflated prices and devaluation of the guarani, but also to increased co-operation of all colony members. H.J.

Friesland Colony, Paraguay, was founded in 1937 by dissatisfied settlers from the Fernheim Colony in the Paraguayan Chaco, when 144 families with 748 men, women, and children left the Chaco, thinking to improve their economic lot, a hope which was not realized.

Friesland is located on the east bank of the Paraguay River, approximately 70 miles northeast of Asuncion, from where it is reached by river boat and horse- or ox-drawn carriages or by use of small planes, since they maintain a good though small air strip. It contains 19,250 acres of land, of which 38 per cent consists of dense forests, 7 per cent of "high-camp" fit for cultivation, 38 per cent of "low-camp" good for grazing, and 7 per cent swampland on which some rice has been grown. The average annual rainfall is 60 inches, compared to 28-30 inches in the Chaco. Cleared forest land is preferred for farming and yields as a rule two crops annually.

Having the same privileges granted by the Paraguayan government to the Chaco colonies, Friesland enjoys complete freedom from military service, has its own schools, and virtually governs itself by a system of one delegate representing every ten citizens of each village under a village mayor, who in turn is responsible to the colony mayor. In 1953 there were nine villages with 202 families, or 1,046 souls.

The dwellings are made of adobe, the Zentralschule and the two churches of burned brick, all three buildings having been built with funds coming from friends in North America. The building housing the Cooperativa Agricola, which takes care of the colony's trade, imports, and exports, is of wood construction.

After the first group of immigrants coming from Europe after World War II had been temporarily housed in Friesland in 1947 because the revolution in Paraguay made transportation to the Chaco impossible, the MCC also began to take an interest in Friesland and has since assisted the colony in a number of ways, such as building and developing a lumber industry, and building roads and the hospital. The latter, built in 1949, had by September 1953 admitted 2,560 patients, 1,037 of whom required surgery; the rest were for the most part maternity cases. An additional 3,300 patients have been cared for with ailments ranging from smaller infections to snake bites and the very prevalent discomforts caused by various types of tropical worms. Only about 20 per cent of the patients come from the colony itself; the other 80 per cent are native Paraguayans.

In 1938 two schools were built. At present there are five schools with a Zentralschule in the central village for those who successfully complete the six-year course offered by the five village schools.

Denominationally Friesland's people are divided between the Mennonite Brethren with 224 members and the General Conference Mennonites with 220 members (in 1953). Problems common to both groups are referred to the *KfK* (Commission for Church Matters).

Friesland is largely an agricultural colony. Seven acres of forest land and five of "high-camp" make up a farmstead (*Wirtschaft*). The average yield on cleared forest land is as follows: maize and kafir corn 7-10 tons per acre, manioc, if harvested the first year after planting, 50 tons, and cotton 3½-5 tons per acre. The livestock industry, as in the rest of Paraguay, is probably the most profitable, but for lack of grazing land cannot expand in Friesland. There were in 1953 about 4,600 head of cattle, 600 horses, 480 hogs, and about 6,000 fowl. Fruit growing is also successful. The 1953 census shows 5,000 citrus fruit trees (oranges, lemons, limes, grapefruit, and tangerines), 4,000 mango, papayo, and peach trees, 4,000 banana plants, and 1,150 grapevines.

The present development of Friesland like that of the other Mennonite colonies in Paraguay has been made possible only through the generous assistance from North America. In spite of this the standard of living, as in the rest of Paraguay, is extremely low. Educational and cultural facilities are hardly offered in Paraguay. For those reasons there is a constant emigration to Brazil, the Argentine, and if at all possible to Canada. The men responsible for the welfare of the colony are of the opinion that if the colony is to succeed friends in North America must assist it in stabilizing its economy. This could perhaps be done by building and developing sugar mills to utilize the best-yielding product of the colony, and then to assist the colony in marketing as well as in imports.

Under the influence of Nazi propaganda, a considerable number of Mennonite young people returned to Germany just before World War II, together with some entire families. A.FA.

J. W. Fretz, *Pilgrims in Paraguay* (Scottdale, 1953).

Friesland Mennonite Brethren Church, located in Colony Friesland, near Puerto Rosario in Alto Paraguay, is a member of the South American District Conference of the Mennonite Brethren Church and since 1948 also a member of the General Conference of the Mennonite Brethren Church of North America. It was founded on Oct. 3, 1937, under the leadership of Kornelius Voth, assisted by Heinrich Braun, by members that had left the older Chaco settlements to establish a new colony in east Paraguay. Its members are largely farmers. The original membership was 153, increased by 1953 to 234. The church is served by six ministers and three deacons. Services are held regularly every Sunday in the village schools; however, construction has been begun on a new brick church in the village of Grossweide, with a planned seating capacity of 400. The first Sunday of each month is set aside for a special meet-ing of church members only. Saturday evening meetings as well as ladies' aid work and other phases of church life are carried on conjointly with the Mennonite Church. The congregation, however, has its own youth and choir work program. Footwashing is practiced. The leader is still the founder, Kornelius Voth, Grossweide, Friesland; since 1947 he has also been the leader of the Friesland Mennonite Brethren Church in Colony Volendam. J.F.

Friesland Mennonite Church, located in Colony Friesland near Puerto Rosario in Alto Paraguay, is a member of the South American Mennonite District Conference (since 1949) and also a member of the General Conference Mennonite Church. The church was organized on Oct. 10, 1937, with 30 members under the leadership of Abram Penner, assisted by Heinrich Wiens and Isaak Goerzen, adopting the motto, "For other foundation can no man lay than that is laid, which is Jesus Christ" (! Cor. 3:11). Its members are a part of the total colony group that migrated from the Chaco to East Paraguay in 1937 and founded Colony Friesland. Leaders have been Abram Penner (to 1945), Abram Harder, and Johann Federau (present); the membership is 220, served by five ministers and two deacons. Worship services are held every Sunday in co-operation with the Mennonite Brethren Church, except the first Sunday of each month when only members meet, at first in the five village schools, and after 1951 in the brick church built in Central, seating capacity 400. Sunday schools are held as well as daily vacation Bible school. Weekly young people's meetings and choir work are carried on separately as a church program. Communion services are held two or three times a year. A.A.H.

Friesland, Sociëteit van Doopsgezinde Gemeenten in (Conference of Mennonite Congregations in the Dutch Province of Friesland), usually called *Friese Sociëteit* (F.D.S.). This conference was founded in 1695 after other conferences had been founded in North Holland (the Frisian Conference and Waterlander or Rijper Conference) and in South Holland. A tour of Friesland by Jan van Ranst (*q.v.*) of Rotterdam seems to have contributed much to the foundation of the Friese Sociëteit (*DB* 1872, 64). The first meeting of the Friese Sociëteit was held on May 16, 1695. The aims of this conference were from its beginning to maintain love and peace among the congregations, to take care of poor congregations, and especially to subsidize the congregations which were unable to pay the salaries of their ministers. In later times new tasks were undertaken; pensioning of aged and ill ministers, of the widows and orphans of ministers (*Weduwenfonds* 1804), and a study fund (*Friesch Studiefonds* 1859, *q.v.*).

Initially the F.D.S. was subdivided into four *Klassen* (groups)—Harlingen, Franeker, Dokkum, and Sneek; but this division was soon abandoned, only a number of congregations in the southwest part of the province forming a special group, the Zuiderklasse (*q.v.*). In 1706-72 this Zuiderklasse acted as an independent conference. From the beginning the F.D.S. met annually at Leeuwarden, 1695-1710 on the first Wednesday after Pentecost, 1710-1804 on the first Friday after Pentecost, from then on the first Thursday after Pentecost. The conference has a board, first of 8 representatives of the congregations, now of 10.

In 1695, 47 of the congregations of the province of Friesland joined the conference. In course of time another nine congregations joined, those of Balk and Ameland not before 1855. Since then some congregations have died out or merged. Now all 44 congregations in the province of Friesland are members of the F.D.S. From 1695 until about 1800 also two congregations in the province of Groningen, i.e., Groningen, United Flemish and Waterlander congregation, and the Flemish congregation at Sappemeer, were members of the F.D.S. The work of this conference has proved to be of great importance. Though it could not prevent the dissolution of a number of churches, it has contributed much to the solidity and harmony of the congregations in Friesland. It generously supported the relief work in behalf of the Swiss and Prussian Mennonites in the first decades of the 18th century. A special meeting of the conference was held when in 1739 two Mennonite ministers of Friesland were suspended by the government (see **Wytze Jeens** and **Pieke Tjommes**). Then the F.D.S. sent a petition to the States of Friesland. After Johannes Stinstra (q.v.), Mennonite minister of Harlingen and president of the Friese Sociëteit, was suspended by the States of Friesland in 1742 another special meeting was held and a petition sent to the States of Friesland, which, however, was unsuccessful.

In 1797 the board of the F.D.S. declined an invitation of the government of Friesland to appoint at their own cost a theological professor to the University of Franeker, because the board was of opinion that the Amsterdam Mennonite Seminary was adequate to supply the needs of training their ministers. Until 1859 the F.D.S. sometimes also appointed *proponenten* (ministerial candidates) after they had been examined by a committee. After 1859 no candidates were appointed any more, the conference of Friesland leaving this matter to the A.D.S. (Dutch General Conference). The oration delivered on June 6, 1895, by P. W. Feenstra, on the occasion of the bicentenary of the F.D.S., was published in *Doopsgezinde Bijdragen* 1895.   vdZ.

Inv. Arch. Amst. I, Nos. 952-58; Blaupot t. C., *Friesland*, 183-91, 193, 195, 197 f., 199 f., 202-5, 209-11, 213, 220 f.; *DB* 1895, 1-33.

Friezen: see **Frisian Mennonites.**

Frisch, Hans, an Anabaptist of Horb, Württemberg, Germany, where he had been baptized by Wilhelm Reublin. From the fall of 1529 he lived in Strasbourg, Alsace. Here he was seized and subjected to cross-examination (Nov. 23, 1534) in which he made some noteworthy statements about the Anabaptists of the city: there were three branches, with the views of Hofmann, Kautz, and Reublin respectively. Frisch himself was a deacon of the Reublin congregation; and it was his duty to announce the meetings which were held in the homes of the members of the church. He had also visited the Brethren in the vicinity of the city to collect money from them. Many foreign artisans, especially from Holland, had been with them and carried on a profitable business.

NEFF, vDZ.

A. Hulshof, *Gesch. van de Doopsgezinden te Straatsburg* . . . (Amsterdam, 1905) 154; *Ztscht f. d. hist. Theol.,* 1860, 79; *ML* II, 12.

Frischau, a village and county in Moravia, about 15 miles east of Znaim. In the 16th century it changed owners a number of times. In 1581 Peter of the Tschertorej family settled the Hutterian Brethren on his estate, who built their Bruderhof "on the open field." As in Frischau, Hutterian Brethren were also found in the village of Maskowitz (q.v.). With a short interruption (1597-98) the Brethren remained in Frischau until the beginning of the Thirty Years' War; July 30, 1619, the house was plundered by the troops of Ferdinand II, and Aug. 2 burned down.   LOSERTH.

Wolkan, *Geschicht-Buch;* Beck, *Geschichts-Bücher* 276, 300, 324, and 326; Wolny, *Topographie von Mähren* (2nd edition) III, 207; *ML* II, 12.

Frischlin, Nikodemus (1547-90), classical philologist and Latin poet of Württemberg, Germany. In 1568 he was a professor at the University of Tübingen, and later the court poet of Duke Ludwig. In consequence of quarrels with other professors and the nobility he went to Laibach to become the head of a school in 1582. In 1584 he returned, but left again in two years to evade his enemies. After an eventful life in Prag, Wittenberg, Brunswick, and elsewhere, he was arrested in 1590 because of a challenging open letter he had addressed to the Württemberg government, and died in an attempt to escape from prison.

Among his poetic works his comedies are most important. One of them, presented in 1580 in Tübingen before princes and lords, printed several times between 1592 and 1619, twice in German translation (in 1606 by Johannes Bertesius and in 1613 by Arnold Glaser), is *Phasma, Comœdia posthuma, nova et sacra de variis hæresibus et hæresiarchis,* in Latin with German additions. An Anabaptist, Melibœus by name, an adherent of Carlstadt and Müntzer, stands in the center of the first and second acts. To his wife he defends in a rude tone of voice communism of possessions and of women, and in an argument with Luther he rejects infant baptism, oath, and government; he has sold his possessions and is going to Moravia. In the two following acts the Catholics are presented, as well as Zwingli, Karlstadt, and Schwenckfeld, while Brenz, the reformer of Württemberg, associates with Luther. In the last act Frischlin, although he occasionally has more liberal religious ideas, has all non-Lutherans, including our Anabaptist, condemned to hell by Christ, who is accompanied by Peter and Paul. Of the choruses between the acts, one is directed against heretics, and another contains requests to the government against the Anabaptists.   E.C.

D. F. Strauss, *Leben und Schriften des Dichters und Philologen Nicodemus Frischlin* (Frankfurt, 1856) especially pp. 125-30; the translation of the first acts of the

Phasma by Immanuel Hoch (Stuttgart, 1839) under the title, *Die Religionsschwärmer oder Mucker; als da sind: Wiedertäufer, Nachtmahlsschwärmer und Schwenckfelder;* K. Goedeke, *Grundriss zur Geschichte der deutschen Dichtung* II 2, ed. 2 (Dresden, 1886) 140 and 386; *ML* II, 12 f.

Frisian Islands (Dutch). To the Dutch province of Friesland belong three islands, Ameland, Schiermonnikoog, and Terschelling. Ameland (*q.v.*) had a population of 2,258 in 1947, of whom 311 were Mennonites. There are three congregations: Ballum, Hollum, and Nes. Schiermonnikoog had (1947) a population of 767, including 12 Mennonites. Terschelling (*q.v.*) had a population (1947) of 3,544, of whom 264 were Mennonites. It has one congregation with a meetinghouse at West-Terschelling. In the 17th century there was a small congregation here, belonging to the Jan Jakobsz group. Jacob Claassen, an elder 1612-38, baptized five new members here at one time. Further records do not exist. (*ML* II, 8.)   K.V.

Frisian Mennonites (Dutch, *Vriezen, Friezen;* German, *Friesen*), a branch of the Dutch Mennonites in the past, which originated in 1566 in opposition to the Flemish group and was also transplanted to West Prussia. After a number of Mennonites had moved from Belgium to the Netherlands, differences arose at Franeker (*q.v.*), Dutch province of Friesland, between the newly arrived Belgian (Flemish) brethren and the local Frisian Mennonites. The Frisians took offense at the dress and manners of the Flemish, which they thought too worldly and too sumptuous, whereas to the mind of the Flemish the Frisians were not sober enough as to the furnishing of their houses. Other circumstances as well as personalities made the schism inevitable, especially since Dirk Philips (*q.v.*) was on the side of the Flemish, and Leenaert Bouwens (*q.v.*) on the side of the Frisians. In June 1567 the parties separated and banned each other. All over the Netherlands, indeed, from Flanders to West Prussia, the Mennonites were divided into Frisians and Flemish, these names indicating not so much geographic descent, but rather becoming merely party names of two different Mennonite branches. Attempts made in 1568, 1574, 1582, and 1589 to bring about peace and union between the two bodies completely failed. (For a detailed account on the origin and development of the schism, as well as of the attempts at reconciliation, see the article **Flemish Mennonites,** and also *DB* 1893, 1-90, and Kühler, *Geschiedenis* I, 395-435.)

Neither the Flemish nor the Frisians remained one united body. As long as Jan Willemsz (*q.v.*), an outstanding Frisian leader, who had been very active in trying to reconcile the Flemish and Frisian groups, was alive, a split among the Frisians was averted, but soon after his death the Frisians divided. For many years great differences had been apparent in the Frisian group: some leaders like Jan Jacobsz (*q.v.*) and Thijs Gerritsz (*q.v.*) were austere and very conservative; they maintained that the (Frisian) Mennonite Church was the only real Christian church, stressed a strict practice of banning and shunning, and vindicated the old doctrine of Incarnation as taught by Menno Simons. Other lead-

ers like Lubbert Gerritsz (*q.v.*) were moderate, did not seriously oppose marriage outside of the congregation, and admitted that the true church could also be found in other groups. These two wings of the Frisians divided. In 1589 Lubbert Gerritsz and his followers were banned by Thijs Gerritsz, Jan Jacobsz, and Joost Eeuwouts at Harlingen, because they had neglected to practice shunning of the banned spouse in marriage. From then there were two Frisian wings: one conservative, called *Harde Vriezen* (Strict Frisians), or sometimes known as *Oude Vriezen* (Old Frisians), and one more progressive, called *Jonge Vriezen* (Young Frisians), or *Zachte* (*Slappe,* or *Tere*) *Vriezen* (Moderate, Weak Frisians).

Among the Old Frisians several schisms followed soon after their separation from the Young Frisians, and this group was splintered into many subdivisions, e.g., Jan Jacobsgezinden, Thijs-Gerritszvolk, Pieter-Jeltjesvolk, etc. Most of their small congregations soon died out or merged with other Mennonites; the Jan-Jacobsgezinden (*q.v.*) maintained themselves on the island of Ameland until 1855.

An outstanding leader of the Old Frisians, who were very numerous in the province of North Holland, was Pieter Jansz Twisck (*q.v.*), an elder of the congregation of Hoorn in the first decades of the 17th century. Outstanding leaders among the Young Frisians were Pieter Willemsz Bogaert (*q.v.*), Hoyte Renix (*q.v.*), and Lubbert Gerritsz (*q.v.*).

In 1591 and the following years most Young Frisians united with the High German Mennonites on the basis of the Concept of Cologne (*q.v.*). Some of them too merged with the Waterlanders. Lubbert Gerritsz too joined the Waterlanders and became their preacher in Amsterdam.

Mention should also be made of the *Bekommerde Vriezen* (*q.v.,* Concerned Frisians), a group which was found in Harlingen and also in Danzig and other towns, who, deploring the schisms among the Mennonites and disapproving the mutual banning, but being too conservative to merge with High Germans and Waterlanders, united with the Flemish. At Harlingen this happened about 1610.

The old Frisian branch founded a *sociëteit* (conference) of Frisian congregations about 1630 in the province of North Holland, which existed until 1841 and then merged with the Rijper (Waterlander) Conference. Outside the Netherlands there were found a few Frisians in Antwerp, and among the Mennonites in Prussia.

The split lasted longest in Prussia and among the emigrants to Russia. Variant practices in the observance of communion and baptism could still be noticed at the beginning of the 20th century. In the Flemish congregations (Heubuden, Fürstenwerder Ladekopp, Tiegenhagen, Rosenort, and Elbing-Ellerwald) the preachers read their sermons while seated (*Menn. Bl.,* 1912, 5), whereas in the Frisian congregations the sermons were not read (Thiensdorf, Markushof, Montau-Gruppe, Schönsee, Tragheimerweide, and Obernessau). In the Flemish group the baptismal candidate had to name two character witnesses, whose names were read from the pulpit; they baptized by pouring, and the

Frisians by sprinkling. In the communion ceremony the Flemish elder distributed the bread to the members, who remained seated; in the Frisian congregations the members filed past the elder, who put the bread on the handkerchief of the member. In Friedrichstadt the unification occurred in 1698, in Danzig not until 1808 (Mannhardt, 89, 104). In West Prussia the ministers and elders of the two groups held annual conferences together beginning in 1772. The first instance of reception into the other group without rebaptism occurred in 1768. After the great Flemish conference at Petershagen on Feb. 9, 1778, where the question was discussed, but blocked by the Flemish, intermarriage between the two groups was quietly accepted.

In Russia, in accordance with an old Flemish regulation, only the elders, not the preachers, were ordained by the laying on of hands; this practice continued in some Flemish congregations until 1900. At the time of the original settlement in Russia (1789) the opposition between the two groups was still so sharp that the Flemish organized themselves into the Chortitza congregation and the Frisians into the Kronsweide congregation, and maintained strict separation between the two. The Dutch Mennonites made a futile appeal in a letter dated May 10, 1788, to the new settlers to unify: not until decades later did this happen, and then only gradually. (See **Flemish Mennonites.**)   NEFF, vDZ.

DB 1912, 60-73; *Ned. Archief voor Kerkgesch.* XI (The Hague, 1914, issue 3) 185-240; Kühler, *Geschiedenis* I, 431-34, 458-60; II, 71, 191-92; *Inv. Arch. Amst.* I, Nos. 480, 482, 486-88, 522, 524, 528, 532 f., 546, 557, 558I, 568, 570, 572, 601, 605 f., II, Nos. 1406-12; H. G. Mannhardt, *Die Danziger Mennoniten-Gemeinde* (Danzig, 1919); Friesen, *Brüderschaft,* 44; *ML* II, 8 f.

Frock Coat. In Colonial America the dress coat of men was a long-tailed coat, with split tails for horseback riding; having no lapels it buttoned up to the top in front. There were no outside pockets. By the end of the 18th century the collar had risen as high as it could on the back and had turned over to make the modern lapel, which lapel still carries the buttonhole and notched corners of the old frock coat. During the 19th century the frock coat slowly passed out of general use in American society. In a general way the Mennonites (MC) tended to follow the changes in convention but only after their general adoption. Sometime during the 19th century Mennonite bishops began to accept baptismal candidates who wore coats with lapels. In the Franconia, Lancaster, and Washington-Franklin Mennonite conferences (MC) the ministers are still expected to wear the Colonial frock coat, while some of the laity wear a modern coat with lapels, and others wear a modern sack coat but without lapels, retaining the straight collar of the Colonial coat. Elsewhere Mennonite ministers (MC) generally wear the "plain" coat which has the short tail of the modern sack coat but the plain collar of the Colonial coat. Thus Mennonite ministers outside eastern Pennsylvania are indistinguishable from that portion of the laity which wear the "plain" coat. Fifty years ago there were a few Mennonite ministers who did not wear the "plain" coat: Bishop Martin Rutt (1840-

1905), who wore a cutaway coat which had lapels, and Christian Brackbill and Frank M. Herr, both of whom preached over a decade in the Lancaster Conference before adopting the plain coat about 1911. John H. Oberholtzer's (*q.v.*) initial refusal to adopt the required coat was one of the factors leading to the division of 1847 in the Franconia Conference, although he ultimately did wear it. J.C.W.

J. C. Wenger, *Historical and Biblical Position of the Mennonite Church on Attire* (Scottdale, 1944); *idem, Separated unto God* (Scottdale, 1951) 81-86.

Froh Brothers Homestead, a Mennonite (MC) home for the aged, located about three miles east of Sturgis, Mich., on U.S. route 112, is operated by the Mennonite Board of Missions and Charities, Elkhart, Ind. The home is licensed by the State of Michigan as a nonprofit home for the aged and a convalescent home.

The institution was formerly a county home for the aged but was sold by the county to Clifford and Alfred Froh, who own the surrounding farm land, and named "Froh Brothers Homestead." In August 1952 the Mennonite Board of Missions and Charities purchased the home and 80 acres of land. The Homestead was remodeled throughout to provide care for about 31 guests in addition to living quarters for the staff. Dedication services were held on Nov. 8, 1953.

A staff of about twelve serve at the Homestead under the direction of Ben and Laura Yoder, superintendent and matron. The Homestead is administered by a Board of Directors appointed annually by the Mennonite Board of Missions and Charities. Guests cared for in the home come from Mennonite churches and from the surrounding community.

H.E.B.

Fröhlich, Samuel Heinrich (1803-57), founder of the Apostolic Christian Church (*q.v.*) or *Neutäufer,* was born on July 4, 1803, at Brugg, canton of Aargau, Switzerland. He stemmed from a French Huguenot family named De Joyeux who fled from their homeland when Louis XIV revoked the Edict of Nantes, and settled in Switzerland where they translated their name to Fröhlich.

Fröhlich studied theology at Basel and Zürich universities. He was ordained in the Reformed Church and served the congregations at Wagenhausen, canton of Thurgau, and Leutwil, canton of Aargau. Wherever he preached he caused a spiritual revival. In 1830 a catechism was put into use in the Reformed Church that he felt reflected a naturalistic or rationalistic religion to which he could not subscribe. The following year he was dismissed from the Reformed Church ministry. During this time he was in contact with the Continental Society of London who had missionaries in Geneva. In 1832 he was baptized by sprinkling by a missionary of this society. In 1831-32 he made four missionary journeys through Switzerland. The first one was in Aargau. He preached to his former church at Leutwil as well as to others whom he could interest. The second journey was through the Bernese Oberland and the city of Bern, in July and August 1832. His third missionary journey during August and

September 1832 centered in the Emmental, where he preached to the Mennonite congregation. He found fertile ground for his teachings in the ministers Christen Gerber and Christen Baumgartner and some 61 other members of the congregation who felt that the spiritual life of their church was very low. During the following years they formed a new congregation. Fröhlich's contacts with the Mennonites also had an influence on him. He accepted their teaching on nonresistance. In October and November 1832 his fourth missionary journey took him to Zürich and eastern Switzerland. Here he met Susette Brunschwiler of Hauptwil, canton of Thurgau, whom he married in 1836. In January 1833, upon the invitation of the Continental Society of London, he went to England for a stay of five months. He then returned to the cantons of Aargau and Zürich where he preached and taught in the face of growing persecution from the state church authorities. In March 1843 he was expelled from Zürich as a sectarian. His marriage was never recognized by the Swiss authorities because it was not performed by a minister of the state church. Fröhlich moved to Strasbourg in June 1844 where he continued his activities of directing the work in Switzerland by letter and also by infrequent visits. He suffered much from sickness. He died on Jan. 15, 1857. He held up to 450 meetings per year. Though he was often so weak that he had to be led to the pulpit, his strength always returned as soon as he began to preach. He wrote annually between 200 and 300 letters in duplicate besides keeping a diary. The grave of Samuel H. Fröhlich is marked to this day by a plain gravestone in the St. Helena Cemetery in Strasbourg.   D.L.G.

Herman Ruegger, *Apostolic Christian Church History* (1949) 36-72; idem, *Aufzeichnungen über Entstehung und Bekenntnis der Gemeinschaft Evangelisch Taufgesinnter* (Zürich, 1948); *U.S. Bureau of the Census, Religious Bodies,* 1936; *ML* II, 13.

Frölich, A., a pastor in Hürtigheim, Alsace, France, author of the book, *Sectentum und Separatismus im jetzigen kirchlichen Leben der evangelischen Bevölkerung Elsass-Lothringens* (Strasbourg, 1889), which discusses the Mennonites (pp. 14-23). In the introduction he calls them "the peaceful descendants of the once wild and rude Anabaptist mobs," of whom he presents a completely false caricature. He explains that these Anabaptists found Alsace-Lorraine "probably because here there were still some remnants of older sects, and also because people were more tolerant here. This was particularly true of Strasbourg, where the synod of 1533 sought to prevent sectarianism. Through Menno Simons the movement was led into quieter channels." Then an attempt is made to describe their prosperity in Alsace-Lorraine and their experiences under pressure and persecution, in addition to their doctrines; but nothing new is presented. Of interest are the accounts of contemporary Mennonitism in Alsace-Lorraine, which are quoted in the article **Alsace.** (*ML* II, 13.)   NEFF.

Frölich, Georg, "known as Letus from the Lömnitz, native of Vogtland," born in Egerland, Bohemia, on the Bohemian border not far from Lomnitz, probably in 1500, was city recorder first in Nürnberg (1524), and then in Augsburg (1536), where with a few interruptions he was still living in 1554, the publisher of a book, *Das fürtreffenlich buoch Isocratis, vom Reich zu Nicocli dem Künig in Cypern geschriben (Isokrates, de Regno) . . . yetzt erstmals treülich verteutscht. Allen Oberkeiten nützbarlich onnd notwendig zu wissen* (Augspurg, 1548). According to Calvary, *Mitteilungen aus dem Antiquariate* (Berlin, 1870, *Verzeichnis* V and VI, p. 49), the author opposes persecution of the sects and offers noteworthy data on the status of the Anabaptists in the Swabian regions. A copy of the book is in the British Museum. (*ML* II, 13.)   NEFF.

Frölichin (Zieglerin), **Dorothea,** a member of the Anabaptist congregation of Augsburg (*q.v.*), Germany, a widow, was branded on both cheeks and banished from the city on April 21, 1528, because she was baptized and had lodged Anabaptists in her house.   HEGE.

Fr. Roth, *Ztscht des hist. Vereins für Schwaben und Neuburg* XXVII (1900) 30; *ML* II, 13.

Froschauer Bibles and Testaments. This term is used for the German Bibles and Testaments published by Christoph Froschauer (*q.v.*). They were very popular because of the clear type, pictorial decoration, and popular language. The following Froschauer Bibles are known: 1524 to 1529 fol., 1527-1529 in 16 (in these two editions the separate parts appeared at intervals), 1530 in 8, 1531 fol., 1534 in 8, 1536 fol., 1538 in 8, 1540 fol., 1542 in 8, 1545 fol., 1545 in 8, 1550 in 8, 1552 in 8, 1553 fol., 1556 fol., 1560 in 8, 1561 in 8, 1565 fol., 1570 in 8, 1571 fol., 1580 fol., 1586 fol., 1589 in 4. Froschauer New Testaments appeared as follows: 1524 in 8, 1524 fol., 1525 in 8, undated in 16 (1528?), 1533 in 16, 1534 in 16 (?), 1535 Latin and German in 8, 1542 in 16, 1557 in 8, 1565 in 8, 1570 in 8, 1574 in 8, 1581 in 4.

The Froschauer Bibles and Testaments were originally reprints of Luther's translation, altered in word order and vocabulary, more rarely in the text itself. Until 1525 they have Swiss vocalization; e.g., Rom. 12:20, *So wirstu führige kolen vff sin houpt samlen.* In 1527 the New High German diphthongs, *au, ei,* and *eu* were adopted. Since the Prophets were still lacking in Luther's translation, the Zürich preachers in 1529 issued this part of the Old Testament in a special translation, based on the translation of Ludwig Haetzer and Hans Denk, which had been published in Worms in 1527, and which the Zürich preachers considered a faithful translation from the Hebrew. Thus it came about that in 1529 a complete translation of the entire Bible was printed by Froschauer, several years before Luther's complete Bible appeared. From the continual revision of this combined Bible rose the actual "Zürich Bible," whose text deviated more and more from Luther's, without, however, losing all traces of its original dependence.

Among the people, especially the Anabaptists, the first editions of the Froschauer Bibles and Testaments were greatly loved. Thus the remarkable thing happened that in the course of the centuries those old editions were several times reprinted word for word. The oldest of these reprints known to us is "Das gantz Neuw Testament grundtlich vnnd wol verteutschet . . . . Gedruckt zu Basel durch Leonhart Ostein 1588," the basis of which was the (16 mo) edition of 1533. A further edition is said to have been published in 1647, also at Basel. In 1687 it was again reprinted by Hans Jacob Werenfels in the print shop of the bookbinder Jerome Schwarz, in an edition of 1,000 in octavo. Of the next reprint by the Basel printer Johann Jacob Genath for the bookbinder Caspar Suter in Zofingen in an edition of 1,500 printed in 6 mo in 1702, only the title is known: "Das gantze neüwe Testament unseres Herren und Heylands Jesu Christi."

Very likely the undated reprint with the title, "Das gantz nüw Testament Vnsers Herrn Jesu Christi, Recht grundtlich vertütscht," was also printed in Basel, in 1729. Its basis was the Froschauer New Testament of 1525. All of these reprints were forbidden in Bernese territory as Anabaptist Testaments, and wherever found they were confiscated. Repeatedly the Bern council appealed to the Basel authorities to punish the publishers and printers of these Testaments. The following reprints bear the same antique title, including the former symbol of the printer Niklaus Brylinger (three lions with an hourglass), also found on the Basel reprints of 1588 and 1687; instead of the place of printing is found "Frankfurt und Leipzig anno 1737" (1790 and 1825). The last are known as the *Täufer-Testamente*, which were likewise doubtless printed in Basel. In 1744 a reprint of the entire Bible, i.e., the folio edition of 1536 was issued. The book was printed in Strasbourg "bey Simon Kürssner, Cantzley-Buchdrucker." In the foreword the reason for the reprint is stated; namely, that the edition of 1536 was in great demand for its faithful translation and had now become very rare. In 1787 the Froschauer New Testament was reprinted at Ephrata, Pa., by the Cloister Press, for the Pennsylvania Mennonites.† A.FL.

J. J. Mezger, *Geschichte der deutschen Bibelübersetzung in der schweizerischen reformierten Kirche* (Basel, 1876); Ad. Fluri, *Luthers Uebersetzung des Neuen Testaments und ihre Nachdrucke in Basel und Zürich 1522-1531 (Schweizerisches Evangelisches Schulblatt, 1922, Nos. 35 ff.); Ad. Fluri, Bern und die Froschauerbibel mit besonderer Berücksichtigung der sogenannten Täufer-Testamente* (supplement of *Bernische Geschichte*, 1922), and *Das Täufertestament von 1687* (supplement of *Bernische Geschichte*, 1923); Chr. Hege, *Die Täufer in der Kurpfalz* (Frankfurt, 1908); J. Gasser, *Vierhundert Jahre Zwingli-Bibel 1524-1924* (Zürich, 1924); *ML* II, 14.

Froschauer, Christoph, renowned publisher of Zürich, Switzerland, born in Neuburg near Oettingen (Bavaria), acquired Zürich citizenship Nov. 9, 1519, as a gift "for his art." His earliest dated books bear the date 1521. He early attached himself to the Reformation; in 1522 he was one of the chief transgressors against the fasting laws. He published principally writings of Zwingli, Bullinger, Leo Jud, Rudolph Gwalter, Theodor Bibliander, Conrad Pellican. He won great renown for his numerous beautifully executed Bibles. "What Lufft was in Wittenberg, Froschauer was in Zürich." Most of the Bernese Reformation writings were also printed by him, since there was no printer in Bern until 1537.

Froschauer had no children. He therefore took his brother Eustachius and his nephews Eustachius and Christoph into the business, which he enlarged in 1532 by the purchase of a paper mill. He died April 1, 1564. His nephew Christoph took over the printing business, Eustachius the paper mill. Christoph Froschauer II likewise had no children. After his death, Feb. 2, 1585, the heirs carried on the business until 1590 and labeled their products "Gedruckt in der Froschow."   A.FL.

S. Voegelin, *Christoph Froschauer* (Zürich, 1840); *idem,* "Die Holzschneidekunst in Zürich im 16. Jahrhundert," in *Neujahrsblätter der Zürcher Stadtbibliothek 1879-82;* E. C. Rudolphi, *Die Buchdrucker-Familie Froschauer in Zürich* (1869); P. Heitz, *Die Zürcher Büchermarken* (1895); Ulrich Zwingli, *Festschrift zur Gedächtnis der Zürcher Reformation* (Zürich, 1919); A. Fluri, *Die Beziehungen Berns zu den Buchdruckern in Basel, Zürich und Genf* (Bern, 1913); P. Leeman, *Die Offizin Froschauer* (Zürich, 1940); *ML* II, 13f.

Fröse (Froese, Frös, Froes, Froesen, Frese, Vreesz, Fresz, Friese), a Mennonite family name in West Prussia, appearing in rural Frisian congregations and at Danzig. It was first mentioned 1655. In the earlier forms this family name cannot clearly be distinguished from the name Friesen; possibly both names developed from the same root. In 1776, 59 families of this name were counted in West Prussia (without Danzig), 254 persons in 1910, 195 persons in 1935. Peter Fröse (*q.v.*) of West Prussia was a Mennonite writer and elder.

At least 11 Froese Mennonite ministers were serving churches in 1953. Six of these were in Manitoba, two in Brazil, one in British Columbia, one in Saskatchewan, and one in Ontario. In the United States, at least 17 Froese families were living in the Buhler-Inman, Kan., area in 1949.   G.R.

Fröse, Peter (d. 1853), elder of the Mennonite congregation of Orlofferfelde, West Prussia, Germany, author of the booklet, *Liebreiche Erinnerung an die mennonitischen Glaubensgenossen in Hinsicht des Artikels von der Wehrlosigkeit. In Einfalt, aber aus Liebe und guter Absicht mitgeteilt* (Tiegerweide near Tiegenhof, West Prussia, 1850).

The foreword of the 38-page booklet is signed by the ministers of the Mennonite church at Orlofferfelde in May 1861. In addition to a detailed Biblical foundation for nonresistance it presents from Gottfried Arnold's *Wahre Abbildung der ersten Christen* testimonies of the Church Fathers Tertullian, Irenaeus, Hilary, Origen, and Chrysostomus, as also the ideas of the Waldenses and Menno Simons' views on nonresistance from Hermann Schijn's history of the Mennonites. Fröse closes with an ardent appeal to Mennonite elders and preachers to hold fast to this important doctrine. (*ML* II, 15.) NEFF.

Fuchsberger (Fuchsperger), **Ortolf,** a lawyer and imperial councilor, who lived in Bavaria and Austria during the Reformation. He was a native of Tittmoning, studied at the University of Ingolstadt, and after a brief residence in Altötting he became court judge and secretary in the Mondsee (or Manse, Mänse) monastery. His first publication was a small text for the study of Latin, his last, *Teutscher Jura regulae*. The first book on logic in German and the first German translation of the *Institutiones* of Emperor Justinian were written by him. On Jan. 17, 1528, he published in Landshut a *Kurtze schlossrede wider den jrsall der neügerottenn Tauffer*. It was addressed to Ernst Wolfgang Schwartzdorffer at Straubing, Bavarian treasurer, in order to show him with what arguments the abbot had brought some Anabaptists back into the Catholic Church. He concludes that since baptism takes the place of circumcision, baptism must like circumcision be performed in infancy, and proves his contention with references to the Bible, Origines, Augustine, Raimundus Lullus, and the imperial law. He tries to prove that baptism does not assume express faith on the part of the infant, and to weaken the objection that circumcision cannot be used as an argument because it concerned only boys, whereas baptism concerns all children. (*ADB* VIII, 174 f.; *ML* II, 15.)   E.C.

Fulda. In the government district of Fulda, Germany, which once included 18 towns and 20 districts around the old cathedral city Fulda, Anabaptism found entry in its earliest period. It was propagated from the south and west of Germany and from Thuringia by migrating preachers. Especially Jörg or Georg of Staffelstein (*q.v.*), and Nikolaus Schreiber, a former Protestant preacher at Hünfeld, were prominent. They succeeded in establishing a large Anabaptist congregation in Grossenbach, a village near Hünfeld, in 1529. They lived a quiet retired life. Their religious services they held in the homes in the evening. Usually they met in the house of the brothers Hans and Heinz Meister, and here they observed communion. The record states that Georg broke several bites of bread, dipped them in the wine, blessed them, and gave them to others. Baptism was performed either by making the sign of the cross(?) on the forehead of the baptismal candidate (presumably with water) or by pouring water three times over his head. All that pertained to the world was forbidden, such as wedding celebrations and attendance at the state church. Simplicity of dress, moderation in eating and drinking, penitence and peaceable living, mutual love and benevolence were their characteristics. Their greeting was, "The peace of the Lord be with you!"

Soon bloody persecution broke upon the Fulda Anabaptists. In 1529 ten members of the congregation at Grossenbach were seized and on Dec. 7 cross-examined. This was repeated a week before Christmas on the rack. Four others were arrested. It was learned that a large part of the village adhered to the Anabaptists. After the third trial, on Jan. 4, 1530, the prisoners recanted. The following names are known: Velten Romeisen, Hans Lober, Adam Meister, Hans Knoth, and Matthias Werner.

Later in the same year, 1530, 19 Anabaptists of Grossenbach were arrested, five of whom had recanted the year before. They were probably executed. The Henneberg chronicle records that Abbot Johannes of Henneberg had ordered several Anabaptists at Fulda to be beheaded in 1530. In other villages Anabaptists were also arrested, as in Biberstein, Rimels, Treichfeld, Soisdorf, Gersdorf, Schlitz, and Mues.

After 1532, according to the report of J. Kartels, seditious tendencies were noted in the Anabaptists of Fulda. Their leaders were reported to be Hans of Fulda and Peter the Anabaptist. Although men like Hans of Kaiserslautern, Hans of Kreuznach, and Hans Beck of Büdingen are named, there were not likely any Münsterite Anabaptists among them, for in these places there were apparently only quiet Anabaptists. Robbers and arsonists like Hans Krug and Hans Schott were criminals who used Anabaptism as a shield for their evil deeds.

On March 25, 1532, at Spahl in the Rockenstuhl district about 40 persons, some of them Anabaptists, some of them curious spectators, were surprised at a meeting, overpowered, and taken to Fulda, where they are reported to have conducted themselves very fanatically. Those who did not recant were executed (Wappler, 82 ff.).

Eberhard Arnold (*q.v.*) established a modern Hutterite Bruderhof in the Rhön district near Fulda in 1923, called the Rhönbruderhof (*q.v.*), which continued until it was dissolved by the Hitler government in 1937.   NEFF.

J. Kartels, "Die Wiedertäuferbewegung im ehemaligen Hochstift Fulda," in *Fuldaer Geschichtsblätter* I (1902) 3-20. As sources he names Schannat, *Historia Fuldensis* (Frankfurt, 1720), the literature in the Fulda library, and the Anabaptists' trial records of the Marburg state archives; P. Wappler, *Die Täuferbewegung in Thüringen von 1526 bis 1584* (Jena, 1913); *ML* II, 15 f.

Fulton County, Ohio, is in the northwestern part of the state, bordered by Henry County on the south and by Michigan on the north. The Mennonite settlement of this region, consisting in 1955 of more than 2,600 baptized members, centers at Archbold in German Township, in the southwest corner of the county. From German Township it extends westward into Williams County, south into Henry County, north into Franklin and Dover townships, and east to Wauseon, the county seat. Archbold is 40 miles west of Toledo and 26 miles east of the Indiana state line.

The early settlers were French and Alsatian Amish Mennonites from the region of Montbéliard and Mulhouse, the first of whom arrived in 1834. By 1850 many families had arrived, including such names as Beck, Frey, Lauber, Rufenacht, Rupp, Stuckey and Wyse. The main body of the settlement eventually affiliated with what came to be the Ohio and Eastern A.M. Joint Conference of the Mennonite Church (MC). The first meetinghouse was the Central Amish Mennonite Church, erected in 1870, two and three-fourths miles northeast of Archbold. In 1908 two new meetinghouses were added: West Clinton, six miles southeast of Central; and Lockport, six miles west, in Williams County. In 1956 there were eleven meetinghouses, representing seven independent congregations and four mission stations, extending from suburban Toledo to Hicksville near the Indiana border, with a total of *ca.* 1963 members in the Ohio and Eastern Conference. The first minister was Christian Beck who had been ordained in Switzerland. Well-known

28

Fulton County bishops in the later period were Christian Stuckey (1841-1907) and Elias L. Frey (1856-1942).

In 1956 the Fulton County settlement also included one small congregation of the Reformed Mennonite Church; one of the Church of God in Christ Mennonites with 33 members; and two congregations of the Conference of Evangelical Mennonites (formerly Defenseless Mennonites), one in Archbold and the other in Wauseon, with a combined membership of 621 (1955 statistics). All three of these groups were originally formed in the 1860's.

In 1956 the Fulton County Mennonites had representatives on the foreign mission field in Africa, India, and Japan. The local mission congregation was serving the needs of the Mexican farm laborers who reside in the community. In 1956 the secretary-treasurer of the Congo Inland Mission was Harvey A. Driver of Wauseon, of the Conference of Evangelical Mennonites.

Fulton County leadership was largely responsible for the founding of Little Eden camp at Onekama, Mich., in 1945. From an economic point of view the Fulton County settlement is unique because of its large number of small community industries, such as woodworking, meat packing, and the manufacture of farm machinery.   G.F.H.

Funck, Heinrich (d. 1760), a European Mennonite settler who located along the Indian Creek in what is now Franconia Twp., Montgomery Co., Pa., about 30 miles north of Philadelphia. He married Anne, daughter of immigrant Christian Meyer and they became the parents of ten children, including Preacher Henry Funck and Bishop Christian Funck (1721-1811), the latter being the founder of the Funkites (*q.v.*), who withdrew from the Franconia Conference in 1778 because they favored recognizing the independence of the American Colonies before the end of the Revolutionary War. Funck was a farmer, miller, and bishop. He wrote two books, *Ein Spiegel der Tauffe* (Mirror of Baptism) in 1744, and *Eine Restitution, Oder eine Erklaerung einiger Haupt-puncten des Gesetzes* (Restitution, or an Explanation of Several Principal Points of the Law), the latter being left as an unpublished manuscript at his death in 1760; his children arranged for its publication in 1763. Funck collaborated in sponsoring the publication of the 1748 German *Martyrs' Mirror,* and he and Dielman Kolb read the proofs page by page as they came off the Ephrata presses. Funck was the most important writer among the Mennonites in Colonial America. His grave is lost, but it is known that he was intimately associated with both the Salford and Franconia congregations of the Franconia Conference. (*ML II,* 17.)   J.C.W.

Fundament, Dat, *des Christelycken leers,* by Menno Simons, or *Fundamentboeck:* see **Foundation.**

Fundamentalism, a movement in conservative American Protestantism in the first half of the 20th century of reaction against the growth of theological liberalism and modernism, derived its name largely from two sources: (1) the publication in 1909 of a series of 12 small volumes in defense of conservative

theology called *The Fundamentals,* of which almost 3,000,000 copies were circulated (2,000,000 in America and 1,000,000 in the wider English-speaking world), and (2) the World Christian Fundamentals Association, which was organized at Philadelphia in 1919 and continued in existence until its merger in 1950 with the Slavic Missionary Society. At its organizing meeting the W.C.F.A. adopted the following statement of Christian fundamentals as standards of evangelical orthodoxy:

I. We believe in the Scriptures of the Old and New Testament as verbally inspired of God, and inerrant in the original writings, and that they are supreme and final authority in faith and life.

II. We believe in one God, eternally existing in three persons—Father, Son, and Holy Spirit.

III. We believe that Jesus Christ was begotten by the Holy Spirit, and was born of the Virgin Mary, and is true God and true man.

IV. We believe that man was created in the image of God, that he sinned and thereby incurred not only physical death but also that spiritual death which is separation from God, and that all human beings are born with a sinful nature, and, in case of those who reach moral responsibility, become sinners in thought, word, and deed.

V. We believe that the Lord Jesus Christ died for our sins according to the Scriptures as a representative and substitutionary sacrifice; and that all that believe in Him are justified on the ground of His shed blood.

VI. We believe in the resurrection of the crucified body of our Lord, in His ascension into heaven, and in His present life there for us, as High Priest and Advocate.

VII. We believe in "that blessed hope," the personal, premillennial, and imminent return of our Lord and Saviour Jesus Christ.

VIII. We believe that all who receive by faith the Lord Jesus Christ are born again of the Holy Spirit and thereby become children of God.

IX. We believe in the bodily resurrection of the just and the unjust, the everlasting blessing of the saved and the everlasting conscious punishment of the lost.

The evangelical movement of protest against the inroads of modernism began long before the W.C.F.A., and was far more widespread than this organization, but the W.C.F.A. focused the movement and for a time gave it greatly increased vigor and influence. It had its earlier roots in interdenominational Bible conferences and Prophetic conferences, and it found organized expression in several of the larger Protestant denominations, particularly, Baptist, Methodist, Disciples, and Presbyterian. Numerous other interdenominational conservative organizations and institutions, such as the widespread Bible institutes and numerous local and regional Bible conferences as well as a considerable amount of periodical and pamphlet literature, contributed to the strength of Fundamentalism. A number of smaller orthodox denominations joined the movement en masse. The outstanding Fundamentalist leader was W. B. Riley of Minneapolis, president of the W.C.F.A. throughout its history, and militant advocate of its cause, founder and long-time president of the Northwestern Bible Institute.

The movement reached its height during the period of 1925-30, after which it declined rapidly in volume and strength. Part of the loss in strength was due to excessive polemicism and a certain hyperfundamentalism which proved unattractive to the masses and quite unsatisfactory to moderate conservatives. The strong emphasis on nondenominationalism alienated others. In the large denominations the Fundamentalists failed in their intent to capture the organizational machinery, and consequently many Fundamentalists withdrew from the denominations to form independent fundamentalist churches and affiliations. Furthermore, the growing tide of Neo-orthodoxy in the second quarter of the century displaced much of outright modernism in the denominations. By 1955 only a small remnant of organized Fundamentalism remained, its most polemic and vocal wing, represented chiefly by the rather small American Council of Christian Churches. The smaller evangelical denominations, which had sympathized largely with Fundamentalism, organized the National Association of Evangelicals in 1942, which has several times the constituency membership of the A.C.C.C.

American Mennonites, historically fully evangelical and orthodox, and deeply loyal to the Bible, were not unaffected by the organized Fundamentalist movement. Here and there individual Mennonite pastors joined the local or regional and national Fundamentalist organizations, and occasionally served as leaders in them. Most Mennonites sympathized warmly with the struggle against modernism, although modernism had had only small success in infiltrating the several Mennonite denominational bodies. Some Mennonite colleges were for a time under considerable suspicion, criticism, and attack for liberal tendencies. By and large, however, the Mennonite groups did not formally join the Fundamentalist ranks, although they almost without exception held to the fundamentals and considered themselves to be fundamentalists in a descriptive sense. When the N.A.E. was organized the only Mennonite body to join it was the Mennonite Brethren Church. Grace Bible Institute, an inter-Mennonite educational institution, founded at Omaha, Neb., in 1945, undoubtedly owes its existence in a large part to the Fundamentalist spirit in several Mennonite bodies. The more conservative Mennonite bodies were aided in their resistance to Fundamentalist influences by their traditional objection to outside influences and contacts, and by their strong insistence upon nonresistance, which the Fundamentalists usually sharply rejected (many Fundamentalists manifested a strongly militaristic spirit). In a few cases, however, schisms occurred in local Mennonite congregations over fundamentalist-type issues, some as late as 1954-56, the withdrawing groups at times dropping the name Mennonite altogether.

Considerable Fundamentalist influence has been exercised upon some Mennonite bodies through attendance of their young people at Fundamentalist Bible institutes. The close union of Premillennialism and Dispensationalism with Fundamentalism has contributed to the considerable growth of these systems of thought in some Mennonite bodies, again often through the Bible institutes. The polemic spirit of Fundamentalism has also at times infected Mennonites and contributed to tension and contention. That certain Calvinistic doctrines such as eternal security have been adopted by some Mennonites is due almost entirely to Fundamentalist influence, Fundamentalists being largely Calvinistic in theology.

From the vantage point of 1956, with a considerably faded Fundamentalism and a generally subsiding Fundamentalist influence, Mennonites, though generally continuing to insist upon a conservative evangelical theology and resisting Modernism in any form, see more clearly than before that they belong neither in the Modernist nor Fundamentalist camps, but have a satisfactory Biblicism and evangelicalism of their own with its unique Anabaptist heritage.

H.S.B.

S. G. Cole, *The History of Fundamentalism* (N.Y., 1931); Daniel Kauffman, *The Mennonite Church and Current Issues* (Scottdale, 1923), Chap. III; John Horsch, *Modern Religious Liberalism* (Scottdale, 1920); idem, *Is the Mennonite Church Free from Modernism?* (Scottdale, 1926); J. L. Stauffer, "Fundamentalism and Fundamentalists," *Sword and Trumpet*, April 1933, 16-20; idem, "Faulty Fundamentalists," *ibid.*, October 1931, 13; Gerald Studer, "The Influence of Fundamentalism on the American Mennonite Church" (unpublished thesis Goshen College Biblical Seminary, 1949); idem, "Is Fundamentalism Enough?" *Gospel Herald* XLI (1948) 486 f.; H. S. Bender, "Outside Influences on Mennonite Thought," *Menn. Life* X (1955) 45-48.

Funeral Customs of the Mennonites throughout the centuries have not yet been studied. The following are some observations pertaining to the Mennonites of Prusso-Russian background. In the days of persecution and martyrdom the experiences, faith, steadfastness, and suffering of the Anabaptists were recorded in the form of poems which found their way into early hymnals. To what extent this practice is connected with that of recording the life work and faith of outstanding leaders in a poem written at the close of a life and sung as a hymn at the funeral, has not been established. However, this was an early practice among the Dutch and Prussian Mennonites. A biographical sketch of Giesbrecht Franssen was narrated in a song at the close of his life and was printed in the Jacob Jacobsz *Liedeboek* in 1604.

H. G. Mannhardt made some relevant observations on the funeral customs of the Mennonites of Prussia and Danzig. He believes that they did not use their churches for funeral services, but met in homes; and that funeral sermons were not preached before the beginning of the 19th century, the service consisting rather in singing a song composed for the occasion by a friend or relative. The Danzig Mennonite Church had a number of Dutch and German songs written for such occasions in the 18th century. Thus at Elder Dirk Jantzen's death Gergen Berentz wrote "Een Lied over het afsterven van den lieven Oudsten Dirk Jantzen" consisting of 28 stanzas, the singing of which could have consumed as much time as a funeral sermon. Hans van Steen, Jr., wrote a funeral song of 14 stanzas for Elder Hans von Allmonde, who died 1753. For Hans von Steen's funeral Jan Lambertz wrote a song of 16 stanzas. At the death of Elder Hans von Steen in 1781, one of the first funeral songs in the German language was used, written by Hans Momber and consisting of 24 stanzas.

This tradition continued in modified form among the Prussian Mennonites up to World War II. Well-known hymns were printed especially for the occasion. Numerous copies have been preserved. The congregations also printed smaller song books for special occasions, such as *Sammlung Christlicher Verlobungs-, Trauungs-, Jubiläums- und Begräbnis-Gesänge* (Ebing, 1908) and *Christliche Trauungs-und Begräbniss-Gesänge* . . . , the fourth edition of which appeared at Danzig in 1858. Judging by the fact that non-Mennonite prayer books and liturgical aids have been preserved in Mennonite homes, it may be assumed that they were used occasionally in times of bereavement.

The modified form in which the practice of composing a hymn or poem at the time of death continued among the Prussian Mennonites up to recent times was known as *Grabschrift* and consisted of a poem. Mannhardt presents some of them in his book *Die Danziger Mennonitengemeinde* (p. 116). The Prussian Mennonites had a special church office for the purpose of announcing and inviting relatives and friends for funerals, weddings, etc., and the person in charge of this office was called the *Umbitter* (*q.v.*). This office gradually disappeared during the 19th century. The various editions of the Mennonite ministers' manuals in Germany, Holland, and America make provision for the use of certain forms in conducting a funeral service. (See **Burial** and **Cemeteries**.)   C.K.

Kanselboek ten Dienste van de Doopsgezinde Gemeenten in Nederland; The Minister's Manual (Newton, 1950); Handbuch zum Gebrauch bei gottesdienstlichen Handlungen zunächst für die Aeltesten und Prediger der Mennoniten-Gemeinden in Nord-Amerika (Berne, 1921); R. C. Kauffman, "Our 'Christian' Funerals," Menn. Life III (July 1947); H. G. Mannhardt, Die Danziger Mennonitengemeinde (Danzig, 1919).

Funk (Funck), name of a Swiss Mennonite family, native to the canton of Zürich, probably in the Kronau district, found in the Palatinate in the 17th and 18th centuries. Henry Funk, a preacher of the canton of Bern, was scourged and expelled from Bern about 1671. Mennonite Funks appear in the records in the vicinity of Heidelberg as follows: Michelfeld 1662, Schaffhausen 1685, Richen 1717, Reihen 1724, Rohrbach 1752, and later in Eppingen 1778, where families of Funcks are listed from that time on until recent times. In every generation there have been preachers and elders among them. In 1710 Hans Funk was one of the original settlers in what is now Lancaster (*q.v.*) County, Pa. Pioneer Henry Funck (*q.v.*, d. 1760) located in what is now Franconia (*q.v.*) Twp., Montgomery Co., Pa., in 1719. A Jacob Funck was living in the Palatinate in 1753. The name Funk is fairly common among South German Mennonites today; Christine Funck of near Heilbronn in Württemberg

married the church historian John Horsch (*q.v.*, 1867-1941). In America Henry Funck of Franconia served long as bishop in the Franconia Conference, and was the author of two books, *Spiegel der Taufe* (1744) and a posthumous work, *Eine Restitution* (1763). His son Christian Funk (*q.v.*, 1731-1811) was a Mennonite minister in the Franconia Conference (1756-?) until the Funk schism, when he was excommunicated with his uncle Christian; he later served as a minister in the Virginia Conference (MC), having moved to Virginia in 1786. The latter's son Joseph (*q.v.*, 1778-1862) became "the father of song in northern Virginia" (among the Mennonites), establishing his music publishing house at Singers Glen in Rockingham County in 1847, which firm ultimately became Ruebush, Kieffer and Co. But by far the most distinguished descendant of Pioneer Henry Funck was John F. Funk (*q.v.*, 1835-1930), born in Bucks Co., Pa., but who did his lifework in Elkhart Co., Ind. Launching the *Herald of Truth* and its companion *Herold der Wahrheit* in 1864, Funk was soon a powerful influence in the Mennonite Church (MC). He was ordained a preacher in 1865 and a bishop in 1892. He organized the Mennonite Publishing Co., Elkhart, Ind., in 1875. The Mennonite Publication Board bought Funk's publications in 1908 and the *Herald of Truth* was merged with the new *Gospel Witness* (*q.v.*) to form the organ of the denomination (MC), the *Gospel Herald*. There have been numerous other ministers named Funk among the American Mennonites. Mention should also be made of Isaac Kauffman Funk (1839-1912), of Funk, Wagnalls, and Co., who was of Mennonite descent. The founder of the noted Funk Hybrid Corn Company of Bloomington, Ill., was a son of a Mennonite formerly in Baden-Württemberg.

The name Funk (Funck) was also found in West Prussia, appearing in all Frisian as well as in the Old Flemish congregations. At Danzig it has been mentioned since 1674. In 1776, 15 families of this name were counted (without Danzig); in 1935, 35 persons (including Elbing). Stephan Funk (*q.v.*) was a prominent 18th-century Prussian Mennonite minister. In 1953 seven Funks were serving as Mennonite ministers in Canada, five in the United States, and seven in Paraguay. A principal center of the Funk family is Hillsboro, Kan., where 37 were listed in the 1949 telephone directory.

The relation to the Swiss Mennonite Funk family has not been clarified, but it seems probable that immigrants from Switzerland, South Germany, or Moravia carried the name to Danzig, since the name is otherwise not found in Holland or North Germany. One theory holds that the West Prussian Funks derive from Hutterite immigrants from Moravia. The name appears in the Thorn area in 1700. Another theory holds that they derive from Swiss Mennonite immigrants to Lithuania. The Waterlander (also called Frisian) congregation of the Kleine Werder near Elbing, which was formed directly of immigrants from Lithuania in 1732, had several Funck preachers: Peter Funck, after 1755, and Adam Funck after 1751. (See the *Naamlijst* of 1757 and 1766.)   J.C.W.

A. J. Fretz, *A Brief History of Bishop Henry Funck
. . . and a . . . Family Register* (Elkhart, 1898); *ML*
II, 16.

Funk, Christian (1731-1811), b. in Franconia Twp.,
Montgomery Co., Pa., the son of Bishop Henry
Funk. He married Barbara, daughter of Preacher
Julius Cassel, in 1751. Nine children were born to
this union. His father ordained him to the ministry for the Franconia circuit about 1756. He was
confirmed as bishop in 1769. According to the letter of 1773 addressed to the Mennonites of Holland,
which was probably written by Christian Funk, the
bishop district included the congregations of Franconia, Plain, Salford, Rockhill, and Line Lexington.

Christian Funk was an able leader with very decided views, which finally led to the first schism
among the American Mennonites. The American
Revolution with its problems for nonresistant Mennonites formed the background for this division.
Most of the Mennonite leaders strenuously opposed
the oath of allegiance required by all Pennsylvania
inhabitants by an Act of the Assembly, June 13,
1777, on grounds of Scriptural principle, as well as
their loyalty to the king, to whom they had promised allegiance. They also opposed the payment of
a special war tax of two pounds, ten shillings, levied
in 1777. They considered Congress a government
in rebellion. Christian Funk agreed with his fellow
ministers that "as a defenseless people, the Mennonites could neither institute nor destroy any government." But after Funk read a copy of the Pennsylvania Constitution, and noted its guarantees of
freedom of worship and freedom of conscience on
the matter of bearing arms and oath taking, he began to express his conviction that Congress should
not be denounced as rebellious. He also urged the
payment of the special war tax, and took no stand
against the oath of allegiance. These views brought
Funk into direct conflict with his fellow bishops
and ministers. He was deposed from his office as
bishop, silenced as a minister, and excommunicated.
After the war ended a reconciliation was attempted,
but was unsuccessful, as Funk refused to be admitted as a transgressor.

Funk and several followers continued to worship
as a separate group, which organized at least four
congregations. Various factors, such as poor leadership, the Herrite influence, and the Oberholtzer
schism, led to the final disintegration of the "Funkite" group by 1855. In that year the meetinghouse
near Harleysville was torn down and rebuilt at the
Delp's burial ground. Tradition holds that Funk
lies buried in this cemetery, though no marker has
been found. He died in 1811.

Our principal source for the history of the "Funkite" controversy is Christian Funk's own treatise,
Ein Spiegel für Alle Menschen . . . (published at
Reading, 1813 and in English, *A Mirror for all
Mankind* . . . , Norristown, 1814). It is admittedly
a strong polemic in defense of Funk's position in
the issues involved. It is also an invaluable contemporary source for our knowledge of Mennonite
church life and practices of the late colonial period.
(See **Funkites.**) (*ML* II, 18.)   Q.L.

Funk, Heinrich H., was born Dec. 28, 1880, in the
village of Neuenburg, province of Ekaterinoslav,
Ukraine, Russia, the son of Heinrich A. Funk and
Katharina Friesen. He attended the Chortitz Zentralschule for four years. Having been granted a
scholarship provided by the churches he studied at
the Theological Seminary (Predigerschule) in Basel,
Switzerland. After graduating he accepted the position of teacher of religion and German literature at
the Zentralschule of New York, one of the villages
of the Ignatyevo settlement in the province of Ekaterinoslav. Here in 1908, he married Susanna Rempel; he had four children, two daughters and two
sons.

He taught in New York for nearly 20 years. He
was elected minister and later elder of the New
York Mennonite Church. Since the latter appointment was made during the communist regime it
necessitated his withdrawal from teaching in school.
In 1929, on the eve of his intended emigration to
America with his family, he was arrested and exiled
to the Far North. In 1937 he was allowed to return
to the South, and since his wife had died and his
children scattered during his absence, he resided
for some time at Karaganda, in the Kazakhstan
region of Asiatic Russia, where his youngest daughter taught at a high school which Funk served as
secretary. In 1940 he was banished to the North a
second time and since 1941 has not been heard from.

Funk was known for his inspiring work as a
teacher and for his effectiveness as a minister and
elder of the church. His considerable influence
came from his attractive personality which combined a natural, polished manner and warm
Christian solicitude for those in his charge and all
others he met. Wherever he went, even in his exile,
he was appointed to important work. Thus, during
the first period of his banishment he was attached
for some time to an American geological mission
studying in Russia. He is reputed to have greatly
influenced his many students to love the noble and
the good.   H.D.D.

Funk, John Fretz (1835-1930), probably the outstanding leader of the Mennonite Church (MC) in
the 19th century, great-grandson of immigrant
Bishop Heinrich Funck (d. 1763), son of Jacob
Funk and Salome Fretz, was born April 6, 1835, on
the family homestead in Hilltown Twp., Bucks Co.,
Pa., where he spent the first 22 years of his life.
His only higher education, two terms at Freeland
Seminary (now Ursinus College), prepared him for
a career of public school teaching in his home community, but after two years in that profession, he
entered the lumber business in Chicago (arriving
April 11, 1857) with his brother-in-law Jacob Beidler (later in partnership with John F. Rittenhouse),
in which he continued successfully for ten years.
On April 6, 1867, he moved to Elkhart, Ind., with
the printing and publishing business he had established in Chicago Jan. 1, 1864. Here he spent the
rest of his long and active life, dying Jan. 8, 1930.
He is buried in the Prairie Street cemetery. He was
married to Salome Kratz Jan. 19, 1864. One of his
two daughters, Phebe, married A. B. Kolb.

The ten years in Chicago were decisive in Funk's life. Here in 1858 he was converted in a Presbyterian revival, here he met and associated intimately with D. L. Moody (1861-67), to whom he attributed much of the influence which moved him into active Christian service with progressive ideas in Sunday school, evangelism, and religious publication, far in advance of the lethargic mid-century Mennonite (MC) Church of his fathers. His decision to cast his lot with this church (he returned to Bucks County for baptism in 1860, and was ordained as a minister for the struggling Cullom, Ill., congregation some 50 miles south of Chicago in May 1865) and assume aggressive leadership was an event of major significance for the North American Mennonitism far beyond the bounds of his own brotherhood, for besides being a pioneer Mennonite publisher, he played a major role in the immigration and colonization of the Russian Mennonites in the United States and Canada 1873-80, and in effect became the publisher for the Manitoba Mennonites. He did not become a bishop until June 6, 1892 (rendered inactive Jan. 31, 1902, when his active career as a church leader came to an end), but he was by all odds the most influential leader for 30 years (1870-1900), shaping the course of the Mennonite Church.

His base of operation was his publishing house, established at Elkhart as John F. Funk and Brother 1867-75, then incorporated as the Mennonite Publishing Co., 1875-1925, with widely held stock ownership. (Unfortunately a bank failure in 1903, which cost him a personal loss of $40,000, and a fire in 1906 caused the company to become bankrupt in 1906, a blow from which he never recovered, although he continued in business selling book stocks and doing some publishing of reprints of older titles until the age of 90 in 1925.) His great influence through the church paper *Herald of Truth* (German edition, *Herold der Wahrheit* 1864-1902) was supplemented by his wide traveling and speaking, conference work, and personal influence. He gathered a group of progressive younger men around him and made Elkhart the strong center of church leadership and growth. He brought J. S. Coffman, the noted evangelist, to Elkhart as an editor in 1879; John Horsch, a writer and historian, in 1887; G. L. Bender, a mission leader, in 1890. H. A. Mumaw, the ultimate founder of the Elkhart Institute-Goshen College (1894), was attracted. In Elkhart the mission headquarters of the Mennonite Church was established (1892); here the Mennonite Aid Plan was founded (1882); from here the first foreign missionaries were sent out to India (1898) at a meeting presided over by Funk. Here the first relief agency was organized (1897). In the church which Funk founded and of which he was the pastor (1871-1902) the first young people's meeting was established (1890?), and one of the first Sunday schools (1870). In 1872 Funk, with Daniel Brenneman, conducted the first evangelistic services (Masontown, Pa., in 1872) in the Mennonite Church (MC). He wrote the first Sunday-school helps (1880), published the first Sunday-school magazine.

In all these good forward steps Funk was a leading figure, if not the actual innovator, moving cautiously, often with great courage, against much opposition, using the columns of the *Herald* in vigorous promotion.

One of Funk's great contributions was his creative combination of conservatism and progress. He had a deep historical sense and anchored the church firmer in its great historic heritage. He published *Menno Simons' Complete Works* in English (1871) and German (1876) early in his career and the *Martyrs' Mirror* likewise in German (1870) and in English (1886), in addition to a vast amount of historical articles on the Anabaptists and Mennonites (largely by John Horsch), and built up an excellent Mennonite historical library (the core of the Goshen College M.H.L.). He himself wrote *The Mennonite Church and Her Accusers* (Elkhart, 1878), a defense against the attacks of the Reformed Mennonite writer Musser against the Mennonite Church. He stood firmly against the Methodistic type of more emotionalized piety (Brenneman and M.B.C., 1875) and equally vigorously resisted the reactionary type (Wisler, 1871). He guided the church in gradual change down the middle of the road, and is more responsible than any other one man (teamed with J. S. Coffman) for the general character of the Mennonite Church (MC) in the 20th century in its middle-of-the-road position between tradition on the one hand and undirected progress on the other. He also played a wise and good role in preparing the reunion of the Mennonite and Amish bodies, which came to full fruition 1915-25.

Funk's contribution as a publisher is remarkable. His major periodical publications include *Herald of Truth* (1864 until its merger with *Gospel Witness* to form the *Gospel Herald* in 1908), *Mennonitische Rundschau* (1878-1908), *Mennonite Sunday School Quarterly* (1890-1908, several levels). He published in repeated editions the prayer books, hymnbooks, catechisms, and confessions which became the household books of Mennonites (including the Russian Mennonites and the Amish) in the second half of the 19th century.

Funk's role in the great Russian immigration was outstanding. Peter Jansen wrote, "My Father, Cornelius Jansen, always said you were more responsible than any other man." His home in Elkhart was the first stopping place, not only of the 12 delegates from Russia in 1873, but of hundreds of immigrants in 1874 ff., who stayed at his home or were quartered in the Prairie Street Church. He was the channel of contact with U.S. senators and the great railroads. He personally conducted the delegates on their tours to Minnesota, Dakota, Nebraska, and Kansas. He helped to organize the great aid agency, *Mennonite Board of Guardians* (q.v.), of which he served as treasurer for many years. He negotiated reduced rates for transportation by steamship companies and railroads, and raised both loan funds and relief donations for the needy settlers in their first hard pioneer years. His name was a household word among the Mennonites of Manitoba, who had read his *Rundschau* for two generations, and for whom he published their confession, catechism, and hymnbooks for 50 years.

Fortunately Funk's great work was done by 1902, when through unwise methods of working as a bishop, and through mismanagement of his publisher-church relations he was forced into an unworthy retirement at the age of 67 (1902-8). Fortunately also his publishing work was salvaged by the organization of a conference (MC) Publication Board (1908) and Publishing House; the school which he had first encouraged (then opposed), Goshen College, stepped into the place of progressive leadership, and the General Conference (MC) which he long and vigorously advocated (though later failed to support) became the unifying factor in his church.†   H.S.B.

A. C. Kolb, "John Fretz Funk, 1835-1930: An Appreciation," *MQR* VI (1932) 44-55, 250-63; K. Schnell, "John F. Funk, 1835-1930, and the Mennonite Migration of 1873-75," *MQR* XXIV (1950) 199-229; *idem*, "John F. Funk's Land Inspection Trips as Recorded in His Diaries," *MQR* XXIV (1950) 295-311; *ML* II, 19.

Funk, John F., & Brother, *"Booksellers, Publishers and Bookbinders,"* 157 Main St., Elkhart, Ind., the name of the Funk publishing agency 1869-74. It had previously (1864-69) been known as John F. Funk, and was afterward (1875-1925) called the Mennonite Publishing Co., Inc. The brother was Abram K. Funk. It was this firm which published the German *Martyrs' Mirror* in 1870, the English *Complete Works of Menno Simons* in 1871, Dirk Philips' *Enchiridion* in German in 1872, began the Mennonite *Family Almanac* and *Familien-Kalender* in 1870, and published many Mennonite hymnbooks, prayer books, and catechisms. A total of 27 titles published by the firm are listed in Bender's *Two Centuries,* 34-40, all of which are to be found in the Goshen College Library.   H.S.B.

Funk, Joseph (1778-1862), of Singers Glen, Va., a pioneer Mennonite publisher and music teacher in America, established the first Mennonite printing house in the United States in 1847 (see **Joseph Funk Press**). He was the son of Henry Funk and Barbara Showalter, born April 6, 1778, in Berks Co., Pa., and a grandson of Bishop Henry Funk, who came to America in 1719 and became the founder of a long line of Funks. Early in his boyhood the family, 13 children, moved to Rockingham Co., Va., where Joseph spent his lifetime. He married Elizabeth Rhodes, Dec. 25, 1804, and raised five children. His second wife was Rachel Britton; they raised nine children. In 1847 Joseph Funk established a hand printing press in his log springhouse at Mountain Valley (Singers Glen), Va., which has the distinction of being the first Mennonite printing house in the United States. Funk had unusual ability in collecting songbooks, revising sacred melodies, and conducting singing schools. He and his sons organized singing schools by the dozens in at least eleven counties in Virginia.

The writings and compilations of Joseph Funk as far as known include the following seven books and periodicals: (1) *Choral Music* (Harrisonburg, 1816), pp. 88, a collection of German hymns.

(2) *A Compilation of Genuine Church Music* (Winchester, 1832), pp. 208. After the fourth edition the name was changed to *Harmonia Sacra*. This was Funk's most popular and famous songbook. Over 20 editions have been printed, the last edition in 1951. (3) *The Confession of Faith* (Winchester, 1837), pp. 461, containing also Peter Burkholder's "Nine Reflections," translated by Joseph Funk. (4) *A Collection of Psalms, Hymns, and Spiritual Songs* (Winchester, 1847), pp. 364. Reprints: Singers Glen, 1851, 1855, 1859, 1868, 1872; Lancaster, 1862, 1864, 1869. This book was compiled by a committee of Virginia Mennonites and has the distinction of being the first hymnbook to be published on a Mennonite press in America and the first English hymnbook used by American Mennonites. It is sometimes called the *English Mennonite Hymnbook.* (5) *The Reviewer Reviewed* (Mountain Valley, 1857), pp. 309, a theological discussion defending his grandfather Henry Funk's *A Mirror of Baptism* against the review of the same by Elder John Kline, a leader in the (Dunkard) Church of the Brethren. (6) *The Southern Musical Advocate and Singer's Friend* (Mountain Valley), a 16-page monthly periodical produced and published by Joseph Funk & Sons; 21 issues appeared altogether, the first in July 1859, and the last in March 1861. (7) I. and D. Brenneman, *Hymns,* pp. 10. The authors are the noted John M. and Daniel Brenneman (*q.v.*).

Joseph Funk died Dec. 24, 1862. He was a faithful member of the Mennonite Church (probably the Weaver congregation) and was in his day cherished by thousands for his contribution to sacred song. He has left a lasting imprint on the Mennonites of the Shenandoah Valley.   J.A.H.

J. W. Wayland, *Joseph Funk, Father of Song in Northern Virginia* (Dayton, Va., n.d., 1908, reprint from the *Pennsylvania German*); G. P. Jackson, *White Spirituals in the Southern Uplands* (University of North Carolina Press, 1933); J. A. Hostetler, "Joseph Funk: Founder of Mennonite Publication Work, 1847," *Gospel Herald* XL (Dec. 23, 1947); *ML* II, 19.

Funk, Joseph, Press (1847-62), of Singers Glen (formerly called Mountain Valley), Va., established the first Mennonite press in the United States. The press was installed in the top story of a springhouse in 1847. The fourth edition (1847) of *Harmonia Sacra* (*q.v.*) and four other editions (1851, 1854, 1856, 1860) were printed on this press. The second outstanding songbook printed here was *A Collection of Psalms, Hymns and Spiritual Songs* (*q.v.*, 47 and three more editions: 1851, 1855, 1859). Other books published were *A Mirror of Baptism* (1851), a translation of *Spiegel der Taufe* (1744) (Bender, *Two Centuries,* 23); Joseph Funk, *Reviewer Reviewed* (1857) (*op. cit.*, 26); and J. and D. Brenneman, *Hymns* (1859). A periodical, *The Southern Musical Advocate and Singer's Friend* (*op. cit.*, 27), was printed 1859-61. After the death of Joseph Funk, his sons continued the business under the name "Joseph Funk Sons." (The sons were not Mennonites.) In 1878 Ruebush-Kieffer purchased the press, and the Mennonite interests were taken over by J. F. Funk, Elkhart, Ind. The original Funk printery, now in Dayton, Va., continues as Joseph K. Ruebush Co. An imprint of the *Harmonia Sacra* of 1847 lists Solomon Funk as "printer." (For bibliography, see **Funk, Joseph.**)   J.A.H.

Funk, Stephan, a preacher of the Mennonite congregation near Thorn, West Prussia, presumably an immigrant from Moravia, became known through his contact with King Charles XII of Sweden in connection with the siege of Thorn in 1703. When the king heard of Funk and learned that the Mennonites rejected warfare, he ordered Funk to preach a sermon in the camp in his presence and prove his principle of nonresistance from the Bible. Funk complied. After the sermon the king inquired whether all wars were unconditionally condemned in the Scriptures. Funk answered, "If anything could be allowed in the Holy Scriptures, it must be that a king who is attacked in his own realm might defend himself; but that a king march into another realm to conquer and devastate it, for that there is no freedom in the Scriptures; on the contrary, it is absolutely opposed to Christ's teaching." This is recorded by W. Mannhardt on the basis of the church record kept by Heinrich Donner (*q.v.*) at Orlofferfelde.   HEGE.

A. Brons, *Ursprung, Entwickelung und Schicksale der . . . Mennoniten* (Amsterdam, 1912) 312; W. Mannhardt, *Die Wehrfreiheit der Altpreussischen Mennoniten* (Marienburg, 1863) 43 f.; *ML* II, 19.

Funkites, the name given the followers of Bishop Christian Funk (1731-1811), who withdrew from the Franconia (*q.v.*) Conference in 1778 because of his sympathies with the seceding American colonies, while the Conference favored continued loyalty to the British Crown in view of their previous promise (oath) of loyalty. Funk was the son of Bishop Henry Funk (d. 1760) and father of a large Funk (*q.v.*) family in America. He was ordained as a minister in 1756 and as a bishop in 1769.

All went well between Funk and his fellow ministers and bishops until the issue of American independence arose. At first he also was of one mind with them on that issue: nonresistants ought not support a rebellion. But when he read the Pennsylvania constitution, and saw to his great joy that it gave full religious liberty, and even promised not to compel nonresistants to take up arms or to swear an oath, Funk began to look at the matter differently. There were, said he, "already four republics, and perhaps America would be another." He also favored paying a (war) tax to the American government which the other ministers opposed. The climax came in 1778, when Funk was deposed from office by the other bishops of the conference. Funk's relatives and some other supporters persuaded him to become their minister. At first the schismatic "Funkites" held their services in the Franconia meetinghouse on alternate Sundays when it had not been used, but soon they were locked out. In the course of time Funk ordained his brother John as a minister, and his son-in-law, John Detweiler, as a deacon. His older brother Henry, a minister from 1768, also stood with him.

Between 1804 and 1806 the leaders of the Franconia Conference sought to restore Funk to full fellowship in the church, but they refused to recognize the offices of John Funk and John Detweiler. The bishops also wanted to receive Christian Funk as a transgressor, a demand which he was unwilling to comply with. After Funk's death in 1811, the "Funkites" erected four or five church buildings in Montgomery Co., Pa., between 1812 and 1815. But lacking a real leader, the group became progressively weaker and smaller. Funk's brother Henry moved to Virginia, and another Funkite minister, Jacob Detweiler, settled in Ontario, where he served in his office in the Ontario Conference. Two of the Funk meetinghouses were torn down, one was rebuilt and is now used for occasional funerals in the community, and one or two came into the possession of the Church of the Brethren. By the middle of the 19th century the group had disintegrated. Some of the Funkites eventually united with the Church of the Brethren, some with the "Herrites" (Reformed Mennonites, *q.v.*), and a few families found their way back into the Franconia Conference. Apparently some members of these families joined the Oberholtzer group in his secession of 1847 from the Franconia Conference.

From the incomplete records of the Funkite division it appears that Funk was a vigorous and intelligent leader with foresight and ability, but somewhat lacking in humility and patience. On the other hand, history has vindicated Funk's judgment that the American colonies might well become "one more republic"; i.e., that they would win the war with Great Britain for their independence. Between 1778 and 1806 ten Franconia Conference bishops died, and six new ones were ordained; the young bishops who had not been involved in excommunicating Funk were unable to win him back into their fellowship, perhaps partly because of Funk's tendency toward self-justification.   J.C.W.

Christian Funk, *Spiegel für alle Menschen* (Reading, 1813); English edition, *A Mirror for all Mankind* (Norristown, 1814); J. C. Wenger, *History of the Mennonites of the Franconia Conference* (Telford, 1937) 260, 261, 345-51; *ML* II, 19-21.

Furniture. Mennonites as a rule do not have furniture different from their neighbors, with exceptions from time to time when they were transplanted from country to country, and retained and developed patterns of their former home, just as they did in the realm of agricultural (*q.v.*) practices, architectural (*q.v.*) patterns, and other forms of culture. The fact that they usually came from a country with a higher culture into areas where they were pioneers necessitated their producing their own furniture, since markets were not accessible, or their pioneer conditions did not make it possible for them to buy expensive furniture. This must have been the case in Prussia when, during the 16th century, Dutch Mennonite settlers established themselves along the Vistula River, and again when their descendants began to move into Poland and Russia. In the prairie states of America, this tradition was soon given up for various reasons. In the early days in Manitoba, Mexico, and Paraguay, the

Furniture of
Mennonite Home
in Russia

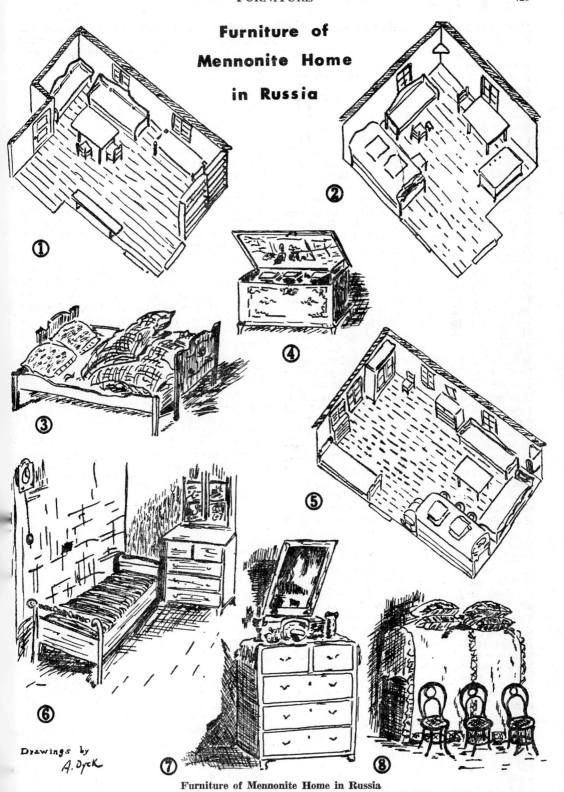

Furniture of Mennonite Home in Russia

1. *Kleine Stube*—Children's room; 2. *Eckstube*—Bedroom; Bench and china cabinet; 7. *Kommode*—Chest of drawers
3. *Schlafbank*—Bed opened for the night; 4. *Truhe*—Dowry 8. *Bett in der grossen Stube*—Bed in parlor.
chest; 5. *Grosse Stube*—Parlor; 6. *Ruhbank und Glasschapp*—

Drawings by A. Dyck

Mennonites continued to make their own furniture after traditional patterns.

The furniture used in traditional Mennonite homes of the Prusso-Russian background is closely related to the pattern of the house. Each room serves a special purpose and has its corresponding furniture, which is always the same. Only slight and gradual deviations occur depending on economic conditions and size of family. Some of the best descriptions of interior arrangements and furniture of this tradition can be found in Arnold Dyck's *Verloren in der Steppe* and Peter Epp's *Eine Mutter,* as well as in the article by W. Schmiedehaus, "Mennonite Life in Mexico" (*Menn. Life,* April 1947, 29).

Entering a traditional Mennonite home of Prussia, Russia, Manitoba, Mexico, and Paraguay through the front door, one enters the front hall (*Vorhaus*), from which one proceeds to the back hall (*Hinterhaus*), which leads into the kitchen and into the *kleine Stube* (see drawing No. 1). This room is usually occupied by day and night by the youngest children, has a table and two beds called the *Schlafbank,* which during the day are used as benches. At night the lid is opened and the benches are pulled out and serve as double beds (see drawing No. 3). The next room is the *Eckstube* (see drawing No. 2). This is the bedroom of the parents. It has a bed in which the bedding is kept, topped by the two pillows. For the night it is pulled out to make a double bed just like the *Schlafbank* (see drawing No. 3). In this room there is also a *Ruhbank,* a bench located under the window and used for sitting and resting, a large traditional dowry chest containing heirlooms, etc. (see drawing No. 4), a table, and some chairs. From this room one proceeds to the parlor or *grosse Stube* (see drawing No. 5), which is used only when exceptional guests come. It contains, right next to the brick stove which heats all three rooms, a bench called the *Ofenbank* which is used for resting. Right above the bench is a traditional Mennonite clock (*q.v.*). At the other end next to the wall is the china closet, called *Glausschaup* (see drawing No. 6), containing traditional china inherited from the parents to which occasionally items are added as a birthday present. Between the windows toward the front yard stands a chest of drawers, above which hangs a large mirror (see drawing No. 7). Toward the inner wall stands a bed filled almost to the ceiling with bedding and topped with pillows (see drawing No. 8); in front of it are some chairs. This is used when guests come. This room also has a table. Next to it in the corner is the wardrobe, called *Kleedaschaup,* where the family's Sunday clothes are kept. The closet is made after patterns dating far back into the early history of the Mennonites in Prussia. Another door from here leads to the front hall. Next to the front hall on the opposite side is the room for the grown boys, called the *Sommerstube,* which contains a bed, table and chairs, and possibly some tools for carpenter work.

All this furniture was made in the home carpenter shops. Not every farmer was a carpenter but some who had the inclination, ability, and time made these pieces of furniture for themselves and also for their neighbors. In some communities there were carpenter shops which served the entire community. This is also the case in Manitoba, Mexico, and South America. Naturally, with economic progress, some families preferred to buy the furniture in use in their respective countries. This was the case to some extent in Russia, but particularly in the United States, and also in Canada. To what an extent the Mennonites of Prussia had retained these patterns or when they disappeared or where modified is still to be investigated. (See also **Architecture.**) C.K.

Fürsorge-Komitee (Guardians' Committee) was the name of the agency established by the Russian government in 1818 to succeed other agencies to supervise the foreign settlements in Russia, and be responsible for their progress and administration. The full name was Guardians' Committee of the Foreign Colonists in the Southern Regions of Russia (German, *Fürsorge-Komitee für die Kolonisten der südlichen Gebiete Russlands*). It had its seat originally at Kherson, later at Ekaterinoslav, and finally at Odessa. It had three branch offices; Ekaterinoslav, Kherson, and Bessarabia. At first the Fürsorge-Komitee was subject to the Ministry of the Interior. In 1837 it became subject to the Ministry of Royal Estates. Both agencies were located in St. Petersburg. In 1871 the Fürsorge-Komitee was abolished and the foreign settlers, including the Mennonites, became subject to the provincial and local authorities of their respective settlements and communities (see also **Government of Mennonites in Russia**). C.K.

A. Ehrt, *Das Mennonitentum in Russland . . .* (Langensalza, 1932); D. G. Rempel, "The Mennonite Colonies in New Russia . . ." (unpublished doctoral dissertation at Stanford University, 1933); Franz Isaac, *Die Molotschnaer Mennoniten* (Halbstadt, 1908).

Fürst, Lorenz, of Bülach, Switzerland, an Anabaptist martyr. Because he taught that "neither the flesh nor the blood of Christ is in the Mass," and said that "he had permitted himself to be rebaptized, and Conrad had baptized him at Wasserberg, and he counted infant baptism as naught, but as false and of no value," he was sentenced on Aug. 17, 1529, at Zug in Switzerland, to be executed by being cast into the sea with bound hands and feet. NEFF.

R. Nitsche, *Geschichte der Wiedertäufer in der Schweiz zur Reformationszeit* (Einsiedeln, 1885) 97-98; ML II, 21.

Fürstenland, a daughter settlement of the Chortitza Mennonite settlement in Russia, was founded 1864-70 and consisted originally of six villages known by the following numbers and names: No. 1, Georgstal, 30 farms; No. 2, Olgafeld, 28 farms; No. 3, Michelsburg, 35 farms; No. 4, Rosenbach, 18 farms; No. 5, Alexandertal, 23 farms; No. 6, Sergeyevka, 20 farms. In 1923 the village Karlovka with 10 farms was added. Each farm consisted of approximately 175 acres. This land was rented from the Grand Duke Michael Nikolaevitch, hence the name "Fürstenland," and was located south of Chortitza in the

Melitopol district, Taurida, volost Verkhne-Rogat-chik. The settlement consisted of approximately 19,000 acres, which was originally rented at the price of one ruble and 25 kopecks per dessiatine, which by the time of World War I was raised to 14 rubles per dessiatine (*ca.* $2.75 per U.S. acre).

The land was under the administration of Moritz Schumacher at Grushevka and had been rented through the mediation of Peter Dyck, a chairman of the Chortitza Agricultural Society, who became the *Oberschulze* of the settlement. Each village had a school at which worship services were also held. Before the emigration to Canada in the 1870's, the Fürstenland Mennonite Church was independent. After Elder Johann Wiebe emigrated to Canada in 1875, with about one thousand persons, Isaac Warkentin was leading minister and the congregation was again a subsidiary of the Chortitza Mennonite Church. In 1910 the Mennonite Brethren at Olgafeld erected a meetinghouse with a seating capacity of three to four hundred. Johann Enns (1850-1934) was leader of the Fürstenland M.B. Church for 40 years. The membership in 1914 was 63. The settlement developed some industries, such as two flour mills and factories of which the Jacob Niebuhr (*q.v.*) factory was most outstanding.

In the great emigration of 1874 ff. from the Ukraine, about 1,100 Fürstenländers migrated to Manitoba, where they settled in the West Reserve, forming about one third of the original settlement.

After the Revolution, in 1924-26, the majority (about 160) of the families of Fürstenland sold their property to families coming from Volhynia and emigrated to Canada, leaving only some 14 Mennonite families in the villages. Soon the collectivization of agriculture was carried through. Before the German invasion of the Ukraine in 1941 some men had been exiled. During the German retreat the Mennonites of Fürstenland made their trip westward on covered wagons; some of them were forcibly sent back by the Russians; the remaining have reached Canada and South America.

C.K.

Jacob Niebuhr Questionnaire; *Mennonite Weekly Review*, Feb. 22, 1951, p. 6; Friesen, *Brüderschaft*; *ML* II, 21.

Fürstenwerder (see **Bärwalde**), a village in the former Free State of Danzig, 12 miles east of Danzig, with a Catholic, a Protestant, and a Mennonite church, on the Elbing Vistula, near the "Danziger Haupt" (see map of Danzig). Fürstenwerder is the name (since about 1830) of an independent Mennonite congregation, which formerly belonged to the "Flemish Mennonite congregation in the Grosse Werder" and was called the "Bärwald'sches Quartier"; from 1809 on was known as Bärwalde and had its own elder (Isaac Schulz, 1809-34).

Since 1768 there has been a meetinghouse in Fürstenwerder, which has been preserved without any important alterations to the present. In that year the bishop of Culm, who in the name of the King of Poland had supreme ecclesiastical authority in the Grosse Werder, had permitted the overgrown Mennonite congregation to erect four meetinghouses, whereas up to this time the Flemish Men-

nonites had only the church built in Rosenort in 1754. The new buildings were begun in Tiegenhagen, Ladekopp, Fürstenwerder, and Heubuden, on the condition that the Mennonites build and perpetually maintain a Catholic chapel on Möskenberg at Petershagen. The buildings were progressing well, when in the summer of 1768 the bishop suddenly forbade and forcibly prohibited their completion. The reason was this: Anna Steffen, the only daughter of Jakob Steffen, a Mennonite resident of Tiegenhagen, was with her own consent abducted by Catholic nuns with aid of the Tiegenhagen priest, taken to Culm, and married to a Pole. Since the girl was still a minor, the parents demanded her surrender, and finding no hearing from the bishop they appealed to the King of Prussia, who had control of the Elbing region as a special right from Poland. The king ordered the bishop to release the girl; but now the bishop visited his wrath on all the Mennonites of the Grossen Werder, by prohibiting the completion of the four buildings, and declared that he would not consent to having them finished until they stopped bothering him about Steffen. At the end of October he gave his consent and the buildings were finished. The Catholic chapel in Petershagen, which was finished at the same time, was burned down by lightning in 1778 and was not rebuilt. The Mennonites terminated their obligation by paying a lump sum.

In 1853 Claas Epp, the Schulze of Fürstenwerder, emigrated to the province of Samara (Am Trakt settlement), followed in 1859 and the following years by the preacher Cornelius Classen and finally also Elder Johann Wiebe to the Alt-Samara settlement in the same province.

The Fürstenwerder congregation was incorporated in 1880. In 1924 it had a membership of 540 souls. According to the *Gemeinde-Kalender* of 1941, the number of souls in 1940 was 556, of whom 450 were entitled to vote, and 106 were unbaptized children. The elder was Jakob Jantzen (preacher from 1894, elder 1911); preachers were Heinrich Dau (ordained 1912), Johannes Dyck (1919), Ernst Dyck (1928), Heinrich Wall (1934); the deacons were Gustav Wiens (1923) and Gustav Schulz (1928). Jakob Jantzen died an accidental death in 1942, and was succeeded as elder in 1943 by Johannes Dyck. The congregation was extinguished by evacuation westward before the advancing Russian army in 1945.

H.G.M.

Ernst Crous, "Vom Pietismus bei den altpreussischen Mennoniten," in *Gesch.-Bl.* XI (1954) 13; *Mitteilungen der Konferenz der ost.- und westpreussischen Mennonitengemeinden*, Nos. 1-3 (September 1943, November 1943, and February 1944, a mimeographed copy in the Research Center at Göttingen); *ML* II, 21 f.

Füsslin, Johann Konrad (1704-75), a Swiss Reformed clergyman and research scholar in history, pastor in Veltheim, canton of Zürich. His writings are distinguished by his wide reading as well as a thorough knowledge of the sources and an objectivity rare at the time. His greater work has the title, *Staats- und Erdbeschreibung der schweizerischen Eidgenossenschaft*. For Anabaptist history two of his works come into consideration:

(1) *Beyträge zur Erläuterung der Kirchen-Reformations-Geschichten des Schweitzerlandes, enthaltende authentische bishero zum theil ungedruckte, zum theil gantz rare Urkunden, öffentliche Vorträge, Gutachten, Ratschlüsse, Manifeste, Missive, Unterredungen, Verträge, Lehrsätze, Confessionen, Schutz- und Streitschriften, Darinnen die Zwistigkeiten der Römisch-Catholischen, der Lutheraner und der Reformierten, wie auch der Wiedertäufer und anderer Sectierer, auf das klarste an den Tag gelegt werden. Nebst Historisch-Critischen Anmerkungen zur Beschützung des Seeligen Reformationswerckes herausgegeben von Johann Conrad Füsslin*, 3 vv. (Zürich and Leipzig, 1741-49).

(2) *Johann Conrad Fuesslins Cämmers des Capitels zu Winterthur neue und unpartheyische Kirchen- und Ketzerhistorie in der mittleren Zeit* (Frankfurt and Leipzig, 1770-74).

The first work contains a mass of historical notices as well as council protocols, orders, and provisions of the Swiss governments concerning the beginnings and the earliest period of the Anabaptist movement, which constitute a valuable supplement to Egli's Aktensammlung. Very worthy of note are the critical notes and commentaries, although in many respects his judgment has been corrected by more recent research.

In the second book the author reveals himself as the Swiss Gottfried Arnold (*q.v.*). Under the collective term "Sonderlinge" he discusses the Manichaeans, Cathars, Albigenses, Bogomiles, Waldenses, Mystics, Beguines, Hussites, Adamites, Taborites, Materialists, Pantheists, etc. He discusses the *Deutsche Theologie* (*q.v.*) at length. The rise of Anabaptism he traces back to Müntzer as he had already done in the earlier work: near the end of 1524, while Müntzer was staying not far from Eglisau, he met with Hubmaier, and especially with Felix Manz, Conrad Grebel, and Wilhelm Reublin. "Here adult baptism was agreed upon." But this is not correct (see **Grebel**). On the whole Füsslin tries to do justice to the Anabaptist movement. He writes, "Some time ago I was involved in a controversy concerning the Anabaptists. The question in dispute is whether the Anabaptists should be reckoned among the anti-Trinitarians and whether Servetus should be reckoned one of them. I denied this categorically and therefore was contradicted by the publisher of the *Musaei Helvetici* and the deceased chancellor von Mosheim. . . . I have in my possession various printed and unprinted Confessions of Faith of the old and the new Anabaptists from Switzerland, Alsace, and the Netherlands, in which they express themselves in such a way on the Trinity of the Godhead, that they can be reckoned among the anti-Trinitarians only with the greatest unreasonableness. . . . Bullinger incorrectly called Servetus an Anabaptist. He erred and did these people (the Anabaptists) a grave injustice. He made the serious mistake of classing all who separated from the Roman Church but did not join the Reformed as Anabaptists" (III, 238).

Anyone who wishes to study the origin and early period of Anabaptism in Switzerland dare not overlook these works of Füsslin. (*ML* II, 22.) NEFF.

G

Gaaikema, a Dutch Mennonite family found in the province of Groningen. Nearly all of them were farmers. Johannes Harkes Gaaikema (1747-1825) and his son Luurt (1786-1848) lived in the hamlet of Gaaikemaweer near Niehove; both were deacons of the Humsterland (*q.v.*) Old Flemish congregation. To the same family belonged Luurt Luurts, a farmer and preacher (1738-87) of the Old Flemish congregation of Houwerzijl (*q.v.*), and also Tiete Popkes, a farmer at Oldehove, preacher 1721, and after 1732 elder of the Old Flemish congregation of Humsterland (Blaupot t. C., *Groningen* I, 131). Tiete Popkes died in 1773. His grandson Tiete Popkes (b. Dec. 25, 1772, at Oldehove, d. soon after 1830) took the family name of Gaaikema as did many of his relatives. This was the ancestor on the maternal side, the paternal ancestor being Harm Gaaikema, a farmer at de Waarden near Grijpskerk. At present two descendants, brothers, are Mennonite pastors: Harm H. Gaaikema, b. 1904 at Noordhorn, who first studied law and then theology, serving the congregations of Dantumawoude 1935-46 and Harlingen 1946- ; and Menno J. J. Gaaikema, b. 1909 at Noordhorn, serving Uithuizen 1933-47 and Zijldijk 1947- .   vdZ.

Gabor Bethlen: see Bethlen Gabor.

Gabrielites, an early Anabaptist group in Moravia and Silesia, led by Gabriel Ascherham (*q.v.*). It began in 1527, merged later with related groups in Moravia (Philipites and Hutterites), broke away again, and entered into many an unpleasant controversy, mainly with the Hutterites, whose practice of community of goods they opposed. The story of this group up to the death of their leader in 1545 is told in the article **Ascherham,** which also reports that toward the end of his life more and more brethren fell away from his spiritualistic leadership, apparently seeking closer ties with the genuine Anabaptist way of life. His minimizing of adult baptism and all the other orders or regulations of a disciplined brotherhood were obviously not to the liking of these less sophisticated brethren. At the end of his life Ascherham is said to have been a "shepherd without sheep."

After Ascherham's death (1545) the group disintegrated. Those who had fled to East Prussia (*q.v.*) in 1535-40 seem to have united with the Mennonites of that area. Those in Silesia most likely joined with the Schwenckfelders, with whom they had many tenets in common. But the greater part of the Silesians returned to Moravia and joined the Hutterites. In Moravia proper some settlements had existed since 1533 (if not earlier) and had weathered the severe persecutions of 1535. At first Ascherham prevented any negotiations with the Hutterites, whom he detested; but when he died, the way was opened to an organic unification of the two Anabaptist groups. Of this the Hutterite chronicles give us a detailed story (*Geschicht-Buch,*

195-200). They report how several Gabrielite brethren had come to the Hutterites to find out about their teachings and the reason for the erstwhile division. "They asked for information about our main tenets (*Hauptartikel*) and received a declaration of five points, concerning (*a*) baptism, (*b*) community of goods, (*c*) marriage, (*d*) authorities or (*e*) false brethren and separation from the world" (text in the *Geschicht-Buch*). After studying these articles and talking them over, the Gabrielite visitors joined the Hutterite community on Jan. 16, 1545, and submitted to the discipline of the entire brotherhood. Still more followed this example; from Silesia alone 300 brethren are said to have come to join with the same group.

Only three Gabrielite groups in Moravia remained independent: in Kreuz near Göding, in Znaim, and in Eibenschitz. In the latter place a debate took place in 1559 with representatives of the Moravian or Bohemian Brethren (from Bunzlau) with a view to possible unification. But these talks eventually failed because the Gabrielites insisted upon adult baptism while the Moravians defended the practice of infant baptism. In 1565 the last three groups also joined the Hutterite brotherhood, and as such ceased to exist as a separate group.   R.F.

Wolkan, *Geschicht-Buch;* Loserth, *Communismus;* W. Wiswedel, "Gabriel Ascherham und die nach ihm benannte Bewegung," *Arch. f. Ref.-Gesch.,* 1931, 100; J. Th. Müller, "Die Berührung der alten und neuen Brüderunität mit den Täufern," *Ztscht für Brüdergesch.,* 1910 (a very important research study); *ML* II, 24 f.

Gäde, Gerhard J., b. in the Molotschna settlement, Russia, attended the Gnadenfeld Zentralschule, taught at Lichtfelde, Molotschna, and later at the Davlekanovo Zentralschule, Ufa. In 1911-15 he taught at the Omsk Zentralschule, Siberia. In 1925 he attended the Mennonite General Conference (Bundeskonferenz, *q.v.*) in Moscow. He was a very gifted educator with artistic inclinations and a severe critic of the weaknesses in Mennonite culture and practice.   C.K.

A. A. Töws, *Mennonitische Märtyrer* (Abbotsford, 1949) 332 ff.

Gadwal Mennonite Brethren Mission Station, India, located in the Gadwal Samista, Raichur District, 100 miles southwest of Hyderabad, was built by the American Baptist Mission, which occupied this field at first, but in 1937 transferred the field and work to the M.B. Mission. On the mission premises are a residence for the missionaries, a church and school building, a hospital with a number of ward buildings, and some smaller buildings.

Resident missionaries stationed here are Mr. and Mrs. A. A. Unruh, Margaret Willems, and Edna Gerdes. The station has for some time been supervised by J. A. Wiebe and by J. J. Dick. Activities include regular church services, a primary school, and a dispensary. The Gadwal field, comprising 1,200 square miles, has a population of 200,000. Response to the Gospel message has been very good, and in 1949 there was a total church membership of 3,500.   J.H.L.

Gaeddert (Gäddertz, Gödert, Goedert, Gederts, Gedert, Geddert) is a Prussian Mennonite family name, the earliest available record of which dates back to 1630. In the *Montauer Dorfbuch* of 1630 appears the name of Wilhelm Gäddertz, together with 20 other Mennonite family names. Montau was the oldest Mennonite settlement of the Sartowitz-Neuenburger lowlands near Culm, dating back to 1567. Since then the name appears occasionally in the records of the Mennonite settlements along the Vistula River in the settlement records of Central Poland and Volhynia, later in those of Russia, and finally in the Mennonite records of North and South America. The church records of the Frisian Church at Montau-Gruppe, of the Frisian and Flemish Church at Schönsee, and of the Frisian Church at Obernessau contain the names "Goedert" and "Geddert."

It seems that the name was difficult to translate. The same author first translates it correctly in the Danzig church records (according to Gustav E. Reimer) as "Gotthard," then incorrectly as "Gerhard" and "Gideon." Various spellings of the name appear in the records.

Dietrich Gaeddert (*q.v.*) was one of the most widely known members of this family. He was a minister of the Alexanderwohl Mennonite Church, Russia, and founder of the Hoffnungsau Mennonite Church near Buhler, Kan. Albert M. Gaeddert, the present pastor of the church, and Gustav R. Gaeddert, an educator, have been active in CPS and MCC work.   G.R.G.

H. Wiebe, *Das Siedlungswerk niederländischer Mennoniten im Weichseltal zwischen Fordon und Weissenberg bis zum Ausgang des 18. Jahrhunderts* (Marburg, 1952) 47, 140, 145, 148, 151-53, 159; G. E. Reimer, *"Die Familiennamen der Westpreussischen Mennoniten"* (Weierhof, 1940) 98, 100; Chr. Hege, "Mennonitenfamilien in Zahlen," in *Menn. Gesch.-Bl.* V (August 1940) 29; Alexanderwohl Church Record (microfilm, Bethel College Historical Library).

Gaeddert, Dietrich (1837-1900), a Mennonite (GCM) minister, was born March 2, 1837, at Alexanderwohl, Russia, the oldest son of Jacob Gaeddert and Elisabeth Ratzlaff, both of Alexanderwohl. His teacher was Heinrich Buller. Gaeddert taught school for eleven years in Paulsheim, Rückenau, and Fürstenwerder, Russia. On June 4, 1856, he was baptized in the Alexanderwohl Mennonite Church and on Dec. 14, 1867, he was elected minister of the church. He married Maria Martens in 1859. Of their thirteen children six died in infancy and the others came with them to America. After the death of his wife in 1874 he married Helena Richert (1858-1953) in 1879. To this union thirteen children were born, of whom two died in infancy.

Gaeddert was chosen delegate to investigate the prairie states and provinces in America for settlement, but was unable to go. In 1874 he became leader of a group of Alexanderwohl immigrants to America who crossed the Atlantic on the *Teutonia* and settled in Harvey, McPherson, and Reno counties, Kansas. He organized the Hoffnungsau Mennonite Church, became elder in 1876, and served the group till his death. The detailed diary of Dietrich Gaeddert, which he kept in Russia and America, is a valuable record pertaining to the coming of the Mennonites to America and the early experiences in this country.

Gaeddert assisted in the founding of Bethel College, Newton, Kan., and was on its board of directors from its founding until his death. He served the Home Mission Committee of the Western District Conference and assisted in organizing a number of congregations of this committee, often serving with baptism and Lord's Supper. He died Dec. 31, 1900, and was buried in the Hoffnungsau cemetery, where the church has erected a memorial.

A.J.D., G.R.G.

"Obituary," *Christlicher Bundesbote*, Jan. 24, 1901, 6-7; *Alexanderwohl Church Record,* Bethel College Historical Library; Dietrich Gaeddert, *Diary.*

Gage County, Neb., is located in the southeastern part of the state, with Beatrice (pop. 12,000), the county seat, near its center. There are two Mennonite (GCM) churches with 512 members (1953), the First Mennonite (328) and Beatrice Mennonite (174). The Beatrice Mennonite Hospital is also located in the county. The Mennonite settlement is concentrated west and largely within a 12-mile radius of Beatrice. A few scattered families live farther west and north extending into Jefferson and Saline counties.

The first Mennonites to buy land in this county were 12 Prussian Mennonite families of Mount Pleasant, Iowa, who settled in Gage County in early 1877. They obtained good quality unimproved land for five to six dollars per acre. In 1878 another group of 34 families settled here, and in 1884, 10 families from Russia. Other families have migrated to the county from Germany and Russia since these early settlements, but not in large numbers. (See **Beatrice** Mennonite Church and **Beatrice** First Mennonite Church, and **Beatrice**, Neb.)   D.P.M.

Gainsborough, a city (1951 pop. 12,604) in east central England, county of Lincoln, in the neighborhood of which a Separatist congregation formed about 1600. Shortly after its inception John Smyth, a former Anglican clergyman and "a man of able gifts and a good preacher," was chosen pastor. Smyth's early writings, which include a kind of church polity entitled *Principles and Inferences Concerning the Visible Church* (1607), reveal that in principle and organization the Gainsborough group closely resembled the Brownist and Barrowist congregations, already forming for more than a decade.

The membership of the congregation included some Separatists who later were among the Pilgrim Fathers. William Bradford in his chronicle, *Of Plymouth Plantation* (1630-50), although he does not mention Gainsborough by name, refers to the original congregation as those who "joined themselves (by a covenant of the Lord) into a church estate, in the fellowship of the Gospel, to walk in all His ways made known, or to be made known unto them, according to their best endeavours, whatsoever it should cost them, the Lord assisting them." The same source states that they held meetings regularly for about a year, "notwithstanding all the diligence and malice of their adversaries, they seeing they could no longer continue in that condition, they resolved to get over into Holland as they could. Which was in the year 1607 and 1608."

The writings of both Bradford and Smyth indicate that the membership was scattered in various towns and villages, "some in Nottinghamshire, some of Lincolnshire, and some of Yorkshire," since the borders of the three counties join near Gainsborough; also, there was no one place of meeting. Shortly after forming, the congregation, for the sake of convenience, divided into two parts, the one gathering at Gainsborough under Smyth, and the other at Scrooby under Richard Clyfton. At the time of leaving for and upon arrival at Amsterdam both groups thought of themselves as belonging to one congregation.

At Amsterdam Smyth and his followers set up a congregation independent of the one already established there in 1593 by the English Separatists under the leadership of Francis Johnson and Henry Ainsworth. Instead they made contacts with the Dutch Mennonites, and several of the group joined them. Smyth himself agreed with their principles and therefore wished to introduce baptism on confession of faith in his congregation. In 1609 he baptized himself, then Thomas Helwys and John Murton, as well as 40 other members of his congregation. This congregation planted on Dutch soil by the Separatists from Gainsborough thus became the original congregation of the Baptists (q.v.). In 1612 Helwys and Murton returned to England with their followers and founded the congregations from which the General Baptists sprang. Most of the followers of Smyth who remained in Amsterdam joined the Mennonite Church after his death.

The Scrooby leaders, arriving at Amsterdam somewhat later than Smyth, broke company with him, due to the contention and the acceptance of what Bradford calls "some errours in the Low Countries." After a year, in 1609, with John Robinson as pastor, they moved on to Leiden. The congregation at Leiden as well as the later Plymouth covenant of the Pilgrim Fathers reveal a close kinship to the mother congregation at Gainsborough. The only evidence of Separatism at Gainsborough after 1608 is recorded by Hanserd Knollys, who states that during the years 1625-29 he knew a Brownist there "who used to pray and expound the Scriptures in his Family, with whom I had Conference and very good Counsel." I.B.H.

W. T. Whitley, ed., *The Works of John Smyth* (London, 1915); S. E. Morison, ed., *Of Plymouth Plantation 1620-1647, by William Bradford, sometime Governor thereof* (New York, 1952); C. Burrage, *The Early English Dissenters in the Light of Recent Research* (1550-1641) I (Cambridge, 1912) 229-35; E. A. Payne, *The Free Church Tradition in the Life of England* (London, 1951), 41-46.

Galahad United Missionary Church, Galahad, Alberta, had a membership of 31 in 1953. D. C. Eby was its pastor.

Galax, Va., the site of Civilian Public Service Camp No. 39, which was approved in May 1942 and was closed in May 1943. Operated by the Mennonite Central Committee, the camp was a National Park Service camp, located 15 miles south of Galax on the Blue Ridge Parkway. When the camp was closed the men were moved to Three Rivers, Cal. M.G.

M. Gingerich, *Service for Peace* (Akron, Pa., 1949) 149-50.

Galenists (Dutch, *Galenisten*) were the followers of the Dutch Mennonite leader Galenus (q.v.) Abrahamsz de Haan. They were also called Lamists (q.v.).

Galenus Abrahamsz de Haan (*Geleyn de Haen*), physician and preacher of Amsterdam, was born Oct. 8, 1622, at Zierikzee, Zeeland, the Netherlands. His parents were Abraham Geleynsz and Katrijntje Gillis, the latter a granddaughter of Gillis van Aken (von Aachen). In Zierikzee Valerius de Schoolmeester had died as an Anabaptist martyr, who in his book *Proba Fidei* (1568) asserted that man can contribute to his cleansing from sin toward an evangelical perfection. Galenus also later emphasized sanctification.

The Mennonite congregation of Zierikzee avoided taking sides in the controversy between the Flemish and Frisians and published a booklet along these lines: *Een Christelijcke Proeve ende overlegginge ofte rekeninge, waerin dat allen Broeders ende Susters vermaendt worden tot een scherp ende neerstich ondersoec haers selfs* (1570). Since they did not take sides they were called *stilstaanders* by the others and were banned both by Flemish and Frisians. Galenus also did not consider as Mennonites only those who subscribed to confessions of faith. He insisted that each had the freedom not to sign those articles of faith which are not prerequisite for salvation. The Zierikzee congregation had a specific way of life. One spoke little and deliberately and adhered to simplicity of dress and household furnishings. Galenus also emphasized a way of life of earnestness and simplicity. François de Knuyt, elder of the congregation, who wrote the book *Corte Bekentenisse onses geloofs* (1618?), taught young Galenus, who later concluded from this book that not every word of the Bible has the same value and that only the sayings of Christ are the Word of God.

After completing the Latin school Galenus went to Leiden in 1642 to study medicine. Here he met Pieter Jansz Moyer, elder of the Flemish church, who in 1626, when he was still a Mennonite minister in Amsterdam, had been the coauthor of the *Olive Branch,* the confession which had united the Frisian, Flemish, and High German Mennonite groups. This contact must have strengthened Galenus' desire to see all Mennonites united. On March 2, 1645, he was graduated as Doctor of Medicine.

Early in 1646 Galenus began practicing medicine in Amsterdam, and on Sept. 16 he married Saertghen Bierens, a daughter of Abraham Dircksz, who was also a coauthor of the *Olive Branch.* In 1648 he was elected preacher by the United Mennonite

Church which was meeting in the "Het Lam" church, the present Singelkerk. When he accepted the ministry, doubts had already arisen regarding his orthodoxy in matters pertaining to the doctrine of satisfaction. Galenus left the impression that the death of Christ was more a proof of the truth of his teaching than an act of satisfaction, which view had also been expressed by some martyrs.

One of the first tasks confronting the young minister was to reply to the Waterlanders, who were proposing closer co-operation between the two groups. They had suggested in 1647 that each group should retain the freedom to formulate its own beliefs, avoid disputes along these lines, but they would have unity through the Word of God in the Bible. Although such a proposal would have been acceptable for Galenus a few years later, he then, in March 1649, wrote a letter declining such an invitation. He must have done so because he still saw the Waterlanders through the eyes of the Flemish, who considered them too tolerant toward non-Mennonites.

Soon after this he was delegated to Texel to defend Elder Claes Arentsz, who in a dispute with the Reformed had aroused the anger of the Calvinists by speaking slightingly of infant baptism. This mission shows that he had the confidence of his coministers. In June of that year he was present at a meeting of the delegates of Flemish congregations at Haarlem which strongly opposed union with the Waterlanders. These experiences must have raised the question in Galenus to what degree elders and congregations may exercise authority. His doubt whether any human being or any human authority ever could determine what someone else had to believe was intensified through his association with the Collegiants. They formed a group in Amsterdam under the leadership of Adam Boreel, whom Galenus befriended, which did not recognize any church as the true church of Christ. Among the Collegiants, many of whom considered the "college," a voluntary organization of "interdenominational Christendom," above their own special church, were also Socinians (q.v.). Those who thought that Galenus was also Socinian accused him in 1655 in a pamphlet Commonitio of this despised and feared heresy. In spite of the fact that on Easter Monday 1655 Galenus declared that not in a single issue in which the Anabaptists differed from the Socinians did he "fully" agree with the latter, the suspicion remained. A meeting of the ministers and deacons of the Lamist congregation became necessary.

Before this meeting took place Galenus and David Spruyt had on Jan. 11, 1657, presented to their coministers the "Nineteen Articles," in which they discussed the question whether any church could claim to be the true church of the Lord. The authors denied this possibility and refused to bind the conscience of human beings to the authority of an office, whose bearers were fallible men, to definite doctrines formulated by men, and to ordinances which are always administered by men. These views were exactly the opposite of what a group of ministers of the Lamist congregation considered sacred. They thought that the confessions which had been written in the beginning of the 17th century were the exact summary of the faith which all Mennonites had confessed from the beginning. Galenus pointed out that the martyrs had not died for a faith in which there had been no deviation and that in the writings of Menno Simons a change in the concept of the church is noticeable. He preferred to use the Bible as the guide for faith and life and to let every man interpret it.

An attempt to solve the tensions caused by this development was made at a general conference of Mennonite congregations held in June 1660 at Leiden under the chairmanship of Thieleman Jansz van Braght, at which it was decided to ask Galenus and Spruyt to give up their views or to discontinue their ministry. The two accused men, however, refused to accept this verdict, believing that only their congregation could dismiss them and not a meeting of congregations. An attempt to have the ministers of the Amsterdam congregation deprive them of their office was unsuccessful since many members shared their views.

It seemed for a time that the Concept van Verdrag of Jan. 31, 1662, had restored peace. However, two newly elected ministers caused a new outbreak of unrest. Pieter van Locren, who shared Galenus' views, preached on Oct. 1, 1662, that in the Final Judgment the question would not be what man had believed, but what man had done. On Oct. 15 Samuel Apostool, who represented the other side, stated that no one could ever do enough good works to be justified in the sight of God and that only faith in the satisfaction through Christ could save men. In the afternoon service Galenus warned against this "misleading" teaching which might cause people to stop wrestling with sin. The tumult which resulted from these discussions in the pulpit in Amsterdam spread throughout all Mennonite congregations in Holland, and even in foreign countries sides were taken for or against Galenus.

Laurens Hendricksz, a deacon of the Lam congregation and a strong opponent of Galenus, appealed to the court of Holland to have Galenus banned from the country because of Socinian views. This failed, as did other attempts to have him removed, because the majority of the members of the congregation favored Galenus. The final stage of the disagreement, which a contemporary satirically called the Lammerenkrijgh (War of the Lambs), centered around the Lord's Supper. Galenus was willing to admit everyone regardless of possible deviations in religious concepts as long as he lived an irreproachable life. His opponents refused to admit those who in their estimation did not fully believe in the vicarious death of Christ. There was also a difference of opinion regarding the support of widows and orphans of former ministers. When the burgomaster, who was asked to help straighten out the difficulty, did not succeed in restoring the peace, one fourth of the members of the congregation rented a building at the end of May 1664, which they arranged for a church. On June 22 the first service was held in this church and thus a new congregation was organized. Since the building in which they worshiped was known as "de Zon," the group became known as Zonists. For a long time Galenus tried to win the Zonists back to his congregation. Since he did not succeed, there was now no reason why his congregation should not unite with the Waterlanders. They, like Galenus, considered the general confessions as human formulations of faith and practiced tolerance regarding deviating views which could be based on the Bible. Thus the Amsterdam Waterlander congregation which met at the "Toren" (Jan Rodenpoortstoren) united with the Lamist congregation on June 1, 1668. This example was followed by other Waterland and Flemish congregations.

The Zonists, too, eventually attracted some Waterlanders to them. On July 18, 1674, the Mennonite congregations which had sided with Apostool united in the Zonist Sociëteit, which was based on the *Oprecht Verbondt van Eenigheyt* of 1664. This *Verbondt* takes the general Mennonite confessions as a basis and states that no ministers who do not agree with them can be admitted to congregations of the Sociëteit. On Nov. 27, 1674, a Lamist Sociëteit was also organized for mutual assistance in matters pertaining to vacancies and religious instruction. Galenus wrote the catechism for this Sociëteit, *Anleyding tot de kennis van de Christelijke Godsdienst* (1677).

Gradually all Dutch Mennonite congregations belonged either to the Zonists or Lamists. When the Lamist and Zonist congregations in Amsterdam finally united in 1801 the unity of the Dutch Mennonites of the middle of the 16th century was restored. This happened on the basis advocated by Galenus, that subscribing to a formulated confession of faith is unnecessary and that each congregation practice complete autonomy.

In 1680 the Lamist congregation of Amsterdam authorized Galenus to train preachers. In 1692 a training school for ministers was established, of which Galenus was instructor until his death (April 19, 1706). This training school developed into the present Mennonite Theological Seminary. Outstanding students of Galenus were Abraham Verduyn, Joannes Houbakker, and Adriaen Spinniker.

The foundation of Galenus' basic beliefs is the Bible, in which the New Testament gets preference above the Old. The Bible is necessary for salvation and is the rule for faith and life. The human mind illuminated by God is in position to understand the true meaning of the Bible; obscure parts must be interpreted in accordance with the teachings of Christ, whose holy and blameless life is the foundation for faith. The Bible is also the source for his statement of the characteristics of God. Most important is the experience of God's fatherly love and for that reason the knowledge of God can never be purely intellectual. It must be coupled with trust, in fact even a sacred and pure "being in love" with God.

Christ is the Son of God, but Galenus does not want to discuss His possible oneness with the Father,

the relationship of His two natures, and the secret of His Incarnation, because Christ Himself was satisfied with the simple statement in Matt. 16:16. God anointed His Son with the Holy Spirit so that He could save the world through His teaching. His teaching includes claims and promises. Galenus strongly stresses the way of life required by God. He devoted the book *Christelijke Zedekonst,* which was published after his death, to this topic. God's promise is in harmony with His divine nature, which men can approach step by step. He elaborated on this in his exegesis on the Beatitudes entitled *Acht trappen ter Saligheyd*. This thought he likely borrowed from Coornhert. The potent means for achieving this is prayer which draws divine grace to the one who is praying. The experience of this grace is for him the center of spiritual life. To illustrate this he used selections from letters of the martyrs which he added to two of his books. His *Verhandeling van de Redelijk-bevindelijke Godsdienst* demonstrates how strongly he emphasized experience.

Galenus did not develop a special church concept. All who possess a genuine faith and obedience to God and are reborn through His Spirit belong to those whom Christ is gathering about Him. The best description of this he found in Erasmus' *Ratio seu methodus compendiosa perveniendi ad veram theologiam* (*Opera* V. Col. 84 b-d). The Mennonite congregations are to strive to attain this state. The leaders are to take a position of serving, and not ruling or certainly not of rank. It is the right and duty of every Christian to teach and preach after a reasonable preparation, upright living, practice of knowledge, and after an express call of the entire congregation, as he stated in a writing against Laurens Hendricksz. Through baptism, which is a publicly given proof of the acceptance of Christianity, one joins the general Christian Church and not any particular congregation. Water baptism is not necessary for salvation; the only prerequisite for that is baptism by the Holy Spirit, but it is helpful because it reminds the Christian that he has committed himself to lead a God-pleasing life. The Lord's Supper is not essential either but it aids in remembering the inexpressible love of God which was most gloriously revealed in the death of Christ on the cross. At the end of life the Christian expects judgment over what he has done during his life. The disobedient will receive punishment depending on the degree of unrighteousness. Those who have had unwavering faith shall through grace receive eternal life.

Galenus' writings appeared as follows: *Negentien Artikelen* with "Nader Verklaringe" and "Wederlegginge van Laurens Hendricksz" in 1659; *Brief aan C.S.* (Claes Stapel), 1677; *Anleyding tot de kennis van de Christelijke Godsdienst,* 1677; *Kort Begrijp,* 1682; *Beknopt vertoog van de gelijkluijdende Getuygenissen der Heilige Schrift,* published in 1684, contains Bible references for the two previously mentioned writings. A dedicatory sermon which Galenus preached for the new church at Zaandam, *Anspraak an de Vereenigde Doopsgezinde*

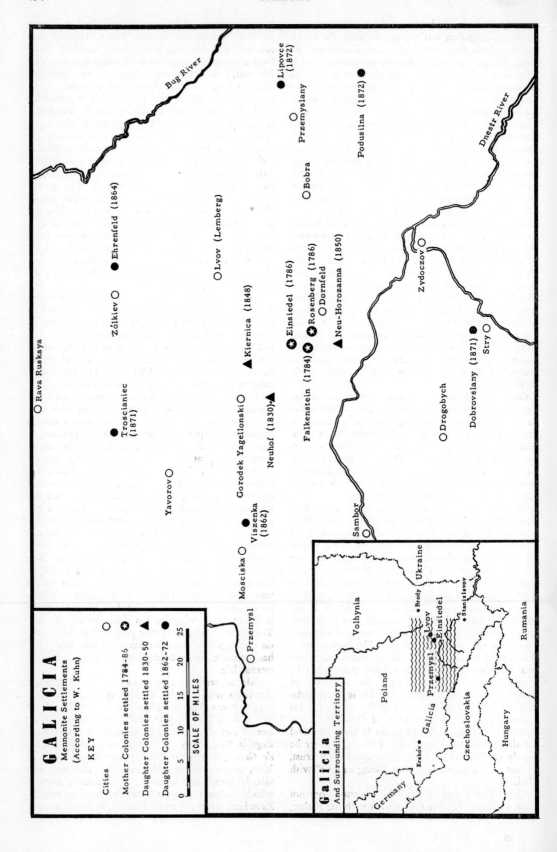

GALICIA
Mennonite Settlements
(According to W. Kuhn)

KEY

○ Cities

Mother Colonies settled 1784-85

Daughter Colonies settled 1830-50

Daughter Colonies settled 1862-72

SCALE OF MILES
0   5   10   15   20   25

Galicia
And Surrounding Territory

Gemeente te Zaandam, to which he added *Acht trappen ter Saligheyd* and *Tegens den Indrang van het Hedendaagze Pausdom* (possibly written by Adam Boreel), was published 1687. His most important work is *Verdédiging der Christenen, die Doopsgezinde genaamd worden, beneffens Korte Grondstellingen van hun gelove en leere,* which appeared 1699. After his death three additional writings of his were published (in 1707) by Wilhem van Maurik: *Veertien Predikatien over de gelijkenis van den Verloren Zoon, Christelijke Zedekonst,* and *Verhandeling van de Redelijk-bevindelijke Godsdienst.*† H.W.M.

Inv. Arch. Amst. I, Nos. 667, 700, 701, 797; II, Nos. 780, 838, 905, 1185-87, 1244, 1301, 1304, 1321, 1393-94, 1398, 1403, 1522, 1762, 1764, 2043-46, 2629, 2630, 2694, 2818; II, 2, Nos. 259, 588; *DJ* 1837, 45, 104, 107; 1840, 65 f.; *DJ* 1850, 88 ff.; *Doopsgez. Lectuur* 1858, 88 ff.; *DB* 1863, 137, 147; 1873, 142; 1875, 27 f.; 1884, 34; 1887, 121; 1888, 103 f.; 124; 1892, 104; 1900, 1 ff., 88; 1901, 119 ff.; 1902, 89, 94 ff.; 1909, 158; 1916, 148 ff., 158 ff.; 1918, 49 ff.; *Catalogus Amst.,* 117, 133, 153, 207, 217, 230, 242, 257, 258; *Biogr. Wb.* III, 166-71; H. W. Meihuizen, *Galenus Abrahamsz* (Haarlem, 1954); K. O. Meinsma, *Spinoza en zijn kring* ('s Gravenhage, 1896); S. Cramer, "De vereeniging der twee Amsterdamsche gemeenten in 1801," *DB* 1898; C. B. Hylkema, *Reformateurs* (Haarlem, 1900, 1902); W. J. Kühler, *Het Socinianisme in Nederland* (Leiden, 1912); J. Lindeboom, *Stiefkinderen van het Christendom* ('s Gravenhage, 1929); C. W. A. Roldanus, *Zeventiende-eeuwsche Geestesbloei* (Amsterdam, 1938); N. van der Zijpp, *Geschiedenis der Doopsgezinden in Nederland* (Arnhem, 1952); besides these see *Catalogus Amst.,* 113-33, for the collection of pamphlets; *ML* II, 26-29.

Galicia, until World War I a part of the Austro-Hungarian Empire, thereafter Polish until 1939. About 3,300 German families, including 28 Mennonite families, settled in the vicinity of Lemberg (*q.v.*), when Emperor Joseph II invited colonization in the patent of Sept. 17, 1781. They came for the most part from the Palatinate. The oldest church record states that they came from various parts of Germany, and were of Swiss origin. In 1784 they lived in three newly laid out neighboring communities, Einsiedel (18), Falkenstein (7), and Rosenberg (3 families). All three places were in the county of Szczerzec (Shchirets), about three miles southwest of Lemberg.

These Mennonites were assured of religious liberty and freedom from military service by a decision of the chancellory, which was announced to the government of Galicia and which designated the following conditions:

(1) They were to be treated as Lutherans, since their case was not regulated by a public law, but they were silently admitted as settlers without being required to join one of the recognized creeds.

(2) Like other non-Catholics they would be permitted to build their own little church as soon as they had 100 families.

(3) They and their descendants, as long as they remained Mennonites, should be exempt from military duty, but no other Mennonite immigrants would be admitted; no member of a tolerated church was permitted to join the Mennonite congregation (*Menn. Bl.,* 1858, 51; 1887, 37).

Some of the new colonists were disturbed by political conditions. Among the native population a conspiracy against the new settlers threatened to grow, and it was feared that it would not be possible to buy more land later. Therefore eleven families, including perhaps all the Amish, sold their possessions and migrated across the border into Russia, to the Hutterian Brethren from Hungary and Moravia, who had already settled in Vishenka, province of Chernigov. They did not stay here long, but soon settled in the province of Volhynia. Nearly all of their descendants emigrated to America in 1875.

The Mennonites remaining in Galicia prospered. In 1800 there were at least 87 members, probably about 100 souls in 15 or 16 families. Their exemption from military service, though sometimes threatened by subordinate officials, was always confirmed by the authorities; this happened in 1812, 1828, 1832, and 1848. After the introduction of universal military service they had the right, as in Prussia, to choose noncombatant service.

Their numbers grew rapidly through their high birth rate; in 1868 their preacher Johannes van der Smissen gave the membership as over 80 families with 400 souls. The official census, which usually reported figures too low, shows 61 families with 362 persons. For the increase subsidiary settlements were founded; in 1830 at Neuhof with about 500 acres, divided into 12 farms; in 1848 at Kiernica with 3,200 acres and Horozanna with 740 acres; in 1864 Ehrenfeld-Blyszczyvody with 2,500 acres, and besides these a number of estates which several families took up and divided. These subsidiaries sometimes formed congregations in themselves.

In 1878-83 a new emigration took place. Seventy-five families, half of the settlement, emigrated to America, principally to Kansas and Minnesota. These were on the whole the poorer members of the congregation.

The remaining members now began to rent land in addition to what they purchased. Between 1866 and 1870 four families moved in. The official report states that there were in Austria-Hungary 490 Mennonites in 1890, 497 in 1910; but these figures are too low. In 1914 there were about 600 Mennonites in the country—200 children and 400 baptized members. They were scattered in more than 100 localities. About one half were leaseholders and had leased over 30,000 acres. The others owned a total of over 130,000 acres. Several young men had adopted city vocations. Over 30 had attended the Gymnasium or Realschule, and about 12 the university.

Religious services and schools for children were at first held in private homes. In 1816 a school was built at Einsiedel and services held there; in 1839 the school was rebuilt as a church. In the subsidiary congregations services were held in the homes of the preachers; some meetinghouses were also erected—Neuhof 1865, Kiernica 1860 (*Menn. Bl.,* 1887, 39), Ehrenfeld-Blyszczyvody 1865. In 1914 there were meetinghouses in Einsiedel, Neuhof, and Kiernica. Services were held in each about six times annually. In 1909 a legally incorporated congregation was formed, called Lemberg-Kiernica (*q.v.*). In 1911 a house was bought in Lemberg containing a chapel, a parsonage, an office, and living quarters for the chairman (*Kurator*) of the church council. In 1910 an association was organized with the name "Mennonit," to promote the cultural and social interests of the Galician Mennonites.

Since in Austria civil marriages were not recognized, the ministers were obligated to keep exact records of births, marriages, and deaths, which were state documents. From the beginning of the settlement until the accession of Francis Joseph these books were kept by Catholic parish priests; but most Protestant churches kept their own in addition. The Mennonite church records were begun about 1805. They were the most valuable treasure in the Mennonite archives. In April 1913 the Galician Mennonites began the publication of the *Mennonitisches Gemeindeblatt für Oesterreich* (*q.v.*). World War I early prevented its further publication.

In the 1880's and toward the end of the 19th century a considerable number of Galician Mennonite families emigrated to the United States. They constituted the major portion of five congregations of the G.C.M. Church, namely, Arlington and Hanston, Kan., Butterfield and Westbrook, Minn., and Perry, Okla. The Hanston congregation was the first, established in 1885; it bore the name "Einsiedel" 1885-1952. In 1880 and the years immediately following, 70 Galician families out of 144 left for America, a total of 369 persons out of 718 in Galicia in 1880.

World War I brought much tribulation and suffering to the Galician Mennonites, since this area was repeatedly in the battle zone. Numerous members lost their lives or disappeared, and there was much destruction of property. The Polish-Ukrainian war (1918-19) and the Bolshevik invasion of 1920 added to the troubles. Austrian sovereignty came to an end in November 1918, and Galicia became a part of the new Polish state in May 1919. Relations between the Polish government and the Mennonites were always very good. In 1925 a home for students (*Schülerheim*) was established in Lemberg, led by Mr. and Mrs. Wilhelm Schroeder from the Molotschna settlement in Russia, in which most of the children of the widely scattered families lived while they attended school in Lemberg.

The first theologically trained (partly) and supported minister was Heinrich Pauls, who served 1908-20. He was followed by Pastor Gsell 1920-27. The church then paid for the theological training of Arnold Bachmann, who served from 1932 until the expulsion of the Germans from the Lemberg area in 1939. In that year the congregation had a population of about 550 souls living in 100 different localities. Through mixed marriages many husbands and wives as well as children were Catholics.

The economic and occupational life of the Galician Mennonites underwent great changes after 1885. The main settlements originated in 1784-1830 and daughter settlements were established in 1830-85. The period 1885-1918 marked the disintegration of the old settlements. After half of the Mennonites had gone to America, others began to occupy large estates, mostly as renters. Of the 116 Mennonite families in Galicia in 1914 half were renters and only one sixth lived in the original settlements, while in 1884 half of them had been living there. Occupations other than farming, such as teaching, law, and medicine, became common. With an increased number receiving higher education, more and more moved into cities. Many adopted the Polish culture. Intermarriage with other Protestants and even Catholics became common. Many efforts were made to counteract these disintegrating forces. Particularly the Lemberg church, the "Schülerheim," the social organization (Geselligkeitsverein Mennonit), and the *Gemeindeblatt* served this purpose.

World War II quickly brought an end to Galician Mennonitism. In 1939, as a result of the Russo-German treaty, Lemberg and the surrounding territory was taken by Russia and all Germans were evacuated. Beginning in late September 1939 and ending by Jan. 1, 1940, all the Galician Mennonites were resettled in the region of Thorn and Posen in West Poland, by then occupied by the Germans. When the Russian armies in 1945 defeated the Germans and occupied this territory also, the Galician Mennonites again had to flee westward into Western Germany. About 30 per cent of the entire group lost their lives in this period.

The remnant of the Galician Mennonites have resettled with the Danzig Mennonites in Uruguay (1951), where they have held together as a religio-cultural segment in the several congregations there.

H.Pa., C.K.

P. Bachmann, *Mennoniten in Kleinpolen, 1784-1934. Gedenkschrift zur Erinnerung an die Einwanderung der Mennoniten nach Kleinpolen (Galizien) vor 150 Jahren. Im Auftrage der Mennonitengemeinde zusammengestellt* (Lemberg, Verlag der Lemberger Mennonitengemeinde, 1934); attached to this book in a separate folder is *Stammbäume der mennonitischen Familien in Kleinpolen;* "Erste Nachrichten von unseren Rücksiedlern aus der Lemberger Gemeinde," *Menn. Bl.,* January 1940; "Die Rücksiedlung der Neuhöfer," *ibid.;* "Die schweizerische Herkunft der Galizischen Mennoniten," *Der Mennonit* II (1949) 74 f., 94-96; W. Kuhn, "Swiss-Galician Mennonites," *Menn. Life* VIII (January 1953) 24; Martin Schrag, "Swiss-Volhynian Mennonite Background," *Menn. Life* IX (October 1954) 156; *Naamlijst* 1787, 63; *DB* 1865, 95-108; *ML* II, 29 f.

Galle (Gally), a South German Mennonite family of Swiss origin. An Anabaptist preacher with the name Gally participated in the religious disputation on Jan. 16, 1613, at Wädenswyl in the canton of Zürich and was later sentenced to galley slavery. As far as is known Peter Gally or Galle was the only member of the family to emigrate to the Palatinate; as a young man he settled in Erbesbüdesheim near Alzey. (Uncorroborated tradition has it that bearers of the name went down the Rhine as far as the Netherlands.) Peter Galle probably had only two sons, one of whom, Peter, took over the Geistermühle in 1734. He was married to Anna Kolb of Wolfsheim (probably the younger sister of Dielman and Martin Kolb) and had nine children, all of whom married Mennonites and settled in the vicinity with the exception of Peter, who is said to have emigrated to America. The family is found chiefly in the Uffhofen and Weierhof communities and has produced some important preachers: Peter Galle, d. 1762; Jakob (1734-1801); Johannes (1766-1838); Peter (1758-1825). Today (1953) there are about ten Galle families with about 50 souls living in the Palatinate and Hessen. On Sept. 12, 1850, Jakob Galle, the great-grandson of the first miller, emigrated to America from the Geistermühle with his children. Kansas has several families with this name.   C.G.

Müller, *Berner Täufer;* S. Geiser, *Die Taufgesinnten-Gemeinden* (Karlsruhe, 1932) 372.

Galle, Jakob (1732-1801), of Uffhofen (*q.v.*), Germany, a preacher of the Mennonite congregation at Erbesbüdesheim (*q.v.*) 1762, elder 1767, who dedicated the new church at Sembach, Jan. 1, 1778 (Brons, 216), did much to sustain and revive his congregation. His son Johannes (1766-1838), "a man of zeal for the customs and discipline of the fathers" (*Menn. Bl.,* 1855, 52), was preacher of the congregation of Oberflörsheim (*q.v.*). He also served many years as elder of the church at Weierhof (*q.v.*), but separated from it and the other large congregations in Hesse and the Palatinate when they began to engage educated ministers for a salary. He also opposed the introduction of the new hymnal and catechism. He apparently clung to the old *Ausbund* (*q.v.*), for in his letters he frequently lamented that the martyrs' hymns were being abandoned. Van Braght's *Martyrs' Mirror* he valued very highly. He must have been a gifted speaker. His extensive correspondence with brethren in America, Switzerland, Bavaria, and Alsace reveals an unusual knowledge of the Bible. His most faithful adherents he found in Heppenheim a.d.W., Oberflörsheim, Uffhofen, Kühbörncheshof, and Neudorferhof. These five congregations formed a close union under his leadership, published the Deknatel catechism and the 35 questions and answers by Gerrit Roosen anew, held their own meetings, and energetically resisted all innovations (mixed marriages, foreign mission, etc.). After the death of Galle this division among the Palatine-Hessian congregations gradually disappeared.   NEFF.

A. Brons, *Ursprung, Entwicklung und Schicksale der . . . Mennoniten* (Amsterdam, 1912); *ML* II, 30.

Galleys, long, narrow, two-masted medieval war vessels with 26 benches for oarsmen, on each of which five galley slaves sat in chains to perform their arduous task. As a rule they were criminals condemned for life to this unbearably hard work. Punishment on the galleys was one of the severest penalties imposed by the seafaring peoples like France and Italy. It was also used in punishing heresy. France was the first to do this in condemning the Huguenots to lifelong galley service. Anabaptists also shared this sad fate.

In 1540, 90 Anabaptists were taken from prison in Falkenstein (*q.v.*) in Austria to Trieste by King Ferdinand, to be delivered as galley slaves to the Doge of Venice, Andrea Doria. They managed to escape. Twenty were recaptured and ended their lives at the galleys (Beck, 147; see also **Aschel-**

berger). On May 12, 1562, at Utrecht Willem Willemsz was condemned to six years of galley service (Vos, 240).

Nearly 75 years later in the canton of Zürich (Switzerland) three Anabaptists, Hans Landis, Galli Fuchs, and Stephan Zehender, were sentenced to the galleys and were taken bound to the French ambassador in Solothurn, where they were freed with the aid of their brethren in Bern (Müller, 216). In the canton of Bern punishment at the galleys for Anabaptists was expressly rejected; but in 1648 it was applied against two Anabaptists, and in 1671 it was actually carried out against six. In two years they returned home. In 1714 five others were sent to the galleys. Two of them died at sea, but the other three were released in January 1716 at the intervention of the Dutch Mennonites. When in the following year four were again sentenced in Bern to service as galley slaves, the States General in Holland intervened and had them freed.

The sentence of galley service remains a blot of religious intolerance and violent persecution on the record of the Protestant states.   NEFF.

Beck, *Geschichts-Bücher;* Müller, *Berner Täufer,* 215-32; *Menn. Bl.,* 1913, 15; J. Huizinga, *Stamboek van Samuel Peter en Barbara Fry* (Groningen, 1890) 119; *DB* 1906, 6; K. Vos, *Menno Simons* (Leiden, 1914); *Inv. Arch. Amst.* I, Nos. 1250, 1254a, 1371, 1375-85, 1780-82; *ML* II, 26.

Gallitz (also *Gollitz,* now *Skalica*) is a county and village (pop. 600) in the former Znaim (Znojmo) district of Moravia between Austerlitz (Slavkov) and Stiegnitz, four hours from Znaim. In 1563 the Anabaptists erected a Bruderhof there, which became one of the chief Hutterite households (*Geschichts-Bücher,* 215). In the Bohemian revolt it was severely damaged by Dampierre's troops in 1619, and again in 1623 and 1662.   LOSERTH.

Wolkan, *Geschicht-Buch,* 314, 539, 592, 649, 658 f.; Beck, *Geschichts-Bücher,* 215, 418, 504; *ML* II, 34.

Gallneukirchen in Upper Austria was shortly after 1530 the center of a live Anabaptist movement. (Wolkan, *Lieder,* 24.)   vDZ.

Gallus, Carolus (1530-1616), a Dutch Roman Catholic priest at Deventer, then Reformed pastor, deposed as priest in 1561 for heresy, at the request of Count Johan of Nassau undertook the task of introducing the Reformation in Gelderland in 1578. He was appointed professor of theology in the University of Leiden. Released from his position in 1592, he became a Reformed preacher at Oldenbroek, where he died. He was a violent antagonist of Anabaptism. Two of his writings bear witness of this: (1) *Lehre des Christelicken geloovens in veer boecken tegen den wedertöpern erdommen* (Bremen, 1577); and (2) *Malleus anabaptistarum. Een hamer op dat hoeft aller wederdoperschen secten* (Arnhem, 1606). (*ML* II, 34.)   K.V.

Gallus Kleermaecker (tailor), an Anabaptist martyr, who was executed at Antwerp in 1573 together with Sijntgen van Rousselare (*q.v.*) and Maeyken Gosens (*q.v.*). The *Martyrs' Mirror* gives a letter of consolation and admonition, which is signed,

"By me your weak brother and servant, to the utmost of my ability." (*Mart. Mir.* D 644-46, E 695-97.)   NEFF.

Gamerslach, Jacques van de, a Dutch Mennonite preacher of the Flemish congregation at Leiden. In the afternoon service held on April 27, 1664, after a communion service had been held in the forenoon, T. J. van Braght (*q.v.*), elder of Dordrecht, preached a sermon. Then before the whole congregation van de Gamerslach made a confession of his faith and was thereupon ordained as elder (*leraer in den vollen dienst*) by the laying on of hands by van Braght. Before this time he had been a preacher. After July 23, 1680, his name is no longer found in the records; so we may assume that he died about that time. Van de Gamerslach, who took a strict stand, e.g., repudiating marriage outside the church, successfully managed the union of his congregation with the conservative Zonists (*q.v.*). He was one of the representatives of Leiden who signed the *Oprecht Verbond van Eenigheydt* in 1674, and was one of the *buitenmannen* (leaders from outside) called in to settle the schism at Utrecht 1661 against W. van Maurik (*q.v.*) and his friends, when he likewise represented conservative views.   vDZ.

L. G. Le Poole, *Bijdr. tot de kennis van het Kerkelijk leven onder de Doopsgezinden* . . . (Leiden, 1905) *passim; DB* 1916, 170 ff.

Gammeren, Abraham van, a member of the Huiskoper (Danzig Old Flemish, *q.v.*) congregation of Haarlem, Holland, was excommunicated in 1741 because of his sympathy with the Moravian Brethren (*q.v.*). Dirk van Gammeren, who translated the sermons of the Moravian leader Count of Zinzendorf (*q.v.*) into Dutch in 1758, may have been a relative of Abraham van Gammeren.   vDZ.

W. J. Lütjeharms, *Het philadelphisch-oecumenisch streven der Hernhutters in de Nederlanden in de 18de eeuw* (Zeist, 1935) 134, 239.

Gam(m)eren, Adriaen van (d. 1725), was an elder of the Danzig Old Flemish Mennonite congregation of Amsterdam. He may have been a descendant of Jacob Gijsbertsz van Gameren (*q.v.*), one of the early Anabaptists of Amsterdam.   vDZ.

Ganglofs, Claes, an author and elder of the Flemish Mennonite congregation at Emden at the end of the 16th century and the beginning of the 17th, who played a role in the Huiskoper (*q.v.*) dispute at Franeker in 1588, which dispute split the Flemish into two divisions, a strict one and a more lenient one. Ganglofs was one of the elders appointed to mediate the quarrel and traveled with the group to Haarlem, where they presumably reached an agreement on the position they would take. He sided with the strict party and worked in East Friesland, Westphalia, Groningen, and Overijssel, opposed the attempt at unification made by Lubbert Gerritsz in 1604, applied the ban in marriage with absolute severity, opposed mixed marriages, and required rebaptism of persons wishing to join his congregation. He wrote the following works: *Proeve des Geloofs*

(1570, reprint 1610); *Antwoort ende verclaringhe op de presentatie tot vereeninge* (1605, 1626, 1631); *Nieu Geestelyck Liedboecxken* (Groningen, 1593, 1606, 1615, 1633); *Dat gebedt ons Heeren Jesu Christi* (1593, 1623); *Grondich Bewijs van Gods Gemeynt* (1599, 1605, 1626); *Vermaning en zendbrief aan zyn huisvrouw* (1605, 1633); and a letter to his brother which contains 29 songs. Some of the songs are about persons in Almelo, Bocholt, and Leer. Some of these writings were published by J. de Buyser in the *Christelyck Huysboeck* (1643), 854-76, in which he attacked the views of Claas Claasz of Blokzijl. Presumably either Ganglofs himself or his ancestors came from Flanders; in 1655 a Joorys Gangeloof of Flanders (*DB* 1877, 11) was a member of the congregation at Aardenburg, Zeeland.   K.V., vDZ.

Inv. Arch. Amst. I, Nos. 477, 558; *DB* 1865, 68; 1900, 74; *N.N.B.Wb.* IV, 628; *Biogr. Wb.* III, 178 f.; *Groningsche Volksalmanak* 1919, 147-53; *Catalogus Amst.*, 104, 185, 224, 269; *ML* II, 34.

Gansfort, Johan Wessel (1420-89), precursor of the Reformation in the Netherlands, born at Groningen, educated in the school of the Brethren of the Common Life at Zwolle. He became the bosom friend of Thomas à Kempis, the famous author of *The Imitation of Christ.* Throughout Europe he was respected as a man of extraordinary learning. He traveled in France and Italy and visited the papal court. His liberal views, deviating from those of the Catholic Church, led to his dismissal from the faculty at Heidelberg. After this event he lived again in Groningen, and regularly visited the noted school at the near-by abbey at Aduard. In consequence he exerted unusual influence on the clergy of Friesland and Groningen, thus preparing the way for the Reformation in these parts. His heretical concept of communion he stated in a book, *De coena Dei* (The Lord's Supper). Two scholarly Dutch Humanists, Hinne Rode and Cornelis Hoen, acquainted Zwingli with Gansfort's ideas. From them Zwingli derived his doctrine on the communion. Thus the concept of the Dutch Mennonites concerning communion is not taken from Zwingli, but was taken directly from Gansfort by Frisian preachers.   K.V.

M. van Rhijn, *Wessel Gansfort* (The Hague, 1917); J. Lindeboom, *Het Bijbelsch Humanisme in Nederland* (Leiden, 1913) 39-55; *Groningsche Volksalmanak* 1920, 148-53; *ML* II, 35.

Gantz-Hernley Mennonite Church (MC), of the vicinity of Manheim, Pa., a member of Lancaster Conference, worships in two meetinghouses. The Gantz meetinghouse, a brick building 40 x 60 ft., located 3½ miles northwest of Manheim, was built in 1915 on the site of the first church, which had been purchased in 1880. The Hernley church was built one mile north of Manheim in 1745 on land contributed by the Penns and was enlarged in 1919. Sunday school and worship services are held every Sunday alternately in the two churches. The membership in 1955 was 256; the ministers were Abram M. Risser and Clyde L. Metzler; the deacons were Isaac E. Tyson and John R. Nissley; the bishop in charge was Homer D. Bomberger. An early division resulted in a considerable loss into the Church of the Brethren. I.D.L.

Gar Creek Mennonite Church (MC), now extinct. About 1854 Mennonites first settled at Gar Creek, a village eleven miles northeast of Fort Wayne, Ind. Among them Michael Rothgeb, Abram and Jacob Bixler, John Federspiel, Hezekiah Rothgeb, and Nancy Lowery. Services were held in Bethel Chapel, a union building. There was no resident minister. Eli Stoffer, a minister in the Hudson (Ind.) congregation, and others conducted occasional services. In 1900 there were 20 members. After the establishing of the Fort Wayne Mission in 1903, the mission workers assumed responsibility for the services at Gar Creek. On Oct. 22, 1905, the building was rededicated for church services. Regular services were discontinued about 1910. H.L.O.

Garber Mennonite Church (MC), of Lancaster Mennonite Conference, is located five miles northeast of Hanover, York Co., Pa., in Richard Danner's bishop district. By 1814 the scattered members had a church-schoolhouse built in the village of Menges Mills. By 1889 the present house was built. The membership in 1953 was 30, with William H. Martin as pastor, and John L. Ruppert as deacon. Joseph Hershey, at least by 1806, was a resident minister in this middle district, which also included Hershey and Bair's Codorus until a recent date. Summer Bible school has been held since 1951, with 235 in attendance. I.D.L.

Garbrant Gabbisz (Gerbrand Gabesz) *van der Scellingh* (from the island of Terschelling?), a Dutch Anabaptist martyr, was sentenced to death by the sword on April 15, 1540, at Alkmaar, province of North Holland, because he had been rebaptized and did not believe in the "holy sacrament of the Mass." He is thought to have been a follower of the revolutionary Anabaptist leader Jan van Batenburg (*q.v.*). (*Inv. Arch. Amst.* I, No. 748, 2; *DB* 1909, 24; Mellink, *Wederdoopers,* 173.) vDZ.

Garden City, Mo., a village (pop. 590) in Cass County, approximately 50 miles southeast of Kansas City. Mennonites (MC) moved into the community in 1860 and eight years later organized a congregation. There have been four congregations in the community, Clearfork (MC) 1868-76, Clearfork (GCM) 1876-85?, Sycamore Grove (MC) 1816- , and Bethel (MC) 1885-1947, which merged with Sycamore Grove in 1947. In 1954 the Mennonite population of this area was approximately 300. J.D.Y.

Garden Mennonite Church (GCM), about halfway between Moundridge and Halstead, Kan., was organized in 1887, by about 15 families (51 charter members), of Garden Twp., Harvey Co. D. W. Schmitt and Jacob Vogt, Sr., planned the building, and Katie M. Krehbiel of Halstead donated the plot for the church, which was dedicated on Sept. 9, 1888.

The first deacons were Jacob Vogt, Sr., D. T.

Eyman, and John Dettweiler. Among the early settlers were names such as these: Leisy, Schmutz, Schmitt, Eyman, Dettweiler, Schowalter, Latchar, Berger, Bachman, Vogt. A number of these early settlers later moved to the west coast.

On Aug. 30, 1890, S. S. Baumgartner began his service of nearly 20 years as minister and elder, during which the membership grew to 147. Other ministers serving this church were A. A. Sommer, H. P. Peters, N. R. Kaufman, J. R. Duerksen, J. M. Janzen, A. J. Dirks, and Victor Graber. The membership in 1955 was 90, with Virgil Dirks as pastor. L.C.R.

Gardner Mennonite Church (MC), now extinct, was established near Gardner, Grundy Co., Ill., in perhaps the early 1860's by families moving there from Pennsylvania and Ohio. Among the families were Buckwalter, Showalter, Tinsman, Kulp, Shelly, Whitmore, and Bachman. The first minister, John G. Bachman, an aged man, was ordained in 1863. Two years later John F. Funk and Henry Shelly were ordained to preach in English and German respectively for the congregation. Once a month Funk came from Chicago to preach for the congregation. Several years after the organization of the congregation, a white frame church was built about two miles west of Gardner. Some time after 1885 the last remaining family, the Lewis Culps, moved to Elkhart, Ind., after which the church was sold. M.G.

H. F. Weber, *Centennial History of the Mennonites of Illinois* (Goshen, 1931) 174-76.

Garfield County, Okla., with Enid as its county seat, has four Mennonite congregations in or near Enid, with a total of about 550 members in 1954, two thirds of whom are M.B. (Enid 210 and North Enid 189) and one third G.C.M. (Bethel 30 and Grace 126). H.S.B.

Garrett County (Md.) Old Order Amish Settlement. Garrett County is in western Maryland bordering Somerset Co., Pa. The settlement consisting of about 75 communicant members is located several miles south of Oakland. The first to locate there came probably sometime before 1850; among them were the families of Pfeil, Gortner, and Miller from Germany, and Yutzy, Slabach, Selder, Beachey, Gnagey, Schrock, and Petersheim from Somerset and Cambria counties, Pa. The congregation was probably organized in 1855. Through the preaching of John Holdeman several families left, including two preachers. Daniel Beachey was the first bishop in the congregation. After his death in 1897, bishops from the Somerset churches served the congregation until 1908. Lewis M. Beachey, the present bishop, was ordained at that time. The settlement has always considered itself as one church district, even though in the early days of the settlement several families lived about ten miles west of Oakland, near Aurora and Eglon, W. Va. The congregation worships regularly in a meetinghouse built in 1949. L.M.B.

Gartental is the second Mennonite colony established in Uruguay. Most of the 431 Mennonites who arrived in Uruguay on Oct. 19, 1951, are living there. About 330 of them are from Danzig and Poland, while the rest are from Russia. Gartental includes approximately 4,400 acres 30 miles from the city of Paysandu on the Paysandu-Mercedes highway. The San Pedro River bisects the land. It is 45 miles from El Ombu, the first Mennonite settlement in Uruguay. The land is gently rolling, with soil from sandy to heavy black. Crops are wheat, oats, rye, barley, corn, sugar beets, and flax. The purchase price was 648,000 pesos ($272,350). Funds from North American Mennonites were loaned to the colony to make the down payment.

The Gartental Mennonite Church was organized almost immediately with Rudolf Hein as elder, and Ernst Enss and Johannes Bergmann as preachers, all having been ordained earlier in Europe. This congregation was one of the three to organize the Uruguay Mennonite Conference on Feb. 21, 1953.   E.Sch.

Gärtnerbrüder (Gardener Brethren), an ancient name for members of the "old evangelical" churches, which was also applied to the Anabaptists (especially in Augsburg in 1530; Keller, *Reformation*, 11, note 8). The real name was "Gartbrüder" from "gartenn," to wander. (*ML* II, 35.)   Neff.

Gaspard Deken (de Decke), an Anabaptist martyr: see **Jasper de Schoenmaker.**

Gast, Johann (d. 1552), of Breisach, Reformed parson and prolific writer at Basel, Switzerland, disciple of Oecolampadius. His diary, preserved only in excerpts (by Tryphius) and as manuscript (a translation by Buxtorf-Falkeisen appeared in Basel in 1856), and also his book, *De anabaptismi exordio, erroribus, historijs abominandis, Confutationibus adjectis* (Basel, 1544), are the most important sources for the history of the Anabaptists in Basel. Since he speaks polemically and in addition copies much from others (especially Zwingli's *In catabaptistarum strophas elenchus*) he must be used with caution. He is a violent opponent of the Anabaptists, and sees in them only obstinacy and hypocrisy. In *Beiträge zur Kenntnis der Mennoniten-Gemeinden* (Berlin, 1821), by Reiswitz and Wadzeck, his name is incorrectly (p. 231) given as Johann Gustius, and his book inexactly.

Hagenbach describes Gast as having a sharp, malicious tongue, in whose diary everybody is defamed. And Hase says that his book is a confused collection, in part based on records, and in part on Swiss anecdotes to defame the Anabaptists, though they actually (unintentionally) frequently honor the Anabaptists.   E.C.

K. Gesner, *Bibliotheca instituta et collecta* (Zürich, 1574 and 1583); P. Burckhardt, *Die Basler Täufer* (Basel, 1888) p. X; K. R. Hagenbach, *Johannes Oekolampad* (1859) 382; K. Hase, *Das Reich der Wiedertäufer* (Leipzig, 1860) 148; *ML* II, 35.

Gasteiger (Gasteyer, Gastaiger), **Christian,** a Hutterite martyr, a smith by trade, was seized May 30, 1586, at Ingolstadt, Bavaria, Germany. Two days

later two Jesuits and the city priest appeared in his cell to talk to him about his faith. But he refused to renounce his faith. Three weeks later the Jesuits appeared again, with the same negative result. Two days later the priest and a doctor of the Holy Scriptures discussed infant baptism with him; he met their assertions with Scripture. They pronounced him a heretic. The judge who visited him on the following day, and told him that he had received orders from the court, if Gasteiger did not accept the faith in which his parents had died, he must be placed on the stake. But Gasteiger replied that he was prepared to die from day to day and would not deviate from the truth. From his prison he wrote the brotherhood an epistle, urging them to trust him, for he would fight well for the eternal crown.

After an imprisonment of 12 weeks in Ingolstadt Gasteiger was welded upon a cart and on Aug. 25 taken to Munich. There he was sentenced on Sept. 13 to die by the sword. The prince, Duke William, was not at home, the chief judge had died, the subordinate judge refused to pronounce the verdict, the mayor and many councilors opposed it, but the Jesuits insisted. When he reached the site of execution he expressed his joy at the nearness of the martyr's crown. The executioner and the Jesuit made another attempt to bring him to recant, but he refused, knelt down, and presented his neck to the sword. His martyrdom is commemorated in the song of the five brethren who were executed for their faith in Bavaria, "Himmlischer Gott und Herr, lass dich erbarmen schier." It is found in Th. Unger, "Ueber eine Wiedertäuferlieder-Handschrift des 17. Jahrhunderts," in *Jahrbuch der Gesellschaft für die Gesch. des Protestantismus in Oesterreich* XIII (1892) 144-53.   Loserth.

Beck, *Geschichts-Bücher*, 299 f.; Wolkan, *Geschicht-Buch*, 423 f.; *Mart. Mir.* D 755, E 1062; Wolkan, *Lieder*, 235; Wiswedel, *Bilder* II, 117; *ML* II, 35 f.

Gätte (Gäta and Göda; now *Kuty*) in Czechoslovakia (formerly Hungary) near the Delta of the Thaya and the March, was in the 16th century a part of the Holitsch domain. In the great persecution of 1550, say the chronicles, there was in Gätte in Hungary a Bruderhof with 150 children, also many sick, lame, and blind. But they were ordered to leave the estates of Berthold von Lipa, and wandered about at the mercy of the populace. In 1552 four deacons were confirmed at Gätte. Then the Bruderhof is not mentioned until 70 years later. On April 15, 1627, Croatian horsemen from Moravia plundered it.

LOSERTH.

Wolkan, *Geschicht-Buch*, 241, 249 f., 208, 606; Zieglschmid, *Chronik*, 319, 331, 341, 808; Beck, *Geschichts-Bücher*; *ML* II, 36.

Gayman, Christian (1825-98), of Cayuga, Ont., was ordained minister about 1863, and bishop about 1875, and became one of the active leaders of the Old Order Mennonite schism in the Ontario Mennonite Conference (MC) in 1889. At the 1888 conference he openly stated that he wished to form a conference of his own and did so in May 1889, at the Wideman Church at Markham, Ont. He was joined by Bishop Abraham Martin of Waterloo County, and Bishop Christian Reesor of Markham. Gayman's home congregation was the Cayuga Church near South Cayuga, in Haldimand County, near the shore of Lake Erie. H.S.B.

Geary First Mennonite Church (GCM) in west central Oklahoma, a member of the Western District Conference, was organized on Aug. 15, 1897, five years after Mennonite settlers had moved into the area, with 22 white and 3 Indian members. In 1953 there were 95 members. The church property consists of a brick veneer church completed in 1929 and a parsonage finished in 1948. Ministers who have served the congregation are J. S. Krehbiel 1897-1916, Henry Riesen 1917-24, Henry D. Penner 1926-33, P. E. Franz 1936-41, H. N. Harder 1943-45, A. H. Peters 1946-52, and Henry Hege 1952- .
A.H.P.

Geauga County, Ohio, Old Order Amish Settlement, consisting of eleven districts and approximately 1,000 baptized members who live in Geauga and the adjoining Trumbull Co., Ohio. The first Amish family to move into the area was that of Samuel Weaver, from Holmes Co., Ohio, in the spring of 1886. In 1887 Simon Mast from Holmes County and ministers Dan Byler and Jacob Byler and families moved to Geauga from Lawrence Co., Pa. A congregation was organized in 1887 with ten families from Holmes County and several from Lawrence County. Isaac Hershberger, a deacon from Indiana, joined the settlement in 1888.

The eleven districts in 1953 with date of formation are as follows: North Parkman 1953; South Parkman 1944; Troy 1897; South Middlefield East 1900; South Middlefield West 1946; Huntsburg 1921; Burton Station 1937; East Middlefield; Mast 1921; Mesopotamia South 1940; Mesopotamia North 1940. The latter two districts are in Trumbull County, but belong to the larger Geauga County settlement. The entire settlement has 10 bishops, 13 deacons, and 20 ministers. J.A.H.

Y. J. Byler, "First Amish Settlers in Geauga Co., Ohio," *The Budget*, Jan. 26, 1950, Feb. 2, 1950.

Gebhardt, (Heinrich) Ernst (1832-99), a Methodist minister of Germany, spent some time in South and North America and England accompanying R. Pearsall Smith as song leader at his evangelistic meetings. Gebhardt wrote many original hymns and translated over fifty Gospel hymns from English into German, most of them Moody and Sankey songs. They appeared in his *Frohe Botschaft* and *Evangeliums-Lieder* (C. F. Spittler, Basel), which were distributed in Europe and America in innumerable volumes. He was the compiler and editor of many other songbooks.

Gebhardt's translations of such songs as "Rock of Ages"—"Fels des Heils," and "Oh, Have You Not Heard"—"Ich weiss einen Strom" seem to have more poetic quality than the English. His contribution to the spread of Gospel songs among German-speaking Mennonites of Europe and America can hardly be overestimated. (See **Hymnology**.) C.K.

Lester Hostetler, *Handbook to the Mennonite Hymnary* (Newton, 1949) 90, 144; *RGG* II, p. 906.

Gebietsamt (Russian, *Volost;* i.e., district government) was the name (German) of the authority established by Mennonites in Russia to govern a large settlement consisting of a number of villages; its head was the *Oberschulze* (*q.v.*). This form of Mennonite district self-government was transplanted from the Mennonite settlements in Russia to Manitoba, Mexico, and South America. (See also **Government of Mennonites in Russia**.) C.K.

E. K. Francis, *In Search of Utopia* (Altona, 1955) 84 f., 90-96.

Gebietsvorsteher: see **Oberschulze**.

Gebser, August Rudolf (1801-74), in 1828 professor at the University of Jena, Germany, in 1829 superintendent and cathedral preacher, 1830-56 professor of theology at the University of Königsberg. Later he lived in Weimar, Kösen, Eisleben, and Halle, where he died. His manifold works, mostly theological, are predominantly occasional writings. In his *Commentatio de primordiis studiorum fanaticorum Anabaptistarum saeculo XVI,* which appeared anonymously at Königsberg in 1830, he tried to prove that the Anabaptist movement emanated from Nikolaus Storch (*q.v.*). A copy of this rare book is found in the Amsterdam Mennonite Library and in the university library of Göttingen. (*ML* II, 41.) E.C.

Geel (Geelen), Jan (Johan) van: see **Jan van Geelen**.

Geeraardsbergen, a town in the Belgian province of East Flanders, about 1560 a center of Mennonite activity. At this time a number of brethren were arrested, but escaped with the aid of the jailer. It is not known whether or not there was a Mennonite congregation there. (Verheyden, "Mennisme in Vlaanderen," ms.) vDZ.

Geeraerdt van de Walle, of Hansbeke in Flanders, who was arrested and tried in November 1590 at Gent, Belgium, evidently was a Mennonite preacher. His trial gives an interesting account of the character and the principles of the Mennonites in Flanders. As early as 1578 Geeraerdt participated in the Mennonite meetings, but not until 1587 was he admitted to baptism on faith by Hans Busschaert (*q.v.*). He related that meetings in Gent were held in weavers' workrooms; the women sat near their spinning wheels; a number of men, some from outside the city, entered, but not at the same time. He admitted that he had written letters to the Dutch province of Zeeland; and that he also had sometimes explained "the doctrines of Menno Simons." A New Testament which he possessed was taken away when he was arrested. Geeraerdt was a simple brushmaker and farm laborer. The extant documents do not tell the outcome of the trial. (Verheyden, *Gent*, 69; *idem*, "Mennisme in Vlaanderen," ms.) vDZ.

Geeraert Saelen (Sielen, Zeelen, Zielen), an Anabaptist martyr, originally from the vicinity of Maastricht, Dutch province of Limburg, was burned at the stake at Brussels, Belgium, on March 2, 1568.

He was about 23 years of age. He refused to betray the names of other Mennonites in the city. During his trial he gave some interesting information about the baptismal practices of the Mennonites. (Verheyden, *Courtrai-Bruxelles,* 73, No. 40.) vdZ.

Geerken Vrancken, a sister-in-law of the martyr Metken (*q.v.*), was also an Anabaptist martyr. She was probably drowned on Aug. 28, 1547, at Echt, at that time belonging to the duchy of Gelder, now the Dutch province of Limburg. Particulars about her were not available. vdZ.

W. Bax, *Het Protestantisme in het Bisdom Luik . . .* I ('s Gravenhage, 1937) 326, 399.

Geerloff Gerritsz (Hemelinck), a martyr, was hanged at Utrecht in the Netherlands on April 20, 1570, for the simple reason that he had been present at a religious meeting held at night at Bunschoten, province of Utrecht, his home, and had listened to a sermon by a Mennonite preacher. It is not clear whether he was a Mennonite himself or not. vdZ.

I. M. J. Hoog, "Onze Martelaren," in *Ned. Arch. voor Kerkgesch.* I ('s Gravenhage, 1902) No. 71.

Geert Cornelis, wife of Frans Philipsz of Leiden, was put in a sack and drowned near the Schooltoren in the moat of Delft, Dutch province of South Holland, on Jan. 24, 1539. (The year 1538 given by Brandt is wrong; it must have been 1539.) Brandt mentions that this woman, who was a follower of David Joris (*q.v.*), was of lax sexual morals; during the trial she gave information about the sex behavior of the Davidjorists with words that, as Brandt says, should not contaminate the paper. It was largely rumored that among the Davidjorists there was much immorality. In most cases these rumors have proved to be false or at least inaccurate and much exaggerated. But there was a germ of truth in those reports, as the case of Geert Cornelis proves. vdZ.

G. Brandt, *Historie der Reformatie* I (2d ed. Amsterdam, 1677) 134; *DB* 1917, 162.

Geert H. (exact name is unknown), a Mennonite from Danzig, East Prussia, a follower of Dirk Philips (*q.v.*), apparently a preacher or elder, who in 1567 was delegated by the Danzig congregation, together with Dirk Philips and Hans Sikken, to settle the quarrels which had arisen in the Netherlands between the Flemish and the Frisians (see **Flemish Mennonites**). (*DB* 1893, 54, 63 note 3, 64.)

Geert Jansdochter (Guert Jan Mickersdochter) of Alkmaar, Dutch province of North Holland, was put to death together with her mother Stijntgen, Jan Mickers' widow (*q.v.*), because she had been (re)baptized and did not believe in the sacrament of the Mass. Both women were drowned at Alkmaar on April 16, 1540. They are supposed to have been followers of Batenburg (*q.v.*). (*Inv. Arch. Amst.* I, No. 748, 2; *DB* 1909, 24.) vdZ.

Geertgen Cort Pietersd of Leiden was drowned at Delft, Dutch province of South Holland, on Jan. 23, 1539, with three other women, because she had been (re)baptized. They were probably followers of David Joris (*q.v.*). (*Inv. Arch. Amst.* I, 749.) vdZ.

Geertgen Geluwers of Zwolle was tortured and drowned on June 3, 1539, at Haarlem, Dutch province of North Holland. She may have been a follower of David Joris (*q.v.*). For particulars see article **Lambrecht Duppijns.** vdZ.

Bijdr. en Mededelingen Hist. Genootschap, Utrecht XLI (Amsterdam, 1920) 21, 208, 210.

Geertken Erasmusdochter, an Anabaptist martyr, a native of Maastricht, was burned at the stake on Sept. 11, 1538, at Vught near 's Hertogenbosch in the Dutch province of North Brabant. She was one of the nine members of Paulus van Drunen's (*q.v.*) congregation, who were executed at Vught on Sept. 9 and 11, 1538. (*DB* 1917, 189.) vdZ.

Geertruidenberg, a town in the Dutch province of North Brabant, where in former times there was a small Mennonite congregation, closely connected with those of Breda (*q.v.*) and Oosterhout. It belonged to the Flemish Mennonites, and in 1665 joined the Zonist (*q.v.*) branch. Deacons at this time were Jan Jansz van Langereyt and Augustijn Gerritsz Hulstman. It seems to have had no preacher at that time. Blaupot ten Cate (*Holland* II, 43) informs us that this congregation died out before or about 1750; but it probably dissolved much earlier, for after 1674 no mention of it is made in the records of the Flemish church of Rotterdam, which used to keep a careful eye on a number of small Flemish congregations in the surroundings. Geertruidenberg now has a population of 3,344 souls, 85.2 per cent of whom are Roman Catholics. No Mennonites are found now in this town. vdZ.

Geertruydt (or Geertruy Jansdochter), the wife of Menno Simons, whom he married in 1536. In 1554 (*Opera,* 259a) he wrote that he and his wife had been refugees for 18 years. This marriage very likely took place in Groningen where he resided temporarily in quietness. Vos's assumption that Geertruydt came from Witmarsum and was the daughter of Herman Hoyer has not been established. Fiction writers have gone into great detail in covering this phase of Menno's life, but the actual information about his wife and family is extremely scarce. Geertruydt's sister Griet was married to Rein Edes. Menno wrote Griet a letter, from which Vos (Krahn, 37) drew erroneous conclusions regarding further family relationships.

Life as a wife of a refugee preacher was not easy. In 1544 Menno reported that he had been unable to find a hut for as long as a year or even half a year for his "poor wife" and their small children (*Opera,* 521). Repeatedly Menno writes about his "poor sick wife" (*Opera,* 259a, 234a). In a writing to a Lasco in 1544 he speaks of "our small children" (*Opera,* 521). They must have had at least two daughters (*Opera,* 392b), and according to Vos (p. 4) they had a son Jan. Geertruydt must have died between 1553 and 1558. In 1553 Menno sent greetings from his wife (*Opera,* 456b) while in 1558 he included regards from his daughters only (*Opera,* 392b). Their son had probably died by this time. One daughter reported details of her father's life to P. J. Twisck (Vos, 14). **C.K.**

C. Krahn, *Menno Simons* (Karlsruhe, 1936) 97 ff.; K. Vos, *Menno Simons* (Leiden, 1917) 3-6, 66, 266, 317; *DB* 1906, 3; *ML* II, 85.

Geertruydt Adriaens de Roevre (Geertken Erasmus-dochter of Tricht), wife of Wouter Hoogendoren, a Dutch Anabaptist martyr, was sentenced to death and burned at the stake at Vught, province of North Brabant, on Sept. 11, 1539, with three other martyrs; the day before, four martyrs had been burned, among whom was Paulus van Drunen (*q.v.*), the bishop of their congregation. Van Braght includes a report on the martyrs of Vught in which he places their martyrdom wrongly in the year 1538; he also says that 12 Anabaptists were executed, whereas the records name only eight. Some of the names given in the records are found in the *Martyrs' Mirror* but other names are not handed down by van Braght. The name of Geertruydt, mentioned in the official records, is not found in the *Martyrs' Mirror*. It is rather surprising that she is found in the Reformed martyrbook by Adriaen van Haemstede (*q.v.*), *De Geschiedenisse ende den doodt der vromen Martelaren,* of 1559. Haemstede no doubt considered her as Reformed, which is an error. She was an Anabaptist, as the records clearly show. (*Mart. Mir.* D 41-42, E 447; *DB* 1917, 189; see also 's Hertogenbosch, and Vught.) **vDZ.**

Geertruyt Faes, an Anabaptist martyr, was executed at Antwerp, Belgium, on Jan. 18, 1577, together with Mayken Truyens and Laureys Janssen. The method of execution was not stated in the records. Geertruyt was charged with the crime of having received (re)baptism and attended the meetings of the Mennonites. Geertruyt and the two other martyrs executed on the same day were the last Anabaptists to die for their faith at Antwerp. (*Antw. Arch.-Blad* XIII, 211; XIV, 98-99, No. 1122.) **vDZ.**

Geertruyt Jansdochter (surnamed Kemster), a Dutch Anabaptist martyr. It is assumed that her surname means that she was a native of Kennemerland, a district of the province of North Holland, north of Haarlem. She was arrested at Haarlem on May 24, 1539, and after torture on May 28 was drowned there on June 3, 1539. She may have been a follower of David Joris (*q.v.*). For particulars see **Lambrecht Duppijns.** **vDZ.**

Bijdr. en Mededelingen Hist. Genootschap Utrecht XLI (Amsterdam, 1920) 200-01, 208, 210, 211, 218.

Geervliet, a town in the Dutch province of South Holland on the island of Putten, formerly the seat of a small Flemish Mennonite congregation. It seems to have formed one congregation with the neighboring towns of Heenvliet, Spijkenisse, and Zuidland; was also called "het Brielsche land" congregation; later it was usually called Spijkenisse (*q.v.*). Of the origin of this congregation nothing is known. It may have been founded by Anabaptist refugees from Flanders. It was represented at the Flemish conference at Leiden in 1660 by its preachers Huygh Barentsz van der Klock, Leendert Pietersz, and Adriaen Jansz. In 1674 it joined the stricter branch

of the Zonists (*q.v.*). For many years it was financially supported by the church of Rotterdam. In 1671 Jan Abrahams was chosen as a preacher, but he served for only one year, moving to Brielle in 1672. After this the pulpit was nearly always vacant. In 1733 and again in 1736 it contributed a small amount to the Dutch Fund for Foreign Needs in behalf of the Prussian refugees; so it still existed at this time; but soon after, in any case before 1760, it must have been dissolved.

The martyr Jan Jansz Brant (*q.v.*), a native of Zuidland, was executed at Geervliet on Nov. 29, 1559 (*Offer,* 550; *Mart. Mir.* D 243, E 617). Whether there was already at this time a congregation cannot be determined. **vDZ.**

Geestelijck Liedt-Boecxken, *een, inholdende veel schoone sinrijcke Christlijcke Liedekens: oock troostlijcke Nieuwe-Jaren, Claech- unde Lof-Sanghen, ter Eeren Godes: Alle oprechte Godt-meenende Liefhebberen der Waerheyt Christi, Olden unde Jonghen seer dienstlijck, deur D. J.* (n.p., n.d.). This Anabaptist hymnbook in the Low German language was published at the end of the 16th century. The author is David Joris (*q.v.*). It was probably published by Gillis Roman (*q.v.*) at Haarlem, Holland. There is also a second edition, enlarged by two hymns; this second edition was in the Dutch language. A copy of the first edition is found in the Royal Library at The Hague, one of the second edition in the Library of the University of Gent. The hymns, for a large part composed by David Joris himself, deal with Anabaptist martyrs of the period 1529-36. The fourth hymn is dedicated to Anneken N., viz., Anneken Jans of Rotterdam. This hymn was also included in the *Offer des Heeren* of 1562. Many of the hymns contain an ecstatic apocalyptic mysticism, as taught by David Joris. **vDZ.**

Wolkan, *Lieder,* 58 f.; F. C. Wieder, *De Schriftuurlijke Liedekens,* (The Hague, 1900) 165-67.

Geestelijcke Bijenkorf, title of a Dutch Mennonite hymnbook published in 1637 at Alkmaar, of which, as far as is known, no copy is extant. **vDZ.**

Geestelijke Belangen, *Adviescommissie voor de* (Advisory Committee for Spiritual Matters), a Dutch Mennonite committee, which gives advice to the executive board of the A.D.S. (Dutch Mennonite Conference), especially in matters of spiritual interest. It was established in 1941; its members are appointed by the A.D.S., and all kinds of Dutch Mennonite activities and spiritual movements are represented in this committee, which meets six to seven times a year. The board appointed to compose a preachers' manual (*Kanselboek, q.v.*) was a subcommittee of the *Geestelijke Belangen* committee. **vDZ.**

Geestelijke Goudschaale, De, a Dutch Mennonite hymnbook. Of the first three editions no copy is extant. The first edition appeared in 1662 at Franeker, the second at Leeuwarden in 1683, but the date of the third is not known. The fourth edition, enlarged and edited by Wiger Jansen, was published at Leeuwarden, 1751. It has three parts, containing respectively 95, 76, and 17 hymns, all without notes. This hymnbook was used in some Mennonite congregations, e.g., on the island of Ameland (*q.v.*), until about 1850.   vdZ.

DJ 1837, 63; *DB* 1889, 10; 1891, 7; 1900, 85 f., 97-99; M. Schagen, *Naamlijst der Doopsgezinde Schrijveren* (Amsterdam, 1745) 43.

Geestelyke ofte Nieuwe Herpe Davidts, a Dutch Mennonite hymnbook, published at Amsterdam in 1752; it contains 284 hymns on 554 pages and a suffix of 17 hymns (all without notes). This hymnbook is a modified and enlarged reprint of the last edition (1724) of *Veelderhande Schrifftuurlyke Liedekens* (*q.v.*). The edition of 1752 under its new title was intended for use in the congregations in Prussia.   vdZ.

Geesteranus, Johannes, b. 1586 at Alkmaar, a member of a Dutch family of which many members served the Reformed Church as pastors, was a Reformed pastor himself, serving at Vreeland 1609-17?, and Alkmaar 1617?-19. In this year he was dismissed on the charge of Socinianism (*q.v.*). He soon joined the Rijnsburg Collegiant (*q.v.*) movement and was the first to receive baptism by immersion at Rijnsburg. He declined an appointment as rector (president) of the Socinian College at Rakow, Poland. After his dismissal he had made his living by weaving. When action was taken against the Socinians in the Netherlands Geesteranus settled at Norden, East Friesland, Germany. Here he met with two other ex-Reformed ministers, both also dismissed—his brother Petrus Geesteranus, and Dirk Rafaelsz Camphuysen (*q.v.*), to whom he was bound by a warm friendship. In 1622 Geesteranus, his wife, and his only son died of the plague at Norden. Geesteranus is said to have shared the Anabaptist view that a Christian should not assume a government office. (*N.N.B.Wb.* III, 190-92; *DB* 1883, 70.)   vdZ.

Geestlicke Liederen, Vijf, is a small volume of Dutch hymns published by Jan Theunisz (*q.v.*) at Leiden in 1600. All songs are signed with the motto "Jaecht naer best" (Striving for the best).   vdZ.

Gehman (Geeman, Geyman, Gayman, Gahman, Gaueman), Bernese family name now having representatives in various districts of the Mennonite Church in North America, especially in the Lancaster, Franconia (MC), and Eastern District (GCM) conferences of southeastern Pennsylvania. The progenitors of most or all of these Gehmans were the brothers Christian and Benedict Geeman, who arrived at Philadelphia on the ship *Samuel* on Aug. 11, 1732, accompanied by their sister Anna Geeman. Immigrant Christian purchased land in Berks Co., Pa., while Benedict located in Lehigh County. The descendants of these pioneers are strongly represented in both the Lancaster and Franconia conferences. Lancaster has had about a dozen deacons and ministers by the name of Gehman, and Franconia thirteen. The first Franconia preacher by the name of Gehman was Abraham Gehman (d. 1792) of the Rockhill congregation, a son of immigrant Christian; both father and son

are buried in the Rockhill cemetery. Preacher Abraham in turn was the father of Preacher Samuel Gehman (1767-1845). Daniel Gehman of Berks County (d. 1809) served in the Gehman congregation of the Lancaster Conference, first as a deacon as early as 1774, and after 1792 as a preacher. His great-great-grandson Moses Gehman, ordained in 1912, frequently writes for the *Gospel Herald,* and for a generation has been the senior minister in the Weaverland-Groffdale district, to which the Gehman congregation belongs.

When the Mennonites located in Lincoln Co., Ont., at the "Twenty," beginning about 1800, one of the settlers was named Gehman. In 1862 a Christian Gayman (*q.v.,* 1825-98) at Selkirk, Ont., was ordained as a preacher, and in 1875 was made a bishop. After several years of tension he withdrew from the Mennonite Conference of Ontario in 1888 and served in the Old Order Mennonite Church when it was organized in 1889 in Ontario.

The General Conference Mennonite Church, Eastern District, had difficulty with a minister named William Gehman (*q.v.,* 1827-1918), ordained preacher at Upper Milford in 1849. After several years of tension on the issue of prayer meetings (promoted by Gehman), he and 23 others, mostly laity, were expelled in May 1857. Gehman's group, in which he served as an elder, took the name Evangelical Mennonites (*q.v.*). This group eventually merged with other small Mennonite bodies to form the Mennonite Brethren in Christ (now known as United Missionary Church except in Pennsylvania). William Gehman's son, William G. Gehman (1874-1941), of Bethlehem, Pa., served as an M.B.C. presiding elder 1905-36.

Mennonites named Gehman have also been found in a few other states besides Pennsylvania, especially in Iowa. Ernest G. Gehman, formerly of the Franconia Conference, has taught at Eastern Mennonite College in Virginia for many years. Although a Mennonite named Gehmann appears in a 1759 Palatinate census list (at Neidenfels), the name seems not to have played much of a role in European Mennonite circles.   J.C.W.

Gehman, William, a descendant of Christian Geeman who arrived in Philadelphia in 1732, b. Jan. 22, 1827, in Hereford Twp., Berks Co., Pa. He grew up on the farm and later learned the trade of a miller. He was married to Anna Musselman; they had nine children, including W. G. Gehman, presiding elder of the Pennsylvania Conference (MBC) 1905-41, and Allen M. Gehman, treasurer of the same Conference 1902-28.

Gehman was a minister and co-worker of John H. Oberholtzer and in 1849 he was ordained at Zionsville, Pa., by the General Conference Mennonites. Disagreeing with his leader on the subject of prayer meetings, he in 1857 organized the Evangelical Mennonites, a group that later helped to form the Mennonite Brethren in Christ Church. He was thus the first to start the movement which resulted in the organization of the M.B.C. Church.

In 1858 Gehman erected at Zionsville the first M.B.C. Church. In 1879 he was elected the first presiding elder of the Pennsylvania Conference, which office he held until 1892, when he retired from active service.

"Father" Gehman, as he was known, never lost his interest in the church. He attended every annual conference up to the time of his death. Altogether he was present at 106 semiannual, annual, special, and general conferences without missing one session. At 29 of these he served as chairman.

He was noted for being punctual in the Sunday school, and kept his place in his class up to the last Sunday before his death. He died April 12, 1918, in his 92nd year. His body lies interred in the M.B.C. cemetery at Zionsville.   E.R.S.

Gehman Mennonite Church (MC), located near Adamstown, Brecknock Twp., Berks Co., Pa., is a member of the Lancaster Conference. The first Mennonites to settle here were a group of Swiss, who came in 1754-58, among them Niklaus Schantz, Hans Schantz, Joseph Wenger, Jost Schoenauer, Hans Burchalter, Hans Moser, and Christian Gehman. The congregation was probably organized in 1760. It worshiped in private homes until 1846, when the first meetinghouse was built, which was replaced in 1913 by a larger frame meetinghouse. Christian Bauman (1724-90) was the first minister, Joseph Wenger first deacon. Daniel Gehman was an outstanding man in this congregation (1774 ord. deacon, 1792 ord. minister, d. 1809). Ever since 1774 there has been a Gehman as minister or deacon in this congregation. In 1955 the membership of the congregation was 90, with Paul Z. Martin and Benjamin S. Zeiset as ministers.   A.M.W.

Geiger Mennonite Church (MC), located on Bleam's Road two miles south of Baden, in Wilmot Twp., Waterloo Co., Ont., was organized by Bishop Benjamin Eby in 1831. The members first worshiped in a schoolhouse; a meetinghouse was built in 1842, replaced in 1874 by a frame building. Remodelings followed in 1913 and 1940. A large buggy shed was built in 1930. The deacons who served here were Ulrich Steiner (1800-57), ordained 1831; Amos S. Cressman (1834-1909), ordained 1864; John Nahrgang (1839-1912), ordained 1872 and about 1899 went to the Old Order Mennonites and served in upper Waterloo (South Peel); Osiah Cressman (1866-1933), ordained 1902; Eli Good (1862-1934), ordained 1904; Abraham Good, ordained 1932; Joseph Cressman, ordained 1944. Ministers who served were Abraham Honsberger (1801-38), ordained at the organizing of the church; Ulrich Geiger (1797-1864), ordained 1838; Amos S. Cressman, ordained 1867; Osiah Cressman, ordained 1903; Moses H. Roth (1898-), ordained minister in 1931, and bishop in 1937. Early bishops were Benjamin Eby of Berlin and Henry Shantz of Wilmot. Amos S. Cressman became bishop in 1875 to relieve Henry Shantz. After him for more than 20 years neighboring bishops served until Moses Roth became bishop. Sunday school was organized in 1901. By 1934 the enrollment was 91 and in 1953 it is 120. Church membership was 31 in 1890, 61 in 1934, and 92 in 1953. Until about 1935 preaching appointments on Sunday mornings alternated with

Biehn's congregation. Young people's meeting continued to do so.

In early years Geiger's was a parent church for scattered congregations several townships north.
          J.C.F.

Geil, John, Mennonite (MC) leader and preacher, b. April 9, 1778, in New Britain Twp., Bucks Co., Pa., d. Jan. 16, 1866, affiliated with the Franconia (MC) Conference (q.v.). His father, Jacob Geil, had emigrated with his parents from Alsace or the Palatinate at the age of eight. John married Elizabeth Fretz (1781-1849) on April 22, 1802; she was the daughter of Mark Fretz (1750-1840), deacon of the Lexington congregation. They were the parents of eight children. Although John went to school but six weeks he was able to write both German and English. He was gifted with a keen mind and a remarkable memory. Ordained in 1810 or 1811 he served in the congregation at Line Lexington, Bucks Co., Pa., as a beloved and influential minister for over half a century. He farmed near the Fretz mill in New Britain Township and attended market in Philadelphia. Physically he was tall, slender, erect, well-proportioned, and had a high forehead. As an aged man he wore his white hair almost to his shoulders. In disposition he was modest and quiet and a man of strict simplicity. In the pulpit he was logical and fluent. His farewell address to his congregation in 1852 (published as a broadside with the title *Abschiedsworte*) is a model of pastoral love and concern. His brother Jacob Geil (1771-1856) was a Mennonite minister in Fairfield County, Ohio.   J.C.W.

John F. Funk, *Biographical Sketch of Preacher John Geil* (Elkhart, 1897).

Geisberg, a French Mennonite congregation, a member of the Alsatian conference, located on the northern Alsatian-Palatine border, two miles southeast of Wissembourg, until the end of World War II a part of the Deutschhof-Geisberg (q.v.) congregation, with origins reaching back to 1760. The earliest settlements were at Schafbusch and Niederrödern, later Geisberg and Deutschhof, and the congregation changed its name after these localities several times. Until 1849 the services were held at Schafbusch just west of Geisberg. In that year a meeting room was constructed in the entrance portal of the Geisberg castle (*Schloss*). In the fighting of 1944-45 the Geisberg castle was largely destroyed. With the aid of American Mennonite relief and reconstruction workers stationed in Wissembourg the meeting room was rebuilt and rededicated on Aug. 3, 1947. In 1953 the baptized membership of Geisberg was 63, with 13 unbaptized children. The elder was Philipp Hege (Schafbusch) since 1928, preacher Fritz Hirschler (Geisberg) since 1937, deacon Jean Hirschler (Geisberg) since 1921.
          H.S.B.

Philipp Hege, "Das kriegszerstörte Gotteshaus zu Geisberg (Elsass) wieder hergestellt," *Der Mennonit* I (1948) 58.

Geiser (Geyser, Gyser), a Mennonite family name originating in Langental, canton of Bern, Switzerland, probably dating back to the 14th century with persons whose occupation was goat herding.

The first recorded bearer of the name who was connected with the Anabaptists was a Gabriel Geyser, who was fined in 1685 by Bernese authorities because it was suspected that he had connections with the Anabaptists. Early in the 18th century some members of the Geiser family who espoused the Anabaptist faith moved from Langental to the Jura where as early as 1724 Johannes Geiser and his wife Anna Jorg and four children were residing on the Sonnenberg Mountain in the commune of Corgémont. A list of 1768 names some members of the family living at Aux Convers. By 1823 most of the family lived in the vicinity of La Chaux-de-Fonds where Johannes Geiser (b. 1756) was a minister. In the early 1830's members of the Geiser family moved to the Sonnenberg settlement in Wayne County, Ohio, where a number have been prominent in church activities. Today in the Jura Geiser is one of the most prominent names among the Mennonites, six of their ministers carrying this name. Best known is Elder Samuel Geiser of Brügg, who wrote *Die Taufgesinnten-Gemeinden,* a history of the Swiss Mennonites, upon the request of the Swiss Mennonite Conference, for many years secretary of the conference. Elder David Geiser (d. 1950) long served the congregation at Chaux d'Abel, Elder Louis Geiser serves at Les Bulles, and Elder Samuel Geiser of Les Fontaines serves at Jeangisboden.

D.L.G.

Samuel Geiser, *Die Taufgesinnten-Gemeinden* (Karlsruhe, 1931).

Geiser, Abraham (1857-1928), elder of the Mennonite congregation in Chaux d'Abel in the Bernese Jura of Switzerland, was born on April 13, 1857, at Mont Cortébert, and grew up on Mont-Soleil near St. Imier, one of 12 children. Since his parents were pioneers in this remote settlement his education was limited to just a few weeks. At the age of 18 he was converted, and, feeling an urge to preach the Gospel, attended the Bible Training School of St. Chrischona for two winter terms. In the autumn of 1879 he married Katharina Gerber; they had four children. For 22 years he lived on a farm near Les-Bois, farming as well as preaching. In 1890 he was ordained as elder. He was one of the most influential Mennonite preachers of his time in Switzerland and was for several years president of the Conference of the Swiss Mennonite churches. In 1918 he sold his farm and with his oldest son and the son's family settled in Pays de Gex, 10 miles from Geneva, in France. Here, in St. Genis, there was a small congregation of Protestants, which was on the point of dissolution. It was soon arranged that this group would meet in Abraham Geiser's house. Several other Mennonite families from the Jura moved into the area, thus forming the nucleus of the present Pays de Gex Mennonite congregation. Later this congregation was in the care of his youngest son. After the close of World War I Abraham Geiser received an invitation from the Conference of Mennonites in Alsace to settle in Alsace, whereupon he and his oldest son Japhet leased a large farm near Colmar and settled there in 1924. In the spring of 1928 he died. He was buried in a cemetery in the Pays de Gex community.†

S.G.

Geistliche Lieder, Sieben, a booklet of seven hymns, translated from the *Groote Liedenboeck* (*q.v.*) of Leenaert Clock. There are at least five editions: Amsterdam, 1664, 1691, and 1711; Basel, 1822; and Giessen, 1834. They are added to T. T. v(an) S(ittert), *Christliche Glaubens-bekentnus.*

vDZ.

Geistliches Blumengärtlein, a rare devotional book published anonymously in Amsterdam 1680, which contains reprints of a number of Anabaptist and half-Anabaptist tracts and also a lengthy doctrinal work entitled *Schriftmässiger Bericht und Zeugnis betreffend die rechte christliche Taufe, Abendmahl, Gemeinschaft, Obrigkeit, und . . . Ehestand, samt einer Bekentnis der Artikeln des christlich-apostolischen Glaubens. Erstlich geschrieben anno 1526 von H.D.* Between its articles II and III a *Danklied* is inserted which has Hans Hut (*q.v.*) as its author, while as conclusion a hymn is printed which is a versification of the Apostles' Creed, said to have either Peter Riedemann (*q.v.*) or Siegmund Wiedemann (*q.v.*) as its author.

It is certainly surprising that all of a sudden such a number of Anabaptist writings should be published in Amsterdam, in the German language, at the end of the 17th century when Anabaptism in its classical form had practically died out. The only explanation could be that a pietistically minded author discovered somewhere in Amsterdam old pamphlets or perhaps a Hutterite manuscript book, as we know that the Mennonite Library of Amsterdam has at least one such Hutterite codex, and more of them must have been in circulation in Holland, due to Dutch relief work among the Hutterites. Searching for new devotional material the author gladly took hold of this unknown and fresh literature. Now he offered it to the reader quite harmlessly as a pietistic devotional book under the popular title of *Geistliches Blumengärtlein* (Spiritual Flowergarden; concerning this title see **Geistliches Lustgärtlein**). The once obnoxious connotation of "Anabaptist" origin had long since been lost, and the devout reader could meditate on these ideas without becoming too aware that these tracts contain much more than mere edification. In fact one is surprised to find in this volume (in the *Bericht*) an article defending community of goods (*q.v.*) and another defending nonresistance (*q.v.*), doctrines which must have appeared to Pietists almost as revolutionary. Yet by 1680 the mood of Protestantism had changed to such an extent that Anabaptist writings were actually welcomed as an enrichment of available devotional literature, in the same way as Mennonites of all branches now zealously read Lutheran, Calvinist, and Schwenckfeldian writings for their own enjoyment and edification (Friedmann, *Mennonite Piety,* 25).

The *Blumengärtlein* contains writings by Hans Denk (*q.v.*), Hans Hut (*q.v.*), Jörg Hauck von Juchsen (*q.v.*), Eitelhans Langenmantel (*q.v.*), plus the afore-mentioned *Schriftmässiger Bericht,* and two hymns. The unknown editor did not know how to identify the last-mentioned tract, and—apparently merely guessing—put down, "For the first time written by H.D. in 1526" (the initials standing for Hans Denk). In 1891, Ludwig Schwabe published this doctrinal tract in the *Zeitschrift f. Kirchengeschichte* (XII, 466-93), attributing it to "Hans Denk," who thus became a teacher of the ideal of communistic living. The existence of this Hutterite practice was then (1891) very little known, whereas Hans Denk had become popular through the writings of Ludwig Keller (*q.v.*). In 1931 Robert Friedmann identified this *Bericht* as an abridged version of the great *Article Book* (*q.v.*) of the Hutterian Brethren, dating from about 1547; as far as is known it had never been published in print, hence the editor must have used a Hutterite manuscript book. It is even possible that all the other tracts were also taken from the same codex, as we know that the Hutterites had the custom of such combination books. In any case, the transformation of a genuine 16th-century collection of Anabaptist tracts into a pietistic devotional reader deserves our greatest attention.

The *Schriftmässiger Bericht,* however, fits no other known version of the "Article Book," and for that reason is a valuable addition to our knowledge of Anabaptist literature and its manifold recasting. Its nearest model is an Anabaptist codex in Wolfenbüttel of 1582, which suggests the approximate date of the original copy of our tract. It goes without saying that Hans Denk had nothing to do with it, never taught community of goods, and is quite foreign to the entire genius of this remarkable doctrinal writing. The *Geistliches Blumengärtlein,* however, apparently never became very popular—perhaps it was yet too strong a drink for that rather soft period. The main significance of the book, however, rests in the fact that it is a testimony to a certain kinship, external though it seems to be, between Anabaptist and pietistic writings. While their genius is different, a mutual appreciation was nevertheless possible, particularly at a time when the original Anabaptist thought had almost completely died away. Copies of the *Blumengärtlein* are to be found in Göttingen, Munich, Berlin, and Dresden.

R.F.

L. Schwabe, "Ueber Hans Denck," in *Ztsch. f. Kirchengesch.* XII (1891) 466-93; R. Friedmann, "Eine dogmatische Hauptschrift der Hutterischen Täufergemeinschaften in Mähren," in *Arch. f. Ref.-Gesch.* XXVIII, 1931, 80 ff.; idem, *Mennonite Piety Through the Centuries* (Goshen, 1949) 25 f.

Geistliches Lustgärtlein (*hortulus animae*), a very popular title for devotional books ever since the Middle Ages, the idea being that the soul or the mind ambles in a lovely flower garden while reading the prayers and devout meditations of such a book. The number of books with this or similar titles is fairly large, both of Catholic and Protestant origin. Particularly during the period of Pietism (*q.v.*) this type of devotional literature became exceedingly well liked, the most outstanding example of it being the hymnal of Gerhard Tersteegen (*q.v.*), *Das geistliche Blumengärtlein inniger Seelen*

of 1729, with many reprints both in Europe and in Pennsylvania.

Among Mennonites two books of this or related title are known and once were much in use: (*a*) Johann Philip Schabalie (*q.v.*), *Lusthoef des Gemoets,* 1638, consisting originally of two parts, the second of which is the famous Biblical history, *The Wandering Soul* [first published separately in 1635]. The first part, a book of "spiritual exercises" (*geestelijke oeffeninge*), was soon published also independently as the very *Lusthoef* itself, and passed through innumerable editions both in Dutch and in High German. It proved to be a really popular religious reader of high value, with all its wealth of edification, information, and imagination. However, no American edition is known.

(*b*) Perhaps still more popular was another devotional book of this title, *Neu vermehrtes Lustgärtlein frommer Seelen, das ist heilsame Anweisungen und Regeln zu einem gottseligen Leben,* ... first edition 1787. No author is named, and the origin of the book is rather obscure though it may be safely assumed that it is of non-Mennonite (possibly Lutheran) origin. No reference to this book could be found anywhere; and yet it is one of the most successful devotional books among European and American Mennonites (particularly among the Amish). It had eight editions in Europe between 1787 and 1854, and thirteen or more editions in America between 1824 and 1941. The first part of the *Lustgärtlein* (i.e., *Heilsame Anweisungen,* etc.) appeared, as far as research could ascertain, first as an appendix to the *Ernsthafte Christenpflicht* (*q.v.*), the well-known Mennonite prayer book, in Herborn, Nassau. A chart with a complete survey of all editions may be found in Friedmann, *Mennonite Piety,* 212, demonstrating the tremendous appeal of this book, in spite of its otherwise surprising obscurity. It is quite uncertain whether the book is found in any European collection of devotional books (thus far inquiries have been negative); on the other hand Goshen College Library has a great number of well-worn copies, collected from Mennonite and Amish homes. It is still being published.

The book is divided into two unequal parts: (*a*) a collection of rules and counsel for the conduct of a pious life "agreeable to God," and (*b*) a collection of prayers for everyday and for holidays, also an extensive formulary for the Lord's Supper. The appropriateness of these prayers and counsel (for which the "Book of Proverbs" is quite frequently quoted) for many occasions, or just for general edification, may explain why this strange book became so unusually popular among Mennonites in spite of the fact that certain passages (e.g., concerning infant baptism) run directly counter to Mennonite tradition. Today the book is still in use among the Amish, and it might even be conjectured that there were Amish groups in Hessen and Waldeck which originally adopted this book for their use, although also Mennonites in the Emmental (Switzerland) and in Bavaria soon became fond of it.

The fact that the oldest known edition bears the title, *Neu vermehrtes . . . Lustgärtlein,* seems to indicate that an earlier (thus far unknown) edition existed, presumably of 1750-70, which was later enlarged and published prior to the Mennonite edition of 1787. The entire tone of the book is extremely pietistic, emphasizing thoughts on death and dying, typical of 18th-century devotion. R.F.

R. Friedmann, *Mennonite Piety Through the Centuries* (Goshen, 1949—see index; the idea of *Lustgärtlein* in general is discussed in a footnote on p. 208). Reference to the idea of *Lustgärtlein* may also be found in Hermann Beck, *Die Erbauungsliteratur der Evangelischen Kirche Deutschlands* (Erlangen, 1883—16th century only) and by the same author, *Die religiöse Volksliteratur der Evangelischen Kirche Deutschlands* (Gotha, 1891).

Geistreiches Gesangbuch, *worin nebst den Psalmen Davids eine Sammlung auserlesener alter und neuer Lieder zu finden ist, zur allgemeinen Erbauung herausgegeben* (chief compiler Hans van Steen, an elder in the Flemish congregation at Danzig), the first German hymnbook of the West Prussian Mennonite churches, first edition at Königsberg in 1767, was long used in West Prussia, then in Russia, Manitoba, and in Mexico, where it is still in use. Further editions were published in West Prussia as follows: Königsberg 1775; Marienwerder 1780, when the title was changed to *Geistreiches Gesangbuch zur Oeffentlichen und besonderen Erbauung der Mennonitischen Gemeine in und vor der Stadt Danzig,* with an appendix, *Anhang einiger Gebethe zur Kirchen- und Haus-Andacht,* Elbing 1794; Marienwerder 1803, again with altered title, *Gesangbuch, worin eine Sammlung alter und neuer Lieder zum gottesdienstlichen Gebrauch und allgemeinen Erbauung ausgegeben, Ps. 104 v. 33;* Marienwerder 1819, when the title was changed a third time to read *Gesang-Buch worin eine Sammlung geistreicher Lieder befindlich. Zur allgemeinen Erbauung und zum Lobe Gottes herausgeben;* Elbing 1829; Marienburg 1838, *"durchgesehene und verbesserte Auflage";* Elbing 1843; Graudenz 1845; and Danzig 1864. The Elbing edition of 1843, the ninth, was reprinted in Odessa for the Russian Mennonites in 1844, 1854, 1859, and 1867. A fifth undated Russian edition was printed in Leipzig, undated sixth and seventh editions again in Leipzig, the last distributed in Halbstadt. In 1843 (Elbing) the word "worin" in the title was changed to "in welchem."

The Mennonites who emigrated from Russia to Manitoba in 1874 had eight unchanged editions published at Elkhart, Ind., by the Mennonite Publishing Company, 1880, ——, 1889, 1895, 1903, 1909, 1916, 1918. Editions were published in 1926 and 1937 (*durchgesehene amerikanische Ausgabe*) by the Mennonite Publishing House at Scottdale, Pa. When the Old Colony Mennonites went to Mexico in 1922 they took this book along as their hymnbook, and there published two editions (1940, 1943). Three further editions for Mexico appeared at Scottdale (1944, 1949, 1954).

The contents of this hymnal have been changed but slightly during the entire period of 200 years. It never had any musical notation. The predecessor of this book was the Dutch *Veelderhande Schrifttuurlijke Liedekens . . .* (*q.v.*), used in West Prussia 1724-69, which had been in use in Holland since the days of the Reformation.

Originally the *Geistreiches Gesangbuch* contained 505 songs and 150 Psalms, selected and translated from Dutch songbooks in use and chosen from the Halle, Stargard, Quandt, and Rogall songbooks. The Psalms were omitted with the third edition, which contained 620 hymns in 652 pages. In the sixth edition a second part (*Zweiter Teil*) was added making the total of 725 songs. The *Geistreiches Gesangbuch* has the unusual record of having been in use for nearly 200 years, going through 11 editions in Prussia, 7 in Russia, 11 in America, and 2 in Mexico, a total of 33 editions ranging from 3,000 to 5,000 copies each, making it the most widely used hymnbook of the Prussian-Russian Mennonites. (See article **Hymnology** of the Mennonites of Prussia and Russia.)† C.K.

Gelassenheit, self-surrender, resignation in God's will (*Gottergebenheit*), yieldedness to God's will, self-abandonment, the (passive) opening to God's willing, including the readiness to suffer for the sake of God, also peace and calmness of mind, in Dutch devotional literature *leijdzaamheid* (*MQR,* 1950, 22, note 17, suggests about 15 possible translations, none perfectly fitting). Only if man relinquishes his self-will may he become an instrument of God. The main Biblical locus seems to be Rev. 13:10, "Here is the patience [RSV has 'endurance'] and faith of the saints," even though Gelassenheit goes further than patience and endurance.

The mystical literature of the Middle Ages abounds in the description of this quality, deemed necessary for the contemplative life. Occasionally the mystics speak here also of the "mystical death" of the self. However, mystics understand this term primarily in a passive sense, for without such passive self-abandonment the craved union with God could not be attained.

Among the "Spiritual Reformers" of the 16th century (Spiritualists, *q.v.*) the term Gelassenheit appears again, but now with a more active connotation, closer to the divine principle of love. Rufus M. Jones recognizes here rightly a kinship to the ideas of the Quakers. It was above all Hans Denk (*q.v.*) who became a telling witness to this more positive interpretation of Gelassenheit. "If I run in the truth, that is if I run sufferingly (*leidenderweis*), then my running will not be in vain" (*Was geredt sey,* Schwindt, 34). "If man shall become one with God, he has to suffer what God intends to work in him" (*Ordnung Gottes,* Schwindt, 46). "There is no other way to blessedness than to lose one's self-will" (*Was geredt sey,* Jones, 23).

It was most likely Denk who made this idea popular among the Anabaptists. They had good reasons to accept it: their own teaching of obedience and discipleship (*q.v.*) almost required this attitude as the precondition of a reborn soul to walk the narrow path. The idea of martyrdom (*q.v.*) becomes bearable only on such a basis of self-surrender and joyous acceptance of God's willing. Only through Gelassenheit may suffering become the royal road to God. A beautiful example for this idea may be found in Michael Sattler's (*q.v.*) well-known letter to the brotherhood at Horb, sent out of his prison in May 1527. "In this peril I completely surrendered myself unto the will of the Lord, and . . . prepared myself even for death for His testimony. [Yet] I deemed it necessary to stir you up to follow after us in the divine warfare" (quoted from *Martyrs' Mirror*).

Perhaps the most outspoken representatives of Gelassenheit among early Anabaptists were the Philipite Brethren (*q.v.*) in Moravia, the rival group to the Hutterites, in the 1530's. It might even be claimed that Gelassenheit in a more passive connotation of quiet acceptance of suffering for the Lord's sake was the distinguishing doctrine of this group. Their strongest leader was most likely Michael Schneider (*q.v.*), of whom Wolkan has this to say: "[In his hymns] he is more profound [than the other brethren]; doctrinal questions do not concern him much, the idea of discipleship, however, seems to have influenced him most. Gelassenheit fills his mind: he is ready to suffer calmly, and even in the last hour he remembers his enemies, and he prays to God for them, for the highest virtue to him is brotherly love" (Wolkan, *Lieder,* 36). Gelassenheit and martyrdom belong then closely together.

Out of this Philipite group came the remarkable tract *Concerning the True Soldier of Christ* (*q.v.*) by Hans Haffner (*q.v.*) of about 1534. Its major idea is Gelassenheit, the victory over "world, flesh and the Devil." "The world truly accepts Christ as a gift, but does not know him at all from the point of view of suffering" (*leidenderweis,* the same term which Denk used a few years earlier). "When we truly realize the love of God, we will be ready to give up for love's sake even what God has given us." It is by this Gelassenheit that a true disciple is first recognized. Only by overcoming all selfishness will a community of love become possible.

In continuation of such thoughts, the Hutterites made the term Gelassenheit their own in a more earthly sense: the relinquishing of one's worldly possessions, in other words "absolute personal poverty," and subsequently the sharing of all earthly goods by the entire group. In fact, thus interpreted Gelassenheit becomes a central teaching of the Hutterite brethren. The great Article Book (*q.v.*) of about 1547 and its abbreviated version, the *Five Articles . . .* , are very outspoken in this regard; e.g., the third article is entitled, *Von der wahren Gelassenheit und christlichen Gemeinschaft der Güter* (*Geschicht-Buch,* 219). The idea is repeated in numberless tracts. Here hardly any mysticism is left; Gelassenheit is rather brought into close proximity to brotherly love which, the teaching goes, requires complete communal life. That Gelassenheit as preparedness to martyrdom was not forgotten, either, can likewise be proved from Hutterite literature. The *Klein-Geschichtsbuch der Hutterischen Brüder* mentions Gelassenheit at seven different places, from 1529 to 1792 (see Index). On page 16, for instance, we read, "We should expect the Lord's work and Cross daily, as we have surrendered unto His discipline (*Zucht*) and have agreed (*verwilligt*) to accept whatever He may send

upon us with thanksgiving, and to bear it with patience" (1529).

Naturally also the *Martyrs' Mirror* of 1660 abounds in quotations indicative of this basic attitude of the Anabaptists. A particularly fine example of it is contained in a letter which the brother Hans van Overdam wrote from his prison to the authorities of Gent in 1550. "We would rather through the grace of God suffer our temporal bodies to be burned, drowned, racked, or tortured, as it may seem good to you, or be scourged, banished, or driven away, or robbed of our goods, than to show any obedience contrary to the word of God, and we will be patient therein, committing vengeance to God, for we know that He says vengeance belongeth to me, I will recompense." Orley Swartzentruber, who quotes this passage (*MQR,* 1954, 139), calls this attitude "eschatological patience," that is, a patience born of an eschatological hope and expectation. This attitude, he thinks, belongs to the eschatological idea of the kingdom of God, which is "near" both in time and in spirit.

It would not be difficult to multiply these quotations from all branches of the Anabaptist movement. Actually the entire tract of Menno Simons, *"The Cross of Christ"* (1555, new Eng. ed. 1946), is basically nothing but an elaborate meditation on the virtue of *leijdzaamheid*.

In the period of Pietism (*q.v.*) the term Gelassenheit assumes again a new meaning, somewhat nearer to the mystical concept than to the Anabaptist interpretation. J. von Lodenstein (*q.v.*) and Gerhard Tersteegen (*q.v.*) are particularly fond of the term which now means the unperturbed calmness of the soul (*Seelenfrieden*) in the contemplation of divine grace. This new interpretation is definitely quietistic, but as such an element of genuine piety. The "Stillen im Lande" practice Gelassenheit, that is, aloofness from the turmoil of life and strife. The world is left to itself, and all activism, i.e., the application of love to the shaping of life, becomes reduced to a mild morality. Suffering is now understood sentimentally, but a certain longing toward unity with the Divine somehow recalls the outlook of the medieval mystics. In England, the Quakers continue the line of the "Spiritual Reformers," approximating the idea of Gelassenheit with their term "opening of the mind."

Present-day Mennonitism has lost the idea of Gelassenheit nearly completely; yet with the recovery of the ideal of discipleship also Gelassenheit may be revived.   R.F.

Article "Gelassenheit" in *RGG* II, 968-70; R. Friedmann, "Concerning the true soldier of Christ," *MQR,* 1931, 91 ff.; idem, "Anabaptism and Protestantism," *MQR,* 1950, 22-24; Rufus M. Jones, *Spiritual Reformers of the Sixteenth Century* (London, 1914, 1928); A. M. Schwindt, *Hans Denck* (Schlüchtern, c. 1922); Wolkan, *Lieder;* idem, *Geschicht-Buch;* Zieglschmid, *Das Klein-Geschichtsbuch* (Philadelphia, 1947); O. Swartzentruber, "Piety and Theology of the Anabaptist Martyrs in Van Braght's Martyrs' Mirror," *MQR,* 1954, 1, 2.

Gelder, van, a Dutch Mennonite family, whose ancestor was Dirk van Gelder (b. 1685 at Kampen, Dutch province of Overijssel, and d. there 1762).

He was a member of the Reformed Church, but his wife, Machteld Bruins, is supposed to have been a member of the Mennonite congregation. Their son Arend van Gelder (b. 1709 at Kampen and d. 1772 at Zaandam) was baptized in his childhood in the Reformed Church at Kampen. As an adult he moved first to Amsterdam and later to Zaandam, where he operated a grocery store. In Amsterdam he was married to Alida Nieuwenhuizen, who was a Mennonite, and van Gelder himself also joined the Mennonite Church, receiving baptism upon his confession of faith in the Zon (*q.v.*) meetinghouse at Amsterdam in 1734. Hendrik van Gelder (*q.v.*) was born of this marriage.

The Mennonite minister Arend Hendrik van Gelder (*q.v.*) was born of the third marriage of Arend van Gelder with Susanna Oortman. Pieter Smidt van Gelder, a son of Pastor Hendrik van Gelder and Maria Smidt (b. 1762 at Ouddorp, d. 1827 at Zaandam), settled at Wormerveer in the industrial Zaan district north of Amsterdam and ran a paper mill, which was continued in the world-renowned Royal Dutch Paper Manufactories *van Gelder Zonen,* a big business which is still carried on by members of the van Gelder family. This Pieter Smidt van Gelder, who became a wealthy man, was also sheriff and assistant-burgomaster of Wormerveer. Hendrik Arend van Gelder (*q.v.*), a Mennonite minister, was his grandson. The van Gelder family at Wormerveer has become allied by marriage with other Mennonite families of this district, such as Boekenoogen, Cardinaal, and Kaars Sypesteyn.

It is not clear whether Pieter van Gelder and Jan van Gelder, who were deacons of the Mennonite congregation at Utrecht about 1651-79 (*DB* 1916, 165 ff.; *Inv. Arch. Amst.* II, No. 2293), belonged to the same family.   vDZ.

J. M. van Gelder, *Stamboek der familie van Gelder* (Amsterdam, 1899); *Ned. Patriciaat* IX (1918) 104-17.

Gelder, Arend van, a Dutch Mennonite minister, son of Preacher Hendrik van Gelder (*q.v.*) and Maria Smidt, b. 1756 at Ouddorp, d. 1798 at Groningen, was baptized at West-Zaandam in 1783. Having been trained for the ministry by his father, he passed his examination to become a ministerial candidate in 1785 before the board of the Mennonite church of West-Zaandam. Thereupon he served the congregations of Norden, East Friesland, Germany, 1785-95, and Groningen (United Waterlanders and New-Flemish in the Pelsterstraat) 1795-98. Then he resigned because of bad health and died soon after. He was married first to Dirkje Bakker of Norden and afterwards to Catharina Vissering of Leer.   vDZ.

Gelder, Arend Hendrik van, the son of Arend van Gelder and Susanna Oortman, was born on Jan. 11, 1756, at Amsterdam, and died there unmarried on Aug. 18, 1819. He was the minister of the Mennonite congregation in Middelie in 1773-79, West-zaan-Zuid 1779, Amsterdam (de Zon and from 1801 the United Mennonite Church) 1779-1819. At Amsterdam he was very active in bringing about the union of the two Mennonite churches, which

was achieved in 1801. He was particularly zealous in promoting the association *Nut van't Algemeen.* He wrote *Redevoeringen over onderwerpen uit de natuurlyke historie* (2 vv., 1813 and 1816). In addition he was one of the compilers of the *Groote Bundel,* in which 25 hymns of his composition were included. Many of them are also found in the *Leidsche Bundel.* The *Doopsgezinde Bundel,* the hymnal now used by the Dutch Mennonites, contains only one song composed by van Gelder. When the A.D.S. (*q.v.*) was founded in 1811, van Gelder was a member of the first executive board. K.V., vDZ.

N.N.B.Wb. III, 198 f.; *DB* 1898, 2 ff., 24 ff.; *ML* II, 47.

Gelder, Hendrik van, b. 1737 at Amsterdam, d. Oct. 3, 1808, at Zaandam, the son of Arend van Gelder and Alida Nieuwenhuizen, was called as pastor of the Mennonite congregation at Ouddorp in 1759, Enkhuizen 1765, Enschede 1771, and West-Zaandam 1781-1808. He was married to Maria Smidt, a daughter of Petrus Smidt, a professor at the Zonist Seminary. Their son Pieter Smidt van Gelder was the founder of the paper factory that still bears their name. Another son was Arend van Gelder (*q.v.*). Hendrik van Gelder was the author of the following: *Davids dankbaarheid . . .* (Amsterdam, 1784), a sermon preached in the Mennonite church at West-Zaandam on March 14, 1784), when a pipe organ was installed in the church; *Lyk-rede op S. Hoekstra Wz* (West-Zaandam, 1786); *Het voorregt der openbare godsdienst-oeffeninge* (Amsterdam, 1787), a sermon preached on Nov. 4, 1787, the centennial of the dedication of the West-Zaandam church; *Het leven van Joannes den Dooper in leerredenen* (West-Zaandam, 1803). For a number of years van Gelder was secretary of the Zonist Conference. He also diligently studied Mennonite history, as appears from a manuscript found in the Amsterdam Mennonite Library. He also composed the *Naamlijst* of 1815.   K.V.

Inv. Arch. Amst. I, Nos. 759, 937; *N.N.B.Wb.* III, 200; *DB* 1869, 25; *Naamlijst* 1808, 73 f.; 1810, 72; *Catalogus Amst.,* 153, 254, 311; *ML* II, 47.

Gelder, Hendrik Arend van, a Dutch Mennonite minister, son of Hendrik van Gelder and Aagje Mats, b. 1825 at Wormerveer, d. 1899 at Haarlem, studied at the Amsterdam Mennonite Seminary and then served the congregations of Mensingeweer 1851-53, Medemblik 1853-55, Drachten-Ureterp 1855-58, Bolsward 1858-63, and Haarlem 1863-84. In 1853 he married Rinske Feikema of Franeker. He was a learned man, whose learning was honored by an appointment to membership on the board of the Teylers Theologisch Genootschap. He also wrote a history of the Mennonite congregation of Haarlem, which, however, was never published.   vDZ.

Gelderland, a province of the Netherlands (1949 population 1,057,941, with 3,403 Mennonites), in which the Anabaptist movement found little footing in the first half of the 16th century, with the exception of the towns of Arnhem, Nijmegen, Zutphen, and Harderwijk, and the vicinity of Winterswijk. The number of congregations has always been small. In the 17th century there were still congregations at

(Zalt) Bommel and at Harderwijk. The weakness of the movement here was doubtless due to the severe persecution by Duke Karel van Gelder, who issued a stern edict against them on April 12, 1539. The present (1956) congregations in this province are at Apeldoorn, Arnhem, Nijmegen, Wageningen, Winterswijk, and Zutphen. The Brotherhood House of Elspeet is also in this province.   K.V.

Ned. Archief v. Kerkgesch. X (1913) 252 ff.; Inv. Arch. Amst. I, Nos. 268, 291, 349; ML II, 47.

Geleyn Cornelis, an Anabaptist martyr, a shoemaker by trade, from Middelharnis, Dutch province of South Holland, was seized on Aug. 5, 1572, on the *Nieuwvaert* at Klundert near Breda with six brethren and several sisters who were engaged in worship. There were perhaps 100 brethren and sisters together, but most were able to escape; the captured women also escaped. After ruthless, brutal torture by Alba's executioners the six were burned at the stake Aug. 7 at Breda. (*Mart. Mir.* D 603-5; E 930 f.; *DB* 1912, 30-48; *ML* I, 370.)   NEFF.

Geleynsz, Jan: see Jansz, Geleyn.

Gellius Snecanus, the "Reformer" of Friesland, was a priest at Niekerk, and after 1565 Reformed preacher at Leeuwarden, d. about 1600. He was a violent opponent of the Anabaptists and published against them the Latin polemic *Methodica descriptio* (Leiden, 1584), which was translated into Dutch in 1588 with the title, *Ordentlijcke beschryvinge ende fondament van dry gemeyne plaetsen der H. Schrift.* The synod of Bolsward meeting in 1588 commissioned him to investigate Menno Simons' *Fundamentboek* (see **Foundation Book**). The consequence was that some group had the original edition of the *Fundamentboek* reprinted in order to show that the revised edition of 1558 (?) omitted certain statements about the Münsterites. (*N.N.B.Wb.* III, 204-8; *DB* 1911, 42 f.; *ML* II, 47 f.)   K.V.

Gellner (Kern), **Rupp,** one of the Anabaptists of the Lower Rhine living around Kreuznach and Worms known as the Swiss Brethren (*q.v.*), who, dissatisfied with the doctrine and life of these brethren, went to Moravia to join the Hutterian Brethren after the Hutterite apostle Hans Schmidt (*q.v.*) had given them a copy of a *Rechenschaft* of seven articles (*Geschicht-Buch,* 272-77). This union took place in 1556. Rupp Gellner was chosen preacher Jan. 8, 1568, at Nembschitz. On Jan. 17, 1572, he was ordained in the service of the Gospel. He died at an advanced age, March 17, 1608, at Frischau. In his last years he had become too weak to fill his office. (Wolkan, *Geschicht-Buch; ML* II, 48.)   LOSERTH.

Geloofsbelijdenis, de Nederlandsche (Dutch Confession of Faith). This outstanding confession of the Reformed Church in the Netherlands was composed in 1561 by Guy de Bres (*q.v.*) in French. The next year it was translated into Dutch and was soon adopted by a number of Calvinist churches in the Netherlands. It was officially approved and accepted by the Dutch national (Reformed) Synod, held at Dordrecht 1618-19. This confession contains 37 articles. Articles 34 and 35 deal with Anabaptism. Article 34 says that the Anabaptists erroneously condemn the baptism of children, which baptism is right and Biblical, because the baptizing of children is the continuation of Old Testament circumcision. Article 36 rejects the doctrine concerning public authorities of "the Anabaptists and other rebellious people . . . who wish to overthrow justice, to introduce community of goods and who trample down all chastity."

These two articles, which are applicable only to Münsterite and Batenburg (*q.v.*) Anabaptism, but not to Anabaptism in general, as must have been known to the Synod of Dordrecht, were often used against the Mennonites in the 17th and even the 18th centuries and formed the basis on which the Reformed Church built its attempt to prevent the Mennonites from building up their congregations.   vDZ.

Geloofsbelydenis voor den Doop. This Dutch Mennonite confession of which a printed copy is found in the Amsterdam Mennonite Library (n.p., n.d., about 1650) is a booklet of 64 pages. The title page is missing. Obviously it is a confession drawn up by a private person, who writes in a preface, "Here I publish a confession, which is to be used in our Mennonite congregations." (*Catalogus Amst.* 172.)   vDZ.

Geloofsbelydenis der Doopsgesinden *van de Socyteit oude Vlamingen genaamt, opgestelt in Vragen en Antwoorden* n.p., n.d. (18th century). This confession or rather explanation of the confession originated from the Groningen Old Flemish (*q.v.*) Mennonites in the Netherlands. It contains 25 chapters on 134 pages.   vDZ.

Geloofsbelydenisse der Doopsgesinden, *bekent onder de naam van Oude Vlamingen. Hunne Societeits Vergaderinge houdende in de Botteringe-straat te Groningen.* Of this confession of the Groningen Old Flemish (*q.v.*) group there are four editions, all at Groningen—1755, 1774, 1805, n.d. (early 19th century). The last edition contains an appendix containing a number of questions and answers drawn up by Cornelis Pietersz Sorgdrager (*q.v.*).   vDZ.

Gelouwe, Arnout van, an opponent of the Protestants and Anabaptists, known as "the Flemish peasant," b. 1604 at Ardoye, a village between Rousselare and Thielt, became a weaver. In Delft, Dutch province of South Holland, where he settled, he acquired a thorough knowledge of the Bible, then joined the Catholic Church and used his gifts in attacking Protestants as well as Anabaptists. In 1648 he betook himself to the Mennonite church in Aardenburg, and at the close of a religious service in the presence of the assembled congregation challenged the preacher Boudewijn de Meijer to a disputation. The rumor spread through the city that a Catholic priest had appeared in the Mennonite church and was trying to convert them; such a crowd gathered before the little church that the meeting had to be adjourned, and the disputation continued at the preacher's house. In 1651 also a violent polemic against the Mennonites came from

Gelouwe's pen, attacking the book of the Mennonite preacher Francois de Knuyt (*q.v.*), *Eene corte bekentenisse onses gheloofs,* etc. Its verbose title reads, *Een onverwinnelycke schrift-matighe Roomsche Catholycke belijdenisse des gheloofs, van Godt den Vater, Godt den Soon, Godt den H. Geest, den Kinderdoop, ende van het wettelyck eedtsweeren, ende van het ampt der Christelycke Overheydt, ofte een schrift-matighe teghen-gift, ghesteldt teghen de onschriftmatighe belijdenisse der nieuwghesinde Wederdooperen, voor desen uytgheeven tot verleydinghe van de eenvoudige onnoosele herten door François de Knuyt.* (*DB* 1877, 25 ff.; *ML* II, 48.)

NEFF.

Gelre (Gelder, Geldern), a former duchy consisting of Lower Gelre, now the Dutch province of Gelderland (*q.v.*), and Upper Gelre, now part of the Dutch provinces of Limburg and North Brabant and the adjacent part of Germany. In the German part of old Gelre is found the city of Geldern, the home of the dynasty of the dukes of Gelre. In Lower Gelre only a few traces of Anabaptism are to be found in the 16th century (see **Gelderland**). In Upper Gelre Anabaptism-Mennonitism was rather widespread. The "Wassenberger Predikanten" (*q.v.*) were active here, and Menno Simons preached in this region (see **Illekhoven** and **Visschersweert**).

vDZ.

Gem Mennonite Brethren Church, located at Gem in central Alberta, had its beginning in November 1928, when 25 Mennonite families, immigrants from the Ukraine and Siberia, settled here, some of whom were the Mennonite Brethren, some Evangelical Mennonite Brethren, and some General Conference Mennonites. On June 2, 1929, the M.B. congregation organized with 35 members and with H. K. Siemens as leader. They met in the school every Sunday for worship together with the members of the other two branches.

In 1932 a church was built, which was enlarged a few years later. In 1952-53, because of its unsatisfactory location and poor condition, it was sold and a new one was erected. An important milestone was the opening of the Bethesda Bible School on Nov. 12, 1933, which with a few interruptions has served until the present. On Dec. 16, 1934, P. P. Doerksen was chosen as leader of the congregation.

The membership in 1953 was 130. The congregation has continued to grow, in spite of the fact that the subsidiary congregation in Countess became an independent congregation in 1939, and many members have gone to British Columbia. In 1942 all the members of the E.M.B. congregation formally united with the M.B. congregation.   H.H.S.

Gemeenschap voor Doopsgezind Broederschapswerk. This Dutch Mennonite association has operated under different names. It was founded in 1917 as *Vereenigung voor Gemeentedagen van Doopsgezinden,* then it was called *Elspeetse Vereniging,* until it received its present name after World War II. For its history and activities, see **Broederschapswerk.**   vDZ.

Gemeentedagbeweging, the popular name of the former Dutch Mennonite Association *Vereeniging voor Gemeentedagen voor Doopsgezinden* (now *Gemeenschap voor Doopsgezind Broederschapswerk*): see **Broederschapswerk,** *Gemeenschap voor Doopsgezind.*

Gemeindeblatt der Mennoniten, a biweekly periodical, the organ of the *Gemeindeverband* of Baden, Württemberg, and Bavaria (*q.v.*). The paper owes its origin to the awakening that took place in the congregations of Baden in the middle of the 19th century. In the 1860's several leading ministers became aware of the necessity and benefit of such a publication for the South German congregations. In particular Christian Schmutz (*q.v.*) of Rappenau was zealous in promoting the project. At that time the only German Mennonite periodical was the *Mennonitische Blätter,* which had been published since 1854. The records of the meeting of the elders on Oct. 14, 1869, state briefly, "Brother Ulrich Hege of Reihen proposes that a church periodical be published for our congregations. This meeting gives its consent to the proposal and commissions him to be the editor."

Beginning in 1870 the *Gemeindeblatt* was published monthly first as a four-page, and later as an eight-page paper. In 1896 the masthead read, "Published—with the co-operation of several preachers and with the consent of the *Aeltestenrat*—by Ulrich Hege in Reihen." In the earlier years this statement was correct, for a series of important articles was contributed by Christian Schmutz of Rappenau, who was a leader in the awakening in the congregations of Baden. His articles on church discipline, mixed marriages, and communion were thus to become effective in wider Mennonite circles. The frankness with which all questions of church life were openly discussed is striking. This frankness is also to be noted in the 1880's when the matter of union with the *Vereinigung der Mennoniten im Deutschen Reich* was debated; the *Gemeindeverband* did not join the *Vereinigung.* Elder Ulrich Hege (*q.v.,* 1812-96) was distinguished by his interest in Mennonite history, combined with a strong publicistic interest. He published excerpts from Menno's works on baptism, communion, etc. Also writings of Hans Denk (*Von der wahren Liebe und Ordnung Gottes*) and of Hubmaier (*q.v.*) were published. In the 1880's when the works of Ludwig Keller (*q.v.*) were stimulating research in Mennonite history, each of his books as it appeared, was discussed in the *Gemeindeblatt.* Also the personal connections of Schmutz occasioned many an article. Frequently there was material from the *Martyrs' Mirror* or one of the martyr hymns. The *Gemeindeblatt* sponsored a movement toward Mennonite union, viz., the Conference of the South German Mennonites (*q.v.*), to which all the South German congregations now belong. Connections with West Prussia were given special attention. There was also correspondence with Mennonites of other countries (America, France, Switzerland, and Russia). From the beginning there were reports from the missions on Sumatra and Java.

The lifework of the first editor of the *Gemeinde-blatt* can best be stated in the words of the number celebrating the fiftieth anniversary of its founding: "Precisely the first volumes of the *Gemeindeblatt* prove that the paper was not the hobby of a few people, but met a real need in spite of much opposition. From North and South Germany, from Switzerland, and from Russia come voices asking to be heard. Sometimes the ideas expressed were in diametric opposition to each other, and for the editor it must have been by no means an easy matter to arbitrate and prevent the expressions from leading to divisive strife, but especially in those questions that dealt with fundamentals to lead to mutual understanding. A decisive attitude was taken against both the influence of rationalism and a petrified formalism. The earnest striving and longing for a spiritual revival in the Mennonite brotherhood stood in the foreground; likewise the effort to bring back to the consciousness of our church members the teaching and faith of our forefathers."

What seemed to Ulrich Hege to be his chief task he expressed in the motto on the masthead of the first issue in 1871: "That ye be perfectly joined together in the same mind and in the same judgment" (I Cor. 1:10). The paper strove in the first place to promote and preserve the spiritual life in the congregations on the foundation which has Jesus Christ as its cornerstone. Its next task was to contribute "to a union and unification, pleasing to God, of our greatly scattered congregations, not only with respect to space, but also with respect to the inner mind, the various views, and organization. Although they are united in the confession of the principal doctrines, because of a few deviating views they are in part so distant to one another and take such a cold attitude to each other, showing little brotherly love" (*Gbl.,* 1873, 3).

At an advanced age, after serving as editor for 26 years, Ulrich Hege passed the office on to his son, traveling evangelist Jakob Hege of Reihen (1848-1911). From now on, historical articles retired to the background. The devotional aspect became dominant. Otherwise the form of the periodical remained the same (news from all the congregations of Germany and from foreign countries). The co-operation of fellow ministers decreased. It is apparent that the time of the first love was past for the paper. The publisher must rely more upon himself. "For my brother the assumption of the editorship in addition to his work as traveling evangelist denoted a great burden, especially since there was at times a dearth of colaborers" (*Gbl.* 1919, 2).

Beginning in 1901 the *Gemeindeblatt,* in agreement with the general wish, became a biweekly four-page paper, and in this form it has continued to serve the Mennonite brotherhood to the present. It was intended to serve as a Sunday paper for members living widely scattered and to create a closer bond in general by its more frequent appearance (*Gbl.,* 1900). That the paper continued to satisfy an inner need is shown by the fact that the number of subscribers rose to 1,200.

Jakob Hege published the paper until his death in 1911. In the first decade of the 20th century there was a lively debate among the South German congregations on the subject of the Conference of the South German Mennonites (*q.v.*). Because of the active connections of the publisher with the Mennonite preachers in the Palatinate, the contributions of articles from the congregations on the left of the Rhine were especially numerous.

In 1911 the editorship was given to the youngest son of the founder of the *Gemeindeblatt,* Philipp Hege (1857-1923) of Stuttgart, the third and last member of this family to serve in that office. The years before the war reflect the high points of the conference work of South Germany, when E. Händiges as traveling evangelist rallied the Mennonites of South Germany, in particular those of Bavaria. The paper was able to appear throughout World War I.

Worthy of note are the regularly appearing articles, "Concerning the War," later called "Rundschau," which afforded an excellent survey of the contemporary situation and testified to the healthy, long-range vision of the writer. The paper gave information concerning the situation of congregations in the homeland and in foreign lands, reports on the suffering of the Russian brethren after the Revolution, and the rising relief work known as *Mennonitische Flüchtlingshilfe,* and later the *Deutsche Mennonitenhilfe.* The devotional character of the paper retired to the background, while historical matters of the past and present came to the fore. It is significant that already under the previous editor the congregational affairs were no longer publicly discussed. The periodical has taken on the character of a Sunday religious journal.

Philipp Hege was taken from the churches by death in March 1923. He was followed in office by Gysbert van der Smissen of Heilbronn (1859-1923). By December of the same year the paper was again orphaned by the unexpected sudden death of the editor. In 1924 the council of elders of Baden assigned the task to Walter Fellmann of Mönchzell, and in 1925, when Fellmann joined the faculty of the missionary seminary of Wernigerode, the council appointed Christian Schnebele, the leader of the Mennonite Bibelheim Thomashof near Durlach, who was still the editor in 1956. The place of publication was transferred from Sinsheim a. Elsenz to Karlsruhe, Baden, in 1926, where it has since been printed by the Mennonite printer Heinrich Schneider.

Due to the war situation the *Gemeindeblatt* was suspended from 1941 (last number Jan. 1, 1941) to 1948 (first number April 1, 1948).

As the organ of the *Verband* of Baden-Württemberg-Bavaria, the paper is read in most of the Mennonite families of these areas. It is also read in the Palatinate and in Bavaria, and was to some extent read in North Germany, especially in West Prussia, when these congregations were still in existence. (*ML* II, 57 ff.) W.F., H.S.B.

Gemeindeblatt und Waisenheim, established in 1895, was the organ of the Krimmer Mennonite Brethren Conference and the Industrial Home (*q.v.,* Waisenheim) near Hillsboro, Kan. Some of the editors were Heinrich Wiebe, Gerhard Dalke, Jakob Z. Wiebe, and Jakob G. Barkman. It was an 8-page monthly (in 1899 a few issues contained 12 pages) and was published in Hillsboro. H. H. Fast was the printer for a while. In the June 1, 1904, issue the Publishing Committee, consisting of Joh. J. Friesen and A. A. Klassen, announced that the editorship was to be transferred to Weatherford, Okla. It is not known how long the paper appeared after this. In March 1906, the *Industrial Home Journal* (*q.v.*) took over the interests in the Waisenheim, and in 1915 the *Wahrheitsfreund* (*q.v.*) became the official conference paper without any reference to the *Gemeindeblatt*. The Bethel College Historical Library has a nearly complete set of the *Gemeindeblatt* from 1897 to 1904.   C.K.

Gemeinde-Kalender: see **Christlicher Gemeinde-Kalender.**

Gemeindeordnungen, ordinances and regulations of the Hutterite brotherhood, also their church disciplines (although different in character from the conventional type of such documents, since church activities and everyday living were identical for the Brethren). They were issued by the bishop (*Vorsteher*) of the brotherhood. Some 30 such Ordnungen are known from 1561 to 1665, and again 1762, 1793, and later. They are among the most original creations of the Hutterites and are in many ways unique documents, revealing the strong consciousness of the brethren that they had to follow a very strict and austere way of life, the "narrow path," and that deviations must be stopped.

These Ordnungen are spiritual and moral as well as practical in nature (to the minutest detail). They are hortative, yet never threatening, admonishing all members of the church to co-operate most carefully and soberly in the great enterprise of brotherly living in community of goods, both in consumption and production, in the way which Christ and the apostles established. In this sense it is not incorrect to call the Anabaptist church in general, and the Hutterite brotherhood in particular, a "church of order" (see article **Church** and R. Friedmann, *MQR*, 1950, 21), i.e., a disciplined and regulated church in which this order is voluntarily accepted by all. God speaks through the bishops, who thus assume a charismatic authority.

In many regards these ordinances suggest the rules and regulations of medieval monasteries, with which the Hutterite organization has many traits in common (the principle of merit is, however, completely absent here). In some other regards these ordinances are reminiscent of the medieval guild regulations, although their outspoken Christian emphasis distinguishes them again from these secular documents.

The Ordnungen may be classified into two kinds: (*a*) those dealing with the general organization and discipline of the community (*Gemein,* Bruderhofs), its morals and its spiritual guidance, also the formulation of the general genius of the group; (*b*) regulations dealing in particular with the special functions of the various members of the group, with the administration of crafts and other occupational

tasks and their most careful and economical fulfillment. In this group regulations for millers, cutlers (*Messerer*), barber-surgeons, potters (*Hafner,* see **Ceramics**), the various kinds of smiths, buyers, stock clerks (*Ausgeber*), stewards, and farm foremen (*Weinzierl*) appear more often than for other occupations. It seems that in these areas temptations were particularly strong to indulge in self-interested extra activities which could easily injure the group and spoil its good name.

The main tenor of all the Ordnungen is the battle against *Eigennutz* (selfishness, greed, profit-motive), and the admonition to live up to the requirements of a life in perfect community of goods. Austerity, puritanical simplicity, even a degree of ascetic living were enjoined time and again, and thus inculcated in the mind of every member. The education of the youth dared not be soft in any way, for they were to be trained for trying times and must then know why to suffer and be able to bear such situations. The reading of the old writings (epistles, confessions, hymns) was advised as helpful. All handiwork was to be diligent, solid, and reliable, carefully done without waste. Work should be done every day including Saturday, without haste but also without loafing; luxuries must not be allowed, likewise no private possessions of any kind. Ehrenpreis (*q.v.*) declared expressly, "Inheritance shall remain abolished as of old; if someone dies, everything he has used shall revert to the community, even his books" (*Klein-Geschichtsbuch,* 526). It should be remarked, however, that the latter point is no longer in practice today; books are now the only possession of a brother or sister which may be left to one's children.

The Ordnungen offer an extremely valuable insight into the inner life of the brotherhood from 1561 on (when the first ordinance of this kind was laid down by the Vorsteher Lanzenstiel, *q.v.*). Before that year we have only Riedemann's *Rechenschaft* of 1540 (*q.v.*) and the epistles (*q.v.*), mainly by Jacob Hutter, or the oral tradition.

In the main, four great Vorsteher distinguished themselves in the drawing up *Gemeindeordnungen*: Peter Walpot (*q.v.*) 1565-78, Klaus Braidl (*q.v.*) 1583-1611, Sebastian Dietrich (*q.v.*) 1611-19, and Andreas Ehrenpreis (*q.v.*) 1639-62 but actually leading the brotherhood since 1633. Although the first-named two men contributed much to this tradition, the great Ordnungen were yet to come: Dietrich's general ordinance of 1612 (which fills 22 leaves in one manuscript) and Ehrenpreis' general ordinance of 1651 (which fills 14 pages folio size small print of the *Klein-Geschichtsbuch,* 519-32). That we are so well informed about all these writings is due to the tradition-mindedness of Ehrenpreis and his unusual sense for the orderly collection of all rules existent before his days, together with the contributions of his own spiritual government. In one handwritten book of 1640 (Codex III, 198 of Esztergom, apparently Ehrenpreis' own copy), with additions up to 1650, this Vorsteher put together nearly everything that had been said before and also that which he himself had presented to the brotherhood since 1633. There is, to be sure, also some repetition, but always with some new angles not stressed before.

This codex has never been published; one copy of it is in the Beck collection (*q.v.*) of Brno, Nr. 87, another, also done by Beck in longhand, is deposited in the Mennonite Historical Library of Goshen College. Beck in his *Geschichts-Bücher* prints only the *Bader-Ordnung* of 1653 (ordinance for the barber-surgeons, actually a repetition of an earlier ordinance of 1633 in Beck, 485-87; English in *MQR*, 1953, 125-27) and a *Weinzierl-Ordnung* (order for the farm managers) of 1650 (Beck, 478-79).

A number of hitherto completely unknown Ordnungen were made public for the first time when A. J. F. Zieglschmid's edition of the *Klein-Geschichtsbuch* came out in 1947. Not only does the Johannes Waldner text (*q.v.*) contain two remarkably strong instructions by Ehrenpreis: (*a*) concerning absolute nonresistance (1633; *Klein-Geschichtsbuch*, 168-72, English in *MQR*, 1951, 116-27), and (*b*) concerning the mating of young people, also against the bad practice of unchecked match-making (*Kuppelei*), which recently had entered the brotherhood (1643; *Klein-Geschichtsbuch*, 215-18). But the most outstanding Ordnung of all is the great ordinance of 1651, which Zieglschmid prints in an appendix from a copy still preserved and in use by the Brethren today (*Klein-Geschichtsbuch*, 519-32). It contains a comprehensive instruction which touches practically every aspect of life, stern in character and yet with a loving concern. Among other things also the idea of shunning (*Meidung*) is enjoined; it must not be allowed to be taken lightly or to be denied altogether. The Ordnung of 1651 contains actually a complete "philosophy of life" in the minutest detail, and for that reason deserves particular attention. A footnote says that it was read before the assembled Brethren in Slovakia as well as in Transylvania year after year, and that it was reread to the brotherhood for the last time as late as 1734. Besides this Ordnung, the larger Chronicle of the Brethren, the *Geschicht-Buch*, contains also two letters to the Brethren in Transylvania of 1642 (Zieglschmid, *Chronik*, 831-37) and of 1649 (*ibid.*, 847-56), again by Ehrenpreis and with similar advice and admonitions.

"Be faithful and loyal, even unto the smallest detail," that is in a nutshell the message of Ehrenpreis, by which he wanted to strengthen the somewhat weakened brotherhood of his time, imbuing it with the spirit of the founding fathers. The scope of his concern is amazing. In retrospect we may say that his work has been fairly successful, even though a certain formalism became dominant as the living spirit faded out more or less. The organization and the genius of the Hutterites today is to a certain extent based on these Gemeindeordnungen, which give to the brotherhood such directions that temptations will be met and as far as possible reduced. And yet, these regulations are by no means dictatorial in character; they are presented with a generally accepted authority of the bishops, and they breathe the spirit of brotherly love and concern in maintaining the way which the Brethren considered the true form of Christian discipleship. (See **Braidl, Dietrich, Ehrenpreis, Bruderhof, Community of Goods, Crafts, Eco-**nomic History of the **Hutterian Brethren,** also **Church.**)   R.F.

Loserth, *Communismus*, 252 ff.; also Loserth's articles on Dietrich (*ML* I, 442-43) and Ehrenpreis (*ML* I, 530-32), where details of these ordinances are given. Also R. Friedmann, "An Ordinance of 1633 on Nonresistance" *MQR*, 1951, 116-27, and J. L. Sommer, "Hutterite Medicine and Physicians," *MQR*, 1953, 125 ff. No special study of these ordinances has ever been made.

A chronological list of all the Hutterite Ordnungen follows:

Time of L. Lanzenstiel
1561 Ordnung of the shoemakers
Time of Peter Walpot
1568 Ordnung for the schools (Kindergarten through grades)
1569 Ordnung enjoining greatest economy at the Bruderhofs
1571 Ordnung for the millers
1574 Ordnung for the carpenters
Time of Claus Braidl
1585 Ordnung for the dyers
1588 Ordnung for the millers
1588 Ordnung for the schools, repeated 1593 and 1596
1591 Ordnung for the shoemakers
1592 Ordnung for the barber-surgeons
1599 Ordnung for the buyers (*Einkäufer*)
1603 Ordnung concerning dress
1610 Ordnung for the millers
Time of Sebastian Dietrich
1612 General Ordnung to be read yearly, concerning the bringing up of the youth, simplicity of life, economy and the right conduct of the Bruderhofs
1612 Ordnung for the stewards, shoemakers, buyers, potters, and cutlers
1612 Ordnung for the potters, concerning the precious, expensive ceramic wares
1612 Ordnung for the hoofsmiths, scythesmiths, coppersmiths, bladesmiths, cutlers, casemakers, watchmakers, and potters
1617 Ordnung repeated
Time of Andreas Ehrenpreis
1633 Ordnung for the barber-surgeons
1633 Ordnung concerning absolute nonresistance
1637 Ordnung for the barber-surgeons, repeated
1639 General Ordnung for the brotherhood (first draft)
1640 Ordnung for millers, stewards, and store clerks (*Ausgeber*), farm managers, buyers, teamsters, seamstresses, and cellar masters
1640 Ordnung also for the Diener des Worts (ministers), likewise for those who are sent out as missioners to visit the people of the world
1641 Ordnung for the cutlers
1641 Ordnung for the potters, repeated
1642 Letter to the Brethren in Transylvania
1642 Ordnung for the stewards (*Haushalter*)
1643 Ordnung concerning matching young people
1649 Letter to the Brethren in Transylvania
1650 Ordnung for the farm-manager (*Weinzierl*)
1650 Ordnung for the cutlers
1651 The great general Ordnung (*Klein-Geschichtsbuch*, 519-32) comparable to the general Ordnung of Dietrich of 1612. This Ordnung was repeated almost every year, both in Slovakian Bruderhofs and in Transylvania, also later in Russia and now in America.
1654 Ordnung for the barber-surgeons
1655 Ordnung for the cutlers (repeated)

––––––––––

1762 Ordnung for stewards, farm managers, the distribution of the food at the tables, overseers of the granary (*Kastner* or *Rentmeister*), cooks and caretakers of the linen, also for dishwashers (*Klein-Geschichtsbuch*, 535-39)
1773 Ordnung concerning uniformity of dress, etc., etc., up to
1873

––––––––––

Gemeindeverband (*Badischer Verband,* or simply *Verband*), terms used to designate the Badisch-Württembergisch - Bayrischer Gemeindeverband (*q.v.*).

Gemeinschaftsbewegung (movement for fellowship, community), the term used to designate the circles of earnest Christians arising in the Lutheran and Reformed state churches of Germany under the influence of Pietism (*q.v.;* P. J. Spener, 1680 ff.) and more particularly the Moravians (*q.v.,* from 1727) and J. A. Bengel (1687-1752) of Württemberg. These earlier groups, called "Old-Pietist" (*Altpietistische*) Gemeinschaften and found mostly in Württemberg and Baden, in 1881 organized an association, the *Verband der Altpietistischen Gemeinschaften,* with some 630 local circles in 1935. In addition to this group are the less numerous circles of the "Hahn" (named for J. M. Hahn, *q.v.,* 1758-1819) Gemeinschaft, which two Baden Mennonite congregations joined in 1858. The Gemeinschaft movement was closely related also to the Inner (Home) Mission movement (J. H. Wichern, 1808-81), which began *ca.* 1835, especially in the earlier period. The Protestant Union for Home Missions in Baden (*Evangelischer Verein für Innere Mission in Baden*), organized in 1848, and its daughter groups in the Palatinate, Hesse, etc., were particularly strongly involved in the Gemeinschaft movement. The St. Chrischona "Pilgermission" group, founded 1841, was also a part of this development. The Altpietistische Gemeinschaft remained formally inside the state church, although maintaining a strong separate fellowship life in the local circles with regular meetings. They had in general a sober, earnest, quiet though intensely devout character.

The modern Gemeinschaft movement in Germany dating from 1875, owes its rise largely to English-American influences such as the Plymouth Brethren of England, and the American Robert Pearsall Smith (d. 1898) and W. E. Boardman (d. 1886), whose influence was mediated in part through Otto Stockmayer, Jellinghaus, Rappard (St. Chrischona), Christlieb, and Elias Schrenk, the great evangelist. This movement was varied in character, but was characterized generally by an aggressive mass evangelism, a holiness emphasis, a millennialistic eschatology, and a Methodistic piety. It was in general more separatistic than the Old Pietists; many new Gemeinschaft circles were now founded and the whole Gemeinschaft movement was greatly enlarged. The new movement, which absorbed or transformed some of the older Old Pietist circles, created an all-over organization in 1888, called the "Gnadauer Verband."

About 1900 a serious division in the movement occurred, in which the Darbyite (Plymouth Brethren) more reactionary, strongly millennialist-dispensationalist and separatistical influences became dominant. This phase of the movement was centered in the Blankenburg Alliance (*Blankenburger Allianz, q.v.*), whose annual conferences at Blankenburg, beginning in 1886, were very influential. Ernst Modersohn (b. 1869) and Ernst Stroeter (d. 1922) were strong leaders, Modersohn being the most influential writer of the entire modern Gemeinschaft movement.

A wing of the Gemeinschaft movement, taking a strong anti-state church position, developed circles which withdrew completely from the state church and in effect became nondenominational independent groups of Plymouth Brethren character and connection. The center of this group has been the Bible School (*Allianzbibelschule*) founded in Berlin in 1905, but located in Wiedenest since 1918, with Joh. Warns and Erich Sauer as prominent leaders.

A related movement which also absorbed some Gemeinschaft groups is that of the Free Evangelical Churches (Freie Evangelische Gemeinden, Eglise Libre) of Germany, Switzerland, and France. It was modeled at first on the Eglise Libre Evangélique of Geneva (founded 1846). The first local church of this group was organized in 1854 in Elberfeld-Barmen, an area which has remained the center in Germany and the seat of the Association (*Bund*) of the Free Churches. Its Bible School was founded in Vohwinkel in 1912.

The Baptist (since 1834) and Methodist (since 1831) churches of Germany have been similar in character to the Gemeinschaft movement, and often closely related to it, but in a sense also competitors to it.

The Gemeinschaft movement has undoubtedly been a powerful influence, mostly for good, in Germany, although it has often met opposition from official church circles. It has gathered into local and larger fellowships countless thousands of earnest Christians eager for a deepening of the spiritual life and a more dedicated type of Christianity than the typical state church type has afforded. It has also furnished a large opportunity for lay participation.

The Gemeinschaft movement has characteristics which are similar to the original Anabaptist movement in the 16th century, although some of its features and emphases, in doctrine and piety, are quite un-Anabaptist. It has had considerable influence in the past 75 years upon the Mennonites of South Germany and Switzerland, as well as in South Russia. Numerous Mennonites from these areas attended the conferences in Germany, particularly of the Blankenburg Alliance. Some of the leaders like Stroeter traveled among the Mennonites of Russia and influenced particularly the Mennonite Brethren there and in North America. Jakob Kroeker (*q.v.*) was an active leader in the Gemeinschaft movement, and mediated its spirit among the Mennonites of Germany, and earlier in Russia. The evangelists of the movement like Elias Schrenk (d. 1913) and Jakob Vetter (d. 1918) (also Pastor Böhmerle) had considerable influence in certain South German and Swiss Mennonite circles. A considerable amount of the revival of spiritual life and activity in these areas has been due to the influence of leaders and literature of the Gemeinschaft movement (writings of Otto Funcke, d. 1910) and the influence of schools which Mennonites have attended, such as St. Chrischona (1840 ff.), Baptisten Seminar in Hamburg-Horn (1881 ff.), Missionsanstalt Neukirchen bei Mörs (1882 ff.), Evangelische Predigerschule in Basel (1876 ff.), Allianzbibelschule (Berlin 1905-18, Wiedenest 1918 ff.).

Although the hymnbooks of the German and Russian Mennonites did not adopt many of the Gospel songs of the Gemeinschaft movement, the typical hymnals of the movement, *Reichslieder* and *Siegeslieder,* were widely used in certain Swiss, Alsatian, South German, and Russian Mennonite congregations and families.

The "Conference for Faith" (*Glaubenskonferenz*) which was sponsored annually by the missionary society "Licht im Osten" (*q.v.*) of Wernigerode a.H., Germany, under the directorship of Jakob Kroeker, was closely related to the Blankenburg Conference and inspired by the Gemeinschaftsbewegung. One of its major purposes was to promote support for the work of "Licht im Osten." H.S.B.

P. Fleisch, *Die moderne Gemeinschaftsbewegung in Deutschland* 2 vv. (1912-14); E. Crous, "Mennonitentum und Pietismus (IV: Die Gemeinschaftsbewegung)," in *Theologische Zeitschrift* VIII (1952) 279-96; *ML* II, 65 f.

Gemeinschaftliche Liedersammlung, Die, zum all-*gemeinen Gebrauch des wahren Gottesdienstes aus vielen Liederbüchern gesammelt, und mit einem Inhalt sammt Register versehen.* This small (12 mo., 320 pp.) hymnbook without music, was the third compiled and published by American Mennonites, and served the Ontario Mennonites as long as the German language was in use. It is still used by the Old Order group in Ontario, the latest edition being 1950. It was first published at Berlin (Kitchener, Ont.) in 1836, with reprints there 1838,·1841, 1849, 1857, 1883, 1892, 1908. The reprints of 1860 and 1870 at Lancaster, Pa., suggest it was also used in that area for at least a time. The second edition was slightly enlarged with an appendix (*Anhang*), which became a larger *Zugabe* with the third edition, both editions having a double index (*Register*). From 1857 on the reprints were identical at 388 pages. Probably edited by Bishop Benjamin Eby (*q.v.,* 1785-1853), the book took two thirds of its 205 hymns from the Lancaster Conference hymnal, *Unpartheyisches Gesangbuch* (*q.v.,* first ed. 1804), and most of the rest from the Franconia Conference hymnal, *Kleine Geistliche Harfe* (*q.v.*). H.S.B.

Gemmingen, an old noble family in Kraichgau, Germany. At the time of the Reformation the family was already sympathetic to the Anabaptists. The Anabaptist evangelist Philip Weber (*q.v.*) received an audience in 1527 from the barons of Gemmingen, who owned the villages of Fürfeld and Bonfeld in Württemberg and half of Ittlingen in Baden (Hege, 62). But he had no lasting success here, for persecution soon set in, which made it impossible for him to remain. The villages were then reformed by Martin Germanus (Stocker, 56). After the Peace of Westphalia the estates of the family again offered refuge to the Mennonites exiled from Switzerland in the 17th century. In the Gemmingen family archives are still to be found the "Bestandsbriefe für die Mennoniten Heinrich Beer und Jakob Ebe" of 1763-65 of Bonfeld, Dammhof, and Fürfeld. Other Gemmingen estates which have in part been leased by Mennonites until recent times are Rappenau, Treschklingen, Hösselinshof, Stockbronnerhof, Mi-

chelfeld, and Unterbiegelhof (the latter since 1888 the property of the family). HEGE.

Chr. Hege, *Die Täufer in der Kurpfalz* (Frankfurt, 1908); C. W. F. L. Stocker, *Familien-Chronik der Freiherren von Gemmingen* (Heilbronn, 1895); *Ztscht für die Gesch. des Oberrheins* LXVIII (1924) appendix; *ML* II, 66.

Gemüthsgespräch: see **Christliches Gemüthsgespräch.**

Génard, Petrus (b. 1830 at Antwerp, d. there 1899), archivist and librarian of the city of Antwerp, Belgium, published in the *Antwerpsch Archieven-blad,* vv. VII-XIV (Antwerp, 1864 ff.), all the extant documents concerning persons who were judicially persecuted in the 16th century because of religion. The documents, which contain detailed and valuable information, are found in Vols. VII-XIII (Antwerp, 1864 ff.). Vol. XIV, pp. 1-127, has a chronological list of over 1300 "heretics." vDZ.

Genealogy. Genealogy and family history are closely related and often combined in the same study. While genealogy is part of family history, not all family history is genealogy. The following bibliography of Mennonite genealogies includes published books in which ancestors and descendants are listed in the natural order of succession. In some instances the books listed are basically family history rather than genealogy, but genealogical charts accompany the book. In the American section of the bibliography titles have been included only if the progenitors in America were Mennonite; there has been no attempt to include every genealogy in which a Mennonite appears. The American section has been based upon the historical collections at Bethel College, North Newton, Kan.; Bluffton College, Bluffton, Ohio; and Goshen College, Goshen, Ind., checked against some lists from other libraries and private collections. The Dutch and German sections were based upon these same collections, the 1919 *Catalogus* of the Amsterdam Mennonite Library, Adolf Schnebele's unpublished bibliography of German Mennonite imprints, and information supplied by individuals in these countries. The total number of titles listed is 310; 265 North American, 30 Dutch, 15 German.

It is immediately evident that much more genealogical work has been done by American than by European Mennonites. This may be explained in part by the natural starting point which the American genealogist finds in the date of arrival in America of the progenitor of the family. In America the first books to appear were those related to the Levering and Schnebele families, both appearing in 1858. From 1870 to the present there has been a continuous growth in American Mennonite genealogical publication with an early peak in the 1890's and a slight recession during the 1930's. The early peak in the 1890's was due to the intense research of one man, A. J. Fretz, a Presbyterian minister-farmer, who compiled eleven genealogies of Mennonite families published between the years 1890 and 1906, many of which he published privately. These books range in size from 80 to more than 870 pages and contain an amazing amount of information concerning many of the individuals listed. It is not unusual to find in the Fretz genealogies rather complete biographical sketches of persons who contributed in a special way to church and community. The number of families which Fretz treated was possible in part because of interlocking family relationships, but even so his work is monumental for one individual.

Interestingly, the increase in the number of American genealogies published in the last two decades can be attributed to two distinct groups—families which are predominantly Amish Mennonite (Old Order) and the families of descendants of Mennonite immigrants from Russia since 1873. Before 1930 this latter group was represented by only one small booklet (Deckert family), probably published before 1895. No further genealogies from this group appeared until 1930, with the majority published since 1948. It is evident that genealogical research among the descendants of these immigrants from Russia has been spurred by the imminent passing of the last generations born in Russia.

The bibliography includes materials ranging from broadsides printed on one side to volumes of more than one thousand pages. Some give little more than names and relationships. Others include data as to place of residence, occupation, church membership, and significant accomplishments. Most report life dates of individuals. A few are profusely illustrated with photographs of members of the family, notably the Brillhart book.

Since many of the genealogies have been published privately, they often lack important bibliographic features. It has been very difficult to state the place of publication accurately in many instances. The place of printing may be given, but it is obvious that the printer is not the publisher. A book may have a title page bearing one title, while the binder's title may be completely different and the better known of the two. The author's name as given on the title page may differ from that given in the body of the genealogy. The date of publication is often lacking. In many instances title page information is supplied on the cover only. In others, title page information is completely lacking.

Just as the genealogies vary in quality, they vary in ease of use. Some have ingenious numbering systems to show relationships. No numbering system, however, can take the place of a careful and complete index which locates every individual in the genealogy. Indexes are completely lacking in some of the books. Others index only those persons who are in the blood line and heads of families. Many break up the genealogy into branches of the family with a separate index for each. Indexing may not follow strict alphabetic principles. It is evident that compilers of genealogies are in urgent need of an advisory service to help them plan some of the details of their books before publication.

In the following list of titles the number of pages, where known, is given immediately following the place and date of publication. The titles are short titles only.

A. North American Families:

ACKERMAN: Sabina Claire Vliet, *The Ackerman Family Association ... Descendants of George Ackerman ... and some of the Descendents of Stephen Ackerman ...* (Ackermanville, Pa., 1950) 258; ALBRECHT: Clara (Zierlein) Blake, Harriet (Martin) Albrecht and Frank Smucker, *The Albrechts, 1836-1936* (n.p., 1936?) 39; ———: Lena Albrecht et al., *The Albrechts, 1836-1952* (n.p., 1952?) 48; AUGSPURGER: *Genealogy of the Augspurger Family* (Franklin, Ohio, 1921?).

BACHTEL: see *Schnebele;* BARTEL: Lawrence Alfred Bartel, *Genealogy of the Bartel Family ...* (Zanesville, Ohio, c1950) 99; BASINGER: Edna Frances Samsal, *Descendants of Christian D. Basinger ...* (Bluffton, Ohio, 1955) 56; BAUER: Lister Oliver Weiss, *A History and Genealogy of Hans Bauer ...* (Akron, Ohio?, 1952) 126; ———: see also *Stauffer* and *Strassburger;* BAWEL: John B. Peachey, *Record of the Descendants of Philip and Grace Bawel* (Belleville, Pa., 1950) 34; BEACHEY (PEACHEY): Samuel M. Peachey, *A Memorial History of Peter Bitsche, and . . . His Lineal Descendants . . .* (Allensville, Pa., 1892; reprint: Grantsville, Md., 1953) 205; BEACHY (BEECHY): William D. Beechy, *Descendants of Benjamin Beachy ...* (Nappanee, Ind., 1950) 153; ———: Lucy C. Lambright, *Family Record of Samuel J. Beachy and His Descendants* (Millersburg, Ind., 1918) 28; ———: Lucy Eash and Ida Beachy, *Family Record of Samuel J. Beachy ...* (Millersburg, Ind., 1946) 80; BEERY: Joseph H. Wenger, *History of the Descendants of Abraham Beery ...* (South English, Iowa, 1905) 328; ———: Joseph H. Wenger, *History of the Descendants of Nicholas Beery ...* (South English, Iowa, 1911) 496; BEIDLER: A. J. Fretz, *A Genealogical Record of the Descendants of Jacob Beidler* (Milton, N. J., 1903) 549; BENDER: C. W. Bender and D. B. Swartzendruber, *Descendants of Daniel Bender* (Berlin, Pa., 1948) 192; ———: Jacob Bender and David Bender, *Familien-Register von Jakob und Magdalena Bender ...* (n.p., 1897) 12; ———: David M. Bender and Noah R. Bender, *Family Record of Jacob and Magdalena Bender ...* (Tavistock, Ont., 1925) 61; ———: Jacob R. Bender, *Genealogy of Jacob and Magdalena Bender ...* (Tavistock, Ont., 1947?) 91; BERGEY: David Hendricks Bergey, *Genealogy of the Bergey Family . . .* (New York, c1925) 1150; BERTOLET: Daniel H. Bertolet, *A Genealogical History of the Bertolet Family ...* (Harrisburg, Pa., 1914) 260; BLAUCH: Daniel D. Weaver and D. D. Blauch, *History of ... Samuel Blauch ... and His Descendants* (Boswell, Pa., 1921) 45; BLICKENSDERFER: Jacob Blickensderfer, *History of the Blickensderfer Family ...* (Lebanon, Mo., 1899?) 56; BLOSSER: Sarah (Yoder) Blosser, *Blosser Family History* (North Lima, Ohio, 1937?) 29; BOESE: J. A. Boese, *Boese Family Tree* (Springfield, S.D., 1931) broadside; BORKHOLDER: Andrew S. Borkholder, *Family Record of John J. Borkholder ...* (Bremen, Ind., 1942) 36; BORNEMAN: J. H. Borneman, *The History of the Borneman Family . . .* (Boyertown, Pa., 1881); BORNTRAGER: Sam R. Borntrager, Mary R. Glick, and Katie S. Mast, *Family Record of Daniel J. Borntrager ...* (Haven, Kan., 1942) 48; BORNTRAEGER (BONTRAGER, *etc.*): John E. Borntreger, *Descendants of Martin Borntraeger . . .* (Scottdale, Pa., 1923) 291; BOWSER: A. B. Bowser, *The Bowser Family History* (Chicago, 1922) 310; BOYER: Charles C. Boyer, *American Boyers* (Allentown, Pa., 1940) 663; BRENNEMAN (BRENEMAN): Charles D. Breneman, *A History of the Descendants of Abraham Breneman* (Elida, Ohio, 1939) 566; ——: Albert H. Gerberich, *The Brenneman History* (Scottdale, Pa., 1938) 1217; BRILLHART: John A. Brillhart, *A Pictorial History of the Brillharts of America* (Scottdale, Pa., 1926) 268; BRUBACHER (BRUBAKER): Jacob N. Brubacher, *The Brubacher Genealogy* ... (Elkhart, Ind., 1884) 243; ——: Claude J. Rahn, *Genealogical Information Regarding the Families of Brubaker, Bomberger, Fogelsanger* ... (Vero Beach, Fla., 1952) 105; BULLER: John A. Boese, *John A. Buller Family* (Springfield, S.D., 1930) broadside; ——: Henry B. Koehn, *A Compilation of the Genealogical ... Record ... of Henry J. Buller* ... (North Newton, Kan., 1952?) 32; BURKHOLDER: *Report of the ... Burkholder Family Reunion, 1926-1934* (Harrisburg, Pa.) 8 vv.; BYLER: Phoebe Byler, *Descendants of Christian Byler* ... (New Wilmington, Pa., 1946) 63; ——: Amanda D. Mast and Barbara (Mast) Swartzentruber, *Descendants of Jacob Byler* ... (Dover, Del., 1949) 114.

CASSEL: Daniel Kolb Cassel, *A Genealogical History of the Cassel Family* ... (Norristown, Pa., 1896) 463; CHUPP: Barbara (Chupp) Hochstetler and Anna (Beachy) Chupp, *Family Record of Eli and Nathan Chupp* (Middlebury, Ind., 1951) 110; CLEMENS: Jacob Cassel Clemens, *Genealogical History of the Clemens Family* ... (Lansdale, Pa., 1948) 56; ——: see also *Strassburger;* CONRAD: S. E. Conrad and L. E. Conrad, *Conrad Family Tree from 1753-1910* (Sterling, Ohio, 1910?) 39; ——: Martha E. Graber, Mary Ellen (Conrad) Krabill, and Harmon D. Schmucker, *The Joseph Conrad Family* (Canton, Ohio, 1937) 16; ——: Henry C. Conrad, *Thones Kunders and His Children, Also a List of the Descendants ... of ... Henry Cunreds* ... (Wilmington, Del., 1891) 105, 23; ——: see also *Yoder;* CUSTER: Milo Custer, *The Custer Families* (Bloomington, Ill., 1912) 22; ——: Agnes Williamson Storer, *Elenore C. Custer, Her Family and Connections* (New Brunswick, N.J., 1937) 215 *(includes information on Kolb and Hunsicker families).*

DECKER: T. T. Johnson, *Geschlechtsregister von unserm Grossvater Andreas Decker* ... (Elkhart, Ind., n.d.) 10; DETER: Eunice Deter, *The Deter Family History* ... (Morrison, Ill., 1941) 48; DETWEILER: Lizzieann J. Hostetler, *Descendants of Gideon Detweiler* ... (Volant, Pa., 1940) 58; DILLER: J. L. Ringwalt, *Descendants of Casper Diller* (n.p., 1877) 56; ——: J. F. Ringwalt, *The Diller Family* (New Holland, Pa., 1942).

EASH: Levi T. Eash, *Descendants of ... Jacob Eash* ... (Middlebury, Ind., 1934) 639; EBERHART: Uriah Eberhart, *History of the Eberharts* ... (n.p., 1891) 263; EBERSOLE (EVERSOLE, ETC.): Charles E. Ebersol, *The Ebersol Families* ... (Lansing, Mich., 1937) 281; EBY: Ezra E. Eby, *A Biographical History of the Eby Family* ... (Berlin, Ont., 1889) 144; ——: Jacob Eby, *A Brief Record of the Ebys* ... (Lancaster, Pa., 1923) 50; ——: Franklin Stanton Aby, *The Eby Family Bulletin* (Chicago, 1923-24) 4 vv.; EICHELBERGER: Abdiel Wirt Eichelberger, *Historical Sketch of Philip Frederick Eichelberger ... and of His Descendants* ... (Hanover, Pa., 1901)

162, 77; ENGLE: Morris M. Engle, *The Engle History and Family Records* ... (Hummelstown, Pa., 1927) 161; ——: S. H. Engle, *The Melcher Engle Family History and Genealogy, 1730-1940* (n.p., 1940) 489; ——: Herbert C. Engle, *A Record of the Descendants of Jacob S. ... Engle* (North Canton, Ohio, 1955); ERNST: E. Z. Ernst, *A Condensed Genealogical Record ... of Sebastian Ernst* (Los Angeles, Cal., 1927) 22; ESH (ESCH): Benjamin L. Blank, *Genealogy of the Descendants of Christopher Esh* (New Holland, Pa., 1949) 200; EWERT: Benjamin Ewert, *Ewert-Stammbaum* (Winnipeg, Man., 1951?) 39; ——: Milton H. Ewert, *The Ewert Family Tree* (n.p., 1952) 19.

FARNEY: Laura E. Farney and Julius Farney, *Genealogies of Three Large Families* (Watertown, N.Y., 1933) 448 (includes information on the Virkler and Zehr families); FLICKNER: Katie B. Graber, *The Flickner Family Record* ... (Milan, Kan., 1942) 18; FREED: Jacob A. Freed, *Partial History of the Freed Family* ... (Souderton, Pa., 1923) 113; FRETZ: A. J. Fretz, *A Brief History of John and Christian Fretz* ... (Elkhart, Ind., 1890) 607; ——: A. J. Fretz, *A Brief History of John and Christian Fretz* ... (Milton, N.J., 1904) 125; FREY: Daniel D. Frey, *Descendants of John Frey* (n.p., 1927); ——: Mrs. Dan B. Hostetler, *Descendants of Samuel D. Frey* (Est. Manuel, Tamps., Mexico, 1955); FUNK: A. J. Fretz, *A Brief History of Henry Funck* ... (Elkhart, Ind., 1899) 874.

GEHMAN: Anna M. Gehman, *The Gehman-Gayman Family History* (Mohnton, Pa., 1954) 92; GEIL: Joseph H. Wenger, *History of the Descendants of J. Conrad Geil* ... (Elgin, Ill., 1914) 275; GERBER: E. P. Gerber, *Historical Sketches ... Descendants of ... Michael Gerber* ... (Kidron, Ohio, 1938?) 283; GILLIOM: Peter Gilliom, *Gilliom Family Record* (n.p., n.d.) 40; GINGERICH: Nettie Beachy, *Family Record of Daniel J. Gingerich* ... (Scottdale, Pa., 1930) 58; ——: Mr. and Mrs. David R. Bontrager and Mr. and Mrs. Amos D. Bontrager, *Family Record of Jacob Guengerich* ... (Millersburg, Ind., 1949) 92; GINGRICH: Simon Henry Irick, *The John Gingrich II Family Record* ... (Berne, Ind., 1953) 79; GNAGEY (GNAEGI): Elias Gnagey, *A Complete History of Christian Gnaegi* ... (Elkhart, Ind., 1897) 197; GODSHALK: H. G. Allebach, *Who's Who in the Godshalk Family* (n.p., 1910) 90; ——: Abraham Godshalk, *A Family Record* ... (Harrisburg, Pa., 1912) 304; GOERING: David J. Goering, *The Goering Genealogy* ... (n.p., 1940); ——: Jacob J. Goering, *Anna Schrag Goering and Her Descendants* (Moundridge, Kan. 1945?) 51; ——: Jacob M. Goering and Anna (Graber) Goering, *The Jacob H. Goering Family Record* ... (Galva, Kan., 1948) 85; GOLDSMITH: Helen (Miller) Graber and John W. Gingerich, *Joseph Goldsmith ... and His Descendants* (Kalona, Iowa, 1955) 95; GOOSEN: Alvin Buller, *The Heinrich Goosen Genealogy* (n.p., 1953) 40; GOTTSHALL: N. B. Grubb, *A Genealogical History of the Gottshall Family* ... (Philadelphia, Pa., 1924) 112; GRABER: Peter M. Graber, *History of the Graber and Stoll Families* (Canton, Ohio, 1917) 28; ——: Jacob M. Goering and Anna (Graber) Goering, *The Peter Graber Family Record* ... (Galva, Kan., 1948)

444; GROENING: Jacob Z. Wiebe, *Genealogy Record of the Groening and Wiebe Families* (n.p., n.d.) 79; GROVE: see *Stukey*.

HAGEY: King Albert Hagey and William Anderson Hagey, *The Hagey Families ... and the Dulaney Family* (Bristol, Tenn., 1951) 714; HALLMAN: Eli Schmitt Hallman, *The Hallman-Clemens Genealogy* ... (Tuleta, Tex., 1949) 80; HARDER: Menno S. Harder, *The Harder Book* (North Newton, Kan. 1952?); HARLEY: J. R. Witcraft, *Heiligh and Harley Family* (n.p., 1914) 31; HARNISH: J. G. Francis, *The Harnish Friendschaft* ... (Gettysburg, Pa., 1955) 541; HEATWOLE: D. A. Heatwole, *A History of the Heatwole Family* ... (Dale Enterprise, Va., 1882) 24; ———: Jacob Heatwole, *Chronicle of the Heatwole Family* (n.p., 1901); ———: Cornelius Jacob Heatwole, *History of the Heatwole Family* ... (New York, 1907) 274; HEGE: *Genealogical Register of the ... Descendants of Hans Hege and Also of ... Henry Lesher* ... (Chambersburg, Pa., 1859) 46; HEISE: Henry R. Heise, *Heise Family Record* (Gormley, Ont., 1925) 8; HELMUTH: Joseph P. Helmuth, *Family Records of Friedrich Helmuth* ... (Arthur, Ill., 1933) 138; HERR: Theodore Witmer Herr, *Genealogical Record of ... Hans Herr* ... (Lancaster, Pa., 1908) 785; HERSHBERGER: Eli P. Hershberger, *History, Descendants of Peter Hershberger* ... (Elkhart, Ind., 1950?) 139; HERSHEY: Scott Funk Hershey, *History of the Herschey Family* (New Castle, Pa., n.d.); ———: Henry Hershey, *Hershey Family History* (Scottdale, Pa., 1929) 291; HERTZLER: John G. Hertzler, *A Brief Biographic Memorial of Jacob Hertzler and a Complete Genealogical Family Register ... Also, an Appendix of the Christian Zug Family* (Elkhart, Ind., 1885) 368; HERTZLER (HARTZLER): Silas Hertzler, *The Hertzler-Hartzler Family History* (Berne, Ind., 1952) 773; HESS: John H. Hess, *A Family Record of the Hess Family* ... (Lititz, Pa., 1880) 68; ———: John H. Hess, *A Genealogy of the Hess Family* ... (Lititz, Pa., 1896) 248; ———: Frank G. Roupp, *Hess Record; Descendants of John R. Hess* ... (Fall River, Kan., 1949) 100; HOCHSTETLER (HOSTETLER): Harvey Hostetler, *Descendants of Jacob Hochstetler* ... (Elgin, Ill., 1912) 1191; ———: Mrs. Amos D. Hostetler, *Descendants of David J. Hochstetler* (Nappanee, Ind., 1953) 99; HOLDEMAN: Edwin L. Weaver, *Holdeman Descendants . . .* (Nappanee, Ind., 1937) 574; ———: Obed Johnson, *A Compilation of the Genealogical and Biographical Record of the Descendants of David S. Holdeman* ... (North Newton, Kan. 1951) 178; ———: see also *Shaum;* HORNER: Viola (Gates) Horner, *Descendents* [!] *of Jacob Horner* ... (Converse, Ind., 1949) 51; HORST: Hettie K. (Horst) Hess and Lydia Ruth Hess, *John Horst Family* ... (n.p., 1940) 149; HOSTETTER: *The Hostetter Family* (n.p., n.d.) (Chart printed on both sides); HUBER (HOOVER): Harry M. Hoover, *The Huber-Hoover Family History* ... (Scottdale, Pa. 1928) 335; HUNSBERGER: Byron K. Hunsberger, *The Hunsbergers* (Norristown, Pa., 1926; rev. & enl. ed.: Norristown, Pa., 1941) 2 vv.; HUNSICKER: Henry A. Hunsicker and Horace M. Hunsicker, *A Genealogical History of the Hunsicker Family* (Philadelphia, 1911) 358; ———: see also CUSTER.

ISAAK: Peter Isaak, *Stammbuch meiner Voreltern . . .* (n.p., n.d.) 89.

JANZEN: Kathryn Klassen et. al., *The Peter Janzen Family* (n.p., 1948?); JUST: L. R. Just, *Just Family History* (Hillsboro, Kan., 1947) 103.

KAEGY (KEAGY, *etc.*): Franklin Keagy, *A History of the Kägy Relationship* ... (Harrisburg, Pa., 1899) 675; KAISER: Thomas E. Kaiser, *The Kaiser Families* ... (Oshawa, Ont., 1931) 20; KAUFFMAN: Daniel W. Kauffman, *History of the Kauffman Family* (Omaha, Neb., 1888) 32; ———: Charles Fahs Kauffman, *A Genealogy and History of the Kauffman-Coffman Families* ... (York, Pa., 1940) 775; ———: Joel C. Beachey, *Family Record of Moses and Katie Kauffman* ... (Arthur, Ill., 1941) 65; ———: Mannoah A. Kauffman, *Abraham Kauffman Family History* ... (Fresno, Ohio, 1949?) 100; ———: Barbara (Kauffman) Gingerich, *Family Record of Jacob Kauffman* ... (Arthur, Ill., 1952) 16; ———: see also *Shetler;* KELLER: E. S. Shumaker, *Descendants of Henry Keller* ... (Indianapolis, Ind., c1924) 594; KEYSER: Charles S. Keyser, *The Keyser Family* ... (Philadelphia, 1889) 161; KING: Isabelle (King) Yoder, *Centennial Memoir; the Life Story and Genealogy of Abraham and Mattie King* (Harrisonburg, Va., 1949) 49; KLOPFENSTEIN: John Henry Klopfenstein, *Klopfenstein Family Record . . .* (Grabill, Ind., c1926) 68; KOEHN: Mr. and Mrs. Henry B. Koehn; *Descendants and Relation Circle . . .* (North Newton, Kan., 1955); KOLB: see *Custer, Kulp, and Strassburger;* KRATZ: A. J. Fretz, *A Brief History of John Valentine Kratz* ... (Elkhart, Ind., 1892) 314; KREHBIEL: *History of the Valentine Krehbiel Family* ... (n.p., 1902?) 12; ———: W. J. Krehbiel, *History of One Branch of the Krehbiel Family* (McPherson, Kan., 1950) 100; ———: Jacob M. Goering, *The Jacob Krehbiel, Sr., Family Record* (Hillsboro, Kan., 1951) 133; KULP: Daniel Kolb Cassel, *A Genealogical History of the Kolb, Kulp or Culp Family* ... (Norristown, Pa., 1895) 584; KURTZ: Alta Kurtz Christophel, *Ascending and Descending Genealogy of the Children of Joseph Kurtz and Lydia Zook* (Mishawaka, Ind., 1941?) 26.

LANDES: Henry S. Landes, *Descendants of Jacob Landes* ... (Souderton, Pa., 1943) 24; LANDIS: D. B. Landis, *The Landis Family of Lancaster County* ... (Lancaster, Pa., 1888) 90; ———: Norman A. Landis and H. K. Stoner, *The Landis Genealogy* ... (Berlin, Pa., 1935); ———: Ira D. Landis, *The Landis Family Book* (Lancaster and Bareville, Pa., 1950-54) 4 vv.; ———: Mary (Landis) Hoover, et al., *Landis Family* ... (n.p., 1951) 14; ———: see also *Strassburger;* LANTZ: Jacob W. Lantz, *The Lantz Family Record . . .* (Cedar Springs, Va., 1931) 265; LAPP: *Genealogy of the Descendants of Isaac and Barbara (Stoltzfus) Lapp* (n.p., 1941) 115; LEATHERMAN: I. John Letherman and Emma Leatherman Candler, *All Leatherman Kin History* ... (Nappanee, Ind., 1940) 1146; LEDERACH: see *Strassburger;* LEHMAN: Laura (Lehman) Mellenbruch et al., *The Genealogy of the Lehman Family* (Willcox, Ariz., 1943) 107; LEHMANN: Peter S. Lehmann and Peter Gilliom, *Eine kurze Chronik der Familie Lehmann* (Berne, Ind.?, 1914) 37; LEISY: E. E. Leisy, *Leisy*

Family Tree (n.p., 1954); LESHER: Lydia Ruth Hess, *John Lesher Family* (Marion, Pa., 1939) 64; ———: see also *Hege;* LEVERING: H. G. Jones, *Wigard and Gerhard Levering and Their Descendants* (n.p., 1858) 193; ———: J. Levering, *Levering Family History and Genealogy* (n.p., 1897) 975; LONGACRE (LONGAKER, LONGENECKER): *History of the Long-acre-Longaker-Longenecker Family* (Philadelphia, 1902?) 310.

MARKLEY: Henry S. Dotterer, *Descendants of Jacob Markley . . .* (n.p., 1884) 36; MARTIN: John D. Risser, *Family Record of Abraham Martin . . .* (Hagerstown, Md., 1940) 48; ———: Adam R. Martin and Kenneth E. Martin, *Family Record of Jacob M. Martin . . .* (Hagerstown, Md., 1947) 168; MAST: C. Z. Mast, *A Brief History of . . . Jacob Mast . . .* (Elverson, Pa., c1911) 822; ———: Moses C. Mast and John P. Weaver, *Mast History of Eli D. Mast . . .* (Cadwell, Ill., 1952) 63; ———: Henry J. Otto and Mary (Gingerich) Otto, *Descendants of Jacob D. Mast . . .* (Nappanee, Ind., 1952) 79; MAURER: Frank T. Kauffman, *Family of Abraham and Susanna Maurer and Ummel Relatives . . .* (Richmond, Cal., 1953) 30; MAUST: Jonas D. Gnagey, *A Complete History of Jonas Maust and His Father's Family* (Parnell, Iowa, 1935); MAZELIN: D. D. Mazelin, *The Mazelins in America . . .* (Berne, Ind., 1941) 262; METZGER: see *Tanger;* MEYER (MEYERS): see *Moyer;* MILLER: C. J. Miller, *Memorial History of John F. Miller . . .* (Arthur, Ill., 1906) 9; ———: Harry D. Miller, S. S. Yoder, and Earl Miller, *Miller Family History . . .* (Middlebury, Ind., 1927) 92; ———: Allen H. Miller, *Yost D. Miller Family Record* (Pekin, Ill., 1927) 46; ———: Walter Speas and Esther (Yoder) Speas, *Family Record; Jacob J. and Anna (nee Schrock) Miller . . .* (Kalona, Iowa, 1942) 80; ———: Emanuel J. Miller, *Family History of Joni Miller . . .* (Wilmot, Ohio, 1942) 123; ———: Emanuel J. Miller, *Family History of the Descendants of Jeremiah Miller . . .* (Wilmot, Ohio, 1943) 69; ———: Emanuel J. Miller, *Family History of the Descendants of John F. Miller . . .* (Wilmot, Ohio, 1943) 105; ———: Henry D. Miller, *Descendants of John C. Miller* (Nappanee, Ind., 1952) 51; MOYER (MEYER, MYERS): A. J. Fretz, *A Genealogical Record of the Descendants of Christian and Hans Meyer . . .* (Harleysville, Pa., 1896) 739; ———: A. J. Fretz, *Genealogy of the Moyer Family* (Milton, N.J., 1909) 144; ———: Edna Ruth Mueller, *Moyer Family History* (Halstead, Kan., 1948) 34; MULLET (MOLLAT): Joyce Nadine (Mullet) Getz, *We Would Remember . . . Genealogical Compilation of the Mollat Immigrants . . .* (Dayton, Ohio, 1950) 264.

NASH: A. J. Fretz, *A Genealogical Record of the Descendants of William Nash . . .* (Milton, N.J., 1903) 88; NEFF: Elizabeth (Clifford) Neff, *A Chronicle . . . Regarding Rudolf and Jacob Näf . . . and Their Descendants . . .* (Cincinnati, Ohio, 1886) 352; NISSLEY: *The Nissley's* (Prospectus with genealogical chart) (Mount Joy, Pa., 1918) 23; ———: Harry Hoyt Nissley, *A Chronologically Arranged Collection . . . Descendants of John Nissley . . .* (Detroit, 1949?) (broadside printed on both sides); NISWANDER: Inez Ernzen, *Hands Across the Years; a Historical Genealogy* (Beloit, Kan., 1953) 163 (Includes information about the Sherk family).

OBERHOLTZER: A. J. Fretz, *A Genealogical Record of the Descendants of Martin Oberholtzer . . .* (Milton, N.J., 1903) 254; ———: Elisha S. Loomis, *Some Account of Jacob Oberholtzer . . . and of Some of His Descendants . . .* (Cleveland, Ohio, 1931) 414; OTTO: Annie E. Gingerich, *Family Record of Daniel D. Otto . . .* (Arthur, Ill., 1929) 16.

PANKRATZ: Helena (Schroeder) Schmidt, *The Jacob Pankratz Genealogy* (Canton, Kan., 1940) 60; PAULS: Jacob B. Neufeld, *The Pauls Family Record* (n.p., 1952) 131; PENNER: Mrs. Robert Lee Koehn, *A Compilation of the Genealogical and Biographical Record of the Descendants of Henry Penner . . .* (North Newton, Kan., 1954) 32; PENNYPACKER: S. W. Pennypacker, *The Pedigree of . . . (the) Sons of I. A. Pennypacker . . .* (Philadelphia, 1892); PLANK: *Sixth Annual Plank Reunion . . . 1903* (n.p., 1903) 40; ———: Charles Plank, *Descendants of Isaac J. Plank* (Lyons, Kan., 1938) 26; PREHEIM: Jacob M. Goering, *The Peter Preheim Family Record . . .* (Hillsboro, Kan., 1953) 130.

RABER: John A. Raber, *Family Records of Jacob Raber . . .* (Sugarcreek, Ohio, 1915?) 78; ———: Daniel J. Raber, *Raber Family History . . .* (n.p., 1937) 20; REESOR: L. J. Burkholder, *The Reesor Reunion of 1928 and Family Chart* (Markham, Ont., 1928) 16; ———: *Reesor Family Reunion, The Reesor Family in Canada . . .* (n.p., 1950) 160; REIST: Henry G. Reist, *Peter Reist . . . and Some of His Descendants* (Schenectady, N.Y., 1933) 118; RICHERT: Maria Dora Richert and Edna Richert Sawatzky, *Jacob A. and Anna Kliewer Richert Family* (Newton, Kan., 1955); RITTENHOUSE: Daniel K. Cassel, *A Genea-biographical History of the Rittenhouse Family . . .* (Philadelphia, 1893-97) 6 vv.; ROSENBERGER: E. Matthews, *Rosenberger Family . . .* (n.p., 1892) 60; ———: A. J. Fretz, *A Genealogical Record of the Descendants of Henry Rosenberger . . .* (Milton, N.J., 1906) 336; ———: Paulyne Grace (Mickley) Kramer, *A Genealogical Record of the Descendants of Joseph Detweiler Rosenberger* (Perkasie, Pa., 1953) 32; ROTH: Harvey Reeser and Norma (Hamilton) Reesor, *The Genealogy of Christian and Catherine (Rich) Roth* (Brownsville, Ore., 1953) 17; ———: Ruth Caroline Roth, *A Genealogical Study of the Nicolaus and Veronica (Zimmerman) Roth Family* (Elkhart, Ind., 1955) 331; ROYER: J. G. Francis, *Royer Family in America . . .* (n.p., 1928) 654.

SCHARTNER: Eldon Smith, *The History and Record of the Schartner Family* (n.p., 1953) 190; SCHLABACH: Emanuel J. Miller, *Daniel Schlabach Family History . . .* (Wilmot, Ohio, 1942?) 32; ———: Mahlon C. Schlabaugh, *A Memorial History of Daniel and John Schlabach . . .* (Kalona, Iowa, 1945) 58; SCHMIDT: J. Boese, *Schmidt Family Tree* (Avon, S.D., 1931) broadside; ———: Jacob Alvin Schmidt, *Schmidt Family Record . . .* (Vermillion, S.D., 1948) 35; ———: H. U. Schmidt, *A Record of Schmidt's* (n.p., 1951) 23; SCHNEBELE (SNIVELY): J. Snively, *Genealogical Register of the . . . Descendants of John Jacob Schnebele . . . and also of . . . Samuel Bachtel* (Chambersburg, Pa., 1858) 31;

SCHNEIDER (SNYDER): Joseph Meyer Snyder, *Hannes Schneider and His Wife ... Their Descendants ...* (Kitchener, Ont., 1940?) 499; SCHNELL: Hervey Schnell and Frances (Schnell) Lehman, *Schnell-Bader Family* (Orrville, Ohio, 1946) 29; SCHRAG: Edwin P. Graber, *Memoirs of ... John Schrag and Family* (n.p., 1952) 108; SCHROCK: Silvanus Yoder, *A Brief History ... With a Complete Genealogy of the Descendants of Peter Schrock* (Scottdale, Pa., 1923) 101; ———: Martha A. Schrock, *The Tobias Schrock Family Record ...* (Decatur, Ind., 1950?) 83; SCHROEDER: Henry R. Schroeder, *The Heinrich Schroeder Family Record* (n.p., 1952) 24; SCHWARTZ: Anna D. Schwartz, *Descendants of Johannes Schwartz* (Berne, Ind., 1949) 243; SENSENIG (SENSENICH, SENSENEY, etc.): Barton Sensenig et al., *The "Sensineys" of America* ... (Philadelphia, 1943) 159; SHAUM: Catharine Mumaw, *Shaum Family History* (Wooster, Ohio, 1915?) 60; ———: Harvey S. Rutt, *History of Chester Township, Wayne County, Ohio, and the Genealogy of the Shaum and Holdeman Families ...* (Smithville, Ohio, 1930) 155; SHERK: see *Niswander;* SHETLER (SCHOETTLER): Samuel D. Guengerich, *A Memorial History of Daniel Schöttler, Sr. ... and also of Jac. & Rebecca Kauffman ...* (Wellman, Iowa, 1910) 119; SHIRK: Henry Yocom Shirk, *The Shirk Family History and Genealogy ...* (Elkhart, Ind., 1914) 137; SHOEMAKER: Benjamin H. Shoemaker, *Shoemaker Pioneers ...* (Philadelphia, 1955); SHOWALTER: Preston M. Showalter, *Family Record of the Showalters* (Maugansville, Md., 1943) 95; ———: Elizabeth Anna Showalter, *Our Family; Facts of the George B. Showalter Family* (Scottdale, Pa., 1955) 30; SLONAKER (SCHLONAKER, SLONECKER, SLONEGER, SLONIGER, etc.): James Rollin Slonaker, *A History and Genealogy of the Slonaker Descendants ...* (Los Angeles, 1941) 732; SLONEKER: *A Short, Simple, Story, Modestly Told* (n.p., 1903); SMILEY: see *Yoder;* SPRUNGER: Abraham J. Sprunger and Samuel F. Sprunger, *Geschlechts- und Namens-Register der Familie Sprunger* (Berne, Ind., 1890) 67; STAUFFER: Henry S. Bower, *A Genealogical Record of Daniel Stauffer and Hans Bauer ...* (Harleysville, Pa., 1897) 203; ———: (STOVER): A. J. Fretz, *A Genealogical Record of the Descendants of Henry Stauffer ...* (Milton, N.J., 1899) 371; ———: Ezra N. Stauffer, *Stauffer Genealogy* (Goshen, Ind., c1917) 179; STEINER: Eunice Deter, *Decendants* [!] *of Ulrich Steiner ...* (Morrison, Ill., 1947) 85; STEMEN: *History of the Stemen Family ...* (Fort Wayne, Ind., 1881) 45; STOLL: see *Graber;* STOUFFER: David Stouffer, *The Genealogy and Historical Sketch of the Stouffer Family* (Toronto, 1918) 30; STOVER: see *Stauffer;* STRASSBURGER: Ralph Beaver Strassburger, *The Strassburger and Allied Families of Pennsylvania* (Gwynedd Valley, Pa., 1922) 520 (While the Strassburger family treated here is not Mennonite, a number of Pennsylvania Mennonite families are included: Bauer, Landis, Kolb, Ziegler, Clemens, and Lederach.); STRAUSZ: Jacob M. Goering and Anna (Graber) Goering, *The Jacob Strausz, Sr., Family Record ...* (Galva, Kan., 1948) 76; STRICKLER: Harry M. Strickler, *Forerunners; a History or Genealogy of the Strickler Families ...* (Harrisonburg, Va.,

c1925) 425; ———: Abigail (Hull) Strickler et al., *Stricklers of Pennsylvania ...* (Mt. Joy, Pa., 1942) 420; STUCKY: Harley J. Stucky, *The Joshua P. Stucky Family Record ...* (North Newton, Kan., 1952?) 8; STUKEY: Elmer Leonidas Denniston, *Genealogy of the Stukey, Ream, Grove, Clem and Denniston Families* (Harrisburg, Pa., 1939) 591; STUTZMAN: Harvey Hostetler, *Descendants of Barbara Hochstedler and Christian Stutzman* (Scottdale, Pa., 1938) 1391; SWARTLEY: A. J. Fretz, *A Genealogical Record ... of the Swartley Family ...* (n.p., 1906) 81; ———: Samuel R. Swartley, *Genealogy Record of Descendants of Elizabeth Gehman and Abraham R. Swartley ...* (Lansdale, Pa., 1916) 60; SWARTZENDRUBER (SCHWARTZENTRUBER): (P. Swartzentruber), *Peter Swartzendruber (and) Wilmina Eash Genealogy, 1777-1955* (Westmoreland, N. Y., 1956) 127.

TANGER: Frederick Sheely Weiser, *The Tanger-Metzger Genealogy* (Gettysburg, Pa., 1955); TREICHLER: Melissa J. (Treichler), *History and Family Record of John Treichler ...* (n.p., 1906) 60; TROYER: *Descendants of Abraham A. Troyer* (n.p., 1951) 12; ———: Eli J. Troyer, *Troyer Family Record ...* (Howe, Ind., 1952?) 32; ———: Hiram B. Troyer, *Descendants of Michael Troyer* (Nappanee, Ind., 1953) 37.

UMMEL: see *Maurer;* UNRUH: J. A. Boese, *Unruh Family Tree* (Avon, S.D., 1932) broadside; ———: Peter U. Schmidt, *The Peter Unruh Genealogy ...* (Goessel, Kan., 1941) 128; ———: Abraham J. Unruh and Verny Unruh, *The Tobias A. Unruh Biography ... and Family Record ...* (Pulaski, Iowa, 1950) 49.

VIRKLER: see *Farney.*

WEAVER: Esther Susan Weaver, *Descendants of Henry B. Weaver* (Ephrata, Pa., 1953) 35; WEBER (WEAVER): Ezra N. Stauffer et al., *Weber or Weaver Family History* (Nappanee, Ind., 1953) 197; WELTY: Samuel H. Baumgartner, *Brief Historical Sketches of Eight Generations, Descendants of Ulrich Welty ...* (Indianapolis, Ind., 1926) 395; WENGER: Jonas G. Wenger, Martin D. Wenger, and Joseph H. Wenger, *History of Christian Wenger ...* (Elkhart, Ind., 1903) 259; WIDEMAN: Ida (Wideman) Reesor, *The Family Chain ... Henry Wideman ...* (Claremont, Ont., 1931?) 12; WIEBE: see *Groening;* WISMER: A. J. Fretz, *A Brief History of Jacob Wismer and a Complete Genealogical Family Register ...* (Elkhart, Ind., 1893) 372.

YODER: Christian Z. Yoder, *Genealogical Records of Descent from John Yoder, Jacob Zook, Daniel Conrad and Nathan Smiley ...* (Wooster, Ohio, 1932) 122; ———: Tillie M. Beachy, *Family Record of Moses and Barbara (nee Miller) Yoder ...* (Arthur, Ill., 1934) 71; ———: Marie Agnes (Beachy) Miller, *Family Record of Moses and Barbara (nee Miller) Yoder ...* (Centerville, Mich., 1951) 80; ———: Sarah B. (Frey) Hostetler, *Descendants of Jacob J. Yoder* (Nappanee, Ind., 1951) 105.

ZEHR: see *Farney;* ZIEGLER: see *Strassburger;* ZOOK: (ZUG): see *Hertzler, Kurtz,* and *Yoder.*

Ezra E. Eby's two-volume *A Biographical History of Waterloo Township* (Waterloo County, Ontario) (Berlin, Ont., 1895-96) and Joseph B. Snyder's *Supplement* to Eby's history (Waterloo, Ont., 1931) contain extensive genealogical material concerning Mennonite families in this area.

B. Dutch Families:

BEETS: A. A. Vorsterman van Oyen, *Genealogie van het Geslacht Beets* ('s Gravenhage, 1884); BRUYN: J. G. de Groot Jamin, Jr., *Geslachtslijst van de Familie Bruyn* (Amsterdam, 1886).

CATE, TEN: G. ten Cate, *Geslachtslijst van den Frieschen Tak der familie ten Cate* (n.p., 1896); COOLMAN (KOOLMAN): (J. Huizinga), *Stamboek of Geslachtsregister der Nakomelingen van Fiepke Foppes en Diever Olferts . . . (Geslacht Coolman)* (Groningen, 1887); COOPMANS: see *Koopmans;* CORVER: G. Vissering, *Geslachtslijst van de familie Corver 1590-1847* (n.p., 1936).

DELDEN, VAN: P. Moussault, *Het Geslacht van Delden* (Laren, 1954); DYSERINCK: A. A. Vorsterman van Oyen, *Het Geslacht Dyserinck* (Amsterdam, 1885).

EEGHEN, VAN: F. K. van Lennep, *Verzameling van Oorkonden betrekking hebbende op het Geslacht van Eeghen in Nederland* (Amsterdam, 1918).

FONTEIN: J. G. A. Fontein, "Genealogie van het Geslacht Fontein," in *Jierboekje fan it genealogysk wurkforban* (Ljouwert-Leeuwarden, 1953).

GELDER, VAN: J. M. van Gelder, *Stamboek der Familie van Gelder . . .* (Amsterdam, 1899); GEUNS, VAN: (A. M. Cramer), *Brief betreffende den Stamvader der Familie van Geuns . . .* (n.p., n.d.); GLERUM: C. P. Glerum Jzn, *Het Zeeuwsche Landbouwersgeslacht Glerum 1580-1940* (Overveen, 1940).

HALBERTSMA: (G. ten Cate), *Geslachtslijst van de Familie Halbertsma* (n.p., 1897); HEYNINGEN, VAN: *Geslacht-lijst van de Familie van Heyningen* (Amsterdam, 1817); HOEKSTRA: A. H. Stikker, *Een Familie van Galjootschippers, Commandeurs op Groenland en Friese Vermaners: Baske-Hoekstra-Veenstra* (n.p., n.d., 1943); HUIDEKOPER: E. Huidekoper, *Huidekoper Holland Family 1730-1924* (n.p., 1924); HUIZINGA: (J. Huizinga), *Stamboek of Geslachtsregister der Nakomelingen van Derk Pieters en Katrina Tomas . . . (geslacht Huizinga)* (Groningen, 1883).

KOOLMAN: see *Coolman;* KOOPMANS: W. J. J. C. Bijleveld, *Geslacht Coopmans (Koopmans)*, repr. from *De Nederlandsche Leeuw*, 1930; KUYPER: Jan Aten, *De Doopsgezinde Krommenieër Zeildoekfabrikeurs-familie Kuyper* (n.p., n.d., 1952).

LEENDERTZ: *Stammbaum der Familie Leendertz* (n.p., 1907); LENNEP, VAN: F. K. van Lennep, *Verzameling van Oorkonden, betrekking hebbende op het Geslacht van Lennep 1093-1900*, vol. I (Amsterdam, 1900); LOOSJES: *Geslachtsboek van de Familie Loosjes* (Haarlem, 1905); ———: Gerrit Jan Honig, *De Zaanlandsche Geschied- en Plaatsbeschrijver Adriaan Loosjes en zijn geslacht* (Zaandijk, n.d.); LUYKEN: P. van Eeghen, *Jan Luyken en zijne Bloedverwanten* (Amsterdam, 1889).

MEIHUIZEN: Jacob Huizinga, *Stamboek of Geslachtsregister der Nakomelingen van Samuel Peter (Meihuizen) en Barbara Fry . . .* (Groningen, 1890); ———: J. Meihuizen Szn, *Het Geslacht Meihuizen 1622-1922* (n.p., n.d., 1937); ———: (J. Meihuizen), *Stamboek van het Geslacht Meihuizen*

1400-1945 (n.p., n.d.,); MESDAG: G. Mesdag Kz, *Het Geslacht Mesdag* (Groningen, 1896); ———: G. van Mesdag, *Het Gestacht Mesdag* (n.p., 1943) 46; MULLER (MUELLER): J. W. Müller, *Das Geschlecht Müller aus Gerolsheim* (Oegstgeest, 1926); ———: G. Kalff, Jr., *Samuel Muller en zijn acht kinderen* (n.p., 1941); ———: H. Muller, *Onze stamvader Prof. Samuel Muller en zijn vrouw Femina Geertruida Mabé* (Amsterdam, 1944); ———: J. W. Muller, *Het Geslacht Muller (Müller) . . .* (Amsterdam, 1951).

NEUFVILLE, DE: A. C. de Neufville, *Histoire Généalogique de la Maison de Neufville . . .* (Amsterdam, 1869); NIEUWENHUYZEN: A. A. Vorsterman van Oyen, *Genealogisch Overzicht van de Familie Nieuwenhuyzen* (Amsterdam, 1884).

PAMA: C. Pama, *De Pama's te Surhuisterveen* ('s Gravenhage, 1942); PAUW: H. N. Slinger, *Het Doopsgezinde Geslacht Pauw* (Alkmaar, 1938).

SALM: W. (J. J. A. Wijs), *Stamboom van de familie Salm* (n.p., 1936); ———: (J. C. te Winkel-Losen), *De eerste Bewerkers van het Stamboek (der Familie Salm)* (Amsterdam, 1917); SLEUTEL: J. G. de Hoop Scheffer, *Het Geslacht Sleutel* (Leeuwarden, 1867); STUURMAN: F. J. Stuurman, *Het Geslacht Stuurman* (Zeist, 1941).

TEYLER *(Teyler van der Hulst): Stamboek der Teyler's of Geslachtsregister der Nakomelingen van Thomas Teyler . . .* (Haarlem, n.d.)

VEEN: E. A. Veen, *Een Friesch Koopmansgeslacht, het geslacht Veen* (Amsterdam, 1947); VEENSTRA: see *Hoekstra;* VEER, DE: *Geslachtsregister van Cornelis Isaac de Veer* (n.p., n.d.); VELDEN, VAN DER: *Genealogische Geschriften over de Familie van der Velden* (n.p., n.d.); VIETOR: Hendrik Haitzema Viëtor, *Het Geslacht Viëtor* (Steenwijk, 1910); VISSERING: G. ten Cate, *Geslachtslijst van de Familie Vissering* (n.p., 1903); VLIET, VAN DER: W. J. J. C. Bijleveld, *Genealogie van het Geslacht van der Vliet* (The Hague, 1924); VONDEL: A. A. Vorsterman van Oyen, *Joost van den Vondel en zijn geslacht* ('s Gravenhage, 1887); VRIES, DE: J. H. de Vries, *De Amsterdamsche Doopsgezinde Familie de Vries* (Zutphen, 1911).

WAARDE, DE: *De Waarden en het Geslacht de Waard* (Groningen, 1937); WARNAARS: J. H. Warnaars, *Het Geslacht Warnaars* (Amsterdam, n.d., 1921); WILLINK: P. B(eets), *Stam-boek der Willingen of Geslacht-register der Nakomelingen van Jan Willink . . .* (Deventer, 1767); WOUTERS: A. Haga, *Bijdrage tot de genealogie van het Doopsgezinde Sneeksche geslacht Wouters* (n.p., 1941).

Concerning the following Dutch Mennonite families genealogical data with their family coats-of-arms are found in A. A. Vorsterman van Oyen, *Stam- en Wapenboek van aanzienlijke Nederlandsche Familiën:* Vol. I (Groningen, 1885): van Aldewerelt, Blaauw, Blijdenstein, Brants, Bruyn, Bruyning, de Clercq, Dyserinck, van Eeghen, van Eik, de Flines, Fontein, de Haan. Vol. II (Groningen, 1888): van Halmael, van Heukelom, van Heyningen, van Heyst, ten Kate (Cate), Koopmans, van Lennep, van der Mersch, Messchert, de Monchy, de Neufville. Vol. III (Groningen, 1890): Portielje. Rahusen, Roeters van Lennep, Sieuwertsz van Reesema, van Vollenhoven, Vreede, and in appendix Fontein, Hesselink, Mesdag.

A valuable source of genealogical information is *Nederlandsch Patriciaat,* first issued in 1910 at The Hague. The following Dutch families, which have been entirely or partly Mennonite, are found in the *Ned. Patriciaat:* van Alde(r)werelt, VII (1916) 8-14; XLII (1956) 23-43; Blaauw, VII (1916) 48-52; X (1919) 21 f.; Blijdenstein, XXXIII (1947) 7-34; Brants, V (1914) 47-52; Bruyn, IV (1913) 78-84; Bybau, V (1914) 68-72; XXXII (1946) 48-55; Cardinal, VIII (1917) 95-102; X (1917) 68 f.; ten Cate, XVII (1927) 109-14; de Clercq, II (1911) 60-68; XI (1920) 43-53; Craandijk, XXXVI (1950) 91-103; Doyer, XXX (1944) 32-68; Dyserinck, II (1911) 116-21; XL (1954) 97-107; Ebeling, XV (1925) 114-20; van Eeghen, II (1911) 121-28; X (1919) 96-105; Flines, de, VII (1916) 174-79; Fock, VIII (1917) 148-53; van Gelder, I (1910) 152-63; IX (1918) 104-17; van Geuns, XIV (1924) 89-107; van Gilse, XXXIX (1953) 87-98; de Haan, II (1911) 175-80; X (1919) 120-26; XVII (1927) 179; XXXV (1949) 47-61; Halbertsma, V (1914) 172-81; XII (1921-22) 206-17; XV (1925) 135 f.; XL (1954) 174-98; van Halmael, XXVI (1940) 60-64; Hannema, XVIII (1928-29) 313-24; van Heukelom, IV (1913) 174-81; XXVII (1941) 140-57; van Heyst, XXXVI (1950) 188-93; Huidekoper, XVII (1927) 206-16; Hulshoff, XXVIII (1942) 78-105; Jannink, XIV (1924) 155-64; Jeltes, X (1919) 136-42; Kaars Sypestein, XVII (1927) 339-44; Kool, XVIII (1928-29) 97-116; Koopmans (Coopmans), XI (1920) 124-32; Kops, X (1919) 190-200; XL (1954) 206-28; Laan, XII (1921-22) 171-86; Leendertz, XIX (1930) 120-42, 290 f.; Lely, XLII (1956) 213-24; van Lennep, IX (1918) 231-52; Loder, VI (1915) 225-28; Loosjes, XIV (1924) 180-88; Lugt, XXIX (1943) 291-318; van der Meersch, II (1911) 329-33; van der Mersch, VIII (1917) 298-302; Messchaert (Messchert), XVI (1926) 212-36; Mol (1), X (1919) 272-81; de Monchy, III (1912) 263-75; XXV (1939) 142-62; Müller (Muller), XIX (1930) 152-62; de Neufville, VI (1915) 275-78; van der Pals, V (1914) 312-16; XVI (1926) 237-42; Patijn, I (1910) 334-38; IX (1918) 280-84; van der Ploeg, XVII (1927) 282-93; Pol, XXVIII (1942) 227-44; le Poole, X (1919) 354-59; XLI (1955) 291-305; Portielje, VI (1915) 314-16; Prins, XII (1921-22) 120-30; Rahusen, V (1914) 326-30; Rueb, II (1911) 413-19; XV (1925) 435-45; Scheltema, XXVII (1941) 218-88; XXVIII (1942) 368-70; Schimmelpenninck, I (1910) 410-13; XIII (1923) 322 f.; van Schouwenburg, XIV (1924) 267-83; Sieuwertsz van Reesema, V (1914) 336-39; de Stoppelaar, XXVIII (1942) 287-304; Uitterdijk, XI (1920) 289-92; de Veer, XXV (1939) 270-313; Vissering, XXIV (1938) 300-18; van der Vliet, XI (1920) 320-31; Vollenhoven, XI (1920) 332-37; van Vollenhoven, XVI (1926) 278-340; Vreede, XLI (1955) 341-70; de Vries, V (1914) 439-49; XXVII (1941) 370-92; Warnaars, IV (1913) 431-35; Westendorp, IV (1913) 445-49; Willink, XXXVI (1950) 368-78.

Data concerning the following Dutch noble families, which were Mennonite or of Mennonite descent, are found in the *Nederlandsch Adelsboek* (The Hague): Hartsen (1929) 168-70; Rutgers (1916) 421-30; Schimmelpenninck (1917) 67-76.

C. German Families:

BACHMANN: Peter Bachmann, *Mennoniten in Kleinpolen,* 1784-1934 (Lemberg, 1934). The second appendix, "Stammbäume der mennonitischen Familien in Kleinpolen," consists of genealogical charts for the following families: Bachmann, Bergthold, Brubacher, Ewy, Forrer, Hubin, Jotter, Kintzi, Klein, Laise, Linscheid, Merk, Müller, Rupp, Schmidt, Schrag, and Stauffer; BECKERATH: Heinrich von Beckerath, *Stammbaum von Beckerath nebst Deszendenz* (Krefeld, 1903); ———: Oskar von Beckerath, *Familie von Beckerath* (vol. II) (Krefeld, 1936); BERGEN (BARGEN): Fritz van Bergen, *Der Berg; Sippenzeitung der Familien van Bergen, van Bargen, 1933?-1940?* (Frankenau/Gutfeld, Ostpreussen); BERGTHOLD: see *Bachmann;* BRUBACHER: see *Bachmann.*

CONWENTZ: Margarete Boie, *Hugo Conwentz und seine Heimat* . . . (Stuttgart, 1940) 284.

DELDEN: P. Moussault, *Het Geslacht van Delden* . . . (Laren, 1954) 283; DIRKSEN: George Conrad, *Geschichte der Familie Dirksen* . . . (Görlitz, 1905) 2 vv.; DRIEDGER: Gustav E. Reimer, *Die Familiennamen der westpreussischen Mennoniten* (Weierhof, 1940; *Schriftenreihe des Mennonitischen Geschichtsvereins,* Nr. 3). The appendix of 12 pages is entitled "Beiträge zur Stammtafel der Familie Driedger."

EPP: Kurt Kauenhowen, *Mitteilungen des Sippenverbandes der Danziger Mennoniten-Familien Epp-Kauenhowen-Zimmermann, 1934?-1943?* (Göttingen); with volume 7 this becomes simply *Mitteilungen des Sippenverbandes Danziger Mennoniten Familien.* While the Epp, Kauenhowen (Couwenhoven), and Zimmermann families receive primary emphasis, there are occasional genealogical articles relating to other Mennonite families with a Danzig background. Ewy: see *Bachmann.*

FIEGUTH: Abraham Fieguth, *Stammbuch der Familie Fieguth* . . . (Marienburg, Wpr., 1938) 45; FORRER: see *Bachmann;* FUNCK: Herman Funck, *Familie Funck-Richen Stammbaum* . . . (Schorndorf, 1939) 23.

HEGE: Christian Hege, *Chronik der Familie Hege* . . . (Frankfurt am Main, 1937) 55; HUBIN: see *Bachmann.*

JOTTER: see *Bachmann.*

KAUENHOWEN: Kurt Kauenhowen and Walter Kauenhowen, *Die Kauenhowen; Mitteilungen aus der Geschichte und dem Leben des Geschlechtes Kauenhowen, 1926* (vol. I, Nr. 1) (Verden) no further issues published; ———: see also *Epp;* KINTZI: see *Bachmann;* KLEIN: see *Bachmann.*

LAISE: see *Bachmann;* LEYEN: Wilhelm Kurschat, *Das Haus Heinrich und Friedrich von der Leyen in Krefeld* (Frankfurt, 1933) 33; LINSCHEID: see *Bachmann.*

MERK: see *Bachmann;* MUELLER: Heinrich Müller, *Versuch an Hand des Stammbaumes der Familie Müller* . . . (Frankfurt a.M., 1919?) 50; ———: see also *Bachmann.*

ROOSEN: Berend Paulus Roosen and Otto Roosen, *Stammbaum der Familie Roosen* (Hamburg, 1875); ————: (Berend Carl Roosen), *Geschichte unseres Hauses* (Hamburg, 1905) 118; ROY: Curt von Roy and Roderich von Roy, *Die Familie des Peter von Roy . . .* (Oppeln, 1918) 50; RUPP: see *Bachmann.*

SCHMIDT: see *Bachmann;* SMISSEN, VAN DER: (Klenze), *Familien-Chronik der Familie van der Smissen* (Danzig, 1875) 146; ————: Heinz Münte, *Das Altonaer Handlungshaus van der Smissen, 1682-1824 . . .* (Altona/Elbe, 1932; *Altonaer Zeitschrift für Geschichte und Heimatkunde*) 178; the first 48 pages contain the van der Smissen genealogy; SCHMUTZ: *Zweihundertvierzig Jahre Familiengeschichte, ein Stammbaum der Familien Schmutz* (Leuterstal, 1936) 281; SCHRAG: see *Bachmann;* STAUFFER: see *Bachmann.*

WIEBE: *Nachrichten über die Familie Wiebe und einige mit ihr in Verwandtschaft stehende Familien* (Berlin, 1872).

ZIMMERMAN: see *Epp.*

Kurt Kauenhowen of Göttingen, Germany, has devoted a great deal of time to research in Mennonite family history, particularly the Mennonite families of West Prussia. His "Das Schrifttum zur Sippenkunde und Geschichte der taufgesinnten niederländischen Einwanderer (Mennoniten) in Altpreussen und ihrer Abzweigungen" in *Mitteilungen der Niederländischen Ahnengemeinschaft e.V.,* I:66-109 (May 1939) includes 34 references to monographs and articles on 21 Mennonite families. In 1954 he compiled a manuscript bibliography of materials relating to 101 "nordostdeutschen" Mennonite families, including branches of these families which had migrated to Russia and to North America. Most of his entries are periodical articles, many of them from his own *Mitteilungen* (see *Epp* above). Walther Risler, in his "Quellen zur Geschichte der Krefelder Mennonitenfamilien" in *Beiträge zur Geschichte rheinischer Mennoniten* (Weierhof, Pfalz, 1939), lists materials relating to 17 Mennonite families in Crefeld. Many of the items he lists are articles published in *Die Heimat: Mitteilungen des Vereins für Heimatkunde in Crefeld, 1921-?* (Crefeld). In *MQR,* April 1949, Gustav Reimer reports extensive West Prussian Mennonite genealogical materials which he was able to take with him on his flight from Marienburg in 1945. The exact location of these materials at present is not known. N.P.S.

Genemuiden, a town in the Dutch province of Overijssel, situated on the Zwarte Water. At Bergklooster, not far from here, a large number of Anabaptists, having come from North Holland and crossed the Zuiderzee by boat en route to Münster, were taken prisoner on March 23, 1534. See for particulars **Bergklooster.**   vDZ.

General Conference Mennonite Church (formerly the General Conference of the Mennonite Church of North America), the first American Mennonite general conference organization and now the second largest Mennonite body of America, was organized May 28, 1860, at West Point, Iowa, by three small Mennonite congregations. By 1955 it had grown to 244 congregations with a membership exceeding 50,000, located in the United States, Canada, and South America.

Background. The first period of Mennonite history in America roughly coincides with the colonial period. This was a time of immigration, beginnings, and setting of patterns. Although there was great appreciation of the freedom in the new country, there was also a deep consciousness of separation from the surrounding world, due to difference in religious convictions and practices, and to some extent in language and customs. Outside pressure, especially as expressed by aggressive Scotch-Irish neighbors, urging political participation, and military service as they faced the Revolutionary War, caused much concern among Mennonites.

After the Revolution (1789) to about the middle of the 19th century the continued lack of Old World contacts and increasing isolation in America gradually tended to congeal the patterns of life and thought among the American Mennonites. During this second period of American Mennonite history, with largely older and untrained leadership, patterns of custom and tradition became increasingly set and authoritative. Slowly blood relationship, the family ideal of religion, a cultural church, separation on a social as well as religious basis, tended to crowd out the personal, voluntary, glowing spiritual life of the "new creature in Christ" which had been so real and vital in earlier days.

John C. Wenger writes as follows of these early Mennonite days in America: "Their Christianity was not that of 'radical' Christians; it had settled down to a comfortable, conventional, denominational type. There was no thought of evangelistic work, no need for any kind of mission work, no occasion to alter any of the set patterns of worship. The faith and practice of the immigrants was good and satisfying; why change? From 1683 to the ordination of John H. Oberholtzer, almost 160 years later, no significant changes were made, and no one intended to make any. The Bible had not changed; why should anyone introduce any innovations? Only with great effort would it be possible to introduce Sunday schools, evangelistic services, Bible study and prayer meetings, evening services, and church boards of charities, publication, education, and missions. This was the situation 160 years after the thirty-five Krefelders arrived at Philadelphia on the good ship *Concord,* October 6, 1683."

About the new life under these conditions H. P. Krehbiel writes as follows: "During that period a number of persons being spiritually awakened, recognized the lethargic condition of the church and endeavored, though not wisely, to awaken the church from its drowsy spiritual stupor. Unfortunately the effect was schismatic . . . . Yet there was hope in the stir and commotion."

John H. Oberholtzer (*q.v.*), a young school-teacher and minister who later also became a businessman (locksmith) and publisher, was the leader of a more progressive group in Pennsylvania. After he and 15 other ministers were excommunicated by the older group for insisting on a written constitution, they

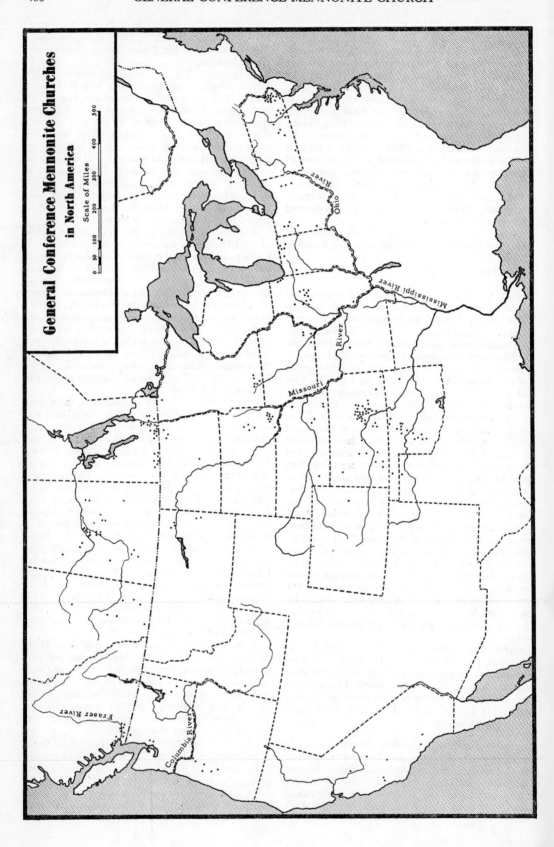

General Conference Mennonite Churches in North America

organized the "East Pennsylvania Conference of Mennonites" (*q.v.*) on Oct. 28, 1847. Besides the adoption of a written constitution they advocated dropping the collarless ministerial coat, keeping minutes of meetings, publishing a catechism, Sunday-school work, free association with other denominations, mission work, etc.

In 1852 Oberholtzer began publishing the *Religiöser Botschafter* (*q.v.*), the first continuing Mennonite periodical in North America. In 1858 the new conference adopted a resolution strongly favoring mission work. European Mennonite contacts were renewed. Ministers were appointed to visit congregations in the interest of spiritual growth. In 1866 a mission society was established and city mission work begun. Oberholtzer served as chairman of this conference from 1847 to 1872 practically without a break.

Two unfortunate minor schisms occurred within the first ten years of the new group's history. The first was the breaking away of a small group in 1851 led by Abraham and Henry Hunsicker, bishop and preacher respectively, who, excommunicated by the new conference, continued for a time a small group known as the Trinity Christian Society, which ultimately disappeared. The second schism was that led by William Gehman in 1857 as a result of the prohibition of prayer meetings by the new conference, followed by the excommunication by the conference of Gehman and 23 others. This group, first called the Evangelical Menonites (*q.v.*), later merged with other similar groups in Ontario, Ohio, and Indiana to form the Mennonite Brethren in Christ (*q.v.*).

A second center of new life developed among the Mennonites who had migrated from Pennsylvania to Ontario for economic reasons, but also to keep their promise of allegiance to the English Crown. Here Daniel Hoch (*q.v.*) of Vineland in Lincoln County was leader. Because of aggressive itinerant evangelistic work, he with other leaders was excommunicated by the Ontario Mennonite Conference in 1849. Long before this, Mennonites had also settled in Ohio, where Ephraim Hunsberger (*q.v.*), who also knew Hoch, became the leader. In 1855 "The Conference Council of the United Mennonite Community of Canada-West and Ohio" was formed, a very small group with three small congregations, with Hoch and Hunsberger as leaders. Here, too, the cause of missions was urged. In 1858 this Canada-Ohio Conference met at Wadsworth, Ohio, to which the Pennsylvania group was also invited. The following year this conference created a "Home and Foreign Missionary Society of Mennonites." Unfortunately Hoch later withdrew from the group to join the Mennonite Brethren in Christ, and the Ontario parts of the conference disappeared.

About the middle of the 19th century several groups of Mennonites from Bavaria and the Palatinate emigrated to America, most of them settling in Illinois and Iowa. They were acquainted with mission and publication work and were otherwise rather progressive. Soon contact was made with the Oberholtzer group in Pennsylvania, the Hoch group in Canada, and the Hunsberger group in Ohio.

Daniel Krehbiel (*q.v.*) was the leader of the Iowa-Illinois group, which at that time was unaffiliated.

Organization, Growth, and Activities. The various Mennonite groups interested in union were invited to send representatives to a conference which was to meet May 28, 1860, at West Point, Lee Co., Iowa. At this meeting, with three congregations participating, Oberholtzer was elected chairman, and Christian Schowalter (*q.v.*), a teacher in the Iowa community, secretary. A committee of five was elected to work out a "Plan of Union" and report the next day. This the committee did. The conference, after some discussion, adopted the plan, and "The General Conference of the Mennonite Church of North America" was under way. The second meeting was held at Wadsworth, Ohio, May 20-23, 1861, with eight congregations responding. Gradually the movement grew. Later most of the 19th-century immigrants from Russia, Prussia, Poland, and Switzerland, joined the Conference. In 1953 the Central Conference Mennonites (*q.v.*) came in as a district conference, merging with the Middle District Conference in 1956. At General Conference sessions individual congregations have been coming in. The name was changed in 1953 to "General Conference Mennonite Church."

Present organization provides that each congregation has direct relation to the General Conference. At the triennial meeting of the Conference each congregation has one vote for every 30 members or fraction thereof. The accompanying chart indicates the present organization and areas of activity.

In the interest of democracy, no person can succeed himself more than once in any office, committee, or board; with certain exceptions no person can hold a position in more than one standing board or conference office at one time. The conference officers, plus two representatives from each of the four standing boards, form the executive committee which acts for the conference between sessions. The Council of Boards and standing committee meet conjointly once a year (usually in December) for consideration of common problems.

There are six district conferences within the General Conference: Eastern, Middle-Central, Northern, Western, Pacific, and Canadian. The congregations have a direct relationship to their respective district conferences. However, the district conferences have no direct organizational connection with the General Conference. Each congregation, as well as each district conference, is more or less autonomous. The General Conference assumes only an advisory, not a legislative, relationship to the congregations and the district conferences. From the very beginning the emphasis has been on "unity in essentials; liberty in nonessentials; and love in all things." However, the boards are directly responsible to the General Conference, and are not autonomous.

The Great Commission of our Lord has from the beginning been considered the basic task of the Conference and the congregations belonging to it. The first American Mennonite mission work was established by the General Conference in 1880. The missionary was S. S. Haury (*q.v.*) of Summerfield, Ill., and the field was among the American Indians in

Oklahoma. In time (1900 and later) foreign mission work was begun in India, China, South America, Africa, Japan, and Formosa. Even before the foreign work was begun, home mission work was done, mainly with the thought of gathering together scattered Mennonite families. Altogether, some 250 missionaries have been sent to foreign lands and some 200 persons have been employed as home mission workers.

Publication and education were emphasized from the beginning. During the years some twenty-five different publications have come into being, only about one half of which are still in existence. *The Mennonite* (*q.v.*) and *Der Bote* (*q.v.*) are the official English and German Conference papers. Sunday-school and young people's material, church hymnals, and a variety of other Christian material is produced. Three bookstores are operated by the Conference (Newton, Kan.; Berne, Ind.; Rosthern, Sask.). The following schools are serving the Conference constituency and report to its triennial sessions: Mennonite Biblical Seminary in Chicago (which is under a board elected by the General Conference); Bethel College in North Newton, Kan.; Bluffton College in Bluffton, Ohio; Freeman Junior College in Freeman, S.D.; Rosthern Junior College in Rosthern, Sask.; Mennonite Collegiate Institute, Gretna, Man.; and Canadian Mennonite Bible College in Winnipeg. In addition to these there are a number of academies and Bible schools. Approximately one thousand General Conference young people annually attend the above conference-related schools.

A third area of activity pertains to relief and peace. Besides carrying on its own program in these areas, the Conference helped to organize the Mennonite Central Committee in 1920 and ever since has been affiliated with it in work of general relief, Civilian Public Service, colonization, peace education, etc. Hospitals and homes for the aged are maintained in various areas by district conferences or local groups. The Mennonite nonresistant faith finds positive expression in relief work and voluntary service.

Cultural Background. All American Mennonites are either of Swiss-South German or Dutch-North German background. There is no other Mennonite conference that has such a variety of groups with different cultural backgrounds as the General Conference, which is composed of many shades of these two main cultural groups. We mention briefly a few facts concerning each.

Swiss-South German Background. 1. The descendants of those who came out of the Mennonite Church (MC) with Pennsylvania-German background at present largely constitute the membership of 28 congregations, mostly in Eastern Pennsylvania.

2. The descendants of those who came to America from South Germany in the 19th century constitute most of the membership of 12 congregations. This group earlier exerted great influence in directing the organization and development of the General Conference. The congregations at Donnellson, Iowa; Summerfield, Ill.; Halstead and Moundridge, Kan.; Reedley and Upland, Cal., are some of those belonging to this group.

3. The descendants of those who came directly from Switzerland to Ohio and Indiana in the 19th century at present constitute the major part of the membership of 11 congregations, e.g., Berne, Ind., and Bluffton, Ohio.

4. The descendants of the Swiss who came from South Germany and France, via Volhynia, Russia, arriving in 1874, now constitute the major part of the membership of 12 congregations. The Eden Church at Moundridge, Kan., belongs here; also the congregations at Freeman, S.D.; Pretty Prairie, Kan., and others.

5. The descendants of the Swiss who came from South Germany via Galicia now largely constitute

The General Conference Mennonite Church Organization

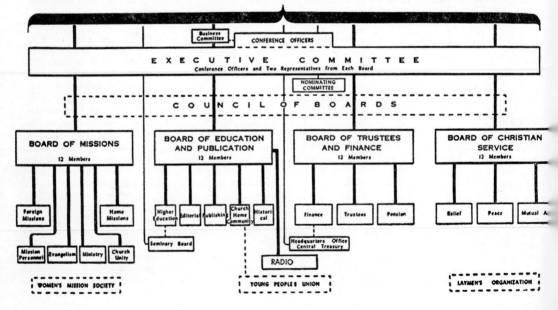

the membership of 5 congregations located at Arlington, Kan.; Butterfield, Minn., and elsewhere.

6. The descendants of Amish background now largely constitute the membership of 27 congregations mostly in the Central District Conference, largely in Illinois and Indiana, formerly (before 1872) affiliated with the Amish Mennonite (MC) group.

7. The descendants of Hutterite background now largely constitute the membership of 7 congregations, mostly in South Dakota.

Dutch-North German Background. 1. The descendants of the Dutch who came via Prussia in 1874 now largely constitute the membership of 6 congregations. Among them there are churches at Beatrice, Neb., and Newton and Whitewater, Kan.

2. The descendants of the Dutch who came via Prussia and South Russia, arriving in America in 1874 ff., constitute the major part of 70 congregations. This is the largest cultural group in the General Conference. The congregations are scattered all over the West. Many are located in Kansas, Minnesota, and Canada. Alexanderwohl at Goessel, and Hoffnungsau at Inman, Kan., are two of the original settlements in the United States, from which have come a number of younger congregations. In Canada the large Bergthal congregation in Manitoba and the Rosenort congregation in Saskatchewan belong to this group.

3. The descendants of the Dutch who came via Prussia and Polish Russia in 1874 now largely constitute the membership of 11 congregations. Among them are Gnadenberg at Elbing, Johannesthal at Hillsboro, and churches at Canton and Pawnee Rock, Kan., and Meno, Okla.

4. The descendants of the Dutch who came via Prussia and South Russia, arriving after World War I (1922-25, 1930, and 1948-53), now largely constitute the membership of 40 congregations, practically all in Canada.

Mixed Background. More than a dozen congregations already have such a mixture of members of various Mennonite backgrounds as well as some of non-Mennonite background that it is impossible to classify them. The Bethel College congregation at North Newton, Kan., is an example of this. Many congregations, through individual family migrations, are becoming more and more mixed.

In the past the various General Conference Mennonite groups lived in different countries, separated from each other for many decades at a time; thus each developed its own peculiarities, not only in dress and food, but also in point of view and world outlook, in language and social customs, as well as in Biblical interpretation and religious practice. However, in essentials they are one; and because of their feeling of kinship and the desire to work with each other, they have been drawn together since coming to America and have been influenced by the social process involved.

Characteristics of General Conference Mennonites. Renewed attention is given today to the nature and function of the church. It is spoken of as an outpost —a mission station—in the world to win the lost to Christ. Increasingly the church is thought of as the very body of Christ in a given community, and as the visible reality of our Lord in the world. As His body the local congregation, as well as the over-all organization, is to serve as His hands and feet, and with His mind and heart spend itself in ministering to those for whom He died. If the church is the body of which Christ is the head, that body cannot be divided; hence the current ecumenical interest. Only as the body of which Christ is the head can the church fulfill its appointed mission—"that the world may believe that thou hast sent me" (John 17:21).

This concern for the faith was one of the main reasons for the organization of the General Conference. The Conference constitution, in all revisions, as also that of 1950, in Article III speaks of the origin and growth of the Conference as a result of "a deeply felt desire for closer union of individual congregations in order: (1) to establish more firmly and to deepen the basic Christian faith and (2) to testify to its relevance to all of life."

This "basic Christian faith" is further elaborated in Article IV, under the heading "Our Common Confession," as follows:

"The General Conference believes in the divine inspiration and the infallibility of the Bible as the Word of God and the only trustworthy guide of faith and life; and in Jesus Christ as the only Saviour and Lord. 'Other foundation can no man lay than that is laid, which is Jesus Christ' (I Cor. 3:11).

"In the matter of faith it is, therefore, required of the congregations which unite with the Conference that, accepting the above confession, they hold fast to the doctrine of salvation by grace through faith in the Lord Jesus Christ (Eph. 2:8, 9; Titus 3:5), baptism on confession of faith (Mark 16:16; Acts 2:38), the avoidance of oaths (Matt. 5:34-37; Jas. 5:12), the Biblical doctrine of nonresistance (Matt. 5:39-48; Rom. 12:9-21), nonconformity to the world (Rom. 12:1, 2; Eph. 4:22-24), and the practice of Scriptural church discipline (Matt. 18:15-17; Gal. 6:1).

"The General Conference believes that membership in oath-bound secret societies, military organizations, or other groups which tend to compromise the loyalty of the Christian to the Lord and His Church is contrary to such apostolic admonition as: 'Be ... not unequally yoked ... with unbelievers' (II Cor. 6:14, 15), and that the church 'should be holy and without blemish' (Eph. 5:27)."

A second characteristic of the conference is the emphasis on freedom and autonomy—Christian freedom, not license, for the individual, and autonomy for the congregation. Each believer stands before God Himself in faith as a free individual, uncoerced by other believers. Each individual soul, created in the image of God, is competent and responsible to deal directly with God through Christ, without intervention of parent, priest, sacrament, church, or state. This personal responsibility to God is the basis for freedom of conscience. This is true, within limits, in both faith and practice.

The chief interest in autonomy is not in property rights, or any other material aspect. It is rather a matter of the spirit. The local congregation must be free and autonomous "so that it may move to some mountain of transfiguration or to some upper room at Pentecost." Nicholas Berdyaev is reported to have said that "freedom is a burden rather than a right, a source of tragedy and untold pain." Freedom is not only to be free from something, but also to be free to something. This involves duty and responsibility.

Of the larger free churches in America, General Conference Mennonites in polity are probably most like the Baptists and Congregationalists. The feeling of affinity with these groups is indicated by the fact that their colleges and seminaries have often been the choice of Conference young people not attending their own, both in earlier years before General Conference schools existed and even now. A number of early and later Conference leaders attended schools at Oberlin, Rochester, and Chicago. Some Methodist schools, such as Garrett, have also been chosen, but very few have gone to Presbyterian or Southern Baptist schools as is the case in some other Mennonite groups.

In recent years the Conference has been moving toward a closer and more integrated organization, including headquarters and executive secretaries, all of which was needed, but which also has its distinct dangers.

The Conference began with unity of all Mennonites in America as one of its goals, as is indicated by the very name that was adopted. It has always been in the forefront in inter-Mennonite co-operation, such as hospitals, old people's homes and orphanages, Civilian Public Service, relief work of various kinds, all-Mennonite conventions, and Mennonite cultural conferences.

The fellowship with other Mennonite groups as well as with non-Mennonite Christians, is indicated by the practice of open communion and the former membership in the Federal Council of Churches (q.v.). General Conference ministers usually participate in local interdenominational ministerial associations, and congregations fellowship with others in summer Sunday evening services in most towns where they are located. The colleges regularly employ teachers not only of other Mennonite groups but also some non-Mennonite Christians.

An open fellowship has its dangers. Because of this the Conference has been more open to some of the non-Mennonite ideas and practices that have here and there caused dissension in congregations, such as child evangelism, eternal security, dispensationalism, materialistic millennial interpretations, various Calvinistic, modernistic, and Fundamentalistic interpretations of Scripture, as well as materialistic influences and trends toward worldliness and secularization.

A fourth characteristic of the General Conference Mennonites is a spirit of dynamics or ability to change. Christian respect for personality is the basic assumption of democracy. The respect for the individual personality underlying democracy is of highest value from the Christian point of view. In democratic America, Mennonites were free to reject change and did so. Because of this inertia they were finally in danger of dying. Oberholtzer and his group recognized this and were willing, at considerable cost, to bring about needed revitalization.

In line with this Christian respect for personality most General Conference congregations are giving women as well as men the right to vote. Laymen as well as ministers have a share in the councils of the church. Delegates to conferences are men and women, young and older people, and far more laymen than ordained ministers.

A noticeable change has been taking place from a plural, untrained, unsalaried ministry to a single, salaried, trained minister for each congregation; from an elder in charge of more than one meeting place to an elder for each congregation, and from different levels of ordination as evangelist, preacher, and elder to one full ordination. Socially the Conference has changed from the position that life insurance and political voting were evil and thus to be shunned, to where these are considered not only good, but to be embraced as a Christian duty. The rural-urban trend with all its implications and many other changes are affecting the Conference.

Finally and above all, from the very formation in 1847-60 until now, the General Conference Mennonites have always been characterized by a deep sense of mission. As a part of this sense of mission there has been a strong emphasis on consistent everyday Christian living of every Christian all through the history of the General Conference. It is considered important to believe right, but this faith must also issue in living and doing right. This living right goes deeper and means more than conforming to any outward rules and regulations. Not that one can earn anything in God's sight by living right, but it is an expression of gratitude for salvation through Christ Jesus. He is not only our Saviour but also the Lord of everyday decisions and ordinary living. The Gospel is not only to be brought into all the world geographically, but also to penetrate all levels and areas of personal and corporate life on earth.

Conference Leadership. It is impossible to list all who have served as leaders in Conference affairs in one area or another. Here follows a partial list with some attempt to classify them according to the area in which they rendered outstanding service.

Conference Leaders: P. R. Aeschliman, John B. Baer, J. J. Balzer, Peter Balzer, Jacob Buller, Walter Dyck, Benjamin Ewert, Allen M. Fretz, Dietrich Gaeddert, David Goerz, W. S. Gottshall, Daniel Hege, Michael Horsch, Ephraim Hunsberger, Cornelius Jansen, Jacob H. Jansen, Maxwell Kratz, Christian Krehbiel, Henry J. Krehbiel, Olin Krehbiel, W. W. Miller, John Moser, John H. Oberholtzer, H. D. Penner, Johannes K. Penner, Abraham Ratzlaff, P. K. Regier, Heinrich Richert, P. R. Schroeder, Andrew B. Shelly, Anthony S. Shelly, Christian Schowalter, C. H. A. van der Smissen, I. A. Sommer, Samuel F. Sprunger, Joseph Stucky, Jacob Stucky, L. Sudermann, J. J. Thiessen, David Toews, Emmanuel Troyer, B. Warkentin, P. P. Wedel.

Leaders in Missions, Education, and Publication: Henry J. Brown, N. E. Byers, D. H. Epp, H. H. Ewert, H. A. Fast, I. I. Friesen, S. J. Goering, Mrs. R. A. Goerz, N. B. Grubb, Gustav N. Harder, J. E.

Hartzler, G. A. Haury, Mrs. S. S. Haury, Samuel S. Haury, N. C. Hirschy, Lester Hostetler, Ed. G. Kaufman, Frieda Kaufman, John W. Kliewer, Cornelius Krahn, H. P. Krehbiel, A. E. Kreider, J. H. Langenwalter, J. F. Lehman, Samuel K. Mosiman, S. F. Pannabecker, Peter A. Penner, Peter W. Penner, Rudolphe Petter, Jacob Quiring, L. L. Ramseyer, J. M. Regier, J. G. Rempel, Peter H. Richert, C. J. van der Smissen, C. Henry Smith, J. N. Smucker, J. R. Thierstein, John Thiessen, John Unruh, Catherine Voth, Henry R. Voth, Abraham Warkentin, C. H. Wedel, D. C. Wedel, Peter J. Wiens.

STATISTICS OF G.C. CONGREGATIONS AND MEMBERSHIP

District	Congregations		Membership			
	Conf.	Non-Gen. Conf.	Conf.	Non-Gen. Conf.	Children (Unbaptized)	Total Population
Canadian	49	22	12,810	1,195	28,425	22,430
Central	19	1	3,020	?	642	3,662
Eastern	28	0	4,558	0	1,519	6,077
Middle	20	0	5,258	0	1,951	7,209
Northern	26	5	5,605	395	2,926	8,926
Pacific	21	2	3,280	64	904	4,248
Western	66	0	13,584	0	5,045	18,625
	229	30	*48,115	1,654		
South America	5	0	1,989			
			48,115			

North American Total 49,769 21,412 71,181

* This is not an accurate figure as 6 churches did not report. The total membership is probably somewhat over 50,000.   E.K.G.

Constitution of the General Conference Mennonite Church (Newton, 1950); J. W. Fretz, "Reflections at the End of a Century," *Menn. Life* II (July 1947); *General Conference Handbook of Information* (Newton, 1956); Ed. G. Kaufman, *The Development of the Missionary and Philanthropic Interest Among the Mennonites of North America* (Berne, 1931); idem, "The General Conference of the Mennonite Church of North America," *Menn. Life* I (July 1947); H. P. Krehbiel, *The History of the General Conference of Mennonites of North America* I (St. Louis, 1898); II (Newton, 1938); S. F. Pannabecker, "The Anabaptist Concept of the Church in the American Mennonite Environment," *MQR* XXV (January 1951); J. C. Wenger, "Mennonites Establish Themselves in Pennsylvania," *Menn Life* II (July 1947); S. F. Pannabecker, "The Development of the General Conference of the Mennonite Church of North America in the American Environment" (Yale University Ph.D. dissertation); idem, "John H. Oberholtzer and His Time— A Centennial Tribute 1847-1947," *Menn. Life* II (July 1947); Paul R. Shelly, *Religious Education and Mennonite Piety Among the Mennonites of Southeastern Pennsylvania: 1870-1943* (Newton, 1952); C. Henry Smith, *The Story of the Mennonites* (Newton, 1950); ML I, 29-32.

Geneva (*Genève, Genf*), a canton of Switzerland, area 107 sq. miles, pop. (1950) 201,505. Its capital, **Geneva**, lies at the source of the Rhone in Lake Geneva, and has a population of about 124,000. During the Reformation the city was not untouched by the Anabaptist movement, although under the autocratic rule of Calvin (*q.v.*) it was unable to assert itself.

In 1532 two foreign Anabaptists, tortured at Basel, revealed that the Anabaptists were increasing in number along Lake Geneva; but they were uncertain whether there were any Anabaptists in the city at this time.

In February 1537 two Dutch Anabaptists Herman de Gerbihan and Andry (Andre) Benoit of Engelen in Brabant came to Geneva. They spread their principles, and on May 9 appeared before the Council of Two Hundred and declared their intention to hold a disputation with the reformers. Farel and Calvin, who had already been attacked by many Genevans, took advantage of this opportunity to oppose these foreign adversaries. The council requested them to present their proposals in writing, and when this was done, it decided that the newcomers receive a hearing before the council; for the credulity of the people made it dangerous to hold a public disputation. On May 14 the principles of faith were read aloud; Farel demanded a public discussion, but the councilors objected, saying, "We know well that you will be the victors, but you may be sure the populace will hear the errors of the Anabaptists more greedily than your truths: to proclaim the untruth to the people is sufficient to create a taste for it." Calvin replied, "You are quite right. But if we now refuse the disputation the Anabaptists will boast that we are defeated and do not dare to defend our faith. Of the two evils it is better to choose the lesser." The council finally consented to grant this request of the reformers and also the Anabaptists. The public disputation began May 16, 1537, in the monastery of Riva (*de rive*) and lasted two days. Without doubt it dealt principally with the question of baptism, the Anabaptists insisting that disciples of Christ may be baptized only when they are capable of giving an account of their faith.

The rug dealers and other persons of rank who made up the council and who believed that they possessed all the knowledge needed to distinguish between doctrines, apparently did not favor this public disputation. On May 18 they met and decided that the disputation would lead to strife rather than to unity and would more likely cause faith to waver than strengthen it; it must therefore be discontinued. These persons should be ordered to leave the city and its canton. All notes taken during the disputation were to be turned in to the city hall and destroyed, lest any of them appear in print. The Anabaptists should no longer be called brethren, because they were not in harmony with the church and were unwilling to worship with its adherents.

The council summoned the two Anabaptists and told them it would be glad to give them a hearing, for it gave everyone a hearing; but because their doctrines were not founded on the Scriptures they must be declared false. It asked them if they were ready to recant, return to God and beg His forgiveness. The Anabaptists replied that they would in no case recant. On May 19 they were again summoned and questioned. They answered that their conscience did not permit them to take any other position; they were then ordered to leave the city permanently. They betook themselves to the canton of Bern.

On May 30 Johannes Bomeromenus, a printer, and Jean Tordeur (Stordeur), both from Liége, who had declared themselves willing to die in defense of the doctrine that infants should not be baptized, were expelled from the canton.

On Sept. 7 Farel and Calvin notified the authorities of several citizens who persisted in holding Anabaptist ideas. The council decided to prosecute them. On Sept. 11 a dealer in caps, named Guider, who was suspected of Anabaptist ideas, recanted.

Jacob de Lesture, suspected of Anabaptism, refused to appear before the council, and was banished. This sentence was opposed by Georges de Lesclef, Jean Philippe, and the councilor Lullin. On Sept. 28 Jane, a glover, was expelled from the city for life because she persisted in her Anabaptist faith; but on June 7, 1538, after the banishment of Farel and Calvin, the council permitted her to return if she would obey the laws.

In spite of persecutions a considerable number of citizens went over to the Anabaptists: Jean Japin, called Cologny, a citizen of Geneva, one of the originators of the Reformation, made a public statement in favor of the Anabaptists, and was consequently sentenced to a year in prison on bread and water so that he would no longer trouble the preachers.

Two of the declared adherents of Anabaptist doctrine were Jacob de Meraulx and Jean Moynier. Their secret fellow believers were probably numerous, for on Oct. 8, 1537, the council expressly ordered the preachers not actually to refuse the sacraments to the Anabaptists, and to let simple admonition suffice. On Jan. 14, 1538, Farel lamented the victory of several Anabaptists.

The theological discussions with the Anabaptists, by opening people's eyes, produced a ferment among them. Farel and Calvin, feeling themselves deserted by a portion of public opinion, and wishing to execute a great coup, had all the inhabitants subscribe to an orthodox confession of faith in order to separate the sheep from the wolves. But the populace distrusted these measures; and hostile magistrates were appointed, who opposed Farel and Calvin. The conflict grew so serious that the council decided to expel Farel and Calvin. The latter retired to Strasbourg, where he married Idelette de Bure (van Buren) (q.v.), the widow of a Dutch Mennonite, and where he lived until 1541. In the meantime public sentiment in Geneva had changed; friends of Calvin had again come into power and recalled him to organize and lead the new church. Calvin returned as a victor and gave the Genevans a new constitution. By means of these regulations the church attained supreme authority and Calvin was its undisputed head until his death in 1564.

Under the scepter of the all-powerful Calvin, who had Michael Servetus killed at the stake in 1553, and who sternly suppressed any attempt to cause a division in the church, there was obviously no room in Geneva for Anabaptists.

Like Luther and Zwingli, Calvin also attacked the Anabaptists. In one of his works, *Bréves instructions pour armer tous bons fidéles contre la secte commune des anabaptistes,* dedicated to the preachers in the county of Neuchâtel, he declared, "To write against all the false opinions and errors of the Anabaptists would be so long a story, almost a hell, from which one could not emerge,—for this vermin is different from all other people in that it not only errs in certain points, but has also caused a sea of nonsensical talk." Here are a few additional specimens of Calvin's opinion of the Anabaptists: "They conclude that all use of arms is of the devil. . . . It is certain that it is the intention of these wretched fanatics to condemn all fortifications, munitions, and all bearing of arms. . . . But the Christian not only does not offend God in seizing a weapon, but really has a divine calling to do so, which cannot be refused without blasphemy.— A man who had only an ounce of brain, would he talk like the Anabaptists?—It is easy to see that these unfortunate fanatics will attain no other end than to reduce everything to turmoil, set up community of goods, in spite of the fact that they fully and completely deny it.—Or they will not be content until they have persuaded all rulers to resign, in order to step into their positions and establish themselves there as in an unowned possession.— These unfortunate persons spit out many of the most irrational blasphemies: the government of the councillors is according to the flesh, they say; that of the Christians according to the Spirit.—As concerns the faith which they claim to have, I want to say that they make of themselves enemies of God and of the human race.—These poor insane people accept as revelations from heaven all the fables they have heard their grandmothers tell.—If the animals could speak, they would talk more sensibly than they. These crazy persons want to take the Lord with them in order to have Him quickly defend their idle talk. Their basis for a change in this command (concerning Jesus' teaching on the oath) is an obvious blasphemy; for it would follow from it that Jesus Christ had rescinded that which had been established by God, His Father, which can surely not be tolerated."

He expresses himself similarly in the *Traité contre les anabaptistes.* But the above citations are sufficient to characterize the work in which Calvin attempts to refute the chief Anabaptist doctrines, such as baptism, oath, discipline, communion, relation to government, the bearing of arms, and the nature of the soul. Theodore von Beza asserted that Calvin was completely victorious in this matter. The reading of these lengthy pages has not made the same impression on us.

It seems that since Calvin's time there has not been a Mennonite church in Geneva. At any rate no trace of any has been found. Not until World War I was there a small contact between Geneva and the Mennonites. In 1912 a French Mennonite, Pierre Kennel, who was the descendant of Bernese

Brethren who were expelled at the end of the 18th century and fled to France, settled in Geneva to enter upon his vocation as a university teacher. As professor at the university he lectured on biology. Then came the war. Proud of being true to his Christian conviction, his social concepts and the inherited traditions, he refused to obey the French mobilization orders. . . . Thereupon on May 7, 1915, the city council and the university demanded that he withdraw from his academic work.

In 1926 about 20 Mennonites were living in Geneva and its vicinity, but without forming an organized congregation. Their names were Geiser, Kennel, Wenger, and Wüttrich. (See **Gex.**) P.K.

Dean Antoine Gantier, *Histoire de Genève;* A. Roget, *Hist. du peuple de Genève* (7 vv., 1870-82); J. R. Gaberel, *Histoire de l'Eglise de Genève* (3 vv., 1853-62); A. L. Herminjard, *Correspondance des reformateurs dans les pays de langue francaise* (9 vv.); P. Charpenne, *Histoire de la reforme et des Reformateurs de Genève* (Paris, 1861); Baroche, *Dictionaire historique de la Suisse;* Eug. Choisy, *La Theocratie à Genève;* Calvin, *Oppuscules francaise,* 579-646; S. Geiser, *Die Taufgesinnten-Gemeinden* (Karlsruhe, 1932) 164; *ML* II, 66 ff.

Gent (English, Ghent), present capital of the Belgian province of East Flanders, pop. (1949) 166,797, with suburbs 218,328. With the exception of Antwerp no other city in Belgium had as long a list of Anabaptist martyrs as Gent. The Anabaptist and Calvinist martyrbooks together list 110 victims; van Braght's *Martyrs' Mirror* lists 92 Anabaptist-Mennonite martyrs. The research of V. van der Haeghen published in *Bibliographie des Martyrologes Protestants Néerlandais* (The Hague, 1890) proved that the number of victims was much higher, and A. L. E. Verheyden (*Het Gentsche Martyrologium 1530-1595,* Brugge, 1946), who studied the sources, lists a total of 252 victims, subdivided in five groups: 51 Iconoclasts, 30 Calvinists, 146 Anabaptist-Mennonites, 23 heretics, 2 Lutherans. So the Anabaptist-Mennonites are by far the largest part of the executed. And of 146 Anabaptist-Mennonite martyrs no fewer than 105 or 72 per cent were burned at the stake; of the Calvinists only 23 per cent were executed in this cruel way. K. Vos (in *ML* II, 69) stated the surprising fact that the names of the victims found in the official records at times greatly differ from those mentioned in the *Offer des Heeren* and the later martyrbooks, including the *Martyrs' Mirror.* He concluded:

"This deviation is in part explained by the use of secret names. For many of these martyrs the names are scarcely known. For instance, in 41 cases the principal source of our knowledge is a song composed on their death by a poet of Gent; it is found in the *Offer des Heeren,* 649-54, and includes martyrs of 1562-69, according to eyewitness accounts. The song was already printed by 1577. It contains a few errors because the poet had to rely entirely on his memory. A second song, *Offer des Heeren,* 556-59, lists 12 martyrs of 1559. A song found in *Veelderhande Liedekens* of 1569 reveals that these martyrs were betrayed by a Beguine and arrested while they were eating a meal."

Verheyden made a thorough study of the materials; although the records of the sentences are incomplete (until 1538, during 1540-55 and 1568-71 lacking), Verheyden by using other old books and documents succeeded in procuring a nearly complete list. The first Anabaptist martyr of Gent, Willem Mulaer, was executed on July 15, 1535; the last ones, Bartholomeus Panten and Michiel de Cleercq, both suffered death on Sept. 15, 1592. The most important martyrs and leaders of the congregation were Hans van Overdam and Hans Keeskooper (d. 1551), Claes de Praet (d. 1556), Joost de Tollenaar (d. 1589), and Michiel de Cleercq (d. 1592).

There must have been an important and at times very numerous congregation at Gent. Anabaptists may have been at Gent as early as 1530, and very likely a congregation came into existence soon after. Not much is known of this congregation. Occasionally the trials of the martyrs supply some facts, and it is mostly from the official records and the martyrbooks that its history is known. They used to meet in secret places, sometimes in the houses of members, sometimes also in grainfields or wooded spots in the neighborhood of the city, usually in numbers not larger than 25 or 30. Meetings are said to have been held every day.

During the first period (1530-40) a certain revolutionary spirit seems to have prevailed in the congregation: this fact can be concluded from the deaconship of Mahieu Wagens (executed Aug. 15, 1538), a revolutionary. But in general the church followed the paths of the movement in Holland, those of a peaceful Anabaptism-Mennonitism. David Joris, who visited the Gent congregation, had scarcely an adherent in this congregation. The congregation—also in the following periods—seems to have consisted more of refugees seeking shelter here rather than of citizens of Gent.

In the following period (1540-73) the congregation was usually served by outside elders from Antwerp or even from Holland, e.g., Gillis van Aken, Cornelis Claissone from Leiden, Jan van de Walle, Christiaen (may be identical with Chr. Janssens Langedul from Antwerp) and Joachim Vermeeren from Antwerp, later also Hans Busschaert, Paulus van Meenen, and Hendrik van Arnhem. Of great blessing were the sojourns of Leenaert Bouwens at Gent. He visited the congregation several times in 1554-56 and 1557-61 and baptized 116 or 129 persons here.

The congregation of Gent had its own preachers and deacons, but no elder of its own. That they desperately wanted one is shown by a letter written by Adriaen van Kortrijk to the church of Antwerp in the name of the principal Flemish congregations. In this letter, which is undated but must have been written about 1545, Adriaen points out that the congregation is like a flock of sheep without a shepherd; the congregations of Flanders are all said to be young, and have too infrequently been visited by elders from Holland. So Adriaen insists that a bishop be sent. It is not known whether this request was granted. The time of prosperity of the church about 1550 was at the same time a period of terrible martyrdom. Many members were executed and many left the city, fleeing to England

(London), Holland (especially Haarlem), and Emden in East Friesland.

In 1566 rising Calvinism became active in Gent; in this year a number of Catholic churches were plundered and images of saints destroyed. The Mennonites, maintaining their principle of nonresistance, did not co-operate with the Calvinist iconoclasts. Notwithstanding their nonparticipation they were terribly persecuted in 1567-73 during the reactionary and implacable Catholic government of the Duke of Alba: within those six years no fewer than 49 members were put to death. The congregation, which is said to have numbered 400 members in 1567, greatly decreased in the following years, both by execution and flight. But church life was still very active; secret meetings continued, and a solid organization is proved by the activity of the deacons.

In 1577-84 Calvinism reigned in Gent. Under the supremacy of the Calvinist government the Mennonite congregation too had a time of rest and security; no one was executed, only a few were banished from the city. But equality with the Calvinist church was not yet obtained: Calvinism considered the Mennonites as heretics just as Roman Catholicism had done before. This is proved from the fact that a debate between Calvinist and Mennonite leaders held in the fall of 1581 was fruitless; and a request of the Mennonites presented to the city government in February 1582 to obtain the use of one of the former Catholic churches taken over by the Calvinists was refused.

The Calvinist government lasted only a few years. In September 1584 the Spanish Stadholder Alexander Farnese conquered the city and the Calvinist magistrates were replaced by Roman Catholics. The new government was rather moderate toward the Calvinists, permitting them, if they wanted to keep their faith, to sell their property and leave the city. But the Mennonites, whose number is said to have been "not small," usually were handled with less moderation. So persecution again came over the congregation. A number of its members died as martyrs, others escaped and came to Holland. On March 15, 1585, nine Mennonites were arrested in the home of Jan de Cleercq. They were probably all deacons, constituting the board of the congregation of Gent. In 1589 and 1592 all the leaders of the congregation were in prison and suffered martyrdom. Then all records become silent; but the congregation still existed. It was led by a deacon preacher, who sometimes received gifts from Holland for the poor and the relatives of those who had been put to death, and who also preached if conditions made it possible to have a meeting. Though there is little positive information extant, the congregation continued to live; in 1609 an elder of Haarlem visited the church of Gent. The members were no longer living in the city, for the meeting was held at Lovendegem, a village near Gent. Here, as well as in Zomergem, another village in the neighborhood, Mennonites continued to meet. Until 1629 they met at Zomergem in a loft. But in this year a house was adapted for the meetings, which soon proved to be too small for the number of members. In this time most members were rather well-to-do merchants. Their preacher was Jacob van Maldegem and twice a year an elder came over from the Dutch province of Zeeland. They also participated in the meetings which were held at Aardenburg, just across the border on Dutch territory. For a number of years this congregation had held its meetings without attracting the attention of the government, but in 1630 the magistrates became aware of it; then it became impossible to hold meetings and about 1634 the congregation was dissolved. Its members migrated to the Netherlands; most of them settled in Aardenburg and Middelburg in the province of Zeeland.

While the congregation of Gent was still in existence the quarrels arose in the Netherlands which divided the Mennonites into different groups—Waterlanders, Flemish, and Frisians. These differences did not stir up the church in Flanders as they did the Dutch congregations. Yet there were in Gent two separate congregations—one, likely the largest, Flemish, and one Waterlander. Representatives of the latter were present at the Waterlander meeting at Amsterdam in March 1581, where it was decided that Albrecht Verspeck should visit the Gent congregation. Further particulars about the differences were not available.   vDZ.

A. L. E. Verheyden, "De Doopsgezinden te Gent 1530-1630," in *Bijdragen tot de Gesch. en de Oudheidkunde van Gent* (1943) 97-130; *idem*, "Een Episode uit de Gentsche Kerkhervorming* (June 1566-February 1567)," in *Rapport-Bulletin van de Vereeniging v. Gesch. van het Belgische Protestantisme* (Brussels, 1945, reprint); *idem, Het Gentsche Martyrologium* (Brugge, 1946); *DB* 1877, 80, 82, 87; 1884, 57 note 2; *ML* II, 68-71.

Gent, Carel van: see **Carel van Gent.**

Gent, Een Liedeken *van XIJ vrienden van,* is found in the *Liedtboecxken van den Offer des Heeren* (reprint *BRN* II, 556-59). It begins "Ick moet een liet beginnen dat sal ick gaen heffen aen." In this song 12 martyrs executed at Gent, Belgium, in 1559 are celebrated. Their names are not found in the song itself, but a marginal note reads: for the names see the confession of Hans de Vette.

The 12 martyrs were Peter Coerten from Meenen, Kaerle Tancreet from Nipkercke, Proentgen his wife from Belle, Jacob Spillebout, Abraham Tancreet, and Maeyken Floris from Nipkercke, Anthonis van Cassele, Hans de Smit, and Marcus his brother, Hans de Vette and Miertgen his wife from Waestene, and Tanneken, wife of Hans de Smet.

This song (also found in Wolkan, *Lieder,* 62, 71) was found already in the *Nieu Liedenboeck* of 1562. Another song celebrating these martyrs, "Een eeuwighe Vruecht die niet en vergaet," is found in *Veelderhande Liedekens* of 1569. For particulars about the 12 martyrs, see Verheyden, *Gent,* and related articles in this ENCYCLOPEDIA.   vDZ.

Gent, Een liedeken *van XLI vrienden binnen Gent gedoot tusschen tjaar LXIJ ende LXIX,* is an old martyr song, beginning "Als men schreef duyst vijfhondert Jaer/ ende tweeentsestich mede/ sachmen te Gent dits openbaer/ vrome Christenen ontleden." The song is included in the *Liedtboecxken* *van den Offer des Heeren* of 1578 (second edition of this year) and following editions. It is reprinted in *BRN* II, 649-54. Between a devotional preface and epilogue the 41 martyrs are briefly mentioned. The names were collected from various sources; they were copied by van Braght in the *Martyrs' Mirror*. Occasionally mistakes were made both in the names and the years of martyrdom, as has been proved by A. L. E. Verheyden's study of the sources (see **Gent**).   vdZ.

Gentman, Cornelis (1617-96), a Dutch Reformed minister at Utrecht, who stemmed from a Mennonite refugee family from Flanders, was the moving force in 1659 in the city government's persecution of the Dutch Mennonite preachers Goris van Aldendorp, Arent van Heuven, Johan Andries van Aken, and Willem van Maurick. This dispute gave him occasion to publish several hate-filled booklets. Gentman is thought to be the author of the 12 questions on the basis of which the Mennonites of Utrecht (in 1655 and 1661), Deventer (1669), and Middelburg (1665) were to be examined by the city governments. The questions are found in Blaupot t. C., *Groningen* II, 205-13. (*Biogr. Wb.* III, 214-15; *DB* 1916, 156, 163, 180, 189; *ML* II, 71.)
                                                  K.V., vdZ.

Gentner, Hans, of Sulzfeld in the government district of Eppingen in Baden, Germany, where the parson Gallus, a friend of Johannes Brenz (*q.v.*), had early turned to the Reformation together with his patron, Göler von Ravensberg, was won to Anabaptism by Philip Plener (*q.v.*) and Blasius Kuhn (*q.v.*) or Kumauf, who had been very active in and around Bruchsal. With Plener he went to Moravia and served as a preacher under the Philipites. But when he became acquainted with the principles of the Hutterian Brethren in Moravia he left the Philipites and joined the Hutterites. Among the Philipites his withdrawal aroused great offense, which found expression in Blasius Kuhn's accusation that Gentner had not been honest with money entrusted to him. He must have succeeded in acquitting himself, for he received a position of confidence among the Hutterian Brethren.

In 1539 Gentner was sent to his former friends in Württemberg and the Palatinate with the prayers of his brethren. In Malsch (Wiesloch district), in co-operation with Wendel Metzger of Heidelsheim, he baptized men and women, some of whom were imprisoned. This mission indicates that he must have been an ordained minister. The brotherhood was so well pleased by his success that in 1540 they sent him again to the Swabian Unterland and to Württemberg, then into northern Württemberg, the near-by Palatinate, and Baden. This time he succeeded in persuading a considerable number to emigrate to Moravia. In 1541 he was again sent to Württemberg and also to Hesse.

The high regard of the brotherhood for Gentner was revealed in 1542. The charge of moral misconduct brought against Christoph Gschäl, a missionary in Carinthia, compelled the brotherhood to have a conference of preachers summoned by the new bishop, Leonhard Lanzenstiel, and his assistant Gentner, whereupon Gschäl was expelled from the brotherhood.

Another journey to Württemberg in 1543 with the deacon Michael Kramer brought Gentner into serious difficulty. He met a number of Schwenckfeldians, who believed that Jesus brought His flesh from heaven and did not receive it from Mary. Their leader was Jörg Nörlinger. Since their doctrine in general was in harmony with that of the Hutterian Brethren, Gentner, on the advice of Kramer, remained silent on this point, for he hoped that their peculiar ideas would naturally disappear if they joined the brotherhood in Moravia. But when Nörlinger arrived in Moravia and tried to come to an agreement with the elders, he stated that Gentner had not opposed him on this point. Hans Feuerbach, a recent convert, was then sent to Württemberg to summon Gentner and Kramer to Moravia. Gentner was deprived of his preaching office and Kramer was also punished (*Geschicht-Buch,* 190-93).

Gentner, however, soon regained the confidence of the brotherhood. For in 1545 he was sent with Georg Liebich (*q.v.*), who had proved his faithfulness in a long prison term at Innsbruck, to Silesia, to inform Gabriel Ascherham's numerous adherents (about 300) that the Gabrielites had joined the Hutterites after the excommunication of their leader.

In 1548 Gentner died in Schäckowitz, a half mile from Auspitz. The *Geschicht-Buch* (242) calls him "a faithful servant of the Word of God and His Church," who "had to endure much sorrow and many a struggle and battle for the sake of the Lord."   G.Bo.

Ztscht für die Gesch. des Oberrheins, 1905, 75; Beck, *Geschichts-Bücher,* 193; Wolkan, *Geschicht-Buch; ML* II, 71 f.

Georg von Chur: see **Blaurock, Georg.**

Georg van Pare, an Anabaptist martyr, a Dutch physician who lived in London and was burned at the stake there in 1551. Zur Linden counts him among the Melchiorites who fled to Holland. Georg Weber calls him a unitarian.   NEFF.

F. O. zur Linden, *Melchior Hofmann* (Haarlem and Leipzig, 1885) 419; G. Weber, *Gesch. der Altkatholischen Kirchen und Sekten in Grossbritannien* II (Leipzig, 1845) 106; *ML* III, 335.

George I (1660-1727), King of Great Britain and Ireland 1714-27, the son of Duke Ernst August of Hannover and Princess Sophie of the Palatinate, a granddaughter of James I of England. This German prince on the English throne was especially interested in the oppressed Mennonites in Switzerland and the Palatinate. Shortly after his coronation he tried to aid the Mennonites who, persecuted and imprisoned by the Swiss government at Bern, were finally released through the mediation of Dutch Mennonites and for the most part settled in the Palatinate. George I issued an urgent invitation to the Mennonites in the Palatinate to settle in the English colonies of America, offering them favorable terms for their transportation. To each family settling west of the Alleghenies in Pennsylvania he offered a gift of 50 acres of land and the permission to cultivate as much additional land as they wished without making any payments for ten years, after which period a small rental was to be paid (Cassel, 278). In 1717 a conference of elders at Mannheim decided to accept the offer and settle in America. In March 100 persons, led by Elder Benedikt Brechbiehl (*q.v.*), emigrated and were followed three weeks later by 300 more. No further emigrations of Palatine Mennonites took place until after George's death. HEGE.

Inv. Arch. Amst. I, 2254-56; W. A. Knittle, *Early Eighteenth Century Palatine Emigration* (Philadelphia, 1937); C. H. Smith, *Mennonite Immigration to Pennsylvania* (Norristown, 1929); D. K. Cassel, *Gesch. der Mennoniten* (Philadelphia, 1890); *ML* II, 72.

George Christian, Prince of East Friesland, Germany, 1660-65, brother of Enno Ludwig (*q.v.*), granted the Mennonites a letter of protection June 2, 1660, upon payment of 1,000 talers and a so-called gift of 100 ducats to his wife, Christine Charlotte, a princess of Württemberg. The Uckowallists (*q.v.*), who had on May 29 requested a letter of protection like that granted by Enno Ludwig, received it on June 26 upon payment of 500 talers. New extortions followed. During the brief reign of the prince the Mennonites were fined 1,200 talers for performing a baptism, which they felt they were entitled to do on the basis of the letter of protection. George's son Eberhard Christian was born posthumously. During the latter's minority his mother reigned, following the pattern her husband had set in regard to the Mennonites. (*ML* II, 72.) NEFF.

George Frederick (1539-1603), Margrave of Brandenburg, at Ansbach and Bayreuth, Germany, a zealous promoter of Lutheranism and rigorous opponent of Anabaptism. When he took over the reign of the duchy of Prussia from his feeble-minded cousin Albrecht Friedrich, the Mennonites there requested permission to settle in Königsberg and other cities and towns. He replied in the decree of Jan. 8, 1579, that it was his duty as a Christian ruler and for him a matter of conscience to see to it that unity of faith prevailed among his subjects, as the constitution of the land already specified. But the confession of faith presented by the Mennonites showed that in many points they did not have the true Christian faith, also in the matter of police and the family they did not agree with the Augsburg Confession or the Prussian *corpus doctrinae,* and primarily in the holy sacrament of infant baptism their attitude was very offensive. Therefore the prince was unable to grant their request; instead all Anabaptists were to leave the country by the first of May (Mannhardt, *Wehrfreiheit,* 110). This mandate was renewed and intensified in 1585 and Nov. 12, 1586, making it punishable by death and confiscation of goods for any "who would not adhere to the church books of the country" to remain in the country; but the tradesman was to have free access by water or land to carry on his business (Hart-

knoch, 497). These mandates were evidently not strictly enforced, for Mennonitism maintained itself in the duchy of Prussia. NEFF.

W. Mannhardt, *Die Wehrfreiheit der Altpreussischen Mennoniten* (Marienburg, 1863); Hartknoch, *Preussische Kirchen-Historia* (Frankfurt, 1686); *ML* II, 73 f.

George the Bearded (1471-1539), Duke of Saxony, in 1500 assumed the reign over the Saxon-Albertine hereditary lands in Germany. He opposed the Reformation. Nevertheless the new doctrine managed to spread in his realm.

He was particularly severe in his measures against the Anabaptists, whom he wished to wipe out. Under the influence of Johann Eck (*q.v.*), he was one of the most fanatical opponents of Anabaptism in the era of the Reformation (Gess, 811). On Dec. 31, 1527, he issued a Draconian mandate against "the old, damned heresy of the Anabaptists" (according to Jacobs, 426, reprinted in *Codex Augusteus,* the great Saxon collection of laws, I, 433 ff., and Wappler, *Thüringen,* 266). Since death was the penalty for adhering to the doctrine of adult baptism, the Anabaptists avoided publicity, propagating their faith silently (Jacobs, 426). It is supposed that the Anabaptists withdrew in part into the Schwarzburg district of Frankenhausen (Jacobs, 430).

But the movement was not broken in Saxony, as is apparent from the fact that Duke George issued a new mandate against the Anabaptists Dec. 23, 1534. It surpasses all previous mandates issued against the Anabaptists in Germany and Austria by its base appeal to the avarice of the populace. Not only the clergy, but also secular officials and all subjects were urged to co-operate in the persecution of the Anabaptists. Anyone who considered infant baptism and the sacraments as naught or expressed himself unfavorably about them, and on the other hand recognized baptism of believers and "similar unchristian ideas" as correct, should be drowned; if there was no suitable water at hand he was to be beheaded; his property should be confiscated. Life and possessions were already lost "if they cannot deny that they have written seriously about it or taken part in it and not opposed it." Even by recanting they could not save life or property. The entire population was challenged to participate in this religious persecution. Anyone who seems lax in the capture of persons suspected of Anabaptism shall be punished; anyone who on the other hand distinguishes himself shall be rewarded with one third of the property of the condemned one. (*Codex Augusteus* I, 433-36; Jacobs, 438; Wappler, *Thüringen,* 383.) This mandate became in part a pattern for the extension of the later imperial laws of 1544 and 1551 against the Anabaptists. Thus no alternative remained for the Anabaptists, in consideration of their relatives and friends, than to seek out infertile regions and live for their faith in solitude; many hid in the depths of the Hohenstein Harz and in the desolate "Schraubishain," also called Schraubenstein, east of Sangerhausen between Riestedt Blanckenhain and Beiernaumburg, where they lived under the open sky and assembled for worship from far and near (Jacobs, 439).

The measures of persecution undertaken by Duke George were not limited to his own realm. He was also the moving power in the annihilation of the Anabaptists in the region of Quedlinburg, as well as in the counties of Mansfeld, Schwarzburg, Stolberg, and Hohnstein in the south Harz. Most zealous in the pursuit of Anabaptists was George's cousin, Cardinal Albrecht; in Halberstadt he discovered two families in September 1535 (Knobloch and Heune), who had left the forest to avoid the inclement weather because of the expected confinement of the mothers. The statements of the prisoners reveal the high moral standards required of the Anabaptists and their deeply felt religious faith. They died as martyrs to their faith. In the following years further executions followed, which are ascribed to the personal intervention of the duke (Jacobs, 493; Wappler, *Inquisition,* 91). Even those who would have recanted found no mercy. Anabaptists who had recanted but had again left the Catholic Church had their hands cut off before drowning (Wappler, *Thüringen,* 161 and 430). The duke "considered the substitution of death by the sword for death by fire as adequate clemency" (Dollinger).

George later learned from experience what it means to have one's family dispersed by death. The last years of his life were saddened by the death in rapid succession of his wife (1534) and nine children. For grief he let his beard grow, thus acquiring the epithet "the Bearded." His inheritance, which he had wished to give Ferdinand of Bohemia, went to his brother Henry, who introduced the Reformation in the duchy. From now on nothing is heard of Anabaptist executions in the country. HEGE.

E. Jacobs, "Die Wiedertäufer am Harz," in *Ztscht des Harzvereins für Gesch. und Altertumskunde* XXXII (Wernigerode, 1899); P. Wappler, *Die Täuferbewegung in Thüringen von 1526-1584* (Jena, 1913); idem, *Inquisition und Täuferprozesse in Zwickau zur Ref.-Zeit* (Leipzig, 1908); F. Gess, *Akten und Briefe zur Kirchenpolitik Herzog Georgs von Sachsen* II (Berlin, 1917); R. Dollinger, "Memminger Sektenbewegungen im 16. und 17. Jahrhundert," in *Ztscht für bayrische Kirchengesch.* XII (1937) 131; H. Becker, *Herzog Georg von Sachsen als kirchlicher und theologischer Schriftsteller* (Leipzig, 1928); H. von Welk, *Georg der Bärtige* (Braunschweig, 1899); *ML* II, 73.

Georges Bare (Barre), an Anabaptist martyr, burned at the stake at Kortrijk (Courtrai) in Flanders, Belgium, on Feb. 5, 1556. Bare was quite impetuous, for in prison he broke an image of the Virgin off the wall. His brother, who was Catholic, visited him in prison and sought to deflect him from his faith, but in vain. The efforts of the Catholic churchmen as well as torture were likewise fruitless. Bare remained steadfast in his faith. After a month of solitary confinement he was executed. His property was confiscated. Bare was born near Rijssel (Lille) in France and lived in Kortrijk. (Verheyden, *Courtrai-Bruxelles,* 32, No. 4.) vDZ.

Georges, E. F., a Dutch artist who in 1849 made a bust of Menno Simons, following a painted portrait, formerly the property of Marten Schagen (*q.v.*), and now found in the room of the church board at Utrecht (*DB* 1890, 75). vDZ.

Geraert (Geert) **Passamentwerker** (official name, *Geraerdt Franssens*), an Anabaptist martyr of Thienen, Belgium, was burned at the stake at Antwerp on Dec. 16, 1558. He remained steadfast in his suffering and is celebrated in the song "Aenhoort Godt Hemelsche Vader" (Hear, O God, heavenly Father), in the *Liedtboecxken van den Offer des Heeren* (No. 16). vDZ.

Offer, 566; *Mart. Mir.* D 202, E 583; *Antw. Arch.-Blad* VIII, 454, 466; XIV, 24-25, No. 273; Wolkan, *Lieder,* 63, 72; *ML* III, 384.

Geraert Sieryns, an otherwise unknown Anabaptist, is named in the last stanza as the author of the hymn "Mijn heer, mijn God, mijn Vader, groot van machten" (My Lord, my God, my Father, great of power), found in the Dutch hymnbook *Het Tweede Liedeboeck* of 1583. (Wolkan, *Lieder,* 70.) vDZ.

Gerbel, Nikolaus (d. 1560), a humanist and convinced Lutheran, professor of law at the University of Strasbourg, Alsace. To him is frequently ascribed a booklet described as nonextant, *De anabaptistarum ortu et progressu.* It is erroneously referred to in *Beiträge zur Kenntnis der Mennoniten-Gemeinden* (Berlin, 1821) by Reiswitz and Wadzeck (231), where it is confused with a work by Joh. Gast (*q.v.*). Büchle considers it doubtful that Gerbel wrote the booklet mentioned above. It is his opinion that the assumption is based on a false interpretation of the passage in Zeltner's *Theatrum* concerning Gerbel's rare book, *Novum Testamentum Graece ed. Nicolaus Gerbelius, Hagenoae, in aedibus Thomae Anselmi Mentio Martio. Anno salutis 1521.* This can, however, hardly be the case, for this work appeared in 1521, before there were any Anabaptists. Wilhelm Horning evidently has no knowledge of Büchle's book. He says (p. 33): "Concerning the origin and spread of the Anabaptists, Gerbel wrote *De anabaptistarum ortu et progressu.* This booklet has disappeared (Geigel should probably be Geiger). Here—he writes on one occasion—all is quiet and peaceful. Two Anabaptists, Hoffmann and Hieronymus Frei, are still held in prison. I do not hear, however, that their ideas are improving. Each holds obstinately to his opinion." NEFF.

A. Büchle, *Der Humanist Nikolaus Gerbel aus Pforzheim* (Durlach, 1886); W. Horning, *Humanist Nikolaus Gerbel, Förderer der lutherischen Ref. in Strassburg (1485-1560)* (Strasbourg, 1918); Varrentrap, *Nicolaus Gerbel* (Strasbourg, 1901); *ML* II, 74.

Gerbens, a Mennonite family at Grouw, Dutch province of Friesland. Ruurd Gerbens, after 1680 elder of the Jan Jacobsgezinden at Leeuwarden, wrote *Korte Belijdenisse des Christelijken Geloofs* . . . (Leeuwarden, 1698, 2nd ed. Groningen, 1717; see *Biogr. Wb.* III, 216). In Grouw during the 18th century this family belonged to the Groote Huys (Waterlander) congregation. There some of them were deacons; e.g., Sjoerd Gerbens, who was among the first Mennonites to take a government office (1795) and who was an ancestor of the Binnerts (*q.v.*) family. About 1800 some members of this family adopted Grouw as their family name.

Ruurd Gerbens van Grouw (d. 1806), likely a brother of Sjoerd, was a preacher of his home church 1763-97; in 1797 he moved to Berlikum. In 1796-1806 he served the congregation of Molkwerum, where he was the last untrained minister. (*DB* 1895, 116.)

Tjalling Gerbens van Grouw (another brother?) served the congregation of Zutfen 1762-63, Middelharnis 1764-70, and den Hoorn on the island of Texel from 1770 until his death in 1810 (*Inv. Arch. Amst.* II, Nos. 1971-75, 2112-15, 2117, 2417; *DB* 1873, 145; 1881, 49). Cornelis Gerbens van Grouw, apparently another brother, served as preacher at Berlikum in 1783-90 and at Pieterzijl 1790 - *ca.* 1812.

Joannes Gerbens van Grouw was a (untrained) preacher of Berlikum 1754-60, Dokkum 1760-71, and De Rijp 1771-79. He died in 1779 of an epidemic raging in this town (*DB* 1917, 22, 61).

Romke Gerbens (another brother?), who later assumed the family name of Zuiderbaan, served in 1785-93 as a (untrained) minister in his home church (Groote Huys) at Grouw. He was active in the political movement of the Patriots and came in conflict with the district government and fled to Emden. Here, though he was already at an advanced age, he attended the Latin school, then studied at the Amsterdam Mennonite Seminary, and served the congregation of (unknown) 1797-1802 and of Blokzijl from 1802 until his death in 1803. Other ministers of this family were Kornelis Gerbens van Grouw, about whom nothing further is known, and Gerben Kornelisz van Grouw (died after 1815), preacher at Berlikum 1783-? and Pieterzijl 1790- *ca.* 1812.   vdZ.

F. H. Pasma, *De Doopsgezinden te Grouw* (Grouw, 1930) 16 ff.; several issues of *Naamlijst*.

Gerber (Gärber, Garber, Garver), a Mennonite family originating near Langnau, canton of Bern, Switzerland. The name denotes the occupation of tanner. There are two very old tanning establishments in Langnau today. The Langnau Gerber family is one of the most numerous in the canton of Bern today.

Members of the Gerber family who were Mennonites left the Emmental for the Jura as early as the middle of the 16th century. This family figured in all of the Swiss Mennonite migrations and especially the one directed to Wayne County, Ohio, 1817 ff. Some of the leading Mennonite farmers and preachers of the Jura bear the name today.

Wälti Gerber of Röthenbach was one of the earliest and most prominent Anabaptist ministers in the Emmental, taking part in the disputation at Bern in March 1538. He preached fearlessly, although forbidden to do so by the state, and baptized many. He was imprisoned at Burgdorf, escaped, but was captured and executed at Bern on July 30, 1566.

This name has been represented in the ministry in the Jura and Emmental from early times to the present. Michael Gerber, a deacon living in the Jura, emigrated to Wayne County, Ohio, in 1822 and became the ancestor of most of the Gerbers in that area. Christen Gerber from Giebel near Langnau, ordained to the ministry in 1821, became influenced by the preaching of Samuel Fröhlich and helped lead half of the Emmental congregation to form the first congregation of Neutäufer (see **Apostolic Christian Church**).

About 1735 three Mennonite Gerbers came to America from Switzerland, and settled in Lancaster Co., Pa., and in the Shenandoah Valley of Virginia, where the name was changed to Garber. In York Co., Pa., the Garber Church was erected in 1814. In Virginia many members of this family have united with the Church of the Brethren.

The name Gerber was common among the Amish of Alsace during the 18th and 19th centuries. Their descendants (some of whom use the form Garber) are to be found today in Ontario, Indiana, Ohio, Kansas, Illinois, and Missouri.

Today there are seven Mennonite ministers in Switzerland who bear the name Gerber. The present (1954) president of the Swiss Mennonite conference is Elder Samuel Gerber.

Seven brothers named Gerber who lived at Les Joux near Les Genevez in the Bernese Jura became outstanding farmers and leaders in their community from 1870 to 1930. Their story as well as picture was published in several Swiss agricultural periodicals at the beginning of the century.

D.L.G.

In July 1711, when a large number of Bernese Mennonites were expelled to the Netherlands, there were a number of Gerbers among them. Hans Gerber, a preacher of the Reist (see **Reist, Hans**) congregation in the Emmental, refused to go; he was arrested and sentenced to the galleys (*q.v.*). Peter Gerber of Langnau left the ship at Breisach, Germany, returned to Switzerland, was arrested there and chained; apparently he was also sent to the galleys. One of the Swiss Mennonites who came to the Netherlands was Claas (Nicolaas) Gerber, who served the "Nieuwe Zwitsers" (*q.v.*) as preacher in 1739-61.   vdZ.

E. P. Gerber, *Descendants of Deacon Michael Gerber, 1763-1938* (Kidron, Ohio, 1938); *Gem.-Kal.* 1924, 77; 1925, 87; D. L. Gratz, *Bernese Anabaptists* (Scottdale, 1953) *passim* (see index, 210); Daniel Kauffman, *Mennonite Cyclopedic Dictionary* (Scottdale, 1937) 119-20, 125-26; *Inv. Arch. Amst.* I, Nos. 1317, 1322, 1334, 1352-54, 1358 f.; J. Huizinga, *Stamboek van Samuel Peter (Meihuizen) en Barbara Fry* (Groningen, 1890), see Index, 124. *ML* II, 74 f.

Gerber, Johann, known as Stockhannes (1838-July 8, 1918), living "im Stock" near Langnau, Switzerland, of a well-to-do farmer family. Shortly after 1870 Gerber, who until then was a "worldly man," was converted. In August 1875 he was ordained as preacher of the large but decadent congregation of the Emmental, and was soon after appointed elder. Through his piety, his love for the church, and his activity he greatly built up the congregation. Two meetinghouses, at Kehr in 1888 and in Bowil-Bomatt in 1899, were built during his eldership. Johann Gerber, though a man of little education, was a great blessing to the Mennonite church. The *Martyrs'*

Mirror and the faithful loyalty of the martyrs were always a powerful inspiration for him.   vDZ.

S. Geiser, *Die Taufgesinnten-Gemeinden* (Karlsruhe, n.d.-1932) 478; Delbert L. Gratz, *Bernese Anabaptists* (Scottdale, 1953) 118.

Gerber, Samuel, a son of Jacob and Catherine (Ropp) Gerber, was born near Carlock, McLean Co., Ill., Sept. 8, 1863. As a boy he moved with his mother to the vicinity of Tremont, Tazewell Co., Ill. He was married to Magdalena Sears of Tiskilwa, Ill., Dec. 30, 1886. Two sons and three daughters were born to them. He was a member of the Pleasant Grove Amish Mennonite congregation, near Tremont, was ordained to the ministry there on May 2, 1897, and ordained bishop May 21, 1911. He was also bishop of the Hopedale (Ill.) congregation 1921-25, and a number of other congregations in the Western A.M. Conference. He served as secretary or assistant secretary of the Western A.M. Conference 1902-05 and 1908, assistant moderator 1911, 1912, and 1920, moderator 1913-19. He was on the merger committee which effected the dissolution of Western A.M. Conference and the reorganization of Mennonite district conferences west of Indiana 1920-21, moderator of the merged Illinois Mennonite Conference 1925, secretary of the Mennonite General Conference 1907, and member of the first Illinois District Mission Board. He was also active in evangelistic work. He was a farmer throughout his life near Groveland, Tazewell Co., Ill. He died Oct. 28, 1929, and was buried in Pleasant Grove Mennonite Cemetery near Tremont.   N.P.S.

Harry S. Weber, *Centennial History of the Mennonites of Illinois, 1829-1929* (Goshen, 1931) 607.

Gerber, Wälti, of Röthenbach, a Swiss Anabaptist martyr, a respected and outstanding Swiss Brethren preacher in the Emmental, attended a disputation in Bern in 1538, presumably the great disputation of March, records of which are in the state archives. These records name "Welltti Gerwer" in a list of Swiss and Bavarian Anabaptists. He escaped from prison with the aid of an Anabaptist locksmith of Burgdorf. He remained true to his faith and preached and baptized. He stressed the teaching that the Christian cannot be a ruler. The Bernese government was not able to apprehend him until they offered a reward of 100 guilders for his capture; he was executed July 30, 1566.

In the first edition of the *Martyrs' Mirror* (1660), van Braght does not name Wälti Gerber, although he must have known of his death from a letter written by the elders of Alsace, listing 42 martyrs in the canton of Bern. He omitted the names of the Bernese martyrs of 1566 intentionally, for he feared "it might cause them (the brethren in Bern) greater persecution, from which they are not yet entirely free." But he is listed in the German edition of Ephrata (*q.v.*) in 1748.   A.-T.

A. Fluri, *Täuferhinrichtungen in Bern im 16. Jahrhundert* (*Berner Heim* 1896, 301); *Chronik* of Haller and Müslin (Zofingen) 111; Müller, *Berner Täufer*, 75; Th. de Quervain, *Kirchliche und Soziale Zustände in Bern* . . . (Bern, 1906) 150, 156; "Acta des gesprächs zwüsschen predikanten unnd Touffbruderenn . . ." in Bern archives; *ML* II, 75.

Gerbert, Camill (1860-1918), studied at the universities of Strasbourg, Zürich, and Tübingen; in 1886 he was made pastor in Saarebourg (Lorraine) and in 1898 accepted a call to Biebrich a. Rh. At the outbreak of World War I he went to Belgium as a chaplain. In January 1918, at the request of his congregation, he returned to Biebrich, where he died May 27, 1918. He is the author of the meritorious work, *Geschichte der Strassburger Sektenbewegung zur Zeit der Reformation 1525-1534* (Strasbourg, 1889). It is based on thorough research in the sources and is a valuable study of Anabaptism in Strasbourg, though it is now superseded, especially by Hulshof's (*q.v.*) work. The author's viewpoint is that of the Protestant Church, but he treats the Anabaptists with a refreshing objectivity, even though he does not do justice to some individual leaders like Hans Denk. The book marks great progress from the research done by T. Wilhelm Röhrich; therein lies its lasting significance.   NEFF.

A. Hulshof, *Geschiedenis van de Doopsgezinden te Straatsburg van 1525 tot 1557* (Amsterdam, 1905); T. W. Röhrich, "Zur Gesch. der Strassburger Wiedertäufer in den Jahren 1527 bis 1543," in *Ztscht f. d. Hist. Theol.*, 1860; *ML* II, 75.

Gerbéviller, a town eight miles south of Lunéville, France, where a Mennonite congregation was formed in 1908. It was, however, short-lived. Until 1914 the elders Pierre Sommer and Joseph Schmouker served it. After the outbreak of World War I religious services were omitted, for the region lay in the battle area. The town was completely destroyed, and most of the Mennonites moved away. (*ML* II, 75.)   HEGE.

Gerbrand (Gerbrandt), a Mennonite family name occurring first in 1711 in Danzig, 1727 in the Danzig area, especially at Einlage and Walldorf. Before World War II there were only nine Mennonites with this name, who lived in the region of Elbing and Thiensdorf-Rosenbart. Jakob Gerbrandt of the Ufa (*q.v.*) settlement in Russia was appointed as traveling elder about 1910, and served widely scattered settlements in Siberia with baptismal services, ordinations, and communion. John Gerbrandt (*q.v.*) was an elder of the Drake Mennonite Church, and his son Jakob Gerbrandt is secretary of the Canadian Mennonite Board of Colonization.   H.P.

G. E. Reimer, *Die Familiennamen der westpreussischen Mennoniten* (Weierhof, 1940).

Gerbrandt, Jakob, from Grossweide, Molotschna, Russia, attended Bethel College, North Newton, Kan., 1897-1902, and returned to Russia where he became an itinerant minister of the *Allgemeine Bundeskonferenz* (General Conference) for the Mennonite settlements in the province of Ufa and in Siberia. He was an elder at Barnaul, Siberia. Nothing is known of his later life and work. (Friesen, *Brüderschaft*, 716, 718; *Unser Blatt* I, 45.)   C.K.

Gerbrandt, John (1854-1938), a Mennonite (GCM) elder and leader, the son of Johann and Katharina Gerbrandt, was born Dec. 23, 1854, in Schwiniar, near Gombin, Poland, his ancestors having come from Marienwerder, West Prussia. He was baptized and received into membership of the Wymysle Mennonite Church in Poland by Elder Gerhard Bartel. In the spring of 1875 he immigrated to the United States with his parents and two sisters, settling in Marion Co., Kan., a mile north of the present town of Hillsboro. On Dec. 26, 1880, he married Helena Klassen of the Gnadenberg Mennonite Church east of Newton. To this union seven children were born.

He was an active member of the Johannesthal Mennonite Church north of Hillsboro (GCM). In 1887 he was called to the ministry and on Dec. 22, 1890, he was ordained elder of his church. He also took an active part in organizing the Friedensthal Mennonite Church north of Durham, Kan.

In 1904 he joined a land inspection delegation to Saskatchewan, where free homesteads of 160 acres were being offered by the Canadian government. He selected homesteads not only for himself and his two sons, but also for a number of relatives and church members in what is now the Drake, Sask., district. He emigrated to Saskatchewan with his family in 1905 and was followed by a number of families from Kansas and Oklahoma. On Feb. 12, 1906, he organized the North Star Mennonite Church at Drake with 20 charter members, and became its first elder. These charter members came from the Johannesthal, Bruderthal (Kan.), and Alva, Okla., churches. By 1931, after 25 years, the membership had risen to 277.

Gerbrandt took a keen interest in the educational and conference activities of the General Conference churches in Western Canada. He was chairman of the Canadian Conference for four years and its vice-chairman for seven years. In addition he was an active member of its committee on home missions for many years. He died at Drake on Aug. 16, 1938.   J.G.

Gerdes, Daniel, b. April 19, 1698, at Bremen, Germany, d. Feb. 11, 1765, at Groningen in the Netherlands, served from 1736 until his death as professor of theology at the University of Groningen and editor of a number of theological writings. For Mennonite history he is of interest because of his disputes with Joannes Stinstra (*q.v.*), the Mennonite minister of Harlingen, who had in 1740 published a *Deductie* in behalf of the freedom of Mennonites to preach without being authorized by the government. Gerdes in his *Elenchus veritatum* (Groningen, 1740) stated that freedom of conscience should be granted but not freedom of preaching, since teaching of false dogma means licentiousness. In his *Twee Godgeleerde Verhandelingen* (Groningen, 1741) Gerdes deals with Socinianism (*q.v.*) and states that Socinians cannot be considered Christians. In his *De Vrijheid des Geloofs* (Groningen, n.d.-1741), he directly attacks Stinstra, accusing him of anti-Christian teachings. Especially in the last-named book Gerdes proves himself an intolerant and implacable Calvinist.   vnZ.

Biogr. Wb. III, 216-22; Chr. Sepp, *Joh. Stinstra en zijn tijd* (Amsterdam, 1865-66) I and II, *passim.*

Gerdt (Gerhard, Gerryt) **Eilkeman** (Eikelman) of Coevorden, Dutch Province of Drente: see **Peter van Norg.**

Gerig, an Alsatian Mennonite family of the Mulhouse, France, area, several members of which emigrated to the United States about the middle of the 19th century, locating in Ohio, Indiana, and Iowa. Two sons of Jacob Gerig (d. 1850 in Mulhouse), Sebastian (*q.v.*) and Benjamin, leaving Alsace in 1856 and 1860 respectively to escape military service, became bishops in the Mennonite Church (MC) in the United States, the former at Wayland, Iowa, 1879-1930, the latter at Smithville, Ohio, 1896-1913. Sebastian's grandson Vernon Gerig has been bishop at Wayland since 1953, and Benjamin's son Jacob S. Gerig has been bishop at Smithville since 1913. D. S. Gerig (d. 1955), a brother of Jacob, was a long-time professor and registrar (also briefly acting dean) at Goshen College. A nephew of Sebastian, C. R. Gerig, was bishop (MC) at Albany, Ore., 1907-42. Another branch of the family was prominent in the Salem Evangelical Mennonite Church at Gridley, Ill. Of this line was Elder Joseph K. Gerig (*q.v.*, d. 1944), prominent leader in the Evangelical Mennonite Conference, Emerald Gerig at Woodburn, Ind., and Gaylord Gerig at Pioneer, Ohio. C. L. Gearig was long a minister in the Church of God in Christ Mennonite congregation at Wauseon, Ohio. Whether the name Gering, found among the Volhynian Swiss Mennonite congregations of the G.C.M. Church at Moundridge, Kan., Freeman, S.D., and elsewhere, was originally the same as Gerig is not certain, but probable.   H.S.B.

Gerig, Joseph K. (1868-1944), elder in the Evangelical (Defenseless) Mennonite Church, was born on Oct. 28, 1868, at Grabill, Ind., the fourth of ten children of Joseph and Katie Nofziger Gerig. He was married to Leah B. Gerig on Dec. 5, 1889; one daughter was born to them. He began his ministry in 1898 as assistant pastor of the Defenseless Mennonite congregation of Woodburn, Ind. In 1908 he took charge of the Salem Gospel Mission in Chicago, serving actively and effectively for 21 years. He was ordained as elder on Oct. 2, 1917. He was also appointed church evangelist for 18 months and superintendent for the Indiana, Ohio, and Michigan district. For one and one half years he was pastor of the congregation in Pioneer, Ohio. His outstanding spiritual ministry ended in his death on April 7, 1944. He was buried at Woodburn. (*Zion's Tidings* XXIV, No. 11, May 15, 1944.)   Ch.L.R.

Gerig, Sebastian (1839-1924), bishop of the Sugar Creek Mennonite Church (MC), Wayland, Iowa, from 1879 to 1924, was born in Pfastatt, Alsace, the son of Jakob and Elisabeth (Zimmermann) Gerig. He united with the Amish Mennonite Church in France at the age of 17, and in 1856 emigrated to America to escape compulsory military service. After spending a few weeks in Ontario he traveled to Iowa, living in Davis and Lee counties for six years and in Ohio approximately two years. After his marriage to Magdalena, youngest daughter of Bishop Joseph Goldsmith (*q.v.*), he established his home in Henry Co., Iowa, where he lived the rest of his life. To this union were born twelve children, all of whom became members of his church. Three of his grandsons are in the ministry of the Mennonite Church (MC): Vernon Gerig, Wayland, Iowa; Willard Leichty, Wayland, Iowa; and Maynard Wyse, Archbold, Ohio.

Gerig was ordained to the ministry in the Sugar Creek Amish Mennonite Church in 1869 and ten years later to the office of bishop. In 1916 he ordained his successor Simon Gingerich. Gerig was a leader in the Western District Amish Mennonite Conference, serving either as moderator or assistant moderator in 1897, 1900, 1904, 1905, 1906, 1908, and 1909. A man of sound judgment and keen insight, he led his congregation through the changes brought about by the introduction of Sunday schools, young people's meetings, evangelistic services, and the English language. (*Gospel Herald,* April 17, 1924, 63.)   O.G.W.

German Teachers' Association: see **Mennonite Teachers' Association.**

German Teachers' Institute (Kansas) was organized through the efforts of H. A. Goerz, Peter Balzer, H. D. Penner, and others. The first Institute met Aug. 6, 1894, at Hillsboro for two weeks. After the first session of the Institute the Mennonite Teachers' Association (*q.v.*) became the sponsor. Its officers were also the officers of the Institute. A curriculum (*Lehrplan*) for the Institute was produced and revised a number of times. The attendance at the Institute ranged from 25 to 57 during the years 1894-1905. Sessions took place at Hillsboro, Bethel College, Newton, and Buhler. Mennonite congregations contributed toward the financing of the Institute. Later teachers lectured without compensation.

The purpose of the Institute was to foster and promote the German schools and to raise the educational and spiritual level of the Mennonite constituency by reassuring the teacher in what he already possessed, by making him conscious of his need for further study, and by training him in the art of teaching. It also aimed to achieve uniformity in methods of teaching and to make the teacher aware of the fact that teaching is a profession. The Institute usually was held in August. A three-year curriculum was covered during the session including Bible, psychology, grammar, principles of education, history of education, methods, etc. Demonstration lessons were presented on various levels in Bible and church history for observation and criticism.

In 1908 the two-week term was reduced to one week. Sunday-school teachers and other Christian workers were also invited to attend. Later the term was reduced to three days. During World War I the Institute was discontinued. German and Bible were now taught in summer Bible schools where mostly voluntary workers with little preparation were employed. Gradually the change from German to English was completed. The German Teachers' Institute fulfilled well a difficult task during the days of pioneer education and the transition period.
                                                        C.K.

H. P. Peters, *History and Development of Education Among the Mennonites of Kansas* (Hillsboro, 1925) 85 ff.; *Lehrplan für das Deutsche Lehrer-Institut.*

German-English Academy, former name of Rosthern Junior College (*q.v.*) of Rosthern, Sask.

Germantown (Pa.) Mennonite Church (MC), the first Mennonite congregation in America, observed its first baptism and communion service in 1708, but congregational life began at least as early as 1690. In that year a visiting Reformed minister from Holland, Rudolphus Varick, found the Mennonites there worshiping every Sunday, with "Menist" Dirck Keyser of Amsterdam reading a sermon from a book by Jobst Harmensen. For a time the Mennonite settlers here, who first came in 1683, had worshiped with the German Quakers, who in the early years constituted the majority of the settlement. In 1690 (or 1698; the manuscripts differ), Willem Rittenhouse (d. 1708) was chosen as first preacher and Jan Neuss as deacon. In 1702 a second election was held, when Jacob Gottschalk and Hans Neuss were chosen preachers. In early 1708 the newly arrived (1707) Palatine Mennonite families united with the Dutch-speaking church, as a result of which three deacons (Isaac van Sintern, Heinrich Cassel, and Conrad Jansen) and two preachers (Harmen Karsdorp and Martin Kolb) were chosen from the newer immigrants. About the same time, when the membership was 34 (in 1712 it was 99), eleven new members were baptized by Jacob Gottschalk, who thus began serving as the first Mennonite bishop in America. Gottschalk's brief sketch of the early history of the congregation to 1712 (preserved in Michael Ziegler's historical letter of 1773 to Holland; see Wenger, 395) is the only extant source for the early years. In 1708 also the first log meetinghouse was built on land donated by Arnold van Vossen in 1703. In 1770 this building was replaced by a stone building, which is the oldest Mennonite meetinghouse in America still in use. At that time the membership was 25, but in 1789 it had grown again to 46. By 1798 the monthly services were being conducted by visiting ministers from the Franconia district churches. By 1839 the congregation was "facing dissolution," but it survived and in 1863 was reorganized as a member of the Eastern District Conference (GCM). (See **Germantown** Mennonite Church, GCM.) In the early 19th century apparently the relations to the Franconia Conference (MC) had become so tenuous that the congregation was in effect an independent congregation.

The first Mennonite conference session in America was held at Germantown in 1725. At this session the Dordrecht Confession of 1632 (18 articles) was adopted as the official confession of the American Mennonites, and was printed two years later (1727) in English to communicate to the English-speaking populace the Mennonite articles of faith.
                                                        H.S.B.

H. S. Bender, "The Founding of the Mennonite Church in America at Germantown 1683-1708," *MQR* VII (1933) 227-50; *idem*, "Was William Rittenhouse the First Mennonite Bishop in America?" *MQR* VII (1933) 42-47; J. C. Wenger, *History of the Mennonites of the Franconia Conference* (Telford, 1937), with chapter I (Part II, Congregational Histories) "Germantown," 87-95.

Germantown Mennonite Church (GCM). During the early 1800's the old Germantown congregation gradually declined. In the division of 1847 in the Franconia Conference the remaining handful of members sided with the new Eastern Conference led by John H. Oberholtzer and Abraham Hunsicker. In 1851, when the Hunsicker group broke with the new conference, the congregation stayed with Hunsicker. During the next years the preachers were Abraham Hunsicker, Henry Hunsicker, F. R. S. Hunsicker, and Israel Beidler. In 1863 the congregation was formally reorganized with 13 members. Finally in 1876, after the death of Beidler, the congregation returned to the Eastern District Conference and has continued weekly worship throughout the years since then. Ministers since 1876 were John A. Haldeman, N. B. Grubb, W. MacArthur, H. Frederick, A. Funk, S. M. Grubb, S. Musselman, F. Gabel, J. Bayley, A. S. Shelly, H. Landes, W. Wolfe, and R. Brewer.

The 1770 meetinghouse, the oldest Mennonite meetinghouse in America, is located with its ancient burial ground along historic Germantown Avenue at Herman Street (6100) in Germantown, now incorporated in North Philadelphia. In 1916 an addition was built to the meetinghouse. Though the membership today is only 37 there has been a renewal of interest and life in the congregation. The interior of the meetinghouse was largely restored to its colonial simplicity in 1952. To preserve and promote it as a Mennonite "shrine" the incorporate ownership of the meetinghouse and grounds has recently been transferred into the hands of a joint board composed of representatives of the congregation, the Eastern District Conference, and the General Conference Mennonite Church.

J.H.F.

N. B. Grubb, *The Mennonite Church of Germantown* (Philadelphia, 1906); D. K. Cassel, *History of the Mennonites* (Philadelphia, 1888).

Germantown (Pa.) **Mennonite Settlement,** the first permanent Mennonite settlement in America, was established Oct. 24, 1683, six miles north of the then one-year-old town of Philadelphia. The first Mennonite group settlement in America, however, was that established by Plockhoy (*q.v.*) in 1663 with Dutch settlers at Horekill (*q.v.*) on the Delaware some 70 miles south of Germantown, which was destroyed by English raiders a year later. Earlier even than this, scattered individual Dutch Mennonite immigrants or traders were found at New Amsterdam and Gravesend (Long Island), but they did not form a congregation and left no trace.

Germantown (also called Germanopolis) was founded personally by the Pietist scholar Francis D. Pastorius (*q.v.*) who, as agent for the pietistic Frankfurt (Land) Company, purchased 15,000 acres from William Penn's agents at London in May 1683 and proceeded to Pennsylvania in June to locate the land. He had previously (March 1683) spent a week at Kriegsheim (Kriesheim) in the Palatinate visiting the Quakers there, certainly in regard to their interest in settling in Pennsylvania (they came to Germantown in 1685). In March 1682 three Crefeld Mennonites, led by Jacob Telner who had visited New York and Pennsylvania at least once in 1678-81, had purchased 5,000 acres each to aid their needy coreligionists at Crefeld to find new homes. Ultimately none of the Frankfurt Company ever came to Pennsylvania except Pastorius, and no settlers were secured through their agency. But on July 24, 1683, 13 Crefeld German (Dutch-speaking) families including 33 persons sailed from Gravesend (London) on the "Concord," arriving at Philadelphia on Oct. 6, 1683. They were largely poor people, weavers, who had scarcely enough money to reach the new world. On Oct. 24 the townsite of Germantown was laid out along a single village street, lots being drawn to decide the allocation of the several plots of land to the individual families.

Two smaller Mennonite groups joined the Germantown settlement from other localities: (1) from Hamburg-Altona, Germany, eight Dutch-speaking families came in 1700—two Karsdorp families, two van Sinteren, and one each of Roosen, Berends, Klassen, and van Vossen; (2) from the Palatinate (Kriegsheim-Mannheim, Germany), five German-speaking families, in 1707—Kolb, about this time or earlier, Kassel, Bowman, and Graf, and a Clemens in 1709. Of these 13 families Roosen and Berends soon returned to Germany. Apparently the descendants of the Hamburg families did not remain permanently in the Mennonite fold, but the Palatine families, apparently all farmers, remained and all became prominent in the life of the Franconia district settlement and elsewhere. Thus a total of roughly 40 Mennonite families settled in Germantown in the first 25 years 1683-1708. In the latter year the Mennonite congregation here, when it built its first meetinghouse and held its first communion service, had 45 baptized members, of whom 11 were added by baptism just before the communion. By April 6, 1712, the total number was 99, including the Skippack settlement some 12 miles farther north in the open country. Who the additional 54 members received in 1708-12 were is not known, except that some new settlers came from the Palatinate, most of whom, being farmers, went directly to Skippack. The Mennonite immigration from Crefeld-Lower Rhine had ceased by 1708 or earlier. It is possible that the two Connerts families, listed in one source as Germantown Mennonite members in 1708, were related to Thones Kunders, one of the 13 Crefeld families. Gorgas, another Mennonite family from Germany, was in Germantown in 1709.

Until William I. Hull proved that most of the original (1683) families were an interrelated group of Quakers, it had been assumed that the group was Mennonite. But since only one family (Jan Lensen) of the original 13 remained Mennonite, while the other 12 appear in the Quaker meeting records, and since most of them had signed a Quaker marriage certificate at Crefeld in 1681, it is safe to assume that this first group of Germantown settlers was essentially a Quaker movement. There was a Quaker congregation in Crefeld 1667-86, all former Mennonites. A total of 15 Quaker families came from Crefeld to Germantown, all by 1686. Later two of the first 12 Quaker families, Abraham and Hermann op den Graeff, reverted to the Mennonites.

A total of 16 Mennonite families ultimately came from Crefeld to Germantown as follows: 1683—Lensen, 1684—van Bebber, 1685—Telner (returned soon to Crefeld), Umstat (Umstead), and Jansen, 1687—van Bebber and Streypers, 1688—Sellen, 1690—Neuss (Nice), 1693—Kuster (Custer), 1702—Hosters, 1703—Neuss (Nice), (?)—Tyson. Two additional families came from the Lower Rhine, 1691—Kasselberg, 1702—Godschalk from Goch. Five additional families probably came from the same general region although their exact residence is unknown, 1685—Papen, 1698—Engel, before 1702—Krey, before 1707—Jansen. Of this total of 23 Crefeld-Lower Rhine families, few have had permanent representatives in later American Mennonitism (Updegrave, Umstead, Johnson, Nice, Tyson, Godshalk, Engel, Sellen). Three other Dutch Mennonite families, directly from Amsterdam, William Rittenhouse and Dirk Keyser and his son Peter, arrived in 1688. Peter Keyser joined Alexander Mack's Dunkards in 1719. Rittenhouse was the first Mennonite preacher (1690 or 1698) at Germantown.

It has often been asserted that the first Mennonites came to Germantown because of a direct personal invitation from William Penn, but this is incorrect. Penn never visited Crefeld, and there is no record of his ever visiting any Mennonites in Germany. He may have met some Mennonites when he visited the Quakers in Kriegsheim on Aug. 23 and 26, 1677, three years before he applied for the grant of Pennsylvania, but the tension between the Quakers and Mennonites there at that time renders this dubious. There is no trace of any correspondence between Penn and any Mennonites who lived in Germany or who came to America. In the pamphlets published by Penn and his agents on behalf of the colonization of Pennsylvania, not the slightest reference is ever made to Mennonites. Penn's alleged invitation to Mennonites in Germany to come to Pennsylvania, personally or by publication, is purely legendary. The Mennonites (and Quakers) who came from the Lower Rhine area came to Germantown to escape oppressive persecution. Those who came from the Palatinate and Switzerland to Germantown from 1707 on also came to find greater religious freedom and to take advantage of the economic opportunities which the rich colony afforded. Many others besides Mennonites and Quakers of course came to Germantown in 1683-1709. Hull lists a total of 397 immigrant persons (excluding children) with provenance as follows: Holland—63, Crefeld and Kaldekerk—96, Kriegsheim and neighborhood—41, other Germany—49, uncertain Holland or Germany—120, other European countries—11, Great Britain—17. It is clear that the Mennonites were not more than 15 per cent of the Germantown population in 1708, the Quakers possibly a somewhat larger proportion. Germantown was a German settlement, but it was not essentially a Mennonite settlement; nor was it primarily a Crefeld settlement.

The Mennonite settlement in Germantown never prospered greatly, apparently never exceeding 100 baptized members in size. It was too much under the influence of the stronger Quakers and other environment and was not able to retain its own natural increase. Besides, the main stream of Mennonite immigrants from Germany and Switzerland, being farmers, passed it by for settlement on the land. Apart from the conference held in the Mennonite meetinghouse here in 1725, the first Mennonite conference in America, which adopted the Dordrecht Confession of Faith, nothing of significance happened in Germantown, and the settlement did not exercise any particular leadership among the Mennonites in the following years. The up-country Franconia settlement and the inland Lancaster settlement, both rural and German, became the significant Mennonite centers in America. Dutch language Germantown Mennonitism was only a small pocket, with the honor of having been the first settlement, with the first meetinghouse, first preacher and bishop, and first organized congregation. The tradition of connection with the Dutch Mennonites of the Lower Rhine and Holland was kept alive for several generations, and did serve the Franconia Mennonites in a minor way by giving them the Dordrecht Confession and the *Martyrs' Mirror*. For the history of the Germantown Mennonite congregation see the preceding two articles.   H.S.B.

W. I. Hull, *William Penn and the Dutch Quaker Migration to Pennsylvania* (Swarthmore College, 1935); C. Henry Smith, *The Mennonite Immigration to Pennsylvania* (Norristown, 1929); idem, *The Mennonites of America* (Goshen, 1909); idem, *The Story of the Mennonites* (Berne, 1945); S. W. Pennypacker, *The Settlement of Germantown* (Philadelphia, 1899); idem, *Hendrik Pannebecker* (Philadelphia, 1894); Wilhelm Hubben, *Die Quäker in der deutschen Vergangenheit* (Leipzig, 1929); C. F. Jenkins, *The Guidebook to Historic Germantown* (Germantown, 1904); J. L. Rosenberger, *The Pennsylvania Germans* (Chicago, 1923); Fr. Nieper, *Die ersten deutschen Auswanderer von Krefeld nach Pennsylvanien* (Neukirchen, 1940); K. Rembert, "Zur Geschichte der Auswanderung Krefelder Mennoniten nach Nord-Amerika," in *Beiträge zur Geschichte rheinischer Mennoniten*, No. 2 of the *Schriftenreihe des Menn. Geschichtsvereins* (Weierhof, 1939); H. S. Bender, "The Founding of the Mennonite Church in Germantown," *MQR* VII (1933) 227-50; Ernst Correll, article "Germantown," *ML* II, 76-81, with older literature cited.

Germany. *Introduction.* Modern Germany, established as a nation in 1871 by the Treaty of Versailles following the Franco-Prussian War of 1870, suffered considerable territorial loss in the East as a result of defeats in World Wars I (area 180,999 sq. mi. in 1919) and II (136,462 sq. mi. in 1946) and now has no territory east of the Oder-Neisse River line. All the German population, with small exceptions, living east of that line was evacuated or expelled westward and has now been added to the population of the truncated Republic of Germany, with a (1946) population of 65,151,019 excluding the Saar. All the Mennonites who had lived in Danzig and East and West Prussia, as well as those in the three congregations in Poland (*q.v.*), were transported westward in this action, some of them later emigrating to Canada and Uruguay. In 1956 the country was still

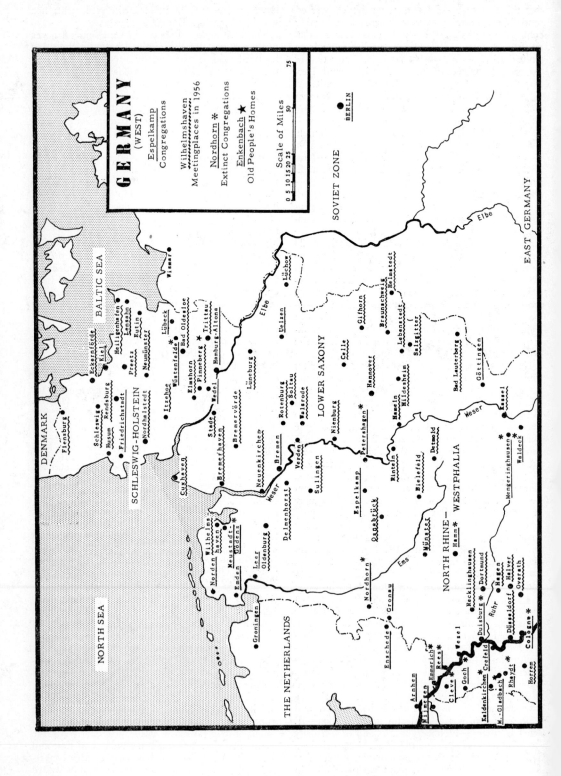

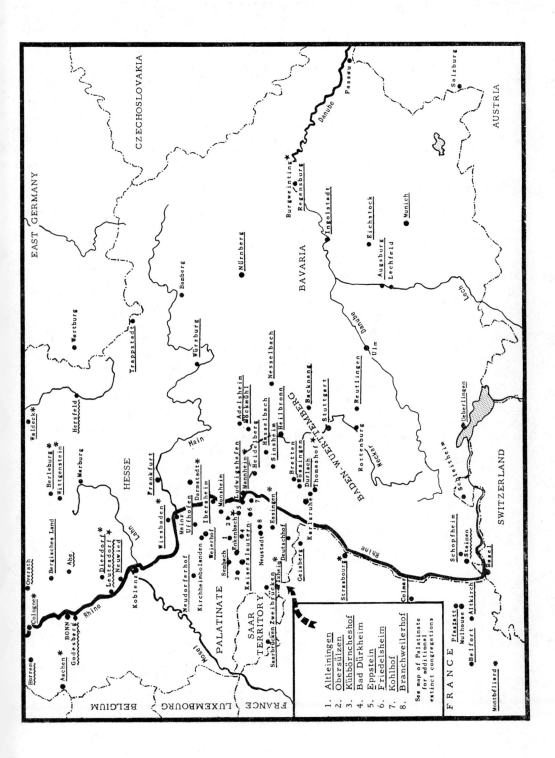

divided into East Germany (Russian Zone) with a population of some 18,000,000, in which there were possibly a maximum of 800 Mennonites (souls) of former West Prussian residence, but no organized congregations or ordained ministers, and West Germany with about 47,000,000 and some 15,000 Mennonites (souls). The total number of baptized Mennonites in 1955 in Germany is about 11,500 in 60 congregations. Of these, 18 congregations with some 7,200 baptized members (total 8,700 souls) are in North Germany (above Frankfurt), 36 congregations are in South Germany with about 4,500 baptized members (5,400 souls), of which 18 are in the Palatinate and Hesse with 2,400 members, 9 are in Baden, 6 are in Württemberg, 8 are in Bavaria, and one in Frankfurt, these last 24 congregations having a total of 2,100 members. Of the congregations in North Germany 9 are refugee congregations of former Danzig-West Prussian origin established since 1945. Many such refugees have also become members of the old established congregations in both North and South Germany.

The German Mennonite congregations are all (except Frankfurt) members of one of two conferences: (1) Vereinigung der Deutschen Mennonitengemeinden (q.v.), mostly North Germany with the Palatinate and Hesse, and (2) the Verband Badisch-Württembergisch - Bayrischer Mennonitengemeinden (q.v.), almost all of whose congregations are in the three last indicated territories. In addition, the Süddeutsche Konferenz (q.v.) includes practically all the congregations in the Palatinate and Hesse and in the Verband, although this conference is not quite the same in character as the other two. Most of the congregations of the Palatinate and Hesse are members also of a local conference called the Pfälzisch-Hessische Konferenz. The refugee congregations of the former Danzig-West Prussia area are represented in a ministerial committee called "Aeltestenausschuss der Konferenz der west- und ostpreussischen Mennonitengemeinden." A committee for co-operation in North Germany (Gemeinden-Ausschuss in Norddeutschland) has been formed to help the 9 old North German congregations and the 9 new North German refugee congregations to work together. A "Mennonitischer Zentral-Ausschuss" serves as liaison between the German conferences and the MCC of North America, which has conducted relief work in Germany since 1946 and now has permanent German and European headquarters in Frankfurt (Eysseneckstrasse 54). Four other organizations have been formed which represent or serve all Mennonites in Germany regardless of conference affiliation: (1) Mennonitischer Geschichtsverein, (2) Mennonitisches Altersheim, (3) Mennonitische Siedlungshilfe, (4) Deutsches Mennonitisches Missionskommittee.

The only current German Mennonite church paper is the Gemeindeblatt der Mennoniten, published since 1870 by the Verband. Der Mennonit (founded in 1948), though printed (at Karlsruhe) and edited in Germany, is published as an international European Mennonite journal by the MCC. Full information about the German Mennonite congregations, organizations, and institutions is found in the yearbook, Mennonitischer Gemeinde-Kalender, pub-

lished since 1892 by the South German Conference. The Mennonitische Geschichtsblätter, founded in 1936, is the organ of the Mennonite Historical Society (Mennonitischer Geschichtsverein).

German Mennonite institutions include four old people's homes in Germany—Leutesdorf (q.v.), Enkenbach (q.v.), Pinneberg (q.v.), and Burgweinting (q.v.); two relief agencies, Mennonitisches Hilfswerk "Christenpflicht" (q.v.) founded in 1924, and Hilfswerk der Vereinigung der Deutschen Mennonitengemeinden (q.v.) founded in 1947. There is also a Genossenschaftliches Flüchtlingswerk (q.v.) to aid in resettlement of refugees in Germany. Only the Verband has a deaconess (q.v.) work. The Mennonite board of directors of the former Weierhof school (Verein für die Anstalt am Donnersberg) operates a student house (Schülerheim) connected with the public high school (Gymnasium) at Kirchheimbolanden near Weierhof. The Verband has a significant institution in the Bibelheim Thomashof (q.v.), founded in 1920, a spiritual retreat center.

ANABAPTISM IN GERMANY, 1525-1650

At the time of the rise of Anabaptism (1525-35) what is now called Germany was a collection of 256 autonomous political units within a loosely organized Empire, called the Holy Roman Empire. Although Switzerland, the Netherlands, and North Italy were technically within the empire, they were actually independent, and the Hapsburg dominions, including Bohemia, Moravia, Silesia, and Lusatia, were outside the orbit of Germany proper. The account of the Anabaptist movement in this article will therefore exclude all these territories. The area "Germany" in the 16th century as it is used here had therefore much the same boundaries as modern Germany 1871-1914, although, not having a unified government, it was broken up into many separate governments with varying religious policies.

The soil in Germany had gradually become rather well prepared for a new religious movement. Already in the late Middle Ages sectarian tendencies had entered Germany (Waldenses, q.v., 1211-1480; Brethren of the Common Life since 1401; etc.). Erasmus and Luther, each in his way, were outstanding advocates of church reform. In the early twenties of the 16th century Carlstadt, Müntzer, and the Zwickau Prophets (Storch, etc.) each propagated a reform of his own, which were often wrongly called Anabaptist. Yet it was not the criticism of infant baptism which was decisive, but the introduction of adult baptism. So Anabaptism proper, arising out of Zwingli's reform, was part of the original Reformation movement.

A. South and Middle Germany. Anabaptism entered Germany first from the South (Switzerland), where it began in Zürich in January 1525. Wilhelm Reublin (q.v.), appearing in Waldshut from Zürich in April 1525, baptized Dr. Balthasar Hubmaier (q.v.), the pastor of the Lutheran Church there, and they together baptized most of the congregation, some 360 persons in all. In July Hubmaier published his Von dem Christlichen Tauff der Gläubigen. Other pamphlets by him followed. But in December of that year the Austrians conquered the city and forced Hubmaier to flee, practically ending the Anabaptist congregation. Hubmaier went to Augsburg (*q.v.*) next, where early in 1526 he established an Anabaptist congregation which became very large and influential, but he went on to Moravia, leaving Augsburg in the hands of Hans Denk (*q.v.*), whom he had baptized in May 1526.

Augsburg and Strasbourg (*q.v.*) now displaced Zürich and Switzerland as the centers of the growing Anabaptist movement, remaining so for some years. Michael Sattler (*q.v.*), a noble man of God, became the chief leader in this area of southwest Germany until his execution at Rottenburg in May 1527. He was no doubt the leader of the Schleitheim conference, the first Anabaptist conference, of February 1527, and the author of the notable confession which it produced, the *Brüderliche Vereinigung* (*q.v.*). Hans Denk, who moved about in the area Augsburg-Basel-Strasbourg-Worms, was the leader of a somewhat more mystical-spiritualist wing, but died at Basel in November 1527. He was related in spirit to men like Johannes Bünderlin (*q.v.*) of Linz, a more radical spiritualist and only for a short time an Anabaptist (1527-29), Entfelder (*q.v.*), likewise only briefly in the movement, and Jakob Kautz (*q.v.*) of Worms. The Sattler and Denk groups remained separate at Strasbourg, and probably constituted two distinct bodies. Denk preferred the "Inner Word" to the "Outer Word," and taught Christ as a teacher to follow and imitate rather than as a redeemer whose atonement saves men. Jakob Kautz's *Seven Theses* of June 7, 1527, at Worms also carry this position. Sattler was a full Biblicist and a thorough evangelical.

Meanwhile in 1526-27 Hans Hut (*q.v.*; d. December 1527 in prison in Augsburg where he had been arrested in September) had become a most effective evangelist for the Anabaptist cause, winning many converts in Swabia, Franconia, Bavaria, Salzburg, and Tirol. In Augsburg men of note became leaders of the Anabaptist congregation in 1527-30, like Sigmund Salminger (*q.v.*) and the patrician Hans Langenmantel (*q.v.*). A noted conference was held here Aug. 20, 1527, often called the "Martyrs' Synod" (*q.v.*) because so many of the missioners sent out from there lost their lives as martyrs within the following years.

Another early center of Anabaptism was found in Hesse, Thuringia, and Franconia, where Thomas Müntzer had had some influence in 1523-25. Melchior Rinck (*q.v.*) was the first Anabaptist leader here in 1528-31 (in prison 1531-51, where he died) near Hersfeld (*q.v.*) and Sorga, where there was a congregation. Moravian Anabaptist (Hutterite) influences were strong here for a time, numerous missioners coming here from the base in Moravia, including the noted Peter Riedemann (*q.v.*), who wrote his great *Rechenschaft* (*q.v.*), in prison near Marburg (Wolkersdorf) in 1540-41. Anabaptists were in considerable strength in Hesse (*q.v.*) as late as 1578, when Hans Kuchenbecker and his brethren drew up an elaborate confession of faith for the authorities (*MQR* XXIV, 24-34). Their criticism of the poor quality of life in the state church contributed greatly through Bucer to the introduction of the ceremony of confirmation, which passed from here into other Lutheran and Reformed state churches.

The next outstanding leader to arise was Pilgram Marpeck (*q.v.*) of Rattenberg on the Inn, converted an Anabaptist in 1528, living in Strasbourg 1528-32, then chiefly in Ulm and Augsburg until his death at the latter place in 1556. He was the most notable doctrinal writer of the South German Anabaptists (see his *Vermahnung* of 1542 and *Verantwortung* of 1544, both against Caspar Schwenckfeld, and his *Testamentserläuterung* of much the same time). He was the leader of a strong group, as the recent discovery of some 42 letters by him (found in a Bern library) attests.

As soon as the German authorities, both Catholic and Protestant, became aware of the rising Anabaptist movement, they used every means at their command to destroy it. The first Anabaptist mandates by the Hapsburg rulers appeared in 1527. The notorious edict of the Diet of Speyer, ordering the extermination of the Anabaptists throughout the Empire, was issued April 22, 1529. In explanation of the attitude of the authorities, the close connection between the territorial government and the local church, which was already true at that time, must not be overlooked. It might have been possible to reform the whole of any given territorial church, but only as a whole and only in so far as the authorities thought fit. Luther and Zwingli and their followers had to learn that, and only as far as they learned it did they succeed at least partly. Hubmaier and the Münster (*q.v.*) Anabaptists tried to go the same way, but they failed. And neither a congregation of saints nor the baptism of adults could win public opinion; nonconformity and nonresistance, the refusal of oaths, nonpayment of war taxes, and refusal of public offices, sometimes a leaning toward the revolutionary peasants, sometimes the hope that the coming of the Turks would announce the coming of Christ, made them suspect. And the magistrates felt responsible for the spiritual as well as for the physical welfare of their subjects. The Anabaptists' high morality, courage, and unflinching fidelity to their convictions impressed many again and again, but these were not sufficient to change the attitude of the others in general. So the advice of the Lutheran and Reformed theologians guided by their own creed, and the decisions of the lawyers guided by their tradition, resulted in a persecution with all the cruelty of medieval law and punishment (e.g., to counterfeit a coin was punished by burning at the stake). Hege (*ML* III, 6 and 7) for the first 20 years (1525-44) alone enumerates 110 mandates against the Anabaptists: 27 Swiss, 27 Austrian, 15 Bavarian and Swabian, 16 Franconian, Hessian, Saxon, and Thuringian, 6 Alsatian, 4 Palatine, after 1530 also 8 in the north, besides 7 of the Emperor and the Empire in general. But though the principle of persecution was more or less the same, everywhere the practice showed much variation. The number of mandates also illustrates the number of Anabaptists in the one and the other area. Apart from Reformed Switzerland, the keenest persecutors were the Catholic King

Ferdinand I of Austria and the Catholic dukes of Bavaria. Among the Protestant princes the electors of Saxony, supported by their theologians, did not shrink from capital punishment (first case 1530 at Reinhardsbrunn in Thuringia, *q.v.*), whereas the Landgrave of Hesse never had an Anabaptist executed and even in cases when Saxony was also concerned he prevailed upon the elector to be content with imprisonment for life (e.g., Fritz Erbe, *q.v.*, 1532-48 at the Wartburg near Eisenach and not far from Reinhardsbrunn). The Counts Palatine in 66 years (1544-1610) several times changed their creed (3 times Lutheran, 3 times Reformed), but the report of 350 killed in the one year 1529 in the Palatinate (at Alzey) is an error, though a smaller number were killed there indeed. The imperial cities followed different policies and were often influenced by the princes near by. At Nürnberg, Franconia, as early as March 26, 1527, an Anabaptist (Wolfgang Vogel, *q.v.*) was executed, at Schweinfurt in February 1529 another (Georg Braun, *q.v.*). In the bishoprics of Bamberg and Würzburg half a dozen were executed in 1528, and in the margravure of Brandenburg (Ansbach-Bayreuth) also about half a dozen in the same year.

The century from the middle of the 16th to the middle of the 17th records the decline of the Anabaptist movement; the persecution gradually reached its goal. From 1548 to 1650 there were (Hege) only 78 mandates (in sharp contrast to the 110 for only the 20 years 1525-44), the centers being the same as before; e.g., 24 Austrian and 16 Swiss mandates. In 1592 the last execution occurred (Thoman Haan of Nikolsburg, *q.v.*) in Bavaria, in 1618 the last executions (Jost Wilhelm and Christine Brünnerin, *q.v.*) at Egg near Bregenz in Vorarlberg (Tirol), also the last in the Holy Roman Empire. All three were connected with the Hutterites who up to 1620 sent many missionaries from Moravia to the West, as also many from the West at this time fled to Moravia (*q.v.*).

Strasbourg long remained a chief meeting place of the Anabaptists. Here important conferences were held in 1555 and 1557, in which the Northern (Menno Simons) doctrines of the Incarnation and of the ban were repudiated by the Southern brethren. The Strasbourg conference of 1568, attended by many ministers and elders from all over southern Germany, dealt chiefly with certain rules of discipline. In 1557 and 1571 there were disputations with the Lutheran and Calvinistic authorities respectively of the Palatinate, the former at Pfeddersheim (*q.v.*) near Worms, the other at Frankenthal (*q.v.*). The protocol of the latter was printed in 1571. Among the 15 Anabaptist participants one came from Andernach in the north, two from Alsace in the south, half a dozen from the Palatinate, one from Heilbronn, and one from Salzburg; two others and two Hutterites served as observers, so to speak.

The story of the Hutterites (*q.v.*) is a chapter of its own, not to be told here. The history of the Anabaptists in Thuringia came to its end in 1584 (Wappler, *Täuferbewegung in Thüringen*), that of the Palatinate in 1610 (Hege, *Täufer in der Kurpfalz*), that of Tirol in 1626 (Loserth, *Der Anabaptismus in*

Tyrol). By the time of the Thirty Years' War practically all the Anabaptists in South and Middle Germany had been converted, exiled, or executed.

It is rather easy to tell the story of the Anabaptists in North Germany separately from that of those in South and Middle Germany, though of course there are connections, Strasbourg especially being the meeting point.

B. *Northwest Germany.* (1) *Lower Rhine.* In Northwest Germany much the same tendencies are found as in the South. As early as 1522 Dr. Gerhard Westerburg, a patrician of Cologne, was visited by Nicholas Storch, who influenced him against infant baptism. A little later he came in contact with Carlstadt, whose sister he married and whose pamphlets and ideas he propagated. In the autumn of 1524 he even paid Zürich a short visit. But in general the question of baptism became important later in the North than in the South. The first martyrs of the Reformation were Adolf Clarenbach (*q.v.*) and Peter Fliesteden (*q.v.*), both subjects of Jülich-Berg, but executed at Cologne in 1529; at least Fliesteden had a moderate touch of Anabaptism. About the same time (1530) Melchior Hofmann (*q.v.*, 1495-1543) brought to this area from Strasbourg the idea of Anabaptism and of a special doctrine of the Incarnation initiating Anabaptism here and founding a congregation at Emden, and soon reaching the Netherlands also.

It is characteristic of the situation on the Lower Rhine that the dukes of Jülich-Cleve-Berg-Mark-Ravensberg (Johann III, 1521-39, Wilhelm V, 1539-92, Johann Wilhelm, 1592-1609) as well as the elector (archbishop) Hermann of Cologne (1515-47) were influenced by Erasmus and tried to follow a middle line between Luther and the Roman Catholic Church. But this middle party of reformers failed: the turning point was the war (1543), when the Emperor defeated Wilhelm V, gained Geldern for himself and so for the Netherlands, and enforced a Catholic polity. Later reform endeavors also failed, especially because Wilhelm V was handicapped by an attack of apoplexy in 1566. (It is significant that Wilhelm V was a brother-in-law for some time of Henry VIII of England and Francis I of France, later of Emperor Maximilian II and of Elector—later Duke—John Frederick of Saxony, who in 1547 was defeated by the Emperor.)

The "Aemter" and "Unterherrschaften" into which the duchies of Jülich, Cleve, and Berg were divided allowed the nobility a rather independent position. So the Aemter of Born, Millen, Heinsberg, Wassenberg, and Brüggen in the northwest corner of the duchy of Jülich adjoining the present Dutch province of Limburg along the Maas from Venlo to Sittard became a center of the Anabaptist movement. In 1529-32 especially the court of the high bailiff (Drost) Werner von Pallant (*q.v.*) at Wassenberg was a meeting place for several clergymen, most of them from the bishopric of Liége (Campanus, Slachtscaep) and the duchy of Brabant (Roll, Vinne), also from Westphalia (Klopreis), known as the "Wassenberger Prädikanten" (*q.v.*). Klopreis (*q.v.*, d. 1535) had been in touch with Clarenbach; from the common prison at Cologne he was rescued and brought to Wassenberg as the first of this group. Here again the influence of Erasmus is found together with that of Luther and Zwingli, and also spiritualistic tendencies and the rejection of infant baptism. With the exception of Campanus (*q.v.*, d. after 1574), the leader, they went from Wassenberg to Münster in 1532-34, were baptized there, and then were sent as apostles of the kingdom of the saints to Westphalia (Slachtscaep, *q.v.*, d. 1534, and Vinne, *q.v.*, d. 1534) and to the Rhineland (Klopreis and Roll, *q.v.*, d. 1534), all ending as martyrs to their belief.

After the first congregation at Emden (1530), the Lower Rhine-Maas congregation at Maastricht (1530-35), Cologne (1531), Aachen (1533), and Emmerich (1534) must be recorded. The first martyr of this region who is mentioned in van Braght's *Martyrs' Mirror* is Vit to Pilgrams (*q.v.*) at München-Gladbach (not 1532, as is said there, but 1537).

At Münster (Westphalia) at first a local movement for religious and social reform was started by the Lutheran pastor Bernhard Rothmann (*q.v.*) and the merchant Bernhard Knipperdolling (*q.v.*). Roll as the first of the Wassenberger preachers had already introduced their vision in 1532. Then, after Melchior Hofmann was imprisoned (for life, as it turned out) at Strasbourg in 1533, the Dutch Anabaptists took the lead. As Hofmann had thought of himself as Elijah and Strasbourg as the New Jerusalem and of the millennium immediately following his imprisonment, now the baker Jan Matthijsz (*q.v.*) of Haarlem declared himself to be Enoch, and Münster the New Jerusalem. The Anabaptist movement here became militant, and at the same time baptism became a political rather than a religious symbol. In February 1534 Matthijsz himself arrived at Münster (which now was besieged by the Catholic and Protestant princes of this region), and was killed in action at Easter (April 5) 1534. But one of his disciples, Jan Beukelszoon (*q.v.*) of Leiden, a tailor, full of eloquence and courage, under war conditions set up a dictatorship as King David of Zion. Discipline was enforced, communism and polygamy introduced, help asked from abroad. The fact that "banners were to fly in Friesland and Holland, Limburg and Jülich," shows what districts were expected to support the enterprise. But through famine and treason the city fell on June 25, 1535. Münster became Catholic again and many executions followed; Beukelszoon and Knipperdolling died not before Jan. 22, 1536. The Münster catastrophe once more strengthened the hostile attitude of public opinion and of the authorities against Anabaptism of all kinds.

It was Menno Simons (*q.v.*, 1496-1561) in Holland and North Germany who after the debacle gathered the nonresistant Anabaptists (for him they were named Mennonites after 1544). Soon he had to leave the Netherlands and found a refuge in East Friesland, where in January 1544 he had a disputation with John á Lasco (*q.v.*), the reformer of the district. Then he had to leave East Friesland and went to the Lower Rhine-Maas area, where the endeavors to introduce the Reformation had not yet come to an end. Menno stayed and worked "in the

diocese of Cologne" in 1544-46. In vain he strove for a disputation with the "scholars" at Bonn (electorate of Cologne) and at Wesel (duchy of Cleve). But about 1545 he lived with Lemken (see below) at Illikhoven (one part belonging to the Amt Born, duchy of Jülich, another part belonging to Roosteren in the duchy of Geldern) and Vissersweert on the Maas (Amt Born), now both in the Dutch province of Limburg. He preached in the environs of both places and also reached Roermond and may have founded the Anabaptist congregation of Illikhoven-Vissersweert. At any rate after the Wassenberg preachers and their adherents had left for Münster, and Menno had visited the region, organized congregations remained or were founded anew.

Roelof Martens, usually called Adam Pastor (*q.v.*), had been ordained as elder by Menno (in 1542?) and excommunicated by Dirk Philips and Menno in 1547. Nevertheless he continued his work in his district from Overijssel in the Netherlands to the county of Mark (Hamm) in Westphalia, having his seat at Odenkirchen (exclave of the electorate of Cologne), and at Well on the Maas (duchy of Geldern), here and there under the protection of a member of the van Vlodrop family. Menno and Adam diverged from the orthodox Christology in opposite directions. In Jesus Christ Menno, following Melchior Hofmann and Obbe Philips (*q.v.*, d. 1568), overstated the divine nature, and Adam the human one. The idea of a pure congregation called for a divine head of the church; the idea of an imitation of Christ called for a human head. Matthias Servaes (*q.v.*), ordained by Zillis (see below), and Heinrich von Krufft (*q.v.*) worked especially in the area of München-Gladbach; Matthias Servaes worked also at Cologne, where he was executed in 1565.

More to the South, in the Aemter Born, Millen, etc., of the duchy of Jülich the records show an office of teaching and baptizing and of deacons for the poor. About 1550 an elder Leitgen died, and in 1550 the "principal teacher" Remken Ramakers (*q.v.*) was executed at Sittard, Amt Born. They were succeeded by Theunis van Hastenrath (*q.v.*), who had his seat at Illikhoven and worked from the Maas to the Rhine (from Cleve to Essen and from Maastricht to Bonn), being executed at Linnich on the Roer in 1551. He was succeeded as elder by Lemken (*q.v.*), formerly deacon at Vissersweert in 1547 and at Illikhoven in 1550, working at first in the western Aemter of the duchy of Jülich and along the Maas, later also in a wider area.

Farther to the South, in the Amt Montjoie in the Eifel Mountains, Zillis (*q.v.*), another elder, is found who together with Lemken (and the Dutch Waterlanders and the South German Anabaptists) fought the rigid attitude of Menno concerning excommunication and shunning from 1557 to 1560, when Menno excommunicated Lemken and Zillis as well as the Waterlanders. Thus Menno and his friends on the one side, and the Waterlanders, the "High Germans" (Lemken and Zillis in Jülich), and the Southern Anabaptists on the other side, were separated. Zillis worked in the duchy of Berg on the right side of the Rhine as well as in the duchy of

Jülich on the left side. There were martyrs, e.g., Palmken Palmen (*q.v.*, 1550) at Born, Maria of Montjoie (*q.v.*, 1552) at Jülich, and Conrad Koch (*q.v.*, 1565) at Honnef in the duchy of Berg. Thomas von Imbroich (*q.v.*) from Imgenbroich near Montjoie was executed at Cologne in 1558. Some Hutterite missionaries were executed in 1558-59 at Aachen (*q.v.*).

In spite of such sacrifices (or because of them) the congregations on the Lower Rhine in general held their own to the end of the 16th century and into the 17th, not being exterminated as was the case in Middle Germany and to a large extent in South Germany. In May 1591 a decisive meeting took place at Cologne under the guidance of Leenaerdt Clock (*q.v.*). Congregations of the Upper Rhine, Breisgau, Alsace (Strasbourg, Weissenburg), and the Palatinate (Kreuznach, Landau, Landesheim, Neustadt, Worms) were represented. Of the Lower Rhine the congregations of the city of Cologne, of the electorate of Cologne (Odenkirchen), of the duchy of Cleve (Rees), of the duchy of Jülich (area of Millen and Maas, München-Gladbach), and of the duchy of Berg were represented. Practical questions prevailed, but some doctrinal questions appear in the first part of the Concept of Cologne (*q.v.*). If on the one side the Trinity was confessed, on the other side the Holy Spirit was described as a power of God (and so not as the third person of the Trinity). He who was baptized according to Anabaptist order was not to be rebaptized.

The 17th century put these congregations under new conditions. Anabaptists were in general expelled in 1601 from the cities of Aachen and Cologne, in 1614 from Burtscheid (then belonging to the Imperial Abbey of Cornelismünster, now incorporated into Aachen), and in 1628 from Odenkirchen. In 1614 the united duchies were divided into tolerant Cleve under the Hohenzollerns and intolerant Jülich-Berg under the Wittelsbachs. From 1600 on the county of Mörs with the dominion of Crefeld for a century belonged to the tolerant House of Orange. Thus, early in the 17th century a congregation was founded at Crefeld, which now became the place of refuge for Mennonites on the Lower Rhine, as well as some congregations in the duchy of Cleve (Goch, Cleve, Emmerich, Rees, Duisburg). It is worthy of note that the founder of the congregation of Crefeld, Hermann op den Graeff (*q.v.*, 1585-1642), together with a second representative, Wilhelm Kreynen (*q.v.*), signed the Confession of Dordrecht in 1632.

(2) *East Friesland* remained a place of refuge for the Anabaptists, first in the country, especially near Krummhorn (*q.v.*). Later there were three congregations of importance besides Emden: Norden (*q.v.*), Leer (*q.v.*), and Neustadt-Gödens (*q.v.*). In 1612 there were a total of about 400 Anabaptists in East Friesland. There were also some across the eastern border in the county of Oldenburg (*q.v.*). Among the first grants of toleration for Mennonites is that given by Count Rudolf Christian in 1626 for his country. Emden reached the climax of its history in the 16th century. Situated next to the Netherlands, but maintaining its independence, it was again

and again (like Wesel in a similar situation) used as a starting point by the Anabaptists for influencing the Netherlands from the outside. In 1568 and 1579 meetings of the Waterlanders (*q.v.*) were held at Emden. In 1571 a Reformed synod took place there. In 1578 there was a religious disputation between the Flemish Anabaptists (*q.v.*) and the Reformed, of which the *Protocol* was published in 1578; from Cologne and Groningen Anabaptist elders were present. For years Leenaert Bouwens had his headquarters at 't Falder near Emden, and baptized 320 persons here alone, in other places of East Friesland also 323, but during 1551-82 many more in the Netherlands and a few also in Cologne, Holstein, and Mecklenburg. It is also probable that many refugees from here found their way eastward—a few, as said before, to the adjacent Oldenburg, but practically none to the district between the Weser and the Elbe (the archbishopric of Bremen).

C. Holstein and Prussia Proper. But the two duchies of Schleswig and Holstein, the dominion of Pinneberg, and the two imperial cities and Hanseatic towns of Hamburg and Lübeck were the goal for many. The first place in this area where Anabaptists were to be found was Lübeck (*q.v.*). Here in 1535 the burgomaster Jürgen Wullenweber (*q.v.*, d. 1537) took a friendly attitude toward the Anabaptists. As early as 1532 Cord Roosen (*q.v.*, 1495-1553 or 1554) of Korschenbroich near Grevenbroich (near München-Gladbach), had found his way to Lübeck. His sons and a grandson were, surprisingly, powder manufacturers. In 1546 Menno Simons held a meeting here concerning David Joris (*q.v.* d. 1556), and in 1552 concerning Adam Pastor. In the winter of 1553-54 Menno was living at neighboring Wismar (*q.v.*) in Mecklenburg, where he debated with the Reformed preacher Micron (*q.v.*, d. 1559). Here the Wismar articles were adopted in 1554. Later Menno, with the Anabaptist printing plant recently founded at Lübeck, went to Fresenburg (*q.v.*) near Oldesloe between Lübeck and Hamburg. Here arose the first congregation (Flemish) in this area; and here Menno found an abode undisturbed by the authorities for his last years (1554-61).

In the second half of the 16th century the Anabaptist impact more and more shifted from the eastern to the western part of this area. During the same time here and often elsewhere it also changed its character more and more: Anabaptists were becoming Mennonites. The struggle for a new vision was disappearing, though the loyalty to convictions remained. While Baptists and Quakers soon undertook to propagate the one or other of these convictions, the Mennonites were content to have permission to live according to their convictions, and in addition to be good manufacturers or farmers and citizens. This development may be the consequence of a colonial existence, of a flight into another country, where first a living had to be made.

On the west coast of Schleswig-Holstein the first Mennonites (as we now may call them) appeared sometime before 1566 when five of them had already been exiled, on the peninsula of Eiderstedt (*q.v.*) in the duchy of Schleswig, not far from the border of the duchy of Holstein, belonging to the

Gottorp portion. Soon there were wholesale merchants, among them Johann Clausen Codt (also Kotte, Cotte, Cothe, Coodt, *q.v.*), a dike-reeve who, like Marpeck, early in the 17th century sustained the religious wishes of his fellow believers by protecting the land and so being very helpful to the country. In 1621, when Duke Frederick III of Holstein-Gottorp (*q.v.*, 1616-59) founded Friedrichstadt (*q.v.*) east of Eiderstedt as a Dutch place of refuge, he gave the Mennonites very liberal privileges. Some years earlier already (1616) the king of Denmark, who with the Gottorps and (until 1640) the counts of Schauenburg (dominion of Pinneberg) shared the whole country, had founded Glückstadt on the Elbe, south of Friedrichstadt, as a place of refuge; here from 1623 on Mennonites were accepted as citizens and from 1631 on were mentioned in a grant of toleration for "the Dutch nation" in the city. But the greatest importance for the Mennonites in this area was gained by Hamburg (*q.v.*), the imperial city, and the adjacent Altona (*q.v.*), first a village of fishermen, since 1604 a borough in the county of Pinneberg under the Schauenburgs, after 1640 under the kings of Denmark, after 1664 a town under municipal law. By 1575 Mennonite families were found at Hamburg (de Voss, Quins, etc., coming from the Netherlands), and 1601 at Altona (François Noë II, *q.v.*, whose father had come from Antwerp to Hamburg, originally from Flanders). At Hamburg the Mennonites made a contract with the city in 1605 (renewed in 1635). Noë as a wholesale dealer had come in touch with Ernst, Count of Schauenburg, and was allowed with others to settle on the "Freiheit" next to Hamburg. He obtained a "privilege" for his coreligionists in 1601 (renewed in 1635 and again in 1641). Though living in different states (until 1937, when Altona was incorporated into Hamburg), the Mennonites of the two places had no separate congregations.

A still larger colonization enterprise of Dutch Mennonite refugees were the settlements in Prussia proper, the German melting pot. In Ducal (or East) Prussia the Duke, himself excommunicated by the Pope and outlawed by the Emperor, even had councilors with an Anabaptist past, from 1536 Christian Entfelder, the pupil of Denk, from 1542 Gerhard Westerburg, the pupil of Storch and Carlstadt, baptized at Münster in 1534. Immigrants were Schwenckfelders (*q.v.;* since 1527), Dutch Sacramentists (*q.v.;* since 1527), Gabrielites (*q.v.,* 1535), Bohemian Brethren (1548), and from *ca.* 1535 Dutch Anabaptists, who settled especially at Königsberg and in the district of Preussisch Holland (*q.v.*) near the border of Royal (or Polish or West) Prussia. After the church inspection (the duke was now following a Lutheran course) in 1543 they were exiled; only a few remained. As the devastation in consequence of the "Reiterkrieg" (1519-25) opened the door for immigrants into East Prussia, so the floods of the Vistula (1540-43) did the same in West Prussia; here the immigrants were expected to drain the inundated land. The first contract was made in 1547 for the Danzig Werder or delta (Reichenberg, etc.) by Philip Fresen of Edzema (*q.v.*), another in 1562 for the Great Marienburg (Unter) Werder by the Loysen (*q.v.*) brothers at Tiegenhof. In the same period Mennonite settlers reached the cities of Danzig and Elbing as well as the lowland to the left and the right of the Nogat (Ellerwald, Little Marienburg Werder) and somewhat later also the pastures of the Great Marienburg (Ober) Werder at Heubuden. Rather early there were Mennonites also along the Vistula up to Thorn. Menno visited "the elect and children of God in Prussia" in the summer of 1549 and wrote them a letter in the autumn of that year. Later Dirk Philips (d. 1568), its founder, was at the head of the Danzig congregation. A successor of his, Quirin Vermeulen (also "van der Meulen," *q.v.*), in 1598 published a stately edition of the Bible in Dutch translation (the Biestkens Bible, *q.v.*).

In 1608 at the diet at Graudenz, the Bishop of Culm, Poland, Laurentius Gumbicki, made a statement to the effect that the Marienburger Werder was filled with Anabaptists. Yet it is reported that at least 80 per cent of the Mennonite farmers had perished of marsh fever in connection with the work of draining and clearing the land. In 1642 King Ladislav IV of Poland (1632-48) gave the Mennonites a grant of privileges in which he declared that King Sigismund Augustus (1546-72) had summoned the Mennonites into a district "which then was a desolate swamp and not used. With great effort and large expenditure they had made this district fertile and profitable by turning woodland into arable land and establishing pumps in order to remove the water from the inundated grounds covered with mud and to erect dikes against the floods of the Vistula."

MENNONITISM IN GERMANY, 1650-1800

We have already observed that from the second half of the 16th century the Anabaptist type more and more died out in Germany and was replaced by the Mennonite type. As evangelization and with it conversion and martyrdom disappeared, with later generations rebaptizing disappeared also, occurring only here and there within the Mennonite groups and being plainly replaced by adult baptism of the following generation when grown up. Thus the imperial mandate of 1529, so to speak, lost its objective; in 1768, for instance, the Imperial Court at Wetzlar even recommended that the affirmation of a Mennonite might be regarded the same as the oath of another. Thus the original endeavor to better the Christian testimony to the world, so much resented by this world, was toned down into the desire of a small religious group to be allowed to live for itself, yes, according to its tradition. And this nonconformity to the world was precisely what made these believers the best farmers, artisans, manufacturers, etc., now highly esteemed by the rulers in this period. So wanderings continued from territories where the Mennonites were persecuted as heretics to other territories where they were welcomed as good citizens. The interest of the world turned more and more from religious problems to economic ones, the Thirty Years' War being the boundary between the older and the newer attitudes.

Migrations. Going from southwest to northeast, there are the migrations of the Swiss Brethren to the Palatinate (*q.v.*), where after the devastations of the Thirty Years' War Elector Karl Ludwig (*q.v.*, 1617-80) gave them a privilegium in 1664. As early as 1652 they are found near Sinsheim (*q.v.*; east of the Rhine, Kraichgau, now Baden-Württemberg) and soon afterwards on the Ibersheimer Hof (*q.v.*; west of the Rhine, now Rheinland-Pfalz). The nobility of the Kraichgau (*q.v.*) between Heidelberg and Karlsruhe opened their domains to the Swiss refugees, as did also Alsace (*q.v.*) and at least from the beginning of the 18th century also the margraves of Baden-Durlach (*q.v.*).

For many of the Swiss emigrants the new home was of rather short duration because of the war of the Palatine Succession (1688-97). The French invaded and devastated the territory once more, and notwithstanding the privilegium oppressions were frequently applied. So from 1707 on many of them searched and found a more lasting place of refuge in Pennsylvania (*q.v.*). But many also remained in Germany, some in the Palatinate, some (mostly Amish) crossing the Rhine and the Main to the north and founding (*ca.* 1750 and later) settlements in Nassau and Hesse (*q.v.*), in the county of Wittgenstein (*q.v.*; now in Westphalia) and in the county of Waldeck (*q.v.*; now in Hesse). Soon afterwards others (Mennonites) turned to the east, to the bishopric of Würzburg (*q.v.*; now Bavaria) and the duchy of Württemberg (*q.v.*). And when Emperor Joseph II, after gaining Polish Galicia (*q.v.*) in 1772, invited colonization there in 1781, since the new subjects needed instruction in agriculture, 28 families, most of them Palatines, some of them Alsatian Mennonites and Amish, settled near Lemberg (*q.v.*) in 1784.

Farther to the north as early as the 17th century the Mennonites of the duchy of Jülich (1654 from München-Gladbach, 1694 from Rheydt), often linen weavers, found their way to the place of refuge in this region, Crefeld. In addition the (great) Elector of Brandenburg in 1654 and 1660 issued mandates favorable to the Mennonites for his duchy of Cleve, quite contrary to the intolerant mandates of the Wittelsbachs in Jülich. Even in the county of Mark, now also inherited by the Hohenzollerns, a small congregation existed at Hamm (*q.v.*, now in Westphalia). A center of its own was Neuwied (*q.v.*), founded in 1652 on the Rhine as the new residence of the counts of Wied. Even from the very beginning immigrants of the northern group of Mennonites (Jülich, etc.) and of the southern group (Switzerland, Palatinate) met here. In 1680 they were given a privilegium, and in 1768 the Count even helped them to get a church, opposite his castle and in the same rococo style of architecture.

Then in the east there was the migration from West Prussia to East Prussia (from 1713 on to the area of Tilsit, *q.v.*, and from 1716 on to Königsberg, *q.v.*), the attitude of the kings changing, but the local authorities continuing to favor the Mennonites. Later on the Mennonites also moved to the southeast along the Vistula *ca.* 1750 into Poland proper (Deutsch-Wymysle, *q.v.*, and Deutsch-Kazun, *q.v.*) to the west in 1765 into the province of Brandenburg (Neumark; *q.v.*).

Most settlements in this period secured legal toleration by a grant called a "privilegium" (concession). Some of these concessions were given by the following rulers: (1) Duke Friedrich III of Holstein-Gottorp, dated Feb. 13, 1623, for Friedrichstadt in Schleswig; (2) Count Rudolph Christian of East Friesland, May 26, 1626, for his country; (3) King Christian IV of Denmark, June 6, 1641, for Altona in Holstein; (4) King Ladislav IV of Poland, Dec. 22, 1642, for his country; (5) Elector Karl Ludwig of the Palatinate, Aug. 4, 1664, for his possessions; (6) Count Friedrich of Wied, Dec. 16, 1680, for Neuwied on the Middle Rhine; (7) King Friedrich Wilhelm I of Prussia, Jan. 30, 1721, for Crefeld. These documents have been preserved in the original or in copies in various archives, most of them also in printed form, some in several editions.

Sometimes older "privileges" were renewed or extended, and also here and there they underwent certain revisions. Sometimes they were limited to a single place (Friedrichstadt, Altona, Neuwied, Crefeld). Elector Karl Ludwig expressly mentioned the protracted war and its effects, and King Christian the importance of the immigrants for trade and commerce. Count Friedrich became the model for other princes of the Empire; he founded the town of Neuwied in the interests of his small territory specifically as a place of refuge for tolerated as well as "privileged" religious groups, hoping to secure as settlers at least part of those "useful" people who had to leave ruined homes elsewhere. The Mennonites were here allowed to conduct their own worship, though it had to be in secret and without making proselytes by "sweet words" (as it is stated in the Altona privilege), and were exempt from attending the worship of the established church, holding public office, bearing arms, and taking the oath. They were even protected against "mockery" (as it is stated in the Friedrichstadt privilege). For all this they only had to be recorded in special registers and to pay a special tax.

The situation of the princes of the Empire in this time as well as their opinions and intentions are rather remarkably revealed by the Neuwied privilege of 1680. The count had asked the Mennonites to attend the official (Reformed) services, but they had asked him to release them from this obligation. So the count pondered and said in his privilege: He was entitled to enforce his requirements, for the imperial law of 1529 expressly forbade tolerating Mennonites in the Roman Empire, and the Peace of Münster of 1648 only permitted Roman Catholics, Lutherans, and Reformed, and even the Imperial Court when authorizing this new residence did not include the Mennonites. But on the other hand they were living quietly, the electors of Brandenburg and the Palatinate and the duke of Holstein and others occasionally tolerated them and so disregarded the law of 1529, and at least he was a free "Imperial Estate" as well, and so by tacit understanding empowered to do the same. And so he gave the privilege in the face of the imperial laws which had settled the problem otherwise. Not the Empire, but the individual territory possessed the real power.

To understand the system of privileges within the

territories it must be pointed out that in this period people did not live under equal rights for all, but that rights were differentiated according to the political, social, ecclesiastical, and economic position of the person in question. Thus at Crefeld, e.g., there was no difficulty in releasing the Mennonites from the oath, since the Reformed clergy were liberated from this obligation also, as is seen incidentally from a report concerning the oath of allegiance. Besides, such privileges gave the princes an opportunity to secure able artisans, etc., and in this time of mercantilism it was quite common for princes to attract such persons from one another. Just as arbitrarily as privileges were given, citizenship was also transferred: at Elbing (*q.v.*) as early as 1585, at Tönning (*q.v.*) in Eiderstedt in 1607, at Crefeld (*q.v.*) in 1678, at Königsberg and Marienburg (*q.v.*) *ca.* 1750, at Danzig (*q.v.*) and in Bavaria (*q.v.*) not before 1800.

Though much scattered by the migrations, under these conditions the Mennonites of Germany reached the culminating point of their history in this period as far as economics were concerned. It may here be sufficient to name David Möllinger (*q.v.,* 1709-86), "the father of the agriculture of the Palatinate," the von der Leyens (*q.v.*) and the silk industry at Crefeld, the Roosens (*q.v.*) at Hamburg, and the van der Smissens (*q.v.*) at Altona, shipowners and whalers of the first rank; or also the gifted mechanic and clockmaker Peter Kinsing (*q.v.,* 1745-1816) at Neuwied, and the strong Bouman family with its manifold trade at Emden. A real host of Mennonite entrepreneurs at many places promoted the economic advance of their respective areas; kingly merchants they often were, especially in the Lower Rhine district and on the Lower Elbe.

Spiritual Life. As to the spiritual life, the northern settlements (Holstein, etc., and Prussia proper) in the beginning were dependent on the Netherlands, and the southern (Palatinate and its daughter colonies) on Switzerland. The Lower Rhine and East Friesland in their turn were already geographically as neighbors in constant contact with the Netherlands. Visits and exchange of preachers for a long time helped in this direction.

When in the north, e.g., Gerhard Wiebe (*q.v.,* Flemish elder of Elbing 1778-98) had documents copied (*Heubudener Urkundenbuch*) which he regarded of particular importance also for his congregation and his time, there were among these documents some relating to the division of 1557 (Menno against the Waterlander, Jülich, and South German-Swiss leaders), that of 1567 (Flemish against Frisian), and that of 1586 (Contra-Housebuyers against Housebuyers). In the case of Quirin Vermeulen and Hans von Schwinderen (*q.v.*), elder and preacher of Danzig (1583-88), and for a later controversy at Haarlem in 1631, the documents show a vivid interchange of opinions and judgments.

So even in 1759 the Dutch divisions were still maintained in East Friesland, in the Holstein region, and in Prussia proper. Old Flemish of the Groningen branch had congregations at Emden, Leer, Neustadt-Goedens (*q.v.*), and Norden in East Friesland, and at Przechowka, etc. (*q.v.*), near Schwetz in Prussia proper. Those of the Danzig Old Flemish branch appear at Danzig, Elbing, Gross-Werder (*q.v.*), Heubuden (*q.v.*), Königsberg, and Nieschewski (*q.v.*) near Thorn, all in Prussia proper. The Flemish (alone or combined with Frisians and Waterlanders) had congregations at Emden, Leer, and Norden in East Friesland, at Friedrichstadt and Hamburg-Altona in the Holstein region. Finally the Frisians or Waterlanders (the names change) were represented at Danzig, the Gross Werder (later Orlofferfelde, *q.v.*), Lithuania (*q.v.;* the Tilsit region), Montau (*q.v.*), and Schweinsgrube (*q.v.;* later Tragheimerweide) in Prussia proper. At Emden and Hamburg-Altona the congregations had joined the conservative Zonists (*q.v.*) in 1674 and 1682 respectively. But at Emden and Leer in 1767, at Norden in 1780, and at Danzig in 1808, the congregations were again united.

In 1739 and following years a discipline controversy about wigs, shoe buckles, etc., at Danzig was settled after the Dutch brethren had been asked for their judgment. In 1776 at Hamburg a German translation of the Ris confession of faith (*q.v.;* 1766 at Hoorn) was published, which remained in use in German congregations until the 19th century.

But soon an independent spirit announced itself among the German Mennonites alongside of the dependency on Dutch developments, especially in literary productions by the settlements on the Elbe and on the Vistula. In 1660 the first German confession of faith appeared at Danzig. Georg Hansen (*q.v.,* d. 1703), a shoemaker, from 1655 deacon and preacher and 1690-1703 elder of the Flemish congregation at Danzig, published a catechism in 1671 and a confession of faith in 1678. Gerrit Roosen (*q.v.,* 1612-1711), a merchant, from 1649 deacon, from 1660 preacher, from 1663 elder of the Flemish congregation of Hamburg-Altona, in 1702 also published a catechism (*Christliches Gemüthsgespräch*) and an apologetic (*Unschuld und Gegenbericht*). Heinrich Donner (*q.v.,* 1735-1804), Frisian elder of Orlofferfelde since 1772, and Gerhard Wiebe (see above) in 1778 and 1783 published a catechism, which as the Elbing-Waldeck-Zweibrücken catechism was one of the most widely used in Europe and in America. In 1792 Gerhard Wiebe also published a confession of faith.

A new influence from the Netherlands began with the introduction of trained and salaried ministers, e.g., at Crefeld since 1770, who received their education more and more at the Amsterdam Mennonite Seminary, established in 1735.

In the South the Palatine Mennonites also showed a continued dependence on Switzerland. Peter Ramseyer (*q.v.,* b. 1706), from 1730 preacher and from 1732 elder of the Jura congregation, for 20 years (1762-82) again and again traveled to the Palatinate to settle dissension there. The Amish (*q.v.*) division of 1693 especially affected the settlers in the Palatinate. Amish congregations arose by migration from the Netherlands to Volhynia; the most northern points they reached in Germany were Mengeringhausen (*q.v.*) in Waldeck, and Petershagen (*q.v.*) in Minden west of Hanover. The Amish remained in strong contact with each other, at least from Alsace to Waldeck, at meetings where "Ordnungsbriefe" supplemented earlier decisions on discipline. Hans Nafziger (*q.v.*), from 1731 preacher and later elder at Essingen (*q.v.*) in the Palatinate, a central figure in his time, held such meetings at his place in 1759 and 1779. In 1765 he traveled to the Netherlands to settle dissension among the Amish there. In 1780 he published the only edition of the *Martyrs' Mirror* in German in Germany at Pirmasens, together with Peter Weber (see below). In 1781 he wrote a letter to the Amish in Holland as a kind of formulary for baptism, marriage, and ordinations.

Outside Influences. As religious discrimination from 1650 on gradually lost much of its former intensity, the Mennonites could come into contact with religious movements outside their group. In fact, the Mennonite congregations not seldom proved themselves to be a fertile ground for such movements. Among the outside influences were (1) Quakers, (2) Dompelaars, and (3) Pietists.

(1) The Quakers (*q.v.*) appeared at Kriegsheim (*q.v.*) in the Palatinate soon after the Mennonites, gained some of them for their convictions, and had a congregation of their own there 1657-86, when they emigrated to Pennsylvania. They also appeared at Hamburg-Altona in 1659, but not being allowed to stay there soon left again, taking with them some Mennonites, among them the preacher Berend Roelofs (*q.v.*). They were at Crefeld also in 1667-83. In the latter year they induced 13 families (formerly Mennonites) to emigrate to Pennsylvania, where they founded Germantown (*q.v.*)—only one remained Mennonite in the long run; it was the first group of Germans to reach the later United States of America.

(2) The Dompelaars (*q.v.*) were found at Hamburg-Altona in 1648-1746, having their own congregation alongside the Mennonite congregation from *ca.* 1656 on, their own church building from 1708. Their most prominent preacher was Jacob Denner (*q.v.*, 1659-1746) from 1684, at Lübeck 1687-94, at Friedrichstadt 1694-98, at Danzig 1698-1702, and then again at Altona until his death. He preached for an interdenominational audience. Perhaps the group was influenced by the Dutch Collegiants (*q.v.*) or by the English Baptists (*q.v.*). The Dompelaars found at Crefeld in 1705-25 were of another kind, viz., Dunkers (*q.v.*), who in 1719 also turned to Pennsylvania. In the Mennonite congregation at Crefeld for some time one preacher, Gossen Goyen (*q.v.*, 1667-1737), advocated baptism by immersion, himself being rebaptized in 1724 in the Rhine, and another, Jan Crous (*q.v.*, 1670-1729), advocated baptism by sprinkling.

(3) The Pietists (*q.v.*) exercised an especially long and far-reaching influence upon the German Mennonites. It came both from the outside and also through Mennonite channels. In Holland the outstanding Mennonite Pietist was Jan Deknatel (*q.v.*, 1698-1759), from 1726 the minister of the congregation 't Lam at Amsterdam, converted (in the Pietist sense) in 1734 and standing in close relations with the Moravians (*q.v.*) and the Methodists (*q.v.*). On the Lower Rhine Gerhard Tersteegen (*q.v.*, 1697-

1769), Reformed, from 1725 an interdenominational spiritual adviser, gained a similar position.

In 1735-69 Tersteegen was in close contact with the Crefeld Mennonites and later also with Lorenz Friedenreich (*q.v., ca.* 1728-94), from 1758 elder of the Mennonite congregation at Neuwied. Friedenreich, in this time of letter writing and traveling and exchange of books and pamphlets, served as a liaison officer in all directions. In his last years Deknatel became instrumental in the conversion of Peter Weber (*q.v.*, 1731-81), a weaver and from 1757-58 until his death preacher of the Mennonite congregation of Höningen near Altleiningen (*q.v.*) in the Palatinate. Abraham Krehbiel (*q.v.*, d. 1804), farmer and preacher (from 1766) of the Mennonite congregation at the Weierhof (*q.v.*), was also from his ordination on in contact with Weber, Tersteegen, and Deknatel's son. It was as in a missionary family, and thus also the name-lists (*Naamlijst*), which at Deknatel's instigation were published at Amsterdam from 1731 on, and the endeavor to make them complete, widened the circle more and more. Under the pietist influence even a correspondence between Prussia proper and the Palatinate, so far distant from one another, was started (1768-73). Hans van Steen (*q.v.*, 1705-81), elder of the Flemish congregation at Danzig from 1754, and Martin Möllinger (*q.v.*, 1698-1774), brother of David Möllinger, preacher of the congregation at Mannheim (*q.v.*) from 1753, were the principal writers. Some letters also came from Gerhard Wiebe (see above) and Frienenreich, Weber, etc. Pietists in West Prussia were Isaak van Dühren (*q.v.*, 1725-1800), converted in 1772, from 1775 preacher of the Danzig Frisian congregation, who in 1787 published a German extract from the *Martyrs' Mirror,* and Cornelius Regier (*q.v.*, 1743-94), from 1764 preacher, 1771 elder of the Heubuden congregation. On the Elbe a stronghold of Pietism was the van der Smissen family, particularly Gysbert III (*q.v.*, 1717-93) and his son Jacob Gysbert (*q.v.*, 1746-1829), who already in 1766-68 on his cavalier's tour with his cousin Hinrich III (1742-1814) visited in England the great evangelist and cofounder of Methodism George Whitefield, and in Germany Tersteegen and the Moravian settlements, Herrnhut and Niesky. At his advice this cousin in 1781 engaged as a tutor for his many children Johann Wilhelm Mannhardt (*q.v.*, 1760-1831), a member of the Tübingen Stift, who in 1790 married one of his pupils, thus combining these two families, which were prominent among the German Mennonites, especially in the 19th century.

Assimilation. In addition to these relations with more or less kindred movements the Christian church in general, and the great world also, entered the scene. Gerrit Roosen (see above) had already taken a position as a conservative as well as irenical trying to recommend the controversial Mennonite teaching to society as "harmless": Mennonitism in assimilation. At Friedrichstadt two Ovens (*q.v.*), father and son, were during 1711-82 successively one of the two burgomasters of the town: public offices were no longer abhorred. In London in 1766 the young van der Smissens (see above) enjoyed seeing English soldiers at drill; at Neuwied the young men of the Mennonite congregation in 1804 wanted to meet their new prince on horseback, with swords buckled on, like other young citizens: the principle of nonresistance was at least softened. And even Gerhard Wiebe (see above) in his confession of faith of 1792 dropped the idea of a visible congregation of saints and accepted that of an invisible church.

Whereas at Danzig in 1697 the painter Enoch Seemann (*q.v.*, b. *ca.* 1660) was banned for painting portraits (Second Commandment), at Hamburg-Altona Balthasar Denner (*q.v.*, 1685-1749) and Dominicus van der Smissen (*q.v.*, 1705-60), the son and son-in-law of Jacob Denner (see above), were "the last German portraitists of international importance." After the Swedish General Stenbock had burned the town of Altona in 1713, Hinrich I van der Smissen (*q.v.*, 1662-1737, father of Gysbert III) rebuilt it, thus becoming known as "the city builder." Berend Roosen (see above) discovered the famous architect Sonnin and had him build his home, one of the finest in Hamburg in the 18th century. Later the great Mennonite manufacturers gave Crefeld its architectural character by their monumental homes, one of their homes even being called "the castle" (now the town hall).

In 1687 and 1688 the Danzig congregation helped the Jesuits and the Lutherans respectively to build their churches; in 1750-51 the Hamburg-Altona congregation helped to rebuild the Lutheran St. Michael's Church; in 1779 the Emden congregation shared in the costs of a Reformed peace festival. In 1732 the Danzig Mennonites made a contribution for the Salzburg (*q.v.*) exiles; for decades the Friedrichstadt Mennonites had done the same for the poor Lutherans of their town. In Crefeld the van der Leyens (see above) in 1738 had Roman Catholic, Lutherans, and Reformed among their laborers and in 1789 promoted social contacts between members of different denominations.

In this course of events it is not astonishing to see also the Mennonite church buildings and services adapted to the surrounding culture. Many of the new church buildings—in 1751 Orlofferfelde, 1754 Rosenort (*q.v.*), 1768 Fürstenwerder (*q.v.*), Heubuden, Ladekopp (*q.v.*), and Tiegenhagen (*q.v.*), 1776 Gruppe (*q.v.*), 1783 Ellerwald (*q.v.*, all in West Prussia), 1778 Sembach (*q.v.*), 1779 Eppstein (*q.v.*), 1784 Heppenheim (*q.v.*, all in the Palatinate); also the old churches—1586 Montau, 1618 Schönsee (*q.v.*), 1638 and 1648 Danzig, 1675 and 1715 Altona, 1693 Crefeld, 1769 Emden—indeed were modest buildings. But Elbing (1590) and Friedrichstadt (1708) were fine patrician buildings, and Norden (1796) was even a finer one in a splendid rococo style. The Spitalhof (*q.v.*, 1682) held its services in a beautiful old Gothic chapel. The church of Neuwied (1768) has already been mentioned. Organs were first admitted to German Mennonite churches at Altona (1764) and at Norden (1797).

Language was long a great barrier between the immigrant German Mennonites and the native Protestants or Catholics. This was not so true in the South, where the Swiss dialect was apparently soon given up and the High German literary idiom commonly used from the start, but in the North things were more complicated. The Mennonites from Holland of course brought the Dutch church language of their old home with them into the new one. The congregations on the Dutch-German border so close to the Netherlands, which was enjoying its political and cultural Golden Age in the 17th century, naturally also felt the Dutch influence in the matter of language. Yet naturally in the course of time the Dutch language for church services, in partly alien, partly changed surroundings, with no support from the language in general use, declined and was pushed aside. It is easy to understand that this development took place most rapidly at the most advanced Anabaptist-Mennonite outpost, in West Prussia around Danzig. By 1671 Georg Hansen (see above) lamented that the young people read German better than Dutch. So in the rural congregations at Heubuden in West Prussia in the 1750's and the city congregation at Danzig in the 1760's and 1770's the ministers began to preach their sermons in German. Farther to the west the proximity of the Netherlands was of strong influence; also the fact that the educated ministers called by these congregations had to be obtained from the Netherlands or had to get their training in the Dutch universities and especially in the Mennonite Seminary at Amsterdam. In 1786 at Hamburg and Altona Reinhard Rahusen (*q.v.*, 1735-93) first began the use of High German in the newly introduced weekday services; in general the High German language was not used here in sermons until 1839 and in the church records not until the 1880's. Crefeld used German after 1818, Friedrichstadt after 1826.

MODERN MENNONITISM IN GERMANY, 1800-1950

Nonresistance, etc. For the history of the Mennonites in Germany a turning point came when the French Revolution did away with local independence and local privileges, in 1789 proclaiming "Liberty, Equality, Fraternity" as the rights of all men, and in 1793 introducing universal compulsory service. Napoleon moderated this law in 1800 by allowing substitutes under special conditions, but enforced it anew in 1806. Since the treaties of Basel (1795) and of Campo Formio (1797), the Rheinbund (1806), and the treaty of Tilsit (1807) ceded the left border of the Rhine to France and placed practically all Germany west of the Elbe under the control of Napoleon I, similar decrees followed, especially in the South German states.

In the face of this danger to nonresistance the Mennonites of the Palatinate as early as 1802 sought contact with those of the Netherlands. In 1803 and 1805 at Ibersheim representatives of Rhenish congregations professed anew their adherence to the principles of nonconformity and nonresistance. Several delegates were sent to Paris on behalf of their privileges. In vain; no exceptions were allowed, only perhaps substitutes. But to obtain substitutes was rather expensive. Some congregations even regarded paying substitutes as contrary to nonresistance. For some time some of the congregations paid for the poor members who could not pay the substitutes. But later on this practice was discontinued, since nonconcerned members opposed it. So, on the one hand many emigrated to America in 1830-60; on the other hand, as the conditions continued, those remaining in South Germany gradually gave up the principle of nonresistance. The catechisms of the Palatinate and Hesse (i.e., old Palatinate on the left border of the Rhine) of 1861, and of Baden (i.e., old Palatinate on the right border of the Rhine: the Kraichgau and Baden-Durlach) of 1865 had already tacitly dropped the principle. Early in the 20th century, when Georg Wünsch (*q.v.*) asked a young farmer in Baden why he did not follow the traditional order, this Mennonite answered, "When every man goes, we can't stay at home."

In North Germany the kingdom of Prussia after the peace of Vienna in 1815 comprised the following Mennonite population: East Prussia 678; West Prussia 12,497; Brandenburg, etc., 692; Rhine Province and Westphalia 1,289, making a total of 15,156 Mennonites (souls). In the Rhine Province alone in 1812-27, in the government district of Düsseldorf (Crefeld, etc.), Aachen, and Cologne, there were about 883; of Coblenz (Neuwied, etc., and Trier) about 353, including some Amish, making a total of about 1,236 Mennonites (souls).

As to the western provinces of Prussia, their different parts had belonged to various states and were only now united into a larger political body. Since the eastern provinces lived under older decrees (see below), the government, after the Prussian military law of 1814 was promulgated, tried to find a similar status for those of the west. A first report was given by the Minister of the Interior in 1817, a second by a commission of the Royal Council in 1819 (Menno, several confessions including that of Dordrecht and that of Ris, the Latin history by Schijn, works on Mennonites by Zeidler in 1698, Rues in 1743, Crichton in 1786, and Starck in 1789, and other general works were cited). There was a lively correspondence between King Frederick William III and the Oberpräsident on the one side, with the congregations, especially Crefeld, on the other. Even a small Amish group at Offhausen (Altenkirchen district) received an answer from Chancellor Hardenberg. In 1826 the king ordered that all heads of Mennonite families be questioned about their position on nonresistance. In 1830 the law on the rights of the Mennonites (and Quakers) in the western provinces and Brandenburg was published. Most of the families asked accepted military service and thus became ordinary citizens. The smaller part refused military service, and were obliged to pay a special income tax of 3 per cent, were not allowed to acquire new property, and were admitted to communal, but not to state offices; new settlements were forbidden. Thus the new legal status was established. In the North as well as in South Germany many, particularly the Amish, emigrated to America in 1830-60, particularly from Nassau, Hesse, and Waldeck. Among those who remained in Germany there were frequently cases—at Friedrichstadt, at Hamburg-Altona, and in the 1820's even at Crefeld—when individuals more or less successfully tried to evade military service. In Hamburg occurred the remarkable case that in 1818 a Mennonite Lieutenant Jansen complained to the military authorities of being excommunicated by the congregation on account of his military service; it was rather surprising to him that the authorities advised him to return to civilian life. Yet the Hamburg congregation lost ground notwithstanding. Whereas in 1837 they had asserted that substitutes were as objectionable as personal service, by 1851 they had to be satisfied with avoiding personal service by the use of substitutes.

Little by little, as in South Germany, the attitude of the Mennonites in North Germany concerning nonresistance changed. Already in 1831 the congregations of East Friesland (in 1815-66 belonging to the Kingdom of Hanover) had relinquished this principle, as they then officially declared to the authorities.

In 1848 the first German parliament in the Paulskirche at Frankfurt became something like another turning point in nonresistance. A Mennonite banker of Crefeld, Hermann von Beckerath (*q.v.*, 1801-70), a member of this parliament (and of the Prussian parliament as well) and of its committee for the constitution and even one of its ministers, discussing the fundamental laws, on Aug. 28 declared: "I think myself fortunate in belonging to one of the freest denominations. The time of privileges is gone. The modern state requires equal rights for all citizens. So the Rhenish Mennonites with only few exceptions are rendering their military service. Nonresistance with them is no longer an integral part of their creed." So an amendment in favor of nonresistance for the Mennonites offered by the members from Danzig was lost. Many applauded: a real confession! Indeed, these Mennonites of West and South Germany now regarded nonresistance no longer as a fundamental article of their creed, but as a privilege no longer tolerable because it was injurious to the rights of fellow citizens.

In 1867 even the conference of Offenthal (*q.v.*; near St. Goarshausen on the Rhine in Nassau), where Mennonites and Amish of the Palatinate, Neuwied, Nassau, and Hesse (the duchy of Nassau and the electorate of Hesse having just been added to Prussia) met to come to an agreement, though confessing nonresistance as an article of the creed, ruled: "But how each congregation and each young man will indeed prove our old-Mennonite nonresistance, in order to satisfy his own conscience and the demands of the authorities, we leave to the judgment of each of them." This was the formula later often repeated to save the principle and at the same time abandon it.

The situation in Prussia proper was more fortunate. In the same year (1818) when at Hamburg Lieutenant Jansen sought in vain to return to his congregation in spite of his military service, the same thing happened to a David van Riesen of Elbing who had served in the Wars of Liberation and had nevertheless also tried to return to his congregation with the help of the courts. The emigration to Russia from 1788 on alleviated the economic difficulties (as the buying of property here was also limited) for those who remained. Besides, the "everlasting" privilege of 1780 gave a matchless support. But after 1848 the Mennonites of Prussia proper also had to realize the change of the times. There was the new Prussian constitution which proclaimed equal rights and equal duties for all (Dec. 5, 1848). At Frankfurt in August 1848 the Danzig members of the parliament (Martens and Osterrath) had in vain pleaded for the Mennonite privilege of nonresistance, pleading for tolerance. The West Prussian congregations met on Sept. 14, 1848, at Heubuden and sent a petition to Frankfurt to recognize their convictions, but in vain. At Berlin in February 1849 delegates of the congregations met the Prime Minister of Brandenburg and at least obtained a postponement. But the discussions about the nonresistance of the Prussian Mennonites, their special tax and their limitations in buying new property continued. Peter Froese (*q.v.*, d. 1853), elder of Orlofferfelde 1830-53, wrote a pamphlet in 1850 once more defending nonresistance as an article of the Mennonite creed, and Wilhelm Mannhardt (*q.v.*, 1831-80), the noted folklorist, in 1863 did the same by means of thorough historical research (*Die Wehrfreiheit der Altpreussischen Mennoniten*).

Even in 1867 the Prussian government proposed, in a bill concerning military service, exempting the members of those Mennonite and Quaker families who by laws or privileges were released from direct service, but obliging them to furnish an equivalent. Yet on Oct. 18, 1867, the first Imperial Diet of the North German Confederation (the nucleus of the later German Empire) rejected this paragraph so that now all Mennonites had to serve in the army. Gerhard Penner (*q.v.*, 1805-78), the elder of the Heubuden congregation 1852-77, was informed of this vote the same day by wire. On the 23rd representatives of the Prussian congregations met in his house at Warnau (Koczelitzky) and a delegation of five set out at once for Berlin and on the 24th called on the Minister of War (Roon). Nevertheless the law was published on Nov. 9, 1867. Summoned by the members of parliament of their region in February 1868 the five traveled to Berlin once more and for a whole week (Feb. 18-26) called on the king and the crown prince, ministers and privy councilors, members of the parliament, etc. Most impressive was what the crown prince said; viz., that the whole royal house was trying to help them; he warned them against emigration to Russia and advised them at least to reserve a return for their children, as probably in Russia matters would soon turn the same way. In this very week, on Feb. 20, the ministers of War and of Interior in a common report recommended that the members of the older Mennonite families who were not willing to serve with arms might be trained as nurses, wagoners, etc., only. These proposals were sanctioned by the Order of Cabinet of the king on March 3, 1868. As a consequence of the new course the limitation as to property and the special tax on the Mennonites were rescinded.

The Prussian Mennonites reacted in several ways to these transactions and decisions. A smaller part emigrated to Russia (1853 f.) and to America (1873 f.). Those remaining were divided into a group which strongly clung to the Order of Cabinet, and another which was willing to serve with arms. The congregation of Montau-Gruppe was split into two for half

a century on this question. In 1909-14, of the 200 young Mennonites of Prussia proper in contact with their congregations nearly one half followed the Order of Cabinet, and the rest served with arms. In this respect for West and East Prussia World War I signified the end of nonresistance. In 1933 when the curatorium of the Vereinigung discussed the question of a new universal compulsory service nobody proposed asking for another "privilege." Even the confession of faith of the Mennonites in Prussia (1895), which forbade revenging oneself on one's neighbor, merely urged its members as far as possible to avoid the outrages of war. The German martyrs of nonresistance in World War II included only one Lutheran and many Jehovah's Witnesses, but no Mennonites. After the war American and Dutch Mennonite influences, as well as the impressions of the war, resulted in a new nonresistant trend. The new German constitution of 1950 makes provision for alternative service for conscientious objectors.

As to the problem of the oath, regulations exempting Mennonites in the courts and as officials were made in Württemberg in 1807, in Bavaria in 1811, in Nassau in 1822, in the older provinces of Prussia in 1827, etc. Under Hitler it was rather easy to get such exemptions for soldiers in the army as early as 1935. But in certain other respects there was a long struggle, the oath being regarded by the National Socialists as a special foundation of the state; hence many had to render an oath, as the authorities ordered, even by radio, and many did so without scruples, although ultimately the requirement was waived for Mennonites.

As to public offices, for the 19th century at least two South German Mennonites may be named besides Hermann von Beckerath (see above) in the North, namely, Peter Eymann (*q.v.*, 1788-1855), a miller of Sembach (Palatinate), assistant preacher of his congregation, who was mayor of Frankenstein and in 1849 a Liberal member of the Bavarian parliament, and Jacob Finger (*q.v.*, 1825-1904), a lawyer of Monsheim (Hesse), in 1862-65 a member of the Hessian parliament and in 1884-98 minister of state. A look at the Mennonite *Adressbuch* of 1936 reveals all the difficulties of the question of officeholding in a modern state such as Germany. Mail, telegraph, and railways are managed by the state, and many schools and libraries also. But is working in them a public office in the sense of earlier times? And if we find a good many Mennonites in these offices, what about Mennonites in the administration of customs or in the revenue department? But then it is only a step to the courts and the police and then again only one more to serving as captain or admiral. At any rate, the principle of avoiding public offices was nearly forgotten. Sometimes and in some places (Berlin, Crefeld) there were Mennonites in an amazing number of public offices.

In 1874 a Prussian law allowed Mennonite congregations to incorporate. After 1924 Gustav Reimer (1884-1955) in a series of lawsuits liberated the Mennonites of Prussia proper (including the Free City of Danzig) from the obligation of paying taxes to the Protestant established church.

As to nonconformity nobody wanted to be very

conspicuous, different, or shocking. At the end of the 19th century nonconformity was gradually dropped even by the Amish. On the other hand, even between the world wars, e.g., 1918-39 in the Palatinate, it was a problem whether girls might be allowed to bob their hair. Sometime later even the older women had bobbed hair. Technical progress often did away with traditional fashions. Thus the world overcame nonconformity.

Foreign Influences. But also spiritual influences of the surrounding life helped to bring about change in the character of the Mennonite congregations in Germany. There was the Reveil (*q.v.*) in Holland in the early 19th century with its interest in missions and Bible distribution. Even in Crefeld in 1818-34 the minister Isaac Molenaar (*q.v.*, 1776-1834), in close contact with Holland, was a spokesman of this renewal of Pietism. The English Baptist William Henry Angas (*q.v.*, d. 1832) visited West Prussia in 1823 and the Palatinate in 1824 to make propaganda for the missions which the Baptists had started with William Carey in 1792. The Basel Mission (founded in 1815) in the South, the Berlin Mission (founded in 1824) in the North, and later (1847 ff.) the Mission of the Dutch Mennonites also were supported by the offerings of the German Mennonites. At present there is a German Mennonite Committee for Missions as a branch of an all-European Mennonite Mission Board (see **E.M.E.K.**). There was the "Gemeinschaftsbewegung" (*q.v.*) in the late 19th century with its Gospel songs which won the South more or less, in West Prussia particularly the Thiensdorf-Preussisch Rosengart (*q.v.*) congregation. Pietistic influences in general came especially from St. Chrischona (*q.v.*, founded in 1840) and many similar schools. From 1858 on the Hahnsche (*q.v.*) Pietists of Württemberg with their universalism reached two congregations of Baden. As the Northwest German congregations (Lower Rhine and East Friesland) were in character like the Dutch congregations, quite different influences are found here. From the Netherlands and from the universities rationalism, liberalism, and modernism found their way into these congregations. Gustav Kraemer (*q.v.*, 1863-1948) in Crefeld (from 1903) and J. G. Appeldoorn (*q.v.*, 1862-1945) in Emden (1904-16) were prominent representatives of these tendencies, the one coming from the German Protestant Church, the other from Holland, to which he later returned. A milder liberalism had appeared earlier in Prussia proper with Carl Harder (*q.v.*, 1820-96), pastor at Neuwied 1857-69 and at Elbing in the progressive town congregation 1869-96, and with Hermann Gottlieb Mannhardt (*q.v.*, 1855-1927), pastor at Danzig from 1879. In general confessional boundaries have become lax in certain areas. So we find non-Mennonite pastors of Mennonite congregations (Crefeld, Monsheim), and the opposite as well (Kiel).

The pietistic wing of the German Mennonites was since 1857 in constant contact with the Evangelical Alliance (*q.v.*), represented for instance by Pastor H. van der Smissen of Hamburg. The South German Conference (see below) was represented at the World Conference for Faith and Order at Lausanne, Switzerland, in 1927 (Benjamin H. Unruh). The Vereinigung has belonged officially since 1930 to the World Alliance for International Friendship through the Churches. In 1947-48 the Vereinigung became a member of the World Council of Churches and one of the founders of the Committee of Christian Churches in Germany. In the World Council meeting at Amsterdam in 1948 it was represented (Ernst Crous and Otto Schowalter).

It must be admitted that there was a great change from the 16th-century Anabaptists to the 19th-century Mennonites and from the old Mennonites to the modern Mennonites in the 19th century. But we may also acknowledge that these changes in some respects at least have been helpful. We cannot deny that the little river ran through the centuries again and again in several smaller branches and two bigger ones, that the number of Mennonites in Germany absolutely and relatively diminished, and that much of the best substance was lost by so many emigrations. But it is nevertheless a fact that even under such conditions until our own time the Anabaptist-Mennonite vision, old and new, has in one way or the other accomplished something in the brotherhood.

In economic life it is worth noting that numerous Mennonites of the city congregations of Crefeld, Emden, Gronau, Hamburg, and Danzig became successful and wealthy merchants and manufacturers, but that the Mennonites of West Prussia and South Germany remained essentially farmers and achieved a splendid reputation in this field.

Internal Migrations. As the emigrations to Russia and to America weakened the position of the Mennonites in the homeland, so also the inland migration dispersed the few remaining over a larger area. There were movements to the East especially in South Germany, 1802 along the Danube, from 1818 and again since 1880 to Upper Bavaria. There was also the tendency to leave the rural areas and settle in the large cities. In Berlin (*q.v.*), for instance, there has been a congregation since 1887, in Munich one since 1893, in Stuttgart one since 1933. A large number of German Mennonites are now living far away from their home congregations. The statistics show a steady relative decline, e.g., in Prussia proper from a ratio of 127 in 1816 to 70 in 1858 to a population of 100,000; and absolutely, e.g., in Bavaria (without Palatinate), from 1,053 in 1875 to 783 in 1910. In 1910 the census gives the number of Mennonites in West Prussia as *ca.* 10,000, in the rest of North Germany *ca.* 4,000, in the Palatinate *ca.* 2,500, in South Germany east of the Rhine also *ca.* 2,500, in Alsace-Lorraine *ca.* 2,000. A real catastrophe was the flight and expulsion from West Prussia proper in 1945. This great tragedy meant unnumbered tragedies in single families and individuals; many perished, even by suicide. For some time many that fled to Denmark were kept there. In 1948 and 1951 more than 1,000 emigrated to Uruguay. In Western Germany refugee congregations had to be founded: Göttingen (*q.v.*) in 1945, later Bremen (*q.v.*), Bergisches Land (*q.v.*, near Cologne), Kiel (*q.v.*), Uelzen (*q.v.*), etc.; Frankfurt on the Main (*q.v.*) was revived in 1948. Berlin was much enlarged (1940—406, 1955—1,122), also Hamburg (from 338 to 935), Crefeld (*ca.* 800 to 1,880), and Neuwied (*ca.* 20 to *ca.* 500). One thousand turned to the Palatinate. In 1955 the German congregations with membership (total 14,068 souls) were, according to the *Mennonitischer Gemeinde-Kalender*, as follows (the word "souls" meaning total population including unbaptized children):

North Germany—8,694 souls

Old Congregations		New Congregations	
Berlin	**1,122**	Bergisches Land	275
Hamburg	935	Bremen	500
Friedrichstadt	39	Espelkamp	135
Neuwied	500	Göttingen	543
Emden	280	Kiel	436
Leer	50	Lübeck	189
Norden	155	Uelzen	465
Gronau	110	Schleswig-Holstein	380
Crefeld	1,880	Westphalia	700
	5,071		3,623

South Germany—5,374 souls

Palatinate-Hesse		Gemeindeverband	
		Palatinate	
Friedelsheim	180	Branchweilerhof	65
Kohlhof	70	Deutschhof	122
Ibersheim	185	*Baden*	
Eppstein	120	Adelsheim	41
Ludwigshafen-		Bretten	32
Friesenheim	90	Durlach	131
Monsheim	310	Hasselbach	94
Obersülzen	221	Heidelberg	42
Kaiserslautern	91	Schopfheim	31
Kühbörncheshof	209	Sinsheim	120
Zweibrücken	245	Ueberlingen	87
Saarland	87	Wössingen	64
Sembach	400	*Württemberg*	
Neudorferhof	138	Backnang	235
Altleiningen	40	Heilbronn	177
Weierhof	560	Möckmühl	25
Uffhofen	58	Nesselbach	32
Bavaria		Reutlingen	131
(Bavaria, not in the		Stuttgart	135
Verband)		*Bavaria*	
Eichstock	32	Augsburg	60
Munich	185	Ingolstadt	135
Regensburg	156	Nürnberg	30
	3,277	Trappstadt	65
Frankfurt on the		Würzburg-	
Main	170	Giebelstadt	73
	3,447		1,927

E.C.

LITERATURE OF THE GERMAN MENNONITES

The literature of the Mennonites in Germany, excluding the 16th-century Anabaptists and omitting small pamphlets and ephemeral literature, falls into six categories: (1) reprints of Dutch Mennonite books; (2) sermon collections; (3) devotional literature and church manuals such as confessions, catechisms, and prayerbooks; (4) historical writings; (5) hymnbooks, and (6) general theological and Biblical literature.

Of the last category remarkably little has been produced by native German Mennonites; they seem to have produced no substantial general writers throughout their history. The entire list includes only five writers: (1) Gerhard Ewert, Gross-Lunau near Culm (*Sieben Betrachtungen*, 1843); (2) Peter Froese, elder at Orlofferfelde (*Liebreiche Erinnerung . . . von der Wehrlosigkeit*, 1850); (3) Karl Harder, preacher at Neuwied and Elbing, who published (with the help of others) three volumes of *Blätter für Religion and Erziehung*, 1869-71; (4) Philipp Kieferndorf, preacher at Monsheim (*Der Eid*, 1891); and (5) Horst Quiring, preacher at Berlin (*Grundworte des Glaubens*, 1938, a theological dictionary). Jakob Kroeker (1872-1948), an outstanding writer with over 20 titles of quality to his credit (e.g., *Das lebendige Wort*, 14 vv. of O.T. exposition), was a Russian Mennonite who came to Germany permanently in 1910 and served as an interdenominational speaker and writer without membership in any German Mennonite group.

(1) The list of German translations of Dutch Mennonite authors is extensive: Menno Simons, *Ein Fundamentbuch* (n.p., 1575; 2nd ed. undated), *Die Fundamente* (Danzig, 1835), translated by P. van Riesen, *Ausgang aus dem Papsttum* (Frankfurt and Leipzig, 1700), and *Kurzer Auszug* (Büdingen, 1758 and Königsberg, 1765); Dirk Philips, *Enchiridion* (1715, with three smaller tracts) and *Von der Ehe der Christen* (1765); T. J. van Braght, *Tugendschule* (1743) and *Märtyrer-Spiegel*, reprinted from the Ephrata, Pa., 1748 edition at Pirmasens in 1780; H. Schijn, *Erster Anfang von dem christlichen Gottesdienst* (1743); J. Deknatel, *Anleitung zum Christlichen Glauben*, a catechism (Amsterdam, 1756; reprints Neuwied 1790, Worms 1829, Alzey 1839); two confessions: (*a*) Dordrecht of 1632 in German first at Amsterdam, 1664 and 1691, then n.p., 1686, 1711, and 1742, further at Zweibrücken in 1854 and Regensburg in 1876; (*b*) Cornelis Ris confession of 1766 at Hamburg 1776 and 1850; the first (*a*) becoming the confession of the Amish, the second (*b*) that of the North German Mennonites. Deknatel's sermons were also published in German translation at Büdingen in 1757. J. P. Schabalie's famous *Wandelnde Seele* had at least nine European German editions, among them Basel 1741, 1770, 1811, Frankfurt and Leipzig 1758, 1770, and 1860.

(2) The printed sermon collections were fairly numerous, seventeen of more than two sermons being listed in 1730-1909 in the exhaustive "Annotated Bibliography of Published Mennonite Sermons" (*MQR* XXVII, 1953, 145-49), beginning with Jakob Denner of Hamburg and including Rahusen of Leer, I. Kröcker of Königsberg, L. Weydmann and Isaac Molenaar of Crefeld, I. A. Hoekstra of Hamburg, H. Reeder of Weierhof, J. Molenaar of Monsheim, C. Harder of Neuwied and Elbing, H. G. Mannhardt of Danzig, J. P. Müller of Emden, and three series of sermons by various preachers (*Menn. Bl.* supplements 1887-89, *Predigten aus Mennoniten-Gemeinden 1891-99*, 9 vv., and *Predigten vorgetragen in den Mennoniten Gemeinden Westpreussens 1906-09*, 2).

(3) The devotional literature and church manuals include, besides the Dordrecht and Cornelis Ris

Dutch confessions and Deknatel's Dutch catechism, the following confessions and catechisms: the first German confession (possibly translated from the Dutch) of 1660 at Danzig (United Flemish, Frisian, and High German Mennonites), *Confession oder Kurtze und Einfältige Glaubensbekentniss,* to which were attached beginning 1690 the catechism *Kurtze Unterweisung* and *Formular etlicher christlicher Gebete;* another West Prussian *Confession oder Kurtze und Einfältige Glaubensbekenntniss* of 1678 (Georg Hansen, elder of the Danzig Flemish congregation); *Glaubens-Bericht vor die Jugend* of 1671 (the first German publication of its sort) and *Erklärungen der Antworten* of 1678 (both also written by Georg Hansen); *Confession or Kurtzer und einfältiger Glaubens-Bericht der* (Danziger) *Alten Flämischen of 1768* (comprising the confession of 1730 and the catechism of 1768); the very popular Elbing catechism of 1778 of the Flemish elder Gerhard Wiebe (Elbing) and the Frisian elder Heinrich Donner (Orlofferfelde), *Kurtze und Einfältige Unterweisung,* which became the catechism of the Amish and, reprinted first at Waldeck (1797), was often called the "Waldeck catechism," with many German reprints for the Amish, four French editions, and many editions in America as well as many reprints in West Prussia and numerous reprints in Russia; the confession of Gerhard Wiebe (1792) and the new West Prussian of 1895. Gerrit Roosen's justly popular *Christliches Gemüthsgespräch* (Ratzeburg, 1702), which went out of use in Germany after 1838 but was widely used in America (14 German editions, 1769-1938, and 6 English editions, 1857-1941); attached to the *Gemüthsgespräch,* strangely enough, was the Prussian catechism of 1690, *Kurtze Unterweisung;* Leonhard Weydmann's *Christliche Lehre* (Monsheim, 1836, and Crefeld, 1852); Johannes Molenaar's *Katechismus der christlichen Lehre* (Leipzig, 1841); the *Christliches Lehrbüchlein* of the Verband (Heilbronn, 1865). (For a complete account of all German confessions and catechisms see the article on these topics in Vol. 1 of this ENCYCLOPEDIA.) The chief prayerbook (*q.v.*) was the *Ernsthafte Christenpflicht,* first published at Kaiserslautern in 1739, reprinted many times in Germany, 1753, 1781 (Pirmasens), 1787 (Herborn), 1796, 1816 (Zweibrücken), 1832 (Basel), 1837 (Zweibrücken), 1840 (Reinach), and 1852 (Regensburg), and many editions in America, largely used by the Amish. (For a fuller discussion of prayerbooks and devotional literature see Friedmann, *Mennonite Piety,* particularly the chapters "Mennonite Prayerbooks, Their Story and Meaning" and "The Devotional Literature of the Mennonites in Danzig and East Prussia.")

(5) The hymnbooks of the German Mennonites were basically few in number. In 1564 was published *Etliche schöne Christliche Geseng, wie sie in der Gefengkniss zu Passaw im Schloss von den Schweitzer Brüdern durch Gottes gnad geticht vnd gesungen worden.* About the same time, probably 1563/64, in the Lower Rhine area was published *Ein schön Gesangbüchlein Geistlicher Lieder, zusammen getragen auss dem Alten und Neuen Testament durch fromme Christen vnd Liebhaber Gottes,* reprinted

twice with additions, the third edition being made by Leenaerdt Clock. Since 1583 the first of these hymnals is the second part of the *Ausbund,* whereas a number of hymns of the second hymnal appear in the first part of the *Ausbund,* which has become the hymnal of the Amish (first edition with this title 1583, n.p., 2nd ed. 1622, n.p., with later editions probably all at Basel, last there in 1838). The first German hymnbook of the Prussian Mennonites (they had used Dutch hymnals before) was the *Geistreiches Gesangbuch* (*q.v.,* Königsberg, 1767), which went through 9 German editions, last at Elbing in 1843, and went on to long use in Russia, Manitoba, and Mexico where it is still being used. Meanwhile it was replaced in West Prussia by a new book, *Gesangbuch für Mennoniten-Gemeinden in Kirche und Haus* (1869, with its 5th ed. in 1922). The Danzig congregation had its own hymnal from 1780 on, also called *Geistreiches Gesangbuch,* displaced in 1854 by a new book called *Gesangbuch zur kirchlichen und häuslichen Erbauung,* reprinted in revised form in 1908. The Northwest German congregations long used Dutch Mennonite hymnals and then replaced them with modern state-church books. But the South Germans, after first using state-church hymnals, created their own hymnbooks. The first one, *Christliches Gesangbuch,* appeared at Worms in 1832, with a revised edition at Würzburg in 1839. The second and final one, *Gesangbuch zum gottesdienstlichen und häuslichen Gebrauch,* appeared at Worms in 1854, with new editions in 1876, 1910 (revised), and 1950. A separate book was published by the Amish in Hesse and neighboring areas at Wiesbaden in 1843 (reprint Regensburg, 1859), under the title *Gesangbuch zum Gebrauch bei dem öffentlichen Gottesdienst.* . . .

The hymns in all these books were largely taken from the older German treasury of hymns and chorales, with few additions of the late 19th-century "Gospel song" type (see **Hymnology**).

(4) The historical literature produced by the German Mennonites includes the following: Wilhelm Mannhardt, *Die Wehrfreiheit der Altpreussischen Mennoniten* (Marienburg, 1863); A. Brons, *Der Ursprung, Entwicklung und Schicksale der Taufgesinnten oder Mennoniten* (Norden, 1884, new ed. 1891 and 1912); Christian Hege, *Die Täufer in der Kurpfalz* (Frankfurt, 1908); Christine Hege, *Kurze Geschichte der Mennoniten* (Frankfurt, 1909); J. P. Müller, *Die Mennoniten in Ost-Friesland* (1881 and 1887); B. C. Roosen, *Geschichte der Mennoniten-Gemeinde zu Hamburg und Altona,* 2 vv. (Hamburg, 1886-87); J. t. Dornkaat Koolman, *Kurze Mitteilungen aus der Geschichte der Mennoniten-Gemeinden in Ostfriesland* (Norden, 1903); idem, *Mitteilungen . . . Gemeinde zu Norden* (Norden, 1904); E. Weydmann, *Geschichte der Mennoniten bis zum 18. Jahrhundert* (Neuwied, 1905); H. G. Mannhardt, *Die Danziger Mennonitengemeinde* (Danzig, 1919); L. Stobbe, *Montau-Gruppe* (Montau, 1918); E. Händiges, *Die Lehre der Mennoniten in Geschichte und Gegenwart* (Kaiserslautern, 1921); Chr. Neff, ed., *Gedenkschrift zum 400jährigen Jubiläum der Mennoniten* (Ludwigshafen, 1925); Chr. Hege, *Ein Rückblick auf 400 Jahre Mennonitischer*

Geschichte (Karlsruhe, 1935); W. Quiring, *Deutsche erschliessen den Chaco* (Karlsruhe, 1936); idem, *Russlanddeutsche suchen eine Heimat* (Karlsruhe, 1938); Horst Penner, *Ansiedlung Mennonitischer Niederländer im Weichsel-Mündungsgebiet* (Karlsruhe, 1940); idem, *Weltweite Bruderschaft, Ein mennonitisches Geschichtsbuch* (Karlsruhe, 1955); Herbert Wiebe, *Das Siedlungswerk niederländischer Mennoniten im Weichseltal* (Marburg, 1952); B. H. Unruh, *Die niederländisch-niederdeutschen Hintergründe der mennonitischen Ostwanderungen im 16., 18. und 19. Jahrhundert* (Karlsruhe, 1955). The greatest historical work of the German Mennonites has been the *Mennonitisches Lexikon* (1913-) edited by Christian Hege and Christian Neff, since 1947 by E. Crous (and H. S. Bender), now at the letter *R*. The publications of the Mennonitischer Geschichtsverein (founded 1933), edited by Christian Hege and since 1950 by Horst Quiring (*Mennonitische Geschichtsblätter* 1936-, and *Schriftenreihe des Mennonitischen Geschichtsvereins* 1938-) have been notable. The Mennonite Research Center at Göttingen, directed by Ernst Crous, was created by the MGV in 1948. The *Mennonitische Blätter* (1854-1941) carried much historical material. The *Gemeindeblatt der Mennoniten*, published since 1870 by the Verband, and the *Mennonitische Jugendwarte*, published by the Youth Commission of the South German Conference 1920-39, also contained some historical material. Much more has been contained in the *Christlicher* (now *Mennonitischer*) *Gemeinde-Kalender*, published since 1892 by the South German Conference. The *Mennonitisches Adressbuch* (Frankfurt, 1936) tried to give complete names and addresses of all Mennonites living in Germany in 1936, by congregations. H.S.B.

In addition to the titles in the section on literature above and the bibliographies under the various articles on subsections of Germany, the following should be noted: A. H. Newman, *A History of Anti-Pedobaptism ... to 1609* (Philadelphia, 1897); C. Henry Smith, *The Story of the Mennonites* (Berne, 1945); John Horsch, *Mennonites in Europe* (Scottdale, 1942); F. H. Littell, *The Anabaptist View of the Church* (1952); R. Friedmann, *Mennonite Piety Through the Centuries* (Goshen, 1949); H. S. Bender, "The Zwickau Prophets, Thomas Müntzer and the Anabaptists," *MQR* XVII (1953) 3-16; Wiswedel, *Bilder*; R. Dollinger, *Geschichte der Mennoniten in Schleswig-Holstein, Hamburg und Lübeck* (Neumünster, 1930); C. Krahn, *Menno Simons* (Karlsruhe, 1936); H. S. Bender and J. Horsch, *Menno Simons' Life and Writings* (Scottdale, 1936); Rembert, *Wiedertäufer*; P. Wappler, *Die Täuferbewegung in Thüringen* (Jena, 1913); Chr. Hege, "Early Anabaptists in Hesse," *MQR* V (1931) 157-78; C. Neff, "Mennonites of Germany, including Danzig and Poland," *MQR* XI (1937) 34-43; J. C. Wenger, "Life and Work of Pilgram Marpeck," *MQR* XII (1938) 137-66; idem, "Theology of Pilgram Marpeck," *ibid.* 205-56; R. Friedmann, "Spiritual Changes in European Mennonitism, 1650-1750," *MQR* XV (1941) 33-45; J. C. Wenger, "The Schleitheim Confession of Faith," *MQR* XIX (1945) 243-53; H. Penner, "Anabaptists and Mennonites of East Prussia," *MQR* XXII (1948) 212-25; E. Crous, "Mennonites in Germany since the Thirty Years' War," *MQR* XXV (1951) 235-62; D. Cattepoel, "Mennonites of Germany 1936-1948, and the Present Outlook," *MQR* XXIV (1950) 103-10; O. Wiebe, "Die Mennonitengemeinden in Nordwestdeutschland vor 10 Jahren und heute," *Gem.-Kal.* 1956, 34-42; *TA Württemberg; TA Hessen; TA Bayern* I and II; *ML* I, 422-29.

Gerobulus, Johannes (Dutch, *Outraadt*), b. 1540 at The Hague, d. there 1606, was a Dutch Reformed minister at Delft, Vlissingen, Deventer, Harder-wijk, and The Hague. In the fall of 1579 he held a dispute with representatives of a Mennonite congregation called the "footwashers," at Wester-Souburg near Vlissingen in the Dutch province of Zeeland. His principal opponent in the dispute was Hans de Ries (*q.v.*), who was at this time staying in Zeeland. (*Biogr. Wb.* III, 222-26; *DB* 1863, 112-13.) vDZ.

Gerolsheim, a village in the Palatinate, Germany, not far from Frankental, where the Mennonites were early found. Before the Thirty Years' War few clues can be found. A Jakob Raab of Ginsheim settled here; on Dec. 9, 1581, he renounced his faith and presented his four unbaptized children for baptism (Hege, 137). It can safely be assumed that there were Anabaptists in Gerolsheim at that time, for there were many in the vicinity. Through persecution by the government and the horrors of the Thirty Years' War most of them perished. Two families may have survived, who are mentioned in the first list of Mennonites of the Karlsruhe *Generallandesarchiv* of 1664—Heinrich and Julius Cassel. Their origin is not known. The former was a Mennonite preacher (see **Cassel, Heinrich**). In 1685 and 1697 the lists name eight Mennonite families in Gerolsheim. The village belonged to the Barons of Dalsberg. Therefore the Mennonites were excused from the payment of protection fees in 1700-59. In the list of 1759 the following are mentioned: Peter Schmid, a son and three daughters; Jakob Peters' (?) widow, a son and two daughters; Jakob Hirschler, three sons and four daughters; Ulrich Borckholder, three sons and three daughters; and Christian Müller's widow, a daughter. The Mennonites of Gerolsheim had merged with those at Heppenheim an der Wiese (*q.v.*) and Obersülzen (*q.v.*) in a single congregation. Services were held in succession in these places, in Gerolsheim in a hall furnished for the purpose and later in a chapel, the property of Preacher David Kaegy of Bolanderhof. After the erection of the church in Obersülzen (1868) services were no longer held in Gerolsheim.

After 1702 Hans Burkholder (*q.v.*) served the congregation as preacher until his death in 1752. In 1758-82 Jakob Hirschler was elder, followed by Johannes Lehmann. The Mennonites living in Dirmstein (*q.v.*) and Offstein (*q.v.*) worshiped with this congregation, which in 1732 consisted of 40 families (Müller, *Berner Täufer*, 211). In 1833-54 Johann Borkholder was their preacher. According to Frey the Mennonites in Gerolsheim numbered 32 souls in 1806 and 36 in 1834. In 1845 the families of Heinrich Burkholder, Stefan Göbels, Johann Schowalter, Johannes Schowalter, Jakob Suter's widow, Jakob Burkholder, and Stefan Hirschler were living there. A memorandum by David Kaegy (Offstein) says: "House, barn, stable, yard (*Hof*), and garden in Gerolsheim I gave my daughter Barbara and her husband on Aug. 3, 1843. But since the Mennonite congregation has the upper room for a place of meeting, even if the congregation no longer wishes to use it and the owner himself uses it, the owner must pay the congregation 100 guilders and give up the chairs, stoves, table, and benches in the upper room and the smaller room without remuneration. The furniture belongs to the congregation."—In 1926 there were two families left—Schowalter and Suter.

NEFF.

The Mennonite archives at Amsterdam contain about 80 letters written by Gerolsheim Mennonites to the Amsterdam congregation, specifically to the secretary of the Fonds voor Buitenlandsche Nooden (*q.v.*) (*Inv. Arch. Amst.* I, Nos. 1420, 1422, 1454-67, 1474-75, 1483-1537, 1539-41, 1547-48, 1550; II, Nos. 687, 690). The first of these letters is dated Sept. 28, 1689 (written by Heinrich Cassel); the last is dated July 12, 1783. These letters, containing much information on the coming of the Swiss Brethren to Gerolsheim and the Palatinate, are very valuable for the light they throw on the social and political conditions of the Palatine Mennonites in the 18th century. The letters also contain information on the Gerolsheim congregation and its preachers. In 1730 the congregation was obliged to pay a fee of 1,500 guilders for the coronation of the new elector (in addition to their regular poll tax). In 1741 the elector doubled the poll tax. In 1744-45 they were disturbed by the French, English, and Austrian armies. In 1744 there was also much trouble with the government; they were not permitted to bury their dead in the cemeteries, and their marriages were hindered. Many wanted to emigrate to the Netherlands or to Pennsylvania. In 1744 they were afraid they would be expelled from the country. In 1744 also they wrote that they had vainly appealed to the mercy of Lord Dalensberg, to whom Gerolsheim had been allotted. There were troubles within the congregation. The Amish, who boasted of their *Feinheit*, were (1744) intolerant and merciless toward Hans Burckholder and his followers, who were *ziemlich grob* (less strict), Rudolf Egli was a spendthrift, and Hans Landis, who had gone to Holland to collect money, was a deceiver. Christian Burckholder, the son of Hans (1764) and deacon of the Gerolsheim congregation, had embezzled the poor-funds and retained for private use the contributions sent by Amsterdam in 1762-63, and had been dismissed and banned. Christian himself wrote on Feb. 27, 1765, a letter of regret and repentance to Amsterdam. The Committee for Foreign Needs at Amsterdam gave financial aid a number of times. It contributed to relief for losses from rinderpest, crop failure, flood, fire, and sickness. On Oct. 7, 1776, Jakob Hirschler wrote that the meetinghouse built about a century ago had been severely damaged by a storm, and that they wanted to have a new one built. The Gerolsheim congregation, he wrote, had 32 families and 100 members; he asked for financial aid, which was given. In 1783 Amsterdam also contributed to a new meetinghouse built in Heppenheim. Most of these letters were written by Heinrich Cassel (2), Hans Burckholder (49), Christian Burckholder (13), and Jakob Hirschler (4), who also signed a number written by Hans and Christian Burckholder.   vDZ.

Müller, *Berner Täufer;* Frey, *Versuch einer geographisch-historisch-statistischen Beschreibung des königli-*

chen bayerischen Rheinkreises (Speyer, 1836); **Chr. Hege,** *Die Täufer in der Kurpfalz* (Frankfurt, 1908); *ML* II, 81.

Gerrets, Vrou, van Medenblick (Medemblik, Dutch province of North Holland), composed a small songbook, *Een nieu Gheestelijck Liedtboecxken,* of which there were three editions—1607, 1609, and 1621. (*Catalogus Amst.,* 270.)   vDZ.

Gerretsz, Claes, a book printer at Amsterdam, who published some of the works of Dirk Volkertsz Coornhert (*q.v.*) and Sebastian Franck (*q.v.*), and also reprinted Melchior Hofmann's *Die Ordonnantie Godts* in 1611. (*BRN* V, 134 f.)   vDZ.

Gerrit van Benschop (Gheryt Ghijsen, or Gheryt van Wou), a Dutch Anabaptist leader in 1534-35; in his home town of Benschop (Dutch province of Utrecht) his influence was so great that Benschop became an Anabaptist center. Here and in other towns he baptized a large number of persons. Whether he was infected with the revolutionary principles of Münsterism (*q.v.*) and by his activities responsible for the revolts at Hazerswoude (*q.v.*) and Poeldijk (*q.v.*), is not quite clear. In February 1535 he stayed at Amsterdam and joined the group of Anabaptists who walked naked along the streets (see **Naaktlopers**). During this event he was taken prisoner and beheaded at Amsterdam on Feb. 25, 1535.   vDZ.

DB 1917, 11, No. 22; Grosheide, *Verhooren,* 57-58; Mellink, *Wederdopers,* see Index.

Gerrit Boeckbinder (Geryt boeckebinder van Nyewenhuys), identical with Gerrit thom Closter, a Dutch Anabaptist leader. In the fall of 1533 he was sent from Amsterdam to Münster by Jan Matthysz (*q.v.*). He belonged to the revolutionary wing of Anabaptism, stayed for some time in Münster (*q.v.*), but came back to Amsterdam. Here and at other places he baptized. Probably he was put to death at The Hague on Feb. 15, 1535. (*DB* 1909, 11; 1917, 80, 100, No. 4; Mellink, *Wederdopers,* see Index.)   vDZ.

Gerrit van Byler, a Dutch Anabaptist imprisoned in London. The *Martyrs' Mirror* contains an excerpt from a letter written by Gerrit van Byler in September 1575 in the Newgate prison in London, which his son Jan handed to van Braght. In it van Byler related that as the congregation was assembled at Easter in a suburb of London it was surprised and 20 members imprisoned. He recounted his trial under "His Majesty's bishop." "Day after day they announced our execution, by hanging and burning; but the Lord strengthened us, to His name be praise." Having heard that Hendrik and Jan were "led to the slaughter," he quoted a few songs, and closed with the words (in Latin), "My hope is in God." Concerning the fate of these Anabaptists, two of them, Hendrik Terwoert and Jan Pietersz, were burned at the stake in Smithfield on July 22, 1576; one of them died in prison, fourteen women were expelled from the city, a young man was whipped, and two, including van Byler, were discharged "after enduring much misery."

These Anabaptists had fled to England from Flanders because of "severe tribulation and small opportunity for making a living." (*Mart. Mir.* D 604-98, E 1008-12, 1022-24; *ML* I, 314.) vDZ.

Gerrit van Cempen, an Anabaptist martyr: see **Kempen, Gerhard von.**

Gerrit (Gheryt) **Claesz,** from Oude-Niedorp, Dutch province of North Holland, an Anabaptist martyr, was beheaded at Amsterdam on May 15, 1535, together with Adriaen Cornelis and Jan Jacobsz. He had been (re)baptized at "de Rijp binnen Oude Nyerop" in March 1534 but did not know the man who baptized him. The sentence is found in van Braght, *Martyrs' Mirror*. (*Mart. Mir.* D 412, E 764; Grosheide, *Verhooren,* 70-72; *ML* I, 359.) vDZ.

Gerrit Cornelisz (Boon), an Anabaptist martyr, a young boatman and a citizen of Amsterdam, was imprisoned because he "was unmindful of his soul's salvation and the obedience which he owed our mother the holy church and to his imperial majesty, as his natural lord and prince, rejecting the ordinances of the holy church, has been neither to confession nor to the holy sacrament for ten years past, and has further dared repeatedly to go into the assembly of the reprobated sect of the Mennonites or Anabaptists, and has also eight years ago, renouncing and forsaking the baptism received by him in infancy from the holy Church, been rebaptized and afterward repeatedly received the breaking of bread according to the manner of the aforesaid sect, and also attended the assembly," as his sentence of death reads (*Mart. Mir.* D 540, E 876). The most brutal persecutions he endured steadfastly; he would not betray his brethren. On June 26, 1571, he was executed by burning. At the stake he prayed the moving prayer, "O Father and Lord, be gracious unto me, let me be one of the least of Thy least lambs or the least member of Thy body! O Lord, who lookest down here from on high and art a discerner of the hearts and of every hidden thing, before whom all things are to be accounted as nothing, Thou knowest my simple love towards Thee, accept me and forgive them that inflict this suffering upon me." A song on his martyrdom is found in *Het Offer des Heeren* and begins "Als men duysent vijfhondert heeft ghe-schreven en eenentseventig Jaer." (*Offer,* 654-58; Wolkan, *Lieder,* 69; *ML* I, 371.) Neff.

Gerrit Dirksz (Gerrit Wevers or Gerrit the Weaver), an Anabaptist martyr, was sentenced to death at Amsterdam on Jan. 16, 1553. He was a native of "Raesdorp," probably a town in Münsterland, Germany, rather than Ransdorp near Amsterdam. He had been (re)baptized and confessed that he had heard Gillis van Aken preach twice. Because he recanted he was not burned at the stake, but beheaded. (Grosheide, *Bijdrage,* 162, 309.) vDZ.

Gerrit Ghijsen: see **Gerrit van Benschop.**

Gerrit van Grol (Geert van Grolle), a Dutch Anabaptist, burned at the stake at Antwerp in 1538 (exact date unknown). He was arrested in March 1538 and tried in the same month. His confession reveals interesting particulars about Anabaptism in Amsterdam, especially on the *Naaktlopers* (*q.v.*) and the uprising of May 1535. From this confession on April 17, 1538, we learn the difference between peaceful and revolutionary Anabaptism. Gerrit van Grol belonged to the peaceful group. He had been (re)baptized in Amsterdam by Jan Matthysz. vDZ.

Inv. Arch. Amst. I, Nos. 192, 193; *DB* 1919, 171-72; *Antw. Arch.-Blad* VII, 39; XIV, 16-17, No. 166.

Gerrit Hazenpoet (Hasepoot), an Anabaptist martyr, a tailor, was burned at the stake at Nijmegen, Dutch province of Gelderland in 1557, exact date unknown (not 1556 as van Braght, *Mart. Mir.,* states). When, after torture, he was sentenced to die, "his wife came to him . . . to speak with him once more, and to take leave and to bid her husband farewell. She had in her arm an infant, which she could scarcely hold, because of her great grief. When wine was poured out to him, as is customary to do for those sentenced to death, he said to his wife, 'I have no desire for this wine; but I hope to drink the new wine, which will be given me in the kingdom of my Father.' Thus the two separated with great grief . . . ; for the woman could hardly stand on her feet any longer, but seemed to fall into a swoon through grief. When he was led to death and having been brought from the wagon upon the scaffold, he lifted up his voice and sang the hymn, 'Oorlof aen Broeders en Sisters gemeen' (Farewell to all brethren and sisters). Whereupon he fell on his knees, and fervently prayed to God. Having been placed at the stake, he kicked his slippers from his feet, saying, 'It were a pity to burn them, for they can be of service still to some poor person.' The rope with which he was to be strangled, becoming a little loose, having not been twisted well by the executioner, he again lifted up his voice, and sang the end of said hymn." Neff.

Mart. Mir. D 173, E 560; *DB* 1874, 3; P. C. G. Guyot, *Bijdragen tot de Gesch. der Doopsgez. te Nijmegen* (Nijmegen, 1845) 19-23; *ML* II, 263.

Gerrit Jan Mickers, an Anabaptist martyr who, according to an account found in a list in *Inv. Arch. Amst.* I, 748, was beheaded at Alkmaar, Dutch province of North Holland in February 1538, because he had been (re)baptized. But this must be an error; the person meant is the martyr Guert Jans Mickers, beheaded because she had been (re)baptized at Alkmaar on Feb. 6, 1538. (Mellink, *Wederdopers,* 173.) vDZ.

Gerrit (or Gheraert) **Janssen Duynherder,** an Anabaptist martyr, born at Tongherloo in Brabant, was burned at the stake with Hendrik Alewijns (*q.v.*) and Hans Marijns (*q.v.*) on Feb. 9, 1569, on the square at Middelburg in Zeeland after being strangled. He was seized one night at Souburg, not far from Middelburg, and was severely racked on Sept. 14, 1568. He was about 50 years old. Neff, vDZ.

Mart. Mir. D 389, E 742, 758; *DB* 1908, 16; K. R. Pekelharing, *Bijdr. tot de Gesch. der Hervorming in*

Zeeland (Archives VI of the *Zeeuwsch Genootschap,* Middelburg, 1866) 77, 85-86; *ML* I, 497.

Gerrit van Mandel, an Anabaptist martyr: see **Gerrit Vermandele.**

Gerrit Siebenacker, of Sittart near Maastricht, now Dutch province of Limburg, the otherwise unknown author of the hymn, "Gnad und Fried vom Herren," which bears his name in acrostics. (Rembert, *Wiedertäufer,* 494; Wolkan, *Lieder,* 100.)

Gerrit (Gheert) **Vermandele** (van Mandel), an Anabaptist martyr, was burned at the stake in Antwerp on March 30, 1569, together with Willem de Clercq and Pieter Verlonge. He was a weaver, originally from Kortrijk, Flanders, 26 years of age; he lived for a number of years at Borgerhout near Antwerp; he had been (re)baptized four years before by Hendrik van Arnhem (*q.v.*) in a wood near Antwerp. He and his companions were arrested while holding a meeting in the house of Jan Poote (*q.v.*) at Borgerhout. Gerrit refused to give details about the congregation. He remained steadfast in his faith and died faithfully.   vDZ.

Mart. Mir. D 415, E 766; *Antw. Arch.-Blad* XII, 341, 369, 393, 439; XIV, 64-65, No. 713; *ML* III, 11.

Gerrits (Geerts, Gerts, Gertz, Gerzen, Goertz, Goerz, Görtz, Görz), a Mennonite family name: see **Goerz** and **Görz.**

Gerrits, Brixius, an elder in the Flemish Mennonite church in Groningen in 1566 (Vos, 257), a learned man versed in Latin, Greek, and Hebrew, and well-informed in other fields of knowledge, worked with Peter of Cologne (*q.v.*) with great zeal for the unification of the Flemish and Frisian branches of Mennonites. Together they took part in the conference in Emden in 1578 to ratify the "Humster Peace," and then signed the Flemish peace proposal to the Frisians, April 2, 1578 (*Menn. Bl.* 1858, 28). Together they also took a prominent part in the great disputation in Emden (*q.v.*) that lasted from Feb. 27 to May 17, 1578. In 1583 Brixius was expelled from the city of Groningen by the Catholic government. In 1589 he was again summoned to arbitrate difficulties among the Flemish and for this purpose traveled to Haarlem. The difficulty in question was the Huiskoper (*q.v.*) dispute concerning a house purchased in Franeker in 1586, which resulted in the division into two groups; viz., the Zachte (mild) Flemish or Contrahuiskopers, and the Old Flemish or Huiskopers. Not long afterward he, who had formerly represented the very blunt, conservative view, was banned by his own church for his lenience, and joined the Frisians.

A letter from Brixius Gerrits, with signatures also by Hans Busschaert, (Paul) Backer, and Christiaen Adriaensz, "written to his dear Brethren of the Church of God in Prussia, together with its elders and preachers," written at Harlingen on Oct. 9, 1578, is included by J. de Buyser in his *Christelijck Huysboek* (pp. 344-47).   NEFF.

K. Vos, *Menno Simons* (Leiden, 1914) 257, 307; *Menn. Bl.,* 1858, 28; *ML* I, 271; *Inv. Arch. Amst.* I, 470, 473, 477b, 558 IIIb; Blaupot t. C., *Groningen* I, 55, 81, 275, 295.

Gerrits van Emden, Jan, b. April 30, 1561, probably at Emden, was of a serious nature from his early youth; at the age of 36 he was made preacher of the congregation at Appingedam (*q.v.*). Nine years later, driven away by the Spanish war, he settled in Haarlem, where he again preached. His service there was saddened by strife in the congregation, which he vainly attempted to settle. He then undertook a journey to the Prussian and Austrian congregations in Moravia. In 1607 he was appointed as preacher of the United Frisians, High Germans, and Waterlanders at Danzig, and about 1612 became elder at Marcushof, serving with great blessing to Danzig and the neighboring churches until his death on April 7, 1617. During his eldership the Polish Brethren or Socinians (*q.v.*) of Danzig, whose leader was Ulrich Pius Herwart, caused him much concern. They tried to merge with the congregation of Jan Gerrits, but the Mennonites, who rejected Socinian doctrines, tried to keep aloof; Jan Gerrits wrote a number of letters to the Dutch Waterlander leader Hans de Ries, asking his advice and requesting him to come over to Danzig to aid them in the disputes with the Socinians, which de Ries, however, declined to do. After his death some books and two letters were published, *Vijf stichtelijcke predicatien* (1st ed. lost; 2nd Amsterdam, 1650). One of the letters is addressed to all his children, the other to his oldest son in Haarlem. "Both letters are full of fatherly, sincere, and emphatic words of comfort." His sermons testify to a zeal to win souls to Christ by God's grace; they deal exclusively with eternal ruin of man and the saving grace of God, based solely on the sacrificial death of Christ. He is also thought to have been the author of *Stichtelijke Gebeden en Meditatien, dewelke mede ter zee gebruikt kunnen worden* (n.p., n.d.), which others ascribe to Hans de Ries, and of *Een Vermaen-Boeckjen . . . met 42 Schriftuurlycke Liedekens* (Amsterdam, 1641, 2d ed. 1648, 3d ed. 1655), of which also Jan Gerrits (*q.v.*), the old Flemish minister of Amsterdam, is said to have been the author.

In the 1650 edition of his sermons and letters three other sermons besides a very interesting formulary for baptism and communion, and several inspirational prayers of unknown authorship have been added. With all his simplicity of spirit he was not hostile to science. Thus, though uneducated, he knew the German and Latin languages in addition to his native Dutch.   NEFF.

BRN VII, 190-91; *Inv. Arch. Amst.* I, No. 472; II, Nos. 2624 f., 2925-27, 2931-35; II, 2, No. 691; *Biogr. Wb.* III, 227; *Menn. Bl.,* 1860, 12; 1904, 3; Schijn-Maatschoen, *Uitvoeriger Verhandeling,* . . . III, 42 ff.; Kühler, *Geschiedenis* II, 53-54; idem, *Het Socinianisme in Nederland* (Leiden, 1912) 106-08; *ML* II, 83.

Gerrits, Jan, a preacher of the congregation at Uithoorn (*q.v.*), Dutch province of North Holland. He and E. A. van Dooregeest were in the group delegated by the Zonists (*q.v.*) to negotiate with the Lamists in 1688 with the view of uniting the two groups. The negotiations, however, failed. (*Inv. Arch. Amst.* I, Nos. 424, 26.) vDZ.

Gerrits, Jan, in the first half of the 17th century a preacher of the Uckowallists (Groningen Old Flemish) in Amsterdam, who had separated from the Flemish at Groningen in 1637. He was one of the speakers on the side of Jan Luies in the debate against Pieter Jansz Twisck at Hoorn in 1622. In 1641 he published *Een spieghel des gheloofs,* in which is found a Confession of the Groningen Old Flemish, and in 1641 also *Een Vermaen-boeckjen* (which some scholars attribute to Jan Gerrits van Emden, *q.v.*). (*Biogr. Wb.* III, 226; *DB* 1876, 39; *ML* II, 83.) K.V.

Gerrits, Tijs (or Thijs) (d. Dec. 15, 1601), one of the outstanding leaders of the *Harde* (Strict) Frisian Mennonites in the Netherlands, who separated in 1589 from the *Zachte* (Mild) Frisians (under the leadership of Lubbert Gerritsz, *q.v.*). In 1587 he was a preacher at Hoorn, later elder at Medemblik. He originated the expression, "Shall we allow ourselves to be governed by the congregation?" He accompanied Elder Jan Jacobsz (*q.v.*) on his journeys to the North Sea islands and to Groningen. In 1599 when a quarrel arose among these strict Frisians between Jan Jacobsz and Pieter Jeltjes, Tijs Gerrits took the side of the Jan Jacobsgezinden. But about 1601 a new quarrel within the Jan-Jacobsgezinden group caused Tijs Gerrits and his adherents to separate from Jan Jacobsz and his followers. Gerrits's followers were called the T(h)ijs-Gerritsvolk. K.V.

Inv. Arch. Amst. I, 478; *DB* 1876, 30; 1893, 80 f.; J. Loosjes, "Jan Jacobsz en de Jan-Jacobsgezinden," in *Ned. Archief vor Kerkgeschiedenis* XI (The Hague, 1914) 189 f.; *ML* II, 84.

Gerritsz, Dirk (1565-1626), a Mennonite preacher of the Frisian congregation in Wormerveer (*q.v.*), Dutch province of North Holland, for many years. After his death a volume of his writings was published, containing two devotional tracts and a number of songs. The (abridged) title reads as follows: *Twee corte vermaen brieven . . . aen sijn Kinderen, met drie Schriftuerlijcke Liedekens* (Hoorn, 1629). He must have been a capable and very influential leader far beyond his home church. By trade he was a merchant. Of his six sons two were deacons and two preachers of the Wormerveer Frisian congregation. His youngest son was Oom Jacob Dirksz (*q.v.*). (*Biogr. Wb.* III, 226-27; *Catalogus Amst.,* 228, 272.) vDZ.

Gerritsz, Lubbert (official family name *Yserman*), a Dutch Mennonite leader in the second half of the 16th century, characterized by his tolerance, the good friend and co-worker of Hans de Ries, with whom he composed the Waterlander confession of faith which was published at Alkmaar in 1610. He was born at Amersfoort, Dutch province of Utrecht, in 1534; by trade he was a weaver. About 1556 he was converted to the Mennonite principles and soon played a role in the small

Amersfoort congregation. In 1559, when persecution arose in this town, he fled to Hoorn, Dutch province of North Holland, where he was ordained in the same year as elder by Dirk Philips. He was one of the delegates appointed in 1567 to arbitrate the difficulties that had arisen in Friesland which occasioned the great schism between the Frisians and the Flemish. His congregation being on the Frisian side, he became the minister of the Frisian congregation at Hoorn. Attempts at reconciliation were futile. On the questions of the ban, avoidance in marriage, and mixed marriages he took the more lenient position. A peace conference in 1578 failed. The stricter views predominated, and he was banned. In 1589 he became the leader of the more lenient (*Jonge*) Frisians at Amsterdam. Here he published *Verantwoordinghe op die seven Artyckelen.* The "Jonge" Frisians in 1591 united with the High Germans, and two years later with the Waterlanders. In 1597 the Reformed Church tried to force him to take part in a disputation; but the mayor Hooft intervened. In 1604 he made another attempt to unite the Flemish and Frisians by writing an epistle to the elders of the Flemish. He died at Amsterdam on Jan. 12, 1612. Anthoni Jacobsz Roscius (*q.v.*), physician and preacher at Hoorn, and Lambert Jacobsz (*q.v.*), the well-known painter and preacher at Leeuwarden, were his grandsons.

Besides the above *Verantwoordinghe* Lubbert Gerritsz published the following writings: *Sommige andachtighe ende leerachtige gheestelicke Liedekens ende Psalmen Davids,* followed by two letters to the *Gemeente Godts in Pruissen* (Amsterdam 1597, 5th ed. 1649); *Sommige Christelijcke sendt-brieven, ghesonden aen diverse particuliere personen . . .* (Amsterdam 1599, reprinted 1611 and 1646). In these reprints are also found *Vier brieven ende een Tractaet van de Uytterlijcke Kercke.* His portrait, painted 1607 by Michiel J. Mierevelt (*q.v.*) or his co-workers, is now found in the *Rijksmuseum* at Amsterdam. Joost van den Vondel (*q.v.*) dedicated a laudatory poem to him.† K.V., vDZ.

Inv. Arch. Amst. I, Nos. 483, 486-88, 504, 510, 524, 528-31, 641; II, Nos. 1194-96, 1359, 1362, 1366; Schijn-Maatschoen, *Aanhangsel . . .* (Amsterdam, 1745) 1-41; *Biogr. Wb.* III, 227-29; *DB* 1864, 23 ff.; 1872, 59; 1876, 30 ff.; *BRN* VII, 62 ff.; Kühler, *Geschiedenis* I, *passim*; *Winkler Prins Encyclopedie* IX, 417 (Amsterdam, 1950); *ML* II, 83 f.

Gerryt mitten Baerde, an Anabaptist leader, who preached at a meeting in June 1533 at Alkmaar, Dutch province of North Holland, and explained the Scriptures from eight o'clock in the morning till four or five o'clock in the afternoon, is likely identical with Gerrit Boeckbinder (*q.v.*). (*DB* 1909, 11.) vDZ.

Gerryt Jansz and his brother Herman Jans (*q.v.*) were beheaded on Oct. 24, 1536, at Leeuwarden, Dutch province of Friesland, because they had lodged Menno Simons in their home. vDZ.

Inv. Arch. Amst. I, No. 747; *DB* 1864, 135, note; 1906, 3; K. Vos, *Menno Simons* (Leiden, 1914) 230.

Gerspitz, a village in Moravia near Austerlitz (*Slavkov*) with a Hutterite Bruderhof. It belonged to the feudal estate of Ulrich von Kaunitz, who caused the Anabaptists severe oppression. He made them responsible for economic losses he suffered, took away their grain and cattle, deprived weavers, barbers, and tailors of their trade, so that the Anabaptists threatened to emigrate. A large part of them actually left in the summer of 1603. Those who remained suffered severe loss during the Bohemian revolt. The Chronicles report, "On Dec. 29, 1620, early in the morning before dawn, the Bruderhof at Austerlitz and Gerspitz was unexpectedly attacked by several hundred horsemen who hastily plundered the place; many brethren, sisters, and children ran into the pond, which was not yet frozen over, and two sisters and a child were drowned. The next year, on Feb. 2, Poles attacked Gerspitz, shooting the housekeeper and burning the gardener." LOSERTH.

Wolkan, *Geschicht-Buch,* 405, 407, 469, 541, 556 f.; Beck, *Geschichts-Bücher,* 335; Wolny, *Die Markgrafschaft Mähren* II, 1, 157; *ML* II, 84.

Gerstungen, a town (pop. 3,433) in the Thuringian Forest, Germany, 11 miles west of Eisenach on the Werra. It is frequently mentioned in the history of the Thuringian Anabaptist movement. The earliest mention is made in 1527. Here Anabaptist doctrine was rather widely spread, for the town was under the jurisdiction of Saxony and Hesse, and the pastor, as Justus Menius stated in his church inspection report of June 25, 1533, to the young Elector John Frederick, "together with the vicar at Herda will not accept correction in the matter of impropriety and disorderly conduct, but always refer to the Hessian church inspection whenever it serves their purpose." On May 1, 1533, Margarethe Koch, who had been imprisoned at the same time as Fritz Erbe (*q.v.*) in the Wartburg, was cross-examined by the parsons Conrad Buchbach at Gerstungen and Martin Berstadt of Berka; she declared her opposition to infant baptism and the bodily presence of Christ in the communion emblems. Christina Strobel or Helwig, who was executed by drowning at Mühlhausen Nov. 8, 1537, was also imprisoned in Gerstungen. A violent opponent of the Anabaptists was the tax commissar Wolf Blümlein of Gerstungen; in a trial of Anabaptists in 1544, he joined Justus Menius in demanding the death penalty for seven steadfast Anabaptists. It was, however, never carried out, for Philip of Hesse refused to give his consent. A church inspection conducted by Menius in January 1544 found 50 persons in Gerstungen who did not go to church or take part in communion services, "out of sheer carelessness or hostility, or because they have been waiting to learn of a council." They, however, promised to fulfill the requirements of the church. HEGE.

G. L. Schmidt, *Justus Menius, der Reformator Thüringens* (Gotha, 1867); P. Wappler, *Die Stellung Kursachsens und des Landgrafen Philipp von Hessen zur Täuferbewegung* (Münster, 1910); *idem, Die Täuferbewegung in Thüringen* (Jena, 1913); *ML* II, 84.

Geryt (Gheryt) **van Campen,** a physician from Kampen, Dutch province of Overijssel, belonged to the revolutionary wing of Anabaptism and being involved in the Münsterite revolt was sentenced to death by the sheriff at Amsterdam on May 8, 1534. (*Inv. Arch. Amst.* I, 744 f.; Grosheide, *Verhooren,* 226.)   vDZ.

Geryt Jansz, of Amsterdam, Anabaptist who was sentenced to death by the Court of Holland because of involvement in the Münsterite uprising and beheaded at The Hague on Feb. 15, 1535. (*Inv. Arch. Amst.* I, Nos. 744 f.; Grosheide, *Bijdrage,* 303.)   vDZ.

Geryt Meynerts, a goldsmith of Amsterdam, was one of the first Anabaptists in the Netherlands. He was charged with *lutherie* (heresy) and rebaptism, and although he recanted he was sentenced at The Hague on Dec. 5, 1531, together with Jan Volkertsz Trypmaker (*q.v.*) and other Anabaptists. (*DB* 1917, 159.)   vDZ.

Gesangbuch, Christliches, *zunächst für den Gebrauch der Taufgesinnten in der Pfalz,* published at Worms, Germany, in 1832, contains 383 hymns with notes. It was soon replaced by a larger book, entitled *Gesangbuch zum Gottesdienstlichen und Häuslichen Gebrauch in den Evangelischen Mennoniten-Gemeinden* (Worms, 1856), which contained 600 hymns with notes. However, a modified reissue of the 1832 volume was made in 1839 at Würzburg under the title, *Gesangbuch, Christliches, zunächst für Mennoniten zum Gebrauch beim öffentlichen Gottesdienste und bei häuslichen Andachtsübungen* (Herausgegeben von der Mennoniten-Brüder-Gemeinschaft in Unterfranken des Königreichs Bayern).   vDZ.

Gesangbuch *zum gottesdienstlichen und häuslichen Gebrauch in Evangelischen Mennoniten-Gemeinden* (Worms, 1856) is the hymnbook of the conference of South German Mennonites which was prepared with the co-operation of A. Knapp. A second edition followed in 1876. The third edition was revised and appeared with 575 hymns, both with and without four-part music (Ludwigshafen, 1910); a fourth revised edition appeared in 1950 at Ludwigshafen.

In 1873 the General Conference Mennonite Church of North America reprinted the songbook adding 22 songs and dropping the word "Evangelischen" in the title and the appendixes. In 1890 a considerably revised edition of this book was published under the title, *Gesangbuch mit Noten,* which experienced 15 editions (50,000 copies) between 1890 and 1936, when it was replaced by the present *Gesangbuch der Mennoniten* (1942) and English hymnals. (See also **Hymnology.**)   C.K.

Gesangbuch zur kirchlichen *und häuslichen Erbauung für Mennoniten Gemeinden* (Danzig, 1854) was the second German hymnal of the Danzig Mennonite Church, replacing the *Geistreiches Gesangbuch* (*q.v.*) of 1780. Containing 702 hymns, it was replaced by a revised edition in 1908 with only 445 hymns. (See **Hymnology** *of the Mennonites of Prussia and Russia.*)

Gesangbuch für Mennonitengemeinden in Kirche und Haus was the second German songbook of the Mennonite churches of West Prussia, published in 1869 to replace the *Gesangbuch, in welchem eine Sammlung . . . (q.v.)* and the original *Geistreiches Gesangbuch . . . (q.v.)*. The book had 700 hymns, a collection of prayers, and indexes to which in the fourth edition (1901) were added 40 religious folk songs and Psalms of the Prussian Mennonite *Choralbuch*, published in 1898. This songbook was widely used among the Mennonites of Russia and America. The first three editions (Danzig 1869 and 1873, Elbing 1888) consisted of 8,000 copies and the fourth (Gütersloh 1901) and fifth (1922, n.p.) of 6,000 copies.

Gesangbüchlein Geistlicher Lieder, *Eine schön* (n.p., n.d.-*ca.* 1563/64) was the hymnal of the Lower Rhine Anabaptists, appearing at the same time as the first edition of the *Ausbund* (1564), the hymnal of the Swiss Brethren. Two later enlarged editions appeared—(1) with 133 hymns after 1569 and (2) with 140 hymns *ca.* 1590. (See **Hymnology of the Anabaptists.**) H.S.B.

Gesangh-Boeck: see **Ghesangen, Het Boeck der.**

Gesangh-Boeck *van Hans de Ries,* a Dutch Mennonite hymnal: see **Hans de Ries.** *Gesanghboek of Gesanghen, om op alle feestdagen voor en na de predicatie in de Vergadering te singhen,* a Mennonite hymnbook, two volumes in the Dutch language, printed at Hamburg, Germany, in 1685 and used in the Flemish congregation of this town. (*DJ* 1837, 65.) vDZ.

Geschicht-Buch: see **Chronicles, Hutterite.†**

Geschichte der Bernischen Täufer *nach den Urkunden dargestellt* (Frauenfeld, 1895, 411 pages) by Ernst Müller, a Swiss Reformed pastor in Langnau, Emmental, Switzerland, is a most valuable historical work on the Bernese Anabaptists, which led in part to the honorary doctor's degree for its author in 1904 from the University of Jena. The spirit of the author is well communicated by his preface, in which he says, "The justification of this work lies in the fact that this section of Swiss church history has never before been treated, and therefore a gap will be filled, not only in this field, but also in the history of that great spiritual movement of the Reformation known as Anabaptism. . . . This is a martyr church, which has its justification and its strength in its history. The willingness to sacrifice and the dedication to ideal values which those manifested who suffered for their faith deserves to be snatched from the forgotten past as a monument to the character of this people."

In 20 thoroughly scholarly chapters, based on primary sources, the author traces the Bernese Anabaptists from the canton of Bern in 1525 to the early 19th century in North America. The first 90 pages are occupied with the 16th-century movement in Bern, followed by a short chapter on Bernese Anabaptists in Moravia and Russia (Hutterites). The major section of the book, pp. 104-313, is devoted largely to the persecution of the Anabaptists-Mennonites by the Bernese authorities and their emigration to Basel, Alsace, Palatinate, Holland, and Pennsylvania. Further chapters treat the Amish division, the fate of the Swiss in Holland, Prussia, and Neuenburg, the Anabaptist hunters (*Täuferjäger*), the Swiss Mennonites in North America, and a brief account of the Bernese Mennonites in their native canton in the 19th century.

The author is remarkably objective and sympathetic. He does not spare his own church and government. A valuable feature of the book is its exploitation of the rich materials in the Amsterdam Mennonite Archives on the Swiss and Palatine Mennonites of the years from 1650 to 1750. (*ML* III, 176.) H.S.B.

Geschichte der Märtyrer *oder kurze historische Nachricht von den Verfolgungen der Mennoniten* (printed by G. L. Hartung, Königsberg, 1787). The preface (31 pages) was written in 1782. Although the author and compiler of this abridged history of the martyrs, based on Tieleman J. van Braght, does not give his name in the book, it is known that it was Isaac van Dühren (1724-1800). He states (p. 191) that the selection of the stories is not only based on the *Martyrs' Mirror* by van Braght, but also that they are taken in the order in which they appeared in the large volume. Investigation as to selective process, abbreviation, and presentation of the material has not yet been made. The book consists of 190 pages of text not including the preface and index, and has on its title page a vignette consisting of a mirror, lights, books, and a laurel wreath. The introduction gives an account of church history dealing mostly with the introduction of infant baptism at the time of Cyprian (*q.v.*). The author claims that the Mennonites are descendants of the Waldensians and opposes the claim that they were followers of Thomas Müntzer or stemmed from the Münsterites. The first part of the book treats the persecution of the Mennonites by the Catholics; the second, a much smaller part, the persecution by the Lutherans; and the third part, by the Reformed. In an appendix the commonly used arguments for infant baptism are refuted.

It appears that two editions of the book must have appeared in succession—the first in 1787 and the second in 1788 (*ML* I, 91). An edition, with a special 6-page extra preface, published mainly for the Mennonites of Russia, appeared in 1863 (printed by J. F. Steinkopf, Stuttgart, Germany). The appendix is followed by a poem. These editions were widely used among the members of the Kleine Gemeinde (*q.v.*). In 1939 a fourth edition "of the Mennonite congregations in Manitoba" appeared at Winnipeg (printed by the Rundschau Publishing House) with a special preface. (*ML* II, 91; see also **Isaac van Dühren** and **Kleine Gemeinde.**) C.K.

Geschriftjes *ten Behoeve van de Doopsgezinden in de Verstrooiing,* a set of short writings in the Dutch language, which were sent to Mennonites living in the Netherlands in places where there was no Mennonite church. The *Geschriftjes* were at first edited and published by a committee, then by a union founded for the sake of maintaining contact with these Mennonites (see **Verstrooiing**), and later by the A.D.S. A total number of 61 writings have appeared, the first published in 1897, the last in 1941. The booklets, written in a popular style, deal for a large part with Mennonite history; Nos. 4, 34, and 42 are reports on the activities of the union; Nos. 11, 22, and 38 contain sermons.   vDZ.

Gespauwde Klauw (*Cloven Hoof*). In the fall of 1534 a dispute took place at Amsterdam between the Anabaptist leaders Jacob van Campen, Obbe Philips, and Hans Scheerder. The theme of discussion was the question whether the Scriptures stand on "one hoof" or on "two hoofs," i.e., whether one should believe "that all that has happened in the Old Covenant corresponds with the New Covenant," meaning that the prophecies of the Old Testament will be realized in the New Testament, or that the Scriptures of the Old Testament are plain, not supposing a fulfillment in the Christian era. This theme is also repeatedly discussed by Melchior Hofmann, who defends the cloven hoof. "Ein ider muss der gespaltnen clawen wol warnemen. Denn alle Gottes wort doppelt oder zwiffach seint" (zur Linden, *Melchior Hofmann*, 430). The expression "cloven hoof" is derived from Lev. 11:3 and Deut. 14:6; the theme is important inasmuch as the problem disturbed Anabaptism in the Netherlands in its early period and Hofmann's theory, adopted by Jacob van Campen and also by Cornelis wt den Briel and later by the Münsterite leaders, opened the door wide for an unsound and dangerous typologizing and for the idea that the kingdom of God should bear the traits of the earthly kingdom of Israel, as Jan van Leyden (*q.v.*) taught. On the other hand Obbe Philips could not believe that the Scriptures have a double meaning, asserting that the Scriptures stand on "one hoof." So he is a forerunner of Menno Simons, who was averse to mystics and false allegories, and who states contrary to the Münsterites and Davidjorists that the Scriptures are plain, and that one should teach and believe the express words of Christ. On this question see the writings of Melchior Hofmann. (*BRN* V, 167, 177, 188, 189; VII, 137; *DB* 1917, 133-35.)   vDZ.

Gespräch zwischen einem Pietisten *und einem Wiedertäufer,* a booklet of 314 pages by the (Reformed) minister Johannes Jakob Wolleb of Thenniken (Switzerland), published in Basel in 1722. It is of interest because of the controversy, due at that time, between old-fashioned Anabaptism (as represented by the Swiss Brethren in the Emmental and the Jura area) and the newly arisen Protestant piety of subjectivism and emotional warmth called Pietism (*q.v.*). The author came from an old Basel family of theologians; at the time of the publication of the book he seems to have been under the influence of Spener and Francke; later he leaned more toward Zinzendorf and the Moravian Church.

The main argument in this fictitious discussion between a Pietist and an Anabaptist centers around the question as to how one could know or demonstrate that the "spirit" which fills the soul of the believer is genuinely derived from the Holy Spirit and not a mere fancy or imagination. Naturally, neither side could undisputably prove its point, but the churchman Wolleb claimed to see the genuine Gospel spirit rather in his church than in that of the Anabaptists. Nevertheless, the author is rather fair in his portrayal of the "Anabaptist," even allowing him long and rather good speeches. Throughout the book Wolleb is afraid of false enthusiasm (*q.v.*) (*Geisttreiberei*) and of confused inspirationalism, the old temptation of all Left-Wing Protestants. The booklet closes with a sermon against the oath. In general, an irenic spirit prevails and the new Pietism seems to be open-minded to learn also from the once slandered Anabaptists. Today the book is extremely rare; only three copies are known—one in the Goshen College Library, one in the Library of the Mennonite Church in Amsterdam, and one in Basel.
                                          R.F.

R. Friedmann, *Mennonite Piety Through the Centuries* (Scottdale, 1949).

Gesprächbüchlein. *Ein christliches vnd trosthafftiges, so mit etlichen der Widertauffer öbristen Rabonen oder Vorsteher gehalten. Darin gantz Christlich von allen Artickeln, so vor je wider den Kinder Tauff sein angezogen worden gehandelt würt den heiligen Kinder Tauff damit zu erhalten und der Gottlosen falsche Heuchlerey zu erlegen,* by Jobst Kinthis (Freinsheim, 1553?). The only known copy is in the Speyer (Palatinate) Landes-Bibliothek; the date 1553 is stamped on the binding. It is dedicated to Frederick II, elector Palatine, who is called upon in the foreword to exterminate "all false devilish and idolatrous teaching and rebellious heresy."

The brief condemnation of Anabaptism at the beginning of the book is strange and disappointing; it offers new evidence of the confused ideas current about the movement. The author correctly points out the great differences in the various kinds of Anabaptists, distinguishing six different branches: "Some are in agreement with Balthasar Hubmaier, Melchior Rinck, Hans Denk, Hans Hut, and Ludwig Haetzer on baptism and the preacher's calling. These do not want an interpretation of the Holy Scriptures, but build alone on the printed letter; they have the four Gospels, the epistles of Paul, James, and Peter, and the Acts and Revelation. All other writings such as Jerome, Augustine, Ambrose, and Bernard they consider human work." This is, on the whole, correct, but applies more specifically to the Swiss Brethren than the Anabaptists of South Germany, whose leaders named here rather insisted on a spiritual interpretation of Scripture and attacked adherence to the letter.

"The others boast of the third David, have much in common with Mahomet Ismanelita, perhaps arisen under Heracletus A.D. 612. They have many wives like the Münsterite king Johan van Leiden, A.D. 1534. These boast of Hofmann, who calls his church the New Jerusalem." In a similarly incomprehensible manner points three and four lump the Anabaptists with the Wicliffites, the Lamperian (?) sect, and with Thomas Müntzer and his following. The author does not state his sources.

Of greatest interest to us are the final characterizations of the Anabaptists. "The fifth stay around St. Gall in Switzerland and Appenzell. . . . These have attached many of this country to them, but not a sect. For the Swiss consider it far more unchristian than our people do. I have made a collection of their opinions." If this information is reliable, it has great historical value. We gather from it that Anabaptism in the Palatinate is of Swiss origin. It is surprising that the emissaries to the Palatinate were from St. Gall and Appenzell.

"The sixth kind are those who boast of Michael Sattler, Jörg Wagner, and Leonhard Kaiser, perhaps the most pious and Christian of them all. Concerning their sect . . . one finds information in the small concordances. The leader (*Vorsteher*) of this brotherhood requires two things: First, the separation of their ordained . . . pastors in their parishes; likewise non-participation in all the sacraments, all association or neighborliness, wedding . . . on penalty of the ban; likewise to speak disrespectfully and defiantly to all authorities and other persons, show no honor, consider themselves alone holy and all the rest ungodly. The second, their leader forbids the brethren to reveal to anyone outside their sect concerning their faith, doctrine . . . , also not to name their preachers and leader; requires to flee our church order, preaching, and the practice of the sacraments as ungodly work because they are idol houses made with human hands, wherein God does not dwell; also our clergymen do not teach or preach right, nor conduct services right, and are themselves sinners since they preach but do not perform, and the common people will not mend their ways therefrom because of their great avarice. But Christ commands that we shall beware of such hypocrites as of false prophets (Matt. 7) and we shall prove the spirits, whether they be of God or not." This description is accurate from the point of view of an opponent; it is apparently based on personal acquaintance. It is only puzzling that the author presents the Swiss Brethren and Michael Sattler's group as two distinct branches; they cannot have been separate groups in the Palatinate. The Swiss Brethren also carried out separation rigorously. Grouping Sattler with Jörg Wagner and Leonhard Kaiser does not agree with historical facts. Kaiser was a Lutheran martyr, and Wagner was more closely related to Denk than to Sattler.

Now Kinthis lists "the leading articles of the Anabaptists." There are 13 of them: (1) rejection of infant baptism; (2) rejection of the true deity of Christ; (3) rejection of the true humanity of Christ, to the extent that He did not receive human nature from Mary; (4) rejection of the merits of Christ; (5) rejection of the sacramental character of the holy communion; (6) they break marriages for "insignificant cause"; (7) rejection of military service; (8) chiliasm; (9) rejection of government office; (10) "some agree with the Donatists and say that preaching and the sacrament are naught if the minister is not upright and holy"; (11) "some believe that before the end of the world the church will be as in the days of Noah"; (12) rejection of original sin and the assertion that those who fall after receiving baptism will not be forgiven, a doctrine they have in common with the Novatians and Cathars; (13) "some of them believe (like Origen) that in the end the devil will be saved with all the ungodly." Kinthis makes not the slightest reference to their rejection of the oath.

The *Gespräch* (conversation), in the form of statement (Anabaptist) and counter statement (Kinthis), has four divisions, and constitutes a comprehensive defense of infant baptism; but it rarely touches the root of the matter. The Anabaptist always insists on the simple meaning of Scripture; his statements are agreeably short and logical, whereas his opponent unfolds a long-winded dialectic skill. He presents the customary evidence for infant baptism and explains at great length that even very young infants also have faith, which God Himself works in them. There are very few historical facts in the book. Once Kinthis sharply attacks emigration to Moravia.

Concerning the author's personality not much is revealed. He says specifically, "I am not a theologian, but a simple layman without understanding." But he shows an extraordinary knowledge of theology. He is especially familiar with the works of the Church Fathers; he also knows the writings of Brenz, Bucer, Bullinger, and Pellikan. Luther he calls "our beloved honorable father . . . in Christ"; but he shows some Calvinism (?) in confessing himself to be a Predestinarian. "God has in His eternal counsel already determined which child shall be saved or damned." The Anabaptist is also a learned theologian, with a command of Latin and a knowledge of the Church Fathers. On one occasion Kinthis accuses him, "You learned that in the University of Brno." This indicates that the Anabaptist was a Hutterite missionary on a mission in the Palatinate; he shared the opinion common among the Anabaptists of that time, that infant baptism was introduced by Pope Nicholas I, and that children should not be baptized before about 12 years of age.

In the fifth section Kinthis discusses the question whether children who are born dead are saved; and in the sixth section he answers the question affirmatively, saying that God in His mercy imparts faith to them.

In the epilogue the author briefly states the occasion for writing the book. Because some fanatics had settled in the Palatinate who criticized the holy baptism of infants, seduced the populace, and moved away with wife and child, thus creating dissension and disorder, he felt called to write, in order that these people might be persuaded to return to the true church. (*ML* II, 103 f.) NEFF.

Gesselsdorf, a Bruderhof of the Hutterian Brethren in Hungary: see **Kesselsdorf.**

Getrewe Warnung *der Prediger des Evangelii zu Strassburg über die Artickel, so Jakob Kautz, Prediger zu Wormbs, kürtzlich hat lassen ausgohn, die frucht der schrifft und Gottes worts, den kinder Tauff, und erlösung unsers herren Jesu Christi, sambt anderm, darin sich Hans Dencken, und anderer widertäuffer schwere yrrtumb erregen, betreffend. Beweren die geyster, ob sie aus Got sind, dann es sind vil falscher propheten inn die welt ausgangen. I. Johan. IV.* (Strasbourg, 1527). This is the title of a booklet in quarto with 47 unnumbered pages. It was written by the Strasbourg reformers, especially Bucer (*q.v.*). The contents are a factual refutation of the seven theses which Jakob Kautz (*q.v.*) posted in Worms. The authors complain that Kautz did not dispute with them in writing, for in the year before he had written quite honestly and fraternally to Wolfgang Capito (*q.v.*); the latter had replied and urgently warned him. Since then (said the authors) he had not been heard from. The booklet considers Hans Denk the actual originator of the doctrines promoted by Kautz, and violently attacks and misjudges him (see **Denk**), whereas it gives Michael Sattler (*q.v.*) very favorable comment. Ludwig Haetzer is also mentioned; the Anabaptist movement is briefly characterized, thus giving the book a certain value for Anabaptist history. (*ML* II, 105.)   Neff.

Getuygenisse, 't, *Ende de Naeghelaeten Schriften van Christiaen Rijcen,* a rare book, published by Gillis Rooman at Haarlem, Holland, in 1588, contains sixteen letters and seven songs written by the martyr Christiaen de Rijcke (*q.v.*), executed in 1588. In addition this volume contains three letters of the martyr Adriaen Jansz; at the end of the book is found a song by Carel van Mander in commemoration of Christiaen's martyrdom. A copy is found in the Amsterdam Mennonite library.   vDZ.

Bibliographie des Martyrologes Protestants Néerlandais I (The Hague, 1890) 321-31.

Geuns, van, a Dutch Mennonite family, whose ancestors were apparently as follows:

(1) *Steven Freriks* (or Fredriks), a landowner, b. 1625 at Holwierde, Dutch province of Groningen, who about 1657 moved to Dyckhusen near Neustadt-Goedens in East Friesland, Germany. Here he married Lysabeth Dircksdochter, from Pilsum, East Friesland, and died in 1679. One of his sons was (2) *Jan Steevens,* b. in Dyckhusen 1660 and d. in Neustadt-Goedens 1716. He was a landowner and a businessman and a deacon of the Old Flemish congregation. He was married to Gepke Lubberts Cremer of an old Mennonite family (see **Cremer** family). One of his sons was (3) Elder *Lubbert Jans Cremer* (*q.v.*), who adopted his mother's family name, as was then very commonly done both in Friesland and East Friesland.

(4) *Steeven Jans Cremer,* another son of Jan Steevens, b. 1696 at Neustadt-Goedens, migrated about 1740 to Groningen in the Netherlands. He was a cloth merchant and rather well-to-do. He

seems to have loosened his ties with the Old Flemish Mennonite congregation, because he played an important role among the Collegiants (*q.v.*) in Groningen, being their leader for a number of years. This Steeven Jans called himself S. J. van Geuns, i.e., from (Neustadt) Goedens and this became the family name. He was married first to Dieuwertje Roos of Groningen and then to Dieuwertje Alringh of Leer. He died in 1737.

One of his sons was (5) *Matthias* (Matthijs) *van Geuns* (1735-1817) (*q.v.*), a medical professor at Harderwijk and Utrecht. This Matthias had a number of children; one of them was (6) *Steven Jan van Geuns* (1767-95), who was a medical professor at the University of Utrecht at the same time as his father (*N.N.B.Wb.* I, 933); other sons of Matthias were (7) *Jan* (*q.v.*), a Mennonite minister, and (8) *Jacob* (1769-1834), first a physician at Groningen, then the founder of a bank in Amsterdam.

A son of Stevens Jans (4) was (9) *Jan Stevens* (1722-80), an iron dealer in Groningen, warmly interested in his home church (*Inv. Arch. Amst.* I, No. 677), father of the Mennonite minister (10) *Matthias van Geuns* (*q.v.*) and grandfather of (11) *Cornelis Sytze van Geuns* (*q.v.*) and (12) *Bartel van Geuns* (*q.v.*), and great-grandfather of (13) *Matthias C. van Geuns* (*q.v.*), all three Mennonite ministers. A large number of members of this family were noted physicians, lawyers, and businessmen. Mention should be made of (14) *Jan van Geuns* (*q.v.*), medical professor at the University of Amsterdam, (15) *Matthias van Geuns* (1802-?), director of the *Associatie Kassa* at Amsterdam, (16) *Albert van Geuns* (1806-79), founder of the Banking Company Luden en van Geuns at Amsterdam, all three sons of Jacob van Geuns (8); (17) *Jan van Geuns,* son of Pastor Matthias van Geuns (10) (1799-1865), at first apothecary at Amsterdam, whose daughter Margaretha was married to Pastor Adriaan Loosjes (*q.v.*). This Jan van Geuns founded the first rubber factory in the Netherlands at Haarlem about 1828 (*N.N.B.Wb.* IV, 650); (18) *Isak Matthias van Geuns* (1772-1804), son of Matthias van Geuns (5), studied law and afterward entered diplomatic service (*N.N.B.Wb.* IV, 648); (19) *Jacob van Geuns* (1847-1909), son of Jan van Geuns (14), physician at Amsterdam, one of the first scholars to study the medical questions connected with life insurance (*N.N.B.Wb.* IV, 649). Many of his descendants emigrated to the United States at the end of the 19th century; (20) *Steven Jan Matthijs van Geuns* (1795-1849), son of Steven Jan van Geuns (6), was a lawyer at Utrecht and a member of the city council and of the provincial States of Utrecht.   vDZ.

"Geslachtslijst van de familie van Geuns," manuscript now in the Amsterdam Mennonite Library, *Catalogus Amst.,* 45; A. M. Cramer, *Brief betr. den stamvader der familie van Geuns hier te lande* (n.p., n.d.); *Ned. Patriciaat* XIV (1924) 89-107.

Geuns, Bartel van, the son of Matthias van Geuns (preacher at Haarlem), b. Aug. 5, 1805, at Haarlem, was called in 1828 as minister to serve the

Mennonite congregation at Akkrum, and to West Zaandam in 1830. The addresses given on the occasion of the union between the Frisians and the Flemish in 1841 by C. Leendertz and van Geuns have been published. Van Geuns retired on Aug. 7, 1870, and died at Arnhem on Feb. 24, 1873. He published a description of Zaandam and also a catechetical booklet, *Gods Openbaringen* (Zaandam, 1851). He was married to Hermina Juliana ten Cate of Enschede. 			K.V.

Biogr. Wb. III, 236 f.; N.N.B.Wb. VIII, 600; *Catalogus Amst.*, 323, 326; ML II, 105.

Geuns, Cornelis Sytse van, brother of the foregoing Bartel, b. 1794 at Haarlem, d. 1827 at Leeuwarden. After finishing his studies at the Amsterdam Mennonite Seminary he served as a pastor for the congregations of Nijmegen in 1819(?)-22 and Leeuwarden 1822-27. He wrote a paper entitled "Over den Oorsprong der Doopsgezinden van de oude Waldenzen," which was published after his death in *Vaderlandsche Letteroefeningen*, 1829. He was married to Barbara van Hees. 		vDZ.

Biogr. Wb. III, 237; N.N.B.Wb. VIII, 600; *Naamlijst* 1829, 43; *Catalogus Amst.*, 10, 323, 325; ML II, 105.

Geuns, Jan van, b. 1764 at Groningen, son of Matthijs (Matthias) van Geuns, studied at the University of Harderwijk in 1780-89, obtaining his Ph.D. degree on April 21, 1789, on the same day as his brother Steven Jan. Soon afterward appointed ministerial candidate, he served the Mennonite churches of Leiden 1789-1814, and Amsterdam 1814-29. He seems to have been a man of warm piety and great learning, but of poor eloquence, so that his services, especially in Amsterdam, had low attendance. He died at Nijmegen in 1834. He published a large number of philosophical, historical, and political writings and papers, such as *Brief aan het Committé ter regeling van de Grondvergaderingen der Gemeente van Leyden* (Leiden, 1795) and *Over den Slaavenstand* (Leiden, 1797). He generously contributed to the Mennonite hymnbook *Uitgezogte Liederen* (Leiden, 1810). He was married to Geertruida van Heukelom of Amsterdam. 			vDZ.

Biogr. Wb. III, 237 f.; N.N.B.Wb. IV, 649; DB 1901, 24; 1897, 169; 1898, 111-12, 116; 1901, 24; *Catalogus Amst.*, 298, 311, 312, 319, 325, 329.

Geuns, Matthias C. van, b. 1823 at Leeuwarden, son of Cornelis Sytse van Geuns (*q.v.*), d. there 1904, was a Mennonite pastor at Noord-Zijpe 1845-50, and Leeuwarden 1850-88. He had a large sphere of influence, not only by his preaching, but also by his secretaryship of the *Friesche Doopsgezinde Sociëteit*, 1875-97. In Leeuwarden he was so highly respected and beloved that during a socialistic disturbance, when a large number of windows were broken, the leaders of the uprising emphatically warned their following not to damage the house of Pastor van Geuns. At first he followed his father as a moderate evangelical; about 1860 he successively turned to modernism (liberalism) and a rather radical rationalism. In this movement he became an influential leader. He published a number of sermons and a volume of lectures, entitled

Ondeugende Scherts (Leeuwarden, 1871). His portrait is found DB 1903 and DJ 1906. 		vDZ.

Biogr. Wb. III, 238-39; N.N.B.Wb. VIII, 600; DB 1903, 119-23; 1904, 239 f.; DJ 1906, 23-27; *Catalogus Amst.*, 315, 321.

Geuns, Matthias Jansz van, son of the iron dealer Jan Stevens van Geuns at Groningen, b. there 1758, d. 1839 at Haarlem, served the following Mennonite congregations as a pastor: Makkum 1783-87, Harlingen 1787-92, and Haarlem 1792-1828. He published *Kort Verslag aangaande den Toestand van het Doopsgezind Kerkgenootschap* (Utrecht, 1793). He was married to Tryntje Cornelisd. Sytses of Leeuwarden. Two of his sons, Cornelis Sytse (*q.v.*) and Bartel (*q.v.*), were also Mennonite ministers (*Naamlijst* 1829, 25; *Catalogus Amst.*, 152.) 			vDZ.

Geuns, Matthijs (Matthias) van, son of Steven Jansz (van Geuns), b. Sept. 2, 1735, at Groningen, d. Dec. 9, 1817, at Utrecht. His wife was Sara van Delden of Groningen. He was a student of the noted Professor Petrus Kamper at the University of Amsterdam, and in 1761 began to practice medicine at Groningen. His call to the University of Amsterdam could not be accepted, because he was a Mennonite. Five years later he became professor of medicine, chemistry, and botany at the University of Harderwijk. His work during the epidemic of 1783 was outstanding. In 1791 he was called as professor to the University of Utrecht. 			K.V.

N.N.B.Wb. I, 931; DJ 1840, 113; DB 868, 94; 1898, 116; 1900, 119; ML II, 105.

Geuns, Pieter van, who in the first decades of the 18th century was a preacher of the Old Flemish congregation at Norden, East Friesland, Germany, belonged to the large van Geuns family, but the degree of relationship could not be determined. (*Inv. Arch. Amst.* II, Nos. 2824, 2827, 2836, 2838.) 			vDZ.

Geur van geestelijke Specerijen, a Dutch Mennonite songbook, containing 57 songs without notes. It was published at Haarlem (n.d., obviously early 17th century). DJ 1837, p. 65, mentions an edition at Haarlem in 1701, but no copy of this edition has been found. Among the composers of the songs are Achior van den Abeele (*q.v.*), Frans Hoefnagel, Jacob Jansz Kat (*q.v.*), and Anna van der Smisse. 			vDZ.

Geurts, Marten, an elder of the Flemish Mennonites in Holland in the middle of the 17th century. He died shortly before 1687. He lived at Veenendaal (also called Rijnsche Veen), was an opponent of the Collegiant innovations. In the conflict of the conservative Mennonites at Utrecht (*q.v.*), and the Galenists in 1661 and the following years, the conservatives refused to accept him as an intermediary, because he was too moderate. He wrote the following: (1) *Tractaet dienende tot beweeringe der sichtbare Gemeynte Gods tegen alle die hedensdaechsche Nieuwigheden en Dwalingen* (Utrecht, 1662); (2) *Aenmerckingen over den*

Handel en Mislagen van eenige Mennoniten binnen Utrecht (Utrecht, 1662). (*Inv. Arch. Amst.* I, No. 452; *DB* 1916, 161, 166, 174; *ML* II, 105.)

NEFF, VDZ.

Geuzenvragen, the designation by the Dutch Mennonites of the 12 questions which the magistrates of Utrecht, Deventer, Middelburg, and other towns in several cases laid before Mennonites to examine their faith and to check on possible Socinian (*q.v.*) or other heresy. The Mennonite ministers usually refused to answer these questions (see **Adriaan van Eeghem**), arguing that the government had no authority in matters of faith and no right to examine the consciences of its subjects. It is assumed that the questions were drawn up about 1655 by the Reformed clergyman Cornelius Gernman.

VDZ.

Gex, a district of the French department of Ain, which was ceded by Switzerland to France in 1601. In the 20th century a congregation with name "Pays de Gex" was formed there in the town of Thoiry, eight miles from Geneva, by Swiss Mennonite emigrants under the leadership of Abraham Geiser. The congregation joined the Swiss Mennonite Conference in 1925; in 1926 it numbered about 50 souls; in 1955 it had 64 baptized members. (*Zionspilger,* March 9, 1924, 39; *Almanach-Mennonite,* 1951, 14; *ML* II, 105.) HEGE, H.S.B.

Geyersbühler, Nikolaus (Niklas Geyersbichler), a Hutterite Anabaptist, named for his birthplace, Geyerbühel in the district of Kitzbühel, Tirol, Austria, a miller by trade, therefore also called Müller. He was received into the Hutterian brotherhood by Peter Riedemann at Freischütz on the Hungarian border (Sobotiste), and was persuaded by his brother Wolf to emigrate with his wife to Moravia. He settled on the estate of the nobleman Sigmund Helt of Kement, near Seelowitz, Moravia. On Epiphany 1563 he was one of four brethren chosen as deacons. Three years later, though he was illiterate, he was sent to the Tirol to lead Anabaptists from there to Moravia. He dedicated himself to his task under difficult circumstances in the vicinity of his home town, but was seized with seven other Anabaptists in 1566 and transferred to Innsbruck.

His statements, which have been preserved in a Hutterite codex under the title, "Bruder Nikolaus Geyerspichlers Verantwortung vor besetztem Gerichte zu Innsbruck gründlich und peinliche Besprechung verfasst 1567, 29. Tag Aprilis," describe the circumstances of the Anabaptists in Moravia and also of the migration of the Tirolean Anabaptists to Moravia. In the case of the former, the conditions are less favorably presented than in other sources. He stated, of course, that he was not familiar with all the places in which Anabaptists lived, for some places were as much as 29 miles apart; furthermore, the Anabaptists were often driven from place to place. The routes to Moravia usually followed the Inn and the Danube. Boatmen accepted them without question if they merely paid the fee.

Geyersbühler lay in the Kräuterhaus (Innsbruck) and was often admonished there by priests to recant. After a final examination on the rack on forty-seven questions he still persisted in his faith. The principal points of questioning concerned obedience to the state, confessions of faith, and infant baptism. He defended himself against the assumption that his coreligionists were a sect; he did not believe in total depravity; unbaptized children (he believed) are saved. The sacraments are baptism (of adults), communion, and marriage. He rejected oral confession, adoration of images, and the intercession of the saints. He stated that Sunday was kept holy, that communion was held in Moravia in the large Bruderhofs, whereas in Tirol they were limited to the services held in woods and fields. They did not render an oath. This was his confession, and he would stand by it. Then, say the chronicles, the Jesuits treated him mildly and rudely, but he did not permit himself to be moved from his faith. Condemned to death, he was beheaded and then burned (1567).

LOSERTH.

Beck, *Geschichts-Bücher,* 249-51; Wolkan, *Geschicht-Buch,* 324; J. Loserth, *Der Anabaptismus in Tirol* (Vienna, 1892) 213 f.; *Mart. Mir.* D 345, E 703, where he is called Nic(h)olas Geyer; *ML* II, 110 f.

Gezangen, Christelijke, two volumes of hymns usually called *Oude Amsterdamsche Bundels* were published at Amsterdam in 1848, and were used by the Amsterdam Mennonite church until they were replaced (1871) by the *Christelijke Liederen* (*q.v.*) or *Nieuwe Amsterdamsche Bundels.* The *Christelijke Gezangen* also were in use in a number of other Mennonite churches. (*Catalogus Amst.,* 329.)

VDZ.

Gezangen, Christelijke, *voor de openbare Godsdienst-oeffeningen; ten dienste der Mennonite Gemeente te Hamburg en Altona.* This hymnbook, also called *Altonasche Gezangboek* or *Hamburgsche Liederen,* printed at Amsterdam in 1802 with 666 pages without music, contained 254 hymns, including a number of Psalms, and a suffix of 19 hymns composed by P. Beets, elder of the Hamburg congregation, all in Dutch. Some of these hymns were inserted in the new hymnbook of the Haarlem congregation in 1851.

VDZ.

Gezangen op de Christelijke Feesttijden. This small volume, containing only 15 hymns, was put in use in the Mennonite Zonist congregation at Amsterdam on Oct. 16, 1762, and later was also used in a number of other Dutch congregations. There are at least three editions, two in 1762 and one in 1775.   VDZ.

Gezangen, Christelyke, *ten gebruike der Doopsgez. Gemeente . . . te Amsterdam,* a Dutch hymnbook: see **Bundel, Kleine.**

Gezangen, Christelyke, *voor de openbaare Godsdienstoefening,* a Dutch hymnbook: see **Bundel, Groote.**

Gezangen en Liederen, Christelijke, is the title of a Dutch hymnbook adopted in 1804 or 1805 by the Haarlem Mennonite congregation and some other congregations. There are two editions, both of 1804. It was used in Haarlem until 1851, when it was replaced by the *Christelijke Kerkgezangen* (*q.v.*). (*DB* 1861, 159; 1900, 102, 110.)   vDZ.

Gezangen en Liederen *der Vereenigde Doopsgezinden te Rotterdam,* a Dutch Mennonite hymnbook. On May 28, 1775, at the dedication of their new church, the Rotterdam congregation introduced the Psalms in the rhymed version of the Reformed Church; in 1776 it adopted the new hymnbook, *Gezangen en Liederen,* which was published in 1775 and contains 27 hymns, for a large part borrowed from the old songbook *Lusthof des Gemoeds* by Claes Stapel (*q.v.*). (*DB* 1900, 94.)   vDZ.

Gezangen, Opwekkende. The Mennonite congregation of Haarlem re-edited the Amsterdam hymnbook *Oude Liederen* (*q.v.*) of 1684 under the new title *Opwekkende Gezangen* (1st ed. about 1712; 2nd ed. Haarlem, 1763). In 1776 a third edition of this hymnbook was published at Haarlem, entitled *Liederen en Gezangen op de Chr. feesttijden, bij de Gemeenten der Doopsgezinden en Remonstranten te Haarlem en elders in gebruik.* The next year a supplementary volume appeared under the old title *Opwekkende Liederen, Tweede Stuk* (Haarlem, 1777). (*DB* 1900, 88.)   vDZ.

Ghatula, a village 41 miles southeast of Dhamtari, Madhya Pradesh, India, at the edge of a rich agricultural valley, was a Mennonite (MC) mission station established in 1916 under the direct management of George J. and Esther E. Lapp. The Bible training school for Christian workers was moved from Rudri (*q.v.*) to Ghatula the same year. Ultimately on the station ground of seven acres living quarters were built for missionaries, employees, Christian workers, and Bible school students, as well as a Bible school, a medical dispensary, and nurses' quarters; on an adjacent plot was built a primary school for village children with Christian teachers. The Ghatula field covered more than 2,000 square miles. There were opportunities for Indian Christians to obtain employment and purchase land in Ghatula and surrounding villages, with the result that a substantial Christian community with a well-organized church was established, which in 1955 had 81 members.

In 1929 the Bible school was merged into the Bible department of the Christian Academy at Dhamtari, from which time Ghatula was more particularly an evangelistic and primary educational center. In 1929-39 a girls' industrial school was operated, giving instruction in handwork, homemaking, field work, and elementary subjects. The industrial school was under the management of Minnie Kanagy and Gladys Weaver.   G.J.L.

Gheerardyne Ryckelmans, an Anabaptist martyr, wife of the martyr Adriaen van Daele (*q.v.*), was burned at the stake at Antwerp, Belgium, together with Peryne de Corte on June 6, 1573. She was charged with the crime of having been rebaptized

and having attended Mennonite meetings. (*Antw. Arch.-Blad* XIII, 122 f., 178; XIV, 92 f., No. 1033.)   vDZ.

Gheertsz, Jan, an Anabaptist martyr: see **Jan Geerts.**

Gheese Aelbrechtsdochter, an Anabaptist martyr, wife of Lambrecht Duppijns (*q.v.*) of Haarlem, Dutch province of North Holland, was arrested there on May 23, 1539, when a meeting of Anabaptists in their home was surprised by the officials. She was severely tortured and was executed by drowning on May 29, 1539. Like her husband and the group meeting with them, Gheese was probably a follower of David Joris (*q.v.*), for in their home were found about 500 copies of a book by David Joris.   vDZ.
Bijdr. en Mededeelingen van het Historisch Genootschap te Utrecht XLI (Amsterdam, 1920) 201, 208-10.

Gheestelijck Bloem Hofken, 'T, *beplant met veel lieflijcke Bloemkens van verscheyden coleuren, tot dienst van alle Liefhebbers der Cantijcke Soetgeurigheydt,* a Dutch Mennonite songbook, published at Haarlem in 1637, containing 128 songs without notes, arranged alphabetically.   vDZ.

Gheestelijck Kruydt-Hofken, 'T, *inhoudende veel schriftuerlijcke Liedekens by verscheyden Autheuren ghemaeckt ende nu tot stichtinge van een yegelijck t' samenghestelt,* a Dutch hymnbook, which was very popular among the Dutch Mennonites of the 17th century. It contains 159 hymns without notes. Copies of the following editions have been preserved: 3rd edition, Amsterdam 1637; 6th edition, Haarlem 1647; 8th edition, Saerdam (i.e., Saandam) 1669; 9th edition, Saerdam 1683; 9th (should be 10th), Saerdam 1693. The edition of 1637 contains an appendix called *Kleyn-Achter-Hofken, Beplant met verscheyden Gheestelijcke Liedekens tot stichtinge der Jeugt,* containing 22 hymns. In the following editions this appendix is called *'t Vermeerderde Achterhofken,* containing 47 hymns.

There is also a 1664 edition of the *Kruydt-Hofken,* published at Alkmaar under a somewhat modified title and containing an appendix entitled *Groot Achter-Hofken* (containing 90 hymns). This Alkmaar edition of 1664 is said to be the 9th edition, which must be a mistake.   vDZ.

Ghele Hame, a native of Friesland, was beheaded at Kampen, Dutch province of Overijssel, on Feb. 15, 1535, after having renounced his faith. His confession before his judges is very informative. He had received (re)baptism in 1534, two weeks before Christmas. He did not believe in the Catholic doctrine of the Mass, did not accept fasting as a Christian doctrine, and believed, as Melchior Hofmann and also Menno Simons taught, that Jesus did not receive His flesh from Mary (see **Incarnation**). (*DB* 1875, 60.)   vDZ.

Gherlandi, Giulio (Guirlando, also Julius Klemprer), an Anabaptist martyr, born *ca.* 1520 at Spresiano near Treviso in Venetian territory, Italy, was intended by his Catholic father for the priesthood but fell into evil ways. He was troubled in conscience at the contradiction between his Christian pretensions and the actual character of his life, and his reading of Matt. 7:15, 16 led him to break with the Roman Church. Around 1549-51 he joined that group of evangelicals in Venetia who are commonly called Anabaptists but who at that time were veering in the direction of anti-Trinitarianism. He was baptized by Nicolo of Alessandria, a member of he anti-Trinitarian community in Treviso, and later he baptized several persons himself. When the renegade Pietro Manelfi (*q.v.*) exposed the evangelical movement to the Inquisition in 1551, leading to its near-destruction, Gherlandi left the radicals and looked about for more compatible society. With Francesco della Sega (or Saga, *q.v.*) he learned about the Hutterites sometime in the 1550's and was admitted to the brotherhood at Pausram, Moravia. He was not required to be rebaptized. In Moravia he engaged in his craft of making lanterns, but soon asked for and was granted permission to bring word of the Hutterites to his former associates in north Italy. In March 1559 Gherlandi went to Italy bearing a letter from Sega to a fellow believer in Vicenza, as well as a general letter of introduction from the Moravian brotherhood to the Italian evangelicals. This letter explains the occasion of the trip, i.e., to make known the nature of the Hutterite community to other Italians, but stipulates that only those Italians would be welcomed as new members whose minds were not contaminated with false doctrines about the nature of Christ, the resurrection from the dead, angels, devils, or other matters (obvious references to the doctrines approved by the Venetian council of 1550; see **Manelfi**). The letter also contains a statement of the Hutterite articles of belief. Gherlandi also bore a list of names of more than one hundred Italians living in over sixty localities in north Italy and the Grisons. On March 21, 1559, he came to official attention because he refused to swear to port authorities near Venice that he had no disease. He was soon released and we find him a few days later in Treviso publicly criticizing the Roman Church. This led to his arrest and examination at Treviso and transfer to prison in Venice, from which he managed to escape and return to Moravia. He was in Italy again at Christmas of 1560, and in October 1561 was captured once again at Treviso and imprisoned more securely in Venice. From his prison he wrote on Oct. 4 or 14, 1561, a letter (never delivered, and now in the archives of Venice) to Leonhard Lanzenstiel, bishop of the Moravian Hutterite community. This document explains his predicament, but shows a courageous spirit and a firmness in the faith that testify to the genuinenes of his religious conviction: "Do not for a moment doubt that there will be given to me in that hour, according to the true divine promise, wisdom, against which all the adversaries shall not be able to resist." A few days later (Oct. 23) Gherlandi prepared a comprehensive confession of faith in which he explained the circumstances surrounding his departure from Catholicism and his joining of the Hutterites, and described the beliefs and practices of the latter. He closed with these moving words: "That is my

simple confession. I ask that it be accepted with indulgence, for I am no orator, writer, or historian but only a poor lantern-maker—I am however not truly poor, since I am indeed content with my fate." On Nov. 16, 1561, Gherlandi was examined by three theologians, who, after lively discussions, concluded that the prisoner remained "obstinate in the crime of heresy." The issue between the two parties rested squarely on the question of authority of the church, with Gherlandi holding steadily to the Scriptures. During the ensuing several months he was left to languish in the prison but occupied himself with efforts to convert his fellow prisoners. When admonished by a priest concerning this he refused to beg pardon from the court, saying, "To God alone ought I to bend the knee and not to worldly men" (Sept. 19, 1562). During this same month Gherlandi was joined in his prison by his old associate Sega; the renewed contact strengthened both in their faith. On Oct. 15, 1562, the court sentenced Gherlandi to be drowned; it informed him of his fate on Oct. 23, and he was executed soon thereafter. His last word was a greeting to the Hutterite community which Sega managed to record in a letter that paid glowing tribute to Gherlandi's splendid martyr example.

DeWind.

Beck, *Geschichts-Bücher*, 239-40; V. Bellondi, *Documenti e aneddoti di storia veneziana* (1810-1854), *Tratti dall' Archivio de' Frari* (Florence, 1902); K. Benrath, "Wiedertäufer im Venetianischen um die Mitte des 16. Jahrhunderts," in *Theol. Studien und Kritiken* LVIII (1885) 9-67; *idem, Gesch. der Reformation in Venedig*, No. 18 of *Schriften des Vereins für Ref. Gesch.* (Halle, 1887); E. Comba, *I nostri protestanti* II, *Durante la riforma nel Veneto e nell' Istria* (Florence, 1897) 555-87; H. DeWind, "Italian Hutterite Martyrs," *MQR* XXVIII (1954) 164-71; *ML* II, 112.

Gherwen, Abraham van, compiler of a Dutch Mennonite songbook entitled *Tot des Heeren Lof heb ick U (Ghod-vresende Zanger) dit Liedboecxken ghejont, ghenaemt: De Ghulde Fonteyne waer duer ick wensche dat veel fonteyntjes (dat zijn ghelovige harten) mede ghewonnen mochten worden . . .* (Ghoude, i.e., Gouda, 1618). This songbook, containing 144 songs on 288 pages, was not intended for use in the public services but for private and family use. Of the compiler van Gherwen nothing further is known.   vDZ.

Gheryt, a Dutch Anabaptist from Deventer, who took part in the Anabaptist revolt and assault on the town hall at Amsterdam, May 10-11, 1535. He was executed on May 14 in a bestially cruel way. Gheryt had been baptized by Jacob van Campen (*q.v.*) in the fall of 1533 in his own house at Amsterdam. (Grosheide, *Verhooren*, 62-64.) vDZ.

Ghesangen, Het Boeck der, the title of three Dutch Mennonite hymnbooks. (1) A hymnbook used by the Waterlander congregations, compiled by Hans de Ries. This hymnbook went through at least seven editions under different titles. The oldest edition, 1582, is entitled *Lietboeck* (see **Hans de Ries**). (2) A hymnbook containing the Psalms in the rhymed version of Petrus Dathenus (*q.v.*) and *Lof-sanghen ende Geestelijcke Lieden,* an anthology of hymns from the *Lietboeck* (1582) of Hans de Ries (*q.v.*), followed by the Confession of de Ries and Lubbert Gerrits. It was published in Hoorn in 1618. This edition was formerly called the *Hoornsche Gesanghboeck*.

(3) A hymnbook containing the Psalms in the rhymed version of Petrus Dathenus (*q.v.*), parts 2, 3, and 4 of the *Liedtboeck* (1582) by Hans de Ries (*q.v.*), followed by the Confession of de Ries and Lubbert Gerrits; it was published at Amsterdam (B. Otsz, voor Claes Jacobsz in de Rijp) in 1624. Later editions of (2) appeared under the title *Gesangh-boeck, vervaet in vier Delen*, . . . ; there are known editions of 1648 (de Rijp), 1658 (de Rijp; printed at Hoorn), and 1684 (de Rijp). The edition of 1684 does not contain the Psalms. This hymnbook was usually called the "Rijper" songbook. (*Catalogus Amst.*, 267 f.) vDZ.

Gheylliart (Gheillyart), **Jan**, a printer of Dutch Bibles at Emden, East Friesland, Germany: see **Mierdemann** (Mierdman), **Steven**.

Ghysbert Jansz, a Dutch Anabaptist martyr, burned at the stake at Amsterdam on March 20, 1549. He was a native of the town of Woerden, province of South Holland, and had been baptized by Gillis van Aken. Together with Ghysbert seven other martyrs, five men and two women, were put to death. They are celebrated in a song, "Tis nu schier al vervult ons broeders getal" (The number of our brethren is now almost complete), which is found in *Veelderhande Liedekens* of 1556, 1566, and later editions. (*Mart. Mir.* D 82, E 483 f.; Grosheide, *Bijdrage*, 308.) vDZ.

Gibson (Miss.), Old Order Amish community, now extinct, was established in the winter of 1895-96 when nine Amish families from Newton Co., Ind., settled in western Monroe County and eastern Chickasaw County. Families from other Amish communities later moved into the settlement, so that with those who were married in the congregation the number reached approximately 25 families. Several families moved away before the last settlers arrived. In 1903-5 the settlement disintegrated, the families moving to Arthur, Ill.; Indiana; Custer Co., Okla.; Anderson Co., Kan.; Reno Co., Kan.; and to Michigan. J.J.Y.

Gichtelianer, a brotherhood founded by Johann Georg Gichtel (1638-1710). He was educated at the University of Strasbourg, studying theology and jurisprudence, became a lawyer in Speyer, Germany, and later in Regensburg, where his receptive religious sense was deeply stimulated by the Hungarian Baron Justinian Ernst von Weltz. He accompanied Weltz to the Netherlands, and in Zwolle made contact with Friedrich Breckling, a mystical Lutheran pastor. This was the turning point of his life. He became involved in extreme, mystical, theosophist thought. He waited in prayer for hours to find God's will. Outward religious services he considered a hindrance to inner communion with God. He felt himself called to denounce the false worship of the Lutheran Church, in which he felt a lack of earnest self-denial. He was in consequence barred from practicing law in Regensburg, deprived of his citizenship and possessions, and expelled from the city.

After a short residence in Gernsbach, Baden, Germany, and in Vienna, Austria, Gichtel returned to Zwolle. Here he was also banished and, at odds with Breckling, went to Amsterdam via Kampen. He became acquainted with Jakob Boehme's writings and lived entirely in the world of Boehme's ideas, which he sought to develop in speculation and to transfer into practical living. He developed a rigid asceticism, rejecting marriage.

Peculiar to Gichtel was the idea of the priesthood of Melchizedek. "God had given him and his followers the power to present one's soul to God as a sacrifice for other lost souls through prayer and concentration on the blood and death of Christ." To him this was a continuation of the high-priestly work of Christ, "the evidence of full communion with Him, the highest point of experience of the love of God, and the symbol of the most intimate contact with wisdom" (*HRE* VI, 660). Gichtel's adherents were scattered through Holland, Hamburg-Altona, Berlin, and South Germany; but they were not numerous and soon died out. He himself had not intended to form a separate group and took no part in related religious phenomena. He sharply attacked the Mennonites, and was answered by Galenus Abrahamsz (*q.v.*) and other Mennonites (Hylkema, 125, 428). Conrad Beissel (*q.v.*) had some contacts with Gichtel.

Among the Mennonites of Russia a brotherhood was organized in Felsenthal (*q.v.*), who had some peculiar points of contact with the Gichtelians. The famous Jan Luiken (*q.v.*) must also have been influenced by Böhme and Gichtel (*ML* II, 700).

NEFF.

C. B. Hylkema, *Reformateurs* (Haarlem, 1902) 125, 428; Friesen, *Brüderschaft*, 133; Fr. Nieper, *Die ersten deutschen Auswanderer von Krefeld nach Pennsylvanien* (Neukirchen, 1940) 153, 169; *ML* II, 112.

Giebelstadt, a village in Bavaria, Germany, 12 miles south of Würzburg, where a Mennonite congregation was established about the middle of the 19th century. The first families settled on leased estates around Zell (Hettstädter Hof in 1803) and Rottenbauer near Würzburg. In Rottenbauer a congregation was organized in 1810, which grew rapidly. After the 1830's religious services were held alternately there and in Giebelstadt, and the congregation was named Rottenbauer-Giebelstadt. The members came originally exclusively from the Sinsheim district of Baden. The most common names were Bachmann, Bähr, Borkholder, Bühler, Fellmann, Heer, Hege, Hodel, Horsch, Hunsinger, Landes, Lichti, Mosemann, Musselmann, Schmutz, and Zeiset. In 1867 a meetinghouse was built in Giebelstadt at a cost of 2,000 guilders, for which Preacher Jakob Horsch and his sons Johannes and Jakob donated the land. It seated 100 persons. A list of 1881 states the number of souls in the congregation as 172. In the following years the congregation declined heavily through emigration to America and southern Bavaria; in 1927 only five or six Mennonite families were living in Giebelstadt out of a total of 122 souls in the congregation.

Since most of the members were then living in Würzburg, regular services were begun there in a rented hall. In consequence the congregation became known as the Giebelstadt-Würzburg, (*q.v.*) congregation (*ML* II, 112). In 1941 the congregation had only 51 souls, with a meeting in Würzburg every Sunday and at Giebelstadt on the first Sunday of the month. In the 1951 *Gemeinde-Kalender* the name had become Würzburg-Giebelstadt, and the meetings were held in Würzburg on the first and third Sundays of the month and at Giebelstadt on the second Sunday in the home of a Landes family. In 1955 the number of members in the congregation was 61. Almost from the beginning the Giebelstadt congregation regularly had two elders. The list of elders includes the following (with terms of service in the office): Jakob Horsch (?-1888), Johannes Landes (1839-?), Jakob Fellmann (1876-1905), Jakob Hege (1880-?), J. Hunsinger (1894-1910), G. van der Smissen (1894-1914), M. Fellmann (1907-36), J. Landes (1907-18), J. Hege (1914-29), Johannes Schmutz (1933-). In addition there were usually two other preachers and one deacon. The noted Ingolstadt elder, Michael Horsch, was earlier a member here and was ordained preacher here in 1909, moving to Hellmannsberg-Ingolstadt in 1913. (*ML* II, 112 f.)   Hege, H.S.B.

Giekerk, a village in the Dutch province of Friesland. Forty-five Mennonites living here in 1947 formed a Mennonite circle (kring), attending the church services at Veenwouden (*q.v.*) and Dantumawoude (*q.v.*) by bus. In Giekerk itself the members of this circle meet regularly, and there is also a ladies' circle with 11 members. Giekerk kring is a part of the congregation of Veenwouden. In 1955 the membership of the circle was 33.
                                                    vdZ.

Gielis van Aerde, an Anabaptist martyr, born at Lier (Belgium), was taken prisoner together with Govert Mertens, Marie Vlaminx, and Tanneken van Roosbroecke. After a severe cross-examination on the rack, in which he publicly confessed his faith, he was hanged and burned at Lier on Jan. 31, 1551 (not 1550; see *Offer* 569, note). Hans de Vette, who witnessed their execution, composed a song about these four martyrs of Lier, that starts with the words: "Als men schreef duyst vijfhondert" (*Liedtboecxken van den Offer des Heeren,* No. 17).   vdZ.

Offer, 568-77; *Mart. Mir.* D 96 f., E 1, 111 (van Braght calls these four martyrs Gilles, Govert, Mariken, and Anneken); Wolkan, *Lieder,* 63; Wackernagel, *Lieder,* 126; *Antw. Arch.-Blad* VIII, 393; XIV, 18 f., No. 196; *ML* I, 73.

Gielis Bernaerts, an Anabaptist martyr: see **Michiel Beernaerts.**

Gielis van Gent, an Anabaptist martyr, executed by beheading at Antwerp, Belgium, in 1559. His name (No. 46) is found in "Aenhoort Godt Hemelsche Vader," printed in the *Liedtboecxken van den Offer des Heeren,* 1562. Particulars are lacking, unless he is identical with Michiel (Jelis)

Bernaerts (*q.v.*). Gielis van Gent is not found in van Braght, *Mart. Mir.* (*Offer,* 566.)   vdZ.

Gielis de Gusseme, an Anabaptist martyr: see **Gillis de Gusseme.**

Gielis (de) **Hevilé** (Heville), an Anabaptist martyr, put to death at Antwerp on Feb. 17, 1573, with four other victims. Gielis had been rebaptized, but refused to name the elder who had baptized him. He remained steadfast and loyally suffered his cruel death. (*Antw. Arch.-Blad* XIII, 104 f., 173; XIV, 90 f., No. 1008.)   vdZ.

Gielis (Gilles, Jelis) **Mattysz** (Matthijsz), an Anabaptist martyr, a surgeon at Middelburg, Dutch province of Zeeland, who was put to death there with Willeboort Cornelisz on Oct. 26, 1564. He said he lay imprisoned over two years. The execution took place at night for fear of the populace. The *Offer des Heeren* and van Braght print three of his letters. One is addressed to the congregation whose pastor he was. It is a pastoral letter of unusual beauty, urging his members to be faithful and walk uprightly. The others were written to his wife, to comfort her and encourage her to have patience and perseverance in a pious life, well-pleasing to God. The *Offer des Heeren* celebrates him in a song, "Mijn jock is soet, mijn last is licht" (eight stanzas). (*Offer,* 448-77; *ML* III, 60; *Mart. Mir.* D 306, E 671-80; Wolkan, *Lieder,* 68.) Neff.

Gielt Eelckezoon, an Anabaptist martyr, burned at the stake at Leeuwarden, Dutch province of Friesland, on March 5, 1555. He had been rebaptized and sharply denounced the Catholic doctrines, saying that all that goes on "in the Catholic Church is idolatry."   vdZ.

J. Reitsma, *Honderd jaar uit de Gesch. der Hervorming in Friesland* (Leeuwarden, 1876) 63; *Inv. Arch. Amst.* I, No. 746.

Giesbrecht (Giesebrecht), a Mennonite family name, which is first found in West Prussia in 1607, Heinrich Giesebrecht being listed in Scharfenberg and Peter Giesebrecht in Reichenberg, both of which were Dutch villages in the Danzig Werder. In that year Peter Giesebrecht, a carpenter, received from the council of the city of Danzig the commission to build two sluices near Pasewark in the Danzig lowlands. He was promoted to the position of mill-builder, settled on a farm in the lowland, sold the farm two years later to a Mennonite named Bestvater, and moved up the Vistula into the neighborhood of Mewe. In 1612 an Abraham Giesebrecht was Schulze of the village of Scharfenberg in the Danzig lowland. His descendants can be traced in the village until 1763. The name was also found in other villages in the Danzig lowland. In 1623 a Peter Giesebrecht is one of a group of Mennonites arraigned before the Danzig city council by the Protestant pastor of Schönbaum for refusing to pay the required fees.

In 1680 an Abraham Giesebrecht of Schöneberg in the Gross-Werder entered the German preparatory school of the Elbing Gymnasium. Other Mennonites with this name were members of the Flemish Mennonite congregations in Danzig, the

Gross-Werder, and Elbing. There were also isolated occurrences of the name in the Frisian congregation of Montau-Gruppe. In 1789, before the great emigration to Russia, the Giesebrechts are listed in the Mennonite register. In 1936 there was no longer a bearer of this name in West Prussia.

In Russia a Jacob Giesebrecht was one of the first members of the newly established Mennonite Brethren Church. His name is found as signatory of the applications to the government in Odessa and St. Petersburg. He later emigrated to the Kuban and in 1875 became Oberschulze of the Kuban Mennonite settlement.

Some bearers of this name emigrated to Canada and South America. This name is not found among the Mennonites of the United States.   H.P.

G. E. Reimer, *Die Familiennamen der westpreussischen Mennoniten* (Weierhof, 1940).

Gieseler, Johann Karl Ludwig (1792-1854), a church historian, professor of theology at the University of Göttingen, author of *Lehrbuch der Kirchengeschichte* (Bonn, 1840-53), English translation, *A Textbook of Church History* (N.Y., 1868), which contains a treatise on the Anabaptists (III, Part I, 196-200) and one on the Mennonites (Part II, 90-102), stating in terse and objective terms what was known by scholars at the time, and citing an amazing number of sources, including even the works of Menno Simons. He does not, of course, give a true picture. He traces the rise of the Mennonites to Thomas Müntzer. In the divisions of the Dutch Mennonites he sees the "repulsive picture of raw piety, crossed by vanity and self-assertion of the most petty kind," and concerning the Swiss Anabaptists he says, "Among them remnants of their original fanaticism continued a long time, and they differ in this from the Mennonites, who nevertheless regarded them as their brethren in faith and frequently had letters of intercession written by the States General to the cantons, as to Zürich in 1660, and to Bern in 1718." On the whole, this history shows clearly what great progress research had made in the field of Mennonite history. (*ML* II, 113.)   NEFF.

Giethoorn, a town in the Dutch province of Overijssel, pop. about 2,500, of whom about 500 are Mennonites, since olden times the seat of a Mennonite congregation. Between 1563 and 1565 Leenaert Bouwens (*q.v.*) visited this congregation and baptized five persons. It is striking that many family names at Giethoorn consist of two syllables and end in a silent *e*: Doze, Haxe, Gorte, Hase, Kleine, Wuite. Blaupot ten Cate (*Groningen* II, 220-21) was of opinion that the congregation descended from the Flagellants. (The Flagellants were a medieval sect, which laid much stress upon asceticism and mortification of the flesh; in the 14th century they marched in large groups through Western Europe, flagellating their bodies; a number of them are said to have been directed to Giethoorn by the Bishop of Utrecht in order to break up the peat-moors here.) This is not very likely, but it is a fact that the congregation of Giethoorn, a picturesque village situated in a lake district,

with its canals, its numerous small and high bridges, its old-fashioned houses, both by its history and the characteristic manners and customs still in use in this town, takes an exceptional place among the Dutch congregations. In former times Giethoorn was a predominantly Mennonite town. As late as 1838, 50 per cent of the population was Mennonite, but now (1955) only 20 per cent.

By the end of the 16th century the congregation of Giethoorn was divided in two congregations, South Giethoorn and North Giethoorn. The smaller North congregation then belonged to the conservative Huiskopers (*q.v.*); in the 17th and 18th centuries it belonged to the Danzig Flemish Mennonites (*q.v.*), and maintained close connections with the church of Danzig. Sometimes elders came from Danzig to Giethoorn to perform baptism and the Lord's Supper. This North congregation maintained the old practices of the ban and the simple life and clothing and never admitted trained and salaried ministers. In 1631 and again in 1646 its members were exempted from serving in government offices on paying a fee.

It maintained some contacts with the conservative congregation of Balk. In 1834 its membership numbered about 60. It possessed a small meetinghouse, which was damaged in 1825 by a flood of the Zuider Zee. The last elders were Hendrik Sijmens Bakker (?-1852) and Gerrit Sijmens Bos, elder from 1838 until his death Jan. 14, 1875. From then on the pulpit was vacant, and the remaining members, only nine, joined the congregation of South Giethoorn in 1890. The meetinghouse, restored in 1854, was torn down in 1894.

The congregation of South Giethoorn always was the larger one. It belonged to the Flemish branch, and was sometimes called the New Flemish Church. It was less conservative than its sister congregation, but in the 18th and early 19th centuries more conservative than other Dutch congregations. Silent prayer was in use until about 1780, and in 1811 the congregation adopted the principle of strict nonresistance, asking absolute freedom from military service. The last unsalaried preacher was Harm W. Dam (1778-1873), who served ?-1850, assisted by K. Hovens Greve, preacher of Zuidveen (*q.v.*), who served from 1826 to 1851. In this year Greve's son A. K. Hovens Greve became the first trained pastor of South Giethoorn. He was followed by W. Jesse 1858-62, A. van Gulik 1863-66, J. A. Oosterbaan 1866-76, J. F. Bakker 1877-81, H. Koekebakker 1881-86, A. van der Goot 1889-92, H. Schuurmans 1894-1910, T. O. M. H. Hylkema 1911-29, M. J. Kosters Gz 1929-33, A. J. van der Sluis 1936-39, Abr. Mulder 1941-46, and F. H. Sixma from 1948.

Concerning the meetinghouse not much is known. The old meetinghouse was remodeled in 1856. A new one, still standing, was built in 1871 and dedicated on Christmas Day of this year. Statistics of membership were not available before 1834, when the membership numbered 314. It must, however, have been much more numerous in the 17th and 18th centuries. In 1861 the membership was 468, in 1900, 490, in 1955 about 365. About 1870 modernism (liberalism) entered the church. Most members of the church are farmers, but the farms are usually small. Besides the farmers there are a larger number of farm laborers, who formerly were often unemployed in winter. Hence the congregation had to take care of them; in 1915 it spent 4,000-5,000 guilders for the care of the poor. About 1920 the church board at the instigation of Pastor Hylkema carried out some plans of providing work, e.g., poldering swampy fields. Now conditions are much better because of the government unemployment benefits. Near Giethoorn are found two Mennonite recreation centers, "Samen Een" and "Kraggehuis," both situated on the lake.

Church life is very active here. Giethoorn was among the first Mennonite congregations to start a Sunday school for children, opened in 1895. Now there are two, one in South Giethoorn, one in North Giethoorn, comprising 200 children. A choir, founded 1914, now consists of 40 members; Bible circles, both in South and North; youth clubs; a gymnastic club (300 members), a basketball club, etc. The number of catechumens in 1955 was 177.   T.O.H., vdZ.

Blaupot t. C., *Groningen* I, *passim; Inv. Arch. Amst.* II, No. 1736; *DJ* 1850, 40 f.; *DB* 1861, 173; 1872, 195; 1873, 196; 1878, 2, 10, 14 ff., 23, 27; 1890, 142; 1892, 79, 81 f.; 1897, 83; 1898, 71; 1901, 2, 16, 47; F. A. Hoefer, "Historische Aanteekeningen omtrent Giethoorn," in *Verslagen en Meded. Overijssels Regt en Geschiedenis* XXX, 33-53; *ML* II, 113-14.

Giger, Gabriel, an Anabaptist of St. Gall, Switzerland, who joined the newly established brotherhood in Zürich in its earliest days. In the cross-examination of Feb. 25, 1525, he said that when the Spirit of God came upon him he hastily ran to Felix Manz's house, and there he was baptized by Conrad Grebel. Upon promising the court to desist and paying the costs he was dismissed. Soon afterward he was arrested again. In the trial of March 16, 1525, he stated that infant baptism was introduced by the pope; for this reason he had let himself be baptized by the godly baptism. He himself had never baptized, but would do so upon request. . . . He was not his own; what God commanded he would do.

Giger's letter written in August 1525 to the Swiss Brethren in Zollikon says, "Peace and grace be with you from God the Father and our Lord Jesus Christ, who gave Himself for our sins, that He might redeem us from this present awful world. . . . Do not take it ill of us that we did not write for so long; for there is not a week when we do not have to appear before the wolves. But we want you to know, dear Brethren, that God is working in a wonderful manner among the common people. I believe that there are many who have been baptized in Christian baptism in St. Gall, in the canton of Appenzell, and in the abbot's jurisdiction. . . . Pray to God for us that He may not withdraw His grace. Amen. Greet Uli Meyer, Heini Gigli, Jörg Schad, Ruotsch and Jakob Hottinger, and all the Brethren at Zollikon. There are probably 500 persons baptized in the Christian faith in the city and the canton." In December 1525 he was greeted in a letter by Niklaus Guldi.   NEFF.

E. Egli, *Die Züricher Wiedertäufer* . . . (Zürich, 1878) 26, 29; J. K. Füsslin, *Beyträge* . . . (Zürich, 1741) 369; *TA Zürich,* 49, 52, 62, 73-75, 80, 120; *ML* II, 114.

Gijsbrechtsz (Gijsbertsz), **Hendrik,** an elder of the Dutch Mennonite congregation of Gouda who adhered to the strict Mennonite principles; in 1660 he was present at the Flemish conference held at Leiden (see **Leidsche Synode**), which appointed him and three other ministers to visit Galenus Abrahamsz (*q.v.*), preacher at Amsterdam, to ask him to change his opinions or to suspend his ministerial duties. In 1665 we find Gijsbrechtsz with the Zonist wing opposing the Galenists (or Lamists), and traveling to Zeeland with the Zonist leader Samuel Apostool (*q.v.*) to persuade the congregations in this province to join the Zonists.   vdZ.

H. W. Meihuizen, *Galenus Abrahamsz* (Haarlem, 1954) 74, 106 f.

Gijselaar (de) (de Gyselaer), a family found from the 16th century on in Dordrecht, Dutch province of South Holland; they were prominent citizens of Dordrecht, well-to-do and usually cloth merchants. Since the end of the 16th century the members of the family have belonged to the Reformed Church. This may be the de Gyselaar family to which several Mennonite martyrs belonged: Cornelis Cornelisz (*q.v.*), a cloth-shearer from Dordrecht; Michiel Gerritsz (*q.v.*) of Prinsenhage, Dutch province of North Brabant, an uncle of Cornelis, who had married the widow of Valerius de Schoolmeester (*q.v.*); and Adriaen Jacobsz (*q.v.*), the son of Jacob Cornelisz of Dordrecht, a weaver at Dordrecht and owner of a farm near Klundert (*q.v.*), in the neighborhood of which all three were arrested in 1572, while attending a Mennonite meeting. (*Ned. Patriciaat* IV, 1913, and XVIII, 1928-29, 78 f.; *DB* 1912, 30-48.)   vdZ.

Gillis van Aken (not identical with Giesbert van Ratheim or Gys van Rotheim, who was also called Giesbert von Breberen for his birthplace; see **Ratheim**). Gillis van Aken was born about 1500 in or near Susteren in the Jülich district of Born (now Dutch province of Limburg), a gathering point of the recent Protestant movement. The *Jülicher Erkundung* says of Born, "One named Herr Gillis, a neighbor child, also preached here." In the examination (*Verhandlung*) before the magistrate of Born on June 16, 1533, one Gielis van Dilsen admitted that he had consented to having "Heer Gilis" preach in Susteren, and had heard him. Since he is addressed with the title "Heer" he may, like Menno Simons, have been a priest. In 1531 he was already traveling as an Anabaptist preacher through Limburg and must also have worked in Aachen, from which town he received his name. For a long time he was on the side of Menno Simons and became "a head and bishop of the Anabaptists." Two sisters of Illekhoven on the Maas testified at a trial in 1540 that Gillis was pale, of average height, with a pointed brown beard and large eyes. At times he wore his hair long, at other times cut. At a meeting in Goch in 1542 Menno Simons confirmed (ordained) him as an elder at the same time as Adam Pastor and Antonius of Cologne.

From this time on, Gillis was one of the outstanding Mennonites, took part in various important meetings of the elders, and traveled over a large part of Holland and Germany. He must have baptized a great many, for no other is named so frequently by the martyrs as the one who baptized them. In 1552 he was "banned" by Menno and his followers at a meeting in Mecklenburg because of adultery, but was reinstated in 1554 upon confession. Subsequently the Mennonites were frequently reproached (not without some justification) with this. On the occasion of the division in 1555 on the question of the shunning of banned marriage partners, he appears to have been very rigid and thus was a factor in the separation of the Waterlanders and High Germans from the main body.

Gillis was captured in 1557 while preaching in Willeboortsveld near Antwerp. For fear of death he recanted and offered to promote Catholicism in the very places where he had formerly preached, but he escaped only the stake thereby. On July 10, 1557, he was beheaded, his right hand cut off, and his body broken on the wheel. Because of his recanting, van Braght did not include him in the *Martyrs' Mirror*. His son Gillis was a preacher in Amsterdam, and the well-known Galenus Abrahamsz de Haan (*q.v.*) was his grandson.

K.V., W.N.

K. Vos, "Gillis van Aken," in *De Tijdspiegel* (August 1905); K. Vos, *Menno Simons* (Leiden, 1914) 95-99 (Vos attempted to prove that Gillis van Aken was identical with Ghielis von Ratheim or Rotheim); Rembert, *Wiedertäufer*, 339-42; Redlich, *Jülich-Berg, Kirchenpolitik* II, 1, pp. 92 and 314. W. Bax, *Het Protestantisme in het bisdom Luik en vooral te Maastricht* I (The Hague, 1937) 52-57 *et passim* (Bax also identifies Gillis van Aken with Gys van Rothem); C. Krahn, *Menno Simons* (Karlsruhe, 1936); *Antw. Arch.-Blad* VII, 435, 438, 440; XIV, 22 f., No. 251; *Inv. Arch. Amst.* I, Nos. 354, 361, 367, 370, 392, 399; *DB* 1918, 138 f.; *ML* I, 2 f.

Gillis (de) Graet (Jelis de Groot), a Dutch Anabaptist martyr, was burned at the stake at Kortrijk (Courtrai), Belgium, on Feb. 18, 1559 (*Mart. Mir.* erroneously 1558, without exact date). He was a native of Lendele, Flanders. After he had been arrested the officers considered transferring him to the Doornik prison, because they were afraid that the populace of Kortrijk would try to liberate him. But the transfer did not take place. Gillis was kept in prison for 13 months. Then he faithfully suffered martyrdom. There were also other Mennonites in the de Graet family. A Jan de Graet of Kortrijk was charged with Anabaptism as early as 1538. Syntgen de Graet (see Jozijne Steeghers), an old woman, and her son Steven de Graet (*q.v.*) died for their faith at Gent, Belgium, in 1564.

vDZ.

Mart. Mir. D 367, E 616; Verheyden, *Courtrai-Bruxelles*, 33, No. 6; *ML* II, 187.

Gillis de Gusseme, a Dutch Anabaptist martyr, was arrested at Merelbeke, Flanders, where he was taken prisoner with other Anabaptists, including Jacob (van) Curick of Cleve and Willem de Brouwer of Leiden, and imprisoned at Gent. Both Jacob and Willem recanted and were beheaded at Merelbeke on July 11, 1551. Gillis and also Lysbeth Piersins (*q.v.*) remained steadfast. Gillis, Lysbeth, and Jacob Curick had been baptized by Gillis van Aken (*q.v.*). Gillis was a native of Merelbeke. He and Lysbeth were sentenced to be executed there, but because the Council of Flanders feared that en route to Merelbeke they would address and stir up the people, they were burned at the stake on the Veerleplein at Gent, on July 21, 1551. A song commemorating the death of Lysbeth and Gillis, "Alsmen schreef vijftien hondert jaren en een en fijftich daertoe voormaer," is found in the *Liedtboecxken vanden Offer des Heeren* (1562), No. 8. Gillis's wife and his 17-year-old son Lievin were also examined, but, though it became evident that they were only halfhearted Catholics, they were obviously not Anabaptists and were set free. (*Mart. Mir.* D 105, E 502; Verheyden, *Gent*, 17, No. 32; Wolkan, *Lieder*, 63.) vDZ.

Gillis van Havre (Havere), an Anabaptist martyr, burned at the stake on May 9, 1571, at Antwerp, Belgium. Gillis van Havre, who is said to have been a young man, was sentenced to death because he was (re)baptized, and because he was not willing to recant. Apparently this martyr is the same person as Jelis Claversz (*q.v.*) and Jelis de Metselaer (*q.v.*), who are listed in van Braght's *Martyrs' Mirror* as different persons. vDZ.

Mart. Mir. D 201, E 872; *Antw. Arch.-Blad* XIII, 53, 63; XIV, 76 f., No. 899.

Gillis (Gieles) Outerman(s), an Anabaptist martyr: see **Jelis Outerman.**

Gillis Rooze, an Anabaptist martyr, b. at Bellegem, near Kortrijk in Flanders, belonged to the congregation at Brugge, Belgium, which was led at this time by Jacob de Rore (*q.v.*). Several times he had taken part in the meetings held in the house of Maillaert de Grave. He was arrested in Brugge in February 1568 and between April 13 and July 28 of this year he was executed here at the stake. His wife Jacquemyne de Wilde (*q.v.*) died as a martyr a short time after him. Whether this Gilles Rooze belonged to the well-known Mennonite Roose (Roosen, *q.v.*) family is not certain, but it is probable that he did. (Verheyden, *Brugge,* 53, No. 50.)

vDZ.

Gillis Schrijver, a Mennonite elder of Flanders, Belgium, came several times in 1566-67 to Harlingen, Dutch province of Friesland, in order to settle the Flemish-Frisian quarrel (*DB* 1893, 26-51, *passim*). In the 17th century a Schrijver family is found in the Netherlands, one of whom was Pieter Schrijver (*q.v.*), a Mennonite preacher at Hoorn and Amsterdam. vDZ.

Gilse, van, a Dutch Mennonite family. As early as 1415 Jan van Gilse is found in the neighborhood of Breda, Dutch province of North Brabant. Obviously he or one of his ancestors received his name after the village of Gilse (now Gilze), situated in the same area. After the Reformation the van Gilses are found in Rotterdam and Schiedam. In the 17th century they are said to have been Remonstrants (*q.v.*).

The first Mennonite of this family seems to have

been (1) Cornelis van Gilse, b. 1717 at Schiedam, d. 1796 at Rotterdam. He was a surgeon, married to Geertruy van Maurik from Utrecht, and a deacon of the congregation of Rotterdam in 1749-53. His son was (2) Jan van Gilse, b. 1756 Rotterdam, d. 1782 at West Zaandam, who was trained for the ministry by Pieter Beets (*q.v.*), the preacher of the Hamburg-Altona Mennonite Church, and appointed ministerial candidate in 1774 by the church board of this congregation. In December 1774 at the age of only 19 years he was called to the ministry by the congregation of West Zaandam, where he served until his early death in 1778. He was married to Agatha Middelhoven. His philosophical essay, *Over Gods Voorzienigheid*, was given an award by the Teyler Theological Society. He also published a sermon, preached July 8, 1781, on I Thess. 5:12, 13, *Redevoering over de Agting . . .* (Amsterdam, 1781). (*Biogr. Wb.* III 253 f.; *DB* 1864, 105 f.; *Catalogus Amst.*, 253 f.)

His only son, (3) Jacob van Gilse, b. 1779 at Zaandam, d. there 1835, was a lumber dealer and owner of a sawmill, married Jannetje van Neck, and was the father of (4) Jan van Gilse (*q.v.*, 1810-59), Mennonite preacher and professor at the Amsterdam Mennonite Seminary. Of the children of this Jan we name (5) Jacob van Gilse (*q.v.*, 1836-1917), Mennonite minister, and (6) Alexander Gerard van Gilse, b. 1847 at Amsterdam, d. 1928 at Hilversum, served as Mennonite pastor of Wormer-Jisp 1871-72, Westzaan-Zuid 1872-78, Leer in East Friesland 1878-90, and Zwolle 1890-1922. In 1922 he resigned. He was married (1880) to Henriette J. Brouer of Leer. Jacob's children were (7) Jan van Gilse (1861-1935), a lawyer and member of the *Tweede Kamer* (House of Representatives), (8) Johan Adam van Gilse (1863-1931), a grain merchant at Groningen, and (9) Jacob van Gilse (1868-1946), police inspector at Rotterdam. A son of Alexander Gerard (6) is (10) Peter H. G. van Gilse, who was born at Leer, May 13, 1881. He was for many years professor of medicine at the University of Leiden, until he resigned in 1951, and a member of the church board of the Mennonite congregation at Leiden, and curator (governor) of the Amsterdam Mennonite Seminary 1941-51; his son (11) Alexander Gerard, b. 1923 at Haarlem, was the Mennonite pastor of Joure 1947-51 and Amersfoort 1951-53, and since Nov. 1, 1953, director of the Mennonite International Center of Heerewegen (*q.v.*) at Zeist. (For the van Gilse family see *Ned. Patriciaat* XXXIX, 1953, 87-99; *ML* II, 115.)   vDZ.

Gilse, Jacob van, b. Jan. 25, 1836, at Koog aan de Zaan, d. June 8, 1917, at Groningen, educated at the Gymnasium at Amsterdam, the Mennonite Seminary of Amsterdam, and the University of Leiden. After the death of his father Jan van Gilse (*q.v.*), he discontinued his studies to become a ministerial candidate in 1860. In January 1861 he delivered his sermon of installation as pastor of the Mennonite congregation at West Zaandam, and on Feb. 26, 1870, he became pastor of the united Mennonite congregation at Groningen. On May 27, 1906, he resigned in order to devote more time to

the study of Hebrew and to social work. For a number of years he was on the board of directors of the A.D.S. and curator of the Mennonite Seminary at Amsterdam. For more than 30 years he served as secretary of the Sociëteit (Conference) of Groningen and East Friesland. In 1906 he was knighted. In his youth he was an ardent promoter of modernism, which had made its appearance in 1860, and with the Reformed preacher B. J. C. Mosselmans of Groningen he became a founder of the weekly *Hervorming*. The results of his studies in Hebrew and the Old Testament he published in a number of studies and articles which appeared in the *Theologisch Tijdschrift*. Besides this he published *Tien Preeken* (Groningen, 1871). He was married to Anna Petronella Meelboom, daughter of Jan Adam Meelboom, Lord of Kockingen, and Engelina Craandijk.   K.V.

Biogr. Wb. III, 257 f.; Groningsche Volksalmanak 1918, 183-90 with portrait; Catalogus Amst., 286, 300, 315, 356; ML II, 115.

Gilse, Jan van, a son of Jacob van Gilse and Jannetjen van Neck, b. Oct. 19, 1810, d. May 25, 1859, at Amsterdam. He was twice married, his first wife being Jannetje Brester, the second Alexandrina Geertruide Craandijk. In 1834 he became the minister of the Mennonite congregation of Koog and Zaandijk. Two years later he received his doctor's degree with the thesis, *Commentatio exegetica et critica in caput XVII Vaticiniorum Ezechielis.* In 1837 he was called as pastor to Amsterdam and on May 5, 1849, as professor at the Mennonite Seminary at Amsterdam, entering upon his duties on Oct. 9. As a student he had twice won a prize with studies on Obadiah and Sirach. He wrote many articles for periodicals such as *Vaderlandsche Letteroefeningen, De Gids,* and *Godgeleerde Bijdragen.* After his death his writings, including a number of sermons, were published in five volumes with a biography by Professor P. J. Veth (*Verspreide en Nagelaten Schriften van Dr. J. van Gilse,* Amsterdam, 1860-61). He was a member of the Royal Academy of Sciences. He was the second president of the Dutch Mennonite Mission Society and a warm promoter of missions. His premature death prevented his full development, and his influence on the education of young Mennonite preachers was too suddenly removed. His work concerns chiefly the field of Biblical exegesis. W. Steelink engraved a beautiful portrait of him.   K.V.

Biogr. Wb. III, 254-57; N.N.B.Wb. IV, 657; DJ 1850, 184-90; DB 1886, 75-82; 1887, 47; 1898, 153; Catalogus Amst., 283, 315; ML II, 115.

Gingerich (Gingrich, Guengerich, Gingery), a Mennonite family name of Swiss Bernese origin. The name Gündrich, which likely became Güngerich, is found in the Bern records as early as 1389. The family, it appears, originated in the county of Konolfingen, canton of Bern. By 1559 the name was spelled Günderich but did not yet appear in Anabaptist lists. In 1692 the Anabaptist preacher (*Lehrer*) Christian Güngerich escaped from the prison in Schwarzenegg, where he had been imprisoned because of his religion. In 1709 the records of the Palatinate indicate that Barbara Güngerich Tschantz had been involved in Anabaptism. The name is again found in the Palatinate Mennonite census lists of 1744, and appears rather frequently in the 18th century. Hans Güngerich is mentioned around 1711 as one of the Amish leaders seeking reconciliation with the Mennonites. In 1765 Christian Güngerich was mentioned as a leader among the Amish in Waldeck and a year later Preacher Christen Güngerich of Steinseltz near Weissenburg (Wissembourg) in Alsace was among the church leaders visiting the Amish in the Netherlands. At Huninghausen in Waldeck the "Schweitzer Christian Güngerig" rented a dairy farm in 1743. In 1792 the lease to this farm was passed on from Christian to Peter Güngerich, who was the ancestor of many of the Iowa Mennonites bearing this family name. A letter of 1781 mentions a Hans Güngerich who had been serving as preacher in the Weissenburg congregation for more than 50 years. In the 1940 Mennonite census lists of Germany, the name Güngerich appears both in south and east Germany. Paul Güngerich of Remscheid, Germany, gathered Gingerich family records for many years, but unfortunately these were destroyed during World War II. Josef Gingerich (d. 1953) was the last president of the Königsberg, East Prussia, Mennonite Church.

The first mention of the family in America is found in the Conestoga Twp., Lancaster Co., Pa., assessment list of 1724, where the name William Gingerick appears. Johann Gingerich appears in the Warwick Township list eleven years later. Michael Gingerich from Alsace migrated to Lancaster Co., Pa., in 1747. His son Abraham with his wife and ten children moved to Waterloo Co., Ont., in 1801. Numerous descendants of this Abraham are numbered among the Ontario Mennonites. The Gingerichs of Dauphin and Juniata counties, Pa., are very likely descendants of Gingerich immigrants who settled in Lebanon Valley before or in 1747.

In 1831 Johannes Jüngerich and family and his brother Daniel were given a letter of recommendation by a Hesse state official, who wished them happiness in America. This Johannes is the ancestor of Amish Gingerich descendants in Daviess Co., Ind., and in the Arthur, Ill., Amish community. Jacob Güngerich, born near Kassel, Germany, came to America in 1833 and settled in Holmes Co., Ohio. Numerous Amish descendants of Jacob live in Ohio, Illinois, and other states. About the same time Amish Gingerichs settled in Waterloo Co., Ont., among whose descendants is the present Bishop Orland Gingerich of the Steinman Church.

In 1833 Daniel P. Güngerich of Waldeck emigrated to America. He was the father of Samuel D. Guengerich (q.v.). Two years later his half brother, Amish preacher Johannes P. Güngerich, son of the Peter of Waldeck mentioned above, and family arrived in Pennsylvania. Both of them finally settled in Iowa. Johannes is the ancestor of Simon Gingerich, Mennonite bishop of Wayland, Iowa, as well as of a considerable number of other Mennonite ministers and church leaders, including Bishop Fred Gingerich of Canby, Ore., Preacher J. C. Gingerich of Dagmar, Mont., Preacher Amos Gingerich of Parnell, Iowa, and Professor Melvin Gingerich of Goshen College.

Among the representative church leaders have been Michael Gingrich (1792-1862), first Mennonite bishop in Lebanon Co., Pa.; his nephew Isaac (-1892), the third bishop in Lebanon Co.; Abraham Gingerich (1856-?), Mennonite bishop in Ontario; Jacob Gingerich (1840-1920), Mennonite minister in Ontario; John Gingrich (- 1845), Mennonite bishop who emigrated to Illinois in 1839; Christian Gingerich (1820-1908), bishop of the South Danvers Mennonite Church; his son John Gingerich (1856-1931), bishop of the Danvers Church; and S. D. Guengerich (1836-1929), lay leader in the Amish Church.

The Gingerich family is widely scattered in America and evidently descended from a considerable number of immigrants not closely related to each other. Twenty-nine obituaries in Mennonite periodicals between 1866 and 1915 show that they lived in Pennsylvania, Ohio, Maryland, Ontario, Indiana, Illinois, Iowa, and Nebraska. In 1954, 46 ordained Gingerichs were serving in the Amish and Mennonite churches of America.   M.G.

Nettie Beachy, *Family Record of Daniel J. Gingerich and His Descendants* (Wellman, Iowa, 1930); Mrs. David R. Bontreger, *Family Record of Jacob Guengerich and Barbara Miller and Their Descendants* (Millersburg, Ind., 1949); Simon H. Irick, *Descendants of John Gingerich II* (Frankfort, Ind., 1952).

Gingrich Mennonite Church (MC), a member of the Lancaster Conference, is located a few miles south of Annville, Lebanon Co., Pa., on a beautiful knoll, with a walled cemetery near by. The first church, built in 1792, served the congregation until 1920, when the present larger brick church was built on the same site. Lebanon County had some of the overflow from Lancaster County in the latter half of the 18th century and again in the last ten years, almost replacing the descendants of the earlier settlers. The first Sunday school was held in 1893. In 1954 the congregation was under the care of Simon G. Bucher as bishop, Daniel D. Wert and Elmer Showalter as ministers, and Harold Frey as deacon; the church membership was 64. I.D.L.

Girls' Homes, also called Girls' Centers, are centers of fellowship and spiritual ministry, sometimes with rooms for rent and boarding facilities, for Mennonite young women who come to the larger cities for employment, especially as domestics. Four of these homes have been established by the Canadian Mennonite General Conference—Mary-Martha Girls' Home (q.v., founded 1935) at Vancouver, B.C., "Ebenezer" Girls' Home, Winnipeg, Man., the Saskatoon Girls' Home, Saskatoon, Sask., and the Calgary Girls' Home at Calgary, Alta., under the leadership of J. J. Sawatzky, the local minister, founded approximately in 1945 (see Scarboro Mennonite Church). The Mennonite Brethren Church has three such homes—the Mary-Martha Girls' Home (q.v.) of Winnipeg, founded in 1925, the Bethel Girls' Home (q.v.) of Vancouver, founded in 1931, and the M.B. Girls' Home of Saskatoon. In the Mennonite Church (MC) there are two such homes—

the Mennonite Girls' Home, founded in 1935 at Reading, Pa., and the Mennonite Girls' Center at Goshen, Ind., founded in 1948. The girls' homes commonly are operated by a matron under either a district mission board (as in M.C. homes), a district conference (as in M.B. homes), or a local committee (as in G.C.M. homes). Usually a local pastor is assigned as spiritual adviser. H.S.B.

Gisbert Dircusoen, the author of the martyr hymn, "Ghy Broeders al tesamen," as proved by its acrostic. He is otherwise unknown. The hymn is found in *Veelderhande Liedekens* (1580) folio 104, verso. (Wolkan, *Lieder*, 79; ML I, 449.) vdZ.

Gladbach: see München-Gladbach.

Glade Mennonite Church (MC) near Accident, Md., had its origin about 1890 as a mission Sunday school established from the Casselman Valley district under the leadership of Preacher Henry H. Blauch of the Springs congregation, although Amish people had moved into this region as early as 1776. Early settlers were Brenneman, Bender, and Ash. Sunday school was begun in the Beachy Schoolhouse, later known as the Forks, but the meetinghouse (26 x 40 ft.) was not built until 1908. At first there was no resident ministry, the congregation being served by the Springs ministers. Bishop Isaac K. Metzler moved into the congregation in 1935 and still serves (1954) as pastor, with Sherman Tressler (ordained 1932) as deacon. The membership in 1953 was 59, about the same as for the past 40 years. H.S.B.

Gladwin (Mich.) Mennonite Brethren Church, now extinct, had its beginning in 1914, when a group of German Baptists and Mennonite Brethren who had moved there asked to unite with the M.B. Church Conference. Elder Heinrich Voth of Minnesota organized them into a local congregation, with P. E. Penner as its first pastor. For some time the church grew and then began to decrease, and discontinued in 1947. Other ministers of the church were D. F. Strauss, Ewald Rohloff, and J. J. Reimer. H.E.W.

Gladys (Va.) Conservative Amish Mennonite Church, with a membership of 20 in 1953, originated in 1944, when the D. K. Yoder and C. L. Ressler families moved into the area and soon began to hold regular religious services in Ressler's home. In 1955, now called Bethel, the church had 20 members, with C. L. Ressler and M. Hostetler as ministers. C.L.R.

Glait (Glayt, Glaidt, sometimes also called Oswald von Jamnitz after his last place of sojourn), Oswald, an Anabaptist martyr. He was born in Cham, Upper Palatinate, Germany, and was originally a monk or priest. Early in the 1520's he joined the Lutheran Church, went to Austria, and became for a while a minister in Leoben, Styria. Expelled from there and "from all of Austria for the sake of the Word of God," he turned to Nikolsburg (*q.v.*) in 1525, where the Lutherans had organized a church under the protection of Leonhard von Liechtenstein, led by Hans Spittelmaier

(*q.v.*). Glait now became the assistant minister of this congregation. Nikolsburg was at that time a real haven for all kinds of non-Catholic groups such as Bohemian Brethren (formerly Hussites), Lutherans, and the more spiritualistic minded "Habrovans." In 1526 Glait supported an attempt by the Moravian nobleman Jan Dubčansky, to unite all these "evangelical" parties. With the consent of several Moravian noblemen Dubčansky called a "synod" to Austerlitz which Glait also attended. The latter's report of this event was printed with the title, *Handlung yetz den XIV tag Marcij dis XXVI jars, so zu Osterlitz in Merhern durch erforderte versammlung viler pfarrer und priesterschaften, auch etlicher des Adels und anderer, in Christlicher lieb und ainigkeyt beschehen und in syben artickeln beschlossen, mit sambt derselben artickel erklärung. I. Cor. I.* (only known copy in the National Library in Vienna). This synod was certainly a great event: on the one side were more than one hundred "Utraquist" ministers (Bohemian Brethren), on "our" (Lutheran) side were many more. At the center sat the nobles, Dubčansky and other manorial lords of the area. Appointed commissioners called attention to the differences of doctrine and requested a comparison, so that the poor populace might not be bewildered. The decision must be left to the clear Word of God; human rank and descent should play no role. Of the seven articles discussed (Wiswedel, 553-5) the fourth might be mentioned: "No one should be admitted at the Lord's Table unless he be born again before, through the Word of God." In general, the type of faith defended was closest to the Zwinglian. Agreement was finally reached, and every participant added his signature (date: March 19, 1526).

A few weeks later Hubmaier arrived in Nikolsburg as a refugee. His reputation must have preceded him, for he found a great following right from the beginning. The town now became to the Anabaptists "what Emmaus was to the Lord. . . ." Apparently Glait also received believer's baptism. In Glait's room Hubmaier finished (July 1526) his book, *Der uralten und neuen Lehrer Urteil, dass man die jungen Kinder nit taufen soll bis sie im Glauben unterrichtet sind.* Hubmaier set to work to replace the former Lutheran congregation by an Anabaptist brotherhood, with the approval of the Lord of Liechtenstein. This stimulated Glait to do more writing. In 1527 he published his second tract, *Entschuldigung Osbaldi Glaidt von Chamb . . . etlicher Artickel Verklärung so ihnen von Missgönnern fälschlich verkehrt und also nachgeredt worden ist* (printed at Nikolsburg by Simprecht Sorg, called "Froschauer," who printed all the Hubmaier tracts). In this tract Glaidt sought to answer the many calumnies of the Barefoot Friars of near-by Feldsberg who had spread all kinds of stories about the "evangelicals" of Nikolsburg and about Glait in particular. "Everyone knows that these things were not true," Glait asserts, "but I would rather be called a 'heretic' with Christ than a 'holy father' with the pope." Since they had charged him with false doctrines, which might confuse the common man, he would now discuss the articles in question. The following points are taken up in the booklet: (1) Faith and its demonstration in good works, (2) the saints and their worship, (3) the giving of alms, (4) and (5) the differences in food and days, (6) the celibacy of the clergy, (7) images, (8) altars, (9) giving offense (i.e., giving up Catholic customs, such as celibacy, eating meat on Friday), (10) burial, (11) the sacraments, (12) baptism, (13) the Lord's Supper, (14) freedom of the will.—It should, however, be admitted that in skill and clarity Glait's book cannot be compared with the writings of Hubmaier.

In 1527, when a dispute broke out in Nikolsburg concerning the use of the sword (defended by Hubmaier) or the practice of absolute nonresistance (defended by Hans Hut), Glait sided with Hut. Dissatisfied with the outcome (Liechtenstein decided in favor of Hubmaier), Glait followed his fugitive friend Hut to Vienna in Austria. Here we find Glait in the Anabaptist meeting in the Kärntnerstrasse, and here it was that Glait baptized the former Franciscan friar Leonhard Schiemer (q.v.), who was soon to seal his faith with a martyr's death. From now on Glait found no place of rest. Hans Schlaffer (q.v.), another well-known Anabaptist martyr and former priest, had contact with him in Regensburg, Bavaria, and testified later to Glait's pious Christian life.

Very little is known about Glait's work in the following years. After Hubmaier's death he turned to Silesia where Caspar Schwenkfeld and his collaborator Krautwald had been working for the Reformation (as they understood it). Around 1530 Glait seems to have published a tract, "Concerning the Keeping of the Sabbath," of which, unfortunately, no copy has been preserved. We learn of its contents only through Schwenckfeld's refutation, dated Jan. 1, 1532, and entitled *Vom Christlichen Sabbath und Unterschaidt des alten und newen Testaments* (the only print known is one of 1589, reprinted in *Corpus Schwenckfeld*. IV, 452-518). Apparently Glait presented the idea that an observance of the Sabbath is binding on the Christians in the new covenant just as it was on the Jews of the old, because it is enjoined in the Decalog. Since Glait and his companion Andreas Fischer promulgated this idea in the area of Liegnitz (Silesia), Krautwald, at the insistence of the Duke of Silesia, wrote a critique entitled *Bericht und anzeig wie gar ohne Kunst und gutten verstand Andreas Fischer vom Sabbath geschrieben* (a copy in the State Library in Berlin).

Glait tried now to work for his faith in Prussia, but an order of Duke Albrecht in 1532 brought about his expulsion also from this territory, together with his friends Oswald of Grieskirchen (an Anabaptist) and Johannes Bünderlin (formerly of Linz, a "spiritual reformer") (q.v.). It is supposed that Glait now went to Falkenau in Bohemia, for we find here "Sabbatarians" as late as 1538. This Sabbatarian movement seems to have also encroached into the Nikolsburg district, for Leonhard von Liechtenstein asked both Wolfgang Capito and Caspar Schwenckfeld for an opinion in this matter (1531). Since Capito was preoccupied

with other affairs, Schwenckfeld undertook the task of judging the booklet of Glait, "with whom I had once pleasant discussions at Liegnitz" (see the above noted tract by Schwenckfeld). Schwenckfeld rejected Glait's main argument for the Sabbath observance (the reference to the Decalog) because logically all the Judaic law would have to be reinstated including circumcision. "The true observers of the Sabbath are those upon whose hearts the law of the Spirit has been written by the fingers of God." In conclusion, Schwenckfeld presented a *Summarium etlicher Argument wider Oswald Glaids Lehre vom Sabbath*, with 18 arguments. But he emphasized that he was careful not to do any injustice to Oswald (*Corp. Schw.* IV, 515-18).

Later Glait must have become the leader of an Anabaptist group around the city of Jamnitz in Moravia, but no particulars are known. The Hutterite *Chronicle* gives only an account of his death of which the Hutterites learned through several brothers who shared Glait's fate (Zieglschmid, *Chronik*, 259 f.): "In 1545 Brother Oswald Glait lay in prison in Vienna for the sake of his faith. The citizens came to him in his prison and asked him kindly and earnestly to renounce it, else they would have to execute him. But say what they would, they could not move him. Two brethren also came to him, Antoni Keim and Hans Staudach [Hutterite Brethren likewise in prison in Vienna for the sake of their faith, and in 1546 martyred], who comforted him. To them he commended his wife and child in Jamnitz. After he had been in prison a year and six weeks, they took him out of the city at midnight, that the people might not see and hear him, and drowned him in the Danube" (autumn of 1546).

A song by an unknown author praises Glait's death as a martyr. It begins, "Ihr Jungen und ihr Alten, nun höret das Gedicht" (*Lieder*, 121 f.). Of Glait himself two hymns are known: one found in a Hutterite manuscript book and still unpublished, "O sun Davidt, erhör mein bitt, und lass dich des erbarmen" (mentioned by Beck, *Geschichts-Bücher*, 161, note), and the other called "Die Zehn Gebote," which begins, "Es redet Gott mit Mose: ich bin der Herre dein," printed 1530 as a pamphlet, reprinted once more in Magdeburg in 1563, and now also to be found in Wackernagel, *Kirchenlied* III, 465 f. (No. 524).

Just as Glait was honored in song after his death, so his services to the Brethren were willingly recognized during his life. Balthasar Hubmaier in his *Ainfeltiger Underricht* (1526) gives him the praise that he "proclaimed the light of the holy Gospel so bravely and comfortingly, the like of which I know at no other place." LOSERTH, R.F.

W. Wiswedel, "Oswald Glait von Jamnitz," in *Ztscht f. Kirchengesch.*, 1937, 550-64; *Die Lieder der Hutterischen Brüder* (Scottdale, 1914); *Corpus Schwenckfeldianorum* IV (Leipzig, 1914); also the excellent study by Loserth, ML II, 117-19.

Glanzer, a family name found among the Hutterian Brethren, which stems from Carinthia (q.v.). Among the exiles who were expelled from Carinthia and taken to Transylvania because of their refusal to return to the Catholic fold was Christian Glanzer, who was settled in Romos, a village west of Hermannsstadt, in October 1755. From here the group went to Alwinc, where they came in contact with the Hutterian Brethren and later united with them. D.D.

Glarean (Heinrich Loriti of Glarus, Switzerland) (1488-1563), able humanist scholar, an important teacher of Conrad Grebel (*q.v.*) during his humanist years in Basel (1514-15) and Paris (1518-20), and along with Vadian (*q.v.*) a major influence on him. Under the influence of Erasmus in Basel (from 1514 on), Glarean became an enthusiastic humanist and opponent of the Reformation. After three years in Basel (1514-17), where he operated a student *bursa* or boarding house with private lessons, he transferred to Paris, where he operated a similar *bursa* 1517-22. Grebel studied Latin and Greek and humanistic studies one year with him in Basel and a short time in Paris (October to December 1518). Through him Grebel was introduced to the outstanding French Humanists in Paris, Faber Stapulensis, William Budé, William Kop, and Nicholas Beraldus. Glarean first made Grebel a humanist in Basel; Vadian continued the development in Vienna. H.S.B.

H. S. Bender, *Conrad Grebel* (Goshen, 1950) 10-17, 29-52; O. F. Fritzche, *Glarean, sein Leben und seine Schriften* (Frauenfeld, 1890).

Glaser (*Hubmayer*), **Bastel**, a Hutterite martyr, one of the Anabaptists connected with Jakob Hutter in 1534-35. His name "Glaser" probably refers to his trade (glazier); the name "Hubmayer," found in the Anabaptist court records in the archives of Innsbuck, is probably the correct one; at any rate he was not related to Balthasar Hubmaier, the Anabaptist apostle in the Black Forest and in Moravia.

We meet Bastel Glaser first in 1534. He was given the task of leading "a people from the Oberland" (Tirol) to Moravia, on the usual route down the Inn and the Danube to Krems, and from there to Moravia. Between Krems and Meissau, in the village of Hohenwart, this group was halted, arrested, and taken to Eggenburg. There they were tortured by "burning the cheeks through." After an extended painful imprisonment, during which Jakob Hutter sent them a letter of consolation (*Epistel an die Gefangenen zu Hohenwart*), they were released, and may have reached Moravia, where, however, persecution was raging more violently than ever.

After three years, during which he was probably preaching, Glaser, together with Hans Grünfelder (*q.v.*), the treasurer of the Anabaptists in Lüsen and in the vicinity of Michelsburg and Schöneck, was captured, taken to Imst (Tirol), and tried. Although Gallus Müller (*q.v.*), noted for his success in leading prisoners to recant, took pains to convert Glaser and his fellow prisoners, Hans Grünfelder and the aged Oswald, he did not succeed. In his cross-examination Glaser confessed that he had not come to this country until Michaelmas. He stayed in the woods most of the time and proclaimed his teaching to several brethren, but baptized nobody.

The report of the death of the above Brethren was written by Griesinger to the brotherhood in Moravia: "Out of sincere love we cannot refrain from reporting on our brethren, Bastel Glaser, Hänsl Grünfelder, and the aged Oswald from the Oetztal. These have with great joy proclaimed the Lord's holy Word and truth, as you probably know. . . . I cannot adequately describe their joy. When Bastel and Hänsl were executed about 1,000 persons were present. Hänsl cried to the people, admonishing and warning; and Bastel too—until their death together with old Oswald." "The people were horrified. . . . It is true, as the wise man says, They will spare neither the aged nor the gray. Their bones could not be entirely burned; they were afterward thrown into the water, and we hope that this witness was not made in vain. The heart of one did not burn; without doubt this was a divine testimony." The date of the execution is unfortunately not given anywhere. Since Gallus Müller wrote on April 4, 1538, that his efforts were not taking effect, the date was probably 1538 (not 1537).

Bastel Glaser is the author of two hymns: (1) "Herr Gott in Deinem höchsten Thron" (15 stanzas); (2) "O Herr Gott, wend mir meine Schmerzen" (23 stanzas). LOSERTH.

Wolkan, *Geschicht-Buch*, 105, 132 f.; Beck, *Geschichts-Bücher*, 116, 181 f.; J. Loserth, *Der Anabaptismus in Tirol* I (Vienna, 1892) 530; II, 149 f.; Wolkan, *Lieder*, 171, 255; *Die Lieder der Hutterischen Brüder* (Scottdale, 1914) 71-74; *ML* II, 119.

Glasgow Mennonite Church (MC), now extinct, was located in Uxbridge Twp., Ontario Co., seven miles northeast of the Wideman Mennonite Church in York Co., Ont. In 1930 a Mennonite family moving into the Glasgow community organized prayer meeting among several homes. In 1932 Sunday school was begun in a local church with occasional preaching by York County ministers. In 1937 Gordon Schrag of Zurich was ordained as pastor. In 1938, 15 baptized members organized into a congregation. With some shift of interested families and a transfer of the pastor to another field regular services discontinued in 1943. J.C.F.

Glasius, Barend (1805-86), Dutch Reformed pastor at Slijk-Ewijk 1828-36 and Geertruidenberg 1836-79, author of an important biographical dictionary of Dutch theologians, the *Godgeleerd Nederland* (3 vv., Hertogenbosch, 1851-56), which includes articles on a number of Mennonites. Of his numerous historical writings mention should be made of *Galerij van Nederlandsche Geloofshelden* . . . (Tiel, 1853-54), a 120-page book written in collaboration with H. M. C. van Oosterzee, in which the (unfinished) 9th chapter deals with the Mennonites. (*Biogr. Wb.* III, 262-69.) vDZ.

Glasmacher (also Huisman), **Peter**, of Telgte, Westphalia, Germany, was an Anabaptist bishop who was active in Liege in 1533 and later in Unna, Westphalia (Keller, 261 ff.). In 1537 he was arrested by the Bishop of Münster with a group of Anabaptists. Among them was Johannes Hasenvot (q.v.), whose testimony has been preserved. Hasenvot had come from the Anabaptists in Soest to establish contact with the brethren in Telgte and Wesel. The Münsterite Peter von Noerich (also Gerhard Eilkeman) named Peter Glasmacher in a trial in 1544 as one of his associates who was also known as "Beichtvater" and had lived for a while in Ibbenbüren.   C.K.

L. Keller, "Zur Gesch. der Wiedertäufer nach dem Untergang des Münst. Königreichs," in *Westdeutsche Ztscht für Gesch. und Kunst*, 1882, No. 4; J. Niesert, *Münsterische Urkundensammlung I* (Coesfeld, 1826) 303.

Glaubensstimme: see **Hymnology** of the Mennonites of Prussia and Russia.

Glen Allen, a small village in Peel Township, six miles west of the northern boundary of Waterloo Co., Ont. In the fall of 1892, according to the *Herold der Wahrheit,* a meeting (MC) was organized here with Waterloo County ministers serving every four weeks. Resident families were Ernst, Reist, Selts, Weber, and Groff. A few years later a church came into use in the village. In 1893 Joseph Nahrgang and Noah Stauffer filled the appointments, the meetings alternating with those in the adjacent Maryboro Township. Communion was served for several years. By 1905 most of the families returned to Waterloo County and meetings discontinued. Since 1945 through summer Bible schools and resettlement by Mennonites a strong Sunday school of 80 and a membership of 35 (1955) has arisen, cared for in a stone parsonage close to the former church and operated under the Mennonite Mission Board of Ontario, with Amos Brubacher as the resident pastor. J.C.F.

Glenbush Mennonite Brethren Church, located near the village of Glenbush in northern Saskatchewan, a member of the Canadian Conference of the Mennonite Brethren Church, was organized on July 15, 1928, under the leadership of N. H. Pauls, with a membership of 17. Its membership in 1954 was 136, and the congregation was still served by its first pastor, N. H. Pauls. The church building was erected in 1930 and has been enlarged four times.   J.H.E.

Glencross, a village with the address of Morden, Man. Here is located one of the 12 meetinghouses of the Rudnerweide Mennonites in Manitoba.
H.H.H.

Glendale Hutterite Bruderhof, established in 1949 near Frankfort, S.D., had a population of 97 in 1950.   M.G.

Glendale Mennonite Church (GCM), of Lynden, Whatcom Co., Wash., a member of the Pacific District Conference, was organized in 1945. In that year a building was purchased and remodeled for a meeting place, and articles of faith were adopted. F. D. Koehn served as pastor until 1947, when his place was taken by Dan Toews. In 1954 the pastor was Myron D. Hilty, and the membership 90.   D.T.

Glenlea Mennonite Church (GCM) is located 18 miles south of Winnipeg, Man. Organized in 1945, its 18 families had formerly belonged to the Schoen-

wiese Mennonite Church of Winnipeg. In 1954 the pastor was J. C. Friesen, and the membership 55.   J.P.

Glick (Glueck, Glück), a Swiss Mennonite family which migrated to the Palatinate. In 1731 there was a Jost Glückli in the Streigenberg congregation near Eppingen (now Baden). In 1940, 24 Glücks were members of four Mennonite congregations in South Germany. In 1954 three Glück ministers were serving in that area, one of whom was Theo Glück of the Durlach congregation, chairman of the Youth Commission of the South German Conference.

Peter Glick, the ancestor of the Amish Glicks, arrived in Pennsylvania in September 1748. Other members of the Glick family no doubt landed in America during that century. Large numbers of their descendants live in eastern Pennsylvania, among them eight Old Order Amish ministers. Five additional Mennonite and Amish Mennonite ministers serve in Pennsylvania and Virginia. Obituary records from 1894 through 1913 show that the family was represented in Pennsylvania, Virginia, and Indiana. Holmes Co., Ohio, also has representatives of the family.   M.G.

Glock, Paul (sometimes called Jung Paul to distinguish him from his father, who had the same name), a poet, and from 1577 a preacher of the Hutterian Brethren in Moravia, born at Rommelshausen near Waiblingen, Württemberg, Germany. According to his own confession he lived frivolously in his youth (*Lieder der Hutterischen Brüder,* p. 727, stanzas 6-8), then appealed to two Lutheran theologians to "teach him Christian morals," but they referred him only to faith (*op. cit.,* p. 710, stanza 15). It is not known who won him to Anabaptism, but it is well known that Württemberg was an active mission field of the Hutterian Brethren.

At the end of December 1550 Glock lay imprisoned in Cannstatt with his father, mother, and wife Else. In January 1551 the leading theologians of the region, Valentine Vannius, at that time pastor in Cannstatt, Matth. Alber, preacher in Tübingen, and M. Martin Cless (Ubinger), preacher at St. Leonhard's Church in Stuttgart, were commissioned to counsel him with kindness; this they did four or five times; but the prisoners rejected the instruction of these preachers, for they (the prisoners) were on the right road, and declared that if the church would practice what it preached, repent and forsake evil living, they would also go into the church, and remain steadfast. Nothing is known of their fate. Very likely they were expelled from the country.

The following years are dark. In 1558 we hear that the wife of the Anabaptist Peter Stürmer told another woman in Rudersberg near Schorndorf, "Your husband helped to capture the pious preacher [meaning Paul Glock]. He would therefore have a difficult position before the Almighty" (Bossert, *Quellen,* 172). This reveals that Glock worked in the vicinity of Rudersberg for the Anabaptists. He himself says that he could proclaim

God's Word for just half a year (*Lieder der Hut-terischen Brüder,* p. 734, stanza 4). After 1558 he was kept in jail continuously. Whether it was during that time that he was painfully racked and much tried by doctors, clergymen, and false brethren, as he states in one of his hymns (the *Lieder der Hutterischen Brüder,* p. 708), is not certain. Because he remained steadfast in his conviction, defending it with vigor, he was sentenced to life imprisonment in the castle of Hohenwittlingen near Urach (Württemberg). But he was apparently in the prison of the Urach castle for some time too (*Lieder der Hutterischen Brüder,* No. 5, stanza 3, p. 722).

At Easter he was given a fellow prisoner, Adam Hornikel or Horneck, called Beck because he was a baker by trade, of Heiningen, with whom he wrote (in 1563) hymn No. 3, "Gott haltet, was er verspricht"; also No. 4, "Herr Jesu Christ in deinem Reich" (*Lieder der Hutterischen Brüder,* pp. 714-18, and 718-21). In September 1559 Duke Christoph learned that these imprisoned Anabaptists were weak with age and ill, and therefore ordered the castle bailiff when he could do so to take them from the prison for three or four hours daily and let them walk in the "Springer" (probably the courtyard of the fortress) and occasionally in the house, but to keep the gates well barred so that they could not escape nor any friend come to them, and not permit them to dispute with the servants and lead them astray, thus spreading their doctrines. In February 1564 Hornikel was taken to Stuttgart, where, after another trial, he was expelled from the country; with two daughters he moved to Moravia.

Now Glock was alone in his cell, but he used his time well in writing hymns and letters to his wife, his brother-in-law, and especially to Peter Walpot, the leader of the Hutterian Brethren in Moravia. Sixteen lengthy epistles (1563-76) full of a fine Christian spirit are known from his pen and two remarkable confessions of faith (1563-73), well preserved in several Hutterite codices and now published in full in G. Bossert's great source publication, *Quellen zur Geschichte der Wieder-täufer* I; *Herzogtum Württemberg* (Leipzig, 1930), 334-477 and 1049-1102. The confessions are contained in letters to Peter Walpot in which Glock reports in lively detail his disputation with several theologians, and show Glock as a very skillful debater, fully certain of his stand and well versed in the Scriptures.

These letters had great influence on the life of the brotherhood (Beck, *Geschichts-Bücher,* 270). In 1562 Glock and Adam Hornikel had jointly drawn up a *Rechenschaft* of their faith before the court in Wittlingen, and in 1573 another. Probably in Wittlingen the court chaplain Lukas Osiander had with some others approached him, and when they were unable to move him, said he did not deserve to be at large, but must be imprisoned for life. (The conversation is reported in the *Geschicht-Buch,* 376 ff.) Otherwise his treatment was humane. The fact that he was able to get paper for letter-writing and to find carriers indicates this. His food was good. Lukas Osiander

said that in 1584, when there was talk of persuading the Anabaptists to recant by means of starvation rations, Glock had as good a diet as if he were in possession of a noble prebend, with good wine and roast meat, and a warm bed, with two small rooms, and if one supposed he was in his room, he had been sent as a messenger over the fields; he was also used for other work in the fields. Indeed as early as 1566 he had acquired the confidence of the bailiff to such an extent that he was sent miles away as a messenger if he merely promised to return (*Lieder d. Hutterischen Brüder,* p. 708).

In 1574 Glock again received a companion in prison—Matthias Binder (*q.v.*), a tailor of Frickenhausen near Neuffen, who had been a preacher of the Hutterian Brethren since 1569, was sent back to his home village as a missionary of the Brethren, and was then imprisoned in Neuffen and tried in Stuttgart. When he refused to promise to leave the country and make no more converts, he was taken to the prison of the Maulbronn monastery in June 1573, where Blasius Greiner (*q.v.*) had lain, and where Binder was now held on short rations and was to be visited frequently by the abbot to discuss his doctrine with him. Binder refused to enter into these discussions, for he had already defended his position before the theologians in Stuttgart. In vain the abbot, the bailiff, and the caretaker showed him how unsuitable prison was for him and that it offered no security against kidnaping. Finally in 1574 he was taken to Hohenwittlingen, where he found his brother in the faith, Paul Glock. In 1574 Glock wrote the hymn, "Kommet her and tut hie losen (hören)" (*Lieder der Hutterischen Brüder,* 726), and in 1576 another, "Preisen will ich den Herren" (*op. cit.,* 734), and "Wie lieblich ist gezieret" (736).

In late autumn 1576 a fire broke out in the Hohenwittlingen castle which both Binder and Glock helped to extinguish. When Duke Christoph heard of this he commanded that they be given the fare for the trip to Moravia. This happened after 19 years of captivity. They reached the brotherhood on New Year 1577, "with good conscience, with peace and joy." On Feb. 12 Glock was chosen as a *Diener des Wortes* (preacher), to serve the brotherhood. Jan. 30, 1585, he died at Schädowitz, Moravia. The Hutterites kept his letters with great care, and the many copies extant prove their great appeal to the Brethren.　　G.Bo.

Beck, *Geschichts-Bücher;* Wolkan, *Geschicht-Buch,* 374-81, bases its story of Glock on his epistles, excerpts from which Wolkan prints in footnote 378-81; Bossert, *TA* I: *Württemberg;* G. Bossert, Jr., "Aus der nebenkirchlich-religiösen Bewegung der Reformationszeit in Württemberg (Wiedertäufer und Schwenckfelder)," in *Blätter zur Württembergischen Kirchengeschichte,* 1929 (esp. 28-31); *Mart. Mir.* D 714, E 1024; Wolkan, *Lieder; Lieder der Hutterischen Brüder* (Scottdale, 1914) 709-37; *ML* II, 123 f.

Glückstadt, a town on the right bank of the lower Elbe near Hamburg (now Germany), was founded in 1616 by Christian IV of Denmark to compete with ambitious and thriving Hamburg, which then no longer belonged to his realm. To attract desirable settlers he gave the city a charter of religious freedom.

The citizenry were divided into three nationalities, which brought about some friction; there were Germans (Lutherans and Catholics), Dutch (Remonstrants, Reformed, and Mennonites), and Portuguese (Jews). Glückstadt was then, besides Friedrichstadt a.d. Eider (*q.v.*), Altona (*q.v.*), and Rendsburg, the only place in North Germany and Denmark with religious liberty, with the exception of several German settlements in Polish territory, like Danzig.

The Dutch and Portuguese enjoyed complete civil and religious liberty, as well as freedom from all military obligations; they had their own judges in civil and commercial matters, and their own arrangements for weddings, baptism, burial, and costume. They could carry on commerce and trade, and exercise any vocation without joining the guilds, which was generally compulsory at that time; and what was most important, they could practice their religious convictions without hindrance.

Very little is known about the Mennonites in Glückstadt, for there are no church records. It is thus not known when the first Mennonites moved into the city; but it is recorded that in March 1623 citizens were accepted without requiring an oath of them. These must have been Mennonites. In the new charter of 1631 the "Mennonists" are specifically mentioned; "They shall live their religion and conscience freely, and not be burdened with any oath, use of arms, or the baptism of their children." For release from military service they had to pay "a suitable annual fee," the amount of which is not known; and at the same time the Mennonites, Calvinists, and Remonstrants together received two acres of land outside the city for burial sites for 50 talers. (The former Mennonite cemetery is now a Catholic cemetery, with no reminders of former times.) The Calvinists and Remonstrants had a church, preacher, and a school in common. There probably never was a Mennonite school; according to a regulation of 1692 they were to send their children to the (Lutheran) city school. The Mennonites of course also bore their share of the common civic expenses, such as in building the city hall in 1642-43. They had to request the renewal of their charter every 10 or 20 years until 1700.

The Mennonites of Glückstadt were considered part of the Friedrichstadt (*q.v.*) congregation, as is shown in the archives of the Friedrichstadt congregation. Gert Henriks, the elder at "Frederikstad," was repeatedly in Glückstadt in 1633-39, to receive new members by baptism. In this connection names like the following are recorded: Albrantz, Ariens, Clasen, Cornils, Hardelop, Jacobs, Jansen, Müllienz, Peters, Siletz; and Christian names like Clas, Dirk, Gerrit, Jan, Jakob, Altje, Gritje, Maartje, Trien—all of them Dutch Frisian names. Discipline was apparently strict; for example, in 1633 a member was excommunicated for misconduct, and in 1645 a woman was expelled for marrying a non-Mennonite. On May 12, 1639, a resolution was passed at a conference in Hamburg to separate Glückstadt from Friedrichstadt; from now on it was a part of the Hamburg (-Altona) congregation, which was much nearer to them, and where Mennonitism could now develop much more freely than formerly. But Glückstadt had its own minister at least at times. In 1641 the Mennonites requested for their preacher freedom from the burden of quartering troops, and refer to a former royal mandate granting this freedom to "one who serves religion." Through visiting preachers connections were maintained with the homeland for a long time; for example, in 1663 Bastiaan van Weenigem, the minister of the Rotterdam congregation, stayed there for a short time when he visited several Low German churches.

The contribution of the Mennonites to the city's progress was probably not slight. In 1635 a Jakob Berentz of Hamburg settled here, whose "people and workers belonged to the Mennonite religion." He was probably a factory owner or a shipper and himself a Mennonite. In 1643 Gysbert van der Smissen II (b. 1620 in Haarlem in Holland, and had been a journeyman baker in Friedrichstadt) moved from Friedrichstadt to Glückstadt with his mother, the widow of Daniel Gysbert van der Smissen. He is said to have organized the guild of cake bakers there. But his chief importance to the city lay in his commercial activities. His ships went to Norway and France; in favorable seasons they penetrated to Greenland to catch seals and whales, an industry which he founded with other wealthy citizens. In the middle of the 17th century Glückstadt was probably at the peak of its importance as the trade center of the lower Elbe, largely through the activities of the van der Smissens. But soon thereafter a rapid decline set in, in consequence of the disturbances of war involving the city (Spanish trade was, for example, constantly disturbed by the outriggers of Dunkirk), for in spite of the urgent advice of the colonists to the contrary, the Danish king had made a fortress of the city.

Gysbert van der Smissen II and probably many others emigrated to Altona, where the family continued to prosper, especially in his son Hinrich (*q.v.*), called "founder of cities" because of his activities in construction and building in Altona. In 1678 Gysebrecht Daniel van der Schmissen (probably Gysbert Daniel) sold his farm at the Kremper Tor. The desire of the colonists to emigrate was strengthened by repeated disregard for their charter, which declared them free for all time from military burdens in the time of war; they sent several complaints and appeals to the king. (In petitions for release from these obligations, they pointed to the beautiful "liberty" in Hamburg and Altona, as a threat of emigration.) These conditions also led to differences between the "privileged" persons and the city government (president, mayor, and council), who belonged to the "unprivileged" German population. To look after their interests the several nationalities or confessions had appointed deputies; it is not known when this was begun. The deputy appointed by the Mennonites in 1685 was Daniel van der Smissen. He also represented the brotherhood in the conflict with the guild of silk and cloth dealers, who were naturally interested in limiting the free trade of nonmembers. The relations of the Mennonites with other religious groups were probably, on the whole, good; only one exception is known. In the winter of 1684-85 the relations were disturbed by a dispute with the Reformed about the cemetery keys, for the income from the cemetery was connected with the possession of the keys. The keys had hitherto been in the possession of the deputies of the nation, who were for a long time two members of the Reformed Church. When, after the death of one of these deputies, Daniel van der Smissen was appointed co-deputy, the Reformed claimed that the keys belonged to them. The president and council sided with the Reformed, but the chancellery, to whom van der Smissen and Lambert Gerts as leader of the Mennonites appealed, decided essentially in favor of the Mennonites. (After the Mennonites died out the cemetery was left in the hands of the Reformed.)

The Mennonites in Glückstadt also took the usual Mennonite position of tolerance toward other faiths. In 1660-61, when many English dissenters fled the Anglican reaction of Charles II and sought protection on the shores of the North Sea, Frederick III issued mandates for his entire realm, forbidding the reception of "banished Quakers or fanatics." The Mennonites were especially mentioned, and were threatened with loss of their privileges if they disregarded the mandates.

Emigration and the dying out of families reduced the number of Mennonites more and more. About 1740 the last one died. The chapel passed into the possession of the Altona congregation; it was remodeled into a dwelling and rented out. In 1792, when royal permission was granted to sell the house, it was already quite dilapidated. Although the charter remained in force in Glückstadt, there were no more Mennonites there afterward. R.Do.

Familienchronik der Familie van der Smissen (Danzig, 1875); Detlefsen, "Die städtische Entwicklung Glückstadts unter König Christian IV.," in *Ztscht der Gesellschaft für Schleswig-Holsteinische Gesch.* XXXVI, 196 ff.; B. C. Roosen, *Gesch. der Mennoniten-Gemeinde zu Hamburg-Altona* I, II (1886 f.); Blaupot t. C., *Holland* I; *Menn. Bl.*, 1858, 35 ff.; *DB* 1891, 94; *ML* II, 124-26; R. Dollinger, *Gesch. der Menn. in Schleswig-Holstein, Hamburg und Lübeck* (Neumünster, 1930).

Glyaden, a Mennonite settlement in Siberia, between Pavlodar, Slavgorod, and Barnaul, about 75 miles east of Slavgorod and 150 miles west of Barnaul. It was founded in 1907-8 by J. N. Dück and K. K. Willms, who were sent by a conference of landless Mennonites (see **Anwohner**) of the Halbstadt and Gnadenfeld (Molotschna) districts to Siberia to look for land. The meeting was held in Lichtfelde; hence the settlement was often called the Lichtfelde settlement. Dück and Willms accepted a tract of about 16,200 acres from the government; it was intended for 95 families with a population of 384; it was divided into villages with 24 farms each; later another farm was added to each village. After the Revolution the land was redistributed, each person receiving 15.4 acres. In 1927 the population was about 1,000.

The settlement had a difficult beginning because most of the settlers were poor and had been manual laborers and day laborers. But their economic life as well as their spiritual life developed rapidly. They attacked their problems with hope and with vigor; in the course of a few years the steppes had been changed into fertile fields, the houses and cottages were lost in gardens, woods were laid out, and each village had a school.

Glyaden had acquired a reputation by the products of its unceasing toil and its social arrangements. Then came World War I. Most settlers were of military age and were drafted; the women stayed at home alone to meet the new difficulties. Money had to be raised to maintain the men in the service. Horses and wagons were levied for military use. The settlement was nearly brought to ruin. For a few years all life was dormant, and all energy and hope had disappeared. At long last the inhabitants found a way to adapt themselves, and now there was a visible revival. The settlement had its own council and two government schools. Two additional schools functioned but received no support from the state. The settlement had a co-operative, a dairy, a cattle and seed association, and a machinery association; a tractor worked the fields. Two thirds of the inhabitants belonged to the Mennonite Church; they rented a hall in which they conducted services every Sunday. Jakob Warkentin was the elder in 1927. The Mennonite Brethren had their own meetinghouse. Jakob Peters was the elder in 1927. Little is known about the fate of the settlement under the Soviets.

D.H.

D. Harder, "Einst und Jetzt," A. A. Friesen Collection, Bethel College Historical Library; *ML* II, 122.

Gmünd, Schwäbisch, a city (pop. 30,748) in Württemberg, Germany, 28 miles east of Stuttgart, in the Rems Valley. It belonged originally to the domain of the Staufers, then became a free imperial city, and in 1802 it was made a part of Württemberg. It was rich in industry, in the Middle Ages strong ecclesiastically, with three monasteries of Augustinians, Dominicans, and Franciscans. The first stirrings of the Reformation took place here in 1523 under the influence of Hans Schilling, a Barefoot Friar in Rothenburg on the Tauber, whose stormy preaching roused the populace to such an extent that he was banished from the city by the council. He then went to Augsburg, where he also called forth a powerful movement; this brought about his expulsion from Augsburg, whereupon he went to Blaufelden and won the people there to the Reformation. Later he was pastor in Grosshaslach until 1549, then preacher in Heilsbronn, 1553-58 superintendent and pastor in Uffenheim. Andreas Althamer (*q.v.*) appeared as assistant to the city pastor in 1524, probably at first with cautiously reformatory sermons, then as the city preacher whom the people paid and whom they accompanied to and from the pulpit to protect him. He performed his own marriage to a young lady of Gmünd. On July 4, 1525, he was, however, forbidden to preach in the city or its territory. Soon afterward he had to flee from the city in a night attack on it by troops of the Swabian League.

The Protestants now met in secret to pray together, sing hymns, and read from the Bible. On Feb. 27, 1527, the council felt it necessary to warn the people of Anabaptism, which had reached its full strength in Augsburg and Esslingen. In Gmünd Martin Zehentmayer, a painter of Langenmoosen near Inchhofen in the district of Aichach, was a significant Anabaptist leader. He is said to have baptized over one hundred persons from the city and vicinity in chapels and private homes and to have celebrated the communion service with them. On the basis of the imperial mandate the council in mid-February 1528 arrested Zehentmayer and 40 of his adherents, including 19 girls and women. They were given only bread and water to make them recant the sooner. The obstinate ones remained in the towers 42 weeks. Among the people there was much sympathy for them. Some women and children climbed the city wall to reach the towers and talk to the prisoners or read and sing to them. This was then strictly forbidden. Zehentmayer was examined on the rack about his faith and his plans. He confessed, according to information given by the city council to the Augsburg city council in November, that he had hoped to secure community of goods. The charge of immoral conduct made by the chaplain Nikolaus Thoman, the author of the *Weissenhorner Historie,* is an unfounded defamation, and is probably based on the provost Aichele (*q.v.*). The Gmünd court records give no suggestion of such a charge, charging the Anabaptists only with their attitude toward the established church.

The prisoners, only two of whom are known by name, i.e., Wolf Esslinger (*q.v.*) and Bamberger, occupied themselves with writing hymns, which are printed in the collection, *Die Lieder der Hutterischen Brüder* (Scottdale) pp. 48-59, together with the songs written about them by their fellow prisoners. The very conservative council did not venture to take the responsibility of judging and condemning the Anabaptists. The mayor Egen secretly appealed to the Swabian League, to send 200 horsemen and 50 footmen to Gmünd to support the council in the punishment of the Anabaptists. The government of Württemberg also received the commission to send well-armed persons, unspotted by the Lutheran faction and loyal to the powers in authority. Scarcely had the armed men arrived when the prisoners were put on trial. But one of the councilors, the glazier Huber, ventured to voice an objection to the court procedure. The prisoners were sentenced to die by the sword, but if they would recant, they would receive mercy. Zehentmayer and four men, a woman, and a 15-year-old boy remained steadfast, and they were executed on Tuesday, Dec. 7. When they were again urged to recant and return to their families, they declared that they had commended their families to God, and He would provide for them. When the first article was read Esslinger said: "As you judge today so shall God judge you when you come before His face; God shall well know

you." When the third article was read, they said: "You stain your hands with our blood; God shall certainly not remit it to you, but require it at your hands." When the fourth article was read, they said: "Today we will testify with our blood, that that wherein we stand is the truth." When the fifth article was read Wolfgang Esslinger said: "Forsake your sins and unrighteousness, and repent, and God shall never remember it to you."

The people, especially the women, cried encouraging words to those who were to die. Some efforts were made at the last hour to induce them to recant. A nobleman rode into the ring to the boy and said to him, "If you will desist from your error, I will give you a stipend and keep you always with me." The boy refused and said, "God forbid! O God, I commend to Thee my spirit. May Thy Son's suffering not be lost in us." All went courageously to their death.

The popular mood was so excited and rebellious against the council that the council did not dare to dismiss the troops of the Swabian League or to execute more Anabaptists. A number of neighboring nobles interceded for them, as well as a part of the community, and the captains and soldiers of the Swabian League who lay in the city besought the council to show mercy to the Anabaptists. The council now summoned Franz Kircher, called Stadian, pastor in Göppingen, a Humanist and an old friend of Melanchthon, to convert the Anabaptists. He cannot have been a Lutheran preacher, as asserted by Debler and Vogt, the Gmünd chroniclers, for under the Austrian government and the strict Catholic spirit of the Göppingen chapter a Lutheran preacher could have asserted himself no more than had the Lutheran preacher Martin Cless, who had been compelled to flee from Göppingen (Hermelink, 211). Kircher was probably an Erasmian. A considerable number must have recanted, for on Dec. 14 the council proclaimed slandering and insulting those who had recanted to be a punishable offense. Calm returned to the community, the troops of the Swabian League were dismissed.

The attempt to win the Anabaptists to the old faith must gradually have succeeded. At least the council had no more trouble from Anabaptists, though it had to combat the Lutherans until the end of the 16th century. On the other hand we hear of several women who fled from Gmünd and its territory to Württemberg and were arrested there for Anabaptist practices: Barbara, the wife of Bonaventura Bopf in Gmünd, who was in prison in Nürtingen on July 2, 1530, and was converted by the Tübingen professor Balthasar Käufelin; Barbara Schleicher, wife of Veit Beck, a smith of Gmünd, who was in prison in Kirchheim early in July, and was converted by experienced and learned men; Ursula Harthmann of Mögglingen, who was in prison in Kirchheim early in July 1530, and like Barbara Schleicher was instructed and recanted; Ursula Spanner of Gmünd, who had married the Anabaptist Konrad Lemlin of Sindelfingen, who was burned in Vaihingen, still lay in prison. Since she was pregnant they did not punish her, but let her swear an oath (Dec. 23, 1531) that she would at once leave the principality and never return.

The Anabaptists were deeply concerned by events in Gmünd. This is shown by the five hymns about them, printed in the *Lieder der Hutterischen Brüder*, pp. 48-59. One of them is also in the *Ausbund*.
G.Bo.

Blätter für württemb. Kirchengesch., 1902, p. 4; *Uffenheimer Nebenstunden* I, 1287; *Beiträge zur bayerischen Kirchengesch.* XVI, 234; *Weissenhorner Historie*, published by Fr. L. Baumann in *Quellen zur Gesch. des Bauernkriegs, Bibliothek des Literarischen Vereins* CXXIX (1876); H. Hermelink, *Die theologische Fakultät in Tübingen 1477-1534* (Tübingen, 1906); E. Wagner, "Die Reichsstadt Schwäbisch-Gmünd in den Jahren 1526-1530," *Württemb. Vierteljahrshefte für Landesgesch.*, 1881, pp. 81 ff.; *Mart. Mir.* D 32, E 439; *ML* II, 126-28.

Gmunden, a town (pop. 10,000) in Upper Austria on Lake Gmunden at the foot of the Traunstein, known for its old salt refineries, was in the late 1520's the seat of an Anabaptist congregation. It is often confused with Gmünd, but neither the Gmünd in Lower Austria nor that in Carinthia was ever the seat of an Anabaptist congregation or the scene of Anabaptist martyrdom. But the Hutterite table of martyrs (*Geschicht-Buch*, 182) shows that in Gmunden two Anabaptists suffered a martyr's death. In Gmunden on Nov. 29, 1529, Peter Riedemann was captured and held in chains; Beck therefore calls him the "martyr of Gmunden." Christoph Gschäl worked here, setting in order the brotherhood in Austria, which had become disorganized (see **Austria**).   LOSERTH.

Wolkan, *Geschicht-Buch*, 65, 73, 178, 182; Beck, *Geschichts-Bücher*, 88; Wolkan, *Lieder*, 24; *ML* II, 128.

Gnadenau (Kan.) Krimmer Mennonite Brethren Church (see **Krimmer** Mennonite Brethren Church) was organized Sept. 21, 1869, in the Crimea, Russia, when 18 were baptized on their faith. To preserve the tenets of their faith this entire group of about 40 members emigrated to America in 1874 and settled in Marion Co., Kan., and named the settlement Gnadenau. They continued to hold their services in the homes or in school. The first church was a small sod building with thatched roof. In 1876 a frame building was constructed and a little later another wing was added, making the building T-shaped. In 1895 this building was torn down and a more modern building was constructed two miles south of Hillsboro, which is still in use by a congregation of 155 members.

Jacob A. Wiebe was the first elder, serving 1874-1900. An outstanding minister was Johann J. Harder 1874-99. Wiebe was followed by Heinrich Wiebe 1900-10, J. J. Friesen 1911-34, F. V. Wiebe 1935-45, Ezra P. Barkman 1946-47, George L. Classen 1948-50, Edward Epp 1950-52, D. V. Wiebe and P. R. Lange 1952-55. In November 1954 the Lehigh Mennonite Brethren Church and the Gnadenau K.M.B. Church consolidated and have since then worshiped as one brotherhood as Gnadenau Mennonite Brethren Church (*q.v.*). The combined membership in 1955 was 155, with D. V. Wiebe as leader.
D.V.W.

A. Pantle, "Settlement of the Krimmer Mennonite Brethren at Gnadenau, Marion Co.," *The Kansas Historical Quarterly* (February 1945).

Gnadenau Mennonite Brethren Church, Marion Co., Kan., was organized in November 1954 by the merger of the Lehigh Mennonite Brethren Church (*q.v.*) and the Gnadenau Krimmer Mennonite Brethren Church (*q.v.*). Its membership in 1955 was 155, with D. V. Wiebe as leader.   D.V.W.

Gnadenau Mennonite Brethren Church, located at Flowing Well, Sask., a member of the Herbert District Conference, was organized in 1910 under the leadership of J. F. Harms, with 38 members. In 1913 they built a church. The congregation has sent out workers both to home and foreign mission fields. J. F. Harms was followed in the leadership by S. L. Hodel, Isaac Toews, John E. Priebe, and W. Buller. The leader in 1954 was William Buller and the membership was 39.
J.I.R.

Gnadenberg (or *Grace Hill*) Mennonite Church (GCM), which is located 8½ miles east and one mile south of Newton, Kan., was founded as a congregation in 1811, near the city of Berditchev, in the province of Kiev, Polish Russia, and was known as the Michalin (*q.v.*) church and settlement, organized under the leadership of David Siebrandt. In the great movement to America the Michalin congregation also chose to emigrate, and arrived in three groups—two late in 1874, and the third in 1878. In 1875 the group was incorporated under the name Gnadenberg. Their church, dedicated in 1882, was still in use in 1953, with the distinction of being the oldest Mennonite church building in continuous use west of the Mississippi River. It was replaced by a new church dedicated in August 1954.

Gnadenberg was a charter member of the Kansas Conference when it was organized in 1877 and took part in the conference sessions of the General Conference at Halstead in 1881. From 1811 to 1941 Gnadenberg was served by three elders: David Siebrandt (minister 1811 and elder 1816), Johann Schroeder (minister 1848 and elder 1852), and Gerhard N. Harms (minister 1888, elder 1901). J. J. Voth served the group in 1937-49, and on May 1, 1949, Herbert E. Miller was installed as pastor of the congregation. The membership of the church in 1955 was 197.   J.F.S.

Gnadenfeld, a common Mennonite village name, found in the Molotschna Mennonite settlement, Russia; Auli Ata Mennonite settlement, Central Asia; Barnaul, Siberia; Alexanderwohl, Kan.; and East and West reserves, Man.   C.K.

Gnadenfeld, a Mennonite village and district (*volost*) of the Molotschna settlement, province of Taurida, Russia, established in 1835. This settlement originated when Wilhelm Lange, elder of the Brenkenhoffswalde (*q.v.*) and Franztal Mennonite Church of Brandenburg, Germany, led his congregation of 40 families to Russia in 1834, where Mennonites of the same background had settled a few years before (see **Alexanderwohl**). Wilhelm Lange, who was of Lutheran background, and his congregation brought new spiritual life and a higher cultural level to the Mennonites of the Molotschna settlement. Soon Gnadenfeld became a center of higher aspiration in the realm of education and a progressive religious life. Wilhelm Lange's (*q.v.*) correspondence, dating back to the time of the immigration to Russia, presents a picture of the religious and cultural life of that day. (The letters have been preserved in the Bethel College Historical Library.)

From the beginning, the town of Halbstadt (*q.v.*) had been the seat of the civic administration of the Molotschna Mennonite settlement. In 1870 Gnadenfeld became the second seat of administration (*volost*), which included 28 of the southeastern villages of the Molotschna settlement. The administrators (*Oberschulze*) who served this district during the first decades were Wilhelm Ewert 1870-71, Franz Penner 1871, Peter Ewert 1871-76, 1877-78, Gerhard Fast 1876-77, David Unruh 1878-87, and Gerhard Dörksen 1887.

A very significant factor in the life of the village and community was the establishment of a *Bruderschule* (parochial secondary school) which was a continuation of a school which the group had in Brenkenhoffswalde. In 1859 this school acquired the right to train teachers. David Hausknecht (*q.v.*) and Heinrich Franz (*q.v.*) were the first teachers of the school, which under their leadership made a lasting impression far beyond the village. The pietistic spirit of the Gnadenfeld community, which had been fostered in the old country through Moravian influence, found new nourishment in the South German evangelist, Eduard Wüst (*q.v.*), of a neighboring Lutheran village. Gnadenfeld became, next to Ohrloff, a center of progressive, somewhat pietistic-revivalistic Christianity. Fr. W. Lange was a personal friend of Eduard Wüst, and officiated at his wedding. By background the Gnadenfeld group had received influences unknown in most of the other Mennonite communities. They were sometimes referred to as "Lutheran Mennonites." The consecration of children, mission festivals, emphasis on temperance, and other practices generally unknown among Mennonites were adhered to in Gnadenfeld. Wüst was a frequent speaker at their mission festivals.

The *Bruderschule,* established in 1857, which acquired the right to train teachers in 1859, became one of the testing grounds on which it was decided in which direction all these influences were to lead. August Lenzmann and N. Schmidt were progressive spiritually minded leaders and sponsors of the school. Jakob Reimer and Johann Claassen were also leaders, but with a different emphasis; they did not approve of Heinrich Franz as a teacher because they thought he lacked the required "piety." Therefore they withdrew and became leaders in a separation movement which resulted in the founding of the Mennonite Brethren Church (1860). Nicolas Schmidt and others had introduced another foreign element by supporting a certain Johann Lange as teacher, who had graduated from a chiliastic school in South Germany and was now promoting the ideas of the "Templers" or "Friends

of Jerusalem." This led to another division (1863) and a temporary closing of the school. In 1873 the school was reopened as a Zentralschule (*q.v.*), which before World War I was changed into a school of commerce (Handelsschule). In 1907 a Mädchenschule (see **Gnadenfeld** Mädchenschule) was added.

The religious life of Gnadenfeld (see **Gnadenfeld Mennonite Church**), in spite of these disrupting early developments, continued without further disturbance. Because of its strong evangelistic, progressive background, disruptive elements caused little dissatisfaction. Gnadenfeld furnished the Mennonites of Russia with their first missionary, Heinrich Dirks (*q.v.*), who went to Sumatra in 1869 and later returned to serve the congregation as elder and promoted the cause of missions among the Mennonites of Russia and Europe. His oldest son, Heinrich Dirks II (*q.v.*), was the last elder of the Gnadenfeld Mennonite church. When in the 1870's a general conscription law was passed, 17 families with 141 persons emigrated to America, a few to Palestine.

Economically, the colony made good progress. Orchards and windbreaks were planted. Until 1881, all the land was considered crown land; it was then sold for a nominal sum to the respective farmers. In 1908 the district of Gnadenfeld had, in addition to the land of the villages which was 1,900 dessiatines (about 5,000 acres), 75 large privately owned estates with a total of 26,537 dessiatines of land or approximately 72,650 acres. In 1926, 632 of the 671 inhabitants were Mennonites. At that time Gnadenfeld constituted a civic unit with the Mennonite village of Paulsheim and the Russian villages of Mokrostrav, Semostye, and Seyony. The former elementary school and Zentralschule (Handelsschule) had been changed to a seven-class Arbeitsschule. The buildings of the former Mädchenschule were used as a training center by the tractor brigade. For a while Gnadenfeld had an agricultural school. It had a hospital, a flour mill, a bank, and a cattle breeding association. The land was very productive. The raising of grain and cattle predominated.

The Gnadenfeld Mennonite church was closed by the government in 1933 and used as a granary and later as a motion picture theater. Of the 550 to 600 members, only some 100 remained members because of the great pressure exercised by the government. Elder Heinrich Dirks perished in exile. Over 50 persons were exiled. When the Germans occupied Gnadenfeld in October 1941, the former way of life was again resumed as much as possible. An 80-year-old minister, Heinrich Boldt, who had survived concentration camp, preached again in the old church, instructed the youth, and baptized 28. On Sept. 12, 1943, the Gnadenfeld Mennonites left their home on more than 100 wagons to flee the approaching Red army, and the village was destroyed by fire. The majority of the Gnadenfeld Mennonite refugees were forcibly returned to Russia. The rest have found new homes in Canada and South America.   C.K.

Friesen, *Brüderschaft,* 79 ff.; H. Görz, *Die Molotschnaer Ansiedlung* (Steinbach, 1950); H. Dirks, editor,

Mennonitisches Jahrbuch (Berdyansk, 1908) 33-46 1911-12, 28-40; 1913, 38-44; Franz Isaak, *Die Molotschnaer Mennoniten* (Halbstadt, 1908); *ML* II, 128 f.

Gnadenfeld Agricultural School, Molotschna, Russia, was organized in 1923 by the Verband Bürger Holländischer Herkunft. In 1925 the school was taken over by the district. The school had an experiment station for which some 300 acres of land were at its disposal. The course of the school was two years.

C.K.

Der Praktische Landwirt (August 1926) 20.

Gnadenfeld Mädchenschule, Molotschna, Russia, was founded and originally sponsored by C. J. Reimer. It was started in 1907 and was forced to close in 1911, but was later reopened. One of the teachers of the school was Katharina C. Reimer, a daughter of the sponsor. The school had a three-year course. After the Revolution it was merged with the Handelsschule of Gnadenfeld (see **Gnadenfeld** and **Gnadenfeld Zentralschule**). C.K.

Friesen, *Brüderschaft,* 627; C. Reimer, "Die Gnadenfelder Mädchenschule," in *Menn. Jahrbuch* 1913, 114-17.

Gnadenfeld Mennonite Church was located in the province of Taurida, South Russia, about 60 miles from the seaport at Berdyansk on the Sea of Asov. In 1835 the congregation as a whole immigrated to Russia from the province of Brandenburg, Prussia, under the leadership of Elder Wilhelm Lange. From the very beginning the congregation was known for its advanced spiritual life. During the middle of the last century the Gnadenfeld congregation became the center of a revival movement which culminated in the founding of the Mennonite Brethren Church in 1860.

The meetinghouse was built in 1854 and was one of the finest older Mennonite churches in the Molotschna settlement with a seating capacity of 500. In 1895 it installed a pipe organ, the only one in a Mennonite church in Russia. The membership was around 300, mostly from the village of Gnadenfeld and some surrounding villages. Prominent elders were Wilhelm Lange, Friedrich Lange, August Lenzmann, Heinrich Dirks, Sr., the first missionary of the Russian Mennonites, Gerhard Nickel, and Heinrich Dirks, Jr.

In 1887 the membership numbered 405 baptized members. The Berdyansk congregation was a subsidiary of the Gnadenfeld Mennonite Church. The interest in education and Christian work was demonstrated by the congregation in many ways. Fifteen of its members went abroad for theological training or a higher education; among them were Heinrich Dirks, father and son, Heinrich Franz, Hermann Lenzmann, W. Neufeld, Abr. Klassen, and Peter Nachtigall.

In 1933, after arresting the last minister, the Bolshevik authorities closed the church and so the existence of the congregation was brought to an end. (See also **Gnadenfeld.**) H.G.

Gnadenfeld Zentralschule, Molotschna, Russia, was preceded by a *Bruderschule* established in 1857, which in turn was a continuation of a school which the settlers had had in Prussia. Because of differences of opinion the school was closed in 1863. When it reopened in 1873 it became known as a Zentralschule (*q.v.*). The first teachers of the Bruderschule were David Hausknecht, Heinrich Franz I, Johannes Lange, and Friedrich Lange; it was sponsored by a group of progressive and pietistically inclined individuals, such as Johann Claassen, Jakob Reimer, Nikolai Schmidt, and August Lenzmann, and supported by voluntary contributions. The aim was to train workers for home missions according to the pattern of the Rauhes Haus, Hamburg.

The first teachers of the Zentralschule were Hermann Lenzmann and Wilhelm Neufeld. They were followed by Abraham Braun 1875-84, P. H. Heese 1877-78, A. Hausknecht 1878-80, D. J. Dück, F. W. Teneta, B. Ratzlaff, J. H. Unruh, Jakob Rempel, Johann Sudermann, and Nikolai Ediger. The school had a three-year course with the usual Zentralschule subjects.

Before World War I the school was reorganized as a school of commerce (*Handelsschule*), patterned after the Alexanderkrone Business School (*q.v.*). The teachers at this time were K. K. Martens, Abraham Bergen, and Isbrand Rempel. After the revolution of 1917 the school went through another transformation. First it was combined with the Gnadenfeld Mädchenschule and later, in combination with an elementary school, it was turned into a seven-class *Arbeitsschule* (see **Gnadenfeld**). C.K.

H. Dirks, ed., *Mennonitisches Jahrbuch,* 1911-12, pp. 28-40; Friesen, *Brüderschaft,* 86 ff., 621 ff.

Gnadenheim, a Mennonite village name of the Molotschna settlement, Russia; Barnaul settlement, Siberia; Menno and Fernheim settlements, Paraguay.

C.K.

Gnadental Mennonite Brethren Church, located in Colony Neuland of the Paraguayan Chaco, was organized provisionally in an MCC refugee camp in Berlin and after emigration to Paraguay in 1947-48, officially established on April 8, 1948, in Gnadental, Neuland, Chaco, under the leadership of Wilhelm Löwen and adopted the name Gnadentaler Mennoniten-Brüdergemeinde. Its members are largely recent immigrants from Russia and Poland via Germany through the MCC and are farmers. The current membership is 317. Church services are held regularly in the school building, as are also Sunday schools, choir work, young people's programs, and Ladies' Aid meetings. Footwashing is not practiced to date but planned for the near future. Church discipline, both excommunication and ban are practiced when necessary. Songbooks are the combined *Heimatklänge, Glaubensstimme,* and *Frohe Botschaft,* and the *Evangeliums-Lieder.* Wilhelm Löwen is still the leader of the group assisted by two ministers and two deacons. W.L.

Gnadenthal, a common Mennonite village name found in the Molotschna settlement, Russia; Baratov; Auli Ata, Central Asia; Barnaul, Siberia; Alexanderwohl, Kan.; West Reserve, Man.; Swift Current, Sask.; Mexico; and Sommerfeld settlement, Villarrica, Paraguay. C.K.

Gnadenthal, a village (pop. 200) situated about seven miles southwest of Plum Coulee, Man., is one of the most progressive of the Mennonite villages west of the Red River, with conveniences such as electrification and telephones. There are two Mennonite churches, one G.C.M. and one M.B., and a two-room public school with qualified Mennonite teachers. The village dates back to 1874-75, when it was settled by Old Colonists from South Russia, who vacated the village in 1923-25 with about 15 other villages in this area, because the Department of Education required the use of the English language in the schools. However, this proved to be a godsend for some of the 21,000 Mennonites who immigrated from South Russia to Canada in 1924, and who now took possession of the land and buildings, most of whom are now well-to-do farmers. Other villages in the vicinity have their own churches, which also belong to the Blumenort Mennonite Church (*q.v.*) as well.

H.H.H.

Gnadenthal Mennonite Brethren Church, located in Gnadenthal, Man., was organized on June 14, 1929, under the leadership of Elder Wilhelm J. Dueck. In 1943 an old house was remodeled into a church with a seating capacity of 200. In 1953 the membership was 28, with Heinrich P. Harder the minister. One missionary, Helen Harder, has gone from this church to the foreign field.

H.P.H.

Gnapheus, Guilhelmus (Fullonius or Willem van Hage), b. 1493, at The Hague, Netherlands, d. 1568 at Norden, East Friesland, Germany, was appointed rector of the Latin School at The Hague in 1522 but already in 1523 was forced to leave because of anti-Catholic ideas. In 1525 he was for some time in prison at The Hague, but was later released. After much wandering he settled at Elbing, West Prussia, in 1531, where he became rector of the Gymnasium (Latin School) in 1535. But in 1541 there was a conflict and Gnapheus moved to Königsberg in the duchy of Prussia (later East Prussia); here he became a schoolteacher and a preacher, but he was dismissed and even excommunicated on June 9, 1547, by the Lutheran government, charged with Anabaptism and fanaticism. After some years he was reinstated, the charges having been proved false. By that time he had already moved to Norden in East Friesland (about 1560), where he became burgomaster. Besides numerous other books, he wrote a fine evangelical treatise, *Een troost ende spiegel der siecken ende derghenen die in lijdn zijn,* first edition in 1531. Gnapheus, who was not an Anabaptist but a humanist, Sacramentist, and adherent of Bullinger (*q.v.*), may by his ideas of toleration have prepared the opportunity for Anabaptists and Mennonites to settle in East Prussia. vDZ.

Biogr. Wb. III, 269-72; *ML* III, 322; F. Szper, *Nederlandsche Nederzettingen in West-Pruisen gedurende den Poolschen tyd* (Enkhuizen, 1913) 62-65, 78, 81-84, 192-95.

Gnieden-Blumenheim Mennonite Brethren Church, located 20 miles from Schönfeld, district of Alexandrovsk, in the province of Ekaterinoslav, South Russia, was organized probably in the 1880's by Mennonite families from the Molotschna settle-

ment. The church took its name from a nobleman, Gnieden, from whom the land was purchased.

Tobias Voth, who after the Russian Revolution died the death of a martyr in exile, was the first minister of the congregation. In 1892, the church had a membership of 15. Until 1898, when the membership had risen to 28, the congregation held its meetings in the farm homes of its members. When one of the settlement moved away, his house was used as a meeting place.

At the turn of the century five families purchased land at Neu-Samara, in the province of Samara, and the Gnieden church began to dissolve. Voth soon thereafter moved to the Memrik settlement, and in 1908 he too moved to Samara. The other families scattered to various parts of the country, some eventually emigrating to Canada after 1923. Several families have settled near Coaldale, Alta. Heinrich Dueck, one of the younger members of the Gnieden church, is now a minister in the Mennonite Brethren Church at Boissevain, Man. I.G.N.

"Go Ye," the official publication of the "Go Ye" Mission, Inc., of Choteau, Okla., published as a 4-page 6¼ x 9½ in. monthly (bimonthly 1946-47), edited in 1954 by Homer Mouttet. The "Go Ye" Mission was organized and directed by Solomon Mouttet to work particularly in the field of "Child Evangelism." H.S.B.

Gobschitz (*Gopschitz*) is a village near Kromau (*q.v.*) in Moravia; here Matthiasch, the captain of Kromau, leased a house to the Hutterites, and they set up a Bruderhof, which is mentioned in the *Geschicht-Buch* for 1547 with other Bruderhofs. They lived here until 1602. The *Geschicht-Buch* comments, "In 1602 the Brethren at Gopschitz (where they lived 49 years) moved away with the Lord's good will on account of the high taxation and trouble with soldiers, which they could not endure." (*ML* II, 129.) LOSERTH.

Goch, a city (pop. 11,798) in the Rhine Province, government district of Düsseldorf, Germany, on the Dutch border. Here the conference was held in 1547 at which Adam Pastor was banned by Dirk Philips and Menno Simons for his anti-Trinitarian views. It is said that Adam Pastor, whose principal field of activity was at Cleve, had also "brought many to rebaptism" in Goch. Theunis van Hastenrath, put to death in 1551 at Linnich, was a preacher in Goch about the same time, but did not baptize there. In the second half of the 16th century there was already a congregation of Anabaptists here, but little is known about its history. Most of the members were weavers; in 1607 the schoolteacher of Goch was a Mennonite. The van Heukelom family, many members of which later lived in Amsterdam, belonged to the congregation at Goch. The membership was always small, but was augmented in the last quarter of the 17th and the first quarter of the 18th centuries by an influx of refugees from the Palatinate. The congregation was supported by that of Amsterdam and in the last part of the 18th century also by Rotterdam. In 1736 it contributed 75 florins to the Dutch Fund for Foreign Needs. In the 18th century it had two (untrained and until 1747 unsalaried) ministers, both of whom served for a long period: Pieter Wendels 1712-60, and Abraham Alders 1729-ca. 72. The first educated minister of the congregation was Gerrit Schimmelpenninck, serving from 1774 until his death in 1792. He was followed by H. van Hinten from 1793 (?) until his death in 1799, and Evert Akkeringa 1800-15, in whose time the membership greatly decreased and the finances collapsed. About 1790 the membership numbered 100, in 1840 only 20. In 1815-18 Jan van Hulst of Cleve also served at Goch. The last minister of the congregation was Hidde Wybe van der Ploeg, 1819-55. After his death (1855) until 1898 it was served by Pastor Leendertz of Cleve. Services were still held in the Dutch language. In 1885 it is said that church and parsonage were in good condition, and there was a considerable property, but no church board (*DB* 1885, 8-9). In 1898 there were 15 members; in 1904 a church board was chosen, and once a month Pastor Kraemer of Crefeld conducted a service, but soon after the congregation became extinct.

Jacob Gottschalk (*q.v., ca.* 1666-1763), the first bishop of the Mennonite Church in America, was a member of the Goch congregation; he received a church letter on June 11, 1701, and presumably emigrated to America in the same year, settling first in Germantown.   K.V., vDZ.

Inv. Arch. Amst. I, 1538; II, Nos. 2571, 2769-87; Rembert, *Wiedertäufer,* 416, 485, 496, 500; W. Niepoth, "Jacob Gottschalk and His Ancestry," *MQR* XXIII (1949), 35-47 contains valuable information on the Gottschalk family and the congregation in Goch; *DB* 1864, 121; 1885, 8 f.; 1895, 184, 1898, 112 f.; 1904, 232; 1906, 191; 1909, 116, 124; *Naamlijst* 1829, 69; *ML* II, 129 f.

Godevaert van Holaer, an Anabaptist martyr, a mason and a native of Mechelen, Belgium, was burned at the stake on the market place at Antwerp on March 3, 1535. Particulars are lacking. (*Antw. Arch.-Blad* VII, 318, 366; XIV, 12 f., No. 136.)   vDZ.

Göding (Czech, *Hodonin* or *Godonin*), a city (pop. 5,000) in Moravia, situated five miles southeast of Brno on the old highway to Hungary along the right bank of the March. It has a long history, for the village, mentioned in the 11th century, belonged to several successive noble Czech families, of whom the barons of Lippa are most prominent in Anabaptist history. From 1762 to World War I it belonged to the Hapsburg family estate. The inhabitants of the city were mostly Protestant in the 16th century. The first Catholic priest was appointed in 1640.

There were Anabaptists in Göding and Tscheikowitz (*q.v.*), which also belonged to this estate, as early as the 1540's. On July 25, 1545, they bought a house there with all its appurtenances and arranged it as a Bruderhof, though of course, under great difficulty, for in that very year, in consequence of the decision of the Diet that only those Anabaptists would be tolerated who did not practice community of goods, the "great tribulation" began which lasted five years. They were driven

from Moravia to Hungary and Austria and back again. In 1564 Hans of Cologne, a mason by trade, was a deacon in Göding. A generation later, Nov. 11, 1593, the brotherhood bought the "Konventshaus" there.

But soon the period of unrest and trouble due to war set in, and frequently struck Göding as a border city. In 1605-6 the Konvent was destroyed in the struggles of the Hungarians against Jörg Basta; it was not rebuilt until 1612. Greater damage was done in the Bohemian revolt, which led to the complete dissolution of Anabaptism in Moravia. Thus on Feb. 7, 1620, the Poles attacked Göding and plundered it so rapidly that no one could withstand them. Three Bruderhofs, Göding, Schädowitz, and Watzenobis (*q.v.*), were plundered and about 20 brethren and sisters seriously injured. Soon the consequences of the battle at the White Mountain were visited upon the Moravian Anabaptist households. The Hutterites at Göding were again sorely pressed and attempted to flee over the border. Three brethren who were sent to Göding the following years were killed by the Poles, and on Aug. 8 Göding was plundered by the Walloons. The Brethren suffered very severely in the struggles against Bethlen Gabor (*q.v.*). They finally withdrew from Moravia so completely that scarcely any reminders of the period of Anabaptism remained in Göding. (*ML* II, 130.)
                                                    LOSERTH.

Godschalks (Godtschalcx), **Jan,** of Elten: see **Elten, Jan Godschalks van.**

Godshalk (Godshall, Gottschall, Gotthall, Gottschalk, Godtschalch, Gaedtschalck), a family name found especially in the Franconia Mennonite Conference (MC) in southeastern Pennsylvania, the progenitor of the family having been an immigrant of 1701 from Goch, Germany, named Jacob Gottschalk (Gaedtschalck), preacher in the Germantown congregation 1702-12 and later at Skippack 1713-63, and first Mennonite bishop in America.

Two Godshalk family histories have been published: *The Godshalk Family History* by Abraham Godshalk (Harrisburg, Pa., 1912), and *The Gottshall Family* by N. B. Grubb, 1924. The family includes a number of bishops, ministers, and deacons. Worthy of mention are the preacher-author Abraham Godshalk (*q.v.,* 1791-1838), Bishop Moses Gottshall (1815-88) of the Eastern District Conference (GCM), and his son, Elder William S. Gottshall (*q.v.,* 1865-1941) of the same district.
                                                    J.C.W.

W. Niepoth, "Jacob Gottschalk and His Ancestry," *MQR* XXIII (January 1949) 35-47.

Godshalk, Abraham (b. Dec. 29, 1791, d. Aug. 19, 1838), Mennonite author and minister in the Doylestown Mennonite Church (MC) of the Franconia Conference (*q.v.*). His wife was Sarah Shrauger, whom he married Oct. 17, 1815. The union was blessed with seven children. Godshalk wrote of himself: "I am a farmer, who was at a pretty early day [about 32] called to be a preacher of the Gospel, and who has not even had the advantage of a good common education." He was ordained as a preacher in the Doylestown congregation in 1824. Shortly before his death at the age of 46, Godshalk wrote a book entitled *Eine Beschreibung der Neuen Creatur* (Doylestown, 1838). He then translated it into English, making "such amendments and additions as to me seemed good." Godshalk wrote in opposition to the perfectionism in certain revivalistic preaching in his day: "Many preach up a kind of regeneration in our day that is not well founded in Scripture; namely, that the change is at once so perfect, that no growth is necessary, or that the regenerated man is at once free from sin" (p. iii). It is believed that the group Godshalk had in mind was the Evangelical Association. Godshalk's treatise takes up the following points on regeneration: its necessity, the means, its nature, and the subject who has been regenerated —what kind of person he is. In his German booklet he spelled his name Gottshall. This was the spelling he used in 1837 when he published a 16-page booklet entitled *Wahre Gerechtigkeit* (Doylestown). J.C.W.

Goebel, Max, German church historian, b. March 13, 1811, at Solingen, d. Dec. 13, 1857, at Coblenz, studied theology at the University of Bonn, served as pastor in Siegburg and Coblenz, where he made friendly contacts with J. G. Lübke at Neuwied and Johannes Molenaar at Monsheim, who later became Mennonite preachers. He is the author of the important book, *Geschichte des christlichen Lebens in der rheinisch-westfälischen evangelischen Kirche* (Vol. I, 1849; Vol. II, 1852; Vol. III edited by Th. Link in 1860 from papers left by Goebel). In this work the Mennonites, especially those of the Rhineland, are given extensive, sympathetic treatment; much new material is presented, making the book an important source for the study of Mennonite history in the Rhineland. Never before had the Anabaptist movement received so thorough a presentation, based on study of the sources, or so just a characterization of its nature (see the excellent analysis of Anabaptism, Vol. I, 134-39, which is still of great value). Of especial interest is the attempt of the author to prove that Pietism in the Rhineland can be traced back to the Anabaptist movement of the 16th century (*Menn. Bl.*, 1858, 9). The *Monatsschrift für die evangelische Kirche der Rheinprovinz,* which Max Goebel edited with C. F. Kling, contains an interesting article from his pen in Nov. 4, 1848, pp. 228-40, "Die oberländischen Mennoniten" (erroneously called Hutterites). They are Amish Mennonites, whom the author describes at first hand. Though some of the material is incorrect and has been superseded by later investigations, on the whole this article has considerable historical value. (*ML* II, 130.) NEFF.

Goechjen Jans (Ghoechgen Jans van Slubich), a Dutch Anabaptist martyr, originally from Lubik near Gouda, Dutch province of South Holland (not Lübeck in Germany), was arrested at Amsterdam and drowned there on April 21 or 22 (van Braght, *Mart. Mir.,* erroneously April 15) together with 10 other Anabaptist women. Particulars are lacking. (*Mart. Mir.* D 413, E 764; Grosheide, *Verhooren,* 67, 70; *idem, Bijdrage,* 62, 305.) vDZ.

Goedereede, Jan Joosten van, an Anabaptist martyr: see Jan Joosten.

Goeree (Goederede), a Dutch island belonging to the province of South Holland, seat of a Mennonite congregation which since the 18th century is called Ouddorp (*q.v.*). (*ML* II, 131.) vDZ.

Goering (Göring, Gering, Gehring), a Mennonite family name. The earliest known record of the name is that of the Swiss printer Ulrich Gering (b. *ca.* 1440; d. 1510, in Paris), who set up the first printing press in France with the assistance of Michael Friburger and Martin Crantz under the direction of Guillaume Fichet, rector of the Sorbonne. Virtually complete genealogical records are extant for the family since issuance of a passport to Moses Gering of Montbéliard, France, on Feb. 8, 1791. Moses Gering is known to have been a member of a group of Mennonites that emigrated from Palatinate, South Germany, to France near the Swiss border about 1673. Moses Gering apparently was born in Montbéliard about 1760. It is also known that his immediate ancestors lived for a time in the canton of Bern, Switzerland. In 1791 Moses Gering moved to Einsiedel, Galicia (Austria), with his family. In 1797 he again moved to Michelsdorf (near Warsaw), Poland. In 1817 the entire family moved to Eduardsdorf (near Dubno), Russia. Some members of the Moses Gering family participated in the founding of the Horodish and Waldheim villages northeast of Eduardsdorf in 1837. In 1860 Eduardsdorf dissolved and Kutuzovka was founded. Included in this group were the majority of Gerings who had remained in Eduardsdorf. In 1874 the Kutuzovka, Horodish, and Waldheim Mennonite settlements dissolved and emigrated to America. The Gerings settled in central Kansas and South Dakota, and subsequently in other states. C. J. Goering was long elder of the Eden Church at Moundridge, Kan., and J. C. Goering was long elder of the First Church of Christian at the same place. S. J. Goering was a missionary in China and business manager of Bethel College. Gering and Gerig have a common source. (D. J. Goering, *Goering Genealogy,* 1940.) R.L.G.

Goerz (Geerts, Gerrits, Gerritsen, Gerts, Gertz, Gerzen, Goertz, Görts, Görtz, Görz), a Mennonite family of Dutch descent, whose members moved from the Netherlands to West Prussia in the 16th and 17th centuries. Many of them served as preachers in Prussian congregations, e.g., in Montau-Gruppe: Dirk Gerts, until his death in 1706; Franz Gertz 1725-d. 57 (elder 1756); Hans Gertz 1756-d. 67; Cornelis Gertz 1773-d. 96; Abraham Gertz 1776-*ca.* 81; Claas Görtz 1782-86; Peter Görtz 1801-d. 13; Franz Gertz 1806-d. 14; Dirk Görtz 1819-d. 42; Hans Goertz (1795-1830), preacher after 1814, elder 1821; Jacob Goertz (1827-98), preacher after 1856, elder in Gruppe 1880; Jacob Goertz (b. 1849), preacher at Gruppe 1879, elder 1900; Johann Goertz (b. 1852), preacher 1897-1934; Gerhard Goertz, preacher 1924-45; Albert Goertz, preacher 1932-45. In the congregation of the Culmsche Niederung, Andries (Andreas) Gertz was a preacher about 1750-65 and Jacob Gertz 1775 until after 1810. In Lithuania, East

Prussia, there were also found some members of this family; in 1732, when a number of them were expelled, among those who migrated to the Netherlands there was Abraham Geerts (Gertz); he soon after returned to Prussia and may have been the same person as Abraham Gertzen, who was a preacher of the Lithuanian congregation 1762-ca. 65. P. S. Goertz was long dean of Bethel College, Newton, Kan.   vdZ.

Inv. Arch. Amst. I, Nos. 1669, 1687; II, 2 Nos. 779, 784; Dutch *Naamlijst;* L. Stobbe, *Montau-Gruppe, ein Gedenkblatt* (1918) 83-87; *Gem.-Kal.*

Goerz, Abraham, for many years a Mennonite elder in Russia, b. 1840 at Gnadenfeld in the Molotschna, d. Jan. 29, 1911 (1913?), was a pupil of Elder Fr. W. Lange (*q.v.*), in 1865 accepted a teaching position at Hochfeld, Melitopol district (South Russia); in 1867-72 he taught in Altonau. For the sake of his health he had to give up teaching, and bought a small farm with a treadmill in Altonau. For two years he served as village mayor and three years as district judge of the Halbstadt district. In addition he was active in various commissions of the community. He was also chosen a member of the committee that in 1874 negotiated with Adjutant General von Totleben concerning military service. He was repeatedly sent to St. Petersburg as a delegate to negotiate with the government. Two weeks before his death he was in Simferopol to call on the governor on the matter of a law forbidding worship periods in Mennonite schools. He succeeded in arranging it in favor of the Mennonite practice. His personality inspired respect and brought him courteous attention even in the highest circles.

On May 5, 1875, Goerz was chosen as preacher of the Orloff Mennonite Church (*q.v.*). After the death of Elder Johann Harder (*q.v.*) he was called as elder of the Orloff-Halbstadt-Neukirch congregation on Dec. 29, 1875, and was ordained in the Neu-Halbstadt church on Jan. 6, 1876. He filled this office until his death. He was an outstanding speaker with many gifts, including tact and foresight. He was the representative of the Molotschna Kirchenkonvent (*q.v.*) in the school council 1876-96. Then he resigned, but in 1906 was recalled to this position by the Halbstadt civil and church authorities. His influence on and services to the educational program of the Mennonites in Russia were outstanding. He succeeded in preserving the church character of the Mennonite common schools, and religious instruction according to Mennonite principles, as well as consideration of the German language, in the face of a government policy of Russianization. From 1906 on he was a manager of the old people's home in Halbstadt. In the last years of his life he was a member of the Glaubenskommission (KfK) of the Mennonites in Russia. In addition Goerz was also often engaged as a surveyor. He was skilled in the use of tools. By his versatility, always mindful of the welfare of his people, he rendered great, unforgettable services to Mennonitism in Russia.†   A.B.

Friesen, *Brüderschaft;* H. Goerz, *Die Molotschnaer Ansiedlung* (Steinbach, 1950); *ML* II, 131.

Goerz, David (1849-1914), a Mennonite (GCM) minister and leader, was born on June 2, 1849, to Heinrich and Agnes Goerz, Neu-Bereslav near Berdyansk, South Russia. He attended the *Vereinsschule* at Ohrloff in the Molotschna settlement. At the age of 18 he was baptized and began to teach school at Berdyansk, where he married Helene Riesen (in 1870 or 1871). He was a close friend of Bernhard Warkentin, who traveled to America on June 5, 1872, and on the basis of the letters which he received from Warkentin spread information about America among the Mennonites of the Ukraine, who had become alarmed by an impending conscription law.

On Nov. 4, 1873, David Goerz arrived in New York and proceeded to Summerfield, Ill., where he taught a Mennonite school. In 1875 he moved with a group of Summerfield Mennonites to Kansas and settled at Halstead, where he served as editor of *Zur Heimath,* manager of the Western Publishing House (*q.v.*), and secretary of the Mennonite Board of Guardians (*q.v.*), the American Mennonite agency set up to aid the newly immigrated Mennonites from Russia. In 1877 Goerz was instrumental in organizing the Mennonite Teachers' Conference (*q.v.*), of Kansas, which led to the organization of the Kansas Conference (*q.v.*) and later became the Western District Conference (*q.v.*). For years, Goerz was secretary or chairman of this conference. He also promoted home and foreign mission work among the Mennonites and organized the Mennonite Mutual Fire Insurance Company (*q.v.*) (Newton) in 1880 (now Midland Mutual Fire Insurance Company). In 1900 he made a trip to India to distribute 8,000 bushels of grain among the starving population, which led to the beginning of the General Conference mission work in India.

David Goerz was one of the founders of the Bethel College Corporation and served as its first business manager until 1910, when his health compelled him to relinquish this work. Under his influence the Board of Directors of Bethel College in 1903 organized the Bethel Deaconess Home and Hospital Society (*q.v.*), which later became an independent institution. In 1878, the Halstead Mennonite Church ordained him as minister and in 1893 he became the pastor of the Bethel College Mennonite Church. He was also instrumental in promoting better music among the Mennonites of the prairie states.

David Goerz was a great organizer, inspirer, and leader in the various realms of cultural, educational, missionary, and relief enterprises of the Mennonites of the prairie states in the pioneer days. What has been realized on a large scale in our day was visualized and planned by him at the turn of the century. In 1910, because of ill health, he made a trip to Palestine and tried to improve his health by retiring to Colorado and later to California, where he died on May 7, 1914.†   C.K.

Dictionary of American Biography VII (1931) 353-54; *Menn. Life,* October 1952, 170-75; *Der Herold,* May 14, 1914; *Bethel College Monthly,* May 1914, 2-4, 12-16; D. Goerz Collection, Bethel College Historical Library; P. J. Wedel, *History of Bethel College* (North Newton, 1954); *ML* I, 131 f.

Goerz, Franz, elder of the Rudnerweide Mennonite congregation, Molotschna settlement, Taurida,

South Russia, was born in 1820 at Rudnerweide, when that village was only one year old. In 1841 he married and after that lived at Gnadenfeld. In 1850 he became minister and in 1861 was ordained elder of his native Rudnerweide congregation. After the death of Elder August Lenzmann (1877) Goerz for five years served also as elder of the Gnadenfeld congregation. In 1891 he retired from his duty as elder because of ill health. He died in 1901 at Gnadenfeld, having served his large congregation 30 years as elder and 10 additional years as minister. In the 1870's during the crisis brought about through the introduction of universal military service in Russia, Goerz was several times one of the delegates sent to St. Petersburg to plead the Mennonite cause. H.G.

Goes, a town (1947 pop. 12,833, with 63 Mennonites) in the Dutch province of Zeeland, seat of a Mennonite congregation. Though no authentic records are available it is a fact that already in the 16th century a Mennonite congregation was found here, which belonged to the Flemish branch. In the 17th century some difficulties arose concerning Socinian (*q.v.*) doctrines. In 1665, when a conflict had arisen in the Flemish Mennonite congregations of the Netherlands (see **Lammerenkrijg**), the municipal government of Goes compelled the preachers, the precentor, and the deacons of the Mennonite Church to sign 12 articles (see **Geuzenvragen**), in which Socinianism was repudiated. Both Joos Baroen, the preacher, and Jan Baroen, the precentor of the congregation, refused to sign, and consequently were dismissed from their office by the magistrates. A quarrel broke out in the congregation, some of the members supporting Joos and Jan Baroen, who were inclined to the ideas of Galenus Abrahamsz (*q.v.*), a rather progressive Mennonite leader. But the majority of the members took the side of Samuel Apostool (*q.v.*), and were not willing to invoke the help of outside church leaders (*buitenmannen*), especially of those who adhered to "the new doctrine of Galenus." Peace was not restored in the congregation until 1680; unfortunately the old book of records, containing the account of these quarrels, was then intentionally destroyed.

On Nov. 17, 1703, the Mennonites of Goes obtained the privilege of performing marriages of their members in their own meetinghouse. As a gift of gratitude the deacons of the Mennonite congregation presented the municipal orphanage with 28 gold ducats. But not many marriages were performed in the Mennonite church, since the membership rapidly decreased. In 1684 the congregation numbered 242 members, in 1721 only 47; in 1733, when an offering was taken for the benefit of the Prussian Mennonites, 115 guilders were collected. The church board apologized for this small amount on the ground of their small number and their poverty. During the 18th century the congregation was served by the following preachers: Pieter Affet 1720-47, Nicolaas Knopper 1748?-52, Klaas van der Horst 1753-57, Gerrit Schimmelpenning 1757-74, and Abraham Staal 1779-87. After the departure of Staal no new preacher was

chosen. In 1796 only three members were left, and the *Naamlijst* of 1815 (p. 107) states that the congregation of Goes had died out. But this is not the case; during the first half of the 19th century the ministers of Ouddorp, Middelburg, and Vlissingen occasionally held church services at Goes. In 1837 the membership had increased to 13. In 1859 a communion service was held and in 1864 a baptismal service, but in 1868 the administration of the property of the congregation as well as the care of church services was given over to the congregation of Middelburg. It was largely due to the assiduity of Tj. Kielstra (*q.v.*), minister of Middelburg, who regularly visited the Mennonites at Goes, that the congregation there was restored to new life; on Oct. 24, 1889, 17 new members were admitted to the congregation by the only deacon left. The old meetinghouse of 1660, situated in the Korte Vosstraat, had been transferred to the Walloon (French Protestant) congregation about 1800. In 1892 the Mennonites acquired a new church, built at the Westwal; it was dedicated on Sept. 27, 1892, by Pastor Kielstra. This building because of its dilapidated condition was torn down in 1934; the present meetinghouse, built on the same place, was dedicated on Sept. 9, 1934.

After its re-establishment in 1889 the congregation was served by Pastor Kielstra of Middelburg; in 1899 it obtained its own minister, together with the congregation of Vlissingen, and was served by S. Spaans 1899-1908 and T. H. Siemelink 1908-19. The assertion (*DB* 1919, 222, 240) that because of lack of finances the congregation was dissolved on Nov. 30, 1919, is not quite true. The fact is that in the spring of 1920 the agreement with Vlissingen was terminated, but in 1921 a new alliance was made with Middelburg, the pastors of Middelburg from that time also serving at Goes. The congregation owes much to A. R. Breetveld, who was (until 1927) for more than 30 years president and treasurer of the church board.

The membership, numbering 26 in 1889, was 36 in 1896, 51 in 1899, 20 in 1919, 29 in 1926, 50 in 1953. The members live partly in the town of Goes, partly in neighboring towns.

The archives of the congregation from 1677 to 1928, described by Abr. Mulder (in *Inventarissen van Rijksarchieven*, Vol. II, sub XIX), are now found in the State Archives at Middelburg.

A.R.B., ABR. M.

Inv. Arch. Amst. I, Nos. 1176, 1180, 1996; II, Nos. 1276, 1737-53; II, 2, Nos. 44, 590, 599; *DJ* 1837, 8.25; 1935, 92; *DB* 1861, 175-76; 1865, 170; 1876, 66; 1889, 11; 1890, 142; 1892, 143; 1893, 137; 1898, 242; 1899, 210; 1919, 222, 240; B. J. H. van Dale, "Bijdrage tot de Gesch. der Doopsgez. Gemeente te Goes," in *Cadsandria* (Schoondijke, 1858); *ML* II, 132 f.

Goes, Antoni Jansen van der, and his wife Magdalena Steenaerts lived in the Dutch town of Goes, province of Zeeland, until about 1651. Then they migrated to Amsterdam. Antoni Jansen was a poet of devotional hymns and moralizing poems of rather mediocre quality. A volume entitled *Zederymen, bestaande in Zangen en Gedigten, Verciert met Nieuwe Muzyk door S. Lefevre* was published (Amsterdam, 1656). Both Antoni and his wife were members of the Mennonite Church. Their son was Johannes Antonides (*q.v.*). (*Catalogus Amst.*, 273; *DJ* 1840, 113.)   vDZ.

Goes, Maeyken van der, an Anabaptist martyr: see **Maeyken Janssens.**

Goessel, Kan., a town (pop. 261) located in east-central Kansas in the southwestern part of Marion County. Approximately 2,000 Mennonites live in the shopping area. In or near Goessel are six Mennonite congregations: three General Conference Mennonite churches—Alexanderwohl, Tabor, and Goessel (the latter is in the town); the Spring Valley Mennonite Church (MC), the Springfield Krimmer Mennonite Brethren Church, and the Meridian Church of God in Christ Mennonite Church. Mennonites have lived in the region since the establishment of the first immigrant house in 1874. Other Mennonite institutions in the town include the 26-bed Bethesda Hospital and the 27-bed Bethesda Home for the Aged. A unique situation exists in the town's Class A public high school in that during most years the enrollment of slightly over 100 is entirely Mennonite.   J.W.L.

Goessel (Kan.) Mennonite Brethren Church, now extinct, formerly known as the Alexanderwohl Mennonite Brethren Church, was begun in 1880 and was for some time an important congregation of the M.B. Conference. In 1888 its membership was 20 and in 1896, 70. Then it decreased and in 1926 discontinued, and the church building was sold. Its presiding ministers were Elder C. P. Wedel, Peter Richert, H. P. Schroeder, J. S. Foth, and J. D. Reimer.   J.D.H.

Goessel Mennonite Church (GCM), a member of the Western District Conference, located in Goessel, Kan., was founded by members of the Alexanderwohl (*q.v.*) (Kan.) Mennonite Church, descendants of Mennonite immigrants who came to Kansas in 1874 from Alexanderwohl (*q.v.*), Russia, on April 15, 1920, with 177 members, because the Alexanderwohl Church had become overcrowded. Meetings had been held for some time in the Goessel Preparatory School. The church building was erected in 1920. P. P. Buller and Peter Buller came into this congregation as ministers when it was organized. P. P. Buller was immediately named leader and served the congregation as elder 1924-50, succeeded by Orlin F. Frey 1950-54 and Leo L. Miller 1954- . The membership in 1953 was 317. Of the 585 who have been members, 278 were baptized here and 307 were received from other congregations.   O.F.F.

Goessel Preparatory School (*Gemeindeschule*), located at Goessel, Kan., was established by the Alexanderwohl Mennonite Church in 1906. The school was responsible to a board composed of members of the congregation. When the Tabor and Goessel Mennonite churches were founded they had representatives on the board and joined in the support of the school. The first teacher was P. P. Buller, 1906-24. In 1912 he was joined by J. J. Banman, 1912-26. In 1925-26 O. K. Galle was principal. The aim

of the school was to teach Bible and German, and to stimulate the talents of the pupils. The curriculum was similar to that of the preparatory schools (*q.v.*) in general. In 1926 the school was changed to Goessel Rural High School, a public school religious instruction is continued in the high-school program.

The enrollment of the Gossel Preparatory School ranged from 40 to 50 pupils. A total of 260 pupils was graduated from the two-year course. Its building was later moved to the Bethel College campus for use as a dormitory, where it is known as Goessel Hall. (*Jahresheft Goessel Vereinsschule,* 1906-26.)
                    C.K.

Goethals, a Mennonite family which emigrated from Flanders, Belgium, to the Netherlands about 1630, and joined the congregation of Aardenburg and Middelburg. The martyrs Joos(t) Goethals (*q.v.*) and Barbelken Goethals (*q.v.*), both executed at Gent, Belgium, in 1569 and 1590, may have been members of this family.   vDZ.

Goetze, Georg Heinrich, superintendent of the Marienkirche in Lübeck, Germany, author of a polemic against the Mennonites entitled *Catechetische Prüfung der Mennonistischen Lehre, welche in Acht Catechismus-Predigten unter Göttlichen Seegen den 12., 13., 15., 16., 19., 20., 22., 23. September An. 1707 in St. Marien Kirche deutlich und erbaulich anzustellen gedenket George Henrich Götze.* Following the five main articles of the small Lutheran Catechism in the form of questions and answers, he tries to refute Mennonite doctrine, and gives expression to some very odd ideas. The whole is a remarkable specimen of the type of material used at that time in the struggle against one's theological opponents. (*Menn. Bl.,* 1880, 85 ff.; *ML* II, 134.)   NEFF.

Goldbach, a village in St. Gall, Switzerland, where the Anabaptist movement found a considerable following in the first years after its origin. (*ML* II, 134.)   HEGE.

Golden Rule Bookstore, 187 King Street East, Kitchener, Ont., a branch bookstore of the Mennonite Publishing House, Scottdale, Pa., was purchased of A. J. Schultz in April 1938. In November 1951 it was moved from 256 King Street East to a new building on 187 King Street East. Managers have been J. C. Fretz 1938-53 and J. W. Snyder since Oct. 1, 1953. A second Canadian branch bookstore by the same name and under the same manager was established at 320½ Dundas Street, London, Ont., in 1955.   H.S.B.

Goldschmidt, Georg: see **Steiner, Georg,** a goldsmith.

Goldschmidt, Heinrich. In spite of the severity of the persecution to which the Anabaptists were subjected in the late 1520's, the movement continued its remarkable growth, as Luther once said, "through the glow of the living and the courage of those dying in fire and water," so that the populace and even the executioners marveled. The zeal of the Anabaptists was quite strong in the district of Sterzing (*q.v.;* formerly Austria, now Italy), where citizens, peasants, and squires were baptized, and the prisons were never empty. Here on Feb. 1, 1528, a number of Anabaptists were pardoned upon recanting, having first been placed on the whipping post and beaten with rods. In addition they had to repeat their recantation on three successive Sundays before the assembled congregation in the church, and to pay the costs of their trial. Heinrich Goldschmidt was one of the Sterzing prisoners, but none of the sources give any further information about him. It is assumed, however, that he was an important person, for he was excluded from the pardon mentioned above, "to make some distinction in the treatment of persons" (Innsbruck Statthaltereiarchiv, *Causa Domini* II, p. 163 f.). He is probably identical with the Goldschmidt mentioned in a letter written by the Innsbruck government Dec. 7, 1527, to the *Landrichter* at Freundberg, "This Goldschmidt recently came to Schwaz and escaped from there with others. The spring of 1529 (Goldschmidt died on April 6) brought him the bloody rose his heart longed for."

LOSERTH.

J. Loserth, *Der Anabaptismus in Tirol* II (Vienna, 1892) 51; *ML* II, 134.

Goldschmidt (Rüdiger), **Ottilia,** an Anabaptist martyr from Mühlhausen in Thuringia. She was seized early in October 1537 with 13 other women and 3 men, including Jakob Storger of Koburg, the preacher of the Anabaptists at Mühlhausen. Upon orders of Duke George of Saxony all the prisoners were to be executed, even if they recanted. If they recanted they were only to be granted instruction and absolution before their execution. But the girls, including Ottilia, were to be shown mercy, for they had in their innocence been persuaded to accept baptism and now desired mercy. Eight women and two men, including Storger, resisted all the attempts of city council and the Catholic clergy to induce them to renounce their faith, and were drowned in the Unstrut between Mühlhausen and Ammern, Nov. 8, 1537.

Ottilia, who had been baptized by Georg Köhler, had at first, in terror of the rack and of a violent death, offered to recant; but she conquered her fear, and remained steadfast in spite of the pleas of the council and the officers. She kept replying that she could not turn back, and was therefore drowned Jan. 17, 1538, at the spot where the others had met a martyr's death. Before she was pushed into the water, a young man stepped up to her and three times offered her marriage if she would recant, but she answered not a word. The promise she had made at her baptism was binding to her.

Ottilia's mother, Katharina, who was also one of the prisoners but had not yet been baptized, recanted and after more than four months in prison was released upon the pleas of her husband.

HEGE.

P. Wappler, *Die Täuferbewegung in Thüringen von 1526-1584* (Jena, 1913); *idem, Die Stellung Kursachsens und des Landgrafen Philipp von Hessen zur Täuferbewegung* (Münster, 1910); *ML* II, 134 f.

Goldsmith (Goldschmidt), a Mennonite family of Swiss origin. More than 200 years ago two (maybe three) Goldschmidt brothers migrated from Richterswil, Switzerland, and settled in the region of Markirch (Sainte-Marie-aux-Mines), Alsace. All of the present Goldschmidts living in Alsace, France, and Switzerland descend from these brothers. One branch of the family settled in the region of Basel, Switzerland, more than a century ago. Fritz Goldschmidt, elder of the Basel Holeestrasse and the Schänzli Mennonite congregation, is a member of this family. Charles Goldschmidt, elder of the Hang congregation, Alsace, is a nephew of Fritz Goldschmidt. Henri Goldschmidt is a preacher in the Pfastatt congregation, Alsace. The great-grandmother of J. S. Gerig, Smithville, Ohio, was Mrs. Christian Gerig, nee Elizabeth Goldschmidt, of Markirch, and therefore the Ohio Gerig families are descendants of the Markirch Goldschmidts.

Joseph Goldsmith (*q.v.*), the fourth child of Konrad Goldschmidt, Markirch, emigrated to America in 1819 and after residences in Pennsylvania, Ontario, and Ohio, moved to Iowa, where he served as a bishop of the Amish Mennonite churches in Lee and Henry counties. M.G.

Goldsmith, Joseph (1796-1876), was born in Alsace, the fourth child of Konrad and Katharine (König) Goldschmidt. In 1819 he landed in Philadelphia. He was married to Elisabeth Schwarzendruber in 1824. Shortly after this marriage they moved to Waterloo Co., Ont. That same year he was ordained a minister of the newly organized Amish Mennonite church in Wilmot Township. In 1831 he and his family moved to Butler Co., Ohio, where he was ordained bishop in 1838. Because of his financial reverses in Ohio, the Goldsmith family moved to a new frontier, Lee Co., Iowa, in 1846. Here he served the Amish church as bishop, and also assisted the churches in Davis, Henry, and Johnson counties in organization, communion, marriage, and ordination services. In 1855, when the Lee County settlement began to break up because of faulty land titles, Goldsmith moved his family to the Amish Mennonite community in Henry County, where he served the church as bishop until paralysis incapacitated him in 1867. He attended the Amish ministers' conference (*Diener-Versammlung*) in 1862 and 1866, participating actively in the deliberations of that body. Among his 12 children were Veronica, wife of Joseph Gingerich, an Amish minister in Johnson Co., Iowa, and Magdalena, wife of Sebastian Gerig (*q.v.*), a bishop of the Sugar Creek Amish Mennonite Church near Wayland, Iowa. Three of Goldsmith's great-grandchildren were in 1954 serving in the ministry of the Mennonite Church and two others on the faculty of Goshen College.

M.G.

Goller, Balthasar, a Hutterite physician in Nikolsburg, Moravia, around 1600 (d. 1619). It is well known that the Hutterite brotherhood held its physicians and barber-surgeons in high esteem; in fact, at the turn of the 16th century one could hardly find adequate medical care in Moravia outside the Hutterite brotherhood (see **Physicians, Hutterite**). It is known that Hutterite physicians were employed by most noble lords of that area, even Emperor Rudolphus II consulted such a doctor twice, and the head of the Catholic Counter Reformation in Moravia, Cardinal Franz von Dietrichstein (*q.v.*), used these men himself and recommended them to his friends, in spite of the fact that he otherwise worked violently against these "heretics."

It seems that Goller was a real doctor (not only a barber-surgeon as most other brethren in this field had been). He lived in Nikolsburg, the manorial estate of the Dietrichsteins, and most likely was for a while the assistant to Georg Zobel (*q.v.*), another outstanding Hutterite physician (d. 1603). Goller distinguished himself as the personal physician of the imperial ambassador to Turkey on the latter's mission to Constantinople in 1608-9. From this trip we have five letters from him to the brethren at home, still extant in one of the Hutterite codices.

From a letter of Dietrichstein of 1618 we learn that he was "chief physician of the brethren." Dietrichstein dispatched him to his friend "even though I needed him badly myself." In 1619, Goller was to meet his tragic fate in the first upheavals of the Thirty Years' War. He was slain by some soldier or officer, and the pharmacy of the brethren in Nikolsburg was likewise destroyed and confiscated. It was but a few years before the entire brotherhood was expelled from Moravia altogether (1622), mainly due to the urging of the Cardinal Dietrichstein. (See also **Dietrich, Sebastian**.) R.F.

R. Friedmann, "Hutterite Physicians and Barber-surgeons," *MQR* XXVII (1953) 129-30.

Golos (Voice), a periodical in the Russian language, was published 1905-12 by the Conference of the Mennonite Brethren Church of North America, printed monthly at Hillsboro, Kan., and edited by Hermann Fast, Sask. The contents were of a devotional character and the purpose of the periodical was to strengthen the spiritual life of the Russian Christians, and also to fill a need for spiritual literature in the Russian language. The approximate number of copies of each edition was 1,500. The first number appeared in 1905. The paper was discontinued in 1912 with a credit balance of $475.75, which sum was donated toward the building of a church of the Russian Christians. H.H.J.

Gom(m)er de Metser (Gomer the mason), in the records called Gommare de Clercq, was an Anabaptist martyr, a mason by trade. He was a native of Lier in Brabant. He was arrested in Antwerp and put to death there on Feb. 1, 1560, together with Pedro de Soza and Jacob Schot. They were executed by drowning in a tub, a method ordinarily used only for women. Gommer remained steadfast. He is celebrated in the song "Aenhoert Godt hemelsche Vader" (Hear, O God, heavenly Father), found in the *Liedtboecxken van den Offer des Heeren*, No. 16. vDZ.

Offer, 567; *Mar. Mir.* D 270, E 640; *Antw. Arch.-Blad*, IX, 6, 11; XIV, 28 f., No. 311; Wolkan, *Leider*, 63, 72.

Good, a German Mennonite family name, originally Guth (*q.v.*). Among the pioneers of the Good family in America were Jacob and Christian Good, who immigrated from the Palatinate in the early 18th century and settled in eastern Lancaster Co., Pa. In this region there is both a village named Goodville in the western part of the county near Elizabethtown, and a Good Mennonite Church (MC). Christian Good (1772-1839), grandson of the first Christian, served as minister at Bowmansville, Pa. Jacob Good, son of the first Jacob, moved to the Shenandoah Valley of Virginia, where his descendants have been active, including Bishop Daniel (1781-1850) and Bishop Christian (1842-1916). Descendants of both Lancaster and Virginia Goods have moved to Mennonite congregations in Ontario, Ohio, Indiana, Illinois, and Missouri. Among the latter were Bishop John S. Good (1811-99) of Page Co., Iowa, Bishop A. C. Good (1881-) of Sterling, Ill., Deacon Sol R. Good of Sterling, Ill., and Bishop Kenneth Good (1910-) of Morton, Ill. Preacher Noah G. Good (1904-) is dean of the Lancaster Mennonite School, I. B. Good (*q.v.*) was a prominent Lancaster County preacher, and Andrew Good (*q.v.*) and C. N. Good (1869-) were outstanding elders in the Mennonite Brethren in Christ Church (UMC).

Some Amish Mennonite Guths who immigrated from Alsace-Lorraine in the 19th century to Illinois and Iowa have retained the spelling Guth. H.S.B.

Good, Andrew, elder and missionary of the Brethren in Christ Church and the Mennonite Brethren in Christ Church, was born Feb. 6, 1838, in Fairfield Co., Ohio, the son of Samuel and Catherine Good. He taught school several years; musically gifted, he also taught singing school. He married Dinah Hendricks on Oct. 4, 1866. Converted at the age of 20, he entered the ministry of the Brethren in Christ Church in 1870, and transferred to the M.B.C. Church in 1885, continuing his ministry. Though most of his ministerial life was devoted to home missions and evangelistic work, he served as presiding elder in the Mennonite Brethren in Christ Church for three years, and pastor for one year. Having lived for a few years in Illinois, the Good family located at New Carlisle, Ohio, in 1882. Their children are Jenny Florence (Mrs. W. J. Huffman), Mary Catherine (Mrs. McHessel), John Wesley, Joseph Hendricks, Lloyd Andrew, and Bertha Elizabeth (Mrs. John Koch). He died at New Carlisle on Oct. 3, 1918. J.A.Hu.

Good, Israel B., an influential minister in the Weaverland district of the Lancaster Conference (MC), born Oct. 2, 1861, in Brecknock Twp., Lancaster Co., Pa., and died April 17, 1945, at East Earl, Pa. He taught school for 26 years, beginning at 18 and ultimately serving as a high-school principal at Terre Hill, Pa. Among his pupils were John M. Sauder, later a Mennonite bishop at Weaverland, and the local historian M. G. Weaver of New Holland. On Sept. 8, 1885, he was united in marriage with Hettie Witmer. In 1899, then a man of about 38, he and his wife were baptized into the Weaverland congregation by Martin Rutt

(1840-1905), who cared for the Weaverland district for a time following the secession of Bishop Jonas Martin (1839-1925). On Dec. 17, 1903, Israel Good was ordained as a preacher. Although he was not a fluent speaker, especially in his early years, he was a deep thinker and a good teacher. He wielded a tremendous influence in Lancaster County, and held a large number of effective evangelistic meetings (one thousand converts). All through his life he read widely; as an aged man he was still reading both philosophical and theological works. During World War I he was very active in behalf of the Mennonite young men who had been drafted, interviewing Congressman W. W. Greist, General Crowder, and even Secretary of War Baker. He was impatient with some of the new influences which he saw entering the brotherhood during his lifetime such as premillennialism, and frequently made statements which caused some criticism, probably mostly by being misunderstood. He was a fast friend of Bishop Benjamin Weaver (1853-1928), his senior ministerial colleague at Weaverland and Conference moderator.   J.C.W.

Good, Solomon R. (1871-1933), a leader in the Illinois Mennonite (MC) Conference, was born at Dale Enterprise, Va., March 3, 1871, the son of Bishop Christian and Anna (Heatwole) Good; died at Sterling, Ill., May 17, 1933; married Jan. 27, 1898, to Martha E. Burkholder (3 children); deacon of the Science Ridge Mennonite (MC) Church 1923-33, he was active in district and general church work. For many years he was a member of the Mennonite Board of Education, and its treasurer for some time. He was also long a member of the General Conference Music Committee, and for some years president of the Illinois Mennonite Mission Board.   H.S.B.

Good Mennonite Church (MC), a member of the Lancaster Conference, built its first meetinghouse about 1815 between Falmouth and Elizabethtown, Pa., four miles from the latter, on land given by Melchior Brenneman, who had moved into the community from New Danville. This meetinghouse was replaced by the present church in 1879. Sunday school was opened here by D. N. Gish and S. E. Ebersole in 1890, following a community union effort. In 1953 the membership was 175. Since 1936 the congregation has conducted a mission Sunday school at Cedar Hill and supported the Steelton mission work, opened the same year. Noah W. Risser and Clarence E. Lutz are the bishops in charge, with Ira Z. Miller as minister and Walter W. Ebersole and Joseph H. Nissley as deacons. The congregation operates a summer Bible school at Cedar Hill.   I.D.L.

Good Tidings was published monthly by the "Defenseless Mennonite Brethren in Christ of North America" (now Evangelical Mennonite Brethren) at Chicago, Ill., as a 4-page 9 x 12 in. journal from July 1919 to August 1921. In September 1921 it was merged with *Zion's Call* (*q.v.*) of the Defenseless Mennonites (now Evangelical Mennonites) to become *Zion's Tidings* (*q.v.*). G. P. Schultz was the editor.   H.S.B.

Good Tidings, "A Religious Message, published quarterly by the Reformed Mennonite Church for the Disseminating of Spiritual Knowledge," was issued from July 1922 to July 1932 as a 32-page 6½ x 10 in. quarterly. Editors were John K. Ryder to October 1926, Frank E. Eshleman to the end.   H.S.B.

Good Works: see **Works.**

Goodrich Mennonite Brethren Church, now extinct, located at Goodrich, N.D., a congregation of the Central District Conference, was organized with 18 members in 1925 by Ludwig Seibel, who served as the first pastor. Later John Siemens ministered to the church for three years. A church building 28 x 36 ft. was erected and served the congregation for a number of years. Most of the members moved away, and the congregation was dissolved.   A.A.D.

Good's Mennonite (MC) Church was established in Clarence Center, N.Y., in 1824 by Mennonites from Lancaster Co., Pa., among them the Leibs, Lehmans, Sherers, Martins. The first minister was Jacob Lapp, who (according to the Hartzler-Kauffman *Mennonite Church History*) came in 1828. John Martin was the first deacon (according to Cassel's *History of the Mennonites,* p. 169). In 1831 Jacob Krehbiel, a Mennonite minister, moved in from Germany. He became bishop in 1839. His son Frederick and Abraham Leib were ordained deacons with the growth of the congregation. They soon built a stone church a few miles west of Clarence Center known as the Good's Church. The congregation prospered both by immigration and by accessions. John Lapp (1798-1878) was ordained as minister in 1828 and as bishop about ten years later. Peter Lehman and Abram Lapp were also ordained ministers. Jacob Krehbiel, Jr., became minister at this place in 1872 but withdrew about 1875, becoming affiliated with the General Conference of Mennonites by the time of their 1884 conference. Jacob Hahn became minister in 1866; he was the father of Sarah Lapp, missionary to India. The *Herald of Truth* in 1872 reported German Sunday school and preaching held every Sunday. John Strickler of the Miller Church near Clarence later identified himself with this flock. Following the active years of Bishop John Lapp the church dwindled, and with the loss of the Krehbiel followers became very weak. The Ontario Conference supplied the ministers for a number of years until about 1920. New families moving in from various states gave rise to a revived congregation in a more easterly location (see **Clarence Center**). The Good cemetery is still the burying grounds for the Clarence Center congregation.   J.C.F.

Goodville (Pa.) Mennonite Church (MC) was organized in 1900 by a number of retired Mennonite farmers as a member of the Lancaster Mennonite Conference. It is located in the strong Weaverland (*q.v.*) district of the beautiful fertile Weaverland Valley on Route 23. The first meetinghouse was greatly enlarged in 1924. In 1953 the total church membership was 113 with A. G. Martin as minister and J. Paul Graybill as bishop. An outstation summer Bible school was held at Bender's Church near Bangor in 1952.   I.D.L.

Goodville Mutual Casualty Company, a mutual automobile insurance agency, was incorporated Jan. 4, 1926, with head office at Goodville, Lancaster Co., Pa. It is in effect a Mennonite organization, all its officers and 12 of its 15 directors being Mennonites and 85 per cent of the 18,000 policyholders being Mennonites. It also serves related groups, in addition to cases assigned to it by the State of Pennsylvania. It area is Pennsylvania and Virginia. It is closely related to Mennonite Mutual Aid, Inc., of Goshen, Ind., an agency under the Mennonite General Conference (MC). It paid approximately $200,000 of losses in 1954.

The company's motto is "Insurance at Cost." It returns the unused portion of premiums to the policyholder at the end of the policy year. This is determined by taking the losses, expenses, and reserves off the premiums collected. The percentage of dividend is then determined. The average dividend is 35 per cent.   H.S.B.

Goor, a town (pop. 4,996) in the Dutch province of Overijssel, with 16 Mennonites, was formerly the seat of a Mennonite congregation. In early times Anabaptists were found here; in 1544 Davidjorists (*q.v.*) were said to be living here (*Inv. Arch. Amst.* I, No. 242). Later on most of the Mennonites were weavers of the Old Flemish wing. The congregation of Goor apparently was a part of the Twenthe (*q.v.*) congregation. Prominent members (deacons?) at Goor in 1610 were Arend ten Cate, Andries Ollenvanger, Hindrik Willemsen, and Willem Hermans. In 1728 the Mennonites living in this town belonged to the congregation of near-by Hengelo (*q.v.*). Whether there was an independent congregation in the course of the 18th century or not, is not clear; in any case it was dissolved by 1787, when a few remaining Mennonites joined the Hengelo congregation.   vDZ.

Blaupot t. C., *Groningen* I, 224; II, 58-60; G. Heeringa, *Uit het Verleden der Doopsgez. in Twenthe* (Borne, n.d.) 132, 134.

Goos was the name of a Mennonite family which played a significant role in the Friedrichstadt and Hamburg Mennonite congregations in Germany. Abraham Goos and his son Isaak (1696-1769) were deacons of the Mennonite church at Friedrichstadt. Another Isaak Goos studied theology and served as the minister of the Mennonite church (1798-1845) of Hamburg, under whom the change from the Dutch language in worship services to the German took place. His son Berend (1815-85) was a well-known artist in Hamburg.   C.K.

R. Dollinger, *Geschichte der Mennoniten in Schleswig-Holstein, Hamburg und Lübeck* (Neumünster, 1930).

Goossen (Gosen, Gossen, Goos), a Mennonite family found in West Prussia. Near Doornik in Belgium a hatmaker Goossen died for his faith in 1558. Four decades later, Sept. 30, 1598, an Abraham Gooss of the Netherlands entered the preparatory

school of the Elbing Gymnasium. In 1658 a Heinrich Goossen was living in Elbing. As early as 1621 a Gert Gosen was one of a number of Mennonites living in Beyershorst in the very low Scharpau in the Gross-Werder.

In the Elbing and Danzig congregations, as well as in several Gross-Werder congregations there were once members with this name. In 1789 the Gosens were listed in the Mennonite directory, a number of whom emigrated to Russia; just before World War II there were no Gosens left. This name was transplanted from Prussia and Russia to the United States (e.g., Beatrice, Neb.) and Canada.
                                    H.P.

G. E. Reimer, *Die Familiennamen der westpreussischen Mennoniten* (Weierhof, 1940).

Goossen, Helena, b. 1889 at Nicolaifeld, Russia, came in 1911 as a nurse to the Dutch Mennonite mission field in Java (*q.v.*). She soon became matron of the hospital at Margaredjo, which office she held until 1922, when she married the medical missionary K. P. C. A. Gramberg (*q.v.*), the director of the entire medical service. At that time the Grambergs lived at Kelet, the site of the principal hospital. Mrs. Gramberg excellently assisted her husband and the medical provision became exemplary; another hospital at Tajoe and a number of polyclinics in the neighborhood were opened and the number of patients rapidly increased. In March 1942, when the Japanese occupied the Dutch East Indies, a trying time began for the mission field. The medical care came to a standstill in August 1943, when the Gramberg family was interned; Helena Gramberg-Goossen died in the camp on Aug. 23, 1945. The Grambergs not only took care of the medical work, but also participated in the spiritual work. So they took part in organizing the Javanese Christians into 10 independent Mennonite congregations (1940).   vDZ.

Goossen de Hoedemaecker (hatter), an Anabaptist martyr, was taken prisoner with five brethren during a service in the Obignies Forest near Doornik, Belgium. They were all sentenced to death and burned at the stake in Obignies in 1558 (see **Egbert;** *Mart. Mir.* D 203, E 584; *ML* II, 136). vDZ.

Goossen (Gosen) of Winterswijk, a Dutch Anabaptist leader, is identical with Jacob van Antwerpen (*q.v.*).

Goot, van der, a Dutch Mennonite family, originally of Akkrum, province of Friesland. Here (1) Jacob Synnes (1703-65), a butter merchant, was a (untrained and unsalaried) preacher of the Mennonite congregation. His son (2) Synne (1740-1818) in 1811 adopted the family name of van der Goot. Sons of Synne were (3) Jacob (1769-1844) and (4) Hidde (1771-1840), both butter merchants like their father and grandfather, and both deacons of the Akkrum congregation. (5) Sine Hiddes van der Goot (1799-1889), son of Hidde (4), was minister of the congregations of Workum 1825-27, Warga 1827-33, Blokzijl 1833-39, and Berlikum 1839-71.

Two sons of Jacob (3), viz., (6) Gerben and (7) Pieter van der Goot in 1806 moved to West-zaan, province of North Holland, where their father had bought an oil mill, but in 1813 they returned to Friesland to hide in order to avoid military service. In 1814 they returned to North Holland and lived at Zaandam. A son of Pieter v.d. Goot (7) was (8) Pastor Pieter v.d. Goot (*q.v.*).

(9) Arnold Hiddes van der Goot (1863-1945), a grandson of Sine (Synne) Hiddes (2), was a Mennonite pastor serving the churches of Giethoorn 1889-92, and Middelie 1892-1930. His son (10) Benjamin van der Goot (b. 1893) was also a Mennonite pastor, serving at Zijpe 1919-24 and Borne 1930-39.   vdZ.

Goot, Pieter van der, b. 1817 at Zaandam, Mennonite preacher at Wormer and Jisp 1841-42, Rotterdam 1842-51, and at Amsterdam 1871-75, where he died in 1877. In Rotterdam he was closely associated with the Dutch Mission Society (founded in 1797) and especially with J. van Oosterzee, one of the best-known Reformed preachers of the time. His interest in mission work, which was later shown in his service as secretary of the Mennonite Mission Society founded in 1847, was aroused here and his spirit, which found no satisfaction in the current hyperrationalism, was completely at home here. When he came to Amsterdam the *Reveil* movement had already passed its prime, but he felt its influence, and many of its leaders, especially da Costa, were often among his audiences. He was a man of warm eloquence, not a strict dogmatician, but rather pietistically inclined. His colleague A. Loosjes, who delivered his funeral sermon (Amsterdam, 1877), especially praised van der Goot's delivery, which was borne by a spirit of warm love that moved his hearers. "The love of Christ constrained him." The memory of his personality is still alive in the Amsterdam congregation, which he served for 24 years. He lamented the critical trend of liberalism which at that time exerted a profound influence on the Dutch brotherhood.

As secretary of the Mennonite Mission Society van der Goot was able to stir up interest in its cause when such interest was as yet quite feeble. He lived with the missionaries, prayed for them in public services, and kept them in his home when they were on furlough. His appeal also reached the Mennonites of other countries, especially Germany and Russia (*Menn. Bl.,* 1854, 46; 1855, 1; 1862, 3; 1865, 6). The mission work in Java and Sumatra owes much to him.

He was also deeply interested in home missions. At this time the Zetten institutions were just being established by O. G. Heldring. Van der Goot was a member of the Amsterdam committee that supported this work. He was also an outstanding philanthropist, deeply moved by the lot of the poor; and with the support of wealthy friends he assisted whenever he was able.

All these activities consumed van der Goot's strength. In the prime of life, at the age of 58 years, he was compelled to resign, and in two years he died. The only writings he left were

Geloofsbeproeving en Geloofskracht bij Christelijke martelaressen (Amsterdam, 1858, and *Opwekkingsrede bij het verslag van de 35ste Openlijke Vergadering der afdeeling Rotterdam van het Ned. Bijbelgenootschap, 18. Oct. 1849* (Rotterdam, 1849). His plan to publish a book of *Pastorale Herinneringen* was unfortunately never carried out.
                                        A.Ku.

Biogr. Wb. III, 306; *Inv. Arch. Amst.* II, 265-68; *DB* 1878, 132; 1886, 73 f.; 1895, 128; 1898, 51; 1901, 21, 26; *ML* II, 136.

Gorinchem (or Gorkum), a city on the Merwede in the Dutch province of South Holland, pop. (1947) 15,321, 34 Mennonites, was an Anabaptist center about 1538, and later the seat of a Mennonite congregation. Leenaert Bouwens baptized 56 persons there in 1563-65. The congregation later joined the Flemish group; Jacob van der Heyde Sebrechts and Jan Jansz van de Kruysen from here signed the Dordrecht Confession in 1632. In 1649 it was represented at the conference of the Flemish at Haarlem. Soon after, the congregation, which was a very small one, had no preacher of its own. It was for more than 40 years served by preachers of other Flemish congregations, especially of Utrecht. The congregation of Gorinchem is not mentioned in the first *Naamlijst* of 1731; hence it must have died out before this year.

Since 1948 there has been a Mennonite circle at Gorinchem, now 21 members, in charge of the congregation of Dordrecht. Together with the Remonstrant group some services are conducted (7-10 each year) in the city orphanage. (*Inv. Arch. Amst.* I, Nos. 93, 200, 207, 215; *DB* 1863, 96, 102; 1917, 122, Nos. 155-58; *ML* II, 136.) W.Ko., vdZ.

Goris, an Anabaptist martyr executed at Antwerp in 1560: see **Joris Leerse.**

Goris (Joris) **Cooman,** an Anabaptist martyr, of Lier in Brabant, Belgium, was burned at the stake on April 11, 1551, at Antwerp, with Naentken (Bornaige), Grietgen (Margriete van den Berghe), and Wouter (van der Weyden). These martyrs are celebrated in a hymn, "Doemen vijftienhondert schreve, daertoe een en vijftich jaer," found in the *Liedtboecxken van den Offer des Heeren* (No. 4).
                                        vdZ.

Offer, 516-21; *Mart. Mir.* D 106, E 503; Verheyden, Gent, 13, No. 21; Wolkan, *Lieder,* 61.

Gorkoya Mennonite Brethren Church, located in the province of Akmolinsk in the vicinity of Omsk, Siberia, was organized in 1903 as a subsidiary of the Tchunaevka Mennonite Brethren Church (*q.v.*). Jakob Friesen was the leading minister. (Friesen, *Brüderschaft,* 444-45.)   C.K.

Gorkoye: see **Friesenov and Gorkoye.**

Gorkum (Gorcum): see **Gorinchem.**

Gormley United Missionary Church, an appointment of the Ontario conference, located at Gormley, Ont., was organized about 1878. The present church was built in 1931 and the parsonage in 1953. Pastors have been A. T. Gooding 1929-34, H.

Shantz 1934-38, I. B. Brubacher 1938-42, W. M. Shantz 1942-43, F. G. Huson 1943-47, P. R. Barley 1947-49, L. K. Sider 1949-52, and C. E. Hunking 1952- . The membership in 1954 was 90. E.R.S.

Gorredijk, a town in the Dutch province of Friesland, seat of a Mennonite congregation, which already before 1700 had united with a congregation at Lippenhuizen (*q.v.*), so that they are always referred to as the Gorredijk-Lippenhuizen congregation. The congregation had two meeting-houses, one in Gorredijk, and the other in Lippenhuizen. The latter was in use until September 1947 and was then sold. Gorredijk acquired a new church in 1940, dedicated April 7.

The origin and early history of the congregation is unknown. Very likely the Mennonite congregation at Gorredijk came into being during the 17th century. The Mennonite settlement at Lippenhuizen may have had its origin in the 16th century. The definite existence of a combined congregation of Gorredijk-Lippenhuizen in 1686 is proved by an entry in the church archives. But there are no records before 1739, with the exception of a few contracts of purchase. From 1739 the records have been preserved, and from 1748 the names of the preachers and members. In July 1711 a number of Swiss Mennonite refugees from the Emmental, Switzerland, a total of 18 persons, with the aid of the Dutch Mennonite Committee for Foreign Needs, were located near Gorredijk, but they did not feel at home here, and in May 1712 they moved to Kampen (*q.v.*). But the Swiss Mennonites living here were Amish and the Gorredijk Swiss brethren were Mennonites (*Rheydtvolk,* i.e., followers of Hans Reist *q.v.*). The latter group in the fall of 1713 emigrated to the Palatinate.

In 1748 the congregation numbered 110 members, in 1838, 118, in 1861, 195, reaching its highest membership of 210 in 1882, then decreasing; in 1900, 166, in 1953, 165.

Not all the members live in Gorredijk; some are scattered over several villages in the southeast of the province of Friesland. A few years ago the members living in Oosterwolde (*q.v.*) organized a Mennonite circle (*Kring*).

The last untrained preachers of this congregation were Pieter Ymes, who in 1810 assumed the family name of van der Woude, a farmer at Lippenhuizen, serving 1782-1805, and Dirk Gerbens Visser 1806-24. During the last decades the congregation was served by the following ministers: J. G. Appeldoorn 1889-1904, J. Koster 1905-9, C. C. de Maar 1910-15, G. A. Hulshoff 1916-27, Miss C. Boerlage 1928-33, A. F. L. van Dijk 1936-38, Miss W. C. Jolles 1938-49, and J. G. van der Bend 1951-56. The pulpit is now vacant.

The congregation owes much to Eesge Ubeles Veenland and Pieter Ymes Veenland, who were treasurer (1868-1915) and president (1915-) of the church board respectively. Church activities include a youth group, children's club, ladies' circles.   G.A.H., vDZ.

Inv. Arch. Amst. I, Nos. 1868 f., 1872, 1881-83; *DB* 1861, 133 f.; 1906, 95; Blaupot t. C., *Friesland,* 189, 200, 247, 254, 306; *ML* II, 137.

Gortchakovo Mennonite Brethren Church near Davlekanovo, province of Ufa, Russia, was founded in the year 1898. Its first leader and cofounder was Wilhelm Baerg of Karanbash. The first ordination, involving two ministers, Heinrich K. Siemens and Heinrich Thiessen, and presided over by Elder De-Fehr of Orenburg, took place in 1907. Baerg soon after this resigned from the leadership and Johann Heinrichs was elected leader. When Heinrichs moved to Siberia in 1909, Jacob J. Martens, superintendent of the *Armenschule* at Berezovka, became leader. After Martens' death in 1922 Heinrich K. Siemens took over. In 1925 Siemens emigrated to Canada and settled in Gem, Alberta. After that the leadership went to G. G. Friesen. During his administration the second and last ordination of ministers of this church took place on Dec. 2, 1927, when H. B. Friesen and H. H. Siemens, son of H. K. Siemens, were ordained. About this time all preachers were disfranchised by the Soviets. H. B. Friesen and H. H. Siemens fled. Friesen found his way to Paraguay, while Siemens managed to join his parents in Canada. The last minister of the Gortchakovo Mennonite Brethren Church was P. Dück, who died in 1932.

In the course of its development this church had branched out into the neighboring localities: Karanbash, Berezovka, Davlekanovo, and Yurmakay. All of them, with the exception of Yurmakay, had their ministers and meetinghouses. Membership of the combined churches grew to approximately 300 souls. Each local church had representatives in the *Vorberat* (preliminary council). Matters of lesser importance were settled by the local church, while questions of wider range were brought before the *Vorberat* and the *Hauptversammlung* (general assembly). Local churches had the following preachers: Gortchakovo—G. Friesen, Sen., B. Friesen, Johann Heinrichs, H. K. Siemens, G. G. Friesen, Jun., H. B. Friesen, and H. H. Siemens; Berezovka—Jacob J. Martens, David Thiessen, J. Isaak, and P. Dück; Karanbash—Wilhelm Baerg and Gerhard Wiens; Davlekanovo—K. G. Neufeld, Heinrich Thiessen, Peter Thielmann, Jacob Friesen, and David Isaak. (*ML* II, 138.)   J.P.R.

Gorter, a common Dutch family name, both Mennonite and non-Mennonite. Not all the bearers of this name are related. Foeke Wiglers Gorter (*q.v.*) was, e.g., not of the same family as Simon Gorter (*q.v.*) and his descendants. A large number of Gorters have been Mennonite preachers. The first one mentioned is Tys Oenes Gorter (1670-?), a preacher at Alkmaar (*DB* 1891, 5, 8). Feiko Wybes Gorter served as a preacher in the congregation at Stavoren in the first quarter of the 18th century. Jan Gorter was the preacher at Bolsward from 1761 to about 1788.

Klaas Oenes Gorter, not a preacher, was treasurer of the Friese Sociëteit from 1788 to 1805, in which year he died. K. Tigler dedicated a Funeral Song (*Grafdicht*) to him (*DB* 1895, 30).

A number of preachers of this name were descendants of Simon Gorter (1778-1862, *q.v.*), who lived in the Zaan district (Dutch province of North Holland) as had his ancestors. Two of his sons, Douwe Simons and Klaas Simons, a grandson Simon Gorter (son of Douwe), a great-grandson Klaas Gorter (1849-89, minister at Borne 1875-79, Zijpe 1879-85, and Hoorn 1885-89), and two great-great-grandsons, S. H. N. Gorter and Klaas Gorter (b. 1911 at Uithuizermeeden, minister at Ternaard 1937-39, Texel 1939-41, Groningen 1941-45, naval chaplain 1945-47, Hengelo since 1948) are Mennonite pastors. (*ML* II, 137.) K.V., vDZ.

Gorter, Douwe Simons, the son of Simon Gorter (*q.v.*) and Tiete van der Zee, was born at Hindelopen on Aug. 3, 1811. In 1834 he was called as Mennonite minister to Stavoren and Warns, in 1854 to Balk, the first trained minister of that congregation, died there on Aug. 27, 1876. He was married to Tryntjen Koopmans. He was the author of the following books: *Onderzoek naar het kenmerkend beginsel der Doopsgezinden* (1850); *Brief aan J. Visscher over de waardeering van den kinderdoop* (1851); *De Christelyke Doop* (1854); *Vruchten van onderzoek en strijd* (1874). He was one of the most erudite preachers of his time. He was also the editor of the *Doopsgezinde Lectuur* (*q.v.*) (1854, 1856, and 1858), to which he contributed many articles, including a study on the martyr Hans van Overdam. K.V.

Biogr. Wb. III, 310 f.; *DB* 1901, 23 ff., 145; *Catalogus Amst.*, 304-7, 310, 327; N. van der Zijpp, *Geschiedenis der Doopsgezinden in Nederland* (Arnhem, 1952) 202, 213; *ML* II, 137.

Gorter, Foeke Wiglers, one of the last untrained Mennonite ministers (*leekeprekers*) in the Netherlands, became preacher at Knijpe in 1783 and in Sappemeer on Feb. 14, 1790. Here he died on May 8, 1836. In 1790 he served as one of the four commissars who supported Wolter ten Cate as manager of the Groninger Sociëteit of the Old Flemish, and after the death of ten Cate (in 1796) he became the manager. He wrote several booklets of religious instruction. K.V.

Biogr. Wb. III, 311; *Catalogus Amst.*, 233, 265, 325; *ML* II, 137.

Gorter, Klaas Simons, a brother of Douwe Simons Gorter (*q.v.*), b. May 19, 1822, at Oosternieland near Zijldijk, became preacher at Den Ilp in 1850, and the first trained preacher at Ameland in 1852. Two years later he managed to bring about a union between the two congregations on this island. He worked here at Hollum until 1895, and died on June 25, 1901. He was married to Tryntje Kat. He published an important study of the Mennonites on Ameland in *DB* 1889-90. (*ML* II, 137.) K.V.

Gorter, Simon, b. March 16, 1778, at Westzaan, Dutch province of North Holland. The family had lived at Westzaan since the time of his great-grandfather Jan Gorter, b. March 13, 1669, whose son Jans, b. Sept. 4, 1705, and grandson, b. Feb. 15, 1741, had been living at Westzaan. He was at first a miller's aid and was educated for the ministry in his evening hours by Gerbrandt Valter. Shortly after the mill known as "De Ruiter" burned down, including all his equipment, he was called as min-

ister of the Zonist congregation at Joure, delivering his first sermon on Sept. 6, 1808. Here he married Tiete van der Zee. He was a man of enormous figure. In 1808 he moved to Hindelopen at Molkwerum, and in 1813 to Zijldijk. He is the progenitor of the numerous Gorters in the province of Groningen. On Sept. 7, 1851, he celebrated the fiftieth anniversary of his ministry. Through his zealous efforts the congregations of Huizinge, Leermens-Loppersum, and den Hoorn were kept alive and at the last-named place a parsonage was built. In addition he was the founder (1835) and the first chairman of the Groningen fund (*q.v.*) for ministers' widows. On July 6, 1856, he retired and on Sept. 11, 1862, he died. His son Douwe Gorter (d. March 17, 1921) was a pillar of the small Zijldijk (*q.v.*) congregation, which he served many years as deacon and treasurer. The sons of Douwe Gorter were also deacons at Zijldijk. (*DB* 1864, 170 f.; *ML* II, 137.) K.V.

Gorter, Simon, b. 1838 at Warns, became the minister at Aalsmeer in 1861 and at Wormerveer in 1863. Because of a long ailment from which he had been suffering for some time, he retired with his family to Arcachon (France) in 1864-66. His excellent articles in the periodical *De Gids* gave him great fame as an author. In 1869 he was compelled by his health to resign from his office, after which he became the editor of the newly founded Amsterdam daily newspaper *Het Nieuws van den Dag.* Here he published a series of excellent editorials which were published after his death in a book, *Een Jaar levens voor de Dagbladpers* (1872). De Hoop Scheffer published his articles in the *Gids* in a booklet *Letterkundige studien,* as well as several sermons under the title, *Ik geloof, daarom spreek ik.* He died June 5, 1871. His wife Johanna Lugt died in 1924. (*Biogr. Wb.* III, 312 f.; *Catalogus Amst.,* 315; *ML* II, 137.) K.V.

Gorter, Simon Henri Nicolaas, b. June 25, 1885, at Hoorn, son of Pastor Klaas Gorter and a descendant of an old family of Mennonite preachers, studied at the University of Amsterdam and the Mennonite Seminary of Amsterdam. He served the congregation of Zijldijk 1910-12, Twisk 1912-14, Sappemeer 1914-16, Rotterdam 1916-46, and Apeldoorn 1946-51. Gorter was a well-known Dutch Mennonite leader, a member of the A.D.S. (General Conference), editor of the *Doopsgezinde Jaarboekje* (*q.v.*) 1932-43, and of the *Algemeen Doopsgezind Weekblad* 1946-50. He was a popular radio speaker. During a number of years he was a coeditor with C. E. Hooykaas, a Remonstrant preacher of Rotterdam, of *De Stroom,* a religious liberal weekly. He was a delegate at the Mennonite world conferences held at Basel 1925, Danzig 1930, and Amsterdam 1936.

His name is gratefully remembered among hundreds of Mennonite emigrants who passed from Russia via Rotterdam to Canada and Brazil in 1928 and following years when he was president of the *Hollandsch Doopsgezind Emigranten Bureau* (*q.v.*). Besides reports published in the records of the Mennonite world conferences of 1930 and 1936, and a large number of articles in various issues of the

Doopsgezind Jaarboekje, Zondagsbode, and *Alge-meen Doopsgezind Weekblad,* he published *Waarom zijn wij nog Doopsgezind* (Rotterdam, 1921); *Doopsgezinde Emigratie* (1934); *Medewerkers,* a farewell sermon, Rotterdam, 1946); *Levende Stee-nen,* a sermon preached at Apeldoorn in 1946 to commemorate the fiftieth anniversary of the founding of the congregation; *Langs de Vloedlijn* (sermons, Zeist, 1941), *Voor de Oude Dag,* a volume of addresses given on the V.P.R.O. broadcast (Amsterdam, n.d., 1953); and *Waarom zijn wij Doopsgezind,* issued by the A.D.S. in 1954.   vDZ.

Gortner Union Church, a congregation in Garrett Co., Md., was organized in the spring of 1893 by the people of the Gortner community. They had a Sunday-school attendance of approximately 40, and some preaching appointments in the schoolhouse by United Brethren and Mennonite (MC) ministers.

In 1898 the Gortner Union Church was built (26 x 42 ft.). Labor and material were donated, and the building was completed at a cash cost of approximately $600, and dedicated Oct. 16, 1898, three different denominations taking part. In the forenoon, D. H. Bender conducted Mennonite services; afternoon, Tobias Fike, German Baptist; and evening, Franklin M. Glenn, United Brethren. During the first year several denominations conducted revivals. S. G. Shetler conducted the first revival by the Mennonites in 1899. The church was remodeled in 1937. In 1954 it had a membership of 17 Mennonites, with D. L. Swartzendruber as pastor.   D.L.S.

Görz, Franz, an elder of the Rudnerweide Mennonite Church, Molotschna, South Russia. He was ordained as elder in Prussia in 1819 and when the Rudnerweide church was organized in 1820 he became its first elder. He died in 1835. (Friesen, *Brüderschaft,* 706.)   C.K.

Göschl, Dr. Martin, one of the notable personalities of Moravia in the early years of the Reformation, provost (from 1524) of the Himmelsrose Nunnery at Kanitz, Coadjutor Bishop of Olomuce (from 1509), who joined the Reformation in 1525. In the spring of 1526 he moved to Nikolsburg, having been forced to surrender the ecclesiastical property and income, which he had tried to retain. He supported the reform efforts of Baron Johann Dubzansky, who had called the synod of March 11, 1526, at Austerlitz, of which Oswald Glait (*q.v.*) wrote a report.

Göschl gave vigorous support to Balthasar Hubmaier when the latter arrived at Nikolsburg later in 1526, who then dedicated two tracts to him. In the foreword he declared Göschl to be the only bishop concerning whom he knew that he had "so manfully and bravely yielded himself to God and His holy Word in this world." The second pamphlet was written at Göschl's express request. It was to be a "catechism or summary" of those articles in which the youth were to be instructed. Göschl participated in person in the disputation held at Nikolsburg between Hubmaier and Hans Hut (*q.v.*) and his followers in 1527, hoping to eradicate the dissension

that was developing among the Anabaptists. Göschl is reported to have threatened to deliver Hut to King Ferdinand (*q.v.*) because Hut had wanted to create disturbance in Nikolsburg; this information caused Hut to flee from Nikolsburg.

According to the Hutterite Chronicles Göschl died in the tower at Kremsier as a martyr to his convictions regarding "the Christian faith and baptism," but he can scarcely be reckoned as a real Anabaptist. He was too much interested in material finances to follow Hubmaier's teaching on the "crucifixion of the flesh." He was imprisoned in 1528.

LOSERTH, H.S.B.

Beck, *Geschichts-Bücher,* 55; J. Loserth, "Bilder aus der Reformationszeit in Mähren: Dr. Martin Göschl," in *Ztscht d. Ver. f. Gesch. Mährens und Schlesiens* I, 65 ff.; Zieglschmid, *Chronik,* 51; *ML* II, 138 f.

Gosen Heymans, an Anabaptist martyr, native of Bunschoten, Dutch province of North Holland, had attended a Mennonite meeting in the home of Steven Pietersz (*q.v.*) at Amersfoort. Later he was also at a meeting in the house of Reyer Rutgersz at Bunschoten. For this he was arrested with his brother Jacob (*q.v.*) on Sept. 20, 1568, and beheaded at Utrecht on July 5, 1569. Whether he was a member of the church cannot be ascertained.

vDZ.

I. M. J. Hoog, *Onze Martelaren,* in *Ned. Arch. v. Kerkgesch. (n.s.* I, 1902) 82 ff.; Gosen is listed here as No. 87.

Goshen, Ind. (pop. 13,000), county seat of Elkhart County, founded in 1831, the seat of five Mennonite churches with a total membership of over 1,600, and shopping center for an area including at least 3,000 more Mennonite and Amish members, hub of a larger area of 20-mile radius with over 11,000 members.

The first Mennonite congregation in the city was the Brenneman Memorial (UMC, 1885), the second the College Mennonite (MC, 1904), the third the Eighth Street (GCM, 1920), followed by North Goshen (MC, 1935) and East Goshen (MC, 1948). Goshen College (MC) was established here in 1903, the Bethany Christian High School (MC) one mile south in 1954. The headquarters of Mennonite Mutual Aid (MC) and Mennonite Aid, Inc. (MC), has been in Goshen since 1947. Here are also located the Mennonite Research Foundation (since 1947), the Mennonite Historical Society (since 1925), the Archives of the Mennonite (MC) Church (since 1940), the *Mennonite Quarterly Review* (since 1927), and the Gospel Book Store (MC), one of the retail stores of the Mennonite Publishing House of Scottdale. See articles on all the above organizations and institutions.   H.S.B.

Goshen College, Goshen, Ind., founded in 1903, was a continuation of the Elkhart Institute (*q.v.*). To induce the school to move to Goshen, the city pledged ten thousand dollars, provided the Board would name the institution "Goshen College" and purchase certain plots in the southern part of the city for a campus. Building operations began in a wheat field at the end of South Eighth Street in June 1903. East Hall, the first campus building, completed in September, served as women's dormitory, dining hall, and lecture rooms until the completion of the administration building in January 1904.

N. E. Byers (M.A. Harvard, 1903), principal of the Elkhart Institute (1898-1903), continued as president of the new Goshen College and C. Henry Smith as librarian and instructor in history, English, and debating, and later as the first dean of the College. Byers served not only as chief administrative officer but also at first as academic dean, registrar, personnel dean, and religious counselor.

Until 1905 the governing body of the College was a self-perpetuating board, but in 1905 ownership of the property was transferred to the Mennonite Board of Education (q.v.), whose members are the elected representatives of the district conferences, Mennonite General Conference, and the alumni associations of the Board's schools. The Board was incorporated in Indiana on Jan. 27, 1906.

When the school moved to Goshen in 1903 the curriculum included junior college, academy, normal school, Bible school, school of business, school of music, school of oratory, summer school, and Bible correspondence department. The college enrollment was less than 20, academy about 60, and the total enrollment in all departments 210. The four-year college course was offered for the first time in 1909 and the first A.B. degree graduates completed the course in 1910. By 1913 college students outnumbered those in the academy, but in 1922 college enrollment was only four times as large as that of the academy. The latter was discontinued after 1933 as an organized department.

In 1913 President N. E. Byers, 1903-13, Dean C. Henry Smith, and Prof. B. D. Smucker resigned to accept positions in the newly reorganized Bluffton College. J. E. Hartzler was elected president to succeed Byers, serving 1913-18. Seconded by J. S. Hartzler, the new president embarked on a program of expansion by purchasing and equipping a farm for agricultural courses and building Science Hall. In January 1918, a heavy debt having accumulated, both J. E. Hartzler and J. S. Hartzler resigned because of the financial difficulties of the school. George J. Lapp, missionary on furlough from India, succeeded J. E. Hartzler as president 1918-20 and the college property was mortgaged to satisfy the creditors. I. R. Detweiler, assisted by G. L. Bender, collected more than $120,000 to meet the more immediate obligations of the Board and the College. In 1919 H. F. Reist succeeded Lapp and early in 1920 secured the accreditation of the College by the State of Indiana. When Reist's health failed in February 1920 the Board elected Detweiler acting president, who served 1920-22. By this time the College was recovering from the effects of World War I, student enrollment was increasing, the financial condition of the College was improving, the curriculum was being expanded, and extracurricular activities reached a high peak of student interest. But the College was still laboring under the burden imposed by various critical charges leveled at the College administrators in the earlier years, and I. R. Detweiler, the acting president, failed to gain the necessary confidence.

When the Board in 1922 elected Daniel Kauffman president, many students and a few faculty members left the institution. At the end of the year 1922-23 the Board, fearing that the next year's student body would be very small and wishing to take time for reorganization, closed the College for one year.

In 1923 the Board elected its president, S. C. Yoder, to serve as president of the College, and continued him in the office 1923-40. The College reopened in September 1924 with Noah Oyer, former dean of Hesston College, as dean, C. L. Graber business manager, and a faculty including only three former faculty members of the institution. Dean Noah Oyer rebuilt the prestige of the College and determined to carry out the Board's earlier directive to build up a strong liberal arts college and a central graduate Bible school. After Oyer's untimely death in 1931 H. S. Bender was elected acting dean and in 1932 as dean. He and Silas Hertzler, registrar and director of teacher training, continued efforts toward accreditation. But always there loomed the apparent impossibility of raising the necessary $500,000 endowment, a prerequisite to admission into the N.C.A. Finally as a result of the depression of the early thirties when endowments no longer were a reliable guarantee of steady income and the N.C.A. made stable income instead of an absolute endowment figure the norm for N.C.A. membership, Dean Bender began a campaign for admission into the North Central Association with the strong support of President Yoder and the faculty.

Other achievements of President Yoder's administration were a gradual winning of the confidence of the constituency, resulting in growth of the student body and in contributions for college expenses and a building program—a large program for that day. With the help of Mennonite Educational Finance, Inc., the Mennonite Board of Education erected John S. Coffman Hall (1929), a dormitory for men; rebuilt Kulp Hall (1930), and erected the Health Center (1939) and the Memorial Library (1940). When President Yoder resigned, he was succeeded in June 1940 by Ernest E. Miller, who served until August 1954.

The president of the College since Aug. 9, 1954, is Paul Mininger (B.D., M.R.E., Ph.D.), a 1934 graduate of Goshen College, past moderator of the Mennonite General Conference (1951-53).

The College was granted membership in the N.C.A. in March 1941. Full-time student enrollment rose from 326 in 1939-40 to 636 in 1948-49 (680 in 1956-57). New buildings, including the annex to Coffman Hall, the College Union Auditorium-Gymnasium, and Westlawn Residence Hall for Women, were erected at a cost of more than $850,000. The campus added about 27 acres and some valuable building lots between 1940 and 1953, and in 1954 the Board added a farm of 77 acres adjoining the campus. In 1954 a further donation of 20 acres of a lake-woods area in Southern Michigan increased the college holdings to 170 acres.

The College furnished significant leadership to other peace colleges in postwar rehabilitation and relief efforts. The president helped to organize the Council of Mennonite and Affiliated Colleges and served for four years as its first president. He also furnished leadership and support in the foreign student exchange program, both in bringing foreign students to study in Mennonite colleges in America and in arranging for Mennonite students to study and travel abroad.

Very significant in this period was the expansion of the curriculum. The years since 1944 witnessed the development of a graduate Biblical Seminary (q.v.), an accredited School of Nursing (q.v.), and the accreditation of the program of teacher education by the American Association of Colleges of Teacher Education. The faculty increased greatly both in number and quality of advanced training. The personnel services of the College were rated superior by the AACTE examiners in 1954. With the growth of the College a system of counseling was developed that furnished intimate personal guidance to the student in campus adjustments, curricular problems, and religious life. A strong campus religious program was developed with emphasis on the Mennonite heritage.

Equally outstanding as its work in the professional field as a Mennonite educational institution was the leadership that the College rendered during the past quarter century in serving the church through research, publication, and the promotion of various types of conferences, such as nonconformity, evangelism, Christian life, foreign missions, and peace. Members of the faculty reorganized the Mennonite Historical Society in 1925 and founded the *Mennonite Quarterly Review* in 1927, recognized among scholars as one of the outstanding religious historical magazines in the United States. The Society is publishing a series of monographs under the general title *Studies in Anabaptist and Mennonite History*. It is also active in building a Mennonite Historical Library of over 12,000 volumes and a serial list of over 200 current publications. Members of the faculty are receiving recognition in the councils of the Mennonite Church (MC), where they are asked to accept positions of major influence and responsibility. A spirit of evangelical Christianity and Christian discipleship on the campus is growing in fervor and intensity.

Over 10,200 students have matriculated in Goshen College and the Elkhart Institute since the founding of the latter in 1894. Because Goshen for many years was the only accredited four-year liberal arts college in the Mennonite Church (MC), students have registered from every section of the United States and Canada and from many foreign countries. Alumni of the College and the seminary are serving in many walks of life and in most of the major areas of the world, their principal fields of service being teaching, preaching, church work, relief work, nursing, medicine, and rural life.

Of the 59 members of the instructional staff in 1954, 26 had a doctor's degree. Of the others only three had less than a master's degree. Eleven had been instructors in the College for more than 25 years, four for 30 years or more. In addition to doctoral dissertations ten members of the faculty had produced 30 major books and numerous pamphlets besides contributing scholarly articles to a variety of magazines in the fields of history, religion, and folklore. Twenty-nine faculty members have studied, lived, or traveled in foreign countries and had been engaged in foreign relief, rehabilitation, and missionary service for periods of one to three years. Dean Carl Kreider was on a four-year leave of absence as dean of the college of liberal arts of International Christian University in Japan.

In a statement adopted on May 5, 1949, the faculty presented its "Concept of Christian Education." This pronouncement says in part: "The guiding principle in determining the values which the faculty considers worth striving for in personal and group living is the concept that the essence of Christianity, as set forth in the Scriptures, is discipleship, the transforming of the whole life after Christ. This Christian discipleship is to be expressed in human relations, in the use of time, energy, material resources, and in devotion to the church and its mission. . . .

"The whole of life is lived in the context of commitment to the will of God; and therefore, every activity, whether work, recreation, social fellowship, prayer, or meditation, has spiritual significance. The highest expression of faith in Christ, who is the way, the truth, and the life, will be found in loving, sacrificial service to one's fellow men. . . . The entire program of Goshen College is planned to help students to know Christ as Saviour and Lord and to become effective witnesses for Him." . . .

The contribution and influence of Goshen College and the Biblical Seminary not only in the field of Mennonite higher education in America, not only in its own direct constituency in the Mennonite Church (MC) but in the Mennonite brotherhood as a whole, has been oustanding in character and far-reaching in effect. It has been without doubt a major influence in directing the course of the life and service of the Mennonite Church into progressive evangelical channels. By its conservative course, its clear theological line, and its staunch Mennonitism, it has done much to mold the thought and action of the brotherhood. It has aided in a strong revival of the historical Anabaptist heritage, and in a strengthening of the nonresistant peace witness. It has been a strong center of missionary spirit and has furnished a large number of the missionaries of the church, as well as leaders in all fields of the church's ministry. (†*ME* I) J.S.U.

Elkhart Institute Memorial (Goshen, 1904); *Fiftieth Anniversary Addresses—Goshen College 1895-1945* (1945); *Goshen College Bulletin* (1903-), contains *Alumni News Letter, President's Annual Report,* annual *Catalog,* and *Golden Anniversary Alumni Directory* (1951); *Goshen College Record* 1903- ; *The Maple Leaf* 1915- ; "Report of Annual Meeting of Mennonite Board of Education" in *Herald of Truth,* 1903-8, and *Gospel Herald,* 1908- ; J. S. Umble, *Goshen College 1894-1954* (Goshen, 1954).

Goshen College Academy (1894-1935). The Goshen College Academy (MC) had its beginning in the Academic Department of the Elkhart (Ind.) Institute, which offered its first diploma in 1898, and which was continued when the Institute moved to Goshen in 1903 and was called Goshen College. The name "academy" was first used in 1905-6 (academy was commonly used for private high schools). The Goshen College Academy was a standard high school as was common in those days. Although the Junior College was added in 1903-4 and Senior College in 1908-9, the Academy remained the largest department in enrollment until 1913-14, when it was outdistanced by the College. The largest enrollment was 100 in 1907-8, the average for many years being 75-85. A total of 373 students were graduated. It finally died for lack of patronage, since by 1935 most Mennonite communities had public high schools available. Principals were N. E. Byers 1898-1906, D. A. Lehman 1906-26, Silas Hertzler 1926-27, U. Grant Weaver 1927-33. The Goshen College Academy served a very useful purpose in furnishing a good high-school education under church auspices for many Mennonite young people who would otherwise have had no opportunity for higher education and it opened the door for a larger life and service for many. In some cases also parental opposition to education compelled young people to wait to attend high school until reaching their legal majority at 21, when they were too old for the local high school. H.S.B.

Goshen College Biblical Seminary is the direct continuation of the Bible School, first organized in 1900 as a division of the Elkhart Institute, Elkhart, Ind., at that time an academy. With the removal of the Institute to Goshen in 1903 and its reorganization first as a junior college, then as a senior college (1910), the Bible School continued to grow. However, until 1933 it actually served only as the Bible department of the college. From the beginning to 1933 the only special curriculum offered was a two-year Bible course leading to a diploma. In 1933 a four-year curriculum leading to the Th.B. (Bachelor of Theology) degree was added, with two years of required advanced Biblical and theological courses based upon two years of Liberal Arts. In 1942 this curriculum was expanded into a five-year course requiring three years of advanced Bible and theology. In 1946 the B.D. (Bachelor of Divinity) degree was added as a graduate degree requiring four years of Liberal Arts and three years of Bible and theology. In 1949 the B.R.E. degree was added as a four-year degree in Christian Education. In 1946 the name "Biblical Seminary" was instituted. In 1955 the Th.B. degree was discontinued and the Seminary program organized into Graduate (B.D.) and Undergraduate (B.R.E.) divisions. In 1944 the school was organized as a separate school within the college, with its own dean. H. S. Bender, who had served as dean of the college and the Bible School since 1931, has served continuously as dean of the Seminary. In 1953-54, 67 students were enrolled. The total number of degree graduates in 1934-56 has been 190, with a total of over 380 students matriculated, almost all members of the Mennonite Church (MC).

The largest number of Seminary graduates enter the pastorate, although a considerable number enter the foreign and home mission fields, and serve in church institutions as teachers, administrators, and writers. The faculty consists of nine fully theologically trained professors. In 1954 these included, besides the dean, Paul Mininger, J. C. Wenger, J. H. Mosemann, H. H. Charles, J. L. Burkholder, C. N. Kraus, P. M. Miller, and J. W. Miller, some of whom were serving part-time in the college proper, in addition to four special lecturers.

The Seminary seeks to fulfill its special calling as a school of the Mennonite Church by appreciation and propagation of the historic heritage of faith and life of the church, by a primary devotion to its contemporary needs for able and faithful workers and sound scholars, and by throwing its aggressive support into a program whereby the church may more effectively serve the modern age and its needs. H.S.B.

Goshen College Bulletin, an official publication of Goshen College, first issued in May 1904. Since 1907 one volume has been issued per year, except in 1923 when the college was closed. The number of issues per volume has varied, but is now 12 or more. The *Alumni Newsletter,* formerly a separate publication, is now issued as a *Bulletin* six times annually. Other issues include reports, announcements, promotional pamphlets, and the annual catalog. N.P.S.

Goshen College Record, formerly Elkhart Institute Monthly, published by the students of Elkhart Institute and then Goshen College. The first issue appeared in October 1898. The name changed to *Goshen College Record* with June/July 1903 issue. It was issued monthly, except for certain summer months, as a literary magazine with some news items, until the late summer of 1937. It changed its form to a 4-page news journal with some literary features in October 1937, since when it has been issued biweekly, except in summer months. It was not published July 1923-September 1924. N.P.S.

Goshen College School of Nursing, Goshen, Ind., opened in 1951 with a four-year curriculum leading to a B.S. in Nursing degree. Beginning with the sophomore year the students commute to the nearby Elkhart General Hospital for part-time clinical experience. Seventy-two Goshen College students were enrolled in the School of Nursing in the 1954-55 school year. Orpah Mosemann is the director of the School of Nursing. M.G.

Goshen Old Order Mennonite Church, located on the Centre Sideroad near the Sixth Concession of Peel Twp., Waterloo Co., Ont., began in a building purchased a few years ago for the benefit of the large number of families moving into this area where farms were still available. In 1955 a large white frame church was built with a seating capacity of 500. The congregation still receives ministerial help from the organized O.O.M. churches of Woolwich.　　　　　　　　　　　　　　　J.C.F.

Gospel Banner is the organ of the United Missionary Church, which was known as the Mennonite Brethren in Christ Church until 1947. The *Gospel Banner* was founded in July 1878 and was published in Goshen, Ind., until 1885, when it was moved to Kitchener, Ont. From 1909 to the present it has been published in the United States, since 1924 under the auspices of the Bethel Publishing Co., the official publishing house of the church, located at 1819 South Main St., Elkhart, Ind. From 1878 to 1880 it was an 8-page monthly, 1880-85 a semimonthly, and in 1885 was increased to 16 pages. In 1892 it was made a 16-page weekly publication. For almost 20 years, beginning in 1879, a German edition was also published under the title *Evangeliums-Panier* (*q.v.*). In 1954 it had a circulation of approximately 3,000. The following have served as editors: Daniel Brenneman 1878-82, T. H. Brenneman 1882-85, Joseph Bingeman 1885, J. B. Detwiler 1885-88, H. S. Hallman 1888-1908, C. H. Brunner 1909-12, J. A. Huffman 1913-24, A. B. Yoder 1925-43, R. P. Pannabecker 1944-51, Everek Storms 1952- .　　　　　　　　　　J.A.Hu.

Gospel Bookstore, 119 E. Lincoln Ave., Goshen, Ind., a branch bookstore of the Mennonite Publishing House (MC) of Scottdale, Pa., was established in 1942. Managers have been Joe Garber 1942-46, Russell Krabill 1946-55, Marion Lehman 1955- .
　　　　　　　　　　　　　　　　　H.S.B.

Gospel Herald, the official organ of the Mennonite Church (MC) began publication April 4, 1908, as a merger of the *Gospel Witness* (*q.v.*, Scottdale) and the *Herald of Truth* (*q.v.,* Elkhart). It is published weekly, 16 pages until 1947 and then 24 pages (occasionally 32), 11¾ x 9 in., at Scottdale, Pa., by the Mennonite Publishing House for the Mennonite Publication Board. The circulation in 1954 was approximately 19,000. It contains articles, news, and promotional matter of special interest to the Mennonite Church. It carries advertising only for the Mennonite Publishing House. There are editorials, pages devoted to missions, schools, church music, peace, church history, and Christian education, a family circle page, a monthly page for shut-ins, a devotional column, a guide to the Sunday-school lesson, book reviews, comments on the world religious scene, poems, prayers and prayer requests. It prints official reports of conferences and boards. Its purpose is to inform, instruct, and inspire in Christian life and work. This periodical has had only two editors: Daniel Kauffman 1908-43 and Paul Erb 1944- . Levi C. Hartzler, director of publicity for the Mennonite Board of Missions and Charities (Elkhart), edits the missions section. John L. Horst and Millard C. Lind are consulting editors.

From April 1916 to the end of 1947 a monthly *Mission Supplement* to the *Herald* appeared, at first 8 pages, then 16, first edited by J. S. Hartzler, after 1944 by J. R. Mumaw. A *Christian Doctrine Supplement* of 16 pages appeared from October 1925 to the end of 1947, first quarterly, then bimonthly, edited until 1943 by Daniel Kauffman, then by Paul Erb. The Peace Problems Committee has supplied a monthly Peace Page for many years, first edited by Edward Yoder, Ford Berg, and since 1955 by Paul Peachey.　　　　　　　　P.E.

Gospel Herald Chapel (MBC), Trenton, Mercer Co., N.J., is a mission station of the Gospel Herald Home Missionary Society of the Pennsylvania Conference. The first service was held in a tent Aug. 8, 1937. L. W. Dinge was pastor in 1953.　　Jo.D.

Gospel Hill Mennonite Church (MC) is located on the western foothills of the Little North Mountain, 2½ miles south of Palos, and 5 miles south of Genoa in Linville District, Rockingham Co., Va. This is the oldest local mission congregation in the Middle District of the Virginia Conference. Services were held first in the White Hall Schoolhouse. A Sunday school was organized in 1907 and the church was built in 1909. In 1956 the congregation had a membership of 79, under the direction of J. Early Suter and Daniel Suter as ministers and D. W. Lehman as bishop.　　　　　　　　H.A.B.

Gospel Mennonite Church (GCM), located in Mountain Lake, Cottonwood Co., Minn., started about 1878 as "Wall's" Church. In 1889 the name was changed to Bergfelder Church. Since 1943 it has the present name. It is a member of the Northern District Conference. The first settlers arrived in 1875 from Molotschna settlement in South Russia. Aron Wall was the first elder. Other ministers have been his brother Henry Wall, Theodor Nickel, and Jacob Harms. Aron Wall was also an able bonesetter (*Knochenarzt*). About 1888 Aron Wall left the church with a group to found the later E.M.B. Church of Mountain Lake. The Bethel Church of Mountain Lake, with H. H. Regier and later J. J. Balzer as leaders, is also a daughter of the Gospel Mennonite Church. The first church was built in 1878, and remodeled in 1913. The church has a beautiful location overlooking the lake. The members are mostly farmers. Preaching is at present in the English language, with occasional German services. In the homes mostly Low German is spoken. The membership in 1953 was 259, with John P. Sudermann as pastor.　　A.A.P.

Gospel Messenger appeared in one issue in 1877 as a private venture to serve the Mennonite Brethren in Christ Church. It failed for lack of support and was succeeded a year later by the *Gospel Banner* (*q.v.*).　　　　　　　　　　　　　　H.S.B.

Gospel Teacher, a four-page monthly, 7 x 12 in., was edited by P. J. Kaufman, a former Mennonite of Wakarusa, Ind., from January 1891 until May 1931. It was published at Foraker, Ind., until 1903, thereafter at Wakarusa. L. S. Hostetler was publisher until 1901, thereafter the editor. In its earlier issues it was quite polemic against the Indiana Mennonite (MC) and Amish churches. There is an extensive file in the Goshen College Library. No issues were published 1893-96.　　　　　　　　　　　W.R.

Gospel Tidings was the name given in 1942 to the *Evangelisationsbote* (*q.v.*), the 4-page, semimonthly (1947-51, 8 pp.) official organ of the Evangelical Mennonite Brethren (founded in 1921). Until 1951 a small part of the journal remained German. Beginning in January 1951 it was a 16-page English monthly with about 900 subscribers. From January to June 1953 it was published jointly with *Zion's Tidings* (*q.v.*), the organ of the Evangelical Mennonite Church, as a 24-page monthly, last issue June 15, 1953. It was succeeded by *The Evangelical Mennonite,* the organ of the merged E.M. and E.M.B. conferences. Editors 1942-53 were H. P. Wiebe, H. F. Epp, and Arnold Wall.   H.S.B.

Gospel Truths, a monthly (8¾ x 11 in.) Mennonite (MC) religious journal published for a short time at Belleville, Pa. (first issue September 1901, last known issue December 1902), edited by Oliver H. Zook of Allensville, Pa., later of Roaring Spring, Pa., assisted by Pius Hostetler of East Lynne, Mo., and Joshua B. Zook of Allensville, Pa.   H.S.B.

Gospel Witness (1905-8) was a weekly (MC) journal published at Scottdale, Pa., by the Gospel Witness Publishing Co. for three years beginning with April 4, 1905, after which it was merged with the *Herald of Truth* published by John F. Funk at Elkhart, Ind., to form the *Gospel Herald.* First published in 8 pages, 11 x 16 in., it was enlarged to 12 pages, 9¼ x 12 in., on Nov. 2, 1905, and increased to 16 pages with the second volume. Daniel Kauffman, the editor, became the editor of the merged journal. The paper was established because of widespread dissatisfaction with the *Herald of Truth,* and financed largely by the Loucks family, in which Aaron Loucks was a leading figure.   H.S.B.

Gospel Witness Company (MC) was organized in 1905 by Jacob S. Loucks, Aaron Loucks, and A. D. Martin at Scottdale, Pa., in order to publish a weekly religious periodical, the *Gospel Witness* (1905-8). At first the business of the company was carried on in the home of Aaron Loucks. Soon a two-story frame building, 30 x 70 ft., was constructed, and two years later an additional three-story brick building 40 x 70 ft. When the *Gospel Witness* was merged in 1908 with the *Herald of Truth* to form the *Gospel Herald,* the assets of the Gospel Witness Company were sold to the Mennonite Publication Board, and the company was dissolved.   P.E.

Gospel Witness to Israel Mission (MB) at Winnipeg, Man., was founded January 1948 by Jacob Pankratz and his wife, who had done mission work among Jews in Toronto, Ont. In September 1948 the General Conference of the Mennonite Brethren Church of North America took over the responsibility for this mission and delegated the work to its City Mission Committee for supervision and financial support. The chief work the Mission is doing among the 20,000 Jews of Winnipeg is house to house visitation, and distributing New Testaments and other literature.   Jo.A.T.

Gosper County (Nebraska) Old Order Amish settlement, 1880-1904. The settlers came from Mifflin and Juniata counties, Pa., in the hope of maintaining their distinct nonconformed church and family life. The settlement at the most consisted of 13 families, mostly Yoders. Yost H. Yoder was the bishop until he died Dec. 11, 1901. The ministers 1900-4 were Yost D. Yoder, Moses D. (E.) Yoder, and Jacob Yoder, brother of Yost H. Yoder.

The address of the Amish settlement was Bertrand, which is located across the line in Phelps County. A few families lived north of the Platte River near Lexington. After several years of pioneering it became apparent that the colony would not survive. As children grew up many left for other Amish settlements. There were only three weddings among the Amish in Gosper County between 1880 and 1904. Jacob Yoder moved to Colorado, then to Custer Co., Okla., where he served as the first minister of the Amish church there. Those who returned to Mifflin Co., Pa., were Mose E. Yoder, Christ Speicher, Yost B. Yoder, Albert Kauffman, and one or two single persons. Minister Yost D. Yoder and family moved to Oscoda Co., Mich., in 1903. The few remaining families in the spring of 1904 moved to North Dakota and to Pennsylvania. There is a small Amish cemetery in Gosper County.

Yost H. Yoder came from Gosper County to Mifflin Co., Pa., in 1881, at the request of the "Samuel King" congregation to assist in a serious church dispute. He ordained David L. Hostetler and Menno L. Yoder to assist Jacob Zook, who was the only remaining church official (deacon) of the one faction. Many families of the Nebraska settlement returned to Mifflin County to join the newly organized group. This Mifflin County congregation has since 1881 been known as the "Nebraska Church," and it is the "oldest order" of the Old Order Amish in America. Its membership in 1955 was 130 baptized members. In 1945 another rupture occurred within the Nebraska group so that there are now two kinds of Nebraska churches in Mifflin Co., Pa.   J.A.H.

Gossau, a village in the canton of St. Gall, Switzerland, in which the Anabaptist movement had a large following in 1525-27, the first years of its existence. On May 16, 1530, an Anabaptist was executed here (see **St. Gall**). Balthasar Hubmaier, who was arrested in the canton of Zürich in 1525, was to be brought to Gossau upon the wish of the magistrate Berger, to recant "in the largest church." Gossau was also the home of Jakob Falk (*q.v.*), the second martyr in the canton of Zürich, who was drowned on Sept. 5, 1528.   Hege.

L. von Muralt and W. Schmid, *Quellen zur Gesch. der Täufer in der Schweiz* I (Zürich, 1952) 89, 143, 187, 257, 278, 289, 290; *ML* II, 145.

Gossner, Johannes Evangelista (1773-1858), a Lutheran writer, born Catholic, studied Catholic theology in Dillingen under Sailer who was in much contact with Protestants. Like Martin Boos he served as a Catholic priest in the same spirit in Dirlewang, Munich, and Düsseldorf. Persecuted here by the

Jesuits, he found a field of service by preaching in St. Petersburg, 1820-24. As a fugitive he stayed briefly in Berlin, Altona, Leipzig, and Silesia. After preaching justification through faith for a long time, he joined the Protestants (1826). He founded the Berlin *Missionsgesellschaft*, which he led actively until his death.

Widely known as a writer of devotional literature (tracts, hymnals, collections of sermons, etc.), Gossner was a guest in many Mennonite homes (*Gem.-Kal.* 1896, 92 f.). Here two of his books were highly regarded:

(1) The *Herzbüchlein oder das Herz des Menschen, ein Tempel Gottes oder eine Werkstatt des Satans in 10 Figuren sinnbildlich dargestellt zur Beförderung des christlichen Sinnes,* published in 1812. Only the text was written by Gossner; the engravings are older.

(2) *Schatzkästchen, enthaltend biblische Betrachtungen mit erbaulichen Liedern auf alle Tage im Jahre zur Beförderung häuslicher Andacht und Gottseligkeit.* This work is Gossner's best-known and most widely read book, the mature fruit of his life of faith, remarkably inspired by the medieval Mystics (Thomas à Kempis and Johann Tauler), by Tersteegen and Zinzendorf, its evangelistic character tested in the struggles with the Catholic Church, a warmly appealing testimony of "Christ for us and in us."

The *Schatzkästchen* came into being during Gossner's stay in Leipzig, the residence of Karl Tauchnitz (*q.v.*), who printed many of his books. Dalton suggested (p. 276 f.) that its beginnings lay in the country home of the van der Smissens, the Mennonite merchant family, where Gossner is said to have resided in 1824 during his months in Altona, a surmise that the *Gem.-Kal.* (1896, 92 ff.) has taken up.

Gossner's relations with the Mennonite van der Smissens are significant. From them and the Wichern family he first sought counsel when he came to Altona (Prochnow II, p. 13); with them he took his first residence (Prochnow II, 29). The van der Smissens were leaders in religiously awakened circles, which were centered in the Moravian Brethren there (Dalton, 266). The head of the family was at that time Jakob Gysbert van der Smissen, and not the son, as Dalton (p. 266) supposes, but the father of Jakob van der Smissen, the pastor of the Mennonite church in Danzig 1826-35 (Mannhardt, 162). The family chronicles report that Kissling, Jung-Stilling (*q.v.*), and Lavater frequented his home; he was a cofounder of the *Basler Sammlungen (Sammlungen für Liebhaber christlicher Wahrheit und Gottseligkeit),* the organ of the *Christentumsgesellschaft,* which had also gained a footing in Altona; there a society known as the *Particulargesellschaft* had been formed (Ostertag, 34). The van der Smissen family already appears in Gossner's letters to Spittler, the business manager of the *Christentumsgesellschaft* in Basel in his Munich period (Prochnow I, 186, 208, 244). At the van der Smissen home Gossner met Merle d'Aubigné, the French Reformed pastor there (Dalton, 267 f.). Dalton names the family as the first

recipient of the circle letter which Pastor Huber of Katharinenstadt (a member of the *Christentumsgesellschaft*) sent to Germany (*Beiträge* IV, 111). Gossner's writings were widely read by the Mennonites of Europe, as well as those of America, particularly those who came to America during the 19th century.   W.F.

J. D. Prochnow, *Johannes Gossner* (2 vv., Berlin, 1864); H. Dalton, *Johannes Gossner* (Berlin, 1874); *idem, Beiträge zur Geschichte der evangelischen Kirche in Russland* (4 vv., Berlin, 1905); *RGG* II, Col. 1311-12; *Gem.-Kal.* 1896, 92-100; H. G. Mannhardt, *Die Danziger Mennonitengemeinde* (Danzig, 1919); A. Ostertag, *Entstehungsgeschichte der evangelischen Missionsgesellschaft zu Basel* (Basel, 1865); *Familien-Chronik der Familie van der Smissen* (Danzig, 1875); *ML* II, 145 f.

Gostal (also erroneously called Grosstal, Czech *Kostl*) was very early in the history of the Anabaptists an important town, ranking with Nikolsburg, Austerlitz, and Auspitz. Kostl, located near Ludenburg, became a possession of the Ludenitz family in the 16th century, and later passed into the hands of the Zierotin family.

The Hutterite chronicles relate that when the Brethren were expelled from Moravia they began to assemble in Gostal and in Rohrbach near Seelowitz, the God-fearing coming with great joy, courage, and zeal, by day and night, wind and rain, cold and snow, to hear the Word of God. In small quarters they thankfully brought their children together and entrusted them to God-fearing sisters. These words indicate the importance given to Gostal in the Hutterite letters. In 1537 Hans Amon was preaching here. In 1557 the "great *Haushaben*" was begun here. Klaus Felbinger (*q.v.*) sent sincere greetings to the brotherhood here from prison in Landshut before his execution. In 1558 Kaspar Hueber and Hans Zwinger were ordained as elders. In 1559 Melchior Wall and Ambrosi Pfeiffer were chosen to the ministry. In 1593 they opened a ceramic (*q.v.*) shop, the best of its kind in Moravia, which produced some outstanding wares (*A.R.G.,* 1931, p. 286). Paul Glock, a member of this Bruderhof, sent some coat material to Gostal for distribution.

The Gostal Brethren frequently suffered violence. Since they could not do anything to aid in warfare, Johann Zierotin in 1576 took eight of their best horses. Cardinal Dietrichstein (*q.v.*) charged the Brethren, who refused to comply with his wishes, with a deterioration of their former dependability. In the disturbances of war in the first decade of the 17th century they fared badly because of excessive taxation. Soon after came the Bohemian Revolt with its terrible consequences. In 1621 the Bruderhof was plundered three times. Finally the cardinal expelled them "with empty hands" from Gostal as well as the other Moravian Bruderhofs. The fleeing Brethren settled in Kesselsdorf (*q.v.*) in Hungary. (*ML* II, 146 f.)

LOSERTH.

Gotebo (Okla.) Mennonite Brethren Church, now extinct, had its beginning in 1902, when a number of families of the M.B. Church settled in that locality and organized a church. The first pastor was Peter Richert; he was succeeded by Benjamin Wedel. A church was built in 1903. Since most of the early settlers left the community, the church was for some time almost completely dissolved, but in 1916 a number of German Baptists joined it, and John Geis became its presiding minister. The church continued as an M.B. congregation until 1942.   J.H.L.

Gotebo Preparatory School (*Vorbereitungsschule*), Gotebo, Okla., was erected in 1910 with H. Riesen as superintendent, to give instruction on the preparatory level, with emphasis on German and Bible. The school was closed about 1917.   C.K.

Gotha, a city (pop. 57,639) and former duchy in Thuringia, Germany, where the Anabaptist movement attained a considerable strength soon after its origin. The events that took place here are of particular interest, because here the reformers for the first time advocated the death penalty in religious matters. The first official records date from 1526; in that year a member of the brotherhood had been baptized. But the movement apparently did not attain any great significance in the duchy, because it was nipped in the bud by the extraordinary severity of the measures used against the new brotherhood.

The suppressive measures began in 1529. Near Gotha, in Reinhardsbrunn near Friedrichsroda, ten persons were arrested "on account of unchristian error toward God, also seriously offensive and seditious plans against their proper government and its subjects," but were released when, after instruction, they gave up their doctrine. Nothing more was said about their "seditious plans." The instructions, however, did not hold, for they soon returned to their brotherhood. Early in 1530 they were therefore again arrested. The cross-examination revealed that they had been conscience-stricken for recanting. Thus Christoph Ortlep, who had been first taught by his cousin Balthasar at Gräfenhain, a village in Sachsen-Gotha, and who had been baptized by an elder named Michael of Uettingen, a village near Marktheidenfeld in Lower Franconia, stated that the doctrine of his brotherhood was the most thorough truth, and that he would give his life for it. He did not regret having to endure the punishment imposed upon him as shame for the sake of Christ; but he did regret recanting and denying what he recognized to be the truth.

After examining each prisoner separately, the judges tried to influence them with admonitions and threats. Out of unusual sympathy—says the court record—the council advised the prisoners "to consider what great danger and ruinous harm would visit them both in body and soul against God and their government out of their obstinacy and unchristian intentions, and also that they were bringing God's judgment, wrath, and anger to their hearts, which would not, like temporal punishment, affect only the body for time, but soul and body for eternity." They were given two or three hours for reflection; then new attempts were made to convert them, with the result that three

prisoners recanted, while Christoph Ortlep and Andreas Kolb, as well as four women, Elsa Cutz, Barbara Unger, Katharina König, and Katharina Kolb, declared that they would persevere in their faith. There is no mention in the record of the trial of any offense against civic order. Nevertheless the six who did not recant were executed a week later, Jan. 18, 1530.

The execution caused a great stir, for it was not a matter of sentencing common criminals to death, but of using the death penalty against dissent in matters of faith in a Protestant country. The leading theologians found it difficult to calm people's minds. Superintendent Justus Menius in Eisenach tried to remove the doubts in a book, *Der Widdertauffer lere und geheimnis* (Wittenberg, 1530), for which Martin Luther wrote a foreword. He asserted in it that these people "were sentenced not alone because of manifold and abhorrent blasphemy and seditious articles of these mobs, but also because they created a public tumult among the people in one of the churches by trying to stone one who was about to renounce their doctrine; and several other transgressions through which they fell into government hands." Any statement describing the nature of the blasphemies Menius omits; nor does he give any information about the civil offenses. From his further discussion it is, however, clear that the latter would not have been stressed if they had recanted. They were simple people, who could not express or defend their faith in learned terms. As the record states, they did not enter into an analysis of their faith, and Menius says of the attempts to convert them, "They found nothing to criticize in our instruction . . . . They also permitted themselves to be instructed. But what shall I say? Before one was aware of it, they fell again and said that although they were unable to show sure Scriptural foundation for their doctrine, there were others who knew it."

Nor did Philip Melanchthon hesitate to sanction the sentence. He wrote in February 1530 to Friedrich Myconius, the superintendent of Gotha, who had some qualms of conscience concerning these executions, that he regretted that he had not advocated the death sentence for Nikolaus Storch, "from whom all these sects of Anabaptists and Zwinglians emanated." He even suggested to Myconius that he intimidate the people with new examples of punishment.

Seven years later at the duke's command, a woman of Gotha, Christina Strobel, was executed by drowning in the Unstrut between Mühlhausen and Ammern on Nov. 8, 1537, with seven other women from Mühlhausen and Frankenhausen, when they refused to recant.

Anabaptism was unable to propagate itself further in the vicinity of Gotha.   HEGE.

P. Wappler, *Die Stellung Kursachsens und des Landgrafen Philipp von Hessen zur Täuferbewegung* (Münster, 1910); *ML* II, 147 f.

Gotthard of Nonnenberg, an Anabaptist martyr, a deacon in the Jülich-Berg, Germany, Anabaptist group, was beheaded about 1558 with Peter Kramer after a long imprisonment. Van Braght relates,

"When all saw their boldness, and perceived that they were upright, pious persons, . . . nearly everyone wept; the steward, the judges, deputy, and executioner, as well as the common people." Gotthard and Peter are commemorated in a hymn, "Merckt auff jhr völker überall," found in the German Mennonite hymnal *Ein schön gesangbüchlein geistlicher Lieder* of about 1580. (*Mart. Mir.* D 207, E 590 f.; Wolkan, *Lieder,* 101; *ML* II, 148.)   vDZ.

Göttingen, a city (pop. *ca.* 78,000, about one third of whom are refugees) in the former Prussian province of Hanover, since 1945 the seat of the first Mennonite congregation of refugees in West Germany (so named because of the residence of Ernst Crous, its founder-elder, and of Gerhard Hildebrandt, pastor since 1953), since 1948 also the seat of the Mennonite Research Center (*Mennonitische Forschungsstelle*) whose director is Ernst Crous. In 1947, in the ancient Göttingen town hall, the Mennonite relief organization for the whole of the British Zone of Germany was started, in co-operation with the MCC. The new Göttingen congregation served 193 locations in an area of *ca.* 80 miles square, then comprising 1,271 Mennonites (souls), most of them refugees, about two thirds of them baptized members: 675 from Russia, 58 from Poland, 538 from West Prussia. Later most of those from Russia and Poland and some of those from West Prussia left for America. In 1955 the congregation had 325 baptized members with circuit meetings in the following places: Göttingen, Braunschweig, Salzgitter-Bad, Lebenstedt, Bad Hersfeld, Kassel, Hildesheim, Bad Lauterberg.

E.C.

Ernst Crous, *Mennonitenbrief aus Göttingen* (periodical 1947-50); Elfrieda Franz Hiebert, "With the Mennonites in Göttingen," *Menn. Life* XI (1956) 73 f.; Kurt Kauenhoven, "10 Jahre Mennonitengemeinde Göttingen," *Der Mennonit* IX (1956) 60 f.

Gottschalk (Gaetschalck), **Jacob** (1666-1763?), b. at Goch in the Duchy of Cleve, Lower Rhine, Germany, immigrant to Germantown, Pa., in 1701, outstanding leader and first bishop of the Mennonite Church in America. Recent research has demonstrated that Gottschalk was born at Goch about 1666, was baptized there on April 7, 1686, that he married Aeltien Hermans there on Feb. 20, 1689, and that he secured his church letter on June 12, 1701. Since his father's name was Gottschalk Theunissen (or Thonis) it is apparent that the name Gottschalk is merely a patronymic, which in America became a family name. The paternal ancestors of Jacob Gottschalk came from München-Gladbach which belonged to the Jülich domain; they apparently migrated from Gladbach when the Elector Palatine ordered all Mennonites to leave in 1654. Besides being a farmer Jacob was also a turner. He had five children: Godschalk, John, Herman, Ann (m. Peter Kuster), and Magdalene (m. Peter Nash).

From a brief sketch of the early history of the Mennonites in America (to 1712) written by Jacob Gottschalk, it is clear that he was ordained preacher at Germantown Oct. 8, 1702, and after the death of Wm. Rittenhouse (*q.v.*) in 1707 served as the sole minister until March 22, 1708, when others were ordained, and from 1708 on as the first bishop of the Germantown Mennonite congregation. In the absence of a bishop to ordain him, Gottschalk assumed the function of bishop at the request of the congregation and conducted the first baptismal and communion services in America at Germantown in May 1708.

When the new settlement was established at Skippack in 1712 Gottschalk joined it, locating in 1713 on a farm in what is now Towamencin Township, Montgomery Co., where he spent the remainder of his long life. On this land the first Towamencin Mennonite meetinghouse was erected in 1728. Gottschalk remained active in his ministerial work at least until 1753, since his signature appears on the Skippack Alms Book annually until that date. He died in May 1763.   J.C.W.

W. Niepoth, "Jacob Gottschalk and His Ancestry," *MQR* XXIII (January 1949) 35-47; H. S. Bender, "The Founding of the Mennonite Church in America at Germantown 1683-1708," *MQR* VII (1933) 227-50.

Gottschall's: see **Eden Mennonite** Church (Schwenksville).

Gottshall, William Shelly (1865-1941), an outstanding Mennonite (GCM) leader and long-time minister—1884-1941, was born near Schwenksville, Pa., the son of Bishop Moses and Mary (Shelly) Gottshall. He married Anna K. von Nieda. He attended Perkiomen Seminary and Ursinus College and graduated from Ursinus Theological Seminary in 1889. He was ordained preacher Oct. 15, 1884, and elder Nov. 24, 1886. He served as pastor in the following churches: Schwenksville, Pa., 1884-1905; Allentown-Upper Milford, Pa., 1905-9; Bluffton, Ohio, the three Swiss churches, 1909-24; Salem, Freeman, S.D., 1924-30; East Swamp, Quakertown, Pa., 1930-38.

Gottshall was widely active in district and general conference work. He was a member of the Home Mission Board for 42 years (1896-1938), serving 22 years as chairman and 12 years as secretary. He was widely known as a Bible expositor and effective preacher and served much in Bible conference work, and was strictly conservative in his theological position.   H.S.B.

Götzke (Goetzke, Goetzki, Jetzke, Goetz) was a Mennonite name of Prussia, Germany. Before World War II there were 48 persons by this name in the Memelniederung (*q.v.*). Arthur Goetzke was a minister of the Prussian Mennonite refugees of Northwest Germany after World War II, and Bruno Götzke was a pastor of the Mennonite refugee congregation at Backnang (*q.v.*).   C.K.

G. Reimer, *Die Familiennamen der Westpreussischen Mennoniten* (Weierhof, 1940); Fr. Crous, "Mennonitenfamilien in Zahlen," *Gesch.-Bl.,* 1940, 26 f.

Gouda, a town in the Dutch province of South Holland, pop. (1947) 37,283, with 89 Mennonites. Anabaptism was found here as early as 1534, and in 1542 the Anabaptist Marijtje Simons (*q.v.*) from Gouda was executed at The Hague. In 1571 Jan Dirksz (*q.v.*) suffered martyrdom at Gouda, and other citizens who had received their baptism on faith were hunted as heretics but escaped. Did a congregation exist here at that time? We cannot be sure, on account of lack of records. The oldest evidence of a congregation dates from 1626; in this year Adriaen Meyndertsz and Adriaen Jacobsz signed the confession of Outerman (*q.v.*). They may be supposed to have been deacons. In 1645 Cornelis Born was a preacher. This congregation, which seems to have been rather prosperous about the middle of the 17th century, belonged to the Flemish wing. Its preachers also took care of the congregations of Boskoop and Schoonhoven. The congregation, of which the strict Hendrik Gijsberts (*q.v.*) was an elder after 1649, and which during the *Lammerenkrijg* (*q.v.*), the conflict between the more spiritualistic Galenists and the rather dogmatic followers of Samuel Apostool, took the side of the "Apostoolsen," joined the conservative Zonist Sociëteit. In the second half of the 17th century the membership rapidly decreased. In 1674 there were found about 50 brethren. So the total membership could be estimated at about 120; they numbered only 50 in 1690. In this year a union was made with the Waterlander congregation.

This Waterlander congregation at Gouda, perhaps older than the Flemish, was always smaller than the Flemish church. In 1675 the membership numbered 20 or 25. Robbert Dam was its preacher about 1650, Isaack van Vrede(n) 1677-80. It joined 1674 the Waterlander (South Holland) Sociëteit. At the time of the union in 1690, the membership numbered about 30. Both the Flemish and the Waterlander churches of Gouda were often supported by other congregations, especially by those of Rotterdam and Amsterdam, as was also the united congregation.

At the time the two congregations united, the minister was Abraham van Loon (*q.v.*), who had first served the Waterlander congregation. Gijsbert Antwerpen was a deacon, first of the Waterlander church (after 1682), then of the United congregation until his death in 1731. He was an influential man, with a warm love for the church, and contributed liberally as did his daughters after his death. Yet the congregation did not flourish. The membership, 44 in 1725, had fallen to 14 in 1770, and in 1795 there were only 10 left. In 1798 the congregation was dissolved and the meetinghouse sold for 800 guilders. This money was given to the Lamist church at Amsterdam, which had given so much support and which assumed the care of a few poor members until their death. So the congregation has died out.

In 1921, 75 Mennonites (baptized) were living in Gouda, in 1947 about 50. A number of years ago these Mennonites formed a circle which organizes church meetings four times a year. The congregation of The Hague (*q.v.*) is in charge of this circle, which numbered 52 members in 1955.

K.V., vDZ.

Inv. Arch. Amst. I, Nos. 109, 247, 613, 708, 778, 781, 846, 907, 1058, 1180, 1248; II, Nos. 1404, 1755-1823, 2063-64, 2224, 2710-12; II, 2 No. 336; *DB* 1864, 121; 1872, 67; 1892, 103, 108, 124; 1896, 48; 1918, 50, 52; *De Zondagsbode* XXXV (1921-22) Nos. 13-17; *ML* II, 150.

Goudeken (Aldegonde) **de Jonc(k)heere,** an Anabaptist martyr, executed on July 21, 1562, at Gent, Belgium. She was 28 years of age, a daughter of Gherolf and a native of Merendree in Flanders. She was burned at the stake together with four other women, among whom were her sisters Vijntgen (*q.v.*) and Janneken (*q.v.*), because they "persisted in their rebaptism." Concerning these martyrs van Braght, *Martyrs' Mirror,* relates: "They confessed their faith without fear and remained steadfast until death." Their names are included in the song "Als men schreef duyst vijfhondert jaer ende twee en tsestich mede," found in the *Liedtboecxken van den Offer des Heeren.* Besides these three sisters, a brother Pieter de Jonckheere (*q.v.*) was executed on March 12, 1562, at Gent.

vDZ.

Offer 650; *Mart. Mir.* D 289, E 656; Verheyden, *Gent,* 29, No. 92; *ML* II, 432.

Goudie, Henry (1851-1942), organizer and first district superintendent of the Canadian Northwest Conference of the United Missionary Church. He was born near Hespeler, Ont., on Jan. 16, 1851, a son of David and Nancy Goudie. In 1870 he was converted and in 1874 became a charter member of the Reformed Mennonites, a group which later united with other groups to form the Mennonite Brethren in Christ Church (now the UMC).

Goudie began to preach in 1877 and was stationed at Port Elgin in 1878, being ordained by the Ontario conference in 1881. He served as pastor at Port Elgin, Breslau, New Dundee, Stayner, Markham, Kitchener (Bethany), Hanover, Shrigley, Toronto (Bethel), Aylmer, and Hespeler in Ontario; and at Mayton and Markham in Alberta. For 14 years he served as district superintendent: five years in Ontario (1900-5) and nine years in Alberta (1907-13, 1916-19). He retired in 1926 after a service of 50 years.

In 1872 Goudie married Sarah Wildfong. They had two sons and five daughters. Following Mrs. Goudie's death he married Mrs. Susannah Lageer in 1923. He died Jan. 19, 1942, just three days after his 91st birthday. He was buried in the Wanner cemetery at Hespeler. E.R.S.

Goudie, Samuel (1866-1951), a minister and leader of the United Missionary Church. He was born in Waterloo County, near Hespeler, Ont., on Aug. 11, 1866, a son of David and Nancy Goudie. On March 20, 1889, he married Eliza J. Smith. Converted at the age of 17, he joined the church in 1885, preached his first sermon that fall, and was ordained by the Ontario conference in 1891.

Goudie gave 54 years of active service to the church. He spent 26 years in pastoral work at Port Elgin, Maryboro, Vineland, Kitchener (Bethany), Toronto (Bethel), and Toronto (Jones Ave.). For 28 years he served as a district superintendent (1905-33). He served well, not only his own conference, but also the church as a whole. For 17 years (1922-39) he was president of the United Missionary Society, and for 31 years (1912-43) was chairman of the executive board. A member of eight general conferences, he was chairman of the

1912 general conference at Bethlehem, Pa. Goudie retired from the active work in 1940 and took up residence in Stouffville, Pa. He died July 2, 1951.

E.R.S.

Goudschaale, de Geestelijke, a Dutch hymnbook: see **Geestelijke Goudschaale**.

Government, Mennonite Historic Position on, and Office-Holding in: see **State**.

Government of Mennonites in Russia had two aspects, viz., the administration of all foreign settlers by the Russian government in Russia, and the self-government of the Mennonite settlements.

Administration of Foreign Settlements. On July 22, 1763, the Russian government established a Bureau of Guardianship (German, *Pflegschaftskanzlei*) of the foreign colonies with its center in St. Petersburg. This office was established long before any Mennonites considered migrating to Russia and was intended for all foreign settlers. On April 20, 1782, when Russia was divided into provinces, the foreign settlements were placed under the jurisdiction of the provincial and local authorities. On March 4, 1797, a government Department of Economy (*Expedition der Staatswirtschaft . . .*) was created in St. Petersburg to supervise the settling of foreigners and help them become successful. In 1800 a Bureau was created in the Ukraine with its center at Novorossisk (later Ekaterinoslav). The "Instructions" of this bureau were to give the settlements suggestions for self-government and for their economic life.

On March 22, 1818, the Bureau was changed to "Guardians' Committee" (*Fürsorge-Komitee*) of the Foreign Colonists in the Southern Regions of Russia and was subordinated to the Ministry of the Interior. The seat of this Guardians' Committee was at first at Kherson and later at Ekaterinoslav with branch offices at Ekaterinoslav, Kherson, and Bessarabia. In 1821 the seat of the Guardians' Committee was transferred to Odessa, where it remained until its dissolution in 1871. In 1837 the Guardians' Committee became subject to the Ministry of the Royal Estates newly created at St. Petersburg. In 1871, when the Guardians' Committee was abolished, the Mennonite settlers became directly subordinated to the local and provincial Russian authorities. The maintenance cost of these various institutions was placed upon the settlers themselves in 1845, each one having at first to pay twenty-one kopeks and later thirty-three kopeks.

Self-Government. According to the Manifesto of 1763 all foreign settlers in Russia were to enjoy complete autonomy in the administration of their own internal affairs forever. In 1800 Paul I issued a series of measures which included the introduction of uniform forms of local self-government based on Prussian forms of local government. Every village had an assembly consisting of a *Schulze* (mayor), two *Beisitzer* (assistants), and a clerk. Schulze and Beisitzer were elected by majority vote of the village assembly for a period of two years. Originally only landowners were eligible to vote and to occupy these offices. The clerk was a hired official. The functions of a constable were performed by several *dyessiatski*. The Schulze represented the village in the district assemblies and before higher government officials. He was responsible for the economic and the cultural welfare of the village. It was his duty to bring about peaceable settlement of disputes between the settlers, or, if this was impossible, to impose public work or fines. He was to prohibit the sale of liquor to villagers who were addicted to drunkenness and he was to enforce simplicity of life, i.e., to prevent the outlay of too much money for the household and entertaining visitors too frequently. The "Instructions" of 1800-1 include a large number of detailed prescriptions which he had to enforce. With the right to interfere in every sphere of the settlers' activity and private life, he could easily become a dictator if the assembly failed to check him. However, since the Schulze was a servant of the assembly, his power was held in check wherever the assembly used its authority effectively. The assembly elected village and district officials, levied taxes, elected schoolteachers, maintained a fire department, regulated the organization of fire insurance and fire prevention rules, matters of inheritance, the care of the aged, etc. All village elections had to be ratified by the Guardians' Committee.

A number of villages comprised a district or volost. A district assembly or volost consisted of one or more representatives from each village. The competence of this body was quite the same as that of the village assembly except that it applied to a larger area. The district office consisted of the *Oberschulze* (district mayor), several assistants (*Beisitzer*), and a clerical staff. The Oberschulze received a token salary. He was responsible for all meetings and for the maintenance of peace and order and exercised police power in the district, and imposed sentences, such as fines, incarcerations, or public labor, but only with the consent of the local Schulze. With the consent of the Guardians' Committee he could even inflict corporal punishment. He and his assistants formed the court of second instance for the prosecution of civil cases.

During their first decade (1874-84) the Mennonites of Manitoba followed exactly the pattern of self-government established in Russia. It was gradually adjusted to the Canadian environment and practices until it finally disappeared. The Mennonites of Paraguay still follow the same old practice which was developed and established among the Mennonites of Russia.

In self-government the problem of nonresistance was lifted out of the realm of theory and principles and put into practice in daily living. It is one thing to believe in these principles and when an extreme case turns up hand it over to a "worldly" authority to settle and wash one's hands of it, and another thing to have to handle it. Here it was thrown right into their laps. They had to solve their own problems. This chapter of Mennonite history furnishes an opportunity for Mennonites everywhere to make a case study as to how workable the principle of nonresistance has been and is, if tested in this manner.

Another aspect which is worth examining is the relationship between this Mennonite self-government and the local church authority. There is here within the Mennonite fold an example of solving the problems pertaining to the relationship of "state" and "church" within the group. Usually there was intimate and harmonious co-operation between the two authorities. At times there were great difficulties. Sometimes the church seemed to be dominating and again the "secular" authorities seemed to be leading. This again brings to light the question regarding the relationship between spiritual and secular authorities even in a Mennonite community based on its traditional principles of separation of state and church. C.K.

A. Ehrt, *Das Mennonitentum in Russland* (Berlin, 1932); D. G. Rempel, "The Mennonite Colonies in New Russia" (unpublished doctoral dissertation at Stanford University, 1933); Franz Isaac, *Die Molotschnaer Mennoniten* (Halbstadt, 1908).

Govert (Godevaert Mertens), an Anabaptist martyr, born at St. Peters near Maastricht, Dutch province of Limburg, living at Lier in Brabant, Belgium, was burned at the stake on Jan. 31, 1551, at Lier with Gillis, Anneken, and Mariken. He testified to his faith with great joy, and strengthened his fellow sufferers, while earnestly warning and admonishing his judges and the spectators. On their death Hans von Overdam wrote the hymn, "Als men schreef duyst vijfhondert En daer toe noch vijftich Jaer," which is found in the *Liedtboecxken van den Offer des Heeren*, No. 17, reprinted in Wackernagel, *Lieder*, 126. NEFF.

Offer 568-77; *Mart. Mir.* D 96, E 495; *DB* 1869, 1, 8; *Antw. Arch.-Blad* VII, 393; XIV, 18 f., No. 198; Wolkan, *Lieder*, 63, 78; *ML* II, 150.

Govert Aertsz, a cobbler, was beheaded at Utrecht in the Netherlands on March 13, 1535, because "he had kept the company of Anabaptists, rejected Purgatory, did not believe in the Holy Sacrament of the Mass, and thought that rebaptism was right." It is not clear that he was rebaptized. Probably he was not. (*Berigten Hist. Genootschap Utrecht* IV, 2, 1851, 130.) vDZ.

Govert Jaspersz, an Anabaptist martyr, was executed by burning at Brussels, Belgium, on Sept. 20, 1567 (van Braght, *Mart. Mir.*, erroneously has 1558, without further date). Govert was a native of Biezelinge, a village in the Dutch province of Zeeland. He was a mason by trade, 40 years of age; he had lived for seven years in Antwerp. During the trial he refused to betray the names of other Anabaptists he knew in Antwerp, Mechelen, Brussels, and in Zeeland. Govert was a preacher; asked by judges why he preached secretly rather than publicly, he answered that Saint Paul also preached in attics. He gave some particulars on the Mennonite baptismal ceremony. Van Braght relates that he formerly had been a lay brother of the Monastery of the Brethren of the Holy Cross at Goes, Zeeland, and that he had been arrested in the field while reading the New Testament. vDZ.

Mart. Mir. D 200, E 582; Verheyden, *Courtrai-Bruxelles*, 71, No. 29; *ML* II, 394.

Goverts (Govertsen, Gowert, Govert), a Mennonite family appearing particularly in Hamburg-Altona and Danzig, usually merchants, ships' chandlers and shipowners, usually of whaling boats. The progenitor of the Altona Goverts family was Peter Goverts of Antwerp (1475-1553). A descendant, Willem Goverts (1531-1608), became an Anabaptist and fled to Fresenburg, Oldesloe, near Hamburg to escape persecution. His son Hans (1578-1639) settled in Altona with other Mennonites and became the ancestor of the Hamburg-Altona Goverts line. He was a successful businessman and a deacon of the Mennonite congregation. His brother Peter was married to a sister of Gerrit Roosen. Peter's son Ernst (1678-1728) was a deacon in the Flemish Mennonite congregation, and caused some disturbance in the congregation by advocating baptism by immersion. He built the Dompelaar (*q.v.*) church on the Grosse Freiheit (*Blaufärber* or Goverts Church) in 1708 and supported its famous minister Jacob Denner (*q.v.*). His brothers Hermann and Gerard Goverts Hermanns, both deacons, were successful businessmen. After their death their business continued under the name "Firma Gerard Goverts Erben." Hermann's two sons left the Mennonite church. Paul joined the French Reformed Church and Hermann's family (11 children) the Lutheran Church. B. N. Krohn (*q.v.*) was the pastor of this Lutheran congregation and the instructor of Hermann's children. (Krohn mentions this experience in the preface of his book.) The name Goverts still appears as a non-Mennonite name in the Hamburg area, but seems to be extinct among Mennonites.

In the Danzig Mennonite church records the name Goverts appears for the first time in 1674. The name had evidently become extinct before the removal of the Mennonites from this area in connection with World War II. It was apparently not transplanted to Russia and America.

In Holland also the name Govertsz (Govers, Goverts) is found among the Mennonites, but as far as could be ascertained they are not related to the German branch. In Haarlem there were in the 17th century a number of members of the Goverts family, some of whom were deacons and trustees of the Mennonite orphanage there. Joost Goverts of Amsterdam is said to have collected accounts on Anabaptist martyrs in Brabant in behalf of the martyrbooks about 1610. In 1658 Goverts, of Leeuwarden, Friesland, established an old people's home in this city. C.K.

Neues Altona II (Jena, 1929) 228-31; R. Dollinger, *Geschichte der Mennoniten in Schleswig-Holstein, Hamburg und Lübeck* (Neumünster, 1930) 86 ff., 146 ff., 170 ff.; *Hamburger Geschlechterbuch* IV; G. Reimer, *Familiennamen*, 108; B. N. Krohn, *Geschichte der fanatischen und enthusiastischen Wiedertäufer* (Leipzig, 1758) 4; Wanda Oesau, *Hamburgs Grönlandsfahrt* (Hamburg-Glückstadt, 1955); B. C. Roosen, *Geschichte der Mennoniten-Gemeinde zu Hamburg und Altona* (Hamburg, 1886 f.); *DB* 1899, 103; Kühler, *Geschiedenis* III, 59; *ML* II, 151.

Govertsz, Joost, a co-worker with Tieleman van Braght in the preparation of the *Martyrs' Mirror* (*q.v.*). For the church at Hoorn Govertsz collected records in Brabant. By this comprehensive work the dependability of the *Martyrs' Mirror* was greatly enhanced; more recent research has frequently confirmed his statements. (*DB* 1899, 103; *ML* II, 151.)

HEGE.

Goverts(z), Tobias, a Dutch Mennonite preacher: see **Wijngaard, T. G. van den.**

Goyen (Gogen, Gojen, Goi), **Arnold** (1699-1762), son of Gossen Goyen (*q.v.*) and a member of the Crefeld Mennonite Church, married Susanna von der Leyen. He was an intimate friend of Gerhard Tersteegen. The Crefeld church has 60 letters written by Tersteegen to Arnold Goyen which reveal the intimate relationship of Tersteegen to the Crefeld Mennonites and particularly to Goyen. Tersteegen visited the Mennonites of Crefeld, and the Goyen family visited Tersteegen in Mülheim. According to Nieper (p. 240), Tersteegen or W. Weck furnished the inscription for Goyen's tombstone. The petition which the Crefeld Mennonites addressed to the King of Prussia regarding religious freedom dated April 13, 1737, bears, among others, Arnold Goyen's signature. 　　　　C.K.

F. Nieper, *Die ersten deutschen Auswanderer von Krefeld nach Pennsylvanien* (Neukirchen, 1940) 209, 233 f., 238-40, 380; Dirk Cattepoel, "Das religiöse Leben in der Krefelder Mennonitengemeinde des 17. und 18. Jahrhunderts," in *Beitrage zur Gesch. der rhein. Mennoniten,* 1939; *ML* II, 152.

Goyen (Gogen, Gojen, Goi), **Gossen** (Gosen, Goessen, Goswin) (1667-1737), married Catharina Lamerts, widow of Herman op den Graeff, in 1696, was minister of the Mennonite Church at Crefeld, Germany, during a time when this congregation was affected by a pietistic revival movement. Among his friends were Johann Lobach (*q.v.*) and Luther Stetius, who had strong Dunkard leanings. Goyen himself must have been baptized by immersion in the Rhine in 1724, but continued to serve the Mennonite congregation at Crefeld, although his fellow ministers Leenaerdt Ewaldts and Jan Kroes (Crous), and the majority of the members did not practice baptism by immersion. He must also have been a friend of Ernst Christoph Hochmann von Hohenau (*q.v.*), who preached in the Mennonite church at Crefeld (Nieper, 217). His son Arnold Goyen (*q.v.*) was a good friend of Gerhard Tersteegen (*q.v.*). His daughter Maria, who was married to Jacob W. Naass, emigrated to Pennsylvania in 1735.

The petition which the Crefeld Mennonites addressed to the King of Prussia regarding religious freedom dated April 13, 1737, bears, among others, the signature of Gossen Goyen (Nieper, 380). Gossen Goyen intermediated in 1715 between the Dutch Mennonites at Amsterdam and the Swiss authorities who kept Swiss Mennonites on the galleys in Italy. In January 1715 he forwarded Dutch money to Torino, Italy, for the purpose of liberating the Mennonite prisoners; and a letter of Oct. 5, 1715, of the French ambassador at Bern, Switzerland, written to Goyen, mentions the liberation of some Swiss Mennonites from the galleys. A letter of Nov. 20, 1715, informs us that more Mennonites were liberated, while still others were to be ransomed. In 1726 (letter of June 4) Goyen was still in correspondence with the board of the Amsterdam Lamist congregation. In this letter he calls himself preacher of the Mennonites at Crefeld.

C.K.

Max Göbel, *Geschichte des christlichen Lebens in der rheinisch-westfälischen evangelischen Kirche* (3 volumes, 1849-60); F. Nieper, *Die ersten deutschen Auswanderer von Krefeld nach Pennsylvanien* (Neukirchen, 1940) 37, 209, 239-40, 273-74; *Inv. Arch. Amst.* I, Nos. 1372, 1376, 1378; II, Nos. 2616; *ML* II, 151.

Goyes, Feycke, elder of the (Flemish) Mennonite congregation at Dokkum, Dutch province of Friesland, who in 1643 caused a division in this congregation; a meeting to settle the quarrel was held at Sneek on May 4 of that year and counsel was asked of the Flemish church at Amsterdam. One of the Amsterdam preachers, Tobias Govertsz van de Wijngaard (*q.v.*), tried to arbitrate the conflict. Lack of material makes it difficult to determine the nature of this division, which also struck the congregations of Sneek and Bolsward, or to follow its course of the conflict. We know about this quarrel only from some letters found in the Mennonite Archives at Amsterdam. (*Inv. Arch. Amst.* I, 607-9). 　　　　vDZ.

Graaf, Lieuwe Willemsz, born 1652 at Harlingen, Dutch province of Friesland, was at first a skipper to Hamburg. He became a Mennonite preacher serving first in his native town and from 1694 on at Amsterdam in the Old Frisian congregation. He died in 1704. By observing the sky on his voyages and by diligent perusal of pertinent literature he acquired a knowledge of the stars unusual for his time. He translated and printed at his own expense a book by Professor Mathias Wasmuth of Kiel, *Kort begrip van de algemeene herstellinge des Tijd.* . . . Believing that he had found an exact method of determining east-west distances, he sold his boat in Harlingen and devoted his time and money to promoting his discovery. He applied to the Dutch States-General for a patent and for financial support to publish the discovery in a booklet. Several times he appeared before them, debating with specialists and with his opponents, and also before the council of the city of Amsterdam. He was finally granted a patent and 2,000 guilders. Then he published his book, *Eenvoudig, en onvervalscht Verhaal . . . ,* in which he gives an interesting account of his appearances before the States-General and the city council and presents his astronomical discovery. In the same year (1689) as the above writing, a second book of his appeared: *De nieu gepactiseerde oeffening der Stuurlieden,* a complete instruction book in the art of steering a boat. Graaf's portrait was engraved by P. Tanjé (published in Schijn-Maatschoen, III, 432), and four short laudatory poems appeared, A. Spinniker (*q.v.*) writing one for the portrait. In Amsterdam Graaf opened a school, apparently for the instruction of navigators. Of Graaf's significance for the Mennonite Church, nothing can be said. While he was still a preacher at Harlingen, he became involved in 1688 in a quarrel with Balthasar Bekker (*q.v.*) on some untheological matter. NEFF, vDZ.

Schijn-Maatschoen, *Geschiedenis der Mennoniten* III, 433-84; *Biogr. Wb.* III, 319 f., 400; *N.N.B.Wb.* III, 485; *ML* II, 152.

Graaf, Volkert (de), a Dutch Mennonite preacher, serving 1728-37 at Zwartsluis and 1737-64 at Blokzijl. Influenced by Joannes Deknatel (*q.v.*), a Mennonite preacher of Amsterdam, he became a follower of Count von Zinzendorf (*q.v.*) and the Moravians, in the Netherlands usually called "Hernhutters." With the Hernhutter preacher Lorenz, a clothmaker, de Graaf traveled through Friesland preaching; as a result a small Hernhutter congregation was founded in Blokzijl, which met for a time in de Graaf's house. De Graaf seems to have entertained the desire to be a Moravian missionary to Surinam, but for some reason this desire was not realized. In 1755 de Graaf left the Hernhutters; a number of members of the Blokzijl Mennonite congregation, among them the deacon Arie Stuurman, however, held to this group.   vDZ.

Naamlijst; W. Lütjeharms, Het philadelphisch-oecumenisch streven der Hernhutters in de Nederlanden in de achttiende eeuw (Zeist, 1935) 62, 82, 84, 103 f., 135.

Graber (Greber, Grayber, Gräber), a Mennonite family name originating in Kirchdorf, canton of Bern, Switzerland. The name likely originated in the 15th century with persons whose occupation was that of digging ditches or trenches. The first mention of a person with this name having been a Mennonite was in 1596 when a certain Georg Graber was dealt with by the Bernese council because he was a member of this forbidden church.

Members of the Graber family were in the mass exodus of Mennonites from the Bernese Republic which took place in 1671 and the years immediately following. They settled near Sainte Marie-aux-Mines (Markirch), Alsace. Again exiled in 1708 they found their homes in other sections of Alsace and especially Montbéliard.

In 1791 a Johannes Graber left Montbéliard with other Mennonites for Poland by way of Austria. They lived in several villages in Volhynia before migrating to Kansas and South Dakota in 1874. Various members of this family have become prominent in church and civic affairs in their communities.

Peter Graber (1741-1805) was the ancestor of most of the Graber family living in the eastern part of the United States. A grandson, also named Peter, emigrated from Montbéliard to Stark Co., Ohio. Another grandson, Christian, settled in Washington Co., Iowa, in 1856. His descendants include C. L. Graber, a minister of Goshen, Ind., and J. D. Graber, bishop and formerly a missionary in India, now in Elkhart. Many of the descendants of the first-named Peter are members of the Old Order Amish Mennonite Church. This name remains a common one among the Mennonites living in Montbéliard and Alsace today. André Graber is an elder of the church at Belfort (*q.v.*).   D.L.G.

Daniel Kauffman, Mennonite Cyclopedic Dictionary (Scottdale, 1937) 135-36; J. M. and Anna Goering, The Peter Graber Family Record (Galva, Kan., 1948).

Grabill (Graybill, Grebiel, Kraybill, Krabill, Krebill, Krehbiel, Krahenbühl, Crayenbühl, and thirteen other minor variants), a Swiss Mennonite family originating in the parish of Grosshöchstetten in the canton of Bern, later prominent in the Palat-

inate and America. In 1682 Peter Krehbiel emigrated to the Palatinate settling on the Weierhof, where the family is still represented. (See the article **Krehbiel** for the history of the family in Europe and America carrying this form of the name.)

When the first member of the family came to America is not clear. An Eva Grabiel was married to a Christian Wenger in Lancaster Co., Pa., about 1728. The first known male immigrant was a John Krehbiel who arrived about the mid-18th century in Lancaster County. His grandson John Grebel moved to Juniata Co., Pa., becoming the first Mennonite minister and bishop there and the progenitor of a large number of descendants who have consistently spelled the name Graybill. Bishops Jacob (1816-92), William (1833-1902), and William W. (1880-   ) are among his descendants. His family who stayed in Lancaster County have largely adopted the spelling Krahbill. That part which moved to Virginia uses the spelling Grabill. Families moving westward to Ohio, Indiana, and Illinois betray their provenance by the form of spelling. The Krabill family in Stark Co., Ohio, and Washington Co., Iowa, is of Amish background, coming direct from Europe, not from Pennsylvania. The family has no connection with Conrad Grebel, the founder of the Anabaptist-Mennonite movement in Zürich, Switzerland, although the pronunciation is similar. Among the currently serving Mennonite ministers of the family are Bishop J. Paul Graybill of East Earl, Pa., Bishop William W. Graybill of Richfield, Pa., preachers J. Silas Graybill of Doylestown, Pa., Russell Krabill of Goshen, Ind., and Martin K. Kraybill of Elizabethtown, Pa.   H.S.B.

Grabill Mennonite Church (EM), Grabill, Ind., had its beginning in 1866 when Bishop Henry Egly withdrew from the Amish Mennonites in Adams Co., Ind., and formed a new church. He influenced similar withdrawals in other communities, among which was one in Allen Co., Ind. These groups became known as the Egly Mennonites and formed a conference body which in 1908 took out a charter in Illinois designating themselves as the Defenseless Mennonite Church of North America. In 1948 the name was changed to the Evangelical Mennonite Church.

The church in Allen Co., Ind., built its first meetinghouse one and one-fourth miles east of Leo on the Leo-Harlan Road about the year 1875 and was known as the Leo Mennonite Church. In 1912 the congregation built a new structure one and one-half miles further east in the town of Grabill. This building was remodeled in 1938 and was then designated as the Mennonite Church of Grabill. Here it attained an active membership of about 135 members.   J.H.S.

Grace Bible Institute, Omaha, Neb., was organized for the purpose of training Christian workers in the Mennonite denomination. The organizational meeting was held on June 1, 1943. The Board of Directors includes leaders from six Mennonite conferences. The student body has increased from 23

(1943) to 325 (1955). The present enrollment consists of young people from 20 denominations, 24 states, and 5 foreign countries. Sixty-five per cent of the student body is Mennonite.

The Grace Bible Institute is accredited by the Accrediting Association of Bible Institutes and Bible Colleges—Collegiate Division. It offers the degree of Bachelor of Arts with a Bible major. The liberal arts courses are fully accredited by the University of Nebraska. The Institute is classified as a professional school in that it is primarily devoted to the training of young people for full-time Christian service. Grace Bible Institute, being an inter-Mennonite school, affirms its stand as true and loyal to the time-honored Mennonite doctrines. H.D.B.

Grace Chapel United Missionary Church, Toronto, Ont., was organized in 1901. The membership in 1953 was 71 with Henry Good serving as pastor.

He.G.

Grace Children's Home, Henderson, Neb., was founded Aug. 1, 1936, and incorporated 1938 as a nonprofit corporation and reincorporated in 1942. It is licensed by the state of Nebraska to care for 35-40 dependent children. The present plant, on the south side of Henderson, was completed in 1948. It is the only home in Nebraska operating on the family system of having no more than seven children per family group, and each family in its own residence. Children of all faiths are admitted, but raised in evangelical Christianity. The home, supported by freewill offerings and private contributions, has as its purpose to minister to the spiritual, social, mental, and physical needs of the child. The president in 1954 was J. R. Barkman and the superintendent Paul F. Barkman, both ordained ministers of the Evangelical Mennonite Brethren Conference.   J.R.B.

Grace Church of God in Christ Mennonite Church, located one mile west of Halstead, Harvey Co., Kan., was organized in 1877. A church was built in 1896 northeast of Halstead, and the congregation was called the "Halstead" congregation. In 1915 this building was moved one mile west of Halstead and was enlarged in 1921. In 1939 a new church building with a seating capacity for 600 was built one mile south of the old site. The past residing ministers Henry A. Schmidt and Henry A. Koehn were ordained in 1882. The latter served the congregation for 24 years. Jacob Dirks was ordained to the ministry in 1896 and served the congregation until his death in 1945, a period of nearly 50 years. Jacob P. Unruh moved here in 1920 ministering to the church until his death in 1947. Carl J. Dirks, the present minister in charge, is assisted by Paul Becker, Kenneth Smith, and Arnold Wiggers. In 1954 the membership was 230. (†*ME* I) C.J.Di.

Grace Mennonite Brethren in Christ Church, located in Reading, Berks Co., Pa., was organized in 1882 under the leadership of W. B. Musselman. In 1953 the membership was 418 with A. G. Woodring serving as pastor. In 1955 a new brick and stone church was dedicated, with P. T. Stengele as pastor.

A.G.W.

Grace Mennonite Church (GCM), located at 4221 South Rockwell St., Chicago, Ill., began in 1917 as the Mennonite Bible Mission, under A. F. Wiens. In 1937, when Wiens died, John T. Neufeld became the leader. In 1940 the Home Mission Board began to help in the support of this work, and the church joined the Middle District Conference. The work is among people of many nationalities, mostly of Central European background. In 1955 the membership was 68, with John T. Neufeld still serving as pastor. A number of its members have served in foreign mission work.   J.T.N.

Grace Mennonite Church (GCM), located at Enid, Okla., was begun as a mission project by the Western District Conference in 1934, when J. B. Frey was instructed to explore the field. H. N. Harder was called to the work in September 1935, and in 1938 the church was organized with 20 charter members. On July 16, 1939, the new church building was dedicated. H. N. Harder left in May 1943 and was succeeded on June 1, 1944, by Ben Rahn, who served until June 1, 1947. Albert J. Unruh has served since then. Membership has grown from 37 in 1940 to 126 in 1955. On Jan. 1, 1954, the church became self-supporting.   J.F.S.

Grace Mennonite Church (GCM), located in Pandora, Putnam Co., Ohio, a member of the Middle District Conference, was organized May 12, 1904, under the leadership of F. S. Sprunger, pastor of the First Mennonite Church of Berne, Ind., with 206 charter members, the great majority of whom had withdrawn from the St. John Mennonite Church near Pandora. The church building, which is still in use, was completed in 1905 with a seating capacity of 750. In 1954 the total baptized membership was 415. Ministers who have served the congregation are Peter P. Hilty, Albert R. Shoremann, Peter W. Penner, Otto Lichti, Albert Schumacher, John T. Moyer, John M. Regier, Paul E. Whitmer, Forrest Musser, and Ernest J. Bohn.   E.J.Bo.

Grace Mennonite Church (GCM), located in Albany, Linn Co., Ore., a member of the Pacific District Conference, was organized June 29, 1931, with 21 charter members, led by John M. Franz, P. R. Aeschliman, and A. J. Neuenschwander. The membership of 117 in 1954 worshiped in a frame meetinghouse which had previously been a Presbyterian church. Ministers who have served the congregation are W. Harley King, William Augsburger, John M. Franz, P. A. Kliewer, Henry U. Dalke, E. J. Peters, and Herbert King, 1955. The Pacific Conference held its session here in 1947. P.A.K.

Grace Mennonite Church (GCM), located in Dallas, Polk Co., Ore., a member of the Pacific District Conference, is an outgrowth of the Zion Mennonite Church (MC), having been organized in 1932 with a membership of about two dozen, under the leadership of Gerhard Bergen, who served as the first pastor. The congregation, with 314 members in 1955, worships in a modern church building which seats about 300. Ministers who have served this congregation are H. E. Widmer, Homer Leisy, John

Hiebert (supply pastor), Jacob J. Regier, Earl M. Peterson, J. M. Franz, and H. D. Burkholder (from Aug. 1, 1955). W.W.J.

Grace Mennonite Church (GCM) of Lansdale, Pa., began in 1928 as a mission work with Thursday evening meetings in private homes for Bible study and prayer. In 1929 this group purchased and renovated an abandoned church on Mount Vernon Street, which is still in use. In 1930 the congregation was organized and the first Sunday school and worship meeting was held in the church.

Most of the 45 charter members were members of the Deep Run church who were living in Lansdale. In 1954 the membership was 290. Ministers have been D. J. Unruh 1930-36, Olin A. Krehbiel 1937-46, J. J. Plenert 1946-53, and Elmer Friesen 1954- .

Over the years the congregation has had a healthy spiritual and numerical growth. A number of the young people have entered Christian service. A larger meetinghouse was built in 1956 at York and Mitchell Avenues. J.H.F.

Gracevale Hutterite Bruderhof, established in 1948 near Winfred, S.D., had a population of 71 in 1950. M.G.

Graef, Elise (*Riemenschneiderin*), an Anabaptist martyr, was drowned in the Unstrut, Nov. 8, 1537, with seven other Anabaptists, between Mühlhausen and Ammern in Thuringia, Germany.

P. Wappler, *Die Täuferbewegung in Thüringen von 1526 bis 1584* (Jena, 1913); ML II, 152.

Graeff, op den (Opdegraf, Updegrave, Updegrove), an old Crefeld Mennonite family, which turned Quaker in part *ca.* 1679-80, four members of which emigrated to Germantown with the first 13 immigrant families in October 1683. Some of their descendants continued in or returned to the Mennonite faith and were found in the Montgomery County congregations of Skippack and Boyertown until modern times. The grandfather of the first Germantown immigrants, Herman, a linen weaver and merchant, was born Nov. 26, 1585, of Mennonite parents in Aldekerk, about 12 miles from Crefeld, moved in 1609 to Crefeld, m. Grietjen Pletjes of Kempen in 1615, died Dec. 27, 1642, leaving 18 children. This Herman op den Graeff was one of two delegates of the Crefeld Mennonite Church to sign the Dordrecht Confession in 1632 and served as preacher in the congregation there.

One son of Herman, Isaac Hermans op den Graeff, b. in 1616, married Grietjen Peters (d. 1679), was converted with his family to Quakerism. His widow, who died in Philadelphia Oct. 19, 1683, his three sons Derick (Dirk) Isaacs, Herman Isaacs, and Abraham Isaacs, and a daughter Margrit (m. later to Peter Schumacher, immigrant from Kriegsheim who arrived in 1685) emigrated to Germantown as part of the 13 famous first families on the *Concord,* arriving at Philadelphia, Oct. 6, 1683, settling in Germantown soon thereafter. Dirk was married in a Quaker ceremony in 1687 in Crefeld, to Nölken Vijtten, probably a daughter of Veit Scherkes, one of the 13 family heads. Herman

had been previously married to Liesbet Isaacs, a daughter of Isaac van Bebber, another of the 13 first families. The op den Graeffs were a family of linen weavers in Crefeld and continued this occupation in Germantown, although the three brothers purchased jointly 2,000 acres of land in Germantown from William Penn's agents in Rotterdam, Jacob Telner and Benjamin Furley.

Dirk op den Graeff was the leader of the 13-family immigrant group and remained prominent in Germantown civic life. He with his brother Abraham signed the famous first petition against slavery in America in 1688. In 1689 he was one of the 11 charter members of the Germantown corporation, in 1692 he was one of the town's six "committeemen," and in 1693-94 he was the bailiff or chief executive (burgomaster). He died childless in 1697. Herman op den Graeff, like his brother Dirk, was a member of the Germantown Quaker meeting, one of the 11 charter members of the corporation, and died childless May 2, 1704, after having moved to Delaware County.

Abraham op den Graeff, the youngest of the three brothers, married to a Catharine (last name unknown), the most skilled as a weaver, was the only one of the family to return to the Mennonite faith, which he did sometime after 1708. (His name is not in the Morgan Edwards list of the Germantown members of that year.) He was also the only one to have children. He died March 25, 1731, leaving four children, Isaac, Jacob, Margaret, and Anne, and was buried in the Evansburg Mennonite cemetery. Since his brothers died childless he inherited their land, but sold his house and 828 acres in Germantown sometime after 1704 and moved to Perkiomen, where he laid out the remaining 1,200 acres of the op den Graeff land. His son Jacob appears as a signer of a petition of 1728 to the governor of Pennsylvania for protection against the Indians. H.S.B.

Rembert, *Wiedertäufer; Die Heimat* (periodical) (Crefeld, 1927) 23; W. I. Hull, *William Penn and the Dutch Quaker Migration to Pennsylvania* (Swarthmore College, 1835) 209-18 with biographies of the three sons; ML II, 152-54, with separate articles on Herman op den Graeff and each of his three sons; S. W. Pennypacker, "Abraham and Dirck op den Graeff," *Penn Monthly* VI (1875) 679-92, reprinted in *idem, Historical and Biographical Sketches* (Philadelphia, 1883) 201-21.

Graess, Heinrich*:* see **Grass, Heinrich**.

Graet, de, a family, originally from Kortrijk (*q.v.*), Flanders, which had three martyrs: Gillis (*q.v.*), Sijntgen (*q.v.*), and Steven (*q.v.*) (see Verheyden, *Courtrai-Bruxelles,* 33). The real name of this family seems to have been not de Graet, as the martyrbooks call them, but Segaert. (Verheyden, *Gent,* 30.) vDZ.

Grafeneck (Graveneck), **Klaus von** (1502-75), a frequently named magistrate of Württemberg; in Blaubeuren 1539-42, in Kirchheim below Teck 1543-50, in Urach 1551-75. He wrote the report of Michael Sattler's (*q.v.*) death in Rottenburg, *Ayn newes wunderbarliches geschicht von Michel Sattler zu Rottenburg am Neckar sampt 9 mannen seiner lere und glauben halben verbrannt und 10* *weyber ertränkt* (1527; there is a copy of this book in the Wolfenbüttel library). He suffered at the hands of both opposing parties in the Peasants War. Klaus von Grafeneck is said to have arisen at midnight every night for prayer and Bible reading in his later years. He died on Jan. 16, 1575.

His two sisters, who had been nuns in Königsfelden, left the convent to marry. It is very likely that Klaus von Grafeneck sent his account of Sattler's martyrdom to one of his brothers-in-law, Balthasar Maler, a printer in Zürich, who had it printed in 1533. In 1533 Grafeneck married Margarethe, the daughter of Peter Scher of Schwarzenburg. She became a devoted follower of Schwenckfeld as was her entire family. She was a sister of A. Blaurer's (*q.v.*) brother-in-law, Peter Scher, Jr. She was the channel for the sending of Paul Glock's (*q.v.*) letters to Moravia. Her daughter Christine also apparently aided Glock. A report given by his nephew Josua Maler (d. 1599) indicates that the Grafeneck home was open to Zwinglians, Schwenckfelders, and Anabaptists. It is very probable that Paul Glock received kinder treatment than was customary because of Grafeneck's intercession for him. Grafeneck employed him in gardening in Dettlingen and sent him on errands to distant places. This freedom ended when Glock engaged in conversation on religious matters with the peasants.   G.Bos.

Urkunden des Staatsarchivs Stuttgart. Oberamtsbeschreibung Münsingen, 532, 610, 632, O.A.B. Rottenburg I, 410; O.A.B. Urach 630; Reutlinger Geschichtsblätter XII (1901) 27, 32, 95; XIV (1903) 54 f.; Hefele, Diözesanarchiv 1884, 74 f., 81 f.; E. Egli, Aktensammlung zur Gesch. der Zürcher Ref. (Zürich, 1879) No. 1100; Württembergische Jahrbücher f. Statistik und Landeskunde 1911, 51 ff.; T. Schiess, Briefwechsel der Brüder Thomas und Ambrosius Blaurer II (Freiburg i.B., 1910) 266, 273, 316; III, 38, 227, 547, 712, 801; V. Ernst, Briefwechsel Herzog Christophs I, No. 879; III, 198; Wolkan, Geschicht-Buch, 379; W. Köhler, Flugschriften aus den ersten Jahren der Reformation II (Leipzig, 1908) 292; Blätter f. württemberg Kirchengesch. 1891, 85; Gabelkover, Collektaneen im Staatsarchiv Stuttgart; Ztscht. f. Gesch. des Oberrheins XIX, 591; ML II, 154 f.

Graft (*Noordeind*), a village in the Dutch province of North Holland, between Alkmaar and Hoorn, which has from a very early date been the seat of a Mennonite congregation. In the middle of the 16th century, according to J. A. Leeghwater, the Mennonites of that area met for worship on an island in Schermer Lake called Matten. The congregation was closely associated with the neighboring De Rijp congregation, and is often called the congregation of Graft en de Rijp. The congregation belonged to the Waterlander (*q.v.*) branch, and existed before 1581, in which year its representatives were present at the meeting of Waterlander churches at Amsterdam. In 1654 De Rijp was completely burned down, and with it the Mennonite church with its archives. Strangely the archives of the Graft congregation have nothing before 1654. Since that date the lists of members and preachers are intact. In 1655 the membership numbered 211, in 1658 even 232. Then it decreased: 1671, 188; 1724, 101; 1730, 77; 1757, 39; 1824, 17. Since then there is again a rapid increase: 1836, 50; 1861, 75; a standstill, 1898, 73; 1928, 75, and a new decline

to about 50 in 1953. The small congregation contributed liberally to the Fund for Foreign Needs in 1733, 1736, and 1744.

Formerly the congregation had a large wooden meetinghouse, which was torn down in 1809 and replaced by a smaller one, also of wood. A brick church was built in 1874 and an organ acquired in 1897. Since 1921 the congregation of Graft has been united with that of Oost- and West-Graftdijk. The last pastors of the independent congregation of Graft were C. Nijdam 1909-12, J. Dirkmaat 1912-14, and Miss J. L. de Eerens 1918-19.

C.N., vDZ.

Inv. Arch. Amst. I, No. 474; II, Nos. 1824-27; DB 1875, 129; 1877, 80; 1878, 111-19; 1882, 108; Blaupot t. C., Holland I and II, passim; ML II, 155.

Graftdijk. Oost- and West-Graftdijk are two small old villages in the Dutch province of North Holland, situated on the great canal between Amsterdam and Helder, nine miles southwest of Alkmaar. Their combined population is about 600, with 44 Mennonites. There was in each of the villages once an old Mennonite congregation. Both congregations belonged to the Waterlander (Rijper) Sociëteit, but turned rather conservative in the second half of the 17th century and also joined the Zonist (*q.v.*) Conference. There was a meetinghouse in both villages. The one in West-Graftdijk, built in 1648, burned down in 1758, and was replaced by a new one, dedicated on Dec. 3, 1758. This typical small frame church, remodeled in 1855, was sold in 1921. In Oost-Graftdijk a brick church was built in 1856, and both the churches of Oost- and West-Graftdijk acquired organs in 1901. The congregations were separate until 1921, but since 1773 had been served by one pastor. Since the two villages are less than a mile apart, it was decided for financial reasons to unite the congregations and to use the small church at West-Graftdijk. It is now called the Graftdijk congregation. In 1921 the congregation of Graft-Noordeind (*q.v.*) was united with the Graftdijk congregation. The membership of the Oost- and West-Graftdijk congregations must have been very large in the 17th century (figures are not available). In the 18th century it declined; in 1833 the two congregations together had 67 baptized members. In 1947 Oost-Graftdijk had 91, and West-Graftdijk 42 members; in 1898 the corresponding figures were 54 and 43; in 1953 the total membership was about 65. Since 1900 the congregation had been served by the following ministers: R. J. de Stoppelar 1900-11, Y. S. Buruma 1912-17, A. Keuter 1917-20, J. H. van der Giessen 1929-34. Since the death of van der Giessen the pulpit has been vacant. Graftdijk has a women's circle.   Y.S.B., vDZ.

Inv. Arch. Amst. I, No. 896; II, Nos. 1828-30; DB 1861, 158; 1917, 47, 61, 62; Blaupot t. C., Holland I and II, passim; ML II, 155.

Grafton Church of God in Christ Mennonite Church, located near Grafton, N.D., dates back to 1891 when Isaac N. Mastre was converted and baptized. He was ordained to the ministry in 1892. At first he held meetings in different schoolhouses but later a mission hall was erected. The enroll-ment has varied greatly; in 1953 there were eight members, with Clifford Mastre as pastor. C.M.

Grahe, Jakob and **Wilhelm,** had themselves bap-tized by the Dompelaars (*q.v.*) of Crefeld in the Wupper River with four other members of the Reformed Church in Solingen, Johannes Lobach (*q.v.*), J. Fr. Henckels, W. Knipper (or Kneppers), and Luther Stettius, and were therefore arrested two years later and taken in chains to Düsseldorf, Feb. 26, 1717. They remained in prison here until autumn. On Dec. 1 they were taken to Jülich, where they spent two years and ten months in damp prison cells at hard labor during the day. Two Mennonites of Rotterdam, Johannes de Koker and his brother Gillis, visited them in prison and drew the attention of the Dutch States-General to this case; on the intercession of Casper Fagel, Grand Pensionary of this body, they were released on Nov. 20, 1720; but they had to leave the coun-try and promise never to return. Wilhelm Grahe wrote a detailed account of this period of suffering, which was published in *DB* 1861, 51-85.

Other Mennonites who visited them in prison were Jan Kroes (Crous), Gossen Goyen, and W. von der Leyen; after their release they found shel-ter with Hubert Rahr of Crefeld. The most com-plete account of the Dompelaar movement is given by Friedrich Nieper. NEFF, vDZ.

M. Göbel, *Gesch. des christlichen Lebens* III . . . (Coblenz, 1849) 238 ff.; *Die Heimat* (Crefeld, 1877) 188 ff.; Fr. Nieper, *Die ersten deutschen Einwanderer von Krefeld nach Pennsylvanien* (Neukirchen, 1940) 201-22; *ML* II, 155 f.

Gramberg: see **Goossen, Helena.**

Gramestetten (*Grametstetten* in the Hutterite *Ge-schicht-Buch*), where three Anabaptists met a mar-tyr's death, is a village in Upper Austria three hours from Linz. (*ML* II, 156.) LOSERTH.

Gran, a city in Hungary: see **Esztergom.**

Gran, *Primatial Library of.* Since 1001 Gran (see **Esztergom**) has been the seat of an archbishop, who is at the same time a prince and primate of Hungary. When the great Anabaptist persecution set in under Maria Theresa in 1757, which ended in a complete liquidation of Anabaptist groups, all their books of instruction or dogma, as well as their private and public correspondence were con-fiscated (Beck, *Geschichts-Bücher,* 578 ff.). On Nov. 8, 1578, order was issued that all suspicious books were to be taken from the brethren in Sobotiste and presented to the authorities for investigation. A similar order was given Dec. 14, 1759, to the Pressburg *Komitat:* a careful search was to be made among the Anabaptists in Gross-Schützen. The confiscated books were not returned to their owners. On April 9, 1760, the government was informed that the orders had been followed and the books and writings taken from the leaders. In the same year a directive was issued to baptize all infants according to Catholic rites; committees were sent out to convert the Anabaptists. With some they succeeded; most of them accepted the

Catholic forms, but remained true to their convic-tions. These conversions mark the beginning of the end of Anabaptism in Hungary; in contrast to for-mer times, the conversions were now to be accom-plished by gentle means. Details are found in the court records, some of which Joseph Beck has pub-lished in the appendix to the *Geschichts-Bücher.* The reports state that many books were success-fully hidden by the Hutterites before the coming of the officers. One of these books was, of course, the official *Geschicht-Buch.*

Most of the confiscated books were put into the Primatial library in Gran, some to the Domkapitel library in Pressburg, some to the Protestant Lyzeal library there, and a relatively large number to the university library in Budapest. The manuscripts in the Primatial library are listed by Beck in his sum-mary of the sources from which he compiled his *Geschichts-Bücher.* Since his edition is no longer to be found in bookstores, the most important of the manuscripts will be listed here with signatures. The following manuscripts contain exclusively mat-ter in the *Geschichts-Bücher.*

(1) Codex G—Graner Chronikel (signature G. J. VI. 27), once the property of Andreas Ehrenpreis, one of the leaders. (2) Codex J—Codex Breitmichl (signature G. J. VI. 25), begun in 1591, extends to April 5, 1668. (3) Codex L—Schad'sche Chronik (signature G. J. X. 11), once the property of Mathes Helm, who headed the brotherhood in 1701. (4) Codex O—Codex Artolf (signature G. J. X. 8), once the property of the weaver, Kaspar Artolf. (5) Codex Q (signature G. J. X. 4) without fur-ther designation. (6) Codex R—Codex Dreller III (signature G. J. X. 5) was written by the book-binder Isaak Dreller in 1647 at Sobotiste. (7) Co-dex T—Codex Ehrenpreis with Hubmaier's motto, "Die Wahrheit ist untötlich." This codex contains a number of brotherhood regulations. The present signature is G. J. VI. 26.

A further list of manuscripts has a mixed con-tent: (1) G. J. X. 9, written in 1574. (2) G. J. VI. 31, containing a defense of the Anabaptists against the charge that they despised government and the ownership of property, and the important letter to the lords of Moravia with a vindication of the faith of the Brethren and their institutions. (3) G. J. X. 33, containing part of an epistle from the Moravian brotherhood to the Swiss Rausenberger in 1601 and a doctrinal statement of the brotherhood. (4) G. J. X. 12 contains an epistle by Andreas Ehrenpreis (also printed in 1652) and the five articles of the great struggle between us and the world: baptism, communion, community of goods, government, and divorce (likewise by Ehrenpreis). (5) G. J. X. 28 contains a report by Hans Schmidt about his imprisonment in Württemberg, then 16 questions on baptism, and a letter by Andreas Ehrenpreis to Daniel Zwicker in Danzig. (6) G. J. X. 14 con-tains the epistle of Andreas Ehrenpreis (see No. 4) and his discussion on baptism. (7) G. J. X. 27 contains a hymnbook of the brethren in Sobotiste. (8) G. J. XI. 29 contains Riedemann's *Rechen-schaft.* Beck adds that he took some documents from the archives in Gran.

From the above it is clear that in spite of Beck's meritorious work a new systematic research of the archives and of the bishopric of Gran according to the sources is necessary to the history of the Anabaptists. (*ML* II, 156.)   LOSERTH.

Grandidier, Philip Andreas (1752-87), an abbot, historian of Alsace. He died on a journey to study the archives in Lucelle (Sundgau). In a posthumously published work, *Oeuvres inédites de Grandidier* (Colmar, 1865-68, 6 vv.), he discusses the Mennonites with pleasant objectivity, thus making his book a notable source for Mennonite history, especially in Alsace (*q.v.*). (*ML* II, 157.) NEFF.

Gran(d)velle, Antoine Perrenot, Lord of Granvelle (1517-86), Roman Catholic bishop of Utrecht 1567, Archbishop of Mechelen and a cardinal, was one of the most influential advisers of Margaret (*q.v.*), Duchess of Parma, since 1559 Regent of the Netherlands (both the present Netherlands and Belgium). He was an opponent of William of Orange and an ardent fighter of "heretics," both Calvinists and Anabaptists, and influenced the regent to maintain the imperial decrees and to take to drastic action. In a letter of 1566 he wrote: If we should give freedom . . . to everyone to believe whatever he wishes, we would have not only 'Hugenots' (Calvinists) . . . but also several kinds of Anabaptists, whose intentions are very pernicious for the Republic (common cause) as one might see by what has happened during our memory at Münster and Amsterdam, and a hundred thousand other monstrous sects."   vDZ.

A. A. van Schelven, *Willem van Oranje* (Haarlem, 1933) 67-99; P. Besson, *Edits de Persécution contre les Anabaptistes des Pays-Bas* . . . (Bern-Neuchatel-Buenos Aires, n.d.) 25-27.

Granger United Missionary Church, located in Yakima Co., Wash., has a seating capacity of 100. In 1955 the membership was 35 with John Detwiler as pastor.   Er.B.

Grant (President) *and the Russian Mennonite Immigration into the United States.* Negotiations of the Russian Mennonites (and Hutterites) with the American government (1873) during Grant's second administration centered about two requests in particular: the acquisition of land (interpreted in the U.S. Senate as a million acres in ten or less solid pieces at a moderate cost) and exemption from military duty. The assumption underlying the former request was that the entire group of Russian Mennonites would transplant their several closed colonies to America to perpetuate their own religious life and culture and the use of the German language, but the main cause for the desire to migrate was not economic opportunity but the abrogation of the long-standing exemption privileges in Russia; and it was hoped that they could secure a "written grant" of privileges and immunities signed by the President similar to the one which had been granted "in perpetuity" to their forebears in Prussia by Catherine of Russia. The following steps of negotiation were taken by representatives of the Russian Mennonites:

(1) A petition for land and exemption was submitted to a U.S. diplomatic officer at St. Petersburg during the middle of 1872. A temporary reply was given to encourage emigration, but later directions from Hamilton Fish, Grant's Secretary of State, were to refrain from making any promises that could not be binding in any event without Senate ratification.

(2) In August 1873 the Hutterites Paul and Lorenz Tschetter, and the Mennonite Tobias Unruh secured a personal interview with President Grant at the White House. Grant was very much in favor of granting the Mennonites some sort of written assurance concerning military service and asked Secretary of State Fish about the possibility of preparing such a statement; but Fish, a man of caution and integrity, warned Grant in a long letter against signing a promise that might later have to be broken in the event state or national legislatures enacted general military conscription laws.

(3) Later in the same year Mennonite Cornelius Jansen secured an interview with Grant; and probably because of Jansen's great diplomatic abilities Grant's interest in the Mennonite request was revived. This time Grant contacted his Secretary of Interior, Columbus Delano; and his concern centered not on military exemption for the Mennonites but on securing for them the land that they desired. The Grant-Delano proposal was submitted to Congress in Grant's 1874 "State of the Union" address, and a bill was subsequently introduced into the Senate which was designed to authorize Delano to withdraw from sale or entry such lands as the Mennonites may have desired to occupy upon arrival, up to 500,000 acres. This bill was debated over a period of several months by prominent legislators, but failed ultimately to come to a vote. The main argument in favor of the bill was not the plight of the Mennonite people in Russia but the advantage of obtaining a large group of what were considered to be high-class agriculturalists. Arguments against the bill were: opposition to the closed community and autonomous Mennonite culture; refusal of the Mennonites to help defend the common country; objection to monopolizing the land together with the possibility of fraud on the part of land agents.

(4) A petition from Mennonite representatives John F. Funk and Amos Herr on behalf of the Russian Mennonites was submitted to the House of Representatives, but was "pigeonholed" for lack of time and support.

Thus the Russian Mennonites received no official encouragement from the United States government to immigrate; and Grant's own personal sympathy with the Mennonite requests must not be interpreted without reference to his general lack of sound judgment on many issues of his administration, which competent historians record had become corrupted with graft and fraud.   L.Ha.

Leland Harder, "The Russian Mennonites and American Democracy Under Grant," *From the Steppes to the Prairies,* edited by Cornelius Krahn (Newton, Mennonite Historical Series, 1949); E. H. Correll, "President Grant and the Mennonite Immigration from Russia," *MQR* IX (1935) 144-52.

Granum (Alberta) Hutterite Bruderhof (Dariusleut, *q.v.*) near Granum, 18 miles northwest of Macleod, founded in 1930. Their preacher Michael

Tschetter, who was chosen to the ministry in the Spink (S.D.) Bruderhof in 1910, led the Spink brotherhood into Canada in 1918 to found the Stand-Off Colony near Macleod, Alberta. From here he went with several families to found the Granum Bruderhof. Michael Tschetter died in 1940. Jakob Hofer was chosen preacher here in 1934 and confirmed in 1938. In 1947 the Bruderhof had 50 baptized members in a total of 125 souls.   D.D.

Grassy Lake Mennonite Brethren Church, located 12 miles south of Grassy Lake in southern Alberta, was founded in 1927 with a baptized membership of seven. From 1936 to 1948 a church basement was used for worship services. A new church was built in 1948 (58 x 28 ft.). In all these years the church has been affiliated with the Coaldale M.B. Church. The first leader was P. Neufeld and the present leader is David Penner, Sr. Ministers who have served the congregation are A. Neumann and David Dyck. The membership in 1954 was 40.
                                                    D.P., Sr.

Grass (Graess), Heinrich (also Johann), a native of Borken, Westphalia, Germany, and a teacher, was a "prophet" in the Anabaptist "kingdom" of Münster, who left Münster in October 1534 as an ambassador of Jan van Leyden, and was arrested at Iburg by the Bishop of Münster. He saved his life by promising to investigate and betray their military secrets to the bishop. He returned to Münster, leaving it a second time on Jan. 2, 1535, to give the bishop the information, through which treachery a number of military projects of Jan van Leyden were prevented. The supposition that the "unknown messenger from Münster" who read Rothmann's book *Van de Wrake* before a meeting of Dutch Anabaptists in Waterland near Amsterdam is identical with Heinrich Grass (*DB* 1892, 11, note) is not very tenable.   vdZ.

DB 1896, 10, 12; Kühler, *Geschiedenis* I, 128, 149 f.; Mellink, *Wederdopers;* C. A. Cornelius, *Berichte der Augenzeugen über das münsterische Wiedertäuferreich* (Münster, 1853) 115-18.

Graudenz, a city (pop. 36,805) of former West Prussia, now Grudziadz in Pomorze, Poland. After the devastating floods of the Vistula River about 1560, large areas of the territory of Graudenz were depopulated. This stricken territory was then largely taken over by Dutch settlers, usually Mennonites, who were granted the privileges of freedom of religion, their own schools, and transporting their products on the Vistula free of taxes. In the 17th century Mennonites predominated in the following villages: Parsken, Kommerau, Klein-Lubin, and Dragass; they were very numerous in the villages of Klein-Wolz, Tresch, Gross-Lubin, and Klein-Lubin. In Graudenz and its vicinity there were until 1945 numerous Mennonites, especially in the congregations of Montau, Gruppe, and Schönsee. In the "Consignation" of all Mennonite families living in "West Prussia" in 1789 (thus outside the city of Danzig and the region of Thorn, both of which were ceded to Prussia in 1793 in the second partition of Poland) only one locality, Parsken with 20

Mennonites, is listed for the Graudenz area. But according to publications of the Prussian census there were in 1861, 67 Mennonites; in 1871, 77; in 1880, 96; 1890, 108; 1900, 159; and in 1910, 230. Of the 230 Mennonites counted in 1910, 164 lived in the city's domain, and 66 in the country.

This conspicuously strong and promising growth was caused by these factors: the development of the city in general; Graudenz was the "city of schools," and centrally located for the three congregations. It thus seemed that in a few years a separate congregation would be organized with its own preaching service. They began by holding services on the second Sunday of every month in the hall of the inn "Zur Heimat." The first conjoint service was held Nov. 11, 1897. Communion was also observed. The congregation was served by the preachers of the three country churches, occasionally supported by guest preachers. The idea of forming an independent congregation and building a church (*Menn. Bl.,* 1905, p. 8, 27, and 34) was never carried out. In consequence of impoverishment many members moved out.

Graudenz was the scene of the memorable meeting between Frederick William III of Prussia and Abraham Nickel (*q.v.*) of Jamrau, the deacon at Culm (Schönsee), Oct. 8, 1806, in the "gouverneur" house, later a school, Nonnenstrasse 5 at the Luisenbrücke.   W.K.

Xaver Froelich, *Geschichte des Graudenzer Kreises* (2 vol., 2d ed. Danzig, 1884-85); F. Szper, *Nederlandsche Nederzettingen in West-Pruisen* (Enkhuizen, 1913) 132; Herbert Wiebe, *Das Siedlungswerk niederländischer Mennoniten* (Marburg a.d. Lahn, 1952) 31-33; *ML* II, 159 f.

Gravenhage, 's: see **Hague, The.**

Gravensteen, Het, a medieval castle at Gent, Belgium, parts of which are still preserved, including the dungeons in which Anabaptists and Mennonites were imprisoned during the 16th century, as well as the courtyard in which a number of them were beheaded or drowned.   vdZ.

Graz, a city (pop. 226,721) in Styria, Austria (also called Bairisch-Grätz to distinguish it from Windischgrätz, as in the Anabaptist chronicles), the capital of the three territories of Styria, Carinthia, and Carniola, all possessions of Archduke Charles of Hapsburg, the youngest son of Emperor Ferdinand I. It enters into Anabaptist history in the 1530's and 1540's, not because it was an Anabaptist center, but because the Anabaptists seized at other places were usually tried and executed there. In the second half of the 16th century the local authorities were more intent than the national or church authorities in keeping Anabaptists out of the country. The famous "Pacification" concluded between these three reluctant duchies and Archduke Karl III at Bruck on the Mur in 1578 granted toleration to the Lutherans, but obligated them not to tolerate "any bookdealer who . . . distributes all kinds of sectarian tracts and books."

In the 1530's and 1540's the great Anabaptist movement came from Upper Austria, chiefly Linz, to Styria; the thorough church inspection of 1528 revealed that the country was no longer free of

Anabaptists. There were already some Anabaptists in Graz; one of them, from Upper Austria, was cross-examined. It was learned that they met in the house of a painter named Kasper (*q.v.*) above the new parsonage. The house was ordered to be razed; but the painter's wife appealed to the authorities that the house was her inheritance from her father, and she herself was not an Anabaptist. The judges and the council reported on Aug. 22, 1530, that one baptism had taken place in the house. The artist himself had been baptized there two years before by a priest named Bernhardin. The house was destroyed.

Seven Anabaptists in the Kapfenberg district were seized there and transferred to Graz. But the cross-examinations did not yield the results desired by the government; therefore Hans Ungnad requested Stubenberger on Jan. 26, 1526, to send him the statements of these Anabaptists and the books in their possession. These Anabaptists were then kept imprisoned in Graz three full years. They refused to be converted, and stressed some of their most important doctrines. The governor, as Michel Meixner wrote to the Cardinal-Bishop Bernhard of Trent, Jan. 24, 1534, "had them taken to the castle . . . and had a preacher preach to them, but none of them would be converted. They stopped before the door and said they would not enter a house of idols; nor did they listen to the sermon, but talked to each other, and comforted and strengthened each other." "The governor then requested the clergymen assigned to the task by the Archbishop of Salzburg to deal with them; he wanted to have nothing more to do with them; he calls them pious, simple people." "Now the provost of Pöllau and the other clergy worked with them two days. If one tries to instruct them in the pure Word of God and convince them of their error, they say they do not need it, for they have been convinced by God. If one says they should call upon God to be enlightened by Him, they do not need that either, for they are already enlightened; in short, one accomplishes nothing with them. If one wishes to apply a serious penalty, it is best to let them go and to expel them from the country."

In another letter—it is the supplement to a report of Jan. 21, 1534—Meixner also states that "no punishments are inflicted on the Anabaptists." It is a burden to him that he must deal with the governor concerning them, who always thought they were simple and pious people. "Recently the Anabaptists who have been so long in prison, have been taken out and preached to. None of them wanted to enter the chapel and when they were admonished and the officers tried to correct them they spoke sacrilegious words against the holy sacrament." Meixner advised that if they were not to be punished, they should at least be expelled, to rid the ruler of the expense.

Unfortunately they were very severely dealt with. The *Geschichts-Bücher* say, "In 1534 Brother Daniel Kropf was one of three seized in Graz in Styria and executed with the sword. At this time four sisters were executed for the sake of divine truth.

All seven of them bravely testified to the divine truth." "Of this Daniel there are still some letters in the brotherhood, concerning baptism and other points, also four Christian songs that he wrote."

Beck mentions one of these writings, the "Confession of faith that he . . . presented to the council at Graz, 1534, . . . why we, having left wife or husband, children, possessions, house and home, were imprisoned as criminals by you, and have now been long imprisoned and tortured." Kropf rejects water baptism and infant baptism. Communion is not "physical but spiritual." In water baptism he sees only a symbol of the covenant God has made with man through Christ. He does not believe that salvation lies in it. Salvation lies in faith in Him whom God sent. Ungnad's letter shows that he was a statesman and friendly to the Reformation; indeed, two decades later he lost his position for the sake of it.

From this time on there is no mention of Anabaptists in Graz except when they are taken through the city, as when the prisoners of Falkenstein are dragged from Falkenstein in Lower Austria to the sea, having been condemned to die as galley slaves. Only occasionally does one remember an Anabaptist who still lies in Graz in prison, like Brother André Keller, of whom the letter of Amon to the brethren at Falkenstein is mindful.

LOSERTH.

J. Loserth, "Zur Geschichte der Wiedertäufer in Steiermark," *Mitteilungen des Hist. Vereins für Steiermark* XLII and L, and *Ztscht des Hist. Vereins für Steiermark* X; idem, *Veröffentlichungen der Historischen Landeskommission* VI, 22; Beck, *Geschichtsbücher*, 115, 116, 278; Wolkan, *Geschicht-Buch*, 48, 158, 182; *ML* II, 161 f.

Grebel, Conrad (*ca.* 1498-1526), can be considered the chief founder of Swiss-South German Anabaptism. Much less widely known than Hans Denk (*q.v.*) or Balthasar Hubmaier (*q.v.*), he is nevertheless historically of much greater significance, for without him Anabaptism in its historical form would probably never have come into existence and he represents original Anabaptism in the form in which it has been perpetuated to the present day, whereas Denk and Hubmaier represent sideward movements from the main stream, both of which diverged significantly on major points and both of which soon died out.

Grebel was viewed as the outstanding leader of original Swiss Anabaptism (properly called the "Swiss Brethren" movement) by his enemies, as well as his followers. Zwingli viewed him as the head of the new heretical faction in Zürich. In January 1525, just after the break with what was destined to become the Anabaptist group, he wrote to Vadian, "Conrad Grebel and a few other less important persons are holding fast to their standpoint." In a letter to Oecolampadius (*q.v.*) and others in November 1526, shortly after Grebel's death, Zwingli referred to Grebel as "the ringleader (*coryphaeus*) of the Anabaptists." Johannes Kessler (*q.v.*) of St. Gall, in his famous Reformation diary, *Sabbata*, calls Grebel the arch-Anabaptist (*Erzwidertouffer*). And the records of a very important disputation (*q.v.*), held in 1538 between the evangelical preachers of Bern and the Bernese Anabaptist leaders, the minutes of which still lie unpublished in the state archives in Bern (labeled *Unnütze Papiere*), indicate that the Brethren counted Grebel as the "first Anabaptist" (*der erste Täufer*). Conclusive evidence of Grebel's position of leadership in the founding of the Anabaptist movement comes from a highly interesting account of the actual birth of Anabaptism which tells us that Grebel performed the first adult baptism in Zürich on the night of Jan. 21, 1525. The story found its way into the remarkable manuscript chronicle of the Hutterian Brethren, known as the *Geschicht-Buch*. In that account of the epochal meeting in the house of Felix Manz (*q.v.*), when 15 brethren were gathered in prayer after the mandate of the Zürich council proscribing the further propagation of their faith, we are told that as they arose from prayer, moved by the Spirit of God, George Blaurock asked Conrad Grebel to baptize him on the confession of his faith, thus recognizing Grebel as the spiritual leader of the little company. This Conrad Grebel did, performing the first adult baptism in Reformation times, the model for millions of similar baptisms since that day.

The attempt to trace the career, theology, and significance of Conrad Grebel is severely hampered by scarcity of sources. His was a short life (*ca.* 1498-1526) with scarcely three years of public activity of a sort sufficiently important to bring his name into public records or into the private correspondence of contemporary leaders, and all that is said of Grebel in both of these sources could probably be written on less than three typewritten pages. The only writing of any sort which he prepared for publication—a brief pamphlet of less than five thousand words—has been lost, and can with difficulty be only partially reconstructed from the translated quotations found in Zwingli's counterattack in the *Elenchus*. Three relatively insignificant short poems have been preserved, and one short petition for safe conduct to the Zürich council in 1525. Fortunately, 69 letters written by Grebel (as well as three written to him) have been preserved. They were written between September 1517 and July 1525, two to Ulrich Zwingli (*q.v.*), one to Thomas Müntzer (*q.v.*), one to a co-worker named Andreas Castelberger (*q.v.*) of Zürich, nine to Oswald Myconius (*q.v.*) of Lucerne, and 56 to Grebel's close friend, former teacher, and brother-in-law, Dr. Joachim von Watt, the reformer of the Swiss city of St. Gall, commonly known as Vadian (*q.v.*). Most of these letters, however, were written during Grebel's student years at Vienna and Paris, and throw practically no light on the important phase of his life as Anabaptist leader. The three letters to Grebel which have been preserved include one from Benedikt Burgauer (1523), a minor evangelical preacher of St. Gall, one from Erhard Hegenwalt, a young evangelical friend in Wittenberg (1525), and one from Vadian (1524). One book of Grebel's library has been preserved in the state library in Zürich.

Conrad Grebel was born about 1498 as the second of six children to Junker Jakob Grebel and his wife Dorothea Fries. For a century and a half the Grebel family had been one of the leading families of the city of Zürich, one of the small number of wealthy patrician families of the lesser landed nobility who had for years directed the political, economic, and military affairs of the city. The family had always had one or more members in the city council and usually furnished the guild-master for one of the aristocratic merchant guilds. Grebels had frequently served as magistrates, and for two generations before the Reformation no important political event took place in Zürich in which a Grebel did not have part. The most influential of all the Grebels was Jakob Grebel, Conrad's father, a wealthy iron merchant, who reached the peak of a successful career in politics in the first years of the Reformation. From 1499 to 1512 he served a double term as magistrate (*Vogt*) of the territory of Grüningen, and from that time on served as a representative of the canton of Zürich at practically all of the meetings of the Swiss Confederacy, as well as serving frequently as plenipotentiary in important Swiss and foreign negotiations.

Jakob Grebel's family also played its full part in the patrician social life of the city of Zürich and northeast Switzerland. The daughters married prominent men, one becoming the wife of Vadian, noted humanist professor and sometime rector of the University of Vienna, later burgomaster and reformer of the city of St. Gall. The two sons of Jakob Grebel, one of whom died young, were given every advantage that wealth and prestige could bring them, one (Andreas) becoming a courtier in King Ferdinand's court in Vienna, and Conrad being sent to the best universities of the time, Basel, Vienna, and Paris.

At the height of prestige, fate struck the family heavy blows. The only surviving son, Conrad, became an Anabaptist heretic, dying as an exile in 1526, while the father was executed in disgrace a few months later on the charge of receiving foreign pensions. However, the family name survived, the sons of Conrad being reared by his surviving relatives in the Reformed faith, and Grebels continued to be prominent in the affairs of Zürich. A grandson of the Anabaptist Conrad, also named Conrad, became treasurer of the city in 1624, and the latter's grandson, another Conrad Grebel, became burgomaster in 1669. A recent member of the Supreme Court of the canton of Zürich was Dr. Hans von Grebel. His son, Hans von Grebel, was in 1954 serving as pastor of the Grossmünster church in Zürich.

Perhaps H. Richard Niebuhr is right in asserting in his book *The Social Sources of Denominationalism* that the Anabaptist movement was a movement of the socially and economically oppressed lower classes, but it is difficult to apply this theory to the founder of the movement, Conrad Grebel, the wealthy, socially elite, university-trained patrician son of an unusually successful father.

Grebel's Education. Conrad Grebel probably grew up in the castle at Grüningen, a few miles east of Zürich, where his father was magistrate during Conrad's boyhood days. His education must have begun in the Latin School of the Grossmünster church in Zürich, known as the *Carolina* because it was supposed to have been founded by Charlemagne. Here he received the typical Latin training of the time, quite in the old-fashioned scholastic spirit.

His university career began in October 1514, when he matriculated for the winter semester at the University of Basel, which was at that time in a very low state, with an average of 50 new matriculants each semester. The newer humanism was just beginning to come in. Glarean (*q.v.*) (Heinrich Loriti), the outstanding Swiss humanist of the younger school, had just come to Basel and established a *bursa,* or boarding academy. Since all the students of the philosophical faculty were required to live in one of the numerous bursae, Grebel joined Glarean's bursa. Fortunately, Glarean was an excellent teacher, and under his tutelage the young Grebel was introduced for the first time into the world of humanist learning and living. Basel was barely beginning to come into its glory as a humanist center. Erasmus (*q.v.*) had come two months before, in August 1514, to remain through the winter. The great Froben had begun his career as an independent printer the year before. Beatus Rhenanus had been there since 1511, Hans Holbein the Younger came possibly during the winter of 1514-15, Oecolampadius came in 1515, Amerbach, Fonteius, and other lesser humanist scholars were already occupied as proofreaders in the great printing houses. The growing humanist life was just organizing itself, the foreigners gathering around Erasmus and Rhenanus in the famous *Sodalitas Basiliensis,* while the lesser Swiss group gathered around Glarean. It was in this latter group that Conrad Grebel moved during the first semester of study, probably scarcely aware of the significance of his environment. Before he could enter fully into this new life, his father transferred him to the University of Vienna, where he had secured a four-year stipend for him from the Emperor Maximilian.

A constant stream of young Swiss students, particularly from Zürich and eastern Switzerland, had been flowing to Vienna for the preceding five years, partly under the influence of Ulrich Zwingli, who had himself studied there in 1501. The center of the Swiss student group in Vienna was Vadian, a famous Swiss humanist professor from the city of St. Gall, who took it upon himself to become the friend and patron of the Swiss boys. Vadian had been in Vienna since 1510, had a doctor's degree in medicine as well as philosophy, was a noted humanist poet, crowned poet laureate in 1514 by the emperor, was appointed professor of rhetoric in 1516 as successor to the great Angelo Cospi, and the same year elected rector of the university.

When Conrad Grebel came to Vienna to enroll as a student in the summer of 1515, to remain for three years until June 1518, he naturally became a part of the Swiss group gathered around Vadian. Indeed, he soon became an intimate friend and protégé of the great professor. The warmth and intimacy of this friendship is elquently attested by the 56 extant letters written by Grebel to his "dear-

est teacher and most faithful friend." Vadian encouraged and promoted the young student in every possible way, recognizing in him outstanding gifts and a splendid personality well qualified for future leadership. He seems to have counted him as the most promising of the Swiss students. Out of this friendship came good fortune for Vadian, for it brought him in the summer of 1519 Conrad's younger sister Martha as wife.

When Vadian suddenly left Vienna in June 1518, partly because of the plague which was raging and partly because he had decided to exchange a professorship in Vienna for the life of a physician and scholar in his native St. Gall, Grebel went with him. However, he remained in Zürich but a short time, for his father had secured a royal scholarship from the king of France for his son—one of the two which were being granted annually by Francis I to each Swiss canton—and in September he set out for Paris on what was intended to be the climax of a successful scholastic career. There he spent two further years, certainly in study, although the rather inadequate matriculation records of the university do not contain his name. He went to Paris with high hopes, being particularly happy again to join the bursa conducted by his former Basel teacher, Glarean, for the latter had conducted a bursa for Swiss students in Paris since 1517.

But the high hopes with which Grebel came to Paris were not to be fulfilled. After three months he became involved in a serious quarrel with Glarean and left him, not to return until an entire year had passed. And in July 1519 a severe plague broke out in Paris which drove Grebel and his friends away from the city for six months. His troubles were further increased when he became involved in several student brawls. He also suffered somewhat from illness due to his loose living, and finally his father, becoming incensed at reports he had received, cut him off from funds. Even Vadian threatened to break off his friendship and practically ceased writing. Under the blows of fate and circumstance Grebel lost heart and returned home to Zürich, his high hopes disappointed, without having completed his studies or secured any kind of degree. It was the end of his student days. He determined to seek a reconciliation with his parents and Vadian, and hoped for some career in his home city, although his self-confidence had been badly shaken and his inner life was full of conflict.

For almost six years Conrad Grebel was a student among the humanists of the universities, and it is of importance to inquire the significance of his training. His chief teachers were Vadian and Heiligmaier at Vienna, and Glarean and Nicholas Beraldus at Paris, of whom Glarean and Vadian alone exerted a significant influence upon him. It is true that in Paris Glarean counted in the circle of his friends the great Budaeus and Faber Stapulensis, but there is no evidence of any sort that Grebel came into contact with them or was influenced by them. Alike in Paris, Vienna, and Basel, Grebel's contacts were primarily with the newer type of transalpine literary humanism, which characterized the better Swiss, French, German, and Austrian humanists. While this humanism was not the immoral, pagan Italian type, it was also not the Christian humanism of the Erasmian type. Vadian and Glarean were solid, stable scholars, whose chief concern in life was to promote the liberal arts, to write poetry, to study geography, mathematics, and natural history, and to enjoy the fellowship of like-minded spirits. They were not greatly concerned about a moral and religious reform of society, for they had not yet been caught in the growing tide of interest in the great Christian Renaissance which Erasmus was promoting with ever-increasing zeal. This is the type of humanism to which Grebel was exposed, and which is reflected in the numerous letters which he wrote to Vadian and Myconius (one to Zwingli) during his student days. At the university he learned Latin, Greek, and probably Hebrew, learned to write Latin well, to appreciate the great classic writers and scholars, but failed to acquire any new religious concerns or attitudes. He did not become a pagan, for he retained his traditional faith in the church and her dogmas, but neither did he become an Erasmian reformer.

If Conrad Grebel ever acquired a humanistic interest in the Erasmian type of reform of religion—which is more than doubtful—it could have come only during the late months of 1520 and 1521 after his return to Zürich. There he sought and found fellowship in the little group of returned students and humanists who gathered with Zwingli to study Greek and Hebrew during the early years of Zwingli's ministry in Zürich; but he found little satisfaction in this activity. At odds with his father, he finally decided to leave home to seek a career as a proofreader in Basel. But this project likewise did not succeed, and after two months in the printing establishment of Cratander in Basel (August and September 1521) he returned to Zürich, hoping to break down the bitter opposition of his parents to his proposed marriage with a girl below his social status. Failing in this, he suddenly went through with the marriage in February 1522, during one of the frequent absences of his father from home. The break with his family was complete, and was only partially restored by the mediation of one of the city pastors, an associate of Zwingli. During this period of stress and strain, lasting a year and a half, Grebel may have been influenced by Zwingli's more religiously motivated type of humanism, but there are no traces of such influence in his correspondence during this period.

As we come to the close of Grebel's humanist period, and see that it made no evident contribution to his religious life or thinking, it may be worth while to point out that this conclusion seriously militates against the theory of the humanist origin of Anabaptism which has recently gained ground. Certainly Conrad Grebel did not become an Anabaptist because he was a humanist. If in the minds of some scholars Anabaptist theology and ethics seem to reflect somewhat Erasmian humanistic Christianity with its emphasis upon Sermon on the Mount ethics, the Erasmian influence certainly did not enter Anabaptism through Conrad Grebel, the founder of the movement.

Grebel as a Zwinglian. The year 1522 marked an epoch for Conrad Grebel which was to lead to a transformation of his entire life. Unfortunately, there is a hiatus in his correspondence for nine months during this vital period, but from the middle of the year 1522 it is evident that Grebel was a changed man. Now he was deeply interested in the progress of the evangelical cause in Zürich; he became an ardent partisan of Zwingli and his reform program. The spirit and atmosphere as well as the content of his further correspondence are so radically different from what they were before that we must believe that a genuine conversion and renewal of life took place during the spring of 1522. The explanation is not far to seek. Grebel was won by the powerful Gospel preaching of Ulrich Zwingli, as many other citizens of Zürich were. From the beginning of his career in Zürich in 1519, Zwingli had carried through a strikingly new program of expository preaching covering many of the books of the New Testament. Like the learned and respected canon, Heinrich Engelhart, who through Zwingli's preaching confessed that he was "changed from a doctor of Roman law to a poor scholar of Christ," Grebel was changed from a loose-living humanist university student to a devout and earnest Christian. Henceforth until his untimely death in the summer of 1526—four short years ahead—he was in the forefront of those who were bringing in the new era, first for a year and a half as an enthusiastic supporter of Zwingli, and then for over two years as the founder of the new Anabaptist movement.

As Zwingli from 1522 on gradually swung into a program of practical reform in Zürich after having laid the foundation through four years of preaching, Grebel went with him. Almost at once he was a leader in the devoted group of younger men who joined Zwingli's side in the conflict. Zwingli recognized and valued Grebel's support and permitted him to publish a vigorous poetic ode hailing the Reformation in his booklet entitled *Archeteles* which was published in August 1522. In October of that year Melchior Macrinus of Solothurn wrote to Zwingli that he had heard that Grebel had developed into an exceptional promoter of the Gospel, a fact which gave Macrinus great joy, for such gifted and learned young men could render the Gospel and the world a great service. During these months a very close friendship developed between Zwingli and Grebel. Zwingli apparently planned to have Grebel appointed to the university or the theological school which he expected to establish. (The theory that Grebel broke with Zwingli, as claimed by Emil Egli and others, because the latter refused to give him the desired appointment is contrary to fact.) A few years later, after the break, Zwingli was very bitter over the broken friendship and complained of ingratitude on the part of Grebel for whom he had done so much.

The close relationship between Grebel and Zwingli was maintained until the second Zürich disputation of October 1523. In this period the views of the two men must have agreed in all essential respects. For instance, in the matter of tithes, one of the burning issues of the hour, Grebel indicated agreement with Zwingli. During this time he also formed a fast friendship with Felix Manz (*q.v.*), young Zürich student just returned from Paris, who had joined the ranks of the Zwinglians, and who was to become in January 1527 the first Anabaptist martyr in Zürich.

Beginning, however, with the October 1523 disputation, a cleavage arose between Zwingli and Grebel, which gradually grew wider during the ensuing months, until in the fall of 1524 it led to a complete break. It went so far as to cause Zwingli to condemn Grebel and his friends publicly from the pulpit as "Satans going about as angels of light," while Grebel responded by condemning Zwingli and his assistants as false shepherds not true to the divine calling and the divine Word.

The October disputation was called to put pressure on the city council to institute immediate reforms in the church life of Zürich by abolishing the mass and doing away with images. Zwingli made valiant speeches during the disputation urging this very thing. But when he saw that the slow-moving city fathers were not ready for such a radical step, he beat a strategic retreat. When Grebel observed the change of front, he at once openly protested and demanded that the city council should not be allowed to decide the matter, since all were agreed on what the Word of God required. But Zwingli would not break with the council. As a matter of fact, the mass was not abolished by the council until May 1525, almost two years later. During all the intervening time Zwingli and others continued to officiate at a ceremony which they had publicly condemned as an unscriptural abomination. This strange compromise was a heavy burden on the conscience of many devout Zürichers, not only of Conrad Grebel, to whom it seemed as though the Word of God was being set aside and made subordinate to the action of a political body. Here then was the issue: should the civil state continue to dictate the faith and life and worship of the church, or should the pastors and laity themselves carry through the necessary reform in church life according to their God-given convictions? Fundamentally, the issue was whether the new evangelical movement was to eventuate in a state church under civil control as before, or in a new type of free voluntary organization. Both Luther and Zwingli, as well as the other reformers, faced this fundamental issue, and decided to continue the medieval state church with a predominant control by the civil state in the life and faith of the church. Perhaps it was a wise and statesmanlike decision, but in terms of absolute principle and plain Scripture teaching it was indefensible. At least so it seemed to Conrad Grebel.

Conrad Grebel and his friends went home from the October disputation shocked and dismayed, feeling that they had been betrayed by the leader whom they trusted. Zwingli, on his part, bearing the burden of actual responsibility, sensing the strength of the Catholic opposition, could not help viewing his critics as irresponsible young radicals who had not yet learned the lesson of patience. The difference in point of view cut deep, and during the winter months an earnest and serious debate was carried on between Zwingli on the one side, and his former friends and supporters on the other, particularly Grebel, Manz, and Stumpf. According to Zwingli's own testimony, these men came to him repeatedly with the proposal that he set up a new kind of voluntary Christian church, one composed of true believers only, willing to live a life of true righteousness before God and man according to the teaching of Christ and the apostles, and in which a Gospel discipline would be maintained. This new church would be freed from state control, although its members would endeavor to secure a true Christian membership on the city council so that the latter would support and not hinder the work of the church. For months the struggle continued, Grebel hoping against hope that Zwingli would adopt this program, for apparently there had been some discussion of these principles earlier, with Zwingli not at all averse to them. (In 1523, for instance, Zwingli had been willing to abandon infant baptism.) But Zwingli had made up his mind that he would not follow the new plan. He feared the consequences. Would there be enough true Christians to carry on the church, and what would happen to the unregenerate mass of nominal Christians? Grebel wanted absolute loyalty to the Word of God regardless of consequences. And he was willing to accept the consequences in his own personal experience.

Those who held to Grebel's position and joined him in the break with Zwingli—a small company of not more than 15 men—did not rush into precipitate action. They met frequently for fellowship and Bible study, Grebel and Manz expounding the Scripture from the Greek and Hebrew text. They meditated, prayed, and waited. But while they waited they sought to find allies outside of Zürich. In this seeking Grebel took the lead. In the summer of 1524 he wrote to Andreas Carlstadt, who apparently had broken with Luther on somewhat similar grounds as Grebel had with Zwingli. And in October Carlstadt himself appeared in Zürich for a short time, obviously to see whether he could establish himself with the Grebel group in a new program. But the bitter opposition of Zwingli, together with the evident weakness of the Grebel group, as well as possible differences of program, no doubt convinced him of the impracticability of the move, and Carlstadt faded out of the picture.

Meanwhile Grebel had heard of another Lutheran preacher who had apparently had a break with Luther—Thomas Müntzer of Altstedt in Saxony. Here might be a possible ally. He secured two of Müntzer's booklets, in which he found much that was good, and some that was bad. But on the whole Müntzer seemed promising. So in September 1524 he wrote to Müntzer in the name of his little group, encouraging him to continue in his opposition to Luther, but warning him of several false steps he was making. (The latest and best edition of this exceedingly important document is to be found in H. Boehmer and P. Kirn, *Thomas Müntzers Briefwechsel,* Leipzig, 1931, pp. 92-101. The only English translation appears in W. Rauschenbusch, "The Zurich Anabaptists and Thomas Münzer" in *Amer. Journal of Theology* IX, 1905, 91-105.) Before the letter was sent off, a Zürich friend returned from Saxony with the information that Müntzer was apparently ready to use violence to promote his program, and on the other hand seemed to be unwilling to dispense altogether with the ancient forms of worship of the church which had no basis in Scripture. So Grebel added an appendix to his letter, chiding Müntzer and expressing concern lest Müntzer should turn out to be a disappointment to those who were dissatisfied with Zwingli and Luther and wanted a true reformation and reconstruction of the church according to the Scripture alone, doing away with all mere customs and traditions of men. Grebel's fears were only too well founded; Müntzer, too, proved to be a broken reed. However, even the hoped-for contact with Müntzer was never established, for Grebel's letter never reached Müntzer, but returned to Grebel and was apparently turned over upon his death to Vadian in St. Gall, where it is found today among the Vadian manuscripts in the St. Gall library. Some scholars have erred in supposing that this letter proved a community of faith and practice between Grebel and Müntzer; it actually proves the opposite. Müntzer probably died without ever having heard of Grebel and his group in Zürich. Later enemies of the Anabaptist movement, following the lead of Heinrich Bullinger (*q.v.*), have insisted that Grebel and his friends frequently visited Müntzer during the latter's brief visit to Basel and southern Baden in November 1524, two months after the above-mentioned letter was written. But there is not the slightest evidence of this. Zwingli never mentioned such a visit in his extensive attack on the Anabaptists, and certainly he would not have failed to connect them with Müntzer's revolution if he could have done so. The legend of the connection of the two is a pious fraud, a pure invention on the part of Bullinger, who was anxious to clear the name of his beloved Zürich from the stain of the Anabaptist heresy and was glad to be able to assign the origin of the movement to an outside source in faraway Saxony.

It is worthy of note that Grebel also wrote to Luther in the summer of 1524, receiving no written answer but the assurance through a mutual friend, Erhard Hegenwalt (*q.v.*), that Luther was not ill-disposed toward Grebel and his group.

Having failed to establish any outside contact, Grebel and his group were forced to rely upon their own resources. The closing months of 1524 were full of increasing conflict for them. Open threats from the pulpit, as well as private warnings, made it all too plain that suffering and persecution awaited them. In a touching letter to his friend Vadian in December 1524, Grebel indicates his fears for the future and his determination to press on unflinch-

ingly upon the course he felt God wanted him to follow. He says, "I do not believe that persecution will fail to come. . . . By their fruits ye shall know them, by persecution and sword. . . . May God give grace; I hope to God that He will grant the medicine of patience thereto, if it is not to be otherwise . . . and may peace, faith, and salvation be established and obtained" (*Vadianische Briefsammlung,* III, 97).

The final break came over the question of infant baptism, although this was in reality merely a reflection of the major issue, which was that of the character of the church. The issue was whether the church was to be a universal organization including the entire population by birth and infant baptism as heretofore, or whether it was to be an organization composed of adult believers only who were prepared to assume the full obligations of discipleship. It was Zwingli and not Grebel who forced the issue in a bitter determination to root out the opposition to his program. The first refusals to baptize infants occurred in the spring of 1524 in the parish of Wilhelm Reublin (*q.v.*), and were not due to Grebel's influence. However, Grebel certainly sympathized with the objectors and without doubt supported them. Zwingli and the council sought to win the objectors to infant baptism by private discussion, but the objectors asked for Scripture proof that infant baptism was commanded, which of course could not be given, and all the devious and specious arguments which Zwingli and his fellow pastors used could not move these simple-minded Biblicists from their fundamental position. It was clear that only vigorous action, including the use of the force by the state if necessary, would suffice to quell what Zwingli called rebellion (*Aufruhr*). So the decision was made to hold a public debate on Jan. 17, 1525, to be followed by a decree of the council on the matter. The story of the debate and its outcome is familiar history. As leader of the dissenting group, Grebel played a major part, assisted by Felix Manz and George Blaurock (*q.v.*). The outcome was two severe council mandates of Jan. 18 and 21, 1525, ordering a complete cessation of activity by Grebel and Manz and their associates, forbidding the Bible study meetings of the group, and ordering immediate baptism of all unbaptized infants on pain of exile from the canton. The final break was at hand. Grebel himself had an unbaptized daughter two weeks old who, as he said, "had not yet been baptized and bathed in the Romish water bath," and whom he did not intend to baptize. No sooner was the issue raised than the answer was given. The Grebel group would not compromise under any circumstance, for their consciences were bound by the Word of God as much as Luther's was at Worms. They felt that they had taken a Scriptural position which had not been refuted from the Word of God by Zwingli and the city council. The Word of God was to be trampled underfoot by the brutal power of the state. Already on the next day after the first mandate Zwingli knew the outcome, for he wrote to Vadian on Jan. 19, "Grebel persists in his stand."

When the little group of Brethren met for counsel to determine their course of action, probably on the evening of Jan. 21, they had no program of introducing rebaptism. In fact, such a thing had never been mentioned in the entire course of the struggle. But in a moment of inspiration by what they confidently believed was divine guidance, adult baptism was introduced in this little meeting, with Grebel performing the first baptism, as related earlier in this article. This was the birthday of Anabaptism.

The story of the Anabaptist movement from this point on is familiar. The little group that had met on the evening of Jan. 21, 1525, went out from their meeting with a sense of divine mission and endowment upon them. Fearing neither Zwingli nor the council, they went from house to house and into the towns and villages of the countryside teaching and preaching and urging men and women everywhere to join them in their new fellowship. The response was remarkable. In spite of repeated arrests and fines and imprisonments, the movement grew. Apparently it was not to be stopped. By Easter time Balthasar Hubmaier (*q.v.*) and practically his whole parish in Waldshut (*q.v.*) had been baptized with three hundred adult participants, and in St. Gall Grebel had great success, so that about five hundred were baptized at one time. In consternation the Zürich council called upon the other cantons of Switzerland to help to stamp out the heresy, for it was spreading to St. Gall, Appenzell, Grisons, Aargau, Basel, Lucerne, Bern, in fact everywhere. Despairing of lesser measures, Zürich finally, in November 1526 established the death penalty by drowning for participation in the new movement. This example was followed widely within and without Switzerland. The movement was checked and soon limited to but a small number of families in scattered places, chiefly in the Emmental (*q.v.*) near Bern, although as late as 1700 there were still a few Anabaptists left in the Zürich countryside.

The strict Zürich mandates made it almost impossible for Grebel to stay in the city, where he was well known, and carry on an aggressive program. Leaving the work in Zürich to less known coworkers, he set out on a mission to surrounding cities to win pastors and leaders to his cause. Several weeks in February 1525 were spent in Schaffhausen (*q.v.*) where it appeared for a time as though he might win Sebastian Hofmeister (*q.v.*), the city pastor. Forced to leave the city, he returned to Zürich for a secret visit. Then followed a call to St. Gall about Easter time, where one of his associates, Wolfgang Ulimann (*q.v.*), whom he had baptized in the Rhine near Schaffhausen in February, was having remarkable success, and where he also perhaps hoped to find at least toleration at the hands of Vadian. After a successful mission there he returned to the neighborhood of Zürich and spent most of the summer preaching with considerable success in the territory of Grüningen just east of Zürich, working much with the village pastors. In October 1525 he was taken captive together with Manz and Blaurock and put in prison

in Zürich on an indeterminate sentence; but by good fortune the entire group escaped in March 1526, after six months' imprisonment, and at once resumed their preaching activity.

During the winter in prison, Grebel evidently succeeded in preparing a brief defense of the position of the group on baptism in reply to the arguments advanced by Zwingli. He had tried during the summer before to accomplish this and to find a printer, but was frustrated in his intentions. It seems that after his escape from prison he succeeded in finding a printer and circulating a small number of the booklets. No copy is extant, but Zwingli attempted to refute the booklet in detail in his *Elenchus* which was published in July 1527.

Worn and weary, in ill health from the long imprisonment and the hardships he had been compelled to undergo, Grebel sought to find a safer field of labor and possibly the rest and quiet which he so sorely needed by going to the region of Maienfeld in the canton of Grisons, where his oldest sister had been living for some time. There is no record of his movements or activities in this region, except for the brief statement in Kessler's *Sabbata* that shortly after his arrival in Maienfeld he died of the plague. Nothing is known of his burial place, nor of the exact time of his death, although it must have taken place about July 1526. He did not die in prison as Neff and others have claimed.

Grebel's Theology. Zwingli considered his struggle with the Anabaptists in Zürich 1524-27 a desperately serious conflict. As early as May 1525 he wrote his friend Vadian that all previous conflicts (referring to the Catholic opposition) were as child's play compared with this one (*Zwingli Werke* VIII, 332). The seriousness of the conflict was due not so much to the number of the Anabaptists as to the power of their ideas and the conviction with which they were held. What were these ideas of Conrad Grebel and his associates which Zwingli feared and with which he differed so radically?

In the first place, they were not ideas referring to the major classic Christian doctrines. It can be said without contradiction that on the cardinal points of Christian theology Zwingli and Grebel agreed, for the former declared that the Grebelites differed from him only on unimportant minor points. In his *Commentario de vera et falsa religione* (*Commentary on True and False Religion*) written in March 1525 he says, "But that no one may suppose that the dissension is in regard to doctrines which concern the inner man, let it be said that the Anabaptists make us difficulty only because of unimportant outward things, such as these: whether infants or adults should be baptized and whether a Christian may be a magistrate" (*Zwingli Werke* III, 872). Zwingli was, of course, mistaken in his judgment that the issues involved concerned only unimportant things, but he was right in denying that the issues concerned the inner aspect of Christian faith or experience. Grebel and his brethren were consistent evangelicals. If we take at face value Zwingli's statement that baptism and magistracy were the chief points at issue, we see that the deeper issues involved were those of the nature of the church and the relation of the Christian to the world. These are of course major theological points.

Grebel's doctrine of the church was substantially that held by the modern nonconformist churches, particularly the Baptists and the Mennonites, and he was the first to hold this position. According to Grebel, the church as a local body comes into existence through the preaching of the Word and its voluntary acceptance, and through the consequent conversion and renewal of life of individual believers. By faith the individual members are united together and incorporated into the body of Christ. This church is in truth a fellowship of brethren in life and suffering, a *communio sanctorum,* which is maintained by the inward bond of faith and the outward bond of love. When a member of the body fails to maintain love toward the brethren or does not order his life according to the Gospel, he breaks the bond of fellowship, and if he will not hear the church and repent and change his life he must be excluded from the fellowship of the believers. New members may be received into the church only upon a confession of faith and separation from sin, upon evidence of a renewal of life and a walk in holiness. The government, ordinances, and activities of the church must be based solely upon the express teaching of the Word of God or the example of Christ and the apostles, with the rigid exclusion of "opinions of men" (a Grebel expression found in his letter to Müntzer, by which is meant a complete break with medieval tradition and a return to the apostolic pattern of the New Testament).

In the second major point, that of the relation of the Christian to the world order, Grebel and his followers occupy a unique position in the history of Protestant doctrine, a position which has not been followed by the nonconformist groups to any extent, and which probably only the modern Mennonites hold. Luther, Calvin (*q.v.*), and Grebel alike condemned the world order as sinful and in need of regeneration, but the three assumed radically different attitudes toward the condemned world order. Luther held that it was futile to do much to change it, and that since it was a necessary evil which one could not well escape, the Christian must compromise with it, participating as necessary in its life and institutions, and finding solace from the conflict by a retreat to the inner life with its experience of the grace of God and the forgiveness of sins. Calvin took the opposite position, namely, that the Christian must not compromise with the world, but must seek to regenerate the world order and make it Christian and thus make the will of God sovereign in all human life and institutions, even though that might mean the forcible suppression of ungodliness. Unfortunately, Calvin relied too much on the Old Testament in addition to the New for the content of the will of God, from which the pattern for human society was to be drawn, and in so doing compromised with the world unconsciously as Luther did deliberately. Grebel agreed with Calvin that the existing

world order needed to be regenerated according to the will of God, but he differed in the method by which it was to be accomplished. He would separate the true Christian from the ungodly world order and its institutions, and resolutely abandon the use of the civil state even in its theocratic form to promote the Christianization of society, rather making the church a light to the world and a salt to the earth. The church should overcome the world by winning members from the ungodly society of the world to the godly society of the church.

According to Grebel, the church has no right to seek to rule society from without or to attempt to control the civil authorities for the benefit of its interests. Rather it should probably expect to continue to be a "suffering church" in the world, as Christ promised His disciples, and never expect the mass of men to enter its portals or to adopt its way of life. However, within the boundaries of the church the will of God as found in the Gospel (not as found in the Old Testament ethic which for Grebel was of inferior value and certainly no longer valid for the Christian) was to have absolute sway. No Calvinist ever taught more rigidly the absolute sovereignty of God over the life of the members of the Christian community than Conrad Grebel and his brethren did. He resolutely refused to make the deliberate compromise with the world which Luther (and possibly Zwingli) made, or the unconscious compromise with the world which Calvin made.

Grebel's absolutism did not make him a social revolutionary, although his program for the Christian was certainly radical for his time, and in fact is still radical for our day. He demanded absolute Christian nonresistance, the complete abandonment of the use of force and of the taking of human life. He was thus the first absolute Christian pacifist of modern times, except for Peter Chilčicky (*q.v.*) of Bohemia, and most of his followers have maintained this principle to the present day. In taking this position, he found it necessary to deny the Christian the right to participate in the functions of the state, for the magistrates were compelled to use force and to take life since the state is ultimately based upon the sanction of force. Again, Grebel repudiated for the Christian the oppressive and unjust economic practices of his day, rejected tithes, and insisted upon the exercise of Christian brotherhood in economic relationships. It is not true, however, that his program included a communistic social order, although the emphasis upon genuine Christian brotherhood did lead to the establishment of pure Christian communism after a few years in one branch of the Anabaptist movement in Austria and Moravia, that known as "Hutterian Brethren."

Conrad Grebel sought after reality in the spiritual life, a reality that was far removed from any mere externalism or legalism. He sought to generate and maintain a deep inner spiritual life through a living faith in Christ and a personal union with Him. He earnestly sought to make this inner spiritual life effective in the daily experience of the Christian believer, in trust in God for daily needs, in love toward the brethren, in separation from sin and the world, and in the life of holiness. He held that alone through incorporation with Christ and the brethren can the individual receive the strength necessary to live the Word of God, to conquer sin, and to maintain love. But by this strength, he and his martyr followers believed absolutely that the individual believer and the church as a whole would be able to bear victoriously "the baptism of temptation and testing," of persecution, suffering, and death, and "pass triumphantly through the testing by fire into the homeland of eternal rest" (quotations from the Müntzer letter).

The most characteristic feature of Anabaptism, following inevitably from its concept of discipleship, was its insistence upon a new church of truly committed and practicing believers in contradistinction to the prevailing concept of the *Volkskirche* or inclusive church of the Reformation and subsequent periods held by Catholics and Protestants (Lutheran and Zwinglian) alike and maintained by the powerful patronage of the state, and to which, by birth and infant baptism, the entire population belonged. It was in the months between October 1523 and January 1525 that the battle between the two diametrically opposing views was fought out in the very heart of the Swiss Reformation. Zwingli, as Professor von Muralt has said, deliberately rejected the Swiss Brethren call for a church of true believers only and established "a church in which all professing Christians, the nominal, lukewarm, and indifferent ones as well as the really live and active Christians are kept together, a church to which the entire population belongs and which is not the church of genuine believers but only an imperfect human institution" (L. von Muralt, "Zwingli als Sozialpolitiker," *Zwingliana* V, 1931, 280). Luther and Calvin made the same basic decision, as did the leaders of the English Reformation, thereby establishing the "Volkskirche" as the official and general pattern for the whole of Protestantism. Only the Swiss Brethren (1525 on) and Dutch Mennonites (1533 on) at this crossroads of Christian history took the road of the free church of committed Christians, thus becoming the fourth major Reformation type.

Grebel's Personal Significance. What personal significance has Conrad Grebel for the historic movement which he founded? The answer is chiefly that he made possible the initial and basic breakthrough. While it is true that during the troubled third decade of the 16th century others longed for and attempted the restitution of the New Testament *ecclesia;* that attempt became successful only under Grebel's leadership in Zürich. Historically the case is clear. The Swiss Brethren movement did begin in Zürich, and it did spread from there throughout Central and West Europe. It began in Zürich not only because Conrad Grebel and his associates clearly envisaged a voluntary Christian fellowship, a "gathered" free church of believers only, committed in earnest loyalty and holy discipleship to follow Christ under the cross and by His way of love, but because Grebel had the courage to make an unreserved personal commitment to this ideal regardless of consequences. To this commitment he held unflinchingly in the crucial moment when, in bitter determination to annihilate their ideas forever, all the power of church and state thundered down upon him and his small band of followers. Once the great and irrevocable step was taken, other faithful and noble spirits, including ultimately thousands of martyrs, followed in Grebel's train; but Conrad Grebel was the first Anabaptist. He performed the first adult baptism in Zürich in January 1525. He was the first to clearly mark the road away from Luther's and Zwingli's mass church into the free church of voluntary commitment, brotherhood, and full evangelical discipleship, of separation of church and state, and of freedom of conscience. Where others shrank from adoption of the full New Testament ideal because of fear that it could not be carried through in practice, as for instance Luther, Grebel acted. He chose to follow the vision without calculation of possibilities or practicalities, believing that the truth commands, it does not merely advise. For him the kingdom of God is to be built here and now in the fellowship of believers, in the beloved community of the disciples of Christ. This conviction was the sole ground for the existence of the Swiss Brethren brotherhood and later related groups. Unlike the other reformers, Grebel's is not a sharply delineated figure because of the brevity of his career, but his basic view of the essence of Christianity and the nature of the church is clear, and his place in church history is secure.

That Grebel and his Swiss Brethren derived their faith solely and directly from the New Testament without any apparent literary or personal antecedents is one of the most striking things about the new movement. Every attempt to trace connections to earlier sources has failed, whether to the Waldensians or the Hussites as Ludwig Keller believed, or to the Franciscan Tertiaries as Albrecht Ritschl suggested. The Anabaptists were Biblicists and it was from the Biblical fountains that they drank. Having taken altogether seriously the *sola scriptura* of the Reformation, they were able to break more completely with the ecclesiastical and sociological forms of the Middle Ages and thus to return to the original ideas of the New Testament. In this spirit Grebel's followers once cried out, "You have Zwingli's word, but we want God's Word" (*Habend ir Zwingli's, wir wellend Gotts wort haben*).

In Conrad Grebel then, the young Zürich patrician humanist turned evangelical under Zwingli's preaching, and become first century Christian as a result of his own devout reading of the New Testament, we have not only the founder of the Swiss Brethren movement and the later Mennonite Church, but also one of the prophetic spirits of Christendom in its great and insistent tradition of reform and revival.   H.S.B.

H. S. Bender, *Conrad Grebel ca. 1498-1526, The Founder of the Swiss Brethren Sometimes Called Anabaptists* (Goshen, 1950), as Vol. I of *The Life and Letters of Conrad Grebel* by Harold S. Bender, Ernst Correll, and Edward Yoder, of which Vol. II, *The Letters of Conrad*

Grebel is still in preparation. (Since a complete Grebel bibliography is found in the above, only certain items will be listed further here.) H. S. Bender, "Conrad Grebel, The Founder of Swiss Anabaptism," *Church History* VII (1938) 157-78; *idem,* "Die Zwickauer Propheten, Thomas Müntzer und die Täufer," *Theologische Ztscht* VIII (1952) 262-78; Walter Schmid, "Der Autor der sogenannten Protestation und Schutzschrift von 1524/25," *Zwingliana* IX (1950) 139-49, which seems to prove that the December 1524 *Protestation* was not written by Grebel as W. Köhler and the editors of *Zwingli Werke* III, 368 ff., where it was published, assume, but probably by Felix Manz; L. von Muralt und Walter Schmid, *Quellen zur Geschichte der Täufer in der Schweiz* (Zürich, 1952); G. Meyer von Knonau, "Konrad Grebel," *ADB* IX (1879) 619-22; C. Keller-Escher, *Die Familie Grebel* (Zürich, 1884) and *Nachtrag* (1887); Max Staub, *Die Beziehungen des Täufers Konrad Grebel zu seinem Schwager Vadian* (Zürich, 1895); E. Arbenz and H. Wartmann, *Die Vadianische Briefsammlung der Stadtbibliothek St. Gallen* I-VII (St. Gall, 1888-1913); Chr. Neff, "Conrad Grebel, Sein Leben und Wirken" in *Gedenkschrift zum 400-jährigen Jubiläum der Mennoniten oder Taufgesinnten* (Ludwigshafen, 1925) 65-133; *idem,* article "Konrad Grebel," *ML* II, 163-99 (appeared in 1928); W. Koehler, "Konrad Grebel" in *RGG* II (1928) col. 1435; J. Ninck, "Konrad Grebel" in *Arzt und Reformator Vadian* (St. Gall, 1937) 109-19; L. von Muralt, "Konrad Grebel als Student in Paris," *Zürcher Taschenbuch auf das Jahr 1937* (Zürich) 113-36; W. Köhler, "Der Verfasser des Libellus Confutationis (Konrad Grebel)," *Menn. Geschichtsblätter* III (1938); Hans Wirz, "Der Ratsherr Jakob Grebel und seine Stiefbrüder Wirz, sein Sohn Konrad Grebel und sein Schwiegersohn Vadian," "Der Zwiespalt im Hause Grebel, die Anfänger der Kampfes zwischen Volkskirche und Täufertum," "Die Zuspitzung der Gegensätze 1525-27, der Untergang von Konrad und Jakob Grebel," *Zwingliana* VI (1936-38) 207-22, 470-86, 537-44; E. Yoder, "Nine Letters of Conrad Grebel, edited with a translation and notes," *MQR* II (1928) 229-59; E. Correll and H. S. Bender, "Conrad Grebel's Petition of Protest and Defence," *Goshen College Record Review Supplement* (September 1926, 33-37); E. Correll, H. S. Bender, and E. Yoder, "A Letter of Conrad Grebel to Zwingli September 8, 1517"; *ibid.,* 33-36, "A Letter of Conrad Grebel to Andreas Castelberger May 1525," *MQR* I (July 1927) 41-53; Ulrich Zwingli, *In Catabaptistarum Strophas Elenchus* (Zürich, 1527, copy in Goshen College Library), a modern reprint in *Huldreich Zwinglis Sämtliche Werke* VI (Leipzig, 1936) 1-196 and an English translation in S. M. Jackson, *Selected Works of Huldreich Zwingli* (Philadelphia, 1901) 123-258, under the title *Refutation of the Tricks of the Anabaptists.*

Grebel, Jakob (1460-1526), outstanding representative of an old patrician family of Zürich, father of Conrad Grebel (*q.v.*), the founder of Swiss Anabaptism. He was a prominent member of the Zürich city council, and a frequent ambassador for Zürich at the Swiss Confederation meetings. While he did not agree with his son, he also did not agree with Zwingli's harsh measures toward the Anabaptists and largely because of his opposition to Zwingli was executed at Zürich on Oct. 30, 1526, on the charge of having received illegal stipends from foreign rulers in 1520-22. H.S.B.

C. Keller-Escher, *Die Familie Grebel* (Frauenfeld, 1884); Hans Wirz, "Der Ratsherr Jakob Grebel und seine Stiefbrüder Wirz, sein Sohn Konrad Grebel und sein Schwiegersohn Vadian," *Zwingliana* VI (1936) 207-22; *idem,* "Der Zwiespalt im Hause Grebel," *Zwingliana* VI (1938) 470-86; *idem,* "Die Zuspitzung der Gegensätze 1525-1527. Der Untergang von Konrad und Jakob Grebel," *Zwingliana* VI (1938) 486-99, 537-44; H. S. Bender, *Conrad Grebel* (Goshen, 1950); *ML* II, 162 f.

Gredig, Valentin, of Savoy, one of the members of the early Swiss Brethren congregation in Zürich, was imprisoned on Feb. 8, 1525, with eight other Anabaptists and released on bail of 1,000 guilders. Soon afterward he was again in prison. In his cross-examination on March 16, 1525, he stated that he had been moved to accept baptism only on the basis of the simple Word of God, which clearly says, "Go ye to all peoples, teach and baptize"; but as to attacking the government, or advocating that it be removed, such an idea had never entered his mind, for he well knew that there must be a government. In reply to the question whether a Christian might bear the sword, he said he would leave it to God, and did not want to interfere with His power. Giving tithes and taxes, he considered right. The baptism instituted by the Almighty he held to be the true baptism; but since his arrest he had baptized nobody. In August 1525 he was arrested the third time, and confessed that he had baptized his wife upon her request. Nothing more is known of him.

NEFF.

Emil Egli, *Actensammlung zur Geschichte der Züricher Reformation* (Zürich, 1879) Nos. 636 f., 674 f., 795; L. Keller, *Die Reformation und die älteren Reformparteien* (Leipzig, 1885) 398; *ML* II, 169.

Greece: see **Thessalonica.**

Green Cross, a Dutch organization for the promotion of hygiene and health in the home: see **Groene Kruis.**

Greendale Mennonite Brethren Church, better known as the Sardis M.B. Church, located at the corner of South Sumas and Sumas Prairie Roads at Sardis, B.C., a member of the M.B. Conference of Canada, was organized in January 1931 with a rather small membership under the leadership of H. G. Dueck. The first meetinghouse, a frame structure with a seating capacity of 250, was erected in 1932 and enlarged in 1940 to seat 600. During the flood in 1948 the church stood in ten feet of water; consequently for two months no meetings were held there. Since 1952 the congregation has had a salaried pastor, H. D. Unger, with H. G. Dueck and Jacob Harder assisting. The membership in 1954 was 345.

J.F.R.

Greenfarm Mennonite Brethren Church, located at Greenfarm, originally Bergfeld, near Herbert, Sask., organized in 1913 under the initiative of J. W. Thiessen, belongs to the Herbert District Conference. During the first years the church services were held in the public school. In 1917 a revival took place and 20 members were added to the church. The following year a church building was erected. J. W. Thiessen was succeeded by Johann Thiessen and Isaac P. Penner. Active workers in 1953 were Johann Thiessen, J. J. Thiessen, and George Penner, leader. The 1953 membership was 56. (*ML* II, 169.) J.I.R.

Greenfield Mennonite (GCM) Church, 13 miles southeast of Carnegie, Okla., was founded Jan. 31, 1914, when a meetinghouse was built, the group having been served for 12 years previously by ministers from the Gotebo congregation. A. W. Froese, the first resident pastor, began his service Feb. 15, 1915. In 1926 the membership was 67 with Froese still serving; in 1955 it was 89 with J. B. Krause as pastor. The congregation belongs to the Western District Conference. (*ML* II, 192.)   DE.N.

Greenland Church of God in Christ Mennonite Church is located five miles southwest of Ste. Anne, Man. The first members moved into the district in 1880, assembling in homes for worship services. The first meetinghouse was built in 1896, and later enlarged; the second was built in 1920, and the third in 1947, which seats 1,100. Martin Penner was the first minister, serving from 1891 until his death in 1928. In 1905 Isaac Penner was ordained as minister, but he with a number of members moved to British Columbia in 1912. Jacob T. Wiebe, a deacon, was chosen for the ministry in 1910 and was the presiding minister 1917-43. John M. Penner, ordained in 1931, has been the leading minister since 1943. The services, formerly held in the German, are now conducted in both the German and English languages. The church had a membership of 285 in 1953. The sewing circle was started in 1935. Young people's meetings are held twice weekly during the winter season. Ministers from this congregation have been holding services at Ste. Anne, Prairie Rose, and Winnipeg for several years.   J.M.P.

Greensburg, Kan., is the county seat of Kiowa County, in the south central part of the state, with a population of 1,724 (1952). It is populated largely by retired farmers and small town businesses. In recent years it has also become quite an industrial city with four large gas pumping stations located near town.

There are three branches of Mennonites in the county, C.G.C.M., M.C., and G.C.M., all located south of Greensburg. The Mennonites have been here since 1908 and numbered approximately 186 in 1952. Only about 45 of this group live in town, most of them employed at the Kiowa County Memorial Hospital, which is the only Mennonite institution in the county. This is a 24-bed general hospital operated by the Mennonite Board of Missions and Charities (MC).   S.J.

Greenwood Conservative Mennonite Church, which is located in Nanticoke Hundred, Sussex Co., near Greenwood, Del., and is a member of the Conservative Mennonite Conference, was organized in 1914 with about eleven charter members. The membership in 1954 was 251, with Eli Swartzentruber and Alvin Mast as ministers, and Nevin Bender as bishop. The first church building was dedicated on July 4, 1920. This was replaced by a larger brick building, which was dedicated on Dec. 14, 1947. The first church building is being used for a junior high school operated by the congregation, which has also had its own Christian day school since 1928.   N.F.B.

Greenwood Mennonite School, located at Greenwood, Del., which is operated by the Conservative Mennonite Church, had its beginning in February 1928. The first 4½ years the school was held in the basement of the church, and then in the fall of 1932 a school building was built. In 1943 the board hired a second teacher, and since that time two years of high school have been offered, and for several years three years of high school. Since 1950 three teachers have been employed, with an approximate enrollment of 70 to 80 pupils in grades one to ten, most of them children of members of the congregation.

In 1953 a committee was appointed to study an expansion program and a possible four-year high school. It is the conviction of the brotherhood that this church-owned and operated school has made a profound contribution toward the spiritual life and growth of the church.

The Greenwood Conservative Mennonite Church has grown to have a resident membership of 230. Approximately 90 per cent of her children of school age attend the church day school.   L.L.S.

Greif, Hans, an Anabaptist emissary, was a beltmaker and citizen of Salzburg, Austria. He was baptized by Leonhard Schiemer (*q.v.*), and sent out by Hans Hut in 1527 to preach the Gospel. But he was soon captured by the Salzburg authorities. His fate is not known. The frequent and sometimes sharpened mandates of the Archbishop of Salzburg against the Anabaptists lead to the surmise that he died a martyr.   HEGE.

"Zur Geschichte der Wiedertäufer in Oberösterreich und speziell in Freistadt," in 47. *Bericht über das Museum Francisco-Carolinum* (Linz, 1889); *ML* II, 170.

Greiff, Cornelius de. On the east wall of Crefeld there has stood since Aug. 22, 1865, a simple monument: a commemorative column in classic form on a square base with bronze bas-reliefs of the goddess of benevolence, an allegory of the city of Crefeld, the coat-of-arms, and the inscription, "In memory of its benefactor, Mr. Cornelius de Greiff, born June 8, 1781, died April 16, 1863, by the grateful native city."

The man thus celebrated was simple, as is suggested by the cap on his head and the stately umbrella under his arm. The contribution he made to the city in unwavering benevolence and the unostentatious generosity of his deeply religious nature is shown by his will of Feb. 25, 1857, which left for benevolent purposes and for the common good a sum hitherto unheard of in Germany: 466,000 talers; i.e., 120,000 talers for the hospital "founded by my mother"; 100,000 talers for a home for needy men and women over 65 years of age; 50,000 talers each for the Catholic and the Protestant orphanages; 50,000 talers for the care of the mentally ill, the blind, and the deaf; 50,000 talers for the support of 50 poor but deserving families having many children to support; 12,000 talers for another mortuary and the beautification of the new cemetery; 26,000 talers to erect a civic building. "I add, as a conclusion to what I have here signed: *An Gottes Segen ist alles gelegen.* May this blessing of the Father not be lacking for the goals striven after, and may much good proceed from them."

The significance of this bequest for a city of 52,700 needs no comment. But it was even surpassed when the niece and heiress of Cornelius de

Greiff, Mrs. Marianne Rhodius (*q.v.*), nee de Greiff, found her sole object in life in serving the needy and suffering. In her will, read on Nov. 2, 1902, she supplemented her uncle's bequest with a legacy of 1,800,000 marks, calling the fund "the Cornelius de Greiff Support Fund."

The grandfather (Johann Philipp) of Cornelius de Greiff acquired citizenship in Crefeld in 1744; his father, Isaac de Greiff (1754-1826), married Anna Floh in 1780, and entered his father-in-law's business (Cornelius and Johannes Floh). As part owner of this important velvet mill he acquired a substantial fortune.

Since Cornelius de Greiff remained unmarried and his only brother, Johann Philipp (1786-1862, married to Marianne ter Meer), preceded him in death, he made his niece Marianne Rhodius, the daughter of his brother, his sole heir; she managed the estates carefully in the intention of her grandmother, nee Floh, as well as her aunt Marianne Jordans, nee Floh. (*Menn. Bl.*, 1888, 124; 1904, 23; *ML* II, 170.)   K.R.

Greiker, Hans, of Heppenheim near Worms, Germany, a participant in the disputation at Frankenthal (*q.v.*). Nothing more is known of him. (*ML* II, 171.)

Grein, a district in Upper Austria, in which there were numerous Anabaptist congregations shortly after 1530. (Wolkan, *Lieder*, 24.)   vDZ.

Greiner, Blasius, the ancestor of the extensive Mennonite family of the Greiners, and his brother Andreas, who was the master of the glassworks at Walkersbach in Württemberg, Germany, which was a church subsidiary of Oberurbach owned by O. A. Schorndorf, were won to the Anabaptist cause in 1562 by the preaching of a leader in the woods at Oberurbach, who preached at night to ten or twelve persons from a pulpit-like stone; after the sermon they fell on their faces, wrung their hands, and finally said, "The Lord be praised." Blasius Greiner greatly influenced not only his family, but also the Oberurbach community, which contained so many Anabaptists that a general inspection lasting months was conducted here in 1598, in which first individuals, and then when the process was taking too long and getting too expensive, families were examined. The Greiner brothers had razed the chapel in Walkersbach, so that about 1548 the pastor of Oberurbach had to hold his weekly Monday services in the homes.

In March 1567 Blasius Greiner was arrested and taken to the prison in Maulbronn, where he was induced to recant in May 1569. His recantation was adopted in 1571 as the model for all Anabaptists. After he had been released he returned to his early convictions, married again, and moved away, and died not later than 1571. In Maulbronn he had violent arguments with the Hutterian Brethren, who accused the Swiss Brethren of disorderly conduct. The Hutterite's name was Jogl; his family name is not known nor is that of his companion. By disorderly conduct they meant a noncommunal life. Blasius' sons were Anabaptists and Schwenck-

feldians; they attended the preaching in the state church, but read Schwenckfeld's books during the sermon. They, however, concealed Anabaptist preachers, such as Bastlin Weber, Veit Gilg, and Hans Büchel (*q.v.*).

An Ulrich Greiner who appeared in the Mainhardt Forest in 1523 called himself a glazier from Schleusingen (Thuringia). He was presumably related to Blasius. Another relative, Jakob, master glazier of Lautertal (Neulautern) under Duke Albrecht of Löwenstein, whose children were forcibly baptized in Löwenstein in 1586, had to leave the vicinity. He perhaps went to Lauscha, Sonneberg area of Meiningen. In 1525 Hans Greiner had established a glassworks in Langenbach near Schleusingen with Swabian glaziers, the beginning of the still thriving Lauscha glass industry. From there it was taken by the Greiners to Bohemia; the Protestants among them were expelled from Bohemia after the battle of the White Mountain, and moved into the margravure of Brandenburg-Ansbach. From them descended the mother of the famed church historian Albert Hauck. The Greiners remaining in Bohemia have become Catholics.
                                                        G.Bo.

Karl Greiner, "Beiträge zur Geschichte der Glasindustrie in Württemberg," *Württemb. Vierteljahrshefte*, n.s. 34 (1928) 70-99; *Schwäbischer Mercur*, Aug. 6, 1920, No. 359; Bossert, *TA* I: *Württemberg; ML* II, 171.

Grellet, Stephen, b. 1773 at Limoges, France, a son of Grellet du Madillier, d. 1855 in Philadelphia. Driven from France by the Revolution, and having lived an eventful life, he joined the Quakers in Philadelphia in 1796, undertook long preaching missions through the United States, and in 1808 visited France. In 1811 he made a second journey to Europe, reaching Munich, where he had a remarkable meeting with King Max I and his son Louis. In Neuwied he visited the Mennonites. More important is his visit with the Russian Mennonites on his third journey to Europe in 1818. On May 23 he arrived at the Mennonite settlement at Chortitz on the Dniepr with Contenius, the chairman of the *Fürsorgekomitee*. Then he went to the Molotschna settlement, where "they have a great cloth mill." Grellet describes the Mennonites in Russia very favorably in his autobiography.

When at the end of May he returned to the Mennonites after a visit to the Dukhobors (*q.v.*) and held meetings with them he wrote enthusiastically, "Oh, what a difference in our feeling when we are with these people from when we were with the Dukhobors! There darkness surrounded us, but here there is light as in Goshen. The presence of the Lord was over us; the Gospel stream of life and salvation flowed freely over the difference in circumstances!"   NEFF.

A. C. Garrett, "Stephen Grellet," *Quaker Biographies* IV (Philadelphia, 1916) 131-256; *Menn. Bl.*, 1879, 21 ff., 68; B. Seebohm (ed.), *Memoirs of the Life and Gospel Labours of Stephen Grellet* (Leiden, 1860); *ML* II, 171.

Gremser, Hansel, an Anabaptist of whom nothing has been handed down except his confession. He was won to the Anabaptists by Jakob Hutter at Vilnöss, Tirol, in 1531. When the Anabaptist persecutions in Tirol were at their height, he was seized and tried. His statements are found in his confession of July 1, 1533. It is located in the episcopal archives at Brixen, Tirol. He admits having been baptized by Jakob Hutter. Twice he has received communion in the manner of the Anabaptists, the first time in Moravia, the second in Vilnöss. The Brethren take communion as a memorial of Christ, but they do not believe that it contains the true body and blood of Christ. They reject the Mass. . . . The mother of Jesus was a virgin both before and after His birth; they hold her in high esteem, though they know no worship of saints. The images in the church they consider idols; he has himself broken one since becoming an Anabaptist. They reject the oral confessional; sins must be confessed to the entire brotherhood. For his part he would not object to confessing to pious priests. The Anabaptists recognize each other in case of question with the words, "I do Christian works." Their greeting is, "The peace of God be with you." They carry no weapons. All things should be in common. They do not reject the government if it supports the good and punishes the bad. Concerning Gremser's fate nothing is known. LOSERTH.

J. Loserth, *Der Anabaptismus in Tirol* I (Vienna, 1892) 517; *ML* II, 171 f.

Gresbeck, Heinrich, a citizen of Münster (Westphalia), a cabinetmaker by trade, had lived outside the city 1530-34, partly as a mercenary, but then returned to the city on Feb. 27, and was baptized on that day. For 15 months he shared the joys and sorrows of the Münster group. He played a subordinate role. During the night of May 23, 1535, he abandoned his post as guard at the Kreuztor and fled. He was seized. Out of pity for his youth his life was spared. In prison he sketched a plan of the fortifications of the city and showed the spot where he had been guard and where the wall could be easily scaled to enter the city. The place he designated was secretly examined, and his assertions were found to be correct. On this basis the attack was planned and executed on the night of June 24. Gresbeck made an essential contribution to the success of this attack. Of particular importance for the history of the Münster revolt is his *Bericht von der Wiedertaufe in Münster.* This manuscript C. A. Cornelius (*q.v.*) published verbatim in his book, *Die Geschichtsquellen des Bistums Münster* II (Münster, 1853) 1-214. (*ML* II, 172.) NEFF.

Gretna, a village in the Red River Valley of southern Manitoba, two miles from the U.S. (N. Dak.) border, with a population of 608, about one third of which are Mennonites belonging chiefly to two congregations of the General Conference Mennonites, either the Blumenort congregation (largely 1922-25 Russian immigrants) or the local unit of the Bergthal congregation (largely 1874-75 Russian immigrants). The entire surrounding area is peopled largely by Mennonites of the 1922-25 immigration who replaced the older Sommerfeld Mennonites who had emigrated to Mexico and Paraguay. Gretna is the seat of the oldest Mennonite school in North America, the Mennonite Collegiate Institute (*q.v.*), founded by H. H. Ewert in 1891. The Altenheim (*q.v.,* Home for Aged) of the Bergthal Church, which was operated here 1918-38, is now a girls' dormitory of the school. (*ML* II, 172.)

H.S.B.

Greuel, Hans, the head of the Anabaptists of Augsburg (*q.v.*), Bavaria, Germany, who took a special interest in his brethren who fled to Augsburg. He was a native of Geltendorf (Bavaria). Among those he baptized were Anna, wife of Thomas Melchinger, who was seized in the Easter meeting at Augsburg in 1528, also the widow Else Knollin in Augsburg about Christmas 1527, and soon afterward in Mindelheim the cobbler Jakob Walch with three other persons, who were for that reason seized by the council of Augsburg. Greuel, who was also being sought by the council, left Augsburg late in the summer of 1528. Nothing more is heard of him. HEGE.

Fr. Roth, *Augsburgs Ref.-Gesch.* (Munich, 1901) 243 and 254; *idem,* "Zur Gesch. der Wiedertäufer in Oberschwaben," in *Ztscht des Hist. Vereins für Schwaben und Neuburg* XXVIII (1901) 7, 37, 84, 125, and 128; *ML* II, 173.

Greuwel der vornahmsten Haupt-Ketzeren, *So wohl Wiedertauffer, als auch andern* (Leiden, 1608), is a translation of a Latin work published in the same year: *Apocalypsis insignium aliquot Haeresiarchium,* by an unknown author who is indicated by the letters "H.S.F.D.M.D." Besides the Latin and German versions, there are also three Dutch editions of this book: *De voornaemste Hooft-Ketteren, Die haer in dese tijden so in Duytslant als oock in dese Nederlanden opgeworpen hebben* (Leiden, 1608); *Grouwelen der voornaemster Hooft-Ketteren* (Leiden, 1623); and a reprint of the latter under the same title (n.p., n.d.). With the exception of this last version, all four editions differ from the original. The Dutch edition of 1623 contains a chapter on Obbe Philips, and in an appendix some information on Menno Simons, Dirk Philips, and their followers. For Mennonite history this book is of no value, but the 17 engravings by Christoffel van Sichem (*q.v.*) which these books contain (the first Dutch edition has only 9) are valuable. Among these engravings there are portraits of Thomas Müntzer, Balthasar Hubmaier, Hans Hut, Ludwig Haetzer, Melchior Rinck, Melchior Hofmann, Jan Matthijsz van Haarlem, Jan Beukelsz (van Leyden), David Joris, and Adam Pastor. Menno Simons and Obbe Philips are not represented. The portraits of course have no guarantee of historical verisimilitude, since they were all made many years after the death of the subjects, and of all but one there were no contemporary representations. VDZ.

Grevinckhoven, Caspar (1550-1606), b. at Dortmund, Germany, a Reformed preacher at Zaltbommel, Dutch province of Gelderland, in 1573, after 1579 in Rotterdam, where he died. He wrote a violent polemic against the Anabaptists: *Grondelijke bericht van den Doop ende Wederdoope* (1599), which contains some important information on Hans de Ries. The assertion that in his old age he became a Mennonite (as stated in *DB* 1908, 27) is an error. (*Biogr. Wb.* III, 336-38; *ML* II, 173.)

K.V., vDZ.

Greyenburger, Veit, the name used in van Braght's *Martyrs' Mirror* for Veit-Grünberger, a Hutterite missionary, who was arrested in Austria in 1570. (See **Grünberger, Veit.**)

Greystone Park (N.J.) CPS Unit No. 77, under MCC direction, established Jan. 19, 1943, and closed August 1946, was attached to the New Jersey State Mental Hospital at Greystone Park, N.J., 40 miles west of New York City. With 5,000 patients it was one of the largest mental hospitals in the country. Leaders of the unit were Lawrence Burkholder, Melvin Funk, Wilton Hartzler, and Harold W. Griest. In July 1945 one hundred CPS men were working here.

H.S.B.

M. Gingerich, *Service for Peace* (Akron, 1949).

Gries, Anthony de, a preacher in the Dompelaar congregation in Hamburg-Altona. Beginning in 1661 he argued orally and in writing with Bastiaan van Weenighem, the Mennonite preacher at Rotterdam, but in vain. He also added an appendix to the attack of his friend Johann Arent, *Eindelycke verklaringe* (1668) against Bastiaan van Weenighem (*q.v.*). The gradual decline of the Hamburg Dompelaars seems to have led him to return to his native Holland, where he died in 1696. (*ML* II, 173.)

R.Do.

Griesbach (not Grichsbach) is mentioned in Wolkan's *Geschicht-Buch* (p. 182) as the place in Styria, Austria, where five Anabaptists gave their lives for the faith. But there is no place with this name in Styria. Beck has correctly placed Griesbach in Bavaria near Passau in his *Geschichts-Bücher*. It is a market village in the government district of Wegscheid, four and one-half hours from Passau and three hours from Wegscheid, situated on a hill which rises from the Danube Valley. Two of the five Anabaptists executed here, Hans Pranthüber, a preacher, and his wife, are named in Codex Kremser (N), dated 1581, now in the library of the Pressburg Domkapitel. (Beck, *Geschichts-Bücher*, 278, note 3; Zieglschmid, *Chronik* 233; *ML* II, 173.)

LOSERTH.

Griesbacher, Wilhelm, of Kitzbühel, Austria. Like many other Anabaptist martyrs, little is known of him beyond his martyrdom and a letter that he sent from prison to the brotherhood by his companion, Hans Donner (*q.v.*) of Wels. Griesbacher, a *Diener der Notdurft*, was seized at Schäkowitz with several of his brethren during the height of the persecution (1536) when Hutter was being sought, and was taken to Brno, Moravia. Here he was cross-examined on the following points: (1) Why did they accept this treacherous faith that was tolerated nowhere? (2) Whether they had an agreement with other sects from whom they received help on occasion (the consequences of the Münster revolt are evident here); (3) Why they would have nothing to do with government; and

(4) Why they attacked the king so rudely in Hutter's reply to the governor. The report of the authorities was followed by a command to try the prisoners on the rack, and if they were obstinate, to use the mandates against them moderately. Only one of them (named Loy) renounced his faith. Griesbacher sent the brotherhood the letter mentioned above, in which he admonished them to pray for the backslider. At the trial under torture Griesbacher was also asked how the exiles fared financially. He replied that they had not left home and land and come to this country for the sake of money, but for the sake of their faith. Griesbacher was sentenced to die at the stake and was burned in Brno.

LOSERTH.

The letter mentioned above is in a manuscript of the Pressburg Domkapitel, and extracts of it are printed in Beck, *Geschichtsbücher*, 119; Wolkan, *Geschicht-Buch*, 77, 78, 115; *ML* II, 173.

Griesinger (Griesstätter), **Onophrius** (Offrus), a Hutterite martyr. Until the death of Jakob Hutter (1536) Tirol was the center of the Anabaptist movement in Austria. This ended now; opposition had become too strong in Austria. Now Moravia became the country from which year after year missionaries were sent out: to Poland and Hungary, into the provinces of Germany, and also to Tirol, where they tried to support their old adherents and win new ones. Not until the "golden age for the brotherhood in Moravia" dawned, did their effort to establish churches in Tirol slacken, for then as many adherents as possible came "down" to Moravia. Hutter's place was taken by Jeronymus Käls and after his imprisonment by Leonhard Seiler. When Seiler also fell into the hands of the executioners the brotherhood in Tirol looked to Onophrius Griesinger, who was then in Moravia, and who had proved his character as an apostle of Anabaptism; he accepted the call.

Griesinger was a native of Frassdorf in Bavaria and before his entry into the Hutterite brotherhood in 1532 had been clerk of a mine in the archbishopric of Salzburg. When he came to Tirol in 1533 he stayed in Weissenbach in the Sarn Valley, and sometimes in the Inn and Puster valleys, where he won many converts and sent them to Moravia.

Soon after being ordained he was captured and taken to Hopfgarten, but managed to make his escape. The government sent out several warrants against him. The warrant of June 8, 1533, describes him thus: "Onoffrus Griesstätter is of medium height, has no beard, wears a rough woolen coat, white trousers, and brown cloth hose. He baptized a considerable number of persons here in Tirol." The warrant of Oct. 8, 1533, describes him thus: "He is wearing a brown tunic . . . and black trousers, and is said to be wandering about in Prixlegg." For his capture a reward of about 100 guilders is offered and the authorities of Sterzing, Gufidaun, Rodeneck, Kitzbühel, St. Petersburg, Ritten, and Linz are required to engage spies to seize him.

But Griesinger eluded his pursuers. At Christmas 1533 he even ventured to hold a large meeting in the Hagau near Rattenberg. He withdrew to Moravia, taking a group (*Völklein*) with him from Rattenberg, and settled in Auspitz with them. Hutter wrote to the prisoners at Hohenwarth, "Brother Offrus has also come with many other brethren and sisters. The Lord led them marvelously. Not many are left in Tirol." After Hutter's death Griesinger continued Hutter's work and took his place at first in the Puster Valley. Amon writes about it to the prisoners in Mödling, "Offrus has come up and many are becoming Christians." During the Easter week of 1536, Christoph Ochs of St. Michaelsburg and Ulrich Gerlinger undertook an examination of the woods on Schönegg and came upon Griesinger with a number of other Anabaptists; but they escaped "because the authorities were not well enough prepared."

But now sharper measures were taken against Griesinger, and searches were instituted on Lüsen and at Greifenstein, as well as around the pass at Thurn. Amon writes to the brotherhood at Böhmisch-Kromau about this time and these conditions, "God the Lord still works daily, also in the upper country, whither our dear Brother Offrus has withdrawn through the will of God; there are many zealous people there, as Jörg (Walpot) can tell you; he can also tell you how Offrus fared in going up." The combined efforts of his enemies finally succeeded in April 1537 in seizing Griesinger with a small group of Anabaptists and taking him to Bozen. But he managed his escape again. The authorities, angry, now offered a reward of 80 guilders for his capture alive, and 40 dead. His escape evoked great joy among the brotherhood in Moravia.

But Griesinger worked on unswervingly near Imst, in the Pitz and Etz valleys and beyond the Brenner. Moving up and down the mountains he preached and baptized; he even visited prisoners, and in the summer of 1538 he observed a three-day communion service with 72 persons. But finally his decisive hour struck too. Betrayed by spies, he was seized during the night of Aug. 29 in a hut of the jurisdiction of Schöneck and taken bound to Brixen. The authorities were warned to watch him with special care, and examine him kindly and on the rack to find out who else belonged "to their sect," and whether they were planning a new revolt. The court was pleased with Griesinger's capture. Ferdinand I kept himself informed on the course of the trial.

With Griesinger, Lienhart Lochmaier's (q.v.) case also came to an end. The former was executed on Oct. 31, 1538, between ten and, eleven o'clock.

Five letters written by Griesinger, the last three in prison, have been preserved. All of them are addressed to the "Gemain Gottes" in Moravia. He also wrote a letter from prison in Lochmaier's name to Bärbel, the latter's wife in Moravia. Griesinger wrote six hymns, all of which except "Loben wöllen wir den höchsten Gott" have been published in *Die Lieder der Hutterischen Brüder* (Scottdale, 1914) 77-82: (1) "Merkt auf, ihr Kinder Gottes rein" (7 stanzas); (2) "Loben wöllen wir den höchsten Gott" (14 stanzas); (3) "O Herre Gott im Himmelsthron" (4 stanzas); (4) "O Vater im Himmelreich sieh darein" (9 stanzas); (5) "O

Gott, erhör mein Klagen" (8 stanzas); (6) "Merk auf, merk auf, o frommer Christ" (11 stanzas).

LOSERTH.

Beck, *Geschichtsbücher*; J. Loserth, *Der Anabaptismus in Tirol* II (Vienna, 1892); *Mart. Mir.* D 43, E 448, where he is called Greizinger; *ML* II, 174 f.

Griet, the wife of Rein Edes, was a sister of Geertruydt (q.v.), the wife of Menno Simons. She had been (re)baptized at Witmarsum, Dutch province of Friesland, by Douwe Schoenmaker (q.v.). Afterwards she became doubtful of the validity of the baptism by a Münsterite (q.v.) and asked Menno Simons to rebaptize her. Menno Simons refused to administer this baptism, as did also Leenaert Bouwens. Menno wrote a letter to his sister-in-law (about 1557), which is found in his collected works (*Opera Omnia*, Dutch ed. Amsterdam, 434; English ed., *Complete Works* II, Elkhart, 1871, 401 f.).

vDZ.

Doopsgezinde Lectuur 1858, 78 ff.; K. Vos, *Menno Simons* (Leiden, 1914) 434.

Griet Jacobs, an Anabaptist martyr, executed at Alkmaar, Dutch province of North Holland, on April 16, 1540. She was a native of the Langendijk near Alkmaar and confessed to have received (re)-baptism. (*Inv. Arch. Amst.* I, No. 782; *DB* 1909, 24.)

vDZ.

Grietchen Bildesnider, wife of Aert, an Anabaptist martyr, burned to death Sept. 8 or 9, 1534, on the Vrijthof at Maastricht, Dutch province of Limburg, together with Henrick Rol. With these martyrs the intensive persecution at Maastricht began, which almost exterminated the young, flourishing congregation.

vDZ.

W. Bax, *Het Protestantismus in het bisdom Luik en vooral te Maastricht* I (The Hague, 1937) 98 f., 124.

Griete and **Femme,** two daughters of Jan Gerroltsma, were executed on April 15, 1535, at Leeuwarden, Dutch province of Friesland, because they had been (re)baptized. Their father had been put to death on the previous day. Particulars are lacking. (K. Vos, *Menno Simons,* Leiden, 1914, 229.)

vDZ.

Griete Arentsdochter (Grietje Arents), an Anabaptist martyr, was banished from Holland for having been (re)baptized, returned, and was arrested at Amsterdam. In the records she is said to have been an old sick and dull woman, refusing to recant. On Dec. 21, 1534, she was sentenced to death by drowning because of heresy and disobedience to the public authorities. Griete was a native of Limmen near Alkmaar, Dutch province of North Holland, a center of ardent Anabaptism in 1533-40. (*Mart. Mir.* D 412, E 763; Grosheide, *Verhooren,* 41-43, 44-45; *ML* I, 81.)

vDZ.

Griete (Grietje, Margriet) **Fransdochter,** an Anabaptist martyr, sentenced on Feb. 17, 1541, at Alkmaar, Dutch province of North Holland, "to be punished to death for the heresy of rebaptism" and for not believing in the Holy Sacrament of the Mass. She had apparently been imprisoned for a long period. Her friends and relatives wrote a letter (May 20, 1540) to the Court of Holland in The

Hague, requesting that the sentence and the execution might be held in secret and not, as was usual, in public. This request was granted. The execution took place in May 1541. vdZ.

Inv. Arch. Amst. I, 748; DB 1909, 24; Mellink, Wederdopers, 173.

Griet(e) Pieter Mollendochter, an Anabaptist martyr, was drowned at Amsterdam on May 21 (van Braght, Mart. Mir., May 15), 1535, together with ten other women. She was a native of Amsterdam. She confessed that she had been (re)baptized by Jan Matthysz (q.v.) of Middelburg in the home of Trijn Jans de Bacxter at Amsterdam in November 1534. Griete said that she did not repent her baptism and died willingly. (Mart. Mir. D 413, E 764; Grosheide, Verhooren, 69, 70; ML III, 147.) vdZ.

Grietgen, an Anabaptist martyr, wife of the martyr Kaerle de Raedt (q.v.), was a Mennonite of Brugge, Belgium. On Ascension Day (May 4) 1570 a meeting of the congregation was held in the woods of Tillegem, near Brugge. This meeting was surprised by the police and a number of attendants were taken prisoner, including Kaerle. Grietgen managed to escape, but she was arrested with her two children on the same night by Maerten Lem, the burgomaster of Brugge. The children, who were young, apparently were taken to a cloister for education. Grietgen, who had not yet received baptism upon faith, was unwilling to recant. So she was sentenced to death for her "obstinacy." About May 20, 1570 (van Braght, Mart. Mir., erroneously 1568), she was burned at the stake at Brugge, with Christijntgen, arrested on the same night. Kaerle had been executed on May 18. (Mart. Mir. D 369, E 725 f.; Verheyden, Brugge, 62, No. 67.) vdZ.

Grietgen, an Anabaptist martyr, was burned at the stake at Belle (Bailleul) in Flanders in 1556 with her aunt Francijntgen (q.v.), and Maeyken Doornaerts (q.v.). In spite of the special efforts to convert her because of her youth, she remained steadfast to the end. (Mart. Mir. D 166, E 553; ML II, 175.) Neff, vdZ.

Grietgen (Grietje van Brussel), an Anabaptist martyr of Brussels, Belgium. Her official name was Margaretha Wynants, widow of Pieter Goossensz. She was burned at the stake at Antwerp on the evening of Pentecost, May 22, 1575, with three fellow believers, with tongue screws. They were put to death, as the sentence states, because they had been rebaptized and had attended Anabaptist meetings. The letters they wrote in prison were destroyed in the Spanish revolt at Antwerp on Nov. 4, 1576. vdZ.

Mart. Mir. D 693, E 1007; Antw. Arch.-Blad XIII, 193, 201; XIV, 96 f., No. 1084; ML II, 175.

Grietgen (Geertruydt), an Anabaptist martyr, wife of Anthonis van Houtere, of Weert, Dutch province of Limburg, was drowned in Antwerp, Belgium, on Dec. 31, 1558, together with Lynken Jacops, Stijntgen van Aken, and Tanneken van Cluyten.

She is listed in the song "Aenhoort Godt, hemelsche Vader" in the Liedtboecxken van den Offer des Heeren (No. 16, and No. 39). vdZ.

Offer, 506; Mart. Mir. D 202, E 583; Antw. Arch.-Blad VIII, 456, 466; XIV, 24 f., No. 276; ML II, 175.

Grietgen (Margriete van den Berghe) of Lier in Brabant, Belgium, an Anabaptist martyr, was seized with three fellow believers (Goris Cooman, Naentgen Bornaige, and Wouter van der Weyden) at Gent, Belgium, in 1555, whither they had all fled from Lier in Brabant. She had been baptized by Gillis den Dooper, presumably Gillis van Aken (q.v.). Because she steadfastly confessed her faith she was sentenced to death by fire, which she cheerfully endured. The death of these four martyrs is sung in a hymn of 24 stanzas, beginning "Doemen vijftienhondert schreve, daertoe een en vijftich jaer," found in Liedtboecxken van den Offer des Heeren, No. 4. vdZ.

Mart. Mir. D 106, E 503; Offer, 516; Verheyden, Gent, 13, No. 21; ML II, 175.

Grietgen Baets, an Anabaptist martyr, was arrested in Gent, Belgium, in 1569 with Christoffel Buyze, Laurens van Rentergem, and Joost Meerssenier. They paid for their joyful confession and steadfastness with their death, and are celebrated with a large number of martyrs of Gent in a song found in the Liedtboecxken van den Offer des Heeren, beginning "Alsmen schreef duyst vijfhondert Jaer, ende twee en tsestich mede." Grietgen is listed here as No. 38. Verheyden (Gent, 56) did not find this martyr in the sources at Gent. (Offer, 653; Mart. Mir. D 407, E 759; ML I, 110.) O.H., vdZ.

Grietgen Bonaventuers (Margriete van Halle, widow of Willem Eggertink), an Anabaptist martyr, was seized May 20, 1559, in Antwerp, Belgium. In the pursuit of an Anabaptist the bailiffs forced their way into homes where Grietgen and five other Anabaptist women were living. Not finding the man they sought, they imprisoned the women. Neither threats nor torture caused them to forsake their faith. They all died as martyrs. Grietgen Bonaventuers was drowned in Antwerp, Oct. 12, 1559, not beheaded as the Groot Offerboek of 1613 and also van Braght, Martyrs' Mirror erroneously assert (DB 1899, 107). In memory of Grietgen and the women who suffered martyrdom with her a song was written, which begins, "Babels raets mandamenten" (Een liedeken van ses vrouwen), and also in the song, "Aenhoort Godt, hemelsche Vader," both found in the Liedtboecxken van den Offer des Heeren (Nos. 16 and 19). O.H., vdZ.

Offer, 566, No. 55, 581-86; Mart. Mir. D. 249, E 623; Wolkan, Lieder, 63, 72; Antw. Arch.-Blad IX, 4, 9, 16; XIV, 26 f., No. 300; ML I, 245.

Grietgen Jans, an Anabaptist martyr, was the wife of Adriaen Heynsius, a weaver of Zwartewaal, Dutch province of South Holland. She was burned at the stake at Brielle (same province) on July 25, 1569, together with Maerten Pieters (q.v.). She was found guilty of heresy, "having united with those called Mennists" and having been rebaptized. (Mart. Mir. D 388, E 740; ML II, 391.) vdZ.

Grietgen van Sluys, an Anabaptist martyr according to van Braght (*Mart. Mir.*), born at Tielt in the Dutch province of Guelderland, was executed at Gent, Belgium, in 1573. According to Verheyden (*Gent,* 61) she is identical with Beelken (*Beliken*) de Jaghere, who was burned at the stake at Gent on March 17, 1573. But it seems more likely that she is the same person as Grietken Heyndrick of Hos near 's Hertogenbosch, Dutch province of North Brabant, who was 23 years old and married to Martin van der Sluys, who lived at Zomerghem near Gent; this Grietken Heyndrick was burned on the same day as Beliken de Jaghere. (*Mart. Mir.* D 647, E 968; *ML* II, 175.) vDZ.

Grietje (Griete) **Maes,** an Anabaptist martyr, widow of Gerrit, was executed by drowning at Amsterdam on May 15, 1535, together with six other Anabaptist women because "they have been rebaptized, holding pernicious views concerning the sacraments . . . contrary to the laws and decrees of his imperial Majesty . . . without having shown penitence." Their property was confiscated. Van Braght (*Mart. Mir.* D 413, E 764) seems to make two martyrs of this person, calling one Grietje Maes and the other Gerrit's widow. (Grosheide, *Verhooren,* 58.) vDZ.

Grietken Govaerts, an Anbaptist martyr, charged with rebaptism and the crime of having attended forbidden meetings of the Mennonites, was burned at the stake at Antwerp, Belgium, on May 20, 1573. (*Antw. Arch.-Blad* XIII, 113 f., 176; XIV, 90 f., No. 1023.) vDZ.

Grietken Heyndrick: see **Grietgen van Sluys.**

Grietken van den Steene, an Anabaptist martyr, was burned at the stake at Antwerp, Belgium, on Jan. 28, 1573, together with Janneken Croecx and Jacques van Hulten. She had been (re)baptized and participated in the meetings of the Mennonites. (*Antw. Arch.-Blad* XIII, 100 f., 171; XIV, 88 f., No. 1002.) vDZ.

Grigoryevka was a Mennonite village in the Ukraine on the southern railway, in the Ezum district of the province of Kharkov; the post office and railway station was Gavrilovka five miles distant. It was founded in 1889 by Mennonites from the leased villages of the Fürstenland settlement and had an area of about 8,000 acres, on which 41 farms were set up. The land was very fertile and the settlement prospered economically as well as culturally. In 1904 a community steam mill was built and from 1906 to 1925 a secondary school in addition to the primary school was maintained. The settlement had 52 farms with 567 inhabitants in 1925. In 1918 Grigoryevka was the scene of fighting between the German and Russian armies. In 1918-20 it was overrun by robber bands, finally by Machno's (*q.v.*) bands. Under the Soviet government many emigrated to other parts of Russia, and some reached Canada. By 1927 Grigoryevka had ceased to exist as a Mennonite settlement. (*ML* II, 175.) H.F., J.B.A.

Grigoryevka Mennonite Church, located in the village of Grigoryevka (*q.v.*), province of Kharkov,

Ukraine, Russia, founded in 1890, had a baptized membership of 184 in 1905, with a total population of 287 in that year. It was a subsidiary of the New York Mennonite Church (*q.v.*), with Heinrich Funk (presumably died in exile) as an elder. C.K.

Grijpskerk, a village in the western part of the Dutch province of Groningen, the center of an extensive Mennonite congregation comprising several original congregations or circles. Many of them are very old. Leenaert Bouwens (*q.v.*) baptized 5 persons in Nieziel, one in Lutjegast, 18 in Visvliet, and 8 in Grijpskerk, making a total of 31 persons. Later all of these groups united in the Pieterzijl congregation, sometime before 1690. In the 17th century this congregation was a member of the Humsterland Flemish Sociëteit. In 1815 a new church was built in Pieterzijl (*q.v.*). In 1826 the congregation participated in the establishment of the Groningen Sociëteit (*q.v.*). The membership was 24 in 1828, 42 in 1835, 80 in 1927, and 48 in 1955. In 1892 the parsonage (which had become dilapidated) and church were transferred to Grijpskerk because of its favorable location. The new church was dedicated on Nov. 30, 1892, by S. F. van der Ploeg, who was pastor of the congregation in 1889-91. He was followed by A. Gerritsma (1894-1935) and Miss C. W. Brugman (1940-45). Since 1946 the congregation has been served by S. S. Smeding of Noordhorn (*q.v.*). (*DB* 1893, 135; *ML* II, 175.) vDZ.

Grijspeert (also Gryspeere, Grisperre, Gryspeer, Grijspaart), a family in Flanders, Belgium, found in the region southwest of Brugge (see Eug. de Seyn, *Dictionnaire Hist. et Géogr. des Communes Belges* XI, Bruxelles, 1933), of whom many joined the Mennonites, fled from Flanders to the Northern Netherlands about 1580, because of religious persecution, particularly to Haarlem. Many members of this family have served as deacons, both in Haarlem and Amsterdam. The preacher Pieter Grijspeer(t) (*q.v.*) belonged to this family.

Fierin Grysperre, living at Hemelghem near Yseghem, who was cited by the Calvinistic church council of Gent, Belgium, on July 19, 1583, to answer for his Mennonite faith, may have been a member of the same family. (Verheyden, "Mennisme in Vlaanderen," ms.) vDZ.

Grijspeert (Grijspeer, Grijspaart), **Pieter,** was a noted preacher of the United Flemish and High German Mennonite congregation at Haarlem in 1625-55. The dates of his birth and death are not known, but he seems to have been chosen to the ministry while he was young, for in his writings he frequently used the motto, "I am young."

He was one of the signatories of the Outerman Confession (1625), presented to the Court of Holland by representatives of nine congregations. He and his colleague Jan Doom represented the Haarlem congregation at the peace conference held at Dordrecht on April 21, 1632, and signed the Dordrecht Confession. Likewise he appeared as the elder of the Haarlem congregation at the conference held at Haarlem in June 1649 for the purpose of forming a union, when representatives were present from Zeeland, Flanders, North and South Holland, Utrecht, and Overijssel. The three previously accepted confessions, Olive Branch, Jan Cents, and the Dordrecht Confession, were presented and quietly adopted, with the understanding that they were still subordinate to the Word of God. In addition many other regulations were passed for the benefit of the union, to serve in the management of the congregations.

These suggestions were published in 1654 by Grijspeert in a volume titled *Een Christelyk Handboekje, gemaakt onder Verbeteringe, hoe men bequaamelyk, als elk zyn Geloove beleeft, en zyne Regeeringe waarneemt, Goddelyk de Gemeente kan regeeren,* without place of publication. The author calls himself a "lover of the apostolic church and of general Christian peace." This can indeed be said of Grijspeert. Already by Maatschoen's time the booklet was so rare (1745) that he included it without any condensation in his *Geschiedenis der Mennoniten* (III, 188-232); not even in the Mennonite library of Amsterdam is a copy to be found. It contained questions to be presented to newly chosen preachers, deacons, and baptismal candidates, gives directions for the baptismal ceremony, the reception of excommunicated members, and marriage, besides thirty rules to be observed in the management of the congregation. In conclusion it contains an excerpt from Paulus Merula's *Tydthresoor* concerning the state and service of the Christian church in the first century, in order to show that it was governed by definite regulations. Maatschoen calls it a most useful booklet and wishes that all Mennonite congregations would on general principles be governed by it; at the same time he notes that many congregations were still living by its precepts.

In addition Grijspeert published a collection of devotional poems, *Sommighe leerachtighe Geestelycke Liedekens, gemaeckt uyt den Ouden, ende Nieuwen Testamente, met ook eenige Psalmen Davids, uyt verscheyden Boecken by een vergadert, om in de vergaderinge der Geloovigen tot des Heeren prys, ende stichtinge onder malkanderen ghesongen te worden.* The addition of the words, *"Vermeerdert met eenighe nieuwe Liedekens door P.G.,"* indicates that he wrote some of them himself. These compose an appendix titled *'s Herten vreucht, inhoudende eenige nieuwe Liedekens, uyt den Ouden, ende Nieuwen Testament by een vergadert tot vermaeckinghe des Gheests.* This little volume contains 12 songs, 11 of which were written by Grijspeert. There is also an appendix of six songs by the martyr Elisabeth (drowned at Leeuwarden in 1549), Menno Simons, Dirk Philips, Joost Ewoutsz, Jacques Outerman, and an unknown author. The hymnbook was published at Hoorn in 1629. A second edition, omitting *'s Herten Vreucht,* appeared at Haarlem in 1638. The last six songs were printed at Amsterdam in 1618, and apparently were added later to Grijspeert's collection. The Mennonite archives at Amsterdam contain two letters written by him.   J.L.

Schijn-Maatschoen, *Geschiedenis der Mennoniten* III, 183-236; *Biogr. Wb.* III, 388 f.; *Inv. Arch. Amst.* I, No. 586; II, Nos. 1387, 1855, 1861; *Catalogus Amst.,* 273; *ML* II, 175 f.

Grimm, Daniel, a Mennonite preacher in the Emmental, Switzerland, a follower of Hans Reist (*q.v.*), was opposed to the emigration of the Mennonites to the Netherlands in 1711. He was banished by the magistrates, but returned and caused much trouble for Runckel (*q.v.*), who was organizing the emigration in co-operation with the Dutch Committee of Foreign Needs (*q.v.*). Grimm is said to have escaped from Switzerland in June 1711. No further information about him is available. (*Inv. Arch. Amst.* I, Nos. 1317, 1334 f.)   vDZ.

Grimmelshausen, Hans Jakob Christoph von (1620-76), author of the famous novel, *Der abenteuerliche Simplizissimus,* published in 1668. In book V, chapter 19, he gives a remarkable picture of "Hungarian Anabaptists" and their communal way of living, and there can be no doubt that Hutterite colonies in Slovakia are thus portrayed. Grimmelshausen tells us that he had discovered "a manner of living for human beings which is more angelic than human. It would happen if a group of men and women, both married and single, would unite and live according to the manner of the Anabaptists. That is, they would have to earn their living with the work of their hands under the guidance of an expert leader, and to spend the rest of their time with the praise and worship of God." And then he continues, "Once I saw such a life in the Anabaptist communities in Hungary [Slovakia]. Were they not involved in heresy I certainly would have liked to join them. At least I would have called their way of life the most blessed in the world." And then Grimmelshausen has no other comparison for these colonies than with the Jewish Essenes as described by Josephus who likewise practiced community of goods. "They have great treasures," he tells us, and modern research bears it out, "and plenty of food, which they, however, wasted in no way. No curse, no grumbling or impatience was heard among them, indeed no idle word at all. There I saw craftsmen working in their shops as if they were hired; their schoolteachers instructed their youth as if they were their own children. Nowhere did I see men and women together; each sex did its definite work at separate places. I found rooms in which there were only mothers of newborn infants, who were well provided for with nursing care, in other rooms nothing could be seen but many cradles with infants cared for by women appointed to this task, so that the mothers did not need to concern themselves except three times a day when the children were brought to them to be fed. The task of watching over the children was assigned to widows; the others had to spin, wash, etc. And thus also among the men; each had his assigned duty. If a man or woman became ill, they had special nurses. They all had definite hours for eating and sleeping, but not a minute for playing or idleness. Only the young people for the sake of their health walked an hour under the supervision of the teachers. There was no anger, no revenge or envy, no jealousy and no enmity among them, also no concern about temporal possessions. In short, there was a lovely harmony which seemed to have no other object than to better the human race and to promote the Kingdom of God. Such a life," Grimmelshausen concludes, "I would have liked to introduce, for it appears to me these people by far surpass in their way the lives of the monks." And then he goes on musing, "I often said if I could only convert these Anabaptists, so that our coreligionists could learn their way of life from them, . . . what a blessed man I should be. Or if I could only persuade my Christian brethren to live lives as Christian (according to appearance) as these Anabaptists." He would have been willing to sacrifice his entire fortune and possession if he thus could establish a Christian community after that pattern, but alas, where would he find such people able or willing to go along such lines?

The question as to how Grimmelshausen got all this information and also his enthusiasm for this way of life has not been completely solved. Some literary historians think it possible that he visited Slovakian Bruderhofs between 1640 and 1645 (the time of the great Vorsteher Andreas Ehrenpreis), but others doubt that he ever traveled. A. J. F. Zieglschmid thinks rather of contacts with the newly established Hutterite Bruderhof in Mannheim (q.v.) (which existed between 1645 and 1684) where Grimmelshausen might have learned all the details described, and also the story of the Hungarian mother colonies. In any case to him it was almost like Utopia come true.   R.F.

A. J. F. Zieglschmid, "Die Ungarischen Wiedertäufer bei Grimmelshausen," *Ztscht f. Kirchengesch.* LIX (1940) 1-36.

Griner Conservative Amish Mennonite Church, located two miles south of Middlebury, Elkhart Co., Ind., was organized in the spring of 1922 as a branch of the Townline congregation. The meetinghouse was formerly a Lutheran church. In 1954 the membership was 192 with Manasseh Miller and Louis Kauffman as preachers, Fred Bontrager deacon, and Sam T. Eash bishop.   S.T.E.

Grisons (Graubünden), a canton in southeast Switzerland, the largest canton, with 2,774 sq. miles and 128,200 inhabitants. During the Reformation it showed many indications of a rapidly growing Anabaptist movement, which was, however, violently suppressed. This was especially true of its capital Chur (q.v.). Two Grisons Anabaptists played an important role in the first Anabaptist congregation in Zürich, Georg Blaurock (q.v.), and Andreas Castelberger (q.v.). They are considered the fathers of the Anabaptist movement in Grisons. At the end of April 1525, expelled from Zürich, they returned to their home with Felix Manz (q.v.). In mid-May they were in Chur and its vicinity; the Reformed took note of their activity and prepared for the conflict. In three months the conflict was on. The Anabaptists had had great success and had been supported by the Catholics. Comander, the reformer of Grisons, was anxious, and on Aug. 8, 1525, urgently appealed to Zwingli for help. The Chur authorities now took a hand. Manz was imprisoned and then expelled; Blaurock escaped from prison. In spring 1526 Anabaptists in the area of Maienfeld and Fläsch were suppressed.

At first they refused to be converted; but when the use of the rack was threatened they recanted. A leader escaped the authorities. Salzmann, the Reformed teacher in the city school of Chur, wrote to Vadian, March 13, 1526, "Wolff Ulimann (q.v.) fled because of pestilence, else he would have been punished. He was fined three pounds." This notice may have been of interest to Vadian (see **St. Gall**). Nothing more is known of the work of Ulimann in Grisons. Supposedly the judges saw in him one of the most dangerous false teachers, who had made himself noticed in the Rhine Valley in Chur.

At Easter 1526 Salzmann complained to Zwingli that the Anabaptists were backsliding (from Anabaptism), but this seems to have been a brief flicker. At the Bundestag at Davos in May 1526 religious freedom was granted only to the Catholics and Reformed; the Anabaptists and other sects were strictly forbidden. E. Camenisch, the church historian of Grisons, estimates "that the Anabaptists at the beginning of 1526 formed a compact separatist brotherhood, differing from the other two creeds by a special concept of faith." After 1526 there were only isolated traces of the brotherhood; the Anabaptists had been robbed of their leaders and threatened by severe edicts of the government, the Reformed Church had been firmly established, and won an equal status with Catholicism. In 1528 the "Catabaptists," led by Castelberger, again stirred in Chur, causing Comander great concern. Then Castelberger disappeared from the scene. Conrad Grebel (q.v.), who was probably about to begin his work in Grisons, was at the gateway to Grisons in the summer of 1526. He died at Maienfeld of the plague. Felix Manz was drowned in Zürich, Jan. 5, 1527, Wolfgang Ulimann was executed in Swabia in 1528, and Blaurock died at the stake at Clausen in Tirol, Sept. 6, 1529. The twelfth of the theses announced by Comander for the disputation planned for Easter Monday 1531 at Chur, which could, however, not take place because of war, read, "Anabaptism is an error and a seduction against God's Word and teaching." This indicates that there were still Anabaptists in the country, but their traces become more scarce.

Martin Seger, magistrate of Maienfeld, in a letter of Sept. 16, 1533, requests Bullinger to send him the book he published against the Anabaptists in 1530. It is not clear whether the reason for this request is renewed Anabaptist activity or the memory of their earlier appearance in Fläsch and Maienfeld. After 1542 the immigration of Italian refugees sets in, among whom there are elements that oppose the Reformed creed and who are called Anabaptists in memory of the doctrines and activities of the Anabaptists in the 1520's; a more accurate name would have been "anti-Trinitarians" (q.v.). They played an important role in the history of the Reformation in Grisons, but they can be only touched upon here. In the conflict between Frell and Gantner (1570) we note a mixture of Anabaptism, anti-Trinitarianism, and Schwenckfeldianism.

From the darkness of the period 1530-70 emerges the figure of a noble Anabaptist, Leopold Scharnschlager, the schoolmaster of Ilanz. He came from

Tirol, had owned a farm in Hopfgarten near Kitz-bühel, but as an Anabaptist had to flee in 1530 with his wife and daughter. Perhaps, like many of his brethren, he had set out for Moravia. In 1535 he was probably no longer there. Pilgram Marpeck, whose acquaintance he had meanwhile made, for-warded letters to him. It can be assumed that, like Pilgram Marpeck, he had ventured to return to his home. It is known from a letter written by his son-in-law, a Moravian Anabaptist, that after 1538 his stay in Tirol was short. In 1544 he was sup-posedly in Augsburg, for there it is known that Scharnschlager and his wife were fined 40 guilders in Bavaria. Scharnschlager also co-operated in writing the *Verantwortung über Caspar Schwenck-felds Judicium* (published in 1928 by Johann Lo-serth). He is named second in the list of authors after Pilgram Marpeck. The epistle to Caspar Schwenckfeld, which precedes that *Verantwortung,* is dated Jan. 1, 1544. In 1546 Scharnschlager and his wife suddenly appeared in Ilanz in the Ober-land of Grisons, where they at last found a quiet place of residence. Their neighborhood did not learn of their Anabaptist faith. Having studied at a Tirolean monastery school or in Innsbruck, Scharnschlager was able to head the country school here. A considerable inherited fortune made him independent of the trifling salary. But his connec-tions with the Brethren in Upper Germany and Moravia he quietly continued. He also put all his strength at the disposal of the brotherhood. In 1558 he copied a book (perhaps the *Verantwor-tung*) and wrote an epistle "Vom Gericht." The Brethren in Augsburg thanked him in a letter signed by Valentin Werner (Aug. 26, 1559). They asked him to continue to serve them with the treasures of his spirit, but "they do not want to overburden his honorable age." In March 1563 Scharnschlager died; his wife soon followed. The lawsuit that developed from their estate (not set-tled until 1566) furnishes these important notes on this Anabaptist leader.

The letter of 1559 by the Augsburg Brethren is addressed to the beloved brethren in Grisons, especially to Leopold Scharnschlager. Thus it is known that there was an Anabaptist congregation in Grisons at that time, which existed in secret. The few notes from the following decade merely say that in the lawsuit mentioned above a tower of Chur, Sebastian Neudorfer, is named, "who carried messages down into the country."

The Chur pastor Johannes Fabricius Montanus had to dispute before the council with an Anabap-tist in January 1560, and evidently used Bullinger's book against the Anabaptists. In the following year the Anabaptists again required his thought. In November 1561 several held meetings in the house of a citizen and baptized two citizens of Chur. Two outsiders in Chur said to the Ana-baptists, Ferdinand had the Anabaptists so severely persecuted with fire and sword that they wished they were in Grisons. Fabricius remarks in a letter to Bullinger of Nov. 28, that they must act quickly. He had held a disputation and had been the victor. Both the Anabaptists have been imprisoned: one of them, a butcher who had learned his trade in

Zürich or had long served there, Tardy by name, was to be expelled (but the sentence was not car-ried out). With the other, a Chur bookseller and bookbinder, Georg Frell, Fabricius had spoken, but without results; Frell referred to the *Paraphrases* of Erasmus. The successor of Fabricius, Tobias Egli, wrote in 1570 that Frell had added Schwenckfel-dianism to his other errors. In the negotiations of 1570 and 1571 there is repeated mention of books by Schwenckfeld that Frell had in stock, and of Schwenckfeldian doctrines that he defended. They mentioned the *Fastnachtsbüchle* or *Vermanungs-büchle* that was distributed in Chur and Prättigau. Egli has shown that at a disputation held on May 19, 1570, Frell took his ideas opposing Zwingli's teachings from Hubmaier's writings. There is here probably an adulteration of Anabaptism that has only occasional contacts with Scharnschlager's type.

The fight about Frell took on larger dimensions when Johannes Gantner, Egli's colleague, took sides with Frell. He opposed the persecution of heretics on the basis of the parable of the tares, but in other points as well he touched Anabaptist doc-trine; e.g., the statements of the Old Testament are not valid, for we are a new people; he who has conscientious scruples against injuring a foe, whom Christ says we must love, even in the greatest dis-tress of the native country should not be compelled to do so; one should not swear, but letting yea be yea and nay be nay is sufficient (concerning the further developments see **Chur**). Frell came back to Chur later and conversed with Gantner openly, but there was no profound movement. The butcher Tardy, who was also expelled, remained for a time in Ilanz, the residence of Scharnschlager ("where he attacked everybody"), but was then permitted to return to Chur, and here committed a murder. On May 9, 1573, he stabbed his stepson on the marketplace; but he escaped and did not reappear.

The last instance of Anabaptism in Chur extends into the 17th century. Stephan Gabriel, who served as pastor of Ilanz from 1593 to 1618 and from 1626 until his death in 1638, stated in 1605 that he fre-quently sought Anabaptists in the great crowds in Ilanz before the Bundestag, convinced them of their error, and converted them. He was even summoned to the Catholic valley of the Lugnez to dispute with two Anabaptists before a great crowd of people, in the presence of six priests. He boasts of being victorious. The town of Ilanz was thus for a long time an Anabaptist center.

In the area of Veltlin, Bormio (Worms), and Chiavenna (Kläven) the Reformation had also gained entry. In these Italian-speaking regions, as well as in the Grisons valleys of Bergell and Pusch-lav, the Protestants fleeing from the Inquisition found a field for work. On the whole their work was fruitful. Only the appearance of several anti-Trinitarians brought confusion and in Chiavenna led to a long-drawn-out church quarrel, involving the congregation there, the Grisons synod, and the Zürich clergy. The principal leader of the radicals, Camillo Renato (*q.v.*), strongly emphasized the authority of the Spirit as above the written Word of God; he questioned the value of the sacraments, rejected infant baptism as a superstitious ceremony, without meaning; salvation, he said, is accomplished not by a historical fact, but by sudden illumination by the Spirit, bringing rebirth.

In the midst of these disputes comes the so-called Anabaptist Council of Venice in 1550. (It was probably rather an anti-Trinitarian meeting, to which some Anabaptists were invited.) The invitations had been issued orally by messengers, who first sought out the churches in Upper Italy, then in Grisons and northern Switzerland as far as Basel and St. Gall. Sixty Anabaptist (?) leaders had assembled in Venice, including 20 or 30 from Switzerland. Unfortunately those from Grisons are not named (il Nero is not Franciscus Niger; see Schiess, *Korrespondenz Bullingers* I, p. LXI, note 5). Titianus, an anti-Trinitarian, had of course worked in the subject cantons (*Untertanenlanden*) and later, in 1554 (Schiess, pp. XXI f.) disputed in Chur with the Grisons reformer Gallicius; he was driven out with lashes. But he cannot be considered the representative of the Grisons Anabaptists. There may therefore have been some of Scharnschlager's type there. The moderate wing left; hence their representatives were not named.

The above-named difficulties in the subject cantons now made it essential for the synod to set up a Confession of Faith and church regulations. In 1552 Philip Gallicius was assigned this task, and he formulated them at once. In April 1553 the *Confessio Raetica* was sent to Bullinger for his perusal, and after it had received his approval and been signed by the Grisons clergy, it was presented to the Bundestag and confirmed by the delegates of both creeds. Of this confession Article II (On the Sacraments) expressly states that baptism is not itself purification and sanctification. Article 18 (On Infant Baptism) says: "It is just as Christian among Christians as circumcision was considered pious by the Israelites." Article 19 says: "He who has once been baptized by a preacher of the Word of the triune God shall not be baptized differently or anew." From the church regulations, articles 37, 40, and 65 should be mentioned: Baptism shall be performed by none but the clergy, since Jesus conferred the office of baptism only on those who have the office of preaching. As the place for baptism the church is designated, and baptism at home is granted only for emergencies. The clergyman shall perform the baptismal ceremony standing, under the appropriate support of the witnesses. "On the other hand, we forbid baptism to be performed seated in barns or in open fields or woods or other unsuitable places as the godless Anabaptists do." All baptisms are to be entered into the church books, as had often been decided before.

When Bullinger worked out the second Helvetian Confession the Grisons Church adopted it without invalidating their own. It was rather considered cantonal law, and with its aid the remnants of Anabaptism and anti-Trinitarianism were wiped out.   J.t.D.K.

E. Camenisch, "Die Confessio Raetica," in *Jahresbericht der hist. antiquarischen Gesellschaft* (Chur, 1914); *idem, Bündner Ref.-Gesch.* (Chur, 1920); T. Schiess, "Aus dem Leben eines Hanzer Schulmeisters," *Bündner Monatsblatt*, 1916, No. 2; "Verantwortung über Caspar

Schwenckfelds Judicium," *Züricher Zentralbibliothek* (Ms B. 72); in the appendix to the former Valentin Werner's letter to Scharnschlager, 489b-92b and a note about the origin of the book, 495 f.; J. ten Doornkaat Koolman, *Leopold Scharnschlager und die verborgene Täufergemeinde in Graubünden* (*Zwingliana*, 1926, 329 ff.); K. Benrath, "Wiedertäufer im Venetianischen," *Theol. Studien und Kritiken*, 1885, No. 1; *idem,* "Gesch. der Ref. in Venedig," in *Schriften des Ver. für Gesch.*, No. 18 (Halle, 1887); Rageth Ragaz, *Stefan Gabriel, der Prädikant und Dichter* (Chur. 1928) 27; T. Schiess, ed., *Bullingers Korrespondenz mit den Graubündnern XXIII-XXV of Quellen zur Schweizer Geschichte* (Basel, 1904-6); P. D. Rosius de Porta, *Historia reformationis ecclesiarum Raeticarum* (Curiae Raetorum, 1771) I; *ML* II, 157-59.

Griswold (Man.) Mennonite Brethren Church was organized June 5, 1926, with 22 members, under the leadership of H. Penner of Alexander, Man. The 1953 membership was 69, all of whom were rural people. In 1929 a church building having a seating capacity of 150 was bought in Griswold. The following ministers have served this church: Jacob Abrahams, Peter Mandtler, Abraham Friesen, Abe L. Klassen, and John J. Krueger. A new meetinghouse was built in Alexander in 1953, when the name was changed to Alexander M.B.   H.C.K.

Gritznis, Wolf von, an Anabaptist preacher who before 1535 worked in the region of Bretten (Badden), Germany, and was executed there, as was stated by Judith Ruemmich, who was imprisoned in Passau, Sept. 14, 1535. She had been baptized by him and was one of a group of 20 brethren who wished to return to their homes in South Germany when they had been expelled from Moravia. Her husband, Hans Ruemmich of Marbach, had been baptized in Auspitz by Blasy Khumbauf in the group led by Philip Plener. Since most of the Passau prisoners, who furnished the core of the *Ausbund* (*q.v.*) with their martyr poems, were adherents of Philip Plener (also called Weber), who was very successful about 1529 in the Palatinate (Hege, 60 ff.), it may be assumed that after settling in Moravia Wolf von Gritznis was one of Plener's adherents in this Upper Rhine region. Nothing more is known concerning him.   Hege.

Wolkan, *Lieder,* 30; Chr. Hege, *Die Täufer in der Kurpfalz* (Frankfurt, 1908); *ML* II, 176 f.

Groede, in Zealand-Flanders, Dutch province of Zeeland, formerly the seat of a Mennonite congregation. Sometimes this congregation is called Cadzand; after 1743 it was usually called the Mennonite Congregation of Nieuwvliet in 't Land van Cadzand. The history of this congregation has been described in the article **Cadzand.** A house in Groede, bought and adapted for use as a Mennonite meetinghouse (1647), was confiscated.

vDZ.

N. van der Zijpp, *Geschiedenis der Doopsgezinden in Nederland* (Arnhem, 1952) 144; *Inv. Arch. Amst.* I, No. 1158; *ML* II, 177.

Groene Kruis (Green Cross), a Dutch society founded in 1900 by the Mennonite pastor F. C. Fleischer (*q.v.*) and Willem Poolman, a physician from The Hague. This association, which was founded for the purpose of improvement of health and domestic nursing, has in the course of the years developed into a large organization. (*ML* II, 191.)

vdZ.

Groff (Graf), **Hans** (1661-1746), the pioneer of 1696, settled first at Paradise and later in Groffdale, West Earl Twp., Lancaster Co., Pa., on 1,500 acres. His first son, Jacob, remained in Strasburg and the rest on the paternal Groffdale acres. The Groffdale church was built on this farm in 1755, the center of a thriving congregation. Hans's sons Peter and David, his son-in-law Henry Landis, together with Hans's brother Martin (d. 1760) as minister, formed the nucleus of this Mennonite community. The first-known bishop of this congregation, Christian Burkholder, married a granddaughter of Hans Groff. Hans and his son David furnished the meeting place for the congregation in the early days in their homes. Many of his descendants with various names have served the church. Abraham Grove of Markham, Ont. (1770-1836), minister here and a molder, was a descendant.

I.D.L.

Groffdale Mennonite Church (MC), located two miles northwest of New Holland, Pa., is a member of the Lancaster Mennonite Conference. The first meetinghouse was built of logs in 1755 on Hans Groff's vast acreage. A stone addition was built in 1823. In 1909 the new brick church was built which was enlarged in 1936. The congregation has co-operated in the Palo Alto Mission from the start, releasing one of its ministers, Lester M. Hoover, to serve there. In 1954 Mahlon Witmer was the bishop in charge, with Eli G. Sauder, Amos Sauder, and John S. Martin as ministers and Floyd Graybill as deacon. Though a large percentage are still farmers, the Old Order Mennonites are buying up most of the land around them. Until 1905 the Metzler and Groffdale congregations were served by the same ministers; since then a gradual separation has been taking place. First they had separate deacons and gradually a separate ministry. In 1953 all except two ministers were serving both congregations. The membership in 1953 was 348. (†*ME* I) I.D.L.

Groffdale (Pa.) Old Order Mennonite Church. In 1895 a frame meetinghouse was built a mile west of the original Groffdale house, for the Martinite division. Joseph O. Wenger and Aaron Z. Sensenig are the bishops; Isaac N. Zimmerman and Eli Hursh, ministers; and Benjamin Hoover, the deacon. This group has no Sunday school, summer Bible school, evangelistic meetings, nor youth activities. It had 325 members in 1955.

In the same house worship the Weaverland Conference group (OOM), who separated from the above in 1926, differing chiefly in permitting the automobile and home conveniences and English preaching. Moses Horning and Joseph Hostetter are bishops; Abram Hoover and Samuel Martin, ministers; and Eli Nolt, deacon. The two groups have well over 400 members. I.D.L.

Grombach, a village (1925 pop. 669, with 12 Mennonites) in the Sinsheim district of Baden, Germany. As early as the 16th century Mennonites were living here. In 1596 Gall Schnaitmann of Fellbach is mentioned. He was an alert man, who left a considerable fortune in his home town, and was baptized at Landau in 1587, after he had studied Menno Simons' *Foundation Book*. He was a wool weaver and had made long journeys; he had also worked in Göding (*q.v.*) in Moravia, where the Hutterian Brethren had a household. In Grombach Schnaitmann took over a mill from the lords of Flersheim. About 1598 the court records mention a sister of Bernhard Bauder of Urbach (Bossert, 271).

There are scarcely any references to other Mennonites in the areas owned by the imperial knights. The few notes handed down from Grombach therefore deserve attention, for in the 16th century no other places in the Kraichgau are known in which Mennonites lived. But from Dutch sources it is known that there were Mennonite churches in that region in the 16th century. The Mennonites in the Neckar Valley in 1575 wanted to unite with the Flemish. Consequently in April three Flemish preachers, Pieter de Leydecker, Hendrik Glasemaeker, and Daniel Graef of Holland were sent to the Neckar Valley to negotiate. They visited all the congregations there, but no union resulted. The Mennonites here gradually died out.

After their expulsion from Switzerland in 1650-1710 the Mennonites found reception and protection in the lands of the local nobility here. About that time four congregations were organized near Grombach, all equally distant from the village. A list of 1731 calls them Zimmerhof, Büchelhof, Hasselbach, and Bockschaft. Several of their preachers lived in Grombach; thus Ulrich Neukomm served Zimmerhof, and Heinrich Kündig served Bockschaft. In the Dutch *Naamlijst der Predikanten* this congregation is mentioned from 1766 on, appearing in the next issues under different names.

In the last quarter of the 18th century the Mennonites in Grombach helped to distribute Gerhard Tersteegen's writings. From a letter by Elder Abraham Bechtel (preacher of the congregation then called Bockschaft-Streichenberg and Wesingen 1752, elder 1770, d. 1794) of Grombach, dated Jan. 20, 1776, it is known that they contributed two "Karolines" to the printing of Tersteegen's books, and that Hans Krehbiel (preacher 1761, elder 1773) of Grombach and Jost Glück (preacher 1756, elder 1773) in Berwangen offered to make contributions to the posthumous editions of Tersteegen's works.

Today only one of the four congregations has survived, namely, Hasselbach (*q.v.*), to which the Mennonites in Grombach belong. (Müller, *Berner Täufer*, 209; *ML* II, 177.) HEGE.

Gronau Mennonite Church, in the city of Gronau (pop. 15,000) in Westphalia, Germany, on the Dutch German border 32 miles northwest of Münster, was established Feb. 4, 1888, by about 20 Mennonite families living in Gronau and Ahaus, under the leadership of Mathieu van Delden (*q.v.*). Services had been held here since 1864 by the pastor of the Enschede (*q.v.*) Mennonite Church. Most of the families were industrialists, proprietors of the large cotton textile mills in Gronau and a jute mill

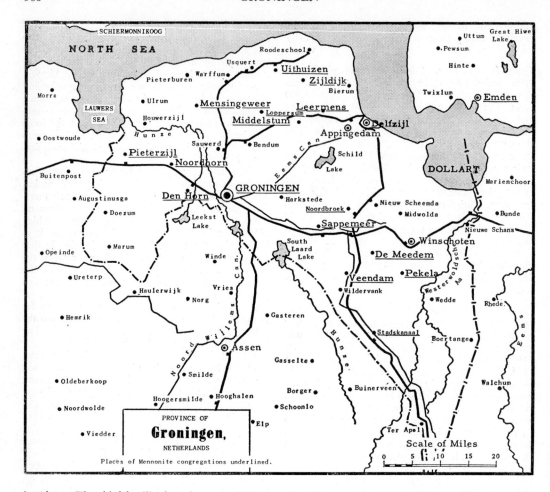

NORTH SEA

SCHIERMONNIKOOG

Morra

LAUWERS
SEA

Oostwoude

Buitenpost

Augustinusga

Doezum

Opeinde

Ureterp

Hemrik

Oldeberkoop

Noordwolde

Viedder

Pieterburen

Ulrum

Houwerzijl

Pieterzijl

Den Horn

Marum

Haulerwijk

Hoogersmilde

Roodeschool

Usquert

Warffum

Mensingeweer

Middelstum

Sauwerd

Noordhorn

Leekst
Lake

Winde

Vries

Norg

Smilde

Hooghalen

Uithuizen

Zijldijk

Bierum

Loppersum

Leermens

Bendum

GRONINGEN

Harkstede

Noordbroek

South
Laard
Lake

Gasteren

Gasselte

Borger

Schoonlo

Elp

Uttum

Pewsum

Hinte

Twixlum

Emden

Delfzijl

Appingedam

Schild
Lake

DOLLART

Marienchoor

Nieuw Scheemda

Midwolda

Sappemeer

De Meedem

Veendam

Wildervank

Winschoten

Pekela

Wedde

Rhede

Walchum

Nieuwe Schans

Bunde

Stadskanaal

Boertange

Buinerveen

Ter Apel

Assen

PROVINCE OF

Groningen,

NETHERLANDS

Places of Mennonite congregations underlined.

Scale of Miles

0   5   10   15   20

in Ahaus. The chief families have been van Delden (*q.v.*), Stroink, Rahusen, Rommelaar, and Goerke, all but the last of Dutch extraction. The leading Mennonite textile firms in Gronau have been M. van Delden & Co. and Gerrit van Delden & Co. Mathieu van Delden, Jan van Delden, Hendrik van Delden, and Julius Stroink were leaders in the congregation, the latter three having been deacons for a number of years. Though incorporated in Germany and a member of the Vereinigung, the congregation was served in the Dutch language exclusively by the preachers of the neighboring Dutch congregation of Enschede from the beginning until 1922. At the end of that year the connection with Enschede was dissolved and Pastor A. Fast of Leer, later Emden, assumed the pastorate as a part of his circuit and has continued to serve until the present (1956). A considerable number of Mennonite refugees from Russia found help and employment in Gronau in the years 1920-25.

The first meetinghouse, erected in 1904, was destroyed in a bombing raid in 1944 and was replaced by a new building in 1950. The membership in 1928 was 32 adults and 14 children; in 1954 it was 62 and 18 children.

In 1946-53 Gronau was the seat of the extensive refugee aid program of the Mennonite Central Committee under C. F. Klassen's direction. The processing office was here as well as extensive housing and hospital facilities of the refugees. Some 1,000 refugees from Russia and several hundred from the Danzig area passed through this center on their way to Canada and Paraguay and Uruguay. A small rest home for incapacitated refugees unable to emigrate to Canada was all that remained in 1954 of the once great work.   H.S.B.

DB 1864, 183; 1889, 136; 1897, 256 f.; 1900, 226; 1904, 227; (G. Heeringa), *Uit het Verleden der Doopsgezinden in Twenthe* (Borne, n.d.) 150-53; *ML* II, 177 f.

Grondt-steen van Vreede en Verdraegsaemheit, *tot opbouwinge van den tempel Christi onder de Doops-Gesinde* (Foundation of Peace and Toleration, in Order to Build up the Church of Christ Among the Mennonites) is a Dutch booklet of 34 pages, printed at Amsterdam in 1674 and reprinted there 1736. It was drafted by four Zonist (*q.v.*) preachers, Pieter Jansz Stapper (Jisp), Jan Jansz Keeskooper (Koog-Zaandijk), Pieter Apostool (Amsterdam), and Engel Arentsz van Dooregeest (de Rijp), and signed at the Zonist Meeting held on Oct. 25, 1674, at Jisp, Dutch province of North Holland, according to the resolution of a conference of preachers and deacons held on July 18, 1674, at Amsterdam.

It was addressed to "the preachers, deacons and members of the Waterlander and Flemish Mennonites, who until now have not joined the Union" (i.e., the Zonist Sociëteit, founded at the meeting of July 18, 1674, at Amsterdam). The *Grondt-steen* was an attempt to unite the Dutch Mennonites; the basis of this union was to be the Confession, viz., the Waterlander Confession of Hans de Ries (*q.v.*) or the *Algemeene Belijdenissen* (*q.v.*). It is said emphatically (p. 19) that it is not enough to accept the Holy Scriptures as the truth; a confession is necessary because of the divergence of opinions. The *Grondt-steen* became the constitution of the Zonist Sociëteit. vDZ.

Groningen, a province in the northeastern part of the Netherlands, area 923 sq. mi., pop. 459,819 (1950) with 4,375 Mennonites. In the Middle Ages this province consisted of a number of different territories: in the north part along the North Sea the districts of Hunsingo and Fivelgo on fertile clay soil, where in early times numerous villages had been built on mounds to protect them from floods; the west part of the province, then called "Westerkwartier," was less fertile; the southeast part (Gorecht and Oldambt districts) was an arid, sandy soil, covered by a thick layer of peat-moor. Shortly after 1400 the city of Groningen became the governing and economical center of all surrounding territories, now forming the province of Groningen, from then on usually called Ommelanden. The north part was often struck by severe floods; this part, now protected from the sea by big dikes, is a center of agriculture at a high level (wheat, pulse, potatoes, sugar beets). Shortly after 1600 a start was made to break up the peat-moors in the southeast of the province, a number of canals were made, and after the peat (used for fuel) was dug out, agriculture was possible in this area (potatoes, rye, oats). Here since the 18th century too a growing industrialization developed, especially in the towns of Hoogezand-Sappemeer and Veendam-Wildervank (straw-board factories, distilleries of brandy and gin, iron works).

Besides in the city of Groningen (*q.v.*) Mennonites in the 16th century were especially found on the fertile grounds of the northern part of the province; they were nearly all farmers (agriculture). The congregations in the former peat-moor district (Sappemeer, Veendam, Pekela, Stadskanaal) are of considerably later date than those on the Hoogeland clay districts.

Concerning the history of the Mennonites, there are large periods with little information. Besides what Blaupot ten Cate gives, there is little material. Hence it is impossible to give a continuous account of its history; the following may, however, be regarded as fairly accurate. As Kühler shows (*DB* 1917, 1-8), four periods can be distinguished here as in the rest of the Netherlands: (1) from the beginning to about 1581; (2) 1581-1672; (3) 1672-1811 (for Groningen 1826 is more accurate); and (4) the modern period.

1. In the beginning of the 16th century the province of Groningen was very favorably situated. It was a part of the territory of the dukes of Gelder-

land, who were represented by Stadholders (some of them quite competent). The government was very tolerant; the Reformation (still intra-church) was able to proceed without interruptions. The humanistic clergy (the influence of men like Wessel Gansfort, *q.v.*, was still felt) promoted it rather than the reverse. Gradually and almost unnoticed Anabaptism also arose alongside of the Reformed movement. Its first appearance can no longer be ascertained. In 1533 Viglius van Ayta, provost in Humsterland, wrote to Erasmus that the sect of the Anabaptists had made great progress in Oldehove and Nijehove and all of Groningen. Where did they come from? It is significant that Groningen forms a bridge between Friesland and East Friesland. It is therefore very likely that the influence of Melchior Hofmann was felt here, or at least that of Trijpmaker (*q.v.*) on his travel through the country en route from Emden to Amsterdam (1530). In 1534 Jacob van Campen (*q.v.*) and Obbe Philips (*q.v.*) stayed here for a time. The latter no doubt founded the congregations in Appingedam and 't Zandt and perhaps also the one in the city of Groningen. The presence of Anabaptists in the city is attested by a record of May 3, 1534, which forbids their presence there. On May 8 the Anabaptists were expelled from the province. But these edicts were indifferently enforced; the severest penalties were fines and temporary exile; only one was put to death in Groningen. Up to this time the movement seems to have been chiliastic, but entirely peaceful in character; even when the Münsterites gained the upper hand, the peaceful element was not submerged. "There were peaceful Anabaptists before, during, and after the Münster episode" (Kühler). The revolutionary movement was brief, but very powerful in Groningen. Twenty-eight emissaries were sent out from Münster in 1534. One of them, Claes van Alkmaer, reached the province of Groningen and found two believers ready to return with him to the New Jerusalem. They were Jacob Kremer of Winsum and Tonnis (Antonius) Kistemaecker of Appingedam. In December they returned to spread Rothmann's *Van der Wrake*, a work of propaganda. Kistemaecker now remained in Appingedam, where there was a considerable Obbenite congregation. He apparently became the originator of the Zandt revolutionary movement, which took place at "de Arcke," the farm of the wealthy Eppe Pieters. About the middle of January 1535 some 1,000 persons assembled here. Hans Schoenmaker proclaimed himself the Messiah; they should kill all priests and government authorities and inherit their kingdom. The local magistrate was powerless to counter the movement. In addition to Schoenmaker, Cornelis in't Kerckhof (Kershof) near Garsthuizen now appeared as "true" Messiah. Now the Stadholder took steps against them; the group itself also turned against Hans. Andries Droogscheerder, with the odd nickname of "Doctor Nenytken," openly expressed his doubt about this Messiah. Hans was imprisoned in Groningen and soon died there, having lost his mind. Cornelis was also seized, but released after giving a confession. The movement can therefore not have been a real threat to the state. Meetings of Anabaptists in Leermens and 't Zandt were dispersed—nothing more happened. In March 1535, when the Frisian revolutionaries stormed the Oldeklooster near Bolsward, the leaders in Groningen also wanted to go there. Seventy men were ready to go, but their wives would not let them go. It was therefore decided to storm the Johannine *Commanderie* at Warffum. The attack failed. Thirty were arrested; Jacob Kremer, the rabble-rouser, was beheaded at the end of April 1535 at Groningen. The rest were released. The influence of Münster in this coup is evident in the fact that on March 25, 1535, eleven boats were ready on the Ems to sail to Münster. Gradually this influence decreased, and the revolutionary character subsided. Batenburg (*q.v.*), who spent the summer of 1535 in Groningen, soon disappeared. His following was slight.

Now the peaceful Anabaptists could come to the fore, especially Dirk Philips and Menno Simons. The former had been ordained as bishop by his brother Obbe in 1536 at Appingedam, but in the next year he moved to Germany (Emden and Danzig). Menno was ordained as bishop by Obbe at Groningen (January 1537) and there baptized a number of persons, including Quirin Pieters, who died as a martyr at Amsterdam in 1545. Menno lived in the province or perhaps in the city "at a quiet place." K. Vos has attempted to show that Menno found a refuge in the home of Christoffer van Ewsum in 1536-43, who was married to Margareta van Dornum. The "quiet place" was located near Middelstum or Rasquert (near Baflo). (See Krahn, *Menno Simons,* 35 ff., 57 ff.)

In general, conditions became unfavorable for the Anabaptists when the strictly Catholic emperor Charles V also ruled over Groningen (1536), although he never dared to show himself quite as fanatical in matters of religion as in his hereditary lands. In consequence of a proclamation (1542) threatening him and his followers with death, Menno withdrew from Groningen to East Friesland. Two or three times he was in the province on journeys across it, as in 1549, perhaps in 1551 (1555) and 1557. A prosperous time dawned for the Anabaptists when Leenaert Bouwens (*q.v.*) began his work. In 1551-82 he served 22 congregations in the province of Groningen, baptizing about 420 persons, 129 in Appingedam alone.

2. In the second period came the consolidation of the individual congregations, which took place very quietly. The congregations must soon have become numerous. At the conference at Haarlem in 1589, which was held to consider the affair of Thomas Bintgens (*q.v.*), 23 congregations of Groningen were mentioned (East Friesland may have been included). Internally the current divisions also took place here at this time, even though they did not take quite so extreme a form as at some other places. Brixius Gerrits (*q.v.*), the elder at Groningen, and Claes Ganglofs (*q.v.*), an elder of Emden, played a role in the Bintgens affair (see **Huiskopers**). Later Ganglofs took a strict position, with the result that most of the Groningen con-

gregations sided with the Old Flemish. He also had a part in the failure of the union of the Vereenigde Broederschap (1601 united High Germans, Young Frisians, and Waterlanders) with the Flemish, which was promoted by Lubbert Gerrits. At the beginning of the 17th century there were in the province Old Flemish, who were most numerous (united in a conference since about 1635); Flemish, especially in the region bordering on Friesland (likewise united in a conference later on). Among the moderate (with respect to the ban and shunning) Waterlanders were a congregation in Groningen and one in Sappemeer; among the Danziger Old Flemish (*q.v.*) there was a congregation in Sappemeer (*q.v.*) and one in Pekela (*q.v.*), which fell into a rapid decline about 1787.

A noted personality of this period was Jan Luies (*q.v.,* for whom the Jan-Lukasvolk take their name). In the conferences at Hoorn in 1622 (against P. J. Twisck) and at Middelstum in 1628 (against Claes Claesz of Blokzijl), he took a rigorous position among the Flemish in Groningen. In Middelstum he opposed the union of the Frisians and the Flemish (in Harlingen in 1610 and 1626) and rudely rejected the hand of peace extended to the Groningen congregations. In 1632, when most of the Flemish and Old Flemish congregations in Holland united, the churches in Groningen did not join this union.

A strict but pleasant personality, who had great influence in Groningen, was Uko Walles of Noordbroek, a pupil of Jan Luies. Like his teacher he held an unusual view of the benefit of Christ's atoning death for his opponents (see **Uko Walles**). He was therefore violently persecuted by the government, at the instigation of the intolerant Calvinist clergy. Even those who did not follow Walles suffered under this persecution. Although not all shared his theological views, he had a large following (conference in Groningen Feb. 23-March 7, 1637). The relationship of his group with the Old Flemish is not entirely clear. In the rural congregations they are probably to be counted identical (all known as Groninger Old Flemish). In the city of Groningen (*q.v.*) they were for a time distinct, but by 1677 they were again united.

The Ukowallists maintained the strict views of Menno and Dirk Philips on the Incarnation. They baptized all that came to them, even though they had previously been baptized in a congregation in another branch. Baptism was usually by immersion. They exercised the ban in its severest form especially in cases of marriage with persons outside the congregation. Old customs that threatened to disappear (such as footwashing) they conscientiously maintained. Also outside of Groningen Uko Walles had a following. The number of Ukowallists in Friesland is estimated at 600.

What was the attitude of the outside world to the Mennonites? In 1568 the War of Liberation against Spain began. Groningen was also severely oppressed by the Spaniards, whose troops were continuously marching through the province. In 1583 the Mennonites were again severely persecuted. In the country they were compelled to attend the

Catholic Church and have their children baptized. In the same year Brixius Gerrits was expelled from the city. In 1594 the Catholics were expelled; the established church was now the Reformed. In 1601 an edict was passed that made the position of the Mennonites even more difficult although the magistrate did not execute it very rigorously. But it is clear that the Mennonites were not very favorably accepted, as the writings of the Groningen chronicler Ubbo Emmius (see his *Rerum Frisicarum, historia* 1616) show. In 1637-61 the government repeatedly opposed Uko Walles, banishing him and creating many difficulties for all the Mennonites, not only for his followers. The congregation at Wildervank-Veendam, which came into being at this time, was thereby seriously hampered. In 1662 an edict permitted the Mennonites to hold their services "as of old." They were given complete toleration in 1672. In this year of distress when the army of the Bishop of Münster made raids upon this province, the Mennonites most convincingly proved their loyalty to the state, and henceforth they were left in peace.

3. The third period (1672-1826), especially in its latter part, is a period of decline. The differences between the old parties in the Netherlands were less sharp. But they were not entirely eliminated, for instance, in North Holland, where in place of the older divisions, the Zonists and Lamists were the opposing parties. In the 18th century there was in Groningen a clearly perceptible difference between the Old Flemish and the Flemish. The latter followed the Lamists. The Old Flemish Sociëteit was so strongly Zonist that it seriously considered uniting with the Zonist Sociëteit (the negotiations in 1766 proved abortive). But even the conservatives did not escape the spirit of the time, which favored softening of lines. Thus the ban was applied less and less, was omitted, or rather leniently enforced, usually only for a short period. Gradually marriage with persons outside the congregation was at least tolerated, if not exactly permitted. In 1743 the Old Flemish decided that members of other creeds who had married into the Mennonite Church should for a certain period be denied spiritual communion. Silent prayer was replaced by audible prayer. In 1749 it was left to the discretion of each individual preacher to decide this question. The authority of the elders decreased. Since 1749 baptism and communion have been in the hands of the congregation. Organs (previously shunned as a sign of worldliness) were introduced in Groningen in 1785, and in Sappemeer in 1808. In 1898 only seven of the fifteen congregations had organs; now there is one in every church. Footwashing—maintained longest by the Old Flemish—was dropped during the second half of the 18th century. Indeed, even the magistrate's office was no longer repudiated. Nonresistance was in danger of being lost, when many volunteers ranked themselves with the "Patriots." Nonresistance as a principle had, strictly speaking, been sacrificed in 1672, when the Mennonites participated at least indirectly in the war. With respect to their standards of moral conduct, they remained true to the faith of

their fathers. Their virtues were acknowledged even by their worst enemies. Their dependability and reliability in business and honesty in dealing were proverbial.

Nevertheless the congregations declined rapidly in numbers. The Mennonites of this province—except those living in the city of Groningen—were almost exclusively farmers, engaged in agriculture or cattle raising. Conditions of agriculture were very bad in the early 18th century and many farmers became pauperized or moved away. Besides this, recurring floods caused tremendous losses to the congregations. A severe flood broke the dikes of the sea at a number of places on Nov. 11, 1686; 80 Mennonites, including 55 children, were drowned, while more than 1,400 head of cattle owned by Mennonite farmers perished. The worst flood was that of 1717. In this year on Christmas day large areas were flooded; 9 brethren, 26 sisters, and 37 children perished; material losses were considerable; houses and barns were destroyed, and Mennonite farmers lost 909 cows, 192 horses, 703 sheep, and 68 pigs.

This meant severe loss for the churches. But there were other reasons why the congregations decreased. Their preachers were unable to compete with the trained ministers of the Reformed Church. Many members transferred their membership to the Reformed Church. The congregations of Bierum, Baflo, and Usquert disappeared altogether. Appingedam was dissolved about 1780; one part settled in adjacent Leermens (about 1700). Ulrum became extinct in 1794; it probably still had a considerable number of members, many of whom joined the Reformed Church. Other congregations, no longer able to maintain their independence, united. Thus the Pieterzijl congregation came into being about 1685, and the union of the Flemish and Old Flemish congregations in Humsterland (since 1838 called Noordhorn) occurred in 1775; Huizinge (now Middelstum), Sappemeer, where the six or more congregations gradually merged with the Old Flemish, Groningen (*q.v.*), and finally Mensingeweer (1818) originated from several unifications. To be sure, there was an influx of Mennonites from the Palatinate (*q.v.*) and Switzerland (*q.v.*). Some of the Palatine Mennonites, expelled from their homes in 1694, and the Swiss Mennonites, expelled from their country in 1710-13, for the most part fled to the Netherlands, and settled principally in Groningen, in the city as well as in the vicinity and in Sappemeer. Money was collected throughout the country to buy farms for them, especially in Hoogkerk and Adorp. These foreigners, who were at first organized into congregations of their own, merged with the Dutch congregations in the first half of the 19th century. There are now among the Dutch Mennonites many descendants of the Swiss refugees, such as the Boer, Leutscher, and Meihuizen families.

Although the progressive Lamists and Socinians were never numerous in this province, there were from early times deviating opinions. This is indicated by the 12 questions (*Geuzenfragen*) drawn up by the state to counter forbidden opinions (used without success in 1660-70). That such opinions also crept into the Mennonite Church is clear in the fact that there was a Collegiant congregation (in the late 17th and early 18th centuries), which, to be sure, had connections with the United Flemish and Waterlanders in Groningen (see **Botterman**). A government resolution of Dec. 6, 1701, calls the Collegiants (erroneously, of course) a new sect of Mennonites. Since the resolutions referred only to the city, the rural area was apparently free of Collegiantism.

At the end of the 18th century the situation was deplorable. Some congregations had disintegrated, many were on the verge of doing so; their churches were dilapidated, their members impoverished, their numbers small; while on the other hand the number of unbaptized persons was uncommonly large. The credit for their ability to survive and even to achieve a revival is due in the first place to the endurance of the people of Groningen, but also to two other factors, viz., the acceptance of preachers trained by the Mennonite Seminary—one of the first in Groningen province was Gerrit Bakker in the Noordhorn congregation (1818-71)— and the establishment of the Groningen Sociëteit (1826).

4. Most of the congregations made a more rapid growth in 1815-50. Thereafter the membership again suffered a gradual decline. The 13 congregations existing at the time of the founding of the Sociëteit (Groningen, Den Horn, Noordhorn, Middelstum, Leermens-Loppersum, Midwolda now Winschoten, Sappemeer, Mensingeweer, Noordbroek-Nieuw Scheemda, Pieterzijl or Grijpskerk, Zijldijk, Uithuizen, and Veendam-Pekela) are all still in existence, though some are very small. New congregations that have been added are Stadskanaal, which branched off from Veendam in 1850 and had a minister of its own (from 1917 to 1950 in combination with Assen), and Pekela, which became an independent congregation in 1852, but has always been combined with Veendam. Recently new congregations have been founded in Haren and Roden.

Almost imperceptibly Modernism overtook the Groningen congregations in the 1870's and later. Only in the city of Groningen was there some difficulty. In the rural congregations many who remained orthodox and did not follow the pastors and the majority of the congregations united with the *Doleerenden* (members of the Reformed Church who had left the main body in 1886) or the Baptists. At present the Groningen congregations are without exception liberal.

There were capable men in the province of Groningen in the 19th century. One of the outstanding men was Simon Gorter (*q.v.*), minister of Zijldijk 1813-56, who saved and brought to new life not only his own congregation, but also the congregations of Uithuizen and Leermens-Loppersum. A. Winkler Prins, the minister of Veendam 1850-82, a versatile scholar, and editor of a general encyclopedia, was another leader.

The first half of the 20th century was for many congregations a period of disintegration. Nearly half of them were without a pastor. Now nearly all the congregations have a pastor, but a number of congregations have merged.

Whereas the population of Groningen is increasing, the number of Mennonites has been declining. The total number of baptized members in this province is now (1953) 2,601; in 1834 it was 4,050. The percentages are as follows: 1733, 4.5 per cent of the population were Mennonite; 1775, 2.3 per cent; 1834, 1.6 per cent; 1900, 0.8 per cent; 1947, 0.6 per cent. This decrease is partly caused by the fact that many Mennonites moved from this province to other parts of the Netherlands.

The following congregations are found in the province of Groningen, with the following memberships:

	1834	1900	1955
Groningen	230	1017	1021
Grijpskerk	42	87	48
Den Horn	95	67	44
Leermens-Loppersum	42	98	90
Mensingeweer	44	100	75
Middelstum	61	74	34
Noordbroek	85	82	28
Noordhorn	56	89	75
Pekela	—	40	45
Sappemeer	255	494	270
Stadskanaal	—	106	85
Uithuizen	30	98	98
Veendam	140	240	127
Zijldijk	61	83	69
Grootegast (Kring)	—	—	13
Haren (Kring)	—	—	111
Oldehove (Kring)	—	—	10
	1141	2675	2243

vDZ.

H. H. Brucherus, *Geschiedenis der Kerkhervorming in Groningen* (1821); *Kroniek van Abel Eppens* (1911); C. P. Hofstede de Groot, *Geschiedenis der Broederenkerk te Groningen* (1832); G. A. Wumkes, *De Gereformeerde Kerk im Ommelanden 1595-1796*, 30-34; Blaupot t. C., *Groningen* I, II; *idem, Friesland;* K. Vos, articles in various issues of the *Groningsche Volksalmanak; idem, Het Honderdjarig bestaan der Societeit van Doopsgezinde Gemeenten in Groningen en Oost-Friesland* (Groningen, 1926); P. G. Bos, "De Groningen Wederdooperswoelingen in 1534 en 1535," in *Nederl. Archief v. Kerkgesch.,* n.s., 6, 1906, 1-17; *Inv. Arch. Amst.* I, Nos. 136, 164, 201, 223, 265, 374, 470, 473, 557, 558, I, II, V, 562-65, 571, 575-77, 579, 590, 594, 597, 600, 605 f., 1069, 1087-91, 1093, 1096-98, 1111-14, 1189, 1608, 1610, 1627, 1636, 1638, 1645, 1664, 1730, 1732-36, 1866 f., 1873-80, 1886-1902; *DB* 1872, 2; 1879, 1-10; 1917, 105; (A. Pathuis) *Inventaris van het Oud-Archief den Ver. Doopsgez. Gemeente te Groningen* (Groningen, 1940); H. Dassel Sr., *Menno's Volk in Groningen* (Groningen, n.d., 1952); C. Krahn, *Menno Simons* (Karlsruhe, 1936); *ML* II, 178-83.

Groningen, the capital (pop. 132,021, with 1,741 Mennonites) of the Dutch province of the same name, situated on the Hunse and the Aa, connected by canals with Dollart and Lake IJssel (formerly Zuiderzee), is the seat of a very old Anabaptist congregation dating back to 1530-34. A city record dated May 3, 1534, contains an order to all foreigners infected with Anabaptist doctrine to leave the city within 12 hours. The edict referred in particular to Obbe Philips, who was staying here in that year. Since the record speaks only of foreign preachers, and does not mention an Obbenite congregation, the group can not have been very extensive or a threat to the state. Furthermore, the magistrate was very lenient and favored the Reformation, even promoting such a Reformation in the Groningen church. The clergy, especially the inspector Willem Fredericks, was also very tolerant. This tolerance was no doubt the legacy of Wessel Gansfort (*q.v.*), who had a marked influence in Groningen. There are no records for 1535-36; in fact, there are large gaps in the known history of Groningen. There are no extant proclamations against the Anabaptists in this period. An edict of May 3, 1536, makes no specific reference to the city; hence it may be conjectured that the city congregation was relatively untouched by the Münsterite movement.

In January 1537 Menno Simons was ordained bishop (elder) of the Groningen Anabaptists by Obbe Philips, but it is not likely that he stayed here very much, though on March 3, 1539, he baptized Quirin Pieters here, who died as a martyr in Amsterdam in 1545. Menno Simons, who had close ties with the Groningen congregation, dedicated to this church two of his writings: *Klaar bericht . . . van der Excommunicatie* (1549 or 50) and *Belydinge van den Drieëenigen God*. An imperial proclamation of Aug. 31, 1544, ordered that the followers of David Joris, Batenburg, and Menno Simons be imprisoned and punished by death. In 1544 a number of followers of the Anabaptist leader Johan Jansen (who is otherwise unknown) were put to death in Groningen. Menno and many of his followers had already betaken themselves to East Friesland; but the city magistrate was more tolerant to the followers of Menno than the Emperor. Again on Jan. 25, 1548, the magistrate ordered the Anabaptists to leave the city or be subject to the death penalty, but this was never enforced, although many remained. Nothing is known of the inner development of the congregation. The number of Anabaptists is estimated at 23 or 24 (letter to the governor Maria), and also at 1,100 with two preachers (Cornelius). Most of the members were craftsmen. In 1551-81 Leenaert Bouwens baptized 66 persons in Groningen (22 in 1551-54). This figure is rather insignificant in comparison with the near-by city of Appingedam, where he baptized 129.

The city of Groningen, which was rather independent until 1576, now fell under the tyranny of Spain. Many "sectarians" who wished a reformation of the Catholic Church were banished and their goods confiscated. This fate struck Willem Lubberts "of the sect of the Anabaptists and Zwinglians." Following the difficult period of 1580-94 under Spanish rule, during which Brixius Gerrits (*q.v.*), elder of the Flemish congregation, was expelled from the city (1583), the city was taken by Maurice of Orange and with the surrounding area added as the seventh province to the united Netherlands. With respect to religion it was decided that the Reformed (Calvinist) religion should be prac-

ticed openly, "but no one should be tested and troubled in his conscience."

But in 1601 the Mennonites were troubled when the government, no doubt at the instigation of the Calvinist clergy, forbade the Mennonites to have religious meetings and to perform marriages, made rebaptism punishable, and excluded unbaptized children from the rights of inheritance. Also in the ensuing period the magistrate occasionally opposed them, although they were on the whole tolerated. Not until 1672, after the Mennonites had assisted in the difficult siege, were they permanently left in peace.

After the divisions in 1556 and the following years that split the brotherhood into several parties, there were in the city of Groningen at least three congregations—Old Flemish, Flemish, and Waterlander. In addition in 1640-73 another arose, most closely associated with the Old Flemish, viz., the Ukowallists, against whom a proclamation was issued in 1662. They were the followers of Uko Walles (*q.v.*), of whom we hear at the great conference of the Old Flemish in 1637 in Groningen (see **Groningen Sociëteit**). In the city accounts of 1663-75 the Ukowallist congregation is listed as independent of the others, and as the largest. It was the bearer of the old unabridged uncurtailed tradition; it was the most determined to hold to the ways of Menno Simons and Dirk Philips. Later it again united with the Old Flemish, or perhaps the latter united with a moderate wing of the Ukowallists. This happened in 1675; two years later they collectively built a church in the name of the Old Flemish on Oude Boteringestraat, where the Old Flemish conference met annually from that time on, and where the Groningen Sociëteit still meets. The chief promoter of this unification was Arent Jans (1610-79), an elder of the Old Flemish congregation since 1636. During the late 17th and early 18th centuries this congregation was very active in giving both moral and material support to the Mennonites of Prussia, Poland, and Lithuania, as well as to the Palatine and Swiss refugees.

This Groningen Old Flemish congregation had some excellent leaders, such as Derk Alles (*q.v.*) and his son and successor in office, Alle Derks (*q.v.*). The former baptized 1,832 persons in 307 baptismal services. Another man of great influence was Aldert Sierks Dyk (*q.v.*), a preacher 1733-79. The Old Flemish congregation used the Biestkens Bible and as hymnals the *Veelderhande Liedekens,* the *Veelderhande Schriftuerlyke Liedekens,* and the *Lusthof des Gemoets*. In 1733 the membership was 291, in 1767 about 200; in 1784, 152, and in 1800 only 138. They had held too tenaciously to the old tradition—even though in the end they had yielded. The office of elder had lost its authority; but to employ trained ministers was contrary to the institutions of their fathers. But the old had also passed away in this respect; the new period following the French Revolution brought new vigor and the Groningen Old Flemish congregation, though weak, was preserved.

The Waterlander congregation, which was represented by Popko Popkes at the well-known conference of the Waterlander congregations at Amsterdam in 1647, and which held its meetings in a house in Pelsterstraat, united with the larger part of the Flemish shortly before 1700.

The Flemish congregation belonged to the Sociëteit of Friesland from the founding of the Sociëteit in 1695 until 1791. Before it merged with the Waterlanders the Flemish congregation held its meetings in a house behind the A-Church. In 1696 they acquired a church on Pelsterstraat. It was a small congregation. In 1695 the congregation numbered about 100 members, in 1721, 123; 1752, 86; and 1809 only 48 members. Eppo Botterman (*q.v.*) was its learned and capable pastor in 1700-14 and 1725 until at least 1752. His being also supervisor of the Collegiants, who met on the Caroli-Weg, involved his congregation in disputes, especially with his colleague Jacobus Rijsdijk (*q.v.*).

The Rijnsburger Collegiants (*q.v.*) had already met Calvinist opposition in Groningen. In 1660-70, 12 questions (see **Geuzenvragen**) were formulated to be used in warding off erroneous doctrine—collectively usually classified as Socinianism. But Christoffel Wensing (*q.v.*), a member of the Old Flemish, had established a "college" (about 1680) and defended a Christianity independent of the church "after the manner of the Socinians." Opposition soon arose, but Wensing did not yield. Apparently there was a rather large number of members who agreed with him (surprising in view of the conservatism of the Old Flemish). The outcome was that Wensing was banned in 1687 with a number of followers. The expelled members now held more closely together than ever; soon the government intervened, urged by the Reformed clergy (1700). The Collegiants drew up a confession of faith which they presented on Dec. 19, 1701. It was declared unsuitable on the grounds that the answers to the questions on the Deity of Christ, etc., were inadequate. On Feb. 15, 1702, the college was closed, and could not be reopened until 1712 in spite of much effort. In 1715 they organized a church. Their elder was the above Botterman who sought to promote his ideas in the Flemish congregation. But because of the accompanying disunity he resigned his office with the Flemish in 1714, but resumed it in 1725 at the request of the congregation. Now his colleague Jacobus Rijsdijk (called from Zwolle in 1728) opposed him. A bitter struggle ensued, which did not end until Rijsdijk moved to Almelo in 1742. The fact that Botterman remained with the congregation until at least 1752 shows that most of the congregation at least tolerated his views, even if they were not in agreement with him. It is therefore not surprising that after the death of Steven J. van Geuns, the Collegiant supervisor, in 1757, when the colleges began to dissolve, most of the Collegiants came into the Flemish congregation.

A new increase came to the Mennonites of Groningen at the end of the 17th century and the beginning of the 18th by an influx of Mennonite refugees from the Palatinate and Switzerland. In 1694 Mennonites expelled from the Palatinate settled in the Netherlands, principally at Groningen. In 1711 and the following years Swiss Mennonites found a friendly reception here. Both Derk Alles and Alle Derks took an active interest in them. The first group coming to Groningen consisted of 30 families, and more arrived in the course of time. An offering was taken and the proceeds used to buy farms in the neighborhood of Groningen for the refugees. As early as 1716 a Swiss congregation, which had merged with the Palatine congregation, was large enough to have an elder of its own. There was also a Swiss congregation at Sappemeer (*q.v.*). Strife within the congregation caused a division into the Old Swiss and the New Swiss about 1720. The immediate cause was actually a minor point, viz., the furnishing of a home; but the basic cause was no doubt deeper. Both parties held their services in a hall located "Achter de Muur" (behind the City Wall) in the "Paltzergang," one in the German language, the other in Dutch. When it was no longer possible to find a German preacher, and David Ricken, the preacher at Sappemeer, had become too old to undertake the troublesome trips to Groningen, the two congregations were again united. Many members had already transferred their membership to the Old Flemish congregation. Their preachers were Izaak Jannes Leutscher until 1810, and Christiaan Jacobs Leutscher 1810-24. In 1809 occurred the union of the "United Flemish and Waterlander congregation of Pelsterstraat with the Old Flemish of Oude Boteringestraat. Until 1815 both churches were used. At that time they decided to build a new church on Oude Boteringestraat since both the old churches were too small. The first service in the new church was held on Oct. 20, 1815. The church on Pelsterstraat was given to the Swiss, who had by this time united and who used it until 1824. Its membership was only 34. In that year it merged with the United congregation. There was now only one congregation in the city. In 1809, at the time of the merger, the membership was 228; in 1838, 365. They now had a considerable growth corresponding with the growth of the city. In 1870 the membership was 566, and in 1900, 1,017; it declined to about 850, but by 1920 was 1,200, of whom 250 lived outside the city; in 1953 the membership numbered 1,208, of whom 173 lived outside the city.

The development in the 19th century proceeded rapidly. When the two congregations united in 1815, the ministers were Pieter Klomp (d. 1832, formerly of the Old Flemish church) and Jacobus David Vissering (d. 1846, formerly of the Flemish and Waterlander congregation). Klomp was the first chairman of the Groninger Sociëteit, which was founded in 1826. Next came Klaas Sybrandi, serving in 1832-38, who wrote a number of hymns, some of which are found in the Haarlem and Leiden songbooks; Wilhelm Gerhards, serving in 1839-64; J. G. de Hoop Scheffer, 1846-49, who later became a professor at the Mennonite Seminary at Amsterdam; J. W. Straatman, 1850-67, who was a radical modernist like his colleague Cornelis Corver, 1865-67, which displeased the congregation, causing both to resign. Their successor J. van Gilse, 1869-1906, was a capable preacher and a noted Old Testament scholar. During his pastorate the *Groote Bundel* of Haarlem was discarded and the *Leidsche Bundel* adopted. Van Gilse was succeeded by Pastor Folkert van der Ploeg 1906-31, O. L. van der Veen 1931-34, L. D. G. Knipscheer 1935- , K. T. Gorter 1942-45, H. Bremer 1946-49, and W. I. Fleischer 1949- .

The church was remodeled and enlarged in 1843; in 1915 two stained glass windows representing Biblical scenes were put in. In 1932 the Mennohuis (rooms for church activities) was built near the church. In 1854 one of the members, G. van Calcar, Jr., presented the congregation with an expensive gift: bread plates, jars, 20 large cups for the communion services, and a jug and vessel for baptismal services, all of silver.

A Sunday school for children was started in 1909, a ladies' circle in 1910, a youth group in 1923. Since 1910 the women of the church can also vote; since 1923 they can also be members of the church board.

A meeting of members on Feb. 23, 1879, resolved that the catechumens (*aankomelingen*) could obtain membership without baptism; though this resolution is still in force, nearly all young members are baptized now. In a meeting of Dec. 26, 1918, it was resolved that not only members of other churches (non-Mennonite) could receive membership without being rebaptized, but also that unbaptized persons who are in sympathy with the church could be accepted as members without baptism.

The congregation has made provisions for its poor and its aged. In 1847 an orphanage was opened and in 1872 a Gasthuis (old people's home), in 1928 followed by a rest home.

During the last decade in some surrounding towns where there are a sufficient number of Mennonites, as at Haren, Zuidlaren, and Roden, Mennonite fellowship groups (Kring) have been founded, which with the assistance of the church board of Groningen are developing into independent congregations.   vDZ.

Mart. Mir. D 73 f., E 474; *Inv. Arch. Amst.* I, Nos. 36, 143, 201, 223, 267, 289, 303, 448, 594, 597, 796 f., 1056-58, 1069, 1074, 1164, 1180, 1329; II, Nos. 1833-47; II, 2, Nos. 49 f.; *DB* 1861, 118 f.; 1864, 135, 140 ff.; 1869, 167 f.; 1869, 157; 1870, 112; 1875, 100; 1879, 3 f., 140; 1883, 72 ff.; 1895, 4 f.; 1901, 15, 28; 1906, 14, 20 f., 23, 27, 139 f.; *Naamlijst* 1810, 80; 1815, 103 f.; 1829, 61; Blaupot t. C., *Groningen* I and II, *passim*; (A. Pathuis) *Inventaris van het Oud-Archief der Ver. Doopsgez. Gemeente te Groningen* (Groningen, 1940); H. Dassel Sr., *Menno's Volk in Groningen* (Groningen, n.d., 1952); *ML* II, 183-85.

Groningen Old Flemish Mennonites (Dutch, *Groninger Oude Vlamingen*), a branch of the Dutch Mennonites. About 1630 the Groningen Old Flemish separated from the Flemish (*q.v.*) in objection to the tendency of Flemish to unite with other Mennonite groups, as had happened at Harlingen 1610. Especially the country churches in the province of Groningen opposed such unions, as is seen from a meeting held at Middelstum (*q.v.*), Groningen, in 1628, where Jan Luies (*q.v.*) combatted the views

of Claes Claesz of Blokzijl and other Flemish leaders who favored the unions. They did not participate in the union of Flemish and Old Flemish at Dordrecht in 1632. After much negotiation especially between the congregation of Amsterdam and the preachers of the country churches in the province of Groningen, the final separation was made.

From then on the Groningen Old Flemish existed as a special group among the Dutch Mennonites; in the province of Groningen they were often called "Uko-Wallists" after Uko Walles (*q.v.*), who, second to Jan Luies, was the most prominent leader of this group. The following 33 congregations belonged to this group in 1710. In the province of Groningen 15—Appingedam, Beerta (also called Klein-Oldampt), Bierum, Groningen, Houwerzijl, Huizinge (also called Middelstum), Humsterland, Leermens, Loppersum, Noordbroek, Rasquert, Sappemeer, Uithuizen, Ulrum, and Zijldijk; in East Friesland 4—Emden and Emdenland, Leer, Neustadt-Gödens, and Norden; in Friesland 5—Drachten, Knijpe, Mildam, Sneek, and IJlst; in Overijssel 4—Borne, Deventer, Hengelo, and Kampen. Besides these, there were Groningen Old Flemish congregations in Enkhuizen, Haarlem, and Zaandam, and also two in Prussia—Kleinsee (*q.v.*, Jeziorka) and Konopath (*q.v.*, Przechowka-Wintersdorf), also later Brenkenhoffswalde-Franztal (*q.v.*). The Alexanderwohl Mennonite Church (*q.v.*) record, which dates back to the 17th century, has the title *Oude Vlamingen oder Groningersche Mennonisten Sociëtaet.* During the 17th century there had also existed the following additional 19 Groningen Old Flemish churches, all of which had been dissolved or merged with neighboring congregations before 1710: in the province of Groningen 10—Baflo, Kloosterburen, Leens, Lutkegast, Meeden, Midwolda, Wold-Oldambt, Scheemder-Hamrik, Vliedorp, and 't Zandt; in Friesland 5—Franeker, Joure, Kollum and Visvliet, Langezwaag, and Oldeberkoop; in East Friesland 1—Oldersum; in Overijssel 1—Kuinre; and besides this at Amsterdam and Middelburg (see *DB* 1879, 2-8).

The Groningen Old Flemish congregations soon united in a conference (see **Groninger Doopsgezinde Sociëteit**). They insisted on strict maintenance both of doctrine and practice; they rejected a trained and salaried ministry, holding to feetwashing when most Dutch Mennonites had dropped it, performing it in connection with the Lord's Supper, which was only held when the whole congregation was at peace. No offerings were taken during the meetings; the meetinghouses were plain with no pulpits and, of course, no organs. The ban was rigorously applied. They stood for plain living and clothing as may be seen from a number of resolutions drawn up by a conference held at Loppersum in 1659, prescribing even the furnishing of the houses and the materials and the cut of the clothes. (These resolutions were published by Blaupot ten Cate, *Friesland*, 307-8.) In 1685 and during the first decades of the 18th century these regulations were repeated several times though less strictly. They only admitted their own members into the communion services, and if a Mennonite of another branch wished to join one of their churches, he had to be rebaptized. They were very active on behalf of the Mennonites who were expelled from Switzerland and those in Prussia who were being persecuted in the early 18th century or struck by floods and crop failures. In this connection the names of Alle Derks (*q.v.*) of Groningen and Steven Cremer (*q.v.*) of Deventer should not be omitted. The Groningen Old Flemish formed a rather closed group, which apart from the joint assistance to the distressed Mennonites abroad did not have much contact with other Dutch Mennonites.

The group mostly provided its churches and members with their own confessions, catechism books, and devotional literature. Mention (chronologically) should be made of "Bekentenisse des Christelycken Geloofs," a manuscript of the 17th century; A. S. D(ijck), *De Heilbegerige Jongeling onderwesen* (Groningen, 1732); Pieter Hendriks, *Korte Schets van verscheydene waarheden des Christendoms* (Groningen, 1743); H. Waerma, *Beknopt Ontwerp van de voornaamste Geloof-zaaken* (Emden, 1744); Pieter Hendriks, *Schriftuurlijke Katechismus . . . nevens een Aanhangsel, behelzende de Schets der Lere van Menno Simons* (Groningen, 1744); *Geloofsbelijdenisse der Doopsgezinden, bekent onder de naam van Oude Vlamingen . . .* (Groningen, 1755, reprints Groningen, 1774, 1805, and a later ed. n.p., n.d.); A. S. D(ijck), *Prove eener kleine catechetize Passischool* (Groningen, 1759); Teunis Clasen, *Verklaringe van de Geloofs-belijdenisse . . .* (Groningen, 1762); H. Waerma, *De evangelische Geloofs-leere der Doopsgez. Christenen . . .* (Groningen, 1768); A. S. D(ijck), *Catechetise behandeling over de Geloofsbelijdenis . . .* (Groningen, 1773).

The most prominent leaders of this group were Uko Walles, Alle Derks, Aldert Sierts Dij(c)k, Wolter ten Cate.

During the second half of the 18th century many of the old regulations were abandoned or laxly maintained. The old principle of not accepting other Mennonites into the church without baptism was gradually abandoned. Both ban and footwashing were dropped and salaried ministry was admitted, e.g., in Groningen in 1772 and in Deventer as early as 1761. The meetinghouse in Groningen acquired a pulpit in 1756, and an organ in 1785. So in this period much of the old strictness was lost, though the Groningen Old Flemish still were among the most conservative Mennonites.

In 1710 (earlier statements are not available) the total membership of the Old Flemish group can be estimated at 2,500 baptized members. This number had decreased to 1,280 in 1767 and about 800 in 1800. During the 18th century many of these congregations were dissolved or merged with other Mennonites, and early in the 19th century, the Groningen Old Flemish Sociëteit having been dissolved in 1815, the remaining congregations of this group were successively absorbed into the main Mennonite brotherhood.   vDZ.

Inv. Arch. Amst. I, Nos. 558 II, 558 V, 559-64, 571-77, 590, 600, 605 f., 614-16, 1067, 1074-79, 1087-91, 1093-94, 1096-98, 1114, 1580-81, 1599, 1610, 1627, 1635, 1638, 1645, 1664, 1730-35; *Inventaris van het oud-archief der ver. Doopsgez. Gemeente te Groningen* (1940); S. F. Rues, *Tegenwoordige Staet der Doopsgez.* (Amsterdam, 1745) 14-67; Blaupot t. C., *Groningen* I and II, *passim;* H. Dassel Sr., *Menno's Volk in Groningen* (Groningen, 1952) 11-17, 24-35; N. van der Zijpp, *Gesch. der Doopsgezinden in Nederland* (Arnhem, 1952) 81, 114 f., 119, 130 f.; *Catalogus Amst.,* 172, 173, 219, 260-62, 264-65; *ML* II, 185 f.

Groninger Doopsgezinde Sociëteit (Groningen Mennonite Conference). In the province of Groningen there were formerly an Old Flemish conference and a Flemish conference (Humsterlandsche Sociëteit, *q.v.*). Now there is only one conference, called the *Sociëteit van Doopsgezinde Gemeenten in Groningen en Oost-Friesland.*

1. The Old Flemish Sociëteit. As early as Sept. 18, 1628, a conference took place in Middelstum, which Blaupot ten Cate (*Groningen* I, 66) considers the first meeting of the Sociëteit. It was called to discuss the attempt at union and to mediate in the disputes between Jan Luies (*q.v.*) and Claes Claesz (*q.v.*). Similar meetings were held in 1633 and 1636. In 1637 (Feb. 26–March 7) a meeting was held in Groningen, chiefly to support Uko Walles in his work. A very important meeting was held at Loppersum on April 20, 1659, at which significant resolutions were passed with regard to the threat of increasing worldliness; the simplest dress and house furnishing was prescribed and all luxury prohibited. Christians were, e.g., not to wear shoes with high heels or edged with white yarn; no paintings or gay colors were to be used in the homes (see Blaupot t. C., *Friesland,* 307 ff.). After 1677 annual meetings were held in the Old Flemish church (on Oude Boteringestraat). Besides 15 Old Flemish congregations in Groningen province, there were in this Sociëteit four congregations in East Friesland, five in Friesland, and seven in North Holland and Overijssel. In 1766 an attempt was made to unite the Groninger Sociëteit with the Zonsche Sociëteit (*q.v.*), but the negotiations were unsuccessful.

The task of the Sociëteit was at first simply to preserve apostolic purity of life and doctrine. This was also the object of the elders in visiting the congregations and holding baptismal and communion services. When several of the active elders had died, the annual meeting appointed a number, usually twice the number to be replaced, as trial preachers. These men traveled through the congregations and preached. Then the membership elected their elders from these candidates. The elders at first had absolute authority; but gradually their power decreased. In 1749 it was decided that every preacher could administer baptism and communion. In 1750 the office of elder was changed to one of supervising, the name *Oudste* (Elder) being changed to *Opziener* (Supervisor); the elders now had only general oversight in matters of church discipline and doctrine. After 1766 the work of the Sociëteit was divided into four classes; each supervisor received a class. Soon the supervisors were called *commissaris.* Beside (or over) them stood for a time the only surviving supervisor Wolter ten Cate, who died in 1796. A new general supervisor was not chosen. The office became extinct.

It was thought that the task of the Sociëteit might be promoted by a confession of faith, especially when zeal began to flag and the old customs were no longer being so carefully preserved. Until about 1750 they got along with a written confession, which differed from one congregation to another. Copies of such written confessions are found in the Amsterdam Mennonite Library (see *Inv. Arch. Amst.* I, Nos. 614, 959, and *Catalogus Amst.*, 172). In 1748 the Sociëteit published the *Kort vertoog rakende het verval en de reformatie der zeden* and soon afterward a confession of faith with a foreword by A. S. Dijk (*q.v.*) in 1755 (3d ed., 1805), which had considerable authority, but was not obligatory. It was frequently reworded without being able to satisfy everybody. The age of fixed paths was past.

Then the second objective was made the primary one, viz., relief. In 1717, when a major flood afflicted many members, the other members gave them good support. The Sociëteit (especially Elder Alle Derks) took charge. From now on until the end (1815) the Sociëteit was faithful to this purpose. In addition it gave financial assistance to foreign Mennonites, as, e.g., the Prussian brethren in 1738 and 1765.

Beginning in 1785 a third purpose was the improvement of ministers' salaries. On this objective not much was accomplished, and by 1811 the A.D.S. assumed this task. Now the Old Flemish Sociëteit had become superfluous. In the last times of its existence it no longer met annually. In 1815 it was dissolved. The last meeting was held on June 18, 1815.

2. In addition to the Old Flemish Sociëteit there was the smaller Flemish one, usually known as the Humsterland Sociëteit. It probably had its beginning not before 1750. It originally embraced ten Flemish congregations in the province of Groningen and until about 1798 the Foppe Ones brotherhood in Ameland (*q.v.*). In 1806 only the congregations of Humsterland, Pieterzijl, Den Horn, and Huizinge were members of the Sociëteit. It met annually in rotation with its constituent congregations. Its initial objective was, like that of the Old Flemish Sociëteit, the preservation of the moral and doctrinal purity of the congregations. Beginning in 1773 an annual offering was taken for the support of the poor and to improve ministers' salaries. For a time it continued to exist without achieving very much. On May 30, 1825, it was dissolved.

3. In 1825, ten years after the Old Flemish Sociëteit had been dissolved, the chairman of the Humsterlandsche Sociëteit, Gerrit Bakker, the zealous preacher of Humsterland, made the proposal that all the congregations be invited to unite in the organization of a general conference in the province of Groningen. On July 26, 1825, a preliminary meeting was held in Groningen. A second meeting was held on Sept. 16, at which it was decided to proceed with the organization. On March 31, 1826, a constitution was adopted and on May 22 the first meeting of the Sociëteit was held. The chairman was P. Klomp of Groningen and the secretary Gerrit Bakker. At this session the constitu-

tion was signed by 13 congregations: Groningen, Den Horn, Pieterzijl, Humsterland (Noordhorn), Mensingeweer, Huizinge (Middelstum), Uithuizen, Zijldijk, Leermens en Loppersum, Sappemeer, Noordbroek, Midwolda, and Veendam-Pekela.

The primary objective of the general Sociëteit was to care for a regular ministerial service. In the congregations which had no minister, the service was taken care of in rotation by those that had ministers. The second objective of the Sociëteit was to intermediate when difficulties arose between preachers and congregations.

In the course of time Stadskanaal (founded in 1848) also joined the Sociëteit. In 1878 the East Frisian congregations, Emden, Leer, and Norden, joined the Groninger Sociëteit. During World War I this tie loosened. Emden and Leer are now merged and have a German-speaking minister. In 1928, however, C. A. Leendertz, then pastor of Norden, was serving in the vacant pulpits of the Groningen congregations. Since World War II the ties between the Sociëteit and the East Frisian congregations have again been strengthened.

In 1835 a Widows' Fund was established on the initiative of Simon Gorter (*q.v.*), the Zijldijk pastor. Also a ministers' pension fund (*Emeritaat en Invaliditeitfonds*) was founded in 1917, and in 1924 a fund for raising the salaries of ministers (*Steunfonds*). The Sociëteit meets annually in Groningen (still in the former Old Flemish church on Oude Boteringestraat). "No great achievements have been made by the Sociëteit, but in our quiet circles it has done excellent work. And in the kingdom of God little things are also of value" (van Cleef).

vDZ.

Inv. Arch. Amst. I, Nos. 614-16, 934, 959-65; *DJ* 1840, 34-52; *DB* 1870, 110-17; 1872, 49-51; 1879, 1-11; Blaupot t. C., *Groningen* I, 66, 125-48; (A. Pathuis) *Inv. van het Oud-Archief der Ver. Doopsgez. Gemeente te Groningen* (Groningen, 1940) Nos. 136-48; Blaupot t. C., *Groningen*; L. van Cleef, Jr., "Feestrede" in *DB* 1877; K. Vos, *Het honderdjarig bestaan der Societeit von Doopsgez. Gemeenten en Oostfriesland* (1926); *ML* II, 185 ff.

Groot Hoorns Liedtboeck, Het, *waer in Eenige Psalmen Davids ende Geestelijcke Liedekens zijn om inde Vergaderinghe der Gheloovigen te singhen etc.*, a Dutch Mennonite hymnbook composed by D. I. and published 1647 at Hoorn by Pieter Zachariaszn Hartevelt. It contains 488 pages with 208 hymns without notes, arranged alphabetically. The copy of this hymnbook in the Amsterdam Mennonite Library contains 16 pages (incomplete) of a suffix entitled *Byvoeghsel van Sommighe Gheestelijcke Liedekens,* printed at Hoorn in 1644. vDZ.

Groot, Jelis de, an Anabaptist martyr: see **Gillis de Graet.**

Groote Bundel, Dutch hymnbook: see **Bundel, Groote.**

Groote Hendrik, an Anabaptist martyr: see **Hendrik Beverts.**

Groote Liede-boeck, Het, van L. C., a Dutch hymnary of which Leenaert (Leonhard) Clock (*q.v.*) is the compiler, is known in only one edition, which appeared at Leeuwarden in 1625. The (abbreviated) title reads as follows: *Het Groote Liedeboeck van L. C., Inhoudende Veelderhande Schriftuyrlijcke Liedekens, Vermaningen, Leeringen, Ghebeden ende Lofsangen . . . mitsgaders het tweede Liedeboecxken van ghelijcken Propooste, ghenaemt Een Hell Cymbaelken des Juychens, waer by nu nieuws ghecomen is het derde Liedeboecxken . . . ghenoemt het nieuwe Hell Cymbaelken des Juychens . . . , mitsgaders Noch ses (liedekens) uyt het cleyn Liedt-boeck van L. C. Item veerthien van andere verscheydene personen.*

From this title we learn that there was also a *Cleyn Liedeboeck* by L. C., but no copy of it is extant. The 1625 edition of the *Groot Liedeboeck* apparently was not the first edition. Part I of the book contains the introduction, dated Jan. 1, 1601, 254 hymns in alphabetic order; Part II, with introduction, dated Haerlem, Aug. 30, 1601, also in alphabetic order, songs Nos. 255-379; Part III, not in alphabetic order, Nos. 380-421 (the last hymn of this part, No. 421, composed by Leenaert Clock himself, is dated Schoonhoven July 1, 1616); Part IV, 14 hymns numbered 1-14.　　　　vDZ.

Grootebroek, a village in the Dutch province of North Holland, near Enkhuizen, where there was formerly a Mennonite congregation, of whose history nothing is known. Leenaert Bouwens baptized 18 persons here in 1551-54 and another 24 in 1563-65. This presupposes the existence of a congregation at this time. In the 17th century the congregation belonged to the Waterlander branch. It dissolved before 1731, since it is not found in the first *Naamlijst* (of 1731). Its possessions and stocks were handed over to the North Holland Waterlander Conference or Rijper Sociëteit (*DJ* 1942, 39).　　　　vDZ.

Gross, a Mennonite family name. On the basis of historical inference, and in the absence of published genealogies, the Gross family name may have had its inception in the Austrian Tirol among the early Hutterites, though this is not established. The name appears among the Hutterites in Russia after the migration of 1770. When, in 1819, the practice of community of goods was abandoned at Radicheva, there were Grosses among those who abandoned the practice. During the immigration of Hutterites to America following 1874 the name Gross appeared among those who settled on non-communal farms in South Dakota.

In the following years independent churches were organized, composed entirely of non-colonist Hutterites. Some of these churches joined the Mennonite (GCM) conference, and a number of their members, leaving the farm for the town, or marrying Mennonites, joined Mennonite (GCM) congregations. The name appears predominantly among South Dakota Mennonites. Harold H. Gross has been dean of Freeman College since 1945.

H.H.G.

A different branch of the Gross family originated with Jacob Gross (*ca.* 1743-1810) who emigrated from either Switzerland or Germany to eastern Pennsylvania about 1763. Jacob became a Mennonite preacher at Deep Run in the Franconia (MC) Conference by 1775, and later was ordained bishop. He was the father of Christian Gross (1776-1865), a minister of Deep Run, John K. Gross (1786-1864), minister of Doylestown, Jacob Gross (1780-1865), bishop in Ontario, and Daniel Gross (1784-1875), deacon of Deep Run. A number of other men named Gross have served in the ministry of the Franconia Conference, including bishops Samuel G. Gross (1839-95) and Joseph L. Gross (1904-　) of Doylestown. Of considerable influence in the Franconia Conference was Mahlon Gross (1873-1937), who left the Methodist Church in which he was a local preacher to return to the faith of his fathers, and was chosen as minister at Doylestown, May 25, 1920.　　　　J.C.W.

Gross, Georg, often called Pfersfelder, was a Protestant baron in the 16th century, who was interested in Schwenckfelder and Anabaptist ideas and defended the victims of persecution in the area of Nürnberg, Germany. For a fuller biographical account see **Pfersfelder, Georg.**

Gross, Jakob (Jakob von Waldshut), a furrier of Waldshut, South Germany, a very successful Anabaptist leader. According to his statements in his cross-examination (Meyer, 245 f.), he received from Conrad Grebel (*q.v.*), whom he called "the student from Zürich," his first suggestion to join the Anabaptists. Balthasar Hubmaier baptized him. He at once went out as an Anabaptist missioner. He was expelled from Waldshut because he refused to support the peasants of Zell in military service. (This he himself said in his trials at Zürich and Strasbourg.)

In autumn of 1525 Gross was in the Grüningen district of the canton of Zürich, Switzerland, and baptized about 35 in one day. Expelled from there in early 1526 he went to the canton of Bern, preaching at Zofingen, Brittnau, and Aarau, baptizing many, until he was imprisoned at Brugg. He skillfully defended Anabaptist doctrine. Devils are driven out of children, said he, although they do not have any. Zwingli and his theologians he reproached with keeping comfortable and rich prebends instead of going out as messengers of God to proclaim the Word and direct the erring to the right way. But those who proclaimed the Word of God without salary, content with mere food, were hunted, arrested, and subjected to all kinds of misery (Egli, 45).

In Lahr, where he soon continued his work, Gross was again imprisoned and then expelled. From Lahr he went to Strasbourg in the summer of 1526. But here he baptized hardly more than three, one of them the furrier Matthis Hiller. His meetings were poorly attended. They were opened with a prayer to ask the presence of God, that He might give strength to bear the cross with patience. Then one of the brethren rose to explain a portion of Scripture, to warn against sinful living, to admonish the hearers not to violate God's commands, to love their neighbors and feed their enemies.

Nevertheless Jakob Gross ranked with Hubmaier and Reublin as one of three most influential in founding the Strasbourg Anabaptist congregation. He was prevented from a more successful ministry by his arrest soon after his arrival. During his cross-examination, Aug. 9, 1526, he expressed some surprise that the Gospel had had so little effect after four years of preaching in Strasbourg. He complained that he was put into prison without a hearing or an admonition. But he was not afraid; for against God's will they could not injure a hair of his head. Even if the life of a Christian might be nothing but persecution and cross-bearing, which was also the lot of the apostles, that should not injure his faith, and if it was God's will he would sacrifice his life, as he had already given up his possessions. Against the Catholic doctrine that baptism washes away original sin he cited the Scripture, "Baptism, not putting away the filth of the flesh, but the answer of a good conscience toward God" (I Pet. 3:21). He would have nothing to do with infant baptism; for baptism is nothing but a change in living, a dying to sensual flesh; and since a little child is not yet master of its flesh it cannot kill the flesh. Furthermore, the Lord's command, Matt. 28, refers only to baptism after confession. In the end everybody must decide for himself whether to be baptized or not; this a child cannot do. Obedience to the government is a duty; for the sword is given it to punish the evil and protect the good. For himself, he wanted to obey all its commands; he would serve as a guard, put on armor, take the sword; but he would refuse to kill anyone, for that was not commanded by God. He would also refuse to swear an oath on the basis of Jesus' command in Matt. 5.

From Strasbourg Jakob Gross went to Augsburg. He may have taken part in the well-known Anabaptist synod here, which took place Aug. 20, 1527, and is known as the martyrs' synod. On Sept. 15, 1527, he was seized with Hans Hut (q.v.) at an Anabaptist meeting in Augsburg. Almost four years he languished in prison, until he recanted, June 22, 1531.   NEFF.

E. Egli, *Die Züricher Wiedertäufer* (Zürich, 1878); L. von Muralt and W. Schmid, *Quellen zur Gesch. der Täufer in der Schweiz* I (Zürich, 1952) 107, 261, 262; H. S. Bender, *Conrad Grebel* (Goshen, 1950) 152; Abr. Hulshoff, *Gesch. van de Doopsgez. te Straatsburg* (Amsterdam, 1905) 18-22; C. A. Cornelius, *Gesch. des Münsterischen Aufruhrs* II (Leipzig, 1860); Chr. Meyer in *Ztscht des Hist. Vereins für Schwaben und Neuburg* (1874) 213 ff.; F. W. Röhrich in *Ztscht für die hist. Theologie* XXX (1860) 33 ff.; Fr. Roth, *Augsburgs Ref.-Gesch.* (Munich, 1901); idem, in *Ztscht des Hist. Vereins für Schwaben und Neuburg* XXVIII (1901) 4 ff.; *ML* II, 187 f.

Gross, Jakob, was born in Germany about 1743, emigrated to America about 1763, settled at Skippack, later moved to Germantown, and finally to Bedminster Twp., Bucks Co., Pa. He was married to Mary Krall; to this union were born six children. Four sons became church leaders: Christian, a minister at Deep Run; Jacob, a minister in Ontario; John K., a minister, and Daniel, a deacon at Deep Run. He was ordained a minister at Deep Run between 1773 and 1775. He preached at Germantown on Nov. 6, 1796. By 1804 he was ordained a bishop of the Deep Run circuit, for in that year he interviewed Christian Funk (q.v.) for possible reconciliation. He was a farmer and shoemaker.

Gross's letter of Sept. 4, 1801, to Lincoln Co., Ont., giving counsel on organizing a new congregation was published in *Briefe an die Mennonisten Gemeine in Ober Canada* (Berlin, Ont., 1840).

A farewell letter written by Jakob Gross to his three churches in 1810 indicates his deep concern for their spiritual welfare, and also reflects the high esteem with which the laity regarded their spiritual shepherd. Bishop Gross died on Dec. 12, 1810, and lies buried in the Deep Run cemetery.   Q.L.

Gross, Paul, chosen Hutterite preacher May 15, 1904, by the Rosedale, Man., Bruderhof, was confirmed March 25, 1906. He died May 2, 1929, in the Iberville Bruderhof in Canada at the age of 60 years, having served in the ministry for 25 years.   D.D.

Gross, Veronika (*Albrechtin*), wife of Jakob Gross (q.v.) and like him a native of Waldshut. She was one of the first women to join the Anabaptist movement. She was baptized in 1525 by a preacher whom she called Wilhelm (Reublin?) in her cross-examination. In Augsburg she and Anna Salminger contributed to the spread and establishment of the Anabaptist congregation by their influence on the women. For a while she and her husband lived (1526) in the home of Eitelhans Langenmantel (q.v.). After the capture of her husband (Sept. 15, 1527) she sought to provide for herself by sewing and spinning. But she must have found it difficult to earn a living, for she sold two of her husband's books, the Prophets—probably the Worms translation—for four Batzen, and a small Testament for 13 Kreuzer. She attended the meetings faithfully, and was one of the 88 participants in the Easter service (April 12, 1528) held in the home of the sculptor Doucher, which was so abruptly ended by the capture of those present. In the cross-examination she stated that she had joined the Anabaptists "since she was convinced that this was the right way." Because she refused to recant she was driven out of the city with lashes on April 30.   HEGE.

Fr. Roth, *Augsburgs Ref.-Gesch.* (1901); idem, *Ztscht des Hist. Vereins für Schwaben und Neuburg* XXVIII (1901) 6 ff.; *ML* II, 188.

Grosse Gemeinde (Big Church) was the name given to a group during the early days of the Molotschna settlement in Russia when the *Kleine Gemeinde* (q.v.) originated under the leadership of Klaas Reimer. Both were nicknames and not official names. The name "Kleine Gemeinde" remained while the name "Grosse Gemeinde" soon disappeared. The Grosse Gemeinde was really the Flemish mother church of the Molotschna, known as the Ohrloff-Petershagen-Halbstadt Church (q.v.). Its first elder was Jacob Enns (1803-18), who was succeeded by Jakob Fast (1818-21). It was during this period that a smaller group separated under the leadership of Klaas Reimer which formed the independent organization known as the Kleine Gemeinde. Under Bernhard Fast (1821-60), who succeeded Jakob Fast as elder of the Grosse Gemeinde or the Ohrloff-Petershagen-Halbstadt Church, the congregation divided because of numerous differences of opinion and practices within the church. The more conservative wing, consisting of about three fourths of the congregation, organized an independent church under Jakob Warkentin, usually referred to as "Grosse Gemeinde" or "Pure Flemish." This became the Lichtenau-Petershagen-Schönsee-Margenau-Pordenau Mennonite Church (*q.v.*). When, in 1842, Warkentin was declared unworthy of his office as a result of conflicts with Johann Cornies, the congregation was divided into three groups: Lichtenau-Petershagen Church, Margenau-Schönsee Church, and Pordenau Church, each one having its own elder. This ended the era during which the name "Grosse Gemeinde" was applicable.

C.K.

H. Görz, *Molotschnaer Ansiedlung* (Manitoba, 1950); Friesen, *Brüderschaft*, 703 ff.

Grosses Werder (Grosses Marienburger Werder, Gross-Werder): see **Marienburger Werder.**

Gross-Lubin in the Graudenz (*q.v.*) district, formerly belonging to Poland, and from 1772 to Prussia, situated on the left bank of the Vistula River, like the adjacent hamlet of Klein-Lubin was from 1591 a *Holländerdorf,* i.e., a village settled by Dutch Mennonite immigrants. In 1623 it obtained exemption from the military tax and from obligatory quartering of soldiers, and in the lease of 1640, was granted freedom of religion, though it was not allowed to erect a meetinghouse. The Mennonites here were members of the congregation of Jeziorken (Kleinsee, *q.v.*). Both Gross-Lubin and Klein-Lubin repeatedly had much to suffer from floods. For this reason and also because the Polish Catholic clergy were very hostile to them, most Mennonites in the 18th century moved from here to other places, e.g., to Brenkenhoffswalde in the Neumark. vDZ.

F. Szper, *Nederl. Nederzettingen in West-Pruisen gedurende den Poolschen tijd* (Enkhuizen, 1913) 130-34; H. Wiebe, *Das Siedlungswerk niederl. Mennoniten im Weichseltal* (Marburg, 1952) 10, 22-24, 79.

Gross-Lunau, Klein-Lunau, and **Horst,** three villages in the territory of the city of Culm (*q.v.*), formerly belonging to Poland, after 1772 to Prussia, and from 1919 to Poland again, situated on the right bank of the Vistula River, were all three *Holländerdörfer,* i.e., villages settled by Dutch Mennonite farmers, who moved here in 1604. (The first lease of 1604 was published in Wiebe, *Das Siedlungswerk,* 92-94.) They are said to have had a Mennonite school at Gross-Lunau shortly after 1604. A meetinghouse was available in the neighboring village of Schönsee (*q.v.*). They were not allowed to proselytize among the Catholic natives or to build meetinghouses. Notwithstanding repeated floods and high rents the Mennonites became rather prosperous. About 1720 a mutual fire-insurance system was organized. In the last decade of the 18th century and the first of the 19th a number of Mennonites from these villages migrated to Russia. vDZ.

Herbert Wiebe, *Das Siedlungswerk niederl. Mennoniten im Weichseltal* (Marburg, 1952) 13, 34 f., 36, 37, 65 (note 48), 82 f., 92-94, 95.

Grosslützel: see **Lucelle.**

Grossmann (Megander), **Kaspar,** born 1495 in Zürich, early a zealous follower of Zwingli. Called to Bern in 1528, he, as a strict Zwinglian, rejected Bucer's mediation on the communion and therefore returned to Zürich as archdeacon and canon at the cathedral. He died Aug. 18, 1545. Conrad Grebel said at his cross-examination in 1525, that Grossmann was also of his opinion, but dared not speak out before Zwingli. This was probably not entirely correct. At the disputation of Nov. 6-8 Grossmann, Leo Judae, and Zwingli defended Zwingli's theses against the Anabaptists. In Bern he frequently had to take a position on the Anabaptist question with other preachers. On April 19, 1531, he took part in the disputation with Hans Pfistermeyer (*q.v.*) of Aarau at Bern, and from July 1-9, 1532, with Haller and Hofmeister at Zofingen. Both disputations have been preserved in print, but the speakers are designated merely as "Prädikant" or "Täufer," hence it is impossible to determine the personal attitude of the individual preachers (see **Hofmeister, Pfistermeyer, Zofingen**). After the disputation Grossmann was appointed to examine the records with the other preachers in Aarau and then have them printed by Froschauer in Zürich. In his *Catechism* of 1536 he interprets baptism entirely in accord with Zwingli's idea, probably because of the need to formulate a clear position against the Anabaptists. In his numerous letters to Zwingli and later to Bullinger he does not mention Anabaptists. L.v.M.

Emil Egli, in *HRE* XII, 501 ff.; W. Köhler and O. Farner, ed., *Zwingli Werke* X (1929) 137, note 1; R. Steck and G. Tobler, *Aktensammlung zur Geschichte der Berner Reformation* (Bern, 1923); *ML* II, 189.

Grossmann, Michael, a Hutterite and writer of hymns, a cobbler by trade, was sent to Prussia in 1602 with Josef Hauser (*q.v.*). When he returned to Moravia he was chosen preacher for the Neumühl brotherhood, Feb. 1, 1604, and ordained on Feb. 5, 1606; then he was made elder at Austerlitz, and died April 4, 1634, at Sobotiste. He is the author of the hymn, "Mich hat die Lieb gedrungen sehr," which contains his name in an acrostic.

NEFF.

Wolkan, *Geschicht-Buch,* 470, 476, 492, 583, and 619; *Die Lieder der Hutterischen Brüder* (Scottdale, 1914) 85; *ML* II, 189.

Gross-Schützen, a Hutterite Bruderhof in Hungary: see **Velké Levary.**

Grossweide, a common Mennonite village name found first in the Marienburg Werder, Prussia, whence it was transplanted to the Molotschna settlement of Russia; Manitoba; Mexico; and the Menno, Neuland, and Friesland settlements in Paraguay.

C.K.

Grossweide, a Mennonite village in the Halbstadt district of the Molotschna, Ukraine, with 51 farms and 2,700 acres. In 1927 the village had a population of 316, most of whom belonged to the Rudnerweide Mennonite Church. A small part belonged to the Mennonite Brethren, who held services in a private home. In the primary school all the village children were taught. The inhabitants engaged almost exclusively in agriculture and cattle raising;

the latter received more attention after the Revolution, since the farms had been radically reduced in size. Though generally thriving the villages experienced some crop failures, as in 1833, 1848, and 1920. On June 16, 1926, the grain was almost completely destroyed by hail. In Grossweide there was for a long time an orphanage founded by A. A. Harder (*q.v.*), in which 50-80 orphans found a home, care, and education. After the Revolution it was taken over by the government. Little is known about the final disintegration of the village under the Soviets. (*ML* II, 189.) N.G.

Grossweide Mennonite Brethren Church, located near Horndean, Man., a member of the Canadian Conference of the M.B. Church, was organized in 1896 under the leadership of its mother church, the Winkler M.B. Church. The membership in 1954 was 164. The first meetinghouse, with a seating capacity of 160, was rebuilt and enlarged. It burned down in January 1953, and was replaced by a new one seating 400, dedicated on Nov. 1, 1953. Jacob Heide was the leader and minister of the church in 1925-44. In 1952 John J. Neufeld was serving as presiding minister and A. W. Klassen as assistant minister, with D. M. Hiebert as deacon. J.J.N.

Groupe des Eglises Mennonites de langue française (Group of French-Speaking Mennonite Congregations) of France and neighboring Switzerland. When the German language had been gradually replaced by the French in a number of congregations they organized a conference in 1907 (called *Association*), which was reorganized in 1927 under the present name. This conference, which meets annually on the Monday after Easter, was at first a part of the conference of Alsace (*q.v.*), but became independent in 1946. vDZ.

Grouw, a town (pop. about 3,000) in the Dutch province of Friesland, southeast of Leeuwarden, picturesquely situated on a lake, seat of a Mennonite congregation. This congregation was probably founded about 1560-70; Leenaert Bouwens baptized 37 persons here in 1563-65. Of its early history nothing is known. A meetinghouse was built in 1659. In 1696 through the activity of its preacher Jan Claesz (or Klaasz, *q.v.*), a more liberal leader, the congregation was divided. The more liberal group, called Jan Claeszvolk and later Waterlanders, was the larger group. This group was in warm sympathy with the Collegiants (*q.v.*) at Grouw and participated in their meetings. Its members mostly lived in town, being navigators, captains, and steersmen on whaling vessels or Baltic freighters, butter merchants like the Koopmans and Halbertsma families, and clockmakers like the Hoekstra family. The smaller group called themselves Flemish; their members were mostly farmers, living outside of the town of Grouw. They maintained the old practices like silent prayer and were averse to a salaried ministry. The Flemish built a new meetinghouse called the "Kleine" or "Oude Huys"; the Waterlanders kept the former meetinghouse, now called the "Groote" or "Nieuwe Huys." In 1829 the two congregations united; the Kleine

Huys was abandoned and the Groote Huys was replaced in 1830 by the present one, which has been built on the same spot and shows the type of the older one, being a hidden church. A pipe organ was acquired in 1872. The number of Mennonites here must formerly have been considerable. The Oude Huys (Flemish) Mennonites at the beginning of the 18th century numbered about 150 baptized members, in 1829, 122; the membership of the Nieuwe Huys (Waterlander) can be estimated at about 320 in 1756, 148 in 1829. These numbers decreased principally because of economic conditions which made many people leave Grouw. In 1839 at the time of the union the membership was 270, in 1861 again increased to 380, reaching its height of 462 in 1889, and then declining: 419 in 1900 and 230 in 1953. Taco Kuiper, who had studied at the Amsterdam Mennonite Seminary, was the first trained minister to serve the (*Groote Huys*) congregation of Grouw (1790-99). J. A. van der Ploeg, also trained at Amsterdam, served the Groote Huys from 1802 and the united congregation 1829-52. With C. Corver (*q.v.*), who served as pastor in 1863-65, modernism (liberalism) entered the congregation. Corver was followed by A. van Gulik 1866-1903, P. Ens 1903-14, H. G. Berg 1915-20, F. H. Pasma 1921-51, and H. R. Keuning 1952- . A new parsonage was built in 1952. Church activities are a Bible group, a women's circle, and a youth group. F.H.P., vDZ.

Inv. Arch. Amst. II, Nos. 1848-53; Blaupot t. C., *Friesland, passim;* J. H. Halbertsma, *De Doopsgezinden en hunne herkomst* (Deventer, 1843) 313 f.; *DJ* 1917, 84-91; *DB* 1887, 51, 53, 79; 1896, 160, 164, 171; 1900, 90, 123; F. H. Pasma, *De Doopsgezinden te Grouw* (Grouw, 1930); *ML* II, 189.

Grouw, Jan Klaasz (Claesz, Claesen) **van:** see **Klaasz, Jan.**

Grouw, Ruurd Gerbens van: see **Gerbens.**

Grouw, Tjalling Gerbens van: see **Gerbens.**

Groveland Evangelical Mennonite Church, located one-half mile east of Groveland, in Groveland Twp., Tazewell Co., Ill., began as a subsidiary of the Wesley City congregation near Peoria, Ill. Meetings were held in homes until the congregation organized in 1878. The meetinghouse has been remodeled twice. Elders who have served are: Peter Hochstettler and Emanuel Rocke; ministers, Ben Birkey, Chris Oyer, Joseph Rediger, Joseph Springer, Moses Ropp, Amos Oyer, and Paul Rupp; and deacons, Andrew Roth, Ben Roth, Daniel Ackerman, and E. E. Zimmerman. Groveland was host to the conference in 1895, 1903, 1907, 1912, 1918, 1925, 1935, and 1943. Fanny Schmallenberger and Mr. and Mrs. Glenn Rocke went as missionaries to Africa, and Ellen Hochstettler to Tennessee. About 1896-1900 some members left to join with the newly organized Missionary Church Association. The membership in 1954 was 149. Milo Zimmerman is the present (1955) pastor. E.E.Z.

Groveland Mennonite Church (MC), also known as the Plumstead Mennonite Church, located in Plumstead Twp., Bucks Co., Pa., is a member of the

Franconia Conference. The first meetinghouse was erected in 1806 for members of the Deep Run congregation living in that area. The present meetinghouse was erected in 1886. Preaching services were held every four weeks by the ministers of Deep Run, Doylestown, or Blooming Glen churches. In 1947 a weekly Sunday school was started, with preaching services every two weeks. Omar Showalter was ordained Aug. 18, 1951, as the first minister and Leidy Myers was ordained March 8, 1952, as the first deacon. The membership in 1955 was 51.   L.M.

Grubb, Nathaniel B., b. July 6, 1850, in Frederick Twp., Montgomery Co., Pa., the son of Silas and Elizabeth Bertolet Grubb, of Pennsylvania-German background. He was married on July 4, 1872, to Salome C. Gottshall, of Tremont, Pa. There were six children, of whom three grew to adulthood. Nathaniel B. Grubb was educated in Frederick Institute (an academy and preparatory school in Frederick Township); and in the Mennonite school at Wadsworth, Ohio (1872).

He was baptized and became a member of the Eden Mennonite Church, Schwenksville, in 1865. On June 30, 1872, he was ordained as assistant to the elder of the congregation. In addition to Schwenksville, he conducted services at Herstines, Bertolets, Skippachville, Rock Hill, and Rich Valley. On Oct. 1, 1882, he became pastor of the First Mennonite Church of Philadelphia, which he served for 38 years and 3 months. On May 28, 1884, he was ordained to the office of elder, or bishop as it was frequently called at that time.

Grubb had a large part in the founding of the Mennonite Home for the Aged at Frederick, Pa., and served on the board of managers of the home for 30 years. He was a member of the Publication Board of the General Conference for 39 years; a Mennonite member of the board of trustees of the United Society of Christian Endeavor for 24 years; a member of the board of trustees of Bethel College, Newton, Kan., for 6 years; and a member of the board of trustees of Perkiomen Seminary (now Perkiomen School), Pennsburg, Pa., for 18 years. He was the first editor of the *Mennonite,* serving as such for six years. He was also the editor of the *Mennonite Year Book and Almanac* for a number of years. During his career he resided in Frederick Township, Schwenksville, and Philadelphia.

Grubb was a very successful pastor, winning many to Christ and the church, and was also active in home mission enterprises and in establishing Sunday school and Christian Endeavor conventions. His avocation was printing and publishing. At one time early in his career he owned a printing office and founded the *Schwenksville Item.*

He died in Philadelphia on April 25, 1938, and was buried in Northwood Cemetery, Philadelphia. An obituary was published in the *Year Book* of the General Conference Mennonite Church for 1939. A historical sketch of his life appeared in *Mennonite Life,* January 1951.†   A.S.R.

Grubenheimer, a name applied to the Waldenses in the 14th century because they were accustomed to assemble in corners and isolated places, in gravel pits (*Gruben*) to escape their enemies. The name seems to have been used for the Anabaptists as well. (*ML* II, 190.)

Gruber, Lamprecht, of Fieless (Villnöss) in Tirol, Austria, a martyr, was one of the groups of Anabaptists at Sterzing who in 1532 went to their death for the sake of their faith. He is one of the rather infrequent examples of Anabaptists who recanted, and then, seized by remorse, atoned for their lapse with death. He speaks openly about it in the letter which he and his fellow prisoners wrote to the church in the Adige; he says he hopes to heal the wound he inflicted on his people through his weakness, and depends on God's help to do it. Otherwise it would not be possible to endure the torture inflicted upon him. In a second letter he gives expression to his joy in receiving word from Austerlitz, and states that he and his five companions, Hans Beck, Lorenz Schuster, Peter Planer, and his former servant, and finally Hans Thaler, hope to discard the hungry, physical body "next Wednesday." They are therefore saying good-by and warn against sleepiness. Then follow greetings to the brotherhood in Moravia, to Lamprecht's wife, to Lienhart and Jörg Zaunring, to Koller's parents, and to Planer's wife. They are glad that the Lord so strongly moves His children to go to Moravia. All of them, says the *Geschicht-Buch,* witnessed with their blood to divine truth.

LOSERTH.

Beck, *Geschichtsbücher,* 105 f.; Wolkan, *Geschicht-Buch,* 74; *Mart. Mir.* D 33, E 440; *ML* II, 190.

Grulla Mennonite Brethren Church, the only Protestant church in Grulla, Starr Co., Tex., a village of 1,800 Latin Americans. It is a member of the Southern District Conference, organized with 12 members on May 22, 1948, under the leadership of the missionary and pastor Ruben Wedel, who is still serving. The membership in 1955 was 42, most of whom were poor people. The first meetinghouse, a new garage which seated about 100, was replaced by a new church dedicated in 1950. Five baptismal services have been held.   R.W.

Grumbach, Argula von (*ca.* 1492-1554), a courageous woman of Burg Ehrenfels near Hemau, Upper Palatinate, Bavaria, Germany, a true follower of Luther, and yet independent in her religious conviction, wishing to be known as "Christian" rather than "Lutheran." She warmly defended those persecuted and oppressed for their faith. In defense of Arsacius Seehofer, a young Luther enthusiast who was compelled to make a humiliating recantation, she wrote a courageous letter to the Ingolstadt city council, to Duke William of Bavaria, and to the University of Ingolstadt, admonishing "all Christian estates and governments to stay by the truth and the Word of God, . . . over which neither pope, emperor, nor prince has any authority." This bold step, unheard of at the time, for a woman to assert herself in writing in ecclesiastical affairs, caused a great stir, and brought her much recognition and admiration, but still more mockery and persecution. Balthasar Hubmaier (*q.v.*) also spoke of her with great respect. In his *Schluss-reden* against Johann Eck (24-26) he remarked that women should be silent in church, but when the men are mute with fear, let the women speak, as Argula did. In a letter to the city council of Regensburg he cites the example of Frau Argula von Stauff (her maiden name), to encourage it to take a bold stand for Protestantism.   NEFF.

S. Riezler, *Geschichte Bayerns 1508-1597* IV (1899) 89; C. Sachsse, *Dr. Balthasar Hubmaier als Theologe* (Berlin, 1914) 12, 85; *RGG* II (1928) 1502; *HRE* XVIII, 779, where bibliography is cited; *ML* II, 190.

Grunauer, Barbara, an Anabaptist martyr, a widow of Salzburg, Austria, was drowned in Salzburg Oct. 25, 1527, with Elsbeth, the cook of Georg Steiner. Johann Eck (*q.v.*) reported this to Duke George of Saxony, Nov. 25, 1527.   HEGE.

F. Gess, *Akten und Briefe zur Kirchengeschichte Herzog Georgs von Sachsen* II (Leipzig, 1917) 812; *ML* II, 190.

Grünberger, Veit (Greyenburger, or Uhrmacher—watchmaker—for his trade), was one of the outstanding apostles of the Hutterian Brethren. Nothing is known of his birth date or early life. The *Geschicht-Buch* states that about 1570, when he was traveling through the Pinzgau, (Salzburg, Austria) with a brother, Veit Schecht, they were spied on by peasants and recognized as Anabaptists by their prayer before meals; they were then turned over to the authorities, tried, and imprisoned in Mittersill, and five weeks later were taken to the city of Salzburg and put in chains. Over 18 months passed before they were given a proper hearing. The record of this cross-examination is given in his most remarkable *Verantwortung*. Without fear he testified to his faith and frequently embarrassed his judges with his replies. When asked to what faith he belonged, he answered, "You know that already. Your lord the archbishop knows it too. Our books have been sent up to the governor; there you may see them. Besides, two of our preachers have been judged, Klaus Felbinger (*q.v.*) at Landshut in Bavaria, and Hans Mändel (*q.v.*) at Innsbruck; these have given a better account of our faith than I can give. Furthermore, the prince must have known before he was made archbishop, how many of our people have been killed in his realm. What he does with us now is his business; with God's help we will hold still. We have read Felbinger's and Mändel's *Rechenschaft* more than once; they are entirely Scriptural; if they are not believed we can do nothing more; the judges know the truth very well; if they wanted to live accordingly they would not need to ask us."

In the cross-examination as reported by the *Geschicht-Buch,* Grünberger asks, "What shall I say? You are the accusers and the judges. What you cannot judge, the executioners must do in your stead. The hangman is your high priest, who helps you hold the field." The disputation covered chiefly marriage, fasts, baptism, and Jakob Hutter's mission. Veit's questions are sharp, his responses sharper. "Veit Urmacher asks the judges whether they consider Paul also an Anabaptist. They said

no. Then he asked them why he commanded the twelve disciples to be baptized when they had already been baptized with John's baptism. This was not adequate for salvation. How much less does infant baptism suffice, which is only of men and not like that of John from heaven. Then they were silent. When they asked him whether Hutter was the Messiah, Veit answered, Christ is the Messiah. I am not ashamed of Jakob Hutter. He was burned at the stake for the sake of divine truth. But you have a fine Messiah in Rome and one here in the city."

Veit's fellow prisoner Schecht finally renounced his faith, but returned to it later with genuine repentance. Veit remained in prison until 1576. He wrote from prison on Feb. 16, 1573, that he had no fears for his life. They had been told that no one wanted to wash his hands in their blood, and everybody knew who they were. He finally succeeded in escaping by letting himself out a window by means of a rope made of old materials. And so he went home to the brotherhood "with peace and joy." The next year he was chosen to the ministry at Neumühl and confirmed three years later. On March 17, 1586, he died at Scheidowitz, Moravia. The story of his imprisonment and that of his brethren Matthias Binder (*q.v.*) and Paul Glock (*q.v.*) and how God helped them escape, is the subject of the hymn, "Merk auf, du wahr' christliche Gemein."   LOSERTH.

Wolkan, *Geschicht-Buch; Die Lieder der Hutterischen Brüder* (Scottdale, 1914) 713-26; J. Loserth, "Zur Geschichte der Wiedertäufer in Salzburg," in *Mitteilungen der Gesellsch. für Salzburger Landeskunde* LII (1912) 35 f.; the text of the *Verantwortung* (1573) is published in extenso *ibid.,* 51-56; *Mart. Mir.* D 501, E 841 f.; *ML* II, 190 f.

Grüneisen, Karl (1802-78), a German theologian, court chaplain and holder of other honorary offices. He is the author of a series of works on theology and art criticism. His "Abriss einer Geschichte der religiösen Gemeinschaften in Württemberg," in *Ztscht für die hist. Theol.* (1841) 63-142, was published in extract as *Geschichte der neuen Taufgesinnten in Württemberg* (1840) and translated into Dutch under the title, *Mennoniten en Doopsgezinden in Wurtemberg* (Amsterdam, 1848). Part I of the *Abriss* presents a noteworthy account of the rise of Anabaptism in Württemberg in the 16th century, and the struggle against it, and then also the rise of the Baptist brotherhood in 1838. (*ML* II, 191.)   NEFF.

Grünfeld, a common Mennonite village name found in the following Mennonite settlements: Schlachtin, South Russia; Barnaul, Siberia; Alexanderwohl, Kan.; Hague, Sask.; Cuauhtemoc and Durango, Mexico; and Menno, Paraguay.   C.K.

Grünfeld, a village in the Barnaul settlement, Siberia, founded in 1908 by Mennonites of Chortitza, South Russia, originally embraced 54 farms with 7,344 acres of arable land and 475 acres of useless land. There were 176 male settlers. In 1912 it was divided into two villages—Grünfeld with 36 farms and Tchernovka with 18. A new school was built in 1926. The Mennonite Church, whose members lived in the villages of Grünfeld, Alexandrovka, Tchernovka, and Rosenwald, was originally attached to the Orlov congregation (later called Schönsee), but because of the great distances it became a separate congregation in 1912 under the leadership of Peter P. Epp. In 1927 it had 186 members, most of whom lived in Grünfeld. It was decided to build a church in the village of Tchernovka, which is centrally located. Nothing is known about the later fate of the village under the Soviets. (*ML* II, 192.)   J.D.

Grünfeld, a village in the district of Krivoy-Rog, Ukraine, with an area of 5,520 acres, founded in 1873 by Mennonites from the Chortitza settlement. The principal occupation was farming on 3,600 acres. The village also had a manufacturing plant for farm machinery, a mill, and a creamery, operated by an agricultural co-operative, and a grocery store. After the Revolution one fourth of the population emigrated to America. In 1928 there were 550 inhabitants. Grünfeld belonged to a compact group of Mennonite villages (Grünfeld, Neu-Chortitz, Gnadental, Steinfeld, and Hochfeld), and had a seven-class school with eight Mennonite teachers, and a Mennonite church. It was also the home of Jakob Rempel (*q.v.*), the elder of the Neu-Chortitz Mennonite Church (*q.v.*).

The collectivization of Grünfeld, which began in 1929, resulted in the exile of a great number of prosperous Mennonite farmers, beginning Feb. 25, 1930. The families of K. Dyck, M. Schmidt, H. Friesen, H. Wiebe, D. Wiebe, P. Fröse, H. Martens, and J. Martens (unmarried) were sent to the Vologda region, and a great number were banished from their home district. In 1931 some were sent to the Ural Mountains. These banishments continued to occur until the Ukraine was occupied by the Germans in 1941. A total of 22 families, about 100 persons, were forced to leave Grünfeld. Among the exiled was Elder Jakob Rempel, who perished like many others. When the German army approached in 1941 some men were evacuated. The land of the collective was now divided among the remaining inhabitants.

The church, which had been used as a dormitory for school purposes and later as a granary, was again used for its original purpose. In 1942 at Pentecost the first baptismal service was conducted. There had been no public worship services since 1929. Peter Sawatzky and Abram Rempel were ordained as ministers, Elder Jakob Penner of Friedensfeld officiating. On Oct. 21, 1943, the inhabitants of Grünfeld and the other villages were evacuated westward by freight trains, some of them being located temporarily in the Warthegau. Numerous Grünfeld persons were among those who were repatriated by the Russians. Eighty-eight reached Canada and 16 Paraguay. (M.E. questionnaire by Sara Kehler and Anna Rempel; *ML* II, 192.)   Hch.L., C.K.

Grünfelder, Hans, an Anabaptist martyr, a native of Lüsen in Tirol, Austria, served first as deacon, then as preacher in his home church and in the vicinity of Michelsburg and Schöneck. At the end of November or the beginning of December 1537 he was seized in the Oetz Valley with Sebastian Glaser and taken to Imst. Dr. Gall (see **Gallus Müller**) was sent to Imst to convert them, but his trouble was in vain. The confession made by Grünfelder reveals that he had joined the Anabaptist congregation two years before and had at first stayed in the Puster Valley. Concerning the death of the prisoners, who were joined by Old Oswald of the Oetz Valley, Griesinger wrote to Hans Amon and Ulrich Stadler and the entire brotherhood in Moravia: "We [Griesinger and Lochmaier] cannot refrain from writing to our brethren. They testified with great joy to the holy Word of the Lord, as you already know, but not in detail. I cannot really describe their joy. When Bastl and Hänsel were executed, about 1,000 persons were present. Hänsel cried out quite loud, admonishing and warning the people. Bastl did too, until his death, together with Old Oswald. The populace was quite horrified. It is true, as the wise man says, Neither the aged nor the gray will be spared. They did not let their legs finish burning, but threw them into the water; we hope that their witness was not in vain." Bastl Glaser is the author of two hymns. Griesinger's account is in part taken verbatim from the *Geschicht-Buch*.

LOSERTH.

Wolkan, *Geschicht-Buch*, 133; Beck, *Geschichts-Bücher*, 132; *Die Lieder der Hutterischen Brüder* (Scottdale, 1914) 71-74; Wolkan, *Lieder*, 171; Loserth, *Der Anabaptismus in Tirol* II (Vienna, 1892) 148; *Mart. Mir.* D 40, E 446; *ML* II, 192 f.

Grünhoffental (*Alexandrovka*), a small Mennonite settlement near the city of Alexandrovsk in South Russia, about four miles from Neuschönwiese, settled in the early 1860's by six men who belonged to the Kronsweide congregation. The village owned 2,187 acres. (*ML* II, 193.)   D.H.E.

Grüningen, a town in the Hinwil district of the canton of Zürich, Switzerland. In 1467 Hinwil had a population of about 2,200. The county of Grüningen, of which the town was the capital, was the part of the canton of Zürich in which the Anabaptist movement found its strongest expression. It can be said that in the years 1525-28 the movement developed here into a real movement of the people. The soil had been truly prepared for it ever since this territory had been incorporated into the canton which had been a center of opposition for those who favored economic autonomy and self-government by the peasants over against the centralization which the city of Zürich was promoting. The opposition was particularly strong against the activity of the district magistrate (*Landvogt*).

The Reformation stirred up this oppositional movement anew. Many preachers complained against their manorial lord, the abbott of Rüti, and in line with the radical wing of the Reformation demanded the abolition of the tithe, grounding their demands in the Gospel. The ferment was so strong, that in April 1525 the peasants attacked and plundered the Rüti monastery. They now added new religious demands to their previous economic and legal requirements: choice of the pastors by the congregations, dissolution of the clerical endowments, secularization of the monasteries, in the hope that the money realized by these measures could be used for the purchase of their freedom from Zürich. The Zürich council promised to examine their complaints, but the peasants were not satisfied. Consequently the government decided, on the advice of the magistrate Jörg Berger, not to yield any further to the demands of the peasants, although they had made concessions to the peasants in other districts. The demand for ecclesiastical autonomy, which had often been advocated by Zwingli, was also not granted. These refusals must have created a strong sense of disappointment in the territory. The people must have felt that they were robbed of their rights in every respect.

It was in such a situation that the Anabaptist movement entered Grüningen. The assertion by Bullinger (*Reformations-Geschichte* I, 261) that the disturbances in the Grüningen territory were caused by the escaped Anabaptists from Zürich I consider untrustworthy. The escape occurred in March 1526 according to the documents. Actually the causes of the peasant movement extend much further back; their immediate motivation, namely, the preaching of the radical preachers, begins at the latest in 1524. These preachers, especially Hans Brennwald of Hinwil, for the most part rejected the Anabaptist ideas. In my judgment the Anabaptists are not responsible at all for the peasant troubles. On the other hand, their teachings concerning the inner conversion, personal sanctification, along with the rejection of all outward forms, the rejection of force (which means the government which was so hated right in Grüningen) found a ready hearing among the peasants. By putting these ideas into practice they could hope for a realization of their earlier demands. We see this in the decision of one of the leaders of the peasants, one called the "Girenbader," to join the Anabaptists in January 1526.

The earliest record of the presence of Conrad Grebel in the territory is found in July 1525. He was the first Anabaptist preacher here and preached in Hinwil and Bäretswil. Probably sensing the mood of his hearers he emphasized that "he had appealed to imperial justice, the divine justice, and also civil justice, but in no case was he given any justice." He claimed to know that Zwingli had advised that the peasants would be brought to the city and shot down. Such statements certainly kept alive the revolutionary mood against the authorities. In autumn the Anabaptist movement grew rapidly. Much information concerning this is contained in the letters of magistrate Berger to the Zürich council. On Sept. 20 he reported concerning two refugees from Waldshut, Ulrich Teck and Jakob Gross, who had been expelled because they refused to carry arms; they had baptized 30 persons before being arrested. They had to pay a fine of five pounds. However, the people stood with them and demanded that the council arrange for a disputation with the Anabaptists. Soon there-

after Blaurock and Grebel appeared. The people of Hinwil refused to arrest Blaurock; so the magistrate and his assistant had to act alone. The crowd followed him, assembling in an open field to listen to Grebel and Manz preach. The leaders must have had an extraordinary influence among the people. Grebel was arrested, but Manz escaped. At the suggestion of the magistrate the court arranged for a trial. The magistrate proposed a disputation, to which 12 impartial men from the district should be invited who would then be able to witness concerning the result of the disputation. The Zürich council agreed to these proposals from Grüningen and arranged for a disputation with the Anabaptists on Nov. 6, 1525.

In spite of the fact that the real leaders were now in prison in Zürich, the Anabaptist movement continued in undiminished strength in Grüningen. Natives of the territory themselves continued the agitation. Both before and after the disputation such charges were raised as that Zwingli would not let the common people speak. The Anabaptists would not admit defeat in spite of the declaration by the 12 representatives that the Anabaptists had been given sufficient opportunity to speak. The representatives sought to work out a compromise between the Anabaptists and the government, but without success. At an assembly of the district legislature 90 Anabaptists remained steadfast in their position, while 13 yielded to the authorities. The magistrate finally succeeded in having a decree adopted to the effect that all persons who would not obey the decisions and mandates of the authorities following the disputation of Nov. 6 but would still continue in their Anabaptism would be incarcerated in the tower or prison on bread and water. But the imprisoned Anabaptists succeeded in escaping out of the tower on Dec. 30. It is worthy of note that Berger recognized the religious needs of his people and tried to do something about them. He proposed a mandate to the effect that each escaped Anabaptist should pay a fine of ten pounds along with the cost of his imprisonment and give a bond for 100 pounds as well as renounce Anabaptism. He proposed granting the common people their request which they had made so often to be allowed to read out of the Gospel for themselves, this in true Reformation spirit.

The Anabaptist movement was much discredited by radical elements. For instance, "Uoli" flung into the face of the magistrate that rebaptism is right. From the pulpit in Hinwil he repeated the charge that the Anabaptists had not received a hearing in Zürich. He moved about the country with a gun and once during the sermon he shot a charge into the roof of the church. At a meeting in a forest in May 1526, 15 Anabaptists were arrested, among them two leading men of the district, Jakob Falk and Heini Reimann. Falk was already in July 1525 a listener to Grebel's preaching and also took part in the disputation of Nov. 6, 1525. Both men had gone to Appenzell in January 1526 after their escape out of the tower in Grüningen. In the summer of 1526 we find traces of Blaurock and Manz. In December 1526 both were arrested by Berger. On Jan. 5, 1527, Felix Manx was put to death by drowning in the Limmat, while Blaurock was beaten with rods and driven out of the city.

The Anabaptist prisoners in Grüningen were not at all impressed by this execution. Falk and Reimann were strongly determined to hold fast to their convictions in spite of the threat of the death penalty. So at the Landtag of May 23, 1527, the council demanded that both Anabaptist leaders should be punished according to the existing mandates. The Anabaptists brought out against this demand the point that they had not been heard at the disputation and demanded that Zwingli should defend himself in writing on the basis of God's Word. The Landtag decided that it recognized the disputations and the mandates of the council but reserved the right to show mercy to the accused. Against this the council claimed a legal right to try the accused before its own court in cases where the Landtag would not execute the mandates. The officials of Grüningen did not want to recognize this right as claimed. The result was a long litigation, which was finally decided by Bern in favor of Zürich.

Why did the Grüningen officials protect the Anabaptists? They agreed with the Zürich government in principle, and only sought moderation of the punishment. It would be wrong to infer from their action a fundamental recognition of the Anabaptists. Their motivation had two further grounds: on the one hand consideration for the many friends and relatives of the Anabaptists, on the other hand a maintenance of their autonomy in criminal trials over against the tendency of the Zürich council to undermine such rights in favor of the centralization of authority. The prisoners were granted the privilege of written defense. As a result their ideas were recorded in a long petition to the Landtag, which is now an important document of the Zürich archives. The contents of this description is briefly as follows: The governmental mandates are contrary to the Word of God and the command of Christ. We must obey God more than man and must baptize according to the will of Christ. Christ calls baptism "a righteousness" and a "counsel of God," a baptism which is to be performed only after repentance and only for believers. It cannot be given to children. Christ gave believers no other disciplinary power than the ban since believers walk in the will of the Spirit. The fruits of the spirit are love, peace, kindness, etc. "Those who walk therein are the church of Christ and the body of Christ and the Christian church. Now we trust you are convinced that we are in the true church. Now they want to force us out of the true church into a foreign church." Circumstance cannot be a ground for baptism. As Abraham was obedient to God, so we now who do not belong to the covenant of Abraham desire to be obedient to Christ. At the end of the petition comes the following proclamation: "Now everyone would really understand from their charge that they call the baptism of Christ rebaptism and for this there is no ground in the Holy Scripture. Now, however, we trust . . . that the baptism which we practice is the baptism of Christ and that infant baptism is rebaptism."

Further noteworthy is the confession of Jakob Falk (*q.v.*). He refused to disclose those whom he had baptized and thus deliver them over to persecution. Rebaptism, as they call it, he considers to be right, while infant baptism is not right. Whoever would come to him and request baptism, such a one he would baptize. For this he was willing to suffer death. "So then when he was asked who had strengthened them and given them help and comfort he said nobody except alone the Son of God who had redeemed him, this one would not forsake him." After the outcome of the trial the two Grüningen leaders were handed over to the authorities and drowned in the Limmat on Dec. 1, 1528. The remaining persons were to acknowledge infant baptism and then would be set free. If they would not do this, they would remain in prison and live on bread and water. Among those who swore to abandon Anabaptism were Heini Karpfis from the territory of Grüningen and Hans Herzog from Stadel. Both, however, rejoined the Anabaptists, were again arrested, and were likewise drowned on March 23, 1532.

The fate of these martyrs broke the power of the movement in Grüningen. In so far as there is further documentary evidence for the later period, only scattered Anabaptists appear in the valley of the Töss. After 1560 some persons living in the Haltberg near Wald are mentioned several times. The pastor of Wald complained that these people never went to church. According to Bergmann the movement gathered renewed strength toward the end of the century under the influence of missionaries sent from Moravia and Holland. In 1601, 15 persons publicly confessed their adherence to the Anabaptists. Many others supported their cause privately and they had so much support among the people that the lesser officials hesitated to take strong measures against them. Again the authorities sought through disputations to suppress the movement. One of these took place on March 3, 1613, in Grüningen. Magistrate Hozhalb gave consideration to the complaints of the Anabaptists. He attempted to improve the clergy and as a result received promise of attendance at the church services. He forbade the public to scoff at the Anabaptists and to offend them. On Aug. 29, 1616, three Anabaptists from the Grüningen district were sentenced to six years' galley service. During the Thirty Years' War the movement grew further since it received little attention from the authorities. But with the beginning immigration to the Palatinate and Holland from 1641 on, the last Anabaptist congregations disappeared from the territory of Zürich.   L.v.M.

Staatsarchiv Zürich, *Akten Grüningen und Akten Wiedertäufer*; E. Egli, *Actensammlung zur Geschichte der Zürcher Reformation* (Zürich, 1879); E. Egli, *Zürcher Wiedertäufer* (Zürich, 1878); R. Stähelin, *Huldreich Zwingli I* (Basel, 1895); C. Bergmann, *Die Täuferbewegung im Kanton Zürich bis 1660* (Leipzig, 1916); H. Nabholz, *Die Bauernbewegung in der Ostschweiz 1524/25* (Bülach, 1898); idem, *Zur Frage nach den Ursachen des Bauernkrieges 1525 in Gedächtnisschrift für Georg v. Below* (1928); A. Largiadèr, *Untersuchungen zur zürcherischen Landeshoheit* (1920); L. v. Muralt, "Jörg Berger," in *Festgabe des Zwinglivereins für Hermann Escher* (1927); idem, *Glaube und Lehre der schw. Wiedertäufer* (Zürich, 1938); *TA Zürich*; *ML* II, 193-95.

Grünthal, a common Mennonite village name found in East and West reserves, Man.; Hague, Sask.; Cuauhtemoc and Durango, Mexico; and Menno, Paraguay. C.K.

Grünwald, Georg, of Kitzbühel, Austria, an Anabaptist martyr. The Hutterian chronicles relate: "In 1530 Brother Georg Grünwald, a cobbler, a servant of the Lord Jesus, very zealous in God, was captured at Kufstein on the Inn for the sake of divine truth, sentenced to death, and burned at the stake. . . . This Grünwald wrote the hymn that is known in almost all countries, 'Kommt her zu mir, spricht Gottes Sohn.' " The only other information we have about him is in connection with the Anabaptists in Kitzbühel, where the Anabaptists found a strong following in the absence of the feudal lords. Kitzbühel was at that time a benefice of the archbishopric of Salzburg. When secular and church authorities began to interfere, they found plenty of work. On May 5, 1528, 200 Anabaptists were investigated. The severest penalties struck the impenitent, and many of them moved away, many leaving their families behind. Among these was Grünwald, who had been made preacher. In September 1529 he was at Lackstatt in Bavaria. The authorities of Rattenstein and Kufstein seized Grünwald, and executed him. He thus, as several old manuscripts say, witnessed with his blood that which he had preached with his mouth. The above-mentioned song, together with the oldest melodies, is found in Böhme's *Altdeutsches Liederbuch* (1677, No. 636) and Wackernagel's *Das Deutsche Kirchenlied* III, 128 and 1252, with all the versions of the poem as found in hymnals of the Lutherans and the Reformed; it is also found in many Anabaptist manuscripts. LOSERTH.

Wolkan, *Geschicht-Buch*, 48; Beck, *Geschichts-Bücher*; J. Loserth, *Der Anabaptismus in Tirol* (Vienna, 1892) 48; Wolkan, *Lieder*, 17, 94; *Monatsschrift für Gottesdienst und kirchliche Kunst*, 1912, 6, p. 197, and *Archiv für Ref.-Gesch.* IX (1911-12) 368; *Mart. Mir.* D 31, E 438; Zieglschmid, *Chronik*, 67; ML II, 195 f.

Gruppe, a section of the Montau-Gruppe congregation in Poland, in the Schwetz-Neuenburg swamp along the Vistula River near Culm, was founded in 1568 by Dutch emigrants. Old documents show that the Polish kings confirmed the lease contract concluded between Hans Dulsky, the heir of Lubochyn, and the Mennonites. The contract was renewed every 50 years, but each time the rental fee was increased; this is evidence that under the skilled hands of the Mennonites the soil increased in value. The church was built at Montau in 1586, and was for 200 years shared by Montau and Gruppe. In this period there are records of visits by preachers from Lithuania, Danzig, Altona, and Harlingen. The congregation belonged to the Frisian (*q.v.*) branch.

The origin of the separate congregation of Gruppe goes back to the erection of a second church in 1776, built in Ober-Gruppe (rebuilt 1865), which was needed because of the great distances within the settlement. From that time on there were two branches, Montau and Gruppe, in the congregation. This was clearly expressed when in 1856 the Montau church was to be completely rebuilt because

of flood damages, and the Gruppe party refused to share the cost. On the other hand, five years later Montau refused to aid Gruppe in the rebuilding of their church. Only the efforts of Elder Peter Bartel prevented a schism. On Oct. 7, 1866, the new church in Gruppe was dedicated. The costs of the building amounted to 6,756 talers.

A second dispute arose from difference in attitude toward the new military law of Nov. 9, 1867, which resulted in a complete break between the two groups. The Montau branch opposed Bartel in three respects: (1) he added acceptance of the military order to the baptismal formula; (2) he required them to add their signature to a regulation expelling those who did not agree with his position; and (3) he changed the place of baptismal instruction from Montau to Gruppe.

But the schism was no sooner formed than an attempt was made to heal the breach. It was begun about 1900 under Bartel's successor Görtz; the church moderated its position on the military law and also granted the admission of new members. And in 1895, when a new confession of faith was drawn up for all the West Prussian churches, Gruppe also accepted it. The formal unification was planned for the winter of 1913, but it was postponed by the war until 1921. Since then the two groups form a single congregation as formerly.—In 1897 Gruppe acquired a new church, and in 1899 a home for the poor; in 1899 an organ was also installed in the church. During the last one hundred years, however, the membership steadily declined, partly because of the events described above, and partly by members moving into the city of Graudenz. Because of the boundaries set by the Treaty of Versailles in 1918 75 members of Gruppe either emigrated or were cut off from the congregation. In 1927 Montau-Gruppe had a baptized membership of about 550 (see **Montau**), in 1940 400. Bernhard Kopper was the last elder, 1934— . O.S.

L. Stobbe, *Montau-Gruppe, Ein Gedenkblatt an die Besiedlung der Schwetz-Neuenburger Niederung (1918)*; ML II, 196.

Gruwel (Grouwel), Barend, prior of the Dominican cloister at Zwolle, Netherlands, was appointed inquisitor of the territory of Gelre (*q.v.*). In this capacity he was active in the trial of Maria and Ursula van Beckum (*q.v.*) in 1544 (*Mart. Mir.* D 65, E 467). He also made investigations into Anabaptist "heresy" at Zutfen in 1549 (*DB* 1909, 109, 112). vDZ.

Gsäl (Gsel), Waltan (*Valentin* or *Balthasar*), an Anabaptist martyr, one of the seven executed in Gufidaun (*q.v.*) in October 1533 (not 1536, as in *Mart. Mir.*). His companions were Hans Beck (*q.v.*), Valser (Balthasar) Schneider, Christian Alseider (*q.v.*), Wölfl of the Götzenberg, Hans Maurer of Flass, and Peter Kranewitter. They died, "mightily admonishing the people to repent, . . . and showing that no impure, false, idle, or heedless hearts can stand the test." One of their epistles advises the Brethren to remove the children living among the ungodly, lest they be ruined. Another epistle reports that ten of them were still in prison, all of whom desired to witness to the Lord with their blood. In a letter from Auspitz, Nov. 21, Hutter laments the death of such excellent companions, especially that of Valtan Gsäl, his faithful brother, who was very dear to him. Unfortunately no further details are given concerning Gsäl, either in the chronicles or (as far as is known) in official court records. LOSERTH.

Beck, *Geschichtsbücher*, 107; Wolkan, *Geschicht-Buch*, 75; J. Loserth, *Der Anabaptismus in Tirol* I (Vienna, 1892) 510; H. Amman, *Die Wiedertäufer in Michelsburg* (Programm, Brixen, 1896); *Mart. Mir.* D 33, E 444; *ML* II, 196 f.

Guardians' Committee: see Fürsorge-Komitee.

Guengerich, Samuel D., was born Aug. 25, 1836, in Somerset Co., Pa., the oldest son of Daniel P. and Susana Miller Guengerich, and died Jan. 12, 1929, near Wellman, Iowa. He married Barbara Beachy, daughter of Joel and Elizabeth Gnagy Beachy. Among his children is William S. Guengerich, minister in the Seventh Street Mennonite Church, Upland, Cal. Although his elementary schooling was somewhat irregular, he decided to become a teacher, acquiring his certificate from Millersville (Pa.) Normal School in 1864. He took his preparation for teaching seriously, as is evidenced by several essays on education which are now in the Mennonite Church Archives at Goshen, Ind. After this he taught in the public schools of Iowa for a number of years. He helped organize the German School Association, which served the Amish churches of Iowa from 1890 to 1916, promoting the interests of parochial education through his writings, speeches, and local leadership of the movement. He paid a service fee of $300 in 1865 for exemption from military duty during the Civil War. He was instrumental in getting a law on the Iowa Statutes granting exemption from jury duty for religious convictions.

When an interdenominational Sunday school was organized in his township in 1870, Guengerich became one of its first teachers. The following year he was the superintendent of a strictly Amish Sunday school in the community. He remained an active promoter of Sunday schools the rest of his life. He was a member of the Upper Deer Creek (*q.v.*) Amish Mennonite Church, north of Wellman, Iowa.

In his later years he had a little shop where he did writing, bookbinding, and printing, and kept a small supply of books for sale. He was instrumental in bringing about the organization of the Amish Mennonite Publishing Association (*q.v.*) in 1912 and served as its manager to the time of his death. He wrote and published a number of leaflets and pamphlets among which was *Deutsche Gemeinde Schulen, ihren Zweck, Nutzen und Nothwendigkeit zum Glaubens-Unterricht, deutlich dargestellt* (Amish, Iowa, 1897). In 1878 he launched the monthly *Christlicher Jugend-Freund* (*q.v.*) in the interest of Sunday schools, serving as editor for a short time. He also was the editor and manager of the Amish *Herold der Wahrheit* (*q.v.*) at its beginning, and at his death at the age of 92 was editor of the German part. In 1892, with the help of his brother Jacob D. Guengerich, he edited and published a German hymnal, *Unparteiische Liedersammlung zum Gebrauch beim Oeffentlichen Gottesdienst und zur Haeuslichen Erbauung,* which was eventually widely used in Amish Mennonite church services.

Guengerich had a great interest in Mennonite history and wrote a number of important manuscripts on Amish history, particularly on the Iowa settlements. His "Brief History of the Amish Settlement in Johnson County, Iowa" was published in the *Mennonite Quarterly Review,* October 1929. Other historical manuscripts from his pen are deposited in the Archives of the Mennonite Church.

Although he was never ordained, perhaps no other member of the Amish Mennonite Church was as widely known during the period 1875-1925 as was S. D. Guengerich. He traveled widely and reported his journeys in the Sugarcreek, Ohio, *Budget* (*q.v.*) and other publications. But he also championed many causes in his writings which appeared in this periodical and in the church papers. Through the *Budget* his appeals for the orphanage work in Armenia and other missionary enterprises reached the eyes and hearts of many Amish Mennonites in all sections of that church. Through many years he championed Sunday schools, religious education, philanthropy, mission activity, improved congregational singing, church literature, and a deeper spiritual life among the Amish. Although his own congregation left the Old Order Amish and joined the Conservative Amish Mennonite Conference after 1912, his influence continued to reach both groups. A.L.S.

Guert Jansdochter (also called Guert Jan Mickersdochter) of Alkmaar, Dutch province of North Holland, was put to death because she had been (re)baptized and did not believe in the sacrament of the Mass. She was drowned at Alkmaar on Feb. 6, 1538. She is thought to have been a follower of Batenburg (*q.v.*), as was her mother, Stijntgen, Jan Mickers' widow, who was drowned at Alkmaar on April 16, 1540. vDZ.

DB 1909, 24, where the name of Guert and the date of her death is incorrect; Mellink, *Wederdopers,* 173.

Guert Willems was put to death at Rotterdam in accord with the sentence of the Court of Holland of April 21, 1558, because he had assisted and liberated a Mennonite at Rotterdam who was to be executed there (see **Jan Hendriks**). Whether Guert Willems was a Mennonite or not cannot be decided. vDZ.

Inv. Arch. Amst. I, No. 384; I. M. J. Hoog, *De Martelaren der Hervorming in Nederland* (Schiedam, 1885) 237-38.

Gufidaun, a village in Tirol, Austria, near Klausen, plays an important role in early Anabaptist history. Anabaptist missionaries came here as early as 1527. In the homes of Gufidaun and in the vicinity shepherd Wolfgang preached, called by the clerk of Gufidaun. The miners of Klausen requested him not to hesitate to do so. Indeed, he preached wherever a congregation requested it.

In Gufidaun Georg Blaurock (*q.v.*) was seized and burned at the stake not far from Klausen,

Sept. 6, 1529. In 1528-29 Jörg Zaunring, called Klesinger, Michel Kürschner, and other missionaries worked. Here Kürschner was executed by burning at the stake. In 1529 Georg von Firmian, the owner of the benefice of Gufidaun, was rebuked by the government because his clerk, Hans Treu, gave support to fugitive Anabaptists. Four years later seven brethren were executed at Gufidaun. Here the brethren also took counsel as to how they could safely aid their members to escape to Moravia, for "in the entire land they had no place to live." In July a group with 25 children started out, and although the roads were guarded by the police of Schwaz and Rattenberg, they arrived safely. The Hutterite *Geschicht-Buch* lists 19 persons who sealed their faith with their blood in Gufidaun.

A special order was given the clerk there on Nov. 5, 1535, to watch for the leaders, especially for Jakob Hutter (*q.v.*), who were now expelled from Moravia. Hutter was actually seized in Klausen and was to be taken to Gufidaun, but because the prisons there were not safe enough he was transferred to Brandzoll. Hutter's wife was kept in Gufidaun to be converted from her error, but with the aid of friends she escaped from the castle tower.

After Hutter's death there were still some Anabaptists in Gufidaun; in 1540 some are reported from Klausen. In October 1540 there is mention of an Anabaptist woman, who, however, joined them only out of ignorance. Four years later 13 others joined them. Gufidaun was the home of Hans Mändl (*q.v.*), one of the most outstanding Anabaptists, not only of Tirol, but of his era. In 1553 Anabaptists were again reported there. Then the movement in Gufidaun apparently died out.

LOSERTH.

Wolkan, *Geschicht-Buch*, 41, 54, 75, 183; J. Loserth, *Der Anabaptismus in Tirol* (Vienna, 1892); *ML* II, 197.

Guillam Roels, an Anabaptist martyr, burned at the stake at Antwerp, Belgium, on Nov. 13, 1571. During the trial he refused to name his fellow members in the congregation. He was unwilling to recant his faith and remained steadfast until his cruel death. (*Antw. Arch.-Blad* XIII, 80, 82, 162; XIV, 86-87, No. 975.)   vDZ.

Guillaume (Guljame) **van Dale** (van den Daele), an Anabaptist martyr, burned at the stake on the Vrijdagsmarkt at Gent, Belgium, on Dec. 23, 1562. His name is found in the hymn "Alsmen schreef duyst vijfhondert jaer ende twee en tsestich mede" of the *Liedtboecxken van den Offer des Heeren*. Guillaume, who was a native of Hansbeke in Flanders, may have belonged to the Mennonite van Daele (*q.v.*, van Dale, van Dalen) family, members of which were later found in the Dutch congregations of Aardenburg (*q.v.*) and Haarlem. (*Offer*, 651; *Mart. Mir.* D 289, E 656; Verheyden, *Gent*, 29, No. 94.)   vDZ.

Guilliame van Robaeys (i.e., from Roubaix, Flanders) was put to death at Commines, French Flanders, in 1552. Particulars were not available. (*Mart. Mir.* D 133, E 526.)   vDZ.

Gulden Fonteyne, De: see **Gherwen, Abraham van.**

Güldene Aepffel in Silbern Schalen, *oder schöne und nützliche Worte und Wahrheiten zur Gottseligkeit,* a devotional book of the Swiss-Mennonite Brethren, most likely of the "Reist Leut" (see **Reist, Hans**), of which three editions are known: 1702 and 1742 (both printed in Basel, although the city is not named), and 1745 printed at Ephrata, Pa. It is a 500-page book, apparently intended for devotional and edificatory purposes, trying to revive the spirit of the early Anabaptists. The anonymous compiler (who used for his title Prov. 25:11) combined in it two very different materials. Part I (403 pages) contains a number of writings of 16th-century Anabaptists: (1) the writings of Michael Sattler (*q.v.*) and the story of his martyrdom (1527); (2) the very popular *Confessio* of Thomas of Imbroich (d. 1558, *q.v.*); (3) "Ein Testament von einer frommen Liebhaberin Gottes," by Soetgen van Houte (d. 1569, *q.v.*); (4) eleven epistles by the Anabaptist martyr Matthias Servaes (d. 1565, *q.v.*), together with (5) two epistles by another martyred brother Conrad Koch (1565, *q.v.*). All these documents are introduced by long and very moving prefaces, likewise of 16th-century origin, thus proving that these materials were simply reprints of old contemporary pamphlets which had been circulating among the brethren ever since the beginning. Now they were combined into one book to provide the persecuted Swiss Brethren with readings which could strengthen them in their tribulations. Part II (94 pages) contains material of much later origin: (*a*) the Dordrecht Confession of Faith (1632) (*q.v.*), reprinted after the manual of T. T. van Sittert (*q.v.*); and (*b*) "Several Christian Prayers" (apparently likewise taken from the 1664 manual but originating with Leenaert Clock, 1625, *q.v.*) enlarged by some more pieces of unknown origin, showing a pietistic slant (pp. 72-94).

The intention of the compiler and editor becomes apparent from his own preface, ". . . It is true that external peace makes the number of those who profess Christian faith increase. But it is also true that at such times of ease for the flesh Satan insinuates to man all sorts of evil suggestions. So depraved is human nature that it cannot endure good days of ease. . . ." And thus he calls for a return to the genuine Christian way of the forefathers, to the idea of the "suffering church" in which faith and steadfastness have to be evidenced. —Part II does not show quite the same spirit, presenting material which originated eighty to one hundred years later. The Anabaptists had no written or printed prayers, but now a collection of 19 prayers is introduced with these words, ". . . My intention is only this that I might help a little those who are unskilled in prayer . . ." (see **Prayerbooks**).

The book is one of the best of the Mennonite devotional literature of the middle and later period. It offers "words and truths unto godliness," partly to revive the old spirit but partly also to meet the needs of the new piety just coming up around 1700 (see **Pietism**). Bishop Henry Funk (*q.v.*) had the book reprinted in Pennsylvania, most likely with similar intentions and out of the same spirit. Even though no further edition ever came out, the many old copies found in Mennonite homes in America prove the great popularity of the book. In Europe things were different: the von Mechel publishing house in Basel was still advertising the 1742 edition in 1822. Later the book was completely forgotten and is today exceedingly rare.† R.F.

R. Friedmann, *Mennonite Piety Through the Centuries* (Scottdale, 1949) see Index; *ML* II, 197 f.

Gulden Harpe, De, a Dutch hymnbook containing 270 hymns without music, alphabetically arranged. The hymns were all composed by Karl van Mander (*q.v.*) and selected from poems published in a number of volumes. The first edition of *De Gulden Harpe* appeared in 1599, followed by editions of 1605, 1620, and 1627. According to Jacobsen there was also an edition in 1626, in which for the first time *Bethelehem Dat is het Broodhuys, inhoudende den Kersnacht* was included, consisting of 15 hymns by the same poet. The *Gulden Harpe* was used among the Old Flemish congregations of Holland and also among the Danzig Mennonites who had the 1620 and 1627 editions.   vDZ.

W. J. Kühler, *Geschiedenis* II, 119; R. Jacobsen, *Carel van Mander (1548-1606) Dichter en Prozaschrijver* (Rotterdam, 1906, 106); Kalff, *Gesch. der Nederl. Letterkunde* III, 394.

Guldin, Nikolaus, an Anabaptist who made his influence felt in the beginnings of the Anabaptist movement in Switzerland, but who caused it serious injury by his attitude. He joined the movement in Zürich in 1525, was seized and expelled from the city after renouncing the faith. In St. Gall he again turned to the Anabaptists. The frivolous nature of his influence is clearly shown in the court records. When he was called to account at Easter 1526 for breaking his recantation, he also recanted in St. Gall, and was released from prison at the intercession of friends and upon his promise never to return.

Concerning other activity among the Anabaptists, it is known that in the spring of 1525 he baptized two women "in the mason's house on the lake." They are perhaps the subjects of the letter, fanatical in tone, published in full in von Muralt-Schmid, *Züricher Täuferakten* (see also Egli, *Die Züricher Wiedertäufer,* 38). Another of his letters was written to Hans Meier, a baker in Aarau.

After his dismissal from prison in St. Gall he entered the ranks of his former opponents, and soon managed to gain the confidence of the leading theologians. They say in his praise that his change of heart was lasting. On Jan. 16, 1530, the preachers of Memmingen, Basel, and Strasbourg interceded for Guldin with the Zürich council when he broke his oath never to return; they say he "is thoroughly converted," and emphasize that they "have never heard anyone so fundamentally converted and with so strong a confession of his error."

Guldin gave information concerning the fanaticism of the St. Gall Anabaptists to Johannes Kessler for his *Sabbata,* which was used as a principal source for the study of the Anabaptist movement in St. Gall well into the 19th century.

In 1535 Guldin took part in the military campaign of Charles V against Tunisia. His notes are found in Vadian's correspondence; Kessler also printed them in part.   HEGE.

J. Schwarzenbach, *Zu den St. Galler Täufern,* in *Zwingliana: Mitteilungen zur Geschichte Zwinglis und der Reformation* II (1905) 19 f.; E. Egli, *Aktensammlung zur Geschichte der Züricher Reformation in den Jahren 1519-1533* (Zürich, 1879) No. 1636; *ibid., Die Züricher Wiedertäufer* (Zürich, 1878); *Johannes Kessler's Sabbata* (1902) 158; *TA Zürich, passim; ML* II, 197.

Gulfport, a city (1950 pop. 22,659) on the Gulf Coast, in Harrison Co., Miss. It is "Mississippi's gateway to world commerce," the nation's largest producer of tung oil, and a heavy producer of pine products.

Mennonites first settled about 20 miles northwest of Gulfport in 1921 on a 5,000-acre tract of land with intentions of farming. Of the 29 families who settled on this tract only four remain, 18 having left the community and the others having moved toward Gulfport. About one third of the approximately 100 Mennonites in the area live in Gulfport or near-by Handsboro. Nearly all belong to the Mennonite Church (MC).

There are two Mennonite (MC) churches in the community. Gulfhaven (*q.v.*) with 63 members is located on the tract originally settled. Wayside (*q.v.*) with 24 members is a mission church organized in 1948, located about five miles north of Gulfport.

In 1945 the Mennonite Central Committee Civilian Public Service Camp #141 (Camp Landon, *q.v.*) was opened at Gulfport. The camp has continuously operated as a Voluntary Service unit since the termination of CPS. Approximately 250 young people have spent from a few weeks to several years in this unit.   O.K.

Gülich van Berch, Hendrik, who lived at Cologne, Germany, and was likely a preacher of the Mennonite congregation of Cologne, published an *Antwordt* (Reply) to a letter written to Marcus (?) by a Mennonite preacher in Friesland. A copy of this booklet is found in the Amsterdam Mennonite Library. The title page of this copy is lost, hence the place and date of publication are unknown. The *Antwordt* is dated Jan. 23, 1577. From the book itself we are informed that the author combats the views of Hans de Ries (*q.v.*) and Dirk Volkertsz Coornhert (*q.v.*). In this book is found a note stating that Hendrik van Gülich died Sept. 7, 1577. Another book by van Gülich is found in the Amsterdam Mennonite Library, entitled *Ein Versamlung oder Zamenfügung, etlicher einheilliger sprüch usz dem Zeugnisz des neuwen bundtz, nach der Orthnung des A.B.C. betreffende so woll die Lher, als den wandel der geheilichten* . . . (n.p., 1592). (*Catalogus Amst.,* 196; *Inv. Arch. Amst.* I, No. 534; *Biogr. Wb.* IV, 485.)   vDZ.

Gulik, van, a Dutch Mennonite family, some of whom have been Mennonites. Willem van Gulik (d. Dec. 4, 1761) was a Mennonite preacher at Zierikzee 1728-61, and Augustus van Gulik (b. 1838 at Blokzijl, d. 1918) was a Mennonite preacher at Giethoorn-Zuid 1863-66 and at Grouw 1866-1903.

vDZ.

Gumbinnen, a government district of East Prussia, Germany. In the northern part of the district there have been Mennonites since the 18th century, to whom King Frederick I (*q.v.*) of Prussia gave some land in the upper lowlands of the Gilge, the southernmost tributary of the Memel, for settlement. The grants were for the most part uncultivated wasteland, that had suffered serious damage in the Swedish war. To induce the Mennonites to settle there, the king promised them complete religious liberty and freedom from military service. He applied to the government of Bern, which was subjecting them to severe oppression, and secured permission for them to emigrate. In 1711, 42 Mennonite families settled in Jedwilleiten in the area of Linkuhnen; these were followed in 1713 by 18 additional families, who took over the Kallwen estate.

From the region of Culm several Mennonite families of Dutch descent settled in Lithuania in 1713; the three estates in the Kammerwerk Kukerneese (Alt- and Neu-Schöpen, as well as Neusorge) were leased to them. With great industry they converted the land into fertile fields. There were no ditches or dikes. As early as 1718 they protected themselves against floods of the Old Gilge with dikes and drained the lowlands with ditches, all built at their own expense. They were chiefly engaged in cattle raising; they made profitable use of their skills in cheese making acquired in Switzerland and Holland, and built up a thriving business. In 1724 there were 105 Mennonite families in the Tilsit lowlands.

The incidents growing out of the forcible recruiting of soldiers for the Potsdam guard caused the Mennonites of Kukerneese and Tilsit to move to the Gross-Werder and the vicinity of Thorn, for they feared further violations of their liberties. The families remaining behind—40 families were settled on estates at Waldburg—scattered throughout the country, were to be expelled from the country on the basis of a royal decree of Feb. 22, 1732, after an invitation had been issued on Feb. 2 to the Salzburg emigrees to settle in Lithuania. A statement presented by the Chamber of War declared to the king that "the Mennonites were of great benefit to the country both as industrialists and as farmers." By banishing them the state would suffer obvious injury, since "there is a lack of such people here who understand these things" (i.e., draining and making the soil arable). But this protest was made in vain; the Mennonites were expelled.

King Frederick II (*q.v.*) made the first attempt to bring the Mennonites back into the country. In 1740, 60 families of the region of Elbing leased the estates Seckenburg, Polenzhof, and Ginkelsmittel in the Friedrichsgraben district. But the land had been so badly damaged by previous floods that it did not yield enough to meet obligations on it. The farms were therefore leased to other colonists in 1840, "who would belong to the church in Lappehnen." At that time there were apparently Mennonites only on the estate of Plauschwarren in the

Ballgarden district, for which 12 Mennonite families applied. In 1776, 16 families with 77 souls were living here. In that year they were most numerous in the Linkuhnen district, with 27 families and 151 souls. In the Tilsit district there were 16 families with 80 souls, in the Winge district six families with 21 souls, in the city of Tilsit four families. Statistics of 1810 (*Festschrift zur Einweihung des Regierungsgebäudes zu Gumbinnen,* 1911, 195) registered 463 Mennonites in the district of Gumbinnen. The highest total was reached in 1890, with 743. Since then there was a steady decline. The church was located in Adlig Pokraken (built in 1831). The membership in 1940 was 450, which included 120 unbaptized children. The last elder was Bruno Götzke (preacher 1931, elder 1932), now at Backnang (*q.v.*).

Census figures show the number of Mennonites in the Gumbinnen district as follows (the Lyck, Lötzen, Sensburg, and Johannisburg areas were after 1905 a part of the newly organized government district of Allenstein, which was composed of parts of the former districts of Königsberg and Gumbinnen; furthermore, in consequence of the Treaty of Versailles a division of the partly ceded areas of Heydekrug, Ragnit, and Tilsit was necessary. Heydekrug was united with the Lowland area, and the remaining portion of Ragnit and Tilsit became the Tilsit-Ragnit district):

Districts	1861	1871	1880	1890	1900	1910	1925
Niederung (Lowland)	456	487	563	628	557	369	329
Tilsit-City	29	39	27	22	74	100	85
Tilsit-Ragnit	49	50	91	69	44	49	50
Pillkallen	..	..	1	..	..	8	..
Stallupönen	..	3	4	..	..	..	5
Gumbinnen	1	..	..	6	2	..	1
Insterburg-City	1	..	2	3	2	3	1
Insterburg-Rural	..	..	..	1	..	..	1
Darkehmen	2	2	2	..	1	..	5
Angerburg	9	6	5	2	..	..	6
Goldap	..	..	..	1	..	4	7
Oletzko	..	..	..	..	..	..	1
Belonging to Allenstein after 1905							
Lyck	1	..	..	2	6	1	..
Lötzen	2	3	3	8	5	16	2
Sensburg	5	2	1	1	1	1	3
Johannisburg	..	..	..	..	..	3	4
	555	592	699	743	692	554	500

HEGE.

Erich Randt, *Die Mennoniten in Ostpreussen und Litauen bis zum Jahre 1772* (Königsberg, 1912); W. Mannhardt, *Die Wehrfreiheit der Altpreussischen Mennoniten* (Marienburg, 1863); Anna Brons, *Ursprung, Entwickelung und Schicksale der ... Mennoniten* (Norden, 1912); *ML* II, 198 f.

Güns (Hungarian, *Köszegh*), in the Eisenburg area of Hungary, at the edge of Austrian Burgenland, had several Anabaptists among its inhabitants in the 1660's, who came from Techtitsch, not far from Tirnau, and from Kobelhof in Upper Austria. The evidence is found in the register of the Roman Catholic parish there. The information was furnished by the Protestant pastor Seregély at Unterschützen. (*ML* II, 199.)

LOSERTH.

Günzburg, a city on the Danube in Bavaria, Germany, was in the 16th century the scene of six Anabaptist executions. Details have not been preserved about these deaths, nor about those in the neighboring cities of Dillingen, Lauingen, and Höchstadt, in each of which two Anabaptists were martyred. The only information is that given by the martyr-list of the Hutterian Brethren. (Wolkan, *Geschicht-Buch,* 183; *ML* II, 199.)   HEGE.

Günzlhofen, a town near Fürstenfeld-Bruck on the Amper in Upper Bavaria, Germany, where the first Anabaptist congregation in the duchy of Bavaria came into existence, and which also produced the first Anabaptist martyrs in Bavarian territory. Here the noble family of Perwanger had its seat, living in an old castle, in which religious services were also probably held. Augustin von Perwanger, the head of the family, had had some disagreement with his pastor Georg Küttl, whom he had himself proposed for the position in 1508, when he wanted to appoint his own vicar in the subsidiary Hattenhofen, feeling entitled to do this as lord of the manor. When he found himself without the support of either the Duke of Bavaria or the Bishop of Freising, he published an account of the incident in an open letter of 16 pages. His congregation shared his view, thus strengthening his position. Later he withdrew from the Catholic Church.

About 1526 he joined the Anabaptists. It is very probable that he soon made contacts with their outstanding leaders, like Hans Denk, Balthasar Hubmaier, and Eitelhans Langenmantel, who came from this region, and that other members of his former parish joined him; for a considerable number of persons from the vicinity of his residence suffered and died for their faith in Munich and Augsburg. Georg Wagner (*q.v.*) of Emmering, who was at that time employed in the neighboring monastery of Fürstenfeld, and who died a martyr's death at the stake with admirable courage on Feb. 8, 1527, at Munich, was probably one of these. A number of those captured on Easter morning in 1528 at the home of the sculptor Doucher (*q.v.*) were natives of villages near Günzlhofen. Many Anabaptists fled over the border from the neighboring Jesenwang when the inquisitor Martin Pasensner went from village to village in the name of Duke William of Bavaria.

At the end of December 1528 Augustin von Perwanger and his younger brother Christoph, who had also become an Anabaptist, were beheaded in Munich because they were members "of the terrible Lutheran heresy of Anabaptism," as a chronicle puts it, although they had recanted, and in spite of the intercession of friends. This deed put an abrupt end to the Anabaptist movement in Günzlhofen.   HEGE.

J. Lehner-Burgstall, "Altbayerns Burgenkranz," in *Altheimatland* III (Munich, Oct. 17, 1926) 114, where the village is erroneously called Günzelkofen; Fr. Roth, "Zur Geschichte des Marktes Bruck an der Amper," in *Beiträge zur bayerischen Kirchengesch.* XXII (1916) 124, 125, and 212; *ML* II, 200.

Gurdau, a village near Auspitz in Moravia, which in the 17th century belonged to the noble family of Lippa, who were friendly toward the Hutterian

Brethren. The village church is said to have been built in its present form as a fortress in 1404. In the spring of 1541 the Anabaptists purchased a house through Hans Amon, a preacher, and Jakob Kircher, a deacon at Gurdau. There in 1547 three brethren were chosen to preach: Hans Greckenhofer, Wolf Sailer, and Peter Hag. The last two were also known as writers of hymns. Hag wrote a hymn about the brethren held in the Falkenstein, and Sailer a number of hymns.   LOSERTH.

Die Lieder der Hutterischen Brüder (Scottdale, 1914) 97, 133, 161, 178; Wolkan, *Geschicht-Buch,* 178, 208, 240; Beck, *Geschichtsbücher,* 168; *ML* II, 200.

Gurtzham, Hans, a cobbler, was a member of the Anabaptist group at Ortenburg in Carinthia, whose leader was Michael Matschidl, called Kleinmichel. In 1546 he was seized with Matschidl and his wife Lisbeth; the three were examined by two priests, but stood their ground so well that "the others had to retire with shame." The captives were put in chains and taken via Spittal to Drauburg, where they lay in prison for a time, and were then transferred to Vienna. In prison they met the Anabaptist Hans Staudach (*q.v.*) and three other brethren who were executed on St. Matthew's Day. Hans Gurtzham glorified their death in a hymn. The others were held about three years.

From prison Matschidl wrote a letter to the brotherhood in Moravia, stating their intention to remain true to the end. But Matschidl's end was a peaceful one. A great fire broke out in Vienna, and, as was the custom, the prison doors were opened. Matschidl and his wife escaped to Moravia, but Gurtzham returned to prison. Here he wrote two hymns, "Die Harpfen" and "Das Ortenburger Lied." In the former he describes his own capture and the martyrdom of Staudach. Gurtzham was drowned in the Danube, June 27, 1550. The *Geschicht-Buch* reports the rumor that before the drowning he was led into a warm room, and as he was sitting behind the stove he quietly left this life, whereupon his corpse was cast into the river. (Wolkan, *Geschicht-Buch,* 267 f.; Beck, *Geschichts-Bücher,* 167, 194; *ML* II, 200.)   LOSERTH.

Guth (Gut), a Mennonite family name officially reported among the Mennonites in the Swiss canton of Aargau as early as the late 16th and early 17th centuries, chiefly in the villages of Hinderwyl, Muhen, and Uerkheim. A Jakob Gut of Oftringen near Zofingen was one of a group of ten Anabaptists—some of them leaders—expelled from the canton on Sept. 9, 1660, after a period of confinement in the penitentiary at Bern.

Among the Mennonites of the Palatinate the first of the name Gut to be named was a Jakob Gut in Hilsbach near Heidelberg in 1685. It has not yet been shown whether he was identical with or related to the above Jakob Gut. In 1716 there was a Johannes Guth among the Mennonites on the Branchweilerhof; in 1724, 1738, and 1743 Jakob Guth (a son of the above Johannes) is listed. In the records of 1716 appears Hans Guth, and of 1759 Isaak Guth on Scharrau near Friesenheim (*q.v.*).

In 1738 and 1742 a Jakob Guth family is mentioned in Kaiserslautern. It is possible that the

Heinrich Guth, who was born at Obermehlingen near Kaiserslautern in 1747 (or 1742?) and who died on the Ransbrunnerhof near Pirmasens in 1809 after a temporary residence in Alsace, is a descendant of this family. His son John, born in Sulzthal in Alsace, was the ancestor of all the families of this name that are today found in the Palatinate and adjoining regions, all of whom belong to the Amish branch. Of his sons, Johannes founded the line on the Bärenbrunnerhof, Georg that on the Freudenbergerhof, and Joseph the line formerly living in Alsace, whereas Peter emigrated to America about 1850. Likewise, Joseph Guth emigrated to the United States from the Bärenbrunnerhof in 1885.

Several members of the family were elders or preachers of the Amish congregation at Ixheim (*q.v.*), or the small group at Fleckensteinerhof, e.g., Joseph and Johannes Guth of the Bärenbrunnerhof, and Christian Guth of the Kirschbacherhof, later Freudenbergerhof (from 1870 owner of this farm).

The best known was Christian Guth, b. in 1879 on the Grafenweierhof near Bitsch, Lorraine. He was educated at St. Chrischona, near Basel, ordained as minister in 1907 and as elder in 1912 for the Ixheim congregation, and in 1923 assumed the duties of traveling evangelist (*Reiseprediger*) and secretary of youth work for the conference of the South German Mennonites. From 1926 to 1933—at that time an innovation for the German Mennonites —he conducted the annual student camps (*Schülerfreizeiten*) on the Neudorferhof. A lengthy period of assisting in the communion services and baptism (1929) of the Mennonite congregation at Lemberg united him with this group until the time of their exile (1940), especially when many former members of the congregation found a refuge in the camp at Backnang near Stuttgart. He died after a three-year retirement at Neckargemünd near Heidelberg in 1952.

At present (1953) there are in Europe 31 Mennonite families with the name Guth, especially in the Palatinate in the Saar region and the adjoining area of France. Nine families of Mennonite descent are today members of the Protestant state church. By far most of the families of this name have remained loyal to their ancestral calling as farmers or millers. Some have been particularly successful in animal breeding. Most of the American descendants of the Guth family spell the name Good (*q.v.*), although a few in Illinois and Iowa, of Amish background, still use Guth. P.S.

Mennonite records in the Karlsruher *Generallandesarchiv;* Erna Guth, *Familien-Stammbuch,* Eschringerhof (Saar); J. Heiz, *Täufer im Aargau* (Aarau, 1902); *Christ Seul,* 1931, Nos. 7 and 9; *Gemeindeblatt* 1952, S. 103 (Nachruf); Müller, *Berner Täufer.*

Guthwohl, Heinrich, an Anabaptist martyr of Lehnmer in the Knonau district of Switzerland, who died in 1639 in the prison of the monastery of Othenbach at Zürich. (*Mart. Mir.* D 816, E 1115; *ML* II, 213.)

Guymon Mennonite Church (MC), near Guymon, Texas Co., Okla., was never officially organized. Will Helmuth was ordained minister Dec. 27, 1908, but moved to Missouri in the fall of 1909. Of the six families that settled near Guymon, only the Felty J. Kauffman family remained. This settlement began in 1907 and was affiliated with the Missouri-Kansas Conference. A.H.E.

Guyon, Madame (Jeanne Marie Motte-Guyon, nee Bouvier) (1648-1717), a French mystic, who preached and practiced semi-quietism, and by her writings exerted influence in Germany on Tersteegen (*q.v.*), Gottfried Arnold (*q.v.*), the Moravian Brethren, and also on pietistically inclined Mennonite circles. Her most read books were *Leben heiliger Seelen* and *Heilige Liebe Gottes mit Sinnbildern.* The latter, published in 1717, translated from the French by Tersteegen (*q.v.*) and published in 1751 at Mühlheim a.d. Ruhr, was reprinted in 1828 in Lancaster, Pa. NEFF.

R. Friedmann, *Menn. Piety Through the Centuries* (Goshen, 1949) 214 f., 218; *ML* II, 213.

Gysbrecht Aertsz of Koudekerk, a Dutch Anabaptist martyr, was burned at the stake on April 25, 1534, at The Hague or Haarlem. He had participated in the journey to Münster (*q.v.*) and was arrested at Bergklooster (*q.v.*). (*Inv. Arch. Amst.* 1, Nos. 744 f.; *DB* 1917, 121, No. 137.) VDZ.

H

Haag, den, Netherlands: see Hague, The.

Haan (Haen), de, a Dutch Flemish Mennonite family, originally living at Sweveghem, near Kortrijk (Courtrai) in Flanders. Pieter de Haan emigrated because of his faith to Haarlem, Holland, where he died in 1617, and where his descendants lived, most of whom were merchants, and many of whom were deacons of the church. Collateral branches were found in Amsterdam and Leiden. Here David Bierens de Haan (1822-95) (a son of Pieter de Haan, 1757-1833, banker and cloth manufacturer at Leiden, and Wijna Bierens of the Amsterdam Bierens family), who was a professor of mathematics and physics at the University of Leiden, was a deacon of the Mennonite congregation 1866-95. Anthony de Haan Pz, who was a deacon of the Amsterdam congregation 1835-39 and 1846-48, was one of the founders of the Dutch Mennonite Mission Association. It could not be determined whether there is relationship between this family and the well-known Dutch Mennonite leader Galenus Abrahamsz de Haan (*q.v.*, 1622-1706). vDZ.

Ned. Patriciaat II (1911), 175-80; X (1919) 120-26; *Inv. Arch. Amst.* I, 598 f.; *DB* 1885, 55 f.

Haan, Galenus Abrahamsz de: see Galenus Abrahamsz.

Haan (Han), Thoman, an Anabaptist martyr of Nikolsburg, Moravia, was seized May 12, 1592, at Freiburg in Bavaria, cruelly tortured, and beheaded and burned on June 18. He endured his martyrdom singing and praying. His death is the subject of two hymns. One of these, with 38 stanzas, contains the acrostic, "Thoman Han," and begins, "Thuet losen, was ich singen will, den Fromen zu trost und zu muete"; the other, which also deals with the martyrdom of Matthäus Mair (*q.v.*), has the acrostic, "Thoman Han, Matheus Mair," contains 20 stanzas, and begins, "Trost, Fried und Freud, Standhaftigkeit im Herrn." NEFF.

Wolkan, *Lieder*, 236; *Die Lieder der Hutterischen Brüder* (Scottdale, 1914) 792-98; Beck, *Geschichts-Bücher*, 315 f.; Wolkan, *Geschicht-Buch*, 774; Wiswedel, *Bilder* II, 162; Zieglschmid, *Chronik*, 562-64; *Mart. Mir.* D 787, where he is called Thomas, E 1089; *ML* II, 213.

Haarlem, Netherlands, a city (pop. 166,000, 3 per cent of which is Mennonite) since 1345, which became the capital of the province of North Holland in the 19th century. A considerable number of industries are located here, especially the famous printing house "Enschede." The city also has several Mennonite publishers: N. V. Erven Bohn and H. D. Tjeenk Willink en Zoons Uitgevers Mij N.V. Haarlem is also the center of the Dutch flower bulb culture, which is centuries old, and in whose history we also find Mennonites such as Voorhelm and Schneevoogt. The city has experienced times of growth and decline which have influenced the life of the various Mennonite congregations located here, of which the two surviving

in 1784, the Flemish (Klein Heiligland) and the Waterlander (Peuzelaarsteeg), merged to form the United Mennonite Church. In 1671 there were 1,868 members in the Heiligland congregation. If the members of the Waterlander and other smaller congregations are included, the Mennonite proportion of the city's population at that time would certainly have been 15-20 per cent. In 1640 the Mennonite population was estimated at nearly 5,000 baptized members. The city was known as "the Mennonite Haarlem" because there were many prominent and influential citizens among them.

The present Haarlem congregation is scattered over the several civic areas of Haarlem, Heemstede, Bloemendaal, and Zandvoort, while others are living in the flower bulb districts. The congregation has a meetinghouse in the center of the city built in 1683 with a seating capacity of 700. In 1955 a second church, Noorderkapel, was dedicated. The city of Haarlem itself has 166,000 inhabitants, not including the suburbs, which have 58,000. Of this total population of 224,000 the Mennonite congregation in 1954 had 3,391 members, 1,337 men and 2,054 women. The congregation is divided into four districts, each district having a preacher and a district committee. Several of the districts are further subdivided. Once a month services are held in Heemstede, Bloemendaal, Haarlem-Noord, and Haarlem-Oost. During the winter there are also district evening meetings in which a topic is discussed. The following services or organizations are sponsored by the church council or the deacons: (1) a "deacon ministry" (*diaconie*) in which the work is carried on by a welfare worker; (2) a Mennonite nursing service with a district nurse; (3) a Mennonite family aid service with two family social workers; (4) a Mennonite school with eight teachers; (5) a relief fund for lodgings for the aged.

Closely connected with the congregation but autonomously administered are a number of Mennonite institutions and foundations: (1) the Mennonite Orphanage, administered by a board of regents, which has nine children under the direction of a housefather and housemother; (2) the Mennonite rest home "Spaar en Hout," an institution with a capacity of 46 persons founded by the orphanage and administered by its regents; (3) four Mennonite almshouses (*hofje*) in which 34 elderly sisters of the congregation have their private dwellings — Bruiningshofje (established in 1610), Blokshofje (1634), Zuiderhofje (1640), and Wijnbergshofje (1662); (4) the Mennonite rest home for the aged at Heemstede, property of the Gallenkamp Foundation, with a capacity of 140 persons.

The congregation has nine Sunday schools for children from 9 to 10 years of age, a young people's church for children 11-15, Mennonite Pathfinder groups for boys and girls of 8-17, a Mennonite youth fellowship for young people 15-20 called Elfregi, a Mennonite young people's circle (*Kring*) for ages 20-30, a study circle for young people, and a study association for men. It has further a circle for members 35-65 years of age, called *De Medewerkers,* a circle for members 50 years and older, a Mennonite circle for the aged, and 13 sisters' circles. There is also a local unit of the Mennonite Association for the Spread of the Gospel. The ushers (*Collectanten*) also have their own organization. There is also a Mennonite choir (1894) which is however not a church choir.

The congregation is governed by the "Large Church Council" (*Groote Kerkeraad*), whose members hold office for life. This council is composed of 15 members including the four active ministers and the retired minister living at Haarlem. It meets usually three times a year. Current matters are handled by the "Serving Church Council" (*Dienende Kerkeraad*), consisting of 17 members, which likewise includes the four active preachers and the retired preacher. The four active preachers constitute the executive committee of both church councils. Two of these ministers are annually elected as chairman and secretary of the two councils. All matters concerning the support of needy members lie in the competence of the board of deacons consisting of 12 members who are also members of the "Serving Council." The preachers may not belong to the board of deacons. The deacons are assisted by a board of deaconesses (5 members) and the welfare worker. The board of deacons also controls the current financial affairs of the congregation. The management of the various endowments is handled by autonomous trustees who are members of the Large Church Council.

The congregation is a member of the A.D.S., to which it appoints four delegates, and of the North Holland Ring, and also of the Association for the Support of Mennonite Orphans of Needy Congregations. The congregation also has its own monthly periodical which contains reports on the work of the church councils and the various congregational organizations.

History. About 1530 there were already Anabaptists in Haarlem. Court trials of Anabaptists took place here repeatedly about that time, although these brethren and sisters came from other sections of the province of Holland. It is clear also that among those on trial were some who either played a part in the Münster affair or were involved in it. Jan Matthijs himself was from Haarlem. A large number of Anabaptists were arrested in March 1534 at Spaarndam north of Haarlem, victims of the unscrupulous Jan van Leiden. Anabaptists were to be found in the whole district around Haarlem, in Kennemerland and Waterland. After the Münsterite affair it is reported that a congregation was formed in the city of Haarlem, although we have no direct evidence of this. It is known that the city authorities of Haarlem in the early years did not always obey the instructions of the national government; later this was changed. On April 26, 1557, the bookseller Joriaen Simonsz was first strangled and then burned at the stake, as was also Clement Dirksz, while a fellow prisoner, Mary Joris, likewise sentenced, died in childbirth. Before the trial of these first two martyrs there was a meeting in the Schouts Street in which a certain

Bouwen Lubbertsz preached "without fear or fright." In his last will and testament to his son Simon, Joriaen Simonsz tells his son not to have any fellowship with "Lutherans, Zwinglians or such others," but "search out a little flock whose whole rule of life agrees with the commandments of God. They also have preachers." From this and from the fact that Leenaert Bouwens baptized 11 persons at Haarlem in 1551-78 it is clear that there was a church here by 1560 and possibly earlier. To what extent this congregation or its ministers played a part in the meeting of 1557 at Harlingen is not known. However, from the connection with Leenaert Bouwens we should assume that the strict party had the upper hand.

In the meantime the Anabaptists of Haarlem were persecuted. The sheriff Jacob Foppens, assisted by a spy called Aagt, was able to arrest several members, particularly in 1570. Among these were Anneken Ogiers, daughter of Jan Ogiersz, wife of the potter Adriaen Boogaert, who was sentenced to death by drowning on June 17. She had been baptized in 1557 at Amsterdam. Other victims were Barber Jans, Allert Jansz, Andries N., Adriaen Pietersz, and Barber Joosten. Soon thereafter (1571) Alba's Spanish troops occupied the city. Then came the rebellion of 1572 when the city took the side of the Prince of Orange, followed by the siege in 1573, which ended with surrender to Don Frederik. It was only after the Treaty of Veere in 1577, which granted toleration to both Roman Catholics and Reformed, that Haarlem again could open its gates to Protestant refugees from Flanders, among whom were many Mennonites. This number increased after the fall of Antwerp in 1585. One of these refugees was the well-known poet and painter Karel van Mander, author of the *Schilderboeck* and two books of poems, *De Gulden Harpe* and *Bethlehem.* He lived in Haarlem 1583-1603. Among other Mennonites of this time should be named the families of de la Faille, Anselmus, Hartsen, Hoofman, Coppenol, Verkruissen, Verbrugghe, Messchaert, Apostool, Boeckenhove (Boekenoogen), and Bodisco. Refugees from other sections and other countries also sought and found permanent refuge in Haarlem, among whom were the Willinks from Winterswijk, and Thomas Teyler from England, ancestor of the well-known Pieter Teyler van der Hulst. One should also name here another Fleming, Hans de Ries, who also must have lived for a time in Haarlem. Whereas he was a man of toleration, the opposite was the case with the Fleming Hans Doornaert, a weaver and formerly a preacher in the congregation at Gent. He and Jacob Jansz Schedemaker got into a dispute over the question of prayer (1587), a matter in which Dirk Volkertsz Coornhert, the secretary of the city, also took part.

But now we have come to the time of the many congregations. In addition to the Flemish congregation there were a Waterlander, a Frisian, and a High German. Each has its own separate history, although little is known of the earlier years. The Flemish and the Frisians seemingly developed into separate congregations about 1567. The Waterlanders, however, had probably been in existence ten years earlier as followers of Schedemaker. The High Germans formed a separate congregation on the basis of their national origin. The Flemish had undoubtedly the largest congregation in Haarlem. The writer of the letter of 1740 to Pastor Martinus Schagen (*DB* 1863) confirms this. The letter also indicated that since 1589 the Old Flemish, also called "Huiskopers" (*q.v.*), had their own congregation at "De Vier Heemskinderen" on the Helmbreekerssteeg near Spaarne. The Young Flemish who were more moderate, whose minister was the well-known Jacques Outerman, by 1614 had a large church building in the Groenendaalsteeg near the Smalle Gracht.

The Old Flemish had as their preachers Vincent de Hont, Phillips van Casele, and later Lucas Philips. The first and the last of these fell into a quarrel *ca.* 1620 concerning the question of whether a bridegroom who had intimate relations with his bride before the wedding day was to be subject to punishment or not. Vincent was strict, and so a division came about in the Haarlem congregation between the Vincent de Hont group and the Lucas Philips group or "Borstentasters" (*q.v.*). The latter continued to meet in the Helmbreekerssteeg, while the followers of Vincent met in the Oude Gracht near the Raaks. The two congregations continued to be irreconcilable even though they were declining. The Lucas Philips group died out about 1700. The Vincent de Hont group or Old Flemish held out longer. In the 18th century they sought contact with the Danzig Mennonites and also with the congregations at Blokzijl and Sappemeer. Eduard Simons Toens, Pieter Boudewijns, and Abraham Tieleman were their last ministers. Many of the members withdrew to join either the Heiligland congregation (the continuation of the Young Flemish) or the Waterlander group at Peuzelaarsteeg. In 1773 the last members joined their fellow believers at Amsterdam. Separate from the latter group, but with much in common, was a congregation of the Groningen Old Flemish, whose ministers were Evert and Pieter Mabé, and which met in the Lange Margarethastraat. This congregation ceased to exist after the death of Pieter Mabé in 1781.

The Young Flemish in 1604 bought a building in the Klein Heiligland called the "Olyblock." In 1626 a church was built (enlarged in 1650) which served until 1795. This congregation was originally the most important one in Haarlem, and was called commonly the "Block" or "Flemish Block." In 1671 the congregation had 1,868 baptized members. Before following its history, however, it is necessary to look at the course of affairs in the High German, Frisian, and Waterlander congregations. In 1602 these groups united; that is, the Mild Frisians joined the other groups. Their meetinghouse stood close by the Gasthuisvest between the Grote Houtstraat and Heiligland with an entrance on the Houtstraat. Leenaert Clock, the preacher in the High German congregation, had promoted the union. But he and Claes Wouters Cops in 1611 separated from the group, and with their followers formed the United High German and Frisian congregation. The other group re-

mained for a time under the name United Congregation of High Germans, Frisians, and Waterlanders. They had by far the majority and kept the old name. From 1611 to 1617 the two groups had to use the meetinghouse alternately, but in the latter year a new meetinghouse was built right behind the old one to serve the Waterlander group, with its entrance at the Klein Heiligland, so that after 15 years there was again a complete division. This new group was the one which grew in numbers and in 1683 built the church in the Peuzelaarsteeg. In 1617 it had 290 members whose names are known. The Leenaert Clock group continued independently until 1638, when it united with the Flemish congregation (*Block*) on the basis of the Olive Branch Confession. Among the preachers of the High Germans and Frisians were Isaac Snep and Coenraad van Vollenhoven. In the Flemish congregation was Pieter Grijspeert. In addition to these "united" congregations and the previously named congregations of Vincent de Hont and Lucas Philips there was a congregation of the Little Frisians which met in the Zijlkerk, and a High German congregation which met in the Wijnberg in the Barrevoetestraat, where it had a meetinghouse. The former died out, while the latter also united with the "Flemish Block" congregation in 1651-52.

We now turn our attention to the two largest congregations. The Waterlander congregation had a sturdy growth, but the Flemish Heiligland congregation did not. The tensions and the strife between the Amsterdam preachers Galenus and Apostool, the War of the Lambs (*Lammerenkrijg, q.v.*), had led to a similar division in Haarlem. The cause of this was the fact that ten Flemish members had taken communion in the Waterlander congregation. When they were called to account by the strict party of Isaac Snep an uproarious tumult developed in which the followers of Snep shouted loudly and jumped down from the balconies to the main floor. The quarrels continued until 1655. Already quite a number had left the congregation to join the Waterlander congregation, among them the preacher Hendrik van Diepenbroek. Due to the intervention of the city authorities a division came about. The party of Isaac Snep and Pieter Marcus had 1,360 supporters, while that of Coenraad van Vollenhoven had 508. Once again the two groups had to hold their services alternately in the same building. Van Vollenhoven considered the grounds for the division to be insufficient, but Snep and his party, strengthened by ministers of other congregations, demanded their rights in a petition of April 1669 to the authorities. After vain attempts at a reconciliation the city officials on Aug. 18, 1671, ordered a partition wall built into the church. The larger northern part of the building was given to Snep and his followers, the southern part to van Vollenhoven. There was also a division of the property. In 1672 the Waterlander congregation united with the van Vollenhoven group, so that their part of the meetinghouse became too small. Plans for a new church building could not be carried out until 1683 as reported above.

A new quarrel divided the Flemish congregation, where Thomas Snep held the scepter. His co-minister Jan Evertsz had married as his second wife a woman who had many debts. He was now accused of being a "bankrupter." Again the authorities intervened, and in 1681 Evertsz and his group left to hold their meetings in the "Glashuys" in the Bakenessergracht. In 1684 this group, which had 728 members, built a new church in the Kruisstraat. The group of Thomas Snep, which had 382 members, continued to meet in the "Flemish Block" meetinghouse, which was now much too large. Again the necessary division of property caused much difficulty, but finally the orphanage and the Zuiderhofje were given to the Kruisstraat congregation. Attempts at a reunion made by the Waterlanders in 1688 and even by the Flemish Heiligland congregation in 1689 were rejected. Finally in 1747 the congregation was dissolved and the members joined the Heiligland congregation. Now comes the time when the smallest congregations died out, and finally in 1784 the two largest congregations united on the basis of the *Acte van Vereeniging*. After more than two centuries of divisions with the resulting large loss of members, peace had returned. In Haarlem for a longer or shorter time there had been 20 different Mennonite congregations, with 14 different meetinghouses.

Originally all the congregations had lay preachers, whose number is too great to be listed here. The first salaried preacher was Pieter Schrijver, who came to the Flemish congregation from Hoorn in 1706. In the Waterlander congregation it was Nicolaas Verlaan, who came from Rotterdam in 1729. It was natural that after the establishment of the seminary the Haarlem congregations secured their preachers from this training school.

In addition to the regular Sunday services and the catechetical instruction of the youth, the deacons took care of the needy members and of the ordinary education of their children. Each of the two large congregations originally had an orphanage, as well as one of the almshouses which belonged to the various congregations. In 1782 a separate house was built, called the "Armen-" or "Bestedelingen-Huis" (poorhouse) to provide for the old, poor, and infirm members who had been taken care of for many years in private families. The building included a school for the children of parents cared for in the house. Soon others asked for admission for their children. Thus arose a separate school in the Groot Heiligland alongside of the poorhouse, which was later called the *Kinderhuis*. This school, which was rebuilt several times, was closed during World War II and sold to a hospital, and was finally closed in 1952. A second school, built in 1893, was still in use in 1955.

As the older institutions and arrangements became out-of-date others were called into being: district nursing, family care, sending needy members to the brotherhood houses for rest, a new home for the aged (1955), and numerous kinds of youth work. Special mention should be made of the welfare worker.

Since 1945 the congregation has been served by four preachers; previously there were always three.

In 1784, when the two congregations united, the following preachers were serving: Martinus Arkenbout 1757-90, Klaas van der Horst 1762-1803, Petrus Loosjes Adrz. 1762-1810, Cornelis Loosjes Adrz. 1763-92, Bernardus Hartman van Groningen 1770-1806. Their successors were Kornelis de Haan 1792- , Matthijs van Geuns Jansz 1792-1823, Abraham de Vries 1803-38, Sybrand Klazes Sybrandi 1807-49, Klaas Sybrandi 1838-71, Sytze Klaas de Waard 1828-56, Willem Carel Mauve 1839-63, Hendrik Arend van Gelder 1863-83, Jeronimo de Vries Gz. 1872-1908, Jacobus Craandijk 1884-1900, Leonard Hesta 1890-1901, H. J. Elhorst 1900-8, B. P. Plantenga 1901-27, A. Binnerts Szn. 1907-32, C. B. Hylkema 1908-36, J. M. Leendertz 1927-50, J. G. Frerichs 1932-46, J. IJntema 1936-44, S. M. A. Daalder 1945- , C. P. Hoekema 1945- , Miss C. Soutendijk 1946- , J. A. Oosterbaan 1950-54, A. J. Snaayer 1954- .   C.B.H.

The history of the Haarlem congregation has not yet been written. Much material is to be found in the Haarlem congregational and city archives, in *Inv. Arch. Amst.* I and II, and in the *Naamlijsten,* and in the *DB,* especially for 1863, pp. 125-64, which contains a letter of 1740 concerning the Mennonites at Haarlem. Material on the orphanages is contained in the memorial volume, *De Weeshuizen der Doopsgezinden te Haarlem 1634-1934* (Haarlem, 1934). See also *ML* II, 213-15.

Haarlemmermeer, formerly a lake, now a polder, situated between the cities of Haarlem, Amsterdam, and Leiden in the Dutch province of North Holland. The lake was impoldered in 1848-52. The fertile soil of the polder (about 4,500 acres), surrounded by a dike, is 10-15 feet below sea level. Fifty-two per cent of it is arable land (cabbage seed, wheat, flax, potatoes; also some vegetables and flower bulbs) and 15 per cent is pasture. The principal town is Hoofddorp (pop. 3,700). Most of the Mennonites living in this polder formerly belonged to the congregation of Haarlem; some of them also were members of the church of Aalsmeer. They usually also joined the *Nederlandsche Protestantenbond,* a union of liberal Protestants founded at Hoofddorp on Sept. 24, 1890, by L. van Cleeff, the Mennonite pastor of Aalsmeer. In 1912 the congregation of Haarlem founded a church for this group, with a building dedicated on Feb. 25, 1912, by Pastor W. Luikinga of Aalsmeer. In 1946 this group was organized as an independent Mennonite congregation and called as its pastor in the same year Miss T. G. Siccama, who had already served as a pastor of the Protestantenbond since 1945. She served until 1949, and was succeeded by N. Treffers-Mesdag in 1953. The membership in 1955 was 165. There is a women's circle, a choir, and a Sunday school for children. (*DB* 1912, 223; *ML* II, 344.)   J.IJ., vDZ.

Haarlemsch Martelaarsboek, also called the *Groot Martelaarsboek,* a name often used for *Historie der Martelaren ofte waerachtighe Getuygen Jesu Christi,* published at Haarlem, Holland, in 1615.   vDZ.

Haarlemsche Bundels (Hymnbooks of the Mennonite Congregation of Haarlem). There are a number of *Haarlemsche Bundels:* (1) *Liederen en Gezangen* (Haarlem, n.d., 1713). This hymnbook was a reprinted and enlarged edition of the *Oude Liederen* of 1684, a songbook used in Amsterdam. In this Haarlem edition a number of Psalms were replaced by versions rhymed by various poets as Vondel, Hooft, Westerbaen, Rooleeuw. It had since 1729 also been in use in de Rijp. It was reprinted at Haarlem in 1756, 1763, and 1776. This 1776 edition, which was also in use in the Remonstrant Church of Rotterdam, was given a somewhat modified title. (2) *Christelijke gesangen en Liederen* (Haarlem, 1804), usually called *Oude* (Old) *Haarlemsche Bundel.* (3) *Christelijke Kerkgezangen* (Amsterdam, 1851). (4) *Doopsgezinde Liederen* (Haarlem, 1895), known as *Nieuwe* (New) *Haarlemsche Bundel.*

Nos. 2, 3, and 4 were also used in some other Mennonite congregations. All these songbooks are now out of use, having been replaced in 1945 by the *Doopsgezinde Bundel* (*q.v.*).   vDZ.

Catalogus Amst., 277, 329, 330; *DB* 1861, 159 f.; 1865, 70-72, 76-79, 91-94; 1895, 180 f.; 1896, 111, 132-34; 1900, 117.

Haarlemsche Vereeniging: see **Vereeniging van Doopsgezinde Gemeenten.**

Habaner, originally a nickname for the Hutterites in Slovakia, used by the Slovakian peasants; later the general name for those Hutterites who after about 1760 turned Catholic and as such were permitted to continue to live in their existing Bruderhofs on a semi-community or co-operative principle. These Habaners are still living in a few villages of Western Slovakia today; in 1925 the older people were still speaking German. Today they have become almost completely Slavicized, and their old traditions, customs, and skills are nearly gone, although remnants of their former community organization still exist. The name "Habaner" has been differently explained: as deriving from "Haben," a section of Velky-Levary (*q.v.,* the former Gross-Schützen), or from "Haushaben" (another term for Bruderhof), which the neighbors abbreviated into Haben. The latter interpretation would correspond to the usage of neighbors in America who call the Hutterites "the colony people."

History: The violent conversion of the Brethren by a strengthened absolutistic government under Empress Maria Theresa (1740-80) and the greater Jesuit missionary activity then permitted in Hungary is graphically described in the Hutterite *Klein-Geschichtsbuch* (230-39). Around 1700 their former community of goods was widely abandoned, yet the Bruderhof organization still remained under a central leadership, with communal bakeshop, blacksmith shop, slaughterhouse, school, and common pastures and ponds. After 1726 infants were generally, although not always, baptized. The last active *Vorsteher* of the brotherhood was one Zacharias Walter, 1746-61, but eventually he could no longer stand the brutalities of his persecutors, and turned Catholic. The next *Vorsteher,* Heinrich Müller, died steadfast in a monastery 1762. After 1757-58 all Anabaptist books were confiscated by Jesuits and later sent to Bratislava, Esztergom, and even Budapest. In 1769 the entire population of

the Bruderhofs in Sobotiste, Velky-Levary, St. Johann, and Trenchin were compelled to attend Catholic services. The methods used were rather brutal: children were taken away from their parents and put into Catholic orphanages, and the men were dragged into monasteries until they accepted the Catholic faith. In the 1780's (time of Joseph II) a second wave of book confiscation set in. Recent reports, however, show that nevertheless a good number of their precious handwritten books were kept and hidden. In the 1890's, when an old house was torn down, books were found behind the plaster of the walls. It was not until 1863 that all fields were completely parceled out into individual lots. But even in 1925 they had something like a community chest and a few other co-operative activities on their Hofs.

Many Brethren tried to emigrate to the Ukraine (Little Russia), where those Brethren who had lived in Transylvania had found a new refuge. But this was more difficult than anticipated, the authorities being extremely vigilant and permitting no emigration whatsoever. Strangely enough, Emperor Joseph II (1780-90), generally known as an "enlightened" ruler, who issued the famous Toleration Edict of 1781, and who in 1782 had a long conversation with a group of petitioning Brethren (*Klein-GB,* 364 f.), still refused to give the Brethren freedom of worship, and demanded that they stay in their new Catholic faith. During the 1780's the Brethren in the Ukraine five times sent missionary teams to Slovakia to induce emigration, but in spite of the desire of nearly all Habaners to return to their former faith, the results were rather poor. The *Klein-Geschichtsbuch* (p. 374) lists a total of eleven families with 56 souls who actually managed to reach the Ukrainian Bruderhofs. Among them was also one Jacob Walter, of probably the oldest Hutterite family in existence (since the 1590's). After the promulgation of the Toleration Edict in 1781, many Habaners declared themselves no longer willing to go to a Catholic church, but their resistance soon broke down. In 1793 another team arrived from Russia, but it failed completely in its purpose. One hundred years later the Brethren now in America again invited the late descendants of these Brethren in Slovakia to come over and begin anew a life in the brotherhood. One Ignatz Pullman came in 1892, bringing a number of rare codices and books along (no longer of value to him) but soon left again. Today the Habaners have almost completely lost knowledge of their own earlier history as Hutterites. Occasional visitors (Dutch Mennonites in 1910, Hutterites from America in 1936, also a few interested scholars like Beck and others) told them their own history, yet hardly awakened any reaction to it.

Description of the Habanerhofs. Today there exist only two such Hofs in Slovakia, namely, in Sobotiste and in Velky-Levary. They represent closed settlements with handsome whitewashed, one-story houses (built of sun-baked clay brick), arranged in a square around a central courtyard, very clean and so solidly built that most of these houses still stand as they were built soon after 1621. Remarkable are their high thatched roofs which are almost fireproof because the straw on the inside of the roof was worked through and covered with clay so that no straw is visible at all (a good protection also against heat and cold, and even dirt). At the ground level are found all those rooms which once served brotherhood activities such as worship, eating, cooking, children's and sick rooms. The floor of this level is of stamped clay covered with yellow sand—a practice which the Brethren also continued even in their American houses until a few years ago. The attics have two stories with the bedrooms, called *Oertl* or *Stuben*. Besides the square, around the courtyard there are other buildings such as the mill, the forge, butcher shops, and in Sobotiste also a remarkable clock tower.

Famous were the crafts of the Habaners. Still today one house in Velky-Levary shows the tiled sign of a potter's "firm," J. H. 1781, which stands for Joseph Hörndl, the *Krügelmacher* (Beck, 620, *Klein-GB,* 355), a man known for his stubborn allegiance to the old faith, who wrote to the Ukraine for help. Their ceramics, called "Habaner-Fayence," were of the highest quality and still are the pride of museums (see **Ceramics**).

Today this craft is no longer practiced. Their other outstanding craft was the making of fine steel knives; it, too, is dead today. Only minor crafts such as shoemaking, tanning, etc., have survived and found a good market both in Slovakia, and before 1918 in Lower Austria.

The most remarkable fact is that in spite of re-Catholization and de-Germanization, a skeleton organization still has survived to this day. In 1936, when two Hutterite elders from Canada visited these places, they were warmly received, shown around, and even some faint memories of old stories came to the surface. In fact, in one chest some old books were still discovered, and a few of them were even taken to America. R.F.

Photographs of the Habanerhofs in Lydia Müller, *Der Kommunismus der mährischen Wiedertäufer* (Vienna, 1928) and in R. Friedmann, "Die Habaner in der Slovakei," in *Wiener Ztscht f. Volkskunde,* 1927. A short description also by R. Friedmann in *Proceedings of the 5th Annual Conf. on Menn. Cultural Problems,* 1946, 61-65. For history see Beck, 584 ff., also 302, note 2, and Zieglschmid, *Klein-Geschichtsbuch,* 230-39, 355-75. For older descriptions of the Hofs (1802, 1810) see *ML* II, 217. Concerning book confiscation see Friedmann, *Arch. f. Ref.-Gesch.,* 1929, 166-68. An extensive description in the Slovakian language is presented by Frantisek Kraus, *Nove Prispevky k Dejinam Habanov na Slovenska* (Bratislava, 1937), with very fine illustrations. The description of the trip of the two Hutterite elders (Michael Waldner and David Hofer) to Slovakia in 1936 exists only as a typescript, extant in several Canadian Bruderhofs. *ML* II, 216 f.

Habegger (Habecker, Hawbecker), a Mennonite family originally from Trub, canton of Bern, Switzerland. The name means "a person from Habchegg" (Hawk Ridge), the name of a place between Trub and Langnau. The first record of Anabaptists having the name was in 1564, when the wife of Vincentz Habkegkers was fined for her beliefs. In the early 18th century some members of this family emigrated to the Palatinate, while others went to the Bishopric of Basel for refuge. In 1737 nine persons of this name left the Palat-

inate and traveled on the same boat for America. These became the ancestors of the Habeckers and Hawbeckers of Lancaster and Franklin counties, Pa. Jacob C. Habecker became a minister of the Habecker (MC) congregation near Mountville, Pa. David Habecker (1791-1889) moved to Niagara Co., N.Y., from Lancaster Co., where he was ordained to the ministry in 1834. He died at the age of 98, having been in the ministry for 64 years. The Habeggers in the Jura area of the canton of Bern lived on the Münsterberg and in Chaluet near Court. In 1708 Peter Habegger was an Anabaptist minister. Records of 1764 mention Ulrich Habegger as a minister. In the migration of 1852 from the Jura to Adams Co., Ind., several families of this name were included. Among them was a gifted young minister Peter Habegger (1821-99), who had been ordained only four years before. He was ordained as bishop in 1853. The main centers where this Mennonite family is found today are the Bernese Jura, Adams Co., Ind., and Lancaster Co., Pa. D.L.G.

S. Geiser, *Die Taufgesinnten Gemeinden* (Karlsruhe, 1931) 452, 455, 470-71; M. G. Weaver, *Mennonites of Lancaster Conference* (Lancaster, 1931) 97, 100, 420.

Habermann, Anstatt, an Anabaptist preacher in the Kurpfalz (today Baden) who took part in the disputation at Frankenthal (*q.v.*). He was a native of Heimsheim (perhaps Heinsheim) near Mosbach. Nothing else is known of him. (*ML* II, 217.)

Habets, Joseph (1829-73), a Dutch Catholic priest, archivist of the province of Limburg, chairman of the Historical Society of Limburg-Roermond, wrote *De Wederdoopers te Maastricht tijdens de regierung von Karel V* (Roermond, 1877), which gives a thorough and authentic account of the rise and suppression of the fanatical Anabaptists of Münster in and about the city. (*N.N.B.Wb.* VIII, 653 f.; *ML* II, 217.)　　　　NEFF.

Habsburg: see **Hapsburg.**

Hackfurt, Lukas (*Lux Bathodius,* Latin), an upper-class citizen of Strasbourg, a civil custodian of alms, was a respected member of the Anabaptist group in the Reformation period. His name recurs frequently in the records of council proceedings concerning the earliest Anabaptist movement in Strasbourg. He was apparently a strong supporter of the group and of pronounced influence on its leadership until he recanted in 1531 (Adam, 204).　　　NEFF.

C. A. Cornelius, *Geschichte des Münsterischen Aufruhrs* II (Leipzig, 1855-60) 270; T. W. Röhrich, *Zur Geschichte der strassburgischen Wiedertäufer* (reprint from *Ztscht f. Hist. Theol.,* 1860) p. 15 f.; A. Hulshof, *Geschiedenis van de Doopsgezinden te Straatsburg* (Amsterdam, 1905) 85; Joh. Adam, *Evan. Kirchengesch. der Stadt Strassburg* (Strasbourg, 1922); *ML* II, 218.

Hadewyck (Hadewijk), a Dutch Anabaptist woman. Her husband, a soldier, being compelled to be present at the execution of the Dutch Anabaptist martyr Sicke Freerks (*q.v.*) at Leeuwarden, was so outraged by this fact, that he accused the Catholic Church and had to flee to save his life. After the flight of her husband (1531) Hadewyck became converted and united with the congregation of

Leeuwarden, was arrested there in January 1549 with Elisabeth Dirks (*q.v.*), but escaped.   vDZ.

Blaupot t. C., *Friesland,* 74; *Mart. Mir.* D 156-58, E 546; *ML* I, 696.

Hadjin, a city in interior Turkey, located in a pocket in the mountains of the Taurus range about 100 miles inland from Adana. Christian missionary work was begun here about 1850 by the American Board. A smaller but significant mission effort known as the United Orphanage and Mission, which was largely sponsored by the Mennonite Brethren in Christ, began in 1898 when Rose Lambert (later Mrs. David Musselman) and Mary A. Gerber arrived. Within a year they had gathered 175 orphans and opened two homes, one for boys and one for girls. By 1905 there were 305 orphans, with an extensive industrial training program and evangelistic work. A total of over 20 missionaries were sent out but several of them served only a short time because of ill health or death. Work was closed in 1914 with the outbreak of World War I. In 1919 three missionaries were sent back and work resumed only to be closed again the next year by the Turkish Nationalist siege of the city. Some of the missionaries carried on work among Armenian refugees in other centers, especially Damascus, but never again in Hadjin. As a matter of fact the Armenian population of Hadjin was practically annihilated through a series of massacres and deportations centering in the years 1896, 1909, and 1920.   S.F.P.

Rose Lambert, *Hadjin and the Armenian Massacres* (N.Y., 1911); Mrs. D. C. Eby, *At the Mercy of Turkish Brigands* (New Carlisle, 1922); J. A. Huffman, *History of the Mennonite Brethren in Christ Church* (New Carlisle, 1920); Julius Richter, *History of Protestant Missions in the Near East* (Edinburgh, 1910).

Haemstede, Adriaen Cornelis van (1525-62), of noble lineage, attended the University of Louvain, where he published in 1552 *Tabulae totius juris canonici, . . . Livino Bloxenio á Burgh dicatae* (copy in the State Library at Munich). He apparently joined the Reformed Church soon after. From Emden he was sent to Antwerp at the urgent request of the Reformed Church (dated Dec. 17, 1555), and preached there in homes and out-of-doors. From autumn 1557 to February 1559 he spent a second period in Antwerp, full of danger and difficulty.

In this period he wrote his chief work, the martyrbook, *De Gheschiedenisse ende den doodt der vromen Martelaren, die om het ghetuyghenisse des Evangeliums haer bloedt ghestort hebben, van de tyden Christi af, tot ten Jare M.D.LIX toe, byeen vergadert op het kortste, Door Adrianum Corn. Haemstedium. An. 1559 den 18. Martii.* The book is of great value, with its carefully collected and highly reliable reports, and was reprinted at Dordrecht 1657, Brielle 1658, Dordrecht 1659, Amsterdam 1671, Doesburg 1870-71, Doesburg 1883. His influence on Tieleman van Braght's *Martyrs' Mirror* (*q.v.*) is unmistakable.

In his report on Anthonie Verdickt, who died in Brussels Jan. 12, 1559, there was in the edition of 1559 (p. 449) a statement of Verdickt's very liberal view on early or late baptism, which has been deleted from all subsequent editions. Sharpened denominational sensitivity is also shown by the fact that because of Haemstede's mild judgment of the Anabaptists his name has been omitted from all the editions of his book since 1566 (Dresselhuis, 67; Sepp, 12). Worthy of note is also Haemstede's *Confession of Faith for the Reformed in Aachen* (1559) (Goeters, *Theologische Arbeiten,* 82 and 91). The following Anabaptist martyrs are found in Haemstede's martyrbook: Wendelmoet Claesd., Anneken vanden Hove, Sybrand Jansz, Janneken de Jonckheere, and Laurens Schoenmaker.

Fleeing from Antwerp, Haemstede led 13 merchant families to Aachen in February 1559 (not 1558; see Goeters, 55 ff.; 1907, 27), obtained permission to let them enter, preached to the citizens, had dealings with the Anabaptists, and preached in Jülich (Redlich, II, 375-81).

When Elizabeth assumed the British throne he sought refuge there for his fellow believers. In May 1559 Haemstede was in London, and was given the right to preach to his countrymen in Christ Church or St. Margaret's. In a letter to Palatine Elector Frederick III (Sept. 12, 1559) he pleaded for intervention in behalf of the Reformed in Aachen and sent a very instructive confession of faith for them (*Nederl. Archief,* 1907, 46 ff.; *Theologische Arbeiten,* 1906, 85 ff.). But he soon became involved in a serious dispute on account of his mild judgment of the Anabaptists. On July 3, 1560, the church council of the greatly increased congregation charged Haemstede with offering the hand of brotherhood to several Anabaptists, though they rejected him; on the question of the incarnation he confessed his ignorance and declared that he would not for that reason reject the Anabaptists. Indeed, he had to intercede for them to the magistrate, to the bishop in London, whom the queen had appointed as supervisor of foreign groups, as well as to the Low German Reformed Church. They did not teach, as the Münsterites had, community of goods or of women; he would not judge them harshly. An anonymous petition was actually presented to the bishop of London, Edmund Grindal, to tolerate several who were unable to unite with the Reformed group. On Sept. 4 the bishop sent it to Petrus de Loenus and Jan Utenhove for their opinion (Strype, *Grindal,* 62 f.). Haemstede admitted that he had promised to speak for them, not because he sanctioned their doctrine of the incarnation, but because he hoped they would see the light; at any rate, they were weaker members of Christ. They replied with the reproof that to underestimate error is to confuse the believers, strengthen the opposition, and make the church suspect in England and elsewhere. Instead of making the confession of guilt required of him, Haemstede declared that persons who acknowledge Christ as priest and intermediary, desire the Holy Spirit in order to work righteousness, are founded upon Christ, the only foundation. Hence he hoped for the best for them as for all his dear brethren. Even if they built on this foundation with wood, hay, straw, or stubble, they could partake of salvation. Their great ignorance did not exclude them from salvation. The truth should be presented to them in friendliness, but to judge and condemn them as ungodly was of the flesh and forbidden. Gal. 5; Matt. 7. This judgment refers not to all, but to the good among the Anabaptists, who err in simplicity (*Kerkeraadsprotokollen*, 448). The council replied that then no church discipline could be exercised toward those who joined the Anabaptists. Whoever rejected the incarnation, infant baptism, the oath, and government, refused to join the church, could not possibly be considered a brother. Haemstede agreed with a document of this nature, but added: the question of the method of incarnation was only a minor point in the article that the Son of God truly appeared in the flesh. To separate on this point would be to cast dice for the garment and to neglect the Crucified, or to quarrel about the color of the garment.

On Aug. 5, 1560, Haemstede was suspended from the office of preaching. He replied, "Do these things, it is well, I thank you; this is what I seek. Christ ought always to suffer at the hands of the scribes and Pharisees; his ministers suffer likewise. But I must preach the Gospel; the Lord will provide the place for me" (*Kerkeraadsprotokollen*, 455).

In further negotiations before Bishop Grindal on Sept. 16 Haemstede signed a correct confession of the incarnation, but refused to make a confession of guilt, and was therefore excommunicated on Nov. 19, 1560, and expelled from the country. His adherents long maintained that he had been unjustly sentenced, and were themselves excommunicated. Among them were such distinguished men as Acontius, the historian Emanuel von Meteren, Antonius Corranus, and Cassiodorus de Reyna.

Haemstede went to Holland, where he worked in The Hague, East Friesland, and later in Groningen. There is also record of a trip to Cleve (121). In Antwerp a document in his defense was circulated (170). Also in the church council of Emden opinion was in his favor, and they wrote to the London church and to Grindal to have the case reopened. But when Haemstede appeared in London on July 19, 1562, to preach, and looked up his followers, he was arrested on July 22. Grindal rejected as inadequate and ambiguous the confession of guilt presented by Haemstede and presented to Haemstede a formula of recantation (Strype, *Grindal*, 469 f.), in vain. An edict of the Privy Council to the church commissioners, Aug. 19, 1562, ordered him to leave England within 15 days or forfeit his life. He died in Friesland in that year.

The influence of Haemstede's attitude toward the Anabaptists continued not only in England. In Holland and East Friesland voices were heard in their defense. A very similar case soon after this is that of the Walloon preacher, Adrian Gorinus.

W.G.G.

Haemstede's *Geschiedenisse* is found in *Bibliographie Neerlandais* II (The Hague, 1890) 269-378; Chr. Sepp, "Geschiedenis der Martelaaren door Adriaan van Haemstede," in *Geschiedkundige Nasporingen* II (Leiden, 1873) 269-378; H. T. Oberman, "De betrouwbaarheid der Martelaarboeken van Crespin en van Haemstede," in *Nederlandsche Archief v. Kerkgesch.* IV (1905) 74-110; Daniel Gerdes, *Historia reformationis* III (Groningen, 1744-52) 270 ff.; E. Meiners, *Oostvrieschlandts Kerkelyke geschiedenisse* I (Groningen, 1738) 371 ff., 396; "Ab Utrecht Dresselhuis," in *Archief voor Kerkgeschiedenis*, 1835, 41-150; Chr. Sepp, *Geschiedkundige Nasporingen* II (Leiden, 1873) 9-136; Fr. Pijper, *Jan Utenhove* (Leiden, 1883); M. F. van Lennep, *Caspar van der Heyden* (Amsterdam, 1884); F. L. Rutgers, *Calvijns invloed* (Leiden, 1899); W. G. Goeters, "Adrian van Haemstede's Wirksamkeit in Antwerpen und Aachen," in *Theol. Arbeiten aus dem Rheinischen Wissenschaftlichen Predigerverein*, 1906, 50-95; 1907, 25-29; idem, "Documenten van Adrian van Haemstede, waaronder eene gereformeerde geloofsbelijdenis van 1559," in *Nederlandsch Archief*, 1907, 1-64; F. de Schickler, *Les Eglises du refuge en Angleterre* (Paris, 1892) 117 ff.; A. A. van Schelven, *De nederduitsche vluchtelingenkerken der XVIe eeuw* (The Hague, 1908) 120 ff.; *Memoires pour servir a l'Histoire litteraire des dix-cent Provinces de Pays Bas* (by Paquot) (II, 1768) 342-44 (erroneously considers Haemstede an Anabaptist); Th. Petrejus, *Catalogus Haereticorum* (Cologne, 1629) 82, lists a sect of Haemstede's followers; *DB* 1916, 114 ff.; *Biogr. Wb.* III, 439-46; *N.N.B. Wb.* I, 1013-16; F. Pijper, *Martelaarsboeken* (The Hague, 1924) 34-72; *ML* II, 218 f.

Haetzer, Ludwig (he himself spelled his name "Haetzer," whereas his contemporaries use the spelling "Hetzer"), was born in Bischofszell in the canton of Thurgau of Switzerland about 1500, apparently descended from a respected family. That he was of Waldensian descent, as Ludwig Keller believed, cannot be proved; according to his own testimony he was educated in the faith of the medieval church, probably early intended for the priesthood. He was educated in the school of the *Chorherrenstift* of St. Pelagius. In the fall of 1517 he was matriculated in the philosophical faculty of the University of Basel, but never acquired an academic degree. His education was humanistic, for already by 1523 he was versed in the three classical languages. This is in agreement with his formal high evaluation of Holy Scripture, his view of Christ as an example, and his predominantly ethical understanding of the Christian faith, features which mark the first recognizable phase of his theology.

After the conclusion of his studies, about 1520, Haetzer probably was consecrated as a priest in Constance, which was the seat of the bishop. Then he was given the position of chaplain in Wädenswil at Lake Zürich (in a territory which was politically attached to Zürich). However by 1523 he left this position to go to Zürich. The reason for this move was very likely his inclination toward the Reformation.

With his first book, *Ein Urteil Gottes unsers Ehegemahls, wie man sich mit allen Götzen und Bildnissen soll, aus der Hl. Schrift gezogen durch L. H.*, published at Zürich by Christoph Froschauer and dated Sept. 24, 1523, Haetzer enters the clear light of history. In three theses, which were proved with many citations from the Bible, he advocated the rejection of images in the Christian churches and argued for their removal as a command of God. In conclusion he refuted four possible counterarguments (the text found in W. Köhler, No. 164, pp. 126-28). This booklet was intended to defend the repeated acts of iconoclasm which had taken place in Zürich during this month, and to assist in hastening reform. Haetzer also tried to work personally for the Reformation. In October 1523, for instance, he interrupted the pastor Konrad Heffelin of Maschwanden, a village on the Zürich border in the direction of Zug, in a sermon, with the result that the council of Zürich occupied itself with this affair on Oct. 22, 1523, and later again on March 21, 1524. Heffelin was deposed from his position; Haetzer was exonerated.

Following the first Zürich disputation of Jan. 29, 1523, the question of images and the Mass took first place in the Reformation movement. Upon the request of the city pastors, Zwingli, Jud, and Engelhard, the council held a second disputation in Zürich on Oct. 26-28, 1523. On the first day Leo Jud spoke on the images and on the second and third Zwingli discussed the Mass and the Lord's Supper. Haetzer was present at the debate and twice asked for the floor. The council then commissioned him to draw up the report, in which task Georg Binder, the schoolmaster of the Grossmünster church, was to help him. The records of the disputation, examined and approved by a council commission, were published on Dec. 8, 1523, by Froschauer: *Acta oder Geschichte, wie es auf dem Gespräch der 26., 27. und 28. Tagen Weinmonats in der christlichen Stadt Zürich vor einem ehrsamen gesessenen grossen und kleinen Rat, auch in Beisein von mehr also 500 Priestern und viel anderer biederer Leute, ergangen ist. Betreffend die Götzen und die Messe* (reprinted in *Zwingli's Sämtliche Werke* II, 671-803). The foreword by Haetzer praises the majesty of the Word of God, which is to decide ecclesiastical disputes. The Zürich council appeared as the example of a Christian government. In connection with these events Haetzer also published a second edition of his booklet on images. In the matter of church politics during these months he sided entirely with Zwingli, who was still urging immediate reform. His theology is an extreme Biblicism, which betrays Zwingli's influence and has definite reform in view. His later understanding of the Apostle Paul in a reformatory sense is not yet present in his thinking.

Haetzer's next work was the translation of a medieval document to be used for the conversion of the Jews, which was printed by Silvan Otmar in Augsburg on Jan. 2, 1524, with the title: *Ein Beweis, dass der wahre Messias gekommen sei, auf den die Juden noch ohne Ursache in der Zukunft warten, geschrieben durch Rabbi Samuel [Maroccanus] . . .,* which Haetzer probably did on a commission. In 27 chapters the correctness of medieval church doctrine against Jews is proved out of the Old Testament. Many of the offensive Catholic statements Haetzer softened by the use of marginal notes. The second edition of this booklet, which appeared on March 12, 1524, published by Johannes Hager in Zürich, contains an insert (text in Goeters), which in Zwinglian formulation attacked the offerings and chants of the Mass, and its numerous prayers. In view of the fact that for the time being the old church order was still in force in Zürich, the critical note of the pamphlet is noteworthy.

The first document indicating an inner estrangement of Haetzer from Zwingli is his exposition of the New Testament epistles from Ephesians to Hebrews: *Eine kurze wohlgegründete Auslegung der zehn nachgehenden Episteln S.Pauli, erstlich im Latein durch Johannes Bugenhagen aus Pommern, Bischof zu Wittenberg, geschrieben und von L. H. verdeutscht.* This book was published by Otmar in Augsburg, the foreword dated June 29, 1524 (text in Goeters). In this book the Reformation is sharply accused of not having applied the Word of God with all strictness and decisiveness. Zwingli himself, though not named, is frequently attacked. The booklet states that a second reformation is expected, which would for the first time produce the true church of confessing Christians. These documents make it clear that Haetzer was being attracted to the circle around Conrad Grebel and Felix Manz. Since we have no extensive sources from this circle at this time, Haetzer's testimonials give an excellent picture of their position. They show that the estrangement from Zwingli was brought about not by dogmatic reasons (now the reformatory understanding of Paul is evident in Haetzer also), but by consideration of church policy. A marginal note on Eph. 5:22 ff. gives the first literary evidence that the common church practice of infant baptism had become dubious to the Grebel circle.

In June 1524 Haetzer traveled to Augsburg with a letter of recommendation from Zwingli to Johannes Frosch, to supervise Otmar's publication of his book on the epistles. Also a translation of Bugenhagen's commentary on the Psalms had been planned, which, however, was not carried out. In Augsburg Haetzer won the friendship of the reformer Urbanus Rhegius. A fateful incident was the beginning of an acquaintance with the merchant Georg Regel, whom he accompanied to his country estate. When soldiers of the Duke of Bavaria took the Regels as prisoners from their castle at Lichtenberg on the Lech because of their support of the evangelical cause, he scarcely escaped arrest and fled to Augsburg. About October he returned to Zürich.

Meanwhile the problem of baptism had become a public matter in Zürich. The circle of opponents of infant baptism had grown to a considerable number; there were connections with Carlstadt. The leaders of the group upon their request were given the opportunity to express themselves on the question of the permissibility of infant baptism in private conversations on two Tuesdays. On the side of the opponents of infant baptism Haetzer also participated in these conversations, and challenged Zwingli with sharp logic in the latter's exposition of Bible passages. He was also present at the disputation before the council on Jan. 17, 1525. Together with Reublin, Brötli, and Castelberger he was expelled from Zürich on Jan. 31 as a noncitizen. But he did not, as did the other members of the Grebel group, accept the baptism of faith in these days, because he disapproved of this act. To be sure he definitely rejected infant baptism, as the fragment of a letter written to Balthasar Hubmaier shows, which must date from this period (text in Goeters), but he was not ready for rebaptism. In fact there is no evidence that he was ever baptized. He definitely did not join the Anabaptist group in Zürich.

From Zürich Haetzer went to Constance. Here the bishop was engaged in a struggle with the council, which was advocating reform. Haetzer was among the clergy who, on April 29, 1525, took the oath of obedience to the council. But his days there cannot have been of long duration. Fridolin Sicher's *Chronik* claims that Haetzer stayed for a while in

Swabia and participated with Christoph Schappeler of Memmingen in the composition of the Twelve Articles of the Peasants. Soon he was in Augsburg again and entered the service of the publisher Otmar as a proofreader. In Otmar's shop then appeared his booklet: *Von den evangelischen Zechen und von der Christen Rede aus Hl. Schrift* (text in Goeters). The word "Zechen" refers to meetings of Protestant-minded members of the trade guilds, such as were being held in this time of religious and social disputes, and may often have ended in wild drinking parties. Haetzer testified that he himself had taken part in such occasions. In this booklet he severely criticized these meetings. Not Christ but Bacchus, he said, was leading people together here. Instead of brotherly edification and admonition, calumnies and warlike counsel reigned. For Christians, who are to live a spiritual life of moderation according to God's will and according to the example of Christ, and who are to have naught but God's Word in their mouths, participation in such meetings is inappropriate. At this time Augsburg was deeply involved in social unrest and in a dispute about communion. Most of the preachers were preaching Lutheran ideas, for which reason many citizens turned away from them and assembled instead in smaller circles. In these conventicles, which followed the teaching of Carlstadt and Zwingli on the Lord's Supper, Haetzer played an important role. In September 1525, when the clergy of the city were on the point of gaining the upper hand in this dispute about the Lord's Supper because of the intervention of Wittenberg (*q.v.*), Haetzer, in a letter dated Sept. 14 (reprint in *ZSW* VII, No. 383, pp. 360 ff.), demanded of Zwingli that he compose a counter booklet which Haetzer would have published in Augsburg. Shortly after this Haetzer had a clash with Rhegius, when he depreciated and tried to refute among his friends Rhegius' Lutheran sermon on John 6:63. He was thereupon challenged by Rhegius to a disputation, but failed to appear. Then he was expelled from the city as a disturber of the peace. Haetzer did not advocate Anabaptist teachings in Augsburg, even though the later Anabaptist congregation here had its origin in these conventicles.

About the middle of October 1525 Haetzer went to Basel by way of Constance, where he had some theological discussions with Ambrosius Blaurer, and in Basel was received by Johannes Oecolampadius. Through Oecolampadius he sent greetings by letter to Zwingli, and on Oct. 17 wrote a letter himself to Zwingli (reprint in *ZSW* VIII, No. 393, p. 389 f.), seeking to regain the latter's favor. Meanwhile he translated Oecolampadius' important book on the Lord's Supper, *Vom Nachtmal,* together with two sermons by the same author on the same subject. But the reconciliation with Zwingli did not take place until he made a journey to Zürich on Nov. 5, on which occasion he took part in the Anabaptist disputation of Nov. 6-8, 1525, held in the Grossmünster church. There he is reported to have publicly confessed his error and even to have attacked the Anabaptists. A personal conversation with Zwingli resulted in a theological understanding between them. Haetzer, who had not received the baptism of faith, recognized the admissibility of infant baptism as an external sign corresponding with the circumcision of the Old Testament. Like Zwingli he made a sharp distinction between the impartation of the Spirit and the reception of the sacraments. The motivation for this agreement is to be found in the status of the dispute on the Lord's Supper. Thus he now again enjoyed the full confidence of Zwingli, who also sanctioned his translation of Oecolampadius' book on the Lord's Supper. This booklet appeared at the end of 1525, published by Froschauer, with the title: *Vom Sakrament der Danksagung. Von dem wahren natürlichen Verständnis der Worte Christi: Das ist mein Leib, nach der alten Lehrer Erklärung.* The foreword (reprint in Staehelin, I, No. 319, pp. 437-47) rejected as Catholic superstition the view of the real presence of Christ in the communion emblems. The idea that the sacraments bring about the forgiveness of sins and the assurance of faith is definitely attacked, thus probably showing the spiritualizing influence of Carlstadt. Furthermore a long list of contemporary opponents, from Luther to Erasmus, are depreciatingly characterized. This foreword contains in addition a justification by Haetzer of his position on the question of baptism (p. 444), which deserves particular attention. At Zwingli's request he was present in Basel participating in the call of Conrad Pellikan to the Zürich pulpit (letter to Zwingli dated Dec. 30, 1525, in *ZSW* VIII, No. 431, p. 482 f.). In the middle of February 1526 he was back in Zürich to supervise the publication of another writing by Oecolampadius on the Lord's Supper. At the time of the disputation of Baden he was living in Basel. The council delegated him to Baden, but he apparently did not take part in the disputation. Meanwhile he was engaged in the translation of writings by Oecolampadius. At the end of July 1526, appeared in the printing house of Thomas Wolfe in Basel the booklet *Der Prophet Maleachi mit Auslegung Johannis Oecolampadii, durch ihn im Latein geschrieben, mit Fleiss verdeutscht durch L. H.* (reprint in Staehelin, I, No. 413, pp. 565-67). The foreword of July 18, 1526, shows a transition in Haetzer's thinking. Scripture and spirit become the principal theme. Biblicistic tones are still noticeable, but at the same time there is a spiritualistic tendency, which is revealed even in his concept of the sacrament. A translation of Oecolampadius' commentary on Isaiah was announced. Shortly afterward there appeared in the same printing shop a translation of Oecolampadius' second booklet on the Lord's Supper entitled: *Vom Nachtmal. Beweisung aus evangelischen Schriften, wer die seien, die des Herrn Nachtmahlswort unrecht verstehen und auslegen,* which, however, was probably written before the translation of the commentary on Malachi. The foreword, dated Aug. 5, 1526 (reprint in Staehelin, I, No. 419, p. 572 f.), again rejects the real presence, and spiritualistic tendencies are also visible here. The depreciation of all learnedness is reminiscent of the ideas expressed by Carlstadt.

But suddenly this leisurely literary activity came to an end. Haetzer had been guilty of a moral offense with a maid in Basel. In order to evade exposure he left the city. Probably for this reason only a part of the planned translation of the commentary

on Isaiah, *Das 36. und 37. Kapitel Jesaja des Propheten, ausgelegt durch Johannes Oekolampad,* appeared, published by Otmar in Augsburg in 1526.
His name is not mentioned in the booklet nor is
there a foreword.

In Strasbourg Wolfgang Fabritius Capito received
Haetzer in his home and supported his scholarly
interests. Haetzer was still planning the translation
of the commentary on Isaiah, but then soon turned
directly to the Hebrew original text. Capito, who
was one of the outstanding Hebraists, or Hans Denk,
with whom he entered into a friendly relation during these weeks, may have persuaded him to do
this. By Denk he was drawn into the Anabaptist
disturbances in Strasbourg. With Michael Sattler,
who already at Zürich in November 1525 had taken
the opposite Anabaptist side, Haetzer had a conversation which ended in disagreement. In a debate
between Martin Cellarius-Borrhaus and Denk he
sided with the latter. When Denk was expelled
from Strasbourg on Dec. 23, 1526, Haetzer, who was
suspected by the reformers of Strasbourg of being
a secret Anabaptist and a friend of Denk, remained.
But when new disturbances took place in the middle
of January 1527, caused by the news of the death of
Manz, he became involved in a quarrel with the
city preachers concerning Zwingli's attitude. He
left the city voluntarily, following his friend Denk
to Worms. A letter of farewell to Capito (reprint
in Röhrich, 459 f.) assures Capito of his forgiveness
and arranges for the disposal of his possessions.

In Worms Haetzer co-operated with Denk in the
translation of the Prophets, which appeared on April
13, 1527, published by the printer Peter Schöffer
under the title: *Alle Propheten, nach der hebräischen
Sprache verdeutscht.* The keen foreword of April
(reprint in G. Baring, *Die Wormser Propheten*)
shows Haetzer to have been the chief translator
and gives Denk the rank of an important co-operator. This volume, which was often reprinted in the
following years, was the first translation of the
Prophets of the Reformation period, which fact gives
a good testimonial to the philological training of the
author. The Zürich translation of 1529 used the
Denk-Haetzer edition more than did the Luther
translation of 1532. Meanwhile an Anabaptist congregation was also formed in Worms, which came
to public attention on June 9, 1527, through the articles of Jakob Kautz. The extent of Haetzer's co-
operation in the establishment of the congregation
is not entirely clear. After a futile attempt by the
council to settle the matter the leaders were expelled.
Denk and Haetzer had just previously left the city.

Again Haetzer went to Strasbourg. An attempted
reconciliation with Capito failed, because in the
meantime Haetzer's misstep in Basel had become
known. In August he met Denk in Ulm and with
him traveled to Augsburg. During the "Martyr
Synod" of August 1527 he stayed in the city, but did
did not participate in the meeting. He was acquainted with Hans Hut, and probably had during these
weeks also a meeting with Caspar Schwenckfeld, at
least according to a report by the latter. Even before
the beginning of the persecution in Augsburg,
Haetzer and probably also Denk had left for Donauwörth. From there they reached Nürnberg, where

Hans Schlaffer saw them together; then their ways
parted. About Sept. 1, Haetzer, according to a statement by Jörg Dorsch, was in Wiebelsheim in Franconia. At the end of October 1527 he was in Regensburg and took part in the establishment of the local
Anabaptist congregation. Here he baptized four
persons; this is the only information in the sources
that he ever baptized anyone. Even before Nov. 15
he had left the city and returned to Augsburg, probably by way of Nürnberg. Here he seems to have
spent the winter; an old bit of information says that
he left Augsburg in April 1528 when the new Anabaptist persecutions began. Then all trace of him
is lost. He presumably returned to his home in
Bischofszell, in order to devote himself in peace to
his literary plans. In the winter of 1527-28 he seems
also to have married. His wife was Appolonia, a
maid in the house of Georg Regel, who had been
baptized as an Anabaptist.

Haetzer's relationship with Anabaptism is not
quite clear. He certainly never belonged to the Biblicistic congregationalistic wing of the Swiss Brethren.
After his residence in Strasbourg and through his
friendship with Denk he had close connections with
the spiritualistic wing, which predominated in South
Germany. He was never active as an Anabaptist, nor
promoted Anabaptist teaching, with the exception of
the baptisms in Regensburg. In his later writings the
problem of baptism plays no role. Also in his trial
at Constance no charge of Anabaptism is mentioned.
Until new hitherto unknown sources make a different judgment necessary he will have to be considered
as only a marginal personality in the early Anabaptist movement. During the latter years of his life
he was a spiritualist who sought refuge in Anabaptism because he was in disagreement with ecclesiastical parties.

As a continuation of the translation of the Prophets, there appeared in the spring of 1528, published
by Schöffer, a translation of part of the Apocrypha:
*Baruch der Prophet, Die Historie Susannas, die
Historie vom Bel zu Babel, alles neulich aus der
Bibel verdeutscht.* Sebastian Franck, who probably
was personally acquainted with Haetzer, reported
he had also begun a translation of the apocryphal
book of Jesus Sirach, but this was never printed;
the Baruch book was the only completed part of the
planned translation of the entire apocrypha. The
foreword (text in Goeters) attempts to justify the
publication of the apocryphal book and attacks the
conception of the canon held by the reformers. In
opposition to the doctrine of the Scriptures held by
the Reformation, Haetzer now manifests an extreme
spiritualism which would devaluate the external
word in the form of Scripture and preaching in favor
of the immediate witness of the Spirit. Faith now
appears as an inner experience. Apocalyptic expressions are now found more frequently. In choice of
words and formulation of thought mystic influences
are unmistakable. There are evidences of the influence of Denk and also of Hut.

Also the edition of the *Theologia Deutsch,* which
was printed by Schöffer with the title: *Theologia
Deutsch, neulich mit grossem Fleiss korrigiert und
gebessert . . . ,* was probably revised by Haetzer,
as his motto, "O God, redeem the prisoners," at

the end of the book, indicates. The attached *Haupt-reden* probably came from Denk, who died in November 1527. Through Denk Haetzer probably became acquainted with the *Theologia Deutsch* and thereby also with mysticism.

One other writing of Haetzer's must have appeared in print, which has, however, not yet been found. It bears the title *Reime, bzw. Lieder unter dem Kreuzgang,* and was no doubt a collection of songs with mystical thought content. The only known fragment (text according to Franck in Goeters), which ridicules the church doctrine of the Trinity, indicates close contact with chapter XXX of the *Theologia Deutsch.*

Haetzer wrote two other booklets which were not printed. The one was called by his contemporaries "the booklet of the schoolteachers" and was apparently directed against all learned scholarship. (A short summary of the content, according to Johannes Gast's *Exordium,* found in Goeters.) Of greater importance is the other writing, "the booklet of Christ." In it he seems to have attacked the deity of Christ and to have established his doctrinal view with citations from the Bible. Other indications of the content are lacking, but his contemporaries unanimously called Haetzer an Arian. Any doubt of this seems to be unfounded, since in his early writing on christological matters there is a conspicuous haziness. The stress always lies on the human appearance of Christ. Both manuscripts fell into the hands of his opponents at his trial and were later destroyed.

In the middle of November 1528 Augsburg demanded that the council of Constance arrest Haetzer. This could at first not be carried out because the man sought was no longer in the city, but on Nov. 28 Haetzer was finally arrested. Inquiries were sent to Zürich, Basel, Strasbourg, and Worms, which show that he was accused of breaking the peace and of an immoral life. Only from Strasbourg did a reply come, which revealed the misstep mentioned above. And so the charge of instigation of disturbance of the peace was dropped and the trial concentrated on the charge of immoral conduct. In Augsburg it was asserted that he had taken as his wife the wife of Georg Regel, Anna nee Manlich, although he himself was already married, and had received from her a wedding ring and some financial loans. He had therefore caused Anna Regel to commit adultery and had injured Georg Regel in body and possessions. All this he was said to have justified with pseudotheological reasoning. Nevertheless the trial came to a rapid conclusion. In December Augsburg sent Dr. Gereon Sailer as the prosecutor to Constance. Sailer for the first time brought Haetzer's writings with him, which showed Haetzer to be a teacher of error. Here especially "the booklet concerning Christ" is to be thought of. Finally on Feb. 3, 1529, he was sentenced to death for adultery.

Much remains unclarified concerning this trial. The court records of Augsburg on this matter are still unknown; they might perhaps reveal the background. Many contemporaries cite Haetzer's christological errors as the reason for the death sentence. It is conspicuous that Anna Regel was not summoned. Nor was Georg Regel, the husband concerned, the plaintiff, but instead the Augsburg council. Just at this time Regel seemed to have been reestablishing himself in Augsburg. The death sentence is quite unusual. Persons guilty of adultery at this time in Constance were punished with fines and imprisonment. One is involuntarily inclined to assume that the intention was, under the charge of adultery, actually to remove the teacher of error.

To undertake to clear Haetzer entirely from the charge of immoral conduct is a futile undertaking. The misstep in Basel has been well attested. Also he seems to have made a confession in Constance. In Augsburg he met frequently with Anna Regel, and one of his songs contains her maiden name as an acrostic. Anna Regel also seems not to have led an altogether blameless life, as one can gather from a letter written to her in 1543 by Schwenckfeld.

Haetzer's death walk on Feb. 4, 1529, has the effect of reconciling the spectator with the unfortunate end of his life. Composed and reconciled he went to the site of execution, upon which already a John Hus had died, admonishing those present in moving addresses. Then his head fell under the executioner's sword. Anabaptist historical tradition counts him among its martyrs. Thomas Blaurer, the councilor of Constance, described his end in an epistle to Wilhelm von Zell, Haetzer's friend ("How Ludwig Haetzer, executed with a sword at Constance, departed out of this time," published at Constance by G. Spitzenberg in 1529; Krebs, No. 467, pp. 460-68).

Haetzer was one of the outstanding authors of songs; his compositions found their way into early Anabaptist hymnology. The following of his songs have been preserved for the most part in Hutterite records and later served other poets as models (see Wolkan, pp. 12 ff.):

(1) "Erzürn dich nit, o frommer Christ." This is a rhymed version of Psalm 37 in 23 stanzas, probably written in Haetzer's later years.

(2) "Gedult sollst han auf Gottes Bahn." Three stanzas with the acrostic: *Gedult bringt Erfahrung* (Rom. 5:4a), also probably from Haetzer's later years. A fourth stanza in the Hutterite version on Rom. 5:5a is a later addition. Both songs have been taken into church hymnals.

(3) "Lug, Herr, wie schwach ist mein Gemüt." Six stanzas with the acrostic: *Lu-de-wi-g Haets-er,* surely from the time of his imprisonment shortly before his death. A seventh stanza in the Hutterite version is an addition.

(4) "Ach Gott, erhör mein Seufzen gross." Three stanzas with the acrostic: *A-na Manlich,* probably coming from the same period.

(5) "Will', Sinn und Gmüt richt auf zu Gott." Four stanzas with the acrostic: *Will-helm von Zell,* probably a poetic version of Zell's letter to the imprisoned Haetzer. The genuine fifth stanza gives Haetzer's reply to the letter and comes from the time of his imprisonment shortly before his death.

(6) "Die Lieb' ist kalt jetzt in der Welt." In the *Ausbund* it is attributed to Leopold Scharnschlager (*q.v.*); in the Hutterite tradition it is however ascribed to Haetzer. It has seven stanzas, of which two to six are a rhymed version of I Cor. 13:4-8 with many allusions to Haetzer's writings of 1525, for which reason it is concluded that it probably

stems from that time and was written by him. Three additional stanzas in the Hutterite version are an addition.

(7) "Sollst du bei Gott dein Wohnung han." It is sometimes attributed to Leonhard Schiemer (*Lieder der Hutterischen Brüder,* 28 f.). It has nine stanzas, one to six of which are a poetic revision of a song by Hans Witzstat with the acrostic *Sophia.* There are good reasons for ascribing it to Haetzer; in that case it probably comes from later years of his life. It is also found in church hymnals.

(8) "Ach, fröhlich lasst uns heben an." In the current version it does not have Haetzer's name, but is ascribed to him by Wolkan because of his motto at the end of the seventeenth stanza. But this is also found in the case of other poets, so that this cannot indicate the contrary. Compare in this regard also the lost "Lieder unter dem Kreuzgang."

Haetzer's significance does not lie in his historical effectiveness; this is exceedingly slight. He was an industrious translator and author, who was known personally by many important contemporaries; and as the first demonstrable anti-trinitarian of the German language in the Reformation time, he has been preserved from complete oblivion. His martyrdom and his songs have made him useful to the Anabaptists. It is doubtful whether the portrait etched by Christoph van Sichem in 1608 is genuine.   G.G.

Details and references in G. F. Gerhard Goeters, *Ludwig Haetzer, ca. 1500 bis 1529, eine Randfigur der frühen Täuferbewegung* (Zürich theological dissertation, 1955); Seb. Franck, *Chronica, Zeytbuch und Geschichtbibel* (1531) 416 f.; *H. Zwingli's Sämtliche Werke* (in *Corpus Reformatorum*), ed. E. Egli, G. Finsler, W. Köhler, I ff. (Leipzig, 1904 ff.); Tr. Schiess, *Briefwechsel der Brüder Ambrosius und Thomas Blaurer* I (Freiburg, 1908); E. Staehelin, *Briefe und Akten zum Leben Oekolampads* (Leipzig, 1927-34); M. Krebs, *TA* IV: *Baden und Pfalz*; Th. Keim, *Ludwig Hetzer,* in *Jahrbücher für Deutsche Theologie* I (1856) 215-88; F. L. Weis, *The Life, Teachings and Works of Ludwig Hetzer* (Strasbourg theological dissertation) (Dorchester, Mass., 1930); Wolkan, *Lieder*; *ML* II, 225-31.

Haffner, Georg, an Anabaptist preacher who baptized Hans Betz (*q.v.*) in 1530 above Donauwörth, Bavaria. (Wolkan, *Lieder,* 31; *ML* I, 213.)

Haffner, Hans, of Riblingen, near Schwäbisch Hall, Württemberg, Germany, an Anabaptist of the Philippite (*q.v.*) brotherhood in Moravia in the 1530's, and the author of a remarkable devotional tract. He had been baptized at Auspitz by Adam Schlögl in 1533. In 1535, when persecutions in this country became almost unbearable, the entire Philippite group left this land (in contrast to the Hutterites) and planned to return to their native Württemberg. On their way the greater part of this brotherhood was seized and the brethren were imprisoned in the castle of Passau on the Danube (1535). There they were tortured to betray information; many died in the dungeons while many others languished for many years under unbelievable conditions. In 1540 or 41 Haffner finally recanted together with his wife Angella (or Agnes?), whereupon both were released. He then disappeared from the records; most likely he had returned to Württemberg.

In the *Ausbund* (*q.v.*), the oldest part of which was composed by these brethren in the Passau

prisons, in the hymn No. 100, "Mit Freuden wollen wir singen," the 11th stanza is signed "H. Haff," which Wolkan (*Lieder,* 39) rightly assigns to Hans Haffner. Haffner is the author of a tract, *Concerning the True Soldier of Christ* (*q.v.*), an unusually noble and profound confession to the principles of Anabaptism, above all to that of *Gelassenheit* (*q.v.*). It is found in only one Hutterite codex.   R.F.

R. Friedmann, "Concerning the True Soldier of Christ," *MQR* V (1931) 87 f.; Wolkan, *Lieder,* 28 f.

Häftler (hookers), the nickname given to the Amish in the 18th century and later in South Germany and neighboring territories to distinguish them from the Mennonites who were called *Knöpfler* (buttoners). The Amish retained the use of hooks (*q.v.*) and eyes to fasten clothing after their use was displaced by buttons. The German has two words for hook, *Hafte* and *Hake, Hafte* being more common in the Palatinate and Alsace. (*ML* II, 231.)   H.S.B.

Haga, a Dutch Mennonite family of Sneek, Friesland. Bauke J. Haga (1789-1874), married to Hillegonda Veen, was a deacon of the Mennonite congregation of Sneek. His son Hendrikus Haga (b. 1814 at Sneek, d. 1889 at Arnhem) was a Mennonite minister, serving at Oldeboorn 1837-55 and at Arnhem 1855-87. Bauke Haga (the son of Hendrikus, b. 1849 at Oldeboorn, d. 1937 at Nijmegen) was a Mennonite minister at Warga 1874-81, Witmarsum and Pingjum 1881-82, Tjalleberd 1882-88, Almelo 1888-91, and Nijmegen 1891-1917. Antonie Haga (1834-1902), a brother of Hendrikus, rose to the high military position of commander of the Dutch army in the East Indies (1887-89).   vDZ.

Hagen, Karl (1810-68), a renowned German historian, the son of a local minister, at his death was a professor at the University of Bern, Switzerland. As a private lecturer in the University of Heidelberg he wrote a historical work in three volumes, *Deutschlands literarische und religiöse Verhältnisse im Reformationszeitalter* (Erlangen, 1841-44). The last volume deals with the Anabaptist movement; in the second volume Hubmaier is briefly mentioned in the discussion of liberty of conscience. In the introduction to the third volume the author says, "My chief object in this third volume was to demonstrate how the Protestant Church, through limitation of new doctrines, through intolerance, charges of heresy, etc., departed from the principles of the Reformation as early as the third decade of the 16th century, and that they could therefore later on scarcely claim the name Reformation or at least only in a few connections, and that on the other hand the concepts of the Reformation were represented by the heretical sects and parties, which at that time stood in the same relationship to the orthodox Protestant party as at present that of the more liberal religious wing to Pietism and to the general reigning religious view. Those heretical sects have hitherto been far too little considered, in respect to their influence on public opinion, either by their views or by their practical effectiveness. Recently, to be sure, attention has been called to them, as for example by Ranke in the third volume of his German history."

Thus Hagen discusses the Anabaptists from the liberal point of view with amazing historical fidelity. His presentation is based on special study of sources, which at that time occurred rarely or never. It has been superseded by more recent investigation. His evaluation of the Anabaptist movement in its one-sided liberal viewpoint is also corrected to a degree thereby. But as the first liberal presentation of Anabaptism, breaking with the traditional historiography and seeking to do justice to the movement, it has value alongside of the presentation by Max Goebel (*q.v.*), which came out a few years later from the orthodox point of view and gave a quite true historical account. (*ML* II, 231.) NEFF.

Hägerley, a Swiss Anabaptist martyr: see **Högerli.**

Hagerman Mennonite Mission (MC) is a small assembly five miles southwest of Markham, York Co., Ont., and ten miles north of the East Toronto Mennonite Mission. It was founded in 1934 in the local school as a Sunday school, and organized as a mission in 1937 under the Mennonite Conference; Floyd Schmucker was ordained as pastor. A basement church was built in 1944. In 1953 the membership was 17.   J.C.F.

Hagerstown, Md., was the location of Civilian Public Service Camp No. 24, consisting of five units operated conjointly by the Mennonite Central Committee and the Brethren Service Committee. Units 1, 3, and 4 were administered by the MCC. The three MCC units were located on farms in the northern part of the Cumberland Valley in Washington Co., Md. The farms were owned by agencies of the MCC constituent churches. Each unit had approximately 35 men, whose work was in the area of soil conservation. During 1944 two special schools were held at Unit 4, which was located about five miles north of Clearspring (*q.v.*). These were the Farm and Community School and the Christian Workers' School. Unit 24 was approved by Selective Service in December 1941 and closed in September 1946.   M.G.

M. Gingerich, *Service for Peace* (Akron, Pa., 1949).

Hagerstown, Md., is the county seat (pop. 26,000) of Washington County (*q.v.*), in the west central part of the state. Two of the eight Mennonite churches in the county, Reiff (*q.v.*) and Paradise (*q.v.*), with a membership of 375, have a Hagerstown address. Brook Lane, a mental hospital operated by the Mennonite Central Committee, was established near here in 1949.   M.G.

Hagey-Blair, a community in Waterloo Township, seven miles southeast of Kitchener, Ont., which had some followers of the Canada West-Ohio movement designed for unification, evangelization, and education. Daniel Hoch took the leading part in forming in 1855 a "Conference Council of the United Mennonite Community of Can. W. & O." Hoch is said to have been related to the Kinzies of the Hagey congregation, who agreed with him.

Daniel Hege of Illinois, secretary in 1862 of the General Conference, wrote an explanatory letter from Blair while resting at the home of S. B. Baumann, when Hege and Ephraim Hunsberger of Wadsworth, Ohio, were touring eleven churches of Canada West, and calling on numbers of persons. Canadian funds gathered for the Wadsworth School were heaviest in the Waterloo area. No organized church can be named for this community. Meetings were held in the Carlyle School at Blair.   J.C.F.

Hague, The (Dutch *'s Gravenhage* or *Den Haag*), capital of the Dutch province of South Holland and seat of the Netherlands government, has a population (1947, without suburbs) of 532,989, of whom 3,719 are Mennonites.

As early as 1534 Meynaert van Emden went to The Hague from Deft to perform baptism. Cornelis Kelder, whom he had baptized and who was condemned to death on Oct. 11, 1536, was from The Hague. On Sept. 9, 1538, Adriaen (or Paulus Adriaensz) from The Hague was burned at Vught. This could indicate that a congregation existed at this place, which met in a home at the Spui. In 1557-61 Leenaert Bouwens baptized seven persons (according to another list 14), and in 1563-65 thirty-one more. This is evidence that a Flemish Mennonite congregation of some size must have existed here, which at the beginning of the 17th century met at the Kort Achterom and after 1642 in the house "de Rosencrans" on Herdersstraat. Evidently the congregation had no elder, since on Jan. 6, 1643, Tobias Govertsz van den Wijngaert of Amsterdam was asked to come to perform baptismal services. During the middle of the 17th century the congregation was without a minister for some time. Before 1679 the congregation united with the Waterlander church of The Hague through the mediation of its elder Maerten Pieterze. This united congregation remained for some time. In 1730 it made its meetinghouse "de Rosencrans" available to the Reformed, and on Jan. 18, 1752, when David Koster, the sole surviving member, died, he willed the property of the congregation to the Mennonite Church of Leiden.

In 1879 it was apparent that there was a sufficient number of Mennonites living in The Hague to start worship services. Upon instigation of H. M. de Vries, S. Hingst, J. Kalff, G. de Vos, and H. L. Boersma monthly meetings were started in September of that year and held in the Remonstrant church. C. Sepp, pastor of the Leiden Mennonite Church, was the leader of the group and on March 14, 1880, he performed the first baptismal service. After Sept. 11, 1881, the group met biweekly and on Sept. 27 of that year the congregation was organized with 47 charter members. Before the end of the year it had a membership of 130. The church council of the Leiden congregation which had managed the property of the former Hague congregation now returned it to the new Hague congregation. On April 1, 1883, S. de Waard of Westzaan became the minister of the congregation and on Sept. 5, 1886, the congregation had its first worship service in its new church located on Paleisstraat. When de Waard resigned on Oct. 7,

1894, a call was extended to D. Kossen from Den Helder who began his service on May 5, 1895, but left the congregation on Jan. 2, 1898. He was succeeded by H. J. Elhorst from Arnhem who served the congregation from June 26, 1898, to Nov. 4, 1900, who in turn was followed by S. Lulofs of Deventer on May 5, 1901. Under his leadership the congregation grew rapidly and on May 1, 1910, G. Wuite Jzn of Arnhem began his service as second minister of the congregation. On Oct. 21, 1911, they started using an educational wing which had been erected behind the church. On Sept. 9, 1929, S. Lulofs, who had died on Sept. 5, 1927, was succeeded by A. Keuter of Akkrum. On Jan. 4, 1944, he was arrested by the German occupational authorities and died in the concentration camp Bergen-Belsen on March 10, 1945. On May 12, 1946, he was succeeded by J. E. Tuininga of Arnhem, who resigned in 1955.

Under the ministry of Lulofs and Wuite the congregation experienced its best growth and when Wuite retired Oct. 25, 1938, it was desirable to have two ministers take his place. On Nov. 20, 1938, P. Vis of Arnhem and H. W. Meihuizen of Veendam began their ministry. The need for additional room for congregational activities such as administration, deaconess work, young people's meetings, and choir practice, was met when a house next to the church was purchased for this purpose. When P. Vis died on Aug. 13, 1942, no one was called to fill the vacancy because of the uncertain conditions during the German occupation. After Pastor Keuter's arrest O. T. Hylkema was called from Bussum and began his ministry on April 16, 1944.

Soon after the organization of the congregation its membership was 150; at its twenty-fifth anniversary it was 1,200, and at the fiftieth anniversary it was 3,000 (1931). The largest membership was reached in 1943 with 3,200 members. Since that time the number has slightly decreased and is now a little over 3,000 (1953). Since 1911 the congregation has published a *Maandblad* containing information regarding congregational activities, which was combined with the paper of the Leiden congregation from 1942 to March 1947. Since that time the reports appear as an insert in the *Algemeen Doopsgezind Weekblad*. From 1911 the ministers of the congregation served a group of Mennonites at Delft which became an independent congregation in 1923. Since 1946 a group of Mennonites in Gouda is being served. The field of service of the congregation extends not only over the city but also includes Scheveningen, Wassenaar, Leidsendam, Voorburg, Rijswijk, Zoetermeer, Loosduinen, and a part of Westland. This territory is divided into 44 districts in which special meetings are held.

Other expressions of congregational life are Sunday school, three groups of the Menno Simons Kring for younger people and two for older members, which bear the name of the first and the last martyr of the congregation, Cornelis Kelderkring and Albert Keuterkring. There are four ladies' groups, a choir, and various organizations for special causes. During the winter months various courses are offered and six congregational evenings

are held. The presentation of a Christmas pageant has become a tradition.

The founding of the congregation at The Hague stimulated the Mennonites of Berlin, Germany, to establish a congregation (*De Zondagsbode*, Feb. 3, 1889). H.W.M.

Inv. Arch. Amst. I, Nos. 20, 30, 83, 203, 216, 314; II, Nos. 1831-32; II, 2, Nos. 45-48; *DB* 1880, 166; 1882, 128; 1883, 59; 1887, 149-50; 1892, 126; 1896, 36-79; 1907, 210; 1918, 52; G. ten Cate, *Geschiedenis van de Doopsgez. Gemeente te 's Gravenhage* (Leiden, 1896; 2d ed. The Hague, 1908; 3d ed., enlarged by H. Veth, The Hague, 1914); L. G. le Poole, *Bijdragen tot de kennis van het Kerkelijk leven onder de Doopsgezinden te Leiden* (Leiden, 1905) 203-13; *ML* II, 160.

Hague, Sask., a town (pop. 400) about 40 miles north of Saskatoon. The railroad station was built in 1898, then in 1900 was moved half a mile north of the first site. Nearly all the first residents of Hague were Old Colony Mennonites. Ten years later people of other denominations moved in. In 1911 the Rosenort Mennonite Church was built, then enlarged in 1929 when additional settlers from Russia arrived. A Lutheran church has also been erected in the town. J.G.R.

Hague and Osler, Sask., about 12 miles apart and 30 miles from Saskatoon, were settled as a whole by Old Colony Mennonites. In 1895 the first settlers from Manitoba unloaded their belongings from the railway, for there was no station or any building in the town. Only a sign with the name Hague was to be seen. The first village was Neuanlage, 6 miles south of Hague, 5 or 10 families settling here in that year. The next villages built were Reinfeld, Hochfeld, Reinland, Blumenstein, Blumenthal, Neuhorst, Chortitza, Rosengart, Hochfeld, Osterwick, Schönwiese, Grünfeld, Grünthal. On the other side of the South Saskatchewan River is the village Edinburg. When the Mennonites from Russia came in 1923, the Old Colony Mennonites were at their height in numbers, because the majority of the children remained in the villages, the total number at Hague and Osler being about 2,000. A part of this number were Bergthaler Mennonites. Some were dissatisfied with conditions here, mainly because the German language was hard to maintain; so nearly half of the population moved to Mexico and Paraguay. The houses and land of the emigrants were then taken over by Mennonites who came from Russia in 1923 and later. J.G.R.

Hahn, Eduard von, a Russian statesman. After the death of General Insov, Czar Nikolas I appointed Eduard von Hahn, a young official of his chancellery, as president of the *Fürsorgekomitee* (*q.v.*) for the German settlers in South Russia, with its headquarters in Odessa. The emperor made this appointment in the early 1840's at the suggestion of Princess Helene Paulovna, who at the time played an important role in Russian court affairs. The charge to Hahn included the Mennonite settlements; here he brought about order with a firm hand. He frequently removed elders from office. Thus on May 20, 1842, he deposed Elder Jakob Warkentin in Halbstadt, and informed all the congregations of this event. This deed naturally produced some disquiet among the Mennonites of Russia; for it was unheard of that a government official would so rudely meddle in church matters. But in the end the people had to yield, for Warkentin had been guilty of civil offenses in interfering in government orders, in inciting disobedience to the local civil authorities, especially in the punishment of a member of the church, for whom the elder offered to take upon himself the labor imposed upon the offender; and in illegal operations in the election of an *Oberschulze,* and finally in unfounded and completely untenable charges against the local government (*Gebietsamt*).

In 1844 Elder Peter Schmidt of Waldheim was deposed because he baptized a Lutheran boy and received him into his congregation without government permission, and because he received into his congregation members expelled from other congregations contrary to the wishes and advice of the latter.

Furthermore, in 1847 Elder Heinrich Wiens of Gnadenheim was banished over the border into Prussia, because he excommunicated three members of his congregation for inflicting corporal punishment on an offender on command of the *Schulzenamt.*

Eduard von Hahn early recognized the importance and capability of Johann Cornies (*q.v.*) and gave him far-reaching authority; thus he contributed most effectively to Cornies' reformatory work and to the rapid cultural and economic progress of the Mennonite colony on the Molotschna, as the records in the archives of the Molotschna Agricultural Association show. Hahnsau (*q.v.*) of the Trakt settlement was named after Hahn. (*ML* II, 232.)

D.H.E.

Hahn, Joh. Michael, b. Feb. 2, 1758, at Altdorf near Böblingen (Württemberg), d. Jan. 20, 1819, a simple peasant who had also learned the trades of butchering and clockmaking, the founder of the brotherhood of the "Hahnischen" or "Michelianer," and the author of a number of books explaining his speculative theosophical system of doctrine. In 1777, while working in a field, he had a vision of three hours' duration. Inwardly converted, he withdrew from all associations and attended the meeting, where he soon acquired great influence. In 1780 he had a second vision, which lasted seven weeks. He received a "central insight," and "looked into the innermost birth and heart of all things." From now on he proclaimed his doctrine as a fluent, inspiring speaker and a profound author.

After 1794 Hahn found an asylum in Sindlingen near Herrenberg on the estate of Franziska, Duchess of Hohenheim, where he devoted the rest of his life to his spiritual work. The Holy Scriptures, which were his unquestioned authority, he interpreted somewhat allegorically. The world, ruined by sin, will be transformed by the redemptive work of Christ into a spiritual body. He urged complete sanctification and separation from the world. His eschatology was especially highly developed, as well as his teachings on the first resurrection, on the places of purification and the interim state in the Beyond, on the expectation of the Antichrist, of the millennium, and the restoration of all things. He was also the author of sacred hymns. Three of his (approximately 2,000) hymns were taken into the hymnal of the South German Mennonites. The membership of the brotherhood founded by him was estimated in 1920 at about 15,000. His views were favorably received in two Mennonite congregations in Baden, Dühren (*q.v.*) and Heimbronnerhof (*q.v.*), which separated from the *Verband* (*q.v.*) in 1858. His numerous writings were posthumously published in 13 volumes (Tübingen, 1819-41). (See **Michelians.**) NEFF.

Die Hahn'sche Gemeinschaft (2 ed., Stuttgart, 1949; *Hahns Leben,* 5-30, *Hahns Lehre,* 31-139); *ML* II, 232 f.; III, 124-26.

Hahnsau, the first village of the Trakt (*q.v.*) Mennonite settlement in the province of Samara, Russia, was founded in 1854 in the Malyshevka district by settlers direct from Prussia. The original village had 25 Mennonite families with a total population of 163, all farmers. The village was named after Councilor Eduard von Hahn (*q.v.*). The first group of settlers included a minister and two teachers. The establishment of the Hahnsau village succeeded well and rapidly, since most of the settlers were well-to-do; they had not only the 350 talers required by the Russian government of its immigrants, but also sufficient funds for building. The settlers Claas Epp, Sr., former *Dorfschulze* in Fürstenwerder (Danzig), and Johann Wall, a minister, had brought considerable capital with them. They were the delegates who had previously traveled to Russia to arrange the settlement with the government.

Of essential significance to the settlement and its later development were the excellent traits of character, such as diligence, of the colonists and a good business sense, as well as the education they had acquired at home. From this village the emigration to Turkestan took place in 1880 and 1881 under the leadership of Claas Epp, Jr. (*q.v.*), which caused the disintegration of Hahnsau. (*Am Trakt,* North Kildonan, 1948, 7-10; *ML* II, 233.)

D.H.E., C.K.

Hahnsau and Popovka Mennonite Brethren Church was located at Hahnsau (*q.v.*), Trakt settlement, Samara, Russia. It was begun about 1860 by B. Bekker, Jacob P. Bekker, H. Bartel, and Otto Forchhammer. In 1874 the group was accepted into the Mennonite Brethren Conference as the Hahnsau and Popovka M.B. Church. Hahnsau was a village of the Trakt Mennonite settlement and Popovka was a Lutheran village in the vicinity. It was here that differences of opinion existed as to whether the Holy Kiss (*q.v.*) or Sister Kiss was to be practiced between brethren and sisters. Among the leaders were Eckert (*q.v.*), Hahnhart, and Borchdorf. The first two were leaders also in Kansas. In the 1870's most of them came to Kansas, settling near Marion, where some of them joined the Mennonite Brethren Church and others the Baptist Church. Those remaining in Russia joined the Baptists. By 1885 the Hahnsau and Popovka Mennonite Brethren Church no longer existed. However, a new Mennonite Brethren group has apparently been started there in later years, about which little information is available. Before World War I, itinerant Mennonite Brethren ministers visited the settlement and organized an M.B. group.

C.K.

P. M. Friesen, *Brüderschaft*, 429 f.; *Am Trakt* (North Kildonan, 1949) 49 f.; Jacob P. Bekker, "Anfänge der Mennoniten Brüdergemeinde in Russland" (manuscript in BeCL).

Hainaut (Dutch, *Henegouwen;* German, *Hennegau*), now a province of Belgium. Although records of Anabaptists here are sparse, many Anabaptists must have lived here in the first decades of the Reformation. In 1535 about 1,000 inhabitants of Hainaut were prepared to take part in the attack on Amsterdam; nothing more is known about them. The only recorded execution of a Hainaut citizen was that of Cortoys, who was beheaded in Utrecht on June 11, 1539.

It is very probable that most of the Anabaptists here as elsewhere joined the Calvinists, for when persecution began anew about 1550, it was mostly Calvinists who were executed in Doornik (Tournai) and Mons (Bergen). But between 1551 and 1557 Leenaert Bouwens (*q.v.*) baptized here; hence there must have been some Anabaptists. In Doornik he baptized 31 persons. Through his visit the number of Anabaptists grew again. They also became better known thereby, for persecution soon struck them. In addition to the many Calvinists who suffered a martyr's death, it is also reported that six Anabaptists were burned at the stake in Hainaut in 1558: Lambert van Doornik, Adriaen van Hee, Joos Meeuwesz, Egbert Goossen, and Willem de Hoedemaker. The first was a native of Doornik; the others were Flemish. They had attended an Anabaptist meeting in the woods of Obignies, and when they were seized they yielded without resistance. They were executed in Obignies. In Mons, the capital of the province, Jan Fasseau of Giory was beheaded in 1555 or 1556 for the sake of his Anabaptist faith. One of the last Anabaptist martyrs in Hainaut was Maeyken Boosers (*q.v.*), who was burned at the stake at Doornik, Sept. 18, 1564.

After this there is no further mention of Anabaptists; but the Protestants here were so severely persecuted that according to the memoirs of van Vaernewyck the city of Doornik was practically deserted in July 1568. The books of martyrs present only a partial list of the victims; 30 are named there, whereas recent research has revealed that by 1570 at least 227 persons had been killed in Doornik for their faith. J.L.

Mart. Mir. D. 302-4, E. 667-69; F. vander Haeghen, Th. Arnold, and R. vanden Berghe, *Bibliographie des Martyrologes Protestants Neerlandais* II, 663, 683, 699, 703, 739; Meyhoffer, *Le Martyrologe Protestant de Pays-Bas*, index, "Hainaut"; Vos, K., *Menno Simons* (Leiden, 1912) 258; *ML* II, 284.

Haintzeman, Konrad, a cobbler by trade, a preacher of the Hutterian Brethren in Moravia, was captured in 1558 in Stain near Krems, Austria, on the Danube, when he was about to go to Moravia from Germany with a company of brethren, and was taken to Vienna, where he spent more than a year in terrible imprisonment. Bishop Anton Brus wished to have him executed in secret, since he refused to renounce his faith; but on the intercession of the Lutheran pastor Pfausinger, who had learned of the preparations, King Maximilian released him. He went to his brethren in Moravia; in 1560 he was chosen preacher and two years later ordained in this service. He died eight years later, in 1568, in the thermal springs of Teplice in Hungary, where he sought a cure for the ills acquired during his imprisonment. He is the author of two epistles written to the elders in 1558.

NEFF.

John Horsch, *Kurzgefasste Geschichte der Mennoniten* (Elkhart, 1890) 129; Beck, *Geschichts-Bücher*, 210, 214, 219; Wolkan, *Geschicht-Buch*, 300; *ML* II, 233.

Hairdressing. The more conservative Mennonite groups have shown during their history a marked resistance to cultural accommodation to the surrounding society's mores, conventions, and fashions. They based this nonconformity to the "world" upon such Biblical passages as "Be not conformed to this world." In both Europe and America there has been conviction against the cutting ("bobbing") of women's hair in the decades following World War I. This conviction was based in part on deep-seated aversion to any sort of conforming to the fashions of the "world," and in part on the specific reference of the Apostle Paul concerning a Christian woman's hair being "shorn," indicating that this constitutes a "shame" (I Cor. 11:6), and that woman's long hair was given to her (by God) for a "covering" (I Cor. 11:15). Such Mennonites not only object to cut hair, however, but also to all forms of highly artificial and fashionable coiffures, basing their position on the teaching of the Scriptures against worldly conformity in general, and on such passages in particular as I Tim. 2:9 and I Pet. 3:3, both of which condemn the arrangement of the hair in what J. B. Phillips renders "an elaborate coiffure." In the stricter groups such as the Old Order Amish, Old Order Mennonites, the Church of God in Christ Mennonites, the Evangelical Mennonites (Kleine Gemeinde), any marked deviation from what the church regards as acceptable hairdressing would involve church censure and exclusion from the Lord's Table and ultimately excommunication. In the Mennonite Church (MC) efforts are made by public teaching and pastoral counsel to secure a more perfect conformity to the standards of the group in regard to hairdressing. In the other Mennonite branches the matter of a woman's coiffure is regarded basically as her private concern, although the church is concerned to teach the principle of nonconformity to the world. The conservative groups in Canada, however, still maintain the older forms of hairdressing. In Switzerland there is strong resistance to the cutting of woman's hair, and to a lesser degree in France and the more conservative churches of South Germany.

J.C.W.

Haitjema, a Dutch Mennonite family, living at Balk, Friesland, where Klaas Haitzes (Haitjema) and Tjeerd Haitjema were among the last lay preachers and elders, Klaas serving 1809-*ca.* 40 and Tjeerd 1829-49. The Balk (*q.v.*) congregation maintained the old Mennonite manner of living and dressing until a large proportion of its members left for America in 1854. Tjiets Haitjema (1853-1939) (*DB* 1902, 26-28, where her picture is found), married to G. van der Sluys, wore her plain dress until 1872. Another member of this family is Th. L. Haitjema, now Reformed Professor of Theology at the University of Groningen. vɒZ.

Halberstadt, a city in the former Prussian government district of Magdeburg, where there was in 1535 a small congregation of Anabaptist refugees from the territories of Duke George of Saxony. Two families settled here in 1535; their leader was Georg Knoblauch. He collected a small group of men and women, including Hans Heune (or Höhne) of Seehausen near Frankenhausen, Christoph Thalacker, Georg Möller, Hans Birkhan, and Hans Hesse of Riestedt, several of whom died as martyrs. Services were held in Knoblauch's house in the Willows behind the cathedral at Halberstadt. Here transient brethren also found shelter.

The Brethren here were truly pious. The official, Heinrich Horn, who listened in on one of their meetings and gave a report to the bishop's authorities on Sept. 9, 1535, said, "Within a mysterious murmuring is held; it was not possible to understand what it was, since it took place behind barred doors and closed windows. The men occasionally came into the yard, knelt and prayed with folded hands." Petronella, a woman who was arrested later, stated, "The brethren and sisters prayed four times daily, also before and after meals. They usually get up twice at night to pray and praise God." At the communion service, which was held a short time before the harvest, the preacher washed the feet of the participants and kissed them; each broke off a bit of the bread, ate it in commemoration of the death of Christ, and confessed that he would gladly die for His sake. Whoever considered himself unworthy of the meal did not take part. Baptism was also performed in Knoblauch's house; thus on July 10, 1535, he baptized Hans Heune's wife Grete, Hans Kraut (the tailor), the brothers Georg and Jobst Möller, as well as Wolf Goldener. Even weddings were performed in the quiet little house; there is record of that of Georg Knoblauch's daughter Ursula with Hans Möller.

The Anabaptists in Halberstadt are sad evidence of the difficulty and danger attending membership in an untolerated brotherhood in the 16th century. To escape persecution they lived under the open sky and the forest wilderness. In order not to subject their children to the inclement weather and to give their women the necessary care in confinement they sought protection in the city. When the owner of the "house among the willows" learned that an infant born there was not baptized, she dispossessed the group. They then found refuge in the unoccupied Grauer Hof in Halberstadt in mid-August. But on Sept. 13 the police found two women, Anna Knoblauch and Grete Heune, with six children; soon they also seized Hans Heune, who had just returned home, and Petronella, a baker's wife, who had been baptized five years previously by the schoolmaster Alexander (executed in 1533).

The prisoners openly confessed their faith. Nevertheless they were tried under torture on the orders of the cardinal. On Sept. 20 Adrian Henckel (also called Adrian Richter) and Anna Reichard (Hermann Gerucher's wife) were also arrested. Since the prisoners refused to renounce their faith, Bishop Heinrich von Ackon decided to have various scholars attempt to convert them. They had partial success. Two mothers of newborn babies agreed to recant, probably to preserve the lives of their children, while Adrian Henckel and Hans Heune, as well as Petronella, persisted in their faith and declared to the judges that they were happy to suffer death for Christ's sake. On Oct. 8 Cardinal Albrecht gave the secular authorities the order to sentence them to death; they were to be taken to Gröningen, placed in a sack, and drowned; they were then to be interred in unhallowed ground by the executioner. Hege.

The statements of the victims have been published by E. Jacobs in "Die Wiedertäufer am Harz," in *Ztscht des Harz-Vereins für Gesch. u. Altertumskunde* XXXII (1899); see also P. Wappler, *Die Täuferbewegung in Thüringen von 1526-1584* (Jena, 1913); *ML* II, 233 f.

Halbertsma (Halbetsma), a Dutch Mennonite family, formerly living in the province of Friesland, now spread throughout the Netherlands. From the side of the mother this family became Mennonite. Dr. Scipio Halbetsma, a lawyer at the Court of Friesland, in 1669 married Catharina Rinia Stinstra (Mennonite) of Dokkum (daughter of Joost Rinia and Antje Hendricksz Stinstra). Their son Hidde Halbetsma (1685-1762) was a silversmith and a member of the congregation of Gorredijk (*q.v.*). Their son Joost (1723-88), b. at Gorredijk, moved to Grouw (*q.v.*), where this family resided for many generations and where are still found the Halbertsma woodworking factories. Joost's son was Hidde (1756-1809), a merchant and officer of a volunteer corps. This Hidde was the father of Pastor Joost Halbertsma (*q.v.*, 1789-1869). Like him his brothers Tjalling (1792-1852), a merchant, and Eeltje (1797-1877), a physician, both living at Grouw, were active in promoting the Frisian language and culture. Their popular literary work in the Frisian language was compiled in the collection of *Rimen en Teltsjes* (Rhymes and Tales), of which a fifth edition appeared at Leeuwarden in 1918.

These Halbertsma brothers have a large progeny, many of whom served in several Mennonite congregations as deacons. Lieuwe E. Halbertsma (b. 1824 at Grouw, d. Lippspringe, Germany, 1854), a son of Tjalling, mentioned before, went into the ministry after having been trained at the Amsterdam Mennonite Seminary. He served the congregations of Ternaard 1850 and Emden, East Friesland, 1850-54. vɒZ.

Ned. Patriciaat V, 1914, 172-81; XII, 1921-22, 206-17; XI, 1925, 135 f.; XL, 1954, 174-98.

Halbertsma, Justus Hiddes, b. Oct. 23, 1789, at Grouw, d. Feb. 14, 1869, at Deventer, served as Mennonite pastor at Bolsward 1814-21, and Deventer 1821-56, when he resigned to devote himself to writing. One of his works was *De Doopsgezinden en Hunne herkomst* (Deventer, 1843), in which he attempted to prove a Waldensian origin for the

Mennonites. The book is of value for its information on the liberal ideas of Halbertsma and many Mennonites of his time. The book also contained some sermons, which were sharply criticized by Samuel Muller in the Dutch periodical *Vaderlandsche Leteroefeningen* of 1843 and 1844 (reprint, *Beoordeeling van eenige Kerkredenen van J. H. H.,* Amsterdam, 1844).

Halbertsma studied the Nordic languages, especially his native Frisian, and became a specialist on Gysbert Japiex (1603-66), a Frisian poet. He cooperated with his brothers Eeltje, who was a physician in Grouw, and Tjalling, in publishing Frisian verse and tales, which were eagerly read and thus influenced Frisian life. He also translated the Gospel of Matthew into Frisian (1858). The complete Frisian works of the Halbertsma brothers were published in 1871 titled *Rimen en Teltsjes* (5th ed., Leeuwarden, 1918).   vDZ.

Inv. Arch. Amst. II, No. 2530; *Biogr. Wb.* III, 457-61; W. Eekhoff, biography of Halbertsma in *De Frije Fries,* 1873; *N.N.B.Wb.* III, 528 ff.; *DB* 1901, *passim; DJ* 1912, 21-41 with portrait; Wumkes, introduction to *Rimen en Teltjes* (5th ed., Leeuwarden, 1918); *ML* II, 234.

Halbstadt, a common Mennonite village name transplanted from the Prussian Marienburg Werder to the Molotschna Mennonite settlement. The name also appears in the following settlements: Barnaul, Siberia; Manitoba; Mexico; and Menno, Neuland, and Sommerfeld settlement of Villarrica, Paraguay.
                                                    C.K.

Halbstadt, village and district of the Molotschna (*q.v.*) settlement in South Russia, was founded in 1804 together with eight other villages by Mennonites emigrating from Prussia and was named after a village in Prussia. Leaders were Klaas Wiens and David Hübert. Originally the village owned 3,829 acres of land or 21 full farms with 189 acres each; later 945 additional acres, or 25 small farms of 38 acres each were added. (A. Braun states that Halbstadt owned about 5,500 acres.) The importance of the town within the Molotschna villages lay at first in the fact that it was made the seat of the district administration (1816) of the Molotschna settlement.

Of the 60 Mennonite villages of the Molotschna settlement, Halbstadt had the largest number of industries. In the course of time there developed, in addition to the smaller shops, a cloth factory (1815-16), a brewery (1809), three vinegar factories, two large steam-power mills, a starch factory, a barley mill, a motor factory, two tile factories, two oil presses, and the "Raduga" print shop. In connection with this growing industry, Neu-Halbstadt (*q.v.*), an adjacent workers' settlement, was established in 1842.

Of special cultural significance for the Mennonites of South Russia were, next to the elementary school, the Halbstadt Zentralschule (*q.v.* founded 1835), which was the teacher-training institute, the Halbstadt Kommerzschule (*q.v.,* founded 1907), and the Halbstadt Mädchenschule (*q.v.*). The Kommerzschule was originally a Realschule, and after the Revolution it became an agricultural school (1923).

Originally made up of only Mennonite families, Halbstadt gradually took in various elements of the population in consequence of the addition of factory workers and the Revolution. Even before the Revolution, non-Mennonites were in the majority. After the Revolution it became difficult for the Mennonite minority to assert its social and cultural character. The total population was 1,455 in 1925, of whom 482 were Mennonites, 118 other Germans, 675 Ukrainians, 120 Russians, 19 Jews, and 41 Poles, Bulgarians, and Greeks.

Under the Soviets all industries of Halbstadt as well as the land were nationalized. The collectivization process and the antireligious policies caused the exile of many Mennonites. During the outbreak of hostilities between Russia and Germany in World War II many were evacuated to Siberia. Those remaining left Russia for Germany in a trek under German army escort in 1943. Many of the Halbstadt citizens who escaped from Russia after World Wars I and II have found new homes in Canada and South America. (See also **Molotschna, Halbstadt** Mennonite Church, and **Ukraine;** *ML* II, 234 f.)   ABr.K., C.K.

Halbstadt Kommerzschule (School of Commerce), Molotschna, South Russia, was established as a private Realschule in 1907 sponsored by the Mennonite Educational Association (Mennonitischer Schulverein). Since it was under the supervision of the Russian Department of Education the name was changed to "Kommerzschule des Mennonitischen Bildungsvereins" in order to enjoy greater freedom and flexibility under the Department of Commerce. It retained the curriculum of the Realschule and added a year and some commercial subjects to the curriculum. Students from the regular Zentralschulen (*q.v.*) could enter a preparatory class of the school. The school consisted of the upper four grades of a regular Russian eight-grade school of commerce. Two foreign languages were taught. In 1910 the enrollment was 124. The school occupied the former starch factory of Halbstadt and had a dormitory for students from distant communities. The director of the school was chosen by the executive committee of the Educational Association (*Bildungsverein*) and approved by the Department of Commerce. In the early days J. J. Sudermann of Apanlee was the chairman of the executive committee and P. J. Wiens the director of the school. Some of the teachers were A. A. Friesen, P. P. Letkemann, and B. H. Unruh.

During the revolution and the following years the school went through great difficulties. In 1923 it was changed into an agricultural school.   C.K.

H. Görz, *Die Molotschnaer Ansiedlung* (Steinbach, Man., 1951) 160; P. M. Friesen, *Brüderschaft,* 627 ff.; *Menn. Life* VI (July 1951) 28.

Halbstadt Mennonite Church was originally a part of the Ohrloff-Petershagen Mennonite Church (*q.v.*) of the Molotschna settlement in South Russia, with one church at Ohrloff and one at Petershagen. The first two elders were Jakob Enns 1805-18, and Jakob Fast 1818-21. From this, the oldest congregation of the Molotschna, the "pure Flemish" congregation of Lichtenau, with strongly conservative tendencies, separated about 1824 under the leadership of Jakob Warkentin. The remnant of the congregation under the leadership of Elder Bernhard Fast retained its name (Ohrloff-Petershagen) until 1858, when a new church was built in Halbstadt (Neu-Halbstadt) to replace the old one in Petershagen, and the congregation was called Ohrloff-Halbstadt. From 1863, when a third church was built in Neukirch for the benefit of distant members, until 1895, it was known as Ohrloff-Halbstadt-Neukirch. The three elders who had charge of the congregation during this time were Bernhard Fast 1821-60, Johann Harder 1860-76, and Abram Görz 1876-95. In 1860-84 the congregation had in its midst Bernhard Harder (*q.v.*), a warmly revivalistic preacher, teacher, and poet, and one of the most important pulpit orators among the Mennonites of Russia, known far beyond his own congregation.

In the course of three decades the three parts of the congregation had grown to such proportions that it was difficult for the single elder, Abram Görz, to give it the necessary spiritual leadership. When he resigned in 1895 the Halbstadt group followed its long-cherished desire for independence, and with the consent of the Molotschna Mennonite *Kirchenkonvent* (*q.v.*) it organized as a separate congregation. The choice of elder in that year fell almost unanimously upon Heinrich Unruh (*q.v.*) of Muntau, who had served them as minister since 1870. He served as elder 20 additional years (to 1915), until his physical weakness prevented his further service in the office. He died in 1927. The local minister, B. Harder, was then given temporary charge. In 1918 Abraham Klassen (*q.v.*), who had hitherto been a minister of the Gnadenfeld congregation and a teacher in the Halbstadt schools, was chosen elder and served the congregation until 1930. He died in exile. The membership reached its highest point in 1910-19. Since then it decreased by about one third through emigration to Canada and the loss of the members living outside the Molotschna district. In 1926 the total membership was about 1,200, of whom 653 were baptized members.

The Halbstadt congregation had been leading in singing among the churches of the Molotschna. In 1919 Heinz Unruh, a son of Elder Unruh, a musically very gifted young man, became leader of the church choir. With youthful enthusiasm he reorganized and enlarged the choir and soon oratorios by Handel, Bach, and Mendelssohn were sung at the Halbstadt church. The choir also made frequent singing tours to other churches of the Molotschna.

In 1921 the Halbstadt Mennonite church building became state property, but even now for a while services went on unmolested. After 1927 religious persecution gradually set in, taxes on churches and ministers became increasingly severe, so that at last church activities became almost impossible. But in spite of all difficulties services at the Halbstadt church continued until January 1931, when on New Year's Day the last service was held, and the church was officially closed by the government. The two

ministers, Klassen and Harder, were arrested by the local authorities. For several weeks they were imprisoned at Halbstadt and then tried. Harder was sentenced to banishment to Siberia, but fell ill and died one day before the execution of his sentence. Klassen was sentenced to seven years' imprisonment in Melitopol. After three years he was released, but in 1941 was again arrested, and sentenced to Siberia, but died on the way in a freight car. In 1938 the Halbstadt church building was torn down and the bricks used for other buildings. The cemetery across the street from the church with its many beautiful marble monuments was also demolished and the grounds used for other purposes. An adopted daughter of Abraham Klassen is now living at Winnipeg, Man.

In its relationship to other congregations of the Molotschna settlement the Halbstadt congregation represented a moderate position and always defended the right of other groups to be independent in doctrine and organization, and had leaders who willingly granted the right of freedom and tolerance to other branches. In the period of confusion attending the withdrawal of the Mennonite Brethren (*q.v.*) it could therefore preserve a calm, thoughtful position and lend a hand of mediation. As a matter of principle it did not rebaptize persons transferring their membership from other Christian denominations. The fact that Elder H. Unruh, who was always above party spirit and of a very pacific temperament, was the chairman of the Molotschna Mennonite *Kirchenkonvent* for more than a decade made itself felt and prepared the way for an understanding between the various branches. (See also **Halbstadt, Molotschna,** and **Ukraine;** *ML* II, 235 f.) ABR.K., C.K.

Halbstadt Zentralschule, Molotschna, Russia, founded in 1835, was the second Mennonite secondary school in Russia. The initiative for the founding of the school was given by Faddeyev of the Department for Foreign Settlers to train teachers, secretaries, and to promote the Russian language among the Mennonites. Orphans and children of poor parents received free training, for which they were obligated to serve the community for pay for a number of years. At first the school was dependent on the *Oberschulze* of the district and the level of education was rather low (1835-70). Among the teachers of this period were Johann Neufeld, Abraham Ediger I, Johann Voth, Peter J. Neufeld, Jacob Wiebe, and Gustav Rempel. Some of the outstanding graduates during this time were Daniel Fast, Johann Claassen, and Bernhard Harder.

In 1869 the school became subject to the newly organized Molotschna school board (*Molotschnaer Mennoniten Schulrat*). Before this time the school offered a two-class course consisting of four years. Now two years were added. The graduates received a certificate. The standard of education was raised considerably. In 1878 a two-year teachers' training course was added. The Neu-Halbstadt elementary school became the "model school" (*Musterschule*) in which the students did their practice teaching beginning in 1879-80. The two basic classes (*Grundklassen*) of the Zentralschule, consisting of two years each, were changed into three-class courses, each consisting of a year (1884-85). Some of the outstanding teachers before World War I were Kornelius Unruh, Peter J. Neufeld, P. M. Friesen, Heinrich Franz II, H. A. Lenzmann, P. A. Ediger, D. H. Hamm, W. P. Neufeld, P. P. Fast, Cornelius Bergmann, D. J. Klassen, Hermann Penner, Abraham Klassen, Abraham Töws, and P. J. Braun.

In the beginning Russian had been taught as a foreign language. Around 1890 all subjects except the German course and Bible were taught in Russian. After the Russian Revolution (1917) all subjects with the exception of the Russian and the Ukrainian languages and literature were taught in German. In 1921 the Teachers' Training Institute was perfected and became known as the *Molotschnaer Mennonitisches Lehrerseminar.* Teachers at this time were P. J. Braun, Peter Epp, Aaron Toews, P. P. Sawatzky, B. B. Wiens, and Abraham Klassen. Its director, P. J. Braun, reported in 1922 that 400 teachers had been graduated during the period of 44 years (since 1878) and that they were serving in most of the Mennonite settlements of European and Asiatic Russia. Many of them were ordained to the ministry or were leaders in the economic and cultural life of the Mennonites. After the Revolution the school fought a losing battle with the Communist government and philosophy. Gradually most of the teachers were forced to resign; many left for America, others were exiled, and a few managed to find other occupations. The Halbstadt Mennonite Zentralschule and the Teachers' Training Institute did much to raise the spiritual, cultural, and economic level of the Mennonites of Russia. (See also **Education** *Among the Mennonites in Russia* and **Zentralschule.**)　　　　C.K.

Friesen, *Brüderschaft*, 596-612; P. Braun, "The Educational System of the Mennonite Colonies in South Russia," *MQR* III (1929) 168-82; P. Braun, "Das Molotschnaer Mennonitische Lehrerseminar in Halbstadt, 1878-1922," manuscript, Bethel College Historical Library; Leonhard Froese, *Das Pädagogische Kultursystem der mennonitischen Siedlungsgruppe in Russland* (Göttingen, 1949).

Haldimand County, Ont., is situated 50 miles southeast of Waterloo County, at the outlet of the Grand River into Lake Erie. Across Lake Erie to the south can be seen the ridge of Pennsylvania bordering the lake near Erie City. Having a heavy clay soil in many parts, it is suited to the cultivation of grain, hay, and livestock. It was one of the earliest Mennonite settlements of Ontario. To this area came the Hoovers (Hubers) about 1790, from York Co., Pa., or near Gettysburg. Fuller accounts will be found under **Rainham, South Cayuga, Selkirk** (MC).　　　　J.C.F.

Halewijn (French, *Halluin*), a town (pop. 13,000) just across the Belgian border in northern France, which in the 16th century belonged to the Southern Netherlands, was the scene of Anabaptist activity in the middle of that century. In 1561 there seems to have been a congregation here, several members of which were executed in 1563 (see **Jan de Swarte**).　　　　vDZ.

Half-Anabaptists, people (mainly of Switzerland) who sympathized with the Swiss Brethren and supported them without, however, themselves ever joining their brotherhood. "Great is the number of those who are suspended between heaven and earth, and know not what to do," writes a Bernese observer around 1690. As is well known the Swiss authorities harshly persecuted the Brethren throughout the country, in particular in the canton of Bern. These persecutions, however, were by no means popular, as it was widely known that the Brethren were as good, if not better, Christians than the majority. Thus many people helped them, gave them food and shelter, and shielded them against the official "Anabaptist hunters" (*Täufer-Jäger*), often endangering themselves. Bernese mandates expressly condemned and threatened these "sympathizers."

The Brethren themselves were split in their attitude toward these friends, or "true-hearted people" (*die Treuherzigen*) as they called them. In the Amish split of 1693 the Reist people contended that the "true-hearted ones" would be saved, while Jakob Ammann in his unyielding sternness denied this (*MQR* 1937, 244, note 29). In contemporary literature these Half-Anabaptists are occasionally mentioned. George Thorman's *Probierstein des Täufertums* (*q.v.*, Bern, 1693), though it was a polemical book against the Anabaptists, still had to admit that the Brethren were highly thought of by the population at large. "They [the Half-Anabaptists] remain with us," he writes, meaning with the established church, "but they are fully persuaded that it would be better for them to cast their lot with the Anabaptists." If they refrained from doing so, it was because of fear, as they were not ready to accept suffering and tribulation.

Around 1700 Hans Reist (*q.v.*), the leader of the milder branch of the Swiss Brethren, composed and published a prayer, *Das Gebätt,* in which we read, "We also pray to Thee on behalf of all those people who do so much good unto us with food and drink and house and shelter, and who produce and show unto us great love and loyalty" (Friedmann, *Menn. Piety,* 185). Again we read in the *Ernsthafte Christenpflicht* (*q.v.*), the first complete Mennonite prayerbook of 1739, several such prayers for the Half-Anabaptists, "the goodhearted people who love us and do good unto us and show mercy, but have little strength to come into the obedience of God" (*ibid.,* 191-212). Such supplications are made at six places.

That in spite of all the superhuman hardships the Brethren were never completely exterminated in Switzerland is at least in part due to the efforts of these Half-Anabaptists.　　　　R.F.

John Horsch, "The Half-Anabaptists of Switzerland," *MQR* XIV (1940) 57-59; D. Gratz, *Bernese Anabaptists* (Scottdale, 1953) 49; R. Friedmann, *Mennonite Piety Through the Centuries* (Goshen, 1949) 185, 191; M. Gascho, "The Amish Division of 1693," *MQR* XI (1937) 244; *ML* II, 234.

Hall (or Schwäbisch-Hall), a city (pop. 15,165) of Württemberg, Germany, 35 miles northeast of Stuttgart, charmingly situated on the Kocher, with its splendid church of St. Michael. Until 1504 Hall was ecclesiastically a subsidiary of Steinbach, which belonged to the Komburg monastery, but it had an independent right in the preaching office, to which Johannes Brenz (*q.v.*) was called in 1523. Together with his friend Johann Isenmann, who was called to the pastorate in 1524, Brenz effected the Reformation in the city. Judging from the funeral address of Bidembach, the Anabaptists in the region of Hall caused them some concern. But the only one known by name is Melchior Hofmann (*q.v.*), who worked for the Anabaptist movement from Livland, Kiel, and East Friesland to Strasbourg and there died in prison. The council of Hall issued a mandate to warn its subjects of the leaven of the Anabaptists; this was surely done at Brenz's instigation. In 1530 Hall could venture to write to the emperor that with true diligence and God's aid they had averted the Anabaptist sect (Hortmann und Jäger, I, 290).

The statement made by the Chronicler Herolt that in 1534 many peasants with their families, who had been Anabaptist adherents, had emigrated to Moravia in the hope that they might there become better Christians (*Württembergische Geschichtsquellen* I, 255) evidently had reference to those who came into the Rhine region from the Palatinate, concerning whose migration Kirchberg reports (see **Hohenlohe**), rather than to peasants of Hall. The isolated case of Katherine Hoffmann of Reinsberg as an Anabaptist is mentioned in 1555 (Gmelin, *Hallische Geschichte,* 736). Her kinship with Melchior Hofmann, which Gmelin assumes, is very unlikely. On the other hand, there are indications that the Hutterian Brethren sent men into the Hall region to gain adherents for their brotherhood. The *Geschichts-Bücher* records on p. 235, "In this year Brother Paul Schuester, a preacher, fell asleep with a peaceful heart in the district of Hall." Paul Schu(e)ster had been chosen to the ministry in 1551. There is no information concerning later Anabaptists in the district. It is very likely that there were none.   G. Bos.

G. Bossert, Sr., *TA:I: Württemberg;* G. Bossert, Jr., "Aus der nebenkirchl.-relig. Bewegung der Ref.-Zeit in Württemberg (Wiedertäufer und Schwenckfelder)," in *Bl. f. Württemb. Kirchengesch.,* 1929, 1-41; J. Hartmann and K. Jäger, *Johannes Brenz* I (Hamburg, 1840) 290; J. Gmelin, *Hallische Geschichte,* 735 ff.; *ML* II, 236.

Hall (now called *Solbad Hall*), a city (pop. 10,535) in the lower Inn Valley, Tirol, Austria, the old capital of the Inn Valley, the seat of the district court, on the left bank of the Inn, 20 miles east of Innsbruck, with which it carries on a lively trade. It has a rich past in the history of Anabaptism in Tirol, which has been better preserved in archive materials than in the chronicles of the Hutterian Brethren. In 1521 Dr. Jakob Strauss was already working to reform the ceremonies and practices of the church, preaching against corruption in the confessional, calling the monks misleaders of the world; but he was not in agreement with the Wittenberg Reformation either. His successor Urban Rhegius also worked with the same idea; thus the Anabaptists in Hall and vicinity found a well-prepared field.

Not only Hall, but also the suburb Mild soon became a center of the Anabaptist movement. The martyr list of the chronicles, to be sure, records only two executions, whereas 68 are recorded for Kitzbühel. The movement evidently moved from Hall to other places which seemed safer at the moment. The town on the Inn also attracted them as the route of many Anabaptists on their way to Moravia.   LOSERTH.

J. Loserth, *Der Anabaptismus in Tirol* (Vienna, 1892); G. Loesche, "Tirolensia, Täufertum und Protestantismus," in *Jahrbuch der Gesellschaft für die Gesch. des Protestantismus in Oesterreich* XLVII (1926); *ML* II, 236.

Hallau, a village in the Klettgau district of the canton of Schaffhausen, Switzerland, not far from Waldshut, since 1525 a possession of the city of Schaffhausen. During the period 1524-25 it was subject to a variety of revolutionary and Anabaptist ideas. It took the lead in the revolt of the Schaffhausen peasants. Hans Rüeger, the cabinetmaker of Hallau, was active here in promulgating the ideas of Thomas Müntzer, who had come into the territory near by in the fall of 1524; he advocated community of goods and took part in the peasant disturbances. In a later court trial he admitted that he had desired that the peasants should be on top and the lords underneath.

It is difficult to say to what degree the true Anabaptist movement was involved in the uprising of the Klettgau peasants. On Feb. 5, 1525, Johannes Brötli (*q.v.*) preached in Hallau for the first time. He is no doubt the founder of an Anabaptist congregation of the Zürich type. He had signed the letter of Grebel and the Zürich Brethren to Müntzer in which they protested against the use of force. His letters to the Brethren in Zollikon indicate that he preached the Gospel as interpreted by the Zürich Anabaptists, who certainly had no part in revolutionary activities. His preaching, however, no doubt contributed to the intensification of the hopes of the peasants for better conditions in the future. The city of Schaffhausen, at the request of Zürich, sought to arrest Brötli, but the peasants forcibly prevented this, apparently considering Brötli as their leader. Almost the entire population of the village was baptized by him. The Anabaptist movement continued strongly for a time. On Nov. 13, 1527, Hans Rüeger was executed as an Anabaptist. By 1529 the majority of the people are reported to have returned to the church, but in 1531 again we find the list of Hallau people who were fined because of attendance at Anabaptist meetings. Thereafter the traces of the movement became progressively weaker. In 1534 there was some discussion in the Schaffhausen council concerning Anabaptists. Later a George Sattler of Oberhallau appears in the report of a Zürich trial of 1548 as an Anabaptist preacher and leader of secret meetings in the Klettgau. Nothing further is known about the movement here.   L.v.M.

H. Nabholz, *Die Bauernbewegung in der Ostschweiz* (Bülach, 1828); C. Bächtold, *Die Schaffhauser Wiedertäufer* (Schaffhausen, 1900); *ML* II, 236 f.

Halle, Bartholomeus van: see Bartel Boeckbinder.

Haller, Berchthold (1492-1536), the reformer of the Swiss canton of Bern, was of a gentle disposition, which he also revealed to the Swiss Brethren. He insisted that it was impossible to eradicate error; that should be left to God. Persecution merely increased the following of the Anabaptists. He therefore wanted to grant them religious freedom if they would be quiet, and punish only those who created a public disturbance. To Zwingli he wrote in 1527: "We know, of course, that the council is quite ready to banish the Anabaptists. But it is in our place to judge all things with the sword of the Spirit, either from the pulpit or in conversation." The council, however, disregarded Haller's admonitions and had two Anabaptists drowned in the Aare in 1529 or 1530 (Thudichum, 225). He also took part in the discussion with the baker Hans Pfistermeyer (*q.v.*). To Zwingli he wrote that he could not convince himself that it was permissible to punish Anabaptists with the sword, so much the less because they strictly avoided wickedness, whereas so many even of the ruling men were, on the contrary, so indifferent and careless (Müller, *Berner Täufer,* 24).

Haller states his attitude toward the Anabaptists still more clearly in a letter to Bullinger, Nov. 16, 1534 (see the letter of Sept. 12, 1532). He says that he had been requested by the city of Bern to offer an opinion on the suppression of the Anabaptists. They had expected that he would sponsor the death penalty, but he could not do this. He pointed out to the council the basis of the evil namely, that when many preachers serve their belly more than their duty, it is not surprising that we are called false prophets; when one sees in the magistracy so much pomp, luxury, and greed, and such disregard of the divine Word, the simpler folk are easily persuaded that we have an unchristian government; when false oaths are not punished and offensive cursing is tolerated, it is easy to see why they do violence to the Scripture in forbidding all oaths; when one sees the young people, whose baptism is demanded, growing up in all evil, they can easily decide to reject infant baptism. He had long since proposed that one should not be so quick to shed Anabaptist blood, while the Papists, who do much more harm to the temporal and Christian state, are spared.

Such a gentle and friendly judgment of the Anabaptists and the reasons for the movement was quite extraordinary. Yet Haller was unable to prevent a relatively large number of Anabaptist executions in Bern. His was a yielding temperament, which was almost dominated by Zwingli. One of his great services for the introduction of the Reformation was his participation in the great Bern disputation of Jan. 6 to 26, 1528.   NEFF.

Fr. Thudichum, *Die deutsche Reformation* II (Leipzig, 1909); H. Hoffmann, *Reformation und Gewissensfreiheit* (Giessen, 1932) 22, 37; C. Pestalozzi, *Berthold Haller* (Elberfeld, 1861); *ML* II, 237.

Hallman, Eli S. (1866-1955), a prominent Mennonite (MC) bishop in Saskatchewan, born near Washington, Waterloo Co., Ont., married Melinda Clemens in 1893, had seven children (beyond infancy). Ordained to the Mennonite ministry on June 17, 1897, he served the First Mennonite Church, Kitchener, Ont., until 1905, when he was sent to Guernsey, Sask., as pastor of the newly founded Mennonite settlement there, the Sharon Mennonite Church, and bishop of all the Mennonite congregations in the Canadian West. In 1912 he moved to Goshen, Ind., to serve as financial field secretary for Goshen College, which post he held till 1916. Following this he lived for two years at Grand Bay, Ala., near Gulfport, Miss., then until 1920 at Allemands, La., in both places assisting new congregations. In 1920-28 he served again at Guernsey, then at Falfurrias, Tex., 1928-32, and at Tuleta, Tex., 1932-50, until his retirement to Akron, Pa.   H.S.B.

E. S. Hallman, *The Hallman-Clemens Genealogy with a Family's Reminiscence* (Tuleta, 1949), largely autobiographical.

Hallman, H. S. (1859-1932), U.M.C. minister and editor, was born Aug. 5, 1859, near Kitchener, Ont. On Feb. 18, 1881, he married Maria Rosenberger, to which union nine children were born. Converted at the age of 14, he entered the ministry in 1881, and was ordained in 1885 by the Ontario Conference of the United Missionary Church. He held pastorates at Port Elgin and Elmwood, Ont.

Elected editor of the *Gospel Banner* in 1888, Hallman served in this capacity for 20 years, and also as publisher from 1899 to 1908. Under his leadership the paper became a weekly publication in 1893. He also published several tracts, books, hymnbooks, and periodicals, and became the founder and first publisher of the *Scripture Text Calendar* which he continued to edit until his death in 1932.

Hallman was secretary-treasurer of the Ontario Conference Mission Board 1898-1910, and president 1910-17. He was the first president of the Ontario Conference city mission work. He was secretary of the Ontario conference for 15 years and also secretary of five general conferences of the denomination (1888-1904 inclusive).

In the latter part of his life Hallman became active in the Christian and Missionary Alliance, although retaining his membership in the United Missionary Church. For some years he was superintendent of the C.M.A. publishing business in New York City, later serving as pastor of Alliance churches in Brantford and Toronto, Ont. He died in Toronto on Oct. 13, 1932.   E.R.S.

Hallum, a village in the Dutch province of Friesland, not far from the North Sea, since the 16th century the seat of a Mennonite congregation. Anabaptism was rooted here already in the earliest period; the martyr Frans Claesz (*q.v.*), executed in 1539 at Leeuwarden, and also the martyr Joriaen Simonsz (*q.v.*), who is said to be from Hallmen in Friesland, burned at the stake at Haarlem in 1557, were natives of this town. In 1568-82 Leenaert Bouwens (*q.v.*) baptized here no fewer than 226 persons. The Mennonite congregation, however, at this time had its center not in Hallum, but in Hijum, about 1½ miles west of Hallum. Of its oldest history very little is known. It did not join the Mennonite Sociëteit (Conference) of Friesland when this was founded in 1695. In 1713 it numbered only about 15 members. In 1779 the old meetinghouse at Hijum was abandoned and a new one built at Hallum, because most members now lived in this town. Then the congregation was called Hallum. From about 1604 until about the beginning of the 18th century there was in addition a second congregation at Hallum, belonging to the Jan Jacobsz group (*q.v.*). Between 1604 and 1643 the traveling elders of this group baptized 159 persons at Hallum, but since then no traces any more are found of the Jan Jacobsz group at Hallum. Its last members may have merged with the congregation of Hijum, which joined the Mennonite Conference of Friesland in 1713 as a united congregation. Even after its transfer to Hallum the congregation did not prosper, remaining very small in membership—20 in 1838, 88 in 1861. The last untrained preacher was Johannes Uiltjes Stinne, a cobbler. He served 1783-1818 and was followed by Roelof Schuiling, serving 1818-57, who at the same time also served the congregation of Oudebildtzijl (*q.v.*). In 1858 a new parsonage was built. An organ was purchased in 1879, in 1906 replaced by a larger one. In 1896 it was discussed whether the congregation, which then numbered 36 members, would be dissolved, but Pastor Sjoerd Wartena, serving here from 1897 until 1910, succeeded in raising the membership to 100 in 1910. S. Wartena was followed by the pastors M. J. Kosters Gz 1911-17, H. J. Busé 1917-22, S. D. A. Wartena, a son of Sjoerd Wartena, 1922-36, C. P. Hoekema 1936-45, and A. Veldstra since 1949.

The membership increased to 138 in 1922, 175 in 1954. A new meetinghouse was built in 1912. In the same year two sisters were chosen on the church board as deaconesses. The congregation possesses a small archive; the oldest document is of 1776. The following activities are now (1954) found in the congregation: a Menno Kring (youth group), Menniste Bouwers (age 13-18), Sunday school (age 6-12), and a ladies' circle.

S.D.A.W., vdZ.

Blaupot t. C., *Friesland, passim; Inv. Arch. Amst.* II, Nos. 1888 f.; *DB* 1910, 121-41; J. Loosjes, *Jan Jacobsz en de Jan-Jacobsgezinden*, in *Ned. Archief v. Kerkgesch.* XI (1914) 229, *ML* II, 237 f.

Halmael, van. This family, now extinct, was in the 17th-19th centuries found among the members of the Mennonite churches both Lam and Zon, at Amsterdam, where they were mostly engaged in banking. Francois van Halmael (Halmale), b. about 1530, a descendant of an old family, emigrated from Belgium. He was a soldier and was active during the capture of Brielle, Holland, in 1572. In his old age he joined the Mennonite Church, retired from all political and military business, and resided at Wesel on the Rhine, Germany. Of his children, who were cloth-merchants, five moved to Holland, Israel van Halmael to Rotterdam, where he became a preacher of the Flemish congregation until he resigned in 1645 at an old

age; Abraham, Jacob, Otto, and Isaak van Halmael moved to Amsterdam. Abraham (b. 1573?) became a deacon of the Amsterdam Old Flemish congregation "bij de Kruikjes" in 1616 and a preacher in 1619, and served until 1624, when he moved to Utrecht. He died there in 1630. (Kühler, *Geschiedenis* II, 131, note 2.) Another Abraham van Halmael was preacher of the "Lam en Toren" congregation at Amsterdam from 1675 until his death in 1679. This family, which was very influential in the Amsterdam business life in the 17th and 18th centuries, and related by marriage to a large number of prominent Mennonite families, provided many deacons. Jacob Otto van Halmael, a deacon in the Amsterdam Flemish congregation, sided with Galenus Abrahamsz (*q.v.*) in the "Lammerenkrijgh" (*q.v.*), a quarrel in this congregation, and with Michiel Comans published three pamphlets in 1664 (*Waerschouwinge; Antwoordt op de Waerschouwinge;* and *Tweede Waerschouwinge*). Hendrick van Halmael (1654-*ca.* 1720), a grandson of Jacob, wrote a number of tragedies.   vdZ.

Ned. Patriciaat XXVI (1940) 60-64; *Inv. Arch. Amst.* I, Nos. 1715 f.; II, Nos. 115 f., 314, 1459 f.

Halstead, Harvey Co., Kan., a town (pop. 1,300) located in the central part of the state, was founded in 1872. Of the 500 Mennonites in the vicinity (1954) about 20 per cent live in Halstead. Christian Krehbiel of Summerfield, Ill., accompanying Mennonites from Russia in 1873, liked the land in the Halstead area. A delegation of the Summerfield Mennonite Church (*q.v.*) was then appointed to investigate the land for possible settlement. The delegation was joined by David Goerz, Bernhard Warkentin, and others, making a total of twelve. As a result a Mr. Touzalin of the Atchison, Topeka, and Santa Fe Railway came to Summerfield, and arrangements were made to reserve land for settlement near Halstead. In 1874 a group was sent to make the final selection of the land which was chosen between Halstead and Moundridge. The town to be established was named Christian (*q.v.*).

Warkentin (*q.v.*) built a mill on the Arkansas River at Halstead and also conducted an agricultural experimental station, particularly to promote and select the hard Red Turkey Wheat which he imported from the Ukraine. In 1876 David Goerz (*q.v.*) established in Halstead the Western Publishing Company (*q.v.*), where he published *Zur Heimath* (*q.v.*). In 1882 the Halstead Seminary (*q.v.*), which became the nucleus of Bethel College, was established. Peter Wiebe founded a lumber business in 1874. Numerous other Mennonite families of the Summerfield Mennonite Church settled in and around Halstead founding the Halstead First Mennonite Church (*q.v.*) on March 28, 1875. The Grace Mennonite Church (CGC), a mile west of town, was founded in 1880. The first Mennonite relief agency, the Mennonite Board of Guardians (*Fürsorgekomittee, q.v.*), of which David Goerz was secretary, had its headquarters in Halstead. For a while it seemed that Halstead would become the center of the Mennonite settlements in Kansas. Gradually, however, Newton won in popularity. Warkentin and Goerz moved their major interests to Newton. Later the town became noted for the Halstead Hospital and its founder, Dr. A. E. Hertzler, who was of Mennonite descent.   C.K.

C. Krahn (ed.), *From the Steppes to the Prairies* (Newton, 1949) 35 ff.; Frank W. Blackmar, *Kansas . . .* I (Chicago, 1912) 802.

Halstead (Kan.) **First** Mennonite Church (GCM). In 1874 a group of 30 brethren from Summerfield, Ill., purchased land in the vicinity of Halstead and held the first church service in a schoolhouse on Jan. 11, 1874, with Christian Krehbiel in charge. On March 21, 1875, a constitution was drafted, and a decision reached to elect a minister and deacons and to celebrate the Lord's Supper on Easter Sunday, March 28, 1875; Valentine Krehbiel was elected as minister. The congregation met in homes and schools until the church building was dedicated, Jan. 1, 1878. The present church was erected in 1885, and remodeled and enlarged after World War II.

Although the Halstead church has grown steadily, it has never become large. It has rather furnished the nucleus from which the following churches were formed: West Zion of Moundridge, Kan.; Garden Township of Hesston, Kan.; Bethel College Church of North Newton, Kan.; Burrton, Kan.; and Geary, Okla. It has sponsored some unusual organizations, such as the Leisy Orphan Aid Society, the Mennonite Board of Guardians to help immigrants, and the Mennonite Charity, which took over the Halstead Hospital begun by Dr. A. E. Hertzler. In addition the church has carried on special work with the American Indians.

In its first 75 years nine ministers served: Valentine Krehbiel 1875-79, David Goerz 1878-97, Christian Krehbiel 1879-1907, J. H. Langenwalter, J. E. Amstutz 1911-21, H. J. Unruh 1922-35, D. C. Wedel 1936-46, Loris Habegger 1947-54, and Roland Goering 1954- . At least seven other ministers for a time had their church home here, mostly before being ordained. The late Sister Frieda Kaufman of the Bethel Deaconess Hospital and Sister Clare Kuehney, missionary to India, came from this church. It has produced a number of physicians and college teachers: H. H. Ewert, H. A. Kruse, W. J. Baumgartner, M. D. Baumgartner, E. B. Krehbiel, D. R. Krehbiel, and J. H. Langenwalter. Two members have served as state legislature representatives, H. P. Krehbiel and J. A. Schowalter. P. J. Galle served as district judge. D. Goerz published here the German paper *Zur Heimath,* which was a forerunner of the church paper, *Christlicher Bundesbote.* Bernhard Warkentin was a pioneer in the milling business, establishing the first water mill at Halstead. In 1953 the congregation had 346 members.   D.C.W.

C. E. Krehbiel, *Historical Sketch, First Mennonite Church, Halstead, Kansas* (Newton, 1925).

Halstead Seminary. The Halstead College Association was incorporated May 5, 1883, with B. Warkentin as president and D. Goerz as secretary. The Association was to furnish a rent-free building for five years to the Kansas Conference (GCM) School which became known as Halstead Seminary. The school, which was controlled by the Kansas Conference and located at the western edge of Halstead, Kan., opened on Sept. 19, 1883, with 12 students, but increased to 76 during the first year. H. H. Ewert was the principal.

The purposes of the school were: (1) to prepare teachers for the elementary schools, the English public school, and the German parochial school; (2) to prepare students for college entrance; and (3) to offer general liberal arts training to any who desired an education beyond the elementary stage. To attain these objectives three different "courses" were offered: a teachers' course, a German-English academy course, and a college preparatory course.

In 1885 in co-operation with the mission board, a special department for Indian students was set up at the Seminary with 15 Indians attending. The arrangement did not work out, for it really meant two schools, the seminary controlled by the conference school committee, and the Indian school controlled by the mission board. After two years the Indian school was removed to the Christian Krehbiel farm east of Halstead where it continued a few more years.

Progress of the Seminary was encouraging although there were also financial and other difficulties. As the movement in behalf of Bethel College at Newton got under way the school interest also gradually shifted from Halstead to Newton. From 1883 to 1893 the total enrollment at Halstead was 515 with 30 graduates.

In 1892 the Conference voted to close the Halstead Seminary with the end of the 1892-93 school year. In the fall of the same year Bethel College under the auspices of a Mennonite corporation opened its doors and became the successor to the Halstead Seminary.   E.G.K.

P. J. Wedel and E. G. Kaufman, *The Story of Bethel College* (North Newton, Kan., 1954).

Hamberg, a Mennonite village in South Russia in the Gnadenfeld district of the Molotschna settlement on the Tokmak River, not far from the railway station of Stulnevo. The village, founded in 1862 by farmers from older villages, was laid out in 26 full farms with 175 acres each, and three small farms of 40 acres each, on a total of 4,684 acres. It soon achieved prosperity, but suffered greatly in the horrors of the Civil War in 1917. Over 300 shots fell into the village, damaged the buildings, and killed cattle, though no human lives were lost. The village was repeatedly plundered by roaming bands of robbers; five persons were killed. Twenty-three adults succumbed to the typhus epidemic. With few exceptions the inhabitants were members of the Schönsee Mennonite Church (*q.v.*). (*ML* II, 239.)   D.H.E.

Hamberge, a village west of Lübeck, Germany. Here and in the adjacent Hansfelde, Mennonite families were living in the middle of the 18th century. The only names known are Wienantz and Wibbe, whose bearers were already resident here in 1700.

A significant concession was made to the Mennonites here sometime before 1654, when they were given a part of the cemetery for the burial of the Mennonite dead of Hamberge, Hansfelde, and also Lübeck. The preacher Herman Hermansen (Harmen Harmens) was buried here in 1713. The earliest information concerning this cemetery is given by the Lutheran Pastor Christian Rodatz, who was in Hamberge in 1645-66, and took a more friendly attitude toward the Anabaptists than his colleagues (see **Lübeck**). His successor, Michael Leopoldi, was of a somewhat different mind, as the inspection report of Christian von Stökken, the Superintendent of Eutin, shows—". . . only that the Anabaptists have their own burial here in the cemetery, which they bought with money, for which everything can be had today." The dead were also carried through the church, in at the south door and out at the north. Besides the purchase price they had the usual fees to pay; they had "to pay to the pastor the quarterly fee and offering, as well as to the sexton the proper dues at definite times, and probably more than others paid" (according to later information they paid a double fee). When the Mennonites became fewer their burial site was reduced. In 1734 the parson required them to repair the fence; Wiebert Wiebe appealed in the name of the group to the *Domkapitel,* probably with success. That is the last we hear of them.

Like the Mennonites of Lübeck, those of Hamberge and Hansfelde disappeared, partly by dying out and partly by emigration. (*ML* II, 239.) R. Do.

Hamburg (*Hamberg*), a common Mennonite village name which appeared first in the Molotschna settlement, Russia. From here it was transplanted to the following settlements: Borozenko, province of Ekaterinoslav; Omsk, Siberia; East Reserve, Man.; and Cuauhtemoc, Mexico.   C.K.

Hamburg-Altona (Germany) Mennonite Church. This congregation, begun in 1601, whose meetinghouse has always been in Altona, was called "Altona" until toward the middle of the 19th century, when it was called "Gemeinde zu Hamburg und Altona." The first printed use of this second name was in J. Mannhardt's *Namens-Verzeichnis* of 1857. This is also the name used in B. C. Roosen's *Geschichte* (1886-87). The modern name Hamburg-Altona appears for the first time in the *Christlicher Gemeinde-Kalender* for 1899. The old Dutch seal of the congregation carries the name *Mennoniten-Gemeente tot Hamburg en Altona.* The Dutch *Naamlijst* of 1731-1829 used only "Altona by Hamburg" or "Altona" alone. The first meetinghouse, destroyed by bombing in World War II in 1944, erected in 1674 and rebuilt in 1717 after the burning of the city by the Swedes in 1713, stood in the street called "Grosse Freiheit" in Altona, with an attached cemetery. The new meetinghouse (built 1915) with parsonage, is located at Mennonitenstr. 20 (Langenfelderstr. 100/102) in Altona, the cemetery at Holstenkamp 80/82 also in Altona. The baptized membership in 1953, greatly increased over that of 1941 (300, plus 38 children) because of the postwar refugees from the Danzig area, was 681, plus 236 unbaptized, total 917. The membership of the congregation is scattered throughout both cities and the suburbs and more distant towns,

and since the refugees have joined, still more widely scattered in a radius of 50-75 miles. More distant refugees are attached to the neighboring and newly organized congregations of Bremen (*q.v.*), Friedrichstadt (*q.v.*), Kiel (*q.v.*), Lübeck (*q.v.*), and Uelzen (*q.v.*).

Hamburg and Altona, though actually one large community, have always been two distinct political entities, with Altona much the smaller of the two. Hamburg, until 1933 a city state with a total area of 160 sq. mi., founded by Charlemagne in 811, became an independent Hanseatic City in the late 13th century, and has remained ever since a leading economic and cultural center of Germany. In 1600 it had a population of 40,000, in 1939, 1,143,000 in the city proper, but in the total area of the former free state, 1,682,200, of which over 80 per cent were Lutherans. Altona is a city of 185,653 in the province of Schleswig-Holstein, Germany, immediately adjacent to Hamburg on the west and closely associated with it, but with a separate political and religious history. Through the admission of Reformed, Mennonites, and others, under the rule of the Counts of Schauenburg the population of Altona increased to such an extent that the village became a market-town in 1604. After the Schauenburg line became extinct, the rule passed to the Danish crown in 1640, which held Schleswig-Holstein until 1863, when it passed to Prussia (1866). In 1664 Altona received the rights of a city and was made the first free harbor of Europe, to enable it to compete with the much larger Hamburg.

The admission of Mennonites into Altona occurred under Count Ernst in 1601. The document is no longer in existence, but the terms are known. Every Mennonite householder had to pay an annual fee of one Taler as protection money; in return the Mennonites were permitted to establish themselves in the district called "Grosse Freiheit," to carry on trades, and to bury their dead; but the services had to be conducted quietly. The successors of the Count permitted them to hold their services openly. The name "Freiheit" is derived not from freedom of religion, but from freedom of occupation, which the inhabitants enjoyed. After the transfer to Danish authority the charter had to be renewed with every change of the throne. These originals are still in the archives of the church.

The Mennonites developed home industry and trade to a high level. To the first Mennonites settled in Altona were added the remnants of the Mennonite Church at Fresenburg (*q.v.*) which was destroyed in the Thirty Years' War. From Glückstadt (*q.v.*), where there was a church until 1800, the well-known van der Smissen (*q.v.*) family came to Altona in 1683. Home industry, i.e., weaving, was engaged in especially by the de Voss family, shipping and commerce by the Goverts (*q.v.*), Roosen (*q.v.*), van der Smissen, and de Vlieger families. After the great fire of 1713, when the Swedish General Magnus Steenbock reduced the city to ashes, many trading-houses transferred to Hamburg, where some Dutch Mennonites had settled before 1600. At least it is known of Hans

Quins (Wins?), an ancestor of the well-known preacher Gerhard Roosen, that he had fled about 1570 from Brabant or Flanders to Hamburg and died there of the plague in 1597.

It was as a consequence of the events of Münster that the strictly Lutheran city of Hamburg together with the "Wend cities" (*q.v.*) issued repeated edicts against the Anabaptists. In 1555 the authorities of Hamburg, Lüneburg, Rostock, and Wismar passed measures designed to keep Menno from entering their territories (Mannhardt *Jahrbuch* 1883, 84). The settlement of a few families in the city by 1575 was possible only because they energetically assured the clergy that they had no connections with the Münsterite Anabaptists. Their ability as merchants also made them desirable citizens. In 1605 a formal agreement was drawn up with the 130 Dutch immigrant families (including such names as de Voss, Siemons, Stockman, Lammers, Amoury, de Buyser, Harmens, and Janssen). In return for the obligation to keep themselves quiet(!) and to pay taxes and fees, they were to be admitted without giving an oath of citizenship. This contract was renewed for the last time in 1635, for the Lutheran clergy vigorously opposed it.

Hamburg would have had no Anabaptist movement if it had not come in from the outside. The regions most desired by the refugees from the severe persecution then raging against all non-Catholics in the Netherlands, were the Rhine region, where the Anabaptist movement had grown strong, especially in the duchy of Jülich and later the Holstein area. It is thus easy to understand that there were several Anabaptist groups of whom the Flemish (*q.v.*) were the strongest and most influential. The Noë, Quins, Goverts, and van der Smissen families were among them. From 1639 the Flemish Mennonites of Glückstadt (*q.v.*) were combined with them. The congregation of the united Mennonite groups later adopted the *Olyftacxken* (*q.v.*) as their confession of faith. The strict Frisians required Flemish Mennonites who united with them to be rebaptized. By 1671 the Frisian congregation died out, chiefly through transfers of membership to the Flemish. Their meetinghouse stood in the Roosenstrasse in Altona.

Also the Huiskoper (*q.v.*) group (see **Bintgens**) was thus disbanded; their preacher was Jan de Buyser (*q.v.*). The High Germans were the smallest group; Johann Peltz(er) (d. 1600) is named as their "priest." From about 1682 there was only the one united congregation in Hamburg-Altona. The Mennonites of Altona (*q.v.*) are always to be included, for they never had a congregation of their own.

It was not to be expected that the Mennonites could settle and develop a congregation without a struggle; indeed the struggle with secular and religious authorities lasted a long time. In 1672 Emperor Leopold threatened the city with a lawsuit on the ground that 300-400 were living there, contrary to the treaty of 1648. In this case, to be sure, the senate defended the Mennonites, stating that they were peaceful and also competent citizens, who had nothing to do with the Anabaptists of Münster but instead prayed for the government in their church prayers.

Several decades of peace followed, but in 1706 the Mennonites again became the objects of ecclesiastical and secular sessions. The occasion of the controversy was the greatly gifted preacher Jakob Denner (*q.v.*), whose sermons were attended by many non-Mennonites, simple people as well as educated. Several senate decrees, issued upon the insistence of the clergy, did not succeed in preventing this. Hence the Lutheran church authorities decided to discipline its "obstinate children" on the following grounds: "running out" (to Altona) is contrary to God's command; beware of false prophets; it is contrary to city law, which forbids attendance even at Lutheran services outside the city, to say nothing of fanatical services; it leads to contempt for the office of preaching and to their own injury and false guidance. This threat of exclusion from the confessional and communion was apparently not very effective. Another circumstance that contributed to this state of affairs in 1711-12 was the warlike condition that made it impossible to attend the Mennonite church. The religious authorities suggested that the Mennonites could now attend the Protestant Church "unless they imagined themselves holier than others." The Mennonites then reminded the senate that in former disturbed times they had held their quiet worship services, if not by law, at least by tacit consent, and asked for liberty of conscience to hold their meetings in some secluded attic without singing. This was apparently done, in spite of the declaration of the church authorities that connivance in this case was contrary to conscience, and the worship contrary to the divine Word. A renewed protest in 1715 was apparently equally fruitless.

Even more dangerous to the Mennonite congregation than these threats from without were the internal conflicts. Especially the separation of the Dompelaars (*q.v.*), who in addition to immersion required footwashing, and who celebrated communion at night and with unleavened bread. Repeated attempts to arbitrate, both from without and within, even by the Lutheran clergy, failed, although the Dompelaars, for want of suitable preachers in their own group, had to employ non-Mennonite preachers. This group experienced a time of growth at the beginning of the 18th century under Denner, whose sermons were attended even by "pious Catholics." The deacon of the main Mennonite body, Ernst Goverts, obtained royal permission in 1708 to build a Dompelaar church on the Grosse Freiheit to seat 300; he gave the beloved preacher an annual salary of 500 marks. Still it took decades with all sorts of experiences with the Moravians and other Separatists before the group dissolved by gradual return to the old church. Denner, whose collection of sermons (1630) is still to be found in many Mennonite homes, was its last preacher (see **Weenighem, B. van**).

According to the *Naamlijst* of 1743 there were at that time two congregations in Altona, one of which was Flemish. In 1731 and again in 1755 only one is mentioned. Was there a temporary split? The church was further weakened in the 1750's by the Quakers (*q.v.*), who agreed with the Mennonites on some points, such as the rejection of warfare and the oath. Eleven members, including the minister Berend Roelofs (*q.v.*), were lost. Also the notorious Antoinette Bourignon attracted some members to her fanaticism. In addition, there were at times differences in teaching between the preachers and the congregation, e.g., concerning the doctrine of Christ (Riewert Dirks), and among the preachers; the dissension between the Lamists and Zonists of the Netherlands (see **Amsterdam**) raged here, the decision finally favoring the Zonists. Jakobus Kornelius van Campen used the pulpit to attack his colleague Jan de Lanoy, who favored the less strict Lamist wing. Not until 1705 was reconciliation achieved.

Active connections with other countries were also maintained, especially with the Netherlands, from where many of the Hamburg preachers came and many guest preachers visited them. Relations with Friedrichstadt (*q.v.*) were similar, both for business and for the arbitration of church difficulties. Brethren from Fresenburg (*q.v.*) also requested help in 1656, when they were ordered by a royal mandate to leave the city within a week; the intercession of Jan de Buyser (*q.v.*), the preacher of the Huiskoper group, was probably successful. Connections were also maintained with West Prussia, Danzig, the Palatinate, and England. In 1711 a collection of 1,470 florins was made for the persecuted Swiss Brethren, in spite of financial difficulties at home.

The organization of the church was on the presbyterial pattern. The ministers, chosen by the congregation, were "in half service," their chief function being to preach. They could function at baptismal and communion services only after a further solemn act, ordination into "full service." The minister must first have been a deacon (*q.v.*). Hamburg also had deaconesses, though on a voluntary, unorganized basis. The church council was composed of preachers and deacons. The most prominent of the deacons and ministers of the Hamburg congregation was no doubt Gerrit Roosen (*q.v.*), who besides preaching also wrote against such things as fashions and wigs, and against Quaker inroads. Not until the 18th century were unsalaried lay preachers gradually replaced by salaried ministers trained usually at the Mennonite seminary in Amsterdam. It was a sign of the economic strength of the Mennonites that they in 1749 could engage four well-paid ministers, with two assistants. In the service of the deacons there was also a change, in that they were appointed for one year instead of a lifetime; there were, in accord with apostolic example, seven deacons. The church council was responsible for the lay meetings of male baptized members, whose business it was to choose the ministers proposed by the church council. In the 18th century it met annually.

At that time their church services began at nine in winter and at eight in summer. Singing was led by a chorister until 1764, when an organ was installed. Midweek services, together with the Bremen hymnal, were introduced in 1786 by Reinhard Rahusen (*q.v.*); but at the same time a Dutch hymnbook was in use. As late as 1802 a new Dutch hymnal was compiled for the congregation, entitled *Christelijke Gezangen voor de openbaare Godsdienstoeffeningen, ten dienste der Mennoniten Gemeente te Hamburg en Altona* (Amsterdam, 1802). This songbook was, however, not used long, and preaching in the Dutch language was replaced by German preaching in 1817 (*DB* 1901, 47). Services for children were begun in 1719; they were actually a questioning of the children in the presence of the church board. Discipline was strictly observed. Marriage outside the brotherhood was punished by the ban. In 1702 this practice was discontinued, but the promise to train the children as Mennonites was required. After 1750 all discipline for "mixed marriage" was abandoned because of the rapid recession of the congregation. Military service was strictly prohibited. Shippers and whalers were required to sell their boats rather than arm them in warlike· times.

Since it was illegal in Hamburg for the Mennonite ministers to perform marriages, the Mennonites went to Altona for such services. In 1753 the regulation was passed that the Mennonites must before marriage secure a state certificate for 1.50 Talers. From 1723 on, with some interruptions, they had their own school. The first teacher was a member of the congregation, who at the close of the week could look back upon 52 hours of teaching. The small salary was raised by collection. The school, which engaged four teachers, closed in 1795. For a long time the Mennonites and Reformed shared a cemetery. In 1677 Christian V granted the Mennonites permission to open a cemetery of their own; Hermann Goverts, a deacon, gave half the land for the burial ground, which was located in Altona, and which also served the Separatists. During the war the Mennonites built a cemetery in Hamburg (Oelmühlenkirchhof). The clergy saw to it that funerals were held in accord with the Peace of Westphalia, i.e., without the ringing of bells or other ceremony.

The achievements of the Mennonites of Hamburg in cultural matters were significant; they would not have been possible without their financial strength, which was founded upon their economic activities. Also their skill in the various crafts is worthy of note. In the weaving of wool they were unsurpassed, and furnished the cloth needed by the Schauenburg court; thereby they were not subject to guild pressure. They established connections with the Leipzig Fair and with Russia. Imported hides were tanned in their own tanneries. Jakob Denner was a dyer; his church was therefore popularly called the "Blue-dyer Church" (*Blaufärberkirche*). Retail trade was also promoted. There was less opportunity to engage in agriculture; nevertheless, a number of families owned large farms. Their extensive overseas trade was very strong. The Roosen and de Vlieger families were prominent in the whaling industry, which in the face of the political uncertainty of the time, required a venturesome spirit. Equipment was built along the Elbe for working and packing the products of the whaling industry. Even if the residents of Altona surpassed those of Hamburg economically (Hinrich van der Smissen, *q.v.,* "builder of the city," was a resident of Altona), those of Hamburg must not be underestimated.

This growth of Mennonite industry, which was of benefit to the entire city, was accompanied by improved relations with the government. In Altona all friction with the state was eliminated in the course of the 17th century. In Hamburg the secular authorities were much less biased than the Lutheran church authorities. To the great annoyance of the latter, the secular authorities disregarded the absence of recognition of Mennonites in the Peace of Westphalia by permitting them to hold services in Hamburg in times of war as far back as 1686 when the Danes were besieging the city, and also by excusing them from swearing an oath. It is significant that at the beginning of the 18th century two thirds of the congregation was living in Hamburg.

A catastrophe for the twin cities, especially Altona, and also for the Mennonites, was the war between Sweden and Denmark 1712-13. Trade became difficult; epidemics raged; fires, set by Stenbock's troops, leveled homes and breweries. The people were impoverished; the church mortgaged its property. It would have been small wonder if the congregation had disbanded.

The century following this catastrophe has a character of its own. Progressive tolerance led to civil equality; friendly relations with the state softened the old principles; internally a calmer development took place, the age of division and schism was past.

After the war the state authorities were interested in restoring economic conditions as rapidly as possible. The Mennonites took advantage of this in having their old liberties confirmed; to the right of free trade and religion was added release from taxes for the proposed new church and school, for the parsonage and the homes for the poor, and in particular, release from all future war taxes and other "extraordinary burdens." The *privilegium exemtionis* confirmed at the change of government in 1715 granted the Mennonites all of this. The church building was begun at once; private rebuilding was also undertaken. Hinrich van der Smissen, with his characteristic energy, rebuilt the burned breweries, some of his houses, besides new dyeing works, sawmills, smithies, forges, shipbuilding etablishments, etc.; he was a member of the city building committee of Altona (the van der Smissensallee was later bought by the city).

Other important names in the congregation of the two cities were Roosen (*q.v.*), Goverts (*q.v.*), de Vlieger (*q.v.*), Linnich (*q.v.*), Beets (*q.v.*), especially Gerrit Beets, the "Apollo" of the congregation, Rahusen (*q.v.*), de Voss (*q.v.*), and Goos (*q.v.*).

There is a dearth of statistics of membership in the congregation. In 1716-17 the heads of 123 households took part in the building plans for the church; that would indicate a total membership of about 620; in 1809, 15 families were counted in Altona; in 1814 Hamburg had 40 members; in 1840 the combined membership was reckoned at 125. The causes of this retrogression were emigration (to Pennsylvania *ca.* 1700), and transfer to other denominations, the most serious of which was the defection of the Goverts brothers. Severe losses were also caused by mixed marriages, which until 1800 were permitted by the state only with the promise of training the children as Lutherans; after the congregation had dwindled in size, this was no longer considered a threat to the Lutherans. The Mennonites still had to pay their fees to the Lutheran pastors—because the salaries of the latter were in part dependent on these fees, which were rated according to the number of houses in the parish. The Mennonites did not object to this fee; on the contrary, in 1750-51 they made a contribution of 5,810 Marks to the city for the restoration of the church of St. Michael.

Thus it came about that relations with the outside grew obviously more favorable. The Mennonites were now publicly recognized for their contribution to the common good, and the clergy had to discard their idea of equating them with the Münsterites. This increasing recognition of "unorthodox" creeds was due in large part to Rationalism, and reached its culmination in the 1820's. Napoleon had dictatorially introduced French laws, which declared the civic equality of all citizens of the state regardless of creed. This was the occasion in 1813 for the consideration by the Hamburg clergy of the weighty question: hitherto only "the Mennonites, who were worthy of respect," had been tolerated, whereas other non-Lutherans were usually shunted off to Altona. In 1814 a proposal was made to drop the fees required of the Mennonites; the clergy offered no objection. The mayor also wanted to include in the new statute "the quiet, responsible, outwardly excellently upright Mennonites." In October 1814 they were pronounced a recognized religious society and were given the right to hold office and to vote. Elder Isaak Goos replied for the congregation that its only wish was to have its quiet existence protected, and pointed out that their religious principles prevented them from accepting certain judicial positions or participation in war affairs. The joy in the new-found freedom was somewhat dimmed by the fear that the old principles would now be broken. Two centuries earlier the Mennonites had been regarded as a threat to church and state; now they had the same equal privileges that their brethren in Altona had enjoyed for two hundred years.

The 19th century, however, brought a period of severe conflict, caused by the growing nationalism among the nations. In 1803 a conference of elders and preachers meeting at Ibersheim had advocated strict adherence to nonresistance. After ten years of negotiation, the Altona Mennonites succeeded in maintaining this right in return for a fee and a fine of 1,600 Talers. In Hamburg too the request of the small congregation was for a long time disregarded. A lieutenant who was expelled from the congregation in 1818 was released from his military duties. New, considerable difficulties arose again by the military regulations of 1821, which made no provision for religious objection. Thus, in 1837, when the son of Elder Goos was drafted into the army, the request for his release could no longer be based on precedent; his request contained not only a willingness to pay a fee, but also a veiled threat of emigration. The *Kollegium* of the Hamburg clergy granted the request. But in 1845, when a young Mennonite was again called, a petition succeeded only in releasing him from personal service, not from guard duty. The Altona Mennonites had been released from military duty by the provisional government. But in Hamburg a number of men continued to be conscripted in spite of protests. Not until 1851 did a general petition, which threatened moving into adjacent Altona, make an effective impression. By abandoning a principle maintained until then (that service by a substitute is service), the Mennonites could secure the release of their young men. In 1867 the privilege was completely lost; the only way out was by serving in the medical corps or the like. But in the meantime, Mennonitism had undergone a change, especially under the influence of Wilhelm Mannhardt of Berlin (*q.v.*), in the direction of the old principle of personal liberty.

The inner development of the congregation in the 19th century proceeded without interruption. The state saved the congregation by annulling the prohibition of mixed marriages, but numerically it declined. After 1817 there was only one preacher, now called pastor because of academic training. Berend Carl Roosen (*q.v.*), pastor after 1845, awakened interest in the history of the congregation. His successor, Hinrich van der Smissen, was pastor 1885-1928. After 1839 the language of the services, which had been Dutch, was exclusively German. The parochial school, which was revived for 13 years, passed into private possession. Connections with Holland grew weaker; those with Friedrichstadt were maintained for some time. The Hamburg-Altona church was given an important position by being made the seat of the *Vereinigung* (*q.v.*) in 1885.

Until 1675 religious services were held in a rear building on Roosen land on the Grosse Freiheit (free trade); in that year a church was built, paid for by a contribution of 5 per cent of the proceeds of the whaling industry for one year. This church was burned down in 1713. On its site a new church was dedicated in 1715. The aftereffects of World War I resulted in great losses to the Mennonites of Hamburg-Altona. However, before the end of the war the congregation erected its splendid new church, parish house, and parsonage (1914-16) in Altona, Mennonitenstrasse 20. It also has a rather extensive archives; its library, which was begun in 1747 with the legacy of Pastor Rahusen's books, is the richest of all Mennonite libraries in Germany.

On several occasions the Hamburg congregation, usually in connection with the Dutch Committee of Foreign Needs, raised funds for the Mennonite refugees displaced by persecution; e.g., in 1690 for those in the Palatinate, in 1710-12 for Switzerland (collection 631 guilders), in 1733-35 for those from Lithuania (collection 3,352 Dutch guilders), in 1766 for

Polish Prussia. In 1710-11 the church board of Hamburg approved a plan to colonize the Swiss Mennonites in East Prussia; but this project was not carried out, both because of the aversion of the Swiss Mennonites and also because of the opposition of the Amsterdam Committee.

Hamburg-Altona suffered most severely during World War II, especially during the air raids in July 1943. One third of the Mennonites lost their homes, most lost property, and some lost their lives. The well-known van der Smissen Allee, the Dennerstrasse, the old Mennonite church in the Grosse Freiheit, the chapel in the cemetery, etc., were completely destroyed. Fortunately, the new church and the other buildings, including the valuable library, although somewhat damaged, were not destroyed. By 1946 the church could be used and by 1948 it was fully restored.

Ministers of the church since 1801 have been Isaak Goos until 1845; Berend Carl Roosen, 1845-82; Hinrich van der Smissen, 1885-1928; Otto Schowalter, 1928- .

The third old people's home of the German Mennonites, called "Abendfrieden," was established in 1952 in a suburb of Hamburg, Pinneberg-Rellingen.

Regular services are held by the Hamburg pastor in Altona, Bad Oldesloe, Trittau, and at the old people's home.

The Hamburg-Altona congregation has taken over the patronship of the Menno Simons Monument at Bad Oldesloe.

The Mennonite Central Committee with headquarters first in Kiel (1946-47) and later in Hamburg (1948-52), did much to alleviate both the physical and spiritual suffering of the Mennonite refugees from the east in the area of Schleswig-Holstein, where a total of 4,300 were resident in 1950. The MCC program of relief, with large distribution of food and clothing, ministered to many more non-Mennonites as well. (†*ME* I.)

R.Do., H.vDS.

E. Wichmann, *Geschichte Altona's* (Altona, 1865); B. C. Roosen, *Gesch. der Menn.-Gem. zu Hamburg und Altona* 2 vv. (Hamburg, 1886); H. Münte, *Das Altonaer Handlungshaus van der Smissen, 1682-1824* (Altona, 1932); R. Dollinger, *Gesch. der Menn. in Schleswig-Holstein, Hamburg und Lübeck* (Neumünster i.H., 1930); O. Schowalter, "Die Mennoniten zu Hamburg," *Menn. Life* V (April 1950); *Inv. Arch. Amst.* I, Nos. 567, 578, 797, 1058, 1062, 1108, 1114, 1155, 1177, 1186, 1271, 1319 f., 1328, 1355, 1422 f., II, Nos. 2788-91; *ML* I, 46 f.; II, 239-44.

Hamelmann, Hermann (1525-95), Lutheran superintendent at Oldenburg, Germany, after serving for a time as Catholic priest in the church of St. Servatius in Münster, and later as a Lutheran clergyman at Lemgo. He wrote the book, *Ecclesiasticae historiae de renato evangelio et motu postea incepto in urbe Monasteriensi explicatio brevis, sed integra.* This book offers important data, not given anywhere else, and collected with great care, and is thus an important source for the history of the Anabaptists in Münster. But because Hamelmann assembled the material uncritically, without inquiry into its authenticity, he is not entirely dependable. At any rate his statements should be accepted with caution. This was convincingly demonstrated by C. A. Cornelius in the introduction to his book, *Die Geschichtsquellen des Bistums Münster* (Münster, 1853). Also F. O. zur Linden agrees that Hamelmann's presentation of the origin of Anabaptism in East Friesland is incorrect.   NEFF.

M. Goebel, *Geschichte des christlichen Lebens der rheinisch-westfälischen Kirche* (Coblenz, 1849) 499; F. O. zur Linden, *Melchior Hofmann, ein Prophet der Wiedertäufer* (Haarlem, 1885) 181; *ML* II, 244.

Hamilton Avenue United Missionary Church, located on Hamilton Avenue, Flint, Mich., an appointment of the Michigan conference, was originally a city mission in charge of deaconesses. The first minister was W. O. Cline, who was stationed there in 1913. In 1954 there were 90 members and the Sunday-school attendance averaged 150.

The following have served as pastors: W. O. Cline 1913-18, J. A. Bradley 1918-21, R. D. Dean 1921-25, J. A. Avery 1925-26, B. Douglass 1926-30, E. W. McClintock 1930-33, J. A. Bradley 1933-36, H. C. Eagle 1936-43, W. K. Burgess 1943-47, L. L. Surbrook 1947-52, G. N. Bridges 1952- . E.R.S.

Hamilton Chapel United Missionary Church, near Dowagiac, Mich., had 13 members in 1954, with Russel Wright serving as pastor. The new church, dedicated on Nov. 7, 1954, is unique in, its architectural style, having a round roof.   R.P.P.

Hamm, Westphalia, Germany, where there was once a small Mennonite congregation (*Inv. Arch. Amst.* I, 1101-2). The *Naamlijst* of 1731 states that the pulpit was vacant at that time. Since the following *Naamlijsts* do not list the congregation, it was obviously extinct.   vDZ.

Hamm (Ham) is a Mennonite family name of Dutch-Prussian background. The name can possibly be traced back to Johan de Mepsche op den Ham from Groningen, the Netherlands, an Anabaptist who fled to Danzig, where he died in 1588. Urban Ham is mentioned in a record as a resident of Orlofferfelde, Prussia, in 1601. The Danzig church record lists the name since 1676. The name appears also in the records of the following congregations: Tiegenhagen, Ladekopp, Rosenort, Fürstenwerder, Heubuden, Elbing, Montau-Gruppe, Deutsch-Kazun. From Danzig and Prussia the name was transplanted to Russia (Chortitza, Samara), the United States (Beatrice, Neb.), Canada, and South America. Some outstanding representatives are Dietrich Hamm, David Hamm (*q.v.*), Dr. David H. Hamm of Hague, Sask., and H. H. Hamm of Altona, Man.   C.K.

Horst Penner, "The Background of a Mennonite Family—Hamm," *Menn. Life* IV (July 1949) 16.

Hamm, David, born in Prussia, was elected as minister of the Köppental-Orloff Mennonite Church (*q.v.*), Trakt settlement, Samara, in 1853, and served as elder 1858-84. During his eldership the congregation was greatly disturbed by the activities of Claas Epp, Jr. (*q.v.*). When Epp published his *Die entsiegelte Weissagung des Propheten Daniel*

und die Deutung der Offenbarung Jesu Christi Hamm wrote the preface (1877) emphasizing the second coming of Christ, at which time He would find only "a little flock" of faithful followers. He states that Epp was "compelled by the spirit of God" to write this book. The Mennonites of the Trakt settlement in general had been influenced by Jung-Stilling, Christian Clöter, and other chiliastic writers before they left Prussia (Bartsch, *Unser Auszug*, p. 7). However, when Claas Epp, Jr., became more and more extreme in his proclamations the sounder elements of the congregation under the leadership of Hamm opposed his views (Bartsch, p. 25), and Epp and his group withdrew from them and removed to Central Asia.

David Hamm was instrumental in establishing the *Allgemeine Mennonitische Bundeskonferenz* (*q.v.*), for which he preached a much-appreciated conference sermon at Halbstadt in 1883 proclaiming the motto of the conference based on I Thess. 5:12-15 as being "Unity in major issues, freedom in minor questions, and charity in everything." In 1869 the Köppental and Alexandertal congregations of Samara sent letters to the Prussian congregation stating that they could not have fellowship with those that accepted the edict providing for noncombatant service. It is likely that David Hamm took the initiative in this matter. His signature stands first on the list. David Hamm compiled the *Choral-Buch für den Kirchen-Gesang der Mennoniten-Gemeinde an der Wolga* (Danzig, 1859).

C.K.

Franz Bartsch, *Unser Auszug nach Mittel-Asien* (Halbstadt, 1907); Friesen, *Brüderschaft*, 119; H. Ediger, *Beschlüsse . . . der Konferenzen . . .* (Berdyansk, 1914) 1 ff.

Hammer Creek (Pa.) Mennonite Church (MC), a member of the Lancaster Mennonite Conference. Until 1819 the Mennonites of the Hammer Creek-Denver district met in eight private homes for worship. Deacon Christian Eby was successful in keeping the children of members for the church during and after the Revolutionary War. The first two bishops were both named Christian Bomberger. From this congregation came Bishop Peter Eby of the Pequea and Bishop Benjamin Eby and the Ebys, Snyders, Brubakers, etc., who emigrated to Ontario in the first two decades of the 19th century. Since 1913 the congregation has had a large brick church. Amos S. Horst and Mahlon Zimmerman are the present (1954) bishops. Noah Hurst and Parke Heller ministers, and J. Henry Eshleman deacon; the membership is 182.   I.D.L.

Hammerstein, a village about 10 miles east of Neustettin, province of Pomerania, Germany, where one of the three camps was located (the others being Mölln and Prenzlau) in which a part of the 4,000 Mennonite refugees fleeing Russia in November 1929 were quartered by the German government until they could emigrate to Brazil and Paraguay, which they did in the first half of 1930.   H.S.B.

Hammon Cheyenne (Indian) Mennonite Church (GCM), located one mile north and one-half mile east of Hammon, Custer Co., Okla., was organized

Feb. 11, 1906, when four Indians were baptized by Rodolphe Petter. The mission had been established by H. J. Kliewer in June 1898. Services were held in the mission house until the chapel was built in 1902. Religious services were also conducted at the Red Moon Government Boarding School near by. By 1949 the number received as members was 129, and the membership was 75. H. J. Kliewer served as pastor 1898-1927, J. B. Ediger 1927-47, and Arthur Friesen 1947- .   A.F.

Hamster, Hans, an Anabaptist martyr, a peasant of Reinsdorf near Zwickau, Germany, brother-in-law of Georg, Heinrich, and Jobst Möller (Müller) (*q.v.*); after their martyrdom, at the age of 30, he joined the Anabaptists. When the lord of Weida at Wildenfels refused to tolerate this step, Hamster fled to the region of Jörg Uttenhofer on the Silberstrasse, and associated with the tailor Hans Steinsdorf (*q.v.*) at Schneeberg, they mutually strengthening each other. Both considered infant baptism without value, denied original sin, declared the sacrament to be mere bread and wine, recognized the government and the obedience due it as long as it performed God's will. They rejected community of goods, but held that those who have much should share and not permit their neighbor to suffer want. On July 20, 1538, Steinsdorf and his apprentice were arrested, and on Aug. 24 the same fate befell Hamster. He was tried Aug. 26 and 27 (court records in Wappler, 110-12). He confessed that he had not been rebaptized; but he believed that his baptism 33 years previously had no value because he had not understood it. And if sin had been taken from him at that time he would not have been a bad boy.

Hamster was now transferred to the Zwickau prison, where Steinsdorf also lay. But they were not put together. Repeatedly they were examined or "instructed in the faith." Hamster said he would gladly be wherever God the Almighty put him; even if he were to be expelled from the country he would not swear, for God had forbidden it; he would rather stay with his family and provide for them with labor, as he had always done. He did not believe in the resurrection of the flesh; for the spirit had come from the Father and would return to the Father; but flesh and blood had nothing to do with the divine Father.

When all efforts to convert them proved futile, their confession was sent to the Elector of Saxony with the comment, "They are laymen; neither can read or write; they are little versed in the Old and New Testaments, but place their faith on the spirit which they boast they have from God the Father." The elector relegated to the court at Wittenberg the matter of sentencing them. The court had difficulty in reaching a decision and repeatedly questioned the prisoners. "But they persisted in their faith." They were probably beheaded near the end of 1538.   NEFF.

P. Wappler, *Inquisition und Ketzerprozesse in Zwickau zur Ref.-Zeit* (Leipzig, 1908); *ML* II, 244 f.

Hamswerum, a town in East Friesland, Germany, where Leenaert Bouwens baptized eleven persons in 1551-61. Since nothing is known of the existence of a congregation in this town, the members apparently joined the congregation in Emderland.
                    vDZ.

Han, Thomas, an Anabaptist martyr: see **Haan, Thoman.**

Handbüchlein, Kleines: see **Kleines Hand-Büchlein.**

Handbüchlein wider den Prozess, *der zu Worms am Rhein wider die Brüder so man die Hutterischen nennt ausgangen ist im 1557 Jahr,* a Hutterite polemical writing, considered with the *Rechenschaft* by Peter Riedemann (*q.v.*) and the *Article Book* (*q.v.*) as one of the most significant doctrinal books of the Hutterites of the 16th century. It was an official pronouncement of the brotherhood, prompted by a document which a number of Lutheran theologians (Melanchthon, Brenz, Andreae, etc.) had issued at Worms in 1557 (see **Bedenken**). In this document, the *Prozess wie es soll gehalten werden mit den Wiedertäufern* (in Württemberg also called *Bedenken* . . . , published by Bossert in the *TA Württemberg* in 1930), the Anabaptists are accused of a number of damnable doctrines and practices (see John Oyer's analysis); their teachings are declared blasphemous; hence Lev. 24:16 (death penalty) should be applied. Toward the end of this document also the upbringing of children in the communistic colonies in Moravia is briefly but violently attacked as a devilish institution (*teuflische Communion . . . wider die Natur und alle Rechte;* Bossert, p. 166, lines 14-19).

The Anabaptists in Germany felt the need of defending themselves against these accusations, which were much stronger than Melanchthon's attack of 1536 ("Several Unchristian Points Which the Anabaptists Advance," *MQR* 1952, 268), although by 1557 Anabaptism had already lost some of its prime vigor. At a conference in Strasbourg the Swiss Brethren decided to produce an answer (see letter to Menno Simons, 1557), but apparently this plan was never carried out. At the Frankenthal (*q.v.*) Disputation in 1571 the *Prozess* was mentioned but no reply was given.

The Hutterites, on the other hand, although less involved (as they lived in faraway Moravia, where the Lutheran theologians had but a minor influence), nevertheless produced an elaborate answer in which they developed at some length their own doctrine and position. This answer was then called *Handbüchlein wider den Prozess,* but neither author nor year is mentioned in it. One would not err too much in assuming that this book was written between 1558 and 1560, and although it was a document issued by the entire brotherhood in Moravia, it seems to have been drafted by Peter Walpot (*q.v.*), then by far the most outstanding spiritual leader of the Hutterites (see Friedmann in *Arch. f. Ref.-Gesch.,* 1931, 105). As far as Anabaptist manuscript literature is known, this book is the strongest polemical writing of the Brethren against the Lutherans, and has always been understood by the Brethren in this spirit.

The *Handbüchlein* is subdivided into 12 sections called "books" which answer point by point the specific accusations of the Worms theologians; viz., (1) concerning worldly authority and whether such an authority can be a Christian; (2) concerning the use of law courts and lawsuits; (3) concerning the taking of an oath; (4) concerning the Anabaptist claim that whoever does not belong to their church (*Gemeinschaft*) is condemned and not saved; (5) concerning infant baptism; (6) concerning the Lord's Supper; (7) concerning original sin and whether children have it; (8) concerning the necessity to preach and to hear the Word of God; (9) concerning the Holy Trinity, whether Christ was the Son of God; (10) concerning whether rebirth prevents any backsliding hereafter; (11) concerning justification, whether man is justified through Christ or by his own endeavor; (12) concerning the upbringing of children in communal establishments.

A comparison of these "books" with the *Prozess* shows that the latter condemns the Anabaptists only on seven points (see Oyer's analysis) while the *Handbüchlein* answers in 12 points. Some of the additional five items were taken from the 1536 accusations of Melanchthon. Item 12 concerning the children is mentioned in the *Prozess* only casually (in Bossert's print only five lines, though sharp in tone), yet the Hutterites felt particularly sensitive in this area, since they were very conscientious with regard to the upbringing of children, and wanted to make it clear to everybody that children were to them the most precious things in the world, and their proper upbringing was one of their most important tasks. We might here remember that it was Peter Walpot who in 1568 wrote a very thoughtful and much advanced *School Discipline* for the Hutterite schools (see **Education**).

The *Handbüchlein* answer to the Worms theologians is a rather skillful and effective work. The arguments are thoroughly but soundly Biblical as was the Anabaptist way of thinking; the words are straightforward, yet never acid (as most polemics of the 16th century were). The author (Walpot?) also quotes amply from old authorities such as Origen, Jerome, Augustine, the Councils, and recent authorities such as Luther (*Deutsche Messe*, 1526), Zwingli (*Contra Fabrum*), and Cellarius. It is most likely that the learned book by Christoph Eleutherobios (*q.v.*), *Vom wahrhaftigen Tauff Joannis, Christi und der Aposteln. Wann und wie der Kindertauff angefangen und eingerissen hat* (*How Infant Baptism Originated*) (1528, sec. ed. 1550) was much used, mainly for "book" five. It is found in many Hutterite manuscripts.

The chapter "Concerning original sin" is one of the most decisive sections of the *Handbüchlein* and expresses a viewpoint accepted by practically all Anabaptists. The Brethren declare: man as a child of Adam stands under the general curse of original sin; hence physical death. But Christ *is* the reconciliation of this world including small children. The mere "inclination" to sin (which is inborn in all of us) does not yet condemn man. Only the doing of sin will cause eternal death.

Moreover, the Scriptures declare that the children will not bear the consequences of the bad deeds of their fathers, rather everyone dies for that which he has perpetrated himself (Ezek. 18:17, 20). This argument, incidentally, is the main argument suggested by Peter Riedemann in his *Rechenschaft* of 1540 (*MQR*, 1952, 214). The *Handbüchlein* closes this chapter by declaring that if the inclination to sin is not carried out into works of sin, it does not harm man and does not cause eternal death. "Whosoever is born of God does not sin" (I John 3:9).

Strange to say, the *Handbüchlein* is nowhere mentioned in other Hutterite writings, not even in their *Gross-Geschichtsbuch*. But from the *Klein-Geschichtsbuch* (ed. Zieglschmid, 1947) we learn that the knowledge of it was kept very much alive in Hutterite tradition. Johannes Waldner (*q.v.*), the author of the *Klein-Geschichtsbuch*, tells us that in 1756 when the Lutheran transmigrants from Carinthia came to Transylvania and there showed the greatest interest both in Hutterite life and Hutterite doctrines the Brethren gave them Riedemann's *Rechenschaft* and the *Handbüchlein* to read. "In this little book the Lutheran Church is sharply attacked and its false teachings and errors are clearly brought to light" (*Klein-GB*, 274). It appears that the arguments of the *Handbüchlein* as well as those of the *Rechenschaft* impressed the newcomers so profoundly that they decided to join the Hutterites and to embrace completely their teachings.

The original of the *Handbüchlein* is no longer extant. That no Hutterite codex in European libraries contains it accounts for the fact that it was completely unknown to scholars like Beck, Loserth, and Wolkan. The oldest copy is one made in Velke-Levary in 1637 and now in Paraguay. Several copies of this manuscript were made, of which one is in Canada, and one in the Goshen College Library (produced by the late Elder Elias Walter, and donated to Christian Hege).　　　　R.F.

W. Wiswedel, *Bilder* III (1952) 171-83 (Wiswedel used the Hege copy, now in Goshen); W. Wiswedel and R. Friedmann, "The Anabaptists Answer Melanchthon," *MQR* XXIX (1955), an English translation of the above study plus additional pertinent material by R. Friedmann; Zieglschmid, *Klein-Geschichtsbuch*; R. Friedmann, "Eine dogmatische Hauptschrift der Hutterischen Täufergemeinschaften in Mähren," *Arch. f. Ref.-Gesch.* 1931, 105, 107, 111; the text of the *Handbüchlein* is to be published in the second volume of Lydia Müller, *Glaubenszeugnisse Oberdeutscher Taufgesinnter*, in 1955; John Oyer, "The Writings of Melanchthon Against the Anabaptists," *MQR* XXVI (1952) 210-15.

Handelinghe der Doopsgesinde, *ghenaemt de Vereenigde Vlaamsche en Duytsche Gemeynte, gehouden tot Haerlem anno 1649 met de dry confessien aldaer geapprobeert*. Of the acts of this Dutch Flemish conference there are three editions: n.p. 1649, Amsterdam 1664, and Vlissingen 1666. The edition of 1666, published by Geleyn Jansz, is of great importance for Dutch Mennonite history, because in the same volume are inserted a number of other documents. The 1664 edition only contains the acts of the meeting. The 1666 edition contains (1) *Voorrede* signed by the delegates of a number of congregations in Zeeland: Vlissingen, Middelburg, Veere, Zierikzee, and Brouwershaven; (2) the resolutions of the Haarlem meeting; (3) the *Olyf-Tacxken* (*q.v.*) confession; this edition is more complete than that of *Algemeene Belydenissen* (*q.v.*) of 1665, because it also contains the second and third question and the *Brief tot Vreed-Bereydinge* and *Presentatie,* which are not found in the *Algemeene Belydenissen;* (4) *Vrede-handelinge* at Amsterdam 1630, and confession of Jan Centzen; (5) *Copye ende Seecker Antwoordt van de Switser broeders ofte Hooghduytschen . . . over gegeven aan de Poolsche betreffende . . . de Menschwordinghe ende der Godtheydt Jesu Christi,* an account drawn up in 1592 at Strasbourg by a meeting of Mennonite leaders; (6) *Copye Emanuel,* an account of the United High-German and Frisian Mennonites of Hoorn, Holland, 1630; (7) Confession of Adriaen Cornelis (*Dordrecht Confession*) of 1632.

To the volume are added the *Concept of Cologne* of 1591, with an introduction, which is not found in the *Algemeene Belydenissen,* the Confession of Jacques Outerman of 1626 with introduction, and *Eenighe Aenteykeningen uyt de Aenporringhe.*
vDZ.

Handclasp or **Handshake:** see **Oath.**

Handlung *oder Acta gehaltener Disputation und gespräch zu Zoffingen imm Bernner Biet mit den Widertöuffern geschehen 1532* (Zürich, Chr. Froschauer, 1532), a copy of which is found in the AML and GCL: see **Zofingen.**

Handt-Boecxken, *ofte: Concordancie, Dat is: De Ghelijckluydende plaetsen der Heyliger Schrift by een vergadert* (n.p., 1576; 2d ed. Rotterdam, 1614) is a concordance of the Bible by an unknown Mennonite author. It is the oldest of Mennonite concordances, and likely also of all Dutch Protestant concordances. Both editions are found in the Amsterdam Mennonite Library.
vDZ.

Hanekuyk, a former Mennonite family at Harlingen (*q.v.*), Dutch province of Friesland, related by marriage to other well-known Harlingen Mennonite families, such as Fontein, Oosterbaan, and Hingst. Aagjen Douwes Hanekuyk (1737-1813) of Harlingen, married to Heere Oosterbaan (*q.v.*), was preacher at Makkum and Harlingen and later professor of the Amsterdam Mennonite Seminary. Hylke Everts Hanekuyk (*ca.* 1745-1824) of Harlingen was a friend of Pastor Freerk Hoekstra (*q.v.*) of Harlingen. A theological study written by Hylke E. Hanekuyk, entitled *Verhandeling over de voortreffelijkheid van de Christelijke geloofs en zedeleer,* was edited after his death by Hoekstra.
vDZ.

Hang, Le, an Amish congregation in Alsace, in the upper Bruche Valley (Vosges), sometimes called Bourg-Bruche. Hang is a little valley surrounded by woods, with about 12 farms. Here a number of families expelled from Switzerland settled in 1770-75; e.g., Bacher, Augsburger, Eymann, Ulrich, Schuerch, Lehmann, Mosimann, Dellenbach. Information on this period is completely lacking, since the local clergy, who kept the registers, did not register dissenters, and the group kept no records.

If remoteness from the world was at first an asset, it became a handicap in the time of freedom. Separation from the church as a whole, difficult transportation, and the inadequate educational opportunities on the linguistic border hindered its development. Nevertheless there were still in 1920 about 35 families with 105 souls in a radius of two hours in the vicinity. Religious services were then held once a month, conducted by brethren from Colmar, with meeting place in a farm home. In 1951 the congregation built its first meetinghouse, with aid from the United States, and meetings are now held every 1st and 3rd Sunday in the month. The membership in 1953, including children, was 125, with Charles Goldschmidt as resident pastor and elder. The congregation has its own burial ground in L'Evreuil. (*ML* II, 249.) H.V., H.S.B.

Hannema, a Dutch Mennonite family of Harlingen (*q.v.*), province of Friesland. This family, which has lived at Harlingen at least since 1530, became Mennonite in the 18th century, when Sjoerd Hannema (b. 1721 at Midlum, d. 1794 at Harlingen), founder of the Sjoerd Hannema Trading Company, was baptized upon confession of faith in the Harlingen Mennonite congregation on Jan. 30, 1752, together with his wife Elisabeth Scheltema, whose father and grandfather were merchants and Mennonite preachers at Franeker (*q.v.*). Sjoerd Hannema himself and many of his descendants served the church as deacons. Sjoerd Hannema, apparently a grandson of the above Sjoerd Hannema, was the (untrained) preacher (1800-8) of the small congregation of the Jan-Jacobsgezinden (*q.v.*) at Baard, Friesland (*Naamlijst* 1810, 77); he died in February 1808.
vDZ.

Hannover (English, *Hanover*), the capital (pop. about 400,000) of the former province of Hannover, had about 40 Mennonites before World War I. In 1891 they united with the support of the *Vereinigung der Mennoniten im Deutschen Reich* to hold regular annual religious services. These were conducted by the preachers of Emden, Hamburg-Altona, Leer, Norden, Crefeld, and Friedrichstadt in the home of the merchant J. Schütt. On Nov. 8, 1908, a committee of three was chosen (Th. Brons, W. Riewesehl, J. Schütt) to arrange for monthly services. After the death of J. Schütt (Aug. 8, 1909) the group met in the Logenhaus, Schiffgraben 8, for several years. Since 1913 there have been no services. On April 8, 1929, the annual meeting of the Curatorium of the *Vereinigung* was held in Hannover. In connection with this session a service had been held on the day before in the auditorium of the Psychological Institute, which was attended by nearly 40. The hope was expressed that regular services could again be arranged, but this was not realized until after World War II when many refugees from the Danzig area located in this area and a meeting in Hannover was placed on the preaching circuit of the Göttingen congregation. (*Menn. Bl.,* 1891, and other years, especially 1908, 96; 1929, 49; *ML* II, 249.) NEFF.

Hanover Mennonite Church (MC), located in Hanover, York Co., Pa., built its first meetinghouse in 1870, and the present one on Broadway in 1881. Hanover is in a circuit of the Lancaster Mennonite Conference with Bair's Hanover and Hostetter. In 1953 the church membership for the circuit was 108. Richard Danner was the bishop; Harvey S. Grove, Amos D. Shank, and R. Norman Bange the ministers; and Melvin J. Shank, deacon.

I.D.L.

Hanover Municipality in the East Reserve (*q.v.*) of Manitoba was settled by Bergthal Mennonites from Russia in 1874.

Hanover (Ont.) United Missionary Church was erected in 1904 with a seating capacity of 100. In 1953 the congregation had 49 members with S. S. Shantz serving as pastor.   W.J.P.

Hans, an Anabaptist martyr; see **Hans de Goudsmid.**

Hans, *the servant of Jan Cooman* (official name *Hans Moens*), was burned at the stake at Antwerp, Belgium, on May 25, 1569, because he had been rebaptized. With him were executed Jan Cooman, Jan van Hasebroek, and Herman de Timmerman. (*Mart, Mir.* D 415, E 766, *Antw. Arch.-Blad* XII, 382, 401; XIV, 66 f., No. 757.)   vdZ.

Hans de Bakker (official name *Jehan Jan Gielis,* alias *Hans de Backe*), an Anabaptist martyr of Jumay, Belgium, was secretly drowned in a tub in the Steen prison at Antwerp, Belgium, on Jan. 20, 1560. His name is found in the song, "Aenhoort Godt, hemelsche Vader" (Hear, O God, heavenly Father), No. 16 in the *Liedtboecxken van den Offer des Heeren.*   vdZ.

Offer, 567; Mart. Mir. D 270, E 640; Antw. Arch.-Blad IX, 6, 10; XIV, 28 f., No. 306; Wolkan, Lieder, 63, 72.

Hans Barbier, a Dutch Anabaptist leader: see **Hans Scheerder.**

Hans van Borculo, also called Hans (or Jan, Janne) Collen (or Colien, Coken), an Anabaptist martyr, a weaver by trade, was burned at the stake at Antwerp, Belgium, on Dec. 16, 1558. He is named in the hymn beginning "Aenhoort Godt, hemelsche Vader" (Hear, O God, heavenly Father), No. 16 in the *Liedtboecxken van den Offer des Heeren.* The records of the Margrave of Antwerp state that his wife, whose name is not given, had been executed in 1559; but nothing further is known of this execution.   vdZ.

Offer, 566; Mart. Mir. D 202, E 583; Antw. Arch.-Blad VIII, 454, 465, 470; XIV, 24 f., No. 272; ML I, 301.

Hans Borduerwercker (official name *Hans Verhoeven*), an Anabaptist martyr, who was burned at the stake at Antwerp, Belgium, on Aug. 27, 1555. His name is found in the song, "Aenhoort Godt, hemelsche Vader" (Hear, O God, heavenly Father) of the *Liedtboecxken van den Offer des Heeren,* No. 16.   vdZ.

Offer, 564; Mart. Mir. D 161, E 550; Antw. Arch.-Blad VIII, 426, 429; XIV, 20 f., No. 229; Wolkan, Lieder, 63, 72; ML I, 246.

Hans Bouwen, a Flemish elder: see **Hans Busschaert.**

Hans Bret, an Anabaptist martyr, the son of the Englishman Thomas Bret and Elisabeth Akers van der Does of Dordrecht. By trade he was a confectioner. Through betrayal he was seized on May 6, 1576. He was severely treated, being cast into a dungeon. He was frequently examined. Since he was well educated—he had a mastery of Latin—he was well able to withstand the inquisitors. In spite of his youth he remained steadfast, and died at the stake in Antwerp on Jan. 4, 1577, at the age of 24. The tongue screw with which the executioner closed his mouth to prevent his speaking was hunted out of the ashes by the well-known preacher Hans de Ries (*q.v.*). This tongue screw with a certification by Trijntje Simons is preserved in Amsterdam, and has been handed down from generation to generation in the possession of the de Hoop Scheffer family.

The charge made against Bret was that he possessed forbidden books, that he had been rebaptized and had frequently attended the forbidden meetings of the Anabaptists, each Sunday morning giving religious instruction to a group of baptismal candidates (*aankomelingen*). Bret had been a servant of Albert Verspeck (*q.v.*), who later was a preacher of the Waterlander Mennonites in Holland (*BRN* VII, 248). Hans de Ries (*q.v.*), who was a friend of Bret, and who had been present at the execution of his friend, married Bret's mother soon afterward. Hans's brother David Bret lived in England, where his father came from. From prison Hans wrote a number of letters to his family, to the congregation of Antwerp, and to friends, the first of which is dated Monday after Pentecost 1576, the last August 1576. In these letters he complained that he lacked writing paper. He wrote that there were imprisoned with him more of Menno's "Volk" at that time; singing of hymns, which would have given them much comfort, had been forbidden. Soon after his death a volume was published under the title *De Christelijcke Seyndtbrieven gheschreven door eenen vromen Christen genaemt Hans Bret,* printed in 1582 (n.p., likely at Antwerp; a copy is in the library of the University of Gent, Belgium). This volume contains 18 letters by Bret and 6 letters addressed to him in prison, three of which were probably written by his friend Hans de Ries; besides these letters this book contains Bret's death sentence and two songs celebrating his sufferings. Of this collection six letters are found in van Braght's *Martyrs' Mirror;* viz., the first three, the tenth, and the last two. Three of these were written to his mother, one to his brother David, one to his sister, and one to Hans de Ries.   K.V., vdZ.

Mart. Mir. D 727-46, E 1037-54; Antw. Arch.-Blad XIII, 210; XIV, 98 f., No. 1117; Bibliographie I, 689-702; ML I, 266.

Hans Busschaert (*Bouwer,* or *de Wever*), a co-elder with Menno Simons, was born at Dadisele (Dudzele) near Brugge, Flanders, Belgium. His special field of activity was Flanders, preaching and baptizing mostly at Gent. In 1566 he was one of the elders called to Harlingen, Dutch province of Friesland, to try to settle the dispute between Frisian and Flemish Mennonites (*q.v.*). In 1567, when the separation of the two groups became final, he was in Emden, East Friesland, and took the side of Dirk Philips and the Flemish. In 1568 he was again present when another vain attempt was made to reconcile the parties. (*DB* 1893, 31-44, 68, 72.) vDZ.

Hans Busschaerts-volk, a name given to the followers of Hans Busschaert (*q.v.*) de Wever, a group of Flemish Mennonites. This otherwise unknown name is used in a letter written by the Dutch congregation of Vlissingen to that of Amsterdam (June 19, 1622). (*Inv. Arch. Amst.* I, No. 559.) vDZ.

Hans Cassier: see Ries, Hans de.

Hans (Jan) van Coelen (not identical with the following martyr), an Anabaptist martyr, was executed at Amsterdam on July 28, 1535. He was charged with participating in the Amsterdam Anabaptist uprising of May 10-11, 1535; he admitted that he had been aware of this revolt, but insisted that he had not taken part in it. Hans, who had also lived at Groningen, had been (re)baptized in June 1535 at Gheyn (near Cologne, Germany) by Peter van Geyn. (Grosheide, *Verhooren,* 125, 131-34; Mellink, *Wederdopers, passim,* see Index.) vDZ.

Hans van Collen (van Coelen), a Dutch Mennonite martyr, identical with Hans van Borculo (*q.v.*). vDZ.

Hans (Jan) Corneliszoon (Hans de Ruytere), an Anabaptist martyr, born at Rheden near Arnhem, Dutch province of Gelderland, burned at the stake at Antwerp, Belgium, on Jan. 4, 1577. He was charged with having been rebaptized and delivering addresses. He was thus apparently a preacher. According to the account of van Braght (*Mart. Mir.*) his wife and daughter were executed with him, but Génard did not find them in the records. vDZ.

DB 1899, 108; *Mart. Mir.* D 748, E 1,056; *Antw. Arch.-Blad* XIII, 210; XIV, 98 f., No. 1118.

Hans van Dantzig: see Dan(t)zig, Hans van.

Hans Doornaert, an early Dutch Anabaptist preacher, was originally a weaver of Gent, Belgium, and a preacher (*Vermaner*) of the local Anabaptists, but later emigrated to Haarlem, Dutch province of North Holland, with many of his brethren. Here he served as a preacher of the Waterlander congregation, opening and closing their services with a call to silent prayer. Since this was permitted only to regularly ordained preachers of the congregation, Doornaert was vigorously opposed by the regular minister, Jacob Jansz Schedemaker (*q.v.*), whereas others approved, inasmuch as Doornaert performed this service in a much more inspiring way than they were accustomed to. In 1587 a conference was called on this matter in Haarlem, which was attended by preachers and delegates from Alkmaar, Amsterdam, and some congregations in Waterland. But it did little good, and there would

no doubt have been a division in the Waterlander congregation if Dirk Volkertsz Coornhert (*q.v.*) had not succeeded in bringing about a reconciliation and therewith also outward peace. J.L.

Blaupot t. C., *Holland* I, 123, 1-4; *DB* 1877, 81; 1897, 93; Kühler, *Geschiedenis* I, 368-71; *ML* I, 466.

Hans de Druckere, an otherwise unknown Anabaptist martyr, who was sentenced to death at Antwerp, Belgium, on Sept. 23, 1552. He was to be burned alive, and his head was then to be put on a stake. (*Antw. Arch.-Blad* VIII, 420, 422; XIV, 20 f., No. 217.) vDZ.

Hans den Duytsch (official name *Hans Pfleinshorn*), an Anabaptist martyr, a native of Nürnberg, Germany, was beheaded at Antwerp, Belgium, at the Steen prison on Oct. 26, 1558, and his body thrown into the Schelde River. His death is commemorated in the song, "Aenhoort Godt, hemelsche Vader" (Hear, O God, heavenly Father), found in the *Liedtboecxken van den Offer des Heeren,* No. 16. vDZ.

Offer, 565; *Mart. Mir.* D 202, E 583; *Antw. Arch.-Blad* VIII, 451, 465; XIV, 24 f.; *ML* I, 250.

Hans Flamingh: see Vlamingh, Hans.

Hans Georgen (John George), an Anabaptist martyr, a count from Italy, who had joined the Mennonites. He had gone to Germany, but was betrayed, arrested, and brought back to Italy. On the sea trip near Venice, without trial, he was thrown into the sea. This martyrdom took place in 1566. (*Mart. Mir.* D 344, E 703.) vDZ.

Hans de Goudsmid (also called *Hans de Zilversmid* or *Hans van Osnabruggen,* i.e., of Osnabrück in Hannover, Germany), an Anabaptist martyr, was executed at Antwerp, Belgium, by drowning on Oct. 31, 1562. Van Braght names a martyr Hans, who is obviously identical with this martyr, and gives the day of his death as Aug. 15, 1561. But this must be wrong; according to the official records studied by Génard, no martyr was executed at Antwerp on that date. Hans de Goudsmid and six other martyrs, executed at Antwerp about the same time, are celebrated in a song found in the *Nieu Liedenboeck* (1562), which begins "Lieve Broeders, ick groet u met sanghen." The song was published by Wackernagel. vDZ.

Mart. Mir. D 288, E 655; *Antw. Arch.-Blad* XIV, 32 f., No. 269; Wackernagel, *Lieder,* 140; *ML* II, 250.

Hans van Gulik (Mellink, *Wederdopers,* 264) may be identical with Hans Scheerder (*q.v.*).

Hans Inghelberts (Engelberts), an Anabaptist martyr, originally from Deventer, Dutch province of Overijssel, was burned at the stake in Antwerp, Belgium, together with three other martyrs, on May 26, 1573, because he had attended Mennonite meetings. He had likely not yet been baptized on his faith. (*Antw. Arch.-Blad* XIII, 116, 117, 177; XIV, 90 f., No. 1026.) vDZ.

Hans Jacopsens (Jan Jacobsz), an Anabaptist martyr, son of the martyr Jacob Dirksz (*q.v.*), was executed together with his father and his brother

Andries (Adriaan) at Antwerp, Belgium, on March 17, 1568. Hans was a native of Utrecht and a tailor by trade. (*Mart. Mir.* D 370, E 724; *Antw. Arch.-Blad* X, 14, 68; XIV, 54 f., No. 631.)   vDZ.

Hans Keeskooper, an Anabaptist martyr: see **Jannijn Buefkijn.**

Hans Knevel, an Anabaptist martyr, a tailor's apprentice of Antwerp, was burned at the stake there in 1573. He had at first fled to Hamburg with his friend Steven Jansz Dilburgh, when he became aware of immediate danger, but returned to Antwerp and was soon seized. At his cross-examination he defended himself and his faith with unusual adroitness. For three days he was taken to a priest to be convinced "of his dangerous error." Hans Knevel answered with a superior knowledge of Scripture. When he asked the priest why he had come, the priest replied, "To win your soul." "Then he told him, if he sought to win souls, to go around in the city, in the brothels, the tippling houses, tennis courts, and to those who shed so much innocent blood, and to seek to win their souls. His own soul Christ had already won." When he was accused with insubordination to the government, he replied, "We will gladly obey the authorities in all taxes, customs, and excises; yea, we should be sorry, if we should withhold one stiver of what is their due." When his faith was likened to that of the Münsterites he said "his faith was as different from the Münsterite sect as heaven is from the earth."

Van Braght's account concludes, "This account we have chiefly taken from Hans Knevel's own letter, which he wrote at Antwerp from prison to his dear brother Steven Jansz Dilburgh and his wife Leentjen at Hamburg, in which he communicates at length the firm foundation of his faith and living hope in God's grace and blessed promises." Van Braght mentions 1572 as the year of his death, but according to P. Génard, who studied the documents, no Anabaptist martyr was put to death at Antwerp in 1572. But Génard found a large number of victims put to death in 1573 who are not found in the *Martyrs' Mirror*. Hans Knevel may be identical either with Hans der Weduwe (*q.v.*) or Hans van Munstdorp (Manstrop) (*q.v.*), both burned at the stake on Feb. 17, 1573. (*Mart. Mir.* D 621, E 945; *ML* II, 514.)   NEFF, vDZ.

Hans Korbmacher (Dutch *Mart. Mir., Hans Mandemaker*), an Anabaptist martyr executed at Innsbruck, Austria: see **Mandl, Hans.**

Hans Keune (Kuene), an Anabaptist martyr, unmarried, concerning whom all further particulars are lacking, was burned at the stake at Antwerp, Belgium, on March 14, 1570, together with Carel (Caerle) Thys, because he had been rebaptized. (*Antw. Arch.-Blad* XII, 446, 453; XIV, 72 f., No. 803.)   vDZ.

Hans van Leeuwarden, an Anabaptist preacher at Amsterdam 1534-35, who performed baptism in the house of the deacon Jan Paeuw (*q.v.*). He was a locksmith or a maker of bags by occupation. Mellink supposes that he is identical with Hans Scheerder

(*q.v.*); but it is also possible that he is the same person as Jan van Geelen. (A Jan van Leeuwarden is named at the same time in Amsterdam, whose wife was Fenne, which was also the name of Jan van Geelen's wife.) At any rate he was a rather influential leader of the revolutionary wing of Anabaptism, who was also active in the Dutch province of Groningen. (Grosheide, *Verhooren,* 23, 46, 47, 172; Mellink, *Wederdopers,* see Index.)   vDZ.

Hans (Hansken) Lisz, an Anabaptist martyr, burned at the stake at Brugge, Belgium, on Dec. 11 (*Mart. Mir.,* Dec. 10), 1561. He belonged to the congregation of Brugge, of whom a number of members were arrested while holding a meeting. Twelve of them were executed. Verheyden, who studied the documents, did not find the name of Hans Lisz among them; so he supposes that Hans Lisz may be identical either with Jehan (Hans) Cant (*q.v.*) of St. Winnoxbergen in Flanders, or with Jehan Bertheloot (*q.v.*) of Cassel, Flanders, who were both executed on Dec. 11, 1561. (*Mart. Mir.* D 288, E 655; Verheyden, *Brugge,* 50, No. 42 f.; *ML* II, 660.)   vDZ.

Hans van der Maes, an Anabaptist martyr: see **Hans Vermeersch.**

Hans van Mandel, an Anabaptist martyr of Flanders: see **Hans Vermandele.**

Hans Marijnsz (Hans Marijnsz van Oosten, or Jan Marinissen), an Anabaptist martyr, burned at the stake on the market square of Middelburg, Dutch province of Zeeland, on Feb. 9, 1569, together with the preacher Hendrik Alewijnsz and Gerrit Duynherder. Hans was about 30 years of age and a cartwright. (*Mart. Mir.* D 389, E 742; *DB* 1908, 16; *ML* III, 57.)   vDZ.

Hans van Monster (of Münster, Westphalia, or from Monster near the Hague?), an Anabaptist martyr, was imprisoned in the castle of Berchem near Antwerp, Belgium, and beheaded there about 1550. Together with him Oude Jacob (*q.v.*) and Bartel (*q.v.*) were executed. (*Mart. Mir.* D 102, E 500; *DB* 1899, 153 f.; *ML* III, 161.)   vDZ.

Hans van Munstdorp, an Anabaptist martyr, who was burned at the stake at Antwerp, Belgium, in 1573. Van Braght's *Martyrs' Mirror* gives the date of the execution as September, but according to the Antwerp documents it took place on Feb. 17. Hans and his wife Janneken were arrested together. Janneken (*q.v.*) was put to death on Oct. 6, 1573, after she had given birth to a child.

A letter written by Hans to his wife in prison is printed by van Braght (*Mart. Mir.* D 664, E 983 ff.) in which he assured his wife that his intention to stay by the eternal truth was unchanged, he hoped to see her in the everlasting kingdom of God, and encouraged her to be true to the end. "Adieu and farewell, my lamb, my love; adieu and farewell to all that fear God. Adieu and farewell, until the marriage of the Lamb in the New Jerusalem. Be valiant and of good cheer; cast the troubles that assail you upon the Lord, and He will not forsake you. . . . Love God above all; have love and truth;

love your salvation, keep your promises to the Lord!"

In the records of Antwerp P. Génard found a martyr called Hans van Manstrop (Menstrop), who was burned at the stake at Antwerp on Feb. 17, 1573, because he had been rebaptized, and whose goods were confiscated. This martyr is apparently identical with Hans van Munstdorp, and may be the same person as Hans Knevel (q.v.). (Antw. Arch.-Blad XIII, 104 f., 173; XV, 90 f., No. 1009; ML III, 183.)

NEFF, vDZ.

Hans van Overdam(me), an Anabaptist martyr, executed at Gent on July 9, 1551 (van Braght, Martyrs' Mirror, 1550), with Hans Keeskooper (Jannijn Buefkijn, q.v.). He was a native of Gent and unmarried; he had been baptized by Gillis van Aken. Already in 1545 he had been sought for heresy, and was then banished from the territory of Gent. The Lietboecxken van den Offer des Heeren (1562, No. 17) contains a song by Hans van Overdamme in honor of Govert Mertens, Marie Vlamincx, Tanneken van Roosbroecke, and Gillis van Aerde, all of Lier, who had been executed on Jan. 31, 1551. Hans himself is commemorated in a song, "Ick weet, die Godes woort bekent, Dat hij ter wereld moet lijden" (I know that he who confesses the Word of God must suffer in this world), also found in the Offer des Heeren. Both Offer des Heeren and the Martyrs' Mirror contain a confession by Hans van Overdamme and two letters, one sent to the congregation of Gent, which tells how he was arrested, and one addressed to the city officials of Gent, which, with a severity unusual among Mennonite martyrs, censures the magistrates for their false religion and their satanic persecution of the children of God.

Hans and his companion Jannijn Buefkijn died steadfast. They had arranged that when they came to the scaffold Jannijn Buefkijn would slowly take off his hose, while Hans van Overdam addressed the crowd assembled around the place of execution; this they did. Thereupon they suffered death, each bound at a stake.

A novel by Kristen Loer, Strijd om het geluk (1949), has Hans van Overdamme as its principal character.

Offer, 98-120, 565, note 4; Mart. Mir. D 86 ff., E 486 ff.; Verheyden, Gent, 15, No. 27; ML II, 69; III, 283, 331; Wolkan, Lieder, 63, 78; Wackernagel, Lieder, 126.

Hans van Oznabrugge (Ozyerbrugge), an Anabaptist martyr: see **Hans de Goudsmid.**

Hans de Potbeckere, an Anabaptist martyr, a native of 's Hertogenbosch, Dutch province of North Brabant, was burned at the stake in Antwerp, Belgium, in 1538 or 1539, because he had been rebaptized. (Antw. Arch.-Blad VII, 444 f.; XIV, 16 f., No. 169.)

vDZ.

Hans Reyst-volk, followers of Hans Reist (q.v.) of the Emmental, the leader of the main body of Swiss Mennonites who refused to follow Ammann in 1693. Hans Reyst-volk were among the Swiss Mennonite immigrants in the Netherlands in the 18th century. The name died out since the group

considered itself the main body of Swiss Mennonites, treating the Amish as the separated group. Hence of the two parties at the time of the Amish schism the Reist following continued as the main body.

H.S.B.

Hans de Ries, Dutch Anabaptist leader: see **Ries, Hans de.**

Hans de Ruyter, an Anabaptist martyr: see **Hans Corneliszoon.**

Hans Scheerder, a Dutch Anabaptist leader, who was very active in propagating a revolutionary type of Anabaptism. In the fall of 1534 he baptized in Amsterdam. Here he met with Jacob van Campen, Jan Paeuw, Cornelis Pieters wt den Briel, and other leaders; about Easter 1535 he was in the province of Groningen as an accomplice of the Münsterite leader Jan van Batenburg (q.v.). After this he is found at the conference held at Bocholt in 1536, and in 1537 he operated as a church-robber near Cleve and Wesel. So "the former Obbenite (follower of the peaceful Obbe Philips) of 1534, the Münsterite leader in the Ommelanden (of Groningen) of 1535, became after Bocholt a Batenburger church-robber" (Mellink, Wederdopers, 396). Then he disappears from sight. Hans, who was a native of Leeuwarden, Dutch province of Friesland, had been baptized there in January 1534, together with Obbe Philips (q.v.), by Bartholomeus Boeckbinder (q.v.). On the next day both Obbe and Hans had been ordained elders by laying on of hands. Hans Scheerder is also called Hans Barbier (barber), but this is an error because Scheerder means wantscheerder, i.e., shearer of cloth. Hans van Gulik may be identical with this Hans Scheerder. He is also called Hans Wantscheerder "uit Appingedam." vDZ.

BRN VII, 118, 129, 367; DB 1916, 116, No. 60; 119, No. 98; Mellink, Wederdopers, passim, see Index.

Hans de Schoenmakere, who was a cloth dyer by trade, an Anabaptist martyr, born at Kortrijk (q.v.), Flanders, was burned at the stake at Antwerp on July 17, 1553. (Antw. Arch.-Blad VIII, 421, 423; XIV, 20 f., No. 225.) vDZ.

Hans Sikken, a Mennonite preacher of Danzig, Prussia, who came to the Netherlands in 1567 together with Dirk Philips and Geert H. to settle the Flemish-Frisian quarrel (see **Flemish Mennonites**). While Dirk Philips remained in Emden, Sikken went to meet the representatives of the Frisian group at Appingedam, Dutch province of Groningen. Here he pronounced the ban upon the Frisian group. Of Sikken nothing more is known, but the Hans S. who was present in April 1556 at a discussion at Wüstenfelde between the Dutch-North German and the South German Mennonite leaders on avoidance in marriage was Hans Sikken. On this trip to the Netherlands he wrote a letter to Steven Vaader, the elder of the Danzig Mennonite Church, which is mentioned in the Danzig Mennonite Church Record, 1667-1830, now in Bethel College Historical Library. vDZ.

Menno Simons, Opera Omnia (Amsterdam, 1681) 489; DB 1893, 54, 64 f., 77; 1894, 37.

Hans de Smet (official name Jan Symens), an Anabaptist martyr, was burned at the stake on Aug. 7, 1559, at Gent, Belgium. He was a native of Waasten (Warneton) in Flanders and a cloth dyer by trade. He was arrested at Gent on Friday after Pentecost, together with a large number of members of the Gent congregation. Hans remained steadfast, as did his wife Tanneken Gressy, executed at Gent on June 27, 1560, after she had given birth to her child. The names of Hans and the other martyrs executed at Gent in 1559 are found in a song, "Ick moet een liet beginnen" (I must begin a song), which is found in the *Liedtboecxken vanden Offer des Heeren,* No. 14. (*Offer,* 348, 556 ff.; *Mart. Mir.* D 246, E 620; Verheyden, *Gent,* 25, No. 63; *ML* II, 250.)   vdZ.

Hans de Smid, an Anabaptist martyr, executed in November 1558 at the Steen prison at Antwerp, Belgium. His official name was probably Hans Janssens, of Kruiningen (Dutch province of Zeeland). He is celebrated in the song, "Aenhoort Godt, hemelsche Vader" (Hear, O God, heavenly Father), which is found in *Liedtboecxken vanden Offer des Heeren,* No. 16.   vdZ.

Offer, 566; *Mart. Mir.* D 202, E 583; *Antw. Arch.-Blad* VIII, 452, 465; XIV, 24 f., No. 268; Wolkan, *Lieder,* 63, 72.

Hans Smit, an Anabaptist martyr: see **Schmidt, Hans.**

Hans Speck: see **Jan Specke.**

Hans van der Stra(e)ten, an Anabaptist martyr, arrested at Antwerp, and burned at the stake at Brussels, Belgium, on March 28, 1571. He was 31 years of age and had been married only six weeks when he was imprisoned. His wife, Tanneken van den Broucke, b. at Mechelen, 17 years of age, was arrested together with Hans. In prison when she was tried, she recanted and was put in a cloister at Breda, in the Netherlands, but soon managed to escape; then she traveled to Danzig in Prussia, where she joined the Flemish Mennonite Church. Hans belonged to a family that had many "heretics," some of whom joined the Mennonites and died as martyrs; a brother of Hans, Martin van der Straeten (*q.v.*), was executed at Gent in 1572, and their father Josse (Joost) (*q.v.*) suffered martyrdom for his faith in Antwerp in 1571.   vdZ.

Mart. Mir. D 540, E 875; Verheyden, *Courtrai-Bruxelles,* 101, No. 147; *idem, Gent,* 60.

Hans (Jan) van Straten, an Anabaptist who lived in England and was arrested in London in 1575 with some other Anabaptists, two of whom were put to death; viz., Hendrik Terwoort (*q.v.*) and Jan Pietersz (*q.v.*). Hans after a long and severe imprisonment was set free. (*Mart. Mir.* D 694-712; E 1009.)   vdZ.

Hans Suikerbakker, an Anabaptist leader who was in prison at Antwerp, Belgium, in March 1538 (*Inv. Arch. Amst.* I, 192), and is obviously identical with Joachim Vermeeren (*q.v.*).   vdZ.

Hans de Swarte, an Anabaptist martyr, was burned at the stake at Lille, France, on April 27, 1563. He was a son of Jan de Swarte (*q.v.*). See also **Swarte, de,** family. (*Mart. Mir.* D 299, E 664.)
vdZ.

Hans (Jan) Symonsz (erroneously also called Simon Janssen), an Anabaptist martyr, was burned at the stake at Antwerp, Belgium, on Sept. 13, 1567. He was a wholesale dealer and a preacher of the Antwerp congregation. In 1566 he had been in Friesland to settle the Flemish-Frisian quarrels (see **Flemish Mennonites**). The *Martyrs' Mirror* contains two letters written by Hans in prison. vdZ.

Mart. Mir. D 345-46, 351-56; E 704, 709; *Antw. Arch.-Blad* IX, 460, 462; X, 65; XII, 462; XIV, 46 f., No. 523.

Hans, Theodor, was a pastor of the Moravian Brethren in St. Petersburg, Russia, who rendered important services to the deputies (see **Deputations**) of the Mennonites of Russia in the early 1870's when they sought exemption from military duty. Pastor Hans's home soon became the information center for Mennonites for questions concerning the new military law that was being formulated in the Ministry of War, and since he had good connections with the upper governmental circles he was able to assist them in obtaining audience and in supporting them in general. When the presence of Mennonite representatives in the capital was demanded or desired he summoned them by telegraph or letter, and when none was present he protected their cause.

Hans probably had a greater influence on the Mennonites of Russia than the casual contacts may seem to indicate. In the days when St. Petersburg seemed an unfriendly capital and it was anticipated that all peace-loving Mennonites would have to leave the country, he received the delegates in his home, helped them to establish the necessary contacts, and above all stimulated them with regard to their Mennonite conscience and Christian responsibility. "You cannot simply leave the country without having been inwardly and completely absolved from your calling [in Russia]. Thus the question of leaving the country for conscience' sake becomes the question of remaining in the country for conscience' sake." "Russia needs you, and the responsibility God has given you for the country is great." Admonitions like these, which were received in letters and reread and printed, must have had a considerable influence.

D.H.E., C.K.

Friesen, *Brüderschaft,* 506-9; D. H. Epp, *Die Chortitzer Mennoniten* (Rosenthal bei Chortitz, 1887) 150 ff.; Abr. Görz, *Ein Beitrag zur Geschichte des Forsteidienstes der Menn. in Russland* (Gross-Tokmak, 1907); *ML* II, 249.

Hans (Jan) Vermandele (in *Mart. Mir.* called *Hans van Mandel*), an Anabaptist martyr, burned at the stake at Antwerp, Belgium, March 19, 1569. He had been arrested with a number of other members of the Antwerp congregation, when a meeting was held in the house of Jan Poote (*q.v.*). He was 25 years of age and a weaver, originally from Kortrijk in Flanders (*q.v.*). He lived at Dambrugge near Antwerp and was married to Betken, whom he had married in a meeting of the congregation outside of the city. He had been baptized upon his faith in Antwerp in 1566. Even while cruelly tortured he refused to name the person who had baptized him and the place where the baptism took place. (*Mart. Mir.* D 415, E 766; *Antw. Arch.-Blad* XII, 337, 368, 398, 440; XIV, 64 f., No. 711.) vdZ.

Hans Vermeersch (thus called in *Groot Offerboek* of 1615 and later in martyr books, including van Braght, *Mart. Mir.*; in *Offer* his name is *Hans van der Maes*), an Anabaptist martyr, executed at the end of 1559 at Waastene (Warneton) in West Flanders, Belgium. About this martyr nothing is known but a letter he wrote in prison, which is found in *Offer des Heeren* and all following martyrbooks, including van Braght's *Martyrs' Mirror*. He states that he was taken from prison to the inquisitor, and gives a detailed account of his trial, both the inquisitor's questions and his answers. In the *Offer* this letter is followed by a hymn concerning Hans beginning "Tyrannich werck spoortmen nu alle weghen" (Tyrannic action is now found everywhere). In the 17th century members of a Vermeersch family were found among the Flemish Mennonite congregation of Haarlem, while Gielis Vermeersch was a deacon at Harlingen about 1690. It could not be determined whether or in what way these families are related to the martyr Hans Vermeersch. (*Offer*, 358-66; *Mart. Mir.* D 259, E 631; Wolkan, *Lieder*, 67.) vdZ.

Hans de Vette, an Anabaptist martyr, was executed at Gent, July 5, 1559. With his wife and eleven other Anabaptists, including Hans de Smet (*q.v.*), he was thrown into prison at Gent on Friday after Pentecost in 1559, when their meeting had been betrayed. They were executed on different days. All remained true to their faith. Hans de Vette wrote a "confession" in prison, in which he describes his trial in detail. Hans was a native of Waastene (Warneton) in West Flanders, and a dyer by trade. His wife Miertgen (*q.v.*) was executed on June 27, 1560. A song on Hans is found in *Offer der Heeren,* which begins "Hebt goeden moet, o broeders van weerden." A hymn commemorating the whole group is found in the *Liedtboecxken vanden Offer des Heeren* (No. 14), "Ick moet een liet beginnen." vdZ.

Offer, 348-57, 556-59; *Mart. Mir.* D 246 ff., E 620 ff.; Verheyden, *Gent,* 25, No. 60; Wolkan, *Lieder,* 62, 67, 71; *DB* 1908, 51; *ML* II, 69, 250.

Hans Vlaming(h): see **Vlamingh, Hans.**

Hans de Wantscheerder, a Dutch Anabaptist leader: see **Hans Scheerder.**

Hans der Weduwe(n), an Anabaptist martyr, burned at the stake in Antwerp, Belgium, on Jan. 31, 1573, because he had been (re)baptized and had attended the forbidden meetings of the Mennonites. Either Hans Knevel (*q.v.*) or Hans van Munstdorp (*q.v.*) may be identical with this Hans der Weduwen, of whom nothing further is known. (*Antw. Arch.-Blad* XIII, 102 f., 172; XIV, 88 f., No. 1005.) vdZ.

Hans van der Weghe, an Anabaptist martyr, was arrested at Gent and burned at the stake with two girls, Janneken van Hulle and Janneken van Rentegem. From prison he wrote four letters which admonish his relatives and friends to a life of penitence and faith, that they might be partakers of eternal life. Hans was a native of Ronse (Renaix) in Flanders. His brother Jacob van der Weghe was burned at Gent in 1573. vdZ.

Mart. Mir. D 528, E 865; Verheyden, *Gent,* 56, No. 195; *ML* II, 70, 250.

Hans de Wever, an Anabaptist elder: see **Busschaert, Hans.**

Hansen, Georg, an elder of the Old Flemish (*Klerkse, Klärische*) Mennonite congregation in Danzig, was made deacon in 1655, preacher in the same year, and elder in 1690, serving until his death, Jan. 16, 1703. He was a cobbler by trade, widely read and gifted in speech and writing. He made the notes in the archives of the church in Danzig which report on important events in the congregation from 1667 on, which furnished the basic data for the later Danzig Mennonite Church Record 1667-1836, which, among other things, gives a complete list of ministers of the church since the days of Dirk Philips.

Hansen is also the author of several important books. One was *Ein Glaubens-Bericht vor die Jugend durch einen Liebhaber der Wahrheit gestellt und ans Licht gebracht* (1671), a book of 276 octavo pages (reprinted by the Mennonite Publishing Co., Elkhart, in 1893?). By clever choice of Bible verses the Christian doctrines of God and Christ and the Holy Spirit, and the Mennonite doctrines of baptism, footwashing, mixed marriage, the ban, avoidance, revenge, and the oath, are graphically presented to the children. In the foreword to this book Hansen makes the interesting observation that the youth of Danzig read German more fluently than Dutch (*Menn. Bl.,* 1857, 61); nevertheless the Dutch was retained in church services for another century. A more extensive book, which he finished in 1699 in the Dutch language, and which was published after his death in Amsterdam (1705), was *Spiegel Des Levens, Geschreven door George Hansen, In sijn Leven Outsten der Gemeynte Godts tot Danzigh, Maar nu door eenige Beminders der Waerheyt ter eeren Godts ende stichtingh haers Naesten in Druck uytgegeven.* It deals in the main with regeneration, its nature and effect. Hansen was also the author of *Einfältige Antwort der Mennoniten die man Clercken nent auf den Erforscher der Wahrheit* (n.p., n.d.), in which he attacked the booklet *Erforscher der Wahrheit,* printed in 1680. The *Einfältige Antwort* was not published until 1706. Hansen also published in the Dutch language the *Fundamentboek,* printed in 1696 at Amsterdam. It was translated into German by Elder Isaak Peters and published at Elkhart, Ind., under the title: *Ein Fundamentbuch der Christlichen Lehre, welche unter den Mennoniten in Preussen (die man zu Danzig "Clerken" nennt) gelehrt wird.* The contents of this book had been approved and agreed upon by the Prussian elders on Jan. 20, 1680. Hansen also compiled the confession of faith that is known under the title, *Confession oder Kurze und einfältige Glaubensbekänntnisse derer Mennonisten in Preussen, so man nennet die Clarichen.* Of this book, Schagen (*Naamlijst der Doopsgezinde Schrijveren,* Amsterdam, 1745, 44) mentions an edition of 1678, entitled *Confessio aut Breves ac Simplices Fidei Articuli illorum Mennonistarum in Borussia, qui vulgo Clarici vocantur.* His *Bekenntnis des George Hansen und sein Examen* was printed in German and Latin, presumably by a member of the Commission which examined him. In 1768 the Flemish congregation of Prussia published Hansen's confession of faith with a catechism and several other additions. (*Menn. Bl.,* 1857, 7, 39, 63; *ML* I, 159 f.)

In 1678, when at the orders of King John Sobiesky, 1674-96, a religious cross-examination was held with the Mennonites of Danzig before Bishop Stanislaus Sarnowski and other spiritual dignitaries, Hansen spoke so successfully (Jan. 20) for the Flemish group that they were absolved of all suspicion of spiritual relationship with the Arians or Socinians.

Hansen placed the painter Enoch Seemann under the ban because he painted portraits. In vain Seemann protested this narrow-minded measure; he wrote a very bitter book, *Offenbarung und Bestrafung des Georgen Hansens Thorheyt, Jedermann zur brüderlichen Vermahnung und getreuen Warnung wohlmeinentlich an Tag gegeben durch einen Liebhaber der Wahrheit* (Stoltzenberg, 1697). The congregation supported its elder. NEFF, vDZ.

H. G. Mannhardt, *Die Danziger Mennonitengemeinde* (Danzig, 1919) 73, 77 ff.; R. Friedmann, *Mennonite Piety Through the Centuries* (Goshen, 1949) 130-34, 137, where Hansen's books are analyzed as to their spiritual contents; *ML* II, 250.

Hansen, Joseph (b. 1862), a German historian, director of the historical archives of Cologne, wrote numerous books and articles on the history of the inquisition and witch-hunting, on the Counter Reformation, and on the older and more recent history of Westphalia and the Rhineland, among which his treatise, "Die Wiedertäufer in Aachen und in der Aachener Gegend" in *Ztscht des Aachener Geschichtsvereins* VI (1884) 295-338, is of importance for the history of Anabaptism. (*ML* II, 251.) NEFF.

Hansen, Reimer (1853-1926), professor at the Oberrealschule in Oldesloe, Germany. Of simple rural origins, the gifted youth acquired a thorough education by study at the University of Kiel as well as by private study. His particular field was history. Later he became famed for his research in the history of Schleswig-Holstein, and especially of his home Dithmarschen. For Mennonite history two of his articles, written with objective scholarship, are of significance: "Wiedertäufer in Eiderstedt" (until 1616) in the *Schriften des Vereins für schleswig-holsteinische Kirchengeschichte,* series II, vol. 2; "Menno Simonis in Holstein" in *Die Heimat,* 1907. For the *Mennonitisches Lexikon* he wrote an article on the Danish Prince Frederick. (*ML* II, 251.) R.Do.

Hansfelde: see **Hamberge.**

Hansijtten (or *Hanssytsche Mennonieten*), a name sometimes used during the 17th century in the Netherlands to indicate the Waterlanders (*q.v.*), and especially the adherents of Hans de Ries (*q.v.*). vDZ.

Hans(ken) van Audenaerde (Oudenaarde), an Anabaptist martyr, burned on the Vrijdag market place at Gent, Belgium, on March 17, 1573, together with Beliken de Jaghere (*q.v.*) and Grietgen van Sluys (*q.v.*). Hansken was born at Geeraerdsbergen, Flanders, a son of Joris, a hatmaker, lived in Gent for two years, and was only 18 years of age. (*Mart. Mir.* D 631, 647; E 968; Verheyden, *Gent,* 61, No. 214; *ML* III, 330.) vDZ.

Hansken van den Broecke (vanden Broeke, vanden Brouck), an Anabaptist martyr, was burned at the stake at Brugge, Belgium, on Oct. 15, 1558, after being strangled. Van Braght's *Martyrs' Mirror* mentions that he had come to Brugge from Oostende to hear the preaching of the Gospel, and that he was arrested with some others and executed about June 12, remaining steadfast in his faith. Verheyden has published more exact and exhaustive data. He was a linen weaver by trade, had been baptized at Gent in 1556, lived in Oostende for some time, and had moved from this town to Brugge in the spring of 1558 together with Jacob de Swarte (*q.v.*) who was burned at the stake at Brugge on Aug. 15, 1558. (*Mart. Mir.* D 202, E 583; Verheyden, *Brugge,* 47, No. 30; *ML* II, 250.) vDZ.

Hansken van Frubergh, an Anabaptist martyr of whom nothing is known but that he was burned at the stake at Antwerp, Belgium, in 1558. (*Antw. Arch.-Blad* VII, 439; XIV, 17 f., No. 165.) vDZ.

Hansken Henricx (Bosseneerken, i.e., from 's Hertogenbosch, Dutch province of North Brabant), an otherwise unknown martyr, was burned at the stake in 1557 at Antwerp, Belgium. (*Antw. Arch.-Blad* VIII, 417 f.; XIV, 20 f., No. 216.) vDZ.

Hansken van Oudenaerde, an Anabaptist martyr: see **Hansken van Audenaerde.**

Hansken Parmentier, an Anabaptist martyr, was burned at the stake on Dec. 11, 1561, at Brugge, Belgium. Verheyden, not finding this name in the records, suggests that Hansken Parmentier is identical either with Jehan Bertheloot (*q.v.*) or with Jehan (Hans) Cant (*q.v.*), both executed on Dec. 11, 1561, at Brugge. (*Mart. Mir.* D 288, E 655; Verheyden, *Brugge,* 50 f., Nos. 42 and 43; *ML* III, 335.) vDZ.

Hansken in't Schaek (Hans Schaek, or Koordedrayer), an Anabaptist martyr, burned at the stake on May 18, 1570, at Brugge, Belgium. Hansken, who was born at Kortrijk, Flanders, was a member of the congregation at Brugge; while attending a meeting of this congregation on Ascension Day (May 4), 1570, in the woods of Tillegem near Brugge, he was arrested with a number of other members during a police raid. He remained steadfast and refused to name other members of the church, and consequently had to suffer death. He was executed with Kaerle de Raedt (*q.v.*) and Willem Vernon (*q.v.*). (*Mart. Mir.* D 369, E 725; Verheyden, *Brugge,* 61, No. 66.)   vDZ.

Hansken Schalijdecker, an Anabaptist martyr: see **Jan Jansze.**

Hansma, Leendert, b. 1861 at Dokkum, d. Dec. 5, 1940, at Assen, a Dutch Mennonite bookseller and printer at Assen. He published the *Doopsgezind Jaarboekje* (*q.v.*) from its beginning (1901). He helped to establish a Mennonite fellowship circle, and soon after, a congregation at Assen, and for a number of years served as its secretary (1896-1926). He not only published the *Doopsgezind Jaarboekje* but also contributed to its contents; in a number of issues sketches are found signed H.V.A. (i.e., Hansma, van Assen). (*DJ* 1942, 17 f. with portrait.)   vDZ.

Hansmann, Hans, a purse maker of Basel, therefore usually called Seckler, was one of the first Anabaptists of Switzerland and filled a place of leadership among them, which was, however, of short duration, for he was one of the first Anabaptists to suffer a martyr's death in Bern. At first he worked in Basel, but the mandates issued in 1526 against the Anabaptists by the Basel government apparently caused him to leave. In 1527 he settled in Bern with Jakob Hochrütiner (the son of Lorenz Hochrütiner of Zürich). With the other leaders of the Bern Swiss Brethren he was arrested in the spring of 1527 and cross-examined. (The protocol is still in the state archives at Bern; see Quervain, 120.) The council favored expulsion, and the clergy undertook public attempts to convert them. A confession of faith discovered in the search of a house was sent by Berthold Haller (*q.v.*) to Zwingli on April 25; by April 28 Zwingli had already presented a refutation of Anabaptist doctrine. Hansmann and Hochrütiner could, however, not be deflected from their faith. Since they did not render an oath they were put in neck-irons and on May 1 expelled from the canton. The other prisoners recanted to escape expulsion (Quervain, 121; Müller, 25).

Hansmann returned to Bern for the great disputation (see *ML* I, 17 f.) of Jan. 7-26, 1528, which was to be decisive in the Reformation of Bern. With him came seven other brethren, including Georg Blaurock. They were, however, not admitted to the proceedings, but were interned for the duration. Shortly before the close of the session they were called to the Rathaus, where five theologians, including Zwingli and Conrad Schmid, publicly disputed with them. The speakers on the Anabaptist side were Hansmann, Blaurock, and Hans Pfistermeyer. The council declared that the learned doctors had adequately convinced the Anabaptists of their error with the Holy Scriptures; but since they persisted in their opinion they were to be expelled from the canton, and if they were ever seen there again, to be "drowned without mercy in that very hour." The safe conduct to the border guaranteed to them was granted (Müller, 29 f.).

Concerning this disputation one of the four presidents at the disputation, Conrad Schmid

(*q.v.*), published a booklet entitled, *Die predigen so vonn den frömbden Predicanten, die allenthalb här, zu Bernn uff dem Gespräch oder Disputation gewesen, beschehen sind,* (with) *Verwerffen der articklenn und stucken, so die Widertöuffer uff dem gespräch zu Bernn, vor ersamem grossem Radt fürgewendt habend* (Zürich, Chr. Froschauer, 1528, copy in Goshen College Library). This first book on the Bern Anabaptists can make no claim of reliability. "The booklet," says Ernst Müller, "not only swarms with epithets from the animal world, but also with distortions and misconstructions" (p. 46). Rather remarkable, however, is the reproach made by the theologians of Zürich and Bern, that the Anabaptists refused to repeat the Ave Maria, since the Reformed Church later took the same position on this point.

Where Hansmann went from Bern is not certain. In the spring of 1529 he was again imprisoned with Hans Dreier (*q.v.*) and examined on the rack on several points: infant baptism, whether a Christian can hold a magistrate's office, the oath, community of goods, tithes and interest, community of wives, and separation from the church. Hansmann (here called Seckler) was tried first. The record states that he said, "Infant baptism is a principle of the pope and because it is not done away with there can be no Christian Church, for it is not instituted of God." Then Hans Dreier was examined. On the question of baptism he said briefly, "I stay with baptism like Seckler." Concerning separation, he said he would not attend church because he was separated from those who do not confess Christ. The confessions made by Seckler and Dreier were signed by them. On May 24, 1529, several other persons were tried before the prebendary on the same points. First came the hatter Heini Seiler (*q.v.*) of Aarau. His answer was like that of the other two, and he "would leave his life for it and testify to it with his blood. . . . He had not gone to church for a long time nor to any other preaching, for one must be taught alone by God."

A letter of self-vindication written by an Anabaptist, which Fluri found in the state archives in Bern and identified as Seckler's, gives his belief clearly. He says that in the old covenant God had removed the temple of Solomon; in the new one the believers are the temple of the living God, wherefore no one could compel him to enter the temple (the church). Further he testifies that he had held no secret meetings, but when anyone requested the reason for his faith, "I revealed my faith to him through the Scripture." Infant baptism has no foundation in the Word of God, and was "instituted without the Word of God," and must be regarded as a plant, according to Matt. 15, "which my heavenly Father did not plant," and which should therefore be uprooted. "But those who commit themselves by baptism into the death of Christ are my fellow members, of which body Christ is the head." The government, in which a Christian might participate, should be obeyed; not by compulsion, however, but voluntarily. The oath is contrary to the word of Christ; whatever the government required he would perform as long as it was not contrary to God's Word. He did not reject private possession of property; in the first church all things were common, but there was no command. "Tithes and all fees imposed by the government a Christian will pay as far as it concerns body and goods; but a Christian will not take them." This was also his idea on the taking of interest. Separation from the church was due to idols; he had no objection to the teaching of the preachers whom God calls and who point out much that is right (Müller, 42 f.). He had baptized only seven persons in the town of Bern; may the Lord preserve these souls in their faith to His praise to the end. A *Verantwortung* by Hansmann was also discovered in the archives of Bern by Adolf Fluri (Quervain, 151).

After these trials the clergy informed the council that the Anabaptists intended to adhere to their belief and testify to it with their blood. On June 8 the council decreed that the three (Hansmann, Dreier, and Seiler) should be drowned if they still persisted in their Anabaptism after another attempt to convert them (*Ratsmanual* 222/153). The sentence was executed above the present railroad bridge at the "blood tower"; they were cast into the Aare in mid-July 1529. They were the first victims of the Anabaptist persecution in Bern.   HEGE.

A. Fluri, "Täuferhinrichtungen in Bern im 16. Jahrhundert," in *Berner Heim* 1896; Müller, *Berner Täufer*, 24 ff. (p. 42 gives the record of the trial); Theodor de Quervain, *Kirchliche und sociale Zustände in Bern unmittelbar nach der Einführung der Reformation* (Bern, 1906); *ML* II, 251 f.

Hanston Mennonite Church (GCM), formerly known as the Einsiedel Church, located 1½ miles north and 2½ miles west of Hanston, Hodgeman Co., Kan., is a member of the Western District Conference. The original name "Einsiedel" was chosen in memory of the church in Galicia (*q.v.*) from which seven of the first eight families immigrated to Hanston in 1885, the eighth being a related family from the Palatinate. The eight family heads were two Johann Müllers, Johann Linscheid, Johann Ewy, Heinrich Rupp, Johann Brubacher, Peter Ewy, and Christian Hirschler. Johann P. Müller was preacher 1885-1915 (elder from 1899); Christian E. Hirschler served as preacher and elder 1915 until his death. In 1888 the first church was dedicated. In 1902 it was destroyed by a tornado, but was rebuilt from lumber salvaged from the wreckage. In 1924 this building was replaced by a larger one, still in use. The pastor in 1955 was Menno Ediger; the membership was 67. (*ML* I, 548.)   E.E.H.

Hapsburg (Habsburg), an old ruling family or dynasty in Austria, Germany, and Spain, most ardent champions of the Catholic cause, at least after the family inherited the Spanish throne in 1516. Since the middle of the 15th century all rulers of the Holy Roman Empire were Hapsburgs. During the age of Reformation Emperor Charles V (*q.v.*) tried in vain to fight Lutheranism; in 1555 he had to admit the right of the German princes to decide the religion of their land for themselves. Yet in a number of momentous mandates (*q.v.*) he laid the legal groundwork for the persecution of the "heretical" Anabaptists. More immediate were the activities of his brother Ferdinand I (*q.v.*), first Archduke of Austria, after 1526 also King of Bohemia and Hungary (where he had little influence), and then after 1556 Emperor. His fight against the Anabaptists, along with the counter-reformatory activities of the Roman hierarchy and the Jesuits, was violent and relentless, and, to a certain degree, also successful. The Hutterite chronicle lists no fewer than 2,169 martyrs during the reign of Charles V and Ferdinand I. Only in Moravia could the Anabaptists persist, protected there by the nobles who, though Catholic, were loath to lose the profits accruing from these industrious settlers. During the time of Emperor Maximilian II (*q.v.*) a milder period set in at first (called in the Hutterite chronicles the "Golden Age"). But by the turn of the century, under the reign of the somewhat enigmatic Rudolphus II, persecution set in again with doubled effort, though only in those countries in which the emperor had full jurisdiction (i.e., the *Erblande* or Hapsburg domain, Austria, Tirol, Styria, etc.). Once a Hutterite physician cured the emperor, but it did not help the brotherhood as a whole very much. With the initial success of the Thirty Years' War (1618-48) the Hapsburgs gained also great power in the kingdom of Bohemia, particularly in Moravia. Under the regime of Ferdinand II (1619-37) the Anabaptists were now definitely expelled from Moravia (1622). Fortunately, the power of the Hapsburgs in Hungary was very limited. This kingdom had fallen to the Hapsburgs in 1526, but the Turks soon took over the greater part of the country (including the suzerainty of Transylvania), and the nobility in the remaining part (today Slovakia) was ready to accept the Anabaptists on their estates, as they were excellent workers. Most of these nobles were Calvinists. Thus the Hutterian Brethren could enjoy a comparatively quiet period in these eastern parts of the Hapsburg Empire, where the power of the Counter Reformation was effective only to a small extent. Soon after Emperor Leopold I (1658-1705) came to power, he even issued a special privilege of protection for the Brethren in three counties in Slovakia in 1659, most likely upon the urging of the manorial lords of that area (Beck, 496).

Around 1700 the Turks were completely expelled from Hungary and Hapsburg's power became effective also here. In general, the 18th century is called the century of enlightenment and toleration, yet little of either was felt in the huge Hapsburg realm. The great Empress Maria Theresa (1740-80) did much to strengthen her realm, but neither Lutherans nor Anabaptists were tolerated. It was under her reign that Lutherans of Carinthia (*q.v.*) had to transmigrate (in 1755) to far-off Transylvania (*q.v.*), a country which, though belonging to the Hapsburg realm, yet was judged too distant to have any "detrimental" influence on the realm in general. These transmigrants came into contact with the last remnants of the Hutterites, and revived their brotherhood to new life. But the Jesuits (though in other countries hard pressed themselves; the Jesuit order was officially suppressed by the pope in

1773) were determined to eradicate the "sect" altogether. Mainly one Father Delphini became of evil repute among the Brethren for his activities. Emigration (to Russia) was the only way out. The same enforced conversion to Catholicism happened also in Slovakia (then Hungary) during the time of Maria Theresa. In the 1750's and 1760's children were taken away, men were imprisoned, books were confiscated, until finally the backbone of these brethren was broken. Those who turned Catholic are now known as "Habaner" (*q.v.*). Even the last Hapsburg ruler to be considered in this rapid survey, Emperor Joseph II (*q.v.*), 1780-90, famous in history as an "enlightened despot," and rather indifferent to religion, was in no way better than his forerunners with respect to things Anabaptist. The *Klein-Geschichtsbuch* reports an interview of the Emperor with a Hutterite brother (of Carinthian descent) in which the question of the property of the transmigrants was discussed. Joseph refused to yield, and the brethren lost everything that had once been theirs.

However, there is at least one positive note in this theme of Hapsburg's attitude toward radical Christians. In 1775, at the first partition of Poland, Maria Theresa received a large area of territory, partly Polish, partly Ukrainian, called Klein Polen or Galicia (*q.v.*). Since it was then but sparsely populated, Joseph II issued a special patent or decree to stimulate colonization of this country. This enabled Mennonites from the Palatinate to migrate to this eastern country and to settle in the vicinity of Lemberg (1784). Their thriving colonies existed there up to World War II (see **Ferdinand I, Maximilian II**, and **Leopold I**).   R.F.

W. Wiswedel, "Kurze Charakteristik etlicher Herrscher Oesterreichs hinsichtlich ihrer Stellung zum Täufertum," in *Der Sendbote* (Cleveland) 1937, 191; Beck, *Geschichts-Bücher;* Zieglschmid, *Klein-Geschichtsbuch; ML* II, 217 f.

Harbin (Manchuria) **Refugees.** In the early 1920's a settlement of Mennonites from West Siberia was established along the Amur River in Far Eastern Russia on the border of Manchuria, hoping for better living conditions and more freedom from Communist oppression. After a few years, however, the group decided to flee from Russia and in the middle of winter crossed the Amur into Manchuria and finally reached Harbin. Here through a Mennonite physician, J. J. Isaac (d. 1956 at Vallejo, Cal., having reached the United States in 1952), they made contact with Mennonite relief organizations in Europe and the United States. Given German passports, some 200 were admitted to the United States in the spring of 1930, most of them settling in the Reedley area of California. A small settlement made in Eastern Washington near Roseo failed. H. P. Krehbiel was active in assisting the Harbin movement to California and Washington.

The remainder of the Harbin refugees were finally moved to Paraguay and Brazil in 1932, with the aid of the Nansen International Office for Refugees under the sponsorship of the League of Nations, and a loan from the Protestant Aid Office, headquarters in Geneva, Switzerland, and the Mennonite Central Committee. The first group of 373 Mennonites was settled in Fernheim Colony, Paraguay, in the "Harbin Corner," while 397 Lutherans were settled in Brazil. In 1934, 180 Mennonites were settled in Brazil, also 100 others.   H.S.B.

A. Loewen and A. Friesen, *Die Flucht über den Amur* (Steinbach, 1946); W. Quiring, *Russlanddeutsche suchen eine Heimat* (Karlsruhe, 1938).

Harde Vriezen (*Friezen*), also called *Oude Vriezen,* a branch of the Mennonites in the Netherlands: see **Frisian Mennonites.**

Hardelop (Hardloop, Hardeloep, Harrloop, Harloop, Harrlop) is a Mennonite family name in Eiderstedt, Stapelholm, and Hamburg. Gerrit Hardelop was received by baptism at Glückstadt in 1634, by the elder of the Friedrichstadt Flemish Church. Jacob and Jan Hardelop, without doubt brothers, members of the High German congregation, lived in Witzwort. The former carried on a thriving export trade in cheese, bacon, and wool with Hamburg and other towns in 1658 and after.

Claas Hardelop lived in the Süderstapel parish, Stapelholm district. In 1683 the officials of the church and school demanded of the Anabaptists living in the parish the same fees as the Lutherans paid. As spokesman for the group Hardelop appealed to Duke Christian Albrecht; orders were then given that the Anabaptists should not be burdened but protected in coming there.

Johann Hardelop was a deacon of the Flemish congregation in Hamburg. Jacob Hardelop in the Groothusenkoog of Eiderstedt was one of the very few Mennonites to hold public office; in 1736-44 he was "overseer of the beach"; his oath of office was a "Christian yea and nay." The Hardelop family was probably lost to the church through marriage. At any rate it is no longer found in the Friedrichstadt church books after 1700.

About 1675 Pieter Ariaens Hardloop and a group of members of the Waterlander congregation of Wormerveer, Dutch province of North Holland, insisted on a more conservative policy in maintaining the confessions and accused the church board of Socinianism (*q.v.*). (*Inv. Arch. Amst.* I, Nos. 900-5; *ML* II, 252.)   R.Do.

Hardenberg (Ritzes), **Albert** (1510-74), a Reformed theologian, born at Hardenberg, Dutch province of Overijssel, was educated at the Aduard Monastery near Groningen and Louvain, Belgium. After some time at Wittenberg he went to the Archbishopric of Cologne to help Hermann von Wied with the Reformation (1544). It was during the same time that Menno (*q.v.*) Simons worked in this area. John a Lasco, a friend of Hardenberg's, stopped here twice during this time. They corresponded about Menno's activities. Hardenberg also wrote to Vadian about Menno's successful work in this area. No doubt Hardenberg was also in touch with the Mennonites during his activities at Emden, where he served as a minister from 1567 until his death on May 18, 1574.

Of interest is what Hardenberg says about Menno: "One who has had stupid teachers during his studies hardly teaches with understanding. Those who have left monasteries without study and without correct understanding or are self-taught have done much damage to the church. Such a one is a certain Menno Simons, whom I knew as a rural priest, who after reading fanatical books indiscriminately and taking the Bible into his hands without judgment and formal education has done much harm among the Frisians, Belgians, Menapiers, Saxons, Cymbrians, over all Germany, France, Britain, and all surrounding countries, so that posterity will not be able to shed sufficient tears on this account."   C.K.

"Hardenberg (Albertus Rizaeus of Ritzes)," *Biogr. Wb.* III, 504; Bernhard Spiegel, *D. Albert Rizaeus Hardenberg* (Bremen, 1869) 117; C. Krahn, *Menno Simons* (Karlsruhe, 1936) 59, 62 ff.

Harder (Haerder) is a common Mennonite name of Prussian background. The Danzig church record first lists the name in 1677. It also appeared in the records of the Mennonite churches of Tiegenhagen, Ladekopp, Rosenort, Fürstenwerder, and Heubuden. In 1940 it took the eighth place as to frequency of Mennonite names in East Germany, having a total of 184 bearers. From Prussia the name was transplanted to Russia, the United States, Canada, and South America.

Who's Who Among the Mennonites (1943) lists B. W. Harder, minister; H. N. Harder, minister; and M. S. Harder, professor at Bethel College. See also names of the numerous outstanding representatives of the name below.   M.S.H.

Reimer, *Familiennamen,* 109; Franz Crous, "Mennonitenfamilien in Zahlen," *Gesch.-Bl.,* August 1940, p. 41.

Harder, Abraham A. (1866- ?), the founder of the Mennonite orphanage at Grossweide, Molotschna Mennonite settlement of South Russia, was born Sept. 29, 1866, at Hierschau, Gnadenfeld district, the son of Abraham Johann Harder, who was a teacher in the village school. After he had completed his schooling, his parents moved to a farm at Alexanderwohl. He was baptized after catechetical instruction when he was about 21 years old and joined the Alexanderwohl Church, of which his father was a preacher.

When Mennonites began to settle in the Crimea, Abraham A. Harder joined the movement, settling at Neu-Toksaba, about 27 miles from the seaport Evpatoriya. Here Harder and his wife were rebaptized by immersion and joined the Mennonite Brethren Church at Spat, Crimea, near Simferopol, but about 1900 moved back to the Molotschna settlement, making his home at Rosenort. Following an inner call to care for Mennonite orphans Harder used the proceeds from the sale of his farm in the Crimea to buy a house in Grossweide, which he turned into an orphanage in 1906. In later years a large modern school building with a boys' dormitory was added. Many Mennonite orphans educated here became valuable citizens of Mennonite communities. The orphanage, however, was taken over by the Communists after the Revolution. Mrs. Harder died in an underground hut at Spat, where she and her husband had fled to escape the terror of the Communists. Harder was still living in Tchongrav, Crimea, during World War II and is thought to have been exiled with many others to Central Asia when the German army invaded Russia, but has not been heard of since then. (*ML* II, 252 f.)   Er.H.

Harder, Bernhard (1832-84), an outstanding Mennonite minister, teacher, and poet of the Molotschna, Russia, was born March 25, 1832, the eighth son of Abraham Harder and his wife Marie Heide Harder (according to Friesen, 743, nee Berg). His mother made an ineradicable impression on him. He lost his father at the age of 12.

Early in his childhood Harder felt called to teach and preach. He was accepted as a pupil at the age of ten in the newly established Halbstadt Zentralschule, from which he graduated after six years. For a while he served as secretary of the *Gebietsamt* (county seat). Finally his heart's desire was fulfilled and he became a teacher, serving in the elementary schools of Yuschanlee, Halbstadt, Blumstein, Friedensruh, and Alexanderwohl. During his teaching career he was chosen minister by the Ohrloff-Halbstadt Mennonite Church (*q.v.*) at Christmas 1860. Friesen (*Brüderschaft,* 744) states that he accepted this call "not with fear, tears, and complaint, taking upon himself the 'heavy office and cross' as it was customary at that time, but with rejoicing and tremendous energy he became a servant of his Saviour." For 15 years he combined the offices of teaching and ministry and the care of a large family.

On March 16, 1854, Harder married Katharina Boschmann. They had eleven children, four of whom preceded him in death. His wife died Oct. 13, 1878; he married Helena Ewert on Feb. 13, 1879. Three daughters were born to them.

He had already "given his heart to the Lord" when he attended the Zentralschule (Friesen, 744). His son Gerhard states, "After four years of teaching, the Lord succeeded in making of him His disciple. This happened at Blumstein where Elder Johann Harder lived" (Harder, XI). A. Harder's preaching was revolutionary, inspiring, and most successful. He broke with the tradition prevalent among the Mennonites of Russia of reading a sermon from a manuscript. His ideals were Elder B. Fast (*q.v.*), Halbstadt, Ludwig Hofacker, and Eduard Wüst (*q.v.*), who influenced Harder's spiritual awakening and activities greatly. He had been one of Wüst's listeners and admirers since 1850. With great zeal and a thundering voice Harder opposed everything he thought to be ungodly, but most of all he protested against formalism which threatened the very life of the church. He was motivated by an ardent love for the Saviour and for lost sinners, trying "to reach the hearer through eye and ear." When he preached he preached with his entire being. His live enthusiasm and clear convictions made his sermons particularly effective. Untiringly he preached from various pulpits and as an evangelist in numerous settlements and villages.

Friesen says, "Multitudes of people who found salvation through Harder could not understand how he could criticize his church so severely without leaving it" (as many did who joined the Mennonite Brethren). Harder did more than anyone else during the second half of the past century to revive the spiritual life of the Mennonites in Russia and to prevent unbalanced and unsound elements from taking advantage of the situation. He was the greatest evangelist and pulpit orator the Mennonites of Russia produced. His son Gerhard says, "Had Harder, with his great love and zeal to win souls for the Lord, had the same measure of gift to evaluate situations and people and had he had more emotional stability and pedagogical wisdom, his work in church and school would have been even more blessed" than was now the case. The fact that he was strongly evangelistic and defended the sound practices of the newly organized Mennonite Brethren Church caused criticism by representatives of the Mennonite Church. On the other hand, the Mennonite Brethren criticized him because he did not join them. He visited numerous meetings of the Mennonite Brethren and reported his impressions, some of which were published (*Menn. Bl.,* February 1863, 15 ff.). His strength and contribution lie in the fact that he followed an independent, warmly evangelistic course within the entire brotherhood, aiming to lift its spiritual and cultural aspects, thus making a singular contribution comparable to that of Johann Cornies in the economic realm.

In 1872 Harder discontinued teaching and spent three years as traveling evangelist, in which capacity he was supported by a group of friends. After this term he taught again for three years at Alexanderwohl. In 1879-80 he served as secretary of the *Gebietsamt* at Halbstadt, after which he taught Bible for one year at the Zentralschule at Halbstadt. The last three years of his life he again devoted entirely to his task as traveling evangelist (*Reiseprediger*), being again supported by a group of friends. Four months of each year he worked in his home congregation at Halbstadt.

From his early youth Harder showed poetic inclinations, which increased in maturity. He composed many poems for special occasions; many of them were collected and edited by Heinrich Franz, Sr., and published in 1888 under the title *Geistliche Lieder und Gelegenheitsgedichte,* with 584 songs (Part I) and 539 poems for various occasions (Part II). The book contains a valuable biography of the author written by his son, Gerhard (VIII-XXIV). Another son, Peter B. Harder, selected and edited from this collection 213 songs which were published by J. Friesen under the title *Kleines Liederbuch. Geistliche Gelegenheitslieder* (1902). Thus Harder was also a pioneer in the realm of the literary activities among the Mennonites of Russia.

In addition to the many trips as a traveling evangelist Harder was also called upon to represent various Mennonite causes and groups. In 1867 he was sent to Petersburg to investigate settlement possibilities in Turkestan. Again in 1882 he made the same trip. In 1879 he was twice sent to Odessa to interview von Totleben regarding Mennonite alternative service. He also visited the Mennonites in the Volga region in 1868 and in Prussia in 1873. On Sept. 27, 1884, he returned from a journey to Zagradovka, ill with pneumonia. He had preached strenuously four times daily. On Oct. 1, 1884, he died.†   C.K.

Friesen, *Brüderschaft,* 211 ff., 743-54; G. Harder, "Mittheilungen aus dem Lebensgange des Verfassers," in B. Harder, *Geistliche Lieder* (Hamburg, 1888, VIII-XXIV); *ML* II, 253 f.

Harder, Cornelius D. (1866-1946), was born at Blumstein, Molotschna, South Russia, on Dec. 1, 1866. He grew up in the Zagradovka settlement, and attended and later taught school there. On Feb. 22, 1890, he was married to Katharina Janzen. Fourteen children were born to them. In 1896 the family moved to the Suvorovka Mennonite settlement in the Caucasus, where he was elected minister July 6, 1897. On Feb. 17, 1912, they went to Siberia to the village of Schönsee, Slavgorod district. On Oct. 7, 1912, Harder was ordained elder of the Orloff Mennonite Church of the Barnaul settlement by Jakob Gerbrandt. In 1926 Mrs. Harder and two children went to Canada, and the following year he followed them. He became elder of the Bergthal Mennonite Church of Didsbury, Alberta. In 1937 he went to Rosemary, Alberta, where he organized the Westheim Mennonite Church and the Conference of Mennonites in Alberta. He died there on Oct. 3, 1946.   C.K.

J. G. Rempel, *Fünfzig Jahre Konferenzbestrebungen 1902-1952* I (1954) 244-46.

Harder, David, teacher and minister, was ordained in 1909 and served as leading minister of the Glyaden Mennonite Church, Slavgorod, Siberia (Friesen, *Brüderschaft,* 718)). Dirks (*Adressbüchlein,* p. 7) lists him in this capacity in 1913. On Sept. 10, 1923, he wrote a report on conditions of the settlement, entitled "Einst und Jetzt." (Copy in Bethel College Historical Library.)   C.K.

Harder, David E. (1872-1930), a Mennonite (KMB) teacher and minister, was born April 2, 1872, in the village of Annenfeld, in the Crimea, South Russia, the youngest of the six children of Johann and Elisabeth Fast Harder. In 1874 the family joined the Russian Mennonite migration to America and settled in the village of Gnadenau, which was established near Hillsboro, Kan., under the leadership of Elder Jacob A. Wiebe, the founder of the Krimmer Mennonite Brethren Church. When the village system of life was found impracticable in America, the Gnadenau village was dissolved and the Harder family moved to their farm 2½ miles south of Hillsboro.

David Harder received his elementary education in the parental home where his father conducted a private school until school districts were formed and public schools organized. When he reached the age of 15, he attended the Hillsboro High School for a few months. He obtained a teacher's license, and began to teach in a rural school near Goessel, Kan. For several spring and summer terms he attended McPherson College, McPherson, Kan. During the school years 1898-1900 he attended Bethel College, and in 1927 he received his Master's degree at the University of Oklahoma. In June 1897 he was married to Margaret Flaming.

To this union five children were born—Menno, David, Rozella, Theodore, and Joseph.

David E. Harder served on the faculty of a number of Mennonite colleges: Tabor College, 1909-22; Bethel College, Newton, Kan., 1922-27; Freeman College at Freeman, S.D., 1927 until his death in October 1930. He served the teaching profession 35 years.

As a minister Harder was in great demand. In 1914 he became moderator of the Krimmer Mennonite Brethren Conference, and was re-elected to this position 12 consecutive times. Under his leadership the Conference experienced growth in membership and great extension of its services. His "History of the Hutterian Brethren" is still an unpublished manuscript.†   M.S.H.

Menn. Life I (July 1946); *Tabor College Herald*, November 1930.

Harder, Ernst (1854-1927), a German Mennonite leader, was born Nov. 29, 1854, at Königsberg in Prussia, the son of Karl Harder (*q.v.*). He studied history and modern languages, and for a time served as tutor in the home of the British ambassador in Lisbon. Later he was an editor on the staff of the *Tägliche Rundschau* in Berlin, as well as a teacher of Spanish and Portuguese. As one of the first students of his noted brother-in-law Martin Hartmann, he finally devoted himself entirely to the study of Arabic. He was one of the founders of the Berlin Mennonite Church, serving on the church board from 1904 to his death, and as chairman of the board the last two years. In 1912 he compiled the *Festschrift* celebrating the twenty-fifth anniversary of the founding of the congregation. He died at Charlottenburg on Sept. 15, 1927.
E.C.

E. Crous, *Karl und Ernst Harder* (Elbing, 1927); *ML* II, 254.

Harder, Gerhard (1857-1931), evangelist and minister of the Halbstadt congregation, Molotschna, Taurida, Russia, was born in 1857 as fourth child of Bernhard Harder, well-known minister, teacher, and poet of Halbstadt. Gerhard was educated at the Halbstadt Zentralschule and pedagogical classes and—after teaching in an elementary school until 1883—at St. Chrischona near Basel, Switzerland. Harder then took a private course in Russian and became a teacher of the Halbstadt Musterschule (*q.v.*) connected with the pedagogical classes of the Halbstadt Zentralschule, serving here for five years (1885-90). He then became a minister of the Ohrloff-Halbstadt congregation and was appointed evangelist (*Reiseprediger*) by the Mennonite General Conference (*Bundeskonferenz*). He wrote a biography of his father Bernhard Harder in the volume *Geistliche Lieder und Gelegenheitsgedichte* (Hamburg, 1888).

Gerhard Harder was married to Justina Peters Harder; they had four sons. His son Johannes graduated from the Teachers' Institute at St. Petersburg and taught at the Halbstadt Zentralschule from 1909 until his death during the Revolution. Harder was arrested in January 1931 together with Elder A. Klassen, spent several months in jail at Halbstadt, was sentenced to banishment to Siberia but fell ill and died at the Muntau hospital the day before the execution of the sentence. Earnestness and at the same time a great kindliness were outstanding features of his character and work. (Friesen, *Brüderschaft.*)   H.G.

Harder, Gustav (1856-1923), pastor of the Emmaus Mennonite Church (GCM) near Whitewater, Kan., was born March 19, 1856, in Heubuden, West Prussia, the son of Bernhard and Agatha Wiebe Harder, Chorister (*Vorsänger*) of the Heubuden congregation. His mother died when he was five years old. At 16 he was baptized.

When the Mennonites of Prussia were faced with compulsory military service, a number of Heubuden families, including the Harders, emigrated to America, and settled about 15 miles east of Newton. In 1877 the Emmaus congregation was organized and Gustav Harder was chosen as chorister. Seven years later he was ordained as pastor and in 1902 as elder of the congregation. Four years after coming to America, Gustav visited his former home in West Prussia, and met Helene Kroeker to whom he was married on May 20, 1880. They became the parents of two children, Helen and Bernhard.

Gustav Harder had great interest in missions. In 1890 the General Conference elected him on the Foreign Mission Board. Soon thereafter this board chose him as its treasurer, which position he held to his death. Emergency relief greatly interested him and his congregation, especially on behalf of the Mennonites of Russia.

Gustav Harder was also active in the establishment of Bethel College and for many years served as a member of its board of directors. He also served as a member of the board of directors of the Bethel Deaconess Hospital. He never fully recovered from the death of his wife in 1919, and died on June 16, 1923, at the age of 65. Both he and his wife were buried just across the road from his home in the small Harder cemetery. (*ML* II, 254.)   E.G.K.

Harder, Johann (1811-75), a Mennonite elder in the Molotschna, South Russia, was born Sept. 18, 1811, in the Blumstein settlement, Halbstadt district, and died on Sept. 10, 1875. He was ordained as minister of the Ohrloff-Halbstadt congregation in 1855 and as elder in 1860 to replace Bernhard Fast (*q.v.*), who had retired. He was characterized by great talents, gentleness, and kindness. The beginning of his service coincided with the rise of the Mennonite Brethren. In their struggle for recognition he was conciliatory, and to him belongs the credit for the peaceful outcome of the separation. Many of his letters regarding this matter were published in the *Mennonitische Blätter* (February 1863, pp. 13-16), by Isaak, P. M. Friesen, and others. Some of his unpublished letters have been preserved in America. He served as elder for 15 years, and died at the age of 64 with the affectionate regard of both the Mennonite Church and the Mennonite Brethren.   D.H.E.

Friesen, *Brüderschaft*, 195, 198, 200, 212-14; Fr. Isaak, *Die Molotschnaer Mennoniten* (Halbstadt, 1908); *ML* II, 254 f.

Harder, Johann J. (1836-1930), Mennonite Brethren pioneer minister, the son of Johann Harder (1811-75), was born in Blumstein, Molotschna, Russia, on Aug. 20, 1836, attended the local school, and was for one year a pupil of the well-known Bernhard Harder (his father's uncle). On Nov. 16, 1858, he married Elisabeth Fast, daughter of Johann Fast. After having taught the Friedensruhe school for three years he taught the Schönau school for another four years.

In 1865 Johann Harder joined other landless pioneers who moved to the Crimea. In 1869 he and his wife and 17 others were rebaptized by Jacob A. Wiebe and thus became members of the newly organized Krimmer Mennonite Brethren Church. The correspondence between him and his father, a leading minister of the Molotschna Mennonite Church during this time, gives valuable insight into the spiritual atmosphere and struggle of that time. In 1871 Harder was elected to the ministry and assisted Jacob A. Wiebe in the organization of the church. Having had more education than Wiebe he played a major role in the early years of the group. In 1874 he emigrated to America, settling first in the Gnadenau village near Hillsboro, Kan. In 1900 he returned to Russia for a visit. He died Feb. 23, 1930. He was the father of David E. Harder (*q.v.*). M.S.H.

Harder, Karl (1820-98), a Mennonite preacher in Prussia, was born in Königsberg, and died on March 4, 1898, at Elbing. He was by trade a lithographer, but wanted to study theology. His wish was fulfilled with the support of Hermann Warkentin (*q.v.*) of Königsberg and a financial grant of the Danzig Mennonite Church. He studied at the universities of Danzig and Halle.

In 1845 Harder returned to his home. A number of members of the Elbing congregation wanted him to become their pastor, but he accepted a call to Königsberg. Thereupon about 24 families of the Elbing-Ellerwald congregation built a small church and joined the Königsberg congregation. In 1857 Harder went to Neuwied on the Rhine, and for 12 years served here as pastor and kept the scattered Mennonite congregation intact. He was also the tutor of Prince Hermann of Wied, and thus became the teacher of the highly gifted Elizabeth, who later was Queen of Rumania, and who became famous as a poet under the *nom de plume* of Carmen Sylva. Until her death she corresponded with Harder. In 1868 Harder was called as pastor to Elbing, and served here for 30 years, taking an active part in the life of the city. He established and presided over a trade school for girls. For his services to city and state he was honored with the Order of the Red Eagle. In 1846-48 he published *Monatsschrift für die evangelischen Mennoniten.* Harder was also the author of the following works: *Das Leben Menno Symons* (Königsberg, 1846); *Predigten* (10) (Neuwied, 1859); *Blätter für Religion und Erziehung* (3 vv. 1869-71); *Die Christliche Religion* (Elbing, 1896); *Kurzgefasste Geschichte der Elbinger Mennonitengemeinde* (Elbing, 1883); and posthumously, *Das Leben—Ein Gebet, Für meine lieben Kinder und Freunde*

(*Rauschen in den Sommerferien* 1891 and 1892). Harder also frequently wrote articles for the *Menn. Blätter* (1858, p. 60; 1888, pp. 2, 70, 117; 1890, p. 51; 1892, pp. 3, 18; 1893, p. 15; 1896, p. 51; 1898, p. 25), admonishing warmly to unity in love and peace. NEFF.

A. Siebert, *Rede zur Einweihung des Denkmals für Karl Harder* (Neuwied, 1899); Ernst Crous, *Karl und Ernst Harder* (Elbing, 1927); *DB* 1868, 136; 1885, 10 f.; 1886, 9, 21, 49, 51, 53, 55; *ML* II, 255.

Harder, Kornelius, a leading minister of the Nikolaifeld Mennonite Church in the province of Stavropol, Caucasus, Russia, from 1897. He was also a member of the local Mennonite school board. (Friesen, *Brüderschaft,* 717.) C.K.

Harder, Peter B., a Mennonite educator and writer, was born July 15, 1868, at Halbstadt, Molotschna, Taurida, Russia, a son of Bernhard Harder, prominent minister, teacher, and poet. P. B. Harder was a schoolteacher for 36 years and wrote a German grammar which was used in most Mennonite schools in Russia. Of his literary works the best known are the novel *Die lutherische Cousine,* and *Lose Blätter,* a collection of short stories and poems in which Harder with great ability and power of observation portrays Mennonite life in Russia in his time. The latter appeared in *Aufwärts* (*q.v.*). A larger work, also about Mennonite life, ready in manuscript, could not be published because of the outbreak of World War I. Peter B. Harder selected and edited 213 of the songs written by his father Bernhard Harder, which were published by J. Friesen in 1902 with the title *Kleines Liederbuch. Geistliche Gelegenheitslieder.* Because of his small salary and large family Harder through all his life had to battle against poverty and died of starvation on Sept. 15, 1923, in the province of Ufa in northern Russia, where he was teaching school. H.G.

J. H. Janzen, "The Literature of the Russo-Canadian Mennonites," *Menn. Life,* January 1946, 22 f.; *Aufwärts* (ed. K. G. Neufeld); H. Görz, *Die Molotschnaer Ansiedlung* (Steinbach, 1951) 167; *ML* II, 255.

Harderwijk, a town (1947 pop. 11,124, with 15 Mennonites) in the Dutch province of Gelderland, was once the seat of a small Flemish Mennonite congregation. In 1649 the congregation sent no representative to the Flemish conference at Haarlem; it is thought to have had no ministers at that time. Apparently it died out soon after. Of its history nothing is known. About 1540 there were some slight traces of Anabaptism in this town. vDZ.

C. Hille Ris Lambers, *De Kerkhervorming op de Veluwe* (Barneveld, n.d., 1890) 23, 36, 75, CIX, CXII-CXVII.

Haren, near Groningen city, Dutch province of Groningen, the seat of a Mennonite fellowship (*kring*) of members of the Groningen congregation. A first meeting was held here in 1923; an occasional service was held in 1936; a ladies' circle was founded in December 1936. Since April 11, 1937, services have been regularly held in a building belonging to the Liberal Reformed Church. At first services were conducted by Pastor Knipscheer of

Groningen. In 1939 the church board of Groningen appointed a minister specifically for the care of its members living at Haren: J. Meerburg Snarenberg 1939-40, J. S. Postma 1940-42, A. H. van Drooge 1946-51, and since 1951 Miss C. E. Offerhaus. When the group was founded in 1937 its membership numbered 97; it is now (1954) 102.   vdZ.

Harich, a village in the Dutch province of Friesland, where Leenaert Bouwens (*q.v.*) in 1563-65 baptized 13 persons. A congregation was not found here. Those baptized by Bouwens may have joined the Balk (*q.v.*) congregation.   vdZ.

Haring (Haaring, Haaringh), a Mennonite family name found at Zaandam, Dutch province of North Holland. In the 17th and 18th centuries the Harings were shipbuilders at Zaandam. Jooris Dirksz Haaringh, d. May 19, 1729, was a preacher of the Frisian congregation (*Oude Huijs*). Other members served as deacons.   vdZ.

S. Lootsma, *Het Nieuwe Huijs* (Zaandam, 1937) 47, 190, 193.

Häring(in), Christina, an Anabaptist martyr, a member of a "zealous" Anabaptist family, for her brothers Christian and Thomas had a good reputation in the Moravian brotherhoods. Of Christina the *Geschichts-Bücher* state that she was seized and put in chains at Kitzbühel. She remained steadfast. Because she was pregnant she was permitted to go home until her confinement. Though she could have escaped during this period, she remained. When she was returned to Kitzbühel she still persisted in her faith, and was therefore beheaded, "Which is unusual for a woman," as the chronicles remark. Her corpse was burned. Her brothers escaped to Moravia. Christian, who is mentioned in the chronicles in connection with the martyrdom of Thomas Herrmann (*q.v.*), was made deacon in 1552 (not 1550) and Thomas in 1568 (not 1567); the latter was also a preacher after 1572, and died in 1593 at Altenmarkt near Lundenburg, after he had been a "brother" for 53 years.   Loserth.

Beck, *Geschichts-Bücher*, 107 f., 198, 253, 260, 297, 319; J. Loserth, *Der Anabaptismus in Tirol* (Vienna, 1882) 509; Zieglschmid, *Chronik; Mart. Mir.* D 34, E 441; *ML* II, 255 f.

Harleysville, a town situated in Lower Salford Twp., Montgomery Co., Pa., on Route 63 at the intersection with State Route 113, pop. 900, named after Samuel Harley who built a tavern here in 1790 and is regarded as the founder of the town. It is surrounded by a Mennonite rural community; within shopping distance there are six Mennonite churches: Salford (MC) with 425 members, Franconia (MC) with 845 members, and Towamencin (MC) with 223 members, Eden Mennonite Church (GCM) with 275 members, a Mennonite Brethren in Christ church with 59 members, and the Calvary Mennonite Church (independent) with 158 members. Mennonites have lived in this area for two hundred years. Christopher Dock (*q.v.*), the pioneer Mennonite schoolmaster, bought a farm a few miles from this place from the sons of William Penn in 1734. The farm is owned today (1953) by

Elmer Wolford, Salfordville, Pa. A white oak, labeled the "Dock Oak," is still standing on this property.   J.C.C.

Harleysville (Pa.) Mennonite Brethren in Christ Church had a membership of 59 in 1953, with Ernest B. Hartman serving as pastor.

Harlingen, a seaport (1947 pop. 10,865, with 562 Mennonites) in the Dutch province of Friesland, in which there have been Mennonites from early times. Though the origin of the congregation is unknown, there was a congregation here at the time of Menno Simons, who visited this congregation in 1556, while Leenaert Bouwens (*q.v.*) baptized a considerable number of persons here (80 in 1551-54; 40 in 1554-56; 88-90 in 1557-61; 648 in 1563-65; 324 in 1568-82, making a total of 1180-82). Leenaert Bouwens lived about 15 years in the neighborhood of Harlingen. By this influx of members the Harlingen congregation, at the same time largely increased by the emigration of Mennonites from Flanders, was the largest in Friesland. In 1566 there were about 450 male members, and about 1680 it is said that more than one fourth of all the citizens of Harlingen were Mennonites.

In the meanwhile the Harlingen congregation had been divided into a number of branches, as had occurred in all the Dutch congregations in this period. With Franeker the Harlingen congregation played an important role in the Flemish-Frisian schism of 1566-67, and numerous meetings, at which the congregations in Flanders and North Holland were also represented, were held in Harlingen.

By the close of the 16th century there were found here at least six separate congregations: (1) Waterlanders, mostly called "de Keetsche Gemeynte," after their meetinghouse, which was a *keet* (former salt barrack), dedicated June 17, 1632, by Idzart van Hettinga, preacher of this congregation, of which Yeme Jacobsz de Ringh (*q.v.*) was an elder; (2) Frisians; (3) Flemish; (4) High Germans, often called "Blaauwe Schuur Gemeente" (after their meetinghouse "the blue barn," built in 1614 and enlarged in 1641); (5) Huiskopers; (6) Jan Jacobsgezinden. As early as 1603 a number of High Germans (4) united with the Waterlanders (1). In 1610 the Flemish (3) formed a union (*Harlinger Vrede, q.v.*) with the Frisians (2). The High Germans (4) (those who had not united with the Waterlanders) merged with the Flemish (3) in February 1643. About this time, or perhaps one or two decades before, a number of conservative members in the Flemish congregation had organized as a separate church, calling themselves (7) Old Flemish and were usually called Ukowallists. Soon after, the Huiskopers (5) merged with the Old Flemish (7). When the High Germans had united with the Flemish in 1643 the meetinghouses of both former groups were in use until the former Flemish church was sold in 1677. This united congregation was a rather large one. Its deacon was Claes Huyberts, who in 1672 presented to the government of Friesland an amount of 500,000 guilders, raised by a collection taken in all the Mennonite congregations of Friesland and loaned to the government for the building of warships. In this year the Waterlanders (1) united with the Flemish-Frisian-High German congregation; both meetinghouses, the "Blaauwe Schuur" and the "Keet," were used until in 1695 the latter was put out of use, causing some dissension in the congregation. This congregation also possessed an orphanage and a house for the poor, which in 1688 were granted freedom from taxation.

About 1700 there were still in Harlingen—(a) the United Church (1, 2, 3, 4), (b) Old Flemish (5 and 7), (c) Jan Jacobsz group (6), (d) "Jan Tammes-volk" (followers of Jan Tammes), which was a splinter of the Jan Jacobsz group (6), and of which Jan Jansen Blauw became a preacher in 1708; nothing further is known about it; (e) "Het Kleine Hoopke," a small group of conservative Mennonites separated about 1696 from the United Church (a), of which Douwe Feddriks (q.v.) was the preacher. In the Jan Jacobsz group (6) Lieuwe Willems Graaf (q.v.) and Lambert Klaesz Aker were preachers. Aker served until his death in 1690. It is not known when this congregation died out, but since it is not found in the first *Naamlijst* of 1731, it was by that time at least no longer in existence.

The Old Flemish congregation (b), which in the 18th century was often called the congregation "in de Nieuwe Kerk" (in the new meetinghouse), was until its end served by untrained and unsalaried ministers. It was very conservative and never joined a conference. It died out about 1796.

The United congregation (in the 18th century usually called the congregation "van de Oude Kerk," i.e., of the Old Meetinghouse) was among the first to promote the Mennonite Conference of Friesland in 1695. Gillis Vermeersch of Harlingen was its first treasurer from 1696 until his death in 1721. Three following treasurers were also members of Harlingen: Simon Johannes Stinstra 1722-39, Robijn Arjensz 1749-70, and Claas Fontein 1771-87. The congregation seems to have been rather liberal even in this period. A Remonstrant (q.v.) minister was admitted to the pulpit as early as 1705. Incidentally we are informed that under the influence of Collegiantism (q.v.) baptism was several times performed by immersion. The old meetinghouse, "de Blaauwe Schuur," was replaced by a larger one in 1706, which was used until 1857 and then replaced by the present meetinghouse, dedicated Sept. 17, 1858, by P. Cool.

During the first decades of the 18th century the congregation contributed liberally for the Fund of Foreign Needs and in 1711, 21 Mennonite Swiss refugees were provided with shelter and even farm land.

Among the Mennonite families of Harlingen we find since the 17th-18th century in the records the following names: Boomsma, Braam, Dreyer, Fontein, Hannema, Hingst, Huidekoper, Menalda, Oosterbaan, Stijl, Stinstra.

The membership of the United Church, which numbered about 560 in 1695, decreased in the 18th

century. In 1838 it numbered 272; in the 19th century it increased again, 1861, 437; 1900, 556. Then in the 20th century, paralleling the decline of Harlingen as an import and export center, the membership declined to 324 in 1930, rising by 1954 to 375. Often it was served by prominent preachers: Reiner Clasen Fontein (1655-1727), a merchant, served from 1694(?) until his death; Joannes Stinstra (q.v.) 1737-85, who was suspended by the government of Friesland 1742-57 on charges of Socinianism (q.v.); Jan Boelaart 1744-56; Cornelis van Engelen (q.v.) 1748-58; Jan Franken 1756-63; Nicolaas Klopper 1764-86; Heere Oosterbaan, formerly professor of the Amsterdam Mennonite Seminary, from 1786 until his death in 1807; Matthijs van Geuns 1787-92; Freerk Hoekstra 1792-1836; Pieter Cool 1836-72; J. Boetje 1872-84; J. W. van der Linden 1884-1912; E. Engelkes HGzn 1918 until his death in 1929; A. L. Broer 1929-38; J. P. H. Grootes 1939 until his death in 1945, and H. H. Gaaikema from 1946 to the present (1954). There is now a ladies' circle, youth group, Bible circle, and Sunday school for children. A large part of the membership lives in the villages outside Harlingen.

The archives of the congregation contain records (membership, resolutions, etc.) from 1632 and a large number (about 400) of separate documents. vdZ.

Blaupot t. C., *Friesland, passim;* see Index; *Inv. Arch. Amst.* I, Nos. 522, 523, 539, 557, 558V, 1180, 1216, 1871 f., 1881; II, Nos. 1523, 1890-1904; *DB* 1861, 135; 1877, 115-32; 1878, 78-97; 1880, 1-41; 1893, 1-90 *passim;* 1909, 147; J. Loosjes, *Jan Jacobsz en de Jan-Jacobsgezinden,* in *Nederl. Archief v. Kerkgesch.* XI (1914) 3, pp. 229-31; P. Cool, *De stichting der nieuwe Doopsgezinde kerk te Harlingen. Redenen en geschiedkundige mededeelingen daartoe betrekkelijk* (Harlingen, 1858); *ML* II, 256.

Harlingen liederen (Harlingen hymns), six hymns from the old Haarlem Mennonite songbook, revised by P. Cool (q.v.) and his Reformed colleague M. A. Jentink, and printed at Amsterdam in 1856. These hymns were formerly used in Harlingen and some other congregations. (*DB* 1865, 74-76.) vdZ.

Harlinger Vraagenboek, thus is usually called the Dutch Mennonite catechism *Vraagen over den Godsdienst tot onderwijs der jeugd, Geschikt door de Leeraaren der Christelijke Doopsgezinde Gemeente te Harlingen.* It was published at Harlingen in 1751, reprinted at Haarlem and Amsterdam in 1776. This catechism, to which Joannes Stinstra (q.v.), minister at Harlingen 1733-85, was the prominent contributor, contains in its first edition on 214 pages 931 questions. It is written in a moderate and somewhat rationalistic tone, and influenced by the practical philosophy of English philosophers like Clarke (q.v.) and Tillotson. Chr. Sepp in his biography of Stinstra is of the opinion that the *Harlinger Vraagenboek* depreciates "the dogma of God's mercy in Christ as the source of new life." This catechism was much used in Dutch congregations, often even until 1860. vdZ.

C. Sepp, *Joannes Stinstra en zijn tijd* II (Amsterdam, 1865) 267; *DB* 1867, 94; 1868, 76, 107, 109.

Harlinger Vrede (Peace of Harlingen). On Oct. 25, 1607, the Flemish congregation of Harlingen (*q.v.*), Dutch province of Friesland, wrote a letter to a number of other Flemish congregations which had elders, saying that they, like the Frisian Mennonites in their town (see **Bekommerde Friezen**), believed that the division of 1567 between the Flemish and the Frisians was wrong and regrettable and that peace should be made between the two groups. The answers made by the Flemish elders to this letter are not known, but in Harlingen peace was concluded in 1610, and the Flemish and Frisian congregations united. A number of Flemish elders, like Pieter Jansen Mooyer at Amsterdam and Claes Claesz of Blokzijl, welcomed the union, but others, especially Jan Luies (*q.v.*) and a number of congregations in the Dutch province of Groningen and elsewhere, condemned this "false peace" and even banned those who favored the union. For two decades the Flemish congregations in the Netherlands were stirred up by the *Harlinger Vrede,* which was the precursor of other unions between the divided Mennonites. (*Inv. Arch. Amst.* I, Nos. 522-23, 539, 557, 558V, 560-64, 571; II, Nos. 1232-41, 2310.)   vDZ.

Harman Coenraetsz (Herman van Kelder), a Dutch Anabaptist who was a native of the district of Cleve, Germany, was sentenced to death by the Court of Holland on Jan. 7, 1539, because of being rebaptized. He was executed by beheading at Delft, Dutch province of South Holland, together with ten others. According to his own confession he had practiced polygamy. Obviously he and his companions were followers of David Joris (*q.v.*).   vDZ.

G. Brandt, *Historie der Reformatie* I (2nd ed., Amsterdam, 1677) 134; *Inv. Arch. Amst.* I, 749; *DB* 1899, 158-60; 1917, 115, No. 51, 160-67.

Harman Hoen, a Dutch Anabaptist martyr, a native of Zwolle, baptized by Hans Speck at Deventer in the fall of 1534, was in a revolutionary group of Anabaptists in the province of Groningen in April 1535 and shortly after in Amsterdam, where he was arrested in May 1535 after the Anabaptist attack on the city hall had failed. During his trial Harman confessed that he had been aware of the intended attack but that he had not participated in the revolt. He was executed by beheading on July 28, 1535, at Amsterdam. (Grosheide, *Verhooren,* 125, 134-40; Mellink, *Wederdopers, passim,* see Index.)   vDZ.

Harman Jansz van Sellem, an Anabaptist martyr: see **Herman Jansz.**

Harm(en) Schoe(n)maker, a Dutch Anabaptist, who by his unsound bigoted fanaticism (he called himself the Messiah and even God the Father) caused a tumult at 't Zandt, Dutch province of Groningen, in January 1535. On the farm called "De Arke," owned by Eppe Pietersz, a wealthy farmer, a large crowd gathered, over 300 of whom were baptized in one night by Schoenmaker, assisted by Cornelis int Kershof (*q.v.*). Schoenmaker was arrested and put in prison in Gro-

ningen, where he soon died insane. He clearly took the Münsterite views and initially considered himself an elect to bear the banner of God from Groningen to Münster; i.e., to be the leader of the revolutionary Anabaptists of the Groningen region to the New Zion, which Jan van Leiden had erected in Münster.   vDZ.

P. G. Bos, "De Groningsche Wederdooperswoelingen," in *Ned. Archief. v. Kerkgesch.* (N. S. VI, 1909); Kühler, *Geschiedenis* I, 145-48; Mellink, *Wederdopers,* 66 f., 74, 257-60.

Harmen de Verwer (House painter), an Anabaptist martyr, found in van Braght (*Mart. Mir.* D 552, E 885); this "Verwer" is an error of van Braght; from the documents it has become evident that he was not a painter, but a weaver. (See **Harmen de Wever.**)   vDZ.

Harmen de Wever (*Harmen de Verwer,* i.e., the Dyer, in van Braght's *Martyrs' Mirror* and *Harmen der Färber* in *ML* II, 256), an Anabaptist martyr, a weaver by trade, of Deventer, Dutch province of Overijssel, was burned there between May 24 and June 16, 1571. On March 11, 1571, he was arrested together with 11 other members of the congregation by the Spanish soldiers of Alba (*q.v.*). When in prison he at first recanted, scandalizing his fellow prisoners by his dice-playing, but soon he regretted his apostasy and finished his earthly life by suffering bravely and steadfastly. On the scaffold he was gagged in order to prevent his speaking to the crowd. (*Mart. Mir.* D 552 ff., E 885; *DB* 1919, 29 ff.; *ML* II, 256.)   vDZ.

Harmonia Sacra, a hymnbook published in 1832 by Joseph Funk (*q.v.,* 1778-1862) of Mountain Valley near Harrisonburg, Va. Remembered as "the father of song" in Northern Virginia, Funk was a pioneer leader, teacher, author, translator, and publisher of music. The book originally bore the title, *A Compilation of Genuine Church Music* (Winchester, Va., 1832, pp. 208 long octavo), but was renamed *Harmonia Sacra* in the 5th edition (Mountain Valley, 1851) with the first title continued as subtitle. This music textbook, now in the 21st edition (Harrisonburg, 1952), has reached a total issue of approximately 85,000 copies.

Designed for use in singing schools, the book contained a variety of meters, all harmonized for three voices (four since the 11th or 12th ed.) together with "a copious elucidation of the science of vocal music." Four syllables, *faw, sol, law, mi* (the master note), seven since the 1851 printing, were used. As an aid to reading the notes in the various keys the compiler invented "patent" or character notes, a different shape for each syllable, which with slight modifications persist in a number of modern hymnals.

In addition to the theoretical part, the book is composed almost entirely of hymns and anthems, a considerable portion of which is of very high quality. Many of the songs look at the Christian life as a pilgrimage and in joyful mood anticipate heaven.

In 1847 a hymnal adapted for church use was compiled from selections drawn from the book and published under the title *Psalms, Hymns, and Spiritual Songs*. This new book was used widely in Mennonite churches and became a source from which in 1902 the *Church and Sunday School Hymnal* was compiled. The Old Folks' Singing movement, originating in 1902 and held annually on New Year's Day at Weavers Mennonite Church near Harrisonburg, Va., together with similar singings held elsewhere, has kept alive the spirit and vision of the *Harmonia Sacra*. C.K.L.

Harms (Harm, Harmssen, Harmsen) is a Dutch-Prussian Mennonite family name which is still common in the Netherlands as a given name (Harm). The name occurred in the Mennonite congregations of Danzig, Elbing, Thiensdorf, Orlofferfelde, Tragheimerweide, Montau-Gruppe, and Deutsch-Kazun. From these congregations the name was transplanted to Russia, United States, Canada, and South America. Outstanding representatives are G. N. Harms (*q.v.*), elder of the Gnadenberg Mennonite Church; J. F. Harms (*q.v.*), educator and editor, Hillsboro, Kan.; Orlando Harms, editor and manager of the M.B. Publishing House, Hillsboro, Kan. *Who's Who Among the Mennonites* (1943) lists A. J. Harms, minister; E. M. Harms, M.D.; Ervin F. Harms, minister; F. L. Harms, M.D.; H. H. Harms; J. H. Harms, M.D. C.K.

Harms, John F. (1855-1945), educator, editor, and minister of the Mennonite Brethren Church, was the only son of Jacob and Anna Foth Harms. He was born at Kleefeld, Molotschna Mennonite settlement, South Russia, April 29, 1855. After his elementary education he attended a school in Steinbach for two years and the Zentralschule at Halbstadt for one year to prepare for the teaching profession. He taught school in the village of Lichtfelde, 1873-78. In the fall of 1873 he married Marie Isaak. To them two children were born, but in the spring of 1876 both the children as well as his wife died. In the fall of 1876 he married Margaret Isaak. To them five children were born.

In the summer of 1878 the family emigrated to America, locating at Mountain Lake, Minn., where they lived two years. In 1880 Harms went to Elkhart, Ind., where he assisted John F. Funk in his printing establishment. At this time the *Mennonitische Rundschau* began to be published, and Harms became its editor for six years. For two years he attended an Evangelical college at Naperville, Ill.

In 1884 Harms moved to Canada, Kan., joined the M.B. Church west of Marion, and began to publish the *Zionsbote*, which soon became the official organ of the M.B. Church. He also conducted a Bible school in his own home for some time. Shortly after this he established his own printing house at Hillsboro, Kan., where he continued his publication work.

Having been used extensively for preaching, Harms was ordained to the ministry in 1896. During the winter 1897 to 1898 Harms made a trip to Europe with his wife, and visited many congregations in Russia and Poland. Upon their return they settled at Medford, Okla., where Harms continued the publication of the *Zionsbote* until 1906, when it was given over to the M.B. Conference.

Harms was one of the most noted M.B. Conference workers for many years, serving as its general secretary as well as member of its Foreign Mission Committee. The cause of education in the conference found in him one of its strongest advocates.

Because of his wife's ill health the Harms family moved to Canada in 1906, and after living in Edmonton, Alberta, two years, settled in the vicinity of Herbert, Sask. Here Harms earned his living by farming and taught Bible classes during the winter months. He was one of the founders of the Herbert Bible School and one of its first teachers. In 1918 the family lived in Seattle, Wash. After that they made their home in Reedley, Cal., until the spring of 1921, when they returned to Hillsboro, where his wife died a few weeks after their arrival. On Nov. 27 of the same year he married Mrs. Adelgunda Jost Prieb. She preceded him in death in 1935.

At Hillsboro Harms again entered publication work, assuming the position of assistant editor of the *Zionsbote*. He also contributed many articles to the Hillsboro *Vorwärts*. His most valuable writing is the *Geschichte der Mennoniten Brüdergemeinde, 1860-1924*, a work of 342 pages. In 1943 he published *Eine Lebensreise*, an autobiographical discourse on his early life. After World War I he took a very prominent part in gathering support for the relief work for the suffering Mennonites in Russia. He died at Hillsboro, Jan. 7, 1945, and was buried at the local M.B. cemetery. (*Hillsboro Journal*, Jan. 11, 1945; *ML* II, 256.)† J.H.L.

Harms, Peter, a Mennonite preacher in the Tilsit lowlands, then Lithuania, (*q.v.*), wrote a letter to the Amsterdam Committee of Foreign Needs on Jan. 28, 1724, giving important information concerning the persecution of the Mennonites in this district by Frederick William I of Prussia, which led to their expulsion. (*Inv. Arch. Amst.* II, 2, No. 715.) vDZ.

Harnish Mennonite Church (MC), now extinct, was a preaching station of the Lancaster Mennonite Conference near New Bloomfield, Perry Co., Pa., in 1881, taken care of by William Auker who lived in Pfoutz Valley and Juniata brethren. In 1861 Christian Harnish with a large family joined the earlier families of Forrey, Miller, and Ayles. They converted a dwelling into a meetinghouse where services were held for some decades. I.D.L.

Harp, Maerten (1650-1736), physician-preacher of the Mennonite congregation at Zaandam-West and Den Ilp (Waterlander congregation) in the Dutch province of North Holland. He is the author of *Lijk- en Pligtpredikatie over Gerrit Dirksz* (Amsterdam, 1701), and *Troost in droefheit wegens de sterfte van het Runtvee en reden van blydschap voor lievelingen Gods wegens de geslootene vreede met de koningen van Vrankrijk en Spanje* (Amsterdam, 1717). (*Biogr. Wb.* III, 530 f.; *ML* II, 257.) vDZ.

Harpe, De, *of des Herten Snarenspel,* a Dutch Mennonite hymnbook, published in 1609 by Gillis Rooman at Haarlem, contains 136 hymns without notes. There was a reprint (Rotterdam, n.d.).

Harper (Kan.) United Missionary Church had a membership of 35 in 1949, with C. A. and Mrs. Neil serving as pastors.

Harper County, Kan., is located in the south central part adjoining the Oklahoma line. It was organized in 1873, but its organization did not become legal until 1878. The county seat is Anthony. Being in the bread basket of the world, it ranks thirteenth in the value of wheat produced among Kansas counties. It is also adapted to diversified farming. Several nationally known dairy herds are found in the county.

Harper County is the home of three Mennonite congregations. Pleasant Valley (MC) was organized in Pilot Knob Township in 1888. The Crystal Springs (Amish Mennonite) congregation was organized in Lake Township in 1904. The Mennonite Brethren in Christ (UMC) congregation in Harper Township was organized about 1890. The total membership of the three congregations is 339 (1953).

The chief trading centers of Harper County are Danville, Harper, Anthony, Crystal Springs, and Attica. Mennonites trade at all of these centers.

G.G.Y.

Gideon G. Yoder, "The Crystal Springs, Kansas, Community," *Menn. Community,* June 1948.

Harriett United Missionary Church, located near Hillsboro, Marshall Co., Ohio, was organized in 1900. The church building, erected in 1903, has a seating capacity of 125. In 1954 the membership was 20, with L. Sydenstricker serving as pastor.

F.A.H.

Harrisburg (Pa.) Civilian Public Service Unit No. 93 at the Harrisburg State Hospital was opened in April 1943 and was closed in August 1946. During its existence, 69 men were assigned to the mental hospital unit. In 1944-45 a Christian Workers' School was conducted in the unit. The *Anniversary Review—Mental Hygiene Number* (May 1945) gave a history of the unit.

M.G.

M. Gingerich, *Service for Peace* (Akron, Pa., 1949).

Harrisburg Conservative Amish Mennonite Church, located 2½ miles northeast of Harrisburg, Linn Co., Ore., unaffiliated, was organized in August 1911 with nine families, under the leadership of Daniel J. Kropf and Peter Neuschwander, who served as the first pastor and deacon. The present membership (1955) is 110, consisting of rural people. The first meetinghouse, built in 1915 and enlarged in 1935, was destroyed by fire in 1944. A new church with a seating capacity of 300 was dedicated on Nov. 22, 1945.

Bishops who have served the church are Daniel J. Kropf, Joseph C. Hostetler, and John P. Yoder; ministers Enos Hostetler, Joseph Schrock, Jacob Roth, Levi D. Kropf, Jacob S. Roth, and Noah D.

Miller; deacons Peter Neuschwander, Joseph C. Hostetler, John P. Yoder, and Ira J. Headings. The present (1953) bishop is John P. Yoder and the minister Levi D. Kropf. At one time there were 14 deaf members in the congregation, but at present there are only seven members who use the sign language; they participate in the worship services through an interpreter. During World War I, because of its nonresistant faith, the church was locked up and also damaged. During World War II the church was destroyed by fire for the same reason. Activities of the church include preaching services, Sunday school, young people's Bible meetings, midweek prayer service and Bible study, summer Bible schools, mission Sunday schools, and a sewing circle.

F.D.K.

Harrisburg (Pa.) Mennonite Brethren in Christ Church had a membership of 108 in 1955, with N. H. Wolf serving as pastor.

Harrison (Mich.) Church of God in Christ Mennonite Church was organized in 1912. For a period of years services were held in the Amble School 7½ miles northeast of Harrison, Clare Co., Mich. The 1956 membership was 59. A new church was dedicated in January 1952. Wilbert Koehn is leader of the congregation.

Ch.B.

Harrisonburg, Va., the county seat (pop. 12,000) of Rockingham County, is located in the heart of the Shenandoah Valley. In 1880 Harrisonburg was made a town by act of the Assembly on 50 acres of the Thomas Harrison Plantation. By 1916 the town had grown to such an extent that it could qualify for a city charter. The city manager form of government was adopted in 1950. The city is supplied with good water from Riven Rock on the foothills of the Shenandoah Mountain west of Harrisonburg. It is a prosperous city with good stores, factories, hospital facilities, and 19 churches, three of which are Mennonite (MC), Chicago Avenue, Broad Street, and Ridgeway. It has two colleges—Madison College, a state college for women, and Eastern Mennonite College, located in a suburban town 1½ miles northwest of the courthouse. Harrisonburg is the shopping center for the largest settlement of Mennonites (MC) in the Valley.

H.A.B.

Harteveldt, P. Z.: see **Zachariasz, Pieter.**

Hartford, a small town in Lyon Co., Kan., located in the northeast corner of Elmendaro Township near the Coffee County line, the site of a former Amish Mennonite congregation. A few Amish settlers located near Hartford about 1880. During the early eighties several Amish Mennonite settlers also arrived. Most of these came from Iowa and Pennsylvania. In 1885 a large part of the congregation in Union Co., Pa., moved near Hartford, and a new congregation was organized with Andrew Miller and David Stoltzfus as ministers. Joseph Schlegel of Nebraska served as bishop of the congregation during the early years. A younger Joseph Schlegel of Hartford was ordained a minister and later a bishop of the congregation. He spent the last years of his life at Hydro, Okla. Because of church dissension and crop failures, the congregation became extinct, the last members leaving about 1910. Hartford was the chief trading center of the Amish and Amish Mennonite settlers.

G.G.Y.

J. S. Umble, "Mennonites in Lyon County, Kansas: 1880-90; A Memoir," *MQR* XXV (July 1952) 232-53.

Hartigveldt, Joan, b. 1616 or 1617 at Rotterdam, Netherlands, d. there Oct. 22, 1678, was descended from a Reformed patrician family, studied law at the University of Leiden, entered a diplomatic career at London and Paris, and was converted shortly after 1645. He then abandoned all posts of honor and retired to a farm near Brielle, province of South Holland, henceforth living soberly and wearing plain black clothes. He gave serious consideration to joining a Christian church, but both the Reformed and the Remonstrants seemed to him to have forsaken the Christian simplicity of life and church ceremonies found among the earliest followers of Christ. He laid much stress upon the claim that in the meeting of Christians everyone was competent to preach the Gospel, not only the ministers appointed to this end. He rejected baptism as an obsolete ceremony. About 1650 he joined the Rijnsburg Collegiants (*q.v.*) and soon became an influential member of the "college" at Rotterdam, which was also attended by a large number of Mennonites, both of the Flemish and the Waterlander congregations. These Mennonites, influenced by Hartigveldt, tried to introduce his ideas in the congregations (free speaking, open communion, baptism by immersion and even joining without baptism). This caused trouble in the Flemish congregation (in 1652) as well as in the Waterlander congregation of Rotterdam (in 1661 and 1672-73). Anonymously Hartigveldt wrote a book, in which he tried to promote a union between the Remonstrants and the Mennonites: *Schriftuerlijke waardeeringe van het hedendaaghse Predicken en Kerckgaan,* . . . (Rotterdam, 1672). He was a man of noble character and rejected government offices, repudiated war, and championed an absolute nonresistance. He was very charitable; he gave away nearly his entire fortune, left to him by his mother, and willed his remaining property to the Collegiant orphanage.

Of some interest to Mennonite history is his book, published posthumously: *De recht weerlooze Christen. Of Verdediging van het gevoelen der eerste Christenen en gemartelde Doopsgezinden; Weegens het Overheyds-ampt, Oorlog en geweldige teegenstand* (Rotterdam, 1678). vDZ.

Biogr. Wb. III, 531-34; J. C. van Slee, *De Rijnsburger Collegianten* (Haarlem, 1895) see Index.

Harting, Dirk, a Dutch Mennonite theologian, b. 1817 at Rotterdam, d. 1892 at Enkhuizen, studied philology and later theology, was the minister of the Enkhuizen congregation 1840-88. From his pen flowed a number of important scholarly works, many of them in the field of the New Testament; in 1848 a treatise on the genuineness of Ephesians (received a prize from the Hague Society), and in 1863 a Greek-Dutch Dictionary of the New Testament. He also participated in the new translation of the Bible instituted by the Dutch Reformed Church. His versatility is shown in numerous articles in periodicals. He was a journalist in the best sense of the word, e.g., one of the founders of the *Enkhuizer Courant* in 1870. He wrote excellent articles on music. He was also familiar with the field of Mennonite history. In 1850 he published *De Munstersche furie of het oproer der Wederdoopers.* In 1861-71 he and P. Cool (*q.v.*) edited the *Doopsgezinde Bijdragen,* in which a number of his articles are found. He also wrote a *Levensbericht* (Leiden, 1870) of his friend G. Vissering (*q.v.*). His services to scholarship are generally acknowledged. He was a member of the Royal Academy of Science, and in 1849 he received an honorary doctor's degree from the university of Utrecht. His service for and influence on elementary education was recognized by his appointment as an honorary member of the Dutch Educational Association. In 1888 he retired. When he died in 1889 the world lost a versatile scholar, a truly "cultured man." He had occupied a position of honor in the Mennonite churches of the 19th century. vDZ.

Winkler-Prins, Levensberichten Mij van Nederl. Letterkunde (1892) 150; *N.N.B.Wb.* III, 544 ff.; *DB* 1901, 21 and 24; *ML* II, 257.

Hartitsch, Dietrich von, captain of the Hungarian city and district of Oedenburg, and provost of Lower Austria. In the Habsburg domains of Austria there was in the 16th century a police officer, the provost, who served as a security and court officer in civil as well as military service. It was the duty of this officer to clear the country of disorderly elements, such as vagrants, retired soldiers, etc. He was also to serve as informer, and to report on the state of roads and bridges. For police duty he was given as many as 50 peasants to assist him. In Styria he had halberdiers at his side. Two horses were assigned to him; as a salary he received the considerable sum of 1,200 guilders, from which he paid also his aides.

At the end of the 1520's the provost had a difficult task in ferreting out and delivering all elements suspected of heresy. In the days of Hut and Hubmaier Dietrich von Hartitsch played an important role as a persecutor of the Anabaptists. The Hutterite *Geschichts-Bücher* say, "In 1528 in the first week of Lent, King Ferdinand sent the provost to Lower Austria. He now and again caused great indignation, sorrow, and persecution. For he put some into prison, and if he seized anyone in the field or on the streets he had him beheaded; those in the villages who would not renounce their faith he hanged on the pillars of the gates. Then many people were moved to go from Austria to Nikolsburg. Many also fled to the mountains with wife and children."

This was the execution of the royal mandate of Feb. 26 and March 20, 1528: "We have sent Dietrich von Hartitsch to eradicate heretical and seductive sects and doctrines, to spy out the ringleaders of the Anabaptists and such persons as have accepted their sect, and to proceed against the ringleaders straightway, without any mercy and without the dignity of law."

This action cost many bloody sacrifices. Many Anabaptists fled over the border of Austria to Moravia, where persecution had ceased for the moment. But in a forest near Lengbach a group of 35 fell into the hands of the provost; 17 of them were killed, the others branded through the cheeks. At other places Hartitsch acted in similar fashion. The above commands of King Ferdinand were followed on April 12 by a directive to the governor of Lower Austria to have a gang of scouts ferret out persons moving away from the places where Hartitsch was in action. At the same time the courts of Lower Austria were shown the characteristics by which the Anabaptists might be recognized.   Loserth.

Beck, *Geschichts-Bücher,* J. Loserth, *Balthasar Hubmaier und die Anfänge der Wiedertaufe in Mähren* (Brünn, 1893); Zieglschmid, *Chronik; ML* II, 257 f.

Hartknoch, Christoph (1644-87), a Prussian historian, professor at the Gymnasium in Thorn, and the author of *Die Preussische Kirchen-Historie* (1686), which is still valid as a collection of source material for the 16th and (especially) the 17th centuries. This is true also for the history of the Prussian Mennonites, who are here treated for the first time, but from a biased, ecclesiastical viewpoint. (*ML* II, 258.)   Neff.

Hartman, an American Mennonite (MC) family appearing first as immigrants from the Palatinate, Germany, 1832-40, and locating (after stops in Lancaster Co., Pa.) in Ashland Co., Ohio (1835 ff.), from where some pushed on to Tazewell Co., Ill. (Peter, who came from Germany in 1837) and to Elkhart Co., Ind., e.g., Adam (1811-94), who left Germany in 1832, came to Ashland County in 1835 and settled in the Yellow Creek (Ind.) area in 1849, and Valentine (d. 1886 in Elkhart Co.), who left Germany in 1837. Peter, of Washington, Ill., was the father of Preacher John Hartman of Ashland County and Bishop Emmanuel Hartman (1849-1912), who served as bishop of the Washington Mennonite Church 1877-97, then transferred to the Apostolic Christian Church (*q.v.,* "New Amish"). The Hartman family was closely associated with the Bally and Beutler families in the emigration from Germany and settlement in Ashland County. Other known Hartman immigrants to Ashland County were Samuel and Henry. The only identification of the exact German origin is that Adam Hartman came from the Kaiserslautern area.

Another Hartman line, that of Harrisonburg, Va., apparently having no connection with the Ashland County line, is that of David Hartman (1812-81), the father of Peter S. Hartman (*q.v.*), whose origin is unknown. He may have come from Lancaster Co., Pa., where a Henry Hartman, a lifelong member of a congregation in East Lampeter Township, died in 1867 at the age of 90. The Virginia Hartmans all descend from him.

The origin of the Hartman name is puzzling,

since it is not found in the earlier Swiss or South German Mennonite records and practically unknown in European Mennonite circles today. In 1936 there was only one Mennonite in Germany bearing the name, a member of the Friedelsheim (Palatinate) congregation. It is possible that the family transferred from a Lutheran background to the Mennonite Church in the Palatinate about 1800 and that the entire family connection emigrated to America.   H.S.B.

J. Umble, "Extinct Ohio Mennonite Churches, Ashland County," *MQR* XIX (1945) 41-58, 215-37.

Hartman, Peter S. (1846-1934), the son of David and Elizabeth Burkholder Hartman, was a successful farmer, businessman, and lay church worker of Harrisonburg, Va. Though he at first opposed the Sunday-school movement, he later became an active leader and teacher in the Sunday school. He was the first solicitor for the Eastern Mennonite College and was one of its founders and ardent supporters. He was an enthusiastic speaker and the talk which appealed most to the students was entitled, "Reminiscences of the Civil War." Students knew him as "Uncle Pete." He served as a member of the General Mission Board for a number of years. He was a strong temperance advocate.   H.A.B.

P. S. Hartman, "Civil War Reminiscences," *MQR* III (July 1929) 203-19; H. A. Brunk, *Life of Peter S. Hartman* (Scottdale, 1937?)

Hartman, Pieter, b. 1736 at Barsingerhorn, d. Feb. 6, 1810, at De Rijp, a lay preacher of the Mennonite congregation of De Rijp (*q.v.*), Dutch province of North Holland, author of the "folk-book" *Hendrik en Anna* (2 vv.), which was awarded the unusual silver medal by the society *Tot Nut van't Algemeen* in 1792. Hartman served as the preacher of the Mennonite congregation of Barsingerhorn-Kolhorn 1773-80 and De Rijp from 1780 until he became blind and resigned in 1805.   vDZ.

DJ 1837, 115 note; *Biogr. Wb.* III, 544; *DB* 1880, 92, 95 and 1917, 61 f., 64; *Naamlijst* 1810, 68; *ML* II, 258.

Hartmann, Heinrich. Neither the Hutterian "Väterlied," which is not sparing in its expressions of praise, nor the *Geschichts-Bücher* have much to say about Heinrich Hartmann, the head of the entire brotherhood in Hungary. On March 17, 1631, he was ordained preacher with two other brethren; he served "about 28 years." The *Geschichts-Bücher* report that after the death of Valentin Winter (*q.v.*), all the preachers and deacons and many other trusted Brethren assembled at Sobotiste and after adequate deliberation unanimously entrusted the leadership to Hartmann on Dec. 3, 1631. The "Väterlied," however, says he was elected by a majority vote rather than a unanimous vote. Great difficulty befell the brotherhood in the following year, when Niagy Michaly Ferencz, part owner of the household at Sobotiste, tried to compel the Brethren to perform gratuitous labor, contrary to the terms of the contract given them. Hartmann was most rudely treated. With two other Brethren he was placed in a dark, stinking, filthy chamber. Even the intercession of the

Palatin benefited them little, for Ferencz openly scoffed at the right of anyone, whether Palatin or even the king, to interfere with the rights granted him by Hungarian law. Hartmann was finally released, of course upon payment of a sum of money. The *Geschichts-Bücher* discuss this incident at great length, in order (they say) that their descendants may see what Hungarian laws can accomplish. Heinrich Hartmann died Sept. 29, 1639. (Beck, *Geschichts-Bücher*, 363, 440 ff.; *ML* II, 258.)

LOSERTH.

Hartog, a Dutch Mennonite family, originally of farmers in the province of North Holland, has produced a number of Mennonite preachers.

The first known is Jacob Hartog Jansz, b. 1656, Mennonite minister of Middelie about 1710-40. His son Jan Jacobsz Hartog (de Jonge), b. at Middelie about 1706, d. at Beemster February 1772, served the congregation of Middelie 1727-47 and then that of Oosthuizen (later called Beemster) from 1747 until his death in 1772. Klaas Hartog, who was a preacher of Middelie 1720-ca. 70, may have been his brother. Another Jan Jacobsz Hartog was serving at Middelie 1727 until he resigned about 1780. He died in 1783. A son of Jan Hartog de Jonge was Jacob Hartog, b. April 17, 1734, at Middelie, d. Dec. 9, 1808, at Beemster, who served the congregation of Oosthuizen (Beemster) 1764-93. In 1795 he was a representative of the Dutch National Assembly; this fact caused some trouble in his congregation. As a preacher he was assisted and followed by his son Jan Hartog, b. Feb. 3, 1772, at Beemster, d. there April 16, 1840. The Amsterdam Mennonite library (*Inv. Arch. Amst.* II, 2, No. 20) possesses a manuscript by this Jan Hartog, containing historical particulars concerning the congregation of Beemster and Oosthuizen. These preachers were all farmers and not specially trained for the ministry. Another Jan Hartog was a (also untrained) preacher of the Frisian congregation of Wormerveer 1745-ca. 60. Jacob Hartog Jansz (1803-94), a son of Jan Hartog (1772-1840) of Beemster, was a preacher at Westzaan op het Noord 1828-70. His son was Jan Hartog (*q.v.*), the first trained minister from this family. A son of this Jan Hartog, Marc Leonard Hartog, b. March 9, 1862, at Westzaan, d. Dec. 30, 1929, at Oosterbeek, studied at the University and the Mennonite Seminary of Amsterdam and served the congregation of Noordhorn 1889-91 and Joure 1891-1928. (See various issues of *Naamlijst*.) vDZ.

Hartog, Jan, b. 1829 at Westzaan, Dutch province of North Holland, d. 1909, became a minister of the Mennonite congregation at Joure in 1853, Zaandam-Oost in 1859, Utrecht in 1861, retired in 1899. He was a popular preacher of the conservative wing of Mennonites and had made extensive studies in the history of preaching, the results of which he published in *Geschiedenis van de predikkunde en van de evangelieprediking in de Protestantsche kerk van Nederland* (1861). A revised edition appeared in 1887 with the title *Geschiedenis van de Predikkunde*. It is an excellent work. Aside

from his own views he gave a clear picture of the development of preaching and its position in the Protestant Church in the past and present.

Of his innumerable other articles in periodicals, and especially his historical writings dealing chiefly with the 18th century, these should be mentioned: *De spectatoriale geschriften uit tweede helft der achttiende eeuw* (Utrecht, 1872, 2d ed., 1890), and *De Patriotten en Oranje van 1647-1787* (Amsterdam, 1882). His knowledge of the "Patriot" period was very wide and intensive. He was a man of industrious and especially critical scholarly work. The theological school of the University of Utrecht awarded him an honorary degree in 1878.

On Mennonite history Hartog published the following booklets and papers: *Levensbericht van Jacob Honig Jzn Jr* (Leiden, 1871); *Menno Simons, persoon en werk* (Utrecht, 1892); "Uit de Broederschap der Doopsgezinden," in *Geloof en Vrijheid* XXX, No. 12 (Rotterdam, 1896); and in *Doopsgezinde Bijdragen* he published "Iets van de publieke opinie over de Doopsgezinden in het midden der 18de eeuw" (1867), "Uit de aanteekeningen van Joannes Cuperus" (1868), "De laatste resolutie van den magistraat te Deventer tegen de Doopsgezinden in die stad" (1870), and "De ergernissen van Antje Dirks" (1872). vDZ.

J. Craandijk, *Levensberichten Mij van Nederl. Letterkunde*, 1904 f., 54 ff.; *Biogr. Wb.* III, 544-47; *N.N.B.Wb.* IV, 712 ff.; *DB* 1901, 36; *ML* II, 258.

Hartsen, a former Mennonite family in Holland. According to a family tradition they came originally from French Flanders and in the 16th century were living at Antwerp, Belgium, where Jacob Hartsen was a burgomaster about 1530. From Antwerp the Hartsen family, according to the tradition, moved to Haarlem, Holland, because of religious persecution. But this tradition is not very exact. As the ancestor of this family we may consider Jacob Hertzen (Hartsen) of Goch, who was a Mennonite, and who moved about 1600 from Goch to Haarlem, where he was married to Antoinette Anselmi, a Mennonite refugee from Antwerp and a relative of Joost van den Vondel (*q.v.*). Their son Anselmus Hartsen moved from Haarlem to Amsterdam and was employed by the cloth merchant and well-known Mennonite preacher Cornelis Claesz Anslo (*q.v.*) and was married to his daughter Maria. Their children and grandchildren were merchants and came to great prosperity. A number of them served the Amsterdam Lamist congregation and after 1801 the United congregation as deacons, among whom were Anthony Hartsen, b. 1719 at Amsterdam, d. there 1784, who besides being a merchant and a deacon was also a poet. One of his poems, "Aen onze Doopsgezinde Gemeente, ter nagedachtenis van onzen leeraar Klaas de Vries . . . ," is found in A. Hulshoff, *Lykrede op Kl. de Vries* (Amsterdam, 1766).

Cornelis Hartsen (1823-95) was a minister in the Department of Foreign Affairs. He also served as a deacon at Amsterdam (1858-63, 1868-72, 1878-82). In the 17th century this family was ennobled by the queen of Sweden and in the 19th century also by the Dutch king. Now most members of this family belong to the Reformed Church. (*Nederland's Adelboek* 1909, 189-93; 1954, 206-8; *DJ* 1840, 113; *N.N.B.Wb.* X, 333 f.)   vdZ.

Hartshuizen (Hartshuysen), a village in East Friesland, Germany, where Leenaert Bouwens in 1551-65 baptized 14 persons, who may have joined the Emderland (*q.v.*) congregation, since there is no indication that there was a congregation at Hartshuizen.
          vdZ.

Hartville Mennonite Church (MC), located 1½ mile south and ½ mile west of Hartville, Ohio, a member of the Ohio Mennonite and Eastern A.M. Conference, was organized Dec. 10, 1944, under the leadership of Bishop O. N. Johns and H. N. Troyer, with 49 charter members. The first meetinghouse, 40 x 60 ft., was built in 1945. This was a basement church. The present building, 40 x 90 ft., with a Sunday-school wing 40 x 30 ft., was built in 1951. In 1956 the membership was 242, with Lester A. Wyse as pastor.   L.A.W.

Hartwich, Abraham, a historian of West Prussia, Germany, was called on Aug. 4, 1698, from Königsberg to Lindenau in the Gross-Werder of Marienburg to serve as Lutheran pastor, after he had taught in the local school in Löbenicht at Königsberg for five years. On June 20, 1712, he accepted the pastorate in Barenhof. He wrote a description of the Werder (river islands), a preliminary account of which he had written in 1719. After his death the book was printed and published in Königsberg in 1722. Part I presents the geographic and historical description of the Werder. Part II deals with the religion and the divine services of the Catholics and the Protestants, the Lutheran church regulations, churches, and preachers, and the Reformed, the Mennonites, and the Quakers. Reformed preachers and laymen worked in Danzig, Marienburg, and Elbing as well as in the country from 1650 to 1750, but were gradually crowded out. In Marienburg, the Werder, and along the Vistula, in Elbing and Danzig there were Mennonites in the first half of the 16th century, who (1581) held meetings in various villages. In 1646 they were expelled from all Poland by the diet at Warsaw, but by paying large sums they were given permission to remain. The author also mentions two confessions of faith, one printed at Hoorn in 1640, one written in 1698; and a catechism with about 26 questions and answers. He writes about their ideas on baptism and communion, their doctrine, services, preachers, the ban, and their resistance against paying fees to the Lutheran preachers, and records a few transfers to the Lutheran Church.

Part III deals with government, housekeeping, war, and damage by fire and water. (*ML* II, 259.)
          A.D.

Hartzler: see also **Hertzler.**

Hartzler, Chancy A. (1876-1947), bishop in the Illinois Conference (MC), son of Bishop John J. Hartzler, was born in St. Joseph Co., Mich., on May 5, 1876, grew up in Cass Co., Mo., married

Mary Neuenschwander Dec. 23, 1900, had one son, John. Ordained preacher at the Sycamore Grove Church (MC) in Cass Co., Oct. 22, 1906, he served 1908-12 as a worker and then superintendent of the Kansas City (Kan.) Mission, then 1913 (1914 ord. bishop)-1947 (d. Oct. 15) as pastor of the Willow Springs (Tiskilwa, Ill.) Mennonite Church. He was active in Illinois Conference work, serving as moderator and secretary, as well as in the General Mission Board (Elkhart) and in the Mennonite Board of Education.   H.S.B.

Hartzler, John J., bishop of the Sycamore Grove (Mo.) Mennonite Church (MC) for more than 40 years, was born May 3, 1845, in Mifflin Co., Pa., died Aug. 11, 1936, at the age of 91 years, the son of Abraham and Magdalene Zook Hartzler. When he was nine years old his parents moved to northern Indiana and later to Michigan, where he grew to manhood. He was married to Magdalene Mast Feb. 25, 1872, in Elkhart Co., Ind. Eight years later he with his family of four children moved to Cass Co., Mo., near Garden City, where he resided the remaining 56 years of his life.

Hartzler was converted when a young man, and united with the Amish Mennonite Church. In 1894 he was ordained bishop in Cass Co., Mo. Besides his home congregation he had charge of churches in Johnson Co., Hickory Co., and Vernon Co., Mo. He also helped to organize churches in Arkansas, Oklahoma, and North Dakota. He was of a quiet and unassuming disposition, yet his work took him into many homes. He officiated in 82 marriages, and baptized over 300 persons in his home community and quite a number in other churches, and also officiated at a number of ordination services.

He was a farmer all his life. In Missouri he purchased a small farm and always supported himself and his family, and was always ready to sacrifice his time and service. In his early ministry his preaching was all in German, but he lived through the transition to English language, and in his later years preached in the English language.

Two of his sons were bishops (MC): Chancy A. Hartzler of Tiskilwa, Ill.; Joseph D. Hartzler of Flanagan, Ill. He is buried in the Clearfork (Mo.) cemetery.   J.D.H.

Hartzler, Jonas S. (1857-1953), Mennonite (MC) author, teacher, and preacher, was born near Topeka, Ind., on Aug. 8, 1857, the eldest son of Samuel and Sarah (Smucker) Hartzler, and died at the Mennonite Home for the Aged near Rittman, Ohio, on April 1, 1953. His maternal grandfather was the immigrant minister Christian Brandt (1783-1866), who moved to Wayne Co., Ohio, from the canton of Bern, Switzerland, in 1818. Reared on a farm, Hartzler early became interested in education, attended Wooster College and the Cook County (Ill.) Normal, and taught school in Noble and Lagrange counties, Ind., before he was called to the Elkhart (Ind.) Institute as instructor in Bible in 1895. There and later at Goshen College his industry, his practicality, and his varied talents and endowments enabled him to render a unique service to the educational, missionary, and organizational activities of the Mennonite Church as minister, teacher, business manager, treasurer, and secretary. He had been ordained minister in 1881 and became known as an exhorter, evangelist, and Bible teacher even before coming to the Elkhart Institute. At this school and later at Goshen College he served as instructor, but he also helped to carry a large share of the heavy financial burdens of the Board of Education and its schools for nearly a quarter of a century. He was the first pastor of the Goshen College congregation, served as secretary of the Mennonite General Conference from the date of its organization in 1898 until 1924, was secretary of the Indiana-Michigan Amish Mennonite Conference from 1888 to 1896, when his connection with the Elkhart Institute dictated the advisability of uniting with the Prairie Street Mennonite Church, secretary of the Indiana-Michigan (united) Mennonite Conference from its formation in 1916 until 1924, member of the Mennonite Board of Education 1895 to 1917 and treasurer (and member of the executive committee) of the Mennonite Board of Education from 1907 to 1917. Always keenly interested in foreign missions, he began in 1911 a long period of service as a member of the Mennonite Board of Missions and Charities. After ending his connection with Goshen College in 1917 he returned to Elkhart where, in 1923, he accepted the pastorate of the Prairie Street Mennonite Church and served until 1940. For many years he was editor of *Rural Evangel,* published by the Indiana-Michigan Conference. He was the author (with Daniel Kauffman) of *Mennonite Church History,* published in 1905, and (with J. S. Shoemaker) of *Among Missions in the Orient and Observations by the Way* (1912). In 1921 he wrote *Mennonites in the World War or Nonresistance Under Test.* He was twice married: in 1880 to Fannie Stutzman (1857-1929) of Johnson Co., Iowa, and 1930 to Mrs. Catharina (Christophel) Bauer, who survived him. He had one son Vernon (1881-1907).† J.S.U.

Harvest Festivals. The observance of harvest festivals among the Mennonites in the United States and Canada is of comparatively recent origin, in most cases apparently beginning during the first third of the 20th century. Today harvest festivals are widely observed in the United States and Canada, especially among the Mennonite Brethren and General Conference churches. In some churches the present observance seems to be an outgrowth of an earlier Thanksgiving Day worship service. In other instances Mennonites imitated the pattern established by other Protestant churches. In eastern Pennsylvania, for instance, the harvest festival is widely observed in Lutheran and Reformed churches by annually placing the best fruits of the harvest on the altar of the church in connection with a worship service.

The harvest festivals today in Mennonite churches seem generally to represent a combination of mission and relief interests. Most churches observing this occasion arrange services for a special Sunday, usually in October or November. In some places there are two or three services, usually with a noon or an evening fellowship meal. It is the common practice for one session to be devoted to inspirational messages centering around the theme of missions and another session around the theme of sharing. Outside speakers and visiting missionaries and ministers are often a feature of the harvest festival. In many churches the special day is marked by appropriate decoration of the church with colored leaves, fruits, cereals, and other items symbolic of the harvest of the various regions. In all of the churches special emphasis is placed on giving. Offerings that have been strongly encouraged for weeks are received at each service for worthy causes such as missions, relief, and peace activities of the church. Many churches seek to make this a high point in the church year in generous giving.

Some churches use this occasion to dramatize the special projects which individuals and groups in the church have carried on during the year, as for instance, the "God's acre" plan, by which members of the church, individually or collectively, contribute the crop from an acre of ground to the work of the church. In many churches the gifts-in-kind are brought for the festival to be sold later and the proceeds given to the church. In every instance the purpose of the harvest festival is to encourage the outreach of the church through missions, relief, and other service phases of the church's work in addition to being a corporate expression of gratitude. The observance of the occasion seems to be spreading to many churches, and the enthusiasm for the festivals seems to be growing. J.W.F.

Harvey County, Kansas, is the center of the largest concentration of Mennonites west of the Mississippi River. The General Conference Mennonites have their headquarters in Newton, the county seat, and there are eight G.C.M. churches in the county: First Mennonite Church of Newton, Bethel College Mennonite Church, First Mennonite Church of Halstead, Garden Township Mennonite Church, Burrton Mennonite Church, Walton Mennonite Church, Gnadenberg Mennonite Church, and Hebron Mennonite Church. Bethel College, also a General Conference institution, is located here. There are two other Mennonite groups in the county—the Church of God in Christ Mennonites have a church near Halstead, and the Mennonites (MC) have two churches, the Hesston Mennonite Church and the Pennsylvania Mennonite Church near Hesston, and also Hesston College and Bible School at Hesston.

The early history of the county is closely connected with the Santa Fe Railroad which by July 1871 had pushed its tracks as far west as Newton, which was named after Newton, Mass., a suburb of Boston, where many of the stockholders of the Santa Fe lived. For a number of years Newton marked the northern end of the Texas cattle trail, known as the Chisholm trail, and was the toughest cow town on the frontier. A number of other towns were laid out along the Santa Fe tracks—Walton in December 1871, Halstead in the spring of 1873, and Burrton in the summer of 1873. In addition to these, Harvey County presently includes the towns of Sedgwick, Hesston, and the villages

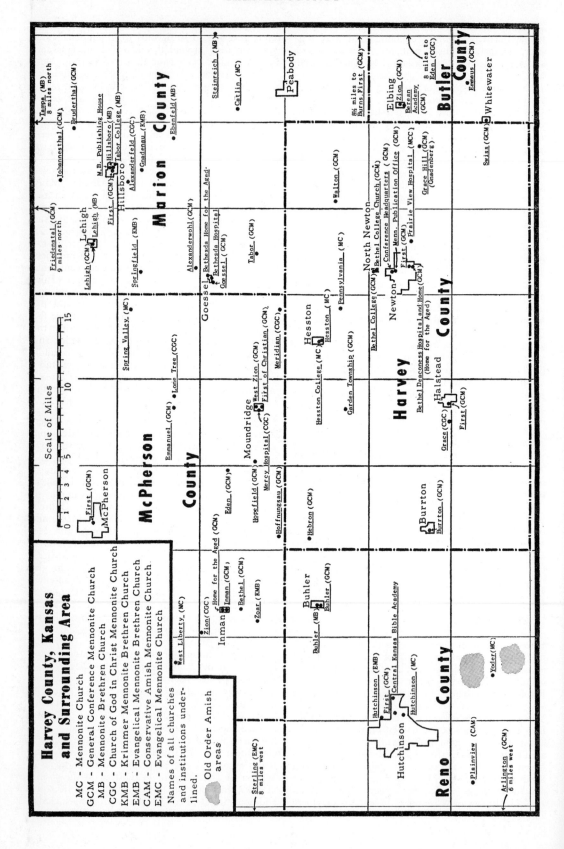

Harvey County, Kansas
and Surrounding Area

MC - Mennonite Church
GCM - General Conference Mennonite Church
MB - Mennonite Brethren Church
CGC - Church of God in Christ Mennonite Church
KMB - Krimmer Mennonite Brethren Church
EMB - Evangelical Mennonite Brethren Church
CAM - Conservative Amish Mennonite Church
EMC - Evangelical Mennonite Church.

Names of all churches
and institutions under-
lined.

Old Order Amish
areas

of Zimmerdale, Patterson, Annelly, McLain, and North Newton. The bill which formed 13 townships into Harvey County (there are 15 townships in the county today) was passed by the Kansas State Legislature and became law on Feb. 29, 1872. The county was named in honor of James M. Harvey, governor of Kansas at the time.

The Santa Fe Railroad and the towns of Peabody, Newton, and Halstead are closely associated with the coming of the Russian Mennonites in the great migration of 1873-75 and in later migrations. The region was then the frontier, with the Santa Fe owning alternate sections of land, most of which had not been touched by plow. The Mennonites came by rail to either Peabody, Newton, or Halstead and thence settled in the region north of Newton, between the Arkansas and Cottonwood rivers, in the counties of Marion, McPherson, and Harvey. The Santa Fe sold thousands of acres of land to the Mennonites, assisted them by erecting immigrant houses in numerous places, and brought carload after carload of implements and other supplies to Peabody, Newton, and Halstead, where they were purchased by the Mennonites. One hardware store in Newton, for example, established a national retail record for the number of plows sold in one year, and some years later sold over 200 binders in a single season.

Harvey County in 1953 had a population of about 23,000 (of whom over 12,500 were living in Newton) with a Mennonite population of probably 5-6,000. It is located somewhat to the southeast of the geographic center of the state in the heart of a rich farming area. The land is relatively flat, and climatic and soil conditions are specially suited for wheat and other small grains. The Mennonites, particularly Bernhard Warkentin, are credited with introducing Turkey Red hard winter wheat to Kansas. Warkentin, who visited the region in 1871 and selected a site at Halstead, where in 1873 he established the first mill in the county, encouraged wheat production by securing several thousand bushels of seed in South Russia and shipping it to Newton, where it was distributed among the early settlers. The Santa Fe Railroad gave the new grain a boost by making markets accessible, and wheat raising quickly spread from the central counties to all sections of Kansas, Oklahoma, and Nebraska.   H.J.S.

Harvey Mennonite Brethren Church, located 11 miles southwest of Harvey, N.D., is a member of the Central District Conference. This church was organized in 1898 with 13 members. Christian Reimche, the first pastor, served the church for about 30 years. The first church was built in 1900. This was enlarged in 1918 and again in 1943. Recently a new church was constructed in Harvey and services are now conducted in both places with a joint service each month. Other ministers who have served this church are Peter Wiens, Dr. L. J. Seibel, H. H. Hiebert, G. Warkentin, and the present pastor Loyal Funk. The deacons J. C. Seibel and Jacob Zweigle served the church for 32 years and the present deacons, H. H. Delk and Dan Bich,

since 1929. Robert Seibel, ordained to the ministry in this church, served as an MCC worker in Brazil in 1947-49. At present (1954) the membership is 210 and consists mostly of rural people. A.A.D.

Harwood United Missionary Church is located in the Harwood community, about seven miles west of Yakima, Wash. In 1954 it dedicated a new parsonage and church. It has a membership of approximately 40, but an average attendance of 160. Donald Mikel from the Indiana Conference is the pastor (1954).   K.G.

Harz, a mountainous region in Middle Germany, partly in Thuringia and partly in Hesse. Anabaptism was transplanted into the Harz by missionaries from Upper Franconia (Jacobs, 430). In the South Harz Anabaptists appeared as early as 1527. They are representatives of the quiet, suffering group who insisted on pure conduct. Their leader was Alexander, a teacher, probably a native of Stolberg, where he often spent the night in the house of his brother-in-law. He was one "of the noblest figures in the Anabaptist movement" (Wappler, 100), who won adherents in Emseloh, Lengefeld, and Sangershausen. He was beheaded in 1533 at Frankenhausen. With him worked Jacob Schmiedeknecht. According to tradition two Anabaptists were drowned in the "Wiedertäuferteich" (Anabaptist Pond) near Liebenrode in 1530.

But cruel persecution did not succeed in wiping out the movement in the Harz. In summer and fall of 1534 they met in a mill near Zorge in the South Harz. Martin Herzog, a carpenter who had been baptized by Alexander, the preachers Klaus Berner (*q.v.*) and Balthasar (*q.v.*) der Futterschneider, Peter Reusse (*q.v.*), and especially Heinz Kraut (*q.v.*) who succeeded Alexander, found temporary residence here and from here made their way into the Harz and Thuringia. When their residence here was betrayed by captured brethren, especially Klaus Schaff, they had to abandon it. They now met at night on the Schraubenstein, a desolate place between Riestedt and Emseloh. In Riestedt on Sept. 2, 1535, the Anabaptists Georg Köhler (*q.v.*) and Georg Möller (Müller) were arrested, taken to Sangershausen and beheaded.

In the North Harz the Anabaptist movement also spread. Georg Möller and other brethren temporarily stayed in Quedlinburg. They felt secure for a time in concealment at Halberstadt. Here Georg Knobloch (*q.v.*) had rented a place in the so-called Pfaffenhäuslein in the willows behind the cathedral. Here the Anabaptists held their services, including baptism, communion, and a wedding. They had to leave this house when the owner noted that a child born there was not baptized. They now transferred to the "Grauen Hof" belonging to the monastery Michaelstein in Halberstadt. On Sept. 13, 1535, an investigation of the persons living here was made. They found the wives of Georg Knobloch and Hans Höhne (*q.v.*) and six small children. The questioning of the women led to suspicion, and the Hof was watched. When Hans Höhne and an Anabaptist woman, Petronella (*q.v.*), returned home and saw what had happened they fell on their knees and cried to God, and then sang Luther's hymn, "Ach Gott von Himmel, sieh darein und lass dich dess erbarmen." They were taken to prison at once. Cheerfully they followed the police and sang along the way. On Sept. 20 another man and woman came to the Grauen Hof; they were Adrian Richter (*q.v.*) and Anna Reichard, wife of Hermann Gereumes (Geruchers) of Kleinschalkalten. The former was also taken to prison, singing all the way. When Hans Höhne heard the song he cried, "There I hear the cheerful voice of my dear brother, praised be God!" When the officials inquired who the singer was he replied, "It is my dear brother Adrian. For as he who is of God knows God's voice, so I also know the voice of my dear brethren." In spite of torture Hans Höhne, Adrian Richter, and Petronella remained steadfast, and were drowned in the Bode, Oct. 8, 1535.

Concerning the further fate of the Anabaptists in the Harz little is known. On Dec. 4, 1537, Hans Linsenbusch was beheaded for his faith at Brücken on the Helme. His cousin, the schoolmaster Johann Zollener, recanted on Nov. 16, 1538 (Jacobs, 493), and was released. About ten years later the reformer Tileman Plathner was successful in the commission given him by Wolfgang Count of Stolberg and Wernigerode to turn Anabaptists from their faith. Those who returned to the church were pardoned, the others expelled (Jacobs, 493).

The numerous court records give rather exact information on the doctrine and life of the Anabaptists in the Harz. Penitence, complete separation from the world, and surrender to God, were required of all who wished to join them. By baptism they were received into the brotherhood. Georg Köhler (Jacobs, 469) reports, "When one wishes to be baptized, he comes to the baptizer, kneels, and says, 'Dear brother, I desire the bond of a good conscience with God and ask for baptism.' The baptizer replies, 'Do you believe that Christ is the only begotten Son of God and eternal, do you want to yield yourself to Him alone, obey Him as God and Lord, and, if necessary, die for His sake?' If the baptismal candidate answers in the affirmative . . . the brother performs the rite, reading . . . the baptism of John word for word. Then he wets a finger three times in water, makes three crosses on the brow and head of the candidate, and says, 'I baptize you in the name of the Father, Son, and Holy Ghost.' He then earnestly admonishes him again to obey the covenant, be obedient to God, avoid sin, and yet always consider himself a sinner in the sight of God." Baptism was sometimes performed by pouring (Wappler, 122). With rebaptism they would have nothing to do, for there is only one baptism; infant baptism is not baptism. Children are clean, without hereditary sin until they reach understanding; the kingdom of heaven is for children dying without baptism.

Communion was not a sacrament to them, but a symbol of their membership in Christ and the church and the obligation of a life of obedience until death. It was conducted with solemnity. A communion service held in Knobloch's house in 1535 began with Peter Reusse washing the feet of the others and kissing each. Then he cut bread into wine and each took a piece, broke it and ate it upon the death of Christ, to testify that he, like Christ, was ready for life or death (Wappler, 128).

Marriage they considered a sacred ordinance of God; it is necessary because of fornication, but to be unmarried is better. Spiritual brotherhood stood above marriage. Where people could not become one in faith they should separate. It occurred that a man left his wife and children because they would not accept his faith, and vice versa.

Prayer they exercised diligently, obeying the admonition to pray without ceasing. Free prayer was usual; but fixed prayers, Biblical or traditional, were not rare. The Lord's Prayer was commonly used. The fourth petition was, "Our true bread, Thy eternal word, give us today."

In the Apostles' Creed they changed "under Pontius Pilate" to "under the covenant of Pilate." Köhler explains it thus: "Because the covenant of Christ, which He made with the Father, was completed through His suffering and death." Höhne declared, just as the Jews had made a covenant concerning Christ with Pilate, so the wicked now make their alliances against true Christians.

Besides preaching and prayer, hymn singing was important in their worship services. Alexander confessed that after the sermon they prayed the Lord's Prayer and sang psalms. They did not always have a sermon; they conversed with each other concerning God and divine things, concerning the wonderful leading of God both toward themselves and others (Jacobs, 478, note 3). They rejected the confessional before men and absolution by the priests. Toward the government they required implicit obedience except in matters of faith. The idea that they had a secret sign or watchword they denied emphatically; but they could be recognized by their simple conduct. Community of goods they did not have; but each should use of his earthly goods only what he needed for himself and his family; the rest he should distribute to needy brethren. They practiced the greatest hospitality and mutual aid support. They liked simple, dark clothing. Georg Möller cut up a good red coat because it had been made for pride, and had it dyed black, to give no occasion for pride. They made no distinction in food; for all is created by God and serves man, who accepts it with gratitude. The observance of Sunday they left to the individual conscience. They considered it a day of reconciliation. The sins committed during the week should be made right with God on Sunday; for this purpose God instituted it.

They lived a strict moral life, which made a deep general impression. Adulterers, gamblers, drunkards, etc., were not tolerated among them. They thus became shining examples of their time. Their suppression is therefore a matter of regret from the viewpoint of the welfare of the people, and has certainly bitterly avenged itself.　　　　Neff.

E. Jacobs, "Die Wiedertäufer im Harz," in *Ztscht des Harz-Vereins für Geschichte und Altertumskunde*

XXXII (1899) 423-536; P. Wappler, *Die Täuferbewegung in Thüringen von 1526-1584* (Jena, 1913); ML II, 259-61.

Hase, Karl August von (1800-90), a Lutheran church historian, professor of theology at the University of Jena, 1830-83. In his historical writings he also dealt with the Anabaptists, but without doing them justice. To his book, *Neue Propheten* (1851), he added a section called "Das Reich der Wiedertäufer," which was published in 1860 as the third part in a new edition, after a Dutch edition, *Het Rijk der Wederdoopers,* had appeared in 1854. The book deals principally with the excesses of the Münsterites, and is based on the incorrect premise that the Anabaptist movement was founded in 1521 by the "new prophets" in Zwickau. The quiet Anabaptists were briefly touched without differentiation. Even though he recognizes the demand of the Anabaptists for the "strict heroic morality of original Christianity," Hase nevertheless sees a danger in this "heresy," "because most of its adherents could depend on the sanctity of their conduct" (second edition, 12). His descriptions pursue a definite objective: in his mind the recollection of the "old Anabaptism" seemed instructive at a time "when a newly rising Protestant orthodoxy gives new justification to Anabaptism" (Foreword to the second edition of *Neue Propheten,* 1861, p. X).

In his *Kirchengeschichte auf der Grundlage akademischer Vorlesungen* only the Münsterites are given extensive discussion, while the quiet Anabaptists are passed by and the results of recent research are ignored. Even in the edition of 1891 he says, "Nowhere is a founder of the Anabaptists named" (Part III, section 1, p. 285), although Hase had in his book *Das Reich der Wiedertäufer* (p. 174) called attention to the forthcoming publication of the second book by C. A. Cornelius, *Geschichte des Münsterischen Aufruhrs* (Leipzig, 1860), which gives an authentic account, based on sources, of the origins of the Zürich Anabaptists in 1525. Hege.

H. Hermsen, *Die Täufer in der deutschen Dichtung,* Stuttgart, 1913; ML II, 261.

Hasel, name of a Swabian family of Württemberg, of which a number became Anabaptists; one of them was an early martyr while others emigrated to Moravia where they became active in the Hutterite brotherhood.

The earliest representative of this family was a Hans Hasel (of Neckarrems or Riembs) who was baptized in 1530 at Ossweil near Esslingen but suffered martyrdom for the sake of his new faith only one year later (1531) in Pfalz-Neuburg.

Around 1555-57 a relative of this man, Peter Hasel of Rudersberg near Schorndorf (Württemberg), together with his wife Barbara and four small children emigrated to Moravia, where they joined the Hutterites. The father died in the following year but his three sons in due time became outstanding members of the brotherhood. Their names were David, who in 1581 became *Diener des Wortes* (preacher), was sent to Württemberg as a missioner, and died in 1599; Peter, who became *Diener der Notdurft* (steward) and supervisor of many farm economies of the brethren around Schäkowitz, Moravia, and died 1597; and Michael, who also was sent out as a missioner (*Sendbote*) to his native Württemberg, where he was soon caught, made prisoner, and kept in the castle of Hohenwittlingen (where once Paul Glock, *q.v.,* had been a prisoner) until his death in 1592. By profession he was a weaver, hence is often called Michael Weber.

Of the next generation we learn in the Hutterite Chronicle of two more Hasels, one Kaspar (d. in Moravia 1619) and one Thomas (d. also in Moravia in 1622 at the time of the complete expulsion of the Hutterites from that country). Both were *Diener der Notdurft* and obviously quite important members of the community.

The best known of these men is Michael Hasel, a true witness to his faith. At his death, the reeve of the castle (*Burgvogt*) of Hohenwittlingen remarked that "if such a man did not go into heaven, he himself would not dare to knock at its door. Yea, if he knew the end would be like Hasel's, he would rejoice even now" (*Geschicht-Buch,* 437; *Mart. Mir.,* E 1951, 1088 f.).

There are three Hutterite manuscript books extant signed M.W. (Michael Weber) and we may rightly assume that he either merely owned these books or was also the copyist of them, as we know that such book-writing was a favorite activity among the brethren. All three codices contain the great *Article Book* (*q.v.*), either complete or in a shortened version. The one codex in the State Library of Wolfenbüttel (*Bibl. Augustana*), dated 1582, says expressly that it was written by this brother. It contains only three of the five articles, and in addition to them an outstanding epistle by Peter Walpot (*q.v.*) to the "Swiss Brethren" in the Rhineland (1577), his farewell address before his death, some prayers and 20 hymns by different authors, five of which have not yet been published (the codex has 235 pages and is written in careful penmanship with red letters for titles and initials). The other codices are in Olmütz (Olomuce, Moravia) 1582, and Bratislava (Slovakia), in the State Archives, dated 1583.

Michael is also the author of two hymns which he wrote in prison 1590 f., "Merkt auf ihr frommen Gotteskind" and "O edler Gott und höchster Hort" (*Lieder der Hutterischen Brüder,* Scottdale, 1914, 798 and 800). R.F.

Wolkan, *Geschicht-Buch;* Beck, *Geschichts-Bücher; TA Württemberg;* Wolkan, *Lieder;* Zieglschmid, *Chronik; Mart. Mir.* D 787, E 1088; *ML* II, 262 f.

Haslibacher, Hans, and **Haslibacher Lied.** Hans Haslibacher, an Anabaptist preacher of Sumiswald in the Emmental, Bern, Switzerland, active as early as 1532, a participant in the great Bern disputation of 1538. He suffered severely for his faith. He was exiled and his property of 500 gulden confiscated, and upon return to his home (his son, of the Reformed faith, was fined heavily on Sept. 2, 1571, for receiving him) was executed by beheading on

Oct. 20, 1571, in Bern as the last Anabaptist martyr in that canton.

A vivid description of Haslibacher's imprisonment and death is given in a 32-stanza poem composed, as the last verse states, in prison by another Anabaptist prisoner (not necessarily a fellow prisoner of Haslibacher in 1571). The poem reports that after torture and strong attempts by the Reformed preachers to cause him to apostatize, which were steadfastly resisted, Haslibacher dreamed that he would be beheaded, and that three divine signs would accompany his execution, viz., his severed head would jump into his hat and laugh; the sun would turn crimson like blood; and the town well would give forth blood. The poet claims that all three happened.

The Haslibacher poem was first published in pamphlet form (6 pages and title page), with the title, *Ein Schön Geistlich Lied von dem Hasslibacher, wie er von dem Leben zum Tod ist hingerichtet worden. In der Melody: Warum betrübst du dich mein Hertz,* etc. As such it was bound with (but not printed in) a copy of the *Ausbund* (*q.v.*) which was published after 1614 (it contains a hymn on the martyr Hans Landis who was executed in this year) but certainly in the early 17th century, probably soon after the dated *Ausbund* edition of 1622. It next appears as hymn No. 140 in the first (1742) American edition of the *Ausbund* at Germantown, Pa., with exactly the same title and content as the above pamphlet. It appeared in all later American editions of the *Ausbund,* but in no European editions. The (1748) Ephrata German edition of the *Martyrs' Mirror* (938 f.) tells the story of Haslibacher from the hymn and prints stanzas 21-32. The Pirmasens (1780) *Martyrs' Mirror* and all later German language editions follow suit, but the Elkhart (1886) English *Martyrs' Mirror* (and all later English editions) published the entire hymn. Nothing of Haslibacher is found in the Dutch *Martyrs' Mirror* of 1660 and 1685. The Swiss devotional book, *Kleines Hand-Büchlein* (first edition n.p., 1786, second edition at Basel, 1801), prints the entire hymn with the slightly revised title, *Ein schön Geistlich Lied, von dem Hanss Hasslibacher, aus der Herrschaft Sumiswald, in der Schweiz zu Hasslebach, welcher von dem Leben zum Tod ist hingerichtet worden. In der Melody: Warum betrübst du dich mein Hertz,* etc. The title reflects information taken from the (1780) Pirmasens *Martyrs' Mirror.* In modern times it has been published as follows: *Mennonite Yearbook and Almanac for 1911* (pp. 24 f.) in English translation by Governor (of Pennsylvania) Samuel W. Pennypacker (done March 8, 1904) from the *Ausbund;* reprinted in S. Geiser, *Die Taufgesinnten Gemeinden* (Karlsruhe, 1931) 185-87; *Im Röseligarti,* a Bernese folksong periodical, prints 12 verses with the music; C. Henry Smith states (*The Story of the Mennonites,* 3rd ed., Newton, Kan., 1950, p. 116) that the Haslibacher hymn, though in the *Ausbund,* "is no longer sung in [Amish] religious services but, strange to say, at weddings and other festive occasions." According to the article "Eine alte interessante Bibel," published in *Der Zionspilger* (Langnau i.E.) VIII (1889) No. 17, pp. 1 f., Haslibacher's Bible (Zürich, 1553), with many underlinings showing typical Anabaptist emphases, was still in 1889 in the possession of his descendants bearing the family name and living on the original homestead, though not Mennonites.

H.S.B.

S. Geiser, *Die Taufgesinnten-Gemeinden* (Karlsruhe, 1931) 183-87; C. Henry Smith, *The Mennonites of America* (Goshen, 1909) 433-35; *Berner Biographien* I (Bern, 1887) 604 f.; A. Michiels, *Les Anabaptists des Vosges* (Paris, 1860) contains the Haslibacher story ("Le Martyre d'Hasslibacher") told in French but taken apparently from the Pirmasens (1780) *Martyrs' Mirror* owned by Elder Augsburger of the Salm (Alsace) congregation; *ML* II, 263 f.

Haslinger, Leonhard, an Anabaptist martyr, a furrier at Wels (Upper Austria), was one of the ten Anabaptists who were put to death at Wels according to the "list of the brethren and sisters who were executed in many places for the sake of their testimony to divine truth." The first were two shoemakers, both named Wastl; on the Friday after Pentecost 1528 the following were also beheaded and then burned: Hans Neumair; Leonhard Haslinger, a furrier; Hans Steinpeck, a mason; Jörg Zacherle, a furrier of Krems; M. Perger and Jörg Kreutzinger, servants; on the following Monday two women were drowned, Barbara, Haslinger's wife, and Barbara, Zacherle's wife. A report of the captain of June 8, 1528, says, "They would not give an affidavit nor swear an oath, also rejected infant baptism, the sacrament of the altar, and the confessional, but still were not mob-leaders or preachers, baptized nobody, and confessed no other covenant than that they said they wanted to desist from evil and help their neighbors as much as possible, and be obedient to the government with body and goods." Of Hans Steinpeck's wife the report says, "She is pregnant—shall be postponed until she has given birth to the child."

LOSERTH.

Beck, *Geschichts-Bücher,* 280; J. Jäkel, "Zur Geschichte der Wiedertäufer in Oberösterreich," *47th Annual Report of the Museum of Linz;* *ML* II, 264.

Hasselbach, a village (1925 pop., 239) in the Sinsheim district of Baden, Germany, three miles northeast of Steinsfurt, the seat of a Mennonite church, concerning whose origin little is known. The fact that in 1575 the Dutch Mennonites sent three preachers to the brethren in the Neckar Valley (see **Grombach**) proves that there were Anabaptists here in the 16th century. Another clue to the existence of this early congregation is the name *Wiedertäuferkirche* given to part of a forest an hour northeast of Hasselbach (*Gem.-Kal.,* 1904, 142). During the period of persecution and before they were tolerated they seem to have met for services in remote places.

In the 17th century the Anabaptists in the Sinsheim district were still compelled to hold their meetings secretly in forests. Thus in 1653 the parson Johann Friedrich Schärer of Hilsbach reported to his inspector in Sinsheim that the Mennonites were planning a marriage ceremony in a forest. That they met in forests was also confirmed by the leaders of a Mennonite meeting attended by 53 persons in Steinsfurt at nine on the evening of March 2, 1661, in the home of a widow, which was disbanded by the authorities when they began to sing. Five of the participants had to be security for all the rest, whose names were listed, and to vow to present themselves for punishment. On March 29 they explained to the authorities at Hilsbach that they had come into the country with their brethren in 1655, all of whom came from Switzerland, and that they had frequently during the summer assembled quietly in the forests near Steinsfurt, without informing anyone. They would not cease to hold meetings; they would prefer to emigrate. The government fined them (July 6, 1661) 100 Reichstaler for meeting secretly. But they continued to meet every Sunday. In reply to an inquiry by Inspector Peter Grill in Sinsheim, Nov. 16, 1661, whether he should let the Mennonites continue, Elector Karl Ludwig ordered (Jan. 4, 1662) that the Mennonites should no longer be forbidden to meet, in spite of an opinion by the church council of Dec. 6, 1661, recommending the contrary. But every participant was to pay a fee each time he attended a meeting. An electoral concession of Aug. 4, 1664, ended the taxation of their services, but not more than 20 persons were permitted to attend (Mennonite court records in the *Generallandesarchiv* at Karlsruhe).

The Mennonites living in Hasselbach and vicinity today are all of Swiss descent. When their ancestors were expelled from Bern at the close of the 17th century they were received on the estates of the knighted nobles. Most of these estates were farmed for generations by Mennonites, as in Ehrstädt, Helmstadt, Grombach, Ober- and Unterbiegelhof, Rauhof, and Wagenbach. A congregation was formed in Hasselbach; the earliest reference to it is in 1731, when it numbered 18 families, whose heads are named by Ernst Müller (*Berner Täufer*, 209). Their preacher was Abraham Zeisset of the Rauhof, who frequently visited the Swiss churches (church records of the Sembach Mennonite Church, p. 260) and maintained connections with the churches of the Palatinate and in Danzig (*Gem.-Kal.*, 1896, 89; see also 1930, 140-42; also Müller, 212 f.). The Büchelhof (*q.v.*) and Helmstadt (*q.v.*) congregations later merged with the Hasselbach congregation.

The Dutch *Naamlijst*, which calls this congregation "Hasselbach, Martishof, Helmstein, and Senfeld," lists the following preachers in the 18th century: Hans Kaufmann from 1754, Hans Grebeil (Krehbiel) from 1761, Abraham Schmutz and Christian Schmutz from 1764, Abraham Krehbiel and Johannes Bechtel from 1767, Georg Hotel from 1786, and Jacob Funck from 1792.

In the 19th century the congregation was the center of the Mennonites of Baden. Its elders Ulrich Hege of the Unterbiegelhof and Heinrich Landes of Ehrstädt, with Christian Schmutz of the neighboring church at Rappenau, were the most prominent leaders of the churches in Baden. In

the 20th century the Hasselbach congregation suffered a decrease by emigration to other districts. Many Mennonites in Württemberg and southern Bavaria are descendants of former Hasselbach members. With Ober- and Unterbiegelhof the village of Hasselbach had 45 Mennonites in 1821. It was thus the fourth largest congregation in Baden: Mannheim had 93, Dühren 54, and Ittlingen 46 members. In 1925 there were only 19 Mennonites living in Hasselbach, 33 in Ehrstädt, 22 in Helmstadt, 21 in Neckarbischofsheim (the part of Helmhof in Baden), 12 in Grombach, 5 in Flinsbach, and one each in Babstadt and Obergimpern. The six Mennonites living in the Hessian enclave of Helmhof were also members of the Hasselbach congregation, which in 1935 numbered 135 souls. In 1953 the baptized membership was 86, the elder was Heinrich Funck (ordained 1943), deacon David Moser (ordained 1939). Since 1846 the congregation has had its own meetinghouse, until recently the only Mennonite meetinghouse in Baden-Württemberg. Services are held every Sunday and holiday. HEGE.

Die Religionszugehörigkeit in Baden in den letzten 100 Jahren (Karlsruhe, 1927) 74; Müller, *Berner Täufer*; *ML* II, 264 f.

Hasselt, a town in the Dutch province of Overijssel, on the Zwarte Water. It was at Bergklooster near Hasselt that the boats landed on March 24, 1534, which had transported 3,000 Anabaptists from North Holland en route to Münster (*q.v.*). They were all arrested here. (See **Bergklooster.**) vDZ.

Inv. Arch. Amst., I, Nos. 22, 23, 30, 32, 45; Kühler, *Geschiedenis* I, 94, 102; Mellink, *Wederdopers*, 31-39, 106, 158.

Hast, Johan (1808-52), a German Catholic scholar, author of *Geschichte der Wiedertäufer zu Münster von ihrem Entstehen zu Zwickau in Sachsen bis auf ihren Sturz zu Münster in Westfalen* (Münster, 1836). The reader who judges from the title of the book that this is a traditional treatment of the subject is pleasantly surprised by the contents. Even if the author incorrectly derives the Anabaptists from the Zwickau "prophets" and logically has them end in the Münster revolt, he nevertheless shows an admirable understanding and evaluation of this religious movement, tries to interpret it in the light of its noble religious motives, and describes it (from a Catholic point of view) in a highly objective manner, on the basis of sources, which he, however, unfortunately sometimes fails to cite. NEFF.

Sonntagsblatt für katholische Christen (Münster, 1843) 638; E. Rassmann, *Nachrichten von dem Leben und den Schriften Münsterländischer Schriftsteller des 18. u. 19. Jahrhunderts* (Münster, 1866) 140; *ML* II, 265.

Hastenrath (Hastenraedt, Haustelraed), **Theunis** (Thönis, Teunis, Tonnis) **van,** an Anabaptist elder and martyr, burned at the stake at Linnich on the Roer, Germany, on June 30, 1551. Theunis van Hastenraedt, who is identical with Anthonis von Asselroye or Assenray, was a native of Hastenrath, Germany, near the Dutch town of Roermond. After his conversion he studied the Holy Scriptures for

15 years, during which time he seldom preached. He also read the books of Menno Simons. As an elder he preached and baptized after 1545 in many towns of the duchies of Jülich and Upper-Gelre. Among the places where he was baptizing, he himself mentions Illikhoven, Loevenich, Hastenrath, Weert, Maastricht, Cologne, Monschau, Cleve, and Goch. In 1547 he was present at a meeting of Mennonite elders at Goch, where Adam Pastor was excommunicated. His interesting confession at his trial appeared in *DB* 1909.   NEFF, vdZ.

DB 1890, 58-59; 1894, 18; 1909, 120-26; W. Bax, *Het Protestantisme in het Bisdom Luik* I (The Hague, 1937) 306-09, 406-10 and Index; *Mart. Mir.* D 97, E 495; *ML* II, 265.

Hastings (Neb.) Mennonite Brethren Church, now extinct, was a small congregation existing from 1878 to 1920. Ministers who served it were Johannes Brehm and Adam Ross.

Hat. The history of costume (*q.v.*) in the Mennonite Church has not yet been exhaustively studied. From the very beginning of the Anabaptist movement in Switzerland and the Netherlands in the 16th century considerable emphasis fell on simplicity of life including attire. Within a century or thereabouts the tendency appeared in some areas for the church to freeze for greater or longer periods the more conservative forms of clothing.

A. *Women's Hats.* Among the more conservative groups in America the matter of women's headgear ultimately became a major concern. The Swiss Mennonite women of southeastern Pennsylvania undoubtedly wore plain and simple headgear from the first, likely a form of beaver hat, or the old flat hat which in some parts of Europe (in England, e.g.) were the predecessor of the bonnet. It appears that under the influence of the Society of Friends in the Philadelphia area, the Mennonite women of the Lancaster Conference and of much of the Franconia Conference adopted the "Quaker bonnet" perhaps early in the 19th century. Some of the more conservative areas of the Franconia Conference showed some resistance to the adoption of this plain bonnet. The mother of the late bishop George J. Lapp (1879-1951) and wife of Deacon Samuel W. Lapp (1833-1926) of the Lexington congregation in Bucks Co., Pa., never wore this Quaker bonnet until her family moved to Nebraska in 1878. She had felt that such bonnets were worn for "pride." It was not until 1912 that the Franconia Conference finally fell in line with the other district conferences of the Mennonites (MC) by making the wearing of a bonnet a test of membership. During much of the 19th century, and in some areas until the present, the wearing of the bonnet is made a test of church membership (MC). Since 1920 or earlier there has been discontinuance of the bonnet in many of the conferences west of eastern Pennsylvania, although the church has stressed the wearing of simple headgear, and although many ministers continue to protest against the wearing of "hats," viz., forms of headgear with brims or ornaments. The Mennonite women of Ontario did not adopt the "Quaker" bonnet but wore the "English" or "Queen Victoria" type of

hat (or bonnet). Under the influence of the United States Mennonites this hat was gradually supplanted in the first quarter of the 20th century by the "American" or "Dutch" bonnet, which in turn is again disappearing and being gradually replaced by more conventional headgear. (See **Bonnet**.)

The Old Colony Mennonites of Mexico still wear flat broad-brimmed straw hats of a shape similar to the flat beaver hats of 18th-century Pennsylvania. (See *Menn. Life* for January 1952, which presents several photographs of these hats.) *In the Dutch Country* (Lancaster, 1953) carries (p. 11) a picture of the 18th-century Pennsylvania flat hat. The museum of the York Co., Pa., Historical Society contains several sketches by Lewis Miller (1796-1882) purporting to portray Mennonite costumes for both men and women of the time of his youth (*ca.* 1810), which show the broad flat hats on both men and women. S. F. Coffman's (1872-1954) article, "Mennonite Dress Customs" in the *Mennonite Historical Bulletin* for January 1955, tells of the earlier wearing of the broad-brimmed beaver hats in the Vineland, Ont., community as reported by the older people in 1895. A Pennsylvania Amish discipline of 1809 prohibits the wearing of hats. (Priscilla Delp, "History Makes Bonnets," *Christian Living* II, 1955, 14-22.)   J.C.W.

B. *Men's Hats.* The history of the Mennonite men's hat is somewhat similar. The eastern Pennsylvania men, including the Amish, generally adopted the "Quaker" broad-brimmed, flat-crowned (uncreased) hat, although this was not commonly done farther west or in Ontario. In the 20th century the style was supplanted, except among the eastern Pennsylvania Amish, by the conventional American men's hat, though usually the crease was omitted by the preachers. In other sections no distinctive hat was worn by either laity or ministers. However, until recently it was common practice for the ministers to wear only black hats. For a time in some sections, at least in Ontario in the second half of the 19th century, the "high hat" or topper was worn by a number of Mennonite men to funerals, weddings, and even to church services. The Old Colony Mennonite men of Manitoba and elsewhere resisted the introduction of hats, wearing instead the peasant type of cap worn in Russia. In South Germany during the mid-19th century the more conservative men wore the French type 3-cornered hat long after the remaining population had abandoned this style.   H.S.B.

Hatfield Mennonite Brethren in Christ Church, located in Montgomery Co., Pa., was organized in 1879. In 1953 the congregation had 130 members with W. A. Heffner serving as pastor.   H.K.K.

Hattavier (Hattawer), **Izak,** a Dutch merchant of Amsterdam, where he died 1657, was a member and likely a deacon or elder of the Reformed (Walloon) or Lutheran church of his home town. Through his business connections becoming acquainted with the troubles of the persecuted Anabaptists at Zürich, Switzerland, he informed the Mennonites of Amsterdam concerning the fate of their Swiss brethren about 1643. Thereupon the

Amsterdam Mennonites through the intercession of Hattavier sent 200 Talers to Zürich for their co-religionists. A proposal was made to have them migrate to Holland, but this was fruitless. Hattavier corresponded with J. H. Ott (Ottius) in Zürich in 1645 and asked whether the rumors that the Anabaptists there were severely persecuted were true or not. Ott answered that the accounts were true but largely exaggerated. Hattavier was not a Mennonite as Anna Brons states. Van Braght, who mentions (*Mart. Mir.* D 805, E 1,104) that Hattavier was present when Hans Landis was decapitated in Zürich in 1614, also says (D 820, E 1,119) that in 1642 the city government of Amsterdam wrote a letter to the government of Zürich in behalf of the presecuted.   vDZ.

J. H. Ottius, *Annales Anabaptistici* (Basel, 1672) 302 ff., 327 ff.; A. Brons, *Ursprung, Entwicklung und Schicksale . . . der Mennoniten* (3rd ed. Amsterdam, 1912) 189 f.; Müller, *Berner Täufer,* 178; *ML* III, 327.

Hauck, Albert (1845-1918), a Protestant theologian, professor of theology at the University of Leipzig. He edited the second and third editions of the *Realenzyklopädie für protestantische Theologie und Kirche,* in which the Anabaptists are given thorough historical treatment and a just evaluation. He also gives the Anabaptists proper consideration in his book, *Ueber Trennung von Kirche und Staat* (Leipzig, 1912). On the maternal side Hauck was a descendant of the Mennonite Greiner family of Württemberg (see **Blasius Greiner**). (*ML* II, 265.)
                                        NEFF.

Haug (Hauch, Haugk, Hawg), **Jörg,** of Juchsen (Thuringia), a friend of Hans Hut (*q.v.*) and the author of a devotional tract of 1524 which became very popular among the Anabaptists. About his life we know only what Hans Hut stated at the hearing before the city court of Augsburg in 1527. During the time of the great Peasants' War in Thuringia (1524-25) the peasants had burned down the castle of the lord of Bibra, and had made Jörg Haug (apparently he himself was also a peasant from near-by Juchsen) the preacher of the village of Bibra. Late in May 1525, soon after the final collapse of the peasants, Haug invited Hans Hut, the former sexton of that parish, to preach to his congregation about baptism, a theme everyone was most eager to learn about (Meyer, 250).

Haug's tract bears the title, *Eine christliche Ordnung eines wahrhaften Christen zu verantworten die Ankunft seines Glaubens* (or shortened: *Anfang eines christlichen Lebens*), 1524, a pamphlet of 12 leaves 4°. Its motto is I Peter 3:15, so popular among Anabaptists. The idea of the tract is that a Christian life has to run through different stages of growth in order to arrive finally at the point of perfection where the mind becomes completely conformed to Christ, and may now experience "the right Sabbath where the Spirit resteth" (Is. 11). The gradual ascent to this goal is described by seven types of mindedness or spirit; viz., the spirit of reverence, of wisdom, of understanding, of counsel, of strength, of patience, and of godliness. Haug concludes with the following summary (Müller, 10):

Gott fürchten von Herzen ist Weisheit,
Das Böse meiden ist Verstand,
Verstand göttlicher Liebe gebiert Glauben,
   und ist gut denen, die ihn tun,
Sich nicht verrücken lassen ist Rat,
Sich selbst überwinden ist Stärke,
Alles in Gott richten und tragen ist Kunst,
Christo Jesu ähnlich werden und gleichgesinnt
   sein, ist Gottseligkeit.
Da ruhet alles und ist der rechte Sabbath,
   den Gott von uns erfordert, dem
   die ganze Welt aber widerstrebt.

The tract is remarkable in many ways. Written in 1524 at the height of the peasants' success, it completely neglects their revolutionary ideas and turns radically to the teaching of spiritual growth in love and obedience. "The fear of God brings forth obedience. Love brings forth the right faith, and faith worketh through love. Love, however, is the fulfillment of the law" (Müller, 8). This speaks strongly for an understanding of the peasant movement of the 1520's not primarily as a socio-economic affair but as a deeply religious longing for the right Christian way. As Hut stated in the report (above), "They were running after him to learn about [right] baptism, and everybody wanted to be instructed on that point." Second, the book was written before genuine Anabaptism began; the influence of Thomas Müntzer is possible but not certain. Yet its spirit of obedience, love, and self-conquest (*Geist der Stärke*) is exactly the spirit of the later Anabaptism. And what Haug calls *Geist der Kunst,* namely, to bear everything in God, is rather close to the idea of *Gelassenheit* (*q.v.*) or self-surrender, again central in Anabaptist thinking.

Thus it is not surprising that the booklet saw four editions (Keller, *Reformation,* 433), and was also copied many times by the Hutterites. From such a Hutterite manuscript book (in Esztergom) Lydia Müller published excerpts in her *Glaubenszeugnisse;* unfortunately, no complete modern reprint is available.   R.F.

L. Müller, *Glaubenszeugnisse oberdeutscher Taufgesinnter* (Leipzig, 1938) 3-10; Ch. Meyer, "Die Anfänge des Wiedertäufertums in Augsburg," *Ztscht des Hist. Ver. f. Schwaben* XIX (1874) 250 (document XIX); Keller, *Reformation,* 433.

Haury (Hauri), a Mennonite family stemming from the Aargau, Switzerland. Since a very early date the Hauri family living in Hirschtal, Lenzburg district (as distinguished from the Hauri family living in Reinach), belonged to the Swiss Brethren. After the Thirty Years' War a number of Haurys, under the pressure of persecution to which they were subjected in Switzerland, emigrated to South Germany. On one of the four boats that left Switzerland for the Netherlands in 1711 there was a weaver by the name of Hans Haury from Hirschtal and his family.

There are still numerous bearers of the name in Switzerland, South Germany, and North America. The ancestor of the Mennonites among them is Jakob Haury, presumably a descendant of the above Hans Haury, who came as a farmer from Bruchhausen near Mannheim to the Bolanderhof near Kirchheimbolanden (Palatinate) in 1745 and married the widow of Christian Stauffer. Jakob Haury (d. 1789) was an elder of the Weierhof Mennonite congregation. Some of his progeny settled in Bavaria in 1820 (Eichstock congregation) and later emigrated to America; others went directly to America. Among his descendants were S. S. Haury (1847-1929) and Gustav A. Haury (1863-1926).

During the middle of the past century members of the Haury family from Germany settled in Mennonite communities in Illinois (Trenton and Summerfield). Daniel Haury, a member of the Mennonite church at Summerfield, Ill., joined Christian Krehbiel when he moved to Halstead, Kan. Richard S. Haury, a practicing physician in Newton, Kan., was his son. S. S. Haury (q.v.), a graduate of Wadsworth Seminary, also went west and became the first missionary of the General Conference Mennonite Church. Later he practiced medicine. Gustav A. Haury (q.v., 1863-1926) was a teacher at Bethel College, North Newton, Kan., as was also his son G. A. Haury, Jr. Another son of G. A. Haury, Emil W. Haury (b. 1904), is head of the Department of Anthropology and director of the Arizona State Museum. Most of the Haurys of Mennonite faith now live in Kansas and are descendants of the Haurys who settled in Illinois a century ago.   HE.H., C.K.

J. A. Heiz, *Die Täufer im Aargau* (Aarau, 1902); Müller, *Berner Täufer*.

Haury, Gustav A. (1863-1926), Mennonite (GCM) leader and teacher. He was born in Franklin, Lee Co., Iowa, on Jan. 15, 1863, died in Newton, Kan., on June 18, 1926. He moved to McPherson Co., Kan., in 1879, attended Halstead Seminary 1887-88 and the University of Kansas 1888-90, after which he was principal of the Hillsboro public schools 1890-92 and instructor in the Halstead Seminary 1892-93. On June 11, 1891, he married Clara Ruth. Of his four sons, Irvin and Gustav A., Jr., also taught at Bethel College. Emil is a noted archaeologist in Arizona.

G. A. Haury was one of the educators responsible for moving the Halstead Seminary (q.v.) to Newton to establish Bethel College in 1893, remaining on the faculty of the school until the end of his life. He taught Latin, German, English, and other subjects, served as secretary of the faculty (dean), and was editor of the *School and College Journal*, later the *Bethel College Monthly*, which carried many of his articles. From 1910 he was treasurer and business manager of the college. He was highly esteemed as a teacher, and was a man of keen intellect and a strong personality. Upon his death the college established a memorial chair, the G. A. Haury Professorship in Classical Languages and German.   C.K.

Mennonite Yearbook and Almanac (Berne, Ind., 1927) 45 ff.; P. J. Wedel, *The Story of Bethel College* (North Newton, 1954) 40, 83, 109, 112, 139, 173, 198, 303, 313; *Mennonite Weekly Review*, June 30, 1926, p. 3; *Bethel College Monthly* (Newton, Kan.) June 15, 1926, p. 1 ff.; Oct. 15, 1926, p. 1 ff.

Haury, Samuel S. (1847-1929), Mennonite (GCM) missionary, was born Nov. 21, 1847, near Ingolstadt, Bavaria, Germany, emigrated with his parents to America in 1856, and settled on a farm near Summerfield, Ill. He was married to Susie L. Hirschler in November 1879. Seven children, four daughters and three sons, were born to this union.

Haury received his elementary education near Summerfield, Ill., and then entered Wadsworth Seminary when it opened its doors in 1868, and was graduated in 1871. Later that year he went to Barmen, Germany, to take a theological course and was graduated from there in 1875. He then entered Jefferson Medical College at Philadelphia, Pa., but his studies were interrupted when he became ill with spinal meningitis. After serving in the mission field he entered St. Louis Medical College (Washington Medical) and received his degree in 1889.

Haury was the first missionary sent out by the General Conference Mennonites. In 1879 he and J. B. Baer visited Alaska as a possible mission field for the Conference. He entered mission work among the Arapahoe Indians in Indian Territory (Oklahoma) in 1880. Here he served for seven years as the first missionary not only of the General Conference but of all Mennonites of America. He was the author of a number of pamphlets: *Briefe über die Ausbreitung des Evangeliums in der Heidenwelt* (Heilbronn, 1878); *Bericht von dem Missionar Haury an die Mitglieder der Missions-Behörde* (1882); *Die Wehrlosigkeit in der Sonntagschule* (Dayton, 1894).

After graduating from medical college he practiced medicine in Moundridge, Kan., until 1894, and in Newton until 1913, when he moved to Upland, Cal., remaining there with his family until his death on May 19, 1929. (*Mennonite Yearbook*, 1930; *ML* II, 265.)   E.G.K.

Hauser, Josef, originally a clergyman in the canton of Bern, Switzerland, then a teacher in Zofingen. In 1588 he was deposed from this position and the next year went to Moravia, where he joined the Hutterites. His wife Anna Abdorf was permitted to live in Bern with their children. In 1590 Hauser returned to Zofingen, was seized and taken to Bern. Released, he went back to Moravia, where he was chosen preacher of the church at Neumühl, March 9, 1594, and confirmed Jan. 18, 1596.

In 1603 he was sent with five other brethren to Prussia to "look through these countries with the Gospel" (*Geschichts-Bücher*, 337). "There they found many Mennonites, who were, to be sure, also divided among themselves, known as Hard Frisians, House-Buyers (*Huiskoper, q.v.*), Klärische (q.v.), Mundauer, Bekumberte (see **Bekommerden**), Waterlanders, and *Abgeteilte*" (*Geschicht-Buch*, 470). Two of his companions were Michael Grossmann (q.v.) and Karl Schneider. They traveled from Danzig to Denmark. There they visited several persons, and because they did not know the language they returned to Danzig, and from there to Moravia in the fall. In the following year (1604) Hauser was again sent to Prussia with seven other brethren and their wives and children (a total of 37 persons). "They made contact with Klaus Philip, a Mennonite lacemaker of Elbing, to get permission to settle in Elbing and vicinity, since they had heard that in Prussia everybody had religious freedom. Upon presenting a petition to the city for admission, they were asked whether they had found anyone who wished to join them in Elbing. They replied that there were such persons in and about the city, as well as on the Marcushof and Wengeln, two villages in the Marienburg district, which belonged to Poland. On Oct. 11 the brethren were informed that they could not count on tolerance in the city. On Oct. 16 they presented a new appeal to the council, to which they received the reply on Oct. 28 after their return from Danzig that the council would adhere to its previous decision" (*Geschicht-Buch,* 470).

The Hutterite chronicles call Hauser a highly gifted man, well versed in Hebrew, Latin, French, and German. He is the author of a manuscript, *Unterrichtung, dass die Gemeinschaft der zeitlichen Güter eine Lehre des Neuen Testaments sei und von allen Gläubigen erfordert werde* (1605, in Budapest); and of two hymns, "Ein Lied der 1605 nach Preussen ziehenden Brüder" (16 stanzas) and "Jetzt ist die Zeit beikommen" (11 stanzas). He died Jan. 3, 1616, at Pribitz in Moravia.   NEFF.

Beck, *Geschichts-Bücher;* J. A. Heiz, *Die Täufer im Aargau* (Aarau, 1902) 56; Wolkan, *Lieder,* 240; Loserth, *Communismus,* 106; L. Neubaur, "Mährische Brüder in Elbing," *Ztscht f. Kirchengesch.* XXXIII (1912) 447-55; *ML* II, 265 f.

Haushaben, a name often used for the Hutterite Bruderhofs: see **Households** and **Bruderhof.**

Hausknecht, David, a Mennonite teacher in Russia, born in Switzerland, who came to Russia during the great immigration near the turn of the century and conducted a private boys' school at Einlage on the Dniepr in the 1830's. Since there were few Russian schools in this region, many Russian nobles and merchants entrusted the education of their sons to Hausknecht. His principles of instruction and education were suggestive of Pestalozzi's ideas. He even used pictorial illustrations and other auxiliary material.

Hausknecht was a serious student of nature, and with his students wandered through the interesting vicinity of the school to make botanical, zoological, and mineralogical studies. Even astronomy was not foreign to him. He lived entirely for and with his pupils, and as an excellent teacher held their interest in education. He was the first teacher of a secondary school in the Chortitza region. After his death Heinrich Heese (*q.v.*) continued the school. His son, D. Hausknecht, was the first teacher of the *Bruderschule* at Gnadenfeld (*q.v.*).   D.H.E.

Friesen, *Brüderschaft;* A. Neufeld, *Die Choritzer Zentralschule* (Berdyansk, 1893); *ML* II, 267.

Hausrath, Adolf (1837-1909), a Protestant theologian, professor of New Testament exegesis and church history at the University of Heidelberg. Under the pseudonym of Georg Taylor he wrote

several historical novels and tales. One of them, *Klytia* (1883), treats Anabaptism in a sensitive and attractive spirit. The miller Werner, who plays a subordinate role in it, is a splendid Anabaptist figure. (*Menn. Bl.* 1910, 93 f.; *Comeniusblätter,* 1920, 121.) Of Hausrath's other books mention should be made of *Weltverbesserer im Mittelalter* (3 vv., 1891-95), and the novel, *Die Albigenserin* (1902). *Klytia* was reprinted after World War I by H. P. Krehbiel at Newton, Kan. (*ML* II, 268.)   NEFF.

Haute-Marne, a departement in eastern France, formed from parts of the earlier provinces of Champagne and Bourgogne. Several rivers, the Aube, Marne, and Meuse, have their source here and form fertile valleys with rich pasture land, well adapted to cattle raising. But grain cultivation is also a prominent occupation.

The Mennonites of this region live for the most part on large farms, far apart, surrounded by Catholics. Here and there they have contacts with individual Protestant families, usually Swiss, who work in the numerous cheese factories. The first Mennonite families came in the middle of the 19th century from the departements of Meuse and Vosges, and soon formed a congregation. Their first elders were Goldschmidt and Rediger. Since that time there has been a persistent urge from eastern France to move westward, which brings in new families with a definite tendency to settle in the interior of France.

The church known as "Assemblée de la Haute-Marne" numbered (1925) about 40 families with 160 souls, who lived scattered throughout the departement and beyond. Meetings were held every two weeks in the homes of the members. Services were formerly followed by a common meal, since most had to come from a distance. Often members came on Saturday and returned home on Monday. The use of automobiles now facilitates attendance. Frequently the round trip covers 140 miles or more.

Originally the services were conducted in German, and the *Ausbund* (*q.v.*) was the hymnal used, but this congregation was the first to use French; religious instruction was given in French about 1850. Like all the congregations in France, this congregation was originally Amish. In 1953 the membership was about 100 souls, with four elders, all Kennels, and four preachers, all Kennels but one, viz., Pelsy. (*ML* II, 268.)   P. So.

Hauteryve, van: see **Outrijve, van.**

Havelte, a town in the Dutch province of Drente (*q.v.*), where until 1650 were found a number of Mennonites. In 1608 the Reformed pastor of Havelte made a complaint at the synod that Mennonites of his town refused to have their children baptized. Nothing is known about a congregation in Havelte.   vDZ.

Reitsma-van Veen, *Acten der provinciale en particuliere Synoden* VIII (Groningen, 1899) 90; *ML* I, 478.

Hawkesville, a village in Waterloo Co., Ont., situated five miles northwest of St. Jacobs. The St. Jacobs Mennonite (MC) congregation undertook an outpost Sunday school here about 1930. For three years the enrollment held between 30 and 44. The Ontario Mennonite Conference assigned ministers to fill preaching appointments until local interest was lost due to activity of a Brethren group. About 15 years later the Mennonite Conference through the St. Jacobs congregation purchased a church in the village and organized a congregation. The membership in 1953 was 120, the minister Paul Martin, and the deacon Oscar Snyder.

J.C.F.

Hawkesville Old Order Mennonite Church, one of the three meetinghouses of the David Martin O.O.M. group, is located near Hawkesville (*q.v.*), Waterloo Co., Ont.

Hawthornden State Hospital, a modern mental hospital located about half way between Cleveland and Akron, Ohio, was the place of service of CPS Unit No. 72, approved by Selective Service in November 1942 and closed Oct. 1, 1946. The unit, under the direction of the MCC, performed a variety of tasks, but about half of the men were attendants on the wards.   M.G.

Melvin Gingerich, *Service for Peace* (Akron, 1949) 226.

Haxenberg, Willibald von, chamberlain of King Ladislas IV of Poland, in 1642 received from this king all the properties of the Mennonites in Prussia, both in the cities and in the country, because "this people has settled in our country without permission and are harming the trade of our citizens." Von Haxenberg took advantage of his privilege to extort 80,000 guilders annually from the Mennonites. By supplications and large gifts to the king, the Mennonites secured from him in December 1642 the cancellation of the privileges given to von Haxenberg. The good will of the king to the Mennonites lasted only until 1647, and after the death of Ladislas IV, von Haxenberg again contacted the Mennonites asking them for two guilders pro "Hufe" under the pretext that he would procure freedom of religion for them. The Mennonites, upon complaint to the new King John II Casimir, were on July 16, 1650, granted an edict which ordered that no one should extort from the Mennonites under the pretext of their faith.

vpZ.

F. Szper, *Nederlandsche Nederzettingen in West Pruisen gedurende den Poolschen tijd* (Enkhuizen, 1913) 210-15.

Hay (Township) Amish Mennonite Church, Huron Co., Ont., was established by settlers from Waterloo County in 1848, when Bishop John Oesch (d. 1850) arrived. Early families were Baechler, Gingerich, Kuepfer, Erb, Gerber, Gascho, Schantz, Bender, Egli, Schwartzendruber, and Wuetherich. The meetinghouse was built in 1884. The first preacher ordained was Joseph Wutherich (ord. 1849), the second John Egli, who moved away in 1860. John Gascho served as preacher 1876-1908. The small congregation was served by bishops from Waterloo County except when Bishop Eli Frey of Wauseon, Ohio, served 1915-23. In 1908 some 50 members transferred to the Mennonite

Church (MC), which constituted the beginning of the Zurich (*q.v.*) Mennonite congregation. In 1954 the Hay A.M. membership was 72, with Ephraim Gingerich serving as pastor. The congregation is a member of the Ontario Amish Mennonite Conference.   H.S.B.

L. J. Burkholder, *A Brief History of the Mennonites in Ontario* (Markham, 1935) 238-42.

Hay (Township) Mennonite (MC) Church, near Zurich, Huron Co., Ont., became extinct about 1900, although one surviving member was incorporated into the new Zurich (*q.v.*) congregation established at about the same location in 1908. The community was settled in 1835-60 by Mennonite families from the Waterloo County and Markham communities: Wideman, Otterbein, Vincent, Detweiler, Lehman, Wambold, Martin, Clemens, Bechtel, Reesor, Baer, Newschwanger. A meetinghouse was built about 1864, three miles south of Zurich. The first minister was Daniel Brundage 1850-58, the first deacon Abraham Vincent, ordained in 1851. Henry Newschwanger served as minister about 1857-70, Henry B. Detwiler 1874-93. Without a resident minister from 1893 on, the membership, which was 35 in 1883, dwindled and finally disappeared. The congregation was a member of the Ontario Mennonite Conference.

H.S.B.

L. J. Burkholder, *A Brief History of the Mennonites in Ontario* (Markham, 1935) 37, 101, 125.

Haycock Mennonite Church (MC), located near Applebachsville in Haycock Twp., Bucks Co., Pa., member of the Franconia Conference, originated in 1937. It was at first a mission outpost with services conducted in a schoolhouse; a church building was erected in 1941. The first minister, Stanley Beidler, was ordained in 1942 (bishop, 1943). By 1940 the membership was 10. In 1953 it was 77.   J.C.W.

Haze Claesdochter of Poeldijk, Dutch province of South Holland, an unmarried woman, joined in the Anabaptist revolt at Poeldijk (*q.v.*) in February 1536 and was drowned (likely at The Hague) on March 18, 1536.   vpZ.

Inv. Arch. Amst. I, No. 745; E. van Bergen, "De Wederdoopers in het Westland," in *Bijdr. v.d. Geschiedenis v.h. Bisdom Haarlem* XXVIII (Leiden, 1903) 278 f.

Hazelton, Iowa, the address of two Old Order Amish Mennonite church districts in Buchanan Co. (*q.v.*), Iowa.   M.G.

Hazenpoet, Gerrit, an Anabaptist martyr: see **Gerrit Hazenpoot.**

Hazerswoude (formerly usually called Hasersouw), a village in the Dutch province of South Holland, where strong Anabaptist activity of the revolutionary type was found in 1535, resulting in a revolt in the last day of that year, in which 60 persons, both men and women, participated. The revolt was rigorously suppressed by the government and most participants were killed or executed some time after. About 1650 and apparently much earlier there were two Mennonite congregations at Hazerswoude, of which there is only sparse information. Both were small; one belonged to the Flemish branch, the other to the Waterlanders. They seem to have merged at the end of the 17th century. This united congregation, which for more than a hundred years was considerably supported by the congregations of Rotterdam, Haarlem, and Amsterdam, belonged to the Zonist (*q.v.*) Conference. In 1726 it liberally contributed to the need of Mennonites in Prussia. In 1792 it numbered only eight members and in 1797 it died out. The last preacher was Aris Baas 1769-95; his predecessor, Adriaan Koenen (*q.v.*) 1725-ca. 67, was appointed in 1740 to go to Danzig, Prussia, to settle the quarrels which had arisen in that congregation. vDZ.

Inv. Arch. Amst. I, Nos. 143, 145, 150, 152-55, 157, 159, 162, 167, 1164; II, Nos. 1808, 1811, 1905, 2141; II, 2, Nos. 82-97; Kühler, *Geschiedenis* I, 186 f., 199; *ML* II, 268.

Head Covering: see Prayer Veiling.

Heatwole (Hütwohl, Hetwol, Hetwold, Heetweel, Hutwell, Hiedwohl, and Heatwol), a Mennonite (MC) family name. It appeared in the 17th-century records with Johann Georg Hutwohl at Steeg near Bacharach on the Rhine, the father and grandfather of Mathias Heatwole, the progenitor of nearly all the Heatwoles in America today, who came to Pennsylvania in 1748. His son David Heatwole, a shoemaker by trade, moved south to Franklin Co., Pa., and then to Virginia, and became the ancestor of the Heatwoles of Virginia. The Heatwole family has produced more than its quota of leaders and distinguished men—educators, physicians, and churchmen. Two bishops (L. J. Heatwole, 1852-1932, *q.v.,* A. P. Heatwole) and at least eight ministers and two deacons with this family name have served or are serving the Mennonite churches in Virginia. Bishop J. A. Heatwole (1871-1940) served churches in and around La Junta, Col.; R. J. Heatwole (1847-1921) was a prominent pioneer in Kansas.

In the 17th and 18th centuries there were members of this family living in the Palatinate (see **Huthwohl**).   H.A.B.

D. A. Heatwole, *A History of the Heatwole Family* (Dale Enterprise, Va., 1882); C. J. Heatwole, *History of the Heatwole Family* (n.p., n.d., 1907).

Heatwole, Jacob A. (1871-1940), a Mennonite (MC) bishop of Colorado, son of Joseph F. Heatwole, was born in Harrisonburg, Va., Sept. 28, 1871. On Dec. 30, 1888, he was received into the Mennonite Church (MC) by Bishop Samuel Coffman. In 1890 he attended school at the Peabody Teachers' Normal at Harrisonburg, Va., and 1892-94 the West Central Academy, Mt. Clinton, Va. He taught school for 12 years in Rockingham Co., Va. On Dec. 25, 1895, he was married to Bertha Showalter, who died May 24, 1934. This union was blest with four daughters and two sons. In March 1907 he and family moved from Harrisonburg to La Junta, which was his home until the time of his death. During this time, because of his friendly and sociable disposition, he became widely known in the community.

J. A. Heatwole was ordained to the ministry Jan. 2, 1902, by Bishop Anthony Heatwole and to the office of bishop at La Junta, on March 16, 1919, by Bishop D. H. Bender. While in Virginia he worked in the ministry with his father and A. D. Wenger in the West Virginia mountains and at the Clinton, Weaver, Bank, and Pike churches. In the La Junta Mennonite Church he served as minister and bishop, and as bishop of the East Holbrook, Limon, and Manitou churches.

In October 1912 Heatwole was elected by the Kansas-Nebraska Conference as a member of the Local Board of the Mennonite Sanitarium and on Nov. 6, 1912, in the organization of the board he was elected vice-president, and on Sept. 9, 1921, president of the board. He served in this capacity to the time of his death.   A.H.E.

Heatwole, Lewis James (1852-1932), a Mennonite (MC) bishop and writer, the oldest of the eleven children of David A. and Cathrine Driver Heatwole, was born Dec. 4, 1852, at Dale Enterprise, Va. On Nov. 11, 1875, he married Mary Alice Coffman, the daughter of Bishop Samuel Coffman (*q.v.*) and sister of John S. Coffman, the pioneer Mennonite evangelist. To this family were born a son and six daughters. He received his education at the Normal School in Bridgewater, Va. He lived all but three years of his life at Dale Enterprise. He was ordained to the ministry at Weaver's Church near Harrisonburg in 1887, and as a bishop in Cass Co., Mo., in 1892, where the family lived in 1890-93. After the death of his father-in-law he became bishop of the congregations of the Middle District in the Shenandoah Valley, Va., which office he held until his death on Dec. 26, 1932.

Besides his ministerial duties L. J. Heatwole was also an astronomer, a calculator of almanacs, a teacher in the public schools, and an official observer for the U.S. Weather Bureau, keeping records of temperature and rainfall for 52 years. His influence was strong in the founding and the establishing of the Eastern Mennonite School. For a number of years he served on the faculty of the Bible term of this school. At conferences and at board meetings his voice was always gladly heard, for he was mild-mannered and conciliatory, and at the same time practical. The titles of his published works indicate the variety of his interests: *Baptism Shown to Be a Ceremony of Consecration* (Elkhart, 1902); *Key to the Almanac and the Sidereal Heavens* (Scottdale, 1908); *Mennonite Handbook of Information* (Scottdale, 1925); *Moral Training in the Public Schools: A Treatise Designed for Teachers* . . . (Scottdale, 1908); *The Perpetual Calendar* (Dale Enterprise, 1911).
                                          E.H.G.

Heatwole, Lydia Magdalena (1887-1932), daughter of Reuben J. and Margaret (Kilmer) Heatwole, was a pioneer Mennonite (MC) nurse. She grew to womanhood in a devout Mennonite home in Harvey Co., Kan. Her service in the Old People's Home near Rittman, Ohio, and later in the Kansas City Mission deepened her conviction to enter nurses' training, but in order to help her parents she took up a homestead in eastern Colorado. In 1918 she graduated with the first class from the Mennonite Training School for Nurses at La Junta. After further training at Agnes Memorial Hospital in Denver she returned to La Junta as superintendent of nurses. She set a high Christian standard for the training school and saw it grow from one supervisor and a few students to ten supervisors and officers and 36 students. Her outstanding contribution to the nursing profession in the Mennonite Church was her emphasis on the spiritual and religious service of the nurse to her patient. J.S.U.

Heatwole, Reuben J. (Feb. 27, 1847-June 7, 1921), the son of John S. and Nancy Heatwole, was born at Rockingham Co., Va. On Feb. 27, 1873, he married Margaret Kilmer, and was the father of seven children—Henry, Anna, Sarah, Susanna, Mary, Martha, and Lydia. In early manhood he took up a homestead in Marion Co., Kan. In later years he with his family lived in Harvey County, and Mc-Pherson County near Windom, Kan. He was an outstanding active Mennonite (MC) layman on the Kansas and Colorado frontier. He taught singing schools, helped organize Sunday schools and churches, served on the Evangelizing Committee, and he assisted many ministers materially in preaching appointments and evangelistic services. His missionary zeal was a positive influence of permanent value to central Kansas and Colorado Mennonite (MC) congregations. M.M.T.

Hebberecht, a Mennonite family in Flanders which emigrated to Aardenburg, Dutch province of Zeeland. Christoffel Hebberecht, a cloth merchant of Gent, Belgium, obtained citizenship in Aardenburg in 1633, and became a deacon of the Aardenburg Mennonite congregation. His son Ghysel (or Gillis) Hebberecht, also called Gillis Aelbrechts, a well-to-do cloth merchant, married Susanna de Meyere, was a preacher of the Aardenburg congregation from 1651 until his death, shortly after Sept. 21, 1680. He played a prominent role in the difficult period when the government vigorously opposed the Mennonites, chiefly at the instigation of the Calvinist preacher Buce. With calm firmness and warm faith he led the church wisely. When the authorities called the Mennonites as civil guards (1657-58), and accused them of disloyalty to the country because they could not for reasons of conscience accept the service, Hebberecht after many discussions finally obtained an agreement in 1663 that the Mennonites should pay a "guard fee" in return for exemption from service. A charge of Socinianism (q.v.) made against Hebberecht in 1660 was dismissed by the magistrate. When the city was besieged by the French in 1762, Hebberecht again became the soul of the congregation. Ready to stand by the city in trouble, the Mennonites nevertheless adhered to their principle not to fight with arms. Contemporaries, among them Hunnius, the Reformed pastor of Oostburg, praised him for his faithfulness to principle and his leadership through the period of confusion. Under Hebberecht the Aardenburg church experienced a period of great development. vDZ.

DB 1876, 81, 105; 1879, 14 ff.; 1881, 1 f., 27-29; 1883, 11, 13-17, 18, 22; 1884, 32-34; *Biogr. Wb.* III, 601 f.; F. K. van Lennep, *Verzameling van Oorkonden, betrekking hebbende op het geslacht von Eeghen* (Amsterdam, 1918) see Index; *ML* II, 268.

Heberle, Urban (1812-66), a Lutheran church historian of Württemberg, Germany. As deacon in Blaubeuren 1843-49 and archdeacon 1847-57 in Tübingen, he published important articles relating to Anabaptist history of the 16th century, showing himself an expert in the field. His important works were (1) "Johann Denk und sein Büchlein vom Gesetz Gottes" (*Theologische Studien und Kritiken*, 1851, 121-94); (2) "Johann Denk und die Ausbreitung seiner Lehre" (*op. cit.*, 1855, 817-90); (3) "Leonhard Kaiser, lutherischer, kein anabaptistischer Blutzeuge" (*Ztscht für Protestantismus und Kirche*, 1856); (4) "W. Capitos Verhältnis zum Anabaptismus" (*Niedners Ztscht für die hist. Theol.*, 1857, 285 f.); (5) "Die Anfänge des Anabaptismus in der Schweiz" (*Jahrbuch für deutsche Theologie*, 1858). Especially the last article is of outstanding importance historically. No student of Anabaptist history can afford to overlook it. (*ML* II, 269.) NEFF.

Hebron Mennonite Church (MC) is a rural mission church located about four miles southeast of Fulks Run, Rockingham Co., Va., under the Virginia Conference. About 1850 Abraham Brenneman, and perhaps others, moved from Linville Creek Valley into Brocks Gap, situated behind the first range of the Appalachian Mountains, about seven miles west of Broadway, Va. Sometime later preaching services were held near there. In 1881 the Mennonites in partnership with the United Brethren built a meetinghouse about 1½ miles south of Fulks Run, where services were held for a number of years. The church building then passed into the hands of the U.B. Church. Later services were again held in two schoolhouses in the same neighborhood several miles east and northeast of Mt. Carmel, the first meetinghouse. A frame building called Hebron was built in 1915 on the Shoemaker River about four miles southeast of Fulks Run to serve the then growing congregation. Membership in 1954 was 66; the pastor was Lewis P. Showalter. T.S.

Hebron Mennonite Church (GCM), located five miles east of Buhler, Kan., a member of the Western District Conference, was founded in 1879 with Bernhard Buhler (q.v.) as elder. From the beginning the congregation made the mode of baptism optional, administering it by sprinkling or immersion. Buhler was baptized by sprinkling and ordained as minister by Leonhard Sudermann. The Hebron Mennonite Church is an exception in that it practices more than one mode of baptism. In 1882 a church building was constructed, which was replaced in 1900 by the present building. Bernhard Buhler served Hebron as elder 1879-1906, succeeded by A. M. Martens 1906-23. Other ministers were J. B. Dick 1900-17, Peter Lohrentz 1888-1924, David Penner 1879-95, Cornelius Froese 1879-1902, P. E. Frantz 1925-29 and 1931-36, P. S. Goertz 1930-31, T. A. van der Smissen

1937-46, J. W. Nickel 1947-48, Elbert Koontz 1948-53, and O'Ray Graber since 1954. The membership in 1955 was 207.   C.K.

C. C. Epp, "Early Hebron Mennonite Church," *Menn. Life* VIII (April 1953) 86 ff.; *Year Book of the Hebron Church,* 1941, 4 ff.

Hechtlein (not Hechtler), **Hans,** a parson at Schalkhausen near Ansbach, Germany, was arrested in 1530 on the charge that he had accepted rebaptism. At his cross-examination he openly confessed that not only he, but also his wife and his mother, had been baptized on confession of their faith. Even on the rack he denied having spread seditious doctrines. He was therefore expelled. Nothing more is known of him.   W.W.

K. Schornbaum, *TA* II: *Brandenburg;* E. Teufel, "Der Täuferprozess gegen Pfarrer Hechtlein in Schalkhausen 1539-40," in *Ztscht für Kirchengesch.* XVIII (1949); W. Löhe, *Erinnerungen aus der Reformationsgeschichte von Franken* (Nürnberg, 1847) 109; *ML* II, 269.

Heems, Abraham, a Dutch Mennonite of Haarlem, Holland, married to Johanna van Dalen, of a Flemish emigrant family, silk manufacturer, d. after 1747, was the author of a number of religious poems. Among his publications were *Absolon of de gestrafte Heerschzucht* (Haarlem, n.d.); and *Bijbelpoezy in Alleenspraken, Tafereelen, Uitbreidingen en Zedelessen* (Amsterdam, 1729).

Heems's daughter Femina (1724-81), married to the Mennonite merchant Gerard Hugaart of Haarlem, also published a number of poems. Heems died in 1756. The Heems family, a number of whom served as deacons or as regents of the Mennonite orphanages, was in the 17th and 18th centuries rather numerous in Haarlem.   vDZ.

M. Schagen, *Naamlijst van Doopsgezinde Schrijveren* (1745) 45; *Biogr. Wb.* III, 603; IV, 787.

Heenvliet, a village on the island of Voorne-Putten, in the Dutch province of South Holland. In the 17th century there was a small Mennonite congregation at Heenvliet, which was closely connected with the Mennonites in the neighboring villages of Geervliet and Spijkenis. It belonged to the Flemish branch. In 1733-34 it contributed to the needs of the Prussian Mennonites, but soon after it must have died out. (*Inv. Arch. Amst.* II, Nos. 896, 1180.)   vDZ.

Heere, de, a Dutch Mennonite family, originally living in Flanders, Belgium, whose members moved from there to Friesland to escape persecution. Whether Philips de Heere, formerly a sheriff at Kortrijk (Courtrai) in Flanders, who fled to Franeker (Friesland), was a Mennonite or not could not be ascertained. In any case the noted poet Lucas de Heere (1534-84), who was also a painter, the teacher of Karel van Mander (*q.v.*), was not a Mennonite. It is not clear whether Philippus de He(e)re, who in 1672 married Antie Jans Agricola (Mennonite) at Franeker, was a descendant of Philips de Heere of Kortrijk. This Philippus de Heere was the ancestor of the Dutch Mennonite de Heere family, a number of whom bear the name of Scheltema de Heere. (See also **Scheltema.**)

It has been proved that Jan Jacobsz (*q.v.*), who was a well-known Mennonite elder, did not belong to the de Heere family as was formerly generally believed.   vDZ.

Ned. Patriciaat XXVII (1941) 218-20; *Biogr. Wb.* III, 604 ff.; *DB* 1867, 54.

Heeren, an old Mennonite family of Aalsmeer, Dutch province of North Holland, still found there; in the 17th century some of them were preachers of the Waterlander congregation. vDZ.

Heerenveen, a town in the Dutch province of Friesland, founded in the second half of the 16th century as a peat-digging center. Already in this period Mennonites were found here; in 1563-65 Leenaert Bouwens (*q.v.*) baptized 14 persons at Oudeschoot, about three miles south of Heerenveen. Soon after 1600 there was at least one Mennonite congregation at Heerenveen; probably there were several. At any rate in the second half of the 17th century there were five or even more congregations: one Waterlander, one Frisian, one of the Jan Jacobsz (*q.v.*) group, one Flemish, and one Old Flemish. It is also possible that there was a congregation of the Twisck (*q.v.*) group, but further information about this congregation is lacking.

The Jan Jacobsz group had a large number of members in Heerenveen and its neighborhood; in the early part of the 17th century it had two meetinghouses, but the congregations died out before 1729. The Frisian congregation, called "Heerenveen en Lange Lilo" in the *Naamlijst* of 1731, died out about 1750 or merged with another group.

The Groningen Old Flemish congregation existed until about 1800. It was a conservative group. Age Jouckes, one of its preachers, was banned in 1687 and then joined the Waterlanders. Most of the Groningen Old Flemish members lived outside of Heerenveen. In the 18th century this congregation is usually called "Knijpe en Mildam" (*q.v.*).

The Flemish congregation merged with the Waterlanders in 1741; it then numbered 37 members. Its meetinghouse was located in the Kakelsteeg.

The most important was the Waterlander congregation. From about 1650 it had two meetinghouses, one in the town on the Agterom bij de Dragt, and one on the Boven-Knijpe. In 1706 the total membership numbered 167. From this year the history of the congregation is well known, for in 1706 a church record (*Menniste Christen Karcken Boeck*) was begun. In 1741, in the merger with the Flemish, the old Agterom meetinghouse was abandoned. The congregation then held services in the former Flemish Kakelsteeg meetinghouse. This being too small for the congregation, a new meetinghouse was erected in 1761 (still in use) on the Vermaningssteeg. Until 1765 it had only untrained ministers chosen out of the congregation. Among them were Jan Thomas (*q.v.*), Wiebe Pieters Zeeman, Pieke Tjommes, and Wytze Jeens Brouwer (*q.v.*). All of these men were suspended by the Frisian government on charges of Socinianism—Jan Thomas in 1719, and the other three in 1738.

Johannes Sytzes Hoekstra, called in from Burg on the island of Texel, served here from 1765 until his death in 1776. He was followed by Hendrik Jans Blauw 1776-82, who had previously served at Norden, Germany. During his ministry the congregation by brotherly agreement was divided into two congregations, one at Heerenveen and one at Bovenknijpe (q.v.). The Heerenveen congregation then numbered about 200 members, that of Bovenknijpe 92.

The ministers after Blauw were Gentius Wybrandi 1782-88, Jan van Calcar 1788-1821, R. J. Keestra 1821-66, A. Vis 1866-1901, Tj. van der Ploeg 1903-8, S. D. A. Wartena 1909-22, A. Vis 1922-25, J. Koster 1926-37, S. Gosses Gzn. 1938-42, S. I. van der Meulen 1943-54, and R. Hofman 1954- .

The membership was about 200 in 1780, 144 in 1837, 260 in 1860, 235 in 1900, 207 in 1954. Church activities include a Sunday school for children, ladies' circle (52 members), men's circle (18 members), choir, and Bible study group. vdZ.

P. H. Veen, *De Doopsgezinden in Schoterland* (Leeuwarden, 1869) *passim;* J. Loosjes, *Jan Jacobsz en de Jan-Jacobsgezinden* in *Ned. Archief v. Kergesch.* XI, 3 (The Hague, 1914) 231; *DB* 1870, 108-18; *ML* II, 269.

Heerjansdam, Dutch province of South Holland, south of Rotterdam, where in the 17th century there was a small Mennonite congregation of the Flemish branch, which must have died out soon after the middle of the 17th century and about the history of which nothing is known. vdZ.

Heerlen, a town in the Dutch province of Limburg, center of the important coal-mining district, seat of the Mennonite congregation of southern Limburg. Since 1926, through the activity of A. E. Dinger and J. L. Swart-Posthumus Meijes, monthly services have been held in a hall at Treebeek near Heerlen, and a congregation was founded on Nov. 19, 1934. In 1936 S. M. A. Daalder became the pastor of the young congregation, serving at the same time at Eindhoven (q.v.). In 1939 the congregation obtained a fine meetinghouse, dedicated on Nov. 19, 1939, adorned with a beautiful stained glass window by the artist C. Baljet.

The membership, numbering about 80 when the congregation was founded, had increased to 160 by 1954; the following pastors have served: S. M. A. Daalder 1936-42, Th. van Veen 1942-47, P. van der Meulen 1947-49, G. A. Maathuis 1949- . Besides in Heerlen services are held at Geleen. Activities: West-Hill Sunday school for children at Heerlen, Geleen, and Treebeek; ladies' circles at Heerlen and Treebeek. vdZ.

Heese, Heinrich (1787-1868), an outstanding Mennonite teacher of Russia, a Prussian and a Lutheran by birth. As a youth he fled from French recruiting to the Mennonites in South Russia and accepted their faith.

Heese came first to Chortitza, where he took a position as secretary in the local government. In 1829 he was called by Johann Cornies to teach in the Ohrloff Vereinsschule, a secondary school headed by the Cornies family. For 12 years he taught about 60 pupils of a wide variety of ages all that he and Cornies considered essential for a Christian farmer. In his spare time he was Cornies' secretary, looked after his Russian correspondence with the authorities and supported him in his various reforms. In 1840 he was requested to teach Russian in the school about to be opened in the Chortitza. He worked out the regulations and a schedule of classes and expenses, and began to teach in a house assigned to him. The initial work was very difficult. It was not easy to find the necessary number of students or to gain adequate support from the parents and the church.

In addition to the work in and for the school, in which he also attempted to fit the less capable for a useful life, Heese worked on a plan to increase the yield of crops, made suggestions to improve the relations with Russian servants, gave advice on the improvement of dairy stock and the planting of trees, etc. So many demands of this kind were made upon his time and strength that he could not devote as much time as he wished to the school.

Heese considered the school a seedbed for the development of a feeling of community among the young people. In agriculture he saw the basis of the entire structure of the state; where agriculture is neglected the people grow poor and their culture disintegrates. Mennonites should be model farmers, if only in gratitude to the government. He advocated better equipment, methodical cultivation of potatoes, deep plowing, rotation of crops, letting at least 10 acres lie fallow but under constant cultivation, and the use of fertilizers.

In spite of his great services to the Mennonite settlements Heese met much hostility. In 1846 he had to yield his position to the youthful Heinrich Franz (q.v.). In 1849 he moved to Einlage, took over the headship of a boarding school, and at the age of 62 passed the Russian teachers' examination at Ekaterinoslav. His students were for the most part the sons of Russian nobles. On April 12, 1868, he died, having previously written his own funeral sermon. D.H.E.

A. Neufeld, *Die Chortitzer Zentralschule* (Berdyansk, 1893); Friesen, *Brüderschaft;* D. H. Epp, "H. Heese und seine Zeit," *Botschafter* V (Ekaterinoslav, 1910) *idem, Heinrich Heese* (Steinbach, 1952); *ML* II, 269 f.

Heese, Heinrich, b. 1846 in Russia, d. March 3, 1903, at Ekaterinoslav, Russia, was a grandson of the educator Heinrich Heese (q.v.). Heese was the owner of a large milling establishment in Ekaterinoslav, a member of the Duma, a member of the board of directors of the city branch of the federal bank and of many private banks (see also **Ekaterinoslav**). C.K.

H. Dirks, *Menn. Jahrbuch,* 1903-4 (Gross Tokmak, 1905) 28.

Heese, Peter (1852-1911), an outstanding Mennonite in Russia, was born June 2, 1852, in Ekaterinoslav, Ukraine, and was educated in the Chortitza Zentralschule, the Gymnasium in Ekaterinoslav, and the University of Moscow. In the school year 1877-78 he taught in Gnadenfeld, Molotschna, and the next school year at the Ohrloff Vereinsschule (mathematics). In 1880 he was made co-president of the Ohrloff Vereinsschule with Joh. Klatt (*q.v.*), and was soon afterward chosen a member of the Molotschna Mennonite school board, and served as its president alternately with Klatt 1889-96.

Peter Heese was a man of extraordinary gifts and a commanding as well as winsome personality. In him the cause of education had an excellent promoter and counselor, on the character of the school as well as on the principles of education, but also an expert in the science and methods. Therefore the Heese-Klatt period is called the Golden Age of education among the Molotschna Mennonites. The most important achievement was the reform of the elementary village schools. New methods in the teaching of Russian, a German reader, outlines for Bible history, church history, and German grammar, and the use of Russian in arithmetic characterize this period.

Peter Heese's independence, his private financial means, and his generous liberality toward benevolent and educational institution causes gave him a name second (probably) only to that of Johann Cornies (*q.v.*). He took an important part in the establishment of the school for the deaf in Tiege, called the Marientaubstummenschule (*q.v.*).

Because he was unable to carry out all of his educational ideas, he left the school board in 1896 and in bitterness withdrew from Mennonite fellowship. In 1906 he published a Russian newspaper in Ekaterinoslav. Until his death he devoted his strength and fortune to sacrificial, unceasing service to his fellow men. (*Menn. Jahrbuch,* 1910, 102; *ML* II, 270.) A.B.

Hege, a widely ramified family in South Germany, which settled here after the Thirty Years' War. The earliest traces lead to the Swiss canton of Aargau, where the name occurred frequently among the Swiss Brethren. At the end of the 16th century there were still some members of the family among the Swiss Brethren; they emigrated when the government tried to compel them to join the state church. Among these was Ulrich Hege of Leerau.

The emigrants seem to have settled first in Alsace, but definite facts about the family are not known before the Peace of Westphalia. It appeared then in the Palatinate. The earliest information comes from Dühren in the Sinsheim district, where Rudolf Hege had gone from Switzerland about 1656. On March 2, 1661, he took part in an evening service of Mennonites in Steinsfurt, and was therefore questioned by the authorities (see **Hasselbach**). In the government records he is not otherwise mentioned. In the church book begun at Mutterstadt in the Palatinate in 1676, his name was entered for the first time in 1697; it is a notice of the birth of Christian Hegi, the son of the surgeon Jakob Hegi (d. about 1733) and his wife Katharina. The spelling Hegi indicates Swiss origin; it was not changed to Hege until 1753. But it is not clear that these Hegis are Mennonites; for the family is not mentioned in the government lists for Mutterstadt, which generally list all the Mennonites in the Palatinate, whereas in the family list of 1724 the Mennonite Hans Kaegy is named as the renter.

Information concerning the spread of the Mennonites in the Palatinate is always given in the inventories of the government, which watched that they did not exceed the set number of 200 families. The official lists are still preserved in the General-landesarchiv of Baden at Karlsruhe. The first mention of the name Hege appears in it in 1716. At that time Daniel Hege was living in Branchweilerhof (*q.v.*) near Neustadt; he is also named in the registers of 1724, 1738, and 1743 as part renter of the farm. He died in 1748. Seven sons survived: Christian, Johannes, Daniel, Heinrich, Samuel, Jakob, and Ulrich, as well as a daughter who married Melchior Fellmann. Their descendants are in part still living in the Rheinpfalz, in Branchweilerhof and in the churches of Deutschhof (*q.v.*) and Kohlhof; but a large part have emigrated. In the government lists of the Kurpfalz, only the oldest, Christian, and the youngest, Ulrich, are named. Christian Hege was hereditary lessee of the Branchweilerhof and is named as such in the family lists of the government in 1752, 1759, and 1769. He represented the Mennonites of the left side of the Rhine at the conference of Oct. 14, 1782, at the Immelhäuserhof, called by Abraham Zeisset, the elder of the Hasselbach (*q.v.*) congregation, to settle a dispute (Müller, *Berner Täufer,* 213).

In the government list of 1769 the name Hege is entered for the first time in Mutterstadt. At that time Ulrich Hege, probably the youngest brother of the Christian Hege at the Branchweilerhof, lived at Mutterstadt. Ulrich was born about 1735 at Branchweilerhof, and about 1762 leased a farm in Mutterstadt. About 1770 he moved to Eppelheim near Heidelberg, where he died about 1783 at the age of 47 years. He is the ancestor of the line that settled in Baden, Württemberg, and Bavaria and from which a large number of preachers and elders of the Mennonite churches there were derived. His oldest son, Daniel Hege, b. 1765, leased an estate in Schwetzingen and in 1811 in Mauer near Meckesheim, and in 1822 took over the leased estate of Oberbiegelhof near Neckarbischofsheim, which was farmed by the family nearly 100 years (see **Unterbüchelhof**). He had been deacon of the Meckesheim congregation; he died in 1728 at the age of 73 years.

Of his sons, Ulrich Hege†, b. April 7, 1808, at Schwetzingen, was one of the leading elders of the Mennonites of Baden. He was ordained preacher in 1838, and elder in 1843. He was aware of the weaknesses of his congregation and worked successfully with the elders Christian Schmutz and Heinrich Landes for a spiritual revival. Although he had no theological education, he was an outstanding preacher. His sermons were simple, but powerful. From them spoke a thorough knowledge of Scripture, deep feeling, and a penetrating understanding. His great emphasis was the personal attitude of the individual to God and to Christ. He was therefore less concerned with increasing the membership than with harmonizing personal life with the Word of God. Hence it occurred that he did not baptize an applicant if he noticed in the baptismal instruction that a serious intention to live a new life was lacking. Two letters have been preserved which he wrote with his brother elders in July 1862 to David Sherrick and Elias Eby of Canada, and which Elder David Sherrick published in a booklet in Preston, 1863 (Bender, *Two Centuries*, 29). His position in the churches of Baden is indicated by the foreword of the elders in *Leitfaden zum Gebrauch bei gottesdienstlichen Handlungen* (Sinsheim, 1876), which states that they wished to avoid the legal rather than evangelistic spirit of the old *Formularbuch:* "We could undertake this task on the basis of the Holy Scriptures so much the more joyfully because we found ourselves in this connection in agreement with the elders Christian Schmutz of Rappenau and Ulrich Hege of Oberbiegelhof, who passed away a few years ago" (p. VI). Ulrich Hege died Nov. 8, 1872 (*Gbl.,* 1872, 86). Seven sons and four daughters survived.

After his death most of his sons continued in the spirit of their father as elders of South German churches. Five of these were:

(1) Christian Hege, b. Aug. 15, 1840, d. April 18, 1907, was renter in Breitenau near Willsbach (Württemberg), after Oct. 19, 1890, preacher of the Lobenbach church (later merged with the church at Heilbronn), and after Jan. 28, 1894, elder, author of a book, *Einst und Jetzt oder Vergangenheit und Gegenwart unserer Mennoniten-Gemeinden* (Reihen, 1890). In 1904-7 he was the representative of the Weinsberg district in the Landtag of Württemberg (*Gbl.,* 1907, 40; *Gem.-Kal.,* 1909, 47-54, with picture).

(2) Jakob Hege, b. Sept. 18, 1844, d. May 9, 1926, was first renter of the large Lautenbach farm near Neckarsulm, then renter in Hettstadterhof near Würzburg, then emigrated to Wisner, Neb., in 1893, went to Aberdeen, Idaho, and died in Paso Robles, Cal. On Aug. 9, 1874, he became preacher, May 23, 1880, elder of the Lobenbach church, and 1880-92 he served the Giebelstadt church, and in America the congregations at Aberdeen (*q.v.*) and Paso Robles. In 1897 he published *Christliche Gemeindezucht* (*Gbl.,* 1926, 78).

(3) Johannes Hege, b. April 5, 1847, d. Feb. 20, 1911, rented in turn the Oberbiegelhof, Buchenhof near Römhild (Thuringia), and Liebenstein near Lauffen a. N. On July 16, 1876, he was ordained as preacher of the Hasselbach church, and later as elder. From 1886 to 1898 he served the congregation of Bildhausen-Trappstadt, and after 1898 the Heilbronn congregation (*Gbl.,* 1911, 26).

(4) Philipp Hege, b. April 15, 1848, d. May 1, 1908, rented the Oberbiegelhof, was ordained preacher June 22, 1873, and elder Oct. 23, 1887, for the Hasselbach congregation (*Gbl.,* 1909, 44).

(5) Daniel Hege, b. Sept. 6, 1836, d. May 5, 1900, rented successively a farm in Neuhaus near Grombach (Baden), Bonfeld near Heilbronn, and Hettstadterhof near Würzburg. In 1880 he moved to Munich, and from there directed the emigration of Mennonites from Baden to southern Bavaria, and helped to bring about a union between them and the Mennonites who were already living here, having emigrated from the Palatinate early in the 19th century. This union resulted in the organization of the church in Munich in 1892 (*Gbl.,* 1900, 27; *Menn. Bl.,* 68, with picture).

Also three sons-in-law of Ulrich Hege served as elders in the churches: (1) Daniel Bähr (1834-1905) was chosen preacher June 11, 1871, and elder June 14, 1874, of the Rappenau (Baden) congregation, and after 1897 served the Munich and Eichstock congregations (*Gbl.,* 1905, 62; *Menn. Bl.,* 76, with photograph). (2) Abraham Schmutz (1849-1924) was made preacher April 15, 1883, and elder Jan. 28, 1894, of the Ittlingen congregation (now Sinsheim a. E.) (*Gbl.,* 1925, 4). (3) Daniel Lichti (1849-1928) was made preacher of the Giebelstadt-Rottenbauer church (now Würzburg) Jan. 18, 1880, and later elder of the Donauwörth church (*Gbl.,* 1928, 84).

The second son of Ulrich Hege of the branch in Baden, Christian Hege (1768-1838), settled in Bockschaft near Kirchardt. His son Ulrich Hege in Reihen (b. Jan. 13, 1812, d. June 13, 1896) was elder of the Ittlingen congregation, and founder and for many years the editor of the *Gemeindeblatt der Mennoniten* (*q.v.*). In the name of the *Aeltestenrat* he published the new edition of the *Leitfaden* in 1876 (*Gbl.,* 1896, 74). Of his sons, Jakob Hege† (b. Dec., 1848, d. Aug. 26, 1911) was traveling evangelist of the Mennonites of Baden, Württemberg, and Bavaria from 1876 on. At the same time he renewed connections with the Mennonites of Switzerland, and beginning in 1883 he promoted the spiritual life of the churches there by arranging and usually conducting regular Bible conferences. In the churches of Baden he occupied a leading position after the death of the older elders. He officiated at most of the baptisms, marriages, and funerals in the Baden churches. After the death of his father in 1896 he was put in charge of the *Gemeindeblatt* (*Gem.-Kal.,* 1913, 47-59, with picture, *Gbl.,* 1911). His brother Philipp Hege, b. Nov. 7, 1857, d. March 7, 1923, was elder of the Heilbronn church and edited the *Gemeindeblatt* during the trying war years with skill and understanding. At the same time he was very active in the field of home missions (*Jugendpflege*), as well as caring for the Mennonite refugees from Russia.

At the time of the mass emigration of Mennonites from the Palatinate to America in the first third of the 18th century some members of the Hege family joined the party. The first emigrant was Hans Hege from the region of Zweibrücken, who sought a new home in Lancaster Co., Pa., with his brother-in-law, Hans Lehmann. They arrived in Philadelphia Sept. 27, 1727, on the "James Goodwill." *The Genealogical Register of the Male and Female Descendants of Hans Hege* (Chambersburg, 1859) states that the Hege family there is of Swiss origin; several descendants of Hans Hege were preachers in Mennonite (MC) churches, among them W. W. Hege of Marion, Pa.

On Aug. 28, 1750, Nicolas Hegi landed on the shores of America (Smith, 213). Today the anglicized form of the name occurs frequently as Hegy or Hagey. The Hagey Mennonite (MC) Church of Preston, Ont., was named after two Hagey brothers (Jacob, deacon 1832-93, and Joseph, bishop 1851-76) who came with their parents in 1822 from Montgomery Co., Pa., to the Preston neighborhood. The Hagey family is still prominent in the congregation.

One of the outstanding early leaders of the General Conference Mennonite Church in the United States was Daniel Hege (*q.v.*) of Klein-Karlbach near Grünstadt in the Palatinate, who emigrated to Summerfield, Ill., where he served as preacher from 1859, then as traveling evangelist for the conference until his untimely death in 1862.

HEGE.

J. Heiz, *Die Täufer in Aargau* (Aarau, 1902); C. Henry Smith, *The Mennonite Immigration to Pennsyvania* (Norristown, 1929); Chr. Hege, *Chronik der Familie Hege*, Heft 1 (Frankfurt a.M., 1937); K. A. Hagey and W. A. Hagey, *The Hagey Families in America* (Bristol, Tenn.-Va., 1951); *ML* II, 271-73.

Hege, Christian (1869-1943), outstanding German Mennonite historian, coeditor of the *Mennonitisches Lexikon* 1913-43, was born Dec. 20, 1869, at Bonfeld, Württemberg, the son of Daniel Hege and Magdalena Schmutz, moved with his parents to Munich in 1880. After completing the Realgymnasium in Munich, he studied at the University of Munich 1890-93 in the fields of history, economics, and trade, and at the age of 24 in 1893 was appointed financial editor of the outstanding Frankfurt newspaper, *Frankfurter Nachrichten,* a post which involved daily attendance at the stock exchange and which he filled for 40 years with distinction until his retirement in 1933. In the 1890's he also founded and edited for a time a successful monthly, *Frankfurter Frauenzeitung.* He was married to Christine Fellmann on Sept. 22, 1895.

But Hege's real lifework was the service of his church, which he loved with all his heart. This work he carried out chiefly in the field of historical research and writing on marginal time along with his profession. After his retirement he spent the last ten years (1933-43) of his life in full-time research and writing, with the aid of a stipendium from the *Badischer Verband* (*q.v.*). He lived all his adult and married life, after the completion of his studies, in Frankfurt a.M., except the last four months, which he spent in Eichstätt, Bavaria, after fleeing Frankfurt because of the incessant bombings. Of five children, only his daughter Adele survived him.

Hege's literary career began in 1891 with articles in the *Gemeindeblatt* and in 1893 in the *Mennonitische Blätter*. His first and largest book was *Die Täufer in der Kurpfalz* (Frankfurt a.M., 1908). In 1935 appeared his booklet, *Ein Rückblick auf 400 Jahre mennonitischer Geschichte* (Karlsruhe). *Chronik der Familie Hege,* edited and largely written by Hege, was designed as a quarterly periodical, but only the first number appeared in 1937. He discovered in Zürich in 1925 the lost *Vermahnung* of Pilgram Marpeck, which he edited for publication in the *Gedenkschrift zum 400-jährigen Jubiläum der Mennoniten* (Ludwigshafen, 1925). He was also responsible for the publication

of Pilgram Marpeck's *Verantwortung* by Johann Loserth in 1929 (Vienna and Leipzig, 1929). He was the chief promoter and founder (with Christian Neff) of the *Mennonitischer Geschichtsverein* (est. 1933) and served until his death as treasurer and editor of its publication, *Mennonitische Geschichtsblätter* (5 volumes 1936-40) and as the general editor of the *Schriftenreihe* (3 numbers appeared 1938, 1939, 1940).

But Christian Hege's greatest work, his real lifework, was the *Mennonitisches Lexikon,* of which he was coeditor and publisher with Christian Neff. Of this work he was the prime mover, and the managing editor from 1913 until his death. He also wrote a vast number of articles, chiefly though not exclusively in the field of Anabaptist and early Mennonite history. An exhaustive bibliography was prepared by Christian Neff and published posthumously in *Mennonitische Geschichtsblätter* VI (1949) 23-27, under the title "Bibliographie von Christian Hege." The same number contains two bibliographical sketches, one by Christian Neff, "Zum Gedenken an Christian Hege," and one by his daughter Adele Hege, "Gedenkworte für die Generalsammlung des Mennonitischen Geschichtsvereins 1947." Prof. Walther Köhler of Heidelberg published a warm tribute to him in the *Theologische Literaturzeitung,* 1944, Nos. 1 and 2. Ernst Correll wrote a biography and appreciation in the *Mennonite Quarterly Review* (1957).

Although Christian Hege produced no great historical works, he was a thorough and devoted scholar, whose many smaller contributions have lasting value, and whose editorial enterprise and financial sacrifice on behalf of Mennonite historical research and publication have produced great and lasting benefits in the cause of Anabaptist-Mennonite historiography. Personally he was a man of great depth of character and dignity, and of striking presence. He lives on in the life and work of many others whom he inspired and to whom he gave an unblemished example of selfless devotion and complete Christian integrity.† H.S.B.

Hege, Christine (1871-1942), wife of Christian Hege (*q.v.*), was born July 23, 1871, in Grombach, Baden, near Sinsheim, daughter of Heinrich Fellmann, married Christian Hege in 1895. Of unusual intellectual and spiritual gifts, she was an intimate colleague of her husband in his work as a Mennonite historian. Herself learned in Mennonite history, she won the prize offered in 1908 by the *Vereinigung der Mennonitengemeinden im Deutschen Reich* for a general book on Mennonite history with her *Kurze Geschichte der Mennoniten* (Altona, 1909). She died March 3, 1942, in Frankfurt a.M. at Rothschildallee 33, where she had spent most of her married life. H.S.B.

W. Fellmann, "Christine Hege," *Menn. Geschbl.* VI, 1949, 21-23.

Hege, Daniel (1826-62), one of the outstanding early leaders of the General Conference Mennonite Church in North America, was born Dec. 26, 1826, at Klein-Karlbach near Grünstadt in the Palatinate, the son of John and Margaret (Bergtholdt) Hege, and emigrated to the United States in 1851. After learning the trade of bookbinding he was educated at the Academy at Schiers (Canton of Graubünden), Switzerland (1848-50), also at the Evangelical Seminary at Marthasville, Mo. (1852-55). He taught in a private school near Bloomington, Ill. (1855-56), and at West Point and Oskaloosa, Iowa (1856-59). He also preached some for the Mennonite congregation at West Point, Iowa (1856-59). He married Barbara Lehman July 19, 1857. In 1859 he was called to be the pastor of the Mennonite Church at Summerfield, Ill. With a great vision of a united and progressive Mennonite Church in the United States, he devoted himself from the very outset of his ministry to the general work of the church. He was one of the delegates to ratify the charter constitution of the new General Conference of the Mennonite Church of North America at Wadsworth, Ohio, in 1861, where he was also elected secretary of the conference. Later he was elected traveling evangelist or home missionary (*Reiseprediger*), the first to hold such an office among the American Mennonites. He was to serve the scattered congregations and members of the small new conference by preaching and pastoral visits in the homes, and to promote the cause of union and higher education. He was a vigorous advocate of higher education and was active in raising funds to establish such a school in his conference (the Wadsworth School, *q.v.*). He returned from Iowa, where he was soliciting funds, to Summerfield seriously ill with typhoid fever, and died prematurely on Nov. 30, 1862.   D.L.G.

H. P. Krehbiel, *The History of the General Conference of the Mennonite Church of North America* (n.p., 1898) 93-113, 414-16; *Das Christliche Volksblatt* VII, No. 11 (Dec. 24, 1862) 42-43; *ML* II, 273.

Hegge, Jakob (Jakobus), of Danzig, hence called Jacobus Dantiscanus, a follower of Melchior Hofmann, a participant in the Flensburg Disputation (April 8 and 9, 1529), was later induced to recant by Bugenhagen in Hamburg.   HEGE.

B. N. Krohn, *Geschichte der fanatischen und enthusiastischen Wiedertäufer* (Leipzig, 1785) 152 f. and 197 ff.; F. O. zur Linden, *Melchior Hofmann* (Haarlem, 1885) 146; *ML* II, 273.

Hegler, Alfred (1863-1902), professor of church history at the University of Tübingen. His father was a lawyer, but both grandfathers were ministers in Württemberg and exerted a great influence on his future course. He was educated in the seminaries of Maulbronn, Blaubeuren, and at the Stift in Tübingen. After a brief period of ministry in the country and at the Hofkirche at Stuttgart, he studied theology and philosophy a half year in Berlin, having written an excellent doctoral thesis on *Psychologie in Kants Ethik*. In 1889-92 he lectured on philosophy. He planned to become an instructor of philosophy.

But in 1892 Weizsäcker won him over to church history. After he had taught a course on the "enthusiasts" (*Schwärmer*) in the Reformation period, he established himself with his book, *Geist und Schrift bei Sebastian Franck, eine Studie zur Geschichte des Spiritualismus in der Reformationszeit* (1892).

The idea of the subjectivity of religion seemed to him to be the center of Franck's thoughts and the source of his criticism of theology and church institutions. Hegler agreed thoroughly with Franck's ideas of tolerance.

Now he arrived at a plan for a lifework, viz., to write a history of spiritualism in the era of the Reformation. He meant to begin with Eckhardt, Tauler, Ruysbroek, *Nachfolge Christi, Deutsche Theologie,* then treat Carlstadt and the Anabaptists, as well as Schwenckfeld, follow spiritualism up to the time of Pietism, in Germany, France, Italy, Holland, and England. His ambitious program, for which he did a vast amount of research in archives and libraries, would have occupied a long life, but he was able to publish articles only on Campanus, Davidis, Hans Denk, Sebastian Franck, Gichtel, Gonesius, Ludwig Haetzer, Melchior Hofmann, Hubmaier, Hans Hut, the Inspired, Joris, Kautz and Marsay in *Protestantische Realenzyklopädie*. But his program, published posthumously by Walther Köhler, in his edition of Hegler's *Beiträge zur Geschichte der Mystik in der Reformationszeit* (1906), pp. XXVI f., must sooner or later become realized. In 1894 Hegler was made associate professor, and after Weizsäcker's death (1900) full professor. On Dec. 4, 1902, he succumbed to kidney trouble. (A biography by W. Koehler in Hegler's *Beiträge zur Mystik,* 1906.) (*ML* II, 273.)

Hegler's idea of a history of "Spiritualism" in the age of Reformation has partly been carried out by the outstanding leader, of the American Quakers, Rufus M. Jones, in his standard book, *Spiritual Reformers of the Sixteenth Century* (London, 1914). Since the term "spiritualism" might be misunderstood (over against its clear meaning in German), the term "spiritual reformers" as introduced by R. M. Jones has generally been accepted.   G.Bo.

Heher, Hans, an Anabaptist martyr, a cobbler, the treasurer of his congregation at Steyr (*q.v.*), captured in 1527 and released after recanting. When he returned to his faith he was sentenced to three months in prison. But King Ferdinand insisted on a death sentence. Heher was accordingly executed in May 1528.   NEFF.

A. Nicoladoni, *Hans Bünderlin von Linz . . .* (Berlin, 1893) 84 f.; *ML* II, 273.

Heidanus, Abraham (1597-1678), professor of theology at the University of Leyden (Holland). By his tolerant attitude and courageous defense of his theological position in the various quarrels of his time he won great respect. Because of his frank book, *Consideratien* (1676), he was deprived of his professorship, but retained his position as parson until his death. He wrote several letters to the authorities in Bern in warm defense of the harassed Mennonites there, thus securing permission for them to leave the country. (Müller, *Berner Täufer,* 173 and 181; *ML* II, 274.)   NEFF.

Heidanus, Caspar (Jasper van der Heyden) (1530-86), a native of Mechelen, Belgium, who had been rejected by his family for turning Protestant, prepared for the office of preaching by Johann a Lasco, came to Frankenthal, Palatinate, in 1564, where he settled as successor to Petrus Dathenus (*q.v.*) until 1574. After a brief sojourn in Antwerp, he took part in the Frankenthal disputation (1571), served as preacher in Middelburg and Antwerp, as inspector in Bacharach, and died there May 7, 1586. He was a sharp defender of Calvinistic doctrine against Catholics, Lutherans, and Mennonites. Against the Mennonites he wrote *Cort ende claer bewys van den heyligen doop* (Antwerp, 1582). (*DB* 1908, 19, 33, 35, 42; *Biogr. Wb.* III, 807-16; *ML* II, 274.)

NEFF.

Heide, Klaas, was born in Manitoba(?) and died in Mexico, October 1926. Heide was a leader of the Old Colony Mennonites, and was repeatedly delegated to negotiate with the Canadian government and to investigate settlement possibilities. In 1919 Heide and Cornelius Rempel, both of Manitoba, Julius Wiebe and David Rempel of Swift Current, and Johann P. Wall and Johann Wall of Hague, Sask., went as delegates to South America to find a place of settlement for the Old Colony Mennonites of Canada. In 1920 Heide again took part in the investigation of settlement possibilities in Mexico, was instrumental in purchasing the land, and was one of the leaders during the settlement period. (See also **Old Colony Mennonites and Mexico**.)

C.K.

Heidelberg, Baden, Germany (pop. 115,750), formerly the capital of the Palatinate, seat of the oldest German university (founded in 1386), has been the seat of a small Mennonite congregation since 1921, which in 1953 had 38 baptized members and 4 children, with Richard Wagner as elder from the beginning. The congregation meets on the first Sunday of the month. The Anabaptist movement was widespread in the Heidelberg area in the late 16th century, "particularly in Rohrbach, Leinen, Kirchheim, Nussloch and Wiesloch. Most of the members emigrated to Moravia (1603)" (Hege, 173). It died out about this time. The Baden-Pfalz volume of Anabaptist documents contains references to Anabaptists in the general area from 1568 on. The new Mennonite settlement in the region was established by immigrants from Switzerland about 1660. Since they were exclusively farmers they did not settle in the city proper, although some rented farm estates belonging to the city such as the Gutleuthof. The congregation in the immediate neighborhood was called Bruchhausen-Rohrbach, or at times Bruchhausen (*q.v.*) or Rohrbach; it existed from about 1664 to about 1880, when it dissolved. Huntzinger's *Religions-, Kirchen- und Schulwesen der Mennoniten* (Speyer, 1830) listed a total of 14 families with 71 souls as living in the Heidelberg district in the locations Nussloch, Handschuhsheim, Grenzhof, Rohrbach, St. Ilgen, and Gutleuthof, with only one member living in the city proper. Many mandates and regulations were issued from the electoral chancellery in Heidelberg, which was the capital of the Palatinate until 1720.

H.S.B.

C. Hege, *Die Täufer in der Kurpfalz* (Frankfurt a.M., 1908); M. Krebs, *TA IV: Baden und Pfalz.*

Heide-Neufeld und Reinländer Waisenamt is the name of one of the two companies organized by the Old Colony Mennonites to purchase and distribute the land of the Manitoba Mennonite settlement (*q.v.*) at Cuauhtemoc, Chihuahua, Mexico. C.K.

Heijnric Willemse Saelmaker, an Anabaptist martyr, executed on March 14, 1536, at The Hague, Holland. He was charged with participation in the revolt at Poeldijk (*q.v.*). Heijnric said that he had not been present at the meeting in the home of Jutte Eeuwouts (*q.v.*) because the leader of this meeting, Adriaen Adriaensz, did not admit him. He denied that he had anything to do with the affair, but admitted that he had been aware of it. For this reason, and because he had lodged an Anabaptist elder, he was beheaded. He apparently belonged to a revolutionary group of Anabaptists. vDZ.

Inv. Arch. Amst. I, No. 745; E. van Bergen, "De wederdoopers in het Westland," in *Bijdr. voor de Geschiedenis van het Bisdom Haarlem* XXVIII (Leiden, 1903) 273-75; Mellink, *Wederdopers,* 220 f., 341.

Heilbronn, a city (pop. 45,000) of Württemberg, Germany, until 1802 a free city, charmingly situated on the Neckar, 27 miles north of Stuttgart, an important manufacturing and trade city.

The Reformation was introduced here by Johann Lachmann, a son of the famed bell-caster Bernhard Lachmann, with strong support from the people and the guilds. In March 1526 are found the first Anabaptists trying to gain adherents in Heilbronn; they had come from Esslingen. Their high moral standards made a deep impression. In 1530 Wertz, Besserer, and Mettel Endris met at Anabaptist meetings. Wertz, who had been won to the movement by his cousin Gertrud, the daughter of Marx Hecker of Eppingen, preached to the people in vineyards and huts, sang psalms with them, and took a very hostile attitude toward Johann Lachmann. Their meetings were attended by 30 or 40 persons, some worthy and some unworthy. A Claus N. of Esslingen preached them a sermon, but was then banished from the city. Near Heilbronn a Frau von Neipperg favored the Anabaptists and permitted them to hold meetings. Wertz and Besserer were arrested and cross-examined. Because they refused to swear that they would desist, both were expelled from the city, but were soon readmitted, upon the intervention of neighboring nobles and upon their recantation.

From the court records on the prisoners in Passau (see **Hohenlohe**) these facts are known: (1) A widow Margarete of Heilbronn was baptized in 1529 by a Hans N., who died after recanting; (2) Judith, the wife of Hans Kimmich of Morsbach near Künzelsau, was baptized in 1532 by Wolf of Gritzingen (Grötzingen), who was executed in Bretten; (3) Anna, the wife of Bernhard Schrot, had been baptized by Hans of Pibrach (Biberach, Heilbronn district); and (4) Dietrich of Heilbronn, baptized by Andreas N., soon recanted. In 1533 all those suspected of Anabaptism were summoned before a committee consisting of Lachmann, Menrad Molter, and the councilor Heinrich

Zünderer. They denied being Anabaptists; but the shoemaker Jobs Fritz offered to "overthrow" the new preacher with the Word of God. He was warned to avoid the Anabaptist sect, to desist from arguing and preaching, or interrupting the sermons of the preachers, and to stop sheltering other Anabaptists on penalty of severe punishment.

In 1536 it was said in Strasbourg that there were about 40 Anabaptists in the vicinity of Heilbronn, who assembled in a forest. Their leader was Adam Siegel. Schuckhans of Landshausen was baptized in Heilbronn by Blasius Kuhn (Hulshof, 168). In the frequent cases occurring until 1540 the following characterizing points may be observed:

(1) The impulse toward sectarianism almost always comes from persons coming from the outside, seeking a following.

(2) All that deviates from orthodox Protestantism is Anabaptist unless it is Catholic; hence the opposition to Protestant preachers in other points than baptism, such as neglecting church services, refusal to render an oath; indeed, according to the confession of an imprisoned Anabaptist they were accused not only of religious errors, but also of revolution and common criminal views.

(3) It is characteristic that members of the shoemakers' guild are found among the sectarians (1533, 1540).

An unusually favorable soil for Anabaptism was found in Neckargartach in 1534, where the imperial knights refused to tolerate any Protestant preacher; likewise in Flein because of the resistance of the Heiliggeist Spital in Wimpfen against the Reformation.

The council repeatedly issued sharp mandates against the sectarians and against the reception and shelter of outside Anabaptists, and had its countermands sometimes read from the pulpit. Suspects were summoned, examined, and if found guilty expelled. Those who submitted and recanted could easily receive pardon and readmittance. There were two formulas of recantation, which expressed the promises that: (1) They would adhere to "the first infant baptism," which was held by the apostles and the Christian church. (2) They would believe the Gospel as it was taught at Heilbronn. (3) They would receive the Lord's Supper properly according to the teaching and institution of Christ and Paul in the Christian church. (4) We are not pure and without sin; therefore we pray with the apostles, as Christ taught us, Forgive us our sins. The more wordy of the two formulas was drawn up by Menrad Molter.

In 1545-57 there was quiet. In 1557 the council again issued an edict against sheltering outside Anabaptists. In 1558 and 1564 Duke Christian of Württemberg reported to the council that Anabaptists were holding meetings in a small forest near Gruppenbach, in which inhabitants of Heilbronn and Böckingen participated. The council offered to investigate and take necessary steps. Soon all traces of the Anabaptist movement disappeared. In 1609 the Anabaptists met every three weeks in the Spitalwald of Heilbronn; there were subjects of Württemberg, from Grossgartach, among them.

For the modern Heilbronn Mennonite congregation see the next article.   G. Bo.

Urkundenbuch der Stadt Heilbronn IV (1922); *Württembergische Geschichtsquellen* XX; *Beschreibung des Oberamts Heilbronn*, Part I (1901) 124 ff.; Jäger, *Mitteilungen zur schwäbischen und fränkischen Ref. Gesch.*, I (1828) 248 ff.; court records of Passau in the Reichsarchiv in Munich; *TA Württemberg*, 814, note 29; A. Hulshof, *Geschiedenis van de Doopsgezinden te Straatsburg* (Amsterdam, 1905); *ML* II, 275 ff.

Heilbronn (Germany) Mennonite Church, organized in 1890, is a member of the *Verband badisch-württembergisch-bayrischer Mennonitengemeinden*. With a membership (1953) of 122 and 35 children it is the largest congregation in the *Verband*. Elders are (1954) J. Musselmann (1937), Walter Landes (1943), Friedrich Schneider (1948). The congregation long met (since 1914 exclusively) in a rented hall in Heilbronn, but since 1948 has had its own meetinghouse in the form of a Swedish Red Cross barracks-church which was imported by the Mennonite Central Committee and used as headquarters for the committee's relief program conducted here 1947-52. Heilbronn has been the spiritual center for the *Verband* for many years and has been the most common meeting place for the meeting of its quarterly elders' and ministers' conferences. In 1918-40 meetings of the South German Conference were held frequently here also. In December 1944 it was severely bombed, being 80 per cent destroyed. However, most of the members being farmers, only one member lost his life in the catastrophe.

The congregation now called Heilbronn has, however, a much older history than its founding date of 1890 would indicate. It is actually the modern center of the easternmost end of the extensive eastern Palatinate Swiss Mennonite settlement, which, beginning around Mannheim and Heidelberg as early as 1664, had spread across the 20-30 miles to Wimpfen and Mosbach by 1731, with centers at Zuzenhausen, Sinsheim, and Hasselbach. The eastward movement apparently did not cross the Neckar until about 1770. The Dutch *Naamlijst* of 1769 lists "the other side of the Neckar" with Eibingen as the name of the location (congregation) with Hans Kauffman and Abraham Krehbiel as preachers. By 1780 the *Naamlijst* calls the congregation "Roschingen," with David Musselmann as preacher. From 1786 on to 1810 the congregation is called "Willenbach, Prutzenhof, Durrhof, and Roschingen," with an Abraham Zeisset listed as elder in 1784 (elder since 1749) and a second Abraham Zeisset elder from 1790 on. A. Huntzinger's *Religions-, Kirchen- und Schulwesen der Mennoniten* (Speyer, 1830), with a statistical table of all Mennonite locations in Baden, omits all four of the above names in the Willenbach congregation, and reports Lobenbacherhof (near Willenbach) with 3 families and 21 souls; J. Mannhardt's *Namens-Verzeichnis* of 1857 reports a Lobenbach congregation with 40 baptized members, lacking an elder but with a Christian Funk of Kochendorf preacher (ordained 1848), and adds that the services were held alternately in the homes of two members (Deacon Daniel Neukem lived at Loben-bach). H. Mannhardt's *Jahrbuch* of 1888 calls the congregation Lautenbach-Lobenbach with 52 baptized members and 21 children, and lists Christian Funk of Kochendorf as still preacher, with also Heinrich Fellmann of Lobenbach (1885) and Heinrich Landes (d. 1918, elder in 1885) of Lautenbach, services being held on alternate Sundays at the two large estates of Lautenbach and Lobenbach. Christian Hege of Breitenau became elder in 1890. The congregation is çalled simply Lobenbach at the first (1898) listing of congregations in the *Gemeinde-Kalender*. By 1904 it is called Lobenbach-Heilbronn, by 1915 Heilbronn alone. The high point of membership before World War II was reached in 1914 with 166 souls. Philipp Hege was a prominent elder in the Heilbronn congregation 1904-23. The Stuttgart congregation was formed out of Heilbronn in 1933. A prominent lay member in the 1920-45 period was Gustav Lichdi, founder of the large Lichdi grocery chain store system, still carried on by his son Kurt, now a preacher in the congregation.

The change in name of the congregation over a period of a century is explained by the fact that most of the members were renters of large estates, which were somewhat scattered and occasionally changed leases, hence they met as circumstances dictated in conveniently located farm homes. The congregation was then named after the most commonly and frequently used homes such as Willenbach, Lobenbach, and Lautenbach, all large farms within a few miles of each other and 5-10 miles northeast of Heilbronn. After 1914 the meetings were held exclusively in Heilbronn, which was a convenient railroad center. The number of Mennonites living in the city itself, and mostly engaged in trade or professions, increased as follows: 1890-5, 1905-5, 1910-22, 1925-47. However the backbone of the congregation has remained on the rented farm estates such as Lautenbach (*q.v.*), Willenbach, Breitenau, and Liebenstein (*ML* II, 275-77).

H.S.B.

Heiloo, a village in the Dutch province of North Holland, south of Alkmaar, where 144 Mennonites, members of the Alkmaar congregation, formed a *Kring* (circle) in 1947. Services are sometimes held by the pastor of Alkmaar in a hall of the Reformed Church. There is also a ladies' circle.

vDZ.

Heilsamen, a Mennonite group belonging to the Flemish (*q.v.*) branch of the church, which was found at the close of the 16th century at Danzig, Prussia, and of which Paulus Bussemaker was leader. He was banned by Hans Busschaert (*q.v.*) and Jacob Pieters van der Meulen (*q.v.*). About the group of the *Heilsamen* no further information was available. It may soon have merged with another group of Mennonites. (*Inv. Arch. Amst.* II, 2, No. 691; *BRN* VII, 70; *ML* I, 304.) vDZ.

Heilsbote. The first literature of the Defenseless Mennonite Conference (now Evangelical Mennonite, *q.v.*) was a report of its first session held at Berne, Ind., Oct. 14-17, 1883. The first real effort of publication was a songbook called *Glaubens-Lieder*. In 1898 a resolution was passed by the conference to start a German paper under the name of *Heilsbote*.

In 1898 C. R. Egle (*q.v.*) of the Salem Church near Flanagan, Ill., purchased a printing press. The conference appointed him as editor of the *Heilsbote*, with Peter Hochstettler and Joseph Rediger as assistants, the first issue appearing in 1898. The purpose of this publication was to help unify the church and help create an interest in mission work which had been started in Africa. Egle was the editor until the paper was discontinued in December 1917. It was a four-page monthly, and during the last years of publication was printed by the Berne Witness Company. The English paper, *Zion's Call* (*q.v.*), was also started in 1898 in the interests of the Salem Children's Home. In 1913 it was made the official organ of the conference. It has undergone several changes, the name being altered about 1921 to *Zion's Tidings*. Since July 1953 it has been called the *Evangelical Mennonite* (*q.v.*), published jointly by the Evangelical Mennonite Conference, and the Evangelical Mennonite Brethren Conference. E.E.Z.

Heimath, Zur: see **Zur Heimath.**

Heimatklänge: see **Hymnology** of the Mennonites of Prussia and Russia.

Heimbronnerhof (Haimbrunn), an estate in the Bretten district of Baden, Germany, owned by the Counts Douglas. Since 1822 the estate has been leased to Mennonites, formerly to the Funck and Horsch families, since 1916 to the Fellmann family. From about 1858 to 1916 biweekly religious services were held at the Heimbronnerhof, since during this period the families were members of the Hahnische (*q.v.*) Mennoniten (see **Baden**). (*ML* II, 279.) W.F.

Heinrich, Jakob, an Anabaptist of whom nothing is known except that he is the author of the hymn, "Ick roepe tot v wt dieper noot," and probably also "Ick moet eens gaen vertellen." (Wolkan, *Lieder*, 80; *ML* II, 279.) NEFF.

Heinsius, Anthonie, b. 1641 at Delft, d. 1720 at The Hague, a Dutch statesman (1689), Grand Pensionary of the territory of Holland and co-operator with Stadholder William III of Holland who in 1689 also became King of England. Heinsius, who played an important part in European politics, especially against the supremacy of France, and who belonged to the Reformed Church, should be mentioned here because of his loyalty and help to the Mennonites. He protected the Mennonites of Holland against oppressive measures of the Reformed ministers, and in 1710, informed by the Mennonite ministers Cornelis Beets of Amsterdam, Matthijs Diepenbroek of Haarlem, and Adriaen van Alkmaer of Rotterdam of the troubles which the Bernese Mennonites had with their government, he instructed (March 14, 1710) the registrar François Fagel (*q.v.*) to draw up a strong protest, which was approved by the States-General of the Netherlands on March 15, and was sent to the city council of Bern, Switzerland. In this address a protest is made against the Bernese policy of punishing the Mennonites in this territory with imprisonment, exile, galley slavery (*q.v.*), and even death. This protest is found in *Inv. Arch. Amst.* I, No. 1759 and published in *DB* 1909, 132-35. Again in 1711 Heinsius acted in behalf of the persecuted Bernese Anabaptists. (*N.N.B.Wb.* I, 1058-61; *DB* 1909, 130, 141, 149; 1912, 97.)   vDZ.

Heiz, Jakob, Reformed pastor in Othmarsingen, Switzerland, author of *Täufer im Aargau* (Aarau, 1902), a booklet of 101 pages, published as a separate reprint from the *Taschenbuch der Historischen Gesellschaft des Kantons Aargau pro 1902.* It offers a welcome supplement to Ernst Müller's *Geschichte der bernischen Täufer.* (*ML* II, 279.)
                                                           NEFF.

Held, Matthias, a statesman in the ecclesiastical service of Emperor Charles V. He was a native of Arlon (Belgian Luxemburg). In 1527 he was made assessor in the court of chancellery in Speyer. When Charles V made his preparations for the Diet of Augsburg he summoned Held and in 1538 gave him the important office of chancellor; he was qualified for the position both by his knowledge of law and his zeal for the Catholic cause, and under his leadership the politics detrimental to ecclesiastical innovations were strongly promoted. A determined opponent of ecclesiastical attempts to come to an agreement, Held counseled against concessions to the Protestants. This policy won him the favor of the Catholic imperial estates, such as George of Saxony, Joachim of Brandenburg, Heinrich of Brunswick, etc. As leader of the imperial chancellery he accompanied the emperor on his campaigns to Italy and Spain, and on April 17, 1536, received the rank of knight in Rome. On the question of calling a council, which the Protestants rejected, he took a very partisan position. It was his objective to unite the Catholic estates in a consolidated union in order to achieve a unified position in opposition to the Schmalkaldian League. Thus in 1538 the *Nürnberger Bund* was founded, which was on the one hand to repel the Protestant estates, and on the other to promote the Catholic plans of Charles V (the Catholic reformation), but which found opponents within the Bund itself. In the end Held succumbed to the influence of Granvella, lost his position, withdrew into private life, and took up residence in Cologne. He died in 1563.   LOSERTH.

Max Maurenbrecher's article in *ADB* II, pp. 672-84, where other literature is cited; *ML* II, 279.

Helder (or Den Helder), a town (1954 pop. 41,199 with 337 Mennonites) in the Dutch province of North Holland, now the most important base of the Royal Netherlands Navy, consists of three parts —the old town of Huisduinen, Den Helder, and Nieuwediep. In Huisduinen (*q.v.*) there has been a Mennonite congregation from very early times, at first called Flemish, later also called Frisian. It

had apparently come into being by the merging of the Flemish and a Frisian congregation. Of this Frisian congregation nothing is known. Of the Flemish church there is only scarce information: it was a small congregation, whose members were mostly poor fishermen. The congregation was represented at the Flemish conference at Haarlem in 1649 and Leiden in 1660. The Flemish-Frisian congregation was merged in 1731 with a Waterlander congregation at Den Helder; at the time of this union the membership of the Huisduinen congregation was 60 baptized members, that of Den Helder only 25. The united congregation was rather poor in the 18th century; it was regularly subsidized both by the Amsterdam Lamist congregation and the Frisian Conference (*Vriesche Sociëteit*) of North Holland. The Huisduinen congregation had a brick meetinghouse, that of Den Helder a frame one erected in 1702. After the union of 1731 both meetinghouses remained in use until 1788, when the Huisduinen church was torn down and that of Den Helder replaced by a new brick church. This church was sold in 1853 after a new church had been built at Nieuwediep which is still in use. In the 18th century this congregation is usually called Huisduinen and Helder, in the 19th century Helder and Huisduinen, and now only Den Helder. In 1811-13 the meetinghouse was occupied by French soldiers until June 30, 1814. The membership, numbering 85 in 1731, increased to 132 in 1847, 179 in 1861, 227 in 1954. In 1922-41 the church of Den Hoorn on the island of Texel (*q.v.*) merged their preaching services with Helder.

Pastors who served here in the last century were P. Douwes Dekker 1844-61, J. Dyserinck 1861-79, J. P. van der Vegte 1880-88, D. Kossen 1891-95, C. B. Hylkema 1896-99, J. Keulen 1900-9, J. Koster 1909-26, P. J. Smidts 1927-41, Miss T. Rothfusz 1946-48, J. J. J. van Sluys 1949-54; the pulpit has been vacant since September 1954.

Church activities include a Sunday school for children (since 1896), ladies' circle, men's circle, church choir, Bible group.   J.J.J. v.S.

Inv. Arch. Amst. II, Nos. 1906-23; II, 2, No. 98; *Naamlijst* 1815, 89 f.; *ML* II, 279.

Helferich, Franz Joseph (1806-81), once a Catholic priest, became a Protestant pastor at Beedenkirchen, Hesse, Germany. He wrote the booklet, *Die Kindertaufe oder eine offenherzige Ansprache an die Mennoniten Deutschlands von einem Freunde des Hinankommens zu einerlei Glaube und Erkenntnis des Sohnes Gottes* (Mainz, 1865), of 28 pages, in which he discusses baptism from the Protestant viewpoint and makes an unskilled attempt to refute the Mennonite position, and then urges the Mennonites to join the state church in order to strengthen it in its common struggle against Rationalism.   NEFF.

Menn. Bl., 1865, 77; 1866, 13, where counter arguments are presented; also the booklet by Wilhelm Fischer, *Pfarrer Helferich, ein rheinhessischer Glaubenszeuge* (Darmstadt); *ML* II, 280.

Hell. The New Testament speaks clearly of the final judgment which will bring about the great separation: eternal life for believers in Christ and eternal destruction for unbelievers and ungodly. The question that has always occupied serious minds is essentially whether this destruction or punishment is really eternal; i.e., to be considered unending or as temporary, even though of long duration, to be followed by complete annihilation or eternal salvation. The most important Bible references are Matt. 25:46; Mark 9:43, 44; II Thess. 1:9; and Heb. 6:2. The opponents of eternal punishment in hell understand the word "everlasting" to mean "of immeasurable length"; but this would then also apply to eternal life, which is expressly opposed to eternal destruction. A more profound objection to the idea of eternal punishment in hell originates in the thought that God is love. He cannot eternally be angry; this contradicts His nature, which is love and mercy. He does not "have pleasure in the death of the wicked; but that the wicked turn from his way and live."

This was Hans Denk's (*q.v.*) concept. He points out Bible references like Jer. 3:12; Ps. 77:8; Rom. 5:18; 11:32. All of God's punishments, hence also hell, have the purpose of bringing about the lasting salvation of men, and of all mankind (see **Universalism**). This idea of Denk's was, however, by no means common to the Anabaptists, as the Confession of Augsburg apparently assumes when it says (Art. 17): "Therefore the Anabaptists are rejected, who teach that the devils and damned persons do not have eternal pain and torment."

All Mennonite confessions of faith teach expressly in the words of the Bible, that the ungodly will suffer eternal punishment in hell. The Confession of Cornelis Ris says (XXXVI, *Of Eternal Punishment*): "This condition will consist in a total absence of God, of all good, all comfort and all salvation, as also in the feeling of the insufferable wrath of God and His avenging righteousness, both in soul and body, without any hope of release or alleviation into all eternity. . . . What makes this unblessed state most desperately terrifying is the fact that the Holy Scriptures give not the least ground for expecting release; on the contrary calling it everlasting pain, the punishment of everlasting fire, a worm that dieth not. . . ." The Dordrecht Confession of 1632 teaches: "that in contrast (to eternal life) the wicked or ungodly will be cast into outer darkness as cursed ones, yea into everlasting pain, where their worm will not perish nor their fire be extinguished, and where they (according to the Scriptures) can expect no hope, consolation, or salvation in eternity." (*ML* II, 340.)
NEFF.

Hellertown, a village (borough) in Lower Saucon Twp., Northampton Co., Pa., not far from Bethlehem. Near the village but now within the city limits of Bethlehem stands a building which was once a school and church building, shared by the Mennonites and the Baptists as a place of worship. Apparently services were conducted here beginning sometime before 1800, although interments were made in the adjoining cemetery as early as 1769 or before. A building was erected in 1802, burned and rebuilt in 1854, and rebuilt again in 1891. Nothing is known of an organized Mennonite congregation in the area, but the 1790 U.S. census lists such Mennonite names in Lower Saucon Township as Bachman, Baer, Boyer, Derr, Geissinger, Gross, Heebner, Landis, Snyder, and Weaver. The building, now known as the Limekiln Schoolhouse, has been converted into a private dwelling.
J.C.W.

Hellmannsberg, a large estate located about ten miles northeast of Ingolstadt, Bavaria, residence of Elder Michael Horsch 1913-49, longtime seat of the relief work known as "Christenpflicht" (*q.v.*), of which Horsch was chairman.

Hellrigl (Helrigling), **Ursula,** is mentioned first in the court records of June 3, 1539, when the Innsbruck authorities reported to Ferdinand I that a peasant girl of 18 years, a native of the Upper Inn Valley, had been in prison at St. Petersberg nearly 15 months. In pity for her youth and sex, attempts had been made by Dr. Gallus Müller (*q.v.*) to convert her. Though she was not versed in the Scriptures, she clung to her faith because her coreligionists lived less frivolously than the world. Her mother, an Anabaptist, had died in prison. One of her three brothers had recanted, and was now pleading for his sister's release. Ferdinand was inclined to grant the request, but feared that such a release would strengthen ignorant persons in their error. He ordered that she should be further instructed. In the following year her family appealed again. On Aug. 13, 1540, the king ordered her sent to Italy, where she would not know the language. Thus she came to Sigmundskron, and in 1543 she was finally pardoned "for the sake of her youth and the petitions of her friends," Peter Müller of Silz having promised to pay the costs of the case, and returned to her people. The Hutterian chronicles report that she was tied to the feet of Brother Liebich when he was racked. But neither of them recanted. "What the devil and his children wished to see happen is easy to imagine. But they were honorable and pious, and did not let any temptations cause them to sin." She is credited with the hymn, "Ewiger Gott vom Himmelreich" (13 stanzas).

Daniel Hellrigl, an Anabaptist, who died at Nikolsburg, April 3, 1615, "an aged preacher," was probably a relative of Ursula's. Zacharias Hellrigl (1580-1630) is the author of five hymns: "Die Danksagung des Morgens"; "Elend hat mich betroffen"; "Erheb meine Seel den Herrn"; "Vom Leben und Tod des Frommen"; "Es ist nun um die Vesperzeit."
LOSERTH.

Beck, *Geschichts-Bücher,* 157-59; J. Loserth, *Der Anabaptismus in Tirol* (Vienna, 1892) 241; Wolkan, *Lieder,* 178; *Die Lieder der Hutterischen Brüder* (Scottdale, 1914) 838-46; *Mart. Mir.* D 64, E 466 f.; *ML* II, 280.

Hellum, a village in the Dutch province of Groningen, where Leenaert Bouwens baptized 16 persons in 1557-65. A congregation at this place, however, was not found.
vDZ.

Helm, Matthias, the head of the Hutterian Brethren 1701-24. The *Väterlied* gives a few data of his life. He died in 1724 at the age of 87. He was chosen probational preacher May 6, 1688, and confirmed March 15, 1689, at Sobotiste; he served the brotherhood in this capacity for 36 years. He was by trade a scythe-smith.

The *Väterlied* gives him the tribute of having been an upright man, understanding and wise. When as an old man, oppressed by ill health, he felt his death imminent, he urged the Brethren to choose Jakob Wollmann as his successor. It is rather remarkable that in 1678 the *Schadsche Chronik* (Beck, *Geschichts-Bücher,* p. XVII) was in Helm's possession.

Since the Wolkan edition of the *Geschicht-Buch* closes with 1665, Beck's edition of the *Geschichts-Bücher* must be used for this period. The most important source is the continuation of the *Väterlied,* pp. 563 and 565 in Beck. The *Väterlied* is also in the *Lieder der Hutterischen Brüder* (Scottdale, 1914) 878. The *Klein-Geschichtsbuch* (Phila., 1947) does not mention him at all. (*ML* II, 280 f.)

LOSERTH.

Helmstadt, a village (1925 pop. 1,111) in the Sinsheim district of Baden, Germany, with 22 Mennonites. In the Mennonite lists of the Palatinate Helmstadt is mentioned for the first time in 1717 with eight Mennonite families. In *Goldruthen zur Geschichte von Helmstadt* (Karlsruhe, 1867, 21), Pastor Ludwig says that in 1727 a Mennonite, Hans Schmutz, settled in Helmstadt; his descendants farmed the estate "Wasserschloss," belonging to the counts of Berlichingen, until the beginning of the 20th century. About 1731 there was in Helmstadt a Mennonite congregation of 12 families; their preachers were Hans Schmutz (presumably the above-mentioned) and Christian Schmutz (Müller, *Berner Täufer,* 209). Later the church was merged with the Hasselbach congregation. In the last quarter of the 19th century the meetings of the Badischer Verband elders were held almost exclusively in the "Wasserschloss" at Helmstadt. (*ML* II, 281.)   HEGE.

Helwys, Thomas, one of the founders of the Baptist Church, b. *ca.* 1570 near Broxtowe Hall, 40 miles west of Gainsborough, England, son of Edmund Helwys, of an old baronial family. Edmund Helwys had Puritan convictions. He died in 1590 and left Thomas as his sole heir. Thomas attended Gray's Inn in London as a law student. He was soon known as a Puritan and Nonconformist at Broxtowe Hall and received and advised members of various confessions (see **England**). About 1606 he came under the influence of John Smyth (*q.v.*), having already withdrawn from the Anglican Church, and became pastor of the Nonconformist Union at Gainsborough (*q.v.*).

About 1607 Helwys was in complete agreement with Smyth. To escape the oppression instigated by Bancroft under James I, he emigrated to the Netherlands with the members of the Gainsborough and Scrooby groups. In Amsterdam he apparently sided entirely with Smyth in the differences of opinion that had developed there between Johnson and Ainsworth. The schisms in Smyth's

party had begun in 1609. Baptism, church capital, and ordination had been recognized by some, who also rejected adult baptism. Several months later, when Smyth himself had come to the conclusion that it was an error to re-introduce baptism and leaned toward union with the Mennonites, Helwys charged him with apostasy and sinning against the Holy Spirit (under whose guidance the group had previously claimed to act), and wrote an urgent appeal to the Mennonites not to accept Smyth and his followers as brethren.

Helwys presented a brief confession of faith and published a clear exposition of the points in which he agreed with the Mennonites. These points were the general doctrine of redemption in contrast to the Calvinistic unqualified predestination and eternal damnation, as well as a rejection of infant baptism. Like the Mennonites he denied the right of the political authorities to limit religious liberty; on the other hand, he did not agree with them in their view on capital punishment and participation in government. Also the true Adamic nature of Christ and the apostolic succession were points of conflict. On the oath and military service he differed from the Mennonites, and charged Smyth with placing too high a value on the apostolic succession, which charge Smyth, however, denied.

Helwys then wanted to be convinced that he and all those who had fled to the Netherlands had erred, or perhaps sinned, in avoiding persecution. The evangelicals in England were now without a leader who would oppose the fallen, corrupted church. Followed by John Murton (*q.v.*) and a small group of followers he returned to England late in 1611 or early 1612, and settled in London, where he had influential relatives. The small congregation was severely persecuted, but still succeeded in maintaining itself. About 1626 there were four associations, from whom the General Baptists originated (see **Baptists**): London, Tiverton Sarum, Coventry, and Lincoln. Dissensions on the deity of Christ and other points were still an issue. Both sides appealed to the Dutch Mennonites for counsel and moral support.

Shortly before his return to England, Helwys published two books in defense of his concept of salvation and adult baptism. In England he published *A Short Declaration of the Mystery of Iniquity* (1612). Little is known of his later life. He apparently died before 1616. John Murton was now recognized as leader of the party and with other Baptists he published several tracts on freedom of conscience. (See also **Baptists, Brownists, Smyth.**)   A.H.N.

W. T. Whitly, *The Works of John Smith with Notes and Biography* (2 vv., Cambridge, 1915); W. H. Burgess, *John Smith, the Se Baptist, Thomas Helwys* (1912); B. Evans, *The Early English Baptists* (2 vv., London, 1862-64); De Hoop Scheffer and Griffis, *History of the Free Churchmen* (Ithaca, N.Y., n.d., 1902) 148 ff., 169 ff.; A. C. Underwood, *A History of the English Baptists* (London, 1947); *ML* II, 281 f.

Hembling, a "preaching appointment" (MC) in Woolwich Twp., Waterloo Co., Ont. William Hembling from England homesteaded here about

1831. He was ordained deacon of the Mennonite Church in 1858. The North Woolwich appointment was first known as Hembling. It is presumed that services were conducted in his home before the building of the church in 1872. The meetings were listed at four-week intervals. About 1875 Hembling associated himself with the Mennonite Brethren in Christ movement. After the schism of 1889 the North Woolwich church was used exclusively by the Old Order Mennonites. The Mennonite Church (MC) built its meeting-house a few miles south at Floradale in 1896. Early ministers were Abraham W. Detwiler (1828-1912) and Joseph Gingerich (1842-1912). Peter Bowman became deacon in 1876.   J.C.F.

L. J. Burkholder, *A Brief History of the Mennonites of Ontario* (Toronto, 1935) 69, where a picture of Hembling is found.

Hemelum, a village in the Dutch province of Friesland, where there was a Waterlander Mennonite congregation from the 16th century until it joined the near-by congregation of Warns about 1700. (Kühler, *Geschiedenis* II, 65; *DB* 1903, 82.)
vDZ.

Hemert, Gerardus van (den), b. 1698 at Middelburg in the Netherlands, d. there 1759, a Reformed minister of Hellevoetsluis 1720-21, Voorschoten 1721-22, and Middelburg 1722-59. He refused a call as professor of theology at the Utrecht University in 1737. Van Hemert was a violent antagonist of the Mennonites. He attacked Gerardus de Wind (*q.v.*), the Mennonite preacher of Middelburg, in his booklet, *G. de Wind . . . uit zyne Verhandeling van Godts Algemeene Genade ontmaskert, . . .* (Middelburg, 1730). After G. Maatschoen (*q.v.*) had translated Schijn's history of the Mennonites from the Latin into the Dutch language, van Hemert published: *Brief . . . aan den Here G. Maatschoen Betreffende voornamelijk den oorsprong en betrekking der Mennoniten of Doopsgezinden in opzigt tot de Munstersche en andere oproerige Doopsgezinden . . .* (Middelburg, 1744). (*Biogr. Wb.* III, 658-60; *DJ* 1840, 128; *DB* 1891, 66.)
vDZ.

Hemme Hauxkens (*Haucx*), a member of the Waterlander Mennonite congregation of Workum, Dutch province of Friesland, was in 1578, at the age of 75, chosen burgomaster of the town of Workum (*DB* 1899, 58, 60). Though it was unusual that Dutch Mennonites in this early period, and even in the following centuries, accepted government offices, some government officials were found among the Waterlanders, as this case proves.
vDZ.

Henderson (Neb.), was established as a Mennonite community in 1874 by 35 families (207 persons) coming from the Molotschna settlement, South Russia, who purchased land in York and Hamilton counties from the Burlington and Missouri Railroad Company. The first group of settlers bought 6,008 acres at $3-$9 per acre, reserving 900 additional acres for relatives. By 1882 some 140 families had settled there. At present the population has increased to nearly 3,000. The first settlers lived in an immigrant house about a mile east of the present site of Henderson. Some sod houses were erected which were replaced after a few years. The first houses and villages were patterned after those which they left behind in Russia; but this practice was soon discontinued. In 1887 the Northwestern Railroad Company built a branch line running through the town of Henderson, which had been established in 1878 in the heart of the Mennonite settlement. All the business in the village is conducted by Mennonites. As a result of the severe drought and the depression following World War I many of the farmers began irrigation farming, which has proved to be successful. Regarding education, religious life, and other questions pertaining to the settlement, see **Bethesda** Mennonite Church, **Henderson** Mennonite Brethren Church, **Ebenezer** Evangelical Mennonite Brethren Church, **Henderson** Bethesda Preparatory School.
C.K.

Theodore Schmidt, "The Mennonites of Nebraska" (thesis, University of Nebraska, 1933) 13 ff.; J. J. Friesen, "Remaking a Community—Henderson, Nebraska," *Menn. Life* V (October 1950) 10 ff.

Henderson Bethesda Preparatory School (German, *Fortbildungsschule*), located at Henderson, Neb., began as a secondary school built in 1902. The two-year course of study was modeled after the Hillsboro (Kan.) Preparatory School (*q.v.*) conducted by H. D. Penner. Christian Hege and J. J. Friesen were early teachers. When the public school began to offer full high-school courses (1911), attendance at the church school gradually declined, and the curriculum was limited more to Bible and German. The school was closed in 1932 and reopened as the Bethesda Bible School (Schmidt). In addition to this school there has also been a Henderson Bible School since 1933 under the leadership of J. R. Barkman. The list of schools under **Bible School** (*ME* I, p. 332) also mentions a Henderson Bible School of the General Conference started in 1942. This school has also been discontinued. Religious training is taken care of in special classes during the regular Sunday-school hour. (See **Preparatory Schools.**)   H.D.E.

Theodore Schmidt, "The Mennonites of Nebraska" (thesis, University of Nebraska, 1933) 43 ff.; *Katalog, Bethesda Fortbildungsschule,* 1902 ff.

Henderson (Neb.) **Bible School** began in 1902 as a secondary school, called the "Fortbildungsschule." The course of study was modeled after a school in Hillsboro, Kan., conducted by H. D. Penner. The Henderson school was built and supported by the Bethesda Mennonite (GCM) church of Henderson. The highest enrollment, 69, was in the beginning when two divisions were offered. When the public school began to offer a full high-school course, *ca.* 1911, the attendance at the church school declined. About 1924 a change was made in its curriculum, instruction being limited to Bible subjects, and the name was changed to "Bible School." This school was discontinued in 1952. The plan now is to have special classes during the regular Sunday-school hour to supply the instruction intended by the Bible School. (See preceding article.)   H.D.E.

Henderson (Neb.) Mennonite Brethren Church began in 1876 when seven M.B. families settled in York and Hamilton counties, Nebraska. The church was organized the next year with 30 charter members. Peter Regier and Heinrich Nickel were their leaders and became ministers. John J. Regier (d. 1902) was the first elder. By 1880 the church membership was 120, and by 1888 it had increased to 226. In 1887 a church 40 x 80 ft. was built three miles northwest of Henderson, which was replaced in 1926 by a church in town. In the early years the church endured severe testings through strange teaching on divine healing, sanctification, and Seventh-Day Adventism, but weathered them through the wise counsel and guidance of Elder Regier.

In 1902 the church elected John J. Kliewer as presiding minister and leader and two years later as elder, serving until 1924. He was followed by the ministers Gerhard Wiens and John Abrahams. Other ministers who have served the church as pastors are David Hooge, B. B. Fadenrecht, H. B. Kliewer, H. E. Wiens, Art. Flaming, and H. R. Berg. The membership in 1954 was 275.

A number of missionaries and other Christian workers have come from this congregation. Among these should be mentioned the evangelist J. S. Regier, and the foreign missionaries, Mr. and Mrs. F. J. Wiens, Mr. and Mrs. B. F. Wiens, Mrs. J. S. Dick, Miss Tina Kornelsen, Mrs. P. V. Balzer, and Mrs. J. J. Kasper.   H.E.W.

Hendrick: see also **Hendrik, Henric, Heyn(d)rich.**

Hendrick Alewijnsz (Heijndrick Walewyns), an Anabaptist martyr. He was a native of Aelburch, in the district of Heusden, Dutch province of North Brabant, by trade a maker of bags or knapsacks. Being thus a simple artisan, he is called by his Catholic opponents a *"professoor ende leeraar van den secte van Menno."* He lived in Vlissingen, Dutch province of Zeeland, and was active in preaching on the island of Walcheren, was banished in 1567 but remained and continued his activity until he was arrested at Souburg near Vlissingen in August 1568. He was put in prison at Middelburg, the capital of Zeeland, and tortured on Sept. 13, 1568. Remaining steadfast in his faith he was strangled and then burned at the stake on Feb. 9, 1569, with Gerrit Duynherder (*q.v.*) and Hans Marijnsz (*q.v.*). Alewijnsz was 36 years of age when he died. In prison he wrote some devotional letters. These were soon published: (1) *Veele schoone grondige leeringen wt des Heeren woort,* 1577, n.p.; (2) *Een vaderlyck Adieu, Testament en sorchvuldighe onderwysinghe, . . . aan zijne Kinderen,* published by Nicolaas Biestkens (*q.v.*) at Amsterdam in 1578 and included by van Braght, *Martyrs' Mirror;* (3) a reprint of (1), n.p. (apparently by Gillis Rooman at Haarlem 1581, followed by six letters "written in my prison at Middelburg," the first of which is dated Aug. 18, 1568, the last Jan. 20, 1569). This volume, which is found in the Amsterdam Mennonite Library, also contains two songs made by Alewijnsz. "Och wilt u doch eens schamen, ghy roemers al te samen" (Oh, be

ashamed, ye boasters all together), and "Hoert mijn Adieu myn vrienden doch" (Hear my farewell, my friends), included in Wackernagel, *Lieder,* 203-5; from this book a letter, "Een gantsch Christelijcke groet," and his confession have been copied in the Dutch martyrbooks, including van Braght, *Martyrs' Mirror;* (4) Nos. 1 and 3 were reprinted together at Hoorn 1611 by Zacharias Cornelisz. A French translation of Alewijnsz' booklet *Veele schoone grondige leeringen* was published in 1626 n.p., under the title *Ensuivent Plusieurs belles Instructions,* as an appendix to the French edition of Dirk Philips' (*q.v.*) *Enchiridion.* The *Martyrs' Mirror* contains a letter of November 1569, his confession, and his farewell letter to his children.   vDZ.

Mart. Mir. D 389-405; E 742-57; *Bibliographie des Martyrologes Prot. Neerl.* I, 1-10, 645 f.; *Biogr. Wb.* I, 83 f., III, 676 f.; K. R. Pekelharing, *Gesch. der Hervorming in Zeeland 1524-72* (1866) 73-86; *DJ* 1840, 64-65; *DB* 1870, 51; 1899, 77 f., 90 f., 138; 1908, 16, 62; *ML* I, 20.

Hendrick Kistemaecker (Henrik van Zutphen), a Dutch Anabaptist leader, adherent of Jan van Leyden and the Münsterite (*q.v.*) principles, was active in Groningen and Deventer in 1534-35, where he baptized. By trade he was a tailor. At the conference of Anabaptist leaders at Bocholt in 1536 he still defended the Münsterite principles. (*DB* 1917, 114, No. 46; 1919, 13; Mellink, *Wederdopers,* see Index.)   vDZ.

Hendrick Simons, coauthor with Willem Seghers (*q.v.*) of the song "Wij clagent o Heer, ons doch verhoort." (Wolkan, *Lieder,* 70.)

Hendrick Willems(z): see **Heijnric Willemse Saelmaker.**

Hendricx, Joost: see **Hendriksz, Joost.**

Hendrik, a Dutch Anabaptist martyr named by van Braght, *Martyrs' Mirror* (D 288, E 655) may be either Hendrik van Dale (*q.v.*) or Hendrick de Raymakere (*q.v.*).   vDZ.

Hendrik Aerts, an Anabaptist martyr, a hatter of Halewijn (Halluin), Belgium, was taken prisoner at that place together with his wife Janneken Cabeljaus and eleven others by the notorious inquisitor Titelman (*q.v.*), and was brought to Rijssel. Among the group was the preacher Jan de Swarte (*q.v.*). Hendrik was burned at the stake on March 17, 1563, at Rijssel with five others of this group; the others were executed later. Hendrik was a native of Driel, Dutch province of Gelderland. (*Mart. Mir.* D 299-300, E 665; *ML* I, 86.)   vDZ.

Hendrik Anthonisz, an Anabaptist martyr, was captured with five fellow believers in 1552 at Amsterdam. Before the council they declared that they intended to remain loyal to their faith. The government ordered him and Reyer Egbertsz to be tortured on June 28. Because they did not recant then, they were condemned to die at the stake on Aug. 6, 1552. Hendrik confessed that he had not been baptized, but was "ready for it." Their property was confiscated. On the same day all of the group met their death at the stake. (*Mart. Mir.* D 142 f., E 536; *ML* I, 75.) O.H.

Hendrik Arents, an Anabaptist martyr, a carpenter by trade, was seized in Brielle near Rotterdam while engaged in repairing a ship. He did not know that it belonged to pirates. Nevertheless he was taken to Rotterdam with the pirates, where they were sentenced to death by hanging. From a petition in which Hendrick stated his innocence, the governor noticed that he was dealing with an Anabaptist. Hendrik was again examined, openly confessed his faith, and was condemned to die at the stake; after a two weeks' imprisonment he bore his suffering with great courage. (*Mart. Mir.* D 383, E 736; *ML* I, 81.) O.H.

Hendrik van Arnhem (Henric van Aernem), "with the crippled foot," a tailor from the district of Cleve, Germany, was an elder in the Anabaptist congregation at Antwerp, Belgium. The martyr Bartel (*q.v.*) had a conversation with him there about Mary van Beckum. Little is known about this elder. He was apparently prominent. The Amsterdam authorities had put a price upon his head, which was raised in 1566 to 200 Caroli-guilders. Among those he baptized were the martyrs Jan Ghijselinck, Gheert Vermandele, Martijn-ken Meere, and Belijnken de Jaghere, in the presence of about 20 other Anabaptists. He also played the role of arbitrator in the dispute between the Frisians and the Flemish, having been called for that purpose as a *buitenleraar* (*q.v.*) to Friesland several times during the winter of 1566-67. He sided with the Flemish, but was accused by some fanatics of sympathy for the Frisians. In 1570 he was still an elder. vDZ.

K. Vos, *Menno Simons* (Leiden, 1914) 146; *BRN* VII, 64; *DB* 1893, 31-76, *passim;* A. L. E. Verheyden, "Mennisme in Vlaanderen," msc, p. 32; *Mart. Mir.* D 103, E 500.

Hendrik Bauwens, an Anabaptist martyr, was burned at the stake at Gent, Belgium, at eleven o'clock, July 28, 1573, on the Vrijdagsmarkt. He was a native of Mechelen, a lace-maker by trade. His name is not found in van Braght, *Martyrs' Mirror;* but the names of Jacob van der Weghe and Fransoys van Leuvene, who died as martyrs with him, are given there. For that matter van Braght is not quite complete in respect to the martyrs from Gent. (Verheyden, *Gent,* No. 226, 63.) vDZ.

Hendrik Beverts (Groote Hendrick, or Henric van Deventer), an Anabaptist martyr, by trade a goldsmith or silversmith, was burned at the stake at Antwerp on Sept. 1, 1551, together with Jeronimus Segersz, who wrote a letter to him in prison while he was also a prisoner. He experienced "much severe torment and examination on the rack," but could not be deflected from his faith. Unafraid he approached the stake to which he was then tied to be burned. vDZ.

Offer, 151, 152, 175; *Mart. Mir.* D 107, E 514; *Antw. Arch.-Blad* VIII, 402, 414, 417; XIV, 18 f., No. 201.

Hendrik Biesman (Henrick Byesman), an Anabaptist martyr, was put to death at Amsterdam on March 6, 1535, with eight others, among them Jan Paeuw (*q.v.*). He was born in Maastricht, Dutch province of Limburg, where he associated with the Anabaptists in September 1534, and also held meetings in his house. He was arrested and tried at Maastricht on Oct. 28, 1534; here he apparently recanted and was released. Soon after he probably went to Amsterdam, perhaps by way of Antwerp, where he also saw Anabaptists. vDZ.

W. Bax, *Het Protestantisme in het Bisdom Luik* I (The Hague, 1937) 85, 88 f.; *Mart. Mir.* D 412, E 763; Grosheide, *Verhooren,* 52 f.

Hendrik Busch Varcken, an Anabaptist martyr, a lawyer, b. in Brussels, betrayed by Reynier Willems, who was a follower of David Joris (*q.v.*), was beheaded at Alkmaar on Jan. 23, 1541, although he confessed that he was sorry that he had accepted baptism. vDZ.

Hendrik Cramer (official name, *Henrick Evert Valckerzoon*), a native of Zutphen, Dutch province of Gelderland, an Anabaptist martyr, was executed at Amsterdam on July 28, 1535, after he had been tortured three times. In the charge brought against him, the following items are catalogued: he had been rebaptized at Coesfeld by Henrick Slachtscaep (*q.v.*); he had associated with these Anabaptist heretics; he had as a peddler (*cramer*) visited Münster and left the city with Jan van Gheel (van Geelen, *q.v.*) and two men from Friesland, transporting to Deventer in his peddler's pack some Anabaptist books printed in Münster, he had been aware of the Anabaptist assault (May 10-11, 1535) on the town hall of Amsterdam, without informing the city government. (Grosheide, *Verhooren,* 141-44, 160; Mellink, *Wederdopers,* see Index.) vDZ.

Hendrik van Dale, an Anabaptist martyr: see **Heyndrick van Dale.**

Hendrik van Echtelo (*Eckelo, Eeclo(o),* also called Heyndrik de Schoenmaker), an Anabaptist martyr, was a young man, who according to van Braght, *Martyrs' Mirror,* was beheaded in 1572 at Gent, Belgium, on the Vrijdag market place. Verheyden, studying the sources, found a heretic, not especially denounced as an Anabaptist, called Hendrick van Eecloo, who was a weaver and who was hanged on May 29, 1572, outside the Muyden Gate at Gent. Verheyden is doubtful whether these two accounts can refer to the same person and states that the problem of Hendrik van Eckelo (van Eecloo) cannot be clarified. Van Braght reports that Hendrik is the author of a song beginning "Aenghesien de nature mij dit te mercken doet" (Because nature makes me know this). This song is found in *Sommighe Stichtelyke Liedekens bij diverse personen gemaeckt* (Hoorn, 1632) 64. (*Mart. Mir.* D 566, E 896; Verheyden, *Gent,* 58 f., No. 204; *ML* I, 502.) vDZ.

Hendrik Eemkens (Henrick Emken), an Anabaptist martyr, a native of Loquard in East Friesland, Germany, a tailor, a simple man unable to read or write; but he defended his faith with amazing skill, clearness, and conviction against a monk sent to convert him. Eemkens was baptized by Joost Verbeek in 1561. He was executed on June 10, 1562, at Utrecht. His death is described by van Braght (*Mart. Mir.* D 294, E 660) with an etching by Luyken. His wife Anna was baptized with him and was likewise captured and tortured; but nothing is known concerning her death. (*DB* 1903, 12 ff., 51; *ML* I, 507.)   NEFF.

Hendrik Eeuwesz, an Anabaptist martyr, the husband of the martyr Claesken (*q.v.*) and the brother-in-law of the martyr Jaques d'Auchy (*q.v.*), was secretly executed with them on March 14, 1559, by drowning in a tub in prison at Leeuwarden. (*Mart. Mir.* D 242, E 611; *Offer,* 268 note, 324, 330, 336 f., 341; *DB* 1899, 36, 38; *ML* I, 507.)   NEFF.

Hendrik van Etten, born at Breda, Dutch province of North Brabant, Anabaptist martyr, seized with his friend Abraham Picolet (*q.v.*) by soldiers of Duke Alba, and although they had not yet been baptized, they were burned at the stake at Antwerp in 1569 together with Maeyken van der Goes (*q.v.*) after a frank confession of their faith. In prison van Etten wrote several letters which have been lost, in which as an ex-soldier he exhorted his friends to persevere in the battle assigned to them. (*Mart. Mir.* D 475, E 818; *ML* I, 614.)   NEFF.

Hendrik Goedbeleid (Goedtbeleed), a Dutch Anabaptist, was killed during the assault on the town hall of Amsterdam on May 10-11, 1535. He was a native of Amsterdam, belonged to the revolutionary wing of Anabaptism, and was an accomplice of the Münsterite leader Jan van Geelen (*q.v.*), with whom he traveled to Brussels (April 1535) to contact the imperial government concerning transferring the city of Münster into the domain of Emperor Charles V. His confession is important as to the activities of the Münsterite movement. vpZ.

Grosheide, *Verhooren,* 17, 21-22, 77, 80, 82, 117; Mellink, *Wederdopers,* see Index.

Hendrik Gutwol, an Anabaptist martyr: see **Guthwohl, Heinrich.**

Hendrik Gysbrecht (Hendrik van Kampen), an Anabaptist martyr, a native of Kampen, was seized at Hoorn, Dutch province of North Holland, with Sybrand Jansz, Steven Benedictus, Femmetje Egbertsdochter, and Welmoed Jansdochter, and sentenced to death on June 7, 1535, on the charge made by Anton Sonck that they had been rebaptized. The men were beheaded, their bodies broken on the wheel, and their heads set on poles; the women were drowned.   K.V.

Mart. Mir. D 36 f., E 443; *Inv. Arch. Amst.* I, No. 131; Mellink, *Wederdopers,* 168 f.; *ML* II, 213.

Hendrik Hendricksz (Henrick Henricxz), a native of Maastricht, Dutch province of Limburg, an otherwise unknown Dutch Anabaptist, was exe-

cuted at Rotterdam, Holland, on March 13, 1535. He belonged to the Münsterites (*q.v.*) and was not a citizen of Rotterdam. (*DB* 1905, 171; Mellink, *Wederdopers,* 224 f.)   vpZ.

Hendrik Hendriksz, a tailor at Amsterdam, a Dutch Anabaptist, was one of the *Naaktlopers* (*q.v.*) and was beheaded at Amsterdam on Feb. 2, 1535. (Grosheide, *Verhooren,* 57 f.)   vpZ.

Hendrik van Hilversum, an Anabaptist leader: see **Henric Rol.**

Hendrik Koel van Gelder (Hendrik Pietersz), a Dutch Anabaptist, beheaded at Delft, Dutch province of South Holland, on Jan. 10, 1539, was an ardent follower of David Joris (*q.v.*). He was a fanatical zealot who believed that the Holy Ghost rested on David Joris and that his writings emanated from the Holy Ghost. (*DB* 1917, 115, No. 22.)   vpZ.

Hendrik Leer(ver)koper, a leather merchant at Antwerp, Belgium, an Anabaptist martyr, was beheaded at Antwerp on Oct. 8, 1558. The goods he left were confiscated. His official name was Hendrick Dache(?), a native of Fleru (Fleurus?). His wife was drowned because of "Anabaptist heresy" at Antwerp on March 19, 1559. The name of Hendrik is found in the hymn "Aenhoort Godt, hemelsche Vader" (Hear, O God, heavenly Father), included in *Liedtboecxken van den Offer des Heeren,* No. 16.   vpZ.

Offer, 565; *Mart. Mir.* D 202, E 583; Wolkan, *Lieder,* 63, 72; *Antw. Arch.-Blad* VIII, 450, 464; IX, 17; XIV, 24 f., No. 264; *ML* II, 626.

Hendrik van Maastricht (also called Henrick Caerdemaker), a Dutch Anabaptist belonging to the revolutionary wing of Anabaptism. He had traveled widely, and places of his activity were Goch, Cleve, Antwerp, Edam, Monnikendam, Amsterdam, and the Gooi-district near Amsterdam. He was arrested in Amsterdam in February 1536. Several times from February 26 until April 29 he was tried and sometimes tortured. His confessions reveal many interesting particulars about the Anabaptist movement in the Netherlands. He had joined the Anabaptists in March 1534, not by being baptized, but by laying on of hands by Claes van Enchuysen.   vpZ.

DB 1917, 111, No. 23; Grosheide, *Verhooren,* 19, 168-77; Mellink, *Wederdopers,* see Index.

Hendrik Maelschap (Maesschop, Maelschalk, Maerschalk), an Anabaptist martyr, burned at the stake on the Veerle square at Gent, Belgium. He had been arrested on his way to a meeting with Jan van Parijs, Peter van Cleve (Pieter Aelbrechts), and Laurens Pietersz; they had not yet been baptized, but they wished to be faithful and confessed their faith "without fear," and were therefore sentenced to death in 1568. As they were to be burned they sang together, "Ick roep v, o Hemelsch Vader, aen, wil myn geloove sterken," and were therefore beaten by the Spaniards. Steadfastly they endured their cruel martyrdom. In prison Maelschap wrote a letter on Jan. 26, 1568, to a friend Goelken, stating that they were all in good spirits and wanted to remain faithful to the Lord until death, and admonished her and all his friends in Biblical terms to live a Christian life to the end. In addition he sent her three songs as a friendly and sincere greeting; "Although they are simple, accept them with thanks, for they were sent in love, Farewell to eternity. Amen." In a postscript written on the next day he describes the cross-examination they had to endure. When he was asked whether he would desist from his faith, he answered that he had desisted from lies and was now following the truth; he hoped to stay by the truth through the grace of the Lord. These martyrs are commemorated in the song "Alsmen schreef duyst vijf hondert jaer ende twee en tsestich mede," which is found in the appendix to the *Lietboecxcken van den Offer des Heeren*.   NEFF.

Offer, 652; *Mart. Mir.* D 367 ff., E 723 ff.; Verheyden, *Gent*, 43, No. 138; *ML* II, 711.

Hendrik van Maren: see **Maren** (Maeren), **Hendrik van.**

Hendrik (de) Naeldeman (Naeldemaker), a Dutch Mennonite elder living at Franeker, Dutch province of Friesland; Karel Vos concluded that he was a tailor. He was one of the men involved in the dispute among the Dutch Mennonites in 1555 on the strict or lenient application of the ban (which was really a question of individual liberty versus obligation to the brotherhood). In opposition to Leenaert Bouwens (*q.v.*), he advocated a triple warning before the use of the ban; in other words, he regarded the ban as a means of discipline. In Waterland, North Holland, Gillis van Aken (*q.v.*) forced the issue, and brethren in other places also were divided; but Menno Simons (*q.v.*) managed to preserve unity in Waterland by a visit to Waterland (1555) and a letter to the brotherhood in Franeker (1557), where the moderate wing was led by Naeldeman and Joriaen Heynsz. But when Leenaert Bouwens enforced the strict ban in Emden, and Heynsz and Naeldeman were put in the ban, the conflict arose again, also in Franeker. In 1557 Menno again attempted to bring about a reconciliation, and was at first apparently successful. But at the conference held in Harlingen Leenaert Bouwens and Dirk Philips carried the day with their strict interpretation of the ban, and unity was ended. Naeldeman wrote a letter to Menno, which deprived Menno of his last hope of reconciliation. The moderate "Franekeraars," commonly known as the Waterlanders, whose position was shared by the South German Anabaptists, went their own way. In 1620 there was still a group of Mennonites in Middelburg (*q.v.*) known as the *(Hendrick) Naeldemans-volk.*   VDZ.

BRN VII, 54 f.; *DB* 1894, 32, 36, 39, 41-44; K. Vos, *Menno Simons* (Leiden, 1914) 132, 135, 137, 191, 257; Kühler, *Geschiedenis* I, 316 f., 319-24; *ML* III, 197.

Hendrik Niclaes: see **Niclaes, Heinrich.**

Hendrik Pruyt (Spruyt), an Anabaptist martyr, was put to death in 1574 at Workum, Dutch province of Friesland. Hendrik, a bargeman of Harder-

wijk, Dutch province of Gelderland, was arrested by the Spanish soldiers, when he passed by Workum with his boat. As the soldiers approached he said to his wife Trijntje Jans: "Dear, there comes the wolf." Hendrik was imprisoned for some time in the military office of Workum and after it had been proved clearly that he was a Mennonite he was sentenced to death without a regular trial. His death was very cruel. He was stripped, tarred, and thrown into a little boat, hands and legs bound together. When ebb tide set in, the boat was set on fire and Hendrik floated away with the stream. Half burned, his ropes loosened by the fire, he sprang into the sea; but then soldiers following him in another boat killed him with their spears. His wife managed to escape. (*Mart. Mir.* D 691, E 1005; *DB* 1895, 55-58; *ML* III, 403 f.)   VDZ.

Hendrik Rol: see **Henric Rol.**

Hendrik Slachtscaep (Heinrich, Henric von Tongeren), one of the "Wassenberg preachers" (*q.v.*), born *ca.* 1470 at Tongeren, bishopric of Liége, a former Catholic priest, came more and more to Protestant convictions, which he preached in popular style with great force and success. Of especial interest are his tracts, *Der Trostbrief,* and the epistle *Aen myne liefte broeders en susters tot Sustern* (Rembert, 357). He was a determined opponent of infant baptism. In 1531 he preached in Wassenberg, Coesfeld (*q.v.*), Aachen, and Maastricht (*q.v.*). Against him and Campanus (*q.v.*) was issued the edict of the government of Düsseldorf of Nov. 1, 1532 (Keller, 295). Invited by Bernhard Rothmann (*q.v.*) by letter, he betook himself to Münster (1534) and was baptized there. Then he was sent out with the other "Wassenberg preachers" as apostles; he was executed as a martyr at Soest on Oct. 23, 1534.   NEFF.

L. Keller, *Geschichte der Wiedertäufer und ihres Reiches zu Münster* (Münster, 1880); Rembert, *Wiedertäufer; DB* 1917, 120, No. 109; W. Bax, *Het Protestantisme in het Bisdom Luik* I (The Hague, 1937) 50-52 and *passim*; Mellink, *Wederdopers, passim,* see Index.

Hendrik Spruyt: see **Hendrik Pruyt.**

Hendrik Terwoort, an Anabaptist martyr, about 26 years of age, was burned at the stake at London, July 22, 1575, together with Jan Pietersz. Hendrik, who was a goldsmith, was a refugee from Flanders, likely from Gent; he was charged with the crime of having held Anabaptist meetings in a private house in Aldersgate at London. He remained in Newgate prison for a long time with a number of other Mennonites, of whom one died in prison and all others finally were set free except Hendrik and Jan. These two martyrs wrote two letters to their friends, the last on July 21, the day before their death. These letters are found in van Braght's *Martyrs' Mirror,* who gives detailed information about this martyrdom, including a letter written by Jacques de Somer, a Calvinist, to his mother in Gent, Belgium. A petition written by Hendrik Terwoort and Jan Pietersz and others and sent to Queen Elizabeth of England, in which they stated that they cannot believe otherwise than that "they feel in their conscience," was fruitless.

The *Confessio* of Thomas van Imbroek (Imbroich), martyred in 1558 at Cologne, printed at Gent 1579 (German edition about the same time or earlier), contains a song on these two martyrs, beginning "Aenhoort met neerstichden [i.e., neerstigheden], menschen verstaet wel mijn" (Hear attentively, ye people, understand me well). (*Mart. Mir.* D 694-712, E 1008-24.)   vDZ.

Hendrik Verstralen, an Anabaptist martyr, executed in 1571 in Rypermonde (Rupelmonde) in Flanders, Belgium. There is not much information about this martyr; even the three letters found in *Offer des Heeren* and following martyrbooks do not give many particulars. He found it difficult to leave his wife Janneken and again and again asks her to kiss his children for him. He expected the congregation to take care of his family after his death. He was imprisoned in the castle in iron shackles; Maeyken Deynoots (*q.v.*) was in prison at the same time. In prison he wrote three letters—two to his wife, the first of which was undated, the second dated Palm Sunday (March 2), 1571; one letter, dated *Jorisdach* 1571, i.e., April 23, is written to the congregation. These letters, together with those of Maeyken Deynoots, entitled *Twee schoone Brieven,* were published in 1577 and in 1579, and perhaps as early as 1571 (see *Bibliographie* I, 465). The Amsterdam Mennonite Library has a copy of the 1577 edition. The letters were also included in a 1578 edition of the *Offer des Heeren.* Hendrik was the author of three songs, of which only the first is found in the *Offer des Heeren.* It begins, "O Heere Godt van grooter machte" (O God, Lord of great might). The two other songs begin: "Genade ende Vrede van Godts bermharticheyt" (Grace and peace of God's mercy) and "O Heere van Hemel en aarde mee" (O Lord of heaven and earth). They are found in *Twee schoone Brieven,* in the *Hoorns Liedt-boeck* (*q.v.*) of 1630, and reprinted in Wackernagel, *Lieder.*   vDZ.

Offer, 628-45; *Mart. Mir.* D 542, E 877; Wackernagel, *Lieder,* 104 f., 205-7; *Bibliographie* I, 643 ff., 674 f.; *Catalogus Amst.,* 100.

Hendrik (Hendrick, Henric) **van Vre(e)den,** a Mennonite elder, co-worker with Menno Simons, ordained by Menno and Dirk Philips in 1542. Of his work almost nothing is known. His field of activity seems to have been Westphalia, Germany. He was present at the conference of Mennonite elders in Emden in 1547 and likely at that of Goch in the same year. The superintendent of police who examined the martyr Jacques d' Auchy at Leeuwarden in 1558 reckoned Hendrik van Vreden among the most important Anabaptist leaders (*Offer,* 274).

In an old Dutch list of elders, *Copia der Outsten* (Vos, 256-57) is found, "1550 Hindrick van Vreede is afgevallen." This does not necessarily mean that he had recanted or left the church; it probably means that he was no longer in harmony with Menno. Nothing is, however, known of such discord.   vDZ.

BRN VII, 50 f.; *DB* 1894, 18, 22; K. Vos, *Menno Simons* (Leiden, 1914) see Index.

Hendrik van Zutphen: see **Hendrick Kistemaecker.**

Hendriks: see also **Hendriksz.**

Hendriks (Hendricx, Henrixen, Hendrikse), **Jacob** (later called Jacob Hendrics Smit), until his death in 1724 a Mennonite preacher of the United Flemish and Waterlander Noorderkaai congregation at Blokzijl (*q.v.*), Dutch province of Overijssel, was charged by the Reformed classis of Vollenhove with Socinianism (*q.v.*) and suspended from his ministry by the States of Overijssel on Aug. 1, 1684. In 1686 he was allowed to preach again but in 1699, after publishing a catechetical book, *Onderwijs na den weg ten hemel* (1698), he was summoned before a Reformed Synod at Zwolle. Because Hendriks refused to sign a statement drawn up by this Synod he was imprisoned in January 1700. After half a year he was released; since he refused to pay the required fine, his furniture was publicly sold. He continued to preach and is likely the author of *Praetje bij de weg,* in which he gave a critical report about his troubles. These troubles also disturbed the congregation; because of his liberal ideas the more conservative part separated from the main body to found a new congregation about 1700. (*Biogr. Wb.* III, 674-76.)   vDZ.

Hendriks (Hendricksz), **Laurens,** appointed deacon of the Amsterdam Mennonite congregation "bij 't Lam" in 1656, was a violent antagonist of Galenus Abrahamsz (*q.v.*), playing an important role in the *Lammerenkrijgh* (*q.v.*), the struggle between more progressive and more conservative views, Hendriks strictly holding to the conservative principles. When after a fruitless discussion between the two parties Galenus and his copreacher presented to their opponents a copy of their *XIX Artikelen* (January 1657), Hendriks unfairly published this document with his additional refutation, *Antwoorde bij forme van aanmerkingen . . .* (Amsterdam, 1659). Galenus then published *Wederleggingen van Laurens Hendriksz* (Amsterdam, 1659). In 1660 and again in 1663 Hendriks tried to have Galenus suspended from his office. In 1664 Hendriks published *Vrede-presentatie aan Galenus Abrahamsz en zyne Medestemmers.* When in 1664 this congregation of Amsterdam divided into a Lamist and a Zonist congregation, Hendriks joined the Zonist branch, serving as a deacon until his death in 1667.   vDZ.

Inv. Arch. Amst. II, Nos. 143, 174, 218, 1244; *Biogr. Wb.* III, 673 f.; H. W. Meihuizen, *Galenus Abrahamsz* (Haarlem, 1954) see Index.

Hendriks, Laurens, a Mennonite preacher at Nijmegen, Dutch province of Gelderland, from 1690 until about 1714. A number of Swiss Mennonites who were being transported from Switzerland to England were liberated en route at Nijmegen on April 6, 1710, and were received by Hendriks and members of his congregation in their homes with much hospitality. In the Amsterdam Mennonite library is found a copy of a letter written by Hendriks, dated April 9, 1710, to Isaak Seckes (?), giving a circumstantial account of the liberation of the Mennonites at Nijmegen, most of whom returned to the Palatinate. His son Hendrik Laurens, ordained on March 18, 1714, by Elder Jan Kroes (Crous) of Crefeld, was the minister of the Nijmegen congregation 1714-59. vDZ.

Inv. Arch. Amst. II, 2, No. 866; *DB* 1869, 7-10; 1874, 31; 1875, 68-70, 78 f.; 1895, 71.

Hendriks, Pieter, was a preacher of the (Groningen) Old Flemish Mennonite congregation at Sappemeer, Dutch province of Groningen. Particulars about him were not available; even in the *Naamlijst* his name is not found. He died before 1754. He defended the doctrine of the Trinity against Johannes Stinstra and published *De vier Uytersten des Menschen* (Groningen, 1741); *'t Geslagte Lam of de Lijdende en verzoenende Hogepriester* (Groningen, 1741); *Korte Schets van verscheiden waarheden des Christendoms* (Groningen, 1743); *Schriftuurlyke Katechismus, waarin de Grondlere der Doopsgezinden in 't Gemeen, dog der sogenoemde oude Vlamingen in 't bysonder met den Woorde Gods opengelegd is* (Groningen, 1744, the 2nd ed. Groningen, 1747, also contained a sketch of the doctrines of Menno Simons); *De redelyk bevindelyke Godsdienst der weerlooze Christenen* (70 sermons) (Groningen, 1747). (*Biogr. Wb.* III, 677; Blaupot t. C., *Groningen* I, 133.) vDZ.

Hendriksz, Jan, a Dutch Mennonite elder, was present at a conference held at Harlingen on Dec. 19, 1566, to settle the Frisian-Flemish quarrels. Later on Hendriksz belonged to the Frisians, being a partisan of Lubbert Gerritsz (*q.v.*) and the "Mild Frisians." In 1590 he was banned by the strict Old Frisians. He became elder at Schiedam, Dutch province of South Holland, having been the preacher of this congregation since 1579. (*DB* 1893, 39, 81; 1909, 156 f.) vDZ.

Hendriksz (Hendriks, Hendricksz, Hendricx), **Joost,** b. 1592, d. March 2, 1644, at Amsterdam, was a preacher of the Flemish Mennonite congregations of Harlingen 1626-31 and Amsterdam 1631-44. Joost Hendriksz was very active in making peace between several divided groups of the Dutch Mennonites. The serious attempts made to unite the High Germans and Frisians with the Flemish at Amsterdam and the invitation of 1626 of the Flemish preachers of Amsterdam to other Mennonites to unite with them (see **Olijftacxken**), were quite after his own heart. About these unions he published *Vredehandelingh . . . Alsmede Noch Eenes Vreed-lievenden Ernstighe Aenmaninghe tot gemeynschap der Heyligen* (Amsterdam, 1630), and an *Aen-Spraeck op het Olijf-Tacxken* (Haarlem, 1636). Against Denijs van der Schuere and Jacob Cornelisz he wrote *Eenige Extracten . . .* and *Nader Bericht . . .* (both Amsterdam, 1640). With P. Bontemps (*q.v.*), French Reformed pastor at Haarlem who had opposed and attacked the Mennonites, he became involved in a paper war, publishing *Wederlegginge van de argumenten voorgestelt door P. B.* (Amsterdam, 1643) and *Spongie tot afwasschinge van de vuyle vlecken, die P. B. de Mennisten nu weder heeft aenghewreven . . .* (Amsterdam, 1643). He also published *XXXVIII corte*

stichtelijcke Predicatiën (Amsterdam, 1646) reprinted at Amsterdam 1647, 1650, 1652, 1666, and Franeker 1668. The title of the third edition was *XXXIX corte Stichtelijke Predicatiën* and of the fourth and following editions *XXXX Korte en stichtelijke Predicatiën*. The second and following editions also contain a treatise on how a member who was banned because of outside marriage should be received. Joost Hendriksz's devotional works have been eagerly read. They were used in the congregation of Balk, Friesland, until the 19th century and were even popular among the American Mennonites. On March 1, 1773, Andreas Ziegler, Isac Kolb, and Christian Funk, bishops at "Schippack, Indian Krik and Blen," in a letter to Crefeld and Utrecht asked to have Joost Hendriks' books sent. vDZ.

Schijn-Maatschoen, *Uitvoeriger Geschiedenis* II, 646-48; *Biogr. Wb.* III, 677-80; *DB* 1863, 133; 1892, 75; 1916, 147; R. Friedmann, *Mennonite Piety Through the Centuries* (Scottdale, 1949) 115, 142; *MQR,* October 1929, 231; *Inv. Arch. Amst.* I, No. 558 V; *ML* II, 282.

Hendriksz, Pieter, a Mennonite, member of the Amsterdam Lamist congregation, who, influenced by the Quakers in his view on the church, attacked Galenus Abrahamsz (*q.v.*), the leader of the Lamist church, in a booklet *Een Ernstige bestraffinge aen de Vlaemsche Doopsgesinde Gemeynte tot Amsterdam* (Amsterdam, 1670), accusing him of laying too much stress upon form, especially in maintaining the old customs of baptism and communion. vDZ.

H. W. Meihuizen, *Galenus Abrahamsz* (Haarlem, 1954) 112 f., 154.

Henegouwen (German, Hennegau): see **Hainaut.**

Hengelaer, Gerrit van, a deacon of the Mennonite congregation of Utrecht in the Netherlands, with conservative views and opposed to the Galenists (*q.v.*) and W. van Maurik (*q.v.*), author of *Een Morgen-Wecker,* an important pamphlet (128 pp., Utrecht, 1673) in which he tried to undo the quarrels and the separation which had struck the congregation. The booklet, an admonition to peace and unity, is followed by a short confession of five articles. (*Inv. Arch. Amst.* II, Nos. 2315; *DB* 1916, 191; *Biogr. Wb.* III, 693; *N.N.B. Wb.* VII, 558.) vDZ.

Hengelo, an industrial, rapidly growing town (1953 pop. 52,474) in the Dutch province of Overijssel, noted for textiles and iron works, has 475 Mennonites, is the seat of a Mennonite congregation. In the 17th century Mennonites living in Hengelo and in Borne (*q.v.*) and Goor (*q.v.*) formed a congregation of the Groningen Old Flemish branch. In 1728 this congregation was divided into two congregations, one at Borne and one of Hengelo-Goor. During the 17th century the Hengelo Mennonites attended the meetings at Borne or Zenderen or Twekkelo, but since about 1709 meetings were also held at Hengelo in the private home of Berend ter Horst and his descendants. In 1792 Wolter ten Cate gave the congregation a meetinghouse at Hengelo. Though he lived at Hengelo, having been the promoter of its textile industry, he was a member and elder of the Borne congregation. The meetinghouse—so ten Cate ordered—should be plain and without luxury. It was remodeled in 1855, 1883, and 1953. An organ was put in in 1874.

In the 18th century the core of the Hengelo congregation was formed by the ter Horst, ten Cate, and Nijhoff families. During this century preachers were regularly chosen from the membership, the last being Engbert Nijhoff, 1757-1805. Its first trained minister was Govert Jans van Rijswijk, 1800-6. He was followed by Barend Rusburg 1807-23, Jan Visscher 1824-28, H. ten Cate Hzn 1829-64, A. Ballot 1864-71, I. H. Boeke 1872-78, H. Boetje 1879-1911, G. Heeringa 1912-40, P. J. Smidts 1941-47, and K. T. Gorter 1948- . The membership was 87 in 1733, 80 in 1767, 85 in 1840, 60 in 1861, 170 in 1898, 390 in 1925, 347 in 1954.

Church activities include a Sunday school for children, a ladies' circle, and a choir.   vᴅZ.

Inv. Arch. Amst. II, Nos. 1924-25; II, 2, 99; *DB* 1879, 7; 1884, 152; *Uit het Verleden der Doopsgezinden in Twenthe* (Borne, n.d.) *passim; ML* II, 283.

Hennebo, a family of Mennonite refugees from Flanders, Belgium, to the Netherlands; its members were found especially in the Flemish congregations of Leiden, Haarlem, and Amsterdam, where many of them served as deacons.   vᴅZ.

Hennegau (Henegouwen): see **Hainaut.**

Henric (Hendrick) **Dirksz,** an Anabaptist martyr, was apprehended in Leiden, Dutch province of South Holland, in 1552 together with Dirk Jans (*q.v.*) and Adriaen Cornelisz (*q.v.*) and executed on Nov. 24, 1552. When the sentence was pronounced he stepped forward and said, "Blessed are they that weep now; for they shall laugh, and be rewarded with shining robes; yea, with an eternal crown, if they strive steadfastly. This is the sabbath of the Lord, which I have long desired; not that I am worthy to suffer for His name, but He has made me worthy; and thus we suffer not for theft or murder, but for the pure Word of God." Their death is commemorated in the hymn, "Ick mach wel droeflich singen," found in the *Liedtboecxken van den Offer des Heeren,* No. 6. (*Offer,* 526, 578 ff.; *Mart. Mir.* D 133, E 526; *ML* I, 450.) Neff.

Henric(k) Rol, an Anabaptist leader and martyr, b. at Grave, Dutch province of North Brabant, who is found under different names: Henric (Hendrik) van Hilversum, Hendrik de Gooilander, Hendrik (van) Wassenberg, Henrich van den Grave, Henricus der Hollander, Henrich de Carmelyt, was burned at the stake at Maastricht, Dutch province of Limburg, in September 1534. He had been a Carmelite monk at Haarlem, but soon became interested in the Reformation. In 1530, while he was still the Catholic chaplain of Gijsbrecht van Baeck (*q.v.*) at IJsselstein, he is thought to have visited Augsburg, Germany, about the time that the Lutheran Confession was presented to the Emperor Charles V, and to have been in Strasbourg, becoming acquainted with Bucer, Capito, Bernt Roth-

mann, and Caspar Schwenckfeld; but any visits to Augsburg and Strasbourg are doubtful. In 1531 he lived in Wassenberg (*q.v.*), where he met Dionysius Vinne, Klopreis, and the other "Wassenberger Predicanten." In the summer of 1532 Rol came to Münster in Westphalia. He was not yet an Anabaptist, though he shared their views about baptism and communion. In 1533, as preacher of the St. Ilgen Church, he ardently opposed infant baptism. In October 1533 he signed the confession called *Bekentnisse van beyden sacramenten Doepe unde Nachtmael* with Rothmann and other Evangelical preachers. On Nov. 6, 1533, he was banished from Münster; he then visited Holland and Friesland, but on Jan. 1, 1534, he preached a sermon in Münster. He now joined the Anabaptists, being baptized on Jan. 5, 1534, by Bartel Boeckbinder or Willem Cuyper, who had been sent to Münster by Jan Matthysz. Rol baptized Gerhard Westerburg in January at the house of Knipperdolling. On Feb. 21, 1534, Rol left Münster to win recruits to join the "New Jerusalem" at Münster. Rol first went to Wesel (*q.v.*), where he baptized a number of persons; then he likely visited Holland. On Aug. 2, 1534, he arrived at Maastricht, where he found a group of Sacramentists (*q.v.*) who had left the Catholic Church, rejecting the Catholic views of the church and the sacraments, especially the Mass. Among this group, usually meeting in the house of the cobbler Jan van Genck, Rol taught the Anabaptist principles and baptized the believers. While holding a meeting he was arrested here on the evening of Sept. 2, 1534, and soon after executed.

The person of Rol has found a varied appreciation. Mellink considers Rol to have been a Münsterite leader, with the revolutionary views of Jan van Leyden; Sepp, Rembert, and Kühler thought him to be a peaceful Anabaptist. Kühler, who calls him the most noble representative of Anabaptism, suggests that Rol left Münster in February 1534 because he did not agree with the principles and policy of Jan Mattysz and Jan van Leyden.

Rol is the author of *Die Slotel van dat Secreet des Nachtmaels* (The Key of the Mystery of the Communion), written in 1531 or 1532 in East Frisian or Low German, a remarkable and profound treatise which totally rejects the Catholic and Lutheran views and describes the communion as a meal of rejoicing in which the redeemed of the Lord may partake. Rol also wrote *Eyne ware Bedijnckijnge hoe dat hoochweirdich lichaam Christi, van unsen unweirdigen lichaam to underscheiden isz, doer Vrage ende Antwoorde* (A True Consideration How The Blessed Body of Christ Is Different from Our Unworthy Body, In Questions and Answers). In both writings, but especially in the last named, Rol describes faith as the personal conviction of the believer; he does not want a church or an authority to lean upon, or to prove his faith. Baptism and communion are not necessary to obtain salvation and to enter upon the joys of heaven. Both writings were re-edited with introduction and commentaries by S. Cramer in *Bibliotheca Reformatoria Neerlandica,* Vol. V. An anonymous letter "Aen mijn liefste broeders und susters tot Süstern und omgelegen plaitzen, ouch tot Mastricht, und allen fromen christenen" is, according to Forsthoff and Rembert, to be ascribed to Rol, whereas Habets considers Slachtscaep (*q.v.*) as the author.   vDZ.

BRN V, 1-123; J. Habets, *De Wederdoopers te Maastricht* (1877) 102 ff., 220 ff.; Chr. Sepp, *Kerkhistorische Studien* (Leiden, 1885) 1-90; Rembert, *Wiedertäufer*, see Index; H. Forsthoff, *Rheinische Kirchengeschichte* I (1929) 145, 147; Kühler, *Geschiedenis* I, 74 f., 80 f., 88 f.; W. Bax, *Het Protestantisme in het Bisdom Luik en vooral te Maastricht* I (The Hague, 1937) 93-100 and *passim;* Mellink, *Wederdopers,* see Index.

Henric van Tongeren: see Hendrik Slachtscaep.

Henrick Henricxzn (Henric Verckendrijver, or Hendrik Kuiper), a Dutch Anabaptist, who was very active among the first Anabaptists of Holland. He was baptized at Amsterdam in 1531 by Jan Volkertsz (Trypmaker) (*q.v.*) and traveled widely in the country. He was a fervent follower of Melchior Hofmann, expecting that this leader by the power of God would be liberated from his prison at Strasbourg to "erect the banner" (to establish the kingdom of God) at Amsterdam. In May 1535 he was arrested in Amsterdam. Asked by his judges whether he did not repent his rebaptism, he answered that he repented all that was done against God, but that he could not consider his (re)baptism as against God. He denied that he had taken part in the revolt (May 10-11) at Amsterdam. It is not known how this suit ended and whether Henrick was sentenced.   vDZ.

Grosheide, *Verhooren*, 93, 114-16; Mellink, *Wederdopers,* 104, 121.

Henrick Herckemaiker (Hendrik Herckmaker), a Dutch Anabaptist, originally from Giethoorn, Dutch province of Overijssel, was beheaded at Leeuwarden, Friesland, on Sept. 27, 1544. He had been baptized 10 years before by Henrick van Zutphen (see **Hendrik Kistemaecker**) as a follower of the revolutionary leader Jan van Batenburg (*q.v.*). After Batenburg's death (1538) he had adopted the views of David Joris (*q.v.*). (*DB* 1917, 86, 88, 119, 140 f.; Mellink, *Wederdopers,* 253, 410.)   vDZ.

Henrick de Raymakere, an Anabaptist who was in prison at Antwerp, Belgium, but about whose fate nothing is known. (*Antw. Arch.-Blad* IX, 117, 120, 123; XIV, 30 f., No. 336.)   vDZ.

Henrick Simons and *Willem Seghers,* about whom there is no further information, wrote the hymn "Wy clagent u Heer, ons doch verhoort" (We lament it to Thee, Lord, hear us), found in the Dutch hymnal *Het Tweede Liedeboeck* of 1583. (Wolkan, *Lieder,* 70.)   vDZ.

Henrick van Wechel, an otherwise unknown Anabaptist martyr, a native of Betborch (?), was executed at Antwerp, Belgium, apparently in 1551. (*DB* 1864, 99.)   vDZ.

Henrietta (Tex.) Mennonite Brethren Church, now extinct, was organized in 1910. The members came from the German Baptists. The minis-

terial leader of the congregation was Christian Kaefer. This church was dissolved in 1915.

H.H.Hie.

Henry County, Iowa, located in the southeastern part of the state, is bordered by Washington County (*q.v.*) on the north and Lee County (*q.v.*) on the south. Its county seat is Mt. Pleasant, the site of a state mental institution, where a Civilian Public Service unit served during World War II, and more recently a unit of I-W alternative service men.

Amish Mennonites first settled in Henry County in the late 1840's, in the northwestern part. By 1860 the following families had settled here: Conrad, Eicher, Roth, Bechler, Rich, Klopfenstein, Goldsmith, Gunden, Christner, Widmer, and Wenger. The first Amish minister in the county was Bishop Joseph Goldsmith (*q.v.*) who moved there from Lee Co., Ia., in 1855, and ministered not only to this settlement but also to the one ten miles north in Washington County. Goldsmith had organized a congregation in the Henry-Washington County area in 1852 or 1853. The growth of the two settlements made possible the organization of two congregations in the 1860's, one in Trenton Twp., Henry Co., and the other in Marion Twp., Washington Co. Under the leadership of Benjamin Eicher (*q.v.*) the Marion Township group withdrew from the Amish conference and eventually joined the General Conference Mennonites. Some members of the Washington County settlement, however, maintained their connections with the Henry County group and when the center of Amish population moved north, the Henry County congregation in 1871 built its first church, Sugar Creek (*q.v.*), 1½ miles southeast of the village that is now called Wayland (*q.v.*), and thus north of the original Trenton Township settlement. Prior to 1900 the Eicher (GCM) group began to conduct services in Wayland as well as in their Marion Township church. In 1900 the Wayland group dedicated its first church building and organized a separate congregation. The two Henry County churches now have a combined membership of 747, Sugar Creek (MC) with 462 and Wayland (GCM) with 285, although some members of both groups live in neighboring Washington County. (See Johnson-Washington County map.)   M.G.

M. Gingerich, *The Mennonites in Iowa* (Iowa City, 1939).

Henry Hannon, an Anabaptist martyr, was burned at the stake at Antwerp, Belgium, on Feb. 28, 1573, together with Lynken Baillaerts. He was charged with attending forbidden meetings (of the Mennonites), and possessing and reading forbidden books. He was not yet baptized, but confessed that he desired (re)baptism. (*Antw. Arch.-Blad* XIII, 108, 110, 175; XIV, 90 f., No. 1016.) vDZ.

Henry the Pious (1473-1541), who succeeded his brother George (*q.v.*) as Duke of Saxony in April 1539, had been interested in Protestantism as early as 1529, and laid the foundation for the introduction of the Reformation in the duchy of Saxony. On July 10, 1539, he had his instructions for inspectors prepared, on the basis of Melanchthon's inspection booklet. It specified that "Anabaptists and the adherents of other sects abandon their false doctrine or leave the land."   HEGE.

J. Issleib, "Herzog Heinrich als evangelischer Fürst," in *Beiträge zur sächsischen Kirchengeschichte*, No. 19, 1905, 168 ff.; *ML* II, 279.

Henslein of Stotzingen, an Anabaptist martyr, who was beheaded at Zabern in Alsace, France, in 1528. The *Martyrs' Mirror* gives an admonitory address that he made on the way to the site of execution. He is the author of the song, "Nun heben wir an in Nöten" (No. 42 in the *Ausbund*). (*Mart. Mir.* D 17, E 427; Wolkan, *Lieder,* 146.)   NEFF.

Hentrock, Hans, an Anabaptist martyr of Ammern in Thuringia, joined the Anabaptists in 1534, but was induced by friends and relatives to leave them, was baptized July 30, 1537, was seized in October of that year; under torture he begged for mercy and declared himself willing to recant. He was, however, not released, and soon regained his conviction; he died a martyr's death with a joyful confession of his faith before the assembled crowd by drowning in the Unstrut between Mühlhausen and Ammern, Jan. 17, 1538.   NEFF.

P. Wappler, *Die Täuferbewegung in Thüringen von 1526-1584* (Jena, 1913) 158, 162-65; *ML* II, 284.

Hepburn, Sask., a village in the heart of a large Mennonite community, 26 miles north and 2 miles west of the city of Saskatoon. The railroad branch line running through the Mennonite towns of Dalmeny, Menno, Hepburn, Waldheim, and Laird was built in 1908 and it was during this year that Hepburn had its beginning. The population (1955) is about 300. Since most of the early settlers were of Mennonite Brethren background, the town has only one church, with a membership of about 275.

Hepburn has for many years been the head office of the North Saskatchewan M.B. Conference and the M.B. missions of Saskatchewan, formerly known as the Western Children's Mission. It is also the home of the Bethany Bible Institute. The Mennonite Mutual Hail Insurance Company with an extensive business beyond Mennonite circles has its office here.

J.H.E.

Hepburn Mennonite Brethren Church, located in Hepburn, Sask., a member of the Canadian Conference of the Mennonite Brethren Church of North America, was organized by P. J. Friesen on July 15, 1910, with a membership of about 114. Most of the members came from Nebraska. P. J. Friesen became the first pastor. Other leaders and ministers were D. Schmor, H. H. Fast, J. P. Dyck, J. B. Toews, F. J. Baerg, and J. H. Epp. In 1954 the membership was 263. The frame structure which was built at the time of the organization has been rebuilt and remodeled and still serves. Services are conducted in both English and German. The congregation has a young people's fellowship, Christian Endeavor, Ladies' Aid, and Ladies' Auxiliary as well as a choir.   P.R.T.

Heppe, Heinrich Ludwig Julius (1820-79), a German theologian and church historian, professor of theology at the University of Marburg. In his *Kirchengeschichte beider Hessen* (Marburg, 1876, vol. I, pp. 261-64, 469-71 and vol. II, p. 187) he touches on the Anabaptists. He presents in the main a brief résumé of the thorough research by Hochhuth (*q.v.*), to which he refers. In one instance he makes a valuable addition (vol. I, p. 471) in offering the letter of Oct. 5, 1569, by Landgrave Wilhelm, which definitely opposes forcible baptism of the children of Anabaptists. "Now we know," says the letter, "that the church has been commanded to compel them to come in, but such compelling is to be accomplished not by force of arms, but by the force of the Word. For it is never the duty of the church to pursue political force; the true church must suffer persecution." Also worthy of note is Heppe's statement (p. 471), "The difficulty which the church encountered in the Anabaptist movement gave the church authorities their first instigation to introduce church records. The first pertinent regulation was set up in the *Kirchenordnung* of 1566 (part III, c. 15 and 16). Here the setting up of baptismal registers, which were also to serve to record confirmations, was commanded. The *Kirchenordnung* of 1573 also prescribed the use of marriage registers. The keeping of death registers was not required until the *Kirchenordnung* of 1657 was passed." (*ML* II, 284.)   NEFF.

Heppenheim im Loch, a village near Alzey, Rhenish Hesse, Germany, in which Swiss emigrants settled as early as 1664. The Mennonite lists of the Karlsruhe *Generallandesarchiv* name the Martin Weber family here in 1664, Matthias Dahlem in 1685, and four Weber families and Heinrich Landes in 1738. In 1742 the Johann Rupp family was added, and in 1768 Jakob Hahn. In 1929 two Biehn families were living here, members of the Monsheim (*q.v.*) congregation, whereas those living here earlier were members of the Oberflörsheim congregation. (*ML* II, 284 f.)   NEFF.

Heppenheim auf der Wiese, a large village near Worms in Rheinhessen, Germany, known for its wealth of fruit and grain. From Worms (*q.v.*) the Anabaptist movement early came to Heppenheim. Dr. Johann Marbach, the reformer appointed by the Palatine Elector Otto Heinrich, on his church inspection tour in the Palatinate disputed with an Anabaptist of Heppenheim who had migrated to Moravia and had returned with commissions from the Moravian Anabaptists (Hege, 88). Thus it is known that by the middle of the 16th century contacts had been established between the Moravian and Palatine Anabaptists. A Hans Greiker of Heppenheim participated in the Frankenthal disputation (*q.v.*) in 1571. In July 1588 the Reformed church council complained to the government authorities in Heidelberg, that 17 Anabaptists in Heppenheim were a burden to the pastor; for 40 years, in spite of all the mandates, they had remained in the community. In reports of Oct. 25 and Nov. 9, 1601, Titus Wittich of Dirmstein, the inspector, complained bitterly about the obstinacy of the Heppenheim Anabaptists. Particularly their spokesmen, Michael Reb, Hans Dix, and Philipp Schneider, caused him much trouble.

In 1608 there were still some Anabaptists in the vicinity (Hege, 175). It is possible that remnants maintained themselves through the Thirty Years' War.

After the war new settlements were made by Swiss emigrants. According to the first Mennonite list of the Karlsruhe *Generallandesarchiv* in 1664, ten Swiss Mennonite families had settled here; among them are found the names Hirstein, Blum, and Schuhmacher. During the later war with France, which caused much suffering to the population here, nearly all of them emigrated, most of them to America. Apparently only one family remained; others came later. In 1737 Joh. Krämer, and in October 1738, Jakob Joder were accepted as renters of the ducal estate of Schönborn; also the families of Wilhelm Gerber, Joh. and Gerhard Becker, Fritz Braun, and Ulrich Stauffer are named in 1738. In 1749 were added Isaak Hiestand, Jakob Gram, Müller, and Christian Roth. The families of Gerhard Hüthwohl and Joh. Lehmann followed. In a petition of Feb. 14, 1769, the Mennonites of Heppenheim a.d.W., Obersülzen, and Flomersheim complained that in addition to their high "protection fee" they were also compelled to pay 3 fl. per household for the use of water and pasture; the request for exemption was granted. On Dec. 23, 1748, upon their request, they were given permission to purchase "a little place between the houses" in which to bury their dead, "without, however, calling it a churchyard or using the least ceremony, much less erecting grave stones."

For a long time Heppenheim was the center of the combined congregation of Heppenheim-Obersülzen-Gerolsheim (*q.v.*), as well as for the Mennonites living in Dirmstein and Offstein (*q.v.*). In the first three places services were held in rotation; in Obersülzen and Gerolsheim in suitable halls, in Heppenheim in a church building erected in 1783, services having previously been held in the home of the preacher Gerhard Hüthwohl. In the Ibersheim Resolutions of 1803 the combined congregation is listed as Heppenheim; Gerhard Hüthwohl signed the protocol as their preacher. Their elder was for a time Jakob Kaegy of the Bolanderhof (d. Nov. 9, 1852). In 1853 Daniel Hirschler was chosen preacher and Christian Krehbiel elder (*Menn. Bl.,* 1855, 39). In 1929 there were only a few Mennonites living in Heppenheim a.d.W.; these belonged to the Obersülzen congregation. Four times a year the preacher of Monsheim held services in the church building at Heppenheim.   NEFF.

Chr. Hege, *Die Täufer in der Kurpfalz* (Frankfurt, 1908; Müller, *Berner Täufer; ML* II, 285.

Herald Book and Printing Co.: see **Herald Publishing Co.**

Herald Bookstore, 220 Main St., Souderton, Pa., a branch bookstore of the Mennonite Publishing House at Scottdale, Pa., was established in 1935; managers have been Silas Graybill 1935-50 and Claude Shisler 1950- .   H.S.B.

Herald of Truth (1864-1908), the first religious periodical published in the Mennonite (MC) Church, first issue January 1864, 4 pp., 10½ x 15½ in., published by J. F. Funk in Chicago, Ill., until 1867, thereafter at Elkhart, Ind., until its sale and transfer to Scottdale, Pa., in 1908. At first a monthly, the journal finally became a weekly. In April 1864 it was enlarged to eight pages. With reduced size (9 x 11½ in.) it was increased to 16 pages in January 1867. In May 1867 the place of publication was changed to Elkhart, where Funk had set up a printing establishment of his own. The printing had been done before this time by Chas. Hess of 93 Randolph St., Chicago. In February 1869 Abram K. Funk entered into partnership with his brother and the publishing firm became John F. Funk & Bro. In 1875 a stock company was organized to take over the assets and work of the firm, the Mennonite Publishing Company. In 1878 the journal was enlarged to 20 pages, still a monthly. In January 1882 it became a semimonthly with 16 pages. In 1896 the page size was again enlarged to 10¾ x 14½, while in 1903 it became for the first time a weekly with eight pages. For one year, March 29, 1906, to March 21, 1907, it appeared as a 10-page weekly, returning to eight pages for the rest of its career. The last issue appeared on April 9, 1908, after which it was combined with the *Gospel Witness* to appear as the *Gospel Herald,* published by the Mennonite Publication Board at Scottdale, Pa. Editorial changes to be noted were as follows. J. F. Funk was sole editor to 1882, when the name of J. S. Coffman appears as assistant editor. In 1889 the name of A. B. Kolb was added as second assistant editor. The name of Coffman was dropped at the end of 1895, and that of Funk in January 1897, so that from Feb. 1, 1897, A. B. Kolb was sole editor. He was displaced from Feb. 15, 1904, to Aug. 17, 1905, by D. H. Bender. From this time on until the end J. F. Funk and A. B. Kolb were joint editors. Thus except for a brief period of less than nine years, Funk edited the journal. A German edition, *Herald der Wahrheit* (*q.v.*), was published by Funk 1864-1901.

The *Herald of Truth* had a very great influence upon the Mennonite Church and its development throughout the entire 44 years of its existence. Through it Funk promoted Sunday schools, evangelism, missions, Mennonite history, unity, and other good causes. The paper remained Funk's personal organ, but it became a common household paper throughout the Mennonite Church (MC) both east and west, both Mennonite and Amish, losing influence only in the last years of its existence when Funk got into trouble in his home district and lost general confidence.   H.S.B.

Herald Publishing Company, Newton, Kan., a nonprofit organization, was incorporated April 7, 1920, under a Kansas charter for the purpose of supplying "such specialized literature as will meet the needs of the Mennonites (GCM) of the Central West." The first board of directors, elected at an organization meeting held April 19, 1920, were: H. P. Krehbiel, C. J. Goering, W. B. Unrau, G. Regier, C. C. Wedel, J. P. Andres, H. J. Dyck, P. H. Richert, and G. A. Haury. Officers chosen at a subsequent meeting on the same date were H. P. Krehbiel, chairman, C. C. Wedel, vice-chairman,

W. B. Unrau, secretary, and C. J. Goering, treasurer. Books, office, and printing equipment (and with it the German publication *Der Herold*) were bought for $8,473.88 from the Herald Book & Publishing Co., a private Stock company, which was then dissolved. Capital funds were obtained through sale of $25.00 "memberships" to over 300 interested persons, all of them General Conference Mennonites and residing mostly in central Kansas. *Herold* editors and general managers were: H. P. Krehbiel, April 1920 to December 1921; C. Frey, January 1922 to June 1922; J. B. Epp, July 1922 to September 1923; H. P. Krehbiel, October 1923 to September 1935, G. H. Willms becoming assistant *Herold* editor in 1923 and also serving as assistant manager 1926-35. In 1923 the English publication, *Mennonite Weekly Review,* was established and A. J. Krehbiel engaged as first editor. Upon his resignation in 1925, H. P. Krehbiel assumed also the *Review* editorship, continuing until 1935. Assistant *Review* editors were Abe Epp, 1925-26; Menno Schrag, 1927-28, 1931-35; and F. J. Wiens, 1929-30. In September 1935 G. H. Willms was appointed general manager and *Herold* editor and Menno Schrag assistant manager and *Review* editor. In June 1938 the company moved from its earlier locations at 107 East 7th Street and 722 Main Street, Newton, to its newly purchased building at 129-133 West 6th Street, Newton. Under difficulties brought about by World War II, *Der Herold* was discontinued December 1941. On April 20, 1946, book stock and a portion of printing equipment was sold to a newly organized private concern, the Herald Book & Printing Co. Menno Schrag, the *Review* editor, then assumed the Herald Publishing Company management, with J. Richard Blosser assistant manager and associate editor of the *Review*. Company activity now centers mainly on publishing of the *Mennonite Weekly Review,* circulated nationally among most branches of the Mennonite Church.   M.S.

Herbert is a town (pop. 1,200) on the Canadian Pacific R.R., 125 miles west of Regina, the capital of Saskatchewan. The first Mennonites came to this place from Manitoba in 1904. They were mainly Mennonites of the Canadian Conference (which started in 1903) and from the Mennonite Brethren Conference. Some Mennonites joined the New Jerusalem (Swedenborg) Church. In 1954 this church was bought by Lutherans. In the depression of the 1930's many Mennonites moved away. In recent years the land has been irrigated. There is a Canadian Conference church, a Mennonite Brethren church, a United church, a Lutheran church, and a Catholic church in the town. There are also Sommerfelder Mennonites, but they have no church. The Mennonite Youth Society has an Old People's Home here.   J.G.R.

Herbert Bible School, an institution of the Mennonite Brethren Church, is located in the town of Herbert (*q.v.*), Sask., about 125 miles west of Regina. The school was founded in 1913 by J. F. Harms. During the first year there were 18 students in the school. The highest enrollment was 72 stu-

dents. In the school year of 1954-55 there were 16 students with two full-time and two part-time instructors. The principal is C. Braun.   J.G.R.

Herbert Mennonite Brethren Church, located in the town of Herbert in southern Saskatchewan, was organized in 1908 with a membership of 68 under the leadership of Jacob J. Martens. The membership in 1953 was 180. The church building, still in use, was built the year the church was organized. The following ministers have served as leaders and pastors during the course of the years: H. A. Neufeld, J. P. Wiebe, Henry Regehr, Isaac Epp, Daniel Wiebe, Alfred Kroeker, and John M. Neufeld.
                                    J.H.E.

Herbert (Sask.) Mennonite Church (GCM) was organized by Mennonite settlers arriving in 1904; in 1908 they built the first Mennonite church. Two ministers came to this place from Manitoba in 1905: Frank Sawatzky (d. 1931), who later was elected as elder, and Jacob M. Wiens (d. 1933). At present (1954) there are two ministers: Isaac H. Wiens, son of the above Jacob M. Wiens, and Cornelius J. Wiebe, who is the leader. Jacob H. Klippenstein, also a member of the Herbert Mennonite Church, lives near Rush Lake. The present baptized membership is 127. Originally there were twice this number.
                                    J.G.R.

Herbéviller, located in France between the Alsatian border and the Moselle, the seat of a Mennonite congregation which died out in the 19th century. (See **France;** also *Almanach Mennonite du Cinquantenaire,* p. 35.)

Herding(h), a former Mennonite family, apparently immigrants from Flanders, living particularly at Leiden, Holland, where they supplied 10 deacons to the congregation (first to the Flemish, then to the United congregation). Some of them served for four or even five periods. They were mostly well-to-do cloth merchants. One member of this family, Vincent Herdingh, was a preacher of the Flemish congregation from 1686, and from 1700 of the United congregation at Leiden; he served until his death on Aug. 24, 1731.   vdZ.

L. G. le Poole, *Bijdr. tot . . . het kerkelijk leven onder de Doopsgezinden . . . te Leiden* (Leiden, 1905) 11 and *passim.*

Hereford Mennonite Church (MC), located in the village of Bally, Washington Twp., Berks Co., Pa., a member of the Franconia Conference. The first meetinghouse is supposed to have been built here in 1732, replaced by a larger log structure in 1755, enlarged in 1790, and used continuously until 1899 when it was razed, and succeeded by a stone structure plastered both inside and out. As in many other congregations of the Franconia Conference, English was first introduced about 1900. The Hereford congregation was never large, seldom being much over 100 even including those who worshiped in the Boyertown (*q.v.*) meetinghouse. (The Bally and Boyertown worshipers constituted but one organized congregation historically, and were served by one set of Sunday-school officers.)

Members worshiping at Hereford in 1956 numbered 95, while 33 worshiped at Boyertown. Elias W. Kulp was the pastor in 1956, assisted by Paul Longacre; the deacon was Abram M. Ehst.

In the division of 1847 one of the Hereford ministers withdrew from the Franconia Conference and took a portion of the members with him into Oberholtzer's new conference. In 1851 this Hereford GCM congregation (*q.v.*) ceased to use the old meetinghouse on alternate Sundays as they had done since 1847, having built a new meetinghouse. It became much larger than the old group, reaching 202 members by 1895.   J.C.W.

A. Gehman and M. Bower, *History of the Hereford Congregation at Bally, Pennsylvania* (n.p., 1936).

Hereford Mennonite Church (GCM), located at Bally, Berks Co., Pa., named for the township in which it is located, dates back before 1725. Originally the area was within the Manatawny, then Colebrookdale, then Hereford, now the borough of Bally in Washington Township. The first ministers of the "Manatant" congregation were Jacob Bechtel and David Longenecker. The first resident ministers (1728) were George Bechtel and Peter Noll. Since the division of 1847 there are two congregations, the smaller group adhering to the Franconia Conference (MC), the other incorporated since 1893 as Hereford Mennonite Church, a member of the Eastern District Conference. In 1955 the membership was 282, and the pastor was Henry G. Grimm.   E.E.S.J.

Heresbachius, Conradus (Conrat Hertzbach) (1496-1576), a humanist and counselor in the service of the Duke of Cleve (*q.v.*), Germany. He was a friend of Erasmus (*q.v.*), to whom he owed all his public positions, the last being that of tutor at the court of Cleve. In this position he was able to accompany the expedition against the Münsterite Anabaptists (as a spectator). He wrote his account of it in two confidential letters to Erasmus (November 1534 and July 28, 1535. The book *Conradi Heresbachii I. C. Historia Anabaptistica de factione Monasteriensi anno 1534 et seqq . . . epistola formae anno 1536 descripta nunc demum . . . edita . . . Amsterdami 1637* is the work of a compiler, and contains much historical source material based on these letters, which is not found elsewhere. A copy is in the Goshen College Library.   NEFF.

K. W. Bouterwek, *Conrad Heresbachii historia factionis exidiique Monasteriensis* (Elberfeld, 1866); C. A. Cornelius, *Berichte der Augenzeugen über das Münsterische Wiedertäuferreich* (1853) p. LXXXVII; *ML* II, 286.

Herk (Aert, Orck) **Dirksz** (Herck van Texel), a Dutch Anabaptist, of Burg on the island of Texel, province of North Holland, who preached and baptized at Brielle, Dutch province of South Holland, in the house of the martyr Anneken Jans and who was executed at The Hague on Sept. 15, 1535. He belonged to the revolutionary branch of Anabaptism.   vDZ.

Inv. Arch. Amst. I, No. 243; *DB* 1917, 115, No. 48; Mellink, *Wederdopers,* 169.

Herman, an Anabaptist martyr: see **Herman Buens.**

Herman van den Berge, a farmer living at Roosteren, now Dutch province of Limburg, was executed (likely at the stake) at Montfort about 1540, because Smeken van Tricht (apparently Jan Smeitgen, *q.v.,* of Maastricht) had preached on his farm. Though particulars are lacking, Herman was probably a member of the congregation.   vDZ.

W. Bax, *Het Protestantisme in het Bisdom Luik en vooral te Maastricht* I (The Hague, 1937) 399.

Herman Buens (Bienes), in van Braght's *Martyrs' Mirror* called simply Herman, was an Anabaptist martyr, burned at the stake at Rijssel (Lille), France, on April 27, 1563. According to *Bibliographie* he was a native of Borchloon and a son of Hendrik Aerts (*q.v.*). By the zeal of the ardent inquisitor Titelman, after a Catholic priest, N. van Casteele, had denounced them, 12 Anabaptists at Halewijn (*q.v.*) in Flanders had been arrested and put in prison at Rijssel. Then some brethren and sisters had come to Rijssel and "called to the prisoners over the fortification, for their consolation." One of those visitors was Herman, whose father likely was among the prisoners. Having been seen by a policeman, Herman was arrested, and "holding immovably to the mercy of God" suffered martyrdom. (*Mart. Mir.* D 300, E 665; *Bibliographie* II, No. 299; *ML* II, 287.)   vDZ.

Herman Dirksz, of Achtersloot near IJsselstein, Dutch province of Utrecht, a Dutch Anabaptist, was beheaded at Utrecht on June 27, 1545. He was an adherent of the Münsterite leader Jan van Batenburg (*q.v.*) and one of the last of his followers to be executed. (*Inv. Arch. Amst.* I, No. 329; Mellink, *Wederdopers,* 240, 411.)   vDZ.

Herman and Gerrit (Gerryt) **Jansz,** brothers, Anabaptist martyrs, were sentenced to death at Leeuwarden, Dutch province of Friesland, on Oct. 24, 1536, because they had lodged Menno Simons. They lived in or near Witmarsum where Menno Simons had been a priest, leaving the Catholic Church on Jan. 31, 1536. In October of this year Menno paid a secret visit to his friends, which brought death to these two brethren.   vDZ.

Inv. Arch. Amst. I, No. 747; *DB* 1864, 135; 1906, 3; K. Vos, *Menno Simons* (Leiden, 1914) 230.

Herman Hermansz (Hermanssone), an Anabaptist martyr, was burned at the stake at Antwerp, Belgium, on June 27, 1570, because he had been rebaptized. Nelleken Jaspers (*q.v.*) suffered martyrdom with him. (*Antw. Arch.-Blad* XIII, 1, 61; XIV, 76 f., No. 852.)   vDZ.

Herman Jansz (Harmen Huyckemaker, i.e., maker of long hooded cloaks), originally of Sollem (Zelhem in the Dutch province of Gelderland), and plying his trade at the corner of the Popelsteech at Amsterdam, was burned at the stake at Amsterdam on Jan. 16, 1553, together with four other Mennonites. In the sentence he is called an Anabaptist and a disciple of Gillis van Aken (*q.v.*). Van Braght in the *Martyrs' Mirror* relates that he was a candidate for baptism upon his faith. All attempts made to move him to apostasy failed and this simple martyr of his Lord died faithfully. (*Inv. Arch. Amst.* I, No. 370; *Mart. Mir.* D 147, E 538.)   vDZ.

Herman van Kelder, a Dutch Anabaptist and follower of David Joris (*q.v.*), was beheaded at Delft, Dutch province of South Holland, on Jan. 7, 1539. (Mellink, *Wederdopers,* 216 f.)   vDZ.

Herman Sassen, a Dutch Anabaptist, active in Deventer, Dutch province of Overijssel, in the spring of 1534. He may be identical with Herman Schroer (*q.v.*) of Deventer. (*DB* 1917, 117, No. 69.)   vDZ.

Herman Schroer (Scroer), an Anabaptist martyr of Deventer, Dutch province of Overijssel, a tailor, was beheaded there on Feb. 6, 1535. Herman was a member of a rather large Anabaptist congregation at Deventer, which was much influenced by Münsterite principles. (*DB* 1919, 7 f.)   vDZ.

Herman van Tielt, a Mennonite elder, originally from Flanders, who lived in Wismar, Germany, about 1553. In January and February 1533 he was an intermediary between Johannes a Lasco (*q.v.*) and Menno Simons, who also lived in Wismar at this time. Herman was also among the seven elders meeting at Wismar in 1554 who drew up nine articles for the believers as a rule of life (see **Wismar Resolution**). In 1555, when the Mennonites were expelled from Wismar, Herman van Tielt must also have left the town. About May 1556 he was present in the home of Menno Simons at Wüstenfelde, where Zylis and Lemke, as representatives of the High Germans, had a discussion with Menno about avoidance in marriage. Nothing more is known about Herman van Tielt.   vDZ.

DB 1894, 37; K. Vos, *Menno Simons* (Leiden, 1914) 114, 117, 119, 127, 135, 147.

Herman (Harman) (de) **Timmerman** (Herman van der Greyn), an Anabaptist martyr, after threefold torture burned at the stake at Antwerp, Belgium, on May 25, 1569, together with three other martyrs. Herman, who was a native of Borchher in the bishopric of Liége, was arrested at Antwerp, where he lived as a carpenter, shortly after March 3, 1569. He was 35 years of age and had been baptized at Berchem near Antwerp by Lenaert "a countryman" (Leenaert Bouwens?), in 1556, when he was 23 years old. During his trials he denied the validity of infant baptism, since only believer's baptism is Scriptural; he had been chosen as deacon (*dienaer der aermen*) by the congregation, and for want of preachers he also delivered sermons (*vermaningen*), but he never baptized or laid hands upon a person. During his tortures he prayed, "O Lord, keep my mouth closed," and did not betray any of the brethren. So he died as a hero, loyal and faithful.

Some doubt has arisen whether this Herman Timmerman the martyr might be the same person as the Elder Herman de Timmerman. They are probably identical, though it is somewhat strange

that an elder never baptized or administered communion, ordained new preachers or elders, as Herman said in his confession. S. Cramer (*BRN* II, 623) calls him elder of the Waterlanders at Antwerp; according to K. Vos (p. 191) he was not an elder but merely a preacher. Of his activity as elder or preacher not much is known. In 1568 he performed the marriage of Pieter Verlongen (*q.v.*) at Antwerp. He may have been ordained in 1566. During the schism in this year between Frisian and Flemish Mennonites in Friesland (see **Flemish Mennonites**) Herman took a moderate view as he had done before (in 1560) when Menno Simons and Dirk Philips decided for a strict practice of banning and shunning, enunciated in Menno's *Een gans grontlycke onderwijs oft bericht van der excommunicatie* (1558) and Dirk Philips' *Een lieflijke Vermaninghe* (1558). Then Herman countered with *Een verklaringhe: hoe en in wat manieren de Heere Jesus zijnen Jongeren in der af-zonderinge macht gegeven haeft, om die onbekeerige Overtreders zijne goddelycken woorts . . . hare sonden hier op der aerden te binden . . .* (published Jan. 28, 1560, n.p., and reprinted 1618 at Haarlem).

Besides this book Herman also wrote *Een corte Bekentenisse ende grondighe aenwijsinghe wt der H. Schrift dat Godt (Vader) Soon ende Heylighe Gheest een onverscheyden Godt is . . .* (1577, n.p., likely edited by Nicolaas Biestkens at Amsterdam), reprinted 1578 and inserted in van Braght, *Martyrs' Mirror.* Herman Timmerman is also thought to be the author of a song celebrating 41 martyrs who died in Gent 1562-69. This hymn was included in his *Een corte Bekentenisse* and is also found in the *Liedtboecxken van den Offer des Heeren* (1578 and following editions). Cramer, the editor of the *Offer des Heeren* and *Liedtboecxken,* supposes that Herman de Timmerman is not the author of this hymn.   vDZ.

Offer, 623, 649 note; *Mart. Mir.* D 415-19, E 766-70; *Bibliographie* I, 161-69, 656, 709-13; *Antw. Arch.-Blad* XII, 364, 371 ff., 382, 400, 405, 436; XIII, 23; XIV, 64 f., No. 724; *Biogr. Wb.* III, 742 f.; K. Vos, *De Doopsgezinden te Antwerpen* (1920) 332 f., 351-54; idem, *Menno Simons* (Leiden, 1914) see Index; Kühler, *Geschiedenis* I, 327, 350; *DB* 1864, 126; 1881, 39; 1882, 53; 1894, 58; *BRN* X, 23, 34 f., 654.

Herman van Vlekwijk (Vleckwick), an Anabaptist martyr, burned at the stake at Brugge, Belgium, on June 8, 1569. He was born at Kervendonck in the Duchy of Cleve, Germany, and was a tailor by trade. In Brugge he attended the Mennonite meetings in 1561, but upon being arrested he recanted. However, he soon repented of his apostasy. Then he left Brugge and traveled around. In 1562 he was baptized at Gent by Hans Busschaert. During the following years he was on the road, sometimes in Brugge or other towns in Flanders, but mostly staying in the territory of Cleve, where he participated in the Mennonite meetings. In 1565-68 he lived in Brugge. But in 1568 he had to flee because of persecution and again he turned to Germany; the next year he planned to make a short trip to Brugge to settle his affairs, having resolved to stay in Cleve for the future, leaving his wife and five children at Cologne. On his way to Flanders he met Jacob de Rore (*q.v.*) in Nijmegen; together they journeyed to Brugge, but arriving here they were immediately arrested and put in prison. Herman was tortured several times but remained steadfast and refused to betray his fellow members. On May 10, 1569, he had a long dispute with the Franciscan friar Cornelis Adriaensz (see **Broer Cornelis**), who tried to bring him back to the Catholic Church, which has been printed in van Braght's *Martyrs' Mirror*. Herman and Jacob de Rore died together at the stake.

In the disputation between Herman and Broer Cornelis, the friar accused Herman of anti-Trinitarianism. Hans Alenson (*q.v.*) related that Herman was a follower of Adam Pastor (*q.v.*) and a unitarian (*BRN* VII, 196). The matter is not quite clear.

Very likely Herman van Vlekwijk, like most Mennonites and nearly all the martyrs, objected to the word "Trinity," since this is not found in the Scriptures. He preferred Scriptural terms and avoided theological or philosophical terminology. At any rate he was not a Unitarian, for he positively confessed the deity of Christ.   vDZ.

Bibliographie des Martyrologes Prot. Neerl. I, 703 cites a booklet, *A Dialogue between a Dutch Protestant and a Franciscan Friar of Dort* (London 1784, repr. Birmingham 1812), which is the disputation of Herman with Broer Cornelis; *Mart. Mir.* D 424, 437-52, E 774, 785-98; Verheyden, *Brugge,* 57 f., No. 62; G. Brandt, *Historie der Reformatie* I (2nd ed., Amsterdam, 1677, 501-7); *Bibliographie* I, 733; Kühler, *Het Socinianisme in Nederland* (Leiden, 1912) 32 f.; *idem, Geschiedenis* I, 289; *DB* 1899, 144-52; *BRN* VII, 147, 194-96.

Herminjard, Aimé Louis (1817-1900), Professor of Church History at the University of Lausanne, Switzerland. With his brother Henri he published *Correspondance des reformateurs dans les pays de langue française* (nine volumes, 1866-97), extending to 1544. Two final volumes are to cover the material to the death of Farel (1565). This historical work includes some source material on the Anabaptists. (*ML* II, 288.)   NEFF.

Herold Mennonite Church (GCM), located three miles east and five miles north of Cordell, Okla., a member of the Western District Conference, was organized in 1899 in the home of Jacob Jantzen with the help of three elders, Christian Krehbiel, Peter Balzer, and Jacob Toews. At this time the church building (built about 1897) on the Jantzen farm was purchased from the Sichar congregation, and the Sichar congregation moved to another site. It was replaced in 1915 by the present church building.

Michael Klaassen, ordained elder in 1901, served until 1918, when he moved to Canada with 28 members on account of military service. He was followed by Jacob Jantzen, who served 40 years as minister, including 18 years as elder. Since this resignation the church has had four ministers: J. R. Duerksen (1940), C. B. Friesen (1943), Paul Dahlenburg (1946), and Richard Tschetter (1951). The church membership in 1955 was 231. (*ML* II, 288.)   R.T.

Herold, Der (1909-41), the name given *Post und Volksblatt* (est. 1903) (first called *Das Kansas Volksblatt, q.v., 1900-2) in 1910 when the publishing company changed its name from Western Book and Publishing Co. (*q.v.*) to Herald Book and Publishing Co. (from 1920 on Herald Publishing Co., *q.v.*), but always published at Newton, Kan. At first a 5-column 8-page weekly, in 1904 it became a 6-column 8-page 18 x 22 in. paper. This publication, always published by General Conference Mennonites and largely for members of that group in the Newton area, was a pioneer in Mennonite journalism with its program of combining religious and secular interests into a weekly Mennonite family newspaper. H. P. Krehbiel was closely associated with the *Herold* from the beginning until a few years before his death. C. E. Krehbiel served as editor until July 1920, H. P. Krehbiel October 1920-January 1922, C. Frey January-June 1922, J. B. Epp July 1922-September 1923, H. P. Krehbiel October 1923-September 1935, G. H. Willms September 1935-December 1941.   H.S.B.

Herold der Wahrheit (1864-1901), the German edition of *Herald of Truth* (*q.v.*), was published by John F. Funk at Elkhart, Ind. (first in Chicago, Ill., 1864-67) as an 8-page 10½ x 15½ in. monthly (first 3 issues January-March only 4 pages) 1864-66, then 16 pp. at 9 x 11½ in. until 1878, then 20 pp., then from January 1882 a semimonthly with 16 pp., in 1896 again a 16 pp. monthly, but on April 15, 1899, an 8 pp. semimonthly until its last issue Nov. 1, 1901, when it was merged with the *Mennonitische Rundschau*. Editors were as follows: J. F. Funk, 1864-98; G. G. Wiens, 1898-1901; A. B. Kolb, assistant editor 1888-1901; John Horsch, second assistant editor 1891-95. Much of the material published consisted of translations from the *Herald of Truth,* but there were also original German articles, especially when Horsch was serving on the staff.   H.S.B.

Herold der Wahrheit (1912-), a 32-page 6¼ x 9½ in. semimonthly periodical "published in the interest of the Amish Mennonite Churches known as the Old Order Amish and the Conservative Amish Mennonites," by the Publication Board of the Amish Mennonite Publishing Association, printed at Scottdale, Pa., by the Mennonite Publishing House from Jan. 1, 1912, the first issue, until June 15, 1956, and at Kalona, Iowa, since July 1, 1956. The periodical has always carried an approximately equal division of German and English material. The English editors until 1955 were Jonas B. Miller 1912-48 and his son Evan J. Miller 1949-55. With the issue of Feb. 1, 1955, the Conservative Church dropped out and henceforth the periodical was solely Old Order Amish, with Ervin N. Hershberger as English editor. German editors have been S. D. Guengerich 1912-29, L. A. Miller March 15, 1929—Nov. 1, 1951, and Raymond Wagler Nov. 15, 1951- . On Sept. 1, 1954, the size was reduced to 16 pages.   H.S.B.

Herr, a Mennonite family coming originally from St. Gall, Switzerland. They were in the group that immigrated from the Palatinate to Lampeter,

Lancaster Co., Pa. Hans Herr, the patriarchal pioneer, who died in 1725 had a family of six boys and a daughter. The *Herr Genealogy* (1908) lists over 13,000 descendants of Hans Herr, naming as ministers not only Hans and his son Christian, but also as bishops—Christian, two Johns, and Benjamin; preachers—Amos (*q.v.*), Christian, and Jacob (of Cumberland County), Christian S., Frank M., and Emory H., as well as numerous deacons and outstanding farmers. John Herr (1782-1850, *q.v.*) founded the Reformed Mennonite Church. I.D.L.

T. W. Herr, *Genealogical Record of Reverend Hans Herr and His Direct Lineal Descendants* (Lancaster, 1908).

Herr, Amos (Feb. 13, 1816-June 19, 1897), a Mennonite preacher in Lancaster Co., Pa., wrote the beloved hymn, "I Owe the Lord a Morning Song," one Sunday morning when the snowdrifts would not permit even horseback riding to church. He was a son of Christian Herr of Pequea, a Mennonite bishop, who, as did Amos, always lived on part of the original Herr acres (of 1710), along the Beaver Valley Pike, Lancaster Co., Pa. Ordained a preacher in 1850, he was an ardent advocate of English preaching and of Sunday school. He was the first always to preach in English in the Lancaster Conference, and with his aid the conference in 1871 adopted the Sunday-school movement. Thereupon his school in the Brick congregation was the first to be started with Conference approval. In 1880-81 his home and his pen aided the committee very materially in the production of the first Mennonite (MC) Sunday-school materials, *The Question and Answer Books*. Married Nov. 17, 1840, to Betsey Rohrer, his family consisted of three daughters and a son. His work was a blessing to the church of his district and beyond.   I.D.L.

Herr, Christian (b. Oct. 31, 1780, d. June 23, 1853), a bishop of the Lancaster Mennonite (MC) Conference. On April 8, 1800, he was married to Anna Forrer (1783-1831), by Peter Eby (*q.v.*), and became his successor as bishop. He was by vocation a farmer along the Beaver Valley Pike, living on the original Herr tract in Lancaster County. He served as a deacon, minister, and bishop for a combined period of 30 years, in the Brick, Strasburg-New Providence charge. He was unusually gifted and influential in both church and community, interested in the education of youth, perhaps not eloquent, but a contender for the faith both by tongue and pen. A collection of German hymns of his production was published. He contributed a brief sketch, "History of the Mennonites," to I. D. Rupp's *History of the Religious Denominations* (Philadelphia, 1844). His family of eight children included Benjamin Herr, a bishop, and Amos Herr (*q.v.*), a preacher.   I.D.L.

J. F. Funk, *A Biographical Sketch of Bishop Christian Herr, Also a Collection of Hymns Written by Him in the German Language* (Elkhart, 1887).

Herr, Hans (Sept. 17, 1639-Jan. 21, 1725), with his wife Elizabeth Kendig, at the age of 72 brought his family across the Atlantic to free them from oppression in Europe, settling near Willow Street in Lancaster, Pa., in the fall of 1710. Seven children, Abraham and Samuel of Manor, Christian, John, Emanuel, Henry, and Maria, the wife of Bishop Benedict Brechbill, living between Lampeter and Strasburg, also settled within the second decade of the 18th century in Lancaster County. This family was a real asset in establishing this colony in the backwoods of Pennsylvania. Herr was their spiritual leader and for 14 years stamped his guiding principles deeply upon this new foreign colony. His son Christian signed the 1725 edition of the Dordrecht Confession (published at Philadelphia in 1727) and built the Christian Herr house in 1719 along the Conestoga Road, the oldest dwelling and church house west of Germantown, sometimes erroneously attributed to his father. I.D.L.

Herr, John (1782-1850), founder of the Reformed Mennonite Church, b. Sept. 18, 1782, son of Francis Herr (1748-1810) and Fanny Barr Herr, d. May 3, 1850, in Humberstone Twp., Welland Co., Ont. His father, having been expelled from the Mennonite Church in West Lampeter Twp., Lancaster Co., about 1800 for dishonesty in the sale of a horse (as reported by the Mennonite [MC] Church), or having withdrawn from the church after having received a refusal of his demand upon the conference for reforms (as reported by the Reformed Mennonite Church), began to conduct religious services in his home as a lay brother. He died in 1810, leaving a family of eight children, none of whom had been baptized as members in any church. Among those who associated with him in his lay services were Abraham Landis and David Buckwalter, both of whom had withdrawn from the Mennonite Church. After Francis Herr's death the meetings continued and his son John was asked to lead the services, although he was not yet baptized. In a meeting on May 30, 1812, at John Herr's home John was elected pastor and bishop, and Abraham Landis was elected to baptize him. Herr in turn baptized Landis and Abraham Groff, Groff being elected deacon. Soon thereafter Abraham Landis was chosen preacher, followed by John Groff as preacher. John Herr baptized 41 persons soon after May 22. On Nov. 7, 1812, the first meetinghouse was dedicated, called Longenecker's.

Herr, a man of considerable gifts, became a vigorous leader of the new group. His attacks upon the old church from which his family and most if not all the members of his group had descended were vigorous and even bitter. He accused it of being spiritually dead and corrupt, and having departed from the teachings of Menno Simons, of having no real discipline. He himself professed to base on teachings of the Bible and Menno Simons. He traveled much, especially to Western New York and Ontario, where congregations of his group were established. It is clear that he built up his group almost exclusively from ex-Mennonites or proselytes from the Mennonite Church.

Herr published in his lifetime six small books and pamphlets which were collected and published in one volume in 1890 as *John Herr's Works*. The separate writings were: *The True and Blessed Way* (Harrisburg, 1816, German edition at Lancaster,

1815); *A Brief and Apostolic Answer to a Letter Written by a Minister of the Moravian Church* (Lancaster, 1842?, German ed. 1819); *The Illustrating Mirror* (Lancaster, 1834, German ed. Lancaster, 1827); *Letter from John Herr to a Number of Converts in Erie Co. N.Y.* (1833); *A Remarkable Vision* (1835). Herr also published the first English edition of Menno Simons' *Foundation* at Lancaster in 1835. It is possible that he also had a hand in the publication of the first English edition of the *Martyrs' Mirror,* published at Lampeter Square in Lancaster County by David Miller in 1836.

The Life of John Herr, published as a reprint from *John Herr's Works* in 1890, contains a brief autobiography (23 pp.) by Herr himself, first published as an appendix to the 1827 *Erläuterungsspiegel,* plus *A Few Facts Concerning John Herr* (6 pp.) taken from Daniel Musser's *The Reformed Mennonite Church, Its Rise and Progress* (Lancaster, 1873), whose chapter VII contains (pp. 295-315) the only known account of the origin and organization of the Reformed Mennonite Church, giving certain information about Herr. John F. Funk's *The Mennonite Church and Her Accusers* (Elkhart, 1878) reports the attacks of John Herr, and especially Daniel Musser, upon the Mennonite Church, and contains certain information about Francis Herr. I. D. Rupp, *An Original History of the Religious Denominations at Present Existing in the United States* (Philadelphia, 1844) contains a section (pp. 502-10) entitled "Reformed Mennonite Society," "which has the sanction of the Rev. John Herr of Strassburg, a bishop of this society." It contains meager items about John Herr and the origin of the Reformed Mennonites and their doctrines. (*ML* II, 289.)   H.S.B.

Herrison, Hendrick Jansz, publisher of Menno Simons' works, which he had printed at Amsterdam in 1681 by Joh. van Veen with the title, *Opera Omnia Theologica of alle de Godtgeleerde Wercken van Menno Symons, t' Samen bijeen vervat, en nu op nieuws door eenige Beminnaers der Waerheydt, ter eeren Godes en hares Naesten welvaert in Druk uytgegeven, verrijckt met vier Registers, en eenige andere schriften van den Autheur, voor desen nooyt in Druck geweest; alsmede voor yder Tractaet sijn eygen Tytel en Voorreden gestelt, en getrouwelijk in onse Neder-duytsche Spraecke overgeset.* Herrison's edition is almost complete. It is chiefly a reprint of the *Opera oft Groot-Summarie* of 1646. After the introduction Herrison put in everything that he knew of Menno's productions. His edition is rather slovenly; there are many errors, a number of sentences are completely mutilated, the translation of Menno's tracts from Low German (Oosters) is sometimes unintelligible. It is clear that Herrison was a man of little education. Nothing is known of Herrison himself. Hylkema discovered that he was a citizen of Amsterdam and that he traveled or lived in Friesland in 1684-88. He was a friend of the well-known pietistic poet and etcher Jan Luyken. Herrison was a servant of Ch(arles) van

Boneval, to whom he gave a letter in 1682 which was written by Menno's own hand, and which is now in the Hamburg Mennonite Library.   vDZ.

DB 1865, 118, 121; 1885, 7 f.; 1904, 27; K. Vos, *Menno Simons* (Leiden, 1914) 297, 301; *ML* II, 291.

Herrites, the name often given to the followers of John Herr (*q.v.*), who are officially called Reformed Mennonites (*q.v.*).

Herrmann, Jerome, of Mondsee. The chronicles of the Anabaptists name Jerome of Salzburg as a companion of Hans Hut (*q.v.*) in Austria, probably because Salzburg was the scene of his martyrdom. Hans Hut had won a number of converts in Styria, where he had come about June 15, 1527; among them was "Hieronymus Herrmann von Mansee," who had previously been a monk at Ranzhofen and pastor in Braunau. He was chosen by lot under Hut's direction as one of four apostles to be sent out, the others being Leonhard Schiemer (*q.v.*) of Vöklabruck, Leonhard Dorfbrunner (*q.v.*) of Nürnberg, and Jakob Portner (*q.v.*) of Meissen, chaplain and preacher in the castle of the Lord von Rogendorf in Styria. Portner went to Freystadt in the mill quarter, Herrmann to Mondsee and Salzburg, and Schiemer to Vöklabruck and Gmunden. They preached Hut's doctrine, spreading it from Upper Austria to Salzburg and Bavaria. Herrmann therefore no doubt rejected the use of force and advocated community of goods. The reports of Wolfgang Künigl, the public prosecutor, indicate that many listened to his sermons, without, however, adopting Anabaptism. He was seized in Salzburg, and like Carius Binder and Wolfgang Wimmer, was burned at the stake.   LOSERTH.

Beck, *Geschichtsbücher,* 57; J. Jäckel, *Zur Frage über die Entstehung der Täufergemeinden in Oberösterreich* (Freistadt, 1895); idem, *Zur Geschichte der Täufer in Oberösterreich und speziell in Freistadt* (47. *Jahresbericht des Linzer Museums*); A. Nicoladoni, *Johannes Bünderlin von Linz und die oberösterreich. Täufergemeinden in den Jahren 1525 und 1531* (Berlin, 1893); *ML* II, 287.

Her(r)mann, Thomas (Thoman), of Waidhofen, Bohemia, an Anabaptist martyr. In the late 1520's Kitzbühel became a refuge for Anabaptists fleeing from Salzburg and other towns of Tirol. Some of them were seized in March 1528, and tried according to regulations; their confessions roused the sympathy of a large number of the common people.

Among those seized was Thomas Herrmann, who was led into captivity and martyrdom by an odd incident. On May 9, 1528, Hans Schweighofer and Hans Platzer of Aschelberg ("der Aschelberger"), besides several others, were committed to the court as Anabaptists. The jury, composed of citizens of Innsbruck, Hall, Rattenberg, and Freundsberg, found them guilty, and the condemned men were executed Aug. 12. When Schweighofer and Platzer were taken to the site of the execution, someone derisively cried out that the Anabaptist leaders spared themselves, while sacrificing their flocks. Herrmann then pushing through the crowd exclaimed, "What I have taught you is divine truth, and with God's help I will testify to it with my blood." He was consequently seized on Aug. 19.

The court record says, "He was a true insurrection-
ist and an Anabaptist, who had led many in this
country into this error."

On Aug. 28 he appeared before the jury, who
had received orders, even if he should recant, to
condemn him to death. They complied under protest. Herrmann was burned at the stake on the
same day, "as the song records, which he is said to
have composed on his last trip" (i.e., to his execution): "O Gott, ich tu dich bitten wohl hier zu
dieser Stund." It was soon related in Anabaptist
circles that his heart refused to burn and was cast
into the near-by lake. (Beck, *Geschichts-Bücher,*
55 f.; *Mart. Mir.* D 11, E 422; *ML* II, 287.)

                                        LOSERTH.

Herrnhuter (Dutch, Hernhutters), a name much
used in Germany and Netherlands for the Moravian
Brethren (*q.v.*) (*Unitas Fratrum*).

Hersfeld, a village in Hesse, Germany, near which
an Anabaptist group had formed at the beginning
of the Reformation. Their leader was Melchior
Rinck (*q.v.*), who had previously been a schoolteacher and chaplain. Active in the congregation
were also Niklas Schreiber, Georg von Staffelstein,
Hans Roth, and Katharina Valebs, who was executed in Frankenhausen in 1530. Hersfeld was
the home of Margarete Koch (*q.v.*), called "die
alte Garköchin," who was for many years in prison
in Eisenach with Fritz Erbe (*q.v.*), and whose
execution was the occasion for an extensive correspondence between the Hessian and Saxon governments. In 1525 Adam Kraft, who later became a
professor at the University of Marburg, court chaplain, and church inspector, was pastor at Hersfeld.
Pastor Balthasar Raidt, also of Hersfeld, was often
engaged by the authorities to convert the Anabaptists; he reported that by 1544 he had dealt
with over 300 Anabaptists, trying to win them into
the state church.   HEGE.

P. Wappler, *Die Stellung Kursachsens und des Landgrafen Philipp von Hessen zur Täuferbewegung* (Münster, 1910); *ML* II, 291.

Hershberger (Hersberg, Hersberger, Herschberger,
Hirschberger, Harshberger, Harshbarger), a Swiss
family name today rather widely spread in the
United States among Mennonite and especially Old
Order Amish congregations. The earliest mention
of the name in Anabaptist history occurs in Basel
in 1529, when many Anabaptists in the canton
found themselves in prison. Among the staunch-
est adherents of the faith, says Paul Burkhardt in
Die Basler Täufer, were the Hersbergers of Thürnen und Läufelfingen. One of them was Elsbeth
Hersberger, a midwife, who influenced numerous
parents not to have their children baptized.

On Dec. 29, 1529, Hans Hersberger, a miller of
Läufelfingen, appeared with 10 other Swiss Brethren preachers in a disputation with Oecolampadius
and the Basel reformers. On one occasion Hans
had taken part in a forbidden communion service
at Aargau. On Jan. 12, 1530, he was sentenced to
death. Following a supposed recantation the sentence was commuted to a fine of 20 gulden and
court costs, after which he and his wife Barbara

were banished from the territory. They were soon
back in Läufelfingen with their children, however,
and in July 1531 were imprisoned in Basel. Hans
remained in prison until Dec. 3, 1533. Barbara was
released at the end of seven months, but from September 1532 to December 1533 she was with her
husband in prison again.

The records also mention a Heini Hersberger
at Dornach in 1530. In the summer of 1531 Jackli
Hersberger of Thürnen was apprehended for refusing to participate in the military campaign of his
community. On July 14, 1535, Jacob Hersberger
(who most likely is the same person) had his
tongue and two fingers cut off by the authorities
for his failure to remain out of the territory after
having been banished. Apparently he now left the
territory, but in April 1537 he was back again and
was once more apprehended by the authorities.

In 1581 another of the Läufelfingen Hersbergers,
also named Hans, was brought before the authorities
for his faith. Four years later he spent eight weeks
in prison and was then banished, leaving his wife
and five children unable to keep themselves on their
little place. In 1588 Heini Hersberger, apparently a
son of Hans, was brought before the court. In 1616
Fridli, another son of Hans, and his wife were
arrested, taken to the border, and banished. They
were soon back again, however, and the authorities
seem to have left them alone. In 1678 another Fridli
Hersberger, perhaps a son or nephew of the former
one, was arrested and brought to Basel for a hearing.
The authorities found him well-instructed and steadfast in the Anabaptist faith. He was banished, with
instructions never to return again; then he went to
Alsace where he made his home among the Anabaptist communities, which continued to have close
connection with their brethren in Basel. It may have
been a sister of the Fridli Hersberger of 1678 who
won her husband Jacob Oberer to the faith in 1680,
who joined the brotherhood in Alsace.

For four or five generations the Basel Hersbergers
are known to have persisted in the Anabaptist faith.
Members of this and perhaps other Hershberger
families evidently spread through Alsace and the
Palatinate. In 1716 Martin Hirschberger is listed in
the census records as residing at Böhl near Neustadt,
Palatinate. In the middle of the 18th century the
Hershbergers shared the great Mennonite migration
to Pennsylvania. On Sept. 9, 1749, the ship *St. Andrew* landed at Philadelphia with a large contingent
of Amish and Mennonites, including Casper and
Jacob Herschberger. The ship *Brothers,* Sept. 30,
1754, had a Johannes Herschberger on the passenger
list. The Palatine state archives at Speyer record
that in 1768 the Mennonite Henrich Hirschberger of
Eppstein was permitted by the authorities, upon payment of a tax, to migrate to Pennsylvania, taking
with him the fortune of his three brothers who had
preceded him.

In 1754 the oldest Amish congregation in Pennsylvania along the Northkill in Berks County had a
Christian Hershberger in its number, and by the
close of the 18th century the name Harshbarger was
found among the Mennonites of Virginia. Hershbergers were among the pioneer Amish settlements
in practically all of the states west of Pennsylvania.

Obituaries in Mennonite periodicals from 1867 to 1918 include 104 Hershbergers in Pennsylvania, Ohio, Indiana, Illinois, Virginia, Michigan, Iowa, Missouri, Nebraska, Oklahoma, and Oregon.

Paul P. Hershberger (1840-1908) was a minister and promoter of Sunday schools among the Iowa Amish Mennonites in the 1870's and later moved to Seward County, Neb. Christian Hershberger (1844-1919) was ordained a minister in Iowa in 1874. Jonathan Hershberger (1829-1902) and W. C. Hershberger (1867-1951) were ministers in the Johnstown, Pa., district. A. W. Hershberger (1875-1943) was a well-known minister in Ohio and Virginia. Edwin J. Hershberger (1893-1952) was an Old Order Amish bishop in Iowa. A Missouri family of Hershbergers gave three sons to the ministry: W. Raymond (1902-54), bishop at Garden City, Mo.; Elmer D. (1900-), bishop at Detroit Lakes, Minn.; and Owen O. (1897-), minister at Hesston, Kan. In 1954 a total of 29 ordained Hershbergers were serving the congregations of America, 10 of them in Mennonite congregations, and 19 in Amish congregations. Emmett L. Harshbarger (1901-42) was a professor of history at Bethel College and active in peace education. Guy F. Hershberger (1896-) is a professor of history at Goshen College and the author of several books on nonresistance. Ezra S. Hershberger (b. 1904) is an artist on the Goshen College faculty.   G.F.H.

Eli P. Hershberger, *Descendants of Peter Hershberger and Elizabeth Yoder 1810-1950* (n.p., n.d.).

Hershey, a Mennonite family which emigrated from the Emmental, Switzerland, to Friedelsheim, Palatinate, Germany, in the early 1670's. Three brothers who were all preachers joined their father Christian (d. 1720) in 1717 and 1739, in settling in Lancaster Co., Pa. Bishop Benjamin Hershey (*q.v.*) with his four sons, Christian with his nine, and Andrew his twelve, made quite a contribution to Mennonite and United Brethren history. Among the Mennonite ministers were bishops Benjamin I and II, Jacob, and Joseph, and preachers Benjamin of Manheim, Isaac, Jr., Jacob (2), Jacob R., and Jacob H. in Lancaster County; Isaac, Jr., Jacob, and Joseph I and II in York County and today Martin R., Noah L., and Sanford. The congregation east of Intercourse and one in central York County are still called Hershey. In the Welland Co., Ont., community the members of the Hershey family who were Mennonite ministers were Christian, Benjamin, and John B. T. K. Hershey was a pioneer Argentine missionary. Milton S. Hershey, known for his chocolate factory, founded the philanthropic-industrial town of Hershey, Pa., was a son of members of the Reformed Mennonite Church. Gen. Lewis B. Hershey of the U.S. Army, long-time (1940-) director of the U.S. Selective Service system, was a grandson of Mennonites (MC).   I.D.L.

H. Hershey, *Hershey Family History* (Scottdale, 1929).

Hershey, Benjamin (1697-July 29, 1789), came to Pennsylvania with his father Christian, his mother Oade, and his brother Andrew, emigrating from Friedelsheim, Palatinate, Germany, whither he had fled from Switzerland about 1671. They arrived in America about 1717 and Benjamin settled "one mile west of Lancaster Town" on the Marietta Pike in the same community as the Hans Brubakers and Peter Swarr. He was early a minister, signing the 1725 edition of the Dordrecht confession (published 1727 at Philadelphia) for the Lancaster area, became bishop and established the Abbeyville congregation and the churches to the northwest. He was moderator of the Lancaster Conference during the Revolution and the stormy days following. The name occurs on some extant documents. He steered the church through the divisions of Francis Herr, the United Brethren, and the Brethren in Christ schisms. His children were Christian, Bishop Benjamin II (d. 1812), who became his successor, and two daughters. He was the author of the petition of 1775 to the Pennsylvania Assembly for release from military service, *A Short and Sincere Declaration* (in GCL).   I.D.L.

Hershey, Eusebius, was born near Manheim, Lancaster Co., Pa., on Aug. 14, 1823. Converted at the age of 18, he joined the United Brethren Church and began to preach for them in 1842. After a few years he joined the Evangelical Mennonites, which later became a part of the M.B.C. Church. He spent 43 years in evangelistic work mostly among non-Mennonites in the eastern part of the United States and Canada, making 13 trips to Canada.

Hershey felt the call to Africa, and on Nov. 1, 1890, sailed from New York, arriving at Sierre Leone after 38 days. He preached through an interpreter for six months, then took sick, and after an illness of seven days died on May 24, 1891. He was the pioneer of all foreign missionary work of his own church, and the first foreign missionary of all American Mennonites.   J.A.Hu.

Hershey Mennonite Church (MC), originally known as the Hess Church, located in Salisbury Twp., Lancaster Co., Pa., is a member of the Lancaster Mennonite Conference. Christian Hess, Jr., and Abraham Hershey were the trustees who purchased the land for the first meetinghouse in 1814, which was used both as a school and as a church. The second church was built by 1837, and a new brick on the present site in 1862, which was replaced by the fourth church in 1879, remodeled during the winter of 1947-48. It was a part of the Pequea ministerial circuit almost to the present. It is now a part of the Old Road-Meadville circuit, but gradually it is becoming a separate congregation. Peter Eby was the first bishop when the congregation still worshiped in homes. In 1953 G. Parke Book was the bishop; Martin R. and Sanford E. Hershey the ministers; and Willis L. Hershey with his father Landis Hershey, deacons; the membership was 196. Meadville (*q.v.*) and the Intercourse Mission Sunday School, begun 50 years ago, were outgrowths of this congregation.   I.D.L.

Hershey Mennonite Church (MC), located three miles north of Thomasville, York Co., Pa., was founded in the 1740's by the Hershey, Roth, Brubaker, and other families from Lancaster County, who organized as a congregation in 1753. The membership in 1886 was 45. The first meeting-house was built in 1825 on grounds donated by John Brubaker. This building was destroyed by a storm in 1896, and the present sandstone church was built. This was closed for a few years and then reopened in 1948. Daniel Bare, Josiah and Benjamin Hershey, Isaac Kauffman, Jacob Hershey, and S. L. Roth have served as ministers here. It is a part of Richard Danner's bishop district. In 1955 there were 22 members; the minister was B. Harnish Noll.   I.D.L.

Hershey Reformed Mennonite Church, Derry Twp., Dauphin Co., Pa., was established about 1833. John Hershey (1801-51) of this community was quite active in building up the congregation. It has never been strong. M. Hershey donated grounds for a meetinghouse in 1871. The 1948 membership was 11, with no local minister.   I.D.L.

Herstein's Mennonite Church (MC), originally an outpost of the Skippack (MC) congregation of the Franconia Conference. The Herstein's school and meetinghouse with cemetery is located in Limerick Twp., Montgomery Co., Pa. The first building seems to have been erected in 1803, and was enlarged in 1917. The high point in number of members was 30, sometime in the 19th century. Services were always suspended during the winter months. For some time, beginning in 1934, a non-sectarian minister conducted services in the "Herstein Chapel." In 1954 the Franconia Mennonite Mission Board (MC) opened work in the ancient building to re-establish a Mennonite congregation at Herstein's.   J.C.W.

's Hertogenbosch, capital of the Dutch province of North Brabant (1953 pop. 61,143; largely Roman Catholic; only a few Mennonites), was in the 16th century a center of Anabaptism. Bartel Boeckbinder (*q.v.*) and Leentgen Hendricksz (*q.v.*), who were executed because of Anabaptism, were natives of 's Hertogenbosch. About 1538 there was a congregation, of which Paulus van Drunen (*q.v.*) was an elder. Eight members of this congregation, including van Drunen, were put to death in September 1538 or 1539 at Vught near 's Hertogenbosch, but in later times also there was a congregation. About 1544 there was here some activity of the adherents of Jan van Batenburg (*q.v.*) and of David Joris (*q.v.*). Magdalena from Waterland (near Amsterdam), a follower of David Joris, was executed at Vught on Aug. 14, 1544. Elder Gillis van Aken (*q.v.*) performed baptism here in the home of a shoemaker in June 1545. According to the confession of Jan van Sol in 1550 Hughe Matthyszoon had preached in 's Hertogenbosch; Leenaert Bouwens (*q.v.*) baptized 35 persons here in 1557-61 and 32 in 1563-65. In December 1569 or January 1570 on his journey from Flanders to Cologne the Elder Hans Busschaert visited 's Hertogenbosch. The congregation still existed but was in a rather sad condition as he states in his letter of Jan. 29, 1570, to Antwerp. Soon after it must have disappeared. Since 1944 there has been a Mennonite fellowship (*Kring*) of 30 members at 's Hertogenbosch-Vught, served by the preacher of

Eindhoven (*q.v.*). Services are held usually monthly in the Lutheran church. There is also a ladies' circle.   vDZ.

Inv. Arch. Amst. I, Nos. 76, 215, 287; *DB* 1917, 137, 186 ff.; 1918, 138; Mellink, *Wederdopers,* 62, 311-15, 414.

Hertzler (*Hartzler*), a family name found among the Amish Mennonites in the canton of Bern, Switzerland, in the Palatinate, in France, and perhaps in other communities in Europe, before 1750. In 1749 Jacob Hertzler, the first Amish Mennonite minister and bishop in the United States, landed in Philadelphia, Pa. In 1750 he, with his wife, three sons, and one daughter, settled on a farm two miles west of Hamburg, in Berks Co., Pa. At least three other Hertzlers arrived in Philadelphia between 1749 and 1761, and still others came later. Some of them were not Mennonites.

According to the *Hertzler-Hartzler Family History* (1952) there are now 8,757 families of descendants of Jacob Hertzler. The family in America covers eleven generations, with a total of 36,548 individuals. They live in all of the 48 states, in 5 provinces of Canada, in 7 nations of Latin America, in 4 countries of Europe, and in 8 other nations of the Near and Far East.

Family heads followed 533 occupations. They belonged to 79 denominational and nondenominational religious bodies. There were 359 Christian ministers in 29 different Protestant churches. Of this number, 254 were members of various Mennonite bodies. There were 97 bishops in eight different Christian churches. Of this number all but eleven were representatives of some branch of the Mennonite faith. There were 47 foreign missionaries located in Bulgaria, Sweden, Ethiopia, Tanganyika, Syria, Lebanon, India, China, Japan, and Argentina. There were 74 nurses reported. There were 60 physicians and dentists. There were 80 members of the family who had earned Master's degrees. Twenty-four had earned Ph.D. degrees, two had earned S.T.D. degrees, with three more having honorary D.D. degrees. Five had biographies given in *Who's Who.* Sixty-four were instructors in colleges, in addition to three college deans, and seven presidents, of seven different colleges. Four of these schools were Mennonite colleges. Five of the presidents were Mennonite men.

Among the Mennonite (nearly all MC) leaders and workers with the name Hertzler or Hartzler have been: Jacob Hertzler (*q.v.,* 1703-86), first Amish bishop in the United States; Christian Hertzler (1800-78), Amish Mennonite preacher at Morgantown, Pa.; Isaac D. Hertzler (1852-1926), preacher at Denbigh, Va.; John Hertzler (1815-88), A.M. bishop at Belleville, Pa.; John J. Hartzler (1845-1936), A.M. bishop at Garden City, Mo., for 42 years; J. S. Hartzler (*q.v.*) (1857-1953), Elkhart, Ind., Mennonite preacher for over 60 years, prominent official and Bible teacher at Elkhart Institute and Goshen College (1895-1918), secretary of the Mennonite General Conference for many years; C. A. Hartzler (*q.v.*) (1876-1947), Mennonite bishop at Tiskilwa, Ill.; J. D. Hartzler (1884-   ), Mennonite bishop at Flanagan, Ill.; E. F. Hartzler (1886-   ), Mennonite bishop at

Marshallville, Ohio; J. G. Hartzler (1880-), Mennonite bishop at Windom, Kan.; J. E. Hartzler (1879-), Goshen, Ind., former president of Goshen College (1913-18), of Bethel College (1920-21), of Witmarsum Theological Seminary (1921-31), professor at Hartford Theological Seminary (1936-53); R. L. Hartzler (1893-), Bloomington, Ill., preacher in the Central Conference; Silas Hertzler (1888-) and H. Harold Hartzler (1908-), professors at Goshen College.   Si.H.

John Hartzler, Sr., *A Brief Biographic Memorial of Jacob Hertzler and a Complete Genealogical Family Register of His Lineal Descendants* (Elkhart, 1885); Silas Hertzler, *The Hertzler-Hartzler Family History* (Goshen, 1952).

Hertzler, Jacob (1703-86), an Amish Mennonite bishop. He was presumably born in the canton of Bern, Switzerland, where his son John was born. It seems likely that here his first wife died, and that he married Catharine Reugy before religious persecution forced him and his family to emigrate. He first moved near Kaiserslautern in the Palatinate, where also there was a large settlement of Amish Mennonites. Two sons, Jacob and Christian, and a daughter Fannie were the children of the second marriage.

On Sept. 9, 1749, Jacob Hertzler and his family landed in Philadelphia. On Jan. 9, 1750, he received a warrant for 100 acres of forest land in Pennsylvania near the Blue Mountain, which he converted into a farm called "Contentment." This farm is located two miles west of Hamburg in what is now Berks Co., Pa. A few Amish Mennonite families had reached America before Jacob Hertzler arrived.

No accurate record is available concerning the ordination of Jacob Hertzler, but on arrival he at once became the minister and bishop of what came to be known as the Schuylkill Amish Mennonite congregation. In 1766 Richard and Thomas Penn donated 20 acres of land adjoining the Hertzler farm for church purposes. On this property was erected a log school building for the education of the children of the congregation. Part of this property was used for a burying ground. Here Jacob Hertzler, his wife, and his son Jacob are buried.

Tradition shows Jacob Hertzler as a frugal, hardworking, energetic farmer and manual laborer. In church work his reputation was that of a conscientious, untiring Christian leader, teacher, preacher, and disciplinarian. He traveled long hours by horseback and on foot to meet his preaching appointments. For many years he was also bishop of a prosperous Amish Mennonite congregation at Malvern, Pa., where probably was built the first Amish meetinghouse in the United States.   Si.H.

John Hartzler, Sr., *A Brief Biographic Memorial of Jacob Hertzler* (Port Royal, Pa., 1885); Silas Hertzler, *The Hertzler-Hartzler Family History* (Goshen, 1952); "Jacob Hertzler, 1703-1786, First Amish Bishop in America," *Gospel Herald*, Jan. 24, 1929; C. Z. Mast and Robert E. Simpson, *Annals of Conestoga Valley* (Scottdale, (1942) 92-98, 213-18; *ML* II, 291.

Herzenberg (later *Alexandrovka*), a Mennonite village established in 1880 in the district of Pavlo-

grad, province of Ekaterinoslav, Ukraine, Russia, by Mennonites from the Molotschna settlement. They purchased 8,000 acres of land at the price of about 31 rubles per acre from a nobleman after whom the village was named. Crops during the first years were poor. Later the village prospered particularly in sheep raising. The first school building erected in 1885 was replaced in 1912 by a massive structure. In 1889, 95 children died of diphtheria and in 1919-20, 18 adults died of typhoid fever. During the political unrest of 1905 buildings on several farms were destroyed by fire. In connection with the Revolution of 1917 the village was robbed and eight persons killed. Little is known about the final fate of this village under the Soviets.

About one third of the settlers of the village belonged to the Mennonite Church, which was a subsidiary of the Ohrloff Mennonite Church. The first minister was Kornelius Siemens ordained in 1881. In 1905 Johann Wölk, ordained in 1882, was the minister. The group was organized in 1881 and had a membership of 31 in 1905 with a total population of 80. The Mennonite Brethren group was a branch of the Rückenau Mennonite Brethren Church. Its first leader was Jakob Dirksen, who was succeeded as leader by Dietrich Friesen, ordained as minister in 1895. This congregation, organized in 1880, had a membership of 79 and a total population of 180 in 1905.   C.K.

Friesen, *Brüderschaft*, 417, 444, 704; H. Dirks, *Statistik*, 1905, 15, 50, 62, 67; *ML* II, 292.

Herzenberg and Alexandrovka Mennonite Brethren Church, located near Pavlograd, province of Ekaterinoslav, Russia, was founded in 1880 by Jakob Dirksen and Johann Kliewer. Wilhelm Bärg served the congregation for a number of years. In 1913 H. T. Kliewer was the leading minister. In 1905 the congregation consisted of 79 members with a total population of 180. Little is known about the later developments and the fate of this congregation (see also **Herzenberg**).   C.K.

Friesen, *Brüderschaft*, 417, 444; Dirks, *Statistik*, 67; D. H. Epp, *Adressbüchlein* (1913) 4.

Herzhorn, a parish in southwest Holstein, Germany. The local pastor reported after the Thirty Years' War, "that members of foreign religions like Anabaptists have settled here . . . but these have all died out; their children and descendants have, however, come into our church." In near-by Glückstadt (*q.v.*) the Anabaptists had lived three decades; during the disturbances of the war they had also settled in the surrounding country, without benefit of a special charter.   R.Do.

Detlefsen, "Geschichte des Kirchspiels Herzhorn," in *Ztscht der Gesellschaft für Schleswig-Holsteinische Geschichte* XXXIII; *ML* II, 292.

Herzog, Hans, of Stadel, Switzerland, an Anabaptist martyr, was drowned March 23, 1532, at Zürich, Switzerland. He was a native of the Grüningen (*q.v.*) district, had under government pressure left the Anabaptists, but joined them again later. (*TA Zürich*, Nos. 342, 348; *ML* II, 292.)

Herzog, Johann Jakob (1805-85), a Protestant theologian, became professor of church history at the University of Lausanne, Switzerland, in 1853, which position he had to resign when he sided with the Free Church in Waadtland in its struggle for independence from the state. In 1854 he became professor of Reformed theology at the University of Erlangen, Germany. He was the founder of the *Realenzyklopädie für protestantische Theologie und Kirche,* which is of value even today, having been published in three editions. In it Mennonite history is given authentic treatment by Mennonite and Protestant authorities (e.g., Prof. Cramer, *q.v.*). Other works by Herzog deserving consideration are *Das Leben Oekolampads und die Reformation der Kirche zu Basel* (Basel, 1843) and *Die romanischen Waldenser* (Halle, 1853). (*ML* II, 292.)   NEFF.

Hespeler, a town (pop. 4,000) in Waterloo Co., Ont., nine miles southeast of Kitchener. Textile mills have been a leading industry. In the early 19th century the Mennonites (MC) met in the home of Samuel Bechtel near this place, until the Wanner Mennonite Church was built two miles from town. Joseph Bechtel was one of the first Mennonite ministers in Ontario and served widely among the churches. For fuller records see **Wanner** Mennonite Church. The town is named after Jacob Hespeler, a brother of William Hespeler (*q.v.*).
                                        J.C.F.

Hespeler Mennonite Brethren Church (since 1953 merged with the Kitchener M.B. Church), located in Hespeler, Waterloo Co., Ont., a member of the Canadian Conference of the Mennonite Brethren Church and also of the General Conference of the Mennonite Brethren Church of North America, was organized on Nov. 20, 1932, under the leadership of J. Bartels. The membership in 1948 was 19. The congregation met in a rented hall with the members of the United Mennonite Church. The ministers who served the church were Jacob Wiens, Dietrich Klassen, Isaak Ewert, and Jacob Sudermann.   H.H.J.

Hespeler (Ont.) United Missionary Church was organized in 1898 with D. Fretz as the first pastor. In 1922 a meetinghouse was purchased. In 1950 the congregation was a member of the Ontario Conference of the United Missionary Church and had 75 members, with Ernest Lucas serving as pastor.   ER.L.

Hespeler, William (1830-1921), was a Lutheran, born in Baden-Baden, Germany, and trained in the Polytechnic Institute in Karlsruhe. In 1850 he emigrated to Preston, Waterloo Co., Ont., where he joined his brother in business. He became Commissioner of Immigration and Agriculture at Winnipeg (1873-83) and later acted as Consul of the German Empire for Manitoba and the northwest territories (1883-1909). While visiting in Germany in 1872 he learned that large numbers of Mennonites living in southern Russia were considering migration to North America. Soon after he had reported this to the Canadian officials, they author-

ized him as a Special Emigration Agent to proceed to Russia, there to assure the Mennonites of a welcome in Canada. After visiting some of the Mennonite settlements his purposes were suspected by the Russian government and he was forced to leave that country. At this point, according to C. Henry Smith, at a meeting in November 1872 at Odessa "with the Bergthal and Molotschna representatives he suggested that they appoint a delegation of competent men to investigate the lands in Canada . . . . The advice was followed the next year. From this time on Hespeler was the representative of the Canadian government in everything that was connected with the immigration of the Russian Mennonites to Canada and their settlement upon their chosen lands." That this was the important position Hespeler filled is attested by the large number of reports, letters, and telegrams by him in the Public Archives of Canada concerning the Mennonite immigration.   M.G.

C. Henry Smith, *The Coming of the Russian Mennonites* (Berne, 1927) 49-50; E. H. Correll, "Mennonite Immigration into Manitoba, Sources and Documents," *MQR* XI (1937) 196-227, 267-83, XXII (1948) 43-57.

Hess, a Mennonite family descended from Hans Hess (d. 1733), a Swiss Mennonite immigrant, who is buried near Baumgardner, Lancaster County, Pa., and had a numerous progeny, including many preachers in the Lancaster (MC) district and elsewhere. The Kraybill district of the Lancaster (MC) Conference had Bishop Samuel Hess (d. 1819); Cumberland County had a preacher Samuel Hess, and Hammer Creek a preacher John Hess. Today Lancaster Conference has preachers Amos L. Hess, Jacob G. Hess, James H. Hess, John S. Hess, John W. Hess, Maris W. Hess, and Richard B. Hess, with two deacons. John H. Hess, minister of the First Mennonite (MC) Church of Kitchener, is a descendant. A. L. Hess (*q.v.*), a layman, who left Lancaster County and settled in Harvey Co., Kan., in 1884, after whom the village of Hesston is named, was one of the founders of Hesston College.   I.D.L.

John H. Hess, *A Family Record of the Hess Family* (Lititz, 1880, 2nd enlarged ed., Lititz, 1896).

Hess, Abraham Lincoln, b. April 10, 1861, at Lincoln, Lancaster Co., Pa., d. Dec. 30, 1920, at Hesston, Kan., the son of John R. and Annie E. Stauffer Hess. On Aug. 17, 1883, he was married to Anna B. Pfautz. From 1884 until his death A. L. Hess lived on a farm near what is now Hesston, at first called Eliven. He was a member of the Pennsylvania Mennonite Church near Hesston until the congregation in Hesston was organized, when he transferred his membership to the Hesston Mennonite Church. He assisted in the founding of the Hesston State Bank, of which he was president for some time. His practical faith in young people was expressed by his contribution of 80 acres of land for the beginning of Hesston College and Bible School (*q.v.*). He was buried in the Pennsylvania Cemetery.   W.E.O.

Dora and Frank Roupp, *Hess Record* (Fall River, Kan., 1949).

Hess, Hans Jakob, a Swiss Mennonite preacher in the canton of Bern, Switzerland, was imprisoned three times for his faith in 1637-39, but escaped twice. Finally he was put in chains for 16 weeks; he endured this martyrdom until his death. His property was sold, but none of the 4,000 fl. of proceeds was given his heirs. His wife was also imprisoned in the same year (1639) and died after 63 weeks in prison. (*Mart. Mir.* D 816, E 1115; *ML* II, 292.)   NEFF.

Hesse stands near the top among the German territories in which Anabaptism became widespread in the very first years of its rise. The history of the movement in this territory, which at that time contained not only the later Grand Duchy of Hesse but also the greater part of the modern Prussian Province of Hesse-Nassau, furnishes a typical example of how theologians, princes, statesmen, and jurists united to combat a brotherhood which thought it could not find the true primitive Christian life in the state church. Nevertheless Hesse has a special place in the history of the Anabaptist movement since in this territory, in contrast to the other Protestant territories, death sentences on account of faith were not passed on the Anabaptists. The clergy in Hesse were not able to put across their viewpoint on the suppression of those who held to the baptism of faith on account of the position of Landgrave Philip of Hesse (*q.v.*). He preferred as more Biblical the method of free exchange of opinion. The results of the discussions with the Anabaptists were of real importance not only for the Hessian state church, but also for Protestantism at large.

Landgrave Philip appreciated the religious sensibilities of his subjects. To a certain extent he sympathized with the views of the Anabaptists. For this reason on Feb. 20, 1530, he wrote to his sister: "I see more real Christianity among those who are called fanatics than among those who are Lutheran." The Lutheran theologians, as well as the authorities of Saxony, were aware of Philip's attitude and this may have been one reason why Justus Menius dedicated to him his book on the Anabaptists, entitled *Der Widdertauffer lere und geheimnis aus heiliger Schrift Widderlegt* (Wittenberg, 1530), to which Martin Luther wrote the foreword.

Philip, realizing that it was impossible to secure agreement on every question of doctrine, was ready, at first at least, to grant tolerance to all the various faiths, with the exception of the Catholic Church. It was only upon pressure from the Saxon authorities that he allowed himself to be moved from his progressive attitude. But in the matter of the punishment of the Anabaptists, he never forsook his original point of view. He looked upon Anabaptism as only a "degenerated child of the Reformation" (*entartetes Kind der Reformation*) and hoped to be able to bring them into the state church.

Since the neighboring territories issued very strict mandates against the Anabaptists, they fled into Hesse. From the middle of 1528 on, the center of this movement was the region of Hersfeld (*q.v.*),

especially the village of Sorga. The spiritual leader here was Melchior Rinck (*q.v.*), who was a priest at Hersfeld in 1523 and who became a very active leader in the Anabaptist movement after joining it in 1528. Philip spared no pains to bring about Rinck's return to the state church; but neither Balthasar Raidt, the pastor at Hersfeld, nor the professors of theology in the University of Marburg were able to make him change his position. He was imprisoned until May 1531, and finally expelled from the country, with the command never to return to Hesse or Electoral Saxony. Nevertheless Rinck returned to Hesse that very year. On Nov. 11, 1531, as he was preaching on the command of Jesus to baptize, he was arrested together with eleven hearers as the result of a search instituted by the council of Vacha. Since the arrest took place in the township of Hausbreitenbach, which was in the joint jurisdiction of Landgrave Philip and the Elector of Saxony, a lively dispute arose between the two states as to the punishment of the prisoners. John of Saxony demanded the death penalty on the basis of an opinion which was submitted to him by his counselors and the scholars at Wittenberg, moved also by the regulations laid down in the decree of the Diet of Speyer of April 23, 1529. Philip preferred a milder treatment.

In order to free himself from the charge that he had done nothing to stop the spread of Anabaptism in his territory, Philip issued a regulation about the middle of 1531, which placed the major emphasis on the reconversion of the Anabaptists. If there was suspicion that an inhabitant of the country was inclined to accept the views of the Anabaptists it was first of all the duty of the pastor to diligently question him. If the questioning revealed an inclination to leave the faith and an unwillingness to modify his attitude, a report was to be submitted to the superintendent of the district. The latter was then to instruct the person in question in the presence of several learned pastors. If he then accepted the teachings of the state church, he was to be released. If he were caught a second time, he was to confess his error in the church and promise to become a full participant in the church organization and not to admit Anabaptists into his house or to associate with them. If he should backslide again, he was nevertheless to be accepted if he should recant the third time, as in the preceding case, but he was required to sell half of his goods and give the receipts to the treasury for the poor.

But if anyone should refuse to yield to this instruction, the regulations prescribed further that in case he were a preacher of the Anabaptists or had baptized others, he should be expelled from the country under threat of death until he should repent and make public confession. This regulation was based upon the assumption that such a preacher had illegally assumed the office of preacher and had illegally undertaken ceremonial procedure. If the preacher would accept these requirements he should be restored to the church. Those who had merely been baptized and had not preached were required to sell their lands and buildings and all property and to submit to the same regulations as the Jews, who were not permitted to possess land in the country. If the wives and children of the accused parties would return to the state church, they should be permitted to recover the lost property. Whoever was expelled from the country but nevertheless would return and not keep his oath, the same should be handed over to the civil authorities "to receive what was due him."

Melchior Rinck, who had violated his oath and refused to be moved in his convictions, was sentenced to life imprisonment. This Philip reported to John of Saxony on Jan. 3, 1532. In 1540 Rinck's punishment was lightened as a result of the intervention of Martin Bucer. Since John, on the basis of the imperial decrees, insisted upon the punishment of the rest of those who had been arrested at Hausbreitenbach, he and Philip agreed to divide the prisoners and permit each prince to apply whatever punishment he saw fit to those that he took. The prisoners who were assigned to Hesse recanted and were released. On the contrary, the Saxon authorities immediately executed three Anabaptists, Hans Eisfart, his wife, and Berlet Schmidt. In Anabaptist circles these executions aroused great indignation and merely stirred them to still greater zeal for their faith. Even those who had recanted now spoke out boldly in the presence of the commissioners of the Saxon and Hessian governments in favor of baptism on confession of faith. John Frederick, who became Elector of Saxony in 1532, insisted like his father upon the execution of the Anabaptists who had been arrested at Hausbreitenbach, basing his position upon a legal opinion of the high court at Leipzig.

The spread of the Anabaptist movement in Hesse led to further pressure upon the Landgrave by the neighboring states. In 1536 a group of 30 Anabaptists were surprised at a service in an abandoned church near Gemünden on the Wohra (district of Kassel). Ten of these Anabaptists were imprisoned at Wolkersdorf (now Oberförsterei in the Frankenberg circuit, district of Kassel), with four of the leaders: Georg Schnabel (q.v.), previously an official of the church in Allendorf, Peter Lose of Gemünden, Hermann Bastian, printer (supposedly from Marburg), and Leonhard Fälber (q.v.) (Rembert, 450) of Jülich. They had previously been repeatedly expelled, but always returned and therefore were now subject to the penalty which the last mandate prescribed, but which Philip hesitated to carry out, requesting an opinion from the evangelical lawyers and theologians of other countries on the basis of a law issued by the previous Landtag. On May 24, 1536, the request for the opinion was sent out to Duke Ulrich of Württemberg, Duke Ernst of Lüneburg, the lawyers of Strasbourg, Ulm, and Augsburg, and the theological faculty of the University of Wittenberg. The response received merely strengthened Philip in his previous attitude, for several reports opposed the death penalty in matters of faith, as for instance the opinion of the mayor and council of the city of Ulm and that of the theologians at Strasbourg. The other theologians demanded the death penalty, as for instance the theological faculty of Tübingen, Martin Luther, Johann Bugen-

hagen, Caspar Cruciger, and Philip Melanchthon for the theological faculty at Wittenberg, and Urban Rhegius for the Duke of Lüneburg. In verbose statements Rhegius declared that the worldly temporal authorities could execute with a good conscience the "accursed heretics" who seemed to him to be worse and more deserving of punishment than the most notorious criminals, since the state had the power to do this (Hochhuth, 1858, 556-78). The Wittenberg reformers declared that it was the duty of the secular authorities to kill obstinate dissenters. Philip summoned his counselors and theologians, together with the representatives of the nobility and the cities, to a conference at Kassel on Aug. 7, 1536, to discuss the future policy in the punishment of the Anabaptists. His first act at this conference was to read the opinions which he had just received; then each of the delegates was asked to state his opinion. This procedure naturally developed opposing opinions, but the outstanding influence of the attitude of the ruler of the land was quite evident. There were some, to be sure, who demanded the death penalty for the Anabaptists and pointed to the example of the Emperor Honorius of the Western Roman Empire. However, the more extreme views were not accepted by the conference. One delegate wanted to have the death penalty for those Anabaptists who should return after they were expelled; these would not be executed for their faith, but for disobedience to the authorities. Others demanded life sentence at hard labor. The extreme opinions of the reformers, however, found no support. Among the theologians only Pastor Justus Winther of Rothenburg favored the death penalty on the basis of the laws of the empire.

The theologians who were of a milder opinion recognized the weaknesses of the state church, especially from the point of view of the religious life among the people, and were quite aware of the strength of the oppressed Anabaptists who baptized upon confession of faith. For this reason it was proposed to institute a general prayer throughout the country for the conversion of the Anabaptists, and to endeavor to have the people renounce their sins in order that the Anabaptists should no longer have reason to stay away from the church. Adam Kraft, the noted preacher who had been professor of theology at the University of Marburg since 1528, and who was also inspector of the churches and therefore had good opportunity to learn to know the reasons why the Anabaptists stayed away from the church, expressed his opinion that the Anabaptists would return to the state church as soon as the more offensive sins and vices of the members of the state church should be done away with. Pastor Johann Lening of Melsungen said, "We should pray God that the people change their manner of life, and admonish the Anabaptists kindly and lovingly, and even if everything which the Anabaptists teach is wicked, yet we must use caution and use every means to convert them before we reach for the sword." And the chaplain Melander said, "The Anabaptist sect represents an affliction from God; for this reason general prayer should be ordained, the preachers ought diligently to preach against sectarians, the people should be admonished to improve their lives and should be told that sins will not remain unpunished, in order that the Anabaptists will find no cause in us to establish a new church. It is the duty of the authorities to punish all the evils and to punish each according to the degree of his sin" (Hochhuth, 1858, 594).

Several delegates insisted upon improvement of the existing regulations, and attacked certain persons in the church whose conduct was offensive to the Anabaptists. What the Anabaptists sought to attain out of inner conviction, namely, a pure life, this the state church should try to accomplish in its members by pressure from the authorities.

The next step was to select a committee composed of several delegates to prepare a new regulation against Anabaptists. The regulations which were adopted the following year in the *Visitationsordnung* of 1537, marked an intensification of the previous regulations and prescribed the death penalty for the Anabaptists. One can see, however, how much the civil and ecclesiastical authorities endeavored to meet the demands of the Anabaptists in wanting to have religious fellowship only with persons of morally irreproachable character. The pastors and officials were required to exercise careful oversight in regard to all persons of immoral tendencies and it was made their duty to punish acts of immorality whenever they occurred.

According to the new regulations the following practices were not to be tolerated in the "Christian church": the rejection of infant baptism and the repetition of baptism; the view that a Christian cannot accept civil office, cannot punish evildoers, cannot partake in just war, cannot receive or give interest or tithes, and cannot swear proper oaths; the view that the incarnation of Jesus was not accomplished by the work of the Holy Spirit; the denial of the forgiveness of mortal sin after baptism; the acceptance of communism of goods; crimes against marriage (bigamy, or separation on the ground of divergence of faith followed by remarriage). The following acts were threatened with the death penalty: unauthorized preaching or conducting of services in the forests in out-of-the-way places, or in isolated houses, and the intentional attendance of such meetings; rejection of civil authority, rejection of obedience to the authorities; return after expulsion (Hochhuth, 1858, 598). The threatened penalties were not actually carried out with great severity. The penalties were in fact due to a confusion of religious and political concepts. It is evident that these regulations were due to the influence of persons who attempted to make the ruler fear that his throne would be endangered if the Anabaptist movement should grow.

Whoever was suspected of transgressing one of the regulations was first of all to be brought to the nearest pastor and to be instructed by several learned theologians. If the attempt to enlighten and convert the erring one would be without success, then according to the regulations the persons involved should be delivered to the superintendent of the district (in Marburg, Kassel, Eschwege, Darmstadt, or St. Goar) and examined by the state counselors of the ruler, and instructed. Whoever admitted his error was required to recant in public. Whoever had previously recanted but had backslidden, and now again repented, was compelled to make a contribution to the treasury for the poor. Those who persisted in remaining true to their faith were treated with greater severity, but the ruler hesitated to actually apply the extreme penalty—death. "No Anabaptist shall be executed, even if the sentence has already been passed, without reporting the matter to us first." In the instructions to the officials a difference was made between the preachers and lay members, as well as between native and foreign persons. The foreign preacher was to be beaten with rods, branded on the cheek, and expelled from the land forever, with a threat of death penalty if he should return. Were he to return, a criminal prosecution was to be initiated against him and he was to be dealt with "according to the present regulations and the imperial laws." The native preachers were to sell their property. If they did not do so within the fixed time, their houses were to be locked, the fire put out, and the property sold. The income from the sale was to be preserved until they should demand it again (which no doubt assumed a return to the state church). They were also required under threat of death to leave the land "forever." They were to be driven out with rods and branded on the face. Whoever should return the third time was to be tortured and executed.

The lay members who were "perhaps misled due to ignorance" were to be expelled from the land if they were foreigners. If they should be caught a second time they were to be driven out with rods and branded. If caught a third time, they were to be put to death. They could however save their lives if they would recant. Native lay Anabaptists were first to be given a month's time for consideration, in which they were to be instructed by the local pastor and other clergymen. "Whoever would not listen to the instruction and join the state church was to sell his property. If this punishment should not avail, then he was to be driven out of the country with rods, but not to be branded on the cheek "because of his ignorance," and if this punishment should be without success, he was to be sentenced to imprisonment and kept there "until perhaps God should give him grace to repent and be converted." Prisons were to be built for these, where they were to be provided with slight food supplies, although they were to be permitted to have spiritual instruction, to hear the proclamation of the Word of God by a pastor of the state church, "so that God might grant His grace to them." Minor children and husband or wife who were not Anabaptists were to be dealt with as mildly as possible.

The officials dealt very leniently with those who were sentenced. The magistrate of Wolkersdorf permitted the wives of the prisoners to visit them in prison. It even became possible for the prisoners to enlarge the hole through which they received their food, by means of a saw which had been smuggled in, so that they could get out. They did not flee, but simply went in and out, sometimes remaining outside for weeks, during which time they would do their work at home, preach, and baptize, although they always returned to prison. This procedure was carried on for almost a year before it was discovered. During this time for instance Jörg Schnabel baptized almost 30 people.

In August 1538 Philip sent Gerardus Noviomagus, professor of theology at the University of Marburg, to go with Peter Dietrich Fabritius of Stadt-Allendorf to Wolkersdorf to convert the imprisoned Anabaptist preachers, Jörg Schnabel, Peter Lose, and Leonhard Fälber. (The fourth leader of the Hessian Anabaptists, Hermann Bastian, was in Marburg.) They discovered a booklet which Jörg Schnabel had written for the brotherhood answering the charges brought against the brotherhood in the *Visitationsordnung* of 1537. Schnabel especially denied that they practiced community of goods and that they rejected civil authority and had peculiar notions about marriage. In this booklet, which bears the title *Verantwurtung und Widerlegung der Artikel, so jetzund im land zu Hessen über die armen Davider, die man Wiedertäufer nent, ausgangen sind,* he defends the Scripturalness of several Anabaptist principles with remarkable evidence of familiarity with the Bible (Hochhuth, 1859, 167-81).

In this writing by Schnabel repeated mention is made of the booklets written by Peter Tasch who originally came from Jülich (Bucer mentions four writings, Lenz I, 50), and who had preached and baptized in the Lahn Valley. Schnabel was in correspondence with him. A letter was also found in which Peter Tasch gave information about the quiet progress of the Anabaptist movement in England. This letter caused Philip to send a letter in his name and that of John Frederick to Henry VIII of England, calling his attention to the spread of Anabaptism in his kingdom. A copy of the letter by Tasch was sent to Martin Luther and Philip Melanchthon. The latter was requested to prepare the letter to be sent to Henry VIII. In this letter Melanchthon spoke of the Anabaptist pestilence which was active in Germany in many places and which did not preach the pure doctrine of the Gospel; but in those regions "where the Gospel truth is preached in its purity, praise God, the people voluntarily flee from this pest because they are made secure against errors by mature doctrine." These remarks by Melanchthon were not quite satisfactory to the Hessian chancellor, Feige, wherefore the letter as written by Melanchthon was modified in many points, so that it was no longer so extreme (Lenz I, p. 320). In its new form as modified by the Hessian chancellor the letter was sent to Henry VIII on Sept. 25. Notable is an appendix which the Landgrave added to the letter as follows: "The Anabaptists are not all alike, a portion being simple, goodhearted, misled people, while another portion are dangerous, wicked, stiff-necked fellows." The Saxon translator omitted this appendix. The English government undertook

severe action against the Anabaptists upon the receipt of the letter. On Oct. 1, 1538, the chancellor Thomas Cromwell issued an order to punish "the stiff-necked Anabaptists." Many of them lost their lives at the stake. (See **England**.)

The discussions which Noviomagus and Fabritius had on Aug. 9, 1538, with the prisoners at Wolkersdorf were a failure. The instruction of the theologians made no impression on the Anabaptist preachers. Leonhard Fälber replied with a lengthy discussion about the power of the living Word which could transform a man from evil to good and completely renew him. In the church he said the dead word was taught which did not check the sinful life of the members. Peter Lose expatiated in bitter expressions about the offensive manner of life of the Hessian preachers and teachers. In consequence the theologians could come to no agreement with the brethren. The prisoners were now taken to Marburg and put under the supervision of Statthalter George von Kolmatsch. Here likewise officials and scholars attempted to work upon them, but everything was in vain. In the meantime the movement was spreading throughout the country. Chancellor Feige, who had also conversed with the brethren, was aroused by their resistance and by the openness with which they attacked the sinful life of the members of the church. He urged the Landgrave seriously to take the matter in hand himself "and lay aside all other affairs."

Philip now sent a writing to the imprisoned preachers in which he accused them of having deceived him in that they frequently were absent from prison. He had now good reason, he said, to use severe measures against them, but he wanted to be gracious once more and give them a last opportunity to let themselves be set right by a "God-fearing man."

So a final attempt was made to convert the Anabaptists to the state church by means of a discussion (*Religionsgespräch*) which was held at Marburg Oct. 30 to Nov. 1, 1538, in the presence of several scholars together with the city council and delegates of the guilds in Marburg. The debate covered these topics: the ban, the church, usury, baptism, magistracy, and the incarnation of Christ. Those who took part were Martin Bucer and the imprisoned Anabaptist preachers Schnabel, Fälber, and Lose. Hermann Bastian was also present. (Hochhuth, 1858, 626-44.) At first they were asked to give Biblical grounds for their separation from the state church. Schnabel, who was asked by Bucer to speak on behalf of the group, explained that he had first accepted the Lutheran teaching and had become at once an official in charge of the treasury for the poor. In the course of his work he noticed that the management was not always carried on in the Biblical spirit. He raised objection to his pastor but received no attention for his criticisms about usury and the practice of the ban, as well as his remarks about the bad conditions in the church. He felt his conscience was bound in the sight of God, and so he could not bring himself to the point where he was willing to loan out the money of the church for interest, while many of the poor people in the community were in great need. For that reason he told the pastor, the mayor, and the council of Marburg, that they were not doing right in the matter of usury and the ban. For that reason he separated himself from them.

Bucer denied that the Anabaptists had the right to separate from the church. He said that a separation from the church could be brought about only by the church itself when it expelled those who were not willing to listen to its admonitions. Jörg had committed an error by dealing only with the pastor and failing to report to the church the evils which he had criticized to the pastor. When he was not willing to listen to the sermons any more he had not only shunned the pastor, but the pastor's work. Let him furnish a passage of Scripture on the basis of which he would be justified to shun the pastor, the pastor's work, and the whole church, before there had been a public excommunication. There was no justification for shunning the church nor a preacher nor any other official just because the church did not throw a sinner overboard. "Even though officials should be found negligent in punishing evil, yet it was not proper for any particular member to shun them or to hold them worthy of shunning," if the church did not excommunicate them.

The Anabaptists showed no appreciation for such views. Jörg declared that the church had not dealt with him and his brethren in the spirit of the Bible. It had taken their books "and plunged them into darkness"; it had driven them from house and home, "and if one should ask the council and citizens of Marburg they would say of those who had been banished that they did not deserve it and they would recognize them as pious people" (Hochhuth, 1858, 633). Although Bucer was not willing to admit that the church in Hesse had dealt unjustly with the Anabaptists since, as he insisted, it was not the church but the authorities which had imprisoned them on account of the discord, yet Jörg's argument on this point was not without influence on Bucer's attitude for the future. "We would not want to justify injustice in the church," said Bucer. The church desired "to be one" with the Anabaptists. Bucer endeavored to compromise with the views of the Anabaptists. He stated that he did not reject the ban and that the church did not want to approve of usury. He even was willing to grant the right to refuse obedience to the authorities for conscience' sake, but he said, "If a subject should know that the authorities would demand of him to do that which is wrong he should not obey" (p. 637). Bucer's explanations that little children were baptized in the time of the apostles made no impression on the Anabaptists. Jörg declared, "I prefer to stand by what I am sure about, namely, that the apostles baptized those who repented. I prefer to let go points on which I am uncertain." In the matter of the incarnation of Christ he explained that he would abide by the article in the general confession of faith on this point, but he believed "that God would in time help him to understand what he did not understand now."

Even though no agreement was reached on all the points under discussion, and in particular in the matter of baptism, in which the prisoners maintained their position, they ultimately agreed to let themselves be influenced to resume their connection with the state church. The ecclesiastical officials hoped that now all the Anabaptists would join the state church. Possibly the concession they made to the Anabaptists in the matter of baptism, namely, the introduction of confirmation, by which they hoped to bridge over the gap between the two views, was the method by which they hoped to bring about the reunion.

In his discussion on the question of baptism, Schnabel had emphasized the point that in the church the children were only baptized and nothing more was done; the children were not taught repentance and oneness of life. Bucer could not deny this fact. He therefore agreed with Schnabel and admitted that something would have to be done in this matter, namely, "the children should be catechized diligently when they came to an age of accountability and should be taught to observe everything that the Lord had commanded" (Hochhuth, 1858, 637). The accusations which Schnabel brought against the state church were now to be met by the introduction of a procedure hitherto unknown in the churches of the reformation, namely, the introduction of general instruction for the youth, followed by confirmation, in order that the Anabaptists might no longer be offended by the neglect of the religious care of the youth. Bucer wrote to Philip on Nov. 17, 1538, from Wittenberg, whither he had gone after the discussion at Marburg, that the Anabaptists could not be dealt with in a way that would be of more use to the church and at the same time the common people more effectively guarded against them, "than by a better organization of Christian life and the more earnest application of Christian discipline" (Lenz I, p. 53).

The Anabaptists did not join the church without conditions. Following the discussion at Marburg they submitted a writing to the Landgrave on Dec. 9, 1538, entitled *Bekenntnis oder Antwort etlicher Fragestücke oder Artikeln der gefangenen Täufer und Anderer im Land zu Hessen* (Hochhuth, 1858, 612-22). In this writing they pointed out once more how the church was lacking in its conflict against sin among the people and did not bring up the people to thankfulness and love toward God and to the praise of the Gospel. They expressed to him their conception of baptism, of the Lord's Supper, of the ban, and of swearing of oaths, and finally declared, "as soon as we feel that all possible diligence is used to apply the ban according to the ordinance of Christ and the apostles, we are willing with our whole heart to gladly enter into fellowship with the church, even though perfection may not be attained at once (p. 620). . . . We promise to conduct ourselves toward the whole church and toward everyone in a free, brotherly, just, and serviceable fashion, just as we desire that everyone should conduct himself toward us" (p. 622). This writing, which was signed by Peter

Tasch, Jörg and Ludwig Schnabel of Allendorf, Leonhard Fälber, Thonig Möler, Christian of Odenhause, Jungheim of Geyssen, Cautz Schmyt of Horbach, and Peter Lose of Gemünden, was turned over by the Landgrave to his theologians for examination (Martin Bucer, Johannes Kymäus, Dionysius Melander, Johannes Pistorius, and Justus Winther). In their reply it is interesting to note that they scarcely contradicted at all the shortcoming and failings of the pastors which the Anabaptists attacked, but much rather expressed themselves in regard to those points which dealt with the doctrine of faith and good works. On this point they hoped that "there are not many among the preachers of our confession who did not frequently and faithfully preach after this fashion. But we do not desire to defend ourselves nor others any further (p. 623) . . . and therefore have no quarrel with them in this first point, but rather agree in Christian peace" (p. 624).

The theologians complained of a shortcoming in the statements of the Anabaptists in that "they were not willing to confess more expressly and willingly their sin and grievous wickedness which they have been guilty of against the church and the congregation of Christ and its ministers and members, along with all sorts of not insignificant errors and false teachings, but rather laid the entire blame for their separation from the church on us and our shortcomings" (p. 625). But if the Anabaptists should desist from their meetings and teachings, should attend the services of the church, should cease to despise and object to infant baptism, should let their children be baptized "since these are born into the church still more than unto their parents," take the oath, assume the obligations of citizens in military service and other matters, and reunite with the church, then they should be accepted with the patience and love of Christ in the hope that they would "by their Christian and kindly association, their faithful admonition, and their devoted living, help to edify the church indeed and bring about true church discipline and the exercise of the Christian ban." Furthermore, no pain should be spared in the church to make matters right and wherever neglect should appear and the Anabaptists or any other persons should call attention of the leaders in the church to the matter, "we faithfully promise to do our best by the grace of God so that men may see that we are concerned about Christian discipline" (p. 626). "These brethren," as the Anabaptists are now called, "should be gladly forgiven for everything they have ever done against the church. On the other hand, the Anabaptists should also forgive if they feel that they have been dealt with too severely."

This opinion of the theologians stands in sharp antithesis to the previous attitude of the Hessian clergy. In it a high regard for the attitude of the Anabaptists can be recognized, a response which was bound to make an impression on the Anabaptist leaders as soon as they were able to realize the emphasis which was being put upon their endeavor to promote holiness, and how much good effect on the church was anticipated as a result of

their co-operation. From this point of view it would not be right to say that it was only the noted dialectical ability of Martin Bucer which was the cause of the bridging over of the differences in the discussions with the Anabaptists, but rather the sincere endeavor of the theologians to make available to the state church the teachings of the Anabaptists which seemed to them to be worthy of acceptance.

The new discipline for the Hessian church was undertaken at once. By the end of November 1538 the synod met at Ziegenhain and adopted the new discipline. It appeared in print in the following year. In this discipline it is quite easy to see the influence of the discussions with the Anabaptists. The discipline required that "all children as soon as they are old enough should be sent to the catechetical instruction which shall be arranged at each place at such a time that it will not be a burden to send the children" (Diehl, p. 17).

With this regulation which rose out of the struggle between the state church and Anabaptism, the Hessian state church created an institution which was introduced at first in the evangelical state church in Hesse and then in the following three centuries gradually into all the evangelical churches of Germany under the name "confirmation," that is, a ratification of the baptism which had been performed upon infants which were as yet unaware of what was being done.

The attitude of Philip to the reforms which arose out of the discussions with the Anabaptists is of importance. In his instruction to the government he said:

"My dear counselors and retainers: We have read the decisions of the synod which has just met at Ziegenhain concerning the ban, confirmation, and the Anabaptists and desire to make known that we are graciously pleased with the decisions, but we have noticed several points which seemed thus to be in part unbalanced and in part possibly not clear.

"As regards the application of the ban, especially at the beginning, in the attempt to prevent a falling away from the Gospel, prevent strife and offense, we have fears that this may be misused just as was the case in former times, and that the ban may not be applied with Christian sympathy and modesty. We also fear that not all preachers and pastors have equal gifts in the matter of teaching or in common sense or in Christian modesty, and feel therefore that the ban should be introduced everywhere in all parishes at once, but should first be applied in the cities and villages where the most able and most learned preachers are to be found, as for instance at Kassel and at Marburg, so that we can see how things go and so that the other preachers and pastors who are not so able should observe and learn thereby how the ban should be exercised. . . . We express ourselves thus also because we have heard that the scholars who were present at the synod are also of this opinion and feel that so far as the ban is concerned, it should not yet be publicly announced in the church or in printed form, but should first be tried out in the various places as mentioned above.

"In the matter of the Anabaptists and their punishment, it will be necessary that you, our Chancellor, should go into this matter and should prepare a proper regulation in accordance with our command which everyone may clearly understand and accept. It shall have the following form: If an Anabaptist should do this, he should be punished for it; if he should do that, he should be punished with a more serious punishment. Further, it is necessary to note that when Anabaptists are about to be punished or sentenced they will probably cry out in public and say, for they are well able to speak, 'Dear people, we are suffering very much today on account of our faith, and on account of righteousness.' Thereupon the poor, common, ignorant people will no doubt be much offended and embittered in spirit. Therefore it would be better not to sentence an Anabaptist unless it is made known in advance to our counselors at Kassel and Marburg, and furthermore that they should not be sentenced anywhere except at Kassel and Marburg. Further, if such a one should be sentenced, several officials must be on hand to explain to the people that we are punishing the Anabaptist for this or that transgression, and the preachers are to publicly proclaim to the people that the Anabaptists are in error on this or that point and are misleading the people. All this should be done in order that the people may hear that the Anabaptists are not being punished for the true Christian faith and for righteousness' sake but because of their transgression and disobedience, and also that they may learn that the Anabaptists are in error in this and that point and are unrighteous, in order that these errors may become offensive to the people and that they may learn to save themselves from them. In Kassel the following persons should do this, namely, the Chancellor and two or three of the most able preachers, such as Dionysius Melander and Johannes Pistorius, while at Marburg it is to be the Statthalter and two or three of their most learned preachers, such as Master Adam and others."

These decisions and regulations give abundant evidence of the extent to which the struggle against the Anabaptists influenced the religious and moral life of the country. The officials desired to really educate and train the populace in the proper manner but were aware of the difficulties attending such endeavors. This is the reason for the cautious method of introducing the ban. Compulsory membership in the state church was incompatible with the application of the ban according to the principles of the Anabaptists. For this reason one of the two had to be dropped if there was not to be continual conflict. The principle of the Anabaptists which was based upon the assumption of freedom in religious matters simply could not be applied without modification of the state church. For this reason the introduction of the ban in the Hessian church never got beyond the stage of experimentation.

The Anabaptists in the country appear to have taken a distrustful attitude toward the assurances which had been given their leaders at Marburg. They could not reconcile the threats of punishment in case of refusal to rejoin the state church with their conception of freedom of faith and conscience. They hesitated to enter into permanent union with a church in which the sword of civil authority exercised dominant influence in matters of faith. Martin Bucer understood their attitude as is evident from the proposal which he made to Philip on Nov. 4, 1538, to send out the Anabaptist preachers who had already entered the state church as missionaries to win over their followers. In this proposal he says: "There are more of the Anabaptists in your Highness' land than I had supposed and among them are many goodhearted people who are so suspicious of us preachers that they will not accept anything or at least very little from us. If therefore they are threatened with punishment the result is that the most pious among them will simply be strengthened in their attitude, for they will thereby think that they are suffering for the Lord's sake, whereas those who yield, usually do it against their conscience and for this reason they will not remain steadfast in their new faith or will forsake all religion and thereby become the most infamous people which can be found, just as I have experienced in many cases" (Lenz, p. 51).

According to Bucer's report Peter Tasch is said to have prevailed upon about 200 members of the Anabaptist group to return to the state church. We learn later of various other commissions which Tasch, Bastian, Jörg Schnabel, and Peter Lose received in the matter of winning back their previous comrades in faith for the Hessian church. However, they were not able to accomplish any great success (Lenz I, 325). Peter Tasch followed Bucer to Strasbourg. What Bucer had said to the Landgrave concerning such Anabaptists who yielded to pressure against their conscience (in his letter of Nov. 4, 1538) was demonstrated in his case. Tasch not only gave up his faith but later the ethical principles of Anabaptism as well. He led an extravagant life, fell into debt, deceived his creditors, and finally disappeared from the city about 1560 (Rembert, 457).

The Anabaptist movement in Hesse was by no means suppressed by these measures. Quite a number of Anabaptists remained steadfast to their faith. On Jan. 22, 1544, Philip wrote to Master Adam that he intended "to drive out of the country the Anabaptists who were not willing to accept the articles which had been accepted by Schnabel, Tasch, and others" (Hochhuth, 1858, 181).

In order to escape the continued pressure by civil and ecclesiastical authorities, many Anabaptists migrated to Moravia, where they joined the Hutterites, whose missionaries for a long time regularly visited their coreligionists in Hesse. For instance in July 1544 a company of 12 travelers whose leaders, Peter and Jacob, had already suffered several imprisonments in Hesse on account of their teaching and baptizing, were arrested by Hessian officers (Hochhuth, 1859, 208). They had decided to emigrate on account of the order which they had received to participate in the war, which was against their faith.

Although Philip was very anxious to restore unity of religious faith in his country and made severe threats against all those who resisted his program, he nevertheless did not permit himself to be brought to the point where he gave his consent to the actual application of the death penalty. At the end of his long reign (he died on March 31, 1567) he could set down these words in his last will: "We have never killed a human being because he did not believe aright." He admonished his sons to follow his example.

After Philip's death his country was divided into four districts. Wilhelm received the principality of lower Hesse with its capital Kassel, Ludwig received upper Hesse with its capital Marburg, Philip received the lower county of Katzenellenbogen with St. Goar, while George received the upper county of Katzenellenbogen with Darmstadt.

In the *Reformationsordnung* of 1572 which included regulations taken from the mandate of 1539 against the Anabaptists, Landgrave Wilhelm fixed the highest penalty against Anabaptists as expulsion from the country. These regulations also provided that if the instruction of the Anabaptists should be in vain the superintendent should sell the property of such persons within 14 days. However, in contrast to the usual practice in other countries, the guilty persons retained the right to dispose of the proceeds. If the property was not sold within the set time of 14 days the officials were required to sell it at the best possible price and hand over the proceeds to the guilty persons as soon as they had passed a point 12 miles outside of the border. However, if the guilty persons should voluntarily leave the country on request they were permitted to retain their property and rent it and later sell it. If they should return to the state church, their transgressions should be forgiven them.

Landgrave Wilhelm had previously manifested his more tolerant attitude toward the Anabaptists when the synod of Kassel laid before him in 1569 the question whether children of Anabaptist parents should be forcibly baptized. Wilhelm had received several opinions from his advisers. For instance, superintendent Dr. Johannes Marbach of Strasbourg, who had participated in the debate with the Anabaptists at Pfeddersheim in 1557, and who had published a book entitled *Prozess* in which he recommended to the authorities the death penalty for Anabaptists, recommended that the children of Anabaptists should be forcibly baptized against the will of their parents. Matthias Flacius Illyricus gave the same opinion. Landgrave Wilhelm however could not accept this point of view. It appeared to him that there were more arguments from human reason in the opinions than proofs out of the Bible. According to him, although the authorities had the power to compel their subjects to obey, he thought that it was quite questionable whether this power extended so far as to control the conscience which God alone was to judge. The Landgrave therefore had serious doubts about applying forcible baptism. In his mind a Christian ruler frequently had to make concessions to prevent harm and to maintain Christian love. To drive out of the country the "poor misled folk" or to inaugurate compulsory baptism might encourage Catholic princes to similar procedure against the evangelicals. He was supported in his opinion by the opinion which the Hessian superintendents Johannes Pistorius of Nidda and Johannes Gidarius submitted. Both of them pointed out the prevailing disorderliness among the members of the state church, which was frequently advanced by the Anabaptists as the reason for their separation from the church (see **Heppe,** *ML* II, 284).

It is worth while noticing in this letter several expressions by Anabaptist leaders. For instance, Martin Richter declared to the superintendents and preachers: "The teaching on infant baptism is incorrect, and likewise there is little improvement in life to be noticed among the members of the evangelical church." Even threat of punishment against him made no impression, so that he finally said he could not give up the truth which he had accepted but must be patient and suffer whatever he was to suffer. He requested however that he should be dealt with according to the regulations of the ruler and should be permitted to leave the country with his wife and child. Another Anabaptist, Hans Kuchenbecker of Hatzbach, expressed himself as follows to the Chancellor, preachers, and counselors at Marburg, on Feb. 5, 1577: he had observed very little improvement of life among the preachers and their hearers, and he did not desire to belong to such a crowd.

The remnants of the Anabaptist church in Hesse were not wiped out until the Thirty Years' War and their influence continued even beyond that time. The superintendent, Dr. Karl W. H. Hochhuth, the first scholar to work through the Anabaptist archives in Hesse, asserts "that the principle of ethical mysticism which lay at the roots of the Anabaptist movement could not be suppressed, and that it is impossible to deny the influence which certainly contributed a great deal toward reinvigorating church life and strengthening the grasp on old and almost forgotten redemptive principles" (Hochhuth, 1859, 234). A later scholar, Eduard Becker, writes as follows in a monograph on *The Anabaptists in Upper Hesse (Die Wiedertäufer in Oberhessen):* "It is noteworthy that a considerable number of villages which were known to have been centers of Anabaptism later became centers of pietism and in our day are now centers of the Gemeinschaften" (*q.v.*).

Although Anabaptism was suppressed, it exerted its influence upon the public life of Hesse. A modern scholar in church law, Dr. Walter Sohm, comments as follows on the consequences of the reunion of the Anabaptist leaders with the State Church: "It is impossible to fail to recognize that Bucer and the Landgrave accomplished an extraordinary thing in this reunion . . . their procedure did not mean the destruction of the movement as was the case in Electoral Saxony; it meant the fortunate assimilation of the movement, the winning over of opposing forces and the exploitation of the movement with all its strength for the promotion of the purpose of the church. Nevertheless Christian society did not come out of this struggle without a loss. The Anabaptism which had been suppressed breathed something of its spirit into the body of the whole Hessian church life. . . . The conception of the pastoral office as having for its sole function the preaching of the Word was restricted by adding to it a disciplinary task in the church of Christ which was quite un-Lutheran. This was done by the inauguration of the church ban which was set up in the disciplinary regulations of 1539 adopted at Ziegenhain . . . . The legitimate state church movement and the sectarian side movement were united. In this act the last and decisive word was spoken as to the public character of the Hessian church society in so far as it undertook at all the education of its Christian subjects . . . . The suppressed Anabaptist revolution had its effect in the life of Hesse. It left a heritage therein which bore its characteristics" (Sohm, 163-66). (See also **Rhenish Hesse.**) HEGE.

E. Becker, "Zur Gesch. der Wiedertäufer in Oberhessen," *Archiv f. hess. Gesch. u. Altertumskunde,* Neue Folge X (Darmstadt, 1914); E. H. Correll, *Das Schweizerische Täufermennonitentum* (Tübingen, 1925); W. Diehl, *Zur Geschichte der Konfirmation* (Giessen, 1897); H. L. I. Heppe, *Kirchengesch. beider Hessen* (Marburg, 1876); K. W. H. Hochhuth, "Mittheilungen aus der protestantischen Secten-Geschichte in der Hessischen Kirche," *Zeitschrift für die historische Theologie,* 1858, 538-644; 1859, 167-234; 1860, 258-84; Max Lenz, *Der Briefwechsel Landgraf Philipps mit Bucer* (Leipzig, 1880); F. O. zur Linden, *Melchior Hofmann* (Haarlem, 1885); Rembert, *Wiedertäufer;* Walter Sohm, *Territorium u. Reformation in der hessischen Geschichte 1526-1555* (Marburg, 1915); A. Trieb, *Ibersheim am Rhein* (Eppelsheim, 1911); P. Wappler, *Die Stellung Kursachsens und des Landgrafen Philipp von Hessen zur Täuferbewegung* (Münster, 1910); Franz, *TA: Hessen;* Chr. Hege, "Early Anabaptists in Hesse," *MQR V* (1931) 157-78; T. Sippell, "Confession of the Swiss Brethren in Hesse 1578," *MQR XXIII* (1949) 22-34; *ML II,* 294-303.

Hesse-Nassau, formerly a province of Prussia, area 6,504 sq. miles, pop. 2,688,922, which was formed in 1866 principally from the former duchy of Nassau, the landgraviate Hesse-Homburg, and the free city of Frankfurt a. M., as well as the electoral principality of Hesse-Cassel, administratively divided into the two government districts of Cassel and Wiesbaden. In the treatment of the Mennonites by the governments these regions have in the course of centuries shown great contrasts. In the 16th century the Anabaptists were systematically suppressed by the governments, but favored in the 18th and 19th. In both eras, in spite of their small numbers, they exerted a lasting influence on the development of the country; in the 16th century in the sphere of religion (see **Hesse**) and in the 18th, of economics.

In the 18th century the Mennonites became pioneers in a new type of agriculture. The Anabaptists of the 16th century had long since been driven out and suppressed; they were replaced in the 18th century by persecuted Swiss Mennonites, who found their way into Hesse-Nassau after temporary residence in Alsace and the Palatinate. The first immigrants settled in Nassau at the end of the 18th century; they were farmers from the vicinity of Heidelberg and Mannheim. Highly pleased, von Kruse, the provincial governor, who was himself a capable agriculturist, received the Mennonites, and in 1783 he leased his estate Mosbach near Wiesbaden to Valentin Dahlem (*q.v.*), who later became the preacher of the congregation

at Wiesbaden. The estate soon became the first of the larger Mennonite model farms in Nassau-Usingen. The remaining families had received in lease from the government, farms in the districts of Wiesbaden and Idstein, where there was frequently much waste and other uncultivated land. Baron von Kruse planned systematically to turn this region, especially around Wiesbaden, where there were still hundreds of acres of waste land, into fertile land.

The achievements of the Mennonites in the culture of the soil in a short time are evident in the reports on the state of the country by the two ministers of state, von Marschall and von Jagern, to the Duke of Nassau. "Agriculture remains the chief source of German prosperity. If it were not of such high quality, how could our nation have endured so many hardships (i.e., the continental blockade). . . . Especially our Anabaptists have set a good example, neighbors from the former Lower Palatinate, and in competition with them progress has been made everywhere. The cultivation of clover has aided us. Uncultivated land grows less. Cattle-raising is thriving."

The Mennonites were now actually used as teachers of the peasants. About 1830 there were in the duchy of Nassau 14 Mennonite families with 80 souls and 17 Amish families with 130 souls (see table of distribution in *ML II,* 303).

From here several families settled in the electoral principality of Hesse-Cassel, the later Prussian district of Cassel. In the 1880's a member of this group, J. Schlabbach, was elected to the Prussian parliament.

At the close of the 18th century the Mennonites living around Wiesbaden organized a congregation, with Valentin Dahlem as their elder, but dissolved after his death in 1840. The Amish group met at various places for their religious services. About 1890 this congregation also became extinct.

During the 20th century a decline in numbers and a transfer of residence to the cities became evident. About 1870 the census enumeration shows 204 Mennonites in the province of Hesse-Nassau, that of 1925 only 135, of whom 72 lived in the cities of Frankfurt, Wiesbaden, and Cassel. According to the statistics of the census in Berlin, the Mennonites were distributed through the various areas (see table in *ML II,* 303).

At the end of 1926, in the south of the Fulda area near Neuhof a Bruderhof was formed, under the leadership of Eberhard Arnold, which represents the principles of the first Anabaptists, was interested in evangelization, and in the spirit of the Hutterian Brethren has carried out a community of goods, of life, and of work. In addition to a library of approximately 5,000 volumes there were here numerous copies from old court records, *Rechenschaften,* letters, and songs of the 16th century Anabaptists, especially of the Hutterian Brethren. The *Eberhard Arnold-Verlag* was located here. A further enterprise was the children's community of the Bruderhof (see **Rhönbruderhof**) with its own elementary and secondary school; it has also accepted a number of poor and neglected children. At the beginning of 1930 the brotherhood numbered 70 souls. The group was expelled from Germany in 1935.

A congregation was established in Frankfurt (*q.v.*) in 1948, after meetings had been held regularly since 1913. (For the small Amish settlement which existed near Marburg *ca.* 1780-1850, see **Waldeck-Hesse Amish.**)   HEGE.

E. H. Correll, *Das schweizerische Täufermennonitentum* (Tübingen, 1925); A. Hunzinger, *Das Religions-, Kirchen- und Schulwesen der Mennoniten* (Speyer, 1830); *RGG*, 562, where the Hutterites are confused with the Quakers; C. Spielmann, "Die Mennoniten und ihre Bedeutung für die Kultur für Nassau," *Annalen des Vereins für nassauische Altertumskunde und Geschichtsforschung* XXVI (1894) 137-44 (reprinted in *Menn. Bl.*, 1895, 19 ff.); *ML* II, 303 f.

Hesseling, Pieter Andriesz, usually called simply Pieter Andriesz, b. 1588 at Rotterdam, d. 1645 at Amsterdam, preacher of the Waterlander congregation at Amsterdam. A tailor by trade, and evidently the son of poor and non-Mennonite parents, he became acquainted with Hans de Ries, and was baptized by him; Hans de Ries must have taught him Latin.

While he was living in de Rijp he married Adriaantje Willemsdr of Amsterdam, Feb. 17, 1613. She was baptized in January 1612. She was an older sister of the wealthy grain dealer, Joost Willemsz Nieukerck (a brother-in-law of the poet Joost van den Vondel) and of Hester Willemsdr (the mother of the poet Reyer Anslo). In 1613 he obeyed the request of the Waterlander preachers to settle in Amsterdam.

Hesseling was at once chosen preacher and was ordained on Feb. 5, 1617, by Hans de Ries and Reinier Wybrantsz. On Dec. 30, 1615, he signed (with Reinier Wybrantsz and Nittert Obbesz) a book titled *Vreede-schrift of eene Christelijke Vermaaning en Andwoord, 't welk van de Vereenigde Gemeente binnen Amsterdam geschreeven en aan Eenigen, die zonder genoegzaame oorzaake van de Gemeente afgeweeken (zijn) en eene bijzondere vergaderinge aangesteld hebben, over geleverd is,* . . . (Amsterdam, 1616). This work deals especially with the ban in mixed marriages, the Incarnation, and the baptism of those who had been baptized as adults by the Reformed. They took a moderate position, as they also did in the second booklet, *Noodwendige Verklaaringe,* . . . (Amsterdam, 1616). Pieter Andriesz stepped into the fore especially in the dispute with Preacher Nittert Obbesz, who differed from the other preachers in his faith. After Nittert Obbesz had severely criticized a sermon by Pieter Andriesz in 1624, and at a meeting on Nov. 25, 1625, had called another sermon by Pieter Andriesz "stupid tricks," the latter induced the others to exclude Obbesz from communion. Then Jan Theunisz, who was on the side of Obbesz, created an offensive disturbance at the service conducted by Pieter Andriesz. In connection with this quarrel Pieter Andriesz, Reinier Wybrantsz, and Cornelis Claesz Anslo wrote *Apologia ofte verantwoordinghe . . . tot onderrechtinghe van alle oprechte Broeders en Zusters sijnde in deselve Gemeente, diemen oock Waterlanders noemt* (Hoorn, 1626). The quarrel took its course in public view through the 13 articles of peace set up by Nittert Obbesz.

About this time Pieter Andriesz must also have been involved in a quarrel about the confiscation of some wax. He did not carry out his intention to settle in Danzig. In 1628 he disputed with Pastor Abdias Widmarius at Uitgeest. In the report by Widmarius, written in detail, but not in favor of his opponent, he calls the latter the "bishop of the Mennonites of Amsterdam."

Pieter Andriesz was a cloth merchant and lived at the Nieuwendijk at Amsterdam. He was a "very peace-loving and pious preacher, in matters of minor import conciliatory, who, with all his meek gentleness, proper in a preacher, held fast to the sound doctrine of the truth and piety, although he had to endure much scorn and shame for it" (Maatschoen III, 85). His portrait, with a signature by Spinniker, engraved by J. Folkema, is found in Schijn-Maatschoen, III, 80. There is also a portrait of him made by Chr. van der Passe.

H.F.W.

Schijn-Maatschoen, *Geschiedenis der Mennoniten* III (1745) 80 ff.; *Memoriaal van Reynier Wybrandsz* and *Banboek* in the Mennonite archives at Amsterdam; van Douwen, *Socinianen en Doopsgezinden,* 147 ff.; Blaupot t. C., I, 273; (*Jan Theunisz*), *Teghenlooper Ontmoetende den Meester van den voorlooper* (1626); Jan Theunisz, *Een Vraghe van Nittert Obbesz* (1627); Knuttel, *Pamfletten-catalogus,* No. 3711; N. W. Posthumus, *De nationale organisatie der lakenkoopers* (1927) 249 and 289; Kühler, *Geschiedenis II, passim;* H. F. Wijnman, "Jan Theunisz," in *Jaarboek-Amstelodamum* (1928) 78 ff.; idem, "Pieter Andriesz Hesseling" in *N.N.B.Wb.* VIII, 757 ff.; *Inv. Arch. Amst.* II, No. 1024; *DB* 1864, 49, 51, 62 ff.; 1907, 51, 55 ff.; *ML* II, 293.

Hesselink (Hesseling, Hesselingk), a Dutch Mennonite family. A branch of this family lived in the city of Groningen where they usually belonged to the (Groningen) Old Flemish Mennonite congregation: Willem Jacobsz Hesselink (d. 1720) was a preacher of this congregation 1694-1720, as was his son Jacob Willemsz Hesselingk (d. 1760) 1725-*ca.* 54; Willem Arendsz Hesselink (1707-68) also served this church as a preacher 1753-54, while many members of this family served as deacons, not only of the Old Flemish congregation, but also after this congregation had merged in 1809 with the Waterlander-Flemish congregation; e.g., Albert Hesseling, deacon 1782-1802, and Jan Hesselink 1826-30. Jacob Derks Hesselink (d. 1878) bequeathed a considerable amount of money to the congregation to build an old people's home, *Hesselink-stichting.*

From this Groningen branch also descended Gerrit Hesselink (*q.v.*) (1755-1811), Mennonite minister and professor. Other ministers bearing this name were Wybo Hesseling, b. at Groningen, d. 1778 at Leiden, who studied at the Amsterdam Mennonite Seminary 1762-67 and served the congregation of Leiden 1768-77. Matthijs Hesselink, b. at Groningen, was educated at the Seminary 1773-77 and served as minister at Huizen 1777-88, Emmerich 1788-96, Zutphen 1796-1802, Westzaandam "Oude Huys" 1802-5. In 1805 he resigned. In 1809 he made a plan to found a fund for pensioning the widows of Mennonite preachers.

Whether Pieter Andriesz Hesseling (*q.v.*) (1588-1645), preacher of the Waterlander congregation of Amsterdam, belonged to the same family, could not be ascertained.   vDZ.

Hesselink, Gerrit, b. Oct. 23, 1755, at Groningen, d. Nov. 7, 1811, at Amsterdam. After securing the Ph.D. at the University of Groningen in 1778 he studied at the Mennonite Seminary at Amsterdam, and served as preacher at Bolsward 1781-86. In 1786 he was appointed to a professorship at the Mennonite Seminary in Amsterdam, demonstrating in the office his great energy and many-sided learning. For a time (1797-98) he also taught the Remonstrant students. He also (1800) lectured in mathematics, logic, metaphysics, even physics. Cramer says (*DB* 1901, 18) that he was more of a natural scientist and philosopher than theologian. Of his many writings in various fields of science, we mention only *Uitlegkundig woordenboek ter verheldering van de schriften des Nieuwen Verbonds* (Amsterdam, 1790, 2nd ed. 1804). He was a keen thinker. As an exegete he used the grammatico-historical method. His free and independent judgment led him often on new paths. His love to the Mennonite brotherhood is evidenced by his attempts at unifying the congregations and his collaboration in the founding of the A.D.S. in 1811. He was a modest and helpful man, in spite of his unusual learning, and won the hearts of his students through his personal fellowship with them.

vpZ.

B. Glasius, *Godgeleerd Nederland* II ('s-Hertogenbosch, 1853) 88-91; *Biogr. Wb.* III, 780-85; *Inv. Arch. Amst.* I, Nos. 686 f.; II, Nos. 618, 2507; *Naamlijst* 1815, 47-49; *DJ* 1850, 122-44; *DB* 1872, 8 f.; 1901, 18; *ML* II, 293 f.

Hesston Mennonite Church (MC), located in Hesston, Harvey Co., Kan., a member of the South Central Conference, was organized on Sept. 9, 1910, with six families and several students then attending Hesston Academy. J. D. Charles served as the first pastor. The group first met in the assembly room of Green Gables, and later in the chapel hall of the administration building on the Hesston College campus. The following have served as pastors and bishops of the congregation: J. D. Charles, D. H. Bender, Noah Oyer, Milo Kauffman, Irvin Burkhart, M. A. Yoder, Jess A. Kauffman, John P. Duerksen, and Ivan Lind. The membership in 1956 was 270. A new church was dedicated in 1956.   J.A.KA.

Hesston College and Bible School (MC) developed from an appeal to the Kansas-Nebraska Conference in 1907 for a Mennonite (MC) school west of the Mississippi "in which Bible would be made a specialty." Many parents and church leaders of the early 1900's were ready to comply with the current trend toward general high-school attendance; they saw the need of fitting young people for positive living in church service and chosen vocations but they demanded the assurance that such training be received under Christian influences.

During its 44-year history the institution has held sacred this wish of its founders. The Bible department of 1909 began as a two-year course on a high-school level and has continuously readjusted itself to fit the developing curriculum. At present the college gives a B.R.E. course on a four-year college level. By an agreement between the two colleges, effective 1942-54, three years of the five-year Th.B. course offered at Goshen College Biblical Seminary could be given at Hesston for later transfer to Goshen.

The institution opened Sept. 22, 1909, on a site adjoining Hesston, Kan., an 80-acre donation by A. L. Hess. There were 21 students and four faculty members—D. H. Bender principal, J. D. Charles, J. B. Kanagy, Estella Cooprider—and one building, now a dormitory for high-school girls.

In 1914-17 the Administration Building was added; in 1946-47 Hess Memorial Hall, an Auditorium-Gymnasium; in 1948-52 the J. D. Charles Hall of Science and Arts; in 1954-56 a chapel-church—Bible department building. An accommodating cluster of practical arts shops, dormitories, offices, health unit, home economics workrooms, and faculty homes have grown up around these major buildings.

In 1909 the institution was an academy; during 1912-13 it was state accredited; in 1915-16 college work was first given. In 1918-27 four years of college were given (a total of 29 B.A. graduates); in 1925 a junior college organization was substituted and is now accredited by the Kansas Board of Education and the University of Kansas. The present curriculum offers the terminal courses in vocational education and the liberal arts program. In 1951-52 the high-school department was admitted into the North Central Association.

The first faculty had four members, one with an M.A. degree. In 1953-54 there are 27 members with 18 Master's degrees and three who have almost completed the work for Ph.D.'s (*H.C.B.S. Handbook,* 1953-54).

The institution has had three presidents: D. H. Bender, 1909-29; Milo Kauffman, 1932-51; Roy D. Roth, president-elect 1951-53, president 1953- . There have been seven deans: J. D. Charles, 1919-23; Noah Oyer, 1923-24; Edward Yoder, 1924-26, 1929-32; Paul Erb, acting dean 1926-29, dean 1933-41; Ivan Lind, 1941-49; Walter Oswald, 1949-53; Justus Holsinger, 1953- .

In pace with the steady growth of the institution the area of its influence has widened. In 1909 the school opened with 21 students and the first graduating class in 1911 had five members. In 1951-52, 520 students of all grades were enrolled and 102 were graduated. Although most of the students come from the states west of the Mississippi, an increasing number of high-school students come from Ohio, Indiana, Illinois, Puerto Rico. Each year, too, there is a scattering of Canadians, Negroes, and foreign exchange students from Europe or Asia.

A 1952 check on alumni vocations gives evidence that the institution has kept faith with its founders. In church institutions and activities, Hesston College alumni are in front-line service. Ten are on the Goshen College instructional staff, 15 on the Hesston College faculty, three at Eastern Mennonite College, seven on the official staff at the La Junta Mennonite School of Nursing, and seven on the Mennonite Publishing House editorial staff. In the foreign and home mission outposts—in India, Africa, Japan, South America, Puerto Rico—in MCC services, and in pastorates and teaching positions in home congregations Hesston College alumni fill responsible positions.

The 1953-54 faculty signed this pledge to send to its constituency: "We, recognizing a divine call to serve on the Hesston College and Bible School faculty, dedicate all our energies to Christ and His Church to teach in harmony with, and nothing contrary to the doctrines of the Word and the historic principles of the Mennonite Church, to be active in leading students to deeper experiences with Christ so that they may respond to His call to fellowship and service, and to do our best to maintain a fervent spiritual and evangelistic atmosphere on the campus." (†*ME* I)   M.M.

Hesston College and Bible School Bulletin, the official publication of Hesston College (formerly Academy) and Bible School, Hesston, Kan., published continuously since May 1915. It appeared quarterly 1915-30, bimonthly 1931-39, and monthly 1940-52. As the school's official publication, the *Bulletin* was devoted largely to reports and announcements, with alumni numbers added in 1940. In 1953 many features of the *Bulletin* were incorporated in a new publication, *This Month at Your College.* The *Bulletin,* now published at irregular intervals, includes such features as the annual catalog, annual report, and alumni numbers. The number of pages and size of page vary.   N.P.S.

Hesston College Journal, first issue March 1914 as the *Hesston Academy Journal,* was first a 16-page monthly periodical. The name was changed to the *Hesston College Journal* in February 1919. It remained a 16-page monthly, with the exception of the year 1925 when it contained 24 pages, until the fall of 1942 when it was changed to a four-page biweekly newspaper.

During the early years of its publication the editorial staff and reporters consisted of both faculty and students. The first editors were M. D. Landis, 1914-15; J. D. Charles, 1915-17; Paul Erb, 1917-18; and Edward Yoder, 1918-23. The first student editor was J. D. Graber in 1923, the position being held by students ever since.   W.E.O.

Hesta, Leonardus, a Dutch Mennonite minister b. May 9, 1856, d. April 14, 1901, at Haarlem. He studied at the universities of Utrecht and Amsterdam, became a ministerial candidate in 1881, and served the congregations of Rottevalle in Friesland 1880-84, Norden in East Friesland, Germany, 1884-89, Sneek in Friesland 1889-90, and Haarlem 1890 until his death. His contributions to his congregations and to the Mennonite brotherhood were varied and significant. He was a member of the executive board of the A.D.S. (Dutch General Conference) and treasurer of the Fund, later the Association in Behalf of Mennonite Orphans. For many years he was the active leader of the committee for the Mennonites in the Diaspora (see **Verstrooiing**). He was a collector of Mennonite writings and well versed in its history. In 1887 he became one of the first editors of the *Zondagsbode* (*q.v.*). He pub-

lished a historical paper in the *Doopsgezinde Bijdragen* of 1892, and three German sermons: *Die Christliche Hoffnung* (Altona, 1887); *Predigt über Phil. 1, 25* (Norden, 1888), and *Gedächtnisrede über 2. Sam. 1, 26a* (funeral sermon for J. Pol) (Norden, 1888). (*DB* 1901, 127 ff., where his portrait is found; *Biogr. Wb.* III, 787 f.; *N.N.B.Wb.* VII, 785-87; *ML* II, 306.)   vdZ.

Heubuden (*Heuboden*), a common Mennonite village name which was transplanted from Prussia to Russia and America. The name appeared in the following settlements: Bergthal, Russia; East and West reserves, Man.; Jansen, Neb.; Cuauhtemoc, Mexico; and Menno, Paraguay.   C.K.

Heubuden, a village in the former Free City of Danzig three miles northwest of Marienburg (1929 pop. 395) the seat of the former Mennonite congregation Heubuden-Marienburg, which was the largest rural congregation of East Germany. In 1929 the membership was 1,092 besides 358 children under 15. The members were mostly farmers and owned a total of over 25,000 acres. Most of them lived in the southern part of the Gross-Werder, a smaller part in Marienburg and east of the Nogat in former West Prussia, and several at Dirschau (Tczew) west of the Vistula on Polish territory. The ancestors were almost exclusively Dutch immigrants. In 1565 there were in the area of Heubuden some Mennonite renters who were making their payments to Koczelitzki. Until the middle of the 17th century the congregation apparently had no preacher and was served by the ministers of other congregations, especially Danzig. In 1662 Herrenhagen was settled. Mennonite settlers with hereditary leases settled on the former estates of the Teutonic Knights such as Leske, Diebau, Kaminke, Kalthof, Klein-Montau, Sandhof, Laase, and Schroop; similarly on lands owned by Marienburg in Dammfelde and Stadtfelde; they also purchased pieces of land in the *freikölmisch* villages or bought new estates on lands farther removed from the villages. So there were at a very early time Mennonites in Koczelitzki, Altenau, Klein-Lesewitz, Halbstadt, Tralau, Lichtenau, Simonsdorf, Gnojau, Kunzendorf, Altmünsterberg, Mielenz, Schönau, and Wernersdorf.

The manager of the estate belonging to the Marienburg castle about 1584 settled a number of immigrants from Brabant and Schottland on the estate lands. Among them there were some Mennonites. Upon the complaints of the citizens and the command of Sigismund III, these were denied all civil rights; but the manager in spite of manifold objections from the citizens settled craftsmen and tradesmen here again and again. Especially after 1672 the lowlands around the castle were settled by foreign, particularly Mennonite, tavernkeepers, *Höcker,* and craftsmen. In Kalthof the manager rented out lands owned by the city and permitted Mennonite potters and merchants to set up business there; thus in 1767 a Mennonite established a vinegar brewery. In the Werder gristmills were built, the oldest ones in 1747 at Koczelitzki and Leske. In 1748 the city of Marienburg leased the castle lowlands, and the Mennonites were now given the rights of citizenship.

Frequently the delegates at the various Landtags protested against toleration of the Mennonites (Mannhardt). As late as 1700 a resolution was drawn up forbidding Mennonite meetings in the Vorschloss (a street in Marienburg) and in the castle warehouses.

The Mennonite worship services were not public. In the 17th century they likely sang little at their meetings; but they had hymnbooks such as van Mander's *Gulden Harpe*. In 1724 and 1752 Dutch hymnbooks were printed at Amsterdam for the Prussian congregations. After the beginning of the 18th century there was singing at their meetings, the singing conducted by a chorister (*q.v.*). For their meetings they chose "either in the wintertime large rooms on the farms or in the summer good barns and large cow stables which were carefully cleaned and decorated with greenery. The preacher, when he preaches, sits on a high-backed chair and the hearers sit round about him" (Hartwich). "The preacher delivered his long address of two hours in the Dutch language seated and without an outline before him." It was the custom that each sermon was delivered on three Sundays. Already in 1671 Georg Hansen wrote that the youth could read German better than Dutch; nevertheless the Dutch language remained in use until 1750-60. In those years a beginning was made in preaching in German from notes and in a standing position. In 1767 German hymnbooks were introduced; nevertheless soon after the beginning of the 18th century Lobwasser's *Deutsche Psalmen* were used, which were incorporated into the first editions of the German Mennonite hymnal.

In the wars between Sweden and Poland the Mennonites "suffered severely under many war disturbances and extortion of money by Swedes, Russians, Saxons, and Poles, but always preserved their freedom of conscience and religion as far as was permitted in Catholic countries" (Donner). On July 18, 1626, the Marienburg castle surrendered to the Swedes. In 1656 Marienburg was besieged by the Swedes, in 1659 by the Poles. In 1698 began the quartering of soldiers in the third Swedish-Polish War, which continued in this region until 1715. The people of Heubuden had to deliver horses, grain, and other produce, as well as money payments. Marienburg and the Werder were occupied and plundered in turn by Swedish, Polish, Russian, and Saxon troops. In 1765 the people of Heubuden protested against oppressive Russian quartering which was illegally imposed on them.

Breaks in the dikes of the Vistula and Nogat caused great floods—1622 and 1652 at Wernersdorf, 1717 at Kalthof, 1786 at Gross-Montau, 1816 at Wernersdorf, 1839 at Kalthof, 1845 at Schönau, and the last and greatest on March 28, 1855, at Gross-Montau. In 1620 a plague raged in Marienburg, in 1624 in the Klein-Werder, and in 1710 in the Gross-Werder.

In 1638 the Jesuits had acquired the clerical lands in Koczelitzki. On Dec. 12, 1701, the Jesuit priest registered a complaint to the royal judge in Marienburg that the people living at Heubuden were refusing to pay the tithe, asserting that they had never paid it and besides paid conscientiously the fees for baptism, marriage, and burial, and in every respect submitted to the community law. On July 7, 1755, there was again a complaint, since according to the rescript of Aug. 2, on April 3, 1699, the Mennonites were to pay the pastoral fees for the liberty to baptize, marry, and bury, and especially they were to be present within a week from the birth of a child the permission for baptism. They were ordered to pay the fees of one florin for permission to baptize and for the right to marry and bury, as had been customary from olden times. "But with regard to the forbidden burial of unbaptized children among the baptized in the Mennonite cemetery, a special place beside the regular one where baptized Mennonites are buried shall be assigned to them and shall be fenced off by a fence." According to Hartwich, they buried their dead quietly in the Catholic cemeteries about 1700; they had to pay a high price for the lots to the Catholic priest. Not until 1775 were they released from payment of fees to the Catholic priests. The cemetery beside the church at Heubuden is mentioned for the first time in 1755. It was plotted and kept up by Mennonite owners of the land in the surrounding villages. In 1905 the congregation took over the burial place.

Until 1728 the congregation was served by the elders of Danzig and the Werder; by the Danzig elder demonstrably since 1694, while Elder Dirk Siemens of the Werder served the Elbing congregation. In 1728 Jacob Dyck was chosen as the first elder in Heubuden and confirmed in the office by Isaak de Veer of Danzig. He died in 1748. As early as 1741 upon the wish of the 81-year-old Elder Dyck, another elder, Gerhard von Bergen, had been chosen. In addition to the two elders there were now six preachers and one or two deacons in service. After the death of Elder von Bergen in 1771, Cornelius Regier was chosen as elder. He was succeeded in 1795 by Peter Braun. Preachers to be chosen were first called as deacons. From the ranks of the deacons the preachers were then chosen in the second stage of the election, and from among the preachers the elder was chosen. The right to vote was possessed by all male members above 21. According to the constitution adopted when the congregation became incorporated, preachers were to be chosen from among the membership.

By 1744 the congregation was so large "that they had preaching at two places on Sunday." For the members living further removed from Heubuden, services were held in the homes of members in Marienburg (Sandhof), Wernersdorf, Klein Lichtenau and Lesewitz in rotation every fourth Sunday and on the first of the holiday days. In 1774 when 14 Mennonite families had been settled by King Frederick II in Czattkau near Dirschau, these families joined the Heubuden congregation in 1778. Among them, as in the other outside locations, services were regularly held, so that there were now services every Sunday at two places, every fourth Sunday at three places, and on the first holiday day at six places. After 1700 the Flemish Mennonites living among the Frisians in the vicinity of Stuhm and Marienwerder became a subsidiary congregation, Jerczewo, united with the Heubuden congregation (see **Pastwa**). This congregation had its own preachers and deacons but was served by the elder of the Heubuden congregation and had a common treasury with Heubuden. In 1854 the congregation built a church in Pastwa. This sub-congregation with 81 members and over 20 children united with the Frisian congregation of Tragheimerweide in 1899.

A Privilegium granted by the Bishop of Culm on June 17, 1768, gave the Heubuden congregation and three other Mennonite congregations the right to build a church of wood 40 ells long, 22 ells wide, with walls 7 ells high, with a thatched roof and a chimney towering over the roof. The building was begun on July 19, 1768, but after considerable progress had already been made, it was forbidden by the bishop and after renewed efforts and expenses released again on Nov. 2 (see **Fürstenwerder**). When the work was halted, members of the congregation took individual parts of the church home and worked on them, so that rapid progress was made when the building was renewed and services were held in it at Christmas time. In 1853 the church was lengthened 14 feet and jacked up two feet and a masonry foundation laid. In its final stage it seated an audience of 800.

The congregation owned two houses each containing four apartments known as "hospitals" for poor members. They are listed for the first time in 1773 in the Prussian land records. An area of 6½ acres of cultivated land belonged to the "hospitals."

The Heubuden congregation, like those of Danzig, Gross-Werder, and Elbing, belonged to the Old Flemish branch (Danzig Old Flemish, *q.v.*). In the 18th century or perhaps at the end of the 17th, these congregations formed a Flemish conference with seven congregations in Holland, namely, Amsterdam, Haarlem, Rotterdam, Blokzijl, Zuidveen, Giethoorn Northside, and Oldemarkt. The Dutch language was used for church services in Heubuden until about 1770. The oldest confession of faith, as far as is known, was that of Georg Hansen, published in 1667 in the Dutch language. In 1730 it was signed by the elders and preachers of the Danzig, Heubuden, Gross-Werder, and Elbing congregations, then sent to the Dutch congregations in the conference, where it was copied and returned. They declared, "Although we have been parted for more than 100 years, nevertheless our confession has remained unchanged." This confession was printed in German in 1768 and used in the congregation until 1861. Beginning in 1862, the congregation used the confession of 20 articles worked out by Gerhard Wiebe of Elbing-Ellerwald in 1792. On Feb. 14, 1897, the congregation decided to adopt the confession worked out together by the Flemish and Frisian congregations.

For the instruction of baptismal candidates the congregation used the (Elbing) catechism compiled in 1778 by the elders Heinrich Donner of Orlofferfelde and Gerhard Wiebe of Elbing-Ellerwald, in 1929 in its ninth almost unchanged edition, in

1935 in a 10th (shortened) edition, there were, however, as early as 1700 instruction books in the form of questions and answers.

In the union of the Flemish congregations of 1730 one of the stipulations was that no one should be accepted in the brotherhood without baptism unless he had already been baptized in one of these united congregations. Members of a Frisian congregation were therefore rebaptized before being received into the Heubuden congregation. This custom was maintained until 1770, when the person to be received was admitted by simply answering some questions before the congregation if he had already been baptized. After 1819, an admission into the congregation was simply announced to the congregation. If anyone from another creed under the Polish government wished to unite with the Heubuden congregation, he had to travel to the Netherlands, be baptized there, and return as a Mennonite. After 1744 the latter could also be baptized in Königsberg, since there was a Mennonite elder there. Under the Prussian government the Mennonites were free to take in members of other confessions with the government's permission. This was later made almost impossible by the edict of July 30, 1789, according to which a person transferring from the state church no longer could retain all the privileges of citizenship (*kantonfrei*); however, in 1824 and 1828 concessions including all the rights of the (*kantonfrei*) Mennonites were still made. In 1910 in a meeting of the congregation, it was decided to admit persons of other Christian churches at their request without baptism.

Marriage with members of other churches was not permitted, and until 1775 marriage with Frisian Mennonites only when the latter joined the congregation. In the time of the strictest church discipline, a broken engagement was dealt with so severely "that not only was marriage forbidden to both, but the one breaking the engagement was excommunicated and not received again until the other died." A widower was also not permitted to marry the sister of his wife; if it happened, he was excommunicated as long as the marriage continued. This rule was dropped in 1826. Remarriage of divorced persons was not permitted. In the 1920's, however, several instances occurred in which the innocent member remarried.

Footwashing was practiced until about 1750, and especially "when an elder or teacher was called or sent into another congregation by God, so that his feet are washed when he arrived; also when a member of one congregation enters another congregation to remain."

Church discipline was carefully administered. In several meetings at the end of the 18th century and the beginning of the 19th, it was decided "to see to it that no member betray the smallest article of our faith unpunished." In cases of lesser disobedience, the one concerned had to appear before the church officers, in more serious instances, before the brotherhood; if there was no improvement, or if there were grievous offences, excommunication followed. A list of excommunicated members kept by the elder in 1805-99 still existed in 1929. After that, excommunication was not practiced.

"It was not customary for us to keep a systematic church book, and not necessary because the Polish government never demanded birth or death lists or birth, marriage, or death certificates. Each elder listed only as much as he needed for his own system." In 1775 the congregations were ordered by the Marienburg government "to draw up a list of those who were born in our congregation, had died, were married, or had attended communion." The church possessed a list of those baptized since 1771, church books on births, marriages, and deaths since Dec. 1, 1771, and a list of participants in communion since 1851. In the summer of 1799 they received instructions from the government to report all births, marriages, and deaths to the pastor of the state church. This regulation remained in effect until the introduction of the civil register in 1874.

"Since all of Polish Prussia was occupied by the King of Prussia on Dec. 13, 1772, and a day of homage was to be observed in Marienburg on Dec. 27 following, Peter Regier called the West Prussian congregations to a meeting at Tralauerfeld, to which the Flemish as well as the Frisian teachers came." Until then the officers of the Frisian and Flemish congregations had usually held separate meetings. Only at special occasions, as, for example, the granting of the Privilegiums of the Polish kings and bishops, did they appear together, because this was always very expensive. From this time on there were regular meetings for both areas, often several in the year. Because of the central location of the Heubuden Church most of the meetings were held in its territory. Of the two meetings in 1802 and the eight in 1813, six were held in the Heubuden Church.

On Aug. 22, 1774, the first taxes were collected by Preacher Hans Klaassen in Heubuden from all East and West Prussian congregations. Of the total of 13,495 souls, 1,831 were from Heubuden without Jerczewo. 503 of the 2,170 parcels (*Hufen*) of land were from Heubuden, and of the total sum of 30,624 guilders, 5,343 were from Heubuden. In the village of Heubuden, 67 Mennonite homes occupied 63 2/3 parcels of land.

In 1788, 17 families left the congregation with the first emigrants to Russia. No record was kept of further emigrations. According to the treasurer's books, there were frequent contributions for emigrants to Russia, especially in 1803, 1819, 1858, and 1869. On March 14, 1794, Elder Cornelius Regier and the preacher (*Lehrer*) Cornelius Warkentin traveled to South Russia to organize and establish the newly formed congregations there. Regier died on May 30 in South Russia. In 1795 the Heubuden congregation chose Peter Braun as elder. After his death, on June 11, 1803, Abraham Regier was chosen as elder on Jan. 6, 1804. After he had faithfully served the congregation for over 47 years, he died on Aug. 8, 1851. On May 20, 1852, Gerhard Penner was chosen as elder, serving until his emigration to America on May 30, 1877. Wilhelm Fast served from Oct. 28, 1877, to his death on Sept. 6, 1903. He was followed by Bernhard

Klaassen from Jan. 31, 1904, to March 8, 1927. Heinrich Dyck served 1924-35, and Bruno Ewert 1935-45. Gustav Reimer served as deacon 1919-45.

In 1807 began for the congregation the difficult times of the French occupation. Heubuden village had to raise 22,249 florins from June 6, 1807, to June 5, 1809, for the French occupation forces; in addition the individual families were heavily burdened by quartering French and Russian troops. For the fund of 187,439 florins for the release of Mennonites from duty in the army, Heubuden had to pay 28,582 florins according to the assessment that took place in the church. With such a burden, there were but few funds for the congregation itself.

The contributions for congregational needs were raised according to land acreage owned by the members; those who lived in towns were taxed according to their wealth and the size of their businesses, in proportion to the charge on the land. In 1794, the assessment per *Hufe* was 4 florins, in 1796, 6 florins, in 1820, 3 florins, in 1852, 2 talers per *Hufe*. After 1873 congregational funds were raised by assessments through taxes on land, buildings, trade, and income. In business affairs all male members who made financial contributions had the right to vote; independent women who contributed to the congregation could be represented by a male member who had a right to vote.

The great religious and intellectual movement of the early 19th century had also affected wide circles of the congregation. As early as 1817 connections were established with the Bible Society in Berlin, and contributions were sent in. In 1822 contributions were received for foreign missions. In 1823 the English Baptist missionary Angas (*q.v.*) visited the West Prussian Mennonite congregations in order to gain their participation in the work of foreign missions; they sent 635 talers to London. On Nov. 7, 1826, the Christian school at Rodlofferhuben (Kalthof), founded by members of the congregations of Heubuden and Danzig, was dedicated by Elder Jakob van der Smissen of Danzig. Here Mennonite boys were trained in a positive Christian atmosphere. The first teacher, Lange, was very competent. The school was transferred to Bröskerfelde (*q.v.*) in 1836. In the school at Rodlofferhuben, soon after its opening, monthly missionary meetings were instituted which were kept up in the homes of the members after the transfer of the school. The Missionary Association formed by Mennonites and some Protestants celebrated its first anniversary in the school in 1830. From 1837 to 1884 these celebrations were held at the homes of members in the barns or granaries, and from 1885 to 1891 in the Protestant chapel in Marienburg. Participation was active. These festivities for a long time furnished a gathering point for many friends of mission work from near and far. In addition there existed an association for home missions (a Bible, Tract, and Abstinence Association). The contributions were contributed to the Protestant mission until 1854, when they were sent to the Dutch Mennonite missions in Java and Sumatra. In 1892 the first missionary festival was celebrated in the church of Heubuden. From now on missionary activity was applied to the Dutch Mennonite Mission, for which the congregation had instituted collections ever since 1880. The monthly missionary meetings were held from 1895 to 1923 in the church, and after 1924 with very great participation again in private homes. Besides the collections the members of the congregation furnished the salary for two native missionary helpers in Sumatra.

In 1836 a Christian Reading Circle was organized in Heubuden by Jacob Regehr together with Mennonite friends and two Protestant teachers. Originally mostly missionary periodicals were read, but soon books were procured, chiefly entertaining literature on a Christian basis. By 1929 there were 1,100 volumes on hand in addition to a number of bound periodicals on family, missions, and Mennonite subjects. In 1886 there were 36 members in this association; in 1929, 52 members. In 1905 a library of Mennonite publications was established in the congregation.

Since the middle of the 19th century singing was cultivated by means of special choirs. In January 1865 it was decided to compile a new hymnal. The old hymnal (*Geistreiches Gesangbuch, 1780*), now 100 years old, had become quite voluminous through several appendices in nine editions. A committee was chosen to select the hymns; after completion, the new songbook (*Gesangbuch für Mennoniten-Gemeinden, 1869*) was accepted into use on the first advent Sunday of 1869. In 1890 the first organ was installed.

In the first decades of the 19th century, the members of the congregation who held pieces of land in perpetual lease (emphyteutic) had very great difficulty in maintaining them. According to the legal stipulations of 1811 to 1816 the emphyteuse was to be turned into private property, but the authorities did not allow the Mennonites who were exempt from military service to acquire this land and even threatened to withdraw the pieces of land from them if they would not assume military duties. After much negotiation, therefore, the king extended the lease contracts by the Order of Cabinet of Feb. 13, 1825, first until 1845, and on Dec. 3, 1838, finally to the end of 1864. Meanwhile on the basis of a new law of land purchase clearance the Mennonites succeeded in acquiring ownership of these emphyteutic pieces of land. The clearance fee expired in Heubuden in 1912 after 56 years.

The cancellation of release from military service through the law of Nov. 9, 1857, called forth a serious crisis in the West Prussian congregations, which, especially in the Heubuden congregation, lasted a long time and became very divisive. The elder, preachers, and a section of the congregation rejected the acceptance of military duty in any form in the hope that the military law could still be changed. The largest part of the congregation, however, was ready to assume noncombatant military service in the form designated in the Order of Cabinet of March 3, 1868. Thus a deep, painful gash was torn into the congregation; from autumn 1874 to summer 1876, no communion services were held. In 1876 there were only five baptismal candidates, the others having been baptized in other congregations. On May 30, 1877, Elder Gerhard Penner (*q.v.*) emigrated to Nebraska; the preachers and all but two of the deacons, the choristers and a part of the congregation left the church and began to hold services in private homes. The rest of the congregation, under the leadership of Elder Claass Friesen of Rosenort, chose preachers and deacons on Oct. 28, 1877, and on that date decided that the members of the congregation should be permitted to fulfill their military duties according to the stipulation of the order of cabinet. As elder they chose Wilhelm Fast on Oct. 25, 1878. From 1876 to 1892, 55 families and 29 individuals from the congregation moved to Kansas and Nebraska. Therewith the emigration which had lasted over 100 years came to its conclusion.

In consequence of the opening of railway bridges at Marienburg and Dirschau in 1857 and still more by means of the building of paved highways the church could be easily reached at any time even by members who lived rather far away. Upon their wish services were discontinued in Czattkau in 1897, in Wernersdorf and Lesewitz in 1907, in Klein-Lichtenau in 1911. For the members living in and around Marienburg a meetinghouse with a seating capacity of 350 was built in Marienburg in 1906-7, and dedicated on June 23, 1907. In 1919 there were 333 members of the congregation living here in 122 households.

During World War I 257 members were drafted. On the battlefield 25 brethren lost their lives, in whose memory a monument was erected in the cemetery in 1920. During the war and after, several other brethren died in consequence of military service. As a consequence of the treaty of Versailles the members of the congregation were living in three different countries (Free State Danzig, Germany, and Poland) with compulsory passport regulations at the borders and several kinds of money. Thereby communication was made very difficult. Members from Germany could not come to Poland without an expensive visa, and vice versa; nevertheless the feeling of belonging together did not diminish, but was rather strengthened.

The centuries old conflict with the Protestant State Church parishes on account of the tax requirements levied on Mennonite property owners was revived in 1920. A decision by the jurists of the University of Königsberg, arrived at in 1929 on a scientific basis, put an end to any such obligation.

The congregation was a member of the Conference of the West Prussian Mennonite Congregations, and since 1913 of the Vereinigung der Mennoniten Gemeinden im Deutschen Reich. It was incorporated in 1904. In the churches at Heubuden and Marienburg worship services were held (in 1929) on every Sunday and holiday. Communion was observed twice a year, and baptism on the second holiday of Pentecost at Heubuden. The congregation was served (in 1929) by an elder, six preachers, and three deacons. Financial and legal matters were managed by a committee of 12 district leaders with 6-year terms.

The number of souls in the congregation in the course of the century has been subject to great variations. The figures were as follows:

Year	Souls	Births	Baptisms	Marriages	Deaths
1774	1831	64	32	15	43
1789	1441	56	29	13	40
1804	1643	67	30	24	29
1846	1225	41	29	10	29
1864	1309	62	21	14	30
1881	1142	37	35	15	20
1910	1520	53	41	8	14
1929	1450	16	36	14	18
1941	1500				

Under Hitler the congregation experienced great changes under the influence of the current political and social philosophy. However, only eight families left the church. During World War II 200 to 250 young men were in service—they received a monthly bulletin from the congregation. Of this number about 100 died as war casualties and about as many were taken prisoner or were missing at the end of the war. When the Russian army occupied the community in early 1945 nearly all the men left at home and many of the girls and women were sent into forced labor in Siberia. Some later returned and reached West Germany. Numerous members of the congregation fled to Denmark during the approach of the Red army, and from there have gone to West Germany, Uruguay, and Canada. The last elder of the congregation, Bruno Ewert (1935-45), as well as the deacon, Gustav Reimer, Sr., emigrated to Uruguay in 1950. The church building has been turned into a Catholic church.

The Heubuden Church had a branch (with meetinghouse) in Marienburg (*q.v.*). It had two homes for the aged and two cemeteries. Before World War II the total Mennonite population of the congregation was around 1,500, of whom 360 were children. (†*ME* I.) A.D.

W. Mannhardt, *Die Wehrfreiheit der Altpreussischen Mennoniten* (Marienburg, 1863); A. Hartwich, *Landesbeschreibung der drei Werder* (Königsberg, 1722); H. Nottarp, *Die Mennoniten in den Marienburger Werdern, eine kirchenrechtliche Untersuchung* (Halle, 1929); idem, *Ergänzungsgutachten* (Königsberg, 1931); Reiswitz and Wadzeck, *Beiträge zur Kenntnis der Mennonitengemeinden in Europa und Amerika* (Berlin, 1821); Bruno Ewert, "Four Centuries of Prussian Mennonites," *Menn. Life* III (April 1948) 10-18; idem, "From Danzig to Denmark," *Menn. Life* I (January 1946) 37; *Gem.-Kal.,* 1941, 143; Ernst Crous, "Vom Pietismus bei den altpreussischen Mennoniten . . . ," *Menn. Gesch.-Bl.,* 1954; *ML* II, 306-12.

Heukelom, van, a Mennonite family, since the end of the 17th century found at Leiden, Dutch province of South Holland, and since the 18th century also in Amsterdam. Their ancestor Hendrik van Heukelom, of Goch, Germany, in 1615 left the Roman Catholic Church and joined the Mennonite congregation of Goch. He was married, first to Janneken Hol, then to Grietje Kops of a well-known Mennonite family living in the Lower Rhine district (see **Kops** family). Until the 19th century the family name of van Heukelom was very common in the Goch congregation. At least two great-grandchildren of Hendrik van Heukelom, Matthys and Johannes, moved from Goch to

Leiden. His son, Matthijs van Heukelom, b. 1663 at Goch, d. 1725 at Leiden, married to Trijntje Floh of Crefeld, was a deacon at Leiden 1692-94, and 1697-1704, and 1714-18, and then the manager of "De Hoeksteen," a home for the aged. He was a merchant and woolen weaver, as were many of his descendants, nearly all of whom also served the church as deacons or as managers of the Hoeksteen home. One member of this family, Frans van Heukelom (1738-87), married to Elisabeth Hartsen, moved from Leiden to Amsterdam; he and his descendants were merchants and bankers.

Many of the van Heukeloms were prominent in the leadership of the Dutch Mennonite Church. Walraven van Heukelom (1775-1853) of Amsterdam was treasurer of the A.D.S. (General Dutch Mennonite Conference), as was his cousin Hendrik Pieter van Heukelom (b. 1868), during the years 1907-41. Jean Charles van Heukelom (1840-1912) of Amsterdam was treasurer of the North Holland Mennonite Widow's Fund and the *Verhogingsfonds* (*q.v.*), and Lodewijk Casper van Heukelom (1847-1920) of Amsterdam, director of the Netherlands Bank, was also treasurer of the *Verhogingsfonds*. vDZ.

Ned. Patriciaat IV (1913) 1741-81; XXVII (1941) 140-57; *DJ* 1850, 143, 179; *DB* 1898, 112; 1907, 145; 1912, 220.

Heuning, Roelof, b. at Westzaan, d. Jan. 25, 1801, at Groningen, a Dutch Mennonite preacher who served the congregations of Edam 1760-71, and Groningen (Old Flemish) 1771-1804. He was elder and moderator (*Commissaris*) of the Groningen Old Flemish Conference from 1775 until his death. In this function he corresponded with some congregations in Prussia, like Kleinsee (*q.v.*), which had been struck in 1781 by a severe crop failure and was given financial support by the Groningen Old Flemish Sociëteit. Roelof Heuning or Honig(h) may have been a relative of the Honig (*q.v.*) family found in the Dutch Zaan district. vDZ.

Inv. Arch. Amst. I, Nos. 1730 ff.; Blaupot t. C., *Groningen* I, 135; *DB* 1890, 111.

Heusdens, F. C., a Reformed missionary, who after having been active on the Indonesian island of Celebes, was in 1940 appointed as an administrator of the leper colony at Donorodjo (*q.v.*) on the island of Java. This colony was founded and managed by the Dutch Mennonite Mission Society. In March 1942, during World War II, when the Japanese captured and occupied the Dutch East Indies, a crowd of fanatical Mohammedans attacked the leper camp of Donorodjo, and Heusdens was stoned to death. vDZ.

Verslagen van het Doopsgezind Zendingsveld op Java, 1940-47, 2, 12, 14; *Jaarverslag Doopsgez. Zendingsvereniging* 1945-49, 4.

Heuven, Arent van, a silk merchant at Utrecht, in the Netherlands, was 1646-74 a preacher of the Utrecht (*q.v.*) Mennonite congregation. Being an adherent of the moderate views of Galenus Abrahamsz (*q.v.*), van Heuven and his copreachers Goris van Aldendorp, Johan Andries (van Aken), and Willem van Maurik (*q.v.*) in 1658 came into conflict with Robert van Hoogveldt (*q.v.*), also a preacher of the congregation, who was conservative and an antagonist of Galenus. These three preachers published *Een belydenisse aengaende de voornaemste Leer-stucken des Christelycken Godtsdienst* (Utrecht, 1659) and *Wijdt-loopiger Verhael van de beklaeglijcke Onlusten, onder de Vlaemsche Doopsgezinden binnen Utrecht in den jaere 1661* (against Robert van Hoogveldt) (Utrecht, 1662). On a charge of Socinianism (*q.v.*) van Heuven and the three other preachers were suspended from their office by the city government of Utrecht on Aug. 12, 1661. They were allowed to preach again on Aug. 4, 1664, after they had declared that they agreed with the published confession of the Mennonites. In the meanwhile a part of the congregation had begun to meet separately and this division lasted until 1675. A new conflict with the Reformed and the city government arose in 1666. Now van Maurik and van Heuven refused to sign a confession drawn up by the Reformed ministers, but finally the city government was content with a statement made by van Maurik, van Heuven, and Aldendorp. Particulars about van Heuven were not available. His years of birth and death are unknown. (*Biogr. Wb.* III, 806-7; *DB* 1916, 145-95 *passim*.) vDZ.

Heydanus, Caspar: see **Heidanus, Caspar.**

Heyden, Caspar van der: see **Heidanus, Caspar.**

Heyden, Jan van der, b. 1637 at Gorinchem, Dutch province of South Holland, d. March 28, 1712, at Amsterdam, was baptized in the Flemish church "bij 't Lam" at Amsterdam in 1656 and served this congregation three periods as a deacon (1675-80, 1686-91, 1696-1701).

Jan van der Heyden is renowned for his technical inventions: in 1669 he was appointed director of the service of street-lighting and organized a lighting system in Amsterdam that was unique in Europe. He is still more famous for his invention of a fire-engine in 1677. From 1672, in which year he and his brother Nicolaas were appointed directors of fire-extinguishing appliances, they had worked on this invention. Soon after Jan van der Heyden founded a fire-engine factory.

Jan van der Heyden is also known as a painter; and a number of pictures, mostly of buildings, still bear evidence of his skill and artistry. His son Goris van der Heyden was also a deacon of the Amsterdam Lamist congregation, 1701-6. Jan's granddaughter (daughter of his son Jan) Jacoba (1705-31) was married to the well-known Mennonite preacher Joannes Deknatel (*q.v.*). vDZ.

Bericht Wegens de nieuw-geinventeerde en geoctroyeerde Slang-brandspuiten. Uitgevonden door Jan en Nicolaes van der Heyden (Amsterdam, 1677); *Amstelodamum Jaarboek* XI, 1913, 29-118 f.; *Amsterdamsche Stadtsgezichten van Jan van der Heyden,* with introduction by C. J. 't Hooft (Amsterdam, 1912); W. v. Bode, *Die Meister der Holländischen und Flämischen Malerschulen* (Leipzig, 1951) 365-69, 373-78.

Heylbronn, Hendrik van, b. Feb. 4, 1697, at Heilbronn, Germany, d. Dec. 4, 1782, at Almelo, Dutch province of Overijssel, about whose youth nothing is known. His official name was Johann Heinrich

Gramm von Heilbronn. In the spring of 1729 he came from Goch, where he was baptized on his faith, to Almelo, where he married Geessien Warnaars in 1729, and in 1730 became a member of the Mennonite congregation. In Almelo he was a physician. On June 21, 1742, he received his medical doctor's degree from the University of Groningen. Besides his care for his patients he found time to give expression to his passion, the making of clocks. Six clocks, made by van Heylbronn, all very beautiful and giving evidence of great skill, are still in existence. One is found in the Mennonite church of Almelo. His son Peter (1730-76) was a clockmaker by trade. vDZ.

Verslagen en Meded. Ver. v. Overijsselsch Regt en Gesch. LIX, second series XXV (Deventer, 1943) 104-8, with pictures of clocks made by Hendrik van Heylbronn.

Heylken Baillaerts, an Anabaptist martyr, was executed at Antwerp, Belgium, on Feb. 17, 1573, together with four others, because he was rebaptized and had attended the meetings of the Mennonites. (*Antw. Arch.-Blad* XIII, 105 f., 174; XIV, 90 f., No. 1012.) vDZ.

Heyman Jacops van Ouderamstel was appointed sheriff of Amsterdam in February 1534, succeeding Jan Hubrechts, who had been a friend of the Anabaptists. He was ordered to adopt rigorous measures against the Anabaptists, but being unwilling to punish heretics and having been reproved on that account by the imperial stadholder, he soon withdrew from the office (October 1534). In 1535, being a burgomaster of the city, he protected the Anabaptists as much as he could. He is said to have been an Anabaptist himself, but this is an error. (*Inv. Arch. Amst.* I, No. 187; Kühler, *Geschiedenis* I, 93, 134, 177.) vDZ.

Heynderickgen Aert Kielezdochter of Harderwijk, a martyr, was bound in a sack and drowned at Delft, Dutch province of South Holland, on Jan. 17, 1539, together with four other women. She likely was a follower of David Joris (*q.v.*). (*Inv. Arch. Amst.* I, No. 749.) vDZ.

Heyndrick Pietersz, a grain merchant and active in early Dutch Anabaptism (Mellink, *Wederdopers,* 133, 264-65), is likely identical with Hendrik Koel (*q.v.*). vDZ.

Heyndri(c)k van Dale, an Anabaptist martyr, was drowned at Antwerp, Belgium, on April 3, 1562, because he "persisted in his heresy of rebaptism." He was unmarried. He had been baptized by Joachim de Suyckerbacker (*q.v.*). Van Braght's *Martyrs' Mirror,* who calls him simply Hendrik, gives Aug. 15, 1561, as the date of the death of a group of seven martyrs which included Hendrik. This is an error. The song mentioned by van Braght in which Hendrik and other martyrs are celebrated and beginning, "Lieve broeders, wij groeten u met sanghen" (Dear Brethren, we greet you with hymns), is found in the *Nieu Liedenboeck* of 1562 and is included by Wackernagel in *Lieder der . . . Reformierten.* (*Mart. Mir.* D 288, E 655; *Antw. Arch.-Blad* IX, 132, 140; XIV, 30 f., No. 353.) vDZ.

Heyne Walingsz, an Anabaptist martyr, arrested at "Krommenieërdijk in Waterlandt," i.e., near Krommenie, Dutch province of North Holland, was put to death very likely in 1534 (not 1542 as van Braght states). (*Mart. Mir.* D 62, E 464; *DB* 1917, 170.)   vnZ.

Heynes, Richt, an Anabaptist martyr: see **Richt.**

Heyningen, Gerardus van, b. Jan. 11, 1716, at Amsterdam, d. Jan. 3, 1801, at Amsterdam, studied at the University at Utrecht, where he obtained his Ph.D. degree in 1736, then studied at the Amsterdam Mennonite Seminary, was preacher of the Mennonite congregations of Utrecht 1739-58 and Amsterdam "bij 't Lam" 1758-1801. His colleague, H. Tichelaar, on Feb. 15, 1801, delivered his funeral sermon on Rev. 14:13b, *Lijkrede op G. v. Heyningen* (Amsterdam, 1801, with portrait). Van Heyningen was a very active and influential man in the Amsterdam congregation. He tried to promote the establishment of more old people's homes. He had some typical ideas: when the church board discussed projects such as the establishment of a school for the poor children of the Amsterdam congregation, such as was founded in Haarlem, van Heyningen opposed it and the school never came into being. On May 19, 1796, he wrote a letter to the church board announcing that henceforth no more marriages should be performed in the meetinghouse.

Van Heyningen was married to Maria de Heger of Utrecht. He stemmed from a prominent and well-to-do Dutch Mennonite family of Amsterdam, where they have been living since the early 17th century, while other members lived at Utrecht. Gerardus van Heyningen was the son of Gerrit van Heyningen (1688-1749) and Elisabeth de Clercq. Besides his doctor's thesis *De Mente Humana* he published a funeral sermon on the death of his colleague and uncle, Bartholomeus van Leuvenigh (*q.v.*): *Lykrede* (Amsterdam, 1760).   vnZ.

Inv. Arch. Amst. II, Nos. 754, 848, 963 f.; *Naamlijst* 1802, 59; *DB* 1868, 97; 1898, 20, 30 f.; *Biogr. Wb.* IV, 12 f.

Heynrick Cornelisz, an otherwise unknown Anabaptist martyr, arrested at Leiden, Dutch province of South Holland, on the night of Jan. 24, 1535, and beheaded on Feb. 3, 4, or 5 of that year at Leiden. Together with a number of other martyrs Heynrick died singing. He was probably an adherent of Münsterite principles, though this fact is not evident from the sentence. (Kühler, *Geschiedenis* I, 156, Notes 1 and 3.)   vnZ.

Heynrick Willemsz (Willemken van Stellinckwerf), a Dutch revolutionary Anabaptist, follower of Jan van Batenburg (*q.v.*), was beheaded at Utrecht in the Netherlands on July 21, 1544. (Mellink, *Wederdopers,* see Index.)   vnZ.

Heynrick (Heyndric) **Willemsz,** an Anabaptist martyr, a native of Hazerswoude, Dutch province of South Holland, was burned at the stake at The Hague on April 25, 1534. He belonged to a group of revolutionary Anabaptists, whose execution was dated by van Braght (*Mart. Mir.* D 34, E 441) in 1532.   vnZ.

Inv. Arch. Amst. I, 744, 745; *DB* 1917, 121, No. 139; Mellink, *Wederdopers,* 190.

Heyst, van, a Dutch Mennonite family, whose ancestor Michiel van Heyst, b. 1556 at Antwerp, d. after 1627 in Amsterdam, emigrated because of persecution from Antwerp to the Netherlands, first to Haarlem (about 1595) and in 1610 to Amsterdam. His son was Pieter van Heyst, b. 1598 at Haarlem, d. 1647 at Amsterdam, where he was a broker. David van Heyst (*q.v.*), who was a great-grandson of Michiel, was a Mennonite preacher. The son of this David, also David van Heyst (1713-84), founded the former Banking House *Van Heyst en Zoon* at Amsterdam. In the 18th century this family was related with well-known Amsterdam Mennonite families such as Leeuw, van Leuvenigh, Willink, and Blaauw. (*Ned. Patriciaat* XXXVI, 1950, 188-93.)   vnZ.

Heyst, David van, a Mennonite minister, b. 1675 at Amsterdam, d. May 23, 1746, at Maarsen, married to Rebecca Leeuw and through this marriage became a man of means. He was a preacher of the Amsterdam Zonist congregation 1701-16. A conflict with his colleague Harmen Reynskes van Overwijk, who accused van Heyst of sympathizing with the ideas of Spinoza, caused the dismissal of both preachers. Van Heyst accepted a call to Rotterdam in September 1718, but here too he soon experienced some difficulty, being charged by his deacon Jan Suderman of heterodoxy. Van Heyst was called to account for his Spinozism by the burgomaster of Rotterdam and had to present a confession of his faith to the Reformed ministers. This confession was approved in 1719. He seems to have given some offense to his congregation by his sympathy with the Moravian Brethren (Hernhutters) and the Collegiants (*q.v.*); especially his holding meetings on each Monday evening for young Mennonite women who were Collegiants was severely criticized by a large part of the congregation. In 1726 van Heyst resigned. The following books by van Heyst were published: *Onzydig onderzoek uit de H. Schriften van de wyduitgestrekte verlossing door Christus' Rantsoendood* (Haarlem, n.d.); *Onderwys nopens de voornaamste leerstellingen van den Christelyken Godsdienst* (Amsterdam, 1753); *Verzaameling van eenige uitgeleezene Predikatiën* (Amsterdam, 1759).

At the end of his life his sympathy seems to have turned to the Reformed Church; his grandson David van Heyst was a Reformed minister. (*Inv. Arch. Amst.* I, Nos. 713, 927; II, 2, No. 458 h; *Biogr. Wb.* IV, 22 f.; *N.N.B.Wb.* VIII, 769.)   vnZ.

Hickory County, Missouri, in the central part of the state and approximately 100 miles southeast of Kansas City, had three Mennonite churches in the last half of the 19th century. The Amish Mennonite settlement had its beginning with the arrival of Joseph Nafziger sometime before 1856, the year in which the Daniel Raber family from Lee Co., Iowa, arrived and located near several Amish families who had preceded them. The list of Hickory County Mennonite family names includes Christner, Klopfenstein, Gerber, Miller, Yoder, Kauffman, Stucky, Nafziger, Raber, Hochstettler, Neuenschwander, Rufenacht, Lehman, Diener, Schindler, Oesch, Rich, Syler, Aker, Roth, Stoll, Gilliom, Bahler, and Gerster.

In 1867 the *Herald of Truth* reported that there were 15 Mennonite families in Hickory County but that the community did not have a minister. In December 1870 when Preacher Joseph Stucky (*q.v.*) from Illinois visited the congregation Carl F. Kuntz was ordained bishop of the church in Hickory County. After worshiping in homes for many years, the congregation built a church about 4½ miles southwest of Wheatland on land donated by Christian Gerber and therefore known as Gerber's Church, although Gerber had by that time become affiliated with the General Conference Mennonite group in the county.

The Egli Amish (Defenseless Mennonites) also became established in the county, winning some of the Amish Mennonites to their fellowship. Their meetinghouse was built earlier than the Gerber Church and was located approximately one mile north of the place where the Gerber Church was later built. The two groups were settled in the Wheatland prairie, with their farms between points east of Elkton on the south and Quincy to the north.

The General Conference Mennonites had a small congregation in the south part of the county, known as the Elkton (*q.v.*) Church. The few families had services in homes and schoolhouses and for a time were served by Minister Peter S. Lehman, formerly from Berne, Ind. After he left the county, ministers were supplied by the church in Morgan County.

When the settlement was established, land was in open range and comparatively cheap. Because both the northern and southern armies swept through the county in the Civil War days, the Amish settlers were impoverished. The ending of the open range and the scarcity of good soil beyond the limits of the Wheatland prairie brought economic hardships to the settlement that resulted in its extinction. Only a few families remained in the county beyond the first decade of the 20th century. At least as early as 1882 Mennonite families began to leave the settlement for Johnson Co. (*q.v.*), Mo. The H. P. Krehbiel census of 1911 lists only one Mennonite church in the county, the Defenseless Church of nine members with Christian Zehr of Quincy serving as minister.   M.G.

Hiebert (Huebert, Hubert, Hübert), a Prussian Mennonite name first recorded in the Danzig church record in 1679, was found in the congregations of Tiegenhagen, Ladekopp, Rosenort, Heubuden, and Königsberg. From Prussia the name was transplanted to Russia. Outstanding bearers in Russia were Heinrich Hübert (*q.v.*), the first elder of the Mennonite Brethren Church, and Johann Hübert (*q.v.*), a missionary to Java. From Russia the name was transplanted to America, where the following have been prominent in the work of the M.B. Church: John K. Hiebert (1865-1933), Hillsboro, Kan., pastor

at Ebenfeld M.B. church; N. N. Hiebert (1874-   ), Blaine, Wash., pastor; P. C. Hiebert (1878-   ), Hillsboro, long-time (1920-53) chairman of the MCC and sometime president of Tabor College; C. N. Hiebert (1881-   ), Hillsboro, evangelist; G. B. Huebert (1887-   ), Reedley, Cal., pastor; P. N. Hiebert (1890-   ), Bakersfield, Cal., pastor; J. C. Hiebert (1904-   ), missionary to India; G. D. Huebert (1906-   ), Hepburn, Sask., pastor and Bible teacher; D. Edmund Hiebert (1910-   ), teacher in the M.B. Biblical Seminary, Fresno, Cal.; Waldo Hiebert, Hillsboro, pastor; and Lando Hiebert, minister and teacher at Tabor College, Hillsboro. The Hiebert family has been primarily an M.B. family in North America. In 1955 the only Hiebert serving as a minister in any other Mennonite body was J. N. Hiebert, E.M.B. pastor at Dalmeny, Sask.   C.K.

Gustav E. Reimer, *Die Familiennamen der Westpreussischen Mennoniten* (Weierhof, 1940).

Hiebert, John K. (1865-1933), minister of the Mennonite Brethren Church, was born at Einlage, Chortitza Mennonite settlement, South Russia, Sept. 8, 1865, the third child of Cornelius and Katharina Wiens Hiebert. In 1876 the family emigrated to America and settled on a farm southeast of Hillsboro, Kan. Here John grew up and received his education in the Gnadenau school. Through extensive reading he later broadened his education. After his conversion he joined the Ebenfeld M.B. Church through baptism April 16, 1880, and became an active member. On Dec. 15, 1891, he married Sarah Eitzen and established a farm home in the same locality. To them six children were born. The four sons entered the medical profession.

Hiebert was deeply interested in Christian work and very active in church life. In 1904 the church elected him to the ministry and three years later ordained him. In December 1915 the pastoral leadership was entrusted to him, a position he held until shortly before his death.

The M.B. Church found in him a strong advocate of educational advance. In the founding of Tabor College he took a prominent part and became the first chairman of the board of directors of the school, serving 20 years on the board. Hiebert was also a supporter of the Bethesda Hospital, Goessel, Kan., and served on its board of directors for some time. In the M.B. Conference he was an active worker making his most noted contribution in connection with the Publication Committee, on which he served as secretary for 30 years. He died at Hillsboro, Jan. 9, 1933, and was buried at the Ebenfeld M.B. Cemetery.   J.H.L.

Hierschau, a Mennonite village of the Molotschna settlement in South Russia, on the left bank of the Begim-Tchokrak, originally planned as a model village, whence its name. Plantings of fruit trees surrounded the regularly spaced farm buildings with lush green and yielded a considerable annual income. On the opposite side the gardens and the charming grove planted by the settlers were nearly destroyed in the Revolution and suffered from the drought in 1921-22.

Hierschau was founded in 1848 by settlers from the older Molotschna villages. Area, apportionment of land, number of farms, etc., are shown in the following table:

	Acres	Farms	Units (Höfe)	Population
1848	5,216	30 with 174 acres	30	201 Mennonites
1915	6,234	30 with 174 acres	62	427 Mennonites
1926	5,297	22 with 87 acres	62	373 Mennonites

Each full farm was given about an acre of additional land in the original plan to be used as a building site for a half farm; all of these were occupied by the sons of the owners by 1870, so that Hierschau had 30 full farms, 30 half farms, and a school plot, in addition to the original central thoroughfare, which had now also been built up, making a total of 62 farms. The school was built in 1852.

Under the rigid control of the Ohrloff Agricultural Association, the village was very symmetrically built. The houses were all made of burned tile. Besides the very productive soil, Hierschau before the Revolution also owned clay-pits which contributed to the prosperity of the village. The fate of Hierschau under the Soviets and during World War II was the common one of the Molotschna (*q.v.*) villages. (*ML* II, 312.)   D.H.E.

Hiestand (Histand, Heistand, Heystandt), a Mennonite family represented chiefly in the Franconia and Ontario conferences (MC). The progenitor of the American Hiestands was one Abraham Hiestand, a member of the Reformed Church in Switzerland, who was born about 1703, and as a young man emigrated to Pennsylvania. In eastern Pennsylvania he and his wife united with the Mennonite Church. A deacon in the Lancaster Conference (MC) bore the name Hiestand, as did Preacher Jacob Histand (1791-1877) of the Franconia Conference (MC), and his well-known grandson, Bishop A. O. Histand (1869-1943) of Doylestown, Pa. Paul W. Histand, a nephew of the latter, is pastor of the Trevose Heights Mission.
                                                        J.C.W.

High German Mennonites, or Upper Germans, in the Dutch sources called *Hoogduitsche Doopsgezinden* or simply *Hoogduitschers,* sometimes also called *Overlanders,* were a group of Mennonites originally found in South Germany and along the Rhine. This was the group to which the elders Zylis (*q.v.*) and Lemke (*q.v.*) belonged who disagreed with Menno Simons concerning shunning. The conferences held at Strasbourg in 1556 and 1559 were also meetings of the High Germans. Many of these High Germans made contacts with the Swiss Mennonites, especially in South Germany, and soon became one body with them. A number of High Germans, usually merchants, moved to the Netherlands, and were found in cities like Haarlem, Amsterdam, and Leiden. During the troubles when the Dutch Mennonites were divided into several branches "High German" became one of the party names, indicating a rather moderate group, which was averse to severity in banning and shunning. In 1591 a number of German congregations agreed with some Dutch congregations of Young Frisians on several points. The result of this agreement is the Concept of Cologne (*q.v.*). Henceforth in the Netherlands High German congregations began to unite with other groups, first with Young or Soft Frisians (*q.v.*), about 1600 also with the Waterlanders. So the *Bevredigde Broederschap* (group of churches who had made peace) came into being. For a while some troubles in Haarlem and Amsterdam (see **Afgedeelde Broederschap**) disturbed the peace, and though the union of the High Germans with the Waterlanders was criticized by a large number of congregations in the Rhine province of Germany who held meetings at Gladbach in 1608 and Geyn near Cologne in 1616 to protest against unification with the Waterlanders, the unification proceeded. After the United Congregation of High Germans and Frisians at Amsterdam had presented a confession in 1630 (Confession of Jan Cents), serious negotiations were made between this congregation and the Amsterdam Flemish congregation *bij 't Lam* which led to a union of both groups in 1639. From then on the High Germans as a special group disappeared in the Netherlands.   vdZ.

Kühler, *Geschiedenis* I, 322-28, 458, 461; II, 71-74, 89-94, 193-94, 197-99; *BRN* VII, *passim; Inv. Arch. Amst.* I, Nos. 525, 532, 536, 542, 544, 546, 555, 556, 600-2, 605-6, 628; II, Nos. 1193-1203, 1379, II, 2, No. 865b; *DB* 1894, 36-38; K. Vos, *Menno Simons* (Leiden, 1914) 140-43; Blaupot t. C., *Friesland,* 169.

In Germany, at Friedrichstadt a.d. Eider (*q.v.*), the High Germans may have had at their best about 100 members; about them there is less information than about the other groups; the strongest group, the Frisians, numbered about 400 members. Since the increase from the region around the Lower Rhine benefited the Flemish and Waterlanders who had united early, nothing was left for the High German element (with the exception of the Palatine families which strengthened them about five years before the general union of 1698) but the lowland plains, from the uncertainties from which people sought refuge in the privileged free city. Names like Clausen, Peters, and Jacobs have a High German stamp. Since they were least in numbers, union was more essential to them; they felt most closely drawn to the Flemish, whose preachers at a conference held in Hamburg, May 3, 1639, had for reasons of geography broken the previous close ties with the Flemish party in Hamburg and Glückstadt, and allied themselves more closely with their brethren in the adjacent region of Eiderstedt; from 1653 on there was a "Hochduytse en flaemse vereinigde Doopsgezinden gemeynte." In Eiderstedt (*q.v.*), where the High Germans were represented especially in Koldenbüttel and Tetenbüll by farmers, they lost members by transfer; according to the charter they were not permitted to organize a congregation of their own, hence the Mennonites growing up there tended more and more to give up their connections with Friedrichstadt, especially because at this place the Dutch language was retained too long (1828) for divine services. In the country there was therefore increasing conformity to the immediate surroundings.

In Hamburg there was from the beginning a preponderance of Flemish; through transfer to them the Frisian congregation had dissolved by 1671; the High German group suffered the same lot, for they—like those of Friedrichstadt—were not permitted to have their own meetinghouse, but were allowed to have meetings like Bible study groups in private homes; the only preacher named for their group was Johann Peltz(er), who lived in Hamburg and died early in 1660; his widow became a Lutheran, was baptized, and married a Lutheran. (*ML* II, 320.)　　　　R.Do.

High Schools. The term "high school" is a technical one in American education. In the history of American secondary education, Latin schools were slowly replaced by English grammar schools, which came to be known as academies. In New England the academy movement began with the establishment of the Phillip's Academies in 1778 and 1781. By 1833, 14 states had established 497 such schools. The academy movement attained its greatest influence in the period 1830-70. The academy generally was a democratic school, with a broad curriculum, supported by fees and gifts, operated as a boarding school, open to boys and girls, and established by groups of private citizens. The academies were slowly replaced by the "free academies," supported by taxes, and by high schools. In 1821 Boston established an English classical school which three years later came to be known as the "English High School" and which introduced the specific use of the term which has become universal for this type of school in the United States. The essential features of the high schools were support through public taxation and control through publicly elected officials. In time the name was adopted for some Canadian secondary schools, although the more common name is Collegiate Institute.

Strictly speaking Mennonite parochial secondary schools are therefore not high schools, although the term has been used in a number of instances as shown below: Eden Bible and High School (*q.v.*); Alberta Mennonite High School (*q.v.*); Bethany Christian High School (*q.v.*). The term "academy" has been generally used for Mennonite secondary schools (see **Secondary Education**).　　　　M.G.

Highland Bethel Mennonite Church, Ft. Wayne, Ind., is a member of the Evangelical Mennonite Conference. In 1937 a Sunday school was started in a new addition of the city and several months later an auditorium was erected. The first regular service was held in it on Dec. 19, 1937. The church was organized on Nov. 19, 1944, with 21 charter members. By 1948 the membership had increased to 35. Pastors who have served the congregation are Milo Rediger, Paul Rupp, and M. L. Klopfenstein.　　　　M.L.K.

Highland Church of God in Christ Mennonite Church, organized in 1937, is located south of De-Ridder, Beauregard Parish, La. The church had a membership of 105 and a Sunday-school enrollment of 140 in 1955. Weekly Sunday-school and worship services are held, with P. W. Decker as minister in charge, assisted by Chester Johnson.　　　　AL.S.

Hijum, the name of a Mennonite congregation in the province of Friesland. Leenaert Bouwens baptized seven persons here. The first mention of a Hijum congregation is found in the resolutions of the Frisian Mennonite brotherhood in 1713; it consisted then of 15 unsupported members. The name Hijum is also found in the *Naamlijst* of 1784, but no longer in 1786. Blaupot ten Cate and Wartena assume that the Hijum congregation was at that time merged with Hallum (*q.v.*). But in all probability Hijum and Hallum were variant names of the same congregation, the latter being adopted when in 1779 it was decided to build the new church one mile north in Hallum. Hence the present church at Hallum owns the land (6 acres) which had been the property of the Hijum church. There is no further information on the church at Hijum.　　　　S.D.A.W.

Blaupot t. C., *Friesland*, 88 f., 244, 306; *Naamlijst* 1731-84; *DB* 1890, 103; 1910, 124 f., 139-41; *ML* II, 385.

Hikkes (Heckens, Hiekens), **Amme,** was an elder of the Old Flemish congregation at Midwolde in Groningen, Netherlands. Although little is known concerning him, he was without doubt an important and influential person. He attended various meetings at which disputes were settled or important resolutions passed, as the meetings of Nov. 15, 1685, and April 11, 1686, at Knijpe in Friesland, where Age Jouckes had to clear himself of the suspicion of unorthodoxy. His presence was also requested at Groningen, June 2, 1685, to form a resolution concerning the brethren who had participated in the meetings of the Collegiants. (*DB* 1870, 111, 114; 1879, 5, 13; 1883, 75; *ML* III, 312.)　　　　vDZ.

Hilarius, a minister of the Lutheran Church at Worms, Germany, was won over to the Anabaptist views in January 1527, together with his colleague Jakob Kautz. Both had to answer to the city council for their opinions. Kautz later became a convinced Anabaptist, but about Hilarius no further information is available.　　　　vDZ.

Chr. Hege, *Die Täufer in der Kurpfalz* (Frankfurt, 1908) 34 f.

Hildebrand (Hildebrandt, Hilbrandt), a Mennonite name of Prussian background originally found in the congregations Rosenort, Fürstenwerder, Tiegenhagen, and Ladekopp. From here the name was transplanted to Russia and America. In Russia Peter Hildebrandt (*q.v.*) was an outstanding pioneer minister, Kornelius Hildebrandt (*q.v.*) was a pioneer industrialist, and J. J. Hildebrand, now Winnipeg, has written a number of books on the Mennonites. There are also some Hildebrands among the Mennonites (MC) of Virginia. (Reimer, *Familiennamen*.)　　　　C.K.

Hildebrand, Jakob Peter (d. 1867), son of Peter Hildebrand (*q.v.*), living on the island of Chortitza in the Dniepr in South Russia, was ordained as a minister of the Kronsweide Mennonite Church (*q.v.*) in 1825 and as elder in 1826. During his long term of service (1825-67) during the difficult

pioneering years of the settlement, he devoted himself to the development of the congregation. He was a lay preacher, making his living by farming.
J.H.E.

Hildebrand Mennonite Church (MC), located in Augusta Co., Va., ½ mile west of Madrid and six miles north of Waynesboro, took its name from the Hildebrand family who were large landowners in that vicinity and leaders in the church—Jacob Hildebrand serving as minister and bishop for a number of years. Jacob R. Hildebrand was a preacher. The church, likely the first Mennonite church in the Southern (Augusta County) District of the Virginia Conference, was a small log meetinghouse, probably built in 1828. A larger frame church was built across the road from the first in 1876. It is thought that this was the first church in Virginia to be formally dedicated. In 1955 the church had a membership of 56, with Joseph H. Weaver of Waynesboro as pastor. H.A.B.

Hildebrandt, Kornelius (1833-1920), a Mennonite manufacturer of the Ukraine, South Russia, was born on Jan. 21, 1833, on the island of Chortitza (*q.v.*) in the Chortitza Mennonite settlement. He worked for many years as a poor clockmaker. With the rise of industry in the settlement, however, the business flourished, and was established as a firm in 1878. In 1903 he transferred the management to his children; it then had the title, "K. Hildebrandts Erben und Priess." The partner Priess (1863-1922) was Hildebrandt's son-in-law; he was the actual founder and for many years the manager of the firm, which had a capital stock of 500,000 rubles. The factory consisted of two branches, one located in the Chortitza settlement and the other established in 1892 in Schönwiese. At the beginning of World War I the Chortitza branch employed about 80 workers, and the Schönwiese branch 100, with an annual output valued at 500,000 rubles. The firm was engaged almost exclusively in the manufacture of farm machinery, with reapers and drills as a specialty, which were sold as far away as Siberia. (*ML* II, 313.)
D.H.E.

Hildebrandt, Peter, a Frisian Mennonite preacher (Kronsweide congregation), living on the island of Chortitza in the Dniepr, South Russia, son-in-law of the deputy Jakob Höppner (*q.v.*), was in the first train of immigrants from Danzig, and was one of the six men who went ahead of the party to Dubrovka with Höppner to make preparations for the group. His impressions were published in 1888 by A. Neufeld in *Erste Auswanderung der Menniten aus dem Danziger Gebiet nach Südrussland.* As an eyewitness and participant in the historical events of the settlement on the Dniepr in 1789 his accounts are important source material for the student of Mennonite history. He relates in the introduction to his book how he came to put down in writing the events of those years: "Several persons expressed the wish to have the most exact information possible concerning the initial steps and the further course of the emigration from Danzig to Russia. . . . I myself also wanted to record it as a

memorial for my descendants. . . ." Thus P. Hildebrandt became the first historiographer of the Mennonites of South Russia. (*ML* II, 313.)   D.H.E.

Hilfsverein of the Evangelical Mennonite Church (*Kleine Gemeinde*) was established in 1929, to create an agency to make it possible to borrow money within the church at a low rate of interest. A committee of three was appointed to manage the fund. An assessment of ½ per cent on net and clear property was levied on the members (payment was voluntary, however) to establish security for the fund. The first loan to the fund was deposited on Feb. 20, 1929, at the rate of 2 per cent per annum. In 1955 the interest was increased to 3 per cent. Though the amount is not large, it has been a great help to many beginners. At present every district of this church east of the Red River has its own committee member. D.P.R.

Hill City Civilian Public Service Camp No. 57 was located 16 miles northwest of Hill City, S.D. Under the Bureau of Reclamation, the camp had as its chief project the construction of Deerfield Dam for the purpose of furnishing a plentiful water supply for Rapid City and for furnishing a supplemental water supply for 12,000 acres of irrigated land in the valley downstream from Rapid City. Camp No. 57, operated by the Mennonite Central Committee, was approved Sept. 23, 1942, and was closed Feb. 28, 1946. It had a capacity of 200 men. During 41 months the conscientious objectors assigned to the camp spent 50,726 man-hours on the dam and when the camp was closed the project was 97 per cent complete. Deerfield Dam is in one sense a "Monument to Peace." In 1946 the men of the camp published a 60-page book presenting in pictures and text the history of CPS No. 57, under the title *The Voice of Peace.* M.G.

M. Gingerich, *Service for Peace* (Akron, 1949) 162-68.

Hillcrest Home for the Aged, Harrison, Ark., is owned by the county but operated by the Mission Interests Committee of the Old Order Amish Mennonite Church. The seventeen-bed home was opened Aug. 3, 1953. Eli Helmuth of Hutchinson, Kan., has been the administrator of the home since its opening, and his wife the dietitian. In addition two young men (usually on I-W assignment) and four young women complete the present staff. All workers are drawn from the Old Order Amish Mennonite Church. Operating costs are more than met by the fees paid by the guests. A large waiting list has made expansion imperative. H.Gr.

Hillcrest United Missionary Church, located in Springfield, Clark Co., Ohio, was organized about 1925. In 1954 the membership was 17, with Lawrence Frey serving as pastor. The name of the congregation was changed in June 1952 from Hillcrest to Neosha Ave. HA.E.B.

Hille Feicken, an Anabaptist woman, native of Sneek, Dutch province of Friesland and baptized there, married to the Anabaptist Psalmus of Utrecht, enticed by the prophecies of Münster (*q.v.*) as the New Zion left Sneek in 1534 to join the "chosen" at Münster. On June 16, 1534, early in the morning she left the city of Münster with the intention—like Judith and Holophernes (in the Apocryphal book of Judith) of seducing and killing the Catholic bishop of Münster, who had laid siege to the city. Of course this enterprise signally failed. Hille was taken prisoner by the bishop's troops, tried, tortured, and put to death. Her confession, published by Kerssenbroich, Cornelius, and Niesert, contains important material concerning the revolutionary Anabaptist movement. (Mellink, *Wederdopers*, 41-43, 60, 243.)   vᴅZ.

Hillegont Petersdochter of Amsterdam, where she lived in the house "De Engel," had lodged the Anabaptist bishop of Amsterdam, Jacob van Campen (*q.v.*). Because of this fact she was sentenced on June 1, 1535, "to be hanged and strangled before her own door, as an example to others." Hillegont was not a member of the Anabaptist congregation. (Grosheide, *Verhooren*, 110 f.)   vᴅZ.

Hilleken Jacobs and **Anneken**, two Anabaptist martyrs, were executed shortly after Sept. 17, 1571, likely at Breda, Dutch province of North Brabant. Hilleken Jacobs, 25 years of age, unmarried, and Anneken, 58 years, wife of Pieter Pietersz, also a Mennonite who, however, escaped, were arrested on Aug. 29, 1571, at Klundert, Dutch province of North Brabant, where they lived. Both were cruelly tortured. Van Braght (*Mart. Mir.* D 603, E 929), who lists a number of Mennonites arrested while holding a meeting at Nieuwvart (Klundert) near Breda in 1572 (this must be 1571) and put to death at Breda, does not name these two martyrs. (*DB* 1912, 38, 41, 42.)   vᴅZ.

Hiller, Matthias, a furrier of St. Gall, was baptized in Strasbourg by Jakob Gross (*q.v.*), a member of the Strasbourg Anabaptist group, probably left the city with Michael Sattler (*q.v.*), with whom he suffered a martyr's death at Rottenburg a. N. on May 21, 1527. He rejected the proffered pardon, saying that if he had seven heads he would offer them all for the sake of Christ.   Nᴇғғ.

T. W. Röhrich, "Zur Gesch. der strassburgischen Wiedertäufer," *Ztscht für die hist. Theol.*, 1860, 15 and 34; G. Bossert, *Das Blutgericht in Rottenburg am Neckar* (Barmen, 1891); *ML* II, 315.

Hillsboro, a town (pop. 2,200) in Marion Co., Kan., founded in 1879 and named after John Gillispie Hill. The town, predominantly Mennonite, is located on the northern edge of the largest Kansas Mennonite settlement, stretching south beyond Newton. In Hillsboro and the immediate surrounding area there are nine Mennonite congregations: First Mennonite Church (GCM), Hillsboro; Mennonite Brethren Church, Hillsboro; Brudertal Mennonite Church (GCM) (first to be organized); Johannestal Mennonite Church (GCM); Ebenfeld Mennonite Brethren Church; Steinreich Mennonite Brethren Church; Gnadenau Krimmer Mennonite Brethren Church; Alexanderfeld Church of God in Christ Mennonite; and Springfeld Krimmer Mennonite Brethren Church. The Mennonites settling in and around Hillsboro came from various parts of the Molotschna settlement, Russia (General Conference, Mennonite Brethren, and Krimmer Mennonite Brethren groups), from Poland (Johannestal), and a few from Prussia (Brudertal). In addition to the Mennonite churches there are the following: Zion Evangelical Lutheran, Evangelical Church, and Seventh-Day Adventist. Hillsboro is located on the branch of the Santa Fe Railway between Marion and McPherson. It has become more and more the headquarters of the Mennonite Brethren with the Mennonite Brethren Publishing House (*q.v.*), Tabor College (*q.v.*), Mennonite Brethren Board of Missions (*q.v.*), and the Mennonite Brethren General Conference Headquarters. The present Mennonite community hospital was founded by the Krimmer Mennonite Brethren as Salem Hospital (*q.v.*). There is also the Salem Home for the Aged (*q.v.*).

In addition to a number of parochial schools in existence in and around Hillsboro in the early days, H. D. Penner founded here the Preparatory School in 1897 which was private till 1913 and operated by the Mennonite churches from 1913 to 1937 under J. H. Epp (see **Hillsboro Preparatory School**). Among Hillsboro's 140 businesses the Central Kansas Co-operative Creamery and the Buller Manufacturing Company are outstanding.   C.K.

Marion W. Kliewer, "Mennonite Community Settlement," *Menn. Life*, January 1954, 14 ff.; *A Guide to Hillsboro, Kansas* (Hillsboro, 1940).

Hillsboro (Kan.) **First** Mennonite Church (GCM), a member of the Western District Conference, was organized in 1884 by J. S. Hirschler, who served as minister 23 years. He was succeeded by H. D. Penner, who served for 16 years. J. H. Epp became the elder in 1914, holding this position for 26 years. H. T. Unruh served as pastor 1942-52, J. W. Nickel 1952-54, and Elbert Koontz 1955- . The congregation, beginning with 39 charter members, in 1955 had a membership of 356. The church building was constructed in 1886, and since then has been enlarged and remodeled four times, the last being completed in 1950 with a seating capacity of 500.

H.T.U.

Hillsboro Journal, founded in 1903 as the *Hillsboro Vorwärts*, had J. G. Ewert as first editor. In 1939 the name was changed to *Hillsboro Journal*. It was a general newspaper. The size of the paper was 15 x 22 in. It was published weekly, generally with eight pages, containing general news and reports from the different settlements mostly rural and of Mennonite interest. It was owned and published by the M.B. Publishing House, Hillsboro, Kan., though it was not an official organ of that constituency. The English language was generally used in the paper but some German reports found room on its pages. The last editor was Peter H. Berg. The *Hillsboro Journal* was sold to T. G. Hiebert late in 1952 and was merged with the *Hillsboro Star* early in 1953.

P.H.B.

Hillsboro Mennonite Brethren Church in Hillsboro, Marion Co., Kan., with a baptized membership of 827 in 1954, is a member of the Southern District. Organized April 25, 1881, near Hillsboro with 34 charter members as the "Johannestal Church of

French Creek," the congregation met in rural homes until 1882, when a school building was purchased in Hillsboro. The first church, built about 1890, was replaced by a larger church in 1910, which was remodeled and enlarged in 1926 to a seating capacity of 700, with a large Sunday-school building 145 x 40 ft., with an increase of auditorium space of 300 seats. The ancestral background of the membership is mostly Dutch coming from Russia and Poland in 1874-84. One third of the congregation is rural and two thirds urban in a town of 2,000. Originally the Low German dialect was used in homes and German in services, but in the last 15 years both homes and services have changed to the English language. The older people's Sunday-school classes still use German and occasionally it is used in services. Pastors serving the church were John Harms, John F. Harms, P. P. Rempel, P. E. Nickel, J. W. Vogt, and Waldo D. Hiebert. The congregation has two young people's organizations, two women's organizations, church choir, two male choruses, a Sunday school, and a Bible school for the entire congregation meeting on Wednesday. The church practices footwashing, has an electronic organ, and several pianos. **W.D.H.**

Hillsboro Preparatory School *(Vorbereitungsschule),* Kansas (1897-1936), was founded as a private school by H. D. Penner in 1897 with a two-year curriculum to prepare students for elementary teaching and college. In 1913 an association was organized, sponsored by the First Mennonite Church, Johannesthal Mennonite Church, and Bruderthal Mennonite Church of Hillsboro, which made itself responsible for the school. Occasionally members from other communities were represented on the board. J. H. Epp served as principal 1913-27. Other teachers were C. J. Epp, H. C. Voth, Gustav Frey, L. H. Linscheid, J. P. Suderman, W. F. Unruh, and Abraham Albrecht.

In 1927 the name on the catalog was given as Bible Academy, although the contents remained unchanged. The two-year course was designed to give a basis in Bible study, German language and literature, church and Mennonite history and related subjects. Gradually more English was introduced. By 1936 the interest in the parochial school had declined and most parents sent their children to the local high school. The school was closed during that year (see **Preparatory Schools**). C.K.

H. P. Peters, *History and Development of Education Among the Mennonites of Kansas* (Hillsboro, 1925) 150 ff.; Catalogs of Hillsboro Preparatory School 1897-1935.

Hillsboro Vereinsschule: see Hillsboro Preparatory School.

Hillsdale County (Mich.) Old Order Amish Mennonite Community. A small group of Old Order Amish settled near Jerome, Hillsdale Co., Mich., in the spring of 1945. This group included the families of Levi, Albert, and Peter Stoll, and William J. Schrock. In 1955 the resident minister was Amos Stoll, and Albert Graber of Middlebury, Ind., had bishop oversight. The 1949 membership was 39. A.St.

Hilversum, a town (1953 pop. 91,967, with 1,093 Mennonites) in the Dutch province of North Holland, the seat of a Mennonite congregation, formerly at Huizen (see this article, where its history is found until 1878). In 1878 a new meetinghouse was built in Hilversum (dedicated June 30 by Pastor A. Loosjes of Amsterdam) and the congregation was named Huizen-Hilversum, since 1945 being called Hilversum. The congregation rapidly increased: membership 40 in 1878; 225 in 1897; 500 in 1926; 600 in 1940; 780 in 1955. The meetinghouse was completely rebuilt and greatly enlarged in 1940. In 1908 the members of Hilversum living at Baarn *(q.v.)* and Bussum *(q.v.)* founded Mennonite circles, which have since grown into independent congregations.

Preachers of the congregation since it moved its seat from Huizen to Hilversum were (until 1885 vacant) I. H. Boeke 1885-93, J. S. Pekema 1894-1904, F. Dijkema 1905-7, P. Oosterbaan 1907-38, A. L. Broer since 1938. Activities are: Sunday school for children, young members' group, ladies' circle, church choir, mission committee. (*DB* 1879, 140 f.; 1908, 206; *DJ* 1943, 44; *ML* II, 364.)

P.O., vDZ.

Hilzin, Elisabeth, an Anabaptist martyr who languished in the monastery prison of Othenbach in Zürich in 1639 until death released her. Van Braght adds that the authorities extorted a fine of 500 guilders from her surviving husband. (*Mart. Mir.* D 813, E 1112; *ML* II, 316.)

Himmelberg, Anthoni (Anthoni Hinnelberg in van Braght's *Martyrs' Mirror,* also called Anthi Wäber), was a Swiss Mennonite preacher who in spite of 27 months of imprisonment remained true to his faith. He was a native of Wattenwyl in the Seftigen district of Bern. Because he was a zealous defender of Anabaptist principles he was imprisoned in the Bern penitentiary and orphanage on June 24, 1658. He had been in this notorious prison over a year with several other brethren, when the Dutch Mennonites began to intervene for their release (see **Bern**). On Oct. 9, 1659, Abraham Heidanus *(q.v.),* professor of theology at the University of Leiden, at the request of the Mennonites of Holland, wrote to Prof. Christof Luthard, a member of the recent *Täuferkommission* in Bern, which had charge of the orphanage, requesting lenience toward the Swiss Mennonites. On Oct. 24 Hans Flamingh also wrote him a long letter, lamenting reports from the Palatinate and Alsace that the Bern government was imprisoning the Mennonites, naming Anthoni Himmelberg among others.

These letters may have been the reason why on Jan. 20, 1660, several of the Mennonite prisoners were cross-examined. The court records of these trials are found in the Bern archives (*De Anabaptistis Varia. Kirchenwesen* II, 131, No. 16). The questions covered 16 points. The first to be tried was Rudolf Wirtz of Kulm; the second was Himmelberg. "He will do nothing at all or adapt himself in any way, but remains absolutely by his faith. Beyond this he requests pity, but he wants to have patience for whatever God wants to do with them."

His reply to point eight, "whether the Anabaptists would have their marriages blessed by the church," and to point nine, "whether for the furtherance of truth in high, important matters, an oath or pledge could be given," was this: "He would do neither the one nor the other." He also refused to name the other preachers or lay members.

The outcome was that the Mennonites had to return to prison. The committee then debated whether they should proceed by banishing the prisoners or holding them in prison (*Ratszedel* of Feb. 13, 1660). They decided on the latter course on the following considerations: (1) It would be like approval of their sect to send them where their doctrine is openly preached; (2) Those who remained would be strengthened by those who left; (3) Thereby more would be led into error; (4) Exile to their brethren would be too lenient a punishment to deter their spread; (5) Imprisonment is more frightening and also makes it possible to continue efforts to convert them.

In the meantime intervention had been made by the States-General of Holland, and the cities Amsterdam and Rotterdam; the Dutch ambassador de Vreede was permitted to visit the imprisoned Mennonites. The question of exile was again opened, and the Mennonites questioned again. All remained steadfast. When Himmelberg was asked whether he would deny his faith or rather leave the canton, never to return, he replied that on account of physical weakness he begged for mercy, but that he would remain true to his faith and would willingly leave the canton.

When the council saw that their efforts at conversion were of no avail, they decided on Aug. 28, 1660, to expel all the prisoners except Himmelberg, who was too ill. On Sept. 10, 1660, they were taken by boat to Brugg, and from there to the border, where de Vreede presumably received them. The directors of the orphanage were asked to give "Anthoni Himmelberg something more in food and drink for the close of his life" (*Ratsmanual* 139, 323). Broken by his long imprisonment and apparently by malnutrition, he died Oct. 25, 1660, at the orphanage.

One stanza of the "Dürsrüttilied" (*q.v.*) commemorates his death.   S.G.

A. Fluri, *Beiträge zur Gesch. der bernischen Täufer,* No. 2, p. 17; Müller, *Berner Täufer,* 173-91; court records of the Bern *Staatsarchiv* as follows: *De Anabaptistis Varia. Kirchenwesen* II, 131, especially Nos. 14, 16, 33, 37; *Mandatenbuch* 8, p. 189 f.; *Mart. Mir.* D 826, E 1124; *ML* II, 316 f.

Himmelsmanna, Das, a 4-page, 15 in. wide (later increased to 8 pages) monthly Sunday-school paper published by John G. Stauffer from January 1876 to December 1906, at Milford Square, Pa. (1876-80), and Quakertown, Pa. (1881-1906), with a circulation of 5,000. It also appeared in English with a circulation of 8,000 in 1879-1908 under the title *The Manna* (*q.v.*), last issue April 1909. Stauffer (1837-1911) was at first a staunch Mennonite, an associate of John H. Oberholtzer 1856-67 in the *Mennonitischer Druckverein,* but about 1889 lost his interest in denominational Mennonitism and apparently finally his connection also. Neither the

Himmelsmanna nor *The Manna* was in any sense a denominational paper. In 1906 *Himmelsmanna* was purchased by M. S. Steiner, then president of the Mennonite Board of Missions and Charities (MC), "adopted by the Mission Board" to serve as a missions paper (*Gospel Witness,* Scottdale, July 18, 1906, p. 241) and published by it for two years 1906-8, when it was sold to the newly organized Mennonite Publication Board and apparently discontinued. During these two years it was printed by the Gospel Witness Publishing Co. (*q.v.*) at Scottdale, with publication at Bluffton, Ohio, under the following administration: M. S. Steiner, Columbus Grove, Ohio, editor; D. S. Gerig, Goshen, Ind., assistant editor; Aaron Loucks, Scottdale, Pa., business manager. The English *Manna* remained in Stauffer's hands.   H.S.B.

J. Battle, *History of Bucks County* (Philadelphia, 1887) 1067-68 contains a biographical sketch of Stauffer with some account of the *Manna.*

Hindeloopen, a town (1947 pop. 924, with 80 Mennonites), once a prosperous city in the Dutch province of Friesland, an important center of Baltic trade, since the middle of the 18th century steadily declining both in commerce and in population, is a seat of a Mennonite congregation dating back to about 1550. In 1562 Leenaert Bouwens (*q.v.*) visited this congregation but baptized only one member. When the divisions arose among the Dutch Mennonites, the Hindeloopen congregation held to the moderate Waterlanders. Haye Hommes was a representative of this congregation at the large Waterlander delegates' meeting at Amsterdam 1647. (Whether there existed also a High German congregation in 1614 is not clear.)

The Waterlander congregation is said to have numbered 1,000 members in 1653. In this year a new meetinghouse was built, being then the largest one in Friesland. Soon after, a division in the congregation took place, the smaller group being a Waterlander congregation, numbering nearly 200 members, around 1700, and meeting in the Kleine Huys; the other group, more conservative and calling itself *Flemish,* meeting in the Groote Huys, numbering about 600 members at that time. Through the intercession of the Friesche Doopsgezinde Sociëteit (Mennonite Conference of Friesland) the groups united *ca.* 1740, but in 1749 a new schism occurred, which lasted until 1810. In this year a part of the Kleine Huys joined the Groote Huys congregation, while other members of the Kleine Huys turned to the Reformed Church. In the meantime the membership had greatly decreased as a result of the decline in trade and population. The membership of the two congregations combined was about 780 in 1700; decreased to about 200 in 1796 and to only 57 in 1838. Since then the membership has remained small—43 in 1861, 48 in 1900, 70 in 1929, 57 in 1954.

In 1808-17 and 1834-73 the pastor of Hindeloopen also served Molkwerum; in 1870-1949 its pastor served also at Koudum; since 1942 the congregations of Hindeloopen and Staveren have had the same pastor, mostly living in Staveren.

In the last half century Hindeloopen was served

by the following pastors: F. J. de Holl 1900-3, G. A. Hulshoff 1904-10, A. de Jong 1910-14, R. Swart 1916-19, B. P. de Vries 1920-23, H. Bussemaker 1926, A. L. Broer 1926-29, Miss J. H. van der Slooten 1932-39, Miss S. E. Treffers (of Staveren) 1942-46, L. Laurense (of Staveren) 1949-53, vacant since 1953. Activities are a Sunday school for children since 1917, a ladies' circle since 1927.

A.L.B., vdZ.

Inv. Arch. Amst. I, Nos. 961, 1162, 1180; II, Nos. 1926-41; Blaupot t. C., *Friesland,* see Index; *DB* 1861, 122, 136; 1870, 34-37; 1874, 87; 1903, 91; *ML* II, 317.

Hingst, a Dutch Mennonite family, originally living at Harlingen, province of Friesland, where Evert Hingst was a deacon about 1690, Sijbrand Hingst about 1785. Another Sijbrand Hingst (b. 1824 at Harlingen, d. 1906 at The Hague), married Jacoba Huidekoper, was burgomaster of Harlingen and a member of the First Chamber of the States-General. Of great importance for the Dutch Mennonites was Sijbrand Jan Hingst, a descendant of the same family. He was a son of Jelle Hingst and Gepke Brouwer, b. 1834 at Amsterdam, d. at The Hague, on Jan. 12, 1890; married M. C. Müller. He studied law at the University of Amsterdam and obtained his doctor's degree at Utrecht in 1859. He was a judge at Amsterdam, and beginning in 1883 a member of the *Hoge Raad* (Supreme Court of the Netherlands) and one of the most learned jurists of his time. Like his father he served the Amsterdam congregation as a deacon (1861-65, 1871-76, 1881-83) and also the recently founded congregation at The Hague. He was also a member of the board of the Dutch Mennonite weekly *De Zondagsbode,* for which he wrote a number of articles, all signed S.H. He had a keen interest in Mennonite history and was a good friend of the well-known historian Ludwig Keller (*q.v.*). The Amsterdam Mennonite Library contains a number of his posthumous papers and notes concerning church history and Mennonite history (oath, disputations, etc.) and also a reprint of the 1887 paper, *Over de Eed.* vdZ.

De Zondagsbode III, No. 12 (Jan. 19, 1890); P. R. Feith, *Levensbericht van Mr. S. J. Hingst* (Leiden, 1890).

Hinkel Mountain is a schoolhouse about 12 miles south of Petersburg, W. Va., where Mennonite services were held for several years to accommodate about a dozen members of the Pleasant Grove (MC) congregation who lived in this isolated community. When the members moved away, services were discontinued. The schoolhouse was last listed in the *Mennonite Yearbook and Directory* in 1948.

T.S.

Hinkletown Mennonite Church (MC), a member of the Lancaster Conference, located on the Lakes-to-Seas Highway, near Ephrata, Pa., where there had been a union church since 1851. The Mennonites had a few services in it at different times but not until the Groffdale-New Holland circuit in 1943 took charge did things really move. Under Mahlon Witmer, bishop, Warren S. Good, minister, and Harry S. Good, deacon, a thriving work has started. A new church was built in 1952. The membership (1955) is 110. I.D.L.

Hinlopen, Dirk Goykes, a dealer in wood at Workum in the Dutch province of Friesland and preacher of the Waterlander congregation, studied under the celebrated Galenus Abrahamsz de Haan (*q.v.*) in 1698-99, delivered his first sermon on Jan. 14, 1700, and remained in this office until his death in 1752. He was generous of heart and peaceable. When the Frisian States, at the request of the Reformed Synod of Harlingen, in 1752 circulated a formulary for the signature of all Mennonite preachers (in part to avoid the spread of Socinian views) Hinlopen not only refused to sign it, but also drew up a document of protest. Hinlopen's descendants were also loyal members of the church, able and willing to contribute many a substantial sum. Simen Dirk Hinlopen (d. 1795) left the church a legacy of 20,000 guilders. Claes Goykes Hinlopen (about 1687-1727), a brother of Dirk, married to Frouwkje Jacobs Braam of Harlingen, was from 1719 treasurer of the "Zuiderklasse" (Mennonite conference of Southwest Friesland); he was a merchant, at first at Workum, and later at Harlingen. (*DB* 1903, 86-89, 114-18; 1905, 4, 6 f., 41; *ML* II, 317.) vdZ.

Hinnelberg, Anthony, an Anabaptist martyr, named by van Braght (*Mart. Mir.* D 826, E 1124): see **Himmelberg, Anthoni.**

Hinrich Ebbinck (*Doktor Klumpe*) is perhaps identical with the elder Hendrik van Vreden (*q.v.*), who was first a co-worker with Menno Simons, but then fell away from him to follow Adam Pastor. It is certain that Ebbinck was in the same region at the same time; we come across him in 1546 in Westphalia and Gelderland. (*DB* 1909, 107; *ML* I, 500.) K.V.

Hinwil, a village in the Grüningen district of the Swiss canton of Zürich, with a population (1950) of 3,000, where the Anabaptist movement appeared soon after its rise. In July 1525 Conrad Grebel (*q.v.*) and Marx Boshart (*q.v.*) preached there with considerable success, and Hinwil soon became an Anabaptist center. Several witnesses reported on a debate between Grebel and the Pastor Johannes Brennwald (*q.v.*) of Hinwil. Grebel lamented to Brennwald that Zwingli had once led him to the truth, but had now "gone backwards" in many respects. When Brennwald on the issue of infant baptism based his position on the imperial mandate, Grebel replied: "You must not regard either my lords nor anyone else, but only do what God has commanded you. And what the mouth of God has spoken, that you must follow after." In conclusion he said, "It is a pitiful thing that I can receive no justice—neither civil justice, nor imperial justice, nor divine justice."

On Sunday, Oct. 8, 1525, Georg Blaurock (*q.v.*) appeared in Hinwil. That was the day of the remarkable scene at Hinwil when Blaurock sent Brennwald from the pulpit and began to preach himself. In the ensuing debate on infant baptism, Blaurock said to Brennwald, "Thus you are the Antichrist and are misleading the people." This somewhat drastic expression on the one hand reveals the fearless mind of Blaurock, and on the other shows the rather violent character of the age.

On Nov. 6-8, 1525, the great disputation on baptism took place in Zürich. Soon there was another scene in the Hinwil church. The Swiss Brethren returning from Zürich complained of their lack of freedom to speak. Brennwald was speaking on the baptism of infants, basing his argument on a comparison with Old Testament circumcision, with reference to John 7, when the Brethren interrupted him and openly complained in the church that they had not been permitted to speak. When Brennwald left the church with the threat that he would report this incident to the authorities, someone, as Brennwald reported, called after him, "He has accused them enough; he should be removed."

The Anabaptist movement was able to maintain itself in Hinwil for some time. In February 1527 over 30 Swiss Brethren were assembled here at one time. Toward the end of 1528 the Swiss Brethren were still meeting in Hinwil and vicinity. On Nov. 26, 1528, the pastor reported to the magistrate Berger that a number of his subjects were not coming to church; among these people were some who had already been in prison in Zürich for neglecting the "Christian Church" and holding to rebaptism. But the movement that had begun so hopefully in Hinwil gradually declined and was ultimately extinguished.   S.G.

Emil Egli, *Die Züricher Täufer* (Zürich, 1878); *TA: Zürich,* see Index; *ML* II, 317 f.

Hippolytushoef (Sint), on the former island of Wieringen, Dutch province of North Holland, seat of a Mennonite congregation, formerly called "Hippolytushoef and Stroe," now usually called the Wieringen congregation. The date of its founding is not known. Leenaert Bouwens' baptismal lists indicate that it must have existed between 1551 and 1578. He baptized 25 persons here in 1563-65, and 10 in 1568-82. Additional information on the early congregational history is found in the membership lists of 1731-1819 and from 1869 to the present (Wiersma in *DB* 1891) and the old record book that was begun in 1721. In the 17th century the congregation belonged to the Flemish branch; it sent a representative to the conference at Haarlem, but in the 18th century it was usually called Frisian. In 1724 trouble arose when one of the members was appointed sheriff, thus accepting government office. Silent prayer was in use until 1728. Not until 1852 were the benches in the meetinghouse replaced by chairs for the women.

In the earlier time the care of the poor was already well developed; even non-Dutch Mennonites were not forgotten. The foreword of the record book lists rather considerable sums contributed to the Lithuanian, Prussian, and Danzig brethren. The earliest minister's name of the Wieringen congregation on record is Albert Pieter Keizer, who was installed in 1690. Other early preachers were Elbert Wognum, who served as preacher 1726-42 and as elder 1742 until his death in 1781, and Cornelis Wagenmaker, preacher 1740-43, elder 1743 until his death 1784. Elder Wognum was at the same time burgomaster. When in the government

meeting an oath had to be taken or a sentence had to be pronounced or military questions were to be discussed, he left the room for a while (Blaupot t. C., *Holland* II, 203, note 2).

The congregation has since early times had three churches; one at "Om Eest," i.e., Oosterland, one in Stroe, and one near Hippolytushoef. The first became decrepit and was sold, the second was renovated in 1738 and was burned down in 1936. From the outside this meetinghouse (*Vermaning*) resembled the farm building that partly concealed it. The meetinghouse near Hippolytushoef, renovated in 1776, was abandoned in 1861, when the new church in the village of Hippolytushoef was built.

Concerning the membership no figures were available before 1815. It then numbered 120, since then increasing: 162 in 1837, 180 in 1861, 275 in 1900, 382 in 1930, 332 in 1954. In the present century the congregation was served by the following pastors: J. P. Smidts 1895-1902, D. Haars 1902-5, M. Onnes Mzn. 1905-9, J. M. Leendertz 1910-23, O. L. van der Veen 1923-29, H. W. Meihuizen 1933-36, H. J. de Wilde 1937-41, P. J. Lugt 1941-45, and A. P. Goudsbloem since 1946.

The following activities are found in this congregation: three women's circles, Bible circle, church choir, library for the youth, and youth group.

Since 1930 Wieringen is no longer an island because of the *Afsluitdijk,* a 20-mile dike extending from Friesland to North Holland (built 1927-33), which has converted the former Zuiderzee into a lake (IJsselmeer), and is connected by the dike with both North Holland and Friesland. (*Inv. Arch. Amst.* I, No. 1,180; *DB* 1891, 42-59; *ML* II, 318 f.)

    O.L.vDV., vD.Z.

Hirschberg-Kirschbach, a Mennonite congregation in the duchy of Zweibrücken, Germany, listed in the Dutch *Naamlijst* for 1784 with Jacob Dätweiler as elder (1760) and Johannes Steinmann (1753) and Jacob Bachmann as preachers. It also appeared in the *Naamlijst* for 1769 with the names of additional ministers, Johannes Steinmann (1753), Andreas Leimberger (1753), and Jacob Thomas (1753). In the list of delegates at the Essingen Amish Mennonite Conference of 1779 this congregation is called the Zweibrücken congregation.

    H.S.B.

Hirschler (Herschler; not Hirschi or Hershey), a Mennonite family stemming from Switzerland, which settled in the Palatinate and in Alsace soon after 1700. The progenitor of the family at Geisberg and vicinity, where there are today several branches of the family, seems to have been Daniel Hirschler, who married Katharina Strickler on June 24, 1730. Another branch of the family flourished in Gerolsheim, where Jakob Hirschler, originally a linen weaver, then a farmer, was chosen as elder. He carried on a correspondence with Hans von Steen at Danzig (*Gem.-Kal.* 1935, 112 ff.) and with the Dutch Committee of Foreign Needs at Amsterdam in behalf of the Swiss immigrants and the needs of his own congregation. (*Inv. Arch. Amst.* I, Nos. 1458,

1463, 1485-97, 1529, 1533-35, 1537, 1539-41.) He may also have been related to Ulrich W. Hirschler, who was chosen as elder of the Friesenheim-Eppstein Mennonite congregation in 1738, or to Hans Hirschi, who is mentioned at Wachenheim in 1716 and 1724. Descendants of Jakob Hirschler are found after 1800 in Quirnheim near Grünstadt, from where a Jakob Hirschler, married to Magdelena Jansen (or Janson), moved to Thaun, Bavaria, in the Eichstock congregation. He is the ancestor of the Hirschler families found today in the various Bavarian congregations. His grandson Abraham Hirschler (1858-1931), after two years of training in the Missionshaus at Barmen, was chosen as pastor of the united congregation of Kühbörncheshof, Heudorf, Neudorf, and Ernstweiler (Kaiserslautern joined later) and lived in Kaiserslautern. He served the congregation for 50 years. In 1900-31 he edited the *Christlicher Gemeinde-Kalender* (*q.v.*).

Abraham's brother Johannes (1856-1933) attended the Seminary at St. Chrischona, Basel, Switzerland, and served the *Gemeindeverband* (*q.v.*) as traveling evangelist until 1885, then became preacher of the Eichstock congregation (from 1893 also Munich) 1887-99, and then was called to the Monsheim and Obersülzen congregations, which he served until January 1926.

David Hirschler was one of the first members of the Zion Mennonite Church of Donnellson, Iowa. Daniel Hirschler, who had settled in Iowa, was one of the founders of the Wadsworth Seminary. David B. Hirschler was for a time a missionary among the Indians in Oklahoma. During the westward move in the seventies and eighties the Hirschlers came to Kansas. John S. Hirschler (1847-1915) of Franklin Center, Iowa, graduated from Wadsworth Seminary and became a leading minister in Kansas (Hillsboro). His son Arnold S. Hirschler (b. 1873) taught mathematics at Bluffton College, Otto T. Hirschler (b. 1889) was a minister of music in various churches and has taught music, and Daniel A. Hirschler was professor of music at Bethel College and at Emporia State Teachers' College. Christian E. Hirschler (1859-1936) of Klosterhof, Palatinate, came to Halstead in 1883 and served churches as minister in Oklahoma and Kansas. Ulrich Hirschler of Bavaria, whose children had preceded him, came to America after World War I and settled at Beatrice, Neb. Most of the Hirschler descendants in America now live in Kansas. P.S., C.K.

E. E. Hirschler, *The Story of a Pioneer Family* (Christian E. Hirschler) (North Newton, Kan., 1937); A. Warkentin and M. Gingerich, *Who's Who Among the Mennonites* (North Newton, Kan., 1943).

Hirschler, John S. (1847-1915), a Mennonite (GCM) minister and leader, was born at Maxweiler, Bavaria, Germany, on July 4, 1847, and in 1856 emigrated with his parents to Summerfield, Ill. In 1868-71 he attended Wadsworth Seminary, Ohio, after which he served the Mennonite Church at Franklin Center, Iowa, for 13 years. Here he married Christine Schmidt. Following a call of the Board of Missions of the General Conference Mennonite Church he went to Hillsboro, Kan., in 1884, where he organized the First Mennonite Church. He traveled much

and spoke on many occasions, especially at conferences and conventions, promoting religious education in the Mennonite constituency. He was a member of the town Board of Education in Hillsboro, was a cofounder of the Mennonite Teachers' Institute, Bethel College, and of the Hillsboro Preparatory School. He also served as secretary of the General Conference and as its chairman in 1902-15, and as a member of its Board of Trustees and its Program Committee. Because of ill health he resigned from his position as pastor in 1906 and went to Upland, Cal., where he continued to serve by establishing a church at Escondido and a tubercular sanitarium at Alta Loma. In 1911-12 he made extensive trips in the northern and western districts to collect funds for this purpose. In 1914 he became ill again, and died May 17, 1915. C.K.

S. S. Haury, "Johann S. Hirschler," in *Bundesbote-Kalender* (Berne, 1916) 30 ff.

Hirschy, Noah Calvin, first president, 1900-8, of Central Mennonite College (in 1913 named "Bluffton College"), was born Feb. 25, 1867, near Berne, Ind. He was married to Augusta Hunsberger of Wadsworth, Ohio, on Sept. 5, 1895. They were the parents of two children: Lois and Hermon (d. March 11, 1925). N. C. Hirschy died at Berea, Ky., on March 13, 1924. From 1885 to 1891 he alternately taught country school and attended normal school. During the year 1891-92 he served as principal of the public schools at Berne.

In 1892 Hirschy received a call to become minister of the Wadsworth, Ohio, congregation (GCM). There he had opportunity to continue his studies at Oberlin College and Seminary, completing his collegiate course in 1897 and the theological course in 1898. From 1898 to 1901 he was principal of the Wadsworth Academy.

On May 6, 1894, he was ordained to the eldership by Ephraim Hunsberger, his future father-in-law. In 1896 Hirschy was chosen a member of the Home Mission Committee of the General Conference. In 1898 he was elected moderator of the Middle District Conference.

During these early years of his ministry N. C. Hirschy was one of the leaders in the movement to establish a conference school. In 1894 he prepared a paper to be read at the Middle District Conference meeting at Bethel, Mo., which was said to be "the first public plea on record for a new college in the Middle District." In 1896-97 he was appointed to committees commissioned to draft plans for a conference college. He delivered the principal address at the laying of the cornerstone of the first building of Central Mennonite College on June 19, 1900. After several entreaties he accepted the presidency in 1900 but did not take up residence at Bluffton until 1901. He guided the college through the troublous initial years, resigning in 1908 to accept the presidency of Redfield College, Redfield, S.D. In 1906 he received his master's degree from the University of Chicago and in 1907 his doctorate of philosophy from the University of Bern in Switzerland. He served as president of Redfield College for five years (1908-13), following which he was financial secretary of Windom College,

Montevideo, Minn. (1913-14), and principal of public schools, Winnie, Tex. (1914-16). In 1920 he joined the faculty of Berea College, Berea, Ky., serving as head of the botany department until his death in 1925. R.K.

C. Henry Smith and E. J. Hirschler (ed.), *The Story of Bluffton College* (Bluffton, 1925), *Bluffton College, An Adventure in Faith (1900-1950)* (1950); H. P. Krehbiel, *The History of the General Conference of the Mennonites of North America* (Canton, 1898).

Hirzel, Rudolf. Three Hirzels are listed in the chronicles of the Hutterian Brethren in the 1620's: the cousins Rudolf and Christoph, and Konrad Hirzel. The best known was Rudolf. When after the death of Ulrich Jaussling on April 8, 1621, the brotherhood had been without a head for four weeks because of the danger of meeting earlier, they chose Rudolf Hirzel to be their leader on May 9. He was apparently not qualified for the position, and soon fell into disrepute in the brotherhood.

The impression that the Hutterites had stored up vast treasure was prevalent in the land, supported by the writings of Christoph Andreas Fischer (*q.v.*). For this reason Cardinal Franz von Dietrichstein had Hirzel and two other brethren seized at Neumühle and taken to prison in Nikolsburg. After several weeks Hirzel was sharply questioned concerning the location of this money, by the cardinal and two other prominent men. If he refused to give this information willingly, they would eradicate the brotherhood from the ground up, beginning tomorrow with Neumühle and Nikolsburg. But if he gave the information, the emperor would protect them as his true subjects and give them liberties. At the same time they promised that the money would not be taken from them, but merely put into safekeeping to keep it out of the hands of the rebels.

Thus they persuaded the leader to deliver the money of the brotherhood, the "hard and sour sweat of so many pious persons," which had been entrusted to him. He thought he was thereby saving the lives of his people, but he reaped only shame and disgrace on every hand; he was deposed from his office and excommunicated. In Jesuit circles it was reported that the money Hirzel had delivered was being used for the imperial army, that this had caused such bitterness in the brotherhood that many moved away, others joined other groups of Anabaptists, and that ten had become Catholic. Rudolf Hirzel confessed his error and repented with tears. He died at Göding in Moravia, April 27, 1622. His successor, Valentin Winter, was chosen on Feb. 22, 1622.

Christoph Hirzel was one of the men imprisoned with Rudolf. Konrad Hirzel, with Franz Walter, a preacher, and 138 men, women, and children, fled before the troops of Buquois to Echtelnitz and Schächtitz, and from there they went to Transylvania and Alwincz to form a settlement. Konrad Hirzel was chosen a preacher in Transylvania, but he was released from this duty after a year, at his "earnest request and insistence." (Beck, *Geschichts-Bücher*, 393-97; Loserth, *Communismus;* ML II, 319.) Loserth.

Histoire des Anabaptistes. There are two books bearing this title, both in the French language. The first, published at Paris in 1695, was written by the Jesuit François Catrou (repr. Paris 1706); the second book is anonymous. It was published at Amsterdam in 1700 and is a partial re-edition of L. Hortensius' (*q.v.*) *Tumultuum Anabaptistarum liber unus.*

Historia Christianorum: see **Herman Schijn.**

Historical Committee of the General Conference Mennonite Church is the continuation of the Mennonite Historical Society (Association) and is the official General Conference organ to "collect, preserve, and make available for research, materials of historical and cultural value to Mennonites." It is "responsible for preserving and maintaining places and items of historical and cultural significance" and is to "promote Mennonite research and recommend desirable materials for publication" (revised constitution of G.C.M. Church, 1950).

The Historical Committee came into being when the Mennonite Historical Society (*q.v.*), which was an independent association within the General Conference since 1911, but always reported at conference sessions, recommended in 1938 that a "standing committee" be created to be responsible for historical interests of the conference and of a Mennonite Historical Institute, which was to be created. As a result the Executive Committee of the conference appointed four members to the Historical Committee, which met for the first time July 11, 1939. Although the Mennonite Historical Institute was not realized, the newly created Historical Committee gradually took over the work and the collections of the Mennonite Historical Society. The new Historical Committee was, at the beginning, directly responsible to the Executive Committee of the conference, but since the adoption of the revised constitution of the conference (1950) it functions under the Board of Education and Publication, which appoints its members, approves the budget, and of which a member serves as chairman of the committee. The materials collected by the former Mennonite Historical Society were taken over by the Historical Committee and are now located mostly in the vault of the Bethel College Historical Library, which houses material of the conference, as well as of its own historical collection. The documents, collected mostly by H. R. Voth and H. P. Krehbiel, pertain, as a rule, to the Mennonites living in the prairie states.

The new Historical Committee, originally under the guidance of A. Warkentin, has been active in collecting, cataloguing, and binding materials which were obtained through donations and purchase. Among the projects carried out by the Committee during the last years are (*a*) the working out of a plan by which the grounds and the church building of the Germantown Mennonite Church would be safeguarded and remain a Mennonite historical marker, (*b*) the microfilming of Anabaptist and Mennonite documents in this country (church records, diaries, correspondence) and abroad (archives containing Anabaptist materials in Holland, Germany, Austria, and others), (*c*) helping to finance the publication of the *Täuferakten*, (*d*) publishing the Mennonite Historical Series (*From the Steppes to the Prairies*, L. Harder, *Plockhoy from Zierik-zee*, etc.). The Historical Committee also helps the Mennonite historical libraries of the Mennonite Biblical Seminary, Chicago, Bluffton College, and Bethel College purchase rare Mennonitica. In 1956 the members of the committee were Don. E. Smucker, chairman; Cornelius Krahn, secretary; and Delbert Gratz, Gerhard Lohrenz, and D. J. Unruh.   C.K.

Historical Committee of the Mennonite (MC) General Conference was established by the 1911 session of the General Conference as a committee of ten with the assignment to prepare a Mennonite church history, and has continued as a standing committee of the conference. In 1937 it was authorized to co-opt additional members and since then has usually had a membership of 12. Officers have been: chairman, S. F. Coffman 1911-47 and H. S. Bender 1947- ; secretary, John Horsch 1911-27, L. J. Burkholder 1927-35, H. S. Bender 1935-47, J. C. Wenger 1947- ; custodian of the archives, H. S. Bender 1940-47 and Melvin Gingerich 1947- ; treasurer, J. C. Wenger 1939-41, 1945-47, Edward Yoder 1941-45, and Ira D. Landis 1947- .

The committee early promoted the building up of a Mennonite historical library at the Mennonite Publishing House, Scottdale, Pa., which was for a time its property, with John Horsch as librarian, but later this library was turned over to the House. The committee appointed historians for the various district conferences to secure material for a history of the Mennonite Church in America. Throughout its history it has from time to time recommended, promoted, and supervised the publication of historical works, and has served as assistant to the Mennonite Publishing House and the latter's Publishing Committee in the choice of historical writers and in the production of historical literature.

A new phase of the committee's work began in 1939 with the organization of the Mennonite Historical Association, whose officers are the officers of the Historical Committee. At the same time it began the publication of the *Mennonite Historical Bulletin* (*q.v.*), which is still published. In 1940, by direction of the Mennonite General Conference, it established the archives of the Mennonite Church (*q.v.*) located in two rooms in the Goshen College Library, at Goshen, Ind., which it continues to operate. In recent years it has generously subsidized the publication in Europe of the series of volumes of Anabaptist documents known as the *Täuferakten*. The committee holds annual business meetings.   H.S.B.

Historical Libraries. Collections of writings on Anabaptist-Mennonite history and of writings by Anabaptists and Mennonites have first of all been made by scholars and writers in the field, then by certain of the older and wealthier Mennonite congregations in Europe, and finally by American Mennonite colleges and seminaries. Extensive special Mennonite historical libraries, well-cataloged and serviced, are of only comparatively recent date, and except for the Amsterdam Mennonite Library are to be found only in a few American Mennonite schools. Most of the personal historical libraries and collections of the historians have found their way into the institutional libraries, hence in 1956 there were no extensive private collections. Numerous catalogs of private and congregational collections in Europe have been published. Only one such catalog has been published in America, that of the Mennonite Publishing House Library, Scottdale, Pa. (1929).

Private Historical Collections. The first of such collections was that of the Dutch Mennonite preacher Marten Schagen (1700-70), who published a list of Mennonite writers and works in 1745 presumably based upon his own collection (sale catalog published in 1771), which was bequeathed to the Utrecht, Holland, congregation, which in turn later presented it to the Amsterdam Mennonite Library. The fate of Gerardus Maatschoen's (d. 1751) large collection (the sale catalog of 1752 contained 258 pages, though not all Mennonite) is not known. The fate of the collections of Steven Blaupot ten Cate (1807-84), sale catalog in 1885, and J. D. Hesselink, sale catalog in 1878, is unknown. Most of W. J. Kühler's (1874-1946) small collection was secured by the Goshen College Library. The smaller collections of the German Mennonite historian Christian Neff (1863-1946) and Christian Hege (1869-1943) have become the property of the German Mennonite Historical Society (*Mennonitischer Geschichtsverein*), the former remaining at Weierhof, the latter now incorporated into the library of the Mennonite Research Center (*Mennonitische Forschungsstelle*) at Göttingen. Ulrich Hege (1808-72) of Reihen had a small circulating library, of which a catalog was published at Leipzig in 1843 (*Verzeichnis der Leih-Bibliothek von Ulrich Hege in Bockschaft*). It was largely pietistic in content; its Mennonite books were secured by John Horsch in 1922. In America J. F. Funk's (1835-1930) extensive collection, largely selected and purchased by John Horsch (1867-1941) in 1887-95, ultimately came to the Goshen College Library. The smaller collections of C. Henry Smith (1875-1948), N. B. Grubb (1850-1938), and C. H. A. van der Smissen (1851-1950) came to the Bluffton College Library. John Horsch's personal collection was incorporated in the Mennonite Publishing House Library and came to the Goshen College Library. S. W. Pennypacker (1843-1916), a former governor of Pennsylvania, had a considerable collection of Mennonitica (auction catalog 1920), much of which was purchased by the Schwenkfelder Library at Pennsburg, Pa. Bethel College obtained the F. C. Fleischer library of the Netherlands, and the collections of C. E. Krehbiel of Newton, Kan., and Cornelius Jansen of Beatrice, Neb., as well as numerous smaller libraries of its constituency of the prairie states. Some of these libraries are preserved as memorial collections. Recently the Franconia Mennonite Historical Society (*q.v.*) has established a regional historical library at Souderton, Pa., and a similar library is being established at Salunga, Pa., for the Lancaster Mennonite (MC) Conference district.

Institutional Libraries. (*A*) *Europe.* The oldest institutional Mennonite historical library is that of the Amsterdam (Holland) Mennonite Church (*q.v.*). The library, which contains much more than

Mennonitica, was established in 1680, although its major accessions of Anabaptistica and Mennonitica came after 1750 and chiefly in the 19th century. Catalogs of the Mennonite publications in the library have been published in 1854, 1888, 1919. In 1919, 3,800 Mennonite titles were listed, not including serials. A catalog of the large archival collection in the library was published in 1883-84. The present director of the Amsterdam Library and Archives is N. van der Zijpp. The small library of the Danzig Mennonite Church (a catalog, *Katalog der Kirchenbibliothek der Mennonitengemeinde zu Danzig,* published in 1869 at Danzig, listed 140 Mennonite titles) was scattered in the fighting of 1945 and following years, some items being brought to the Bethel and Goshen College libraries by returning relief workers and others. The larger library of the Hamburg Mennonite Church published a catalog in 1890, *Katalog von der Bibliothek der Mennoniten-Gemeinde zu Hamburg und Altona,* which listed over 500 titles by and about Mennonites. This library, established at the end of the 18th century by the bequest of the preacher R. Rahusen (1735-93), was attempting in 1890 (according to the foreword in the catalog by the church board of the congregation) to assemble a complete collection of all such writings. It has numerous rare Dutch titles of the 17th and 18th centuries. The library was temporarily stored elsewhere for safety during the last years of World War II and suffered some loss by theft. There have been few accessions during the past 30 years, but in 1916 it had 2,000 volumes, over half of them Mennonitica. The German Conference known as the Vereinigung der Mennoniten-Gemeinden im Deutschen Reich (*q.v.*) attempted to create a theological library, which was added to the Hamburg Mennonite congregational library. The congregations of Crefeld, Emden, and Heubuden had small libraries with Mennonite collections. The Heubuden library, kept in the meetinghouse as a circulating library, was in part destroyed 1945-48, and in part taken over by Polish authorities who may have placed it in the Danzig city library collection. The Weierhof school (Realanstalt am Donnersberg, *q.v.*) had only a small collection of Mennonitica. The Mennonitische Forschungsstelle at Göttingen (est. 1948) is vigorously building up a Mennonite library and now has over 500 titles and numerous serials. It is the only active Mennonite library today (1956) in Europe outside of Amsterdam. The Swiss Mennonite Conference has a small library and archives housed in the Jeangisboden meetinghouse in the Jura district near Tramelan.

(B) *America.* The major Mennonite historical libraries, outside of Amsterdam, are those of the Mennonite colleges at Newton, Kan. (Bethel College) and Goshen, Ind. (Goshen College). The Goshen College Mennonite Historical Library was established in 1907 by the G.C. Alumni Association and developed in a small way by C. Henry Smith until his departure from the institution in 1913. The serious development of the library did not begin until 1929 (holding then *ca.* 200 titles) when Harold S. Bender was given charge of the collection and the Mennonite Historical Society began its substantial support. In 1940 when the collection was placed in the new college library building, it had *ca.* 1,800 volumes. In 1956 its holdings were over 12,500 volumes including serials. The director was Bender and curator Nelson P. Springer, the latter in charge of the library since 1949. The Mennonite Historical Library of the Mennonite Publishing House at Scottdale, founded *ca.* 1908 (librarian John Horsch), reached its height about 1929, when its catalog was published (*Catalogue of the Mennonite Historical Library in Scottdale, Pa.*) containing more than 3,000 items. The catalog lists only some 1,300 titles of books and pamphlets valuable for Mennonite History. Of this number slightly more than 900 (all the foreign language titles and some English) were given in exchange to the Goshen College Library in 1944 where they are shelved as the "John Horsch Collection." The remaining historical materials at Scottdale are now a part of the larger working theological library there serving the Publishing House editorial staff (Alta Erb, librarian). The Goshen library is particularly rich in 16th- and 17th-century Anabaptistica, as well as in Mennonitica Americana.

The Bethel College Mennonite Historical Library, now over 12,000 volumes, including serials (Cornelius Krahn director since 1944), was established by A. Warkentin in 1935 (1,130 cataloged books in 1940), although the collection was begun by C. H. Wedel (d. 1910). The library has grown steadily under the direction of Cornelius Krahn, assisted by John F. Schmidt since 1947. Some 2,000 books and pamphlets were obtained through its director during his sojourns in Europe in 1952 and 1953-54. Larger collections of Mennonitica such as the collection of the Mennonite Historical Association (*q.v.*) have been incorporated, although part of the latter collection went to the Mennonite Biblical Seminary in Chicago. Although the library aims to collect every item pertaining to the Anabaptists and Mennonites in general its holdings are possibly most complete in the realm of Dutch, Prussian, Polish, and Russian Mennonitica. The library is housed in spacious quarters in the new Bethel College Library building, which was completed in 1953.

Additional notable smaller Mennonite historical collections are found as follows: Bluffton College, established as a separate collection in 1928, holdings now about 4,000 volumes; Mennonite Biblical Seminary in Chicago, established in 1944, holdings now about 1,600; Eastern Mennonite College, established *ca.* 1950, holdings now about 1,000 (Irvin Horst librarian since 1955).

The Schwenkfelder Library at Pennsburg, Pa., has a small collection of Mennonitica, mostly American, the core of which it secured from the S. W. Pennypacker collection in 1920. It has attempted to serve as a depository for Mennonite materials from Eastern Pennsylvania, especially Montgomery, Bucks, and Chester counties. The Historical Society of Pennsylvania Library at Philadelphia has a considerable number of Mennonitica Americana, especially Pennsylvania imprints, as does also the large collection of Pennsylvania German imprints in the Pennsylvania German Folklore Center at Franklin and Marshall College, Lancaster, Pa.

The largest collection of Anabaptist material, outside of Amsterdam, Goshen, and Bethel, is to be found in the Prussian State Library (formerly in Berlin, now at the University of Marburg except for unknown war losses), the University of Munich, Germany, and the libraries in Zürich, Switzerland (university, canton, and city). In the United States the Baptist historical libraries at Crozer (Chester, Pa.) and Colgate-Rochester (Rochester, N.Y.) theological seminaries have considerable amounts of Hubmaier and early Anabaptist material. The Union Theological Seminary Library in New York City has the largest general collection of Anabaptist materials in the New World outside of the Mennonite libraries. The Southern Baptist Theological Seminary Library at Louisville, Ky., is building up an Anabaptist collection, as is the Baptist Theological Seminary Library at Zürich/Rüschlikon, Switzerland.

Most of the Mennonite Historical Library collections contain not only printed books and pamphlets, but also periodicals, historical documents, historical manuscripts such as dissertations and papers, microfilms, photocopies, photographs, pictures, recordings, and museum items. Not infrequently denominational archival collections are attached to or housed with or near the collections. Only the Bethel College and Goshen College libraries are attempting exhaustive collections in all fields, languages, and groups. They have established a union catalog. (See **Amsterdam Mennonite Library; Archives;** and the articles **Mennonite Historical Library** of Bethel College, Bluffton College, Goshen College, and Mennonite Biblical Seminary.) H.S.B.

Historical Library (of Mennonite colleges: see **Mennonite Historical Library** (of the colleges).

Historical Societies. In 1956 there were four Mennonite Historical Societies in existence, three in the United States and one in Europe. The Mennonitischer Geschichtsverein (*q.v.*) of Germany, the largest with about 800 dues-paying members, was founded by Christian Hege (*q.v.*) and Christian Neff (*q.v.*) in 1935. It is unique in character as a national organization with a large number of Mennonite ministers as well as laymen in its membership. It publishes (1) a journal, *Mennonitische Geschichtsblätter* (*q.v.*, 1936-), and (2) a publication series, *Schriftenreihe des Mennonitischen Geschichtsvereins,* supports the Research Center (Mennonitische Forschungsstelle, *q.v.*) at Göttingen, and holds annual meetings.

The Mennonite Historical Society (*q.v.*) of Goshen College, Goshen, Ind., is a purely local society of professors and students of Goshen College and Biblical Seminary, with about 100 dues-paying members. Founded in 1920, it was moribund until reorganized in 1924 by Harold S. Bender and Ernst Correll. It publishes the *Mennonite Quarterly Review* (1927-) edits a publication series, *Studies in Anabaptist and Mennonite History,* which it formerly published (up to 1950, since then published by the Mennonite Publishing House at Scottdale, Pa.), holds quarterly meetings during the school year, and supports the Mennonite Historical Library at Goshen College. The Franconia Mennonite Historical Society (*q.v.*), founded in 1930 by John D. Souder and others, is a district society for the Franconia Mennonite

Conference (MC) in eastern Pennsylvania with no dues-paying membership, which holds annual meetigns, supports the Franconia Mennonite Historical Library at Souderton, Pa., and has published J. C. Wenger's *History of the Mennonites of the Franconia Conference.* The Iowa Mennonite Historical Society (*q.v.*), founded in 1948 by Elmer G. Swartzendruber, is a regional society with its center near Kalona, Iowa, with no dues-paying membership, which holds annual meetings. The Mennonite Historical Association (*q.v.*) was created in 1938 by the Historical Committee of the Mennonite General Conference (MC) as a nominal organization of the subscribers of the *Mennonite Historical Bulletin* (*q.v.*). It holds no meetings. The Echo-Verlag (*q.v.*) of Canada, though not called a historical society, is similar to one, with dues-paying members. Earlier, in 1911, H. P. Krehbiel had organized a Mennonite Historical Association (Society, *q.v.*) in the General Conference Mennonite Church, which reported regularly to the triennial sessions of the General Conference and collected a large amount of historical literature and materials, but held no regular meetings. It was replaced in 1938 by the Historical Committee of the General Conference. H.S.B.

Historie der Martelaren, published at Haarlem in 1615: see **Martyr Books.**

Historie van de Vrome Getuygen Jesu Christi, published at Hoorn in 1626: see **Martyr Books.**

Historie der Warachtige Getuygen Jesu Christi, published at Hoorn in 1617: see **Martyr Books.**

Historiography I: Anabaptist. General. Anabaptist historiography was formerly the privilege of its enemies. The Anabaptists could not take part, for from 1528 on the German imperial and national laws threatened death to any defender of Anabaptism. Any attempt to refute false accusations was directly followed by persecution and arrest. Therefore the opponents of Anabaptism were able to spread the most absurd assertions concerning the life and doctrine of the Anabaptists without having to face a rebuttal. They took copious advantage of their position. This violent suppression of the right of self-defense naturally injured the entire Anabaptist brotherhood, for those who were not in a position to draw their own conclusions from observation had to consider them hostile to the state as well as to religion. The few fanatical manifestations among the Anabaptists, which modern research has shown to have occurred largely when their sober leaders had been forcibly removed, were the principal foundation for the attacks of the writers—chiefly theologians—of the 16th century. In their hostile attitude the writers made no distinction between the character of quiet Anabaptism and the extreme excrescences. The few objective contemporary historians like Sebastian Franck (*q.v.*, 1499-1543, *Chronica, Zeytbuch und Geschychtbibel, q.v.,* 1531) were exceptions and exerted little influence. The difficulty of securing a printer also handicapped the Anabaptists in publishing their views. An Amsterdam printer was executed in 1544 for publishing a book by Menno Simons.

This one-sided attitude dominated the body of church historical writings far beyond the 16th century. The very titles of the books dealing with the origin and doctrine of the new brotherhood betray this. One of the oldest writings was Zwingli's *In Catabaptistarum Strophas Elenchus* of 1527; another of the same year was that by Urban Rhegius which appeared in Augsburg: *Wider den newen Tauff-orden, Notwendighe Warnung an alle christ gleubigen durch die diener des Evangelii zu Augsburg*. Also of 1527 was J. Bader's *Brüderliche Warnung für dem newen Abgöttischen orden der Widertäuffer*. In 1528 appeared Philip Melanchthon's book, *Unterricht wider die Lere der Wiedertauffer verdeutscht durch Justus Jonas*, and eight years later the admonition to the princes by the same author, *Das weltliche Oberkeitt den Widertäufferen mit leiblicher straff zu weren schuldig sey*. In 1528 Andreas Althamer also wrote a book, *Ein kurze unterricht den Pfarherrn und Predigern in Brandenburg . . .* ; it draws the conclusion that Anabaptist doctrines carried revolt in their train. In 1531 Heinrich Bullinger wrote *Von dem unverschampten fräfel, ergerlichem verwyrren und unwarhaftem leeren der selbsgesandten Widertouffern;* in 1560 he wrote a second book, *Der widertäufferen ursprung, fürgang, secten, wäsen, fürneme und gemeine irer Artickel*. This method of attack continued in the 17th century. In 1603 Christoph Andreas Fischer published his polemic, *Von der widertauffer verfluchten Ursprung, Gottlosen Lehre und derselber grundtliche widerlegung*, followed in 1607 by his equally venomous book, *Der Hutterischen Widertauffer Taubenkobel*. In 1623 Theobaldus Zacharias wrote *Widertaufferischer Geist, das ist Glaubwürdiger und historischer Bericht, was Jammer und Elend die alten Widertauffer gestifftet und angerichtet* (repr. by W. A. Mayer at Cöthen in 1701). Note also L. Duck's *Adversos impios Anabaptistarum errores* (Hagenau, 1530) and Johannes Gast's *De Anabaptismi exordio, erroribus, historiis abominandis* (Basel, 1544).

These few samples from the literary flood issuing from all the churches are sufficient to show how little interest there was in treating the Anabaptist movement with justice. These works were used as sources by later historians, who took them over without question; very few historians went back to the original confessional writings of the Anabaptist leaders; it occurred to only a few to compare them with the statements of contemporary opponents. Well into the 19th century the great Anabaptist movement of the 16th century was uncritically identified with the Peasants' War of 1525 and the events in Münster; Menno Simons was thought to have gathered the dispersed remnants of the Münster Anabaptists and to have turned them to the ways of peace. But of the persecutions, which lasted in Holland until the last quarter of the 16th century, in Germany until the outbreak of the Thirty Years' War, and in Switzerland until the 18th century, and brought a martyr's death to thousands, practically nothing was said. Not even the imperial laws against baptism upon confession were mentioned.

The inevitable consequence was that these biased presentations could not hold their ground against scholarly investigation as soon as the nature and goals of the Anabaptist movement were clearly recognized. It, of course, took several centuries to reach this point. But when it was reached, an amazing reversal took place in the judgment of scholars regarding Anabaptism. In the meantime many of the Anabaptist ideas, such as liberty of faith and conscience, the rejection of force in religious matters, complete separation of church and state, for which the old Anabaptists had struggled so long and valiantly, had already become so commonly accepted that the movement, so long despised, now attracted the scholar. "Thanks to the research of recent years," writes Adolf Harnack (*Lehrbuch der Dogmengeschichte* III, 1910, 772), "the portraits of distinguished Christians from Anabaptist circles have been given us; and not a few of these honorable and strong-minded men are more comprehensible to us than a heroic Luther or an iron-willed Calvin."

The foundation for this unprejudiced presentation of the Anabaptist movement could not be laid until historians took the trouble of becoming acquainted with the writings of Anabaptist leaders and the testimony of the victims of persecution. There was, to be sure, not a wide selection, but the few writings available were sufficient to enable an unprejudiced scholar to form a judgment. Information on their doctrine was found in the works of Hans Denk, Menno Simons, and Dirk Philips. Their spiritual stature is indicated in their hymns, which were begun in 1535 by the prisoners in the castle at Passau in the oldest Anabaptist hymnal, the *Ausbund*. A collection of the testimony of the martyrs appeared first in the Dutch martyrbook *Het Offer des Heeren* (1562), which Tieleman Jansz van Braght expanded into his *Martyrs' Mirror* (q.v., 1660).

The first writer of church history to make a complete break with the accepted presentation of Anabaptism was Gottfried Arnold (*q.v.*). In his extensive work, *Unparteyische Kirchen- und Ketzer-Historie*, first published in Frankfurt in 1699 (enlarged 3d ed. Schaffhausen, 1740-42), he proves the untruth of a series of false assertions. He was familiar with the writings mentioned above and recognized the injustice of the church toward dissenting Christians. A factor in his interest may have been the fact that he was closely connected with the arising Pietism; through the spiritual relatedness of Pietism with Anabaptism he may have been granted a deeper understanding of it than the theologians of the traditional school. He was reproached with prejudice in favor of the "heretics." But this did not prevent his work from actually forming the transition from the orthodox, limited concept of church history to an objective evaluation of events and processes. Ernst Troeltsch calls Arnold's *Kirchen- und Ketzer-Historie* "a church history which is even today not out-of-date and which can still be compared with modern church historians. It covers an incredibly rich field of material and carries the student into the atmosphere of extra-ecclesiastical Protestantism as no other book does" (*Sociallehren*, 1912, 800).

Nevertheless it took a long time for Arnold's work to find recognition from scholars. The prejudices against circles outside the state church were so deepseated that the principles represented by the Anabaptist brotherhood were intentionally overlooked. German writers of church history were still so much under the spell of the traditional concepts that they could not free themselves for objective reporting, and writers of secular history did not investigate into the religious history of the 16th century deeply enough to recognize the significance of the Anabaptist movement. They saw in it rather a mere secondary phenomenon of the Reformation, which must in the nature of things disappear of itself after the large churches of the Reformation were firmly established. "At the time when the older men of our generation were students," said Walther Köhler in a lecture on Mennonite historical research, "we scarcely heard anything mentioned [about the Anabaptist movement], and if it did happen, a judgment was passed upon it in advance by the use of the word 'fanatics'" (*Gedenkschrift*, 1925, 173). A familiar type of writing about the "heretics" (Anabaptists always one of the chief) was the *Ketzer-Historie* (*q.v.*), *Ketzer-Lexikon,* or *Ketzer-Geschichte* ("Ketzer" being the equivalent of "heretic"), which flourished in the 18th century.

A more careful cultivation of Mennonite history was made first in Holland, where the Mennonites found official toleration earlier than in other countries. Here, after the preliminary work done by van Braght (*q.v.*), the desire for further research was already awakened. The large numbers of Mennonites there—in the 17th and 18th centuries about 10 per cent of the population of Holland belonged to the Mennonite brotherhood—and their economic prominence brought about a greater attention to their own history. In addition the numerous polemics of their opponents compelled them to make an attentive study of the sources. Since in Germany there was no literature of this kind, German writers frequently dealt only with the Dutch Anabaptists.

The oldest historical work produced by the Mennonites was published anonymously in 1615 under the title, *Het beginsel en voortganck der geschillen, scheuringen, en verdeeltheden onder de gene die Doopsgesinden Genoemt worden* (*q.v.*). For a long time it served with *Het Offer des Heeren* and the *Martyrs' Mirror* as one of the three principal sources for the history of the Dutch Mennonites in the 16th century. One hundred years later, in 1720, J. Chr. Jehring published a German translation (*Gründliche Historie*). About this time the works of Herman Schijn, a Mennonite historian, also began to appear. A work of importance was *Geschiedenis der Mennoniten* in three volumes, 1743-45, by Schijn and Gerardus Maatschoen; another was *Nachrichten von dem gegenwärtigen Zustand der Mennoniten,* written by the German historian, S. F. Rues, published at Jena in 1743, and in a Dutch translation in 1745.

In the 19th century new interest awoke in Holland through the influence of Samuel Muller (1785-1875), a professor at the Amsterdam Mennonite Seminary, who published the *Jaarboekje voor de Doopsgezinde Gemeenten* (1837-50). S. Blaupot ten Cate (1807-84) did outstanding regional histories. The historical work of J. G. de Hoop Scheffer (1819-92), also a professor at the Amsterdam Seminary, and the outstanding authority on the Reformation in Holland, was also epoch-making. He brought to light the oldest sources, which he used in many works of lasting value. Alongside of de Hoop Scheffer, Samuel Cramer (1842-1931), professor at the Seminary, deserves credit for his publication of rare 16th-century books dealing with the Anabaptists, in the *Bibliotheca Reformatoria Neerlandica,* the noted collection of works from the time of the Dutch Reformation, which he edited (1903-14).

An abundance of historical treatises appeared in the *Doopsgezinde Bijdragen,* 1861-1919. Dutch Mennonite historiography was brought to a climax with the work of W. J. Kühler (1874-1946) and N. van der Zijpp, both professors at the Seminary. Kühler devoted three volumes to the 16th- and 17th-century Dutch Anabaptists (1932-45) and van der Zijpp presented a brief history of the Dutch Mennonites from the beginning to the present (1952). Cornelius Krahn, the author of the latest complete biography of Menno Simons (1936), summarized the "Historiography of the Dutch Mennonites" in *Church History,* September 1944, and *MQR,* October 1944. Eberhard Teufel presented an annotated bibliography pertaining to the Dutch Mennonites entitled "Täufertum und Quäkertum im Lichte der neueren Forschung" in *Theologische Rundschau,* No. 1 and 2 (1941) 21-48; No. 2 (1948) 161-81. W. Köhler's "Das Täufertum im Lichte der neueren Kirchengeschichtsforschung" (*Archiv f. Ref.-Gesch.* 1940-48) also contains valuable historiographical material on Dutch Anabaptism. (See **Historiography: Netherlands** below.)

In Germany in the 17th century presentations of the whole of Anabaptist history were predominantly in the Latin language. The best-known works are those of A. Meshovius (*q.v.*), *Historiae Anabaptisticae Libri Septem* (Cologne, 1617) and J. H. Ottius (*q.v.*), *Annales Anabaptistici* (*q.v.*, Basel, 1672). Since the middle of the 18th century German research scholars have engaged in the study of Anabaptist history. In his copious collection of sources on Swiss Reformation history (*Beyträge zur Erläuterung der Kirchen-Reformations-Geschichten des Schweitzerlandes,* Zürich, 1741-53), the Swiss scholar J. C. Füsslin (*q.v.*) published valuable materials on Swiss Anabaptist history. On the Anabaptist movement in Bavaria in the 16th century V. A. Winter published in 1809 a fragmentary presentation (*Geschichte der baierischen Wiedertäufer*) based on several archival sources, in which he nevertheless completely misinterpreted their character. He even attempted to justify the Anabaptist persecutions against Kant's conception of the scienceless character of the heresy judges. In the Anabaptist movement he saw only mischief and ruin to the state (p. 162). The results of more recent research were used by Siegmund Riezler in his sensitive presentation in *Geschichte Bayerns* (1903).

The first comprehensive history of the Anabaptists (*Geschichte der Taufe und Taufgesinnten*) was published in 1789 by Joh. Aug. Starck, the Hessian court chaplain. Starck was severely attacked by the rationalistic wing; he called his book a sort of defense of his theological position (p. VI). Beside the writings (1821, 1829) of G. L. von Reiswitz and F. Wadzeck it was the most reliable informative work on the history of the Mennonites in the first centuries up to that time. J. Hast's *Geschichte der*

Wiedertäufer (1836), written by a Catholic, is typical of the early 19th century. The liberal Karl Hagen (*Deutschlands . . . Verhältnis im Ref.-Zeitalter* IV, 1844) and the orthodox Max Goebel (*Geschichte des christlichen Lebens* II, 1848) began a juster objective reporting.

A great impetus was given to the study of Anabaptist history about the middle of the 19th century by the noted Old Catholic historian, Carl A. Cornelius (*q.v.*), who by his thorough research (e.g., *Geschichte des Münsterischen Aufruhrs,* 1855-60) sought to fathom the nature and significance of Anabaptism, and thus came to the conclusion that the movement emanated from more worthy motives than the historians, secular and religious, had up to that time given it credit for.

In rapid sequence thorough investigations of the Anabaptist movement of the 16th century were now published, throwing light upon this hitherto neglected branch of church history. For a while nearly every year produced several works on the history of the Anabaptists in various countries or on leading personalities in the movement. Heberle wrote on Hans Denk (1851 and 1855) and Capito's relation to Swiss Anabaptism (1858), G. E. Röhrich on Hans Denk (1853) and the Anabaptist movement in Strasbourg (1860), K. Keim on Ludwig Haetzer (1856), K. W. H. Hochhuth on the movement in Hesse (1858-60), Friedrich Nippold on David Joris (1863-68), and Chr. Meyer on the movement in Upper Swabia (1874). Later many individual biographies of Anabaptist leaders appeared; e.g., Denk (Keller 1862, Haake 1897, Schwindt 1922, Weis 1925, Coutts 1927, Vittali 1932); Haetzer (Weis 1930, Goeters 1956); David Joris (Bainton 1935); Grebel (Bender 1950); Blaurock (Jecklin 1891, Loserth 1898, Moore 1955); Hofmann (Leendertz 1883, zur Linden 1885); Hubmaier (Vedder 1905, Mau 1912, Sachsse 1914, Wiswedel 1939); Menno (Cramer 1837, Roosen 1848, Vos 1914, Horsch 1916, Krahn 1936).

Some excitement was caused by the research done by archivist Ludwig Keller (*q.v.*) of Münster on the forerunners of the Anabaptists and by his attempt to prove direct connection between them and the old-evangelical parties of the Middle Ages. In his investigations he was led by the idea that the Anabaptists, in whom he recognized a revival of apostolic church life, must be the descendants of those suppressed brotherhoods, and he tried on a large scale to construct an unbroken chain of free evangelical brotherhoods from original Christianity to the present. Even though this attempt failed, nevertheless his book, *Die Reformation und die älteren Reformparteien* (1885), retains its value by virtue of the source material it contains; it was a powerful incentive to further research on Anabaptist history in all countries in which congregations were formed during the Reformation. Even before this book appeared, Ludwig Keller had published monographs on the Anabaptists, for the purpose of serving the truth. His presentation of the life of the Anabaptist leader Hans Denk (*Ein Apostel der Wiedertäufer,* 1882) won wide attention.

In the following years books and articles on the Anabaptists were published as follows: J. Habets on Maastricht (1877), J. Hansen on Aachen (1884), F. O. zur Linden on Melchior Hofmann (1885), Gustav Bossert on the Anabaptist movement in Württemberg (1888 ff.), C. Gerbert, in Strasbourg (1889), Karl Rembert, in the duchy of Jülich (1893 and 1899), A. H. Newman on the Anabaptist movement in the 16th century (1897), Joh. Loserth, in Styria (1894), Eduard Jacobs, in the Harz (1899), Friedrich Roth, in Augsburg and Upper Swabia (1900), Eduard Becker, in Kürnbach (1902), Rudolf Wolkan on the hymns of the Anabaptists (1903) and the Hutterian Brethren in America (1918), Christian Hege on the Anabaptists in the Kurpfalz (1908), Paul Wappler, in Thuringia (1908 ff.), Hermann Nestler, in Regensburg (1926), and Alt, in Kaufbeuren (1930).

The theology of the Anabaptists and their place in the history of Christian thought has received considerable attention in recent years. Ernst Troeltsch's *Sociallehren der christlichen Kirchen und Gruppen* (1912, English 1936) was epoch-making and influential for the typology of the Anabaptist movement. Johannes Kühn's *Toleranz und Offenbarung* (1923) was a further creative and stimulating effort in this direction. Karl Holl, "Luther und die Schwärmer" (*Gesammelte Aufsätze,* 1922), and Ulrich Bergfried, *Die Verantwortung als theologisches Problem im Täufertum des 16. Jahrhunderts* (1938), while containing much valuable information, wrote wholly from the strict Lutheran standpoint with a negative critical outcome, similar to H. Lüdemann's earlier *Reformation und Täufertum* (1896) from the Reformed standpoint. Fritz Heyer, *Der Kirchenbegriff der Schwärmer* (1939) is better but still misconceives the Anabaptist position. Walther Köhler, *Dogmengeschichte als Geschichte des Christlichen Selbstbewusstseins,* II *Das Zeitalter der Reformation* (1951) is the first general history of dogma to give the Anabaptists both space and a fair evaluation. F. W. Littell's *The Anabaptist View of the Church* (1952) is by all odds the best monograph an Anabaptist theology yet produced. John Horsch's *Infant Baptism and its Origin among Protestants* (1917) treats a limited field thoroughly and is important for its assembly of documentary evidence for the emergent years of Anabaptism. Ethelbert Stauffer's important article "The Anabaptist Theology of Martyrdom" brilliantly opens a new aspect. H. S. Bender has set forth the essence of the Anabaptist faith in *The Anabaptist Vision* (reprinted from *MQR* XVIII, 1949). The *Mennonite Quarterly Review's* "Special Anabaptist Theology Number" (January 1950) contains valuable studies. J. C. Wenger published "The Theology of Pilgram Marpeck" (*MQR* XII, 1938, 205-56). The latest study is Peter Kawerau's *Melchior Hofmann als religiöser Denker* (1954).

Modern comprehensive accounts of Anabaptism, following the initial attempt by Anna Brons in her *Ursprung, Entwickelung und Schicksale* (1884), have been delivered only by English and American writers (except for the brief account in Horst Penner's *Weltweite Bruderschaft* of 1955). In English A. H. Newman's *History of Anti-Pedobaptism . . . to 1609* (1897) was the first good account, and is still useful. E. B. Bax, *Rise and Fall of the Anabaptists* (1903), written from the social and socialistic point of view, does not go beyond Münster. E. C. Pike, *The Story of the Anabaptists* (1904), is better but brief. C. H. Smith's general works on Mennonite history (1920 and 1941) give the best comprehensive treatment, although John Horsch's *Mennonites in Europe* (1942) gives more detail, and R. J. Smithson's *The Anabaptists* (1935) is a reliable popular account. Roland Bainton's treatment of the Anabaptists in his *Reformation of the Sixteenth Century* (1952) is the best in any general history of the Reformation or of the church as a whole. At last the true character of the Anabaptists is being reported by the best modern church historians, among whom the American Bainton is a peer. W. Wiswedel's well-written and reliable essays on a large number of Anabaptist leaders and episodes in his 3-volume work, *Bilder und Führergestalten aus dem Täufertum* (1928, 1930, 1952), together with numerous articles in scholarly journals, stamp him as one of the best living scholarly popular writers in Anabaptism. He writes *ex animo*.

In prewar Austria the Hutterian Brethren had their history written by their own chroniclers and distributed by means of copies. To the outside world the brotherhood was shut away for centuries. These valuable documents were published in extracts in 1883 by Josef Beck in volume 43 of the *Oesterreichische Geschichts-Quellen* as *Geschichts-Bücher der Wiedertäufer*. Finally the full publication of the large *Geschicht-Buch* was accomplished by Rudolf Wolkan in 1923 and A. J. F. Zieglschmid in 1943, followed by the *Klein-Geschichtsbuch* by Zieglschmid in 1947. The large Hutterian hymnbook had already been published in 1914; the fully edited scholarly edition by Zieglschmid (manuscript deposited in the Goshen College Library) still awaits a publisher.

There had already been some articles published by Gregor Wolny on the Anabaptists in Moravia (1850) and by von Kripp on the Anabaptist movement in Tirol (1857). The work and collection of materials of Beck was followed by publications by Alexander Nicoladoni on Johannes Bünderlin (1888 and 1893), by Joseph Jäkel on the Anabaptist movement in Upper Austria (1889 and 1895), by the outstanding scholar Joh. Loserth on the Anabaptist movement in Tirol (1892 and 1894), on Balthasar Hubmaier (1893), the Anabaptist movement in Moravia and Styria (1894), on the communism of the Hutterites in Moravia (1894), and on the movement in Lower Austria (1899), besides numerous articles in the *Mennonitisches Lexikon* and in other periodicals. Loserth's work is of the highest quality. Worthy of mention are also the works by Hartmann Amman on the Anabaptist movement in the Puster Valley (1896 and 1897), by Georg Loesche on Anabaptism and Protestantism in Tirol and Vorarlberg (1926), by Robert Friedmann on the Habaner (*q.v.*) in Czechoslovakia (1927), by Lydia Müller on the communism of the Hutterian Brethren in Moravia (1927), by Fr. Hruby on the Anabaptists in Moravia (1935), by Franz Kolb on the movement in the Wipptal (1951), and by Widmoser on Tyrolese Anabaptism (1951). John Horsch's *Hutterian Brethren* (1929) is the only good general work on the Hutterites in English.

A stately series of writings has also been produced in Switzerland, the country of Anabaptist origins. In addition to the studies by Füsslin, pioneer work was done by Emil Egli on the Anabaptists in Zürich (1878) and in St. Gall (1887), and in his important collection of court records regarding the history of the Swiss Reformation (*Actensammlung zur Schweizerischen Reformationsgeschichte,* 1879). Egli's research in the field of church history yielded disclosures fundamental to the study of Mennonite origins. After his death Georg Finsler published (in 1910) the first volume of the history of the Swiss Reformation (1519-25), which Egli had almost completed. Here Egli's research is unusually comprehensive, precisely on the Anabaptist movement. From the socio-economic viewpoint Ernst H. Correll throws light on Swiss Anabaptist-Mennonites (1925); his work was the first thorough presentation of an Anabaptist group in the sociological sense. (See **Historiography: Switzerland** and **Historiography: France** below for further details.)

On the Anabaptist movement in Italy the publications of Karl Benrath, *Wiedertäufer im Venetianischen* (1885) and *Reformation in Venedig* (1887), have been superseded by the work of Henry DeWind "Anabaptism and Italy" in *Church History* (1952), based on his unpublished doctoral dissertation at the University of Chicago, "Relations Between Italian Reformers and the Anabaptists in the Mid-Sixteenth Century" (1951). DeWind has shown that there was no true Anabaptist movement in Italy, Benrath and Comba (*I Nostri Protestante,* 1897) having confused anti-Trinitarians with Anabaptists. (See **Italy**.)

Anabaptism in England will receive full treatment for the first time in Irvin Horst's doctoral dissertation (Amsterdam, 1957).

The chief repository of scholarly articles on Anabaptist history, theology, etc., is the *Mennonite Quarterly Review,* which since its founding in 1927 has published a vast amount of material in this field and seeks to keep abreast of current research. Significant articles have appeared in *Archiv für Reformations-Geschichte* and in *Church History*.

Independent judgments on the Anabaptist movement are found in few handbooks on church history. One of the first objective presentations was that by Max Goebel in his *Geschichte des christlichen Lebens in der evangelischen rheinisch-westfälischen Kirche* (1848). The most thorough evaluations were given by K. Müller in his *Kirchengeschichte* (2nd ed. 1922) and Möller-Kawerau in *Lehrbuch der Kirchengeschichte* (1907). Noteworthy articles appear in *HRE* (3rd ed., 1896-1908), and in *RGG* (2nd ed., 1926).

The historiography of utopian as well as scientific socialism also dealt with Anabaptism. This trend, represented especially by Kautsky (*Vorläufer des neueren Sozialismus* I, 1895) and Bernstein (d. 1932), had two objectives: (1) to explain the Reformation in general according to the principles of materialistic historiography; (2) to see especially in the Anabaptist movement the "forerunners of modern socialism." A critical summary of these attempts was given for the first time in Correll, *Das schweizerische Täufermennonitentum* (1925), p. 6 f.; see also p. 16; see also his sections "Allgemeine his-torisch-soziologische Kennzeichnung des Täufer-tums" and "Ausbreitung und ökonomisch-sozialer Charakter des Täufer-Mennonitentums" with his-toriographical remarks. Socialistic historiography has to its credit the recognition of the distinction be-tween radical and pacifist Anabaptists. Recently East German writers have exploited the Anabaptists for the Communist cause; e.g., K. Kleinschmidt, *Thomas Münzer* (1952).

Finally the religio-sociological standard works by Ernst Troeltsch (*Protestantisches Christentum und Kirche in der Neuzeit*, 1909, and *Die Soziallehren der christlichen Kirchen und Gruppen*, 3rd ed. 1923, translated into English, *The Social Teachings of the Christian Churches*, N.Y., 1936) and Max Weber (*Gesammelte Aufsätze zur Religionssoziologie* I, 1920, and "Wirtschaft und Gesellschaft" in *Grund-riss der Sozialökonomie*, 1922) have removed the last trace of a sectarian judgment. To the same end Walther Köhler (1870-1946), the Zwingli scholar, worked in an eminently objective manner.

For a treatment of bibliographies see the article on this subject in Volume I of this ENCYCLOPEDIA.

Source Publications. The past 30 years have wit-nessed a significant amount of publication of major Anabaptist sources. The first such enterprise was the publication of two Marpeck writings, one, the *Vermahnung* edited by Christian Hege in the *Ge-denkschrift* of 1925, the other the *Verantwortung* edited by Johann Loserth in 1929 (*Quellen und Forschungen zur Geschichte der oberdeutschen Taufgesinnten im 16. Jahrhundert*). Meanwhile the Verein für Reformationsgeschichte, led by Hans von Schubert and Otto Scheel, had undertaken the pub-lication of all Anabaptist archival sources in the German language area, under the series title, *Quellen zur Geschichte der Wiedertäufer* (changed to *Täu-fer* in 1951). The following volumes appeared before 1940: *Herzogtum Württemberg* 1930, *Markgraftum Brandenburg* (Bayern I) 1934, *Glaubenszeugnisse oberdeutscher Taufgesinnter* (Hutterite) 1938. After World War II, the Mennonitischer Geschichtsverein (*q.v.*) now being a partner in the project, the fol-lowing additional volumes appeared: *Bayern* II 1951, *Baden-Pfalz* 1951, *Hans Denk's Works* 1956. Fur-ther volumes are in preparation: *Alsace* I (Stras-bourg), *Glaubenszeugnisse* II, *Württemberg* II, *Hut-terite Epistles* 2 vv., *Austria* 3 vv., *Rhineland* 2 vv.

The *Täuferakten* for Hesse (1527-1626) were also published in 1951 by the Historische Kommission für Hessen und Waldeck, and in 1952 Leonhard von Muralt began the publication of a Swiss Anabaptist source series (*Quellen zur Geschichte der Täufer in der Schweiz*) with a volume on Zürich, to be fol-lowed by a volume containing the *Berner Gespräch* of 1538, and at least two other volumes.

The two great Hutterite chronicles have been pub-lished, the first in two editions (Wolkan, Vienna, 1923, and Zieglschmid, Philadelphia, 1943), the sec-ond, again by Zieglschmid, in 1947 at Philadelphia. Riedemann's *Rechenschaft* was reprinted twice (in 1903 at Scottdale, Pa., and in 1938 in England), then published in an English translation in England in 1949. The *Mennonite Quarterly Review* has pub-lished a series of English translations of shorter docu-ments and tracts by J. C. Wenger, such as the *Schleitheim Confession*. The American Series, *The Christian Classics*, published in 1956 one volume on the Anabaptists and related groups.

There has been extensive use of the Anabaptist theme in literature, with the Münsterites used most often. Two doctoral dissertations surveyed this field up to 1913: W. Rauch, *Johann von Leiden, der Kö-nig von Sion, in der deutschen Dichtung* (Leipzig, 1912), and H. Hermsen, *Die Wiedertäufer zu Mün-ster in der deutschen Dichtung* (Stuttgart, 1913). Elizabeth H. Bender published a series of articles on Anabaptists and Mennonites in German and Ameri-can literature in the *Mennonite Quarterly Review* 1943-46, and Mary E. Bender's doctoral dissertation (Indiana, 1957) surveys the field since 1900.

The hymnology of the Anabaptists received an out-standing treatment by Rudolf Wolkan in his *Die Lieder der Wiedertäufer* (Berlin, 1903). The great German hymnologist, Philipp Wackernagel, treated Anabaptist hymnology twice. His *Lieder der nieder-ländischen Reformierten aus der Zeit der Verfolgung im 16. Jahrhundert* (Frankfurt, 1867) is largely de-voted to Dutch Anabaptist hymns, reproducing a total of 79, while volume III of his *Das deutsche Kirchenlied* (Leipzig, 1870) reprints 45 hymns of German Anabaptists (441-86). (See **Hymnology**.)

The only comprehensive treatment of Anabaptist historiography to date is that by Christian Hege in his article **Geschichtsschreibung** in *ML* II, 96-101, to which the present article is much indebted. H.S.B.

Historiography II: Switzerland. *General Histories.* The best general accounts of the Anabaptist-Men-nonite movement in Switzerland are those by C. Henry Smith, *The Story of the Mennonites* (3rd ed. 1950), and John Horsch, *Mennonites in Europe* (2nd ed. 1950). Samuel Geiser, the only Mennonite his-torian of Switzerland, published a very valuable history of the Swiss Mennonites under the title *Die Taufgesinnten-Gemeinden* (1931, pp. 496), but as the title suggests it is not limited to the Swiss, only pp. 126-214 and 369-486 being devoted to this group. Anna Brons, *Ursprung, Entwickelung . . . der Men-noniten* (1884) has a generous section on Switzer-land. Ernst Correll, *Das schweizerische Täufer-mennonitentum, Ein soziologischer Bericht* (1925, pp. 145), includes France and South Germany. Ernst Müller's *Geschichte der Bernischen Täufer* (1895, pp. 411) and Delbert Gratz's *Bernese Anabaptists* (1953, pp. 205) are thorough regional histories, Gratz including emigrant settlements in Europe and America. All general surveys of Anabaptism and Mennonitism must of course pay attention to the history of Swiss Anabaptism as the initial aspect of the whole movement and need not be further men-tioned here; likewise general or cantonal histories of Swiss Protestantism. However, A. H. Newman's *A History of Antipedobaptism . . . to 1609* has a very good section on Swiss Anabaptism, pp. 88-152; J. H. Ott's *Annales Anabaptistici, hoc est Historia Universalis de Anabaptistarum origine, progressu . . .* (1672; pp. 360) reports chronologically year by year, consists largely of quotations from sources, and does not segregate Swiss material, though containing much of it. J. Heberle, "Die Anfänge des Anabaptismus in der Schweiz," *Jahrbücher für deutsche Theologie* III (1858), 225-79, and C. A. Cornelius, *Geschichte des Münsterischen Aufruhrs* II, *Die Wiedertaufe* (1860, pp. 413), 1-30 and 240-50, are excellent. Special monographs on Swiss Anabaptism include: H. S. Burrage, *A History of the Anabaptists in Switzerland* (1882, pp. 230); Gottfried Strasser, "Der Schweizerische Anabaptismus zur Zeit der Reformation," in *Berner Beiträge zur Geschichte der Schweizerischen Reformationskirchen* (1889, pp. 168-245); and Richard Nitsche, *Geschichte der Wiedertäufer in der Schweiz* (1885, pp. 107). L. von Muralt gives a valuable summary of Swiss Anabaptist doctrines in *Glaube und Lehre der schweizerischen Täufer in der Reformationszeit* (1938, pp. 49), while H. Lüdemann, *Reformation und Täufertum in ihrem geschichtlichen Verhältnis zum christlichen Prinzip* (1896, pp. 95) sharply attacks the Anabaptist position. Georg Thormann gives a valuable report on the Swiss Anabaptists of the 17th century, particularly in Bern, in his *Probier-Stein oder Schriftmässige und aus dem wahren innerlichen Christenthumb Hergenommene Gewissenhafte Prüfung des Täuffertums* (1693, pp. 610). Robert Friedmann's *Mennonite Piety Through the Centuries, Its Genius and Its Literature* (1949, pp. 287), besides the chapter "The Devotional Literature of the Swiss Brethren 1600-1800" (pp. 154-75), devotes the first part (pp. 3-90) to a treatment of "Anabaptism and Pietism" based largely on a study of the Swiss J. J. Wolleb, *Gespräche zwischen einem Pietisten und Wiedertäuffer* (Basel, 1722, pp. 314). Paul Peachey's *Die soziale Herkunft der Schweizer Täufer* (1954, pp. 157) gives the first thorough report on the social origins of the Swiss Anabaptist population.

Cantonal and Local Histories. Zürich, known as the birthplace of Anabaptism, has received the most frequent treatment. Heinrich Bullinger's two books, *Von dem unverschampten fräfel . . .* (1531, folios 178) and *Der Widerteuflleren Ursprung, fürgang, Secten, wäsen* (1560, pp. 231), while most valuable, are polemical attacks rather than history. The best monograph is Cornelius Bergmann, *Die Täuferbewegung in Kanton Zürich bis 1660* (1916, pp. 176). But see also Emil Egli, *Die Züricher Wiedertäufer zur Reformationszeit* (1878, pp. 104), and Walther Köhler, "Die Züricher Täufer" in *Gedenkschrift zum 400-jährigen Jubiläum der Mennoniten* (1925), 48-64. Fritz Blanke's brilliant *Brüder in Christo* (1955, pp. 88) tells the story of the rise and end of the first Anabaptist congregation at Zollikon, canton of Zürich, in 1525. Paul Kläui, *Geschichte der Gemeinde Horgen* (1952, pp. 746), 185-92, includes the story of the Anabaptist congregation at Horgen. Walter Rauschenbusch, "The Zürich Anabaptists and Thomas Müntzer," in *Amer. Journal of Theology* (1905, pp. 91-106), prints Grebel's letter to Müntzer in 1524 with comments. A report of persecutions in the Zürich territory 1635-45 is contained in an undated pamphlet, *Ein warhafftiger Bericht von den Brüdern im Schweitzerland, in dem Zürcher Gebiet, wegen der Trübsalen,* which has been reprinted (46 pp.) in all American editions of the *Ausbund* beginning in 1742. See also *Wahrhaffter*

Bericht unsers des Bürgermeisters . . . der Statt Zürich . . . unserer Handlungen gegen den Widertäufferen (1639, pp. 71). Other cantonal and local histories worthy of note are Emil Egli, *Die St. Galler Täufer* (1887, pp. 64); Ernst Müller, "Langnauer Täufer vor 200 Jahren," in *Kirchliches Jahrbuch für den Kanton Bern* IV (1893) 63-133; P. Burckhardt, *Die Basler Täufer* (1898, pp. 125); C. A. Bächtold, "Die Schaffhauser Wiedertäufer in der Reformationszeit" in *Beiträge zur vaterländischen Geschichte* (1900, pp. 73-118); W. J. McGlothlin, *Die Berner Täufer bis 1532* (1902, pp. 37); G. Appenzeller, "Solothurner Täufertum im 16. Jahrhundert," in *Festschrift für Eugen Tatonioff* (1938, pp. 110-34) and "Beiträge zur Geschichte des Solothurner Täufertums" in *Jahrbuch f. Sol. Geschichte* (1941, pp. 50-89); A. Fluri, *Beiträge zur Geschichte der Bernischen Täufer* (1912, pp. 69, reprint from *Blätter f. Bernische Geschichte, . . .*); J. Heiz, "Täufer im Aargau" in *Taschenbuch . . . des Kantons Aargau* (1902, pp. 107-205); R. Feller, "Die Anfänge des Täufertums in Bern" in *Festgabe für Heinrich Türler* (1931, pp. 105-12); O. Vasella, "Von den Anfängen der Bündnerischen Täuferbewegung," in *Ztscht f. Schw. Geschichte* (1938, pp. 165-84). T. de Quervain's *Kirchliche und soziale Zustände in Bern* (1906, pp. 286) has a good chapter on the Anabaptists (pp. 120-58) and Max Stiefel's similar *Die kirchlichen Zustände im Knonaueramt nach der Reformation 1531-1600* (1947) has a useful chapter on the Anabaptists (pp. 152-67); R. Wolkan, *Die Lieder der Wiedertäufer* (1903, pp. 295), has considerable sections on the hymns of the Swiss Brethren (pp. 26-56, 118-64). For biographies of Conrad Grebel, the founder of Zürich Anabaptism, see Christian Neff, "Konrad Grebel," in *Gedenkschrift (op. cit.,* pp. 65-133) and H. S. Bender, *Conrad Grebel* (1950, pp. 326). Beatrice Jenny's theological treatment, *Das Schleitheimer Täuferbekenntnis"* 1527 (1951, pp. 81), taken with Fritz Blanke's "Beobachtungen zum ältesten Täuferbekenntnis" in *Arch. f. Ref.-Geschichte* (1940, pp. 242-48) and J. C. Wenger's translation and commentary, "The Schleitheim Confession of Faith," in *MQR* XXIV (1950, pp. 243-53), gives a definitive picture. Milton Gascho's "The Amish Division of 1693-1697 in Switzerland" in *MQR* XI (1937, pp. 235-66) is excellent, based on the sources. Jan Matthijssen gives a good account of the great Bern disputation of 1538 in *MQR* XXII (1948, pp. 19-33). M. de Boer's "Vom Thunersee zum Sappemeer, ein Täufer- und Auswandererschicksal aus drei Jahrhunderten," in *Berner Zeitschrift für Geschichte und Heimatkunde* (1947) 1-24, is a valuable account of the Swiss Mennonite settlement in Holland in 1711 ff.

Source publications. The Swiss Anabaptist sources are to be published in a series of at least four volumes, *Quellen zur Geschichte der Täufer in der Schweiz,* of which Vol. I, *Zürich,* edited by L. von Muralt and Walter Schmid (replacing Egli's *Aktensammlung* of 1879) appeared in 1952 (pp. 428). The next volume (due in 1957) is to be the record of the Bern disputation of 1538. J. C. Füsslin, *Beiträge zur Erläuterung der Kirchen-Reformations-Geschichten des Schweitzerlandes,* 5 vv. (1741-53), contains much material not in von Muralt-Schmid, which stops with 1533. The discussions of the Reformed preachers of Bern with Hans Pfistermeyer in 1531 were printed under the title *Ein christenlich Gespräch* (pp. 90). Oecolampadius' written reply to the Anabaptists Carlin and Hubmaier appeared in 1527 under the title *Underrichtung von dem Widertauff von der Oberkeit, und von dem Eyd, auff Carlins N. Widertauffers Artikel* and *Antwort auff Balthasar Hümeiers Büchlein wider der Predicanten Gespräch zu Basel von dem Kindertauff* (pp. 103). The only other public Anabaptist disputation to be published was that of Zofingen of 1532 (*Handlungen oder Acta der Disputation gehalten zu Zofingen, 1532*, folios 154).   H.S.B.

Historiography III: France. No adequate treatment of the history of Anabaptism or Mennonitism in France has been published, and the French Mennonites have produced no thorough historians. Pierre Sommer (1874-1952), long a leader in the French Conference, did more than anyone else to gather and publish historical materials. (See *Pages choisies de Pierre Sommer précédées d'une Esquisse Biographique, 1955*, pp. 143). With Valentin Pelsy he published *Précis d'Histoire des Eglises Mennonites* (1914, new ed. 1937, pp. 162), but the section "Les Mennonites en France" contains only nine pages (119-28). His most extensive work was done in a historical series in *Christ Seul*, which he founded in 1907 (preliminary publication 1901-7), published 1930-33 in 49 articles with separate historical sketches of all existing and extinct Mennonite congregations in France. His successor as editor of *Christ Seul*, Pierre Widmer, is also historically active, having published *Almanach Cinquantenaire (1901-1951)*, with much historical material. Pierre Sommer also contributed numerous articles to the *Mennonitisches Lexikon* including the one on France. C. Henry Smith, John Horsch, and Anna Brons have little on the history of the French Mennonites in their general volumes.

The history of Anabaptism in Alsace has been treated in all the general works on Anabaptism, and also in monographs, the best of which is A. Hulshof, *Geschiedenis van de Doopsgezinden te Straatsburg van 1525 tot 1557* (1905, pp. 262). Louis Hauth, *Les Anabaptistes à Strasbourg au Temps de la Reformation* (1860, pp. 34), although a Strasbourg dissertation (B.Th.), is unimportant. Much more valuable is the work of T. W. Röhrich, "Zur Geschichte der Strassburgischen Wiedertäufer in den Jahren 1527 bis 1534," in *Ztscht f. hist. Theologie* (1860, pp. 3-121), and particularly Camill Gerbert, *Geschichte der Strassburger Sectenbewegung . . . 1524-1534* (1889, pp. 200). See also X. Mosemann, *Les Anabaptistes á Colmar 1534-35*. Robert Kreider, "The Anabaptists and the Civil Authorities of Strasbourg 1525-1555" in *Church History* (1955, 99-118) has much to contribute, as does Christian Neff's article **Martin Bucer** (*ME* I, 455-60).

On the Mennonites of France in the last 250 years see *Les soirées Helvetiennes, Alsaciennes, et Fran-Comtoises* (1772), A. Michiels, *Les Anabaptistes des Vosges* (1860, pp. 333), and Ch. Mathiot, *Recherches historiques sur les Anabaptistes de l'Ancienne Principauté de Montbéliard, d'Alsace et des Regions*

voisines (1922, pp. 158). "Anabaptistes" in these titles refers to modern Mennonites, since the latter term had not come into general use in the French language until recently. Correll's *Das schweizerische Täufermennonitentum* (1925) has a strong section on the modern French Mennonites, "Die Täuferemigranten im Elsass, in Baden und der Kurpfalz (der 'elsässische' und 'pfälzische' Mennonit im besonderen)" pp. 75-135, with special emphasis on the sociological and agricultural aspects. Paul Leuillot, "Les Anabaptistes Alsaciens Sous le Second Empire d'après une Enquête Administrative de 1850" in *Journal d'Alsace* LXXXVII (1947) 207-11, calls attention to a valuable governmental report. P. Marthelot, "Les Mennonites dans L'Est de la France" in *Revue de Géographie Alpine* XXXVIII (1950) 475-91, is a useful socio-geographic account of the Mennonites in Alsace and Lorraine, emphasizing their agricultural contribution.   H.S.B.

Historiography IV: Netherlands. *Introduction.* Anabaptism in the Low Countries began predominantly as a movement among the lower classes of the cities. In the Netherlands the Mennonites shunned the "world" more consistently and extremely than anywhere else, but being mainly urban and sharing the wealth and opportunities of the Golden Age of the country, the more progressive factions of Dutch Mennonitism gradually become secularized. They began to take part in all the functions of the social, cultural, economic, and political life of the country. Soon we find among them men like the great writer Joost van den Vondel, and the poet and painter Carel van Mander. Thus it is not surprising that scholarly inquiry into the beginnings of their own history could grow and develop.

When a movement originates in struggle and persecution there is little time for retrospection and objective description of facts. This was especially true in the case of the Dutch Anabaptists, who for a long time were persecuted, gradually tolerated, and finally granted freedom. The early literature relating to them, as during the first centuries of the Christian church, was produced by both friend and foe. Controversy is the characteristic of all historic literature of this period. And Anabaptism had to struggle not only with the foe outside the flock but also the foe within the brotherhood. The attempt to establish a church "without spot or wrinkle" caused the internal controversy. Accordingly, before entering the field of modern historiography, it is necessary to follow the high lights of this controversial literature as far as it has value for the historian of Mennonitism.

Controversial Historical Literature (1530-1740). 1. *External Controversy.* Before Menno Simons withdrew from the Catholic Church and became the leader of the Dutch Anabaptists he wrote "a very clear and explicit" pamphlet against Jan van Leiden, the king of the New Jerusalem (1535). But Menno Simons was involved in religious discussions with more worthy opponents than Jan van Leiden. John a Lasco, reformer of East Friesland, had a religious debate with Menno Simons in Emden in 1544, after which Menno presented to him his confession of faith (*Opera omnia*, 517-42; *Complete Writings*,

419-54). A Lasco replied to this (J. a Lasco, *Opera,* ed. A. Kuyper I, 1866, 1-60). Gellius Faber, who had participated in the debate, wrote a pamphlet against the Anabaptists in which he denied the proper calling of the Anabaptist minister (*Eine antwert . . . vp einen bitterhönischen breeff der Wedderdöper,* Magdeburg, 1552). In answering this challenge Menno gives the most detailed and valuable information concerning his development as a priest and consequent conversion to Anabaptism (*Een klare beantwoordinge over een schrift Gellii Fabri, Opera,* 225-324; *Complete Writings,* 623-781).

An early and outstanding Catholic opponent of Menno Simons and the Anabaptists was M. Duncanus (*Anabaptisticae haereseos confutatio et vere Christiana baptismi ac potissimum paedobaptismatis assertio, adversus M. Simonis Frisii virulentas de baptismo blasphemias* 1549). The strongest attack by a representative of the Reformed Church of this time was made by Guido de Bray (*La racine, source et fondement des anabaptistes ou rebaptisez de nostre temps,* 1561). A number of reprints of a Dutch translation appeared, and an English translation at Cambridge, Mass., in 1668. The great Reformed theologian Dathenus (*q.v.*) was not only the chief opponent of the Anabaptists at the Frankenthal debate (1571) but also a writer against them. Gerhard Nicolai translated Heinrich Bullinger's *Adversus anabaptistas* into the Dutch and added a refutation of Dutch Anabaptism (*Inlasschingen in het vertaalde werk v. Bullinger: "Teghens de Wederdoopers,"* Embden, 1569, reprinted in *BRN* VII). The complete record of the religious debate held at Emden (1578) between representatives of the Reformed Church and the Mennonites continuing through 124 sessions (see *Emden* Disputation) was published. A similar debate consisting of 156 sessions, held at Leeuwarden in 1595 (see **Leeuwarden** Disputation), was also published. Pieter van Keulen was the outstanding Mennonite representative at both places.

J. P. van der Meulen wrote the *Successio Apostolica* (1600) to prove that the Anabaptist church was in direct lineal descent from the Apostolic Church. A Catholic priest (Simon Walraven) answered this in the *Successio Anabaptistica* (1603), which proved to be an important source for Mennonite history, and was reprinted by S. Cramer (*BRN* VII). H. Faukelius, a Reformed minister, wrote *Babel, d. i. Verwerringhe der Weder-dooperen onder malkanderen* (1621), in an attempt to produce evidence of the weakness and heresy of Anabaptism because of its numerous divisions. This was answered by A. Roscius, among others, in *Babel, d. i. Verwerringe der Kinderdooperen onder malcanderen* (1626). He pointed out that on the same grounds the believers in infant baptism must be guilty of greater heresy, since there were more divisions among them than among the Anabaptists. J. Cloppenburch was another minister who wrote against the Anabaptists (*Gangraena Theologiae Anabaptisticae,* 1645). A well-known source on Anabaptism is *Grouwelen der voornaemster Hooft-Ketteren . . .* (1623) which was originally published in Latin and translated into German and Dutch (*Catalogus Amst.,* 7). J. Hoornbeek, a Reformed theologian, wrote numerous books concerning the Ana-

baptists, among which *Summae controversarium Religionis* (1658) is outstanding. His colleague F. F. Spanheim also participated in this controversy. His book, *Selectarum de religione controversiarum elenchus* (1687), was answered by the Mennonite minister Engel Arendszoon van Dooregeest, in *Brief aan den Heer F. Spanhemius Prof. der H. Godsgeleertheyt en der Historien tot Leyden.* Another outstanding defender of the Mennonite cause was the well-known physician and minister of the Mennonite Church at Amsterdam, Galenus Abrahamsz de Haan, in his *Verdediging der Christenen die Doopsgezinde genaamd worden, beneffans korte grondstellingen van hun gelove en leere* (1699). Among the many books of devotional, controversial, and historical character written by Pieter Jansz Twisck we mention in this connection his *Chronijck van den Onderganc der Tijrannen* (2 vols., 1619-20).

About the middle of the 18th century a revival of controversy occurred, when the Mennonites were accused by their Reformed neighbors of harboring Socinian beliefs. This accusation centered mainly around the gifted Mennonite minister, Johannes Stinstra. A case similar to Stinstra's was that of A. van der Os. A detailed account of this controversy was given in Chr. Sepp's *Johannes Stinstra en zijn tijd* (2 vv., Amst. 1865-66); W. J. van Douwen's *Socinianen en Doopsgezinden* (Leiden, 1898); W. J. Kühler's *Het Socinianisme in Nederland* (Leiden, 1912); and J. C. van Slee's *De Geschiedenis van het Socinianisme in de Nederlanden* (Haarlem, 1914). (For further literature on it, see *Catalogus Amst.,* 109-46.) The article "De Nederlandsche gereformeerde synoden tegenover de Doopsgezinden (1563-1620)" by F. S. Knipscheer (*DB* 1910 and 1911) discusses the attitudes of the Reformed synods to the Mennonites. The proceedings of the Reformed synods were published by Reitsma and van Veen in *Acta der Provinciale en Particuliere Synoden* (I-VII, 1892-98).

2. Internal Controversy. Historical source material can be found in both devotional and controversial literature. Furthermore, in some instances it is hard to distinguish between the two types, since a given book may have both purposes. A number of books by Menno Simons and Dirk Philips deal with matters of internal controversy. Outstanding are questions of church discipline, that is, excommunication and shunning. A valuable account of the origin and the divisions among the early Anabaptists was written by Obbe Philips (*Bekenntenisse,* 1584, reprinted in *BRN* VII). He had baptized Menno Simons and his own brother Dirk Philips, but later withdrew from the brotherhood. A similarly significant source is *Het beginsel en voortganck der geschillen, scheuringen, ein verdeeltheden . . .* (1659, reprinted in *BRN* VII).

The outstanding contribution of the Anabaptists of the 16th century to the field of devotional and historical literature was the compilation and publication of *Het Offer des Heeren* (1562), the first edition of the famous collection of biographies, testimonies, and songs of Anabaptist martyrs (reprinted in *BRN* II). Hans de Ries, the prominent writer and leader of the more liberal Mennonites (Waterlanders), enlarged this collection considerably and had it published in 1615 under the title *Historie der Martelaaren*. P. J. Twisck, a voluminous writer and representative of the more conservative Mennonites (Old Frisians), edited a reprint of this edition for his churches and added a confession of faith (1617). The resulting controversy brought forth a significant description of the inner conditions of the Mennonite church during the latter part of the 16th and early 17th centuries in Hans Alenson's *Tegen-Bericht op de voor-Reden van 't groote Martelaer Boeck der Doops-Ghesinde*, 1630 (BRN VII).

Better known is the enlarged edition of the *Martyrs' Mirror* edited by Tieleman Jansz van Braght under the following title: *Het Bloedigh Tooneel der Doops-gezinde en Weereloose Christenen, die om het getuygenisse Jesu . . . geleden hebben en gedoodt zijn, v. Christi tijt af, tot dese onse laeste tijden toe. Mitsgaders een beschrijvinge des H. Doops en stucken . . . Begrepen in twee boecken. Zijnde een vergrootinge vande voorgaenden Martelaers-Spiegel* (1660). The second edition (1685) was illustrated by the Mennonite artist and poet Jan Luyken. Van Braght's book is not merely a compilation of facts and biographies concerning the Anabaptist martyrs, as the previous edition had been, but an attempt to interpret history. In tracing the history of the martyrs from the Apostolic Church down to the Anabaptist persecution he concludes that the true Christian church has always had its martyrs. He also includes a history of baptism in his book proving that adult baptism was practiced during the first centuries of the Christian church and was later replaced by infant baptism (see **Martyrology**).

Until the middle of the 17th century the internal controversy in Holland centered mainly around questions of the degree of rigidity and strictness of church discipline and the attitude of the church toward the world. This divided the Mennonites into numerous factions such as Waterlanders, Frisians, Flemish, and others, which in turn were again subdivided. Then a great new upheaval overshadowed the former divisions and caused the formation of two main wings. This was caused by the rationalistic-pietistic movement of the Collegiants and the Socinians, mentioned above in connection with the discussion on the external controversy of the Mennonites.

Galenus Abrahamsz de Haan, a brilliant physician and minister of the Flemish Mennonite Church of Amsterdam, became the central figure of the Collegiant movement in the Netherlands. His chief opponent was his colleague, Samuel Apostool, also a physician and minister in the same church. The latter represented the conservative Mennonite groups, while the former, influenced by modern trends and thought of his time, advocated a liberal reformation of his church. Being an outstanding and influential leader he had a large following. The controversy resulted in a split in the Amsterdam church in 1664 which gradually spread throughout the country. The followers of Galenus were known as "Lamists" and those of Apostool as "Zonists" from the names of their respective meetinghouses in Amsterdam. From the flood of pamphlets and writings which resulted from this controversy only a few

typical titles will be given here. Theodore van der Meer wrote *Het Gekraay van een Socianiaanse Haan, onder Doopsgezinde Veederen* (1663). An outstanding anonymous pamphlet was *Lammerenkrijgh* (1663). Most recently this era and controversy has been treated by H. W. Meihuizen in *Galenus Abrahamsz* (1954).

Beginnings of Scholarly Historiography. During the first half of the 18th century the historiography of the Dutch Mennonites became more scholarly. It was, however, not the liberal wing that made the first contribution of this type. To be sure, they had founded a theological seminary at Amsterdam in 1735, but their main interest centered around current problems, such as the relationship of religion to natural science, philosophy, etc. The spirit of unlimited tolerance and increasing indifference which was spreading among them was not conducive to appreciation and study of their past; hence this progressive wing of the Mennonites could not at this time make any significant scholarly contributions in this field. At the threshold of modern historiography in the Netherlands there are representatives of the conservative "Zonists" like Herman Schijn, Gerardus Maatschoen, and Marten Schagen.

Schijn's first book, *Korte historie der protestante Christenen, die men Mennoniten of Doopsgezinden noemt . . .* (1711), was written for the general public. Encouraged by the fact that scholars abroad made wide use of it, he wrote a Latin version of his book (*Historia Christianorum qui in Belgi Foeder. inter Protestantes Mennonitae appellantur*, 1723), which was followed by a second volume (*Historiae Mennonitarum plenior deductio*, etc., 1729). M. van Maurik translated these two volumes into Dutch (1727 and 1738). Maatschoen, like Schijn, a minister and physician at Amsterdam, made another translation and added a preface, annotations, illustrations, and a third volume (*Geschiedenis dier Christenen, welke in de Vereenigde Nederlanden onder de Protestanten Mennoniten genaamd worden*, 1743-45). Although these men were not scholarly historians in the modern sense of the term, they produced a significant piece of work in compiling much valuable material. They viewed past and present controversial matters objectively and encouraged others to continue along these lines. Another ardent collector of Anabaptistica and the author of a book on the Waldenses was Marten Schagen, linguist, book dealer, and minister. He was the translator of F. S. Rues's *Aufrichtige Nachrichten von dem gegewärtigen Zustande der Mennoniten . . .* (Jena, 1743) into Dutch (*Tegenwoordige Staet der Doopsgezinden of Mennoniten, in de Vereenigde Nederlanden*, 1745), to which he added material of his own. The extent of the libraries owned by Rues and by Maatschoen, as revealed in the printed catalogs, indicates their extraordinary interest and knowledge in this new field of study. Non-Mennonite writers who should be mentioned in addition to Rues are Jakob Mehrning (*S. Baptismi Historia: Das ist, Heilige Tauff-Historia . . .*), the Remonstrant historian Geeraert Brandt (*Historie der Reformatie*, 4 volumes, 1671-1704), A. Moubach and B. Picard (*Naaukeurige Beschryving der uitwendige Godstdienst-plichten*, 6 volumes, 1727-38).

The second half of the 18th century is marked by a general indifference and decline in Dutch Mennonite church life. Both numerically and spiritually the group reached its lowest level at the end of the century. To be sure, in 1778 the noted Teyler Theological Association (Teyler's Godgeleerd Genootschap) of Haarlem was founded and has contributed, especially of late, to the promotion of research in the field of Anabaptistica. At that time, however, in accordance with the general spirit of the age, the relationship of religion to the natural sciences and philosophy was the main concern of the organization. Thus Mennonite historiography received a setback from which it did not recover until the beginning of the 19th century.

A Century of Historiography (1840-1940). The beginning of the 19th century marks a new era in the history of Dutch Mennonites. The most sincere and loyal among them realized the necessity of uniting the scattered churches and the divided forces of the small brotherhood. After a number of local unions had been formed, the Dutch Mennonite conference, *Algemeene Doopsgezinde Sociëteit* (A.D.S.), was organized in 1811, which included nearly all the Mennonite congregations of the Netherlands and the adjacent German Mennonite churches. The general and main purpose of this organization was to care for the spiritual and economic welfare of the churches and to prevent further decline. To accomplish this the newly established A.D.S. accepted the supervision of the Mennonite Theological Seminary at Amsterdam, which had thus far been taken care of by the local Amsterdam congregation, and gave financial support to small churches which could not provide for themselves.

The revived church life as well as the newly established church unions aroused historical interest. From this time on the Mennonite Theological Seminary of Amsterdam was the center of Mennonite historical research. Efficient professors and librarians collected and preserved, in the library and archives of the Mennonite Church of Amsterdam, what is now known as the best collection of Dutch Anabaptistica. The first of the professors to pioneer in this field was Samuel Muller. He introduced a course in Mennonite history at the seminary and founded and edited the *Jaarboekje voor de Doopsgezinde Gemeenten in Nederland* (1837-50). In addition he wrote numerous articles and collected much material. Furthermore, he inspired his students in theology to continue his work. A. M. Cramer wrote the first comprehensive biography of Menno Simons (*Het leven en de verrigtingen van Menno Simons,* 1837). S. Blaupot ten Cate was the author of an extensive and scholarly history of the Mennonites of the Netherlands which is indispensable even today, *Geschiedenis der Doopsgezinden in Friesland* (1839); *Geschiedenis der Doopsgezinden in Groningen, Overijssel en Oost-Friesland* (1842), *Geschiedenis der Doopsgezinden in Holland, Zeeland, Utrecht en Gelderland* (1849). J. G. de Hoop Scheffer, professor and librarian at Amsterdam, was editor of the *Doopsgezinde Bijdragen* (published 1861-1919) and a pioneer historian. Christiaan Sepp also carried on extensive research in the field of Anabaptist history.

(*Geschiedkundige Nasporingen,* 3 vv., 1872-75; *Johannes Stinstra en zijn tijd,* 2 vv., 1865-66.)

1. *The Origin of Anabaptism.* The relationship between the Münsterite Anabaptists and Dutch Mennonitism had always been a touchy subject for the earlier Mennonite writers. From the time of the writings of Menno Simons against Jan van Leyden and Menno's *Fundamentboek* until the history of the Mennonites was written by Schijn-Maatschoen, the main object was defense. The opponents emphasized the similarities which pointed to a common origin with the fanatical elements in Anabaptism, while the Mennonite writers denied or minimized this and attempted to prove the Biblical character of their church, which they traced back, hypothetically, to the Apostolic Church. The interpretation of the history of the Mennonites by T. J. van Braght in the *Martyrs' Mirror* has been mentioned. In this theory of the *Successio Apostolica* the Waldenses furnished a welcome link. Outstanding among those who did research in the history of the Waldenses and their supposed connection with the Anabaptists was A. M. Cramer in his book on Menno Simons (1837). Neither he nor S. Blaupot ten Cate found any definite evidence of a direct lineage from the Waldenses to the Anabaptists. J. H. Halbertsma based his theory of historical connection on the similarities between the Waldenses and the Anabaptists (*De Doopsgezinden en hunne herkomst,* 1843). This proved to be a challenge for further research in that field. Blaupot ten Cate wrote *Geschiedkundig onderzoek naar den Waldensischen oorsprong van de Nederlandsche Doopsgezinde* (1844), while others made contributions of lesser importance to this field. However, even after the Dutch Mennonite historians had given up this theory, a staunch advocate arose in the German historian and archivist Ludwig Keller. In his numerous writings, he advocated the theory of the direct descent of the Anabaptists from what he called the pre-Reformation Old-Evangelical Brethren Churches. In this chain of evangelical churches, the Waldenses formed an important link (*Die Reformation und die älteren Reformparteien,* Leipzig, 1885, and other publications).

It must be noted that it was the research of the Catholic scholar C. A. Cornelius, which changed the approach to the problem radically (*Berichte der Augenzeugen über das Münsterische Wiedertäuferreich,* Münster, 1853; *Geschichte des Münsterischen Aufruhrs,* 2 vols., Leipzig, 1855-60). From that time on both Catholic and Protestant scholars gradually gave increasingly unprejudiced consideration to the Anabaptist movement of the 16th century.

The manner in which the assertion of a connection between the Mennonites and the Münsterite Anabaptists was revived in our own century is an irony of history. This time it was not a debate between an "orthodox" Catholic or Protestant and a "heretic" Anabaptist, but a lively and lengthy discussion between the two leading Dutch Mennonite historians, viz., Karel Vos, minister and historian, and W. J. Kühler, professor in the Mennonite Theological Seminary and the University of Amsterdam. In 1917 Vos published (in *DB*) "Kleine bijdragen over de Doopersche beweging in Nederland tot het optreden van Menno Simons." Influenced by the materialistic and socialistic interpretation of the Münster incident, Vos does not hesitate to consider the chiliastic and revolutionary element of Anabaptism, as it found its most extreme expression in the "kingdom" of Münster, as genuine original Dutch Anabaptism. According to this interpretation, the Biblicist peaceful element became dominant after the Münster catastrophe by falling from one extreme to another. Kühler replied to this in his article, "Het Nederlandsche Anabaptisme en de revolutionnaire woelingen der zestiende eeuw" (DB 1919). This in turn was answered by Vos in "Revolutionnaire Hervorming" (De Gids, LXXXIV, 1920). Kühler concluded the controversy with his "Het Anabaptisme in Nederland" (De Gids, 1921). In his article, as well as in his subsequently published history of the Mennonites in the Netherlands, Kühler emphasizes that the Biblicist peaceful type of Anabaptism, without the practicing of adult baptism, existed in the Netherlands before the preaching and baptizing by Melchior Hofmann in 1531 (in the Sacramentist movement, the Brethren of the Common Life, etc.). Hofmann and his preachers were reaping without sowing. After Hofmann's arrest the Anabaptist movement split into two groups: the left wing of Münster, and the right wing of Obbe and Dirk Philips, Menno Simons, and others. No doubt Kühler came closer to the historical truth than Vos, even though he probably overemphasized the independence of the reformatory movement in the Netherlands. One of the studies that have since appeared dealing with this subject is A. F. Mellink's De Wederdopers in de Noordelijke Nederlanden 1531-1544 (1954), which follows the Vos-Kautzky line, whereas N. van der Zijpp thoroughly criticized Vos' thesis in "Menno en Munster," in Stemmen (1953).

2. General and Local History. In addition to these histories on the origin of the Dutch Anabaptists some earlier and some recent monographs and studies of a general character deserve mention. The Mennonite historians of the 19th century, Samuel Muller, de Hoop Scheffer, Samuel Cramer, and others, furnished a number of articles on the Mennonites, Menno Simons, etc., for the internationally known encyclopedias of different countries. De Hoop Scheffer's article, "Korte geschiedenis der Mennoniten en Doopsgezinden" (DB 1882), translated from the second edition of the Real-Encyclopädie für protestantische Theologie und Kirche (see also Chr. Sepp, Bibliotheek, 387-89), and Cramer's article, "Mennoniten," in the third edition of this work, deserve special mention. The latter also wrote, among other contributions, a significant study, "De Doopsgezinde Broederschap in de negentiende eeuw" (DB 1901), and a survey of Dutch Mennonite statistics of the 19th century (DB 1902). The most significant history of the Mennonites of the Netherlands, after that by S. Blaupot ten Cate, was Anna Brons's Ursprung, Entwickelung und Schicksale der altevangelischen Taufgesinnten oder Mennoniten in kurzen Zügen übersichtlich dargestellt (1884), which covers the history of all Mennonites in all countries.

The need for a scholarly Dutch history of the Mennonites of the Netherlands grew more and more urgent. W. J. Kühler published Geschiedenis der Nederlandsche Doopsgezinden in de zestiende eeuw (Haarlem, 1932), which was continued in 1940 when the first half of the second volume appeared, now entitled Geschiedenis van de Doopsgezinden in Nederland (Tweede deel, 1600-1735, eerste helft). After Kühler's death one chapter of Vol. II, Part 2, "Gemeentelijk leven," appeared (Haarlem, 1950). N. van der Zijpp published the first modern complete history in Geschiedenis der Doopsgezinden in Nederland (1952). A general survey of early Anabaptism, including the Dutch, was written in England by R. J. Smithson entitled The Anabaptists, Their Contributions to our Heritage (London, 1935), and in America by H. E. Dosker, The Dutch Anabaptists (Philadelphia, 1921). C. Henry Smith's Story of the Mennonites (1941) and John Horsch's Mennonites in Europe (1942) give major attention to the history of Anabaptism in Europe, particularly in Holland, and later Dutch Mennonite history.

A. L. E. Verheyden has published considerable material on the Anabaptists in Flanders in addition to his major work, Het Mennisme in Vlanderen, which awaits publication in English and Dutch. Among his publications are Doopsgezinden te Gent (1943), and Anabaptist Martyrologes for Brügge (1945), Gent (1945), and Courtrai-Brussels (1950). Most valuable is Bibliographie des Martyrologes Protestants Néerlandais (2 vv., 1890) and Jean Meyhoffer, Le Martyrologe Protestant des Pays Bas 1523-1597 (1907). For further literature consult the Catalogus of the AML (146-55, 287-97).

The Lower Rhine and Northwest Germany until recent time were culturally in close contact with the Netherlands. Besides the works of Goebel (1848) and Rembert (1899), an outstanding contribution is the series of articles by Ernst Crous in Der Mennonit, May-August, 1956, "Von Täufern zu Mennoniten am Niederrhein."

3. Biographies and Genealogies. Melchior Hofmann was the medium through which Anabaptism was spread from South Germany to the Low Countries. He expounded his teachings in a number of books. For these reasons considerable literature about him is available. Teyler's Godgeleerd Genootschap awarded prizes for two biographies and published them. One was written by W. I. Leendertz entitled Melchior Hoffman (1883), and the other by F. O. zur Linden entitled Melchior Hofmann, ein Prophet der Wiedertäufer (1885). Samuel Cramer's edition of Melchior Hofmann's writings, with a valuable introduction, was published in 1909 as Volume V of BRN. The most recent publication is Melchior Hofmann als religiöser Denker by Peter Kawerau (1956). The latest biography which lists all the literature by and about David Joris, who for a while lived and worked in the Netherlands, is written by Roland H. Bainton and entitled David Joris Wiedertäufer und Kämpfer für Toleranz im 16. Jahrhundert (Archiv für Reformationsgeschichte, Ergänzungsband VI, Leipzig, 1906).

Throughout the century of Mennonite historiography no other leader was the object of as many studies as Menno Simons. A. M. Cramer pioneered in this field by presenting a thorough study, Het leven en de verrichtingen van Menno Simons (1837), on the occasion of the third centennial of Menno Simons' conversion. Of those who made special contributions in this field we mention J. G. de Hoop Scheffer, *"Eenige opmerkingen en mededeelingen betr. Menno Simons"* (*DB* 1864, 1865, 1872, 1881, 1889, 1890, 1892, 1894); G. E. Frerichs, *"Menno's taal"* (*DB* 1905); "Menno's verblijf in de eerste jaaren na zijn uitgang"(*DB* 1906), and Karel Vos, *Menno Simons, 1496-1561, Zijn leven en zijne reformatorische denkbeelden* (Leiden, 1914), which is well documented and gives evidence that the author is the best authority on the sources in that field. Two years later, John Horsch published *Menno Simons, His Life, Labors, and Teachings* (Scottdale, 1916).

About 1848 two German biographies of Menno Simons appeared. B. C. Roosen wrote *Menno Simons den evangelischen Mennoniten-Gemeinden geschildert* (Leipzig, 1848) and C. Harder *Das Leben Menno Symons* (Königsberg, 1846). On the fourth centennial of the conversion of Menno Simons, Cornelius Krahn presented his study, *Menno Simons (1496-1561), Ein Beitrag zur Geschichte und Theologie der Taufgesinnten* (Karlsruhe i.B., 1936). The first part is a biography of Menno Simons and the second an interpretation of the theology of the Anabaptists as compared with that of the reformers of the 16th century. Recent American brief biographies are *Menno Simons, Apostle of the Nonresistant Life* (Berne), by C. Henry Smith, and *Menno Simons' Life and Writings* (Scottdale, 1936), by Harold S. Bender and John Horsch. In this connection "De portretten van Menno Simons (Met 12 afbeeldingen)" (*DB* 1916) by G. J. Boekenoogen should be mentioned. Menno Simons' writings have been published in the Dutch, German, and English languages. However, a scholarly edition of the original writings of Menno Simons has not yet been published. The Mennonite Publishing House of Scottdale, Pa., published in 1956 in a revised translation, *The Complete Writings of Menno Simons* edited by J. C. Wenger, the first absolutely complete edition in any language.

The writings of Obbe Philips (S. Cramer in *BRN* VII, 1910), Dirk Philips (F. Pijper in *BRN* X, 1914), and Adam Pastor (S. Cramer in *BRN*) have been edited by S. Cramer and F. Pijper, who wrote introductions which contain the best available information concerning their lives. A. H. Newman wrote "Adam Pastor, Antitrinitarian Antipaedobaptist," in *Papers of the American Society of Church History* V (1917). Complete biographies of these and other co-workers of Menno have not yet been written.

More than thirty biographies, partly illustrated, of the great Mennonite leaders of the first century are given in the second and third volumes of Schijn-Maatschoen's previously mentioned history of the Mennonites. K. de Wit published 30 pictures of leading men in *Verzaameling van de afbeeldingen van veele voornaame mannen en leeraaren* (Amsterdam, 1743), each illustration accompanied by a short poem written by men like J. van den Vondel and Adr. Spinniker. The biography of Galenus Abrahamsz de Haan (1622-1706) was presented by H. W. Meihuizen (Haarlem, 1954). Important material about Mennonite Collegiant connections is found in van Slee, *De Rijnsburger Collegianten* (Haarlem,

1895), and C. B. Hylkema, *Reformateurs* (2 vv., Haarlem, 1900 and 1902).

4. *Characteristics and Principles.* We shall not attempt to mention all of the literature which deals with Mennonite tenets, beliefs, teachings, and principles, but merely name a few outstanding titles of the past and present centuries. J. H. Scholten's *De Leer der Hervormde Kerk,* in which he characterized the Anabaptists, was the reason for the writing of D. S. Gorter's *Onderzoek naar het kenmerkend beginsel der Nederlandsche Doopsgezinden* (1850) and S. Hoekstra's *Nog iets over het eigenlijke wezen van den Doopsgezinden Christen* (1851). All this was just a prelude to the most significant work written on this subject by a Dutch theologian, viz., *Beginselen en leer der oude Doopsgezinden, vergeleken met de overige Protestanten* (1863), by Sytse Hoekstra Bz. Hoekstra, the author of numerous books in systematic theology, made a thorough comparative study of the Mennonite and other Protestant teachings and principles.

We shall not here attempt to present the interpretations of the essential principles of Anabaptism as they are given by the well-known historians, Albrecht Ritschl, Ludwig Keller, Karl Holl, Ernst Troeltsch, Max Weber, Walther Köhler, and others, but will merely mention a few significant recent publications in this field. An outstanding treatise is Ethelbert Stauffer's "Märtyrertheologie und Täuferbewegung" (*Zeitschrift für Kirchengeschichte*, XV, 1933, 545-98; English also in *MQR* XIX, 1945, 179-214), which presents the outstanding characteristic of Anabaptism as the willingness to suffer for the Lord. The martyrs went through a threefold baptism—with the spirit, with the water, and with the blood. The willingness to suffer, which the Dutch call "lijdzaamheid," finds expression in the principle of nonresistance. How this principle was given up by the Dutch Mennonites is described by J. Dyserinck in "De Weerloosheid volgens de Doopsgezinden," in the journal *De Gids* I (1890) 104-61 and 303-42, by S. Cramer in "Hoe een van onze vroegere kenmerken is te niet gegaan" (*DB* 1898), and by Vos in *De Weerloosheid der Doopsgezinden* (1916). A recent Dutch study of this field was made by N. van der Zijpp in *De vroegere Doopsgezinden en de krijgsdienst* (1930). The most thorough study based on Dutch sources is *Die Wehrfreiheit der Altpreussischen Mennoniten* (Marienburg, 1863) by W. Mannhardt.

N. van der Zijpp published the only general study on Dutch confessions: *De Belijdenisgeschriften der Nederlandse Doopsgezinden* (1954); English translation in *MQR* XXIX (1955) 171-87.

The most detailed Dutch account of the development of modes of baptism was given by J. G. de Hoop Scheffer in his "Overzicht der Geschiedenis van den Doop bij Onderdompeling" (*Verslagen en Mededeelingen der Koninklijke Academie van Wetenschappen,* Afd. Letterkunde, 2.reeks, dl. XII, Amsterdam, 1883). Karel Vos wrote "De doop bij overstorting" (*DB* 1911).

Menno Simons and his followers shared the peculiar conception of the incarnation of Christ held by Melchior Hofmann. Krahn in "Der Gemeindebegriff Mennos im Zusammenhang mit seiner Lehre von der Menschwerdung Christi" (*Menno Simons,* 1936) attempts to point out the connection between this doctrine and their conception of a church "without spot and wrinkle." Irvin E. Burkhart wrote "Menno Simons on the Incarnation" (*MQR IV,* 1930, VI, 1932). The most recent treatment of this question was presented by H. J. Schoeps in *Vom Himmlischen Fleisch* (Tübingen, 1951).

Regarding the Mennonite principle of nonconformity a few titles deserve special mention. P. Langendijk gives an account of the complaints of the Swiss Mennonites who settled in the Netherlands about the worldliness of their Dutch brethren (*De Zwitsere Eenvoudigheid, klagende over de bedorvene Zeden veeler Hollandse Doopsgezinden,* 1713; see also *Mennonite Life* X, July 1955). C. N. Wybrands portrays the cultural and ethical standards of the past conservatism of the Dutch Mennonites in *Het Menniste Zusje* (1913).

F. S. Knipscheer wrote an exhaustive study concerning the controversy on silent and audible prayer in "Geschiedenis van het stil en het stemmelijk gebed bij de Nederlandsche Doopsgezinden" (*DB* 1897, 1898, *Catalogus Amst.,* 188). In "Reizen naar de Eeuwigheid" (*DB* 1896) J. J. Honig Jz. makes a study of one of the most popular devotional books entitled *Wegh nae Vredenstadt* (1625) by Pieter Pietersz. The most complete study of this subject was made by Robert Friedmann in *Mennonite Piety Through the Centuries* (Goshen, 1949). Books in the field of devotion and theology are listed in the *Catalogus,* pp. 212-39, 306-10. Sermons are found on pp. 239-56 and 310-24. The extensive literature in the field of religious education is given on pp. 256-65 and 324-29.

The Dutch Mennonites had their own Bible translations. Samuel Muller wrote on this subject the article "Het onstaan en het gebruik van Bijbelvertalingen onder de Nederlandsche Doopsgezinden" (*Jaarboekje voor Doopsgezinde gemeenten,* 1837). Also the articles *Bible Translations,* and *Bibles used by Anabaptists* (*ME*) give information along these lines. Pieter Jansz Twisck, one of the most prolific Mennonite writers of the 17th century, wrote a Bible concordance entitled *Concordantie der Heyligher Schrijtvren enz.* (Hoorn, 1615), which was generally used. He added a second volume, *Bybelsch Naem- ende Chronyck-boeck* (Hoorn, 1632).

Libraries and Archives. The most complete collection of books and documents on Dutch Anabaptistica is to be found in the Library and Archives of the Mennonite Church of Amsterdam. Smaller collections are located in the libraries of the universities of Amsterdam, Leyden, Groningen, and Kiel, the Royal Library at the Hague, the British Museum, and certain church and private libraries among the Mennonites of the Netherlands and Germany. Most of the archives have been microfilmed by the Historical Committee of the General Conference Mennonite church. The microfilms are located in the Bethel College Historical Library.

The collections of Dutch Mennonitica in America are growing. Special efforts are being made to preserve and collect everything in connection with the history of the Mennonites, including the Dutch, by the Mennonite historical libraries of Bethel College

and Goshen College. These two libraries have next to the Library of the Mennonite Church of Amsterdam the largest collections of Dutch Mennonitica.

C.K.

Historiography V: North Germany including West and East Prussia, and Poland. The Mennonites of Germany in general were later in joining scholars in Mennonite research than the Dutch. Gerrit Roosen was an exception when he published his *Unschuld und Gegen-Bericht der Evangelischen Tauffgesinnten Christen . . .* (1702). Little was written or published along these lines by German Mennonites until the middle of the past century when, under the influence of their Dutch brethren and scholars like Ludwig Keller, they too began to investigate phases of their history and principles and publish articles and books. The Mennonites of northern Germany were the first to do work along these lines. B. C. Roosen wrote *Geschichte der Mennoniten-Gemeinde in Hamburg und Altona* (2 vv., 1886-87) and did also some genealogical research. The *Familien-Chronik* of the van der Smissens (1875) was published, and monographs and articles dealing with various phases of the Mennonites in the Schleswig-Holstein and Hamburg area appeared in a number of periodicals. Most significant was Robert Dollinger's *Geschichte der Mennoniten in Schleswig-Holstein, Hamburg, und Lübeck* (1930), which contains a fairly good bibliography dealing with this area. Heinz Münte presented *Das Altonaer Handlungshaus van der Smissen 1682-1824* (1932) with a bibliography on the subject. Wanda Oesau wrote *Hamburgs Grönlandfahrer auf Walfischfang und Robbenschlag vom 17.-19. Jahrhundert* (1955). Scattered information about the Mennonites can be found in all major writings dealing with the economic life of the cities of Altona and Hamburg, such as A. Lichtwark's *Das Bildnis in Hamburg* (2 vv., 1898) and P. Th. Hoffmann's *Neues Altona* I (1929) 217 ff.

Some of the outstanding writings on the Anabaptists and Mennonites of East Friesland are J. P. Müller, *Die Mennoniten in Ostfriesland* I (1887); II (*Jahrb.* IV, Emden); C. A. Cornelius, *Der Anteil Ostfrieslands an der Reformation bis zum Jahr 1535* (1852); E. Kochs, "Die Anfänge der ostfriesischen Reformation" I and II, in *Jahrb. d. Ges. f. bild. Kunst u. vaterl. Altertümer zu Emden* XIX, 109-273 and XX, 1-125; H. Reimers, *Die Gestaltung der Reformation in Ostfriesland* (1917); J. ten Doornkaat Koolman, *Kurze Mitteilungen aus der Geschichte der Mennoniten-Gemeinde in Ostfriesland . . . und der Norder Gemeinde . . .* (1903); *idem, Mitteilungen aus der Geschichte der Mennoniten-Gemeinde zu Norden im 19. Jahrhundert* (1904); Blaupot t. C., *Groningen, Overijssel en Oost-Friesland* I and II (1842). Abraham Fast wrote *Die Kulturleistungen der Mennoniten in Ostfriesland und Münsterland* (1947).

The Mennonites of the Lower Rhine were first extensively treated by Karl Rembert in *Die "Wiedertäufer" im Herzogtum Jülich* (1899). The Mennonites of Crefeld were featured in *Beiträge zur Geschichte Rheinischer Mennoniten* (1939). W. I. Hull treated a phase of the Crefeld Mennonite Church in his *William Penn and the Dutch Quaker Migration to Pennsylvania* (Swarthmore College, 1935). A related study is Friedrich Nieper's *Die ersten deutschen Auswanderer von Krefeld nach Pennsylvanien* (1940). The economic significance of the Crefeld Mennonites was recently investigated by Gerhard von Beckerath in *Die wirtschaftliche Bedeutung der Krefelder Mennoniten . . .* (1951). The Mennonite textile manufacturers of Gronau are represented in V. Muthesius, *100 Jahre M. van Delden & Co.* (1954), and *Das Geschlecht Van Delden* (1954).

In addition to what has been said about the Anabaptism of Münster and Westphalia in the Dutch section of the historiography it should be stated that P. Bahlmann compiled a bibliography on this subject which was published under the title, "Die Wiedertäufer zu Münster" (*Ztscht f. vaterl. Gesch. u. Altertums-Kunde*, 1893; Part I, pp. 119-74). Outstanding are the source collections and writings on the Münsterites by J. Niesert, C. A. Cornelius, L. Keller, Kl. Löffler. Fiction writers and artists continue to deal with this subject. Among the dissertations dealing with the belles-lettres on this subject should be mentioned: W. Rauch, *Johann van Leyden, der König von Zion, in der Dichtung* (1912) and H. Hermsen, *Die Wiedertäufer zu Münster in der deutschen Dichtung* (1913). A recent treatment of the Reformation of Westphalia, including the Anabaptists, is Fr. Brune, *Der Kampf um eine evangelische Kirche im Münsterland 1520-1802* (1953), which contains a valuable bibliography.

The Mennonites of the Vistula area were originally featured mostly by non-Mennonites in books like W. Crichton's *Zur Geschichte der Mennoniten* (Königsberg, 1786), Reiswitz and Wadzeck's *Beiträge zur Kenntnis der Mennoniten-Gemeinden . . .* (2 vv., 1821, 1829), and Max Schön's *Das Mennonitentum in Westpreussen* (Berlin, 1886). However, through the *Mennonitische Blätter,* started by Johann Mannhardt in Danzig in 1853, which carried many articles pertaining to the Mennonites, and the historian Wilhelm Mannhardt, who wrote the book, *Die Wehrfreiheit der Altpreussischen Mennoniten* (1863), interest in their own history was created among the Mennonites of Prussia. The first fruit was the brief *Kurzgefasste Geschichte der Elbinger Mennoniten-Gemeinde* (1883). Bruno Schuhmacher (*Niederländische Ansiedlungen . . . ,* 1903) and Felicia Szper (*Nederlandsche nederzettingen . . . ,* 1913) investigated the Dutch Mennonite settlements in Prussia, which subject is included also in B. H. Unruh's *Die niederländisch-niederdeutschen Hintergründe der Mennonitischen Ostwanderungen . . .* (1955). Walter W. Mitzka made a linguistic study, *Die Sprache der deutschen Mennoniten* (1931?). H. G. Mannhardt did the history of the Danzig Mennonites, *Die Danziger Mennonitengemeinde* (1919). Horst Penner made a study of settlements along the Vistula, *Ansiedlung mennonitischer Niederländer im Weichselmündungsgebiet von der Mitte des 16. Jahrhunderts bis zum Beginn der preussischen Zeit* (see also *MQR* XXI, October 1949), and Gustav Reimer presented *Die Familiennamen der westpreussischen Mennoniten,* both of which appeared as No. 3 of *Schriftenreihe des Mennonitischen Geschichtsvereins* (1940). Herbert Wiebe's *Das Siedlungswerk nieder-*

ländischen Mennoniten im Weichseltal . . . was published in 1952. H. Nottarp wrote *Die Mennoniten in den Marienburger Werdern* (1929) and L. Stobbe published *Montau-Gruppe . . .* (1918). Horst Penner gives the best over-all summary in "Anabaptists and Mennonites of East Prussia," *MQR* XXII (1948) 212-25 and in his book, *Weltweite Bruderschaft* (1955). William T. Schreiber's booklet, *The Fate of the Prussian Mennonites,* summarizes the history up to the present (1955). Numerous articles on the Prussian Mennonites have appeared in *Mennonitische Blätter, Mennonitische Geschichtsblätter, Christlicher Gemeinde-Kalender,* and *Mennonite Life.*

Poland is one of the most neglected areas of research so far as the Mennonites are concerned. Walter Kuhn wrote some articles in *Deutsche Blätter in Polen* (Posen, 1928) and in *Mennonite Life* (April 1953). A summary of his research was presented in "Deutsche Täufersiedlungen im westukrainischen Raume" (*Zeitschrift für Ostforschung* IV, 1955, 481-505). The *Mennonitische Blätter* and the *Mennonitisches Gemeindeblatt* of the Galician Mennonites carried articles pertaining to this group. P. Bachmann presented a complete history of the Galician Mennonites from 1784 to 1934 in *Mennoniten in Kleinpolen* (Lemberg, 1934) with numerous genealogies. The Swiss Mennonites of Volhynia have been treated in a number of booklets written by descendants in America in a commemorative style. A complete scholarly presentation is still not available. The Low-German Mennonite settlements and congregations of Poland proper (Michalin, Deutsch-Wymysle, Deutsch-Kasun, etc.) have occasionally been dealt with in articles or in family and congregational histories. No complete and thorough study is available.

C.K.

Historiography VI: Russia. The Mennonites of Russia found early historians in the following: A. Klaus, *Unsere Kolonien* (Odessa, 1887), dealing particularly with the Hutterites; P. Hildebrandt, *Erste Auswanderung der Mennoniten aus dem Danziger Gebiet nach Süd-Russland* (Halbstadt, 1888), and D. H. Epp, *Die Chortitzer Mennoniten* (Odessa, 1889). The history and the sources pertaining to the Molotschna settlement were presented by Franz Isaak in *Die Molotschnaer Mennoniten* (Halbstadt, 1908). D. H. Epp wrote *Die Memriker Ansiedlung* (Berdyansk, 1910). The history of the Mennonite Brethren, in the framework of the total Mennonite history of Russia, was written in a nearly one-thousand-page volume, *Die Alt-Evangelische Mennonitische Brüderschaft in Russland 1789-1910,* by P. M. Friesen (*q.v.*) (Halbstadt, 1911); it is an extremely valuable collection of source material. Monographs appeared on subjects such as alternative service by A. Goerz (*Ein Beitrag zur Geschichte des Forstdienstes der Mennoniten in Russland,* Gross-Tokmak, 1907), *Johann Cornies* by D. H. Epp (Berdyansk, 1909), *Die Mundart von Chortitza* by Jakob Quiring (Munich, 1928), *Unser Auszug nach Mittelasien* by Franz Bartsch (Halbstadt, 1907).

S. D. Bondar wrote on the Mennonites in Russia in *Sekta Mennonitov v Rossii* (Petrograd, 1916). From a Communist point of view A. Reinmarus (Penner) wrote *Anti-Menno* (Moscow, 1930), V. Schirmunski, *Die deutschen Kolonien in der Ukraine,*

Geschichte, Mundarten, Volkslied, Volkskunde (Moscow, 1928), and B. Bartels, *Die deutschen Bauern in Russland* (Moscow, 1928). At the beginning of the Communist regime articles and books on the "German Red Cow" (D. V. Elpatevsky) and the contributions of the Mennonites in agriculture and other economic areas appeared by S. P. Sorokin, K. Lindemann, and others.

Valuable historical materials pertaining to the Mennonites of Russia are contained in Mennonite periodicals and yearbooks such as *Der Botschafter* (1905-14), *Mennonitisches Jahrbuch* (1905-13, H. Dirks), *Unser Blatt* (1925-28), *Der praktische Landwirt* (1925-26) published in Russia, and *Unser Blatt* (1947-50) published at Gronau, Germany, by the MCC for the Russian refugees.

The most fruitful and significant contribution in the realm of research and the publication of monographs, studies, and materials pertaining to the Mennonites of Russia was begun after the emigration from Russia, particularly after World War I. The first phase of this movement of Mennonites to America and their descendants of the prairie states and provinces has been studied and presented by numerous American writers such as C. Henry Smith in *The Coming of the Russian Mennonites* (1927), Georg Leibbrandt and E. H. Correll in the *MQR* (Oct. 1932, Jan. 1932, July 1935, July and Oct. 1937), in *From the Steppes to the Prairies* (1939), Carl Dawson in *Group Settlement . . .* (1936), Heinz Lehmann in *Das Deutschtum in Westkanada* (Berlin, 1939), and in numerous other books and articles. Gustav E. Reimer and G. R. Gaeddert presented *Exiled by the Czar: Cornelius Jansen and the Great Mennonite Migration, 1874* (1956), and E. K. Francis features the Mennonites of Manitoba in *In Search of Utopia* (1955).

The largest wave of emigration of Mennonites from Russia after the Revolution (1920-25) stimulated and resulted in many publications in Germany, Canada, and the United States. Adolf Ehrt's *Das Mennonitentum in Russland . . .* (1932) is one of the best studies of the economic and social life of the Mennonites of Russia, containing a very valuable bibliography. Prior to this a popular summary with maps and illustrations had appeared, entitled *Die Mennoniten-Gemeinden in Russland* (1921), which had previously been published in the Dutch language. D. Neufeld wrote three booklets pertaining to his experiences during the Russian Revolution. The Deutsches Ausland-Institut of Stuttgart published numerous books on the German element in Russia including the Mennonites. Of special value is the yearbook *Der Wanderweg der Russlanddeutschen* (Vol. IV, 1939), which contains many maps and statistics. Otto Auhagen, who as a German agricultural expert in Moscow witnessed a flood of refugees coming to that city in 1929, described their fate in his book, *Die Schicksalswende des Russlanddeutschen Bauerntums in den Jahren 1927-1930* (1942), which appeared in the *Sammlung Georg Leibbrandt,* in which Hans Rempel's *Deutsche Bauernleitung am Schwarzen Meer* was also published. (The whole edition was destroyed during the war.) K. Stumpp's *Bericht über das Gebiet Chortitza . . .* (1943), which contains extremely valuable statistical material and a map of the Chortitza settlement in Russia before the German invasion of Russia (1941), also appeared in this *Sammlung. Die Deutschen Siedlungen in der Sowjetunion,* a series *Für den Dienstgebrauch,* lists all German settlements of European Russia and shows them on maps (*Sammlung Georg Leibbrandt,* 1941). W. Quiring's *Russlanddeutsche suchen eine Heimat* 1938) and *Deutsche erschliessen den Chaco* (1936) deal with the Canadian and Russian Mennonite immigration to Paraguay.

During this period of interest in genealogical research, much valuable material was published in Germany in books and periodicals pertaining to the German element abroad, which usually included the Mennonites. Some of the German periodicals which regularly carried articles pertaining to the Mennonites of Russia and their descendants were *Deutsche Post aus dem Osten, Mitteilungen des Sippenverbandes der Danziger Mennoniten-Familien* (edited by K. Kauenhoven, Göttingen), and *Mitteilungen der Niederländischen Ahnengemeinschaft* (Hamburg). The latter, compiled by K. Kauenhoven, published in 1939 the most exhaustive bibliography on the Mennonites of Prussian and Russian background available (I, 1939, 66-109).

Among the Mennonites of Russian background in Canada and the United States the literature pertaining to their history in Russia and their new country is increasing steadily. A valuable unpublished study of the Mennonites in Russia was made by David Rempel (doctoral dissertation, Stanford University, 1933), "The Mennonite Colonies in New Russia," which contains a valuable bibliography. The *Mennonitische Volkswarte* (1935-38) and the Echo-Verlag (1944- , Steinbach, Man.) have published much material along these lines. The series of books of the latter publisher includes histories of the following settlements: Terek, Zagradovka, Trakt, Molotschna, Kuban, Central Asia, and biographies of Cornies, Heese, and Wiebe. *Der Bote* (Rosthern, 1924-) and *Die Mennonitische Rundschau* (1880- , since 1923 in Winnipeg) contain much valuable information about the Mennonites in Canada, South America, and Russia. The *Altona Echo* and the *Steinbach Post* carry information pertaining to the Mennonites of the 1870's in Manitoba, as well as Mexico and South America. In the United States the following periodicals have devoted considerable space to the Mennonites of Prussia, Russia, Poland, the prairie states and provinces, Mexico, and South America: *Mennonite Life* (1945-), *Mennonite Quarterly Review* (1927-), *Hillsboro Journal* (Vorwärts), and *Mennonitisches Jahrbuch* (1948-).

The most helpful bibliographies on the Mennonites of Northern Germany, Poland, and Russia can be found in *Mitteilungen der Niederländischen Ahnengemeinschaft* (1939) written by K. Kauenhoven, in the books listed above written by Robert Dollinger, Heinz Münte, Friedrich Nieper, Adolf Ehrt, in C. Henry Smith's *Story of the Mennonites* (rev. ed. 1950), and in every April issue of *Mennonite Life* since 1947 and in the Bibliographical and Research Notes of the *MQR*. Regarding publications pertaining to hymnody, art, cooking, periodicals, yearbooks, etc., see the literature under the respective articles. For a list of bibliographies and catalogs see Cornelius Krahn, "The Historiography of the Mennonites of the Netherlands," *Church History* XIII (1944) or *MQR* XVI (1944). C.K.

Historiography VII: North American Mennonites. The writing of history by North American Mennonites, either of the history of the Mennonites in their own land, or of Europe, was a late development. The lack of trained men, whether ministers or scholars, the rural conservatism combined with traditionalism and preoccupation with pioneering problems, readily account for this. It was only at the end of the 19th century and especially in the first quarter of the 20th that substantial and worthy history writing began, with C. H. Wedel (1862-1911), John Horsch (1867-1941), and C. Henry Smith (1872-1948) as the first capable historians. Before that time the few volumes which appeared as history were chiefly apologetic or polemic and occasioned by schisms. These include: Christian Funk's *Spiegel für alle Menschen* (1813, 54 pp.), Jakob Stauffer's *Eine Chronik oder Geschicht-Büchlein von der sogenannten Mennonisten Gemeinde* (1859, 439 pp.), John Holdeman's *A History of the Church of God* (German 1875, English 1876, 303 pp.), Daniel Musser's *The Reformed Mennonite Church, Its Rise and Progress* (1873, pp. 608), and John F. Funk's reply to Musser's sharp attack on the "old" church in his *The Mennonite Church and Her Accusers* (1878, pp. 219). Of these only Holdeman and Funk contain a significant amount of information of historical value. Benjamin Eby's little *Kurzgefasste Kirchen Geschichte und Glaubenslehre der Taufgesinnten Christen oder Mennoniten* (Berlin, Canada, 1841, 16mo. historical part 164 pp.), though often reprinted, was only a frontier preacher-schoolteacher's attempt to assemble a modicum of information about Mennonites in various parts of the world. The very first bit of American Mennonite history written was that by Jacob Gottschalk in 1712 (see H. S. Bender, "The Founding of the Mennonite Church in America at Germantown, 1683-1708," *MQR* VII, 1933, 227-50).

General Works. The first American Mennonite historian, D. K. Cassel of Germantown, self-taught writer, produced two books devoted to the Mennonites of America: *History of the Mennonites* (1888, 450 pp.) and *Geschichte der Mennoniten* (1890, 545 pp. but containing almost twice the information of the English book), containing much valuable undigested and unorganized information, gathered largely from primary sources. John Horsch's *Kurzgefasste Geschichte der Mennoniten-Gemeinden* (1890, pp. 146) is chiefly valuable for its remarkable Anabaptist bibliography. C. H. A. van Smissen's *Kurzgefasste Geschichte und Glaubenslehre der Altevangelischen Taufgesinnten oder Mennoniten* (1895, pp. 251) is avowedly based on secondary sources, chiefly the German Anna Brons (*Ursprung, Entwickelung,* etc., 1884, which contains only 34 pp. out of 444 on the American Mennonites) and has next to nothing on America. Johannes Bartsch's *Geschichte der Gemeinde Jesu Christi, das heisst, der Altevangelischen und Mennoniten-Gemeinden* (1898, 207 pp.) is little better. C. H. Wedel's

training and scholarship was registered in his useful four-volume *Abriss der Geschichte der Mennoniten* (1900-4, total 756 pp.), but only 80 pages of the last volume were devoted to America. C. Henry Smith's Ph.D. dissertation (he was then a professor of history at Goshen College) *The Mennonites of America* (1909, pp. 484) was the first and to date only scholarly general history of the American Mennonites. He reworked this material twice in combination with a general Mennonite history, once in his *The Mennonites* (1920, pp. 340), and again in his *The Story of the Mennonites* (1941, pp. 823, revised in 1950). His booklet *Mennonites in America* (1942, pp. 71) condensed this material for CPS men. The only other extensive general history of the Mennonites of North America yet published has been Part II of P. M. Friesen's monumental work on the Mennonites of Russia, *Die Alt-Evangelisch Mennonitische Brüderschaft im Russland* (Halbstadt, 1911), covering 154 large pages in three sections: *A.* Mennonite Brethren; *B.* The General Conference Mennonites; *C.* The "Old" Mennonites. The work is more descriptive than systematic. Friesen's source was largely Cassel's *Geschichte der Mennoniten,* with C. H. Wedel's *Abriss,* the *Mennonitische Rundschau,* and private correspondence with M. B. Fast and John Horsch. W. S. Gottshall's *Mennonite History* (1921, pp. 84) and Daniel Kauffman's booklet by the same title (1927, pp. 147) are minor popularizations. J. C. Wenger's *Glimpses of Mennonite History* (1940, pp. 126) devotes pp. 38-54 to American Mennonites, while the revised edition of 1947 devotes pp. 101-36 to them. J. J. Friesen's *An Outline of Mennonite History* (1944, pp. 114) is very general. P. J. Schaefer's *Woher? Wohin? Mennoniten* (pp. 491), intended as a high-school text for (German) Mennonite schools in Canada, was published in four parts: I. Western Europe (1942, pp. 66); II. Russia and the United States (1942, pp. 82); III. Canada (1946, pp. 187); IV. Mexico and South America (1954, pp. 115). The third volume is the only general work on Canadian Mennonite history yet published. Horst Penner's *Weltweite Bruderschaft* devotes 45 of its 224 pages to North and South America. H. S. Bender's *Mennonites in America* is to appear in 1957.

Denominational Histories. The following histories of individual Mennonite groups have appeared: H. P. Krehbiel, *History of the General Conference of Mennonites of North America* I (1898, pp. 504), II (1938, pp. 682); Klaas Peters, *Die Bergthaler Mennoniten* (1924, pp. 45); J. S. Hartzler and Daniel Kauffman, *Mennonite Church History* (MC, 1905, pp. 422); J. A. Huffman, *History of the Mennonite Brethren in Christ Church* (1920, pp. 282); J. F. Harms, *Geschichte der Mennoniten Brüder-Gemeinde* (1924, pp. 342); W. B. Weaver, *History of the Central Conference Mennonite Church* (1926, pp. 254); J. H. Lohrenz, *The Mennonite Brethren Church* (1950, pp. 335); Walter Lugibihl and Jared Gerig, *Missionary Church Association* (1950, pp. 164); J. G. Rempel, *Fünfzig Jahre Konferenzbestrebungen* (1902-1952), *Konferenz der Mennoniten in Canada* (GCM 1952, pp. 491); J. J. Wiens, *The Mennonite Brethren Churches of North America* (1954, pp. 192), consists of pictures of meetinghouses with brief sketches of congregations.

Regional Histories. A series of regional or district conference histories of the Mennonite Church (MC) have appeared during the past 25 years, several of them outstanding in quality, including doctoral dissertations (marked herein with an asterisk *) at leading universities: M. G. Weaver, *Mennonites of Lancaster Conference* (1931, pp. 496); H. F. Weber, *Centennial History of the Mennonites of Illinois* (*1931, pp. 680); L. J. Burkholder, *A Brief History of Mennonites in Ontario* (1935, pp. 358); J. C. Wenger, *History of the Mennonites of Franconia Conference* (*1937, pp. 523); E. J. Hirschler, *Centenary History of the Swiss Mennonite Churches of Allen and Putnam Counties, Ohio* (1937, pp. 150); Melvin Gingerich, *The Mennonites in Iowa* (*1939, pp. 419); John Umble, *Ohio Mennonite Sunday Schools* (1941, pp. 522). Several interesting county, local, or congregational histories should be mentioned, some quite brief; W. H. Grubb, *History of the Mennonites of Butler County, Ohio* (1916, pp. 49); Samuel Peachey, *The Amish of Kishacoquillas Valley* (1930, pp. 48); F. P. Schultz, *The Settlement of German Mennonites from Russia at Mountain Lake, Minnesota* (1938, pp. 123); Eva Sprunger, *The First Hundred Years, A History of the Mennonite Church in Adams County, Indiana (Berne)* (1938, pp. 344); C. Z. Mast and R. E. Simpson, *Annals of the Conestoga Valley* (1942, pp. 689); Edward Yoder, *The Mennonites of Westmoreland County, Pennsylvania* (1942, pp. 64); R. M. Yoder, *Clinton Frame* (Ind.) *Sketches* (1944, pp. 106); J. J. Gering, *After Fifty Years, A Brief Discussion of the History and Activities of the Swiss-German Mennonites Who Settled in South Dakota in 1874* (1924, pp. 58); Jacob Rupp, *Entstehung und Auflösung der Gemeinde zu Maxweiler bei Neuburg an der Donau in Deutschland, und erste Pionierjahre in Amerika* (1924, pp. 24); C. E. Krehbiel, *Historical Sketch of the First Mennonite Church, Halstead, Kansas* (1925, pp. 53); P. B. Amstutz, *Geschichtliche Ereignisse der Mennoniten-Ansiedlung in Allen and Putnam County, Ohio* (1925, pp. 411); J. G. Rempel, *Die Rosenorter Gemeinde in Saskatchewan* (Rosthern, 1950, pp. 183). Numerous county histories contain valuable material on the history of early Mennonite settlements in America.

Immigration and Colonization History. Several excellent volumes have been devoted to immigration and colonization history: C. Henry Smith, *The Coming of the Russian Mennonites* (1927, pp. 296); *idem, The Mennonite Immigration to Pennsylvania* (1929, pp. 412); P. J. Kaufman, *Unser Volk und seine Geschichte* (1931, pp. 168, tells of Volhynian Mennonites settling in the United States); S. C. Yoder, *For Conscience Sake: A Study of Mennonite Migrations Resulting from the World War* (1945, pp. 300); Delbert Gratz, *Bernese Anabaptists and Their American Descendants* (1953, pp. 219); E. K. Francis, *In Search of Utopia, The Mennonites in Manitoba* (1955, pp. 294); J. W. Fretz, *Mennonite Colonization* (1944, pp. 80); *idem, Mennonite Colonization in Mexico* (1945, pp. 43); C. Krahn, Editor, *From the Steppes to the Prairies* (1949, pp. 115); G. E. Reimer and G. R. Gaeddert, *Exiled by the Czar, Cornelius Jansen and the Great Mennonite Migration 1874* (1956, pp. 205); note also J. H. Langenwalter's earlier brief summary, *The Immigration of Mennonites into North America* (1914, pp. 100).

A considerable number of monographs have been published on special phases of Mennonite history, work, life, and thought in America, some of them outstanding in quality.

Missions. Building on the Rock (MC mission in India, 1926, pp. 200); *Twenty-Five Years with God in India* (GCM mission, 1929, pp. 250); Ed. G. Kaufman, *The Development of the Missionary and Philanthropic Interest Among the Mennonites of North America* (1937, pp. 224); Alta Erb, *Studies in Mennonite City Missions* (1937, pp. 224); Ira D. Landis, *The Missionary Movement Among Lancaster Conference Mennonites* (1937, pp. 119); *The Gospel Under the Southern Cross* (MC mission in Argentina, 1943, pp. 272); W. B. Weaver, *Thirty-Five Years in the Congo* (Congo Inland Mission, 1945, pp. 241); E. R. Storms, *What God Hath Wrought* (MBC-UMC foreign mission work, 1948, pp. 164); *The Love of Christ Hath Constrained Us* (MC mission in India, 1949, pp. 63); Emma Oyer, *What God Hath Wrought* (MC Home Mission in Chicago, 1949, pp. 186); G. W. Peters, *The Growth of Foreign Missions in the Mennonite Brethren Church* (1952, pp. 327); Mrs. H. T. Esau, *First Sixty Years of Mennonite Brethren Missions* (1954, pp. 552).

Relief. D. M. Hofer, *Die Hungersnot in Russland* (1924, pp. 575); P. C. Hiebert and Orie O. Miller, *Feeding the Hungry* (1928, pp. 450); M. C. Lehman, *The History and Principles of Mennonite Relief Work* (1945, pp. 48); W. H. and Verna Smith, *Paraguayan Interlude* (1950, pp. 184); Irvin Horst, *A Ministry of Goodwill, A Short Account of Mennonite Relief 1939-1949* (1950, pp. 119); J. G. Holsinger, *Serving Rural Puerto Rico* (1952, pp. 232); J. D. Unruh, *In the Name of Christ, A History of the Mennonite Central Committee and Its Service 1920-1951* (1952, pp. 404).

Peace and Nonresistance. J. S. Hartzler, *Mennonites in the World War* (1921, pp. 145); John Horsch, *The Principle of Nonresistance as Held by the Mennonite Church* (1927, pp. 60); G. F. Hershberger, *War, Peace, and Nonresistance* (1944, pp. 415, revised editions 1946 and 1953); *idem, The Mennonite Church in the Second World War* (1951, pp. 308); Melvin Gingerich, *Service for Peace* (1949, pp. 508); Willard Hunsberger, *Franconia Mennonites and World War II* (1951, pp. 30).

Education. H. P. Peters, *History and Development of Education Among the Mennonites in Kansas* (1921, pp. 221); J. E. Hartzler, *Education Among the Mennonites of North America* (1925, pp. 195); C. Henry Smith and E. J. Hirschler, *Story of Bluffton College* (1925, pp. 296); *Bluffton College, An Adventure in Faith* (1950, pp. 268); Marie Waldner, *For Half a Century, The Story of Freeman Junior College* (1951, pp. 103); P. J. Wedel, *The Story of Bethel College* (1954, pp. 632); John Umble, *Goshen College 1894-1954* (1955, pp. 284).

Miscellaneous Topics. H. S. Bender, *Mennonite Sunday School Centennial* (1940, pp. 64); J. C. Wenger, *Historical and Biblical Position of the Mennonite Church on Attire* (1945, pp. 32); Ira D. Landis, *The Faith of Our Fathers on Eschatology* (1946, pp. 423); Robert Friedmann, *Mennonite Piety*

Through the Centuries (contains several chapters on America, 1949, pp. 287); J. W. Fretz, *Christian Mutual Aid* (1947, pp. 88); Paul R. Shelley, *Religious Education and Mennonite Piety Among the Mennonites of Southeastern Pennsylvania* (1952, pp. 193).

Biographies. M. S. Steiner, *John S. Coffman, Mennonite Evangelist* (1903, pp. 139); M. G. Brumbaugh, *The Life and Works of Christopher Dock* (1908, pp. 272); *Memoirs of Peter Jansen, An Autobiography* (1921, pp. 140); P. A. Wiebe, *Kurze Biographie des Bruders Jacob A. Wiebe* (1924, pp. 27); H. A. Brunk, *The Life of Peter S. Hartman* (1937, pp. 73); John Umble, *Mennonite Pioneers* (collected M.C. missionary biographies, 1940, pp. 211); J. W. Kliewer, *Memoirs or From Herdboy to College President* (1943, pp. 150); Paul Schaeffer, *Heinrich H. Ewert* (1945, pp. 161); M. G. Ramseyer, *Joseph E. Ramseyer* (1945, pp. 293, founder of the Missionary Church Association); Lambert Huffman, *Not of This World, Biography of J. A. Huffman* (1951, pp. 159); J. Paul Graybill, *Noah H. Mack* (1952, pp. 177); Alice K. Gingerich, *Life and Times of Daniel Kauffman* (1954, pp. 160); G. E. Reimer and G. R. Gaeddert, *Exiled by the Czar, Cornelius Jansen and the Great Mennonite Migration, 1874* (1956, pp. 205).

Reference Works and Bibliographies. L. J. Heatwole, *Mennonite Handbook of Information* (1925, pp. 187); Daniel Kauffman, *Mennonite Cyclopedic Dictionary* (1937, pp. 443); H. S. Bender, *Two Centuries of American Mennonite Literature 1727-1929* (1929, pp. 180); John A. Hostetler, *Annotated Bibliography on the Amish* (1951, pp. 100); A. Warkentin, *Who's Who Among the Mennonites* (1937, pp. 221); A. Warkentin and M. Gingerich, *Who's Who Among the Mennonites* (1943, pp. 428).

Periodicals. The only strictly historical American Mennonite periodical has been the *Mennonite Quarterly Review* (1927-), published by the Mennonite Historical Society of Goshen College, which has carried a large number of scholarly articles on Anabaptist and Mennonite history, thought, and life.

Mennonite Life (1945-), published by Bethel College, is an illustrated quarterly magazine featuring the Mennonites the world over. It has carried many briefer historical articles. In a way it is the continuation of the *Monatsblätter aus Bethel College* and *Bethel College Monthly* (1903-18), in which C. H. Wedel and others published many historical articles. The several conference yearbooks and almanacs have often carried valuable historical material and shorter articles, such as the *Mennonite* (MC) *Family Almanac* (1870-1955), the *Mennonite* (MC) *Yearbook and Directory* (1905-), *Bundesbote Kalender* (GCM, 1886-), *Mennonite* (GCM) *Yearbook and Almanac* (1895-1930), *Yearbook of the General Conference Mennonite Church* (1930-46), and *Mennonitisches* (GCM) *Jahrbuch* (1948-). *The Proceedings of the Conference on Mennonite Educational and Cultural Problems* (1942-) frequently contains solid historical papers.

The following books on the Mennonites in Mexico and South America should be noted: Walter Quiring, *Deutsche erschliessen den Chaco* (1936?, pp. 207); *idem, Russlanddeutsche suchen eine Heimat* (1938,

pp. 192); *idem, Im Schweisse deines Angesichts,* largely a picture book (1953, pp. 150); A. E. Janzen, *Glimpses of South America* (1944, pp. 130); Walter Schmiedehaus, *Ein feste Burg ist unser Gott. Der Wanderweg eines christlichen Siedlervolkes* (1948, pp. 307); S. C. Yoder, *Down South America Way* (1948, pp. 148); Gladys Widmer, *We Enter Puerto Rico* (MC Mission History in Puerto Rico 1946-51; 1952, pp. 95); J. W. Fretz, *Pilgrims in Paraguay, The Story of Mennonite Colonization in South America* (1953, pp. 247).

In this historiographical report numerous and important periodical articles, as well as sections in books on the colonial history of Pennsylvania such as Seidensticker, Kuhns, and Pennypacker, have been omitted.   H.S.B.

History Liedboeck. A Dutch hymnbook under this title is mentioned by van Braght (*Mart. Mir.* D 147, E 538). It is not clear what hymnbook van Braght means. A book under this title is unknown.

Hoadley (Alberta) United Missionary Church was organized in 1945. In 1948 the congregation had six members, with Lloyd Torgerson as pastor. L.T.

Hobelmacher *(Zimmermann),* **Lux,** a citizen of Strasbourg, a member of the Anabaptist congregation there, in whose house meetings were held. In 1528-29 he was several times cross-examined, once on the rack; he was to confess that "they have the women in common," but he firmly denied the charge. (*Ztscht für die hist. Theol.,* 1860, pp. 36, 48; *ML* II, 319.)

Hoburg, Christian (1607-75), a mystic theologian, preacher of the Dompelaar (*q.v.*) Mennonite Church at Hamburg, had an eventful life. Orphaned early, he entered the University of Königsberg under great difficulty, left without completing his course, became a private tutor at Lauenburg, then cantor and assistant preacher, studied the works of Arndt and Schwenckfeld, and fought to prevent the ruin of his church. In 1640 he was proofreader and assistant preacher in Uelzen, was dismissed from his church office, took a position as tutor in Hamburg, then proofreader in a Lüneburg print shop, wrote here under the pen name of Elias Prätorius his most important work, *Spiegel der Missbräuche,* and under the pen name of Bernhard Baumann (*q.v.*), *Das ärgerliche Christentum.* Under Duke August of Wolfenbüttel he received the pastorate at Borne, from which he was rudely deposed. In a complicated financial state brought on by his charities he left Brunswick and secured a position as chaplain on an estate in Geldern. This position he also had to give up because of his attacks on the church. He then served as preacher of the Reformed Church at Latum (Rhineland) for 16 years until his mysticism brought him into conflict with this congregation.

After a temporary residence in Amsterdam, he spent the rest of his life as a Mennonite preacher in Hamburg. His critique of the church and the era are significant. He stands on a high tower, and shows an unusual insight and vision. He was without doubt a highly gifted man, with the purest of motives, who, however, lacked the spiritual calm and strength to develop his teaching and carry it to a successful conclusion (*ADB; Menn. Bl.*, 1854, 11). His books (not including those published under a pseudonym), *Theologica Mystica: Das ist geheime Kraft-Theologie der Alten anweisende den Weg* (Lüneburg, 1650); *Der unbekannte Christus, Das ist gründlicher Beweiss, dass die heutige sogenannte Christenheit in allen Sekten den wahren Christus nicht recht kennen* (Frankfurt and Leipzig, 1720) (with an interesting account of David Joris, *q.v.*), were also widely read in the Mennonite families of the Palatinate.

NEFF.

RGG II, where the following are cited: *Biographisch Woordenboek van Prot. Godgeleerden en Neerl* IV, p. 49; Gottfried Arnold, *Kirchen- und Ketzer-Historie* II, 17, chapters 1, 38; 6, 11; III, 13, 14-37; A. Ritschl, *Geschichte des Pietismus* II (Bonn, 1884) 61; Rud. Winkel, *Mystische Gottsucher der Nachreformationzeit* (1925) 31; E. Seeberg, *Gottfried Arnold* (Meerane, 1923) 343; E. Kochs, "Das Kriegsproblem in der spiritualistischen Gesamtanschauung Chr. Hoburgs" (*Ztscht f. Kirchengesch. XLVI*, 1927) 246; *ML* II, 319 f.

Hoch (High), **Daniel** (1806-78), lived near Vineland, Lincoln Co., Ont. In 1831 he was chosen as minister in the local Mennonite (MC) congregation and in the following years became leader of a prayer-meeting group in his church which emphasized the use of the mourners' bench, immersion, open communion, true repentance, and holiness. A division between his party and the church resulted in 1848. Hoch was ordained by J. H. Oberholtzer (*q.v.*) as bishop in 1851 and from 1853 on was engaged in itinerant work among scattered congregations. He was active in early union efforts among Mennonites and served as chairman of the second General Conference (GCM), held in Wadsworth, Ohio, in May 1861. After 1869, Hoch and his churches withdrew from the General Conference and apparently were drawn into the "New Mennonite" movement in Ontario which was one of the parties that eventually produced the Mennonite Brethren in Christ. S.F.P.

Religiöser Botschafter, May 16 and July 11, 1853, June 25, 1855; A. Eby, *Ansiedlung und Begründung der Mennoniten Gemeinde in Canada* (1872); J. H. Oberholtzer, *Aufschluss der Verfolgungen gegen Daniel Hoch* (1853); H. P. Krehbiel, *The History of the General Conference* (Canton, 1898).

Hochburg, an Amish Mennonite congregation, named after the village of Hochburg in Baden, Germany, in the Eltz Valley a few miles east of Emmendingen, was founded by families expelled from Alsace in 1712, probably from the congregations near Colmar such as Baldenheim, Ohnenheim, and Jebsheim, and also from Markirch. Hochburg was represented in the conferences held on the west side of the Rhine, such as those at Essingen in 1759 (by Jacob Rupp, who also was part of a delegation to Holland in 1760) and 1777 (by Jacob Muller). Both of these men must have been elders. Bentz Koenig of Nimburg was ordained elder in 1802. The last elder, a Zimmermann, moved from here in 1845 to Ueberlingen on Lake Constance. Some members moved to the neighborhood of Durlach, Baden. The congregation soon thereafter became extinct. (Taken from P. Sommer's "Assemblée de Hochburg," *Christ Seul*, June 1932, 6.) H.S.B.

Hochfeld, a common Mennonite village name which occurred in the following settlements: Don region, Russia; West Reserve, Man.; Hague, Sask.; Cuauhtemoc and Durango, Mexico; and Menno and Bergthal settlement Villarrica, Paraguay. C.K.

Hochfeld, a village in the province of Ekaterinoslav, Ukraine, South Russia, 12 miles from the station Sofievka, founded by Heinrich Thiessen, a mill owner, who in 1848 bought 5,000 acres of land and settled his children on it. In consequence of the nationalization of all land in 1917 ff., this Mennonite settlement has been dissolved. (*ML* II, 321.) D.H.E.

Hochfeld (*Morozovo*) was a village of the Yazekovo Mennonite settlement (*q.v.*) near Chortitza, Russia, established in 1869. In 1918 it had 92 farms and 5,070 acres of land which was reduced to about half that acreage under the Soviets at the time when the village was farming its land collectively. In 1914 the population was 313 and by 1941 it had increased to 608. In 1919, 19 persons were murdered and in 1929-41, 53 were exiled. At the outbreak of the war with Germany in 1941, 12 persons were evacuated eastward. During the German occupation the community had a church, a choir, and a school with three teachers and 77 pupils. When the Germans withdrew the population was taken along; some were returned to Russia by the Red army, while others reached Canada. C.K.

Hochfeld, a village near the station Akimovka in the district of Melitopol, Ukraine, South Russia, founded in 1832 by Thomas Wiens from the Altonau settlement (Molotschna), who bought 8,000 acres of land here and divided it among four descendants. In consequence of the nationalization of land in 1917 ff., this settlement disintegrated in 1921. (*ML* II, 321.) D.H.E.

Hochhuth, Karl Wilhelm Hermann (1823-93), a Protestant theologian. In his studies in church history one of his interests concerned the brotherhoods outside the state church at the time of the Reformation. With his "Mitteilungen aus der protestantischen Secten-Geschichte in der hessischen Kirche," which he published in the *Ztscht für die hist. Theologie* (1858, 538-644; 1859, 167-234; and 1860, 258-84), he made the first attempt to present an account of the Anabaptist movement in a German state based on court records. It was his aim to do justice to the significance of the Anabaptist movement for the Hessian state church. In this study he was able to correct many errors and omissions in former publications. On the other hand various errors crept into his copies of the records, which have in part been rectified by Lenz. Hochhuth's work offers a wealth of material on the history of the Anabaptist movement in the 16th century that has frequently been made use of in the literature on church history. HEGE.

Blaubuch des Corps Teutonia zu Marburg 1825-1925 (Elberfeld, 1925) 69; "Hessenland," *Ztscht für hessische Geschichte und Literatur* VII (Kassel, 1893) 191; M. Lenz, *Briefwechsel Landgraf Philipps des Grossmütigen von Hessen mit Bucer* I (Leipzig, 1880); *ML* II, 321.

Hochmann von Hohenau, Ernst Christoph (1670-1721), grew up in Nürnberg, Germany, as a Lutheran, was awakened while a student at the University of Halle (1662) by August Hermann Francke, in 1697 became associated with Gottfried Arnold, and was thereafter an active Separatist, without however joining a church brotherhood, zealously proclaiming the Gospel when he was not prevented by imprisonment and persecution of all kinds. In his creed of 1702 he said, "Concerning water baptism I believe that Christ instituted it only for adults and not for children, for there is found in all of the Holy Scriptures not an iota of an express command. Faith and baptism belong together." His position on government is also akin to that of the Mennonites; for he acknowledges it as a divine ordinance, but "things which conflict with the Word of God and conscience and against the liberty of Christ . . . it has been granted no authority." When a group of his adherents led by Alexander Mack, yielding to the influence of the English Baptists, regarded immersion as the only true baptism and necessary to salvation, and therefore required a second baptism of those who had been baptized as children, he took a moderate position (Max Goebel comments, "agreeing with Mennonite doctrine"), namely, that the sprinkling performed on children was valid and sufficient, if it was only followed later on by rebirth or the baptism of the Spirit.

It is therefore not surprising to find that Hochmann made contacts with the Mennonites. Goebel states (13) that in his speeches and writings he made many references to Menno Simons. In Crefeld he was given friendly reception by the Mennonite congregation and its three preachers (Gosen Goyen, Leonhard Ewald, Joh. Crous), and preached in their church. In the Palatinate he also frequently visited the Mennonites in Zuzenhausen, Eppstein, Guntersblum, Mutterstadt, and Lambsheim, and preached for them. Though the members of these congregations living now have no knowledge of his visits, his influence must have been deep and lasting. He is said to have preached with such power that "his hearers felt themselves lifted above the earth, as if eternity were dawning." His influence on the religious life of the Rhineland was fraught with extraordinary blessing. This is attested by both Jung-Stilling, who set him a memorial in *Theobald oder die Schwärmer,* and Gerhard Tersteegen, who wrote the verse found on his tombstone. NEFF.

M. Goebel, *Geschichte des christlichen Lebens in der rheinisch-westfälischen evangelischen Kirche* II (Coblenz, 1852); *HRE* VIII, pp. 162 ff.; *RGG* II; (2nd ed.); D. Cattepoel, "Das religiöse Leben in der Krefelder Mennonitengemeinde des 17. und 18. Jahrhunderts" in *Beiträge zur Gesch. der rhein. Mennoniten,* 1939; Fr. Auge, "Acht Briefe Ernst Christoph Hochmanns von Hohenau" in *Monatsbl. für rhein. Kirchengesch.* XIX (1925) 133 ff.; Fr. Nieper, *Die ersten deutschen Auswanderer von Krefeld nach Pennsylvanien* (Neukirchen, 1940) 126, 151, 201 f., 217 f., 275 f.; H. Renkewitz, *Hochmann von Hohenau* (Breslau, 1935); *ML* II, 321.

Hochrütiner, Jakob, the son of Lorenz Hochrütiner (*q.v.*), came to Bern, Switzerland, with other Anabaptists in the spring of 1527, and was expelled under oath from city and canton. Because he refused the oath he was placed on the pillory and

led out (May 1, 1527). Soon he was back in the city. At the petition of his wife his life was spared, "if from prison he leaves the city and canton, or he will be executed without mercy." (Müller, *Berner Täufer,* 24 f.; *ML* II, 322.) NEFF.

Hochrütiner, Lorenz, one of the founders of the Zürich Anabaptist brotherhood. He was a weaver of St. Gall, and early joined the Protestant movement. For taking part in destroying the crucifix at Stadelhofen near Zürich he had to leave the city in November 1523, and returned to St. Gall, where Conrad Grebel (*q.v.*) appealed to his brother-in-law Vadian in Hochrütiner's behalf. In St. Gall he won converts for the Anabaptist movement in 1524. In a Bible class led by Johannes Kessler, when the passage in Romans VI about baptism on the death of Jesus was read, he spoke in opposition to infant baptism. Upon his return to Zürich he was baptized with George Blaurock (*q.v.*), Jan. 21, 1525. Then he betook himself to Basel. At a meeting in the house of Michel Schürer of Freiburg he was arrested and on Aug. 23, 1525, expelled from the city on penalty of death. The next year he was back in Basel, where his family had probably remained. He was banished anew (July 24, 1526). His wife and children were to be sent after him within a week. At this point all trace of him vanishes. NEFF.

E. Egli, *St. Galler Täufer* (Zürich, 1887) 17 f.; P. Burckhardt, *Die Basler Täufer* (Basel, 1898) 131; *ML* II, 322.

Hochstädt, a common Mennonite village name found in the following settlements: Barnaul, Siberia; East Reserve, Man.; Hague, Sask.; Cuauhtemoc and Durango, Mexico; and Menno, Chaco, Paraguay. C.K.

Hochstett, a former Amish Mennonite congregation in France, became extinct in the 19th century. It was located about 10-15 miles northwest of Strasbourg, near the towns of Brumath and Hochfelden (*Almanach Menn. du Cinquantenaire* 1901-51, 35). The list of congregations represented at the Essingen Amish Mennonite Conference of 1779 includes a Hochstettler congregation represented by Christian Schenk and Hans Höfle (*Menn. Gesch.-Bl.,* 1938, 54, where Hochstätten near Münster a. Stein, Germany, is suggested as the location of the congregation). The text of the Essingen discipline as published in *MQR* XI (1937) 167, however, names a Hoffstetter congregation represented by Andreas Imhoff and Christian Schantz. It is not clear whether the two (or three) congregations are identical. H.S.B.

Hochstettler: see Hostettler.

Hochwald, a former Amish Mennonite congregation in Alsace in existence at least as early as 1770, which became extinct about 1837, after most of the members had emigrated to America. Most of those remaining joined the new Protestant congregation, which was organized in that year. (*Menn. Bl.,* 1898, 73, which calls it "Hohwald"; *ML* I, 561.) H.S.B.

Hoefnagel, Pieter, a Mennonite preacher in the Kruisstraat congregation (conservative Flemish) of Haarlem, Holland, published the following: *Zedige*

Bedenkingen over het bitter Lyden onses Heeren en Zaligmaakers Jesus Christus, followed by some hymns (Haarlem, 1701, repr. 1714); *Ondersoek op't Merkwaardige Getal 666* (Haarlem, 1715); *De Schaduw en het Ligchaem der Profeetsyen Vertoond in het boeck der Openbaaringen van Johannes* (Haarlem, 1717; an addition to this book appeared in 1732); *Melchizedek beschouwt in zyn eeuwig Priesterschap* (Haarlem, 1730). Hoefnagel died in 1737; he was married to Hilleke Amelsdonck Leeuw of Nijmegen. vDZ.

Biogr. Wb. IV, 66 f.; M. Schagen, *Naamlijst der Doopsgezinde Schrijveren* (Amsterdam, 1745) 47.

Hoejewilt, Hendrik Albertsz, b. 1606 at De Rijp, Dutch province of North Holland, d. there Feb. 14, 1667, known as "de Rijper poëet," a Dutch poet, a large number of whose hymns have been inserted in the *Rijper Liedtboecxken* (q.v.) of 1669 and following editions. He also published *Vermaning aen de Jeugt* (De Rijp, n.d.) and *May-Gift van verscheyde Vogelen* (Amsterdam, 1737). vDZ.

Doopsgezinde Lectuur III (1858) 195; van der Aa, *Biogr. Wb. der Nederlanden* VIII, 2 (Haarlem, 1867) 857; M. Schagen, *Naamlijst der Doopsgezinde Schrijveren* (Amsterdam, 1745) 47 f.

Hoek (Hoeck), **van,** a Dutch Mennonite family living at Amsterdam in the 17th century, members of the Waterlander congregation (deacons Anthonie van Hoek 1639-50, 1657-62, and Leonard van Hoek 1668), and after the union of the Waterlander and the Flemish congregations, members of the United congregation (deacons Adriaen van Hoek Azn 1674-79, 1684-89).

Of importance for Mennonite history are Dirk van Hoek, his son Jan van Hoek and his grandson Jan van Hoek Jr., who moved as merchants and bankers from Amsterdam to Danzig, Prussia, where they became members of the "Vereenigde Vlaemsche Vriesche en Hoogduytsche Gemeynte te Schladal." Dirk van Hoek must have moved to Danzig about 1670. He died shortly after 1680. His son Jan van Hoek, who was married to Elisabeth Rutgers, whose father Isaack Rutgers also had moved from Amsterdam to Danzig, died 1732 at Danzig. He had some troubles in 1726 with Hendrik van Dühren (Duren), elder of the Danzig congregation, because of wearing a periwig. (*Inv. Arch. Amst.* II, 2634.)

Dirk van Hoek and the two Jan van Hoeks (father and son) served as intermediaries of the Dutch Mennonite Committee of Foreign Needs and the Prussian Mennonites, who in cases of persecution and extortion by their rulers, of removal to other districts, of emigration, of devastation because of wars, of floods, of crop failures, briefly in all kinds of difficulties, were liberally supported by the Dutch Mennonites. Bills of exchange were sent from Amsterdam either to Jan Bruinvisch (q.v.) at Königsberg or to Ludwig Rump (q.v.) at Elbing or to the van Hoeks at Danzig and paid out by them to all who needed money. This caused an ample correspondence both with the Prussian congregations and the Dutch committee at Amsterdam. In the Amsterdam archives are found a large number of letters written by or sent to the van Hoeks. The first document of this kind is an account of the laying out of Dutch money by Dirk van Hoek,

dated June 19, 1680. The first letter of Jan van Hoek Sr. is dated Aug. 12, 1711; the last one of Jan van Hoek Jr. June 24, 1746. vDZ.

The most important of these letters are *Inv. Arch. Amst.* I, Nos. 1234 f., 1571-89, 1601, 1605 f., 1611 f., 1615, 1618-20, 1622-28, 1632-69, 1676, 1679 f., 1682 f., 1697, 1699; II, 2, Nos. 699, 714, 716, 719, 725, 730, 743, 751, 767, 786, 788, 793-95; concerning the van Hoek family at Danzig and especially their troubles with Hendrik van Dühren, *Inv. Arch. Amst.* II, Nos. 2632-43.

Hoek, Kornelis van, belonged to a Rotterdam branch of the foregoing family. He died at Rotterdam in 1722. He was a member of the Rotterdam Waterlander congregation, but seems to have left the congregation in 1695, when the deacons had thwarted the Collegiants (q.v.), who had been holding their meetings in the Waterlander meetinghouse. That Kornelis van Hoek was an ardent Collegiant is proved by a number of books and pamphlets published by him. He especially attacked the conservative Zonist (q.v.) views of Lambert Bidloo (q.v.) and Herman Schijn (q.v.). Of his publications, which were eagerly read by Mennonite liberals, we should mention: *Lykreden op J. Oudaen* (Rotterdam, 1695); *Christelyke bedenking over en tegen . . . de aanmerkingen op het formulier van Benoodiging van H. Schyn* (Amsterdam, 1701); *De Christelyke verdraagzaamheit verdedigt tegen H. Schyn en Bidloo* (Rotterdam, 1701); *Ongebonden licentie, de grondslag der Rhynburgsche verdraagzaamheit* (Amsterdam, 1702); *Nadere verdediging der Christelyke verdraagzaamheit tegen de laatste Wederspraak van H. Schyn en L. Bidloo* (Rotterdam, 1703), and a devotional book, *De vernederde en verhoogde Christus* (Rotterdam, 1716).

A cousin of this Kornelis van Hoek was Jan van Hoek, a member of the Mennonite congregation of Rotterdam and an antagonist of liberal principles. His son Sander van Hoek (b. 1757) left the congregation and became a Reformed minister. vDZ.

K. Vos, *De Doopsgez. in Rotterdam* (Rotterdam, 1907) 27; *Biogr. Wb.* IV, 70-71; Schijn-Maatschoen, *Geschiedenis* II, 664; J. C. van Slee, *De Rijnsburger Collegianten* (Haarlem, 1895) *passim,* see Index.

Hoek, van der, a Mennonite family living at Broek near Joure, Dutch province of Friesland, many of whose members have served as deacons of the Joure congregation. The ancestor was Homme Jeltes, b. at Irnsum, Friesland, in 1575. In 1813 they adopted the family name of van der Hoek. Two members were preachers: Atze Wybes van der Hoek, d. 1835, untrained minister serving Edam 1791-96 and Twisk-Abbekerk 1796-1835, and his cousin Wybe Hommes van der Hoek, b. 1790, d. Aug. 15, 1875, at Wolvega, appointed ministerial candidate by the church board of Twisk in 1812, serving Aalsmeer as a candidate 1812-14, as a minister 1814-15, Grouw "Kleine Huis" 1815-19, Wieringen 1819-23, and Kromwal Ytens 1823-62. In 1831-38 he also served the Kleinzand congregation of Sneek (*DB* 1890, 120-23). In 1849 he addressed the Executive Committee of the Conference in Friesland on behalf of provisions to be made for Mennonites living in towns where there was no congregation. (*DB* 1894, 73.) vDZ.

Hoeksteen, De (Cornerstone), a Dutch Mennonite 8-page (sometimes 6, 10, or 12 pp.) monthly periodical, published by the Youth Association (*Doopsgezinde Jongeren Bond, q.v.*), first number October 1935. vdZ.

Hoekstra is the name of two Mennonite families in the Netherlands, many members of which have served as preachers. The ancestor of the one family was Sytse Benedictus Hoekstra (1698-1768), whose biography and descendants are given in the article under his name. Important members of the other Hoekstra family were Freerk (*q.v.*, 1760-1837), and his grandson Johannes (1836-1908), preacher at Middelstum (1861-74) and Wolvega (1874-79), where he promoted the restoration of the meeting-house and dedicated it in 1875. In 1879 he retired to Apeldoorn where he organized a chapter of the Nederlandsch Protestantenbond (*q.v.*) and shared in the founding of the Mennonite congregation. (*N.N.B.Wb.* I, 1120 f.; *Biogr. Wb.* IV, 87.) vdZ.

Hoekstra, Freerk, b. 1760 at Dokkum, studied at the Mennonite Seminary in Amsterdam 1780-85 under Prof. H. Oosterbaan, and on June 18, 1786, became the Mennonite minister at Holwerd. From here he went to Zaandam in 1791 and then to Harlingen in 1792, where he served until his retirement in October 1836. He died March 31, 1837. He was married to Ynske Terpstra. In 1827 he achieved a union between the Witmarsum and Pingjum congregations. He was also one of the founders of the *Friesch Weduwenfonds* (1805).

He is best known as a writer of children's literature (P. Cool wrote an extensive treatise on F. Hoekstra as a children's author, *DB* 1869, 56-89). For children he wrote *De geschiedenis van Jesus, in gesprekken* (Harlingen, 1825, reprinted 1842); *De geschiedenis der Apostelen* (Harlingen, 1818); *De gelijkenissen van Jesus* (Haarlem, 1821); and *De Wonderwerken van Jesus* (Haarlem, 1833). A catechism which he published in 1804, *Vragen en antwoorden over den godsdienst* (3 editions), was widely accepted. In addition to numerous occasional sermons he also published *Kerkelijke redevoeringen* (Groningen, 1816, reprinted 1837), *Lijkrede op Heere Oosterbaan* (Amsterdam, 1807), *Verhandeling over de waarheid van den Christelijken godsdienst,* and *Verhandeling over de voortreffelijkheid der christlijke zedeleer* (Haarlem, 1825); also *Zedelijke en godsdienstige vertoogen* (Arnhem, 1827-31).

His grandson Johannes Hoekstra (1836-1908) served the congregations of Middelstum 1861-74 and Wolvega 1874-79. At Wolvega he promoted the restoration of the meetinghouse and dedicated it in 1875. He retired in 1879 and moved to Apeldoorn, where he was active in founding first a section of the Dutch Protestant Union and in 1896 a Mennonite congregation.   J.L.

A. van Steenderen, *Iets ter nagedachtenis van Freerk Hoekstra* (Franeker, 1839); *Biogr. Wb.* **IV,** 76 f.; *N.N.B.Wb.* **II,** 1119 f.; *DB* 1869, 56-89; *ML* **II,** 323.

Hoekstra, Johannes Albertus, a Dutch Mennonite preacher, the son of Sjoerd Hoekstra and Maria Jans Valk, b. June 28, 1763, at Emden. He studied theology at the Mennonite seminary "de Zon" in Amsterdam; in 1784 he was called as pastor to the Edam church. He remained here until January 1786, served a year at Westzaan-Nord, then went to

Utrecht, and in 1793 to Altona, Germany, where he remained until his death (Dec. 7, 1817). The funeral sermon delivered by J. Goos, and a booklet, *Ter nagedachtenis van J. A. S. Hoekstra,* by J. Schultz, both appeared in Altona in 1817. He was a member of the directorate of *Tot Nut van't Algemeen* (*q.v.*).

A collection of sermons preached by J. A. Hoekstra and his father Sjoerd Hoekstra, *Plegtige leerredenen te Emden en Utrecht,* was published in Utrecht in 1790. He also wrote *Leerredenen en bedestonden* (Utrecht, 1787); *Twee leeredenen bij den doop, en afscheid van Utrecht* (Utrecht, 1793); *Iets ter handhaaving en bevordering van waarheid en plicht* (Altona, 1794); *Iets over Gods grootheid* (Altona, 1797); *Dichtkundige menglingen* (Amsterdam, 1800); *Dank- und Ermahnungs-predigt* (Altona, 1801); *Jubelpredikatie wegens 25 jarige ambtsverrichting in onderscheiden Doopsgezinde gemeenten, gehouden te Altona am 8. October 1809* (Altona, 1809). In addition he published with G. Karsdorp and J. de Jager, *Leerredenen. Met een vertoog, dat genade en plicht, de leer van Jesus en zijne apostelen, ook de leer van Menno en de waare Mennoniten is* (Altona, 1794), and with G. Karsdorp, *Stand- en Gedachtenisrede over Jan de Jager, Prediger zu Hamburg und Altona* (1802) and with J. Goos, *Ter gedachtenis van Gerrit Karsdorp,* a preacher at Hamburg and Altona, who died on Oct. 11, 1811. (*Biogr. Wb.* IV, 77 f.; *N.N.B.Wb.* I, 1121; *ML* II, 323.)   J.L.

Hoekstra, Sjoerd, a Dutch Mennonite preacher, the son of Jakob Hoekstra, was born Jan. 20, 1805, at Den Helder, and studied at the University and the Mennonite Seminary at Amsterdam. In 1829 he went to Medemblick, and from there in 1835 to Twisk; here he was in active service until his retirement in 1881. He died Aug. 1, 1894. Hoekstra is known best for his investigations on the principles of Anabaptist life. J. H. Scholten, the well-known professor at Leiden, had previously discussed Anabaptist principles in *De leer der Hervormde kerk;* this book was refuted by D. S. Gorter (*q.v.*), and more extensively by Hoekstra, under the title *Nog iets over het eigenlijk wezen van den Doopsgezinden Christen* (Hoorn, 1851). He discussed the oath in *Doopsgezinde Lektuur* II, in an article titled "Het Doopsgezind gevoelen omtrent den eed, opnieuw ter toetse gebragt." In addition he wrote the following: *Leiddraad voor eenvoudigen in het afleggen van belijdenis* (Medemblik, 1836); *Jesus in Zijne verhevenheid* (2 vv., Medemblik, 1838); *Het Evangelie. Een onderwijsboek* (Amsterdam, 1848); *Nieuwe beschouwingen van Jesus' persoon en werk* (2 vv., Medemblik, 1852); *Feestrede bij 25jarige Evangeliebediening* (Amsterdam, 1854), besides various articles in the *Jaarboeken voor Wetenschappelijke Theologie.* (*Biogr. Wb.* IV, 78 f.; *N.N.B.Wb.* I, 1121; *DB* 1894, 172; *ML* II, 323.)   J.L.

Hoekstra, Bzn, Sytse, professor at the Mennonite Seminary and the University of Amsterdam, one of the outstanding theologians of his day. He was born on Aug. 20, 1822, the son of Benedictus Hoekstra and Aafje Pruit, at Wieringerwaard, where the parsonage of the Oudesluis congregation

—now Noord-Zijpe—was located. To his mother (d. 1855) Hoekstra owed much of his education. In 1840 he attended the Athenaeum at Amsterdam, studying with the Orientalist Taco Roorda, and at the same time finished the theological course at the Mennonite Seminary, becoming a ministerial candidate on June 15, 1845. He served the Akkrum congregation as pastor until 1852, and then the Rotterdam congregation until 1857.

On Nov. 26, 1856, he was appointed by the A.D.S. to succeed Samuel Muller (*q.v.*) as professor in the seminary, at Muller's own suggestion, who had been his teacher. He received an honorary doctor's degree from the University of Leiden on Feb. 3, 1857, and two weeks later he delivered his inaugural address, *Oratio de summae veritatis cognoscendae ratione et via* (Amsterdam, 1857), translated into Dutch by J. van Gilse, *De weg der wetenschap op godgeleerd en wysgeerig gebied* (same date and place). From 1877 on, when the Athenaeum was converted into a university, he lectured on Christian doctrine, ethics, and philosophy of religion, and also had charge of Biblical theology. At times he also lectured on logic. He retired in June 1892, and died at Ellecom on June 12, 1898. On July 21, 1873, he married Rebecca Anna van Geuns (d. 1909). He was a member of the Association of Dutch Letters (1857), Teyler's Theological Association (1858), and the Royal Academy of Science (1865); in 1874 the king gave him the rank of knight of the Dutch Lion.

Hoekstra was characterized by Samuel Cramer (*q.v.*) as "probably the keenest thinker that Holland produced in his field in the 19th century." His spirit is best revealed in three of his works: *Het geloof des hartens volgens het Evangelie* (Amsterdam, 1856, 2d ed. 1857); *Bronnen en grondslagen van het godsdienstig geloof* (Amsterdam, 1864); and *De Hoop der Onsterfelijkheid* (Amsterdam, 1867). In the first of these Hoekstra was a supranaturalist, closely related to the ethicist Chantepie de la Saussaye (professor at the University of Groningen). He accepts the pre-existence, the miraculous birth and the miracles of Jesus, declaring, "Such a person as Jesus must do wonders, if He was not intentionally to conceal the divine life that was in Him." He gradually changed his views and became a theological liberal. He formulated a theory of faith in God, the immortality of the human spirit, and the supersensual character of the moral law. In opposition to the empiricism of Opzoomer he set his ethical idealism; in opposition to Scholten's theocentric theology and definite determinism he defended an anthropocentric theology and a psychological indeterminism. Hoekstra said, "All faith in a supersensual world is based on faith in the truth of our own inner being," so that we cannot base the understanding of our spiritual life alone on sensual perceptions, but especially on spiritual experience. "The ineradicable needs and strivings in man cannot deceive us concerning the deepest reality." In the area of religion, "faith in ourselves" is an infallible rule, and he endorses Pascal's statement, *"Le coeur a ses raisons, que la raison ne connait pas."* The needs of life awaken faith in a higher world order and faith finds in these needs also its justification. That religion and ethics are interrelated Hoekstra is firmly convinced. "The fear of God is, if not one of the components, at least a necessary condition or the basis of all higher ethics."

His book, *De Hoop der Onsterfelijkheid,* was called by van der Wyck, the professor of philosophy, "the most beautiful book that Hoekstra has written." Here too hope is rooted subjectively in faith, and is not based on scientific evidence. A healthy human soul must understand that spiritual development is its goal in life, and for the genuine life of the spirit, a belief in immortality is essential. This human life cannot be comprehended if this is the true life rather than the introduction to another life.

As opposed to Scholten's determinism, Hoekstra wrote *Vrijheid in verband met zelfbewustzijn en zonde* (Amsterdam, 1857). The freedom of the will is for him the deciding "factor of dawning morality." In the period of the formation of the moral character man has the capacity to choose between motives that act upon him. Not even the most powerful motives must of necessity control him; he can choose one and discard the other. The heroes of history he did not consider as products of their time, but as personalities from whom a decisive influence has emanated upon humanity. At the end of his life he published *Zedenleer* (3 vv., Amsterdam, 1894); then *Wijsgeerige godsdienstleer* (2 vv., Amsterdam, 1894 f.); *Geschiedenis der Zedenleer* (2 vv., Amsterdam, 1896); and *De Christelyke Geloofsleer* (2 vv., Amsterdam, 1898). These books, actually theological lectures, are inferior to his earlier works; while he was working on them he was already struggling with physical ailment.

Hoekstra always remained a Christian philosopher, who did not detach faith from historical Christianity and from Jesus, but he did not want to present a rounded system of the concepts of faith. He illuminates a question from all sides, but does not find it necessary to come to a conclusion. Paradoxes, such as God's foreknowledge and the freedom of our will, God's foreknowledge and answer to prayer he leaves side by side. He did not found a theological school, for he did not want to be a leader of a wing; he was rather a pure scholar, not popular, not even with his students, with whom he associated little.

Nevertheless his influence was profound in circles of many kinds; his clear sermons made a deep impression, his catechetical booklet was widely used for mature students. His first writings, such as *Geloof en leven des Christens* (Sneek, 1852, republished 1855 and 1862); *Levensvragen over den weg des heils in Christus* (Sneek, 1853, reprinted); *De leer des Evangelies, voor beschaafde en nadenkende christenen ontwikkeld* (2 vv., Sneek, 1854 f., reprinted 1858); *Het Evangelie der genade in de gelijkenis van den Verloren Zoon* (Sneek, 1854, reprinted 1860); *Het geloof des harten en Bronnen en grondslagen van het godsdienstig geloof,* gave a clearer insight into the Bible, not only to theologians, but to a wide circle of readers. His students also carried his views into many Mennonite congregations. Even the theologians of our day have recognized the high worth of his views. Eerdmans observed that it would not have been to the disadvantage of modern theology if it had moved more in the direction given it by Hoekstra; and Prof. Roessingh laments that the Dutch theologians did not more basically seek to solve the problems of theology along the lines that Hoekstra pointed out.

Even though Hoekstra became known as a philosophical thinker, he was in fact a universal scholar; in every field of theological scholarship he was more or less at home. Born of a genuinely Mennonite family, he was excellently versed in the history and teaching of the fathers, as is shown in his book, *Beginselen en leer der oude Doopsgezinden, vergeleken met die van de overige Protestanten* (Amsterdam, 1863). He contested their Waldensian origin, considering them rather as the original and faithful representatives of the Reformation of the 16th century in the Netherlands. Their fundamental principle was the building of a spotless church of God, and their other characteristics were accordingly more essential or more accidental. Among the relatively accidental characteristics he counts baptism upon confession of faith, which is by many considered the principal tenet. Their importance he also sees in their tendency to the practical, but they have thereby presented only "one side of the Christian spirit and that only imperfectly." The church can fulfill its task best when it keeps itself free of an exclusive community spirit.

Hoekstra was a good man, sincere, willing to help, and very benevolent. Spiritual pride was foreign to him, sharp criticism did not wound him, he could not hold a grudge. Nor was he calculating, and therefore he frequently uttered all too heedlessly what his sense of humor dictated, and the tone in which he said it at times caused offense. Nor was he a master of language, and was therefore unable to clothe his developing ideas concretely.

Hoekstra wrote an unusual amount, and many articles he wrote for periodicals are well worth reading. He published them in *Theologisch Tijdschrift; Licht, Liefde, Leven; Doopsgezinde Lectuur*, of which he was for a time an editor; *Verslagen en Mededeelingen van de Koninklijke Academie van Wetenschapen; De Gids; Godgeleerde Bijdragen; Nederland; Christelijk Album; De Referent; Christelijke Huisvriend; Evangelisch Tijdschrift;* and *Taal des Geloofs*. Besides these works already mentioned he published the following: with M. A. Amshoff *et al.*, *De feestvierende Christen* (Amsterdam, 1855); *De triumph der liefde in alle beproeving, bezongen in het Lied der liederen* (Utrecht, 1856); *Inhoud en doel der Evangelieprediking, Leerrede over Titus 3:8 en 9* (Amsterdam, 1857); *Waarheid in liefde. Afscheidsrede over 2. Joh. 3* (Rotterdam, 1857); *De twee getuigenissen van den lijdenden Jesus aangaande zichzelven. Leerredenen* (Amsterdam, 1860); *Wedergeboorte. Leerrede over Joh. 3:1-9* (Amsterdam, 1858, reprinted); *De weg tot Evangeliekennis. Leerrede over Gal. 1:11 en 12* (Amsterdam, 1859); *Grondslag, wezen en openbaring van het godsdienstig ge-*

loof volgens de H. Schrift (Rotterdam, 1861); with J. Tideman *et al.*, *Zestal leerredenen* (Amsterdam, 1861); *De Zoon des menschen, de Heiland der wereld* (Amsterdam, 1861); *De ontwikkeling der zedelijke idee in de geschiedenis* with the supplement, *De zondeloosheid of volmaakte rechtvaardigheid van Jesus* (Amsterdam, 1862); *De benaming "de Zoon des menschen," historisch-kritisch onderzocht* (Amsterdam, 1866); *Des Christens godsvrucht naar de eigne leer van Jesus* (Amsterdam, 1866); with van Bell *et al.*, *Voorlezingen over bijbelsche berichten aangaande het leven van Jesus* (Amsterdam, 1866); *De vervloeking van de vijgenboom* (Haarlem, 1871); *De tegenstelling van Optimisme en Pessimisme. Academische redevoering op 21. Sept. 1880* (Amsterdam, 1880); *Het jaarcijfer 81 als getuige van de beteekenis des geloofs* (Amsterdam, 1881).†

J.L.

J. Molenaar, "Professor Hoekstra," in *Mannen van Beteekenis*, 1897; *Theologisch Tijdschrift*, 1898, 448-54; van der Wyck, "Levensbericht van S. Hoekstra," in *Jaarboek der Koninkl. Academie van Wetenschappen*, 1901; *DB* 1898, 150-62; 1901, 27; *DJ* 1903, 25-34 (with portrait); 1943, 61-67; K. H. Roessingh, *De Moderne Theologie in Nederland. Hare voorbereiding en eerste periode* (1914) 166-82; Gorter's *Doopsgezind Lectuur* III (1858) 13 f., 33; W. F. Golterman, *De Godsdienstwijsbegeerte van S. Hoekstra Bz* (Assen, 1942); *Biogr. Wb.* IV, 79-87; *N.N.B.Wb.* I, 1122-26; *HRE* VIII, 195 ff.; *DB* 1898, 150-62; 1901, 27; *DJ* 1903, 25-34 (with portrait); 1943, 61-67; *ML* II, 323-25.

Hoekstra, Sytse Benedictus, b. 1698 at Oudega near Witveen, Dutch province of Friesland, d. July 13, 1768, at Den Burg on the island of Texel. He did not receive a special training for the ministry; before and also during the first years of his ministry he was a farmer. He was the progenitor of a large family of Dutch Mennonites, which has produced many preachers. He was minister at Witveen 1722, Veenwouden 1726, Kollum 1736, Kollum and Buitenpost 1742, Burg op Texel 1753 to his death. He wrote *Bespiegelnde en practische onderwijzingen uit Genesis* III (expanded and published by his son, Zaandam, 1756), and *Beknopte antwoorden op vragen voor den Doop* (Zaandam, 1766). (*N.N.B.Wb.* I, 1126; *DB* 1868, 90 f.; 1890, 108-10.) He was married to Joukje Egberts, was the father of five daughters and six sons, all of whom became preachers in the strict Zonist Mennonite branch:

I. Benedictus (1722-79), preacher at Buitenpost 1743, den Ilp 1746, and Westzaan (Frisian congregation) 1754-79. He published a funeral address for his father (Zaandam, 1768); *Vragen met korte antwoorden over den Doop en het Avondmaal* (Zaandam, 1771), and *Het antidox character van Justus Benevolens* (Zaandam, n.d.). (*Biogr. Wb.* IV, 75 f.; *N.N.B.Wb.* I, 1119; *Inv. Arch. Amst.* I, No. 711).

2. Egbertus (d. 1798), minister at Goedereede 1745 and at Groningen (United Flemish and Waterlander congregation) 1754-98 (*N.N.B.Wb.* I, 1119; *Inv. Arch. Amst.* I, No. 1056).

3. Sjoerd (d. 1789), preacher at Aalsmeer 1748, Ouddorp 1754, and Emden 1759-89. His son published a collection of sermons delivered by his father and himself, *Plegtige leerredenen te Emden en Utrecht*. Sjoerd was married to Maria Jans Valk and had a son, Johannes Albertus (*q.v.; N.N.B.Wb.* I, 121).

4. Wytse, b. about 1728 or 1729 at Veenwouden, d. March 27, 1801, at Rotterdam, was married to Jannetje C. Loos of Blokzijl (*N.N.B.Wb.* I, 1126; *Biogr. Wb.* IV, 76). He was preacher at Veenwouden 1751, Blokzijl 1753, where he united the Flemish and Danziger Old Flemish congregations, and Rotterdam 1786. He wrote *Leerzame en vertroostende gedachten.* His son Sytse Wytses (1757-86), married to Elisabeth van Cleef, was preacher at Den Ilp, June to December 1780; Kampen 1780; West-Zaandam 1782-86. He wrote *Over de natuur van onzen Middelaar Jesus Christus,* published with the funeral address delivered at his death by H. van Gelder (Amsterdam, 1768). (*N.N.B.Wb.* I, 1121; *Biogr. Wb.* IV, 87.)

5. Hidser, b. March 14, 1730, at Veenwouden, d. Sept. 7, 1772, at Sneek, preacher at Burg op Texel 1761, Harlingen 1763, Sneek (Kleinzand Old Flemish congregation) 1764-72 (*N.N.B.Wb.* I, 1120; *DB* 1890, 107-10). His son Sytse Hidsers, b. 1757 at Den Burg, d. there on June 7, 1814, married to Neeltje Jacobs Baske, was preacher at Den Helder 1777, and Texel 1790-1814 (*N.N.B.Wb.* I, 1122; *DB* 1873, 151-54. Sytse had two sons: (*a*) Jacob, b. about 1779 at Den Helder, d. May 12, 1850, at Kampen, preacher at Hoorn op Texel 1812, and Den Helder 1815-39. His son was Soerd (1805-94, *q.v.*); (*b*) Benedictus, b. March 5, 1793, at Den Burg, d. Jan. 19, 1872, at Barsingerhorn, married to Aafje Pruit. For his theological training he was not sent to the Amsterdam Mennonite Seminary, because his father did not like the liberal teaching of Prof. Hesselink (*q.v.*). So Benedictus Hoekstra was trained for the ministry by Preacher H. Veenstra of Texel (*DB* 1898, 161). He was preacher at Oudesluis 1813, and then 1828-63 at Barsingerhorn (*N.N.B.Wb.* I, 1119). His son was Prof. Sytse Hoekstra Bzn (1822-98, *q.v.*).

6. Johannes, b. at Kollum (?) about 1740, d. at Heerenveen in 1776, was preacher at Burg op Texel 1764, and Heerenveen 1765-76. (*ML* II, 322.)

                             J.L., vDZ.

Hoen, Cornelius Hendrickz, d. before April 1524, lived at Delft, Dutch province of South Holland, lawyer of the Court of Holland at The Hague. At Delft Hoen heard the preaching of a Dominican monk Wouter, known as "the Lutheran monk," who "gave him the sense of truth." This may have happened about 1510, though it is more likely that Hoen became averse to Roman Catholicism shortly after 1517. Reading the writings of Erasmus, Gansfort, and Luther, he more and more rejected the Catholic doctrine of transubstantiation, no longer believing that the real flesh and blood of Christ were present in the host. Hoen exposed his new views in *Epistola Christiana,* in which he wrote that communion should not be a sacrament in the Catholic sense, but merely a commemoration of the death of Christ; the bread should be understood as a symbol. The word "is" in Christ's words "this is my body" has not the sense of "this really is," but "this means," as when Christ says, "I am the vine." This letter by Hoen was brought to Luther by Hinne Rode in 1521, but Luther rejected Hoen's symbolical conception, because he wished to maintain the real presence of Christ in the sacra-

ment. Two years later, in January 1523, Rode visited Oecolampad in Basel, who read the letter with much interest and advised Rode to travel to Zürich and present the letter to Zwingli. Zwingli, whose doctrine of the communion at this time was still somewhat uncertain, was very receptive to Hoen's views. "In this letter," he writes, "I found a pearl of great value; *is* has the sense of *means."* Zwingli soon adopted Hoen's views, which in this way also became the Anabaptist concept. In the meantime Hoen was arrested (February 1523) for heresy. Before he came to trial he died.

Hoen's *Epistola Christiana* was published by Zwingli in 1525 and re-edited by W. Eekhof at The Hague in 1917.   vDZ.

Biogr. Wb. IV, 90-92; J. G. de Hoop Scheffer, *Geschiedenis der Kerkhervorming in Nederland* . . . (Amsterdam, 1873) *passim,* see Index; L. Knappert, *Het ontstaan en de vestiging van het Protestantisme in de Nederlanden* (Utrecht, 1924) *passim,* see Index; *DB* 1910, 110 f.; Kühler, *Geschiedenis* I, 57.

Hoeve, Vincent van der, sheriff of the city of Amersfoort, Dutch province of Utrecht, was publicly beheaded at Utrecht (city) on Aug. 25, 1569, because he had favored the Mennonites at Amersfoort, tolerating them and permitting them to hold meetings. This protector of the Mennonites was apparently not a member of the church. (*DB* 1863, 94; 1918, 123 f.)   vDZ.

Hofer, name of a Hutterite family of wide ramifications. The Hofers originated in Carinthia, Austria, where they had been staunch Lutherans, for which reason they were exiled by Empress Maria Theresa to Transylvania in 1755. The founder was a Johannes Hofer of St. Peter, with his wife, five sons, and two daughters. Besides we hear also of two brothers Matthias and Michael Hofer, who left their parents and a brother and joined the transmigrants. These Hofers were strong characters unafraid to oppose the authorities whenever demands were made impinging upon their freedom of conscience. The result was conflict and jail (in Hermannstadt, Transylvania) almost from the beginning in 1756. Michael died there in 1757. Matthias spent a total of 16 years (1756-72) in this jail, composing there 30 hymns and many Biblical tracts. In the meantime the entire brotherhood had migrated to the Ukraine, where Matthias eventually joined his brethren. Unfortunately, he was a man of strange ideas, very headstrong. Although he was highly regarded for his straightforwardness and profound familiarity with the Scriptures, he soon became a thorn in the flesh of the brotherhood, requiring midnight prayers, forbidding singing while at work, not greeting anybody who was not a brother, etc. Eventually he had no choice than to leave his family and the brotherhood. He wandered to Prussia, where he visited the Mennonite Elder Gerhard Wiebe (*q.v.*) of Ellerwald (Johannes Waldner in the *Klein-Geschichtbuch* says that in this way the contact with the Prussian Mennonites was established), then went on to Hamburg, perhaps to go to Pennsylvania. But he had no money, and returned again to Prussia, where he died among Mennonites in 1786.

Of the five sons of Johannes, the eldest son, also named Johannes, is described in the *Klein-Geschichtbuch* likewise as a headstrong man with queer ideas. In 1784, when peace could not be achieved in the colony in Vishenka, Ukraine, he, too, left the brotherhood, and went first to Sobotiste, and then to Silesia. Here he proposed to the authorities the establishment of a new Bruderhof, which was welcomed. But he did not find followers, and the brethren in the Ukraine did not want to have any dealing with him. Thus he failed and soon after disappeared. The brethren heard nothing more from him.

The other Hofer sons, Michael (d. 1793), Christian (d. 1802), Paul (d. 1790), and Jacob (d. 1811), were highly regarded among their brethren. But none of them had a leading position. Of the second generation we hear of one Jacob Hofer, who together with Michael Waldner (*q.v.*) re-established community of goods in Hutterdorf, Southern Ukraine, in 1859 (the *Schmiede Leut*). One year later, in 1860, Darius Walter, a preacher, established another Bruderhof in Huttertal, where community of goods was again established anew, after it had been discontinued in Russia for over 40 years (the *Darius Leut*). The preacher Jörg Hofer was among the first to join this new group. In 1864 more such colonies were established with David and Peter Hofer among the constituents. David died in 1868; Peter came to America with all the other brethren.

Of the family of this Peter the Chronicle has a sad story to tell. Three sons, David, Josef, and Michael, were called to serve as United States soldiers during World War I. They refused to compromise, and, since adequate provisions for CO's did not exist, were sent first to the ill-famed federal prison at Alcatraz, Cal., and then to the not less ill-famed prison at Leavenworth, Kan. Here they were submitted to nearly unbelievably cruel treatment; Josef and Michael died here in 1918, while David survived (*Klein-Geschichtbuch,* 482-86).

Today Hofers are found on many Bruderhofs in Alberta and Montana, many in leading positions. One preacher David Hofer traveled to Europe with Michael Waldner in 1937-38 to assist the New Hutterites (*Arnold Leut*) in their exit from Germany, and also to visit the old places of their ancestors. His very interesting travel report exists only in mimeographed form but would deserve publication. One Hofer family separated and started a small brotherhood of their own, called "The Hutterian Fellowship" (Brocket, Alberta). A number of Hofers moved away from the brotherhood altogether and joined the Krimmer Mennonite Brethren, with one mission station in Chicago, of which D. M. Hofer (*q.v.*) was the pastor for many years. Others joined the General Conference Mennonite Church, in which there were several Hofer preachers in 1954.

It should be mentioned that one Preacher Peter Hofer continued the *Klein-Geschichtbuch* where Johannes Waldner had left it, that is, for 1802-77. But his work is rather inadequate and merely annalistic. (Zieglschmid, *Klein-Geschichtbuch.*)

R.F.

Hofer, David, chosen to the ministry of the Hutterian Brethren for the Rockport Bruderhof, S.D., on June 13, 1897, and confirmed by Michael Stahl, elder of the Darius branch on Nov. 25, 1900.

D.D.

Hofer, David, chosen Hutterian Brethren preacher of the Milltown Bruderhof June 2, 1907, confirmed Oct. 10, 1909. He died April 6, 1941, in the James Valley Bruderhof in Canada at the age of 64, having been in the ministry for 33 years. D.D.

Hofer, David M., K.M.B. evangelist, editor, city missionary, and relief worker, b. July 24, 1869, in Johannesruh, Russia, d. Dec. 31, 1944, in Chicago. In 1879 he emigrated to the United States with his parents, Michael and Mary Gross Hofer, and settled on a farm near Bridgewater, S.D. In 1893 he married Barbara Hofer. In 1902-14 he was engaged in the grain and banking business; 1914 he left the business field and answered the call into the ministry. With Joseph W. Tschetter as associate he founded the Lincoln Avenue Gospel Mission in Chicago in 1915. He edited the *Wahrheitsfreund,* the organ of the K.M.B. Conference 1917-33. In 1922-23 he served as American relief administrator in Russia. He was the author of *Die Hungersnot in Russland und unsere Reise um die Welt* (Chicago, 1924). J.S.M.

Hofer, George, chosen preacher of the Hutterian Brethren in Russia (probably in 1857), date of confirmation unknown, died in the Wolf Creek, S.D., Bruderhof Jan. 5, 1882, at the age of 64 years, having served in the ministry for 25 years. D.D.

Hofer, Jakob, a Hutterian Brethren preacher chosen in Russia in 1859. He died in the Milltown Bruderhof in South Dakota in 1900 at the age of 70. He served as preacher for 41 years. D.D.

Hofer, Peter, chosen a preacher of the Hutterian Brethren, March 29, 1857, and confirmed Dec. 22, 1857, at Huttertal in Russia, by Peter Wedel, an elder of the Alexanderwohl congregation. D.D.

Hoffmann, Christoph (1815-85), the founder of the brotherhood of the *Deutscher Tempel,* grew up in Korntal near Stuttgart, Württemberg, Germany, which his father had founded. He was a delegate to the parliament of Frankfurt, in 1848 founded the *Evangelischer Verein,* which established a school for evangelists to revive the church, withdrew from it in 1853, served for a short time as inspector at St. Chrischona near Basel, in 1854 called a meeting of the *Jerusalemsfreunde* (Friends of Jerusalem) at Ludwigsburg, and in 1861, on the Kirschenhardthof near Marbach he founded the *Deutscher Tempel zur Ausführung des Gesetzes, des Evangeliums und der Weissagung,* which found adherents in Württemberg, Russia, North America, and Palestine. On a trip to Russia he and his friend Christian Paulus (1861-63) gained a following among the Mennonites, giving rise to a Tempel movement. Many of Hoffmann's adherents among the Russian Mennonites, however, left him when in his open letter of 1877-82 he abandoned his Biblical position for a rationalistic one. The periodical of the movement, *Süddeutsche Warte,* was also read by the Mennonites of Russia.

Gnadenfeld (*q.v.*), where a movement originated which gave life to the Mennonite Brethren, was also the scene of the origin of the Tempel movement in Russia. Johannes and Friedrich Lange, who had attended the *Paulusinstitut* of the Templers in South Germany, became teachers in the Gnadenfeld Bruderschule, promoting a pietistic rationalistic chiliasm with a strong emphasis on the significance of education. Parallel with the Mennonite Brethren movement this caused a great disturbance in the Molotschna Mennonite brotherhood. In 1863 the group withdrew from the Mennonite Church under the leadership of Nikolai Schmidt and organized as a separate church, which established the Tempelhof settlement in the Caucasus in 1868. The group also became known as *Jerusalemsfreunde,* a sort of Mennonite Zionism which caused some of them to emigrate to Palestine. The Alexandrodar Mennonite Church of Jerusalemsfreunde consisted of 148 persons in 1905, with Isaak Fast as elder.   NEFF, C.K.

H. Görz, *Die Molotschnaer Mennoniten* (Steinbach, 1951) 86-90; H. Dirks, *Statistik . . .* (1905) 69; Friesen, *Brüderschaft,* 88-91; Chr. Hoffman, *Mein Weg nach Jerusalem* (2 vv., 1881-84); Fr. Lange, *Geschichte des Tempels* (1899); E. Rohrer, *Die Tempel Gesellschaft* (1920); Heinrich Sawatzky, *Die Templer mennonitischer Herkunft* (Winnipeg, 1955); *ML* II, 325 f.

Hoffnungsau Mennonite Church near Buhler (*q.v.*), Kan., was organized on Feb. 22, 1875, after the arrival of a group of immigrants who originally belonged to the Alexanderwohl Mennonite Church (*q.v.*) in Russia. They crossed the Atlantic on the *Teutonia* under the leadership of Dietrich Gaeddert, arriving in New York on Sept. 2, 1874, settling on some 35 sections of land in Harvey, McPherson, and Reno counties near Buhler. After their arrival the meetings were held in the immigrant house (1874-80), which was destroyed by a tornado. On Oct. 2, 1880, the cornerstone was laid for the first building made of adobe, which was completed on Dec. 19. This building was replaced in 1898 by a wooden structure, which was destroyed by fire in 1948 and replaced by a brick building in 1949. The change from the use of the German to English in worship took place after World War I.

The congregation was the first Mennonite church in the Buhler-Inman area; from it have been organized the Buhler Mennonite Church (*q.v.*), 1920, and Inman Mennonite Church (*q.v.*), 1921. Dietrich Gaeddert (*q.v.*) was elected elder on April 19, 1876, and served the congregation in this capacity until he died Dec. 4, 1900. Since that time the following have served as elders: Abraham Ratzlaff 1901-24, A. J. Dyck 1925-46, and Albert Gaeddert 1946- . The congregation had a membership of 369 in 1954.   C.K.

A. J. Dyck, "Hoffnungsau in Kansas," in *Menn. Life,* October 1949, 18 ff.

Hoffnungsau Mennonite (GCM) Church (Mennonite Fellowship), Cuauhtemoc, Chihuahua, consists of a few GCM families who came to Mexico after World War I. Most of the immigrants have meanwhile moved to the U.S. and Canada. Some Old Colony Mennonites fellowship in the Hoffnungsau Church.

H. P. Krehbiel was invited by the group to organize a church in 1938. For a while J. H. Janzen, who was ordained to the ministry within the group by J. M. Regier, served the congregation. Frank Dyck also served. Since 1950 B. H. Janzen has been serving the church, sponsored by the Mission Board of the General Conference Mennonite Church. During the extreme drought the congregation played a significant role in giving spiritual and material aid to the Old Colony Mennonites (*q.v.*) of the area. In 1954 there were 37 members with a total of 73 associated with the congregation.   C.K.

Hoffnungsau Preparatory School was located in McPherson Co., Kan., near the Hoffnungsau Mennonite Church (GCM). It was organized in 1906 and continued to give instruction until 1929, when it was discontinued. The curriculum was composed of Bible courses and some of the courses commonly taught during the first year of high school. The school was established primarily to offer to the young people of that community instruction in Bible and some of the basic non-Bible courses before public high schools were established in that area. The school enjoyed adequate support from its friends. The average attendance was between 25 and 35 students. The following teachers served it during its existence: J. H. Epp 1907-14, Abraham Albrecht 1914-20, Edward E. Flickinger 1920-22, A. J. Dyck 1922-25, Henry Hege 1925-26, and P. T. Neufeld 1926-29.   M.S.H.

Hoffser, Jürg, of Obergallbach, Signau district of Switzerland, an Anabaptist martyr, executed on Aug. 28, 1537, at Bern.

Mart. Mir. E 1129, note; A. Fluri, *Beiträge zur Geschichte der bernischen Täufer* (Bern, 1912) 14; *ML* II, 326.

Hofkes, former Mennonite family in the Netherlands, now extinct. Its members were especially found in the congregations of Winterswijk and Almelo.

Hofmann, Melchior, the noted early Anabaptist leader, was born about 1495 at Schwäbisch-Hall. He received a good elementary education and learned the furrier's trade. He was early interested in religious literature, especially the writings of the mystics, Tauler, *Deutsche Theologie,* etc. He also acquired a thorough knowledge of the Bible. The writings of Martin Luther moved him deeply and he became Luther's zealous follower.

In 1523 business took him to Livland; here he was soon drawn into the religious movement of the Reformation. In the shortage of Protestant preachers, Hofmann entered this service and preached at Wolmar until persecution caused his imprisonment and expulsion from the country. Nevertheless his influence here must have been lasting, for even from Sweden he wrote admonitions to his Wolmar friends. In the fall of 1524 he came to Dorpat where he preached against the use of images. This led to a fateful wave of iconoclasm (Jan. 10, 1525), in which he, however, did not participate (Leendertz, 26). The populace successfully opposed his arrest by the church authorities; this constituted a victory for the Protestant cause.

In the new state of affairs the city council was doubtful about permitting the furrier to continue his preaching, and demanded an approval of his doctrine by recognized theological authorities. He therefore betook himself to Riga where the Protestant preachers Knöpken and Tegetmeier gave him this approval. Hofmann then went on to Wittenberg to get Luther's confirmation of his preaching. He arrived there about the middle of June and was joyfully received by Luther. Luther and Bugenhagen together wrote to the churches in Livland *Ein christlich Vermahnung von äusserlichem Gottesdienst und Eintracht an die in Liefland, durch Martinum Luther und Andere* (Wittenberg, 1525), to which Hofmann added a letter of June 22 (Krohn, 51-57) with the title, "Jhesus. Der christlichen gemey zu Derpten ynn Lieflandt wunschet Melchior Hofmann gnad und fride, sterkung des Glaubens von Gott dem vater und dem Hern Jhesu Christo. Amen." This is Hofmann's earliest known writing. In addition to a strong emphasis on justification alone through faith, the author already stresses the sanctification of life, which must be shown in all the fruits of the Spirit. He opposes the "fanatical spirits" who make themselves illegal executors of God's judgment; for "he who takes the sword shall perish by the sword." In this letter Hofmann's allegorical interpretation of the Bible and his chiliastic ideas are already evident. (Leendertz considers it unlikely that Hofmann met Schwenckfeld and Andreas Carlstadt in Wittenberg, but believes that he became acquainted with Carlstadt's writings here, pp. 41 ff.)

With Luther's written recommendation Hofmann returned to Dorpat in the late summer of 1525. His self-esteem had risen considerably, making his relations with the Lutheran clergy intolerable. They refused to recognize Luther's authorization, whereas Hofmann accused them of self seeking and of denying by their life the faith they preached. He declared that they did not have the divine call to preach, and that they were incapable of understanding the simple word of Scripture. He considered himself a prophet called to testify to the imminence of the final judgment by a stirring cry for repentance. Again and again he referred to Enoch and Elijah, the two witnesses of Christ's return, and with increasing strength the idea possessed him that he was one or the other of the two. His most violent opponent was Tegetmeier, who published a polemic against him, making his position in Dorpat untenable and compelling him to leave the town again.

From Dorpat Hofmann went to Reval in the fall of 1525. Here the Reformation had been introduced and the preaching offices were filled. "There I was made the servant of the sick," he writes. Unselfishly he devoted himself to the service of the church. For his preaching service in Dorpat he accepted no salary, but supported himself with his own labor (Leendertz, 14 and 53). But before long the Lutheran clergy in Reval accused him of heresy because in addition to faith he insisted on the necessity of holy living. His views on communion also differed from Lutheran doctrine. On the other hand, the absence of the fruits of faith in the Lutheran brotherhood raised doubts in Hofmann's mind as to whether it was the true Christian church; the idea of separation from it seems to have occurred to him at this time. He was expelled from Livland.

The prospect of success in Hofmann's trade took him to Sweden. The German Lutheran Church in Stockholm conferred the office of preaching upon him early in 1526. He married and a son was born to him there. He perhaps hoped that his position would be permanent. But King Gustav Vasa, fearing that the stormy nature of the preacher might embarrass the young government, requested his resignation (letter of Jan. 13, 1527), and Hofmann was compelled to move on.

Melchior Hofmann wrote three booklets in Stockholm. The one on the judgment day is lost. The second has the title, *An de gelöfigen vorsambling inn Liflant ein korte formaninghe, van Melcher Hoffman sich tho wachten vor falscher lere de sich nu ertzeighen unde inrithen under der sthemme götliker worde* (1526). The first part of this booklet is to reveal the "Hiddenness of God," and deals largely with the declaration of the last things, while the second practical part is an argument with his opponents in Livland. The other book offers an exposition of Daniel XII: *Das XII. Capitel des propheten Danielis ausgelegt, und das Evangelion des andern sondages, gefallendt inn Advent, und von den zeychenn des jüngsten gerichtes, auch vom sacrament, beicht und der absolution, eyn schöne unterweisung an die in Lieflandt und eyn yden christen nutzlich zu wissen* (1526). This important book falls into six parts; the first contains a complete exposition of Daniel 12, verse by verse; the second explains the Gospel for the second Sunday of advent; the third demonstrates that laymen should also be preachers; the fourth deals with communion, the fifth with the confessional, and the sixth with the office of the keys. Of special interest for us is Hofmann's teaching on communion. For him communion is a memorial of the death of Christ and at the same time a celebration of closest union with Christ, which is the product of faith. Conspicuous is this early agreement with the Anabaptists in their rejection of all force in matters of faith and the oath. The end of the world is to occur in 1533.

From Sweden Hofmann returned to Germany, temporarily to Lübeck. It is possible that his ruthless, passionate defense of the Reformation here drew upon him persecution by the city council. Only by hasty flight was he able to avoid a tragic death. Early in 1527, with his wife and child, he arrived in Holstein territory, which was at that time Danish. At first he was unable to establish himself here. In May he made a second trip to Wittenberg, visiting en route at Magdeburg, Luther's friend Nicolas Amsdorf. He evidently wrote

Amsdorf of his intention to visit him, for Amsdorf inquired of Luther how to receive this "prophet" and was advised to give him a cold reception and to advise him to return to his trade. Amsdorf consequently rudely showed him the door. In Wittenberg Hofmann was also rejected. Bitterly disappointed he started back; at Magdeburg en route he was jailed and robbed. He placed the blame for this on Amsdorf who had published a violent polemic against him. In Hamburg his poverty compelled him to accept alms from the pastor Zegenhagen.

But when Hofmann arrived in Holstein, great success awaited him. Frederick X, the Danish king, was pleased by his sermons and had him given a position as preacher at the Nicolaikirche at Kiel along with the pastor Wilhelm Pravest. But he lacked the qualifications needed to conduct a quiet and orderly pastorate. He continued his allegorical exegesis of Scripture, finding in every detail of the Ark of the Covenant profound, divine meaning. His favorite topic was "the last things." Without moderation he attacked the senators of Kiel, calling them rogues and thieves from the pulpit.

With his colleague Pravest, who was not of the highest character, his relations were never entirely friendly. Pravest wrote to Luther for advice on the attitude he should take, and received the reply that M. Hofmann, the furrier, should be silenced, for he was neither competent nor called to preach. When Pravest made dishonorable use of this letter, Luther rebuked him in a second letter and to a certain extent defended Hofmann. In a letter to the mayor of Kiel Luther also remarked that Hofmann's intentions were good, but that his acts were hasty.

But Luther's favorable opinion was of short duration. When Hofmann was engaged in his ink-campaign against Amsdorf, Luther wrote to Duke Christian of Denmark, expressing the wish that Hofmann refrain from preaching until he should be better informed. Even more fraught with disaster for Hofmann was his conflict with the Lutheran clergy of Holstein concerning the communion. The bitterness was so deep that the king agreed to proclaim a public disputation.

This disputation was held in the spring of 1529 at Flensburg. Carlstadt, invited by Hofmann to help him, was unable to do so, for Hofmann was unable to secure a safe conduct for him. A stately audience of 400, including the nobility and clergy, met in the church of the monastery of the Barefoot Friars. On the preceding day Hofmann had handed Luther's *Vom Missbrauch der Messe* to the duke, as support for his concept of communion. On the same evening the duke pleaded with him to yield; when this proved vain he threatened Hofmann with banishment. Hofmann replied that all the scholars of Christendom could not justly do him any harm; but even if God should permit violence to be done to him, they could take from him only his old robe of flesh, which Christ would replace with a new one at the judgment. The duke expressed some surprise that Hofmann would dare to speak so boldly to him, whereupon Hofmann

replied, "If all the emperors, kings, princes, popes, bishops, and cardinals should be together in one place, nevertheless the truth shall and must be known to the glory of God; may my Lord and God grant me this." On the next morning, when the duke asked Hofmann about his adherents, he answered, "I know of no adherents; I stand alone in the Word of God, let each do likewise."

Duke Christian presided. Bugenhagen, who was to function as referee without participating in the debate, spoke the opening prayer while the audience kneeled. On Hofmann's side Jan van Campen, Jakob Hegge of Danzig, and Johann Barse spoke; then the disputation was closed. The next day the king presided as the verdict was read, which was solemnly proclaimed in the Franciscan monastery three days later: Melchior Hofmann and those of like opinion must leave their home towns within two days after arriving there, and leave Danish territory within three additional days. Hofmann complained that he had been expelled with wife and child, his house plundered, and an estate of 100 guilders in books and printed matter taken; "even his life was in danger, but God helped him" (Leendertz, 119-35).

From Holstein Hofmann went to East Friesland. En route he met Carlstadt (*q.v.*), and the two arrived there in late April or early May. At this time Count Enno II (*q.v.*) was about to reinstate Lutheranism in the place of the Reformed faith. Carlstadt opposed this plan with passion, agitating against Luther "from fortress to fortress, from parsonage to parsonage." Hofmann was probably staying quietly at the castle of Ulrich von Dornum (Leendertz, 141), engaged in writing his *Dialogus* on the Flensburg disputation. He was kindly accepted as a colleague by the Reformed preachers. He was, however, unable to oppose Enno's plans actively, for he again found himself in embarrassing circumstances and left the country in haste.

Hofmann now betook himself to Strasbourg, where he was received with open arms at the end of June 1529 as a champion of Zwingli's teaching on the communion (letter by Bucer to Zwingli, July 30, 1529). At first he kept very quiet, staying in the house of Andreas Kleiber and his wife Katharina Leid, a gifted woman, who joined the Anabaptist brotherhood in 1532. He published his account of the Flensburg disputation under the title: *Dialogus und grüntliche berichtung gehaltener disputation im land zu Holstein underm künig von Denmarck vom hochwirdigen sacrament oder nachtmal des Herren. In gagenwärtigkeit kü. ma. sun hertzog Kersten sampt kü. räten, vilen vom adel und grosser versamlung der priesterschaft. Jetzt kurtzlich geschehen den andern donderstag nach ostern im Jar Christi als man zalt 1529.* He made his first contacts with Kaspar Schwenckfeld, without, however, accepting his ideas. He continued to go his rather solitary way and to construct his own peculiar allegorical-spiritualistic doctrine. The theologically trained reformers of Strasbourg, unimpressed, advised him to return to his furrier's craft and stick to it. But Melchior Hofmann was convinced that the Holy Spirit fully compensated for any lack of education;

book learning was a hindrance rather than a help. He therefore devoted himself to the publication of several booklets, which appeared early in 1530: (1) *Weissagung auss Heiliger Götlicher geschrift. Von den trübsalen diser letsten zeit. Von der schweren Hand und straff Gottes über alles gottlos wesen. Von der zukunfpt des Türkischen Thirannen und seines gantzen anhangs: Wie er sein reiss thun und vollbringen wird unns zu einer straff und rudten, wie er durch Gottes gevalt sein niderlegung unnd straff empfahen wird . . .* (1530); (2) *Prophezey oder weissagung uss warer heiliger götlicher schrift. Von allen wundern und zeichen bis zu der zukunft Christi Jesu unsers heilands an dem jüngsten tag und DEr welt end. Diese prophecey wird sich anfahen am end der weissagung (kürtzlich von mir aussgegangen in eime andern büchlin von der schweren straf Gottes über alles gotloss wesen durch den Türkischen tirannen* (1530); (3) *Auslegung der heimlichen Offenbarung Joannis des heyligen Apostels unnd Evangelisten* (1530). This last pamphlet was printed in Strasbourg by Balthassar Beck. (He was an Anabaptist according to zur Linden, p. 191, note 1, and was sentenced to prison for printing Hofmann's works without permission.) One of Hofmann's most significant works, this pamphlet had an especially disastrous effect through its glowing description of the return of the Lord. It was dedicated to the king of Denmark. The title page vignette is interesting, representing, as it does, Christ as judge of the world, with Elijah and Enoch as witnesses, and the sun-clad woman riding on the dragon (Rev. 12). In this book Hofmann divides church history into three periods, the first from apostolic times to the reign of the popes, the second the period of the unlimited power of the popes, and the third, already prepared by Hus, beginning with the Reformation, in which the pope is deprived of all power, and the office of the letter is turned into spirit. Then the two witnesses of the last day appear. To destroy them the adherents of the letter will combine with the papists; the two witnesses will suffer death, and the spiritual Jerusalem will be destroyed by the Turks. Prostration will last three and one-half years. Finally Christ will appear, hold judgment, and renew heaven and earth.

Meanwhile Hofmann had made contacts with the Anabaptist movement, and found what he was seeking. Their earnest piety, their simple Biblical faith, their religious mind, open to mystical and chiliastic ideas, attracted him. He became interested in Lienhard and Ursula Jost (*q.v.*) of Strasbourg, both of whom boasted of visions and revelations. He published their collected visions in two books; the first of these has the title, *Prophetische Gesicht unn offenbarung, der göttlichen würkung zu diser letzten zeit, die . . . einer gottes liebhaberin durch den heiligen Geist geoffenbart seind. . . .* (1530). The other, proclaiming the prophecies of Lienhard Jost, has been lost. In spite of their confused ideas, these two books made a deep impression even in Holland (Hulshof, 118).

Hofmann had not actually joined the Anabaptists, when he took the unheard-of step of presenting a petition to the council (April 1530) demanding that a church be assigned to the Anabaptists. He demanded not only toleration for them, but also equal rights with the state church. He was obviously moved to this step by his warm sympathy for the suppressed brotherhood.

In 1530 Hofmann took the formal step of joining the Anabaptist brotherhood by baptism. But his residence in Strasbourg was of short duration. It is not likely that he became closely associated with Kautz (*q.v.*) and Reublin (*q.v.*), who were living there at the time, for they were greatly superior to him in theological training. Nor was he the equal of Pilgram Marpeck. In clearness of spirit and depth of understanding of the Scriptures, Marpeck far outranked Hofmann. The city council issued an order of arrest against Hofmann because of his petition and on account of lesé-majesté in his exposition of the Revelation; he left the city hastily on April 23, 1530.

Hofmann now betook himself to East Friesland again, arriving there in May 1530. Luther, hearing of it, sent a letter warning the authorities in very sharp terms: Hofmann had long since been committed to Satan, and was filled solely with fanatical speculations, for the sake of which he let the cause of Christ perish. In June 1530 Hofmann appeared in Emden as a preacher. He gathered the elements dissatisfied with the established churches ("simple souls and the quiet in the land," Leendertz, 217) and through his eloquence acquired a large following. He can be considered the founder of the Anabaptist congregation at Emden (*q.v.*), which is still in existence. In the city church of Emden, which the clergy had evidently given him, he is said to have baptized 300 persons. This created a great stir, and the council compelled Hofmann to leave the city. Hofmann left Jan Volkertszoon (*q.v.*) (Trijpmaker) in charge as preacher.

Hofmann now turned again to Strasbourg, impelled by worry concerning his wife and child (as zur Linden assumes). Along his route up the Rhine he won adherents for the new *Bundesgemeinde*. This term appears first in his most important and best work, the *Ordonnanz Gottes*, in which he presents his Anabaptist point of view for the first time. The title of this booklet is *Die Ordonnantie Godts, De welche hy, door zijnen Soone Christum Jesum, inghestelt ende bevesticht heevt, op die waerachtighe Discipulen des eewigen woort Godts* (1530). The term "ordinance of God" means to him Christ's baptismal command, Matt. 28:19. In opposition to justification he stresses sanctification (*q.v.*), the "imitation of the life of Christ." As Jesus was tempted in the wilderness after His baptism, so all those who "in the endtimes" are entrusted to Him in baptism by His true apostles, should follow Him in being led to the spiritual wilderness there to prove their steadfastness in the face of temptations. Here they must spend "forty days and forty nights in spiritual fasting"; not until they are complete in the favor, spirit, and will of Jesus Christ, and have fought to the end and have conquered, and in all the tests have remained faithful and unblamable, "is their justification perfected." Baptism, which should be

the symbol of the covenant with God and the Lord
Jesus Christ, shall be administered only to adults
who can understand the Lord's teaching. But
minor children, lifeless bells, churches, or altars
shall not receive baptism; for not a single letter of
the Old or New Testament can prove that infant
baptism is commanded by God or was practiced by
the apostles. After the presentation of his concept
of communion, as it differed from that of Luther
and Zwingli, he discusses the strict requirement of
church discipline (*BRN* V, 127-70).

This time Hofmann remained in complete concealment in Strasbourg. The government was not
aware of his presence there. He left the city with
his family before the end of 1530.

In the course of 1531 he visited Holland; he stayed
some time in Amsterdam, where he is said to have
baptized 50 persons, and could move about unmolested. Though there is no information, he may also
have visited other towns of Holland. Soon after
his departure from Amsterdam conditions became
much less favorable for Anabaptism. Volkertszoon
and eight other followers of Hofmann (later called
Melchiorites) were beheaded in The Hague on Dec.
5, 1531. Nevertheless the brotherhood persisted, at
first, of course, very quietly. Melchior Hofmann
now decided to postpone baptism for two years and
confine himself to preaching and admonishing; the
construction of the Old Testament temple had also
suffered an interruption of two years on account of
resistance by the Samaritans (Ezra 4:24).

This order of delay Hofmann issued from Strasbourg, whither he had gone the third time in 1531.
In this Strasbourg period he wrote a series of booklets: (1) *Verclaringe van den gevangenen ende
vrien wil des menschen, wat ooc die waerachtige
gehoorsaemheyt des gheloofs ende warachtighen
eeuwighen Evangelions sy* . . . (*BRN* V, 171-98).
He takes a different position here from that in his
exposition of Dan. VII (1526), and skillfully blends
Luther's idea with Denk's, taking a position between them. (Details in Leendertz, 239 ff.) (2)
*Warhafftige erklerung aus heyliger Biblischer
schrifft, das der Satan, Todt, Hell, Sünd, un dy
ewige verdamnus im ursprung nit auss gott, sunder
auss eygenem will erwachsen sei* . . . . (3) *Das
freudenriche zeucknus vam worren friderichen
ewigen evangelion* (Rev. 14), *welchs da ist ein
kraft gottes, die da sallig macht alle die daran
glauben, Rom. 1, welchem worren und ewigen
evangelion itzt zu disser letzten zeit so vil dausend
ketzerischer irriger lugenhaftiger zeucknas gegen-
standt. Nim war die postbotten seint draussen und
schreien und die fridtbotten wynen bitterlich* . . .
(zur Linden reprints this pamphlet in his appendix,
429-32). Here is found the passage where Hofmann recognizes nobody as a preacher of the truth:
"Alas, what a terrible time is this, that I do not yet
see a true evangelist, nor know any writer among
all the German people who witnesses to the true
faith and the everlasting Gospel." (4) *Von der
wahren hochprächtlichen einigen Maijestat Gottes,
und von der wahrhaftigen Menschwerdung des
Weigen worts und Sohns des allerhögsten, ein
kurzes Zeugnis. Selig bistu Simon Jonas Sohn,
dann Fleisch und Bluth hat dir das nicht offen-*

bahrt, sondern mein Vatter im Himmel . . . . In
this booklet Hofmann teaches the Triune God; he
can therefore not be reckoned among the anti-
Trinitarians (*q.v.*), as Trechsel states in his *Anti-
trinitarier* (I, 34). He did, however, maintain that
prayers should not be addressed especially to Christ
or the Holy Spirit, but only to God (Leendertz,
142).

A new order of arrest by the city council again
compelled Hofmann to leave the city. Whither he
went is not definitely known. He traveled through
Hesse, where Landgrave Philip heard him preach.
He also stayed in the Netherlands in 1532, at least
at Leeuwarden, the capital of the province of Friesland, where he had a number of adherents, including Obbe Philips (*q.v.*).

In addition this man of inexhaustible energy had
time for writing. He now published his exposition
of the Epistle to the Romans: *Die eedele hoghe
enn trostlike sendebrief, den die heylige Apostel
Paulus to den Romeren gescreven heeft, verclaert
enn gans vlitich mit ernste van woort to woorde
wtgelecht Tot eener costeliker nutticheyt enn troost
allen godt-vruchtigen liefhebebbers er eewighen
onentliken waerheyt* . . . (1533). In this book,
particularly in chapter XIII, Melchior Hofmann
reveals himself as an advocate of quiet Anabaptism.
He rejects the bearing of arms, and definitely demands unconditional obedience to the government for God's sake. The book concludes with
these words: "By the mercies of God it is a
small matter to me at this time to become a sacrifice to the All-High when God's work is completed through Christ. My rebukes and accusations
are not made in fleshly envy and hate. God is my
witness, that in the depths of my heart I hate nobody. And if it were God's will that all be united
in the truth, I would gladly serve them day and
night as the lowliest servant; for their blindness
grieves my heart, and day and night I sigh in my
heart about it. In so far as any preacher is in the
right I stand by him; but in the wrong no support
does any good eternally; much rather would I lose
my life a thousand times."

This willingness to die Hofmann was soon to
prove in prison. His thoughts were centered on the
imminent end of the world. He was firmly convinced that he was called to take a part as Elijah
in the return of Christ. He was confirmed in this
idea by the prophecy of an old Frisian Anabaptist
that he would lie in prison half a year, and would
then at the head of his adherents lead Anabaptism
to victory over all the world.

In an exalted mood he entered upon his trip to
Strasbourg. In the spring of 1533 he arrived there.
Now he no longer remained in concealment. To
be sure, he avoided appearing in public meetings,
and he tried to avert the suspicion that he was
fomenting insurrection; but in the house of the
goldsmith Valtin Duft where he was staying his
adherents streamed together. The city council
maintained silence, and tolerated this activity. For
two months he was unmolested; then he himself
approached the council as if to have himself arrested. In May 1533 he sent a letter to the council,
with a booklet, *Vom Schwert*, which has been lost,

explaining that the kingdom of Christ would begin in Strasbourg, but it would be preceded by a terrible slaughter of (unbelieving) men; he awaited the fulfillment of these events here, and until that time would go about with bare head and bare feet, taking only bread and water.

The council met the prophet's desire, and in May 1533 had him arrested. Melchior Hofmann rejoiced. Now the awaited great time was at hand. Upon his imprisonment he thanked God (zur Linden, 322). Now his arrest was truly a mistake and a grave injustice, for insurrection and revolt were not to be feared from Melchior Hofmann. On the contrary, if anyone could have done so, he would have been able to direct the entire movement in Holland and Münster in peaceful paths.

The books Hofmann wrote during this time had in part a fantastic religious character. (1) *Der Leuchter des alten Testaments ussgelegt, welcher im heyligen stund der hütten Mose mit seinen siben lampen, blumen, knöpffen. . . . Und alles das such reicht uff die siben versamling des nuewen Testaments.* The book on baptism (2): *Erklerung des waren und hohen bunds des allerhöchsten* has been lost. It was presented to the Strasbourg synod in 1533. (3) *Wahrhaftige Zeucknus gegen die Nachttoechter und Sternen das der Gott Mensch Jhesus cristus am Kreuzs und im Grab nit ein angnomen Fleisch und Blut aus Maria sey, sunder allein das vaure und ewige wortt und der unendliche Sun des Allerhöchsten.* (4) *Eine rechte warhafftige hohe und götliche gruntliche underrichtung von der reinen forchte Gottes ann alle liebhaber der ewiger unentlicher warheit, aus Götlicher Schrifft angezeygt zum Preiss Gottes unnd heyll sines volcks in ewigkeyt . . .* (1533).

The severity of Hofmann's position on disorderly conduct is shown by his attitude toward Claus Frey (*q.v.*), whom he expelled from the brotherhood because of his fanatical conception of marriage which led him into polygamy.

Hofmann's confinement was at first mild. His friends were permitted to visit him and receive from him oral instruction and written information. In May 1533 he had to undergo two hearings. He defended himself successfully against the charge of having seditious plans. His defense was approximately as follows: He did not claim to be a prophet, but a witness of the supreme God and an apostolic teacher. This honorable title did not apply to the regular preachers, for all of them preached themselves rich. He did not oppose the office of preaching as a matter of principle; but pastors should be chosen from the oldest and most honest, and these should be permitted to own a home to shelter poor traveling brethren. But an apostle may own no property; he must always be ready to go wherever God may send him to proclaim the Word; his preaching would contribute only to his poverty; for he would have to leave all his possessions in exchange for a constant prospect of stocks and pillory.

Hofmann was also questioned (June 11-13) on the occasion of the General Synod of Strasbourg in June 1533. He clearly stated his faith. Bucer recorded these proceedings in his booklet, *Handlung* (1533), which was also translated into Dutch and distributed in the Netherlands, where it roused a storm of disappointment among the Anabaptists. For example, Cornelius Poldermann (*q.v.*) wrote a letter to the Strasbourg city council, asserting that he could produce 100 letters and books to prove that Bucer was in error in supposing that he had refuted Hofmann. Leendertz is of the opinion that he referred to two books that Hofmann had written in prison, and had sent to him through the warden's maid. These books are in the library of the University of Utrecht. Their titles are: (1) *Eine rechte warhaftige hohe und götliche gruntliche-underrichtung von der reinen forcht Gottes an alle liebhaber der ewiger unentlicher warheit, auszz götlicher Schrift angezeigt zum preisz Gottes und seines volcks in ewigkeit. . . .* (2) *Ein sendbrief an alle gotsförchtigen liebhaber der ewigen warheit, in welchem angezeigt seind die artickel des Melchior Hofmann, derhalben ihn die lerer zu Straszburg als ein ketzer verdampt . . .* (1533). The foreword of this book is signed "Caspar Becker," Hofmann's pseudonym.

Bucer's book relates that Melchior Hofmann expected Strasbourg to be besieged about July 1533 before the return of Christ, whom he hoped to meet at the head of the 144,000. When Bucer called this to his attention, Hofmann postponed the date to a later time, but clung to the idea itself. Nor did an illness that struck him cause him to waver. The bitterness of his adherents, who were constantly increasing in number, was deep when they were denied the privilege of visiting and comforting their Elijah in his serious illness (Leendertz, 304).

Why the council did not release this harmless man, or in accord with custom banish him from the city as a foreigner at the close of the examination, is incomprehensible. Only the hope that he might eventually be converted saved him from execution. Even Bucer apparently counseled against releasing him, for a letter from Melanchthon, Oct. 10, expressly approves of the severe measures of the council against Hofmann (zur Linden, 344). Hofmann made the serious charge against the Strasbourg clergy (1536) that they had wanted to deliver him to the executioner. He reminded them that a court trial could be instituted against an elder, which he was in the eyes of God, only on the basis of two or three witnesses, and pointed to the example of Zwingli, who had to pay with his life for the blood of one man, that of the Anabaptist Felix Manz; they should lay aside all carnal hate and as soldiers of Christ fight only with spiritual weapons.

On May 4, 1534, Hofmann presented a petition to the magistrate, that he be cast into the dungeon, where neither sun nor moon could shine, until God would have pity and bring the affair to an end, which would occur in 1534. In July of this year he wrote some pamphlets, which have been lost, under the pseudonyms of Caspar Becker and Michael Wächter; he was cross-examined about them on Sept. 9. His prison conditions were made more severe, but by bribing the wife of a guard he was able to maintain active communication with his group through books and letters.

In the spring of 1535 Hofmann thought there were indications that his redemption was near. On April 15 he requested the authorities to provide the city with food, for it would suffer hunger and want; in the third year of his imprisonment the Lord would come. During the siege the city need have no fear of its Anabaptists; only the masses who lusted for the estates of the priests should be feared. The Anabaptists, who, like him, would not bear a sword, should be assigned to the walls. Great tribulation was to fall upon the imperial cities, and Strasbourg would be a seal for the rest, for it would be the first to unfurl the banner of divine justice.

But this expectation also ended in disappointment. In April 1536 he complained about the severity of his jailers. He was in an unwholesome cell in the top story of the tower of Strasbourg, and had to live on inedible bread and water. He was completely isolated from the outside world. For lack of paper he filled the covers and blank parts of his books with writing. When these were removed he wrote his ideas down on 24 cloths, which were preserved in the Strasbourg archives until they were burned in the siege of the city in 1870. (For particulars about them see zur Linden, 380 ff., and Leendertz, 315 ff.) He requested alleviation of his difficult situation, a conversation with the Strasbourg preachers, some writing paper and ink. Nothing was granted.

On May 5, 1539, he had a talk with Peter Tasch (*q.v.*) and Johann Eysenburg, Anabaptist leaders who had left the brotherhood. In the spring, when he had suffered an attack of swellings on his face and legs, he had been moved into a more wholesome cell, and here the two men visited him in the hope of converting him; but the six-hour conversation was fruitless. Four additional conversations of five hours each followed. The rumor was spread among his adherents that he had recanted. (Hulshof discovered in Strasbourg a purported recantation by Hofmann in 1539, in which he sacrificed his rejection of infant baptism, and his teaching that sins committed after conversion could not be forgiven. See Hulshof, 180 f.)

Because of this rumor the Anabaptist Konrad v. Beghel or Bühel (*q.v.*) risked his life to ask him whether he still held to the faith he had confessed eight years before, or had fallen from it as Tasch and Eysenburg claimed. Hofmann assured him that he was faithful to the truth as before, and warned Bühel to seek piety, live a quiet life, keep his marriage pure, and not cause any mobs, for he had no call to do so. Bühel should pass this admonition on to the brethren, warning them against holding secret meetings in the woods contrary to government orders, and holding up the Peasants' War, Zwingli, and the Münster revolt as warning examples. In general he should insist that they respect the government, especially in Strasbourg, for it was a pious government.

In June of 1539 the four Strasbourg preachers (Bucer, Capito, Hedio, and Zell) conferred with Melchior Hofmann, as they thought with success. But in November the prisoner informed the *Ammeister* of the city, on bits of paper cut from books, that the city should provide itself with food and munitions, for there would be great suffering in the coming siege; he had received high revelations, which he could give the council if they would furnish him paper and ink. These were refused, and his remaining books taken from him.

For two years (1540-42) there is almost complete silence on Melchior Hofmann. He was said to have annoyed Hans Kunlin, a messenger of the council, by singing and shouting. Once again his hope for the future flickered up when, through bribery of the guards, his friends visited him and brought him good news of the Anabaptist movement. He thought his release was at hand; but the reverse happened. In January 1543 the council made his confinement still stricter. His cell was to be locked, the key kept in the chancery, and the door opened only in the presence of a member of the council. Food should be let down through the ceiling in a basket. Those who had accepted the bribe should be suitably punished.

On April 16, 1543, Hofmann asked the council to let him out into the air once more, and this request was granted. He also had temporary relief in June while repairs were made in his cell. In the autumn of 1543 he became so seriously ill that he was unable to receive his food. The council therefore had him transferred to the higher, better room, which the patient gratefully accepted. But Hofmann's health was broken and continued to deteriorate. On Nov. 19 the council ordered that he be given the linens necessary to his care. Before the end of 1543 the sufferer died, a martyr to his faith.

Melchior Hofmann was an unusual person, a man of extraordinary gifts, of a consuming selfless zeal for the cause of the Lord Jesus, of a rare eloquence, combined with moral earnestness and a genuinely truthful character. This accounts for his mighty influence and great success with the masses. The amount of writing he could do in his unsettled life is amazing. Aside from his unbridled fantasy, his arbitrary interpretation of Scripture, and his fanatical view of the end-times, his writings contain a wealth of sound Christian ideas and sober thoughts (see Cramer's article in *BRN* V, 127 ff.). His favorite ideas, (1) the hope of the imminent return of Christ and (2) his view of the Incarnation (*q.v.*), that Jesus took His flesh not from Mary but out of her, were not generally accepted by the Anabaptists, although Menno Simons did adopt his view of the Incarnation. On the other hand, his determined insistence on freedom of religion, on evidence of the fruit of the Spirit, on sanctification of life, on believers' baptism, and on nonresistance, made essential contributions to the strengthening of Anabaptism. His teaching on the communion is still prevalent among the Mennonites of the Palatinate. The oath he at first rejected unconditionally, but later permitted it under certain circumstances, or even made use of it himself (zur Linden, 220). (If, however, Obbe Philips is the only authority for this statement, it is still open to question.) For the Münster affair Hofmann is no more responsible than Luther is for the Peasants' War. Granted that some of his teachings, such as the Incarnation and the imminent return of Christ, were carried into Münster by the "Wassenberg preachers" (Rembert, 299, 360 f.), nevertheless the fact remains that the social and moral aberrations in Münster find no source nor echo in either the life or teaching of Melchior Hofmann. His lasting significance lies in the fact that he transplanted the Anabaptist movement from the South to the North. Cramer calls him the father of Dutch Anabaptism.

Melchior Hofmann, even before his recantation, spoke of the Swiss Brethren in terms of disapproval and reproach. He sided with their opponents by holding them responsible for the well-known fratricide of Thomas Schugger in St. Gall, a man who was not an Anabaptist at all. Hofmann made the assertion that before the beginning of his labors no one had proclaimed the true Gospel. From his prison he sent word to the Swiss Brethren in Strasbourg, admonishing them to "stand still," and not to come together for worship without the consent of the authorities. As for the attitude of the Swiss Brethren toward Hofmann, they declared in the debate held in Bern in 1538 not only that he was not of their brotherhood but that his teaching was resisted by them "with all earnestness." NEFF.

W. L. Leendertz, *Melchior Hofmann* (Haarlem, 1883); F. O. zur Linden, *Melchior Hofmann, ein Prophet der Wiedertäufer* (Haarlem, 1885); Cramer in *BRN* V; A. Hulshof, *Geschiedenis van de Doopsgezinden te Straatsburg van 1525 tot 1557* (Amsterdam, 1905); Rembert, *Wiedertäufer; DB* 1919, 124 ff.; B. N. Krohn, *Gesch. der fan. u. enthus. Wiedertäufer vornehmlich in Norddeutschland* (Leipzig, 1785); H. J. Schoeps, *Vom himmlischen Fleisch Christi* (Tübingen, 1951) 37 ff.; E. B. Bax, *Rise and Fall of the Anabaptists* (London, 1903) 95 ff.; C. A. Cornelius, *Geschichte des Münsterischen Aufruhrs* II (Leipzig, 1860) 75 ff., 282 ff.; Kühler, *Geschiedenis* I, 52-77; *Biogr. Wb.* IV, 121-34; Peter Kawerau, *Melchior Hoffman als religiöser Denker* (Haarlem, 1954); *ML* II, 326-35.

Hofmeister, Sebastian, b. 1476 in Schaffhausen, Switzerland, a Barefoot Friar, took his doctor's degree in Paris, and early advocated and promoted the Reformation in Schaffhausen. He took part in both of the Zürich disputations in 1523, in the second as chairman. Like Zwingli he wavered on the question of baptism in early 1525. Conrad Grebel tried to win both Hofmeister and his colleague Dr. Sebastian Meyer, pastor in Schaffhausen, to Anabaptism by personal discussion in Hofmeister's home in late January or early February 1525, when he spent the two months of February and March in the city (Bender, 39 f.). Johannes Brötli tells in a letter of March 1525 to the brethren in Zollikon how he, Reublin, and Grebel were guests of the two doctors one evening, and declared that "Doctor Sebastian agrees with us in the matter of baptism." Felix Manz also visited Hofmeister in Schaffhausen. The attempts were, however, not ultimately successful. Hubmaier states in his book (1526), *Der alten und neuen Lehrer Urteil . . .* that Hofmeister had written him, "We were not ashamed to testify openly before the council of Schaffhausen, that our brother Zwingli strays from the goal and does not walk in accordance with the truth of the Gospel if he wants the infants to be baptized" (Bächtold, 87). In his testimony as a witness in the Anabaptist trial of 1525 Hofmeister

said that he rebuked Grebel and showed him by proofs from the Scripture that he erred and was mistaken (Egli, 309). In Schaffhausen the Catholic party won the upper hand in the peasant revolts of 1524-25. Hofmeister was considered a fomenter of disturbances. In August 1525 the council sent him to the University of Basel to be examined on his (Catholic) orthodoxy. On Aug. 10, 1525, the council wrote to the university that Hofmeister had often preached from the pulpit that the Mass was an invention of the devil, and that infant baptism was not valid (Bächtold, 93).

Hofmeister was not questioned in Basel and was not permitted to return to his home town. He found reception in Zürich. There he conducted the disputation with the Anabaptists of Nov. 6-8, 1525. He was considered an exceptional debater. In 1528 he was called to Bern, and given the assignment to introduce the Reformation in Zofingen. On April 19, 1531, he was again in Bern as a debater in the disputation with Hans Pfistermeyer (*q.v.*) of Aarau, probably having been appointed by the council. He and the other preachers succeeded in bringing about Pfistermeyer's recantation. Hofmeister's influence at the disputation of Zofingen (*q.v.*), July 1-9, 1532, was no doubt also outstanding. Since the records of this debate merely name the preachers and Anabaptists, the personal position of individuals cannot be ascertained (see **Kaspar Grossmann**). Hofmeister died in Zofingen, Sept. 26, 1533.   L.v.M.

M. Kirchhofer, *Seb. Wagner genannt Hofmeister* (Zürich, 1808); J. Wipf, "Sebastian Hofmeister, der Reformator Schaffhausens," in *Beiträge zur vaterländischen Geschichte* (1918); article by Bloesch in *HRE* VIII, 241 f.; C. A. Bächtold, "Die Schaffhauser Wiedertäufer," in *Beiträge zur vaterländischen Geschichte*, No. 7, 1900; H. S. Bender, *Conrad Grebel* (Goshen, 1950); *ML* II, 335.

Hofstede, Petrus (1716-1803), a Dutch Reformed minister at Anjum 1739, Steenwijk 1743, Oost-Zaandam 1745, and Rotterdam 1749-70, an intolerant and fanatical man, one of the last Calvinists in the Netherlands to attack the Mennonites in his writings, particularly Johannes Stinstra (*q.v.*), preacher of Harlingen, Friesland, in his poem (1742), *De Waarheid in Friesland tegen de aanslagen der ketterij verdedigt*. In 1781 in a booklet against F. G. C. Rütz, the Lutheran minister of The Hague, he again attacked Stinstra.   vDZ.

Biogr. Wb. IV, 138-52; *N.N.B.Wb.* IV, 762-65; Chr. Sepp, *Johannes Stinstra en zijn tijd* II (Amsterdam, 1866) 86-89.

Hofstetter (Hoffstetter), a Mennonite family name originating in Langnau, canton of Bern, Switzerland. It means "caretaker of orchard or farm." The family found its way from the Emmental to the Bernese Jura in the early part of the 18th century with many of their coreligionists. Members of the family lived near Bevillard and Delsberg in 1824. The first mention of a member of the family as an Anabaptist was in 1672, when a person with this name was imprisoned for returning to Switzerland after having been deported for belonging to this forbidden religion. The brothers Nicolas, Peter, and Christian Hofstetter came with their families from the Bernese Jura to the Sonnenberg settlement in Wayne County, Ohio, in 1824, and became one of the leading families of the community. Reuben Hofstetter is the present bishop of the Kidron Mennonite Church near Kidron, Ohio. The names Hofstetter and Hostettler (*q.v.*) did not originally come from the same name.   D.L.G.

Högerli (*Hägerly*), an Anabaptist martyr, was arrested in 1532 in Aarau with a fellow believer called "the tailor," was kept in prison 13 days and then taken to Bern, where he was executed for his faith. The *Martyrs' Mirror* on page 1129 erroneously gives 1529 as the date of his death, and calls him Haegerley of the Alburg district. His name Högerli is that of a farm near Aarburg, which was favorably located for Anabaptist meetings.   NEFF.

J. Heiz, *Täufer im Aargau* (Aarau, 1902); *Mart. Mir.* E 1129; *ML* II, 335.

Hohenberg, formerly an Austrian dependency or territory in southwest Germany, since 1806 a part of Württemberg. The main cities are Horb (*q.v.*) and Rottenburg am Neckar (*q.v.*); the latter was also the seat of the regent or governor who ruled in the name of the (Austrian) Hapsburgs. During the first half of the 16th century the counts of Zollern held this office (Joachim 1525-37, Jos Nikolaus 1538-58), yet they were rather passive in their duties if not downright negligent. Much more zealous was King Ferdinand (*q.v.*) and the provincial government of Innsbruck (Tirol) which at that period administered also the county of Hohenberg (part of Vorderösterreich). They insisted upon the suppression of all non-Catholic movements, both Lutheran and Anabaptist, and sent out stiff mandates to allow no leniency.

The most outstanding victim of these orders was Michael Sattler (*q.v.*), the former prior of the monastery of St. Peter, who was the saintly leader of the new Anabaptist movement around Horb and Rottenburg. The trial of Sattler and his co-workers is a memorable event in Anabaptist history, mainly for Sattler's noble defense. In 1528 these brethren were executed in a most cruel manner in the city of Rottenburg. The great stir which this event provoked (a pamphlet with the story of Sattler soon spread all over Germany) made the government somewhat more cautious in its endeavor to suppress the new Anabaptist movement. Eventually, however, the Counter-Reformation (*q.v.*) succeeded in bringing the entire population back to their former Catholic faith. It is remarkable that in the southern part of the county of Hohenberg, which is adjacent to Switzerland, no centers of Anabaptism are known, while in the northern part, around Horb and Rottenburg, numerous such centers thrived until the middle of the 16th century, apparently as a result of Sattler's activities and testimony. (*ML* II, 336.)   G.Bo., R.F.

Hohenlohe, a principality (32 sq. mi.) in northeast Württemberg, Germany, to which it has belonged since the beginning of the 19th century. In 1555 it was divided between the brothers Ludwig Kasimir and Eberhard into the gravures of Hohenlohe-

Neuenstein and Hohenlohe-Waldenburg. Whereas nothing is heard of the stirrings of the Reformation in the district until 1540, and it was not actually instituted there until 1556, there are indications that as early as 1530 the Anabaptist movement from Heilbronn had acquired some influence in the town of Künzelsau and on the near-by farms and hamlets. The first official mention of them occurs in an order of Count Albrecht to all officials, May 25, 1533, to warn their subjects against receiving into their homes Anabaptists expelled from other places, against tolerating any meetings or "corner sermons," providing them with food and drink, or listening to their sermons (Wibel, 299 ff.). Magistrate Bonifatius Wernizer of Kirchberg, which had been pawned to Dinkelsbühl, Hall, and Rothenburg, reported on March 17, 1534, to the mayor and council of Rothenburg, after an inquiry in Hall and Dinkelsbühl, that many Anabaptists had crossed through the land in groups of 20 or 30 with wagons and carts, women and children, without being molested. They were permitted to eat, for they paid. Their goal was Moravia, where 5,000 or more were together, having been expelled by the bishop of Gran, which was, of course, an error. Anabaptists could be identified in that they did not give the customary greetings, or wish one a good morning or a good evening (state archives of Nürnberg, *Kirchberger Akten* II).

The next bit of information is given by an inquiry of Count Albrecht to an unnamed jurist in Rothenburg o.d. Tauber, April 6, 1534. He wrote that wicked persons of the new sect (Anabaptists) were breaking into the area, requesting a night's lodging of the poor people on farms and in the villages. If it was granted, they were orderly and humble; they read books, taught that evil should be abstained from, and misled their hearers under the guise of the teaching of these treacherous preachers that the people should leave the church and call the church a temple of idols; for the temple of God was in the heart. They rejected the Mass, considered infant baptism invalid; some refused to swear an oath and use weapons. Some of the people moved away with wife, child, and servants, leaving much food behind, which the barons then claimed as being forfeit; the count tells of an instance of this and requests the lawyer's speedy judgment (Nürnberg *Staatsarchiv, Konsistorialakten* I). The reply is not known. The case in point must have referred to the farm and other goods of Georg Lang of Etzlenweiler, which Count George confiscated, but which his brother Johann induced him to give to Lang's son-in-law, Balthasar Weiss, in Ingelfingen (Wibel, I, 749).

In 1534 a number of Anabaptists were found in Künzelsau and punished by the authorities; they were to abandon their faith and pay a pledge of 100 florins. They left Künzelsau and did not request readmission until 1539. After numerous requests by the nobility and the community they were admitted on the following conditions: (1) on a day previously announced, at a signal given by the pastor, they must acknowledge their error before all the people and ask forgiveness; (2) they must adhere to Christian order, as it was observed in Künzelsau; (3) they must hold no secret meetings or prayers, and adhere to no Anabaptist sect; (4) in their life and conduct they must avoid any suggestion that they were still spotted with this error (Weikersheim Archives, *Künzelsauer Ganerben Verträge*).

In 1535 King Ferdinand expelled the Anabaptists from Moravia. They tried to return to their homes or to enter Württemberg, which had recently become Protestant, but were intercepted in three groups in Passau. Almost all of them were natives of the Künzelsau region, most of them from small farms and hamlets. Most of them had been baptized, en route to Moravia, in Donauwörth by Adam Schlegel, and some in Auspitz by Philip Plener (*q.v.*) or Blasius Kuhn (*q.v.*). There they had settled in compact groups. In Passau an attempt was made to make them recant, but all clung to their convictions. Only Hans Höfner and his wife, of Reublingen, recanted at the end of 1540 or in early 1541 and were released.

At the church inspection of 1571 it was stated that the farmer of the Dörrhof had with his wife gone to the Anabaptists five years previously, as had also some others from Jungholzhausen. Anabaptists continued to cross the country, stopping in Nesselbach, where the innkeeper's wife entered into conversation with them, thus arousing the suspicion that she was about to go with them. After her death the innkeeper was ordered to receive the Anabaptists only to give them food or a night's lodging, but not to discuss their doctrine with them. In Ingelfingen the carpenter Brentz had been with the Anabaptists a while, but had returned without having gone to their communion.

There is no further information on the Anabaptists in Hohenlohe.   G.Bo.

J. C. Wibel, *Hohenlohische Kirchen- und Ref.-Historie* III (4 vv., Ansbach, 1752-54); *ML* II, 336 f.

Hohenwart, a parish in Lower Austria on the boundary between Krems and Meissau. The Anabaptists of Tirol, on their trips to Moravia from Stein, where they left the ships, frequently stopped here. In 1534 Bastl (Sebastian) Glaser, who was leading a company from Tirol to Moravia, was seized with his party. Jakob Hutter wrote a letter of consolation to them (Wolkan, *Geschicht-Buch,* 105). The prisoners were transferred from Hohenwart to Eggenburg; here they had their cheeks burned and were then released. The same fate befell Hans Peck of Gredins, who was also halted in Hohenwart. (Beck, *Geschichts-Bücher,* 116; *ML* II, 337.)   LOSERTH.

Hohenwittlingen, a castle in the Urach district of Württemberg, 2,259 ft. above sea level, on a cliff that projects like a promontory into the Ermstal, 25 minutes from the village of Wittlingen. The castle was built about 1100. When Joh. Brenz (*q.v.*) was compelled to flee from the emperor's wrath in 1548, Duke Ulrich concealed him in Hohenwittlingen. There under the pseudonym of Joh. Wittlingius he wrote his exposition of Psalms

94 and 130, and the treatise, *An magistratus iure possit occidere Anabaptistas aut alios haereticos* (*Whether a magistrate has the legal right to execute Anabaptists or other heretics*) (Koehler, Nos. 163 and 261, p. 69 and p. 117).

Under Duke Christoph Hohenwittlingen was made a prison for poachers, who instead of being blinded were now given a life sentence, and for Anabaptists who refused to be converted. Thus in November 1555 Barbara Löffler, an Anabaptist from Stuttgart, was imprisoned in the castle but released when she recanted; and after Easter 1557 Adam Hornikel, a baker of Heiningen, Göppingen district, was held there. With him Paul Glock (*q.v.*), who had probably been taken to Hohenwittlingen before this, wrote a *Rechenschaft* of their faith in 1562 (*TA Württemberg,* p. 1049) and also two songs, "Gott haltet steif was er verheisst," and "Herr Jesu Christ in deinem Reich" (*Lieder der Hutterischen Brüder,* 714 and 718). On Feb. 11, 1564, Hornikel was taken to Stuttgart for a new cross-examination and was then expelled from the country; he went to Moravia. In 1574 Matthias Binder of Frickenhausen, a tailor and preacher, was taken to Hohenwittlingen. He had previously been held a long time in the dungeon at Maulbronn, where Blasius Greiner (*q.v.*) had also been. In 1573 and several following years the prison also held Leonhard Sommer of Necklinsberg, Jakob Gantz of Ossweil, and Martin Klopfer.

When in the late fall of 1576 a fire broke out in the castle, Glock and Binder took an active part in extinguishing the flames, and were released by order of the duke, to go to Moravia. The castle was repaired and the prison continued to be used. The following were imprisoned there: Simon Kress (*q.v.*) of Gündelbach 1582-96; Michael Hasel (*q.v.*) of Gudersberg, 1588-92; and in 1590 Franz Feyerabend of Oppelsbom. From 1574 to 1594 the pastor of the adjacent village of Hengen was Stephan Geer, the father of the Anabaptist leader Georg Geer. It is possible that youthful impressions of Hohenwittlingen contributed to his decision to join the Anabaptists. Hans Dauber of Illingen, who had been imprisoned six years on Hohenurach and released in 1588, and who had merely attended the preaching in Illingen, not the communion, was in Hohenwittlingen in 1596. In that year he and Kress were permitted to attend church services. They sang with the audience, indicated their approval by nodding their heads, and their disapproval by averting their faces. This conduct caused the congregation to doubt the Scripturalness of the pastor's teaching; their attendance at church was discontinued. The castle superintendent, Claudius Robert, thought they should turn the wasteland before the castle into meadowland, for they would be more easily won by the pick and hoe than by the Bible. Hoes and spades were also recommended in 1612 by the church authorities for the treatment of Dauber, who is mentioned as late as 1617 as an obstinate Anabaptist (*TA Württemberg*).

The castle governors Hans and Jakob von Talheim, and Robert and Glas Miller treated the Anabaptists kindly. Glock had absolute freedom of

movement and was used as a messenger. Likewise
Kress moved freely in 1582 and worked in front of
the castle. Under Duke Christoph in 1559 they had
been permitted to move several hours, fastened only
to foot-irons. Glock was satisfied with the food;
the court chaplain Lukas Osiander in 1584 thought
it was as good as that of a benefice. Exceedingly
laudatory is the testimony the castle governor gave
the deceased Michael Hasel (*q.v.*). In 1608 the
castle governor Miller was even under suspicion of
Anabaptist leanings because of quiet conduct (*TA
Württemberg* 308).

After the beginning of the Thirty Years' War
there were no more Anabaptists in Hohenwittlingen.   G.Bo.

W. Koehler, *Bibliographia Brentiana* (Berlin, 1904);
G. Bossert, *TA* I: *Württemberg; Lieder der Hutterischen
Brüder* (Scottdale, 1914); Beck, *Geschichts-Bücher;* Ziegl-
schmid, *Chronik;* ML II, 337 f.

Hohenzollern. The reign of the rulers of this
Prussian royal house (1701-1918) was of essential
significance to the development of Mennonitism in
East and West Prussia in the 18th and 19th centuries. In general, the Mennonites enjoyed toleration under them, particularly on the principle of
nonresistance and the appreciation of their agricultural capability.

This friendly attitude found expression in the
intervention in 1710 of the first Prussian king,
Frederick I (1701-13, *q.v.*), with the Swiss government in behalf of the persecuted Swiss Mennonites
and in settling a number of them in Lithuania, together with some Mennonites from the Elbing and
Culm marshes. The achievements of the Mennonites in cultivating and draining the land, in
cattle raising and cheese manufacturing were, in
return, of benefit to the state. If the Mennonites
suffered under Frederick William I (*q.v.*) for their
maintenance of nonresistance, they were so much
the more benefited by the religious tolerance of
the reign of Frederick the Great (*q.v.*). Of greatest value to the Mennonitism of East and West
Prussia was the *Gnadenprivilegium* (charter of
favor) of March 29, 1780, with the assurance of
freedom of religion and conscience and of protection in the exercise of their former crafts. Under
his successor, Frederick William II (*q.v.*), to be
sure, the Mennonites were limited in their acquisition of land to that which had already been in
Mennonite hands or was not subject to military
duty. This limitation of land ownership was the
chief cause of the emigration of a number of West
Prussian Mennonite families to South Russia from
1789 on.

In spite of the fact that Frederick William III
(*q.v.*) and IV (*q.v.*) renewed the charter of privileges, since they wished to keep these economically
capable citizens in the country, the principle of
complete religious freedom collapsed in Prussia in
the middle of the 19th century. It was no longer
tenable when universal military service was introduced in the interest of nationalism, and the absolute power of the king was restricted by popular
representation. In 1868 the Mennonites living in
the jurisdiction of the North German League were
obliged to accept some form of military service (see
Prussia). Since this fact also eliminated the basis
for the restriction of civil rights for the Mennonites,
the law of June 12, 1874, regulating the legal status
of the Mennonites removed these restrictions and
opened to the Mennonites the possibility of acquiring corporation rights. (*ML* II, 338.)   E.G.

Höhne (Heune), **Hans,** an Anabaptist martyr, by
trade a maker of strawhats, native of Seehausen near
Frankenhausen, Thuringia, Germany, moved with
his wife Grete Reusse to Halberstadt, where they
were seized in September 1535. His wife recanted;
but he remained constant, and was drowned on
Oct. 8 in the Bode with Adrian Richter (*q.v.*) and
Petronella (*q.v.*). His two trials, Sept. 14 and 21,
1535 (Jacobs, 512 and 520), are not unimportant
for the understanding of the Anabaptists in Thuringia.   NEFF.

P. Wappler, *Die Täuferbewegung in Thüringen von
1526-1584* (Jena, 1913) 117; E. Jacobs, "Die Wiedertäufer am Harz," in *Ztscht des Harz-Vereins f. Gesch.
u. Altertumskunde,* 1899; ML II, 338.

Holdeman (Haldeman, Holdiman, Holderman, Hal-
teman, Halterman, Haldiman, Haldenmann), an old
Swiss Mennonite family, now no longer found
among the Mennonites of Switzerland or Germany,
but widely represented in the United States. The
names first appeared in Anabaptist records in Switzerland in 1538 at Eggiwil, canton of Bern, when
Thuring Haldemann was ordered deported. In
1670 a Hans Haldemann was banished from Hotchi-
kon, Bern, and in 1671 a Katharina Haldemann of
Hochstetten, Bern, migrated to Holland. Nicholas
Haldeman of the canton of Bern immigrated to
Montgomery Co., Pa., in 1727 locating in Salford
Township. His brothers Hans and Michael, who
came the same year, located in Coventry Twp.,
Chester Co., whither Nicholas later moved also.
Nicholas was a trustee in the Salford Mennonite
(MC) Church, and had many descendants in the
Franconia Conference (MC) district, including Abra-
ham Haldeman, bishop 1830-65 first in Chester
County, then in Juniata County, Christian Halde-
man, preacher at Salford 1791-1833, John M. Halde-
man, preacher at Line Lexington 1869-76. Christian
Haldeman (and other Holdemans) moved from
Bucks Co., Pa., to Wayne Co., Ohio, near New
Pittsburgh in 1827. His widow, with ten sons,
moved to Elkhart Co., Ind., in 1849, at about the
time when other Holdeman families came. The
Holdeman (MC) meetinghouse near Wakarusa was
built in 1857 on land given by one of these families.
John Holdeman (*q.v.*) founder of the Church of
God in Christ Mennonite Church in 1859, was of the
Wayne County branch; he began the new church at
New Pittsburgh. David S. Holdeman moved from
Medina Co., Ohio, to McPherson Co., Kan., in 1873,
where many of his descendants are still living. He
was treasurer of the Kansas Relief Committee and
a vigorous supporter of the work for the incoming
Russian Mennonites in 1874 ff. The only ministers
bearing the name in 1956 were George W. Holder-
man of Eldorado Springs, Mo., and Paul Holdeman of Denver, Col., both of the Mennonite Church
(MC).   H.S.B.

E. L. Weaver, *Holdeman Descendants . . . of Christian Holdeman 1788-1846* (Nappanee, 1937); Obed Johnson, *Record of the Descendants of David S. Holdeman* (N. Newton, 1951).

Holdeman, John (1832-1900), founder and elder of the Church of God in Christ, Mennonite, a son of Amos and Nancy (Yoder) Holdeman, was born Jan. 31, 1832, at New Pittsburg, Wayne Co., Ohio. He was married in June 1852 to Elizabeth Ritter. Six children were born to them, of whom three grew to maturity. At the age of 12 he was converted, at 21 he reconsecrated his life, and in October 1853 he was baptized by Bishop Abraham Rohrer of Wayne Co., Ohio. At this same time he felt that God was definitely calling him to the ministry. In reply to this conviction Rohrer is said to have remarked, "It may well be that from your birth you were called into the ministry as was Paul." Not being ordained to preach by the old church, he started out on his own to preach in 1859. This may be taken as the beginning of the denomination which he founded.

Though without academic opportunities Holdeman was self-educated. He devoted himself to the study of German and English, and also gave some attention to Dutch and Greek. Following his conversion and baptism he felt strongly constrained to study the Scriptures. He also studied the writings of the Church Fathers, including those of Menno Simons and Dirk Philips, and was thoroughly acquainted with the *Martyrs' Mirror*. Through his studies he became convinced that the Mennonite Church had greatly deviated from the truths and precepts as given by Christ and the apostles, and as upheld by the forefathers. With deep concern he sought co-operation of the leaders in order to re-establish the fundamental doctrines which he held to be the true foundation upon which salvation is attainable, but met little response. Therefore he found it necessary to build anew on an evangelical basis, and to exercise discipline according to the Scriptures as had Menno Simons and many of the forefathers, in order that the faith and the true lineage of the church might be maintained. All efforts to bring about a reconciliation with the mother church (MC) having failed, yet with the assurance that he was called of God to preach the Gospel, he applied himself to the ministry with much earnestness. It was his desire to bring to his hearers the truth and the whole truth. He placed special emphasis on the necessity of the new birth and separation from the world. Many were awakened, and accepted Christ. He organized churches in the United States and in Canada (Manitoba), where he won over the bishop of the "Kleine Gemeinde" and half of the group of members there. He won over some of the Russian Mennonites in Kansas (Marion Co.), including Tobias A. Unruh of the General Conference group. He served the church, which he named the "Church of God in Christ, Mennonite," as pastor, evangelist, elder, moderator of general conferences, and first editor of its official periodical *Botschafter der Wahrheit* from June 1897 until his death in 1900.

He was an extensive writer, writing the following books and treatises: *The Old Ground and Foundation,* in both German (1862) and English (1863); *A Reply to the Criticisms of John Roseborough* (1864); *Eine Vertheidigung gegen die Verfälscher unserer Schriften* (1865); *A History of the Church of God,* German (1875) and English (1876); *A Treatise on Redemption, Baptism, and the Passover and the Lord's Supper* (1890); *A Treatise on Magistracy and War, Millennium, Holiness, and the Manifestation of Spirits* (1891); *Eine gründliche Abhandlung von dem schriftwidrigen Entstehen der Siebenten Tag Adventisten und ihrer unevangelischen Lehre* (1892); *Ein Aufsatz von Unmöglichkeiten* (1893); and the extensive work, *Ein Spiegel der Wahrheit* (1878; English, 1956).

He lived on farms in various states, including Jasper Co., Mo., but gave most of his time to the ministry. He died on March 10, 1900, near Galva, McPherson Co., Kan. (*ML* II, 338 f.) F.H.W.

Holdeman Mennonite Church (MC), located one and one-fourth miles northwest of Wakarusa in Olive Twp., Elkhart Co., Ind., is a member of the Indiana-Michigan Mennonite Conference. The first meetinghouse, a log building, was built in 1851 and was replaced in 1875 by the present frame structure, which was remodeled in 1913 and again in 1951. During the early years all the Mennonites in the western part of the county were considered members of the Yellow Creek Church (*q.v.*); regular Sunday services alternated between Yellow Creek and Holdeman. By 1875, however, the separation into two distinct congregational organizations had been well established. The congregation was host to the first regular session of the Mennonite General Conference in 1899. Ministers who have given longer periods of service to the congregation include Jacob Freed, Jacob A. Beutler, Henry Weldy, and Silas Weldy. The membership in 1955 was 234; Simon Gingerich was pastor. L.V.C.

Centennial History of the Holdeman Mennonite Church (Wakarusa, Ind., 1951); *MHB,* January 1952.

Holidays and Anniversaries. European Mennonites and those American Mennonites who have kept closer to their European background pay more attention to the holidays of the church year than the American Mennonite groups with a longer American history. However, most American Mennonite groups have no consciousness of a "church year."

Among the older Mennonite churches in America, Good Friday, Ascension, and Pentecost are no longer observed (except for possibly using the day for special programs unrelated to the real meaning of the day), and seldom is Christmas Day observed with church services. In Ontario there is more observance of such days, except by the Old Order Amish. Recently the observance of all or part of Passion Week by special church services has been growing among Mennonites.

The Old Order Amish, having retained more of the older traditions, manifest a different pattern. They celebrate a "second Christmas" Jan. 6 in addition to Dec. 25, known in their German as "Alt Christtag" (Old Christmas). They celebrate this day, as well as Good Friday, Ascension, and Pentecost, with fasting, i.e., omitting breakfast, but without church services, and follow by visiting relatives and friends on these days. Pentecost Monday and Easter Monday are also observed as holidays, but with visiting only and not fasting.

Because of the somewhat military character of the observance of Independence Day (July 4) and Memorial Day (May 30) most Mennonites dislike to join in the common observance of these civil holidays. A considerable number of congregations have at one time or another deliberately placed special church meetings on one or both of these days to counteract the influence of the common type of celebrations. Sunday-school or congregational picnics are often held on July 4.

The use of the Christmas tree in connection with the Christmas season is seriously objected to by the more conservative groups, as was formerly the case among practically all the American Mennonites, as a pagan survival which has no place among Christians.

Most European German, Swiss, and French Mennonites customarily observe the following holidays, usually with a church service in the morning: Christmas, Good Friday, Easter, Ascension, Pentecost, "Buss- und Bettag" (Day of Repentance and Prayer). At Christmas, Easter, and Pentecost, the day following is also celebrated as a holiday, but without services.

In the Dutch Mennonite congregations services were formerly held on Good Friday evening, at which communion was usually observed. On Ascension Day church services are held only in a few congregations. Days of Repentance and Prayer are unusual among the Dutch Mennonites. On the day following Christmas there is often a Christmas celebration for children in the churches. On New Year's Eve services are held in all the churches; services on New Year's Day are very rare.

Anniversaries are not celebrated in America nearly as frequently, nor with as much emphasis, as in Europe. Particularly in Germany anniversaries (25th, etc.) of pastoral service, weddings, birthdays, ordinations, dedications, etc., have often been observed with much ceremony, and even by ministers with special sermons and publications, and by gifts or medals from the congregations.

The Mennonites of Prussian background in Prussia, Poland, Russia, and America have as a rule observed the Christian holidays of Protestantism, viz., Christmas, Good Friday, Easter, and Pentecost. The Mennonites broke completely with the Catholic tradition of observing the festivities connected with the saints and other occasions of the Catholic church calendar. In Russia they never adjusted themselves to the observance of the holidays of the Greek Catholic Church in as far as they differ from Protestant holidays, although they used the Julian calendar. As a rule Mennonites observed the customary number of holidays of the country in which they lived. In Prussia, Poland, and Russia they celebrated Christmas and Easter for three days. Gradually the third day was not strictly observed. After the immigration to America the number was reduced to two days. At present only rarely is a second day observed. Some churches still have worship services on the second holiday, sometimes in the German language.

As a rule the worship centers around the event of the holiday. In the afternoon and evening relatives visit each other, often traveling long distances for this occasion.   H.S.B.

Holiness Movement. The logical tension between recognizing the Christian believer as a regenerated and cleansed child of God, and at the same time as sinful and unworthy of God and His grace, has driven some Christian teachers to one or other of two extremes: (1) to hold strongly to justification through the imputed righteousness of Christ, with an inadequate emphasis on becoming a new creature in Christ, sometimes even to the radical extreme of a form of antinomianism which does not regard as sin those wrong acts committed "in the flesh"; and (2) to teach that it is possible by the grace of God and the renewal of the Holy Spirit to attain such a degree of holiness as to no longer have any struggle with the flesh or the carnal nature. This state is often thought of as being attained instantaneously by an act of faith, subsequent to conversion and receiving the gift of salvation. This second definite experience is called the "second work of grace" or "holiness" or "Christian perfection" by its adherents. This theory of holiness is really Wesleyan, but it gained acceptance in some groups of Mennonites within the past hundred years. This is best illustrated in the United Missionary Church, formerly known as the Mennonite Brethren in Christ (which name is still retained in the Pennsylvania Conference of the group), and in the Brethren in Christ, commonly called "River Brethren." It is the teaching of these bodies that salvation is received in two steps—first, the new birth and the gift of salvation through repentance and faith, but which ordinarily leaves the new convert less than a fully victorious child of God; and second, the second work of grace, or holiness, in which the Holy Spirit miraculously gives full deliverance from the power of sin. The believer is then regarded as "relatively perfect" in life. He is still tempted by Satan, and by the evil forces of the world, but he no longer has to suffer from the sharp inner struggles with his own carnal nature which formerly plagued him.

There have been a few ministers in other Mennonite bodies such as the Mennonite Church (MC) who have more or less adopted the Wesleyan doctrine of holiness, and in some cases minor secessions have resulted; as in Harvey Co., Kan., 40 years ago, when J. M. R. Weaver and others withdrew from the Mennonite Church (Weaver returned).

One of the results of the Holiness movement in Kansas, which affected various Mennonite leaders (MC), was the teaching that nonconformed Christian men ought not to wear neckties. Prior to this time, black bow ties (earlier, the old neckcloth or *Halstuch*) had been universally worn in the Mennonite Church, ministry and laity alike. In spite of the opposition of such leaders as John F. Funk (*q.v.*), editor of the *Herald of Truth,* who openly and in print opposed the anti-necktie sentiment, this view gained ground until many ministers and some lay members (MC) ceased to wear ties. In recent years, however, this attitude has faded.

In recent years there appears to be a moderating of the more extreme views of holiness in the United Missionary Church and in the Brethren in Christ. Although some ministers teach the old-fashioned doctrine of a "second work of grace" in just the same fashion as did the leaders of a generation or two ago, other ministers are becoming less vocal on the point, and in many cases have begun to stress "Christian growth" rather than the more distinctive doctrine of "holiness."

Among European Mennonites Perfectionism (*q.v.*), or the doctrine of "total eradication" has had little influence, although the Anabaptists were often accused of holding this position because of their staunch insistence on holy living. J.C.W.

Holitsch (*Holic*), a town in Slovakia (formerly in Hungary) not far from the Moravian border, where a Hutterite Bruderhof was established in 1547 on the estate of a nobleman Peter Bakich de Lak. The brethren had sought refuge here from the unusually heavy persecutions in Moravia, and at first the manorial lord was well disposed to accept these brethren who were generally known as excellent farmers. But soon he changed his mind, mainly under the influence of the harsh mandates of King Ferdinand (*q.v.*) who would not tolerate "heretics" either in Moravia or in Hungary. Thus Bakich undertook severe and drastic measures against the brethren who were quite at a loss where to turn to. The Chronicle reports these events with these words, "They were driven from Moravia to Hungary, from Hungary to Moravia, from there to Austria, and again back to Moravia. In short, there was no place at all for the God-fearing people" (*Chronik*, 337). These persecutions lasted for five years (1548-53). Afterwards the situation changed to the better, and from then on the brethren could enjoy relative peace in their Slovakian colonies.

LOSERTH, R.F.

Details of the persecutions around Holitsch are recorded in the *Geschicht-Buch* (Wolkan) 241-50, or in Zieglschmid, *Chronik*, 319-39; *ML* II, 339.

Holl, Folpmer Jacob de, b. 1869 at Utrecht, d. Dec. 19, 1934, at Baarn, Dutch Mennonite pastor and theologian. After studying at the University and Mennonite Seminary at Amsterdam, he served as pastor at Mensingeweer 1897-1900, Hindeloopen and Koudum 1900-3, Den Ilp 1903-5, Medemblik 1905-13, Borne 1913-26, Purmerend 1926-29, and Leermens-Loppersum 1929-34. In 1933 he was appointed lector of the Amsterdam Mennonite Seminary, to teach ethics to the theological students, but his teaching was only for a short period, ending by his sudden death in 1934.

De Holl was a very learned man. He was a disciple of de Bussy (*q.v.*), his teacher at the Seminary, who estimated him highly. De Holl published only one book, *De Kennis van goed en kwaad; een gedachtewisseling met de professoren Heymans en Kranenburg* (Amsterdam, 1928). Besides this he wrote a number of critical reviews of books on ethics in a number of Dutch periodicals. His historical study on Jan de Liefde (*q.v.*) was published in *Doopsgezinde Bijdragen* 1901.

De Holl was an amiable man, who was loved by many and whose influence reached much further than the small congregations he served. / vDZ.

De Zondagsbode, Jan. 6 and 13, 1935; *DJ* 1936, 17-28 with portrait.

Holland, the popular name for The Netherlands (*q.v.*). Two provinces also carry the name, North Holland (*q.v.*) and South Holland (*q.v.*). The language of the country is called Dutch, occasionally in America called "Holland Dutch."

Hollandsch Doopsgezind Emigranten Bureau (Dutch Mennonite Emigration Office), a committee founded in June 1924 on the initiative of the Mennonite Church Board of Rotterdam, and supported by the Mennonite Committee of Foreign Needs (see **Fonds voor Buitenlandsche Nooden**), sponsored by the A.D.S. (Dutch Mennonite General Conference). The first trustees were S. H. N. Gorter, president-secretary; J. Th. de Monchy, treasurer; J. Thiessen, M. P. Schütte, J. N. de Jong, all of Rotterdam, and Pastor A. Binnerts Szn and J. W. van der Vlugt of Haarlem. Soon Z. Kamerling became secretary, followed by C. S. Altmann of Rotterdam, who both as secretary and treasurer 1927-37 (together with Pastor Gorter) did much for the Mennonite refugees. The services rendered by the committee were fivefold: (*a*) collecting money, clothing, and medicines in the Netherlands; (*b*) (especially during the first three years) sending food rations to Russia; (*c*) boarding the Russian Mennonites passing through Rotterdam, who had to wait there even for months; (*d*) shipping the refugees to North and South America; (*e*) aftercare of those who immigrated to South America (this care was given on a large scale to the Mennonite settlements in Brazil after 1930).

The refugee rush reached its peak in 1928-30. By 1930 more than 1,000 Mennonite refugees from Russia had passed Rotterdam. After 1930 the number soon decreased and the committee could give full attention to the needs and problems of the Mennonites in Brazil. By 1936 the activities of the committee had practically stopped. More than 220,000 guilders have been collected and spent on this work of Christian and brotherly charity. vDZ.

Archives of the *Hollandsch Doopsgezind Emigranten Bureau,* found in the Mennonite Archives of Rotterdam; *De Zondagsbode* from July 1924 on; *DJ* 1926, 53-62; 1931, 67; 1935, 69-76; *Mennonitische Welt-Hilfskonferenz, Danzig 1930* (Karlsruhe n.d.) 28, 65 f., 90-94; *Der Allgemeine Kongress der Mennoniten, gehalten in Amsterdam, . . . 1936* (Karlsruhe, n.d.) 143-46.

Hollatz, David (d. 1771), a Protestant theologian of Pomerania, Germany, and author of devotional literature, pastor in Güntersberg from 1730 on. His books, some of which are still read, were also used by pietistically inclined Mennonites in the Palatinate, chiefly *Evangelische Gnadenordnung* (Basel, 1894); *Gebahnte Pilgerstrasse nach dem Berge Zion* (Basel, 1866); and *Verherrlichung Christi in seinem theuren und unschätzbaren Blute* (Basel, 1894). The *Gnadenordnung* (with *Pilgerstrasse*) was reprinted a number of times in the United States, first in Philadelphia in 1810. The second edition was reprinted by the Mennonite printer Heinrich Eby at Berlin, Canada, in 1844 under the title *Heils und Gnaden Ordnung*. (ML II, 339.)   NEFF, H.S.B.

Hollum, a village on the Dutch island of Ameland in the province of Friesland, the seat of the largest of the three Mennonite congregations (Hollum, Ballum, and Nes) on the island. Leenaert Bouwens (*q.v.*) visited Ameland a number of times on his journeys in 1551-82 and baptized at Hollum and Ballum a total of 99 persons; hence it is likely that there was a congregation here in those early days. The several congregations on the island are due to divisions in the 16th century; there were two at Hollum: the "Blue Barn" or Waterlander, and the "Jan Jacobsgezinden" (*q.v.*) or Old Flemish.

Both congregations were served until into the 19th century by unsalaried preachers. In the Waterlander congregation, which was much the smaller and had been receiving support from Amsterdam since 1709, the first known preacher was Douwe Abes Tichelaer, 1709-46, and the last preacher was J. H. Costers (retired in 1854). The Jan Jacobsgezinden group was very strict regarding the ban and avoidance; the government finally intervened and in 1608 passed such severe regulations that the congregation spoke of being persecuted. Their first elders (1650) were Jacob Janssen and Cornelis Jannsen, who were permitted to conduct baptism and communion; they were assisted by two trial preachers (*proefdienaars*), from whose ranks the succeeding elders were chosen. Noted elders were Jacob Jobs 1769-1804, and Cornelis Sorgdrager 1793-1826, the latter of whom was the first to give religious instruction to the children.

In the middle of the 19th century a desire to have a trained minister became evident here; the two elders were aged, and none of the members was willing to be chosen to the office. The A.D.S. at Amsterdam sent proponents (*q.v.*) to help them in 1850-52; then the congregation called K. S. Gorter as its minister, who served 1862-95. In 1854, when J. H. Costers of the Waterlander congregation retired, all the Mennonites on Ameland were united for a time in a single congregation, which at this time numbered 175 members. In 1870 the congregation divided into three separate congregations, served by two preachers, one serving at Nes and one at Hollum and Ballum. Gorter was followed by the preachers A. Stiel 1898-1905, J. M. Erkelens 1906-8, J. Loosjes 1909-14, J. E. van Brakel 1914-28, W. Schopenhauer 1928-32, W. Broer 1933-41, H. D. Woelinga since 1947. Since 1933 there has been only one minister on the island; he lives at Hollum and serves the three congregations. In 1857, 16 members left the church to join the followers of the pietistic Jan de Liefde (*q.v.*), who had founded a Free Evangelical Church on the island of Ameland. A new meetinghouse was built in 1867. The members are partly farmers, partly navigators. The membership, 175 in 1854, was still 175 in 1900; since then it has steadily decreased to 113 in 1954. Church activities include a Bible circle, ladies' circle, and girls' club,   vDZ.

DB 1861, 145 f.; 1868, 167; 1889, 1-50 *passim;* 1890, 1-38 *passim; ML* II, 340 f.

Holly Grove Mennonite Church (MC), located near Westover, Somerset Co., Md., a member of the Ohio Mennonite Conference, was organized as a congregation of 27 members in April 1919 by Bishop John S. Mast of Elverson, Pa., in the home of I. M. Kauffman. In 1909 the D. P. Yoder family had settled here with others following from Michigan, North Dakota, Pennsylvania, Virginia, and Missouri. The first Sunday school, held in a schoolhouse, was organized by Amos C. Ogburn in 1916. The present structure, enlarged and remodeled in 1951, was erected in 1920. Those who have served the congregation as bishops are John S. Mast and Geo. M. Hostetler; as ministers, Aaron Mast, Geo. M. Hostetler, A. Roy Payne; as deacon, Amos C. Ogburn. Now serving are Ira A. Kurtz, Amos C. King, and Harold Hostetler. Present membership (1956) is 86.   A.C.K.

Holmes County in east central Ohio, the location of early Amish and Mennonite settlements, was formed from Wayne, Coshocton, Tuscarawas counties in 1824, and was organized the next year. The section is very hilly with few railroads and most of the highways follow the winding course of some stream. Amish families named Troyer, Hochstetler, Weaver, and Gerber moved into the Walnut Creek and Sugar Creek valleys with the first settlers in 1809. Following the better farming areas they have now spread north into Wayne County and east and northeast into Tuscarawas and Stark. The first Mennonite settlers came from Bucks Co., Pa., settled near Wilmot in 1812 and erected two small meetinghouses—Kolb's (*q.v.,* of logs, erected 1833; pronounced Kulps), and Longenecker's (*q.v.,* hewn logs erected 1834). After an early period of great interest and growth during which two frame meetinghouses were erected the congregation declined. The Shoups and Mumaws moved to Wayne Co., Ohio, and Elkhart Co., Ind. Attempts by nearby Amish Mennonites to revive the work have met with only spasmodic success. Members of the Amish Church in the Walnut Creek Valley organized or participated in Sunday schools held in schoolhouses as early as 1859. Holmes County with Wayne was one of the centers of controversy between the more progressive Amish who were ready to allow a few cultural changes, to erect meetinghouses, and to make slight changes in the worship service and those who insisted on the strict old order. In the ministers' conference held during the early 1860's certain progressive leaders tried to introduce a less conservative interpretation of the Scriptures. The others made a strict adherence to the old rules and regulations—*die alten Regel und Ordnungen*—an absolute requirement of fellowship. Out of the controversy arose the Amish Mennonite and the "Old Order" Amish. Leaders of the opposing groups in Holmes County were "Big" Mose Miller and "Little" Mose Miller, the former insisting on progressive measures. Amish Mennonites established their first congregations at Walnut Creek and Martin's Creek. These have now grown into four regular congregations and a mission, and with Longenecker's had a combined membership of 1,414 in 1953, and three mission stations with 25 members. The congregations are Walnut Creek, Farmerstown, Martin's Creek, and Berlin, Longenecker's, and the mission Gray Ridge near Millersburg. All these belong to the Ohio and Eastern Mennonite (MC) Conference. A 1923-25 schism in the Walnut Creek congregation resulted in the organization of a General Conference congregation in Sugarcreek just across the border in Tuscarawas County. The Old Order Amish membership in Holmes County and contiguous areas in Tuscarawas, Stark, and Wayne counties is over 4,000, with 43 "districts" or congregations. This is the largest Old Order Amish settlement in North America.

In recent years two Conservative A.M. congregations have been organized in the county, Pleasant View and Maysville, with a total membership of 340 in 1953. Thus the total Mennonite and Amish baptized membership in Holmes County and its immediately adjacent territory, all of whom, except Longenecker's, are the descendants of the original 1809 settlers and their later associates, equals in 1956 approximately 6,000.

A Beachy Amish mission and a Church of God in Christ mission have recently been established.

J.S.U.

Holmes County (Ohio) Old Order Amish settlement is the largest Old Order Amish community in the United States. Founded in 1809 by settlers coming from Somerset County, Pa., in 1955 it has 43 congregations with 4,354 baptized members and approximately 1,600 families. In addition there were in the community one Beachy Amish congregation with 28 members, two Conservative Amish congregations with 428 members, six Mennonite (M.C. Ohio Conference) congregations with 1,312 members, and one General Conference congregation with 235 members, all of whom with few exceptions descend from the original Amish constituency in this area. The Amish community, which is in the eastern half of the county, roughly east of Route 76 and the county seat of Millersburg, has "spilled over" into Coshocton County on the south and Wayne County on the north. It always has also covered the western part of Tuscarawas County lying immediately east of Holmes County. In the heart of the settlement the land is almost solidly occupied by Amish or Mennonite farmers. From east to west the Amish shopping centers are Sugarcreek (Tuscarawas Co.), Walnut Creek, Berlin, and Millersburg.

The Old Order Amish of Holmes County are no longer fully unified. A stricter group of congregations, which practices shunning sharply against members transferring to other Amish or Mennonite congregations, has no communion fellowship with the other Amish congregations. This includes several subgroups: the "Swartzendruber" or "Sam Yoder" group of five congregations, and the "Stutzman" group of two congregations. Some of these strict congregations are not in communion with each other.

The first division in the community, that between the Old Order and the progressive group (Walnut Creek congregation) which joined the Mennonite (MC) Conference, occurred in 1862. The Conservative division occurred about 1915. The small Beachy congregation was started in 1941. A Church of God in Christ mission, called the Rock of Ages Mission, which was established recently among the Amish near Maysville, had won a small number of Old Order Amish and a few more Old Order Mennonites and others.

Parochial schools have developed more widely in the Holmes County Amish community than anywhere else among the Old Order Amish. For the school year 1955-56 there were ten such schools, with a total enrollment of 344, each operated by its own Amish school board, the first established in 1945. Two of these offer nine grades, thus including the first year of high school.

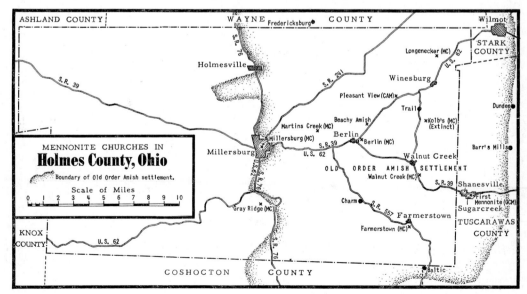

MENNONITE CHURCHES IN
Holmes County, Ohio
Boundary of Old Order Amish settlement.
Scale of Miles
0 1 2 3 4 5 6 7 8 9 10

The typical congregational organization of the Holmes County Amish consists of one bishop, two preachers, and one deacon. There were in 1955 in the 43 congregations 39 bishops, 80 preachers, and 36 deacons, or a total of 155 ordained men. There is no church activity in the congregations except a Sunday morning church service every two weeks. Some of the members support the work of the Mission Interests Committee (*q.v.*). J. A. Raber of Baltic, Ohio, has operated a small bookstore at his home, and has occasionally issued publications, including even an edition of Menno Simons' Works in German (1926). He has published the *Neuer Amerikanischer Calender* annually since 1930. This *Calender* contains an Amish "ministers' list" with years of birth and ordination indicated for each one.

The Holmes County Amish settlement is a typical close-knit Amish community, somewhat less tradition-bound than the more conservative Lancaster County settlement, and very similar in spiritual and cultural level to the Elkhart-Lagrange County settlement in northern Indiana. In recent years the Brunk Brothers' revival campaign and similar campaigns by other Mennonite evangelists held in the vicinity have had some influence, although the most common result has been the transfer of awakened members to a Conservative congregation or to an Ohio Mennonite congregation.

Beginning with 1953, Ervin Gingerich, an Old Order Amish deacon, has been publishing annually an *Ohio Amish Directory,* since 1956 in two volumes, the first of which gives complete ministerial and membership statistics and names for all Amish congregations in the Holmes County settlement, including also parochial school statistics. Vol. II does the same for all other Amish congregations in Ohio. *The Budget,* a weekly newspaper published at Sugarcreek, Ohio, since 1920, has long been "the Amish newspaper," not only for Holmes County but also for the entire United States with a circulation of well over 8,000. It contains a remarkable amount of Amish local news "correspondence" from many Amish communities, as well as special articles of interest to the Old Order and Conservative groups. For over 30 years (1890-1920) the paper was edited and published by S. H. Miller and J. C. Miller, the former an Amish Mennonite minister of Shanesville.

In spite of the long history and size of the Holmes County Amish settlement practically nothing has been published about it. Two unpublished M.A. theses on this region have been recorded by John A. Hostetler in his *Annotated Bibliography on the Amish* (Scottdale, 1951): Lyle Fletcher, "The Amish People of Holmes County, Ohio: A Study in Human Geography" (Ohio State University, 1932, pp. 98) and Velma Leeper, "The History, Customs, and Social Life of the Amish of Ohio with Special Reference to Holmes County" (Kent State University, Kent, Ohio, 1936, pp. 180).   H.S.B.

A. P. Karch, "The Amish of Holmes County, Ohio," in *The Standard Atlas of Holmes County, Ohio* (Cincinnati, 1907); S. H. Miller, "The Amish in Holmes County, Ohio," in *Mennonite Yearbook and Directory* (Scottdale, 1918) 31 f.; John H. Yoder, "Caesar and the Meidung," *MQR* XXIII (1949) 79-98, treats a case of a lawsuit regarding "shunning" in the Holmes-Wayne County settlement.

Holmfield and Lena Mennonite Brethren Church, a congregation having two meetinghouses, one in the village of Holmfield, the other near Lena, Man., a member of the Northern District Conference of the M.B. Church, was organized under the leadership of H. Unger on March 11, 1928, with a membership of 24. The membership in 1949 was 63, all of whom are rural people. Both churches were built in 1944, each with a seating capacity of 250. In 1949 P. Schultz was the leader of the group at Holmfield, and J. F. Poetker at Lena. H. Derksen also served as minister. In 1951 the two groups separated, each becoming an independent congregation, Holmfield being organized with 26 members and P. F. Sawatsky as pastor. In 1954 Holmfield had 27 members, with Peter P. Schulz as pastor. The Lena group had 40 members at the time of separation. In 1955 it had 58, with J. F. Poetker as pastor.   J.F.P.

Hollsopple, Somerset Co., Pa., a mining village of 1,000 inhabitants, located about 10 miles south of Johnstown, is the post-office address for a very large part of the Johnstown district Mennonite (MC) settlement, particularly the four older congregations, viz., the Stahl (1 mile distant), Kaufman, Blough, and Thomas congregations, with a total of about 650 members (1956), and is therefore a very familiar address. It is, however, on the south edge of the settlement and is not the shopping center for the Mennonite community.   H.S.B.

Holstein. The duchies of Holstein and Schleswig were divided under Christian III (d. 1559) in such a way that the Duke of Gottorp and the king had sole jurisdiction over a part of each, while some districts remained under joint jurisdiction. The difficulties resulting from this arrangement were of benefit to the spread of Mennonitism.

With dukes Hans and Adolf, the king issued severe edicts against the Mennonites who had settled in Oldesloe (*q.v.*) and in the east at Steckelsdorf as powder manufacturers, linen weavers, and cover makers. In the cemetery "thor Krempe" (today Altenkrempe) there was a great number of "such false rabble," including women and girls, who "live well and some among them go with golden chains." At the "lower mill" near Lütjenburg a meeting of 900 had taken place at night. This is the complaint of the Statthalter Bertram von Anevelde (Ahlefeldt) in 1554 to the king, whom he besought to expel them not only from this district, but also from Lübeck. The memory of events in Münster in 1535 was still fresh. Duke Adolf proposed to his brother that they issue an edict against dangerous heretics to be posted on all church doors. They were thinking in particular of Bartolomäus of Ahlefeldt (*q.v.*), who was their common subject, and upon whose estates at Fresenburg (*q.v.*) near Oldesloe Mennonites were living. In 1533 and in September 1555 an edict was issued by Christian III warning that Anabaptists, because they caused insurrection, should not be employed (see **Denmark**).

On their account Adolf ordered a church inspection in 1557 and had a pastor deposed who was suspected of Anabaptist leanings. These measures were not unsuccessful. Nothing more is heard of Mennonites in East Holstein. Nevertheless Menno Simons could spend the last years of his life, 1554-61, quietly in Wüstenfelde.

In the south of Holstein there were a few Mennonites in the towns of Pinneberg and Wandsbek, who were not subject to any marked hostility. In the next century Fresenburg is again on the scene. Very suddenly in July 1656 the order was issued by both rulers to Joh. von der Decken, the owner, to remove "the ungodly rabble" from his jurisdiction within a week, on penalty of a fine of 3,000 talers; for "as soon as they get enough air and opportunity, they will rebel against the God-ordained government, revolt, and draw entire nations into insurrection and ruin, as the examples of the previous century show." Three families felt this blow; Jan de Buyser (*q.v.*), the "Huiskoper" (*q.v.*) preacher of Hamburg, drew up a petition for them, pointing out the toleration the ancestors of these families had enjoyed. They were very likely permitted to remain.

In the southwest of the duchy, many Mennonites immigrated in the 16th century to the marshes of Krempe and Wilster, and were of no little importance to the country. Actual places of freedom, where they were granted special privileges, were set up in 1623 in Glückstadt (*q.v.*) and in 1601 in Altona (*q.v.*) where they were valued for their industry in the crafts. In the north the marsh borders on Dithmarschen. The assumption that Anabaptists had also gone there is supported by the "Landrecht" of 1567, article 2 of which opposes the Anabaptists. In addition a royal decree of 1637 forbade secret conventicles in the south of Dithmarschen.

Mennonitism in Holstein gradually declined. The descendants of the immigrants joined the state church; e.g., Jacob Lammerts, the only Mennonite living in Rendsburg after 1800. In 1834 distinctions in active and passive franchise on the basis of creed were removed. A regulation of 1863 permitted Mennonites to settle anywhere in the duchies.

A large number of refugees from the Danzig area settled in the Schleswig-Holstein area in 1945-46. The Kiel (*q.v.*) congregation was organized in 1949.   R.Do.

B. C. Roosen, *Gesch. der Menn.-Gem. zu Hamburg-Altona* (2 vv., Hamburg, 1886-87); Ernst F. Goverts, "Das adelige Gut Fresenburg und die Mennoniten," in *Ztscht der Zentralstelle für Niedersächsische Familiengesch.*, No. 3-5, 1923; Ludwig Harboes, *Det Siellandske Clerisie Eller Eiteretning Om De Bisko* . . . (Copenhagen, 1754); R. Dollinger, *Gesch. der Menn. in Schleswig-Holstein, Hamburg und Lübeck* (Neumünster, 1930); *Menn. Bl.*, 1904, 29 ff., 76; *ML II*, 341.

Holt Hutterite Bruderhof, established in 1949 near Yarrow, Alberta. It had a population of 57 in 1950.

Holwerd, Dutch province of Friesland, seat of the congregation of Holwerd-Blija, formerly called Holwerd, de Vischbuurt, and Blija; de Vischbuurt in 1850 became the independent congregation of Ternaard (*q.v.*). Until 1935 church services were also held in Blija (*q.v.*); now only in Holwerd. Holwerd is a town of about 2,000 inhabitants. Its Mennonite congregation must have been established about 1563; Leenaert Bouwens baptized a total of 234 persons here (67 in 1563-65; 167 in 1568-82). Of the history of this congregation not much is known. A meetinghouse was built in 1629 (this old meetinghouse was still in use in 1930 as a non-Mennonite kindergarten); the membership then numbered about 180; 241 in 1861, 260 in 1900, only 85 in 1954. A new meetinghouse was built in 1850, rebuilt in 1927. An organ was installed in 1906.

Holwerd was one of the first rural congregations to call a minister trained at the Amsterdam Seminary, viz., Pieter Feenstra, who served here 1792-97. Since this time the congregation has always been served by a trained minister. Ministers of the last decades were A. H. van Drooge 1897-1901, H. C. Barthel 1902-13, G. A. Hulshoff 1913-16, W. Hilverda 1916-50, A. J. van der Linden 1950-54.

Church activities include a ladies' circle since 1920; Sunday school for children since 1902; youth group, *Menniste Bouwers* group.   W.H., vdZ.

Blaupot t. C., *Friesland,* see Index; *Inv. Arch. Amst.* II, No. 1942 f., II, 2, No. 100; *DB* 1861, 136 f.; 1906, 195; *ML II*, 342.

Holwierde, in the Dutch province of Groningen, where Leenaert Bouwens (*q.v.*) baptized ten persons in 1563-65. Since there was no congregation here, the newly baptized must have joined neighboring congregations, either Appingedam or Bierum.   vdZ.

Holy Spirit. Main-stream Anabaptists as orthodox Trinitarians confessed both the personality and the deity of the Holy Spirit, avoiding both unitarianism and tritheism. Grebel in his letters and defenses assumed the accepted doctrine of the Holy Spirit as the third Person of the Trinity (Bender, 287). Sattler began the Schleitheim Confession in true Trinitarian fashion, speaking of the Spirit as the One "who is sent from the Father to all believers for their strength and comfort and for their perseverance in all tribulation until the end" (Wenger, *Doctrines,* 69). Menno Simons wrote, "We believe and confess the Holy Ghost to be a true, real, or personal Holy Ghost, and that in a divine way—even as the Father is a true father, and the Son a true son; which Holy Ghost is a mystery to all mankind, incomprehensible, inexpressible, and indescribable, . . . divine with His divine attributes, going forth from the Father through the being of the Father and the Son" (*Works* II, 186). Riedemann said of the Holy Spirit, "Thus we acknowledge Him, with the Father and the Son, to be God," and emphasized the unity of the Godhead, using the illustration of "fire, heat, and light" to show that the three persons of the Trinity are inseparable, so that "where one is, there are all three, and when one is lacking, none is present" (*Confession,* 37).

Marpeck like Menno Simons and Riedemann emphasized the importance of the Holy Spirit in the Christian life. The Holy Spirit in His relation to the believer effects regeneration, assures of salvation, guides into truth, activates the conscience, purifies the heart, comforts, produces love, and gives power and joy in service (Wenger, *Marpeck,* 214). The Anabaptists never identified the Holy Spirit with reason, or with emotion, or with the conscience, resisting the positions of rationalism and mysticism, but declared the Holy Spirit to be objective reality, revealing Himself to the believer in the Gospel (Friedmann, 82). In His relation to the Scriptures, the Holy Spirit was not considered to be a separate and independent "inner light" or "inner Word" whose authority might contradict and supersede the "written Word" as spiritualists taught. Anabaptists held that the Holy Spirit as the true author of Scripture is also the true interpreter of Scripture who does not contradict Himself. Concerning this Marpeck wrote, "We say again that there are not two, but there is only one Word of God, and the word of divine evangelical preaching . . . is truly the Word of the Holy Spirit and of God, for the Holy Spirit, who is God, has spoken through and out of the heart and mouth of the apostles" (Horsch, 351 f.).

While neither the Dordrecht nor the Ris Confession has a separate article on the Holy Spirit, both stress the importance of the Trinity and of the place of the Holy Spirit in Christian faith and experience. Ris declares, "The Holy Spirit belongs, as a divine entity, to the essence of God. He is as well the Spirit of the Father as of the Son and proceeds from the Father and from the Son as the mighty worker of all divine and spiritual things" (Ris, 4 f.). Acknowledging the equality of the persons of the Trinity he adds that "equal honor and equal service are due them."

The *Shorter Catechism* briefly affirms faith in the Trinity and in the Holy Spirit, while the *Waldeck Catechism* gives a more detailed description of the operation of the Holy Spirit, noting that "He testifies of Jesus; He comforts believers; He sanctifies them, and leads them into all truth; and through the Holy Ghost, the love of God is shed abroad in the hearts of believers" (Wenger, *Doctrines,* 104). *The Roosen Catechism* discusses more extensively the nature of God, stressing the unity of the Godhead to the extent that it appears anti-Trinitarian. Commenting on Matt. 28:19 Roosen says, "From this it must not be understood that there are three beings, or three persons, much less that there are three Gods in heaven. But these names are thus differently expressed in consideration of the work of redemption and the salvation of the human race; as the Father, the origin; the Son, the means of redemption; and the Holy Ghost, sanctification and confirmation in salvation" (Wenger, *Doctrines,* 125 f.). In the light of its historical context and the writer's lack of theological training this statement may be accepted as Trinitarian in spirit though it lacks the precision of a trained theologian (Wenger, *Doctrines,* 125 f.).

American Mennonite groups, generally accepting the historic position, are largely agreed on the doctrine of the nature of the Holy Spirit as personal and divine but they reflect some differences in the relative emphasis given to the work of the Holy Spirit in Christian experience. Distinctive emphases may be noted in the following groups. The Brethren

in Christ Church has "for many years made much of the influence and operation of the Holy Spirit," including an emphasis on the doctrine of sanctification (Climenhaga, 296 f.). While this group is not unanimous in its interpretation of sanctification, it seems to be agreed on its importance as a separate work of the Spirit. The Mennonite Brethren in Christ Church (now the United Missionary Church) officially affirms the doctrine of "entire sanctification," which is "an instantaneous act of God, through the Holy Ghost, by faith in the atoning merits of Christ's blood, and constitutes the believer holy" (Huffman, 163). The Defenseless Mennonite Church (now the Evangelical Mennonite Church) includes in its statement of faith a separate article, "The Baptism of the Holy Ghost," which it calls "a distinct operation of the Holy Ghost, separate from His regenerating work, . . . an experience always connected with . . . equipment for testimony or service" (Manual, 27).

Distinctive emphases in the doctrine of the Holy Spirit also occur among the French Mennonites. The Mennonites of Holland reflect various views on the Holy Spirit, some of which reject traditional Trinitarianism and represent a revival of spiritualistic tendencies of earlier centuries (Meihuizen, 259-304).

E.W.

H. S. Bender, *Conrad Grebel* (Goshen, 1950) 287; J. C. Wenger, *The Doctrines of the Mennonites* (Scottdale, 1950) 69, 104, 125 f.; *idem,* "The Theology of Pilgram Marpeck," *MQR* XII, 4 (October 1938) 214; Menno Simons, *Complete Works II,* 186; Peter Rideman, *Confession of Faith* (London, 1950) 37; R. Friedmann, *Mennonite Piety Through the Centuries* (Goshen, 1949) 82; J. Horsch, *Mennonites in Europe* (Scottdale, 1942) 351 f.; Cornelis Ris, *Mennonite Articles of Faith* (Berne, 1918) 4 f.; A. W. Climenhaga, *History of the Brethren in Christ Church* (Nappanee, 1942) 296 f.; J. A. Huffman, *History of the Mennonite Brethren in Christ Church* (New Carlisle, 1920) 27; H. W. Meihuizen, "Spiritualistic Tendencies and Movements Among the Dutch Mennonites of the 16th and 17th Centuries," *MQR* XXVII (1953) 259-304.

Holzkamp, an estate near Lübeck, which about 1555 was leased by members of the Mennonite Roosen (*q.v.*) family, especially by Geerlinck, a refugee from Jülich. They were apparently not only farmers, but also tanners at a time when they were everywhere exposed to fines and expulsion.

B. C. Roosen, *Gesch. der Menn.-Gem. zu Hamburg und Altona* (Hamburg, 1886-87); C. H. Starck, *Lübecker Kirchen-Historie* I (1724); *ML* II, 342.

Home and Church, a 12-page monthly organ of four General Conference Mennonite congregations in eastern Pennsylvania, viz., Deep Run, Perkasie (Bethel), Springfield, and Bowmansville, edited by the pastor Allen M. Fretz, beginning in 1920 and continuing at least to 1929.

Home and Foreign Relief Commission was originated under the auspices of the Mennonite Evangelizing and Benevolent Board (*q.v.*), the mission board of the Mennonite Church (MC), by John F. Funk, G. L. Bender, George Lambert, C. K. Hostetler, and seven others (most of them associated with the Mennonite Publishing Company, *q.v.*) at Elkhart, Ind., March 2, 1897, for the immediate purpose of famine relief in India. Funds were gathered and grain was purchased, the latter being shipped to India as parts of cargoes sent by various relief agencies. In April 1897 George Lambert (*q.v.*) was sent to India to supervise the distribution of the HFRC funds and the grain for which it was responsible. Lambert returned in November 1897, reporting the presence of 20,000 famine orphans in mission orphanages requiring continued support. By the close of 1897 the HFRC had collected more than $20,000 for India relief.

For a time the HFRC assumed a quasi inter-Mennonite character. While it was initiated under M.C. auspices, and while this group made the largest financial contribution to the work, practically all Mennonite groups shared in the contributions. From the beginning D. F. Jantzen, representing the "Russian" Mennonites of the prairie states and residing in Elkhart as editor of the *Mennonitische Rundschau*, was associated with the movement. Jantzen was a member of the publicity committee and for one year served as secretary of the HFRC. The generous support of the Mennonites of the prairie states was largely due to his influence through the *Rundschau* (and other periodicals).

In November 1897 the HFRC withdrew from the auspices of the MEBB, although continuing to work closely with it. For a time consideration was given to a constitutional provision that all branches of Mennonites supporting the work of the HFRC be represented on its board of directors. In August 1898 a group of 23 persons, including 9 from other Mennonite groups, met at the call of the HFRC to give further consideration to the constitution and also to consider the possibility of an inter-Mennonite foreign mission program, several of the General Conference Mennonite Church representatives being interested in this proposal. The meeting concluded, however, that to take this action would not be advisable at this time. At the annual meeting in November 1898 the various groups were again well represented, David Goerz (*q.v.*) of Kansas, representative of the General Conference Mennonites, being elected vice-president of the HFRC, and H. H. Regier of Mountain Lake, Minn., a member of its executive committee. The announcements of the HFRC published in the various Mennonite periodicals continued to say that all branches of Mennonites had contributed to its relief funds and that as soon as Mennonite missions were established in India the HFRC would support the orphanage and relief work of all such missions.

By the close of 1898 the MEBB had appointed its first missionaries to India, who then opened the work at Dhamtari (*q.v.*) in November 1899. In 1899 also the G.C.M. group organized its own Emergency Relief Commission (*q.v.*), which sent David Goerz to India in 1900 as a relief commissioner and to take the first steps in locating a mission. Later that year the first General Conference missionaries sailed, establishing their mission at Champa in 1901.

The HFRC continued to collect funds for another five years, supporting various benevolent and mission projects including orphanage work in India. By 1902 these funds had reached a total of more than $45,000. With two Mennonite missions in India,

however, as well as two relief agencies at home, the inter-Mennonite character of the HFRC declined. Beginning with the annual meeting of 1901, all officers of the HFRC were representatives of the M.C. group, although that year G. G. Wiens was re-elected to the board of directors. From this time the Commission served more as a companion organization of the MEBB, and with the merging of that organization with the Mennonite Board of Charitable Homes (*q.v.*) to form the Mennonite Board of Missions and Charities (*q.v.*) in 1906, the HFRC ceased to exist. In 1917 the Mennonite Commission for War Sufferers (*q.v.*) was created as a companion organization of the MBMC, and can be thought of as a kind of successor of the HFRC. In 1926 the MCWS was absorbed by the MBMC and eventually came to be known as the Mennonite Relief and Service Committee (*q.v.*) of that board. Renewal of an inter-Mennonite relief program came with the organization of the Mennonite Central Committee (*q.v.*) in 1920.

The HFRC published a monthly 4-page periodical for a short time in 1901 (nine issues apparently), first issue April 1901, under the title *The Mennonite Missionary Messenger,* "Devoted to the interests of Home and Foreign Missionary Work in General and especially to the care and support of orphans." It was edited by the HFRC secretary A. C. Kolb, who was a leading spirit throughout HFRC history.

G.F.H.

Home for the Aged, located in Inman, Kan., was founded in 1946, when Mrs. Maria Vogt, a 72-year-old resident of the Inman community, offered her ten-room residence to the churches of the community as a home for aged people. An organization was formed and plans were made to remodel and enlarge the house, to make room for 15 residents and about 5 workers. The home is controlled by a board of nine members, who appoint a management committee of three to supervise the work. Most of the contributions and the larger number of residents have come from seven of the Mennonite churches of this area, representing three conferences.

The home was dedicated on June 15, 1947. Residents pay for their rooms and care, so that the home is largely self-supporting. However a gift day is observed annually and smaller gifts come in quite often. P.T.N.

Home for the Aged of the Mennonite Brethren Pacific District Conference, located at Reedley, Cal., was established in 1942 after a committee had been working on the project since 1938. Mr. and Mrs. A. R. Jost were the house parents. A committee of five, elected by the Conference, supervises the institution. In 1948 a new and larger home was built. In 1952 there were 48 guests. (Annual Reports in *Handbook of the Pacific District Conference of the M.B. Church.*) C.K.

Homes for the Aged, the designation for institutions operated for the care of older people unable to care for themselves and yet not requiring hospital attention. In May 1954 there were 38 such institutions sponsored by Mennonites of the United States and Canada, 3 in Germany, 1 in France, and about 20 in Holland. There had earlier been at least two in West Prussia and one in Russia.

The primary purpose of these homes is to provide care for the older members of the churches—generally over 70 years of age—in a Christian, homelike atmosphere. It is recognized that in modern society there are many older people who are not able to care for themselves and who do not have relatives or friends who can assume the responsibility. While the state has provided emergency care, the feeling has been that the church has a responsibility of Christian sharing.

There was probably less need for homes for the aged in the colonial period of Mennonite history. In the establishment of Mennonite homesteads, provision was made for the care of the aged. Some groups of Mennonites still take care of the aged, primarily through the family. The Old Order Amish, for instance, still maintain the practice of building a small apartment onto the main house, or a separate but closely connected small house, in which the parents or grandparents retire when the time comes. This is called the "grossdoddy" house. However, increases in population and the infiltration of a more urban culture made a consideration for the aged necessary. The first home for the aged sponsored by American Mennonites was the Salem Home at Hillsboro, Kan., established in 1894 by the Krimmer Mennonite Brethren. The second was the General Conference home at Frederick, Pa., established in 1896. The third was the Welsh Mountain Samaritan Home established by the Lancaster Conference (MC) in 1898, and the fourth the Bethesda Home (GCM) at Goessel, Kan., in 1899.

The slow growth of an awareness of the need for institutional care for the aged was reflected by the fact that in the first two decades of the 20th century only three homes were established. In the next two decades six more were opened, making the total in operation in 1940 twelve.

The sharp upturn in opening homes for the aged came in the 1940's, during which decade eleven were established. During the present fifth decade eight have already been opened, and several more are under consideration. Some are being expanded.

Possibly primary among the factors accounting for this increase in homes for the aged is the growing awareness of the need for a church-wide sharing in meeting the unique problems of the aged. One significant factor has been a change from the large farmhouse to a smaller one in or near a town or city. Space became an issue. Of course, the sheer fact of more older people has brought the problems of the aged to the forefront.

Another trend which has stimulated the increase in institutions for the aged has been a larger share of financial responsibility assumed by governments. In some sections, homes for the aged can be operated by payments from the guests received through old-age pensions. Also, some governments have been willing to assume part of the cost of construction. The provincial government of Ontario, for instance, contributes $1,000 per bed.

In May 1954 there were 38 (statistics are available for only 34) homes for the aged operated by Mennonites in eleven states in the United States and in four provinces in Canada. Five different Mennonite conferences operated homes for the aged. The total capacity of the homes was 977, and 247 workers were employed. The total property valuation was $1,756,000.

There are four major types of Mennonite-operated homes for the aged. First is that under direct conference supervision, in which the board of directors is elected by the conference and the conference assumes ultimate financial responsibility. The second type is the private corporation where a legal group is formed for the purpose of operating the home and the corporation has direct responsibility in all things. The third type is the privately owned type home. Here the individual Mennonite assumes full responsibility for the operation of the home as a vocation. The fourth is the community type where a community operates the institution and the community is made up predominantly of Mennonites.

Having had almost 60 years' experience, American Mennonites have been evaluating their efforts regarding homes for the aged. Five trends can be discerned. First, there is the rapid movement toward self-supporting operation. In the earlier years homes were supported by freewill gifts from churches. More homes now fix charges with a view of covering costs; individuals who need subsidizing are aided separately. However, with old-age pensions and county grants an institution can usually be self-supporting. Second, the need is felt to do more for the guests in our homes. Often the work has been to provide only the basic necessities until death. A new emphasis on spiritual ministry and meaningful activity is in evidence. Third is a movement toward more adequate personnel. Workers are studying their tasks and leaders who have special training and talents are sought. Fourth, the present trend is away from the large institutional type of care. One beginning has been made in a cottage type. Here couples (or single individuals) live in cottages on the grounds as long as they are able; later they are moved to the central building. Fifth, in some areas communities are finding they can solve the problem by wide cooperation. It appears that the number of community homes will grow in the future.

Following is the list of the 38 Mennonite homes for the aged in operation in 1954, with date of founding where known:

Mennonite (MC): 14

Welsh Mountain Samaritan Home, New Holland, Pa. (1898)

Home for the Aged, Rittman, Ohio (1901, 1939)

Mennonite Home, Lancaster, Pa. (1903)

Home for the Aged, Eureka, Ill. (1922)

Mennonite Old People's Home, Maugansville, Md. (1923)

Braeside Home, Preston, Ont. (1942)

Eastern Mennonite Home, Hatfield, Pa. (1942)

Eastern Mennonite Convalescent Home, Hatfield, Pa. (1942)

Mennonite Home for the Aged, Albany, Ore. (1946)

Rest Haven, Gassville, Ark. (1950)

Sunset Home for the Aged, Geneva, Neb. (1951)

Froh Brothers Homestead, Sturgis, Mich. (1952)

Rockome, Arcola, Ill. (1952)

Virginia Mennonite Home, Harrisonburg, Va. (1954)

General Conference Mennonite: 9

Mennonite Home for the Aged, Frederick, Pa. (1896)

Altenheim der Bergthaler Menn.-Gemeinde in Manitoba, Gretna, Man. (1918-38)

The Mennonite Home, Meadows, Ill. (1923)

Rosenort Home for the Aged, Rosthern, Sask. (1945)

Bethania Home for the Aged and Infirm, Winnipeg, Man. (1946)

Home for the Aged, Inman, Kan. (1947)

The Tieszen Home, Inc., Marion, S.D. (1947)

Home for the Aged, St. Catherines, Ont.

Mennonite Memorial Home, Bluffton, Ohio

Mennonite Brethren: 7

Tabor Home for the Aged, Morden, Man. (1921)

Mennonite Home for the Aged, Reedley, Cal. (1944)

Sunshine Mission Home, Buhler, Kan. (1945)

Corn Home for the Aged, Corn, Okla. (1947)

Altenheim, Winkler, Man.

Home for the Aged, Coaldale, Alberta

Mission Home, Yarrow, B.C.

Church of God in Christ, Mennonite: 1

Bethel Home for the Aged, Montezuma, Kan. (1948)

Reformed Mennonites: 1

Reformed Mennonite Home, Waynesboro, Pa.

Mennonite Community Homes: 4

Bethesda Home for the Aged (GCM), Goessel, Kan. (1899)

Bethel Home for the Aged (GCM), Mountain Lake, Minn. (1921)

Bethel Home for the Aged (GCM), Newton, Kan. (1926)

Salem Mennonite Home for the Aged (GCM), Freeman, S.D. (1949)

General Community Homes: 2

Salem Home (KMB), Hillsboro, Kan. (1894)

Mission Home, Hillsboro, Kan. (1942)

A recent development has been the establishment of "Convalescent Homes." (The name is a euphemism since the inmates are largely bedfast old people who come to the home to die.) Most of these homes are privately operated for profit, but there is at least one conference home, the Franconia Mennonite Convalescent Home near Souderton, Pa. (MC). A.R.S.

A. R. Shelly, "An Evaluation of Mennonite Social Welfare Institutions," *Proceedings . . . Ninth Conference on Mennonite . . . Cultural Problems* (North Newton), 1953.

Homes for the Aged in Europe. The care for the aged, indigent, ill, and orphaned has always been an integral part of the religious and social life of the Mennonites, although the forms have changed with circumstances. In the early days of persecution it was impossible to establish special homes for the needy; later on, since most of them were rural people, parents were generally taken care of in the homes of their children. Often they would live in a small house especially built for them on the home place. If necessary, the congregation would help to care for them. In Switzerland homes for the aged have never been established among the Mennonites, and in South Germany and France, only since World War II. The city congregations of North and East Germany had in some cases established homes for the aged and needy. The founding and early history of most of these is obscure and has never been investigated.

The Crefeld Mennonite Church originally had an orphanage next to the church on Königstrasse. Later the orphanage was changed into a home for the aged. The home was financed by small contributions from the inmates and the income from the von der Leyen endowment. The church custodian also lived in this building. During World War II the numerous buildings of the congregation, including the church and the home for the aged, were destroyed.

The Crefeld Mennonite Church built an old people's home in 1906. Since provision had been made for the poor of all creeds by the Cornelius Foundation given by Cornelius de Greiff (*q.v.*), the Crefeld old people's home was intended for unattached women who had some money (married couples were not necessarily excluded), for whom rent, light, and heat were furnished free. Each apartment was made as private as possible.

The Mennonite congregations of Emden and Norden each had an *Armenhaus* (home for the needy), in which old and needy people were cared for. However, as early as the 19th century these homes lost their original character and significance. The house in Emden was destroyed during World War II, but the one in Norden is still in existence. Although the Mennonite Church of Hamburg-Altona has always had a sense of responsibility toward the needy in the congregation, a home for the aged was never established.

The congregation of the Gross-Werder, West Prussia, had a home for the aged about which H. G. Mannhardt reported in *Mennonitische Blätter* (1896, p. 87). The Mennonites of Danzig had institutions called "Hospital" which cared for the aged and needy for a period of more than 300 years. The Frisian congregation had an *Armenhaus* next to its meetinghouse since 1638, and the Flemish congregation established one large enough to house 30 aged persons ten years later. During the Russian occupation of Danzig in 1734 it was destroyed, but was later rebuilt. In 1795 the congregation with a membership of 700, including children, supported 95 aged and poor. A collection for this purpose was usually held in connection with the observance of the Lord's Supper, which on July 7, 1765, amounted to 16,660 guilders. Again in 1813 during the occupation of Danzig, church and hospital were destroyed. A new home for twenty-four poor and aged persons was built in 1816 even before the church was erected. In 1902 it was replaced by a new building with eight small apartments, the home of the church custodian, and an auditorium (*Gemeindesaal*), which was severely damaged during World War II. The Königsberg Mennonite Church had two almshouses, which also cared for the aged, next to its church building since 1769, in which there was room for six families.

The first home for the aged in Russia was established in Rückenau, Molotschna, by the Mennonite Brethren in 1895, when P. M. Friesen donated a house for this purpose which provided room for 15 people. A larger project was started in 1903 by the Molotschna Mennonites in commemoration of the 100th anniversary of the settlement. This home was erected on 90 acres of community land on the Kurushan River at a cost of 41,000 rubles raised through collections and taxes. The home was opened in 1906, had 50 inmates in 1908, and was to be enlarged to accommodate 100. The cost of maintenance for 50 inhabitants amounted to 6,000 rubles per year.

As a result of World War II, two thirds of the German Mennonites became homeless and lost much of their possessions. In order to help the aged among them an organization called "Mennonite Homes for the Aged" (*Mennonitisches Altersheim*) was founded June 17, 1949. Successively the following homes for the aged were opened: Dec. 28, 1949, "Marienburg" at Leutesdorf near Neuwied on the Rhine; Oct. 20, 1950, "Friedenshort" at Enkenbach, Palatinate; and on Dec. 6, 1952, "Abendfrieden" at Pinneberg, near Hamburg, with 101, 72, and 22 inmates respectively in 1952. Contributions for maintenance of the homes in 1952 were DM 19,630 from the Mennonite Central Committee, DM 3,049 from the German Mennonites, and DM 14,018 from their own production. Each of the homes has one or two trained nurses. Only a few of the inmates are in a position to pay for their maintenance. Most of them depend upon government support and an additional allowance from the homes, which is raised within the Mennonite constituency. On Dec. 31, 1952, the organization had a membership of 1,047, which had contributed DM 34,282 in money and DM 20,430 in gifts-in-kind. The executive committee of the organization consisted at that time of Fritz Hege, Josef Gingerich, Richard Hertzler, Gertrud Schowalter, and Paul Kliewer.

In Burgweinting (*q.v.*) near Regensburg, Bavaria, there is a home for the aged owned by "Mennonitisches Hilfswerk Christenpflicht," established in 1922, managed by Sister Elise Hochstettler. Most of the occupants are non-Mennonites.

The French Mennonites established a home for the aged at Valdoie near Belfort in 1953, operated by the Association Fraternelle Mennonite.   C.K.

In the Netherlands there are two types of homes for the aged, those founded in the 17th and 18th centuries, and those established in recent times. The former, usually called "Hofje," were homes for the poor members of the church; most of them were founded by wealthy members of the church, sometimes named for their founders, and managed by a board in which both the founders or their descendants and the church board appointed their representatives. Now most of these homes are managed directly by the church boards. There are still a number of these homes: at Haarlem the Blokshofje,

Bruiningshofje, Wijnbergshofje, and Zuiderhofje; at Leiden the Bethlehemhofje; at Amsterdam the Rijpenhofje, Zonshofje, De Lelie, and De Vogel; at Leeuwarden the Marcelis-Goverts Gasthuis, at Koog aan de Zaan the Johanna Elisabeth-stichting. Formerly there were more, but they have either been closed or merged with others.

In the 20th century a number of new Mennonite homes for the aged have been founded in the Netherlands; these were not in the first place meant for poor members, but for those for whom it was difficult, particularly after World War II, to obtain a proper residence. These new homes are Mooi-land at Doorwerth, near Arnhem, Doopsgezind Rusthuis at Bolsward, Doopsgezind Gasthuis en Hesselinkstichting, Doopsgezind Tehuis voor Ouderen, Doopsgezind Rusthuis, all three at Groningen; Johanna at Heerenveen, Spaar en Hout at Haarlem, Huize Salland, Colmschate near Deventer, and De Olyftack at Haarlem. Schaerweyde near Zeist, Avondzon at Velp near Arnhem and the Klokkenbelt at Almelo are operated in co-operation with other churches. In the near future other homes for the aged will be opened in the Netherlands, one near The Hague; others are planned.   vdZ.

Menn. Bl., 1896, 87; 1902, 12; H. Görz, *Die Molotschnaer Mennoniten* (Steinbach, 1950) 150; Friesen, *Brüderschaft*, 661-63; *Um den Abend wird es licht* (Neustadt); R. Hertzler and Fritz Hege, *3 Jahre Altersheim* (Ludwigshafen, 1953); *ML* I, 38 f.

Home Mission Board *of the General Conference Mennonite Church.* One of the first acts of the small group that founded the G.C.M. Church in 1860 was to adopt a resolution: "That hereafter Home and Foreign Missions shall be carried on according to ability by our denomination." It took some time for the movement to gain momentum and strength. A foreign mission field was planned among the American Indians. In 1872 L. O. Schimmel of Pennsylvania, Ephraim Hunsberger of Ohio, and Christian Krehbiel of Kansas were appointed by Conference to look after the scattered churches and groups of Mennonites that needed shepherding. There was no united planning and so each one worked independently in his own region. The conference seemed to be satisfied with the start that was made. Perhaps because they were burdened by problems in other fields, the Home Mission Committee was permitted to lapse.

In 1878 conference considered it necessary to elect a new Home Mission Committee and engaged as a permanent worker in 1887 J. B. Baer, trained in Union Theological Seminary, New York. At the very next conference session Baer presented various concrete needs to the home congregations. His work in Manitoba, where he visited the hardpressed immigrants, was indeed encouraging in that a new spirit of determination, evangelism, and devotion became apparent. Next Baer followed churches in Minnesota and the Dakotas, and on to the Pacific. In the strictest sense of the term, this was church extension work, rather than the conventional type of Home Mission work. Many churches in the Northern District and in the Pacific District (all the older churches) owe their start to Baer's wise and energetic direction. In order to share the joy of the fruits with the home churches, and to enlist their aid in prayers and gifts, Baer spent considerable time visiting all the older congregations.

During the past two decades the Board of Home Missions has carried on church extension work in rural and urban centers in the United States. Workers in addition to Baer were engaged from time to time. In some of the rural areas, congregations required aid for only a rather short time until they became self-supporting. City mission work was started in Chicago and Los Angeles and later in Hutchinson, Kan., and other places. It is a source of satisfaction that the congregations in the last two cities have become strong enough to stand alone and in turn help others through their gifts. A few rural stations were abandoned when the families moved elsewhere.

Canada. The northward and westward movements of Mennonites were also manifested in the Canadian Prairie Provinces. Some of the new settlements were formed by farmers from Manitoba and from the United States who were looking for cheaper land and more room. Because of the background of the German and Russian immigrants, congregations frequently had two or three ministers, the Board of Home Missions inaugurated the itinerant type of work since extra preachers were available. Most preachers in Canada were farmers and it was found to be comparatively easy for them to spend part time in visiting smaller scattered settlements. In the earlier days economic conditions were uncertain; so in order to help needy ministers the Board of Home Missions engaged men and paid them the equivalent of three months' full pay, divided into 12 monthly payments. Many congregations in the large Canadian District are indebted to the Board of Home Missions for aiding them in getting established.

In Canada city mission work took a unique course. Mission churches and girls' homes developed hand in hand in Winnipeg, Man.; Saskatoon, Sask.; Calgary, Alberta; and Vancouver, B.C. The long winters and the need to earn money to repay obligations forced many families to move to these cities. Canadian Mennonite families are usually large, and in many homes girls could work out to earn money to help with the family needs or repay the travel debt. Jobs are located through the matrons of the homes. From the time a girl arrives in the city and comes to the girls' home, the matron plays the part of mother. Thursday evenings the girls usually spend socially in the home, with an hour of Bible study conducted by the pastor of the local mission church. The missions and the girls' homes are a blessing to each other and the result is a faster growing city congregation and many a Christian home is established through the channels of these girls' homes.

During the large Canadian immigration 1923-30, when 20,201 came, every phase of Home Mission work had to be intensified and some new phases of work had to be opened. The Board of Home Missions sent special workers into Canada to assist in church music and young people's work for a number of years. Canadian Mennonites responded quickly to the musical training, and in 1952 a Canadian music leader paid a return visit to some United States communities. The young people responded well through their Provincial Retreats. A goodly number of decisions for mission work and full-time Christian service have been made the last five years. Today the first of these are already on their way into our Foreign Mission fields and others are filling pulpits and other places of leadership.

The Board of Home Missions has felt deeply convinced that the best investment is to help small and young groups to grow in grace, faith, and numbers, so that in due time they might in turn be the ones to help furnish their portion in the prayer and finance support for our whole conference program. A strong home base makes a far outreach for Christ possible.

South America. Mennonites in South America, except the Old Colony groups from Canada, are all refugees from Russia or the Danzig areas, either from World War I or II. Approximately 40 per cent of these Mennonites lean toward or already belong to the General Conference. Being refugees, they are naturally short in funds, and it is most essential to aid them in their economic as well as spiritual life. The Mennonite Central Committee is definitely committed to extending economic aid, while the different conferences help with the establishing and maintaining of schools, Bible schools, and general church work. Pioneering is always difficult in each of the countries where our Mennonites have settled, but since Paraguay has been held back by stronger neighbor-nations, it is most difficult here. Testimonies have come to the Board again and again that, if it had not been for the spiritual aid given in the form of German literature, along devotional lines, visits from leaders in North America, they would have felt like giving up. A warm and vibrant faith in Christ strengthens and steadies in any circumstance of life. Much has been done in the past years, but much still remains to be done. Our aim in giving aid has always been to help them to help themselves in their spiritual and economic conquest. Ministers are given part salary for their service so that they can hire help to tend their farms, when they do church work. Without this undergirding, many would be unable to give the needed time or effort to do the spiritual work the Lord called them to render. Students are aided to get theological training. Aid is also given when a new church is to be built.

New Phases of Work. For a number of years, members of the Home Mission Board felt that the conference should do its part in endeavoring to ease tension conditions in certain areas of our country. We have entered the southern mountain area to bring the Gospel to the neglected people in this region by establishing some mission stations and doing Bible story and memory work with children in the public schools. A special phase of the children's work is the annual camp held in the summer months. Large numbers of children take part in these camps and it is encouraging to know that many decisions for Christ have been made and others indicate a desire to become full-time Christian workers. City work, where problems are innumerable, was undergirded by sending summer volunteer workers to help in conducting summer Bible schools and in directing recreational work. We have also been helping in the "larger city parish plan," where many workers join hands in making a united onslaught against the forces of evil. In a large city a single worker is often almost swallowed up, even though he may be doing an excellent piece of work. An effort has also been made in certain cities to form Mennonite fellowships, by bringing Mennonites from different branches together for worship and getting acquainted. Fellowships are often made up of students, individual Mennonite workers in these cities, and also some families who have come to the city to pursue some specialized line of work. In recent years one of these Mennonite fellowships has developed into a congregation. The dire need of our large migrant population was another call, which was answered by securing two trailers and workers to labor among the cotton workers in Arizona. In 1950 the new General Conference constitution was adopted and all General Conference mission work was put under the Board of Missions. The men who served on the Board of Home Missions in the past 25 years, 1925-50, are, W. S. Gottshall, A. S. Shelly, J. E. Amstutz, David Toews, S. S. Baumgartner, J. M. Regier added in 1925, H. A. Fast in 1932, A. J. Neuenschwander in 1935, John J. Plenert in 1938, W, Harley King in 1941, C. E. Krehbiel in 1945, G. G. Epp in 1947, Ben Esch in 1947. A.J.N.

Home Missions Board *of the General Conference of the Mennonite Brethren Church of North America* (officially *Board of Home Missions*) serves as an advisory and co-ordinating body. The conference statistical work is assigned to this Board. For more effective work in the field of home missions the conference is divided into four district areas and all the home missions activities are assigned to the district conferences. All of the churches in Canada compose one district and the United States is divided into three district areas.

The organization for home missions in the four districts is very similar and the activities are the same in all: (1) co-ordinating of the program for the traveling evangelists in the member churches; (2) establishment and maintenance of city missions in larger cities of our land; (3) extension service by conducting Sunday schools, vacation Bible schools, etc., in the immediate neighborhood of our churches. This latter has resulted in the establishment of a number of mission chapels in the various districts, which are expected eventually to become self-supporting member churches.

Some of the districts have a three-member board; others have three-member committees for each major activity, which together comprise the District Board for Home Missions. The total budget for home missions of the four districts is (1953) approximately $100,000 annually. A.A.SCH.

Homestead Mennonite Church (MC) 1911-14, in Benzie Co., Mich., now extinct, was organized by Bishop J. P. Miller of Kent Co., Mich., who placed Deacon Harvey Sarver in charge of the congregation. The membership was 15, mostly from Middlebury, Ind., and Kenmare, N.D. Sarver served a year, 1912-13; and was succeeded by John M. Yoder who served in 1913-14 as minister and then also moved away. The Homestead congregation participated in union Sunday-school and church services and had no building of its own, although organized as a congregation. The year 1918 marked the departure of the last Mennonite family from the area. J.C.W.

Homeville Mennonite Mission meets in a formerly unused church near Cochranville, Chester Co., Pa., where in 1945 the Millwood District of Lancaster Conference opened a mission outpost. The membership (1953) is 37, the Sunday-school enrollment 85 with an average attendance of 69, and a summer Bible school of 114. The minister is Ephraim Nafziger, and John A. Kennel and LeRoy Stoltzfus are the bishops. Kennett Square is now an outpost of Homeville. I.D.L.

Homma, Wilhelm Jacobs, a preacher of the "Lam en Toren" Mennonite congregation at Amsterdam in 1681-d.1705; particulars about this man were not available. Long's assertion that Homma translated the New Testament from the Greek into the Dutch language has been proved to be an error. Homma was the editor of two translations from the Greek into the Dutch, of A. Boreel's translation of *Matthew* and *Romans* (Amsterdam, 1693) and of R. Rooleeuw's translation of the New Testament (Amsterdam, 1694). vDZ.

Izaac le Long, *Boekzaal der Nederlandsche Bybels* (1732) 843; *Biogr. Wb.* IV, 197 f.; *Inv. Arch. Amst.* II, No. 1682.

Hondscho(o)te, a town (pop. 2,800) in Flanders, during the 16th century belonging to the Southern Netherlands, now in France. In the 16th century its population was much larger than now, and the town was an important center of wool weaving. There was once a Mennonite congregation here, which supplied a number of martyrs. In 1558 a young man named Wouter was burned at the stake. Four years later seven were seized, apparently when a religious meeting was surprised. Five of them were burned; two married women were secretly drowned in 1562. Their names were Karel van den Velde of Gent and his wife Proentgen, Frans de Swarte of Bailleul and his wife Klaesken, Jasper de Schoenmaker, Charlo de Wael, unmarried, and Martijntgen Amare (*Mart. Mir.* D 297, E 663). The last was without doubt the Martijntgen Aelmeers (*q.v.*) whom van Braght mentions as a martyr. In *Veelderhande Liedekens* is found a song on her death, "Genade ende vrede moet godvreezende zijn." Her brother Nicasen was also burned at Brugge in 1562. In 1587 the preacher Christiaen de Rycke was seized. He had previously been active in Leiden. A booklet of 15 letters written by his hand is reprinted in part in the *Martyrs' Mirror* (D 757 ff., E 1063 ff.). He was burned at the stake April 7, 1558.

Jacob de Rore (*q.v.*) addressed his fifth letter to the congregation of Hondschote. Of this congregation not much is known. It may have existed about 1540-87. A letter of Adriaen van Kortrijk, deacon or preacher of Gent, addressed to the congregation of Antwerp about 1545, is also signed by the congregation of Hondschote. This letter says that the congregations are "young" and want visits of an elder.

In 1561, when the congregation of Ypres (Ieper) had been destroyed by the drastic measures of the inquisitor Titelman (*q.v.*), its members fled partly to Armentières, partly to Hondschote. As has been said, Christiaen de Rycke was for some time its preacher. After his arrest the congregation may have been destroyed or its members moved to other towns. In the Frisian-Flemish troubles the congregation of Hondschote took the side of the Flemish and was very rigorous as to banning and shunning.   K.V., vDZ.

Kühler, *Geschiedenis* I, 439; A. L. E. Verheyden, "Mennisme in Vlaanderen," ms.; *ML* II, 342.

Hondt, Vincent de, an elder of the Mennonite Church at Haarlem, Netherlands, who in 1620 by his implacable attitude caused a division among the Old Flemish or "Huiskopers" (*q.v.*), who had already been weakened by the secession of the "Bankroetiers" (*q.v.*). Vincent de Hondt put out of the church a young man who had illicit relations with his fiancee. His copreacher Lucas Filips did not agree with de Hondt's act. This led to a division. Part of the congregation remained loyal to de Hondt. Attempts at reconciliation made by Claes Claesz (*q.v.*), a true apostle of peace, failed (*Propositie of Voorstelling dat de eens geloofsgezinde Christenen niet behooren gescheiden te blijven,* Haarlem, 1634). Equally unsuccessful was a letter, *Vredesbode* . . . , sent by numerous delegates from the churches assembled at Utrecht in 1633 and presented with the *Propositie.* Among Vincent de Hondt's writings were *Korte Bekentenisse des Geloofs* (1626, n.p.; 2d ed. Haarlem, 1630) and *Een korte en grondige Verklaring van de vrede Godts* (Haarlem, 1732). A treatise by de Hondt on the Trinity, the office of the ministers, baptism, the church, the Lord's Supper, marriage, the magistracy, shunning, etc., is found in *Christelyck Huys-boeck* (1643) by J. de Buyser (*q.v.*).

Vincent de Hondt's group at Haarlem, at first usually called "Vincent de Hondt-volk," merged with the Danzig Old Flemish about 1760.   vDZ.

BRN VII, *passim; DB* 1863, 58, 135, 156; *Biogr. Wb.* IV, 225 f.; 1876, 35; 1898, 6; Blaupot t. C., *Holland* I, 319; *idem, Groningen* I, 63; *Inv. Arch. Amst.* II, 2, No. 571; *ML* II, 342.

Honert, Jan van den (1693-1758) (son of Taco Hajo van den Honert, who was a Reformed preacher and a professor of theology at the University of Leiden), was a Dutch Reformed clergyman 1719-27 at Katwijk, Enkhuizen, and Haarlem, then professor of theology at the University of Utrecht 1727-34 and the University of Leiden 1734-58, achieved some importance for the Mennonites of Holland through the pen war he carried on (1740-42) with Johannes Stinstra against Stinstra's defense of re-

ligious freedom. Van den Honert charged Stinstra with Socinianism (*q.v.*), and Stinstra repudiated the charge. It was certainly the work of van den Honert that the government of Friesland on Jan. 13, 1742, suspended Stinstra from service and suppressed his book, *Natuur en gesteldheid van Christus koningrijk.* With all respect for the scholarship of men like Hoornbeek and van den Honert, the impression remains that witch-hunting and tracking down unorthodox Socinian views among Mennonites became second nature to them. vDZ.

DB 1868, 62, 64 f.; *N.N.B.Wb.* VIII, 816; *Biogr. Wb.* IV, 226-32; 233-46; Glasius, *Biographisch Woordenboek* II, 144 f. Chr. Sepp, *Johannes Stinstra en zijn Tijd* (2 vv., Amsterdam, 1865, 1866); W. J. Kühler, *Socinianisme in Nederland* (Leiden, 1912) 264-67; *ML* II, 342.

Honich, Tymen Claesz, b. about 1550, d. between 1605 and 1612, was a follower of Robert Robbertsz (*q.v.*). He may have been a sailor. He apparently lived at Amsterdam as a member of the Frisian congregation, from which he was banned because of marrying a nonmember of the group. He published some pamphlets: *Eene grondelijcke verklaringhe van den echtelijcken staet* (about 1591), in which he defended intermarriage; in his *Gedeeltheyt der Tongen int leeren vant Ampt der Overheyt* (1596) he defends his view that no church is the true Christian church; his *Christalijnen Bril* (1602, repr. 1612) sharply attacks the Calvinist ministers Geldorp and Bogerman, who had insisted that the government persecute the Mennonites.   vDZ.

Honig (formerly also *Honigh* and *Honingh*) is the name of one of the oldest and best-known Mennonite merchant families of the Zaan district of the Dutch province of North Holland. The earlier members were principally engaged in the manufacture of paper and oil pressing. In Koog a.d. Zaan there is still a large Honig plant for the manufacture of starch, flour, soups, and other products.

Jan Symons Honigh is named in the 17th century as a paper manufacturer at Koog aan de Zaan. His grandson Jacob Cornelisz Honigh at Zaandijk was likewise a manufacturer of paper and at the same time a shipowner in the whaling industry. With three older members of the united Waterland and Flemish Mennonites at Koog and Zaandijk he formed a committee to take charge of the erection of a new church, which is still used. In 1692 he was chosen deacon, an office which many of his descendants have filled, down to the present. One of his descendants, Jan Jacobsz Honigh (1792-1863), deacon and secretary of the consistory, did valuable work in the church archives.

Klaas Jansz Honig, b. July 6, 1769, at Zaandijk, was made substitute preacher of the Koog and Zaandijk congregation, Oct. 18, 1792. To commemorate this event a silver coin was struck with the inscription, "De ware wijsheid is de kennis van God; De beste wegen zijn, o Jeugd, die van wijsheid en van deugd. 1792." On June 23, 1793, he was called to preach for the congregation at Oude Sluis (Noord Zijpe). On June 15, 1794, he accepted a call from the church at Purmerend, where he died, March 10, 1832. By his competence and his virtuous character he won general respect and affection. He was a zealous member of the organization, *Tot Nut van't Algemeen*. In addition to the sermon he preached on the occasion of the thirtieth anniversary of the settlement of Purmerend in honor of this charitable association on May 2, 1814, he published *Redevoering over het Nut van Heuchlijke gebeurtenissen plegtiglyk te herdenken* (*N.N.B.Wb*. VIII, 821; *Biogr. Wb*. IV, 247).

Jan Jansz Honig, Jr., b. May 27, 1847, at Koog aan de Zaan, attended the Mennonite seminary in Amsterdam (1866-71), was made preacher of the church at Poppingawier in 1871, in Baard in 1873, and in Balk in 1875. From 1899 to his death he was a member of the directorate of the A.D.S. as the representative of the Friesche Sociëteit. He died at Balk on March 17, 1902. J. J. Honig wrote in the *Doopsgezinde Bijdragen* the articles, "Het Gezangboek der Gemeente te Balk voor 1854" (1887); "Een Zondagmiddag onder de fijne Mennisten te Balk" (1892); "Reizen naar de Eeuwigheid" (1896); "Bij het Portret van Mej. T. R. Haitjema" (1902).

Meindert Honigh, a member of a younger branch of the family, the son of a farmer near Purmerend, studied at the Mennonite seminary in Amsterdam (1892-96), in 1897 was made preacher of the congregation at Uithuizen, and in 1900 went to Franeker, where he served until his death. He published the following: *Leerboek der Formeele Logica, bewerkt naar de dictaten van wijlen Prof. Dr. C. Bellaar Spruyt* (Haarlem, 1903); *Feestrede ter gelegenheid van het 100jarig Bestaan van het Departement Franeker der Mij. Tot Nut van't Algemeen, 1809-1909;* "De oudere en de jongere generatie," *Tijdschr. Teekenen des Tijds*, 1909; "De Toekomstige Eeuw de Psychologie," *Tijdschr. Teekenen des Tijds*, 1911; "De jongste proeve van idealistische philosophie in ons vaderland," *Teylers Theolog. Tijdschr.*, 1911.

Gerrit Jan Honig (b. 1864), lived at Zaandijk, a deacon of the congregation of Koog-Zaandijk and representative of this congregation in the A.D.S. (Dutch General Conference) for 30 years, had published a large number of articles on the history of the Zaan district and also on the Mennonites in this region. Gerrit Honig of Zaandam was the first secretary (appointed in 1926) of the *Doopsgezinde Jongeren Bond* (Dutch Youth Association) and a founder of the Elfregi (*q.v.*) Youth group at Zaandam in 1929. He is also a deacon of West Zaandam and a member of the A.D.S. (*ML* II, 343.)   G.J.H., vDZ.

Honnoré, Jan, a Dutch Mennonite of Amsterdam, was a son of Abraham Honnoré and like his father a deacon of the Amsterdam Lamist congregation. Abraham Honnoré (d. 1680) served 1676-80 and Jan 1695-1700, 1707-13, and 1719-25. Jan Honnoré was a member of the Dutch Committee of Foreign Needs, in which he took an important place as treasurer; the Amsterdam Mennonite archives contain a number of documents bearing witness to his activities on behalf of the suppressed brethren in the Palatinate, Switzerland, Prussia, and Lithuania. (*Inv. Arch. Amst.* I, Nos. 1211, 1360.)   vDZ.

Honorius (384-423), Emperor of Rome, became the first emperor of the Western Roman Empire at the age of eleven, upon the death of his father, Theodosius I (d. 395). He was educated monastically and was later completely controlled by his surroundings. During his childhood the church acquired its great influence on legislation. Only two months after he assumed the reign the bishops were given jurisdiction over ecclesiastical affairs and heresy (*q.v.*) was declared a civil crime. Severe measures were undertaken to suppress the Manichaeans and Pelagians (Buchberger, 2016).

A law passed in 413 in the reign of Theodosius II of the Eastern Roman Empire, who succeeded his father on May 1, 408, as a seven-year-old, forbidding rebaptism, was used by the Protestant theologians of the 16th century to suppress the Anabaptists. In their official opinions to the rulers the German reformers advocated punishing Anabaptists with death; this was done by Luther, Melanchthon, Bugenhagen, and Cruciger in their opinion of Landgrave Philip of Hesse, on June 5, 1536 (Hochhuth, 563), and Urban Rhegius on the same occasion (Hochhuth, 575); also Dr. Eisermann at the diet at Cassel, Aug. 7, 1536.

The decree of the two emperors specifies, "If anyone is denounced or seized in baptizing again any of the servants of the Christian Church, he shall be punished with death together with the one who has carried out this criminal act, in so far as the one who was persuaded is by his age capable of crime." Thus there was no consideration of a universal punishment of a repetition of baptism. Johannes Brenz had as early as 1528 in his *Unterricht Philips Melanchthon widder die leere der Widderteuffer* stressed that this imperial decree did not have reference to all Christians who were baptized a second time, but only to servants of the church; the regulation was merely intended to prevent a repetition of baptism in those cases where the baptism already administered was beyond doubt. This was assumed as certain in the case of church officials. That many members of the church at that time were uncertain whether or not they had actually been baptized in infancy is seen in the discussions of the fifth council of Carthage in 401. It was decided here that all who did not definitely know that they had been baptized should be baptized again (Sachsse, 37).

A regulation similar to that of Honorius and Theodosius had already been issued by the emperors Valentinianus (d. 375) and Gratianus (d. 383), which specified, "We hold as unworthy of the priestly office the bishop who has improperly rebaptized" (Brenz). But the terrorizing method of capital punishment was not yet employed. HEGE.

Buchberger, *Kirchliches Handlexicon*, 1907; J. Hartmann, *Joh. Brenz* (Hamburg, 1840) 304; K. W. H. Hochhuth, "Mitteilungen aus der protestantischen Secten-Geschichte in der hessischen Kirche," in *Ztschr für die hist. Theol.*, 1858; Carl Sachsse, *D. Balthasar Hubmaier als Theologe* (Berlin, 1914); W. Sohm, *Territorium und Reformation in der hessischen Geschichte 1526-1555* (Marburg, 1915); *Codex Theodosianus*, Book 16, chap. 6 (*Ne sanctum baptismaiteretur*); *ML* II, 343 f.

Hont, Vincent de: see **Hondt, Vincent de.**

Hoofddorp: see **Haarlemmermeer.**

Hoofman, a Dutch Mennonite family, formerly found at Haarlem, where they were businessmen and members of the Mennonite Church, both Flemish and Waterlanders. Many of them served as deacons or were trustees of the Mennonite orphanages and old people's homes (*Hofjes*). Cornelis Hoofman (b. 1672 at Haarlem) studied law at the University of Leiden and founded a trading post and a banking house at Königsberg, East Prussia. He also wrote some Dutch plays. His sister Elisabeth Hoofman (b. 1664 at Haarlem), married to Pieter Koolart, published a number of poems in the Dutch language. She died at Kassel, Germany, in 1734, where her husband had established a bank. (Church records of Haarlem; *N.N.B.Wb.* IV, 770 f., 857 f.) vpZ.

Hoog, Isaac Marius Jacob (1860-1928), was a Dutch Reformed minister. He was the author of *De Martelaren der Hervorming in Nederland tot 1566* (Schiedam, 1885) and "Onze Martelaren," in *Ned. Archief voor Kerkgeschiedenis* I (1902) 82-116. Both publications are of high value for the history of Anabaptist martyrology. vpZ.

Hoogduitse Doopsgezinden, or *Hoogduitschers:* see **High German Mennonites.**

Hoogeveen, Dutch province of Drenthe, where a Mennonite fellowship group (*Kring*) was founded in 1946; in 1954 it numbered eleven members and was served by the pastor of Meppel. Services are held in the Remonstrant church four times a year. vpZ.

Hoogezand, a town in the Dutch province of Groningen, which, together with the adjoining town of Sappemeer (*q.v.*), is the seat of a Mennonite congregation. (The history of this congregation will be found under **Sappemeer.**) In the town of Hoogezand and vicinity Mennonite farmers settled early in the 17th century. In 1711 a number of Swiss Mennonite immigrant families settled at Hoogezand, at near-by Kalkwijk and about 1721 nine Mennonite families moved from Deventer to Hoogezand. (*DB* 1919, 74-76, 96-109.) vpZ.

Hooghe, Romein de (1645-1708), a Dutch artist who made a portrait of Menno Simons, which is found in a Dutch edition of Gottfried Arnold, *Historie der Kerken en Ketteren* (Amsterdam, 1701; Vol. II, page 533). This engraving by de Hooghe seems to have followed a portrait by an unknown artist, made after 1650. (*DB* 1890, 71; 1916, 99.) vpZ.

Hooghveldt (Hoogvelt), **Robbert van,** was a preacher of the Flemish Mennonite congregation of Utrecht in the Netherlands 1646-63. He held stern views concerning banning and intermarriage and in 1659 disagreed with his copreachers Willem van Maurik, Goris van Aldendorp, Arent van Heuven, Johan (Jan) Andries van Aken, and a number of deacons, who took a more moderate view. The troubles led to the excommunication of van Maurik and the other moderate preachers and to a division in the congregation, which was not healed until 1675. In these quarrels van Hooghveldt played an important but not very fair part. He denounced his antagonists to the city government, accusing them of Socinianism, and invoked the help of the Reformed pastors against them.

During this conflict van Hooghveldt published the following writings: *Korte doch Noodighe Waerschouwinghe* . . . (n.p., 1659); *Copye van de Beschulding* . . . (n.p., n.d.); *Kort verhael van 'tgene verhandelt is* . . . (Utrecht, 1661); *Kort bericht* . . . (Leeuwarden, 1669).

The Hoogvelt family is also found in Amsterdam; some of them served as deacons in the Lamist Mennonite congregation in the 17th and 18th centuries. (*DB* 1916, 152-88, *passim; Biogr. Wb.* IV, 266 f.) vpZ.

Hoogkarspel, a town in the Dutch province of North Holland, where Leenaert Bouwens baptized 35 persons in 1563-65. This large number indicates the existence of a Mennonite congregation in this town, of which, however, nothing is known and in any case dissolved before 1650. vpZ.

Hoogkerk, a town in the Dutch province of Groningen, five miles west of the city of Groningen. Here and in surrounding villages of Leegkerk, Dorkwerd, and Adorp the Dutch Mennonite Committee of Foreign Needs bought and rented some farms in 1711 for Swiss immigrants. vpZ.

Inv. Arch. Amst. I, 1097; J. Huizinga, *Stamboek . . . van Samuel Peter en Barbara Fry* (Groningen, 1890) 43 f., 57, 77 f., 105 f.

Hoogmade, van, a Dutch Mennonite family belonging to the Waterlander congregation at Leiden, Dutch province of South Holland. Gerrit Frankensz van Hoogmade, a merchant, in 1630 founded Bethlehem, a home for the aged, which he gave to the Waterlander congregation. His son Salomon Gerritsz van Hoogmade was a deacon of this congregation, as were some of his descendants. vpZ.

L. G. le Poole, *Bijdrage tot de kennis van . . . de Doopsgezinden . . . te Leiden* (Leiden, 1905) 50 *et passim.*

Hoogsaet (Hooghsaet), a Dutch Mennonite family of Amsterdam in the 17th century. Cornelis Claesz, at first a sailor and later a wood-dealer at Amsterdam, assumed the family name of his mother, who was a daughter of the Mennonite preacher Dirck Pietersz van Nierop (*q.v.*). His son Jan Cornelisz Hoogsaet, b. 1654 at Amsterdam, d. there about December 1733, was a painter and though he is not much known, he was very popular during his lifetime and received important assignments, e.g., he worked in the Amsterdam town hall (now Royal Palace). Catharina Hoogsaet, another grandchild of Dirck Pietersz van Nierop (daughter of Jan Dircksz Hoogsaet, who was a maker of compasses), married to Hendrik Jacobsz Rooleeuw, preacher of the Amsterdam Waterlander congregation 1626 until his death in 1656, was painted by Rembrandt in 1657.

Jan Ysbrandtsz Hoogsaet, a well-known shipbuilder, who was baptized in the Waterland congregation of Amsterdam in 1743, was likely also a grandson of Dirck Pietersz van Nierop. (*N.N.B.Wb.* VIII, 829 f.) vpZ.

Hoogstraten, Anthony Lalaing, Duke of (1480-1540), one of the confidential agents and co-operators of Charles V, was in 1522 appointed stadholder of the provinces of Holland and Zeeland, in 1528 also of Utrecht. Being an orthodox Catholic he was a violent opponent of heresies; he especially took severe measures to extirpate the Anabaptist movement at Amsterdam in 1534-35.   vdZ.

J. S. Theissen, *De regeering van Karel V in de Nederlanden* (1912) *passim;* Kühler, *Geschiedenis* I, 90, 134-36.

Hoogstraten, Dirk van (1596-1640) and his brother **Samuel,** two Dutch painters. Dirk was a grandson of François van Hoogstraten, who emigrated from Antwerp, Belgium, on account of his Mennonitism and settled in Dordrecht, Dutch province of South Holland, where Dirk was born. Dirk was one of the few painters who joined the Anabaptists. He was at first a silversmith, but after a journey through Germany he felt drawn to painting and engraving. Of his works only a few have been preserved. One of his pictures, "Mary and her Mother and the Christ child," is in the Rijksmuseum in Amsterdam. Dirk van Hoogstraten was the father and teacher of the better-known painter Samuel van Hoogstraten (born in 1627 at Dordrecht, d. there 1678), who was also a disciple of Rembrandt. On a long voyage in 1651-54 he visited Rome and also Vienna. In 1662-66 he was often in London. Dutch and foreign picture galleries possess pictures painted by him. He was the author of *Inleyding tot de hooge Schoole der Schilderkonst, anders de zichtbare werelt* (Rotterdam, 1678). He also was the author of a songbook and two tragedies. He was a member of the Dordrecht Mennonite congregation until he was banned for marrying outside the brotherhood. He then joined the Reformed Church. Frans van Hoogstraten, a son of Samuel, was a bookdealer in Rotterdam; he too left the Mennonites about 1660 to become a Roman Catholic. Jan and David van Hoogstraten, sons of Frans, who were respectively a bookdealer at Gouda and a medical doctor and senior master of a Latin school at Amsterdam, are known as poets.   vdZ.

W. Martin, *De Hollandsche Schilderkunst in de 17e Eeuw* II (3rd ed., Amsterdam, 1944) 299 f., *et passim;* G. Kalff, *Gesch. der Nederl. Letterkunde* (Groningen, 1910) IV, 483, 568, 570; *ML* I, 467 f.; II, 344; *N.N.B.Wb.* IV, 779; VIII, 831 f., 833, 836-38.

Hooley (Hoelly, Holly), a Swiss family name occurring among the Mennonites of America. Among the immigrants bearing this name were two brothers, Michael and Andreas Hooley, the latter having with him a son John, who arrived in Pennsylvania (Philadelphia) Nov. 3, 1750. Andreas was an Amish Mennonite, and located in what is now Lebanon County, Pa. His son John (1739-1805) married Catherine Blank, and lived for a time in Berks County, Pa., later in Mifflin County, Pa. He was an Amish Mennonite preacher. Some of his descendants later (1844) settled at West Liberty, Ohio. The Hooley family is now found in many states, chiefly Pennsylvania, Ohio, Indiana, Missouri, and Oregon. Among the ordained members of the family may be mentioned Joseph Y. Hooley, a deacon ordained in the

Forks, Ind., congregation (MC) in 1906, and Orvin H. Hooley, minister ordained in the Locust Grove, Mich., congregation (MC) in 1945. A German immigrant named Holly, who came from Hesse, served as one of the early ministers in the Tiskilwa, Ill., congregation (MC), possibly in the 1840's.   J.C.W.

Hoop, de, a Dutch Mennonite family, originally from Workum, province of Friesland, where they were lumber merchants and owners of a lumber mill called "de Hoop" (the hope), from which they took their family name. Jan Douwes de Hoop played a role in the "Patriot" disturbances about 1785 and later moved to Harlingen. He had been a deacon at Workum. His son Douwe (1800-30), was an artist of promise. Taedse Jakles de Hoop, b. at Workum 1753, also was a member of this family. He studied at the University of Franeker and the Amsterdam Mennonite Seminary and then served the congregation of West Zaandam Oude Huis for nearly 62 years, 1777- d. 1838.   vdZ.

DB 1905, 24 ff., 38, 41; S. Lootsma, *Het Nieuwe Huys* (Zaandam, 1937) 162; *Biogr. Wb.* IV, 269 f.; *Inv. Arch. Amst.* I, 1749 f.; *Hulde aan T. J. de Hoop, bij gelegenheid van het 50-jarig jubelfeest van deszelfs predikdienst* (Zaandam, 1827); a funeral sermon by B. van Geuns, *Herinneringen aan T. J. de Hoop* (Amsterdam, 1838).

Hoop Scheffer, Jacob Gijsbert de, b. Sept. 28, 1819, at the Hague, d. Dec. 31, 1894, at Amsterdam. His parents were not Mennonites, though his grandmother was Aagje Houttuyn (of Hoorn) of the well-known Mennonite Houttuyn (*q.v.*) family. From his fourth year, after his father had died, he was educated by a relative, Jacob de Hoop, whose family name was added to that of young Jacob Gijsbert, his father only bearing the name Johannes Scheffer. He studied theology at the universities of Leiden and Utrecht and the Mennonite Seminary at Amsterdam. In 1843 he was appointed ministerial candidate and soon answered a call of the Mennonite congregation of Hoorn to be its minister. He served at Hoorn 1843-46, Groningen 1846-49, and Amsterdam 1849-60. In this year he became a professor of the Amsterdam Mennonite Seminary, teaching exegesis of the Old and New Testaments, Mennonite history and homiletics. In 1877, when the Athenaeum (Latin School) of Amsterdam became a university, de Hoop Scheffer was also appointed professor of this university and called to teach church history. He resigned in 1890.

In his youth de Hoop Scheffer was much interested in Dutch mdieval literature and published a number of literary papers. In 1860 he took up his professorship with an address in Latin: *De providentia divina Teleiobaptistas Neerlandicos ab exitio vindicante* (The Divine Providence Protecting the Dutch Mennonites from Extinction), a revised translation of which was published in Dutch in 1861: *De Doopsgezinde broederschap in Nederland voor vervloeiing en ondergang bewaard.* His most important publication was a book published at Amsterdam in 1873, *Geschiedenis der Kerkhervorming in Nederland van Haar ontstaan tot 1531,* of which a German translation (by P. Gerlach) appeared in 1886: *Geschichte der Reformation in den Niederlanden von ihrem Beginn bis zum Jahre 1531.* De Hoop Scheffer's paper of 1881 on the Brownists (*q.v.*) at Amsterdam: *De*

Brownisten te Amsterdam gedurende de eerste tijd na hunne vestiging, in verband met het ontstaan van de Broederschap der Baptisten, is still of outstanding significance. This study, edited by W. E. Griffis, appeared in 1922 at Ithaca, N.Y., under the title *History of the Free Churches, called the Brownists, Pilgrim Fathers and Baptists in the Dutch Republic 1581-1701.* But the most important field of de Hoop Scheffer's study was the history of the Mennonites, especially of the early period of Dutch Anabaptism and Mennonitism, on which he published a large number of papers in the *Doopsgezinde Bijdragen;* the most extensive of these papers is the study on "'t Verbond der vier Steden" in *DB* 1893.

De Hoop Scheffer, who also was director of the Amsterdam Mennonite Library, compiled in two volumes a catalog of this library, which appeared in Amsterdam in 1885 and 1888. He also worked on the Mennonite archives and compiled a catalog, *Inventaris van Archiefstukken, berustende bij de Vereenigde Doopsgezinde Gemeente te Amsterdam* (2 volumes, Amsterdam, 1883-84).

In 1870-93 he was editor of the *Doopsgezinde Bijdragen.* In 1852-94 he was a member of the board of the A.D.S. He was a member of a number of learned associations, such as the Society of Dutch Literature and the Royal Dutch Academy of Science. His learning was recognized by the University of Leiden, which honored him with the degree of *Doctor Theologiae honoris causa* in 1870.

His grandson J. G. de Hoop Scheffer (b. 1884), a lawyer and bank manager at Amsterdam, was a member of the A.D.S. 1929-55; in 1929-51 he was its treasurer, and 1946-51 a member of the board of the Mennonite Seminary.   vDZ.

De Zondagsbode, Jan. 7, 14, 21, 1894; P. Feenstra Jr., *Wettig gekroond,* a memorial sermon preached in the Amsterdam Singel Church on Jan. 7, 1894; A. Winkler Prins, *Levensbericht van J. G. de Hoop Scheffer* (Leiden, 1894); H. C. Rogge, *Levensbericht van Jacob Gijsbert de Hoop Scheffer* (Amsterdam, 1895); *N.N.B.Wb.* III, 1129 f.; *DB* 1894, 1-10; 1901, 34 f.; *DJ* 1904, 21-29.

Hoorn, a Dutch city (1947 pop., 13,420, with 209 Mennonites) on the former Zuiderzee in the province of North Holland, is the seat of a Mennonite congregation. Little is known of its early history. No church records were kept until 1706, when the Waterlander congregation began one. Presumably there were advocates of adult baptism in Hoorn before 1550. The chronicler of Hoorn recorded that on June 7, 1535, five Anabaptists, including some women, were put to death on account of their faith. In 1542-43 the Anabaptists of Hoorn organized a congregation, which was visited by Menno Simons on his journey through North Holland. The noted elder Leenaert Bouwens (*q.v.*) baptized 25 persons in 1551-56. The congregation grew rapidly from the influx of refugees from the rest of Holland and Zeeland, among them many shippers and merchants. Leenaert Bouwens is said to have stopped here 12 times in 1556-67 and to have baptized a total of 165 young people.

In 1566, when the wave of iconoclasm broke out, the Catholic authorities passed very severe measures and limited the freedom of the Anabaptists in holding services. Unfortunately divisions were taking place here as elsewhere in the country. Tradition says that there were 13 different groups of Anabaptists in Hoorn. A deacon who was born in 1677 relates that at his time there were only six left. They had the following names: Frisian; Old Frisians or Jan Jacobsgezinden (after their founder Jan Jacobsz); Waterlanders (practiced footwashing); Flemish; High Germans; and "Plempschen" (probably so called because their church stood on a canal that had been filled [geplempst]; these "Plempschen" were also called the "Pieter Jansz Twisck gezinden" after their elder, P. J. Twisck, *q.v.*); the Rijnsburger Collegiants (who had much in common with the Anabaptists and whose meetings were also attended by many Mennonites); the name "Robbertgezinde" also occurs, whose founder in 1590 was a teacher of sailing and a printer of books in Hoorn.

Attempts to bring about a union had of course been made, at least by a few groups. In 1566 such an attempt was made by Jan Willemsz and Lubbert Gerritsz, elders of the Frisian and Flemish congregations. It failed and was repeated in 1576, again in vain. Union was not achieved until 1692.

In 1724 the Pieter Jansz Twisck group or Old Frisians united with the Frisians. From then on, there were only two congregations—a Waterlander and a Frisian—whose relations were friendly. In 1698 the Waterlanders invited the Frisians to cooperate in merging their services, so that the members of both groups could attend services in both churches. This suggestion was rejected, but was successfully repeated in 1706. In 1723 a Frisian elder had charge of the worship of the Waterlander congregation. An attempt made in 1727 to unite the congregations failed, although the elders of both congregations were holding baptismal and communion services in both churches. On Dec. 17, 1747, the two congregations were merged, with Jacob Fortuyn as preacher and Cornelis Ris as elder. Beginning in 1700 the membership had greatly receded, partly because the city was declining, and partly on account of indifference.

Although the Frisian and Waterlander congregations had united, they kept their own churches until 1800, when there was danger that the less used of the two would be used for military training purposes. The nonresistant Mennonites would have nothing to do with such a cause, and tore down their church. The remaining church, which belonged to the Frisians, stood until 1865, when it was replaced. The membership in 1931 was 200.

Formerly Hoorn was an important center of Mennonitism, both by its large membership and its influential leaders. Jan Willemsz and Lubbert Gerritsz of Hoorn were called to Harlingen (*q.v.*) in 1567 in a futile attempt to settle the conflict between the Frisian and the Flemish Mennonites; a large conference of North Holland leaders was held in Hoorn 1568, where the conduct of Dirk Philips, who had banned Willemsz and Gerritsz, was censured; in 1576 a number of elders and preachers of the Waterlanders met at Hoorn to make peace with the Frisians—a fruitless effort; a meeting of the principal leader of the Old Frisians, Pieter Jansz Twisck, elder at Hoorn, and some conservative Flemish leaders took place here in 1622.

The Waterlander congregation of Hoorn was more conservative than Waterlander congregations usually were. It laid much stress upon the confession and took measures to keep out of the pulpit the preachers from outside who sympathized with Collegiantism. After the congregation had united with the Frisians, its preachers published a booklet for the catechumens *Vraagen over de Grondwaarheden des Christelijken Geloofs,* . . . (Hoorn, 1768). Shortly before (1766) the elder of Hoorn, Cornelis Ris (*q.v.*), had produced a Confession, approved by the Zonist (*q.v.*) Mennonite Conference.

In the 18th century after the union of Waterlanders and Frisians the congregation was a member both of the Frisian Conference of North Holland and the Zonist Conference. Important preachers in that century were Pieter Beets, Peter Houttuyn, Willem Houttuyn, Adriaen Houttuyn, Jan Beets, Jacob Houttuyn, Cornelis Ris, and Jacob Spits, who was the last unsalaried minister of Hoorn. He died in 1810, at the age of 90 years.

Notwithstanding these prominent preachers the membership declined considerably, both because of the decline of Hoorn as a trade and navigation center and also because of the indifference of the Mennonites to their brotherhood in the 18th century; during this century many Mennonites transferred their membership to the Reformed Church.

About 1700 (figures of an earlier period were not available) the total number of (baptized) Mennonites in Hoorn was 500, in 1747, when the Frisians and Waterlanders united, it had decreased to 212 members, about 119 in 1840, 142 in 1900, 165 in 1954.

The ministers during these 150 years were Jacob van Zaanen 1805-13, Jacob Pol 1814-43, J. G. de Hoop Scheffer 1843-46, J. Kerbert 1846-67, J. H. Uiterwijk 1867-70, A. W. Wybrands 1870-82, J. W. van der Linden 1883-84, K. Gorter 1885-89, J. Pottinga 1890-93, M. Uiterdijk 1894-1932, B. P. de Vries 1933-48, W. Broer 1949- . Since 1933 the pastor of Hoorn has also served at Enkhuisen (*q.v.*).

In 1952 a group left the main body of the congregation because of the rigorous orthodoxy of Pastor Broer. This group, now 45 members, has made contacts with the Beemster congregation; it holds separate meetings and has a ladies' circle of its own. The Hoorn congregation, which was very wealthy in the 18th century, has since lost most of its means. Church activities now (1954) include a Sunday school for children since 1896, a ladies' circle, and a Bible group.   M.U., vDZ.

Inv. Arch. Amst. I, Nos. 131, 396, 480, 502, 531, 558, 708, 781, 868-72, 888, 1154, 1180, 1408, 1415; II, Nos. 1944-46; II, 2, Nos. 101-218; Blaupot t. C., *Holland* I and 11, *passim; DB* 1861, 161; 1867, 58, 66, 77-90; 1873, 52 f.; 1879, 94; 1882, 116 f.; 1883, 72; 1892, 103 note 1; 1893, 37 f., 58 f., 61 f., 78, 81; J. C. van Slee, *De Rijnsburger Collegianten* (Haarlem, 1896) 188-94; *ML* II, 344 f.

Hoorn, Den, a village of 550 inhabitants in the southern part of the island Texel in the Dutch province of North Holland. On the island the Anabaptist movement found early entry (*ca.* 1534). Leenaert Bouwens (*q.v.*) visited the island twice (1560). The martyr Jan Gerritsz (*q.v.*) and Elder Simon Fijts (*q.v.*) are also known,

In 1709 the congregation at Hoorn dissolved its union with Burg, Waal, and Oosterend. It has a church record, begun in 1753 by the preacher Johannes Cuperus (*q.v.*). From 1709 to 1922 it existed as an independent congregation. In the latter year it joined the Helder (*q.v.*) congregation in the engagement of a minister. This union lasted until 1941. Then the congregation of den Hoorn united with that of Burg on the island of Texel, all Mennonites of this island now belonging to one congregation, called that of Texel (*q.v.*).

In the 16-17th century the congregation of den Hoorn belonged to the Waterlander branch of the Mennonites. Den Hoorn has a meetinghouse of 1850; an organ was acquired in 1896. The membership was always small: 42 baptized members in 1861; 42 in 1900; 43 in 1940.

The last minister of the independent congregation was R. Kuperus (1919-20). From 1922 to 1941 it was served by the pastor of den Helder. (*Inv. Arch. Amst.* II, Nos. 1947-76; *DB* 1873, 140-58 *passim; ML* II, 345.)   J.Y., vDZ.

Hoorn, Den, a village in the Dutch province of Groningen, formerly the seat of a Mennonite congregation of the Flemish branch. Of the origin and history of this congregation there is little information. In 1717 the congregation was badly hit by a flood of the North Sea, in which many were drowned in this part of the province, and many farms were destroyed, as well as the meetinghouse of Den Hoorn.

About 1770 the congregation numbered 100 souls, about 50 baptized members, meeting in a plain meetinghouse erected in 1718. In 1792 its last preacher died, its membership decreased, and in 1816 the congregation united with that of Rasquert (*q.v.*) and Obergum (*q.v.*), forming the congregation of Mensingeweer (*q.v.*). After the building of a new meetinghouse at Mensingeweer in 1819, services at Den Hoorn were discontinued and the old meetinghouse was razed.   vDZ.

Inv. Arch. Amst. II, Nos. 1841, 1977-79; Blaupot t. C., *Groningen* I, 149, 202 f.; *DB* 1906, 46.

Hoorn, van, a Dutch Mennonite family, from the end of the 17th century, found in the northeastern part of the province of Groningen, originally all belonging to the Groningen Old Flemish and numerously found among the membership of the congregation of Zijldijk, Middelstum, and Leermens. In the 19th century they spread all over the Netherlands.

Another van Hoorn family, not related to the former, is found at Leer, East Friesland, Germany. This family, according to a family tradition, moved to East Friesland in the 16th century from Hoorn in the Dutch province of North Holland because of religious persecution. Among them were a large number of deacons of the Mennonite congregations of Leer and Emden. They became related with other Mennonite families like Vissering, Rahusen, Zytsema, and Alring. The van Hoorns were usually engaged in business; e.g., the Reinhard van Hoorn Sons tobacco business at Leer. Apparently Jacob van Hoorn, preacher of the Mennonite congregation of

Burtscheid-Maastricht ?-1710 and the Amsterdam Lamist congregation 1710-28, belonged to neither of these families. vdZ.

Hoornbeek, Johannes (1617-66), a Dutch Reformed theologian, appointed professor of theology at the University of Utrecht in 1644, and at Leiden in 1654. Among his numerous writings is the stately compendium of five volumes, which also touches upon the Mennonites, *Summae controversiarum religionis* (Utrecht, 1658). Among the writers opposing Anabaptism he has received considerable recognition. vdZ.

Biogr. Wb. IV, 277-86; BRN VII, 95; Kühler, Geschiedenis II, 14; DB 1883, 9; ML II, 345.

Hoorns Liedt-boeck, *vergadert uyt verscheyden gedruckte boecken waer by ghevoeght syn eenighe nieuwe Liedekens,* a Dutch hymnary printed by Isaac Willemsz and published by Zacharias Cornelisz, both at Hoorn. Only one edition, that of 1630, is known. It contains 474 pages and 214 hymns in alphabetical order without music. The hymns, as is indicated, could be sung to familiar melodies of both secular songs and hymns. vdZ.

Hoornsche Gesanghboeck, a name often used for a Dutch Mennonite hymnal, *Het Boeck der Ghesangen* (q.v.), printed at Hoorn in 1618.

Hoosen (Hoozen, Hoose, Hose), a Mennonite family, which according to tradition emigrated in the 17th century from Switzerland to Giethoorn, in the Dutch province of Overijssel. Some of the members served as preachers and elders of the Danzig Old Flemish congregation of Giethoorn ("Noord"), i.e., Jan Hoosen 1744-69(?), and both his sons, Gerrit Jans Hoosen 1796(?)-1812(?) and Pieter Jans Hoosen about 1802-?. Jan Jansz. Hoosen of Giethoorn, who is not the same person as the foregoing elder of Giethoorn, but likely also a son, was elder of the Swiss emigrant congregation at Kampen about 1805-22. He was a shoemaker, was b. 1758 at Giethoorn, died there 1834. vdZ.

J. Huizinga, Stamboek . . . van Samuel Peter and Barbara Fry (Groningen, 1890) 67; DB 1878, 28; 1880, 103 f.; several issues of Naamlijsten; DB 1881, 103 f.

Hoover (Hover, Hoober, Huber, Huver, Hueber), a Swiss family name found among the Mennonites of Germany and America. A Swiss Anabaptist named Ulrich Huber was executed in 1538, and Hans Huber, a German Anabaptist, was put to death in 1542 at Wasserburg on the Inn. The Hutterite Chronicle contains the martyr record of Wolfgang Hueber, who was executed in Bavaria in 1559. A number of Huebers are mentioned in the Chronicle; for example, Caspar Hueber who was ordained as a preacher in 1557.

More than 50 Hubers emigrated to America before the Revolutionary War, who represented at least four faiths: Mennonite, Lutheran, German Reformed, and Moravian. The ancestor of many of the Mennonite Hoovers was the immigrant Hans Huber (ca. 1670-1750), a Swiss who was married to Margaret Koch. After living for a period in the Palatinate he came to America in 1710 or soon

thereafter and settled at Mill Creek, Lancaster Co., Pa. Today the Hoover family is spread rather widely in the United States and Ontario. More than a dozen Hoovers have been ordained in the Mennonite Conference of Ontario (MC), and a smaller number in Indiana (MC). Bishop Martin Hoover (MC) settled in Elkhart Co., Ind., in 1845, four years before his death; he had immigrated from Europe and had lived in Lancaster Co., Pa., Markham, Ont., and Ohio. Noah S. Hoover (MC) served long as a deacon in the Yellow Creek, Ind., congregation 1887-d.1913. The name Hoover also occurs among the Brethren in Christ; their second Overseer in the Indiana District was a Martin Hoover who evidently served in the second half of the 19th century. Paul Hoover is a minister of the Old Order Mennonites (Wisler) near Goshen, Ind. J.C.W.

Harry M. Hoover, The Huber-Hoover Family History (Scottdale, 1928).

Hope, a Dutch family. A number of members of this family of bankers and wholesale dealers, which came from England to the Netherlands and settled at Rotterdam, belonged to the Mennonite Church. The first member of the Hope family in Rotterdam was Archibald Hope (d. ca. 1743), who was married to Anna Claus. He may have moved to Rotterdam about 1680. He soon became very prosperous; in 1716 he built the country seat Lindenhof at Kralingen near Rotterdam. By the last decade of the 17th century he was conducting an important trade to England, Ireland, and America. Both he and his wife were members of the Mennonite congregation. His son Isaac Hope (d. 1767) was baptized in 1729 and was a deacon of the Rotterdam congregation 1735-39; his brother Zachary (d. 1770) was baptized in 1733, and served 1739-43, and another brother, James, was deacon 1751-55. In 1735 Archibald Hope and his son Isaac transported 180 Swiss emigrants (probably Mennonites) to Pennsylvania, and again and again they carried emigrants to the English colonies in America, e.g., 3,000 persons in 1753, and 4,000 emigrants from the Palatinate in 1765. Among those there may also have been a number of Mennonites. The Hopes were friends of the Bisschop (q.v.) family of Rotterdam; after the death of Jan Bisschop in 1771, Jan Hope inherited the painted portraits of the Bisschop brothers, Archibald Hope, Jr., the rich collection of coins, while Adriaan and Jan Hope bought the considerable collection of paintings gathered by the Bisschops. During the 18th century some of the Hopes moved to Amsterdam. They were—in contrast to most Mennonites, who were Patriots (q.v.)—at the close of the 18th century nearly all convinced followers of the Prince of Orange. vdZ.

Hope Rescue Mission, the first rescue mission operated by the Mennonite Board of Missions and Charities (MC), opened on Feb. 28, 1954, at 530-32 South Michigan Street, South Bend, Ind., because of the great need in that city. Men from surrounding churches donated over 1,750 man-hours of labor to clean and renovate a dilapidated tavern and gambling hall, transforming it into one of the most attractive rescue missions in the country.

During the first month an evening service was held on five nights of the week. Today one public service and two classes are conducted daily in the mission. Thirty different church groups participate in the evening services. The facilities consist of a chapel seating 125, prayer room, dining room, kitchen, laundry, shower rooms, housing facilities for 45 transient men and women, and quarters for staff workers. The mission serves two meals daily to transients, distributes clothing daily, and operates a medical clinic, a barber shop, and an employment service.   T. E. Sch.

Hopedale Mennonite Church (MC), approximately 2½ miles southeast of Hopedale, Tazewell Co., Ill., a member of the Illinois Conference, was originally named the "Delavan Prairie Church." Preceding the merging of the Amish with the Mennonites of the state, it was known as the Hopedale Amish-Mennonite Church and by the general public as the German Church. Some of the first settlers were Joe Litwiller 1854; Peter and Christian Nafziger 1856, Christ Slagel 1857, David Springer 1858, Simon Bechler 1862, and Christ Birky 1862. Services were held every two weeks in the homes in 1854-76. The first church building was erected two miles southeast of Hopedale in 1876. Additions to the church were built in 1884 and 1906. A new building, still in use, with a seating capacity of 450, was erected in 1926.

Christian Nafziger (1819-99) was ordained as the first minister in 1856 and as bishop in 1860. John C. Birky served as bishop 1896-1920, Samuel Gerber 1920-25, and Simon Litwiller 1925-56. Others who have served as ministers are Joseph Litwiller, Simon Bechler, William Unzicker, Joseph Hochstetler, J. Nafziger, Noah Augsburger, Andrew Birkey, Joseph Birky, Daniel Grieser, J. Birkey, John Egli, Joseph Egli, Joseph Springer, Daniel Nafziger, Ben Springer, and Ivan Kauffmann, who was installed as pastor in 1956. The membership in 1956 was 370. The first Sunday-school services were held in 1885 and were conducted in German.   I.K.

H. F. Weber, *Centennial History of the Mennonites of Illinois* (Goshen, 1931).

Hopefield (Hoffnungsfeld) Mennonite Church (GCM), located four miles west of Moundridge, McPherson Co., Kan., a member of the Western District Conference, is one of the oldest Mennonite churches in Kansas. It was founded in October 1874 under the leadership of Elder Jacob Stucky (*q.v.*), by a group of 64 Swiss Mennonite families who had emigrated as a congregation from Volhynia, Russia, in August 1874. The congregation adopted the name Hoffnungsfeld but in 1880 it was chartered as the Hopefield Society of the Mennonite Church. Eight churches in central Kansas have been organized wholly or in part by members and descendants from the original Hopefield congregation. The original and present frame structure was built in 1882. Recently the building has been completely remodeled and redecorated. The 1953 membership was 100, with Archie Kliewer as pastor.
                                                 D.D.S.

Hopewell Mennonite Church (MC), located near Hubbard, Marion Co., Ore., a member of the Pacific Coast Conference, was organized in the fall of 1899 by George R. Brunk, a minister of the Kansas-Nebraska Conference. J. D. Mishler, then of Eugene, Ore., was the first bishop. The membership in 1953 was 56. The present meetinghouse, the second built on the same site, is a frame structure with a seating capacity of 200. Ministers serving this congregation are N. L. Hershberger, James Bucher, and Jacob Roth; O. W. King is the deacon.
                                                 O.W.K.

Hopewell Mennonite Church (MC), located in the village of Kouts, Porter Co., Ind., is a member of the Indiana-Michigan Conference. The original Mennonite settlers in this area came largely from Hopedale, Ill., and Nebraska, beginning in 1916. They built their first meetinghouse in 1919, just south of the village, and in 1952 a new house of worship at the northern edge of the village. The most outstanding leader of the church was Bishop Jacob Z. Birky (1855-1926), who was born at Morton, Ill., and ordained preacher in Nebraska in 1895, and bishop in 1902. He located at Kouts, Ind., in 1920. He was a brother of Bishop John C. Birky (1849-1920) of Hopedale, Ill. The membership in 1954 was 207, pastor Samuel S. Miller.
                                                 J.C.W.

Hopi, a tribe of less than 4,000 Pueblo Indians inhabiting about 986 square miles of arid land in the northern Arizona highland, which was until the end of the 19th century less touched by contemporary culture than the larger tribes. Its customs and morals, its culture and religion were therefore preserved in their original form. The Hopi live in seven villages in northeastern Arizona on the elevations between the Rio Colorado and the Colorado Chiquito on the same area on which the Spanish Conquistadores found their ancestors in 1539. Even at that time their villages, consisting of stone houses, were apparently very old. In 1893 the General Conference Mennonites opened mission work among the Hopi, when H. R. Voth (*q.v.*) settled in Oraibi, the largest of the villages, having at that time a population of about 1,000. The work was difficult, but was continued with persistence and eventual success. A second mission station was opened in Moencopi (*q.v.*) and a third one in Hotevilla (*q.v.*), which had been established in 1906 by the Hopi inhabitants of Oraibi. During 60 years of missions (1893-1953) about 150 Hopis were baptized.

One of the early difficulties was the lack of ability to communicate, since there were no written materials to facilitate learning the Hopi language. The missionaries, however, produced some literature, including a Bible history and a translation of the Gospels. The three stations had a combined membership of some 50 in 1931.   Hege.

J. B. Epp, *Bible History in the Hopi Indian Language* (Los Angeles, 1916); H. R. Voth, *The Oraibi Powamu Ceremony* (Field Museum of Natural History, Anthropological Series III, 1901); *idem, Traditions of the Hopi* (Field Museum of Natural History, Anthropological Series VIII, 1-319, 1905); Laura Thompson, *Culture in*

Crisis, A Study of the Hopi Indians (New York, 1950); *ML* II, 345 f.

Höppner, Jakob, appointed with Johann Bartsch (*q.v.*) as a deputy of the West Prussian Mennonites; they traveled to Russia in the fall of 1786 to investigate the offer for colonization made by Catherine II. Under very difficult circumstances they performed their task. The outcome was the emigration to Russia beginning in 1788. Their services were miserably rewarded. When the emigrants reached the colonization site at Chortitza, all the resentment of the disappointed settlers, who had expected better land, was heaped upon Höppner and Bartsch. Höppner was expelled from the Flemish congregation. He was accused of misappropriation of funds and imprisoned in Ekaterinoslav, and was to be deported to Siberia. When Emperor Paul I died and was succeeded by Alexander I, Höppner was pardoned and released after a year's imprisonment. Meanwhile his property had been sold. Finally he was received into the Frisian church at Kronsweide, where he quietly spent the last years of his life. After his death a beautiful monument was erected in his honor on the island of Chortitza. (Friesen, *Brüderschaft,* 72, 95 ff.; *Unser Blatt* I, 205 ff.; *ML* II, 346.) D.H.E.

Höppner, Jakob, b. Aug. 10, 1850, on Chortitza Island, South Russia, d. Nov. 16, 1936, at Winkler, Man. He was the great-grandson of the Jakob Höppner (*q.v.*) who was sent to Russia by the Danzig Mennonites to inspect the land. He was married to Aganetha Dück in 1873. In 1876 he emigrated to Manitoba, where he was elected minister of the Bergthal Mennonite Church (*q.v.*). In 1887 he was ordained minister and on April 14, 1903, he was ordained elder. C.K.

J. G. Rempel, *Fünfzig Jahre Konferenzbestrebungen, 1902-1952* I (Steinbach, 1954) 15.

Horb, a town (pop. 2,800) of Württemberg, Germany, situated on the Neckar, had a tempestuous period in the early decades of the Reformation. From December 1522, to the beginning of March 1523, Karsthans, who was probably Johann Murer (Maurer), a native of Horb, worked here for the new (Lutheran) faith as a lay preacher and won some adherents. In addition, the Protestant schoolteacher, Aegidius Krautwasser, praised by Joh. Eberlin as an exponent of the Gospel, had come to Horb from Stuttgart. A canon of the *Heiligkreuzstift,* Konrad Starzler, had expressed his Protestant convictions in three pamphlets, but later recanted.

Concerning the imprisoned Karsthans, of whom he expected constancy in the faith, Sebastian Lotzer (*q.v.*), a furrier and a native of Horb, wrote from Memmingen in the middle of March 1523: *Ain hailsame Ermanung an die ynwoner zu Horw, das sy bestendig belyben an dem hailigen wort gottes mit anzaigung der göttlichen hailigen geschrift.* He admonished his countrymen that he who had two coats should sell one and buy a New Testament. Then he examined fasting, holy days, indulgences, and the worship of the saints in agreement with Luther's interpretation. When his father wrote him that his pamphlets had aroused much antagonism among the populace, he wrote a second pamphlet entitled *Ain christlicher sendbrief, darin angezaigt wirt, ds die layen macht und recht haben von dem hailigen wort gots reden, leren und schreiben . . .* (1523). He points his father to Christ as the Saviour, distinguishes clearly between the church faith and justifying faith, which is proved by good works. Against the assertion of his opponents that the layman must not concern himself with the Scriptures because he does not understand them, he cites the promise: Every one that asketh receiveth; and he that seeketh findeth. Then in opposition to the natural man's fear of suffering he demands open confession of faith, even if it is dangerous. Waiting for a decision of council is superfluous for him who hears the Word of God and buys a New Testament; that is sufficient council. The government does not approve of laymen's discussing and writing on sacred subjects. Lotzer's writings must have made considerable impression on Horb, for on Sept. 30, 1523, the Hofrat in Innsbruck reported to Archduke Ferdinand that the Protestant movement was making rapid strides in Horb.

In the spring of 1526 Wilhelm Reublin (*q.v.*), of Rottenburg, came to Lotzer's home town and won many friends for the Anabaptists. In Horb, too, he found many adherents; he baptized in 25 homes. Ludwig Scheurer of Reutlingen was baptized at a well in a field near the Neuneckerhalde, dipping water with his hands and pouring it on Scheurer's head. Then he called his friend Michael Sattler (*q.v.*) from Strasbourg to Horb.

In the middle of February the government became aware of the Anabaptists. Reublin escaped to Reutlingen and to Esslingen. But his wife, Sattler and his wife, Veit Feringer, and Matthias Hiller, a furrier of St. Gall, were seized at the end of February. Because the authorities feared that the multitude of adherents might create a disturbance, the prisoners were taken to Binsdorf. After eleven weeks of imprisonment Sattler, Feringer, and Hiller were taken to Rottenburg with an escort of 56 foot soldiers. Sattler died at the stake there on May 21, 1527; three of his adherents including Hiller were beheaded, and his wife was drowned in the Neckar on the next day; Feringer had recanted, but withdrew his recantation and was held thirteen and one-half years imprisoned in Schömberg. Reublin's wife and child lay in prison in Ihlingen and Horb.

On May 31, 1527, Capito (*q.v.*) wrote to the council in Horb, that they should defend the prisoners against the Austrian government; though they erred in some points they were not blasphemers whom the government had to punish, unless it was blasphemy to avoid gambling, excessive drinking and eating, adultery, war, killing, slander of one's neighbor, and living according to the lusts of the flesh. At the same time he wrote to the prisoners, urging them to desist from their error concerning the oath, holding government office, and the rejection of force, but comforted them in their suffering and encouraged them to pray for their enemies and to lose all hate for them. These letters of Capito's are examples of the most beautiful testimonials of the Christian spirit (Baum, *Capito,* 371; Hulshof, *Geschiedenis,* 66 ff.).

Nowhere is there a suggestion that Reublin showed any concern for his wife; but on June 19, 1527, Zürich sent a request to the authorities of Horb on behalf of their fellow citizen Adelheid Lehmann. The letter played up her foolish simplicity; she was only a poor woman who had been misled by her husband. The Austrian government had no inkling that the woman in question was Reublin's wife. On June 21 the Horb authorities replied that the woman was in the prison of the prince and out of their jurisdiction (Egli, *Akten.* pp. 210 ff.). Many petitions for clemency were presented. On June 14 the government gave the information that those who had escaped must surrender unconditionally and could not sell their possessions. At the same time an attempt was made to lure them home; for it was hoped that with their help the Anabaptist leaders might be betrayed into government hands. They even promised that any who delivered Bällin and Küeffer to the authorities would be unconditionally pardoned.

On July 17 court was again held in Horb, guarded by 90 foot soldiers. Twenty-four men and women were accused of Anabaptist adherence. All of them were led to recant. On the market place a framework was set up, and there the defendants had to swear before a notary and trustworthy witnesses that they would abandon their error and faithfully and zealously adhere to the holy Christian Church and its regulations to the end of their lives. On the next seven Sundays they were to gather at the altar at the early Mass, with bare feet, bare heads, and loose hair, in gray wool apparel on which the baptismal font was painted in white, and in the customary procession walk around the church before the cross. As a sign of penitence they had to carry in their left hands a rod, in their right a lighted candle, and after the procession kneel before the altar; there they should receive absolution from the priest with three blows, and remain on their knees until the end of the Mass. Their gray clothing they must wear a year and a day. On certain days they must go to the confessional and to communion. For the rest of their life they must avoid all public and private society in or outside the houses, could carry no weapons but a broken bread knife. Finally they could not without permission leave the town of Horb. The fine levied upon them was heavy.

That which the Anabaptists could be compelled to yield to was merely the ceremony of the church and submission to the priest. A clear confession of their error, a renewed love for the church, whose service was hard, could not be secured by compulsion. We do not hear that the clergy were requested to win their spirits by indoctrination.

Many Anabaptists had fled from Horb, especially to Strasbourg. Jörg Lederlin, whom Reublin had baptized, was there. In his house the Anabaptists met. He rejected communion, because Christ had not commanded that His example be followed. Hans Frisch of Horb was the treasurer of the Ana-

baptists in Strasbourg; Thomas Schomer's property was confiscated; but his clever mother had all his movable goods taken to her house at night and sent on to Strasbourg. In Switzerland a Hans from Horb appears as an Anabaptist (Egli, *Wiedertäufer in Zürich,* 88).

The government had indeed been victorious over the Protestant and Anabaptist movement; but it could not be sure that no new opponents of the old church would appear, and had to observe that a wildness took possession of the populace, and murder increased, while the Anabaptists in the Hohenberg could not be charged with wrongdoing, deceit, thievery, drunkenness, or vice.   G.Bo.

E. Egli, *Die Züricher Wiedertäufer zur Ref.-Zeit* (Zürich, 1878); *TA Zürich;* A. Hulshof, *Geschiedenis van de Doopsgezinden te Straatsburg* ... (Amsterdam, 1905); *Bl. f. württemb. Kirchengesch.,* 1887, 9 ff., 25 ff., 89 ff.; 1888, 65; 1889, 83; 1892, 82, 90; *ML* II, 346-48.

Horn, Den, a hamlet in the Dutch province of Groningen, seat of a Mennonite congregation, formerly also called Zuidhorn (as in *Naamlijst*). Originally the congregation, which existed already in the early part of the 17th century, but of whose history nothing is known, belonged to the Flemish branch. Until 1829 it was served by untrained and also unsalaried preachers; the first preacher to receive a small salary was the untrained preacher Jan Geerts, serving here until 1788; the last untrained minister was Jan Tjerks Vermanje, serving 1799-1829. During his ministry the number of members increased from about 50 to 90. The first minister here who had been trained at the Amsterdam Mennonite Seminary, serving in 1835-44, was Jacob Dirks Huizinga (*q.v.*). A new meetinghouse was built in 1861, an organ was not acquired until 1906. Ministers serving during the last half century are F. F. Milatz 1905-10, H. Schuurmans 1910-12, J. A. P. Bijl 1914-27, R. Boersma 1928-36, J. S. Postma 1936-40, and S. J. Verveld 1940- . The membership, numbering 95 in 1861, decreased to 53 in 1954. There is a ladies' circle and a youth group.   vDZ.

Blaupot t. C., *Groningen* I, 206, 238; *Inv. Arch. Amst.* II, No. 1842; *Naamlijst* 1829, 67; *DB* 1861, 149 f.; 1901, 122; 1906, 46, 195; *De Zondagsbode* III, No. 30 (May 25, 1890).

Horn, Georg H. (1620-70), a German historian, professor of history at the University of Leiden in Holland, the author of the book, *Historia ecclesiastica et politica* (Leipzig, 1677, new revised edition, Frankfurt, 1679), a book of 442 pages dedicated to Karl Ludwig, the Palatine elector. In compressed form it deals with the history of the church from the creation of the world to the 17th century. The author's statements about the Anabaptists, whom he derives from Thomas Müntzer, do not differ from the contemporary and traditional presentation. The book is of no historical importance. What he has to say about the Anabaptists in England is more extensive and is more deserving of consideration, even though he offers little that is new even here. (*ML* II, 348.)   Neff.

Hornbach. In the *Naamlijst* of 1769-75 is found a congregation Freudenberg-Hornbach-Kirchheimerhof. This congregation was in the duchy of Zweibrücken, Germany. Joseph Schnebele, preacher 1762-67, was elder since 1767; preachers were Johannes Lehman from 1745, Rudolph Schmidt from 1755, and Peter Böer also from 1755. In the *Naamlijst* of 1780 and following this congregation is not found any more.   vdZ.

Horning Mennonites. Following a dispute over the introduction of a pulpit in place of the traditional preachers' table at the Lichty meetinghouse, Weaverland circuit, Lancaster Conference (MC), Lancaster Co., Pa., in 1889, Jonas Martin led a conservative schism in October 1893, popularly called "Martinites." This group in 1926 suffered another schism under Bishop Joseph Wenger, who led a still more conservative faction, commonly called "Wengerites." The Martinite group have had Moses Horning as their bishop since 1914, and since 1926 have been popularly called "Horning people," although their official name is Weaverland Conference of Old Order Mennonites. Their membership (1955) numbers 1,710, with congregations at Weaverland, Groffdale, Martindale, Bowmansville, Churchtown, Pequea, Meadow Valley, and Springville in Lancaster County; Fairview and Myerstown in Lebanon County; and Witmer and Stony Brook in York County. About half of their services are still conducted in German. They have no missions, Sunday schools, summer Bible schools, nor youth activities. They have automobiles, but paint the bumpers black and are therefore sometimes termed the "Black Bumpers." They are chiefly farmers and live mostly in the northeast sector of Lancaster County. The present bishops are Moses Horning, Joseph Hostetter, and Joseph O. Weaver. The conference also includes (1953) eleven ministers and eight deacons.

This group has joined with the 1889 Martinite division of Waterloo County and elsewhere in Ontario and the Wisler division of 1873 in Elkhart Co., Ind., to form the Old Order Mennonites (*q.v.*). The Old Order church is found elsewhere in Markham Twp., Ont., Dayton, Va., Wayne County and Mahoning County, Ohio, numbering 5,277 baptized members all told. It is not to be confused with the Old Order Amish Mennonites. It does not require beards and hooks and eyes and uses meetinghouses.   I.D.L.

Horozanna wielka (i.e., Great Horozanna), a Ruthenian village in the district of Rudki, about 22 miles south of Lemberg in Galicia. In 1850 some Mennonites from the first settlements at Einsiedel, Falkenstein, and Rosenberg, whose names were Bergthold, Ewy, Rupp, and Schmidt, bought about 800 acres of the Horozonna estate and settled there on individual farms with their families. According to a note in the oldest church record of the Galician Mennonites, the first prayer meeting was held in Horozanna on April 25, 1852. In 1857 the settlers called as their preacher Johannes van der Smissen, and formed a subsidiary congregation. It did not exist long, however, for the farms were sold one by one and the families migrated to other localities in Galicia or to America. In 1931 only one Mennonite family was living in Horozanna, the Ewy family, who belonged to the Kiernica-Lemberg Mennonite Church. (*ML* II, 348.)   J.Ru.

Horqueta is the name of a town in East Paraguay about 25 miles east of the city of Concepcion which is located on the Paraguay River approximately 200 miles north of Asuncion. A narrow-gauge railroad, one of the few railroads in Paraguay, operates from Concepcion through Horqueta to a few miles beyond. Hardly had the Russian Mennonites settled in the Fernheim colony in the Chaco when, for various reasons, some became dissatisfied and began to cast about for other places to which they might move. Early in 1931 a committee composed of Gerhard Isaak and a certain Langemann investigated several areas in East Paraguay including Horqueta where a few German-speaking families were already settled. Langemann recommended moving to Horqueta, but Isaak advised against it. In 1932 a few families, including Langemann's, moved to Horqueta and started a new Mennonite colony. Others followed in the next few years until about 20 families were located there. The group did not prosper, however. In addition to having some difficulties with Paraguayan neighbors, there was a lack of unity in the colony. Gradually families began moving away —some back to the Chaco, some to the newly formed Friesland colony, a few to near-by Concepcion, and a few to Asuncion. The last family moved away in 1945.   W.H.S.

Fr. Kliewer, *Die Deutsche Volksgruppe in Paraguay: Eine siedlungsgeschichtliche, volkskundliche und volkspolitische Untersuchung* (Hamburg, 1941).

Horsch, a South German (Badischer Verband) family, presumably of Swiss origin, which has produced many preachers. The earliest record of the name is that of Hans Horsch in the Büchelhof congregation near Wimpfen in 1731 (Müller, *Berner Täufer*). In the Mennonite census lists of the Palatinate Joseph Horsch appears at Mauer near Heidelberg 1738-59 and a Jakob Horsch at Schatthausen near Heidelberg in 1759. One branch of the family settled near Giebelstadt, Bavaria, about 1810, from which descended four elders in succession (with one break): Jacob (d. 1873), Jakob (d. 1888), Michael (d. 1949), Hellmut (still living). Another branch continued at Hasselbach and elsewhere in Baden. In 1956 a Johannes Horsch was preacher in Hasselbach and David Horsch was preacher at Bretten. David Horsch of Lamprechtshof near Durlach was long a preacher of the Hahn'sche Mennonites there, and a cofounder of the Bibelheim Thomashof. Michael Horsch (1872-1941), who came to America in 1887, was for over 40 years a minister in the General Conference Mennonite Church and an active general leader, for some years field secretary of the conference. John Horsch (1867-1941), who came to the United States in 1887, was a well-known writer and historian in the Mennonite Church (MC), resident at Scottdale, Pa., 1908-41.
                                                     H.S.B.

Horsch, John (1867-1941), a leading historian and writer of the Mennonite Church (MC) in America, was born in Giebelstadt near Würzburg, Germany, on Dec. 18, 1867, the fourth of nine children born to Elder Jacob Horsch and his wife Barbara Landes; m. Christine Funck of Neipperg near Heilbronn, Württemberg; was the father of four children—Elizabeth (Mrs. H. S. Bender), Walter, Menno, and Paul; died Oct. 7, 1941, at his longtime home at Scottdale, Pa. Intended by his father to be a farmer he studied two years at the Bavarian State Agricultural School at Würzburg, securing the diploma in 1886. Having meanwhile come to accept the full nonresistant position he emigrated to America to avoid military service, arriving in New York Jan. 3, 1887.

January to May 1887 Horsch spent at Halstead, Kan., attending the Indian Mission School conducted by Christian Krehbiel (to learn English), then moved to Elkhart to enter the employ of John F. Funk in the Mennonite Publishing Co., where 1887-95, with intermittent absence to attend several colleges, he did much of the editorial work on the *Herold der Wahrheit,* the *Familien-Kalender,* and the German Sunday-school quarterlies. This was the beginning of a long career of 55 years of editorial work, historical research, and historical and theological writing. During these eight years at Elkhart he also collected a large Mennonite historical library, and established a lifelong connection with the Hutterites in South Dakota.

Between 1888 and 1898 Horsch spent almost four years in study in various colleges and universities (Evangelical Theol. Seminary at Naperville, Ill., Valparaiso University at Valparaiso, Ind., Baldwin-Wallace College at Berea, Ohio, and the University of Wisconsin, Madison, Wis.). In 1898-1900 he engaged in a private publishing business at Elkhart, publishing the monthly *Farm und Haus* (first number September 1898). In 1900-8 he was associated with J. A. Sprunger (*q.v.*), the owner and operator of the Light and Hope Publishing Co., at Berne, Ind., Cleveland, Ohio, and Birmingham, Ohio. Sprunger, formerly a minister in the Berne Mennonite (GCM) Church, was at this time loosely affiliated with the Missionary Church Association. In May 1908 Horsch moved to Scottdale, where he served the Mennonite Publishing House as German editor of several publications and carried on private research and writing in Mennonite history and the theological field until his death in 1941.

The awakening of John Horsch's historical interest was the result of the intellectual movements in the Mennonite Church in Germany during his youth. His father had a not inconsequential library and subscribed to the two German Mennonite periodicals: the *Mennonitische Blätter* (*q.v.*) and the *Gemeindeblatt der Mennoniten* (*q.v.*), both of which carried many historical articles in the 1880's particularly 1885-86. The first adequate Mennonite history in German had just appeared in 1884, written by Anna Brons (*q.v.*). But the decisive influence on Horsch's interest in Mennonite history was the archivist and historian Ludwig

Keller (*q.v.*), with whom he continued in close touch for ten years (1885-95), even after his emigration to America, and who directly influenced him to dedicate his life to a revival of the ancient Anabaptist principles in the Mennonite brotherhood, in spite of the fact that Keller considered the principle of nonresistance a handicap to be discarded. Keller had begun to publish his books on Anabaptist history in 1880 with a book on the Münsterites, followed by his biography of Hans Denk in 1882, and was an almost constant contributor to the *Mennonitische Blätter.*

In his early period in America, from 20 to 30 years of age, Horsch had not altogether found himself. During this period he did publish (1890) his valuable brief history of the Mennonites in German, *Kurzgefasste Geschichte der Mennoniten-Gemeinden* as well as his English booklet, *The Mennonites, Their History, Faith, and Practice* (1893), in addition to countless periodical articles. But his program of reviving the church through writing was also partially frustrated due to three factors: (1) his lack of intimate knowledge of the American Mennonite Church, its leadership, and its problems; (2) his want of a complete and independent mastery of Anabaptist history and theology and the full inner meaning of its program, due partly to the dominance of Keller's unbalanced interpretation; and (3) the difficulties with Bishop Funk and his editorial staff at Elkhart, including a disappointment with the somewhat legalistic program of the church there. The net result of the early years was disheartening, and he found no other connection by which he could effectively work for his program than that which he reluctantly surrendered at Elkhart. Nor was the connection with J. A. Sprunger a solution, for Sprunger had no vital connection with any church body, still less with any Mennonite body. Horsch's library was in Funk's hands at Elkhart, and he had no adequate stimulus to creative scholarship, although he did publish during this time his book, *A Short History of Christianity* (1903).

But with the coming to Scottdale in 1908 Horsch found himself again. Here in the old church, he found inspiration, challenge, and opportunity. In the next 35 years he gave himself without reserve to Mennonite historical research and writing, producing a series of valuable studies: *Menno Simons* (1916); *Infant Baptism, Its Origin Among Protestants* (1927); *The Principle of Nonresistance as Held by the Mennonite Church, An Historical Survey* (1927); *The Hutterian Brethren: A Story of Martyrdom and Loyalty, 1528-1931* (1931); and *Mennonites in Europe,* posthumously published in 1942. In addition many historical articles came from his pen in both scholarly and popular journals, some published in the *Mennonite Quarterly Review,* 1927-40. He has the credit of discovering the modern Hutterites and their historical manuscripts and introducing them to modern scholarship, particularly to Wolkan in Vienna. He was the channel through which their large hymnal, Riedemann's *Rechenschaft,* and the Ehrenpreis *Sendbrief* were published.

For a number of years, 1917-26, Horsch was deeply stirred by the Fundamentalist-Modernist controversy in America and was drawn away somewhat from his historical studies into a position of semi-participation in this controversy. One fruit of this was the writing of an influential book called *Modern Religious Liberalism,* a scholarly exposé of modernism which became quite popular in Fundamentalist circles, going through three editions (1920, 1924, 1938) with a total sale of over 10,000 copies, and being used as a text in several seminaries and Bible institutes. One edition was published by the Moody Bible Institute Colportage Association. It was preceded in 1917 by a booklet, *The Higher Criticism and the New Theology.* In this period Horsch also assailed the milder forms of liberalism which had begun to infiltrate into American Mennonite educational circles through a few men trained in liberal seminaries, writing the pamphlets, *The Mennonite Church and Modernism* (1924), and *Is the Mennonite Church of America Free of Modernism?* (1926).

Being convinced about the same time that the Mennonites of America needed a strengthening of their nonresistant position, Horsch also performed valiant work in this field through publication of booklets and articles, including the book, *Die biblische Lehre von der Wehrlosigkeit* (1920) which was also published in Germany, and the pamphlets, *The Principle of Nonresistance as Held by the Mennonite Church* and *Symposium on War* (1927). Horsch's writing on modernism and nonresistance, intended both to awaken the Mennonite Church (and others) and to ward off theological and historical enemies, was frequently of necessity polemic and controversial.

In the last years of his life Horsch again returned fully to his first and major love, Mennonite historical writing. Having received a commission from the Mennonite General Conference to write a history of the Mennonite Church in Europe, he devoted himself to this task and succeeded in completing the manuscript in 1939 in all essentials before the final illness which cut short his career—*Mennonites in Europe,* which will remain his greatest monument.

One of John Horsch's lasting contributions to historical scholarship was the collection of an unusually rich library on early Anabaptist history. At the age of 17 he was seeking to secure books of Hans Denk, and to the end of his life he sought to assemble the tools necessary to scholarship in a good library. The Horsch Collection, as it is now called, is especially rich in early Swiss, German, and Dutch Anabaptistica. A study of the *Catalogue of the Mennonite Historical Library,* prepared by Horsch and published at Scottdale in 1929, and of the final contents of the collection as it was incorporated into the Mennonite Historical Library of Goshen College in 1945, reveals its uniqueness. It was for Horsch a working collection; the many marginal notes, underlinings, and indexes of subjects and names on the flyleaves speak of his assiduous use, as do also numerous notebooks and scrapbooks filled with copious extracts; the extensive documentation of his writings with source

references likewise proves his thoroughness. The gleaning in the sources which Horsch did will not need to be repeated.

Horsch is best known for his outstanding work in the field of Mennonite history, by which he won wide recognition in two continents. He was a thorough and painstaking research scholar, capable of the most intensive and sustained effort in the exploitation of original sources, competent in several languages and an able and prolific writer, although he lacked formal advanced training in history. But the deepest interest and greatest passion of Horsch's life was not history, but the church, the Mennonite Church. He strove to help her to attain and maintain the ideal of a church "without spot or wrinkle," wholly devoted to her Lord.

Horsch's historical interest was not merely antiquarian, nor one of pure scholarship. He found in Anabaptism the prototype of his own faith, and he sought with all his heart to revive and make effective this faith in his own Mennonite brotherhood and beyond. History was to be an instrument for evangelism in the truest and best sense. It is this frankly propagandistic strain in his writings, often with a polemical slant, that at times annoyed his readers and irritated his critics. It must be remembered, however, that the ancient perversions of Anabaptist history were still dominant and that a vigorous challenge to this historical error was necessary. Much of Horsch's brilliant energy was devoted to the fight to rehabilitate the Anabaptists in the world of scholarship. He lived to see the verdict largely reversed, a reversal to which he made no small contribution.† H.S.B.

The July 1947 issue of the *MQR* was a special *John Horsch Memorial Number* containing the following articles: H. S. Bender, "John Horsch, 1867-1941: A Biography," 3-16; E. Correll, "Notes on John Horsch as a Historian," 17-22; J. C. Wenger, "The Theology of John Horsch," 23-31; R. Friedmann, "John Horsch and Ludwig Keller," 32-46; E. H. Bender, "The Letters of Ludwig Keller to John Horsch, 1885-1893," 47-76; Edward Yoder, "A Bibliography of the Writings of John Horsch," 77-100. These materials were also issued in book form as *John Horsch Memorial Papers* (Scottdale, 1947).

Horsch, Michael (1871-1949), an outstanding elder and leader of the Mennonite churches of the Badischer Verband (*q.v.*), South Germany, was born of a long line of elders and preachers of two old Swiss-Baden Mennonite families, which settled in Giebelstadt near Würzburg, Germany, soon after 1800 (Horsch and Landes). Born the son of Elder Jakob Horsch, Jan. 15, 1871, he grew up on the estate at Gelchsheim rented by his farmer father, which he with his mother took over at the death of his father when he was only 17. The rest of his life Michael Horsch was a farmer, purchasing the large estate of Hellmannsberg near Ingolstadt where he lived from 1914 to his death. He was married to Maria Schmutz in 1898; one of their 10 children is Elder Hellmut Horsch of Ingolstadt. Michael was ordained preacher of the Giebelstadt-Würzburg congregation in 1909 and elder of the Ingolstadt congregation in 1923.

Michael Horsch, though without formal higher education, displayed a remarkable breadth of interest, vision, and ability as a leader. Conservative in theology, and a devoted Mennonite, he was not denominationally narrow nor bound by tradition. He founded (January 1922) and led as chairman until his death the South German Mennonite relief organization known as Christenpflicht (*q.v.*). He was a prime mover in the founding of the Bibelheim Thomashof (*q.v.*) near Durlach. He was an active promoter of the deaconess work and a supporter of missions and evangelism. Many Bible conferences (*q.v.*) were held at Hellmannsberg. He died Oct. 13, 1949, and was buried at Hellmannsberg.†

H.S.B.

Jakob Landes, "Michael Horsch, Aus seinem Leben und Lebenswerk," *Gem.-Kal.* 1954, 19-53.

Horst (Hurst), a well-known family name among Mennonites in Pennsylvania, Maryland, Ohio, Kansas, Iowa, and other midwestern and far western states. The ancestors of these people emigrated from Europe in 1731. They sailed from Rotterdam on the Brittania, which arrived at Philadelphia on Sept. 21, 1731, with 108 Palatinates and their families on board. The Horst family was composed of Barbara, a widow of 40, and three sons—Michael, 18, Joseph, 8, and Peter, 2. To pay their passage Barbara bound out the two elder sons as redemptioners. Joseph's master was Hans Groff, a pioneer settler of Groffdale, Lancaster Co., Pa. When Joseph reached maturity, he married Mary, a daughter of Samuel Groff, a grandson of Hans Groff. Samuel Groff deeded to Joseph 150 acres of land. Joseph Horst continued to live in the Conestoga Valley until his death in 1804, at the age of 81 years. He is buried in the Groffdale cemetery. He is the ancestor of most of the Horsts in the Mennonite Church today. In 1750 Michael located in Lebanon Valley, where he owned nearly 500 acres of land. He died in 1772, leaving a large family, some of whom now live in Dauphin Co., Pa. Peter settled southeast of Lancaster, then sold out and joined the migration to the west after 1800.

Among the ordained men furnished to the Mennonite (MC) Church by this family have been the following bishops: Michael Horst (1825-1900) and Moses Horst (1882-), both of Maugansville, Md., Michael Horst of Dalton, Ohio (1832-1916), John L. Horst of Scottdale, Pa. (1889-), and Amos S. Horst of Akron, Pa. (1893-). Michael Horst (1854-1915) was preacher at Peabody, Kan., for many years. Levi Hurst (1903-) and Simeon Hurst (1913-) are missionaries to Tanganyika, Africa. A number of other members of this family are serving in the Mennonite ministry in the United States and Canada. Irvin Horst is a professor at Eastern Mennonite College.   J.L.H.

Horst, ter, a Dutch Mennonite family, originally living at Hengelo, province of Overijssel, where its members together with the ten Cate (*q.v.*) family, predominated in the congregation during the 18th century. About 1600 Jan ter Horst at Hengelo was a Mennonite and a weaver by trade. At the beginning of the 18th century the meetings of the congregation were regularly held in the house of Berend ter Horst, also a weaver. Many of this family were deacons, among whom should be mentioned Abraham ter Horst (1715-79), who was a pillar of the congregation. Since the end of the 18th century members of this family have spread all over the Netherlands.   vDZ.

Uit het Verleden der Doopsgezinden in Twenthe (Borne, n.d.) 14, 115 f., 137 f.

Horst, Klaas van der, b. 1731 at Amsterdam, d. May 1, 1825, at Haarlem, studied at the Amsterdam Mennonite Seminary 1747-52 and was a minister of the Dutch congregations of Goes 1752-57, Zwolle 1757, Leiden 1757-61, and Haarlem—Flemish-Waterlander congregation (Peuzelaarsteeg congregation) 1761-84 and United congregation of Haarlem 1784-1803. He published only a sermon, which had been preached on the occasion of the union of the two Mennonite congregations of Haarlem into one on Nov. 7, 1784. A sermon on John 15:14, preached on July 5, 1767, is found in manuscript in the Amsterdam Mennonite Library. vDZ.

Biogr. Wb. IV, 314 f.; *Inv. Arch. Amst.* I, No. 725; *Naamlijst* 1804, 63 f.; 1829, 25.

Hortensius, Lambertus (1500-74), a Dutch historian, studied at the school of St. Jerome at Utrecht, then at the University of Leuven, in 1527 was employed as a teacher in the school of St. Jerome, was here dedicated as a priest, served from 1544 as rector of the Latin school at Naarden, in 1572 lost his entire estate by plundering Spanish soldiers, and died on the near-by country estate "de hooge Eng" or "Crayl" in 1574.

One of his several works is of interest to us: *Tumultuum anabaptistarum liber unus* (Basel, 1548). This booklet of 84 pages is dedicated to the mayors and the council of Amsterdam. It endeavors to increase the fame of the council by bringing into prominence its wisdom and energy in mastering the Anabaptist attempt at a coup d'état, in contrast to the negligence and foolishness of the government of Münster. After a brief reference to the origins of the Anabaptist movement, which he finds in a miscomprehension of Luther's *Von der Freiheit eines Christenmenschen,* Hortensius presents a detailed account of the events in Münster in a smooth and skillful style in Latin, without division into chapters or sections. The result is a graphic and impressive description of the affair, which explains the remarkable influence the book enjoyed for centuries. Its historical value is slight. The first Dutch translation, *Het Boeck . . . van den Oproeren der Weder-dooperen* (Enkhuizen, 1614), quarto size, 53 pages, contained 8½ remarkable full-page hand-colored illustrations in five colors (copy in Goshen College Library). Later Dutch editions appeared in 1624, 1660, 1694, and 1699. The *Histoire des Anabaptistes,* published anonymously at Paris in 1695, is in effect a translation of Hortensius.   NEFF, H.S.B.

C. A. **Cornelius,** *Die Geschichtsquellen des Bistums Münster* II (Münster, 1850) II, p. XXVIII; Mees, "Lambertus Hortensius . . . als geschiedschrijver," *Nieuwe Verh. v.h. Prov. Utr. Gen. XI* (Utrecht, 1838); *ML* II, 348.

Horton Mennonite Church (MC), located at Whitmer, Randolph Co., W. Va., is a mission church of the Middle District of the Virginia Conference.

The meetinghouse was originally a Presbyterian church, but when the large sawmill operations were discontinued in that area, and people left the community by the hundreds, the Presbyterians sold their church to the Mennonites for fifty dollars in 1930. It has since been repaired and remodeled— the front lobby over which the bell tower and bell were placed was removed and a new entrance made which was more in keeping with the Mennonite faith and practice. In 1953 the congregation had a membership of 24, with Olin McDorman serving as pastor. H.A.B.

Hosauer, Sigmund (also Hasauer or Hassauer), a preacher in the Hutterite brotherhood. In 1555 he witnessed the martyrdom of Hans Pürchner (*q.v.*) of Saalen near Bruneck, who was seized at Kortsch near Schlanders in the Adige Valley, and was so severely racked during his trial that he was unable thereafter to use his hands or feet, and was finally beheaded. His death was commemorated by Hosauer in the hymn of 44 stanzas, "Fröhlich wollen wir singen jetzt," which describes all the details of the torture and death. It is found in the *Lieder der Hutterischen Brüder,* 436-41. Here are also three other hymns by Hosauer (pp. 446-50): "Hör, o Himmel, und Erd merk auf," 18 stanzas; "Mein Sinn dahin steht alle zeit bereit," 11 stanzas; "Merk auf, o Gott, lass dir mein Stimm," 9 stanzas. In 1557 he was called as preacher; he received a final greeting of the martyr Klaus Felbinger (*q.v.*), and died in 1564 at Gosstal in Moravia. LOSERTH.

Wolkan, *Geschicht-Buch,* 306-7; Beck, *Geschichts-Bücher;* Klaus Felbinger's letter to Leonhard Sailer is published by Loserth in *Ztscht für allgemeine Geschichte* I, 451-54; *ML* II, 348.

Hosius, Stanislaus (1504-79), cardinal-bishop of Culm in West Prussia, Germany. He was noted for his hatred of the Protestants; he discusses Menno Simons in his book, *Confutatio Prolegomenon Brentii* (Antwerp, 1561). He names Hubmaier as the founder of the Anabaptist movement and ridicules the Biblical faith of Menno Simons, who seems "to surpass all his fellow believers in scholarship." He also discusses the Anabaptists in his *De origine haeresium nostri* (Louvain, 1559). NEFF.

K. Vos, *Menno Simons* (Leiden, 1914) 322; *DB* 1872, 89; *ML* II, 348.

Hospitals. As followers of Christ, Mennonites the world over have always heeded the admonition that "faith without works is dead" (James 2:20), and that faith works by love (I Cor. 13). They have therefore always sought opportunities for service.

Through the years they have not only taken a vital interest in the work of hospitals but have also made it a major part of their conference and mission work. They saw in it opportunity to discharge their obligation to the sick by ministering to their physical needs, and at the same time to their spiritual needs; for when the physical needs of the body are met, the soul is in a receptive mood for those things which are eternal. Also they saw in the work of hospitals a field of service. Since they taught that a vital Christian life must express itself also in sacrificial service to others the work of hospitals offered a splendid field for this type of service and many have found opportunity to dedicate their lives to God in this field of activity.

The Mennonites of Russia were the first Mennonites to establish hospitals for their communities. Chortitza had a district (*Zemstvo*) hospital which, with its staff of doctors, was maintained by the Mennonite district (Chortitza volost). The Chortitza Mennonite industrialists maintained a doctor for their laborers. In the early days the hospital had ten beds, the number being increased later and a special maternity ward being added. Some of the doctors were Jakob Esau, Theodor Hoffmann, David A. Hamm, and Peter Zacharias. During World War I the Chortitza Mennonites maintained a 75-100 bed Red Cross emergency hospital in addition to the regular hospital. After the Revolution of 1917 these hospitals were nationalized.

In the Molotschna settlement the first hospital was established in 1880 by Franz Wall in Muntau. Under the able leadership of Dr. Tavonius this work expanded and became a great blessing to the community. Somewhat later Warkentin and his wife built a hospital in Waldheim, Molotschna. For some time this work was carried on, although under difficulties, but discontinued its services after World War I. With funds received from the H. H. Reimer estate the benefactors built a beautiful hospital in Ohrloff, Molotschna, which was opened for service on Jan. 7, 1910. In the same year a hospital was erected in Neu-Samara and about the same time Bethania (*q.v.*), a mental hospital, was established at Alt-Kronsweide, Chortitza. All of these institutions were nationalized by the Soviets after the Revolution.

In Holland and Germany the Mennonites limited their efforts in the care of the sick and the work of hospitals largely to the services which their deaconesses rendered.

In the United States the Mennonites have been quite active in this field. The first General Conference hospital, Bethesda, was established at Goessel, Kan., in 1900. Bethel Hospital was opened at Mountain Lake, Minn., in 1905; Bethel Deaconess Hospital at Newton, Kan., in 1906; the Mennonite Hospital at Beatrice, Neb., in 1911; the Mennonite Hospital at Bloomington, Ill., was taken over by the Central Conference Mennonites in 1919. The Mennonite (MC) Church established the Sanitarium and Hospital in La Junta, Col., in 1908. They have also taken over the administrative responsibility of a hospital at Greensburg, Kan., and one at Lebanon, Ore. They further established a mental hospital, "Philhaven," at Lebanon, Pa., in 1952. The Krimmer Mennonite Brethren established the Salem Hospital at Hillsboro, Kan., in 1917. The Church of God in Christ Mennonites established Mercy Hospital at Moundridge, Kan., in 1944.

In Canada the Mennonites (GCM) established Concordia Hospital at Winnipeg in 1928. Since then Bethania Hospital at Altona, Man., in 1936, Bethesda Hospital, Steinbach, Man., in 1937, and Bethel Hospital at Winkler, Man., in 1935, have been established, and also the Bethesda Home for the mentally ill at Vineland, Ont.

The work of hospitals also plays an important part in Mennonite mission work. The Mennonites (MC) have established hospitals in connection with their mission work in India, Africa, Puerto Rico, and Ethiopia. The General Conference also maintains hospitals in connection with its mission stations in Africa and India, as well as in China until that work had to be discontinued. The Mennonite Brethren have hospitals in India and Africa. The Dutch Mennonites had hospitals in their missions in Java (q.v.).

Another phase of the Mennonite hospital program was brought about by the work of the Mennonite Central Committee, which helped to establish hospitals for the Mennonite refugees who migrated to Paraguay.

In 1950 there were five colony hospitals in Paraguay: Fernheim (org. 1932) with 42 beds; Menno (1947) with 30 beds; Neuland (1948) with 40 beds; Volendam (1948) with 20 beds; Friesland (1949) with 20 beds; Primavera, the Hutterite hospital (1941), with 10 beds. The Krauel settlement in Brazil had a hospital at Witmarsum, established with the strong aid of the Dutch Mennonite relief organization.

A new interest was awakened in hospitals for the mentally ill after World War II, during which time many of the young men of military age did alternative service in our mental hospitals. As a result the MCC, upon authorization of its constituent groups, has sponsored the building and operation of three such hospitals. The first one, Brook Lane Farm, located at Hagerstown, Md., was opened in 1949. Kings View Homes at Reedley, Cal., was opened in 1951. Prairie View Hospital at Newton, Kan., was opened in 1954.   H.J.A.

ML II, 556; M. Hottmann, "Dr. Theodor Hottmann," Menn. Jahrbuch 1953, 39-48.

Hostetler (Hostetter, Hochstetler, and many other variations), a family name occurring frequently among Mennonites (MC) and Amish in America. The earliest trace of the name appears in Switzerland, in the town of Guggisberg (canton of Bern) and the neighboring communities of Wahlern and Albigen. According to Christian Lerch, State Archivist at Bern, all Anabaptist-Mennonites of this name come from this locality, but only a small proportion of the Hostettlers (as it is spelled currently in Switzerland) were *Täufer*. The forms Hofstetter (q.v.) and Hostettler originated independently of each other, though the spellings appearing in early records are never consistent; it is a matter of speculation whether both come from the same root, i.e., "orchard." The first syllable of the name was written "Hoch" by those who went to Germany. The long-standing Hochstättlers of Münsterhof in the Palatinate and those in Regensburg in Bavaria trace their ancestry to Jakob, born at Lautenbacherhof near Strasbourg about 1765, and his father Isaak, who died at Neuhof near Strasbourg. Mennonites with this name are extremely rare in Europe today, and live chiefly in Bavaria near Regensburg. Two well-known Amish Mennonite preachers were Jacob Hochstättler of Münsterhof

of Palatinate, and Peter Hochstetter (1814-85) of Regensburg, Bavaria.

Jacob Hochstetler (1704-76), an Amish Mennonite who boarded the English ship *Harle* at Rotterdam, came to Philadelphia in 1736 with 388 persons from the Palatinate and adjacent places, and settled north of Reading, Pa. The family suffered severely from an Indian attack near North Northkill in Berks Co., Pa., in 1757. The story is told in Harvey Hostetler's *Descendants of Jacob Hochstetler*. He is the ancestor of most of the large number of Amish Mennonites and Amish bearing the name. Families bearing this name are scattered all the way from Pennsylvania to Oregon.

The Hostetters in the Lancaster Mennonite (MC) Conference district must descend from a different immigrant from the Jacob mentioned above. A congregation of this conference near Hanover in York County is called Hostetter's (q.v.).

Among members of the family prominent in church life and work have been Bishop Jacob Hostetler (d. 1761) of the Hammer Creek district in Lancaster Co.; Bishop Jacob Hostetter (1745-1826) of the same conference, Manheim district; Bishop Jacob Hostetter (1774-1865), moderator of the Lancaster Conference; Bishop John Hostetler (1791-1866), of York Co., Pa.; Bishop Oscar Hostetler (MC) of Lagrange Co., Ind.; Amos Hostetler, a minister in Topeka, Ind., secretary of the Mennonite General Conference (MC) 1923-53; B. Charles Hostetter, a minister in Harrisonburg, Va., evangelist and radio preacher; J. J. Hostetler, a longtime city missionary (MC), Bishop John G. Hochstetler of Creston, Mont. (MC), Bishop Eli G. Hochstetler, Wolford, N.D. (MC), and Lester Hostetler, Freeman, S.D., a minister in the General Conference Mennonite Church. Prominent in the Brethren in Christ Church is Bishop C. N. Hostetter, Jr., President of Messiah College, Grantham, Pa., his father Bishop C. N. Hostetter, long president of the mission board, and his brother, Bishop Henry N. Hostetter, executive secretary of the mission board.   J.A.H.

Two monumental genealogies were compiled by Harvey Hostetler: *Descendants of Jacob Hochstetler* (Elgin, Ill., 1912), and *Descendants of Barbara Hochstedler and Christian Stutzman* (Scottdale, 1938). Barbara was the youngest daughter of the 1736 immigrant Jacob. See also Mrs. Amos Hostetler, *Descendants of David J. Hochstetler* (Nappanee, Ind., 1953).

Hostetler, Pius (1867-1937), was born in Elkhart Co., Ind., on July 23, 1867, the seventh son of Christian J. and Magdalena Hershberger Hostetler. He was married to Ella Zook in Mifflin Co., Pa., on Feb. 15, 1892. They raised a family of two boys and three girls. He took a short normal course, taught school in the elementary grades, and was Sunday-school superintendent and chorister in his church. He wrote two books: *The Life, Preaching and Labors of John D. Kauffman* (1916), and *Drifted* (1916). He lived in Cass Co., Mo., from his youth until 1910, when he moved to Pryor, Mayes Co., Okla. In 1912 he moved to Shelby Co., Ill., where he died on July 2, 1937, and where he was buried.   H.H.

Hostetler's Meetinghouse in Wilmot Twp., Waterloo Co., Ont., is the place of worship of a Reformed Mennonite congregation having approximately 50 members. The church was established in 1844.

J.L.K.

Hostetter Mennonite Church (MC), established in Union Twp., Adams Co., Pa., in 1845, is a member of the Lancaster Conference. The church has a cornerstone marked "Manosimon Meetinghouse Built A D 1854; Rebuilt 1899." This beautiful farming community was settled by Mennonites two centuries ago. The congregation met in private homes with Bair's Hanover and later a schoolhouse until 1854, when Bishop John Hostetter gave land for a church, and the first meetinghouse was built, later replaced by the present one. Services are held here every four weeks. It is part of the Hanover-Bair's Hanover circuit. In 1955 it had 111 members.

I.D.L.

Hotevilla is a settlement on the third mesa in the southern half of the Hopi reservation, seven miles from Oraibi (*q.v.*), made up of those who were driven out of Oraibi in 1906 by Hopis that were friendly toward the government. The work there had been begun by Marie Schirmer, with the assistance of John R. Duerksen who moved to Hotevilla in October 1919. He built a chapel and mission house near the village. Marie Schirmer resigned in August 1919, and the work of both Hotevilla and Bacabi was left to the Duerksens until 1929 or 1930. After that J. P. Suderman was responsible for this station and from 1949 Daniel Schirmer was there for several years. In 1953 Walter Goossen was stationed at Hotevilla. He was followed in 1955 by Herbert Peters.

W.K.

Hottinger, Hans, the night watchman of Zollikon in the canton of Zürich, and at the beginning of the Anabaptist movement allied himself with it. The court records name several persons of the widely ramified Hottinger family, who joined the Swiss Brethren. As a zealous advocate of church reform Hans Hottinger participated in the storming of the images in the church at Zollikon. Because of this act he had to defend himself before the court in December 1523.

After it had come to a break between Zwingli and some of the Brethren and they began to practice adult baptism, many inhabitants of Zollikon were baptized, Hottinger among them. Soon the government took steps to suppress the movement. Twenty-four Anabaptists were imprisoned in the Augustinian monastery until they were tried on Feb. 7, 1525. Hans, Jakob, and Conrad Hottinger and several companions stated that they had been baptized and were "servants obedient to God"; they wanted to do what God's Spirit directed them to do, and not allow any temporal power to force them from it. Where the Word of God did not interfere, they would be obedient to my lords.— They were then dismissed upon Urfehde and payment of costs and security of 1,000 guilders. They were also to be warned and rebuked for having done wrong and having acted "against God and against their neighbor with offense."

About this time a conference was held between Zwingli and the Anabaptists. Soon afterward, when the Brethren were conversing about the course of the proceedings, Hans Hottinger said Zwingli had asserted that there is no instance in the Bible that anyone had been baptized twice. But when the Brethren showed him the passage (Acts 19), he admitted it, indeed he had been partly convinced and would accept for himself "this godly life." When Hans Asper defended Zwingli and expressed his pleasure with Zwingli's sermons, Hottinger remarked, "I do not know why I should be happy. Today he preaches one thing, and tomorrow he retracts it. Years ago he preached that little children should not be baptized, but now he says they should be baptized. And when he says God has commanded that children be baptized, he lies like a rogue and a heretic." For this statement Hottinger was brought to trial on Feb. 25. He was released on promise to do better, but dismissed from his position as watchman.

In the following month (March) we find Hans Hottinger as a defendant in the great Anabaptist trial. With Manz and Blaurock, who had not been convinced of wrongdoing, he does not want to be considered in the wrong either. No one had instructed him "but Christ and His teaching, which is the true Word of God." He did not know whether he had been baptized as an infant, and had therefore let himself be baptized. At the close of the discussions, which lasted several days, Hottinger is said to have stated that he was satisfied with Zwingli's teaching and promised to be obedient to "my lords." It seems that he kept this promise and gave the authorities no trouble for several months.

When at the turn of the year 1525-26 Balthasar Hubmaier appeared in Zürich, he soon made his influence felt. In the court proceedings in the trial of Hubmaier in January 1526, Heini Aberli stated that the watchman Hottinger had received Hubmaier in his house. Then he related how the two (Aberli and Hottinger) had journeyed to Waldshut, and at a well Hottinger had said to him, "Who has anything against my being baptized?" Aberli then asked him whether he "believed in his heart." Hottinger answered affirmatively and fell on his knees, and asked him "with weeping eyes through God's will" to baptize him. He did so. From that date some of Hubmaier's influence may have remained with Hottinger, whose acquaintance he had made in Waldshut. When Hubmaier appeared in Zürich, Hottinger was one of the courageous advocates of believers' baptism. He was also among those sentenced on March 7, 1526, to imprisonment in the tower on bread and water, and beds of straw. In a book Hubmaier wrote against Zwingli, *Ein Gesprech Balthasar Hubmörs von Friedberg auf Mayster Ulrichs Zwinglens Taufbüchlein,* he describes the awful conditions of the imprisonment and names several of the prisoners, among them "Hansen Hottinger." On March 21, two weeks after the sentence, Hottinger is said to have returned again to the established church. Did he perhaps emigrate to Moravia? Loserth (*Communismus,* 42) mentions a Hans Hottinger of

Brinelsdorf near Zürich, who lived at Scheidewitz in Moravia. (*TA Zürich; ML* II, 349.)   S.G.

Hottinger, Jakob, of Zollikon, Zürich, a sponsor of church reform, as early as 1523 opposed the doctrine of transubstantiation and demanded the two forms of communion. Without consideration of circumstances he challenged the populace no longer to participate in the Mass, since the priests had hitherto deceived the people with it. There had been enough "looseness and idolatry." For this conduct he was punished with a prison sentence and a fine.

His radical view on the administration of the sacraments was not accepted by the church; he therefore joined the Anabaptists. When Kaspar Grossmann in a sermon on Jan. 16, 1525, defended infant baptism, Hottinger interrupted him and took issue with him on this point. The court records of the Anabaptist trial of Feb. 7, 1525, report that at a meeting of the Anabaptists in the home of Ruedi Thomann, Felix Manz baptized Jakob Hottinger and others with a dipper of water in the name of God the Father, God the Son, and God the Holy Ghost. There is also record of a meeting in Jakob Hottinger's house, where Conrad Grebel spoke on baptism and communion. They had then observed communion together. Grebel cut the bread and distributed it with the admonition that all who partook "should henceforth live a Christian life." In several weeks another meeting was held in Jakob Hottinger's house, at which Blaurock baptized Heinrich Aberli (*q.v.*) with a handful of water, after Aberli had confessed his faith in the finished sacrifice of Christ.

A distinguishing feature of these meetings is the emphasis placed on the inner state of faith before baptism or communion, not only by the leaders, but also by the rank and file. We read, for example, that Jakob Hottinger and Blaurock met in the evening in Aberli's house and conversed "about divine things" and then observed communion. One of those present had requested them to pray for him that God might strengthen him in the faith, so that he might be worthy to approach the Lord's table. Jakob Hottinger also stated that anyone who falls back into sin after baptism must according to Scripture be punished with the ban. "It is not the sphere of any government to administer the Word of God with force, for it is free" (Egli, *Züricher,* 96).

In a few instances Hottinger also baptized; one of these he baptized was his wife in Zollikon. In March 1525 he promised before the council to amend his conduct. But in June he was already publicly warning the churchgoers of the parson, the false prophet; he was punished by strict confinement on bread and water. After a period in prison Hottinger requested an audience before the clergy to discuss baptism with them. On this occasion he promised again to go to church, with the reservation that if the sermon did not seem Scriptural to him he would be permitted to discuss it with the preacher after the service. Under the date of June 1526 the records state the following:

"Jakob Hottinger, who about a year ago was converted from Anabaptism in writing and made a recantation in Zollikon, has recently been seized for falling back into Anabaptism. He says he ascribes it to God, who had at that time let him fall and then raised him up again; he would stay by Anabaptism."

He remained true to this intention for a long time. The last report we have of him is dated April 4, 1528: "Jakob Hottinger, who has long been confined on water and bread in the new tower on account of his participation in the disturbances of the Anabaptists, now promises to reform." He was released upon payment of a fine of five pounds, defraying his expenses, and the customary oath, with the urgent admonition "that he keep his sons, his wife, and servants from Anabaptism."

    S.G.

E. Egli, *Die Züricher Wiedertäufer zur Ref.-Zeit* (Zürich, 1878); Fritz Blanke, *Brüder in Christo. Die Geschichte der ältesten Täufergemeinde (Zollikon 1525),* (Zürich, 1955); H. S. Bender, *Conrad Grebel* (Goshen, 1950); *TA Zürich; ML* II, 350.

Hottinger, Johann Heinrich (1620-67), a Swiss scholar who played a role of some importance in the negotiations between the city council of Zürich and the Dutch government on the persecution of the Anabaptists. In 1653, in the commission of the Zürich council, he presented his official opinion on the letter of a "sectarian from The Hague" to the four Protestant cities (Zürich, Basel, Bern, St. Gall), which sharply opposed religious persecution. In December 1663 he was authorized to send a letter to the States-General in Holland, defending the proceedings against the Anabaptists. He pointed out that toleration of the Anabaptists would jeopardize the national security and the existence of the Reformed Church. When in 1664 he was sent to Holland on a political mission he came in touch with the Mennonites living at Utrecht. They handed him a petition addressed to the Zürich council in favor of their persecuted brethren, whom he promised to support. Cornelius Bergmann assumes that he also negotiated with the Mennonites in the Palatinate. The subject deserves investigation.   NEFF.

C. Bergmann, *Die Täuferbewegung im Kanton Zürich bis 1660* (Leipzig, 1916) 149, 155 ff.; *ML* II, 350.

Hottinger, Johann Jakob (1652-1735), a Swiss church historian, the son of the above. He continued Joh. v. Müller's *Geschichte der Eidgenossen* and is the author of the book, *Compendium historiae anabaptisticae,* which does not claim special importance. (*ML* II, 351.)   NEFF.

Hottinger, Klaus, one of the most zealous advocates of the Reformation in Zürich, participated in the destruction of the crucifix in Stadelhofen before the city gate, was consequently banished from the city for two years on Nov. 4, 1523, died at the stake cheerfully in Lucerne, March 26, 1524, as the first Protestant martyr of Switzerland.

He was closely associated with the founders of the Anabaptist movement, and it can be assumed that if he had lived longer he would certainly have joined it. Neff.

E. Egli, *Schweizerische Ref.-Gesch.* I (Zürich, 1910) 254 f.; *ML* II, 351.

Hotz, Hans, an Anabaptist martyr, a native of the Grüningen district of the canton of Zürich. He was probably baptized by Georg Blaurock. It is possible that Hotz was converted in 1525, during Blaurock's successful missionary activity in Grüningen. From that time on Hotz was an inspired defender of Anabaptism. Through the work of such men as he and Jakob Falk (*q.v.*) and Heini Reimann, the movement continued to gain ground in Grüningen so that great numbers of people flocked to hear them preach.

Meanwhile the Zwinglian church had established itself as a state institution and attacked "corner preaching and rabble-rousing," which had grown to considerable proportions in Grüningen. The council of Zürich also decided to put an end to the "Anabaptist mischief" in the Zürich Oberland. The leaders of the movement were arrested, tried, and sentenced. It is not definitely known that Hans Hotz was one of those sentenced by the council of Zürich on March 7, 1526 (see **Blaurock**). It is nevertheless safe to assume that in 1526 he was still in prison with Georg Blaurock; for in the court records of a later trial is found the following statement: "Hans Hotz in the Ketzerturm says: 'Blaurock first taught him and also strengthened him, likewise Felix Manz. Thus they all encouraged one another in the tower. He holds infant baptism to be an error, and rebaptism right.'"

As soon as the prisoners were released from the Ketzerturm they renewed their missionary work. It cannot be definitely determined when Hotz was again arrested. In August 1528 he was cross-examined with several other brethren, after an imprisonment of nearly one and one-half years. Hans Hotz confessed that infant baptism was the false baptism and was not right; he had once called infant baptism right, but was now very rueful; nor did he want to hear the preachers. All the others likewise repented having called infant baptism right; it is an abomination before God, and baptism on faith is a command of God.

All the prisoners confessed that in prison they had strengthened and encouraged each other, well or sick, to be steadfast. They were therefore isolated in the various towers and monasteries in the city. For two weeks they were kept on bread and water. The leaders Falk and Reimann were then sentenced to death by drowning and were executed on Sept. 5, 1528. At a further trial the others were urged to be converted and return to the pastor in the church, to hear the Word of God and to recognize infant baptism. Probably the following undated notice in the records refers to this trial: "Hans Hotz said he considers the baptism with which he was baptized in his youth, as wrong and useless; but the other baptism that he received was right, and he does not suppose that he has done wrong. Nor did he want to go to church to hear words of idolatry." Those who refused to be converted and like Hotz persisted in Anabaptism should be kept in the tower on bread and water another month to think it over, and should then be tried again and sentenced. The final verdict concerning Hotz is not known. But it is certain that in spite of long incarceration he held fast to his faith.

But Hans Hotz did not share the severe struggles of the Anabaptist brotherhood only in his own community; his activity extended far beyond the borders of this canton. In the disputation at Zofingen (*q.v.*), July 1-9, 1532, as well as that in Bern (*q.v.*), March 11-17, 1538, Hotz was the spokesman of the Swiss Brethren. The adamant character of this warrior was so developed by experience and suffering that he became a quick-witted opponent of the church party. Unfortunately the records of these debates rarely name the speaker. One of the most important points the Brethren had to answer in Zofingen was "the divine call to the office of preaching." The preachers had charged the Brethren that their commission to preach the Gospel was not of God. No wonder that they answered their opponents that because they were not sent according to apostolic custom, their mission was not of God! Hans Hotz placed special emphasis on his belief that before a preacher could proclaim the Word he must experience a conversion or renewal of heart and he must then also be found blameless in his life. Those who were divinely called, were called by a believing brotherhood and not by a government.

Hans Hotz adroitly discussed the question of baptism. He admitted that baptism is the sign of a Christian people, with which we are received into the church of God. But this does not belong to little children, but only to those who experience salvation through faith. Hotz said, "It has not yet been proved that those shall also be received who do not have the faith; for baptism is always the sign of the renewed man, buried in the death of Jesus Christ, and always a certain announcement or testimony of resurrection through the death of Jesus Christ."

In the same tone Hotz defended baptism on faith in the disputation in Bern in 1538. The court record says, "This confession of Hotz was read to them, and then the presidents questioned the Anabaptists one by one. They all were satisfied and confirmed it; none rejected it." After further debate Hotz said, "Therefore we hold baptism in the Christian brotherhood . . . as taught by Christ and practiced by the apostles. If anyone can prove otherwise by Scripture, we will wait for it."

Apparently the authorities were not pleased with the outcome of this disputation. The council decided that the nonresidents (of whom Hotz was one) should be escorted over the border, subject to death by beheading if they crossed it again, because they were "leading people astray." Nothing is known of Hotz's life after this disputation.

S.G.

E. Egli, *Die Züricher Wiedertäufer zur Reformationszeit* (Zürich, 1878); *TA Zürich;* Müller, *Berner Täufer; ML* II, 351 f.

Houbakker, Joannes, a Dutch Mennonite preacher, b. April 18, 1685, at Amsterdam, d. there Dec. 14, 1715, who in spite of an early death occupies a place of honor in the Mennonite brotherhood of Holland. At the age of 20, having attended the lectures of Galenus Abrahamsz (q.v.) 1699-1705, he was provisionally appointed preacher of the United Flemish and Waterland congregation in Amsterdam (Lam and Toren congregation); he received the position permanently in 1711 after he had declined an offer from the Rotterdam church. He was known as an excellent pulpit speaker. After his death three volumes of his sermons, *Predikatien over verscheide texten der H. Schriftuur,* were published in 1730, 1732, and 1735. His picture in a steel engraving is found in *Verzaameling van de Afbeeldingen van veele voornaame Mannen en Leeraaren* (Amsterdam, 1743).   vdZ.

Schijn-Maatschoen, *Geschiedenis der Mennoniten* III, 492-97; *Biogr. Wb.* IV, 325 f.; *Inv. Arch. Amst.* II, 686; *DB* 1918, 64, note 2; *ML* II, 352.

Houbraken, a Dutch Mennonite family of artists living at Dordrecht, province of South Holland. In the records of the "Lam and Toren" Mennonite congregation of Amsterdam, there are also found some van Houbrakens who were members of this congregation. Arnoldus Houbraken, b. 1660 at Dordrecht, moved to Amsterdam 1708, d. there 1719, wrote *Groote Schouwburgh der Nederlandsche Konstschilders* (1718, repr. 1758 and 1943). He also painted a number of portraits. His son Jacob Houbraken (1698-1780), who is well known for his engraved portraits, was Reformed.   vdZ.

Schijn-Maatschoen, *Geschiedenis* III, 492; *Biogr. Wb.* IV, 325 f.; *Inv. Arch. Amst.* II, No. 686; *DB* 1918, 64 note 1.

House-Buyers, a group of Dutch Mennonites: see **Huiskopers.**

Households of the Hutterian Brethren: see **Bruderhof.**

Houten, Samuel van, a Dutch statesman, derived from an ancient Mennonite family. He was the son of Derk Hindriks van Houten and Barbara Elisabeth (Samuels) Meihuizen, and a direct descendant of the well-known Samuel Peter and Barbara Frey, who in 1714 emigrated from Gontenschwyl near Lenzburg, Switzerland, and settled in Holland with several other families for the sake of their faith (Müller, *Berner Täufer,* 322).

Samuel van Houten was born Feb. 17, 1837, at Groningen, received his *Doctor juris* in 1859. He was at first a barrister, and became a very well-known Dutch political leader. In his native Groningen he was a member of the church and city council. From 1869 to 1894 he was a member of the second chamber of parliament, 1894-97 Minister of the Interior, and 1904-7 a member of the first chamber of parliament. He was a liberal statesman in the style of 1848. Inflexible and independent, he never tried to favor any person or party. He was the instigator of the social laws of the Netherlands. When he was in the cabinet he initiated the election

law named after him (de kieswet-van Houten). In 1866-73 he was a member of the A.D.S. (q.v.). He died in The Hague, Oct. 14, 1930. (*ML* II, 352 f.)   J.Y.

Houttuyn, a Dutch Mennonite family, originally found at Hoorn, Dutch province of North Holland, of which some members were preachers in their native town and also at Amsterdam. Pieter Adriaensz Houttuyn (1683-1736) and Willem Houttuyn, a physician (1692-1756), were elders of the Frisian congregation of Hoorn (Willem serving 1721-56), while Adriaan Houttuyn (ca. 1700-77) was a preacher of the Waterlander congregation at Hoorn 1732-77.

This Adriaan Houttuyn was an adherent of Collegiant principles, and of baptism by immersion. He published *Eenige redenen om de in- of onderdompeling te verkiezen boven de besprenging* (Hoorn, 1752). He preached a sermon, *Redevoering over Handelingen XVI:30-34,* at Rijnsburg on June 2, 1770, when he baptized by immersion (published Rotterdam, 1770).

When the Frisian and the Waterlander congregations of Hoorn had merged in 1747 Willem Houttuyn and Adriaan Houttuyn were its preachers, and also Jacob Houttuyn, a son of Pieter Adriaensz, b. 1711 at Hoorn, d. there 1789, serving in 1746-89. A Frans Houttuyn of Hoorn (year of birth unknown), who may have belonged to this same family, settled in Amsterdam as a book printer and was a lay preacher of the Amsterdam Frisian ("Arke Noachs") congregation 1750-52, and after this congregation had merged with the Zonist congregation (1752) until his death in 1765. His son Martinus Houttuyn was a physician at Hoorn.

In Hoorn and Amsterdam a number of members of this family were deacons. The grandmother of J. G. de Hoop Scheffer (q.v.), noted Mennonite minister, historian, and professor of the Seminary and the Amsterdam University, was Aagtje Houttuyn of Hoorn (1752-1818), a daughter of Preacher Jacob Houttuyn. Pieter Houttuyn of Hoorn was an ardent Patriot (q.v.), who in 1787 together with P. Bel, another member of the congregation of Hoorn, fled from Hoorn to Brussels because of their anti-Orange principles. He was chorister (*voorlezer en voorzanger*) of the Hoorn congregation.   vdZ.

Houttuyn family: *DB* 1867, 57, 70; 1898, 119; Pieter Adriaensz Houttuyn: *DB* 1887, 130 f.; Frans Houttuyn: *Inv. Arch. Amst.* II, No. 1409; *DB* 1896, 12; Pieter Houttuyn: *Inv. Arch. Amst.* II, 2, No. 178; Willem Houttuyn: *Biogr. Wb.* IV, 338; *DB* 1887, 130 f.; Adriaan Houttuyn, *Biogr. Wb.* IV, 337-38; J. c. van Slee, *De Rijnsburger Collegianten* (Haarlem, 1895) 193, 211.

Houwerzijl, a hamlet around a dike-lock in the Dutch province of Groningen, where already in 1660 and apparently much earlier there was a congregation of Groningen Old Flemish Mennonites. In this congregation of farmers in the 18th century the Rietema family produced three generations of preachers: Kornelis Jacobs, his son Jan Kornelisz, b. 1689, serving 1730-ca.1760, and his grandson Jacob Jan 1757-83.

The membership of Houwerzijl, about 70 in 1710, had by 1767 already decreased to 15 members, but seems by 1790 to have increased somewhat. During a terrible flood of the North Sea, which struck this part of the province of Groningen on Christmas Day 1717, 12 members and 7 children of the congregation perished. In 1773-78 the congregation merged with Ulrum (*q.v.*), but by 1794 the united congregation dissolved.   vDZ.

Blaupot t. C., *Groningen* I, 127, 140, 142, 202; *Inv. Arch. Amst.* II, No. 2287; *DJ* 1840, 43; *DB* 1879, 4; 1906, 46.

Hove, Peter *(Pieter)* **ten.** Van Braght's *Martyrs' Mirror* relates that Peter ten Hove, Huybert op der Straten, and two women, Trijnken, Huybert's wife, and Lijsken of Linschoten, were arrested, whipped, and expelled from Wittgenstein, Germany, by Johann, Count of Steyn. This account is, however, not clear. First it is rather strange that these four Mennonites with their typical Dutch names were living in Germany, but secondly, as Crous has indicated, Count Johann of Wittgenstein died in 1551 and the ruler in 1601 was Count Ludwig the Older, who with the aid of Olivianus (*q.v.*) gradually Calvinized the duchy.   NEFF.

Mart. Mir. D 803, E 1,102; Georg Hinsberg, *Sayn-Wittgenstein-Berleburg* I (Berleburg, 1920); *ML* III, 352.

Hovens, a Dutch Mennonite family, of which there were in the 17th century two branches, viz., at Haarlem and Utrecht. Later a lateral branch of the Utrecht family was also found at Haarlem. In 1632 Daniel Hovens, a deacon, signed the Dordrecht Confession for the Utrecht Flemish congregation. He became a minister in 1640, and retired in 1652. Johannes Hovens was a deacon of the Utrecht congregation 1680-82. The family was found there until the end of the 18th century. Daniel Howens Korn.zn. was a deacon of the Amsterdam Lamist congregation 1708-14. He was also a member of the Committee of Foreign Needs and its treasurer 1715-21. Enoch Hovens (1661-1742) and Daniel Hovens were preachers of the United Flemish-Waterlander congregation of the Peuzelaarsteeg at Haarlem, Enoch serving 1685-1735 (he died 1742), and Daniel 1731-ca. 1760. Enoch Hovens is the author of an important account of the history of the Mennonite congregation of Haarlem. This account, a letter to M. Schagen (*q.v.*), dated April 15, 1740, was published in *Doopsgezinde Bijdragen* 1863, 129-52. A preacher, Daniel Hovens Hz (*q.v.*), d. 1795, another member of this family, served a number of congregations. A side-branch of this family is the Hovens Greve family, of which there have been deacons until now. Koenraad Hovens Greve (1779-1874) of Haarlem served as pastor at Nijmegen 1812-14 and Zuidveen (since 1848 called Steenwijk) 1814-62. He served also at Giethoorn-Zuidzijde 1826-51, when he was succeeded by his son Abraham Kornelis Hovens Greve (1817-57), who had previously served at Noord-Zijpe 1850-51.   vDZ.

Hovens, Daniel, a Dutch Mennonite preacher, b. 1735 at Haarlem, d. 1795, married to Susanneke

Nieuwenhuyzen in 1755, became the preacher of the Frisian congregation of Barsingerhorn, province of North Holland, serving 1755-57. His conflict with a Reformed colleague on account of a Reformed girl who joined his congregation, shows him to have been peaceful but determined. He later served the congregations of Sneek 1757-61, Monnikendan 1761-64, West Zaandam "Oude Huys" (Frisian) 1764-70, and Leiden 1770-89. After 1789 he no longer exercised his preaching office, having accepted a political office in Rotterdam. During his term at Leiden he performed at least one (1777) baptism by immersion.

Among his colleagues he holds a high place in scholarliness and mental acuteness. His treatise *Over het onderscheidende kenmerk der christelijke openbaring en derzelver verband met de Natuurlijke en Joodsche Godsdienst* was awarded the gold medal by the Teyler Theological Association in 1781. The subject indicates the intellectual atmosphere in which Hovens lived. The same spirit is shown in a catechism he wrote: *Lesboek voor de Kinderen der Christenen . . .* (Leiden, 1787, 1794). He also published *Onze tegenwoordige Toestand vergeleken bij dien onzer Voorouders in en omtrent het jaar 1574 . . .*, and two addresses (Leiden, 1782). He served as a director of the *Maatschapij tot nut van't-Algemeen* in 1784, the second year of its organization. He had planned to enter the book business, but under the influence of Collegiant meetings, he devoted his life to theology.   vDZ.

Biogr. Wb. IV, 342-44; L. G. le Poole, *Bijdrage tot . . . het kerkelijk leven onder de Doopsgez. . . . te Leiden* (Leiden, 1905) Index; *DB* 1880, 84-90, 95; *Inv. Arch. Amst.* I, No. 693; *ML* II, 353.

Howard (Pa.) CPS Unit No. 40, under MCC direction, attached to the U.S. Government Soil Conservation Service, was established in June 1942 and closed in June 1943. Leaders were in order Ralph Hernley and Jesse Short. The work consisted chiefly of operating the Howard Nursery of the Soil Conservation Service. The unit had *ca.* 50 men. H.S.B.

M. Gingerich, *Service for Peace* (Akron, 1949) 122.

Howard (R.I.) CPS Unit No. 85, attached to the Rhode Island State Hospital for Mental Diseases, under MCC direction, was established in February 1943 and closed in October 1946. Directors were in order Earl Heisey, Warren Leatherman, Willard Hunsberger, and Ernest Goertz. A special feature of this unit was the Relief Training unit January 1944-February 1945. A report in book form (*The Seagull*) was published by the unit.   H.S.B.

M. Gingerich, *Service for Peace* (Akron, 1949) 228 f.

Howard-Miami County (Ind.) Amish settlement, north of Kokomo, was founded in 1848, largely by settlers from the Holmes County (Ohio) region. The division between the "Old Order" and "progressive" factions, which spread throughout the country, took place in the new settlement sometime between 1856 and 1863. The Old Order community almost died out but began to revive in 1887-90. It has never been large, and in 1955 had only two small congregations with a total of 88 members. The two Mennonite (MC) congregations of the area had 422 members, while the Beachy Amish congregation, organized in 1939, had 49 members. A small Conservative Amish congregation organized a few years before the Beachy Amish division failed to thrive.   H.S.B.

Howard-Miami Mennonite Church (MC), located about 12 miles northeast of Kokomo, Ind., on the Howard-Miami county line, a member of the Indiana-Michigan Conference, was organized in 1848 by Amish settlers from Tuscarawas and Holmes counties in Ohio. The Sunday school was organized in 1869. The present building was remodeled in 1917. In 1946 the congregation began a mission station in near-by Kokomo. The settlements at Fairview and Pleasant View, Mich., were made by members from this congregation. In 1955 the total baptized membership of this congregation and its mission outpost was 422. The present bishop is Anson Horner; the ministers are Niles Slabaugh and Emanuel Hochstedler.   E.S.R.

Mennonite Church History of Howard-Miami Counties, Indiana (Scottdale, 1916).

Howl Ranch (Tschetter), a Hutterite Bruderhof established in 1948 near Irricana, Alberta. It had a population of 76 in 1950.

Hoyte (Hoite, Huyte) **Riencx** (Renix, Renicx, Rienicks, Reincx), also called Hoyte Renix Santvoort, a Dutch Mennonite elder, a cobbler. The years of birth and death unknown; he died after 1600. Hoyte Riencx was ordained as an elder in 1555 by Leenaert Bouwens (*q.v.*), who had baptized him and of whom Hoyte remained a loyal follower. He lived at Bolsward (*q.v.*), a Dutch town in Friesland. K. Vos surmised that Riencx was present at the Mennonite conference of elders held at Wismar in 1554 or 1555, and may also have been present at a meeting of elders in Harlingen in 1557, where Menno Simons and Leenaert Bouwens disagreed on banning and shunning. K. Vos also supposed that a letter by Menno Simons (printed in *Opera Omnia,* 1681, 392) was addressed to Hoyte Riencx. In 1566-67, during the Frisian-Flemish troubles, he took the side of the Frisians, as did Leenaert Bouwens. In 1590, when the group of the moderate Young Frisians (*q.v.*) was founded by Pieter Willems Bogaert, Lubbert Gerritsz, and Jan Hendriks of Schiedam, Hoyte also joined this group. He was attacked by the Reformed ministers of Stavoren and Grouw, and in 1600 by Johannes Bogerman (*q.v.*) and Gosuinus Geldorp, Reformed ministers of Sneek.

Doreslaer-Austrosylvius mentions (pp. 151, 154) a writing by "H.R." of 1563, which had been approved by the Mennonite leaders of "Vrieslant, Hollant, Brabant, Groeningerlant ende Emderlandt." These initials apparently mean Hoyte Riencx.

Hoyte Riencx, though he played an important part in the Frisian-Flemish schism, seems not to have been a highly gifted man; his antagonists have described him as a haughty, narrow-minded man.   vdZ.

BRN VII, 51, 62, 67 f.; K. Vos, *Menno Simons* (Leiden, 1914) *passim,* see Index; Kühler, *Geschiedenis* I, *passim,* see Index; *DB* 1893, 12-79 *passim;* A à Dooreslaer and P. J. Austro-Sylvius, *Grondighe ende Clare Vertooninge* (Enchuysen, 1637).

Hrubcice (also *Hrubschitz*): see **Rupschitz.**

Hubbard, Oregon, a village (pop. 493) in the Willamette Valley in Marion County. Approximately 500 Mennonites live in the general area, largely of the M.C. group, and some of the General Conference Church. Most live east of Hubbard in two areas: one surrounding the Hopewell (MC) and the Zion (MC) congregations and the other about three or four miles further east near the Bethel (MC) congregation about 10 miles east of Hubbard. Only about 5 per cent of them live in or near Hubbard. The General Conference Church is near Barlow and Canby to the northeast. The area in which the Mennonites live is one of diversified farming and dairying, which includes berries, cherries, and other fruits, and small grains with some corn for feed; milk is sold on the Portland market about 30 miles to the north. Two tile and brick factories are owned and operated by Mennonites in the Zion community. A few are engaged in the lumbering industry; one large mill is owned by a Mennonite. Mennonites first came to this area in 1892 and held the first services in their homes. Some of the early names still found in the membership are Roth, Kropf, King, Hostetler, Lais, Yoder, Kenagy, Schultz, Strubhar, Burkholder, Hamilton, Nofziger, Rogie. The soil is very productive and well drained, and the climate is moderate with very few freezing days in the winter and few hot days in the summer.   P.E.Y.

Huber, a name used early in the 19th century for the Mennonite (MC) settlement in Haldimand Co., Ont., near Lake Erie, where the Hoovers (Hubers) pioneered before 1800. The cemetery at the lake shore southeast of Selkirk village continued to be known as Huber far into the 19th century (see **Rainham** Mennonite Church). Preacher Jacob Swartz is recorded as buried at the Huber church in 1866.   J.C.F.

Huber, Hans, a saddle maker of Strasbourg, one of the first members of the Anabaptist group at that place. He was baptized by Jakob Gross (*q.v.*). Because of his Anabaptist faith he was imprisoned at Lahr and then expelled from the city. At his trial in Strasbourg in 1527 he presented his views on the ban: Christians who do not live in accord with Christ's command should be expelled from the brotherhood, because one should not have fellowship with them. (Röhrich's article in *Ztscht für die hist. Theol.,* 1860, 30, 35; *ML* II, 353.) HEGE.

Huber, Hans, an Anabaptist martyr of Braunöken (probably Brauneck in Upper Bavaria, Germany), a cobbler, was seized at Wasserburg on the Inn in 1542 under Baron von Oettingen, having been recognized as an Anabaptist. All attempts to move him from his faith were futile; he was sentenced to death by fire. Even in the face of the terrible torture he remained true to his confession. On the fagots, when his hair and beard were already singed off, he was once more offered freedom if he would return to the Catholic Church. But he refused this pardon and died a martyr. (Beck, *Geschichts-Bücher*, 152; *Mart. Mir.* D 63, E 466; *ML* II, 353.)   HEGE.

Huber, Ulrich, an Anabaptist martyr of Rötenbach, Signau district, Switzerland, was executed at Bern for the sake of his faith in 1538.

Mart. Mir. E 1129; A. Fluri, *Beiträge zur Gesch. der Täufer* (Bern, 1912) 14; *ML* II, 353.

Huber, Wolfgang, an Anabaptist martyr, was executed in 1559 at Titmoning (Bavaria) with Wolf Maier (*Mart. Mir.* D 243, E 617; see *Die Lieder der Hutterischen Brüder*, 623, where two hymns written by the latter with a later supplement about their death are printed, both with the title, "Wo soll ich mich hinkehren"). (*ML* II, 353.)

Huber (MC), a "preaching appointment" in York Co., Ont., which appeared in the *Calendar of Appointments* for 1854. In 1858 the meeting place was given as Whitchurch Twp., which is north of Markham. The Mennonite minister Martin Huber (Hoover) resided near the present village of Gormley for several years before moving to Indiana in 1857. It appears that services were held in or near his home before he left this section. The name Stecklin is later used in referring to this settlement. Stecklin alternated in services with Huber before the building of the Almira Mennonite Church in 1860. The Steckley pioneers lived a few miles east of Huber at Bethesda village. (See **Stecklin.**)   J.C.F.

Hübert, Heinrich (1810-95), the first elder of the Mennonite Brethren Church, was born in Münsterberg, one of the newer villages of the Molotschna settlement in southern Russia. From here he moved to Liebenau, where he became the manager and owner of a treadmill, and served as presiding officer of the village council for a number of years. In 1861 he sold his business interests at Liebenau largely because of the pressure of his creditors, no doubt due to his affiliation with the newly organized Mennonite Brethren Church. Later on he changed his residence to Blumenort, and from there moved to the new Kuban settlement in 1873.

Hübert received his education in the Zentralschule of Ohrloff under Tobias Voth, who inspired in Hübert a love for music, poetry, and nature study. Hübert was a habitual reader of the new books from the circulating library sponsored by Voth, and was inspired by the writings of men like Hofacker, Krummacher, and Spurgeon. In his home congregation, the Ohrloff Mennonite Church, he was held in high esteem until he became a signatory of the *Ausgangs-Schrift* of the newly formed M.B. Church on Jan. 6, 1860. Hübert's part in the first struggles of this new movement is not exactly known, but his name is affixed to such documents as the *Ausgangs-Schrift*, addressed to the Mennonite elders of the Molotschna; the explanation of the

Brethren written to the leaders of the churches of Ohrloff and Halbstadt on March 19, 1860, in which they replied to the charges that the new group was interpreting the Bible one-sidedly, and respected no existing church organization; the explanation to the *Fürsorgekomitee;* and the inquiry directed to the Mennonite elders of the Molotschna on Jan. 1, 1861, requesting permission to move away from the Molotschna settlement.

May 30, 1860, was designated by the new church for the election of ministers in the home of Jakob Reimer, where 27 members cast their votes, 24 for Heinrich Hübert as the first preacher of the M.B. Church. Hands were laid on Hübert by the oldest brother of the group, Franz Klaassen, of Elisabethtal. He was ordained elder in 1868 in the home of Cornelius Neufeld in Neukirch by Johann Fast of Rückenau.

Movements of a highly emotional nature (*die Fröhlichen*), which threatened to make inroads upon this new group, were firmly restrained and in 1862 officially condemned by Heinrich Hübert and his assistant, Jakob Becker.

When Hübert was imprisoned at Tokma by the Russian government on a false charge that he had baptized a Russian, the emotional forces gained control and dismissed Hübert from his office. His case was reviewed, however, in 1865, and repentance on the part of those responsible for ousting Hübert opened the door for his reinstatement. The group, not knowing what to do, cast lots which turned in favor of Hübert's reinstatement. When released from prison he resumed his duties until he emigrated to the Kuban settlement, after having ordained Abraham Schellenberg, the elder of the M.B. Church in the Molotschna. In the Kuban area he was leader of the M.B. Church until May 1877, when he ordained Daniel Fast as his successor and retired because his health had been seriously impaired during the ten months of imprisonment. In 1895, at the age of 85, he died.

Hübert is said to have been the deepest thinker in the Brethren group of that time, and, although he was handicapped in his public ministry because of a weak voice, his sincere faith more than compensated for this deficiency and succeeded in inspiring faith and Christian living in the newly formed M.B. Church.†   J.J.T.

Friesen, *Brüderschaft*, 776, 154; Johannes F. Harms, *Gesch. der Menn.-Brüdergemeinde* (Hillsboro, 1924) p. viii and p. 342; P. Regier, *Kurzgefasste Gesch. der Menn. Brüder-Gemeinde* (Berne, 1901) 97; F. Isaak, *Die Molotschnaer Mennoniten* (Elkhart, 1908) 354; P. E. Schellenberg, "Makers of Our Church," *Tabor College Herald* I, No. 1 (October 1930) 21-27.

Hübert, Johann (d. 1944), was born in Steinthal, Russia. After some study in Russia and Holland he was sent out in 1893 by the Dutch Mennonite Mission Association to its missionary fields in what then was called the Dutch East Indies; he settled at Kedungpendjalin on the island of Java, where he was active in teaching and evangelizing without interruption for a period of more than 15 years. He also founded a little hospital at Kedungpendjalin, of which he was the manager until 1938. In September 1908 he returned to Europe, visiting

Holland, Germany, and Russia. In April 1910 he again went to his post. In course of time his field considerably expanded, a number of new posts at Margakerto and other places being founded. In 1938 Hübert resigned because of advanced age. He was succeeded in this territory by Otto Stauffer (*q.v.*). When Stauffer was arrested in 1940, Hübert served again until the Japanese invasion of Indonesia made all activities impossible in 1942. He died in Indonesia in 1944.   vᴅZ.

Reports of the *Doopsgezinde Vereeniging tot . . . Evangelieverbreiding.*

Hubmaier (Huebmör), **Balthasar** (1480?-1528), an Anabaptist leader 1525-28, particularly in Moravia, where he was the head of a large congregation 1526-28, outstanding for the number and importance of his writings, but of no great permanent influence on the later Anabaptist-Mennonite movement, since he diverged from the main line of Anabaptists on the question of nonresistance, and his group of "Schwertler" did not survive his death more than one or two years. He has been variously evaluated. Some have judged him solely by his attitude in the confusion of the Peasants' War, others see him only in his reformatory work in the church. The Baptists in general have viewed him as their great hero among the Anabaptists and celebrated the 400th anniversary of his martyrdom with a special observance in Vienna in 1928. The following presentation, which is based on an objective examination of his works, and which does not leave his opponents out of consideration, will show that he did not advocate radical views, either in the realm of society or the church. His motto was "The truth is immortal." He strove toward it. The truth, he says, occasionally lets itself be captured, yea lashed, crowned, crucified, and buried, but on the third day it will rise victorious, and reign in triumph. This striving of his for the truth becomes evident in his course in life and his teaching, and for it he went to his death with courage.

I. *Hubmaier's Life and Teachings.* The date of Balthasar Hubmaier's birth is not known. It is assumed that it was in the early 1480's. His native town was Friedberg near Augsburg. His contemporaries called him Pacimontanus after the former, or Augustanus after the latter. He called himself usually Huebmör (as the *Geschicht-Buch* spells it) or Huebmör von Friedberg. He probably received his early education at home; he attended the Latin school in Augsburg. To his contemporaries we owe a description of his appearance and his personality. He was of short stature and swarthy; when he is described as being proud, it must not be overlooked that this description was given by an opponent.

At Easter 1503 Hubmaier matriculated at the University of Freiburg, Germany, where Eck, later the opponent of Luther, acquired powerful influence over him, and praised him for his rapid progress. In genuine devotion he pursued his theological studies. Lack of funds compelled him to accept a position as a schoolteacher (1507) in Schaffhausen, but he soon returned to Freiburg, took his baccalaureate in 1510, and was ordained

to the priesthood. When his teacher Eck went to Ingolstadt, he followed; and there he received the honor of a licentiate, then of a Doctor of Theology. In 1515 he was prorector of the university, and a year later, because of his pulpit eloquence, he was given the honorable position of pastor and chaplain in the ancient cathedral in Regensburg. The populace of Regensburg was involved in a dispute of long standing with the Jews; in it Hubmaier took an active part. It ended in the expulsion of the Jews and the razing of their synagogue; in its place a chapel "zur schönen Maria" was erected, where according to the credulous public there was no lack of miracles; this led to a great concourse of pilgrims and rich gifts for a church. Hubmaier, as the first chaplain of the chapel, kept a record of the supposed miracles. The pilgrimages to Regensburg caused some excitement which resulted in some coarse abuses, for which Hubmaier blamed the eccentric character of the pilgrims.

These events in particular, then also the insecurity of his position, led Hubmaier to accept a pastorate in Hapsburg territory, in the town of Waldshut in Breisgau, situated at an important ford in the Rhine. He preached his first sermon there in the spring of 1521. He was still loyal to his Catholic faith when the Reformation movement had made itself felt in all parts of the Holy Roman Empire, punctiliously observing all the customs of the church, and won the complete confidence of his congregation. But by the summer of 1522 he had begun to change. He studied Luther's writings, made connections with the friends of the Reformation, and engaged in a study of the Pauline epistles. Soon a new call to the Regensburg church reached him and he accepted. But there was already some evidence of his leanings toward the new doctrine. His position became equivocal, and even before the year contracted for had expired he returned to his pastorate at Waldshut, which had been held open for him.

The change in his religious convictions, which drew Hubmaier in the direction of the Swiss rather than to Luther, he now expressed without hesitation. He opened correspondence with the Swiss reformers and in 1523 discussed with Zwingli the passages of Scripture on baptism. "Then Zwingli agreed with me, that children should not be baptized before they are instructed in the faith." Then he began some innovations in Waldshut. Of decisive importance was his participation in the disputation held by order of the Zürich council in the city hall on Oct. 26-28, 1523. Here Hubmaier expressed himself sharply in opposition to the abuses in the Mass and the worship of images. He declared that the Bible alone must decide such questions; the Mass is not a sacrifice, but a proclamation of Christ's testament, which commemorates His bitter suffering and His sacrifice of His life; as a sacrificial offering the Mass benefits neither the living nor the dead. "Just as I cannot believe for another, neither can I hold a Mass for another." Concerning the worship of images he cited the Scripture that a carved or graven image is an abomination to God.

As a pulpit orator Hubmaier received great applause. His attitude in Zürich met with the disapproval of the Austrian government, which painfully watched the progress of the new ecclesiastical movement in its outlying lands. But Hubmaier continued on his way. In the spirit of Zwingli he delivered his 18 *Schlussreden* concerning the Christian life, which he hoped would win the clergy of Waldshut. The citizenry was already on his side. His connections extended over a large portion of South Germany. But the Catholic party was not idle. Sharply worded letters from secular as well as spiritual authorities demanded the removal of Hubmaier. So much the more expressly he worked for the Reformation in Waldshut, conducting the religious service in German, and abolishing the laws on fasting and the celibacy. He married Elisabeth Hügeline, the daughter of a citizen of Reichenau, who willingly and bravely shared his later lot. All the attempts of the government to restore the old order of things in Waldshut failed; it therefore decided to compel the city to obedience by the use of force. Then Hubmaier requested his own dismissal.

On Sept. 1, 1524, he left Waldshut for Schaffhausen. But he was not safe there either. "Very soon," he wrote, "warnings were brought to me that I was to be arrested." The government opened negotiations with Switzerland, but since Hubmaier had settled in Schaffhausen "in der Freiung" the city refused to deliver him into the hands of Austria. In three written *Erbietungen* he declared himself ready to defend what he had been teaching for two years; and in order to defend himself against the charge of heresy he wrote his booklet *Von Ketzern und ihren Verbrennern.* His opponents were meanwhile incessantly working to have him extradited. Not feeling secure "in der Freiung" he returned to Waldshut. The city, threatened with a heavy fine by the government, and hoping to find outside assistance, was now in open opposition to the government. Hubmaier became the soul of its resistance, and now completed the Reformation of the church in Waldshut.

He still adhered to Zwingli's party. But Zwingli was already meeting opposition in Zürich; his opponents accused him of not holding earnestly to the cause, and wanted him to separate from the ungodly and to gather a brotherhood of the true church of God. The leaders among his opponents were Conrad Grebel (*q.v.*), Felix Manz (*q.v.*), Georg Blaurock (*q.v.*), and Wilhelm Reublin (*q.v.*), who, according to the *Geschicht-Buch,* "did not recognize infant baptism as a true baptism and demanded that one must and should be baptized in accord with Christian order and the institution of the Lord," i.e., be taught, and then baptized.

These Anabaptists found in Hubmaier their champion. On Jan. 17, 1525, the well-known disputation was held in Zürich to settle the question, which, though its outcome was officially a victory for Zwingli's side, nevertheless won new adherents to the Anabaptist movement. Hubmaier now also in actual practice dropped infant baptism, baptizing only the children of such parents as were still weak in the faith and therefore desired baptism for their children. Anabaptists came to Waldshut and on Feb. 2, 1525, Hubmaier published his *Oeffentliche Erbietung,* offering to prove in a public debate that infant baptism had no foundation in Scripture. But his request for a disputation was apparently not granted. Hubmaier's step had the support of a large part of the citizenry, but drew upon him the hostility of the Swiss reformers. He undertook further reforms in the order of divine service; after a period in which he conducted the Mass in German, he abolished it altogether and had the altars removed from the church, observed communion as practiced by the apostles, and finally, in accepting baptism by Wilhelm Reublin at Eastertime, openly joined the Anabaptists.

The opposition of the Anabaptists had made of Zwingli an avowed champion of infant baptism. In reply to his book, *Von der Taufe, der Wiedertaufe und Kindertaufe,* Hubmaier wrote his booklet, *Vom christlichen Tauf der Gläubigen,* which is correctly regarded as the classic presentation of his teaching on baptism and as one of the best defenses of adult baptism ever written. It was directed against Zwingli, although it does not mention him by name, and made a profound impression on both friend and foe. Zwingli took up arms against it, and the council of Zürich thought it necessary to arrange another disputation, which was held on Nov. 6. Public opinion acclaimed Zwingli as the victor. Grebel, Manz, and Blaurock were summoned before the council and warned to desist from their teaching, and because they did not heed the warning they were taken to prison, so that if they persisted in separation, they should be most severely punished. Adult baptism and the postponement of infant baptism were forbidden. Zwingli's booklet against Hubmaier is dated Nov. 5, and Hubmaier's refutation, Nov. 30, but the latter was not published until the following year at Nikolsburg in Moravia, after misfortune had descended upon Waldshut and its preachers.

Of equal significance with his religious activity was Hubmaier's political position. There is no doubt that he encouraged the city of Waldshut in its resistance against the Austrian government which led to armed intervention, and himself took part in the preparations for battle. Contemporaries and later writers have actually considered him the instigator of the Peasants' War. Thus the chronicler Letsch says, "and if one thinks this matter over properly, this Doctor Balthasar is a beginner and originator of the whole Peasants' War."

Wherever Hubmaier turned his steps later, this ill fame pursued him, and it did no good to resist it. In his booklet *Eine kurze Entschuldigung,* he said, "In being represented as an agitator, I fare as Christ did. He too had to be a revolutionary, and yet I testify with God and several thousand persons, that no preacher in all the regions where I have been has taken more pains and done more work by writing and preaching than I have that the government be obeyed; for it is of God. As concerns interest and tithes, I said that Christ also gave a third or a fifth. But the fact is: they tried to compel us to abandon the Word of God with force and contrary to law. This has been our only complaint." Likewise the people of Waldshut wanted to obey the house of Austria in all things, as their *Erbietung* says: "If there were a stone ten fathoms deep in the earth that was not truly Austrian," they would scratch it up with their nails and cast it into the Rhine.

Hubmaier expressed himself similarly in other writings. It has, of course, been demonstrated that he was not an instigator of the Peasants' War; nevertheless it is a fact that in Waldshut he was in close alliance with the peasants, supported them, and was aided by them. He assisted the citizens of Waldshut with counsel and helped them compose letters. He enlarged the peasants' Articles that came to his hands through the army, interpreted them, and told the people to accept them as Christian and reasonable. Much has been laid to his charge by his enemies, of which he was innocent. In Waldshut the point at issue in the entire conflict was not the removal or alleviation of feudal burdens, but, as Hubmaier expressly stated, the freedom of Protestant doctrine. If the people of Waldshut would only be granted religious liberty, they would be ready to fulfill all their obligations as Austrian subjects. But the government sought with a single blow to strike the peasants as well as the citizens of Waldshut who were fighting for the Gospel. It succeeded. First the peasants were defeated at Griessen, and then Waldshut was conquered.

With difficulty Hubmaier succeeded in escaping on Dec. 5, 1525. In flight and with tattered garments he went to Zürich. The city refused to comply with the demand of the Austrian government to extradite him, kept him in light confinement, and arranged a disputation between him and Zwingli, which was held on Dec. 21, 1525, but ended inconclusively. The city demanded that he recant, and he complied on April 15—not without severe qualms of conscience; for while he was on the point of renouncing his teaching on baptism he prayed that God might again establish the two bonds of the Christian faith, baptism and communion; even if through fear of man and weakness of mind he was forced to yield these points by tyranny, torture, sword, fire, or water, he prayed the merciful Father in heaven to raise him up again and not permit him to part from this world without this faith.

In spite of his recantation his position in Zürich was precarious, for he was in danger of falling into the hands of imperial or Swiss enemies. He finally managed to leave Zürich secretly. He went to Constance and from there to Augsburg, where he associated with zealous Anabaptists, and in the summer of 1526 he turned his steps toward Austria, via Ingolstadt and Regensburg. His goal was Moravia, where several creeds lived side by side without molestation. In Augsburg, among others, he baptized Hans Denk (*q.v.*).

Early in July 1526 Hubmaier arrived at Nikolsburg, which through his influence became for a time the center of the Anabaptist movement. Contemporary reports state that Hubmaier's presence there brought about an extraordinary influx of Anabaptists. About 12,000 are said to have gradually collected there and in the vicinity. The *Geschichts-Bücher* of the Hutterian Brethren also report, "In 1526 Balthasar Huebmör came to Nikolsburg in Moravia, began to teach and to preach, but the people accepted his teaching and in a short time many were baptized." This Moravian town became to the Anabaptists "what Emmaus was to the Lord, when He was asked to stay there." From all of South Germany they gathered and spread their teaching over all southern Moravia. Here they found the soil well prepared. The Protestants had formed a church here two years before, under the protection of the feudal lord, Leonhard von Liechtenstein; Hubmaier now made contacts with the preachers of this church, Hans Spitalmaier (*q.v.*) and Oswald Glait (*q.v.*). The provost Martin Göschl of Kanitz also promoted his cause. Anabaptists of established reputation, including some who suffered a martyr's death for their faith, like Hans Hut (*q.v.*), Leonhard Schiemer (*q.v.*), and Hans Schlaffer, came to the community. The printer Simprecht Sorg of Zürich, called Froschower (*q.v.*), who had been staying in Styria for some time, was now called in by Leonhard von Liechtenstein, brought his entire print shop with him, and published all the works Hubmaier wrote after leaving Zürich. Most of them are dedicated to the heads of the Moravian nobility, with the intention of winning their favor to the Anabaptist cause.

Not all the Anabaptists remained true to Hubmaier. Among his opponents was Hans Hut (*q.v.*), an apostle of the Anabaptists in Upper and Lower Austria, with whom many of Hubmaier's former friends sided, because in their opinion Hubmaier's program was too moderate. Hut had even before the Peasants' War preached the coming of the last day; he adhered to these chiliastic views, and opposed Hubmaier especially on the questions "of the sword," and whether war taxes should be paid. Hubmaier tried to remove the tension by means of a disputation, which was held at Bergen, a village near Nikolsburg. The discussion centered on community of goods and war taxes. The Anabaptists were faced by a dilemma by the demand for war taxes, for on the one hand they were compelled by law to pay them, and on the other hand their religious principles forbade warfare or the payment of taxes to wage war. The disputation did not achieve the desired result of unity. A second disputation ended similarly. Hans Hut was "held in the castle against his will by the lord of Liechtenstein, because he would or could not agree with him to bear the sword"; he was, however, released at night by a friend. Hut's opposition caused Hubmaier to speak of it openly once more in the "Spital," and in his final book he again discussed this controversy: he rejected all violence, to which Hut was evidently inclined, and told him and others this to their faces. From the cross-examination of an attendant at the Nikolsburg disputation it is learned that other subjects were also discussed there: baptism, communion, the Last Judgment, the end of the world, the new kingdom, and the coming of Christ. The Nikolsburg disputation attracted attention far beyond the borders of Moravia, as can be seen in the

"Articles from Moravia," which claim to be the teaching of the Anabaptists, but which mingle much that is false with the truth.

The conflict between Hut and Hubmaier resulted in Hubmaier's publishing his teachings in a series of pamphlets; but, assured of the powerful support of the nobility he was also able to refute earlier rumors spread by his opponents. Thus in the short period of one year he published no fewer than 18 works, some of which he had written before coming to Nikolsburg. The first, probably finished at the end of November 1525 and published in July 1526, was his *Gespräch auf Meister Ulrich Zwinglis Taufbüchlein von dem Kindertauf.* When he wrote it he evidently did not yet know of Zwingli's sharp reply to his book *Vom christlichen Tauf* (see above), since he did not mention it. He complained about the severe suffering he endured in Zürich, where he "wished to present the proof in the divine Word that infant baptism is a work without any foundation in the divine Word." He complained further of Zwingli's severe attitude toward the Anabaptists, who, he (Zwingli) preached, should be beheaded. At Zwingli's instigation about 20 Anabaptists had been put into prison, there to die. At the same time an edict was issued which threatened all Anabaptists with drowning. In this manner he overcame the Anabaptists, but not a Scripture did he produce against them; instead, as he admitted in his booklet *Von den aufrührigen Geistern,* those who baptized children had no foundation for it in Scripture. "In my teaching," continues Hubmaier, "the Holy Scripture shall be the judge, in temporal affairs the government, to whom God has given the sword, to protect the godly and to punish the wicked." He did not want to take revenge on Zwingli, but only contribute to the re-establishment of the church. Four other booklets which were already finished, were to deal with these subjects: (1) a catechism or *Lehrtafel,* what a man should know before he is baptized with water; (2) what Christian water baptism is; (3) a Christian church order; and (4) a reply to the mocking speech of some preachers in Basel. Hubmaier had great expectations from this polemic against Zwingli: in six years no article had been published which offered clearer proof that infant baptism should not be permitted.

The booklet itself consists of five parts, of which the third is the most important, maintaining that one can become a disciple of Christ only by teaching and faith. When Jesus commanded that all believers should be baptized, all those were excluded who had not been instructed in the faith. To Zwingli's "most powerful argument," that the baptism of children (like circumcision with the Jews) is "an *anhebend* sign" whereby we obligate ourselves, Hubmaier replies: The child weeping in its cradle knows nothing of a sign, or a duty, or a baptism. In summary, Hubmaier teaches: (1) no element, only faith, cleanses the soul; (2) baptism cannot wash away sins; (3) it is therefore only a testimony of the inner faith and a sign of the obligation of a new life; (4) whether infants are God's children may be left to God; (5) Noah's ark rather than circumcision is a figure of baptism; (6) only

adult baptism is founded upon Scripture. Infant baptism is not of God. Hubmaier asked where there is mention in the Bible of a godfather.

The four booklets mentioned are directly connected with this polemic against Zwingli. But first Hubmaier published a booklet dedicated to the provost Göschl, *Der uralten und gar neuen Lehrer Urteil, dass man die Kinder nicht taufen solle, bis sie im Glauben unterrichtet sind.* It is a collection of quotations which prove that in all periods outstanding men of the church have preferred adult baptism to infant baptism. Since every Christian must be instructed before he is baptized, Hubmaier wrote *Eine christliche Lehrtafel, die ein jeder Mensch, bevor er im Wasser getauft wird, wissen soll.* The foreword is dated Dec. 10, 1526. This *Lehrtafel* was intended to in general remove ignorance, namely, among the clergy. The depth of this ignorance he reported from his own experience: "With my own blush of shame I testify and say it openly, that I became a Doctor in the Holy Scriptures without understanding this Christian article which is contained in this booklet, yea, without having read the Gospels or the Pauline epistles to the end. Instead of living waters, I was held to cisterns of muddy water, poisoned by human feet." In the form of a dialogue between Leonhard and Hans (the Christian names of his sponsors in the house of Liechtenstein) he discussed the articles of the Christian faith.

The next book has the title *Von der brüderlichen Strafe;* it may be the same book that he had earlier called *Eine Ordnung christlicher Kirche,* and brought to Nikolsburg completed. It deals with the need for church discipline, and gives instructions for brotherly admonition. It was printed with *Vom christlichen Bann* early in 1527. It was followed by *Grund und Ursach, dass ein jeglicher Mensch, der in seiner Kindheit getauft ist, schuldig sei, sich recht nach der Ordnung Christi taufen zu lassen, ob er schon 100 Jahre alt wäre.* It was dedicated to Johann von Pernstein auf Helfenstein, the governor of Moravia. In it Hubmaier presented 13 reasons that obligate men to be baptized according to Christ's order, even if they had already been baptized in childhood. This book is a supplement to his *Taufbüchlein,* and was in all likelihood finished before 1526. It was not published until the following year.

The last book, the outline of which was drawn up in Switzerland, is the reply to the well-known book by Oecolampadius, and has the title, *Von dem Kindertauf; Oecolampadius usw., Ein Gespräch der Prädikanten zu Basel und Balthasaren Huebmörs von dem Kindertauf.* It is a refutation of the book by Oecolampadius, *Ein Gespräch etlicher Prädikanten zu Basel, gehalten mit etlichen Bekennern des Wiedertaufs,* which was published at Basel in 1525. Hubmaier defended his teaching that Christ ordained baptism for believers, and not for infants. He replied to Oecolampadius's objection that councils, St. Augustine, and the tradition of the church confirm infant baptism, with the argument that faith must be founded not on councils, nor on tradition, but on the Holy Scriptures. "If you can show me a single instance of infant baptism in the

Bible, I am defeated. Anabaptist doctrine is therefore not new, but derives from Christ."

One of the books which Hubmaier brought to Moravia more or less completed has no polemic character. It is *Zwölf Artikel des christlichen Glaubens zu Zürich im Wasserthurm betweis gestellt,* Hubmaier's confession of faith. Here too his teaching on baptism and communion formed the basis for his arguments. He fervently prayed that God might re-establish the two bonds with which He has girt the church, viz., baptism and communion. The book was written April 15, 1526, and printed in 1527.

Written after this book, but published before it, was his *Entschuldigung an alle christgläubigen Menschen, dass sie sich an den erdichteten Unwahrheiten, so ihm seine Missgönner zulegen, nicht ärgern,* printed in 1526. It is a defense against the many untruthful charges made against him in four years. To this point he had patiently borne them, and would continue to bear them, but because so many spirits were offended by them he found it necessary to defend his innocence. He was accused of dishonoring the mother of God, of rejecting the saints, of discarding prayer and the confessional, fasting, the Church Fathers, the councils, etc., in short, of being the archheretic. He replied that his teachings were not innovations; he preached Christ and the Gospel, considered Mary both before and after the birth a pure virgin, honored the saints as God's tools, taught prayer without ceasing, fasted daily; confession must be made hourly; i.e., mourn one's sins; a rattling confession would of course not do; the teachings of the Church Fathers, councils, etc., he tested by the touchstone of the Holy Scriptures. He did not regard monks and nuns, taught the true baptism of Christ, which is ruined by infant baptism; the latter is a misuse of the name of God and a disparagement of Christ; of the Mass the Scriptures contain nothing; the "Pfaffenmesse" is of no more avail than the "Frankfurter Messe"; for at both one can buy and sell every day. If he was called an insurgent and a misleader of the people who preached against the government, he could testify with God and a thousand witnesses that he held the people to obedience toward the government; for it is of God. Without murmuring one must give the taxes, tithes, and tributes and pay it honor and reverence. He then enumerated the persecutions to which he was subjected by the Austrian government, and the slanders broadcast during his stay in Regensburg and Ingolstadt. He protested against the charge that he was a heretic, lamented Zwingli's tyranny without mentioning him by name. This book doubtless originated during his residence in Nikolsburg; it must have been of importance to him to prove that the slanders spread abroad were unfounded.

A considerable number of the works of Hubmaier that follow have didactic contents. His *Kurzes Vaterunser* (Nikolsburg, 1526) is a devotional booklet. In his *Ein einfältiger Unterricht auf die Worte, das ist der Leib mein im Nachtmahl Christi* (Nikolsburg, 1526) he shows "that the breaking, distribution, and eating of the bread is not the breaking, distribution, and eating of the body of Christ, who is in heaven seated at the Father's right hand, but that it is a memorial of His body, an eating in the faith that He suffered for us. And as the bread is 'the body' of Christ in memorial, so is also the blood of Christ a memorial." The book is dedicated to Leonhard von Liechtenstein, to whom a few words of appreciation are addressed, and Nikolsburg is compared with the Biblical Emmaus. In it Hubmaier opposed Luther's concept of communion no less than Zwingli's.

The next book, titled *Eine Form zu taufen in Wasser die im Glauben Unterrichteten* (Nikolsburg, 1527) and dedicated to "Johann Dubschansky von Zedenin und auf Habrowan," contains the baptismal ceremonies "as we apply them at Nikolsburg and elsewhere." Whoever wished to be baptized must notify the bishop, so that the latter might examine him to see whether he had been adequately instructed in the articles of the law, the Gospel, and the doctrine, whether he could pray, and with understanding state the doctrines of the Christian faith. If this was the case, the bishop presented him to the congregation, and urged all the believers to ask God to grant him grace. Then followed the formula of the prayer and the baptismal vow, then the baptism, laying on of hands, and the reception of the candidate into the congregation.

A similar purpose was to be served by *Eine Form des Nachtmahls Christi* (1527). It is dedicated to Lord Burian of Cornitz, a Moravian nobleman who was zealously devoted to the cause of the Reformation, and was sent to him by the (Bohemian) Brother Johann Zeysinger. Hubmaier referred to his booklet, *Ein einfältiger Unterricht,* as a dogmatic presentation of communion, and here presented "in what form communion is held in Nikolsburg." The church was to be called to a fitting place at a suitable time, the table set with ordinary bread and wine, which requires no silver goblets. The priest reminded the audience of their sins, explained the Scriptures that deal with reformation of life and the new birth, asked them individually whether a proper understanding was still lacking, and instructed them, then took the passage on communion and closed, "Let him who would eat of this bread arise and perform his duty of love with heart and mouth, declare his intention to love God and his neighbor, obey the government, submit to brotherly reproof, and desire to eat at the Lord's table." With a prayer of praise and thanks the communion was then taken. Then the congregation again assembled for the closing prayer and the repeated admonition to live a Christian life.

The booklet *Von der brüderlichen Straf* (Nikolsburg, 1527), which is probably identical with the *Ordnung der christlichen Kirche,* and was thus written in Waldshut, proceeds from the idea that "all labor and toil is in vain, baptism and communion futile, if church discipline is not practiced in the church as ordained by Christ; this has been clearly seen in the past few years, when the people, without changing their conduct in life, have learned nothing more than two things. One group says that faith alone saves; the other, that we of ourselves can do nothing good. Both statements are true, but under cover of these truths malice, faithlessness, and unrighteousness have become prevalent, and brotherly love has cooled off more than in 1000 years before. There is only one remedy: Openly committed sins must be punished as a deterrent to others; for such sins eat like a cancer if they are not rooted out; for what one does, the other considers permissible. Secret sins must be punished in secret, as the Lord commands; first before one person, then before two or three witnesses, and finally before the entire congregation. If the question is raised where anyone gets the authority to punish his brother, the answer is, from the baptismal vow, in which each obligates himself to live according to Christ's ordinances. When the brother has been punished in accord with Christ's regulation, and if he still will not forsake sin, then according to the command of Christ he must be excluded from fellowship and banned."

The booklet *Vom christlichen Bann* (Nikolsburg, 1527) appropriately continues the subject of punishment. It is therefore, says Hubmaier, necessary to know what the ban is, the source of the authority of the church, how banning should be carried out, and what to do with the excommunicated member. The ban is the public excommunication of the obstinate sinner from the Christian brotherhood, to the end that he will not give offense in the church, but will rather confess his sin and reform. Christ employed the ban both in word and deed and left it to the church, which then excludes the wicked, unfaithful, and disobedient from the Christian brotherhood. Concerning the form of the ban Hubmaier says that the brother to be expelled has broken the vow he made at his baptism and communion. Therefore the church is excommunicating him. With the expelled member no fellowship may be had henceforth; yet he shall not be treated as an enemy, beaten or killed, but avoided, for the punishment is not given in hatred, but in Christian love for the benefit of the sinner. Hubmaier does not neglect to point out the flagrant abuses that the clergy have practiced with their anathemas, usually pronounced with unchristian motives. If one did not immediately believe what church law commanded, he was from that hour placed under the false ban instead of the Christian, and the secular arm had to be his constable. The man, continues Hubmaier, is released from the ban when he confesses his sin and repents. Naturally if the great lords, nations, and cities refused to accept this regulation of brotherly punishment and of the Christian ban, then it is difficult to set up a Christian regime there.

With nearly the same words as in the book on brotherly punishment Hubmaier in his book *Von der Freiheit des Willens* (Nikolsburg, 1527), dedicated to Georg, Margrave of Brandenburg, says that the people have learned only these two things from the preaching of the Gospel: faith saves, and we have no free will. These statements are only half-truths, from which only a half judgment can be formed. Such half-truths do more damage than complete lies, for they are rated by their appearance of whole truths. People then push their guilt upon God as Adam did upon Eve, and she upon the serpent. To root out such blasphemy is the object of this book; this concept includes how and what man is and can do within and without the grace of God. Man consists of three parts, body, soul, and spirit. Therefore three wills must be recognized, that of the flesh, that of the soul, and that of the spirit. Before the sin of Adam all three parts of man were free and good. After his fall he lost this freedom: as a vassal who is untrue to his lord loses his fief not only for himself, but also for his heirs, so the flesh has lost its freedom through Adam's fall and must return to the earth whence it came. The spirit has remained good, but as a prisoner of the flesh had to eat too; the soul, becoming ill through Adam's disobedience, has lost the knowledge of good and evil and is powerless to carry out the good. Since the fall of man the flesh is useless, the spirit willing to do good; the soul stands between in concern; but, healed by Christ, it has again acquired its lost freedom and can willingly obey the spirit and will the good. Thus it depends only on the soul. According to its decision man is saved or damned. Through Adam's fall man received two wounds, an inner one, which is the inability to recognize good and evil; and an outer one, in doing and carrying out. The former is healed through the law, which teaches him to distinguish between good and evil; the other is healed through the Gospel. Thus no one can use lack of liberty as an excuse; for what Adam lost, Christ brought back.

Das andere Büchlein von der Freiwilligkeit des Menschen (Nikolsburg, 1527) was finished on May 20, 1527, and dedicated to Duke Friedrich von Liegnitz und Brieg. It shows, as is said in the title, that God through His Word gives men the power to become His children and commits to them the decision to will and to do good. It contains the passages of Scripture that show that before the fall man had the grace to keep God's commands and be saved; then those passages that show that man has regained the freedom lost through Adam. In the second part follow the conclusions, which show the purpose of the book most clearly. Some of these are as follows: He who knows what the new birth is will not deny the freedom of the human will. He who says that the flesh does not need to will contrary to its natural will or perform the will of the soul that has been awakened by God, gropes along a wall in midday. That lord is foolish who sets a goal for his people and says, "Go on, run that you may win," when he knows that they are in chains and are incapable of running. All things happen in accord with God's will: the good in the power of His word, the evil to punishment. God wills that men should do good; He also wills that he who will not do good be the master of his own works and do evil, that the forsaking of the good may be punished in him. We do not know whom God has elected and which of the two He will give, blessedness or damnation. In the third part he discusses the objections that have been made. He explains 16 situations. Thus if one says to him: God has mercy on whom He will and hardens whom He will, he replies: There is an absolute will of God which is subject to no rule, and a revealed will, which wants all men to be saved. Of course,

God does not have two wills; this is a figure of speech so that we may understand.

Already in his *Kurze Entschuldigung* Hubmaier had expressed himself on the attitude of men to their authorized government and defended himself against the charge that he was a rabble-rouser and heretic. He develops this further in his *Vom Schwert* (1527), which he dedicated to Lord Arkleb von Boskowitz und Tschernahora auf Trebitz, chief Landeskämmerer of Moravia. He wished to present in it what had always been his conception of government. More earnestly than any other preacher he observed the Scriptures on government, but he also pointed out to the tyrants their vices. Hence the envy, hate, and hostility to him. Hubmaier first treats those passages with which his enemies attack him and then cites those which form the basis of his attitude. His opponents, for example, point out the passage, My kingdom is not of this world. If the kingdom of Christ is not of this world, then he would not be permitted to bear the sword. But the passage merely states that our kingdom should not be of this world. But alas, it is of this world, as we ourselves pray in the Lord's Prayer: Thy kingdom come. Or the opponents quote: Put up thy sword. But here Christ was merely saying that those should not bear the sword who are not entitled to do so; else they will perish by the sword. In the same manner all the passages are explained. For the affirmation of government among Christians Hubmaier cites the verse: Let every soul be subject to the higher powers. For there is no power but of God. This passage alone is sufficient to establish the government against all the gates of hell. Subjects should, of course, examine the spirit of their governments, whether they rule out of pride, envy, hatred, or self-seeking rather than for the common welfare and peace. This is not bearing the sword against the government. But when the government punishes the evildoers to create peace for the good, then help, then advise, then support, as often as it is asked of you. Only when the government is childish or foolish or cannot reign wisely, then if one can legally escape it is good to do so, for God has often punished an entire country on account of a bad government. But if it cannot be done without insurrection, then endure it. No doubt this booklet was intended also to make good the impression that the Nikolsburg disputation must have made on the ruling classes.

II. *Hubmaier's Arrest, Imprisonment, and Martyrdom.* While Hubmaier was increasingly promoting his teaching, the Anabaptist movement with its elemental force spread throughout the Austrian hereditary lands. From all sides reports reached the government on the success of the Anabaptist movement and advice for its suppression. Ferdinand I had after the death of King Louis of Hungary and Bohemia in the battle of Mohács acquired these lands and it was doubtful that he would deal as tolerantly in Moravia as his predecessors had done. He was particularly disquieted by the reports he received from the Austrian authorities. He did not fail to issue edicts for the suppression of the Anabaptists. On Aug. 12, 1527, he sent a letter to the citizens of Freistadt in Upper Austria with the command to seize Hans Hut, Hubmaier's former associate. But more important to the government than Hut's capture was the capture of Hubmaier, its old opponent from the time of Waldshut, to whom, according to a contemporary eyewitness, masses of people were streaming from the adjacent regions. Hubmaier had no intimation of the danger hovering over him when he signed the foreword of his book on the sword. Four weeks later he found himself imprisoned in Vienna. The details of his capture are not known. The *Geschichts-Bücher* only record that Ferdinand I had cited Hans and Leonhard von Liechtenstein to Vienna together with their chaplains. "From that hour Balthasar Huebmör with his wife was seized and sent to the Kreuzenstein castle." Hubmaier's extradition was not so much a consequence of his religious work as of his political activity in Waldshut; for the persecution of Anabaptists was not permitted in Moravia until after the edict of the diet in March 1528. Some manuscripts of the chronicles state that Hubmaier was forged to a wagon when he was seized in Nikolsburg, and was thus taken to Vienna. That in the Hubmaier affair the primary issue was his political activity in Waldshut is seen in the command Ferdinand issued to his government in Ensisheim to conduct a careful investigation of Hubmaier's actions in Waldshut, where he caused insurrection and revolt among the common people. His teachings occupy a subordinate place; certain individuals in Waldshut are to be questioned about them. The government in Ensisheim as well as that in Innsbruck complied with the order. Two "witnesses" in Hubmaier's own hand are sent in, one of which had much to say "against Luther"; the second indicated "that his spirit had tended to awaken insurrection against the government"; those in Waldshut had been the first and the last to persist in it and conduct themselves according to the Doctor's teaching.

Kreuzenstein is a castle in Lower Austria, now newly rebuilt from its ruins, three quarters of an hour north of Korneuburg. When Hubmaier was taken there is not certain. It is only known that he lay in prison in Vienna several weeks. But at the turn of the year he was in Kreuzenstein; for from that place on Jan. 3, 1528, he sent his booklet, *Eine Rechenschaft seines Glaubens,* to Ferdinand I. Kreuzenstein was at that time a possession of Niklas, Duke of Salm, but was used as a state prison, and was in a bad state of repair.

Stephan Sprugel, the contemporary and eyewitness of Hubmaier's execution, reports that Hubmaier enjoyed numerous visits by learned men of good repute, who, with good intentions and sympathy urged him to renounce his errors. Hubmaier himself bemoaned his strict confinement. Illness and other difficulties had come upon him, and he suffered from want of books. The prospects for release were not favorable, even if he would recant, because of his activity in Waldshut.

In his need Hubmaier cast his longing glances upon Johannes Faber (*q.v.*), his erstwhile fellow student and friend, but now his opponent, and addressed a petition to King Ferdinand to grant him a conference with Faber. This was granted. Faber described the course of his conversation in his booklet, *Adversus D. Balthasarum Pacimontanum . . . orthodoxae fidei catholicae defensio*. He had gladly acceded to Hubmaier's wish, for he had known him for years and had cultivated friendly intercourse with him while he carried on his studies with him, being still of irreproachable character. Faber was accompanied to Kreuzenstein by Markus Beckh of Leopoldsdorf and Ambrosius Salzer, the rector of the University of Vienna.

During the conversation Hubmaier said: What I have hitherto taught and written, I have not taught for the purpose of securing privileges for myself, but because, as I think, God's Spirit seized me. The colloquium, which took place in late 1527 lasted several days—on the first day until after midnight. Topics under discussion were the exposition and correct understanding of the Bible tradition and infant baptism; on the second day the altar sacrament, sacrifice of Mass, intercession of saints, and purgatory; on the third day faith and good works, Christian liberty, freedom of the will, the worship of Mary, the last things, penitence and confession, the power of the keys, Lutheran and Zwinglian doctrine, and the Councils.

At the close of the conversation Hubmaier declared his intention of presenting his confession of faith to the king. He carried out this intention without delay, and wrote the *Rechenschaft seines Glaubens*. He requested that the king most graciously listen to it and grant him grace and mercy. The *Rechenschaft* contains 27 articles, most of which are so worded that any Christian could subscribe to them; and in the two most important points, not so worded, he is willing to submit to the decision of a council, but in the meantime "stand still" on these points.

Hubmaier was mistaken in supposing that his defense would ease his situation. Precisely on the two points mentioned the authorities had looked for unconditional yielding, and said that he had expressed only half an opinion and had not presented a complete revocation. During the last days of February 1528 he wrote a second booklet, which is unfortunately no longer in existence, in which he discussed both points again. But since this document did not contain the required recantation either, Hubmaier was led back to Vienna, and before the heresy court tried on the rack; when this did not produce a recantation he was sentenced to die at the stake. His wife encouraged him; she was, as Sprugel comments, even firmer in her faith than her husband. When Hubmaier was taken to the site of execution, on March 10, 1528, he spoke words of comfort to himself by reciting Bible verses. When he arrived at the scaffold, accompanied by a great crowd of people and followed by an armed company, he raised his voice and cried out in the Swiss dialect, "O my gracious God, grant me grace in my great suffering!" Turning to the people he asked pardon if he had offended anyone, and pardoned his enemies. When the wood was already in flames, he cried out, "O my heavenly Father! O my gracious God!" and when his hair and beard burned, "O Jesus!" Choked by the smoke, he died. To the spectator it appeared that he felt more joy than pain. As the *Geschichts-Bücher* relate, he sealed his faith with his blood like a knight. His wife, the Waldshut citizen's daughter, did likewise. A few days later she was thrown from the large bridge over the Danube with a stone tied about her neck and drowned.

The men who had been seized with him recanted, except two who likewise died in flames on March 24. On the pyre they sang, "Come, Holy Spirit."

Hubmaier's death aroused consternation not only in Lower Austria and Moravia, but far beyond their borders. Because it was said in many places that he had been unjustly treated and was a martyr before God, and like John Hus innocently burned, Faber had a pamphlet printed in 1528 with the title, *Ursach, warumb der Widertauffer Patron und erster Anfänger Doctor Balthasar Hubmayr zu Wien auf den zehnten Martii anno 1528 verbrennet sei*.

Hubmaier's large literary output has been listed above. Two of his hymns were known by the Hutterian Brethren, but only one has been preserved, which is based on his constant motto, "God's truth will stand eternally," and begins, "Freut euch, freut euch in dieser Zeit." If the *Geschichts-Bücher* do not record much about Hubmaier, it must be remembered that he was not only not a member of the Hutterian Brethren, but was in opposition to a central doctrine of the group, namely, nonresistance.

The question of the influence of Hubmaier on Peter Riedemann (and thereby the Hutterian Brethren) has been thoroughly examined by Franz Heimann ("The Hutterite Doctrines of Church and Common Life, A Study of Peter Riedemann's Confession of Faith of 1540," *MQR* XXVI, 1952, particularly pp. 142-45, and 160). He says:

"The remark of Johann Loserth [*Communismus*, 226], that Riedemann's *Rechenschaft* closely follows the writings of Hubmaier, is by and large correct as far as the teachings of baptism, Lord's Supper, and ban are concerned, even though in these points there is no literal identity. Hubmaier's influence upon the Anabaptists with regard to baptism and Lord's Supper is clearly recognized at one place of the Hutterite *Chronicle*. At the occasion of Hubmaier's martyrdom and death, the Chronicle writes:

"'Two hymns are still in our brotherhood which this Balthasar Hubmaier composed. There are also other writings by him from which one learns how he had so forcefully argued the right baptism, and how infant baptism is altogether wrong, all this proved from the Holy Scriptures. Likewise he brought to light the truth of the Lord's Supper, and refuted the idolatrous sacrament and the great error and seduction by it' [Zieglschmid, *Chronik*, 52].

"There exists a common Anabaptist understanding both in Riedemann and Hubmaier as far as they deal with the fallen state of man, the inner rebirth in faith, and the testimony of this faith in confession and life, presupposing the freedom of man to obey God's commandments. Beyond that also the teaching concerning the right sequence of preaching the Word, hearing, change of life, and baptism, seems to be derived from Hubmaier. In addition, Riedemann seems to have borrowed from him almost in its entirety the polemic against infant baptism (70-77) with all its numerous arguments and reasons, in which polemic Hubmaier nearly exhausted his theological capacity. There is also a fairly complete agreement of the *Rechenschaft* with Hubmaier's teachings concerning the 'Fellowship of the Lord's Table,' whose inner communion must already be present prior to the breaking of the bread. Likewise we find already in Hubmaier the teaching of the Christian brotherhood or church (*Gemeinschaft*), which exercises inner discipline by brotherly punishment and the ban. It seems fairly apparent that Riedemann knew and used Hubmaier's tracts and books such as: *Eine christliche Lehrtafel; Ein einfältiger Unterricht auf die Worte: das ist mein Leib, in dem Nachtmahl Christi; Eine Form zu taufen in Wasser; Eine Form des Nachtmahls Christi; Von der brüderlichen Strafe;* and *Vom christlichen Bann.* Riedemann used these books primarily for his chapters 'How One Should Baptize,' 'The Misuse of the Lord's Supper,' 'Concerning the Supper of Christ,' 'Concerning Exclusion,' and 'Concerning Readmission.'

"The closest contact between Riedemann and Hubmaier is to be found in the concern for the awakening of the Christian individual and for the brotherhood which in Anabaptist thought coincides with the church in general. In the center of Hubmaier's religious thinking stands the inwardly united 'Fellowship of the Lord's Table,' which breaks the bread as a sign of love and readiness for sacrifice (Hubmaier, *Eine Form des Nachtmahles Christi,* Nikolsburg, 1527). The religious ideal of Riedemann, on the other hand, is more the spiritual fellowship of the body of Christ, or the Holy Church without spot or wrinkle, into which the individual who is longing for Christian fellowship is accepted by the right sequence of hearing the Word, believing, rebirth, and baptism. By this the church becomes a true 'fellowship of committed disciples.' In Riedemann's vision it is in the idea of discipleship of Christ that the unity of the Spirit takes on flesh and blood and becomes a true church.

"Concerning 'brotherly punishment' and 'Christian ban,' Hubmaier sees in them the means to secure the purity of the 'Fellowship of the Lord's Table.' Riedemann would agree, but he sees the fellowship 'of the children of God' much more concrete and wide, and he interprets the ban much more radically in view of the purity and sacredness of his community. In the *Rechenschaft* the doctrine of the fellowship of the Lord's Table is closely connected with the doctrine of separation from the world, in complete agreement with the Schleitheim Articles. The latter require expressly in Article II that the ban be employed prior to the breaking of the bread, 'so that we may break and eat one bread with one mind and in one love, and may drink of one cup.' Likewise in Article IV the complete separation of the children of God from the wickedness of this world is required.

"The idea of an absolute contrast of the pure church of the children of God to the impure 'world' is basic for the Hutterite brotherhood. From it all further characteristic traits derive, and upon these, it should be emphasized here, Hubmaier's ideas had no influence whatsoever. It was, we should remember, Jakob Hutter who took the step of organizing the final brotherhood and of establishing the way of life in complete communion of goods as the expression of brotherly love and self-surrender (143-45)."

Heimann concludes: "In general it can be said that the teachings of Hubmaier concerning baptism and the Lord's Supper are reflected in the *Rechenschaft* of Riedemann; in fact, they represent teachings espoused by practically all evangelical Anabaptists. Beyond that, however, Hubmaier had no tangible influence upon Riedemann's thinking. With the arrival of Jakob Hutter in Moravia, late in 1529, the time of compromise had come to an end, and the spirit of strict and committed discipleship, the 'narrow path,' became dominant."

A complete translation into English of all Hubmaier's extant writings has been made by William O. Lewis and deposited in the William Jewell College Library at Liberty, Mo. A microfilm copy of this manuscript is found in the libraries of Bethel College and Goshen College.

The Amsterdam Mennonite Library has the following books by Hubmaier: N. Prugner and B. Fridberger, *Acht unnd dreyssig schluszrede so betreffende ein gantz Christlich leben war an es gelegen ist* (n.p., 1524); B. Fridberger, *Achtzehen schluszrede so betreffende ein gantz Christlich leben* (n.p., 1524); *Schluszreden die Balthazar Fridberger dem J. Eckio die meysterlich zu examinieren fütbotten hat* (n.p., n.d.); B. Frydberger, *Ain Summe ains gantzen Christlichen lebens* (n.p., 1525); and written copies made in the 19th century of B. Huebmör, *Von Ketzern und iren Verbrennen* (1524); *Ein gesprech . . . auf Mayster Ulrichs Zwinglens Taufbüchlein* (1526); *Der Uralten und gar neuen Leerern Urtail* (1526), and *Zwölf Artickel Christlichen Glaubens zu Zürich im Wasserturm gestellt* (1527).† LOSERTH.

C. Sachsse, *D. Balthasar Hubmaier als Theologe* (Berlin, 1914); a book also very likely written by Hubmaier, *Ein warhafftig Entschuldigung und Klag gemeiner Stadt Waldshut von Schultheis und Rat aldo an alle christgläubig Menschen ausgangen anno 1525* (printed by J. Loserth in "Die Stadt Waldshut und die vorderösterreichische Regierung in den Jahren 1523-1526" in *Archiv für österreichische Geschichte* LXXVII, pp. 1-149); *Die Lieder der Hutterischen Brüder* (Scottdale, 1914); Wolkan, *Geschicht-Buch;* Beck, *Geschichts - Bücher;* H. Schreiber, "B. Hubmaier," in *Taschenbuch für Geschichte und Altertum in Süddeutschland* (Freiburg, 1839); F. Hosek, *Balthasar Hubmaier a pocatkov en ovo Krestenstva na Morave* (Brno, 1893); W. Mau, "B. Hubmaier," in *Abhandlungen zur mittleren u. neueren Gesch.*, No. 40 (Berlin and Leipzig, 1912); H. C. Vedder, *Balthasar Hubmaier, the Leader of the Anabaptists* (New York and London, 1905) in *Heroes of the Reformation,* contains a portrait of Hubmaier, which is probably not contemporary; S. Sprugel, "Bericht über Hubmaiers Tod" in *Acta facultatis artium* IV, 149b (university archives in Vienna) reprinted in Mitterer, *Compectus hist. Univ. Viennensis* (1724); A. Stern, "Ueber die 12 Artikel von 1525 u. ihre Verfasser," *Hist. Ztscht* XCI; G. Wolny, "Die Wiedertäufer in Mähren," *Arch. f. österr. Gesch.* (1850); W. Wiswedel, *Balthasar Hubmaier, der Vorkämpfer für Glaubens- und Gewissensfreiheit* (Kassel, 1939); idem, "Dr. Balthasar Hubmaier," *Ztscht f. bayr. Kirchengesch.* XV (1940): 2 Halbbd. (reprint Gunzenhausen, 1940); ML II, 353-63.

Hübner, Johannes (1668-1731), a noted Lutheran educator, teacher at the University of Leipzig for a time, 1694-1711 rector of the Merseburg (Germany) Gymnasium, 1711-31 rector of the Hamburg Johanneum, important in church history only as the author of *Biblische Historien* (1714), which enjoyed over 100 editions in Europe (Germany) and was translated into five foreign languages. The book also was reprinted at least 81 times in America (first edition at Harrisburg, Pa., in 1826), and at least four times (1887, 1889, 1891, 1909) by John F. Funk at Elkhart, Ind., and once at Scottdale in 1936, which indicates its popularity among the Mennonites in America. It was the first German book to publish Biblical material for children in story form instead of catechetical or text form. The title of the first Funk edition was *Biblische Geschichten des Alten und Neuen Testaments durch Bibelsprüche und zahlreiche Erklärungen erläutert.* (222 pp.). The original German title was *Zweimal 52 Biblische Historien und Fragen* (Leipzig). It is still sold by booksellers for the Amish, e.g., by J. A. Raber of Baltic, Ohio.   H.S.B.

Hubrechts, Jan, a sheriff of Amsterdam, was in sympathy with the Anabaptists and obstructed the policy of the government concerning their persecution. When the representatives of the Court of Holland came to Amsterdam (November 1531) to arrest a number of Anabaptists, Jan Hubrechts sent them a warning by his maidservant so that they could escape. Jan Hubrechts was dismissed on Feb. 25, 1534. Though an opponent of Roman Catholic practices, he was not an Anabaptist. He is called a *nieuw-gesinde,* i.e., a Sacramentist (*q.v.*).   vDZ.

Inv. Arch. Amst. I, Nos. 18, 187; *DB* 1917, 195 f.; Kühler, *Geschiedenis* I, 64-68, 93.

Huf, Lorenz, an Anabaptist of Sprendlingen in Rheinhessen, a member of the Kreuznach congregation "who are called Swiss." "He was evidently an elder, and as such he, with Rupp Gellner (*q.v.*), Matthes Stroh, and Wilhelm Henchen, was offended by the doctrine and conduct in his congregation." "Although they have learned that a believer should sacrifice himself with all that he has to God and His saints, they have contrary to their own teaching granted in life that each man use his goods for himself and give to the poor only what they need. Besides they have taught concerning the brotherhood that no one should have property, but what one has should be held in common, his neighbor's as well as his own. And, at the same time, when anyone needed anything he had to buy it of others. In the third place, concerning original sin, that they do not teach the right according to the truth, pay taxes for war and sacrifice to idols, do not earnestly rebuke unclean dealing in business and wrongdoing, but rebuke privately so that it does not become known among the populace. Nor do they have true separation from the people, but in many respects mingle with them."

The demand for complete community of goods is foreign to the Swiss congregations; it is Hutterite. On the other hand, the question of strict church discipline and separation not rarely gave occasion to disunity and strife. An extensive account is given of the manner in which dissatisfied members joined the Hutterian Brethren. When one of them, Thoman Neumann, a cobbler of Wolfsheim, a village not far from Sprendlingen, heard that "there is a group in Moravia that lives in brotherly unity and true fellowship, he made up his mind not to give up until he came to the church of God in Moravia, learned the foundation of the truth and offered it again to his friends" (*Geschicht-Buch,* 272). This led to thorough and repeated discussions among them. They finally agreed to ask Hans Schmidt (*q.v.*), a missionary of the Hutterian Brethren who was traveling in Hesse, to come to talk the matter over with him. He presented to them the creed of the Hutterian brotherhood, concerning the call of their preachers, their offices, brotherhood, church regulations, marriage, and separation from the world. On several points, viz., marriage, taxes, separation, the food and drink of the preachers, sacrifice to idols, and why one should emigrate to Moravia, they asked more information, and Lorenz Huf was commissioned with other judicious brethren to carry on the above points. When this reply came (*Geschicht-Buch,* 273-77) they met, discussed it point by point, and found themselves in agreement with it. This was reported to Moravia, and the union was agreed upon on Nov. 26, 1556, with Hans Schmidt. "Then they moved in to the church of God," and Lorenz Huf was made their preacher. He died four years later at Stiegnitz. He is the author of the hymn, "Lugt auf, ihr Christen alle," which has 20 stanzas with the acrostic, "Lorenz Huf von Sprendeling." (*ML* II, 363.)   NEFF.

Hugaart-Heems, Femina: see Heems.

Hügeline, Elsbeth (Elisabeth), the wife of Balthasar Hubmaier (*q.v.*), was the daughter of a citizen of Reichenau on Lake Constance, whom he married on Jan. 13, 1525. She was an energetic and courageous woman, who shared the very sad fate of her husband with devoted love and faithfulness. When he was seized and after cruel torture condemned to death, she spoke words of comfort to him. Three days later she also suffered a martyr's death in Vienna. With a stone tied to her neck she was thrown from the large bridge over the Danube on March 13, 1528, in Vienna. (*ML* II, 363.)   NEFF.

Hughestown, a Mennonite Brethren Mission station in India, located in the northeastern suburbs of Hyderabad city in Madhya Pradesh (formerly Central Provinces), was purchased by J. H. Pankratz in 1913, and at that time included three compounds —one with a hall for church and school, and the other two with bungalows for missionaries and living quarters for workers. Since the mission at one time intended to discontinue the station and transfer to another locality, it sold two of these compounds and retained the one with the larger bungalow. In 1927 it was, however, decided to retain Hughestown as a center for work in the field southeast of Hyderabad.

Missionaries who have worked here a longer period of time are Mr. and Mrs. J. H. Pankratz, Anna Suderman Bergthold, Katharina L. Schellenberg, Anna Hanneman, and Elizabeth D. Janzen. The station has been without resident missionaries much of the time and was supervised by missionaries of other stations. Mr. and Mrs. J. H. Lohrenz of Shamshabad have long had charge of the work.

Activities have included regular church services on the station and evangelism in the city of Hyderabad and its environs as well as in the villages. The station field has an area of 1,200 square miles and a population of 200,000. Of the Christian community, which numbers 1,000 communicant members, about 400 live in the city and 600 in the villages. A primary school has been conducted since the beginning of the station. A new church was built in 1952.   J.H.L.

Hugwald, Ulrich (1496-1571), a native of Wylen near Bischofszell in the canton of Thurgau, Switzerland, a student under Vadian, matriculated at the University of Basel in 1519. As a proofreader in the print shop of Adam Petri in Basel, he published three Latin works: *Dialogus studiorum suorum prooemium et militiae initium, Ad sanctam Tigurinam ecclesiam epistola* (1521), and *Tres epistolae, quarum ultima legunt qui hodie Euangelistas persequuntur et caveant, ne lacessitus ad arma deposita redeat* (1521). Calvary's statement (*Verzeichnis*, 9 and 28) that these books show that already at that early period he was a follower of Denk and the Strasbourg Anabaptists is chronologically impossible. Paul Burckhardt correctly says that in these pompous writings there is no trace of old-evangelical heresy. They are rather the ideas of Erasmus; i.e., a blending of humanism with the Gospel. In 1522 Hugwald published a booklet, *An alle, die Christum oder das Reich Gottes von Herzen suchen* (Clemen, 72 and Wernle, 266). The same year saw the publication, without his knowledge, of 134 theses by him under the title, *Est tibi lector brevissimo compendio per U. H., unde hominum perditio, in quoque sit eorum salus. . . .* Theses 42-46 deal with baptism. Hugwald vigorously defends infant baptism. He wrote the foreword to several booklets of Luther's, showing himself to be an enthusiastic adherent of the German reformer, whereas he never formed an attachment to Zwingli (Wernle, 265).

At the end of 1524 or the beginning of 1525 Hugwald joined the Anabaptists, and was baptized. He seems to have attached himself to Thomas Müntzer when the latter made a brief visit to Basel. "It is extremely instructive to follow the road that leads from glowing love for Luther to Anabaptism," writes Wernle. At an Anabaptist meeting in the home of Michel Schürer, a tailor of Freiburg, he was seized with 25 others, and released on Aug. 23, 1525, upon an oath of *Urfehde* "in the best and strongest form." He remained for a time an adherent of the Anabaptists, abandoned his scholarly career and took up turning and agricultural tasks, but then left them, became a schoolmaster at Burg and later professor at the University of Basel.

NEFF.

Keller, *Reformation*, 374; O. Clemen, "Der Wiedertäufer Ulrich Hugwald," in *Beiträge zur Reformationsgeschichte* II (1902) 45-85; R. Thommen, *Geschichte der Universität Basel* (Basel, 1889) 352; Calvary, *Verzeichnis wertvoller und seltener Bücher* (Berlin, 1870); P. Burckhardt, *Die Basler Täufer* (Basel, 1898); Paul Wernle's article in *Basler Ztscht*, 1918, 255, 265 ff., and 286; *ML* II. 363 f.

Huidekoper, a Dutch Mennonite family, originally from Harlingen, province of Friesland, where Anne Jans Huidecoper, a merchant of hides, from which trade he received his family name, was born about 1640. Both he and his son Jan Annes Huidekoper (d. 1746) were loyal members of the Mennonite congregation of Harlingen. A grandson of Jan Annes, Harm Jan Huidekoper, b. 1776 at Hoogeveen, migrated to the United States in 1795, where he first was a clerk of the Holland Land Company and then an industrialist. He did not join the Mennonites, but in Meadville, Pa., where he died in 1854, he founded a Unitarian church, which caused some trouble. He published a number of theological works. He became the founder of the American branch of this family (*N.N.B.Wb.* VIII, 884).

A half brother of Harm Jan was Jan Annes Huidekoper (b. 1766 at Berlikum, d. 1835 at Amsterdam), who was married to Geertruy Margaretha Stinstra. This Jan is the founder of the Amsterdam branch of the Huidekoper family. By his important businesses and high positions he was a very influential man; he was a member of the municipal board of Amsterdam and member of the board of directors of the "Great Fishery," of the Levant Trade, of the Amsterdam Chamber of Commerce, later also its president. Notwithstanding his many offices he served the Mennonite congregation of Amsterdam two periods as a deacon, 1796-1801 and 1811-15.

Jan's four sons were all men of great importance: (*a*) Anne Willem (1796-1841) studied law and was a judge at Amsterdam and member of the Second Chamber of the States-General; he was much interested in improving the conditions of prisoners and served the Mennonite congregation of Amsterdam as a deacon 1821-25 and 1831-35. He was unmarried. (*b*) Pieter (1798-1852), member of the municipal board of Amsterdam, of the Second Chamber of the States-General, mayor of Amsterdam 1841-49. Besides all this he was a banker and leader of a trading company. He was married to Sara Geertruida van Eeghen and was a deacon of the Amsterdam congregation 1826-30 and 1841-42. (*c*) Jan (1803-76), married to his niece Catharina Huidekoper from Harlingen, became a merchant at Harlingen. (*d*) Albert (1807-54), married to Aletta Jacoba Rahusen, also a businessman and deacon at Amsterdam 1836-40. The Huidekoper family had a country house at Breukelen, which was known for its art treasures.

Of the late Harlingen branch should be mentioned Anne Willem Huidekoper, son of Jan (*c*); he was born Aug. 23, 1836, at Midlum near Harlingen and d. April 7, 1900, at Arnhem. After studying at the Amsterdam Mennonite Theological Seminary he became a preacher of the following Mennonite congregations: Burg, Waal, and Oosterend on the island of Texel 1861-63, Bolsward 1863-

73, Koog-Zaandijk 1873-77, and Almelo 1877-78. In 1878 he left the ministry to found a banking house at Amsterdam. He was married first to Susanna Jacoba Portielje (d. 1836) and then to her sister Cornelia Maria Portielje. vdZ.

Ned. Patriciaat XVIII, 1927, 206-16; Edgar Huidekoper, of Meadville, Pa., *Huidekoper Holland Family* (n.p., n.d.).

Huig, Jorisz, an otherwise unknown Anabaptist martyr, who was beheaded with his brother Quirijn Jorisz on Jan. 22, 1550, at Delft, Dutch province of South Holland, because of being an Anabaptist. They were natives of Delfshaven near Rotterdam. Their goods were confiscated. About these martyrs we only know by the statement of account of the sheriff of Delft. (*Inv. Arch. Amst.* II, 2, p. 162, No. 362.) vdZ.

Huins, a hamlet in the Dutch province of Friesland, where Leenaert Bouwens in 1568-82 baptized seven persons. They may have joined a congregation in the neighborhood, since there has never been a congregation at Huins. vdZ.

Huisduinen, formerly a fishermen's village at the tip of the Dutch province of North Holland, now a part of the town of Den Helder. A Mennonite congregation of merged Flemish and Frisians existed here until 1731, when it merged with the Waterlander congregation of Den Helder (*q.v.*). Its meetinghouse was in use until 1788. vdZ.

Huisinga Bakker, Pieter, b. March 24, 1714, at Huizinge (*q.v.*), Dutch province of Groningen, d. Oct. 22, 1801, at Amsterdam, was a merchant. He wrote three volumes of poems, published under the title *Poëzy* (Amsterdam, 1773, 1782, and 1790); he translated the works of John Milton into Dutch and wrote a biography of the Dutch historian Jan Wagenaar (1776), to whose sister Elizabeth he was married. He was a descendant of the Huizinga (*q.v.*) family and was the first to publish a genealogy of this family, entitled *Stamboek of Geslachtsregister van Derk Pieters en Katrina Thomas* (Groningen, 1775). vdZ.

N.N.B.Wb. VI, 67; J. Huizinga, *Stamboek . . . van Derk Pieters en Katrina Thomas* (Groningen, 1883) pp. VI, XI, and 4; DB 1896, 12.

Huisko(o)pers (House-Buyers) is the name of a party of Flemish Mennonites, which arose in Franeker, Dutch province of Friesland, in 1586, when Thomas Bintgens (*q.v.*) bought a house, the deal involving some implications of dishonesty. A division of the Flemish group followed, with the Huiskopers (Bintgens and his followers) on one hand and the Contra-Huiskopers (*q.v.*)—Jacob Keest, Joos Jans, and Jacob Berends with their adherents on the other. The elders from Haarlem, Amsterdam, Groningen, and elsewhere, who had met to settle the dispute, returned without having achieved their object.

The schism was not confined to Franeker. Its rapid spread is evidence that it was not merely a matter of the sale of a house. The issue was actually strictness or laxity of moral conduct; i.e., the retention of the concept of a church without spot or wrinkle, or its abandonment. Another attempt made in Haarlem in 1589 to heal the breach ended in failure; Amsterdam decided against Bintgens, while Haarlem decided in his favor.

The Contra-Huiskopers are identical with the "Young" or "Soft" Flemish Mennonites, and the name Contra-Huiskopers soon disappeared. The Huiskopers were identical with the Old Flemish Mennonites. After most of these Old Flemish had merged with the Flemish on the basis of the Dordrecht Confession of 1632, the name Huiskopers was often used for another group of Flemish Mennonites which arose about this time in the Netherlands, namely, the Danzig (*q.v.*) Old Flemish Mennonites. In the 18th century their congregations were still called Huiskopers, and not only as a nickname by their antagonists, as is shown by a catechism of 1708 of the Danzig Old Flemish, of which R. A. Joncker is the author, entitled *Mennoniste Vrageboek . . . als . . . in de vergaderinge der Doops-gesinden: genoemt de Huys-kopers geleert wort.* vdZ.

DB 1912, 49-60; *Inv. Arch. Amst.* I, Nos. 477, 558, 578, 593, 1122; II, Nos. 2689 f.; ML II, 267.

Huizen, a town in the Dutch province of North Holland, east of Amsterdam, formerly the seat of a Mennonite congregation, sometimes also called the congregation of Huizen and Spakenburg (*q.v.*). It belonged to the Waterlander branch of the Mennonites; at the large Waterlander conference at Amsterdam in 1647 this congregation was represented by Pieter Reyniersz; it must therefore have been in existence in this period and perhaps long before. There are no documents older than 1681. In 1731 it received from Jacobus van Hoorn of Amsterdam a rather valuable piece of land (since called "Hoornschehout") and other assets. The membership was small; no exact figures were available before 1792, when it numbered 35, unbaptized children included. The last minister was Jacobus van Moerbeek 1790-1834(?). Since 1834 no meetings have been held, and in 1843 an agreement was reached with the Amsterdam congregation concerning the administration of the properties of the Huizen congregation. The church, now converted into a private house, still stands, and an inscription, *Religioni consecrata,* recalls its former use.

In 1878 the sleeping congregation awoke and came to new life. A meetinghouse was built at Hilversum and the name of the congregation became Hilversum-Huizen. For the history of this congregation since 1878 see article **Hilversum.**

P.O., vdZ.

Inv. Arch. Amst. II, Nos. 1980-2006, II, 2, Nos. 2, 219; DJ 1837, 16; DB 1879, 140 f.; 1907, 113; ML II, 364.

Huizinga (formerly also Huysinga and Huisinga), a widely diffused Dutch Mennonite family, whose ancestor was Derk Pieters (d. 1566 or 1567), a farmer, married to Katrina Thomas, and living on the old "heert" (a castlelike farm building) of Melkema near Huizinge in the Dutch province of Groningen. He was apparently the owner of this stately farm. He was in all probability a Mennonite, as many of his descendants have been. In the

17th and 18th centuries most members of the family belonged to the Groningen Old Flemish branch. Many of them served the church as deacons and preachers or elders. Jacob Derks (1560-1620, a son of Derk Pieters), a farmer at Maarhuizen near Winsum, was in 1585 chosen as a preacher of the congregation of Rasquert.

The name Huizinga was already used by a great-grandson of Derk Pieters, namely, Jacob Derks Huizinga (1659-1736), a merchant living in the city of Groningen, the son of Derk Syerts (1608-78).

The following Mennonite ministers of the Huizinga family have been found: Luirt Luirts (d. 1674), farmer and elder of the congregation of Westeremden, ordained 1655 (see the interesting account of his journey of 1645 with Derk Syerts through the Old Flemish congregations, in *DB* 1879, 86-94); Derk Syerts (1608-78), Tamme Pieters (d. 1684), ordained elders in 1655, and his son Derk Tammens (d. 1728), all three farmers and preachers of the Huizinge congregation; Jacob Lippes (1660-1735), farmer and preacher at Baflo; Klaas Jans (1701-77), farmer and preacher at Zijldijk 1756; Andries Huizinga was preacher of the Flemish congregation of Obergum-Winsum 1740-ca.50 (*Inv. Arch. Amst.* II, No. 1843); Tammo Huizinga (1711-70), farmer and preacher at Baflo (later Rasquert) 1741-70; Jacob Tietes (1734-1821) born at Gaaikemaweer near Oldehove and living at Terhorne near 't Zandt, a farmer, assuming in 1811 the official family name of Huizinga, which was his wife's name, served from 1764 as a preacher of the congregation of Leermens and Loppersum. He married Trijntje Tammes Huizinga. His son Dirk Huizinga, b. Jan. 29, 1772, near 't Zandt, d. Jan. 31, 1843, was trained for the ministry privately by Gerbrand Valter, preacher of Westzaan-Zuid, and served the congregation of Midwolda-Beerta-Meeden 1793-1802, Norden 1802-9, and Westzaan-Zuid 1809-43. He married Trijntje Jurjens Coolman. Their son Jacob Dirks Huizinga (*q.v.*) was also a Mennonite minister.

Doewe Sieuwertsz Huizinga, b. Dec. 14, 1820, at Loppersum, d. 1907, studied at the Amsterdam Mennonite Seminary and served the congregation of Mensingeweer 1847-49 (as an assistant pastor), Hoorn on the island of Texel 1849-53, Westgraftdijk 1853-68, and Wieringen 1868 until he retired in 1887 (*Biogr. Wb.* IV, 400).

Menno Huizinga, a grandson of Jacob Dirks Huizinga, b. 1876 at Harlingen, studied at the Amsterdam University and the Mennonite Seminary there and was a pastor of Nes 1902-10, Zwartsluis 1910-14, and Noord en Zuid-Zijpe 1914 until he retired in 1918.   vdZ.

The genealogy of the Huizinga family was first published by Pieter Huisinga Bakker (*q.v.*) under the title *Stamboek of Geslachtsregister der nakomelingen van Derk Pieters en Katrina Thomas . . .* (Groningen, 1775), then in a much enlarged edition by Jacob D. Huizinga under the same title (Groningen, 1883) (see also *DB* 1879, 3-6, *passim*, and various issues of the *Naamlijst*); *ML* II, 365.

Huizinga (Huysinga), Jacob Derks, b. Jan. 9, 1659, at Huizinge, d. Dec. 24, 1736, at Groningen, a member of the Dutch Mennonite Huizinga (*q.v.*) family. Jacob Derks Huizinga was not a farmer like his forefathers, but a merchant. He settled in the city of Groningen, first as partner of the well-known Jan Arents "in 't Block." He married twice: in 1681 Janneken Lubberts Cremer (see Cremer) of Neustadt-Gödens (*q.v.*), who died in 1701, then in 1702 Stijntje Mattheusd. van Calker of Deventer, who died in 1731. At first he was a loyal member of the Groningen Old Flemish Mennonites, but in course of time friction arose because Huizinga was less conservative than the Old Flemish. He sympathized much with the Collegiants and seems to have left his church to join the Collegiants, who had a considerable group in the city of Groningen with a meetinghouse of their own.

Huizinga wrote a family book in which he wrote "memorable occurrences from my time 1672-96," which gives some valuable information on Mennonite history. His *Lyckreden op het Christelijk en zalig afsterven van . . . Albert Jansen* was published at Groningen (n.d., 1727). A curious letter by Huizinga as a marriage broker is found in Gorter's *Doopsgezinde Lectuur* 1858, 329 ff. (*Biogr. Wb.* IV, 404 f.; *N.N.B.Wb.* VIII, 886 f.; *DB* 1883, 73.)

vdZ.

Huizinga, Jacob Dirks, b. June 3, 1809, at Norden, d. Aug. 12, 1894, at Groningen, son of Pastor Dirk Huizinga and Trijntje Jurjens Coolman, studied at the Amsterdam Mennonite Seminary and served the congregation of Knollendam 1832-35, den Horn 1835-44, and Burg on the island of Texel 1844 until he retired in 1879. He was well versed in Mennonite history and the Amsterdam Mennonite archives owe to him a number of important documents on the history of the Mennonites, especially from the province of Groningen. Besides a catechism, *Hoofdwaarheden der christelijke Godsdienst* (Burg, 1852, reprinted at Sneek, 1863), and a paper on the history of the Mennonites on the island of Texel in *Doopsgezinde Bijdragen* 1873, he published genealogies of the Huizinga, Coolman, and Meihuizen families: *Stamboek der nakomelingen van Derk Pieters en Katrina Thomas* (Groningen, 1883); *Stamboek . . . der nakomelingen van Fiepke Foppes en Diever Olfferts* (Groningen, 1887); *Stamboek . . . der nakomelingen van Samuel Peter (Meihuizen) en Barbara Fry* (Groningen, 1890). Especially the Meihuizen genealogy is of interest for Mennonite history for its account of the emigration of the Swiss Mennonites to Holland, studied from the sources found in the Amsterdam Mennonite archives. Jacob Huizinga was married to Aaltje Samuels Meihuizen of Hoogezand. (*Biogr. Wb.* IV, 405 f.; *N.N.B.Wb.* VIII, 885 f.; *ML* II, 365.) Their son Derk Huizinga (1840-1907) first studied theology at the Amsterdam Mennonite Seminary; he was appointed ministerial candidate in 1862; but since the ministry did not appeal to him, he studied science and in 1867 became a teacher in physics and chemistry. In 1870 he was appointed professor of physiology on the medical faculty of the University of Groningen (*N.N.B.Wb.* IV, 789).

Johan Huizinga (1872-1946), a well-known professor of history at the University of Leiden, was a son of Derk and a grandson of Jacob Dirks Huizinga. Johan Huizinga was not a Mennonite. vDZ.

Huizinge, a small town in the Dutch province of Groningen, which already in the 16th century was a Mennonite center, with a congregation of Groningen Old Flemish, known by various names— Huizinge, Westeremden, Middelstum, and Huizinge and Westeremden. A meetinghouse of this congregation was built in Huizinge in 1815, but in 1863 the seat of the congregation was transferred to Middelstum (*q.v.*), where a meetinghouse and parsonage were built in 1863. vDZ.

Huizum, Dutch province of Friesland, where Leenaert Bouwens baptized seven persons in 1563-65, who may have joined the congregation of adjacent Leeuwarden. vDZ.

Hulka (Holka, now Velká) is a town in Moravia, two miles east of Strassnitz with a population of about 2,000, of whom about 300 belong to the Reformed Church. The Anabaptists owned a renowned mill there. The market belonged to Strassnitz, and thus to the famous Moravian noble family of Zierotin. The records do not state when the Anabaptists came to Velká. The *Geschicht-Buch* merely remarks (p. 441), "We lived there many years." In 1595 they were compelled by Arkleb von Kunowitz for selfish reasons to move out. They suffered great losses, but the withdrawal cannot have lasted long, for by 1610 they were again in Velká, in the complete possession of the grace of Johann Friedrich of Zierotin, who was a special benefactor of the Hutterites. (Wolkan, *Geschicht-Buch;* Beck, *Geschichts-Bücher; ML* II, 365.) LOSERTH.

Hulle, van, a Dutch Mennonite family, formerly found in Haarlem. This was a refugee family. Jan Hulle, a Mennonite martyr of Ieper and executed there in 1561, may have belonged to this family, as obviously did Jehanne van Hulle and Cataline van Hulle, Mennonites who had left Gent in 1568, their property being confiscated. Jehanne seems soon to have returned, for Janneken van Hulle (*q.v.*), who died as a martyr at Gent in 1570, is identical with Jehanne. Cathalyne van Hulle (baptized about 1581 at Gent by Paulus van Meenen, who soon after performed her marriage with Jacob Martins), apparently not the same person as Cataline mentioned before, was a Mennonite banished from Gent in 1592 (Verheyden, "Mennisme in Vlaanderen," ms.).

Denys van Hulle, son of Michiel van Hulle, living at Haarlem about 1610, was apparently a preacher there. It could not be ascertained in which congregation he served. He was a man of moderation, opposing the strict principles of Leenaert Clock (*q.v.*) and others. (*Inv. Arch. Amst.* I, Nos. 482, 519, 525, 535.) vDZ.

Hulshof, Abraham (b. 1874 at Borne, d. 1954 at Utrecht), though spelling his name with one *f*, belonged to the large Dutch Mennonite Hulshoff family. He studied theology at the University of Amsterdam and the Amsterdam Mennonite Seminary and became a ministerial candidate in 1902, but never went into the ministry. In 1922 he was appointed director librarian of the University of Utrecht. Among his many publications, mostly papers published in various periodicals, should be mentioned his doctor's thesis, *Geschiedenis van de Doopsgezinden te Straatsburg van 1525 tot 1557* (Amsterdam, 1905). vDZ.

Hulshoff, a Dutch Mennonite family, whose members are still found in a large number of Mennonite congregations. The ancestor of the family was Berend Jansz (b. August 1635, d. April 1694), whose father had moved to the "Hulshoff," a farm near Zenderen in the district of Twenthe, Dutch province of Overijssel. Berend Jansz, who was a spinner and weaver (and apparently also a farmer), and who was married to Geessien Hendriks, was an elder of the Groningen Old Flemish Mennonite congregation at Borne, as were his sons Hendrik Berends Hulshoff (*q.v.*) and Goossen Berends Hulshoff, serving 1695-ca. 1727. Another son of Berend Jansz was Abraham Berends Hulshoff, b. 1674 at Zenderen, d. 1759 at Groningen; he was a merchant and a manufacturer in the city of Groningen, and was the ancestor of the Groningen branch of this family. His grandson was Allard Hulshoff (*q.v.*). Arent Berends Hulshoff was also a son of Berend Jansz. He was apparently a weaver or merchant of woven materials in Twenthe; he accompanied his brother Hendrik Berends in 1719 on his voyage to Prussia and Poland; his son Berend (Barent) Arents Hulshoff (*ca.* 1697-1779) married Geertje Pol Jansdochter and was a preacher of the congregation of Borne 1736-79, as was the son of Berend Arents, Arent Hulshoff (b. 1728 at Borne, d. 1802 at Hengelo), who founded a textile factory at Hengelo and served as preacher 1770-1802. The son of Hendrik Berends was Gerrit Hendriks Hulshoff; he moved to Wildervank (*q.v.*) and was a preacher of the congregation of Wildervank-Veendam from 1752 until his death in 1781. His sister Fenneken Hulshoff was married to Jan Jansz Pol, preacher at Borne about 1710-17. All these ministers, except Allard Hulshoff, were untrained. The following Mennonite ministers, trained at the Amsterdam Mennonite Seminary and the University of Amsterdam, were descendants of Hendrik Berends: Allard Abraham Hulshoff, b. 18— at Amsterdam, d. Feb. 22, 1875, served Akkrum 1839-45, and Leeuwarden 1845-70; Gerhard Adam Hulshoff, b. 1836 at Borne, d. there 1901, served Knollendam 1864-90, and Enkhuizen-Medemblik 1890-94; his son Gerhard Adam Hulshoff, b. 1874 at Knollendam, d. 1938 at Borne, served at Hindeloopen 1904-10, Terhorne 1910-13, Holwerd 1913-16, and Gorredijk-Lippenhuizen 1916-27; Isaac Hulshoff, b. 1869 at Borne, d. at Zeist 1951, pastor of Baard 1895-1901, Noordbroek 1901-3, Irnsum 1903-14, and Workum 1914-35; Jacob Hulshoff, b. 1875 at Sneek, d. 1938 at Amersfoort, pastor at Rottevalle 1902-9, Makkum 1909-20, Oldeboorn 1920-30 and Ternaard 1930-37. vDZ.

Nederl. Patriciaat XXVIII, 1942, 79-105; *Uit het verleden der Doopsgezinden in Twenthe* (n.p., n.d.) 76-78; *ML* II, 365.

Hulshoff, Allard, b. Feb. 20, 1734, at Groningen, d. July 30, 1795, at Amsterdam. He studied philosophy at the University of Groningen, obtaining his doctor's degree in 1755. He began his theological studies in 1756 in the Mennonite seminary at Amsterdam. In 1759 he was made preacher of the congregation at Makkum and in 1760 he was called to the "Lam en Toren" congregation at Amsterdam. His eloquence as a pulpit speaker is attested by the collection of his sermons (*Kerkelijke rede-voeringen,* 4 vv., Amsterdam, 1796). He wrote numerous philosophical works, which earned him much recognition. He was also successful in the field of pedagogy. He was married to Anna Debora van Oosterwijk. His son Willem van Oosterwijk Hulshoff (*q.v.*) died ten weeks before his father. Besides this son he had a daughter Aletta Maria (1781-after 1850), who was an ardent Patriot (*q.v.*) and caused a lot of trouble to the government. She seems to have been very unbalanced; in 1810 she made an attempt on Napoleon's life when he visited Amsterdam; only by fleeing abroad could she save her life; by many she was celebrated as a heroine.   vDZ.

W. de Vos, *Leven en Character van A. Hulshoff* (Amsterdam, 1796); *Biogr. Wb.* IV, 412-18; *N.N.B.Wb.* II, 619; *Naamlijst* 1796; *Inv. Arch. Amst.* I, No. 724; *DJ* 1850, 112 f., 125 f.; *DB* 1868, 95, 97; 1898, 20, 26; *ML* II, 365.

Hulshoff, Hendrik (1664-1745), usually called Hendrik Berents, was a spinner and weaver, married to Jenneken ten Cate of Groningen, and lived in "het Paschen" at Zenderen near Borne in the district of Twenthe in the Dutch province of Overijssel. From 1690 on, he was an elder of the Groningen Old Flemish Mennonites. This group also had a congregation in Twenthe, which split in 1728 into the Borne (*q.v.*) and Hengelo (*q.v.*) congregations. As elder he made official trips to the Old Flemish congregations; in 1719 he made a journey all the way to Polish Prussia. On May 22, accompanied by his brother Arent Berends, he started out on a trip via Groningen and Harlingen, to Vlieland, and from there by boat to Danzig, where they arrived on June 28. Here he met with Mennonite leaders, including Jan van Hoek and Anthony Janssen, but he did not preach. In Gruppe he visited Jacob Bertelt (Bartel), "being a man of the other Mennonites" (i.e., Bertelt belonged to the Waterlanders), for whom he had brought a letter and a "great basket full of books" from Holland. On July 5 the travelers arrived at Przechovka or Przysierk, later called Wintersdorf, not far from Schwetz. (In the *Naamlijst* of preachers of 1755 the congregation is called "In't Colmsche op Kunpad en Przekowsky.") Here Hulshoff took up his residence in Elder Benjamin Wedel's (*q.v.*) house. This was also a Groningen Old Flemish congregation. Hulshoff visited many members and preached several times; and on Thursday, July 13, he officiated at the ordination of the two preachers, Jacob IJsaäks (Isaak) and Abraham Onrouw (Unrau). On the following Sunday he officiated at the reception into the congregation by baptism of at least 31 baptismal candidates, to whom he had given baptismal instruction on the previous Monday. They also visited the brethren in Wolz(?) and Schönsee. On Saturday the matter of the discipline of Hans Voet (Voth) was acted upon, and on Sunday, July 23, he conducted communion and footwashing. On Tuesday, July 25, he preached once more. On this occasion many persons came from other places, even from the other side of the Vistula.

Afterward Hendrik and Arent Hulshoff took their departure. On the return journey they spent a night with a member at Montau, Pieter Baltzer (Balzer) of the Frisian branch. After a short stay in Danzig, where the brothers had business—our elder managed very eminently to combine the spiritual calling with the material—they traveled overland via Berlin, Hamburg, Bremen, Lingen, and Noordhorn back to their home, arriving there on Aug. 13.

The travel account was written up by Hendrik Berends Hulshoff himself, and was published in 1938 with an introduction by H. Ch. Hulshoff. Among the important items included is a list which Hulshoff received from his fellow elder Alle Derks (*q.v.*), and one which he himself made of the members of the congregation in "Persighofke en 't Koenpat (Przechowka)." Presumably Hendrik Berends made a second journey to Prussia and Poland.   vDZ.

H. Ch. Hulshoff, "Bezoekreis van Hendrik Berents Hulshoff aan de Doopsgezinden Gemeenten der Oude Vlamingen in Pruisen in Polen in 1719" in *Bijdragen en Mededeelingen v. h. Hist. Genootschap* LIX (Utrecht, 1938) 32-82; Herbert Wiebe, *Das Siedlungswerk niederl. Menn. im Weichseltal* (Marburg a. d. Lahn, 1952).

Hulshoff, Sybrand Klaas, b. May 4, 1849, at Leeuwarden, d. April 5, 1897, at Utrecht, a son of Allard Hulshoff, studied medicine, then devoted himself to diseases of the eye and later after a journey abroad to pediatrics. The erection at Utrecht of the first children's hospital in Holland is due to his initiative; he served as its managing physician. He is also the author of several scientific studies. (*Nederlandsch Tijdschr. v. Geneeskunde,* 1897, 565; *N.N.B.Wb.* IV, 790 f.; *ML* II, 365.)   vDZ.

Hulshoff, Willem van Oosterwijk, son of Allard Hulshoff (*q.v.*), b. March 6, 1771, at Amsterdam, d. there May 17, 1795, studied at the Amsterdam Mennonite Theological Seminary and became a ministerial candidate in 1792. The ministry, however, did not appeal to him, and so he studied philosophy at the University of Utrecht. Having always been frail, he died at the age of 24 years. Yet his name was very well known in the 19th century for his publications: *Vertoog over het Wederzien* (Amsterdam, 1795); *Josef in sijne Kinderliefde en trouw ter naarvolging aangepresen* (published 1796 by the "Genootschap tot verdediging van den Christelijken Godsdienst"), and especially *De Geschiedenis van Josef voor Kinderen* (Leiden, Amsterdam, 1796); this last book, crowned by the "Maatschappij tot Nut van 't Algemeen," was used until 1857 in nearly all elementary schools in the Netherlands; a new (17th) edition appeared as late as 1886.   vDZ.

Biogr. Wb. IV, 418 f.; *DB* 1869, 56, 59, 83.

Hulst, van, a Dutch Mennonite family, probably from the Lower Rhine district in Germany, in the last part of the 17th century residing at Nijmegen, Dutch province of Gelderland, where Laurens (Lourens) van Hulst was appointed deacon in 1697. His son Caspar van Hulst and grandson Jan van Hulst (d. 1809) were also deacons. A son of this Jan van Hulst, also named Jan (d. Nov. 13, 1821, at Cleve), became a Mennonite minister. After having been trained at the Amsterdam Mennonite Seminary, he served the congregation of Cleve 1804-21.

His cousin Jan van Hulst, b. Aug. 24, 1779, at Nijmegen, d. Nov. 12, 1846, at Norden, a son of Lourens, studied at the Amsterdam Seminary and served the congregation of Kampen 1802-9 and Norden 1809-44; in 1944 he resigned. He published *Korte Geloofsbelijdenis in vragen en antwoorden ten behoeve van Min-geoefenden in den Godsdienst* (Norden, 1816), also some German and English theological works in Dutch translations. Two of his sons went into the ministry: Laurens van Hulst, serving the congregation of Emden 1826-50, in which year he resigned to become director of the Teyler Foundation (*q.v.*) at Haarlem, and Willem van Hulst (d. 1885), serving at Bolsward 1831-58.

Whether Coenraad van Hulst, baptized at Amsterdam in 1793 (Lamist congregation), d. 1844, who was a famous actor, was a member of this family or not, could not be ascertained.   vDZ.

Inv. Arch. Amst. II, 2028-29, 2608-13; *DB* 1874, 31; 1875, 68, 71, 81, 90; *Biogr. Wb.* IV, 435-36; several issues of *Naamlijst,* especially 1829, 39, 68 f.

Hulst, Pieter Teyler van der: see **Teyler, Pieter.**

Humanism, since the middle of the 15th century the designation of an intellectual movement, which in many respects prepared the way for the Reformation and in contrast to medieval theology placed man in his natural and intellectual development in the foreground, sought to free him from all hierarchical and scholastic restraints and endeavored to build a new culture and *Weltanschauung* on the foundation of the purely human.

As the basis of education Humanism valued the "humanities" (*studia humaniora*), especially as they were presented in the works of classical antiquity and to whose content scholars devoted themselves with a new zeal. To be sure, the writings of the Greeks and Romans were not entirely neglected in medieval times; Aristotle indeed had a profound effect particularly on formal education; but on the whole they were only of secondary importance, and science remained dependent upon the church and philosophy was regarded as the "handmaid of theology."

The second half of the 15th century brought with it a fundamental change in this respect. Its point of orientation the Humanistic movement took from Italy. At the time of the "Council of Union" (1439) important Greek scholars from the Orient had come to Florence and exerted their influence on the western world. After the conquest of Constantinople by the Turks (1453) many Greeks fled to Italy. Through their influence first in the field of art, a conscious connection was made with antiquity which was united in the Renaissance with the new feeling of life of the greatest Italian painters; in philosophy Humanism triumphed as the new intellectual movement.

The principal nurseries of this movement were the princely courts of the Medicis in Florence; but the new spirit also penetrated into the highest circles of the hierarchy and the Curia at Rome. Classical learning was accompanied by antique heathenism and a refined syncretism in the secularized church, and occasionally could be heard the pulpit greeting, "Beloved in Plato." For Christianity the Italian Humanists had only a historical or aesthetic interest, in so far as they were not completely indifferent or actually hostile to it.

Much deeper was the development of the Humanistic movement in the countries north of the Alps, where it achieved its greatest significance and where it found a soil prepared for its coming in the schools endowed by Gerhard Groote of the Brethren of the Common Life (*q.v.*), especially at Deventer in the Netherlands and later at Schlettstadt in Alsace (Jakob Wimpfeling). Humanism reached its decisive influence when it passed from the Latin schools into the universities and was zealously cultivated there: first in Vienna (Celtes), then in Basel, Freiburg, Heidelberg (Agricola), Tübingen, Ingolstadt, Erfurt (Muth), Leipzig, etc. Everywhere a new spirit of research awoke, and through the invention of the art of printing about 1450 the Humanistic ideas found rapid dissemination, especially among the educated classes, the patricians in the cities (Augsburg, Nürnberg, Strasbourg), as well as the nobility of Germany (Ulrich von Hutten, Franz von Sickingen).

The cry, "Back to the sources!" was now applied not only to the study of the old classics; it became the stimulus for the eager study of the original text of the Bible and the writings of the Church Fathers, especially of Augustine. The outstanding representatives and leaders of Humanism were Johann Reuchlin (*q.v.,* d. 1522) and Desiderius Erasmus of Rotterdam (*q.v.,* d. 1536). Reuchlin's most meritorious service was in the field of the original language of the Old Testament; his Hebrew grammar was long the only textbook of this language. Erasmus published the first critical edition of the New Testament in 1516; the second edition (of 1519) was used by Luther as the basis of his translation. Philip Melanchthon succeeded in harmonizing the rich Humanistic intellectual training of the time with the new theology filled with Luther's gospel and making them serve the purposes of the Reformation. Luther himself remained spiritually aloof from Humanism; he felt the difference in spirit. He violently attacked the dominating influence of Aristotle in theology. "From Aristotle back to Paul and Augustine!" was the watchword with which he led the new "Wittenberg theology" into sound paths.

The positive effect of Humanism came to the surface in the open break with the former world of culture. The reign of Scholasticism fell, and science was freed from the guardianship of the church. From serfdom the people and the individual awoke to maturity, to a clearer awareness of self and to personal responsibility, also in matters of faith. Through occupation with religious questions and through the reading of religious pamphlets and books a new lay piety arose. In opposition to the claims of Rome a new national feeling grew stronger. In rude popular wit and biting satire the intrigues and the monastic narrowness of the priesthood were uncovered and mocked. Against the intolerance of the obscurantists a sharp pen war was carried on. The cry for a reform of the church in its leadership and laity grew more common and could no longer be suppressed. Through all of this, Humanism helped to pave the way for religious renewal.

But the negative side of Humanism must not be overlooked. Humanism was not able to penetrate the core of the Gospel. It was more concerned with the education of the spirit than with a renewal of the heart. It remained uninterested and politely indifferent to. the actual questions of salvation. In addition to morally outstanding representatives who led an exemplary life, there were others who felt themselves above all moral restraints. Many Humanists rejected the absoluteness of the Christian religion and placed the ethics of Plato and Cicero or the Stoics on the same plane as Jesus' Sermon on the Mount. Syncretism and Pelagianism, indeed often heathen superstition (magic, alchemy, fear of witches), were not lacking. Powers much deeper than and very different from those shown by Humanism were required to produce an inward renewal and transformation of religious and spiritual conditions among the Western peoples. They were not found in Humanism, but in the new comprehension of sin and salvation of the Reformation with its cardinal question, "How can I acquire a merciful God?" Humanism could only serve by preparing the way.

As Humanism in some respects was in general of service to the Reformation, it also in a certain sense helped to break a path for the Anabaptist movement. There was, however, no close connection between Humanism and Anabaptism. But in the field of formal scientific training many an Anabaptist, like Conrad Grebel, Felix Manz, Balthasar Hubmaier, Hans Denk, etc., owed a good share of his sound education to Humanism.

Conrad Grebel (q.v.) acquired a comprehensive knowledge of Latin, Greek, and Hebrew during his student years in Vienna, Paris, and Basel. Theology was still remote from his interests, and yet "it would be an error to reckon him as one of the adherents of Humanism antagonistic to Christianity." His fundamental religious views, which he put into reality in the founding of the brotherhood in Zürich, are rooted in his later conversion and are determined only by the words of the Holy Scriptures.

The same is true of Felix Manz (q.v.). He had pursued Humanistic studies in Basel and had a thorough mastery of the classical languages. With Zwingli he read the Old Testament in Hebrew; his expositions of the Bible at their meetings are based on the original text of the New Testament. But his preaching showed no trace of Humanistic influence, but was thoroughly Biblical and theologically orientated.

Hubmaier (q.v.) had a brilliant Humanistic education at his command, the foundation of which had already been laid in the Latin school in Augsburg. At the university of Freiburg he completed it with deep seriousness. Among his teachers Dr. Eck, Luther's later opponent, exerted the greatest influence on him. Hubmaier speaks of Eck with gratitude. "It is wonderful to say," he says, "with what care and eagerness I took up the philosophical ideas, how carefully I listened to my teacher and how zealously I took down his lectures—an industrious reader, an untiring listener, and a busy teacher of the other hearers. So I won the master's degree with the highest praise . . . . What progress I made is attested by my learned lectures, my sermons before the people, and my scholastic exercises" (Loserth, 15). Hubmaier's later works show a comprehensive knowledge of patristic literature. Thus in his booklet, *Der uralten und gar neuen Lehrer Urteil* of 1526, he bases his teaching on baptism upon the teachings found in Origen, Basil, Athanasius, Tertullian, Jerome, Cyril, Theophylactus, Eusebius, the *Corpus juris Canonica;* but the more recent authorities are also used by him, in the first place the great Humanist Erasmus (Loserth, 143 ff.). But even though his opponents marvel at his classical education, Fabri calls him a "man of select spirit and outstanding education," and von Watt a "highly eloquent and in a high degree humanistically educated man" (*eloquentissimum et humanissimum virum*), for Hubmaier all of this was only of formal significance. Humanism furnished him only with the weapons for his fight of faith. His religious life was rooted in his experience of salvation in Christ; the "touchstone" by which he tested all things and on which he based his teaching was the Bible.

Hans Denk (q.v.) also owes his scholarly preparation largely to Humanism; in religious matters, however, he went his own way. Nevertheless his teaching on the freedom of the will, his demand for unconditional liberty of faith and conscience, and his principle of tolerance show the influence of Humanism. In Basel he got into close touch with Oecolampadius and applied himself to the study of the classical languages, especially Hebrew. He was also one of the close circle of students, with whom Erasmus associated. But there is no evidence of any deep influence of that great Humanist upon Denk. A splendid product of his knowledge of Hebrew is the translation of the Old Testament Prophets from the Hebrew, which Denk and Ludwig Haetzer together published in Worms in April 1527. The content of Denk's sensitive contemplative ideas is derived from Christian mysticism, especially from Tauler's sermons and from the *Deutsche Theologie,* which Luther had published. Denk's doctrine of regeneration and his requirement of discipleship of Jesus in daily life is far above the moral average of his contemporaries.

The relationship of Anabaptism to Humanism may be summarized as follows:

In common with Humanism Anabaptism is characterized by a fearless critique of the traditional ecclesiastical system, a break with the medieval hierarchical concept, a demand for a completely new order in church conditions, a return to the sources of original Christianity, the responsibility of the individual for his own decisions, the demand for complete liberty of faith and conscience and the principle of religious tolerance.

But the ways by which these aims were to be accomplished and the fundamental temper in which it was done were different. Humanism hoped to be able to attain them by humanitarian means; Anabaptism insisted on a renewal of heart, rebirth, and discipleship in daily life. Humanism is basically anthropocentric, Anabaptism Christocentric. To Humanism the actual questions of salvation were unimportant; to Anabaptism the doctrine of salvation had the key position. Humanism regarded the Scriptures as a historic document; Anabaptism held them as the only guide for faith and conduct. Humanism seeks the truth by way of intellectual understanding; Anabaptism looks for it only through divine revelation. To Humanism Christ is a teacher and example among many others; to Anabaptism He is the Son of God and the only medium of salvation. Humanism is concerned with the creation of a new culture; Anabaptism with the realization of the kingdom of God, including the relations of earthly life. To Humanism knowledge was an end in itself; to Anabaptism it was merely a tool of preparation. Humanism promotes the feeling of life and aesthetic enjoyment of life; Anabaptism demands self-denial and willingness to bear the cross to the point of martyrdom. In many of its representatives Humanism teaches that what pleases is permissible; Anabaptism requires fulfillment of the divine commands in the obedience of faith. Humanism pursues a philanthropic ideal and creates an elite of the spirit; Anabaptism seeks a reconciliation of differences in love to the brethren. Humanism is generally indifferent to the Christian ordinances; Anabaptism recognizes in the ordinances of Christ and the apostles a means for the realization of the New Testament church.

In an objective evaluation of given relationships and existing influences and in a critical weighing of inner conflicts, collective Protestantism and with it Anabaptism must not fail to recognize how much it owes to Humanism, especially in its German interpretation. In its positive and negative effects it was an important factor in the historical development of church conditions and in its transition from an old to a new era.   E.H.

O. Clemen, "Humanismus in Religion," in *RGG;* W. Windelband, *A History of Philosophy* (2d ed., N.Y., 1901); Wuttke, *Christliche Sittenlehre* (3rd ed., Leipzig, 1874); Loofs, *Dogmengeschichte;* Springer, *Die Rennaissance in Italien* III; H. Hermelink, *Die religiösen Reformbestrebungen des deutschen Humanismus* (Tübingen, 1907); Robert Kreider, "Anabaptism and Humanism: An Inquiry into the Relationship of Humanism to the Evangelical Anabaptists," *MQR* XXVI (April 1952) 123-41; *ML* II, 365-68.

Humberstone Reformed Mennonite Church in Welland Co., Ont., was established about 1825. It was later absorbed by Port Colborne, and is now known by that name. The membership of the Port Colborne congregation was 43 in 1954.   J.L.K.

Humsterland, a district in western Groningen, Netherlands, where Anabaptists have lived from the beginning. In 1574 an agreement was formulated here between the Frisians and the Flemish, known as the Peace of Humsterland (*Humstervrede, q.v.*). In 1578 another meeting was held here after fruitless discussions at Emden. There were in Humsterland two groups, the Old Flemish and the Flemish, which extended over several villages. The Old Flemish congregation was always small. In about 1775 it united with the Flemish, which must always have been much larger, and was the center of the Humsterlandsche Sociëteit. In 1838 the combined congregation acquired a new church in Noordhorn, and in 1839 changed the name to Noordhorn.   vDZ.

Blaupot t. C., *Groningen* I, *passim; DJ* 1840, 27, 43; 1850, 60; *DB* 1879, 4; 1906, 46; *ML* II, 368.

Humsterlandsche Sociëteit: see **Groninger Doopsgezinde Sociëteit.**

Humstervrede (Peace of Humsterland). About 1550 divisions began to take place among the Dutch Mennonites. About 1566 the great division between the Frisians and the Flemish occurred at Franeker and Harlingen, and soon spread throughout the country. Violently and irreconcilably they opposed each other. The peaceable, who watched with pain, spared no efforts to heal the breach. Jan Willems was finally successful in establishing a temporary easing of tension on the basis of several articles; the agreement was signed in Humsterland (near Noordhorn) in the province of Groningen, and hence was called the "Peace of Humsterland." The Frisians especially expected much of it, and for a while it seemed that the discussions following it at Hoorn (1576) might bring peace. But the attitude of the Flemish elders was such that all further attempts at peace (1578 at Emden and Hoorn) failed. The question at issue was the application of the ban. The conflict remained sharp and the number of separations increased. Peace did not come for more than a century.   vDZ.

Inv. Arch. Amst. I, Nos. 467, 470, 473; *BRN* VII, 547 f.; Blaupot t. C., *Friesland,* 109-11; *DB* 1893, 81; Kühler, *Geschiedenis* I, 425, 447; *ML* II, 368.

Hungary, originally an independent kingdom (after A.D. 1000) outside the Holy Roman Empire, with the Danube River crossing the great plains, which are surrounded by the densely wooded Carpathian Mountains. In 1526 the last Hungarian king fell in a battle against the Turks and the kingdom was now inherited by the Hapsburgs (*q.v.*); however, it was not until 1700 that the Turks were driven out completely. From then on Hungary was ruled by the government in Vienna, more or less in an absolutist fashion. After 1867 Hungary again had its own government, and the Hapsburg territory was then named Austria-Hungary. In 1918 this kingdom broke up into the following parts: Republic of Hungary (capital Budapest); Slovakia (capital

Bratislava), as a part of the Czechoslovakian Republic; Transylvania (capital Cluj, formerly Klausenburg), as part of Rumania; and Croatia, Slavonia, and the Bata, as part of Yugoslavia.

During the Reformation era the manorial lords (called magnates) turned to a very large extent to the Calvinist or Reformed faith. They were quite independent of the Viennese court, and it was not until the 18th century that this court could attempt greater centralization of the empire. A parliament existed in Budapest since the Middle Ages, mainly as an aristocratic assembly. An elected Palatine functioned as viceroy and representative of the Hapsburgs in Hungary and as a representative of the aristocracy in Vienna.

Anabaptists (Hutterites) lived in only three districts (comitates) of Western Hungary, now Slovakia, after 1546 (see **Slovakia**), and here enjoyed a relative internal peace under the magnates (externally the numerous Turkish Wars brought much hardship). It was only in the 18th century, under Maria Theresa (1740-80), that enforced conversion by Jesuits (*q.v.*) was carried out (see **Habaner**). In Transylvania (inhabited by Rumanians, Magyars, and colonial Germans, called Saxons) the Brethren had only one large settlement near Alvinc (1621-1767). It, too, had to be abandoned when systematic persecution set in in the 18th century, and thus the great trek began into Walachia and Russia. (See **Alvinc, Ehrenpreis, Habaner, Jesuits, Sobotiste, Transylvania, Velke Levary**, also **Hapsburg**.)
R.F.

Hungerl, Peter, "the servant" of Peter Planer, an Anabaptist martyr, after severe torture beheaded in 1532 at Sterzing, Austria. In the *Martyrs' Mirror* van Braght calls him "Pieter the servant of Peter Plaver." His martyrdom was shared by Hans Beck, Lambrecht Gruber, Peter Planer, Lorenz Schuster, and Hans Thaler.					vDZ.

Loserth, *Anabaptismus*; Zieglschmid, *Chronik*, 102 f.; Beck, *Geschichts-Bücher*, 108 f.; *Mart. Mir.* D 33, E 440; *ML* I, 149; III, 368.

Hunsberger, a Mennonite family, evidently Swiss in origin, found in the Franconia (Pa.) and Ontario districts of the Mennonite Church (MC). Bishop Henry Hunsberger (1768-1854) of the Blooming Glen, Pa., Mennonite congregation (MC) was assistant moderator of the Franconia Conference in 1847 by virtue of being second in seniority in years of service as a bishop. Because the moderator, Bishop John Hunsicker, who died Nov. 17, 1847, sympathized with the vision and concerns of John H. Oberholtzer and sat with the Oberholtzer party who occupied one particular section in the Franconia meetinghouse on Oct. 7, 1847, when the final secession of the Oberholtzer group occurred, Hunsberger served as moderator of the October 1847 session of the Franconia Conference. Jacob B. Hunsberger (1836-1919) served as preacher in the Coventry and Vincent congregations of the Franconia Conference from 1877 until his death over 41 years later. Christian R. Hunsberger (1823-1906) was a preacher in the Upper Skippack congregation (MC) of the Franconia Conference 1879-1906.

Among the Ontario Mennonite (MC) preachers may be mentioned Abraham K. Hunsberger (1827-89) of the Moyer congregation, and Noah Hunsberger, ordained preacher in 1903, who served at Sherkston and Waterloo. Bishop Ephraim Hunsberger (1814-1904) of the Eastern District Conference (GCM) served as preacher at the Hereford (GCM) congregation 1849-52 when he removed to Wadsworth, Medina Co., Ohio, where he organized a congregation which he served for 50 years.
J.C.W.

B. K. Hunsberger, *The Hunsbergers, Part II, The Descendants of 31 Christian Hunsberger* (n.p., 1926); idem, *The Hunsbergers* (Norristown, 1941).

Hunsberger, Ephraim, was born near Bally, Berks Co., Pa., Nov. 18, 1814, died at Wadsworth, Ohio, Feb. 21, 1904. He was married to Esther Bechtel in Montgomery Co., Pa., on Dec. 23, 1838. To this union 12 children were born. After the death of his first wife he married Elizabeth Overholt of Medina County on March 17, 1862. Three children were born to this union. His father, Abraham Hunsberger, was a teacher and gave his son an education in German and English. Ephraim learned the trade of carriage making. On Oct. 18, 1849, he was called to the ministry by lot as assistant to Christian Clemmer, pastor of the Hereford Mennonite (GCM) Church, and on Oct. 10, 1852, ordained elder. Immediately following this ordination, upon the call of four families, he moved to Wadsworth, Medina Co., Ohio, where a congregation, now known as the First Mennonite Church (GCM) of Wadsworth, was organized. For the next half century Hunsberger gave his life in service in this area. One phase of his activity was the organization of a Sunday school in 1854. He continued as pastor until 1892, when N. C. Hirschy became his successor.

Hunsberger was a central figure in the organization of the General Conference Mennonite Church 1859-65. He was overseer of the erection of the Wadsworth School (*q.v.*) and served as president of the Board of Supervisors from 1863.					A.S.R.

H. P. Krehbiel, *History of the General Conference* (Canton, 1898); Rachel Kreider, "One Hundred Years at Wadsworth," *Menn. Life* VIII (1953) 161-66; *The First Hundred Years* (Wadsworth, 1952).

Hunsicker (Hunziker, Unzicker, Hunzinger, Hunsinger, Honsaker), a Swiss family from the region of Aargau, represented today in Alsace, the Palatinate, and America. The Hunsickers left Switzerland because of religious persecution about the middle of the 17th century. One of the well-known European representatives of the family was Abraham Hunzinger (1792-1859), author of *Das Religions-, Kirchen- und Schulwesen der Mennoniten* (Speyer, 1830). Valentine Hunsicker (1700-71) emigrated from Europe to eastern Pennsylvania in 1717 and served as deacon in the Skippack congregation (MC) of the Franconia Conference about 1739. Three of the more prominent American Hunsickers were Bishop Henry Hunsicker (1752-1836) and his sons, Bishop John Hunsicker (1773-1847), senior bishop of the Franconia Conference in 1847 (he seceded with John H. Oberholtzer), and his younger brother, Preacher Abraham Hunsicker (1793-1872), who also seceded in 1847, and who with the help of his son, Henry A. Hunsicker, established Freeland Seminary in 1848. Henry A. Hunsicker served as principal of Freeland Seminary from 1848 until 1865. (The name of the school was changed to Ursinus College in 1869; the institution had not long remained Mennonite, but had become a college of the Reformed Church.) Oberholtzer's conference ordained Preacher Abraham Hunsicker a bishop in 1847 and his son Henry A. Hunsicker a preacher in 1850, but in 1851 expelled them both. They then carried on a sort of non-sectarian work. The Unzicker families of the midwest, especially in Illinois, are 19th-century immigrants from Europe, and included a number of Amish Mennonite ministers. The best-known layman named Hunsicker was Leidy D. Hunsicker (1878-1954) of the Blooming Glen, Pa., Mennonite Church (MC), a noted chorister for 40 years.

J.C.W.

H. A. Hunsicker, *A Genealogical History of the Hunsicker Family* (Phila., 1911).

Huntersville Mennonite Church (MC), Menahga, Minn., was established as a mission church in 1942 and is sponsored by the district mission board of the North Central Mennonite Conference. It was an outgrowth of a service unit from the Franconia Mennonite Conference in 1949-50. The 30 members, mostly of Finnish background, worship in a basement. The pastor (1955) is Clyde Allebach. C.A.

Huntington Avenue Mennonite Church (MC), formerly the Newport News Mennonite Mission, located in Newport News, Va., was begun in 1928 by the Warwick River Mennonite congregation (*q.v.*). In 1936 the mission was turned over to the Virginia Board of Missions and Charities, and a year later a brick meetinghouse was built. In 1951 the mission was organized as an independent congregation under the Virginia Conference (MC). In 1955 Andrew M. Hartzler was the minister and the membership was 31. C.N.K.

Hunzinger, Abraham (1792-1859), a German Mennonite writer, was born May 22, 1792, at Wimpfen, Germany. He was the author of a booklet, *Das Religions-, Kirchen- und Schulwesen der Mennoniten oder Taufgesinnten: wahr und unpartheiisch dargestellt und mit besonderen Betrachtungen über einige Dogmen und mit Verbesserungs-Vorschlägen versehen von einem Mennoniten* (Speyer, 1830). The booklet is dedicated to the Grand Duke of Baden, Ludwig Wilhelm August, and was accepted by him in a letter by his own hand Jan. 13, 1829. An American edition of the book appeared at Milford Square, Pa., in 1862.

After a foreword and an interesting table of subscribers, containing only a few Mennonite names, Part I, Section 1, contains a brief, often inexact and incorrect account of the history of the Mennonites; Section 2, several confessions and a description of the contents of the *Christliches Gemüthsgespräch* (*q.v.*) whose appended "Kurze Unterweisung" is presented *verbatim;* Section 3, an extract from the Dahlem *Formularbuch* with a short notice on other customs; Section 4 reports on the "Kultus und die Liturgie der amischen Mennoniten," who are erroneously also called Frisians; Section 5 deals with the Flemish or more lenient Mennonites — he means the Reist-Mennoniten; Section 6, of the election of preachers and elders; Section 7, of religious instruction; Section 8, of the errors and abuses and their consequences, which are rigorous church discipline, rejection of scientific study.

Part II deals with the distinctive Mennonite doctrines: (1) baptism; (2) oath; (3) divorce; (4) bearing of arms and warfare; (5) occupying government positions; and (6) marriage with members of other churches. The last four Hunzinger wants changed, and presents detailed proposals for improvement, which consist in the appointment of a salaried church council, approved by the ruler, as the highest authority of the Mennonites in every country, the employment of salaried, educated preachers and morally sound, properly trained schoolteachers, introduction of special church synods, introduction of suitable religious instruction, which is to be continued in Sunday schools to the eighteenth year, and proposals for raising funds, with the support of the state and the other churches.

Of the supplements, the statements of the government decisions of Baden and the statistics have a certain historical value. On the whole, the entire treatise, breathing the current spirit of Rationalism, has had no significance for the Mennonites.

In 1817 he changed his name from Hunsinger to Hunzinger, its original form. Abraham Hunzinger had six sons and two daughters, whom he had baptized into the Protestant church. Three of his sons became Protestant pastors in Hesse and Mecklenburg; a grandson Prof. Aug. Wilhelm Hunzinger (d. 1920) was the head pastor of St. Michael's in Hamburg, the author of a series of important books, mostly apologetics. (*ML* II, 368 f.) Neff.

Huron County, Mich., a rich farming section located in the east-central part of the state. Approximately 370 Mennonites are scattered over an area about 20 miles long and 10 miles wide in the western part of the county. Three families live in adjoining Tuscola County as home missionaries. Approximately three fourths of the settlement is of the Conservative Amish Mennonite branch and the remainder of the Mennonite (MC) branch of the church. The first settlers arrived from Ontario about 1888 or earlier and later organized what is now the Pigeon Mennonite Church. The settlers who later organized the Pigeon River Conservative A.M. Church began to arrive in 1900. The Fairhaven Mission was begun as an outpost of this church in 1934. R.B.

Huron County, Ont., comprises the central townships in Ontario lying along the east shore of Lake Huron. Its maritime climate makes it suitable for raising a variety of bush and tree fruits as well as mixed farming and stock raising. The first Mennonites to migrate westward beyond Waterloo County, settling in Hay Township (*q.v.*) about 1840, were Amish; about 1850 the Mennonites also settled there and with help from itinerant ministers from Waterloo County assemblies were started in the townships of Hay, Stanley, and Grey. Daniel Brundage (*q.v.*), who moved from York Co., Ont., about 1850, was the earliest resident minister. The first deacons were Daniel Lehman, Samuel Reesor, Henry Baer. (See **Hay; Stanley; Clemens; Zurich, MC.**)   J.C.F.

Huron Hutterite Bruderhof 12 miles northeast of Huron, S.D., founded in 1906 by ten families from the Bon Homme Bruderhof and their preacher Joseph Waldner, who was chosen to the ministry in 1905 in the Bon Homme colony. In 1911 Michael Waldner was chosen to the ministry. In 1918 the Bruderhof sold its property and migrated to Canada, founding the Huron Bruderhof (*q.v.*) in Manitoba.   D.D.

Huron Hutterite Bruderhof, four miles north of Benard, Man., founded in 1918 by 19 families with their preachers Joseph and Michael Waldner, who were brothers. The colony sold its holdings in South Dakota, 12 miles northeast of Huron and gave the new Bruderhof the same name. The reason for the migration was the more liberal provisions made for conscientious objectors to military service. On Feb. 14, 1926, Joseph Glanzer was chosen preacher and confirmed in office on Dec. 9, 1934. Preacher Michael Waldner was chosen on March 3, 1940. In 1947 the Bruderhof numbered 163, of whom 64 were baptized members. D.D.

Husum, a city (pop. 23,551) in Schleswig-Holstein, Germany, 20 miles west of Schleswig. In the early 1600's Jan Clasen, called Rollwagen (see **Acronius**), the ducal dike-master, planned to build some dikes south and north of Husum. Although Husum never had special religious privileges, it is known that two Mennonites were citizens there in 1702 and 1737 practicing their dyer's trade; viz., Johan Claesen van Aken and Franz Claasen van Aken, probably father and son; their descendants, if there were any, were lost to the state church through mixed marriage. Twice Husum again plays a slight role in Mennonite history. In 1850 C. J. van der Smissen, pastor of Friedrichstadt, fled to Husum with the church records when Schleswig-Holstein shelled its own city during the Danish occupation. The last preacher of the Friedrichstadt (*q.v.*) church, an Ellenberger, made his living as a bank official in Husum, because the church had lost its assets in the catastrophic inflation of German currency in 1922-23. (*ML* II, 369.)   R.Do.

Hut (Hutt, Huth, Huet), **Hans,** is correctly known as the apostle of the Anabaptists in Upper Austria, although his work and influence extended far beyond its borders, at first in his home country, Franconia, then in Bavaria and Salzburg, Moravia, and Silesia. He was a native of Haina near Römhild in Thuringia. The year of his birth is not known. For four years before 1517 he was a sexton in the service of the knights Hans and Georg von Bibra-Schwebenheim in the village of Bibra near Meinin-

gen. There he had property of his own. By trade he was a bookbinder, but he worked also as a book salesman. As such he traveled about the country distributing pamphlets propagating the new evangelical Lutheran faith. Thus he came to Würzburg, Bamberg, Nürnberg, Passau, and as far as Austria. For several years he was a frequent visitor in Wittenberg (Meyer, 223).

His appearance is described in a kind of poster issued by the council of Nürnberg on March 26, 1527, which says: "The highest and chief leader of the Anabaptists is Johannes Hut, a well-educated, clever fellow, rather tall, a peasant with light brown cropped hair and a blond mustache. He is dressed in a gray, sometimes a black, ridingcoat, a broad gray hat, and gray pants."

About 1524 he met in Weissenfels with three other craftsmen, a miller, a tailor, and a weaver of wool. They argued on baptism. Their objections to infant baptism caused him to reflect. He sought enlightenment in Wittenberg. The information he received there in support of infant baptism did not satisfy him; it was outweighed for him by such Bible passages on baptism as Matt. 28:20; Mark 16:16, and Acts 19:3. Christ and the apostles baptized no children; they should therefore not be baptized until they have acquired understanding for a truly Christian life and for the sufferings that accompany it. He was also confused by the fact that the preaching of the Wittenberg theologians did not produce a reform of life.

When Hut had returned to Bibra, he refused to have his newborn child baptized. He declared that he had been shown no proof in the Bible that infant baptism was necessary. Then the lords of Bibra ordered a disputation, but at the same time they demanded that he have his child baptized within eight days or sell his property and move out. He chose the latter course and left his home with wife and five children. He probably betook himself to Nürnberg where he met Hans Denk (*q.v.*), who received him in his house. He also met Wolfgang Vogel (*q.v.*), pastor at Eltersdorf; later he preached in this village and baptized Vogel and two others. Vogel also visited him in Nürnberg and talked with him about the Gospel.

While peddling his books between Wittenberg and Erfurt, Hut heard that the Peasants War had broken out near by. He immediately betook himself to Frankenhausen (Thuringia) where the army was stationed, hoping to earn much money selling books and pamphlets (1525). Here he heard Thomas Müntzer (*q.v.*) preaching against the lords; apparently he was profoundly impressed by all that he saw and heard here. Especially the thought of the imminent coming of Christ kindled in him a sort of enthusiasm for this war. When on the next day the peasants marched to battle, he at first went up the hill with them, but because "the shooting was too thick," he hastened back to Frankenhausen where he was later seized by the Hessian authorities. Although many peasants were executed on that day, he was fortunate in being released.

Now he returned to Bibra, and stayed there for

some time. Müntzer also went there on his flight and spent a night and a day in his house. He gave Hut his exposition of the first chapter of the Gospel of Luke to be printed; they had had no other dealings. Hans Hut stated expressly at his later trial that he had not been an adherent of Müntzer; "he did not understand him." In Bibra Jörg Hauck (*q.v.*) invited him to preach. On May 31, 1525, Hut then preached on baptism, communion, idolatry, and the Mass. He made some grave statements about the holders of benefices, who served the Gospel for the sake of their belly. "The Almighty God will punish them and all who oppose the truth; they will all perish in disgrace, and it is now the time when they will be defeated, and the peasants have the power" (Meyer, 251). He explained that he had meant the end-times, and thought they had come. But he had erred and knew better now.

After the complete defeat of the peasants and the bloody suppression of the revolt Hut could no longer stay in Bibra. He was again forced to flee. He turned his steps to Augsburg, where he again met Hans Denk. Denk and Kaspar Färber (*q.v.*) persuaded him, after long hesitation, to join the Anabaptists. On May 26, 1526, Denk baptized him in a little house before the Heiligkreuz gate.

Now Hut worked with unprecedented success for the establishment and spread of the new brotherhood. "Very quietly, but indefatigably he went from place to place in Bavaria, Swabia, Franconia, and Austria, a popular preacher of deepest effectiveness, everywhere proclaiming Anabaptist doctrine, immediately baptizing those he convinced, and sending out individuals as apostles. Especially in the ranks of the artisans he found many adherents" (Wappler, 28). In the period of a few months he succeeded in winning a great number of converts.

His confessions and those of his adherents offer rather exact information on his preaching. He usually began with the words, "Go ye into all the world and preach the Gospel to every creature. He who believes the Gospel and is baptized will be saved; and this is the baptism—to endure anxiety, want, sorrow, and all tribulations in patience." With glowing words he proclaimed the imminent coming of Christ. He divided his sermons into four parts: (1) the judgment upon the house of God; (2) judgment upon the world; (3) the future; and (4) the resurrection. On the basis of Matt. 24; Mark 13, and Luke 17 he explained the signs of the times. The threatening Turkish tribulation was to him a certain sign of Christ's imminent return. But other great tribulations would also occur: revolt, earthquakes, wars, and plagues, so that scarcely one man in three would survive. For three and one-half years more the Lord had given time for repentance, as shown in Rev. 13 and Dan. 12. He who was converted to repentance would be persecuted, as is stated in II Tim. 3:12. But those who repented in these last times would not perish, but survive, and after the day and the judgment of the Lord would possess and rule the earth and would not die (I Cor. 15).

Thus it is evident that Hut's preaching on the return of Christ was entirely based on the Bible and was purely religious. He kept himself aloof from any political or revolutionary tendencies. Statements to the contrary taken from the confessions of his adherents either are erroneously interpreted or are forced by the torments of the rack. He expressly asserted that he knew of no coming of Christ but the one indicated in the Holy Scriptures; it would not be a physical, but a spiritual kingdom. He also denied the imputation that he considered himself a special prophet; he was only a preacher of the Gospel. Nor did he boast of special visions or revelations. God, however, imparted His revelations to the elect sometimes by visions and dreams. There are, he said, three kinds of dreams. Some come from the flesh, from the daily conduct. These are worthless. Some are from the devil; the evils with which one has had contact during the day appear again at night. These are also worthless. Some come from God; they are revealed to human beings by the strength of the Holy Spirit through certain signs and words. He who understands may accept them, and much is revealed to him, as is promised in Num. 12.

Hut also taught that government is instituted by God and implicit obedience is its due. He rejected community of goods. He persuaded no one to sell his goods, but taught that anyone who had a superfluity of goods should help the poor.

In the center of his preaching was the confession of Christ Jesus, the Son of God, who was true God and true man, and who has paid the price for the sins of the whole world and has redeemed us. "He and Denk preached of the crucified Christ, how He suffered and was obedient to His Father unto death," says one of his confessions.

Infant baptism he repudiated; it was not instituted by God; not a word is found about it in the Holy Scriptures. One must not be baptized until he can with full understanding assume the responsibility of living a Christian life, as shown by the Word of God, and for God's sake to suffer all that is laid upon one. Three kinds of baptism are known—baptism by spirit, water, and blood; the three are one and bear witness on earth (I John 5:6-8). The first, the spirit, is the assurance and the assent to the divine Word, that he will live as is proclaimed to him by the Word. This is the covenant of God, which God makes with them through His Spirit and their hearts. Beyond this, God has given water as a sign of this covenant, with which one testifies that he will live in true obedience toward God and all Christians, and lead such a life that he is blameless. But he who does not live right, and deals contrary to God and to love, shall be rebuked by the others; this is the ban that God describes; this is a sign before the church. The third is the blood; this is the baptism that Christ indicated to His disciples; "Ye shall be baptized with the baptism that I am baptized with." This is the baptism that testifies throughout the world, wherever such blood is shed.

Concerning the Lord's Supper Hut did not hold that the body of Christ is in the bread, or the blood of Christ in the cup; it is nothing other than it has always been, namely, bread and wine; for Christ said to His disciples, "I will not drink henceforth of this fruit of the vine, until that day when I drink it anew with you in my Father's kingdom"; and likewise, when they had all drunk from the cup, "This is my blood of the new testament, which is shed for many." These words Christ spoke *after* the eating and drinking, and also shed His blood afterwards; therefore he believes that Christ gave bread and wine to His disciples as a memorial of His suffering, and not His body and His blood.

From Augsburg Hut probably went first into Franconia. In his native town of Haina he won the cooper Georg Volk Kolerlin; in the vicinity he also won many adherents, among them Kilian Volkaimer, Eucharius Binder (*q.v.*), and Joachim Mertz, who became zealous representatives of the Anabaptist cause. Near Erlangen he held a conference, which was broken up by the Nürnberg authorities; several of his adherents were seized, but were soon released and expelled from the city. Now he made his way to Swabia; the council of Nürnberg sent warnings to Augsburg, Ulm, and Regensburg. Hut moved on to Austria and Moravia.

In the spring of 1526 Hut again spent about ten days in Augsburg. He lived in the home of Eitelhans Langenmantel (*q.v.*), and won him to the Anabaptist cause, as also the monk Sigmund Salminger (*q.v.*), the painter Peter Scheppach, and others. He organized the young congregation in Augsburg, giving it a firmer footing. He conducted the choice of leaders. The lot fell on Sigmund Salminger; his substitute was Jakob Dachser (*q.v.*). Hut also arranged for the care of the poor.

At the end of 1526 Hut came to Nikolsburg, where he met Balthasar Hubmaier. They were of different temperaments. Hubmaier would have nothing to do with Hut's chiliasm, nor with his opposition to the government. Hubmaier tried to eliminate the difficulties by the usual disputation. The first one was held in Bergen, a village near Nikolsburg. They discussed community of goods and taxes for resisting the Turks. Since the Anabaptists were committed against warfare or furnishing funds for it, they faced the dilemma either of sacrificing their principles of faith or of refusing obedience to the government at a time when the cry arose, "The Turk is marching upon Vienna!" In addition, the Moravian diet had pronounced all those as dishonorable who managed to be released from these taxes. In the Nikolsburg Anabaptist congregation the rigorous party insisted on exact obedience to their principles and found a leader in Hans Hut. Hubmaier and his adherents were less strict. Thus, as could be expected, the first disputation was fruitless.

The second disputation, held in the Nikolsburg castle, likewise did not lead to union. Hut, who voted "against the sword," was now forcibly detained in the castle. A friend helped him to escape through a window. In this disputation also other subjects were discussed. Hans Nadler (*q.v.*) of Erlangen enumerated seven points under discussion: (1) baptism; (2) communion; (3) God's judgment; (4) God's sentence; (5) the end of the world; (6) the new kingdom; (7) the return of Christ (Schornbaum, 153).

In former times this disputation of 1526 was usually associated with the "Nikolsburg Artikel," a document which brought the Anabaptists into serious disrepute. (It was even deemed important enough to be put on the Index of Forbidden Books in Rome.) Hut at his trial emphatically denied any part in its composition and guessed that perhaps Hubmaier forged it out of jealousy. Today it has been proved that it was forged by enemies of the Anabaptists, most likely by Urbanus Rhegius, the Lutheran preacher at Augsburg, to discredit the Anabaptists, and has nothing to do with Hut or Hubmaier (see **Nikolsburg Articles**).

In the conflict between Hut and Hubmaier, Oswald Glait was one of those on Hut's side; he soon accompanied Hut to Vienna. In Vienna the Anabaptists held a meeting in a house on Kärntnerstrasse. Here 50 persons, including Leonhard Schiemer (*q.v.*), were baptized by Hut. From Vienna Hut went to Melk, where he made contacts with Anabaptists and baptized 15 persons.

On June 15, 1527, Hut arrived secretly in Steyr (*q.v.*), Upper Austria, with two companions, Hieronymus (probably Hieronymus Hermann of Mondsee, a former monk from Ranshofen) and Karius (probably Eucharius Binder), and was introduced into the company of respected citizens by Frater Jakob (Portner), the chaplain of Count Rogendorf. On the following Sunday he held a meeting in the house of Veit Pfefferl at the Grünmarkt; later on he baptized and administered communion also outside the city. Among those baptized were Leonhard Dorfbrunner (*q.v.*), a former priest, and a chaplain of Pechlarn. When the city council was informed of these meetings, it issued a prohibition and ordered the arrest of the preachers. Hut escaped, but his patrons and those he had baptized were arrested, tried, several executed, and the others expelled; only those who recanted were released.

Hut now fled to Freistadt (*q.v.*), Upper Austria. Here too he met Anabaptists. Near the city, in the home of Baron von Zelking, Hans Schlaffer (*q.v.*) had already been active in 1526. In Freistadt Hut baptized ten or twelve persons. From there he went to Gallneukirchen, where he won ten members to the cause, and thence to Linz (*q.v.*), preaching and baptizing everywhere. It is known that he was active also in Passau. Finally traces of his work are found in Schärding, Braunau, Laufen, and Salzburg. In Salzburg he stayed longer, preaching in the house of a citizen Georg Goldschmidt (*q.v.*), whom he won with his wife and six others to the Anabaptist cause.

From Salzburg Hut returned to Augsburg, where he participated in the "Martyrs' Synod" of 1527. Here he was later seized and tried for the first time on Sept. 16, 1527. From his admissions it is seen how extensive his field of influence was, especially in Moravia. After this trial he was given several others, some on the rack. Exact information was given on his life in Bibra, Nürnberg, Salzburg, Moravia, Franconia, and Austria.

Concerning Hut's death there are two reports. According to one he apparently had a premonition of death by violence, and decided to escape by flight. He managed to make a light, and wrapping it in rags, produced much smoke, and cried out, hoping that his irons would be opened by the iron-master. He planned to take the keys and escape. But the guard arrived too late; Hut was nearly asphyxiated, and died Dec. 6, 1527, "as God wished." The second account, found in the *Geschicht-Buch* (Wolkan, 47), was given by his son Philipp. It states that "Hut was racked in the tower, and then released. He lay like one dead." They went away, leaving a candle in his cell, which ignited the straw. When they came to the tower they found him dead.

In either case, sentence could be pronounced only on his corpse. The officials took the dead body to court on a chair, tied the chair to the executioner's cart, sentenced it to die, and burned it at the stake on Dec. 7.

Hans Hut had five children. A daughter died on Jan. 25, 1527, a martyr to her faith; she was drowned in Bamberg. A son Philipp died in Moravia as a member of the brotherhood (Beck, 35).

Not a few mourned Hut's innocent death, gathered his ashes, and took them away as sacred relics. Thus Hut, "a well-educated and clever fellow," as Urbanus Rhegius called him, considered by his brethren an elect instrument of God, who had in scarcely two years won more adherents to Anabaptism than all the other leaders together, laid down his life. Hut was obviously one of the most important leaders of the great Anabaptist movement in the 1520's. He was able to hold his own against great speakers in his own group like Hubmaier. Today the opinion prevails that he was one of the leading and most forceful Anabaptists of the earliest period who influenced that movement, both in Bavaria and Austria by his activities as well as by his writings.

Of these writings only two tracts and two shorter pieces have become known, besides a number of hymns of permanent value. (1) The book *Vom Geheimnus der Tauff* is found in many Hutterite manuscript books (but without naming its author). According to Roth (1900) it is identical with the book Hut himself mentioned at his trial in November 1527 as *Von dem Buch mit den sieben Siegeln, wie in Apocalypsi steht geschrieben* (a msc. supposedly in the city archives of Augsburg). The brethren called it "the book with the seven seals." L. Müller, *Glaubenszeugnisse*, 12-28, prints it from a Hutterite manuscript. (2) *Ein christlicher Unterricht wie göttliche Geschrift vergleicht und geurteilt soll werden*. This tract was published in 1527 by Johannes Landtsperger (*q.v.*); L. Müller, *Glaubenszeugnisse*, 28-37, prints the main part of it; it was also published in the *Mittheilungen aus dem Antiquariat S. Calvary* (Berlin, 1871; there under the name Landtsperger). It is likewise found anonymously in many Hutterite manuscript books. At his trial on Nov. 14, 1527, Hut mentioned this tract as a "booklet on three articles of faith, for which Landtsperger set the title" (and changed it at not less than 20 places). L. Müller recognizes in it a certain dependence on Denk's book, *Unterricht wie das Gesetz Gottes aufgehebt und doch erfüllt muss werden* (something which Sebastian Franck

had called the *Schriftkrieg*—the paradoxes within the Holy Scriptures and their solution).

A third booklet of Hut's was a pastoral epistle beginning "To all good-hearted Christians I Hans Hut wish the pure fear of divine wisdom . . ." (dated "at the cave of Elias"; this is supposedly a typical term of Thomas Müntzer, according to L. Müller), written in Augsburg. When it became known to the Lutheran preacher Urbanus Rhegius (*q.v.*) of Augsburg, he immediately replied with a pamphlet in quarto, *Sendbrief Hans Huthen etwan ains Fürnemen Vorsteers im Wiedertaufforden. Verantwortet durch Urbanum Rhegium* (Augsburg, 1528). From it L. Müller, *Glaubenszeugnisse*, 12, note, prints the main section of the epistle.

A fourth Hut publication was the *Rathsbüchlein* (1526-27). It was found in a pocket of Eitelhans Langenmantel (*q.v.*) when arrested, and is made up of a catechism, a prayer before meals, and a concordance (with 78 items). F. Roth published it in his study of Langenmantel (*Z. d. Hist. Ver. f. Schwaben*, 1900, 39 ff.). At his trial Hut admitted that he had compiled close to one hundred concordance items in his Bible, which he left to his son (Meyer, 236).

It must be regretted that the work of Hut has not yet been studied and analyzed from the standpoint of a history of Anabaptist ideas. As Hut was an important agent of this new movement, valiantly suffering for the nonresistant attitude of true discipleship, but, on the other hand, perhaps somewhat too strongly emphasizing the eschatological-chiliastic angle, such a study would be highly needed. The work by Neuser (1913) has unfortunately never been published in full.

Hut was also a rather successful writer of hymns which found later entrance even into Lutheran and Reformed hymnals. Two or three hymns became known from Hutterite manuscript books, two more are known through the work of Wackernagel, *Das Deutsche Kirchenlied* (see Wolkan, *Lieder*, 15). (1) The best-known hymn is the *Danksagung* "which we sing when celebrating the Lord's Supper" (Beck, 35, Wolkan, *Geschicht-Buch*, 47). It begins, "Wir danksagen dir, Herr Gott der Ehren . . ." and has seven stanzas. Wackernagel (III, 507) erroneously ascribes it to Thomas Müntzer. According to Beck (649, note 2) it was still in use 1650 by the Brethren, and might even today be sung at the Bruderhofs (*Lieder der Hutterischen Brüder*, 38 f., from an old msc. book). Wolkan remarks that this hymn was possibly still older, and was only reworked by Hut. (2) The hymn, "O Almechtiger Herre Gott, wie gar lieblich sind Deine Gebot," is well known from the *Ausbund* (all modern editions, 49-51), 12 stanzas. It is also present in several Hutterite manuscript books, and published by Wackernagel (III, 508) and in the *Lieder der Hutterischen Brüder*, 39 f. (3) This *Lieder der Hutterischen Brüder* prints one more hymn (40) of five stanzas, *Die Danksagung genannt* ("Der wahre Fels ward da geschlagen . . ."), but Hut's authorship is uncertain (again reference is made to Beck, 649, note). The next two hymns are not found in Hutterite codices. Wackernagel prints them (III, 509 and 510 f.) from the *Salmingersche Gesangbuch* of 1537. (4) "Lasst uns von Hertzen singen." As its author Hut is expressly named. (5) "O Herre Gott in deynem Reych . . . ," a paraphrase of the eighth Psalm, was printed 1527, 1529, and 1537. Hut's authorship is not absolutely certain, but most likely. It has eight stanzas (1527), but only seven in later editions. Wackernagel (III, 511) prints this later edition which begins, "O Herre Gott in Ewigkait, wie ist dein nam so sunderlich. . . ."   Loserth, R.F.

Chr. Meyer, "Die Anfänge des Wiedertäuferthums in Augsburg," *Ztscht d. Hist. Ver. f. Schwaben*, 1874, 207-56, with a complete publication of the court records at Augsburg, 1527; W. Neuser, *Hans Hut, Leben und Wirken bis zum Nikolsburger Religionsgespräch* (Berlin, 1913) (the complete dissertation has never been published; Lydia Müller, *Glaubenszeugnisse oberdeutscher Taufgesinnter* (Leipzig, 1938); F. Roth, "Zur Lebensgeschichte Eitelhans Langenmantels zu Augsburg," *Ztscht d. Hist. Ver. f. Schwaben*, 1900 (here the *Rathsbüchlein*, 38-40); F. Roth, *Augsburger Ref.-Gesch.* (2nd ed. 1901); other literature in *ML* II, 370-75.

Hutagodang, a mission station on the island of Sumatra (*q.v.*), formerly Dutch East Indies, now Indonesia, operated by the Dutch Mennonite Mission Society, was founded in 1912 by Peter Nachtigal (*q.v.*). In 1938 this station was transferred to a German mission association.   vDZ.

Hutchinson, Kan. (pop. 34,000), is the county seat of Reno County. The earliest settlements of Mennonites near Hutchinson took place between 1874 and 1883 when groups of the Amish came from Pennsylvania and Illinois and settled south and west of the city near the present village of Yoder. Today these Amish settlements constitute three groups: the Old Order Amish, the Conservative Amish, and the Mennonites (MC). The Conservative Amish have a meetinghouse at Partridge, Kan.; the group that has become affiliated with the Mennonite Church (MC) has its church one mile north of Yoder, Kan. This latter church has a membership of 280 at present.

Throughout the years, many Mennonites (GCM, KMB, MB, CGM, EM, and MC) have moved into Hutchinson from surrounding communities such as Pretty Prairie, Burrton, Buhler, Inman, and Sterling. Many of these have relinquished their Mennonite affiliation; still others continue to worship in their home churches. Four Mennonite churches have been established in the city of Hutchinson to minister to Mennonites in the city; viz., the Mennonite Mission Church (MC; present membership 125), the First Mennonite Church (GCM; present membership 200), the Orchard Park Church (KMB; with 31), and an E.M.B. church (with 26). An inter-Mennonite Bible academy named the Central Kansas Bible Academy is also located in the city of Hutchinson.   V.S.

Hutchinson County, in southeastern South Dakota, is the most heavily Mennonite populated county in the state. Beginning in 1874 until the early 1880's a heavy stream of Mennonites settled in the county, all coming from Russia. Freeman (pop. 1,000, about two-thirds Mennonite) very early came to be an active center of Mennonite life. In this city there are many Mennonite business establishments, a Mennonite home for the aged, Freeman Junior College (*q.v.*), and a General Conference Mennonite church. Many Mennonites from the surrounding territory have come to Freeman to retire. There are in the county six Mennonite churches—one Mennonite Brethren, one Krimmer Mennonite Brethren, and four General Conference Mennonite, all but one of which are rural, and three Hutterian Brethren Bruderhofs, all located along the James River, with a population of 275. The estimated 1,700 Mennonites in the county constitute approximately 14 per cent of its total population. J.D.U.

Hutchinson Evangelical Mennonite Brethren Church, called Crestview Bible Church, on the corner of 17th and Crestview, Hutchinson, Kan., was organized in 1954, when the meetinghouse was erected, although the first meeting of the group was held on Dec. 2, 1953. The membership in May 1955 was 26, with Vernon Harms as pastor. H.S.B.

Hutchinson First Mennonite Church (GCM) at 725 E. 7th St. in Hutchinson, Kan., is a member of the Western District Conference. The first service was held on April 20, 1913, and a site was purchased in 1914. Sponsorship of the church was transferred to the Home Mission Board in 1917. A church was dedicated on March 28, 1920, and a congregation organized in 1922. The congregation became independent in March 1936. In 1955 the membership was 192, with Leonard Metzker as pastor.   V.S.

Huthwohl (Hüthwohl), a Mennonite family found in the Palatinate and Rheinhessen, Germany, in the 17th and 18th centuries. Valentin Huthwohl of Kriegsheim, probably a preacher, wrote a letter to the Mennonites in Amsterdam in 1671, informing them that 430 Swiss Mennonite refugees had come to the Palatinate, and asking their financial aid, which was liberally granted. Again in 1695 he asked for support. Gerhard Huthwohl was a preacher or elder of Heppenheim (*q.v.*) an der Wiese; in 1784, after the congregation for a long period had held its meetings in his house, he received support from the Dutch Mennonites to build a meetinghouse; again in 1802-6 he asked the Dutch Mennonites for advice in meeting the requirements of the French occupation army, which compelled them to do military service. David Huthwohl was a preacher of the Erbesbüdesheim (*q.v.*) congregation in 1769-? and (obviously another) David Huthwohl of the Weierhof (*q.v.*) congregation 1791-?.

In the 18th century most members of the Huthwohl family emigrated to the United States, where they are called Heatwole (*q.v.*).   vDZ.

Inv. Arch. Amst. I, Nos. 1059, 1198, 1248, 1406, 1416, 1547, 1551; II, Nos. 2682-84.

Hutscher, Ulrich, an Anabaptist from Tieff near Windsheim in Lower Franconia, Germany, was arrested early in April 1531 and taken to the mountain castle Hoheneck, together with the wife of Julius Lober. Lober himself shortly met the same fate. On April 16 the prisoners were cross-examined by several priests. Hutscher confessed that two years previously the wife of Georg of Passau had been baptized in Tuchscherer's house at Windsheim. Asked why he had forsaken the pure doctrine he replied: May God forbid that he forsake the pure true doctrine of Christ. He had just entered the pure doctrine of Christ, and he was surprised that they wanted him to abandon it, for faith is the gift of God. Georg of Passau had taught him to forsake sin and to live a true Christian life. He had repented and then been baptized on confession of his faith. Formerly he had been deep in sin, but now he stood in God's grace. In November the prisoners were still in prison. The outcome of the trial is not known. (Wiswedel, *Bilder* II, 34-36; *ML* II, 384.) W.W.

Hutter, Jakob. It is a false assumption to consider the simple and unlearned hatmaker Jakob Hutter the founder and beginner of the Anabaptists in Tirol; for the Anabaptist movement had long been thriving when Hutter entered it. But it is certain that none of his predecessors or successors in the eastern Anabaptist movement equaled him in importance; for none was so successful in creating and reforming. He not only afforded the cause a strong support when it had begun to waver in the extremely difficult times; he was also the founder of that peculiar organization which preserved itself in Moravia with its communistic character to the end, the founder of the brotherhood named for him, which still has shoots growing on the American continent. It is therefore easy to understand when the *Geschichts-Bücher* of the Anabaptists speak of him in highest praise, beginning, "At that time one came, by the name of Jakob."

He was a native of the hamlet of Moos near St. Lorenz near Bruneck in the Puster Valley of Tirol. Scantily educated by the school at Bruneck, he went to Prague to learn hatmaking there. Then he began his extensive journeys for the sake of his trade and finally settled at Spittal a.d. Drau in Carinthia. In Klagenfurt he probably made his first contact with the teachings of the Anabaptists, which became so significant for his inner development. He was never in Silesia or Bavaria, and learned of Gabriel Ascherham (*q.v.*) and his Silesians only when in 1529 he came to Moravia to find a quiet place for his little congregation. It is not known when he was baptized, but after he had "accepted the covenant of grace of a good conscience in Christian baptism with true resignation to lead a godly life and God's gifts were richly felt in him, he was chosen and confirmed in the service of the Gospel."

In this position he first traveled through the Puster Valley, Tirol. One of the first small congregations he headed was that at Welsperg. Here his adherents assembled alternately in the house of his relative, Balthasar Hutter, or Andreas Planer, a scythe-smith. At the latter place he baptized ten persons on one day. The government had word of this "synagogue" in May 1529 and now ordered Christoph Herbst, the sheriff at Toblach-Welsberg, to surprise and seize the Anabaptists. Some were captured, but Hutter and others escaped. The statements of the prisoners were sent to Innsbruck.

They gathered from them that Jakob Hutter, a real leader, "baptized the others for money"; what is meant is that each had to make a contribution to the common treasury.

Though the leader escaped this time, the authorities seized his sister Agnes in 1529. She had a short time previously been pardoned, but had at once returned to the brotherhood. By this act her sentence was already pronounced. The persecution of the "pious in the land" gradually grew intolerable. On every side one saw the blood of the martyrs and the burning stakes, prisons filled with captives, children forsaken and starving at home, with never a ray of hope except in God.

Then some recalled that the Lord of Hosts had gathered a people in His name in the city of Austerlitz in Moravia. The elders decided to send Brother Jakob and Sigmund Schützinger to them to gather information. After hearing his favorable report the brotherhood in Tirol decided to join the one in Moravia. Hutter appointed this co-worker Jörg Zaunring (or Zaunried) to lead them, and sent one small group after the other to Moravia. Most of them were members of Blaurock's (*q.v.*) orphaned congregation (he had been burned at the stake at Klausen on Sept. 6, 1529). Singly and in groups, driven by the persecution prevailing throughout the land, the Anabaptists sought the road to Moravia. There was hardly an alternative. The government pointed out in a letter to King Ferdinand in Vienna that for two years hardly a day had passed in which Anabaptist matters had not come up in the council; "and more than 700 persons have been in part executed, in part expelled, in part have fled into misery, who left their property as well as their children behind." All the rulings were of no avail. "These people not only have no horror of punishment, but even report themselves; rarely is one converted; nearly all only wish to die for their faith."

Here Hutter worked on without fear. In the early summer of 1530 he wrote a letter about it to Moravia. But while he was devoting all his energy to the care of his brethren at home, conflicts arose in Austerlitz in the winter of 1530, which threatened the very existence of the congregation, and finally split it into two hostile camps. The causes of this division were misapplication of church regulations by ordained ministers, irregularities in church discipline, mismanagement of possessions, lack of tact in critical cases, the ambition of certain individuals, all of which Reublin (*q.v.*) sharply criticized in his letter to Pilgram Marpeck of 1531.

A part of the congregation then went to Auspitz, but not without having sent a messenger to Hutter, asking him to investigate the difficulty. The Austerlitz group did the same. Therefore Hutter and Schützinger went back to Moravia, investigated "where the error in dispute lay, and found that the Austerlitz group was most to be blamed." After they had settled the quarrel they returned to Tirol, but had to go back to Moravia the next year to establish order once more. At this time Anabaptism came to full bloom in Moravia. From Silesia, Swabia, the Palatinate, and Tirol came a long procession to Moravia.

At this time begins the struggle of the Tirolean Anabaptists for their existence. The year 1533 marks the climax of the persecution of the Anabaptists in Tirol, for the government neglected no measures for their suppression. Special efforts were made to capture Hutter, "who had brought so many people of the district into the sect." But no one was found who could claim the reward offered for his capture. When it was finally decided by the Anabaptists in the Gufidaun region that tyranny had reached the highest degree, so that it was no longer possible for "the saints" to live there, Hutter was commissioned to go to Moravia to prepare a new home for the emigrants.

On Aug. 11, 1533, he arrived in Auspitz with one companion. The majority of the brotherhood there wished to accept Hutter, who was known for his energetic action, as their leader, but this ran counter to the wishes of their current leaders, Schützinger, Philipp, and Gabriel. And yet in view of the continued friction in the congregation, there was imperative need for clear-sighted leadership. These leaders had shown themselves incapable of energetic execution of original Anabaptist doctrine. They had no clear grasp of true brotherhood, and tended to cling to family ties, which were incompatible with unadulterated Anabaptist doctrine. Reublin's complaints about the education of the children, the difference in the treatment of the members in food and clothing and in respect show how inadequate their leadership was.

Hutter's attack on the problem was different. The court records relate that he distributed to the poor the money collected from the members: "This Jakob," say the Geschichts-Bücher, "also brought a temporal gift, a sweet sacrifice, a little food, so that they could repay their debt of the time of need." More important to Hutter than choice by the lot was inner awakening: "The Holy Spirit called him for leadership." He could not escape it. It was his duty to reform matters. He stated this emphatically in his first address before the brotherhood. After a few days he began the improvements. But he was opposed by Schützinger, who claimed the office of leadership on the strength of his election by the brotherhood. He therefore betook himself to Gabriel in Rossitz. "He wanted to see clearly whether the people wanted him as their leader or not. To be quiet and not perform the duties of his office he was not free to do before God. If he was not needed, he would move on, wherever God directed him." With great difficulty he managed to have the brotherhood recognize him as leader, "that he be our bishop and shepherd."

The Hutterites now formed a brotherhood and Hutter was able to lead them with a firm hand. The Geschichts-Bücher say, "He put the true church in pretty good order by the help and grace of God, hence we are still called the Hutterites." The loss created by the withdrawal of Schützinger and of the dissatisfied elements under his leadership was replaced by fresh additions from Tirol. In a letter written immediately after the separation Hutter named 120 to 130 persons who had come in the last few weeks. The reports he sent from the "holy" church at Auspitz to Tirol caused a veritable mass migration of Anabaptists to Moravia; they came singly and in groups.

To provide for the continued growth Hutter was compelled to look about for new homes; thus in the same year (1533) Schäckowitz, a half mile south of Auspitz, was settled. The only serious difficulty arose from their relationship with the adherents of Philipp, his opponent, who also lived in Auspitz. The additions from Tirol continued in increasing numbers; even Tirolean noblemen, like Sigmund von Wolkenstein, made pilgrimages to Auspitz. At the beginning of 1534 the movement was general among the Anabaptists of Tirol. Soon the government was shocked by reports that nearly all the valleys in the Sterzing district were full of them; three leaders had come from Moravia and were agitating in the region of Schwatz. Almost at the same time it was rumored that Hans Amon (q.v.) was planning "to send the common people, whom he had misled from the true faith in the Puster Valley and other places," to Moravia in the coming spring. Although orders continued to be issued to guard the boats on the Inn River, nevertheless the emigrants managed to get to Moravia. It can be imagined what pleasure the report—false, to be sure—created in Brixen, that Hutter and Amon had been seized in Linz. A considerable number of brethren were captured at Hohenwart in Lower Austria; to them Hutter wrote a long letter of consolation. Here in Auspitz, he said, there was also great tribulation. In Tirol there were no longer many brethren. These, too, were preparing to go to Moravia under the untiring leadership of Hans Amon.

But in Moravia affairs had also taken a turn for the worse for the Anabaptists. The blow that was to strike them here had long been in preparation and was in essence the consequence of the events that had taken place in Münster; but it did not materialize until 1535. The Moravian diet, which was attended by Ferdinand I in person, acceded to his wish to have all Anabaptists expelled. In vain they lamented that they were illegally being driven from their possessions. No one in Moravia had ever had cause for complaint to the government. But if the sovereign or the feudal authorities demanded tribute or taxes they were willing to pay as much as they were able, if they were only permitted to keep their work and their religion. A petition did indeed reach the court, but was disregarded. Marshall Johann von Lipa, who took them into his protection, was threatened with the disfavor of the king. They had to move out into wretched poverty.

Hutter took his bundle on his back, as did his assistants; the brethren and sisters with their children went in pairs. "They were thus," their Geschichts-Bücher relate, "driven into the field like a herd of sheep. Nowhere were they permitted to camp until they reached the village of Tracht in the possessions of the lord of Liechtenstein. There they lay down on the wide heath under the open sky with many wretched widows and children, sick and infants." In touching words Hutter wrote to the governor Kuna von Kunstadt: "Now we are camping on the heath, without disadvantage to any man. We do not want to wrong or harm any human being, not even our worst enemy. Our walk in life is to live in truth and righteousness of God, in peace and unity. We do not hesitate to give an account of our conduct to anyone. But whoever says that we have camped on a field with so many thousands, as if we wanted war or the like, talks like a liar and a rascal. If all the world were like us there would be no war and no injustice. We can go nowhere; may God in heaven show us where we shall go. We cannot be prohibited from the earth, for the earth is the heavenly Father's; may He do with us what He will." The step merely resulted in greater efforts to capture Hutter.

Now the brotherhood itself insisted on Hutter's leaving. He committed his office to Hans Amon and bade his relatives farewell; with pain and grief they saw him leave. Those remaining scattered, some here and some there. A little group settled at Steinabrunn in Lower Austria, some on the estates of lords who did not feel bound by the latest decree. Hutter's ideal, "the brotherhood," was now broken up, but preserved itself in numerous small groups. Many who were unable to endure the trials of the brethren returned home.

Thus many returned to Tirol. There, led by Hutter, they began anew their evangelization. "The ungodly tyrants," he writes to his forsaken church, "do not yet know that we are here. God grant that they do not find it out." But even before Hutter appeared in Tirol the cry resounded on every hand, "Anabaptists from Moravia are roaming through the country!" Orders were at once issued for their arrest. During the period from early September to the end of November, 1535, Hutter wrote three letters to the brethren in Moravia. In one he wrote, "God has again set up a church. His people are increasing in numbers daily. The harvest is nearly ripe, but the laborers are few"; in another he spoke of the "raging" of the foe. "They threaten with hangmen and bailiffs." "The Sodomite sea is raging madly. I fear it will not come to rest until the pious Jonah is cast into it." He warned the brotherhood of treachery.

Hutter's last letter, written shortly before his capture, indicates the great danger hovering over him. With so many enemies he could not hope to remain undiscovered. When he and his pregnant wife were spending the night in the home of Hans Steiner, a former sexton, at Clausen, they were surprised by the clerk of Seber and the city judge Riederer, and together with Anna Steiner of St. George and the aged wife of the sexton they were taken to the neighboring episcopal fortress of Brandzell. The capture of Hutter was immediately reported to Brixen and from there on Dec. 1 to Innsbruck, where the news was received with pleasure, and orders were issued to transfer Hutter to Innsbruck, for he was not an ordinary prisoner, but a leader; the hearing of his wife was to take place before the city judge in Clausen. In Hutter's bag were found letters from Hans Amon in Moravia, which were sent to Innsbruck with the statements of the arrested women.

Hutter was then taken to Innsbruck under strong escort on Dec. 9 in severely cold weather, and was cross-examined two days later. The attempts made by Dr. Gallus Müller to convert him were fruitless. Even if he had recanted, his tragic fate would not have been averted, for the final decision of Ferdinand I was, "We are determined that even if Hutter should renounce his error, we will not pardon him, for he has misled far too many, but we will let the penalty which he has merited so abundantly take its course." He was to be closely questioned on his activity within and without the land, and precautions taken not to let him be replaced with other leaders from Moravia; orders to this effect had already been sent to Moravia.

Apparently it was expected that Hutter would ultimately be converted, but this was not achieved, neither by the torments of the rack nor by the barbarous whipping. Hutter was firmly resolved not to yield in matters of faith nor to betray his brethren. He endured every degree of terrible torture and "remained steadfast to the end." The sentence condemned him to death by fire. The court had doubts concerning the advisability of a public execution; but the king would not consent to having him executed with the sword in the quiet of dawn; he insisted on a public execution at the stake. He died on Feb. 25, 1536, and in the words of Hans Amon, "he gave a great sermon through his death, for God was with him." A trusted brother was at once sent to Moravia by the orphaned brotherhood to bear the news of his departure to the brethren there.

Hutter's wife had meanwhile been examined in Brandzell, but as the official report says, persisted "in her obstinate foolish opinion." She was transferred to Gufidaun (q.v.), where a learned and tactful man was assigned to convert her from her error, but she escaped before he arrived. Two years later she again fell into the hands of the government and was executed at Schöneck.

Hutter's death was commemorated in song by his adherents. But his old opponents—a Gabriel Ascherham—carried their rancor beyond his death. Only Philip Plener, also an opponent in Hutter's Moravian period, gave a juster verdict: "No one provided so faithfully for the people in temporal or spiritual matters as Hutter. Never was he found unfaithful. Through him the Lord gathered and preserved His people." In general his brethren recognized his service to the Moravian Anabaptists in re-establishing discipline and order, confirming the "community" in opposition to destructive private ambitions, cleansing it of impure elements, and averting the abuses that brought dissolution of the groups in other places.

The reply to an inquiry concerning the content of his teaching, is to point to the Articles of Schleitheim (*Geschichts-Bücher* 41-44), common to the Anabaptists of South Germany and Austria. Also *Jeronyme Kräls Bekanntnuss und Rechenschaft etliche Artikel christlichen Glaubens betreffend,* which Kräl presented to the government in Vienna in 1536, may be regarded as a reflection of Hutter's own words. His spirit is further revealed in the *Rechenschaft und Zeugnuss* of the brethren who were taken from Steinabrunn to Trieste as galley slaves in 1540; the completion of his doctrinal system is found in the *Rechenschaft unserer Religion, Lehr und Glaubens,* written in 1540 by Peter Riedemann (*q.v.*).

The Hutterite brotherhood, after the death of its founder in Moravia, has developed and maintained its sharply defined communistic character to the present time.

Of Hutter's writings only his eight epistles have been preserved. He has erroneously been credited with (1) Riedemann's *Rechenschaft;* (2) *Anschlag und Fürwenden der blinden, verkehrten Welt und aller Gottlosen gegen die Frommen* (Cod. G. J. VI, 31 in Gran); (3) *Von den 7 Siegeln des verschlossenen Buchs,* by which is meant either Sebastian Franck's book, *Das verbütschiert mit 7 Siegeln verschlossene Buch,* or probably Hans Hut's booklet, *Von dem Buch mit den 7 Siegeln, wie in der Apocalipsi stunde.*   LOSERTH.

Beck, *Geschichts-Bücher;* Loserth, *Anabaptismus; idem, Communismus; ML* II, 375-78. The letter by Wilhelm Reublin to Pilgram Marpeck (1531) mentioned above is printed by C. A. Cornelius, *Geschichte des Münsterischen Aufruhrs* II (Leipzig, 1860) 253 f.; Hans Fischer, *Jakob Huter, Leben, Frömmigkeit, Briefe* (Newton, 1957); Zieglschmid, *Chronik;* Wolkan, *Geschicht-Buch.*

Hutterdorf Mennonite Church (GCM), a member of the Northern District Conference, located near Freeman, Hutchinson Co., S.D., derives its name from the village in Russia from which the settlers came in 1874. Until 1880, when the first school was built, services were conducted in the homes of members by the first ministers, the brethren William Tschetter and David Waldner. The first church, built in 1901, still serves the congregation. John Hofer, Elias Wipf, and Peter J. Stahl have also served as ministers. The latter was ordained in 1917 and still serves. The congregation has an organized Christian Endeavor and an active Sunday school. The membership in 1955 was 50.   J.D.U.

Hutterian Brethren, also called Hutterites, the Austrian branch of the great Anabaptist movement of the 16th century, characterized by the practice of community of goods, as first established in Moravia in 1529 and re-established on more solid grounds by Jacob Hutter in 1533. In contradistinction to the other Anabaptist groups the Hutterites had the unique chance to develop their communal life in comparatively peaceful Moravia where, due to a predominantly Slavic surrounding, they lived in relative isolation from the rest of the world. Thus a rich group life developed with a strong sense for their own history. Remarkable is also their extensive manuscript literature (devotional and historical) which made it possible that their teachings and their history, particularly of the beginnings, should become better known than those of any other group of the Anabaptist movement except the Dutch.

The 1520's saw a lively spread of Anabaptism throughout the Hapsburg territories, Tirol, Austria, Carinthia, etc. In Tirol in particular Anabaptism was by far the strongest trend, and remained so until far into the second half of the 16th century, in spite of a government which ruthlessly fought all "heretics" wherever they could be ferreted out. It was here that Georg Blaurock (*q.v.*) of Switzerland worked successfully as a missioner until his early martyrdom in 1529. Persecutions were extremely bloody. One source (Kirchmaier, 487) claims that prior to 1530 no less than one thousand had been executed, and that the stakes were burning all along the Inn Valley. Yet the number of Anabaptists only grew. Soon the news became known that Moravia (and in particular the manorial estate Nikolsburg of the lords of Liechtenstein) was a haven for all sectarians. Here Hubmaier (*q.v.*) could freely write and print his new ideas concerning adult baptism. In fact, one of the Liechtensteins himself accepted baptism upon faith. Also other manorial lords showed sympathy and toleration, perhaps due to the fact that this country had seen the Hussites (now called Piccards) for nearly a century, and allowed complete freedom of conscience to practically all sorts of beliefs. Naturally from now on a continuous stream of Anabaptists moved toward this "promised land," from Tirol as well as from other Hapsburg lands, but also from South Germany, Bavaria, Württemberg, Hesse, and even from Switzerland.

In 1528 the nonresistant group, called "Stäbler" (staff-bearers), moved away from Nikolsburg, then the center of the opposing group, the "Schwertler" (sword-bearers, the Hubmaier followers), who, however, soon died out. Compelled by the emergency situation, the need of taking care of the many indigent brethren, they pooled all their possessions and money in the manner of the first church in Jerusalem. But this act was at first not understood as a definite step toward complete community of goods comprising both consumption and production. This development came but slowly step by step. The first leader was Jacob Wiedemann, the "one-eyed one"; later leaders were Siegmund Schützinger, Jörg Zaunring, and Gabriel Ascherham (for details see **Moravia, Nikolsburg,** also **Auspitz** and **Austerlitz**). The groups around 1529-33 lived by no means in brotherly harmony; local quarrels over leadership and form of community-life mar these first years in Moravia. Jacob Hutter, an Anabaptist from Tirol (*q.v.*) who had visited the Moravian brotherhoods in 1529, and who worried much about these conditions, first sent his emissary, Jörg Zaunring, but eventually decided to leave Tirol and to try for himself to settle these disputes and rivalries, and to establish more evangelical foundations. Details of this intricate story cannot be told here, but it soon became obvious that Hutter was by far the strongest leader of all. In 1533 the evangelical (nonresistant) Anabaptists of Moravia broke up into three groups: (*a*) Those who accepted Jacob Hutter's leadership and (according to his organization) complete community of goods, called themselves from now on *Hutterische Brüder*. Hutter, himself a very strong prophetic and charismatic leader, had given to this group such definite foundations that it could survive and, in spite of many ups and downs, preserve its basic principles through more than four centuries. (*b*) The Philippites (*q.v.*), named after Philipp Plener or Blauärmel (*q.v.*), a Württemberger. This group left Moravia already in 1535 during the first bitter days of persecution. They returned through Austria to South Germany. On their way many were imprisoned in Passau (see **Ausbund**), while others decided to stay in Upper Austria where still in the 1530's Peter Riedemann (*q.v.*) visited them and managed eventually a merger with the Hutterian Brethren. This group stressed the suffering church in particular and with it *Gelassenheit* (*q.v.*) (see also **Haffner**). (*c*) The Gabrielites (*q.v.*), named after Gabriel Ascherham (*q.v.*). They, too, soon moved out of Moravia back to Silesia, Ascherham's home country. But soon they became disappointed with their leader, who tended more and more toward a vague spiritualism. Between 1542 and 1545 most of these Gabrielites returned and likewise merged with the Hutterites. (The doctrinal basis for this is contained in a document inserted in the *Geschicht-Buch*, Wolkan, 197-200, "Der Gabrieler Vereinigung mit uns.") Other groups of evangelical Anabaptists in Moravia who did not accept community of goods were given the general name "Swiss Brethren," even though they did not come from Switzerland. Also a small group of followers of Pilgram Marpeck (*q.v.*) were found in Southern Moravia under the leadership of Leopold Scharnschlager (*q.v.*). Yet these groups later disappeared, while the Hutterian Brethren managed to maintain themselves through all early hardships and local persecutions.

This may have been due to a large extent to a remarkable number of outstanding leaders: Ulrich Stadler of Tirol (*q.v.*), Hans Amon of Bavaria (*q.v.*), Peter Riedemann of Silesia (*q.v.*), Peter Walpot of Tirol (*q.v.*), Klaus Braidl of Hesse (*q.v.*), not to mention the long array of other brethren, most of whom died as martyrs or suffered long years of imprisonment. Although "expelled" from Moravia more than once upon mandates by Ferdinand (the later emperor), they yet somehow succeeded in finding the sympathy of the manorial lords, who quickly recognized their value as craftsmen and tillers of the soil. Many of these lords were either Protestants or at least in sympathy with the Reformation, and proud of their quasi-independence from the government in Vienna. And thus Moravia remained the one stable place in this century of intolerance and suffering. In 1546 the Brethren also moved east across the border into adjacent Slovakia (then a part of Hungary) where the influence of the Hapsburgs was still weaker, and where a good many of the lords belonged to the Reformed faith.

Jacob Hutter was a leader for only two years (1533-35); he returned to Tirol where eventually he too fell into the hands of his persecutors. In February 1536 he was martyred. Hans Amon thereupon became the *Vorsteher* or head bishop of the brotherhood, 1536-42, being a strong and inspiring leader. In this time organized missionary activities of the brethren set in, perhaps the first such in all of Europe. Missioners (*Sendboten*) were sent out to many places (knowing quite well the fate ahead

of them; 80 per cent of them died a martyr's death), and those in the throes of death were comforted by epistles and visiting brethren (e.g., the case of the 140 Falkenstein Brethren who were sent to Trieste to become galley slaves, 1539-40). One of the strongest missioners of this time was Peter Riedemann, who went more than once to Upper Austria and to Hesse. While in jail in Hesse (1540-42), he drew up that outstanding document which from now on became the very symbolic book of the brotherhood, the *Account of Our Religion* (*Rechenschaft, q.v.*), 1540 (printed 1565, and again in the 19th and 20th century). In 1542-56 he shared the leadership of the brotherhood with Leonhard Lanzenstiel or Seiler.

While elsewhere persecution intensified (Anabaptism had died out by the middle of the 16th century in the Hapsburg domain except Tirol; it declined in Bavaria and other German lands), in Moravia on the contrary it experienced now a kind of flowering. This was particularly true during the reign of Emperor Maximilian II (1564-76), himself rather in sympathy with Protestantism, hence averse to any harsh measures. The Brethren speak of the "Good Period" (about 1554-65) and of the "Golden Period" (1565-90 or 95). Although the Jesuits had been admitted in Hapsburg territories since about 1550-60, they did not find full influence in Moravia until the end of the century. It is true that Nikolsburg had changed hands; the Dietrichsteins (*q.v.*) bought it in 1575, but even though they were more in sympathy with the Counter-Reformation, the Brethren could still persist here, too, relatively peacefully, until the coming of the Cardinal Franz von Dietrichstein in 1599, the very head of the Catholic party.

During the Golden Period the Brethren, now well established all over southern Moravia and Slovakia, found a particularly strong leader in Peter Walpot (*q.v.*), a Tirolean, who led the group in 1565-78, and whose activities added much to further consolidate the brotherhood. A number of regulations were drawn up, both for the general conduct of the brotherhood and for the different crafts or trades. The schools of the Brethren were organized on better defined grounds. Doctrinal and polemic writings (mostly anonymous) were drawn up (such as the great Article Book, *q.v.*, the *Handbüchlein, q.v.*, the book called *Anschläg und Fürwenden*, etc.). A rich correspondence with missionaries all over the countries of German tongue came in and went out (carefully recorded in a *Schreibstube* or *scriptorium*); the great *Geschicht-Buch* was then begun by Caspar Braitmichel (*q.v.*) on the basis of archival material collected almost from the very beginning. In short, it was the peak of Hutterite history. It has been estimated that in Moravia and Slovakia together there existed at that time about one hundred Bruderhofs or farm colonies, with a population estimated at between 20,000 and 30,000. (Certain estimates go as high as 70,000, but that figure is most unlikely.) (See the accompanying maps.) While Anabaptism elsewhere (except for the Netherlands and Prussia) was on a sharp decline, in fact nearly disappeared as an articulated movement in the latter half of the 16th century, in remote Moravia and Slovakia it was almost on its way to becoming a distinct denomination (were it not that the sect-principle, that is, brotherhood-living, continued to be dominant).

Very remarkable of that time are also contacts with the anti-Trinitarian Polish Brethren (Socinians) who in Racov (Poland) tried to set up their "New Jerusalem" (see **Anti-Trinitarianism**), somewhat along lines which they had been studying at the Moravian Hutterite communistic colonies. Visitors and correspondence witness to this contact which, however, never became very warm, due to basic differences both in doctrine and intellectual background.

Contacts with Swiss Brethren, in Switzerland and elsewhere, continued to be intensive; missioners were sent out and a good number of Brethren from Switzerland and South Germany joined the church in Moravia. (The later bishop Ulrich Jausling, serving 1619-21, had been such a Swiss newcomer.) Of particular interest is here a long letter (almost a tract) which the *Vorsteher* Claus Braidl sent to a Swiss brother Christian Raussenberger in 1601 defending on Biblical ground the principle of community of goods. Also with the Prussian Mennonites around Elbing and Danzig contacts were obtained around the turn of the century. Even a settlement was attempted in Elbing though without success. In the meantime the peaceful period had come to an end, and severe trials were in store. (*a*) The Counter-Reformation (*q.v.*) became now the cry of the day. Whoever would not be converted to the Roman Church was to leave Moravia. Cardinal Franz von Dietrichstein gave the lead in that movement, supported by a most vigilant government in Vienna and two priests, Christoph Erhard (*q.v.*) and Christoph Andreas Fischer (*q.v.*), in southern Moravia, who supplied the Catholics with polemic material (gross slanders), and cast suspicions of all kinds. They incited the hatred of the poor peasant population all around who naturally could not compete with large-scale rational farm economies (see **Eysvogel** and **Jedelshauser**). In short the situation became ever more precarious. Yet until 1622 they somehow managed to come through, although on a declining scale. (*b*) Turkish wars and invasions added to these internal troubles. Emperor Rudolph II asked for war contributions, and Dietrichstein was to extort them from the Brethren (at one time no less than 20,000 fl. was asked). Needless to say, the Brethren very decidedly declined, accepting all the consequences. In 1605 Turks and their Hungarian allies plundered southern Moravia and many brethren were killed or dragged away into Turkish captivity (see **Böger**). Eventually (*c*) the event, later called the Thirty Years' War, 1618-48, brought the Moravian establishments of the Brethren to a complete end. After the success of the Catholic forces at the White Mountain in 1620, all restraint was dropped; complete expulsion was ordered by Vienna. The *Geschicht-Buch* (570-71) reports that what they lost on inventory (corn, wine, cattle, linen and woolens, groceries, equipment, and furniture) amounted

to about 364,000 florins not assessing any houses and grounds. And all this after only one year earlier (1621) a sum of 30,000 fl. had been taken away from the Brethren by methods of extortion and downright robbery.

With these events the brotherhood begins to show a sharp decline in activities and also in loyalty to the old principles, and even in number of members and colonies (in Slovakia there were only 15 colonies). Although Moravia was now lost, the Brethren could still withdraw to their Slovakian colonies, and since 1621 also to their new Bruderhof in Alvinc, Transylvania (today Rumania). In spite of continued great hardships, mainly through Turkish marauders, the Brethren carried on, and visitors were amazed by their industriousness and diligence (see **Grimmelshausen**). The brotherhood was fortunate enough in getting once more a bishop of outstanding qualities in leadership and spirituality, viz., Andreas Ehrenpreis (*q.v.*), 1639-62, the real leader already since 1630. He was born in a Moravian colony. His work was an effort to revive the brotherhood in many regards: the last mission work in Silesia (contacts with Schwenckfeldians) and Danzig (the Socinians were contacted) was carried out, although with rather moderate success. A short-lived colony was established in Mannheim (*q.v.*) in 1664. Internal discipline was re-established by strict regulations (see **Gemeindeordnungen**). And a rich literature was produced. Of particular value for posterity was also the new custom of writing down all sermons (called *Lehr und Vorred*). The amount of such manuscript material is amazing; there are about 250 such *Lehren* (some quite voluminous books about most books of the N.T., and many of the O.T., mainly prophets, psalms, also about many apocryphal books and pseudepigrapha, and about as many *Vorreden* (shorter sermons). The *Klein-Geschichtsbuch* (204-21) brings excerpts from these sermons. One may safely say that the Hutterian Brethren of today continue the Ehrenpreis tradition at least as much if not more than any earlier tradition (e.g., that of Jakob Hutter). Ehrenpreis' *Gemeindeordnung* of 1651 is still in use, and the sermons of that period are the backbone of all spiritual life of the brethren today.

After Ehrenpreis' death more tribulations made life in community of goods harder and harder until this core element of the Hutterites was partly abandoned, and a semiprivate or semico-operative form of economy was accepted (1685, 1695). The great misery of Turkish invasions with its looting (which the nonviolent Brethren could not stop in any way) impoverished the brotherhood to such an extent that they had to turn to their Dutch Mennonite "cousins" to ask for financial help. The Great Chronicle ends with the letter which Johann Riecker, the successor of Ehrenpreis, wrote to the "Gemeinden in Holland," April 20, 1665. It is known that the Doopsgezinde most generously responded (*Inv. Arch. Amst.* II, 419, a letter of thanks). Yet also this help could not prevent further troubles.

After the defeat of the Turks before Vienna (1683) and their expulsion from Hungary (1700), the Hapsburg government gained strength also in this newly conquered territory. And even though the 18th century is known as one of religious toleration, it was not the same for Hungary. Empress Maria Theresa (1740-80) allowed the otherwise forbidden Jesuits to exert all means to convert non-Catholics back to the Roman Church. And what torture, dungeon, and executioners could not achieve in the 16th century, the Jesuits achieved, at least partly, in the 18th, mainly in Slovakia. Their old manuscript books were confiscated (1757-63, 1782-84); children were taken away from their parents; and the more important male members were put into monasteries until they either accepted instructions and were converted, or until they died. Catholic services were established at the Bruderhofs and every one was compelled to attend. In short, externally the Hutterite population now turned Catholic, although in secret they continued to practice their old beliefs, likewise maintaining their co-operative enterprises. From now on the nickname *Habaner* (*q.v.*) became the general name for these people.

In Transylvania the Brethren had dwindled to scarcely more than a small group of perhaps 30 or 40 souls. Then Lutheran transmigrants from Carinthia (*q.v.*) to Transylvania (they arrived in 1756) came into contact with this remnant of Hutterite life, and felt immediately attracted by this form of Christian communism. They now joined the brotherhood, and thus brought about a rejuvenation of and rededication to the old principles. Naturally, persecutions, mainly by Jesuits, quickly set in here too. After a number of attempts to find other places the Brethren finally decided to flee Transylvania (1767, after a stay of 146 years), across high mountain passes almost without trails, and to enter Walachia (now Rumania) where conditions looked favorable. Another Turkish War (against Russia) again brought hardships, and the great trek continued after three years. In 1770 at the Dniester River the Brethren were received by the Russian general Count Rumyantsov, who offered them an asylum on his own estate in the Ukraine (then a rather sparsely populated area). At Vishenka the Brethren finally settled down for about one generation. In 1802 the colony was transferred to Czarist crown land at Radichev, 10 miles north. It was Johannes Waldner (born in Carinthia) who was then the most outstanding *Vorsteher* of the brotherhood (1794-1824). It was he who between 1793 and 1802 wrote the second big chronicle of the Hutterites, the *Klein-Geschichtsbuch,* a work of great charm and refinement. J. Loserth called Waldner a genuine historian. He was also a genuine disciple of Jacob Hutter, who with all his strength opposed the threatening abandonment of the principle of community of goods, which one group under the leadership of Jacob Walter (formerly of Slovakia) carried out in 1818. This new Walter-group then settled down in southern Russia (Molotschna district, under the sponsorship of the Mennonite Johann Cornies), where for about 40 years it practiced private property. In 1859-60 some leader dared to re-establish communal life as of old,

and soon the new Hutterite villages began to thrive. Then in 1870, universal military conscription in Russia brought an end to all former privileges, and the Brethren saw no other way out than again to migrate—in this case to emigrate to America.

The story of this migration is too long to be retold here in detail. After a trip of inspection and scouting (1873), all the Brethren decided to come to the United States, where they chose the prairie land of South Dakota for settlement (in scenery so similar to the steppe of Russia). They arrived in 1874, 1877, and 1879, settling down in complete community of goods in three colonies near Yankton. According to these three settlements they are still today divided into the *Darius-Leut* (*q.v.,* named after Darius Walter, their leader), *Schmiede-Leut* (*q.v.,* after Michael Waldner, a blacksmith, their leader), and *Lehrer-Leut* (*q.v.,* named after Jacob Wipf, called the *Lehrer*). The last group, when still in Russia, did not practice community of goods but began to do so in South Dakota. Those of their members who were disinclined, however, to accept this new-old form of living and wanted to stay in private ownership, later joined the group now called Krimmer Mennonite Brethren or also the General Conference Mennonites.

The colonies soon grew again under the favorable conditions of American democracy and its freedom, until new suffering occurred during World War I. Then super-patriots could not understand the nonresistant attitude of these Anabaptists, and a great number of young Hutterite conscientious objectors went through almost unbelievable hardships in federal prisons. Two men died there on account of exposure and privations. At that point the Brethren decided to move on to Canada where exemption from military service was granted. They located in southern Alberta, and south central Manitoba. However, one colony, the original one at Bonhomme, remained in South Dakota, and several new ones have been re-established there, while others were established in north central Montana from Alberta.

Today the brotherhood is still growing, and in general their young people stay loyal to their group. In 1954 they have close to 120 farm colonies (Bruderhofs) with almost 10,000 souls (between 50 and 150 souls per colony). Community of goods is practiced everywhere, rather strictly, and seems to result in thrift and general health, both physical and moral. By and large the customs of old are observed, and this reminds the visitor occasionally of similar Amish attitudes. Although the young people learn English in their schools (on each Bruderhof), they yet speak exclusively German at home. Since the days of Ehrenpreis (17th century), mission work has been abandoned. At their services they read the sermons of old, and would not allow any new ones. The use of farm machinery, cars, telephone, and electric light is accepted, but otherwise they share very little in modern American civilization. They continue to copy their manuscript books by hand (in fine penmanship). Only the two Chronicles and their hymnbook have been printed,

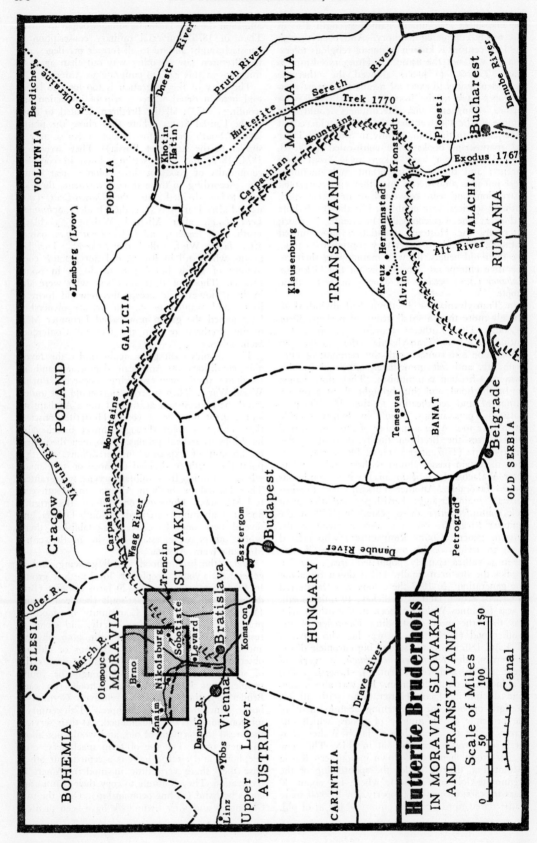

Hutterite Bruderhofs
IN MORAVIA, SLOVAKIA
AND TRANSYLVANIA

Scale of Miles

together with Riedemann's *Rechenschaft* of 1540 and Ehrenpreis' great *Sendbrief* of 1652.

The story of the New Hutterite group (Eberhard Arnold-Leut), originating in Germany in the 1920's, which joined the brotherhood around 1930, and now is settled in Paraguay, England, and recently (1954) also in New York State at Rifton (Woodcrest), cannot be told in this article (see **Eberhard Arnold**, and **Society of Brothers**).

Likewise, this article cannot describe in any way the inner life of the Brethren or their external organization; for these purposes compare the following articles: **Bruderhof, Community of goods, Crafts, Ceramics, Economic History of the Hutterian Brethren, Education — Hutterite, Epistles — Hutterite,** as well as articles on leaders such as **Hutter, Amon, Riedemann, Walpot, Braidl, Ehrenpreis,** and on their books, **Article Book, Chronicles, Handbüchlein, Rechenschaft, Liederbuch.** Finally also the following articles should be consulted: **Gemeindeordnungen,** regarding their regulations and discipline, **Marriage, Medicine among the Hutterites,** dealing with their barber-surgeons and physicians, **Sermons—Hutterite,** and naturally also the article **Habaner** which gives details about those who had turned Catholic in the 18th century.

LIST OF HUTTERITE BRUDERHOFS
1. Moravia, 1529-1622
(According to E. Crous, *ML* III, 420-22. For location of the Bruderhofs see the numbers 1-85 on Hutterite Map II.)

1. Alexowitz (Alecowitz, Olkowitz)
2. Altenmarkt (Zierotin, 1545)
3. Auspitz
4. Austerlitz
5. Bergen (Pergen)
6. Bilowitz (Billowitz, Pillowitz) (1545)
7. Birnbaum
8. Bisenz (Bisentz) (Zierotin, 1545)
9. Bogesch (Bogesitz/Bogenitz)
10. Bohntitz (Bohutitz/Bochtitz-Pochtitz) (1546)
11. Boretitz/Borzetitz (Paraditz) (1545)
12. Budespitz/Butschowitz (Bucovic, Pudespitz) (1536)
13. Budkau (Budkaw)
14. Czermakowitz (Schermankowitz)
15. Damborschitz/Damborzitz (Dämberschitz) (Kaunitz, 1550)
16. Eibenschitz (Lipa)
17. Eibis
18. Frätz/Wratzow (Niary von Bedek, 1547)
19. Frischau (1581)
20. Gobschitz/Gubschitz (1545)
21. Göding (Hodonin) (Lipa, 1545)
22. Gurda/Gurdau
23. Herspitz (Gerspitz)
24. Hosterlitz
25. Hrubschitz (Rupschitz) (1546)
26. Jamnitz
27. Jemeritz (Jemeritz/Jaronowitz)
28. Kanitz
29. Kobily/Kobyli (Kobelitz)
30. Kostl/Kostel (Gostal) (Zierotin)
31. Kreuz (Creutz) (Lipa, 1565)
32. Kromau (Lipa, 1540)
33. Landshut (Zierotin, 1565)
33a. Lettnitz/Letonitz (Lettonitz)
34. Lundenburg (Breclav)
35. Milotitz/Millotitz
36. Mistrin/Mistrin
37. Moskowitz (Maskowitz)
38. Muschau
39. Napagedl (Napajedl) (Zierotin, 1545)
40. Nembschitz/Klein Niemtschitz (east of Auspitz)
41. Nembschitz/Klein Niemtschitz (near Prahlitz) (1562)
42. Nemschau/Niemtschau (Niemtscha) (Kaunitz, 1560)
43. Neudorf near Lundenburg (Zierotin, 1570)
43a. Neudorf, Hungarian-Ostra district (Liechtenstein, 1570)
44. Neumühl (Liechtenstein, 1558)
45. Nikolsburg (Mikulov) (Liechtenstein, Maximilian II, Dietrichstein, 1556)
46. Nikolschitz/Nikoltschitz (Zierotin, 1570)
47. Nusslau (Nuslau) (Zierotin, 1583)
48. Paulowitz/Pawlowitz (Lipa, 1545)
49. Pausram (Zierotin, 1538)
50. Pohrlitz (Zierotin, 1581)
51. Polau/Pollau
52. Polehraditz (Bellerditz, Pettertitz) (1559)
53. Popitz/Poppitz (1537)
54. Pribitz/Przibitz (Zierotin, 1565)
55. Pruschank/Pruschanek
56. Pulgrams/Pulgram (1538)
57. Puslawitz/Bohuslawitz (Postlawitz) (1546)
58. Rackschitz/Rakschitz (Lipa, 1545)
59. Rakowitz (Räkowitz/Rakwitz) (Lipa, 1540)
60. Rampersdorf (Zierotin)
61. Rohatetz
62. Ropitz/Rossitz (Pernstein, Lipa, Zierotin)
63. Saitz (Lipa, 1540)
64. Schaidowitz/Ziadowitz (1553)
65. Schaikowitz (Schaickowitz/Ceikowitz) (1545)
66. Schäkowitz (Schäckowitz/Schakwitz) (Lipa, 1533)
67. (Klein-) Selowitz/Kl. Seelowitz
68. Skalitz (Gallitz) (1563)
69. (Klein- or Gross-) Steurowitz
69a. Stigonitz/Stignitz
70. Swatoborschitz/Swatoboritz
71. Swetlau
72. Tannowitz (Abtei Kanitz, Thurn)
73. Taykowitz/Taikowitz
74. Tracht (1558)
75. Tscheitsch/Ceitsch (Schenkhof)
76. Turnitz-Durdenitz
77. Urschitz/Uhrzitz (Kaunitz)
78. Voit(e)lsbrunn (1557)
79. Watzenowitz (Wacenowitz) (Zierotin)
79a. Weisstätten
80. Welka-Hulka (Zierotin, um 1560)
81. Wernslitz (Wemslitz/Weimis(ss)litz)
82. Wessely (1546)
83. Wischenau
84. Wisternitz
85. Wostitz (Thurn, 1567)

2. Slovakia, 1545-1762
(According to E. Crous, *ML* III, 423. For location of the Bruderhofs see the numbers I-XIV on Hutterite Map III.)

I. Broczko (Protzka; Neutra) (1547)
II. Dejte (Dechtitz; Oberneutra)
III. Dobravoda (Gutenwasser; Oberneutra)
IV. Egbell (Neutra)
V. Farkashida (Farkenschin; Pressburg) (1622)
VI. Holics (Holitsch; Neutra)
VII. Kosolna (Kesselsdorf; Pressburg)
VIII. Kuty (Gätte; Neutra) (1550)
IX. Lévárd Velky-Levary (Gross-Schützen, Lewär; Pressburg) (1588)
X. Pobudin (Popadin, Popodin; Neutra) (Bakisch de Lák)
XI. Rovenszko (Rabenska; Neutra) (1622)
XII. Soblaho (Soblahov, Zobelhof; Trentschin) (Illésházi, 1622)
XIII. Sobotiste (Freischütz, Sabatisch; Neutra) (1546)
XIV. Unter Nussdorf (Deutsch-Nussdorf; Pressburg) (1548)

3. Moravia, by manorial estates, 1619-22
(According to Fr. Hruby, *Die Wiedertäufer in Mähren*, Leipzig, 1935.)

1. *Lundenburg-Billowitz:* Lundenburg, Altenmarkt, Gostal (Ober- and Nieder-Haus), Pillowitz, Rampersdorf
2. *Seelowitz:* Eibes (auch Meubes), Nikolschitz, Nussla, Pausram, Pribitz, Poherlitz
3. *Austerlitz:* Austerlitz and Gerspitz
4. *Nikolsburg:* Nikolsburg and Tracht

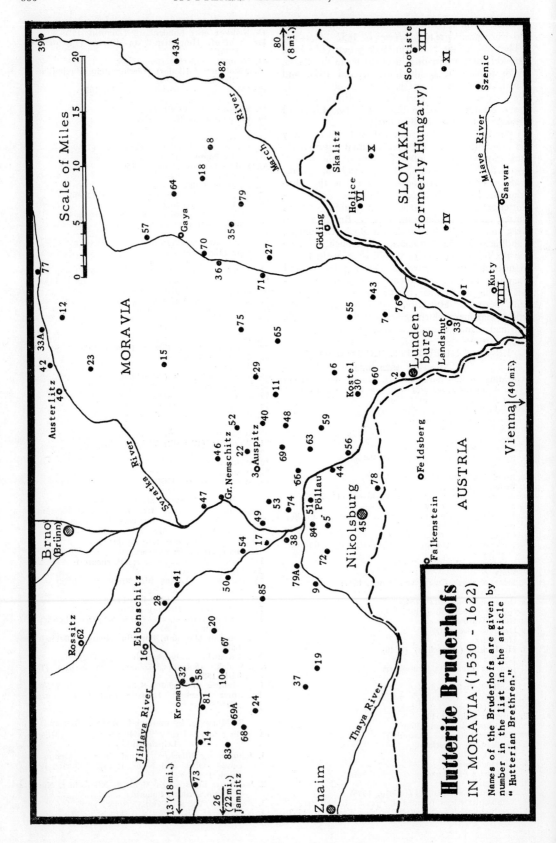

Hutterite Bruderhofs
IN MORAVIA·(1530 - 1622)
Names of the Bruderhofs are given by
number in the list in the article
"Hutterian Brethren."

Hutterite Bruderhofs
IN SLOVAKIA
Key to numbers: see list in article.

5. *Steinitz:* Dämberschitz
6. *Kanitz:* Klein-Niemtschitz (Ober- and Unterhaus)
7. *Landshut:* Landshut
8. *Lettonitz:* Lettnitz
9. *Skalitz:* Gallitz
10. *Wischenau:* Wischnau and Stignitz
11. *Tscheikowitz:* Schäkowitz (Schaikowitz) and Prut-
    schan
12. *Bochtitz:* Pochtitz
13. *Frischau:* Frischau
14. *Göding:* Göding and Koblitz
15. *Mähr. Kromau:* Maskowitz and Oleckowitz
16. *Milotitz:* Wäzenobis
17. *Uhritz:* Urschitz
18. *Wesseli:* Wessela
19. *Ziadowitz:* Schädewitz
20. *Ungarisch-Ostra:* Neudorf
21. *Eisgrub:* Neumühl
22. *Ober-Tannowitz:* Tannewitz
23. *Tulleschitz:* Schermankowitz
24. *Wostitz:* (Wostite), Weisstätten
25. *Polehraditz:* Pellertitz
26. *Tawikowitz:* Teikowitz

4. Transylvania

1. Alvinc, 1621-1767
2. Kreuz, 1761-67
3. Stein, 1761-67

5. Ukraine

1. Vishenka (1770-1802)
2. Raditcheva (1802-42)
3. Hutterthal (1842-57)
4. Hutterdorf (2) (1859-74)
5. Johannisruh (1864-77)
6. Sheromet (1868-74)
7. Neu-Hutterthal or Dabritcha (1866-75)

6. Germany

Rhönbruderhof (1920-37)

7. Liechtenstein

Almbruderhof (1934-38)

8. England

1. Cotswold (1936-40)
2. Wheathill (1942-)

9. Paraguay: Primavera (3), 1940-

(See page 862)

10. North America, 1950, by branches

(According to J. W. Eaton, "The Hutterite Mental
Health Study," *MQR* XXV, 1951, 17-19.)

Name of Colony Address	Yr. Settled	Pop., 1950
DARIUSLEUT, ALBERTA		
1. Camrose, Camrose	1949	83
2. Cayley, Cayley	1937	80
3. East Cardston, Cardston	1918	81
4. Ewelme, Macleod	1928	69
5. Fairview, Ponoka	1949	75
6. Granum, Granum	1930	75
7. Holt, Irma	1949	57
8. Tschetter, Irricana	1948	76
9. New Rosebud, Crossfield	1944	78
10. Lakeside, Cranford	1935	91
11. Beiseker, Beiseker	1926	65
12. New York, Maybutt	1924	110
13. Pincher Creek, Pincher Creek	1926	85
14. Pine Hill, Penhold	1948	86
15. Riverside, Fort Macleod	1933	86
16. Rosebud, Redland	1918	187
17. Sandhill, Beiseker	1936	114
18. Springvale, Rockyford	1918	77
19. Stahlville, Rockyford	1919	98
20. Stand Off, Macleod	1918	76
21. Thompson, Glenwood	1918	76
22. West Raley, Cardston	1918	117
23. Willow Creek, Stettler	1949	89
24. Wilson Siding, Lethbridge	1918	140
25. Wolf Creek, Stirling	1924	76
DARIUSLEUT, MONTANA		
26. Ayers Ranch, Grass Range	1945	54
27. Deerfield, Danvers	1947	65
28. King Ranch, Lewistown	1935	61
29. Spring Creek, Lewistown	1945	26
LEHRERLEUT, ALBERTA		
30. Big Bend, Woolford	1920	129
31. Crystal Spring, Magrath	1937	117
32. Elmspring, Warner	1929	177
33. Hutterville, Magrath	1932	155
34. Macmillan, Cayley	1937	127
35. Miami, New Dayton	1924	103
36. Milford, Raymond	1918	134
37. New Elmspring, Magrath	1918	115
38. New Rockport, New Dayton	1932	113
39. O.K., Raymond	——	96
40. Old Elm, Magrath	1918	151

Hutterite Bruderhofs
in Ukraine
1770 - 1874
Vishenka   1770--1802
Radichev   1802--1842
Molotschna 1842--1874

41. New Dale, Queenstown	1950	60
42. Rock Lake, Wrentham	1935	89
43. Rockport, Magrath	1918	100
44. Sunny-Site, Warner	1935	186

LEHRERLEUT, MONTANA

45. Birch Creek, Valier	1947	95
46. Miami, Pendroy	1948	112
47. (New) Milford, Augusta	1945	105
48. Miller Ranch, Choteau	1949	100
49. New Rockport, Choteau	1948	101
50. Rockport, Pendroy	1947	100
51. Hillside, Sweet Grass	1950	

UNAFFILIATED COLONIES, ALBERTA

52. Felger, Lethbridge	1924	25
53. Hofer Brothers, Brocket	1920	15
54. Monarch, Monarch	1942	31
55. Stirling Mennonite, Stirling	1944	30

SCHMIEDELEUT, MANITOBA

56. Barickman, Headingly	1920	151
57. Blumengard, Plum Coulee	1922	132
58. Bon Homme, Benard	1918	108
59. Elm River, Newton Siding	1934	153
60. Huron, Benard	1918	193
61. Iberville, Headingly	1919	101
62. James Valley, Starbuck	1918	128
63. Lakeside, Headingly	1946	94
64. Maxwell, Headingly	1918	86
65. Milltown, Benard	1918	54
66. New Rosedale, Portage la Prairie	1944	155
67. Poplar Point, Poplar Point	1938	93
68. Riverdale, Gladstone	1946	98
69. Riverside, Arden	1934	98
70. Rock Lake, Gross Isle	1947	85
71. Rosedale, Elie	1918	128
72. Sturgeon Creek, Headingly	1938	118
73. Sunnyside, Newton Siding	1925	93
74. Waldheim, Elie	1935	121
75. Springfield, Vivian	1950	83

SCHMIEDELEUT, NORTH DAKOTA

76. Forest River, Fordville	1950	

SCHMIEDELEUT, SOUTH DAKOTA

77. Bon Homme, Tabor	1874	58
78. Glendale, Frankfort	1949	97
79. Gracevale, Winfred	1948	71
80. Huron, Huron	1944	74
81. Jamesville, Utica	1937	107
82. Maxwell, Scotland	1949	72
83. Millerdale, Miller	1949	54
84. New Elm Spring, Ethan	1936	102
85. Pearl Creek, Iroquois	1949	94
86. Platte, Academy	1949	68
87. Riverside, Huron	1949	48
88. Rockport, Alexandria	1934	84
89. Rosedale, Mitchell	1945	92
90. Spink, Frankfort	1945	94
91. Tschetter, Olivet	1942	94

CONVERT COLONIES

ONTARIO

92. Colony Farm of the Brethren, Bright	1941	46

SOCIETY OF BROTHERS

ENGLAND

93. Wheathill Bruderhof, Bradon, Bridgeworth, Salop	1942	165

PARAGUAY

94. Sociedad Fraternal, Primavera Alto	1942	
95. Isla Margarita Primavera Alto	1942	800
96. Loma Hobby Primavera Alto	1942	

URUGUAY

97. Montevideo

NEW YORK

Woodcrest, Rifton	1954	135

SUMMARY OF HUTTERITE POPULATION BY CENSUS, BY KINSHIP GROUP AND LOCATION

				Total
Dariusleut				
Alberta	2,247	Montana	206	2,453
Lehrerleut				
Alberta	1,852	Montana	613	2,465
Schmiedeleut				
Manitoba	2,272	S. Dakota	1,209	3,481
Unaffiliated colonies				
Alberta	101			101

Total, Kinship Colonies		8,500
Total, Convert Colonies and Society of Brothers	(est.)	1,100
Total No. of Hutterites		9,600

SUMMARY OF HUTTERITE POPULATION CENSUS (1950) BY LOCATION

Montana		819
South Dakota		1,209
Alberta		4,200
Manitoba		2,272
Ontario		46
England		165
Paraguay		500 (est.)
		9,211

Addenda 1955

List and maps correspond to the situation around 1950. From 1950 until early 1955, 14 new kinship colonies were established; the population increased in these 4½ years by more than 1,400 souls to a total of close to 10,000. These new colonies are (according to Rev. Peter Hofer, James Valley):

Dariusleut, Alberta
98 Pibroch, Pibroch
99 Scotford, Fort Saskatchewan
Lehrerleut, Alberta
100 Acadia Valley, Oyen
101 New Milford, Winnifred
102 Rosedale, Etzikom
103 Springside, Duchess
Lehrerleut, Saskatchewan
104 Bench, Shaunavon
105 Cypress, Maple Creek
106 Slade Colony, Tompkins
Lehrerleut, Montana
107 Glacier, Cut Banks
Schmiedeleut, Manitoba
108 Bloomfield, Westbourne
109 Crystal Spring, St. Agathe
110 Oak Bluff, Morris
Schmiedeleut, South Dakota
111 Blumengard, Wecota
The colonies of the Society of Brothers (Paraguay, etc.) have grown in the same period to more than 1,000 souls.

NOTE FOR THE MAPS ON THE FOLLOWING PAGES

Rev. David Decker, Tschetter Colony, South Dakota; Rev. Paul Gross, Pincher Creek Colony, Alberta; Rev. Peter Hofer, James Valley Colony, Manitoba; Rev. Joseph Waldner, Springfield Colony, Manitoba; and Rev. John Wurz, Wilson Colony, Alberta, assisted in preparing a list of Hutterite colonies and determining their location. The maps were prepared under the direction of Dr. Joseph W. Eaton, Dept. of Sociology and Anthropology, Wayne University, Detroit, Mich., with the assistance of Evelyn Plaut; they were drawn by R. A. Morwood of the Dept. of Geography at Wayne University.

The first exhaustive list of Hutterite Bruderhofs in Europe with locations (concerning Moravia and Slovakia, however) is that prepared by E. Crous and published in 1953 in connection with the article *Rabenska* in the *Mennonitisches Lexikon* (Installment 39, pp. 418-23) where two maps are also given, prepared by Dr. Gerhard Wöhlke of the Geographical Institute in Göttingen on the basis of the Austrian Spezialkarte 1:75,000, published 1869-88 by the

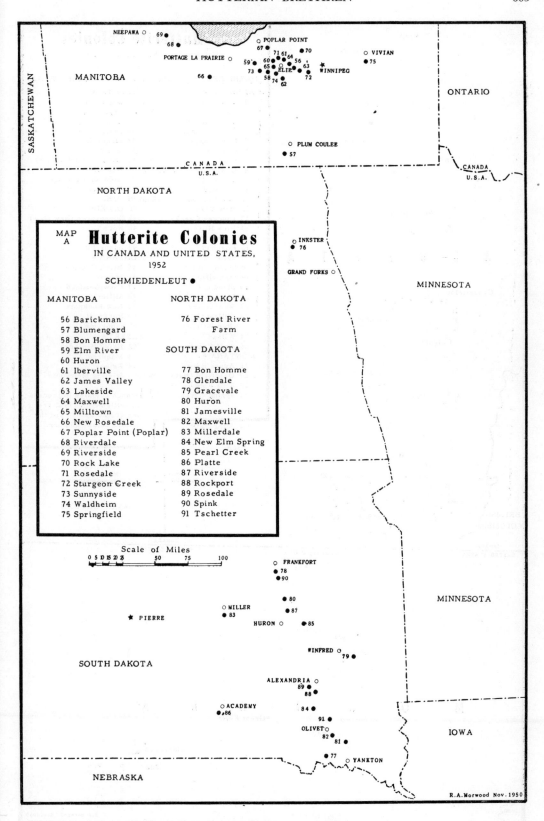

MAP A **Hutterite Colonies**
IN CANADA AND UNITED STATES,
1952

SCHMIEDENLEUT ●

MANITOBA	NORTH DAKOTA
56 Barickman	76 Forest River
57 Blumengard	Farm
58 Bon Homme	
59 Elm River	SOUTH DAKOTA
60 Huron	
61 Iberville	77 Bon Homme
62 James Valley	78 Glendale
63 Lakeside	79 Gracevale
64 Maxwell	80 Huron
65 Milltown	81 Jamesville
66 New Rosedale	82 Maxwell
67 Poplar Point (Poplar)	83 Millerdale
68 Riverdale	84 New Elm Spring
69 Riverside	85 Pearl Creek
70 Rock Lake	86 Platte
71 Rosedale	87 Riverside
72 Sturgeon Creek	88 Rockport
73 Sunnyside	89 Rosedale
74 Waldheim	90 Spink
75 Springfield	91 Tschetter

Scale of Miles

0 5 D 15 2 25   50   75   100

R.A.Morwood Nov.1950

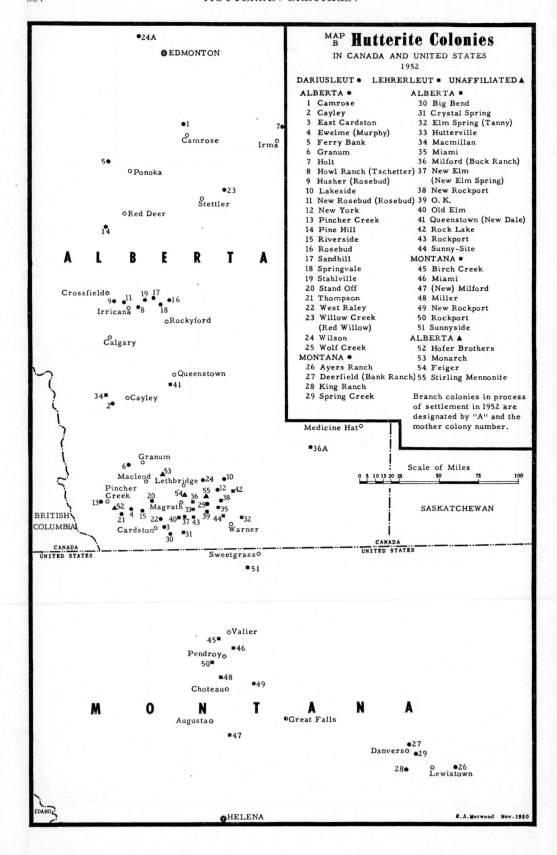

MAP B **Hutterite Colonies**
IN CANADA AND UNITED STATES
1952

DARIUSLEUT ●   LEHRERLEUT ■   UNAFFILIATED ▲

ALBERTA ●
1 Camrose
2 Cayley
3 East Cardston
4 Ewelme (Murphy)
5 Ferry Bank
6 Granum
7 Holt
8 Howl Ranch (Tschetter)
9 Husher (Rosebud)
10 Lakeside
11 New Rosebud (Rosebud)
12 New York
13 Pincher Creek
14 Pine Hill
15 Riverside
16 Rosebud
17 Sandhill
18 Springvale
19 Stahlville
20 Stand Off
21 Thompson
22 West Raley
23 Willow Creek
   (Red Willow)
24 Wilson
25 Wolf Creek
MONTANA ●
26 Ayers Ranch
27 Deerfield (Bank Ranch)
28 King Ranch
29 Spring Creek

ALBERTA ■
30 Big Bend
31 Crystal Spring
32 Elm Spring (Tanny)
33 Hutterville
34 Macmillan
35 Miami
36 Milford (Buck Ranch)
37 New Elm
   (New Elm Spring)
38 New Rockport
39 O. K.
40 Old Elm
41 Queenstown (New Dale)
42 Rock Lake
43 Rockport
44 Sunny-Site
MONTANA ■
45 Birch Creek
46 Miami
47 (New) Milford
48 Miller
49 New Rockport
50 Rockport
51 Sunnyside
ALBERTA ▲
52 Hofer Brothers
53 Monarch
54 Feiger
55 Stirling Mennonite

Branch colonies in process
of settlement in 1952 are
designated by "A" and the
mother colony number.

Scale of Miles
0 5 10 15 20 25   50   75   100

R.A.Morwood Nov.1950

K. K. Militärgeographisches Institut. The Crous lists are here reproduced, but new maps have been prepared by Dr. Robert Friedmann, two of which are based on the *M. Lex.* maps. The first two lists contain all known Bruderhofs of the 16th and 17th centuries, without indication as to the date of dissolution. They therefore do not reveal how many were in existence at any one time, although most were in existence in the "Golden Age" *ca.* 1590. The only such list is the third one, which names the Bruderhofs in existence in Moravia, 1619-22, 1622 being the date when all were expelled from the country.

J. Loserth published the first list of Bruderhofs in his *Communismus* (1894) p. 246. This list he published in *M. Lex.* (1931) **Haushaben,** slightly revised, where 88 locations are named. Fr. Hruby published a list of 43 Bruderhofs in existence in Moravia in 1619-22, in his *Wiedertäufer in Mähren* (Leipzig, 1935), which is reproduced as list no. 3 above. He reports that a considerable number of Bruderhofs were destroyed in 1605. According to Hruby most of the Bruderhofs were in Czech nationality areas; only 9 of the 43 listed areas were in German nationality areas.

Zieglschmid's list of North American Bruderhofs (*Klein-Geschichtsbuch,* 677-80) contains only 64, although it was not quite exhaustive. He reports (p. 471) the growth in numbers as follows: 1878 (3), 1900 (10), 1915 (17), 1926 (29), 1944 (57), 1947 (64). Before 1918 all American Bruderhofs were in South Dakota. The first Canadian Bruderhofs were established in Manitoba and Alberta in 1918, when a mass migration occurred. Zieglschmid (p. 472 f.) gives a genealogical chart of the origin of the North American Bruderhofs of the Schmiedeleut and Dariusleut in existence in 1947. R.F.

R. Friedmann, "Comprehensive Review of Research on the Hutterites, 1880-1950," *MQR* XXIV (1950) 353-63; *idem,* "Die Briefe der österreichischen Täufer" in *Arch. f. Ref.-Gesch.* XXVI (1929) 30-80, 161-87, with extensive bibliography; *idem,* "The Christian Communism of the Hutterian Brethren," *Arch. f. Ref.-Gesch.,* 1955; *idem,* "Christian Love in Action, the Hutterites," *Menn. Life,* July 1946, 38-43; Zieglschmid, *Chronik* (1943); Zieglschmid, *Klein-Geschichtsbuch* (1947), with exhaustive bibliography to that date; Beck, *Geschichts-Bücher;* Wolkan, *Geschicht-Buch;* Loserth, *Communismus;* J. Horsch, *The Hutterian Brethren* (Goshen, 1931); Fr. Hruby, *Die Wiedertäufer in Mähren* (Leipzig, 1935); L. Müller, *Der Kommunismus der mährischen Wiedertäufer* (Leipzig, 1927); *idem, Glaubenszeugnisse oberdeutscher Taufgesinnter* (Leipzig, 1938); Wiswedel, *Bilder* I-III; J. W. Eaton and A. J. Mayer, *Man's Capacity to Reproduce; the Demography of a Unique Population* (Hutterites) (Glencoe, Ill., 1954); Bertha W. Clark, "The Hutterian Communities," *Journal of Pol. Economy* (1924) 357-74, 468-86; J. Heimann, "The Hutterite Doctrines of Church and Common Life. A Study of Peter Riedemann's Confession of Faith," *MQR* XXVI (1952) 22-47, 142-60; J. W. Eaton and R. T. Weil, *Culture and Mental Disorder, a Comparative Study of the Hutterites* (Glencoe, 1954); Hans Fischer, *Jakob Hutter, Leben, Frömmigkeit und Briefe* (Newton, 1957); J. Sommer, "Hutterite Medicine and Physicians in Moravia in the 16th Century and After," *MQR* XXVII (1953) 111-27; R. Friedmann, "Hutterite Physicians and Barber-Surgeons," *ibid.,* 128-36; *idem,* "Economic Aspects of Early Hutterite Life," *MQR* XXX (October 1956) 259-66; *ML* II, 378-84.

Hutterite Family Names. The Hutterite Brethren of today (1954) numbering close to 10,000, belong to not more than 15 different families as follows: Decker, Entz, Glantzer, Gross, Hofer, Kleinsasser, Knels, Mändel, Stahl, Tschetter, Waldner, Wipf, Wollman, Wurz, Walter. These 15 families may be divided according to their origin into (*a*) the "old" Hutterites, (*b*) the "Carinthian" Hutterites (since 1756), and (*c*) former Prussian Mennonites who joined the brotherhood in the Ukraine in the 1780's. (This article does not deal at all with the New Hutterites or "Arnold-Leut.")

(*a*) "Old" Hutterite families may again be subdivided into those (1) who lived in Transylvania (Alvinc) ever since 1621, and from there moved to the Ukraine 1767-70, and (2) those from Slovakia (mainly Sobotiste) who joined the brotherhood only after the 1780's. The assignment, however, to either group is not absolutely certain. (1) From Transylvania come the Stahl and the Wipf families. A Stahl is mentioned in the small *Chronik* as early as 1663 when he was killed by the Turks; of the Wipfs the *Chronik* says nothing, mainly because the writers of this *Chronik* lived in Slovakia and somewhat neglected the story of the Transylvanian (*q.v.*)Bruderhof. (2) From Slovakia (Sobotiste and perhaps Velky Levary) come the families Walter, Wollman, Tschetter, and Mändel. The Walters are no doubt the oldest family of all. One Franz Walter (of Oetisheim, Württemberg: see Bossert, 685, 891 f.), a barber-surgeon, was made preacher in 1597; in 1621 he led a group to Transylvania (Alvinc), where he died six months later. His family continued in Sobotiste. A Zacharias Walter (1700-62), head bishop from 1746, is the ancestor of all the Walters of today. His son, Jacob Walter, went to Russia in 1782 (see **Walter**). As to the Wollmans we read of one Jacob Bollman, Vorsteher 1724-34; in the "Väterlied" (*Lieder der Hutterischen Brüder,* 1914, 878) the same brother is named Wollman. It appears that the names Wollman, Bollman, and Pullman (still today in Slovakia) indicate the same family. A Tobias Pullman, the husband of the daughter of Jacob Walter, came to the Ukraine in 1784. Also the name Walman in the *Chronik,* may be of the descent.

The Tschetters of today come from a family originally named Zeterle or Cseterle. It is possible that they were of Slovakian origin; however, the name Zeterle (Zieglschmid, *Klein-Geschichtsbuch,* 247, note 3) could also be of German origin. They must have joined the brotherhood late, since their name appears only in the *Klein-Geschichtsbuch.* There were Tschetters both in Slovakia and in Transylvania; it is uncertain from which branch the family of today derives, as no family tradition has survived. Finally there are the Mändels. Apparently this family has nothing to do with the old Tirolean Anabaptist name (Hans Mändel martyred in 1561). It originates rather with a Slavic family, mentioned in the *Klein-Geschichtsbuch* as "Mändelig." In 1784 a Paul Mändelig arrived in Vishenka. It is interesting to learn that still today the Mändels are called among the Brethren the "Bohemians" (*die Behm*).

The *Klein-Geschichtsbuch* lists (373-74) all those who had managed to leave Slovakia and to rejoin the brotherhood in Russia. All told there were 56 souls. In this list also an Andreas Stahl is mentioned; whether the Stahls of today go back to him or to Johannes Stahl of Transylvania can no longer be ascertained.

(*b*) Hutterites of Carinthian origin who joined the brotherhood in Transylvania in 1756 are Waldner (*q.v.*), Hofer (*q.v.*), Kleinsasser (*q.v.*), Glantzer (*q.v.*), and Wurz (*q.v.*). The *Klein-Geschichtsbuch* (268-70) gives a list of all those who left Carinthia in 1755, with at least 14 names; only 5 names have survived to this day.

(*c*) Hutterites of Mennonite origin: contacts with the Mennonites of East Prussia began around 1780-81 (see **Hofer**). Today four families exist of that Mennonite extraction: Decker or Dekker (*q.v.*, in 1782, one Els Deckerin joined with her children), Entz (no further information), Gross (joined the Vishenka group in 1781), and Knels (like Els Deckerin, also one Liset Knelsin with two children, joined the brotherhood in 1782, *Klein-Geschichtsbuch*, 369). It is said that the family name of Knels will soon die out among the modern Brethren. A fifth Mennonite Hutterite family name, Jantzen, died out in 1927. Any Mennonites of today who bear a Hutterite name (except for the four names just mentioned, deriving from Mennonite background) are certain to be of Hutterite background, and most likely transferred from a Hutterite group after its arrival in North Dakota 1874-77.

It might be valuable also to record that in Slovakia today among the Habaner (*q.v.*), the following family names have become known: Walter, Pullman, Baumgartner, Tschetter, Bernhauser, Miller and Müller, and Roth.

Another "old" Hutterite family of high standing, the Kuhr family (active in Transylvania), seems to have died out in the Ukraine at an early date.

R.F.

Bertha W. Clark, "The Hutterian Communities," *Journal of Pol. Economy* XXXII (1924) 357-74, 468-86. She was the first to list all existing family names (16 at that time).

Hutterite Missioners (*Sendboten*). While it is characteristic of Anabaptism in general that its very existence is preconditioned by the mission idea (as over against the state and national churches with their comprehensive constituency), this is in particular true of the Hutterites, perhaps the most active and aggressive missioners of the entire 16th century. They acted out of a strong sense of being called to spread the Gospel, to call people to repent and to change their life in a spiritual rebirth, and to invite men and women to follow Christ as true disciples. They "sent brethren every year to lands near and far according to the commandments of Christ and the practice of the apostles, to teach and to preach and to gather for the Lord God's people" (Ehrenpreis, *Ein Sendbrief*, 1652, reprint 1920, 122 ff., *Von der Sendung in die Länder*).

The established churches in Germany contested the right of the Brethren to send out missioners on the ground that they had not been ordained by God to do so. For instance the Calvinist superintendent of Alzey in the Palatinate asked the Hutterite missioner Leonhard Dax (*q.v.*), imprisoned in

1567, who had given him the right and authority to come into the Palatinate to confuse the people. Dax replied that he was not sent to confuse them but rather to lead everybody from error to the right way of Christian discipleship. The Brethren owed it to the world to bring it the pure and unadulterated Word of God. And those who were sent by the brotherhood were properly ordained as "apostles" (*Sendboten*), and must be considered as commissioned by God Himself. Otherwise also the apostolic church would not have done right. (He quoted Phil. 2; Col. 4; II Tim. 4; Titus 3; Acts 11, 12, 13, and 18.) Dax had also been chosen to this service by an orderly established Christian church (*Gemeinde*), whose duty it was to preach faith in Christ and to testify both to repentance and forgiveness of sins in His name, and that not only at one specified place but to the ends of the earth. (Dax epistles, Beck Collection in Brno, file 14.)

In order to be able to fulfill the task laid upon them by the Lord, the congregation semiannually (usually in the spring and fall) chose from the preachers a number of Brethren to perform a widespread missionary service in all directions, to preach the Gospel in accordance with the commandment of Christ, and to lead the converts to the "promised land" or Moravia.

The departure of these missioners was always a most solemn occasion, as everyone was fully conscious of the extraordinary responsibilities laid upon these itinerant preachers, and also of the real dangers involved in this task. We find in one Hutterite codex of 1628 (in Esztergom) two descriptions: "How the Brethren who go into foreign lands take leave from the brotherhood" and "Response of the elders to the Brethren who are about to leave." (A full description may be found in Loserth, 228-31, and Wiswedel, *Archiv f. Ref.-Gesch.* 1948, 119 f.) Words of encouragement, of wisdom, and of trust in God and His guidance are exchanged, and the parting Brethren are then assured of the intercessory prayers of the entire brotherhood while they are away on their dangerous task. At the end, a hymn composed especially for this occasion was sung, "Ein Lied wöllen wir singen und fürher bringen tun" (1568); Wolkan (*Lieder*, 206-9) prints the entire hymn, and the *Lieder der Hutterischen Brüder* (650-52) borrows from him.

Each missioner had his field assigned to him; thus Brethren went out to all parts of Germany (Bavaria, Württemberg, Hesse, Thuringia, Rhineland, also Silesia and Prussia), to Switzerland, to Poland, and in two cases also to Venice, Italy. A few even came as far as Denmark and Sweden, but that was hardly their actual field of work. Each brother had epistles and tracts in his knapsack. The home congregation supported its missionaries not only by prayers but also by writing them letters and, in case of imprisonment, by dispatching Brethren to maintain contact, bring them these letters and receive their replies, also to bring home all news of importance. The missionaries, on the other hand, never tired of writing letters home about their success or, if arrested, their trials and their good cheer and unshaken trust in God.

As a rule the Brethren held their meetings at

night in remote places, often in forests or mountain glens, in lonely mills, barns, stone quarries, and the like. It was not as their opponents asserted (Menius, for example) that they only "sneaked" around in corners because they feared the light of the day or despised church buildings, but merely because they were safer in such places. By chance we learn also how they called such meetings and how they came into contact with possible listeners. T. W. Röhrich published a "letter of invitation" (which by chance was found in the Strasbourg church archives) in which those who arranged the meeting wrote to a couple to come then and there ("in the house where one has been before") and not to be late and also to invite "the old man" to come too (Röhrich, 115, note 73).

As to the exact contents of their message and preaching we do not know too much. We may assume that it was about the same as what we read in their epistles and tracts. In the *Handbüchlein wider den Prozess* (*q.v.*) we read: "An evangelical missioner shall use the sword of the Spirit which reveals to men the sin of their heart, separates them from the wrong, revives the soul and gives assurance of eternal life in the faith of Christ."—"We believe in Jesus Christ," writes Riedemann in his *Rechenschaft,* "and although men cry against us that we seek to become pious and saved by our own works, we say no to that." And Hans Hut (*q.v.*) confessed at his trial that he taught nothing but first repentance, then believing, and finally baptism upon faith. But this baptism imposes also the obligation to live as the Word of God indicates. Without such a life of obedience faith does not save. Above all they stressed discipleship—a message which people could not hear anywhere else. There is no God-fearing life without the "fruits of the Spirit." Hence it is deemed necessary to leave this worldly life and join the brotherhood. People may see for themselves in Moravia how genuine disciples of Christ actually live.

The result of this message was truly amazing. A continuous stream of Brethren moved from all parts toward Moravia, from Tirol, from Switzerland, and also from Württemberg, and the Rhineland, including the Palatinate. It made the authorities of these countries uneasy, and almost everywhere laws were enacted specifying that those who left for Moravia should lose all claim to their parental inheritance. But the price of these achievements was also no small one. Very few of the missioners died a natural death. Most of them ended their lives as martyrs, being burned, beheaded, drowned,. or imprisoned for life. "Thus fare the messengers of God who seek to help people out of ruin," remarks the *Geschicht-Buch.* The memory of these blood witnesses is retained in the brotherhood by word, song, or writings. Time and again we find remarks of that kind in the Chronicle.

The execution of these brave men was quite often a public event shared by a crowd "of thousands." As these brethren went to the place of martyrdom with shining eyes, admonishing people to remain loyal to their faith in God and to follow His commandments, people were profoundly touched, and many turned Anabaptist as a consequence of such an event. And this the Brethren knew and were unafraid of trial and suffering. There was a time, Loserth contended, when almost all of Tirol and Styria were in sympathy with Anabaptism. It was about the same everywhere in southern Germany.

The missionary zeal lessened somewhat toward the end of the 16th century when the situation in Moravia began to deteriorate, hence the incentive to come thither became weaker. But we still hear of mission work in Prussia (Joseph Hauser) and in Silesia in the early 17th century. Even after the Brethren had been expelled from Moravia and moved to Slovakia, they tried to continue their mission work although on a reduced scale. The last mission work was done around 1650-54 in Danzig, where individuals of the Polish (Anti-Trinitarian) Church were contacted (see **Ehrenpreis**).

Perhaps the most successful of all Hutterite missioners was the brother Hänsel Schmidt (*q.v.*) or Raiffer, who was burned at Aachen in 1558. R.F.

W. Wiswedel, "Die alten Taufgemeinden und ihr missionarisches Wirken," in *Arch. f. Ref.-Gesch.* XL (1943) 183-200; XLI (1948) 115-32; Loserth, *Communismus,* 228-31; Wolkan, *Lieder,* 206-9; T. W. Röhrich, "Zur Gesch. der Strassburger Wiedertäufer," *Ztschr f. Hist. Theol.,* 1860 (115 n.); Wolkan, *Geschicht-Buch;* Ehrenpreis, *Sendbrief* (Scottdale, 1920); P. Rideman, *Account of Our Religion* (Bridgnorth, England, 1950): F. H. Littell, "Anabaptist Theology of Missions," *MQR* XXI (1947) 5-17; *idem, The Anabaptist View of the Church* (American Society of Church History, 1952) 94-112, chapter on "The Great Commission."

Hutterthal, a village of the Hutterian Brethren (*q.v.*) in the province of Taurida in South Russia. They came from Vishenka (*q.v.*), province of Tchernigov, in 1843 and established their village on a tract of steppe-land which Johann Cornies (*q.v.*) had leased for a long time previously. At the request of the government Cornies guided the entire venture and became the best friend and adviser of the new settlers. Many were very poor, unable to provide food or shelter for themselves for the winter; Cornies secured the necessary grain as well as a loan of 15,000 rubles from the crown. In 1844, 30 houses were finished, and soon the second village, Johannesruh (*q.v.*), founded. Economic prosperity came soon. By 1846 they had paid off their entire debt to the government. When universal military service was introduced in Russia, the Hutterites again abandoned their homes, and in 1874 emigrated to America. Their villages passed into Lutheran possession. (*ML* II, 384.)   D.H.E.

Hutterthal Mennonite Church (GCM), located in Hutchinson Co., S.D., a member of the Northern District Conference, was organized in 1877 by noncommunal Hutterites under the leadership of John L. Wipf. The first meetinghouse was used from 1877 until 1899, when a new church was built, which was replaced by a modern brick structure in 1953. John P. Hofer, P. P. Tschetter, and Jacob B. Hofer have served as ministers. The 1954 membership is 220, largely rural.   J.D.U.

Hutterthal Mennonite Church (GCM), located near Hitchcock and Carpenter in Beadle Co., S.D., is a member of the Northern District Conference. The congregation was first organized in 1906 under the leadership of Joseph M. Hofer. The original building was purchased from the Methodists and was replaced with a new structure in 1949. The membership has increased from 80 to 176 in 1954. In addition to Joseph M. Hofer, the congregation has been served by Elias J. Wipf, Joseph J. Hofer, and Paul J. R. Hofer, who is the present pastor. J.D.U.

Hutterville, a Hutterian Bruderhof near Magrath, Alberta, founded in 1927 by Brethren from the Rockport commune in South Dakota. Their preachers are Johann Waldner and Michael Hofer. In 1947 the Bruderhof numbered 147 souls with 70 baptized members.   D.D.

Huybert op der Straaten, together with his wife Trijnken, Pieter ten Hove, and Lijsken te Linschoten, was beaten, robbed of his possessions, and banished from Homburg in 1601 because of his Anabaptist faith, at the instigation of Count Johann of Witgenstein. They were obviously of Dutch descent. (*Mart. Mir.* D 803, E 1102; *ML* II, 385.)

Huyberts, Claes, a deacon of the "Blauwe Schuur" (Blue Barn) congregation (United Flemish and High German Mennonites) at Harlingen, Dutch province of Friesland. He served in the second half of the 17th century and promoted the union of 1672 between his congregation and the Waterlander congregation of Harlingen. In 1666 he negotiated with the Frisian government in the name of all the Mennonites of the different branches concerning a loan of 500,000 guilders to be made by the Mennonites of Friesland to equip warships. With much trouble this compulsory loan was raised by the Mennonites, each of them having to pay about a hundred guilders. A letter written by Claes Huyberts in 1666 concerning this loan, which enumerates several Mennonite branches in Friesland and their membership figures, is found in the Amsterdam Mennonite Library. A second loan for the same purpose was contracted in 1672 and again Claes Huyberts was middleman between the government and the Mennonites of Friesland. The son of Claes Huybertsz and his descendants assumed the family name of Braam.   vdZ.

Blaupot t. C., *Friesland*, 163, 176 f., 311; *DB* 1877, 125-27; *Catalogus Amst.*, 348.

Huyge (Huych), **Jacobsz Kraen** (Craen), a Dutch Anabaptist martyr, burned at the stake at The Hague on April 15, 1534, together with two anonymous martyrs; his wife Marritgen had been put to death at Haarlem, Dutch province of North Holland, shortly before by being drowned. Huyge was a native of the Dutch village of Hazerswoude (*q.v.*), province of South Holland. According to van Braght's *Martyrs' Mirror,* which erroneously gives 1532 as the year of his death, he was a peaceful Anabaptist, but the records studied by Vos and Mellink show that he was an adherent of revolutionary principles. In March 1534 he took part in a journey to Münster and was arrested en route at Bergklooster (*q.v.*). With his wife and some others he was first taken to Haarlem, where his wife was executed, then to The Hague. According to Vos he

was a leader of the revolutionary Anabaptists of South Holland. He was a rather wealthy man, which was an exception among the early Dutch Anabaptists.   vdZ.

Mart. Mir. D 34, E 441; *DB* 1917, 121 (No. 134) 124, 171; Mellink, *Wederdopers,* 190; *ML* II, 555.

Huygen, Jan, an otherwise unknown Dutch Mennonite, the author of *Stigtelyke Rymen op Verscheyde Stoffen* (Amsterdam, 1700, repr. Amsterdam, 1738).   vdZ.

M. Schagen, *Naamlijst der Doopsgezinde Schrijveren* (Amsterdam, 1745) 49.

Huygen, Pieter, a Mennonite, concerning whom nothing is known but that he was the author of *Beginselen van Gods Koninkryk in den Mensch uitgedrukt in Zinnebeelden.* This book was formerly very popular among the Dutch Mennonites. There have been at least nine editions (Harlingen 1689, of which there is no copy extant, Amsterdam 1700, another edition of 1700, Groningen 1715, Amsterdam 1724, 1735, 1738, 1740); in the third and following editions are inserted the *Stigtelyke Rymen* by Jan Huygen (*q.v.*), who was probably Pieter Huygen's son.   vdZ.

Huyzen, Kornelius van, b. Aug. 24, 1667, d. Jan. 28, 1721, at Emden, was a preacher of the Mennonite church at Emden in East Friesland from 1701, elder from 1702 to his death in 1721. Van Huyzen was an advocate of audible prayer by the minister (*stemmelijk gebed*), and defended the thesis that the Mennonites are descended from the Waldenses (*q.v.*). One of his numerous works was titled *Historische Verhandeling van de opkomst en voortgang, mitgaders de Godgeleerdheijd der Doopsgezinde Christenen* (2 volumes, Emden-Hamburg, 1712); second edition with foreword by W. Houttuyn (Hoorn, 1734), a work which in a number of respects has value for the study of Mennonite history. It was thought that the book reflected Spinoza's views, giving rise to an unedifying pen-war, of which some writings are still extant. He was especially attacked by Harmen Reynskes van Overwijk (*q.v.*), a Mennonite preacher at Amsterdam, to whom he replied with *Toetz-steen van de Leere der Doopsgezinden* (Amsterdam, 1713) and *De Grondslag van de Leere der Doopsgesinden* (Amsterdam, 1715). Besides this he published *Korte inhoud van de Leere des Geloofs. Geschikt nae de Algemeene Belijdenissen van de Doopsgesinde Christenen* (Amsterdam, 1705) and two sermons: *Ezechiels gehoorzaamheid* (Emden, 1702) and *Paulus Beede,* the sermon preached when he was ordained as an elder (Amsterdam, 1703).   vdZ.

Biogr. Wb. IV, 452-54; *N.N.B.Wb.* VIII, 898; Schijn-Maatschoen, *Geschiedenis* II, 611-27; *DJ* 1837, 96; *DB* 1867, 52-54; 1898, 62, 76 f.; *ML* II, 385.

Hydro, Okla., a town with a population of 750, is located 65 miles west of Oklahoma City on U.S. Highway 66, the "Main Street of America." It is noted mainly for its agricultural products—wheat, cotton, peanuts, and livestock. A small rock mining industry is in operation in a slightly mountainous area south of Hydro. Some General Conference

Mennonites settled south of Hydro in 1904 and Mennonites (MC) established themselves on the level wheatlands north of town soon after. W.W.K.

Hylaard, a hamlet in the Dutch province of Friesland, where Leenaert Bouwens baptized 21 persons in 1568-82; a congregation of Hylaard, however, is unknown; the newly baptized must have joined a congregation in the neighborhood. vdZ.

Hylkema, a Dutch Mennonite family, originally from Friesland. Sjouke Hylkes (whose children assumed the family name of Hylkema) was a farmer and a preacher of Oldeboorn, Nieuwe Huys congregation, in Friesland 1759-ca.1803. Some of his descendants were deacons at Akkrum (near Oldeboorn). The following members of this family went into the ministry after training at the University and the Mennonite Theological Seminary at Amsterdam:

(1) Kornelis (Cornelis) Bonnes Hylkema, b. 1870 at Akkrum, d. 1948 at Haarlem, who served the congregations of Den Helder 1896-99, Zaandam-Oost 1899-1908, and Haarlem 1908-36. He published a number of books: *Reformateurs* I (Haarlem, 1900, his doctor's thesis) and *Reformateurs* II (Haarlem, 1902), which contain important material for Mennonite history; *De Rechtsverhoudingen in de Ver. Doopsgezinde Gemeente te Haarlem* (Haarlem, 1918); *Het predikambt* (Haarlem, 19—); *Werkelijkheids theologie* (Haarlem, 19—). Besides this he published a number of papers on Mennonite history and other subjects: "De afzetting van Jacob Pieters Banning als leeraar te Wormer en Jisp, Anno 1698" (*DB* 1898, 78-106), "Isaak Molenaar aan Willem de Clercq" (*DB* 1911, 63-92), and "Jan Luyken" (*De Gids,* 1904).

(2) Tjeerd Oeda Ma Hylke Hylkema, b. 1888, pastor of the Giethoorn Mennonite Church 1912-29, Amersfoort 1929-36, and Amsterdam 1936-48. At first he was a liberal Christian as most Dutch Mennonites are, but while serving in his first congregation he was converted to a pietistic orthodoxy. Since then he has been active in behalf of what he calls "een belijdende en dienende vredesgemeente des Heeren" (a congregation of the Lord, whose character is peace and which is willing to serve and confess the Lord). Hylkema has been of considerable influence on the Dutch Mennonite brotherhood, both by his activities and his piety. He was (1917) the founder of the *Vereeniging voor Gemeentedagen* (see **Broederschapswerk**), of which association he was president 1917-27; he took the initiative in building the camping houses "Kraggehuis" and "Samen Een" on the lakes of Giethoorn. He was active in behalf of the Russian Mennonites in 1920; he promoted the foundation of the brotherhood-home "Fredeshiem" near Steenwijk in 1929; he was leader of the Mennonite peace movement and president of the Dutch *Vredesgroep* (Peace Group); he was one of the co-operators in the present *Doopsgezinde Bundel* (Dutch Hymnbook). He published a number of books, *Woodbrooke en de Oud-Woodbrookers* (Steenwijk, 19—, reprinted in 1913); *Aan den Arbeid voor de Gemeente* (Wolvega, 1917); *De Geschiedenis van de Doopsgezinde Gemeenten in Rusland* (Steenwijk, 1920, repr. in 1921); also a German translation of the above: *Die Mennoniten Gemeinden in Ruszland* (Heilbronn, 1921); *De betekenis van de Gemeentedagbeweging* (Wolvega, 1922); *Aan den Arbeid voor de Gemeente* II (Wolvega, n.d.-1928); *Dagelijks leven uit het Woord* (1948); *Wat de Bijbel zegt: dienende weerloze liefde ? of niet ?* (n.p., 1953). Together with D. A. Wuite van Maasdijk, he published *Het Evangelie naar de Beschrijving van Lukas met verklarende aantekeningen en uitlegging voor het persoonlijk leven* (Haarlem, 1947).

(3) Oepke Trinus Hylkema, b. 1902 at Amsterdam, serving the congregation of Terschelling 1926-28, Almelo 1928-39, Bussum 1939-44, and The Hague since 1944. He published *Levende Moraal* (Bussum, 1951) and *Wat Hemel en aarde verbindt* (The Hague, 1953). vdZ.

Hymnology of the Anabaptists. Many of the early Anabaptists were hymn writers, at least 130 being identifiable by name. Among them were Felix Manz, George Blaurock, Michael Sattler, Balthasar Hubmaier, Sigmund Salminger, Jacob Dachser, and Hans Hut of the Germans, Menno Simons and Dirk Philips of the Dutch, and of the Hutterites a large number including Peter Riedemann (at least 46 of his hymns have been preserved), Paul Glock, Antony Erdforter, Offrus Griesinger, Hans Schmid or Raifer, Wolf Sailer, Hans Mändl, and Hauprecht Zapf. Many of the hymns of these writers were included in the several German and Dutch Anabaptist hymnals printed soon after the middle of the 16th century (1560, 1562, 1564, 1565), but many others circulated in manuscript form, particularly the Hutterite hymns. A captive Anabaptist of Urbach, Württemberg, in 1598 surrendered two Anabaptist hymnbooks, "a written one and a printed one" (*TA: Württemberg,* 725). Von Liliencron reports an Anabaptist codex in the Wolfenbüttel Library of *ca.* 1578, containing among other items 18 hymns, 8 of which he reprints (*Zur Liederdichtung,* 20-58). Th. Unger reports an Anabaptist hymn-codex of the 17th century in Graz, consisting of 460 folios. The Hutterite hymnal of 1914 (*Die Lieder der Hutterischen Brüder*) is based largely upon three codices of *ca.* 1600, 1650, and 1660. Just what the written hymnbook of 1598 was remains unknown, since the presence of numerous copies of the printed "Anabaptist songbook" in the Urbach area at that time is attested in the court records. (The burgomaster of Urbach bought one for his children.) Earlier (1573) at Maulbronn Matthes Binder had received a hymnbook (letter to Leonhart Reuss, *TA: Württemberg,* 708). This hymnbook and Menno Simons' *Foundation-Book* were the most common (and apparently only or chief) books in the possession of captured Anabaptists around the turn of the 16th century in Württemberg (*TA: Württemberg, passim*).

Many of the early hymns were written by prisoners or martyrs. George Blaurock wrote a hymn just before his death as a martyr in 1529, in which he gives his reason for writing in the final words of the hymn, "Therefore will I sing to the praise of Thy name, and eternally proclaim the grace which appeared to me." The oldest section of the *Ausbund*

(1564) carries a title which indicates that its hymns were "by the grace of God composed and sung at Passau in the Castle by the Swiss Brethren." This occurred in 1535-37, when Swiss Brethren returning from Moravia were imprisoned at Passau en route. Paul Glock related in a letter he wrote in prison in Hohenwittlingen to Peter Walpot in 1573 that he had composed three hymns which he was sending to Walpot for improvement, and reported, "We read and sing to the glory of God and so pass our time" (*TA: Württemberg*, 373). Eager to comfort and encourage the brethren at home, the prisoners and martyrs wrote spiritual songs which became a part of the hymn treasury of the brotherhood.

The unusual number of Anabaptist hymn writers and hymns suggests that these hymns were much used among the Anabaptists for private personal and family reading and singing as well as in the congregations, although of course in times of worst persecution singing was little heard because of the danger. But the Anabaptists did sing; the hymns are assigned tunes in the hymnals, they were not merely literary vehicles. In 1596 it was reported of Peter Ehrenpreis of Urbach that he had won much favor with the people by his manner of life and "with his Anabaptist songs which he is accustomed to sing in his vineyards and elsewhere" (*TA: Württemberg*, 687). Without doubt the hymns were also a factor in Anabaptist evangelism, both read and sung. Christian Neff says (*ML* II, 86), "A flood of religious songs poured over the young brotherhood like a vivifying and refreshing stream. The songs became the strongest attractive force for the brotherhood. They sang themselves into the hearts of many, clothed in popular tunes. They were mostly martyr songs, which breathed an atmosphere of readiness to die and a touching depth of faith. And those that did not report on martyr steadfastness admonished the listener to a devout faith, which was to prove itself in love. Sanctification and its demonstration in life and death is their glorious content." Von Liliencron says (pp. 4-5), "Love is the great and inexhaustible theme of their hymnody; for love is the sole distinguishing mark of the children of God . . . . For the brethren love is the 'chief sum' of their being . . . . So these hymns immerse themselves in the concept of the love which is all in all, which takes up its cross with joy, which gives everything in the service of God and the neighbor, which bears all things, and out of which flows all humility and meekness, mercy, and peace." Seldom do the Anabaptist hymns have a dominant didactic or doctrinal character, although doctrine is not absent. Sebastian Franck's characterization of Anabaptist doctrine as teaching nothing but "faith, love, and the cross" (*Chronica*, 1531) may well be applied to their hymns.

There is evidence that before the production of complete hymnals some Anabaptist hymns were published as single numbers or small pamphlets. An illustration is a hymn by Hans Rogel (*Ausbund*, No. 53), presumably an Anabaptist, which appeared in three printed editions at Augsburg in 1539, and two other hymns by the same author which appeared separately at Augsburg *ca.* 1550 and at Strasbourg.

Apart from manuscript collections, real Anabaptist hymnals did not appear until after the middle of the 16th century. Then five hymnals appeared at almost the same time, two German and three Dutch. The Dutch came first, one a martyr hymnal, the *Lietboecxken van den Offer des Heeren* with 25 hymns (later enlarged), published always with *Het Offer* in ten editions in 1563-99; another, a collection of spiritual songs, *Veelderhande Liedekens*, in six editions (1560, 1562, 1566, 1569, 1579, and 1580) with 257 hymns; the third, *Een nieu Liedenboeck* (1562, reprint 1582) with 289 hymns. Late in the century (1582) the noted Hans de Ries issued his *Lietboeck*, which had many reprints but really falls outside the Anabaptist period.

Germany also had an outspoken martyr hymnal, the *Ausbund*, first edition in 1564 (*Etliche schöne Christliche Geseng*, with 53 hymns), first full edition in 1583 with 130 hymns (later increased to 137), with a third edition in 1622 and nine additional reprints in Europe to 1838, as well as many in America beginning with 1742. It was the Swiss Brethren hymnal, and was used in Switzerland and South Germany until at least 1750-1830 in most places, until about 1900 among some of the Amish congregations in France. It is still used by 15,000 Amish members in the United States. The full titles of the editions of 1564 and 1583 are as follows: *Etliche schöne Christliche Gesang, wie sie in der Gefengkniss zu Passaw im Schloss von den Schweitzer Brüdern durch Gottes gnad geticht und gesungen worden* (n.p., 1564), 53 hymns in 119 folios; *Aussbund Etlicher schöner Christlicher Geseng, wie die in der Gefengnuss zu Passaw im Schloss von den Schweitzern, und auch von andern rechtgläubigen Christen hin und her gedicht worden. Allen und jeden Christen, welcher Religion sie auch seyen, unparteilich und fast nützlich zu brauchen* (n.p., 1583), 80 hymns in 432 pp. The second part of this edition is a reprint of the 1564 book with a slightly modified title as follows: *Etliche sehr schöne Christliche Gesenge, wie diesselbigen zu Passaw, von den Schweitzerbrüdern, in der Gefengnuss im Schloss, durch Gottes gnad gedicht und gesungen worden.* (n.p., 1583), 51 hymns in 347 pp. The 1583 edition is the first to carry the title *Ausbund*, but Petrus Dathenus, the presiding officer of the Frankenthaler Gespräch of 1571, specifically mentions a *"geistliches Liederbuch, der Ausbund"* in the course of the debate. There may be a lost edition between 1564 and 1571, unless the term "Ausbund" was used by the Swiss Brethren to refer to the 1564 edition.

The other 16th-century German Anabaptist hymnal was *Ein schön Gesangbüchlein Geistlicher Lieder zusammengetragen aus dem alten und Neuen Testament durch fromme Christen und Liebhaber Gottes welcher Hiefür etliche seind gewesen aber noch viel darzu getan welche nie in truck ausgangen. In welchem auch ein recht leben und fundament des rechten Christlichen Glaubens gelert wird. Col. 3. Lehrend und ermanendt euch selbst mit gesangen und lobgesangen und Geistlichen Liedern in der gnadt und singend dem Herrn in ewren hertzen.* The first edition with 122 hymns appeared about 1564, possibly in Cologne; the second with 133 hymns was printed after 1569; the third with a somewhat changed title and 140 hymns appeared about 1590.

This last edition incorporated four hymns from the Dutch *Veelderhande Liedekens*. It was apparently the hymnal of the Anabaptists of the Lower Rhine.

Unfortunately very few of the Anabaptist hymns carried over into the later Mennonite hymnals of Holland, Germany, and Russia. The reason for this is, at least outside of Holland, that the Mennonites of the 17th and 18th centuries, having lost much of the martyr spirit and some of the Anabaptist vision, and coming under the influence of Lutheranism and Pietism, or lacking resources ·and opportunities to print their own hymnals, actually used the state church hymnals of the areas where they resided, in many places for over a century. When they then began to compile and publish their own hymnals they naturally preferred to take over the hymns with which they had become familiar; they had lost touch with their own hymnological tradition. To be sure, many of the martyr hymns were too narrative in character to be suitable for worship; but the content of the Anabaptist hymnals was by no means exclusively of this type. Some Anabaptist hymns were included in the earliest German Protestant hymnals such as the hymnbook of the Bohemian Brethren by Michael Weisse (1531), and Joh. Zwick's hymnal published at Constance in 1536, *Neu Gesangbüchle*.

An outstanding early Anabaptist leader and hymn writer was Jacob Dachser (*q.v.*), preacher and leader of the Augsburg Anabaptist congregation from February 1527, when he was baptized and installed as assistant pastor by Hans Hut, to his recantation in May 1531. A graduate of the University of Ingolstadt and a teacher in Augsburg, he composed a number of hymns as an Anabaptist preacher which were published in the Augsburg hymnal of 1529 "and are among the best in the collection" (Hege). He was either the editor or coeditor of the second edition of the Augsburg hymnal in 1532, for which he versified six Psalms. The hymnal of 1537 (*Der gantz Psalter*), published by Sigmund Salminger, also a former Augsburg Anabaptist, contains in addition to several of Dachser's earlier hymns a translation of 42 Psalms by him. In 1538 Dachser published all the Psalms with notes (*Der gantz psalter Davids*), together with an appendix of hymns for church holidays and ceremonies which he wrote. Dachser's Psalter was, to be sure, produced after his recantation, but grew out of what had been begun while he was an Anabaptist preacher.

Chr. Hege has pointed out that the changing relationships of the several major groups of Anabaptists with each other can be traced through the interchange of hymns. In the early days the Swiss Brethren and the Anabaptists in Moravia had many hymns in common. Later the divergence and even opposition between the two groups is reflected in the fact that the Hutterites went their own separate way in the matter of hymns. The exchange between Dutch and Swiss-German groups found expression in their printed hymnals. The *Schön Gesangbüchlein* contained not only Swiss-South German hymns which also appeared in the *Ausbund*, but likewise translations of Dutch hymns. The 1583 *Ausbund* contained improved reproductions of these translated Dutch hymns, obviously taken from the *Schön Gesangbüchlein*. Thus the Swiss-South German Anabaptists-

Mennonites, through the *Ausbund*, received both Dutch and Hutterite influences in the 16th century and later. The Anabaptists of the Lower Rhine region, the producers of the *Schön Gesangbüchlein*, apparently had few hymns of their own.

The outstanding work on Anabaptist hymnology, a most thorough and scholarly treatise, is Rudolf Wolkan's *Die Lieder der Wiedertäufer, Ein Beitrag zur deutschen und niederländischen Litteratur- und Kirchengeschichte* (Berlin, 1903), 295 pp. Besides the chapters, "The Oldest Hymns of the Anabaptists," "The Oldest Hymns of the Swiss Brethren," "Dutch Hymns," "Mennonite Hymns in Germany," "The Later Hymns of the Swiss Brethren," and "The Hymns of the Hutterites," the book includes a list of Anabaptist hymn writers (130 in number), a list of the Dutch Anabaptist hymns mentioned (119 in number), and a list of all hymns of the German Anabaptists (931 in number). Wolkan attempts to give the provenance of all the hymns in the two German Anabaptist hymnals. Philipp Wackernagel's *Das deutsche Lied von der ältesten Zeit bis zu Anfang des XVII. Jahrhunderts*, Vol. III (Leipzig, 1870) contains a section (pp. 441-86) headed "Die Lieder der ersten Wiedertäufer," in which 45 hymns, Nos. 498-542, are reprinted with annotations. The writers of some of these hymns were not really Anabaptists, as e.g., Thomas Müntzer with ten hymns and Ludwig Haetzer with three. The remaining authors in order are Hans Hut (4), George Blaurock (2), Felix Manz, Hans Koch, and Lenhart Meister, George Wagner (2), Hans Langenmantel, Leopold Scharnschlager, Oswald Glait (9), Henslein von Bilach, Leopold Schneider, Hans Schlaffer, Annelein von Freiburg, Jörg Steinmetz, Seven Brethren (2). Wackernagel's *Lieder der niederländischen Reformierten aus der Zeit der Verfolgung im 16. Jahrhundert* (*Beiträge zur niederländischen Hymnologie*, No. 1, Frankfurt, 1867) devotes pp. 79-147 to an exact reproduction of 68 Dutch Anabaptist hymns, 46 from *Veelderhande Liedekens* (edition of 1569), 21 from *Een nieu Liedenboeck* (edition of 1562), and one from Hans de Ries' *Lietboeck* of 1582. On pp. 194-208 Wackernagel reproduces eleven more Dutch Anabaptist hymns, three from the 1570 edition of the *Lietboecxken* of *Het Offer*, and eight from another printed source of 1577. The introductory section reproduces in bibliographically complete form the title pages, prefaces, and conclusions of all the above books. (See Neff, **Gesang** and **Gesangbücher**, *ML* II, 85-91; Hege, **Liederdichtung**, *ML* II, 652 f.) H.S.B.

Wolkan, *Lieder;* Wackernagel, *Kirchenlied; idem, Lieder;* H. S. Burrage, "Anabaptist Hymn Writers and Their Hymns," in *Baptist Hymn Writers and Their Hymns* (Portland, 1888) 1-25; Franklin Johnson, "Some Hymns and Songs of the German Anabaptists," in *The Baptist Quarterly Review* IV (1882) 370-78; A. J. Ramaker, "Hymns and Hymn Writers Among the Anabaptists of the Sixteenth Century," *MQR* III (1929) 93-131; R. Friedmann, "Devotional Literature of the Swiss Brethren," *MQR* XVI (1942) 199-220; H. S. Bender, "First Edition of the *Ausbund*," *MQR* III (1929) 147-50; E. Koch, *Geschichte des Kirchenlieds und Kirchengesangs*, 3d ed., 8 vv. (Stuttgart, 1866-77) with Anabaptist materials in II, 143-45, and VI, 185 f.; Rochus von Lilienkron, "Zur Liederdichtung der Wiedertäufer," in *Abhandlungen der k. bayer. Akademie des W. III. Cl.*, Vol. XIII, Part I (Munich, 1875) 1-58; August Kamp, *Die Psalmendichtung des Jakob Dachser* (Greifswald, 1931); Th. Unger, "Ueber eine Wiedertäufer-Lieder-

handschrift des 17. Jahrhunderts," in *Jahrbuch der Gesellschaft f. d. Gesch. der Protestanten in Oesterreich,*
1892, 1894, 1896, 1897, 1899; S. Cramer, "Bijdragen tot
de Geschiedenis van ons Kerklied en ons Kerkgesang,"
DB 1900, 71-124; 1902, 1-25; F. Mencik, "Ueber ein
Wiedertäufergesangbuch" [*Etliche schöne geistliche Lieder und Lobesang von vilen frommen Zaigen.* Ausge-
schrieben von Melcher Hipscher Anno 1655.] (Prag,
1896, *Sitzungsberichte der k. böhm. Gesellschaft der W.*
1896, XI); J. Loserth, "Aus dem Liederschatz der mährischen Wiedertäufer," *Ztscht des deutschen Vereins f. d.
Gesch. Mährens u. Schlesiens* XXVII (1925) III/IV, 48-
50; K. Rembert, "Die Liederdichtung des sogenannten
Anabaptismus," *Monatshefte der Comenius-Gesellschaft*
XV (1906) 139-49; J. P. Classen, "Taufgesinnte Lieder-
dichter," *Der Mennonit* IX (1956) 100.

Hymnology of the Swiss, French, and South German
Mennonites. The Swiss and French Mennonites
never published a hymnal of their own, except the
Ausbund (*q.v.,* first ed., 1564), until 1955, when they
joined in sponsoring the *Neues Gemeinschafts-Lie-
derbuch* (Basel, 1955). The editorial sponsors
(*Herausgeber*) are listed as the Mennonite Churches
in Switzerland and Alsace, the Pilgermission St.
Chrischona at Basel, and the Association of State
Church "Gemeinschaften" of the Canton of Bern.
Samuel Geiser, one of the elders of the Swiss Mennonite Conference, was one of the chief editors of
this collection. This hymnal with its 436 hymns is
of good quality, including 108 hymns taken directly
out of the 1952 edition of the *Gesangbuch der Evan-
gelisch-reformierten Kirche der . . . Schweiz.*

The *Ausbund* (*q.v.,* see also **Hymnology of the
Anabaptists**) was used until the 19th century in the
Swiss congregations, both Mennonite and Amish, by
the congregations in Alsace and France, which were
almost exclusively Amish, and by the Amish congregations in South and Middle Germany, the last
European editions of this hymnal being issued in
1809 (Basel), 1815 (n.p.), and 1838 (Basel). The
1815 edition bears the title, *Christliches Liederbuch
der Schweizer Brüder.* Between the dated editions
of 1564, 1583, and 1622, all without place, and the
edition of 1809 six other editions appeared, all without place or date, but three each in the 17th and
18th centuries, publication place for some editions
being doubtless Basel. From the 6th edition on the
basic number of hymns was 137. The last four editions added an appendix of five hymns and eleven
Psalms.

The Mennonite congregations of South Germany began earlier to use the hymnals of the state
churches. One of the most popular hymnals, both in
Switzerland and adjacent areas, was Lobwasser's
book of Psalms (first ed. 1573, after 1700 with many
hymns added), while in the Palatinate the hymnal
of the Reformed Electoral Palatinate (first ed. 1749)
was long used. The first Mennonite hymnal of this
area was *Christliches Gesangbuch, zunächst für den
Gebrauch der evangelischen Mennoniten-Gemeinden
in der Pfalz* (Worms, 1832), with 383 hymns, sponsored by the conference of this area, and edited
largely by Leonhard Weydmann, pastor of the Monsheim Mennonite Church. It appeared in two editions. The edition with the above title was apparently issued by Jakob Ellenberger, pastor of the Friedelsheim congregation, since it has a preface by him.
The other edition bears the title *Christliches Gesangbuch, zunächst für die Taufgesinnten in der Pfalz.*

Although many of the hymns were printed with
tunes, many were not given tunes. Hence Ellenberger
published a lithographed book of tunes in four-part
harmony for use with the hymnal. A second hymnal,
containing the majority of the hymns in the hymnal
of 1832, but with other hymns from other sources,
was published by the two congregations of Bildhausen and Rottenbauer in Franconia (northern
Bavaria), with the title *Christliches Gesangbuch
zunächst für Mennoniten. Herausgegeben von der
Mennoniten-Brüder-Gemeinschaft in Unterfranken*
(Würzburg, 1839), with 575 hymns. The introduction to this hymnal refers specifically to the previous
use of the state church hymnal: "For a long time
the hymnal of the Reformed Electoral Palatinate,
published in 1749 at Mannheim and Frankfurt,
served us and our forefathers in public services and
family worship." The final form of the South German hymnal was *Gesangbuch, zum gottesdienstlichen und häuslichen Gebrauch in Evangelischen
Mennoniten-Gemeinden* (Worms, 1854), with 600
hymns, without music, edited by three preachers
(with the help of the hymn writer A. Knapp), J.
Molenaar of Monsheim, J. Risser of Sembach, and J.
Ellenberger of Friedelsheim. It contained an appendix of 32 pages with prayers for family worship, and
an index to the hymn writers, and was reprinted unchanged in 1876 at Kaiserslautern. The tunes were
printed at Dürkheim in 1856 in four-part harmony
under the title, *Vierstimmige Melodien zu dem Ge
sangbuch zum gottesdienstlichen und häuslichen Ge-
brauche in evangelischen Mennoniten-Gemeinden,*
lithographed, reprinted in 1874 at Dürkheim, and
again in 1897 at Waiblingen, slightly revised. The
next edition of the *Gesangbuch,* edited in revised
form by Christian Neff and a "Gesangbuchkommis-
sion," appeared in 1910 at Ludwigshafen with 575
hymns, a new tune-book (*Choralbuch*) accompanying it. This edition was reissued in 1950 at Ludwigshafen.

The only other hymnbook published in South Germany was the one sponsored by the Amish congregations, *Gesangbuch zum Gebrauch bei dem öffentlichen Gottesdienst und der häuslichen Erbauung,
zunächst für einen Teil der Mennoniten-Gemeinden
beider Hessen, der bayr. Pfalz, Rheinpreussens und
des Herzogtums Nassau bestimmt* (Wiesbaden, 1843,
reprint Regensburg, 1859), with 286 hymns, and an
appendix of 102 hymns entitled *Gesänge für Religion
und Tugend,* all set to four-part music. The introduction is at pains to explain why the "old" hymnal,
meaning the *Ausbund,* was no longer serviceable.

Another aspect of the hymnology of Switzerland
and South Germany was the publication of small
separate collections of new hymns in the late 17th
and early 18th centuries. An illustration is: *Zwanzig
neue geistliche Lieder, Das Erste: von einem Drucker
Gesellen Thomas von Imbroich genannt, Aufs neue
gedruckt Anno 1758,* first edition at least as early as
1699. In at least one instance the Dordrecht Confession was combined with a collection of prayers and
a collection of hymns to form a devotional manual,
printed in 1686. The title page runs: *Christliche
Glaubens Bekentnuss . . . wie auch Etliche Christliche
Gebätt . . . worbey gefüget Etliche Geistlich Lieder,
Alles zu Erbawung, Auffmunterung und Lehr, unser*

Jugend zum besten gestellt und geordnet worden.
Seven long hymns constitute the hymn section. Another edition of this same book appeared in 1691. One copy in the Goshen College Library contains bound with it the following hymn collections: *Das Gebätt von Hans Rösch* (Reist?) *her, Darbey auch die fünf nachfolgenden Lieder zu finden; Ein Geistliches Lieder-Büchlein, Darinnen Diese zehen folgende neue Geistliche Lieder zu finden* (after 1709); *Zwanzig neue Geistliche Lieder* (1758); *Ein Send-Brieff samt einem schönen Gebätt und geistlichen Lied, worbey noch etliche andere Christliche Gebätt . . . Wie auch etliche geistliche Lieder.* This section includes *Unterricht vom Christlichen Singen* just preceding the hymns. The GCL has several additional *Sammelband* volumes of similar character, one with many small hymn collections and single hymns, so that apparently this type of combination book was popular. It is possible that these "new spiritual hymns," as they are commonly called, were intended to supplement the *Ausbund,* which had more martyr hymns and fewer "spiritual hymns." It seems most likely that these materials were printed in Basel or Strasbourg from 1660 to 1760. This aspect of Swiss hymnology deserves a thorough study.   H.S.B.

Hymnology of the Mennonites in the Netherlands.
Anabaptists and Mennonites even in the earliest period sang hymns in their meetings when it was possible to do so. Mostly it was impossible to sing together, because in the period of persecution singing would attract the attention of the government officers, who eagerly tracked down the Anabaptists, and there are a few cases of meetings being surprised by the officers because the singing had betrayed them. But among the earliest Anabaptists many songs (*liedekens*) were known. Anneken Jans (*q.v.*) was arrested in January 1539 at Rotterdam, because a "heretical song" that she had sung in the ferryboat had betrayed her. In prison the martyrs often took up a hymn to comfort themselves and each other, and of a number of martyrs it is mentioned that they were singing a hymn while going to the execution places.

As to what kind of hymns they sang no definite answer can be given. Only in two or three cases do we have information. Reytse Aysesz, executed at Leeuwarden in 1574, on the way to his execution began the hymn, "Ic roep U, o Hemelsche Vader aen, Wilt myn geloove stercken" (I call to Thee, heavenly Father, wilt Thou strengthen my faith) (*Mart. Mir.* D 690, E 1,005). Another martyr sang, "Ic arm scaep aen groener heyde" (I poor sheep on the green heath), which is a well-known medieval song.

Soon there were in circulation a number of hymns composed by the martyrs themselves in prison (as is mentioned of many of them), or composed by others, all unknown poets, to celebrate their martyrdom. These hymns, rhymed versions of their trials and accounts of their sufferings and death, must have been clandestinely printed on separate sheets and circulated shortly after the death of a martyr, as is evident in the case of the "liedeken" on Anneken Jans, which was sung on the streets of Hamburg only a few weeks after her death (1539).

In the second half of the 16th century these single hymns were collected and compiled in songbooks. In 1562-63 a collection of hymns by and about martyrs was published, together with the oldest Dutch martyrbook, *Het Offer des Heeren* (*q.v.*). The name of the collection of hymns was *Lietboecxken van den Offer des Heeren* (*q.v.*). This *Lietboecxken* was reprinted together with the *Offer* at least 10 times (last edition in 1599). Besides these historical hymns another type of hymns, called *Schriftuurlijke Liedekens* (Scriptural Hymns), or *Geestelijke Liedekens* (Spiritual Hymns) were used among the Mennonites, and soon pushed aside the martyr songs. As early as 1560 the first hymnary of this type was published by Nicolaes Biestkens (*q.v.*). It is entitled *Veelderhande Liedekens* (*q.v.*). This first edition has been lost, as was also a second edition of 1562; of the following editions of 1566, an undated edition, one of 1569, one of 1579, and one of 1580, copies are still extant. Of a second collection, printed in 1562 by Biestkens and entitled *Een nieu Liedenboeck* (*q.v.*), there is only one copy extant found in the Amsterdam Mennonite Library. This *Nieu Liedenboeck* was reprinted at Amsterdam in 1582 by Biestkens under the title *Het Tweede Liedenboeck* (*q.v.*) (the second hymnary). Van Braght (*Mart. Mir.* D 665, E 683) mentions a *Rotterdamsch Liedboeck.* What kind of hymnary this was is unknown, since no copy of it has been found. These hymnbooks may all have been used in Mennonite congregations. They are all without notes and could be sung according to the melody which is announced at the top of each hymn. In most cases two melodies are given. These melodies are of well-known songs, both secular and spiritual, sometimes of a psalm used in the Reformed Church.

The Dutch Mennonites of the 16th century did not sing psalms as the Calvinists did. Reytse Aysesz about 1570 was accused by a Reformed preacher that whereas they (the Reformed) sang the Biblical Psalms of David, the Mennonites used songs made by man, but Reytse was comforted by the thought that their (Mennonite) hymns were made according to the Scriptures (*Mart. Mir.* D 686, E 1,001).

Among the authors of these *Schriftuurlycke Liedekens* are Menno Simons, Dirk Philips, Joost Eeeuwouts, Jacques Outerman, Hans de Ries, Claes Ganglofs, Leenaert Clock, Jan Jacobsz, and Pieter Jansz Twisck, as well as a large number of anonymous poets.

In the early 17th century the *Veelderhande Liedekens* and other old songbooks were largely replaced. New hymnaries were composed and put into use. It is impossible to enumerate all of them, since more than 100 different hymnaries were published between 1582 and 1790. Some of the most important were Hans de Ries, *Lietboeck* of 1582 (many reprints under varying titles); Carel van Mander, *De Gulden Harpe* (1599); Leenaert Clock, *Het Groote Liedeboeck* (1625); *Het Gheestelyck Kruydt-Hofken* (1637); *Het Rijper Liedtboecxken* (1637); *'t Kleyn Hoorns-Liet-boeck* (1644-45); *'t Groot Hoorns Liedtboeck* (1647); Claes Stapel, *Lusthof der Zielen* (about 1680, 2d ed. 1682, 3rd ed. 1729); *Lusthof des Gemoeds* (1732); *De Geestelijke Goudschaale,* 1st ed. in 1662 at Franeker, 2d ed. 1683 at Leeuwarden,

4th ed. 1751. These songbooks were used in the different branches of the Dutch Mennonites. For example, the Waterlanders used de Ries's hymnal, the Old Flemish van Mander's *Gulden Harpe,* and the Groningen Old Flemish *Lusthof des Gemoeds.* Many of these hymnaries did not contain original hymns, but largely borrowed from each other. With the exception of van Mander's hymnbook the poetical quality of these hymns is rather mediocre or less. As is said in the preface of many of these hymnaries they were intended not only for congregational singing, but also for private use, or to be read "for the edification of souls."

As mentioned above, the early Anabaptists and Mennonites did not sing Psalms, but this changed in the 17th century. Quite early, Hans de Ries, a champion of Psalm-singing, had inserted in the 1624 edition of his hymnary all 150 rhymed Psalms after the version of Dathenus, and from then on singing of Psalms became more and more usual. In the Flemish congregation of Amsterdam about 1630 a fine had to be paid every time the preacher allowed any other hymn to be sung but a Psalm (*DB* 1865, 69). But the clumsy version of Dathenus did not satisfy; so the Lam and Toren congregation of Amsterdam introduced in 1684 a new Psalmbook, rhymed by the Mennonites J. Oudaen, D. R. Camphuyzen, Galenus Abrahamsz, and others. In 1713 the Haarlem congregation replaced Dathenus' version by a psalter rhymed by Vondel, Hooft, Westerbaen, Rooleeuw, and other poets in 1713. Some other congregations introduced either the Amsterdam or the Haarlem Psalter. The Amsterdam Zonist congregation used the Dathenus version until 1762, when it was replaced by a Psalmbook rhymed by the literary association "Laus Deo Salus Populo." This version too was used in a number of Dutch Mennonite congregations. In most cases some other hymnbook was used in addition to the psalter. From the end of the 18th century the singing of Psalms decreased in favor of hymns.

Since the old hymnbooks were no longer available, or were little appreciated, they went out of use, except in a few congregations like Ameland, where *De Geestelijke Goudschaale* was in use until 1818 (*DB* 1890, 7) and in Aalsmeer, Giethoorn, and Balk, which used the *Kleyn Hoorns Lietboeck*—reprinted as late as 1814—until the 19th century, Balk until 1854 (*DB* 1892, 56, 65 f.) and Aalsmeer even until 1862 (*DB* 1862, 147). The congregation at Grouw used the hymnal by Stapel (*q.v.*) until about 1800. A number of new hymnaries appeared, all bearing the traits of that rationalistic time. The congregation of Rotterdam introduced a new hymnary in 1776; the Amsterdam Lamist congregation compiled the *Kleine bundel* in 1791, the Amsterdam Zonist congregation the *Groote bundel* in 1796. Hamburg-Altona, then still using hymnaries in the Dutch language, composed the *Altonasche Liederen* in 1802. Haarlem introduced a new hymnary in 1804, Zwolle one in 1808. All these hymnaries were not only in use in the congregations which had compiled them, but also in other congregations, as was especially a songbook called *Uitgezochte Liederen,* composed by a committee and published in 1809, which was introduced in about 20 congregations. Most of the

hymns of all these hymnaries were borrowed from older songbooks though the words of the hymns occasionally were much altered. Often the same hymns were found in all these songbooks, most of which also contained a number of Psalms. Some Mennonite congregations introduced the Reformed *Evangelische Gezangen* of 1805.

From about 1850 nearly all these hymnaries were replaced by new ones. After an attempt to get only one hymnary for common use by Dutch Mennonites had miscarried, both Amsterdam and Haarlem compiled new hymnaries, Amsterdam in 1848 (*Christelijke Gezangen,* 2 vv.) and again 2 vv. in 1895 (*Doopsgezinde Liederen*), to which a supplement was added in 1916, and Haarlem introduced new hymnaries, *Christelijke Kerkgezangen* in 1851 and *Doopsgezinde Liederen* and the Lutheran hymnbook, both in 1895. Both these Amsterdam and Haarlem songbooks came to be used by a number of other congregations, as was a new hymnary introduced in 1893 at Groningen and Deventer, *119 Christelijke Kerkgezangen.*

In the meantime a number of Mennonite congregations had put into use a hymnary composed by the Union of Dutch (liberal) Christians (*Nederlandsche Protestantenbond*), which had been published in 1882, as well as the two hymnaries of the Remonstrants. In 1897 two Mennonite ministers, J. Sepp and H. Boetje, published *Gezangen ten gebruike in Doopsgezinde Gemeenten.* This hymnary, in 1900 enlarged by an anthology from the Psalms and usually called *Leidsche Bundel* (*q.v.*), became the songbook of many congregations, though it was not introduced in all congregations as the authors had hoped.

In 1900 the following hymnals were in use (some congregations used two or even four different hymnbooks): *Het Boek der Psalmen* (Reformed Psalter) in 82 congregations; *Godsdienstige Liederen* of the "Protestantenbond" in 31; *Leidsche Bundel* in 27; *Groote Bundel* in 26; *Evangelische Gezangen* (hymns of the Dutch Reformed Church) in 18; *Vervolgbundel op de Evangelische Gezangen* (appendix to the hymns of the Reformed Church) in 14; *Uitgezochte Liederen* in 13; *Christelijke Liederen II* (Amsterdam hymnbook of 1870) in 11; *Doopsgezinde Liederen* (Haarlem hymnal I and II, of 1895) in 9; *Evangelische Gezangen, uitgegeven vanwege de Remonstrantsche Broederschap* (Remonstrant hymnaries I and II) in 7; *Kleine Bundel* (1791) in 6; *Christelijke Liederen* (Amsterdam hymnbook I of 1870) in 6; *Christelijke Gezangen uitgegeven door de Synode der Evangelisch-Luthersche Kerk, 1884* (Haarlem hymnal II of 1895) in 5; *Christelijke Kerkgezangen* (Haarlem hymnal of 1851) in 5; *Het Boek der Psalmen volgens de overzetting van het dichtgenootschap Laus Deo Salus Populo* of 1759 in 2; *Zwolsche Liederen* in 1.

In 1940 these figures were: *Godsdienstige Liederen* of the "Protestantenbond" in 73 congregations; *Vervolgbundel van de Godsdienstige Liederen* of the "Protestantenbond" in 60; *Leidsche Bundel* in 45; *Het Boek der Psalmen* in 20; *Evangelische Gezangen* in 7; *vervolgbundel op de Evangelische Gezangen* in 5; *Christelijke Liederen II* in 3; *Doopsgezinde Liederen I* in 3; *Christelijke Gezangen, uitgegeven door de Synode der Evangelisch-Luthersche Kerk* in 3; *Aanhangsel* (Appendix) to the Amsterdam hymnary (1916) in 2; *Groote Bundel, Kleine Bundel,* and Psalms *Laus Deo,* each in 1.

All these hymnbooks were put out of use in 1944, when a new hymnary, entitled *Liederenbundel ten dienste van de Doopsgezinde Broederschap* and commonly called *Doopsgezinde Bundel,* appeared. It came into being by the co-operation of the Mennonites, the Remonstrants, and the Dutch Protestantenbond. The Mennonites use the main body of 250 hymns, followed by a special appendix of 50 hymns, which are not inserted in the Remonstrant and Protestantenbond hymnaries. All Mennonite congregations, except three, introduced this new hymnary.

In the 16th and early 17th century only one hymn was sung at the beginning and one at the close of the meeting, and this remained the custom in conservative groups such as Groningen Old Flemish and Jan-Jacobsz group until the end of the 18th century. About the middle of the 17th century both Lamist and Zonist congregations, obviously influenced by the practice of the Reformed church, sang a hymn at three times. Nowadays most congregations sing a hymn three times during the services, but sometimes also four and five times. From about 1770 the churches gradually installed pipe organs (see **Musical Instruments**) to accompany the singing of the congregation.

Because the Dutch language continued to be used in worship in the Mennonite congregations of Hamburg-Altona and near by until the end of the 18th century, and in the congregations of East and West Prussia and Danzig until the beginning of the 19th, Dutch Mennonite hymnbooks long continued in use in these areas. Although most of these were imported from the Netherlands, some were expressly printed for these congregations in Prussia, and it is possible that two or three were actually printed there. As early as 1597 *Sommige andachtighe ende leerachtige Gheestelicke Liedekens* were published at Amsterdam but intended for the Mennonites in Prussia. Obviously they were used in the Frisian congregations. A 1638 edition of this hymnal (published at Haarlem, Holland) was used in the Frisian congregation of Montau, West Prussia. A *Pruys Liedt-boeck inhoudende schriftuurlijcke nieuwe Liedekens* (Amsterdam, 1604), with an Introduction by I.I. from Danzig, was followed by the *Tweede Pruys Liedtboeksken* in 1607. A number of Dutch Mennonite hymnals, mentioned before, such as the hymnal of Hans de Ries, the *Kleyn Hoorns Lietboeck,* and the *Lusthof des Gemoeds,* were also frequently used in the Prussian congregations. In the correspondence between the Prussian Mennonites and the congregations of Amsterdam and Groningen the request was frequently made to send Dutch hymnbooks to Prussia, and in 1753 (*Inv. Arch. Amst.* I, No. 1600) mention is made of a hymnal for Prussia which was printed in the Netherlands. (For further information on Dutch hymnals in Prussia, see the next article.)

The Flemish congregation of Hamburg-Altona, from 1685, used *Gesanghboek of Gesanghen, om op alle feestdagen en vor en na de predicatie in de Ver-* *gaderingen te singen* (Hamburg, 1685). The *Christelijke Gezangen voor de openbaare Godsdienstoeffeningen* of 1802, usually called *Altonasche Liederen,* was also in the Dutch language and printed at Amsterdam. vDZ.

Inv. Arch. Amst. I, No. 759c; *DJ* 1837, 63-65; *DB* 1865, 67-94, 153-59; 1867, 72-77; 1887, 86-112; 1900, 71-124; 1902, 1-25; Kühler, *Geschiedenis* I, 248 f., 293 f., 348; *idem, Geschiedenis* III, 28-37; N. van der Zijpp, *Geschiedenis der Doopsgezinden in Nederland* (Arnhem, 1952) 110, 112-14, 165, 170, 243, notes 25 and 43.

Hymnology of the Mennonites of West and East Prussia, Danzig, and Russia. In an article entitled "Die Entwicklung des Gemeindegesanges in unsern westpreussischen Gemeinden" (*Menn. Bl.,* April 1931) Abraham Driedger quotes a Danzig Mennonite chronicle for 1780, "In our meetings especially during the past century (17th) there was no singing." Although there were reasons in the days of the "hidden church" for not being too vocal in praising God in order not to attract too much attention to forbidden meetings, the above statement is obviously an exaggeration. The same article states that Hartwich is given credit for the information that the "fine" Mennonites did not sing in their meetings around 1700, while the "coarse" sang "Psalms and other Lutheran songs." This could indicate that the more conservative had some objections to singing in worship. It is also possible that the silence imposed earlier had become a sort of principle.

The same article, however, says that the Mennonites of the Vistula area used Carel van Mander's songbook, entitled *De Gulden Harpe,* published in 1626, which had as an appendix *Bethlehem, Dat is het Broodhuys.* . . . It is possible that this book was in use even before this time. It appeared in Holland first in 1599. Another source takes us even further back. In the list of Georg Hansen's Danzig Mennonite elders and ministers appended to the Danzig Mennonite Church Record, 1667-1836, there is a note in connection with one of its first elders, Giesbrecht Franssen, which reports that he died in 1607 "as it is stated in a hymn written in his memory which appears on page 139 of the Jacob Jacobsz *Liedeboek* and page 116 in the second part." This indicates that Dutch Mennonite hymnbooks were in use in the Danzig Mennonite Church around 1600.

This is very likely the same *Liedt-boeck* referred to by Hansen which he names the Jacob Jacobsz *Liedeboek,* which likely was printed in Danzig or for the Danzig congregation. Jacob Jacobsz (*q.v.*) was elected deacon of the Danzig Mennonite Church in 1606, minister in 1611, and elder in 1640, and died in 1648. In his article **Gesangbücher** (*ML* II, 88), Neff speaks of three editions of the *Pruys Liedt-boeck.* The first one, dated Alkmaer, 1604, by J. J., could be the edition quoted above; the second appeared at Alkmaer in 1607 by S. H., and the third one by H. v.D. (Danzig) without date. Unfortunately Neff does not give his source of information.

In his book, *Das Siedlungswerk Niederländischer Mennoniten im Weichseltal* (Marburg, 1952), Herbert Wiebe reproduces the title page of *Sommigh Leerachtige Gheestelijcke Liedekens* published at Haarlem by Hans Passchiers van Wesbusch in 1638.

876   HYMNOLOGY

A copy of this book was present at Montau. Further investigation, although most of the sources have been destroyed or are not accessible, would doubtless produce further evidence that the Prussian Mennonites used the hymnbooks of their Dutch home congregations from the early days of their settlement along the Vistula until the end of the 18th century. A thorough investigation of the hymnology and the role which singing played among the early Prussian Mennonites has never been made. (See the previous article, **Hymnology in the Netherlands**).

In 1724 the Prussian Mennonites ordered a print of *Veelderhande Schriftuurlijke Liedekens Gemaakt uyt het Oude en Nieuwe Testament, zoo als voor desen in Druk (in verscheyde Boeken) geweest zyn. Beneffens nog eenige, die voor deen nooit in Druk geweest zyn. Nu weer op een nieuw te samen gestelt, om in de vergaderinge der Gelovigen te zingen* (Amsterdam, 1724). In the preface the publishers state: "The reason which caused us to print this book is not that we do not have enough hymnbooks, but it is because of the convenience. Since various books had to be used it was inconvenient to carry them in a pocket." This would indicate that the Mennonites of Prussia at that time were using several hymnbooks and that they solved this problem and arrived at a unification by selecting from the various books those most frequently used, which they compiled in *Veelderhande Schriftuurlijke Liedekens*. Under this title (without the "Schriftuurlijke") Nicolaas Biestkens (*q.v.*) had published a hymnbook in 1560, numerous editions of which appeared in the century and a half following. In 1700 this hymnbook was published at Groningen by Berent Taeitsma, reduced to pocket size, many hymns having been dropped, while others never printed before were added. Some lines were adjusted to the music. The Prussian edition of 1724, printed at Amsterdam, was a reprint of this revised edition of 1700. A second edition was published at Amsterdam in 1752 for the Prussian Mennonites. The editors and publishers state in the preface that the edition of 1724 had been printed in haste, omitting the melody for a number of hymns, and that it was now exhausted. In the new edition they added some melodies in use in their surrounding German communities, omitted some hymns because the melodies were little known, and included other hymns in use, adding an appendix of 14 or 15 hymns. The hymns were arranged, not alphabetically as formerly, but according to topics. The edition consisted of 3,000 copies.

At the middle of the 18th century the change from the Dutch to the German language among the Danzig and Prussian Mennonites was nearly completed. The Dutch Biestkens Bible imported from Holland was replaced by the German Lutheran translation. In the Danzig Mennonite Church Record, 1667-1836, the change from the Dutch to the German language occurs in all entries consistently in 1784. The first German sermon was preached in the Danzig Mennonite Church in 1762, and by 1777 the change was almost complete (Mannhardt, 107). At this time the Dutch hymnbook was replaced by a German hymnal entitled *Geistreiches Gesangbuch, zur öffentlichen und besonderen Erbauung der Mennoniten Gemeinde in und vor der Stadt Danzig*

(Marienwerder, 1780). In the preface the elders, ministers, and deacons state that the book was to a large extent the work of the late Elder Hans van Steen, assisted by Peter Tiessen, Jacob de Veer, and Hans Momber, the latter two furnishing a considerable number of hymns which they had written. Few of the hymns of the Dutch hymnbooks in use, if any, were translated. The editors selected from non-Mennonite hymnals "songs which in doctrine agreed with our faith and if this was not the case they were altered or abbreviated" (*Foreword*, p. 3). The book consisted of 620 songs and index, an appendix with prayers and another appendix of hymns. J. J. Kanter, Marienwerder, printed 2,000 copies.

In 1851 the Danzig Mennonite Church decided to publish a new hymnbook, prepared by a commission of eight assisting the pastor J. Mannhardt and his ministerial assistant, H. A. Neufeldt. It appeared in 1854 printed by Edwin Groening, Danzig, entitled *Gesangbuch zur kirchlichen und häuslichen Erbauung. Für Mennoniten Gemeinden,* containing 703 hymns, an appendix of prayers, biographical sketches of the hymn writers, an index of the hymns, and selected Scripture passages. In 1908 a revised edition was prepared by the pastor of the congregation, H. G. Mannhârdt, who reduced the number of hymns from 703 to 445, of which approximately 100 were new. It appeared under the same title in 1908 at A. W. Kafemann, Danzig, and again in 1926. The appendix contained prayers and an index.

Even before the Danzig Mennonites published the German hymnal, the Prussian Mennonite congregations changed from Dutch to German, replacing the *Pruys Lied-Boeck* of 1752 by introducing the German *Geistreiches Gesangbuch, worinn eine Sammlung aus denen 150 Psalmen Davids, und auserlesenen alten und neuen Liedern zu finden ist, zur allgemeinen Erbauung und zum Lobe Gottes herausgegeben,* printed at Königsberg in 1767 (reprints 1775, 1784, 1794, 1803, 1819, 1829, 1835, 1838, 1843, and 1844, 1845, 1864). The fact that the Heubuden Mennonite Church in 1945 still had copies of the Dutch hymnal of 1752 indicates that the change from Dutch to German came so rapidly that they did not even wait until the old hymnbooks were worn out. In the preface to the German hymnal the editors state, "In order to satisfy the longing [for High German hymns] we have decided to publish the 150 Psalms in a well-known German version, as well as 500 spiritual songs. In this collection there are not only many known Dutch hymns translated into the German, but also many from the Halle, Stargard, Quandt, and Rogall hymnbooks, to which have been added some never printed before." The book contains 505 hymns and 150 Psalms.

Under the influence of the Dutch Reformed tradition the Mennonites of Holland and Prussia used rhymed Psalms for worship purposes. Hartwich (*Menn. Bl.,* April 1931, p. 31) reports that at the turn of the century Psalms were in use among the Mennonites of Prussia. They were Dutch in the version of Dathenus, which were later replaced by the Lobwasser German version of the Psalms. However, the use of the Psalms gradually disappeared, likely under the influences of the surrounding Lutheran population. The second edition of the above hymnal carried only those Psalms which were actually used at that time, but the editor still felt it necessary to apologize for not including all of them. This edition had a preface by G. W. and was printed by D. Chr. Kanter, Königsberg, 1775. The fifth edition (Marienwerder, 1803) has the changed title, *Gesangbuch worinn eine Sammlung alter und neuer Lieder zum gottesdienstlichen Gebrauch und zur allgemeinen Erbauung herausgegeben.* The editor, signing himself P. S., states that the remaining 58 Psalms had been dropped and that a third appendix of hymns was added, making a total of 545. The sixth edition (Marienwerder, 1819), with the preface signed by J. A., containing 550 hymns, adds another part (*Zweiter Theil*), making a total of 725 hymns. In the preface to the seventh edition (Elbing, 1829) J. W. states that the second part had been omitted (there are copies with it). In 1835 appeared a "Neue Auflage mit der Siebenten übereinstimmend," printed by Lohde at Thorn and Culm without preface, which also contains the *Zweiter Theil.* The eighth edition (Marienburg, 1838) reprints the preface to the first edition with a brief additional statement that this was requested, and omits the second part. The ninth edition (Elbing, 1843) retains the first preface, but adds again the *Zweiter Theil,* while a Graudenz edition of 1845, called "Achte Auflage," reprints the preface of the sixth edition without the *Zweiter Theil.* In 1864 the tenth edition appeared in Danzig printed by Edwin Groening, with a special preface stating that there was a plan under way to publish a new hymnbook, but since it was not ready and there was a need for some copies an edition of 1,000 was being printed. This was the last Prussian edition of the *Gesangbuch* which since 1818 (sixth ed.) carried the title, *Gesangbuch worin eine Sammlung geistreicher Lieder befindlich.*

The Mennonites of Russia had been using this *Gesangbuch* since their settlement in the Ukraine. In 1844 they reprinted it in Odessa, calling it the tenth edition and the first in Russia. They added the *Zweiter Theil,* reprinted the preface of the sixth and added their own, signed by B. F. It consisted of 3,000 copies. In 1854 a second edition appeared and in 1859 a third, both printed in Odessa. The preface of the latter states that a total of 15,400 copies had been printed in Russia since 1844. The fourth edition (Odessa, 1867) had a dedicatory poem instead of a special preface. It was followed by undated fifth and sixth editions printed in Leipzig, while the seventh, also undated and printed in Leipzig, was distributed by Jacob Lötkemann, Halbstadt.

At the time when the Mennonites of Russia were about ready to prepare another hymnal the immigrants of 1874 ff. from Russia to the prairie states and Manitoba took with them the old *Gesangbuch* which had originated in Prussia. The first American edition appeared in 1880, being marked as "Erste Amerikanische Ausgabe," which was followed by a second, a third (1889, when "worin" was dropped from the title), and further editions (1895, 1903, 1907, 1916, and 1918), all printed at Elkhart. The Old Colony Mennonites moving from Canada to Mexico reprinted it there at Cuauhtemoc, Chihuahua, in 1940 and 1943, with five editions, a total of 32,000 copies, at Scottdale (1926, 1937, 1944, 1949, 1954). This book is still the hymnal of the Old Colony and Sommerfelder groups in Canada and Mexico.

The bibliographical history of the *Geistreiches Gesangbuch,* tracing it back to its first appearance in the German form and its Dutch predecessor as *Veelderhande Liedekens* to the Reformation in Holland, has been sketched in the preceding paragraphs; however, the extent to which the content of the hymns and its theology and spirit were retained has not been investigated. It is apparent that the *Gesangbuch* deserves as much attention along these lines as the *Ausbund* of the Swiss tradition.

A special hymnbook commission of the General Conference of Mennonite congregations in Russia prepared a new book which appeared under the title *Gesangbuch zum gottesdienstlichen und häuslichen Gebrauch in den Mennoniten-Gemeinden Russlands,* printed by P. Neufeld, Neu-Halbstadt, 1892. The editors state that they have printed many of the hymns from the former *Gesangbuch,* but have added a considerable number. The total of hymns was 725. The next edition was printed in Odessa in 1896 and distributed by David Epp, Chortitza. The fourth edition was printed and published with a brief additional preface by Peter Neufeld, Halbstadt 1903, in a smaller format, and by H. Braun, Neu-Halbstadt 1904, in a larger format. The fifth edition appeared in 1914, published by A. J. Unruh, Tiege; H. Braun, Halbstadt; and H. Born, Chortitza, in an edition of a smaller format with a special preface. The Mennonites migrating to Canada after World War I reprinted the songbook in 1929 in Germany, without a preface, stating that this was the fifth edition.

By 1865 the Prussian Mennonites felt that their old *Gesangbuch* was not quite meeting the needs of the day. A special commission was charged with the responsibility of preparing a new hymnbook, which appeared at Danzig in 1869 under the title *Gesangbuch für Mennoniten-Gemeinden in Kirche und Haus.* The second edition (Danzig, 1873) followed without change. The book consisted of 700 hymns with the traditional collection of prayers and an index of hymns and melodies. The fourth edition (1901) with the special preface contained 35 additional religious folk songs and Psalms from the Prussian Mennonite *Choralbuch* which had been published in 1898. Forty new melodies were added in the enlarged edition. Its preface shows that the new *Gesangbuch* had not only found acceptance among the Mennonites of Prussia, but that it was also used in Russia and America. The first three editions consisted of 8,000 copies, the fourth and fifth (Elbing, 1922) of 6,000.

The chief compilers and distributors of Mennonite hymnbooks in Danzig, Prussia, Poland, and Russia were originally the congregation of Danzig and the congregations of West Prussia, the hymnal of the latter being the most widely used. The Mennonites of Poland and Austria seem never to have printed their own hymnal, but relied on the Prussian hymnbook, as the Mennonites of Russia had in the early days. The Mennonites of the Samara and Trakt settlements in Russia probably used either the Prussian or the Russian songbook; although there exists a collection of hymns under the title, *120 Kirchenlieder zum Gebrauch in mennonitischen Schulen* (Köppenthal, 1876), with ciphers, for use by the Mennonites of the Trakt settlement. As early as 1859 Elder David Hamm (*q.v.*) had a *Choral-Buch für den Kirchen-Gesang der Mennoniten-Gemeinde an der Wolga* printed in Danzig with ciphers, to be used in their congregational singing.

One of the best-known religious poets of the Mennonites of Russia was Bernhard Harder, whose *Geistliche Lieder und Gelegenheitsgedichte* were edited by Heinrich Franz, Sr., and published in 1880 (1,208 pp.), from which Peter Harder, a son of the author, selected some songs for a publication entitled *Kleines Liederbuch. Geistliche Gelegenheitslieder,* published by J. Friesen (Tiege, 1902.)

The Mennonite Brethren of Russia originally used T. Köbner's *Glaubensstimme,* the German Baptist hymnal. Since 1890 they also used *Heimatklänge,* and also *Frohe Botschaft* and *Evangeliumslieder,* both by E. Gebhardt, as well as the *Zionslieder* and others. *Heimatklänge,* first published in Russia for the Mennonites by Isaak Born at Halbstadt, was taken over in 1903 by the Raduga Publishing House of Halbstadt. Seven editions appeared in Russia, after which A. Kroeker published the eighth revised edition in America, in the year 1924, which was followed by a second one (1939?) with notes. In Russia as well as in Canada the three hymnals, *Heimatklänge, Glaubensstimme,* and *Frohe Botshaft,* were often bound together in one volume, mostly without notes. J. Ewert transcribed the notes of the melodies to Gebhardt's *Frohe Botschaft* into ciphers, which were published in *Die Melodien der Frohen Botschaft* (Gnadenfeld, 1884). Born published a monthly periodical with songs with notes for use in Mennonite homes and congregations.

In addition to the regular hymnals, from time to time other aids for singing have been in use in Mennonite congregations, homes, and communities. The *Choralbuch* (*q.v.,* first edition 1898 in West Prussia, reprinted in 1935) was in use in various forms by the Mennonites of Prussia, Russia, and America. The Bethel College Historical Library has many dozens of handwritten songbooks with ciphers which were used by the Mennonites of Russia and in the early days in America. Interestingly a little booklet of hymn texts was printed to accompany the appendix to the West Prussian *Choralbuch* of 1898, and was reprinted three times, 1903, 1922, 1929, with the title *Texte der geistlichen Volkslieder und Chorgesänge im Anhange dis Mennonitischen Choralbuchs,* with hymn texts numbered 703 to 742. Wilhelm Neufeld (and K.W.) edited *Choralbuch, dem neuen mennonitischen Gesangbuche entsprechend, zum Gebrauch in Kirche, Schule und Haus* (Neuhalbstadt, 1897).

In the days of persecution and martyrdom the experiences, faith, steadfastness, and suffering of the Anabaptists were recorded in the form of poems and found their way into early hymnals. This practice of recording the life, work, and faith of outstanding leaders was continued even in more peaceful times. Such a poem written at the close of a life would sometimes be sung as a hymn at the funeral. It has already been pointed out that the life of Giesbrecht Franssen was narrated in a song which was printed

in the Jacob Jacobsz *Liedeboek.* This practice was continued among the Mennonites of Prussia. For example, when Hans van Steen (*q.v.*), a well-known elder, died, his life and activities were commemorated in a song written for the occasion. Poems were sung to known melodies and were written for various anniversaries such as silver weddings, anniversaries of ministers, etc. Later in many cases familiar hymns were printed for the occasion. Numerous copies have been preserved in the Bethel College Historical Library. The West Prussian Mennonite congregations also had smaller songbooks for special occasions, for example: *Einige Trauungs- und Begräbniss-Gesänge von alten und neuen Liedern, die von mehreren Autoren zusammengesetzt und auf verchiedene Fälle zu einem gottgeheiligten Singen gewidmet sind* (Elbing, 1842), with 43 hymns; *Christliche Trauungs- und Begräbniss-Gesänge nebst Tisch und andern geistlichen Liedern. Zum Gebrauch in Mennoniten-gemeinden besonders derer in Preussen und Russland. Vermehrte und veränderte Auflage* (Danzig, 1888), with 83 hymns; *Lieder zum Gebrauch für Missionsgottesdienste* (Heubuden, 1896), with 85 hymns; *Sammlung christlicher Verlobungs-, Trauungs-, Jubliäums- und Begräbnis-Gesänge* (Elbing, 1908); and *Vierundneunzig Lieder für Missionsgottesdienste.* It is possible that many of them were in general use and not always specifically printed for the Mennonite congregations. They evidently were needed to fill in gaps in the standard hymnals. No comparable Mennonite publications appeared in America, but *Der Sänger am Grabe* (Philadelphia) was popular among the Franconia Mennonites through the second half of the 19th century.

"A Frequency List of Hymns in Mennonite Hymn Books" compiled by Walter H. Hohmann shows that the following hymns appear in at least 15 Mennonite hymnbooks out of 24 including all German hymnals in Europe and North America. This gives us an indication as to which of the hymns have been most commonly used among the Mennonites in various countries in a period of over two centuries. They are "Ach bleib' mit Deiner Gnade"; "Allein Gott in der Höh' sei Ehr'"; "Aus tiefer Not schrei' ich zu Dir"; "Befiehl du deine Wege"; "Es ist gewisslich an der Zeit"; "Gott des Himmels und der Erden"; "Herr Jesu Christ, Dich zu uns wend'"; "Komm, o komm, Du Geist"; "Liebster Jesu, wir sind hier"; "Lobe den Herren, den mächtigen König"; "Mache dich, mein Geist, bereit"; "Mir nach, spricht Christus, unser Held"; "Nun danket alle Gott"; "Wachet auf, ruft uns die Stimme"; "Was Gott tut, das ist wohlgetan"; "Werde munter, mein Gemüte"; "Wie schön leucht't uns der Morgenstern" (*Outlines in Hymnology,* 53 ff.).

The hymnbooks of the Prusso-Russian tradition were originally mostly without notes or ciphers and the melodies were transmitted from generation to generation by tradition. The introduction of notes and ciphers came at the beginning of the past century when individuals and groups began to copy melody books for use in home and choir singing. This led to the publishing of special choralbooks for use in school, at home, and in congregational singing. In Prussia the tunes were transcribed by means of the commonly used notes, while in Russia a certain cipher system was in use. The origin of both and their relationship in Mennonite use have not been investigated.

Four-part singing in Mennonite congregations is also of a rather recent date. It started with the introduction of hand-copied collections of songs with notes and ciphers and the publication of the choralbooks (see *Choralbuch*). Four-part singing in congregations was gradually introduced through choirs (*q.v.*), which were first school or community choirs and gradually found their place in the congregational worship. Just as in the case of the use of the musical instruments in Mennonite worship this innovation was not accepted without resistance. Now four-part congregational singing is accepted in all Mennonite congregations except the older conservative groups such as the Old Colony Mennonites.

This is a brief summary of the hymnbooks that have been compiled and used by the Mennonites in Prussia and Russia. No study has been made of the selective process when a new hymnal was to be produced or of the change in the spiritual and theological content of the hymns that has taken place through the centuries. There is possibly no other record that would lend itself as well to a study of the theological influences which the Mennonites have undergone and the views which they have held as the hymnals collected in our historical libraries. They reflect accurately, second only to the devotional books used, the source of their spiritual nourishment. Another valuable research project would be the effect of the change from one language to another upon the spiritual life of the Mennonites as it took place in Prussia and later in America.   C.K.

H. G. Mannhardt, *Die Danziger Mennonitengemeinden* (Danzig, 1919); Wolkan, *Lieder* (Berlin, 1903); H. P. Krehbiel, *History of the General Conference of the Mennonites of North America* I, 155, 174-79; II, 176, 391; Lester Hostetler, *Handbook to the Mennonite Hymnary* (Newton, 1949); Bruno Ewert, "Geschichtliches aus der Mennonitengemeinde Heubuden-Marienburg," *Gem.-Kal.,* 1940, 48, F. C. Wieder, *De Schriftuurlijke Liedekens* (The Hague, 1900); A. Driedger, "Die Entwicklung des Gemeindegesanges in unsern westpreussischen Gemeinden," *Menn. Bl.* (January 1931) 30; S. Cramer, "Bijdragen tot de geschiedenis van ons kerklied en ons kerkgezang," *DB* 1900, 71; *Catalogus Amst.; Danzig Church Record,* 1667-1836; Kühler, *Geschiedenis* II, 117 ff.; R. Jacobsen, *Carel van Mander (1548-1606), Dichter en Prozaschrijver* (Rotterdam, 1906); Herbert Wiebe, *Das Siedlungswerk Niederländischer Mennoniten im Weichseltal* (Marburg, 1952); G. Kalff, *Gesch. der Nederl. Letterkunde* III, 387-413; W. H. Hohmann, *Outlines in Hymnology with Emphasis on Mennonite Hymnology* (1941); *ML* II, 86-91, 652 f.

Hymnology of the American Mennonites.

A. THE MENNONITE CHURCH (MC), INCLUDING THE AMISH. (1) *German Hymnals.* The Early Swiss and Palatine Mennonite immigrants to Pennsylvania brought with them the ancient Swiss Mennonite hymnal, the *Ausbund* (*q.v.*), first published in 1564 in Switzerland. This book was in common use in the early days. An American edition of the book was soon needed, and was the first Mennonite book published in America for Mennonite use. It was published by Saur at Germantown in 1742, and again in 1751, 1767, and 1785. At Lancaster, Pa., it was first published in 1815, reappearing there a total of eight times, last in 1912. Further editions were published

by the Old Order Amish congregations of Lancaster County with the place given as "Lancaster County" in 1935, 1941, 1949, 1952, with an edition at Kutztown, Pa., in 1922. John F. Funk published editions at Elkhart in 1880, 1905, and 1913, obviously for the Amish of the Midwest. The *Ausbund* went out of use in Mennonite congregations early in the 19th century; since that time it has been used almost exclusively by the Old Order Amish congregations of Pennsylvania and west. The Alsatian, Bavarian, and Hessian Amish who settled in Ohio, Ontario, and Illinois from 1824 on brought the *Ausbund* with them (last European edition at Basel in 1838) and may also have purchased some of the Lancaster editions.

The American editions of the *Ausbund* all carry significant additional materials beyond the European editions as follows: a total of 140 hymns rather than 137, an index of hymns by first lines, an index of hymns which can be sung to the same tune, the *Confessio, Oder Bekantnuss* of Thomas von Imbroich (19 pp.), *Ein warhafftiger Bericht, von den Brüdern im Schweitzerland in dem Zürcher Gebiet, wegen der Trübsalen welche über sie ergangen seyn um des Evangeliums willen* (38 pp.), and an appendix called *Anhang von fünff schönen geistlichen Liedern* (40 pp.), first added in 1767, but becoming "sechs" (six) hymns in 1785.

Even before the Revolutionary War, the Mennonite congregations began to use other hymnbooks, particularly one of the Reformed Church, which was called *Ambrosii Lobwasser's Neu-Vermehrtes Gesangbuch* and was popular among the Mennonites in Switzerland in the 18th and early 19th centuries. The first American edition was published at Germantown in 1753, a second edition in 1763. A number of clean, unused copies of the 1763 edition of this Reformed hymnbook were found by the author in the attic of the Groffdale Mennonite Church in Lancaster County, in 1925, mute evidence of their early use there. That various non-Mennonite hymnbooks, in particular the Reformed, as well as the old *Ausbund,* were used in Pennsylvania as late as the turn of the 19th century is indicated by a letter written in 1821 by Deacon Martin Mellinger to relatives in Germany (*MQR* 1931, 57 ff.), which tells about the conditions leading to the preparation and publication of an official Lancaster Mennonite hymnbook in 1803-4. Mellinger says: "And now I want to tell you how it went when the first book was to be printed. Since we had all sorts of hymnbooks, the old Swiss songbooks [*Ausbund*] and Reformed hymnbooks [Lobwasser], and not enough of what we had, our brethren decided to have a hymnbook printed for ourselves. Brethren and choristers were to select beautiful and fitting hymns, after which they were to be collected and given over to three, four, or five men. These men were to select enough of the hymns which had been collected so that the hymnbook would not be too large. After a time two Skippack brethren [Franconia Conference] came together with two of our leading bishops in my house to examine the hymns which had been collected. The Skippack brethren, since they have a large and strong church as well as a large district and are well trained in singing, had collected enough hymns for a complete hymnbook and had taken 3,000 subscriptions in advance. We also had many hymns from Virginia, from Jacob's Creek [Westmoreland Co., Pa.], and from our vicinity, which were to go into the book. So it was feared that the book would become too large. In addition our brethren wanted to include a number of psalms and notes. In short, the difference was so great that the Skippack brethren said that their hymns had been handed in by so many brethren and dared not be omitted, and so many had already subscribed, and there was a lengthy discussion. The second day the Skippack brethren said that they were only delegates, and they saw no other way than to have their book [*Die Kleine Geistliche Harfe,* 1803] printed in Germantown where they had a good printer and bookbinder, which was so handy for them that they could look after everything, and we could print ours [*Ein Unpartheyisches Gesangbuch,* 1804] in Lancaster. And so the outcome was that they had as many printed as we. But that made no difference to us or them, for we love one another, and we visit them and they visit us every year. And still it is a pity that it had to be so. For many years many families have been moving to Virginia, Jacob's Creek, and Canada, and each has his hymnbook and then they have different hymnbooks when they come together. Although you will doubtless know most of the hymns in the books, you will probably find many beautiful and valuable hymns especially in the last appendix, which are unfamiliar to you and have never yet appeared in print" (*MQR* V, 1931, 56 f.). Actually, 56 per cent of the Lancaster hymns appear in the Franconia hymnal, while 48 per cent of the hymns of the larger Franconia hymnal appear in the Lancaster hymnal.

The first original Mennonite hymnbook edited and published in America was the Franconia Conference hymnal, *Die Kleine Geistliche Harfe der Kinder Zions* (Germantown 1803, 472 pp., further editions as follows: Germantown 1811 and 1820, Northampton 1834, Doylestown 1838, Lancaster 1870, Elkhart 1904). It had 40 select Psalms in a first section, followed by 474 hymns (475 from the second edition on) in a second section under a new title, *Sammlung alter und neuer Geistreicher Gesänge.* An appendix of 20 hymns, added in the second edition, grew to 34 hymns by 1870. It had no imitators or condensations as did the Lancaster hymnal. However, when the *Church Hymnal, Mennonite,* was published in 1927 a special edition was furnished with a German appendix of 135 hymns (56 pp.) chosen from the *Harfe* by Bishop Abram G. Clemmer of the Franconia Conference. As late as 1952 1,000 copies of this German appendix were printed and bound in with the *Hymnal* for Franconia use.

The first edition of the Lancaster Conference hymnal, called *Ein Unpartheyisches Gesangbuch* (the word *Ein* was dropped after the second edition), was published at Lancaster in 1804 as a good-sized book of 511 pages. It contained two parts: first 62 select Psalms set to music; second a selection of 390 hymns with a new title page, *Ein Neues, Unpartheyisches Gesangbuch zum allgemeinen Gebrauch des wahren Gottesdienstes. Auf Begehren der Brüderschaft der Mennonisten Gemeinen, aus vielen Liederbüchern gesammelt mit einem dreyfachen Register versehen.*

Later editions added numerous additional hymns in the form of three appendices (1808, first appendix, 35 hymns; 1820, second appendix, 32 hymns; 1829, third appendix, 14 hymns). The compiling committee states that several were selected from the martyr hymns of the earlier church hymnal, meaning the *Ausbund;* actually 64 hymns (45 per cent of the *Ausbund* total) were taken from it, amounting to 17 per cent of the 390 basic hymns in the book. It was apparently the only Mennonite hymnal, European or American, which took over any substantial number of the hymns of the *Ausbund*). This hymnal went through 14 more editions 1808-87, all at Lancaster with a late edition in 1903 at the same place. Mellinger states that the earlier editions were for 4,000 copies each. The hymnal was published again in 1923 and 1941 in a special edition for the Old Order Amish and other branches in Lancaster County which still use the book. It also seems to have been used in Southwestern Pennsylvania, in Ontario, and in Virginia, at least for a time.

In 1839 a condensed version of the Lancaster hymnal, containing 102 of its hymns, small format, was published at Canton, Ohio, printed by "Peter Kaufmann and Co.," under the title *Ein Unpartheyisches Gesang-Buch, zum allgemeinen Gebrauch des Wahren Gottesdienstes,* probably for the newly established Mennonite congregations in Eastern Ohio. The *Gemeinschaftliche Liedersammlung* (Berlin, Ont., 1836), most likely edited by Benjamin Eby (*q.v.*), also small format, took two thirds of its 205 hymns from the Lancaster hymnal and most of the rest from the Franconia *Kleine Geistliche Harfe,* omitting many stanzas. It was reprinted eight times at Berlin (Kitchener) (1838, 1841, 1849, 1857, 1883, 1892, 1908, 1918), twice at Lancaster (1860, 1870), and once at Scottdale (1950). In 1860 another condensation of the Lancaster *Unpartheyisches Gesangbuch* with 152 hymns was printed by John Baer's Sons in Lancaster "for the publisher" under the title, *Eine Unpartheiische Liedersammlung,* small format, which was reprinted eight times by Baer's (1864, 1867, 1870, 1876, 1886, 1891, 1900, 1905), twice at Elkhart (1911, 1929), and eight times at Scottdale 1917, 1924, 1929, 1936, 1941, 1942, 1945, 1954). It is still used by the Old Order Mennonites of Lancaster County and the Old Order Amish ("das dünne Büchlein," in contrast to the *Ausbund,* "das dicke Buch"). This hymnal was published in a revised larger edition with 309 hymns, still small format, by S. D. Guengerich (*q.v.*), an Old Order Amish layman of Amish, Iowa, in 1892 (printed at Elkhart), which used somewhat less than half of the hymns of the older book, with many other hymns, but carried the same title with the addition, "Revidiert und vermehrt" (revised and enlarged). It was reprinted twice at Elkhart (1907, 1916), twice at Arthur, Ill. (1928, 1940), and once at Scottdale (1954). It has been used exclusively by the Old Order Amish in the Midwest and is still used in some places. Sometime before 1929 Guengerich published a 16-page booklet of 12 selections from it entitled *Etliche Schöne Lieder.* The *Unparteiisches Liederbuch* of the Church of God in Christ, Mennonite (Elkhart, 1906, Scottdale, 1915), small format, 353 hymns, has no connection with any of the above hymnals.

Three additional German hymnbooks of the Mennonite Church (MC) deserve notice. John F. Funk published in 1871 at Elkhart (later editions 1877, 1880, 1883, 1885, 1889) *Die allgemeine Lieder-Sammlung zum privat und öffentlichen Gottes-Dienst mit Fleiss zusammengetragen*. It had 329 hymns (2nd ed., 330) and an English Appendix of 23 hymns (1880 ed., 44 hymns). A German appendix of 19 hymns (*Anhang*) was added in 1877. This same hymnal was published in 1901 at Belleville, Pa., under the title *Eine Sammlung von Schöne Lieder zum Gebrauch bei dem Gottesdienst,* evidently for the Amish Mennonites of this community. It was reprinted in 1912 at Scottdale (*Eine Sammlung von Schönen Liedern*) and again in 1931, "With an appendix arranged and enlarged by a committee of the Amish Mennonite Church [tr. from the German] H. S. Yoder, C. W. Bender, J. B. Miller," all of the Conservative Amish Church near Grantsville, Md. The appendix contained German hymns numbered 331-80 (copyright by J. B. Miller) and the English appendix of 44 hymns of the *Allgemeine Liedersammlung,* edition of 1880. *Deutsches Lieder-und Melodienbuch mit einem Anhang englischer Lieder zum Gebrauch in der Gemeinde, der Sonntagschule und dem Familienkreis* (Elkhart, 1895, reprint Scottdale, 1926) was edited by a committee composed of J. S. Hartzler, C. Z. Yoder, J. S. Coffman, John Horsch, A. B. Kolb, W. P. Coffman, and John F. Funk. The preface states that it was published at the request of several conferences. It was the last of the German hymnals of the Mennonite Church (MC). Its English appendix reprinted the 457 hymns of the *Hymns and Tunes* (1890).

In 1855 Samuel K. Cassel edited and published at Skippackville, Pa. (Franconia Conference district), *Der Christliche Sänger, eine Sammlung der vornehmsten und gebräuchlichsten Lieder zum Gebrauch des öffentlichen und privat Gottesdienstes für alle heilsuchende Seelen jeder Christlichen Benennung,* small format, with 228 hymns. The family of Abraham A. Meyer (d. 1877) published after his death *Christliche Lieder gedichtet und zum Theil gesammelt von Abraham A. Meyer an der Deep Run in Bedminster Taunschip, Bucks County, Pa.* (Milford Square, 1877), small format, with 46 hymns, 28 by the author. The executors of Daniel Kreider published after his death *Hinterlassene Lieder-Sammlung* (Lancaster, 1865) with 13 original hymns, small format. George Funk, of Bowling Green, Clay Co., Ind., published *The Little Hymn Book, A Selection of Hymns from Different Authors* (n.d., 1864), with 23 hymns, small format. None of these four hymnals was of any historical consequence.

All of the above hymnals were without notes, except the *Deutsches Lieder- und Melodienbuch,* since the Mennonites and Amish up to the end of the 19th century generally (with increasing exceptions) sang one-part music only, and objected to published notes in their regular church hymnals. The only exception was a few tunes for the Psalms in the Franconia and Lancaster hymnals. All singing in church was a cappella, of course, since musical instruments in the church services were forbidden.

(2) *English Hymnals.* The English hymnals of the Mennonite Church (MC) began with a small format book published at Harrisonburg, Va., in 1847, entitled *A Selection of Psalms, Hymns, and Spiritual Songs. From the Most Approved Authors, Suited to the Various Occasions of Public Worship and Private Devotion of the Church of Christ by a Committee of Mennonites* [Joseph Funk, David Hartman, Joseph Wenger], with 363 hymns. It was reprinted by Joseph Funk at Singers Glen (*q.v.*), Va., six times (1851, 1855, 1859, 1868, 1872, 1877) at Lancaster four times (1862, 1864, 1869, 1875), at Elkhart three times (1880, 1882, 1884), and at Scottdale in 1948. In 1851 the title was changed from *A Selection* to *A Collection* and the number of hymns increased to 402, with a German appendix of 27 hymns, which grew to 37 in 1855, and changed to an English appendix of 48 hymns in 1875. This was the only English hymnal of the church until 1890, when *Hymns and Tunes* appeared at Elkhart. Joseph Funk's *Harmonia Sacra* (first published in 1816 as *Die allgemein nützliche Choral-Music* at Harrisonburg, Va., then in 1832 in English as *A Compilation of Genuine Church Music,* called *Harmonia Sacra* with the fifth edition in 1851) did not become a regular church hymnal, since it was in the long (horizontal) singing-school format and had three-part harmonizations (four-part harmonizations introduced by 1871). It did, however, furnish many of the tunes for the little English hymnal and was very popular. Called the *New Harmonia Sacra* in its 15th edition (1876), it is still being printed (21st edition 1952). A similar book was the *Philharmonia* compiled by M. D. Wenger and published at Elkhart in 1875 (reprint in 1881) under a double title in English and German: *The Philharmonia, a collection of Tunes, Adapted to public and private worship, containing tunes for all the hymns in the English Mennonite Hymn Book, the Gemeinschaftliche, Unparteiische and Allgemeine Liedersammlungen, the Unparteiische Gesangbuch, and the Mennonitische Gesangbuch, with Instructions and Explanations in English and German, also English and German Texts to most of the Tunes, Metrical Indexes, etc., including a greater variety of Meters of Church Music than any other work of the Kind now Published. Compiled by Martin D. Wenger.* (The "all" in this title was an overstatement.) An English Sunday-school hymnal, prepared by C. H. Brunk of Virginia, published at Elkhart in 1883 (reprints 1884, 1888) under the title *Bible School Hymns and Sacred Songs for Sunday Schools and Other Religious Services,* 40 pp., was really a hymnal for children. A similar book, *The Christian Harp and Sabbath School Songster, designed for the use of the Social Religious Circle, Revivals and the Sabbath School,* published in 1866 jointly by Ruebush & Kieffer of Singers Glen, Va., and H. B. Brenneman of Bremen, Ohio (printed by Joseph Funk's Sons at Singers Glen), has also been attributed to C. H. Brunk (*Menn. Cycl. Dict.,* 44).

The first American Mennonite hymnal with printed tunes (for about one half of the hymns) was *Hymns and Tunes for Public and Private Worship, and Sunday Schools Compiled by a Committee* [H. S. Rupp, Samuel Shank, Emanuel Suter, C. H. Brunk, J. S. Coffman] (Elkhart, 1890), with 457 hymns and 216 tunes, sponsored by the Virginia and Indiana Mennonite Conferences. It was a transition hymnal between the German and the English books, especially in the Franconia and Lancaster Conferences, but was displaced in turn by the *Church and Sunday School Hymnal* of 1902.

The fully official English hymnbook of the Mennonite Church (MC) began in 1902 with the *Church and Sunday School Hymnal, A Collection of Hymns and Sacred Songs, Appropriate for Church Services, Sunday Schools, and General Devotional Exercises. Compiled and Published under the Direction of a Committee appointed by Mennonite Conferences* (Elkhart, Ind., and Freeport, Ill., 1902) with 412 hymns and a German appendix of 50 hymns. It also appeared in a word edition without music. It was reprinted at Scottdale in 1911 and 1926 and a number of times since, and in 1911 given a supplement (*Church and Sunday School Hymnal Supplement*), which increased the number of hymns to 532. (*Selections from Church and Sunday School Hymnal* was issued at Scottdale in 1911.) It was finally replaced in 1927 by *Church Hymnal, Mennonite, A Collection of Hymns and Sacred Songs, Suitable for Use in Public Worship, Worship in the Home, and all General Occasions, J. D. Brunk, Musical Editor, S. F. Coffman, Hymn Editor, Published by approval of Mennonite General Conference, First Edition Fifteenth Thousand. Printed in Both Shaped and Round Notes* (Scottdale, 1927). This standard hymnal, with 657 hymns, has gone through thirteen editions, with a total of 120,000 copies issued to 1956. However, the *Church and Sunday School Hymnal* of 1902 continues to be reprinted and enjoys a substantial patronage, with probably 80 per cent of the sales of the *Church Hymnal* of 1927; from 1925 to 1954, 73,000 were printed. *Select Hymns and Gospel Songs Taken from the Church Hymnal for Use in Conferences and Special Meetings*, with 77 hymns, appeared first in 1929, was issued in an enlarged edition with 132 hymns in 1934, and reached its final form in 1953 with 138 hymns, with the title *Selections from Church Hymnal for Use in Conference, Special Meetings*, with a total printing of 20,000.

To meet the demand for somewhat lighter music for Sunday-school use, the Mennonite Publishing House, using manuscript delivered by the Music Committee of the Mennonite General Conference, has published the following songbooks: *Life Songs* (1916) with 271 hymns and *Life Songs No. 2* (1938) with 343 hymns, both books edited by S. F. Coffman, and *Songs of the Church* (1953) with 274 hymns, edited by Walter Yoder. The latter book contains numerous chorales and is definitely of a higher type than *Life Songs. Selections from Life Songs No. 2* was issued in 1943 with 122 numbers. *Sheet Music of Heaven*, compiled by C. F. Derstine, published by the compiler, was printed at Scottdale in 1925 and 1926, with 300 hymns as a Sunday-school type of book, and reached a total of 10,000 copies printed. *Life Songs* appeared in five editions in 1916-30 with *ca.* 20,000 copies, *Life Songs No. 2* in eleven editions, 1938-50, with 96,000 copies, and *Songs of the Church* in one edition with 15,000 copies.

Three hymnbooks for children have been published at Scottdale: *Children's Hymns and Songs* in 1924, with 143 hymns (no tunes), not officially sponsored; *Songs of Cheer for Children, A Collection of Hymns and Songs Suitable for use in the Primary and Junior departments of our Sunday Schools, Authorized by Mennonite General Conference, Compiled by Music Committee* (1929), with 155 hymns (152 tunes); and *Junior Hymns for Juniors in Church, Sunday School, and Summer Bible School* (1947) with 157 hymns and 146 three-part tunes, edited by Walter Yoder. *Songs of Cheer* has had seven printings with a total of 41,000 copies.

No careful study has yet been made of the sources of the hymn selections in either the German or English hymnals of the Mennonite Church (MC). However, it is clear that the English hymnals contain almost exclusively standard English and American hymns, supplemented by the American Gospel songs of the late 19th (with considerable influence from Ira D. Sankey's *Gospel Songs* Nos. 1-5) and early 20th centuries. Very few hymns have been contributed by Mennonite writers. Unfortunately very few of the standard German chorales have found their way into the English hymnals, in contrast to the hymnals of the General Conference Mennonite Church and the Mennonite Brethren Church, although good translations have been available.

In a class by itself is *Amische Lieder*, written and compiled by Joseph W. Yoder (published by the Yoder Publishing Company, Huntingdon, Pa., n.d., 1942). This book contains 114 pages, with 97 hymns, 38 of which are taken from the *Ausbund* (in each case 3 stanzas only) and set to its historic tune (one part only) which Yoder wrote down from actual singing by an Amish song leader. The remaining 59 hymns are taken from what Yoder calls the "Dine Bückley" (thin book), the *Unparteiische Liedersammlung*, which is also used in certain Amish services and sung with "faster tunes," also not printed in the book, and for which Yoder has transcribed the music. Yoder's avowed purpose is to help the Amish to conserve their hymn tunes and to contribute toward uniformity in the various Amish communities. A 14-page section, "Rudiments," closes the book.

B. THE GENERAL CONFERENCE MENNONITE CHURCH (1) *German Hymnals.* The first hymnal of this group, the *Gesangbuch zum Gottesdienstlichen und Häuslichen Gebrauch in Mennoniten Gemeinden* (Philadelphia, 1873), was a republication of the hymnal of the South German Mennonites of 1856 (with the word "Evangelisch" dropped from the title), with its 600 hymns, but without 30 pages of prayers, and with the addition of an appendix of 22 hymns apparently chosen by the committee which the conference had commissioned to prepare a hymnal. It was reprinted in a "second improved edition" at Berne in 1885 with exactly the same content. Meanwhile those congregations in the General Conference which had come from Russia (1874 ff.) continued to use for some time the *Gesangbuch in Welchem eine Sammlung geistreicher Lieder befindlich, zur allgemeinen Erbauung und zum Lobe Gottes*, which they had used in Russia and which was reprinted in Elkhart, first in 1880 and seven times later (—, 1889, 1895, 1903, 1907, 1916, 1918), at Scottdale five times (1926, 1937, 1944, 1949, 1954, total 31,800 copies), and at least twice in Mexico (1940, 1943); and is still in use among the most conservative Mennonites in Canada and in Mexico. The General Conference successfully sought to unite, in church music, its eastern and western wings in the United States by issuing with notes a revised edition of the 1873-85 *Gesangbuch* under the title *Gesangbuch mit Noten* (Berne, 1890) with 600 hymns, of which it had only about half in common with the book of 1873, although it used all the 24 categories of the table of contents of that book. A total of some 50,000 copies of this popular book were distributed in its 15 editions (1890 twice, 1893, 1896, 1898, 1901, 1906, 1908, 1911, 1913, 1914, 1920 [?], 1925, 1927, 1936) and an edition of 1906 by the Mennonite Publishing Company at Elkhart, Ind., for the Amish churches. It was replaced, for the German-speaking congregations, in 1942 by the *Gesangbuch der Mennoniten* (Rosthern, Sask., 1942) with 550 hymns, prepared by a special hymnal commission of the Canadian Conference, but published by the General Conference, which was reprinted in 1944, 1947, and 1949, for a total of 20,000 copies. An appendix, *Anhang zum Gesangbuch*, with 60 additional hymns was published, which led to an edition of the main hymnal called *Ausgabe mit Anhang* (third edition, Newton, 1953). The appendix (*Anhang*) could also be purchased separately.

A selection of 132 hymns from the *Gesangbuch mit Noten* was published in 1892 at Berne by the Christliche Central Buchhandlung, Welty & Sprunger, under the title *Evangelisations-Lieder aus dem Gesangbuch mit Noten, geeignet für Schulen, Bet- und Bibelstunden, u.s.w.*

The *Choralbuch* of Heinrich Franz (Leipzig, 1860, 1880) was reprinted for the Mennonites of Manitoba four times (Elkhart 1878, 1918, and twice in Manitoba). It was further reprinted in condensed form by a group of four men from the Chortitz Mennonite congregation at Steinbach, Man. In 1935 a special *Choralbuch* was published by a commission appointed by the Ministers' Conference of the Conference of Mennonites in Canada. It bore the title *Choralbuch in vierstimmigem Tonsatz zum Gebrauch in Kirche, Schule und Haus der Mennonitengemeinden,* and contained two or three stanzas of 250 hymns with four-part music (ciphers).

Not to be overlooked is the *Kleiner Liederschatz für die Schule und den Familienkreis. Gesammelt und geordnet von einigen Lehrern und Schulfreunden in Kansas* (Newton, Schulverlag von Bethel College, 1901), reprints at Newton 1914 and 1928, with 126 songs. It was copyrighted "by David Goerz, in trust for the Western District Conference of the Mennonite Church of America." The Herald Publishing Company published the editions of 1914 and 1928. A similar booklet of 80 pages is *Der Kleine Sänger* (6th ed., Altona, Man., D. W. Friesen & Sons, 1947).

Meanwhile the *Gesangbuch zum gottesdienstlichen und häuslichen Gebrauch in den Mennoniten-Gemeinden Russlands* (first ed., Odessa, 1842) with its 725 hymns was reprinted in Germany in 1929 for the newer Canadian immigrants from Russia, with the title changed to substitute "Canada" for "Russland" (called erroneously "Fifth Edition").

J. A. Sprunger, formerly a minister in the Mennonite Church of Berne, Ind., after about 1898 a minister in the Missionary Church Association, edited, with H. J. Dyck, a Mennonite minister from Kansas associated with him in orphanage work at Birmingham, Ohio, *Himmels-Harfe für Sonntag-Schulen, Jugendvereine und Evangelisations-Versammlungen* at Birmingham in 1907, with 178 hymns, published by the Light and Hope Publishing Co., a publishing agency created by and largely owned by Sprunger.

(2) *English Hymnals.* The need for an English hymnal in the General Conference Mennonite Church was met by three successive books: (1) *Mennonite Hymnal, Blending of Many Voices, Prepared and Arranged for Use in the Mennonite Churches of the General Conference of North America* (Berne, 1894 and 1905) with 560 hymns; (2) *Mennonite Hymn Book* (Berne, 1927, 1928, and 1929) with 412 hymns, and (3) *The Mennonite Hymnary* (Berne and Newton, n.d., 1940) with 623 hymns. The first was, in spite of the assertion on the title page, only a reprint of the hymnal *Many Voices,* published by the non-Mennonite A. S. Barnes Co. in 1891. The *Mennonite Hymn Book* was the first English compilation by General Conference editors (leading members on the editorial committee were G. A. Lehman, A. D. Schmutz, and W. H. Hohmann), but it never became popular, less than 5,000 copies being sold of the three editions. *A Selection of Songs Taken from the Mennonite Hymn Book* (1929) with 69 hymns was donated to the General Conference session of 1929 by the Berne Witness Co. in an edition of 1,500. A new edition of this *Selection,* but with only 56 hymns, was printed in 1935. More popular was *Treasure Songs for Schools and Churches, Compiled for General Use in All Religious Services,* corresponding to the *Kleiner Liederschatz* of 1901. It was sponsored by the Western District Conference, but published by the Herald Publishing Company at Newton in 1937, in an edition of 2,000 copies. Intended as a supplement to the *Mennonite Hymn Book,* with a lighter type of music, it had 290 hymns including many children's choruses. A selection of 45 hymns of the book was published in 1936 (*sic!*), prepared by the Committee on Schools and Education of the Western District Conference, under the title, *Selected Songs from the New Song Book.* The committee which edited the *Treasure Songs* was composed of P. P. Buller, P. R. Voth, P. J. Wedel, and J. R. Thierstein.

The Mennonite Hymnary of 1940, edited by W. H. Hohmann and Lester Hostetler, was an outstanding success, selling 37,000 copies in nine editions up to 1955. Although all the General Conference hymnals have expressed the desire to carry on the tradition of the German hymn as one of their purposes, the *Hymnary* is most successful in this purpose, with 104 German hymn tunes, 58 of which are classified as chorales. Besides the standard English and American hymns the book has an important section of 26 Psalms and Psalm tunes, and also a good selection of 68 of the better Gospel songs. Although it began as a revision of the *Mennonite Hymn Book,* the *Hymnary* turned out to be a new compilation (about 63 per cent of the *Hymn Book* was taken over, constituting 41 per cent of the *Hymnary*). Lester Hostetler also edited *101 Hymns from the Mennonite*

Hymnary, with actually 113 hymns, in 1947 (2nd ed. 1953). His *Handbook to the Mennonite Hymnary* (Newton, 1949, pp. 425) "seeks to explain, as far as possible, the origin of the words and music of every hymn in the *Hymnary.*" "Without a doubt, the *Mennonite Hymnary* is the best hymnal that the General Conference Mennonites or any other Mennonite conference has published" (Wohlgemuth). It has had great influence on the General Conference Church. *The Mennonite Retreater* was a camp hymnal with 121 hymns, published specifically for use at Camp Wood, Kan., in July 1939.

In 1956 *The Youth Hymnary,* also edited by Lester Hostetler, with 303 hymns, was published at Newton.

C. THE MENNONITE BRETHREN CHURCH. Since this body is wholly of Russian origin, having immigrated to the United States in 1874 ff. and, with a much larger number of immigrants, into Canada in 1922 ff., it has until recently used the German books it brought from Russia, or reprinted in North America, or the songbooks of other related groups, chiefly of the Gospel song type. The first book used in Russia was the *Glaubensstimme,* the songbook of the German Baptists. This was reprinted in 1905 at Medford, Okla., by the M.B. Publishing House, edited by H. W. Grage, under the title *Zions-Glaubensstimme,* with 512 hymns with music. The *Heimatklänge,* by E. Gebhardt, published in seven editions in Russia, was republished twice in America, in a revised edition at Mountain Lake, Minn., in 1924 (?) by A. Kroeker, and in 1939 (?) at Winnipeg. Both in Russia and in America a popular combination was the *Drei-Band* (three volumes) *Heimatklänge-Glaubensstimme-Frohe Botschaft,* all of non-M.B. origin. The Mennonite Brethren Publishing House at Hillsboro, Kan., published the *Sänger-Bote* in at least five editions, *Zions-Klänge* and *Neue Zions-Lieder* (1919) by J. J. Franz and D. B. Towner, and printed A. G. Sawatzky's *Lieder-Quelle für Kirche und Haus,* which appeared quarterly in 1929-30. The *Sängerbote* was a periodical publication of an M.B. Association of Singers (*Christlicher Sängerbund der Mennoniten Brüdergemeinde von Nord Amerika*) beginning in 1912. *Young People's Sacred Songs,* edited by H. C. Richert, also published by the M.B. Publishing House at Hillsboro (1935), is really a collection of 25 numbers of the Gospel song type, partly for special groups, only 15 being of the hymn type for mixed voices.

The first official conference hymnals of the Mennonite Brethren Church of North America, and the only ones to date, are: the *Mennonite Brethren Church Hymnal, A Treasury of Hymns and Gospel Songs Compiled, Edited and Published by the Mennonite Brethren Hymnal Committee . . . Music* Editor, Herbert C. Richert (Hillsboro, n.d., 1953), with 500 hymns; and the *Gesangbuch der Mennoniten Brüdergemeinde Herausgegeben im Auftrage der Bundeskonferenz ausgewählt und zusammengestellt von dem Gesangbuchkomitee der Kanadischen Konferenz* . . . (n.p., n.d., Winnipeg, 1953, with 4th edition in 1955) with 555 hymns. The English hymnal is composed largely of hymns of the Gospel song type of English and American origin; only 34 German hymn tunes appear, among which are only 10

chorales. The German *Gesangbuch* has a larger proportion of hymns of the German chorale type, but the number is still relatively small compared to the number of songs taken from *Glaubensstimme, Reichslieder, Heimatklänge, Ausgewählte Lieder,* and *Evangeliumslieder,* from which many selections were made. The Evangelical Mennonite Church (Kleine Gemeinde) formally adopted the M.B. hymnal in 1955 for regular use in all its services.

D. SMALLER GROUPS. The groups with smaller membership naturally find it difficult to publish hymnals and therefore commonly use books of other groups. The Krimmer Mennonite Brethren German hymnal of 1884, *Die Geistreiche Lieder, Auswahl für Familien und öffentliche Erbauungen mit Sorgfalt gesammelt von der Krimmer Mennoniten-Brüder Gemeinde* (Elkhart, Ind., 1884) with 754 hymns, small format, was a brave venture for a very small group. It was not repeated. The same is true of the Evangelical Mennonite Church's (formerly Defenseless) one hymnal, *Glaubens-Lieder, Eine Sammlung Geistreicher Lieder zur öffentlichen und häuslichen Erbauung und zum Lobe Gottes* (Elkhart, 1890) with 600 hymns, small format, and an appendix of 50 English hymns. The somewhat larger Church of God in Christ Mennonites published their first hymnal in 1952, *The Christian Hymnal, A Collection of Hymns and Sacred Songs Suitable for Use in Public Worship, Worship in the Home, Evangelistic Meetings, and General Occasions* (Hesston, 1952), with 629 hymns, small format, prepared by a hymnbook committee of the General Conference with Harry D. Wenger as chairman. This hymnal shows considerable influence from the *Church and Sunday School Hymnal* (1902) of the Mennonite Church (MC), and also carries largely Gospel songs. A small booklet of 14 pp., called *Der Köstlichere Weg. In Liedern,* was published by Peter Töws of Stern, Alberta, in two editions, 1912 and 1914. Neither the Evangelical Mennonites (Kleine Gemeinde) nor the Evangelical Mennonite Brethren have ever published any hymnals of their own.

The Reformed Mennonites, founded in 1812 in Lancaster Co., Pa., by John Herr (*q.v.*), have had their own hymnals since 1847. In that year *A Collection of Hymns, designed for the Use of the Church of Christ, by John Reist, Minister of the Gospel,* small format, with 197 hymns, was published at Buffalo, N.Y. Reprints appeared at Lancaster in 1858 (bound with it *Eine Kleine Lieder-Sammlung, zum allgemeinen Gebrauch des wahren Gottesdienstes für die Gemeinde Gottes* also published at Lancaster in 1858, which had appeared at Harrisburg in 1837), in 1873 (revised), and in 1895.

The United Missionary Church (formerly Mennonite Brethren in Christ), whose beginnings date back to 1875, has had several hymnals. As early as 1876 Daniel Brenneman, one of its founders, published *The Balm of Gilead: For Christian Workers and Reformers, A Collection of Psalms, Hymns, and Spiritual Songs "Old" and "New," for Public and Private Devotional Exercises. Especially adapted to the use of Revival, Prayer, and Fellowship Meetings; Family Worship, and the Sabbath School* (Orrville, Ohio. H. A. Mumaw, Publisher, 1876), a booklet with 101 hymns. In 1881 the Evangelical United

Mennonite Publication Society published at Goshen, Ind., *A Choice Collection of Spiritual Hymns Adapted to Public, Social and Family Devotion and designed for the use of Evangelical United Mennonites and all Lovers of Zion,* small format, with 834 hymns, prepared by a committee composed of Daniel Brenneman, Solomon Eby, and B. Bowman. A revised edition was published in 1893 at Berlin, Ont., with the number of hymns reduced to 791, but with a separate section added called *Revival Hymns* (189 hymns) with its own title page, which could also be purchased separately. It carried many standard English and American hymns, as did the next hymnal. In 1907 the M.B.C. Church published its *Church Hymnal, A Choice Collection of Hymns and Meters for Public Worship in the M.B.C. Churches,* compiled by Henry S. Hallman, with 774 hymns and 258 tunes, sponsored by three district conferences: Canada, Michigan, and Northwest. It was not reprinted since the denomination soon began to use the popular Gospel song hymnals of other groups, such as *Gospel Hymns, Pentecostal Hymns,* etc. In 1917 the Pennsylvania district conference published its own hymnal, *Rose of Sharon Hymns,* compiled by a committee of which H. B. Musselman was the leader. Its 727 hymns are very largely of the Gospel song type, and quite different from the *Church Hymnal.*

E. The Hutterian Brethren. Before coming to North America in 1874 ff., and in America until 1914, the Hutterian Brethren used only manuscript hymns, of which they had a large number, and which were to be found collected in numerous codices. Examples are: a codex of somewhat before 1600 containing 165 hymns on 550 pages, one of about 1650 with 140 hymns on 800 pages, and one of about 1660 with 80 hymns on 780 pages. These three codices were the chief sources for the first printed Hutterite hymnal, *Die Lieder der Hutterischen Brüder, Gesangbuch, Darinnen viel und mancherlei schöne Betrachtungen, Lehren, Vermahnungen, Lobgesänge und Glaubensbekenntnisse, von vielen Liebhabern Gottes gedichtet und aus vielen Geschichten und Historien der heiligen Schrift zusammengetragen, allen frommen Liebhabern Gottes sehr nützlich zu singen und zu lesen. Herausgegeben von den Hutterischen Brüdern in Amerika* (Scottdale, 1914). This stately quarto volume of 891 pages, two columns to the page, probably prepared by Elias Walter with the aid of John Horsch, contains 276 hymns, written from 1527 to 1762, mostly with many stanzas each (up to 70 and 80 stanzas in some instances), arranged chronologically. It is clear that these hymns were not intended to be sung in full, but are often historical poems, relating the tribulations of the church and the experiences of the martyrs. A second edition of this hymnal was printed by the Christian Press of Winnipeg, Man., in 1953, with 632 pages, identical in content but using smaller type. A. J. F. Zieglschmid had prepared before his death in 1950 a scholarly edition of the Hutterite hymns in manuscript which is deposited in the Mennonite Historical Library at Goshen College.

An altogether different type of hymnal is the *Gesang-Büchlein. Lieder für Schule und Häuslichen Gebrauch Herausgegeben von den Hutterischen Brüdern in Canada,* which has appeared in small format in four editions thus far: 1919 (135 hymns), 1930 (137), 1940 (166), 1950 (186). The first edition had the following title page: *Gesang-Büchlein. Lieder besonders zum Auswendiglernen für die Jugend in der Schule geeignet, meistens aus alten Handschriften gesammelt und herausgegeben von Elias Walter.* The second edition indicates it was published by the Hutterian Brethren in Alberta. Not a single one of the hymns in the large hymnal of 1914 appears in the small book, nor do its hymns have any Hutterite character; rather they seem to be typically Lutheran or even Pietistic in type. There is no connection between this book and any existing German Mennonite hymnal. What manuscripts Elias Walter used is unknown, nor where the 52 additional hymns of the later editions came from, except that the author of the last hymn is given as Rev. A. G. Gross of Brentham, Alberta, in 1909, and the third last hymn is ascribed to Joseph Mändel of Elie, Man., both certainly Hutterites. How this quite un-Hutterite hymnal has come to be the popular book of the modern Hutterites must remain a mystery.

F. Apostolic Christian Church. This group, the "New Amish," had their hymnal *Neue Zionsharfe, Eine Sammlung von Liedern und Gesängen für die Gemeinen der Gläubigen in Christo, Neue Auflage,* with 275 hymns, printed by "John F. Funk and Bro." at Elkhart in 1875. In 1924 (reprint 1941) it appeared in English as *Zion's Harp, A Collection of Hymns and Songs for the Apostolic Christian Church of America, Translated from the German,* with 253 hymns.

G. Gospel Hymn Influences. The American "Gospel" hymn, often referred to in Germany as the "English" type hymn, which arose about the middle of the 19th century and became a widespread and very popular type of hymn and tune in both England and America largely as the result of the great Moody revivals of 1870-90, has also influenced American Mennonite Hymnology, and to a lesser extent that of the German, Swiss, French, and Russian Mennonites. Developing out of the earlier "White Spirituals" and religious folk music of the southern Mountains, and aided by campmeeting and Sunday-school hymns and tunes of the first half of the century, this type of hymn was published in an increasing number of hymnals in large editions from 1875 on. The two most important collections have been *Gospel Hymns and Spiritual Songs* (Nos. 1-6, 1875-94), the famous "Moody and Sankey songbook," and the *Pentecostal Hymns* (1894 ff.) series, published by the Hope Publishing Co. *Gospel Hymns* was translated into German as *Evangeliums-Lieder* (1891) for use in America and Germany. Similar additional Gospel song books published in Germany, some before and some after the *Evangeliums-Lieder,* were *Glaubensstimme, Frohe Botschaft, Heimatklänge, Reichslieder,* and *Siegeslieder.* In Europe it was the more pietistic and *"Gemeinschaft"* (*q.v.*) circles, and the Mennonites influenced by them in South Germany, France, Switzerland, and Russia, which used these books. In America, although some such German books were used by Mennonites, (for instance, all the K.M.B. congregations used the *Evangeliums-Lieder* until they changed to English, and most of the Kleine Gemeinde congregations in Manitoba used this book for Sunday school for the period *ca.* 1915-45, and began to use it in regular church services to displace the old Gesangbuch, *Eine Sammlung geistlicher Lieder,* which had been used from the beginning of their history) it was the English books mentioned above and others like them which had the greatest influence. Hymnals of Gospel songs were introduced directly into many Mennonite (MC) congregations at the time of the transition from the German to the English language from about 1890 on, though almost exclusively for Sunday-school use. Thus many congregations developed the practice of using two hymnbooks, the non-Mennonite Gospel type for Sunday school, the more standard Mennonite type of hymnal for "church" services. Some of the Gospel type books were actually "published" in imprint editions by Mennonite publishers, but most of them were bought directly by the congregations from such publishers at the Hope Publishing Co., and the Rodeheaver House, both in Chicago. The Mennonite Publishing Co. at Elkhart published soon after 1897 *The Gospel Call, A Choice Collection of Standard Hymns and Gospel Songs,* and about 1905 *Songs of Faith and Hope.* The issuance of *Life Songs* and particularly *Life Songs No. 2* effectively replaced the outside publications, and has largely eliminated the use of the cheaper type of Gospel song in the M.C. group. In 1910 the Mennonite Book Concern of Berne, Ind., issued an imprint

edition of *Evangeliums-Sänger,* edited by Walter Rauschenbusch and Allan Sankey. Similar publications by Mennonite Brethren publishers in the United States were *Zions-Glaubensstimme* (1905) and *Neue Zions-Lieder* (1919), the latter edited by J. J. Franz and D. B. Towner. Besides in the complete hymnals mentioned above, the Gospel hymns and tunes influenced American Mennonite hymnology by the deposit of smaller or larger numbers of Gospel hymns in every major English Mennonite hymnal published in America. The widespread use of such hymns and tunes has influenced the piety and even theology of Mennonites toward a heightened emotional emphasis and more emphasis upon subjective religious experience. This influence has been both wholesome and harmful depending upon the form it has taken and the extent of use. It has contributed in some quarters to a progressive detachment from the historic heritage and anchorage of Anabaptist-Mennonite background, accompanying and aiding similar outside influences in other areas of 20th century Mennonite church life, both in America and Europe.   H.S.B.

W. H. Hohmann, *Outlines in Hymnology with Emphasis on Mennonite Hymnology* (n.p., Newton, 1941); Paul W. Wohlgemuth, "Mennonite Hymnals Published in the English Language" (unpublished doctoral dissertation in Musicology, Univ. of So. Cal., 1956, dealing primarily with the tunes); H. S. Bender, *Two Centuries of American Mennonite Literature* (Goshen, 1929); *idem,* "The Literature and Hymnology of the Mennonites of Lancaster County, Pennsylvania," *MQR* VI (1932) 156-68; *ML* II, 86-91.

Illustrations

Contents

1

I. Historic Places: Europe

1. Menno Simons House and Linden Tree, Oldesloe, Ger.; 2. Menno Simons Monument, Witmarsum, Neth.; 3. Wartburg Castle Tower, Eisenach, Ger., where Fritz Erbe was imprisoned 17 years; 4. Lamberti Church Tower, Anabaptist Cages, Münster, Ger.

3

Das alte Rathhaus nach Edlibach.

Verlag von Orell Fü

II. Historic Places: Europe

1. Limmat River Scene, Zürich, Sw., showing Zwingli's church and Scene of Felix Manz' Martyrdom 1527; 2. House "Zur Eintracht," Zürich, home of Conrad Grebel 1508-14 and 1520-25; 3. Rathaus, Zürich, where Anabaptist-Zwinglian Debates of 1525 were held.

4

III. Historic Places: Europe

1. Tower Prison, "Käfigturm," in Bern, Sw., where many Anabaptists were in prison; 2. Emmental, Canton Bern, Sw., home of Anabaptists since 1528; 3. Het Steen Castle Prison, Antwerp, Belgium, where many Anabaptists were executed; 4. Passau Castle, Ger., where Anabaptist prisoners composed one part of the *Ausbund, ca.* 1535.

IV. Historic Places: North America

1. Ephrata (Pa.) Cloister Press, where *Martyrs' Mirror* was printed in 1748-49. Sketch by O. W. Schenk; 2. Conestoga (Pa.) Pioneer Wagons, used in westward migrations. Sketch by O. W. Schenk; 3. Waterloo Co., Ont., Pioneer Memorial Tower near Doon; 4. Swiss-Volhynian Pioneer Memorial Stone, near Moundridge, Kan.

V. Historic Scenes

1. First Immigrant Ship of Russian Mennonites arriving at Winnipeg, Man., in 1874; 2. Immigrant House Interior near Newton, Kan.: Russian Mennonites arriving in 1874.

(*From Frank Lesslie's Illustrated Newspaper*, New York, March 20, 1875)

7

VI. Historic Scenes

1. Chortitza (Russia) "Thousand-Year Oak," Landmark at beginning of settlement in 1739; 2. Mennonitische Flüchtlingsfürsorge Meeting, Oberursel b. Frankfurt, Ger., June 18, 1922; 3. Russian Refugee Camp Prenzlau, Ger., where many Mennonites stayed in 1930; 4. Russian Mennonite Refugees (Volendam Group) en route Berlin to Paraguay in 1947; 5. European MCC Relief Workers Conference, Basel, Sw., 1948.

VII. Homes for the Aged: Europe

1. Haarlem, Neth.; 2. Thiensdorf, West Prussia, Ger.; 3. Enkenbach, Palatinate, Ger.; 4. Valdoie, France.

2—P

VIII. Homes for the Aged: North America

1. Frederick, Pa.; 2. Souderton, Pa.; 3. Rittman, Ohio; 4.   7. Newton, Kan.; 8. Corn, Okla.
Bluffton, Ohio; 5. Eureka, Ill.; 6. Meadows, Ill.

IX.A. Homes for the Aged: North America
1. Reedley, Cal.; 2. Winnipeg (Bethania), Man.

IX.B. Hospitals: General Hospitals
3. Bloomington (Mennonite), Ill.; 4. Newton (Bethel Deaconess), Newton, Kan.; 5. Goessel (Bethesda), Kan.; 6. La Junta (Mennonite), Col.

11

X. Hospitals: General Hospitals

1. Winnipeg (Concordia), Man.; 2. Steinbach (Bethesda), Man.; 3. Winkler (Bethel), Man.; 4. Muntau, Molotschna, Russia; 5. Friesland, Paraguay; 6. Fernheim, Paraguay.

XI. Hospitals: Mental Hospitals

1. Prairie View, Newton, Kan.; 2. Brook Lane Farm, Hagerstown, Md.; 3. Kings View Homes, Reedley, Cal.; 4. Bethesda, Vineland, Ont.; 5. Bethania (Russia) Staff, founded 1911; 6. Philhaven, Lebanon, Pa.

Etliche schöne

Christliche Gesen z/ wie sie in der Gesengkniß zu Passaw im Schloß von den Schweitzer Brüdern durch Gottes gnad getichtt vnd gesungen worden.

Psalm. 139.

Die Stolgen haben mit strickt gelegt/das garn haben sie mir mit seilen auffgespannen / vnd da ich gehen solt haben sie mir Fallen zugerüstet/Darumb sprich ich zum HErRXEN: Du bist mein Gott. ꝛc.

M. D. LXIIII

EXACT FACSIMILE OF THE
TITLE PAGE OF THE ORIGINAL EUROPEAN
EDITION OF THE AUSBUND, REPRODUCED

1

HET RYPER
Liedtboecxken/

Inhoudende

Veel Schriftuerlijcke Liedekens, by verscheyden Autheuren gemaeckt, ende nu tot stichtinge van een yegelijck t'samen gestelt.

Dese laetsten Druck vermeerdert met een byvoeghsel, van verscheyde stichtelijke Liedekens.

Siet/ick segge u/heft uwe oogen op ende siet de Landen over/ want sy nu alreeds wit (ofte RYP) zijn totten Ooghst

t' ALCKMAER,

Voor Iacob Pietersz. Moerbeeck, Boeck verkooper op 't Dronckenoert, Anno 1664.

2

't Kleyn
HOORNS-LIET-BOECK

Inhoudende eenige

Psalmen Davids/

Lof-sangen/en Geestelijcke Liedekens. Seer bequaem om inde Vergaderinge der Geloovigen gesongen te worden.

Col. 3. 16.

Leert ende vermaent malkanderen met Psalmen Lof-sangen en Geestelijcke Liedekens.

Tot Sardam.

By Hendrick Iacobsz Soet, inde Witte Pers, 1646.

3

VEELDERHANDE

SCHRIFTUURLYKE

LIEDEKENS,

Gemaakt uyt het Oude en Nieuwe Testament, zoo als voor desen in Druk (in verscheyde Boeken) geweest zyn. Beneffens nog eenige, die voor desen nooit in Druk geweest zyn. Nu weêr op een nieuw te zamen gestelt, om in de vergaderinge der Gelovigen te zingen.

Leert ende Vermaant Malkanderen met Psalmen Lof-zangen, ende met Geestelyke Liedekens in der genaden: Colos. 3. v. 16.

Ik wil den Naam Gods Loven met een Lied, ende wil hem hooge Eeren met danken, dat zal den Heere beter gevallen, dan eenen Osse, die hoornen ende klauwen heeft Psalm 69. v. 31. 32.

Singt den Heere een nieuwe Liedt, de Gemeynte der Heyligen zal hem Loven. Psalm 149. v. 1.

Gedrukt tot AMSTERDAM, A°: 1752.

4

XII. Hymnbooks

1. *Ausbund* (Swiss) 1564; 2. *Het Ryper Liedtboecxken* (Dutch) 1664; 3. *'t Kleyn Hoorns-Liet-Boeck* (Dutch) 1646; 4. *Veelderhande Schriftuurlyke Liedekens* (Dutch) 1752.

XIII. Hymnbooks

1. *Geistreiches Gesangbuch* (Königsberg, Ger., 1775); 2. *Die kleine geistliche Harfe* (Germantown, Pa., 1803); 3. *Ein Unpartheyisches Gesang-Buch* (Lancaster, Pa., 1804); 4. *A Selection of Psalms, Hymns and Spiritual Songs* (Harrisonburg, Va., 1847), first English Mennonite hymnbook.

15

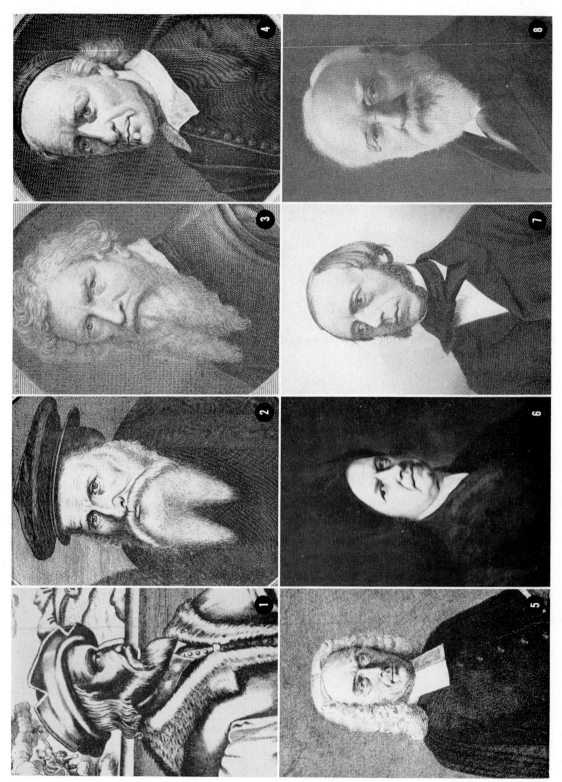

XIV. Portraits

1. Balthasar Hubmaier (1480-1528), Nikolsburg, Moravia;
2. Dirk Philips(z) (1504-68), Danzig, Ger.; 3. Lubbert
Gerritsz (1534-1612), Hoorn, Neth.; 4. Galenus Abrahamsz
(1622-1706), Amsterdam, Neth.; 5. Jeme (Joannes) Deknatel
(1698-1759), Amsterdam, Neth.; 6. Jakob Denner (1659-
1746), Hamburg-Altona, Ger.; 7. Sytze Hoekstra Bz. (1822-
98), Amsterdam, Neth.; 8. Pieter Feenstra, Jr. (1850-1936),
Amsterdam, Neth.

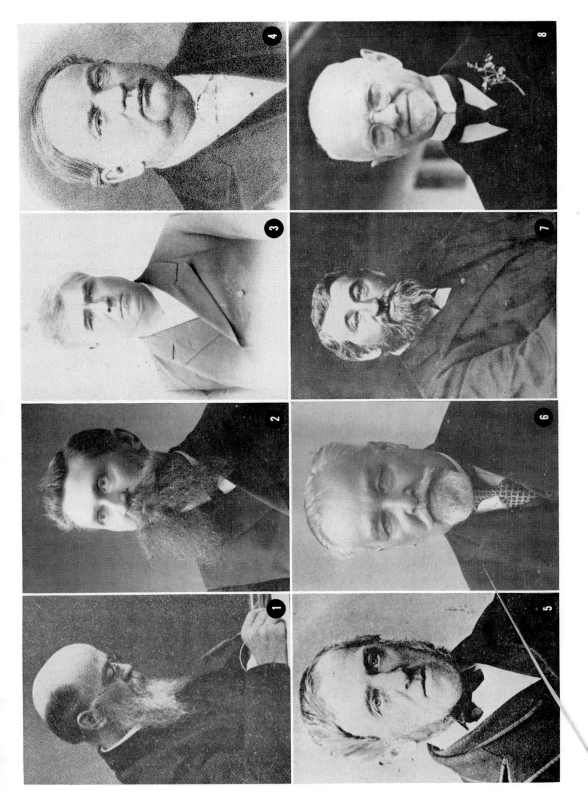

XV. Portraits

1. Peter M. Friesen (EM) (1849-1914), Halbstadt, Russia;
2. David H. Epp (Menn.) 1861-1934), Chortitza, Russia; 3.
Heinrich Dirks (Menn.) 1842-1915), Gnadenfeld, Russia; 4.
Bernhard Harder (Menn.) (1832-84), Moloschna, Russia; 5.
Ulrich Hege (Verband) (1808-72), Reihen, Ger.; 6. Christian
Hege (Verband) (1869-1943), Frankfurt, Ger.; 7. Jakob
Hege (Verband) (1848-1911), Reihen, Ger.; 8. Michael
Horsch (Verband) (1871-1949), Hellmannsberg, Ger.

17

XVI. Portraits

1. Heinrich Huebert (MB) (1810-95), Molotschna, Russia, first elder of the Mennonite Brethren Church in Russia; 2. David Gerhard Duerksen (MB) (1850-1910), Crimea, Russia; 3. Alexander Ediger (Menn.) (1893-?), Berdyansk, Russia; 4. Abraham Geiser (1857-1928), Chaux d'Abel, Sw.; 5. Isaak Dyck (Menn.) (1847-1929), Chortitza, Russia; 6. Abraham Goerz (Menn.) (1840-1911), Orloff, Russia; 7. Henry H. Ewert (GCM) (1855-1934), Gretna, Man.; 8. Nathaniel B. Grubb (GCM) (1850-1938), Philadelphia, Pa.; 9. David Goerz (GCM) (1849-1914), Newton, Kans.

18

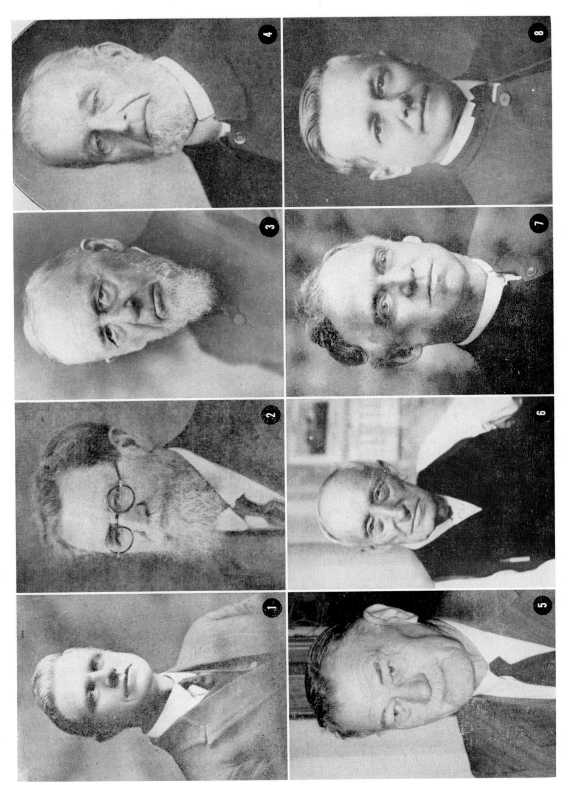

XVII. Portraits

1. David E. Harder (KMB) (1872-1930), Hillsboro, Kan.;
2. John F. Harms (MB) (1855-1945), Hillsboro, Kan.; 3.
John F. Funk (MC) (1835-1930), Elkhart, Ind.; 4. Solomon
Eby (MBC) (1834-1931), Kitchener, Ont.; 5. Dietrich H.
Epp (GCM) (1875-1955), Rosthern, Sask.; 6. Jonas S. Hartz-
ler (MC) (1857-1953), Elkhart, Ind.; 7. Tillman M. Erb
(MC) (1865-1929), Hesston, Kan.; 8. John Horsch (MC)
(1867-1941), Scottdale, Pa.

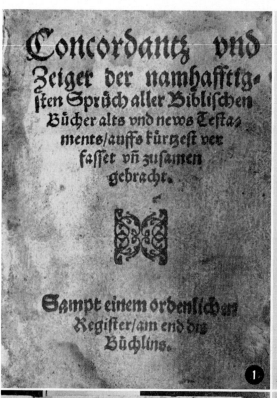

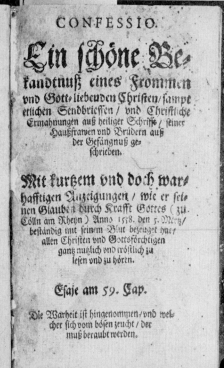

XVIII. Book Title Pages

1. A German concordance (*ca.* 1550); 2. A Dutch concordance by Pieter Jansz Twisck (Haarlem, 1648); 3. A confession of faith of Thomas von Imbroich (Cologne, *ca.* 1558); 4. A devotional book used in America (Ephrata, 1745).

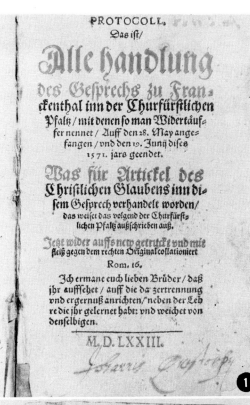

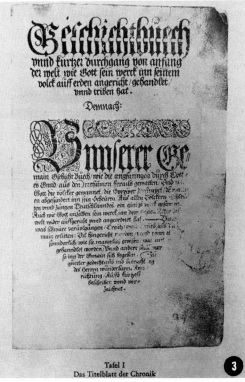

XIX. Book Title Pages

1. Record of the disputation held at Frankenthal, Ger., in 1571; 2. Record of the disputation held at Emden, Ger., in 1579; 3. The *Chronicle* of the Hutterian Brethren; 4. Heinrich Funck's *Mirror of Baptism* (Germantown, 1744).

Index of Illustrations

Asterisk (*) indicates a portrait; *italics*, a book

22

Explanation of Illustrations

The illustrations in the MENNONITE ENCYCLOPEDIA appear as pictorial supplements at the end of each of the four volumes. They are grouped according to the topics they illustrate. For instance, pictures of Mennonite colleges are grouped under the heading "Colleges," and appear in Volume 1, since this volume includes the letter "C." In the case of portraits, however, pictures are presented only for those persons for whom articles appear within the volume. An alphabetical index indicates the location of the pictures by pages in the supplement. In the text of the volume itself, the symbol (†) at the end of the article indicates that an illustration for the article appears in the pictorial supplement of that volume. The choice of illustrations has been limited by availability.

The co-operation of the many individuals and institutions who have secured or contributed pictures is here gratefully acknowledged, even though individual recognition is not given. The larger number of illustrations have been drawn from two chief sources: the Bethel College Historical Library, North Newton, Kan. (Cornelius Krahn, director) and the Goshen College Mennonite Historical Library, Goshen, Ind. (Nelson Springer, curator). In addition the Archives of the Mennonite Church at Goshen College (Melvin Gingerich, custodian), the Library of the United Mennonite Church at Amsterdam, Netherlands (N. van der Zijpp, director), and the Library of the Mennonite Research Center at Göttingen, Germany (Ernst Crous, director), deserve recognition for their contributions. The following periodicals kindly granted us the use of pictures which they had published: *Mennonite Life,* North Newton, Kan., and *Der Mennonit,* Frankfurt a.M., Germany.

The principle of selection of pictures has varied according to the type of matter to be illustrated. Thus, only a few typical dwellings were chosen, in cases where the dwelling represents a distinct type. But in the case of meetinghouses and institutions, age, historic importance, style, and regional and denominational representation, have all played a part in the decision, along with the availability of good photographs. Under "Art" only works of genuine merit, and artists of established reputation, have been chosen. For title-pages chiefly first editions, where available, of titles of historic significance have been used.